Also by Sherwood Smith

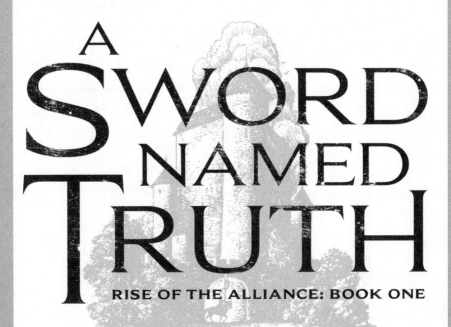

# A SWORD NAMED TRUTH

## RISE OF THE ALLIANCE: BOOK ONE

# SHERWOOD SMITH

## DAW BOOKS, INC.

DONALD A. WOLLHEIM, FOUNDER

1745 Broadway, New York, NY 10019

ELIZABETH R. WOLLHEIM
SHEILA E. GILBERT
PUBLISHERS
www.dawbooks.com

DAW Book Collectors No. 1825.

Published by DAW Books, Inc.
1745 Broadway, New York, NY 10019.

Author's Note: *A Sword Named Truth* takes place at roughly the same time
as *A Stranger to Command*.

First Printing, June 2019
1  2  3  4  5  6  7  8  9

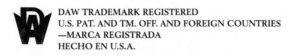

# A SWORD NAMED TRUTH

# Norsunder

**T**HERE are, at present, two records that the world believes lost.

I know where they are. I've sat in the dusty chamber where they lie, my only company spiders spinning cobwebs into spectral lace over the years I was in and out reading both.

One of those records is *The Emras Defense*, a deposition with a later—secret—addition, written by Emras, the mage who wrote on advanced ward magic. The first version, without the addition, was surrendered to the Sartoran mage guild, and buried so deeply in the archives that it requires several levels of inquisition to be permitted to see it. Only a heavily redacted version is studied by senior mage students at present.

The other record predates Emras's confession by four hundred years, written by the man who went down in history as Fox, captain of the ship named *Death*, who sailed under the Banner of the Damned. He did not sign his history, which delves into everyone's thoughts but his, as his purpose was to record how Inda Algara-Vayir changed the world they both lived in.

I am taking him as my model in writing the history of the disparate group later called the Young Allies. I, too, have a purpose beyond autobiography.

This will be unsigned, which permits me the freedom of anonymity.

At least, so is my intention in setting out. As I get farther in, everything might change, except the actual events: the consequences remain to be seen.

Since the war that nearly destroyed Ancient Sartor more than 4700 years ago, Norsunder—the ancient, evil enemy—had, until recently, dwindled from admonitory parable to vulgar epithet.

While assembling my facts for this writing, I was entertained by the various definitions of Norsunder by those who have never ventured to that retreat beyond the limits of the temporal. Most of them described Norsunder as a vast army with a single motivation, an oversimplification that borders on outright lie.

This much *is* true: Those in command of Norsunder withdrew from the temporal after the Fall of Ancient Sartor nearly wiped out magic as well as humanity from the world. So much was lost, including magical abilities that had become innate. With the dwindling of magic, these abilities vanished forever—or so humans thought.

But recently it's become evident that these abilities were only dormant, as magic slowly manifested in the world again before Norsunder was aware or ready, this being the disadvantage of existing outside of time.

Norsunder's center is commanded by two individuals who seldom venture out of their citadel, aided by four others who call themselves the Host of Lords, implying they are part of the inner circle. The struggle for power among these four will be addressed in time; before that, all you need to know is that they assigned much of the grunt work in the temporal world to an Ancient Sartoran who had fought successfully against them until he was captured and turned.

He has operated under a variety of names over the succeeding centuries. Currently he goes by Detlev. Under Detlev—and straining against that short chain of command—is his nephew Siamis, who had been twelve years old when he was seized and used as the bait to entrap Detlev, in those terrible days at the very end of the Fall.

Bringing us to the year 4735.

When a new voice was heard in the mental realm for the first time in over four thousand years, it meant that one of the skills thought lost forever, Dena Yeresbeth—"Unity of the Three," cohering body, mind, and spirit in ways impossible to humans after the Fall—was emerging again. For his first assignment Siamis was sent to track down the child and secure the source of that voice.

Now on the threshold of manhood, Siamis used that opportunity to demonstrate his skills in magic and command by binding entire populations under an enchantment, to cover Norsunder's attempt to create rifts between Norsunder's timeless vantage and the temporal world in order to bring across the armies waiting there.

Siamis was so intent on proving himself by building this web of enchantment that locating and snapping up a ten-year-old shopkeeper's daughter named Liere became a secondary consideration, until she managed to elude capture. Aided by fifteen-year-old newly crowned king Senrid Montredaun-An and a growing host of allies, Liere brought down Siamis's enchantment as rapidly as he had created it.

That was the year previous to the beginning of this history.

In spite of what ballads, speeches, and poems about the Girl Who Saved The World, and new Golden Ages, will tell you, neat, discrete endings to stories don't happen in real life.

Of all the subjects of this chronicle, most of whom were young rulers brought too early to thrones, probably the one most distrusting of the ephemera of Golden Ages and happy endings was Senrid Montredaun-An.

It seems appropriate to begin with him.

# PART ONE
## The Alliance is Born

## Chapter One

MARLOVEN Hess, a kingdom traditionally not given to taking any interest in its neighbors except as prospects for conquering, was still unsettled after the civil war that had removed their hated regent—who had been secretly supported by Norsunder. The Marlovens, never easy to rule even for a powerful and experienced king, found themselves with a fifteen-year-old boy trying to hold onto his throne.

Senrid had first become aware of Norsundrian game plans and stirrings of old powers during the bad days when he and Liere had been on the run from Siamis.

But right now? Norsunder was not his problem.

All his focus was on a boy several years older, who faced him across the stone court in the infamous Marloven military training academy.

At best, it would hurt. A lot. At worst, Senrid would be dead. No, that wouldn't be the worst, Senrid was thinking, because then he'd be gone. Unless he became a ghost, but if ghosts actually existed, he'd never seen any. If dying by violence caused haunts, by rights Marloven

---

\* All month names and festival days in headers given in Sartoran

Hess should be wall-to-wall revenants, and Senrid had never even seen his father's—

Ten years of habit shut away *that* thought. He flexed his hands once, resisting the impulse to wipe them down his trousers, and faced the tall, dark-haired, angry boy who towered over him. Boy? Jarend Ndarga, the leader of the seniors of the academy, had four years and two hands of height over Senrid.

"Fight me," said Senrid.

He knew he hadn't a hope of winning, but since he was an underage king in a land where fighting has always decided everything, and all his future commanders were gathered in this one place staring at him like he was a squashed bug, what did he have to lose?

"Of course I can't fight you," Ndarga said bitterly. "I touch your precious kingly head and you'll have me at the flogging post so fast there won't be time to whistle up a crowd to scoff."

"That," Senrid said, "was my uncle. This is me. When I said anything goes, I meant it. Do you see a uniform tunic?" He lifted his hands and spun around, as if Ndarga hadn't been aware of his plain white shirt tucked into his black trousers. Senrid hoped no one noticed the tremble in his fingers.

"No," Ndarga said slowly.

"Then take off your coat. We're two people, and we're going to scrap."

"Rules?" Ndarga said in a goading voice.

Senrid exulted, in spite of his hammering heartbeat. *I've got him.*

He didn't pause to reflect on how. Who cared? He might not last until the next watch change, but at least he'd go out fighting, a fitting finish to the shortest reign in Marloven history . . . "Anything goes," Senrid said recklessly.

The low whistles and whispered comments from the perimeter were testament not only to how many had gathered on the walls and at the windows, but to what they thought.

"Oh, for certain," Ndarga sneered. "If I kill you, nothing happens to me?"

"Something is certain to happen, but it won't be by my command," Senrid retorted, and breathed out when he heard a ripple of laughter from the spectators. "Seeing as I'd be dead," he added, in case there were some a little short on logic.

Senrid dared not look around to see the reactions. With an effort he kept his gaze steadily on Ndarga's dark eyes.

"Kill him," a senior called from a safe vantage behind.

And as Senrid had hoped, Ndarga's upper lip curled in disgust.

From that same direction behind came a fast, whispered exchange from the crowd:

"Swank!"

"I didn't see *you* walking out there when he called his challenge."

"And have the guard land on me for my pains?"

"He's not here as king."

"He's always king," someone else said.

"What's the matter, afraid of an untrained scrub?"

"We all know he's had training."

"But not with *us*."

Senrid listened without shifting his gaze from Ndarga, who was also listening as he took off the coat that only academy seniors wore, and handed it to a friend to hold. Now they were both committed. They could hear it in the whispers.

Senrid was not the only one who felt that the world had gone smash in the last few years. He didn't need his still-uncontrolled Dena Yeresbeth to know that Ndarga was furiously angry at the situation and at the world. Senrid might not have been traditionally trained at the academy with his future leaders, but the academy's commander had risked his life by personally training him in secret throughout Senrid's boyhood.

They began to circle, each watching the other for tiny signs—the twitch of an eyelid, attitude of shoulder, how a foot was placed.

While they circled, inside the castle, Hibern Askan, a Marloven-born mage student, arrived in the transfer chamber. She stared at the patterned tiles on the floor, different for every transfer Destination. Her joints throbbed in slowly diminishing pangs, protesting being wrenched in and out of the world from a continent away.

She let out her breath, and as she headed for the stairs, she began to consider what to say to Senrid. This was not her usual time for their magical studies, and she knew he liked sticking to a schedule.

She ran up the stairs two at a time, not surprised to find Senrid's study empty.

She was far more unsettled to find the hallway empty, too. Usually there were guards moving on their regular patrols at every landing.

What now? Something violent, of course. Her heart banged at her ribs. It was strange. A few years ago, their respective guardians had expected Hibern and Senrid to someday marry. They were both

Marlovens, and close to the same age, but in every other respect they could not have been more different. As she walked more slowly downstairs, she reflected on the thrill of excitement she'd experienced on discovering the world outside of Marloven Hess.

World? Worlds! The fact that there were seven worlds circling the sun Erhal, and that on three of them humans lived, made her long to read about them. But Senrid—one of the smartest people she knew—was totally indifferent.

Her passion was magic, a passion so strong it had lost her her home. Senrid's passion was his kingdom.

But, she thought grimly as she heard the low mutter of voices echoing along the stone hallway at the ground floor, in many ways she still thought like a Marloven. Maybe just as well. She'd discovered that the world outside her homeland's borders still distrusted her for being one.

A turn of a corner revealed guards talking in a cluster, mostly-blond hair glinting in the beating torchlight.

At the sound of her step, the four guards whipped around, two half-drawing swords. Then they separated and hustled away, presumably to resume patrols they never should have abandoned.

Something was definitely wrong. Hibern reached the landing, and said to the runner stationed there, "I'm looking for Senrid-Harvaldar."

The runner, who was probably twenty-five, looked about ten as he said stiffly, "Went to the academy."

"At this time of night?"

She didn't expect any answer, but the runner seemed to need to talk, as if to pass his tension on to someone else. "They say he went to the senior court."

The words were fraught with extra meaning. Hibern ran downstairs. Three steps in the direction of the academy, and she faltered in the middle of an empty, echoing stone hall. She wouldn't be permitted to set foot in the academy. No girls were, except at the barns, a holdover rule from the regent. Women do not carry weapons. It was said that the regent had killed his own wife . . .

Never *mind* that. Think! Hibern paused before the mighty iron-reinforced door that led in one direction to the tower stairs, and in the other to the ancient tunnel that debouched into the academy, now an inky darkness dimly lit by a distant torch.

The barns—and Fenis. Hibern and Fenis Senelac had played as children. Was Fenis still training horses at the academy barns? She would be if she could, Hibern knew.

Hibern ran, her proud new mage robe flapping at her knees. She encountered no academy boys. They had to be gathered as close as they dared to the senior court, wherever that was. She pounded down torchlit stone corridors between the unembellished sandstone buildings that had trained Marloven commanders for centuries. The sinkhole of the kingdom, that's what the academy was known as outside Marloven Hess. And there had been times, she'd discovered, that it had been known that way inside the kingdom, usually before some great ruction.

She reached the barns, where girls were busy bedding down horses for the night, and asked after Fenis until she was pointed in the proper direction.

She spotted a familiar dark, curly head. Fenis looked exactly like her brothers from the back, but when she turned, Hibern recognized her, though she was dressed much like the younger academy boys in her loose tunic-shirt and long riding trousers.

Fenis stared, brow furrowed. Hibern paused, waiting. She could imagine Fenis thinking: tall, black hair, black eyes, riding clothes, but what's that sky blue robe over them? Mage blue, hadn't she heard something about her old playmate doing magic studies?

Fenis exclaimed, "Hibern! I thought you were . . ."

"Disinherited and driven from home?" Hibern asked in a hard enough voice to hide how it still hurt, all these months later. "Yes, I was. I'm now a mage student."

Fenis made a quick slapping motion in the air, as if to strike the words away. "Magic," she said, and grimaced. "Almost as nasty a subject as the regent."

Hibern knew that any magic but the everyday spells that everyone used without thinking, such as the Waste Spell, or those concerning bridges, roads, and water purity, was a matter of distrust to her fellow Marlovens. And she was not about to explain the difference between the dark magic that Marloven mages had been using for several centuries, and light, which was now her study. "Senrid? They said in the castle that he's here. What's going on?"

Fenis scowled. "They won't let us girls anywhere near." She gave Hibern a grim smile. "But if you really do know magic, maybe you could make us invisible so we can climb to that rooftop there? We could see everything." She pointed toward a glow from many torches.

Hibern didn't bother saying that invisibility was impossible. What she needed was an illusion that would deflect attention from them, and that was easily done—and as easily penetrated if anyone were actually looking for them, illusions being mere tricks of the willing eye.

Illusions were the first thing mage students learned. A word, a gesture, and Hibern said, "Lead on."

Fenis led the way to a fence. Hibern kirtled up her mage robe, and followed Fenis onto the fence, then on a hard, fast scramble onto the slanted roof until they reached the ridgepole.

Hibern clung grimly, hating heights, as she glanced below into a walled square around the perimeter of which a huge crowd of younger boys crouched. Torches had not only been jammed into the sconces at the edges of roofs, but into cracks along the walls. Boy guards stood guard on the wall, but their attention was bent solely on the tall senior and the shorter, blond figure in the gold-lit square. Both boys were shockingly blood-splattered, as was the ground. In that ruddy light, the blood looked black.

"Why doesn't Senrid stop it?" Hibern whispered.

"Don't you see? They're in shirtsleeves. It means the rules are laid aside. Even for a harvaldar." She used the formal Marloven word for 'king.'

Hibern wanted to scream out her sudden upsurge of fury. Senrid, the smartest person her age she knew, was doing the *stupidest thing possible*. He risked his life down there in a useless fistfight when he could command the entire army to stop these obnoxious academy boys. He was a powerful enough mage to cast spells to hide the sun from the entire kingdom—and there he was, letting some brute beat the snot out of him.

She clenched her fists, wanting to drop a stone spell over them both.

In the court, Senrid tried to keep his focus on the blood-smeared face before him, though distracted by the drip from his own nose—did the drips coincide with the throbs?—and the horrible flutter in his muscles that he knew meant he was tiring . . .

Senrid saw the intake of breath, the tightening of muscles a heartbeat before Ndarga swung.

He was fast. Senrid had begun his block, but Ndarga's fist caught the side of his head. He shut his eyes against the pain-flash and used the recoil to torque his block, step, and kick low.

Ndarga shifted. Not quite fast enough. Senrid's boot heel clipped his knee, and he staggered.

That was the last blow Senrid landed for the next thousand years. He had one advantage, but it was untrustworthy at best: he could hear others' thoughts, if he concentrated. Dena Yeresbeth was a new idea, discovered when he and Liere had been on the run the year before.

Ndarga's intent reached Senrid's mind less than a heartbeat before his body acted, giving Senrid very little time to react as he tried to avoid the worst blows.

His strategy, which had seemed like such a good idea before he started, was to use his being smaller and lighter to stay ahead of Ndarga until the older boy wore out. Senrid understood within the first half dozen desperate exchanges how wrong he was to base his strategy on his limited experience of real contact fighting.

Commander Keriam, who had trained Senrid, was in excellent condition—for a man in his fifties. The time it took to cause a man of fifty years to get out of breath was far shorter than that required to tire a nineteen-year-old who had been training hard for the past nine years.

Further—Senrid spared a moment to take in the watchers—his strategy looked like cowardice from the outside.

Think. Keriam had trained them all. Senrid saw familiar patterns in Ndarga's moves. Another thousand years was going to pass, and it was only going to get worse unless he did something . . .

What am I doing wrong? He was using the patterns to evade—

Oh. So think against the pattern.

He reversed. Jumped in instead of to the side, dealt Ndarga a stinging slap over the ear, then followed with a fist to the gut. It was like hitting wood. He danced back, wringing his throbbing fingers. Ndarga took a harsh breath. So the blow did have an effect.

It wasn't much of one, but it was enough to anger Ndarga, who returned with a wicked flurry of feints and strikes.

That was another thing that Senrid's training with Keriam had not taught him. They'd always halted when they began to puff, as Keriam discussed Senrid's errors. There was no halt for discussion now. Senrid crowed for breath, the edge of his vision smeary on one side, glittering on the other. Focus! Break the pattern.

Another half a dozen blows and he fell to his knees once, causing a shout to go up. Some laughter. He rolled, used the anger sparked by that derisive laughter to launch himself straight into Ndarga for a head-butt to the gut.

Ndarga smacked him away. Tears stung Senrid's eyes, his nose throbbing, but he'd heard that grunt. Patterns! Ndarga was taller, and used to hitting high, from the gut up. Senrid feinted high, then came in with kicks. One connected solidly with Ndarga's forward knee, causing him to nearly topple as he brought a fist up under Senrid's jaw.

Senrid threw himself to the side, deflecting most of the force of the blow. Still felt like his neck had broken. Sick, dizzy, desperately thirsty, he knew he was going to lose. The question was how badly.

Listen! He could make one more try. Go out fighting . . .

Senrid sensed that Ndarga's thoughts were nearly as inchoate as his own, but by now Senrid had the patterns. He sidestepped—barely—two blows whizzing close to his ears. Could've crushed bricks. Then Ndarga followed through with what was intended to be the final series: a lunge, uppercut, two side blows.

Senrid put all he had into avoiding the uppercut, but instead of retreating, he whirled into Ndarga, fists together, straight into the point below the breastbone. Being shorter, he had the advantage of thrusting upward. *Thud.* Ndarga's eyes widened, and his breath whistled.

Senrid was aware of a roar. Inside his head or out?

Then Ndarga's hands hit either side of his head and Senrid's vision flashed into scattered lights. He found himself on the ground, arms and legs twitching, the side of his face gritting in dirt. Dust got in his mouth. He groaned, trying to spit it out. Then fingers gripped his shirt collar and yanked him up.

The roar in his ears resolved into voices, then into words as his bleary vision took in Ndarga looming over him. Ndarga was on one knee, swaying. Senrid squinted up at him, waiting for the last blow.

But it didn't come. "Shit," Ndarga muttered, and flung him away.

Senrid landed with a splat, nose first. Pain shot through him. He had just enough strength to flop over and gaze up at the sky, which revolved gently. One by one round brownish blobs appeared. Then a familiar voice . . . "Satisfied?"

Keriam stepped into the court, looking neither right nor left. The boys, out of long habit of obedience, stilled.

"Ndarga. Satisfied?"

Jarend Ndarga was mopping his bleeding nose and looking around as if he'd find his wits among the blood splatters on the stones. "Yes," he said.

Whispers from the walls, but no one moved. The rules held, barely. The boys stilled, a breath away from chaos as Keriam bent over Senrid, and repeated, "Satisfied?" Because that was the rule in these personal scraps.

Senrid struggled to speak. "Yes."

It came out sounding like "Wheh," but Keriam straightened up, and turned his toughest glare around the waiting faces. Then in a field command voice, "Fight's over, both satisfied. Anyone out of place by the time the watch change rings—and I'm sending a runner to the bell right now—wins a breeze from my own hand." He pulled a polished length of ash from his belt and whacked it against his leg.

The rumble and dust of many feet running followed. Clear chain of command, Senrid thought. Keriam ruled the academy. Could he take the kingdom? Yes. No. They'd kill him. *They might kill me.*

He couldn't find a reason to care, as hands took hold of various portions of his body. Now, he knew from experience, was going to be the worst of it. He couldn't speak, but he could sort sensations and interpret their meanings.

Senrid knew who he was. The thing he'd figured out by the time he was eight was that he wasn't the same person to everyone. To Uncle Tdanerend, he was the stupid little boy whose inconvenient birth kept Tdanerend from kingship. As long as Senrid was small, and acted stupid, nothing fatal happened to him.

Now he was going to find out if he was Senrid-the-dead-king, Senrid-the-former-king, or . . .

He was carried, not hauled. He was put on something soft, not flung down into stone and darkness. Without having to make the effort to listen for unspoken thoughts, he knew from the way he was handled that he was still—at this moment—Senrid-Harvaldar.

## Chapter Two

KERIAM followed the runners carrying Senrid, and watched as they laid him gently on his bed.

"Fetch the healer," Keriam said to one, and "Strip him, and clean up the blood," he said to two others.

Keriam had scarcely breathed during the endless agony of that fight. He could have told Senrid all the reasons why it was a bad idea, but Senrid had launched straight out there, driven by a desperation that Keriam understood.

The former regent had so distorted his brother's attempt at re-instituting rule of law that Marloven Hess had been thrown back to the worst days of the old Olavair kings, under most of whom rule by whim had been the norm. Jarls had been petty kings in those days, unanswerable to anyone. The regent, in buying favorites, had been eroding all his brother's hard-won attempts at establishing a justice system that extended to everyone. So here was Senrid, trying to prove that he was fit to rule, young as he was, in the only way that Marlovens would understand: by the oldest tradition.

It had taken all Keriam's control not to interfere.

The runners were quick and efficient, Senrid mercifully unconscious. When they were done, Keriam carefully checked Senrid over.

Long experience with battered bodies convinced him that his first assessment was correct: Ndarga had retained enough self-control not to do permanent damage, though he had used all his years of hard training to make this thrashing as painful as possible. As Senrid stirred, muttering something through puffing lips, the garrison healer arrived, breathless from running.

Downstairs, Hibern arrived from the seniors' private court in the academy. She sent a runner up to Senrid, hoping he was in better shape than he'd looked, then prowled the lower hall, trying to figure out what to do if she was denied. She was on her fifteenth lap (she'd first said she'd give herself ten, then twenty) when the runner reappeared and said, "King will see you."

She ran upstairs to the royal residence on the third floor. Instead of the plain stone walls of the lower floor, here were fine frescoes in shades of gray, depicting running horses and swooping raptors.

When she entered Senrid's bedchamber, she recognized Commander Keriam, the grizzled man in charge of the Marloven military academy. He stood beside the bed, looking tired and exasperated, but Hibern thought she saw something worse in the tightness of his forehead and the deep lines on either side of his mouth. An echo of horror, not quite gone?

A healer in uniform was holding a cup to Senrid's lips. The air in Senrid's bedroom filled with a sharp, distinctive aroma that made her feel slightly heady—green kinthus. Magic could bind bones and teeth so they could heal, but it didn't do anything for pain. The fact that Senrid drank green kinthus, which could be dangerous if drunk in large quantities, instead of the much milder listerblossom, meant that the pain was bad. As if you couldn't tell by the distortion of swellings and bruises all over the parts of him visible above the sheet.

"This stuff will make me go off my head," Senrid muttered as the healer lowered him to the pillow. Senrid's diction was usually crisp, and his speech a headlong reflection of his thoughts, but now his words were slurry and nasal, even plummy. As one would expect from someone whose nose was being held in place by a magic spell.

"You were already off your head," Keriam retorted from the other side of the bed. "What made you do something that stupid, Senrid?" Keriam sat down on the bedside stool that the healer had just vacated. "You couldn't possibly win a real fight, for the same reason he had to win."

"I know." Senrid touched his jaw, and winced. "But they had to. See me try. And see me. Stick to my word."

"Assuming," Keriam said cordially, "you survived."

"Thought he would stick to academy rules. And not kill me."

"So you did have a strategy. Even if it was poorly thought out."

One of Senrid's eyes was puffing up fast, but his other narrowed. Soon the kinthus would have him mentally floating, then he'd drop into sleep. Hibern watched Senrid struggle to hold onto his wits. "The yelling. Did it change?"

Hibern wondered if he'd already lost the battle, but Keriam's grizzled brows lifted. *He* clearly made sense of those words. His gaze went distant, then he said, "I'd say it was even. At best. When you began, probably more for Jarend Ndarga, but you must remember he's been the academy leader for two years."

"End?" Senrid asked, carefully touching his jaw. "Ow."

"By the end, they were mostly yelling for you," Keriam admitted. Then he scowled. "By academy rules—with the four-year handicap on his side—you won by two points. It was that last blow you got in before he let you go. But you are not to consider that a real win. On the field, nobody lets you go because you're too pitiful an object to kill," Keriam said bluntly. "You *know* that. Senrid, don't do that again."

"Shouldn't have to," Senrid said. "See? Took on toughest senior. Nothing happened to him. See?" He winced. "It worked. Didn't it? Did it?" He looked up at Keriam, his one functioning eyebrow puckering anxiously.

"For now." Keriam sighed and then got to his feet. "Hibern is here. Said it was an emergency." He started toward the door. "Don't talk long," he warned Hibern, and left with the healer.

Senrid squinted at Hibern. "Isn't our day. Or time."

"I know. Clair of the Mearsieans asked me to come," Hibern began.

Senrid leaned on an elbow, wincing. "Emergency," he muttered. "Keriam said emergency. My cousin?"

"I'm not here about your cousin. Far as I know, Ndand is perfectly safe."

Senrid blinked at Hibern through his one functioning eye. "What's happened?"

"Today—yesterday, I guess it would be, here, the Chwahir invaded Mearsies Heili."

"Invaded? Wait. Wait. Wait." Senrid clutched his hands to his face. The pain was beginning to recede, to be replaced by the soft cottony blanket of kinthus, which made him feel like his brains were leaking out of his ears. But at least he could talk without his jaw sending lightning through his head at every word. "I don't get it. Chwahirsland is huge."

"Yes."

"It lies at the other end of the continent. *This* continent."

"Yes."

"Mearsies Heili is a small blot, lying across the ocean to the west. Opposite direction of Chwahirsland."

"Yes."

"Why would the Chwahir go all the way there? And no one else noticed an invading force sailing up the strait? Oh, but it would have launched when the rest of the world was under Siamis's enchantment . . ."

Hibern sighed. So the pain relief of the kinthus had temporarily restored Senrid's habit of muttering, his thoughts zipping with frenetic speed. If she waited, he usually returned to the subject, and sometimes managed to answer his own questions.

". . . so people wouldn't have noticed if the warships had galloped up to their doors. But Siamis's enchantment has been over for how many months? How long does it take to reach past the Nob, way up north, then it's all open sea . . . no. The Delfin Islanders would have known. They always know everything in those waters." He looked up at Hibern. "How many warships?"

"Three," she said.

"That's not an invasion. Even for something as small as Mearsies Heili, which is mostly farm. Oh. Right. Didn't the Chwahir already have an outpost of some kind there? But that's real small, too, isn't it? Not much larger than a castle and half a day's ride of bad farmland, under permanent magic-made shadow."

"Yes, and yes."

Senrid peered one-eyed at the huge map of the world up on the wall on the other side of his bedroom. But that wouldn't show much. Mearsies Heili was too insignificant in both size and influence.

Its capital was no larger than a market town in Marloven Hess, but it was distinctive because it had been raised into the sky, surrounded by magical vapor so it looked like a city in the clouds, dominated by a towering palace made of white stone.

"It wasn't an invasion," Senrid stated, this time firmly.

Hibern let out her breath. "That's what *I* said. *They* said that the Chwahir and the Mearsieans are enemies going back for generations. And there is that outpost."

"So what does this have to do with me?" Senrid asked, and added sarcastically, "Don't try to tell me Clair wants my military advice."

"Not in the least," Hibern retorted calmly. "She needs your help to break into the citadel of the King of the Chwahir."

"What?"

Now she had his complete attention.

Hibern took a deep breath, surprised to find it shuddering against her ribs. It felt as if she hadn't breathed for the past . . . how long had it been? "It's even stranger than you think. And I can tell you everything, because I was there."

## Chapter Three

*Same day, earlier*
*Roth Drael*

AT dawn that day, while Hibern had been tossing and moaning in the grip of yet another nightmare, her tutor-mage Erai-Yanya, woken by the noise from across the hall, had decided she might as well get up.

She moved into the oddly shaped remains of a chamber, used to the broken walls and half roof overhead—weather-warded by considerable magic—and touched the glowglobes to light. And there she saw a newly arrived letter on the polished wood tray that she had ensorcelled as her transfer Destination for letters. Her heart wrung as Hibern coughed a low, rib-sucking sob into the bedding.

As she had countless times, Erai-Yanya considered getting doors fitted into those arches. Then she forgot doors, archways, and nightmares when she picked up her letter and read it.

And read it again.

She dropped the paper and stared at the window. The sun was still somewhere behind the thick forest to the east, which meant it was still night in Mearsies Heili, on another continent south and west. How to handle this request from her old mage school comrade-in-sneaking, Murial of Mearsies Heili?

Erai-Yanya was still thinking about it as she trod out in the early morning air to fetch some wild grapes from the garden, and had made no decision by her return.

As she set about making breakfast, at the other end of the hall, Hibern woke at last, and knew from the stinging along her eyelids and the panging of her head that she'd had another nightmare about the home that was no longer home.

Hibern rubbed her eyes, consciously breathing against the hurt in her throat as she listened to the little sounds of breakfast being readied— the click of crockery plates and cups on the table—and smelled the scent of fresh bread, which arrived each day by magic transfer, wafting enticingly to her room.

Hibern grimaced down at her hands when she remembered that this was her day to endure the long transfer to the magic school in Bereth Ferian, the northernmost city in the world. That was the last thing she wanted to do, with this headache, but no one would be interested in her whining.

Marlovens learned early that most people had a limited budget of pity. In the last year, Hibern had found that true outside their border, as well; people might have more conventional expressions than Marlovens did, accompanied by a dip of the head and rueful smiles, but they wanted you to pretend their words did away with the pain and get on with it. Marlovens, in her experience, didn't waste the breath.

She stepped through her cleaning frame, which zapped away the dried tear tracks from her face as well as the normal grime, dressed, and went out to face the day.

Erai-Yanya never paid attention to her appearance, but she seemed even more distracted than usual, her brown hair looking like she'd just woken, the shapeless dress she'd been wearing for a week rumpled. She was surrounded by a moat of open books and scrolls. Hibern suspected that some kind of magical emergency having to do with wards had to be happening somewhere in the world.

"Another nightmare?" Erai-Yanya said, her glance sympathetic.

Hibern opened her hands. And because she knew that all that could be said had been said, "Today is my day to go north. Any messages?"

Erai-Yanya knew that the rational person would have felt only relief to escape Hibern's dreadful home, but emotions were not always rational. She also knew that she, a recluse from a long line of positive hermits, was never going to understand whatever it was that bound families together for good or ill. She had sent her son off to be trained by an excellent mage, and was proud of him having that place, but she wondered if she would have chosen differently if she'd had a daughter.

But those kinds of what-ifs were useless. She said, "I do have a letter for you to carry, as Clair of the Mearsieans apparently did not take her notecase when she went visiting up there. Murial sent this to be handed off to her niece." A quick smile as she pushed a sealed note toward Hibern.

Wondering why Murial didn't send the note to the scribe desk up north, Hibern shrugged. She didn't understand the ways of royalty outside of Marloven Hess, even the royalty of so small a polity as Mearsies Heili. Or maybe 'royalty' was the wrong idea here. Murial, Erai-Yanya had said once, was a regent at a remove, being a fellow hermit-mage living alone somewhere in the wild woods of that country's western border. She watched over the pastoral little kingdom from a distance, avoiding people as much as she could. Her niece, Clair, led the kingdom day to day.

Midway through breakfast Erai-Yanya startled Hibern by clapping a book shut with a soft, "Ha!" She tucked the book under her arm, and trod to the Destination-book to leaf through it for some tile pattern. She muttered the transfer spell and vanished, the air in the room stirring strongly enough to flutter the abandoned pages.

Hibern sat back and breathed. At least breakfast had vanquished the nightmare headache. She picked up her magic study books, and braced for the magic transfer to the north to Bereth Ferian.

She endured the usual joint-wrench, and staggered in the new space, breathing cooler air that smelled of aromatic trees. She sank onto one of the low benches surrounding the tiles until the transfer magic effects had worn off, then left the Destination chamber.

Since she had the note to deliver, she bypassed the hall leading to the magic school and entered the grand marble-floored hall leading inside the palace, where Erai-Yanya's son Arthur studied magic separately.

'Arthur.' It always snagged at her, that foreign-sounding name. She knew it was a nickname given him by some world-gate crossing friends. She was going to have to find out that story someday, she thought as she passed the gorgeous decorative motifs and statuary, gifts from various northern governments over the generations.

Arthur's kingship was fiction in a way that Hibern found difficult to understand, coming as she did from Marloven Hess, where kingship had historically been the center of violent struggles for power. For command. Arthur's title was traditional, a courtesy.

When Siamis had spread his enchantment over a good part of the world a year or so ago ('or so' was the only way to consider a period in which time seemed ephemeral, and people had walked about as if in a dream world, obedient to whatever command Siamis gave them, without remembering any of it), the elderly mage Evend, King in Bereth Ferian, sacrificed his life to destroy Norsunder's rift magic. Everyone accepted Evend's title passing to Arthur even though he was no older than Hibern was. A title with no responsibility, as far as Hibern could discover, except presiding at official gatherings.

The sound of girls' laughter broke Hibern's dour mood. Odd, how a duty visit would turn interesting as soon as she heard someone having fun.

"But once you find people, you have to race them to home base," one of the Mearsiean girls was earnestly explaining as Hibern entered an enormous drawing room lit down one side through tall arched windows by slanting shafts of light.

Arthur stood over by the opposite wall, absently running ink-stained fingers through his short blond hair. His habitually vague expression altered when he saw her, and he beckoned for her to enter. She joined him in a few quick steps.

"Erai-Yanya said the Mearsieans were still here. Why?" Hibern whispered. The noisy Mearsieans seemed out of place in this quiet, archival atmosphere.

"For her," Arthur said, pointing to scrawny Liere, the girl the world had begun calling Sartora. She sat in the circle of girls, her raggedly cut, lank, almost colorless pale hair framing an earnest face dominated by huge light brown eyes. "I asked them if they'd stay. She seems, I don't know, happier, with them around." He sent a puzzled look Liere's way.

Hibern's gaze shifted to Liere, then to the other girls. Young people played games in Marloven Hess. Of course. But the games tended to be competitive, often related to military training. Hibern had hated them from early childhood.

This game the Mearsieans played was messy and complicated—the rules seemed to be changing constantly—but Liere clearly found it funny when a freckled, red-haired Mearsiean girl waddled across the far side of the huge drawing room, waggling her elbows and quacking like a duck. Another girl slithered over the beautifully woven rug, graceful even when pretending to be a snake. In the background, the rest of the Mearsieans made barnyard noises, as Liere shook with silent laughter.

"I won!" the freckled girl shouted, her bristly red braids flapping, arms and legs pumping as she danced around. "I'm It! I'm It!"

Liere watched, lips parted as if she were about to laugh out loud but didn't dare. She looked unchanged since Hibern had met her the previous year, right down to the same worn old tough-woven tunic and riding trousers.

Hibern glanced past her and found Clair, who stood out as the only one with pure white hair.

Clair was short for thirteen or fourteen, ordinary-looking enough except for that white hair. It wasn't the cobwebby, floating hair of the morvende, nor did she have their fish-pale skin or their talons, but her ancestors had to number among the underground people.

Erai-Yanya had told Hibern about Clair's upbringing, how her dejected mother drank wine and took sleepweed until she died. Clair had been educated by her aunt Murial, who started her on magic studies when she was small. "Don't be fooled by her young age. She probably knows more magic than you do," Erai-Yanya had finished.

When Hibern first met the Mearsiean girls, she'd thought one of the other girls the Mearsiean queen, as she was loud and tended to swank about. But when Clair spoke, the way the others instantly deferred made it clear that her gang of runaways and castoffs regarded her as their chief.

Clair must have felt Hibern's gaze, because she turned around and then smiled. "Greetings! Hibern, isn't it? I'm sorry. I didn't see you come in."

"Hibern?" Liere whirled around as if someone had poked her.

"Hi, Sartora," Hibern said.

"Please call me Liere," Liere whispered.

"My pardon, Liere," Hibern said, thinking that mighty mind powers or not, Liere was very odd.

Hibern could not understand why Liere would reject an honor that most would be proud of any more than she could understand why the girl wore ragged old clothes and bare feet, when surely she could ask for anything she wanted in that massive, wealthy palace.

Liere's light brown eyes looked golden in that light. "You're Marloven, aren't you? It's just that I hope everything is all right with Senrid."

"I see him each week for magic studies. Want me to pass on a message?"

Liere's thin fingers twisted together. "Yes. No! It's just that he was my first friend. But I understand. He's a king, so he must be extra busy. Much too busy to visit. It's just that he once said . . . no, forget that."

Her skinny shoulders hitched up near her ears. Hibern suspected Liere had no idea how to get out of that hopeless tangle, so she turned to Clair. "I have a message for you."

Clair took the note and broke the seal. Then she looked up, her hazel eyes wide. "The Chwahir have invaded," she said. Her voice changed, dropping a note or two, as if she had to convince someone. "We have to go *home*. Right now."

"Invaded?" CJ asked, skinny arms wide, her long, straight black hair swinging. She was Clair's best friend. Clair had made her a princess, though she'd been born on another world and brought through a world-gate. "Like, war junk and everything?"

Clair held up the paper. "Three ships of warriors, plus those from the Shadowland outpost, under the direction of the King of the Chwahir."

Hibern made a mental wager that Murial had sent the note begging Clair and these girls to stay here, out of trouble, queen or no queen.

CJ scowled. "I call this completely unfair!" And when everyone turned her way, she pointed at Liere. "Here's the world saved from the villain Siamis by Sartora. We deserve a golden age of peace, like in all the songs! But thanks to the Chwahir, as usual, we get rotten luck instead."

'Luck'? But no one asked what that was as Clair's mouth pressed into a thin, pale line. "The note says the main attack is magic, on our capital. Aunt Murial is there, trying to fight against it. She said we should stay here in safety—"

I was right, Hibern thought.

"—but I have to go home," Clair stated.

"To a magic attack?" Hibern asked, and then it hit her, why Erai-Yanya hadn't told her where she was going. "I think Erai-Yanya went to help." Hibern studied Clair's tense face, knowing the other girl was going to go regardless.

Hibern bit her lip, instinct at war with duty. Erai-Yanya expected her to go to the mage school for her long day of study. But she was learning to become a mage because she wanted to help people, and right now, Clair needed help. She'd let Clair's reaction decide. "Shall I go with you?"

Clair let out a soft breath, her eyebrows lifting in a revealing expression of relief. "I know we'll need any help we can get." She waved the paper. "Aunt Murial can protect the country, if we try to protect the cloud top so she won't have to. Does that sound right?"

Hibern thought, cloud top? She said with more assurance than she felt, "I'll be glad to help any way I can."

Clair turned to her friends, who stood in a tight circle, waiting. "Transfer to the Junky, count five between each, okay?"

Her friends reached inside shirts and dresses for the medallions they wore, then began winking out in transfer magic, each disappearance sending a wild current of air whooshing around.

While they did that, Clair described her home transfer Destination tiles to Hibern. Then, in turn, they vanished.

*Mearsies Heili, cloud city above Mount Marcus*

Erai-Yanya, satisfied that her single student was safely removed from danger, transferred to the Destination in Mearsies Heili and, once she recovered, gazed upward in astonishment.

Her home was in Roth Drael, once a center for Ancient Sartoran magic until blasted in the Fall of Ancient Sartor. It was a ruin, no complete building standing. The fragments left behind indicated the city had been built out of a strange white stone that looked like a blend of ice and metal. She had discovered on her first visit to Sartor that there was a single tower in the heart of its capital, made of the same material. She was reverently told by her guide that this tower was the oldest edifice in Sartor.

Now she was standing in front of an *entire building* built of the same material.

Murial appeared, looking mostly unchanged from their student days, except for strands of silver in her dark hair. "Erai-Yanya," she called, hurrying across the terrace. "You're here."

"I came as soon as I found my mother's old border protection spells." Erai-Yanya brandished her book. "Where're the invaders? Have you contacted the school for help?"

"The Chwahir have already landed." Murial's voice was tense.

That meant ships, warriors, borders breeched. It was now a military matter. Mages took an oath not to meddle in such, not that magic was much use in warfare anyway.

Murial went on, "They entered the Shadowland outpost during the night, but emerged on the mountain road a while ago. They can only be marching on this city."

"Shadowland?" Erai-Yanya looked around. A fountain splashed behind her, and beyond that, a pretty little town seemed quiet, no movement except the stirrings of a breeze in what she suspected were brightly colored flower boxes in windows, though this early before sunrise the world appeared a thousand shades of gray and blue.

Murial pointed down at her feet. "The Chwahir outpost below the city. It's held by Prince Kwenz, brother to Wan-Edhe, the King of the Chwahir."

Erai-Yanya glanced down at her dusty sandals, remembering that the Chwahir king never used his name, only his title—'Wan-Edhe' in Chwahir meaning *The* King, as if there never had been and never would be another. Then she blinked past that, remembering that only this palace was actually located on the mountaintop. The adjacent village extended outward on a magically maintained cloud. Unimaginable magic had raised it in the far past, though for what purpose no one now knew. Mearsies Heili had no importance whatever, either magically or politically.

She scowled down at her sandals, struggling to make sense of the situation. This palace, made of material that only existed elsewhere as ruins—the tiny capital held up by magic equally impossible to mages now—Chwahirsland so very vast, located on the other side of the continent across the sea. Instinct insisted she was missing something important.

"The Chwahir must have set sail during the Siamis enchantment," Erai-Yanya said slowly, considering what she'd learned about the Chwahir from Gwasan, the runaway Chwahir princess she and Murial had been close to during their years at the northern mage school. Until Gwasan was hunted down and killed by assassins sent by the head of her own family, this very same king.

"Murial, what could Wan-Edhe possibly want *here?* If we know, maybe we can form some kind of plan to thwart him, or at least get the right kind of help."

Murial rubbed her forehead in slow circles. "The Shadowland army has tried a couple of times to take our east provinces. They could feed all Chwahirsland if our people were forced to labor for them, growing crops to ship back to their homeland. You know Chwahirsland is ruined. But I don't think Wan-Edhe is after farmland. Why come halfway around the world for that? I think he's after the palace."

Erai-Yanya turned her gaze upward, toward the asymmetrical towers shimmering in the pale predawn light. Knowing that distracting herself from an impossible situation wasn't going to improve it, she still spoke. "When we were girls, you said you lived in a marble palace. And every time I leave here I *remember* it as marble."

Murial stared at her old friend, fighting impatience, because she'd had this conversation before. At least twice, if not more. And Erai-Yanya never remembered it. "We were *told* it was marble. By the time I found out it wasn't, I'd learned not to talk about it." She sighed. "Erai-Yanya, it was here when the first Mearsiean refugees reached this shore, seven hundred years ago. It could be it . . . wasn't here, before that. There are rooms up there that come and go. We never thought much about it, having grown up with it, and furthermore, every visitor, including you, goes away and forgets about it. But right now, *here is what's important*, Wan-Edhe doesn't seem to forget. When he overran this kingdom a few years ago, he was not able to get past the second floor."

"Your wards?"

"No." Murial's thin fingers pressed against her temples, her eyes closed. "I don't know that much magic! Something so old I have no record of it, and so powerful I can't perceive what type of spells, only that they exist."

"Is it possible to extend something off that spell?"

"That's what I was thinking right before you came. But it'll take two of us."

Both found a semblance of relief in talking about what they knew was possible. In cryptic conversation honed over the years, they discussed the intricacies of magic as they hurried inside and upstairs to the library, where Murial began hunting through old tomes.

From long habit, Erai-Yanya reached for the end of her sash and tied a knot, whispering to herself as she did it. She was going to remember this old palace and its mystery, and research it as soon as she got home.

The tall glass windows in the hall outside the library were open to the air, through which came the high sound of young voices. Murial paused in the act of thumbing through an ancient text.

She said with annoyance, "Your Hibern doesn't seem capable of passing on a message," as they hurried out of the library to the window.

They looked down on the tops of three heads: Clair's white, Hibern's dark, with CJ's shiny blue-black locks between them.

Erai-Yanya retorted, "That niece of yours doesn't seem capable of following orders either. Just like someone else I remember."

Murial sighed. "She got my sense of duty, and my younger sister's impulses for poking her nose into trouble, always with the best intent. Let's get back to work before they come inside."

She was right about Clair's sense of duty, and where Clair went, the girls had to go. On the floor below the mages, CJ complained with a graphic list of which muscles and bones hurt worst after that long transfer, and Clair winced and swung her arms.

Hibern breathed away the nausea and ache as she gazed in witless amazement at the palace. The three started up the shallow, wide terrace stairs. When they got inside, Hibern walked to a wall to examine it. She knew this strange material, not quite stone. It was more like ice without the cold—ice and stone mixed with a hint of metal, only with a pearlescent sheen. It was the very same material as the broken building she lived in with Erai-Yanya.

"Oh, no!" Clair cried, and uttered a soft, breathy laugh. "Now I know we're in trouble."

In ran a tall boy, saying breathlessly, "Thought I heard CJ crabbing. I just got here from below. Did you know the Chwahir are marching up the old road right now?" He jerked his thumb toward the window.

In answer, Clair held out her aunt's note, and he bent over it. He was so tall that at first Hibern took him to be older than he was, until she noticed the still-round cheeks over a square jawline, and the gangling proportions of a teen. Though he had brown hair, his face so resembled Clair's he had to be related.

"It's Clair's cousin," CJ whispered to Hibern, as they mounted the stairs. "He doesn't actually live here. He's always on the Wander."

The Wander wasn't a tradition in Marloven Hess, for whatever reason, but along the rest of the vast Sartoran continent, and even on other continents, underage people often traveled the world, working their way along in ships or caravans. Most trade cities and harbors had Wander Houses, where young travelers could bunk. A lot of businesses offered food or goods in trade for the sort of enthusiastic but unskilled labor expected of the young.

CJ went on, "Puddlenose seems to have this . . . this weird kind of sixth sense, where he'll be somewhere traveling around, then he suddenly gets this idea that he has to come home, and it always means trouble."

*Puddlenose?* Hibern repeated to herself, then shrugged it off, attributing the unfortunate name to CJ's penchant for creating nicknames—whether the recipient liked it or not.

". . . had to come by transfer, and I hoped you'd be here," Puddlenose was saying. "I think Wan-Edhe has ordered up every sword in the Shadowland, and they are on their way up the mountain." He pointed at the floor.

The air stirred, bringing an eye-watering whiff through the open windows. It smelled like rusty metal placed too near a fire.

"Dark magic," Clair breathed, then glanced up as the two mages came running down the stairs. "Oh! Aunt Murial—?"

"I sent that message to keep you *safe*—" Murial started, before both Murial and Erai-Yanya stilled, gripping the bannister, as greenish light flared outside the windows. Everyone felt the hairs on the backs of their arms lift.

Then the building shivered all around them.

As one, they moved upstairs to broad windows. Hibern glimpsed another terrace made of the same iridescent material as the walls around her. Beyond this terrace a formation of men gathered. They wore uniforms that looked black in the aggregate, but the strong sunlight revealed some grayish with age, and others' dye tended toward rust or green.

The biggest group surrounded a tall, stooped old man in a night-black robe, with unkempt white hair and beard. He and a slug-pale man stood beyond the terrace on a grassy sward between the palace and the town, the houses mostly whitewashed with colorful tile roofs.

"The Chwahir king," Murial breathed. "Here himself. All right, we're going to have to take a stand inside this palace." To the girls— "*Don't* go anywhere. Watch him. Let us know when he moves. Erai-Yanya, we might be able to get Clair and your student to help us chain a deflection ward . . ."

The two mages dashed back up to the library, talking fast, as Hibern and the Mearsieans hung out the window, too terrified to take their eyes away.

The building trembled again, a significantly stronger rattle.

"Is he doing that?" Clair asked.

No one answered.

"Look." Puddlenose pointed at the Chwahir warriors below.

The ranks shifted, pale Chwahir faces looking around fearfully. Hibern's stomach tightened when she saw their eyes. There was no color, no white, even, visible. Their eyes were all black, as if their eye sockets were empty.

That had to be illusion, she reassured herself, as Clair said, "I think . . ."

Another tremor rumbled through the building, and the warriors below reacted with wild looks and raised hands as if they felt it as well. Hibern's knees locked, and her insides swooped in an odd way that she had not felt since her older brother had pushed her in a tree swing, before their father's spells had made Stefan crazy.

Clair's face had blanched nearly as pale as her hair. "I think we're sinking," she whispered.

At the same moment, inside the library, Erai-Yanya set down her useless book, saying, "Murial? Is this normal?"

"No." It was said on an outward breath.

They rushed back to the windows in time to see another weird flash of magic, more powerful than the earlier flicker: beyond the edge of the terrace the air shimmered with thundercloud green.

Hibern's teeth buzzed as she tried to blink away a blurring shadow in the air. But it did not blink away. The shadow coalesced into a writhing line extending from the sky to the ground, and as they watched in horror, it began to widen into a lightless fissure.

The Chwahir below began to edge away from that pulsating darkness, their voices rising in fear.

"That's a Norsunder rift," Clair cried, leading them back upstairs.

"It can't be," Erai-Yanya said sharply. "Norsunder cannot make rifts anymore. Evend *died* binding that magic."

CJ gasped in horror as a slim young man with short, black, curly hair emerged from that darkness. He stepped onto the grass a pace away from the King of the Chwahir. "That's Kessler!" she hissed, hands pressed to her mouth.

"Who?" Hibern asked.

"Villain." CJ's blue gaze was stark with terror. "Descendant of Wan-Edhe, got away. But they got him in Eleven-Land. And now they've opened up one of those rifts!"

Eleven-Land was a euphemism for Norsunder, Hibern remembered as she shook her head in disbelief.

Murial breathed, "It's illusion. We're to think it's a magical rift."

"*They* are to think it's a magical rift," Erai-Yanya muttered.

Prince Kessler Sonscarna spoke in a soft voice, barely above a whisper, yet it carried distinctly on the air. "Come along, uncle. You made a bargain with Norsunder, and I was sent to collect you."

"Kill him!" The old man waved at the big guards surrounding him, his protuberant eyes wild with rage.

The guards shifted, some with hands to their swords. The renegade Chwahir prince smiled, and the guards looked at one another as they pulled their weapons. But no one dared to take the first step.

The king's face mottled with fury as he raised his hands. Dry old lips muttered behind the yellow-stained mustache, and light glowed around his fingers, but Kessler ignored the magic as well as the guards closing in.

Prince Kessler reached with his left hand and gripped the skinny arm of the King of the Chwahir, who stared aghast. No one had touched him for over fifty years—his formidable personal protections were gone.

"Right hand," Erai-Yanya muttered. "See that?" Something in Kessler's palm glinted in the pale light, too quick to catch.

The prince's teeth showed in a brief laugh as he performed a circle gesture, his fingers wide. A scintillating magical fog curled outward to swallow the slug-pale dungeon master and Wan-Edhe's personal guard and commanders; they appeared to be drawn into the rift, but the experienced mages saw the truth past the illusion: they dissolved into enchantment, not transfer.

And were gone. Prince Kessler and his prisoners vanished less than a heartbeat before the massive transfer spell closed with a snap like a blow to the chest. The stench of burning metal torched the air. Nothing made sense, except one fact that the two elder mages clung to: no one would be able to make a transfer in that spot without burning to ash, maybe for years.

And the danger was not yet over.

The ground jolted again, rumbling through the city. The quake caused Mearsieans hiding inside the houses to creep outside, looking around fearfully.

The grinding rumble seemed to come from everywhere at once, but the towering spires above did not creak or grind. It was more like a deep, uneven hum, punctuated by a shivery tinkle, like a silver hammer tapping on glass.

A man called out orders in Chwahir, a phrase picked up by others. Puddlenose said, "The company captain just ordered the mainlanders back to their ships. Ah, did you do that?" He turned to his aunt. "If not, who did?"

The floor jolted underfoot again, sharper, causing the ground to roll. "No," Murial said. "The city beyond the terrace is sinking. It's not the prince's spell. This is something else entirely."

"The entire city?" CJ said, her voice high. "I thought you didn't have earthquakes here!"

Puddlenose pointed out the window, beyond the Chwahir, who were stampeding away in barely controlled order. "Look. People are coming out, now that the Chwahir commanders are gone and the rest are on the run."

Another quake caused a loose tile here and there to clatter down from roofs. People began to cluster in shrill groups, asking questions no one answered, while others ran around without apparent purpose. A few started toward the palace.

Erai-Yanya said, "If the cloud top is sinking, we need to get out."

Hibern said quickly, "Will you need help transferring people?" At last, something she could do!

Murial turned to them. "Everybody in the city wears a transfer token. It's always been that way, at least since the Chwahir chased our ancestors to these shores to carry on the old war, and established themselves in the Shadowland under us." She pressed her hands against her eyes, then brought them down. "We have to warn people to get out. We don't know how bad it's going to be."

Erai-Yanya turned to Clair and Hibern. "You two do that." She drew Murial back into the library.

Clair grabbed Puddlenose by the arm. "I want you to go warn the Chwahir in the Shadowland that the city is coming down on top of them."

Puddlenose and CJ exclaimed at the same time, "What?"

"You speak Chwahir, Puddlenose. I think the Shadowland people should be warned if the city is really coming down," Clair said. "They are directly underneath. It will crush them."

"Oh, sure, I guess you should warn the ordinary people. They can't help being Chwahir. But not Jilo," CJ said.

"Jilo?" Hibern asked.

CJ scowled fiercely. "Kwenz's heir, our age, and a complete and total villain! If you ask me, he deserves what he'll get."

"He's a person."

"A villain!" CJ shrilled.

"The villains are those who told them what to do. Who kept them living in the Shadowland, and made them act that way. That includes Jilo, who has to do what he's told," Clair said. "You *know* that. You *know* what would happen to him if he didn't obey Wan-Edhe. Puddlenose, go."

Puddlenose made a comical grimace. "Do my best." He vanished.

"You watch. Jilo will be busy plotting something nasty, with Kwenz the Fumbler gloating around right behind him," CJ said. "And if Puddlenose warns him, he'll get a knife in his ribs as thanks."

"Jilo never *killed* any of us," Clair said over her shoulder as she ran toward the stairs. "CJ, we can't do an evil thing just because they did."

"It's not evil, it just makes sense," CJ muttered not quite under her breath as Clair led the way downstairs, followed by Hibern.

"Who is Puddlenose?" Erai-Yanya asked, distracted as the building shook around them, loose books falling from their shelves. "Why do you call him that?"

Murial's tense face tightened into hatred. "That horrible name is from Wan-Edhe. I told you he suborned my brother after he killed Gwasan."

Erai-Yanya remembered something about Murial's brother going to the Chwahir. Willingly, Erai-Yanya thought, but kept it to herself. She had never liked Murial's brother, or her whiny, sullen youngest sister, Clair's mother.

Murial looked around wildly as the building trembled again. The weird tinkling seeming to come out of the air around them. "Puddle-nose is my middle sister Malenda's. We don't know his real name. Malenda was killed before we even knew about the boy. Wan-Edhe apparently uses derisive words instead of names, and—" She slapped her hands together. "Never *mind* that," she said as another tremor ran through the building. "I'm babbling." She gripped her head with her fingers as if to hold her skull together.

"When did you sleep last, Murial?"

The hands came down, revealing ravaged eyes. "I don't know."

"Breathe." Erai-Yanya said with a calm she didn't feel. "Think. You know what Gwasan would tell us if she were here. If you can't do anything about this building shaking, whatever the cause, then we must act where we can."

"Here?"

"Chwahirsland."

Murial's eyes widened. "What?"

"Think about it, Murial. Wan-Edhe, who has ruled over eighty years, which should be an impossibility, is now completely out of reach. He probably transferred straight to his flagship this morning when they docked. Nothing in his history indicates he would risk himself away from his citadel for a four-month ocean journey, or however long it takes to get from the other side of the Sartoran continent to here. So whatever his intent, well, is there a chance we could discover something back in his citadel, if we act now? No one knows that he's gone, except that young Prince Kessler."

"Who could be taking the throne in Chwahirsland right now."

"Perhaps. But he said he was sent, and that was definitely Norsunder magic taking Wan-Edhe away. So we transfer to Chwahirsland, where we're bound to find Wan-Edhe's things awaiting his return." And on

Murial's doubtful look, "Come on. You're the one who did Queen Lammog's Back Door with Gwasan."

Murial nodded slowly. Like Erai-Yanya, she was never able to recollect without sharp regret their wild days as fearless mage students: Murial of Mearsies Heili, Erai-Yanya of Roth Drael, and Gwasan of Chwahirsland. They both knew that the mastery project called Queen Lammog's Back Door was, like so many mastery projects having to do with penetrating or comprehending dark magic, theoretical.

The time had come to see if it worked.

Murial drew in a deep breath. "For Gwasan," she said in a hard voice. "Whatever is going on with this quake is beyond us. The girls can be trusted to get the city evacuated. Let's go to Chwahirsland."

Long ago, the last great Chwahir queen had foreseen the troubles that had isolated Chwahirsland for the centuries to come. As Lammog Sonscarna was also a powerful mage, she had fashioned a magical trapdoor in the fortress central to Chwahirsland's capital, Narad. She had given the key to this backdoor to the Sartoran mage guild to be kept as a secret.

In a sense it was still largely a secret, though the trapdoor gradually had become an intricate magical puzzle for the rare magic journeymage interested in Chwahir history to solve before they could advance to mastery. Murial's friendship with Gwasan had prompted her to take that as her mastery project.

The result was right there in that library. She sprang to fetch the little hand-bound book, and looked down at her girlish handwriting as she repossessed the details.

Then, holding the book out so they both could read it, the two pronounced the transfer words together.

They appeared in another library, the transfer magic worse than either had ever experienced. It took a long time to recover, perhaps the longer because of the atmosphere, a lour of dark magic mixed with stale fug, weightier than the massive stone blocks around them.

Erai-Yanya choked, putting the crook of her elbow over her nose. The stuffy, oppressive air reeked of acrid male sweat.

Murial whispered, "Do you feel them? This place is *coated* with tracers and traps and wards."

"The whole thing is a trap," Erai-Yanya stated, glancing down at the central table. Light distorted, as if the table were farther away than it was. "But look at those books."

Two magic books lay open on the table, as if recently consulted. Erai-Yanya took a cautious step closer. Murial reached toward one book, fingers spread to sense traps on the table itself. She felt nothing, which made sense as it was a work table, but she wouldn't put it past that horrible old man to make and remove traps every time he worked on one of his destructive projects.

She pulled a pen from her sleeve, where she always kept one in reach, and extended it to the book, which was written in Chwahir. The pen wavered as it neared the book, its nib glowing greenish in warning. She snatched it back and squinted down at the books, taking care not to let any part of her clothing brush against the table.

She'd had to learn the rudiments of the Chwahir language to do her project; some of it came back, enough for her to say, "These appear to be written in two different languages."

Erai-Yanya ventured in a circle around the table. Her magical senses wavered, expanded and contracted in a slow, sluggish manner that made her skin crawl and her stomach lurch.

Murial glanced up with her lips crimped as if she were going to be sick. "This is beyond us. Much beyond."

Erai-Yanya nodded. "Let's get out of here. I can't even breathe anymore. I don't think the air in here has changed for a century."

## Chapter Four

ON the mountaintop, another quake jolted the ground, severe enough to make people clutch at one another or hold out their arms for balance. Windows rattled in the houses.

"Spread the word," Clair yelled, her light voice barely audible above the grinding of stone. "The city is coming down. Everyone must leave!"

Hibern stopped on the terrace and gazed upward at the spires overhead. The palace was even more amazing when seen from this vantage, the mystery material nacreous in the spring light. Hibern was afraid that if those impossibly tall spires toppled, the entire town would be crushed.

If the Mearsieans hadn't caused the quake, and the Chwahir hadn't, then who? Who was watching them, and to what purpose? The back of her neck prickled with warning.

She shook off the dread and looked around. The last of the Chwahir were disappearing in one direction, while the Mearsieans dashed back to their houses, yelling at family, friends, and neighbors. Many ran back inside to grab belongings, but here and there people paused, touching bracelets or necklaces, and vanished.

"I'll go tell the staff," CJ offered, hopping anxiously from one bare foot to the other.

"Do. Then go to the Junky." Clair named the girls' underground hide-out. "Meet you there."

As CJ ran off, Clair turned to Hibern, her face almost as pale as her hair. "Did you see where my aunt went?"

"No. But Erai-Yanya seems to be with her."

"They must have gone to the cave. Trying magical protections."

"Cave?"

Clair pointed at their feet. "Below us. In the mountain. Above what we call the magic lake. There are beings in the water. One of the girls is actually from there, wearing human form."

Hibern stared at Clair in astonishment, wondering if this 'cave' was the Toaran Selenseh Redian, one of the mysterious caves full of what looked like, but were not, crystals that shed their own light. Some of the strongest indigenous magic pooled in those caves. As far as she knew there was only one on each continent.

This little kingdom, so small and isolated, tucked up in the right-hand corner of Toar, seemed to be full of mysteries. And the rest of the world appeared to be completely unaware. But then, the indigenous beings, whose magic was far more powerful than anything humans had achieved, had so far demonstrated no interest whatever in human conflicts, governments, or affairs. Except when they were angered by human excess.

Or so Hibern had been taught.

Clair said urgently, "We'd better get people safely away."

"I'll help," Hibern said as they raced together across the terrace, past the fountain, and into the first street of houses.

The rest of the day was spent covering the city street by street, some-times dodging falling flowerpots on window sills, or decorative bric-a-brac along eaves. The quakes were frequent, but never strong enough to knock the girls down as they ran along, flushing people from their homes.

Some were witless with fright, and needed someone telling them to move. Twice they caught thieves lurking on the verge of looting. One look at Clair sent both running off into the gathering darkness.

When the girls reached the last street, they looked back, shocked to see that the palace and its terrace lay far above their heads, broken pavement sliding slowly down raw-looking gouges in the side of the mountain. The palace still stood undamaged, glowing faintly as if the strange material absorbed the emerging starlight. As quakes shook and rumbled, the spires rang glassily above.

Finally Hibern and Clair seemed to be the last ones left. The streets had emptied, and doors stood gaping open in houses, no one inside.

Another quake jolted through, cracking windows. The girls' stomachs dropped as their hands reached wide in instinctive balance.

"The ground is starting to slant," Hibern said shakily, arms out wide.

Clair shouted, "I need to check that the girls got safely to the Junky!" She clutched a medallion on a necklace, and held out her free hand.

Hibern closed her fingers around that small, square hand, hoping whatever transfer magic lay on that medallion was strong enough for two.

One last vicious transfer-jolt, and they fell heavily to the floor. Hibern blinked away the vertigo, to discover herself lying in the center of a brightly woven rug in what appeared to be a cave carved out of soil, with tree rootlets working in and out of the rounded ceiling overhead.

The light from glowglobes fell on furnishings set against the equally rough, curved walls. On these walls pictures had been affixed, obviously drawn by the girls themselves. At either end of the round room tunnels led off, one upward, one downward.

Hibern sat up, her head panging, and saw most of Clair's gang surrounding a figure lying on the smoothed dirt floor near the downward-leading tunnel. This was a lanky teenage boy with limp black hair and the pasty complexion of the Chwahir. He stirred, groaned, then subsided. A lump distorted the side of his head.

"Ugh!" CJ exclaimed as Hibern approached.

"I found Jilo lying on the floor in Kwenz's magic chamber," Puddlenose said. "The other Chwahir had abandoned him. Or maybe they didn't know he was there. I think a bookcase fell on him during one of the quakes. There were books all over the floor, and smashed wood."

"You shoulda . . ." CJ glanced at Clair, halted, and crossed her arms, scowling. "Well, what are we going to do with him?"

Clair shut her eyes. "I don't know."

Puddlenose said cheerily, "Until you do, I'll tie him up and stash him somewhere. Got a handy closet down here?"

"Use my room," offered a tall, soft-spoken girl.

Clair sighed. "I'll think about Jilo later. If only I knew where my—"

Transfer magic buffeted them, forcing them back. Murial, then Erai-Yanya, appeared in the middle of the multi-colored rag rug. Hibern, Clair, and her friends stilled as the greenish-gray complexions of the women mottled. Erai-Yanya swallowed convulsively, and Murial leaned down, hands on her knees as her breath shuddered.

"Aunt Murial!" Clair said, voice high with relief. "Where have you been all this time? Were you in the cave?"

The woman leaned against the archway decorated with clumsily drawn patterns of leaves and four-fold flowers, echoing the time-blurred carvings Hibern had noticed in the archways of that amazing palace on the mountain.

"No," Murial said hoarsely, wiped her shaking hand over her eyes. She cleared her throat, and began again. "Erai-Yanya and I were in Chwahirsland. Then transferred back to the palace before coming here. I would swear we were in Chwahirsland scarcely a turn of the finger glass, but night has fallen."

"Chwahirsland?" Clair repeated, her face blanched nearly as pale as her hair. "Why?"

"We thought to discover something of use, even if only a map indicating Wan-Edhe's plans. But all the books are written in the language of dark magic, and worse, the wards are lethal, far more layered than either of us have experience with."

Clair let her breath out in a long sigh. "Puddlenose told us a long time ago that you need magical protections to survive walking those halls."

Everybody looked at each other, then at Jilo, who was in the process of being dragged away by Puddlenose.

Clair pointed to Jilo's loose hands bumping over the ground before they vanished downward around the corner. She said slowly, "Jilo wears an onyx ring. That must be his protection."

Murial said, "Queen Lammog's spell only gains us access. I'm not the least surprised that moving about requires protection. Just standing there was as much as I could bear."

"I'm going back to Bereth Ferian to report everything we saw to the northern mages," Erai-Yanya said. *And to search the records for explanation of that palace on a cloud.* "As soon as I can stand another long transfer."

Murial was still thumbing her eyes, then dropped her hands. "And I had better see to replacing the border protections that Wan-Edhe destroyed."

They all knew that 'protections' in light magic were really not much better than tracers, warning spells when dark magic has been done. But warning was better than ignorance.

One of Clair's friends brought the two women cups of listerblossom steep.

They drank, exchanged looks, braced themselves in a way that ignited a visceral reaction in the others familiar with magic transfer, then with soft pops of air, they vanished.

Hibern said to Clair, "I don't know how much help this would be, but Senrid knows dark magic."

Senrid's name usually brought either blank looks, or grimaces of distrust.

To Hibern's surprise, Clair's demeanor brightened. "Senrid! Of course! He was a great help against Siamis. Sartora told us how he helped keep her out of Siamis's clutches."

CJ crossed her arms, scowling. "I still don't trust him," she muttered, and while Hibern knew it was a rational response, she couldn't prevent a pulse of resentment.

Clair turned to Hibern. "You know Senrid, don't you? Aren't you from his country? Should we ask him for help?"

Nothing was going as expected, but that didn't mean Hibern couldn't think ahead. Senrid expressed as much contempt for light magic workers as they did for him; he wouldn't be taught by any of them. Though Hibern wouldn't be a full mage for years, he'd asked her to tutor him. "You'll teach me what I need to know without all the blabber about high-mindedness and oh-we-are-so-pure," he'd said, his expression caustic.

And Hibern remembered that the Mearsieans had sheltered his younger cousin, refusing to send her back even after Senrid defeated his uncle.

Hibern blinked, and turned to Clair. "First. About Senrid's cousin Ndand . . ."

". . . and so that's it," Hibern finished relating to Senrid.

Senrid had listened in silence, his fingers pressed against his eyes, one of which was now completely closed. "I guess I could help. Clair isn't so bad. I talked to her a little up north, when we were running from Siamis. She was a whole lot less annoying than the rest of those magic school mages." He looked up, his puffy, bruised face making his expression difficult to read. "But she never sent my cousin home."

"That's next." Hibern flicked her fingers open, showing Senrid an open palm. "I asked about that, last thing. Your cousin Ndand isn't even in Mearsies Heili. She left. Went somewhere else, to study music."

Senrid struggled painfully up on one elbow. "Where? I can—"

Hibern said, "Ndand made Clair promise not to tell . . . anyone where she was going."

"Nobody besides me would ask," Senrid retorted, collapsing back again. In spite of the nasal plumminess of his voice, he still retained enough wit for that. "Tell who?"

"You," Hibern said, hating the conversation. But she and Senrid had always promised the truth to one another. Both had dealt with far too many lies. She hastened on. "Clair wanted you to know this, though. You aren't the problem. It's Ndand's father, your uncle. She's afraid he'll reappear from Norsunder. That you can't hold the kingdom against him. I'm sorry, Senrid."

He said with an attempt at briskness that didn't fool either of them, "At least I know Ndand's still alive. All right. As soon as I sleep off this kinthus. Right now I don't think I could walk across a room, much less smash my way past dark magic wards. But I'll go to Chwahirsland. You if anyone would know why."

Hibern grimaced. Her own father had been an associate of this wretched King of the Chwahir, through whom he'd obtained the experimental mind control spells that the former regent had asked for. *If* Senrid could get into a citadel that no one had broached for at least a century. Hibern made a mental note to ask the details of Queen Lammog's Back Door, and make certain Senrid knew them.

"Come back tomorrow," Senrid said. "It might already be too late, but . . ." He made a weary movement, flicking his fingers.

"Tomorrow," Hibern repeated, and left.

Outside Senrid's room, she drew in a deep breath. Her head panged. Three long transfers in one very long day, and two more ahead. But she'd promised. This was to be her future, if she wanted to be a mage. She had to get used to it.

Anyway, she was just as glad to get away from the hurt that Senrid had tried to hide about his cousin.

Clair had given Hibern her medallion-necklace, bespelled to transfer one directly back to the girls' underground hideout.

When she recovered, Hibern blinked away the tiny stars at the edge of her vision, a warning that she'd been using too much transfer magic. One more, she thought. One more. "Senrid is going to go with me tomorrow." She held out the necklace.

"We got Jilo's ring," Clair said, taking the medallion back from Hibern, then pointing to where a glinting black circle lay on top of a small bookcase.

"I'll return tomorrow, then," Hibern said.

And transferred back to Roth Drael, where she found Erai-Yanya had arrived ahead of her. The senior mage was in the midst of slicing bread and cheese.

"There you are," Erai-Yanya said cheerfully, using the knife handle to brush back an unruly lock of brown hair from her tumbling bun. "I knew those girls wouldn't stay up north in safety. Clair is just like her aunt. Murial was always dashing off home when we were mage students, mostly to rescue her appalling siblings."

Hibern suspected the cheerful talk was meant to distract her from thinking about Marloven Hess. Every mention of home or family hurt, and she suspected would always hurt.

Erai-Yanya pushed a plate of sliced fruit and fresh bread toward Hibern, saying, "For now Wan-Edhe is gone, though if Norsunder has him, he will no doubt be sent back at the worst time."

She glanced at the day glass on its pedestal in the corner, and the hour or two of sands left to trickle through before dawn, and added prosaically, "But not today. So. While you were on your errand, I did my duty and reported to Oalthoreh at the northern school. She said she would pass my report to the Sartoran mages." Erai-Yanya gestured southward with her bread, and then glanced down at her sash, and the knot still tied in it. "You were there when I tied this, right? So much was going on I forgot why I tied it. Can you remember what it was I was supposed to do?"

Hibern gazed in surprise. She knew about Erai-Yanya's habit of tying a knot somewhere to help her remember something she needed to do. But she'd always remembered the knots. "Was it about Wan-Edhe?"

"It must have been," Erai-Yanya said, in a dissatisfied tone. She untied it and smoothed the worn fabric. "So that's that."

"Not quite," Hibern said, and told her what she, Clair, and Senrid had decided, ending, "And so, whatever Senrid learns, he said he'd share. Like everyone keeps saying, our ignorance is the enemy's first weapon. And I have no idea why, because Mearsies Heili is so small, with no strategic importance whatsoever, but Clair said that this wasn't the first time Wan-Edhe moved against them."

'Strategic importance.' Erai-Yanya knew that Hibern wasn't thinking magically, but militarily. She drank some fresh berry juice to hide her grimace. Hibern could not help her upbringing any more than Gwasan had, all those years before.

Gwasan had had the habit of making similar remarks, until she learned better. During their student days, she, Murial, and Gwasan had covered for one another when they'd felt the necessity to steal away in spite of the strict rules. Murial had invariably returned home to deal with whatever disasters her siblings were causing their father, who had had four children over a number of years, all by different mothers.

Gwasan's private excursions had always stayed private, until she left the school for the last time, an assassin from home right behind her.

Erai-Yanya's private expeditions had been ventures into magical experiments that she knew she was ready for, but that the school's strict ladder of permissions forbade.

All three had had what they considered vital reasons for breaking the rules. In retrospect, out of all of them, her own were probably the most dangerous and least well-thought-out, which had proved to Erai-Yanya that the rules were there for a reason.

So when she had taken on this Marloven student, who would have been summarily rejected by both schools because of her birth kingdom, Erai-Yanya had made a vow to avoid setting rules in favor of talking out situations, especially as Hibern had been used to struggling against a nearly impossible situation on her own.

As a result, Hibern talked to her. Erai-Yanya prided herself on that. But there were times when she was not as forthcoming in return. This was one of those times; she knew how Hibern would react if she pointed out how adamant both mage schools would be about preventing Senrid of Marloven Hess from gaining access to what probably was the best collection of concentrated evil intent in the world. So she just said, "Senrid wants to explore in the Chwahir capital?"

Hibern nicked her chin toward her collarbones, fighting impatience. Erai-Yanya wasn't forbidding her, but her long silence, followed by the question in the carefully neutral tone of adults, meant distrust.

It was a justified distrust, Hibern had to admit. If you didn't know Senrid. He'd been raised to think violence the first tool of kings, and when Hibern first met him, they had been enemies. But he had slowly, painfully, begun to change.

"He's in no shape to be raiding Wan-Edhe's library for evil magic, if that's what you're thinking," Hibern said. "Even if he wanted such. He doesn't. He's seen the cost. Lived it. He really does think in terms of defense, knowing what your enemy is capable of. And the enemy he fears is not his neighbors but Norsunder."

Erai-Yanya exerted herself to sound approving. "That is an excellent idea, actually. So excellent that, rather than train you in Queen

Lammog's Back Door, which is complicated and dangerous, partaking of dark magic, I'll go with you. Also because we still cannot explain why Murial and I were gone no more than the turn of the finger glass, but returned several hours later. So I'm going to prepare a time candle."

Hibern exclaimed, "Oh, what a good idea."

Erai-Yanya shook her head. "Everything this day has been disturbing. Some mysterious connection between the Chwahir and Norsunder? Some kind of artifact that swallows a group of people? I have deep misgivings about powerful ancient relics suddenly turning up, when we've gone centuries without 'em."

Busy, determined, the two turned their minds to all these problems, and once again the mystery of the white palace sank below the surface of their thoughts, and faded out of memory.

The day following, Hibern again endured the long transfer to Marloven Hess, though she had misgivings about Senrid's ability to sit up, much less sustain a magic transfer. However, a promise was a promise.

But when she was conducted to his study, there he sat, squinting down at some papers with his one good eye, an empty cup beside his hand. His other eye was swollen shut. His hands looked as raw and bruised and swollen as his face. Hibern smelled listerblossom in the air.

"Are we still doing this?" he asked, his voice plummy.

"Erai-Yanya is already in the Chwahir capital, with Clair."

"You have transfer tokens? I can't make any right now."

She frowned. "Senrid, are you able to transfer? You look—"

"I know what I look like. Let's go."

Transfer magic is always jolting. The farther one goes, the stronger the wrench, though no more time elapses; the distance is felt in the transfer reaction. When you add magical spells forcing past wards, it doubles the intensity.

Hibern and Senrid both emerged staggering. Hibern shut her eyes and gulped for breath, aware of a sour tinge to the air, the smell of a tightly closed room with heaps of old laundry and unwashed bedding, and under that the metallic nastiness of layers of dark magic.

She felt the last tremors of transfer reaction fade rapidly, and turned her head to discover Senrid leaning against the wall, fingers splayed against it, both eyes shut. The little portion of his face that had not been bruised looked distinctly greenish in the pale light of a glowglobe.

She tried to find words to ask if he was all right—words that would not get her nose snapped off—but then his good eye opened, and he said, "Where?"

They turned, to meet the twin shocked gazes of Clair and Erai-Yanya taking in Senrid's battered condition, the thin flame of Erai-Yanya's time candle reflecting in their eyes. But Erai-Yanya was by nature an observer, and seldom spoke before those she didn't trust—and Clair knew how much Senrid hated being weak.

So she only pointed to the inner room, the thick, moldy lour curling its vapors in her throat if she tried to speak.

Senrid walked slowly into what had to be a magic chamber, his hands held out, fingers spread as he used every sense to detect lethal wards. This was certainly a place to expect lethal wards.

And there were. Erai-Yanya had brought an old quill to test for further wards and traps. A long table dominated the room, which was otherwise bare stone age-darkened with mold in the grouting. Around three sides, bookshelves extended nearly to the ceiling, and it was to these Erai-Yanya moved first, testing with her feather, as Senrid drifted toward the table, looking down at the books lying there, some open. It was clear that Wan-Edhe had expected to return.

Senrid began muttering, and the greenish flash of magic strengthened the metallic singe in the air, then all four sensed a chain of wards breaking. A chain. So much magic potential bound for such little purpose.

Senrid rapped the table lightly with his fingertips, and when nothing happened, Erai-Yanya set her little hour candle down in its wooden holder. The flame burned steadily, sometimes flashing greenish, and once, a disturbing blue.

Erai-Yanya thought sourly that that bruised-looking bluish flame was Wan-Edhe's effect on the world in living metaphor. Clair wondered if there was anything in this terrible place that could help them ward against Wan-Edhe when he came back (because she didn't believe for a moment he was gone forever—of course Norsunder would send him back) and Senrid faced the realization that this situation was far beyond his knowledge. He should be studying harder, but when would he find the time?

Erai-Yanya cautiously extended her quill toward the books on the shelves, then lowered her arm and glanced Senrid's way. "Can you remove any wards on these?"

Senrid took a step toward the bookshelves, one hand out, then shook his head. "Only the ones I know. But it'll take time. Every book is separately warded. And there are traps beneath 'em. On top of 'em. And . . ." He raised his head, squinting up at the top shelves. "I think there are even more up there."

Clair pointed at the table. "These must be the books he was using before he invaded Mearsies Heili. What are they?"

"That's what I want to find out." Senrid moved back to the table. "That one seems to be written in Chwahir, I guess, as I've never seen the alphabet. This one here is . . . dark magic. I recognize some of the words . . ."

He looked back at the one written in Chwahir, switching his gaze between the two books. "This one is his experiment book, or one of his experiment books," he said slowly, with an air of uncertainty as he touched the book.

Erai-Yanya eyed him, as questions bloomed in her mind. "You know Chwahir after all?"

"No. But these words are all in Sartoran, the version used for dark magic. And I can see the same number of letters in sentences here and here. Patterns, you might say. So I'm assuming he's chained experiments onto these spells. Experiments."

"What type of experiments?"

Senrid flashed a quick look her way. It was easy to see that she didn't trust him as far as she could throw a mountain.

Hibern and Clair saw him hesitate, though his distorted face gave even less clue to his thoughts than usual. Then he shrugged, and bent over the dark magic book.

The others waited, Clair trying not to breathe too deeply in the poisonous lour, until they understood that he was done talking. Hibern and Clair both suspected the reason, and Clair cast a speculative look Erai-Yanya's way.

The mage sensed the Marloven boy shutting her out, and turned to examine the shelves, to hide her disgust. She had spent a night digging out all her notes from her days of study with Gwasan and Murial, before Wan-Edhe killed Gwasan. She knew she only had a partial list of spells to remove traps and wards, but she began to try those, as behind her, Senrid leafed through the experiment book.

Erai-Yanya successfully removed three wards before she nearly killed herself in a trap. She sensed the building of magic as internal heat, then Senrid snapped, "Don't!"

Erai-Yanya had already abandoned the spell a heartbeat before he spoke, but she said gravely, "Thank you," as an oblique truce.

He heard it as typical lighter condescension, suspecting she'd made a judgment about evil Marlovens before he'd even turned up. Or else why was she even here? It was Hibern who'd asked him to come.

Hibern glanced between them, understanding that nothing was going to be learned. Meanwhile, her head throbbed. "This air is making me sick," she said.

At the same time, Erai-Yanya pointed to the time candle. "It's nearly gone. I think we'd better go." She rubbed her temples, forgetting the quill in her hand, which jabbed her in the ear. Her breath hissed out.

Senrid had been studying the experiment book. He backed away, and approached Clair. "Didn't Puddlenose talk about a boy our age who was Wan-Edhe's current target?"

"Jilo is sort of an heir, but mostly like a hostage," Clair said. "Wan-Edhe would never have a real heir. He wants to live forever."

Senrid snorted in contempt, then muttered, "If you trust the hostage, then tell him to take a look at that page right there, all set up for renewal. I think . . . I'm not sure . . . I think it's the sort of mind control spells my uncle was messing around with. The patterns are familiar—I'm almost certain my uncle got that magic from Wan-Edhe, or his brother."

He stopped then, aware of Erai-Yanya and Hibern looking his way.

"Wan-Edhe and your uncle were allies?" Erai-Yanya asked, eyes stark.

"No," Senrid said shortly.

Clair said peaceably, "Prince Kwenz and Senrid's uncle traded magic books. But that's all I know."

Hibern put in, "Makes no sense to have an alliance, as Marloven Hess and Chwahirsland lie at opposite ends of the continent."

Senrid had gone back to studying the two books, then carefully fingered his good eye, blinking several times.

"I think we are done here," Erai-Yanya said, and waited until Senrid was safely gone before transferring home.

When they recovered, all four got quite a shock: the time candle had been set for half an hour . . . but the entire day had vanished.

## Chapter Five

*Mearsies Heili, the Junky*

NOW I must introduce one who will become an important member of the Young Allies, though no one, he least of all, would have thought of a Chwahir being anyone's ally. Being accepted as anyone's ally.

Another quake rolled through Mearsies Heili.

Jilo, son of Quartermaster Dzan, had been chosen by old Prince Kwenz Sonscarna of the Chwahir for his meticulous bookkeeping and excellent handwriting. Perhaps the old man had seen something of himself in the boy, or perhaps he merely chose him out of idleness, but he'd been training Jilo in magic as well as in running the outpost. He'd even enjoyed sitting up in his magic library, talking about the fundamentals of magic with Jilo, who couldn't get enough of magic studies.

Now, Jilo sat against the dirt wall of the Mearsieans' underground hideout, hands tied behind his back and ankles bound, his head throbbing and his heart beating in his ears as the cave bedchamber around him rumbled. Rocks ground in the walls and dirt ceiling above his head, and tree roots creaked and shivered.

But again, no dirt sifted down from the smooth ceiling, and no roots broke through the walls decorated with pictures. The rumble subsided, as had the many before it. The Mearsieans might be weak and sentimental, their light magic as strong as candle wax, but their spells seemed to be holding this cave chamber together.

Jilo had been trying to puzzle out what had happened, but thought seemed to come slower than ever, a jumble of confusing memories that seemed to have no connection. He tried unsuccessfully to ease his aching arms, then gave up with a sigh.

The world seemed to be nothing but contradiction. Prince Kwenz and his brother Wan-Edhe had both lectured Jilo about how the waxers were stupid, weak, and sentimental, and deserving of being conquered. The Chwahir rulers despised as sentimental and weak those who practiced light magic. The term 'waxer' had started out as slang for the lowest of the low—usually women—who followed nighttime military parades, scraping up the wax drippings from torches, to be used again, dirty as it was.

Worst of all waxers were these Mearsiean brats, entirely ignorant about military discipline or training, and yet they ran around free. They'd even managed to make this underground hideout, which Jilo envied, and wanted almost as much as he'd wanted to be left alone to his studies and sketches.

And here he was.

But a prisoner.

"They are stupid," Wan-Edhe had said repeatedly.

Jilo knew the Mearsieans weren't stupid. The weakness was debatable. Or maybe that was his excuse for his own failures against them. And he *had* failed. He was still alive only because he'd always done what he was told. Another truism of life among the Chwahir was that heirs weren't exempt from extreme disciplinary measures should they disobey orders, or make mistakes.

Especially heirs, for Wan-Edhe had no true heirs, having systematically killed off his entire family save only Kwenz, his brother, and Prince Kessler, who had escaped at a young age—though not young enough to keep a hold on sanity, from all accounts. Wan-Edhe fully intended to live forever. He'd held Chwahirsland in his ever-tighter grip for more than eighty years.

Though Kwenz was the elder, he'd always deferred to Wan-Edhe, which was probably the single reason he was still alive. If he was still alive. The last thing Jilo remembered was Prince Kwenz being sent to do some kind of magic in support of his brother's latest attack against the Mearsieans, though the frail old man could barely move, these days. Jilo had used the chance to nip into the forbidden magic chambers for some unsupervised study, but then there was this loud, grinding noise, the castle stones shifting, and his stool had tipped over, pitching him backward.

Then he woke tied up in this chamber, where he'd been ever since. Except when Puddlenose brought meals, untied him, and lounged in the doorway, sword in hand, until he finished eating. Then it was back to handkerchiefs around wrists and ankles and another stretch of bone-aching tedium. At least he'd been able to feel that lump on the back of his head, and that it was going down.

Jilo tried to ease his stiff neck, stilling as a small quake shivered the cave around him. He sat with his back against the cave wall, his head uncomfortably bent forward to avoid bumping the tender spot on his head against the smooth dirt wall.

He sat between a clothes trunk decorated with painted flowers and a shelf containing ornaments. The Mearsieans didn't even seem to have a prison, at least not in this cave hideout, for they'd stuck him in a bedroom.

He didn't know how long he'd been a prisoner, not that it mattered. Jilo didn't want to think of what disciplinary measures Wan-Edhe would deem suitable for a Chwahir who had let himself get captured. He knew only that if he survived, the punishment would last a long time.

Maybe Clair was trying a hostage exchange. Jilo could have told her it was futile, that Wan-Edhe would sooner see him dead.

Let the Mearsieans find out the hard way. His report to Wan-Edhe would have to begin with scoffing about the ruffle-edged cover on the bed over there, and the awkwardly drawn sketches of animals and people affixed to the dirt walls. Waxer sentiment was also evident in the fact the girl the room belonged to had set the single candle high on a shelf so it wouldn't worry at Jilo's magically altered eyes.

Clair's cousin Puddlenose was another contradiction. Jilo couldn't understand anyone who'd keep a ridiculous name because (he said) it was so much fun to see officious clerks writing it out. Puddlenose seemed to regard that shameful, humiliating name as a badge of triumph.

The kind of mind finding triumph in that was as incomprehensible as the Mearsiean perceptions of the Chwahir. Jilo could not reconcile them. His head hurt inside as well as outside when he tried. How could the Mearsieans laugh at Wan-Edhe's given name, Shnit, one passed down by many Chwahir kings? In Chwahirsland it was now dreaded so much that no one whispered it out loud, as if he had spells that spied if anyone said his name, the way Norsunder was supposed to have. *Everyone* referred to Shnit Sonscarna as Wan-Edhe, *The* King.

While Jilo stewed as their prisoner, in the tunnel directly above him, Clair, CJ, and Puddlenose debated what to do with him.

CJ was in full rant mode. A short, skinny figure even for twelve, she stamped barefooted in a circle around the cousins, who sat on the brightly colored woven rug that covered the smooth cave floor. Nothing about CJ's moods was ever subtle.

". . . and so, I think it's a big mistake to let Jilo go free."

Another quake rumbled through, as if in emphasis to her words. Instinctively they all looked up, though all they could see was the dirt ceiling overhead, marbled by tree roots.

"That one was different," Clair said. "I'd better check."

"Again," CJ sighed.

Clair heard the sighed word a heartbeat before the transfer took her. She could understand CJ's puzzlement. Clair wasn't sure why she had to keep checking. There was nothing she could do, and for such a monumentally dramatic event, there actually wasn't much to see: the white palace seemed undamaged, as far as she could tell, and all one could see of the city was a lot of white fog extending eastward from Mount Marcus. A fog that was lower every time she looked at it.

With Clair gone, CJ scowled down at Puddlenose, who lounged in the middle of the brightly colored patchwork rug on the smooth dirt floor. "You shouldn't have brought Jilo here," she said, fists on her hips.

He only shrugged. As usual. He rarely took anything seriously—not with a wild past like his. He didn't even have a real name, or at least if he did, it had long ago been forgotten, along with his real parents. Puddlenose had heard nothing but insults from Wan-Edhe from his earliest memories, the one used most—for a sniveling, frightened little boy—having been Puddlenose.

After CJ had stamped around the edge of the rug three times, she pointed to the floor, below which their prisoner sat. "I just wish Jilo wasn't *here*. For one thing, I'm scared Clair is going to just let him go."

"What else should she do? Execute him?"

"That would make us just like the Chwahir," CJ retorted. "I think, oh, we should find some spell and turn him into a petunia for a hundred years. Let someone else worry about what to do with him."

At Puddlenose's skeptical look, she relented. "Ten years, maybe. Look, you know as well as I do that Jilo is nothing better than a villain-in-training."

Puddlenose shrugged. "Don't know anything of the kind."

CJ scoffed. "He's a friend?"

Puddlenose shrugged again. "Don't know what to call it, except maybe a truce. Once or twice. When Wan-Edhe had us both under death threats."

CJ scowled down at the rug.

"It was either truce or—" Puddlenose drew a finger across his neck. "And we talked. Sort of. And he looked the other way when I escaped. I don't claim to know much of what he thinks, but I do know he hates Norsunder as much as we do."

CJ jerked her skinny shoulders up and down. "So he hates the eleveners! That just makes sense. But what about us? If we let him go, what's to stop him from coming after us just like Wan-Edhe has sixty billion times?"

"Ben doesn't think Jilo will," Puddlenose said, glancing around the room for the boy who could shape-change into birds or animals. "Ben's the one who listened to Kwenz and Jilo most."

CJ's scowl eased for about a heartbeat. She liked and trusted the boy who had spied on the Chwahir for Clair, but Ben wasn't present in either boy or beast shape.

CJ crossed her arms. "What you want to bet Ben's not coming anywhere near the hideout until we get rid of Jilo, any more than the girls are coming out of their rooms?"

Her goading tone caused nothing more than another shrug. Puddlenose was used to CJ's moods. He thought of them as personal thunderstorms, loud and messy for a time, then soon gone.

"Jilo is our responsibility."

The two turned at the sound of Clair's voice. She walked down the tunnel and plopped on the rug beside her cousin. "As far as I can tell, the cloud city seems to have settled along the east side of the mountain and a ways beyond."

Puddlenose said, "Who wants to bet your plateau was what got lifted into the air in the first place?"

"I think it is too obvious for betting," Clair said in her careful way. "As far as I can tell, many of the buildings lost their windows, and probably glass things inside, and the streets are a jumble of brick and cobblestone. But everything else is still there."

"The white palace?"

"Not even a window broken," Clair said, and returned inexorably to the issue at hand. "Anyway, I think it's time to let Jilo go. I don't see what else we can do."

CJ smacked her hands over her face. "Let him *go*?"

Clair said, "But we don't have to tell him everything—"

"We shouldn't tell him *anything*," CJ burst out, and around they went again.

Clair knew the argument was going in circles, but that was often the only way to achieve consensus. She could see she wasn't going to get it this time.

Everyone knew the final decision was hers, so when she got to her feet, CJ and Puddlenose both fell silent.

Clair said, "I can't do a wrong thing just because I think Jilo might."

She took a step in the direction of the tunnel leading to the lower levels, then paused, arms lifting wide as another strong quake rolled through.

"Wow," CJ exclaimed. "It's been, what, three years? Four? Since I escaped from Earth, and I know you said that magic is supposed to take away the dangerous quakes, but those things still scare me."

"I don't see why the people of Earth don't control quakes with magic," Puddlenose said as they tramped down the tunnel, which curved around, with rooms leading off to the left and right; as they passed, a couple of Clair's gang peered out, saw where they were going, and vanished again behind their tapestry doors.

CJ grimaced. "Reason five thousand four hundred and thirty-two why I hate remembering living on Earth: no magic."

"I find that so hard to believe." Puddlenose shook his head. "No magic. Huh."

"But plenty of smog." CJ snorted.

They reached the flower-and-vine tapestry door to the room Jilo was kept in. CJ and Puddlenose stood aside so that Clair could remove the ward spell protecting the doorway. It vanished with a flash of glittery light, then the tapestry that served in place of a door was batted aside.

Jilo lifted his head and squinted their way as Puddlenose entered, his tanned, square face—usually good-humored, even in a scrap—rueful. At his shoulder was Clair, square-faced like her cousin, but there the resemblance ended. Most noticeable was that weird white hair.

Last came CJ, shorter even than Clair, scrawny and glowering. CJ was, and looked, ready for verbal battle. Jilo hated her more than all the rest of Clair's irritating, obnoxious gang of girls.

"A lot has happened," Clair said abruptly. "I'll start with what everyone knows: your king is gone."

As always, as soon as the enemy was nearby, Jilo found it difficult to think, even difficult to see. It was like thoughts were reduced to one or two fireflies bumbling around in fog. The more he tried to follow them, the worse they winked in and out of existence.

"What?" Jilo couldn't help it. He saw the contempt in CJ's face, emphasized by the scornful crimp in her black brows, but it was no stronger than the contempt surging through him. Why couldn't he think? He really was as stupid as Wan-Edhe constantly claimed.

Clair looked doubtfully down at their prisoner, who stared back, his magically altered eyes squinting, which was a mercy. At least when he squinted they didn't have to see that unnatural blackness, as if he were an empty shell containing only darkness. She didn't like to think that about anyone, but it was hard to tell your mind not to notice what your eyes saw.

Puddlenose said, "Clair asked me to go to the Shadowland under white flag to look for you or Kwenz. And tell your people to evacuate. Kwenz was dead, someone said. Dropped down clutching his heart when the quakes started. I found you lying in Kwenz's book room. So I brought you here."

"As what?" Jilo found his voice. "Wan-Edhe wouldn't trade for my life."

"Wan-Edhe," Clair repeated, "is gone."

"And so is the Shadowland," CJ said in a gloating voice from behind Clair's shoulder.

"Gone?" Jilo repeated, wincing as a pang shot through his forehead. He tried to recapture the sense that he'd been here before, that the conversation had come full circle.

"Squashed flat." CJ clapped her hands, grinning smugly. "The cloud city came down on top of it. All your people skedaddled."

He became aware of the quick patter of footsteps, and opened his eyes to discover a thin, shaggy-haired brown boy more or less CJ's age. Ben was dressed in a rumpled gray lace-up tunic and old, baggy gray kneepants, his feet bare. Ben didn't like to admit to strangers that he could shape-change. He was not about to tell Jilo that he'd been wearing the form of an eagle; that he'd seen Jilo fall, and if Puddlenose hadn't found him, Ben would have seen to it that he'd be found.

"Kessler came for Wan-Edhe. Straight out of Eleven-Land," Puddlenose said.

Eleven-Land, Jilo knew, was the waxer euphemism for Norsunder. He still didn't know why they called it that, and on impulse said, "Why?"

Three faces looked at him as if he'd sprouted wings. "Why what?"

"You say 'eleven' for Norsunder. I've heard you."

Clair's face reddened, and she looked away. Definitely a euphemism, then.

Puddlenose said, "Insult."

Clair glanced at him, then said earnestly, "My aunt says that Norsunder used the number themselves, at first, as a kind of nasty hit against the Ancient Sartoran Twelve Blessed Things. They were going to destroy them one by one. But they never got past eleven for some reason or other, maybe the Fall of Ancient Sartor."

"Or maybe our side lost count," Puddlenose said cheerfully. "At least, if anyone knows what those Twelve Blessed Things are, they do seem to be pretty much . . ." He drew his finger across his throat and made a squelching noise.

Clair finished, "So 'eleven' became the word to say if you didn't like to speak of Norsunder. It's bad manners in some places."

Jilo had asked because he wanted to know if they would answer. Having no interest in Norsunder, old theories of magic, blessed things, or bad words, his thoughts went straight to Prince Kessler, who was the only person Jilo found more terrifying than Wan-Edhe. Warning tightened his neck. Kwenz dead, and Wan-Edhe now in Norsunder? Wan-Edhe had always claimed autonomy from Norsunder, hiding in his fortress protected by decades of carefully interlocked, deadly wards.

But though he was a powerful mage in his own right, eventually you had to pay. Norsunder never forgot bargains.

"Does that mean Norsunder is taking over Chwahirsland?" Jilo asked, though why he asked the Mearsieans, he wasn't sure. But his thoughts seemed to come from farther away than ever, now more like little wormy things groping around in the dark, and less like flies.

"Not yet," Clair said. "But this is what we know," she said, gesturing for Puddlenose to loosen the bonds around Jilo's wrists. "Right now, the Land of the Chwahir has no one on the throne."

Jilo's head felt like it did when someone clapped him over the ears, only this was worse, like an invisible vise was squashing his brain.

Jilo's hands were now free.

Puddlenose tossed the binding onto the bed, and stood back against the curved door frame, his arms folded, the old enemy. Though once or twice, just for survival, they'd had almost what could have been called a truce. Never acknowledged by either afterward.

Jilo hesitated, then with a mental shrug reached to untie his ankles. The Mearsieans didn't stop him.

"There's no place for you here," Clair said. "I think most of Kwenz's warriors left the Shadowland, under the command of someone from

Chwahirsland. They crowded onto the ships the invaders brought from Chwahirsland, and sailed away on this morning's tide."

Jilo felt the last knot give, and he kicked free of the silk.

He looked up. "Wan-Edhe will come back if he can."

CJ crossed her arms, her scowl now a glare. "We know. But if we smell that grunge-bearded old geez, we'll be ready." She flexed her bare toes and made a kicking motion.

Clair said, "In the meantime, let me point out again that there's no one on the throne in Chwahirsland."

"Prince Kessler has to be there," Jilo said.

Clair said, "As of yesterday, no one is. Some friends went to scout, but they only stayed a short time, because there are so many wards and traps. In spite of this." Clair held out a small black circle, and Jilo felt at the base of his little finger.

He hadn't even noticed his ring was gone. Jilo blinked at her as he slid the ring back into place. Though he was taller than the Mearsiean girls, roughly the same age as Puddlenose, Clair and her noisy, irritating gang had always managed to combine and defeat him when he'd tried to find and take this hideout, a perfect retreat where Wan-Edhe would never have found him.

His private conviction was that Clair's gang was more like a Chwahir *twi*—a group of eight, the fundamental unit of Chwahir life—than the false twi, spies all, that Wan-Edhe had formed around Jilo. Now all gone, leaving him to be found by an enemy.

Jilo retrieved enough thought-flies to realize he'd been staring.

His heart thumped as he stood uncertainly, waiting for their laughter if he tried to make a break for the door. What then, the knife? That was a favorite ploy among the Chwahir, to let prisoners think they'd escaped just long enough to make it really hurt when they were brought down again. And again. And again, until they gave up.

So he stared at his enemies, and the enemies stared at his strange black eyes with no hint of white, his lips chapped from too much biting, his greasy black hair hanging lank and unkempt on his brow.

Clair took a step back, holding her hand out toward the doorway.

Jilo took one step. Then another. A third. He heard CJ mutter to Clair, "It seems so weird to let a villain just go."

*A villain.* She meant him. Jilo snorted. A meaningless term, 'villain'— at least, when applied to someone like Jilo, who had always done what he'd been told, and tried to survive. Villains were Norsundrians, the ones with power, the ones who tried to take whole worlds, who consumed souls. Or they were Clair's gang, so galling with their fast talk and incomprehensible private jokes and smug superiority about their underground hideout.

Five, six, eight steps . . . Twenty. Jilo passed CJ, who held her nose, her fierce blue eyes a scowl above the pinching fingers. Much as he despised her, her obvious hatred was oddly steadying. He didn't trust anything else about this situation, but he could trust her hatred to be real.

Clair said, "Before you go, I'd like to ask you a question."

Jilo shrugged. Here was the expected ploy, the slammed door, the real end. "See me stopping you?"

"Are you coming back here with an army?" Clair asked.

Jilo snorted a humorless laugh. "If I understand you, the Shadowland is now crushed under your city. Kwenz is dead, everyone else gone."

Unless she meant . . . She couldn't mean . . . They all expected him to transfer halfway around the world, walk in and take the throne of Chwahirsland itself.

The magnitude of the idea defeated him at first, and he stared at the floor, trying to think, and found that—as always—when he needed clear thought, it would not come.

He looked up. Clair stood before him, waiting.

He remembered her question.

A few facts squirmed their way to consciousness. He said, "It never made any sense to come months' journey by ship just to take this tiny country."

"No," Clair said.

"But that never stopped King Beardo the Stink in Human Form," CJ put in.

"Prince Kwenz said that that was Wan-Edhe's preoccupation with the old enmity between the Chwahir and Tser Mearsies," Jilo said. "I think. If he had any other purpose, he never shared it."

The Mearsieans stood in silence while he grasped that the old goal had gone with Wan-Edhe. He didn't have to do *anything* that Wan-Edhe had ordered.

He was free.

So he said, "No. I would not."

Clair nodded. "Then I have something to tell you. In Wan-Edhe's magic chambers, Senrid, one of the people who went there yesterday, said there is a book on the big table, open to a page you ought to see, first thing."

Jilo found no point in saying anything more. He gathered his concentration enough to make a short transfer spell, to the usual Destination point at the base of Mount Marcus, at the edge of the Shadowland.

The transfer worked, leaving him with the usual vertigo. He blinked, breathing deeply, his eyes tearing up from the strong sunlight. He raised a hand to shade them as best he could, and squinted around.

Instead of the long stretch of darkness to the east, shrouded by the dense vapor-bounded city above, he perceived the sloping line of the mountain, visible in the bright sunlight. Terraced down the east side, the tile rooftops clearly visible from where he stood, was the Mearsiean capital, roads a jumble of brick and tile. It would take a year to clean that up, he thought.

More important, it had completely buried the Shadowland fortress and its outlying buildings. The Shadowland really was gone. A faint pall of dust still scintillated high in the air, and another tiny quake rolled through.

Jilo stared at the aprons of rockfall that had cascaded down the rest of the mountain, smothering scrubby brush. This was all that was left of Kwenz's castle. All Kwenz's belongings. All Jilo's, not that he'd owned much beside the clothes he stood up in. Chwahir prentices were always dependent on their masters. Now all of it was gone.

Where were Kwenz's servants? Though Wan-Edhe would have had no compunctions about squashing them under a mountainside—in fact, he would have enjoyed the prospect—Jilo suspected that the waxers would have a moral objection to crushing enemies who hadn't been on the attack. Oh, yes, Puddlenose had said something about scuttling in all directions.

Now Jilo understood what that meant: the Mearsieans had gone through the Shadowland chasing people out while the cloud was descending.

Jilo squinted up the mountain, the daylight painful on his magically altered eyes. Tears leaked down his cheeks, but he ignored them as he studied the few spires of Clair's castle that were visible from this vantage, glinting in a sky murderously bright.

Wan-Edhe's harsh voice echoed in his ears, *You have a single goal. One goal! To take that white castle. And you can't even do that.*

And Prince Kwenz's snivelly reply, *You don't understand how much magic is on that castle.* To which Wan-Edhe would snarl, *Of course I do. Which is why I want it!*

Jilo turned away, hating the place all over again. Looking at that glaring whiteness in sunlight was like knives stabbing his eyeballs. He'd have to find the spell to restore his eyes to normal, or he'd go blind.

But first, he had to contemplate the idea that he was free.

He belonged nowhere.

He could do anything. Well, except he had only one skill, magic. According to Wan-Edhe he was incompetent at that, because the white castle on the mountain remained unconquered, in spite of all Prince Kwenz's labors and Jilo's mad studying of wards and how to break them.

He turned around slowly. Southward, grassy hills stretched away into the meadows of No One's Land, buffer between the Shadow and Wesset North, the Mearsiean province. To the west, the green line of the vast woodland that occupied the entire center of the kingdom, somewhere in the center of which lay Clair's underground hideout. To the north, the mountain, bulking above him, and right there on his eastern side, the Mearsiean capital with its jumble of colorful tile roofs dotted the mountainside, connected by broken streets. He couldn't see much beyond that.

Jilo thought of the Land of the Chwahir, vast, desolate, its huge army waiting for its master to return from his latest gambit against his old enemies.

Now no one was there.

He gathered his strength, and concentrated, and made the transfer spell to take him halfway around the world.

## Chapter Six

*Narad, capital of Chwahirsland*

THE transfer room in Wan-Edhe's great fortress was empty.

Jilo steadied himself on the wall.

Transfer magic was always wrenching, but for some reason, transferring to Narad hurt so very much worse.

When the black spots faded from his vision, he opened the heavy, iron-reinforced oaken door and took a cautious peek down the torchlit stone corridor. As always the light worried at his eyes, sending stabbing pains through his head, but that was part of life in Narad Fortress. In the Shadowland castle, Kwenz had kept the torches high, above his soldiers' lines of sight. Wan-Edhe would never have made any such accommodation. Flickering light did not bother *his* eyes, and as long as he was comfortable, anything else was pandering to weakness.

If Norsunder had held the city, Jilo knew he would have transferred straight into a trap. Perhaps Norsunder was going to permit Wan-Edhe to return if he performed whatever it was they had required of him. A quick look around disclosed that nothing had changed. The fortress, the city, the kingdom waited, without the tiniest deviation from standing orders, for Wan-Edhe to return.

Jilo had nowhere else to go. Nothing to do. If Wan-Edhe or

Norsunder appeared, he would be dead anyway. So why not see how far he got?

So. The first thing Jilo needed to do was find the spell to restore his eyes to normal. He left the heavy door open and proceeded with care.

Jilo did not know how Clair and her allies had managed to gain entry, but it couldn't have been through the regular transfer room. The way from there to Wan-Edhe's private chambers was so laden with traps that the air felt thick, and smelled of burnt metal. Jilo used one of the secret passages.

How silent the fortress was! It had been afternoon in Mearsies Heili, so it had to be hours short of dawn in Narad, Chwahirsland's capital city.

The weight of stone seemed to press on Jilo's bones. Strange. Jilo had felt no such weight when he was the Mearsieans' prisoner, and yet he'd been underground.

He smelled dust, and mildew, and stone, and steel, and stale sweat: the smells of power, and of fear, familiar as his own hands.

The stone wall of a secret passage slid silently open on judiciously greased pintles. At the top of the narrow stairs, he slid another door open, into an empty corridor leading to rows of uninhabited rooms.

This was the private Sonscarna family wing, where the magical wards had always been thickest, as Wan-Edhe did not trust his own guards in his private quarters. The fortress guard clustered below, company upon company, guarding night and day against an attack that no one had dared to mount since Wan-Edhe had caught his last grandson in a plot, and had him and his twi, and their families' twia, all put to death before the entire city.

Jilo entered the magic chambers. The glowglobes cast blue-white light at the edge of Jilo's tolerance, making that lump at the back of his head throb. The shelves of books seemed untouched, oldest on top, some snow-gray with piled dust. Old records, those. And old lists of proclamations and laws.

On the great work table, just as Clair had said, lay one of Wan-Edhe's private workbooks. There was the tiny, crabbed handwriting, a combination spellbook and diary, which surprised Jilo. Maybe it shouldn't. The only person Wan-Edhe really trusted besides his dungeon master was himself. Of course he would write a journal about himself. Puddlenose had said once that Wan-Edhe found himself the most interesting, as well as the most important, person in the world. *He is*, Jilo remembered saying. Stupidly. *No, he spends a lot of time and power making you think he is*, Puddlenose had said. And then escaped, yet again, helped by some mysterious mage Puddlenose called Rosey.

Jilo had never been able to escape, much less discover who Rosey was and why he aided Puddlenose. Because he was stupid.

A quill lay at an angle across one page, and all the wards had been lifted from the book. Jilo lifted the quill, and nothing happened. He bent to decipher the writing, which was a mix of dark magic language and Chwahir.

The date was three years previous. Someone had been paging through the book.

*Kwenz does not want the loyalty spell on that fool he's training. He will know if I perform it, so I will give the fool this instead. And, after he's proven to be worthless, he will be replaced with someone of my choosing.*

'The fool.' Wan-Edhe had never granted anyone the dignity of their name. He'd always issued a label for others, usually diminishing, mostly insulting. Like Puddlenose. Jilo was *the fool.*

Jilo blinked against eyestrain, a headache already throbbing through his skull as he labored to recover his previous thought. Fool? Names? Oh yes. The book. Eyes. Below that bit pointed out by the quill was a notation, the name of a spell. Jilo looked at the book lying next to the great one. It was an older one, slim, its binding cracked. Jilo followed the cryptic notation—categories of numbers—until he found a match to the notation.

He read the antidote to the spell three times, and then—slowly—performed it. The faint snap made him dizzy and skin-prickly, followed rapidly by a rush of sensation so strong that he stumbled backward into Wan-Edhe's big wingchair, which smelled rank with old grime, sweat, and mildew. He breathed through his mouth, his heartbeat loud in his ears. Sensation streamed through his mind, the mental fireflies so plenteous and bright that he became more giddy, not less. He blinked rapidly, then looked around, dazed. The dull stone, begrimed by centuries, glinted with thousands of subtle shades.

Was he dying?

No. Death could not be this amazing breadth of subtle coloration, the speed of thoughts, the heightened detail of sound: his own breathing, wind soughing against stone, and, beyond the window slits, the rhythmic clatter of marching sentries in one of the stone courtyards far below. Even the variety of odors in the stale air.

The meaning of the note seeped through the sensory brilliance.

He had been enchanted. These things he was seeing, feeling, thinking? This was normal thought and sensation! This was the way he'd been when he was little, when Kwenz had taken Jilo from the lowly Quartermaster Dzan and made him his apprentice.

Wan-Edhe had befogged his mind and his movements, quite deliberately. A fogged mind would never lead a coup. Would never originate one.

Anger burned corrosively through Jilo.

He stood up, and again almost overbalanced. Had his strength increased? He tried jumping around, then slammed his hand on the table. Ow. No, no extra strength. The change was more subtle; he felt easier in his body, a readiness to move. Before, it had taken more thought, more concentration just to walk around without colliding into unexpected doorways, corners, furniture, as his depth perception had been untrustworthy.

Before, he couldn't have even had that thought about depth perception.

Jilo laid aside the book of mind-altering spells for later study, and searched for the spells that altered the physical self. Though he could perceive color, he could also perceive a sense of glare, of visual distortion: the Shadow spell enhancing darkness vision.

His stomach growled, reminding him of the Mearsieans, with their astonishing variety of foods.

No one knew what Wan-Edhe ate because he never ate with anyone, but Kwenz, in recent years, had only taken gruel. Old man's food. Jilo had had a choice: either eat gruel with Kwenz, or go to the mess with the soldiers. Their food wasn't much better, all the ingredients boiled together except for the bread. That was life in the military. Anything else was decadent weakness.

Prisoners got what the soldiers didn't, or wouldn't, eat, days old and cold. Once a day. If that. He wasn't hungry enough to face mess hall food, so he bent over the books again and got to work.

The light of day grayed the narrow slit window out in the hall when at last he found the spell to restore his eyes to normal. He performed it, and pain lanced through his head. When he dared to open his eyes again, the chamber had shadowed to gloom. He swayed, dizzy, then clapped, and the glowglobes brightened.

Color had both intensified and become more subtle in its gradations. Light didn't hurt. He thought of the Shadowland warriors on board ship, and how painful their vision must be out on the water, with little shadow to protect them. He'd have to remove the spell, but he needed strength first.

He walked to the window, and looked down.

There in the great courtyard, the first drill of the day had commenced. Jilo watched the wheeling soldiery marching, turning, raising swords, slashing, all in unison.

It was like a body moving when the head was gone.

He turned around. There lay the great book, it and the antidote to that spell an unexpected gift from Clair of Mearsies Heili, the old enemy. It was an inexplicable gift. She could have kept it from him. Jilo remembered the fogginess of his mind, and shook his head. He never would have found the book, much less the spell: he would have blundered into one of the wards or traps he could feel all around him.

Experience dictated wariness. He'd endured lengthy sessions with Wan-Edhe lecturing about how no one gave gifts without expectation. Life was a struggle for power. Offense, defense.

Jilo looked around, sensing thick skeins of dark magic. A few minor protection wards were gone, but a dense miasma of enchantment still bound the old stone. Wan-Edhe had never trusted anyone; his favorite experiments were control of mind and will. And his favorite victims had been his own family, and then Puddlenose's family, first his uncle. Wan-Edhe had loved the exquisite cruelty inherent in the idea of sending Clair's own cousin against her.

The first thing to do was to find the wards and traps, and then maybe to turn them all against Wan-Edhe. That, too, would take strength. But then, there was no one else to do it. And Jilo had spent ten long, and very hard, years being tutored in one area of dark magic: wards. The idea of turning all that learning against Wan-Edhe instead of that blinding white castle burned through Jilo in such intense joy it made him giddy. Or maybe that was hunger.

As Jilo walked to the door, his stomach growled more insistently. His last meal had been the braised fish and rice with chopped greens that Puddlenose had brought him . . . when? It didn't matter.

He stood there thinking. No one would dare to walk into the throne room at the other end of the wing and sit down. Jilo knew his fellow Chwahir. Wan-Edhe had picked his subordinates for their steadfast, unquestioning obedience, and horrific punishments awaited anyone who erred. Wan-Edhe was also reputed to have spent magic in fashioning spywindows all over the castle, so he could be watching at any time.

But one thing Jilo had learned in his secret reading of Chwahir history: if enough time went by, and things got really bad, there would be mass uprisings. Unless someone stepped in, right now, and took command. Not just of this room, or the fortress.

Right now.

Someone like . . .

Someone . . .

Why not? He loved magic studies, and puzzles, and here was a wealth of both. He had nowhere to go, and nothing to lose. Nothing but his life, and that had been in danger for so long that it was a given.

He walked out of Wan-Edhe's library, his shoes scuffing on the stones. In the heavy, stale, burnt-metal air, the silence reminded Jilo of snakes moving, or of the whisper of bound spirits.

He looked around, but the idea refused to settle into his mind; instead, questions flickered through, leaves on a cold wind, whirling with increasing speed.

He stopped at the great double doors. It took both hands and all his strength to throw back the huge cast-iron bolt. Usually the guard did that in the morning.

Jilo gripped the door, and swung it open. He let it crash into the wall, a dull, flat sound.

Three runners sat silently on their bench, waiting to be summoned. All three looked up in mute question, not quite surprise. The miasma of heavy magic was too dense for that.

"Wan-Edhe is gone," Jilo said, watching them recoil reflexively. "And Prince Kwenz. The Shadowland over on the Toaran continent is no more as well."

Shock stripped all personality from the three faces. The first reaction, when the shock began to diffuse, was fear.

"For now, carry on as before." And then he knew instinctively what his second command ought to be. "Tonight, double rations for all, including ale."

The only reward they'd felt reasonably sure of was food. Promotion had been rare, and arbitrary; much more frequent had been punishment.

Food. Jilo's stomach growled, and he remembered his own hunger, and he thought of what waited down in the kitchens. Food the only reward, and that was stuff that a bunch of barefoot girls in Mearsies Heili—enemies all—would turn their noses up at.

What pitiful lives we have, Jilo thought, continuing past the runners down the stairs to the great halls. He would change that.

He heard whispers, one fierce, another voice edged with nerve-grating anxiety: "What does he mean, Wan-Edhe is gone? Wan-Edhe will never be gone. He said so himself."

And the answer, "It's a loyalty test. Didn't he just say 'carry on as before'?"

"When Wan-Edhe comes back, he'll want to see everything as he left it."

*When Wan-Edhe comes back.*

Jilo walked away, aware of the tightened gut, the tremble in his limbs, the fear gripping the back of his neck, aware that he believed in Wad-Edhe's return as strongly as they did.

Norsunder couldn't stop Wan-Edhe. Nothing could.

*Mearsies Heili, the Junky*

We are coming at last to the birth of the alliance, which was the result of no grand council or far-seeing strategy on the part of the wise and powerful.

Quite the opposite.

As soon as Jilo left the girls' hideout, the rest of Clair's gang began to appear from their bedrooms, until all seven girls joined Clair and CJ. They were a disparate group, ages roughly from eleven to fifteen, from all kinds of backgrounds. All were either outcasts or runaways, adopted by Clair.

Puddlenose and the small, scrawny shape-changer named Ben slipped out of the last room in the tunnel—the lair of Puddlenose and his various traveling companions, and a catch-all for storage—to join them.

"Is he really gone?" one of the girls called.

"Yes! Time to decootie-ize this place!" CJ yelled. She waved her arms as though dispersing a terrible stench, and began stamping around the rug.

Three girls passed out plates and spoons, as the day's cook came around with a pot of oatmeal.

"Jilo did have spells on him to ward initiative." Clair sat cross-legged in the middle of the rug. She dug her spoon into the oatmeal. "Just as I always thought. Senrid found the evidence in Wan-Edhe's personal spellbook, left on a table awaiting his return."

"Urk." CJ stopped stamping, and flopped down to eat. "If there is anything worse than Chwahir, it's Marlovens. I still think it was as big a mistake to bring him in on it as it was to let Jilo know. If Jilo really is as smart as Ben says—"

"He's smart," Ben said, with conviction, as he took a bowl. "I've spent more time spying on him than any of you have. I think Jilo's plenty smart. It's Wan-Edhe's spells that made him go stupid. It was always worst when we were around, or Wan-Edhe was around, or certain words were said. Like Wan-Edhe did it on purpose."

"Of course he did," Clair said.

Puddlenose had already downed his first bowl. As he got up to help himself to more, he said, "I can tell you this, after all my time as Wan-Edhe's prisoner: he was afraid of Jilo. That is, afraid that when Jilo got old enough and learned enough magic he'd depose Kwenz, take over the Shadowland, then come after the homeland. After all, pretty much all the rulers in Chwahirsland over the past couple centuries got their thrones the quick way, rather than waiting for the previous throne-warmer to croak of old age."

CJ glared his way. "I just hope Jilo doesn't pop up on the horizon with a million ships full of Chwahir military loaded with swords and stuff."

Clair shook her head. "I don't think he's going to. I can't say why, I just don't believe he will."

"He wanted to take our Junky," one of the girls put in, pointing dramatically to the braided rug. "How can you forget him and his group of groanboils riding around just to try to catch us sneaking in or out?"

Puddlenose shrugged. "True. But I bet that's because Kwenz wouldn't let him have a hideout like ours in the Shadowland. And pinching a hideout is not conquering. Besides, who could blame him for wanting a place to get away from Kwenz, especially when Wan-Edhe turned up?"

"I still hate him," CJ said.

Clair got up to dunk her empty bowl in the water barrel with its purification spell. As she clacked the bowl back onto the stack, she said, "Aunt Murial is busy trying to replace the old protections, and I think I ought to learn how. The Chwahir might be gone, but there are worse villains."

CJ groaned. "It's not *fair*. I thought we were supposed to have a happy ending, after Siamis got defeated. We deserve a happy ending. We earned it. Yeah, don't say it, villains aren't fair."

"That's why they're villains," a redhead said, raising a forefinger.

Clair smiled as the girls laughed, then turned serious. "Before I go study magic, maybe we should make a patrol through the forest, as we always have. Aunt Murial said we couldn't trust that all the Chwahir went away. She was going to talk to the regional governors about watching for any bands of Chwahir looking for trouble. We can help out by patrolling the woods."

"I'll take to the air," Ben offered. He was wondering what he would do without any Shadowland to spy on.

CJ scowled. "I wish there was some kind of spell that would take an invading army and turn them into a field of petunias." She kicked at the colorful mural that the girls had painted. "But no matter how much magic we learn, it doesn't really stop villains. We need an Idea to Save the World." The capitals conveyed themselves through extra sarcasm and an eye-roll.

The girls jumped up, some glad to be getting outside, especially after their long stay up north.

Puddlenose offered to help, and as the gang started up the tunnel toward the cave exit, he said, "If you see any Chwahir, give a yell. They probably know their king is gone. No one in control. They'll be looking for sport." He made a gesture, drawing his forefinger across his throat.

"Our rules haven't changed," Clair said. "Pairs or threes!"

"Follow anyone we find, then use our transfer medals," Irenne recited, rolling her eyes and flipping back her long light brown ponytail. "Puddlenose, it's *not* like we haven't been doing this for *simply ages*."

Puddlenose patted the air. "I know. I know. What we don't know is if Wan-Edhe's experimental loyalty spells and all the rest of his weird magic and crazy proclamations will still keep 'em afraid to try anything. When those spells do break, the Chwahir are going to be really, really angry."

A short time later, Clair tramped along next to CJ, looking up and down the gentle hillocks and rocky glades, before saying, "While you think up your idea, I'd better find my aunt."

"But the idea is so obvious," CJ said, throwing her arms wide. Birds rose out of a nearby shrub, squawking. "We lived it, there at the end. None of us kids could defeat Siamis by ourselves. But when we worked in a big group, we were great. We worked it all out, some searching, others decoys, you remember!"

Clair said doubtfully, "The nine of us have always worked together."

"I don't mean just our gang. I mean, like a . . . a pact, with other kids. Who could help." CJ smacked the front of her black woolen vest, then said, "There's the stream."

Clair ran beside CJ down a grassy hill. They plunged into the green shadows of a shaded path, and CJ went on. "By others I mean the kid rulers, the new generation, like those old mages called us. Sartora's generation. Yeah, we don't have mind powers like she does." On the words 'mind powers,' CJ whizzed her hands around her head as if she were shooing flies. "But we still are smart. Look how many villains have tried to wipe us out."

"Look how close we've come to being wiped out," Clair said, then shook her head, her blue-white hair a silky curtain around her arms. "No, no, I agree. And I know you're not saying we should go looking for trouble."

CJ whirled so that her green skirt flared and fell back to ankle length as she walked backward. She knew the forest well, and if strangers had been lurking around, the local birds would have been sending up the alarm. "The way I see it is, Eleven-Land is grown-ups who all want power. Siamis is a grown-up, or so close you may as well call him one." She made a sour face. "I don't know if he's younger or older than Disgusting Rel the Disgusting Hero, but anyway. From what everybody said, Siamis was able to pull off his enchantment because grown-up rulers found him so handsome, and so well spoken, and good at everything he did," she warbled in a syrupy coo. "No kid is going to fall for *Oooo, yer so haaaaaaandsome, Siamis!*"

Clair squashed the impulse to remind CJ that they'd met plenty of kids who would have wanted to *be* Siamis, and that she not only trusted but relied on adults, beginning with Aunt Murial. And Janil the Steward, queen of the kitchen, who had seen that Clair ate, bathed, and dressed when she was small, while her mother was drinking or dosing under the effects of sleepweed. And the city's guild leaders, and the oldest of the provincial governors. She was a queen because they let her be one, she thought privately. It was not a new thought.

But she understood CJ, who had come from a home in which the adults were abusive and untrustworthy, and further, she understood what CJ was trying to do. Their group of friends looked out for one another, and so CJ wanted to form a larger group to do the same.

Like . . . an alliance.

"Maybe an alliance is a good idea. I remember Senrid of Marloven Hess saying that he didn't think Siamis was really defeated. He said it was a retreat, that Siamis is coming back."

"Senrid *would* say that," CJ scoffed. "Being a Marloven. He probably *hopes* Siamis comes back, so they'll have an excuse for a lot of battles and military junk. But Siamis skunked so fast he left behind that Ancient Sartoran sword of his, remember? What else can that mean except he's too scared to come back? But. We need an alliance to be ready for the next villain. Because one thing you know about Norsunder is, they have to have a crop of 'em, ready to come boiling out to try their next evil plan."

Clair was nodding slowly. She hoped Senrid was wrong in saying that Siamis's retreat wasn't even a defeat in any real sense, just an abandonment of a plan when it ceased to be successful. She didn't want to tell CJ that she'd been having occasional nightmares about the pleasant, smiling young man who so easily put the world under a web of enchantment. Not horrible nightmares, which somehow made it worse: he always seemed so friendly and kindly. She found that more sinister than evil old Wan-Edhe, who never pretended to be anything but mean, and who had labored for years to create his web of spells over his own people. Siamis had bound people in enchantment in moments.

CJ paced in a circle, one fist pounding the palm of the other hand. "It has to be a kid alliance, ones who aren't villains or power-mad. Friends only! Code names, so anyone nosing in won't know what we mean. And we'll have code words, too, ones that the grown-ups would never pay attention to. And if someone gets into trouble, we all promise to go and help out."

"I'd be glad to send out messages to see who else might like the idea. Whom were you thinking of inviting?" Clair asked.

"Our friends. Ones we know and trust."

"Of course," Clair said. "Beginning with . . . ?"

"Arthur and Sartora up in Bereth Ferian. That is, Arthur would join. He's like us, though he's been learning magic forever, and Sartora might, if she's not too busy being famous."

Clair made a face. "Sartora asked us to call her by her real name."

"Liere, Sartora, it's all the same," CJ said, whirling her hands upward. "We should ask her, too. Of course! I'm just saying she might be too busy being important."

"Is that fair?"

"It's true. They made her a queen up there, after all, and she's got those weird mind powers, and she knows how to use that even weirder dyr thingie from the days of Ancient Sartor, that thing that broke Siamis's enchantment."

"I'm not certain that thing is trustworthy," Clair observed as they turned onto the forest road.

"I agree," CJ said fervently. "After all, if Siamis wanted it, it has to be evil, in spite of all that hoola-loola about how it was made of this mysterious stuff that no longer exists, and it has Great Powers, and all the rest of it. If Detlev used to use one of those things back in the old days, and everybody up north seems to agree that he did, it definitely has to be evil, right?"

Clair said doubtfully, "Maybe not evil, not in ancient days. But old. Really, really old, and no one understands how to use them, or what they're for."

"Except Ancient Sartoran villains," CJ stated.

"And Lilith the Guardian," Clair countered. "Sartora said she's real, not just a story from ancient days."

"Real or not, she never seems to be around when she's needed." CJ sighed.

"Well, I'm just glad Arthur's mother took that dyr away. She'd know where to stash it so it can't do any more damage if anyone does. So, who else in this alliance?"

"The Queen of Sartor, of course," CJ said quickly. "They say she's fifteen. And. You know. Sartor. If the Queen of Sartor joins, then others will follow."

"No argument from me," Clair said, and, relentlessly, "Who else?"

CJ heaved a long-suffering sigh. She knew where this was going. So she sidestepped. "Hibern. Your aunt said that she's really advanced in light magic studies, and that Arthur's mom would only take a really smart student."

"Good. But what about Senrid? He helped Hibern when she asked. And for that matter, he was the one who suggested that plan when Siamis was defeated."

CJ made a face. "Isn't Hibern enough? We don't need any more Marlovens."

Clair said, "Senrid knows more magic than anyone our age. Even Hibern, I think, though it's dark magic. But he's learning ours really fast. And you did make your peace with him."

CJ sighed, rolling her eyes.

"Or is this alliance just supposed to be 'people CJ likes'?" Clair asked.

"That's not fair." CJ scowled.

"You don't look dangerous with that whipped cream mustache still on your upper lip from breakfast." Clair tipped her head to the side.

CJ had to laugh, a big guffaw, startling more birds from the trees.

"You still don't trust Senrid?" Clair asked.

"No."

"I do. I think. Oh, I know that he started out badly. Very." Clair frowned down at her hands, remembering their first meeting with Senrid the previous summer, when he'd snatched one of them for execution, on the regent's orders. "But I think he's changed. The Senrid we dealt with before Siamis came wouldn't have bothered looking for that spell on Jilo, much less warning me to pass it on if I thought it a good idea."

"Maybe. He's still a know-it-all and a bigmouth."

"You mean, as fast as you with a nasty crack?"

CJ's grin was quick and rueful. "Well, maybe it's better to have him on our side than against." As they turned toward home, she added under her breath, "Maybe."

## Chapter Seven

*Three days later*
*Valley of Delfina, home of Tsauderei*

BEFORE I get to how the alliance began to spread, I need to sketch an overview of the mage relationships of that period.

Before Sartor was enchanted the century previous, the magic world acknowledged two leaders. First was Lilith the Guardian, who had fought during the Fall of Ancient Sartor. Since then—like the Norsundrians she had dedicated her life to opposing—she had recourse to refuge beyond time.

Her appearances had been less rare than those of Detlev, but rare enough that many believed she was mere myth. One of her purposes was to seek promising youth and put them in the way of training, though often her next appearance would be decades later, sometimes a century or more after they died.

Next was the Sartoran mage guild led by Chief Veltos Jhaer, oldest guild in the world. Ninety-seven years ago, when Norsunder Base attacked Sartor, the kingdom was frozen in time.

With Sartor inaccessible to the rest of the world, the gap in magic leadership was eventually filled by Evend of Bereth Ferian. He'd nearly gone to the Sartoran mage school, but then the war between Sartor and

Norsunder Base broke out. So Evend's family kept him in the north to study magic, and eventually he became the King in Bereth Ferian (a title that meant little more than presiding over treaty meetings concerning the ancient wards against the Venn) and head of the newly expanded northern school of magic.

Tsauderei, ten years younger, was one of Evend's first students. Tsauderei was so gifted that Evend broke many of the traditions of magic teaching, maintaining that education had to evolve as did everything else. His style of teaching, individual lessons tailored to the interests and abilities of the student, had worked well for the northern school.

Once handsome, vigorous, and strong, Tsauderei at over eighty was still commandingly tall, though gaunt under the robe that had been male fashion in his young days. Every year, as soon as the snows of winter began to melt, Tsauderei had dared to explore as close to Sartor's enchanted border as was safe, which enabled him to discover that the enchantment was gradually receding. This discovery he kept to himself in hopes that Norsunder would overlook it.

His determination strengthened one spring fifteen years ago, when his journey disclosed two living persons in century-old clothes: a palace guard, her wound still fresh, protecting an infant who turned out to be the youngest of the royal children. This baby was the last living member of the ancient Landis family, who had ruled Sartor for a couple millennia.

This girl, nicknamed Atan (for her name was surely warded), had been raised by Tsauderei and taught magic and history according to the northern school's teachings, until the enchantment broke at last, and Atan was joyfully reunited with the Sartorans, who crowned her queen and surrounded her with guardians—and guards.

But once the enchantment was broken, bringing Sartor back into the flow of time, Sartor was striving to reclaim its ancient authority. Its mage school objected strongly to any deviation in their centuries-old tradition of moving students through classes in cohorts, overseen by Sartor's mage guild.

To their objection, Evend had pointed out that they were now a century behind. And so the northern school stayed separate from the Sartoran.

That was one cause of tension. Tsauderei's refusal to put himself under the authority of the outdated Sartoran mage guild was another. He prized his independence and all the knowledge he had learned after decades of watching over enchanted Sartor in his effort to break the enchantment.

And so, after Atan was restored to Sartor, Mage Guild Chief Veltos and the rest of the Sartoran mage guild—though professing gratitude and friendship—effectively shut Tsauderei out.

*Roth Drael*

Erai-Yanya woke up to a friendly note from Tsauderei that from anyone else would be a summons.

Erai-Yanya grimaced. It had to be politics, and she hated politics. She had chosen early to live and work alone largely to avoid mage politics. Further, she knew Tsauderei loathed politics as well, but as the oldest of the senior mages, almost anything he did had political repercussions in the mage world. He had also been her tutor during the time she studied with Gwasan and Murial.

These days, Tsauderei seldom left his cottage on the border between Sartor and Sarendan. His colleagues, new and old, were accustomed to going to him.

As soon as Hibern transferred to Bereth Ferian for her deferred day studying with the northern mage school, Erai-Yanya braced for the long shift from winter to summer. She found herself standing on the grass outside the small one-room cottage with its broad front window. She blinked away the transfer haze, gazing down into the deep blue of the lake at the bottom of the valley, then turned toward the door and walked in.

She glanced around at the three walls filled with books and scrolls as she waited for the transfer-throb in her joints to subside. Why was the sight of books so reassuring? Mages intent on destruction surely had libraries, too . . .

Tsauderei waited until his former student regained her focus and said, "You went to Chwahirsland again?" He leaned forward.

How did he even know? Of course he'd know.

Men had worn beards when Tsauderei was young. His was long, white, and the diamond he wore in one ear glittered against the ordered locks of his long snowy hair. His gaze was reassuringly direct, the many lines in his face emphasizing his ironic view of the world.

"Yes, a useless journey," she said. "More interesting on our return than for anything we discovered."

"Please tell me what happened, even if it was disappointing."

"First you need to know that Hibern and the Mearsiean girls, without consulting Murial, decided that Senrid of Marloven Hess ought to go along, as he could probably read the books."

"Senrid Montredaun-An. Taking an interest in something outside of that benighted kingdom? I might have to meet that boy some day," Tsauderei said, his interest sharpening exponentially as Erai-Yanya reported the rest of the visit.

At the end, she said, "The time candle had burned down and we all felt ill, so I insisted we leave." She let out a breath. "And now we come to the disturbing discovery, that a full day had passed while we were gone, though I had watched that candle. Which I had cut and bespelled myself, binding it to half an hour." She held two fingers apart, indicating the length of the candle.

Tsauderei looked grim. Several possible reasons for the time anomaly occurred to him, all of them dire, but he didn't know enough about dark magic to determine which was right. "That, too, will have to be sorted out, if Wan-Edhe is really gone. Which I don't believe. It's too easy. Right now, I need your advice."

"On what? You know I have nothing to do with so-called world affairs, except magical, and your knowledge outstrips mine there."

"Except in other-world studies," he observed. "But that's a conversation for another day. This is as political as you can get, as is everything having to do with Sartor. But I still think you're the best advisor. Erai-Yanya, I have yet to see Atan. They keep her so busy she can't even visit me. But she writes to me via magic transfer." He leaned out to tap a golden notecase. "She wants a study partner, and asked me to find one."

"She asked you, not the chief mage?"

"Precisely." Tsauderei uttered a soft, sardonic laugh. "Now, if I ask Oalthoreh up at the northern school, she'll send Atan the same sort of student that the Sartoran mages would give her: scrupulous, obedient, careful, and who will think it his or her duty to report every word they exchange. I was hoping you might have a suggestion of a smart, dedicated mage student who'll permit Atan that one hour of freedom from being Queen of Sartor."

At first Erai-Yanya turned her mind dutifully to the northern magic school's seniors, but as she sifted them mentally, the sense of Tsauderei's words sank in, and she laughed at the obvious. "I believe I can help with that. Hibern would be perfect."

"I thought she might."

*Two weeks later*
*Marloven Hess to Sartor*

Remembering how bad Senrid had looked the day they went to Chwahirsland, the next week Hibern dutifully put in her skipped day of northern study instead of going to Marloven Hess for her weekly magic session with Senrid.

The week after that, she transferred to Marloven Hess, having dressed carefully, her best polished cotton robe under her blue mage robe, her hair brushed and braided. But she did not transfer directly to the capital.

She appeared on a low, forested hill from which she could look down at her family's castle, and her old tower room. Now empty. Each time she did this, she promised herself it would be the last, but after a few weeks she couldn't resist another visit, for all kinds of reasons that she knew were weak.

No one moved in the narrow windows, built for archers to shoot through and not be shot. The clear air over the tower indicated that her secret structure, which had taken two years to make, was gone as if it had never happened.

As if *she* had never happened. Except that she could feel the wards against her entry if she began the transfer spell to her old Destination.

No one looked out, and if her father detected her presence, no one was sent to invite her in. Her imagined triumphant conversation with her parents about being invited to be study partner to no less a person than the Queen of Sartor faded like morning mist.

She turned away, knowing it was stupid to keep returning, because it always hurt. "That will be the last time," she resolved. "Absolutely the last."

And she transferred the short distance to Choreid Dhelerei, where she was expected.

Senrid's face had resumed its normal shape, and his skin looked less like someone had thrown a set of paints at him. As she took her seat, she found the resumption of everyday schedule calming, and once again she tidied the pain away.

Ordinarily they argued about magic and history as much past their hour as Senrid had time for, but today, as the castle bells clanged the watch change, echoed from farther away by the city bells, Hibern closed her book. "We're done."

Senrid eyed her. "And you're all dressed up."

"I am." Hibern shook out her robe as she rose. "Oh yes. I forgot to mention when we went to Chwahirsland, but I made a promise to pass this along: the Mearsieans want to start some kind of alliance."

Both knew it wouldn't be military. "This is to prepare for Siamis's return?" Senrid asked.

"That, and to be an alliance between underage enemies of Norsunder, especially rulers and magic students, against whoever else comes along."

Senrid sighed, remembering CJ's annoying rants about how all adults were stupid. Maybe on that weird world she came from they were. He wouldn't have survived if he hadn't had Commander Keriam in his life, but on the other hand, that older generation of lighter mages? Before the defeat of Siamis, those old lighters up at Bereth Ferian had looked at him as if he'd kill them as they stood when they found out he was a Marloven.

"Like who?" he asked cautiously.

"Like you." Hibern held up three fingers. "You inherited a throne, you know magic, and you're an enemy of Norsunder."

He could see that kind of alliance being useful, if it really was an alliance. "What am I expected to do? If it's to waste time at lighter celebrations, listening to forty-verse snores about Golden Ages and Lo, How Great We Be, I'm not doing it."

"Nothing was said about celebrations," Hibern said. "The idea is kind of like what we just did for Clair in Chwahirsland."

Senrid snorted. He'd really gone to find out how far Wan-Edhe had gotten in developing the mind control spells. Looking for some kind of evil plan for taking over Mearsies Heili (as if Wan-Edhe would be idiot enough to write such a thing in a magic book) had been secondary.

But he'd looked, and as a result, had stumbled on that ugly little spell designed for Jilo. Which he duly passed along to Clair once that stiff-necked mage of Hibern's was not listening.

Hibern went on. "If someone in the alliance asks for the kind of help we can provide, we give it."

"That I can do." But Senrid wondered how any of them could possibly help him. Assuming they would want to.

To say that out loud might sound like whining. He'd been up studying far too long the previous night, but had still risen before dawn to practice with bow and knife. As a consequence, his mind was tired, making it more difficult to control his nascent Dena Yeresbeth. So he heard thoughts: Hibern's regret, and from farther away images of Hibern's crazy brother Stefan.

Physical distance didn't seem to matter to Dena Yeresbeth. Stefan himself was at Hibern's family castle, glowering at phantasms that may or may not be there. What snagged Senrid's focus, however, was the strength of Hibern's regret, shame, and bitterness.

Senrid closed off Stefan and listened to the whisper of minds in relative proximity. Jarend Ndarga? Yes, surrounded by other minds, some scoffing, others angry, some laughing. A few afraid. *Nothing good ever comes of tangling with kings, my dad says . . .* And someone else, *Yes. You wait. He's a young scrub, so he might smile and pretend there's no repercussion, but next season, next year, if he thinks he can get away with it . . .*

Senrid knew he shouldn't listen to Ndarga, but he couldn't resist. Just the surface. Ndarga had been so surprised and angry over his own hurts, believing he shouldn't have had any after fighting a scrub of fifteen. He had spent days (Keriam told Senrid grimly) watching for retribution after that fight.

That's who he was to the senior academy boys: a scrub. So much for his ancient lineage . . . Senrid laughed at himself, and then made another reach with his Dena Yeresbeth. It was a long reach, very long, and yet it was so easy: Liere. There she was, far away, struggling with Ancient Sartoran verbs . . .

Senrid shut the mental door. He shouldn't do that. It was wrong. Liere hadn't come to see him because she hadn't. If she'd wanted to, she would have. There was no point in guessing at reasons.

Senrid didn't realize he'd spoken Liere's name out loud until he opened his eyes to find Hibern paused at the door. "Senrid, this is none of my concern, but when I was in Bereth Ferian last, Sartora asked when you were going to visit. It didn't take mind powers to see she was disappointed."

"'Sartora,'" he repeated. "Liere hates that stupid name. Or she did. Anyway, she's got to be surrounded by an army of mages. Heralds. Arthur. All busy stuffing her head with lighter magic and . . ."

The word 'hyperbole' died.

Hibern said, ". . . and?"

Senrid sighed. "She could visit any time she wants."

Hibern said, "I think she misses you. She did say that you were her first friend." She found Senrid's wide gaze disconcerting. "Senrid, I don't know her, but everybody says she came from a family of shop-keepers who don't travel. If that's true, then she would probably never think to invite herself to visit a king. Even one who'd said he was a friend. She's probably been told how little words of friendship mean from nobles, much less anyone who considers themselves above that rank."

"Oh," Senrid said. "Never thought of that." He grimaced, his ears reddening.

"Study those wards!" Hibern said as the last of the castle bell-clangs died in the distance.

Now that she was about to transfer to Eidervaen, ancient capital of Sartor, anxiety tensed Hibern. It was a different sort of anxiety from the sick grief and betrayal of being rejected by her family. For several days she had happily tackled her studies, bolstered by the knowledge that the new Queen of Sartor wanted a study partner, and who had been suggested? Not some favored student at either magic school, but Hibern.

Doubt formed into question about why she'd been chosen. Or maybe she was merely the latest in a very long line already interviewed and sent away again.

All she knew about the new queen was that she was more or less Hibern's age, and a formidable mage student. Nobody seemed to know much else about her, except that she had been raised by Tsauderei, hidden away in a mountain cottage until she and a band of war orphans had made their way into the disintegrating enchantment that had held Sartor beyond the reach of the rest of the world—beyond *time*—and by so doing, broke the last of it so that Sartor could rejoin the world.

After nearly two weeks of wondering, Hibern was about to meet her now.

She clutched the transfer token she'd been given. Magic wrenched her out of Senrid's dusty castle and thrust her into a cool space smelling of an herb a little like cinnamon mixed with lemon, with undertones of beeswax, and faintest of all, a vague scent that reminded her a little of mildew.

As Hibern gasped from the effects of the transfer magic, she looked around the Sartoran Destination chamber. Three walls were plain blue-white marble. The fourth divided into three long panels, a gilt sun placed high above the middle one, with rays slanting down through all three panels. Dragons wound in a sinuous curve up the outer panels, their open mouths reaching up toward the sun.

It was Sartor which, history insisted, brought through the world-gate the notion of dividing the day into twenty-four hours, eight sets of three. Everything in threes. Even the Marlovens had threes, though those were military in nature.

At the exact moment Hibern recovered her breath and could move, a door opened in the middle panel, and a teenage page conducted Hibern out of the Destination chamber. Behind her, someone else appeared by transfer, causing a flurry of air that brought a faint whiff of some unfamiliar place.

The girl leading Hibern wore a gown of soft green under a paneled robe of dark blue edged with white. There was a stylized star worked in white thread along the edges of the white border, the symbol for the Sartoran mage guild. It was small and subtle enough that Hibern only recognized it when the girl was two paces away.

The girl said, "I bid you welcome," as she guided Hibern to a cushioned couch. Conventional greeting, Hibern said to herself. Polite, for the widest circle. The next circle in would have been acknowledged with a polite question about well-being.

Hibern made the conventional response, "I thank you for the welcome," then the girl offered her a tiny cup of fresh steep—the best Sartoran steep, the aroma like summer grass clearing the last of the transfer malaise from Hibern's head. Hibern accepted the cup. It was not too hot or too cold, and tasted fresh and slightly astringent, slightly tart.

A skinny boy appeared, wearing livery edged in lavender, and once again Hibern completed the conventional outer-circle exchange of greetings, after which she said in her best Sartoran, "I am here for my interview with the queen."

The attendant took the empty cup and made a polite gesture to follow.

The hall was also marble, with round windows high above, framed by stylized running vines. They let in summer light indirectly, keeping the air cool.

Hibern breathed in the complicated scents—more elusive spice, a trace of nut oil (furniture polish?)—as they passed a sideboard with no straight lines, and complicated knotwork inlays in various types of colorwood. Then a tapestry depicting some historical occasion, a treaty from the looks of the figures, the long robes and tiny ruffs and rosebud "mouse ear" headdresses the fashion nine centuries previous. To the Sartorans, a nine-hundred-year-old fashion was probably next thing to modern, Hibern thought, turning slightly to take in the last of the silvery blues and golds of the colors.

A broad landing was next, a carved door full of knotted vines in threes, and Hibern found herself inside an interview chamber with an amazing vaulted ceiling. She tried not to gawk, catching a glimpse of a night-blue sky and stars painted on it: so they were in mage territory.

The attendant bent to whisper to the young man at the desk, then gave Hibern a nod and retreated noiselessly as for the third time Hibern was given the conventional greeting, to which she responded politely.

A girl of about twelve appeared through a door at the back of the office, carefully bearing a silver tray, which she set down noiselessly next to the young man. Hibern couldn't help but compare these gliding, quiet runners with those in Senrid's castle, with their clattering boot heels and unmodulated voices and weapons at their belts.

The young man then indicated one of the several empty chairs, all upholstered in pale blue, and said, "If you will have a seat?"

Hibern did, looking askance at the empty chairs. Maybe Erai-Yanya had been wrong, and there was a line of interviewees before her. Or—her heart sank—maybe this wait was some kind of insult because Hibern didn't belong to either mage school, but was taught by Erai-Yanya, the hermit-mage of Roth Drael.

Erai-Yanya had said when Hibern first came to her as a student, "These bare feet of mine? Yes, I find it comfortable to go like this. But there's a reason why I've always gone before various kings and queens with my hair tumbling down, my toes bare, even in winter, and wearing an old gown I carefully preserve for these interviews: it is a reminder that I stand apart from their social and political hierarchies, and I will not be 'managed.'"

Hibern wondered if it was a mistake to come in her best robe. Maybe she should have routed out an old horse blanket.

The orderly quiet of the hall was broken by a quick ticketty-tick sound, followed by the abrupt emergence of Hibern's first sight of one of the southern morvende, the cave-dwelling people. Like the morvende of the northern continent, this boy was pale-skinned, with drifting blue-white cobwebby-hair. He wore a knee-length, sleeveless tunic woven out of a gold-dyed fabric that rippled like gauze. His lower legs and his feet were bare, the talons on his toes ticking on the marble as he walked.

"Greetings and welcome! Prosperity and well-being! You must be the one Erai-Yanya sent to Atan," he exclaimed.

Hibern blinked. How many of Sartor's strictly defined social circles had the morvende blurred with his unexpectedly informal greeting?

"I thank you for your greetings and felicitations," Hibern said, groping for the right words. "But who is Atan? Do you mean the Queen of Sartor?"

"It is short for Atanrael. It is her heart-name. Who would go by 'Yustnesveas Landis the Fifth' if she did not have to?" He flicked his long, thin fingers through the air, the talons at the ends painted a cheery orange. So were his toe talons.

"As for me, you must call me Hin," he said. "For Hinder. You'll meet my cousin Sinder around here somewhere, but she is never 'Sin' to anyone but me. Not to confuse you. Just to help you sort us out," he went on in the same cheerful tone, thereby doing away with all the careful formality on which Hibern had been coached. "Atan is presiding over the high council interviewing the Colendi ambassador. If you can call a formal assembly in Star Chamber a mere interview. I suspect the idea was to intimidate Colend into agreement." He grinned. "We have a saying, 'A juggling snake has no time to bite.'"

*How does a snake juggle?* Hibern said, "There are problems with Colend?" Aside from the gossip about their king being mad, the Colendi were renowned for using politeness as a weapon.

Hin's fingers lifted to the side of his face and twiddled, as if he played a flute.

"Oh," Hibern breathed. "The Music Festival?"

Hin's smile vanished. "That interview was to last a glass." The orange talons flashed as Hinder mimed turning over a small sandglass. "It's been an entire hour."

## Chapter Eight

*Elsewhere in Eidervaen's royal palace*

THE time has come to introduce Atan, saddled with the name Yust-nesveas, queen at fifteen of the oldest country in the world. Therefore her influence would always be disproportional. She knew it. She hated it.

She also hated crying.

When she was small and impatient with chores, in her haste once she'd accidentally splashed boiling water on her hand and wrist. She'd refused to give in to tears while her hand was wrapped with soothing keem leaves, because nowhere in the records she'd been given to study did any queen of Sartor cry.

Tsauderei, her guardian and tutor, had said, "Atan, you keep forgetting that those records you're reading are what people want you to remember about the individuals, not necessarily what they were truly like. Go right ahead and howl, if it helps."

But Atan hadn't. Queens were supposed to have self-control. Their decisions affected a lot of people, so giving in to passion was the next thing to evil.

Even so, there were three occasions when she did cry.

She'd felt the sting of tears when she first walked into the Tower of

Knowledge, known for centuries and centuries as Sartor's mind. But she'd been too hurried and frightened to let the tears fall, for she had to break the cruel enchantment that had been bound to the Landis family (who Norsunder thought had all been safely killed), while Norsundrian warriors were chasing her people into the square below.

The second time she cried happened a few days after Sartor was freed from the enchantment, during her first Restday-dawn walk through the Purrad, the twelve-fold labyrinth in its secluded garden at the oldest part of the royal palace—the place sometimes called Sartor's soul.

She had not expected the ancient silver-barked trees, lit by slanting shafts through time-worn stone traceries, to be so beautiful when seen from all sides as she walked the Purrad's interlocking circles; she had not expected the rush of sorrow and wonder when she imagined her own parents having stepped on these same smoothed pebbles so carefully placed and tended.

The third time she cried was when she walked into her parents' bedroom, and saw the little signs of haste: her mother's nightgown tossed on the rumpled bed, her father's desk scattered with papers and books.

However, she had not cried when she first walked into Star Chamber, Sartor's oldest chamber of governing, known as Sartor's heart. High under the complicated vaultings of the ceiling, windows let in the light at different times and seasons, golden shafts in winter, cleverly multiplied through crystal, and in summer, coolly diffused to silver. At night, or on a gloomy winter's day, floating lights glimmered above in ever-changing patterns, like stars.

It was winter's golden light that she had first seen: so clear, striking the marble and diffusing, so the vast room seemed infinite as sunrise.

The tree-shaped throne where she sat now, an elaborate combination of carved golden marble, real gold, mirror, and magic so that she could be seen from all sides, stood in the center of the room, around which the floor circled in wide, shallow marble tiers on which courtiers could move in the ancient complexities known as Circles.

Right now she was bored, irritated, and increasingly angry as the beautifully modulated, carefully cadenced adult voices murmured in the first circle tier below her throne. The high council was gathered there, where only the duchas and the mage guild head could stand in more formal gatherings.

There stood Chief Veltos, head of Sartor's mage guild, tall, thin, and grim-faced as she glared at the Colendi ambassador. The first time Atan met Chief Veltos, she had insisted on taking Atan to this very room. As they stood beneath the vaulted ceilings in this chamber freighted with history, the chief mage had said in a low, bitter voice, "Everyone knows that our army lost the war with Norsunder, but your father, as commander, is dead, past blame or care." She paused, her tone flattening. "*I* lost the magic battle, for it was my strategy that Detlev of Norsunder ripped apart so easily, before binding us under enchantment. Our first job must be new, and better, protections. Because we must expect Detlev to attack again."

Atan had been too overwhelmed for tears.

Her next visit to this chamber had been her coronation on New Year's Firstday 4735—for the Sartorans, a jump of ninety-seven years— that she only recollected as great noise and color as the remnants of Sartor's Three Circles gathered to see her take her father's place. After fifteen years of secluded life she had been too terrified to raise her head beyond the formidable array of staring faces.

Most recently, Midsummer's celebration felt hollow without the ancient tradition of the Music Festival, which now took place in Colend. As it had for the last ninety years.

She'd been unprepared for the anguish and sorrow in every adult who'd gathered to make the Progress through the Twelve Stations, when for the first time in centuries, it would not signal the start of the Sartoran Music Festival.

*Centuries*, everyone had repeated, their voices ringing with the weight of moral outrage.

So here they were in the summer of the year 4737, and all Sartor wanted the Music Festival back.

The Colendi ambassador's lovely singsong echoed through the chamber now, mellifluous and rehearsed. ". . . And our king is the first to acknowledge Sartor's respect for tradition, but his majesty bade me speak for our own traditions, beginning with honoring the treaties we have made with the Alliance of Guilds. For, if you will permit me to offer a reminder, it is not merely the hostelries and bakeries and eateries and houses of entertainment in Colend, but those along the road leading to us, who have invested much in expectation of the yearly gathering."

The elderly Duchas of Chandos, who stood first within the first circle opposite Chief Veltos, lifted his hand. "I hear no objections being offered to Colend establishing its own music festival in complement, but it seems reasonable to us to expect that the Sartoran Music Festival would continue to be held in Sartor, as it has for centuries."

"What greater way for Sartor to rejoin the world?" stated a baras, her chin elevated, eyes darting glances from side to side. She was in the high council, though as baras she was only third circle, because her daughter was deemed one of Atan's Rescuers.

The dapper guild chief bowed to the duchas, light shimmering along the tiny mois stones embroidered on his formal tunic as he said to the ambassador, "Our Sartoran guilds will suffer greatly if denied the yearly gathering. And we are already sorely burdened due to the war which, for us, was recently lost."

The Colendi ambassador turned to each, his hands and expression apologetic, but Atan suspected that he was not really sorry. His voice was too smooth, the corners of his mouth easy, as he went on in the musical Colendi version of Sartoran, "My king respects Sartor's place in history. Were we not once a part of the Sartoran empire? Did not my own ancestors travel here every summer, claiming their summer sojourn the pinnacle of their year?"

He paused to bow in Atan's direction. "My king commanded me to beg her majesty's forbearance, and assure her that no one understands better than he the difficulties besetting a new monarch, especially in this troubled time."

Though he bowed to her, Atan could see how his attention stayed with the high council as he opened his hands in a graceful gesture, fingers pointed starward, slightly opened. If she stuck her tongue out at him, she suspected he wouldn't even notice.

Chief Veltos would.

"I am enjoined to request a hiatus of five years," the ambassador oiled on, "that our own treaties may be renegotiated, and his majesty also hopes that in that time Sartor will have fully recovered its rightful place in the world."

The bells rang then. Atan wondered if he had chosen his time.

The high council had not risen. They didn't even look at one another, much less at Atan. That meant they'd already agreed to force the interview to last until they got what they wanted.

Atan stirred impatiently. Chief Veltos, at least, should remember that Erai-Yanya's student was coming. No, she was probably already here. But it was Chief Veltos who had said so reasonably, "We will honor you all our lives, your majesty, for yours was the hand freeing the kingdom from the enchantment. However, now that we of the guild are no longer enchanted, we can free you of the necessity for continuing those studies . . ."

And they still had not invited Tsauderei to visit, much less found time in the schedule for her to visit him—the mage who had saved her life when he found Atan as a baby, lying in the border mountains with the wounded guard who had run with her. It was Tsauderei who had tutored Atan as well as guarding her for fifteen years.

Atan meant to be good. She meant to wait for the signal that the interview was over, but she could not contain the surge of resentment at this evidence that they intended to talk through her impending interview as if it did not matter. As if *she* did not matter, as if she were part of the decoration of this ancient room. Perhaps not as important as those decorations, as she wasn't centuries old.

She knew that that was self-pity, but the prospect of a study partner was important to her. And they kept reminding her of her duty as queen.

So . . . maybe it was time to act like a queen.

She put her hands together in the old gesture of peace. It caught the attention of the ambassador, as she had hoped. She then opened her hands and held them out, palm up, the signal that he could withdraw.

She saw at once from the little smile the ambassador gave her as he raised himself from his bow that he had won some kind of contest. Yes, there it was, in the faces of the council, the little narrowing of eyes and thinning of lips that indicated she had done wrong. They all rose as the ambassador touched his fingertips to the air above her palms and bowed, retreated the full twelve steps backward, then bowed again at the door before it boomed shut behind him.

"Five years," the Duchas of Chandos began in a querulous voice.

"'His majesty,'" the Duchas of Mondereas repeated contemptuously. He was one of the few leaders who had survived the war previous to Detlev's enchantment. "Just because we were away a century can he possibly think we are not aware that his king is mad?"

"Who really makes the decisions in Colend?" a duchas asked. She was young, and very new to both her title and her place on the council, as her elders had all been killed in the failed defense of Sartor before the enchantment.

A babble of voices broke out.

Chief Veltos had turned away from Atan as if she really were an invisible part of the throne. But now she placed her hands together and bowed to Atan, saying, "We would not keep you from your interview, your majesty. We will take counsel among one another and wait upon you at your convenience."

In other words, they would tell her what to do.

Atan made her first-circle bow. The high council bowed, heads low until she left the chamber.

She knew she shouldn't complain. She had not been raised as a royal heir, in spite of all of Tsauderei's efforts. Neither he nor Gehlei, the bodyguard who had run with Atan, could train a Sartoran queen the way monarchs had been trained for centuries. She had a lot to learn, and she knew that the high council worked tirelessly to bring Sartor back into a world that had gone on for nearly a century while Sartor was frozen beyond time.

As Atan walked back, she glanced along the corridors, mentally ticking off all the people who watched over her.

First was Chief Veltos, who headed the Sartoran mage guild as well as the high council that governed the kingdom while Atan learned statecraft.

There was the council-appointed herald-steward, who taught her the traditions and protocol of that statecraft.

There was the wardrobe mistress, who chose exactly the right clothing for every occasion and saw to it that everything was fresh, the embroidery perfect, the panels creased.

There was a personal maid whose job it was to brush out Atan's hank of brown hair, trying to coax highlights into it, and dressing it up with pearls and tiny gems worked into butterflies and blossoms. There was a maid whose job it was to expertly twitch away any evidence of a tiny hangnail on her cuticles, to keep her nails buffed and trimmed.

Then there were the scribes, heralds, and pages who inexorably swept her from one event to another all through her day.

There was somehow in her carefully orchestrated schedule scarce time or place for friends.

Hibern's mood had turned uneasy when the morvende boy reappeared. "I found her! They had her closeted with the Colendi ambassador." He said that as he opened a door, and fluttered those distracting orange talons in invitation for Hibern to go through.

Hibern gained a vague impression of a beautiful room, full of light and color, but her attention went straight to the girl her own age who rustled in from another door, her smile tentative until she saw Hinder's orange talons. She laughed, a quick, soft sound. "Orange, Hin?"

"Sin considered purple, then decided your overseers would be even more aghast at orange." He walked out, shutting the door behind him.

The two girls were left alone.

Both Hibern and Atan were used to being the tallest of anyone their age. Their gazes met at eye level, each appraising, and a little shy. Each wanting to like, and to be liked. The two girls took one another in: Hibern a thin girl plainly dressed in cream linen with blue over it; Atan a big girl wearing an elaborate costume consisting of a stiff brocaded under-gown in green, made high to the neck, the lace edging goffered, an over-robe of pure white silk embroidered with stylized patterns of wheat, and over that, a brocade stole of gold, with interlocked patterns connected by stars picked out in gems and tiny pearls. Her brown hair was bound into a coronet made of three braids, threaded through with gold.

"Welcome," Atan said—just one word, no ritual greetings, but the tone made it sound real. "Before we begin I must apologize for keeping you waiting."

Hibern belatedly remembered her bow, and performed it, feeling intensely awkward, as Marlovens did not bow.

"Come within, please, and do make yourself comfortable," Atan said, indicating an oval-backed chair, as she sat in its twin.

Hibern had been warned that most outland rulers would keep visitors standing. In Sartor's history, she'd read, people once had had to kneel before royalty. In Marloven Hess, the throne was on a dais, so the jarls in the back could see the king and the king could see them. As Senrid said, "Kings up on daises were also great for target practice when the jarls wanted a new king."

Hibern sat on the edge of her chair, hands flat on her knees. So far Atan was not using the formalities she had been told to expect. So she must rely on her own eyes and ears.

"I may address you as Hibern?" Atan asked.

"Yes, your majesty."

"And you learn magic from Erai-Yanya?"

"Yes, your majesty."

"Have you studied at all at the northern mage school in Bereth Ferian?"

"I go there once a month. My tutor wishes me to study certain things with the students, your majesty." When Atan seemed to be waiting for more, Hibern said, "Erai-Yanya goes there to visit her son, as well as to lecture to senior students on advanced magic. Arthur was made heir to King Evend. Before Evend died—"

Atan's hand came up. "I'm familiar with the tragic history. That is, I've heard about Evend dying and taking the Norsunder rift with him,

which ended the Siamis enchantment last year. So you learn from these
northerners, and yet, if I'm not misled, you're from the south?"

"Marloven Hess, your majesty," Hibern stated.

Atan's eyes widened. Hibern was distracted by the color of Atan's
eyes, a rare dark blue. One couldn't call such protuberant eyes pretty, but
they were distinctive, a familiar feature of her exalted lineage. Anywhere
else in the world, she'd be called plain—as would Hibern herself.

"How is it that a Marloven came to study light magic? From everything
I've heard, they have been . . ." Atan made a gesture. "Not allies. Your
family differed, or have I been given false information?"

"Yes, and no, your majesty." A gesture invited Hibern to elaborate.
She forced herself to say, "You're not wrong." She'd known this subject
would come sooner or later. May as well get it over with. "My father
practices dark magic. Traditional in Marloven Hess. He was responsible
for spell renewal, wards, and protections. But the regent wanted more,
things like loyalty spells. My father, well, the short answer is, he tried
his best to find such—did some experiments for the King of the Chwahir in return for certain spells—and used the household for the experiments. My brother most of all."

Atan grimaced. "What happened to your brother?"

"He went mad, your majesty. Even worse, the regent was impatient,
as Senrid was learning magic fast, and beginning to question his uncle's
decisions. The loyalty and obedience spells were intended for Senrid.
The regent tried some of those on his own daughter, as he didn't quite
dare to try them on Senrid until he knew they'd work."

"May I inquire after the result? You did say yes and no."

"The 'yes' part of my answer is that one of my aunts is connected to
the local governor, your majesty. She was always giving me books about
history. I told her I wanted to learn magic, to fix poor Stefan, and to
save the rest of us—well . . ." Despite her best efforts, Hibern could feel
her throat tightening. "The short answer is, I began to study light magic.
In secret. To counter my father's spells."

Atan leaned forward. "Who taught you?"

"Lilith the Guardian."

Atan sat bolt upright. "You've *met* her?" The mysterious mage Lilith
the Guardian appeared in the world perhaps once a century, guarding
the world from Norsunder. Though she certainly didn't guard Sartor a
century ago, Atan thought to herself.

"Yes. She found me. I don't know how. Gave me my first light magic
books, and introduced me to history outside our own. Pointed out the

green star, so bright in the sky, and said that it was Songre Silde, a world circling our sun. And that the tiny dull one is Aldau-Rayad, destroyed in the Fall. She told me that we have a sister world—"

"Geth-deles!" Atan exclaimed. "Circling opposite us, so we never see Geth-deles in our skies. Do you find that amazing, too?"

Hibern's tone lightened as she said, "When I first heard about Geth-deles being a twin world opposite ours, I thought that Lilith meant a world exactly like ours, and that there was a Hibern on it, but she moved backward to me, maybe using this hand instead of this." She held up one palm, then the next.

Atan rocked back on her chair, her fabulous silks rustling and crushing as she clapped in delight. "Oh, that's wonderful! So Lilith taught you magic?"

"Well, she gave me my first magic books. Our visits were brief. She warned me they would be. She couldn't always come." Hibern paused to take a deep breath. "She cautioned me about studying secretly, what it might mean if I got caught. By my family. I didn't care. I wanted to fix Stefan, and I knew I was *right* . . ."

Another pause, as she gazed into memory, evoking the pain of the past year. "The regent's rewards to my father turned to threats. The king was getting harder for him to control. He also offered one further reward: to marry me to the king when we came of age. My family has never married into the royal family, but they've served loyally for generations. My family would gain thereby."

"So you would have been married off to an enchanted king."

"Yes, your majesty."

"Go on, please, Hibern."

"I was eleven then. I wanted more study time. I turned an accidental fall into a fake permanent injury. Got a reputation as poor mad lame Hibern. Ah, being physically strong is important in my country. Crippled limbs from war wounds give one prestige, but falling down the stairs makes one despised. I studied in secret, countering my father's spells when I could."

Another deep breath.

"Lilith the Guardian came one last time, to say that Norsunder was rising again, and she could no longer come as she had too many places to watch that might be under imminent attack. She introduced me to Erai-Yanya, to see if we might fit together as tutor and student, then Sartor came back, and Siamis appeared. You know the rest better than I."

Atan leaned forward, her gaze intent. "I know the history of the Si-amis enchantment, though I spent that year enchanted into a dream sleep, like most of the rest of the kingdom. The world. Go on, please."

Hibern went on in her most neutral voice, "Your Sartoran mage guild had sent mages north, so they didn't fall into the enchantment. When they came back, they put out the call for aid. Erai-Yanya said it would be good practice to come here to Sartor, to help your guild close those rifts through which Norsunder could move armies as fast as the Nor-sundrian mages made them."

Hibern dropped her gaze, remembering the Sartoran Mage Chief Veltos exclaiming, *A Marloven? Have we come to such a pass?* Even worse, when Erai-Yanya fell into a dark magic trap, Hibern was the first one questioned, as if she'd been responsible. And even after Tsauderei managed to break Erai-Yanya out, the Sartoran mages still insisted that Hibern be assigned to help the elementary students. She was never let anywhere near the Tower of Knowledge.

But none of that was Atan's fault, Hibern knew.

While Hibern thought, unaware that her pause had stretched almost to a silence, Atan watched Hibern's tightly clasped hands and her low-ered gaze, before Hibern said, "I could only help with elementary spells. When Siamis was defeated and the rift magic destroyed, I returned home."

By then the memories crowding her mind were so strong she was unaware of the pain in her face, and her white-knuckled grip on her hands. She shut her eyes against the betraying sting of tears. "When I got home, I . . . my father had discovered my study. What I had been doing. To counter his wards."

The image of her father's face replaced Atan's, his eyes wide with fury, his mouth twisted with disgust as he screamed at her.

*A vile traitor in my own home? 'Help Stefan'—what do you think I've been doing this past year? What you have done has worsened everything. I could have reversed those spells by now.*

Sick dismay chilled Atan as Hibern's gaze blanked and her voice low-ered to a whisper of pain. "He told me to go. So I left."

Still gripped by memory, Hibern felt the echo of her father's finger poking into her forehead, then his open hand as he slapped her away.

*Get out of this house.* Hibern remembered lying on the floor dizzily, looking up at the vein ticking in his forehead. Then turning to her mother as she cried, *But I wanted to fix things. That's what light magic does.*

Hibern's throat ached as she remembered her mother's furious face, her low, angry whisper, *Then you could have done it another way besides sneaking behind our backs.*

Abruptly Hibern recollected time and place. And shut her eyes, mortified. She strove for a normal voice. "So I live with Erai-Yanya now. And Senrid—our king—asked me to tutor him in light magic. Your majesty," Hibern belatedly remembered.

"Call me Atan," was the answer, with a quick gesture, as Atan looked away, disturbed by the pain her question had caused. "You may drop the 'your majesty' if it's not part of your habit of courtly speech. It certainly wasn't part of my own upbringing."

"I don't have any courtly speech training, your majesty," Hibern said. "Other than being coached to always append 'your majesty' to a response asked for by, well, you."

Atan cast an uneasy look at her hands. "Does your king require such honorifics?"

"We don't have any honorifics such as 'your grace' or 'your majesty.' Titles are part of the holder's name. King Senrid is Senrid-Harvaldar in our tongue."

Atan gave her a sober glance. "I asked Tsauderei for a study partner my age, who wasn't from an exalted family that would expect favors, and who wasn't considered a part of either of the magic schools . . . well, because. Do you have any questions for me?"

"What was it like?" Hibern asked. "Coming back into the world after a century, I mean?"

"I didn't, really. I mean, I did, but as a baby. I was born a century ago. My mother's last act was to send me away, carried by one of her bodyguards. Gehlei fought her way out of the city, and even though she was wounded so badly she lost an arm, she made it with me almost to the eastern border when the enchantment caught us. We were discovered by Tsauderei, lying there on the mountainside. I was a crying baby, and Gehlei's wound was still fresh. He took us back to his valley, which is a very old mage retreat that Norsunder cannot get into. There, I grew up during the last fifteen years of the enchantment. As I was just a baby when it happened, I don't remember anything of the war, or the time before. But I spend all day every day with those who do."

Atan's smile was pensive. "It was so happy, at first. Then . . . then they started learning what it meant for them, that their yesterday had happened close to a century ago in the rest of the world. We had ninety-seven-year-old stores in the cupboards, and all our old ties with the world had been broken. The treasury was completely empty, because of the war my father lost. Trade monies had vanished, treaties no longer had meaning. Reclamation is near impossible from those long dead. People who had relatives outside the country . . . don't. A lot of them had already lost their families in the war."

*Like yours?* Hibern thought, but didn't say it. She'd been bitter about being driven out of her home, troubled as it was, but at least her family was alive. Atan was never going to get her family back.

A distant bell bonged, and Atan sighed. "The steward will send someone to fetch me soon. My duties leave me this one hour a week, and I mean to keep up with my magic studies. I don't want to lose what I worked so hard to gain. I study better if I have someone to do it with. Will you come back?"

"Yes," Hibern said. That would mean several transfers in a day, but from Marloven Hess to Sartor was considerably less than from Roth Drael to Sartor. And she did have to get used to it.

"Thank you," Atan said. "I so look forward to it!"

"So do I," Hibern said, but before she could add anything else, there was an insistent tap on the door.

Atan said, "Enter."

As the door opened, Hibern got to her feet, bowed self-consciously, and slipped past the entering servant, who gave her a stern glance before greeting the young queen in formal language.

Hibern walked slowly back to the Destination, her mind filled with that conversation, so unexpected in every way. Despite all the coaching about protocol, and her knowledge of Atan's prestigious background, it struck Hibern that Atan was a lot like herself.

In a thoughtful mood, she shifted back to Roth Drael.

Erai-Yanya looked up at the flash and air-stirring of transfer magic. She took in Hibern's closed expression and turned back to the letter she was writing to her son.

Hibern went to her room, where she stood, head bowed. Except for that wakening of those horrible feelings of rejection, she thought it had gone well. Enough of that shudder inside remained for her to breathe in and out, reminding herself that she had the life she wanted, and further, the Queen of Sartor had accepted her, despite her background and mistakes, to be her study partner.

She went out to find Erai-Yanya sealing a finished letter.

"Hungry?" Erai-Yanya asked, indicating a covered dish from which steam still trickled. "How did it go?"

"Oh, Atan is great. Her majesty. She wants me to call her Atan." Hibern sat down. "The best moment was finding out we both like history. And the study of worlds. The formal language from the servants was what I expected, public circle, polite and correct, but the moment I met the morvende boy Hin, everything went different."

"How?"

Hibern told her, then added baldly, "I told her the truth about myself. Because that was a promise I made to myself. The queen—Atan—did me the courtesy of listening. And kept herself from saying anything about Marlovens."

Erai-Yanya ran a quill through her fingers. "Pause, Hibern. Do not invest her words with insult that was not there. So begins misunderstanding. I feel fairly certain that the impression she has of Marlovens is that when they are not at war, they practice civility. Sartorans practice courtesy. And the Colendi practice politesse. You do perceive the difference?"

Hibern flushed. "I take it back. When I was done, I guess I hoped it was me she would find interesting, not a Marloven oddity."

"I expect it was both." Erai-Yanya chuckled. "Orange talons! The morvende are doing it to annoy the Sartoran first circle, and maybe even the high council, I should imagine."

"Why?" Hibern's emotions swooped.

Erai-Yanya pursed her lips, still running the feather through her fingers. "Is it not clear? Atan's had a strange upbringing, as she told you herself. What she didn't tell you is that she's next thing to a prisoner." As Hibern gasped, Erai-Yanya stuck the quill into her untidy bun. "Oh, it's not like your kingdom, iron bars, torture chambers—"

Hibern was going to interject that Marlovens, for the most part, despised torture, but kept silent.

"—kings and jarls murdering one another right and left. Everyone in Sartor seems to be doing their duty as they see it, but they have Atan nearly strangled in protocol and obligation, the more so because they're all certain that Detlev of Norsunder, or Siamis, whoever gains the ascendance over the other, is going to come back."

Senrid believes it, too, Hibern thought, but decided against saying it, after that crack about Marlovens. She knew Erai-Yanya didn't intend to be mean, but she was so ignorant about Marloven Hess. And she had no interest in learning about a primarily military kingdom with a problematical past.

Erai-Yanya continued, "The thing to understand is that the young queen's morvende friends are trying to loosen those constraints as best they can, since they have the freedom to do it."

"I've never heard of morvende being in royal palaces like that."

"They usually aren't. Even when they come sunside, they have nothing to do with sunsider governments, and they pay no attention to political boundaries. But in Sartor, it's always been different. And those two, Hinder and Sinder, were part of the Shendoral Rescuers, the youths who helped the queen break the century-long enchantment. They have a special status."

"But the queen—Atan—"

"Call her Atan. She really needs to be Atan to someone, without expectation in return, even if it's only for an hour a week."

"Well, that's easy enough."

"Hibern." Erai-Yanya leaned forward, her expression sardonic. "Nothing is ever easy in Sartor."

## Chapter Nine

*Same day*
*Norsunder Base*

THE alliance, so far, numbered thus: the Mearsieans, whom nobody had ever heard of and nobody would pay attention to if they had; Senrid, whose kingdom everyone had heard of and distrusted; and Hibern, a lowly mage student unclaimed by either school, who had lost her home.

All of them approached the idea of recruitment in significantly varying ways. The single shared conviction was that any alliance must form some kind of defense against Norsunder.

However, 'Norsunder' was no more a unified entity than their alliance.

The same day that Hibern visited Sartor, a week's ride south of Sartor's border, everyone in the vast fortress called Norsunder Base stilled as greenish lightning flashed in windows. The vast granite construct resonated with an abyssal boom more felt than heard.

The burnt-metal smell to the air, gone in an instant, warned the mage Dejain that a mass transfer had been attempted, and had failed. Those who had attempted it had vanished into whatever-it-was between physical locations.

She met the eyes of Lesca, the fortress steward, and sighed. "Why *do* they keep trying to transfer in groups? They know the rifts are gone."

Lesca grimaced. "Because everyone's plots need to have happened yesterday, of course." Her eyes crinkled with amusement, as she sat back comfortably on her chair, a large, curvy woman with a taste for the delicate embroideries and fragile silks of Colend. "I guess I won't be needing to find space for this latest bunch."

"I had better go see what's happened," Dejain said, though she'd just arrived at Lesca's request. "They'll be wanting the mages."

"Do that," Lesca said. "Then come back and tell me everything."

Dejain left the steward's chamber and turned the corner toward Norsunder Base's command center, where she was waved past the sentries. She started down the hall to the room at the other end of the soot-blackened, torchlit hall.

She had expected to be the first arrival, as Lesca's suite was two short halls from the command center in the enormous fortress. But she didn't expect the only two voices in the command center to be speaking in the lilting Ancient Sartoran that Dejain had expended much effort to attempt learning.

Siamis and his uncle Detlev, alone? She glanced back. As expected, the sentries faced outward. All she saw were their backs. She didn't quite understand all that talk about mind-shields, but she knew from personal experience that Detlev really was able to invade someone's thoughts, and so she closed her eyes, and imagined a brick wall encircling her head. When she had that image, she tried to listen from within it, the way one would listen to a conversation from the other side of a fence.

". . . and you were wrong by at least a century." That was Siamis, the handsome young nephew, grown up under the aegis of Norsunder. Everyone knew that Siamis had been taken hostage as a boy of twelve, over four thousand years ago, forcing Detlev to go into Norsunder-Beyond to try to rescue him. What no record revealed was what Ilerian, the most terrifying of the Host of Lords, had done to Detlev to turn him against Sartor.

Siamis's voice was tenor, expressive—a singer's voice, though Dejain had never heard him sing.

"Yes," Detlev said. His voice was just a voice, never very expressive. In her mercifully brief encounters with him, Dejain had never heard him angry, which made some of the things he did far more unnerving. "Which means we have to find it first."

"You must," Siamis retorted.

"I must," Detlev agreed.

What was 'it'? Dejain did not understand the tone. Was that anger or laughter?

Siamis went on in that same tone, "And so. My plan. The spells need alteration, not the strategy."

"Evend may be gone, but Tsauderei is very much alive, Oalthoreh in Bereth Ferian has sent her journeymages through the world to create tracers specifically to reveal your presence, and Sartor has been adapting to a century of change with commendable speed. Today is probably evidence of that."

"My very dear uncle," Siamis drawled. "When you point out the obvious—"

"—it means you have overlooked something obvious. The new orders must supersede the old."

"Are we back to the brats, then? I've seen to it that Liere Fer Eider is afraid of her own shadow. I cannot improve on what you did to Senrid Montredaun-An. Between the two of them, they are sufficiently intimidated into hiding behind childhood. It has even become a fad."

Detlev's voice quieted. Dejain held her breath. "See that it spreads. I need time to investigate the Geth claims. And you must make readiness here your first concern."

"I thought that was *your* first concern." Siamis's retort betrayed nothing but good humor. "Or is my freedom to act conditional after all?"

"I condition for nothing. The Host might see a different view from the Garden of the Twelve—"

Clattering echoed up the stairway opposite Lesca's suite: armed warriors on the way. Dejain must not be seen lurking outside the command center.

Keeping her steps noiseless, she scurried toward the sentries, and just before the new arrivals reached the corner and the sentries she whirled, so she would be seen walking toward command.

Before she stepped over the threshold, she glanced back at the group of warriors. That arrogant young Henerek strode at the front, recognizable instantly by his size and his thick, sandy hair. He was followed by lesser talents and ambitions.

Dejain passed inside the chamber, darting a quick glance at Siamis and Detlev for any sign of awareness of having been spied upon. Detlev stood directly below the big world map on the far wall. He was an ordinary-looking man above medium height, brown hair worn collar length in a military cut, tunic and trousers of so plain a design he would go unnoticed in most kingdoms of the south, and probably in the north as well. His expression revealed nothing.

Beyond him, his nephew Siamis lounged against a table, slim and graceful, his head bent, so all Dejain could see was his fair hair, gilt in the glowglobes' light.

Detlev turned Henerek's way. "I take it you were the fool who just obliterated four well-trained captains by attempting a group transfer. Or was that your intent?"

"They were *my* captains. For the challenge," Henerek retorted, then added sullenly, "There's never been any problem with transferring from Five. I distinctly recollect bringing two others along the last time I transferred."

"That," said Detlev, "was previous to Sartor's mages' recent gift. Or someone's. You did not get the general order: single transfers only, no more than four in a day, then test with a stone first?"

Henerek looked down, then up, his fingers twitching absently at his sword hilt. Or was that a sign of intent?

Siamis bestowed on them his gentle smile. "Henerek seems to feel that he's the exception to general orders. Or we wouldn't be gathered today." He made a lazy wave toward the window, through which Dejain glimpsed the long line of warriors moving into the broad plain where the wargames were held. She remembered that today's wargame was different from the usual: a challenge for command of Norsunder Base—Henerek against Siamis.

Detlev did not acknowledge the interruption. He said to Henerek, "If you were taking the field against Ralanor Veleth today, and four of your captains dropped with arrows in them, would you request a postponement from Szinzar, until such time as you could arrange for replacements?"

The scrape of a foot and a half-suppressed chuckle from the watching circle caused Henerek to glance back, a flush of anger on his heavy-jawed countenance. The avid audience fell silent.

"Regard your failed transfer as a . . . shall we call it a tactical error? Your challenge will go forward as planned."

Siamis sighed, sounding weary and bored.

For the time it took for Dejain's heart to beat three times, no one moved.

Dejain held her breath, aware of the shifts in stance, the brush of hands over hilts, among the watchers. Henerek had gone still, almost rigid. Nobody needed mysterious mind powers to see how much he loathed the two Ancient Sartorans. Though Dejain had never seen Detlev wearing a weapon, and Henerek positively bristled with steel.

Finally Henerek muttered, "I'll see you on the field." He stalked out.

With quick glances in Detlev's direction, the rest of the military clattered after him, leaving Dejain wondering whom they would have helped if Henerek had assaulted Detlev.

She wondered whose aid, if any, Siamis would come to.

With the warriors gone, Dejain saw the two mages who had come in behind the warriors.

Detlev lifted his head. "Dejain. Attend to the transfer problem, please."

Dejain said, "I just came from the steward, who sent for me."

Detlev replied, "Give Lesca anything she wants, of course. Then investigate the transfer problem, and fix it." He vanished abruptly, as usual, not even going to the Destination in order to transfer.

Siamis's gaze lifted from the window. "This should be fun," he said. Gone was the affect of boredom that had so goaded Henerek. His expression was thoughtful as he walked out. Unlike Henerek's, his step was noiseless, but Dejain thought that he was just as dull and simple as Henerek, really. All men were simple, she thought sourly as she faced the two mages still left in the room.

The mages were both men, one old and unfamiliar, and Pengris, young and ambitious. "What happened, exactly?" she asked him. "Were either of you in the Destination chamber?"

Pengris said, "I was. Henerek summoned me to sweep the Destination for traps or wards, which I did. I found nothing amiss. The transfers nearly made it. I saw four silhouettes, then that flash of light. When I could see again, there was no one on the tiles. They were gone."

"Silhouettes," Dejain repeated, her skin crawling. "I've never heard of a transfer failing . . . like that."

"Neither have I," the elder said uneasily. "Who could have warded our Destination?" He turned to the young one. "They were coming from Five, am I correct?"

The Norsunder base on the world the lighters had once called Aldau-Rayad before it was destroyed in the Fall had as much protective magic over its transfer Destination as this one. Because Aldau-Rayad was the fifth world from Erhal, the sun, it was known among them as Five.

Dejain and the gray-haired man turned to Pengris, a weedy, sparse-haired fellow. Dejain had pegged him for the type who often studied magic because they hated people.

He sighed, a loose strand of reddish hair lifting, his eyes shifting in a way that reminded Dejain of a rat caught in a trap.

He was young, but experienced in subterfuge, misdirection, and imaginative nastiness. Right now he was caught square: the Destination at Five was his responsibility.

"The problem is not at this end," Dejain said. Pengris licked his lips, and Dejain knew he was trying to slither out. Transfers hurt, everyone knew it. World transfers hurt far worse. Younger bodies sustained the effects better.

He sighed again, resigned and irritated. "I'll shift to Five to investigate."

"Wait at least two hours. Then use a token," Dejain warned. An already-spelled transfer token had the best chance of escaping any general wards, though they hurt substantially more than established Destination chambers.

He walked out, already nervous as he exited.

How Detlev managed to transfer so easily without Destinations, Dejain wondered, not for the first time. He was so very much older than she was, some would say impossibly old. But then Ilerian, the strangest of the Host of Lords, who seldom emerged from the Garden of the Twelve at the center of Norsunder, was said to be far older. And neither of them looked a day over thirty. Her shoulder blades prickled with a crawly sensation.

Detlev was just a man. They are all the same in essence, she reminded herself as she turned over her hands, so small and youthful-looking.

She'd begun to use dark magic to halt her aging when she turned twenty-two, and so she knew she appeared as she had then, a dainty, blonde figure. Even before that spell had been broken once, nearly killing her, she'd begun to feel the subtle pull of age. It was inescapable, and the best way to keep that pull from becoming direr was to live very carefully. Sometimes she felt ancient, and certainly far more aware than those around her, but Detlev and Siamis managed to make her regain all the awkwardness and uncertainty of youth, without any of its strength.

Still, they obviously had their limits: for all their vaunted powers, they hadn't perceived her listening outside of command.

She smiled as she rejoined Lesca and reported what she'd seen and heard.

Though Lesca was no older than forty, she was far from stupid. To double-check, Dejain finished, "I heard the words, but the context completely escapes me as much as my presence escaped them. Though I'm fairly certain that Siamis is fretting under Detlev's control."

"That's been the case for a year," Lesca drawled.

"But that about 'it.' What can they mean?"

"Something they're looking for," Lesca said, amused.

"The dyra? The lighters got the one, and destroyed the other."

"Why does it have to be a thing? How about a person, an idea? A specific place that gives them military advantage? All I know is, it's more plotting." Lesca yawned. "Present company excepted, I find mages unspeakably tedious, even more than I find politics. Everybody wants something they don't have. Except me. I sometimes wonder if I'm the smartest person in this place, because I am wise enough not to have ambition." Lesca lifted a lazy hand to encompass her comfortable rooms.

"Detlev and Siamis are not like the rest of us," Dejain stated.

"And here's me wondering if Siamis leans right." Lesca tipped her head.

Dejain understood the current idiom, at least among Norsunder's warriors: 'right' meant right hand, sword hand, preference for men. 'Left,' shield hand, ring hand in some cultures, preference for females. Both-handed for interest beyond gender limitation.

"Someone insisted they saw him in one of the more exclusive houses up north somewhere, under a guise. As one would expect with a very young man. I wonder if Detlev is made of wood, and I don't mean that in any interesting way." Lesca chuckled, running her hand through her silky hair, which was now colored a rich chestnut. "This I do know. Neither of them shows the least interest in any of the hirelings I take such trouble to recruit." She shrugged, tipping her head in the direction of the rec wing, across the great courtyard, where Lesca had installed pleasure house workers for those who earned the privilege.

Dejain knew that discipline had been better since Lesca brought them in. Before then, warriors at Norsunder Base, which was considered a way station, were on their own during their liberty watch. No sexual outlets beyond what they could find among one another usually meant more fights, and horrific punishments. The former commander had felt that that made for better fighters. Siamis—young as he was—had told Lesca that fighting was better if there was an immediate reward for exertion, like her present arrangement.

Lesca lifted her upper lip. "Do you think he goes off-world to seek perversions, as they whisper about Efael?"

Dejain grimaced at the name of the youngest of the Host of Lords. In so many ways he was the worst of them. At least the nastiest, and his sister the second worst. If rumor was true, the least objectionable sexual play those two indulged in was with one another. "You would think there would be whispers if he did."

"If Henerek wins, and his face isn't distorted, I'll crook my finger, and he'll be here as fast as he can." Lesca shrugged indolently, and turned her head toward the far wall, which was smooth, painted white. "But if Siamis wins, and I crook my finger, he'll look at me with that air of question. I loathe that. I hope Henerek wins, though Siamis is so much prettier."

Lesca picked up the wand that Dejain had ensorcelled, and pointed it at the wall, whispering. An image replaced the wall, the vantage from the topmost tower of the fortress, with an unimpeded view of the cracked plain beyond, on which no blade of grass had grown for centuries. In ragged lines, the contending forces were drawing together according to each commander's placement.

Dejain had put together the spells: Lesca had only to visit a spot somewhere in the fortress once, look at the view she wished to see, touch the wand, and speak the simple charm Dejain had set up. Thereafter she could sit in her comfortable chamber and watch from that vantage. Dejain had thought at most Lesca would limit herself to three or four views, maybe half a dozen, as the spells pulled a great deal of magic potential.

"How many views have you set?" Dejain asked.

"I've lost count," Lesca said cheerfully.

Dejain suppressed an exclamation. She'd carefully explained how much magic was used for each, but Lesca seemed to have as little regard for magic as Dejain had for sex. No wonder the Destination was becoming more unstable. It probably wasn't Sartor at fault, or Five.

But she did not know for certain. She glanced up, to find Lesca regarding her with that narrow, observant gaze. "Speaking of petrified wood," Lesca said. "Have you considered that those two knew you were listening to them? You know their reputation."

"I think most of that is hyperbole." Dejain settled back on her cushion. "Oh, I know they can speak from mind to mind. And listen. But you will probably have experienced the latter: there's a pang like a needle stuck behind your eyes, and your own words echo inside your head, and that didn't occur while I was eavesdropping just now. As for the talking from mind to mind, surely it must take even more effort than normal listening must."

"At least, outside of the Garden of the Twelve." Lesca's profile was avid as she watched Henerek riding to the front of his force. Though the foot and mounted warriors all carried wooden swords, Henerek brandished naked steel, evidence that he was willing to fight Siamis to the death for command of Norsunder Base. "Ah. There's Henerek, sword a-swing. The show is about to begin. Why is it that the boys can finish a fight with the other sword still a-swing, but the women just want a hot bath?"

Dejain didn't bother making the obvious observation that there were exceptions to everything, even among warriors, whose minds she found dull or repellent.

Dejain glanced to the other side, easily spotting Siamis by his white shirt and blond head. He scorned uniforms, and as the weather, for once, was clement, there he was, without his famous sword. She did not understand why he'd left it in Bereth Ferian after his defeat there. Another game, no doubt. Like his uncle, he seemed to prefer carrying no weapon, a different sort of arrogance.

Dejain listened with the least part of her attention as Lesca began a dispassionate catalogue of various captains' physical attributes and drawbacks. Once, very long ago, Dejain had cared about such things, but that had been in her young days, before she found her way to dark magic. She remembered standing silently as a servant as the baras's daughter and her friend held just such conversations, but of course no servant's opinion would be sought.

Dejain uttered agreements during the pauses, to hide her disinterest. At least the divan was comfortable for her sensitive joints. She cooperatively turned her gaze to the window, but her attention was inward rather than on the two lines racing together as she mentally reviewed varieties of transfer traps, tracers, and wards. She would have to delve into research, once the witnesses' reports had been heard . . .

"Yes indeed," Dejain said again, when she became aware of an expectant pause from Lesca. When you haven't been listening, agreement is almost always safest.

Lesca shot her an inquisitive glance. "But coming back to Henerek. He's willing enough, even delightfully brusque, but I sense he's not seeing *me*. I pride myself on my not-inconsiderable skills, but whose face is he seeing over mine? One wishes to be noticed for one's efforts."

"Most certainly," Dejain said tranquilly, thinking that though Lesca's favorite subject was herself, at least she didn't prate of love.

Lesca sighed.

Men were useful only as toys. For companionship of the mind, Lesca preferred women—but they had to share at least a sense of humor, if not Lesca's interests.

Smart women in command positions were rare at Norsunder Base: Vatiora was dead (and good riddance, as she'd been crazy); Yeres was infinitely worse, but at least she rarely appeared and then only for moments; the new spy, Elzhier, was a smart-mouthed teen and kept constantly in the field; Nath, a female captain with brains, was down there behind Henerek right now, which just left Dejain. Mages were generally unsatisfactory as company, male or female. Their minds were always in magical fogs.

Below, the trumpet blared, the signal to begin.

The neat lines of marching and mounted warriors began to waver, and met. Lesca leaned forward to watch, wishing she could pick out details better. Henerek smashed and clubbed at the center of his line, two big men at either side. Whatever clever strategy he'd come up with had had to be abandoned when he lost his best captains, so he'd fallen back on the old charge, strongest at the midpoint, the intent to cut the opposing line and roll them up separately.

Siamis rode directly behind his main two lines, one making a shield wall and the other armed with cudgels. He looked so easy in the saddle with those graceful straight limbs unencumbered by any weapons. He could have commanded by mental communication. He'd forestalled complaints about advantages by using signal flags, same as Henerek— not that the latter signaled, with his captains gone.

Siamis turned his head, then spoke to one of his outriders. A whirl and dip of the flag, and chosen squads in the reinforcement line formed up into wedges. They muscled up behind their mates in the first two lines, who were still struggling to resist the chaotic charge.

The two lines stirred as squad captains shouted orders. Henerek's chargers, clearly taking this movement for surrender, lost all form as they pressed together, all struggling to be first through the openings, presenting a solid target for the wedges.

Smash! They hit Henerek's straggled line and shattered it and all semblance of order, as everyone began fighting. Those who surrendered fell to their knees.

Henerek stilled, head twisting back and forth, and then Siamis turned his head, beckoned, and pointed.

A familiar short, slim, black-haired figure, also instantly recognizable, launched through the melee like an arrow from a bow. Dejain's heart jolted with fear when she recognized Kessler Sonscarna, the renegade Chwahir prince she'd once worked with on his mad plan to replace the world's most powerful rulers with people of his own training. Dejain had never believed he would succeed, and had betrayed Kessler to save her own skin. As was expected in Norsunder. But Kessler was . . . mad.

He fought his way through Henerek's big guards as if they were straw targets, hitting them with unnerving speed in nerve clusters that caused limbs to freeze in breath-hitching pain. Then he found Henerek.

Lesca was leaning forward, elbows on knees. "Look at him," she said appreciatively. "He's smart, he's fast, and he's brutal. I think he's broken Henerek's arm! This will make him a captain at last, one would think. Why isn't he a captain?"

"Because he's insane," Dejain said.

"But that's so often an attribute." Lesca uttered a deep chuckle as, below on the field, Kessler threw away Henerek's cudgel and attacked with his bare hands. "I heard that Efael himself sent him to bottle up that disgusting old crock in Chwahirsland, but he doesn't seem to be grateful for the privilege, does he?"

"That's because Kessler would have preferred to gut the old crock and watch him die at his feet," Dejain said.

Below, Henerek circled around Kessler, who waited in stillness, only his head moving. Henerek's left arm dangled, but he gripped a sword in his right.

At last Henerek struck. He lasted about four blows, then measured his length in the dust. "Do you think Henerek's dead? No, he's moving." Lesca shook her head. "You worked with him once. What kind of lover does Kessler like?"

"Never saw him with anyone," Dejain said. "I think Kessler's too insane for anything normal like sex."

"They say he never lies."

Dejain understood. The more she warned Lesca away from Kessler, the more interest Lesca would take, especially since Henerek was on his way to the lazaretto, probably for some weeks' stay. "He's a Chwahir," she said.

Lesca grimaced. "I forgot that. He doesn't move like them, or act like them. They're so . . . so furtive," she finished in disgust. "No wonder I've never seen him at the recreation wing."

Dejain didn't bother explaining that she knew little about his life other than that Kessler had escaped Wan-Edhe at age ten, and thus half of his life had been spent away from Land of the Chwahir. The thinking half.

Lesca made a noise of disappointment. "See there! It looks like Siamis is reorganizing them into drill groups. Now he'll work them until they can barely crawl after their commander back to their bunks." She rose. "What a disappointment. I may as well see about the cornmeal shipments, as soon as I know you mages have fixed the transfer. At least we should be able to get non-living things through."

## Chapter Ten

*Bath Rennet (Midsummer), 4737 AF*
*Bereth Ferian*

IN Bereth Ferian's Hall of Light, the music swelled to a glorious climax, four melodic lines braided by women's voices, men's voices, children's, and the soloist as dancers leaped back and forth, their streamers rippling in the air, symbolizing the propagation of world-healing spells.

Every beautiful chord, every repetition of words such as 'glory' and 'peace' needled Liere Fer Eider's spirit.

She squirmed in the great chair that was so much like a throne. She wanted to love the beautiful music and the brilliant dancing, because it was all for her. But she couldn't enjoy it because it *was* for her. That is, it wasn't really for her, it was for Sartora. Someone she wasn't.

The performance closed in a many-voiced *Hail Sartora, who saved the world!* that made Liere prickle painfully all over as if someone had stuck pins in her.

She forced herself to smile, though her teeth felt cold.

She then forced herself to turn in all directions in the way taught her by Arthur, but she looked over the people's heads so she couldn't see their faces, and she shut her mind in tight so she wouldn't hear the thoughts people sprayed all over so freely.

She spoke the words of thanks that Arthur had helped her put together, and tried not to listen to how spindly and high her own voice sounded. ". . . and so I invite you to partake of refreshments in the Hall of Amber." She rushed the final words together, embarrassment making her skin crawl as she whispered *please-don't-bow please-don't-bow.*

A rustle and sigh as all the visiting Venn merchants made a profound, deliberate bow.

It was so sickening, so horribly false, and it wasn't her fault, it wasn't. If she could choose she never would be clumsy, stupid Liere Fer Eider, so boring the Mearsieans had been glad to go home and leave her behind.

Liere forced herself to smile. She got up and extended her hand toward the Hall of Amber, breathing freely once they turned toward the archway leading to the next room. As soon as the guests spied the food and drink, she sensed their attention shifting. A few lingered, apparently wanting to talk to her, but she'd gotten good at evading that.

The visiting Venn were quite tall. She found the tallest, slipped behind him, and waited while Arthur kindly drew attention by pointing out what people could already see: "Here's our attempt at Venn berry drink. Let us know how it tastes? And there are baked cabbage rolls that we are told are a Venn delicacy . . ."

Liere backed up. A quick step behind a substantial man with a complication of lemon-colored braids, a pause behind a carved column, and she was almost free. She tiptoed to the door, the back of her neck tight until she escaped into the empty hallway beyond.

On the other side of the room, Arthur watched her go, and sighed. She'd told him once that he was an "almost," that he might "make his unity," which had something to do with Dena Yeresbeth. If hearing others' thoughts turned one into a nail-biting, anxious mess like Liere, he didn't want this Dena Yeresbeth. In fact, if he detected any mysterious signs of such an ability in himself, he would do anything he could to avoid it.

"We have offended Sartora?"

Arthur turned around quickly, to find the Venn emissary standing there. The man was old, his face lined, his pale hair silvery white instead of the mostly-yellows Arthur saw in the rest.

"Not at all," Arthur said, and because he'd found the emissary easy to talk to, in spite of the Venn reputation for truculence, he added, "She's not comfortable in crowds."

The man inclined his head, the light running along the thin gold band around his brow, not quite a coronet. Arthur had seen that some wore them, some didn't, but he didn't know what they meant. He knew so little about the Venn, who historically never came out of their kingdom except to make war, centuries ago.

"Tell me about this child who can save a world, yet not endure a little conversation. Unless you are being diplomatic, and it is not crowds but Venn to whom she objects?"

"She doesn't know anything about the Venn," Arthur said quickly. "She came from a town where reading, especially for girls, was discouraged, as they were meant to keep shop. She told me she really liked your crown prince, whom she met after she broke Siamis's spell over your country."

The emissary's brows went up, and he smiled. "He is well-beloved, our Prince Kerendal. I shall take your words as truth, then, though it still does not explain why someone who did what she has done will not remain with us long enough to be thanked."

"She doesn't . . ." Arthur began, then halted. Maybe he was saying too much. He had already failed Liere, he felt, though he didn't know how to fix it. All along he'd wondered why she wanted the Mearsieans to stay, some of whom he found tiresome with their endless private jokes that they clearly thought so hilarious.

It wasn't until they'd left that he'd seen in Liere's dejection her hope to be invited back with them.

The sad thing was, though they might be silly or annoying, none of them were snobs. Arthur was very practiced at identifying snobs, after having served as a page and then as King Evend's chosen heir. The Mearsieans didn't think they were better than anyone else. They were a closed group. It didn't seem to have occurred to them that anyone new might want in. Especially Sartora, the Girl Who Saved the World.

The Venn emissary lifted his head. The Venn had divided into groups the way people tend to do in big crowds, a couple of them venturing apart to talk in a stiffly polite way with the magic students on duty.

"It would appear natural," the emissary said as they paced the perimeter of the Hall, "that someone who had done what she did could enjoy the accolades she earned."

"But that's it, she doesn't," Arthur said.

"Why not? She cannot think she failed."

"She was convinced by a friend that Siamis wasn't defeated. That he retreated, and will come again."

The Venn lifted his gnarled hand, his embroidered sleeve dropping back to reveal a diamond of Venn knotwork tattooed on his forearm above his wrist. "Norsunder always returns." Arthur had heard of Venn body art, but had never seen it; then the sleeve dropped back, hiding the mark. "We know that, and perhaps the knowing requires us to celebrate every defeat the more. Surely we would not wish to think, 'why bother?' Sartora does not have wise friends, if she has such an attitude at so young an age."

"It's not that at all," Arthur said. "Her friend is a Marloven."

"Ah-h-h."

The word was exhaled on a different note. Arthur remembered there was some ancient connection between the horrible, warlike Marlovens and the Venn. He had never wanted to meet any of them, though he'd come to rather like Senrid, puzzling as he was.

The emissary stared down at Arthur, an earnest young mage student without a fragment of the experience that had made wily old Evend such a splendid diplomat as well as mage. The emissary reflected that in olden times, before the magical construct called the Arrow had bound Venn magic, the Venn would have overrun this entire region in three days. In truth, they could do it now without magical aid.

But the old queen had spoken: *We will heed the treaty, and thereby we turn dishonor to honor. Norsunder will be back soon enough, and when they come, our former foe shall release the Arrow and welcome us as allies. In the meantime, let us continue to trade.* "So in fact her young Marloven friend feels that if Norsunder does return, Sartora will be looked to for defense, perhaps single-handed?"

"That's it." Arthur gave a sigh of obvious relief. "Oh, and you should hear the stories about her father—" He caught himself. That was gossip, and he knew better.

The emissary's gaze sharpened with interest.

Arthur chewed his lower lip. King Evend had always said that the personal would win over the theoretical in almost any discussion. Arthur hadn't always understood it, as he hadn't understood a lot of what Evend had said while ruminating during or after their lessons in history and magic, but he was discovering how many of Evend's observations about human behavior were true.

"Might that explain," the emissary ventured in a mild voice, while watching Arthur closely, "why Sartora was not restored to the bosom of her family, but lives here among you, young as she is?"

A vivid memory hit Arthur: Liere's sour-faced father who all three times Arthur saw him had been criticizing Liere in a bitter, scolding voice. The first time made sense. No parent would want to see their child looking the way Liere had, her hair hacked off with a knife during her run, wearing the clothes she'd taken from her brother, worn and patched and outgrown.

But the second time, Arthur had heard Liere's father whispering to Liere as he held her skinny arm in a tight grip, "Who do you think you are, mentioning people of rank by their private names, as if you were one of them? We thought you'd grown out of putting on airs to be interesting." And the third time, "Nothing good *ever* comes of girls getting above their place."

That was the one that made Liere go silent for a whole week. Until he met Lesim Fer Eider, Arthur had sometimes wished he had a father. Lesim Fer Eider had interrupted his daughter's every utterance with some criticism, and the morning after his arrival, they'd found him scolding his shrinking daughter for "idling around palaces belonging to her betters," and had issued an order demanding that she "return home to prepare for her future as a shopkeeper's wife," upon which old, sour Head Mage Oalthoreh had retorted, "I never speak against the wishes of families, unless that family is using the bond to propagate ignorance and prejudice. The child has declared her desire to remain here to learn. She may remain here until we have nothing more to teach her."

Having no answer he would vouchsafe to a mage, who might turn him into a tree stump, or worse—and no real value for his tiresome daughter—Lesim Fer Eider had used the transfer token the mages gave him to take himself away, leaving a general sense of relief when he was gone.

Arthur looked up. They'd walked halfway around the room without him being aware. He glanced the emissary's way, to encounter an expression of polite inquiry. He couldn't stop his neck from burning as he said, "Sartora stayed to begin the study of magic."

"A worthy aspiration," the emissary said smoothly as he lifted his head.

One of the castle pages entered, leading a familiar boy, white shirt-sleeves rolled to his elbows, black trousers and riding boots, his yellow hair squared with military precision just above his collar in back, the unruly waves combed back from his forehead, unlike Arthur's messy hair flopping on his own forehead.

"Senrid," Arthur exclaimed in blank surprise.

Heads turned, and Arthur had time to wonder whether it was the name or the person that caught the interest of his Venn guests, before Senrid's quick step closed the distance between them. His searching gaze was just as Arthur remembered, the only difference being the faint marks of healing bruises on his face. Arthur's stomach tightened. He'd heard plenty about those Marlovens.

The emissary studied Senrid with interest, and though Arthur knew it would sound stupid, there was no etiquette for the sudden and unannounced arrival of kings: "How should I introduce you?"

"Senrid Montredaun-An," Senrid said with his quick, wry smile. "Came to see Liere."

That took care of introductions, but not the quandary. What was Arthur's duty? There were invited guests, and here was a king.

"I can wait," Senrid said quickly, and Arthur remembered that Senrid, too, could hear thoughts. His neck burned again.

The emissary said suavely, "Perhaps we might resume our conversation when you have more leisure, your highness?"

Arthur knew what that meant: the man was going to interrogate him later. But that was all right. He'd have time to talk it over with his tutors, or his mother, by letter, and he'd know exactly what to say. He and the emissary exchanged courteous bows, and Arthur turned in relief to Senrid. "She's not in here."

Senrid's brows twitched upward. "Tactical retreat, eh?"

"Yes," Arthur said, though he had no idea what the 'tactical' part of retreat meant. He thought in dismay of all the places she could be in the enormous palace . . . but he knew where she had probably gone. "Come with me."

## Chapter Eleven

IN spite of the thick walls and the magic spells aiding the hot air vents, a wintry current snaked along the marble floor, making Liere shiver. Winters had never been this cold in Imar, nor was it dark from midafternoon to midmorning, the sun, when it appeared, riding low and weak far to the south, the light even at noon a soft bluish shade.

She avoided looking up at the long clerestory windows and ran until she couldn't hear the hubbub from the Celebration Wing. When she reached the huge vestibule with its fine carvings centered around acorns, of all things, she slowed. That way lay the mage school wing, and over this way the living quarters where she had rooms. She still didn't think of that grand suite as hers, and she didn't want to go there now. She was afraid to disturb anything, to make work for the servants, and found the silence unsettling, after growing up in a tiny house with a large, noisy family. And though she loved the fine furnishings and bright rugs with their complicated patterns, she couldn't live among them.

Maybe she should go and stand there, even if she scarcely dared sit. Anything was better than the irresistible urge to see *It*, to make sure *It* was still there. She knew she shouldn't, though she couldn't say why. It was just wrong.

But she had to. Just a peek. Because Senrid had said before he left that Siamis hadn't surrendered that ancient sword named Truth, he'd left it as a warning.

Liere took a step and another across the elaborate mosaic depicting a winged dragon surrounded by flames, or petals, or both. She hunched her shoulders, refusing to look up at the great dome overhead with its many long windows that should be showing sunlight. They were nearly dark, though the ceremony had begun at noon.

She reached the richly gleaming double doors higher than the eaves of her father's shop back in Imar. She ran her fingers along the gold carvings, a riot of flames that Arthur had said represented the Gate between Worlds, whence the dragons had come millennia ago, and through which they'd vanished again, leaving behind the inspiration for strange pieces of art and music and stranger tales about their sojourn in Sartorias-deles.

She yanked her hands down guiltily and scurried inside the ante-chamber before the old throne room.

Arthur had told her that this beautiful building had once been a royal palace, from which kings and queens had ruled over a federation of territories bound together to defend themselves against the ancestors of those very Venn who were eating pastries over in the Hall of Light on the opposite side of the palace, as they talked about trading foodstuffs—hard to grow in the storm-battered Land of the Venn—for their wonderful stoves, beautifully soft yeath fur gathered from the bushes where the animals scraped it off each spring, and wool.

Father was right. Revealing that she'd been born with the ability to hear people's thoughts and remembering everything she'd been told seemed to make her so awful, or boring, or *something*, that no one wanted to be around her. Like the Mearsiean girls. She had spent weeks with them, had done everything they suggested, had laughed at all their jokes, but when Clair got that letter, did they think about asking Liere to join them?

No.

All those girls had been adopted by Clair. They were Liere's age. Senrid had said . . . She sighed. No use in remembering what Senrid had said. She had to stop having imaginary conversations with him.

She tapped the carving in the discreet side door, then held her breath and stepped through. The door looked solid, but Arthur had taught her that this was illusion. Glowglobes much plainer than the pretty ones outside in the silent halls revealed a narrow stone passage. She ran down the stairs to what had once been a treasure room, and before that a dungeon. At the end of the hall, there was an iron-reinforced door, with a magic spell bound into it for extra protection.

Arthur had showed her how to get past the spell, after which she used both hands to lift the heavy latch and ease the door open wide enough to slip inside.

The room beyond was even colder. She clapped on the glowglobe, and let out a breath of relief. *It* was still there, lying alone on a carved stone table. She tiptoed up, knowing she was being silly. That sword would not jump up and slash around the room at the sound of footsteps. But still. She kept her hands laced behind her as she stared at the thing made four thousand years ago.

She tried to imagine Siamis her own age, being given this sword, in a world that shared the same seas and lands and sky, but in all other ways completely different. She tried to imagine having to grow up in Norsunder while thousands of years passed. Her father scolded her, and despised her, but at least he wasn't a Norsundrian villain.

She heard an echo of Senrid's wry voice. *Nobody throws away a four-thousand-year-old sword. He's going to come back for it.*

"Liere?"

Liere knew that voice so well that she thought at first it was inside her head, another memory vivid as life. But the quick step that followed caused her to whirl around, joy and surprise sparking into light inside her. "Senrid!"

Senrid and Arthur stood side by side in the treasure room door, two blond boys of roughly the same age, but to her eye they were utterly unalike: Arthur slightly taller, but slightly stooped, skinny in his formal robe, and Senrid short and slender, his shoulders and hands tension points, his body poised to move. Just as he had when she first met him, he wore a perfectly tailored white shirt with loose sleeves, and black riding trousers with a dull gold stripe down the side, disappearing into high blackweave riding boots.

His reaction to her obvious joy was too quick to catch before he shuttered it away, but she recognized that wry grin of self-mockery.

"I hoped you wouldn't be here," Arthur said. Then he grimaced, knowing he sounded petty, but he was worried.

And he'd forgotten that both the others could hear his thoughts. Liere turned to Senrid as if had been a day or two since they'd last seen one another, instead of months. "Tell him. What you said. Siamis didn't surrender that sword."

"Definitely not." Senrid shrugged, a jerky movement. "Arthur, have your mages checked it over? There's only one reason to leave it behind. Because it's loaded with magical traps."

"They checked it first thing," Arthur said in a defensive tone.

Senrid opened a hand, palm down. "Second reason, maybe he left it here so his uncle couldn't have it." At Arthur's surprised look, Senrid said, "They were squabbling when I was a prisoner in Norsunder. I mean, I only heard it—sort of—once, but everybody in the Norsunder Base gossiped about some kind of trouble between Siamis and Detlev. And you should remember at the end, there, before Evend ended the rifts, your mages were all willing to back Liere in ending Siamis's enchantment. But Detlev didn't back Siamis. Though we don't know why."

The mention of Evend caused a quick contraction of grief in Arthur's face. He was obviously remembering, too. Arthur said, "Oalthoreh and the senior mages think that Detlev abandoned Siamis."

"Or it was a test," Senrid said. *Or a feint.* He didn't want to reveal how much he'd been worrying at that question, knowing it was futile. He simply didn't know enough.

Senrid shrugged tightly. "So I think the sword got left so Detlev can't have it, it being some kind of family heirloom. It even has a name," he added, for Marlovens did not name weapons, considering them extensions of their hands, instruments of will and skill. But Senrid knew that in other lands, weapons had names because warriors felt a kinship with the implement that was expected to defend their lives.

"Emeth," Liere said in a low voice, her gaze fixed not on the sword, but beyond it, into memory. "Ancient Sartoran word for 'truth.' Siamis said once when he attacked me by mind, wasn't it funny that he had a weapon named 'truth' when there isn't any truth. That truth is whatever the strong say it is."

Both boys stared at her. Arthur had never heard her speak a word about the harrowing days when she had been on the run from Siamis and Norsunder, being the only person who could use the dyr, an Ancient Sartoran artifact, to rip apart Siamis's enchantment like a broom clearing moth webbing.

Senrid remembered the chase, remembered the day Siamis had attacked Liere mind to mind, but she had refused then to tell him what was said.

When the pause became a silence, Arthur cleared his throat. "Well, *I* believe he's wrong. Just because he doesn't want to believe there isn't any truth doesn't make it so."

Senrid shrugged, quick and sharp. "What matters here is why he left that sword behind."

Liere stirred, her huge light-brown eyes golden in the shafting light. "I think . . . I think he left it on purpose. As a sort of warning."

Senrid's brows shot upward. "You mean, like throwing down a war banner? Yeah, that I can see."

But Liere gave her head a little shake. "Not that. Not *just* that. Norsunder makes threats all the time, don't they? Everything they do is a threat of war, or attack, or bad things. I think there's something else." She looked up at the boys. "Though maybe you're right about him not wanting Detlev to have it."

"Sounds kind of petty," Arthur said doubtfully. "But maybe they are that petty."

Senrid turned his palm upward. "Not so petty if there's magic on it that even your mages can't find, or there's some power struggle going on in Norsunder, and the sword is part of it."

Senrid knew his speculation was getting wilder with every word, but he pursued it anyway, because he wanted to hear what Arthur, who had the ear of all the senior lighter mages, would say.

But Arthur merely shook his head, and Liere's gaze narrowed. "Senrid, what's that on your face?" She peered at the nearly faded bruises.

He jerked one shoulder impatiently. "Walked into a door." And, "I didn't hear from you. Thought you'd . . ." He flicked a hand up, taking in the palace.

Liere's joy altered to dismay, and Senrid knew instantly that he'd managed to talk himself into misjudging her. ". . . be too busy learning," he amended the sarcasm, striving for neutrality.

"And I thought *you* were too busy. But here you are. You remembered!"

"Remembered?" he repeated.

"You promised. I could visit your country. If things settled down. Have they settled down?"

Senrid was about to say that she could have come to visit any time she wanted, but recollected what Hibern had said. It matched with Liere's anxious twisting of her fingers, her wistful expression. He should have known that she would never ask for something expensive like a transfer token.

The bards could warble about Sartora, the Girl Who Saved the World, but she saw herself as a shopkeeper's brat. She'd been scolded her entire life into believing herself clumsy, stupid, and unimportant.

He knew it better than anybody, but he'd managed to let himself believe she'd swallowed all the twaddle about 'the great Sartora.'

Furious with himself, he said, "Things are . . . things. No use in boring on about home."

Liere said quickly, "I've been learning." Her thumbnail dug at the cuticles on her forefinger in the worried gesture he remembered from the desperate days they were on the run together. "You know how ignorant I am. So I'm going to read everything in the archive. I started with the first shelves, which turned out to be the oldest ones, copies of Sartoran taerans. Do you know that word? It means their old scrolls, and they are ever so difficult. But sometimes there are these events, and Arthur says it's polite and proper to attend . . ."

Senrid was gazing at her, unsettled by how quickly she detected his emotions. He'd forgotten how quick she was, and he wasn't used to anyone seeing past the bland face he'd used as his shield ever since he could remember.

". . . though Arthur said to pretend that Sartora is a role, and I'm on a giant stage, but it doesn't work. When people go to a play, they know that the players wear roles. People who come here expect Sartora to be a real person. Not me," she said in a breathless rush.

Senrid exclaimed, "This is why I don't see any jewels? Royal robes? Isn't that your brother's old tunic? I can't believe there isn't any cloth in the entire north to sew up a new shirt or pair of trousers, at least."

Liere's thin cheeks reddened. "They've given me so many beautiful things! Enough for a family of ten. But I don't really feel comfortable in all that stuff." She looked helplessly at Arthur. "Everyone here is so generous and kind . . ."

So no one teased her? Senrid would fix that. "And it makes you feel even more like a fake. Oh-h-h-h, wo-o-o-o-oe is me!" He grinned when he won a small laugh at that.

He'd meant to make this a short visit. But as he listened to her sudden laugh, he thought about how much he'd missed it, and he had to face the truth: he really didn't want her in Marloven Hess. It was too easy to imagine her looking around in horror, or saying something about warmongers.

Who was being stupid now? He said recklessly, "Come on, let's cure your gloom with some broiling weather."

Liere's lips parted. "What? You mean—"

"Unless you don't want to risk poisoning your purity by setting foot in my evil kingdom, why not come along and watch the academy gymkhana?"

Her joy flared, a flash of sunlight in the realm of the spirit. "I'd love that!"

Liere remembered where she was, and her obligations, and turned to Arthur, who was staring at her like she'd grown an extra arm. "Um, ought I to be back at a certain time? Or—" Liere spread her stiff, nervous fingers.

Arthur gave them a determined grin. "That's the good part about being a symbolic queen. Come and go as you like. Long as you aren't forgetting an appointment to meet with any powerful sorcerers or guild chiefs that you might have made?"

"Just breakfast with Siamis and three other Norsundrian commanders," Senrid put in, his face straight. "I can transfer her back in time for those."

Liere had been shaking her head somberly, but now she looked up, startled, then laughed.

It was the first real laugh Arthur had heard from her, so different from those self-conscious, sycophantic giggles she'd expressed at the Mearsiean girls' antics.

". . . it'll be hot, and dusty, and you're going to see more horses then you've probably ever seen. Or smelled—"

"Could I ride one? I so miss riding."

Arthur stared at Liere, his lips parting to say, *You never told us that.* But Senrid forestalled him. "After the exercises, I'll introduce you to the girls at the stable. How's that?"

Liere whispered, "Don't tell them who I am. Then nobody will pay any attention."

Senrid knew that 'no one paying attention' was impossible for anyone in his position. He was a walking target, at least for talk, maybe for assassination. But he could use his position to keep people at arm's length until she felt more comfortable. If comfort was possible in the Evil Marloven Hess.

"Oh, let's go," she said, sensing his mounting doubts.

They soon transferred away, leaving Arthur wondering what was he going to say to the Sartoran mage guild when they sent their next emissary. *She hates being here, and would rather go watch Marlovens play war and ride horses* didn't sound very diplomatic, even if it was the truth.

The transfer made Liere feel as if she'd been turned inside out, then stuffed back right side in again by an impatient hand, like a pair of socks readied for the washtub.

She found herself in a room with a row of tall windows open to the air. She looked out as she drew in a long, unsteady breath to settle her insides. The windows looked out over some kind of square filled with color, and noise, and a whole lot of shades of brown, gray, and yellow. Gradually the noise resolved into what seemed to be a thousand versions of Senrid, all speaking quick, sibilant Marloven, with horses in a long string at one wall.

Among all the blond heads were ones with dark hair, and red hair; tall boys, short, even a few girls, all dressed pretty much alike; clear consonant-sharp voices in the hot air. They sounded like Senrid because they spoke with his accent, and they kind of moved like him, except none so fast, or with three stiffened fingers, the way Senrid tended to gesture when he was tense.

Because he was definitely tense. She saw it the moment she turned around. She remembered all his sarcastic remarks about Evil Marlovens, and knew instinctively that he was waiting for her to judge. But what was there to judge? When she'd broken Siamis's worldwide spell, she'd had to do it kingdom by kingdom. A light-being called Hreealdar had taken her on that journey, which had lasted several weeks, during which she'd seen people from across the world. All kinds of people. From places famed down the ages to ones no one had ever heard of. But the people in all those places had all shared so many of the same emotions: puzzlement, fear, anger, relief, when the spell restored their minds to them.

To her, Marlovens looked like people.

"Arthur resents your muscling into a title up there in Bereth Ferian?" he asked, startling her out of her reverie.

"Oh, not at all." Liere glanced at him in surprise. "Not at *all*. He is still a kind of king, too, as Evend's heir, and anyway those titles are what they call a courtesy." She squirmed, hating that sense of being a fraud, even if her 'title' didn't actually mean anything.

"What does a courtesy title entail?" Senrid asked, coming to stand beside her at the window.

"Arthur told me that a king or queen in Bereth Ferian can't make laws, or give commands. It's a presiding thing, over the federation, and also over the archive, and all the old magical protections. Did you know the library is the biggest one in all the north half of the world?"

"Not much competition, from what I remember of our run," Senrid said.

"Arthur says that humans are outnumbered by all the other types of beings in the north. It's here in the south where there are more humans," Liere said, looking slowly around the room with interest. "Anyway, I'm not a *real* queen, but Arthur said if the federation ever comes to argument, and I'm presiding, they might think I'll do some kind of mind spell, and I shouldn't tell them I can't. I still don't get that, whether he was joking or not. Like when he said that what he really wants to be is King of the Libraries. I like this room," she exclaimed, taking in the fine desk, the cabinet by it, and the colorful map on the wall behind the desk.

"It's my study." Senrid jabbed the three fingers toward the door. "Come on. I'll give you a tour."

She followed him into a hall formed out of light brown stone, not the expected gray of granite. The sandy color seemed warm, though maybe that warmth was the strong summer light brightening everything, so welcome after the horrible dark and pervasive cold of the far north. Someone had carved reliefs of dashing horses and flying raptors into the plastered walls, in colors of silver and white and gray.

She paused to look more closely, almost touched, then yanked down her hand—her father's scolding voice was never far from memory. She found Senrid looking at her with that peculiar question, his mouth awry, and she said, "These carving things on the walls are pretty."

"The ancestor who put those up was actually from Colend," he said, but dropped the subject when she wrinkled her nose. Mad King Carlael of Colend was not a great memory for her, however brief their contact.

"This way."

They ran downstairs and out to the parade court, then climbed into the stone stands where Marlovens had been sitting for centuries. She could see the dips in the stone worn by shoes down the many years, the benches smoothed by weather.

Senrid gave Liere a quick description of the academy, which turned out to be a school where the Marlovens trained their future army officers. Senrid had mentioned so little about this part of his life during their travels together, though they had talked about everything else, that she had this odd sense that he was revealing something private.

No, that's silly, she thought as he laughed, and gestured, and interspersed the running stream of talk with waves or calls. It wasn't as if you could hide an entire kingdom in a trunk.

She was distracted by a tall older boy with curly dark hair whom Senrid kept glancing at, and when Senrid's head was turned, stared at Senrid. "Who is that?"

In the mental realm, Senrid's reaction was like a flash of lightning, instant, painfully intense, then gone. "Jarend Ndarga," he said, and then, his reluctance obvious, "I had some trouble with him recently. Just local stuff."

Liere nodded, suspecting that asking further would be nosy, especially as she wouldn't know what 'local stuff' meant.

A lot of little boys her younger sister's age ran out to do something or other with loose horses. After them came the excellent, sometimes frightening dash and skill of the gymkhana riders. Oh, how she would love to ride that well! Not doing those tricks, like shooting arrows at a post while galloping—she couldn't see ever needing such a skill—but how easy they looked on the backs of horses, like horse and rider had been born together.

After a last amazing set of stunts involving boys leaping from the back of one horse to another, Senrid kept his promise and brought Liere to a teenage girl with black curly hair and dark eyes. "Here's Fenis Senelac. She can give you your first lesson in riding," he said, and to Fenis, in the Marloven language, "Send someone with her when it's over, will you?"

He flicked up a hand. "We'll eat when you're done," he said to Liere in Sartoran, and vanished into the crowd.

Fenis Senelac's straight brow lifted, and she said, "What do you know about riding?"

A mage had performed for Liere the Universal Language spell. It was not perfect, she'd been told; mages were always adding to it, but some languages were more up to date than others, especially with idioms. But Liere had discovered that if she listened on the mental realm as well as with her ears, she could understand idiom as well as intent. What she had trouble with was pronunciation.

"A little," Liere said carefully, trying to emulate Senrid's accent. "I rode a pony once, for many days, but there were two of us, and we never galloped. Then I rode . . ." She clipped her lips.

"Rode?" Fenis asked, amazed that the king would bring this grubby scrub here, who spoke with such an odd accent. It was a first, for though she had the light coloring one saw a lot of in Marloven Hess, she was obviously no Marloven. Fenis's interest increased sharply when the girl's cheeks mottled red, and she mumbled to the dusty ground, ". . . something like a horse."

Fenis stared. Though the king was closer than a stone about whatever had happened during the Siamis time, gossip from the little neighboring kingdom of Vasande Leror, where several Marlovens had relatives, had brought word of their own king's heroism. You had to call it that, though everyone knew how much Senrid-Harvaldar hated such words.

The thing was, he hadn't been alone when chased by Siamis and half of Norsunder. He'd been with some little girl who turned out to have amazing powers of some kind, enough to vanquish a Norsundrian sorcerer, even if a young one.

Fenis looked at that untidy head, the old clothes, and wondered if she was seeing the same 'little girl.' Part of the rumor put this girl on the back of a horse made out of light.

"Well, we have ordinary horses here," she said. "So let's put you up on a nice, well-mannered mare, and see what you know."

She held out a hand, indicating the barn, and led the way. At first Liere wondered if Fenis was related to the mysterious Jarend Ndarga, but no, her features were completely different, her skin browner. All they really shared was the curly black hair, she decided when she saw Jarend Ndarga walk by.

The tall boy looked so threatening. Was there trouble for Senrid? Liere skimmed his thoughts, catching an angry, confused jumble of a lot of images and words she didn't know, then the horrible jolt of memory: a bloody fist smashing into Senrid's face.

Her stomach lurched. That's what she got for listening. That memory would never go away.

She drew in a slow breath, and discovered Fenis gazing at her, brows raised. Liere's face burned. "They were so good," she said, feeling stupid and awkward. "Leaping from horse to horse like that."

"The girls do that when they're ten," Fenis said with a snort. "But in the bad days, before Senrid-Harvaldar, they never got any credit."

"Is Senrid going to change that?" Liere asked, not knowing how much was revealed in her easy use of Senrid's name with no formal 'harvaldar' attached.

"He says he will, but slowly. Marlovens don't like change. Unless they make it themselves. Jarend Ndarga, who seems to have caught your eye, hates it more than most." Fenis stopped at a stall, and paused, one hand on a halter. "You'll get an earful if you stay around here, how much the men and boys all hate change. How much they all want the good old days back. Only, of course, better." She snorted a laugh. "So. If you're going to learn to ride, you need to learn how we get the horse ready. Here, don't be nervous. You'll make the horse nervous."

Liere had been staring up at the animal in fascinated terror. This was not a fat, placid old pony like her first mount, nor was it like the strange beings in horse form whom she had met up north. Once she'd been this close to a Norsundrian horse, its mind warped with terror and anger. All she'd had to do was touch that mind and urge the animal to run.

But she couldn't do that now. So she put out a tentative hand, laying it on the horse's bony flat head above its nose, and as Fenis said, "Good, good, they like scritchies, calm and steady . . ." Liere sorted through the strange mental landscape, her instinct to hide from danger prompting her to send the thought: *Don't see me, I am invisible.*

The horse promptly began panicking. Fenis broke off her praise with a startled, "Hai, what's wrong?" She gripped the halter of the wild-eyed, plunging horse.

Senrid's thought came from somewhere near, straight into Liere's head: *Don't do that!*

Liere jumped.

In answer to her unspoken question, Senrid's thought blared, too strong and uncontrolled: *It smells you, and hears you, but doesn't see you—you are a threat!*

Liere jerked down her hand and scrambled behind Fenis as she calmed the horse, then sent a wary glance at Liere. "Shall we try that again?"

Liere blinked back tears of shame. "Just tell me what to do," she said.

*Narad, capital of Chwahirsland*
*Roughly the same time—very roughly*

Jilo was so exhausted that he wondered if Wan-Edhe's poisonous enchantment had seeped into his brain and bones again, until it occurred to him that he ought to lie down and sleep. There was no way of knowing how long had passed in this airless, windowless space unless he remembered to go into the hall to see if sunlight came through or not. And he seldom remembered to do that. Time measures, whether candles, sandglasses, or mechanical clocks, never functioned well in Narad's fortress's inner chambers, probably because of the layers of magic.

As he walked to the old room (cell, really, except that it was above ground) where he'd stayed when he and Kwenz were forced to visit, he wondered if he would wake up to discover Siamis there. Or Detlev. Or some other even more terrifying Norsundrian, except if anyone would return from Norsunder to take control of Chwahirsland, wouldn't it be Wan-Edhe?

Or Prince Kessler.

Maybe Jilo should lay warning tracers over the already-thick layer, just to be safe.

When he'd finished that, he fell directly into slumber. He didn't stay asleep, waking often, usually in a sweat, though the room was chill. When he rose at last, the narrow arrow slit he had for a window showed gray light. He frowned, trying to think past the panging in his temples. Was it daylight when he'd gone to sleep?

What about breakfast? He'd had to beg meals from Wan-Edhe, and half the time he was denied on the pretense of some wrongdoing or failure or disappointment. Jilo felt under the mattress. He'd sometimes brought rolls from the Shadowland and stashed them in case; two were there, but they had hardened to rocks.

It didn't matter. He wasn't even hungry.

As always, he had to find out what he could, to protect himself. Being taken by surprise was never, ever, a good thing in Chwahirsland. Wan-Edhe still had not returned. No one was giving him orders.

No one was stopping him from learning. Or removing wards and traps.

He really ought to get something to eat, though the thought of cold food was unappetizing, and anyway there was so much to do before anyone showed up with orders or threats . . .

## Chapter Twelve

*Dyavath Yan (New Year's Week), 4738 AF*

JILO finished checking for wards and traps in Wan-Edhe's library and magic chamber. He knew that next it was time to be systematic about finding out what was on those shelves in the magic chamber. The first book he touched sparked. Blue flame singed his fingers as the book vanished . . . somewhere. He stuck his throbbing fingers into his armpit, and studied the shelf in dismay. If only the air weren't so thick! It was as if he never could get a deep enough breath.

All right, clearly he hadn't removed all the worst wards. Maybe he'd only found the obvious ones. That was dismaying, after all his effort.

He still wasn't sure how much time had passed, but no one disturbed him. Everyone in the castle seemed to be sticking to the schedule as if they expected Wan-Edhe to reappear at any moment. Maybe it was time to see to something else, like removing the spell that rendered the former Shadowland army's eyes a solid black, making sunlight acutely painful. Though he didn't feel any better than he had before he slept, a promise was a promise.

He forced himself to breathe deeply as he picked up Wan-Edhe's book of spells. Balancing that on one hand, he fixed in mind an image of the fleet captain who had brought the Chwahir to the Shadowland. It was dangerous to use a person as a Destination, but it was either that or nothing.

He transferred, and fell with a splat, the reaction nausea worsened by the movement of a ship.

A sentry bent over him and pulled him to his feet, his tight grip loosening when Sentry-Captain Mossler recognized Jilo. "You were sent by Wan-Edhe?" the man asked Jilo fearfully.

"No. The Shadowland Chwahir no longer need the shadow vision." And Jilo began the spell.

It was almost worse than the transfer. From the beginning of the spell, he felt that internal burning of strong magic. Two days ago he would not have been able to hold it. Now he could—barely. But it worked.

"Augh!" Mossler clapped his hands over his eyes.

"You'll soon get accustomed," Jilo whispered.

"But Wan-Edhe," the sentry-captain said, still in that fearful voice. "Is Wan-Edhe still gone? Commander Henjit went with him, and there have been no orders. We're doubled up here with the homelanders." He gestured down the deck, where Shadowland Chwahir rubbed their eyes, or stood with their hands covering their faces. From the looks of things, they had been sleeping on deck.

"I have orders from the throne," Jilo said, having planned that much, and watched the easing in Mossler's sunburned face. "You are to bring them back to the homeland."

Jilo had just enough strength to transfer back to the Destination in Wan-Edhe's chambers, where he fell to his hands and knees, the book thumping onto the grimy floor. He waited until the black spots had swum away from his vision, then sat back, his breath coming in shuddering gasps.

He had to do something about the Shadowland warriors before he forgot. What was it?

He went to the door, and beckoned the waiting runner. "Tell the Quartermaster Commander that the Shadowland Chwahir are to be dispersed, by twi, to reinforce any strongholds shorthanded. They will arrive . . ." When? Already he had lost grip on time. "Soon."

The runner bowed and withdrew.

All right, back to the traps. Jilo turned too quickly. Dizzy, he stumbled down the hall, and fell headlong through the magic chamber door. He knee-crawled to the first bookcase. Before, he'd tested shelf by shelf, but now he was going to have to proceed book by book. He extended a forefinger, not quite touching the first book, waiting to see if he sensed the faint magical burr that probably meant a trap.

And traps he found, as if they'd grown overnight. The process was long and laborious, too dangerous to be boring—lethally tedious. He nearly fumbled into a couple of especially nasty traps, after which he forced himself to take a break.

Both times he slept right there on the floor.

When he remembered meals, he ate methodically, permitting his mind to range over his life so far. With that damping spell gone, he was able to remember more. Even think about it. What he came back to most was the fact that Clair of Mearsies Heili, long regarded as his chief enemy, had helped him.

Time wore on.

He was peripherally aware of the guard going about its daily routine, and surprised when no one came to ask orders. But of course they wouldn't. Wan-Edhe had trained his guards to never interrupt him. Not that they wanted to. If he didn't like what they said, it could be their last words.

"They probably go about their day and hope they never see me," he said to the dead air.

He'd taken to talking out loud. The sound of his voice seemed to break the heavy stillness, as oppressive as the stone. If for only a moment.

But as time labored on, he found it more difficult to think, to rest, to get anything done. It was as if that terrible spell had seeped out of the stonework, taking over his mind again, an invisible and smothering fungus. It wasn't until he sat down to pick up the quill that he caught sight of his own hands.

They looked like someone else's hands. The nails were longish, the beds ridged in a curious way, grayish in color. He dropped his hands to the table, steadying himself by feeling the grain of the wood, and looked at the shelves he'd managed to complete: one and a half bookshelves. Then he looked at the enormous volume of books awaiting him in the rest of the room, and admitted defeat.

He gathered his strength, shut his eyes, and transferred to the old Destination square outside of what had been the Shadowland. Transfer reaction knocked him tumbling. He blinked stupidly. The square was covered with snow and ice. Snow and ice?

He peered upward at a low, gray sky. The air was so cold that it hurt to breathe. Wasn't it . . . warm when he left? When did he leave, anyway? Two days ago? Three? Trying to remember made the headache worse.

So he stood up, brushing snow off with numbing fingers. The area seemed wild, as if the Shadowland had never existed. He couldn't comprehend that, so he braced himself, and transferred to the mountaintop.

Clair's magic did not ward him. If anything, this transfer was far easier. It was only a relatively short distance, but still, it barely hurt, compared to the agonizing transfer from Chwahirsland.

He looked around. The city was different, now that it didn't stretch over a cloud. It lay across the top of the mountain, cut into a gentle slope and connected by switchback streets, the buildings either whitewashed or painted with colorful shutters, now mostly closed, and roofed with patterned tile. The Destination square was still in the terrace before the palace, whose blinding, glaring white no longer tortured his eyes. He stared at towers that looked like they were made of ice.

He tipped his head back, running his gaze up the asymmetrical series of towers. He hated the idea of trying to enter. Wan-Edhe had (briefly) managed to get inside a couple times, but that after endless magic, and not for long, and never past the ground floor.

He dreaded walking into some kind of waxer trap, but if he did, well, life would probably be no odder than it was already. So. He trudged the short distance to the palace, his breathing labored. He halted near the archway, his attention caught by the intertwined carvings, age-softened, of four-petal blossoms of a sort he did not recognize. The walls appeared to be luminous, though he didn't trust his vision when it came to this building.

A step.

Another step.

He was inside! He was actually inside, and no magic, or guards, or anything had stopped him!

He made it about ten steps before he encountered one of the Mearsiean servants, an older man.

"May I—oh, aren't you . . ."

"Jilo." His voice was hoarse. He stood poised to run, to fight, though he really hadn't the strength for that.

"Come this way."

Jilo followed, too weary to question, though a mild surprise bloomed in him when they walked not into the throne room but down a side hall. The enticing smells of warm food of some kind (he didn't even know what it was, just that it smelled so good the sides of his mouth watered) met him before he walked into a warm, bright kitchen.

There CJ sat on a high stool, a bowl of whipped cream next to a silver pot of hot chocolate. A book lay on the table.

She scowled in astonished recognition, poised to fling the hot chocolate at him since she didn't have a weapon. Why hadn't she been
warned? Where was Ben, their trusty spy on the Chwahir? Except that
there was no more Shadowland to spy on, and Ben had traveled off
somewhere with Puddlenose.

Meanwhile, Jilo just stood there, swaying on his feet. To CJ, he
looked terrible. Her alarm forgotten, she said tentatively, "Jilo? You
look like a week-old corpse!"

A spurt of laughter bloomed in Jilo's throat, but it didn't come out.
He could only manage a dusty huff of breath.

CJ raised a finger. "No, I don't know what a week-old corpse looks
like, but if I did, it would look healthier than you. Have you been in
the clink?"

"Clink?"

She waved her hands. "Dungeon. Jail. Where you skunks used to try
to stick us when Kwenz was trying to take over."

"No, I've been busy." That much talk seemed to make him breathless. He gulped in air, and tried again. "Where is Clair? I have a question."

CJ bit down on a retort, so long a habit. She'd promised Clair: assuming they ever saw him again, Jilo had to move first in resuming the
old conflict. And saying he had a question wasn't a gesture of war in any
possible way. "Clair's tobogganing with the girls, and I'm keeping an eye
on things here, just in case." Another glance at that drawn face. "Maybe
you're an 'in case'?" Her thin black brows lifted in puzzlement as Jilo
swayed on his feet. "Are you going to croak right on our floor?" She
dashed across the room, picked up a cup, returned, and poured out a
brown stream of chocolate. "Drink that."

Jilo was beyond questioning. He sipped. The flavor was completely
new, and so delicious he gasped. More, the warmth, the fluidity seemed
to send silver fire all through his veins, chasing out the dust. He drank
it off, then reeled, dizzy.

"Whoa! I think you better sit down. I've never seen anybody get
snockered on hot chocolate before!" Small, insistent hands pushed Jilo
onto a chair, where he collapsed like a bag of old laundry.

When he had blinked the world straight again, there was Clair, wearing a bulky coat. Snow glistened in her white hair. Next to her, CJ
stood, a small, adamant figure wearing the familiar white shirt, black
vest, and long green skirt. Jilo had hated the sight of that outfit, and
that girl, for too long to count. While Clair had been his chief enemy,

CJ had been a personal enemy. But now he couldn't seem to find . . . any thoughts at all.

Clair whispered, "I have never seen anyone actually gray before."

"Is it a sign of good health in a Chwahir?"

"Does he act healthy?"

"Noooo." CJ's quick footsteps departed, returning with the tread of Janil, the Steward, a stout, cheery woman who bustled about, and soon set before Jilo a plate of brightly colored, delicious foods that he couldn't name—but the flavors were indescribable. With it he drank down four glasses of clear, sweet water.

Warmth chased the silver in his veins, and reached his head, clearing it. He felt strange, like someone had replaced his head with a dandelion puff. Other than the wobbly sensation, the feeling wasn't bad. "How long has it been? I can't seem to remember if it's been four days, or five?"

CJ's fierce blue eyes rounded. Clair said carefully, "I don't quite know if it's been four or five days from what, but you left here eight months ago."

"Eight—"

"Months," Clair said. "It's New Year's Week. Jilo, Senrid said there was really heavy magic in that chamber."

"Senrid? Who's that?"

"Better ask *what* is that," CJ said darkly, and when Clair began to protest, CJ raised her hands. "No, no, I couldn't resist the crack. Boneribs is . . . Boneribs. Uh, Senrid," she corrected quickly.

Jilo was too exhausted to listen to CJ, who was always making up names for people.

Clair wasn't listening, either. She gazed past CJ and Jilo both, wrestling mentally with a new idea.

Court historians like to point to ceremonial treaty signings, battles, and royal marriages as turning points in history, but it is the archivist in possession of insights into such moments as this who recognizes the individual decisions that change the world.

So it was now, as Clair drew Jilo into the nascent alliance.

She gave a tiny nod of decision. "Senrid lives in Marloven Hess, on your continent, but at the end closer to us. He knows dark magic, and he's the one who found that terrible spell on you, in Wan-Edhe's experiment book."

Clair waited. Jilo waited. Then he understood she was waiting for permission to introduce him to someone, something he was utterly un-prepared for.

"Ah, yes," he said, feeling stupid.

Clair nodded. This had to be how an alliance really started, not with everybody making promises, but by doing the right thing, an item at a time. At least, she was pretty sure this was the right thing. She had to test the idea herself before trying it on CJ, who she knew would not like the idea of allying with a former enemy.

So she said to CJ, "I'll take him to Senrid." And then, as a hint, "Maybe our alliance is going to need a name?" She went to get a transfer token for Jilo, as she was afraid he couldn't hold a transfer spell on his own.

*Marloven Hess*

Hibern pulled her coat tighter around her, as the distant rhythm of a drum rumbled through the winter windows, followed by the rise and fall of voices in long-familiar martial melody. It was the end of New Year's Week and the Marloven Convocation.

The sound of Marloven singing threw her back to memories of home. She'd managed to stay away from that spot overlooking Askan Castle since the last visit. Erai-Yanya was right, thinking of home hurt a little less, but the difference seemed akin to a hard stab with a knife com-pared to a lot of little cuts. The cuts were questions: Would her mother ever contact her again, or her aunt? Had Father succeeded in removing his spells from Stefan?

When she was honest with herself, she knew why she kept at these study sessions with Senrid, when she could have found someone else for Senrid to study with. Like Arthur. But she wanted word to get out, to her family. If she worked hard, might they be proud of her, ask her to come back, say all was . . .

Was what? She still didn't believe she had anything to be forgiven for.

And yet she knew if her mother required her to beg forgiveness, she would do it, if it meant she would have her family back.

And she *knew* what Senrid would say: "Lighter sentiment and weakness."

She let out a sharp sigh, then entered Senrid's study. He looked up, his slight frown altering to a wry grin. Mind-reading? No, she suspected that it wasn't her thoughts but her expression that had given her away. "That mind-shield thing is hard to maintain," she said.

Senrid jerked a shoulder up. "If you're going to tangle with Norsunder, you lighters are going to have to make the mind-shield into a habit. Siamis made a strategic retreat. Detlev didn't even retreat. They both are Ancient Sartorans, and they know how to listen in on thoughts and dreams from a day's journey away. A continent away."

Hibern's neck prickled with warning. "You're still saying 'lighter' in that tone, as if you're still dedicated to dark magic. If so, why am I here tutoring you in light?"

"Because light magic has its strengths," Senrid retorted. "Dark magic is only useful for brute force. People using either for long enough to build customs around them have managed to make some stupid ones. Dark for mindless destruction, and light for mindless hypocrisy."

"Mindless!" Hibern exclaimed in the same tone of genial sarcasm. "How did I miss the fact that I think exactly like every one of those Sartoran or northern mages, not to mention every hair-colorist or bridge-mender? Oh wait. None of us can think."

"I didn't say they were alike," Senrid shot right back. "I said—"

"You said we're mindless."

Senrid grinned. "Okay," he said. "I take that back."

Hibern sighed, still finding it strange when Senrid used the slang he'd picked up from the Mearsiean girls while they were all in Bereth Ferian. "Lilith the Guardian said to me once that we—humans—are still changing. We lost our civilization in the Fall four thousand years ago. We're still trying to catch up to the place where we lost ourselves."

"A grim thought," Senrid said. "That we need to catch up to the time when we nearly managed to destroy the world." His expression tuned sardonic. "Strange, the idea of her living back then."

"What I think stranger is the idea of being . . . somewhere . . . beyond time, and only coming back every now and then over the centuries, when you're needed," she said. "How could you bear that, knowing that everyone you met would be dead by your next return? How would you even know you're needed? I read about a conversation with Lilith the Guardian in a record written a couple centuries ago, in which she said we can't make the same mistakes our ancestors did, and that what you call lighter hypocrisy is a kind of standard to aim for. If it makes life a little better when we try, the failures don't matter so much."

"There's the moral superiority drumbeat banging my ear," Senrid said, but his tone was no longer as derisive. He jumped up and moved restlessly to peer out his window, then turned. "Everything is about getting power. Keeping it. People can talk themselves into thinking they're worthy, but they want power, same as anyone else."

Hibern wondered what that was about, and then remembered the day. Senrid would have given his speech before the jarls on New Year's First-day, outlining new laws, new policies. When Marlovens squabbled, they didn't argue about who had the moral high ground. Instead, out came the knives. And he was waiting for the first sounds of steel being drawn.

Senrid reached for the books stacked neatly on his desk as Hibern took the hint and brought her own study materials out of her satchel.

Time passed as they studied together, looking at ways to layer building wards. When Senrid asked a question she didn't know the answer to, he waited for her to look through all the notes she'd written in her classes at that mage school up north.

At one point she halted, and her gaze slowly went diffuse.

Senrid was tempted to try to read those thoughts, but he pictured Liere's questioning face. Her disappointment. They'd had enough talk about that. He could hear her pointing out that just because somebody knew how to kill someone five different ways with only their hands didn't mean they should do it.

It was one thing when Hibern was so intent on a subject her mental images and emotions splashed out, like her grief and betrayal and pain for a long time after that idiot mage Askan had kicked his daughter out of his house, as if she were to blame for all the regent's rot. It was another to deliberately invade. He knew how much *he'd* hate it, and she certainly intended no threat to him.

A runner appeared. "Visitors," she said. "Just transferred to the Destination. Said they are here to see you, Senrid-Harvaldar."

"Then we're done." Hibern got to her feet and pointed to the book she'd brought. "Study that, King Mindless Destruction." She hefted her satchel and transferred.

Clair and Jilo found themselves on a hilltop Destination.

A cold wind whipped at them. Jilo shivered in spite of the bulky coat Clair had fetched from Puddlenose's room, and Clair turtled her head deeper into her own coat.

A scarf-muffled guard beside the Destination turned their way. "Go ahead," he shouted against the wind.

Former enemies, Clair and Jilo began trudging down a pathway toward the high walls of a fortress city, barely visible in whirls of snow. They could not have looked more like opposites: she short, sturdy, hair the same white as the snow; Jilo gaunt and gangling, his lank hair blue-black. But their thoughts were not all that dissimilar at that moment, Clair worried about Jilo, who looked so ill, and Jilo worried about pretty much everything.

Clair tried to reassure Jilo with a description of Senrid, but she was wondering if he had the strength to toil through the wind-driven snow all the way to Senrid's castle. Then horseback riders thundered toward them, and reined to a halt.

"The king sent us," said one of the riders.

The two were each pulled up behind a rider, and they galloped the rest of the way, through the massive gates, and up to the castle.

Clair wondered if she'd made a deadly mistake as she eyed the sentries on the walls. Everything looked threatening. Senrid had once said that she was welcome to visit. Maybe he hadn't meant that as a real invitation, but as a kind of dare.

Jilo wondered if this was going to be a deadly mistake. He'd heard of Marloven Hess. Who hadn't? There had been glancing references to some sort of encounter between the Marlovens and the Chwahir in the past, though he'd never found out what happened.

Then he was distracted by the wintry sunlight changing the color of the stone to an almost gold, and by the fine weave of the sentries' uniforms. The histories insisted the Chwahir used to be the finest weavers of sailcloth and related fabrics in the south. If that wasn't all lies, why was everything so shoddy now?

He remembered he was living where a king once had, and might again. In spite of his headache (which was actually rapidly diminishing), Jilo looked around the way he thought a king might. He felt sorry for anybody who would try to attack this city. The walls were high and thick, and the guards walking along them looked alert. The street leading to the royal castle bent to the left, which would make it tougher for attack than a straight street—he'd read that once—and easier for defenders to pick invaders off.

If you listened to Wan-Edhe, the danger wasn't always from the outside. Nobody had tried to attack Chwahirsland for centuries. All Wan-Edhe's magical protections, laws, and rules, were for a single purpose: preserving his own life against conspiracies among his own people. No, two purposes, the second being the gathering of power.

They dismounted in a huge stable yard. It was much larger than any in Chwahirsland, but Chwahir were foot warriors, and the Marlovens were reputed to be mostly mounted.

A waiting runner beckoned for them to follow.

The castle's inside looked luxurious to Jilo, according oddly with what he expected of another military kingdom. The stone wasn't the slate-colored stone he was accustomed to, but something more the color of sand, and the upper reaches inside had plastered walls, with bas-reliefs of swooping, stylized, powerful figures. Jilo longed to stop and take them in, but he'd learned when young to hide his interest in art.

Yet those dashing equine figures, the sweep of raptor wings, stayed with him, kindling the burn of resentment in his middle. All his life he'd heard that art was for the weak, and here were these Marlovens, who got the rep but still got to have art.

But he could have art now. Jilo tested the idea as he and Clair were led into a huge room with actual windows. Maybe the Chwahir wouldn't revolt if they found out there was art in the royal fortress.

Or maybe they would.

Nice rugs, a fine table. These Marlovens had it soft. Clair glanced toward a desk where a short blond boy sat before three neatly aligned stacks of papers.

Jilo turned to stare at their host, who stared back, thinking that their timing could hardly have been worse.

Oh, wait, yes it could. They could have showed up yesterday.

The others saw no sign of Senrid's bitterness as he got to his feet in a quick move. He was shorter than Jilo by quite a bit.

"This is Senrid," Clair said.

"Senrid," Jilo repeated. He looked around, rubbing his temple. "You are a mage student? Mage?"

"Senrid is the king," Clair said. "He's like us. Underaged ruler." And to Senrid, "Jilo has taken over Chwahirsland."

A voiceless laugh escaped Jilo. "I think."

"*Chwahirsland?*" Senrid's eyes had widened. "You led a revolt?"

"No."

"Wan-Edhe didn't kill off all his relatives?"

"Yes. No. I told you before, Kessler Sonscarna is still alive. Or some-where. In Norsunder." Then she remembered that Senrid had been beaten bloody at the time. She decided against mentioning that.

Senrid whistled. "So how did you get the throne?"

Jilo spread his hands. "Walked in."

Senrid stared up at the tall, slope-shouldered, shambling boy with the pasty-pale skin and unkempt black hair who mumbled at his shoes. He was barely holding onto his own throne, and this fellow strolls in and just . . . takes over one of the biggest, nastiest kingdoms on the continent?

At what cost?

Senrid hadn't met many Chwahir, but he was willing to bet anything that Jilo hadn't slept since he'd 'walked in' and sat on that faraway throne.

Clair said, "Senrid, you know I'm ignorant about how dark magic works. That spell you found helped Jilo."

"I didn't really find it," Senrid said, his gaze on Jilo, "as in a search. The book was left open by someone who probably expected to come back to it. All I did was read a few spells, since the language they were written in was the old-fashioned Sartoran everyone uses for dark magic."

Clair flicked a look Jilo's way, and he bobbed awkwardly in assent, then winced as if his head hurt.

Clair went on, "There's something else. It's really creepy. Jilo thinks he was gone a few days. But it was eight months ago."

Senrid's astonishment wiped away all the other reactions. Jilo was fingering his nails, which were an unhealthy shade, even for someone so leached of normal skin tones.

Senrid said, "How many times did you sleep?"

"I don't know. Two or three . . . I don't remember."

"Did you go to sleep at night and wake up in the morning?"

Jilo flushed. "I know it sounds stupid, but I really don't remember."

"How many times did you eat?"

"In Chwahirsland? Um, I didn't. Yes, once. When I first got there. Then I got to work. Then a couple more times. I remember that. But it's been a few . . ." Jilo reddened to the ears as he said on a questioning note, "Hours?"

"Weeks? Months?" Senrid drew in a breath as his nerves tingled cold. "Jilo, unless you're dreaming right now, it sounds like your king managed to distort time's flow."

"What?" Jilo said.

"You can do that?" Clair asked, her green eyes wide.

"It's difficult magic. Probably the most difficult there is," Senrid said. "Think of it this way. It's like creating a piece of Norsunder all of your own. Because that's what Norsunder is. That is, not the Norsunder Base down south below Sartor, but what they call Norsunder-Beyond. It's a place beyond time and temporal constraints."

Jilo said, "I can believe that Wan-Edhe was busy creating a Norsunder of his own. He's been resisting time as hard as he could."

"But that kind of magic needs tremendous power," Senrid said. "So what are you here for?"

Clair said, "Senrid, you're the one who said we should know what dark magic can do, so we can defend ourselves. And this is our chance to see if our alliance will actually work."

"Right." Senrid had completely forgotten the alliance. He said to Jilo, "It looks to me like you need sleep, and in a place outside that magic chamber. Eight months." He shook his head. "Clair and I were there a sand—" He pointed to a small sandglass. "And I felt like I was swimming in mud. Especially my head. How did you endure that? You must be made of iron."

Jilo's ears burned the more. He was so used to insults, derision, and humiliation, that he tried to understand Senrid's words within the context of mockery, then gave up.

"Sleep," he heard himself say. "Oh yes."

Senrid gave him a sardonic grin. "That, I can give you." He touched a stack of reports, on top of which lay a smooth, heavy paper different from the rest, a very expensive, fine paper made from silk and rice. "If I was my uncle, I'd be seeing conspiracies, especially this week. First this letter from someone claiming to be a Renselaeus, and in the name of our supposed mutual ancestors, wanting to send his son to the academy. And the day after I receive that, here's someone I've never met who walked in and took a throne . . ."

He looked up, but saw only polite disinterest in Clair's face, and noncomprehension and exhaustion in Jilo's. It was clear that neither of these two knew anything about the Renselaeus family, whose descendants in the former principality of Vasande Leror had spearheaded the treaty forced on Marloven Hess by its neighbors a couple generations ago. They not only didn't know, they clearly didn't care.

Conspiracy there might be, ten conspiracies, but these two were obviously not part of any of them.

Senrid promised Clair a report, turned Jilo over to a runner to be put in a guest chamber, and dipped his pen, wondering if life would ever be normal again . . . and if it did, if 'normal' would seem unusual.

## Chapter Thirteen

*Y*OU *must be made of iron.*

Was that sarcasm? Maybe it was just an insult, like Wan-Edhe used to use, when he'd strike him across the face and snarl, "Get that into your rock-thick skull."

Jilo woke up ravenous and light-headed, but he knew what time it was: morning. He knew that he'd slept all through the night. And he remembered that conversation the day before, with the king of the Marlovens. A boy his age.

There was a cleaning frame in the room, and also a vent that brought in warm air. He'd been raised to scoff at these things as waxer weakness, so how did that fit the ferocious reputation of the Marlovens?

He made a wager that the food would be as good as the Mearsieans', and, after stepping through the cleaning frame, poked his head out of the room. There was the tower stairway, right where he'd remembered it. Senrid had said something about his being not far from the dining room. Dining? Did the Marloven warriors dine instead of mess?

When he reached the lower level, he found a pair of guards. The older one said, "You're the guest, aren't you? If you go down that hall there, you'll find a runner. But if you don't see one, just follow your nose."

Guest. He was a guest. Jilo tried to get his mind around the word.

He knew what it meant in language, but not in behavior. Chwahir in his experience didn't have guests. They weren't guests. He had no idea what was expected of him.

A runner appeared, a boy his own age. He carried a basket. "If you want breakfast, just duck through that arch there, and you'll find the dining room." The runner passed by on his errand.

Jilo stepped inside, and discovered a room with a table, chairs, and a sideboard laden with dishes, some covered so the food inside would stay warm.

He carefully lifted each lid to sniff the treasure inside. Then he went back and just as carefully picked up one item each from inside those dishes, though one or two burned his fingers.

His first bite into a hot rye biscuit, the crunch of the crust, the softness inside, the delicious sharpness of the rye blending with a trace of sweetness in the bread . . . the explosion of tastes in the potatoes and cabbage topped with crumbled cheese . . . the way the astringent coffee spread over his tongue . . .

Though he savored every bite, his emotions swooped from pleasure to shame. Why shouldn't the Chwahir eat this way every day? Or did they, and he didn't know it? But how could they, when the laws required half of every crop to go to the army, and so much of it was storehoused, then cooked together in a mass . . .

He was so very ignorant. Surely someone was going to walk into the fortress at Narad and have him shot for his temerity. Maybe someone had already taken the throne, and was waiting for him to come straight back to execution.

While Jilo struggled mentally, Senrid rammed his way through his expected tasks so he could leave for the day, if Jilo wanted him to look at that chamber again. Though he wondered—if he left, would he come back to find an assassin waiting? Or a delegation of jarls to demand that he abdicate in favor of one of them? They were probably still arguing over that, elsewhere in his castle. If they weren't plotting an overthrow.

Senrid climbed up to the tower room where Commander Keriam's office was located. One nice thing about being king: when he was tired and full of anxious questions, he didn't have to wait to talk to someone.

Keriam's office was crowded with tall, strong third-year seniors, several flushed, one or two white-faced with anger. Great. More trouble among the academy boys. Jarend Ndarga wasn't among them. Bad or good? Both, probably.

When they saw Senrid, most of them snapped their fists to their chests, one or two belatedly. Senrid made sure he met each of those boys' eyes, and yes, there was anger and resentment. He didn't have to listen on the mental plane. If he did, it would feel like a hammer on his head. Or his heart.

He forced himself to do and say nothing. He was not his uncle.

He had said that a lot to himself over the past year.

"Dismissed." Keriam turned a thumb outward at the boys.

Senrid prowled the perimeter of the room as the seniors clattered out. Keriam looked tired. "Want a report now?"

"Trouble with the exhibition?"

"Trouble because they're listening to those . . . to the jarls."

Senrid flat-handed the subject aside. "Unless it's academy business, or a direct threat, I don't want to know what they say."

Keriam understood the tremendous conflict Senrid had gone through to speak those words. No spies, he'd said after he took the throne. But that had been in the euphoria of winning. No spies, no punishments for speaking their minds, he'd said after the Siamis enchantment was over, and people got their will back, because it had been what Senrid's father Indevan-Harvaldar had said. Although after he'd said it all those years ago, he got a knife in the back. From his own brother.

Indevan was gone, but not forgotten: two days ago, Senrid faced his jarls on the first day of Convocation and told them that he was upholding Indevan's Law, which meant they no longer had the right to execute citizens without royal dispensation. The jarls listened in silence at the time, but now it seemed every corner was filled with angry liegemen talking in knots.

But Senrid had said, *No spying.*

"I understand," Commander Keriam said. "This problem is going to carry to the academy, Senrid, so be prepared."

"I don't care what they say about me, as long as they obey regs."

"I know. The problem really lies in how they handle being disagreed with. You might say the biggest problem is not with you, though they're getting plenty of that at home, but with one another. How do we handle disagreement among peers, if not by duel? Except for your father's too-short reign, it's been generations since we could disagree without it being a matter of steel. Jarls have been ruling like little kings off and on since the Olavairs, encroaching on the throne a little more with each weak king. Your uncle was the weakest in two centuries." Keriam lifted his gnarled hands in a vague circle. "Those seniors? Nothing is going to rein them in short of assembling for punishment. I know you wanted to stop that, but they all expect it, and if we don't, we'll lose them."

Senrid kicked the wall lightly with the toe of his riding boot. "How can watching someone get caned into bloody pulp be 'expected'?" Senrid waved his hand. "I know, I know, we can argue it later. We're all mad, and bad, and dangerous, especially to ourselves. Speaking of that, I'm expecting to have to leave for a glass or two."

Senrid laid a transfer token down on Keriam's desk as he explained briefly about Jilo. Keriam (of course) had heard about the surprise guest. Marloven kings seldom had guests. Tdanerend, as regent, certainly hadn't. But last summer Senrid had brought a famous one, the Little Girl. She'd come a few times since. Everyone had gotten used to the Little Girl who had rid the world of Siamis through some kind of magic. It seemed fitting that she would visit their king.

Keriam liked the Little Girl not because she was famous, but because with her, for the first time, Senrid could be a boy. He'd never had a chance to roust about like other boys, but with the Little Girl, he built big cities out of books and a jumble of items as they argued back and forth and laughed, or they rode, or they just chattered, even if their chatter was in a different language. It was their laughter. Keriam couldn't remember ever hearing Senrid laugh like that, before the Little Girl came.

Senrid finished up, ". . . so if I don't show up within a glass of the exhibition practice, which I very much wanted to see, hold this token and say my name."

Keriam had considered canceling the exhibition and sending the new seniors home, like recalcitrant little boys. But it was so good to see Senrid acting like a normal boy, wanting to see the exhibition. "That will be after the midafternoon bell," Keriam said, making the decision. He'd slam the lid on the seniors' strut some other way.

"Then I'd better go soon."

"Why go at all?" Keriam said, and regretted it. Senrid had probably just told him, somewhere in all that gabble about Chwahirsland and Mearsies Heili that he hadn't really listened to.

Senrid stilled, his lips parted, his gray-blue eyes startled. Then his gaze went diffuse, and Keriam suspected that the question had struck Senrid differently than he'd intended.

He was right.

Senrid stared at Keriam, thinking that he wanted the real reason.

So what was the real reason? Senrid knew the real reason. It was both simple, and impossible, to say out loud: I'm going because Clair of the Mearsieans asked me to.

It would sound so sickening, maybe even sentimental. But there was no sentiment about Clair. She was offering to trust him, by coming to him in this alliance he'd agreed to so carelessly months ago, figuring it was more lighter hypocrisy that would be forgotten as fast as the self-righteous speeches about great Us battling nasty Them. (He did agree about Norsunder's being nasty.)

"Jilo seems to have no one. Can you believe that? No one, except that bunch of Mearsean girls. And they're his enemies, at least former enemies. At least I have you." Senrid's words tumbled quickly. "Here's the irony. I have you, because I know you're the only one who wouldn't conveniently lose the token if I vanish into whatever awaits in that chamber. And it makes me afraid. Yet, here's more irony, you'd be a better king than I am."

"You will be a great king," Keriam said, careful not to show how profoundly Senrid's quick words moved him. "Besides, I've got the wrong name. We both know who of those fools arguing about their inherited rights, as if those haven't changed at least once a century, would try to take this castle if he thought the others wouldn't fight him."

Senrid snapped his fingers. "Then I'd better get to work. While my name still means something besides a catch-all for cursing."

He whirled around before Keriam could answer, and shot through the door as if trying to outrace time.

Senrid found Jilo in the formal dining room, which had been used exactly once so far in Senrid's short reign, the first time Liere came to visit. After they sat uncomfortably across from each other for a tense meal, they had both admitted that they'd rather eat in Senrid's study, or in the kitchens. By her third visit, that was now habit.

But the servants had put this new visitor there. Jilo lurked at a window overlooking the southern part of the city. He was even more unprepossessing in daylight than he'd looked at night, but at least his unpleasantly pasty complexion appeared somewhat more natural, and less like the gray of a corpse.

Jilo glanced up sideways through his lank, unkempt black hair, his manner furtive. Senrid reminded himself that this shambling, slope-shouldered fellow had endured eight months of the poisonous atmosphere of that magic chamber in Narad fortress.

Senrid said, "I've made some magical preparations, in case you still want my help. I'm sure you don't want to get caught again in that time . . ." Senrid didn't even have a word for it. "Smear. And I can't afford to vanish that long. I don't plan on returning in half a year, or longer, to everyone fighting, their only point of agreement that they should execute me."

Jilo shrugged, like execution squads were part of everyday life. Yes, from what Senrid had heard about the Chwahir, especially in the last century, they probably were.

Jilo's shoulders didn't come down out of the shrug, but stayed tense under his ears as he mumbled to the tops of his shoes, "Ah, what is it . . . that you want to do?"

"Find out if there is a time-binding spell. And how it's bound. If we can." Senrid sighed. "This is way, way beyond anything I know. But I think it's the first thing to do."

Jilo ducked his head in agreement, Senrid stuck out his hand, and Jilo understood that he was to make the transfer. He swallowed. "Brace yourself."

Jilo stretched out the hand wearing the onyx ring and clamped his fingers around the other boy's wrist. He muttered the spell, and magic hammered them against a wall, then scraped their components off and flung them into ice to reconstitute. Or that's what it felt like.

They found themselves in Wan-Edhe's magic chamber.

Senrid drew a shaky breath, then nearly choked. He'd forgotten that thin, yet pervasive stench of stale sweat tinged with a musty, animal smell of old, unwashed clothing. There was nothing in the room but the huge central table, made of wood so old it seemed petrified, a chair, and shelves and shelves of books. The stink had permeated the stone, if such a thing was possible. Either that or no one had cleaned the room in decades.

Jilo rubbed trembling fingers across his eyes, then said, "This small book is experimental spells. The large one is Wan-Edhe's log."

Senrid had figured that out on his short visit before, but he didn't point it out to Jilo. It was a way to establish a starting place.

"Here's where I can help, I think," Senrid said. "I learned this ward because of my uncle, who had a habit of protecting all his secrets with traps. It's laborious, but you can find the traps faster than careful feel by fingers."

"I've already searched for traps," Jilo said.

"You really think you got them all?" Senrid countered.

Jilo didn't have to think about it. "No."

Senrid explained his tracer spell. It had to be cast for specific objects as well as specific spells. If there was a hidden fire trap on whatever you touched, you'd see a red flare. A stone spell would make a blue flare. And so on.

Jilo's forehead eased. "So these kinds of tracers do exist. Neither Wan-Edhe nor Prince Kwenz would have let me near any such magic. Though I tried to find it."

"I'll start on this half. You over there."

Jilo ducked his head again.

Senrid worked fast, the spell having become habit during the bad old days before his uncle turned to Norsunder. His mind was free to run with questions. This was an enormous library; there must be at least a thousand books on the nearest wall alone. Some of the ones on the highest shelf looked crumbled. They were most likely records of various types. But somewhere lay the solution to the lethal atmosphere here.

Or maybe not. How long had it been in making? The size of the task ahead of Jilo pressed down on Senrid, making it hard to breathe. No, he could breathe. It was more that he had to think about breathing, that he was aware of all the potential pain his body could be in if he moved wrong. His joints seemed ill-fitted, his skin tender in a way he couldn't describe.

It was a relief when he found himself sucked away and deposited in Keriam's room, where he collapsed onto the floor, head on his knees as his ears roared.

When he looked up, the air in the familiar office smelled sweeter than spring, light as noon, though the sun was weak behind streaky clouds, and low in the sky.

"What a life." He enjoyed the miracle of easy breathing. "Next time I whine about things here, remind me of Chwahirsland."

Keriam did not comment on how very little Senrid whined. "Did you complete your task?"

Senrid made a flat gesture with his hand. "Not even close. But we got a start. The rest is up to Jilo. I think he knows what to do. Better than I. He knows the territory." Then his mood changed. "Let's go watch those seniors, and I can pretend I don't see their fathers glaring at me because I won't let them kill their civilians whenever they get a blister or a bellyache. Hah!"

## Chapter Fourteen

JILO was startled when he noticed that Senrid was gone. A brief pulse of gratitude made him look around to make sure. Jilo wanted to thank Senrid not only for the spell, but for illuminating a hitherto shadowy path of magical logic. He knew what to do, now. It felt so . . . so steadying—was that the right word?—to know what to do.

He straightened up, aware of a sense of malaise sapping at his vitality. After carefully pulling out the last book he had tested, so he could find his place again, he sighted the door, and walked out. It was like walking through . . . fog. No, fog didn't resist you, cold and wet as it might feel.

He noticed the farther he got from the magic chambers, the more easily he moved; one floor down, and he encountered servants. The two he saw looked at him fearfully, one jumping as if prodded.

"Any orders?"

"A meal," Jilo said. "Bring it here."

"A meal?" the young one asked, eyes wide. "Here?"

"Is there a standing order against meals brought here?" The stink of fear was almost as bad as the magical malaise. "Until Wan-Edhe returns," Jilo forced the hated words out, "I will have meals here."

The young one bowed, hands out to his sides and open, as Wan-Edhe had required, showing no weapon. With his head bowed like that, Jilo could see the roundness of his face beneath the pallor and haggardness that marked everyone in the castle. He didn't look all that much older than Jilo himself. Was he worrying about what was going to happen?

Jilo hesitated, then ventured a new idea. "I will be making an inspection, to be ready for Wan-Edhe's return."

Was that relief? Yes. Routine was steadying, and the order clear. And readying the castle for inspection would keep everyone busy.

The meal arrived, and the boiled grain with cabbage and dried fish was as tasteless as the Shadowland food Jilo had eaten all his life. However, it did what it was supposed to do. Or maybe it was the thinner air downstairs. When he returned to the magic chambers, he did not immediately take up the task of checking for traps on the books, but explored the other chambers. There was little to find.

Then he remembered the anteroom off the throne, the one Wan-Edhe had always kept locked to anyone but himself and his dungeon master. Jilo went downstairs to discover the throne room empty and cold. Kwenz must have removed most of the spells on the anteroom door while executing a fetch order from his brother, for there was only a stone spell on the latch, easy to remove.

The room beyond had a table, in the center of which sat a plain wooden frame with what looked like black slate inside it. At the left and right of this framed slate were polished scry stones, each with flickers of movement inside. All different.

Jilo bent over the nearest, trying to see what was going on. He brushed his fingers over the top of the stone to remove a thin layer of dust, and found himself staring at the inside of one of the guard command centers. This time he kept his fingers on the scry stone and heard voices.

". . . I tell you, just fit them in."

"But we are already overcrowded."

"Not down the coast. They're all undermanned."

"Under leaky roofs, without beds or supplies. What are they going to do with two thousand extra mouths to feed and bodies to house?"

The Shadowland Chwahir were already *here!* 'Already'? He'd lost eight months upstairs.

"Do you really want to ask for clarification of orders?"

The youngest said, "If he's truly gone, I will."

They all looked around on the word 'he.'

Then the oldest said, "I'll wager a neckin he's watching you right now."

Jilo said, "Neckin?"

In the command room, all three jumped as if they'd been stabbed. Jilo almost found it funny, except the yellowish fear in their faces was not at all funny.

The three straightened up. One said, "May we request clarification of orders?"

Jilo remembered the relief in the runner's face. "Carry out as specified. But you are to send orders across the land. Everyone ready for inspection. That includes a list of necessary repairs."

Hands snapped out, palms bare, fingers stiff. "It shall be done." Though already the three commanders were worrying about what 'necessary' might mean, and what would happen if they interpreted the word incorrectly.

Jilo touched the scry stone, and a different room appeared. Another touch, a different room. Of course Wan-Edhe would have spent months, maybe years, setting up this elaborate spy system. As for 'neckin,' it obviously was slang.

Jilo stretched out his hand to return to the first room. He could listen to what they said about their orders . . .

No. If he did that once, he'd do it again. And again. And he'd never stop. The words flowed through his head, feeling like an argument. Against whom? There was a sense in his chest, like . . . like a beating was nigh. Like Wan-Edhe was watching. Like . . . threat. He couldn't characterize it beyond that.

So he ran out of the room, pausing only to restore the stone spell. No one should be in that chamber, that much seemed sensible.

As he returned upstairs, he thought about slang, and how he'd known pretty much all the Shadowland slang, but that didn't mean the warriors here shared the same slang, though they shared a language.

Comfort. The slang he knew had to do with sneaking ways to get better food, better everything. Ways around the rules. And of course the shorthand for various punishments.

*We Chwahir have to sneak to get comfort,* he thought grimly.

He left the thought behind. He used one of the secret passageways to reach the magic chamber, and got to work.

Senrid had discovered that even when he was deeply asleep, some part of his mind was awake and aware enough to sense subtle changes.

Something broke into his dreams. When he was small, one of his survival habits had been to remain lying still, his breathing even, when his uncle stole into his room to see if he slept or was conspiring, and later, to attempt magical spells that Senrid had managed to spy out and so had already warded; the only reason he was still here was because the regent had been a terrible mage, and hadn't taken the time to study to become a better one.

Senrid lay still except for one hand. His heartbeat crowded his throat as his fingers wormed under his pillow to close on the hilt of the throwing knife he always slept with.

His door opened a crack wider, the hinges noiseless. Whoever opened it slipped inside equally noiselessly, except he couldn't completely hide the soft sough of breathing.

Senrid sat up, spotted the man-shaped shadow barely visible against the pale wall, and hurled the dagger all in one motion.

"Shit."

The voice cracked. An adolescent voice. This was no sinister Norsundrian spy mage, and anyway a Norsundrian would set off tracers.

Senrid snapped his fingers, lighting the glowglobes, and stared as Jarend Ndarga grimaced, yanked the dagger out of his bicep, then sank onto Senrid's trunk. "Your aim stinks," he said with a fair attempt at a steady voice.

"Didn't aim for the heart. Shoulder," Senrid said, with no attempt at hiding his shaky voice.

"Then your aim still stinks." Ndarga grimaced. "Why don't you have bodyguards?"

"Not going to live like my uncle, always expecting assassins," Senrid said.

"I'm not an assassin," Ndarga retorted in somewhat breathy outrage, his hand clapped tightly over his arm. "If I wanted a fight, it would be—"

"I know, I know, according to the rules," Senrid said, his heart still hammering as he rolled out of bed and reached for his clothes. "Here." He pulled a winter scarf from his bureau and tossed it to Ndarga, who wrapped it around his dripping arm as Senrid yanked on yesterday's trousers and shirt. "So why are you snaking into my bedroom in the middle of the night?"

The look of acute pain that Ndarga shot at Senrid came from something other than a dagger puncture, nasty as that was. Ndarga's surface emotions were like a hammer inside Senrid's skull—regret, anger, anxiety—causing Senrid to wince, and tighten his mental shield.

It took him a few breaths to resist the almost overwhelming temptation to delve behind those surface emotions, but he controlled it. He wasn't good enough not to risk being detected, and he knew how very angry, justifiably angry, that would make Ndarga.

So he said, "Come on. My study is right down the hall."

A short time later, Ndarga hunched on a guest mat, a heavy mug in his hands containing a healthy dose of the sometimes double- or even triple-distilled liquor called bristic, made from rye, with a blend of almond and pepper.

He sipped, blinked rapidly, and some of the blue shade vanished from his lips. Senrid loathed the taste of bristic almost as much as he hated the blurring effect of alcohol, but he knew it could help blunt pain. Listerblossom or green kinthus would be better, but he'd have to send for those, and he sensed Ndarga wanted to keep this interview private.

Ndarga let out a long, ragged sigh, glanced distractedly at the crimson-splashed scarf he'd knotted around his arm, then looked up. "Nothing happened."

Senrid knew exactly what that meant. All these months had passed, with Ndarga neither penalized nor singled out in any way; he was now beginning his two-year stint serving in the city guard with the rest of last year's senior class.

Senrid said, "Won't. Like I said."

"You took away capital rights from the jarls."

"Not completely. Decisions to execute anyone have to be reviewed," Senrid said. "It's not new. The Senrid-Harvaldar I'm named for introduced it when my family got back to the throne five centuries ago. My father reintroduced it under the new regs." When Ndarga raised his hand to speak, Senrid said, "Yes, I know I'm not my father. Underage. Never went through the academy, and you know why."

Ndarga looked away. Then he said, "If I tell you something, will it be a capital case?"

Senrid sighed. "How can I know that before I know what it is?"

"Still. It's about *my* father," Ndarga said. "I'm not going to rat if it will get him put up against the wall."

There again was the impulse to sift through Jarend Ndarga's thoughts, but doing so was like trying to swim in a weed-choked lake, while being screamed at and burned and frozen by the person's emotions. And, of course, Liere would say it was wrong.

Senrid said, "I won't promise anything I don't know about first."

Ndarga let out his breath, trying to think clearly in spite of the

throbbing pain. One thing he was sure of. If the king had agreed immediately, he wouldn't have believed it.

Neither understood the other, and so they sat there like that, at an
impasse, until Senrid said, "You came in here. I didn't yelp for the
guard. So speak your piece, or let me get back to sleep. And you better
get that wrapped properly in any case."

Ndarga spoke reluctantly, as if each word was yanked out of him the
way he'd pulled the dagger from his arm. "My father. And the Jarl of
Waldevan. Others if he can get them. I think Torac will also ride, as he
owes my father for our help against the Gorse Gang—horse raiders—
on the border two years ago. First thaw, they're moving to take the
coast back." He raised a hand. "They know they won't be able to keep
it, that there are international treaties that separated off the Rualese.
But if you have to defend that treaty, which only benefits outsiders,
then they mean to force you back to the old ways, before you can raise
the rest of the kingdom."

"Which old ways would those be? The ones under my uncle, with
executions and floggings any time he didn't like someone's expression?
Or my grandfather, who got us into two wars, which resulted in that
same treaty being made by every other kingdom ganging up against us?"
Senrid retorted cordially, and as Ndarga just shook his head miserably,
Senrid sighed. "Forget that. I know what it is. They want to be petty
kings again. But it isn't going to happen while I'm alive."

Ndarga got to his feet. "If you win. Exile him, or all of us, if you
think that's fair. Whole family. You'll probably want to give Methden
to someone new, and I get that, how it works. I hope it goes to the
Senelacs. But don't execute him."

Senrid grinned. "The Senelacs probably wouldn't take it. Jan and
Fenis both are ridiculously proud of that stupid old saying that Senelacs
are great captains and terrible governors."

Ndarga ignored this attempt to ease the atmosphere, his hand
clutched tightly to his arm. "You still haven't said. Look, Senrid-
Harvaldar, I don't want my father against the wall. Because I ratted
him out."

Senrid clawed his hair out of his eyes, his mind wheeling uselessly
without being able to light anywhere sure. Lying had come easy when
he lived under his uncle's tyranny, and without guilt. Lying fast and
well was a survival tool.

The urge to lie shaped his lips, but he forced himself to meet Ndarga's angry, wary gaze. "I promise you I'm not going to ride down to

Methden waving a war banner and order him shot in his own courtyard, on the strength of 'he might.' I'll wait for action. If he breaks
capital law, not talks about it, but actually breaks it, then, no promises.
How's that?"

A flick of the fingers. "I can take that."

"You know," Senrid couldn't help adding, "If I end up having to send
your father and all his captains into exile, they might make it in Toth,
or Telyerhas, but in Perideth, Marlovens are shot on sight."

"We have relations in Toth," Ndarga said in a gritty voice.

"Right then. Cut along." Senrid lifted his hand.

Ndarga cut. Senrid ran back to his room to clean the gore off his
dagger, and replace it under the pillow. Then he jumped through his
cleaning frame and pulled on socks, boots, and a tunic. As he did, he
rapidly made and discarded plans. His first instinct was to race up to
Keriam's tower.

Then he caught himself up short. He had to start acting like a king,
instead of running to Keriam, or he may as well hand over the throne.

Senrid ran back to his study and snapped the glowglobes to light.

## Chapter Fifteen

SENRID scowled at his desk. He needed more Scouts.

But recruiting the elite group, once known as royal runners before his family regained the throne, and King's Scouts afterward, was a slow process at best. They had to be trustworthy, vigilant, impartial, smart, and they had to go unnoticed. They had to listen, and be loyal to Marloven Hess. So far, most of his recruits were women and girls, who he knew would go unnoticed by even the most suspicious jarls.

He had to be careful about their selection and their deployment. Never far from his awareness was the sinister fact that all his uncle's Scouts (who had been expert spies as well as assassins) had vanished without a trace. Senrid still had no idea what had happened to them. In Marloven Hess, that usually meant they'd been scragged.

It was possible that some had scuttled for the border as soon as the regent was deposed. But all had vanished. Keriam said that argued for concerted action. Senrid found the idea unsettling that someone had the skill to get the drop on them all, as his uncle had recruited his Scouts for their sneakiness as well as their viciousness.

He'd think about Scouts later.

Senrid whirled around and studied the big map on the wall behind his desk, twin to the one in his bedroom. He'd made that map himself, with as much detail as possible. His uncle had thought it a harmless task, not knowing that Senrid had undertaken it to get his own kingdom's landscape thoroughly into his head.

If Jarend Ndarga was right, the Jarl of Methden was going to invade Enneh Rual. Senrid eyed long, thin Enneh Rual. It was a country that existed only as a result of a treaty, but it would be foolish to overlook the sea-trained hardiness of the folk there, whose ancestors were partly Marloven, and partly Iascan, the fisher folk who'd lived there before Senrid's ancestors rode a-conquering out of the north.

Senrid had been listening to the seniors talking about command class ever since he was little, and he'd begun testing all his reading against what he heard. When he looked at the map, the strategy seemed obvious. He could even name a couple of battles in which it had been used. If Waldevan took Tarual Harbor, which dominated the bay, and Methden supported him from the southern end, that would secure both population centers, and the rest of Enneh Rual would fall easily.

But Senrid had learned from Keriam that 'obvious' was not inevitable, or even exactly the same thing to every commander. Senrid considered what he knew of Jarend Ndarga's father. The jarl was tough, hardened from years of riding the southern border in the ongoing effort to curtail the constant horse-raiding going back and forth, but actual battle experience? Senrid was fairly certain that David Ndarga had been an academy scrub, consigned to the horse pickets, when Senrid's grandfather last led the Marlovens against the neighboring countries. He could always ask Fenis Senelac, who seemed to know the history of every battle, as a result of having two older brothers in the academy.

Senrid scowled at the map, then darted for the library, warded and locked, where what remained of the royal records were kept. Marloven rulers who took their thrones by violence had a habit of eradicating all their predecessors' records. Senrid's uncle had been no different, trying to remove Senrid's father from everything but memory, but he'd not succeeded as well as he thought.

Older records were harder to find. The year before, Senrid had made a foray into his ancestral home, deep in the tangled, dark-magic-distorted forest of Darchelde. His ancestors' castle was a ruin, blasted by unimaginable magic, but careful exploration had disclosed an enormous archive filled with books. Most had been destroyed by four centuries of wind and weather. But not all.

Senrid had set teams of young scribes to work sorting them and re-copying the most fragile. The reward was the filling of some of the holes left by long-dead usurpers. Senrid sought some of those now, to read up on how his ancestors had commanded past battles, skirmishes, and routs, successful and not.

He was still at it when Keriam found him lying on the floor in a welter of maps. Senrid looked up, startled to discover wintry light blue in the windows, and Keriam standing at the door, ready for their morning briefing.

"Keriam, Methden is going to war. I have to stop it." And before Keriam could respond, Senrid scrambled to his feet, sending papers flying. "Hibern is due soon. Have the runner tell her we had to leave. She'll understand. I'll meet you in your tower. There's somebody I've got to talk to first."

He bolted out the door and raced down to the academy.

He knew where he was likely to find Retren Forthan, one of his few friends among the academy boys. Forthan was that rarity, a boy from a laborer family. He'd been scooped up during one of the regent's mass conscriptions for building a super army with which to reclaim the Marloven empire of old. Forthan had been assigned with the other laborers' boys to the foot, but he'd proved to be so skillful that he'd been put forward by his infantry captain to be considered for command training at the academy.

Senrid's uncle had been ambivalent, knowing that his cronies among the jarls would not like this precedent, for places in the academy were much prized. Keriam had been insistent. And now Forthan was about to embark on his second year as a senior.

The academy was mostly empty during the winter, but a few boys stayed on. Forthan was inevitably one. Senrid knew he'd find him up early, drilling contact fighting in the same seniors' forecourt where Senrid had gotten his teeth loosened by Ndarga last year.

He hopped up and down, cursing himself for running out without a jacket, then forgot the cold when Forthan appeared, wrestling his clothing straight before saluting, fist to chest.

"I've got a situation," Senrid said in a quick, low voice. "Come on. Let's go where we won't be overheard."

Forthan followed without question, matching Senrid's quick step until they reached the archery yard, empty except for pools of icy slush here and there on the ground. Senrid whirled to face the older boy. "You've probably been reading the same histories I have, right? Of course you have. But you've been getting lectures in the military thinking behind all the glory, and that's what I need, that knowledge. Keriam agrees we need to know our own history better than just singing the same old stupid songs."

Forthan muttered with uncharacteristic ambivalence, "That's so." And to get off the subject of reading, "My father said once that nobody seemed to know any songs but the ones that made their family look good."

Senrid laughed. "True!" He kicked at the slush with the toe of his boot. "But I'm talking about reading. I mean, you can read and read and read. I have. I know. Reading makes you able to quote the significant facts of every battle, but it doesn't make you a commander. I know that. I knew that."

He looked sideways. Forthan could barely make out his expression in the weak light, but he could see the self-mockery in Senrid's tight shoulders, his sharp gestures.

Senrid went on. "Not many have heard this, but it was a near thing with Siamis, there at the end, up in Bereth Ferian. And it was all my fault. Mine was the decoy plan, because those mages up there didn't take anyone our age seriously. Well, they were right not to take *me* seriously."

Forthan gestured with a flat hand, as though pushing something away.

"It's true," Senrid said. "I should have known that Siamis would be ahead of me." He kicked the slush again. "Nobody knows this, either. When I was a prisoner. In Norsunder. Detlev looked right at me, and said that I wasn't worth his time yet. That's why I've done the no-growth spell."

Forthan stared somewhat helplessly. Like most Marlovens, he knew nothing about magic other than the little spells people were raised with, and trusted it less. He did understand that Senrid had done some kind of spell that kept him from aging. He said slowly, "Some people think that you did that spell because you wanted a chance to play, now that the regent is gone. You want a boyhood you didn't get."

"Let 'em," Senrid said carelessly.

"But others think you are running some kind of ruse, only not against us, but against outsiders."

"I suppose that's going to happen. Especially if I . . ." *Win*, Senrid thought. But he couldn't say it. Instead, "The rumor I want going to those outsiders is that first one, at least until Detlev is defeated. He and Siamis read minds like we read books. Forthan, Siamis was a step ahead of me all the time. One step? Ten steps. I fell right into his trap. If it hadn't been for the lighter mages coming to Liere's call, I'd probably be right back in that cell. So let any Norsunder spies hear that Senrid wants to play with the little brats."

Forthan remained silent, feeling very much out of his depth at this careless reference to personal encounters with Norsunder's most sinister villains.

Senrid kicked again at the slush. "I don't want to look like I'm worth Detlev's notice, but I still need to make the jarls see that my father's rules are back. Where was I? History. Reading history." He began to pace back and forth. "Look, Forthan, I've got no *harskiald* whom everyone will follow." Senrid used the Marloven word for supreme army commander, who in wartime was second only to the king. "We both know that we've had no upper rank commanders when we need them often enough that we've got jokes about it: 'the empty tower', and 'waiting for an elgar.'"

"Elgar" was a centuries-old slang term for the heroic commander who won every duel as well as every battle.

"All because of our Marloven would-be kings taking out the opposition's strongest leaders before they strike at the king they want to replace. Or, in my uncle's case, purging the academy of all its smartest seniors, because he'd watched as a scrub as a handful of the smart ones helped my oldest uncle when he tried to take the crown from my grandfather."

Forthan made a vague gesture of agreement. He'd grown up hearing bad or unpopular commanders joked about as 'waiting for an elgar.' It was the next thing to saying they were cowards. Or stupid. And he'd heard some of the jarls' sons repeating gossip about the boy king and his empty tower.

Senrid said, "If I did have a great harskiald, and handed my problems off to him, then I'd probably end up with another regent. Don't want that! So *I* have to learn to command. I've read everything I can find, and I know the details of countless battles, but I can't find *why* they did things, that is, their thinking before they gave the commands that led to wins."

Forthan was still silent. If the king asked directly, he wouldn't lie. But he dreaded making the humiliating confession that he was illiterate, convinced it would end his academy days summarily.

"Our greatest hero, Inda-Harskialdna, left the least direct evidence. All we have of him are the two versions of the Fox record, neither of which agree with the other, and a lot of hearsay and bombast about people who came after, you know, 'hearkening back to the great days of.'"

Senrid threw up his hands, fingers stiff. "In some of the oldest, moldiest stuff, I've found hints that there's a third Fox record. One that has everything. Though I'm sure it's not in this kingdom. Too many have searched for it. Horseshit! There goes the bell. But you don't have to go, right?"

Because the academy was not in session, Forthan wasn't expected anywhere. He flicked his fingers in agreement, and Senrid went on, "Here's why I need you. You know I've been watching the academy games ever since I was little. And I got so I could predict who would lead wins, who wouldn't. What they'd do."

Forthan opened his hands in assent, relieved to find himself back on familiar ground. He and Senrid and Jan Senelac had sat on the seniors' roof many a summer evening, little Senrid avidly listening as the two older boys dissected the games, before the regent put a stop to it. "Academy games are different from a war with Siamis, is that what you're going to say?"

Senrid whirled around, then stabbed the air with three fingers. "But it's the same, really. Isn't it? Siamis plays for keeps, but it's all a game to him, he even said so. And I see that, I do, because what we're talking about are patterns, predicted by the way somebody thinks. The choices they always make. Right? Right?"

Forthan tried to follow the quick voice, and turned up his palm again in silent assent.

"So how do you know how and when to give orders, when in the heat? Because *you* always win."

Forthan scowled into the middle distance, then said, "I don't always win. Well, I guess it's always if I know the ground. Or if I'm up against someone I've been up against before. If I know the ground, and I know them, I pretty much know what they'll do next."

Senrid's breath crowed. "So it's true! What they say about picking your ground. Right?"

Forthan shrugged, acutely uncomfortable at being pulled from familiar to dangerously unfamiliar territory. He wanted to help Senrid, whom he liked and admired, even though he found it difficult to follow Senrid's quick changes of mood and subject. "I know the ground. Here. At the academy," Forthan said stolidly.

Senrid gazed at him, suspecting that Forthan's meaning was metaphorical as well as specific. He grinned, socked Forthan companionably on the arm, and raced off.

He pounded up the stairs to Keriam's tower, and burst in as the man was just being served a cup of freshly ground coffee.

As soon as the orderly was gone, Senrid kicked the door shut, and out it all came, from Ndarga's sudden appearance to Senrid's talk with Retren Forthan, in a headlong cascade. Keriam listened, knowing when Senrid was like this there was no halting him.

". . . and so it must have taken them the better part of two months to put this together. I think I need to confront them on their own ground. Waldevan is a rat, I know that much from my uncle's day. No, rats fight. He's a . . . a beetle. He'll squeak and try to scuttle but if he's penned, he'll go belly up. That's his pattern of behavior! But the Jarl of Methden will go all out, don't you think? And from everything I've seen, it would be a mistake to hit him in his own territory. Like Forthan said, ground is important. Don't you think he'll fight?"

Keriam had gone through the academy with David-Jarl Ndarga of Methden. "Oh yes. He'll fight," Keriam said grimly.

"Then we have to catch him outside Methden, right? Outside his territory, but before he gets to the Rualan border and drags us into war. I have to get there first, so I can pick the ground. It'll be just like the academy, won't it?" Senrid's voice pleaded. "Patterns."

Keriam said, "I can't predict the outcome, Senrid. You've studied Headmaster Gand's command text, from long ago. Think of what the man said about himself. That could speak for me. I'm excellent at analyzing what has happened, but I've never been good at predicting what will happen. The best I can ever give you is a set of possibilities, culled from the records. That's why I teach, and don't command."

Senrid rapped his knuckles on the desk. "How does this sound? You send the order for West Army to split. Give me two wings of horse, no, better make it three, a full company, for Waldevan's got three wings of his own. Then send the rest to ride south for . . . here. Where Methden borders with the Rualans." He pointed to the plain map on the wall adjacent to Keriam's desk. "The West Army winter quarters are closest to Waldevan, which means I can threaten him first, soon's my company gets there. Should only take them a day, or three if the weather is bad. Then I'll transfer down here, and walk the ground, until the rest of West shows up. By then I'll have a plan. I'll pick the ground. I've already been studying the terrain maps, and I think I know where to look, because I know maps never give you a real feel for what's actually there."

Keriam said, "And if Waldevan fights? If he wins?"

"Then I'll probably be dead, and it's up to you," Senrid retorted with a toothy grin.

Keriam stared down into that face. The fair hair came from both Senrid's parents, but the eyes that gazed back at him so intently were Evan's eyes, the Indevan-Harvaldar everyone had loved.

Grim memory seized Keriam, beginning with the days when David Ndarga of Methden had been riding mates with Kendred, the king's oldest son, until Kendred's unsuccessful revolt against his father had caused him to disappear, after which David's loyalty had gone to Indevan. Who had been an excellent king until his younger brother, Tdanerend, (it was everywhere believed) stabbed him in the back.

Tdanerend, as regent for five-year-old Senrid, had ordered the entire city guard out in search for the assassin, and the regent had even put a deserter-turned-thief through a grisly execution, but the man had maintained to the end he wasn't anywhere near the royal castle that night. Everyone believed he'd been a scapegoat, but after Tdanerend had handed out savage floggings for rumor-mongering among castle guards saying so, the rumors went underground.

More than ten years later, Keriam still felt like a coward for not speaking up, and he knew many others did as well, but what could they have done? Accusing the regent would not have brought Indevan back, but it would have touched off civil war. Tdanerend had made concessions and promises to gain powerful support among ambitious jarls, or those who wanted to become jarls, enough to make the outcome uncertain. The only sure thing would have been a high body count.

David Ndarga, like the other jarls, had thereafter been forced to swear fealty to Tdanerend or die with the knowledge that his family would be replaced by Tdanerend's sycophants. And so Indevan's dreams of justice had died on that balcony with him.

Keriam shifted uncomfortably, and Senrid stilled, a rarity for him, and waited as Keriam considered the present. Waldevan, Keriam was sure, would back down. He was a weasel. Had always been one. But David Ndarga of Methden was a wolf: loyal to his old mates and to an image of Marloven Hess that had not existed for ten years; fiercely bitter toward everyone else.

"It might work," he said finally.

## Chapter Sixteen

*Bereth Ferian*

"YOU *are?*" The journeymage named Sigini threw her head back, pale hair rippling, blue eyes wide in astonishment. "*You* are?" No, that wasn't astonishment. That was affront. The senior mage student looked at Hibern as if she'd spat on the beautiful marble floor.

Hibern stared back. Fhlerians were like that, everybody said. Fhlerians sounded arrogant because of those Venn-sharp consonants and the drawled vowels of their version of Sartoran. Because those strong enough to become citizen-warriors, with the right to vote for their own government, considered themselves better than anyone else. They were all that way, it was nothing personal.

Not true, Hibern decided as she met that unfriendly gaze. It didn't take mind powers to guess what this Fhlerian was thinking: *But you're a Marloven.*

Sigini opted for the veneer of politesse as she asked, "Why would the Queen of Sartor pick you for a study partner?" Her fellow mage students crowded around, some sharing her expression of personal insult as she added, "You are her own age. You cannot possibly be ahead of us."

"Not in general studies." Another girl hefted her mage notebook.

"But she must be in non-human magical studies, as she's with Erai-Yanya of Roth Drael."

"Tsauderei probably arranged it," a tall boy interjected, his tone reasonable, but speaking as if Hibern weren't there in front of them. "She's probably a compromise, since either mage school wouldn't like the other being so honored."

Sigini, who looked about eighteen, rolled her eyes. "Of course. That explains the diplomatic side of it."

Hibern breathed out through her nose, trying to rid herself of the irritation Sigini obviously wanted her to feel. Not long ago, Erai-Yanya had told Hibern, "You're going to meet with jealousy, I expect. Remember, no one at either Sartor's or Bereth Ferian's school knows Atan, much less who might be best for her. They are all thinking, quite naturally, that they should have been picked. It's human nature, and if you're going to work with mages of both schools for the good of the world, you must learn how to deflect such slights, and forget them."

Hibern forced a smile at Sigini, who someday might save Hibern's life, or the other way around. "Speaking of diplomacy, I don't want to be late." She walked out of the lecture room.

A couple of Bereth Ferian's mage students walked with her. One of the younger girls said, "Do you transfer all the way to Sartor from Roth Drael? Isn't it brutal?"

"I do it in stages," Hibern responded, walking quicker. "Spend an hour in my home kingdom. Then on to Sartor." At the corner of the hall, she turned away from the archive, knowing that most of the students would be heading that way to get started on their new assignment.

The younger girl cast a quick look back at her seniors, then stayed with Hibern. She matched pace and asked, her voice low, "What's she like? The queen, I mean."

Hibern didn't want to say that she didn't really know. Even though she called the Queen of Sartor 'Atan,' the most personal conversation they'd had so far was at that first interview. Since then, their weekly meetings these past eight months had been strictly about magic.

But Hibern's earliest lessons had been to keep her own counsel, and though this red-haired mage student with all the freckles seemed friendly, Hibern didn't know any of the Bereth Ferian mage students well enough to predict how they would hear her words. So she said, "She works very hard. She's earnest, and quick. She knows more about the history of magic than anyone I've ever met."

"That would be Tsauderei's doing," the student said confidently. "We all hear about how he and Mage-King Evend used to argue about how to teach magic, how Tsauderei felt that history ought to come before basics, not after." She tossed her curls. "As for the queen, she sounds boring."

Hibern didn't find Atan boring. Well, maybe the mask was boring. But the day of her interview, Hibern had glimpsed somebody behind that mask.

The girl went on, "Though she could be a dragon come back and Sigini would have volunteered to tutor her, just for the prestige." The redhead laughed and ran off with a flick of a hand, her silvery-blue mage robe rippling.

It was not actually Hibern's time to go south, but the other students didn't know that. Hibern transferred back to Roth Drael, and shivered at the sudden shock of damp chill. Magic warded the heavy sleety rain slanting down, but not the cold of the late summer storm.

She ran down the short hall, by now so accustomed to the place she no longer noticed the startling jagged lines of the broken walls, some fixed with regular stone centuries ago, others protected by layers of warding spells. She'd learned on her first interview with Erai-Yanya that Roth Drael was one of the few untouched ruins left from the Fall of Ancient Sartor four thousand years ago. Mages had vowed to leave the ruin as a memorial, but an ancestor of Erai-Yanya's had withdrawn from the world to study ancient magic in it, and heeding the vow, managed to make a cozy home of the ruin, using magic to ward weather. Bright woven rugs, comfortably shabby rigged bookcases, and low, cushioned chairs made for ease of reading, with plenty of small tables that could double as desks.

Erai-Yanya sat in one of these old chairs, a lapboard stretched across the padded arms, her bare toes propped on a fender near a leaping fire in the fireplace. Two old-looking scrolls lay half-furled on the lapboard, with an empty mug, an inkwell, and a stack of paper on which the mage was busy writing.

She looked up. "How did it go?"

"Well enough." Overhead, the roar of rain ceased abruptly. Hibern lowered her voice. "We got assigned some reading about magical displacement spells and banks and treaties. The same reading you gave me last year."

"Did you tell them that?"

"I kept it to myself."

Erai-Yanya smiled. "Good. Anything else?"

"Yes. At the end of the lecture, someone asked something about wards. I confess I was only paying partial attention, as I'd already done that reading. But the tutor said something about Sartor, then she pointed at me and told them that I was the new queen's study partner, and perhaps I could better answer their question. They all stared at me."

"And?" Erai-Yanya asked.

"It went pretty much as you predicted. Even who."

"Sigini," Erai-Yanya said unerringly. "Did she, or anyone, ask what you study with Atan?"

"No. But that'll probably come," Hibern said.

"And what will you say?"

Hibern suppressed a sigh. "This is an old lesson. I'll be as brief as possible. Tell them as little as I can. Without claiming great secrecy."

Erai-Yanya dipped her head in a nod. "I beg your forgiveness for being repetitive, but when it comes to Atan, everyone wants to know everything. And one can never quite be sure what people are hearing in the most innocuous-seeming answers."

"What if I tell them that we studied wards? Won't that be innocuous enough?"

"For anyone else, maybe. But someone hears that, and passes it on, and it gets passed farther—because Sartor is always interesting—and before you know it, some diplomat appears before the Sartoran Star Chamber, and demands a treaty to prevent the magic war that rumor has it the queen is about to begin because she's expanding her border wards. Then someone at Twelve Towers, or the Sartoran mage guild, gets busy and traces the rumors back to you."

Hibern sat back. "Muck! I didn't think of that."

"Do," Erai-Yanya said earnestly. "You gained enormous prestige in being picked as Atan's study partner. But prestige . . . well, you don't need that lecture."

"Yes, we Marlovens have the opposite of prestige," Hibern said. "Old news!"

Erai-Yanya smiled, but she did not deny it. Hibern said, "The sun is out. I'm going to take a walk before I have to transfer again."

Erai-Yanya shook her head. "Better not. I noticed a migration earlier."

"Oh." A migration usually meant the Fens, animals of Helandrias, who had been cursed with speech, because of some well-meaning but misguided mage long ago. The animals were very definite about speech being a curse; the mages had discovered that the animals called humans the Snakes with Two Faces.

Hibern grimaced as she hung up her shawl. The Fens might or might not attack her. Better not to tempt them. "This two-faced snake will work, then."

Hibern discovered she still had a turn of the glass before she was due in Marloven Hess.

She walked to her own room, with the old tapestry covering the massive crack in the single wall, and a strong weather-ward making a window of the missing part of the roof. This room had probably been a conservatory once, with its broad windows on three sides, through which Hibern could watch the forest life. She'd decided to live in this room during the summer. During winter she retreated to a smaller, cozy room.

She sat down at her desk, virtuously pulled out her notes from the year before on the incredibly boring subject of banks and displacement wards, then sat back, thinking about what the redhead had said about the Queen of Sartor and Sigini the Fhlerian.

*She could be a dragon come back* . . . The expression had all the cadence of a popular saying. Dragons occasionally appeared in colloquialisms in the world, though no one had seen one for thousands of years. It was said that the Chwahir language was full of dragon references, but that was a secondhand report. Hibern knew no one who spoke it.

When it was time to go, she packed up her books and transferred to Marloven Hess.

Senrid's study was empty. Not only empty, but it looked like a windstorm had been loosed, for books lay haphazardly on the table, and papers had been scattered all over the floor, their edges curling. More books kept them flat, which dispelled her first impression, that someone had ransacked Senrid's study. He was always so tidy. Something had clearly happened, probably bad.

The door opened. A runner stuck his head in and eyed Hibern. "Blue robe. Are you the mage student?" he asked. On Hibern's open-handed gesture of assent, he continued, "I was to tell you that Senrid-Harvaldar and Commander Keriam were called away."

Hibern sighed with disgust. Why hadn't Senrid written her a note and saved her a wrenching transfer for nothing? She knew he had a golden notecase. That had been one of their first projects together. He'd even insisted it actually be gold, though that metal hadn't been used exclusively since centuries ago, back when only the wealthy and powerful could afford to have mages make them. Senrid had been skeptical about the fact that anyone could send a note or a small object if it fit inside the case, as long as the 'sigil,' the notecase's Destination, was known to the sender.

He'd asked for gold simply because it would stand out, as he had no other gold objects. But he still thought like their ancestors, who never trusted magical communications. If he had some emergency, he would go straight to his army of runners, who would carry messages without revealing them to anyone else.

She walked out of Senrid's study and paused on the landing, staring sightlessly at the curving lines of a running horse frescoed on the wall, a raptor wing-spread above its flying mane.

She now had an entire hour to explore Eidervaen, the capital of Sartor and the oldest city in the world. She hadn't been permitted to wander alone during the rift-fighting days, but surely nobody was stopping her now.

She walked back to Senrid's personal Destination, transferred to Sartor, and after recovering, asked the chamber attendant, "Which way is outside?"

A formal gesture toward the opposite archway sent her down a hall with a shiny tiled floor into a vault-ceilinged intersection made of gray, peach, and silver marble.

She tipped her head back to study the tall windows high up on the wall, the strong afternoon light shafting in, lighting up slow-moving dust motes. As she slowed, she became aware of a quick, light sound, followed by the hasty whisper of slippers on marble.

She suppressed the urge to turn and look. There was no danger here. She picked another tile-floored, marble hall, hoping it would lead to the famous dragon door that she'd read about in her studies.

The pitter-patter neared. Hibern whirled, to find herself looking down in amazement at the strangest-looking child she'd ever seen. This girl would have been ordinary enough—brown of skin and hair—save for the wide, slightly protruding eyes with the droopy lower lid that marked her as some relation to the Landis family, and for the fact that she was dressed in some kind of ragged garment that was way too large for her.

"Are you a mage?" the child asked. She couldn't have been more than five.

Hibern said, "I'm a mage student," as she lifted her gaze to the servant, correct in livery, who halted a pace behind the child. This servant, a young woman, clasped her hands tightly, saying in a low, firm voice, "Come, joel, this is not appropriate."

"I am only asking," the child stated, owl-eyed.

'Joel,' Hibern had learned, was a familial honorific, which could also be used for small children. Hibern said, "I am a student of magic, joel." Nobody reacted, so she was not incorrect.

"Teach me a spell to become invisible?"

"Do you know your basics?" Hibern responded.

The child scowled, and the servant stepped up to her. "Come, joel, do you not see? It is necessary to learn your letters."

The child whirled away in a flutter of tatters and uncombed brown hair. "I *won't* do letters," she stated, then ran off without another word.

The servant sent Hibern a look that the latter took as regret and worry, then scurried after her charge.

That was odd. Not just the way the child was dressed, but how much she looked like Atan. And yet Atan had said her family was dead. But then the word 'family' could differ in meaning—to some it meant only parents, guardians, and siblings, and to others it could encompass an entire clan.

Hibern forgot the child when she reached a door, carved around with leaves and flowers but no dragons. She opened it and slipped outside, pulling her coat close about her. So far, no one had stopped her. No wards or alarms, though the Marloven was loose.

The sun was out, so it was comparatively balmy for a winter's day, sunlight shining weakly on a series of broad, shallow steps, worn by countless feet over the equally countless years. She looked down at the pale gray stone, then up, overwhelmed by the profligacy of grace in color, shape, and style: tower, archway, statue seduced the eye, demanding adulation. And the decorative motifs, as if to compete against the monuments of kings! Here was the famous stylized wheat pattern, there a Venn knot in reverse. Above, the sun with the sword rays, and facing it from that tower, the sun with the waving rays . . .

She had an hour. She forced her attention downward to the street, where people came and went, walking and riding in carriages, carts, and pony traps, and driving long wagons full of goods. Where to begin?

"Need transportation?"

The clatter of small hooves neared, and Hibern whirled around to discover a small pony trap pulling up, only the animals were a pair of silky-haired goats. As she stared in amazement, the nearer goat gave her a stern look, and uttered a soft "Mah-a-a-ah."

The boy driving the trap was no older than Hibern, a round fellow with rusty red hair tied back. He wore a thick yellow tunic with a green shoulder-cape and green cuffs, a yellow and gold wheel patch sewn on the shoulder. "Where to? Or are you just lost?" the boy asked, making the polite bow for third circle. "I can give directions. Things are slow today."

Hibern was intensely interested in talking to someone born a century before. "How much to ride around, and maybe get information on what I'm seeing? I have an hour."

The boy's business-smile widened to a grin. "I can get you around the Way in under an hour, if we don't stop, for a sixer. Ask any questions you like. You get your money back if you stump me."

The Way. Hibern knew that had to be the Grand Chandos Way, the street built on the foundations of what had once been the walls of the most ancient part of the city. And 'sixer,' she knew, was idiom for the six-sided brass coin, twelve of which made up one silver. Not to be confused with the six-sided silver coin, half of a gold-piece, that was called a 'six.' Erai-Yanya had counseled her to always carry a few coins in her pocket when transferring, and here she was, needing them for the first time.

Feeling worldly, she said, "I'd like that," and hopped into the trap.

A whistle, and the goats trotted neatly off, their prettily shod hooves clicking on the street paved in chevron brick pattern. "Do you get a lot of custom from the palace?" Hibern asked, to hear his accent again. It was different from Atan's, which was more like Hibern's own.

"Almost none. Those who come to the palace usually have palace business, and go away again either by their own wheelers or by magic. The good trade's at the guild Destinations." He flapped a hand behind them. "The senior wheelers get the best spots. But I like getting foreigners, because they're fun to talk to. As long as I can understand 'em."

As he spoke, he drove them under the enormous windowed archway that connected to a white stone tower. Hibern looked up at that smooth, glistening stone, like ice and yet not. Here was the same strange not-quite-stone of Erai-Yanya's ruin at Roth Drael. Some of the most awe-inspiring, and frightening, stories about Sartoran history involved this tower.

"Mages' Finger, that is, the Tower of Knowledge," her guide said. "Been here as long as the city. Some say longer. Only mages go in. And the royal family. Behind it is first district's labyrinth."

"Is that just for the royal family, too?"

"Oh, no, they have their own on the other side of the palace. Many families have their own. Each district has a public one, maintained by citizens."

The west wing of the palace hid the tower from view. They were making a wide sweep to run alongside the northern branch of the Ilder River. On the other side of the river ranked in elegant rows the famous Parleas Terrace, the aristocratic houses. The boy called off a list of statues and towers, about half of them names she recognized from history.

At the end, he said, "Any questions?"

"I know that kings and queens put up monuments to their rule, here, in Colend, and in many other kingdoms."

"They start thinking about it right when they're crowned. So the stories go," her guide said cheerily. "Some don't last long enough to put one up, and some dithered until it was too late. If there wasn't one put up to honor them, they just become another name in the list."

"So I take it rulers don't remove former monarchs' efforts?"

"Not in Sartor." He sounded surprised that anyone would do such a thing.

"So is this because the Landis line is unbroken here? Or because Sartor hasn't been conquered, outside of a hundred years ago?"

"Oh, there have always been Landises, but I don't know what you'd call unbroken," the guide said. "No, they don't knock down anyone else's monument, but build in front? Around?" He laughed. "I wish you had longer than an hour. I could show you some peculiar ones." He glanced back at her. "They don't build monuments where you come from?"

"No." Royal legacies of any kind in Marloven Hess didn't often survive changes of kings, save the shields and swords on walls, commemorating battles.

He clicked to the goats, who veered expertly between a dashing high-sprung two-seater carriage, pulled by a pair of gray horses, and a slow covered wagon behind a team of oxen. "Things'll be slow today up in the palace for you scribes."

"Slow?" Hibern repeated, not correcting his misapprehension. Erai-Yanya had deliberately given her a robe of a sky blue, different than either the dark blue of the Sartoran mage guild or the silver blue of Bereth Ferian's mage school. Scribes also wore various shades of blue. Scribes and mages had been tied together as long as there was recorded history. And in those histories it was clear that people didn't always like mages.

"Oh, yes." The boy chuckled. "Rumor has it Rel the Traveler himself just arrived. He and the queen'll be talking up old times. He was there, you know, when the queen lifted the spell off us, and broke the hundred-year sleep. Now over yonder, we've King Jussar the Golden, which referred to his singing, not his hair, which was black, and . . ."

Hibern had never met Rel, but she'd heard plenty of gossip about him, mostly praise from those who knew him, except from CJ of the Mearsieans, who seemed to waver between a wary friendship and a scowling conviction that he was an overgrown blowhard. All Hibern knew about him was that he came from some small kingdom in the middle of the Sartoran continent, and that he was often on the Wander.

Hibern waited for the guide to draw a breath after his history of another sword-bearing monarch on a marble horse, and asked, "What did Rel the Traveler do?"

"He got the queen to safety, by way of a morvende geliath. He's friends with them," the guide said proudly. "Not many sunsiders get to say that. He was also there at the end, fending off Norsunder when they tried to kill the queen. Not that I saw it. I was still asleep on the other side of town. But I've met him, twice, when I carried a fare to the garrison while he was visiting. He's friends with what's left of the Royal Guard, being very good with the sword."

Hibern was done with the subject of Rel. To stem the flow of friendly chatter, she commented when he stopped for breath, "I really like the embroidery on your livery. Did you do it?"

"Yes," he said proudly. "My dad taught me. He was a sailor, before the war." His smile lessened. "He was out to sea when Nightland attacked." Hibern was caught by his use of 'Nightland.' She'd read it on old records, a euphemism like 'eleveners.' "So I was gone for a century, but he wasn't," he finished.

"That must be very difficult."

"I'm better off than most. At least I can hope he got a good long life, unlike mates whose families were killed by the Nightlanders. But you wanted a tour of the Way, not of my life." He went on with his recitation of famous sights that Hibern had read about, and some that had local meaning; the patterns of his speech indicated he'd worked hard to memorize it.

When he paused, she asked the history of the various five-story buildings. Presently they rounded through the expensive shop area east of the palace, and curved back along the winding middle branch of the river to their starting point.

She recognized the square as the melodic bell rang the four chords, echoed by other city bells. She was sorry to climb out of the cart. "Thank you," she said, digging for her coins.

"I'll take half," the boy said.

Hibern was startled. "But you answered all my questions. And I know they weren't very good questions. I think I need to spend a week just walking and looking."

The boy leaned on the edge of the cart, his mouth wry. "It's the questions you didn't ask: Where's the spot where King Connar XXIII died, and are the bloodstains still there? Where's the house where Alian Dei entertained the first Connar, before he married her? Where's the stone marking the place where they executed Efran Demitros?"

Hibern smiled ruefully as she handed over the coins. "My unasked questions are all about the white tower, and I know whom to put them to." She belatedly remembered her first-circle bow.

The boy returned her bow from his seat, and she hurried inside, to find the desk attendant peacefully reading his book. Hibern was considering whether to interrupt him and ask for a message to be sent, when Atan's laughing voice preceded her appearance with a very tall, dark-haired fellow with deep-set dark eyes. Though he was dressed plainly in the ubiquitous traveler's loose, belted linen tunic over riding trousers and boots, his size and breadth of shoulder drew the eye.

"Hibern," Atan exclaimed. "I apologize. We went to visit friends over at the guardhouse, and just got back."

Hibern had never heard that happy lilt in her voice before. Atan was usually so serious.

"I hope you didn't wait unduly long," Atan went on. Hibern was opening her mouth to say something diplomatic when Atan bent over the shoulder of the desk clerk, and exclaimed, "Oh, no, you were here an hour ago?"

"I came early because someone else canceled," Hibern said quickly. "And so I wanted to see the famed dragon door—which I didn't see—and the Grand Chandos Way, which I did."

Atan turned a wide-eyed glance up at the fellow. "Rel, did you hear that? Dragons?"

Hibern gazed in surprise. So this was the Rel whom CJ of Mearsies Heili spoke so disparagingly?

Atan turned a hand her way. "This is my study partner Hibern. Let's find Hin and Dorea—no, that's right, the scribes put Dorea on archive duty, did they not? She would love that. Wouldn't want to leave." She turned her gaze from Rel to Hibern as she said with a return of her old, careful, sober manner, "This is *my* hour. Perhaps we could visit Tsauderei. Is that all right with you?"

Hibern didn't need coaching to know that when a queen asks if something is all right with you, you say, "Yes, your majesty." Yet she'd heard a tone in that soft declaration, *this is* my *hour*, as if all the hours belonged to someone, or something, else, and she remembered what Erai-Yanya had said about Atan needing a taste of freedom.

Tsauderei was old enough to find little to surprise him and much to amuse him in the vagaries of human nature. He had expected the newly enchantment-free Sartoran mage guild to be jealous of their prerogatives, which extended to their new young queen. And so it had proved.

Few people in the world were granted immediate magical access to Tsauderei. Atan was one of them. When magic warned him of multiple transfers, with Atan's tracer among them, he waited, ready to drop a stone spell over them in case there was treachery afoot. But a quick glance at the little group recovering in the Destination outside his one-room cottage made it clear that she was with them willingly.

"Tsauderei, I'm so very glad to see you," Atan exclaimed as she led the way inside. "I apologize for not sending a message ahead, but I only have my hour."

"I'm entirely free," Tsauderei said, as Hibern looked around with intense interest at the living quarters of one of the world's most famous mages.

Tsauderei lived in a one-room cottage with a loft above. Three walls were entirely covered with books. The fourth was an enormous glassed-in window looking out over a steep valley above a deep blue lake.

The old mage turned the hourglass sitting on his side table and said, "That'll warn us. So, begin with introductions?"

"Here's Hibern. This is our magic study hour, actually. But she agreed. You've heard me talk about Hinder." The morvende boy flicked a hand in greeting, his talons today painted a distinctly virulent green. "And this is Rel, who helped us against Norsunder." She clasped her hands together. "I remember going through your books about dragon legends when I was ten or so. You used to tell me, when a subject comes up three times during separate circumstances, the wise mage pursues it?"

Tsauderei laughed. "And that subject is dragons?"

"Yes. Is there any truth about their once being in the world? And if not, why do legends about them persist?"

Tsauderei laid his gnarled hands in his lap. "I can answer that. Of course I've never seen one. No one has. But I have seen where they once lived." He paused, and saw four pairs of interested eyes. "As you can see, we are quite high up. Much higher are the mountains between your Sartor and Sarendan below us. Imagine an enormous plateau of heat-blackened stone. It's cold there all year round, with either snow or dry wind. Far in the distance, what looks like small hills are huge caverns, the walls black and glassy, as if melted by fires of unimaginable heat. The plateau is where dragons once perched, and the caverns, we believe, were where they sheltered their young. I spent a very cold summer studying those caverns when I was a journeymage. I wasn't the only one. Despite the thin air and the barrenness and the cold, there were many of us who went over that place looking for any hints of dragons' lives all those thousands of years ago. But all there is to be found are the faint remains of carvings in the rock, made by the humans who lived among the dragons and cared for them. Those carvings are yet to be deciphered, but the carved images make it clear that the dragons chose to be there."

Atan said, "So humans did live with them, even in such a terrible place! Is that the appeal of dragons, then? That they were immense?"

Tsauderei gave a crack of laughter. "Atan. I taught you better than that."

"I know there's seldom any 'simply,'" Atan hastened to say. "But the dragons have been gone so long we don't know anything about them, other than that they were large. And flew, and breathed fire. So I'm thinking that humans seemed to admire large creatures for being large as well as the dangerous predators for their ability to kill."

Rel looked down at his hands.

Tsauderei leaned back, eyeing him. "Your large friend appears to disagree," Tsauderei observed. "Is that due to your size, young man?"

Rel lifted a hand. "Has nothing to do with my size. If you've ever traveled by earning your way cross-country, you'll discover that the easiest job in any city is to work for the Wand Guild. Anyone can wave a magic stick over horse droppings in a street. But the bigger the beast, the bigger the pile, and you soon lose any admiration for size."

He stopped there, shrugging.

Hinder laughed, his cobwebby hair drifting. "I did not think of that. What a nasty job—surely that had to be during the days of slaves, for who else would wand dragon droppings? Not I!"

Tsauderei's smile was sardonic. "Then you'd be wrong. You're forgetting the chief appeal of dragons: their treasures."

"I thought dragon hoards were the false part of the legend," Atan exclaimed. "It makes no sense. What use would an enormous creature like a dragon have for cups of gold, bejeweled crowns, and the like?"

"Cups of gold are certainly the distortion of legend." Tsauderei chuckled. "Dragons breathed fire. They melted rock to make their caves, so what do you think their internal arrangement was like?" He studied the four bewildered faces before him, clapped his hands on his knees, and laughed again. "Their excreta came out as gemstones, my dears. Volcanic glass. Sometimes precious metals, depending, I guess, on what they'd been eating, which was mostly ores of various sorts from mountaintops, left from very old volcanos. Their caves were piled high with the stuff, until humans carted it off."

Atan said, "Why didn't I know that?" Then she winced. "Now I feel stupid. Dragon-stones, dragon-eyes, the rare and expensive gems—those were dragon droppings?"

"Yes." Tsauderei chuckled again. "There are few real dragon gems left, though there are numerous types of rock misnamed dragon-eye and the like, usually rocks with a thin layer of some other substance compressed in the middle."

"'Greed and beauty. Two human traits,'" Atan quoted as she moved to the little kitchen arrangement in the corner opposite the door.

Tsauderei delighted in how unconsciously she resumed old habits, but it was not an unmitigated pleasure. Atan had not changed at all since he'd seen her last, which meant she had not only performed the Child Spell, keeping her from maturing to her adult form, she was holding onto it. It would be too simple to assume she had done it to keep her court from negotiating a marriage. He suspected her reasons were more complex than that, connected to the emotions Atan seemed to be trying to hide.

He could have told her that emotional attachments were not avoided by doing the Child Spell, only the physical component of such attachments. Even in this short visit it was clear that she was developing feelings for Rel, and that Hibern, the age-mate whom he and Erai-Yanya had so carefully chosen for her, seemed oblivious.

As for Rel, there was no more heat in his gaze than there was in hers, but then, big as he was, his cheeks were still smooth. That sun for him was clearly still below the horizon, as it was for her.

Well, and if the sun came up, so what? The passions of the teen years were like thunderstorms, wild for a short time, soon gone. Rel seemed an excellent young man for Atan's first experiments into relationships, whenever she decided to step over that threshold. But he foresaw yet more conflict from the Sartoran first circle, who could not be prevented from talking about a future royal marriage.

He watched from under hooded eyes as she went about preparing hot steep. She knew all the spells. The firestick under the tiny grate had probably been made by her, one of a magic student's first projects, to repeat, over and over, the spell to capture the sun's heat.

Unaware of his scrutiny, Atan was trying to recapture the sense of being Tsauderei's student again. It was good to be here again, and with people she liked, and yet that sense of goodness was so conscious. She knew it would end soon, which hurt.

She glanced a fourth time at the sand trickling relentlessly through the glass, and scolded herself. She would never want to go back to the days when Sartor was enchanted, never, never, never. She was *happy* to be able to make steep with fresh leaf, because Sartoran leaf was growing again on the northern slopes, and she should celebrate that its trade all throughout the world would help fill an empty treasury.

"Hot steep in moments," she said with forced cheer, bringing the tray of cups to hand out.

The water boiled. Atan poured it through the new leaf, filling the cottage with a delicious summery smell. She sniffed it in, hoping the aroma would chase the resentment out of her heart.

Hinder held out a hand. "Steep I can get any time. Everybody says that people can fly in this valley."

"They can," Tsauderei said, pointing to the ledges and small plateaus around the steep slopes above the lake, on which could be seen, amid the trees, tile roofs. "It's the way the villagers get from ledge to ledge. By ancient magic, beyond anything we are capable of now."

"I want to try flying," Hinder said, bouncing gently up and down so that his painted toe talons clicked on the clean-swept stone floor.

Tsauderei said, "Here's the magic word and sign." He demonstrated. "Perform them at the same moment, then spring up. You should figure it out fast enough—"

The door closed on the last word. The others watched Hinder through the great window. He did the magic while running, then flung himself over the side of the cliff, causing Hibern to suck in her breath, the backs of her knees gripping sickeningly, the way they did when she was confronted with heights.

The boy vanished, then he reappeared, hands outflung, the wind ripping through his snow-white hair and his tunic as he shot skyward, cartwheeled clumsily, began to fall, righted himself, then arrowed off to the west and vanished from view.

"Now we'll never get him back in time," Atan said, hating how she could not keep her heart from twisting anxiously as the sand spilled inexorably into the lower chamber in the glass, already much less above than below.

Tsauderei smiled. "I can send him along when he's finished flying." He then filled the remaining time with easy questions about Atan's and Hibern's studies and Rel's travels.

When the last sands ran out, they got up to leave. He noted the regret Atan tried to hide, and said merely, "Come again when you can." So she didn't want to talk about whatever was bothering her. He reminded himself that it was right and good for her to cleave to her Sartorans. She would always be his student, but they'd talked frankly about the fact that if the enchantment did break, and Sartor was freed, he would cease being her guardian.

"I will," Atan promised, hating the way her throat tightened. She refused to add, *If I can.*

She, Rel, and Hibern transferred to Sartor in time to hear the bells of the hour ringing melodiously.

The break from the customary hour of scholarship had caused Hibern to remember outside affairs—specifically Clair and the prospective alliance.

She turned to Atan. "Have you met any other rulers our age?"

"I haven't met any at all," Atan said. "I know there are several, many due to troubles with Norsunder, and others due to civil disturbances. Have you met them? Besides the king of your country?"

*Bong-g-g-g!*

Hibern said quickly, "Clair of Mearsies Heili. She mentioned some time back that she wishes to start some kind of alliance, among only people our age. Mutual help."

Rel said, "That sounds like Clair."

Atan gave him a glance of surprise. "You know her?"

"Pretty well. I travel a lot with her cousin. I haven't been back this year, but this doesn't surprise me at all."

*Bong!* As the last ring died away, the door opened to a silent waiting steward, bringing the invisible yoke of duty to tighten around Atan once more.

"Tell me about it next time," she said, walking backward, and to Rel, "Where will you be?"

Rel said, "I'm off to visit Mendaen and the others. Do you want me to carry any messages?"

Atan lingered in the doorway, and as they talked quickly about people Hibern had never heard of, she decided not to interrupt them. She transferred back to Roth Drael, her emotions in turmoil.

Tsauderei was wrong about her obliviousness. Hibern had immediately been aware of the difference in Atan's behavior, the way she glanced at Rel when he spoke, and the way he looked at her.

Hibern hadn't the experience to be certain about the bond that she perceived, but she could guess. She could also guess how much trouble there might be because of it. In spite of Atan's wish to be regarded as an ordinary person, she wasn't ordinary, would never be ordinary, because Atan was one of a kind: the last Landis of a very, very long line, Queen of Old Sartor.

Whereas Hibern knew she herself was one of many, and disinherited at that. But she had the freedom to pick any friends she wanted. There was no family to care, no council to disapprove. Atan was so special that every aspect of her life was inspected by her formidable household and council, and so it was only when she escaped to Tsauderei's that she could behave like an ordinary girl who liked a boy.

Since Atan hadn't said anything about it, Hibern kept these observations to herself when Erai-Yanya asked for her report. Hibern talked about dragons, and described the encounter with the odd little girl.

To her surprise, Erai-Yanya's brow lifted. "Ah, you've met Julian Dei, Atan's cousin."

"Julian Dei?" If there was any family as famous as the Landises—some might say infamous—that would be the Deis.

"Atan promised to adopt her, but she is a troubled child, some think from events before the war ever happened. She balks at any notion of education or even social polish. I'm told she didn't speak for months, she was so determined against any education."

"Is that why they called her 'joel' instead of 'princess'?"

"Yes. A nice compromise."

"How old is she?"

"No one knows. Records about her were destroyed, probably by her mother, who, it's rumored, had to sign a marriage treaty that cut her and her offspring from the line of succession. There was a scandal with one of the Deis before the war, but as all of the individuals concerned are now long dead, the details don't matter. Anyway, the child was hidden away with other refugee children."

She paused, noting the tension in Hibern's brow, and suspected it had nothing to do with Julian Dei. "If you are not writing down all your observations after these visits, you should start the habit. You don't have to show them to me. The idea is to chart your self-reflection as well as keep track of details while dealing with powerful people."

"That's just it," Hibern exclaimed. "Though she's Queen of Sartor, Atan doesn't seem to think she's powerful at all."

"She's still young. But that," Erai-Yanya stated, "will change."

# PART TWO
## The Alliance Grows

## Chapter One

*Arad (Secondmonth), 4738 AF*
*Marloven Hess*

SENRID let Chwahirsland and the alliance slip to the back of his mind. No outsider would be the least help if Marloven Hess was in trouble. The Marlovens had never had allies, but then Senrid was well aware that their worst enemies were themselves.

Through all the violent upheavals of Marloven history there was one constant: you obeyed orders, or you died.

Another constant was knowing which rules could be bent, and how to bend them. A wing—three flights, or nine ridings, or eighty-one warriors—of horse and foot taken to a conflict without duly informing the king came under the heading of treason. But any less was deemed enough to defend against hill brigands, horse thieves, or the like.

Therefore, strictly legal were the two flights apiece of horse and foot that the Jarls of Methden and Torac were bringing to the border of Enneh Rual. (The third flight followed at a distance to 'maintain the supply line.')

If they attacked the Rualese, that would be war in the eyes of the world. Marlovens would see it differently. If the attack was successful, fellow jarls would hail their success as a just recovery of ancestral lands—and many would no doubt soon be planning similar sorties.

If they lost, diplomatic legalities would be the least of their worries.

So the two jarls had reasoned before issuing orders to their followers.

David-Jarl Ndarga of Methden was aware of a divisive atmosphere among his ranks, signaled at the beginning of their ride from Methden Castle when someone way back in his double column whistled a few notes of a compelling melody, instantly recognizable: the Andahi Lament. No one *ever* sang that in battle. It was for memorials.

This was nothing less than an exquisitely insubordinate condemnation of the orders.

The jarl heard both flight captains riding down the column to deal with the individual, restoring superficial obedience, but the fact of the whistle disturbed the jarl. In his experience, the lower ranks only dared such insubordination when they had sympathizers.

Traveling from Methden's castle to the border in winter took a few days. The jarl used the daylight to enforce strict columns, the foot marching in rhythm, to reestablish one mind obedient to his will.

His captains, under his direct orders, were on the watch for disobedience, which would earn immediate and sharp punishment. There was none. Everyone knew what happened if they did not follow orders.

Likewise, nothing untoward happened when Torac and his two flights joined them two days from the border.

They camped early the day before they were to reach the hilly ridge that marked the border, their third wings joining them with the supplies. The jarls spent the last watch of light drilling in preparation for any resistance, not that Methden expected much. The Rualans had once been Marlovens when the rest of the subcontinent was ruled by Marloven Hess, but they had stolidly and stubbornly kept to their Iascan roots as much as they could, their customs inclined toward the sea.

The jarls set out early in the morning under a reasonably clear sky, and Methden, as leader, was reviewing flag signals with his fellow jarl and their captains when one of the outriders came galloping back.

"It's Senrid-Harvaldar," the outrider reported. "Sitting athwart the road with several wings of the West, from the banners, and more on either side of the bluffs above the road."

The words caused absolute silence from behind, save only the jingle of gear and the clop and whuff of fresh horses eager to move.

Torac muttered a curse, scowling at the outrider as if he were the cause of this unexpected wrinkle. Methden knew better than to expect anything but oaths and empty threats from Torac, who had been a follower since their academy days, of each prince in succession. No ideas could be expected from him, and sure enough, he looked back at Methden, blue eyes angry, but empty of intent. He, too, was waiting for orders.

"We'll flank 'em," Methden said. And when the outrider made a movement, his horse's ears twitching, "Or?"

"There's at least a riding tracking me."

That meant that this encounter was no happenstance. The boy Senrid had—somehow—got hold of their plan. Lookouts would be posted far to either side. There'd be no surprise flanking maneuver, and a charge would be impossible over such difficult terrain.

"Who leads?" Methden asked.

"Keriam is no commander," Torac said, and spat into the snow.

The outrider said flatly, "Senrid-Harvaldar."

Torac uttered a derisive laugh, and scorn was Methden's immediate reaction, followed by uneasiness. Senrid might be riding in command position, but who was really in command?

A short time later, Methden glared down the road at the fair-haired boy in the center of the mounted warriors, ranged behind the front three rows of foot warriors who stood ready and waiting, shields locked together. Sentiment had no place in ruling the Marlovens. Evan's boy had never been to the academy, the reason whispered being weakness.

Methden wished he had his own son at his side, but Jarend was doing his two years in the guard, and had received direct orders from this boy king to serve under Senelac in East Army, on the opposite border, for the rest of the winter.

Obey or die.

Senrid watched Methden's and Torac's force pull up. He'd picked the ground after hours of agonizing, and here they were. He gulped air, trying to still his thundering heart. He knew he shouldn't be listening on the mental realm, but he was. Not that anything was clear. He may as well have been standing in the middle of a shouting crowd, only this was worse because of the bombardment of emotion-drenched images, against which he had no defense when he lowered his mental shield.

"What orders?" the wing captain asked, breaking into his streaming thoughts.

Senrid listened, and sensed his intent to obey in spite of skepticism about whether or not a boy could lead. But so far, everything was right.

*So far, everything was right.* Senrid shivered, though his nerves were on fire. He'd only had to ride back and forth before Waldevan's gate three times, his force arrayed behind him, before the parley flag was sent out, at which time Senrid knew he'd subdued Waldevan without shedding a drop of blood.

Now, here were the other two errant jarls. If Methden wished to engage with the cavalry lined along the bluffs, his riders would be forced to ride uphill. And Methden was definitely in command. Torac kept looking his way.

What orders? Senrid said the obvious, to be clear. "If they kill first, then it's a capital matter. After which you're justified in fighting to finish."

He listened again on the mental realm, then shut out the hammer-blow of emotion. The visible signals were clear enough: tight mouths, gloved hands gripping weapons. The shift of horses, sensitive to their riders' emotions: ears alert, snorts and tossed heads.

Senrid could see the effect of his words on his own force. Waiting for Methden to kill first meant that someone here had to die. Senrid could see righteous anger kindling, and sensed the bloodthirsty determination to break bones and dump Methden's and Torac's men out of saddles before letting one of those strutting cockerels get steel into a riding mate's gut. Much less one's own.

Senrid's hands sweated inside their gloves. His toes curled in his boots. He'd transferred back twice to talk out the plan with Forthan, drawing out the terrain on the slate floor in one of the lecture rooms at the academy, and moving rocks and coins around as they talked out endless combinations, but here he was, he didn't know the pattern, he wasn't sure when to loose his people . . .

Methden's force stirred as if a breeze had gone through them. Senrid sensed a corresponding tightening all around him, and *knew*. "Now," he said, his voice cracking in a ridiculous squeak.

He cleared his throat to repeat, but the drum of hooves smothered his shout, and then two masses met in a violent meshing of individuals, voices howling in anger and anguish amid the clang and clatter of staves and swords.

Senrid gave up trying to make sense of the conflict, which so far was not quite battle, but more heated than a wargame. Each side was waiting for the other to deal a death blow, while doing their very best to knock one another out of the saddle, or whack each others' knees out from under them.

He had to hold his mount, which had been trained to charge, but Senrid had no experience with lance, and very little with sword. He could shoot to precision, but had forbidden arrows to his own side in this exercise. He was equally skilled with knives, but did not want to kill his own people. He'd defend himself, if attacked, but he found four riders from West Army grimly ringing him in guard position, probably on Keriam's orders.

Liere had once said, *It's just like sorting through a crowd of voices for those you know, only you're listening with your mind instead of your ears.* Senrid shut his eyes and listened.

There. He sensed more than saw the instinctive division in Methden's ranks: there were many, maybe most, who labored under sharp misgivings.

He clapped his legs against his mount's side. The mare leaped forward; the ring of guards followed a heartbeat after, the captain roaring something Senrid did not try to distinguish. It was enough. Cleaving clean through the Methden force, he led his own in an arrow formation—

His nerves flared painfully: intent. On him. A glance. Over there, a Torac man drawing bow. The honor guard that rode so tightly around Senrid made him an easier target in this crowd, Senrid saw in a heartbeat. Instinct was faster than thought. He snatched the shield hanging at the saddle, whipping it up.

Thunk! The arrow hitting the shield was surprisingly loud. Senrid recoiled, heels locking down hard in the stirrups so he wouldn't fall as his guards cried out, two going after the Torac man, the others motioning more around Senrid—

And the jarl's men fell back.

They fell back!

Senrid had already forgotten the Torac man as he sustained the mental bombardment of frustration, the barely-controlled urge to kill. His own force was the worst, the dangerous anger of self-justification, which the leaders were expressing with deliberately broken bones, filling the air with dust and the rumble of hooves, the thuds of blows, cracks, clangs of steel, and cries of pain and outrage.

Senrid shut them out, his thoughts racing: the jarl had lost before he began—act now or it will turn lethal—save honor—

Senrid kneed his horse once again, trusting in his ring of guards, and plunged into the middle of the melee. "Weapons down!" he shouted, hating how shrill he sounded. "Weapons down!"

As he hoped, the guard took up the shout, their bigger voices ringing outward through the entire body. To his captain, Senrid said, low-voiced, "Cut Methden out."

A nod, a gesture, and with a token resistance, the Methden personal guard fell back—again, nobody willing to kill outright, though from the looks of some, there were bad wounds and breaks.

Senrid found his throat dry as the dust hanging in the air. "Form an honor guard around the Jarl of Methden and we'll return to Choreid Dhelerei." Senrid addressed the tall captain of the foot warriors with the rust-red hair. "Captain Marec, you'll escort Methden's people home. At a sedate walk, your pace. Take as long as you like."

Captain Marec's lips twitched; these Methden turds were going to be eating their own belts before they reached their home castle. He cast a fast, expert glance over the wounded, the worst already dealt with. He recognized from his years of equally rough games during the bad times under the regent that no one was in immediate danger, and struck his fist against his chest, mentally formulating his orders. Methden and his fools could stand around in the cold contemplating their own stupidity while his own people saw to the animals and ate a good meal.

But first.

"What about Torac?" a cavalry captain asked, sending a glare in the jarl's direction, and Senrid, his nerves unsheathed, winced under the impact of the man's fury. It was echoed in many, and he caught a stray whisper, "Did you see that boy whip up that shield? He wasn't even looking . . ."

Senrid wanted justice. Justice, or revenge, or something. He wasn't certain now which man had tried to shoot him, any more than he knew if that had been on orders or impulse. All he'd sensed on the mental plane was the intent.

"Captain Sereth will escort the Jarl of Torac and his ridings back," he said, and saw a glance of understanding—of grim intent—pass between Marec and Sereth. They were going to take their time. Good. Torac and his followers wouldn't enjoy the trip, but it would give everyone a chance to cool off, to think.

It would give Senrid time to think.

A fierce whisper serried through both ranks. He heard words: "shield"—"betrayed"—"Scouts?"

Senrid tried to calm his drumming heartbeat. He'd survived. He'd live another day. Let them think that his Scouts had winnowed out the truth about Methden's plan. Senrid would not tell them that the Scouts were all outside the kingdom, because one thing for certain, the Rualans would not be sitting on their hands, and he knew he'd have to deal with beyond-the-border trouble over this mess.

## Chapter Two

*Sartor*

ON the third day of Rel's stay in Eidervaen's huge, rambling royal palace, the elderly steward in charge of the visitors' wing came to Rel's room himself. The man made a first-circle bow, and then asked if everything was all right, if anything could be fetched. The briefness of Rel's responses ("Yes, thank you," and "No, thank you") seemed to inspire the steward to longer inquiries: could he order a meal, would Rel be traveling, could they arrange horses for carriage or riding, recommend posting houses?

Rel repeated, "No, thanks."

The steward put his hands together. "It is our privilege and pleasure to heed the queen's command that any and all of the Rescuers be housed in this wing, but at the same time, we owe duty to those illustrious guests who have traveled from afar to rediscover, and reconnect, with Sartor . . ."

The soft, pleasant voice went on about how vital communication and trade was, ending with eternal gratitude toward the Rescuers, especially Rel, who had selflessly risked his life though he owed no allegiance to Sartor.

'Rescuers.' This was a heroic name for the band of refugee children smuggled by an old mage out of the city when Norsunder invaded. He'd taken them to the forest of Shendoral, where Atan met them in her journey to the capital to break the enchantment. Some had helped her, others had been less helpful, but all were hailed as heroes by the Sartorans. That was all right. Rel had learned that it was good to have heroes, sometimes.

Rel patiently waited the steward out, thanking the man at each pause—assuming that that was what he wished to hear. Finally the steward withdrew, and Rel glanced around the room in puzzlement.

What was that all about? It wasn't as if he asked for anything, ever. He scarcely left a trace in the room, for he always made up his own bed wherever he stayed, and as for his belongings, they remained neatly folded in his pack so he could grab and go.

He shook his head as he headed out. Atan, he knew, was scheduled tightly all day, but Rel had friends to visit. If it wasn't for Atan's insistence, and for the fact that it was difficult to catch Hinder anywhere else, he wouldn't stay in the palace. He didn't like palaces, or at least, he wasn't used to them. That odd conversation was one of the reasons he didn't like them.

Halfway to the garrison, he stopped short on the bridge leading out of the elite first district, and gazed back at the palace towers jutting above the jumble of city roofs.

Had he just been invited, in the nicest way possible, to leave?

Thoroughly uncomfortable, he resumed his walk into the southern half of the second district, which was shared between the mages and the garrison in a silent struggle that went back centuries.

At the old garrison, he found Mendaen, another of the Rescuers, a tall, weedy fellow with clubbed black hair, who was verging on adulthood.

Rel always exercised with the guard, which had been severely diminished not only by the war, but also by edict of the royal council.

As with his previous visit, Rel stood in the back of the yard, knowing that his size drew the eye. Though Mendaen was a couple years older than Rel, everyone assumed it was the opposite. It was easier to go to the back, to avoid attention. From the back he could also see the interactions of the others as they worked through a warmup drill set more than a century ago, everyone's breath clouding the cold air.

Mendaen took his place next to Rel. As they swung their swords to loosen up muscles, and stamped to waken their feet and legs, Mendaen said, "I've applied for leave to go to Khanerenth's military school."

Rel hid a grimace, then spoke the truth. "Not a good idea."

Mendaen gave him a pained glance as he switched the hilt to his other hand. "But it was your idea. Leastways, I remembered you telling me you had a season there."

"And I should have had longer," Rel said ruefully.

"You're better than most of us," Mendaen said.

"Mainly because I'm bigger than most of you," Rel said. He sensed by the cants of heads, and the stiffness of arms, that many were listening. "I'm good enough to fight off a brigand or two. Which is my only aim. I'm not going for a life in the military."

"But you do get people trying to recruit you?"

Rel couldn't prevent the flash of memories: on his first journey being jumped by Kessler Sonscarna's recruitment gang, and waking up to Kessler's mad blue stare as he talked about killing off the decadent, useless world leaders who got crowns through inheritance, and replacing them with people promoted by merit—these meritorious new leaders trained and promoted by Kessler. Though Kessler had also hated Norsunder, Rel was secretly relieved that Kessler ended up there after he was defeated.

Rel had encountered him again when Kessler was sent by Norsunder to kill Atan before she could end the century-long enchantment. Rel still had nightmares about losing his fight with Kessler. The only thing that fight accomplished was winning Atan enough time to end the enchantment . . .

Rel shook away the memories, recollected the question that had prompted them, and said easily, "What do you expect, when you're my size?"

Mendaen sighed. "I'd love someone to recruit me."

Rel knew that Mendaen would hate being recruited by force, but kept his peace.

"Reaaaaaady!" the drill captain called from the front.

Mendaen and Rel began working through what Rel thought of as the standard set of block-and-lunge, feint-and-backswing moves that were common all across the continent, even Chwahirsland, which he'd been to a couple times, disguised as a flatfoot, the common infantry soldier.

The front rows wore livery, not uniforms. The back rows were a mix of guards-in-training, like Mendaen, and guild guards sent to exercise with the palace guards. The Royal Guard was all but gone, having been the first line of defense when Norsunder had invaded. None of the many dead had been replaced, because the mage guild had decided that they were useless, and that the only real protection was magic. So the bulk of defense spending went to the mages, who labored to find ways to thwart Norsunder's magic. Meanwhile, many of the former guard had gone to the guilds, which didn't bother trying to fight the council. They simply beefed up their private security—as evidenced by familiar Guard faces now wearing those guild colors.

When they broke up to work in pairs, everybody separated off into their own particular groups. Mendaen looked at Rel expectantly, and as they pulled on their practice pads, Mendaen said, "Tell me, why isn't it a good idea to go to Khanerenth?"

"I left because there was political trouble," Rel said. "Reaching into the school. Not a good time to be a foreigner."

"Oh," Mendaen said, disappointed. Then, "Well, seems to me we need more training, because as our captain says, what if Siamis comes back again, only this time at the head of an army? The mages all think magic is the answer, but it wasn't, was it?"

"What about the military school at Obrin, over the mountains? Isn't the trouble ended in Sarendan?" Rel asked.

"Everybody says Obrin is closed to outsiders."

"Century-old 'everybody says' or recent?" Rel asked, and Mendaen's lips parted, but he was forestalled by a bawled command to stop yawping and attack.

As the yard filled with fighting pairs and trios, gradually conversation returned. Rel listened, picking up a general dissatisfaction among the Royal Guard, even bitterness about the mage guild's regarding them as not worth the tax money to maintain.

At the end of drill Mendaen had to go off to duty in the armory, so Rel walked along what the Sartorans called the middle river, his coat pulled up tight to his chin, until he reached Blossom Street, where Hannla Thasis, another of the Rescuers, lived. Hannla's aunt ran a pleasure house.

Hannla greeted Rel with a happy smile. Hannla was the oldest of the Sartoran-born Rescuers, sixteen or seventeen, and genuinely popular. Rel had discovered on his previous visit that Hannla's aunt's pleasure house was the unofficial meeting place for all the Rescuers who weren't aristocrats. Rel was always assured of a free bed, especially as he offered to turn his hand to any task needing doing.

After he'd finished bringing up the last of the jugs of cowslip wine (the label dated a century ago), carried down stacks of washed and clean old jugs, rotated the barrels of ale, and helped sweep the stone floor, he went up to find a substantial meal waiting, and Hannla sat down to keep him company.

"How'd you find Mendaen?" she asked. "Is he going outside the borders, then?"

"I may have talked him out of that."

"Why?" Hannla's face was heart-shaped, her eyes wide, her hair a curly brown. The rest of her was as charmingly round . . . Rel's gaze caught, then he hitched it upward again, to find her grinning.

She'd always liked his thick, glossy dark hair, a little unkempt above his collar in back, his dark eyes deep set under equally dark brows, the strong bones of his face tapering to a truly heroic chin. The rest of him was both trim and powerful under the old travel-worn tunic and baggy riding trousers.

She put her cheek on her hand and said, "You ready for upstairs, then?"

Rel's reaction was a mix of curiosity and something else too subtle to define, but which he recognized as attraction, though it still hadn't warmed into the urgency his guardian had told him about when they'd discussed these matters. "Not yet," he said.

Hannla's eyelids flashed up. "Don't tell me. You, too, did the Child Spell? You?"

Rel chuckled, a low sound deep in his broad chest. "My guardian told me once I'll probably grow another half-finger before I have to do the beard spell. But yes, I found a mage to do the Child Spell on me."

"Why?" Hannla put both elbows on the table to support her chin.

Rel lifted a shoulder. "Promise I made to myself when I first set out, to find my father first. That was before I discovered the benefit of being a youth on the Wander. Most places, there's little prejudice against the young wandering. Whereas a man without a home or employment is often looked at with a suspicious eye."

"Of course," Hannla exclaimed. "That makes perfect sense. But . . ." She paused, considering how to express her doubt.

He flashed a brief grin. "No, it doesn't always work for me. Even though I'm not full age, just because I'm tall, I can't tell you how many stints in lockups I've done for vagrancy, though it's pretty much always in places where they seem to need free labor for road repair or construction. And in other places you can find yourself summarily recruited into someone's army."

Hannla's eyes widened. "You never told us any of that. All you said was that you weren't a duchas or a prince in disguise."

Rel had to laugh. "Nobody asked. Except Atan. Mendaen, too, though at that time, he didn't have much interest in anyplace beyond Sartor's border."

Hannla's expressive smile turned rueful. "Mendaen. I meant to talk to you about him, then got sidetracked by your pretty face." When Rel blushed to the ears, she rocked with silent laughter, which faded too soon. She said with an air of regret, "Atan's told you, right? That the mages now have total control of wherewithal, what little there is, for defense? That the Guard is reduced to patrolling the outer city and the southern border to watch for anyone riding out of Norsunder Base?"

"Yes. Result of losing so badly in the war, though I don't see how the mages did any better, considering they didn't stop Norsunder's attack any more than the army did, and they, too, ended up enchanted for a century."

Hannla shrugged. "That, I can't tell you. Doubt Atan even hears the inner councils. But this I know. Everyone is looking around the next corner for that horrible Siamis to return, or his uncle, the villain Detlev. That's the worst of them, they hide in Nightland and don't die!"

Rel fervently agreed, thinking of his own brushes with Norsunder.

"But with Mendaen, there's the personal reason he wants to go outside the border for training."

"Personal?"

"Yes. Like a lot of others, he's trying to find out if his father had a family. You knew his father was a sailor, right?"

Rel began mopping up gravy with a piece of bread. "Mother in the queen's guard, killed defending the palace. Father was at sea when the enchantment happened. Right."

"Well, Atan's probably told you that the entire kingdom is still trying to fit itself back in the world. When all the poems and songs were over, what was left? As my aunt says, 'All the vexations of broken families, trade agreements, inheritances.' For Atan, it means the mages and diplomats and that sort of thing, but for Mendaen, it would cost far, far more money than he or his two orphaned cousins have, trying to trace relatives who were shut out a century ago."

Rel grimaced. "I never thought of that. And it has to be expensive, paying someone to sort through records. That's a lot of work."

"It's even more work if you have to trace a sailor on a ship, especially if the ship was attacked by pirates. The scribes at the archive told him he might have to apply at a lot of countries, or pay to have the scribes do it."

"Mendaen didn't tell me that," Rel said. "Maybe it's not for outsiders."

"He doesn't talk about it to anyone outside his family. He knows all his friends would give him money if they had any. He doesn't want them to feel obliged. I know because his younger cousin works at the pastry shop we deal with when patrons order fancy baking beyond our menu, and she talks a lot."

Hannla got up from the table, dashed off, then returned with a folded piece of paper. "So I'm asking you, and Mendaen will never know and feel embarrassed. But in case you happen to be anywhere where you might find something out," she said. "On that is written his father's name, the name of his last ship, and what he did on board. The year they think might have been the pirate attack, and the location."

Rel slid the paper into his tunic pocket. "It's easy to check for someone else while I do my own search."

"So you're still wandering the world to look for your father?"

"Yes."

"Did you have a wicked guardian?" Hannla asked, eyes wide.

"No." He didn't mind talking to Hannla, who was so ready with genuine sympathy. "Excellent guardian. Like a father in all ways except the one."

"Well, why won't this guardian tell you about your father?"

"Because he promised he wouldn't."

"Why?"

"I don't know. But think about it. Why would anyone keep that secret, especially if he'd gain nothing by it?"

Her brow puckered, then cleared. "To protect him, or to protect you."

"Right. Here are the clues I've gathered: My father does something dangerous. He's not from any royal family. Actually, there's some hint about a disgrace. Last and most important: he found me the best place he could before he left."

Hannla jumped up and kissed his cheek. "Of course your guardian was a good man. A wicked man would not raise a darling! Make sure when you're ready for upstairs that you come to us, mind. Half of 'em want to be your first, and do you think you like men or women? Both would be charmed." Hannla chuckled.

Rel didn't see her. He saw Atan, so earnest and studious and capable, and how her entire demeanor changed with her sudden laughter. He wasn't sure exactly what the hollow feeling behind his ribs meant—it wasn't the same as that mild warmth when Hannla leaned forward, or smiled at him.

Rel was fairly certain that his attractions were slanted toward women, but he was reluctant to talk about such things lest the talk somehow point at Atan. Hannla, he knew, was very observant. So he said, "Not sure," and Hannla sighed, then offered him another slice of cake.

"I don't need that, thanks, but maybe you can tell me the real meaning behind a conversation I had this morning." And he repeated the entire exchange with the steward.

When he finished, he could see by the way Hannla looked down at her hands that he'd actually guessed right. "What is it?" he asked. "Did I break some rule of etiquette? I know Atan wants me to stay."

"And that's the problem," Hannla said.

"Then all that about cherishing the heroic Rescuers is a lie after all?"

Hannla made a quick gesture. "No, it's true. But. You have to remember who Atan is. The high council has to be talking about whom she will marry."

Rel shifted in his seat, but the hollow feeling in his chest now felt more like a stone had taken up residence. A boulder. "I know that one day she'll be expected to make a dynastic marriage, and that those have nothing to do with personal choices. But that's a long way off, yet."

"Not for them." Hannla shook her head. "I'll wager you anything they're up there right now, worrying about when she'll lift the Child Spell. And watching all her relationships. Especially with foreigners."

"And so that's why all those questions this morning," he said, and with reluctance, "This is the fourth day of my stay as her guest. I'm going to guess that three days is their limit. I guess I'd better leave."

"Perhaps it's best. But come back next season. Really, if you turn up now and then, stay for two or three days only, then they won't fret so much," Hannla said earnestly.

"Thanks," he said, not wanting to load her with his bad mood.

He walked back toward the palace, determined to get control of his annoyance before he saw Atan again. Much as he might have liked to rant to Atan, he knew she already felt hemmed in, and it wasn't as if the high council was a bunch of Norsundrians in disguise. They meant well, and they had a wreck of a kingdom to deal with, along with a very young queen who hadn't been raised to her job.

The council was going to plan Atan's future, because that was what Sartoran first circle nobility did.

He waited patiently until he caught Atan between scheduled activities, said he had to get on the road before the weather changed, grabbed his pack, and walked out.

"You'll come back when you can?" she asked.

"I will," he promised.

That chest boulder resolved into the ache of loss as Rel walked away from the city a day later. He paced steadily northward, already planning his return.

In spite of his mental turmoil, habit ever since the days of Kessler Sonscarna's recruitment attempt kept him wary. As he climbed and descended the gently rising hills toward the border mountains, he always found a vantage from which to look ahead and back without being seen, and discovered among the various carts and coaches and travelers on horse and foot a single constant over three days: a lone figure, male in silhouette, matching his pace. It was quite likely that he was being followed.

He kept watch until he reached the last market town before the steep road to the pass that marked the border. The possible tail was still there, but too far back to be seen.

Rel looked around the widening road as he plodded through the slush. It was far too cold up this high for sleeping under the stars, so taking off cross-country was out. As he walked past the slant-roofed buildings edged with icicles, he reflected on how often he traveled this road, knowing which inns had beds long enough for him. He chose his favorite, a large place bustling with custom.

His tail had blended into the city traffic, as expected.

Rel wasn't worried about being attacked in Sartor. The roads were busy, the patrols intermittent but frequent enough. But Oneh Kaer on the other side was another question, for an old treaty required Sartor to patrol the three roads that branched from the border pass. But Sartor was not patrolling.

The traffic along the three roads, most of it north toward Mardgar and the biggest harbor on the Sartoran Sea, or northeast toward Colend, and a very few west toward the ancient aristocratic estates along the rough coast, abandoned after the war, tended to move in well-guarded caravans, which made the lone traveler vulnerable to attack.

Rel opened the door to a hostelry he'd used before and liked. He breathed in the warm complexity of human scents and spices. After a polite exchange with the boy at the counter, he paid down his money for a bed, adding a coin for the tuft-haired urchin who offered to take his knapsack upstairs. From the common room, the hubbub punctuated by the clatter of cutlery indicated the evening meal had begun, so Rel hung up his hat on one of the pegs inside the porch to avoid issues of etiquette involving whom he should doff to and whom he shouldn't. Sartorans could be prickly about customs that had changed up north.

He paused in the doorway to give the crowded room a quick scan. He recognized the old timers, each in his or her usual place, and moved his gaze past; all over the continent, regardless of kingdom, locals who met regularly seldom welcomed interlopers, and never liked it if someone presumed to take a seemingly empty chair, if that chair was in the middle of their invisible boundary of privacy.

"Welcome, tall stranger," one of the oldsters called, beckoning Rel to the table.

Rel hesitated only a heartbeat. Now everyone was looking his way. He saw no signs of hostility. Curiosity, yes. The empty chair the man indicated was not a place he would choose—he hated having his back to the door—but he shrugged away instinct. Whether he had actually been followed or not, it was highly unlikely he would be attacked in this mob.

So he took the chair, touching fingers to his heart as he swept his gaze around the circle. He spared a thought to the irony that the exact same gesture considered respectable for a stranger would be perceived as a dismissive insult between high-circle acquaintances.

"Haven't I seen you passing through here before?" the oldest, a tall, gaunt man, asked.

"Might have," Rel said.

"Tried to get work with the guard, have you?" a gray-haired old woman asked, as she worked swiftly at a piece of crewel. She chuckled, shaking her head. "We coulda told you nothing but moths in the guards' pay, is what we hear from Eidervaen."

The oldest man shook his head slowly.

"The mages are fools. It's an invitation for brigandage," a balding glazier said, making a spitting motion, as the innkeeper brought a plate of the day's meal.

The vegetables might be withered, but the rice was fluffy and the braised fish smelled of wine and garlic. Rel dug in as the glazier went on, "These hills yonder are full of brigands, ever since the soul-rotted magic lifted. Now everyone wants guarded caravans."

"Where can a fellow go to get work as a caravan guard?" Rel asked.

The old folks laughed. They'd clearly established Rel's intention the moment he walked in. "You go over to the Main Square Hostelry. *You'll* get snabbled up quick enough." He jerked a gnarled thumb over his shoulder back toward Sartor. "And if you like it, why, the Duchas of Oneh Kaer will be looking for hires soon's he declares himself king."

"He's going for a crown, is he?" Rel asked, when he saw expectancy in the faces.

A miller at the other end of the table said, "A lot of talk about loyalty and honor and that, but what it comes down to, and everybody know it, if the duchas makes himself a king he can keep the taxes. Then maybe we'll see the roads cleaned up at last."

Rel didn't pause in his eating. "Is that a fact, or rumor?"

"Everyone knows," the woman said comfortably. "As much as we know this: if Siamis comes marching back at the head of an army, Sartor won't even be able to protect Sartor, so they won't be looking out for anybody else. That's for certain."

*The next month*

After Hibern's visit to Tsauderei's house, Atan dutifully wrote down what she'd said about the alliance in her private daybook, but in memory she returned most frequently to Tsauderei, the dragon cliff, and to the freedom of talk when she was away from the palace she was supposed to be reigning over.

The girls met the next week, Hibern thirsty for knowledge, reveling in the fact that Atan could summon any mage book she willed, and Atan determined to learn twice as much to make up for their escape the week previous. They met three more times after that.

On the fourth visit, Hibern arrived to find everything changed.

As soon as the door closed behind the young page who always conducted Hibern to Atan's little study, Atan gestured for Hibern to come close, but instead of inviting her to sit down, she reached behind her chair, pulled out two very heavy coats, and silently handed one to Hibern.

Wondering—curious—excitement quickening her heartbeat—Hibern complied, and when Atan pulled from the capacious side pockets of her coat a scarf, a knit hat, and gloves, Hibern checked hers and discovered that she was similarly equipped.

The only sound was the soft rustle and hiss of cloth as they wintered up, then Atan smiled, and held out on her gloved palm a transfer token.

Hibern looked from that to Atan's eyes, which gazed back at her, straight dark brows lifted in question.

Hibern opened her hand in assent, remembered that nobody outside of Marloven Hess gestured a 'yes' in the same way, and brought her chin down in a nod.

The magic shifted then released her with such a powerful buffet that she fell to her knees. An icy wind shrieked overhead, and her eyes stung when she tried to open them. She fumbled the scarf over her face, pulling it up tighter as the wind tried to rip it away.

By then the transfer magic reaction was gone and she steadied herself, still on her hands and knees, and lifted her head. Atan was scarcely more than a shadow a few paces away, also crouched on all fours.

"This way," Atan shouted.

She crawled farther into the gloom, Hibern following. The icy stone ground had long been scoured smooth. They rounded a stone outcropping and the wind lessened abruptly.

"I think we can stand now," Atan said. Her voice echoed.

Hibern got to her feet, shivering inside the bulky coat. Then she forgot the cold when Atan muttered something and glowglobes lit.

Hibern gazed up in amazement at the vaulted ceiling overhead. At first it was difficult to make out the proportions, due to the black stone curving most of the way overhead, shiny as glass.

"You know where we are?" Atan asked. "We're inside the dragon caves. *A* dragon cave. Is this not amazing?"

Both girls looked up, trying to imagine the huge space filled with a dragon. "This way," Atan said. "I think either humans or baby dragons might have lived here." She walked across the smooth stone floor, marbled with thinly branching patterns of minerals glinting coldly. She thought of unknown hands at work here, as she often did when encountering an old road, an ancient building, a crumbling wall with a weathered figure carved in: so many had left their work behind them, but unlike the monuments of Sartoran monarchs, seldom with their names.

The far side disclosed smaller oval chambers that had been scooped or scoured out. These were still sizable—twenty-five or thirty people could have sat comfortably in one—and just as cold, but at least the wind did not reach. They could talk in normal voices.

More glowglobes set around testified to previous visits as Atan said, "I've been sneaking here for bits of stolen time all this past month. Something Tsauderei said gave me the idea."

Hibern said, "To explore these caves? Look for the mysterious writing?" She peered around as she spoke, disappointed not to see any such carvings.

"To get away," Atan said, mittened hands extended. Her expression was difficult to see because of the shrouding scarf; nothing much was visible but those heavy-lidded gooseberry eyes. "Did you know that the mage council did not want me to have you, a Marloven, as a study partner?"

Hibern opened her mittened hands, not wanting to say that that was no surprise.

"After all our sessions, they convinced me it was my duty to tell them every single thing you and I studied. Everything we talked about. It's so funny. I've known Tsauderei all my life, and he's so very old, but the high council considers him too young and dangerously wild in his ideas, you being one of those ideas. The mages on the high council wanted me to study with one of their people. Maybe it's unfair to judge. I know they mean well, but I couldn't bear having every one of my words re-peated, analyzed, discussed. They said it was for safety, that they should know what you were taking away from our sessions."

Atan's words chilled Hibern inside as effectively as any mountain wind. Hibern said, "Erai-Yanya warned me when she first began to train me that people would think a Marloven learning light magic was some kind of spy."

Atan sighed, watching her breath cloud, freeze, fall. "I don't believe the problem is your origins so much as your not being Sartoran, one chosen by them. There's a ledge here, where we can sit. And no one can overhear us."

"Do they really watch you so closely?"

"Everything," Atan responded, tipping her head back. "Everything I do. Everything I say. What books I read. Even how much I eat. It's all for my own good, so what answer can I make to that? I was so very ig-norant about court affairs. Tsauderei did warn me that it might be like that. He got all the records he could, of course, but he didn't have ac-cess to first-circle privities." She made a quick gesture, with thumb and forefinger making a ring shape. "I was so ignorant that I was, and am, grateful to learn. I am! But . . ."

She hugged her arms around herself, and Hibern recognized that shoulder-hunched posture, those tight arms: Atan was holding anger in, the same way Hibern had after being disinherited. An echo of that sick hurt and futile rage pulsed through her, and she tried to breathe it out. Her breath froze and fell before vanishing.

"I *know* they mean well," Atan said again. "Sometimes I almost wish they were evil. No, I don't! That's wrong. It's just that everything I do and say seems to have endless possible dire consequences unless it's precisely what they tell me to do and say. What to think, even. They always sound so reasonable. But I was beginning to have dreams of shrinking so small that I could be locked in a ring box, and thrown down into a vault. So late nights, when they think I'm asleep, I sometimes experiment by myself. The first time I did, I had no nightmare, or not one of *those*."

She reached a stone ledge, turned around, and sat. "I've also been reading about places you and Rel described. Tell me more about this Clair, and her Mearsies Heili. Rel's told me a little, but I want your perspective."

The alliance! Hibern said, "Mearsies Heili is very small, located at the northeast corner of the Toaran continent."

"About which we know so little. Rel said that Mearsies Heili has no court, and no military, just five or six provinces, each with a governor who pretty much sees to things. One or two market towns to each province, one border is desert, and the middle of the kingdom is forest-land. Clair's family is said to originate in the far north, a wooded area called the Shaer, where morvende and dawnsingers both used to live. Clair's family has only been on the throne three or four generations. That tells me so little. What is she like?"

"Clair has one cousin who is always on the Wander, and a group of friends, all sort of adopted by her. I believe they are all either orphans or runaways."

"Ah!"

"They used to patrol to watch for enemy Chwahir at an old outpost, but that's gone, and now they mostly seem to have fun. Except Clair, who studies magic."

"It sounds so . . . so free. So jolly," Atan said, then burst out enviously, "I'm told she even has her grandmother or great-grandmother back again—seemingly her age as she did the Child Spell—so she can be friend and companion, to share the throne."

"Yes," Hibern said slowly, recollecting the things Erai-Yanya had said about the mysterious Mearsieanne. *She might have escaped Norsunder after being imprisoned for all those years*, Erai-Yanya had said, *but she was forever scarred.*

Hibern wasn't going to repeat that. More diplomatically, she said, "Mearsieanne was the first of her family on the throne. She was a seamstress originally, but renamed herself Mearsieanne when she took the throne as a compromise in response to an impasse reached by the noble families of that day. When her son reached our age, she was taken by Norsunder, about the same time as the war here in Sartor. She was enchanted by Detlev in one of his evil experiments, and brought back into the world to be put in Everon. Another of his experiments. That failed, too."

Atan rubbed her mittened hands over her face. "I only know the gist, that the enchantment was the first one broken by that dyr thing that Liere used against Siamis."

"True enough," Hibern said slowly, remembering what Erai-Yanya had also said: *Two queens, even as girls, will eventually be a problem. I hope later than sooner. I'm glad Mearsieanne spends most of her time in Everon and Wnelder Vee at present.*

Hibern did not understand why the rediscovering of a missing relative should be a problem, queen or no, and to bring it up felt like gossip.

"I want to meet them," Atan said. "I want to meet them all." She got to her feet. "The mage guild thinks it a waste of my time for me to keep up my studies of magic, now that I have them." She spread her hands.

Hibern grimaced in sympathy.

Atan said in a rush, "Here's what I truly wanted when I asked for you: someone who'll show me the world that the council will not let me see. And, keeping your alliance idea in mind, we can begin with these Mearsieans."

## Chapter Three

*Spring, 4738 AF*
*Marloven Hess*

SENRID had discovered that the jarls, seated on their benches a few steps below his dais, couldn't see his butt scootched to the edge of the throne so that his feet could be pressed flat against the floor instead of stupidly dangling.

As the captains finished giving their well-practiced reports, Senrid watched the jarls watching him. There wasn't much to be seen in their straight figures, but he was aware of each flicked glance above his head at the enormous black and gold screaming eagle banner that once had been the Montredaun-An's house banner, and now belonged to the kingdom, and at the impassive guards at their stations at either side of the dais, the only people bearing arms inside the throne room. Senrid hoped these reminders bolstered the aura of authority that he knew he so sadly lacked.

He held firm to his determination not to listen to surface thoughts, a determination strengthened by his awareness of his lack of skill. He dreaded discovery. They would, quite rightly, consider it the worst sort of invasion.

Besides, there didn't seem to be any surprises waiting. Everyone knew what was going to happen, but they'd all come as summoned, though they'd come a few months before, for Winter Convocation. But hearing capital cases concerning jarls was their right.

They listened as the captains of West Army reported, followed by both jarls' captains mumbling and stuttering through their reports, all of which established a clear line of command that pointed straight to David-Jarl Ndarga. Torac had owed the Ndarga family allegiance, which technically exonerated him. Senrid wished he could send Torac into exile. He thought the man just as much of a weasel as Waldevan. But he didn't dare.

At the end, Senrid stood, and delivered his carefully prepared speech. "You are foresworn, David-Jarl Ndarga of Methden. As you have broken your fealty to me, mine to you ends. You are now David Ndarga. Methden reverts to the crown, and Marloven Hess is closed to you. I shall detail a riding to accompany you to the border, which you shall not re-cross on pain of death."

After a silence that seemed to last forever, the former jarl said, "My son?"

Senrid let out the breath he discovered he'd been holding. He hoped his voice wouldn't squeak as he delivered the second part of his speech. "I shall appoint an interim captain for the remainder of the year, at which time the question of Methden will be revisited in time for Oath Day during New Year's Week. Jarend Ndarga, who had no part in oath-breaking, will continue to serve as is."

The former jarl's eyes closed for a heartbeat, his face full of pain. His fist came up, froze halfway to his chest, and then he laid his hand flat, the salute of the civilian, and his expression shuttered. The scrape of a foot, an audible indrawn breath, the shift of clothing among the jarls indicated their reactions, and how silent the room had been. Senrid wondered if he had not been alone in holding his breath.

The captain of the guard motioned his chosen escort into place around the former jarl, and out they walked.

Senrid rose, indicating that the convocation was over. He spoke the words inviting the remaining jarls to a meal, seeing in their faces that no one wanted to stay. Good, because if he didn't get out of that room by the count of ten he was going to puke.

When he knew he had himself under control, he walked into his study and dropped onto the floor next to Liere, who scrambled up, her book falling unheeded from her lap.

"You didn't do anything about that nasty Jarl of Torac?" Liere's thin shoulders were tight, hunched up under her ears. "He told a man to shoot you!"

"You listened." Senrid tapped his head.

Liere was small and thin, her single prominent feature a pair of large eyes so pale a brown they looked gold. So when she rolled her eyes, it was a very effective expression. "He was thinking it right *at* you!" Her chin came up. "And it scared him, how you raised the shield to stop the arrow. But Senrid—"

"I can't do anything without visual evidence or witnesses."

Liere's fingers gripped her elbows. "That other one, he thinks you had spies to find out his plot."

"That's better than the truth," Senrid muttered. If Jarend Ndarga hadn't ratted his father out, a whole lot of people would have died. Including the jarl. Because Senrid would have had to throw the entire army at them, or lose the kingdom. And Jarend had known it.

But he didn't want to load Liere down with those worries. "Methden is used to raids, which means a lot of spying back and forth." Senrid sighed. "There's a lot of trouble on the border, mostly horse thieving. Our horses bring a fortune in other lands, especially trained."

"I thought you had border guards," Liere said.

Senrid shrugged. "Well, South Army patrols all along there, but short of standing across the hills that make up the border, fingertip to fingertip, there's no way to guard all the gullies and trickles, especially on moonless nights, the favored raiding time. Then there's the problem with at least half the raiders having relatives on our side of the border, because Toth and Telyerhas both share ancestry with us. There are even some who make a good living being either Marloven or Toth as suits them."

Liere took a chance. "You didn't guard your thoughts, Senrid. I know you want to know who that jarl sent to shoot you."

He grimaced. "The mind-shield isn't quite habit yet. It needs to be, if Siamis comes back. That's what worries me much more than that horseapple Torac, whom even my uncle despised."

Liere couldn't prevent herself from casting a worried glance at the door. She sensed Senrid observing it, and did her best to pass her apprehension off as a question. "What happened with that emissary from Enneh Rual?"

"Oh. He was lurking in the hall when I came out." No need to mention how long Senrid'd had to hide until his stomach stopped twisting itself in knots. Liere had probably heard him, anyway. "As soon as he saw me he spoke his piece about how they didn't want our exiles, and threat, threat, threat, and I said that Ndarga was surely going south, and when he started in again, I told him he and his government were welcome to capture Ndarga and hold an execution if they really wanted one. He stomped away, and I hope he's on his way back home now, because I didn't offer him any meals."

Liere sat up, her gaze distant. "Yes. He's going."

"You could pick out his thoughts from everybody else's?"

"I can pick out anybody's if I know them," Liere said. "I mean, I don't know that man, but I met him, and so I can find his thoughts. He's so afraid of you Marlovens, and hates you so much. But he's going away." She heaved a sigh. "If you want to know how to listen, just send out a tendril," she said.

"Tendril," he repeated. "You say that, but thoughts aren't tendrils. They're loud and jumbled and . . ." Senrid paused, reaching for the words to describe the violent babble intensified with emotional color, sometimes with a physical overlay that he found even more unsettling— even painful—and gave up. "Loud," he finished.

Liere accepted the repeated word with a nod and shrug. She was used to failing to find words for Dena Yeresbeth, which nobody else in the world understood, and it wasn't as if she had great control, herself. Far, *far* from it.

She picked up her book, then said, "I don't see why you had to go through all that. You already knew what everyone was going to say. That Jarl of Methden, I mean, the man who used to be jarl, he's really, really angry."

"He would have been angry no matter what." Senrid sat on his desk and swung his leg back and forth, his heel hitting the wood, tap, tap, tap. "Yep. Every jarl there knew what the reports would say. But everybody heard chain of command, according to law. Methden's. Mine. Have to remember how important obeying orders is here . . ."

Liere nodded seriously, fighting the urge to gnaw her nails. She despised herself for being afraid of these Marlovens who had all these rules for raids, as if raiding were some kind of game.

But Senrid wouldn't let anything happen to her. He wasn't afraid. Why did she have to feel these stupid, useless emotions?

Senrid was still talking. ". . . Keriam thinks Torac won't try any plots on his own. At least, not now. I hope he's right. Here, let's get something to eat. I just discovered I'm hungry, and I'm sure you are, too."

He looked at the book in her hand, and though he couldn't hear her thoughts, there was a quickness in the way that she said, "I've nearly finished it," that served as a kind of signal.

It had become a kind of habit to limit her visits to the time it took for her to work her way through whatever books she brought.

*Mearsies Heili*

Spring rain roared on the ground overhead, a soothing muffled thud familiar to the Mearsiean girls. Ordinarily they saluted the first rains of spring with toasted bread and cheese, but the astonishing news that they were about to be visited by the Queen of Sartor had caused a flurry of excitement.

Now they stood around in the main chamber of their underground cave, staring at the mural that had hung on the back wall opposite the fireplace ever since they'd first made the hideout.

"I think it needs to come down."

"No it doesn't! It's funny!"

"It's mean," tall, quiet Seshe said.

The others looked her way.

"What?"

"What?"

"No!" Irenne crossed her arms in a flounce. "Mean would be if Fobo and PJ ever saw it."

"But we had such fun making it," blue-eyed Sherry, one of Clair's first friends, said wistfully.

This mural had been painted on sailcloth, the only type of canvas that was large enough and sturdy enough. The wrinkled, battered sailcloth was thick with paint, having been corrected and added to by various hands.

The girls stared at the mural, each seeing a different picture. CJ glowered, aware of her inner conflict between pride and the old, old feelings of not being good enough, left over from her terrible early childhood on Earth. Clair had discovered how to go through the world-gate without any idea how very dangerous it was, and offered CJ a better life. CJ had followed her through the world-gate without a backward glance, determined to leave the horrible memories behind, but she'd discovered that even when one is happy, memory can't be snipped and tossed away like toenails and split ends.

She'd come desperate to please Clair's other adopted and rescued friends, offering what she regarded as her only talent: drawing. It was her idea to satirize these ridiculous people who had made Clair's early reign miserable. She'd sketched it out and the girls had worked together to paint it, laughing and adding their own inventive touches. And it had cheered them all up during the awful days when Kwenz of the Shadowland had aided the grasping princess from Elchnudaebb in her efforts to annex Mearsies Heili.

So here was this mural depicting the snooty, ill-tempered princess the girls had nicknamed Fobo, wearing one of her typical court gowns loaded with lace and ribbons, festoons and flosses, bangles and spangles. Beside her sulked her son, Prince Jonnicake—he really was named Jonnicake—decked out in extra jewels, lace, ribbons, and whatnot, as if to hide his scrawny body and pimply face. Around them passers-by fainted at the sight, and above, birds and insects were falling out of the sky.

Seshe shook her head, her long river of ash-blonde hair rippling down her back. "It's mean," she said again, her voice apologetic.

Irenne sighed loudly. "*You* loved it as much as *any* of us did. I remember."

Seshe said, "It was funny when Fobo was acting so horrible. But now that we know that her brother has exiled her from Elchnudaebb's court, I just don't think it's funny anymore. I especially don't think PJ's part is funny. You know how much I felt sorry for him, how horrible it must have been, living with such an awful mother. She bullied him into doing the Child Spell, just so she wouldn't look old. I find that so cruel."

CJ stared in disbelief. To her, the Child Spell was the best thing in a world she loved passionately. "It's not like the Child Spell hurts anybody."

"But nobody should be forced, should they?"

Silence fell.

Seshe said, "Anyway, now that we know that PJ ran away, well, when I see the mural, I can't help but think that it's mean. People change."

CJ was thinking: not us. But she didn't say it, because it wasn't really true. Dhana wasn't actually human, and Falinneh, who had run away from the last remnants of a justly feared magic race, did her best to pretend she wasn't a shape changer—she wouldn't even say if she'd been born a boy or a girl, insisting she didn't remember. That might even be the case.

CJ knew she wasn't the only one with bad memories of her old life. She knew Diana had them as well. Same with some of the other girls. You could say they hadn't changed since they had formed the gang . . . Except, in a way, they had. You had to, if villains kept trying to do villainous things. The girls were good at patrols now, and some were even pretty good at defending themselves long enough to run away. And they were all very fast runners now.

Dark-haired Diana—the only one with weapons training—looked sober, as usual. She said, "Queen of Sartor won't know what it is. So it won't look mean to her."

Everybody listened, because Diana so seldom spoke.

Clair stood at the far end of the circle, her head a little bent so that her waving locks of white hair curtained her face from view. The girls shifted their attention from Diana to Clair to see what she thought.

Clair rarely gave orders to the gang. She liked it when they found a way to agree. "Do we want the Queen of Sartor seeing the mural?" she asked.

Falinneh grinned. "Why not? I'd love to tell the story of Fobo and PJ versus us!"

CJ shifted from foot to foot, digging her toes into the bright rug. "We don't have to change things just to impress her, do we?"

Clair rubbed a knuckle against her lip. "I don't know how to answer that," she admitted. "I know I want her to see Mearsies Heili at its best. I also hope she'll join our alliance. I mean really join. I know Hibern said she would, but since we never heard another word, maybe that was some kind of courtly politeness."

"The alliance is dust anyway," Falinneh said, flapping her hands. "How many people have asked for our help in galoomphing villains? Not one!"

"Jilo came."

"But he didn't really want our help. He went straight to Boneribs in Marloven Hess," someone else put in.

Seshe pointed at the mural. "This picture doesn't really show us the way we are. That is, we're no longer defending Mearsies Heili against Fobo and PJ."

"It's our past, but it's a funny past," Falinneh protested.

Sherry's big blue eyes rounded, and she pointed to the far end of the mural. "But we've already folded over that corner where we'd painted in Jilo."

Everybody stared. They had woken up the morning after Jilo left and found it that way. Nobody had said anything, but they all suspected that Seshe had done it.

CJ glared resentfully at the mural. She hated change, but she didn't want to go back to the bad old days of the Shadowland. She had not minded seeing the Jilo part of the mural folded, even though she had been the one to paint him in, making him look extra stupid and gawky, with a gloppy pie about to fall on his head. But it was kind of nice not seeing those all-black eyes staring out at you, like empty pits. And now that Jilo had removed Wan-Edhe's horrible eye-spell that had characterized the Shadowland Chwahir, the picture was no longer even right. Jilo turned out to have ordinary light brown eyes, not much different from Sartora's color.

Clair said, "How many want the mural to stay?"

Three hands shot up. Irenne crossed her arms, and seeing that, another girl curled her lip and put her hand up.

Diana remembered the exhilaration of belonging to a group for the first time in a very hard life. She lifted her hand.

CJ hesitated. She would feel better if Clair put her hand up. Then she could raise hers as well, because the whole mural had been her idea and she had planned most of it. She sighed, thinking it was more honest to stick with her real feelings, but Clair forestalled her.

"That's a majority, so it's decided." She looked around. "I guess that's it. Maybe we should have an early night, because Hibern and the Queen of Sartor will be here at dawn. It's the only free time the queen has."

CJ grimaced at the rug. The underground hideout was already clean. The girls had swept it earlier that day. CJ couldn't scorn anyone for primping because she'd stood in her own room, looking at the pictures she'd made and trying to decide if she should keep them or make a new one, just to impress this unknown girl because she happened to have been born queen of the oldest country in the world. CJ could tell herself that she merely wanted the gang, and Mearsies Heili, to look their best, but really, showing off was showing off.

Clair said, "If we're done here, I'll go upstairs."

Upstairs was the white palace on the mountain. Clair had made only one request: that she be the first to meet the Queen of Sartor, show her whatever she wanted to see, and then bring her to the underground hideout to meet the girls. "Throwing an entire group at a newcomer might not be the best introduction," she'd said, and everybody agreed.

CJ said, "I'm coming with you."

Clair had layered transfer magic into the medallions all the girls wore. She and CJ each touched their medallions, said the transfer word, and felt themselves snatched out of the world and thrust into the white palace on the mountain.

They went to Clair's room, where CJ flopped on the bed, and Clair stood at the window, gazing out at the rain.

CJ sighed. "You wanted us to take down the mural, didn't you?"

Clair turned around. "I don't know." She made a face. "I have such mixed feelings. I like everything you girls make, and it was such fun when we made it. Also, if they were here, I suspect Puddlenose would have voted to keep it. Christoph, too," Clair named Puddlenose's most frequent traveling companion, a boy who'd come from Earth from a time centuries before CJ's time, nobody knew how or why. "Puddlenose always says he loves coming back and finding things just the same. I don't quite get what he means, because things change every single day, don't they? A tiny bit? Or we'd be like statues in a garden."

"I know exactly what he means," CJ said.

Clair turned around. "Do you?"

CJ sat up cross-legged, her green skirt spread around her. "No icky changes, but most of all, no icky surprises."

Clair walked to the window and back. "Maybe it's just as fake as courtly behavior to want this girl queen to see us at our best. I've been thinking I ought to wear my interview dress," she confessed.

"Why not? It's pretty. Everybody likes wearing something nice, as long as we don't have to every day. As for the rest . . ." CJ snorted loudly. "Falinneh's right. We already *are* our best. Mearsies Heili isn't the largest, or the richest, and it's not famous for anything, but it's still the best. Anybody who doesn't like it, even if she's queen of the universe, is a windbag."

Clair heard the utter conviction in CJ's voice, the loyalty. She smiled. "When you say it like that, I'm a windbag to be worrying about it."

"Never," CJ said, with equal conviction. "Okay. I feel a bit better. See ya." She made the sign and transferred back to the Junky, where she stood in her room, tried to see her artwork as the Queen of Sartor would . . . then laughed at herself and got ready for bed.

## Chapter Four

*Sartor*

IN the heart of Sartor's royal palace, Atan was at that moment lying awake, staring through the east windows at the distant line of mountains, barely discernible as darkness began to lift over the capital city.

She still hadn't decided which room she wanted to be her private space: she couldn't bear to let anyone touch her parents' things in the old royal suite, flung aside so carelessly as war overtook them, though she knew that the Norsundrians had rifled through everything before casting the enchantment. Detlev himself had sat down at Father's desk and penned a threatening message that Atan had found ninety-seven years later, after breaking the enchantment he had cast over the kingdom—she still did not know why that enchantment had been cast. No one did.

Maybe it was that, and not her parents' memory, that kept her out of their rooms.

She had also bypassed the nursery where she'd been an infant for so short a time, next to the larger, airy nursery where her siblings had played together. She had offered the entire nursery to Julian, who had stood there, arms crossed, face sulky, and said, "This is for princesses. I hate it!"

Atan had chosen her mother's winter morning room for her bedroom through the dark months, because the curved bank of windows gave the best view of the dim northern sun in its arc, but now that spring was here, Atan found herself back again in the eastmost room in the royal wing, with its windows that only caught the morning sun. She'd looked in records, discovering that this room had been a bedroom before, as well as a study, a third-circle receiving room, and an antechamber when the big nursery had been a bridal suite.

Sometimes she liked to imagine those ancestors moving through these very rooms. What were they like? What did they talk about when they looked out this window? Which one put the beautiful marble carving of the heron in flight in that little wall alcove, made by a sculptor from Tser Mearsies up north . . .

Her meandering thoughts jolted to a halt when she remembered Mearsies Heili. That's why she'd woken so early! She was going to meet Rel's friends. Not that Atan had gleaned many details. Rel wasn't talkative about other people, or even things he'd done, only things he'd seen.

She bathed, still loving to watch the marble tub fill with steaming water. She plunged into it while the water was still churning from its transfer from the hot spring veining the city far below ground. When she was done, she stepped into the adjoining room where her staff waited to dry her, order her hair, and dress her in a morning outfit chosen for the interviews that awaited.

As she moved through the tightly scheduled day, she was thinking, what to wear to her secret visit? In the wonderful days when she lived hidden in the hermit's hut in Tsauderei's Delfina Valley, she'd had three old shirts, two sturdy sets of trousers, and a dress she'd made herself.

But you can't go back. Clothes were communication. You could pretend to be someone else, but people still looked at you and made judgments about what they saw.

Atan only knew that the Mearsiean girls had been on a surprising number of adventures, and that they lived in a tiny kingdom that the youths in the school for aristocrats up on Parleas Terrace called a *honas*, an outsider. *Selas* were kingdoms big enough for their names to be written inside their drawn borders. *Honas* were too small, their names written with arrows pointing to the correct tiny splotch on the world map; the words reflected the organization of social circles, words Atan (an outsider in just about all ways except birth) thoroughly loathed.

So, what to wear. She would be meeting a fellow queen, but one a couple years younger than she was. From a country that had no court. Atan didn't want to look pompous, but neither did she want to appear condescending.

She worried at the question off and on all day. Most of what she had to do was listen—she was told what she thought, not asked—which caused her to escape inside herself.

When it came time to get ready, she shed her elaborate court gown in favor of an undertunic of plain, cream-colored linen, slit up the sides, with loose trousers of the same fabric, and over it a robe of spring green embroidered with tiny blossoms in cherry and gold. She picked out her plainest gold tiara, knowing it was loaded with protections in case any Norsundrians might be lurking about. She felt . . . bumptious, wearing crowns. But this was a compromise with herself for not telling anyone in the high council or mage guild what she planned to do.

She was ready before Hibern appeared on the first ring of the hour. She wore her usual long tunic over riding trousers under her sky blue robe, and Atan was glad she'd chosen the clothes she wore, which were more or less the same style as Hibern's.

"How do you want me to introduce you?" Hibern asked.

"As Atan," she said, suppressing the urge to wipe her damp palms down her skirt. "They know who I am. But I don't want them seeing Yustnesveas Landis The Fifth of Sartor, I want them to see *me*."

Hibern had misgivings about that, but she said nothing as she handed Atan the transfer token she'd prepared.

The Destination for Mearsies Heili's capital had been set on the white stone terrace before the palace. Atan let the reaction die, and gazed up in astonishment.

The palace was definitely Ancient Sartoran in origin, or at least in design: no attention paid to symmetry. The design was more graceful than that, the complication of soaring arches, towers, and spires angled for exposure to the sun's path at different times of the year.

The topmost spires glimmered against the clouds as Hibern recollected a fact she'd forgotten. "Clair said that they've tried to count all the rooms in the palace, and always come up with a different number."

Atan said, "I believe it. Our tower can make you dizzy, because time isn't always . . ." She reached, not finding the right word, and made a gesture with her hand, waggling it from side to side.

Hibern grinned. "I can't imagine what that's like."

"Remind me some day, and I'll ask the mages to schedule a tour." Atan turned her back to the palace, expecting to see the rest of the cloud top city, and gazed at the little village zigzagging down the mountainside, the steep rooftops catching reddish highlights from the early morning sun rising over the line of the ocean to the east. "This was the cloud city mentioned in the records? This really isn't a city, at least, the way I define city. Nor is it a cloud top, except perhaps in a figurative sense."

"City or village, it was definitely on a cloud. I was there when it began to come down. I believe it took two days to settle. Took them most of a year to rebuild chimneys, reset windows, and redo the roads in these switchbacks you see leading down the mountain. See how young the trees are at the corners? All that is new."

"Who brought down an entire town? For that matter, who put it up in the air in the first place?"

"No one knows on either account. I think that even includes the Chwahir who had come to invade, and that horrible Prince Kessler Son-scarna."

"*He* was there?" Atan turned sharply.

"Oh yes. But only for a moment. It was a very strange day, still a mystery. Erai-Yanya thinks it was some spell made centuries ago, that ended suddenly."

The palace's arched doors stood open onto a vestibule bare of ornamentation, the light falling so perfectly that the space itself was an ornament, filled with the pearly light of early morning. Beyond that, another doorway opened into a magnificent vaulted throne room, empty except for the morning light.

Atan paused. "This palace doesn't seem to be warded at all, at least against us." She walked right up to a wall, and extended a finger.

Now that she was close, she made a discovery: the material wasn't like marble, or even ice, at all. The silver component was much more present, causing that curious glisten. When she bent so close her eyes almost crossed, she perceived specks of all kinds of colors, just like the stone Tower of Knowledge was made from, except the Tower was more like bone, and this seemed . . . almost alive, somehow.

"We'd better go," Hibern said, and Atan backed away hastily. "This is actually a shortcut," Hibern said as they crossed this empty chamber, Atan hesitating long enough to take in the curved balconies above, and above those the arched windows.

"Where is Clair?"

"Probably in the kitchen, though she might be in her study upstairs. But we'll check the kitchen first."

"The kitchen?" Atan repeated. She'd never gone into her own kitchens, except on her first tour through the palace. The cook staff would be scandalized if she set foot there—not that she knew anyone there, or had any reason to go.

"The cook is also the steward, a woman named Janil. Erai-Yanya says she was like a mother to Clair, when her own mother died. Before that, too."

"Was her mother killed by treachery?"

"Erai-Yanya was told by Murial, the queen's sister, that it was a mixture of wine and sleep-herbs. She was reported to be dark in mood, and started early in the day with wine. Clair was about the age of your little cousin when it happened."

How awful, Atan thought, and below that stirred an unsettling thought: Who would stop kings and queens from doing stupid things? Maybe the high council was not such a curse. Unless they did the stupid things.

Several people bustled about the roomy, airy kitchen. At first glance they all looked like servants. Atan's eye was drawn to the one white-haired figure among the ordinary variations of light and dark brown hair. A morvende? No, the white hair, though pure blue-white, was not the drifty cobweb hair of morvende; it fell in waves down below the girl's waist. The girl herself was ordinary, light brown skin, no talons at her fingers' ends, and she wore slippers, which morvende never did. She was dressed in a plain gown reminiscent of Colendi shopkeepers a generation or two ago, the only decoration a ribbon tied around the upper part of the slightly belled sleeves, a round neck, sashed waist, plain skirt.

"Hibern! And . . . how do you wish to be called?" Clair asked, forestalling Hibern's carefully thought-out introduction. "I've never met another queen before, outside of my own ancestor. Are we supposed to bow?"

A year ago, Atan would not have known how to answer that without getting tangled up in confusion. "Atan will do. We can skip bowing, if it's not your custom." When she saw the relief in Clair's serious, squarish face, she added, "I haven't met any other rulers either. Only emissaries, and two new ambassadors, for the old ones fled before the war."

"A century ago, is that correct?" Clair asked.

"True."

"Would you like to meet the other girls, or have the tour first? Um, we were putting together a nice breakfast, then I remembered that it's not morning for you. Are you hungry?"

Atan did not want to waste any of her hour on a meal. "Not really," she said. "Thank you."

"Would you rather have the tour, then? And meet the others?"

Atan heard in Clair's *the tour* that she'd made a plan. So she agreed. It was clear from the slightly self-conscious way that Clair conducted her through parts of the palace that indeed she'd thought it all out. Atan found it strange, to see such simple, relatively modern furniture inside the rooms whose lineaments were pure Ancient Sartor in a way that she'd only seen in archival drawings. But when they came to the library, and Atan saw from Clair's attitude that this was her favorite room, Atan thought, we are a lot alike.

She did not comment on how small the library was, relative to that at Sartor's palace, which had been added to and refined over thousands of years. Clair was proud of her library, and made reference to her studies of magic. Atan envied Clair her quiet life and the chance to study so much. So far, being queen here seemed to be largely symbolic, again like Atan's own position, but Clair appeared to be blessedly free of the demands of symbolic presiding. "Do you see glimpses of the past when you walk about?"

Atan had meant the age of the furnishings, but Clair answered matter-of-factly, "Only upstairs in the towers. There are rooms that we sometimes see, and sometimes don't. We can't always find them again when we go looking—but it's great fun for playing hide-and-seek."

Atan shivered, realizing Clair meant it literally. But . . . hide-and-seek?

The mages did not permit Atan to go alone into the Tower of Knowledge, lest she make an error and slip inexplicably into some fold in time, yet these girls played hide-and-seek in this building that seemed to be made of the same mysterious not-quite-stone. They had *time* to play hide-and-seek. "May I ask about your ancestral background?" Atan asked.

Clair shrugged, her smile fleeting. "I believe we were weavers, from somewhere way, way up north."

"The Shaer?"

"That's the place. Shaer Wood. Mearsieanne had a grandfather with white hair, but nobody else in the family did. The rest pretty much looked like my cousin Puddlenose."

"Puddlenose?"

"We don't know what name he was born with, only the insults Wan-Edhe called my cousin during the time he was a hostage in Chwahirsland," Clair explained as they walked out into a chilly spring wind, and stopped on the Destination.

From there they transferred down to the base of the mountain. For a short time Atan could do nothing but gaze in amazement at the bubbles rising slowly from the waterfall filling the rock-framed pool. The bubbles spun in the air, each flickering with what looked like facets, before thinning and vanishing.

Clair said, "We used to swim in it, though it made us feel drunk. We stopped when Dhana, who wasn't born human, told us we were thrashing through her people. See those wriggling lines, like facets in a gemstone? Those are the people. Dhana said our swimming doesn't harm them in the least, but we hated the idea of swimming through someone." She shrugged.

"The Selenseh Redian," Hibern exclaimed, having kept quiet all this time. But mention of one of the weirdest and most powerful and least understood magical phenomena in the world broke her determination to stay in the background. "Erai-Yanya said to me once that you have one here. Is that true?"

"Oh! The jewel cave. Yes. Right up there," Clair pointed up the craggy cliff above the waterfall. "The jewels have the same lines in them. You can go in, and ask questions, even, and sometimes they kind of put answers into your head . . . but again, it makes you feel drunk."

It *was* the Toaran Selenseh Redian! Atan stared upward, thrilled at the idea of its proximity. To live near one! Tsauderei had taken her via long, wrenching magic transfer to see one once, and Atan recollected the glowing gems inside, facets coruscating like sunlight sparkling on water, though no light source could be seen. The air had been warm, and breathing it somehow made her feel heady, as if the space was much larger than what she saw.

As far as the mages knew, there were only seven such caves in the world, and none—except, apparently, this one—located anywhere near human civilizations. And they could vanish abruptly, if they were disturbed. The archives maintained that Norsunder once expended tremendous effort to invade the caves and dig out the gems, which some believed were living beings, but in any case somehow gave access to tremendous magical power.

But the caves no longer were open to Norsundrians; it was said that dark mages who entered deep within never came out again. When the stones nearer the entrance were threatened, the caves would close somehow, and reappear somewhere nearby, always in mountains.

These Mearsieans don't understand what they have here, Atan thought as Clair said, "If you don't mind another transfer—it's short—it will give us time to visit the others. They wanted to show you our underground hideout."

Atan heard the pride in her voice, and began to imagine a grand, abandoned morvende geliath, full of ancient carvings. In fact, it wouldn't be surprising, because Atan now was certain she understood the purpose behind that palace being built here: its presence had to be connected to the Selenseh Redian directly below it. Maybe even to that lake full of beings, so rare in the south, much more common in the north.

But all three together? As far as Atan knew, there was no such combination in all the *world*.

Did Clair—who had to have morvende ancestors—have an ancient morvende geliath nearby, that the Mearsieans called an underground hideout?

But when the short transfer jolt dissipated, Atan found herself in a cramped, stuffy room dug out of soil. The Mearsieans had made an effort to domesticate it with a clumsily made colored rug, rough wooden furnishings, and a lot of very badly drawn pictures affixed to barren dirt walls that at least had been smoothed by magic.

A host of girls appeared from two side tunnels, smiling with pride, and Atan was stunned at the thought that *this* was their home. Why didn't they live in that astonishingly beautiful palace on the mountain?

Clair stepped forward and introduced each of the girls to Atan. At first there seemed to be too many to count, all talking over each other, but CJ named them one by one, finishing, ". . . here's Gwen, another escapee from Earth, and over there is Falinneh. That's all nine of us."

Hibern had told Atan a little about Falinneh, whom she'd met shortly before Senrid became king. Falinneh was the most colorful as well as the dominant talker: a short, sturdy girl with bright, wiry red hair and thousands of freckles, who wore crimson satin knee pants and a shirt of green and yellow stripes under a blue vest edged with little crimson pompons. "Fal-IN-neh," Falinneh declared, wiggling her red eyebrows. "My name is Fal-IN-neh—everybody always leaves out the AL, and I get stuck with Flinna, which I hate!"

"Oh, don't talk to ME about 'Renna,'" a prissy girl in a very old-fashioned Colendi morning court gown declared, swanning about the room, her long light-brown ponytail swinging. "My name is EAR-ren-neh, please."

Odd, how Falinneh made Atan want to laugh, but Irenne was instantly irritating.

Falinneh said, "Now, about that alliance. We can also show you how to go about defeating villains. We've become such experts that I've decided to write a book, once I finish learning how to write." She hooked her fingers in the armholes of her vest and twiddled her fingers absurdly.

Atan said, "You have instructions? Besides assembling armies of mages and warriors?"

Falinneh waved a freckled hand. "Who needs all that nasty stuff if you can defeat 'em without? Not that wig-lifting or pie-beds will defeat them all," she added. "I suspect Siamis would only laugh if he put his foot through a sheet, or fell out of bed, and he didn't wear a wig, and I wouldn't have dared do anything to that horrible Kessler—"

"Kessler," Atan repeated. "The renegade Prince Kessler Sonscarna of the Chwahir? Hibern said he was here when your city came down."

The girls' smiles vanished at the repeat of the young man's name, and Atan remembered that the Mearsieans had also been mixed up in Rel's bad experiences with Prince Kessler.

"He was sent against us when we were trying to free Sartor from the enchantment," Atan said. "Rel the Traveler, the outlander who helped us, said he had encountered him before."

At the mention of Rel, CJ groaned. "Here we are again, back at the Great Hero. Rel, schmel."

"CJ, Rel's not a villain," Sherry exclaimed.

Atan stared. "Is this another Rel? I understand it's a common enough name on both coasts of the Elgar Strait in particular—"

CJ sighed, her thin black brows a scowl-line above vivid blue eyes. "Taller than a house? A face like a sour lemon, only sourer? Thinks he's the greatest thing ever?" CJ shifted her gaze to Clair, who studied her bare toes, and CJ flushed. "All right, I know that's not fair. It's just that I thought, just once, we could get through a single conversation without the Perfect Rel."

CJ was so busy watching Clair that she did not notice Atan's expression of extreme reserve.

"Rel the Traveler is a friend to Sartor," Atan said in her most polite voice. "He's *my* friend."

CJ sighed, struggling against the old, familiar, hot pit of jealousy. "He's everybody's friend, he's just so perfect," she said in a sprightly voice, trying to sound polite, but she could hear how false her own voice sounded.

And so could everyone else. "Is anybody hungry?" Sherry asked a little too brightly. "I made some berry muffins."

"Did you show Atan the Magic Lake?" Falinneh asked.

"Yes," Atan said.

She knew her answer was short. She felt the pause afterward as a silence, and saw that the others did, too.

This is a disaster, Hibern thought, and to fill the awkward silence, began blabbing about how difficult it was to find histories about parts of the world that didn't have humans. Clair aided this limping conversation.

Because both girls turned toward her, Atan fell back on the politeness with which she'd been raised, and agreed, but she was waiting for CJ to apologize for her crack against Rel.

CJ fumed, wanting to explain, to justify, but she didn't know how to get around Atan's statement, which sounded like an imperial declaration from the Queen of Sartor. So she grinned, and agreed heartily with everything Hibern and Clair said without listening to a word of it, and pretended nothing had happened, hoping everyone else would, too.

Clair had no idea how to resolve the tension she felt, so she kept on talking about magic until her mouth felt dry, and somehow it never seemed right to mention the alliance again.

The hour ended. Hibern and Atan vanished, after the latter thanked them formally for the tour. Just as formally Clair told her she was welcome, and even then, she couldn't bring herself to talk further about the alliance.

Well, Hibern had said Atan would join. There would be other times for figuring out what it all meant, she told herself as everybody went off to eat.

In Sartor, Hibern spotted the approach of the inevitable steward, and said quickly, "I don't think you saw the Mearsieans at their best."

A pause grew into an uncomfortable silence.

Atan frowned at her hands. "Thank you very much for the tour," she said a little too politely.

Sick with a sense of failure, Hibern took her leave, and Atan turned to the steward with an equally intense sense of relief.

As she changed into the proper set of formal robes for a third-circle reception, she struggled with her emotions. She recognized that, aside from the impulse to dislike that CJ for those remarks about Rel, her disappointment at finding the Mearsieans so ignorant was prompted by jealousy. They were such friends. The stories they all shared, even those stupid jokes they all laughed at. You could call them a family.

They didn't realize what they had in any sense, she thought as she stalked out of her bedroom, twitching her brocade over-robe into place. Further, they were self-satisfied in their ignorance, pigging it in a stuffy cavern rather than living in that airy, pretty marble palace, and doing the Child Spell to play, rather than as a defensive measure . . .

What *possible* use was an alliance with *them?*

The bad mood she had tried to scold herself out of was worse by the time she reached the antechamber where the duty page awaited her. She was in a thorough stew of righteous indignation when she glanced down at her golden notecase on the table, and as always, touched it. To her surprise, the cool brush of magic on her fingertip indicated a letter inside. Her mood lightened to anticipation.

All of her correspondence as Queen of Sartor was handled by the scribes. This was her own personal notecase, and few of those she regarded as friends had one. Rel didn't. So she never carried hers, but she'd trained herself to check it when entering the room, though it was usually empty.

Since the duty page was standing there looking expectantly at her, she tucked the notecase into the pocket of her under-gown, and went off to do her duty. It was a reception for the weights and measures branch of the scribe guild, which had finished touring all of Sartor to make certain that officially recognized scales had been calibrated to current international standards.

Atan was glad that some people liked such exactitude in their lives enough to go around seeing that people got honest measure, but she found their anecdotes excruciatingly boring. She saw no reason why she had to preside. The guild could just as easily celebrate on its own. But she had to be there because the high council put her there. It was they who ruled Sartor. She only provided a warm body with the right face to decorate Star Chamber, while they did the real work.

Nobody could really think she understood all the weights-and-measures scribes' arcane references, and she was aware that these people were talking at her, not to her.

But she smiled and made the appropriate formal gestures, and as soon as everyone had had their say, she invited them to partake of refreshments. In the general movement that ensued, she retrieved her letter. It was a note from Tsauderei.

*My dear Atan:*

*Until you command me otherwise, I will claim my privilege as your old tutor to speak up when I feel that you are in error. Though I will admit that the fault is probably my own for having kept you sequestered during your childhood. The need for secrecy prevented you from learning simple, yet vitally important, rules of social engagement, one of the first being: do not neglect your friends until you find you have a need for their service.*

*I was very glad to meet your friend Rel, yet a month and more has passed, and you have not found another free hour to visit your first and oldest friends outside of my valley, Lilah and Peitar Selenna. I never visit Sarendan without either Peitar or Lilah asking for news of you.*

Atan crushed the note into her pocket, her face burning with guilt.

## Chapter Five

*Two weeks later in the world*
*Hours later in Chwahirsland*

THE alliance, still a vague idea to most, and a negative one to Atan, might have died right then, but for two people: Jilo, and Rel.

Jilo had learned to shift out of the magic chambers whenever he noticed his fingernails turning gray. He just had to remember to check.

When he did remember next, a distant pang of shock accompanied the thought, whose hands are these? The nails were ragged, the beds gray. In the dull magical light of the chamber, they looked like old man's hands.

He'd finished the trap removal on another shelf, but none of the books there were the least use. Most were old records. Of the magic books, all he found were magical histories—lists of wards done and by whom—and plenty of elementary spell books. Nothing about binding time.

What was he missing? He stood in the room trying to think until he found himself struggling to remember why he was standing there. The effort to penetrate the fog closing around his skull like an ironmonger's vise reminded him of those days when he'd had that spell on him.

*Go outside. Breathe.* It was less a thought than an unconscious urge, insistent enough to penetrate his mental fog.

He walked out, down the hall, and down the stairs.

When he reached the side court, he blinked. The air wasn't cold, the light daytime under the ubiquitous cloud cover. His hands looked more like normal hands, though his nails were still a dull color. And he'd have to trim them. He wondered if that gray was happening more often, but then time didn't seem to mean anything anymore. He only knew that once he got outside the palace it seemed easier to breathe, and his stomach woke up. He felt real hunger. His thoughts were clearer, or at least he could remember them.

Since the air wasn't cold, he set out to walk into the city. The guards all knew who he was—that is, they took him for Wan-Edhe's mouthpiece— because they snapped rigid when they saw him, eyes straight forward, hands tight on their regulation weapons, or hanging down, open and empty.

When he reached the city, he slipped into a side street and no one paid him any attention. It had always been that way, but before, he'd been under that magical fog, so he hadn't noticed much. Now he could see the uniformity of buildings, all gray granite, the sounds of footsteps or the occasional clop of hooves echoing along the stone canyons. No one spoke unless it was for business, and no woman spoke at all.

For the first time he wondered if people really did obey Wan-Edhe's insane laws. Jilo grimaced at the cobblestoned street, worn almost smooth by ages of tramping boots. He struggled with anger and a sense of humiliation, not wanting to believe that the Chwahir had been reduced to the status of worms, blind to injustice, their entire lives spent in mindless toil as Wan-Edhe's evil perpetuated itself on the strength of invasively malevolent spells.

Jilo's stomach rumbled again. He gave in to impulse and picked a street at random. There were no street signs, but he could orient easily enough on the castle's highest tower, looming above. At the street's end he found what he expected, a way station, for restaurants and inns of the sort to be found in other kingdoms had also been forbidden. Everything in Chwahirsland existed to service the army.

Jilo had no shoulder flashes or armbands. He had never changed out of his probationer's uniform, which Wan-Edhe had required him to wear to remind him of his place.

He ducked his head and sniffed at himself, wondering if he stank as badly as Wan-Edhe. He imagined the stale whiff of old sweat and unwashed laundry trailing after him, after his long toils in Wan-Edhe's chambers, but he also remembered what the barracks had smelled like on a normal day in the Shadowland.

Nobody was going to say anything.

He walked into the way station, and as he expected, the cowled women behind the counter only glanced at his uniform, then away. He moved to the counter. The women waiting to serve rotated in a practiced circle as they ladled boiled oats, boiled beans, and vinegar-dressed spinach onto a plate, then a girl handed him a regulation shallow-bowled wooden spoon wrapped in a napkin.

He took them without meeting anyone's eyes, of course; he did not want to alarm them. In Chwahirsland, meeting the eyes of a superior was rarely a good thing. But as he turned away, he glanced to the side. That snub-nosed girl reminded him of one of Clair's gang, only he caught a glimpse of a ruddy dark braid inside the cowl. The Mearsiean's short hair was light brown, streaked by the sunlight, because in Mearsies Heili, people only wore hats in winter, or for formal occasions.

Jilo found a table at the back and sat down.

The place was nearly empty. He'd caught either the early or the late portion of a service shift, which, he knew, ran counterpoint to the military watches by which the entire kingdom was governed. No one spoke, of course, as Wan-Edhe had strictly forbidden public chatter on pain of a hundred lashes. And he'd enforced it by having his spies also turn in anyone who didn't report infringements.

That had been a sore point between the brothers, Jilo recollected as he dug into the tasteless oats, always getting the worst over with first. Kwenz kept reminding Wan-Edhe that he hadn't enough guards in the Shadowland to have most of them in the lazaretto recovering from punishments, and whom would he put in the field if there were an emergency? Wan-Edhe had always said, *Force them to take duty anyway, and let 'em bleed. It enforces the necessity—the wisdom—of obedience. Idle talk is what leads to conspiracy. There should be no time for idle talk, as well as no place.*

Jilo set his spoon down, aware for the first time of scents, of the food, other people, dust. The small noises of wooden spoons clattering against clay bowls, the hissing shift of a foot, but what was that tiny sound, almost like rain against a window?

He knew better than to look directly. It took a moment or two to figure out what to do. He dropped his spoon, and in the process of retrieving it, got a sideways look at the four people sitting at the table on the other side of the room. They were all in uniform, of course: a grizzled oldster wearing the brown armband of a stable troop, and two youngish men, one wearing the shoulder flash of a horse troop and the other that of a squad leader in the infantry. The youngest, a boy Jilo's age, wore an unmarked gray-black uniform similar to Jilo's own. A trainee.

At first Jilo thought the older man had something wrong with him, the way one shoulder twitched, then the other. It took a second look as Jilo got up to get a biscuit from the bread basket and walked back to notice what was going on: finger taps on the table or one's arm, twitches, touches to chest. All quick, furtive. He would not have noticed if he hadn't been staring. It seemed to be some kind of sign language.

Jilo became aware of his empty plate. He'd eaten his food without noticing. He rose to get another biscuit, and this time took a sideways glance at the women. They stood still, waiting to serve, except for the one who came out from the kitchen with another tureen of oats. Before she turned away, one of the others brushed her sleeve, and the tureen woman rippled her fingers, then wiggled her forefinger three times. She turned away, and vanished back inside the kitchen.

He walked out, and took a long tour of the city, pretending to look at shops, but using the occasional reflective surface to see behind him. Twice he caught forefingers turned his way, making a tiny circle, as someone else turned an empty palm up. Question, and answer? They wanted to know if he was a spy.

Jilo wondered why he hadn't heard about this—why the Court of Rule wasn't lined up with people waiting for punishment. The people must know who the spies are, Jilo thought, and question became conviction when he walked along an armory street at the same time an otherwise undistinguishable man wearing a lowly green suppliers armband appeared. Only because he was watching did Jilo perceive heads dropping minutely, as if a chill wind had blown down the street; gazes dropped streetward, quick as the eye. Hands hung at sides, except when executing business; all words spoken had to do with orders given and received.

They knew who the spies were, and they had a secret language.

Joy suffused him as he walked back to the palace. They had a secret language! He spared a sympathetic thought for the Shadowland Chwahir, now surely absorbed into the massive army structure. He hoped that someone was teaching them the secret language.

Jilo examined his emotions as he trod toward the castle. Pride, and a sense of isolation. He had to do his part, and unravel Wan-Edhe's web of spells. His determination renewed, he turned his mind to reviewing the search he'd made so far. Outside, he could think more clearly. In fact, he could remember his painstaking search among the books, one by one, first to remove wards and traps. He could remember the shelves, even in large part what was on the shelves; yes, he must catalogue everything that was there.

He paused in the forecourt, frowning down at the stones. Wait. Why was it that he could recollect so clearly the archives, the old lists of wards, the elementary spells, but other places were a blur? He'd been over every part of the archive at least three times.

Hidden language, hidden things. We Chwahir hide things. What if Wan-Edhe had hidden his chief treasures where nobody but he could see them, much less touch them?

Oh, yes.

Wherever he had slid past without paying attention, that was where he must begin to search.

*Along the caravan route from Sartor to Mardgar Harbor*

Rel stood in a circle with the other caravan guards. From the uneasy sideways glances and the uncertain stances, he suspected that most were even more inexperienced than he was.

A scruffy woman faced them. She appeared to be somewhere between fifty and sixty. She was short, reminding Rel of a gnarled old apple tree toughened by years of hard weather. She said, "Now that it's just us, here's the truth. Fact is, I been running caravans for forty year, twenty as leader. Been no problems to speak of until lately, after the border opened. Don't mistake me. I'm glad Sartor is in the world again, but." She turned her head and made a spitting motion. "Instead of picking right up with their side o' the treaties, they send us nothing. And so our woods is filled with brigands. Came across 'em twice, now, in only four trips."

Rel knew he should keep silent, but he couldn't bear to have his friends maligned. He didn't want to cause trouble with his new boss, so he raised his hand.

She paused, and nodded curtly. "Something to say, Shorty?"

Some of the others chuckled, apparently never tired of the joke.

"Only that I just came from the Royal Guard at Eidervaen. Have to remember that the war for them was recent. Aren't enough of 'em left alive to defend the kingdom, much less patrol."

"Nobody's forgot when the war was for them." The woman grunted.

"But this is what I'm thinking. If they wouldn't hire the likes o' you, then they must indeed have moths in their purses."

The others chuckled louder, and a weedy fellow said, "It's true. I heard it over in Mandareos. They got no treasury. No hiring at all."

Rel didn't correct the misapprehension that he'd gone into Sartor to look for a job, as the woman said, "Well, that's a big problem, and they have my sympathy that side o' the border, yes they truly do, but the fact is, these here woods north o' us are mostly full o' former border riders who got shorted their pay when the guilds up and decided they weren't going to pay Sartor the old taxes. So here we are, with a lot of 'em lookin' to turn brigand, because it's easier to carry on doin' what you've always been doin' than to look for new work."

She paused, and when nobody argued, she said, "Now the truth is, most of 'em aren't much better than us. So far it's been, make some noise, look tough, and they ride off, looking for easier pickings. But one of these days we're going to come across something better run, and I tell you honest, I know pretty much everything there is to know about tending the horses—I was first a farrier—but as for leading a real defense, well, if any of you has some real training, speak right up."

And all heads turned expectantly toward Rel.

He suppressed a sigh, wondering what would happen if he claimed that his only training was in maintaining Colendi orchid conservatories. But the problem was a real one, and he was the biggest and tallest there. He suspected he would always be the biggest and tallest. So he said, "I did get a bit of training here and there. Can't say I know how to command." He didn't mind mentioning Khanerenth, but he hated mentioning Everon, as he still had regrets about turning down a Knighthood. And he knew he'd sound like he was swanking.

"But you're the biggest," the weedy fellow said doubtfully.

Another fellow, a stout redhead, said, "Leader has to see everything at once. Knows what to do."

Rel gave a nod at the redhead. "All I know is something about defending myself against whoever comes at me with sword or knife."

The woman said, "If you're willing to do point, that is, you take the front position in any squad, and make a lot of noise, and wave that sword of yours around—that's a nice blade, youngster, inherit it?—well, seems to me, that's the next best thing."

Rel did not offer any explanation for the sword that Atan had given him, just shrugged, and everyone accepted that as assent.

The leader said, "Good. Then here's how we'll divide up the watches . . ."

The caravan left at midday, under gentle drifting snow that slowly turned to sleet, then slushy rain, making everyone but the oxen miserable.

By week's end, they had descended far enough down the weather-pitted, neglected road to feel the thaw of spring, which made for somewhat cheerier campfires, at least for the hired guards. One of the two merchants, a young woman, was unrelievedly anxious about her barrels of winter flush Sartoran leaf. It wasn't the best leaf, but even the last winter pickings would bring a tremendous price in a world that had been deprived of steeped Sartoran leaf for a century. The other merchant was more cheery, a plump old bookseller serene with the conviction that few bandits ever showed any interest in books.

Oxen were slow, but their pace guaranteed little jiggling or smashing of contents. Spring storms flooded the ancient wheel ruts in the roads, left bare after three generations of raided flagstones while Sartor was beyond reach. Consequently it was nearly a month after they left the border when the caravan entered the rolling hills that, the caravan leader said cheerfully, meant that they'd soon be at the west branch of the Margren River.

"That means we've left the woods behind, and surely the brigands," the redhead stated, and the others nodded, as if saying it would make it true.

Rel had been placed either at the front or the rear, where he'd be seen by lurking scouts. From either position he had an unimpeded view ahead or behind; he was fairly certain that the caravan had been watched on at least three occasions, and he was definitely certain that a lone horseman was following them in spite of their crawling pace. The only thing he couldn't be sure of was the horseman's target.

When he pointed out the follower to the caravan leader over their meal of pan bread and fried fish, she shrugged. "One shadow, I don't worry about."

Nobody else seemed concerned.

The next night they reached their first market town. After all those weeks of camping (for few of the tiniest southern villages had inns above their taverns, after a century of no travel), it was most welcome.

The next day, two of the caravan guards went missing, but the rest set out without them, made confident by the sight of traffic on the road, and the thought that the Mardgar Harbor was only three days away.

They'd just settled the oxen for the night, and a good fire was going under a kettle of trail soup, when Rel, who had picket duty, noticed all the horses' ears twitching in the same direction.

Rel turned. All he could make out was a hillock topped with an ancient, overgrown hedgerow, marking some long-abandoned boundary. He'd learned that abandoned houses made great hideouts if they were isolated enough.

Drawing his sword, he yelled, "Alert—"

The word was lost in the thunder of hooves. From over the hedge in one direction and around the hill in the other galloped a gang of brigands, swords and knives upraised.

Rel had little practice fighting upward, but he'd learned one trick. Sheathing his sword again, he dashed to the wagon and snatched up one of the poles, snapped it free of ties, and spun it humming as he dashed between the first two riders. He ducked one's slashing sword, knocked the man out of the saddle, and clopped the second rider across the back of the head on the backswing.

He had enough time for a brief spurt of triumph. Grinning, he launched into the thick of the skirmish. For a short burst he was too busy staying alive to be aware of anything beyond a wailing cry; the wagon leader shouting, "Jem, get back here!"; the leaf merchant's hysterical shouts of "Help! Help!"; and the wheezing breathing of the book merchant from under one of the wagons.

We're losing, Rel thought, anger burning through him hot and bright. He'd take as many of them with him into death as he could—

Then the sounds changed, and he stumbled, fighting for breath, aware of a furious increase in the noise of battle from the other side of the shifting, lowing oxen. Rel slung the stinging sweat out of his eyes and pushed himself forward.

Brigands lay dead or wounded, except for a knot still furiously fighting, these all on foot. Rel launched himself at the fight, tossing away the pole and pulling his sword. He got in a kick and warded a blow, then his burly attacker gave a shocked, eye-bulging, mouth-open stare. Foamy blood dripped out of his mouth as he began to topple. He jerked as a sword was pulled from his back.

The burly man dropped dead at Rel's feet. Beyond him, Rel glimpsed a pale Chwahir face flicking a look his way. Shock froze him.

He knew that face. It was Prince Kessler Sonscarna.

The short, slim renegade prince fought with unnerving speed and brutality; with one accord the remaining brigands turned and ran. Kessler chased after the five of them for a few steps, blood-smeared sword raised, then slowed. He stooped, wiping his blade on the jacket of a dead brigand.

Rel caught up, heart beating painfully. "It was you following us?" He might as well get the worst over.

Kessler was breathing hard, his quiet voice husky with spent effort. "No." He reached with his free hand into a pocket of his black tunic, and with an ironic gesture, held up a transfer token. "Had you tailed. He sent for me when you were attacked." He jerked his chin at the brigands.

Rel glanced back. Those left of the caravan were just beginning to pick themselves up, exclaiming questions no one listened to, and checking themselves, the animals, the wagons.

"That was fun," Kessler said, looking up at Rel with that well-remembered flat stare, out of light blue eyes shaped unsettlingly like Atan's, evidence of a long-ago treaty marriage between a Landis and a Sonscarna. "Haven't had a good fight for too long."

Fun, Rel thought, sick with disgust as he glanced down at the dead scattered about in a rough circle around Kessler.

Kessler said, "You had fun, too." His smile was brief. Knowing.

Rel had scarcely exchanged a hundred words with Kessler since their disaster of a first meeting. Since then, instead of words, there'd been a near execution and two sword fights, both of which Rel had lost. Rel's shoulder still ached in cold weather from where Kessler had stabbed him moments before Atan lifted the Sartor enchantment.

He was going to deny having fun, but the vehemence of the urge unsettled him, and he remembered that moment of triumph. He was not going to admit it to Kessler. There could be no possible good result.

"I'd think you can fight any time you want to, in Norsunder," Rel said.

"Not the same," Kessler said, with a slight shrug. "You were seen by my scout in Eidervaen. I had him follow you until I could get the time to interview you. This attack forced things."

Rel's heartbeat thudded in his ears. The first time he'd met Kessler was right after Rel had turned down the Knights' invitation to join them, during his very first journey. He'd just met up with Puddlenose and Christoph on Everon's border when the three of them were jumped by Kessler's recruitment gang, and transferred to a hidden compound that Kessler had set up in some desert, where he was training assassins to take down all the major rulers of the world.

Kessler really hated kings.

Oh yes, and he also hated ugly people.

Rel always reminded himself of that when encountering venal authorities who had inherited positions of power, in case he caught himself ever thinking Kessler's plan the least bit sane.

"You had me followed," Rel said, reaching for the immediate, and the personal. "Are you recruiting again? If so, my answer is still no." Rel forced a shrug. "Sorry you had to go to so much trouble to save me, if you're going to haul me off and finish the execution that got interrupted the last time I turned you down."

Kessler's mouth twitched, and he continued in the same tone as before, as if they sat together over a tankard of ale instead of standing over the fast-cooling body of an unknown man. "I still do not understand what you could object to in ridding the world of corrupt rulers, leaving the way for a system based on skill and brains."

"Because," Rel said, "your plan began with assassination." He didn't mention the wholesale slaughter of ugly people; when he'd asked, during that first interview, "Who decides who is ugly enough to die?" Kessler had replied without a hint of doubt, "I do."

Kessler made that slight shrug again. "Do you think the likes of Wan-Edhe of the Chwahir would relinquish their thrones any other way?"

"Do what you want in Chwahirsland," Rel said. "But I don't believe Clair of the Mearsieans is evil," Rel said, then wished he hadn't brought her name up.

"When I investigated Clair of the Mearsieans, she appeared to be an ignorant brat, unable to rid herself of the senile Kwenz, or even that fool from Elchnudaebb. I underestimated her, as I underestimated her friends' sense of loyalty."

Rel didn't want to cause those girls to become targets any more than they might already be. He said, "Norsunder seems to be the place to recruit for assassination plans."

Kessler glanced sideways as the caravan leader began limping toward them, then shifted from Sartoran to Mearsiean, spoken with a heavy Chwahir accent. "Worse corruption and stupidity there than in the world. Everyone fighting one another for place. Siamis swanking around thinking he can conquer the world by cleverness. Even his uncle is giving up in disgust."

Good, Rel thought, but said nothing.

Kessler said, "The goal is the same, but the game has changed. Your friend King Berthold of Everon might not be corrupt, but his precious Knights are divided, one side ruled by stupidity and privilege, the other half merely obsolete in strategy and tactics. You know that. You saw it. Is that why you turned down their invitation to join the Knights of Dei?"

Rel said nothing. Somewhere behind, the caravan leader called, "Rel?"

Kessler glanced over his shoulder, then said, "Tell your friend King

Berthold that the danger is not from me, or even from Detlev, right now. Ask him if he remembers Henerek."

"You want me to warn him?" Rel asked.

Kessler's teeth showed in what might have been meant as a smile. "Do what you want. If Berthold is ready, Henerek won't succeed."

"Why are you telling me this?"

"Because I want Henerek to die trying." Kessler spun a transfer token into the air, caught it, muttered the spell, and vanished.

Sickened, Rel turned away. He remembered Henerek, a fellow Knight candidate, a bully and a braggart. If Kessler meant that Henerek had made his way to Norsunder, Rel was not surprised. The only question was why he would go to this trouble to give Rel the message to pass on. Rel would have expected that pettiness from Kessler's followers. Kessler's grudges had been reserved for kings.

Then it hit him: if the world was watching Everon, Kessler could attack somewhere else and take his target by surprise.

"Who's your friend?" the caravan leader asked, as she closed the distance. "He coming back?"

"He's not my friend," Rel said.

She grunted. "Friend or not, we could use him, if he does. He musta accounted for half these deaders. I'll give him an entire journey's pay for the next two days. You tell him that."

Suppressing the impulse to declare that he never wanted to see Kessler again, Rel stared at her. The sense of unreality was fast changing to urgency, and even dread. He had to spread the word. He had to . . . "Last night, did anyone say anything to you about the northern route, once we reach Mardgar?"

The caravan leader squinted up at him. She looked old in the flickering firelight. "I thought you was headin' east."

"Changed my mind," Rel said. "Going north first."

She grunted. "Just avoid Remalna, directly next Mardgar, but that's nothing new. Bad king there. Getting worse." She pointed at the burly man lying so still on the ground. "Help me lay out these deaders, so we can describe 'em exact for the Road Guild, or the local magistrate, whichever we find first. Then we'll Disappear 'em, nice and decent. Though I always wonder why we treat 'em decent in death when they didn't treat us decent in life."

## Chapter Six

*Winter, 4739 AF*
*Chwahirsland*

JILO shivered.

Was it really cold, or was it time to go out again? He leaned against a work table, looked around the dim room, and sniffed the stale air. What had Clair said when they were walking toward Senrid's city, talking about his castle up ahead? Something about how clerestory windows could let in light and air, but still leave a place defensible. Jilo looked, imagining windows. Oh, what a good idea.

He shivered again. Surely the air was cold, it wasn't just him. Either way, he had better get out again. He became aware of the familiar drag on bones, teeth, muscles. Breath. Thoughts.

One more search. He'd gotten adept at teasing out the traps and wards as he went over the empty hall finger-measure by finger-measure until he found a space midway down the gloomy, moldy stone hallway between the magic chambers and Wan-Edhe's quarters.

Jilo's heart lump-lumped in his chest. His head panged. He gripped the magic protection-layered token he'd hung around his neck in mimicry of Clair's medallions. He whispered the key words, then staggered back. When he peered into the weird space, he spied a book about as thick as his thumb, its size somewhat bigger than his hand. It seemed to be floating in a thick murk.

Cautiously he extended a finger, wary of yet another trap, though reason would say that having come this far he was safe. But you were never safe with Wan-Edhe—ever.

Closer . . . closer . . . he touched it gently, as if that would matter to magic. The book jolted from the murk and began to fall. He bent to catch it before it reached the stone, his head pounding from the sudden exertion.

It was definitely time to go out.

Clutching the book to him, he made his way down and down, the air colder with each turn in the stair, each door gone through. When he approached the last door, he slowed. From the other side of the iron-reinforced wood came the moan of high winds. The door guards stood inside, which meant winter.

Winter? Already?

But he needed to get out. He thrust the book inside his tunic and signed for the guards to open the door.

The icy wind nearly took him off his feet. He bent into it, each step a struggle, the cobblestones slippery under his feet. His socks squidged, and his toes itched and tingled. His body began trembling, but the headache actually diminished, though his nose and ears and lips were numbing painfully.

He wasn't going to make it to the street, not like this. He raised his head, and descried a sentry box, a gray silhouette barely visible against the outer wall. He fought his way there and stepped inside, surprising the watch gathered around a table. They exclaimed, words cut short as they recognized him.

"What's a neckin?" he asked.

The youngest froze, staring as if he'd been stabbed. The older ones shifted, gazes dropping or sidling.

Jilo said, "This is not for Wan-Edhe. It's for me. What is a neckin?"

The oldest said to the lintel of the door, "It's by way of being a trip to the wall. For two, you might say."

"Trip to the wall? I don't get it."

Jilo gazed in frustration as they tightened into rigidity. They were afraid. Somehow he'd ventured into punishment territory. But then with Wan-Edhe, everything was punishment territory. Whatever it meant, it seemed to have nothing to do with him, and so he said, "I need a place to sit." He pulled the book out of his tunic.

Nobody asked why he didn't find a place to sit in the vast fortress on the other side of the courtyard. Chwahir did not ask questions. Everyone except the two on duty faded through a narrow door on the other side of the sentry box, leading to the covered corridor to the guard station.

Jilo was left to himself. He sat down at the table on the side nearest the little stove, wherein burned a single firestick. He set the book before him, opened it, and stared in amazement.

The words were too uniform to be handwritten, which pointed to a magical cause. He had no idea what kind of spells produced words, other than the copy spells that book makers sometimes used, though it took as much magical exertion to make them as it did the exertions of a copyist. But magic didn't wear down pens or run out of ink.

This book, though, could not possibly be a copy, for its text was nothing more than a list: first a name, then the location of the person. No date.

Jilo scanned the names. Early on, nothing was familiar, except for Detlev of Ancient Sartor. Then there was Kwenz, farther down. Paging on, Jilo found more familiar names: Wan-Edhe's sons, nephews, then grandsons. Gradually the names became more familiar—and then his own name appeared, along with Clair's and CJ's. Paging back, Jilo discovered 'The Brat,' and wondered if that was Puddlenose.

Jilo flipped to the end, to find the pages blank. He paged back until he found text, and as he looked, words appeared at the end of a solid block of notations after Kessler's name: 'Norsunder Base.'

He stared, his nerves flashing hot and then very cold as he comprehended what he had in his hands. This book was a list of all Wan-Edhe's enemies, or people he wanted to track. And each time they transferred by magic to Destinations warded by Wan-Edhe over what must have been decades, their location appeared.

Jilo flipped back, scanning carefully. There was Siamis, mostly Norsunder Base, but many other places. That must have been when he enchanted the world.

Jilo turned back to Detlev's entry. His location was seldom mentioned, and nearly all of those were Norsunder Base. Not all the transfers linked up the way Siamis's did. So the book had some limitations. It never mentioned Norsunder-Beyond, only the Base. Even so? Wan-Edhe was going to want to retrieve it.

The sense of threat pressing down on Jilo intensified as he fumbled his way back inside the castle.

*Colend*

After six months of hard travel, which included visiting harbors along the Sartoran Sea in quest of Mendaen's father lost a century ago, Rel finally cut north into the vast Sartoran continent, which—if Halia, where Marloven Hess lay, was included—reached three quarters of the way around the southern hemisphere.

He rode down the single street bisecting the small market town of Wilderfeld in western Colend. Snow had been swept but ice lurked between the fitted stones in the frigid air.

Like in most places he'd been in Colend, the snow had been formed into neat white walls. Mounds were unsightly.

Rel hunched into his scarf as a cold blast of wind scoured straight off the frozen river alongside the town. Beneath his legs, he felt the horse bunch its muscles as he himself leaned into the wind.

The street abruptly widened into the town square, which was empty of people, snow blankets covering the plots that would be gardens in spring. He expelled a cloudy breath in relief when he found what he had been looking for: a rambling two-story building. Judging by the different patterns to the stones, the lighter growth of ivy up the walls, and the sizes of the windows, it had been added onto at least twice. The sign hanging from the awning over the long porch stated in the flowing Colendi script:

*Wilderfeld Scribes and Messengers*

Puddlenose of the Mearsieans had taught Rel many of his traveler's tricks when Rel began his wanders, such as to always seek out the scribe guild when reaching a new town. Young and friendly scribe students were usually willing to recommend places to go (and places to avoid) to someone their age. In fact, Puddlenose had scribe friends here in Wilderfeld, whom he had introduced to Rel the last time they traveled together. The Colendi scribes Thad and Karhin Keperi were always a valuable source of information, and Karhin in particular seemed to have correspondence friends in every city on the continent.

Rel clicked his tongue, though the horse needed no encouragement to lift its head and pick up the pace, as it smelled a stable. A short time later, Rel stamped his boots at the back door porch, and then walked inside to a rare sight: near emptiness.

The rest of the year the shop was crowded with custom, lines at each of the slanted desks where scribes wrote messages for people, couriers coming and going. Rel stepped inside the long main room, noted the duty scribes—mostly adults, none of the young ones familiar—then took the officially stamped greenweave wallet from his pack and handed it to the duty apprentice scribe who sat at the courier desk, writing in beautiful script.

"This is to go to Alsais," Rel said. "I'm heading northwest."

"You're the first in several days," she said, laying her pen carefully on its holder. "Where from?"

"Lisdan, in Melire," Rel said.

The scribe's thin face brightened. "Oh! My cousin Albet is at Lisdan. Did you see him?"

Rel shook his head. "Not on duty when I was through there, but everyone seemed cheerful. There was a smell of cinnamon buns in the shop that day." Puddlenose, who had initiated Rel into the mysteries of getting bonded as a courier (which basically meant being paid to travel where you were going anyway) had told Rel that scribes liked to hear bits of detail that most people would shrug off.

Sure enough, she thanked him, and when he said, "Is Thad or Karhin about?" she didn't apologetically tell him the siblings were off-duty, which was the Colendi way of brushing one off. She said, "I can send the duty page to see, if you wish?"

Rel thanked her, and waited as the scribe tapped a tiny bell. A short time later, he was ushered into a plain room, where Thad and Karhin both sat on cushions before a low table, finishing their midday meal. Tall, weedy, with bright red hair, they rose and put their hands together and then outward in the graceful Colendi greeting called 'the peace.'

Karhin was the first to smile with recognition. "Puddlenose's friend, I believe? Rel?"

"Yes. The year before the Siamis enchantment you helped me become bonded as a courier for Colend, and I've been grateful ever since."

Colend was so important all across the Sartoran subcontinent that the Universal Language Spell was kept up to date on Colendi idiom more than any other language in the world, except Sartoran. But mere translation did not guard against cultural pitfalls, such as avoiding questions that might require a negative, and other Colendi peculiarities.

When they had gone through the politenesses of Colendi greetings, Thad and Karhin offering food and asking about his journey, and Rel thanking them and replying suitably, Rel brought out the first of his carefully planned requests, worded so that a Colendi could avoid a negative.

"There are two subjects on which I hoped to ask your advice. First . . ." He brought out Mendaen's information. As soon as he said, "Sartoran boy from the old days. Can you tell me where I'd go to begin my quest?" Karhin flicked her fingers outward like a flower opening, a gesture of pleasure, as she exclaimed, "Oh, please, would you honor me with this precious investigation?"

Rel said, "I did not want to burden you with it, only to ask advice—"

Thad grinned. "You must see, it's the very type of task some of our friends like the most. Old Sartor, you know!"

By 'Old Sartor,' Rel knew that they meant Sartor of a century previous, as opposed to Ancient Sartor.

Karhin added, "This is *exactly* the kind of project to gain a scribe student great credit." She bowed over her pressed palms. "Thank you for entrusting it to me."

Rel thanked her on Mendaen's behalf, then said, "There is a second thing. I've been thinking for weeks how to describe it, and maybe it is not possible. I hope you can advise me . . ."

He really had been thinking about it for weeks. The sense of urgency after that encounter with Kessler had driven him to race northward, but as the days slid by while he was first stuck on a boat riding out a series of storms, then at a border that was closed because of trouble, he'd had time to think about the alliance.

He shrugged off CJ's rants about adults. Her reasoning might be faulty, but he believed that the idea of underage rulers uniting to form their own circle of communication was exactly what Atan needed. Especially if he, or any of them, ended up with what might be crucial news like what Kessler had told him about Henerek and a possible invasion, information that they might not be able to get past governmental watchdogs to deliver.

Rel imagined trying to tell Atan's high council about Kessler's warning earlier in spring. It didn't take much imagination to predict the way he'd be ushered right back out again on a wave of polite skepticism. After all, he couldn't prove the truth of anything the renegade prince had said, and he knew what they would say about Kessler as a reliable informant.

Rel described the theory behind the alliance to Karhin and Thad. ". . . so my thought is, if I, or any of my friends, stumble on information that might be important to know, there ought to be a way for us to spread it without having to go before nobles, councils, and others who might see fit to block information before a young ruler gets it and can decide what to do. For example, you might remember a few years ago, Wan-Edhe of the Chwahir tried to invade Colend." Rel lifted his hand northward. "Using magic as well as marching his army over the middle pass. And when the mages united against him, he took a couple of hostages to cover his retreat."

Thad tapped his palms together in the peace, trying to hide his excitement at the idea of being a part of such an alliance.

Rel eyed him uncertainly. He'd learned that the Colendi peace gesture could mean many things, from *Hello and welcome* to *Don't mind my interruption* (or, more bluntly, *We know that*), to *Quiet down, mannerless lout.*

"Puddlenose has told us a little about that story," Thad said, hoping for more—though he could see in his sister's careful politeness that she was uneasy.

Rel eyed her. He rarely talked about his own part in that ugly business, which had happened right before Kessler's recruiting gang had come along. He suspected that the Keperis probably knew the general history, but not that he'd disguised himself as a Chwahir flatfoot in a desperate attempt to rescue the hostages, both of whom were friends.

Rel had to be careful, because it all began with Puddlenose's futile attempt to warn the Colendi king about the invading Chwahir. It had occurred right after Puddlenose made his final escape from Wan-Edhe, knowing that the army was on the march to invade Colend. Yet King Carlael had ignored him with royal and serene loftiness.

Rel knew that no Colendi liked outsiders referring to their king as mad.

Thad raised a hand. "Would your example perhaps relate to Puddlenose's idea of a scribe circle?"

Karhin said helpfully, "Some of whose members are young monarchs who might like to correspond on subjects of mutual interest."

Rel let out a long sigh of relief. "Then he's already talked to you! Ha, it figures. And here I've spent the past several weeks thinking about how to approach the idea."

Karhin said more seriously, "Puddlenose described it as a message relay, saying that he never can keep hold of a notecase. He told us on his last visit he's lost three, and had two stolen. He wanted a way to send us news from any scribe desk if he thought it might be important, and for us to send it on. We can always relay messages without charge, as practice, for us, but when you say 'the relay of information,' that suggests a different purpose."

Rel bent his head, peripherally aware of the rising wind howling outside. "I'm seeing something entirely new. It might not be possible. It might not be useful." He hesitated to mention Atan.

Instead, he recounted his recent journey as a caravan guard, and Kessler's warning about Henerek's impending attack on Everon. "So you see," he finished, "I believe the threat is real. But I can't predict this attack with any certainty. Yet I feel I ought to warn anyone who'll listen, especially at high levels."

He'd come this far, why not tell it all?

"The new king of Erdrael Danara, who is no older than you—" He nodded at Thad. "Was one of those hostages during the abortive Chwahir invasion. He's become a friend, and that's where I'm headed next. I believe he'd welcome such an alliance. And I also plan to ask the princess and prince in Everon."

He couldn't tell if he was making sense or merely sounding pompous. But he had to try, because of Atan's frustration, her sense of being caged by her high council.

There was another quagmire, too. He wouldn't betray Atan's ambivalence about Colend, though on the surface the two kingdoms were firm allies. However, Atan had told him that Sartoran courtiers had begun removing the Colendi lace from their court clothes. Until he'd spent time with Atan, he had been completely oblivious to how galling it was to the Sartorans to have lost the yearly Music Festival to Colend, not only for the sake of music, but because that festival served as the center of cultural exchange for most of the continent, and even farther out.

Thad listened with abating interest. Instead of suggesting a relay crossing countries with news, Rel seemed to want letter writers. It would be a lot of extra work obtaining the expensive paper, and inks, appropriate to royalty, and composing in formal scribe mode for an idea that probably wouldn't last out the winter. Kings writing to kings, relaying through the scribe desk of a tiny outpost such as Wilderfeld? Unlikely! Kings were surrounded by senior scribes, with elite, magic-protected scribe circles.

As Thad's interest waned, Karhin's intensified. She was passionate about being a scribe, and had not only read twice as much scribe history as her brother, she enjoyed voluminous correspondence with scribe students all over, including two new ones, girls from Old Sartor who wanted to catch up with world news, and who'd passed along interesting tidbits of information about the friendship between their young queen and the mysterious Rel the Traveler.

"I'd be happy to relay letters, as part of my service time," Karhin said when Rel finished. "I'll register a sigil with the scribe mage at once, before you depart on your next journey. Please carry it to any of your contacts that you wish."

At last, a success! Even if a small one. Gratefully, Rel began to thank them, but was interrupted by the chimes ringing downstairs.

"Time for tutoring," Thad said apologetically.

Rel thanked them again, and went downstairs to catch a meal at the courier annex, leaving the brother and sister alone.

"You really think we can run a scribe circle for royalty?" Thad asked Karhin as they assembled their study tools. "King of Erdrael Danara—the Queen of Sartor—the royal children in Everon!"

"It's not just royalty," Karhin said. "Rel would be part. And other travelers like him, such as Puddlenose."

"He's cousin to a queen," Thad said.

"But he doesn't tell everyone. His friends are all over, every rank." She indicated them both. "Ah-ye! The question of royal correspondents aside," Karhin said practically, though inside she was thrilled at the idea of being central to so much royal correspondence, "from what Rel describes, it seems they want not just a circle, but a back door scribe-net. Only instead of some senior scribe or noble at the center, *we* shall preside. Think what it would do for our future positions, once we're given permission to reveal it!"

"For you," Thad said, laughing. "You know I haven't any ambition. And this sounds like a lot of work of the sort I like least. Especially if it has to be written out in formal mode, for all those royal eyes."

"I'll handle that part," she promised.

Thad studied the signs of secret pleasure in the quirk of her eyes, the little smile, and comprehended that she truly relished this extra work, if he didn't quite perceive why. Thad was a scribe because it was the family business. He didn't have the passion for the world of paper and words that Karhin had. He was far more interested in people. He only went along because of the prospect of interesting visitors coming by to leave messages.

As they started out of the room, pen cases tucked under their arms, he stretched out a hand to halt Karhin. "There's Puddlenose's request," he said at last.

Karhin's gaze shifted away. Thad recognized in her averted gaze the discomfort he felt: looming unspoken between them was Prince Shontande, heir to Colend, who Puddlenose thought might like being invited into the alliance because he was young.

Their stepmother, before she joined the family, had been a scribe at the royal palace. Of course she said nothing about the personal lives of the king and prince. That oath was drilled into scribes as they practiced their first letters.

But Thad and Karhin were both good at discerning the shapes of silences, and intensely interested in the young prince, who was so rarely seen. They'd gained an impression of a very lonely boy sequestered in his exquisite palace at Skya Lake for most of the year.

The question no one ever asked out loud, but everyone thought, was: is he also mad?

Karhin said, "There are no scribe students at Skya. I asked."

For her, that was clearly the end of it.

Thad lifted his hand. "Leave that part to me." This mystery was the sort of challenge he liked best.

Karhin duly registered the new sigil, gave it to Rel to pass along, and wrote to the contacts whose sigils he had furnished.

*Spring, 4739 AF*
*Marloven Hess*

Senrid seldom remembered to check his golden notecase.

He couldn't imagine writing letters to anyone. And it wasn't as if he didn't have plenty of things to do.

Now that winter was over, the castle staff was cleaning and airing out rooms. As the snows melted in Marloven Hess, they began to fall up north in Bereth Ferian, and Liere came as usual to visit Senrid. She was there when one of the stewards discovered underneath piles of old winter armor some trunks that Senrid's barely-remembered mother had brought from her own land. They turned out to be full of carved and painted toy houses.

Liere was so delighted that Senrid gave orders for the trunks to be brought to his study. The pieces now sat all over the floor, along with the plain wooden blocks that Senrid and his cousin had made castles with when very small.

Liere crouched over the beautifully carved toys, marveling over the detail, round Iascan houses (the doors never face west!), steep-roofed Telyer houses, farms and cottages and even one castle.

She moved them about in cozy patterns, built around squares and circles. She didn't want her town to look like South End, laid out in a strict grid. How did villages and towns and cities grow, anyway? When was a town a city? Well, that might be just a matter of names. The Mearsiean girls called their capital on its mountain a city, but Liere had discovered it was smaller than South End, which was a town.

She sat back, hugging her bony knees against her chest as she wondered how towns began, and if people first chose each other as neighbors before they began building.

If only she weren't so ignorant! She glared at the little town she'd built, wishing she were smart. It had been fun until her mind filled with all these questions. If she could make up answers for herself, it stayed fun, but she knew the real world surrounded her little play town, and in the real world people called her Sartora, as if she knew all the answers to their questions.

Senrid found her sitting there beside the play city, rocking back and forth on the floor, thumbs digging at her cuticles, her skinny arms wrapped tightly round her legs and her chin grinding on her kneecaps. "Liere?"

"Maybe reading every book on the shelves is the wrong way to go at it. Maybe I should start with something like a history of towns," she said. "How they grow."

Senrid sighed, knowing that her anxious mood had to be related to 'Sartora' again.

"I don't think there is such a book." He dropped cross-legged to the floor opposite her. "Except maybe in a general history. Or local histories of a specific place. Towns generally grow beside rivers, or at crossroads, I know that much. Then there are walled towns, like in my country. Here, let me turn this into a Marloven town. I'll show you how we defend them. Did you know that in the old days, the women and girls handled defense while the men roamed around on patrol?"

She watched his quick hands moving the pieces around. She had so little interest in defense that she let his words stream past. Instead, she watched his deft fingers below his wrists with the rope scars. He didn't wear knives strapped to his forearms when he played with her, so she could see the scars, and his strong forearms, below the sleeves he rolled to his elbows. It was interesting, how differently he saw things. He was defending the town, and he didn't even know the families she had imagined in the houses.

He looked up, and recognized her distant gaze. He let out his breath, and clapped his hands to his knees. "You don't want to hear about town defenses."

She blinked, and ground her chin harder on her knee. She knew Senrid would scoff about the Sartora worries. He already had. Not to be mean. It was just that he didn't seem to care what people expected of him, or thought about him. No, she knew that was not quite right. He did care, but he was able to do things. She didn't even know where to start.

How about with what she was most scared of, then. "I want to learn about *me* defenses. If Siamis comes back, and takes away the sword, everybody will want me to defend them, but he's sure to kill me with it first," she said.

"That, we can fix." Senrid grinned. "Why didn't we think of sword fighting lessons before? I need 'em, too. I'm terrible at it, because Keriam didn't dare teach me when my uncle forbade it. Too easy to catch us out, because it's noisy. Contact fighting is quieter."

Liere let out a slow breath. "But I don't have any strength."

"Same as anything, you start simple and build it up. Come on. Let's go get the practice blades for the pups, the ten-year-olds in the academy. They don't arrive until next week, so we have the place to ourselves."

Something new to learn! Liere followed him. Before long they stood in an empty room, wooden swords in hand. Senrid said, "I'll show you the basics. We won't even put on padding. If you take to it, I'll get you proper lessons."

Liere knew by the way he looked upward he was counting the things he needed to be doing, and she thought sadly that it was time to return to Bereth Ferian. Senrid was getting behind in his real duties, and she was terrified of becoming a burden.

Senrid was so busy, and yet he always made time for her. Guilt squeezed all the joy away, because she was sure if she listened on the mental plane, the first thoughts she'd hear would be people annoyed because Senrid was spending time with her that he should be spending on them.

"Liere?"

"I'm ready."

"Here's the stance . . ." When she got that, he demonstrated the four basic blocks for a foot warrior against another on foot.

She picked it up quickly, laughing with him as they slashed the wooden swords through the air. Already her hand stung a little, and her arms tingled.

Then it came time to try the first block. "I'll stab, and you block. Slow at first. Very slow. Then we'll try it a little faster."

Slow was fine. She knew what to do, but the first real strike sent a sting of pain from her hand to her shoulder.

She dropped the sword and wrung her hand.

"Maybe gloves, until you build up some calluses," Senrid said. "I'm sorry."

Liere shrugged. "I asked you to show me." As she stooped to pick up the wooden sword that was used by boys two years younger than she was, she knew she didn't want to learn to fight. She didn't believe that even with practice she'd be any good against a grown man unless she released the Child Spell and grew up.

With that came a memory that always tightened her stomach with horror: she was nine, listening idly to her mother in the mental realm when another woman said, *She's plain as mud now, but you wait. She'll one day be a beauty, and you'll make a fine marriage for her.*

Liere rubbed her hand up and down her skinny leg, loathing the thought of people staring at her.

She jumped when Senrid tugged the sword from her fingers. "Maybe we should stop before you get blisters. They hurt."

"It'll take forever to learn," she breathed.

He had become adept at keeping his mental shield in place, but it didn't take Dena Yeresbeth to hear the fear in her whisper.

"If you don't want to fight, then you learn to hide," he said. "Siamis can't carve you up if he can't find you. So, let's talk about hiding places. I know. Let's play hide-and-find. My cousin Ndand and I used to play it a lot, when my uncle thought we were with the tutors, before he started putting spells on her."

That was a game she'd begun to be good at, thanks to the Mearsiean girls. She grinned. "I'd love that!"

*Everon*

The alliance was spreading slowly, but not all its members defined it the same way. Rel and Puddlenose were the first to realize this, as in

Ferdrian, Everon's capital, the people gathered for a royal exhibition on the royal parade ground.

Trumpets played a sweet fall of notes.

"Wheel left!"

Rel leaned in the saddle, aware of the immediate response from his borrowed mount, aware of his old friends Enthold and Seiran at his left and right, Seiran, his own age, having been a Knight candidate when Rel found himself invited into the elite cadre of military protectors of Everon. He caught her eye. She flashed him the briefest grin, then faced forward, her ornamental lance couched at the correct angle. Rel belatedly adjusted his.

Except for the lance, which he'd drilled with perhaps three times before he turned down the offer to join the Knights, everything else came back as if he'd drilled two weeks ago, and not two years.

It was a brilliant day in early spring, and Rel had enjoyed the journey once he discovered Puddlenose in Erdrael Danara. The two crossed the strait then rode to Everon together, straight to the royal palace in Ferdrian.

Rel knew that in Everon, he would get a hearing. Sure enough, the king listened seriously to Rel's warning, and Commander Roderic Dei invited Rel to participate in the exhibition.

It was good to feel the spring sun strengthening each day, good to be listened to, good to be with friends. And it was good to ride with the Knights again.

Exhilaration flooded through him as the trumpet raced up two chords, and the captain bawled, "Wheel right!"

As the command echoed from company to company, horses and riders wheeled with thrilling precision. Rel gloried in being part of a mighty whole moving as one. The fresh cheers from the sidelines made it clear that Ferdrian's citizenry found the sight just as impressive.

The brisk spring air flirted with ribboned horse manes and tails, and tossed the bright pennants on the pavilions lined along both sides of the grassy sward. This parade ground, generally reserved exclusively for the Knights of Dei, was today open to all, tables of tasty things having been provided by the royal kitchens and the two most popular inns.

The high mood carried Rel through the end of the exercise, and accompanied him to the king's pavilion, where he'd been invited to join the royal party and their guests.

As Rel stepped up onto the platform, ducking under the wind-tossed canvas awnings, he heard Prince Glenn say fiercely, "Let Norsunder come. In fact, I hope they do."

Like a pinched candle, Rel's good mood was snuffed out.

Glenn's sallow, sullen face eased when he saw Rel. He straightened up from his slouch and waved Rel to a seat beside Puddlenose. "Isn't that so, Rel? If Norsunder comes, we'll *thrash* them."

Rel lowered himself onto the cushioned bench next to Puddlenose, who had stretched out his legs and was studying his bare, sun-browned toes. Rel took the time to sort his words, shutting out distractions—the rising wind, the changing light promising rain, the fact that this bench was lower than that of the princess and prince—and finally said slowly, "One thing I learned here is that the Knights are all still new."

Glenn flushed. "It's not our fault we were enchanted—"

Puddlenose's gaze flickered, but he didn't stir, and Rel wondered if he was thinking back to those strange days when evil seemed to shadow them at every turn. Wan-Edhe—Kessler—Norsunder. Only in retrospect was it obvious how many of the things that had befallen them were linked. The only exception being Detlev's experiment with forcing Everon into the same weird enchantment Sartor had been in, placing them beyond space and time. No one knew why he did anything he did—what he had planned to do with enchanted Everon, had not the experiment failed when the magical dyr thing fell into the wrong hands.

Queen Mersedes Carinna leaned over to touch her son on the shoulder. "Glenn. This same observation was put to us by Roderic this very day. It is no cavil, merely observation. Experience will come. It is the way of things. I'd as lief it comes later."

Glenn sent an impatient scowl up past his shoulder at his mother on her throne next to the king, and then at grizzled Roderic Dei, commander of the Knights, who stood at the king's right, where he could signal the trumpeter.

Roderic said, "The queen speaks true."

Glenn's scowl altered to brooding puzzlement, then he swung back to Rel. "Just so you understand. We're not cowards."

"Opposite," Rel said. "I know Harn and Seiran, there in Company Ten. Can think of few braver. And everyone respects Lord Valenn." He pointed with his chin at tall, dark-haired Erhold Valenn of Valenn, who as a newly inherited duchas, was first in rank among the Knights, and usually won firsts in all the competitions. "But each of them will tell you themselves they have yet to face battle."

Glenn chewed his underlip, then glanced warily back at Rel. "And you have?"

"Not war. Brigands only. I hope to keep it that way as long as I can."

Glenn leaned forward, about to protest, but was stayed by his father leaning down to rest his hand on Glenn's shoulder. "No one doubts your courage, my boy," the wine-flushed king said genially. He nodded at the field, his craggy face looking younger as he grinned at someone among the riders lining up for the mock battle.

Glenn crossed his arms, his mouth going from sulky justification to tightly controlled disgust when a curly-haired knight grinned back at the king, the pure white feather on her helm indicating a captain.

Rel guessed that this merry captain was probably the king's newest lover, or the latest one in his favor. He never quarreled with the old ones, Rel had learned (hearing far more than he wanted to about the royals' complicated lives from his friends among the Knights). The king was privately known as 'the butterfly lover.' A light touch, a flutter, and he was gone.

Unlike the queen's lovers, who all seemed to stay in love with her, though none so devoted as Roderic Dei, captain of the Knights.

The queen lifted her hand to the captain, who saluted her respectfully back, hand to helm. Then the trumpet played the charge.

Not hiding his disgust at the secret signaling, Glenn sat back with a snort. "I hope they can beat Norsunder," he muttered under his breath. "If only they'd listen to Valenn! Mama would have done better to . . ."

He shut his mouth, but Puddlenose and Rel had both heard Glenn on this subject: the Knights were an elite group not many generations old, elite in name as well as prowess, their command granted to the Dei family. The Knights had been confined to well-born males who passed stringent tests, until Mersedes Carinna, wearing male guise, had applied, made her way into the Knights, and into the king's heart. As queen, her first proclamation had been to open the Knights to women. And now there were plenty of women among them.

Glenn respected his mother as a person, but he resented her influence. It was bad enough that princesses ranked over princes in all countries influenced by Sartor, just because a million years ago, apparently Ancient Sartor only had queens. He thought that some things should belong to men, like warfare, because they were stronger than women. He was sure the women weakened the Knights. After all, they were smaller, and never as strong as the Duchas of Valenn or even Uncle Roderic.

Princess Hatahra, a year younger than her brother, and perhaps even more unprepossessingly narrow-faced and sallow, turned a scowl her brother's way. Under cover of the adults discussing the complicated maneuver being executed on the grounds below them, she muttered, "Seiran is the second best archer. And the first best is Captain Alstha." She pointed at the white-feathered captain. Both women were common in birth.

Glenn crossed his arms. "Having royal favorites never is good for discipline," he muttered back.

Tahra glanced skyward, sighed, then said, "True. But Uncle Roderic is fair."

Whenever Princess Hatahra spoke, she was listened to: she was, all knew, the royal child who had broken herself free of Norsunder's evil spell all on her own. Her parents, the nobles, Roderic Dei—everybody in Everon respected her for that. They respected the fact that when the evil Siamis and Detlev ranged over the world searching for Liere, it was Princess Tahra they came to first. Even though she did not have Dena Yeresbeth, she was respected as if she did have special mind powers, and she was the one spoken of most often as the possible royal heir.

Tahra, aware of that respectful silence, sat back, and shut up.

She would never tell anyone the real reason she'd broken the spell was through happenstance, just because she hated to be touched. Strong emotion broke the illusion, that much she'd learned in her magic studies since. And illusions were like spider webs—if you broke one, the entire web of illusions tore. It had been the flimsiest of enchantments. Norsunder kept trying to find ways to control minds, she had learned, but all they could do was distract or fool people with these various experiments—Detlev's, Siamis's. All of them broken in the end. Worthless.

She smiled grimly.

Glenn said to Puddlenose, "I really wish you'd join the Knights, even if Rel won't. I've seen you in the practice field. I know you can handle that sword."

"Only if someone threatens to air my innards," Puddlenose said, patting his stomach. "And itch-feet don't make good knights."

"You'd have to change your name, of course," Glenn said louder, aware of the adults listening. "But you should anyway. Pick something honorable, and when you make your oath, you'll no longer be mistaken for a vagabond."

"I like my name." Puddlenose reached into the basket of fresh apricot tarts. "I'm the only one in the world who has it. What could be a finer distinction than that? Even kings can't claim such exclusivity!"

The Queen of Everon chuckled, glancing covertly at her son, whose behavior increasingly worried her. "There is no finer, ha ha!"

Queen Mersedes Carinna was probably the plainest woman there, except when she smiled or laughed, which she did often. That laugh, a gusting waterfall of sound, seemed to come up from her toes, curving her thin lips, turning her close-set eyes into crescents of mirth, and flushing her sallow skin that had been privately sneered at by Colendi visitors as surely inherited from some Chwahir ancestor.

King Berthold also laughed, though only because his wife did. He kept to himself his conviction that it was irresponsible for a prince to shrug off inherited duty, but Puddlenose had aided his children when he himself was under enchantment, and so Puddlenose would always have a welcome in Everon.

The laughter ended when Tahra muttered, "I hate war." She sent a wary, accusing glance Rel's way, as if he'd been encouraging her brother.

The adults were quiet again, considering her words for extra significance.

Puddlenose said, "We all do, Tahra. At least, anyone sane does. Me, when someone wants to throw a war, I do my best to be two kingdoms away, snoring in bed. And if the eleveners come galloping out of one of their black rifts, I'd like to be a continent away."

Everybody laughed, of course. Rel laughed as well, but as he glanced from Puddlenose to the queen, who slapped her thigh and stamped one foot, repeating, "Snoring in bed! Or doing something in bed!" Rel reflected that she wasn't the only one whose entire identity seemed to be bound up in laughter.

But Puddlenose could be serious. Rel had seen him so. Once. Deathly serious, with the deliberate intent to kill. So unfamiliar had been that familiar face that Rel would have walked right past him, had he not recognized the ragged, blood-stained prison clothes he'd been looking at for weeks, and smelled the prison stench: the moment they'd been freed from the prison in Kessler's assassin camp, Puddlenose had headed out, weak as he was, his purpose to kill Prince Kessler's chief lieutenant, who'd renamed himself Alsais, after the capital of Colend. Alsais's penchant for petty cruelty had escalated to torture and murder among the prisoners. Puddlenose could not have survived a fight. He'd had barely enough strength to throw a knife. Which he'd done.

They'd never spoken about that day since. Rel wondered from time to time if Puddlenose remembered it.

Puddlenose's lazy gaze flicked his way, then back again, his smile fading. "Rel?"

Puddlenose was also unsettlingly quick at times.

Rel said, "*Two* continents away."

Tahra lifted her chin. "Perhaps we should invite Sartora here. She might know how to use that dyr thing to protect kingdoms."

"Or she could teach you," the king began.

"Dyr!" The queen turned her head and spat. "Any such magic smacks of Detlev. He made those things, everybody says. Even if that thing served us once, I am certain it was inadvertent. As far as I'm concerned, 'dyr' is another word for 'damnation.'"

Glenn grimaced. "I wish Mother wouldn't spit," he said beneath his breath.

Whether the king heard or not, he clapped his son on the shoulder, and brushed his fingers over the top of Tahra's head, his touch brief and light. Even so, she stiffened.

The king gestured toward the field. "Come, my dears. Enjoy the last of the exhibition! Tomorrow they begin hard training." His smile turned Rel's and Puddlenose's way. "Thanks to our friends, who brought us warning. When Norsunder comes, we shall be waiting."

The next morning, Rel woke early out of habit, aware that he'd heard something. As he pulled on clothes, he identified the sound: a closing door.

He moved to the window and looked through the colonnaded archways into the secluded garden between the guest wing and the residence of the old, rambling royal palace. There was Puddlenose, ten steps from the huge gate that would let him into the big formal garden at the front of the palace.

Rel knew instantly that Puddlenose was heading quietly for the road.

Even kings you've done a good turn for do not like abrupt departures, and so Rel got up and dressed, sought out the royal family, and made farewells for the both of them in proper form.

Mid-morning, Rel caught up with Puddlenose on a bend in the Royal Highway. Puddlenose gave Rel a lopsided smile. There were a lot of things that Rel could have said, but he confined himself to, "Glenn wouldn't let it go, eh?"

Puddlenose heaved a sigh. "Sometimes I think the enchantment is still on him." He kicked at some weeds tufting along the roadside. "Christoph won't come here anymore. Signed on for a cruise with Captain Heraford."

Rel gave a nod. He'd been wondering where Puddlenose's usual traveling companion had gone off to.

Puddlenose bent to pick up a pebble, and shied it along the newly smoothed road, then he sniffed the air. "Ah. Beyond that hill ahead, isn't there a village with a good bakery?"

Puddlenose's method for dealing with problematical people and situations was to walk away from them. They'd told the royal children about the alliance, and they had passed Kessler's warning to King Berthold. Both had witnessed how Everon's court almost welcomed the prospect of a fight. Prince Glenn definitely did.

Maybe that was what you had to do to prepare for what was coming anyway.

But if you weren't a king, and you hated war, sometimes the only thing you could do was walk away.

## Chapter Seven

*Winter-spring, 4740 AF*
*Sartor*

AS the previous year waned into winter, everyone in the alliance was busy.

When so much is happening, record keepers usually begin with Sartor, then spiral outward.

Directly after the festivities of New Year's Week, one of Sartor's mages tasked with monitoring their young queen for her own safety discovered Atan's hoard of transfer tokens, and promptly reported it to the head of the guild, who discussed it with her senior mages before reporting it to the high council. They then waited for her next magic study hour, and sure enough, she was gone, transfer residue left behind in the air for those trained to perceive it.

Naturally the outlander Hibern was blamed.

Atan, at her next session with the high council, was presented with a unanimous recommendation: "We, as your counselors, feel it is best that you limit your magic study hour with the outland student to once a month."

In other words, *we know you have been going outside our borders unguarded.*

Chief Veltos looked into that shocked young face, and added with an attempt at kindness, "But if you wish to study the specifics of Sartoran magic, I can find a volunteer among our students. Or I will take time aside from my own tasks to tutor you myself, your majesty."

*Your majesty.* What a horrid irony. There was nothing majestic about being controlled like an erring child. Atan flushed, and spoke without considering: "I thank you, but I believe I have too many state matters to learn."

"Ah, an astute observation," exclaimed the Duchas of Ryadas, with a deep curtsey.

"I shall see to it that you are provided with tutoring in Star Chamber procedure," the chief of the heralds said, bowing.

"But I do not wish to lay aside my magic studies," Atan said quickly. "And Hibern teaches me what the senior students in the north learn, which no one here knows."

All faces turned to Chief Veltos, who had to admit the truth of that. What Veltos didn't acknowledge publicly was that she meant to change that. She saw the stubborn jut of Atan's chin, and said in her most soothing tones that once a month with Hibern would permit her to continue her studies, but the rest of the month that hour would benefit the kingdom as well as the queen if it went to tutoring in state matters. Oh, that inescapable moral superiority!

Atan managed to accept that, though her throat hurt.

All winter, she and Hibern had faithfully restricted themselves to Bereth Ferian's history and magical practice, which Atan duly reported on to Chief Veltos, in hopes of proving that the monthly hour was not wasted.

Hibern had also spent the winter with a changed schedule. Erai-Yanya vanished on some quest that she was not yet ready to talk about. Hibern spent the winter alone in the strange, cracked building kept warm by magic bindings, except for two days a week when she transferred to Bereth Ferian for her northern school classes, after which she had study time with Arthur. There were also weekly visits with Senrid.

She tried not to be lonely, or to brood about what could not be helped. Study, learning, mastery were the only solutions.

And yet, in spite of her resolve, Hibern was so glad one day early in spring when her next Atan study day arrived again after weeks of incessant rain, that she didn't even mind the prospect of the double transfer as she shifted to Marloven Hess.

She found Senrid's study empty. Hibern knew that he hated tardiness, so there had to be a reason. No, there had to be trouble. Magical or military? His academy had barely begun its season. Surely the trouble couldn't be there?

She walked to the bank of four tall windows, and looked out over the academy. Her eye was caught by a short, slight, white-shirted figure among the many moving around the sandy-stone corridors. There was something about the set of those shoulders that caught her attention, though the curly blond head was exactly like so many others.

She was about to turn away when Senrid's thought overwhelmed her own: *Hibern? I've trouble in the academy. I sent Liere home last night. Next week?*

The words hit her like a mental shout, strengthened by a whirlwind of emotion, most prominent being anger and remorse. Guilt. Fury, which came with an image of a tall, blond boy of about eighteen or so. Self-condemnation. Hibern recoiled, her head throbbing with protest, then as suddenly as it had come, Senrid's thought was gone.

So once again, Hibern was given an extra hour, and decided to use it to take another tour of Eidervaen.

Hibern's guide this time was a cart driver with bright red braids. She gave a practiced patter as the goat cart whisked along the patterned-stone streets of Eidervaen.

". . . and this is Peri's Corner." A quick look from the guide. "Are you interested in romance?"

"Not really," Hibern said. "But tell me anyway. I did ask for famous sites in Eidervaen, where important things happened."

The guide flicked a smile back at Hibern. "This isn't important in the world of kings and queens. But it's important to *us*." The girl indicated the five-story buildings bordering the square, one with carved tree-columns on the first story and gargoyles peering down from under the roof, another with two false spires, a third with patterned stone blocks and colored glass windows, the fourth the plainest, and the oldest. It was below this one that a small fountain had been built, around which scattered flowers lay, petals fluttering in the spring breeze.

"If you want to make a public declaration of courtship, you bring flowers here every day until either you're accepted or turned down."

Public declarations? What if you get turned down just as publicly? The whole idea made Hibern feel squirmy.

As the cheerful guide went on about the history of tree-columns and what they meant during different centuries, Hibern tried to concentrate, but she kept seeing those blossoms, wilted and fresh. Declaration. Challenge. The squirmy sense settled between her bellybutton and ribs. Someday, that might be her. No. She'd never make a private dec-laration in public.

The cart rolled past, and eventually turned back toward the palace.

"You look thoughtful," Atan said when Hibern entered her study as the last echoes of the bell died away.

"I need to learn how to make a mind-shield," Hibern said. "Earlier today I was thinking about Siamis, and Dena Yeresbeth, and what hearing others' thoughts really means. I want to talk to Sartora about mind-shields."

"Yes," Atan exclaimed. "Yes, include me, too." She ran restless fingers along the queensblossom embroidery edging her sleeve and said slowly, "Sartora isn't alone in having this talent, is that right? Your king is another one?" The fingers shifted to tapping. "Have you met Sartora?"

"As it happens, I see her occasionally. Sometimes when she visits Senrid. Sometimes when she's back in Bereth Ferian and I go to study with Arthur."

"She visits your king? I should like to meet them both," Atan said. "I had a bad experience in Bereth Ferian's school, when I was still living with Tsauderei. No one knew who I was, and . . ." She shook her head. "Maybe it was my upbringing, not knowing how to act around people my age in groups. Anyway, I've been reading about Marloven Hess. 'Marloven.' I tracked down the history of the word, and there is 'Venn' in it. Did you know the Venn took their name from Sartoran '*fen*,' meaning 'family,' or 'clan,' and turned it around to mean 'The People,' as if they were elite?"

Hibern laughed. "One of my first mage lessons, learning our history from the outside view. And so we Marlovens became proud of our 'Outcasts of the Venn,' until the word 'Venn' came to imply barbarians and murderers, and the connection with them was frowned upon."

"In Sartoran many words still include 'ven' or 'fen' or 'vaen,' which means 'of the people.' It's odd, how words migrate and then come to mean different things."

Hibern agreed, but she wondered about Atan's experience at the northern mage school. Her tone suggested something unpleasant. Would the two mage schools, both dedicated to the good of the world, ever really be united in more than lip service? She hated it when Senrid was right about the hypocrisies of those who swore to dedicate their magic studies to the good of the world.

Atan shrugged. "Enough of that. The senior mages are busy with some project behind closed doors, so I believe we can resume our escapes for an hour. Have you ever been to Sarendan? Lilah and Peitar were my first friends."

"No." Hibern knew a little of its history. Peitar was another young king, barely adult-aged, unexpectedly inheriting his throne after a terrible revolution. Another for Clair's alliance? She said, "I'd like to meet them."

"I think you'll like Lilah. I've never known anyone who makes friends so easily—when I first left Delfina Valley to release the enchantment over Sartor, Lilah traveled with me. So she's one of the Rescuers. Peitar is so smart he'd be intimidating if he wasn't as friendly as his sister," Atan said as she handed Hibern a token.

They transferred to Sarendan, which lay east of Sartor across the jagged border mountains. It took Hibern longer to recover, as this was her third of the day, but she struggled to hide the reaction, walking to the Destination chamber's window to look out. I have to get used to this, she thought, noting that the building she stood in was positioned along a hilly ridge, a jumble of city rooftops layering away at the extreme edges in both directions. Directly below the sheer cliffs under the window lay a lake, wind rippling patterns across the water that reflected the rapidly moving clouds overhead.

"Ready?" Atan asked, and Hibern remembered they only had their hour.

"Of course," Hibern said, though her head still panged.

A servant took them down a hallway. Waiting side by side in the cheerful room overlooking the long lake below were stocky Lilah, her slanted eyes slits of mirth under her short thatch of rusty red hair, and slender, dark-eyed Peitar, whose only resemblance to his sister was the tilt at the corners of his eyes, and the quick flash of laughter when he smiled.

"Atan!" Lilah exclaimed. "I'm so *glad* to see you again!"

"This is Hibern, Lilah, and Peitar—"

Lilah was bursting with her almost-surprise. "I've wanted for *ages* and *ages* to introduce Derek to you, but I know you're so busy in Sartor, and he's always so busy all over Sarendan, doing stuff for Peitar."

Derek? Hibern's curiosity sharpened when she recognized the name: he had to be Derek Diamagan, the leader of the bloody revolution against the former king. He was also the one who very nearly got himself and Peitar executed.

Atan, aware of time streaming away, said, "Hibern was just suggesting that we ought to learn mind-shields. I think it a great idea, if we're to be facing Ancient Sartorans from Norsunder again."

Peitar Selenna turned to Hibern. "You've met Sartora, right? Perhaps you've heard her mention whether such things as mind-shields can only be used by those who have her ability?"

"I haven't spoken to her long enough," Hibern admitted. "But I wondered about that."

Lilah clasped her hands. "A girl my age defeating nasty villains!" Her face clouded. "Or is she all noble and solemn, only talking in Ancient Sartoran? She can't be a snob, because Derek told me everyone says she came from a little town of shopkeepers somewhere up north."

Hibern thought of that tense little figure with the enormous, staring eyes. "She is definitely not a snob—"

The door banged open, and in strode a shaggy-haired young man, his bony face high with color. He wore a dusty shirt, the laces swinging carelessly at the open neck, baggy old riding trousers covering long legs, and shabby forest mocs on his feet. He brought in the scents of dust, and sweat, and a tinge of horse.

Hibern blinked, disoriented by aromas from home.

Lilah sprang up. "Derek!" she exclaimed happily.

Derek Diamagan flashed a boyish grin at Lilah, then he and Peitar exchanged the open smiles of brotherhood, absent the heat of passion.

Lilah waved proudly at Derek as she said to Hibern, "Derek helped us defeat our horrible uncle, who used to be king."

Hibern nodded, noticing Peitar's wince that Lilah did not see.

As Lilah spoke, Derek was taking in the two newcomers: both tall girls, one with black hair and what seemed to be a scribe's or mage student's robe over ordinary travel clothes, the other in a fine linen gown embroidered in gold with flowers, her shining brown hair bound up in a complication of braids above a pair of distinctive, protuberant eyes.

Into the short silence, he said, "Peitar, I've an idea about how we might get those city urchins off the streets. So many of 'em orphans." He jerked a thumb over his shoulder. "Why didn't we think of this before? They can become an orphan brigade. Maybe we can even resurrect your old Sharadan Brothers name."

Lilah hopped from foot to foot. "Oh! I want to be one!"

Derek laughed. "You are one, Lilah. They all expect you to join them. I've got them drilling in the old coopers' yard down on the east side, near your old hideout."

"Drilling?" Peitar said.

Derek swung his way. "Sure. Learning to work together. To defend themselves and their families."

Peitar sighed. "I thought the goal was to get the sword *out* of everyone's hands. Make negotiation, not force, the way."

Derek held out his hands, palm up. "That's all very well for civilized folks. We're agreed on that, but we're also agreed that Norsunder won't be civilized if they come again." His voice was low, serious, coaxing, gentle. A curiously attractive combination of all, and Hibern watched Peitar's sensitive face change, his brow puckering.

Derek turned to Lilah. "This is why I thought of the Sharadan Brothers, champions of justice for all." He opened a hand toward Lilah, who grinned, drumming her heels against the legs of her chair as Derek took a quick turn around the room. "This isn't a military in the way you fear, Peitar. It's home defense. Readiness. You know we were our own worst enemies during the revolution, because we had no idea how to stand up to your uncle's trained army, or even the city guard."

Peitar said slowly, "Well, we do have a problem with orphans who don't seem to have a place, yet who don't trust us enough yet to come forward so I can help them find one."

"Exactly. I want to draw them out. Give them purpose!"

"Let's talk about it. But later. I don't want to be rude," Peitar said, turning toward the visitors. "This is Atan from Sartor, and here's Hibern from . . . where is it, exactly?"

General attention switched from Atan to Hibern so quickly that only Atan saw Derek's reaction to her name—the crimped upper lip of contempt, and narrow-eyed mistrust.

Mistrust?

Derek's expression smoothed when Hibern said, "I'm from Marloven Hess, but I live in Roth Drael, where I'm prenticed to the mage Erai-Yanya."

Derek leaned against a chair, and began asking Hibern about Roth Drael—where was it, how many people, she lived alone with the mage, really?—and from there, questions about the study of magic, who got chosen, if there were ability tests like some guilds gave potential prentices.

The talk shifted from magic to the history of magic. The Siamis enchantment. Travel. The hour sped by, the conversation so quick and full of laughter that Atan wondered if anyone else noticed that Derek controlled it, and that he was excluding her. He behaved as if she were not even in the room, talking so fast that no one else seemed aware.

A chill branched down her nerves as the idea formed: Derek had done it on purpose. He'd kept Lilah waiting, and Hibern and Peitar talking, in order to cut Atan out of the conversation.

Surely she was misreading him—she felt like Tsauderei's hermit student again, whose early friendships were all people in books. This was the hero of the revolution, the admired Derek Diamagan, who could do no wrong in Lilah and Peitar's eyes. There was no reason for him to be rude.

But then Derek touched Lilah on the shoulder and said, "How about we go and talk to some of the orphans, see what they think of the idea?" and then to Hibern, "Do return again. I want to hear more about magic in the north." Atan felt certain her exclusion had been deliberate.

Had the others noticed? Hibern and Peitar were deep in discussion about the two magic schools. Obviously they'd noticed nothing amiss. Atan reflected wryly on what Tsauderei had once said about how people are sure to notice what impacts precious self, but not so quick to detect slights to others.

"We'd better go," Atan said, and took Hibern's transfer token from her hand.

Hibern broke off. "Already?"

But Atan didn't answer. She was whispering an alteration to the transfer spell on the transfer tokens.

"Come again when you can," Peitar said to them both, but now that she was leaving, he let his gaze linger on Atan.

Atan didn't see that gaze. She handed Hibern her token, and Hibern braced for the wrench of transfer to Eidervaen. But instead, she felt a mere jolt, no worse than missing a step. She blinked, disoriented, until she recognized the round cottage belonging to Tsauderei, and breathed in the colder, thinner air of the mountain heights.

Tsauderei was there in his chair, a lap desk loaded with books and papers. He looked up, bushy brows lifted.

Atan said, "I know this is rude and sudden, but it'll be short. I really, really need your advice." And she summarized the conversation, then said to Hibern, whose expression had rounded in surprise, "Did you notice that? How Derek completely ignored me?"

"No, he didn't," Hibern began, then halted. Thought back. "Well, we were talking about history, magic, and the north . . ." Her expression changed. "All the questions were directed to me." She blushed.

Atan said, "No, don't apologize, or feel badly. Peitar didn't notice, either, and he is usually the most sensitive and discerning of people. I think Derek Diamagan cut me out deliberately."

Tsauderei said, "Of course he did."

Hibern rocked back a step, and Atan let out her breath in a sigh. "Why? What have I done?"

"Nothing. It's what you haven't done, which is to earn your place. No, no." The mage raised his gnarled hands, and pointed his quill at Atan. "Save your breath. Who in the world knows better who you are, how you learned, and what you've done? What's more, Derek Diamagan knows, too. He's heard the story about the freeing of Sartor from Lilah, but in his eyes that doesn't alter the error you made in being born a Landis."

Hibern exclaimed, "But . . . weren't Lilah and Peitar related to a territorial prince? If that isn't royalty, it's the next thing to it!"

"It's nobility, but in any case, Derek makes an exception for them. And he argues with them, his first point usually being, *You nobles cannot begin to understand*," Tsauderei said. "Peitar depends on Derek to argue the position of the commoner."

"Derek speaks for all commoners, and yet he resents a king presuming to do the same?" Atan retorted.

Tsauderei chuckled.

Atan flushed. "I shouldn't have said that. I shouldn't return a hatred he obviously holds for me though I've done him no wrong, because then I'm lowering myself to his standard."

Tsauderei gave a gust of laughter, then wiped his eyes. "I'm glad you came to me first," he said, the laughter fading.

Atan let out her breath again, trying consciously to dismiss her anger. How much of politics came down to personal antipathies, really? "Don't worry. I'm not going to declare war against Sarendan. Even if I could get such a stupid thing past the high council and the three circles."

Tsauderei leaned forward, completely serious now. "Derek is Peitar's most trusted friend and advisor."

"I know that," Atan said, and winced at how petulant she sounded. She made an effort. "I've heard wonderful things about him ever since I first met Peitar and Lilah. And I know he's done a great deal of good—"

"Spare me," Tsauderei said, waving the quill to and fro. "You don't have time for dither. Your people are no doubt looking all over for you—"

"Oh, I'm aware," Atan said, irritated all over again. "To dress the doll for another function at which I will make empty gestures and count steps to and fro, and measure the depth of their bows."

Tsauderei said, "You can sulk later. Right now, you'd better let me finish, since you came here to hear what I have to say."

Atan flushed. "I'm sorry."

Tsauderei went on. "I suspect that you were right that Derek deliberately ignored you. And you're equally aware that you cannot say a word against Derek before Lilah or Peitar."

Atan said, "Of course not."

Tsauderei went on in a milder tone, "I know you won't say anything, and you won't do anything foolish, but this much I know about human nature: within ten years, maybe even sooner, I strongly suspect Derek Diamagan is going to lead another revolution. This time against his 'brother' and friend Peitar Selenna, and oh, it will be for the best of reasons, but it will kill Peitar. Whether or not they put a sword through him, he will never recover from the betrayal."

Atan shivered.

Tsauderei finished inexorably, "And if that does happen—I repeat, I truly hope I'm wrong—but *if* it does happen, then all the other nations will look to Sartor for clues on how to react. You're going to need to think through how you're going to respond."

This is why I stay away from politics, Hibern thought, and when Atan had taken a sober leave of them both, and vanished, she transferred back to Roth Drael.

After she recovered and sat tiredly down at her desk, she remembered the alliance, which she had completely forgotten to ask Peitar about.

Next time, she told herself, though she wondered if it was worth the effort. It didn't seem to be going anywhere.

But she'd promised Clair.

Four days later, Hibern woke up to tiny sounds. Not the sounds of the forest, but the clink of a spoon on ceramic, the rustle of papers, the thud of a trunk closing.

Erai-Yanya was back.

Hibern whirled out of bed and pulled on her robe. She padded barefoot through the archway into the study, and there was her tutor, hair falling down, dressed in an unfamiliar robe rumpled from long wear.

Hibern said, "You're so brown!"

"Hah!" Erai-Yanya exclaimed. "That's because I was on our sisterworld, Geth-deles. Got back last night, after you went to bed."

Hibern stared in astonishment. Though the oldest history books seemed to indicate that shifting between the worlds circling the sun Erhal had been much more common before the Fall of Ancient Sartor, nowadays it took serious magic to transfer between them.

Erai-Yanya said, "It's much warmer there, or at least, where I spent most of my time. Norsunder seems to be stirring there, though what they could want in a world full of floating islands is impossible to guess. I trust it'll turn out to be rumors, but . . ." She shook her head. "Enough of that, until I learn more. I'll have to go back. I hope, I *hope*, for a short time, until we prove the worries are nothing. This I can tell you: it was dreadfully hot and humid." She spread her fingers and ran them through her hair, tangling it even more. "So! Tell me what you've done, and what you've learned . . ."

## Chapter Eight

*Bereth Ferian*

EARLY summer on the Sartoran half of the world was early winter in the north.

Liere listened to the crackle and crunch of her footsteps on ice as she walked the whisper-silent avenue of birch that bordered this wing of Bereth Ferian's marble palace. It was so pretty, the way the bare white limbs stretched up, the branches weaving together, blurred slightly by tiny round nubs that would soon be buds. From a distance the marble palace, seen through the branches, reminded Liere of her grandmother's white silk lace work.

Arthur had told her that back in the bad old days, when everyone leagued together to keep the Venn from overrunning the entire north, the various kingdoms in the alliance were in a silent sort of competition. Each was to contribute to the building of a headquarters that eventually became this enormous palace, one of the most beautiful in the world.

She could attest to that, after flashing from city to city in those awful days when she had to break the Siamis enchantment by visiting leaders, one by one, to disenchant them, and through them, their citizenry. This really was one of the most beautiful palaces, all that luminous marble, the acorn carvings around the windows, the way the tapestries all seemed to form doors into another place, one of past majesty and magic. Even candle sconces were made of gold in the central public areas, and polished brass above, in orderly knotwork shapes that incorporated the unlikeliest elements—vines, blossoms, wheat, and more acorns—but for some reason they drew and kept the eye.

She wished she understood art. Stamping her feet to kill the sense of pins and needles in her toes, she wished she understood people better. Maybe Erai-Yanya was right, and she wasn't going to understand until she lifted the Child Spell and grew up. But the very thought of that made her want to run and hide in the deepest hole she could find.

No, she simply had to learn on her own.

She stamped up the avenue. It wasn't fun to crash the thin ice layer, or to make footprints anymore. She was getting cold in spite of her mittens and scarf and knitted hat pulled down to her eyebrows. Her nose hurt, her fingers hurt, and she tried not to worry about Senrid, from whom there had been silence ever since he'd sent her home in the middle of the night a few weeks before.

All she knew was, there had been trouble in that academy. He'd been white-lipped with anger that night, too upset and angry to remember his mind-shield. So she'd seen what he'd seen: a host of seniors at Senrid's academy fighting, with knives, in a courtyard.

She hadn't understood anything she saw, except that it looked like a war to her—and she'd felt Senrid's sharp fear that civil war would break out if these expertly trained seniors started killing each other.

She'd shut him out, let him give her a transfer token back to Bereth Ferian, and after that, silence.

She tried to understand, but couldn't, how somebody, *anybody* would want to be a king. She longed to run and hide every time they wanted her to preside as Queen in Bereth Ferian, and nobody expected her to pass the smallest law, much less prevent civil war.

"But they expect me to get rid of Siamis, if he comes back," she said to the air, and watched her breath cloud.

Saying his name out loud felt like uttering obscenities. She waved her hand through the already-dispersed cloud of steam as if she could wave the words from having been spoken, and broke into a run to leave them behind.

She found Arthur in the small room they used for mealtimes during the winter. The warmth tingled not unpleasantly on her nose and toes and fingers as she shed the scarf, mittens, hat, and heavy coat.

Arthur sat hunched over an old tome, his feet wound around the legs of his stool, his shoulder blades poking at his shirt as he put his finger on the page and looked up. He had a blue ink-smear on his cheek where he'd scraped his pen when sticking it behind his ear, and brown ink smudged his fingers. She couldn't explain why she liked these smudges any more than she could explain the appeal of art, but they made her smile.

"Warm corn muffins and tartberry jam?" he asked.

Liere grabbed a muffin, tossing it from hand to hand when she discovered it was still hot. As she reached for a knife to cut it and smother both halves with jam, Arthur said, "Hibern made her visit at the school. She stopped by here to talk to you, but you were outside, so she asked me to ask you when you are going to Marloven Hess next."

"I don't know," Liere said. "You remember, I came back because of some kind of trouble. I don't know if it's over."

Arthur sat back. "That place sounds terrible. You really prefer it to here?"

Liere knew that when she wasn't listening in the mental realm, she was not a good judge of character, but the hurt in Arthur's expression was plain to see. "It's not Marloven Hess I go to," she reminded him. "I don't see much of it. It's Senrid. He's like my brothers, only better, because my real brothers thought I was stupid. Well, one did. And the nice one didn't live with us."

Arthur wondered if that was why he was failing with Liere. He'd never had any brothers or sisters to practice on.

"And there are a few Marlovens I like very much," she added, thinking of Fenis Senelac, under whose exacting tutelage Liere's sporadic riding lessons progressed slowly but surely.

But Marloven Hess, like Bereth Ferian, was a place to visit. It wasn't home. Home still brought images of South End, yet Liere never wanted to go back. Maybe the word 'home' was at fault. It wasn't truly a thing word so much as a feeling word. She hated emotions. They were so *useless*. 'Home' was definitely an emotion word. She should never think it or use it.

Arthur perceived her tensing up, and understood with a kind of sick certainty that despite all his efforts, it was clear that Liere was never going to love Bereth Ferian. That's what his mother had said, and she was right.

He couldn't understand it, but he did understand that to pressure Liere with his own sense of failure or fault was unfair. So he pointed at the book. "This fellow is really funny. The translation is Sartoran. Do you want me to read some of it to you?"

"Who's the writer?"

"A long-ago southern king, writing to his descendants. It's called *Take Heed, My Heirs*, and I've been laughing all morning."

Liere had no interest whatsoever in old kings. "I need to practice Ancient Sartoran," she said. "I'm having such trouble understanding a book, and all it's about is farming."

"Ancient Sartoran, that reminds me. Hibern says that the Queen of Sartor seems to want to meet both you and Senrid."

Liere jerked her shoulders up to her ears. "I dunno when I'll go there next."

Arthur did not understand Liere at all, but she was one of his responsibilities. Hoping to ward off one of those awkward silences during which she'd sit there fighting some inward battle while chewing her cuticles bloody, he pretended she'd shown interest in his book, and translated a couple of the funnier incidents from the early years of Prince Valdon's life. His reward was a grin, then a chuckle, and pretty soon she was laughing, and begged him to read more.

*Chwahirsland to Marloven Hess*

Jilo blinked. He stared into the empty closet in horror. The air rippled slowly, the stone walls appearing to be a day's journey away, the floor a thousand paces below. He blinked and they closed in on top of him. Jilo struggled for breath, his heart squeezing in his chest.

The enemy-book in his hands seemed to pull him forward, forward, toward the abyss he could barely sense . . .

He lunged backward, and stared down at the object leached of dimension, of its essential bookness. He blinked at the rough-cut papers pressed between stiffened canvas, stitched on the outside by blackweave . . .

His head began floating off his shoulders. The tiniest dart of alarm brought his attention back long enough for him to glance at the stranger's hand lying on the square thing whose purpose he no longer recognized, gray nails . . .

Gray nails.

He knew that was important. He shut his eyes.

Breathed.

Each simple action required concentration, and appalling effort.

Frightened, he clutched convulsively at the token that thumped against his ribs at every move. Heat flashed through him, shocking him thoroughly awake long enough to clutch the book to him and stumble backward through the door. He shambled down the hall, though his limbs had come unhinged, and his feet had turned to blocks of stone.

When he got outside, he leaned against the rough wall, drenched in sweat as he labored to breathe. Waves of black rolled across his vision, punctured by pinpoints of light. Slowly the darting fireflies brightened, and gathered more brethren from the darkness. Did they form into twia? He should count, see if they darted in eights . . .

One, two, three, hold still . . . Gradually sense returned, and with it, awareness of thirst, weakness in knees and wrists. He had stayed much too long. Oh no. Had ten years passed?

He shoved the book inside his shirt, then walked up to a duty guard he knew. Thought he knew, only he looked so much older. "What is the date?"

The fellow looked at Jilo as if he'd spoken in Norsundrian, fear widening his eyes. "Date?" he repeated.

Jilo tried again. He knew these questions were important. No, it was the answers that were important. No, it was how the fellow didn't answer. "How old are you?" Jilo asked.

The guard said, his tone placating, "I joined at my twelfth year."

Jilo stared at the guard, horror curling inside him, and the guard stared back, his pupils wide and black. Like the Shadowland days, only this was fear. Jilo forced himself to move. He pushed on in search of water and food.

It was easiest to walk into the city, to the place he knew. Habit. That was important. Habit was as strong as . . .

As strong as? Twi. Groups. Loyalty. You stayed loyal to your twi, you survived. Every Chwahir grew up knowing that. Survived what, that was the question for a king to face. Survive an evil king who had no twi, who had killed everyone close to him?

The Mearsiean girls always won. They'd had a real twi, almost the right number, even. They did have the right number when Clair wasn't there, something that had always irritated Jilo, as if they somehow made game of the fundamental strength of Chwahir life. A bunch of silly waxers . . .

As he blew the steam off the soup, his thoughts shambled on.

Waxers. Lighters. Where had he had that conversation? That boy king from, what was it? Somewhere far to the southwest. Senrid, that was it. Tutored in dark magic. Came to help, once. Said to find the source, *and I've found it.*

Jilo left the tasteless food after only two bites and sloped out to the street. He looked around, trying to remember why he was there. Passers-by distracted him, the way they watched one another . . . were they doing the hand-signs? Hands. Talk. Talk? Yes, he was going to Marloven Hess.

He recollected the Destination that Clair had taken him to, braced, and did the magic.

He found himself standing on the windswept tiles, the sun barely risen. He fell painfully to his knees, fighting for breath as black spots drifted across his vision.

Senrid had done his morning drill earlier, so he could take a fast horse out to ride the plains below his city. As the strengthening sun made its way each day a little farther along the distant eastern ridge of mountains, he liked to pause and watch the sky lighten, then the first rays of ruddy light outline the towers of Choreid Dhelerei, his city.

He sighed out his breath. It barely frosted. After a very cold, late spring, summer was coming at last.

The tug of obligation pulled him cityward. The mare, a young one newly released into the garrison stable, sensed his decision, and she tossed her head, sidling. She wanted to run some more, so why wasn't the two-leg giving her the signal?

He obediently tightened his thighs, and she bolted off the mark like an arrow from the bow. And that was what Jilo saw, as he stood there on the Destination below the city wall, horse and boy so well melded in the rhythm of the gallop that they looked from a distance like one of the northern centaurs he'd seen pictures of in some old book.

The round face turned Jilo's way, the horse veered, and clods of mud flew up behind the animal's hooves from the rich soil so different from the sandy clay found in Chwahirsland.

Senrid reined in with an ease that made Jilo's heart yearn for such unthinking skill. He'd always been so awkward on horseback.

"Is that you?" Senrid asked. "Jilo?"

"You said I could come back." Jilo looked around. "Wasn't it snowing last time?"

"So you've solved the time riddle?"

"Not the time riddle," Jilo said painstakingly, picking out each word.

Senrid could see the effort. At that moment, the inner perimeter riders approached, and Senrid motioned for one to surrender his horse.

Jilo grimaced. Here came the humiliation. He wondered how quickly that horse would boost him off at that thunder-and-turf pace.

Jilo scrambled up onto the saddle pad (barely any saddle, he noticed dismally), and clutched the reins desperately, braced for the inevitable fall. Senrid cast him a quick look, then his horse, which had begun to trot, unaccountably slowed to a walk. Jilo's, trained to follow, also slowed.

Senrid said, "Now we can talk. What've you found?"

"I think I've located a . . . I'm not getting the word. It's a locus of power? Where it draws . . ." Jilo breathed hard against the pressure in his throat. "Just thinking about it strangles me." His breath shuddered as he fingered the medallion at his neck. Cold tightened the muscles and nerves along his spine when he contemplated how very close he had come to . . . what? Would the servants who finally dared to come looking for him have found a desiccated body? How long before they would have come?

Or would they?

He was not aware of having fallen into reverie, but Senrid noticed the absent gaze, the squint of oncoming headache, the desperate clutch on the reins. The first thing Jilo obviously needed was a decent meal between his belt buckle and his spine, and then sleep.

They reached the castle and dismounted, and part of the reason for Jilo's oddly stiff, awkward style of riding became apparent. Jilo looked shiftily around, then stuck his hand into his heavy-weave tunic-shirt, and produced a thin book.

Jilo already whiffed of the distinctive burnt-metal stink of intense dark magic, a stench more psychic than physical. When the book appeared, Senrid reeled back a step. "Jilo, whatever wards you put on yourself are killing you."

"Oh." Jilo blinked rapidly, clutched at the medallion, muttered, and took a cautious breath.

The miasma of intense dark magic eased, but did not disappear.

"Come on," Senrid said, resisting the unnerving sense that he was being towed into deep and unfamiliar waters.

Jilo tucked the book under his arm, his head drooping, and he followed Senrid in silence. Along the way, Senrid hailed a runner and gave swift orders for a meal to be brought to the study. As soon as the door was shut, Jilo sank into the chair beside Senrid's desk, then held out the book.

Senrid stretched out his hand, then recoiled from the smell of stale sweat and mildew and dark magic emanating from the thing. "Go ahead." Jilo's voice husked with the effort he made just to speak. "I think I got all the wards and tracers off it. And the wards on me are gone. They were the only protection I had in the King's secret chamber." He tapped the medallion.

Senrid could feel layers of magic from a palm's breadth away. "Are you sure?" Jilo didn't look sure of anything, even his own name. *Be specific.* "What type of spells are in that book?"

"No." Jilo dropped the book onto the desk, leaned back in the chair, and shut his eyes.

"No?" Senrid prompted, clamping down hard on impatience.

Jilo's throat knuckle bobbed in his skinny neck as he said, "Purpose. It tracks the movements of any enemy if they visit designated Destinations. A *lot* of them. And I've added Wan-Edhe's name."

Fire shot along Senrid's nerves. That thing would track enemies who moved about by magic?

He stared at the thin, grubby book, no longer seeing the oily smudges along the edge from frequent openings, or smelling the mildew and the rank odor from that terrible chamber in faraway Narad. Senrid reached convulsively, then stilled, eyeing Jilo, who sat there, eyes closed.

What was the danger? There was no danger.

Even if Jilo weren't obviously exhausted, Senrid suspected he could take him in three strikes. This was Senrid's citadel, he could command the guard, he could drop a stone spell over Jilo and set him aside to deal with some other year.

He could take the book, add Destinations within Marloven Hess, add names of troublemakers, and track every one of his enemies . . .

Once again he reached, his fingers halting a grass-blade's width from touching. He sensed the layers of magic. Maybe Jilo had put protective wards over the thing as a trap. Senrid knew he would.

The door banged open, and in came the runner with a tray loaded with oatmeal drowned in milk, and rye buns, with a little bowl of blackberry jam to spread on them. Since Senrid ate what everyone else ate, from garrison to castle staff, it was easy to dish up extra for a sudden guest.

Hoping his voice sounded normal, he said to Jilo, "Eat up." And to the runner, "Some listerblossom steep. Make it strong."

Jilo's color was never going to appeal to anyone outside of Chwahirsland, but as he worked his way through the food, the pale, pinkish sallow that replaced the mottled gray looked almost healthy.

Senrid possessed himself in patience, but never had a meal lasted so long. Through his mind flitted images, sustained by the alluring, the sweet image of knowing. At all times. Where his enemies were.

When the steep came, filling the air with the astringent summery scent of listerblossom, Jilo gulped it down hot. He blinked away tears from the scalding liquid, and sighed.

"So tell me how this book of yours works," Senrid prompted.

"Go ahead. Take a look," Jilo said.

"I don't want to touch it," Senrid replied, the instinct to grasp and keep it so strong that his voice must have changed, for Jilo looked up, one eye narrowed. Senrid cleared his throat. "There might be other wards on it. Against outsiders. Non-Chwahir. Anyway, I can't read your language."

Jilo's blinks made it clear that he had not thought this far ahead. Flipping the book open, he pointed. "As you can see. Wan-Edhe had a lot of enemies. This book is just the last year. Before he got snatched by Norsunder. There must be pages and pages stored somewhere. Or maybe he burned them. He writes in a name. It shows when and where they transferred by magic."

"It has to be transfers? Can it track them if they travel by horse or walking?"

"Magic transfers only. Specific Destinations."

"Let's get to who. Start with Detlev? He has to be in there."

"Yah." Jilo's ragged, grimy nail pointed to a line. "Few notes, as you can see. Spaces between entries, like holes. Because otherwise, why would it say 'Norsunder Base' four times in a row? He wouldn't be transferring around inside, would he?"

"How about if he transfers to Norsunder-Beyond and then back? Or off-world?" Senrid guessed.

Jilo blinked slowly. "I hadn't thought of that."

Senrid grimaced. "So you just write someone's name in? Or do you have to find the person and bespell them, the way you do if you put a tracer on them?"

Jilo bobbed his head. "There is a very complicated spell, requiring the person to step into a warded Destination. I don't know how he differentiated between people. I just know it works."

Senrid whistled. "My uncle wanted something like this book. Had me working on it from the time I was ten. Best I could do was lacing objects with tracers, then you had to get the person to take the object with them." He whistled again, more softly, as he extended his hand over the top of the book. "There's lethal magic on this thing."

Chill flashed through Senrid to pool in the pit of his stomach as he recollected some of the stuff he'd overheard when he was a prisoner of Siamis's bully-boys. They hadn't known he could understand their language. Most of it had been brag, threats, and lies, but once one of them said, *The Host of Lords sit in the Garden of the Twelve and watch anywhere they want, any time.*

Senrid had shrugged that off as scare-brag, but if the likes of the King of the Chwahir could construct this book, maybe it was real.

Yet even the Host of Lords can only watch one thing at a time.

Right?

Senrid shook off the dread, reached across his desk, and closed his fingers on one of his steel-nib pens.

He pushed pen and ink toward Jilo. "Try an experiment? Write a name in another language. Someone you know enough to make the spell work."

"Who?"

"How about Puddlenose of the Mearsieans?"

Jilo glanced up in surprise. "He's an enemy?"

"No. I just want to see how it works."

"He's already in here. I think he's this one, 'The Brat.'"

"Already in there?" Senrid remembered Puddlenose as a jokester, but there had been some brief, sharp moments hinting at some kind of past. "Someday I want to hear about that. Try Arthur of Bereth Ferian, then. Have you met him?"

"No."

"Try. His real name is Irtur Vithyavadnais, and he's the son of Erai-Yanya, if that helps." And Senrid described Arthur.

Senrid breathed out silently, considering the feeling that he'd dodged a falling rock as Jilo closed his eyes and whispered a long spell. Senrid heard Arthur's name mixed in, but when Jilo wrote the name down, nothing happened. He shut his eyes. "I don't know what I did wrong," he whispered. "I think maybe I need to do the spell again after he steps into one of the warded Destinations?"

All right. It had limitations. Still. Senrid wanted so badly to try it, his fingers twitched toward the pen.

He forced himself to sit back. "Okay. Go hole up. Sleep it out. No one will touch this thing," Senrid added. "Including me."

## Chapter Nine

SENRID'S natural inclination was to turn to Commander Keriam, but not for anything having to do with magic.

His second thought was Hibern, but he suspected she would go straight to her tutor if she had any idea that something like this book existed. He couldn't imagine the lighter mages doing anything other than ganging up on Jilo to take away that book for his own good.

For the rest of the day Senrid's body moved about his various tasks, his mind on that book lying there on his desk, as he asked himself useless questions, such as *Where is Jarend Ndarga's exiled father right now?* And, *How could I locate any conspiracy if I don't know who is conspiring against me?*

He knew the cause of his ambivalence. This desire to possess that book was his uncle's thinking. Tdanerend had always been frantic about conspiracies. Toward the end, he had a full flight of guards on duty around his sleep chamber at night, plus his three handpicked private guards, men he bribed and flattered then changed if he thought that they, too, might be conspiring. Thirty thinking, breathing beings on the watch all night so one man could sleep, and even then, Tdanerend had often been wakened by a noise, and fearing attack from his guards, set up traps, because though he demanded loyalty he never believed he had it. How could he, when he had professed loyalty to his own brother up until he stabbed him in the back?

Senrid tried to shove the book out of his thoughts, but when he found himself thinking about *thinking* about it, he hopped up onto the fence to watch the choosing of colts after summer-long training, and let his mind ride down the what-if trail.

He saw himself taking the book away from Jilo. Learning Chwahir. It shouldn't take long. He was good with languages. And he could easily get proximity to all his targets, in order to bespell book and person, if that's what it took. Warding the city, each jarl's capital, the army garrison Destinations, to begin with.

And then what? Spend the entire day creeping back to check on their movements? Or would he carry the book around with him all the time, and constantly sneak peeks?

That was exactly what Tdanerend would have done. Senrid understood, now that he was king, the relentless desire to know, to brace for attack, to be ready for the knife in the dark. Anywhere he went, he was a moving target.

The colt selection ended. He ran to the quartermaster, who was waiting with reports related to the stables. He was supposed to know all that stuff, so he forced himself to listen and concentrate. When he finally retired, he was still so ambivalent he tossed and turned, finally falling into an uneasy sleep in which he dreamed that he and Liere were lost and Siamis was chasing them, but Senrid's feet had turned to rock and he couldn't run.

Sleep fled at sunup, leaving him groggy. A cold bath shocked him awake. He ran to the garrison side, where he found the sword master waiting. "You haven't tried the sword again for quite some time," the man said, indicating the rack of practice swords. "Or would you prefer our usual?"

Senrid was tired, his mind full of Jilo and his damned book. He eyed the swords, hating his slowness, his clumsiness: by now he'd had enough lessons to know that to be really good he was going to have to unlearn everything that had become habitual with knife fighting. He hated that.

"Knife," he said. "Some castle guards took against my learning the sword," he added when the sword master evinced a little surprise. "Thought it some kind of reflection on their ability to keep me alive."

It was true—in a sense. They'd been mostly joking, when some of the morning shift had come in while Senrid was finishing one of his lessons in basic sword moves, not long after Liere's last visit.

The sword master's brows went up. He opened his hand in assent, accepting Senrid's not-quite-lie, and Senrid sensed the man's opinion of the guard lessening.

Senrid picked up his practice weapons, throat tight with disgust and self-condemnation. Lying was so *easy*. That was another path down which his uncle had gone, only Tdanerend had also lied to himself. Senrid had lied to survive. He could not claim that this lie was even remotely about survival.

Usually Senrid enjoyed these lessons. He reveled in being skilled, and fast. He had to be fast, if he was to defend himself against a grown man, and he usually came out of these sessions less weary than exhilarated, muscles aching enough to free his mind for the day's tasks. But that smarmy lie stayed with him, souring every movement.

He was glad when the watch bell rang and he returned to the residence side, in a thoroughly vile mood.

And there sat Jilo in his study. Senrid nearly stumbled. He'd actually managed to forget all about Jilo during that practice session.

He strove to sound normal. "Breakfast should be along soon. I hope you liked yesterday's, since it'll be the same. Did you sleep well?"

"Your food is much better than ours." Jilo's face was a lot less gray. "Slept very well."

There wasn't any talk during the meal. Both were too hungry. But as soon as his plate was empty, Jilo thumbed his eyes. "Maybe I should stay away for a time. My head's clearer when I get distance."

"Distance from Wan-Edhe's magic chambers?" Senrid asked.

"From the castle. Maybe . . . maybe from the capital." Jilo's gaze strayed to the study windows.

Senrid exclaimed in surprise, "You could leave that long and not come back to find one of your commanders on the throne and an assassination team waiting for you?"

Jilo's gaze returned. "I worried about that. At first. But they know now that Wan-Edhe was taken by Norsunder." He looked down, his embarrassment clear. "They expect him back any day. After eighty years of Wan-Edhe, no one believes he's gone for good. Won't, until his dead body is seen. But I think, from my walks in the city, they only want to get on with their lives. They fear the castle. No one wants to go into it, and risk being his first target when he does return."

Senrid was on the verge of saying, *Why don't you just walk away?*

Jilo went on in his painstaking, monotone mumble. "I think . . . I think I need to find out what they expect from the castle, besides fear.

Wouldn't that be what a king would do, find out? One who wasn't Wan-Edhe?"

Senrid said sardonically, "If they're like people anywhere, one person will say the king ought to lift taxes. The next one will say the king should improve roads. The third will say better patrols against brigands, the fourth will demand exports of Bermundi rugs."

Jilo nodded unsmiling on each point. "Yes, but eventually the demands will repeat. Won't they? Then won't I see how many want the roads, and how many are worried about brigands, and so forth?" He ran his fingers through his lank, unkempt hair. "Won't that give me an idea of what I should be doing?"

"If you have big numbers demanding this or that, isn't rebellion more likely?"

"Maybe." Jilo shifted on his chair. "The way I see it, their idea of the king is in his castle. Doing what kings do. So as long as I'm pretending to be a king, shouldn't I try to be the king they want, and do what they expect me to do?"

Senrid stared at him. It sounded so simple. Simple-minded, even. Tdanerend would have said so.

He could suggest Jilo just walk away, to which Jilo could retort the same to Senrid.

He could do it. If he got up from the table right now, walked through the castle, saddled a horse, and rode for the border, nobody would stop him. Maybe (if they figured out what he was doing) they might even chase him, like the stories about his Uncle Kendred. Senrid still didn't know whether they'd chased Kendred to capture and kill him, or if they'd run him over the border. As always happened to displaced Marloven princes or kings, Kendred had been eradicated from the most accessible records, as if he'd never existed.

Senrid squirmed. He couldn't bear the idea of running. Of being anywhere else. This was where he belonged, the only place he felt like himself. Even if he died staying.

He thought of older writings, the few not destroyed, in which one of his ancestors had defined kingship as an idea shared by the many minds a king ruled. Or he would have to spend all his time forcing his own idea of kingship onto them.

*They just want to get on with their lives.* Senrid's gaze fell on the book, and he shifted uncomfortably as he recollected the headlong plans, images, and thoughts of the previous day. Sickness churned inside him at the awareness of how close, so very close, he had come to following his uncle's path. He knew exactly how it would begin, how you convinced yourself what you were doing was perfectly justified. Sensible. Self-protection. And the only thing that had stopped him was wondering how he could find enough time in the day to check the book.

"Everyone follows the law." He had to stick to it. He'd seen what happens when you don't . . . the seniors at the academy had been extraordinarily subdued ever since the senior revolt in spring, during which Ret Forthan, the best of the seniors, had broken the rules and used steel on the worst of the seniors. The entire academy had been humiliated by the sight of Forthan, the most popular boy, tied to a post and caned before the entire school, though *everyone* knew his action had been justified.

But that was the law.

The scars on Senrid's back crawled. How he hated remembering watching that, knowing exactly how Forthan felt. All these months later fury still burned in him, and beneath that a sense of failure, though he knew it was not his fault. That senior revolt was a direct result of his uncle's lies and playing of favorites among those boys' fathers.

Senrid forced his attention back, and pointed to the book. "Listen, Jilo, I don't know how your king managed to make that thing, but you'd better keep it tight."

"I will."

"I mean really tight. Don't tell anyone about it. I wish you hadn't told me. But if word of that gets out, you're going to have every mage, light or dark, hunting you down." He shook his head. "I don't even know how that king of yours drew enough magic to make that thing. The magic on it is stronger than most kingdom wards."

Jilo's eyes widened. "But I told you. Didn't I? The chamber. I did tell you. You said it was killing me. And you're right. I think I'd be dead if I hadn't made these wards." His fingers clutched the medallion on its dirty string hanging around his neck.

Senrid leaned forward. "We got to talking about the book, and got stuck there." *Or I did.* "What exactly did you find in that chamber?"

"The source of Wan-Edhe's power." Jilo's complexion blanched again, his cracked lips thinning. "He's using the life force of the palace inhabitants. That is, everyone's but his own."

Senrid's head rang as if struck by a bell clapper. "You're sure about that?"

"As sure as I can be. No one has a sense of time passing. And yet they're aging faster than time is passing outside. I asked a guard, one I recognized. Not much older than me when I first met him. He didn't know the date. Or how old he was, but he looks old. Too old. It's like time . . ." He groped. "Inside the castle, we forget time, but they age fast. I believe their lives are being sucked out of them."

Senrid had felt all day as if he were on a rough ride, but Jilo's words sent him tumbling over the metaphorical horse's head. "He what?" He'd already known that there was some kind of weird time distortion in that castle, but that happened naturally in some places around the world. "That king of yours is using *lives* to recreate a simulacrum of Norsunder-Beyond, right there in that fortress."

Jilo mumbled, "I don't know where to begin to fix it."

Senrid said slowly, "This is way beyond me, too. Way beyond."

"I guess I ought to go." Jilo sighed.

"Wait. Wait." Senrid rubbed his eyes, realized he was trying to rub an awareness into his head that wasn't going to come, and dropped his hands. "Is it okay with you if I bring in someone else? Not about your book. You better hide that thing, and pretend it doesn't exist."

"'Okay.' The Mearsieans say that," Jilo observed, oblivious to the advice about his book; hiding it was too instinctive. He blinked rapidly, then said, "Who?"

"Her name is Hibern. She knows more than I do about lighter wards, though I suspect she won't know what to do about yours. But maybe she knows the right archives to search in." When Jilo shrugged, Senrid dug around on his desk, and recovered his notecase.

He found a paper inside, scanned it—from some Colendi stranger about Clair's alliance—and tossed it to the desk to be dealt with some other time. He scribbled a note to Hibern and sent it.

"What is that thing?" Jilo asked, pointing to the case.

Senrid stared in surprise. "You mean to tell me, you've managed to discover a pocket Norsunder, and survived, but you've never seen a notecase for letter transfer?"

Jilo said, "Who would I write to?"

Senrid laughed.

Hibern listened in stomach-cramping shock, and remembered Erai-Yanya saying, *I know you prefer to solve things on your own. I'm that way myself, or I wouldn't be living alone in this ruin. But some problems are beyond you, and recognizing that is part of solving. If that happens, Tsaud-erei explicitly told me that you could contact him any time. Promise me you'll remember.* And Hibern had said, *I promise.*

She looked up. "I think I know what to do."

"Over to you," Senrid said.

Hibern gave Jilo a doubtful glance. He looked like he'd been sick for months. "Jilo, shall we go to someone who might be able to advise us?"

All he cared about was the possibility of help. "Yes."

She didn't think he had the strength to perform transfer magic, so she spelled the transfer token she always carried for an emergency, gave it to Jilo, then fixed on the Destination Erai-Yanya had taught her for reaching Tsauderei.

This Destination was located far from the valley where Tsauderei lived. It was a first line of magical defense. Their pending arrival alerted the old mage, who passed them through his secret wards, and permitted them direct access.

All they experienced was an extra-long and bumpy transfer, then they found themselves standing on a grassy patch outside of a round stone cottage.

Tsauderei opened the door. "Come in, come in," he began, then halted when his magical sense, honed over a lifetime, sustained a tidal wave of toxic dark magic.

The source was the pallid, slumping black-haired boy in his mid-teens, who stood next to Erai-Yanya's student Hibern. Tsauderei spoke swiftly, activating several protections, which caused a startled, uneasy glance from Hibern. The boy just stood there wanly, looking as if a strong breeze would topple him.

Hibern gazed at Tsauderei in question. "Erai-Yanya is gone. Out of contact. She said I should bring emergencies to you. I think this is one." She repeated Senrid's words.

Tsauderei's sense of immediate alarm diminished slightly, but by no means did he relax.

As for Jilo, he was still struggling against transfer reaction. Words jabbered over his head as he gazed at a tall, thin old geezer who at first reminded him unpleasantly of Wan-Edhe. As the transfer reaction slowly dissipated, he recognized that the only characteristics the two had in common were white hair uncut for decades, a tall, thin form, the corrugated face of age, and the old-fashioned robe, popular all over the southern continent a century ago, like beards.

But where Wan-Edhe, with his protuberant, mad stare, had been unkempt, often wearing the same robe for years, this Tsauderei dressed in fine velvet with embroidery at the cuffs and hem, and his beard was clean and braided. In one ear he wore a diamond drop that sparkled with deep lights within, probably magical. His eyes were alert, thick brows quirked at a sardonic angle.

Tsauderei thought rapidly. Chwahirsland and its problems were far beyond his reach, or understanding. The sense of dangerous magic permeating this Jilo so disturbed him he had no idea what to say, so he decided that nothing was safest. "Thank you, Hibern," he said when she finished. "You did the right thing. I'll take it from here."

Hibern stared. Just like that, she'd been dismissed. She wanted to protest. If she'd been talking to Erai-Yanya, she would have protested. But she didn't know Tsauderei well enough, and his reputation was daunting. So she said, "I'd like to learn what happens, and how."

"So you shall," Tsauderei promised, and thinking that it was best to get Jilo out there as soon as possible, leaned forward to touch the boy's scrawny arm in the worn black sleeve.

Transfer wrenched Jilo once again. When he came out of it, black spots swimming before his eyes, he tried to blink them away, and discovered that he was shivering. He seemed to be on another mountain plateau, and next to Tsauderei stood another man, this one huge and powerfully built, with a thick, curly black beard and long black hair.

Jilo's head ached. Though the black spots had faded, the mental fireflies were back, each thought flaring and flying wildly, making it nearly impossible to connect one to the next. He knew that Tsauderei was important. He was Wan-Edhe's enemy. His name was in The Book. That did not necessarily make him Jilo's ally.

Jilo tried to blink the blur from his vision as he took in his surroundings. He sat in the middle of a grassy space in front of a sturdy cottage, high on a cliff. In the hazy distance, meandering streams and canals of gleaming blue stitched farmland in rich shades of gold and green. This could not be any part of soil-poor, parched Chwahirsland, and yet the wind from the west brought familiar scents of old stone, dust, rusty metal, moss.

He was subliminally aware of Tsauderei speaking in a low, rapid voice to Curly Beard, who stepped close and bent down, elbows out, huge rough-palmed hands on his thighs. He peered into Jilo's face.

Jilo's limbs tingled unpleasantly as life returned. He glanced southward at the farmland as he struggled to get up. "Where is that?"

One of those strong hands took hold of his upper arm and lifted him to his feet. Though his body felt heavier than stone, and far more unwieldy, Curly Beard seemed to expend no effort, as if Jilo were as light as duck down.

"That, my boy, is Colend. To be precise, yonder land westward is the duchy of Altan, and there, eastward, lies Alarcansa, two of the greatest jewels in the Colendi crown. The targets of your ancestors, and your king, many times over. And to the north lies the Land of the Chwahir. We are perched on a cliff in the mountains between."

"Border," Jilo murmured, trying to blink away the blur.

"I think he's confused," Tsauderei said from the side, where he sat on a stone bench. "Perhaps you ought to show him."

Curly Beard chuckled, the sound resonating in that mighty chest like a rockfall. "We can call it the border, but it really isn't. Do you see the actual border?"

His hand had not loosened its grip on Jilo. He found himself swung around, so he faced north, and the ranks of mountains, like serrated knives rising up and up. "What do you see?"

"Mountains." Jilo tried to swallow, but his throat was too dry, and the lingering effect of transfer magic made him slightly dizzy.

"What do you see in those mountains? Look closely."

Jilo blinked harder. Gradually detail resolved: the barrenness of the stone, blurred by rare, twisted trees, black with age and . . .

He drew in an unsteady breath. "That's the border."

"Yes. Burdened with magic so strong that very little survives. You know what an Emras Defense is, right?"

A flare of resentment burned through Jilo. He'd sought help, not this interrogation, or this iron hand gripping him like he was about to be tossed off the cliff. "Of course I do. You learn of it in your first year. Strongest ward in dark magic. Spell fashioned some four centuries ago."

"Strongest because it finds the exact balance between light and dark, so *this* doesn't happen." Curly Beard's free hand swept northward. "But your king scorned that balance, and has spent decades layering more wards over wards. One of the virtues, if you can call it that, of your dark magic." And when Jilo didn't answer, he turned his head. "Tsauderei, your turn. Show him."

Tsauderei held up some kind of cloth. Jilo couldn't make out the details, as his vision was still blurry, but he suspected it didn't matter what it was, as Tsauderei said slowly, "This is a piece of my clothing, with a personal ward over it. As far as the border magic is concerned, this shawl is Tsauderei."

He laid it down, put a transfer token on it, and whispered over it. Then he glanced up. "I am now sending my substitute to your capital city."

The shawl vanished. Light flashed over the mountains to the north, followed by a thunderous *voom!* Hot, metallic air buffeted Jilo's face, stirring Tsauderei's long hair and beard.

Then, as Jilo gawked, fire rolled from mountaintop to mountaintop in both directions. The firestorm lasted no more than a heartbeat or two, but when it vanished, it left a thousand tiny fires as the twisted trees, scraggly bushes, and tough grasses burned to ash.

Jilo stared, appalled. "The entire border?" he said in his own language, knowing that they understood—that in fact their version of the Universal Language Spell was better than the dark magic equivalent.

"No," Curly Beard said, letting go of Jilo. "But only because Wan-Edhe was a single person, and hadn't the time to traverse your entire border laying that spell, and also run the kingdom. The wards are worse over the old roads, and lines of transfer to your capital. But as you can see, it's bad enough. If anyone had been on the road below that point, they would be dead. No matter who they were, which includes Chwahir patrollers."

Jilo finally managed to swallow. "That's terrible."

"Yet you've done nothing about it."

"I didn't know."

"How long have you been in Narad?"

The blur was getting worse. Jilo covered his face with his hands. "Time isn't the same," he mumbled through his fingers. "Why I asked for help." He sat down abruptly. The dizziness had also worsened.

Curly Beard hunkered down to peer into Jilo's face. "So you went for help to another user of dark magic, a boy who also answers to no master. Who holds the throne of a large and powerful kingdom. If your two kingdoms weren't almost at opposite ends of the continent, I should think half the monarchs around you both would be quite alarmed."

Jilo stared at the harsh-boned face revolving gently before him. "I, I, I . . ." He shut his mouth and took a deep breath. Again, anger steadied him, enough for him to get the words out: "The first time. I asked Clair of the Mearsieans for help."

As soon as the words were out, he braced for the "Who?" but instead, Curly Beard put his fists on his hips as he exclaimed, "Ah! Clair? Indeed! I shall ask her. Go on."

"She took me to Senrid. He helped me. Twice. When I found Wan-Edhe's hidden chamber . . ." He swallowed again, an action that took concentration. "It's bleeding their lives out. To make that chamber. Slow time."

Curly Beard's heavy black brows shot upward, and he sat back. "Very well. Very well." He laid his hand on his chest. "This is no easy problem to solve. But there might be some ways to begin."

"Who are you?"

The big man laughed, white teeth flashing in the blue-black beard. "You may call me Rosey."

"Rosey," Jilo repeated, and glared at the man, hatred giving him enough strength to fling back his head. During those terrible days when he'd spied on the Mearsieans in order to find out where their underground hideout was, he'd heard references over and over to 'Rosey.' "You're the one who rescued the Mearsieans from Wan-Edhe."

"When I could. When I could. I've had to be very careful to avoid my real identity being discovered by your former king. He's gotten close enough as it is. Now." Jilo was so weary he was not surprised when Rosey shifted to perfect Chwahir, command mode, captain to flatfoot. The language, the mode, reached back into Jilo's earliest memories, and he found it oddly comforting as Rosey said, "You are going to march into that cottage, and lie down. You'll find an extra bed in the loft. It's clean. There's water in the pitcher. When you're slept out, we will talk. Go."

Jilo wobbled inside, clutching the book tightly against his stomach as he tipped his head back and gazed up the ladder to the loft. Those ten or twelve rungs seemed to stretch up forever. He forced each hand and foot to move, but it took all his strength, and finally he fell onto a low bed.

The moment he caught his breath, he took the book out of his shirt and checked the names, though he was fairly certain he'd memorized them all. Yes. Tsauderei was there, near the top. As he'd expected, there was no listing for 'Rosey.'

He ran his gaze down the other names. Detlev: nothing new.

Siamis: nothing new.

Prince Kessler: Norsunder Base, Norsunder Base, Onekhaer, Mardgar, Imar, Everon, Norsunder Base. He'd been moving around a lot since the last time Jilo had looked. And when had that been?

Even thinking about time made Jilo's mind swim unpleasantly. He blinked, and stared down at the book again. What did those spaces between the Norsunder Base entries mean? He remembered what Senrid had said about the named targets possibly going out of the world. Wan-Edhe would not care what they were doing somewhere so far away that he would not feel threatened.

So much of the book was useless. And yet. Jilo clutched it against him, fighting for concentration. Hide it? No. The medallion he wore with its wards might mask the magic, but if Jilo tried hiding the book in this cottage, Rosey was sure to sense its magic. Oh. Old habit: the hollowed tree where he had kept his drawing supplies, back in the days under Kwenz. Drawing was strictly forbidden, one of the many, many forbidden things. So he'd sneaked it.

That tree lay outside of the old Shadowland, so it ought still to be there.

With the last of his strength, Jilo transferred the book to the hidey-hole.

Then he fell back and dropped into sleep.

It had never occurred to Jilo how difficult for others it might be to fashion magical hidey-holes and transfer objects to them. He'd needed it, found a way to learn how to do it, and did it. Such was the pattern of his life.

Rosey—whose name was Mondros—and Tsauderei had watched Jilo slowly climb to the loft, his thin figure bowed as an old man's. As soon as he vanished up the ladder, they spoke in Ancient Sartoran, which had never been added into the Universal Language Spell.

"That horror did not seem feigned," Mondros said.

Tsauderei didn't really know Mondros that well. Mages were notoriously reclusive; you didn't dedicate your life to magic without being somewhat solitary. But he knew less about Mondros than any of the other powerful mages he had dealt with over the years.

He did not understand what drove Mondros to dedicate his life to fighting Wan-Edhe from a distance, as the man was not a Chwahir, but he respected Mondros for it. Everyone else seemed inclined to overlook Chwahirsland, and forget its ancient problems.

He sat down on the stone bench in Mondros's tiny garden. "My predecessor's records indicate two things: that Wan-Edhe of the Chwahir was not much older than this boy when he made his first kill. In defense, yes. And some records even seem to hint that when he started out, he meant well. By the Chwahir, I hasten to say."

"It's true, all of it." Mondros dropped down beside him. "And so, what? Do you want me to go up there and knife that boy in his sleep? How do you justify that?"

Tsauderei gave a snort of disgust. "Of course not. But I mislike this pattern."

"Jilo turning to Senrid Montredaun-An for help? What's the truth about him? His grandfather had a terrible reputation, and so did the oldest son, but the middle son was supposed to have been fairly benign. For a Marloven."

"I was an assistant mage at the border parley when the grandfather was forced by an alliance of all his neighbors to accept the treaty," Tsauderei said, looking back down the years, then shaking his head. "If the grandson is anything like him, we can expect nothing but trouble. But that's the future. Right now, I don't like the way these children are turning to one another, and not to us."

Mondros, he noted, did not ask him to define that 'us.' "You said Erai-Yanya's prentice brought Jilo to you," Mondros said.

"She did." Tsauderei sat back on the bench. "But not because of established procedure. This particular problem seemed beyond her reach. Let's consider what we just heard about your young Mearsiean, Clair. Why didn't she report this Jilo and his actions to you, who saved her from Wan-Edhe's vindictive pettiness? Why didn't she go to Murial, her own blood relation?"

Mondros pointed a thick finger. "Did *you* always turn to the elders? I know I didn't."

"In matters of great import, I did. As did Evend. And even Igkai, who I believe is the most reclusive of all of us. We followed established procedure. Not that we didn't make mistakes. Plenty of them. My point is, we find ourselves with a number of children in key positions. Many of them smart and well educated. And impatient of guidance."

Mondros sighed. "You see Detlev's hand here."

"Possibly," Tsauderei said. "A poke here, a threat there, an experiment over yonder, then fading back to watch a tragedy unfold. That's his usual style, the rare times he comes out of Norsunder."

"That we know of," Mondros said.

"True. So let's look at what we know of Detlev's latest exploits. We know Senrid was Detlev's prisoner during Siamis's enchantment, before the morvende sent Rel into Norsunder Base to rescue one of their friends, and discovered him there. Did whatever happened to Senrid there make him even less trusting of outsiders than Marlovens are reputed to be?"

Mondros's gaze had shifted sideways, and his hands tightened on his knees. But at Tsauderei's question, he sat back and loosened his grip. "You're right. If there is one thing Detlev's known for, it's rarity of visits, and something always happens, usually wide-reaching and devastating. But even Detlev could not have foreseen the emergence of this Dena Yeresbeth after four millennia. That desperate search before Siamis launched his enchantment in '36 indicates Norsunder had no more notion of its re-emergence than we did. I think it took them as much by surprise as it did us."

Tsauderei was silent a long time before he said, "Dena Yeresbeth." His tone made the words a curse. All his life, it seemed that he'd no sooner gain some understand of the world and how to keep it safe from Norsunder, than some new, larger, more sinister threat would appear. This one seemed the worst one yet because the only people who truly understood it were Lilith the Guardian, whose appearance was ephemeral at best—and the Norsundrian Host of Lords, with Detlev as their minion.

Mondros got to his feet. "Well, that's yet another problem for the future. Right now, I have this boy upstairs. The first thing to be determined is if I'll trust him enough to send him back with some carefully fashioned spells. Time bindings using lives! Wan-Edhe's depredations were even worse than I'd thought. If Jilo really does intend to loosen those deadly wards from within Narad, then we'll know how to proceed."

"Good," Tsauderei said, with feeling. "This one is all yours."

## Chapter Ten

WHEN Senrid showed up in Bereth Ferian the day after Hibern took Jilo away, he made no reference to whatever had caused him to end Liere's previous visit so abruptly in the middle of the night. And she, remembering those vivid, horrifying images he didn't know he'd shared, was too afraid to ask.

"Hibern has relatives who knew my mother," he said to Liere as if they had parted the day before, and not a couple of months ago.

Though his voice sounded the same as ever, the quick flex of his hands, the pulse of horror he couldn't quite mask on the mental plane, made her middle tighten with dread. But all Senrid said was, "I guess since I've managed to stay alive so far, or maybe because they wanted to get rid of the stuff and reclaim their cellar, they sent me some art things that my mother had brought from her home country. I remember you liked the blocks. Want to help me sort through this art and see what to keep and what to stick in our cellar?"

"Shouldn't you ask somebody who knows about art?" Liere asked doubtfully.

"Nah." Senrid made that quick motion, his palm down, hand flat, as though shoving something away. "I don't care what some blathering expert on art likes. I have to look at the stuff, not them. So it makes more sense to go through and find what I like. But you have a good eye,

I noticed that before. You'll be able to tell me why I like it. Or not, if you don't want to."

"Oh, it sounds like fun, if you put it that way," she exclaimed.

"Good! And Hibern is bringing the Queen of Sartor to our next tutoring session. They want to learn how to make mind-shields, and asked if you'd teach them."

When Liere began to tense up, Senrid grinned. "Atan—Hibern says she wants to be called that, instead of The Great and Mighty Queen Yustnesveas Landis the 152nd of Ancient Sartor, or whatever her number is. 'Yust-ness-vey-ass!' No wonder she wants to be called Atan. Who wouldn't, saddled with a load like that? Anyway, she's my age. And was raised in a cave, or some such thing."

Liere's doubt turned to perplexity, and Senrid said quickly, "Liere, think about it, would anyone really come to Marloven Hess in a lot of pompous state, spouting speeches and old poetry that nobody can understand, or whatever these Sartorans and Colendi do when kings go calling?" He made a face. "Hah. Come to think of it, I don't think any kings or queens have ever made any kind of visit here, state or not, unless they were wrangled into marrying one of my ancestors. That would be princesses, since nobody ever wanted any foreign princes snouting in."

Liere's tension eased slightly, and he said, "The cook even ordered more of that cocoa to make hot chocolate, just for you."

Liere brightened. "Oh, that is so kind!"

They transferred to Marloven Hess.

And for the rest of the day, as she adjusted to the heat of summer, she hugged to herself the delight over knowing that the cook had ordered hot chocolate. For her.

By the end of dinner, she had come full circle to wondering if another word for 'belonging' was 'expectation.' Was she turning into one of those spoiled princesses everyone hated, who expected special treatment? And she wasn't even a real princess!

And of course, by then, late at night, as she sat in her room trying to read in spite of eyes burning with exhaustion, as Senrid tended to his kingdom affairs, she fell into the old battle against the weakness, the futility of emotion.

She tried wearily to focus on the book she'd brought, which was the next on the shelves she'd been toiling through. And she wasn't comprehending it at all. She blinked at the page. No. Not one word. She'd been moving her gaze over it while feeling sorry for herself.

Aware of that, she sat up straight, and settled the book firmly on her lap. Because of that stupid emotion, she would read twice as long the next day, and give up her ride.

Stupid stupid stupid emotions—worthless, useless, weak emotions. From now on, anything she discovered herself looking forward to, she would cancel.

She firmly turned back to the beginning. This would be useful. This would train her stupid, weak, useless brain.

*Rhythms in Soil Richness.*

*In the north meadow, shall we ever seed with corn, but in the south meadow, shall three-fold the rhythm be: after summer's heat shall be wheat, followed by a spring of sprouts, followed thence by a season of openness to birds of the air . . .*

The second reading really did go easier. She was well into the third year—fifteen pages!—when Senrid returned from wherever he'd been.

"Keriam keeps telling me things my father said, and they sound good, but when I really think about what they mean, how to use them, I don't get it." He sighed and dropped cross-legged onto the other end of the window seat, where Liere sat with her books. "Like the difference between strength and power." He stopped there, aware of her distracted attention.

She was thinking, *More Marloven stuff.* She knew she should take an interest, but it was so hard to, because she knew she'd never need any of it. *Like old-fashioned harvests?* she taunted herself.

"Fenis Senelac is down in the riding ring," Senrid said. "It's a full moon night, and the heat has finally gone. Perfect for riding."

Liere clapped the thin book onto the fat lexicon of Ancient Sartoran, and leaped up happily.

Then she remembered her promise. She sat back down firmly, opened the ancient book, and said, "I can't go riding. I didn't complete my studying."

Senrid looked surprised. "Studying?"

Liere tapped the book. "My project."

"But you can read later. She's got a horse saddled."

Liere shook her head. "I didn't study earlier. I need the discipline."

Senrid sighed.

Liere forced herself to breathe, to calm herself. Rational discourse! "You've got discipline. I need to work on mine."

Senrid eyed Liere. She sat there in the window seat, her fingers gripping that old book from Bereth Ferian's library, her cuticles ragged.

Senrid glanced down at the book. Ancient Sartoran. About farming, of all things.

"If I could go riding any time I wanted," he said, "I would."

Liere looked down, her mouth unhappy. Presented with the top of Liere's head, Senrid noticed that she'd taken a knife to her hair again; it was more ragged than ever. He knew better than to argue, though he thought it was crazy to force herself to read every book in that library, starting with the first shelf and moving through every single tome, just because that sounded orderly. Likewise forcing herself to learn Ancient Sartoran without knowing the modern language first.

When she got like that, he'd discovered, the only way to get her to act like a normal person was to ask her to go with him when he did fun things.

"How about if you lay that aside, and let's try tackling an easier lesson in Ancient Sartoran? It's more like code breaking, then, and less a toil of having to look up every second word," he said.

Liere set aside the dusty tomes, angry with herself for having revealed whatever it was that got Senrid to say that. She would triple the study time on the farming book the next day.

If only she had his sense of discipline, and his lack of stupid emotion. No, he had emotions. She'd seen him angry, ashamed, afraid. Hurt.

But he didn't let any of it out, it didn't get in the *way*. He got things *done*.

Atan anticipated her visit to Hibern's homeland with a pleasure that was the more intense for its being a secret. The more delving she'd done into her ancestors' private archives, the more often she'd discovered far-reaching state matters turning on personalities and private actions—abductions at one point numbering high on the list.

Tsauderei, in his efforts to educate Atan on Sartoran matters when Sartor and its archives were beyond reach, had initiated her into the histories written by scribes. She really liked scribe histories. Most seemed more even-handed than official court histories, and some scribal memoirs gave hints of the sort of thing she was doing, finding ways around the complication of protocol and tradition.

She was going to keep using her free hour for . . . freedom.

As she paced her study waiting for the bells that would herald Hibern's appearance, she wondered why it was that secret things were so much fun. And the idea that she would be the first Sartoran ruler to set foot in a kingdom depicted as full of villains made the fun that much more fun.

Hibern had promised her that Senrid wasn't a villain. At least, he was trying not to be one, though he'd been raised to be. All that made him even more interesting. Atan imagined someone even taller than Rel, more imposing, except blond, because the records indicated that the Marloven forebears were Venn, and everybody knew the Venn were mostly tall and light-haired and very good at war.

When she and Hibern reached Marloven Hess at last, Atan found herself looking down at a boy whose only resemblance to her inner image lay in the light hair. His short, light-boned form reminded her a lot of Hinder, except his quick, nervy movements were totally unlike Hin's casual drift, and there was a hint of more muscle in the bland white sleeves of his shirt and in the dark-covered legs above the riding boots.

Senrid stared up at a girl who was apparently even taller than Hibern, or maybe the effect was caused by the up-and-down effect of the purple silk edging to her robe, which extended all the way to the floor. Marloven formal House tunics always ended at the boot tops.

As Hibern performed the introductions, and Atan took in the little figure half-hiding behind Senrid, once again amazement flooded her. This frail little creature was the famous Sartora? The thin, unkempt child with the wide honey-colored gaze looked like she would have blown away at the first puff of wind, and yet she'd stood up to the evil Siamis!

Liere reddened. "Would you like a tour?"

"I would indeed, thank you," Atan said.

Liere, not Senrid, led the way.

Atan's third impression was that the place smelled awful: the warm, humid summer air brought the distinct tang of horse. Nobody here seemed to know a thing about air or light flow.

They walked past endless rooms of plain sand-colored stone. The monotony was broken along some halls by plaster reliefs in subtle shades of silver and gray depicting flying raptors and running horses. She counted one tapestry, and from the way it was wrinkled, it had apparently just been removed from storage and mounted on this bare wall at the top of a landing.

Senrid hung back during the tour. Before their arrival, remembering the discomfiture he'd experienced at the disgust with which CJ of the

Mearsieans had described his home, he'd said to Liere, "Why don't you show her around? You'll know better than I what non-Marlovens will want to see."

So Liere did. She was nervous at first, then quietly indignant at the drift of Atan's thoughts. She knew she shouldn't be listening, but she could scarcely help it. They came here to learn the mind-shield, she told herself as they walked downstairs. This was why.

While Liere talked to Atan, Senrid spoke low-voiced to Hibern in their own language. "What happened to Jilo?"

"Tsauderei took him somewhere."

"And?"

"Don't know. Tsauderei's note to me that night only said that Jilo was with a mage who could help him. Maybe there's nothing more to tell. But I'll get Erai-Yanya to ask when she returns, if you need to know who, and what's going on."

Senrid scowled at the floor. "Is it you or me they don't trust?"

"They?"

"Tsauderei and whoever else he's drawn in." At Hibern's skeptical expression, Senrid muttered, "Tell me if I'm wrong, but don't these adult mages usually love nothing better than to lecture us about our ignorance?"

Hibern opened her hand. "I've been studying at the mage school in Bereth Ferian while Erai-Yanya is gone, and they haven't heard anything about Jilo. Arthur would hear if anyone was talking about a king our age that far advanced in dark magic. So maybe Tsauderei isn't talking to anyone."

Senrid said, "Where is your tutor? Seems she's been gone a long time."

"She was here, then went back to our sister world, Geth-deles."

"The ocean one? Why?"

"Norsunder is doing something suspicious there."

Senrid drew in a sharp breath. That fit the holes in the transfers of the head snakes in Jilo's book, he was thinking, but he didn't say anything.

When they reached the bottom of the stairs, Liere looked back inquiringly.

Senrid glanced at Atan. "State chambers, maybe?"

Liere led on. When they reached the throne room, Liere pointed inside the massive double doors. "This is where the Marloven jarls gather for Convocation at New Year's Week."

She observed Atan's gaze lifting to the banners on the walls, and the crossed swords below, with other artifacts of the Marloven past. She sensed Atan waiting, and added, "I don't know what those swords are for, or what those crown-like things are."

"Helms." Senrid stayed back in the shadows, watching. "Commanders' helms. Worn at specific battles."

"And those must be their swords?" Atan asked politely.

"Yes and no. Those are surrendered swords. From the defeated commander, some of them crossed by the triumphant commander's sword."

Atan wasn't interested in the swords, helms, or banners. She was more interested in Senrid. He didn't sound all that bloodthirsty, nor was his tone gloating or bragging.

Atan wondered what having these things on the walls here meant to Marlovens. Perhaps these disgusting objects were intended to scare the jarls into obedience. Either that or these objects were supposed to fire the Marlovens with the desire to go out, win battles, and have their own banners and steel stuck up on that stone wall. She hoped that their own homes weren't as ugly as this chamber.

"Very fine," she said in her first-circle voice.

"We're done here." Senrid ducked through the door, his boot heels ringing a quick tattoo on the stone. He was thoroughly unsettled by how much Atan's opinion mattered to him. Why should it? But it did. As if she were inspecting his entrails and finding them wanting, like a suspicious fish laid out at the marketplace. "Rest is the same," he said over his shoulder. "And you came for a purpose, not a hike through my castle."

The others followed, Hibern suspecting and Liere knowing that something had disturbed Senrid.

Liere was glad when they reached the study and Senrid said briskly, "You came here to learn mind-shields. You're better at teaching mind-shields than I am, Liere. Why don't I see about your favorite drink? Atan, do you like hot chocolate, too?"

"Certainly," Atan said in some surprise, and was more surprised when Senrid shot out the door. "What just happened?" Atan asked Hibern.

As they sat down in Senrid's study, Hibern turned a questioning look to Liere, who was not going to tell the Queen of Sartor that she was leaking thoughts.

Liere said, "Teaching you about the mind-shield will be very boring for Senrid to hear again, since he already knows it." She had been through this explanation enough times with the northern mage school, Arthur, Erai-Yanya, and anyone else who asked, that she could teach it fairly swiftly: building a wall in the mind, seeing the wall, concentrating on keeping thoughts behind the wall.

She paused to demonstrate each level, and then said, "That's it."

Atan gazed in surprise. "Really? That's all? I thought this would be a first lesson, that it would take months. Even years. And maybe hurt."

Liere's face turned a mottled red as she tried not to laugh. She said, "Next comes practice. That takes longer. Until it's habit."

"Ah. Of course." Atan nodded. "So tell me this, either of you. Those swords on the wall downstairs. Do those sustain some hidden idea, or a version of loyalty, or oaths, century after century? Hibern, you told me that written records don't often survive one change of king to the next."

Hibern said, "I think you could say that they're a symbol of pride, and power. Order. Much like the statuary in your city. The ones people talk about, I mean, not the ones they ignore."

"And yet those weapons aren't beautiful to look at." Atan raised a hand in the Sartoran gesture of apology. "I ask only to be taught. Do Marlovens look upon those swords as art, or are they symbols to remind them of the battles, the stories behind them?"

"The second," Hibern said. "Stories are important. And while Marlovens don't have written records, we do have ballads." She winced at that 'we' slipping out, because it always brought back her father's thick, angry voice. *Get out.*

"About smiting enemies?"

"About honor and privilege, including the honor, the privilege to go to battle, to die, for the—" *glory* "—preservation of the kingdom." She heard a memory echo of the Andahi Lament, and the back of her neck tightened.

"In Sartor we would call that duty, but no one sings about fighting to keep peace," Atan said, then added quickly, "At least now, they don't. We do have some fairly martial songs in the past." She sounded apologetic, like someone admitting to an error in taste.

Atan studied Liere. "And you, I think you're from Imar?"

Liere ducked her head, her smile vanishing.

Atan gestured apology once again, knowing she had erred, but not how. "I just wanted to ask, do you feel the same as the Marlovens? Are you going to live here?" She bent closer. "What brings you here?"

Liere said, "Senrid." She twisted her fingers together. "He's my first friend. My real one."

"What does that mean, 'real one'?" Atan asked.

In spite of the lessons, Liere was the only one whose mind-shield was in place. She tried not to listen, but the inexact nature of the Universal Language Spell distracted her; she could 'hear' whispers of meaning all around the translated words, and had to concentrate to shut it out. Senrid had told her she really needed to learn modern Sartoran first, the language people actually used. Discomfort tightened her middle, because she knew her wish to master Ancient Sartoran was in part a wish to truly fight ignorance and in part to merely appear less ignorant.

Perhaps that was really a wish to show off.

Unaware of how long she sat in reverie, she finally looked up to discover the older girls waiting. "Senrid never called me Sartora."

Atan stared in surprise. "You don't like that?"

"No. I do not," Liere said, her voice low and unsteady. "I am not Sartora. I am not a world rescuer. It was all an accident. At least, mostly— it was just that I was the only one who could use the dyr, which was a very common thing in the days of Ancient Sartor, so I'm told. And so many people helped me. And I don't live here. I visit Senrid, and he lives here, so here I am. I don't have a home anymore. I . . ." She heard her father's derisive voice about whiners, and how much people despised them, and closed her mouth.

Atan leaned forward. "Sar—ah, Liere, if you want a home, anyone would give you one. Don't you see what being Sartora means? You can have anything you want."

Liere eyed Atan. "No, not really. They call me a queen, but it's only in a symbolic way. I don't have a crown, or an army, or guards, or a treasury. And I don't want them! That beautiful palace in Bereth Ferian doesn't belong to me. It's a place where the mages put me. You might not understand, because you are a real queen. *You* can have anything you want."

Atan said, "I can't have my family back. I can't command Colend to return the Music Festival, which might sound silly to you. It did to me, at first, until I understood how ashamed all the adults are, the people born a century ago, who came back into the world to discover we're a hundred years behind everyone else. The world didn't stop to wait for Sartor . . . oh, never mind all that. I can work on those things, and I will. But you, you're completely free. You can go where you want."

"I can't have everything I want, either."

Atan smiled. "I think the world would give it to you if it could."

Liere bit her nail, then snatched her hand down as if she'd been slapped. She wriggled in her chair, head lowered. "Maybe they would. Now. Until Siamis comes back and I won't be able to do what I did before. How angry will they be that I can't be Sartora, the Girl Who Saved the World, again?"

Senrid had been listening from outside the door. He could hear how close to tears Liere was, even if the others couldn't. He could sense Atan's puzzlement, her striving to understand, and Hibern's uneasiness (because she'd forgotten her mind-shield yet again).

Time to intervene. "The only good thing about Ancient Sartoran Norsundrians is that they usually let a few centuries pass between their visits," he said as he entered. "Siamis is probably holed up tight, and won't pop up again until our great-grandchildren are old and gray. Hot chocolate coming right behind me."

Hibern and Atan stayed long enough to drink a cup. The conversation was resolutely superficial, and they took their leave shortly after.

As soon as they arrived back in Eidervaen, Atan said, "Did that go as badly as I thought?"

Hibern opened her hands. "I don't know Liere at all. But I've seen her get all tied in knots in that same way. It wasn't you. And I don't know why she does it."

Atan tugged gently on a silken tassel hanging from a hassock. "Art. Do Marlovens see art the way the rest of us do?"

Hibern snorted. "Does everyone else see art exactly the same way? No, don't answer, I know what you meant. I think you could say that the idea of art the way you have it here came late for us. Marlovens didn't have houses until they took over the Iascan castles. They didn't even know that the Iascans stripped everything out when they left. My ancestors lived with bare stone for ages and ages, but then they were very seldom inside. Still true. Ornaments tend to be badges of triumph. But art, oh, you could say it's in the songs, and in movement: the perfect gait of a horse, perfect form in shooting, the rhythms in the drums, the sparks shooting upward in the sword dance."

Atan's mouth rounded. "I see. Oh, that is so interesting! All right, last question, or rather, observation. Senrid is so short! He looks about nine, but he's too well-spoken for that."

"He's the same age as me." Hibern grinned. "Father quite tall, his mother small, so I'm told. But yes, Marlovens tend to be shorter. Erai-Yanya thinks it's due to the fact that the Marlovens' ancestors took to horses, and the shorter, lighter families thrived. They were just as fierce as the big Venn warriors."

The bell rang then, and Hibern took her leave.

Atan walked out into the hall, breathing deeply. Then she had to laugh at herself when she whiffed the faint, familiar scent of mildew, which had become so familiar she'd forgotten it. But she had noticed on her first tour of the castle. Despite the servants' constant, rigorous efforts to keep everything scrupulously clean, it seemed to be the inevitable consequence of centuries of little change.

If Senrid was ever to come to her palace, would he think it stank?

## Chapter Eleven

FOR a couple days, it took all Jilo's strength to walk out of Mondros's cottage.

He made it far enough to drop onto the late-summer grass and gaze down into Colend lying peacefully below. He watched cloud shadows ripple over the land, changing colors to blue tones, then the red-gold reappeared, except for the greens, which brightened with a buttery overlay. The long shadows slowly pulling in then moving eastward fascinated him.

The third day, the impulse to sit there forever and watch the sky and the land faded away. He was aware of a stronger pull, a fretful anxiety impelled by fear.

Mondros called him in to breakfast.

"I walked over the border, to assess the state of Wan-Edhe's wards. There was no time to ride to your capital. I wish there were, and of course I dare not transfer. But as little as I saw impressed me mightily," Mondros said when Jilo sat down. "You have improved things."

"Not much," Jilo mumbled. "Not nearly enough."

"Many senior students couldn't do as much as you have. In fact, I don't know anyone, old or young, who's mastered as much about dark magic wards as you have."

"Had to learn it."

"On the run, so to speak. I'll accept that, but if you really don't want to find yourself turning into a replica of Wan-Edhe, then you had better begin your studies in another direction."

"Which?" Jilo asked.

"Is it not obvious? The land. If you want to help the Chwahir, you will have to understand the relationship between land and magic. This corner of the continent has never been easy. Your Chwahir ancestors set out to enhance, to alter, to influence, to change. Well, all our ancestors did. Sartor as well."

"How do I fix that? Every book I spotted is for extending those spells. I know better than to release them all at once, even if I could."

"Smart boy." Mondros frowned at his pan of crushed olive. It had begun to steam, so he tumbled in the potatoes, garlic, and purple onion that he'd chopped.

The smell opened up a yawning cavern inside of Jilo. He had begun to think of cooking as magic. There were so many similarities.

Mondros shook the pan to even out the ingredients, then jerked a massive thumb over his shoulder at the opposite wall of the cottage, which was packed, floor to ceiling, with books. "You're going to have to begin studying light magic. And while you do that, you must begin the process of reversing that benighted sinkhole of evil in your castle in Narad. We will address that. Today, begin with the fundamentals. I set some books on the work table."

Jilo inhaled the delicious breakfast. With the return of energy came commensurate anxiety, proliferating questions. "Maybe I ought to start now."

Mondros could see the fret, and signs of resentment, in the narrow-eyed, speculative glances the boy sent his way. He decided to let Jilo guide the talk as he watched for manipulation, the smiler who tells you what you want to hear. He withheld judgment, aware that survival around Wan-Edhe would warp individuals as much as his magic warped the air.

The day passed in study.

As Mondros fried up the trout he'd caught for their supper, he observed Jilo still bent over the rudimentary magic book, the one given to ten-year-olds who thought they might want to become mages. The boy's lank black hair hung down unkempt, half-hiding his flat cheeks, and his shoulder blades poked the back of his shirt, which had lightened to a dull gray. Jilo didn't appear to notice, or maybe it had yet to occur to him he could wear whatever he wanted. That there were other possibilities besides the badly dyed, one-size-fits-all flatfoot-probationer uniform.

———

A week of hard study passed.

The day came at last when rain on the Colendi side, merely thunder and lightning with no moisture to the north for the parched Chwahir, caused Jilo to say, "I think I ought to go back."

"Very well," Mondros said. "I'm not stopping you."

Jilo's head lifted from its habitual droop. His pale brown eyes met Mondros's, then his gaze dropped again. "That's all?" he said to the scuffed chair leg, and Mondros made a mental note to do some sanding and varnishing. The summer weather, when he moved his furniture outside, was difficult on the wood.

Mondros said, "Did you expect something else?"

"Threats?" One side of Jilo's somber mouth curled up briefly, then he gave in to the resentment that had burned in him for years. "I know I ought not to expect a rescue, like Puddlenose got, time and again, which usually resulted in my being punished. Or Tereneth of Erdrael Danara's rescue."

"Who was a prisoner," Mondros said. "The first was a hostage. You are a Chwahir. Since all my efforts to curb Wan-Edhe's attempts to spread his evil influence had to be done from the outside, how was I to know that you were not in Narad because you wanted to replace Puddlenose as potential errand-boy to Wan-Edhe?"

Jilo could not suppress a recoil of angry revulsion. But he had to admit that from the outside, his compliance might have looked like choice, and not survival.

Mondros saw some of this. "There are two secret exits in your fortress, one established by a Sonscarna mage-queen centuries ago. That one is magical, and I believe you now know of it."

Jilo shrugged jerkily, remembering what Clair had said. Senrid had used it.

"The other was through the dungeon, a very old tunnel. It's how Prince Kessler escaped, and how Puddlenose was able to get away. You should ask him about it." Mondros put his fists on his knees.

Jilo's chin came up. "He might still think I'm a villain. The Mearsiean girls called me a villain."

Mondros said provocatively, "You did some villainous things, if their stories are true."

"I did what I was told to do. You knew what would happen if I didn't follow orders."

"Always?" Mondros countered.

"Yes . . ." Jilo thought back, and a tide of heat burned up his neck and made his ears itch. "Not always." He scowled. "But that was my life. I didn't see anything else."

"You saw the life Puddlenose and the girls led. It was very different."

"They were Mearsieans."

"And you tried at least once to take it away."

"I wanted to have that life, and taking it away was how it was supposed to go," Jilo retorted.

Mondros gave an encouraging nod. "All right. I'll concede that you existed under a cloud of threat at least as palpable as that cloud under which you once lived. But from a distance, you were beginning to look like Wan-Edhe in training, until he put those spells on you."

"Well, I'm not Wan-Edhe. I don't want to be Wan-Edhe. I can't think of anyone I hate more than Wan-Edhe."

"Yes, everyone hated him. But who are you when you are not hating, Jilo? No, don't tell me. Show me. There are no wards keeping you from transferring."

Jilo transferred out a short time later, carrying a basket of Mondros's delicious food, and a carefully copied scroll of light magic fundamentals under his arm. It didn't occur to him to wonder until later, when he sat down to eat the first item in the basket, why Mondros had been watching over Chwahirsland, when he wasn't a Chwahir.

*Late autumn, 4740, Sarendan*

Peitar Selenna, king of Sarendan, had looked forward to Atan's next visit for weeks.

He knew that even if Atan did release the Child Spell and miraculously fall in love with him, that would mean two unhappy people, for there was no future for them unless one of them abdicated.

Yet when Atan appeared with tall, handsome Rel, whom Peitar immediately recognized from Lilah's and Atan's descriptions (and the praise didn't seem exaggerated), the pain was quite sharp.

It was a relief when Lilah leaped up, fired with inspiration. "Oh, Rel, would you come and drill our new Sharadan brigade like you did the Sartoran orphans in the forest?"

Peitar watched Rel covertly. There was no roll of the eyes under shuttered lids, no curl of lip, however brief. The only sign that Rel was not overjoyed to be thus summarily taken off was the quick, amused look he sent at Atan, and the swift, secret smile she returned.

But Atan said nothing. Rel smiled at Lilah's hopeful, expectant face, and said, "I'd be glad to." And he walked off with Lilah as if happy to toil in the bitter weather with a group of strangers.

". . . and I told them you might come some day, because Atan did promise she would bring you," Lilah Selenna chattered on, proud and excited, as she and Rel walked down the steep hill into the eastern part of Miraleste, the capital of Sarendan.

Fire damage still existed here and there, and rubble-strewn empty lots where houses had once stood, but those were rare. Everything else looked newly constructed, or at least refurbished. Even in the bleak lighting under lowering gray clouds, the city was bright and clean.

"Won't your brigade see me as an interloper?" Rel asked.

"Oh, no, not at *all!* They've heard about what we Rescuers did in Sartor, and they all said, if you ever visit, would you come and show them what you showed the Sartoran orphans, in case we have to defend ourselves against the eleveners? I said you would," Lilah finished, her slanted eyes earnest under puckered brows. "That you didn't think the Sartorans better than us."

After that, what could Rel say?

The weather was as bitter as to be expected as the year waned. Maybe none of her orphan brigade would show up. He tucked his chin down into his fleece-lined coat.

". . . and so the guilds all contributed, and they rebuilt the burned-out shop where we four hid while being the Sharadan Brothers, and it's now our headquarters," Lilah was saying proudly. "Sometimes Bren comes and does exercises with them, when he's in the city. Innon has, too."

Rel glanced down at Lilah's friendly face. She still looked like a rust-haired, stocky boy. "I thought Innon was noble-born. Doesn't Derek mind?"

"Derek likes Innon. He worked for the revolution." Lilah rushed on, "And Derek knows all about you, and that you aren't a noble, and he said he would like to meet you. I wish he was here, but Peitar sent him on a mission. Derek is Peitar's most trusted person. Besides me. And Tsauderei," Lilah finished as they turned down a narrow alley with newly laid brickwork instead of cobblestones, the buildings neat.

"All the locals, mostly our age, pitched in to rebuild. Here we are," Lilah finished.

Rel's hopes sank when they passed through a narrow gate into a newly flagged yard crammed with shivery, blue-lipped youth.

They took one look at Rel's size, and Lilah's proud grin, and sent up a cheer.

So Rel fell into his old routine, working them until they were sweating. All the while he wondered what Atan, Peitar, and Hibern were talking about during Atan's precious free hour that he was missing.

In the palace, Hibern began talking about an interesting book she'd discovered in the northern mage school archive. Peitar half-listened while he analyzed the physical sensation of sharp disappointment and regret.

How stupid it was to think that the Child Spell would keep Atan—or her friend—from experiencing the emotions of attraction. These things were not like following a recipe: the spell froze you at whatever age you were when you performed it, but it did not stop your mind from working. In that single quick gaze between Atan and Rel he sensed a natural turning to one another. They might never have kissed. Either or both might not even be consciously aware of their feelings. But they were there.

"Don't you think, Peitar?" Atan asked, and Peitar hastily recollected the thread of discourse, and joined in.

The hour passed far too swiftly, as it always did, from history to historical people to who wrote about famous people to ideas about justice. The discussion turned into friendly debate as they tried to hammer out exactly what 'justice' meant.

"That's one of the reasons why I am glad of my council, constraining as I find them," Atan said earnestly. "They still see justice clearer than I do. I listen, I feel for both sides, they decide, they explain why, later, and I say 'Oh-h-h-h, I did not see that.'"

"Perhaps you didn't interpret it that way," Hibern suggested. "One thing I've learned reading records, everyone sounds reasonable when they explain why they did something. Then you consider *what* they did, and you get the sick feeling." She made a fist and lightly struck her middle.

"And so it is, sitting in on justice." Peitar spoke in a low, ruminative voice, thin hands clasped, long dark lashes shuttering his eyes as he gazed sightlessly at his hands. "There are always two sides, sometimes three, which makes it even more difficult to find a compromise that fulfills the expectations of all parties. If the king has to make a judgment against one when there is no compromise, that party might go away feeling betrayed by what is supposed to be royal justice. The emotional price is one the king pays. It should be that way, or we risk becoming—"

The distant city bells rang.

Atan said, "Peitar?"

He looked up, and shook his head. "I lost the thread. I was blathering. It wasn't worth following."

"The emotional price," Hibern said, thinking of Senrid.

"You're in danger of becoming a tyrant?" Atan prompted teasingly, disturbed by his mood; she couldn't define it, but sensed somberness in the subtle tensing of his shoulders, his hands, his high, intelligent forehead. "But wouldn't a tyrant perpetrate injustice on whim?"

Peitar's hand lifted, palm out, and his smile twisted. "It matters not. I suspect I'm beginning to sound pompous."

Atan jumped up. "Not at all, but I can't stay to argue! We've already figured out that your bells ring noon very little before ours do." She held up two fingers as she turned to Hibern. "Will you be able to bring Rel back, if he wants to return to Sartor?"

"Glad to," Hibern replied.

Atan muttered a quick apology for transferring directly in company, and vanished in a puff of herb-scented air.

Lilah and Rel arrived a short time later. Peitar watched Rel look around, and his expression shutter as Lilah said in the tone of one who had been marshaling every persuasive argument she could, "So can you stay? I know Derek wants to meet you, and it's only two days until we expect him back. Maybe even tomorrow!"

Lilah turned expectantly to Peitar, who said obediently, "You are most welcome. We have plenty of room."

"There, you see?" Lilah exclaimed, bouncing on her toes, her short rust-colored hair flopping on her freckled forehead and over her ears. "You see? Peitar, you should have been there, they *loved* it. They were so *proud* of themselves. Rel, you *have* to show Derek those things you've learned, he's been trying, and trying, but he never had any military training . . ."

Rel looked slowly from one face to the other. He'd heard about Derek from Lilah, and Atan; on the surface, they scarcely seemed to describe the same person. But he knew that people were seldom all good or all bad, and that opinions were rarely uniform.

So. He was curious. He also wanted to keep his promise to Puddle-nose and invite Peitar and Lilah into the alliance, since Atan kept forgetting. Most important, he'd already missed Atan's free hour; if he returned now, he would only have two more days of catching her at odd moments before Atan's noble watchdogs would expect him to be pushing along.

"If you truly don't mind," he said.

"Yah!" Lilah jumped around the room. "It will be such fun!"

*Six weeks later*

*Rel: Will you be here to celebrate the anniversary of the Freeing of Sartor? If so, ask Lilah if she would like to come, since she was a Rescuer, too. I plan some special entertainments just for us. Atan.*

Rel looked up at Peitar, who had just received the note through his notecase. Atan knew that Rel didn't have a notecase, after having lost two on his travels, so she'd sent her note to Rel via Peitar.

His expression didn't change as Rel offered the note back to him. He glanced down at it and then handed it to his sister.

Lilah bounced up and down on her toes. "Oh, may I go?"

"Of course you may," Peitar said, and looked askance at his sister in her ragged old knee pants, scruffy haircut, and incongruously pretty blouse. "Lilah, may I in turn suggest you put on one of your better outfits? You'll be going as Sarendan's representative."

Lilah twitched a shoulder impatiently, but she was too happy at the prospect of seeing Sartor again to argue.

And so, the next day, Peitar gave them transfer tokens.

Peitar was surprised at the pulse of regret he felt when Rel vanished. Rel was smart, competent, easy-going, and utterly without pretense. Peitar had wondered how Derek would accept him, as he was wary around not only aristocrats and royalty, but anyone favored by them. But he'd been watching Derek when Rel said, "Don't expect me to know a lot about commanding, because I don't. All I've commanded have been fellow guards for small caravans when I earned my way through kingdoms. But I've done plenty of drills."

Derek said, "Someone called you Rel the Shepherd's son. Is that true?"

"Don't know." Rel shrugged his big shoulders. "My guardian has never said. But my first job was tending the holding's sheep."

Derek's reserve had vanished in the genuine smile that Peitar knew meant acceptance, and the rest of Rel's visit had gone just as well.

As Peitar returned to his tasks, he found it hurt a little less that Atan would find Rel attractive. He felt it in a mild way himself.

---

Rel and Lilah transferred to the royal palace Destination in Sartor.

A page ran off to report. When they recovered, Lilah was instantly claimed by Hinder. They vanished down a corridor, high voices echoing back, as Rel was conducted by a self-conscious page to Atan's informal receiving room.

When Rel saw her formally dressed in complicated layers of green and gold over ivory, with cherry highlights, the differences in their rank struck him afresh.

She said, "The celebration was Hradzy's idea, actually, that we institute a new festival day, the Freeing of Sartor, and have our candle march. Even though New Year's Week is only a short time off, it still seems fitting."

Rel remembered meeting Hradzy Wendis during a previous visit. One of the youths born a hundred years ago, a skinny fellow with a charming smile, Hradzy reminded Rel a lot of Hannla. From a prestigious family, related to at least three duchas, the sort of fellow they'd want Atan to marry someday, he couldn't help thinking. If they didn't force her to marry some other kingdom's spare prince for treaty purposes.

Atan went on. "I put together this party beforehand, just for the Rescuers. I hired a group of singers to perform for us before they lead the singing on the parade. I don't know if it will take, but it's nice to be queen when you can try to get around something you know is unfair," she added under her breath, and Rel remembered hearing some gossip about how certain important nobles wanted the commoners among the Rescuers to be quietly yet tastefully closed out. "How was your stay in Sarendan?"

He'd been thinking about what he ought to tell her. Atan hated military or war talk, and then there was that business about Derek.

Keep it short, he'd decided. "I ended up traveling around to give the orphan brigade some rudimentary training."

"Did Derek decide you were tainted by my friendship?"

"On the contrary. Invited me." Rel shrugged. "He was the first to admit he's a terrible military leader. I've had enough training to run beginners through the basics. Derek didn't even know that. His style of training was to tell them rousing stories, or make speeches to bind them together at heart, then loose them in a melee, that is, an attack in a crowd." Rel clapped his hands together, twined his fingers, and wiggled them. "No notion of discipline. I think in his mind, the idea of a chain of command was akin to the bad old king."

"Who very nearly had him executed," Atan said, as they paced down to the concert hall. "And Peitar along with. Go on."

"Not much more to say. I convinced Derek to see discipline as the people working together. A commander is there to call directions."

"And not act like a king," Atan said. "Does that actually work?"

Rel spread his hands. "So far."

"So this is a new army?"

"Don't know. Don't even know if their brigades will last out the winter. There was some muttering in some of the still-recovering trade towns about rowdy orphans playing with swords while others did the work to feed them. Criticism that Derek took hard, by the way, because it was from the workers and ordinary folk, not from the nobles."

Atan nodded slowly. "Good. Anything that gets Derek to see people as people, and not as bad-people-with-rank versus good-people-without-rank, will go toward proving Tsauderei's dire prediction wrong. I know he wants it to be."

Rel remembered the wild enthusiasm of the brigades when Derek spoke of raising their banner—defending the kingdom—heroism and fame and glory. He looked down at the trefoil patterns in the mosaic tiles, feeling as if he'd done something wrong, or that he was part of a huge something going wrong, and he had no idea how to fix it. Yet everyone around him believed they were in the right.

It was a relief to reach the concert hall where his Sartoran friends awaited his and Atan's arrival, everyone self-conscious in their best. Mendaen and Hannla closed in on either side of Rel, competing cheerily for news of his latest adventures.

Rel gave them a very truncated version as he looked about for the aristocrats among the Rescuers. None of them were present. And he saw Atan's true purpose: she had arranged this special party, and attended it herself, as a silent rebuke to her high council for planning a festival that only included the high-ranking Rescuers.

*4741, New Year's Week, Marloven Hess to Bereth Ferian*

On the other side of the continent, Senrid watched from his study window as Forthan commanded the third-year seniors in drilling the exhibitions intended as Second Night's entertainment for New Year's Week Convocation.

The exhibition far outstripped the lance demonstration the second-year seniors had been working on during mornings. This carefully choreographed fight on horseback, with real cavalry blades, was insanely dangerous, especially when they insisted on real strikes—'real' meaning sending sparks flying.

But Keriam officially did not take notice, and Senrid watched from a distance, knowing that these determined rehearsals in the face-cracking cold of nighttime were in part a kind of apology, and in part an attempt to shed the last of the shame of the academy troubles during spring.

It would be a relief to disperse those seniors at the end of New Year's Week for their two years of duty with the guards. Keriam had been very careful to split them all up, assigning the worst of the Regent's toadies' sons to the border garrisons, away from their special cronies. Those remaining in the capital, like Forthan, were mostly not troublemakers, save one whom Keriam wanted to keep under his eye.

Senrid nearly turned away, then spotted a lone figure climbing into the stone stands to watch the last of the rehearsal: the foreigner, known only as Shevraeth.

It had been impulse to accede to the surprising letter from that prince in Remalna. The Renselaeus family and Senrid were related way back in the family tree, but that shouldn't matter. Senrid was more nearly related to Leander Tlennen-Hess of Vasande Leror, and it would never have occurred to him to invite Leander to the academy.

Not that Leander would ever accept. He loved studying magic and history as much as he loathed anything military. If he hadn't ended up as king of that tiny polity that once had belonged to Marloven Hess, he would probably be in Bereth Ferian's mage school right now, or in Sartor's scribe school, studying magic at nights so that he could become a herald-archivist in the mage guild.

Shevraeth sat down there alone in the stands, papers and a book tucked under his arm, as he blew on his fingers.

The third year seniors might think Shevraeth was studying, but he was actually waiting for Forthan, as he was tutoring Forthan in secret. Usually early mornings before anyone was awake, except this week, when Forthan was overseeing the second-year seniors' exhibition.

Keriam had said to Senrid, *That is your future army commander. There isn't a better candidate in the entire country. Fix the problem now.*

Officially, Senrid wasn't supposed to know Forthan was illiterate, so he'd sent him to Shevraeth, who had no assignment, but could not go back to his home, where a bad king threatened his life. Turned out the foreigner was a good tutor. If only everything else were so easy to fix—

*Senrid!*

Senrid recoiled violently, then spun around purposelessly in a circle, his fingers whipping out the dagger he wore up his sleeve, as his brain recognized the cry as inward, coming from a distance impossible for the ear: Liere.

Senrid transferred to Bereth Ferian, and staggered against the Destination chamber wall, feeling like he'd fallen from a galloping horse. He heard Liere on the mental plane and ran toward her until he fetched up outside a room he recognized at a glance. Liere stood there, her stiff arms held away from her sides, thin fingers spread like starfish.

"Senrid," she gasped on a high note. "It's gone."

Senrid glanced past her at the table. Siamis's sword was no longer there. On the table lay a jumble of spell books and other stuff as mages in gray and white robes walked around the room, whispering spells.

Terror had widened the pupils in Liere's eyes, making them look enormous in her blanched face.

There was more than met the eye, Senrid was absolutely certain of it. Equally certain that somehow Siamis was watching for reactions, he said carelessly, "Bet you he had a transfer spell on it. He's probably a continent away. More. Sitting in Norsunder Base, swigging bristic and laughing fit to be sick."

Liere's wide, terrified gaze shifted to the table.

Senrid shut up. He stepped inside the room, and saw that what he'd taken as a jumble of light magic stuff was not: the spell books and the old scroll formed a careful circle around a single object, a round gold coin. Senrid's guts tightened as he took another step. Round coins were a northern thing, and sure enough, this one had been hammered with a shape like a hawk's eye.

Senrid knew that shape, that coin. It sported the earliest symbol of the Erama Krona, the Eyes of the Crown during the earliest days of the Venn empire, before the Marlovens left.

This hawk's eye had been adopted by Senrid's own ancestors.

A golden eye . . .

"Shit," Senrid said.

Two of the mages looked around in silent rebuke, and a stern-faced old woman whom Senrid recognized as Oalthoreh, the head of the Bereth Ferian mages, frowned direfully and said, "What is he doing here?"

She talked past Senrid to Arthur, lurking in the doorway next to Liere.

"I called Senrid," Liere spoke up bravely, though her voice quavered. She tapped her head. "This way."

Senrid schooled his expression, though deeply appreciating the effect Liere's gesture had on the mages, two of whom stepped away. As if that would prevent Liere from reading their minds.

"I think it's an ancient Venn coin," Senrid said with what he hoped was a helpful air.

"We know that," Oalthoreh snapped.

Senrid resisted the impulse to bait her, which would be too much like the way Siamis (or his uncle, even worse) was baiting these mages by leaving that coin lying there. A coin that Senrid made a mental wager had lain outside of time since those early days, as it looked newly struck. The only people who might have personal hordes like that were Ancient Sartorans: Siamis. Or Detlev.

So what to do? Get Liere out of there. Senrid's first thought was to take her back with him to Marloven Hess, except it was New Year's Week. She'd been intimidated by the castle full of jarls and their attendants the year before. And then there was that kick in the gut he got when he first recognized the coin.

But. When he took in Liere's blanched face, he said, "Think, Liere. The sword is gone. Siamis isn't here. It's probably just a scare tactic."

Arthur watched in amazement as Liere's face colored up, and she seemed to breathe for the first time that day. "Oh. Oh," she said, her relief obvious. Though Arthur had been saying pretty much that same thing.

"Right. He's not here," she said quickly, her fingers twisting together. "So why is that coin there?"

"An insult, a challenge, another scare tactic. A different kind of being stupid," Senrid said, piling on the sarcasm, sure that Siamis was somewhere about listening. He itched to return to the room and try magic on that coin. But he had to leave it for the more experienced mages.

He tipped his head toward the door. Liere and Arthur followed him out, and they walked in silence until he felt certain there was no chance Siamis could hear them. "Look, it probably means Siamis is coming back, but as he hasn't actually done anything, and seems to want to scare everybody out of their pants with that damned coin, I think you should just go somewhere so you don't have to see it. Those Mearsiean girls seem to collect strays. I'll take you there, if you want to hunker down out of sight. I wanted to ask Clair if she's heard anything lately about Jilo. Or if you don't like going there without an invitation, how about Roth Drael, with Hibern?"

Liere brightened. "I remember that place. It's where we freed the dyr, isn't it? I loved it. Would Hibern mind?"

"I can take you, and we'll ask," Arthur offered.

They walked back toward the treasure room, encountering Oalthoreh and three of her mages coming down the hall, as a fresh group entered the chamber to investigate.

Arthur explained the plan. Neither he nor Senrid missed the obvious relief in Oalthoreh's face at the idea of getting Liere safely away, before she said, "We will continue to test for traps and wards."

As Arthur and Liere walked toward the residence wing, she to collect some things, Senrid took a quick step inside the treasure room to grab another look at that coin. Ancient Venn, definitely. Connection to his own family . . . maybe it was just borrowing trouble, because the first thing anyone does is see themselves connected to whatever is going on.

Yeah, Senrid thought. Like the old saying, he was probably putting one and one together to make eleven.

From Norsunder Base, the elite watched Senrid from the chamber they called the Window. Whenever someone successfully planted a spy-hole in a distant location, this was where they observed.

Siamis presided, urbane as a good host. It was fun seeing grim old Oalthoreh squawking orders like a hen, and the mages scurrying around muttering as they cast spells for traps and tracers.

The real fun for some occurred when the Marloven brat briefly showed up. He himself was disappointing. Looked barely old enough to cut his food by himself, and the only thing he said was so obvious it didn't need saying: "I think it's an ancient Venn coin."

Through the derisive crowing—"You think so?"—"The Marlovens have gone to seed if that's what's ruling them!"—"When Detlev finally gives us our Marloven party we'll clean them up in a day!"—Siamis said cheerfully, "You'll get your own hawkeye soon, Senrid."

The watchers fell silent, one or two telegraphing messages with looks. So, Siamis was poaching on territory Detlev had claimed for himself, was he?

Kessler stood at the back, observing them all. He never laughed. Never commented.

## Chapter Twelve

*Various points around the world, in reaction to bad news*

ONCE more, Hibern arrived in Choreid Dhelerei to be told that Senrid would not be available for study.

The entire castle seemed gripped by tension, the sentries—never lax—wary, with hands on the hilts of their weapons. She knew better than to ask, and hoped the problem was merely more trouble with those teenage boys in the academy.

She arrived in Sartor happily anticipating a free hour to explore.

By now Hibern had ventured into several cities, and was astonished by not just architectural differences, but ways in which otherwise utterly different cities could be alike. She suspected Atan would be appalled, for instance, to have Eidervaen compared to Marloven Hess in that neither capital city had scribble-scrabble words and drawings on walls and fences, as Hibern had found in Miraleste, the capital of Sarendan.

She'd asked Lilah, who explained proudly that Peitar thought it was important for ordinary people to be able to make art and to express themselves. Lilah had added with a brief scowl, "It used to get you in trouble, under my uncle. My friend Bren was *really good* at drawings about how rotten things were then."

Hibern wondered if the so-civilized Colend would hand out death sentences if people marred their walls and fences with slogans and scrawls—except when invited.

She was ready to talk about that after another walk through Eidervaen, but when it was time to go to the royal palace, Atan met Hibern with a solemn face. "I have to give up my hour of frivolity," she said bitterly, then clapped her hands over her face, and dropped them in fists to her sides. "No, that's unfair. It's just that I insisted that I hear the high council's deliberations about what to do . . ."

Hibern was so surprised to be shut out by two study partners in a row that she didn't ask what they were deliberating about. "And so your new schedule doesn't even permit one hour a month?" she asked.

"So they say." Atan sighed. "And I have to accept it, or they'll shut me out of the real deliberations. When I dared to point out it was only one hour a month, they all looked at me like I'm a sulking brat, selfishly taking up time that ought to be put into finding ways to ward Norsunder."

*A brat like Atan's wild little cousin?* Hibern kept her opinion behind a blank expression. Clearly something else more urgent was wrong.

"We'll still communicate," Atan promised.

"Right," Hibern said, wondering what the etiquette was. She suspected that Erai-Yanya would say, "You leave the first letter to the Queen of Sartor."

She was ready to discuss it when she arrived back in Roth Drael, but fence scrawls and Atan's restrictive council went out of her head when she arrived to a waiting missive from Arthur relating the news:

*Siamis took the sword.*

"Horseapples!" Hibern exclaimed in Marloven, and threw herself down at her desk to start writing letters.

*Siamis is back.*

Word spread across the world faster than the sun's daily course, reaching everywhere but the most isolated corners. And Chwahirsland, as who talked to them?

Senrid, who might have, still wasn't used to thinking about communication going outward from him. His notecase sat forgotten on his desk as he conferred with Keriam, and with his army commanders via runner.

Most countries looked to their own defenses—magical wards and tracers, militias mobilized and armies drilled. Diplomats conferred earnestly, referring to defense treaties in hopes that the stronger would protect the weaker.

In Sarendan, Derek paced back and forth along the top rail of an old fence so the crowd of defenders in the city of Miraleste could see him. His face lifted, his eyes wide so the sunlight struck glints of amber in them as he shouted, "It's just as we feared! But we shall fear no more! *Fear no more!*"

"Fear no more!" shouted the brigade.

"We shall not fear, we shall fight!"

"We shall fight!" the brigade echoed back.

Derek swung his sword, sunlight flashing along the steel as he walked. "We know that there's a vast army at Norsunder Base. But vast armies must move like anyone else, that much we won when Siamis was here before. The big rifts between Norsunder and us are gone."

A few shouted, "Gone," but the rest waited, or stirred, or whispered.

Instinctively aware that he'd lost the rhythm, Derek swung the sword higher. "They have to march. And where will they go, to get to the rest of us?"

Now they were paying attention again. "They either march to their west, which means carrying months of water through benighted land. Or they go north into Sartor, and risk magical traps. Or they try to come through us. We're the first line of defense! Sarendan!"

"Sarendan!"

"And it's not our king who can defend us, though he's a good king, the best who ever lived, my friend and brother. But his strength is wisdom and justice. He does not carry a sword. For that, he trusts me. And whom do I trust?"

A more confused response—"Us!" "The brigades!" "City guard?" And even, "King Peitar!"

Derek's voice lifted over the noise. "Do I trust the nobles?"

They knew that one. "No!"

"There aren't enough of them even if they were all united in wanting to protect us. Who has the numbers? *The people!* Who has the will to defend themselves? *The people.* Whom do I trust?"

This time he got the response he wanted, united in a heartfelt body of sound: "The people!"

"So let us train as one heart, one will, and one strong arm, to defend Sarendan!"

In Mearsies Heili, Clair and CJ stood on a balcony high on a spire in the palace on the mountain, looking out over a hushed world of white from an early snow.

"Why is it that everything turns beautiful under snow?" CJ asked, enormously pleased. She'd come from a part of Earth where there was no snow, and subsequently, could not get enough of it. As long as she didn't have to travel in it.

"No idea. But it does." Clair hated to ruin the quiet with anxious things, but even thinking that made her realize that the quiet was already ruined. And so she broached the subject that had made her brood for two days. "CJ, I got two letters, one from Puddlenose's friend Karhin in Colend, and another from Hibern. They both reported that Siamis's sword disappeared from Bereth Ferian."

CJ recoiled. "Does that mean Siamis is back? Where?"

"They don't know. Nobody saw it taken. All the wards were destroyed. They think it's some kind of warning."

CJ's shoulders hunched under her ears. "What are the grownups doing?"

"What they usually do, Hibern said, and I also heard from the new addition to the alliance, Lilah of Sarendan. Plan defenses and drill armies and talk a lot."

"What are *we* going to do? We can't fight those spittoon-brains."

"No. At least Aunt Murial finished renewing the border protections, and this time she taught me as she went along. I know them, now. I have them all written down, and we'll at least have warning if anybody from Norsunder tries to invade. We might have time to get the word out to people to hide."

CJ didn't trust adults or their protections. If protections really worked, none of the villains would be able to attack, right? Wasn't that what 'protection' meant? "Did you hear from Atan about what Sartor's doing?"

"No."

"I knew it. She's too high and mighty for us—"

"CJ."

CJ sighed explosively. "Then why haven't we ever heard from her? Everybody else has written at least one letter to us all, to test the alliance net. Except Senrid, but I don't count him."

"Because she's terribly busy learning to be queen of the oldest country in the world? Because her high council won't let her? Because there's another alliance with Sartor as its center, like it's been in history for centuries? I don't know."

"Clair, Atan came and looked us over. She *did*. And didn't invite us back for a visit. I can see her not inviting me, because she might think I'm not a real princess. But she could have at least invited you."

Clair shrugged. "I don't care. I don't want to go to Sartor, particularly. More important is our alliance. If Atan is really a part of it, that's good for everybody, because Sartor always led the fight against Norsunder in history. But I think we need to work on spreading the alliance. Getting more people."

"Yes." CJ rubbed her hands, then stuck them in her armpits. "And that means finding more kids like us. But how?" She stared at the glimmering white forest far below, then glanced at her blotchy hands in vague surprise. "Hey, I'm cold!" Inside, she said, "Won't Puddlenose be showing up for New Year's Week? Maybe we can ask him if he's got any suggestions for new people, since he travels so much."

"Good idea."

Unaware of any events outside his dire quest, Jilo worked, and time slid past, unnoticed. He worked until colors leached out of the world, leaving it subtle shades of shadow-gray, and voices began to distort until he discovered he couldn't understand anything any guard said. Their voices buzzed like the drone of bees.

But he stayed until he had to write out every syllable, and then read out the spell with his finger on each letter, because he scarcely recognized the sense of the words.

It took the remainder of his dwindling strength to complete the last spell.

But complete it he did.

So when he collapsed, he woke where he had fallen, his head pounding, his mouth dry, but he was alive.

He woke up undisturbed because every guard, cook, and servant also woke up lying on the floor, blood crusted around their noses. They crawled off to recover, and then to assume duty as if nothing had happened. Nobody wanted to risk a flogging, or worse, if they complained.

Jilo staggered up to the desk, aware of the heaviness of the atmosphere. It scarcely felt different. But he'd made a start on breaking the life-draining magic.

At Norsunder Base, Dejain made her way to the Bereth Ferian window, as she had begun doing each day.

She thought it duty to visit when she was most likely to catch the Bereth Ferian mages in the process of searching for the magic that had permitted Siamis egress. The reward had been learning a great deal about their process.

Henerek and a couple of the other captains were there a lot, hugely entertained by the lighters' panic, the squawking, the horrified speculation after their discovery that the sword was missing.

In the days since Siamis had returned from Bereth Ferian, Dejain had noticed some patterns developing among those who habitually watched the lighters in their failed attempts to find the magic that had been slipped into their citadel—such as the spy window they visited each day.

The first thing she noticed was that Siamis was there less and less frequently, and he stayed a shorter time each visit. Second, Detlev never arrived at all.

Third, Kessler had stopped going.

Dejain peeked into the room and glanced at the magical window bespelled against the opposite wall. She recognized three of Oalthoreh's senior mages busy working methodically through magic books, page by page. Their talk centered mostly around some celebration being planned.

Dejain turned her attention to the watchers. Henerek was there, and several of the minor mages.

Dejain left, and went about her business.

One of the most disconcerting things about Kessler was that he didn't have easy patterns. But he did have to move about on his duties, and she knew the few places they would not be overheard either by physical or magical means.

She caught him later that day, as he was leaving the stable.

He paused, silent and still, a study in contrasts: black hair, pale face, flat blue stare; ignoring the general-issue uniform for a plain white shirt and black riding pants tucked into his riding boots. He wasn't all that much taller than she was, slim, and young, but her heart always beat harder when she was around him in a way that had nothing to do with attraction. It was fear. They had once worked together, then, convinced by a third mage that Kessler had betrayed her, she'd helped destroy his plans for ridding the world of kings born to privilege. He knew it, and knew why.

The thing she never mentioned, hoping he did not know, was that the blood-spell on the knife that had cut him, binding him to Norsunder, had been cast by her.

He made a movement to pass by.

She had to get his attention at once, or never. So she revealed the secret she'd been sitting on: "I know you're studying magic. You've been stealing my books, then putting them back. But I have tracers on them."

"What do you want?" he said, his angry light blue gaze direct.

She sure had his attention now.

Extortion would never work on him. "I thought you'd want to learn the ways of the enemy. But you don't watch at the Bereth Ferian window anymore."

His mouth tightened. "It's there to keep us busy."

"How do you come to that conclusion? It took months to build the location spell for it. And nearly that long to successfully place it."

"Yes, but who did the work? Not Siamis. He retrieved the sword, then afterward used the window exactly as long as it took to get Henerek and those other fools listening every day."

"We learn a lot."

The corner of Kessler's mouth curled. "You learn what Oalthoreh wants you to hear."

"So you think they know about the location spell."

"I think they did from the start."

Dejain had suspected that as well. So the question then was, "If you're right, why did Siamis bother at all?"

"To deflect us from what he's really doing," Kessler said, and made to push by.

"Which is what? I overheard him and Detlev talking. They're searching for something. All they said was 'it.' Do you think that refers to that dyr they looked so hard for when Siamis ran his enchantment?"

Kessler said impatiently, "They have to be looking for ways to create rifts. There is no way to bring over the armies stashed in Norsunder-Beyond until they can regain group access."

Dejain nodded slowly. In the meantime, the lighter mages kept finding ways to foul what were, for convenience, referred to as 'transfer tunnels,' though time and space were not so easily holed. People transferring even in small groups of ones or twos had been burning into nothingness if they followed one another too quickly. No one knew why only the ancient Destinations were the most stable, but even those couldn't be overused.

Kessler started away, saying over his shoulder, "And Siamis, maybe Detlev, too, they're not looking on this world."

She extended a hand to halt him, but didn't touch him. He had a nasty way of reacting with extreme prejudice if one crossed that invisible boundary. "Is that what the Geth project is? Looking for rift magic?"

Another expression of derision. "What else could it be?" He shoved past, turned, and said, "You should be watching closer to home. Henerek has been stalking your mages."

"They're not my mages," she said.

He lifted a shoulder, and was gone in a few quick steps.

*Spring, 4741 AF (autumn in northern hemisphere)*
*Marloven Hess*

The first warm night of spring, Senrid left all his windows open when he went to sleep.

He fell into a dream.

Through the door in the dream room he was working in walked a familiar figure, light from somewhere catching in his blond hair, outlining a shoulder, an arm, an empty right hand. The man halted before Senrid's desk in the dream room. He waved a negligent hand, and the jumbled elements of the dream whipped away quick as the wind.

"Senrid." Siamis's voice chided gently. "Are you really that unaware?"

Senrid bolted upright in bed, his heart drumming at a gallop. He flung aside the coverlet, wrestled into some clothes, took up his fighting dagger, then lit the entire upstairs and searched room by room.

By the time he'd done that, and had had time to slow his heartbeat, he remembered his wards and tracers. He returned to his study to check . . .

And found them broken.

So he widened the search. Morning light filled the windows, and the rooms, unnoticed; he missed his drill time on this determined hunt through every room in his castle, though he didn't know what he would do if he found Siamis waiting, sword in hand.

Finally he crossed to the garrison side, and climbed up to Keriam's office.

The grizzled commander sent away a runner and a couple of academy boys, still self-conscious in their new-made military tunic jackets and real blackweave belts. The boys saluted Senrid and clattered down the stone steps.

Keriam looked up from the neatly aligned stacks of papers on his desk, and said, "I was going to send a runner to you. Did you leave this for me?" He moved a stack of papers, revealing a golden coin.

Round, with the hawk's eye hammered into it.

Senrid's breath hissed in. "Where did you find that?"

"Oddest thing, it was on the floor."

"Where exactly?"

Keriam pointed to a spot between his desk and the rows of empty benches upon which during evening lessons sat the specially selected candidates for command class.

"Shit!" Senrid yelped, then smacked his hands over his eyes. He called up a string of complicated tracer spells, and sensed the magic flashing through the surroundings. In his mind's eye, the magic was like liquid lightning, splashing ineffectively from floor, ceiling, window frame, and walls, before vanishing.

Someone had tried to plant some kind of spell, but had been foiled by four-century-old magic. Senrid drew a deep breath, and let it out, glad of the mysterious Colendi mage only known as Emras, who had laid down the protections over the city and castle. History named her evil, but she had protected Marloven Hess.

Whoever in Norsunder had tried to break her wards had not succeeded.

When he opened his eyes, Keriam said, "What's the significance of this coin? It looks a little like one of ours."

"It's ancient Venn, I'm almost certain," Senrid said. "There was another like it left up north, after Emeth disappeared—"

"Emeth?" Keriam asked.

"Not a person. Name of Siamis's sword. Translates to 'truth.'"

"Odd name for a sword," Keriam said.

Senrid scarcely heard. Memory flung him back to the conversation he and Liere had had about that, when he first went to Bereth Ferian to visit her. He also remembered her conviction that there was some symbolic meaning behind the sword being there. Senrid hated symbolic meanings. Lighter hyperbole about golden ages and peace forever signifying their own moral superiority were sickening enough, but he'd take a year of that, non-stop, rather than symbolic gestures from the likes of Siamis.

While Senrid stood there with distant gaze and his mouth a tight white line, Keriam thought of the history of the room he stood in, once known as the harskialdna tower, used by the brothers of kings, by army commanders, and during a brief period by mages. For the past few years it had served as the academy office, as it looked right out over the academy.

Keriam studied Senrid's grim expression. "Is this coin a threat from Siamis?"

Senrid walked around the perimeter of the room. "Let's call it a threat," Senrid said, jerking his chin up. "Siamis, or someone, is either throwing down a war banner, or, more like, giving us the back of the hand. The next one will probably be found on my throne." He remembered the dream invasion. "Or maybe on my pillow."

Keriam swore under his breath. Then he said, "Right. So we'll take it as a warning." And though he hated magic with a passion motivated by fear, because it was nothing he could fight, he was no coward. "Let's see what we can come up with to be as disobliging as possible."

Senrid agreed, and walked out, resolving to be more disciplined about his mental shield all the time, not just when Liere was there—

Oh, shit. He stopped short. Two coins, one here, one in Bereth Ferian. The sword might have been a warning, or even bait. But two coins, one where Liere would see it, and one here—Senrid was absolutely certain that Dena Yeresbeth lay behind all this mystery, which made Liere and him specific targets.

That didn't mean there weren't other targets, too. He spent the rest of the day making a transfer token, then protecting it with several different personal wards. The next day, he chose his moment, when the lower school was playing a war game. This was the best time to catch one of the radlavs—the boy group captains—without witnesses.

Senrid rode along the academy practice fields until he found Shev-raeth, the foreigner. He stood alone on a small tree-lined ridge, watching the little boys under his charge playing capture-the-flags on the grassy meadow below. He looked bored. Why should that bother Senrid?

Because he looked like a bored courtier, Senrid thought as he looped the horse's rein over a branch so the animal could crop the spring grass. Senrid despised courtiers for their arrogance, their assumption of supe-riority in taste, brains, blood, whatever others held dear.

But he knew that Shevraeth had endured a tough year in the acad-emy; in his first weeks, he'd had the snot beaten out of him. But he'd survived, and had not only found his place, but was doing well.

And Senrid was responsible for him.

So Senrid ran up to join him, and handed off the transfer token, which he'd attached to a gold chain from his mother's collection of fine jewelry. Satire? Intent to impress? Shevraeth took it with scarcely a glance as Senrid explained it, then added, "There's evidence that Siamis might return."

He meant to leave, but Shevraeth said, "And you expect to be his initial target?"

"It's not Siamis that worries me. At least, he's a big threat, bigger than I can handle. But there's a worse one."

"There is?" Shevraeth's head canted as he ran the golden chain through his fingers.

Senrid wondered how much the Remalnan boy knew, Remalna being about the size of an inkblot on the continental map. But small did not always mean backward. "Siamis was betrayed to Norsunder when he was a few years younger than us. Some records say it was by Norsundri-ans. Others—the ones I believe—say he was betrayed by his uncle, Detlev Reverael ne-Hindraeldrei. They called him a dyranarya."

Senrid stopped, struggling for words to define something he didn't understand himself.

"What is that?" Shevraeth looked puzzled.

"No one's sure. Except that they controlled people by thought, using these magical objects called dyra. Since Detlev was a dyranarya, it has to be something extra evil even by Norsunder standards."

Senrid suppressed the urge to go into detail about the mysterious Ancient Sartoran artifacts, and how Liere was able to handle a dyr be-cause of her Dena Yeresbeth, and use it to destroy the Siamis enchant-ment. Either he took the time to explain all these terms—which he didn't even begin to understand himself—or he got to the point. "Here's what matters. Siamis and his uncle might come back. I tangled with Detlev once, and he promised me we would meet again. From all I can gather he keeps his word—when it suits his purpose."

Below, the small boys screeched and jumped and shouted, as the last struggle for the flags commenced. Around them the shadows had lengthened, leafing tree branches segmenting the field, light and shadow.

Shevraeth gazed between the screening trees at the little boys shrieking below as they pelted across the field with the enemy flag. His fingers opened, disclosing the medallion on his palm. "I take it I am to wear this?"

"Day and night."

"It seems unfair that the only living Ancient Sartorans would be those one would exert oneself never to meet." Shevraeth put the chain around his head and slipped the medallion inside his tunic. One responsibility covered.

"Oh, there's also Lilith the Guardian, but she's as dangerous, in her own way."

Shevraeth's brows lifted. There was the courtier again. "She's real? I mean, not in the historic sense, but lives?"

The courtier was habit, Senrid reminded himself. Not intent. "She, too, has recourse to someplace outside of time. Because she does live. I've seen her."

Shevraeth whistled, something he'd picked up from the Marloven boys. No courtier would whistle. "And you can read Ancient Sartoran?"

"Some. Barely. Liere and I have been trying to study it. But with all the success of a couple of puppies trying to learn the famed Colendi flower symbols, their ribbon symbols, their fans and the rest of it."

Shevraeth laughed, a sound scarcely louder than a sigh. "I wonder which one is the more obscure, Ancient Sartoran, about which my father had some pungent things to say, when he told my tutor to confine his exertions to modern history, or Colend's court customs."

"Maybe the Ancient Sartorans weren't trying to be obscure. I think they used metaphor for when ordinary vocabulary wasn't working. They seem to have been a lot closer to the non-human beings in this world. Until we humans almost managed to destroy ourselves along with everything else. Anyway, for non-human ideas, human language isn't enough, is it? I mean, how would you describe red to a blind man?"

Senrid couldn't tell from Shevraeth's polite, courtly expression if he believed any of it.

Memory seized Senrid. Gone was the playing field, the courtly boy, birds, trees, flowers. Again Senrid stood on a cliff beside Detlev in the frigid winter wind, the very first day of his reign, as Detlev forced him to watch Norsundrian warriors decimate Marloven Hess's South Army on the border below.

Senrid had been helpless to do anything. South Army as well as himself would be dead now, except that Senrid had been given a name half a year before, a continent away, by a mysterious and ghostly figure, who had said, *When you want my help, Senrid Indevan Montredaun-An, ask for it. Once, only, you may call upon me and I will aid you. Say 'Erdrael,' and I will come.*

Senrid did not believe in ghosts any more than he believed in mysterious offers, but in utter desperation that day on the cliff, he'd shouted the name. It had evoked a blast of magic that effectively blinded the Norsundrians, forcing them into retreat. The remnants of South Army were saved, as was Senrid, leaving him with the bitter conviction he had just served as a pawn in a game so vast, and so old, that he couldn't see but a sliver of it.

He snapped his gaze to Shevraeth's waiting face. "Fall into the hands of Siamis, or worse, Detlev. They'd probably be glad to discourse on the verities of their day, right before they rip your identity from out of your skull, and all without moving their hands. See that you keep that thing always by you. If I do have to transfer you away from here, likely there won't be time for warning."

And he left.

## Chapter Thirteen

*More consequences of bad news*
*Beginning at Sarendan*

IN Miraleste's royal palace, Lilah Selenna flung open the new doors to one of the rooms burned by the revolutionaries, glad to escape the smell of paint into the balmy air of spring. She sprinted across the garden, and was about to hop the low stone fence and drop onto the path that would lead to the palace gates, when she caught sight of Derek Diamagan coming from the other direction.

"Derek!" she yelled, surprised. "I was just about to go to drill practice. Only . . . why are you here?"

"I've been thinking about something Rel said," Derek replied as he drew up next to her. "Here I am, going on about the uselessness of the aristos, which I still believe, but also about the uselessness of the army, because it was commanded by the former king."

Lilah made a sour face. "Ugh!"

Derek grinned as she hopped around in a circle, pretending to shiver and shudder at the thought of her deposed uncle. Peitar might have a lot of sympathy (misplaced, Derek believed) for his uncle, but Lilah unreservedly hated him. "Why would you ruin a perfect spring day thinking about *him?*" she demanded, fists on her hips.

"Not thinking about him." Derek perched on the low wall, fists propped on his knees. "I'm thinking about what Rel didn't say. Much as I hated the king's army, they did know what they were doing. They defeated us without half trying, which is how I nearly got Peitar and me executed." He jerked his thumb toward himself, then up toward the palace on the highest hill. "So I thought, now that they're not commanded by the former king, maybe it's time to go to Obrin and become cadets. Learn something. Want to go with me?"

Lilah's mouth rounded. "Me?"

"Sure."

"But I don't even like army stuff!"

"You've been practicing with the orphans." Derek shrugged, and his expression turned rueful. "Lilah, you know how much I've spoken out against the army. Perhaps not as much since your brother took over as king, but the little I've said hasn't been good. I still object quite strongly to nobles being trained there. They already have enough power. But since Peitar declared that anyone may train there, boy or girl, commoner or courtier, perhaps it's time for me to learn some of the basics. And if you're there to protect me, they won't heave my sorry carcass back over the fence."

"Well," Lilah exhaled on a breath of satisfaction. "If you put it like that. Why not? Let's go tell Peitar, and pack a knapsack. It'll take us a few days to get there . . ."

*Roth Drael to Delfina Valley to Marloven Hess*

Liere enjoyed her stay at Roth Drael so much that she might have felt guilty getting pleasure out of a dire situation had not Hibern made it plain how much she liked having company.

"I thought I'd get used to living alone," Hibern said one morning as they lay side by side on a beautiful old Bermundi rug, a bowl of warm muffins between them. They ate as they gazed straight up through the cracked roof of the white-stone domicile, where the first cold rain of the season ran along the ward that took the place of a roof. This magic was ancient. Hibern couldn't replicate it, though it was one of her many ongoing personal projects.

"It was fine the first month or so that Erai-Yanya was gone," Hibern continued. "Then it got lonely. Especially in winter. Well, you can tell by how many times I came north to visit Arthur. I didn't even mind twice weekly transferring to Oalthoreh and the school."

Liere wrinkled her nose, but didn't say anything. She felt so uncomfortable around those mage students and their teachers, though at least the teachers showed her respect. Maybe too much respect? It was the 'Sartora' thing all over again. Maybe they wouldn't even want her back, now that Siamis's sword was gone, and she hadn't somehow found and vanquished Siamis with some mysterious spell.

She wasn't the only one thinking along a similar path. Not that Hibern thought Liere a fraud. But after a few days around Liere's finger-twisted worries and awkwardnesses, Hibern formed the impression that Liere was more of an ordinary person who might have stumbled into the right circumstances at the right time, and now was paying the price of fame.

As the days turned into weeks, she kept her word and began teaching Liere modern Sartoran in the mornings and Marloven in the afternoons. Instead of complaining the way students usually did about language lessons, Liere soaked in everything Hibern said. Liere also remembered everything the first time she heard it. She asked interesting questions about the origins of words, or word patterns, that Hibern hadn't thought about.

She knew Liere couldn't be slow in mental capacity. Senrid did not include patience among his better qualities. It wasn't that he despised people whose minds didn't crash and carom headlong the way his did, but he tended to avoid spending time around people who couldn't, or wouldn't, keep pace. Liere, though significantly younger than Senrid, didn't seem to have any difficulty in that regard.

But it wasn't until the local morvende (who left Erai-Yanya and Hibern strictly alone) sent a pair of youths on those amazing creatures that took the form of white horses, with an invitation to 'Sartora,' that Hibern began to suspect that Liere was more of a puzzle than she appeared.

Especially when she turned up three weeks later, a garland made of flowers that Hibern had never seen bound around her brow, her escort singing songs in those distinctive braided triplets that never failed to send Hibern's heart racing.

Liere waved a farewell, wandered back in, smiled, and asked how Hibern was. She was speaking perfect Sartoran.

"I'm glad you're back," Hibern said. "I have a feeling that you're going to be needed." Hibern was sorry to see the old, anxious look tighten Liere's face. She said quickly, "Tsauderei wants to meet with Senrid. And I think you should be there."

Liere's eyes rounded. "Me? Why?"

"While you were gone, one of those old Venn coins showed up in Keriam's tower."

Liere blanched.

Hibern said quickly, "Nothing more happened. So far. But after I got the letter from our alliance net, I told Tsauderei, because Erai-Yanya would expect me to. If Senrid's temper goes runaway-horse, it might take both of us to rein him in."

But Senrid didn't argue—at least with others. He'd already been through all the arguments with himself.

Norsunder was coming.

Everyone knew that.

The specifics of why the coin was there didn't matter. The overall message was clear enough: he was one of the pieces on their game board, and swearing didn't fix the fact that he was vastly outmatched in magic, power, brains, military, and experience.

The one most surprised at Senrid agreeing to meet was Tsauderei. He would have liked very much to get a glimpse inside the mysterious Marloven Hess, but Senrid wouldn't go that far. Hibern had explained, "With the military, you try to pick the ground, and if you can't, you try to take the battle to the enemy. That goes for magic, too."

"So I'm the enemy," Tsauderei said, and though he laughed, Hibern sensed he was not pleased.

She said, "Everybody is a potential enemy to him. It's the only way he's managed to stay alive."

Tsauderei grunted. "And so he doesn't want me nosing around his wards. Very well. Bring him here. I will even pass you all through."

So the three transferred across the entire continent. Senrid sensed their being passed through two significant wards, which made him warier than normal as they recovered from the rough transfer outside Tsauderei's mountain cottage, under the deafening crash of a mountain thunderstorm.

Hibern hastily motioned them inside.

Liere, terrified by thunder, shot through first. She hated storms at any time, but had never been on a mountaintop so close to a storm. She stared out the window at the tumble of grayish green clouds that seemed so low she could touch them if she stretched out her hand. When lightning flared, she gasped and backed against the wall, which shivered as thunder exploded right overhead.

Senrid gave his host a grim, assessing look, then turned to sweep his gaze over the floor-to-ceiling bookcases surrounding him on three sides in the one-room cottage.

Tsauderei took a moment to observe the newcomers. He'd briefly met that poor little Liere, who looked as if she'd jump out of her skin if he coughed suddenly. Best to leave her alone for now.

Senrid had a strong look of his grandfather, his expression exactly as wary. When the thunder had rumbled away over the land below, Tsauderei said easily, "So someone planted a Venn coin inside your citadel? What's your defensive strategy?"

Senrid's eyelids flickered up, betraying how tightly he'd been braced for demands, lectures, admonishments. "Detlev once said I wasn't worth bothering with yet. When he decides I am, I want to be very hard to get." He looked down at his callused palms. Then up. "It might not be me they want at all, but the Marloven army. So our strategy has been twofold: to make sure they cannot surprise us on the border again, and to make it tough to take the royal city."

'Twofold.' This little speech sounded rehearsed. "We can discuss your border," Tsauderei said, "but first, permit me to point out that your strategy is shortsighted."

Tsauderei observed Senrid's defensive hostility easing to interest, and said, "Feel free to disagree, but I think the most effective defensive strategy is to determine Norsunder's overall goal, and to deny it to them."

"I know that." Senrid's chin lifted, his expression thoughtful, then the wariness was back. "We know what they want: the world. And tactics will preferably include wholesale slaughter for sport."

"That would be the means, or a means, but I'm not so certain it's the end. Not for the ones who matter most, the Host of Lords. If that were all they wanted, they would have come out of their lair beyond time centuries ago."

Tsauderei paused as green-white lightning filled the room with actinic glare, and Liere covered her eyes, cringing against the battering noise of thunder. She loathed herself for her stupid fear, *wishing* she could be like Senrid, who loved thunderstorms. Or like Hibern, who didn't seem to care.

Tsauderei spoke again, lifting his voice against the steady roar of hail bouncing on the roof: "Is it possible that there are competing strategic aims? Take the invasion, conquering, and enchantment of Sartor, now rejoined the world. That appears to have been a random act, isolated because it devolved into an internal squabble between Norsunder's military commander and the mage Detlev."

Tsauderei had all Senrid's attention now.

Senrid said, "Invasions are never random. Take too much effort. Too much cost. There has to have been some plan. What makes you think there were conflicting strategies?"

Tsauderei said, "The enchantment came at the point the kingdom had been overrun and the Norsundrian force had slipped their leash and were settling in for slaughter for sport, as you say. When the enchantment cleared away, the entire population of Sartor was there, but the Norsundrians weren't. Where did they go?"

Senrid shrugged. "Probably just transferred back to the Beyond through a rift. Because Sartor came out of the enchantment right before the Siamis attack, and the closing of the rifts, right?"

"Except there was no evidence of a rift."

"It had been a hundred years, almost, right?" Senrid retorted.

"Not to the locals," Tsauderei responded. "Not to the locals. They're still mostly a hundred years back. Anyway, my point is that Norsunder seems to have competing commanders. So that would indicate competing goals."

Senrid drew in a long breath, his gaze distant. "Right. Yeah, right."

"So," Tsauderei went on, hiding how pleased he was not at having won his point, which was minor, but in having won Senrid's interest. "I'd hoped, when you found that coin, you'd also find a suitable threat, or warning, or something indicating Siamis's goal. Alas. We'll have to look at patterns of movement, but first, would you tell me about Norsunder's attack on your border, right before Siamis first appeared?"

"Hibern didn't tell you?" Senrid glanced her way.

"Hibern has been here fewer than five times, and has never stayed very long. She is not my student." Tsauderei's voice was sardonic.

Senrid flushed at the implied rebuke, as Tsauderei thought with mordant humor, yes, let us narrow the chasm between Us and You that you seem so determined to dig.

Senrid began to speak in a far less hostile tone. "I'd barely been king for a day. Detlev captured me and—" He decided not to mention Leander of Vasande Leror's annoying sister, who he'd beent traveling with at the time. She was immaterial to what had happened. "Detlev forced me to watch them march a couple of companies over my border. They'd been hidden from view by illusion. I know now that the idea was to shock me into thinking that they'd appeared suddenly. Well, it worked.

Wasn't until later that I learned about the rifts. Norsunder sent 'em over from Sartor's southern rift. I found out that the king of Perideth let 'em march through his kingdom on the understanding they were coming to attack us." Senrid's voice was bitter.

"They were coming to take over your uncle's Marloven Hess," Tsauderei suggested, as lightning flared again, and the hail abruptly ended.

But it was farther away, and Liere let out a trickle of breath as Senrid looked down at his hands, the rope scars on his wrists whitish below the edges of his cuffs.

Senrid appeared to be struggling inwardly, then made a sharp movement with one hand that again called his grandfather to Tsauderei's mind. "The southern companies were shorthanded because of, well, me. Trying to take my throne from the regent, my uncle. Half of them were first-year guards, right out of the academy, with no experience. What made it worse was, magic made the Norsundrians invisible to my army until they attacked. It was a slaughter. Detlev knew it was a slaughter. I think he was *enjoying* it. He forced me to watch . . ." Senrid struggled again. Then looked away. "The short version is, I'd been traveling with Puddlenose of the Mearsieans earlier in the summer. Came across some sort of, oh, magical artifact that thought it would be fun to take the form of a, call it a ghost."

Liere said softly, "Her name was Erdrael. Leander's sister called her an angel."

Senrid's voice was hard. "There is no such thing. It was some sort of magical artifact. It might even have been meant for Puddlenose." Though Senrid remembered Erdrael's words had been specifically for him. "Anyway, that sort of thing never happens twice."

Tsauderei leaned forward. "What exactly did Erdrael do, whatever she was?"

"Mirrored the invisibility illusion, but a lot stronger. It was so strong that Norsunder couldn't see any of my people, and Detlev was forced to withdraw."

Tsauderei let out a long sigh. "Whatever she, or it, was, no, we cannot expect to see that again. 'Erdrael.' I take it you never did figure out the mystery?"

Senrid's struggle this time was shorter. "No. I wasted a lot of time delving for mentions of 'Erdrael' before I discovered that the Sartoran language is full of them. Not surprising, considering there's a continent called Drael. I still have no idea what it means, other than the lighter syrup about blessings and sunlight and so forth."

"It's symbolic," Tsauderei said. "The root appears to be 'rael,' which we are still unable to translate, but the combination of the two syllables would appear to connote your metaphorical syrup."

Senrid grimaced slightly, then opened his hand in a gesture that could have been apology. Then he said, "It can't be too syrupy since the word, or the root, appears in the middle of Detlev's name. Hibern once told me that his family name is Hindraeldrei. Drael is the continent above us, so he lived there, is that it? 'Hin' means 'under,' doesn't it?"

Tsauderei said, "The scribes think the prefix indicates something subordinate, either a personal or familial rank. The 'dray-ee' at the end of the name meant 'oath-of-guardianship.' So, people of the area could say they were from 'ne' Hindrael, but a guardian was Hindraeldrei, or ne-Hindraeldrei."

Hibern spoke for the first time, lifting her voice above the distant thunder. "No maps of Ancient Sartor exist, so we don't know if Drael was even called that in the days before the Fall."

Senrid said, "Anyway, that was the military defense. Magical, we'd only had a single-point Emras Defense protecting the border. It was all I could manage to renew when I was ten."

"Many cannot complete one now," Tsauderei observed.

The implied compliment only made Senrid tighten up again. "Well, this past winter, I did it properly, around our entire border. A hundred anchor points. Took months. So at least I'll have warning if they break it, and I'll know where. But if they aren't conquering for the fun of it, I've got nothing more than you do."

"Ah, but I didn't say we had nothing. I told you we look at patterns of movement."

Senrid's eyes narrowed. "You mean, where someone like Detlev's been, since you can't catch him in the act?"

"We can't follow as closely as that, I regret to say."

Senrid understood then that they hadn't taken Jilo's book away from him. Maybe they didn't even know about it.

Tsauderei went on. "From what Erai-Yanya has managed to gather, Detlev has been seen more times in the past five years than in the past five hundred."

Liere hugged her elbows tight against her body; the low, uneven rumble of thunder sounded sinister.

"Then there's Siamis, whose appearance in the world is new. Why now, after all these centuries? Though it's possible he was around now and again before, there is no sign in any records, and the scribes have been searching patiently."

"So the Ancient Sartorans are out for a reason," Senrid said.

Tsauderei held up two gnarled fingers. "Two of the Ancient Sartorans. There are more, the ones who command them."

"The Host of Lords," Senrid said.

Liere thought that that would be the moment for the thunder to break right overhead, but in fact the rain was diminishing to drips at the corners of the eaves. Shafts of sunlight shot down into the valley, lighting up a lake hereto invisible behind the sheets of silvery gray.

Tsauderei continued. "There's some reason compelling enough to bring these two out of their citadel beyond time. Whether or not their appearance is on orders from the Host, Erai-Yanya believes their current goal is set in our sister world on the opposite side of the sun from us: the world called Geth."

Senrid lifted a shoulder. "Not our problem."

"It might become our problem," Tsauderei said. "But you're right. It isn't our problem at this moment. I asked Hibern to invite you so that we could exchange information, which we have now done."

Senrid eyed him. "That's it?"

"Since you Marlovens, for whatever reason, see fit not to establish diplomatic relations with anyone outside your borders, I hoped you would be willing to share any future discoveries. Insights. Threats." Tsauderei's sardonic smile was back.

"The jarls have never agreed to the Eidervaen Accord," Senrid said. "Yes, I know what it is." He'd learned of it only recently, but he wasn't going to admit that. He sensed he was being tested. "In that treaty, ambassadorial residences are deemed part of the country of origin. Our people can't get past the idea of inviting enemies right into your home to take notes on your defenses."

"And you don't think spies of these potential enemies wouldn't be doing that?"

"Of course," Senrid said, then admitted the truth. "I just learned about it. I don't know what to think. I'm still trying to learn how to rule what I have, before I figure out stuff we don't have. And I know I'm not strong enough to force it on the jarls at Convocation, especially since I don't see what we'd gain. We do have envoys going back and forth for specific purposes." Senrid walked to the window, then turned abruptly. "So what did you do to Jilo?"

"Took him straight to a friend of mine, who has in past years made it his mission to battle the former—I hope he stays former—King of the Chwahir. He was going to teach Jilo some magic specific to the Chwahir plight. I know nothing more than that. But when I do, I can see to it that Hibern learns the information, if you're not in the habit of communicating via notecase." The old mage dug in a pocket in his fine robe, and pulled out a golden case.

"I have one," Senrid said, thinking that Hibern hadn't told him about the kids' alliance net, either. Not that it was much use. His gaze met Hibern's black eyes, and her mouth curled sardonically. Oh, yes, she'd guessed what he was thinking.

Senrid fought the hot prickles of a blush. "I made my notecase myself. But I rarely use it," he admitted.

No surprise there, Tsauderei thought. Like his forebears. Ah, dark magic! So very predictable!

All Tsauderei said out loud was, "Fair enough."

Then Liere breathed, "This is. This is the place. Where you can fly?"

And Tsauderei watched Senrid turn from a tense bundle of distrust into a boy. "What?" His head turned sharply.

Liere didn't waste time on words. She shared memory images from a conversation about Tsauderei's Valley of Delfina.

Unaware of that fast mental communication, Tsauderei laughed. "Go ahead." He gave them the spell.

The door banged shut behind Senrid and Liere. She stumbled to the edge of the cliff, hands clutched together at her skinny chest as she jumped softly up and down, then her face lifted with joy as she floated gently above the new grass. But Senrid flung himself straight off the cliff, tumbling downward, then swooping up, turning end over end and whooping as he figured out how to control his body in flight.

Liere flailed after him, her shrill voice like a gull's cry.

"Go on," Tsauderei said to Hibern.

"I don't like heights," she admitted. "Just looking at them makes my stomach turn. A fast ride, I like, because a horse has at least one hoof on the ground."

Tsauderei laughed. "Then watch them, and rejoice. My guess is that neither of them remembers what fun really is."

When they left, Liere transferred with Senrid.

In his study, Senrid stood looking around, his expression absent. Mildly alarmed, Liere brushed the surface of his unshielded thoughts, to discover a confusion of delight and embarrassment.

"Senrid?"

"I hate being stupid." He turned his head, his face red to the ears. "I keep saying I'm not going to be like my uncle, but then I find out I am."

"No, you're not."

"In certain ways I have been. Stupid ways." He threw himself in his chair, giving a jaw-cracking yawn. In order to meet Hibern he'd had to rise earlier than usual. He looked around the sun-filled study, then let out his breath. "Have you ever had so much fun? Ever?"

"Flying!" She clasped her hands. "It was just like my dreams!"

"You fly in your dreams?"

"Oh, yes. I thought everybody did. Well, I know some do."

"I never have," Senrid said. "Though maybe I will after today." He paused to consider the thrill in flying so high the lake had looked like another sky below, then falling, no, stooping like a hawk, the air pressing his face so hard his cheeks rippled and he had to close his eyes to the merest slits, then arching his back and flinging his arms out a moment before he'd hit the water, and skimming above the surface so close that splashes stung his face, and he could see his own shadow within arm's reach. What was it about speed that was so exhilarating? He felt the same when galloping over the open plain. "We have to do that again."

"Tsauderei did say we can go back." Liere looked wistful. "Though I know you don't like to be away long. Because of your responsibilities."

"But that's just it. That's one way I'm like my uncle, thinking I daren't be gone longer than an hour at most. Then when I do go, like transferring to Bereth Ferian to fetch you, I can't help worrying about what I'll find when I return. Well, we were gone half a watch, and here we are. I hear the boys in the academy. I can see the sentries strolling on the walls. Nothing's changed." He lifted a hand toward the open windows, and the spring air carrying in boys' voices shouting in cadence.

Liere sniffed the air, full of spring scents below the ubiquitous scent of horse. She almost didn't notice that horsey smell anymore.

"And another thing. That notecase," Senrid said as he rummaged through the neat piles on his desk. "I forget about it for months on end. Ah."

He opened it and grimaced when he discovered two notes inside.

"I'm going to have to put an alert spell on it," he muttered as he opened the first note. "Oh. I really am a horseapple."

He held out the papers to Liere. One was written in the beautiful script of a scribe, from Karhin, another from Clair of the Mearsieans.

Inside Clair's note was another, short, written in Marloven, which Liere could read now.

> *Senrid: I am told you are still king. Maybe some day I will come back. But only if I know my father is dead. You and I never really understood one another, or even really liked one another. This makes your having watched out for me mean a lot more, and so I am writing to you what will probably be one last time, to thank you for that. I wish you well, and I hope when you remember me, you will imagine my happiness at having made a life I chose.*
>
> *Ndand*

Liere looked up. "This is your missing cousin!"

"Yes, and I really feel stupid now. Okay, let's see how bad this other one makes me feel."

Senrid read it, and threw it on the desk. "This is the kind of thing I expected. Sort of. That an alliance would mean people might want my army coming in and strutting around and looking tough, or maybe even fighting. To clean up somebody else's mess. And then we go home again, and everybody hates the villainous Marlovens."

Liere said, "That does sound like your uncle."

"Except it's true. That is, in our history it happened over and over again. Both sides of our border."

"Did Karhin ask you for fighting?"

"No. She passed on word from Puddlenose, who says this prince our age wants help with training. Where is Erdrael Danara? Isn't it one of the little splotches west of the Land of the Chwahir? Hah. There's 'Erdrael' again."

Liere said, "Are you going to do it?"

"I think I need to know more, but listen. There's Forthan sitting over there in the guard, bored spitless because he has to do his two years patrolling the city. When he was the senior commander in the Academy, part of his duties was to organize the boys. I'll wager anything he could do that for someone else, what do you think? It might even be fun."

"I like him. He's so nice," Liere said.

Forthan's niceness was not the issue here, but Senrid let that pass. Liere was never going to take any interest in things military. "I was going to put him in charge of handpicking some tightlipped friends to pretend to be Norsundrians and test the defenses of the city. Keriam and I talked about the coin and what it might mean."

Senrid snapped the back of his hand up toward the windows, and imaginary Norsundrian spies. "If Detlev decides he wants me, well, this city is where I live, and if it's the army they want, Choreid Dhelerei has the biggest garrison in Marloven Hess."

"Do you think they will attack?" Liere asked, shoulders hunching as she glanced at the windows.

"If they do want my army, it would be stupid to attack us in force, because all they get is corpses. But if they want to force us to fight for them, then they have to take the commanders, because they have to know that in this kingdom, you obey or you die. So they'll infiltrate, right? Execute snatch and grabs, then force the commanders to issue orders on behalf of Norsunder?"

Liere knew he was not expecting an answer.

He snapped his fingers. "This might even be better. Forthan knows the city. The Norsundrians won't. What if, at least at first, I ask that foreigner Shevraeth to lead the attacks? He doesn't know the city, so he'd be looking at it as a stranger. The city would love it," he added. "When there's an all-city war game, then I have to pay for the supplies, and the day's wages, which they almost always turn into a bonfire party at night."

Party? Liere mouthed the word. Every time she thought she understood the Marlovens better, something like this would make it clear she didn't. Maybe she never would.

Senrid's pen was already dashing fast, a little grin on his face. So she kept her thoughts to herself.

## Chapter Fourteen

*Colend*

BECAUSE Colend was halfway around the world from Mearsies Heili, the three going on the alliance mission—CJ, Seshe, and Puddlenose—had tried to nap during the day, so they'd be awake and alert when transferring at midnight.

The sudden shift from rainy darkness to the clear midday skies of Colend made the town square of Wilderfeld, decorated with streamers, bunting, and silk flowers, look even brighter. Even if it was too early in spring for actual flowers.

But even with a dearth of flowers, little could spoil Flower Day.

Once they recovered from the transfer, the sound of singing drew their attention to a flower-decorated gazebo at the other end of the square. Three people stood there, wearing green and white, their heads crowned by garlands mostly made up of lilies, the Colendi flower.

Voices rose and fell. "What's that?" CJ asked, pointing. "Some kind of celebration?"

"A wedding, looks like," Puddlenose said.

CJ peered under her hand. "But there's three people. And I know they don't have priests or rabbis or religious guys to do the vows here, that if you want somebody Up There listening . . ." CJ pointed heavenward. "You talk directly to 'em. Or you know they're already listening. Clair explained it, once, though I still don't get it."

'Religious guys.' Puddlenose shrugged, figuring this had to be another of CJ's incomprehensible Earth references. "Is there a problem?"

"Three? I guess weirdness like that is typical of Colend."

Seshe hesitated, not liking to contradict a friend, but Puddlenose grinned. "You don't think it happens right at home in Mearsies Heili?"

CJ made a gag face. "If by 'it' you mean sex, I know all about sex. I heard plenty of jokes on the playground, before I came to this world." She snorted, then said in a low voice, "If you mean marriage, I didn't think you could do that with three. On Earth, anyway. And thank goodness! On Earth, marriage really means fighting and arguing, and both take it out on the kids."

"I guess marriage is different on Earth than here," Puddlenose said, with a total lack of interest.

CJ scowled. Two people or ten, any thought of what she termed 'mush' made her squirm with disgust. But she had come all this way as an ambassador to the alliance, so she squashed down the desire to mutter about how three would only make the arguments louder. "Where's Thad's house?"

"Right across there." Puddlenose pointed to the rambling two-story house, with a sign hanging that read *Wilderfeld Scribes and Messengers*. Before they crossed the sward, Puddlenose held out a hand. "Look, CJ. Remember that we're here to make things easier for Senrid and Terry. I know you haven't been in Colend since you and Terry were snabbled as hostages by Wan-Edhe."

CJ scowled, loathing that memory: being captured along with a boy she'd called Terry—Prince Tereneth of Erdrael Danara. He'd barely survived a political coup before he was captured.

"I just want to say that if that should come up, Thad and Karhin— really, everyone in Colend—knows that their king is insane. Doesn't help to talk about it. Okay?"

"Clair already told me to be diplomatic," CJ said.

Puddlenose ducked his head. "Good enough, then." And led the rest of the way across the grass. He said as they stepped onto the porch, "Today being a festival, all the kids will have freedom from work. Thad said to come straight upstairs."

Before they'd gone two steps inside, a slim, graceful teenage girl met them, red braids swinging against her cream-colored scribe student over-robe, her grin wide and merry. "Puddlenose! You're here!"

"As promised, Karhin."

Before Puddlenose could introduce CJ, Karhin looked up at tall, calm Seshe, dressed in a fine linen long robe over trousers. Seshe was the Mearsiean girls' peacemaker, along to help in case she was needed. She'd loved beautiful Colend on her previous visit. As Seshe copied Karhin's peace gesture, Karhin said, "And you brought your princess!"

Seshe dropped her hands and reddened to the ears, which surprised Puddlenose and CJ both, but Puddlenose said quickly, "CJ's the princess." He jerked a thumb her way. "That's Seshe."

Karhin's lips parted, her wide blue eyes apologetic as she said contritely, "I beg pardon. I am so clumsy sometimes. Welcome, CJ, or should I say your highness?"

"Don't," CJ said. "We only do that junk when I'm throne-warming for Clair."

"Very well, then," Karhin said cheerily, smothering her intense curiosity as she gestured for the company to precede them.

Puddlenose bounded up the stairs three at a time. Karhin followed the two girls, observing how Seshe moved like one trained to courtly behavior, whereas CJ thumped up, bare feet twinkling beneath her plain green skirt. Karhin loved a mystery, and here was the oddest one, in a prince who called himself Puddlenose, and who seemed glad to surrender his rank to this girl in the black vest and green skirt, who didn't act, or dress, the least like a princess. And yet this other girl did.

CJ was determined to be a diplomat, but she couldn't help being on the watch for the slightest sign of snobbery or bullying. Her first glimpse of Thad was reassuring, as he was a beanpole of a boy, scrawny and knobby-kneed, with flyaway hair as bright a red as Falinneh's. He clapped his hands together in the peace, his grin merry.

So CJ's mood was high as Thad led the company into a pleasant room filled with comfortably shabby furnishings that had obviously seen plenty of use, the diamond-paned windows opened wide to let in the air wafting in over budding flower boxes.

The newcomers greeted Senrid, who sat cross-legged on the floor, and lanky Terry—King Tereneth of Erdrael Danara—lounging on the other side of a low table from Senrid. Terry was surreptitiously trying to get his bad leg comfortable, as he kept the hand with missing fingers curved protectively against his middle, mostly covered by his loose robe.

Terry wore his brown hair long, parted on one side to hide the awful puckered scar on his otherwise pleasant face. CJ, sitting next to him, glimpsed it and quickly looked toward the window, through which she could hear the melodic rise and fall of children's voices singing wedding songs. As long as CJ didn't have to see any mush, she could enjoy the music.

"Our mothers are down there, with Lisbet and Little Bee." Thad made a gesture toward the window as he named his younger stepsiblings. "And they think we're there, too. So we are free to talk."

"We even have some wedding cakes," Karhin said, triumphantly bearing in a plate of delicious-looking pastries: custard cakes glazed with lemon, puffy tartlets, and what looked like square oatmeal cookies with ground walnuts.

They sat in a circle with the plate in the center. CJ eyed her hosts, waiting for them to move first, Puddlenose having warned her that the Colendi tended to have elaborate customs, like not stepping on their shadows. At least the room was airy and bright, pretty framed mirrors on the walls opposite the open windows making sure there were no shadows.

Karhin gestured to the guests to help themselves, observing Seshe's neat manners, controlled to the fingertips as she took a single cake, contrasting with Puddlenose and CJ piling their plates. Senrid ignored the cakes, and Terry looked away, reluctant to risk making a mess, dealing one-handed with delicate pastry on fine dishes.

Senrid, impatient with politesse, said, "Terry, I understand you want military advice."

Terry sent a panicked look Puddlenose's way, and gestured with his whole hand. "It's . . . not military, in the sense of armies. It's our border guard." He sent another eloquent look Puddlenose's way.

Puddlenose said, "Terry's country had a lot of trouble not long ago."

A breathtakingly bland summary of several horrific years. "We were once three very tiny kingdoms," Terry said. "But the older generation, well, the short of it is that they all decided to grab each other's thrones. Assassinations. Fighting." No, he wasn't doing any better. Either you told it all, or nothing.

Terry shrugged sharply, pulling his marred hand in tighter, and Senrid grimaced, wondering how long he'd endured his injury before he could get to a healer. If he even got to a healer, who ought to be able to bind fingers back to a hand by magic. Assuming the wound was fresh. And the fingers were there.

"The Chwahir didn't make things any better," Puddlenose said grimly.

"Ugh!" CJ interjected, then remembered she was to be a diplomat, and she sat back, face red.

CJ's outburst enabled Terry—who was intimidated to be in Colend, whose customs and manners had been dinned into him as the model for nobility—to say more normally, "The border guards were either lazy, or leading the assassinations. You used to have to be born to the right families to belong. Most of them rode around in splendid uniforms, and that was about it. But there is so much rumor about the Chwahir and trouble there, and Norsunder, and everything else, I think I need somebody to come to the guard to tell them how to train. Oh. So many of them either died or ran off, that there weren't many left, and so I opened it to anyone. Birth rank doesn't matter."

Senrid's wariness thawed with every sentence. "So you really do want trainers, not mercenaries."

Terry looked hopeful. "Puddlenose says you described a training school, people our age, who learn how to have discipline, right? Your people know what to do if there's an attack. They know how to use their weapons properly, and all that."

"'All that,' I can help you with. I even have someone in mind," Senrid said.

As the boys talked, Karhin noted how CJ met one's gaze straight on, whereas Seshe's gaze was a butterfly touch, brief then moving away lest it disturb or intrude. She sat so neatly, legs folded under her.

Karhin made a wager with herself that Seshe even crossed her feet, one big toe over the other, the way the Colendi nobles were taught from childhood. Why was CJ the replacement princess instead of Seshe? All Puddlenose had ever said was that his cousin, a girl queen, collected runaways and adopted them.

Puddlenose popped a last bite into his mouth, and licked his fingers. "So you'll do it, Senrid?"

"Forthan could use the experience." Senrid quoted Commander Keriam. "Yes."

The brother and sister put their palms together in the peace gesture, heads bowing in gratitude.

Karhin indicated the last of the cakes. "Let us celebrate harmonious agreement."

"You mean," CJ said as she lunged forward to grab the chocolate one she'd been eyeing, "the alliance really works!"

There was laughter as everyone agreed.

CJ went on. "So we need to get more kids in. And we need a name! Something that won't cause adults to snout in. Like our underground hideout, we never called a hideout. We called it the Junky, or Junkyard. What grownup would want to nose into a junkyard?"

Karhin said, "Maybe you should be in charge of the names?"

CJ wanted nothing better. "I already have a great idea. We'll call the group Fonebone."

"Fonebone?" the others repeated doubtfully, and CJ chortled, loving how the silly word sounded.

By now, CJ knew that saying *It comes from a magazine called MAD, back on Earth* would cause a zillion questions, beginning with *What is a magazine?* "In my birth language, I used words to make up an acronym, see? Federated Organization to Negate Eleveners By Organizing New Enforcement-tactics." And at their bewildered looks, she waved her hands. "Never mind that. If nosy adults heard you talking about The Secret Organization, or the Sisterhood, or the Kids' Guild, would they ask?"

"Yes." Thad put his hands together in assent. "You must understand that our mothers, in accepting the guild license, made the scribes' vow never to become involved in politics."

"But *we* have not made these vows," Karhin explained. "And we see the alliance as something non-political, a net for the purpose of communication, and defense against Norsunder."

"So our new name is Fonebone," CJ stated, thinking privately that surely such a silly name was certain to keep bad luck away.

## Chapter Fifteen

L IERE went to visit Senrid as summer ended in the south.

Under Hibern's tutoring, she had begun diligently studying the fundamentals of magic, but when she left Hibern, she couldn't resist setting aside the boring basics to delve into Senrid's magic books. He let her read anything she wanted, so, driven by her dread of Norsunder taking her by surprise, she skipped over years of stuff in search of transportation spells, and—the most frightening of all—rifts.

Of course she was not going to try them. The first time she opened one of the books, she tightened her hands into fists, just in case simply reading a spell made it somehow happen.

But she had to know.

And so, on a hot, humid day, with the sounds and scents of the world going about its business carried on the heavy air, she crouched in the window seat and read that anyone who studies the fundamentals of transfer magic, however the spells are formed ('dark' or 'light') learns early that with each successive person added to a transfer there is not just a corresponding reaction, but an exponential one.

All right. She understood that much.

More surprising was the observation that not all space between spaces was the same, no more than the density of objects (air, water, wood, soil, rock, ice, fire) was the same. Certain places had been fairly stable, if transfers were regulated, for centuries; some cities had grown up around such places.

The rest of the world could sustain the occasional transfer, though it was "more keenly felt" but became exponentially more volatile if more than one living being used the same space: they were more likely to come through non-living. If at all.

That was scary.

*The shift of material objects in and out of the physical world, alive or inert, requires exactitude.*

Senrid had underlined that. She wondered how old he had been when he'd studied this stuff.

*Using dark magic to force too much material or especially too many living beings too close together through even the most reliable Destinations can instigate an explosive friction that can destroy not only that which is transferred but anything within a considerable space around.*

That was another one Senrid had underlined.

She closed the book, walked around aimlessly, then came back to it, feeling like she was picking at an invisible scab. But she had to know. Imagination was too frightening otherwise.

*After a double transfer, the Destination needs to be cleared of magic reaction before it's safe to use again. That's more expense. And the reaction for those transferred is unpleasantly strong.*

Well, she'd felt the truth of that.

Reference to a name sent her to another book that covered the history of magic. Paging along, she discovered that as soon as mages had understood how transfer magic worked, dark mages had tried to create ways to transfer armies. They found ways to use magic to rip gaps between spaces, though the edges were very dangerous. These rifts caused other mages to develop wards against their formation. The larger a rift, the more involved the wards against them. In dark magic, those wards could be deadly.

She was working slowly down a page, her finger marking each word, when running footsteps, thumps, and boys' shouting erupted from Senrid's study down the hall.

She dropped her book and sped outside, to find a couple of guards and runners gathered at the door of Senrid's study. She was just in time to see a flurry of papers settling down as Senrid tapped out from his position flat on the floor, a big black-clad boy sitting astride him. Two others stood by, one of them hanging back, betraying uncertainty: Liere recognized Shevraeth, the Remalnan studying at the academy, whom she'd met the year previous. Liere had to look twice. Shevraeth had shot up to be quite tall, and he looked very much like the other Marlovens, except for the graceful way he used his hands.

His expression was a polite chagrin as everybody else in the room grinned in triumph. She knew what was going on. The 'Norsundrians' in the 'city attack' had won their way to the king!

Liere gasped. "I told you," she exclaimed, pointing at Senrid. "I told you!"

At the door, the runner laughed, waving in one of the guards, who from the resemblance was a brother or cousin.

Senrid sat up. Both he and his attacker had bloody noses.

"I told you so, I told you." Liere couldn't seem to stop herself.

Senrid grinned at the three attackers as he mopped his nose with his handkerchief. "Good job, you three."

He got up and started out, Liere following.

The guard, who last year had been an academy senior, closed in on Senrid's other side, saying defensively, "Not fair. No accident they broke through the first day Forthan is back. He knows the castle routine like no soul-sucking Norsundrian will. May as well waft 'em in by magic. We weren't slack."

Senrid sighed. "But that's the whole point. If Norsunder can cheat, they will. Still, report what happened to the guard captain. Tighter patrols are always a good idea."

The guard saluted, fist to chest, and loped off, leaving Senrid and Liere alone.

She followed him to his room. "Senrid, you aren't safe here. If they attack. I told you so."

"Don't you think I know that?" he retorted, carefully fingering his nose and wincing. "All right. I'm still a target, even inside the biggest guarded city on the continent. I think we're going to have to try Keriam's idea, a communication system, so we have a warning and can take action . . ."

*Chwahirsland*

Jilo never remembered walking outside the castle gates.

He barely recognized his lungs laboring and his blood whooshing in his ears past the weird buzzing sound in his head. The buzz gradually resolved back into voices, but they were still too distorted to understand.

The after-effects of two powerful spells counteracting one another had dropped enough people for the city-dwellers to have cautiously crept out to aid sentries they'd seen collapse on the outer wall.

Others had fallen in the street. Jilo, who still wore his shabby flatfoot-probationer uniform, was bundled by furtive hands into a way station, where he woke up the next morning. For a time all he could do was lie there and listen to his labored breathing. Gradually he managed to get enough breath into him to widen his awareness outside himself to others on the cots.

He overheard mumbled fragments of conversation: *What happened? We think Wan-Edhe might be back, but there have been no orders. Oh, right, I should get back to duty. We will all get back to duty.* (This last said in a raised voice, in case they were overheard.) *But first, the mess hall has food.*

Finally it was Jilo's empty belly, lying pinched and flat between his jutting hipbones, that got him to his feet and down an interminable hall of some twenty paces, to the nearest bench. A bowl of thin gruel, a crumbling of egg (one egg shared among four people), and some hot steeped tare-weed woke him up enough to sort out a roomful of people unsure what had happened. But something had happened. Everybody was afraid of what it might mean.

Jilo crept back to the bunk, and fell into it.

When he woke next, it was easier to get to the mess hall, which was half full. The subsequent meal was heartier, and he was able to keep it down without any trouble.

The next day, he made it outside. His plan was to get out of the city, while that mighty spell slowly began to unravel the pocket Norsunder.

He only managed to reach the garrison at the east gate, but that was just as well, as thin, sleety rain fell. Even if he'd felt well, there would be no distance gained if he had to splash through puddles and mud.

By the following day, he felt strong enough to walk. He had his plan ready: he would be a probationary courier, which meant no one would ask for his twi, or rank, or army place. Couriers crossed the country bearing messages that they were not permitted to see, so no one would ask questions, at least not about his supposed messages, especially if he was regarded as probationary. Probationers never carried anything vital.

In this way, he figured, he'd be as good as invisible, and could learn more about the people. He didn't have the strength to go fast, but that was all right. He wasn't doing this to run a distance race. Sitting in mess halls listening was a better way to learn than running to see how far he could get.

Each day that Jilo got farther from the capital, he found himself a little stronger. He walked a little farther. When he stopped at night, he was able to study a little longer, and he remembered more of what he had learned. Meanwhile he gained the victory of being able to see a day begin, progress, and end. Counting them was still beyond him.

By the time he'd reached the outpost halfway between the garrison at Narad and the provincial one farther along the river, he had come to the conclusion that yes, he'd been suffering magical reaction, but it was not entirely due to the spells he hoped he'd completed. The entire city was ill from the effects of Wan-Edhe's magic.

If he really had managed to complete the spells Mondros had taught him, then he should come back to Narad and sense a change. What would that do to the people?

One day at a time.

He was still trying to accustom himself to how sharp sounds were when he joined the outpost mess. No one spoke, except about orders, of course. That regulation was fifty years old. He wanted to hear talk about orders, and gain a sense of who was issuing them. Who was going to try to fill the space left by Wan-Edhe? The clearer Jilo's head, the less he believed that he was going to succeed in his mad attempt to walk through the entire kingdom to learn what the people truly thought.

One day at a time!

He got up to get more to drink, and watched people's hands. Two might have been using that hand language. Maybe only one, and the other was absently tapping his fingers on the table. Jilo was distracted by those hands. Very small for a man.

Jilo got his drink and sat down again. He looked at the various backs and bent heads, all shades of black, from blue-black hair to reddish, and from new, well-woven and dyed uniforms to the dirty gray of a shabby, much-scrubbed tunic years old. The room was silent except for the little noises of eating, utensils ticking unmusically on clay dishes, a snort over here, a cough over there. Cloth shifting. From outside the window, the steady wash of the river.

Everyone appeared to be as isolated as he was. So why was the hand-tapper impatient?

Jilo decided to watch the fellow.

When the two benches filled, Hand Tapper rose to make space. Jilo also rose, and followed Hand Tapper through the low door, down the narrow corridor, which smelled of baked cabbage, to the outer door that looked over the river dock. A thin, bitter rain had begun to fall from under lowering clouds.

Jilo debated retreating to the barracks, as the air flowing off the river was cold and damp, when a small boat tied up at the dock, and Hand Tapper straightened up. A gangling boy waved a courier bag at the sentries at the dock, was passed, and ran up the stairs.

Hand Tapper greeted him with, "What happened? I wanted to get on the road before noon."

"Bridge is out again. We all had to take a watch binding the pontoon."

"Here's Narad." Hand Tapper dropped a slim packet into the newcomer's hand, and whirled around.

Jilo stepped aside, glanced up, and blinked. The fellow had female contours to his face, neck, and chin, though somewhat hidden by the graying hair, and blurred by the pouchy flesh on either side of his mouth.

The newcomer paused to shove the Narad communication into his bulging pouch, and Jilo wondered why Hand Tapper was handing it off one day's journey from Narad. Didn't these couriers cross the kingdom, collecting and dropping off communications?

He tried to formulate a question without actually asking, but before he could find words, the newcomer pushed past him and headed inside.

Jilo abandoned his questions. He had to be more observant, and patient.

By the time Jilo had crossed the country to Burda Garrison in the center of the kingdom, the impossible had altered to improbable, and from there to unlikely-but-possible.

He knew that some of what he heard was the result of his escape from the life-destroying magic in Narad. Everything was clearer, sharper, almost as dramatic a difference as when he first managed to dispel Wan-Edhe's brain-fogging magic. Even with the centuries-old blight leaching life from sky and water and soil, the diffuse light carried subtle variations, the smells a complication of decay and growth, the wind whiffing of brine from the distant sea.

Then there were the sounds. At first he thought the sense of rhythm in the chopping of vegetables, the brush of a horse's hide, the creak of wheels on a cart nothing more than his own burgeoning awareness of the world, but slowly came the conviction that the fact that he heard these things at all, especially in a kingdom where any form of music, song, poetry, or dance had been outlawed on pain of death, was significant.

Then there were the . . . warriors? What ought he to call them?

The law had been strict for generations: females were not permitted in the army.

But Jilo was seeing them.

Girls, women, their hair clipped like men, their uniforms mostly shapeless, though as the distance from Narad increased, the less some of the older ones hid the shapes beneath the clothing. They were referred to as 'he' and they answered to male names.

But they weren't males, and he was fairly sure they weren't what the Chwahir called soft-shells, the women who for whatever reason wished to be transformed into men, and strove to earn enough credit to obtain the complicated, some said painful magic to make themselves into them. (Hard-shells, men who wished to become women, were put to death under Wan-Edhe's law.)

Soft-shells could never hold any position of command even after completion of the magic, they could only serve in menial tasks, but these women hadn't gone through any magic transformation. They used male names, and everybody used male pronouns when talking about them. Some of them were patrol leaders—many were couriers— stable masters. They just didn't go to Narad.

Wan-Edhe could not have known, or they'd all be dead.

## Chapter Sixteen

*Autumn, 4741 AF*
*Norsunder Base*

W HEN Henerek found out that Kessler had been sifting through his carefully chosen and trained company there at Norsunder Base, recruiting his best for purposes of his own, he wasted little time in cursing. He put more time into trying to ambush Kessler, and a great deal of time concocting a parallel track to his plans.

Now everything was carefully prepared.

Unwitnessed meetings between Norsunder Base commanders were never easy to arrange. There must be a balance of power, or what appeared to be a balance of power, because few of these meetings ended up with agreement.

So first you have to catch the target's interest.

Henerek did that by intercepting Kessler at the stable, at a well-known corner inconvenient for fighting. Kessler never let anyone get within arm's reach, but all Henerek had to do was pass within sight, open his hand, and disclose a single twelve-sided onyx stone on his palm.

Kessler stilled.

Into the silence Henerek said, "Hill Five. Now."

Hill Five did not have a Destination, a window, or any other distinguishing feature besides being raised enough for commanders to view the war game field from the other side.

It was one place Norsunder Base's inhabitants could be reasonably assured of privacy. Henerek knew he had caught Kessler's attention, but that didn't mean Kessler would show up. Already there was a fifty-fifty chance he wouldn't, as most commanders who met there for private talks insisted on riding across the field side by side, the better to watch one another for treachery. Nevertheless, Henerek went through the motions: he saddled a horse, told the stable within hearing of several of the internal informers known as rats that he was scouting the field for an exercise, and set out.

When he spotted a lone horseback rider approaching the jumble of rocky hills from an oblique angle, the thrill of the chase burned through his nerves. Henerek urged his horse faster, as if he were worried that Kessler would get there first and arrange some sort of ambush.

Heh. If he was uncooperative, Kessler was going to be the one getting a surprise.

They approached the hill from opposite sides. Henerek tied up his horse and vaulted quickly from rock to rock to reach the wind-flattened top, which afforded a fine view of the rocky plain below. As he expected, there was Kessler, approaching from the other side, hands empty at his sides. His sword, if he had one, left with the horse.

Oh, stupid move.

Henerek resisted the impulse to touch the blood-magic-enchanted blade he carried safely in a sheath. He knew it was there. It hadn't gone anywhere. And best that Kessler thought it an ordinary blade of the sort he carried plenty of. Kessler himself was armed: steel-handled knife hilts winked in the gray light at both boot tops, at his belt, and there were probably more up his sleeves. A lot of good those would do him once the hidden attack team laid him out flat.

"The object-transport stone," Kessler said, coming forward to meet Henerek in the middle of the hilltop. Unimpeded, the wind cut like a steel blade and winter was still a month off. "Where did you get that?"

"One? I have four," Henerek said. He had no intention of revealing the whole of his plan, but he couldn't resist this little flourish. "I've had Pengris searching for a year. Or he's been gone a year. Who knows how long he spent ferreting in Norsunder-Beyond?"

Kessler was so surprised he actually looked surprised. Henerek took in a breath to suppress the laugh threatening to get past his ribs. Kessler said, "What did you promise to get a mage on your side?"

"Said I'd make him head mage when I take Everon."

"Where did you stash the body?"

"Where Siamis will never find him," Henerek retorted, gloating over the fact that Kessler would get the blame if he was found. Henerek didn't like that Kessler had guessed so quickly about Pengris's death. On the other hand, Kessler was fast with a knife. Maybe he expected that in everyone.

To get Kessler off the subject of the mage (and whatever the other mages were going to do if they found Pengris's corpse), "This is what's important. You're aware that over the past year, Siamis has been showing up once every three or four months to look at us."

"And he was here yesterday. Your point?"

"When he comes next, he'll find his precious army dispersed over two continents."

"What kind of transport will that stone bring out of the Beyond?"

"Ship. Four of 'em, actually. Four stones, four ships. Troop-transport ships are what I need to take my company to the east coast of Drael. When Siamis shows up next, I'll be securing a base of operations in Everon. Siamis can sulk, but I'm sure Detlev'll be pleased to see us get a jump on his plan."

Kessler said, "You don't know what his plan is. Nobody does."

"How many variations are there on invasion?" Henerek shrugged, anticipation making him want to protract the moment. Enjoy it the longer. "Those ships might've been transformed into these stones a thousand years ago or more. Wonder what they'll think, coming back into the world again." He paused, but Kessler just stood there. To fill the silence, Henerek got back to the plan. "Bostian says that once I reach Everon, he'll launch his campaign against Sartor. It'll make the lighters panic like a hammer to an ant hill."

"So I'm here because?"

"I want you with me."

"Under your command." It wasn't a question.

Henerek shrugged again. "If you'd laid the plans, then I'd be under yours." A heartbeat, three, four. The only sound, the wind moaning around the rocks. Henerek lifted his voice. "Siamis can sulk if we've shipwrecked his campaign." *Shipwreck* was the attack phrase. "But he should have been here."

Kessler shrugged. "Not interested in 'should have.'" He made a half-turn, about to leave.

Henerek lifted his voice. "So you won't shipwreck my campaign, even if you won't join?"

Where was the ambush team? Henerek's nerves chilled colder than the wind as the impossible became probable. Angry, he pulled the be-spelled knife, and threw it. All he needed was the tiniest nick for the blood-spell to take hold.

Kessler had not completed his turn; he sidestepped, and the knife clattered against a rock. Two, three steps, and Kessler slipped behind an enormous boulder and vanished from sight.

Henerek had placed his men carefully. He ran to the slab behind which the team leader was supposed to be waiting, and stared down at the slumped figure, blood already congealed in a black pool between two cracked rocks. When had Kessler done that? More important, how had he known?

The sound of horse hooves beating a rapid retreat made Henerek recoil wildly, but all he saw was the back of a dark head in the swirling dust kicked up by the wind.

Shipwreck. His hand tightened on the magical artifacts as he faced the fact that his month of careful planning had just been shipwrecked. No, it hadn't. He just had to act faster. The hunt was on!

He laughed, and rapidly assessed the shambles, deciding what to leave and what to keep. He wouldn't be able to wait for the horses being brought in.

He had better get what supplies there were, and march out that night.

*At the same time in Sartor, directly to the north*

Atan had begun to dread Restday ever since the council, singly and collectively, had convinced her that she was wrong to let the morvende take Julian to Shendoral, where she was happiest—but she not only was not getting any education, she also wasn't getting any older because of the way time worked there. The council had made it clear that Atan was the only person who could properly take little Julian in hand.

Atan had begun firmly but lovingly, as they suggested. Not every day, but once a week, that was her compromise.

She had chosen Restday, as it seemed to be Julian's favorite day, the one that saw her around the palace most often. Rather than ruin Restday supper with its wine and bread, candles and songs, she forced herself to go to Julian's room first thing in the morning.

She'd had the tailor make two outfits that would fit the child: a very plain tunic and riding trousers like any Sartoran child would wear, and the most beautiful dress Atan had ever seen. She would have loved it at Julian's age, living as she did in the hermit's cottage: it was a pale blue velvet, the color of the summer sky at dawn, embroidered with tiny birds and blossoms, with diamonds winking at each shoulder.

"Julian, will you choose one of these outfits today?"

"No." Julian scrambled into her oversized robe and long scarf, which at least the servants had been able to put through the cleaning frame while the child was asleep.

"Julian. Will you permit the maid to brush your hair?"

"No."

"How about if I brush it? I will be very gentle. You can stop me if anything hurts."

"No." Julian ran out the door.

That first time, Atan almost chased her, but stopped at the door. She could easily catch up. With all the walking about the palace that she did, and climbing of the dragon plateaus and other places she'd explored, she was strong, with plenty of stamina.

But when she caught up, what then? A screaming, kicking fight in the halls? At least she knew wherever Julian ran to when she disappeared like that, she always came back safe. People all over the city knew who she was, and shared food with her when she was hungry.

The next week, Atan nerved herself to the same conversation, to get the same result. At the end, she forced herself to say in her calmest, firmest, but most loving voice (knowing she was failing with every word, her throat was so tight with dread, and even anger), "Julian. I am going to ask you every week, until you decide it is time to be a person, and not a wild thing."

"I hate you!" And the sound of rapidly vanishing feet.

Atan looked at the rejected clothes, controlling the urge to toss them out the window.

She'd failed again.

She walked down to the steward's chambers, where she found tough old Gehlei, who had been in the queen's private guard in the old days. Gehlei had saved Atan's life, losing the use of one arm in the process.

Gehlei was now her steward. Gehlei had long wanted the position, but when young hadn't had the connections. Busy as she was, she always made time for Atan, not because Atan was Queen Yustnesveas the Fifth, but because they were both as close to family as either had left.

Neither counted Julian as family, not without the mental effort required by duty.

"She was yelling *I hate you*," Atan said.

No need to say whom she meant.

Gehlei shut the outer door. "She says that all the time," she said gruffly. "To the kitchen staff when they don't have her favorite orange-iced pastry at all hours. To the rest of us if we try to stop her. Nobody is going to touch her, and I think she knows that."

"Gehlei, this is a terrible idea, but the council says only I have the authority to do anything about her. I know Hin or Sin will take her back to the forest hideout, but we can't let her live in Shendoral all her life."

Gehlei wrinkled her nose at the thought of the weird forest, where time seemed to stand still. Or even go backward. She tucked a strand of gray hair into her headdress, then said even more gruffly, "Send her to that baras."

"I don't like her."

"I know."

It felt so good to speak plainly, but that wouldn't solve the problem. "I don't trust her, either, even less than I trust Irza." Irza and her sister, the highest ranking of the Rescuers, had taken care of Julian during the days they'd hidden in the forest of Shendoral before the century of sleep was lifted.

As the baras tended to remind Atan, usually after a sickly sweet, "How is dear little Julian? My daughters miss her so very much, and would love nothing better than to have her live with them again." And she'd smile with her elder daughter's smug smirk. "My daughters often tell me little stories about how *good* the dear princess was when they had her under their care," she'd add, or something insinuating like it.

"Were the girls really good with Julian?" Gehlei asked, after scowling into the middle distance.

"As far as I could tell, but you know I joined the forest orphans so late."

Gehlei's mouth thinned. "Then let them have her."

"The baras is going to use Julian for political purposes, just as she was the one leading the campaign to shut out the commoners among the Rescuers. I really hate that. She doesn't care about Julian. How could she? She'd never even seen her until the enchantment broke, and has barely glimpsed her since."

Gehlei lifted a shoulder, as in the distance a bell rang the quarter-hour. "You have an entire council to deal with that. Do you want Julian civilized?"

"Yes. All right," Atan said, giving in. As she always did. "Next time the baras brings it up, I'll tell her to go ahead."

It happened a week later, after a temper tantrum down in the public areas, when one of the servants tried to get Julian to put on shoes before running into the rain. Atan thought later that this was a measure of how fast gossip traveled when the baras brought forth her invitation that very day.

And she watched, her spirits about as low as they'd ever been, as Julian looked back over her shoulder and said triumphantly, "Irza gives me what I want. I love Irza."

Gehlei was standing next to Atan as the baras's carriage rolled away. She smiled grimly.

Atan said, "I feel sick."

"Don't. The child knows the word love. An improvement."

Atan turned away, feeling even worse.

Two days later, she sat on her dais at the back of the public interview chamber, gazing through the colored glass in the windows at the great square as, on the other side of the room, district street and water guild representatives argued in bristlingly formal words, their voices heavy with innuendo. Each tried to imply that paying for the much-needed repair to a six-hundred-year-old fountain was the responsibility of the other.

Atan sat upright when she recognized a tall figure bearing some kind of burden.

The guild chiefs and the city officials paid no attention, of course. Knowing that they would be forced to rise if she rose, she got to her feet. The tedious argument ceased abruptly as everyone bowed.

Atan walked past, guessing how much resentment was constrained in those bent heads. A moment before the door shut behind her, she heard a low, angry, "*Now* see what you did!" from one of the district speakers.

"*I* did?" yelped a water guild representative.

The door snicked shut, and she hurried to meet Rel at the corridors' intersection, returned from his usual visit to Mendaen at the guard. His arms bore a mound of draggling fabric, a hank of tangled brown hair hanging down. Out of the middle of the swathe popped a red face as Julian declared indignantly, "I hate Irza!"

Rel set down the child, who scampered off as Irza herself appeared behind them.

Irza slowed, face red from running. Atan wondered if she'd chased Julian clear from Parleas Terrace to the palace as Irza performed a formal bow that was stiff with fury. "I relinquish her . . . to your care. Your majesty."

"Irza," Atan said. "What happened?"

Irza's face pinched up in an expression very like her mother's. "I do not know . . . what has happened to her since . . . our peaceful . . . days in the forest . . . but she has become ungovernable."

Atan didn't bother trying to deflect this blame. At the other end of the hall behind Irza, a white-haired boy appeared, waved, and retreated. Atan recognized Hinder, who should be underground in the morvende geliath for a family celebration.

Atan made herself speak formal words of thanks to Irza, though she knew it was a waste of time, that Irza and her mother were surely already spreading gossip blaming Atan for Julian's behavior. And Atan thought dismally that it was true. She was to blame as much as anyone.

As soon as Irza was put into a royal Landis carriage for the ride back (Atan knew that it would mollify Irza at least somewhat, being seen in a royal carriage) Atan and Rel began walking upstairs to Atan's private chamber.

"Found her running over the bridge, screeching. I called to her," Rel said. "Surprised when she came, but I think it was only because Irza was about to catch her."

Atan sighed. "I don't know what to do. The servants refuse to go near her."

Rel grinned. "Her hair smells like a bird nest. They can't trick her to step through a cleaning frame?"

"Not anymore. We used to. I don't know why she began putting up such a fuss. At least when the weather is warm she'll swim in the river with the other little ones, or when she goes back to Shendoral, she plays in the streams."

They reached her study, whose perimeter Hinder paced, his cobwebby hair drifting. "Atan," he said the moment she shut the door, "the elders sent me to warn you, and I wanted to tell you first: the Norsunder Base army is on the move."

"Where?"

"They were seen from the southeastern watch post, marching toward the coast."

"How many?"

"Hundreds. You have to remember we can only spy them out from a distance. But they were going toward the eastern coast."

Atan turned to Rel. "Then they must be taking ship. That makes it unlikely they're marching here, or against Sarendan."

At the first mention of Norsunder, Rel's smile had vanished. "I better get my gear," he said. "I promised Tahra I'd return to Everon at the first sign of Norsunder emerging from the Base."

Atan faced him. "How do you know that Everon is the goal?"

"I don't. But like you say, if they're taking ship, then they aren't marching here. King Berthold can decide whether or not to act on such scant information. I feel I ought to provide that information."

"The ambassador will be doing that," Atan said.

Rel smiled. "My three days here are up."

"I can give you a transfer token," Atan said as she reached for the bellpull. "It's time for me to summon the high council . . ." She stopped. "I will, of course. In a moment," she said, staring out the window at the courtyard below as she thought about Karhin's message a few weeks back, about the first alliance mission—Senrid of Marloven Hess sending someone to help train Terenth of Erdrael Danara's Mountain Guard—being a success.

Atan whirled to face Rel, and remembered the beautiful letter that she had received from the scribe named Karhin, who had said that Rel had personally recruited her. "But first I'm writing to the alliance, as I promised," and light filled her inner being at his sudden smile. "And then I'm writing to Hibern. For Sartor."

Senrid was sitting at breakfast, his knuckles throbbing from a good session on the mats, when a runner appeared, followed by Hibern.

"It's Atan," she said, and in Sartoran, "there's bad news on their south border. She wants to talk to you."

"Me?" Senrid said.

"I think she wants military advice, and she asked me to come to you directly, rather than going through Karhin Keperi."

"This is exactly what I didn't want happening," Senrid muttered. But maybe it would only be another chance for Forthan to gain some more experience training foreigners. He'd certainly enjoyed going to Erdrael Danara.

Most important, Senrid had promised.

A short time later, he stood where he had never thought to be: in Sartor's royal palace, parts of which were said to be more than five thousand years old.

The longish walk from the Destination to the interview chamber didn't surprise him, as he'd expected the mosaics, the murals, the patterned marble in the worn floor and all the fancy furniture. Unexpected was the way the low autumnal light slanted in through filigree carvings, throwing patterns on the marble, or reflecting again in long mirrors, so that even though he knew he stood in a stone building, the effect was of lightness and air and color.

Then they reached the interview chamber, and here was Atan and a vaguely familiar tall boy who looked roughly the age of the academy seniors. Was that the sense of familiarity? That he stood like someone trained? No. Senrid had seen him. He just didn't remember where.

Atan noted that Senrid did not bother with formality when visiting any more than he did in his own home: he stood there in a white shirt, riding trousers, and boots, an outfit that her first and second circles would consider positively undressed. At least he wasn't wearing any weapons. Or, he didn't appear to be, she corrected herself as she took in his wary, tight posture.

This conversation was going to be more difficult than she'd thought. "Sartor's army was annihilated a hundred years ago," she said, without any of the politenesses she ordinarily began with. Her single visit to Marloven Hess had made it clear that what worked as social easing in Sartor was pointless dither there. "The mages all think the only way to deal with Norsunder is by magic."

Senrid backed up a step, his palms out. "Why do you want me? I'm no expert in lighter magic. You've got your entire Sartoran mage guild."

"But they didn't protect us a century ago. And," she said quickly, seeing him stir, "I don't want anybody's army coming to our rescue, either. I have a very small palace guard, and scant more at the border, the fewest permitted by some old treaty. And Rel here tells me that their military approach is a hundred years out of date. I don't even know what that means."

Senrid made a warding gesture.

Atan said, "Look, Senrid, we don't have any real defense. Oh, the council will shortly be telling me what to do. And I bow to their wisdom in so many ways. But this situation? I know they won't know any more than I do how we should proceed, and I can't help but hope that the kind of aid you gave to Erdrael Danara might do for us."

"They needed training." Senrid turned up his palms. "You're in need of action, right? You have to defend yourselves."

"How, without serving people up to the slaughter? At least tell me whom to ask? How about the person you sent to Erdrael Danara?"

"I sent someone his age." Senrid jerked a thumb at Rel, who stood silently by. "Ret Forthan will probably be a commander one day, but he'll tell you himself, he's not one now. All he did in Terry's land was give their newly reformed Mountain Guard some ideas about reorganizing, and improving their drills. He showed them some basic ones. Really basic. We Marlovens don't know anything about protecting mountainous land like Erdrael Danara." He made a motion up and down. "Plains horses don't like up and down."

He eyed Atan, who stared back, her desperation battering at Senrid's consciousness because of course she wasn't even thinking about mindshields.

Then she said abruptly, "You're reading my mind. Aren't you?"

Senrid grimaced. "Yes and no. You're sending emotions at me like a charge of lancers, but I'm no good at sieving out sense from the emotions and jumble of memories, the way Liere has been doing from the time she was a baby. You need to practice your mind-shield."

Atan blushed to the ears, her lips compressed.

Senrid said quickly, "Here's the truth. We know war is coming, and we're not sure what will work to protect our kingdom, much less anyone else's."

"War," Atan said steadily, "is here."

Senrid struggled inwardly. He wasn't going to admit to anyone how exhilarated he'd felt after that little brush between Ndarga and his companies from West Army. It would be so easy to find another reason to do that again, especially when he thought he would win.

But that wasn't going to happen in Atan's kingdom. Atan didn't want him leading any battles, not that the Sartorans would follow him even if he did jump on a horse and start waving a sword and yelling orders. She wanted to make sense of something he'd spent his life trying to learn in order to survive.

Even if he didn't quite know what to do about it, yet.

His experiments with the city attack, and the secret communication network this past year, had taught him that much.

"Do you have a map?" he asked.

"This way."

Map-making had been one of the few activities Senrid's uncle had approved of while regent, so Senrid's first sight of the enormous table map of Sartor caused him to whistle in appreciation.

The map was actually a model, set on an enormous round table in the center of a round room, with a mirror set above it. Atan said, "My ancestors have had it remade over the centuries, as it needs constant repair as things change. Herald apprentices spend a year traveling the kingdom as part of their training. They bring back sketches, and the map is adjusted as rivers alter course, streams become rivers, towns add a building here, and take one apart there."

"And after wars," Senrid said.

"Yes. And after wars. You can see from the scars on this one how much was lost before the ninety-seven years of silence. But I cannot bring myself to order it destroyed. The scars here remind us of scars in the hearts of those who endured the attack and the enchantment."

She indicated the places where once had stood tiny porcelain villages and castles, the marred spots etched with stylized flowers. "There's building going on, of course. And a lot of trade coming over the border, which . . ." She paused, shook her head, then motioned for Senrid and Rel to join her at the south end. "Below here is Norsunder Base."

Senrid had been eyeing that gray expanse, with the ugly dark stone fortress made of unfired clay. "How accurate is that?"

"Symbolic only. Lilah told me it's completely wrong. She was a prisoner there before we lifted the spell. Uh, that's Lilah Selenna of Sarendan, whose brother Peitar is the new king. The newest members of the alliance."

Senrid shrugged Sarendan away as irrelevant. "I take it you don't have any inside information on numbers, defenses, that sort of thing?"

Atan's lips parted. "'Inside line of communication.' Is that what you mean? I was talking about that not three days ago in an interview. Quite an interesting fellow. Old. A prince of somewhere quite small, I forget."

Senrid had a feeling he knew. "Renselaeus?"

"I think that was it. I forget how we got onto it, but I asked him to define this phrase after he used it in conversation, and though he was very obliging, time was pressing, and I still don't quite understand what he was talking about, except that it sounded dauntingly military."

Senrid wavered, then thought, *Why not?* "Is he still here?"

"In Sartor? I believe so. He's one of the many who are trying to disentangle century-old trade agreements and funds. Nothing of that sort is done in a day." Atan frowned at the relief map, then said, "In fact, I ought to warn those visitors when I send word to the heralds to warn the city. Thank you. As for what the morvende told me . . ."

Little enough, Senrid soon discovered. He said, "Then here's what I think. Even if you had exact numbers. Capabilities. Intent. There's not a lot you can do in a military way if you don't have a military."

Atan nodded cautiously.

"So you have to use what you've got to make it as tough as possible for the enemy to invade. If you have wards, great. But we all know that lighter wards are mostly good for advanced warning. And it's not that much of an advance. There are very few light magic wards that can keep Norsunder out for very long. The only wards that seem to hold are those bound to magical artifacts of the sort we aren't able to make anymore."

He walked around the table to the southern border. "So, that aside. Is this city the heart of Sartor?"

"Yes."

"Then they will probably want to come up from the south, flank the city, and take it from both sides."

"I think that's what happened a century ago. They crossed the river at two places, east and west corners, and marched up the royal roads. They met my father's army here, and here, slaughtered them all, and then pushed on. It took them mere days." Atan had been an infant, but since she'd freed Sartor from its century of sleep, she had heard stories from elders for whom the grief was still raw.

"The map isn't telling me what kind of terrain, but if this river over here can be diverted to wash out this road, that ought to slow up a column of foot and horse. Water is also notorious for resisting magical manipulation, I'm sure you know . . ."

"I see," she said, her eyes widening. "Yes. I wonder if the magic council tried such things?"

"If they didn't, talk 'em into it. There is no easy save," Senrid said. "Eventually Norsunder'll get to your gates, then you better be ready with the close and personal defense. Though magical traps through the city will help. You know the terrain. They don't." He was silent, then said apologetically, "Though if this city has been squatting unchanged for centuries, they've got to have good maps."

"We can still try the traps," Atan said, her voice flat.

Senrid needed to get away from her whipsaw emotions. "The best person to help you would be Hibern. She and I have talked a lot about this plan for our own border. In my turn, I'd like to meet that prince from Renselaeus. You know where he might be staying?"

"I'm almost certain he's at the Carriage House."

"Carriage House?"

"It has a splendid name, but everyone has called it 'the Carriage House' for generations. Where visiting dignitaries stay if they don't have connections in the city."

"I'll show him." Rel spoke for the first time.

Atan threw him a look of relief. "Thanks, Rel."

Senrid had recovered the memory by now: this was the tall fellow dressed in a stolen Norsunder uniform who had pulled Senrid and that northern girl out of the prison cells at the Norsunder Base, at the beginning of Siamis's enchantment, and whisked them into a morvende tunnel.

Further, this had to be the same Rel that he'd heard about from the Mearsieans, both praise (Puddlenose) and insults (CJ).

A few steps into Sartor's chilly air, and Senrid wished he'd thought to bring a coat, but after matching a few of Rel's long steps, he decided he wasn't going to need one.

"From what I saw at the Norsunder Base that day, and from what Puddlenose has told me, you could take the field against Norsunder all by yourself," Senrid said as they crossed the square toward the bridge leading into the eastern part of the city.

"Puddlenose likes to joke," Rel said.

"So I take it Atan isn't going to be sending you off to the south, waving a sword and acting heroic?"

"The only time she's seen me waving a sword," Rel said in his deep, even voice, "she watched me get trounced by a fellow a head shorter than me."

"I should think most of the world is a head shorter than you," Senrid commented, wondering where CJ got the idea that this Rel was an arrogant blowhard. Of course, everybody had their bad days.

Senrid had been taking in his surroundings. He had to admit he was impressed, even if the first impression was a lot of clutter: statues, fountains, decorative carving that would be the first thing smashed in street fighting. But Sartor was too civilized for that, wasn't it?

Oh, yes. The war in which Atan had lost her entire family wasn't hazy generations ago, but relatively recently, for most of the people walking around before his eyes.

Rel had taken in the direction of his glance, and obligingly furnished names and dates and a brief story behind the local sights. Senrid grinned at the funny ones, and then they were there. The Carriage House was an imposing building on a corner where five streets met, its walls made of marble, with gargoyles and the like carved over all the tall windows.

Senrid was about to thank him when Rel said quickly, "I understand you know magic. Would you send me to that southern harbor so I can do some scouting?"

Senrid squinted up at Rel, a tall silhouette against the low northern sun resting on the city rooftops. "You don't think anyone is going to scout?"

"The mages might. I don't know. But they won't be looking for the same things I would."

Senrid could understand that. "Here's the problem. You say 'southern harbor,' which isn't a Destination. Unless you know there is one, and you can give me the pattern, I can't send you. Beyond my skills."

"No Destination that I know of."

"I think you'd need a mage like Tsauderei."

"Tsauderei," Rel repeated. "Great suggestion. Atan can send me to him. Thanks."

With a casual salute Rel left him, and walked off. Senrid watched for a few steps, wondering why CJ hated this Rel, who made no pompous speeches. He was going to do what needed doing. Anybody else would call that heroic behavior.

He shrugged it off and headed for the formidable building called the Carriage House.

He approached the front desk, whose carved wood depicted a sylvan scene. "I'm looking for the Prince of Renselaeus."

"He is dining in company," was the reply. Interesting, how this fellow's Sartoran was subtly different from Atan's. Regional difference or time difference? "But he has left instructions to pass on messages. Do you wish me to do so?"

Senrid hesitated, wondering if 'dining in company' meant no one was permitted access, or what the etiquette was. He found the whole question annoyingly pointless, but he didn't want to antagonize someone who found such stuff important.

So he said, "Senrid Montredaun-An would like to speak to him."

The smooth-faced man behind the counter mangled Senrid's name with a heavy enough accent to make Senrid want to grin.

A very short time later, he was back, leading a white-haired elderly man who leaned heavily on a cane. Senrid glanced at, then ignored, the fine velvet long coat over an old-fashioned tabard-vest, the loose long trousers and embroidered shoes, and met a pair of heavy-lidded dark eyes.

The old courtier greeted him in a smooth drawl, but the man had never heard of mind-shields, and Senrid braced against the sharp, anxious question.

"Your son is fine," Senrid said. "Right now he's sitting in my castle library, I'm sure, along with several others who stay at the academy year round." And left the question open: if you're so worried about your son, why haven't you brought him home?

"Please. Come this way," the old prince said, gesturing through a pair of tall doors carved to match the relief-work on the panels along the front desk.

Beyond these doors lay a hall, off which opened small, discreet anterooms, each with its tall window that overlooked the five-points intersection. Senrid could make out a couple of the palace spires above the inward-slanted rooftops across the way.

The chairs were big, comfortably cushioned. Senrid sat on the edge of one, glad it was low enough that his feet weren't off the floor, as the elderly prince took a moment to sink into the other.

During the walk, Senrid had been turning over what to say to Shevraeth's father while half-listening to Rel's explanation of the local sites.

Senrid had acceded to the prince's request to invite his son to the academy, but at first he hadn't liked Vidanric Renselaeus, Marquis of Shevraeth, known only as 'Shevraeth' in the academy. Then Liere had made the painful, but true, observation that jealousy lay behind most of Senrid's dislike.

Jealousy because Shevraeth had a living father.

True.

But Senrid had thought about it ever since, and knew that there was also Shevraeth's apparently effortless self-possession, a quality Senrid didn't have, knew he didn't have, and doubted he would ever have.

Well, he'd seen enough evidence that Shevraeth didn't have it all the time—that it wasn't effortless. More like habit, and when he was hurt, he broke like anyone else.

And so here Senrid was, facing Shevraeth's admired, wise, beloved father . . . who was alive. "The Sartoran Queen is going to be letting people know soon that Norsunder is on the march, down below the border," he said.

The prince sighed. "We have been dreading such news, but rumors have been flying too frequently and fast for it to come as surprise. As well I've finished my affairs here. Thank you for informing me."

The question he was too courtly, or too something, to ask, lay heavily in the air. Senrid said, "Your son's doing very well with us. As I think you know from his letters." Senrid made the gesture people recognized as tapping the lid of a notecase. He'd given Shevraeth one so he could communicate with his family.

The prince said, "Affording me the opportunity not only to thank you for this news, but also for providing us with the means for that communication."

The man was a courtier. Senrid should have known not to expect anything but empty flattery put in polite parlance. But in spite of the prince's dignified posture, trained into bone and muscle, Senrid sensed on the mental plane the weariness and anxiety the old man had no idea he was revealing. Remalna might be an inkblot of a kingdom, but it was home to this man and his family, and that home was being squeezed dry of its lifeblood by an evil king.

"So I came," Senrid said, "to tell you that, and also to make an offer. If you happen to know your exact Destination pattern, I can send you home by magic, before I return to my own home."

Surprise and gratitude lifted the weary lids. "Permit me to gather my belongings? It is little enough," the prince requested.

"Certainly. If you'll tell me your Destination pattern," Senrid said, "I can set up the spell. I'm not nearly as fast at sending another somewhere I've never been as my mage friends are."

"The Destination in my own palace, then." The Prince of Renseleaus described the pattern to Senrid, then excused himself with a polite word.

Alone, Senrid decided to test the spell first, though even that much would hurt like a punch to the gut. But he'd feel better if he made a trial.

So he looked around. Someone had set an aromatic plant on a table in front of the window. Senrid pulled off a leaf, set it on the carpet, depicted the Destination, muttered the spell—and withdrew so fast he staggered backward, missed the chair, and fell on his butt. He sat there on the rug, shock ringing through him, then mentally worked backward. The leaf ought to have vanished with a little puff of air. But the stench of burning metal that had smacked him backward meant that a lethal magical trap awaited anyone who used that Destination.

A present for the prince from the evil king, maybe? Senrid waited impatiently until the prince returned, then told the prince in a few words what he'd found.

This time, the courtier mask didn't hold. The prince's face blanched, and he groped behind him, sitting down far quicker than he had before.

"Where else can I send you? That is safe?"

"Perhaps the harbor at Mardgar? I know that Destination. Used it often when I was younger. I can hire transportation to carry me north along the coast."

Another leaf, another test. Poof! They both watched the leaf vanish. The Mardgar Destination was safe.

Senrid transferred the old man. And as soon as he'd recovered, he transferred home. After that much transfer magic, he needed to sit and gather his wits again. As soon as he could move, he went straight to find Keriam.

If it was true that Siamis (or Detlev) wanted a ready-made army, then they'd destroy Senrid's wards and protections and come in intending to take and hold, not slaughter. If that was their initial tactic, Senrid and Keriam had decided the best defense was none—that is, there would be no army, and no academy, to find.

Time to step up the plans.

## Chapter Seventeen

*Chwahirsland*

NO one but the Chwahir would understand resistance to tyranny expressed through nature, covertly and subtly shifted to make music or art.

Such as a dripping water trough.

Jilo entered a tiny village whose inhabitants made quilting for saddles and under chain mail. Everyone worked with the cotton grown on the north faces of the mountains, carefully tended; villagers carried pannikins of water to each plant during the long, dry days between rainstorms.

They lived in dilapidated, unpainted houses, with tiny blocked-in windows to conserve warmth. The way station for couriers was nothing more than a narrow bed of straw beside the stabling for two horses, meeting the minimum required by law. That was all the locals could scratch together.

Jilo had wanted to leave his horse and move on, but there was no fresh horse, the other having a strained hock. And so Jilo perforce must let his horse rest. He was impatient to get to Burda, to discover if there were women pretending to be men in the garrison there, if they had hand language, if they . . .

A woman offered him a bowl of stewed oats with shredded carrot to sweeten it, then withdrew in silence, and Jilo was left to eat where he might. He did not want to sit on that sagging bed made of sagging hemp rope under a thin, mildewing mattress of lumpy quilting, so he wandered around the village, the bowl tucked against him. At least it was warm. The days were definitely colder, the sun dropping lower in the north each day.

Jilo stopped out of the wind beside the last house, indistinguishable from the others but for the noise. He was barely conscious of it at first, though that was how it began with them all, and so he began actively to hunt.

He soon found the warped trough that carried water from the nearby hill to the village. Behind the house the trough dripped through cracks in the old wood. It looked old, broken-down, the big muddy-sided jars beneath the trough apparently abandoned.

Yet droplets from the cracked wood, on falling into the small hole in the enormous jug, plinked in soft melody.

Music. Forbidden on pain of death.

You couldn't hear it well unless you were close by. Jilo turned his head, and discovered open windows all along the back of the dilapidated house.

His shoulders tightened. He glanced behind him, catching no more than a flicker of movement. But retained in the inward eye, much like the distorted glow of lightning after the thunder has died away, remained a face, eyes like pits, mouth round in horror. It was too easy to imagine frightened villagers inside the houses, waiting for him to exclaim, to point, to kick aside the jar or say that he was going to report the trough for its noisy disrepair. But he backed away, and returned to the stable, where he finished the meal.

He returned the bowl. No one spoke. He didn't speak, and the villagers understood his complicity in his silence. His generous, unlooked-for, silence. And word swiftly and silently rang out behind him.

Unaware, he turned away from Burda, and headed toward the tiny town he'd only heard of, where his father's family had been born.

It didn't take long to reach. He'd been skirting the area all along.

As he closed the distance, he worked out a story in case anyone spoke to him. But they wouldn't. The law proscribed that, and everywhere he went, people existed in silent isolation, precisely as Wan-Edhe had wanted them.

But only on the surface.

In the old days, before the crown had assumed all land ownership, his family had worked in the guardhouse for the local *nanijo*, or warlord.

That was a very long time ago, before family names were forbidden. Even so, Jilo remembered the few things he'd learned about the family Back Home. To the Shadowland Chwahir, Chwahirsland was always Back Home, even though the Shadow outpost was several centuries old.

Before Jilo's father vanished, he'd told detailed stories about his single visit to the castle where his ancestors had lived. Jilo recognized the castle the moment it came into view: the twin towers, one crumbling, both overlooking the river road. The confusion of houses built up against the walls, which were honeycombed with passages, the stone removed to reinforce flimsy walls of mud and old wood.

This castle, like pretty much all midlands buildings, showed the cost of many years of drought. The quarries, under Wan-Edhe's orders, supplied the border garrisons against an invasion that never came, and served the coast against his next planned war.

The buildings were as described, but as Jilo entered the castle courtyard, he ran into difficulties with the people. Jilo remembered his father's description of his Uncle Shiam: "He looks much like me, but taller, with a limp from the battle off Imar."

Jilo expected a hale man of thirty or forty, father-aged, but the guard commander was grizzled and stooped. The only thing Jilo recognized was the limp.

Had to be the same man. Jilo mentally added a generation of aging to those remembered features. Then there were the unknown young faces who had to be the cousins of whose existence his father, and therefore he, had been ignorant.

Nobody asked questions. They went about their business, scrupulously quiet, until the silence coagulated in a way that seemed to cut off all the air. The only signs of his connection to this world being glimpses of people with light brown eyes shaped like his, and his father's pendulous ears.

His attention went to those closest to his own age. The girl (cousin?) whisked herself out of sight, quite properly, whenever she saw Jilo walking about, but the livable portions of the castle were so small that the people were in fairly constant contact. Jilo found an old arrow slit while he was poking around, from which he could handily see an inner court between the stable and the garrison kitchen. There he saw the girl cousin in head-bent, earnest conference with a brother who had to be her twin. They were exactly the same size, their hair the same blue-black, somewhat like his own, only thicker. He hadn't known that girl and boy twins could be identical; it wasn't until the vagaries of wind brought their voices, which were so alike he could not tell them apart, that the obvious occurred to him: the supposed boy might actually be a girl.

Interest sharpened. He had to test his theory.

A rainstorm, thick with sleet, provided a convenient reason to postpone his having to carry his false messages onward. It was while he was trying to find another way into the stable, and lost himself in the broken honeycomb of small rooms long since ruined by law-enforced neglect as well as the weather, that he unexpectedly came face to face with the girl.

Girls were forbidden to speak first. He stepped aside (which was strictly against regulations, as it was for females to get out of males' way) and moved on, prompted by a pulse of guilt for spying. But when he reached the extremity of the ruin, which was little more than piles of broken stone rejected for reuse elsewhere, that it hit Jilo. She'd been stalking him.

And here it was again, so unexpected: danger.

For all the years he'd been Kwenz's student, he had lived with danger as his daily companion, far away when Wan-Edhe was distant, brought sharp and close with his proximity. Since Prince Kessler had taken Wan-Edhe away, the danger had been from his magic, and the possibilities that Jilo dreamed up: What if the army revolted? What if the people revolted? What if they caught him (whoever 'they' might be) and squashed him flat for his temerity in pretending to be a king?

He clutched at the ring on his finger, ready to transfer back to Narad, whose poisonous atmosphere was at least a familiar danger.

But while he stood there in the half-sheltered ruin listening to the hissing roar of sleet, and nothing happened, his heartbeat slowed, and his breathing eased from the rasp of fear.

Nothing was going to happen. Now. Wild thoughts of a knife in the darkness assailed him, to be dismissed. That was thinking like Wan-Edhe. It made no sense. Thinking himself threatened made no sense. He was only a courier. This was an unimportant flatfoot garrison. The girl was curious because . . .

Her curiosity sharpened his own. Wan-Edhe's conviction that females, generally born smaller than males, were therefore stupid and useless, had been proven abundantly wrong by the Mearsiean girls.

This girl, possibly a cousin, was curious, and that made her interesting. Jilo had to find out why she was curious.

The bell rang once, a sour iron clang. He made his way around to the mess hall.

Jilo's entrance shut everyone up, and they moved in strict rank order to the long benches. But Jilo kept the image in his mind's eye, the natural groupings that made it clear where the twia were, and further, that family members were bound into some of the twia, though that was also forbidden. Twia were supposed to become patrols or support staff if one member attained officer status, entirely military in purpose.

Jilo was about to enter when he heard a light footstep from behind: the girl cousin again, bearing a tray of food. She stepped against the wall, but did not lower her eyes. Jilo could see fear in the tautness of her high forehead. The tension of her shoulders was not due to the heavy tray she carried.

She licked her lips, and then spoke. "I am Aran." And waited for the axe to fall.

So simple and natural, those words, proscribed by law and regulation. Jilo, thrilled by her daring, said, "I am Jilo."

She gulped in air. The dishes rattled on the tray, and Jilo became aware of rustles and whispers around the corner. That had to be the rest of the females, waiting in line to bring the food.

So Jilo ducked into the mess hall, and awkwardly fumbled his way to the place where couriers always sat. Those seated there quietly made space.

And though everyone's attention appeared to be strictly on his plate as the women and girls served the food, Jilo was sensitive to the weight of their collective scrutiny. The tuneless, random clatter of eating implements on plates, the rustle of cloth, here and there a quick tread did not mask the sense of . . . of a rounded scrutiny, an instinctively arrived-at roundness divisible by eight. Though Wan-Edhe had denied Jilo a true twi of his own, he could see, he could feel, the rightness, the balance of the twia he saw before him.

After the meal, he was climbing up to the rooms over the stable, when he came up short in a low doorway, face to face with the commander himself.

"Has my granddaughter trespassed?" he asked.

Jilo fingered the onyx ring, ready to transfer out. "I think we're related."

The commander said gravely, "You're the son of my nephew Dzan."

He wasn't asking a question, and so Jilo said, "I'm Jilo."

"We know," the commander said even more gravely.

"You do?" Jilo asked. "Oh. Do I look like my father? All of you, that is, many of you, remind me of him."

There was a pause that grew almost to a silence, then the commander said gently, "We know who you are." He amended quickly, "That is, along the courier routes."

The words struck Jilo like a blow to the head, only from the inside. Of course the couriers would talk. Though not to him. They had their twia. They could not, dared not, read the dispatches they carried, customarily sealed with lethal spells against tampering, but just because they were expected to remain silent, that did not mean that every person was not using eyes and ears exactly as Jilo did.

"Why are you here?"

Jilo hunched defensively. "Trying to learn . . ." Words failed him. As always. He looked down, hating his inability to articulate his thoughts. But because Commander Shiam still waited, he said, "Everything."

And because that steady gaze reminded him of Mondros, up there in the distant mountains barely visible to the south, Jilo said, "To see what damage Wan-Edhe has done. If . . . if he doesn't come back. How to fix it."

The commander let out a slow breath. "We call him The Hate. That word cannot be magic-bound against mention."

Jilo still had not managed to ascertain whether or not Wan-Edhe actually had a spell to warn him whenever his name or title was spoken, the way many believed Norsunder was warded. He jerked his head in assent, accepting that a fuller conversation was impossible.

"If he is not dead, and some believe even then, he will return," the commander said.

Jilo shrugged again, more sharply. "I know. I think on that each day." More he dared not say.

He didn't need to. Jilo's demeanor, his lack of regulation reaction, the dropped tone of his voice when he said 'I think on that each day' implied to Shiam that there was more going on than met the eye. It implied that he was not Wan-Edhe's creature, that he was possibly, miraculously, taking steps against the evil tyranny that had begun to seem inescapable. Eternal.

So when Jilo asked the question he had not been capable of considering until he had been days away from Narad's poison—"Does my father still live?"—Shiam did not hide his surprise.

Jilo flushed guiltily, old habit, after using the forbidden words 'my father.' "Prince Kwenz warned me never to ask, for my loyalty might be questioned."

Shiam accepted that, and said in a voice of low regret, "We were told he died in a border dispute with the Danarans. He was in charge of the supplies."

*We were told.* Jilo inclined his head.

They parted then, Jilo to wander over and peer out at the dreary sleet, and occupy himself as he might until the next meal. A gradual awareness of a qualitative alteration in atmosphere resolved into a repeat of the sound patterns he'd noticed on his travels. Furtive, brief: tapped fingers here. The clatter of nut shells on a string, which he discovered suspended high up under a rafter above the scrawny cows. He was very certain he had not overlooked it on his first exploration through the barn.

A whistle, soft and low, that might have been mistaken for the wind moaning through the rocks, but it wasn't. It was too regular and too short for that.

As night fell, and the storm abated to drips and plops along the edges of eaves and overhangs, the shadows closed in, and once more Jilo found himself in the ruins.

This time Aran came toward him deliberately, barely discernable among the deepening shadows.

"Is there anything I can get for you?"

Jilo took another cautious step toward understanding. "Information only."

"As in?" Aran replied.

"Your twin."

Aran stiffened. "What about him?"

Jilo said, "Him?"

That was all. Aran stilled. Jilo could hear her breathing, then she sighed softly, and began to speak in what at first sounded like storytelling mode: "Long ago, it is told in great Chwahirsland, under the great king . . ."

That way every story, false or true, had always begun, fanciful stories being forbidden by Wan-Edhe as frivolous and time-wasting when drought conditions required a steady mind and constant labor. But then she said, "In faraway Shadowland, the law required every family to kill or shell a second girl—"

"That's not true," Jilo interrupted. "I was in the Shadowland. That law was here."

Aran said firmly, "In faraway Shadowland, the law required every family to kill or shell a second girl."

And Jilo had it: the storytelling mode hid a truth behind "in faraway Shadowland" the way his own folk had hidden it behind "long ago."

When he didn't interrupt again, she went on more softly, "There was a family who had two sons. The regional commander spread the word through the land that a third son would gain the family a better placement, and as they had no daughter, the birth of one would not cause lament."

Jilo was silent. He knew about Wan-Edhe's method of dealing with the encroachment of drought upon the resources of a hungry kingdom, where all must support the army above anyone else. Second daughters were a luxury Wan-Edhe decreed the kingdom could not afford.

". . . and so, to this family was born twin girls, named Aran and Kirog. But the decree raised consternation among them, and because twins are rare, word had spread all through the region, unto the ears of the regional commander himself. His merciful solution was to shell Kirog to Kinit—"

Jilo's nerves jolted. Until this moment he had not known that magic could force a person to change gender. He'd assumed the will of the changee must be obtained first.

"—and so the process was begun, but somewhat into it, Wan-Edhe assembled all mages for great purposes of his own, and so the process was incomplete. But Kinit was accepted by the family, and by his twi, and by the regional governor who assigned that twi unto the study and maintenance of horses."

A pause, which became a silence. Jilo stared at the silhouetted girl, his mind proliferating so many questions he had no idea where to begin. Or if he should.

The first being: what did that mean, 'the process was begun'?

Did it matter?

Until now he had not troubled himself thinking about what lay under anyone's clothes, so why should that become an item of interest now? Identity was a matter of mind, that much he had learned from observing those Mearsieans: Falinneh, a Xubarec, who shapechanged between genders as easily as people changed clothes; Dhana, whose natural form looked like a crack in water, but who had decided to experiment with human form, one closest to that of the girls she'd been watching from the water; and even Puddlenose, who had a habit of disguising himself as a girl when he was bent on escape. When he dressed as a girl, people believed he was one, tall and bony as he was.

Enough. The matter was plain: Aran's twin was, to the family, to his twi, and to the world, Kinit the stableboy. No more, no less.

And so Jilo gave the prescribed reply, "Long ago, in great Chwa-hirsland, under a great king, life was truly great."

He expected her to leave him to himself. He would not have minded if she had, because he wanted to think through everything he'd heard.

But she said softly, "Come."

The note of her voice sent a frisson through his nerves, for so profound a change—a girl in effect giving him an order, though her tone was invitation—meant that he had been tested without his knowing, and something else was about to occur.

Then fingers bumped against his arm. He jerked it back, and took a couple of steps away.

Aran said, "I will leave you if you wish, but . . ."

It was that *but*, in the same invitational tone.

Every sense alert, he stepped forward once, twice. This time he reached, and when he encountered the girl's cold fingers, he stilled as her hand patted his arm lightly, then slid under his elbow. And tugged with gentle insistence.

He walked with her through the dripping ruin, into the barely warmer stable, and through that into the garrison mess. But that room, too, was empty, though light spilled, pale gold, down the staircase from above.

On they walked to the kitchen, and through that. Jilo followed in growing surprise as they entered the unlit larder; he fought a sneeze from the sharp scents of dried herbs. Dimly he made out a narrow entrance beyond the barrels of bitter beer.

Down they walked, not into the dankness of rot and moss, but into a malty-warm vapor of ancient brewing. He could see nothing, he could hear nothing, but he knew that the cellar was not empty.

Aran pulled the cellar door closed, and then one by one came the scritch of sparkstones, and light sprang into being: candles wavering here, throwing dramatic shadows up the plastered walls, and in the center a single glowglobe, its magic fading. More candles were lit, and set on a bare little table in the center. Above it someone had hung a cloth so old it was almost rotted, fragile beyond belief, age-spotted.

When Jilo made out the circular pattern on it, shock flared through all his nerves: it wasn't even the forbidden circle symbol of Chwa-hirsland. This was far older, long forbidden, the eight intertwined linden leaves, heart-shaped, the twi symbol that had become Chwahirsland's circle, which in turn Wan-Edhe had forbidden because it implied loyalty to one's group, and loyalty must only go to his person.

Jilo stared up at it, shocked by the trust implied in his seeing this sacred treasure as, in silence, someone ladled something whitish yellow and unfamiliar-looking into tiny bowls that were then passed from hand to hand, the fragrance rising from them delectable.

When a bowl reached him, he stared down at the tangle of nearly translucent vermiform shapes, then he gasped. Rice noodles! Kwenz had occasionally eaten them, in the Shadowland days: Jilo had sometimes slipped in and finished the old prince's bowl if he wandered off, forgetting the meal he'd been eating. They had been delicious.

And they were absolutely forbidden to the ordinary Chwahir, again, on pain of death—a death not only for the eater, but for his entire village. Rice, once the great Chwahir staple, now so precious, had been reserved for the upper echelons for at least four centuries, and in this century, reserved for Wan-Edhe and his elite guard only.

Yet here. In Jilo's hand. Was fragrant rice, beaten with milk into batter, laid out on wooden racks to dry, and then cut into noodles, an act that required secrecy from all involved.

The weight of the village's trust nearly overwhelmed him, the sharing hollowing him with emotions he had no experience with except that they hurt, and yet it was a sweet anguish.

Jilo didn't even know how to eat the noodles; he had no eating sticks, which of course had also been forbidden to the people. Spoons only. No one could assassinate with a spoon.

So he tipped his head back and let the warm noodles slide into his mouth. The pungent flavor was unidentifiable, but it tanged on his tongue, shading to sweet, with a lingering hint of sour. Two swallows, and the little portion was gone.

He opened his eyes and discovered the empty bowls being passed and stacked. He relinquished his.

When all bowls were stacked, the people stepped forward, not in their tidy regulation rows of rank, but forming a circle. What's more, hand moved to hand, linking at elbows, until they stood in two circles, one within the other: females within, males in the greater circle. Aran left Jilo with Kinit, the sister turned brother, whose firm arm interlocked with him on one side, and old commander Shiam on the other, his arm gnarled as the branch of an apple tree.

Jilo scarcely had time to take his place, with these people pressed up against him on either side—strictly forbidden—when the first sounds reached his ears: a soughing, that reminded him of the sea that he had sometimes visited from the Shadowland, half a morning's ride.

Hiss, rush. The people breathed in unison. In benison. Jilo's heart beat in rhythm, his breath sibilated, in, beat, beat, out, thrum, thrum. A little giddy, he let his eyelids fall, and faint as a distant bird's cry far over the water came a high-voiced "Ah-h-h-h."

Thrum, thrum, a low rumble, "Ho-o-o-o-h-h-h-m."

The two voices splashed through the rhythmic tide of hiss, hiss, hrum, thrum, gradually subsiding into harmonic resonance, and cold showered through Jilo's nerves when the truth struck him. They were humming.

Absolutely forbidden! On pain of death!

A new high voice: "Chika-chee, chika-chee, Tsa-tsa-tsa," the mating cry of the marsh river's bird.

New voices joined, "Hoo-wee, hoo-wit!"

"Caw, caw, caw!"

"Orble-roo, orble-roo!"

On Jilo's right, Commander Shiam uttered a subsonic rumble that Jilo felt more than heard, an abyssal fremitus resounding steadfast as mountains, "Hrummmmhrumhrummm . . ."

Here the rhythmic popping noises, made by lips and tongue, the snap of beans and greens, there the chuckle of boiling liquid, sung on a note that blended into the chord that now sustained itself through at least six voices, three male and three female.

"Korroo, korroo," the cry of the rooster.

"Sssssa, ssssa," a winding snake.

Hrumm, thrummm, bound together by the low, eternal rhythm of the sea, the glorious music encompassed the comforting sounds of life and the shared cadences of work: the clop of horse hooves, the keen of the saw, the chink of stone, each voice adding to the rhythm until all found a place in the syntonic chord, a sound that reverberated through his bones, drenching his being with the blessedness of tears.

How Wan-Edhe would hate this flouting of his decrees, the evidence that there was more to life than fighting, and feeding warriors so they could fight! Jilo found himself sustained by the will of the people, unspoken evidence that the Chwahir did not exist to serve Wan-Edhe's will, though he had exerted his vast power to that end.

And they were trusting him enough to count him in the circle.

Trust. How simple a thing. How powerful, when one trusts eight, and each of the eight reaches out to another twi, which becomes sixty-four, and sixty-four becomes four thousand . . .

Jilo's fragile cage of bone and flesh could not contain the intensity of his joy and wonder—and of sorrow, for all they had lost.

Sobs welled up, shuddering against his ribs, and would have sent him running, but those arms held him tight, the sound swelling in glory and pain and brightness and darkness, drowning his own voice with the birth of a new emotion, as yet unrecognized. But it was there.

He got his ragged breath under control, though he couldn't see for the burn of unaccustomed tears, as around him and through his body flowed the Great Hum of the Chwahir, which had never gone silent at all. One by one the voices ceased, except for the rhythmic breathing, and the moment, precious as life, flowered into memory.

# PART THREE
## The Alliance Meets

## Chapter One

*Winter, 4742 AF*
*Unnamed bay east of Norsunder Base*

THE alliance had a name, and a communications center, but as yet it had never met in a body.

It was going to take the advent of war to achieve that, as we shall see presently.

Right now, everyone was busy thinking of home defense, except for Rel, who sat alone on a wintry palisade overlooking the green-gray ocean, watching for Norsundrians.

On his fourteenth early-morning sweep of the horizon, Rel was surprised to discover his first sign of Norsundrians coming from the land, and not the sea.

He'd expected to see the transport ships arrive first, but wariness had forced him to survey in all directions as soon as he opened the flap of his tent.

So though he was surprised, he was not caught by surprise.

Obedient to his promise to Tsauderei, at the first sight of movement cresting the far ridge that stitched the gray, rocky landscape to the equally gray low sky, Rel crawled all the way out of the tent the old mage had given him, and said the words he'd been taught.

The tent's interior had been chilly but livable. The cold struck hard when the tent vanished. Rel hunched into Tsauderei's magnificent yeath-hair coat, yeath hair being extraordinarily hard to glean high in the mountains, the hair scraped off by the animals onto brambles and rough rocks each spring.

The world this far south had dwindled to infinite shades of gray, including the thick hat that Rel had pulled down to just above his eyelids, the heavy scarf he'd wound around his neck and lower face to cover his nose, the mittens, and four pairs of socks stuffed inside his forest mocs.

Forcing himself not to hurry, he crouched to keep from making a silhouette, and lowered himself with painstaking care from upended, treacherously slippery rock to rock. Tsauderei had said that the day the tent reappeared in his cottage, he would transfer Rel away at sundown. A transfer token would easily be traced if mages did a sweep. But if Rel had nothing magical about him, any mages would not find him.

"I watched that harbor for one miserable season sixty-five years ago," Tsauderei had said, "when we were still uncertain whether Norsunder was going to move against Sarendan the way it had against Sartor. The crevasse my predecessor watched from, and showed to me, is the equivalent of two stories up from the sand, which means you will be climbing down the cliff about three stories. You must not descend all the way to the sand, unless you wish to leave footprints. Or wade through the tide. Your limbs will freeze beyond the ability to heal."

Rel had spent lonely days watching the invisible progress of the northerly sun behind the clouds, and observing the milky rime slowly building along the coast and along the old stone jetty put in the natural harbor centuries ago, judging by the long greenish streamers surging in the surf.

To pass the time, Tsauderei had given him a court history of Sartor, which was exactly as boring as it sounded, but from which, the old mage said, "All Sartorans will quote, as they were all brought up on it." He also gave him a gossipy history of Eidervaen written by a retired household goods mover in the century before Sartor was bespelled, which recounted all the local legends that were most definitely left out of court histories. Crammed with stories about the insides of famed houses, this one entertained Rel so much he could ignore the uncomfortably rocky ground, the continual drum of the wind on the tent, and the pervasive chill.

Now those and the tent were gone. He crept down the face of the cliff until he reached the crevasse, whose ancient bracken still held sturdily against wind, weather, and time.

He crouched in the mossy slime, one hand alternating with the other as he peered through his field glass. The free hand, he pressed between his chest and thigh as he perched in the tiny space with his knees up under his chin. His feet had begun the inevitable pins-and-needles prickling by the time the distant movement had resolved into a column snaking its way down the ridge on the extreme southwestern side.

He was still too high to overhear the Norsundrians as they streamed down onto the sand at low tide and marched toward the jetty. He caught the occasional word on the brittle air, mostly curses, as the thickening overcast began spitting slushy rain. Winter was nigh, and the desire to get well out into the water before the first freeze of the coming season was apparent in the way the marchers were crowded up onto the rocks.

A perimeter team made a fast, thorough search along the edge of the sand where it met the rock, and another marched along the top of the ridge. Rel had done his best to make certain he left no prints, never treading on any moss, no matter how thin. Still he held his breath, ducking down when the inner perimeter passed directly below.

The searchers moved on, clapping their arms to their sides, rubbing mottled noses, stamping, and generally making it clear that the cold wind was fast getting even colder as the short day drew swiftly toward its end.

When they rejoined the column picking its way like a trail of lumbering ants along the rocky jetty, Rel relaxed enough to lift his field glass to scan them. It was frustrating to be so near, and yet not near enough to overhear anything. At least he could count up the force.

He had positioned himself in the crevasse so that he could see along the jetty. Thanks to Puddlenose's having introduced him to Captain Heraford, he'd spent a little time crewing on board the *Tsasilia*, which had taught him something about currents and tides.

On the far side of the bay, a lone figure peered down from the crevasse through which the Norsundrians had marched. He made a perfunctory visual sweep, but didn't see Rel. His attention was on Henerek as the husky man moved carefully from rock to rock along the jetty, to where the sea splashed up.

Rel also scrutinized that bundled-up figure, wondering if there was something familiar about the way the fellow moved, or if it was only his imagination.

The man paused on a huge stone jutting out over the seaweed trails in the water, and peered back toward the beach as though measuring something. Then he dug deep in the pocket of his bulky coat, cocked back his arm, and threw something as far as he could out into the choppy waters.

White water boiled up in an enormous splash, and in less than an eyeblink, an entire ship appeared, an old-fashioned thing with an up-curving prow of a kind Rel had never seen before. It rocked danger-ously on the water, sending an enormous greenish-gray wave splashing up onto the rocks to drench the waiting warriors, who gave a huge out-cry. Many fell painfully. Several were knocked from the rocks entirely.

On board the ship, the crew fell to the deck, then struggled to their knees, or grabbed for ropes. Rel knew enough about ships to see the immediate danger: if the crew did not get some sort of sail up, the ship would swamp on the beach.

The captain seemed to recover first, bawling something at the man on the rocks, who had staggered back, dripping wet.

Aboard the ship, the captain began kicking and striking his crew to get them moving. After they had accepted the mysterious Ramis's offer to send them beyond time, the captain had ordered his crew at the first sight of the great crack in the world to lay aloft on yards and mastheads. So when the magic released them, they were already in position. They scrambled into action, unreefing a sail that the crew below sheeted home. The ship came alive, shivering in the water as it moved against the inexorable tide toward the very tip of the jetty.

On the rocks, the man removed his sodden scarf, which he flung down. For a heartbeat his face was visible as he took in the ship from tumblehome to masts, and Rel's breath hissed in when he recognized that arrogant countenance, and the sandy hair: Henerek, the would-be Knight who had been dismissed for too many infractions to remember.

This had to be the Everon attack force that Kessler promised.

Henerek turned away and began clumsily hopping from rock to rock farther along the jetty. He had to be freezing. His waterlogged coat clung to his long body. He, too, had aged from a weedy teen to a man heavy with muscle along chest, shoulders, arms.

At the extreme tip of the jetty, as the ship beat out to take up station a short distance away, once again Henerek threw something. This time, he ducked down behind a rock when the expected wave surged over the jetty. The rest of the Norsundrians having stayed where they were, there was no other damage to those waiting. This ship recovered itself and got a sail up, as the first one lowered a longboat into the water.

Twice more this happened. As the light began to fade, the ships withdrew to a safe distance, sending longboats to the beach to fetch Henerek's waiting force and ferry them back.

They had begun lighting lanterns when abruptly Rel transferred, his cramped, shivering body falling to the thick red and gold rug in Tsauderei's cottage.

The old mage remembered the extreme cold. He had a warm change of clothing, hot food, and drink waiting. When Rel could get his jaw to work without chattering, he gave a concise report.

"Four ships," Tsauderei repeated. "From what you describe, they sound rather like vessels from the bad old days when the Venn ruled the seas. Records insist that Norsunder used to grab pirate ships wholesale, shoving them through powerful rifts, before the mages learned to close those rifts. Now, it seems, they are going to begin reappearing. This is grim tidings."

"So we should look for vast armies appearing on the coasts?" Rel asked.

"It is possible, and yet . . . only four to transport that force. I wonder if this is an experiment by someone higher up the command chain. Yet one would think they would be sparing. The magic that put those ships beyond time has been unreproduceable for centuries."

"Henerek might have stolen the means. He was a thief as well as a bully and a liar."

"Always possible. But even so, the higher-ups have a way of catching out unruly underlings and taking advantage of their resourcefulness." Tsauderei sat back. "Here. Eat the rest of that food. Get a good night of rest up in the loft, where it's warmest. I'll send you directly on to Everon in the morning. Tonight, I have some letters to write."

*Everon*

The next morning, Tsauderei transferred Rel to Everon as promised.

Once he recovered, he was brought by a footman into the royal presence. Though Everon was quite a ways north of the border mountains where Tsauderei's valley was located, to the sun's movement, it was perhaps an hour to the west. The royal family was at breakfast, their faces sharing similar expressions of concern when Rel was conducted in.

Rel made his bow, then once again issued a report, this time with precise numbers.

On the name 'Henerek,' the king reached for the hand bell to summon a page, as Glenn grinned fiercely down at his plate. "Please request the presence of Commander Dei," King Berthold said.

The king left his half-eaten breakfast. The queen went off in another direction, leaving Rel with the royal children.

Glenn threw down his napkin. "They *have* to let me ride with the Knights," he declared, and he, too, ran off.

Tahra scowled at her plate, then looked at Rel. "The alliance needs to know."

Rel said, "I don't have the means to communicate with them."

"My friend Piper is a scribe student, and she writes regularly to Karhin for me," Tahra said as she pushed a last bite of berry tart around on her plate. "Her Sartoran is better than mine." She tapped her fingers twice on the table, the side of her cup, then the table again before looking up. "Do you think the alliance can help us?"

"I'm not sure.," Rel admitted, and when Tahra's thin brows crimped anxiously, he said, "I think it's a good idea, but I don't know how it's supposed to work other than as a way to pass news."

Tahra's long face seemed to lengthen as she glared at her plate. "Glenn is wrong to think everything will be fixed by swinging swords. Norsunder must have millions of warriors, if they never die."

"They can die. Unless they're soul-bound. But then they lose their wills."

"So what happens when they are inside Norsunder? Are they statues?"

"Maybe it's like what happened to Sartor, you just . . . stop. Until you go again."

Tahra folded her arms across her front and ran her thin fingers up her arms, her stomach tight with disgust. "I thought it was horrible when my family was enchanted. But that sounds so much worse. How can anybody even fight them, if they have millions?"

"We don't know that they have millions, and anyway, they aren't in our world. They need rifts to bring them to the world from Norsunder-Beyond. Transfer magic is dangerous, so they can't even bring them in by twos and threes without a safe period in between."

"I know that much." Tahra's straight dark brows crimped, then she turned her head sharply as a page entered. "What is it?"

The page said to Rel, "The king requests your presence."

Rel was shown into the king's interview chamber, where the king himself was busy unrolling one map, the queen another.

They occupied themselves looking at the map of the Sartoran continent, tracing the natural harbor where Rel had spied the Norsundrians, and estimating how long it would take to sail northward. Rel listened, aware that none of them knew the winds and currents enough to be certain of anything.

But it gave them something to do until Roderic Dei arrived, looking as if he had hastened away from his breakfast. Once again Rel gave his report, after which the Commander said, "I'll talk to the fleet captains, but one thing for certain, we'll need to work on shore defenses."

"Yes!" The king slammed his hand down in a gesture of agreement. "That, we can do over winter." He looked up at Rel. "Thank you. I trust you will honor us with your skills?"

Rel had been about to ask to be sent back to Sartor. Except what could he do there? The high council scorned military action. He could march around holding a candle in parades, but they didn't want his help, or even his presence, in Sartoran affairs.

"If you can use me, I'm yours," Rel said.

Roderic Dei smiled, well pleased. Maybe he would gain Rel as a Knight after all. "Come along with me. We'll report your findings, and get you situated."

## Chapter Two

*Roth Drael*

HIBERN woke up late, startled by the internal tick of her notecase. She groped for it, wondering who would send her a note by magic before dawn.

She snapped the glowglobe alight. The note was written in a shaky hand, strong on the downstrokes:

> *Hibern: I am certain Erai-Yanya arranged an emergency signal with you. If your demonstration is prepared, now would be the time to use that signal. I've Atan and Veltos ready to meet tomorrow. Erai-Yanya's presence might make all the difference.*
>
> *Tsauderei*

Hibern scrabbled on desk for the token Erai-Yanya had made. She picked it up, murmured the words she'd been taught, and the thing snapped away from her fingers and vanished.

She heard rustlings from the outer room, and sighed inwardly. Liere, whom she had removed from Marloven Hess at Senrid's request, had rendered the past few days tedious almost past bearing by her stream of questions about magic that was way beyond her level as a beginner.

For someone who claimed she wasn't the least bit special, she certainly seemed to expect special tutoring. Hibern pulled on a wrapper against the cool drafts moving along the floor. Why hadn't the senior mages put Liere in a magic school?

She found the girl hovering over the basket of food transferred daily from the Bereth Ferian palace's kitchen. Liere looked rumpled, as if she'd slept in her clothes and forgotten to step through the cleaning frame, her short, raggedly cut hair sticking out in all directions.

"Why are you up so early?" Hibern asked.

"I was awake a long time," Liere mumbled. "My mother was dreaming bad things about me again. I had to fix things inside her dream. So she knows I'm all right."

Hibern's skin chilled. "You can do that?"

Liere looked startled, as if she'd been caught committing a crime. Her cheeks mottled with color. "Siamis did that to me once, talked to me in my dreams, I mean. When I was with Senrid, running away from the eleveners. When I had the dyr. He tried to scare me into giving it up. I figured, if he can do it, I can. I was used to hearing my mother's dreams. Hadn't known that I might be able to talk to her in them and make it all right."

And that was probably why they didn't put Liere in a magic school. Hibern turned away, hiding her expression of revulsion as she concentrated on her mind-shield. Neither school would want a mind reader among them, much less someone who could wander into dreams and 'fix' them.

"Is the bread still warm?" Hibern asked. "Pass the elderberry jelly."

As the sun began sifting golden shafts between the eastern trees, they finished, worked together in dunking and drying the dishes, then Liere picked up her garden tools and went outside in the clear summer air while Hibern looked at her piles, trying to decide which project would be least annoying to be pulled out of when Erai-Yanya arrived.

A blast of warm, oddly scented air startled her. Erai-Yanya appeared in the corner reserved for magical transfers. She staggered as if she'd run down a couple of steps, sneezed violently five or six times, then lifted a hand to her head. "I'll never get used to how different the air is. Emergency?" she said, rubbing her sun-browned face. She looked unfamiliar, wearing an odd, brightly colored outfit that seemed comprised of three layers of thin cloth.

"In a way. Tsauderei asked me to send for you."

"Do you know what it's about?"

"We've spent the past three weeks talking about almost nothing else."

"We?" Erai-Yanya asked, "You, Tsauderei—"

"And Senrid, and Peitar—"

"Peitar Selenna of Sarendan?" Erai-Yanya rubbed her eyes again. "Please don't tell me he's discovered the sport of kings, and is marching to war."

Hibern said, "Peitar's friend Derek has organized the orphans of Sarendan into defense. But that's made Peitar more determined than he was before to find some way to defend his kingdom without bloodshed."

"All right. *That* sounds like Peitar Selenna." Erai-Yanya sighed. "I'm glad people haven't changed out of all recognition while I've been gone. Tell me your part."

Hibern looked down at her hands, clean and warm right now, but the echo of bitter cold pulsed there as she considered how much to report. And how very important it all was to her—this first time she had been asked to act as a mage, instead of being exhorted to watch and learn as a student.

But what can seem vitally important for all kinds of reasons could sound really boring, especially when performing dangerous and yet tedious tasks again and again, as she and Senrid had endured the late-autumn winds and rain, toiling along Marloven Hess's southern border, where Norsunder had crossed a few years back.

"I worked with Senrid," she said. "Our strategy was that illusion works when it's unexpected. Especially if its traces are subsumed by stronger magic. So we created false roads on Marloven Hess's southern border."

Unlike in Sartor, there was no mysterious forest in Marloven Hess for Senrid to guide invaders to. His illusory roads were meant to guide any attacking Norsundrians onto ground that Forthan and Senrid had chosen, guarded by wings of South Army.

That meant walking the entire area step by step, and altering the landscape one boulder and weed at a time, in order to fool the sweeping eye—taking care never to create an image so out of place that it required a second look.

When they finished, Senrid gratefully went back to his capital, but Hibern was not finished. Once Tsauderei chose the likeliest locale, Hibern had transferred to Sartor, where she spent four long, bitterly cold days in heavy snow grubbing along the southern border. She'd stooped and searched, paused and whispered illusion spells over and over as she broke seed husks in half, and placed moldering bits of brick or wood to mark the place where each illusion would be evoked.

She looked up into Erai-Yanya's waiting face, and it occurred to her for the first time to wonder how many hours, days, months, even years of labor, performed with dread and hope and maybe even glee, but mostly grimly endured tedium, adults did that no one knew about, though it was for the world's benefit.

She squared herself on her cushion, and summed up those untold hours in the cold, her bleeding hands and unexpected bruises, with, "I took what I learned to Sartor, where I transformed the road Tsauderei suggested, masking it and creating a new road to Shendoral. I'm to demonstrate for Atan and Chief Veltos. Tsauderei said you really ought to be there."

Erai-Yanya smiled thinly, in complete understanding. "So . . . you did all the work, but I'm to be there to give your labors a semblance of legitimacy in the eyes of the Sartoran mages?" She sneezed again, nodded, and said, "*Now*, I'll look at my notecase."

She vanished into her own chamber, leaving Hibern to appreciate how her tutor had understood not only everything she said, but everything unsaid.

When Erai-Yanya emerged again, she had brushed out her hair and skewered it neatly on her head, and she wore her usual warm, shapeless robe. She said briskly, "You will not be surprised to learn that I've been invited to join you in your meeting with Tsauderei and Chief Veltos of the Sartoran mage guild on Sartor's border tomorrow."

Hibern flicked up her palm in assent.

"Currently under a blizzard, Tsauderei says. So tomorrow might turn into the day after." Erai-Yanya's thin smile faded, and she indicated the dramatic crack in the wall that served as a window. She gazed out at Liere in the abandoned kitchen garden, who crouched over the now-neat rows, straightened, then walked into the woods with something in her hands before returning. "What's she doing?"

"Carrying snails and caterpillars to the weedy area down by the stream."

"Snails." Erai-Yanya made a warding motion. "One of the many, many things I loathed about gardening was grubbing for snails, and picking caterpillars off the cabbages." She grimaced as an uncomfortable idea occurred. "I suppose she can hear snails' thoughts?"

"Thinking of all the snails you squished?" Hibern asked her tutor candidly. "I did. And I asked her. She said it's not hearing or seeing, but the closest she can come is perceiving tiny, dim lights in the realm of the mind. That's how she finds them so easily."

"Why is she doing it? More of the self-punishment that Arthur can't seem to talk her out of? She can't enjoy it."

"She says she likes doing it because she knows how," Hibern explained. "Tending their kitchen garden was hers and her sister's job where she lived before. But here, nobody criticizes her. I guess her father never noticed anything anyone did, except to criticize." Hibern grinned as she gathered up the breakfast eggshells. "She thought your abandoned garden was hundreds of years old."

"Just twenty." Erai-Yanya huffed out her breath. "Walk with me."

Hibern complied, glad she hadn't begun work.

"My mother gave me that garden to tend when I turned six or seven, saying I needed to understand the connection between human and soil, water, and air. How the Waste Spell we use every day, and the animal droppings we wand, are spread through soil, where they in turn enrich the plants. She also declared that I needed discipline. All I thought about when I flicked snails out of the garden or yanked weeds was how much I hated that chore."

Hibern was grateful for her own escape. She would have done the work if Erai-Yanya had demanded it as part of her magic-learning, but she knew she would have hated it.

They stepped onto the terrace, and turned toward the pathway that would lead to the garden some hundred paces away.

Erai-Yanya continued. "So when she managed to lose herself mysteriously in that struggle over the dyr in Everon, when I was sixteen, I abandoned the garden that day. And Evend, who you know took over tutoring me, didn't say a thing about it. That was one of the reasons I sent Arthur to him when it became apparent that Arthur needed to be around people."

She bunched her skirt in one hand, and Hibern followed, watching birds darting overhead as she crushed eggshells in her palms.

"Patterns," Erai-Yanya said. "My mother was fifty-five when she got me, after disappointment with the brother I've never met, who hated magic and ran off to sea. Her mother was even older when she was born. We who stay here share certain traits, you could say family traits, though not everyone in any family is exactly the same. My mother never knew how to play. She saw only wasted time. I think play has an important place. But she was an excellent mage."

Hibern sensed that the point was coming. Erai-Yanya stopped, and shut her eyes. Hibern wondered if she was having some kind of reaction to her cross-world hop, and then her neck prickled when it hit her: Erai-Yanya was concentrating on a mind-shield. Hastily Hibern reinforced her own, annoyed that she'd let it lapse yet again.

As Hibern began dropping eggshells around the plants, Erai-Yanya said, "My mother spent many years trying to winnow out the truth about the powerful, mysterious dyra of Ancient Sartor." She held up her thumb and forefinger as though holding one of the magical artifacts. "As did some of her foremothers. I inherited that task, and stubbornly stuck to it. And so I came to be recognized as the expert on dyra, though I know little enough." Her voice dropped low, the words coming in a rush. "And that shopkeeper's daughter out there in our garden, who never had a magic lesson in her life—she didn't even know how to *read*—took up the thing, and used it against Siamis as if she'd been trained all her life. Everything is changing into an unrecognizable world, that is going to belong to you young people. But." The sunburned little wrinkles around her eyes shifted as her brows rose. "Hibern. What are you doing with those eggshells?"

"Putting them around the vegetables. Liere says they discourage the snails."

"My mother had me put the coffee grindings on the soil. It sometimes worked, though not when rain was heavy, but I suspect nothing works then. Or are eggshells better?"

"We haven't been at it long."

"I see." Erai-Yanya blinked absently at the green shoots neatly growing sunward, then continued. "But. Back to the dyr. Since Sartor has returned, I've delved in their records, to find nothing. Admittedly the records are sparse, after so very many centuries. Even so, to find nothing whatsoever? Either dyra were so dangerous they were not written about, or they were so much a part of normal life that people didn't write about them any more than we write each day about the air we breathe. But this we know from the Siamis enchantment: those things are dangerous. And maybe poisonous."

She waited as Liere picked another plate of snails from the rows at the extreme edge of the garden, then vanished down the slope toward the stream.

"You know I study patterns. In magic. In families. In everything. Liere demonstrates patterns for . . . oh, maybe I'd better not say it. Most of what I know about her is secondhand. From my son, from the mages up north." She looked troubled.

Hibern shivered. "You think something's wrong with Liere?"

"I think there's a reason she's so frail, so colorless . . ." Erai-Yanya shrugged. "I thought at first her family starved her, but in spite of the fact that everyone who hosts her provides excellent food, and comfort, she doesn't look a whit more healthy than she did when she was running over the world using the dyr to destroy Siamis's enchantment."

"You think the dyr poisoned her?"

"That's my guess. Pending more information. I think she needs to be observed more carefully . . ." Erai-Yanya looked like she was going to say more, but Liere had returned after depositing the last of her snails, and approached them, an inquiring look on her face.

Erai-Yanya smiled at Liere. "Hibern and I need to go south tomorrow. Something about strengthening Sartor's southern border ward. In the middle of a blizzard, as it happens. I suggest you rejoin my son in Bereth Ferian. You like midsummer up there, as I recollect."

Liere said, "Senrid thought I ought to hide here."

Erai-Yanya took in the neat rows in the garden before saying cordially, "I realize that to a certain extent Senrid's life depended on his being able to out-think his uncle, but it does not follow that all adults are as easily out-thought. Or to put it another way: stupid."

Liere flushed. "Senrid doesn't think all adults are stupid." At Erai-Yanya's wry eyebrow lift, Liere turned even redder. "Well, he knows when he's been stupid."

"I don't doubt it, and I have nothing else to say on the subject, having exchanged little converse with him. But I truly believe that Chief Oalthoreh and the entire northern mage school are all capable of keeping you safe."

*Sartor*

What Atan saw when Chief Veltos entered a room was iron discipline, focused austerity, and above all, authority.

What Veltos Jhaer saw in her own mirror was a middle-aged failure.

She yanked down her dark blue robe with its three hard-earned stars, and headed for the Destination, thinking grimly that when she was dead, she hoped it would be said about her that she never shirked her duty. But she suspected that her only claim to fame would be that she lost the mage war to Detlev of Norsunder, causing Sartor to vanish for nearly a century.

Her defensive strategy—the greatest share of her work time was given to this—was to reproduce that spell, only to be used to remove Sartor magically from Norsunder's grip. But such a defense could only work if it was an absolute surprise, which meant keeping it secret.

So far, she had not been able to reproduce Detlev's magic, or even to penetrate his intent. Meanwhile, she must wrest the time from her research to train a young, uneducated queen who knew just enough magic to ask dangerous questions. Veltos had to make certain that the girl didn't become willful, which would make her dangerous herself.

Veltos's head already ached after a restless night. Transfer magic turned her inside out, then thrust her back into the world. She pulled on her thick mittens, her head turtling into the scarf she'd wound around her neck and ears.

A thin silhouette in the bleak, low sunlight resolved into the gaunt form of Tsauderei, seated on a carved stone bench.

As Veltos stepped off the temporary Destination, she controlled the spurt of disappointment. She knew it was unworthy to have deliberately come early, a silent gesture of moral superiority. In her day, only kings and queens kept others waiting.

But here was the old mage. He had chosen the site, traced the Destination magic onto an old terrace, and provided everyone with a transfer token. That meant he had also swept the area for magical traps or tricks, but still she crossed the tile terrace, recognizing the interlocked garland pattern as one popular some nine centuries back, and reached to drop the token into Tsauderei's hand.

"Thank you for timeliness, Veltos," Tsauderei said.

"You will forgive my desire to be sure of her majesty's safety?"

"Contrary. I would expect you to do your duty as you perceive it," he said, and watched as she paced the terrace's perimeter, whispering her tracer spells.

She was aware of his scrutiny, aware of his smile, this elderly man who had been born a generation after her fiftieth birthday while she was senselessly prisoned outside of the world. Having ascertained that no evil spells lurked for the unwary, she looked around. The terrace was the only solid part of what had once been a sizable dwelling overlooking the Hvas River below, beyond which lay the uninhabited lands that eventually led to the Norsunder Base.

"Do you know whose baras-territory this was, and what happened to it?" Tsauderei asked. "The ruin being much older than last century's war."

"All I know is that it had to have been subordinate to Chandos." She was going to add that she had never studied wars, so she didn't know which had resulted in the destruction of what had probably been a beautiful dwelling. Her life had been dedicated to constructive matters. Civilization.

Until she led the mages to defeat, and the kingdom to ruin.

And so she bowed her head, prepared to let this upstart from Sarendan lecture her on her own history, but he said, "I wondered. Found it by accident, when the spell over Sartor began receding. Never mind. It's a perfect spot from which to observe the southeast end of your border—"

He abandoned the rest of his observation as the air flickered and Erai-Yanya appeared, managing to look scruffy to Veltos even in a heavy coat, scarf, hat, and mittens. She was followed by that Marloven girl whom Erai-Yanya had unaccountably selected out of all the possible mage students in the world.

The two looked bewildered, as to be expected; the time difference was not all that much in east-to-west measure, but to them it must look as if the sun had leaped far to the north, plunging them into cold.

Veltos put her hands together in the polite gesture of greeting, then walked away to the edge of the terrace not only to let them recover from the transfer, but to scold herself into composure. She gazed hard at the silvery ribbon of iced-over river below. Erai-Yanya might look like a northcoast beggar, but she was a Vithyavadnais—a formidable line of mages, many of whom had apparently been at least as idiosyncratic. That did not lessen their skill.

There was no excuse for the young queen to have turned to that Marloven girl for aid for this venture. Veltos could only see this unexplainable preference as a covert reminder of her own failure a century ago, and her current inability to secure Sartor against further enchantment.

Erai-Yanya and the Marloven girl began chatting with Tsauderei, their voices distinct, curiously brittle on the frozen air, then they all fell silent at the brief stir of air of a new arrival, and there was the young queen, who insisted on her parents' intimate, family-only heart-name, Atan.

"I hope you will pardon my tardiness," Atan said, and her polite smile widened. "Hibern! You're here!"

"Ready when you are," Hibern said.

"First." Tsauderei thumped his gloved hands on his bony knees, his breath clouding. "Erai-Yanya, is there anything to report from your time on Geth?"

"I could talk for half a day about how differently they do things, and about the difficulties of making oneself clear when the Language Spell turns out to be two centuries out of date. But I won't. We know that Norsunder has been poking around, and the Geth mages think it has something to do with transfer magic."

"They're looking for rift magic," Veltos exclaimed.

"Or ancient, hidden artifacts?" Atan asked, turning from one to another. "The way we've been searching?"

"Little success either will bring, I should think," Tsauderei commented. "My understanding is, that world was mostly settled by runaways from Sartorias-deles after the Fall, who then instituted extreme measures to control magic, so there would never be a repeat of the Fall. The only way they'd have powerful ancient artifacts would be if they brought them, and I defy Norsunder to find what Geth's mages have spent centuries making sure is well concealed."

Erai-Yanya said, "You know the problem with spying on Norsunder, how sparse information is, and that's usually distorted. But I'll give you details later, if you like. When we aren't freezing our noses and ears off." She turned to Tsauderei. "The last time I was here, someone was talking about instituting an Emras Defense, one that is perfectly balanced between light and dark."

Veltos bit her lip. With these two, she did not need to point out the long-standing debate between the Sartoran Council and the Bereth Ferian mages about who Emras's tutor really had been. Whether or not he was actually Detlev in some guise, or a Marloven dark mage, didn't really matter: the best Emras Defense that magic could manage now, with hundreds of anchor points, would only buy time. Magic could always be broken by stronger magic.

She said, "As for hidden artifacts, there is one we all know about, and you have charge of it. You even have someone who does know how to use it, though she is a child." Veltos would not willingly speak that highly inappropriate name 'Sartora,' and she kept forgetting the child's given name.

"I sent Liere away," Erai-Yanya said. "She doesn't understand the dyr any more than we do. Less."

"But she used it."

"For one spell," Erai-Yanya said. "To break an enchantment that built an illusory boundary around minds. The dyr is only useful for that same spell. Liere was relieved when she surrendered it to me, and she has never asked me to bring it out of hiding."

"If she does, don't," Tsauderei cut in. "The magic in the dyr augments these other spells in some way none of us understand. All we know is we cannot control it."

Veltos began a noiseless sigh, halting when the clouding of her breath betrayed her. "But from all reports she has no discipline, no course of study, and is most often to be found in Marloven Hess, of all the inappropriate places." She turned Hibern's way, palms together. "I speak only the truth as I see it."

Atan spoke quickly. "I only met Liere once. She didn't seem undisciplined to me. A little odd, and ignorant, but she was aware of that. She made mention of a lot of reading."

Hibern let out a slow breath of relief as Erai-Yanya said sardonically, "Do you want to lecture a child who can read your innermost thoughts on what you perceive to be her duty?"

Veltos recoiled, then shook her head.

"Exactly," Erai-Yanya said, more cordially. "The fact is, no one quite understands what goes on in her mind. In the meantime my son has done everything possible to make her welcome in Bereth Ferian. As for her friendship with Senrid of Marloven Hess, my understanding is that he was very close to a female younger cousin until she left to study music, and Liere is used to older brothers. She's a sister substitute, he's a brother. No doubt, like all youth, they will grow apart."

Veltos's brows contracted, her gaze downward lest the others somehow see the pain she couldn't quite control, or hear the whispers from her youth about the future King of Sartor, *Prince Connar Landis falls out of love as fast as he falls in it.*

He certainly hadn't fallen out of love with Diantas Dei. And Veltos had never lost her painful, hopeless love for him, even when he was a middle-aged king with thinning hair, a large family, and a war he did not know how to fight. Every time she looked into Atan's face, she had to stop herself from trying to find traces of her father there.

Veltos said to the countryside, "Children need to be learning discipline. They need good examples to emulate. Especially someone with her gifts. Liere's parents relinquished authority, then?"

"If you had met her father, you would understand why no one wished to send the child back to him. In any case, he did not really want her, for the same reason neither one of the schools has tried to take over her instruction." Erai-Yanya tapped her forehead. "Everyone agrees that, pending Lilith the Guardian coming forth from beyond time and directing us, Liere needs to learn to control her gifts before undertaking formal training. And none of us can teach her to do that."

Veltos bowed again.

"Then there's my own worry, one I expressed to Hibern today, after not having seen Liere for months. She looks ill, though she insists she's fine. Given no other discernable cause, I wonder if the dyr poisoned her somehow. Do you really want me bringing that thing out again? Especially if we're expecting a Norsunder attack? How long do you think that child would escape their hands this time? There is certainly no chance they would be surprised again."

Veltos sighed. "They'll probably be after her anyway."

"Bringing us to our meeting now," Tsauderei said. "And the sooner I get my old bones out of this cold, the better. Hibern, tell them your idea."

Hibern said, "It's not a great solution, but if nothing better comes along, well, you've got this weird forest here, that the record books say distorts time."

"Shendoral," Atan, Veltos, and Tsauderei said at the same time.

Erai-Yanya said suavely, "I believe that's the one in which inexplicable things happen if you're within its border."

Tsauderei said, "Correct. If you commit violence, that violence recoils upon you. It is quite real."

"Time is not trustworthy in Shendoral," Chief Veltos said. "Or direction. But what has this to do with this meeting?"

Tsauderei smiled Hibern's way, but smoothed his face as he said to Veltos, "It has to do with our proposed plan, which is to set up careful illusions that will lead Norsunder's warriors into Shendoral."

"Illusions?" Veltos exclaimed. "Those are so easy to dispel."

"Only if you know they're there," said Hibern.

Veltos frowned. "But surely Norsunder will send along mages to perform tracers."

"And they'll sense all these wards meant to deflect, or to swallow, their magic. Illusions are so easy, so deceptive if they're placed right. If they aren't expected, they can be quite effective." Tsauderei grinned. "Hibern, time to demonstrate."

Hibern walked with self-conscious care over the slippery ground toward the extreme edge of the ridge. She slipped off her mitten, pulled from her pocket the handful of carefully preserved seed-halves and rocks, held them on her open palm, and whispered the transport spell over and over as the objects vanished one by one to meet their other halves. As the others watched, the landscape below transformed itself in subtle ways. Illusion can be done by design, like drawing from memory, but it is most convincing when images are made of existing things combined so that the effect is not mirror image.

The mages looked down at new hills, ridges, and thick copses of trees that hid the road, creating a new road over flat areas.

Atan exclaimed, "Oh, Hibern, that's *wonderful!*"

"This is just the bit we can see from here. I don't know your countryside all that well, and I only had a few days. As you can see, my false road gently divides off from the real road by connecting to existing paths. So, the invading army will think they are on the road to Eidervaen, but if they follow the illusory road, they'll find themselves in Shendoral."

"Excellent job," Tsauderei said with a glance Veltos's way.

"The spells would have to be renewed frequently, as they wear off so fast," Veltos said doubtfully.

"Which is easy enough. Of course you marked your locations on a mage's map?" Erai-Yanya said briskly.

"Right here," Hibern said, withdrawing the scroll from inside her coat, with its carefully measured lines, its exact ratio of fingerbreadths to paces, and the magic symbols for her spells at the proper locations.

"You could put your students to that," Tsauderei said to Chief Veltos. "Do the same from the Luyos River. You can even get the magic to last longer by binding it to the moving water of the rivers without the least harm."

"What did you do, precisely?" Veltos asked, peering out over the countryside.

"Create what looks like impassable objects at road crossings, to direct them along the roads you wish. Mask landmarks," Hibern said. "And recreate illusions of famous landmarks where they ought to lie on their maps. Their maps are going to be wrong anyway, as so much repair has been going on." She was quoting Senrid directly.

"It's wonderful," Atan said firmly, and asserted herself again. "I intend to bring this idea before the high council, and then the circles. I trust you will support it, Chief Veltos."

Veltos looked at Atan's long face, but she wasn't seeing the teenage girl. She was thrown back in memory, hearing Connar's warm, husky voice as he bent over his daughter in her cradle, whispering, "I suppose we ought to name her Yustnesveas, which will satisfy several and insult none, but to me, she will be Atanrael . . . Atanael . . . Atanelen . . . what do you think, Dian?"

"Atan," said Diantas Dei, who had legally given up her family name to marry a king. "She is too small for more."

"Ah, love, as always you are right." And he'd straightened up to kiss her . . .

Veltos had to physically turn away from the memory. He was gone. Now a century in the past. And at least all those Deis were gone, too, except for that poor mad child Julian.

She bowed. "I shall, your majesty."

"Then we're done here," Tsauderei said. "Back to defrost my old bones at my fireside."

Atan watched as Chief Veltos and Erai-Yanya walked toward the edge of the cliff, speaking in low-voiced conversation.

Atan said equally low-voiced to Hibern, "This is the first time I've told them what I want to do, rather than them telling me what I ought to do. You did a brilliant job. Thank you!" Then she raised her voice. "Chief Veltos, Tsauderei. You're shivering. You have to be cold. Please return to warmth."

Hibern knew a hint when she heard it. "Erai-Yanya?"

Atan smiled at Hibern, and as the elders vanished, Atan transferred to Miraleste, capital of Sarendan.

Atan had been corresponding with Peitar and Lilah long enough to know not only the time difference, but Peitar's schedule. So much less ritual in Sarendan!

Peitar and Lilah sat at their midday meal, each with a book propped before them. Atan's heart gladdened at the genuine welcome in the two faces, so unalike: Peitar slender, his dark hair waving back from a high brow, Lilah short and square, freckled and slant-eyed, like so many people in both Sartor and Sarendan.

"Atan!" Lilah leaped up. "Want some lunch?"

"I've only a short time before I'm expected back. Am I keeping you?" She looked around, hoping Derek was not nearby. "If you're expecting anyone . . ."

"Aunt Tislah went home in a huff, as she always does after trying to matchmake for Peitar," Lilah said with a grin. "Bren is traveling with Innon, and Derek is at Obrin."

"Obrin? Is that not where the Sarendan army training takes place?" Atan said in surprise.

"Derek has become quite popular with the remnant of my uncle's army, at least at Obrin." Peitar's smile faded into pensiveness.

Lilah put her spoon down. "I went with him to train the summer before last," she said proudly. "They didn't much like him, at first, on account of our civil war. But Derek said we should go to the back row, with all the age tens, and work our way up. That was kind of fun, especially when he made jokes, and told stories in the dorm at night. By the end of that summer, I made it to scout trainee, and Derek got promoted to leader of a foot patrol. Then we returned to Miraleste, and he taught the orphans things we learned. He went back last spring, but I didn't, because I was visiting up in the Valley."

Atan's attention was on Peitar. He listened to his sister with a thoughtful air. Atan knew how much Peitar cherished this friend of his, and how distrustful he was of war preparations, so when Lilah finished, and no one had anything to add about Derek, Atan used the rest of her time to describe how Chief Mage Veltos had reacted to Hibern's demonstration.

At the end, Lilah clapped her hands, and Peitar gave his rare, thoughtful smile. "If Chief Veltos was impressed, then I have more confidence about the illusions I placed around Diannah Wood. I could only get away for a day or two, and then there's the fact that Diannah Wood is not as strange, and as inhospitable to enemies, as Shendoral is reputed to be. But it's a great idea. And if Chief Veltos agreed, well, we can hope the illusions will at least discourage the enemy."

"I know Tsauderei will be giving you his impressions of Hibern's demonstration, but I wanted to tell you first," Atan said.

Actually, she wanted what she'd seen: the genuine glow of friendship in both their faces. They would have accepted Atan the Mage as happily as they accepted Atan, Queen of Sartor. Sometimes she needed that reminder.

Veltos arrived back in her quarters, her head pounding. She tried to walk off her irritation at having found that Marloven girl there, after all the work the high council had done getting rid of her. It was clear that the young queen was corresponding on her own, in spite of all the thought and care dedicated to surrounding her with the very best tutors the kingdom afforded.

Well, if her mages liked the illusionary diversion plan, at least they could dismantle everything the Marloven had done on the southern border, and make their own.

When Veltos had her temper under control, she summoned her mages to report. As she expected, they hailed the illusion plan with cautious enthusiasm, and added a lot of froth about how wonderful it was that their queen, young as she was, showed signs of becoming a fine Sartoran monarch. Veltos endured it in smiling silence.

Over the next few days, she took volunteer mage students to the border. As the young will when inspired, they set to the task with almost frightening alacrity.

And so she was able to return to her normal rounds of duty and study, keeping her thoughts to herself until her brother, a scribe, came to visit her, as he did every week or two. He felt for his older sister, who had lost more than people realized, during the war.

But even so, a short way into their discussion, he exclaimed, "Veltos, remember how much we hated being twitted by our elders? I don't agree that these young folks coming south from other lands have no manners or wits. They're simply different from our day."

Veltos said, "Come here to the window. Look down there. No, that way, at the end of the street. Do you see what's going on there?"

Her brother obliged her, his graying hair brushing his shoulders as he leaned in the thick stone window to peer out. "Someone seems to be getting rid of their furniture, as far as I can tell."

"No." Veltos gripped her elbows. "What you see is a man—a young man, though he's from our day—losing his home. Not just his home, which has been in his family for a very long time, he is losing everything."

"What happened?"

"What else? A hundred years ago, when the word went out that Norsunder had crossed the border in force, he sent his young wife with everything they had to her family somewhere up north, including the house-deed, which he'd made over in her name as a measure of safety. Then he did his duty as he saw it, joining the king to mount the defense. He being an artisan, not a warrior, he was wounded almost at once, and left for dead. He was still wounded when we came out of the spell. When he recovered, he wrote first thing to that family in the north, who, it turned out, no longer lived there. His wife had remarried, thinking him dead with the rest of us, and all his holdings had been passed down through her second family. With those holdings had been the deed to this house. They own it. He doesn't."

Her brother grimaced. He'd thought the busy scene at the end of the street was an everyday occurrence, the sort of thing you could see anywhere at any time. But now the steady stream of workers carrying furnishings out took on a new meaning. "That's horrible. There must be something that can be done."

"The family wishes to bring business, which this country sorely needs, and so two guilds backed the family. His guild offers him a room among the old folks, but as his wound prevents him from doing fine silverwork anymore . . ." She gave a sharp shrug. Her mouth twisted bitterly. "There are those who consider the family generous, as they have given the old furniture they least want to the man. It means nothing to them, of course. Even most of the family relics in the room of honor are also cast aside, except someone told me that they'll keep the most prestigious of them, because after all, where can the man put them in his single room? In so many ways, brother, that man represents Sartor."

Her brother patted her shoulder. "He is relatively young, and he has his training. He'll find a place in the world. As will Sartor."

"I told myself that," Veltos retorted, "until Tsauderei came to us with the news that we're facing another war."

## Chapter Three

*Marloven Hess*

ONCE Hibern and Erai-Yanya had spent a day catching up on Hibern's studies, Hibern transferred to Marloven Hess to keep her promise about reporting on the success of the Sartor border illusions idea.

Senrid wasn't in his study, or in the public rooms. Hibern walked to Keriam's tower, and as always, the moment he saw her, he waved off the cluster of gray-coated boys with which he always seemed to be surrounded.

She asked, "Where's Senrid?"

Keriam pointed a sheaf of papers at the window.

Hibern had already glanced out Senrid's study windows at the bleak winter sky. From Keriam's tower she got a different angle over the plain roofs and dull light brown stone of the academy. This time she caught what she'd missed previously, the small figure sitting on the farthest roof out, his shapeless gray blending with the gray of the sky.

She turned back to Keriam, her question in her face.

"He's watching the lance practice," Keriam said.

"Lance practice? Way out beyond the corrals?"

"Unofficial," Keriam said.

"What does that mean?" Hibern asked, trying to hide her exasperation.

"It means that the boys are forbidden to do heavy weapons training unsupervised, but they are not fighting each other, they are rehearsing a demonstration. Working very hard at it," Keriam added in a reflective tone. "Let's just say they have something to prove, to themselves as well as to the rest of us. As for Senrid, I suspect he could use the diversion."

Sure enough, Hibern thought, the explanation didn't really explain anything other than that there had been trouble among the academy boys. No surprise there! But one thing she did understand: Senrid was fretting.

So she ran down the stairs, bent into the bitter wind, and made her way along the barren stone walls. The air smelled of snow. Senrid perched on the roofpole with his knees drawn up under his chin and his arms wrapped around his legs. He looked over, his face nearly invisible between his scarf and his knit hat, except for a plum-red nose and a pair of narrowed eyes. "Did they go for it?"

"Yes. But Atan and I agreed to leave you out of it. The Sartoran mages think it was my idea, and even then, Chief Veltos eyed me like I'd farted in their Star Chamber. Erai-Yanya reminded me about five times that she does belong to the last century."

"Which means she was probably around at the same time as my un-lamented great-grandfather Senrid."

They considered the songs and stories about the bloody warfare during that reign, Marloven against Marloven, as the Hesean plains jarls and those of the northern reaches led by the Olavair family tried to conquer one another. That particular Senrid-Harvaldar had led a campaign of such destruction that the squabbling northerners had united long enough to fight him to a standstill, forcing him to a treaty.

Senrid went on, "You'd think she'd be able to figure out that I'm not him. I wasn't even named for him."

"I suspect to Sartor, there isn't any difference between the Senrid who reunited the old Marloven Hesea centuries ago and your great-grandfather. How much attention do you pay to Sartoran affairs?"

"I can name maybe ten of their rulers. Point taken. So Erai-Yanya is back?"

"Yes."

"It's about time! Did Tsauderei ask her how the dyr can be used to ward Norsunder?"

Was that the weight on Senrid's mind? "He didn't send for her until now because whatever she's doing on Geth-deles is more important than what's going on here."

"More important than a Norsunder invasion?"

Hibern said, "Yes. But rather than argue about which problem is worse, let me remind you of what Erai-Yanya said before: we don't know how to use the dyr, she can't find anything in the ancient archives on how to use it, and if we try, we're almost sure to draw the likes of Detlev or Siamis like arrows to the mark."

"They can probably smell it from beyond the world," Senrid agreed. "They sure were good at hunting Liere and me down. Shit. I knew it was too easy."

"As for working with the thing, part of the problem is the necessity for Dena Yeresbeth." Hibern touched her mittened fingers to her forehead. "Which you have. If you get an idea, go ahead and talk to her, but you're going to have to convince her that—"

"I would never think of using it for war," Senrid cut in impatiently.

"Convince her," Hibern said with deliberate emphasis, "that war isn't a game."

He eyed her, recognized the Marloven-to-Marloven irony, and said, "But it is a game. It's one we play to win until we're killed."

Hibern knew both the songs he was quoting from. She rubbed her hands together, then stuck them in her armpits as she stared out at the boys on horseback circling around one another, waving long sticks. It looked uncomfortable in the extreme. "Senrid, something's galling you under the saddle."

Senrid struck the roof flat-handed. "I want to know what they want."

They? The boys out there on horses? No. Norsunder. "You know what they want," she said.

"I *don't* know what they want. All Detlev's experiments with mind-magic at high levels, and maybe these weird enchantments that cut whole kingdoms off from the rest of the world, have to be a part of it."

"The scariest thing to me was hearing that he's been in the world more times recently than in the last five centuries," she said.

"Right." He sighed. "I've got my east, west, north, and south armies placed at what we think are best spots for invasion for each border. But where are Norsundrian invaders going to come from in order to get here? They don't sprout out of the ground. If they do manage to punch another big rift in the south, large enough to shove an army through, what's the use of attacking Marloven Hess in the middle of Halia and fighting us to a standstill, which is going to take out half the population?"

"Half?" she drawled, and he flashed a quick grin.

It was gone a heartbeat later. "And those left will be resisting covertly until the last one is dead. Unless the soul-suckers want us as a bloody training ground, it makes no *sense* to come after us, not unless they have armies and armies ready to take the entire continent. If they did, yeah, all my reading says we'd make a perfect foothold, they grab Halia, press east. If they've got enough of 'em."

"We know they've got armies and armies. We even know some of their names."

Senrid's lip curled. "I hope I never actually get to meet great-father Ivandred. He's bound to come thundering through here first in as a warm-up exercise."

Hibern watched as Senrid thumped his fist lightly on the roof tile. In certain moods he could be really annoying, the way he'd carom around a room, rapping lightly on things as he uttered a fast stream of talk. But seeing him so still, wrapped in a little ball like that, was unsettling.

He said, "I don't think they're going to attack us in force."

"You think it's going to be a mage war?"

Senrid turned to face her, his chin grinding on his knee. "I think it's going to be Siamis's plan again, enchanting everyone's brains out when they don't see him coming." He looked away. "Only worse. I remember that Siamis kept refining that enchantment as he went. At first it was a few people, then a village, then a town, and then he was able to enchant entire kingdoms through their loyalties, once he'd hunted down the right person. Yeah, Liere broke the enchantment, but he's had years to learn how to get around it."

*Here it comes*, she thought.

Senrid's voice flattened. "I think their being around so much, and experimenting with magic that messes with minds, has to do with this damned Dena Yeresbeth. That I probably inherited from my mother, she being a direct descendant of the Cassads."

Hibern knew all the stories about the Cassads, or Cassadas, who had ruled before the Marloven invasion, and some stories insisted they were related all the way back to the mysterious Adamas Dei of the Black Sword. The Cassads had been mages, and all the old stories and songs insisted that some of them heard thoughts and talked to ghosts.

She turned up her palm. "If anyone would inherit Dena Yeresbeth, it would be descendants from them. But why 'damned'?"

"Because I don't know how to control it. I don't know how to use it. What if that's what Detlev and Siamis want? What if Detlev gets to me, rips my brains out with Siamis's spell, and forces me to order my own army to cross the border in Norsunder's name?"

"Then you tell everybody if you don't sound like yourself . . ." Her mind raced ahead of her tongue. "Oh."

Every Marloven grew up knowing that you obeyed orders or you died.

Senrid said, "I thought about trying to change a thousand years or so of tradition, naming kings whose orders were flagrantly stupid, but Keriam pointed out to the seniors in command class that when everyone knows that the commander, whether king or riding captain, is responsible for the order, then people obey, knowing that even if they disagree, they're protected. It's those at the top who pay the price for stupidity. Eventually."

"And of course, if you issue a command to ignore you if you sound funny, then any troublemakers can claim you sounded funny if they don't like your orders."

"Right." He said in a low voice, "If Siamis gets to me, I think I'm going to order Keriam to pick up a crossbow and shoot me dead."

Hibern's insides cramped. She pressed her arms across her middle, and reached for logic. "But Senrid, people under Siamis's spell didn't have any volition, they just sort of existed. If you issue commands, you're going to have to sound like yourself, or nobody will believe you. You remember what people under the spell were like? Sleepwalkers."

"That was then. What if he's refined it, either he or his shit of an uncle?"

"Then you prepare a token, give it to some trusted people to drop a stone spell on you, with a transfer to Tsauderei's Valley of Delfina, where the wards are so ancient and so powerful that Norsunder never has broken them. Which is another reason I'm here. I think the alliance should pass the word to hide out there, if Siamis comes back looking for rulers to enchant. We all know people our age would be the easiest targets. If you end up there, Tsauderei will know what to do."

"That's not a bad idea." Senrid's expression eased. "Hibern, that's great. Have you written to Thad and Karhin to sound out the others?"

"Last night. But listen, Senrid. Here's what's important. If you're alive, there's a chance to fix things. If you're dead, you're dead. Would you do that to Marloven Hess, force Keriam to shoot you?"

"Would you be my heir?" His voice was thin, as if the words had been wrung from somewhere deep inside him.

Hiding the surge of nausea those words caused, she struck the air with the flat of her hand. He was unsettled now, but she knew instinctively that he would hate pity as well as sentiment. Much, much better to be brisk, treating the question as a joke. "I turned on you once, to prevent my becoming a gunvaer, remember?"

He grinned. "I thought you turned on me so you wouldn't have to marry *me*."

"You or anyone, I am not the kind of person to become a queen." Hibern managed to laugh, relieved to see him catching himself. It wouldn't do to let Senrid know how disturbing she found this conversation. "Look, nobody would accept me as Hibern-Gunvaer even if I wanted it. The Askans haven't put anyone in the field for generations, and you know how important that is to the jarls."

"I don't have anyone else."

"So, I'm very sorry, but you're just going to have to stay alive."

His gaze flicked back and forth between her eyes. She stared back, her eyes squinted against the cold. She knew her mind-shield was shut tight.

Senrid's quick grin was more pain than humor. "Right." He looked away. "I'm still making plans for possible invasion. Because Siamis took all that trouble to leave that coin here, so why not deny him what he wants most? If my wards vanish I've ordered the entire city guard to melt away—dress civ and become carters or blacksmiths or bricklayers. Same with the academy. And the army. Norsunder won't even get our horses."

"The horses will go into the Nelkereth Plains?"

"Yeah. Soon's we begin seeing grass, the stable girls have their orders to go to the plains and get lost. We're not waiting for word, we've decided the horses would like a summer out there even better than their usual winter."

"If you can get them there before the rains wipe out the trail, it'd take Norsunder Base's entire army just to find 'em and round 'em up."

"That's what Fenis Senelac promised. She's got relatives out there, in old Tlennen territory, and they know even the farther reaches. If my brains are enchanted out of my head, it'll take me time to round everybody up. Maybe by then someone will either shoot me or turn me into a statue."

"Go to Tsauderei's Valley before they can get you."

"Yes." He let his legs down, his heels knocking against the roof. "Is Liere all right?"

"Erai-Yanya sent her up north. Listen. Erai-Yanya thinks Liere might have been poisoned by the dyr. Carrying it so long."

"What?"

"You carried it," Hibern said, as he crouched down again, gazing intently into her face.

"Yes."

"Did it make you feel sick? Or anything?"

"Nothing like that. Well, except when we did the magic. Not sick. It . . ." Senrid shut his eyes, then said after a protracted pause, "It made me feel like my skull had vanished, and my thoughts spread out beyond the sky. Ech, how stupid that sounds in words. Why does Erai-Yanya think Liere is poisoned?"

"Haven't you asked yourself why she looks so . . ." Hibern put her thumb and forefinger together. "Frail, and like a sheet that has been washed too many times?"

"I think that's something she does to herself," Senrid muttered. "But maybe it could be due to the dyr. Except she looked like that when I met her, before we got the dyr. Of course she'd been on the run for months." He climbed quickly down to the wall, hopped to the ground, and walked away with his characteristic quick step.

Hibern sat there on the roof, considering how Senrid's dread kindled hers. It had been great, thinking about how Tsauderei and Erai-Yanya had looked at her with respect after her demonstration in Sartor, but the exhilaration dissipated like her breath in the cold air when she thought about what Senrid feared: a war they couldn't win.

But that didn't mean they couldn't try.

By now, calculating what time it was in various parts of the world took Hibern only a moment or two: it was early for the Mearsieans, but a promise was a promise.

She transferred to the white palace and was sent to the underground hideout, where she found them all at breakfast, including Clair.

The girls listened to the illusion idea, CJ and Clair thoroughly enthusiastic. Then, as usual, the rest of the girls turned the entire matter into a joke, offering silly suggestions like pie fights, or greased stairs, or short-sheeting beds. Hibern waited it out as long as she thought polite, then said she had to contact the rest of the alliance.

"You mean Fonebone," CJ said. "I even made up names for every kingdom, really funny ones, that the villains would never understand.

I've written about these to everybody, but nobody's written back. Maybe if you mention it?"

Hibern suppressed a sigh. Maybe being silly was the Mearsieans' way of dealing with fear. She said with what she hoped was a diplomatic tone, "I think that's your project. Meanwhile, if Siamis comes after you, get yourselves to the Valley of Delfina however you can."

"Okay," CJ said, thumping a thin fist into her palm.

*Norsunder Base*

The Norsunder Base resounded with the sharp voices of those antici- pating action. Gossip flew, and Lesca amused herself at her listening post, reporting to Dejain each night.

One day midway through winter, Kessler abruptly confronted De- jain. "Henerek is on his way to Everon," he said, answering one of the questions everyone had been asking.

She understood immediately that Kessler was following his own rule: even trade, one for one. She had not told anyone he was secretly learning magic. Rather than trying to extract a favor, or threatening to reveal some secret he'd winnowed out about her, like a normal person, he was offering a fact she might not know.

And she hadn't known that. Henerek and his followers had made a large noise about conducting a training mission in the mountains.

"On orders?" she asked, dread crowding her heart at the prospect of Kessler having learned enough magic to determine who had cast that blood-spell on him.

"Absent of," he said.

"Ah." She said, testing, "You could take this base. They'd all fol- low you."

"Why?" His expression didn't change, but he managed to convey contempt in the angle of a shoulder, the slight turn-away gesture of his right hand. "Why would I get them into shape just for Siamis to walk in and take over?"

When Kessler actually conducted a conversation, there was a reason. She ventured a guess. "You're leaving. To take Sartor in spite of Bos- tian?" She named one of the up-and-coming Norsundrian captains— this one obsessed with the desire to conquer Sartor, oldest kingdom in the world.

"He's an idiot," Kessler said. "Sartor is a bowl. Anyone who takes it can squat and say 'I hold ancient Sartor,' but what use is that? And while there aren't enough of 'em to put up much of a fight, I don't ever want to find myself in Shendoral again."

"He's asked me to ward Shendoral Forest," Dejain said, and when Kessler lifted his shoulder slightly and began to turn away, she said, "Chwahirsland?"

He flipped up the back of his hand. "It's a useless ruin. And Efael will one day send Wan-Edhe back."

She hid a flinch at the casual mention of the youngest and nastiest of the Norsunder's Host of Lords. She said, "You want a beachhead. In the east? That would either be Sarendan, or if you have ships, Khanerenth."

She had little interest in military planning, but she'd perforce learned something about it during the time she'd allied with Kessler. She knew he hated stupid questions. It was the sure way to get nothing from him, so she considered swiftly.

Both Sarendan and Khanerenth would put up a strong fight. He would like that, if he was to exert himself at all. Sarendan would furnish better supplies once he won, but there would be those mountains to get over before he could advance into the eastern end of the Sartoran continent, the prize being Colend, the richest country in the east— many said in the entire continent. Khanerenth would give him easier access to Colend, but scarcer supplies, and he would have to get there in ships. "You don't have ships. Or do you? Is that why we found Pengris's corpse at the foot of the mages' hallway? He'd been gloating about some find deep in Norsunder."

"Pengris winnowed out a stash of old transport-object artifacts that Detlev had secreted centuries ago against just this situation. Henerek killed Pengris for them. I just shifted the body, because Henerek set up the murder to point to me."

"Did Henerek get all Pengris's stash?"

Kessler turned away without answering, which she took as a no.

She called after him, "Sarendan or Khanerenth?"

He had nearly reached the end of the hall before he said, "Either promises to be fun, but Sarendan is closer."

## Chapter Four

*Sarendan*

ON a cloudless New Year's Firstday, the northern light shimmered on the ice like hammered silver as Peitar Selenna walked with his sister Lilah and Derek Diamagan into the throne room, which he seldom used, especially in frigid weather.

It was packed solid, which almost took the chill off. The marble columns were slick with moisture from so many breaths as he walked carefully up the shallow steps to the dais. Peitar no longer needed a crutch, or even a cane, but the echoes of old pain still twinged when he mounted steps, especially in the cold weather.

Lilah hopped up, grinning at her friends among the youngsters who'd started out calling themselves the Sharadan Brothers, in honor of Lilah's secret group during the war. The girls among the orphans left by the civil war had changed the name to Sharadan Brothers and Sisters— then Sharadan Sisters and Brothers—and now they were the Orphan Brigade.

Peitar's solemn expression lightened when he saw the eager faces, but then his humor vanished. Derek flashed a grin, and twiddled his fingers at his side, a semi-surreptitious wave, which sent a thrill through the mass of youngsters.

At the right, the King's Army not on duty roaming the borders stood in ranks, their captains at the front.

Peitar hated war. The prospect of it harrowed him to the edge of nausea. He hated the fact that he could do nothing to ward it, nor could he lead a defense.

"If there was anyone else," Derek had said the night before, as the three of them sat in the library, Lilah bouncing on her chair, "I'd happily relinquish command."

"Who else is there but you, Derek?" Lilah asked loyally.

Derek had spread his hands. "I've asked, and I've looked. I know I was no good leading the revolution, but I've learned so much at Obrin."

But had he learned enough? Peitar only knew that war was coming. If Norsunder Base was astir, the first two kingdoms likely to be overrun were Sartor and Sarendan.

So here he was. He stepped to the edge of the dais. His manner caused the front rows to fall silent. Gradually the rustles and whispers died away, and all faces lifted expectantly.

"As you have heard, Norsunder Base is on the march," Peitar said. "This is what Darian Irad, my uncle, had prepared for all his life, and his grandfather before him. But my uncle has gone to our sister-world to help there, and so the trouble has fallen to me, who has no knowledge of warfare."

He paused, and looked out over the straight ranks. "You are what remains of his army. Your commanders went into exile with my uncle, or died, as you all know. But this past year, Derek Diamagan, once considered your enemy, has gone among you to learn your skills."

A rustle from the brigade quickly died.

"I told you when I became king that I wanted no more division among the people of Sarendan, and Derek has done his best to bring everyone together again. The captains at Obrin have met with me, and we are agreed: to face this new threat, we need someone in command whom all will willingly follow. Someone whom you trust. Someone I trust."

Lilah and her friends held their breath.

"And so I come here before you to present Derek Diamagan, who is now Army Commander in Chief—"

His next words were lost in the spontaneous cheer that rose, first the high voices of the Brigade kids, who could not contain their joy. They were joined by the deeper voices of the army ranks.

Derek's grin flashed again, then he turned to Peitar and nodded, almost a bow. Everyone who knew him understood how important this moment was to him, how deeply he was aware of Peitar's trust, and how deep was his own trust in return. The cheering doubled in intensity and volume, going wild when Derek turned, eyes gleaming with tears as he raised his fist and shouted, "The king!"

"*The king! The king!*"

"Sarendan!"

"*Sarendan!*"

"Freedom forever!"

"*Freedom forever!*"

"Death to Norsunder!"

"*DEATH TO NORSUNDER!*"

Peitar's eyes closed. How many of them would be left alive when the coming war was over? The shouting voices brought back the shouting crowd of the revolution, and images of fire, the dead and dying, during those first terrible days of the revolution.

Derek glanced at Peitar's profile, saw the grief there, and raised his hand, tears drying on his lean, sunbrowned cheeks.

The noise died away. "I'll meet with all the captains for a strategy session. Orphan brigade captains, this means you, too. We won't leave you out."

A ragged treble cheer rose, and quickly died.

"We'll set up our defensive plan, and we'll spend the winter preparing, since spring is the most likely time for attack."

Another cheer rose.

When at last it ended, Peitar turned to go. Lilah lingered, looking between Derek, who was surrounded by army captains, and Peitar walking alone toward the back exit, then she ran after her brother. "What is it?" she cried. "I know a lot of people are complaining because our brigades are marching around drilling instead of doing spring planting, but you yourself said we have to defend Sarendan. And Derek is the best one to do it. So why are you upset?"

"I think . . ." Peitar studied his hands as if someone had written a message there. "Because I've seen the fervor of hatred of the former king and the army shift to hatred of Norsunder."

"And that's bad?" Lilah cried, hopping from toe to toe. "Why is that bad?"

"Because harnessing hatred is . . ." Peitar shook his head slowly. "Don't you see, Lilah? Because it's still hatred. It's such a powerful weapon, a poisonous one, and once loosed, can it ever be sheathed?"

*Sartor*

Anyone in Eidervaen could make the napurdiav—walk the palace's Purrad, the ancient labyrinth—except on Restday dawn, when it belonged exclusively to the royal family. That tradition had been ingrained for so many centuries that it carried the force of law.

On non-Restdays, Atan had gradually taken to appearing there before dawn, walking its four three-fold loops among the sheltering silver-leafed argan trees. She walked it in solitude with a candle in hand, but she was finding that frequency did not guarantee peace of mind. Maybe it was the impending war.

She meant to put war, and Julian, and her unspoken tension with the council out of her mind; she understood that she was not going to gain peace and insight if she brought her problems into the sacred space.

Or maybe it was memory. It had been Atan's idea to coax Julian to walk the Purrad with her, promising a reward if she completed it. What did she expect would happen? Atan resolutely forced herself to return to the starting point.

She was bitterly cold, yet tears burned her eyelids when she looked at the now-peaceful patterns of water-smoothed stones worked into the twelve points under the shelter of beautiful trees, and how Julian had run hither and yon screaming, kicking the stones, and yelling "Stupid! Stupid! Stupid!" when she discovered the 'reward' was to be a good feeling inside when the pattern was complete.

Atan stood, her breath shuddering against her ribs. She winked and blinked, trying to control the tears, but they came anyway, and so she gave up. It was already late. There would be no peace today.

She retreated indoors. She'd scarcely gone ten steps when the hiss of slippered feet heralded arrivals from a side hall, and there was Chief Veltos leading a young mage, maybe a few years older than Rel, his curly red hair a pleasant contrast to his blue robe. His greenish-blue eyes were wide as Chief Veltos bowed and said, "Your majesty. Nalar here witnessed a Norsundrian mage breaching the border." And to the mage, "Report."

Nalar bowed, speaking the entire time. "I was assigned to take the fourth-year students to the border to oversee the illusions leading to

Shendoral. I left the students to form a suitably aged-looking stone sign naming the western reach of Shendoral as Leath Wood, and transferred to the border to oversee what we had done."

He paused to glance at the chief, who nodded for him to speak.

"We were told that on no account must we permit anyone to see us. So I hid when I perceived a rider approaching from the south, a woman, wearing a white coat. She rode a gray. Difficult to see against the snow. I hid and watched. She rode alongside the river, with something in her hand."

"Magic?" Atan asked.

"I report only what I saw, which was little enough. However, whatever it was glowed blue briefly at the anchor point for the border protection. She bent and laid something on a rock, then rode the other way, past the bridge, to the west. I moved parallel to observe. When she reached the next anchor point, she laid something down, and then retreated to the bridge and rode across."

"When was this?" Atan asked.

"Not an hour ago," Nalar replied. "I transferred straight to the chief."

Veltos added, "She has broken the border wards with mirror spells. I myself just came from checking. Anyone can now come across between those two markers, without our knowing."

"It's got to be preparation for the invasion," Atan said, sick and cold inside.

"And she's riding ahead. She'll know at a glance what we've done. Whatever she's doing, she cannot discover the illusions," Chief Veltos exclaimed. "Or all our work comes to nothing."

Atan looked from one to the other. "What can we do?"

Chief Veltos said, "Nalar now knows where all our illusions are. I think he must transfer ahead of the woman and remove them all."

Nalar said apologetically, "We can always restore them as soon as she has passed. I know my students would—"

"No students," Chief Veltos said quickly. "This is a matter for mages. Your students may demonstrate what they've done. Then seniors only. If your majesty desires," she appended quickly, turning Atan's way.

Atan had been about to suggest she see for herself. But she knew what she was going to hear: her place was to hide, to stay away, with the useless youth. To agree to the command that Chief Veltos had just uttered, before her *If your majesty desires.*

So Atan did what was expected of her. But then she added, "I want to know what that woman is doing."

Chief Veltos bowed, not hiding her relief. "You shall know first thing."

Atan easily translated that to mean after the senior mages, the high council, and whomever else Chief Veltos deemed more important.

*Off the continent of Drael*

Eight and a half centuries ago, Tosta Orm, captain of the *Grebe's Claw* raider, which was one of the fleet of raiders attached to the warship *Gannet* of Lefsan House, had known that Rainorec, the doom of the Venn, was nigh.

Generations of the orderly Breseng kingship election had been disrupted by murder, followed by whispers about the Dag Erkric, who was said to practice blood magic. When House Lefsan ordered their entire battlegroup across the Sea of Storms to attack the Venn colony for no discernable reason beyond House politics, Orm and eight other raider captains decided to flee.

It was breaking every oath they had made. It meant, if they ever returned, a painful death atop the Sinnaborc Tower, it meant iron-torc shame for the entire family, but what meaning had any of it, if those who ruled no longer honored their own oaths?

When the scar-faced pirate dag named Ramis, master of an ancient drakan-ship, offered to the nine a transfer token out of the world, they had accepted it. In trade they agreed to carry whomever needed carrying once they found themselves back in the world. Two days out of the Land of the Venn, they were on their way to fetch their marine fighters, the Drenga, who had been on a training mission related to the attack. A convenient storm began to rise, and the ships wore out to win sea room while their sea dags shifted to the command ship to confer with the *Gannet*'s dag, who was Erkric's chosen.

This was their moment, or never, in spite of the weather. Nine ships hauled their wind and slipped away, a full sea-voyage of supplies in their holds. Each raider captain used the magical device that Scarface Ramis had given them, touching the fire-eyed gem to his captain's torc. The device created a night-black chasm, ripped between sky and sea. All nine ships sailed willingly into that crack between sky and sea . . .

. . . and Orm's ship emerged into bitter winter, nearly thrown by the frigid seas onto the shore.

Because he had ordered all *Grebe Claw*'s hands aloft before they had sailed into the chasm—expecting anything from ice-demons to firestorm—Orm was able to crack out an order that was instantly obeyed. Barely—barely—they skimmed the jagged rock teeth below the surf and beat out into the tiny bay.

But not before he witnessed, with his own eyes, this black-clad fellow with hair shorn like a thrall toss stones into the water in three different directions. These stones brought three more of his fleet out of the chasm, *Grebe's Eye*, *Grebe's Wing*, and *Grebe's Heart*. Orm's own heart mourned when he saw that his brother Luka, captain of *Grebe's Crest*, was among the five missing.

Who would be stupid enough to cause a sailing ship to emerge nearly on the shore, and on the last of the flood tide? Only the wind howling over the land out to sea, and his sailors' speed and strength, had kept them from beaching on this desolate coast, and all hands drowning.

Stupid as this fool perched on the rocks might be, Orm would keep faith with Scarface Ramis, who had kept his promise, unlike Orm's own people, for he had never seen this rocky coast before. Scarface Ramis's second promise was that they would be free to sail the seas once they completed their obligation.

And so Orm ordered the longboats down, and the three of his fleet who had sailed out of the chasm also lowered their boats. By the time the tide had turned to flow inward again, all those warriors perched upon the rocky jetty, and along the shore, had been brought aboard the ships.

It was then that the fool stamped into his cabin, and uttered a string of words. When Orm shook his head, the fool said distinctly, "Everon."

"Everon?" Orm repeated, wondering if this be name or verb.

Henerek had scowled at the pale-faced, flaxen-haired idiot before him, who didn't appear to understand a word of Sartoran, the most common language in the world, much less Norsundrian—an easy offshoot of Sartoran. Was this ship captain one of those idiot dawnsingers with their eternal, nauseating warbling, flitting around eating nuts and building treehouses?

Henerek glanced impatiently around the cabin, spotted rolled-up papers that had to be maps, and reached for them. "Everon," he stated louder, jabbing his thumb toward those maps.

The maps turned out to be charts, to Henerek a backward sort of map. He made no sense of the big one with the colored lines on it, but he recognized the shape of Drael's coastline above the long strait, and jabbed his finger on the place where Everon should be.

"Ev-er-on," he said distinctly. "Take us there."

Orm gazed at the chart, recognizing the coastline of Ymar. Why would this fellow wish to land above the better harbors at Jaro and Beilann? Though there were a few natural harbors, the coast rose steadily steeper, with treacherous currents around the many islands.

It did not matter. His pact with Scarface Ramis had been to serve as transport for whoever brought them back into the world. And so he would.

Three and a half months later, Orm's and Henerek's opinions of one another had not changed.

Orm took such a dislike to the arrogant young fool Henerek that he avoided direct contact, but he knew that a few of the young sailors had spent time with some of Henerek's younger warriors, trading words by sign, and when they'd found enough common words, they traded stories.

As for Henerek, he thought of ships as wagons on water, existing to ferry goods or transport warriors. He hated these Venn whose food stank of fish and vinegar, and their pale, arrogant gazes.

Three long months and more he had to endure the vile cold and wet of shipboard life, beginning with constant nausea as the ships tried to beat into howling east winds that sent them back again and again. Six weeks until they rounded the southeast corner of the continent, off Sarendan's mountainous coast. He'd expected them to pass that in a matter of days. Then they had to waste another three weeks in a desolate natural harbor while the Venn scavenged wood and rebuilt the masts destroyed in the worst of the storms.

At least the Venn captain obeyed his mandate to preserve the element of surprise by avoiding all other ships.

Or so Henerek assumed.

Orm paid no attention whatsoever to Henerek's orders, even after his youngest crew member, the boy in charge of flag signals, learned enough of the interloper's tongue to communicate. Long before he understood that Henerek wanted surprise, he'd said to his men at the whipstaff, "Keep every vessel that nicks the horizon hull down." And to the lookouts, "Mark any rigging. I want to know who's out there, or what's out there, but don't risk us being seen."

This order soon furnished the disturbing information that no rigging looked familiar: there were no signs of the distinctive Venn profile on the seas, nor the fore-and-aft rigging of the southern ships of their day.

Orm came to the conclusion that Scarface Ramis had caused them to sail beyond their own time long before the flag boy and Henerek's youngest scout found enough common words to trade personal information. They had gone nearly nine centuries beyond their time. Discovering what this new world might offer them must come after they ridded themselves of these warriors.

Orm counted the days.

Henerek counted the days.

The night before the fleet of four expected to make landfall in Everon's main harbor, the Venn flag boy and Henerek's scout sat on the taffrail eating hot, spicy buns and talking, hand motions taking the place of modifiers.

"Why you no survey first?" the Venn youth asked the scout.

"Commander was a boy in that harbor. Says he knows it. Says also, they notice a stranger nosing around." Seeing that most of his words confused the Venn, the scout put his hands up beside his face and spread his fingers. "Surprise!"

"Midday? Not so good. Dawn good," the Venn said, and motioned behind him. "Sun."

The scout shrugged. He didn't care about tides or any of the rest of that. What mattered to him was the fact that he wouldn't get to sneak in and scout out the harbor first, which was his job. But nobody crossed Henerek.

So the scout drilled with the others, each patrol having their own target. And once the harbor was secured, they'd march up the river to Ferdrian, the capital.

"If we're fast, and strike hard, four days will do it," Henerek predicted. "Six at the outside."

The next morning, half of the Norsundrians were puking again, as waves splashed along the heaving deck, and low clouds shot stinging arrows of sleet at sails, ship, sailors, and the massive kelp-veined breakers.

Two days later the storm died away, leaving fretful whitecaps on a running sea. The ships had worn well out into the ocean, making Henerek impatient. After so much toil, and waiting, his hand clenched with the mounting desire to strike his sword through King Berthold's heart.

Should he make the king kneel first? Roderic Dei was going to be kneeling before Henerek cut out his liver before the eyes of his daughters, but the one who was going to linger a very long time was that insufferable snot Valenn. Henerek was going to take out, as painfully as possible, every brooded-over insult and sneer upon the noble Lord Valenn's body . . .

Wind, weather, and tide finally appeared to be cooperating. Orm had been trained to rise well before dawn for the hour of meditation, a time to marshal the will and consider one's decisions, thus inspiring followers with surety and strength.

Orm had been reflecting through most of the night. When he was certain his fellow captains would be awake, he walked out onto his deck, noted everyone in place, discipline tight in spite of all the changes and those unspeakable Norsundrians snoring and farting in the hold, so sick they scarcely had the strength to mutter the Waste Spell.

He ran up the 'captains meet' flag himself, and bade the duty hands to let down his boat without making noise. And, as when they decided to leave the world (except then it had been all nine), he met his fellow captains in the waters between the ships, the boats bumping against one another, as they all knew how sound carried over the sea.

"Midday?" *Grebe's Heart's* captain repeated, hoarse with his effort not to shout his disbelief. "He wants the midday tide, when he has the perfect tide at the perfect time, the sun directly behind him to confuse 'em?"

"Won't listen, won't risk the boats before there's light," Orm said. "Thinks his attack will come as a surprise."

*Grebe's Wing's* captain snorted, his blue gaze wide. "Surprise? There are only two places between those two rivers for an attack. His enemy must be asleep, not to expect them."

The others agreed, for they all had seen the chart. The southeast corner of Everon had flat beaches, but that meant a very long march all across the kingdom to the city now serving as the capital. The only other place was the estuary that opened into the natural harbor. Surely it was guarded. Everywhere else were tall, rocky cliffs, with jagged rocks below. A deadly coast.

They considered that, then they considered their passengers, as the water wash-washed against the hulls of their boats.

"Norsunder," said *Grebe's Eye's* captain. "You hear they are evil," he began.

"Any worse than Erkric?" Orm retorted.

*Grebe's Eye's* captain raised his hands. "I know. I know. All mages seem bent on bringing Rainorec the sooner. My point is, evil they may be, but stupid?"

"Land warriors," said *Grebe's Wing*'s captain. "Arrogant as our Drenga."

"Who at least were Venn, by the Tree!" exclaimed *Grebe's Eye*'s captain, and the others agreed. "But we are oath-sworn to land them, stupid plan or not."

"And this is why I signaled you," Orm said. "I know you will not like this any better than I, but I'd rather lose timber than lives. I say, let them take our boats. We aren't trained in landing attack any more than they are."

"So you are certain there is no surprise, that the defenders are expecting them?"

"Even if they are not, we know how difficult it is to land a force and go straight into attack. We've watched our Drenga drill landings again and again, and even they can suffer accidents. I don't think these know what to do from sea to shore, however good their skills are once they stand on firm ground." Orm shook his head. "I don't foresee anything but trouble, and this is not our fight. Our oath to Scarface Ramis was to bring them to their destination, which we have now done. Let them take our boats. We will build new ones."

The other three agreed, one reluctantly, one angrily. But they agreed.

They were all there watching from the sides, rigging, and yards of their ships as Henerek and his force clambered down into the boats.

Henerek was furious, of course. He'd expected the Venn to row them neatly ashore, then conveniently vanish. But he'd seen them drilling on deck, and knew that a fight would seriously harm his own people. And even if he won, how was he going to force the Venn to get them safely ashore?

The Venn had expected rich amusement from the sight of the Norsundrians clambering down the steep tumblehomes and dropping into the boats tossing alongside. They weren't disappointed. A gratifying number of Norsundrians managed to drop between boat and ship, or overbalance if they made it to the boat, but none of them drowned. Silver drams exchanged hands as a result of wagers.

The Venn also expected some entertainment out of watching Henerek's force attempt the oars. A couple boats spun in circles, oars clattering and clashing amid hot curses, but shouted orders from neighboring boats made it clear that some'd had experience on the water.

Would that experience extend to beach landings, the worst sort of attack short of running uphill? Orm and his captains watched through their glasses, expecting to see a rain of arrows commence at that vulnerable moment when the boats hit the breakers.

And so it would have been, had not Lord Valenn commanded the harbor defense. Orm and his captains noted the uncharacteristic quiet of the ships bobbing in the harbor, yards crossed, no one in sight, the lack of the usual harbor business on quay and jetties. Even the harbormaster's tower flew no flag.

"Lying in wait," Orm said to his second in command.

They watched until their boats, inexpertly rowed by the Norsundrians, reached the breakers. Two boats turned sideways as oars flailed uselessly, and broached to, spilling out warriors. More wager tokens exchanged hands.

Orm cast one last look at those suspiciously empty ships, and smacked his glass closed. "I'd say they're waiting on a signal, and we are not part of this foolery." He motioned to the flag boy. "Signal 'make sail.'"

The Venn ships' yards bloomed, sails catching the wind, the distinctive prow, not seen on that coast for centuries, turning seaward.

Up behind cover, Lord Valenn watched through his glass. "There is no retreat," he murmured. "Unless there are more ships beyond the horizon."

"Oh, let us shoot," Harn said anxiously, taking no notice of the ships. His attention was on Henerek's people forming into groups, weapons ready. "Look at that. There has to be a thousand of them."

"And they're scrambling about, soggy wet," someone else said. "We should attack now, while they're still fishing their fellows out of the water."

Valenn silenced his young knight-cadets with a stern look. "We are Knights. We take no action without honor. As soon as Henerek is on firm ground, we will proceed as planned."

'Honor.' It silenced discussion. If attacking an invading enemy while they were relatively weak was dishonorable in the eyes of their admired leader, well, nobody wanted to be the one to suggest otherwise.

Valenn returned his attention to his field glass, and ah, there he was, just as Rel had said. Henerek was instantly recognizable, though he had changed considerably from the weedy, pouting boy Valenn remembered, always shirking the more boring tasks, always looking for insult, and whining about privilege and rank without ever understanding the weight of duty commensurate with that privilege.

As soon as Henerek reached the shore, Valenn snapped his field glass to, handed it to his squire with a word of thanks, checked to see that his gloves were not awry, and glanced right and left at his flank captains to make certain they knew their orders. When he received short nods in return, he straightened up, walked around the wagon that had served as his cover, and started alone down the quay. His heart thundered, but he breathed deeply, aware of his sword loose in its scabbard.

Henerek marked him immediately, his sharp features aligning into a smirk. Around and behind him, he heard the rustle of cloth and the creak of blackweave straps as shields, slung over backs for the landing, were pulled around.

Surprise was gone. "Surprise," Henerek shouted anyway, a little too soon. His voice was weakened by the shore wind.

Valenn resisted the impulse to call "What?" just to disconcert Henerek. Weak his voice might have been on the wind, but Valenn had heard it, and he would stay strictly within the rules of war.

So he bided his time as he walked up to Henerek, who put out a hand, holding back his dripping force. So far, the rules had been obeyed.

"Henerek. Your quarrel was with me. I challenge you to single combat."

Henerek's smirk widened. "And here I thought you were strutting out to take us all." He glanced to the side, making a long face, and won some snickers from his force. "We were trembling in fear."

Valenn's heartbeat quickened as Henerek took one, then another sauntering step nearer. He seemed no worse for being soaked to the waist, in spite of the cold wind of early spring, and his boots making squelching noises at each step. Somewhere, someone had seen to it that he had developed enough discipline to put on muscle.

Valenn resisted the impulse to clear his throat, and spoke slowly, to keep his voice calm and measured. "If you win, then let battle be joined. If I win, you will return whence—"

Henerek began to shake water from a glove, and as Valenn's gaze flicked that way, Henerek used his other hand, driving a hidden short blade through Valenn's ribs and up in a vicious undercut.

Pain flowered through Valenn, followed by spreading numbness in knees, joints, lips.

"Surprise," Henerek said again, laughing as Valenn fell dead at his feet. "Damnation," he exclaimed, stepping over him. So much for the week of protracted play. Already the plan was going sideways—

Sitting there waiting for Norsunder to attack had been unnerving, but seeing their leader cut down without warning shot red rage through the defenders. The two flank captains were not quite a heartbeat apart in signaling their archers.

A familiar crackling sound followed by a very familiar hissing hum, and here was the steel-tipped rain. Shields whipped up and the hiss became a hammering thud as arrows hit them.

Henerek extended his hand, and the patrols took off to envelop the harbor—the fastest runners jerking in surprise then tumbling to the ground as ropes, hidden in the mud, winched taut.

Henerek's fury ignited. So maybe the Everoneth were not the hapless idiots he'd come to believe. That only made him angrier.

A couple quick steps and Aldi Nath, his senior captain, joined him. She was a square woman with a frizz of light hair, her face seamed by years of sun. "This isn't a day's defense. They've had all winter to dig in." She lifted her chin toward the apparent clutter of wagons, stacked barrels, and dilapidated barns.

Henerek glanced back. The Venn were gone. Half the boats were beached, half bobbing around in the waves. As he watched, shielded groups of Everoneth splashed into the surf and began chopping the centers out of the boats; as his rear guard ran to engage them they scattered, two-legged turtles under their shields.

Henerek's master charge was already disintegrating into fierce little battles everywhere.

Nath's light eyes narrowed.

All Henerek knew about her was that she'd been some kind of guard before she lost her fiery temper once too often, and ended up with a stone spell on her, in some Garden of Shame, until some other Norsundrian went harvesting. "If we take the harbormaster's tower, and set a defensive perimeter," she said, "we can regroup and relaunch."

Henerek gave a short nod. So the Everoneth wanted a fight. Well, he'd never really expected surrender. He'd give them a fight. "Do it."

## Chapter Five

*The Garden of the Twelve, Norsunder-Beyond*

THE garden was beautiful: each blossom perfect, each blade of grass green, each shrub full of shiny new leaves. All frozen by enchantment at the point of death, Yeres had said with her slow smile, just showing the tips of her teeth, the first time she brought Siamis there as a child, before handing him off to her brother's untender lack of mercy.

At that time, he'd been a terrified boy of twelve. Now he found the lovely, dead garden a precious conceit, while still appreciating the implied threat.

Yeres could not get into his mind, though it seemed to amuse her to keep trying. Yeres and her brother Efael had been born on another world, plucked from there by Svirle, who found their inventive viciousness useful and their perversions entertaining. They did not have Dena Yeresbeth, which guaranteed that they would never be equal to the architects of Norsunder, though Yeres expended great effort with magical mind-tortures in an effort to gain similar skill.

Timelessness, Siamis had discovered, growing in fits and starts as four thousand years rolled away beyond Norsunder's gates, could hang curiously heavy in the borderland places where the body was not merely an illusion.

Yeres stepped close to him, tipping her chin back to look up into his face. Seemingly they stood alone in the Garden of the Twelve, but here, no sense could be trusted, even on the mental plane: the layers of lies and deception appeared to be endless, an eternal fall that never reached the ground of truth.

The implication, he knew, was that there was no truth to be found.

"So you'd left your sword behind as a threat? How charming," Yeres said as she traced a finger from the hilt of the now-recovered sword named Emeth to the top of Siamis's hand. He did not respond, but knew better than to move.

She was close enough for him to smell the floral scent that did not quite mask her brother's musk. Siamis's stomach clenched. The physical memories, usually quiescent, stirred briefly, but he was long practiced at shutting those away.

"Not a threat," he said, sidestepping her deliberate ambiguity by assuming the context was Bereth Ferian's mages. "Merely another move in the game."

The corners of her smile tightened. "Provocative."

"Entertaining," he said austerely, taking refuge in obliviousness. When he was twelve she had enjoyed watching Efael toy with him.

His first defense had been to take refuge in their expectations: if he bored them long enough, they punished him for it, but then they went away. "And your little game in Marloven Hess?" she asked.

"I thought that was obvious," he replied. "Detlev wants the Montredaun-An boy isolated and angry, ripe for recruitment when the time comes. That was a gambit to hasten things along." It had also been a gambit to test how closely he was observed.

The answer: right now, very closely indeed.

So, time to be both boring and cooperative. "Oalthoreh and her minions provided a protracted lesson in their current arsenal of wards," he said, and began reciting a catalogue of magical defenses observed through the Norsunder Base window until the Bereth Ferian mages made it a little too obvious they knew they were being spied on. But they had done what Siamis had expected of them until then: kept watching eyes busy.

He could feel Yeres's disinterest in his catalogue, but it, like their apparent isolation in the Garden, could be another deception. Her waylaying him could be mere cupidity or whim, but it was more likely a deflection. And always a test.

Still talking, he took an easy sidestep, and dropped onto the stone bench, where he leaned back and propped one foot on a decorative stone. He clasped his hands around his knee as he kept up the catalogue.

Though he'd never had any interest in the twins' sexual preferences beyond defensive tactics, he had learned that Efael always took his targets off-world, the young ones terrified, the older ones full of fight, the only common pattern being their unwillingness; Yeres had nauseated Siamis long before he had the remotest interest in such things with lingering, lascivious descriptions of what a good lover her brother was, and how that tenderness might be earned. Her tastes were for young men, or boys just barely over the threshold, the prettier the better. Above all, she liked the spice of seduction. Adoration was sweet for a time; the only mood she seemed indifferent to was perfunctory acceptance.

When the tracing finger drew up his leg, he obliged by setting his heel on the grass, his knees wide, as he embroidered the theme of the Bereth Ferian mages' ignorance. He was the very picture of perfunctory acceptance.

When the toying finger lifted, he permitted no reaction, not even an alteration in his breathing. ". . . and it suits us to keep them on the hop."

"Us," she repeated. "You are such a very good boy, aren't you? Running errands for your protector?"

"Detlev is not my protector," he said, permitting a hint of his ready anger to heighten his tone.

Yeres smiled. "And yet here you are, his loyal minion. How sweet is the family bond."

"I like his plans. So I'll obey his orders," he retorted. "Until I don't."

That made her laugh, as she twined her fingers through the lock of hair that had dropped on his forehead. In the Garden, which was mostly her design, she had all the power. All he had were his wits.

She left his hair and the finger traced around his ear as she leaned close. "What does he really want in Geth? Humans have been there half as long as they have here. Not even half."

"Without nearly eradicating themselves as well as magic." He stated the obvious to be boring, to prod her toward her purpose. When her eyelids briefly shuttered, subtle as a butterfly's antennae, he ventured a verbal backstep. "Detlev insists that their transfer magic can be learned and brought here, the intention to force rifts."

"Why have we not heard about this?"

He lifted a shoulder. "Because he's still seeking the fundamentals. If he's right, this method is akin to intensifying the effect of light through refraction, the mirror behind the sconce. Can it be intensified enough to rip a hole in the between?"

Rifts. Even the Host of Lords could not move until the powerful spell that Evend of Bereth Ferian had sacrificed his life in making could be broken, permitting rifts once again between Sartorias-deles and Norsunder-Beyond.

She lifted her hand, and sighed. "You had better get to it, then, errand-boy. Your master is waiting."

He made the sign to transfer to Norsunder Base. As soon as the transfer magic dissipated he walked straight through a cleaning frame, and resisted the nearly overwhelming impulse to step through a second time, as if her touch, and that whiff of Efael, still lingered. But he knew it didn't; a second step-through would do nothing but raise interest, if he was being watched.

He intended to get a meal and listen to a status report at the same time, but the first two sentences spoken by the desk flunky in the command center caused him to abandon his meal untouched: in her last gesture of spite, Yeres had not kept him a few hours, she had kept him for nearly two years. In those two years, the Base had apparently disintegrated into quarreling factions, resulting in Henerek going off to invade Everon, Bostian busy planning to march on Sartor with all the warriors Henerek and Kessler didn't want—all stupid, short-sighted campaigns that made a hash of this crucial stage of Detlev's plans. And no sign of Detlev.

Siamis went to fetch the world transfer token from Detlev's warded room, where he stood, tossing the transfer token on his hand as he considered his next move.

Yeres's purpose had been to anger Detlev. And he would be angry. But she wanted the anger to fall squarely on Siamis.

Power, he had long ago decided, was a fluid concept. In the Garden of the Twelve, it meant privacy. Yeres spied as she willed, and expended much effort in breaking into minds, yet she herself was used by Svirle or Ilerian, whose thoughts, and intentions, were shared with no one.

If Yeres didn't know what Detlev was doing on Geth, then that meant Efael didn't know, either. Efael's most recent surge of malice was probably the result of his being warded from Detlev's project on Five, which meant that Yeres's random pulse of concupiscence was the first move in their latest lethal game.

Well, figuring out that game was for later. Right now? She had yanked Siamis's strings, so he'd better be dancing.

But before he could nerve himself for the bone-socket wrench of world transfer to Five, Detlev himself appeared in a whirl of singed metal smell.

Of course he'd have a window; impossible to know who else did. Siamis sustained the mental contact as Detlev reviewed the memory of the conversation with Yeres. He was clearly irritated at finding Norsunder Base nearly empty, the captains scattered pursuing their own plots.

Siamis was supposed to be holding the Base in readiness. Detlev said contemptuously, as avid eyes all around watched and eager ears listened, "You walked right into that, didn't you?"

Siamis retorted, "I was in Norsunder on your order."

"You may commence your dance." Detlev flicked his fingers. "But leave Marloven Hess to me."

*Sixthmonth, 4742 AF*
*Sartor*

What remained of the Sartoran Guard still patrolled the outskirts of the city, and the southern border, below which Norsunder Base existed in constant threat. Mendaen of the Rescuers, now captain of a small company, was riding the familiar road between the capital and the border when a cloud of dust ahead signified someone galloping belly to the ground.

Mendaen urged his mount to the side, but placed his hand on the hilt of his sword. That hand fell away when he recognized one of his border scouts, a seventeen-year-old redhead, who pulled up, eyes round as robin's eggs.

"They're coming!" the scout gasped.

"Who—what, Norsunder?" Mendaen demanded.

"Yes. Riders and marchers both, in column!"

Mendaen muttered, "It has to be an advance force. Go—" No. He looked at the scout's sweaty horse, then said, "Ride back and tell the patrol to go to ground. Don't attack. Just watch. My horse is fresh—I'll get word to Eidervaen."

The scout wheeled about to obey.

Mendaen kneed his mount into a canter, then let her stretch her legs into a gallop as they rode hard for home. That was orders, any sighting was to be reported. He hated the thought of just standing by, but a hundred Royal Guards scattered from the border to the north of the city was not going to do much against an invading army except serve as target practice.

He didn't slow until he spotted Eidervaen's towers on the horizon. By now he was dodging traffic on the royal road, forcing him to ride up embankments and splash across summer-shallow streams, as the Guard no longer carried pennants that gave them the right-of-way.

Orders were specific: report first to the mages, not to the palace. That wouldn't keep him from yelling the news as he passed down the great parade ground before the palace, if he spotted anyone he knew, who might be able to get to Atan first. But all he saw was poor little Julian, still looking no older than six and filthy and bedraggled as ever, crouched down as she fed bits of something to a flock of birds. Probably her lunch.

Mendaen rode straight to the mage headquarters. He tossed the reins to a waiting apprentice, shouted, "Walk her," past the boy's inquiry after his business, and ran inside. "Where is the mage chief?"

A very short time later, there was Chief Mage Veltos. At least she listened as Mendaen delivered his one-sentence report. Then she turned her head and began handing out orders to the blue-robed mage students crowding around, beginning with, "You. Report at once to the queen."

Once all of the mage students had been sent with orders, Veltos shifted her attention back to Mendaen. "Thank you for being timely. You may go."

Mendaen was now free to spread the news, as the mages, who had been practicing emergency procedures daily, went in ordered haste about their arrangements.

Veltos stood in the headquarters and took a deep breath, mind racing with tasks to protect the city. Presently a young student pattered up in slippered feet, saying, "Chief Veltos! I was sent by Verias at the desk. The alarm protection on South Road, it—"

"Thank you," Veltos interrupted. "Return to your classroom." So, the magic alarm laid over the road was not faster than a human, probably because the magic required proximity, and that Guard's patrollers had seen the evidence of the approaching invaders some distance off. She must remember that.

A short time later, she, Atan, and certain senior mages stood on the cliff where, during winter, they had first planned this elaborate illusion. At the first sight of the long column riding up the road, she suppressed the urge to hide behind a boulder. The mages had already cast illusions before themselves—if the enemy should look up their way, they would only see a blurred reflection of the sky overhead. As long as no one moved, there would be no reason to look hard.

Atan stood by Veltos, her fingers gripped tightly as the black-clad enemies, each holding a spear, rode steadily toward the crucial point. None of them seemed to be looking at any of the illusory terrain.

Closer . . . closer . . .

Without any hesitation, they rode past the true turn in the road, and headed down the false curve. In complete silence, Atan and her mages watched until a forested hill intervened, hiding the enemy from view.

Atan said to Veltos, "I'm going. I have to see." And before the chief mage could voice the objection Atan saw in her face, she touched a transfer token she'd secreted in her pocket, whispered the transfer word, and felt herself jolted from the cliff to a hiding place she'd selected in spring without anyone knowing.

Veltos, furious at the useless risk their young queen was taking, had long since arranged for another vantage from which she could observe the road. Separated in heart as well as by distance, she and Atan watched from behind the safety of trees as, two by two, the invaders rode straight into the sun-dappled shadows of Shendoral Wood.

*Marloven Hess*

Senrid's two visits to Chwahirsland had been a dramatic lesson in the difference between light and dark magic. Light magic was useless for military purposes, no matter how many spells you layered. It would run off harmlessly, like an overfilled bucket. Dark magic was not much better, unless you interlocked dangerously volatile spells that required a terrible cost. Chwahirsland was living proof of that.

Senrid could consult Keriam on everything except magic. That, he alone was responsible for. So he'd decided not to rely solely on the illusions, which were too easy to get rid of once you knew they were there, but to create a spiderweb of tracers along the border. By the time any Norsundrian could dismantle his webwork of tracers, Senrid would know, and could get his secondary plan—equally laboriously put together with Keriam—into action.

He was so certain the threat would come in the middle of the night that he'd taken to sleeping in his clothes, with his notecase next to his dagger under the pillow.

But he was halfway through breakfast on a bright morning that promised a hot summer when the mental poke somewhere behind his eyeballs caused him to look around for a heartbeat. He dropped his bread onto his plate.

"The tracers," he said to the bread crumbs.

He thrust his hand into his shirt pocket, where he had stashed his fast-escape ensorcelled shank button, then he whispered the transfer spell that would pull him to whatever, or whoever, had tripped the tracer.

Shock washed through him with the impact of ice when he came out of the transfer reaction to find himself high on a cliff overlooking a winding river valley that he recognized instantly.

Standing at the extreme edge, looking down, was Detlev.

Senrid clutched his escape shank and said his transfer word. Horror suffused him when he found it blocked.

Detlev said, "Sentiment?" One hand, an empty hand, gestured toward the scene below.

"It is not!" Then the real meaning struck Senrid: Detlev knew very well that sentiment was no part of why Senrid had chosen this cliff to anchor his tracer web. He'd chosen it as a reminder of the humiliating defeat he had suffered while watching his own people being slaughtered by Norsunder.

There'd be no Erdrael now.

Detlev watched the slow river winding down the middle of the valley below, a random updraft stirring the light brown hair on his brow.

Senrid stood poised to run, knowing he probably didn't have a chance. He'd run anyway if he saw even a sliver of opportunity.

Detlev said to the view, "Incompetent in two forms of magic, are you? Now that, I am afraid, can only be attributed to sentiment."

His left hand came into view, also empty, but Detlev didn't need to carry weapons. One thing all the records agreed on, he could kill with a thought.

Detlev glanced upward, then to either side, as if listening to something or someone Senrid could neither see nor hear. His impassive expression altered to faint disgust, as if he regarded shoddy workmanship, then he met Senrid's gaze, the morning sun striking a cold pinpoint of light in the center of his hazel-framed pupils as he said, "It seems there is another demand for my attention. When I do find the time to undertake your education, you will not see me coming."

He vanished. Leaving Senrid to discover that the entire webwork of wards and tracers he and Hibern had labored over so painfully had been swept into nonexistence, like a stick through a spiderweb.

Senrid gave himself a few moments to breathe as his heart thudded in his ears. He dared not transfer with his carefully prepared token, lest Detlev had altered it somehow. He flung it away with all his strength, then stood there with his breath shuddering, his knees watery, as the shank spun end over end until it vanished below.

He braced—and spoke the old transfer spell.

Magic flung him inside out, then restored him in his study. Alive. Unharmed. He forced watery limbs into motion, and presently dashed through Keriam's office door, panting for breath.

Keriam glanced at Senrid's pale face, his pupils huge and black, and his pen dropped. He had never seen Senrid that afraid, even in the darkest days under the threat of his uncle.

"Detlev." Senrid whispered the name, as if the man could hear across time and space. "He was there. My protections . . ." He snapped his hand flat, as though smashing something away. "Give the signal," he croaked. "It's begun."

Keriam strode to the door, beckoned to the runner waiting outside, and said, "Sound the retreat."

Senrid heard the rap of departing footsteps, and within a very short time the tower overhead rang *tang-tang, tang-tang*, the signal for which everyone had been practicing all summer.

Senrid ran to Keriam's tower window, which looked out over the academy. For a heartbeat or two, nothing could be seen. Then as the garrison bell picked up the rhythm, *tang-tang*, and then the south tower, followed by the city bell, Senrid saw orderly lines of boys running low to the ground below a wall. One by one the boys vaulted the wall into the corral, then completely vanished from sight.

Elsewhere, a couple of blond heads bobbed, then vanished abruptly, as if yanked. Senrid imagined lines of boys running low along the fences and vanishing into the practice grounds beyond the stables, and from there following the lines of creeks into wilder country, where he knew that the senior boys in charge of each group had stashed supplies.

All over the castle, the garrison guards had gone into alert mode. Runners would be departing through the gates to warn the army garrisons to vanish. Everything happening just as he'd planned.

It was a relief to see those empty stone corridors, but fear still churned inside him, twisted into worry—what if he was wrong, and Detlev wasn't launching an army over the border? There had been that moment of distraction before he uttered that last threat.

Senrid scowled down at the empty academy. Why else would Detlev come to Marloven Hess? Unless the target was not the kingdom, but Senrid himself. *You will not see me coming.*

"Senrid," Keriam said, more loudly.

Senrid realized the commander had said his name a couple of times. He looked up, as Keriam said gently, "They're gone. Now it's your turn."

*At the same time*
*Sarendan*

The galloper dashed into Peitar Selenna's private family chamber in his palace in Miraleste. The teenage scout, mud-splashed to the waist, nose and ears raw with cold, had ridden through a wild hailstorm to bring the news.

"They're coming," he declared, eyes wide with excitement. Then bowed belatedly, falling against a curve-legged table in his weariness.

Peitar's heart constricted, more at the excitement in the boy's face than at news too long dreaded to be a surprise.

Derek got to his feet. "I'd better join my defenders."

"Wait. Wait," Lilah exclaimed.

"I don't think you ought to ride at night. Especially in this weather." Peitar indicated the rain beating against the windowpanes, as he signed to a waiting servant to take the shivering galloper somewhere and get something hot into him.

"Storm's nearly blown." Derek flashed his careless grin. He was excited, too. "You know I'm used to riding in bad weather." He turned to Lilah. "Norsunder won't wait."

Lilah swallowed, then said stubbornly, "I have to pack."

"Pack?" Peitar and Derek said together.

She forced a nod. "I promised the orphan brigade. I would fight with them."

"Most of the younger orphans are staying right here in the city," Derek said, with a glance at Peitar's distraught expression.

Derek felt the same way about sending children into battle. He eyed

Lilah, a sturdy figure for a child, but in no way ready for what lay ahead. "You haven't been drilling but during summer," he began.

It was the wrong tack. "Same with many prentices," she retorted, bravely meeting that assessing gaze. At least Derek wasn't angry. She had seen him angry, the day he started the revolution, and she dreaded his anger. "They had to divide between work and drill. I *promised*." Her voice rose anxiously as she turned in desperation from one to the other, afraid of a worse thing than bad language and glares: that they were going to laugh at her. Dismiss her promises with a sickening, *But you're just too young.* "I promised."

Derek heard Peitar stirring, but half-raised a hand. "All right, then. If you can beat me in a sword fight, you can go with me."

"Beat you?"

"If you can beat me, then you can beat a Norsundrian," Derek said reasonably. "But if you can't, then all you'll do is serve as target practice, which will make everybody who didn't defend you feel terrible. Want that?"

"No," she said grittily. "All right. Let's go. Right now."

They trooped off to the salle, where Derek chose one of the side rooms, away from the city guard's own drill space. Lilah looked doubtfully at the weapons—real ones, not wood—and said, "How many tries do I get?"

"As many as you like," Derek said.

She picked up a sword, braced, and held it up. And attacked.

He struck the blade out of her hand.

She ran to get it, saying over her shoulder, "I wasn't ready."

"That's all right," Derek said. "Go ahead, strike when you are."

Peitar began to breathe again as three times, Lilah launched herself grimly at Derek, who blocked her moves, then struck the sword out of her hand.

After the third, she sighed, wringing her numb fingers. Her throat tightened with defeat. "If you see any of my friends, tell them I tried."

"None of them will be there," Derek said soberly. "We put all the orphan brigade through a similar test."

Lilah turned away, aware of a sickening sense of relief. It felt like betrayal, somehow.

Derek set out a short time later, his galloper having been fed and issued new, warm clothing and a fresh mount. His news had been lamentably brief, not much more than that a sizable force had been spotted in one of the older mountain passes. Peitar and Derek had hired shepherds to watch all the passes, against this very situation.

As Derek climbed onto his horse, he thought grimly that already they were at a disadvantage. Shepherds were not militarily trained: they didn't even think of counting heads, noting weapons, and so forth. He was going to have to fix that if they survived this attack, he promised himself. He saluted the two anxious faces up in the library window and rode off.

As soon as Derek was out of sight, Peitar withdrew to let Tsauderei know.

Derek's mood rose as he and his scout rode through the city gates. All right, they were through waiting, at least. It was finally time for action, a realization that filled him with fierce joy. This was so much better than the revolution: a clear enemy, and training behind his army.

He and the scout verbally sifted the few words of the brief report for any stray details. So far, at least, everything was going exactly according to plan. He'd put their very best people in the south, camping in Diannah Wood. From there it would be relatively easy to reach any of the southwest passes, as they all debouched roughly in the same area, feeding the rivers that spilled into Tseos Lake below Miraleste.

Derek left the exhausted galloper at the first changing post, then set out alone on a fresh horse under a clear sky. The moon crested the mountains, not full, but casting enough light over a road Derek knew well.

He slept in snatches in the saddle, pausing long enough to get bread and cheese at the posts he'd established along the road in order to change horses.

At noon the third day, he rode into his camp, where he found everyone honing weapons, their voices sharp with excitement. They sent up a cheer when they saw him. "Come," he said to the three captains. "Let's look at the map one more time."

They had worked up contingencies for all the passes, but now that they knew which one would bring them face to face with the enemy, it was reassuring to go over everything again. He felt it, and he could see it in the captains, the old, grizzled one—a stonemason who had fought for Khanerenth in his youth—his son, and the upright captain with the neatly tied-back dark hair, who had been a patrol leader under the old king.

Derek no longer resented the remnants of the king's army. War was really happening, soon. Now that it was close, doubt twisted his guts. He looked at that patrol captain, remembered the inefficient scout report, and once again wished he had the equivalent of the old king's army, with its training and discipline—but without the arrogant nobles.

It was then that they heard noise outside the tent, high voices protesting and low voices arguing. He burst out to discover three boys struggling in the arms of older fellows.

"I promised Ma he wouldn't be here," declared the tallest, a rust-thatched young silversmith, his voice breaking as he fought to contain his eleven-year-old brother, nicknamed Ruddy.

Derek signed for the boys to be let go, then frowned at them. "I told you all to stay in Miraleste. You'll be needed as scouts and errand runners."

"Not if you fight 'em off here," Ruddy said fiercely.

"Lilah said she's coming," a twiggy blond, son of a seal-maker, spoke up.

"She's in Miraleste," Derek said. "She'll be a runner for the king."

A brief silence, then Ruddy burst out, "But she and the real Sharadan Brothers, they were in the revolution. They were *heroes* in the revolution."

"But they didn't fight," Derek said, at the same time as Ruddy's older brother said, "They got information, and thieved from collaborators. Anyways, that was us against us. Not us against Norsunder."

The third boy, the lanky son of a joiner, muttered, "So Lilah is a princess. Of course they'd keep *her* safe. Bren is somewhere fighting, I bet anything."

Derek heard the scorn in the word 'princess,' knowing that the boy was reflecting his own contempt for royalty, nobles, and their attitudes. But now was not the time to be divisive. "Bren is also going to scout, but in his town. Listen, since you sneaked here uncaught, that means you're good at sneaking. We were just saying that we need more scouts up above the pass, to signal us when Norsunder is spotted. The most important post, right now, is that. Go up the trail and report to Granny Innah, who has a magic ring. You say the word 'Sarendan' and touch the stone, and the captain here will know that Norsunder is sighted, so we move into position."

The older captain held up his hand, displaying the ring twin to the one the scout had.

"Now that we know which pass is the one, Granny Innah will probably want you on different cliffs, to make sure we see every possible trail, in order to get the earliest sighting," Derek said. "Get some trail supplies, because she won't have enough for you, and run!"

The three brightened at having real orders, important orders. Within a short time the boys had journey-bread and vanished up a back trail.

The silversmith said to Derek, "Thanks. My brother thinks it's a game. He doesn't remember seein' our dad lying dead in the street, trampled by the mob during the revolution. Wasn't even the king's men that did for him." A brief flick at the dark-haired captain. "All he remembers is, Dad was a hero. But Ma remembers, and she made me promise."

Derek said, "I know. She made me promise, too." Their red-haired mother had been one of his fiercest supporters before the revolution. Until the viciousness of the city battles turned her against both sides, after half of Miraleste went up in smoke.

With the boys safely out of sight, Derek gave the order to break camp and move to the mouth of the pass, which squeezed down to a funnel. They would hide on either side of the tumbling stream, and attack the Norsundrians coming down the last of the rocky, narrow path in ones and twos.

As they streamed along the dappled glades of Diannah Wood past spring goldenrod dancing like candle flames, high in the eastern peaks, Tsauderei cursed under his breath as he put together a few necessities. He did not look forward to several transfers in a row, as he sought the best vantage from which to observe the invaders.

In the pass, Prince Kessler Sonscarna led at the front, walking with the Venn renegade he'd winnowed out of Norsunder itself.

Kessler had occasionally heard reference to the Venn as legendary warriors, but he'd always assumed that was hyperbole. After all, how good was 'legendary?' That meant 'formerly good,' right? From what he could discover, the Venn were now locked inside their borders, which did not signify formidable warriors to him.

But after he'd seen those strange ships appear in the ocean, he wondered about those old Venn. Their language wasn't included in the Universal Language Spell. Mindful of the ship tokens he'd wrested from Pengris, he'd sought out a renegade Venn to teach him some of their language.

The man was a snake, but willing enough to brag about the customs of his homeland, and to teach Kessler the rudiments of Venn, in order to get out of scut work. Kessler had always had a facility for languages, so they were arguing in basic terms the advantages and disadvantages of attacking in column (disadvantage, flank exposed to archers) versus attacking in line (easier to break) when the scouts sent the signal back: *Enemy in sight.*

Up on the trail above, the orphan brigade boys, having eaten all their bread early on, were looking forward to a camp meal as they toiled the last paces to the summit—until Ruddy, in the lead, halted the other two. "Something's not right," he whispered.

The brilliant day abruptly turned sinister for small, twiggy Sig. Lanky Faen scoffed, "What?"

Ruddy muffled his mouth, then glanced at the rocky outcropping that screened them from the cliff. "S'posed to be Granny Innah. There's two voices. Men."

Everyone knew Ruddy had the quickest ears of their group. In silence, the three crept to the nearest mossy rock, and peered beyond. There, they gazed in shock at the blood-covered remains of Granny Innah, and the two gray-clad strangers who stood at the edge, looking down, their backs to the boys.

Ruddy counted three swords. One fellow had a longsword strapped across his back, and a rapier at his hip. They also had bows, arrows, and several daggers. Those were the weapons in view.

So when Faen predictably whispered, "Let's fight 'em," Ruddy put his lips to Faen's ear. "With what?"

All they had were their daggers. Each of the three took another long peek at the pair chatting as though no old woman sprawled in death five paces away. When Ruddy saw a fly wandering over the sightless eyes of a woman who had often made him berry tarts, anger burned inside him.

He motioned Sig and Faen back, well behind the rock, and said, "We'll push 'em off."

"How?" Sig looked frightened. "Have you ever pushed someone? You go forward, too. We'll fall off as well!" He hated heights.

"Not if we use Granny's stick. Sig, you're going to fling dirt straight into the eyes of the left one. I'll get the right. Just like Derek said, working together. And you, Faen, being biggest, you take Granny's walking stick and shove the nearest one off. Sig and I will do for the other one."

Sig didn't want to 'do' anything. The sight of popular Granny Innah all bloody and dead made him sick. His fingers shook as he bent to pick up two handfuls of dust. He didn't feel real, except yes it was real, and he wanted to pee, he wanted to run and run. But if he left Ruddy and Faen, after all the promises they'd made each other, he would be as good as dead.

*As good as dead.*

Derek had said, "You're only as good as your team, when you are small."

The urge to pee was fear, that much Sig recognized. He whispered the Waste Spell, then poised himself to run. When Ruddy nodded, they bolted head down as hard as they could go. The Norsundrians heard the footsteps and turned, hands going to weapons. Ruddy got his man square in the eyes with dust. Sig's splattered across his man's arm, but it didn't matter, because Faen shrieked as he rammed Granny's walking stick directly into the man's chest, and the man toppled over the edge, arms windmilling as he fell.

The second man flung himself away from the cliff edge, swinging his sword in furious arcs as Sig and Ruddy scrambled back. Screaming incoherently, Faen darted in with the stick, which the sword struck with a crack. The stick ripped out of Faen's hands. The man stamped, sword flailing around him as he cursed violently. Ignoring his throbbing hands, Faen scrambled for the stick, and remembered one of the drills. This time, he whirled the stick high so the sword would come at it, then he shot it between the man's legs.

The enemy tripped, falling to one knee.

That was when Ruddy hit him in the face with a huge rock. Swearing in a guttural howl, the man groped for his sword, but Sig picked it up with both hands, and, whimpering, his fingers slippery with sweat, he stabbed it into the man's stomach, then let go, retching at the horror of how that had felt.

He didn't have the strength to do more than break the man's skin, and the sword fell. Faen caught it and stabbed again and again, but the man still wriggled. Ruddy hit him again with a bigger rock, and this time he lay still, stunned. Faen and Ruddy each tugged an arm, getting him to the edge. Faen keened and Ruddy's breathing harshened as they sat down, planted their feet against the Norsundrian's back, then kicked him over the edge.

Sig had moved away, coughing as he tried to control his sobs.

Ruddy straightened, triumph spiraling with fear inside him, making him dizzy. They'd done it! Working together, they'd done it!

But then Faen said in a voice of horror, "Look."

Ruddy joined him at the edge. Sig followed on his hands and knees, peering down, past the two bodies sprawled on the rocks below, at the moving heads in a narrow crevasse, like ants in column.

"The signal," Ruddy said. "We have to let Derek know!"

They sprang to Granny Innah, and stared down at her hand. Sig's stomach lurched again when he saw that the Norsundrians had cut off her finger. The ring was gone. Probably now lying on the rocks below.

The boys looked at each other. "Can we yell?" Sig asked.

"If anyone hears us, it will be them." Faen pointed at the advancing enemy below.

"Then we have to run," Ruddy said, and the boys got their trembling limbs into motion, and bolted back down the trail.

Derek's force moved in a mass.

A scout at the front heard the rhythmic noise of tramping feet above the rush of the tumbling stream. He held up a hand, and when no one paid him any heed, he pushed through the crowd whose voices drowned his own, and ran straight to Derek. "I think Norsunder's already here."

Derek flung his head back to search the cliffs framing the sky, but he saw nothing. Where was Granny Innah?

"Shit." He whirled around.

His sudden movement caused those around him to stop talking, and as reaction ringed outward, he jabbed a hand toward the steep crags above the bottleneck.

Then he pointed violently, deploying his people. They flung themselves behind what cover they could as the first gray-clad enemies emerged.

The air hummed with arrows, causing birds to flap skyward, scolding. Shields came up with a clatter, and the arrows drummed against them like the roar of hail on rooftops. "They're fast," Derek said.

"They expected us," the grizzled stonemason replied, his accent strong.

Derek swallowed. Surprise was definitely gone. He thrust his fist upward, launching the two main forces. The third and fourth scrambled behind rocks and scrubby bushes to provide covering arrows.

Only the covering arrows were mostly bouncing uselessly off the crags, or, even worse, falling among the struggling lines of their own people. Derek hopped on his toes, desperate to see, and the last order he was able to give was the signal to cease the arrows.

After that he couldn't see. Things moved too fast. Everywhere he looked, his people, people he knew, recoiled, screamed, bled, fell, to be lost from view in the mass pushing inexorably forward to help, to see. They crushed together, so that some couldn't raise their weapons; the front fought the more desperately. One, two—five of the gray-clad ones fell. They could be killed!

Then a miracle happened. A horn brayed, and the Norsundrians turned smartly and began retreating back up the rocky slope, the last of them fighting a rear guard action.

Derek shouted, tears of angry joy in his eyes. They were in retreat! It was working!

Far above, Tsauderei watched from a rocky escarpment, his heart grieving as the gray mass spread into the colorful one, causing a crimson froth. Then, with no warning, they reversed. What was this? Tsauderei could see how many Norsundrians still waited in the pass. Was it possible the commander was a coward? He expected moral cowardice from anyone who would cleave to Norsunder, but weren't those who did the fighting bloodthirsty killers?

Something was amiss. He glanced upward, gauging the tumbling clouds with decades of experience. Then he leaned dangerously out as Derek's people gave chase. "Good, hit them hard from the rear," he muttered.

Tsauderei, like Derek, had no military experience, and so they were both stunned when the Norsundrians stopped at the top of the slope spilling out of the bottleneck. Then, in one of those timeless moments, as emotions spiral out end over end, Derek gazed up into the face of the commander, who stood a little apart from his forces, dressed unlike them entirely in black. Derek had expected some monster of a man, grizzled and scarred, but the slim fellow with the short, curly dark hair was his age.

And he knew that face.

His heart gave a sharp rap against his ribs, then thundered with horror. Kessler Sonscarna's face had featured in nightmares ever since Derek's escape from the assassin-training compound.

Kessler Sonscarna's hand went up, tightened into a fist.

His Norsundrians turned, and with withering effectiveness, demonstrated the first truth of mountain warfare, that he who has the higher ground has the advantage.

Tsauderei saw it before Derek did: Derek's people had chased the enemy straight uphill into a trap. It was going to be a slaughter. Sorrow and anger drummed his heart as he looked upward again, this time with intent.

Though light mages very seldom interfere with weather patterns, Tsauderei knew the mountains, the air currents, the patterns of rainfall. A late spring storm was already forming. He drew the currents together with such speed that the resulting thunderstorm shocked both sides below. In moments nobody on either side could see much beyond their own weapon, as hail pelted them, the rocks, and the tumbling stream with the merciless dispassion of nature.

"Retreat." Derek's numb lips could barely move, and as his captain stared uncomprehendingly into his face from two handsbreadths away, Derek made the motion for retreat.

There was no argument: the stonemason bent to pick up the lifeless body of his son, and leaned into the icy shower to stumble down the slope.

## Chapter Six

*At the same time*
*Sartor and Sarendan*

"BUT I warded that damned wood," Dejain protested, as she and Siamis stared down a grassy slope bright with wildflowers toward the dark line of Shendoral Forest. "I traveled up here in winter. I would swear that no one saw me."

"Then you would be swearing to little purpose," Siamis said, and indicated the evidence of muddy footprints in the road below.

Dejain stared from those to the weathered sign that indicated travelers were about to enter Leath. Then she turned back to Siamis, whose light gaze had narrowed, reminding her unpleasantly of his far more dangerous uncle.

"Second question," Siamis said, evenly enough. "Where is Kessler Sonscarna? I cannot believe he was a part of this idiocy." A sharp lift of the hand, indicating all of Sartor, not just Bostian's invasion army now wandering around in the weird forest beyond.

"He is," Dejain said, with a spike of malicious pleasure. "He decided to take Sarendan."

"Yes." Siamis's gaze went distant. "He's holed up in a cave outwaiting a storm. Go fetch him." The gentle voice gentled further. "Now."

"When I do?" Her nevers chilled in spite of the mellow sun of early summer.

"Bring him to Eidervaen."

She vanished, and he signaled to the horsemen waiting at a prudent distance. When they drew near, he motioned for a horse, saying, "I will have to ride in there myself, it seems. Meet me in the city."

And he rode toward the forest alone.

Part of its strangeness was the suddenness of its border, as if an invisible ring had been laid down by some monumental hand. Most forests began with clumps of trees, or with shrubbery that thickens along the road until greenery surrounds the traveler. Sometimes there was a dramatic difference in vegetation between one slope and another, largely having to do with the angle of the sun as well as soil, but here, the road led into a sudden stand of trees that dimmed the light to greenish shadow, broken by slanting shafts of gold.

He entered Shendoral.

Late spring blossoms dotted the glades, a reassuringly normal sight. Siamis found it peculiar, how navigating here was not unlike navigation in Norsunder; it brought to mind the dire consequences of any kind of violence. Humans had not imposed this rule onto Shendoral. He did not know who had. Perhaps the indigenous species, who existed outside of time and space, as did Norsunder; only here, the animals as well as humans were forced to live in peace.

Did this cause surviving predator species to turn to nuts and fruit for sustenance, and had that spread outward, as had the dawnsingers' and morvende embargoes on killing any living creature for food?

He gave himself a moment to appreciate the long view that such changes required, and then it was time for business. He focused on Bostian, the brash young commander who was too eager to make a name for himself by conquering Sartor, and so had ridden past elementary illusions, straight into Shendoral forest and its formidable magic.

This humiliation was going to be salutary.

Siamis found him around the next bend, as he expected, though anywhere else they might have been as much as a week apart in distance. Bostian, a big, burly fellow a year or so older than Siamis, looked almost comically dismayed, a reaction that intensified after Siamis told him where he was, and how long it had been.

"But I've only been in here a day!" Bostian protested. "Look at our stores. We've camped once."

"Yet it has been eight weeks since you crossed the border," Siamis said, his sense of humor tickled at the sight of rows of tough warriors walking their horses, treading carefully lest they step on some small creature unawares, and fall down dead. Shendoral was exact: a life for a life. "We can continue this unedifying exchange outside the forest border, if you wish, lest another couple of months pass while you argue. You can follow me out."

Bostian's interest was entirely confined to the cut and the thrust. As Bostian and his company fell in behind, Siamis focused on the border of the forest—and there it was.

Once they were well away from Shendoral's imperceptible grip, Siamis said to Bostian, "I'm going ahead into Eidervaen, to see if I can rescue this fool escapade of yours from disaster before Detlev gets here."

He watched Bostian's rugged, tanned face blanch, then added, "When you arrive, you will become an occupation force. Everything will be peaceful and orderly as you take charge of the city."

Siamis did not need mind-touch to sense Bostian's anger, frustration, and above all disappointment. He laughed as he left them there, and left to conquer Eidervaen alone.

"They're out of Shendoral," the young Sartoran mage student reported, her eyes huge. "And Olvath, who was on watch duty at the forest road, says she's certain it was Siamis who brought them out." She looked around at Atan, Chief Veltos, and four of the high council.

"Siamis," Atan breathed. "Then he's here. In Sartor?"

Veltos whirled. "Call the high council to Star Chamber. Stay, the entire first circle—" She broke off, and made a profound bow to Atan.

It was sincere, but it was too late.

Everyone knew that only the monarch could summon the first circle of nobles. Atan forced her palms together, opening them outward in the gesture of royal order, an empty gesture as the order had already been given. By someone else. She watched them watch her confirm the order, confirming the fiction that she was the queen, then she said, "I will withdraw while they assemble."

Everyone bowed deeply, and Atan saw in those lowered heads the silent acknowledgement of who really ruled Sartor. It was not Atan.

She went straight to her private chamber, where she looked for her notecase to report the sighting. It was not in its place. She frowned, her hand reaching to summon the duty page, but she hesitated. The pages, the cleaning servants, even Gehlei would not touch it without leave.

Atan wandered about the room, looking from round tabletop to lyre-legged chair to window sill where lay two private histories written by ancestors when they were her age. She remembered laying the books down. She remembered laying her notecase in its place on the table.

Who could have taken it?

She shook her head. Siamis on the way . . . This was not the time to bother with inquiries about absent-minded servants. She should be warning people, like the rest of the alliance. Beginning with Sarendan over the mountains. Since Chief Veltos was summoning the council (Atan sustained a flash of anger, and then determinedly dismissed it), Atan had time. She had the will. And she had the means.

So she transferred to Miraleste in Sarendan. While she was standing on the Destination tiles, she remembered hearing the quick patter of feet down the hall outside her rooms. Julian? Would Julian have taken it? Impossible. Julian wouldn't touch anything that she thought connected in any way with lessons or princesses or queens. With responsibility, Tsauderei had said, when last they talked about her.

". . . there?"

Atan blinked, to discover herself peering into a pair of familiar tip-tilted eyes widened with anxiousness. "Lilah?"

Lilah cast a sigh of relief. "I thought you were Siamised!" Lilah exclaimed. "Did you know a bunch of eleveners attacked us?"

"Siamis himself," Atan said, "is in Sartor."

Lilah gasped, then took Atan's hand. "Come on."

They found Peitar in the residence wing, where Atan stopped short, blinking when she saw Peitar wielding a paintbrush, busy sloshing black paint over a plaster wall. In the ochre light of late afternoon, the streaks in the paint looked oily.

He turned around, and waved the brush in greeting. At the look on her face, he grinned, and Lilah said, "I've been bothering him to redo the throne room all in black marble. You know, veined with gold. It got kind of ruined in the revolution . . ."

"And I'm doing this to demonstrate what an entirely black room might look like," Peitar said.

Atan nodded, thinking that of course he wouldn't order servants to paint it, when he knew very well that it was going to have to be unpainted.

Almost as if he read her mind, he said in a lower voice, "I pick up the brush every time I need to keep myself busy—"

A bustle at the door interrupted him. Lilah flitted to peer out, then turned back, paling beneath her freckles. "Derek is back," she said.

Peitar flung the brush into the bucket, where it sent out a glurpy tide of black onto the floor unperceived. "Success? Success?" He could not bear to say the opposite.

The sharp stink of sweat nearly knocked Atan back, as a cluster of filthy, mud- and blood-splattered men entered Peitar's interview chamber, exhausted after their battle and a three-day headlong gallop.

They collapsed onto the satin-upholstered chairs uninvited, unheeding; so dazed were they that Derek's gaze crossed Atan's and, other than the faintest check, passed on with no reaction.

Lilah gripped Derek's arm. "Atan says Siamis is in Sartor!"

"Peitar," Derek said. "Kessler Sonscarna is the one leading the invasion."

Lilah gazed from one to the other. "Kessler? He's scarier than Siamis," she exclaimed with heartfelt horror. "He chased us in Sartor—" Lilah was about to remind them of those frightening days before Atan ended the enchantment over Sartor, but she saw that nobody was listening to her.

She sighed as Derek said hoarsely, "We would all have died. If it hadn't been for a fierce storm. We ran. We ran and left our dead there." Derek's face puckered. Tears dripped down his face. He thumbed them impatiently away, and his head dropped back tiredly. "I think half are gone. Maybe more. I must go back." His voice roughened. "And Disappear the dead. Do it right."

Peitar said, "The rangers in Diannah Wood will have done that by now, if Norsunder's warriors are no longer there."

"They have to be right behind us," Derek said. "At most a day away, if they were slowed up through the wood. We had our guides, who probably fouled the trails for them."

"Then we have at least one night to prepare," Peitar said. "Captain Leonos will raise the city guard, all watches. Including your defenders." His voice changed to concern. "Derek, you need to get some rest."

"I can't sleep," Derek returned flatly.

Peitar said, "At least eat, then. Mirah-Steward will have seen you enter, and unless I miss my guess, hot food will be along any moment. Surely you will not insult her by turning it down."

"I can't," Derek began—as the door opened, and an impressive row of servants entered, bearing silver trays that trailed enticing smells.

Peitar's gaze shifted as if he sought answers to unspoken questions, then his expression warmed briefly when he caught sight of Atan. "I beg your pardon. What news did you bring?"

Atan told him in a few short words as servants passed round plates, utensils, and food. Atan refused a plate. "I have to get back," she said. "Can you report for me to the rest of the alliance? And don't forget . . ."

"I know. If I lose the kingdom, I retreat to Delfina Valley," Peitar said with a crooked smile. "So I don't lose myself, and the kingdom with it, to Siamis's spell."

Atan walked to the door, then cast a thoughtful look back. Derek yawned between bites, his red-rimmed eyes marked with exhaustion. He seemed too tired to pursue his grudge, which made her own resentment dissolve. They were just two more weary humans, dealing with a new crisis. Why did it have to take a war to get them there?

She slipped into the hall and transferred home, where she plumped down at her desk until the swirl of tiny dots evaporated from her vision. She counted the pangs in her head until they were faint, then stirred her limbs. A last throb, and she could move.

She opened her door. Where was the duty page? A few steps, and she knew by some subtle sense that something was not right. Yet there was no noise, no clamor, no smell of fire. Through the open windows drifted birdsong.

It was the quiet, the empty hall. Halls were never empty. The duty page was missing. No one was in sight.

The back of Atan's neck gripped. She whirled around and ran back to her room, then opened the old servants' door, which led to a narrow stairway, the glowglobes dim. She picked up her skirts and skimmed down the stairs to the stewards' quarters.

Then she froze in the doorway when she saw Gehlei pass through in the direction of the kitchen without looking right or left. Atan took a few steps in her wake, and glimpsed the senior staff moving about, no one speaking. As if asleep.

As if enchanted.

Horror wrung through her. What now? "The council," she whispered. Back she ran, using servants' byways to get to the Star Chamber. She paused outside the door to listen, and heard an unfamiliar man's voice. A tenor voice, like a singer's, pleasantly rising and falling—

A hard tug on her skirt jolted her. She looked down into Julian's face. "Go away," Julian said, clutching her dirty robe to her. "We don't want you."

"We?" Atan repeated, struck in the heart.

"My friends," Julian said, as her quick fingers lifted the latch to the great door and she darted inside.

Atan heard the laughing male voice say, "Ah, here is our little friend back again."

She knew who had to be in there, and the fact that no one reacted, no one even responded, meant she was too late. They were enchanted, and because everyone who really ruled the kingdom was inside that room, it meant that everyone in Sartor had fallen under the soft, dream-like spell along with the council.

Siamis had enchanted Sartor once again.

Atan choked back a sob and mumbled the transfer spell. When the black dots—bigger this time—faded away, she remembered Julian's angry voice, the push of her little hands. The sickening realization that Julian had not fallen under the spell because she had no loyalty whatso-ever to anyone.

Atan covered her face with her hands as sobs wracked her.

"Go ahead. Cry it out." Tsauderei patted his guest chair invitingly. "Then tell me what happened."

Dejain had had magical access to Kessler, back in the days when she was working with him on his mad plot to eradicate bad kings from the world. Since then, she had been very careful not to remind him that she had this access, particularly since she'd found evidence that he was studying magic. Somehow. Without anyone else catching him at it, much less teaching him.

But now there was this direct order from Siamis, who was far too dangerous to cross. She saw no way around transferring directly to Kessler—with a fifty-step margin of safety—if she was to stay out of whatever trouble was brewing, and pretend to be an obedient minion, until she found someone strong enough to take Siamis down.

She transferred. It wasn't a long distance, but the pain was sharp enough. She found herself in a cave behind a waterfall. When she could trust her body to move, she stepped cautiously into the gloom, toward voices. Kessler's face, lit by the ruddy leap of a fire, tightened to anger when he saw her. She held her breath, ready to transfer out if he made a move toward his weapons.

But he jerked his chin in dismissal. His captains withdrew, weapons clanking and boots squelching, into what appeared to be a honeycomb of caves.

She did not make the mistake of assuming she was safe. But she pretended she was, as she looked around and tasted the air, registering the loud roar as a violent rainfall. Then made a discovery. She said to Kessler, "It's not a waterfall, it's a storm. It has magic in it."

"I thought lighters did not do that to weather."

"Someone did." She took a step toward the fire, hating the chill air. "Siamis has summoned you."

"Where?"

"Eidervaen. He should have it pacified by now." She added acidly, "Or so he appeared to think would be the case." And when he made no move, she said, "The palace in Eidervaen."

He said, "Do you know the Destination pattern?"

"Yes." So he was going to cooperate.

"Take me there."

This was going to hurt more. But she could not show weakness.

They transferred, both appearing in the cool blue and white vaulting of Sartor's Destination chamber. The clawing nausea of a double transfer faded enough that she could stalk on watery legs around a corner, then sink against a wall, shivering and shaking. As soon as she could bear it, she used the transfer token in her pocket and returned to Norsunder Base, to recover in peace.

Kessler had already forgotten her. He glanced bemusedly up at the golden sun above the middle panel, the dragons rising on the attack, and a derisive smile twisted his lips. Would they ever want to actually see any of those things? He didn't think so.

He left and began to search for Siamis. People moved sedately, paying him no heed. So the enchantment had happened again. He turned a corner, figuring he'd look for the most important rooms, but when he reached a marble-banistered stair, he was almost knocked over by a small figure hurtling down.

He backed up a step, a hand half raised, then lowered it when he gazed down into a vaguely familiar small face.

"I know you," the child said. She barely came up to his middle. Her brown hair was tangled, full of leaves. She clutched some kind of grimy garment to her, looped and wound around her and dragging behind in a filthy train. "I do! You're the one who almost broke my fingers."

Kessler laughed. "But I didn't." Now he remembered: when he and Dejain were tasked to halt that Landis girl from breaking Sartor's century-long enchantment that was, apparently, already weakening. No doubt the lighters had made a hero of her anyway.

The child went on. "They were talking about you. They thought I didn't listen, but I did, when I was riding on your horse."

Kessler was going to move away, but the girl darted in front of him, her round, droopy eyes intent. "I'm Julian. They want to make me one of Them, and then I'll be dead. You're the prince who ran away so you wouldn't have to be a prince."

He laughed again. "So I am."

"You can do anything you want," she accused.

"I will be able to, soon," he said, entertained enough to lean his wrist on the bannister's marble-carved acanthus leaves, smoothed by generations of touch.

"Can I go with you? Show me how to get what I want. All They do is try to make me do what They want. I hate that. I don't want to be Them. I don't want to be dead," she said, a memory flash of her mother's slapping hands, her low voice when she pinched Julian, whispering in her ear, always that phrase, *You would like to be a princess, wouldn't you?*

Kessler stared down at the child whose eyes were shaped like his own, one of those random features that appeared from time to time in descendants of the Landis family. He liked teaching. He'd always wanted to find young people similar to himself after he'd escaped Wan-Edhe, ambitious.

But there were standards. He said, "You don't even have the self-discipline to clean yourself up. Why should I teach you anything?"

Julian opened her mouth to yell, but he turned away, his indifference plain. So she said speculatively, "If I do that? Will you?"

"Maybe," he said. "But you'd better be fast. I'll be out of here soon. If you're not here waiting before I leave, then you'll have to find your way same as I did."

He walked off, forgetting Julian within a few steps. His search was systematic; he was beginning the second floor when he spotted Siamis exiting a room in the midst of a lot of sleepwalkers. Hatred spiked for Detlev's strutting pet.

Kessler paused to enjoy the spike, to speculate on the success of an attack right now. But Siamis was carrying that sword of his, and a marble hallway was a stupid place for swordplay. Kessler would wait until he found the right ground. "How long before that brat with the dyr thing shows up to blast this spell of yours?"

"Soon, I hope." Siamis smiled. "This spell of mine is only meant to hold them until Detlev finds what he's looking for on Geth."

"Which is?" Kessler asked.

"Rifts," Siamis said equably enough. "They transfer in tunnels, which apparently can be broadened to rifts. As yet I don't know the details. I was kept elsewhere for an appreciable time." He made a large gesture, and then added, "Some don't appear to understand the difference between enterprise and stupidity. I'm surprised to discover you among their number."

Kessler shrugged. "Why not? If nothing else, mounting an invasion gives us seasoning."

"Leave the seasoning to me. As for the idiot who started this stampede. Henerek, as you probably are aware, decided to smite his childhood rivals, and is in Everon botching the job. Detlev wants you to go clean that up."

He walked past, leaving Kessler standing there.

So Kessler transferred back to his cave, where he summoned his captains. "We're done here." Before they could express their disappointment, in which he had no interest, he said, "Though I think, since we're going in that direction anyway, we'll stop in Miraleste first. Resupply. Then we're going to double it across Sarendan, and take ship at the nearest port."

"What's the target?"

"Everon," Kessler said, and smiled.

Julian ran upstairs as fast as she could, giggling with triumph and anticipation. So there! She should have thrown that notecase thing of Atan's down a well long ago. Now everything was going to be fun, if that runaway prince could really teach a person to get everything she wanted.

Julian burst into her bedchamber and looked at the trunk full of clothes that she had refused to touch. She flung her wrap on the floor and took out the first thing on top. It was riding clothes, a top and trousers, not a horrible princess outfit.

Only how were you supposed to pull it on, from the bottom or the top? In the forest, before anyone talked about princesses, all she had was somebody's robe. That had been so easy!

She tried to stick her feet through the top, but the head part wouldn't go past her upper legs. So she kicked it off, laid it on the floor, opened the hem, and crawled into it, feeling the way into the arm holes and head hole. When that was on, she jammed her feet into the trousers and yanked them up. She was about to run through the door, but caught sight of her hair in the mirror, and grimaced. A hairbrush lay on the table below the mirror, never before used.

She had seen people brush their hair. She tried the brush, but it stuck right away, and stung her scalp. Gritting her teeth, she dragged the brush through as much of her hair as she could reach, at least in front. It still looked horrible. So she dug through the drawers in the table until she found winter things—gloves and caps. She shoved all her hair up into a cap, and flung the hairbrush at the mirror as hard as she could. She smiled when the glass cracked like a big spider web.

Then she ran downstairs, where she found the tall friendly one with the sword talking to two more of the ones in uniforms. But the runaway prince with the black curly hair wasn't in sight. "Where is he? He said he'd wait. I went as fast as I could! But he's gone."

The friendly one said, "I fear we all get less attention than we feel we deserve. Except when we don't want it."

Julian ignored his smile. "He didn't wait!" she yelled.

"Who didn't wait?"

"That man. The one who ran away from being a prince. Who can do anything he wants."

"He's gone, I'm afraid. On my orders."

"So he doesn't do what he wants?"

"He would like to. But he must do what I tell him."

"Why?"

"Come along, and we'll talk about it," said the yellow-haired man.

"You won't try to make me a princess?" Julian said suspiciously.

The man sat down on the broad marble steps. "Why wouldn't you want to be a princess?"

"I hate it," Julian said. In memory, there was her mother, with her jewels, and her mad face, pinching Julian hard and hissing, *Don't you want to be a princess?* before telling her to smile at the baby princess, take a flower to the queen, be the first to say this thing, or that thing, to be pretty—*pinch*—smile—*pinch*—be pretty and smile—*tweak*—wear her pretty clothes and smile. "I *hate* it," Julian burst out again.

"Well, then, let's see if we can find a use for you," the man said. "Where nobody will expect you to be a princess."

"Promise?" Julian demanded.

"I promise," he said, laughing. When he got up and walked away, she followed along behind.

## Chapter Seven

*Chwahirsland*

THE alliance began to gather at last.

In Chwahirsland, without any idea of what was going on beyond its borders, Jilo turned a cup around in his hand, then finally said, "What's a neckin?"

Granduncle Shiam glanced up in mild surprise.

Jilo twisted uneasily in his chair, distracted by the patiently painted dots indicating patterns of raspberry clusters alternated with grape around the rim of his cup. "I know it's old army slang for 'a lot,' but why wouldn't someone just say 'a lot,' in talking about a wager? Don't they usually mention an amount for the stake?"

"Because they were really wagering a trip to the wall," the commander said.

"I heard that before." Jilo looked puzzled. "'A trip to the wall' usually meant an execution. They were wagering on deaths?"

"No. Sex." Shiam remembered that Jilo had no close family to explain sex, and of course he hadn't had a twi to exchange information with, much less indulge with in practice sex play. If he was even of age enough for that.

But Jilo had been running around a garrison all his life. "It's sex? Against a wall?"

"Sex in the army was forbidden. 'Neckin' was originally slang for the number of floggings you would get for capital crimes, such as having relationships. The Hate wanted all loyalty strictly to on him. But people, being people . . ." The commander waited for Jilo to ask the questions that would indicate he was ready for the answers. "There was a certain amount of humor in choosing slang for a long punishment resulting from a brief act," he finally said.

Jilo shrugged off the unpleasant subject. Sex as mechanics was familiar. You didn't do stable duty without knowing the rudiments, and the language of it was everyday around rec time back in the Shadowland. The feelings that led to it? Those were as distant as the winter stars.

So he lifted the cup to study the painting around his rim. He wondered if the cup was old, from before the edict against painting things had been issued. Yet another forbidden thing that made life better, if you chose to have it.

Jilo looked up at his granduncle. This was his third visit to his relatives since winter. After lifting the killing wards around the castle Destination, he'd placed tracers on it so if anyone arrived he would know.

His granduncle noticed his interest. "Grandfather Nissler made those cups. He was a potter, before the edicts." Uncle Shiam furrowed his brow.

"Maybe that ought to go on our list? Releasing the edicts binding the potters to the army for ten years."

Jilo had agreed that they ought to release Wan-Edhe's terrible edicts a bit at a time. Food first: this spring, the secondary army fields had been opened under the strict control of local commanders, who measured off spaces for each village and town, a certain amount of ground per household. There had been no riots, though trouble had been threatened over hoarded seed, until Jilo let it be known that seed was coming from overseas. He did not say that he'd used some of Wan-Edhe's terrifyingly immense hoard of gold to buy it—Senrid had set it up through the king of Erdrael Danara, who turned out to be a friend of his.

"Slow," Uncle Shiam said. "Very slow. If people are busy, they will not revolt. If you give them too many choices after no choice at all . . ." He shook his head. "We do not know how to negotiate choices anymore. I've seen death struggles over the possession of extra boot ties, and that in an army where any action whatsoever outside of orders gets you a bloody back."

Jilo swallowed. "Maybe over winter, then—"

His cousin came in carrying a tray of corn cakes, but just as Jilo reached for one, a tracer warning poked him inside his head.

Someone had actually used the Destination he had so carefully de-trapped?

Unless it was . . . "I have to go," he said.

His family reflected surprise, but no one asked. And he wasn't sure what to say. If there were normal patterns of conversation for such moments, he had yet to learn them, a thought that made him feel sorrowful.

"Take a corn cake with you, Cousin Jilo," Aran said practically.

Jilo thanked her, and did. The cake was still hot when the transfer magic left him standing in the castle, making him reflect on how heat transferred as well as bones and skin and clothes.

It had cooled by the time he recovered from the transfer; it had also left a pink spot on his hand, which throbbed faintly. He didn't mind that. It was somewhat better than the way he used to feel when he returned to this castle. There were actual air currents along the lower floors now, and sometimes he heard voices. The time binding was still there, but it had begun to lessen the farther you got from the third floor, and people were showing tiny signs of possible recovery, in very small ways. Like, someone had dared to ask him a question, "Would you like a meal?"

He walked through the Destination chamber door, which he had removed half the wards from. He stopped short when he recognized Senrid of the Marlovens.

Senrid had been looking around the library, but turned at his step. "Haven't you been keeping up with that book of yours?" he asked without preamble.

"It's locked up. While I go places," Jilo said. Then he caught up mentally. "Something happened?"

"Detlev and Siamis are back. Siamis, I heard about. I know Detlev's back. Saw him myself, three days ago."

"At the head of an army?" Jilo braced for worse news.

"No. But he destroyed all my border wards. Everything. Then smoked." Senrid swiped his hand through the air, as if pushing something away. His lip curled. "If he does come back, he's going to have to look hard to find our army." His smile vanished. "Hibern says that Norsunder did launch armies against Sarendan, Sartor, and Everon. And I'd love to know where Detlev smoked to. Can we look in that book?"

Jilo was already moving into the next room. "Wan-Edhe will be back," Jilo said in a weird, flat voice.

The way he said it made Senrid's nerves jump. He knew why.

Substitute 'My uncle will be back,' and there was Senrid's own fear. That was the real horror of Norsunder. Well, one of them. People you saw dragged off, who should be dead and gone, weren't.

"Then you make sure your army isn't there for him to command, at least, as much as you can. But Jilo," Senrid said sharply, and the other boy turned his way, the glassy expression in his eyes turning to worry. At least he was listening. "Siamis doesn't seem to bother with armies. According to Hibern, who got it from Tsauderei, he entered Eidervaen's royal palace, and exited half a glass after, leaving the entire kingdom sleepwalking. It's just like before."

"What do we do?"

"My suggestion is, get yourself out of reach of Siamis, or whoever they might send here, and join us in our alliance fallback." Senrid described the Delfina Valley Destination.

"Me?" was all Jilo could think to say, then reddened at what he knew sounded like witlessness.

"You. Or, better, take this transfer token." Senrid dropped a cheap brass ring of the sort found at festivals onto Jilo's palm. Jilo could feel the tingle of magic on it. "Get yourself to Delfina Valley, where Tsauderei is hiding out. Used to be some kind of lighter mage hideout. Norsunder can't get past the protective wards."

"Are the Mearsieans going to be there? You know they won't want me in their alliance."

"Mearsieans?" Senrid exclaimed, in disbelief. "You mean Clair and the rest of those girls?"

Jilo ducked his head in a nod.

Senrid stared at the kid who had taken over a vast kingdom with a formidable reputation, who had been wrestling single-handed with magic far beyond Senrid's skills. Was Jilo really worried about some bratty girls who couldn't manage a sword between them? "If they don't, then they are an almighty pack of lighter hypocrites. But Clair was the one who brought you to me for help." Or had she thought Senrid would have Jilo put up against a wall? His gut curled at the bitter thought.

"It's not Clair I'm thinking about."

Senrid laughed. "CJ, then? She was the one who said we should recruit. I'm recruiting you. She can like it or shut up."

Senrid flicked the subject of CJ aside impatiently. He wanted, needed, to see that book. "Jilo, listen. If Siamis gets you, then that means he's got your entire kingdom. Whatever you've set up to get around Wan-Edhe, Siamis can make you put it all back again. He can make you do anything, and you'll do it." Senrid's features lengthened with horror. "Nobody can tell me if you feel yourself doing what he wants, or if your mind just goes somewhere else. Either way . . ." He snapped his fingers. "So much for all your plans."

Jilo blinked. "Yes. Right. My Uncle Shiam and I . . . there's an order I can give. It will go through all the captains. The army will go into the fields, because it's our first year of allowing general planting—"

Jilo abruptly stopped babbling, and muttered spells. His 'locked up,' Senrid saw, was in the magical sense. The book appeared in a tiny flash of light and puff of air that smelled of singed paper.

Jilo flipped it open, and stared.

"What does it say?" Senrid demanded impatiently.

"There is nothing for Wan-Edhe," Jilo muttered. "He must still be in Norsunder-Beyond."

"What about the head snakes?" Senrid rapped his knuckles lightly on the table as he fought the nearly overmastering desire to grab the book and transfer out.

"Detlev's last mention was Norsunder Base. That was right after Mar-loven Hess, three days ago." Jilo glanced up briefly. "Siamis has been moving around a lot. A *lot*. Sartor, Imar, a bunch of places I've never heard of—"

"Like?"

Jilo rattled off names, during which Senrid said, "Got to be a scout-ing run," but then a pattern emerged, just as Jilo said, "Mearsies Heili?" He looked up in surprise. "Why would he go there?"

"Bereth Ferian, Roth Drael, Mearsies Heili."

"All in the same day?"

"Yes." Jilo glanced up in question. "He must have the world's worst headache."

"He's hunting Liere," Senrid whispered, raised his hands, and vanished.

Jilo started. Senrid's abrupt disappearance was somehow more un-settling than his news, which Jilo had been dreading since the day he'd first walked into this castle and made his first spell.

He scrabbled among the papers for a pen, dipped it, scrawled the pre-arranged message to Uncle Shiam, then whispered a transfer spell over it. The paper vanished in a tiny puff of air.

He was about to send the book back to its hiding place, but Senrid's words caused him to hesitate. He wasn't used to using it to track other people's enemies, none of whom had shown any interest in Chwahirs-land. However, what if someone else tried to take it?

If he hid it . . .

He placed the book between the two light magic guides given him by Mondros, closed them into a travel bag, and looked around. Enemies—Wan-Edhe—might come. He could do nothing beyond the wards he'd already laid to trap him. Anywhere Jilo went beyond his border seemed to be among enemies. But he had learned there were degrees of enmity.

And maybe things could change.

Like this alliance?

He looked down at the transfer token Senrid had given him. He had to find out.

*Sarendan*

Derek Diamagan had taken the poorest house on the east side of Miraleste as a sort of temporary home. He traveled too much for the idea of 'home' to be much more than a place to store the things he didn't want to take on the road. He'd chosen that sorry little house to demonstrate his contempt for the perquisites of being friends with royalty.

He sometimes bunked at the city guard barracks because it was convenient, but Lilah and Peitar could never get him to stay in the palace except during the worst of winter weather, and then he always stayed with the servants.

Derek's house was meant to be ordinary, but people had gradually, always while he was away, taken to improving it for him. As gifts. So each trip he'd returned to find new articles of furniture, each plain but well-made. Dishes. Curtains. Upholstery on the chairs, then embroidery on the upholstery. Good traveling boots, sized to his footprint in the mud when he left. Then he returned to a lack of mud, the street having been paved with good stone.

Once the house was painted inside and out, and reroofed, the adjoining houses were cleared out and the former owners resettled in good locations. He had to admit it was convenient, because he always had people waiting to talk to him, and they could wait in those houses. He could feed and house the more skittish orphans because he had a fully equipped kitchen and willing hands and donated food as well as those extra rooms.

He protested that it was too grand, but his protests were mild because he could see the pride in the artisans' faces.

Guilt underlay the fury that oppressed him as he walked down the hill away from the palace in the streaming rain, though every bone and muscle in his body ached, and the little casket in his hand weighed as heavily as the guilt and grief, fury and remorse. He longed to shout, "Nobody told me!"

There had been no lessons on fighting in mountains. But the knowledge hadn't been kept from him, because no one in his army had experienced anything like that Norsundrian attack, and as for mountains, they had always been regarded as the kingdom's protection. Battles happened on flat fields, or alongside rivers, or along streets.

He walked faster, thinking furiously. Kessler Sonscarna and his Norsunder force were coming. Maybe not that night. The weather was too bad for that: horses would mire on the road, and he'd already sent people to hack the bridges apart, once the support magic was broken. The Norsundrians would have to ford the high waters, and get shot at from the banks.

But they'd still come. There was little that could divert Kessler, Derek had learned once, a lesson that had nearly cost his and his brother's lives. But he'd learned this much, so he could learn more. If a runaway prince could learn to command like that, Derek could learn faster. And better. Commoners had self-discipline that no noble ever had.

Next time it would be Derek winning.

Anticipation brought him smiling grimly to his street, where he found the rain-washed square full of people waiting. At the front stood familiar faces, clearly hoping for word of their loved ones. Or for personal condolences, for those whose bad news had run ahead.

All right. This was his duty as a commander.

He set the casket on his desk and turned to the first anxiously waiting face, laboring to find words that would hurt less.

There were none.

The man looked into his face, then backed up a step, saying, "No! No! He's just seventeen—"

It was near morning when the last of them departed. Stupid with exhaustion, Derek forced himself into his bedroom, where he discovered a new rug, woven in bright colors. He shut his eyes, which brought the dizziness, and he swayed, then jerked upright.

He would not look at that waiting bed. He picked up the casket again. Inside rattled the coins that had been turned into transfer tokens. Tsauderei had begun making them directly after that battle. Before Derek left the palace, Peitar had made him promise that all the brigade children under thirteen were to be transferred to the Valley.

This promise made sense in all directions. Those loyal children were Derek's future officers. When they all got training along with their strength, it would be them winning against the likes of Prince Kessler Sonscarna.

But that was for the future. He had to deal with them right now. Once Derek got the children to the Valley, Tsauderei would be able to keep them locked down.

A muffled laugh, and the sound of a rock skipping over the stones, brought him to his window. The orphans were already gathering, in spite of the rain that was now tapering off. They were going to be angry with him; they would probably consider it a broken promise when he took them out of harm's way, because he'd so easily promised them all an important role in defending the country.

He knew that no one could reason with youngsters who thought danger would be like the hero songs and tales, or the plays on stage, in which there might be an exciting fight, but only the villain would fall to the boards, and there would be no blood.

Until a week ago, Derek had led them in believing it.

To get away from that thought, he marched outside, oblivious to the rain. Ruddy whistled, and the orphans scrambled into their rows. Derek counted, then counted again. Not including Lilah and her three friends (one of whom was outside the country altogether), ten were missing.

"I have special orders for you," he said. "We have to be fast, which means travel by magic."

The questions burst out. He gave evasive answers as he passed along the rows, handing each kid the thin copper coin called a flim, which had been bespelled into a magic transfer token for one journey. Peitar had reasoned that the flims could then be tendered to pay for room and board.

"Now here's what you do," Derek began, and told them the sign and word that would carry them all directly to the Valley, then he made them count between transfers, giving them a graphic description of what could happen if they all tried to transfer to the same Destination at the same time, even in the Valley. Though Peitar had told him that a mass transfer using light magic wouldn't work, Derek didn't trust magic any more than he trusted kings.

He waited until they had all popped out of existence, one by one in orderly fashion, then followed last.

He found what he expected, a milling group of youths all yelling over one another to be heard. Faen and another boy were already shoving at one another.

"Quiet!" he shouted.

They subsided, and cast quick looks around. They found themselves on a broad cliff, with a cottage built in the middle, surrounded by grass. Tsauderei opened the door and shuffled out, old-fashioned robes swaying in the pearly morning light. There was no storm here.

"What's our special orders?" a girl shouted, her expression a mix of hope and, for the first time, wariness. Derek hated seeing that wariness. He hesitated, too tired to think of special orders that would satisfy his followers.

"Would you like to fly while you wait?" Tsauderei asked.

The children whirled around.

"Fly?" half a dozen voices responded in disbelief.

"I am a mage. I made a spell the lets you fly all over this valley, and the mountains nearby." Tsauderei let that sink in, then said, "Here are the rules. You can fly anywhere you want, but don't disturb the villagers on the lower ledge that way." He pointed down at the circle of houses on the westward slope of the mountain. "Or any other houses. You also stay away from the flowers on the other side of the lake, unless you want to sleep forever."

"Listen to what he says," Derek ordered, but he hadn't needed to.

The orphans were too intimidated to argue. A mage! He could turn them into toadstools, and looked like he might if they sneezed wrong.

The old mage taught them the spell, and as kids launched into the air like so many ungainly birds, Derek looked around for somewhere to sit until Tsauderei could send him back to Miraleste.

"Come along. I've some extra Sartoran steep already made," Tsauderei said, and Derek started. He'd nearly fallen asleep on his feet.

He was going to argue, but couldn't find the words.

It was easier to walk those few steps inside, where vague curiosity flared briefly. He'd never seen the inside of the mage's cottage. It was as plain as any laborer's hut, a single room, with a sleeping loft above the fireplace. Only the books on all the walls but the front, which was all window, differentiated it from a commoner's house. Derek looked around with reluctant approval. He'd assumed mages would whistle up palaces for themselves, and invisible servants to provide for every need.

At a gesture from the mage, Derek sank into an upholstered chair. Tsauderei pressed a cup into his hands. Derek drank deeply, leaning his head back on the chair to appreciate the warmth going down. Maybe now he could think again. Special orders . . . something that would keep that loyalty, so very important . . . loyalty . . . He closed his eyes . . .

And fell asleep. Tsauderei glanced at him askance, then sighed, shaking his head. He didn't particularly want Derek Diamagan in his cottage, and was overdue somewhere else, but from the looks of the boy, he wasn't going to waken any time soon.

He finished his own steep, set down his cup, cast a quilt over Derek, then braced for the long shift north.

*Mearsies Heili and Vasande Leror*

Senrid stepped off the Destination on the terrace before the white palace in Mearsies Heili's tiny capital. He gazed up at the spires of the palace, which owed nothing to symmetry, yet did not look like a random collection of towers. What kind of design was that? It would be impossible to defend in a war. You'd think. Yet it was still standing after unknown centuries.

Not ten steps into the nacreous light of the hall, he shut his eyes hard. Something was trying to make him dizzy. He listened on the mental plane, then recoiled, slamming his mind-shield tight against a subtle shimmer of dark magic, a thin sheen like oil spilled upon a lake.

*Siamis has been here.* Senrid controlled the urge to flee, and ventured farther, keeping his footfalls quiet. All senses alert, he crossed the broad, empty hall to the open doors of the throne room. He'd never seen anyone in that room until now.

Surprised, he gazed at Clair, a small white-haired figure sitting on the carved throne. He had never seen her in her throne room in all his visits.

Did he look as ridiculous perched on his own throne? Probably worse.

He approached. She could have been a square-faced kid statue, her waving white hair falling in ordered locks down to her lap where her hands rested loose, palms upturned. It was so uncharacteristic that his skin crawled: it was too easy to imagine her body hollowed out, brains, wit, and heart removed, leaving this empty shell.

But her color was a normal, healthy light brown with rose beneath, and her rumpled blue tunic stirred slightly with her breathing.

He remembered encountering people under the grip of the Siamis enchantment. They could answer specific questions. But then they would report the conversation, as ordered.

So he wasn't going to mention Liere directly. "Where are the girls?"

"I don't know," Clair stated.

Senrid looked around, and wondered if they'd escaped the spell. Otherwise, wouldn't they be sitting here with Clair, like a row of live dolls? 'Did you send them somewhere?' No, that question might put Siamis on their trail—if he hadn't already asked it. He eyed Clair, then bent closer, perceiving the glint of metal above the first button of her tunic, nestled below her collarbones.

He reached, then pulled his hands back. Those medallions were loaded with magic, and if someone tried to take them from the girls, they'd get a spark of fire on their fingers.

"Will you give me your medallion?" he asked. "I want to look at it."

Clair sat still for a breath or two, as if her thoughts came from very far away, then her hands moved to her throat, and she lifted the chain over her head and dropped the thing onto Senrid's palm with a soft *ching*.

"Thank you. I'll be right back," he said.

He walked out of the throne room to the hall, where he fingered the medallion, then shrugged. Why not try? He whispered the transport spell, picturing the girls' underground hideout, and moments later staggered a few steps forward on the brightly colored wool rug in the main chamber. The stuffy air smelled stale, laden with traces of a long-ago meal.

"Anyone here?" he called.

The quick patter of bare feet on the smooth dirt tunnel heralded one of Clair's friends. Her brows lifted, then snapped together. "What are you doing here?"

"Looking for Liere, so I can get her to safety before Siamis nabs her," Senrid said, and remembered that this particular girl, though she looked ordinary enough—thin, with short hair a soft tint midway between brown and blond, and a light scattering of freckles across her high-bridged nose—was not actually human. He remembered her name then: Dhana.

"Not here," Dhana said with an air of triumph. "None of 'em are."

"They escaped Siamis's spell, then?"

Dhana's changeable expression hardened. "Clair made them promise. If Siamis showed up, and he did. Walked right into the interview room. She couldn't get away. Me and Ben are watching over things. Ben stays in animal shape, and Siamis's magic can't do anything to me," Dhana said. She grinned. "So I got to see Andrea chase the eleveners out of the forest."

"Who?"

"Andrea. The forest ghost," Dhana stated.

Senrid couldn't help the derisive expression the word 'ghost' sparked, but Dhana just laughed. "Go ahead. Call me a liar. I was just talking to her this morning."

"Talking. To a ghost," Senrid said.

Dhana shrugged. "She usually only talks to Seshe. When she appears, which isn't often. Maybe they get foggier over the centuries."

Senrid was thinking that it couldn't be a ghost. Magical anomaly, maybe. But he wasn't going to argue.

Dhana had been eyeing him, trying to figure out what Clair would want. Well, she knew what Clair would want. She knew as soon as Senrid appeared. The problem was, in this instance, what Clair would want might not be what CJ wanted.

But she decided to do it anyway. "They're at Kitty and Leander's. Something about the spell Hibern was going to teach Leander, to break Siamis's enchantment."

Senrid stared, astounded, forced himself not to blurt questions, and said, "Thanks. Here's Clair's medallion." He dropped the thing onto her palm and braced himself for another transfer, to a long-familiar Destination.

When he came out of it, he found himself sitting on the gravel outside a familiar small, square castle, the size of an outpost.

This was the royal castle of Vasande Leror, an inkblot of land adjacent to the northeast corner of Marloven Hess, above the Nelkereth plains. Vasande Leror had once belonged to Marloven Hess. Its king, Leander Tlennen-Hess, was even related to Senrid way, way back in their family trees. And they both had endured similar problems in coming to their crowns.

Senrid got to his feet, shrugging away the ache in his joints from so much magic transfer. It would be harder to shake away the reaction of irritation he'd felt at Dhana's news.

It was strong enough to make him angry, so he took the time to sort it out.

One. There was no reason Hibern ought to have come to Senrid first, if there really was an antidote to Siamis's enchantment. He could easily imagine her saying, "Yes, I could give it to you, and what would you do with it? You'll sit around and watch your academy play games, whereas Leander will go out and use it."

Two. Leander was really good at magic and history, which was why Senrid had made sure that he was invited into the alliance. But Senrid hadn't invited him himself because—

Three. Leander's stepsister, Kyale. She'd once helped Senrid, grudgingly, when he finally defeated his uncle. But she was the most self-involved, annoying person Senrid had ever met.

No help for it. He brushed off the last of the dust, noting that if Leander still had guards, they weren't very competent, and walked in through the barren stone entrance, then turned in the direction of the kitchens, where most often Leander was to be found if he wasn't in his study.

And there was Kyale's high voice echoing down the hall. Considered as a voice, it could have been pleasant, but her constant, simmering anger (akin to his own, he was very well aware) made it shrill. At least he didn't sound self-righteous.

He hoped.

"Leander, really, a king ought to at least receive royalty in a drawing room. Let's get them to move upstairs. It's such a pretty room, and it's silly, sitting there with nobody in it, and here we all are, crammed into that smelly old kitchen."

"The Mearsieans like to gather in their own kitchen, Kitty," Leander said patiently. "And CJ never acts like a princess."

"Well, maybe she should."

"I don't see the purpose in getting the kitchen help to haul all that food and those dishes upstairs, and then haul it all back again, when they've got things to do to get ready for the festival."

"There isn't going to be any festival if Siamis comes!"

This was obviously a private conversation, but Senrid decided it was time to interrupt. "Are the Mearsieans here?" he asked, rounding the corner.

The two turned, Leander as tall as Puddlenose, dark-haired, with bright green eyes that he'd inherited from the ancestor he and Senrid shared. He dressed like a forest ranger, in a rough old long tunic over loose trousers. Kyale was tiny, with silvery hair and light gray eyes, wearing a gown of lace and fragile tissue over satin, festooned with ribbons and bows.

Leander smiled with genuine welcome, and Kyale scowled. "Yes, they are," Leander said. "In the kitchen."

There was no irony in his voice, sparking amazement and admiration in Senrid. Though Leander regarded himself as Kyale's brother, he wasn't. The only relation between them was the disastrous marriage Kyale's mother had tricked Leander's aged father into making before she arranged his murder so she could reign as queen.

But none of that was Kyale's fault. In fact, Senrid's private suspicion was that Kyale might even have been stolen from somewhere else, a conveniently acquired daughter for the ambitious queen.

He showed no sign of these reflections as he followed the two into the servants' mess area beyond the kitchen, Kyale sighing dramatically.

Leander held open the door, whispering, "Maybe you can convince them to get themselves to the Delfina Valley." He sent a glance at the Mearsiean girls, who had crowded around the plain table that Leander and his servants customarily sat at.

Seven faces turned his way. Senrid searched among them, his disappointment so sharp he couldn't keep it from his voice as he said to Leander, "Liere isn't here? Is she safe, at least?"

CJ hopped up, a short figure in her habitual white shirt, long black vest, and green skirt, bare feet planted wide. "Who cares about Sartora?" she demanded, the black line of her brow furrowed over angry blue eyes. "I mean, I care!" She exclaimed, hands going out. "I do! We all do! But she can take care of herself, can't she, with all those mind powers?" CJ's fingers whirled little circles on either side of her head. "Clair got Siamised, because of her. And I want to go back to make sure she's safe." She shifted her glare to Leander. "And to unspell her, if it really works."

"You can't," Senrid said. "Unless you want to walk right into whatever trap Siamis laid. In which case, you'll deserve what you get for willful stupidity."

CJ kicked an imaginary object, then said in a less belligerent tone, "We have to do *something.* We can't just leave her there."

"That's why we have to wait for Hibern," Leander said.

Senrid said, "What's going on?"

Kyale, obviously tired of not being the center of attention, spoke up in a self-important tone, "There's been a horrid war in Bereth Ferian."

Leander said quickly, "Mage struggles. Not armies."

"Should we try to help?" Senrid offered, thinking of Liere in the middle of it, probably believing it her duty, and Arthur struggling to cope, knowing it was his. Though he was merely a mage student.

"I suspect they wouldn't take your offer." Leander's smile turned wry, and when Senrid had to laugh, acknowledging the truth of it, Leander added, "They wouldn't take me, either, I'm sure. Having been largely self-taught."

CJ's fierce blue gaze shifted from one boy to the other, and she said, "You mean they don't want kids. Think we're stupid and useless."

Senrid tried for fairness. "I think it's natural to look to the strongest and most experienced."

CJ crossed her arms with a thump against her scrawny chest. "Did you get that from your stenchiferous Uncle Bully?"

Senrid flushed. "When people—not only Marlovens—can't defend themselves, they look to someone stronger. It's human nature. Not Marloven nature. Or Sartoran nature. Or whatever else you want to call it. A boy to his older brother, the older brother to his father, his father to the jarl, the jarl to the king. Whatever regional authorities are called. And kings turn to their armies, or to their law."

CJ glowered. "I remember your laws," she fired back. "The first time I ever heard of you was when Leander came here to warn us that you were going to come into our country, and drag Falinneh back to yours for execution. Because why? Because she helped some people, and what did Leander say your fine and superior law was? 'You don't cross Marloven kings and live.'"

Senrid flushed to the ears. "Leander didn't know shit about our laws," he retorted, then reined his temper hard, and forced himself to really look at her pale face, at the betraying signs of anger and fear. This was stubborn loyalty he was seeing, not Kyale's equally stubborn wish to be the center of attention. CJ was clearly one spell away from transferring back to rescue Clair any way she could.

Leander walked between them, holding out a tray of fresh cinnamon buns that he must have fetched that moment from the kitchen behind them. "Take one," he invited. "Both of you. And please, don't pull me into your argument." To CJ, "When I told you that, I was ignorant about Marloven Hess. Which has its problems. Did, and does. But, well, I learned that that was never law. More like tradition. *Old* tradition. No longer in force."

Senrid added, "How many times have you crossed me? Enjoying every moment. It seems to me you're still alive."

"Okay. Yeah." CJ grinned, but she still radiated tension. "True! On both counts."

Before anyone else could put in unwanted opinions, a faint sense of magic alerted Senrid.

Leander glanced toward the door. So he'd felt it as well. But whatever tracer had alerted him didn't disturb him unduly, so Senrid relaxed.

Then Hibern walked in, tall and gaunt as always, her long black hair flagging against her blue robe. Her black eyes were marked underneath, indicating too little sleep.

She glanced from CJ squared off to Senrid's tight shoulders and curled lip, and said quickly, "I'm sorry I haven't answered any of your notes. We've been working so hard, and transferring back and forth between Murial's and the northern mage school until Siamis's mages attacked, and I left my notecase . . . well," she stuttered to a stop, seeing impatience in Senrid and subtle signs of tension in the others.

She let out a short breath. They clearly didn't care about the months of study, trial, and error, error, error. She forced herself to skip to what they would care about. "Erai-Yanya," she stated, "has figured out an antidote to Siamis's enchantment."

And everyone started talking at once.

Hibern waited until they stopped exclaiming and shouting questions, then added, "And we just discovered that it works. I was there with Erai-Yanya. We freed Oalthoreh from the enchantment. We left her freeing all the other mages up north. Murial—"

"You mean Clair's Aunt Murial?" CJ interrupted.

"Yes. I think you know that she and Erai-Yanya studied together as students, right? She's been helping all along. Right at this moment, she's still trying to break the magical traps around that palace, and said that you girls should stay away. Erai-Yanya says someone Siamis would never lay magical traps for must go break the enchantment over Clair."

Leander said, "That would be me. Want to come?" He glanced at Senrid, a friendly grin. "Like old times."

Kyale scowled resentfully, as Senrid grinned back. Whenever they could, that first year or so after they both came to their thrones, they'd tried setting magic traps for the other, and breaking them. Win or lose, they'd go back and study. But since those days that now seemed a lifetime ago, they'd had less time for that kind of fun.

Hibern added, "And she also warned that if you break Siamis's spell, he's probably going to be able to trace the magic. And come after you."

Leander said, "I counted on that. Everything is ready here. As soon as we do this, we all have our transfer tokens to get to the Valley of Delfina. Though I doubt he'll bother with Vasande Leror. We're too small."

"And I've given certain orders in Marloven Hess as well. He wants my army? He won't find it," Senrid said. And in a lower voice, "All that's left is the city guard, but they won't take Choreid Dhelerei easily. And Detlev can't get in at all. What about Liere?"

Hibern said, "She and Arthur were swept off by the northern mages to someplace Norsunder can't possibly find them. Without the dyr, Liere can't break that enchantment, though she feels really bad about that."

Senrid said, "This new antidote doesn't need the dyr?" He knew that Liere had to be writhing with guilt and anxiety over not being able to rescue the world, but if there was a new way around that nasty object . . .

"No." Hibern made a negating motion. "We know that Siamis and his evil uncle want the dyr back, very badly. All the mages agree that this magical attack up north was a ruse to flush out Liere and the dyr, so they could grab them both. As I told Leander, the antidote is not easy. First, you have to get the attention of the enchanted person through using a personal object of theirs . . ."

Two conversations were going on, CJ and the Mearsieans dividing off to plan their raid to reclaim Clair, and Hibern instructing Leander and Senrid in the new spell.

Kyale looked from one to the other, and sighed. "I may as well go pet my cats," she said loudly.

Everyone stopped talking. "Let's go," Leander said.

For CJ, the rescue of Clair, her most important priority, was almost an anticlimax. First of all, none of the girls could go near the white palace because of magical traps.

They found Murial alone at the top of what had once been the town square, and now was a broad street leading away from the palace terrace and Destination down the eastern slope into the town, the townspeople keeping a prudent distance. Dhana sat on the terrace steps near the Destination, swinging Clair's medallion on its chain.

When all had arrived one by one, then recovered from the transfer, Leander said, "First I need a personal object of Clair's."

Dhana silently held out the medallion, then joined the anxiously awaiting girls as he and Senrid proceeded cautiously into the silent palace made of strange white almost-stone that somehow always got remembered as marble.

Clair was a still, small figure on the throne, exactly where Senrid had left her. Leander swung the medallion with intent. When Clair's hazel gaze lost its blind affect and her eyes began following the medallion, Leander said the spell.

Sensitive to magic, Leander and Senrid stepped back a pace as a not-quite-blow, not-quite-wind radiated outward. For an instant the air scintillated, then the spell was gone, and Clair stirred, blinked, and said, "How did you two get here?"

Senrid turned to Leander. "Want to explain?"

A short time later the three walked out, and Clair was surrounded by shrieking, jumping girls. Leander and Senrid approached Murial.

"Good," the woman said. "This is our second success. I'll take care to spread it. Now, get out of here. I'm certain Siamis layered traps within that enchantment, which will alert him. I'll prepare some nice surprises if he or anyone from Norsunder does show up."

Murial stepped up to the crowd of girls, who fell silent. She and Clair hugged, then she said to them all, "I want you all to go somewhere safe. Don't tell me where, in case. But I believe I am much safer than you, as I am not Siamis's target. *But listen to me first.*"

Everyone fell silent, Senrid wary.

Murial said, "Keep the antidote spell to yourselves for the moment. It's still new, and while we now know it works, we don't know if, or how, Siamis will retaliate. And we certainly don't want all your friends haring off to try the spell without any plan or protection. It's terrible that people are enchanted, but at least they are in no pain. Correct?"

Clair said, "True. It's like being asleep, kind of."

Murial gave a tiny nod. "So waiting until the senior mages decide how best to deploy it is the best course right now. Will you do that?"

They agreed.

"Then go somewhere safe," Murial said gently.

Senrid longed to check on Marloven Hess, but remembered what Clair looked like sitting on that throne, her expression utterly empty. Asleep or not, he loathed the idea of it happening to him—and of being unable to resist anything Siamis might tell him to do while he was 'asleep.'

He yanked out the token he'd readied the day the bells rang in Marloven Hess, and transferred to Delfina Valley.

Clair met Leander's gaze, and she saw agreement there. She said to Murial, "I'll fetch my notecase. Will you write to me if anything happens?"

Murial said, "You may be sure I will."

## Chapter Eight

*Sharmadi (Seventhmonth), 4742 AF*
*Sarendan and Delfina Valley*

IT was late at night when Peitar Selenna heard footsteps outside his study.

He noted them, hoping Lilah was not awake so late, but this new line of inquiry into the nature of Dena Yeresbeth was so intriguing!

He put his finger on the moldering page he'd been translating mentally from Sartoran. He'd stumbled across the ancient book, which had been completely mis-shelved among books for beginner mages trying to learn the quake easement magic. Its extreme age had caught his attention, an anomaly.

Tiredness vanished as he reread a passage in growing wonder. It really seemed that the translator, twelve centuries ago, had misinterpreted the Ancient Sartoran. Unless the meaning of the word had shifted . . .

"The first," came a pleasant voice. "But the misinterpretation goes back much farther than twelve centuries."

Peitar looked up, startled, at an unfamiliar fellow maybe a year or so younger than he was, wind-tousled wheat-colored hair glinting in the candle light, his white linen shirt dappled with raindrops. "Who—"

"I just arrived from Sartor," the newcomer said with a smile. "Why candles? Where are your glowglobes? Surely they provide better light to read by."

"I made a promise," Peitar said, "not to work long past midnight. So I made time candles. What's your source for the mistranslated word for ancient magic, and how did you find it?" He sat back, pleased at the prospect of discussing magic, his mind open with questions. "Did Tsauderei send you?"

"No," said Siamis, and closed the trap.

He glanced through Peitar's books, then gently shut them all, as Peitar gazed beyond the walls into timelessness. "It's almost a shame you won't remember your discovery," Siamis said, listening on the mental plane as the enchantment ringed outward. Asleep or awake, all those within the border who shared the same loyalty for which Peitar served as symbol slid into that same timelessness.

"Almost," Siamis said, and made that one book vanish. Then Siamis caught Peitar's gaze and issued the instructions that Peitar was to follow.

Derek woke to the rumble of distant thunder. He blinked, his eyes burning. He sat up, rubbing the crust from his eyelids and working his dry mouth. The sound of voices emerged from the fading thunder: Tsauderei's gravely old man's voice, and the nasal honk of a teenage boy.

Derek turned his head, finding a broad window overlooking a sky full of tumbling clouds, gold-lit at one end, purple at the other. A flicker of lightning briefly outlined the clouds as they sailed away.

He sat up, his head pounding. He had slid to the floor, tangling himself up in a quilt.

He flung away the covering and looked around. At the other end of the cottage, the old mage sat with a hunch-shouldered, black-haired young teen whose pasty face was completely unfamiliar. The kid wore shapeless garments of rusty black.

They each looked Derek's way, then Tsauderei said something in another language, his tone kindly.

The teen ducked his head, mumbled an answer, then sloped out the door. He reappeared in the window a moment later, shuffling toward the edge of the cliff the cottage sat on. As Derek watched, he made an ungainly, tentative hop, then came down slowly. He hopped higher, arms wiggling, and floated down. Then he sprang upward, limbs flapping like an ungainly crow as he shot out over the cliff into air. Derek heard a faint, strangled yell through the thick window glass.

Tsauderei approached, leaning heavily on a cane. The old mage's face looked more furrowed than Derek remembered it.

"Who's that?" Derek asked. Even his voice felt crusty.

"His name is Jilo."

"Why is he dressed like that? Someone's livery?" Derek didn't hide the contempt in his voice for whoever would put his servants in such willfully ugly garb.

"Jilo is a Chwahir. They all dress like that."

"Chwahir," Derek repeated. That explained the sickly, pale skin. He'd never seen any Chwahir, but he'd heard jokes about moon- and platter-faces.

"He is, I hope and trust, the first of several refugees from the various kingdoms Norsunder is currently attacking."

"Someone else besides us?" Derek asked.

"Everon," Tsauderei stated, "is at present getting the worst of it."

Worse than the other day? The tide of memory flooded unmercifully, prompting a deep desire for vengeance. "I've got to get back." Derek struggled to his feet, head swimming. He leaned against a bookcase. "I promised Peitar I'd get those youngsters out."

Tsauderei sank into the empty wing-backed chair, and let out a long sigh. "Derek, I have bad news for you."

"Worse than the battle I lost? Another battle," Derek said wryly, lunging toward the door in reflex.

"To a degree it's worse than that." Derek jolted to a stop when Tsauderei waggled a hand back and forth. "After you fell asleep, I had to go to aid my fellow mages in Bereth Ferian. But while I was there, expecting magical attack from Siamis, he was here. In Sarendan. He put Peitar under enchantment, which extends to the entire kingdom."

Lightning shot through Derek's nerves. "I've got to do something!"

"You can stay here. Until the situation is clearer."

"I failed. Again," Derek muttered, his gaze going sightlessly from object to object.

Tsauderei waited for comprehension; Derek glanced up. "But I can't stay here. There are those children still in Sarendan. Including Lilah, Bren, and Innon. I promised Peitar I'd get them to safety here."

"I'm aware."

"The flims you put the magic on are still sitting in my house."

"Most likely."

"So give me the magic to go back and rescue them."

"No. Not yet. Not until I know the nature of the magic on Peitar, and . . ." Tsauderei paused, and decided against explaining how the few mages who as yet knew about Erai-Yanya's antidote were waiting to discover if it held. ". . . and what Norsunder would do."

And Derek didn't care about magic. "You can't keep me here," he stated.

"I can't stop you from walking out," Tsauderei retorted. "It'll take you, oh, maybe six weeks to clamber the mountains to the border. Longer, in the storms I predict as a result of my interference the other day."

Derek remembered the sudden storm, which sparked an older memory: the sudden storm the dawn he and Peitar were marched out to face execution. "That was you?"

Tsauderei brought his chin down, his white beard rippling on his chest. "The local weather will be disturbed for a time, but this is the mountains. Such storms are frequent. It will do little harm. Except maybe to lone travelers scrambling over the cliff faces. I trust any such will be Norsundrian stragglers."

Derek drew in a shaky breath. "Where is that little girl who ended Siamis's enchantment before?"

"She's expected here any time, as it transpires. We will discuss that when she does arrive."

Derek let his breath go. "All right." A plan of action, of sorts. He could live with that. "What can I do?" He added, "Don't tell me I'm useless because I don't know magic."

"There is a very important service you could provide, actually. Those children you brought, added to others who are gathering here, will need organization. This Valley has served as a refuge before, from time to time, and I believe we can accommodate them, but when they tire of swimming in the lake and flying, they will probably get restless. I would not like to see them disturbing the villagers unduly."

Derek gave a short nod. He had a lot to learn before he'd become a good commander. But he did know how to organize a rabble.

"All right," he said. "Where are they? Who claims authority here? Some damned noble, no doubt?"

"'Damned' is not for me to decide," Tsauderei said wryly. "But you may look to me for whatever authority exists. Now, sit down. There's fresh bread on the table over there, and some good goat cheese. If you like Sartoran steep, you may fill the kettle from the pump in that corner. The dried leaves are in that lacquered canister with the flowers painted on it, that Lilah's mother made for me when she was about ten."

Derek was surprised enough to obey without question.

Tsauderei nodded, and smiled benignly. "You can eat, and listen, while I claim the privilege of the old and regale you with the Valley's history so you will understand how things are done here. We need to go far, far back in history, when magic was much stronger in the world. This valley was a home for aging mages, or those who needed to retreat from the world, as well as for the small population of people whose descendants' houses you can see on the other plateaus. . . ."

*Everon*

Princess Tahra Delieth of Everon sat up in bed. There was nothing to get up *for*, but too much to get away *from*.

She swung her feet out of bed, pressing them to the floor at exactly the same moment, all ten toes. Then she got up and walked to her dresser, five steps each side. Even stayed clear. Odd was brown, and brown meant a bad day.

Tahra knew that counting steps and touching her things in the right order didn't make any difference outside her room. Her father had told her. Her mother had told her. Uncle Roderic had told her. Rel had told her. Mearsieanne had told her. Even Glenn had bored on at length.

That was fine. Nothing she did or didn't do in the right way, the right order, affected other things, except she knew if she didn't do them right, she had a bad day. If she did them right, she might have a good day. Might was better than nothing. Clear was better than mud brown.

But all the days had been bad, ever since this war happened. Going on three weeks, now, she and Glenn had to stay in the palace all day, and their parents were always in conference. Always with long faces. Every couple of days there seemed to be new skirmishes somewhere, which meant somebody new was dead.

Here it was, Restday again, the third since the Norsundrians had invaded, killing Valenn and taking over the harbor.

Today was to be the memorial for the latest dead.

Tahra stepped through her cleaning frame, one two, and decided that yesterday's trousers and shirt would do. No one would notice if she put on a proper mourning robe over them. She lifted the white one from the trunk, shook it out twice, then pulled it on, both arms at the same time. Sash, over, over, under, through. The ends . . . yes, they hung together. Clear, so far. Everything in order.

Relieved, she put on stockings and shoes, then brushed her hair, twenty strokes left, twenty right.

When she stepped out, she found her mother having just left her suite, her shining dark hair with white starliss braided into it. "Darling," Mersedes Carinna exclaimed, eyeing her daughter. "I was about to send Jenel to you."

"I'm ready. And my hair is neat. See?" Tahra turned, so her mother could see her ordered hair. Tahra had cut hers to shoulder length, like Glenn's, so she wouldn't have to sit there and endure someone's fingers in it. Just the thought made her skin crawl.

Mersedes Carinna saw Tahra's long face turn obdurate. Her heart already ached at the loss of Alstha, her husband's new sweeting; life was so fragile, she believed that joy should be embraced fiercely wherever it came. Her arms ached to hold her daughter within their circle, but Tahra had pushed her away long ago.

She forced herself to smile, and to say, "You look quite proper. Come, let us not keep Uncle Roderic waiting."

Tahra's maid Jenel was standing by with an understanding smile, holding the dethorned white roses that Tahra would carry. She quietly surrendered them into Tahra's keeping without permitting their fingers to touch, which Tahra was grateful for.

They waited until the king's door opened and he joined them, sorrow carving lines into his face as he reached down to kiss Mama.

Tahra stiffened when it was her turn, and grimaced at the warm, moist pressure of his lips on her cheek, the brush of his beard against her neck.

As the king saluted Glenn, Tahra hastily wiped her cheek against her shoulder, then walked beside her brother behind their royal parents, leading the procession into the court.

There, people waited for them. Tahra looked into each face; last was Uncle Roderic, his head down, only his graying beard visible. It wasn't until she was within ten paces that she discovered it wasn't Uncle Roderic at all, but some gray-bearded man wearing the white robes of the Knights of Dei with the commander's gold trefoil embroidered on the shoulder.

Her parents had been watching. The king flashed a bitter smile at his wife, a shared moment of anticipatory triumph.

Henerek, watching through field glasses from a rooftop in the city, saw that brief grin, cursed, and lifted his hand in a fist, signaling his galloper waiting at the end of Woolens Row: whatever caused that smile, there was a good chance his surprise attack wasn't.

And that meant the Knights—or someone—weren't all ranged down below, but were about to attack his hostage towns.

"Go, go, go," he yelled.

Below, the stately procession followed the four biers along the tree-lined path leading from the palace to the Knights' square. The citizens of Ferdrian tossed showers of white petals, gathered in the dew before sunup.

The royal family and the supposed Knights were barely visible in the soft, fragrant snow of petals, tranquil and melancholy for the space of twenty steps.

*Zing!* Then the first arrow hissed through the air. Shields whipped up, as citizens screamed in terror and outrage. Henerek's assassination team began to converge, to find themselves in turn shot at from behind chimney pots and attic windows that looked down on either side of the royal parade: while they had crept over roofs into position, watching the palace, young Knight candidates had gained their rooftop vantages through the houses, and one by one shot half of Henerek's assassins, Roderic Dei's daughter Carinna leading the team.

A day's fast ride away, Rel sat behind a honeysuckle shrub, watching bees bumble between blossoms as the summer sun rose, baking the back of his head. Down beyond the slope, along a sluggish river, lay the two towns that the Norsundrians had taken when they were driven from the harbor.

Behind Rel, Roderic Dei sat in the lee of a squat juniper, talking quietly to his new captain, another of his weedy teenage daughters serving as squire. She looked as upset as all of them had to feel, not to be present as the rest of Everon sang the memorial farewell to the gallant Captain Alstha and three other Knights. Rel's mind wandered to Atan, far to the south. He hoped Sartor was all right. But he could do little there—the royal council had made it clear that the mages were in charge.

The commander raised a hand, halting the conversation. Everyone stilled as he flicked open his notecase, read, then beckoned to Rel, who was the duty runner for the day.

Rel hunched over, hoping his head and shoulders were not visible above the curling tendrils at the top of the honeysuckle.

The commander said grimly, "It's as the king expected. Henerek has not sufficient a sense of honor to grant us this Restday memorial. Our decoys are busy chasing his assassins over the rooftops right now."

"Ah," said Rel. Not only did that give the Everoneth leave to attack in turn, by their own code, it probably strengthened their resolve to rescue the hapless citizens whose lives the Norsundrians had threatened.

"Also, Henerek is apparently leading the would-be assassins, which means he's not here," Roderic said. "And so, let us put the secondary plan in motion."

Rel nodded his assent, backed away, and returned to his position, which was in line of sight of two watchers. He held up his hand, then pumped it twice, once to each side.

A count of fifty as the signal spread to the other side of the river, and then it was time to move.

Rel hated covert movement. He was not made for skulking. His neck and spine ached by the time he had duck-waddled, hunched over, from bush to bush along a gentle inward slope carved by a chuckling spring that emptied into the river; his shield and sword seemed to grow extra corners just to gouge him in unexpected places. Sweat soaked his clothes and ran down the back of his neck by the time he'd reached the candle-bloom chestnuts along the base of the hill.

They'd nearly reached the village when the first signs of the enemy appeared: archers on the rooftops. A hail of arrows slowed the Everoneth slightly, but everyone had shields up.

Then the first wave of attackers boiled out from between sleepy-seeming cottages, two forces going for the Knights forward of Rel's position. Rel ripped free his sword, whirling it in tight circles to either side as he charged.

A furious battle compounded of dust, sweat, the fierce glint of sun off steel, and he was through the line of Norsundrians, but glimpsed more beyond the houses. Where were the villagers who were supposed to rise against the enemy? A sense of foreboding grew as he loped down a narrow alley between cottages, and he peered cautiously over a projecting porch rail.

The village square was crowded, the villagers gathered in a tight group, ringed by Norsundrians. Swords and knives held at the throats of all the children. Along the perimeter, hidden Norsundrians attacked the occasional Knights who burst through singly or in pairs. Rel dropped back, then retreated at top speed, his breath burning his throat. He caught sight of Roderic and the main body descending in columns fifty paces away.

Rel caught up before Roderic reached his first cottage. In a few gasped words, he repeated what he'd seen.

Roderic's face blanched nearly as gray as his beard. Then he jerked his mailed fist at the signaler. "Sound the retreat."

Nauseated from thirst and heat, Rel fought his way past the laughing, hooting enemy, and at a gesture from his patrol leader, helped to pick up a fallen comrade to carry up the hill.

Stalemate—again. And again, new dead to mourn.

At that same moment, in Sarendan's capital, Miraleste, Kessler marshaled his company.

They'd enjoyed a couple days of rest and relaxation in the enchanted city, while Kessler amused himself with locating Peitar Selenna's annoying sister, one of the brats who had caused him so much trouble in the Sartoran enchantment fiasco a couple years back.

He tested the limits of Siamis's spell to see how it was put together by asking questions, and repeating demands, over and over. Before he left, he laid a blood-enchantment over a blade. All it needed was contact with Derek Diamagan's blood to work. He pressed the enchanted blade into Lilah Selenna's hand, and ordered her to stab Derek Diamagan on sight.

Laughing at the brat's slack face, he summoned his company and said, "To the coast. Double-time. We're off to Everon to have some fun."

## Chapter Nine

*Othdi (Eighthmonth), 4742 AF*
*Delfina Valley*

**"Y**OU'LL stay here," Tsauderei said, as he and Jilo flew past the main plateau of the Delfina Valley. Jilo glanced down at steep roofs made of slate. Otherwise the houses reminded him of those in Mearsies Heili, with colors on the shutters, the doors, and the plastered walls.

Jilo had assumed the old mage couldn't fly, he was so stiff-jointed, but flying clearly made movement easy for him. It was odd, how his body felt bird-light, but his hair and clothes did not float upward, the way they did in water. He wondered how the flying spell was bound, and who had done it.

Tsauderei led Jilo to the largest house in the Valley. It had been built on a plateau of its own, in the midst of a wildly overgrown garden. "This belongs to Peitar and Lilah Selenna," Tsauderei said, his voice low with regret. "It once belonged to their mother. They won't mind its being used."

When they landed, Tsauderei winced as the magic dissipated, the ground again pulling at his joints the moment his feet touched down. He lifted the latch and led the way into a slate-floored foyer, past a beautiful salon done in white and black. "Run upstairs, and pick out a bed," Tsauderei said. "Go ahead. I'll wait, in case you have questions."

Jilo walked from room to room and back again, up the steep stairs and down, just looking at all the colors, and how each fitted well with the next. He found a trunk filled with art supplies next to a bed, the edges of the paper curled from age. He knew an abandoned trunk when he saw it and dared to claim it for his own.

Also in the trunk, he found folded clothing: tunics of various sizes, riding trousers, socks, various types of shoes. All in summer-light fabrics, even colors.

Elsewhere in the room was another bed, another trunk. There were two gabled windows, and between them a desk. On the corner opposite the window, there stood a wooden frame that looked like a window frame with no window. When he approached it, he felt magic. A cleaning frame! For two people? In Chwahirsland, the only ones left were in barracks, for officers.

He ran downstairs. "I found a chamber," he said. "Is there someone living here who does drawing?"

"Bren." There was the regret again. "He won't mind sharing. Whatever art gear he left wasn't what he wanted to take back into Sarendan. In fact, I encourage you to investigate the clothes in the trunk, which are donations from a couple generations of family and guests. Unless you're fond of yours."

"No," Jilo said. "But may I use the cleaning frame?"

"As often as you wish. You might consider resuming your studies. If you do, I recommend visiting Atan, who lives in the hermit's cottage, on the platform at the western end of the Valley."

"Atan?"

"She's your age. An accomplished mage student."

Jilo nodded, but he couldn't get his thoughts past that cleaning frame for a single bedroom. Why wouldn't Wan-Edhe permit people to have cleaning frames? Because he despised the people. Because the onerous task of scrubbing laundry and trying to dry it in the harsh weather kept people busy who might otherwise be fomenting revolt, of course.

Jilo was going to change that first thing when he returned.

"As for meals, I have an arrangement with a colleague at a very popular inn in Colend. We will not burden the locals with feeding the refugees."

Tsauderei had explained on Jilo's first night that under ordinary circumstances the Valley was nearly impossible to get to. Transfers were strictly warded. Access to the Valley was by flying, and the prospective visitor appeared in Tsauderei's scry stone. He could block the magic with a word, and deny their entry.

But for the current refugees, he had created special transfer tokens like the one that had brought Jilo directly to his cottage. Jilo found this demonstration of the power of waxer magic so intriguing he was almost tempted to talk to a stranger, this Atan.

That night and the next, Jilo only saw Tsauderei at meal times. Otherwise he was alone. He dared the trunk, choosing one of those soft shirts, dyed a bright yellow, with blue embroidery in fanciful blossoms down the front. It felt good next to his skin, and he liked the cheerful color, but years of habit were difficult to break, and he didn't want anyone actually seeing him.

Yet when the sun was out, he couldn't bear to be inside. Sometimes he left through the window, because he could. He still didn't like the idea of putting himself into the deep waters of the lake. He had only swum in small ponds during the Shadowland days. He watched from above as other kids swam, always staying away from the far end, where some kind of noxious flowers grew.

And the food! Goat cheese was familiar, but the flavor, so delicate and delicious, wasn't. Jilo knew that this was because the goats ate sweet grass and clover, far better than the bitter, drought-tough weeds eaten by Chwahir goats.

All the food was delicious.

But by the end of that second night the questions began to proliferate, bringing back the old worries: was Chwahirsland safer with him home, or away? If he returned, what could he actually do, if Wan-Edhe was sent back from Norsunder?

He checked the book convulsively. That raised more worries: what if someone found the book? Tsauderei had said that the Valley was laced with very deep protections, ancient ones impossible now to reproduce— like the flying spell. No one could do any sort of magic without Tsauderei knowing. Creating a tiny pocket beyond space and time was (this surprised Jilo to discover) considered a major piece of magical working, and Tsauderei would know immediately. Did that mean he'd know what was in the book? Or demand to know?

The last worry was what would happen when the Mearsieans showed up and found him (ostensibly) part of their alliance. Or maybe they'd think him only a refugee, as Tsauderei did. In all his talk, the old mage never mentioned the alliance, whereas he was clear about this valley having served as a refuge from Norsunder many times in the past.

The third morning, Jilo woke to the sound of high girlish voices elsewhere in the house. He decided he'd better get it over with, dressed, and went downstairs, to discover the Mearsieans newly arrived.

"Jilo! You here?" Falinneh exclaimed, echoed by others.

Falinneh pointed and laughed, almost doubled over, at the idea of Jilo in normal clothes. She didn't intend to be mean, but he just looked so . . . so odd!

Several laughed, surprised to see a Chwahir in anything but rusty black, except for Seshe, the tall quiet girl, who studied Jilo's mottled face and said, "I think it looks nice."

"Yes!" CJ said, bright blue eyes going from Jilo to the tall girl and back. "That is a pretty shirt. Where did you get it?"

Now they all stared at Jilo. He cringed inside, waiting for the punch line of the joke. Or was she accusing him of theft? Of course they were making fun of him. They always had. He'd never understood those girls and their fast games and slang.

CJ tried again. She said to Jilo, "Did that grunge-bearded geez of a king splat back on the throne?"

Jilo stared back, and by the time he understood she meant Wan-Edhe, CJ thought he was ignoring her, and turned away to join the other girls crowding protectively around Clair, all talking at once, as they left the house and took off like a flock of starlings to experiment with flying over the lake.

Jilo fled back to his room, ripped off the green silky shirt, put it through the cleaning frame, then put it at the very bottom of the trunk.

When he was back in his old clothes, he took off again, his intention to avoid any encounters at all by exploring the limits of the flying area.

On his return mid-afternoon, he angled down to the open bedroom window, where he surprised Senrid and a tall, thin, dark-haired boy startlingly symmetrical of feature. No, not just symmetrical, it was the way he was put together. Was this what people called 'handsome'? Jilo discovered an urge to draw him in order to figure out what compelled the eye.

Senrid whirled around, one hand going to the other sleeve, then dropping when he recognized Jilo. "Tsauderei told us to bunk in here with you. They expect to fill up the other rooms. This is Leander."

"Jilo."

"Well met," Leander said pleasantly.

Jilo didn't know what he was supposed to say to that, so he mumbled something and retreated to his side of the room. He'd learned from Senrid that Vasande Leror was a tiny kingdom next to Marloven Hess,

and that its king was a boy named Leander. These two who were historically supposed to be enemies worked together to sling a canvas hammock between candle sconces on adjoining walls. It took the effort of
both boys to get the thing stable, after which began a friendly argument
about who was to get the second bed, and who the hammock.

Senrid said, "Look, the way we've got this thing hung, whoever is in
it is going to have their knees up by their ears. Since you're taller than I
am by at least a hand, that means you'll hang lower, right? I don't want
your butt directly over my head. If you fart, I'll have to kill you."

"So you put your head at that end of the bed," Leander pointed out.
"And we'll cinch this hammock up tighter." He moved to the sconces
and efficiently retied the hammock at both ends.

Then Senrid leaped up and landed in the hammock, which swung
dangerously. The way he grinned, it was clear he liked it, and Leander
gave up, throwing his travel pack on the bed.

The two born princes acted more like the lowest recruits as they
took turns swinging in the hammock and trying to launch themselves
from it to the open window. Jilo watched, fascinated; they laughed as
one or the other got tangled in the hammock, or knocked into the win-
dowsill or wall.

When Leander got himself successfully out the window, he let out a
whoop of triumph, then circled back and peered inside, arms swinging
as he tried to stabilize himself midair. "I'll never use a door again," he
predicted. "While I'm here. I should probably make sure Kitty is all
right, and then how about some exploring? I want to get used to this."

"Your sister will be happy as a bird as long as I'm not around," Senrid
predicted, to which Leander flashed a wry smile. "I'll catch up." And to
Jilo, as Leander skimmed away over the treetops, arms waving awkwardly, "Where is it?"

"Where is what?"

Senrid said impatiently, "You've got two magic study books there on the
table. That means you've got the enemy-tracking book hidden somewhere.
Mattress? Another room? Come on, that's what I would have done."

Jilo grimaced and pulled the book from under the mattress.

"I want to see where the head snakes are."

Jilo opened the book. "Wan-Edhe, no sign. Siamis is in Roth Drael.
Roth Drael?"

Senrid's stomach hurt. "Where Erai-Yanya and Hibern live. He's
probably trying to track them down, if he found out they're the ones
who discovered the antidote to his enchantment."

"Detlev, still nothing," Jilo said.

"I wonder if our guess is right," Senrid mused.

"Going out of the world?"

"Hibern told us that Erai-Yanya thinks he's gone back to Geth-deles. You know, our sister world, the one we never see in the sky because it's always on the other side of the sun. Though I'm told *they* call *us* Darkside."

"Hope he stays there," Jilo said.

"No." Senrid struck the air as if pushing something away from him. "Don't you see? If he's there, and not here handing out commands right and left, then it has to mean he's on the hunt for some kind of magical weapon he can come back and hammer us with."

Jilo considered, then said, "If he is, what can we do about it?"

"Probably nothing." Senrid scowled. "But I have to know."

Jilo was more concerned about the book, and how Senrid had hustled his friend out the window so he could ask about it. Hoping this would prevent trouble, instead of starting it, he said, "Well, you know where I keep it. Look at it any time you like. Just don't let anyone see it."

"I can't read your language. And it's probably as well," Senrid said so quickly that Jilo eyed him uncertainly. "Can I tell Leander?"

Jilo grimaced. "I don't know him."

"I do. You can trust him." Senrid's smile was not particularly humorous. "He's far more trustworthy than I am, but the Mearsieans will tell you that's not saying much. Though they like him."

"I wouldn't ask the Mearsieans anything," Jilo retorted, mentally excepting Clair. And maybe the tall one, Seshe. Maybe. If only he'd had a real twi! How did anyone figure these things out about people? "All right. But only him."

"One more," Senrid said. "Only one. Hibern. When she gets here. She's very good with secrets."

Jilo thought he may as well give in now. "Done. That's it."

"Come on. Show us around."

In the Valley, Atan and Derek existed as polar opposites.

Derek's Sarendan orphans had been taken in by Valley families on the central plateau. Derek drilled them each morning, his determination no more ferocious than theirs.

Derek's anger at his failure had gradually metamorphosed into anger at his lack of training. There were times when he held imaginary conversations with King Darian, whom he had helped to oust, as he lay restlessly in bed through long nights. "I understand now why you wanted the army alert and ready," he once admitted. "You were right. You were right."

At the extreme western end of the Valley, almost not in the Valley at all, lay a single cottage tucked up on a cliff amid thick forest. In centuries past, this was where mages who required solitary tranquility had been housed, leaving a formidable magic library almost as good as Tsauderei's.

Atan had spent her childhood secluded in that house, and here she was again, only without Gehlei, the faithful steward who moved about in an enchanted dream-state in Eidervaen.

Atan wept a great deal those first few days, missing Gehlei and worrying about everyone else; she wept about the hard irony of her ending up back here in this cottage that never quite stopped smelling of mold no matter how vigorously she scrubbed every surface. And she did scrub, but restoring clean and shining order did not take away the truth: she had lost Sartor as assuredly as her father had. At least no one had died on a battlefield. The Siamis enchantment had been broken once before, and by a ten-year-old. That meant it could be broken again. Just not by her.

Tsauderei came to visit her those first couple of mornings. He told her about the shy Chwahir boy who had apparently assumed an infamous throne. But this Jilo did not appear, and Atan was too dispirited to seek him out. What had she to offer him, save lessons in how to lose a throne?

When Tsauderei came the third morning, he said, "Sinking into self-pity isn't going to do you or anyone else any good. Use those skills of yours. Find Jilo, because he really needs help."

She grimaced. "I keep trying to overcome—to plan—but it's impossible."

Tsauderei lifted his hand, gnarled as an apple tree. "Choose a happy memory. Sometimes mine are my best companions. Think of your Sartor in celebration, after the enchantment broke. Imagine how it will be when everyone is free, and you've helped to make it that way."

She admitted, "I've tried to walk the Purrad in my mind, and I remember every step and turn, but it hurts. I don't feel I deserve its peace."

"Tchah!" Tsauderei's expression was so explosive his long, snowy mustache fluttered. "That is exactly why those things were built. You dishonor their purpose, child, with this mood."

He left, and she promptly sat down to make a napurdiav in memory. He was right. If she approached it the way she ought, walking it mentally did lift her spirits. As soon as she was done, she left the cottage, flying by habit toward the village plateau. But when she recognized Derek Diamagan down there, leading children in some kind of exercise with sticks, she couldn't bear to risk his sneers about royal blood and failure, and she retreated again.

She tried again on another day, flying well away from the main plateau. When she caught sight of a group of girls flying over the lake, she slowed and hovered. The one who drew the attention by cartwheeling in a gleefully awkward, limb-flapping manner was a redhead in bright, mismatched clothing. Prominent in the admiring circle were a girl with pure white hair and a smaller one with long black hair.

Sharp disappointment caused Atan to recoil when she recognized the Mearsieans, the Rel-haters. And no word or sign of Rel for months.

Atan retreated to her cottage once again, too angry to attempt a false napurdiav. So she pulled out a book at random to study.

Her solitary struggle was summarily broken early one morning a few days later, when Tsauderei reappeared, this time towing a figure burrowed in a heavy coat still sparking with melting snow.

"Hibern!" Atan exclaimed.

Hibern smiled, making a mental note to remember what she could say and what she couldn't say. That morning, Erai-Yanya had told her, *Now that the antidote is out there, Tsauderei will do much better at herding the cats, that is, dealing with the senior mages, than I ever could. I am going back to Geth-deles. My quest is even more urgent than it was before, and I believe that Roth Drael isn't safe—Siamis might show up looking for the dyr. Tsauderei invites you to join him in the Valley. But remember, no mention of the antidote until he has the senior mages ready to deploy it.*

Forestalling possible questions from Atan, Hibern looked around with an air of interest. "So this is your famous cottage? I would never have left, if I had a library like that."

"Come, get rid of that coat," Atan said. "Where did you come from? Have you eaten?"

"I was up north. Oh, it's a long story. One thing I can say is, I found Arthur and Liere, and gave them transfer tokens. They should be along soon."

Tsauderei said, "Show her around, Atan. There are some friends who have been waiting to meet you, but dislike imposing."

Atan studied the old mage, who smiled back, the diamond in his ear winking in the light of the fire on the hearth. "What does that mean, they think I'm a snob? Too good for everyone else, is that it?"

Tsauderei did not deny it. "Prove them wrong."

Chastened, Atan frowned down at her hands. 'Friends.' Such an easy word to say, but what did it really mean? She knew that her prejudice against the Mearsiean girls was wrong. Rel had said himself that they were his friends. He hadn't explained how he could be friends with that loudmouthed princess who complained about him behind his back, but Atan struggled to dismiss her own prejudice. They were allies against the evil of Norsunder. They had to work together.

"Very well, then." She forced a smile. "The one bad thing about this cottage, buried in the woods as it is, it never gets any sunlight." She indicated the leaping fire. "So getting outside will be good, especially if the weather is fine."

"It is right now," Tsauderei said. "Which probably won't be true by afternoon. So. I have to see about making arrangements for the kitchen at Selenna House, now that we're gathering quite a crowd there. And troll for news," he added.

Atan remembered the Sartoran mage council, yet again caught in a web of magic, and the familiar sick sense of humiliation and defeat tightened around her heart. She caught a sympathetic glance from Hibern. That much, at least, Atan could share. "Do you truly want to hear it?" she asked.

They'd reached the ledge, and as Hibern made the sign for flying, she wrinkled her upper lip. "Please tell me everything. Then I don't have to think about how much I really, really hate heights. Especially with nothing below my feet but air."

Atan unburdened herself as they floated above cliff and crevasse. Hibern listened in sympathy, severely tempted to reveal that the Siamis enchantment could be broken, but she had to keep her promise not to talk about it. *It won't be long*, Erai-Yanya had promised.

Presently they approached the village on the main plateau. Atan would have veered away, but Hibern caught sight of familiar figures. "Hold, isn't that Senrid?"

They were unnoticed by the orphan brigade, who formed up into their lines, as they did every morning at dawn.

The girls watched from above as Senrid sauntered up. "Is this open to anyone?" he asked. He missed his morning exercise.

"Sure," Sig said, remembering how Derek always welcomed new people. He added, "Your accent is funny."

Ruddy put in, "You must be one of the foreigners that old geez said might come."

"Yep," Senrid said.

Someone else shouted, "Derek is coming!"

The lines instantly straightened, and the orphans began doing the warm-up arm swings that they always began with. Senrid took up a place in the back row.

Red-haired Falinneh of the Mearsieans emerged early from Selenna House, seeking breakfast. She always flew over the big plateau if she saw people. When she spotted those uniform lines, most of them boys, drilling in unison, the urge to have some fun with them was irresistible.

She landed in the front, and promptly began copying the drill with loud groans, groaning, making popping noises as if her joints creaked, and falling down.

The rest of the Mearsieans streamed after her.

Derek had pulled a small boy out to demonstrate a better grip on his sticks, and hadn't noticed the addition. When he looked up, irritation flared through him at this garishly dressed urchin making fun of his war refugees. He started toward her, hot words forming, when the rest of the Mearsieans landed.

He glanced their way, then his head snapped back when he recognized CJ.

From the air, Atan and Hibern watched as Derek Diamagan made a profound bow to CJ.

The orphans, knowing how Derek felt about bowing, gaped.

CJ flushed, at first suspecting she was being ridiculed. She gazed warily at Derek, her chin lifted. Then her lips parted. "Don't . . . I know you?" she asked.

"There is no reason you should remember me," Derek said earnestly. "But I will never forget you, the person who saved my brother and me."

CJ blanched as pale as the shirt collar above her black vest.

Derek turned to his orphans. "Some of you had parents who did not believe young people could be useful. To them I always said, 'black wool and ambition.' It was this girl who proved that people your age have smart minds, and brave hearts." And to CJ, "I see that you still wear the vest made from the wool of a black sheep. I never understood what you meant when you said that you were that kind of person, but when I spoke of a uniform for my orphan brigade, here, I thought it should include such a garment, as it symbolized those stout of heart."

CJ scowled at her bare toes, red to the ears, and when Ruddy said, "Tell us what happened!" she muttered, "I hate even thinking about that mess with Kessler."

"I'm starved," one of the other Mearsieans said loudly, sending a worried glance at CJ, who stalked away, then looked back with the oddest expression, a mixture of regret, embarrassment, and concern.

"Is your brother all right?" CJ asked Derek.

Derek said, "He's up north in western Khanerenth, trading for horses. He'll regret not having been here to meet you."

Senrid could see how every word made CJ flinch. Mentally resolving he would get that story out of someone, he drew Derek's attention by saying, "I don't understand using two sticks." He pointed at the pair resting on the grass beside each orphan. "One would be a practice sword, but two?"

Derek smiled. "Welcome! I didn't see you there in the back. No, we do not use swords. The weapons are these sticks. Any sticks. The art of the two sticks comes from Khanerenth. Like many things in that kingdom, it is said to have originated as a form of marine warfare, on ships."

"Oh?" Senrid said innocently, knowing very well that his own ancestor, Inda-Harskialdna—known elsewhere in the world as Elgar the Fox—had spread double-stick fighting to mariners, more than eight centuries previous.

CJ didn't trust Senrid's earnest, inquiring air as far as she could throw him, but she recognized his distraction of Derek away from an embarrassing moment, and flashed him a grim smile of gratitude as she took off.

Derek bent to pick up a pair of double-sticks. "I brought a simplified form here before the new king came to the throne, as commoners were forbidden to possess steel. But any hand can pick up a stick from field or road."

Derek paused, and motioned a pair of his orphans forward to demonstrate. Senrid stood with his hands behind his back, and what he hoped was an interested look on his face. He knew the basics, but until his uncle was deposed, the only hard training he'd had was in archery and hand-to-hand knife fighting. He could tell that Derek had gotten decent training somewhere, though he wasn't very practiced.

Atan offered space in the cottage loft for Hibern, which she instantly accepted. She could hardly wait to get at that library. By afternoon, when thunder heralded a brief storm, she and Atan sat on either side of the leaping fire, absorbed in study.

Or Hibern set out to study. She discovered that the library was mostly handmade copies of Sartoran histories and magic books that she was already familiar with, and a few personal records by unknown mages, obscure and difficult to read. She earmarked the oldest ones for priority reading, but sat back, reflecting on what she'd seen so far.

The alliance was gathering for the first time. But instead of cleaving together in order to combine knowledge and strength, they seemed to be separating out into disparate groups. They had little in common but a shared hatred of Norsunder, she was thinking. And hatred was never a good way to bind people together.

Part of being a mage was trying to negotiate between people. As Hibern stared down at her cup of wild berry juice, she wondered where to begin.

Why not with what she knew? She turned her gaze up to Atan. "Shall we start our studies again? Only not just us. Senrid, you've met. Tsauderei tells me that Jilo is interested, and in desperate need of light magic guidance. I think that kind of help is exactly what the alliance is for. Also, I think you'll like Leander Tlennen-Hess. He loves history, especially how language forms and changes. And he knows as much magic as either of us."

"Study," Atan said, "is exactly what I need. Shall we go find them?"

At first Atan was distracted by the chiseled beauty of the green-eyed, dark-haired Leander Tlennen-Hess. His manner reminded her of Arthur: scholarly, a little absent about his environment. He has no idea how beautiful he is, she thought, and turned to the sallow, awkward Jilo so Leander wouldn't think she was staring.

Though Jilo didn't talk, he soaked in every word of that first discussion.

The day after that, Hibern brought Clair, who was quiet, polite, and burning with interest.

The study group was a success beyond Hibern's hopes. After a shy first day, except for silent, listening Jilo, they began talking so fast their words tumbled over one another as they flung history and magic record citations at one another to bolster their admitted lack of experience. Hibern rejoiced when she saw Atan leaning forward, elbows on knees, arguing with Senrid.

Senrid enjoyed it, too. He considered giving mornings to the study group, but Tsauderei's library seemed to be mainly composed of musty old tomes. Senrid's primary motivation was to research Erdrael, but he hated the thought of anyone discovering what he was doing and asking nosy questions.

Since it sounded like the mages were planning to dispense the antidote to the Siamis spell soon, he would take a short leave from magic studies.

Over the next few mornings, he flew down early to drill with the orphans. By now he was convinced that Derek's double-stick form was a variant of the ancient Marloven plains's snap-staff fighting, an artifact of Inda-Harskialdna's seafaring days. He kept that to himself, and continued to stay in back so he could observe better. But he couldn't hide how well he moved, after all his years of drill in close-in fighting with knives.

Derek, experienced enough now to spot military training, was as interested in Senrid as the latter was in Derek. At the end of the week, on a warmer-than-usual morning, Derek dismissed the brigade early. They promptly stampeded to swim in the lake.

Senrid was going to go with them. Like most Marlovens, any swimming he got was in rivers or ponds at the height of summer, and that rarely. The lake was almost as good as flying.

But when Derek said, "I have some questions," Senrid's interest sharpened.

"So do I," he said. Swimming could wait.

They flew up to sit on the emerald grasses beside one of the two waterfalls filling the lake, under the shade of resiny-smelling, soughing pine.

Derek said, "Ask away!" He proved to be very ready to talk about Kessler Sonscarna's assassination training camp. Senrid learned that Derek had not been abducted, like Puddlenose and Rel—he'd actually been recruited. "I was seventeen, and I thought it was a perfect plan," Derek admitted, the residue of his fanatical fervor bombarding Senrid on the mental plane. "Promotion through pure merit, not birth! The world would be far better, would it not?" he asked mockingly, and then laughed somewhat bitterly.

The problem came when Derek had found himself being promoted rapidly (he had to be a natural leader, Senrid thought, remembering Keriam's lessons on the subject), and of course his popularity was his downfall.

Derek bitterly and lengthily described being set up for betrayal by Kessler's trusted lieutenant, the near execution, and then CJ's intervention.

"Wait. CJ was there? In a military camp?"

Derek nodded. "All of them. Except the white-haired one, who later broke Dejain's magic. Kessler made no distinction between boys and girls, and the younger the better. Fewer bad habits to be trained out of, so he said. He favored the Mearsieans because the King of the Chwahir hated them. There was even a rumor that Kessler wanted to make CJ his heir. But Kessler's second in command, a nasty piece of work who'd called himself Alsais, took against anyone Kessler favored. When she was supposed to prove herself by assassinating the white-haired girl, the Mearsieans disrupted the deployment by interfering with Dejain's magical business—and then Dejain turned on Kessler. That boy they call Puddlenose went for Alsais," he finished up. "Near as I can tell, he got him, too."

Senrid whistled. No wonder easy-going Puddlenose had never talked about that experience.

Part of Derek's gift for leading was understanding that you give before you demand. Senrid saw this, appreciated it, and let himself talk more than he might have when Derek began his own questions. Especially when Derek didn't react with disgust or distrust at the word 'Marloven.'

"That is exactly what Sarendan needs," Derek exclaimed after Senrid described the academy. "Under the old king, they only studied for a season, then they spent the summer playing games."

"Wargames have purpose," Senrid said.

Derek waved a hand. "The way you describe, yes. Without a horde of servants to do all the actual work."

Senrid grinned. "We train people to be self-sufficient because there were never servants on the battlefield. At least, in our ballads, nobody holds up his hand and declares, 'Wait,' to his enemy. 'I need to send someone to fetch my second-best hat.'"

Derek slapped his knee and laughed. "Oh, yes, this is exactly what we need here in Sarendan. I trust we can come to some arrangement, as soon as we rid ourselves of these soul-suckers."

Senrid thought to himself that Retren Forthan would probably love to come work with Derek, and adapt some basic training for Sarendan's infant army to use—Senrid assumed he was talking to a fellow monarch, though Derek thought he was talking to a Marloven academy trainee.

As he flew away, Senrid reflected back, puzzled. He knew there'd been a revolution in Sarendan. Only if Derek was the new king, then who was the anchor for Siamis's enchantment?

## Chapter Ten

*Off the coast of Drael*

W HEN Christoph was a youth in a very small part of Flanders, before the turn of the eighteenth century, he'd learned a motto: *carpe diem*, or 'seize the day.'

A brush with death resulting in a trip through the world-gate had strengthened this attitude. There were mysteries unexplained at work in a universe that he could not understand. So why try? His next brush with death might hurl him into yet another world, or it might smite his body into the four elements and his soul into the ethereal, a prospect that seemed almost as mysterious.

Life therefore was for having as much fun as one could, and on this world, he'd found the next thing to a brother in Puddlenose of the Mearsieans, whom he'd met on his travels. They began traveling together, sharing similar tastes in food, tastes in jokes, tastes for comfortable surroundings with people who knew how to laugh. They talked about everything except serious things. Sometimes they talked around serious things, though never for long. He was fine with that.

They were fresh from one of their favorite midsummer festivals, having discovered the Mearsiean privateer *Tzasilia* in Breis's harbor, off The Fangs at the northeast corner of the long Sartoran continent.

Captain Heraford had promptly hauled Puddlenose along on errands as a convenient message runner, telling Christoph to report on board. Having tossed his knapsack onto a hammock, Christoph was up on deck enjoying the brisk breeze in the sunshine, and regaling his friends among the crew with their recent adventures. ". . . and if the prentices win the games, see, then they get to command their masters. I assure you, there is no finer sight than a parcel of windbag city aldermen having to hop to the meeting hall on one foot, hooting like owls—"

Heads turned, gazes shifting beyond Christoph, who abandoned his tale to see what caught their attention. On the quay adjacent to their pier someone was shoving through the crowd of lounging mariners, passengers, workers, pie-sellers, pickpockets, and patrollers, judging by the way people staggered, jumped, and dropped things; in the wake of the force burrowing its way faint shouts of protest rose.

The crowd boiled, parted, and . . . it was Puddlenose shoving everyone aside, and running at top speed. Puddlenose bounded up the ramp, skirting a line of dock workers bearing the last of the supplies to stow in the hold.

Puddlenose rarely moved faster than a slope-shouldered amble, except when confronted with three circumstances. One was war, and the second and third were persons who happened to be related, though they would kill one another if they could: Wan-Edhe of the Chwahir, and Kessler Sonscarna, his grandson, or grandnephew, or whatever-he-was.

"Uh-oh," Christoph said under his breath.

Puddlenose spotted Christoph's sturdy form and sun-bleached hair.

He galloped straight to him, then leaned over, hands on his knees as he fought for breath. "Kessler." He expelled the word like a curse. "Sure it was him. Description matches, black short hair, pale eyes, black clothes. Wiry build. On some kind of ship with a weird bow. Leading a fleet of five. Weird tree on the foremast sails." He flung a hand upright, hooking the fingers like a dragon prow. "Everyone's talking about it. Passed outside two days ago, heading north. Should have reached The Fangs by now."

Christoph said, "Wasn't that the same kind of ship that everyone said brought Henerek and the eleveners to attack Everon?"

Puddlenose didn't wait for an answer. "We've got to warn Everon."

Captain Heraford, a weathered man, spare of form, had been right behind Puddlenose. He looked from one boy to the other. "Clair gave you one of those notecases. Now would be the time to use it."

"Lost it." Puddlenose grimaced. "And you know Rel. Travels light."

The captain gave a short nod. "Take the boat," he said. "We'll meet up later."

*Off the coast of Everon*

"What do you fight for?"

Kessler leaned against the taffrail next to Luka Orm, the captain of the *Grebe's Crest*, his fingers in reach of one of his knives.

It had been a fast, smooth journey, and he liked the taciturn Venn, even if he didn't understand all that about Venn Doom and damnation. But if this man thought for a heartbeat that Kessler must sustain interrogation before he and his command would be put ashore, he'd kill the man right now, heave him over the side, and take the ships. It wouldn't be easy, but he had no doubt he could do it.

"What do you fight for?" Orm said again, his eyes a paler shade of blue than Kessler's own. Strange, how little they had in common, and yet there was that, and the familiar smell of fish in vinegar, a staple in coastal Chwahirsland. He hadn't eaten it since he'd run from Wan-Edhe, but he remembered the shore villagers who had sheltered him and fed him before he'd managed to escape . . .

A fine splash of spray brought his thoughts back.

"You do not answer. It is orders, then?" Orm persisted. "You do not think beyond orders?"

"They don't think beyond." Kessler tipped his chin toward the foredeck, where his warriors drilled by turn. One command—no more than a raised fist—and they'd turn on the Venn sailors.

"This is why they chose Norsunder to cleave to, because they do not think?"

"Norsunder chose us," Kessler retorted. But that veered too near the personal, so he said, "Many of them like to fight. Most of them like to kill. At least half were adjudged criminals before some court or other, given stone spells and planted in a Court of Shame."

"A what?"

"Ah, that's right, you come from the old Venn," Kessler said with a sardonic twist to his mouth. "You either killed your criminals, or put iron torcs around their necks and made them into thralls. Well, you will discover as you travel about in this enlightened time—" His teeth showed on the word 'enlightened.' "You will discover that in the interim, many kingdoms conceived a way to deal with violent criminals tried and convicted: put a stone spell on them that would last for a century and set them up in a Garden of Shame, as a reminder to the rest of the populace. These Gardens of Shame have gone out of fashion in most places. You can still find them here and there. Norsunder mages recruited by releasing the stone spell and then using an enchanted knife to cut the recruits. Bind them by their own blood." *Like me.* "Such retain free will, but no free rein. Then there are the soul-bound, who are essentially dead, but their bodies kept alive by magic. I don't have any of the soul-bound to show you as example. They're obedient, but profoundly stupid."

Orm listened to the half-understood words, appalled. This was the result of oath-breaking. He must serve such a person.

To ward the question he could see in Orm's expression, Kessler said, "I'd like to take a look at your maps—your charts—again."

Brine dripped off the creaking ropes into Kessler's face, stinging his eyes as they made their way down to the captain's cabin. Orm spread out the chart that displayed the right-hand side of the continent of Drael. Kessler took a moment to appreciate the complication of navigational lines that the Venn had apparently used by magic, and overlaid on these, in different colors, beautiful lines showing the track of the sun in different seasons. It was by these that this captain now navigated, bringing them in sight of The Fangs, off Chwahirsland.

Orm ventured a remark. "Our Drenga would land with the sun behind them. If your enemy is surprised, he cannot count you."

Kessler gave a short nod. Surprise was unlikely. But he would never waste an advantage. "I always fight with the sun behind me if I can. How long before we reach Everon's harbor?"

Luka Orm glanced up at the bulkheads as if he could see the sky and smell the air. "With this wind, some days. Unless it changes to aid us." Then he proceeded to what was most important to him. "We are agreed, then. We have kept our bargain. You will tell your commanders this? We land you at the time and place you wish, and go our way."

Kessler's mouth tightened on the word 'commanders' but he said, "You get us there. Then, as far as I'm concerned, you are on your own."

Captain Heraford's 'boat' was a tender, built for speed.

While Christoph had no liking for Prince Glenn of Everon, he understood the need to warn the king, and he was not about to let Puddlenose sail alone. It took at least two to handle the tender. They traded off sailing and sleeping, scudding before the friendly summer winds sweeping down the strait out of the west.

It was this same wind that caused the Venn ships to tack and tack again, fighting their way northwest toward Drael.

The boys caught up by the second day, and trailed the fleet with reefed sail until well into the night. Dousing their lanterns, they sped silently by as far away as they could while still being able to watch through their field glasses. As it was, all they could see were tiny figures moving about on the deck, and blocking the golden pinpoints of light in the scuttles belowdecks. There seemed to be a lot of people on board.

They'd nearly given up when a sail being changed briefly silhouetted a slight masculine figure who otherwise would have been completely invisible in the gloom. He stood on the captain's deck, at the rail—

Christoph gasped. "He's watching us!"

Puddlenose shrugged. "So? He can't see us any better than we can see him."

"It's Kessler. I'll never forget that silhouette, standing at the top of the dungeon entrance."

"Yeah, but would he recognize us, on this tiny thing? Out of all the people he threw in his dungeon?"

They each tried to convince the other as well as themselves that Kessler couldn't see them, but both were relieved when the ship sank beyond the horizon, leaving them alone under the peaceful summer sky.

The wafting night breezes strengthened into the winds of oncoming weather by morning, bringing up gray, heaving seas with frothy whitecaps. Rejoicing—those big three-masters would lug with the wind directly on their forward beam—the boys felt the tender come alive, surging and plunging into the waves as the taut sail vibrated overhead.

They reached the Everoneth harbor late that night, which looked ruined through the glass. So they bypassed it in favor of one of the smaller coves farther north. They drew into the shallow waters, bowsed the tender up tight, and dragged sea wrack onto the narrow stern in hopes it would remain invisible from the sea.

Then they waded ashore, and grimly toiled up the vertical palisades. As they climbed, they tried to figure out where to go first: up the river to the capital, or the short way to the harbor? But what if the Norsundrians held it?

They were still arguing when they topped the palisade at last, as early dawn light spilled like milk along the horizon behind them. Around a grove of cedar rode a patrol of Knights. The boys dove behind a tangle of flowering vines at the sound of horse hooves, but the sight of the patrol brought them out again, waving and yelling.

After a short exchange, the patrol leader sent Puddlenose with a fast escort toward the capital, and took Christoph up behind her to report to her captain at the harbor.

Puddlenose and his escort reached Ferdrian as the sun set. By then he was nearly fainting with hunger, not having eaten since a scanty meal of stale bread the day before.

The Knights took him straight to King Berthold, who glanced at Puddlenose, red-eyed and fighting yawns. "Whatever it is can wait. You need food and rest."

"No it can't," Puddlenose said, propping his shoulders against a wall in spite of the scandalized glances of the more correct of the two ever-present bodyguards. "Kessler is coming."

"Who?"

Puddlenose groped for words, not knowing where to start.

The king turned to his steward. "Get something hot into him."

Puddlenose was too weary to protest.

By the time he'd wolfed down a substantial meal, he was nearly falling asleep at the table. He sat back, gazing heavy-eyed at the pattern of twined leaves and flowers carved under the ceiling, until familiar voices roused him. He sat upright as the king walked into the dining room, with Christoph and Rel in tow, both mud-splashed to the eyebrows, Rel having been posted to the retaken harbor as a courier, and subsequently tasked to bring Christoph.

The king said, "Now, let us begin again. Who is coming?"

"Kessler Sonscarna," Rel and Puddlenose said at the same time.

Rel added, with a hand turned toward Puddlenose then toward Christoph, "At least, they're pretty sure."

"I saw him," Puddlenose stated. "We both did." A thumb at Christoph, who nodded, his mouth full of pastry. "Yes, it was dark, and the ships were far apart. But I know it was him. I will never forget that silhouette."

Rel agreed with a "Yes," on an outgoing breath.

King Berthold gazed from one to the next. He could not recollect ever seeing Puddlenose serious. "Who is this man? Sonscarna, the 'ssler,' it all sounds Chwahir."

"He is. He wanted to take over the world," Puddlenose said.

King Berthold burst out laughing, but when he saw no corresponding smile in his guests, he looked askance. "You cannot mean to tell me he had a chance."

"He's crazy, but his plan might have worked. For a time." Puddlenose was taken by a sudden yawn. "Rel, explain." He blinked watery eyes.

"Kessler's plan was not to invade with armies. He trained assassins to take out kings—"

King Berthold interrupted, his expression genial. "Who would he put in these dead kings' place? Himself, of course. From where did he plan to rule this empire, or would he hop about as the sun moves?" The king leaned against the table, his silken tabard gleaming in the rich candlelight.

Puddlenose thoughtfully moved a plate of butter away from a careless fold of that silk.

Rel said, "No, he planned to place people on thrones who had demonstrated merit. By his standard."

"Since I never heard about it, I take it he failed." King Berthold laughed indulgently. "Then he couldn't have been very smart, eh? Or let us say, not very experienced? How old is this prodigy?"

Rel said reluctantly, "Not much older than I am."

And watched the king smile and shake his head. "So this formidable world-conquerer is coming by ship as well? Do you think he'll attack the harbor, or will his highly trained teams land along the coast and scramble up the palisades like spiders?"

The king got his expected chuckles from his attendants, and not all of those were obsequious, but when he saw the stolidity in the three faces before him, especially Puddlenose, who was always first with a joke, he relented.

"You came at great cost to warn me, and I will not forget that. Boys, get some rest. You earned it. Rel, return to the harbor in the morning. It's late, and isn't that thunder in the distance? Yes, morning will do. Tell Captain Berneth to send scouts within line of sight along the coast in both directions, equipped with those magic rings. And tell him what you know about this Kessler Sonscarna, so that he may provide a suitable welcome. Will that do?"

Perforce the boys agreed.

The king then turned to one of the equerries behind him. "I want you to apprise Commander Dei, and tell him to be prepared for Henerek to be attacking the harbor from landward, in support of the newcomer. That is probably our biggest worry."

---

Rel couldn't sleep.

He tried. Ordinarily he slept through thunderstorms with no problem. But every flash jolted him from sinking below the surface of constant thought into the dream world of deep sleep. And each jolt was welcome, because he knew that what lay in wait in those depths were not dreams but nightmares forming around memories of the days cooped in an underground cell with Puddlenose and Christoph, waiting for death as they listened to the cadences and clashings of steel as Kessler trained his assassins.

When the storm lifted, leaving the air outside his windows a musical concert of drips, Rel got up and dressed. Being a scout and courier for the Knights, he had access to horses whenever he wanted; rather than rouse up sleepy stable hands, he chose one he was familiar with, strong enough to easily bear his size for a long ride. He saddled up and set out under the full moon high in the sky.

He chased the storm eastward, gradually catching up until the starry sky gave way to a thick layer of clouds that made it seem he would forever ride in semi-darkness.

He was tired enough to be unaware of the time after he'd changed his third horse. It wasn't until he crested a hill and saw the bright glow in the east that he thought gratefully, sunrise at last.

But wait. As the horse slowed, ears alert, head tossing, Rel caught up mentally. Sunrise was long past, he just hadn't noticed the gradual lightening under the gray overcast.

So what was that glow above the harbor?

He clucked at the horse, urgency burning the lassitude from his tired body. The horse pranced nervously, ears twitching, nostrils spread. She snorted explosively. Rel couldn't see anything wrong. He snapped his legs to her sides, and she plunged forward, her gait jerky, ears flattening. When they rounded a curve, Rel stared down into the valley emptying into the river above the harbor, and made out a massive column of brown smoke pushing up against the undersides of the clouds. Flame glowed the entire length of the harbor.

Smoke. That was what the horse smelled, the scent still too far away for Rel to catch, as the wind was at his back.

The horse turned in a circle, fretting; Rel was trying to decide what to do when a couple of horsemen bore down from either direction. He wheeled his mare and kicked her sides, but she was too tired to outrun pursuit, and Rel was surrounded.

One Norsundrian caught the bridle, and the other leveled a crossbow at Rel, who sat back, hands raised, his heartbeat thundering.

"You're wanted," one said in Sartoran, rather than the Fer Sartoran dialect spoken in Everon. That meant they knew he was not a local.

Rel sighed. He hadn't so much as looked right or left in the past few hours. Of course he had been spotted. The worrisome aspect was the possibility he was recognized.

A short ride later, they crested the last hill before the harbor, from which he could see most of the surrounding countryside. They reached a makeshift camp, no more than a fire and bedrolls piled beside a string of horses being saddled. A force of maybe forty sat on rocks or the ground, eating from shallow travel pans as a faint whiff of wild onion carried on the air.

The biggest two of Rel's captors closed in on either side, and all three horses walked a little ways beyond the camp to where a familiar slim, taut figure stood. Sick with helpless fury, Rel recognized Kessler Son-scarna, who stood at the edge of the cliff, sweeping the land with a glass.

At the sound of hoof beats thudding in the turf he turned, and when he recognized Rel, he said, "Ah." He made a quick gesture with two fingers, and Rel's captors turned away, leaving Rel still mounted on his horse, his sword untouched in the saddle sheath.

"You joined the Knights?" Kessler asked, looking interested, the faint orange glow from the distant fires side-lighting the planed bones of his face, the heavy-lidded eyes that were shaped so unsettlingly like Atan's.

"I'm serving as a scout," Rel said.

"And so you rode to the capital to report my landing to Berthold? No, that couldn't have been you on the little boat. Never mind. Whatever orders you bear are immaterial. They're all dead." Kessler jerked his thumb over his shoulder at the harbor.

Rel's throat closed, rendering him unable to speak.

Kessler's lips curved in a humorless smile. "Henerek has run out of time. So they sent me."

Rel fought against shock. "He's no longer in command?"

"He has other things to occupy him right now. Like a broken knee, a fractured jaw, and a set of cracked ribs. He objected to my taking over the command, so I gave him something else to think about."

Rel remembered Henerek: big, husky, brutal. He stared down at Kessler, short, slight, but made of solid muscle.

Kessler's soft, slightly husky voice changed to that reasonable tone he'd always used at his maddest. "The fastest way to clean up his failure is to burn my way to the capital. Put anyone who gets in my way to the sword."

Rel's fury congealed to dread. He knew Kessler would do it without any hesitation.

Kessler ran a hand through his short, curly hair. "Slaughtering civs is boring. There's no sport in it. But some of them think otherwise." He tipped his head toward the camp a few paces away, where Norsundrians went about finishing their morning meal as if nothing had happened.

No, that wasn't quite right. Rel heard the sharpness of tone, the cracking laughter of after-action triumph. Anticipation.

Kessler took a step nearer, and lifted his hand back toward the road. "Run." He swatted the shivering mare's hindquarters.

The horse leaped into a gallop, nearly unseating Rel. As he clutched at the reins, he heard raucous laughter rising behind him.

Rel's dread sharpened to terror, no longer for himself, but for the unheeding people along the east-west road. Kessler never made idle threats, or exaggerated. When he said he was going to burn his way to the capital, he was going to do just that.

Rel didn't waste time trying to figure out why Kessler would tell him, much less save his life. It had to be some kind of game, or contest, or challenge he was playing with the Norsundrians who commanded him—Rel knew that Kessler had not gone to Norsunder willingly.

None of that mattered. What did was getting the word out, as fast as possible.

The royal roads were straighter than the old, civilian roads that wound around hills alongside meandering streams, and circumvented ancient borders. The royal roads tended to avoid villages and towns, whose traffic would slow up couriers.

So Rel turned off the royal road and watched ceaselessly for the first sign of civilization. When he spotted farmland, he left the road and kept his tired horse at her best speed until he came across a small hamlet alongside a river. He dismounted and banged on every door, and when disgruntled people came out with questions and demands, he pointed to the smoke cloud in the east, and said, "They're coming. *Now.*"

In a short time he'd borrowed a fresh horse from someone with animals to spare, who offered to keep the mare from the royal stable with her.

An old baker pointed out the road—not much more than a wheel-rutted path—to the next town, and Rel took off at a gallop, leaving people scurrying to pack what they could, gather their livestock, and head deeper into the hills. He forgot them within moments, goaded by the ghost of Kessler's voiceless laughter.

He crossed three streams, then rode down into a river valley as a rainstorm passed overhead. He forded the slow-moving waters and surged up the riverbank toward the cluster of buildings on the other side.

His new mount, a young stallion, splashed dramatically through puddles into the square, tail high even after that long run.

Rel gathered what strength he had left and bellowed, "Fire!"

A couple of apprentices busy carrying display tables outside paused to laugh. Everyone else, shopkeepers, customers, strollers, stopped what they were doing, with various expressions, hope for entertainment foremost.

Rel tightened his middle and lifted his hoarse voice. "Norsunder has burned the harbor, and they are going to fire their way to the capital. That means you are next. If you don't believe me, climb on the roof of the highest house, and look toward the sea."

His horse circled, head tossing and ears twitching.

Faces changed as the two teenage upholstery prentices dropped their samples onto the display tables and raced one another up either side of the carved supports holding up their awning.

Gathering villagers watched the boys clamber over the gabled windows upstairs, then one boosted the other to the roof, the first reaching to pull his friend up behind him. A clattering of loose tiles, and the two reached the ridgepole.

"He's right!" One boy yelled, his voice cracking. "Smoke all across the sky!"

Voices rose, a couple of worried shouts. Rel cut across them all. "I'm riding to the capital. Send someone to warn your neighboring villages!" He pointed south and north, then nudged the stallion, and rode on.

## Chapter Eleven

*Delfina Valley*

TSAUDEREI would later reflect that it was inevitable that the secret of the antidote to Siamis's spell would get out—and it was probably as equally inevitable that it would be Derek who spread it.

After a week of drill with the orphans, followed by chat with Derek over breakfast, Senrid discovered he was wrong in his assumption that Derek was a king when Derek, fretting over how the days were dragging by and nothing was being done to rescue Sarendan from the enchantment, confided to Senrid the promise he'd made to Peitar.

Thunder rumbled over the distant peaks as Derek and Senrid floated high over the lake, which rippled below, a deep, stormy gray-blue. "Peitar is my oldest friend, better than a mere king," Derek said suddenly, startling Senrid. "He'd put the orphans' lives above his own, if he knew what was going on. I've got to find a way back down the mountain so I can rescue them before the mages get around to breaking the spell on Peitar."

Senrid hesitated, aware that he had the wherewithal to help Derek do both. He wanted to help Derek, who was the kind of person he admired most—fearless, loyal without being sickening about it, always looking to improve, because it was the only way to fight Norsunder.

"Wouldn't Tsauderei be the one to talk to about that?" Senrid asked, hedging.

"Did." Derek shrugged, then stretched his arms over his head and swooped downward, his long, tangled brown hair flagging in the wind. "He's a mage," Derek said over his shoulder as Senrid dove after him. "They jaw on about how they study for years, but all they seem to talk about is caution, watchfulness, and doing nothing."

Senrid wished that Detlev would do nothing, remembering that *You will not see me coming.* Disgust made him fly faster. He hated whining, including in his own thoughts. "Tsauderei has tough wards," he shouted against the wind. "Nobody is going to get in or out without him knowing, unless he's away."

"He goes out a couple times a week," Derek said, swooping close enough for Senrid to see the honest frustration narrowing his brown eyes. "All I need to do is get to Miraleste, grab the youngsters most important to Peitar, and bring them back. I even have a casket of transfer tokens to get them back here. One for each."

Senrid struggled, reminded himself that he had made a promise, and said, "I'll talk to Hibern and Leander."

Derek heard that as agreement.

Senrid saw his chance when everyone broke for lunch before the big tag game the Mearsieans had organized for the afternoon. The study group—Atan, Hibern, Jilo, Leander, Senrid, and sometimes Clair—were picnicking on the roof of Selenna House, because eating on a rooftop was more fun than eating in Atan's gloomy cottage, especially in the bright sunshine and cool breeze, with interesting cloud towers piling up in the west.

Senrid gathered Hibern and Leander with a glance, and flew down to the boys' room in Selenna house. They streamed through the open window. Leander dropped onto his bed, Hibern sat on the edge of Jilo's, and Senrid shot into the hammock as he explained his conversation with Derek.

At the end, Leander said, "I don't get what you're asking."

"It's simple enough. Derek wants to transfer down into Sarendan to break the enchantment over some kids he's sort of guardian for. It would be so easy to help him. Transfer tokens, to and from, he knows the specific locations so we can use that as Destination, in and out."

"How many?" Leander asked doubtfully.

Hibern shook her head. "Didn't we agree—"

"Less than a dozen." A shadow appeared at the window a moment before Derek did.

The three started, Senrid annoyed at his own lack of awareness. But if anyone had the right to nose into this conversation, Derek did.

Then Derek said, "I knew it. I *knew* you had the means to break that damned enchantment. This is why I hate mages, doing absolutely nothing for selfish reasons."

Hibern said, "It's not selfish to wait to see if Norsunder retaliates against *entire kingdoms* after the enchantment is lifted. The antidote is new, so new we don't know if there is other magic we have to watch for."

"I'm not suggesting you mess with entire kingdoms," Derek shot back. "I'm talking about fewer than a dozen boys and girls. None of whom Norsunder has ever heard of."

Senrid looked at Leander, who was smart, dedicated, but a lighter through and through. Leander was clearly hesitating.

Hibern said slowly, "I'd like to rescue a dozen people of any age. But . . ."

"There's no but about it," Derek said. "I can't believe Norsunder mages would put a lot of extra spells on the children of boot-makers and fisherfolk." He added quickly, "I understand old—that is, Tsauderei has a lot of other concerns. He's worried about kings and kingdoms. Rightly so. I'm just talking about a dozen youngsters I was responsible for—and who were lost when I came up here and fell asleep. Sometimes I want to cut my own throat because of my stupidity," he added ferociously.

Senrid certainly understood that, and the other two saw in Derek's face that if he wasn't going to act on his own yet, he was close to it.

Hibern sighed. "Give me one day. Will you? I want to talk out magical problems that I might not see."

"Not Tsauderei," Derek said. "You know he'll nail you down for your own good."

"I was thinking of someone else," Hibern said, and because Derek was still there, blocking the window, she slid off the bed and opened the door.

She left Selenna House, shot into the air, and bypassed a swarm gathering for the tag game to head for Atan's cottage. She found Atan there alone, not interested in tag. Atan had three books spread before her, but she set the one she was reading aside when Hibern entered.

Hibern sat down and, having ordered her thoughts during her flight, began to explain.

Hibern's nightmares usually fell into two categories. There were the nightmares about her home, and then there were the ones where she would be stuck in mud, or weighed down some way, and somehow the more she labored, the less success she had. The harder she strove to explain, the more angry Atan looked, until Hibern—aware that she had repeated herself at least twice—said helplessly, "I guess I'm not explaining well."

Atan had been struggling to keep her temper in check. But at this invitation, she burst out, "Oh, you've explained quite well! You know, all of you know, how to lift that enchantment, and you kept silent?"

Hibern stared in shock. "But we promised."

"Didn't you think *I* could keep a promise?" Atan shot back.

"Of course," Hibern said. "That was never a question. But I don't think anyone believed it would help you to know you had the antidote, but couldn't use it. Sartor would be the first place Norsunder would lay lethal spells, surely you see that? I think everyone assumed it would be better if you didn't know, until it could actually be used."

"How is that better?" Atan cried.

Hibern was so shocked she stared back, hot tears blurring her eyes. She dashed them impatiently away with her sleeve, her throat tight. As she groped for words, Erai-Yanya's calm, practical voice whispered in memory, and she said slowly, "Maybe it's a fault in those of us who become mages. Erai-Yanya says we tend toward a type, the sort of person who prefers book things. Certainly every senior mage I know is single, if not an outright hermit. In fact, Erai-Yanya told me once that your Sartoran school had a reputation for selecting out mage students who showed an interest in political questions and moving them over to the scribes before they started using their magic to meddle in questions of state. You're thinking in terms of state, now."

"And you will no doubt tell me why that's bad?" Atan asked, eyes narrowing.

"It's not bad, it's . . . well, how much do you think your royal council would welcome a mage who was really interested in how kings get and keep their power?" Hibern asked.

It was a wild guess, barely connected, but she saw in how Atan's eyes widened that her stray thought had a powerful effect. "I think that's a fear every government has about mages," Atan said, in a subdued voice.

"So you can see that there are different ways of seeing the world, and trying to serve the world. Right now Erai-Yanya—well, no, she's at Geth-deles, but these others, they're seeing the possible *magical* threats. They can't think about political things. The Siamis enchantment is cruel, but it's not life-threatening, and no one is actually in pain, at least that's what Clair said."

"She knows?" Atan asked.

"Yes—she was the second one we freed, the first being Oalthoreh, who we knew would willingly sacrifice her life in case there were hidden lethal spells."

Atan's mouth thinned. "So the Mearsieans know about this spell, too?"

"Yes, but Murial made them promise not to speak of it, the same promise I had to make. And Leander, who I taught it to, in case something happened to me."

Atan's expression didn't ease, which worried Hibern a little. Atan was thinking that those irritating Mearsieans, out there laughing and playing tag, didn't think about the rest of the world, so long as *they* were all right.

But she didn't say it. There was no use in speaking resentful thoughts, as satisfying as it might feel. "All right, I get it. So Senrid wants to help Derek rescue a dozen children from the enchantment, to make things easier on Peitar. I think I can see it. I absolutely believe that Peitar would be grieved at any of his young friends being imprisoned by that magic a heartbeat longer than necessary. When is this going to happen?"

"Right away."

Atan said, "Why don't you bring the two boys. I want to hear what they have to say."

Relieved to escape, Hibern went to fetch Senrid and Leander, who were hovering on the edge of the tag game.

She passed Jilo, who was making his way to Atan's cottage in search of a book that Arthur had loaned him, that he'd left somewhere. As he went through the stacks, Atan slipped out and awaited the others in midair above her cottage, thinking how wonderful it was to be able to hold conferences in places where one could see in all directions, even beneath.

When Hibern returned with the two boys, Atan raked them all with those gooseberry Landis eyes and said abruptly, "Derek ought to have brought this up to Tsauderei, who is the person most concerned. In fact, I suspect he has, and was turned down."

Hibern said in surprise, "You think so? But why would Derek then turn to Senrid? Derek hates kings."

"For a while there I thought Derek was a king," Senrid said flippantly.

He expected them to laugh at him, but instead Atan's expression shuttered, and Hibern pursed her lips. He gave a mental shrug and went on. "Derek doesn't know who I am, only where I come from. He wants to keep his promise to his king friend, and grab those orphans of his. I don't see anything wrong with that, if we do it the same way we rescued Clair, checking for magical traps first."

Hibern took her bottom lip between her teeth, needing time to work out in her own mind whether or not teaching Senrid the antidote spell and standing by while he transferred with Derek into Sarendan would be considered a trespass against Erai-Yanya's and Murial's implied trust. Because on the positive side, it seemed a right action for the alliance.

She could see impatience in Senrid's face. He flung his hands wide. "It's not like it'll be a secret, now that Derek knows about it! We'll go, find the brats, and get out."

His expression changed as Leander, who faced the direction of Tsauderei's cottage on the other side of the Valley, pointed. "Is that . . ."

Two small figures emerged from Tsauderei's. As the group watched, the figures bobbed up and down, testing the flying spell. Then the taller one launched wildly into the air, arms and legs gyrating as he tried to figure out balance. The smaller figure was slower, limbs stiff.

From above the lake the tag game ended in a flock of girls zooming toward the newcomers, who resolved into Arthur, tousled and ink-splotched, and Liere, skinny as ever, her hair hacked off so unevenly above her ears that she was nearly bald on one side. Atan and her companions shot across the airy expanse to join them.

Senrid grimaced when he saw Liere. "Somebody's been calling her Sartora," he said under his breath.

A group of the orphan brigade followed. They'd been with the Mearsieans, trying to learn the rules of the complicated tag game the girls had invented. One urchin said in disbelief, "That's Sartora? Really? Somebody must have tortured her!"

CJ's fluting voice carried over all, calling happily, "Hi, Sartora! Does this mean we can go home now?"

*Uh-oh.* CJ had managed to say the worst thing possible, though it was clear that nobody knew that but Senrid.

Liere's first reaction to the warm, beautiful Valley and the prospect of flying had been thrill. But CJ's question struck hard, with all its expectation that Sartora had of course Saved The World once again.

"No," Liere said, hating her weakness.

CJ halted in the air, black hair flagging in the wind, her wide eyes as blue as the sky overhead. "Didn't you get rid of Siamis? Isn't that what you've been doing?"

"I've been hiding," Liere said, as all the kids pressed around her.

Senrid tried twice to get past them, then gave up as whispers and explanations rang outward.

CJ goggled, her amazement plain to those watching. Her sharp sense of disappointment, no, of betrayal, smote Liere mercilessly on the mental plane.

"Hiding? But . . . why? You saved the world before! Everyone's talking about Bereth Ferian, and Sartora, and—" CJ heard her own voice rising, and halted. Liere had once been a hero, the first world-renowned girl hero, but now she wasn't. It seemed disloyal to crab about it, but why hide when you've got all those mysterious mind powers?

Liere was going to explain about how she couldn't break the enchantment without the dyr, and she certainly couldn't flash from kingdom to kingdom without that strange being made of light, whom she had no idea how to summon, but at the looks on all those faces, her throat closed and she couldn't get past, "The mages thought I should hide . . ." She hated her bleating voice, and she stopped.

Aware of everyone staring, CJ forced herself to speak cheerfully. "We're going to play a big game of spy-versus-spy. Remember, we played it in Bereth Ferian, only this is going to be even better, because we're in the air!"

As if that served as a signal, everyone began clamoring around Liere, begging her to be on their side. Liere dreaded the inevitable discovery that she was terrible at games, and turned to find Senrid in the crowd, in time to catch sight of him and Leander flying off, talking earnestly.

Liere turned away, sick at heart at the intensity of CJ's sense of betrayal, which the girl had no notion Liere sensed. Liere loathed herself for a coward and a weakling, and she deserved all the disappointment and contempt she was going to get.

"Very well," she said, reaching out to the nearest hand. "Tell me the rules."

At last Senrid had a project, and it had nothing to do with Erdrael or ghosts. His restlessness eased as he threw himself into the tedium of creating transfer tokens, once they elicited exact descriptions from Derek for the location of the first rescue.

Leander had decided to go along with it because he knew Senrid, and suspected that if Senrid didn't have this rescue to work on, he might hare off and do something reckless and dangerous, if only to himself.

So they worked hard through the night, making transfer tokens for four. Leander was going along with Derek and Senrid to demonstrate the antidote spell one more time. They left Jilo sitting alone in their room with the door blocked and the window shut and curtains closed, watching his book. It was Senrid's idea to lay tracer spells on the brass rings they were using as transfer tokens: if Jilo's book said that Siamis or Detlev had transferred into Sarendan, he'd use his ring to send a burst of illusory color to the rings worn by Leander and Senrid. They would all three transfer instantly out.

Their target lived in a village called Riverside, in the principality of Selenna. Derek had described a wooden bridge to use as a Destination, a bridge he knew well, as it had been a meeting place during the bad days before the revolution. They transferred, all three gasping as lowland summer's intensity enveloped them. Heat shimmered off the newly paved stones of the road on either side of the bridge, and broke sunlight into brilliant shards in the river running below the bridge.

"This way," Derek said, looking at the ground. He'd borrowed a battered hat from someone in the Valley, which he'd pulled low over his forehead. He wore a plain-spun thigh-length tunic-shirt, sashed with rope, and his usual saddle-worn riding trousers. Being a brown-haired, sun-browned young man, he looked anonymous enough with his face hidden.

Leander and Senrid took the lead as they tramped down the bridge into a village that seemed to be undergoing vast renovation. Cottages made of stone had been, or were being, freshly thatched, some subsequent to additions. Vegetable plots were framed by flower borders, and everywhere wild olive trees grew.

As in Mearsies Heili, people drifted through their days in eerie silence. The boys overheard no conversation, saw no innovation and no tempers good or bad.

All eyes would watch for whatever Siamis had commanded them, through the enchantment, to watch for.

Derek shuffled along behind the two boys as they crossed the square and then proceeded down a narrow lane bordered with berry shrubs.

"On the right," Derek whispered.

They stopped at a house indistinguishable from the others. The kitchen door stood open. Inside, a woman kneaded bread with slow, absent movements. Leander and Senrid moved past her, blocking Derek from her view. Senrid held his breath as her absent gaze passed indifferently over him.

This enchantment might not look cruel, but he found it obscene, how effectively it wiped out all traces of individual thought and will.

The little hall opened into three small rooms, one of which contained a gangling boy with a rust-colored thatch of short hair. Derek's sudden smile made it clear they'd found Bren. Drawings and paintings covered all the walls, mostly village scenes of people working, dancing, eating. Celebrating. Bren sat on the bed, his hands loose. Drawing on paper, it seemed, did not come under the mandate of the enchantment, though it hurt Derek not to see Bren with chalk in hand, sketching his commentary on life at wall, eave, fence, door.

Leander had to look away from the drawings. The contrast between the papers full of joy, anger, interest, laughter, passion and this blank-faced boy clawed at his heart.

He glanced at Senrid, who leaned his shoulders against the door, blocking it. Derek took up a stance at the window to watch for danger from that angle. He kept his face averted; he couldn't bear to see Bren's slack expression stripped of all personality. It was too much like he was dead.

Leander whispered to Senrid, "You want to try?"

Senrid murmured, "I'll watch. One more time. Next one, I'll do."

Leander cast his eyes over the drawing table angled to catch the window's light, and found what he was looking for, a much-used nub of a drawing chalk.

He picked it up and held it out to Bren, saying in a low voice, "See it, Bren? This is your chalk. Take your chalk and draw a picture. Can you see it? Pick it up."

Bren's breathing changed. Then he stirred, as if some semblance of thought winked into life down deep under the smothering layers of magic.

"Do you know what that is?" Leander persisted.

Bren stirred again, his fingers flexing.

"Does this chalk belong to anyone?" Leander asked.

Bren's lips twitched. His hand made a vague grasping motion.

*Now*, Leander thought, and leaned close to whisper the spell.

Magic shimmered in the room, a quick, vague flash not unlike the reflection of light on water, and Derek instinctively turned around before Leander could finish the spell.

Bren blinked, his gaze widened, his face suffused with red, and he sucked in his breath and shouted a word.

"Get him out of here," Senrid ordered Leander sharply, and to Derek, "That was magic. Go!"

Leander finished the spell. Bren started, gasping and looking around wildly. "What did I do? What did I do?"

"This will get you to the Valley," Leander said, pressing a token into Bren's hand.

Bren jerked his head in a nod and they vanished, followed by Derek. With them safely gone, Senrid was about to use his token when he perceived the dark flicker in air that meant an incoming transfer. He looked at the ring. No Siamis. He could get away from anyone else. Why not see the result?

He flung himself into a corner and threw up an illusion a heartbeat before two Norsundrians appeared, the wind caused by all the transfers sending loose papers flying around.

The Norsundrians briefly scanned the room, their gazes moving past Senrid's corner, which he knew would appear vaguely shadowy as long as he didn't move. One stuck his head out the door; from his vantage, Senrid could make out the woman who kneaded bread.

"Gone. We'd better report," one said to the other.

They transferred away, and Senrid did as well.

In the Valley, the orphan brigade was delighted to welcome Bren. He was delighted to see them, and to return to Selenna House, but as soon as he understood that he'd been enchanted, he looked around anxiously at the unfamiliar faces, and his joy diminished.

"Where's Lilah? Where's Peitar?" When he saw Derek looking to one side, Bren's shoulders slumped. "You got me first."

Derek beckoned, and they flew away in low-voiced conversation.

Tsauderei returned from Mondros's plateau on Chwahirsland's border to find Arthur deep in one of his books, as usual. But he wasn't alone. Hibern was there, waiting.

Hibern cast a glance at Arthur, who was obviously lost to the world. So she lowered her voice and gave Tsauderei a succinct report about the breaking of the antidote spell secret, and the first rescue.

"I should have foreseen it," Tsauderei said when she was done. "Derek, obsessed with his version of making things right, and dismissing the necessity for keeping silent about that antidote spell. And Senrid plunging right in." He sank into his chair, his brow furrowed. Finally he looked up. "I didn't want to warn Derek that if Siamis gets hold of him, he could easily layer an enchantment over him."

"Why not? Surely that would give him pause."

"I'm beginning to wonder if that spell of Siamis's can be altered to take advantage of people's natures. You may have noticed that Siamis did not bother to order Peitar to form up an army. But Derek? What if Siamis could order Derek to lead all Sarendan against Colend? Even if he listened to my conjecture, for we have more truce than trust, I don't think he'd believe me. He's more likely to scoff about the weakness of magic, and declare he could out-think a mere Norsundrian, but might there be a spark of, oh, let us call it ambivalence? It's been plain to me for several years that Derek is happiest when leading a crusade, and of late he's fallen in love with military might."

"Oh," Hibern said, her stomach lurching. "Should I tell Senrid? He and Derek have become such friends."

Tsauderei let out a deep sigh, his gnarled fingers absently tracing the line of his mustache. He said at length, "Your friend Senrid hasn't spoken ten words to me since his arrival, so I cannot answer that."

Hibern got up from her chair. "I think I know what to do."

"I wish I did," Tsauderei said, but after she'd left.

## Chapter Twelve

L IERE liked flying with Hibern and Senrid.

It was quiet. Peaceful. She could enjoy the wind through the pines, the way their branches were in constant rippling movement, like an emerald-green sea. She loved the glinting stripes of muted color in the tumbled rocks, some as big as houses. She loved the towering mountains in the distance, crowned by never-melting snows reflecting the colors of dawn and sunset, for she came out at both times just to watch the change of the sky and the way the land woke up and then shrouded itself at the end of the long summer's day.

She liked the fact that Hibern and Senrid remembered mind-shields, so she was alone with her own thoughts without having to concentrate on shutting others out.

By gritting through morning flights on her own, Hibern had conquered her fear of heights—at least while flying—and had come to love soaring around the lake at the prettiest time of day.

The morning after the rescue of Bren, Senrid told Liere the details, since everybody was now talking about how the enchantment could be broken. Liere had already heard about the rescue the night before, as the orphan brigade made much of Bren. They seemed to admire him almost as much as they admired Derek.

"We decided to wait a day, then go back for the next one," Senrid finished.

"There are more?" Hibern asked.

"Ten."

"Can it be done without Derek along?"

Senrid's sharp "Why?" caught Liere's attention as Senrid shot a considering glance Hibern's way. Then he said, "You're thinking there might be people on the watch for him. Derek being some kind of commander. Though, hoo, he's kind of like one of our academy first-year seniors, from what I can see. You know, pretty fast, really enthusiastic, but he thinks he knows more than he does. Of course, so do I, but—"

Hibern sighed. "I know, I know, I've heard you before about how Commander Keriam says the worst of ignorance is not knowing how ignorant you are. I have no interest in your war blabber. None."

Senrid assumed an air of injured dignity. "I wasn't going to quote Keriam." He dropped the manner. "I was going to say that Derek does know the risks, but as it's only himself—"

"But it isn't." Hibern flew backward, her long black hair snaking around her sides as she held out her arms to balance herself. To Liere, she looked like an eagle, with her fingers outspread and her sleeves snapping, and her blue robe flagging like tail feathers.

Liere said into the silence, "You said Derek is some kind of commander. If people are loyal to him . . ."

"I hadn't thought of that," Senrid admitted. "But Sarendan is already enchanted. Do you think nailing a second leader intensifies the enchantment? Damn, that's vicious."

"When it comes to evil," Hibern stated, "don't underestimate Siamis."

Senrid waved that off, then flipped around to fly face up, eyes closed against the sun. "I'm going to remind Derek of that. I'll wager Tsauderei would agree. Maybe it's time to talk to him. I know he knows what we've been doing—"

"Yes," Hibern said cordially.

Senrid flashed a quick grin. "Well, and he hasn't hauled us in to shake fingers in our faces. Maybe Derek will agree that Leander and I ought to go alone." He opened his eyes. "In fact, I could go myself, after I see one more use of that spell. It'll give me something to do."

Hibern said, "But that goes for you, too. About enchanting leaders."

"Except that I've dispersed the army and academy," Senrid said. "And if I show up acting the least bit weird, Keriam has a token that will drop a stone spell on me. I'll be fine," he added with a hint of impatience, resenting the implication that he hadn't thought ahead.

Hibern said, "Senrid. If you get captured, and Siamis muscles you back to Marloven Hess and enchants you, then *they'll be enchanted too.* Keriam won't be *able* to drop that stone spell on you."

"Then I won't get caught," Senrid retorted. And looked askance. "I wonder if Dena Yeresbeth interferes with the enchantment. Anyway, I have a transfer token. The first I see of any Norsundrian, I rabbit."

Liere's heart squeezed. 'Something to do.' She'd wondered how soon Senrid was going to get bored playing those chase-and-tag games he was so good at. Her joy in playing had vanished that first day when she saw the others' surprise, or scarcely hid disappointment, at how bad she was at it.

She knew why Senrid was the best. No mystery there. After watching the academy boys play similar games ever since he was five, and reading everything he could about strategy and tactics because his kingdom—his life—depended on his knowing, he couldn't help but be better than a bunch of boys and girls who mostly just flew around hooting insults, or yelling orders at each other that no one paid any attention to.

Liere hadn't expected so much competition in games that everyone declared to be fun. She hated competition, especially when unspoken anger and spite and hatred streamed on the mental plane after certain people. It took so much concentration to shut it out, and she knew she shouldn't care, that caring was more evidence of her stupid emotions, which meant she deserved to feel rotten.

"Yep. I'm going to talk to them both." Senrid left.

Hibern was alone with Liere. Something that happened rarely. So she said, "I know you don't like to talk about Dena Yeresbeth, but Atan keeps asking questions. I was wondering if you might answer them yourself."

The Queen of Sartor? Liere felt so shy around her. Somehow Atan's friendliness made it worse. But Liere said, "If you want," because her reaction was a stupid emotion, and she deserved to feel worse for not having controlled it.

When Liere and Hibern reached Atan's cottage, they found her deep in magical studies with Jilo, Clair listening closely.

Jilo flushed and fell silent at the entrance of the newcomers, but Atan said in a coaxing voice, "Go on, if you would. How exactly did you release the time bindings?"

"They aren't completely broken," Jilo mumbled, acutely self-conscious. "I don't know how to do that. Maybe no one can, outside of

Wan-Edhe, because there are layers and layers. But I got it started by weakening the spells that used the life forces of the castle guards . . ."

Liere shuddered at this blithe mention of life forces being sucked out of living beings. No wonder Senrid was so impressed with awkward, limb-tangled Jilo—she could not imagine herself fighting single-handedly against such violently lethal magic.

Not long after, as the others went out to watch a thunderstorm, Liere sank down with her back to the windows. She was startled when Atan emerged out of the gloom. "Now that everyone is busy, may I trouble you with a question?"

"Of course," Liere said, biting back the 'your majesty.' Atan had made it plain that she wanted to be called Atan—that titles and honor-ifics hurt her especially now, when she had lost her kingdom—and she had never said 'Sartora' once. Which was more than Liere got from some of the others, who thought 'Sartora' was a wonderful honor, and that she should love it.

Atan said, "Someone said you can hear people thinking from far away."

"Only if I know them." Liere caught herself picking at her cuticles, and sat on her hands. "And if they don't have mind-shields."

"Oh yes! I forgot about that," Atan returned, looking away. "I apolo-gize if any of my thoughts have been intrusive."

"I try to shut everybody out," Liere said. "But sometimes I get tired . . . well, anyway, I haven't heard yours."

Atan looked back, her expression somber. "Not that I have any real secrets, except feeling sorry for myself about Sartor. I wouldn't want you to have to hear that. I do worry about everyone in Sartor. But I'm also worried about a friend, one you know, who helped me when I broke the century-long enchantment over Sartor, which was so very much worse than this one Siamis has spread everywhere. You met Rel, right?"

"Oh, yes. I traveled with him once. He's a really, really good traveler," Liere said, smiling as she remembered tall, sturdy Rel. He'd reminded her so much of the brother she liked—the one her father had prenticed out to a baker, so she seldom saw him.

"He is. I just want to know if he's all right. Do you think you could find him?"

"I can listen for him, but I did teach him the mind-shield," Liere said. "However, if it isn't habit . . ." She didn't bother explaining, but shut her eyes.

Distance on the mental plane was deceptive, not always measurable in days of travel. There were times when she could hear Senrid, or her family, like they were in the next room, and other times they were more distant than dreams.

She reached a thread, a tendril, toward Rel—and gasped.

"What is it?"

"He's . . . he's . . ." Liere felt him sway as he climbed out of the saddle, felt her dry tongue cleaving to the top of her mouth, felt her eyes burn. She saw the glow of fire like a false dawn in memory, heard the casual voice, low, flat, a little husky, *They're all dead.*

She jerked her thoughts free, then curled up into a tight ball as she fought the resultant vertigo, until she'd sorted her own thoughts from his.

Then she opened her eyes and stared at Atan, her face blanched, eyes huge. "He's in the middle of a war."

A short time later, she, Hibern, and Liere sat in Tsauderei's cottage, as Liere related what she'd seen when touching the surface of Rel's thoughts.

As soon as she finished, Atan said, "What can we do?"

Tsauderei said, "What do you want to do?" And when she didn't answer, he added, "You knew about this attack on Everon weeks ago. Is it suddenly real because someone you know is in the midst of the slaughter?"

Atan's temper flared, and then she remembered her heated accusations against Hibern about keeping the enchantment antidote secret and her brow creased. She saw at once that this was somewhat akin. "Yes. No. It's not more real. War is real, and horrible wherever it is. But when a friend is in the middle, it becomes more immediate. Urgent. Is it because I know I can't stop a war, but maybe I can stop him from being killed in it? I apologize if that's wrong."

"It's not wrong, it's human. So you would have me transfer in, and take Rel away?"

"Yes," Atan stated.

Hibern listened with a growing sense of loss, wondering why the Everoneth princess and prince hadn't contacted anyone. The alliance was definitely falling apart.

Tsauderei said, "But from what Liere tells us, Rel is spreading the word about the imminent attack. He might be the only one carrying that news, if those he was reporting to are all dead. Do you really want me to take him away?"

"No. Yes. Why isn't anyone *doing anything?*" Atan asked angrily.

Tsauderei sighed. "Why do you think I've been traveling so much? Which is not particularly good for old bones. King Berthold immediately attempted to invoke his treaties with his neighbors. The elderly queen of Wnelder Vee, to his north, who was in her nineties when she assumed the throne on the death of her son a couple years ago, fell into a stroke when she heard about the Norsunder attack. She was insensible, and though the healers did their best, she died a week ago. The new king is a boy about your age." He nodded at Liere. "Who is apparently being fought over by various guild factions in Wnelder Vee. Which is largely rural, with no militia, much less an army. As for Imar . . ." He sighed again. "Prince Conrad and Princess Karia—I should say, the new king and queen—officially expressed concern, but. You know the political situation there."

"I remember," Atan said. "The nobles of Imar are like pocket kings in their own land. The monarchy is very weak."

"It doesn't help that King Conrad and Queen Karia, with no real authority, are mostly concerned with social life. Neither of them has the will or the ability to honor the treaty, and the last I heard, the most powerful nobles are all digging in to defend their family holdings if Norsunder comes over the border."

"So Everon is left to itself."

"There is nothing we mages can do. We're forbidden by centuries of treaties to interfere in non-magical affairs. And there isn't much we can do about war anyway."

Liere heard Atan's thought as clear as if spoken: *I am not willing to do nothing.*

Hibern said to Atan when they left the mage's cottage, "There's still the alliance. Not that it seems to have helped so far. But I do know this. Princess Tahra has a notecase."

*Everon*

Mersedes Carinna was increasingly uneasy, but other than the obvious, could not define the cause. She had no success in getting Berthold to listen, and couldn't blame him for kissing her and saying, "It's just the war. Strikes us all differently."

Six couriers arrived, claiming that half the countryside was on fire. Berthold said after the first three, "You know how wild rumor spreads. I will not have people harming themselves through panic. If Roderic hasn't sent anyone from the western border, or Berneth from the harbor, then there is no real news. Just countryside gossip."

Mersedes Carinna tried to believe it until the fourth report, then she took her husband by the shoulders. "Are you certain this is mere gossip? Or is that what you want to believe, so strongly you are trying to make it true through will?"

Berthold covered her hands with his own. She saw in the quick flicker of his eyelids, the jut of his beard, that her guess was right, and she intuited with a thrill of sorrow that he couldn't let himself believe it, because he did not know what to do other than what he had already done.

And so she kissed him, then said, "I hope it's true." She kissed him again, harder, because he was a man underneath the trappings of kingship, a man enduring as much fear as his subjects. More, because they looked to him for a way out. And he had no one to look to.

She ran her hands up his sides to cup his face. "I'll feel better when we hear from Roderic." A third kiss.

A clatter of footsteps announced another arrival; the king's head turned slightly, and she excused herself and sped to her own rooms.

When she came out, she had changed into a riding outfit of dark blue velvet, and had bound up her hair under her coronet. She headed toward the stable, where she nearly collided with Rel.

"The harbor is on fire," he began, and coughed.

"You're the sixth person to come in with that news," she said.

"Why isn't anyone doing anything?" Rel was too exhausted to be diplomatic.

"Because we thought it was rumor. Until now. I was about to ride out to find Roderic myself, but I think that shall have to wait. Rel, if you will help me, it's time to rouse the city. I'll wrangle with the nobles, who'll be watching one another, and talking absurdities about standing and fighting, as if—like my darling son thinks—war with Norsunder will be the same as the Knights' martial displays, only better. Because it's an enemy you can really hate."

Rel was hesitant to agree, but she saw in his lowered gaze what he thought to hide, and she went on, "If you'll begin with the merchants and the older sections. Tell them to take refuge in the hills. It is where we traditionally went, back in the bad old days when the Venn raided up and down this coast. They couldn't kill people they couldn't find. Remind people of that, but if they argue, move on."

Rel held the back of a chair. "Understood."

"I see how tired you are, and if we survive this, you shall be awarded a medal you will probably be embarrassed by, and a grant of land that you won't use."

Her smile trembled, and sorrow constricted her heart at the thought of what the destruction of Ferdrian would do to Berthold. If it came to that. She would rather be the foolish queen who sent the populace of the capital scrambling for the hills than a queen reigning over ghosts. "I'll send another equerry to Roderic, in case your Kessler ordered someone to cut off any communication between us and the Knights flanking Henerek's last position."

She compressed her lips, longing to go kiss her darling, difficult children, but she knew that Tahra would push her away, then feel guilty, and Glenn would fret about his duty as a warrior prince, arguing and sulking, because those emotions were easier to bear than helpless anxiety. "Before you go, please help Puddlenose get my children out of the country. I think they'll listen to you boys quicker than they will to me. If Puddlenose still has the boat he told us about, it would be perfect. You know the path to take, the Knights' trail through the northern forest. Norsunder will probably avoid that, in the unlikelihood they even know about it. Difficult to maneuver in."

"Done," he said.

Mersedes pressed his hands, then dashed away.

Rel forced himself down the hall to the heirs' wing.

He found all four youths together, the boys clustered around Tahra. They all turned, their expressions so individual: Glenn sulky, Tahra stolid-faced, Puddlenose lazily smiling except for his watchful eyes, Christoph clearly wishing himself elsewhere.

"You look like you fought a war all by yourself," Christoph said, running a hand through his short blond curls so they stuck up all over his head. His expression was the habitual mild one, but Rel recognized in that swift gesture the frustration he sought to hide.

Tahra scowled at the ground, unsettled because the world was breaking into angles and uneven numbers, all murky, muddy shades. That morning she'd received a note from the scribe student Piper that their mutual courier friend, who had been translating Tahra's notes into good Sartoran before sending them on to Thad, was dead, killed at the harbor. No one knew when it had happened, but Tahra could assume that any notes she'd written had not been sent on.

Not three glasses after, her notecase, silent for so many weeks, had 'tapped' again. Before Rel could answer Christoph, she said, "I just got a note from Hibern, who was requested by the Queen of Sartor to ask if you are all right." She nodded at Rel, eyes wide with curiosity.

"Atan?" Rel stopped short. "Is she all right?"

"She and many others of the alliance are in the Valley of Delfina," Tahra said. She was embarrassed to admit that she hadn't written directly to any of them because she didn't want them to see her mistakes in Sartoran.

"Cowards," Glenn sneered. "Hiding. They don't have anyone locking *them* in the nursery wing."

It didn't take more than a breath to figure out the truth: Glenn wanted any excuse to go riding off to war, which he believed would be won by the daunting presence of that golden circlet on his brow, and the king had tasked Puddlenose to use his ingenuity to keep the prince in the palace, out from under everyone's feet.

No wonder the queen wasn't there herself. Glenn would spend the entire war arguing with his mother while Ferdrian was attacked from all sides.

Tahra gave a short nod. "Maybe someone ought to send an official letter to that snot Conrad, that the Queen of Sartor is thinking of us, at least."

"What?" Rel asked, remembering the difficult prince from Imar. "What's he done now?"

"Nothing," Tahra and Glenn said together, Tahra adding, "They're supposed to come to our aid. But haven't. I think it's because he's so high and mighty."

"I hate that soul-sucker," Glenn snarled.

While Rel tried to find a way to shift the subject, Tahra said indignantly, "He thinks we Delieths are upstarts, because our dynasty is only four centuries old, and we were originally a fisher fleet."

"As if Winstanhaeme is as old as Landis," Glenn said, kicking the rungs of Tahra's chair.

"Stop that," she said irritably. "They aren't. Their throne has changed hands more often than ours, and the Haeme family was from Sartor, yes, but only through a cousin who had nothing to do with . . ."

As she went on detailing the minutiae of family history that no one else cared about, Rel decided this was his chance.

"As it happens," he said as soon as Tahra stopped to draw breath, "I know that the Queen of Sartor would personally invite you to her. . ." He glanced at Glenn. "To her strategic retreat. Her *royal* retreat." And because he suspected the underlying cause of Tahra's lack of communication, "If you'll permit me to function as your secretary, I'll write to her and I can assure you of a royal invitation to join her."

He saw the effect of these words on the siblings. He knew that most royal children, at least in the south, were taught 'pure' Sartoran. But lessons in a language they didn't use daily didn't make them fluent. Tahra had asked him countless questions ever since she found out he spoke the language.

"You can send it in my notecase," Tahra said. "If you know the sigil to send a letter to the Queen of Sartor."

"I do," Rel said. "And if you'll teach me your sigil, so she can write back, I'll send a note right now."

Rel took up a pen, and sat down at a little distance. Puddlenose, judging correctly that Rel did not want anyone overseeing his words, said to Glenn, "So what would you do to lead the defense?"

Glenn had taken a few steps toward Rel. He turned back. "I wish Uncle Roderic would ask that, instead of you. If they listened to *me*, we would have been rid of Henerek weeks ago. All it takes is a charge with lances . . ."

A short time later, Rel handed Tahra her notecase, shoved the token that had been wrapped with Atan's answer deep into a pocket, and said, "It's even better than I thought. You can write to Prince Conrad that you're invited to visit the Queen of Sartor in the Valley of Delfina. She is in company with several other young rulers. Such as the King of Marloven Hess."

Glenn's head came up at that. "*He's* there?"

"Discussing strategy," Rel said, figuring it had to be true from what little he knew of Senrid. "The Queen of Sartor's issued you an immediate invitation. They'll send transfer tokens to your notecase, Tahra, once they make them." He took a chance. "But you'd better leave the palace now, because the tokens might not get here before the imminent attack."

Glenn said warily, "But my parents? My father might still permit me to ride in command of a company."

"Before I came to this suite I encountered your mother. There are no companies in need of leaders at present, and I believe she would appreciate your making diplomatic connections." With every word Rel felt he was treading closer to becoming the kind of liar he despised. Back to the truth—though the truth they most wanted to hear. "In the Valley are two kings, a queen, and a couple of princesses. All your age. In the alliance. Discussing countermeasures against Norsunder."

Glenn grinned. "*Finally* someone will listen to me! Let's go."

Tahra looked puzzled. "Mother? Wants us to go?"

"You know they will be pleased to hear you taking diplomatic initiative," Puddlenose said, hands out wide. "And you also know they aren't going to let either of you pick up swords. So why not do what you can? Impress them with your resourcefulness?"

"If we leave now, we can reach the coast by nightfall," Christoph put in. "Where we have hidden a fast sailcraft. Why not grab a suitable outfit or two? But no more than you can carry. We'll go by a secret path, because Norsunder would like nothing better than to capture the two of you."

Secret path and the risk of capture? Glenn's expression changed from stubborn to enthusiastic, and the royal pair departed.

Puddlenose turned to Rel. "Captain Heraford said he'd be following us from a circumspect distance. If those tokens take a while to make, we can return the boat to him. It'll be tight, with five of us." He grimaced.

"I'll sleep on deck," Christoph said hastily.

"Just four of you." Rel quickly outlined what Mersedes Carinna had requested of him. Then, "So I'd better get to it. Tell Tahra and Glenn I have courier duty. To the merchants," he added, thinking of Glenn.

Rel ran out, breathing a sigh of relief. He spotted a half-eaten meal sitting in the outer chamber, and paused long enough to pick up a chicken pie, a peach, and a hunk of cheese. He devoured the food as he ran.

He wondered if he should begin with the royal palace, but discovered the queen was ahead of him there. The Sandrial family and all their subordinates, who had been stewards for the Delieths as long as Delieths had been in the royal palace, were buzzing about like bees in a hive, packing for evacuation.

When he reached the high street, the alarm bells in the palace began to ring. People emerged from houses and shops, making his task easier at first: they spotted his mud-splashed white tabard, and crowded around.

Rel repeated over and over, "The queen orders . . ." which they responded to with endless questions.

He answered as patiently as he could, but by the time darkness closed in, he saw that he'd not even completed one street.

He pushed on until he stumbled over the low threshold of an empty house. He sat down with his back to the wall to rest . . . and woke up with an aching head, a fiery thirst, and a driving urgency to carry out his orders.

Rel worked his way from house to house, and street to street, repeating the same words until they leeched of meaning in his head. The responses fell into patterns: pleading, angry, bewildered. Some were shouted in his face, as if asking more forcefully would bring a different answer.

And some he couldn't answer, like "Why didn't the king deal with them earlier?" and "I thought the Knights were invincible!"

When he got to the narrower streets, many people had already heard gossip and had evacuated. He found a woman hastily washing dishes, as if leaving a clean house would somehow guarantee order when she returned. Halfway down the otherwise empty street, he found a family setting up defenses, determined to protect their shop and home. As he moved on, he had to help carry bushel baskets of belongings, tie down furniture jumbled onto carts, and lift squalling children after harassed elders.

"I've lived here girl to widow," an old woman declared, her voice wavering. "And my grandmothers before me. No one crosses this threshold without my permission!"

Rel tried to argue, but the woman shook her head. "Where would I go? How would I travel? I can barely walk to market each day."

"If you come with me to Prince Solenn Road going east, someone will help you," Rel said. "I'll find you someone with an extra corner in their wagon or cart if you'll come now." But she shook her head and shut the door in his face.

He'd been at it a couple days by the time he began finding more empty side streets. Through the middle of the city the royal road leading north toward the mountain filled with streams of people bearing baskets and parcels, and the occasional wagon loaded with the elderly and young, furniture, and baskets of food. Most of those were pulled by family cows, or goats, for all horses had long since been commandeered; many carts were pulled by the families who owned them.

Rel forced himself to the last street at the extreme west end of the city. Darkness had fallen once again, broken by no lights anywhere. He walked into the open door of a cottage, and sank down into a chair by the cold hearth. He leaned on the table next to the chair, which cradled his aching body, the cushions shaped by a generation of some unknown family.

He only meant to rest his eyes a moment . . .

## Chapter Thirteen

*Delfina Valley and Everon*

FLYING was the most wonderful sensation in the world, but Liere discovered that she missed smells. If the wind shifted one way, she could catch a pine scent, and the other way, snow. But it wasn't anything like walking on a road and sniffing fresh bread baking, or wildflowers, or the fragrance of soil and grass just after a rain. Still, she thought as she followed the swarm swooping, diving, chasing, and laughing, she wanted to remember every sensation concerned with flying, because Atan had said this was the only place in the entire world that had this magic. There were, she said, flying people in another range of very high mountains, but you had to be born one.

Liere flew with the chase games to be part of the group, but she never tried to catch anyone, and never tried to be the target. It was more fun to watch the ones who were the most graceful.

She was watching when Tsauderei came out of his cottage and took to the air. He was another who became graceful in flight. Liere watched him go to Derek, which surprised her, because usually the two avoided one another. She realized then that she might be snooping instead of watching, and so she flew in another direction.

Tsauderei was not aware of her scrutiny. He had considered

everything going on, and decided it was time to try talking to Derek. Derek, Senrid, and Leander had been leaving more frequently.

To Tsauderei's surprise, Derek came willingly, and he wondered if this apparent cooperation was due to Derek having his own set of demands.

As soon as they stepped inside the cottage, weight mercilessly pulled Tsauderei's bones. He winced as he sat. Joint pain made him more irascible than he'd intended to be as he eyed Derek standing there, arms crossed, head at a wary angle, then said bluntly, "You know Peitar would hate your risking yourself, so we'll take that as a given. But what you might not know is that both Leander and Senrid are kings, which is something Siamis could use against their kingdoms if they get caught."

Derek's eyes widened. "Impossible."

Tsauderei snorted, his mustache fluttering. "Go right ahead and ask."

"Both of them?"

"Right next to each other. Of course Leander's Vasande Leror has, as far as I know, one tiny town, and the rest of it isn't any bigger than one of the middling counties here in western Sarendan. But Marloven Hess . . . you may have heard of it."

Derek frowned. "Kessler talked about a regent who . . ." He stopped. "Senrid's the crown prince?"

"He's been king for a couple years now."

Derek shook his head. "He doesn't talk or act like any king. Why, when he joined my orphans at morning drill, he went to the back. No prince or king would do that."

"Ask him. Or don't. I don't care. My point remains, if you keep pestering them to go with you into Sarendan, you're risking more than you think. And that goes double for snatching Lilah, if she's being held at the palace, which has to be laced with magical traps. Wait until I can go."

"Why can't you go now?" Derek tipped his head the other way.

"Because we need to free more mages, so that we can break the Siamis enchantment at the same time, all over the world. Then it won't matter if breaking it brings Siamis at the run."

Derek left, brooding. He wasted a breath or two thinking that Tsauderei had to be lying, but why would he? He floated in the sky, watching from a distance as the others played, Senrid faster than anyone except Bren, and better at directing others. Maybe Senrid was like CJ, with no pretenses. Even though he'd been born a prince. As Derek watched Senrid, the thought occurred that if Senrid was really a king, then he could not just talk to whoever was in charge of the Marloven academy, he could make them accept Derek there, so he could learn all they had to teach.

He decided to put it to Senrid after they'd rescued the rest of the kids. But, mindful of Tsauderei's threat, he waited until nighttime, when the boys showed up to plan the next foray.

"You two are kings," he said. "Maybe you should stay here."

Senrid rolled his eyes, looking pained. "Someone got gabby, huh? Look, I've already had this argument. I carry a transfer token with me. If I catch a whiff of Norsunder around, I'll be out of there faster than a heartbeat."

"Most of us are rulers of some sort," Leander said amicably. "That's what our alliance is." He held up his hand. "But Senrid and I are both trained in magic. We'll get out if we have to."

Derek grinned. *I tried, Tsauderei.* "Then let's get back to planning . . ."

They decided to rescue the remainder of the Derek's orphan brigade in one day. Mindful of the kingship argument, Leander and Senrid re-cruited Hibern and Arthur to help. This meant talking Jilo into letting Arthur in on the secret of the book. He gave in reluctantly.

At the other end of the Valley, Atan received a slightly peculiar note from Tahra, stating that they were now sailing aboard a little boat called a tender, and that as soon as they sank the land below the horizon, she and her brother Glenn would use the transfer tokens.

Afternoon had shifted the shadows from west to east when two fig-ures were spotted on the grassy Destination outside of Tsauderei's cot-tage. Atan and the study group went to welcome them.

They found a pair of dark-haired, sallow-complexioned young teens recovering from the transfer. Atan led in speaking words of welcome, then they went around the circle introducing themselves.

Tahra stared from one to the next through droopy gooseberry eyes, marking a connection to the Landis family in her background, then said flatly, "I promised Puddlenose I would tell you that he will come after he sails the tender back to the ship it belongs to."

Glenn waited for her to finish, then stated, "Now that my sister is safe, I'll wait here until Rel sends for me. I told my father I'll lead any company whose commander has fallen."

Silence fell, some exchanging looks, then Arthur said easily, "Why don't we show you where you can stay for now?"

And so the Delieths joined the group.

---

On the surface, that week was uneventful, at first even cordial. Glenn stopped talking wildly about war and duty after a short, pungently expressed set of questions from Senrid about numbers, terrain, and tactical observations, none of which Glenn could answer. After Senrid, with trenchant cheer, admitted that he wouldn't know what to do himself, Glenn stopped talking about commanding wars and contented himself with counting up how many had titles, and ignoring anyone who didn't.

The first evidence of strain occurred when Kitty offered to introduce the Everoneth siblings to the famous Sartora; on hearing herself addressed that way, Liere sidled off as quickly as she could, but not before she heard CJ say, "Sartora was great at world-rescuing one time. But I guess even she can't do it again, in spite of all those mind powers."

It was no more than the truth, but CJ's sharp disappointment acted like a whip to the spirit.

The second bad moment occurred a couple mornings into the newcomers' stay, when Glenn discovered the orphan drill. If Senrid had gotten there first, things might have gone differently; as it was, Glenn landed, surveyed the plainly dressed, barefoot orphans, then marched with princely assurance to the front.

Faen, one of the orphans' leaders, gathered a couple of the bigger boys with a glance, and all three summarily muscled Glenn to the back row with unnecessary vigor. "Beginners start here," Faen said.

"But I'm Prince Glenn Delieth of Everon," Glenn said in a reasonable tone. "Should we not go in order of rank?"

"Well, *I'm* Lord High Emperor of the Brick-Layers, so *I* go first," Faen retorted, to gusts of laughter from the orphans.

"And I'm King of the Silversmith Prentices, so I'm next," Ruddy added, prompting more laughter.

Derek stood to the side, arms crossed, and smiled to see the arrogant young prince get the trimming he deserved.

When Glenn saw Derek's smirk, and realized that he was not going to interfere, he flew away in disgust, and never came back.

Hibern's morning flights had changed.

Senrid now attended the orphan drill every morning, rather than flying with her and Atan, but Liere had taken his place. Liere was now living in the hermit's cottage with Hibern and Atan.

One morning the three flew out at dawn to watch the sun rise over Sartor far beyond the mountains.

"You're both unhappy," Atan observed after a very long silence. She did not want to point out that they looked as unhappy as she felt during this protracted waiting.

Hibern said, "I think it's this waiting. Though I know it's necessary, it isn't good for us. The alliance, I mean. There are some of us who are used to acting on their own, and, well, I'm afraid the alliance is in trouble."

Liere said solemnly, "CJ is angry with me. But I can hear her trying so hard not to be. It's that she wants so strongly for me to be a hero. But I'm not. I try to stay out of her way. I'm sorry if my being here makes the trouble."

"It doesn't," Hibern said quickly. "And CJ isn't the only problem in their group."

All three girls glanced across the valley to Selenna house, where some of the Mearsieans sat on the roof eating breakfast. Sitting with them, her silken skirts spread around her, was Leander's stepsister Kyale, her silvery hair a shining fall down her back. Kyale, who veered between wanting to be called *Princess* Kyale and Kitty, reminded Liere of spun glass—beautiful to look at, but fragile, and sharp-edged.

Atan contemplated Kyale's penchant for sticking to CJ's side, trying hard to create an inner circle exclusively made up of princesses. CJ seemed typically oblivious, trying a little too hard to organize group games whether others wanted to play or not.

Hibern said, "At least Jilo seems to like studying light magic with Arthur. And I was glad to see Clair joining them."

"Who wants to wager," Atan said with a smile, "they're over there right now, half the breakfast things set out."

"Water filled, but the fire forgotten," Hibern suggested.

"Bread sliced, but nobody remembered to make the toast."

Liere chuckled soundlessly. "Yesterday I saw Arthur with the jam pot beside his dish, and a knife, and no bread. Then he got up and went off with Jilo to study something horrible called mirror wards, thinking breakfast was over."

"His theoretical breakfast *was* over," Atan commented.

"What are mirror wards, anyway?" Liere added, with a thoughtful glance.

Atan grimaced. "I don't understand them at all, except that this is very, very dangerous magic."

Hibern said, "Imagine a mirror behind a candle sconce. You've seen that, right?" At Liere's cautious nod, "Well, the magic reflects the image, doubling the power. Especially if you are strong enough to make inter-locking mirror wards, in effect breaking the connection between real and unreal, just as the flame in the candle is real, but the one in the mirror isn't. And yet it reflects light."

"This," Atan said, "is how dark magic distorts time and place. And if you also draw on life itself, you are on the way to creating Norsunder."

"I'm sorry I asked," Liere whispered, and dove down in an effect to let the wind scour away the horror.

But it went right along with her, so she willed it away, and as she, Atan, and Hibern finished their circuit all around the valley, Liere turned her attention to her surroundings in order to impress all the details she could into her mind: the little goats hopping along steep slopes, juts of striated rock glistening in the sun, wildflowers of colors she had no names for. She wanted *these* memories to show up in dreams, after she had to leave. And nothing about mirror wards.

They finished, as usual, at Tsauderei's hut. Hibern caught sight of Seshe's long light hair through the window, and thought that a good sign, as she was hungry. Though she had no objection to fixing break-fast, she wasn't very good at figuring out how to estimate, much less cook, food for more than herself and Erai-Yanya.

She opened the door first, then recoiled when she smelled smoke. Alarm flashed through her, just as Liere darted past her, yelling hap-pily, "Rel, you came!"

Atan was right on her heels.

Except for Seshe, quietly toasting bread at the fireplace, Tsauderei was alone with Rel, who looked unfamiliar in his white tabard edged with midnight blue and gold, the formal wear of the Knights of Dei. Rel wore no device on his chest, as he was not sworn a Knight, but somehow the tabard made his chest look broader, and emphasized his height.

Atan stared. He was thinner, the hard bones of his face pronounced. It struck her that she now knew what he would look like as a man, and as warmth pulsed in her middle, she thought in alarm, not now, not now, I am not ready for that.

"Rel, what happened?" Hibern asked, with the freedom of easy ac-quaintanceship. "I smell smoke."

"Ferdrian is burning." Rel indicated Tsauderei's cleaning frame. "I stepped through that first thing, but before I could, I guess I still stank up this cottage. I've been wearing these clothes for . . ." He thumbed his eyelids in a gesture of tiredness. "Ten days? Two weeks? I've lost count."

He looked around, as Tsauderei made a casual gesture and the side windows to his great bay opened, flashing briefly with magic.

"I've been asking Tsauderei what I should say to Glenn and Tahra," Rel began, but not two heartbeats later the door slammed open, and Glenn flew in.

"I saw you arrive," he said, his eyes wild. "I saw you from the other ledge." He pointed at Rel. "Why did it take you so long to come get me? Where are my parents?"

"I don't know," Rel said, and after a hesitation, "Ferdrian is on fire. I had to leave."

Glenn's face reddened as his angry gaze swept over the faces, then he whipped around and zoomed out again, flitting past the window in the direction of Selenna House.

Hibern made a gesture as if to follow, feeling some sense of responsibility, but Tsauderei said, "Let him be. If he or his sister want help dealing with the news, or lack of it, they'll let us know." He turned his head. "Rel? Tell us what happened."

By now several others, seeing Glenn's wild arrival and departure, had come to see what was going on, including Kyale, whose secret, unexpressed desire was to be accepted into Atan's select group, so that one day she might be invited to Sartor's court. She had a happy vision of stunning the Sartorans with her most beautiful gown—then, afterward, she could come home, and everyone would be impressed when they heard where she'd been, and they would finally give her the due respect of her rank! Only every time she flew out to that secluded cottage, they were talking about such boring magic or history stuff.

She saw Atan's attention on Rel, so she added her voice to those pestering him, "What happened in Everon? Tell us!"

"It fell to Norsunder." He looked around for a subject change. "Is that the house where everybody is staying?"

Hibern leaned out the door, peering toward Selenna House. "Speaking of Everon. Where are Glenn and Tahra? I thought they were coming right back?"

Arthur scratched his head with the inky quill clutched in his fingers, leaving spots of dried ink in his tousled yellow hair, and said vaguely, "I saw Glenn, I think. I was reading this, and didn't really notice." He brandished the scroll he'd been carrying. "Where's Leander? I thought he was right behind me."

Jilo spoke up from behind him, "No. He and Senrid were talking to Glenn when I left."

---

Jilo had finessed that a little.

At Selenna House, Glenn had burst in on the boys while Senrid was dressing for the morning drill, and Leander was assembling his study materials.

"Rel is back," Glenn said, his sallow face blanched to the color of paper. "Ferdrian is on fire. He didn't see my parents. Uncle Roderic. Anyone. I have to go back. Will one of you send me?"

Jilo sidled a glance at Glenn's angry face, faded straight out the open window, and headed for Tsauderei's house.

Senrid and Leander met each other's gazes. Leander said slowly, "He should. Be able to go home."

Senrid knew that Leander was loading the words with meaning, but what meaning? He leaned against the wall, his eyes closed, and reached mentally.

He recoiled at the intensity of Leander's memories from the time Senrid's uncle invaded Vasande Leror. Senrid gritted his teeth, hating his own memories of that shameful episode. Through came Leander's thought: *It was important to be there. Though I could do nothing.*

That, too, hit Senrid hard, in an unprotected place: that inward conviction he'd fought against ever since he was five, that he ought to have been there when his father was killed.

"Let's go," he said, more in reaction to his own memories—the instinct to get away—but once he said it, Glenn's whole demeanor made so dramatic a change that Senrid listened to his thoughts instead of warding them. He heard below the anger and frustration a gnawing anxiety.

"Let me get Tahra," Glenn said, and arrowed out the window.

Leander felt obliged to say, "Tsauderei won't like it," and when Senrid shrugged sharply, "nor will the others. If we find something bad, they'll say our taking them was cruel."

"Let 'em. Glenn wants to be there. He yaps a lot about princely rights, but this is one I agree with."

"And I don't disagree." Leander sighed. "Transfers?"

Senrid picked up the tokens waiting for the orphan rescue the next day. "We'll use these. We can get Arthur and Hibern to help us make new ones tonight."

Tahra and Glenn dashed in, Tahra tousled and heavy-eyed from being wakened. Her mouth was pressed in a thin line.

"Where do we go? Give us a Destination," Senrid said.

Tahra did, with her usual meticulousness. Senrid and Leander altered the transfer spells, changing Destinations. Then Senrid handed the tokens to the siblings. "Don't lose these. There are two transfers on each, there and back here again. Let Glenn and me go first. We'll wait while the Destination clears."

When they arrived in the Ferdrian royal palace's Destination, smoke and heat nearly knocked each pair down. Everywhere flames roared and snapped, withering the textiles that the Sandrials had not been able to remove. They raced down a hallway, dodging small fires and bending low, to fetch up short at the first blood-splattered, hacked body sprawled in death.

Tahra choked. Glenn gripped her hand and tugged her onward before Leander could get the words past his tongue, "We should go back."

Glenn put on a desperate burst of speed. In his father's chambers they found three dead guards, all known to the siblings; one was a cousin. He ran out again, batting furiously at the drifting smoke. Eyes burning, the others followed until he stopped again on the terrace above the square, giving an inarticulate cry.

The king lay below the first step, surrounded by the remainder of his personal guard. All dead, King Berthold with a sword loose in his hand.

Glenn jolted forward as if yanked by invisible strings. His chest heaved on a sob, then he dropped to his knees, and reached a tentative, shaky hand to straighten his father's tabard.

Tahra threw herself down on his other side, heedless of the darkened pool of gore. She kicked the sword angrily. It clattered away, fetching up horribly against a lifeless Knight. Glenn shot her a venomous look, retrieved the sword, and gently laid it by his father's side.

Tahra pulled her father's hands together, then tried to order his hair, but it was filled with spiky black blood from a killing blow to the head. So she smoothed the jagged wrinkles in his clothes, though her joints had turned to water, and the world had broken into rust-colored elevens and sevens.

While Glenn and Tahra laid out their father, Leander and Senrid watched the perimeter, Leander troubled, and Senrid stone-faced.

"Shall we Disappear them?" Senrid asked when the siblings had done what they could.

Glenn's lips moved, but he couldn't speak.

Leander and Senrid stepped carefully to each of the fallen. They left the king for last. Glenn's face was a rictus. He'd given up the fight against weeping, as tears of rage dripped onto his father's chest. The king's body, his kingly garb so lovingly woven and embroidered, and the steel he had borne when he was killed, broke down to their components and vanished into Everon's soil.

Tahra said, "We have to—"

A noise behind caused Senrid to grasp the hilts of his forearm knives, and Leander to grip his transfer token. But they stilled when a bloody figure staggered through the door. "Gone." It was a young Knight-cadet. She stared at the ground, her lips working. "He's gone? I came to . . ."

Glenn closed the distance between them. "Where's the queen, Perles?"

"They say she fell. In the attack on Roderic. Someone else said that they were taken prisoner. She and Commander Roderic." Perles raised her unwounded arm, making a vague gesture at the fire. "Somewhere."

Sickened, Leander said, "Let us go. Perles, is that your name? Do you want to transfer with us?"

Perles backed away, raising her hands. "No. No. Take the princess and prince away. Keep them safe. We fight to the last." She turned away, and was lost in the smoky entrance.

Senrid said, "We can do nothing more here."

Glenn managed a short nod.

One by one, the four transferred out, Senrid going last.

In Delfina Valley, Tsauderei's group had moved outside to discuss where to search for the missing four when light flickered on the other side of the grassy terrace and Arthur said, "Transfer."

One by one, the four appeared, staggered, then took in the circle of faces.

Tahra leaped into the air and flew away. Kyale and one of the Mearsieans peeled off to chase after her, ready to coo and pet as needed. Glenn looked indecisive, then stuck his jaw out and crossed his arms, glowering in spite of the tear tracks still wet on his face.

As the crowd lit on the grassy path beside the cottage, forming a half-circle, Atan said, "Where did you go?"

"Everon," Glenn said in a flat, belligerent voice. "We had a right."

"And so we took them," Senrid said, indicating Leander and himself.

Hibern had heard that tone in his voice before, and seen that nasty grin with too many teeth and no humor. Senrid, for whatever reason, was spoiling for a fight.

Hibern had little expectation that anyone would listen to her, but she raised her voice. "I think we should give Glenn and Tahra the choice whether they want to talk about what happened, or to be private."

"I agree," Atan and Derek said at exactly the same time. Then cast a startled glance at the other.

People took to the air, with many questioning, doubtful glances cast back. Glenn flew off alone. Senrid sensed he was at the end of his self-control, and didn't know whether to go with him or stay. It seemed cowardly to leave him, but he loathed the thought of sticking around unwanted.

He was distracted by Jilo's appearance. Jilo sidled up, glanced furtively around, then muttered, "The book says that Detlev's in Everon."

## Chapter Fourteen

*Everon to Norsunder Base*

DETLEV peered down at the smoking ruins of Ferdrian from the hilltop where Kessler had pitched camp while he waited for the worst of the fires to burn out.

He snapped the glass to. "Where is Roderic Dei?"

Kessler remembered a report in the constant stream, something about Henerek's men hoarding prisoners to play with, but at that time he'd been commanding the last, fierce battle at the Ferdrian palace. "Henerek has him."

Detlev cut in. "You didn't think to ask Henerek where before you rendered him speechless?"

"Nobody gave me orders concerning prisoners." Kessler knew how weak that sounded, though it was the truth.

Detlev said derisively, "That's because those orders came from Yeres. You did know that Henerek is her current toy." His tone implied that it was obvious—and in retrospect, it *was* obvious. Henerek never would have gained this much command without backing from higher up.

Detlev didn't wait for the answer that Kessler couldn't give. "Go back to Base. I'll deal with the detritus."

It had not occurred to Kessler until that moment that he had been set up.

He transferred, and while still recovering, left the Destination at Norsunder Base, and walked the short distance to the command center. The prickling hairs on the back of his neck and the faint but distinct metallic not-quite-scent, not-quite-taste warned of a window opened from Norsunder.

He walked into the command center, and there was tall, dark-haired and sharp-faced Yeres, dressed in crimson, lounging in a doorway from the Beyond—wasting enormous power—in the middle of the room. Because of the way windows were made, no matter where people walked in the room, they saw the same angle, which meant she wanted an audience.

A lot of people had crowded into the command center, clearly expecting entertainment. Siamis did not number among them.

Yeres ran her fingers through a long lock of her glossy dark hair, then said, "Efael is not happy with you at all, Kessler."

Silence.

Yeres spoke slowly, as if to one of the soul-bound. "Everon was Henerek's reward."

Kessler said, "He was losing. I was told to go clean it up."

"Your orders, I believe, were to clean. It. Up. Not destroy everything and everyone in sight. I'm sure it was fun, but Henerek was to capture Roderic Dei for Efael, and to lure Berthold Delieth and his wife from their citadel, so that Detlev could use them. He also wanted whatever artifact they had in that palace that prevented our getting mages in there. Did you find the artifact before you torched the place?"

Siamis had never mentioned any of this. Kessler had been framed, and he knew how much his admission was going to cost, but said it anyway: "What artifact?"

Yeres looked around in mocking disbelief, then put fingers to her forehead. "'What artifact?'" She got the expected laughter from the avid audience, then said, "Did you ask Henerek for his orders? No. Though he can barely speak, he has given me to understand that you did not."

The room had gone silent.

She continued in a sweet, mock-sorrowful tone. "Now, Kessler, everybody likes their fun, and a short temper can be useful, except when you manage to destroy not one." She raised a forefinger, in case there was dispute about the number. "Not two." Up came another finger, the back of her hand aimed at Kessler in deliberate insult, causing snickers around the perimeter. "But three, count them, three people's plans. Detlev's, Efael's, and *mine*. Henerek says he had Roderic Dei, but your followers squabbled with Henerek's leadership—yes, dismal, but at least he understood orders—and the old man hobbled away in the midst of the tiff."

She *tsk*ed, causing another wave of snickers.

She went on in that chiding, slow voice, as though he were a lackwit with no will. "We do not like waste, so you will be given a task that might be easier for you to compass. You are to take that token there on the map desk, and remove yourself to Geth. It seems our two favorite busy bees are not cooperating in establishing their little hive, and Siamis wants a drone to set up and maintain the guard station, which will free him up for important tasks. *Now*."

Kessler took up the token; the moment he touched it, the room vanished, and he found himself enclosed in a bubble somewhere in the weird area on the outer perimeter of the Beyond.

He and Yeres were alone.

She smiled. "If everyone despises you, they do not notice you."

Kessler said nothing.

She said, "Siamis scorns you, and Detlev ignores you. Can't you see what a useful weapon you can be? Go to Geth. We cannot get into the city Isul Demarzal."

Kessler had no interest in Geth-deles, much less any of its islands, but he had to maintain a semblance of obedience because of that damned blood-spell Dejain had inflicted on him. Until he got rid of it, he was Norsunder's minion.

So, "What is Isul Demarzal?"

Yeres smirked, always glad to demonstrate the ignorance of a captive audience. "Isul Demarzal," she stated, "is the oldest city on Geth-deles. All their mages and magic are centered there. You hold Isul Demarzal, and you hold the world. Surely that makes sense to your military mind?"

Kessler stood impassively.

She sighed, cast her eyes skyward, then said, "Siamis managed to lure its leader out, and used that enchantment of his to make them permit him access. He's now inside. He says he's working to break the wards keeping us out, but no one believes that. It's unlikely that you're warded from getting inside, since no one on Geth-deles knows your name, or even that you exist. Siamis wants you to run his guardhouse, but Efael thinks what that really means is, he wants you running backup."

"In?" Kessler asked.

"Efael thinks that this is the battleground Siamis has chosen to fight dear Detlev. You handle the bloodletting, he the magic."

Kessler shrugged, and Yeres sighed. "My very dear boy," she said, though they looked exactly the same age. "It is the first time any of us have breached that city. I want in. Efael wants in. Svir wants in. You achieve that, and you can have anything you want."

She snapped her fingers, and the transfer token hurled him out of the world.

*Delfina Valley*

At Tsauderei's cottage, Senrid stared at the old mage, then exclaimed, "But this is the right time to go to Miraleste for the last rescue, while Detlev's in Everon!" Then he stopped, appalled. How could he be so stupid?

Tsauderei's brows shot upward. "He most definitely is not in Everon. But he was. How did you know that?" He regarded Senrid steadily, as Senrid rapidly formed and discarded lies.

After a silence that felt like two days to Senrid, Leander, and Jilo, the old mage sat back, saying with dry humor, "Well, it takes no intelligence to understand that you youngsters have your own methods of communication. Or you would not have seen fit to take the two Delieths to Everon in the middle of battle. However, no harm came of it, and you did get them back safely. So least said, soonest mended."

He paused as lightning crackled outside the cottage, and a sudden downpour nearly drowned the thunder. He spoke more seriously now. "I know you think that because you've been successful so far, by rights you should be able to get Lilah out of Miraleste. Have you considered that she's the lure to a trap?"

Senrid said, "Of course we have. This is why we saved her for last. We've run ten other rescues, the last two in Miraleste, and nothing's happened. We're really fast by now."

"Miraleste," Tsauderei said, "but not the palace. Correct?"

Derek put his hands on his knees. "I promised Peitar."

He didn't say it aggressively, or angrily, just with that utter conviction that made him so appealing a leader. Tsauderei could see in subtle movements, the lift of chins, the inadvertent smiles, the way the youngsters all faced him, that the kids responded to Derek exactly the way Peitar did: with their trust.

So he came at his objection in another way. "As I said, I appreciate that you youngsters have your own communications—yes, Derek, at my age, I regard you as one of 'em—and I commend you all for keeping within safe margins. If a little closer than your adult guardians, whoever they may be, might have liked. You've seen I've been away on my own concerns. Oalthoreh and I have been rescuing mages from Sartor, one by one. However, when Murial tried to rescue Chief Veltos, she nearly walked into a trap. Actually, she would have, if Veltos had been in another chamber. But the one she sits in happens to have some very old magic left in it, with a protection afforded by an artifact of the kind we cannot reproduce today. It exhibited a warning that only a mage would perceive, before she set foot in what seemed to be an unwarded room. We thought we'd removed all the Norsundrian wards. And there are a lot of them."

He saw the sobering reaction in Senrid and Leander, who understood magic. Derek looked like he was patiently waiting for Tsauderei to finish speaking.

So he tried again. "Lilah will be free very soon, as well as Peitar. Soon—at most, three days. The antidote spell is being taught to all mages who are deft with ward and tracer magic, while other mages do their best to spot and ward hidden magical traps that might bring Siamis back to this world. None of us want *that*, right?"

He looked at each young face, seeing ambivalence in Senrid, but resistance in Derek's tight forehead, the lift to his chin. Bren and Innon both turned pleading eyes to Derek, and Tsauderei knew, with a sinking heart, that they were going to act with or without his leave.

So he said more crisply than he'd intended, "I can't go with you. There is a heavy ward set against me, a mirror ward with a lethal trap built in, so any magical attempt to remove it if I choose the wrong side of the mirror will rebound onto me. As well as alert Norsunder before I can remove it. I've been waiting for one of the stronger mages to have the time to deal with it in tandem with me, but it will take us considerable time to test and remove the traps. We've chosen to work on the universal deployment of the antidote to Siamis's enchantment first."

Derek still sat there, arms crossed, blank of face. Senrid grimaced at the mention of mirror wards, but he said nothing.

Tsauderei gave up. Short of dropping Derek with a stone spell, which would guarantee his followers going wild with what they'd consider a betrayal, there was no stopping him from doing whatever he was going to do.

And then he had it, the motivation underlying everything. The mage rescue could be a matter of hours away, but Derek would contrive to get there first. It mattered to him to be the one to free his particular charges from the enchantment, and he considered Lilah one of his charges.

Tsauderei sighed. "If you're determined to proceed, I suggest you take not one, but three of you to scan for further wards. Each with transfer tokens gripped in your fingers."

He nodded at Hibern, then turned to Jilo and Senrid. "You two are probably familiar with every likely form of dark magic that might be laid down. If you find anything suspicious, promise me you'll transfer immediately."

They promised.

Tsauderei's attention shifted to Jilo, who was more hunched than ever, as if he was a breath away from running out the door. Because he'd been coerced into this reckless plan of theirs? No, he'd entered calmly enough. That tight-shouldered hunch had happened . . . ah. Directly after Senrid uttered his remark about Detlev.

He was going to need to probe that.

But not now. "However, I got sidetracked. Permit me to finish what I was saying about Detlev. I just received a communication, sent between worlds by Erai-Yanya, that Detlev has been seen on Geth-deles a lot in the past few years, ever since Evend destroyed Norsunder's rift magic."

Tsauderei jabbed a finger at them. "Think about that. A man born four thousand years ago, whose appearances in the world are usually once a century, has been spending appreciable time there. If he finds a kind of rift magic that will get around Evend's binding spell, you know he's going to bring it back here."

He stopped there, afraid he'd said too much. But no one seemed to be making the leap to the weaknesses in Evend's binding.

Jilo's eyelids flickered, then he rubbed stiffened fingers down his trouser legs.

Not the rift, Tsauderei intuited. But definitely something, and Jilo was the key. Probably some dire scrying object created by Wan-Edhe, though what it might be, Tsauderei could not imagine. It would have to be extraordinarily powerful (and dangerous) to track the movements of someone like Detlev, and Jilo clearly was wary of sharing it with Mondros, or Tsauderei would have heard about it by now.

"All right, I think that answers your questions," Tsauderei said.

That broke the meeting up, Senrid streaming out with Jilo and Leander, talking in low voices. Hibern followed, and Atan headed after her until she caught Tsauderei's gaze.

She waited behind until everyone else was gone. Tsauderei's expression was grim, which made Atan press her arms tightly against her ribs. Whatever he was about to say was bad news.

Then a horrible idea hit her. "Julian," she gasped. "They found her . . ." The word *dead* could not get past her lips.

"Not that," Tsauderei said quickly, and smoothed his mustache, one of his rare unsettled gestures. "I debated within myself, then decided you would want to know. Siamis seems to have taken her to Geth."

Atan turned away, disheartened and sick with failure. Her one living relative, this small cousin, and Atan hadn't even been able to get the child to acknowledge her as anything but a possible enemy.

She flew through the rain back to her cottage, where she found Hibern setting slices of bright orange cheese on hunks of bread, which were laid out on a pan ready to be set over the fire in the fireplace.

Hibern glanced at Jilo and Arthur sitting at the table at the other end of the room, muttering over 'wards' and 'chained spells,' then back to her work in such a way that Atan suspected something was wrong.

In fact she was certain of it. She hadn't seen the usual group playing around in the rain. "What is it?" she demanded.

The two boys looked up, then down again as Hibern said, "You really want to hear it?"

"Maybe I'd better hear it," Atan said.

"Well, I guess CJ told Rel—"

"Stop." Atan shut her eyes as she flung up a hand. "Stop right there. I changed my mind. I *don't* need to hear it. Here, give me that knife. Let me do something useful. At least I can toast bread."

Hibern set down the hunk of cheese, handed over the knife, and pretended not to hear Atan as she muttered, "I hate that girl."

---

"Bring Lilah right to us, promise?" Bren said, hopping up and down on his toes.

Innon stood next to him, his pale blond hair hanging in his eyes, wet from the lake. Swimming in a thunderstorm was a double pleasure. "She'll want to see us first thing. Especially since Peitar is still in the enchantment."

"I promise," Derek said, holding up both hands. "We'll come straight to you two first. Even before Tsauderei, though if he turns me into a tree stump, be sure to explain to Lilah."

The boys laughed, then took off, arguing happily over what to do first while they were waiting.

That left the four standing in a circle—Hibern, Senrid, and Leander alert and ready, Jilo tense. This would be the first time Jilo wouldn't be monitoring his book during the rescue, but Detlev and Siamis were not even in the world, so it was easier to agree to Tsauderei's stipulation that Jilo aid Senrid in sniffing out dark magic traps at the palace.

As always, Derek had to keep his face well hidden. He'd stuffed his shaggy brown hair up into a winter cap, and pulled the front down to his eyebrows. He wrapped a scarf around his lower face, leaving a thin slit to peer through. He'd look suspicious to anyone not under enchantment, but to the enchanted, he would be unrecognizable.

He'd told the boys the best place to transfer would be the fish market along the docks below the lake. If there were any Norsundrians left in the city, they surely wouldn't patrol there during summer. Bren, with an artist's eye, gave them an exact description of a locale that they could use as a Destination.

Nobody was in sight, except boats bobbing gently on the water as a hot summer wind kicked up. When they recovered from the transfer they found themselves baking in the summer sun, the odor of fish strong. They forced themselves to move at a slow, steady pace.

The only conversation was from Derek, who muttered as they turned up toward the royal palace on a road bare of people, "I will never eat a boiled potato again without remembering this day." He touched his head in its wrappings.

Hibern grimaced with sympathy. She usually wore her hair loose, except in summer. High in the mountains, she hadn't bothered with a braid, but now she wished she had. To avoid the glare of the sun she watched her sandaled feet treading stones placed by unknown hands unknown years before.

Leander, Senrid, and Derek found the quiet eerie. That much reminded Jilo of Chwahirsland, though nothing else about the city did. He stared in astonishment at new buildings jostling old smoke-damaged ruins, everything dappled with painted and chalked slogans and drawings. Some were actually well done, though most were messy scrawls.

The people themselves were also unlike Chwahir. They didn't dart furtive looks around them, or converse in hand signals. They looked like a city of sleepwalkers. He wondered if Wan-Edhe would demand that spell from Siamis, then he remembered that it was predicated on a sense of loyalty to a leader. Wan-Edhe would never lay that enchantment over himself. The thought made Jilo shake with silent laughter.

When they reached the palace gate, Senrid and Jilo both searched for tracers. Nothing happened.

"This way." Derek motioned toward a narrow path between a couple of buildings made of light stone, with fine slate roofs. This was not the main part of the palace, which was built of marble.

He led them along servants' paths. Senrid fingered the silk scarf that he'd been given for the purpose: as soon as they saw Lilah, Senrid, being the fastest, was to bind the scarf around her lower face before Derek came into the room. That way she wouldn't be able to perform any tracer spells that she might have been commanded to use while under the enchantment.

Derek silently pointed to a discreet entrance in what was obviously a wing of the royal residence. No guards in sight. Senrid held out his hands as a signal to tread warily. It stood to reason, you hedged your royal prisoners with either human guards or magical ones.

He and Jilo moved to the front, testing for wards and tracers.

Jilo halted them before the door to the room Derek indicated. He'd already found a bad trap. He whispered another spell, and Hibern saw with her magical sense a flash of green around the door. Senrid reached for the latch, but Jilo shook his head, and Senrid pointed to the latch.

"Nothing here," Senrid mouthed.

Jilo shook his head. He knew he might be slowing them up, but dealing with Wan-Edhe's complexity of deadly wards had taught him about chained spells. He crouched down, holding his hand flat above the floor near the bottom of the door. And once more he whispered. Once more there was a subtle flash of green.

Senrid whistled soundlessly.

"Clear?" Senrid breathed.

"I think so. But . . ." Jilo flicked his fingers outward. Maybe that was the way this particular spell dispersed. It was a nasty one. He had the sense there had been a secondary spell, though there was no trace now.

That was enough for Senrid. "Let's be quick."

Derek gave Jilo a grateful clap on the shoulder, which startled Jilo into jumping backward, nearly colliding with the inlaid buffet outside the door. Senrid and Hibern both caught his arms. He blushed as he righted himself.

Senrid led the way in. Hibern took up a station inside the door, to listen for footsteps or sense magic.

She gazed across the room at Lilah, a sturdy girl of twelve or so sitting decorously at her window. "She's wearing the same clothes she had on that night. When I returned after my defeat at the pass," Derek whispered.

Lilah's head turned. Her eyes were wide and glassy as a doll's. Hibern's heart galloped at the girl's tense stillness. She found it impossible to believe that she'd sat like that for all these weeks, and wondered how time distorted under Siamis's enchantment.

Derek peered in the open doorway, then stepped into the enormous salon with its fine old desk and the comfortable circle of low chairs with embroidered cushions that had somehow survived the revolution. Everything was the way it was supposed to be, except that was not Lilah behind that flat stare.

Hibern shut the door and set her back to it.

Lilah didn't move even when Senrid whipped the scarf around her face, firmly covering her mouth. She just stared.

The boys began picking up objects in the room and holding them before her eyes, but she never gave them a glance. It was as if they were invisible. Lilah's blank gaze was turned toward Derek.

He met that flat gaze and ripped off the mask. It was time to end this nightmare, and get out. He knelt before her chair so she'd see him well enough to focus for Leander's spell.

Lilah brought her hand up in a fast, deadly arc. Senrid was the first to react to the glint of steel, smacking Derek out of the way, the green-glowing tip of the knife cutting the air a fingernail's breadth from Derek's throat. Leander, Jilo, and Hibern all lunged toward them, then stilled as Derek fell back on his butt.

"Lilah?" Derek exclaimed. "It's Derek."

"Somebody took extra time inside the enchantment," Senrid muttered. "Gave her this blood-spelled knife, and commanded her to use it on you."

"Blood-spell?" Derek asked.

"All it has to do is nick you. The magic gets into your blood, and Norsunder can get at you," Senrid said. "Control you." He grabbed Lilah's wrist from behind, and twisted until she dropped the knife onto the floor. "The spell is very hard to make."

"And very hard to break," came a new voice from behind them.

While everyone's attention was on Lilah, the door had opened noiselessly. Hibern felt a strong arm bend her right arm up behind her and a hand clap over her mouth.

Senrid, Derek, Jilo, and Leander whirled around.

"Siamis," Senrid whispered sickly.

Derek's first reaction was disgust at yet another failure of magic, but maybe this was better: hand to hand.

Hibern stomped as hard as she could on the man's instep, but she could feel her sandal sliding over his boot, and Siamis's soft laugh stirred the top of her hair. Then his grip tightened, bending her arm up behind her to an excruciating degree. She groped with her free hand, trying to get her elbow up to dig into his ribcage.

A Norsundrian warrior stepped up to her side, crossbow pointed directly at her ribs, and she subsided, her heart crowding her throat.

Derek rose slowly to his feet, readying for an instant of inattention on Siamis's part. Come on, Hibern—someone—distract him, he was thinking.

Jilo nudged Leander, glancing toward Lilah, who twitched, blinking. Leander softly whispered the antidote spell as Senrid kept one hand on Lilah's wrist, his other gripping the transport tokens so tightly his knuckles crepitated.

Siamis said to Derek, "Well, king-breaker. What's it to be? Her life or yours?"

'King-breaker'? Rage ignited in Derek. He snatched Lilah's knife from where it had fallen and flung it straight at Siamis's head.

But Siamis was faster. In three moves he thrust Hibern stumbling, swept the crossbow from his guard to whack the knife spinning—

"*Now,*" Senrid yelled, his voice cracking.

Siamis shot the bolt as everyone said their transfer words—

Senrid landed hard, rolled, then sprang up, ignoring the transfer nausea as he stared witlessly at Derek, who lay lifeless on the grass outside Tsauderei's cottage, the bolt sticking up from his heart.

Lilah staggered, then flung herself down beside him, crying, "Derek? Derek?" And then, holding tightly to his lifeless hand, she let out a long, desolate howl that soon brought everyone running.

Tsauderei came out, leaning heavily on a stick, and gazed down at Derek's lifeless form. The old mage looked even older, face furrowed with grief and regret. It was Senrid who laid hands to the bolt sticking up so horribly from Derek's chest; everyone flinched as if it were pulled from their own bodies as Senrid drew it out then snapped it angrily over the cliff.

"We have to take him to Selenna house," Lilah wailed.

"We have to get Peitar first, we have to," Bren shouted.

"Yes," Faen cried. "You get the king. We orphans will guard Derek's . . ." He choked on a sob.

Tsauderei put up a hand for silence. "All of you know that Derek Diamagan would prefer being Disappeared in the open air," he said. "And Peitar will prefer knowing everything was done properly, beginning with a cessation of this quarrel over Derek's lifeless body. Lilah, you, Bren, Innon, Ruddy, Sig, the five of you may take him to the village. The rest of you, get yourselves cleaned up, and find candles. There are plenty in the storage cupboard at Selenna House; you needn't raid the villagers for all theirs."

Nobody argued with that.

Someone in the village brought out an artisan's table as a bier, over which the grandmother in the house where Derek had been staying produced an heirloom quilt to cover the table. The five kids—all five still weeping—laid him on that as gently as if he could feel their tenderness, and many hands came forward to straighten his clothes and limbs, and order the long, tangled hair that he had rarely bothered combing in life.

Lilah collapsed by the bier, weeping wildly; Bren keened on the other side, next to Innon, who stood, head bent, tears dripping down his face. Most of the brigade wept with them until the first paroxysm was over, and then, in ones and twos, they all repaired to bathe, and dress in whatever they thought was their best.

Senrid remained behind with Tsauderei to give a report. At the end, he said flatly, "King-breaker?"

Tsauderei gave his head a shake. "You know how Norsundrians look for the worst in people, and then use it to divide others. Let it go. It's immaterial now."

Senrid turned his palm up in assent, but those words—king-breaker—continued to fret him, because once again he sensed knowledge shared by others that they weren't going to tell him. He wasn't sure if this was because he was a Marloven, and therefore not to be trusted, or because Tsauderei and Derek had been antagonistic, but as he turned away he promised himself he would find out.

Ordinarily it was left for the next of kin to do the Disappearance spell, and failing that, the highest-ranking person there. Given the preponderance of those with royal claims, and the fact that Derek's brother was in another country altogether, Tsauderei snuffed the possibility of argument by declaring that he would do the spell himself, as eldest. No one objected to that.

So at sunset he stood at the head of the bier, holding a tall candle in both hands, though one of his knees shot pains up his legs to pool at the base of his spine. But he was determined to see this memorial through with utmost respect. He was grateful that he would never have to hold the conversation with Peitar that he had been rehearsing in his head for a couple of years now—well knowing that it would be useless. Peitar would never have believed ill of Derek. And the worst of it was, Tsauderei was fairly certain that Derek would never have intended ill.

King-breaker. How unsettling, this oblique corroboration from a source such as Siamis. Why would the Norsundrian have said that?

*What did he hear inside Derek's head?*

Tsauderei shifted position minutely, as yet another child stepped forward, clutching a candle in tight, sweaty fingers, to speak a long, disjointed, sob-punctuated memory.

The sun sank beyond the snowcaps in the west overlooking slumbering Sartor, and still they came forward to speak their memories.

The Mearsieans stood in a tight group, eventually their surreptitious nudgings of CJ becoming more obvious, until finally she stepped forward and said in an uneven voice, "I didn't know Derek's name when we all got taken prisoner by that evil skunk Kessler. But I met him when he refused to fight in Kessler's disgusting army, and I . . ."

That wasn't coming out right. She looked back at Clair, who stepped to her side. "CJ saved Derek's and his brother Bernal's lives," she said in a firm voice. "Without knowing who they were. Derek told us that moment was important to him. That showing mercy to a person not because of who they are, simply because they are another person, was important. We don't . . . we didn't know Derek. But we'll always remember that about him."

She and CJ stepped back together, holding hands tightly, as a brief rustle of approving whispers went around the watchers.

Atan, standing at the back with Rel, murmured for his ears only, "That was actually civilized."

Rel shifted, his breathing changing. "You've seen the worst of CJ. You haven't seen the best."

"Is there a best?"

"Yes. You just heard about one incident."

Atan struggled to control the corrosive sense of dislike. It helped no one, it never did anyone any good. "I'd like to hear more," she said. "Not just for me. But because, especially at times like today, there needs to be more best in the world. Peitar is going to be so hurt."

Rel's chin came down. "Yes. He and Derek should have been brothers. Did you know?"

"Peitar and Lilah both told me something about Peitar's mother having loved Derek and Bernal's father, but she was a princess and he was a stablemaster. How sad that is, when stupid rules . . ." She sensed herself nearing uncomfortable thoughts, *personal* thoughts, and said instead, "I hate the idea that Peitar will come out of that enchantment to this news. I wonder if he would like to walk the labyrinth." Then she thought back, and it occurred to her that Peitar had never actually been to Sartor. "I should invite him. When the troubles are over. Don't you think he would love it? He knows so much about history."

Rel said, "From what I saw, I think he would like that very much."

And as the painful memorial went on, Atan called the royal Purrad to mind and set Peitar there, imagining his reaction to the wind chimes, the sough of leaves and branches, the scents, the sound of footfalls on pebbles, the unfolding of quiet beauty all around. Some of the pain banding her heart loosened.

Hibern observed Atan and Rel whispering, then raised her head to take in the alliance all gathered. And no one arguing. She looked down, grief and guilt intensified by a new thought, that it took tragedy to unite them. Her gaze lit on Derek's still profile, and the unsettling way the flickering candlelight made it seem as if he breathed. It took leaders to draw people together for good purposes, she was thinking.

She glanced inadvertently at Senrid, who stood in the second row on the other side of the bier, between Jilo and Leander.

Senrid was unaware of her glance, unaware of anything. He was shut tightly inward, lest Liere hear his thoughts.

Memory and custom both threw him off balance. The sight of Tsauderei standing in a robe of sky blue, embroidered down the front in gold with the ancient symbols of the Twelve Blessed Things, was so unlike Marloven custom, and yet Senrid was thrown back in memory to when he stood at his father's bier, a shivering five-year-old, surrounded by black-clad people tall as the castle towers, the bier framed by leaping torchlight.

In Marloven Hess, a king's memorial was held at midnight, with everyone singing the Hymn to the Fallen. This ancient hymn was accorded all kings, commanders, and jarls, but also every warrior who fell in battle, no matter what his background or degree.

Senrid remembered the deep male voices singing the hymn, and in his own mind, he sang it over again for Derek Diamagan. He shut out the kids' halting, rambling memories, which had no place in Marloven custom: the stories and anecdotes were reserved for the banquet following the burning of the person's private effects by the family.

I know why you did that, Siamis, Senrid thought, ice-cold conviction flowing along his nerves. You didn't want Derek to make Sarendan ready to fight you off. You're the real king-breaker. At least, that's what you intend. But I'm going to make sure you don't get your chance.

I'm going to kill you myself.

Nobody saw that Liere had already slipped away.

# PART FOUR
The Alliance Acts

## Chapter One

GETH-DELES is an azure gem in the night skies of the fifth and third worlds from Erhal, the sun.

Scattered across that blue expanse, a necklace of islands rises on the sea, vanishing in a horizon where the sun burns itself out among the monumental clouds.

The islands offer a marvelous variety, dark forests and grassy plains quilted with ordered avenues of crops, and evenings alive with multi-colored fireflies. White-glare sunlight splashes in shards off the endless sea by day, and silver nights glow on cascades down low mountains, flowing into calm shores along the smooth sweep of the sea.

Humans—mostly Ancient Sartorans, fleeing the cataclysm known as the Fall—are latecomers to this much-populated world, calling it the World of Floating Islands.

Many of these islands, it transpires, truly do float, bolstered beneath by an endless tangle of growth that supports soil and rock, hill and tumbling water, but the rest are true islands, connected to vast elon-gated continental shelves in constant motion. The undersea beings cared nothing for constant quakes; it was the mysterious former surface-dwellers who bound the floating islands, tamed the quakes to gentle rocking, and left here and there monuments whose design united for-ests, sea, sunset, and air into a conspiracy of beauty.

On the largest island of a complicated archipelago sits the largest and oldest city in the world, Isul Demarzal. Here, walled within the city walls, is Charlotte's Palace, a ramble of a low building, patchworked with gardens, housing all the human world's archives and a library, a center of magic and learning, until recently well-protected against Norsunder.

Down the centuries there was little contact between the two worlds revolving opposite one another, until relatively recently, as Sartoriasdeles recovered enough magic for world transfers. Geth's mages, descendants of Sartor but now with their own customs and disciplines of study, fashioned their own methods of transfer.

It was this magic that Norsunder was after.

Liere didn't know that.

She didn't know anything about Geth-deles, except that Siamis was there, and, as frequently happened when shocked or grieved, she heard her father's bitter, scornful voice ranting in memory that she was selfish, stupid, clumsy, and that whatever happened was surely her fault.

So it was time to stop being weak. It was time to be like Senrid, and do something about it. When the memorial was over, and Tsauderei returned to his cottage, she overheard him reading just-arrived messages to Atan and Hibern: Siamis was already back in Geth.

Clarity soothed Liere's jangling nerves. Erai-Yanya, who was Keeper of the Dyr, was on Geth-deles. Siamis was on Geth-deles. Liere knew how to break Siamis's spell by using the dyr. Therefore she ought to stop being weak and selfish, hiding in the Valley while the world's mages struggled to vanquish Siamis's spell, go to Geth-deles, get Erai-Yanya to pull the dyr out of its magical hiding place, give it to her, and then . . .

Well, then she would either win or die.

She considered telling Senrid, but sensed the darkness of his mood. Besides, he'd find all kinds of reasons for her to stay, and really, what they amounted to was that she was weak. And useless. Just as her father said.

But she'd prove them all wrong. Yes. That was the way to think.

She knew that Hibern and Arthur both had the world transfer spell in their books. All she needed was a Destination. She understood that much. So, while the others talked, or consoled the grief-stricken Sarendans, she slipped into Tsauderei's cottage and went through Arthur's books until she found what she sought: the world transfer spell. And in another book, a description of the Gate of Isul Demarzal.

Everything was happening at Isul Demarzal, so that was the place to go.

She fixed the Destination firmly in mind, spoke the spell, and magic seized her.

Atan went to sleep feeling tense and headachy from hiding her reaction to Derek's death. Which had been . . . no reaction. To be truthful, even a little relief, but acknowledging that increased that sick inner sense because she knew that was wrong. So she'd made herself attend the memorial, staring dry-eyed down at Derek's still profile while surrounded by the genuine grief of people she liked, and while she hid her own lack of emotion, she hoped some of their grief would enter her heart and clean out the residual anger.

Hibern spent a sleepless night, her mind insisting on seeing that horrible scene over and over again, beginning with Lilah's crazy-eyed swipe with the knife, and her own futile, stupid leaping forward. And then those hands grabbing her from behind.

She knew that Siamis, and not she, was to blame for Derek's death, but the overwhelming grief and anger sparked a deep conviction of guilt. When a bleak dawn at last lightened the cottage, it was a relief to get up.

She and Atan bundled into their coats. The flying magic kept them from getting drenched and frozen, but the chill gripped them the moment their feet touched the ground, and they hurried into Tsauderei's cottage.

The old mage and Arthur were not alone. The study group stood around feeling, and looking, awkward, and Senrid was there, grim-faced, as Lilah tearfully argued with Tsauderei, "Oh *please*. Just Peitar. Why would it hurt to rescue just one person? Why do you have to wait?"

Tsauderei said, "It's best for the kingdom, for the world, because there is a larger plan."

"But it's horrible!" Lilah sobbed. "That Kessler, he tied me in a chair for *days*, and there was never any dark so I could sleep—"

Tsauderei said, "Lilah, Kessler's Norsundrians were only in Miraleste a day at most before they set sail."

"And you've got no rope burns," Senrid pointed out, indicating Lilah's freckled wrists; the movement slid his shirt cuff back slightly, revealing the white scars of his own rope burns. "What you're remembering is distortion because of the enchantment."

Lilah turned on him. "But don't you *see?*" Another sob shook her. "Don't you see, it *felt* like days and days, so what are they doing to my brother? Right now? It could feel like years and years of telling him over and over to do horrid things."

Tsauderei said, "I'm sorry, Lilah. If it helps at least a little, neither Kessler nor Siamis is in Sarendan. So it is doubtful that Peitar is being told anything."

Lilah's chest heaved and her breath shuddered as tears bounced down her face. "You should have gotten him out first."

She didn't sound angry, she sounded broken, and no one had the heart to say that her rescue was at Derek's insistence.

Atan and Hibern both backed to the door. Arthur followed them, his customary vague expression brow-furrowed with question. "Did either of you move my books?" he whispered.

"Didn't touch them," Jilo said, at his shoulder. "Wouldn't."

"Me either," Clair said softly.

"Nor I, without permission," Atan said.

Hibern said, "Is something missing?"

"No, but my new study book, the one I copied all Erai-Yanya's notes about Geth into, it was moved, and so was my spell book."

Lilah headed for the door, beyond which they stood. She gave another heart-wrenching sob, freckled fingers covering her face. The study group moved aside. Lilah's desolation was reflected in their averted gazes, Arthur absently wiping his inky fingers on the sides of his already-ink-stained trousers. The girls exited, and Arthur withdrew to his pile of books.

Atan and Hibern hunched into their coats, the bitter wind fitting the bleak mood. "I think this might be a day to spend by the fireside reading," Atan said.

As they lifted into the air, a short blond figure chased after them through the sheeting of rain, and Senrid caught up, his yellow hair blowing straight back off his tense forehead. "Have you seen Liere?"

Atan and Hibern looked at one another. "Isn't she with the other girls?" Hibern asked. "She didn't come back with us last night."

"She wasn't at Tsauderei's, either," Senrid said. "If you see her, pass the word that the Mearsiean girls want to have breakfast with her, will you?" He left abruptly.

Hibern and Atan retreated to the hermit's cottage, closing the door hastily to keep the warmth inside. As Atan sliced the last of the previous day's bread, she said slowly, "That does seem a bit odd. That no one can find Liere. But if Senrid, who seems to have appointed himself Liere's big brother, is not worried, then—well, good."

Hibern looked up from glancing at and neatly stacking all the books on the table. "Senrid loathes fuss. Don't assume anything from his demeanor. I think I'm going to take a quiet look around after I finish my toast. I just won't say anything to anyone."

"I'll join you," said Atan, bringing the toasting fork to the fire. "Four eyes being better than two."

As Hibern sliced cheese to bring to the toast now that the underside was done, she thought back through the previous evening, and then exclaimed, "Atan, I haven't seen Liere since the memorial."

Atan looked up from the golden cheese just beginning to bubble. "Nor have I, now that I think about it."

Hibern went on, remembering what Arthur had said, and hating the possible conclusion. "Further, I think Senrid knows that. In fact, I think he knows where she went, but he's being extra careful to make sure."

Atan looked startled. "Where? Back to Bereth Ferian?" She set the fork down, and the two poked the hot bread to their plates.

Hibern reluctantly spoke the words, as if saying them aloud would make it true. "Geth-deles."

"What?" Atan's expression of surprise turned to skepticism. "Liere? That poor little thing is frightened by her own shadow. And she knows no magic."

"She can be very determined, when it comes to what she thinks of as her duty."

Atan drew in a breath. "But still, she doesn't know any magic."

"Yes and no," Hibern said. "She has a perfect memory. I guess because of that Dena Yeresbeth. She successfully used a very complicated spell to bring the dyr out from timelessness, where it had been hidden behind years of protective wards. And she did it by herself. Without knowing how to read. When she was ten."

Atan hastily swallowed the bite she'd just taken. "Would she do something crazy like transfer to Geth? Why?"

A tight voice spoke from behind: "If she thought it was her duty."

Hibern and Atan whipped around to find Senrid standing in the open door. He added, "When I first met her, she thought it was her duty to climb on the back of a horse made out of lightning and go around the world flashing that dyr while half Norsunder was howling after her blood. And yesterday, I'm very sure she managed to convince herself that Derek's death was her fault, and therefore it was her duty to go after Siamis herself because she'd failed the entire world."

The sharp precision of Senrid's consonants revealed how angry he was.

Senrid pointed at the door. "You left it open." He shut it. "Arthur just told me that Tsauderei reported a transfer out of the Valley. He thinks it was one of us on another errand."

"We've got to tell him what happened," Atan exclaimed.

Senrid's teeth showed as he lifted a piece of cheese-topped bread from the plate. "After I'm gone."

"But—"

Senrid cut in. "You know—" He paused, jerking around when the door he'd shut behind him banged open. But when he saw that it was only CJ, not Tsauderei, he continued on, "You know what we'll hear, a lot of horseshit about how children can't do anything, and—"

"And planning, and waiting, and let the adults think it through," CJ said, coming around the side of the battered old couch. "While they take another million years to get around to doing anything. We think Sartora's gone to Geth to chase Siamis. And we're going to help!"

"What can *you* possibly do?" Senrid poked his half-eaten bread at her.

"What we did in Bereth Ferian when Siamis attacked with that enchantment the first time. It was your plan," CJ retorted, crossing her arms, as the Mearsiean girls crowded in behind her, Clair looking troubled. "We can search, or lure Siamis out, or—"

"My stupid plan that nearly got us all killed?" Senrid shot back. "You still don't see that, do you? The only reason why Siamis didn't kill the lot of us was because Oalthoreh and the northern lighters were also decoying him, so Evend could walk into that rift and die closing it."

"But we aren't dead," CJ said, spreading her hands. "Sartora's *alone*. We need to find her. And *help* her. The more we have to search, the better, right? And then we can also break Siamis's spell, if he's spreading it around there."

"Stay here," Senrid said. "There's nothing you can do—"

"Who," she said loudly, "was just blabbing about children can't do anything?"

"You're useless," Senrid said. "Except in making things worse."

"Oh, yeah, Mr. Too-big-for-your-britches? I've been in as many adventures as you have. More! And I never tried to—"

Senrid's temper ignited. "If you try to fling my uncle's penchant for executions in my teeth—"

"You'll do what, execute me?" CJ cut in, and waved a hand. "Save it for Siamis. In fact, if you want to execute him, I'll hold the arrows. I already hated him before he did that to Derek, and now I hate him even more."

She and Senrid glared at each other, both fighting guilt and regret. CJ harbored a secret terror that she might be responsible for Sartora going off like that to another world. She wasn't quite sure why or how. It was just those nasty looks Atan had been shooting at her.

Senrid endured the goad of guilt because he'd known very well that Derek's insistence on rescuing Lilah had been needless, but he'd agreed mostly out of restlessness and boredom. Because the other rescues had been easy—though Tsauderei had warned them more than once that there were probably extra traps waiting.

Clair nodded at Hibern. "Right before the memorial yesterday, Liere was asking me about signs, and how to pronounce certain words, but I thought she was just asking to know. Not that she was going to do anything."

"We've waited around long enough." Senrid pulled a piece of paper out of his pocket. "Arthur taught me the world transfer spell."

By then all the alliance had arrived, and everyone looked at Atan.

She looked back, knowing what they expected—caution, threats to tell Tsauderei, her tutor and first guardian. But all she could think was, *Julian.*

If Liere had gone after Siamis, who had taken Julian . . .

She said to Senrid, "When do we start?"

Senrid gazed back, surprised.

Hibern looked from one to the other, knowing she was missing something, but more important than that, it looked as if a whole lot of people were about to go haring off separately to Geth.

She braced herself, remembering what Erai-Yanya had said about the future, and her place in it. And she raised her voice. "I won't go straight to Tsauderei if you all promise to just find Liere, and bring her back. No chasing after Siamis or trying to end his spells. Geth-deles is not our world. We know nobody there, or how they do things."

CJ looked belligerent, but when Senrid stated, "I agree completely. I don't know why Liere suddenly thinks she has to go rescue Geth-deles, but she can explain it all to us once we get her back."

"Yes," Clair said. "That's the best plan."

CJ sighed. "I'd love to boot the stinkard Siamis right out of the world."

"As long as he gets booted," Senrid said. "Who cares who does it?"

At the back of the crowd, Bren whispered to Lilah, "Sooner they get rid of Siamis, sooner we can free Peitar."

"Then let's go with them," Lilah whispered fiercely. "I *can't* stay here. Everything is memories. Let's go, too. And I am going to pretend that Peitar is with us."

Innon said soberly, "We all will."

Bren jerked his head in a nod, rubbing his red, swollen eyes. "Yes. We'll talk to him like he's with us. And we'll even say what he says back. And then when we get back and he's free, we'll tell him all about the good things he said and did."

As several voiced agreement, Hibern looked at the faces that had been so grief-stricken, now firm with resolve. She knew they were going to go anyway, so the best thing would be to keep everyone together. And maybe two world transfers in a day would land everybody in bed for a week, so they wouldn't try any more stupid ideas.

She raised her voice. "I'll agree, and not tell Tsauderei, if you also agree to take notecases, in case the magic somehow separates us. So get whatever you want to take. We'll find Sartora. And everyone transfers straight back. Agreed?"

Everybody spoke or signaled their agreement. Then the door banged open, and people streamed out.

Hibern said to Senrid, "I mean it about the notecases."

His lip curled, but he patted the pocket in his black uniform trousers. "I've got mine here."

Hibern knew she was right, that she'd caught him before he was about to hare off alone after Liere. "I still think we ought to tell Tsauderei that we're going."

"Why?" Senrid retorted. "We let Tsauderei dictate the plan for rescuing Lilah, and look where that got us."

Hibern flashed back, "That is not true, or fair. He didn't want anyone to go. He wanted us to wait. But when he saw that Derek meant to go anyway, he added those extra cautions."

Senrid jerked a shoulder up. "Then tell me how having Jilo staying here, watching in the book for Siamis transferring and alerting us, was wrong?"

"Book?" Glenn asked.

Senrid's face blanched, and Hibern suspected he hadn't slept at all, or he would never have made a slip like that.

She turned to Glenn. "Magic book." And saw Glenn's complete lack of interest—he was only interested in swords and battles.

Senrid crossed his arms, a sure sign that whatever he was going to say next, Hibern would hate. He shifted to Marloven. "If you're about to yap out that we should tell Tsauderei now, then you can save your breath. How long before he and a posse of mages hunt Jilo down and wrest that book away from him because 'no powerful artifact should be left in the hands of a child?' Don't try to tell me they didn't do that after Liere took the dyr around when Siamis first showed up. They couldn't wait to separate her from the damned thing."

Hibern stood on the low table, and faced everyone. "For the last time. The plan is, we go, we find Liere, we come back immediately."

Leander said, "What Destination?"

Arthur spoke up from the back. "The city everyone is worried about is called Isul Demarzal, but Norsunder is there now, Tsauderei said, so I wouldn't use anything in that city. When Erai-Yanya first traveled there, she used a white sand beach as her Destination. There's one near Isul Demarzal, an unlikely place to find Norsundrians."

"Don't we need tokens?" Atan called over heads, as Rel silently joined her. "This is a world transfer."

"But this spell works differently from ours," Arthur said. "It's kind of like a tunnel, or lights strung along the way. It's . . . different. Everyone who's going, form small circles."

He might have said more, but Senrid had already memorized the spell. He vanished.

CJ had been watching. The Mearsieans grabbed hands, and Clair, who had been practicing silently, did the spell.

Aided by Hibern and Arthur, the others popped into transfer.

Tsauderei was sitting in his cottage, staring in dismay at the note he'd just received from Erai-Yanya, who had transferred all the way from Geth just to send it.

He was pondering what—if anything—to say to that half-grown, half-trained, thoroughly wild bunch of puppies currently eating breakfast in houses around the valley when a tracer alerted him to sudden cluster of transfers.

Instantly suspicious, he hobbled to his door, launched into the air, and scowled at the revealing emptiness all around. He reached the deserted hermit's cottage to discover that even Atan was gone. He cursed himself, suspecting what had happened: he should never have told Atan about Julian being taken to Geth.

He slammed out. As soon as he reached his desk he ignored the rain soaking beard and clothes, pulled out paper, and began writing letters.

## Chapter Two

*Geth-deles, Isul Demarzal*

JULIAN walked down the street.

She liked Geth. It was warm, and the air smelled like gardens and fruits. She liked looking at the houses, so different from what she was used to. She liked the shiny wood that they were made of, and she liked those roofs that sloped at a gentle curve upward to a flat top. Like houses with hats. So much prettier than the slanted roofs in Eidervaen, with gargoyles and things carved around the eaves. And much too high. None of these were high buildings.

Siamis told her they couldn't build high because of all the ground shaking, and the roofs could be flat because it never snowed here. The big thing they called Charlotte's Palace was only one story. She liked that, but she didn't like how you had to walk and walk and walk to get anywhere inside. It was more fun to walk outside, and see how many kinds of wood and how many kinds of houses there were.

But if she tried to go out the Charlotte's Palace Gate and the runaway prince wasn't there, the mean-faces in black or gray slapped her back inside. If he was there, they didn't slap her, but she still couldn't go out.

"Why?" she asked, the first time she saw the runaway prince again.

"Because Siamis wants you here, for now."

She scowled, then said, "You didn't come back for me."

"I did. You weren't there before I had to leave."

Julian eyed him. "He said he gave you orders."

"That's true."

"So he gave you orders to guard this gate?"

"No. This gate is the result of his orders," Kessler said. "Because he lied." Then he rode out to inspect the perimeter teams, leaving Julian standing there.

So she couldn't explore outside the gate. She was stuck with the dream people inside the gates.

At first she'd liked how quiet the Geth people were. How nobody cared when she traded those stupid clothes from the trunk in her room for a long silken thing of crimson and gold with speckled green flowery things, so long she could wrap it around herself and still have long streamers, the way many did here. Nobody noticed when she took a robe thing of bright blue out of someone's house, when it rained and the air turned a little bit cold at night. Nobody noticed if she walked in and took food right off people's plates.

It was just like in Eidervaen, when Siamis had talked those sharp-voiced, frowny grownups like Chief Veltos into smiling and quiet.

She heard noise. Galloping horses. She sighed. That meant more of the mean ones in gray or black. At least they no longer slapped her every time they saw her, like they'd done at first back in Eidervaen, before Siamis told them not to.

She missed those days, when he talked to her a lot. Only he'd asked such boring questions. Not about swings, and living in the forest with Irza and Hinder, but about Atan, and Chief Veltos. After Julian said how much she hated them all for trying to make her into a princess, the way Mother used to, he didn't ask any more. He let her do whatever she liked. He was wonderful!

But he was the only wonderful one. All his followers were worse than Atan, and worse even than Gehlei or the baras Irza was growing up to be, or Chief Veltos, always telling her to brush her hair, and learn letters, and wear stupid princess clothes. The followers didn't do any of those things, but they uttered ugly words when they saw her, and sometimes they would spit right in front of her, or where she'd been. If she didn't want to step in the spit, she had to move away. One time she stepped in it without knowing, until her foot got slippery, so she dropped the clothes right there, wiped her foot on them, and ran off in her skin to get new ones. She heard a woman in gray laughing the ear-hurting kind of laugh as Julian went away, and a man mocking the one who spat, saying, "That puts you in your place."

She hopped to the side of the road so she wouldn't get spat upon, and watched as a bunch of them galloped by. What was that in the front of the middle one? A girl!

Julian stared with interest, getting a good look at a skinny girl with short hair flopping around her face. She had a red mark on one cheek and on her jaw, and a big scratch on her arm.

Julian waited until the last gallopers passed, then she ran after them to see who this visitor was. Another girl would be very nice, if she wasn't bossy. She didn't wear princess clothes, so maybe she wouldn't be bossy.

Julian made it to the big space at the front of Charlotte's Palace. It was so very pretty, made with shiny wood that was mostly a pale gold, that Siamis said came out of the sea.

The horse riders stopped, and one of them pushed the girl off the horse so she landed on her hands and knees.

They laughed as they dismounted, and one (it was the same one whose spit Julian had stepped in) yanked the girl up by her hair, and when she gasped, led the laughter.

Inside they went, past all the lights that hung down with the pretty globes of glass around them, to keep fires from streaming, Siamis had said. When the ground shivered, the lights swayed and swayed, making shadows dance in rhythm.

They passed the first big book room where a lot of the people who lived here went about putting all the books and scrolls back on the shelves after those crabby people in gray had thrown them. Julian had watched them one morning in one of the many other book rooms, moving from shelf to shelf, taking things down, looking, then throwing the books on the floor.

Julian had tried to help by grabbing some books to throw, but they'd screamed at her to go away. Julian hated books, so she didn't understand why they would want to look at them before throwing them. You'd think they'd just throw them if they hated learning, too.

They passed the hall where another three of the crabby gray ones did magical spells and passes. The air glittered here and there, but nothing else happened, and they looked crabbier than ever. Good. Julian didn't like any of them.

Finally they came to the room with the pictures painted on the ceiling, of winged horses and people, and clouds upon clouds, building toward strange stars, as if the ceiling were higher than the sky. Julian liked to lie on the floor and look at this room when no one else was in it.

But right now Siamis was in it, talking to two crabby grays.

He looked up, and smiled as Spit Mouth shoved the girl into the room, followed by the rest of his riders. Julian crept along the perimeter of the room so she could see, as Siamis said, "Liere Fer Eider! I wondered who might be venturesome enough to perform a world transfer directly outside the city gates. This is a surprise. What brought you here?"

The girl's voice quavered. "I came to get rid of you."

That made the followers laugh so hard that Julian hated them all the more.

The girl jerked her chin up. "I did it before."

Siamis smiled his nice smile. "Yes, you did," he said in his nice voice. "And I trust you brought the dyr? No, I can see from the lamentable state of your dress that you were thoroughly searched, and you neglected to bring the most important element of my defeat. Well, we shall have plenty of time to talk about its whereabouts. But not right now. Put her in . . . where? The biggest building I have ever had the misfortune to get lost in, yet no convenient lock-up. One of the cold-cellars will do."

He pointed to a couple of the followers in black, but the girl shrugged them off, pointed to the shiny sword leaning against the table, and said, "Why did you leave the sword named Truth in Bereth Ferian?"

Siamis stopped what he was doing and got very still. The girl also was very still. Julian struggled to understand the silence, then Siamis said in his nicest voice, "It was a gift, Liere."

The girl stiffened as if he'd poked her.

"It was a gift," Siamis said gently, almost sadly.

"And the coins were a gift too?" Her voice shook.

"No, those were in the nature of a warning, exactly as you surmised. Take her away." He flicked his fingers and turned back to the grays.

Each of the followers in black grabbed one of the skinny girl's arms, and they marched off, the girl's feet barely touching the ground.

Julian trotted along behind.

Siamis watched her go, until interrupted by the ambitious young mage who had carefully pointed out all Dejain's shortcomings in order to be assigned to this job. "That urchin will be pestering your prisoner," he said sourly.

"I want her to," Siamis retorted. "Though Julian is as ignorant as a garden slug, she's not stupid. As you ventured to take an interest, and you've been singularly useless in locating anything related to the Geth transfer magic, you will station yourself somewhere nearby, where the urchin cannot see you, but you can hear them both, and you will write down every word they say."

The pair of guards shoved Liere into a cellar room from which everything had been carried out. Here, in the dark, she took stock of her injuries. One elbow throbbed, she had a cut on the side of her face, and her shins were scraped. Everywhere else ached from the gravel she'd fallen on when they knocked her down. She could ignore all that.

What she could not ignore was her self-hatred, her disgust at her own stupidity. She had heard Senrid say so many times that you scout first, and figure out what to do afterward.

But no, she'd blundered straight into the enemy. Of course they'd be guarding the gate of the city they'd already conquered. She deserved exactly what had happened.

For a time she sat there bound so tightly in self-loathing that she wished Siamis would come in and strike her head off with that sword. A *gift!* Somehow that was the worst threat Siamis ever could have uttered, all the worse because she didn't understand at all what made him say that. It could only be for some unexplainable, horrific reason.

Then she thought guiltily how angry Senrid would be if she admitted to wanting Siamis to strike off her head. She could just hear him saying that was the coward's way out, that it wasn't her fault evil people did evil things. Her job—she could hear him, could see him pacing around his study, rapping his knuckles on the sills of the four tall windows, and then the desk, and then the carved map case—her job would be to *resist* evil.

Well. There was one thing she was good at, thanks to her mean brother, and that was, if they sent a bunch of bullies in to rant and rave and threaten, she could lock herself inside her head and she wouldn't hear a thing. Until she came out. But she wouldn't think about that unless she had to.

"Girl?"

That voice belonged to a child.

"Yes?"

"I saw you. Do you want me to ask Siamis to let you out of the cellar?"

"Siamis told them to put me here."

"Did you do something bad? My mother used to put me in the closet when she said I was bad."

At first, Liere thought that the little girl's voice might be some kind of Norsunder trick. But she could hear the emotions under the surface thoughts on the other side of the door. This little girl's memories were sharp and clear, so clear they hurt. Liere saw her mother, a pretty woman with a mean mouth who talked in a hissing whisper. She had jewels set in her fingernails that sparkled when she slapped and pinched . . . Julian. The little girl's name was Julian.

Liere whispered, "I did nothing bad. Siamis will try to make me tell him where—" She halted before mentioning the dyr. She didn't know if Siamis had a daughter. He wasn't old enough for that, surely; maybe this little girl was a spy, or why else would she be permitted to run around? She certainly wasn't dream-walking under the enchantment.

Or, somebody from Norsunder might be listening. Senrid had told Liere once how his uncle used to put prisoners together so they would talk, and reveal things that they wouldn't when interrogated.

Liere said in a firmer voice, "I don't know anything."

"Me either! Learning is stupid and boring," Julian said.

Liere had to laugh, though she wasn't sure why. That sounded more like an ordinary child, not some kind of mysterious Norsunder child spy, if they even had such a thing. "What's your name?" Liere asked, so Julian wouldn't know her thoughts had been listened to.

"Julian. What's yours?"

"Liere."

"If you come down, and look under the door, maybe I could see you."

Liere crouched down, put her throbbing cheek on the cool tile floor of the cellar, and peered under the door. She saw a mat of messy brown hair, and part of one eye. Small, dirty fingers wriggled under the door insistently, and the girl's thoughts came clearly. Liere briefly touched the reaching fingers, and was surprised by the flow of good feeling caused by so simple a touch.

"Would you like me to get you a piece of bread from the kitchen?" Julian asked.

Liere's stomach lurched. Until then she hadn't thought about food. Her last meal had been at noon the previous day, before the terrible news about Derek.

Hunger woke, simple and insistent. Liere remembered what Senrid had once said about being a prisoner in Norsunder Base: your job was to survive, and then to escape. In order to escape, she needed all her strength.

"Yes," she said firmly.

"I'm hungry, too," Julian announced. "I'll come back after I get something to eat. I don't think they should put people in the dark who didn't do anything bad. Is it dark in there?"

"Yes."

"I'll tell Siamis." And the feet pattered away.

*Geth-deles, on a small island south of Isul Demarzal*

And so the alliance took action for the first time, transferring to Geth-deles in order to find Liere. That was the stated goal, the group goal, but as usual, certain individuals had private goals.

Those left behind knew that this was more reaction than action. Tsauderei sent an emergency token to Erai-Yanya, to report that he'd lost them all.

The ground coalesced under Senrid's feet.

Or that's what it felt like. He sensed an intense flash of magic fleeing outward into the air, and wondered who might have tracers in the area.

It wasn't dark magic, so he looked around, finding himself on the beach of a small, crowded inlet. None of the others from Sartorias-deles were with him, but with no definite Destination, he'd expected the magic to scatter them. Just as well. He'd be faster alone.

He fought mild vertigo, but the transfer hadn't wrenched muscles and bones as did long transfers at home. It felt more like he'd been falling down a long, long tunnel, streaming past barely perceived sparks of light, like the ones on the mental plane when he concentrated with Dena Yeresbeth. The falling wasn't the same as diving out of the sky toward the lake as fast as he could go, as he and Puddlenose and Leander had tried in the Valley of Delfina, where his ears whistled, his eyes hurt if he opened them too wide, and the wind battered his face. There was no wind, but he'd felt that sense of sliding down and down and down.

He looked at his boots, half-sunk in white sand. That partly explained the sense of unsteady ground.

He lifted his gaze again, and this time took in more detail: the sand beside a pier, at the seaward end of which clustered long, low, narrow boats. They floated on water of a startling blue even more dense than the blue of Delfina Lake.

The air was also bluish, colors subtly different than what he was used to. The pier joined a sandstone quay surrounded by low houses made of some kind of polished material that resembled wood, except the ruddy brown color was unlike any wood he'd ever seen, more like melted chocolate with streaks of berry juice stirred in.

Lusty male singing soared over the everyday noises of chatter, hammers, and footsteps on the wooden pier. The singing poured through the open doors of a tavern next to the pier. So much for this being a children's world, Senrid thought, as he took in flirting couples, and big dock workers hauling goods back and forth along the pier.

Though youth there was aplenty, he was glad to see, because that meant he didn't stand out. Much. The boys all seemed to be wearing colorful nightdresses. No, they wore light robes, some over the sort of loose trousers he'd seen in pictures of his ancestors, only those had been gathered at the ankle and stuffed into boot tops. Some were bare-legged somewhat like that morvende boy Senrid had seen at Atan's, but the weave and colors were different: the garments had loose sleeves, and were tied with sashes or scarves, and people wore headbands of bright colors. At least nobody seemed interested in him, but he yanked his shirt from his waistband and let it hang over the belt on his riding trousers.

The Universal Language Spell worked better than he'd hoped. Someone had clearly been adapting it. The language itself was pleasant to the ear, with trills and bits that sounded like coughs at the back of the throat. Like the 'ch' in Chwahir. And it was all the same language, not the cacophony of tongues he'd heard in Jaro Harbor during the first Siamis attack.

He saw a row of boys sitting on a rail eating grilled fish on a stick. It smelled of pungent spices; he walked up to the boy on the end. "Have you seen a girl wearing clothes kind of like mine, but gray on top and green trousers? Bare feet, short hair?"

The boy waved a hand in a circle, which Senrid took to mean 'no.'

"I mean, in the last day."

Another negative.

"Where is the magic city, Issal, Isool . . . ?" he asked, to test the Language Spell as well as to orient himself.

The boy turned his head, his dark brows rising as he looked Senrid up and down. "You are a curious one! From a far island, is it? If you

mean Isul Demarzal, you'll be going north." He waved his hand at
the sea.

"Where's your boat?" someone on the end asked.

Senrid waved vaguely in the direction of the water, and went on to
ask people who seemed to live or work there. He'd thought to pick up
Liere's trail first thing, but to his dismay, his description of Liere only
caused incurious stares and negation.

So he ventured father along the shore, and still nothing.

That meant she'd done the worst possible thing: transferred herself
directly to where the enemy was, instead of scouting. He let out his
breath as he turned in a circle.

What now? Find out more. Like, north as in walking, or north as in
another island? Instinct prompted him to look around more slowly,
breathing in the familiar scents of garlic, smoked fish, hemp, and unfamiliar spicy scents.

He turned again, his attention drawn to the pier, and the boats bobbing alongside. He liked boats, liked the pleasant sound of laughter
floating over the water, and the rise and fall of a lone voice in song from
somewhere beyond the end of the pier. A kid's voice.

He turned his steps that way, and stepped up onto the warped
boards, more poured chocolate, unlike the grainy oak or pine that came
from carefully coppiced wood at home.

Each boat had at least one person in it, working away with ropes or
barrels or nets. When he reached the end of the pier, he spotted the
longest vessel. The singer was a girl about Senrid's age, as she sanded
the rail forward.

Senrid caught the gaze of a comfortably plump, grandmotherly
woman who met his gaze steadily, her expression benevolent. She sat in
a kind of hammock chair, slung on the roof of what was probably the
living quarters, rising waist-height from the smooth deck. Now here
was someone who had surely sat right there for a while. Without much
hope, he asked about Liere.

"No, she was not here," the woman answered, her gaze steady and
her tone final.

"Can I get a ride to the magic city, ah, Isul Demarzal?"

"You've a few days' sailing ahead of you."

Senrid stared at her. He'd expected to be a short walk away. How had
he managed to transfer a few *days* off? Clearly a lot of island beaches had
white sand. No wonder no one had seen Liere! "How do I get there?"

She chuckled. "If you step aboard, nothing easier. This vessel is sailed by those your age."

That was far too easy. He backed away, scanning the boat, which was long and narrow, with a tall mast slightly forward of the middle, and a shorter one behind the roof on which the old woman sat. At the bow, three girls and a boy worked at something. They as well as the singer paid no heed to the old woman or Senrid.

It was too convenient. Nothing was more unthreatening than an old woman, except maybe an infant. Senrid knew he'd spoken first because of this assumption; he never would have addressed a brawny man sharpening a sword. Old women didn't raise suspicion.

That in itself spiked his suspicion. So, either he could stand there and dither, or do something. He looked around once more for any obvious threat as he braced his feet on the pier, and then he lifted the habitual mind-shield and focused on the old woman, making an effort to skim the surface of her thoughts.

It was like falling out of the sky into a new world, one that expanded beyond the horizons, flickering with uncountable memories filled with poignant joy, with sharp sorrow, with the calm, infinite waters of peace. A soft inward voice said: *You do need training, do you not, dear boy?*

Senrid would have resented anyone calling him 'dear,' except he could sense that she meant it. Further, that everyone present in that inlet and beyond was dear to her.

And he'd heard that inward voice before—in Liere's shared memories.

"Lilith the Guardian," he breathed. Because life had made him wary, "You just happened to be here?" He spoke in Sartoran.

"No," she answered in the same tongue, but her accent carried an unfamiliar lilt. "Let us say that your arrival by the spell given to Erai-Yanya alerted a number of people, after your young friend Liere's unfortunate arrival before the gates of the city. I was fastest, and I thought you might find this conversation easier if I let you find me, rather than my approaching you."

Senrid's nerves flared at that mention of Liere. But first things first. "And them?" Senrid jutted his chin at the kids working in the bow.

"They are what they seem: a group of your peers. They're on what is called on Sartorias-deles 'the Wander.'"

Senrid shrugged. There had been a time when he'd traveled with Puddlenose and Christoph on the Wander—and not by choice. It was during that journey that he'd encountered the weird whatever-it-was called Erdrael.

He eyed Lilith warily as she indicated the working teenagers at the front of the boat. They seemed completely unaware of her, or Senrid. Lilith said, "The lightest of illusions keeps attention away. You may converse safely." She smiled at the space between them. He stood on the pier, well out of physical reach, though if she were even half as powerful as legend had it, she could probably smite him with a word. A thought.

So she was permitting him to feel in control of the situation, though he wasn't. He wasn't sure how he liked that. "You said Liere's 'unfortunate arrival.'"

The furrows in Lilith's ruddy face deepened to concern. "She transferred directly to the gates of Isul Demarzal. She was immediately seized and taken into the city as a prisoner."

"Shit," he exclaimed in Marloven. "Send me there right now."

"So that you may be taken as prisoner as well?"

"Better two of us than her alone."

Lilith shook her head. "But Siamis would not put the two of you together. From what I have gathered, Detlev has marked you for his future project. Siamis would have to send you along. Do you want that?"

"No." The word was a voiceless exhalation. He didn't even try to hide his horror.

"Then you should gather your friends and go back to your world," she said. "There is nothing you can do here."

"No." Senrid said it sharply. "First, I don't know where they are. We didn't transfer together, and I don't see them. Second, I'm not in command."

"They are scattered between three islands," Lilith said. "You don't know the nature of the magic here. Suffice it to say that world transfer requires magework at this end to complete the, oh, we'll call it a tunnel, to save half a day's digression into magic as used here."

"Scattered on purpose, I take it?"

"Yes. In hopes they will think better of their decision and return home."

Senrid decided against arguing about this piece of high-handed interference. He didn't know the people or the situation here. He was clear on one thing: Lilith was sitting on the top of a boat instead of doing something.

But the answer was obvious. Whatever magic had been laid over that city surely had wards against her magical signature as well as against those of Tsauderei and the rest of them. That was the tough part of being a famous mage: other mages knew your work, and could exert their own powers to keep you from interfering with theirs.

"None of us can act," Lilith said, paralleling his thoughts. "Not only has Siamis effectively and specifically warded all the senior mages of both worlds, but he set the enchanted mages to watch for any appearance of their colleagues, using a lethal mirror ward—yes, I can see you know what that is. It was carefully thought out, and it took appreciable time to lay."

*And you walked right into it, Liere.* Senrid's stomach roiled.

Lilith went on. "There is even a theory that Siamis's enchantment over Sartorias-deles was, at least in part, practice for this very situation. Isul Demarzal is the oldest city in this world, the seat of magic learning."

"I won't let her sit there alone," Senrid stated. "Tell me what I can do, or I'll try to figure it out for myself."

"If you wish to help your friend, you should go home and let those best trained free her."

"No," Senrid said again, more forcefully. "Because you just told me they can't do anything. I'll bet you anything there are no mirror wards, or any wards, against *me*. I could get in and out, probably better than any senior mage they're on the watch for. And I won't use magic. And before you start telling me there are people better trained in sneaking than I am, they don't know Liere like I do."

Lilith was quiet.

Senrid grinned. "I also know the antidote to Siamis's enchantment. You need someone Norsunder doesn't expect to get inside that city. Right? Let me do it. I'm going to try anyway, unless you drop a stone spell on me, but you lighters don't do that, right?" He knew he was goading her, but he was far too angry, and too upset, to stop himself.

Lilith gazed back at him. "We are at an impasse," she said finally. "We do need someone inside who can break Siamis's enchantment—"

Senrid cut her off. "I'll look for whoever the leader is that the spell is anchored on, but I'm going after Liere. I won't let her sit there and rot." *While you lighters run around trying to be fair and nice and moral,* he didn't say.

"Go, then," she said.

Senrid was so surprised, he exclaimed, "What?"

Lilith said distinctly, "Go with my good will. I will speak to the local mages. Perhaps the sharron can find a way to get you inside." She swallowed the 'r,' and emphasized the last syllable, speaking the 'o' a little through her nose.

"'Sharron?'"

"Think of them as the long-separated cousins of the Sartoran dawnsingers, the forest dwellers. The children who sail this boat will tell you all about them. Before you go, you need to know that the First Witch was not just enchanted by Siamis in order to bind the city, we have been able to detect from a distance that she has also been warded. If you walk up to her and try magic on her, you'll kill her as well as yourself," Lilith said. "No magic can be leveled at the city wards until the wards on her are lifted." Her tone, even, reasonable, was more effective than sarcasm: *Did you really think it would be that easy?* "We know that Siamis has used a mirror ward. Do you know how to break it?"

"No," Senrid said. That level of dark magic had a habit of burning up the mages who attempted it. But Jilo had been studying wards. He would definitely know where to begin. If he found Jilo, they could do this in tandem. "First Witch?" he said.

"The woman you could say is in charge. It is a respected title here. No one can aspire to it until he or she has lived and practiced magic for fifty years. The current one is a woman, who resembles me in many ways. She has a distinctive white streak of hair right here." Lilith touched the top of her head. "The rest of her hair being dark."

Senrid said, "I'll find her. After I find Liere."

"There are two more aspects to consider. First, Siamis has set Kessler Sonscarna to guard the city."

Senrid grimaced at the name. "He doesn't know me."

"You don't actually know that," Lilith countered. "Though you have not met him, that doesn't mean he hasn't observed you. Second, we are fairly certain that Detlev is warded as well. So he might conceivably be stirred to investigate, which is another reason why the local mages feel the pressure of time. No one wants to be caught in a possible magic battle between Detlev and Siamis."

Senrid's nerves prickled. "Where's Detlev?"

"At present he is said to be somewhere in the estuary between two hill ranges, called the Marshes. There is magic centered there, akin to what is found in Shendoral and a few other places on our own world, but much wilder. Time and space are problematical."

The prickles turned to that nasty neck-gripping sensation. A sudden spurt of laughter from the tavern overlooking the water startled Senrid. "I want to kill Siamis," he burst out, then braced for the lighter lecture on morals.

Lilith said, "Is that a declaration or a request for permission?"

Senrid flushed, suspecting that his outburst just made him sound like a scrub on the swagger. Here was someone who had lived four thousand years ago. Even though she had escaped the pressure of time, she had seen the real Ancient Sartor. "So you really were there, in what they call the Fall?"

"I was." Her intent gaze softened to sadness. "My view was limited to the struggle I lost, so I cannot answer most questions."

"Maybe you can answer this. In the histories Hibern has given me, written by lighters—that is—"

"I understand your context. What is your question?"

Senrid considered that, and decided against arguing that she didn't know what he meant, but maybe she did. Maybe she could even get it from his memories. He made an effort to shrug that off, and said, "So they warn us that the native beings who have always lived on Sartorias-deles will kill off humans if they transgress enough. Is that just lighter hortatory, *Be good, or else?* I mean, wasn't the Fall about as big a transgression as you can get short of destroying everything?"

"There are two things that took the worst destruction, magic and human lives," she said. "The world was largely unharmed. Not to say that mages don't fear the indigenous life ridding the world of the human stain once and for all. Much has been said over the centuries about that, and no one knows the answer for certain, but this is my own guess: that though human greed and anger and intent to destroy were very much a part of the Fall, it was not caused by humans."

"It wasn't?" Senrid looked askance.

"Humans joined in, as you very well know. But they didn't start it. There is someone, or something, else, from outside our world, something that consumes life in order to, ah, to metamorphose, I guess the word would be. My circle believed that to be the catalyst, if not the cause, of that war, and we think it still dwells at the heart of Norsunder, wearing human guise. If it is there, surely it is waiting to make another attempt. If we are right, humanity's survival is not part of its plan."

Senrid flexed his fingers, feeling out-maneuvered and out-weaponed.

But that could wait. He needed to focus on the present problem: Liere was a prisoner, and he had to try to free her. He would always have to try, until he couldn't anymore because someone had stopped him dead.

Before Lilith could burble about children being unprepared for danger, he said recklessly, "My second question is this. Who, or rather what, is Erdrael?"

Her expression shuttered. Water slapped the sides of the boat, and from a distance came the sound of voices as the kids reworming the foresail rigging passed materials back and forth, and, farther in the distance, the singers in the tavern wailed another ballad.

Then Lilith said, "It was a common enough name in my day. What is the context of your question?" She smiled. "Besides provocation?"

He looked at the sparkling water, reminding himself that she had the kind of Dena Yeresbeth that Detlev did. Being a lighter, she was unlikely to kill at a thought, but she had the same sort of ability. And she was definitely hearing his thoughts. That meant his mind-shield wasn't all that great when he was talking. He'd have to remember that.

But she'd riposted his question with her own, and he really wanted to know the answer. So he said, "Never mind the circumstances. Someone once transferred me to another continent, where I met up with a couple of Mearsiean boys. While we traveled in search of transportation out of there, a . . . thing appeared. Looked like a bad illusion, as it was partly transparent. But it spoke. To us. Me." And—there was the memory of that freckle-faced girl.

Senrid hated remembering the end of that episode six months later, with Detlev on the cliff on that first bloody day of Senrid's reign. That sense of helplessness still haunted him, the despair that forced him to surrender and yell for Erdrael, though he'd had no hope of succor. The memory was as vivid as the day it happened, so he let it come, and sensed Lilith's awareness.

He opened his eyes. "That was Erdrael."

"The magical illusion called 'Erdrael,'" Lilith said, "was fashioned to resemble my daughter, Erdrael, who was killed early in the Fall."

"Your daughter," he repeated, his stomach churning.

"Yes. Age was no defense against Norsunder then, any more than now."

Senrid ignored the implied warning. "So someone was using me to get to you, all this time later?" He knew he was right about being used as a piece in a game, if nothing else.

"I will have to think about what it means," Lilith said. She indicated the kids at the bow. "They'll be finished soon, and wish to set sail. If you're determined to go forward, you should probably go talk to them."

Senrid turned away reluctantly, and approached the teens at the front of the boat. "Where are you going, and can I get a ride?" he asked.

The Universal Language Spell worked oddly, with curious lags, or mental image overlays on some words, making it hard to concentrate. It felt a bit like he was trying to hear a conversation in a noisy room.

But the boat's owner, a weather-browned girl his own age and height, said they were willing to take passengers as long as the passengers were willing to work. Senrid said he had some experience with boats, and he was invited to find a hammock in the crew quarters under their feet.

When he turned toward the hatch leading below the weather deck, he was not surprised to discover that Lilith was gone.

## Chapter Three

*At an enclave, on an island east of Isul Demarzal*

TO Erai-Yanya and the Geth mages, Lilith related the conversation with Senrid, leaving out only the exchange about Erdrael. That, she had not known about, and she would have to contemplate it—when she had the leisure for it.

"And so Senrid is on his way now," she finished. "I suspect if I were to confront the rest of the children from Sartorias-deles, I will hear similar arguments."

"I can yank Hibern out, at least," Erai-Yanya stated.

"Do what you think is best, but I hope you will not do that to Senrid Montredaun-An," Lilith said. "I believe anyone who does will make an enemy of him. That means nothing to you, of course," she said, indicating the five Geth mages. "But it would be a very bad thing for your sister world."

The mages sat in a circle on a shaded terrace in a fragrant garden, regarding her in silence, their expressions ranging from distrust and disgust to worry.

"Senrid," Lilith said, "is going to try to rescue his friend, no matter what anyone says. So you senior mages have three choices. You can use force to take him back to safety. Relative safety. You can leave him alone, which will probably end with his being captured by Norsunder. Or you can lay parallel plans, that is, let him—and those who will follow him, as I suspect most of those youngsters will choose—to provide exactly the distraction we need," Lilith said.

"This goes against instinct," murmured one of the mages. "We do not know these Darksider youths."

The others regarded him with varying expressions.

"They should be taken away for their safety," another, older mage stated. "And returned to Darkside of the Sun."

"If you summarily send them back to Sartorias-deles, you will deeply wound their trust, which is already tentative. Perhaps irreparably," Lilith said. "They are not only testing themselves, they are, in a sense, testing us, the elders, who have not kept them safe in spite of all our efforts."

Erai-Yanya had been nodding slowly. She remembered the trouble that she, Murial, and Gwasan used to get into in their mage student days. "So we have to work around them as well as with them, and keep them as safe as we can, without their knowing?"

"That I believe is the wisest course of action." Lilith indicated the map of Isul Demarzal's island that rested on the table between them. "We are in a situation where the unexpected, which can only be used once, might act in our favor. Here is my suggestion. The young people must be permitted to enter the city, but with a safeguard. Don't tell them it's a safeguard, of course. Convince them that they need illusory disguises, and ask the sharron to weave in certain magical precautions."

Expressions lightened around the circle as they began to plan.

*Various locations on and around the main island*

Kyale wrote:

> *CJ? What happened? We landed on a beach with a village around it. Their houses are really ugly, and the girls are all wearing nightgowns, but they are very nice. Their food is delicious. If they'd told us that it was made from nuts and ground-up ocean plants, I would have refused to eat it, but I didn't know until after we ate.*
>
> *We can kind of understand the people, but when we said that we came to rescue them from Siamis, they said Who?*

*Leander told me Hibern says to go to the east of some big city called Issill Something.*
*Where are you?*

CJ to Kyale:

*We're heading toward some mountains. It looks like forest ahead.*
*We also landed on a beach, but not near any people. It took a while to find some. Clair got a note from Hibern. We're supposed to meet in the forest east of that city. Boneribs has some kind of plan. I don't see why we can't make our own plans, but everybody seems to want to meet up.*

CJ hesitated, then crossed out the last few words, put a period after 'plan,' and sent the note. She'd been sitting on a rock while the others took a break from the hot walk in the sultry air by playing around in a stream. But then Clair beckoned, and everyone joined her.

"Weather here might be different, but at home that flat sheet of puff clouds looks like rain. Shall we try to get there?" She pointed down the slope to where a small village lay on either side of a tumbling waterfall.

Nobody argued. They slipped and slid down a narrow goat path, until they reached the first houses, which looked like others they'd seen: low buildings made out of smooth chocolaty-looking wood that reminded CJ of manzanita. The language the people spoke sounded to her kind of like French—or at least the kind of French they spoke in cartoons, as she had never heard a real French person before she left Earth—and kind of like Hebrew.

As Falinneh and Irenne ran ahead to talk to the locals about staying, CJ walked slowly, brooding about the news Clair had passed on: according to Hibern, Liere was Siamis's prisoner.

When the rain came, they were cozily gathered on a broad porch. The etiquette was, if you didn't have any money, or whatever they used for money, then you had to work to get a meal. That meant not only helping to prepare the food, but entertainment afterward.

Ordinarily CJ loved an excuse to show off some of their favorite songs and plays. Two girls snickered, blonde and red heads together as they shucked beans and pulled silk off corn for the kitchen people. They alternately rehearsed one of Irenne's many plays, and laughed with anticipation over how thrilled their audience would be.

Dhana had gone off dancing in the rain.

CJ fidgeted, knowing that she was going to get stuck with dishwashing. Not that that mattered. If she got everyone to help, it would go faster, because she really wanted to reach that forest before anyone else.

She moved restlessly, hating how everybody had given her the stink-eye, especially that snobby Atan, before they all magicked away. Like Sartora going off to defeat Siamis was a bad thing. Like it was her fault.

CJ wished she had her magic boot, made in the days when Jilo was the worst villain they'd ever faced. Her boot was great for knocking villains off balance with a magic-propelled whoosh of wind. How things had changed! And not in a good way, except that ol' Jilo was no longer on the villains' list.

But his place had been taken by far worse villains, ones you couldn't boot into a mud puddle and expect to slink off to the Shadowland while you laughed loudly. Sartora, with all her mind powers, was the best one to boot Siamis out, right?

CJ resisted the impulse to kick the railing. She was afraid that weird wood might crack, and everybody would give her the stink-eye again. Even if those snobs . . .

She grimaced fiercely, knowing it was no use calling Atan a snob. The Queen of Sartor seemed to like Clair okay, so it couldn't be that she looked down on the Mearsieans in their little country with no court or army. It was that Rel business. Atan really seemed to like the hulking galoot, and CJ knew she couldn't accuse Rel of buttering Atan up because she had a title, because Rel didn't butter anybody up. He didn't even seem to know how to crack a smile.

And I don't hate him. I don't, she thought firmly. She wanted to get to the forest first, before anyone else, so she could be seen giving him a big fat welcome, and also she wanted to be in on any plans to rescue Sartora, just in case they did think she was to blame.

Only why did people have to be so weird?

*Isul Demarzal*

Liere's determination to survive received aid from two unexpected directions.

The first occurred a day later, after Julian threaded through a gaggle of Norsundrians to tug on Siamis's arm. When she got his attention (causing every one of the scouts and flunkeys waiting to deliver reports to wish to be the one he would order to knock the vile brat out of the room) she said, "There's a girl in the cellar."

"Yes." Siamis chuckled.

"Can I talk to her?" Julian thought she was being sly, because she already *had* talked to her. Three times.

"She's all yours."

"Mine?" Julian exclaimed. "Mine? Really?"

"Promise," he said, mock-solemn.

"But she doesn't have anything to eat!"

"Why not?" Siamis asked.

"I can't open the door, and the bread wouldn't fit under it."

Siamis laughed. "We'll see about that."

He summoned the mage, who duly furnished his account of Julian and Liere's conversations (the last two solely on the subject of food), and asked with genial sarcasm, "Don't you think the quality of words might improve if someone troubled to open that cellar door and put in something to eat?"

The mage, who loathed this duty, said, "You gave no orders."

"I am giving some now, and so plainly that I believe even you can take my meaning: see to it that Liere Fer Eider has a jug of clean water, and some food."

Liere had been walking back and forth in her cell, after exploring its dimensions. Remembering what Senrid had said about keeping your strength up for escape, she'd even tried running around the perimeter, but she was so hungry and thirsty it had made her feel dizzy. So she sat down again.

A short time later Liere's door opened, and an armed guard set down a jug of cold water, and a plate of stale bread, the end of a cheese, and the crumbled remains of a vegetable pie. Then the door closed, leaving Liere in darkness.

She slurped down the water, relief pouring through her veins. Then she tore into the vegetable pie.

Strengthened by her meal, Liere listened for Julian's voice on the mental plane. She was with Siamis! "I saw them give her food, but they wouldn't let me go in to talk to her. Why does she have to stay in the cellar? Why can't she come out and talk to me?"

Siamis said, "Detlev wants her for his pet experiment. I might just have to comply, if I lose my gamble. Until then, talk to her through the door all you like, Julian. Ask her about the dyr. It's a magic thing."

"I hate magic things," Julian retorted, thinking of Atan and *lessons*.

"Ask her anyway." Siamis laughed. "Run along."

Liere withdrew her mental tendril and sat back to think. So Siamis wanted them talking about the dyr. No surprise there.

Even if she knew where it was kept she wouldn't talk about it, but there was something she *could* do: figure out why Julian hated Atan, and find out if it had something to do with her terrible memories of being shut in a dark closet by that whispering woman with the jeweled fingernails.

Senrid got himself acquainted with his new travel mates, did what he was told, and, when he could finally get a corner alone, he dug the note-case out of his pocket, pulled out the last note he'd received, and turned it over. He used the pen from the ship's log near the tiller and wrote a quick note. Wondering if the magic would work on this world, he put the note in the notecase and tapped out Hibern's sigil.

The paper vanished.

He went below to climb into his hammock, and dropped immediately into sleep.

Over the next few days, Senrid heard a great deal about Geth and its many islands from his shipmates. The captain whom he'd taken to be an agemate turned out to have done the Child Spell decades ago. You could tell if you got close enough to see the lines in her face that she wasn't fourteen or fifteen. But she sort of acted like it . . . and sort of not. He found the idea somewhat repellent, but then he did not want to spend the rest of his life looking as if he were fifteen.

Senrid could feel the impulses to break the spell holding his physical growth back, but stronger was the conviction that he ought to keep hiding in plain sight to the likes of Detlev, to whom the passing of years had to be meaningless.

Ten days after his conversation with Lilith he was obligingly set down at a point that afforded the shortest path to the forestland directly south of the city. He wasn't there half a morning before he found Jilo sitting dismally at a crossroads, puzzled by which way to turn.

Astounded that Jilo couldn't gauge the geography that seemed so obvious, Senrid pointed him northwards, saying, "The forest seems to lie that way." And, as Jilo had expected the moment they saw one another, "What does the book say?"

"It doesn't say anything, because Wan-Edhe never came here to ward any Destinations."

"Well, chances are pretty good we wouldn't have any idea where any of them would be if it did, since we haven't a map. Right. May as well hide it away again."

Jilo promptly stashed the book inside his tunic, where it pressed comfortingly flat against his stomach. They walked together, as Senrid told Jilo about parts of his interview with Lilith the Guardian. It never occurred to Jilo not to try breaking Norsunder's wards over this Isul place. His life had defined itself since the disappearance of the Shadow-land in trying to break Wan-Edhe's formidable wards. So they spent time talking about what Jilo had learned about lethal wards.

After a day, Jilo and Senrid were found by two of the sharron Lilith had spoken of: dark-haired people, one young and one old, in green and brown clothing. They were very shy, scarcely speaking or meeting any-one's eyes. Not that Senrid or Jilo had much energy for talking, for it took all their concentration to follow their swift, sure-footed guides up razor-edged cliffs and down narrow trails shadowed by gnarled trees of types they did not recognize, or kind of recognized.

When it seemed they couldn't walk another step, they emerged abruptly in a central clearing where they discovered half of the alliance already there, some doing various chores under Rel's direction as they set about cooking fresh-caught trout on sticks. Others made biscuits with the meal that the sharron had given them before departing into the woods.

"Senrid," Hibern said with relief. "Here you are! Everyone is full of questions."

"So the mages haven't broken the mirror-ward over that city yet?" Senrid asked, his appetite waking up with a cavernous gape as the aroma of herb-rubbed fish wafted his way.

"No. Everybody has ideas about rescuing Liere. We wanted to hear what you were told."

Dappled light played over Arthur as he wandered from below the low, spreading branches of a cousin to the chestnut, a book that he'd either found or brought with him tucked under his arm, and a quill pen sticking out from his ear. "All we've seen are the sharron who brought us. They gave us a bag of some kind of meal, and said somebody would come to lead us to the city."

"They don't talk much," Hibern added.

"We noticed," Senrid said, looking around appreciatively. It wouldn't be accident that they'd been ushered to this deserted area, probably unknown to Norsunder's scouts.

Jilo faded to the perimeter as Senrid said, "Here's what I learned."

The alliance gathered over the space of a few days, and fell into a companionable rhythm, with Rel as leader. They had a goal and an interesting new environment, and for some, the onslaught of emotions over Derek's death gained distance.

Not all gained the relative comfort of distance.

Rel was good at camp life. He liked spending the day scouting fallen timber for firewood, and teaching people how to fish and to toast wild tubers that they found growing.

Camp food got even better when Leander arrived. Having spent a lot of his early childhood as a forest-dwelling outlaw with a price on his head, Leander knew how to find and cook tasty greens and wild onions and herbs. He even discovered varieties of sweet berries that they could eat for dessert.

Rel welcomed the work, but in spite of keeping himself busy all day, as soon as he fell asleep his dreams filled with flames and people screaming. It didn't help that those first few days, he could still smell the lingering traces of smoke if he coughed.

He was not ready for the arrival of the Mearsieans, especially when CJ marched up scowling, having discovered that not only were they last to arrive, but someone had gone ahead and made Rel the boss of the camp. He overheard her remark to the air that it seemed all you had to do was be a hulking boy and everybody fell all over trying to put you in charge.

Hibern also heard that, and to forestall anything else from CJ, climbed up on a rock and called out, "Listen! Now that everyone is here, and we know that Liere is a prisoner, we need to figure out what's next, unless anyone wants to return to Sartorias-deles?"

She had hoped that most would raise their hands, the Mearsieans first.

No one did.

She went on firmly, "Rel is in charge of the camp, so listen for your jobs, and everything will be faster."

Rel sighed as he glanced across the fire into CJ's bright, derisive blue gaze. He wished even more strongly that he could have had one night of real sleep before facing CJ's temper.

Atan had been watching. Her own temper simmered.

Hibern took in Atan's anger, Rel's stolid expression, and CJ's lifted

chin, and her heart sank. No matter how far you traveled, even to another world, you brought your trouble with you.

She climbed down, wishing she had kept her mouth shut. Rel sighed,
and stepped up beside the rock.

With that many people crowding around, there was the inevitable
tangle, exacerbated by Kyale, who loathed dirt, eating off sharpened
sticks, and sitting outside, and by Glenn, whose grief found expression
in a series of small irritations, beginning with the lack of proper protocol and ending with his sister's weird, irritating counting of steps and
fussing with twigs and rocks so that they were square or parallel.

Rel attempted to avoid the Mearsieans in hopes they'd go off and
play. But no, Clair kept them waiting for jobs.

Rel thought up some easy ones to get rid of them, but halfway
through, Kitty pushed through, shrilling indignantly, "There are bugs
over there! I can't sleep anywhere with bugs!"

"You can have my spot," CJ said in her most goading voice not two
paces from Rel. "Unless King Rel gets mad, because whatever King Rel
wants is so important."

Rel wasn't aware of the red flash of irritation until it happened. He
reached with his fingers, gave CJ's shoulder a flick as he said, "Just clear
out." He meant to add something about how they'd just arrived, and
they could wait until the morrow to work, but the second his fingers
collided with her skinny little body he knew he'd regret it, that he'd
broken his own code.

CJ had recoiled to avoid his touch, but when two of his fingers collided with her shoulder she was so furious that she sucked in a breath
and shrilled, *"He hit me!"*

On the other side of the fire, Lilah whirled around, her eyes rounding with honest horror.

Rel gritted his teeth. It had been a gesture of irritation, but he may
as well have socked her.

"Sorry," he said, knowing that that sounded as if he really had hit her.
But anything he said would make the situation worse.

Clair said, "Come on, CJ. The sooner we pitch in, the sooner we eat."

"Did you see that? He hit me!" CJ felt the falsity of every word, like
biting into an apple that looked fresh but was rotten. But she couldn't
seem to help herself, as a lifetime of pent-up anger forced her to the
summit of self-righteousness.

"Well!" Kyale's voice rose as she eagerly climbed that summit beside
her. She gloried in all the shocked eyes.

CJ's mind flooded with angry joy, but her triumph—*see? He really is a bully*—died when she caught the contempt in Atan's face before she walked to the other side of the camp, where she sat with Tahra and Arthur, her rigid back squarely toward the Mearsieans.

And here was the most tenderhearted of the Mearsiean girls, her big blue eyes almost tearful as she whispered, "Did he hurt you? I never thought Rel would ever . . ."

CJ sat down next to Clair, her gaze on her lap, her stomach boiling with a sick sense of wrong. She knew what getting hit was like. The actual touch had been barely a flick, but she'd sensed the irritation Rel had tried to hide.

She knew she was being unfair. That she had lied. Somehow that made her even angrier. It was all Rel's fault or she wouldn't have had this problem at all! But . . . that stomach-churning sense that she'd lied, that her sense of moral superiority was completely fake, kept her silent, furious with rage.

She stayed where she was when someone called for music; she forced laughter when Falinneh and Irenne acted out the play they'd worked out over the past few days; she clapped hard when Tahra recited a long, boring poem about some old war in the flattest voice ever; she watched without enjoyment as Dhana rose and danced light-footed around the fire, the flickering light playing over her soaring form as she leaped and twirled.

Finally, *finally* it was all over, and CJ was the first to leave, staking out the soft grass under a broad tree. Gradually the other girls appeared, except for Clair, who remained at the fireside, a small figure staring down into the flames.

Clair became aware of a quiet conversation on the other side of the fire; she lifted her eyes, but her vision dazzled, and all she could see were silhouettes.

". . . know what to do," Atan was saying. "It's like in the forest group in Sartor, one ill-tempered person can break the group into little groups. Kyale likes to see things stirred, and Lilah is upset, which means all her friends are upset. I wish we could send them both away and let them figure it out, except I feel so for Rel, after what happened in Everon."

*Ill-tempered*, Clair was thinking. It hurt the more because right now, it seemed true, if you didn't really know CJ, the most loyal friend ever.

Puddlenose sauntered up to the campfire, the firelight under-lighting his square face. "Put CJ in charge."

He wandered away.

Atan sighed sharply, but Clair understood. "I think he's right," she said, though she hadn't been invited into the conversation. But they were talking about her friend.

Atan sighed again, as if she were trying hard to get rid of her own bad temper. She said, "How is that going to help? Unless she's figured out how to defeat Siamis, rescue Liere, and send Detlev back to Norsunder forever."

Clair sat back, trying to fit words to the emotions she was feeling, then was surprised when Hibern, filled with a kind of cautious hope, said slowly, "There's this ballad where I come from. It's meant to be funny, but it kind of fits. Tomorrow, put CJ in charge of all the camp jobs. Everything that Rel's been doing, or asking people to do."

Atan repeated doubtfully, "Everything?"

Clair said, "I think that will do it."

But she felt like a traitor as she retreated through the quiet, leaf-scented air to the grassy area where the other girls lay. Insects sang and chirruped in the distance as she curled up by CJ and Sherry.

Sherry was already asleep. Clair could see starlight reflecting in CJ's eyes as she stared upward. So Clair rolled over and stared up at the stars through the leaves. She thought she recognized some of the twinkling patterns, though they looked sideways to what she was used to. She still felt a sense of shock at the idea of two moons, but there they both were, on opposite sides of the sky, one small and one big, though only half lit.

Clair whispered, "Are you all right, CJ?"

"I'm fine," CJ muttered. "I just want to find Liere, and go back home."

"We could talk to Hibern. Maybe she'd send us back. I'm sure not all of us are needed."

"No, we better stay. They think everything is my fault," CJ whispered bitterly. "I have to help rescue Liere. In fact, I have to be the one to find her, or I'm a gigantic villain, worse than Detlev, Siamis, Kessler, and all the rest of them combined."

If she brought up Rel, Clair vowed to tell her. But CJ didn't, and Clair stayed silent, hoping that CJ's bad mood would break before morning.

CJ was too angry with everyone, but herself most of all, to speak Rel's name.

Clair's warm hand stole over CJ's. She gave her fingers a gentle squeeze, then Clair sighed and turned over, leaving CJ staring upward.

In the morning, the noise of those early to rise got everyone else stirring, yawning and stretching, talking and laughing as they brushed grass off their clothes. They wandered to the center of the camp, where Atan was sitting on a log. When the Mearsieans approached, she said in a clear voice, "Since you object to whatever Rel does, you can run the camp, CJ."

Atan pointed to an axe by her feet. "You'd better start by fetching the firewood, since we've already burned all the gleanings. There is a fallen log over that way."

CJ looked at the circle of faces, some hard, a few friendly, but nobody said anything until Clair came up beside her. "Want help?"

CJ lifted her chin. "No." She meant to say that anything that galoot can do, she could do better, but the words stuck in her throat.

She grabbed the axe and marched off, glad to get away.

The fallen log lay some hundred paces off. CJ walked around it, trying to decide where to begin. As she did, she argued mentally with friends and enemies, vilifying Atan and Rel and justifying herself, but every word seemed to escape into the air.

Meanwhile, here was this gigantic log.

She hefted the axe, and hit one of the dried branches, which splintered into a thousand bits, splinters hitting her hands and face. Ugh!

She marched to the big end of the log, and swung the axe as hard as she could.

The blade bounced off the log, twisting so hard her fingers stung painfully. She wiped her hands on her grimy skirt, and tried again. This time the blade landed awry and bounced away without leaving a dent. She tried again, and got the blade to stick, but when she tried to pull it out, she had to tug hard.

Three more hits, and she'd made three little gashes that weren't even close together. Her palms were fairly tough from a lot of tree climbing, but even so they were beginning to sting with promised blisters if she kept it up.

But she had to, right? Because . . . *Because it's my fault.*

Smack! A chip flew off, nearly clipping her ear. The axe fell to the grass.

Footsteps whished through the grass, and there was Rel, looming like a mountain. CJ hunched up, braced for war.

Rel sat on the log.

He said, "They think you've got a grudge against me."

"I don't," she shot back.

"Yes," he said. "It's something besides that. I know our first meeting was bad, but you had worse experience with Jilo."

CJ jerked her shoulders in a shrug.

"I think you're envious," Rel said.

"I am not!"

His eyes crinkled briefly, but he didn't laugh. "You're not envious of me. That is, I know you don't want to be me."

"Ugh," she said, crossing her arms.

This time he did laugh, a brief, voiceless huff. "I don't think you want to take away my friends. Or my life. It's what you think I can do, isn't it?"

"How do you mean?" she asked warily.

"You seem to think I should be smiting Norsundrians, but you don't see that I'm not that far ahead of you, except for size and a few years. Or maybe it's the size and the years that's the problem? Someone once said to me that when things like size, and age, and strength are a problem, then maybe they were used against a person, instead of to protect them."

CJ fumed. She suspected that 'someone once said' was really 'when we were talking about you,' but far worse than that was remembering her life on Earth. Oh, yes. Size and strength were *definitely* used against you *there*.

Envy.

She squirmed, hating the word, an old and familiar enemy.

Maybe he was right. To lie to herself was to lie to the world, that's what Clair had said once. She'd seen how envy came out of anger.

CJ sidled a look at Rel, who sat there as patient as a mountain. Waiting. So she looked within herself, past the ugly memories, and forced herself to endure the nastiness.

Anger was like that. She'd think she'd gotten rid of it, but there it was again. It was worse than the time she'd fallen on the sandy blacktop at school and scraped both her knees, then had to run to the restroom and endure the torture of wiping the sand and blood out of the scrapes. Every time she thought she got it all, and she could dare to go back to her classroom (because if the teacher saw she'd get into trouble for running, which was against the rules, and then she'd get into worse trouble at home for being in trouble at school), she'd look down, and there was more blood. And she'd have to use that rough paper towel again, which hurt worse than fire.

"But everybody thinks you're perfect," she said bitterly. "And you are." *And I am so, so not.*

"No, I'm not. I'm good at some things, and bad at others, just like anyone else. I can't learn magic. The strange words don't stick in my head. I can't draw. I could never build a loyal group like you have with the other girls. I don't seem to be able to settle in one place. And as far as size and strength are concerned, they don't guarantee wins. Every time I tangled with Kessler, I lost. I'm only alive because he decided not to kill me. But he could have."

At the mention of Kessler's name, all CJ's anger whipped away like smoke before the wind. "I hate thinking about him," she said fiercely, not wanting to be reminded of the terror of those days.

"But you'll have to. We all do. Senrid said that he's in charge of guarding yon city. If we want to rescue Liere, we're going to have to get past him." He picked up the axe. "That's for tomorrow. Today, this is the sort of thing I'm good at. I'm glad to do what I'm good at. Same as anyone else."

CJ watched him heft the axe and chop the wood in exactly the right place. He'd split off the rotten bits of the branch she'd first attacked, creating a good pile of firewood, before she said, "They want to make me do all the chores."

"Oh, I think if you help me, nobody'll say a word. They're all hungry, and want a hot breakfast more than anything else. And Leander found some wild olives so we can crisp the potatoes."

CJ swallowed. "Let's get to it. Maybe it'll be faster if you chop and I stack."

They did, working in silence. She was relieved at first, but as the stack of firewood grew, so did the thing inside her, until it felt like a stone the size of a bowling ball.

When Rel said presently, "That should be enough," CJ sucked in a deep breath and muttered, "I'm sorry."

Rel took in the tight fists and the black hair swinging, hiding CJ's averted face, and did not make the mistake of taking that surly mutter as insincere. He had a pretty good idea how much that apology cost her, and how humiliated she'd feel if he gave in to the laughter fluttering behind his ribs. Or made a speech.

So he grunted, "We're square."

And saw her skinny shoulders drop away from her ears.

Another silent fifty paces and they entered the camp together, each carrying a stack of firewood. Nobody said anything. Atan watched narrowly at first, but when she saw Rel's brief smile, and heard CJ talking as if nothing had happened, she decided to act as if nothing had happened.

Everybody else fell into their usual patterns, except for Kyale, who found time to whisper to CJ, "I hope you told him off. Those boys are so bossy, but Senrid is the worst of all."

CJ sighed, relieved to have it over. Except it wasn't over, not with Kyale saying things like that, and the looks she got from Atan and others. They thought she was a villain. And, even worse, that tiny voice way, way inside: *I was acting like one.*

To Kyale she said tiredly, "We gotta think about how to get into that city now."

Kyale wandered off, disappointed, and Clair stepped up beside CJ, her smile pensive. "Are you all right?"

CJ side-eyed her. "Why didn't you tell me I was being a bat-head?"

"Because that would have made you madder," Clair answered.

CJ scowled, knowing it was true. "I hate anger. Getting angry makes me angry!" And when Clair snickered, she muttered, "I don't know how to get rid of it."

Clair watched CJ sigh, her bad mood obviously gone as quickly as thunderstorms pass.

If you figure it out, CJ, she thought, you could fix the world.

The group was finishing up clearing their campsite when a sweet, heart-catching cascade of pure, clear notes echoed through the forest.

"Oh," Kyale breathed, sitting down abruptly on the log she'd disdained as filthy the day before. The air scintillated with color, something that usually annoyed her, but this time it and the sounds matched so perfectly that she clasped her hands and stared.

"What is that sound?" Hibern asked.

"Some kind of bird?" Arthur asked, for once not absent.

"I've never heard one like that," Leander said, as he peered under his hand through the bluish-white light shafts in the wooded shadows. "I think it's coming this way."

"Hide," Senrid said.

"I don't think that could come from any Norsundrian," Lilah said. "It's sounds so pretty!"

Atan murmured, "I'll bet that's what people were saying about Siamis right before he took their wits away."

The Mearsieans bolted up trees with the ease of long practice.

The melodic cascade intensified, and CJ hummed a counterpoint below it; that meant she was memorizing that melody, possibly for making a song later. Clair's eyelids prickled, though she couldn't have said why. And over on the rock, Kyale noticed that, as usual, nobody else saw the colors like gleaming ribbons in the air. And she blinked them away as a couple of pale-haired figures walked into the clearing.

Everybody took in the two boys, the taller sturdy one with a round, genial face, dressed in a shapeless long shirt belted by a bit of rope. He carried a pitchfork in one hand, and something greenish poked out of the other sleeve.

The second boy was smaller, his perfectly oval face lifted. The filtered bluish light fell softly on his high, intelligent brow, his definite jawline beginning to emerge from baby-round cheeks. He, unlike the older boy, stood still and alert.

"Hiya Darksiders," the big one called.

"Darksiders?" Kyale popped up, fists on hips. "Do you think we are dark magic villains?"

"No, no!" The taller boy patted the air. "Darkside of the Sun is our name for your world. On account of we can't ever see it."

Kyale crossed her arms. "I assure you, we have just as much sunlight as you do."

"I know! And I understand a very fine place it is. But it's an old name, see? So here's me, to lead a lot of Dar—foreigners to the cave under the city, and all I find is trampled grass. Do I smell?"

He lifted his arm, sniffing at his armpit, then made a show of gagging as he reeled, arms flapping.

Puddlenose almost broke his sinuses holding in a laugh, but when he saw Christoph's red face, it escaped, and he dropped down out of the tree, figuring any kid with a sense of humor would never join Norsunder.

"Who are you? I'm Puddlenose," he said.

"Bena Dak." The newcomer hefted his pitchfork. "But you can call me Dak. That's my brother, Cath."

The green thing in his sleeve moved, slithering out. A snake!

"Hoo," Puddlenose said. "Did you know you had a snake in your shirt?"

"I do?" Dak pretended to be shocked, then laughed. "This is Alivier. She travels with us."

By then, the others were approaching. "What is that?" Dhana asked Cath, pointing to the flute-like object in his hand.

"We call them silverflutes," Cath said. His childish treble was precise. He held out the silverflute on his palms, so those interested could see the pearlescent wood that wasn't quite white, nor silver, though it gleamed at a distance.

"You must've been playing since before you learned to walk, to be that good," Kyale said enviously. She'd tried to learn a couple of instruments, but could never stick with practice long enough to get past the boring basics.

"A year," Cath said.

That left his audience silent as he slid the silverflute into a kind of sheath hanging from his neatly tied sash.

Dak said with his friendly smile, "The sharron sent me, on account of, I know some o' them, and I got to be friends with some mages." The Mearsieans liked his accent, which CJ thought of as sort of French.

"The sharron are in a pucker over these stone-backs. We call the enemy that on account of those gray jackets they wear—"

"We call them Norsundrians," Kyale offered importantly.

Dak grinned. "Well, the sooner we hoof 'em out, the better, is what I'm saying."

"Then lead the way," Hibern said. "We can talk as we walk."

## Chapter Four

*Isul Demarzal*

TALL trees towered overhead, long-lobed leaves of every shade of green, blurring in great swoops back and forth.

Julian was dreaming about the swing again.

Liere liked this dream, or this part of Julian's dreams. All the rest of Julian's dreams were different kinds of horrible. There were the ones where all the furniture was distorted and giant and the walls red, as if seen from the floor. Those were the ones with the whispering woman in them, jewels in her headdress and at her neck and on her fingernails glittering like tiny needles and knives. Those dreams always carried remembered pain.

The forest dreams had unknown children singing or playing games. Sometimes those began as swing dreams, but below those were sharper memories: being interrupted by tall, pretty Irza, who came to take Julian away from Atan, whispering things:

"Atan will make you do your duty."

"I will always give you whatever you want."

"You're our baby, our dolly, our perfect girl."

Liere could hear Irza's thoughts across the distance, brought close and painful. In Irza's memories she didn't think Julian was perfect, she thought she was a spoiled brat, and yet she gave her whatever she asked for, smiling, smiling, smiling.

Atan didn't hurt Liere with distortion because the Atan she saw and heard in Julian's dreams and memories was the Atan whose actual thoughts whispered across the distances.

Liere knew what was dream and what was memory. If someone appeared in her dreams, and she stepped through the mirror into their dreams, she had found that she could think away specific ugly symbols, like red walls, and sometimes the feelings that came with them, and then walk through into a better memory. She had done that for her mother many times.

When Irza turned Julian's dreams sour, Liere thought the dream-Irza away and brought dream-Atan back, and when she did, she brought some of Atan's own memories of the forest glade into Julian's dreams: Her joy in pushing Julian on the swing. Julian's toes twinkling among forest grasses. Julian laughing, her flower garland shedding blossoms on the breeze. Julian warm and happy and clean.

As the days drifted by, Liere, so used to separating out dreams from memories, and memories from thoughts, caught flickers that surprised her. She woke up one day comprehending that Atan was here. On Geth. In Atan's dreams, she searched and searched for Julian, worried and scared.

Liere ventured further and discovered that not only was Atan on Geth, so were many from the alliance. Including Senrid.

Liere promptly shut her mind-shield tight. She was good at dream-walking, but she knew that Siamis was far better, and better yet was the sinister Detlev, whom she had never met, but whose presence sometimes passed through the mental realm like the shadow of a predator bird blocking the sun.

They were here. Because Liere had been stupid and managed to get herself caught. But still, joy closed tight as a flower seed in her heart. She was not alone, and she knew that Senrid would look for her.

Meanwhile, Julian was not conscious of Liere in her dreams. She only knew she was happier. One day she felt so restless she got tired of crouching on the floor to talk, so she ran outside to look at the people and the streets.

She wanted to talk to the runaway prince again.

*Outside the city*

Cath's oddness partly explained itself when Senrid felt a brief, subtle sense of widened perception or echo on the mental plane. He knew that sense. He'd first experienced it with Liere. When he looked around sharply, he met the boy's steady gaze.

*I was asked to listen for the enemy.* Cath's mental voice was as clear and precise as his spoken voice—unlike Senrid's hard-to-control mental contacts.

Senrid said out loud, "We're not enemies. But I'd do it, too, if I had as good a control as you have." Unspoken was the term 'Dena Yeresbeth,' which Cath caught.

Cath's thought came: *I don't know what Dena Yeresbeth is. 'Marsh mad' is what we call it.*

With that came an almost dizzying sense of weird space, full of rich scents, an echo of which Senrid had already experienced.

That was the difference, Senrid perceived. With Cath, it was like their minds met somewhere, and with Liere, it was not a place, but more like in his head.

*Yes,* Cath thought. *I heard that girl. Dak did, too. But we daren't listen long for her. The enemy can hear in the Marsh.*

Dak thumped his pitchfork on the ground. "I was told you want to go in, searchin' for where the stone-backs keep First Witch, which we can't do, because we're warded. But they didn't ward you, because they don't know about you bein' here."

"That's right," Senrid said.

"We'll find her," Hibern promised. "If you can tell us where to go."

"But we don't rightly know that," Dak admitted. "They coulda put her anywhere."

"Then we'll be faster and more efficient if we divide up and hunt through the city," Leander said reasonably.

"Yeah, and we can't run, or change our expressions," CJ said. "We have to act zombified. That's what people look like under Siamis's evil spell."

Dak thumped his pitchfork in agreement on each point, then said, "The Witches said, you need disguises."

Puddlenose walked backward. "I dunno." He scratched his head. "Nobody loves disguises more than I do. An adventure isn't a good one unless I get to wear a false beard, or a fancy dress. But don't you think Kessler would recognize some of us even in disguises?"

"In a city?" Leander asked. "He can't be everywhere at once."

"These would be illusion," Dak said, as Cath lifted his head to watch a flock of long-tailed birds erupt from a flowering vine that had overtaken an old fence.

"I don't want to go looking for some old woman," Glenn muttered. "I thought we were here to kill Siamis. That's what *I* want to do."

Atan said to Dak, "Illusory disguises would keep us from being recognized by any Norsundrian who has seen us on our world, but what about Norsunder's wards?"

"That's been thought of," Dak said, thumping his pitchfork again. "Talk as we walk. They told me to get you to the tunnel by sundown tomorrow."

They camped, and the next morning, Dak led them behind a waterfall in a rocky, rough portion of hill, but instead of the trail skirting the hill, it opened into a tunnel hidden by the falling water. Some found it fun to slip and slide over the green, mossy rock, others picked their way carefully.

Down and down they hiked, until the sound of the waterfall was replaced by the susurrus of a rushing underground stream.

Dak was explaining the general layout of the city as they walked. "Over our heads right now is Weavers' Row. Then comes the park, see the tree roots way up there? Then over here begins what they call Charlotte's Palace. We don't know what part Charlotte actually lived in, it's been rebuilt and added onto so many times, but it's the biggest building I've ever seen. Some say in the entire world! Now, down this here tunnel, and then we're—ak!" Dak stopped short, dropped his pitchfork onto a flat rock, and put his hands on his hips. "There you are, Cath. Good. Right in time."

Cath had brought an older boy, skinny, as brown as the off-world visitors, with jug-handle ears and a big grin.

"Ol' Bones!" Dak exclaimed with pleasure. "Explain to 'em about vagabond magic."

Old Bones faced the allies. "My magic is something new to Geth. It's pretty much illusory, and Les is only teaching it to a few of us. It isn't like regular magic. It fades away on its own, except at sunset and sunrise, and when other kinds of magic are done. They can't put the magic tracers on it, any more than you can shape a statue out of ocean water, no matter how much you use." He turned to the others, without explaining who Les was. "So I can give you any kinda fake face and form you want. 'Long as you don't touch anybody, you'll fool 'em."

The rescuers considered thoughtfully, then CJ said, "I want to try being an old bat. With a warty chin! No elevener will pay any attention to an old bat hobbling around."

"Me, too! Me, too!" Kyale shrilled. "Warts on my chin *and* my nose!"

"I want to be an old geez," Bren declared. "Beard down to here." He indicated his knees as he hunched over and shuffled in a circle.

"Pirate captain!"

"And I'd like to be a raptor," Senrid said. "But we're supposed to be keeping attention away from ourselves. Pirates and a whole lot of warty old people aren't going to go unnoticed."

Dak thumped his pitchfork on the boulder. "Whatever you choose, make it quick, as the day is getting late."

"Line up," Old Bones said.

*Isul Demarzal*

In Charlotte's Palace, Liere and Julian crouched at the doorway.

"Siamis said it is a joke, see?" Julian explained. "He says they named the sword Truth in the old days, but there isn't any truth."

"I know. He said the same thing to me once."

Julian shrugged, uninterested in the subject of truth. "At least he got a sword as a present. In the bad days, *Mother* only let me have *jewels* and *princess dresses*." The emphasized words came out in a tone of sullen resentment, underscored by the memory of terror, which Liere had seen in Julian's dreams.

"I think there's truth," Liere said.

"What is it, then?"

"Well, I think truth is . . . when you make a promise, you keep it. And if you know you can't keep it, you don't make the promise. Truth has a lot of things in it, but one of them is trust. Like, I trust my friend . . . Devon," Liere avoided mentioning Senrid, in case that lurking listener might somehow know that Senrid was somewhere in this world.

Liere had seen him twice in her dreams, once alone, sitting on a boat, looking down at the sea, and another time with Atan and Leander, eating smoked fish off sticks.

"If Devon doesn't know a thing, she says so. If she sees a thing, she tells me what she sees, not what she thinks I want to see. And if she can't keep a promise, she won't make one. Devon speaks truth."

Julian was running her fingers along the underside of the door, back and forth. "Irza didn't keep her promise. She said if I liked her best she would give me whatever I wanted."

"Did she?"

"When we lived in the forest. Those were the good days. But when we had to come into Eidervaen, then she didn't."

Liere thought that over. "Did Atan make promises?"

"She said I didn't have to be a princess."

"Did you believe her?"

"No. Irza said Atan wouldn't give me what I wanted. And she didn't! She tried to give me what *she* wanted. Clothes, and lessons, and stupid things that make princesses. Just like Mother."

Liere thought back through all the dreams. Atan had come all the way to another world to get her cousin free. Liere knew better than to say that; Senrid had said once that the nastiest weapons were the ones you can't fight, and to Liere that meant the way her father always used to finish a scold by adding another scold for not being grateful. "But wouldn't lessons let you be what you wanted?"

For a time all Liere could hear was Julian's breathing. She didn't want to break the mental wall, lest Siamis pounce, but she was tempted. Then Julian said resentfully, "I said I don't want to be a princess. It *hurts*." And there again, sharp as a knife, were the memories of pinching and slapping, enforced by the whispering voice, *If you want to be a princess, you have to smile, and be sweet.*

"So you don't have princess lessons," Liere said calmly. "There are lots of kinds of lessons. You go to the stable for lessons if you want to be a . . . a horse rider. You go to the kitchen to learn how to cook tasty things. There are lessons to be an artist, or make music. Did Atan mean to offer you those?"

Julian said, "I don't know."

She got up and ran away. She hated those old memories. She ran as hard as she could down one long corridor and up another, until the memories turned into questions.

She stopped at the kitchen to get a cake, then took her cake back to the place where Siamis usually could be found. When she saw him, she said, "The runaway prince told me you broke your promise."

Siamis smiled. "I may have."

"Why?"

"Here's a lesson," he said, and Julian looked wary. Lessons again! But he went on, "When you are in power, you can keep promises when it suits you. And ignore them when it suits you."

"What if people don't keep promises to you?"

"Then I destroy them." He laid his hand on the hilt of the sword named Truth, only there wasn't any truth, so maybe he was lying. Then he made that motion with his fingers that meant he wanted her to go away.

Atan doesn't lie, Julian thought as he turned his attention to one of the crabby grays waiting impatiently. In memories and in dreams, Atan just got sad if people broke promises.

Julian wandered off, and watched the cooks make rows and rows of pies. They had power, too, she thought. Everybody needed food. They kept the promise of being cooks by making pies every day. So that was one true thing and it had nothing to do with being a princess.

She pondered asking them for lessons, and wondered what Liere would say about that.

From hidden vantages all around the city, mages from both worlds watched through the illusory magic set up to protect the young allies as they covered the last distance alongside a vast underground pool.

"Here's the stair," Dak said, his voice echoing in the stone cavern. "This stairway will put you in the center of Charlotte's Palace, in the servants' wing. This used to be the laundry, centuries ago, before the mages invented cleaning frames. Me and my brother will wait for you here. Cath is listening for the mages." He tapped the side of his head, then perched on a rock nearby, his pitchfork laid across his lap.

The young allies looked at one another in their illusory disguises, then down at themselves. Hibern saw from Senrid's narrowed eyes, Arthur's thoughtful expression, and Atan's careful testing of the illusion that she was not the only one who felt extra magic worked into the illusion, though it was impossible to categorize. She suspected there was some kind of protection woven into the mysterious 'vagabond magic.'

Hibern walked up the first few steps of the mossy stairway, wondering if Erai-Yanya was somehow connected to the mages behind the extra protection. "We're a decoy," she whispered to Senrid, who was right on her heels. "I feel something under these illusions."

"I don't care." He shrugged. "As long as it doesn't interfere with me finding Liere and yanking her out of here."

Hibern knew Senrid would have walked in without illusion, protection, or anything. She'd chosen the most nondescript form she could think of, which wasn't much different from her real form, except that she looked older, and Old Bones had given her the illusion of a common Geth robe-gown, loose from the shoulders, with a long contrasting swath of fabric draped crosswise around and over one shoulder so the ends hung behind. She'd chosen muted colors.

She looked past Senrid down at the waiting faces on the steps behind her, many unrecognizable in their disguises. Even distorted by illusion, faces betrayed tension and uncertainty.

So maybe it was time to repeat what they already knew, because knowing was a kind of protection against the unknown. "Remember, as well as looking for Liere, we're looking for the First Witch: old, dark hair, white stripe. Fetch Senrid and Jilo so they can break any dark magic wards on her. As soon as she's found, retreat. We'll gather here."

Atan added, "You know what the enchanted look like. Don't stare. Walk slowly. Ignore any Norsundrians as if they aren't there."

"Whether we find her or not, return by sundown," Leander added from the middle of the crowd. He'd chosen a male version of Hibern's nondescript person, complete to robe-gown.

"That's right," Dak called from the other end of the cavern. "The illusions will fade by then. If no one discovers you, we can camp here tonight and try again tomorrow."

A murmur of agreement rose, then by ones and twos they mounted the stairs, counting to fifty between each so no crowd would be seen emerging into what they'd been told was a forgotten stairway at the back end of the palace.

Atan had asked only for an illusory Geth outfit. When she looked down, her hermit's tunic over riding trousers had scarcely altered, the hem of her tunic extending past her knees, her old hermit cottage riding trousers billowing around her ankles in the same dull dun color.

The station she'd volunteered for was the front side of the palace, which Dak had said was a lot of right turns from where they'd emerge. Though she intended to do her part in the search for this mysterious First Witch—and for Liere—she meant to find Julian first. No one else would be looking for her.

She found herself in a narrow hallway. The ground shivered slightly as she walked. Alarm burned through her, and faded: another quake. The tenth one since their arrival. The building creaked warningly around her, but she reminded herself that it had survived this long. It was not likely to fall around her ears now, and all the quakes had been small, no more than the swaying of a small boat on a pond. Surely that had to mean that quakes here were like the ones on Sartorias-deles, lessened by ancient magecraft. But at home, they were made much smaller, so no one felt them.

She emerged from a hall across from an open door, through which she glimpsed neat stacks of various sizes of brooms and mops. The hall stretched in both directions, meeting what looked like other halls. Right turns.

She struck out, meeting another intersection, then another, always turning to the right; she noticed that these were not squared-off turns, which meant she was bending gradually in a long arc.

After the seventh right turn the hall widened abruptly, the floor of reddish tiles becoming a mosaic pattern of twined geometric shapes making forms around fish and blooms and birds.

She peered inside the countless rooms for a blank-faced middle-aged woman with a streak of white in her dark hair. She saw people of every age, some going about simple tasks in a rote manner that made her skin crawl, others sitting quietly, the way people had in Sartor.

None of them fitted First Witch's description, and she wondered if Norsunder had put an illusion over First Witch. She wasn't sure she'd be able to pick out an illusion seen across a room.

She pushed on, until the inner blow of extremely powerful dark magic caused her to stumble, staring around the silent hall.

All over the palace, everyone looked up and around uneasily. The Norsunder mages stopped their search through the libraries, and exchanged glances: someone was in trouble, judging by the power of that impact. They returned to work with a sedulous air. Nobody wanted to become a target.

At the key intersections in the city, and at the gates, the Norsundrian patrollers who had begun another boring day of useless duty among the mindless sheep straightened up, alerted by that sense of teeth-gritting, metallic danger, smelling of burnt steel.

Inside the Palace, Siamis stilled, then dropped the map he'd been rolling. It fell to the table, half on, half off, then slipped to the floor, bringing with it a whispering cascade of papers.

But the cascade went unnoticed. He was already out of the room.

Julian looked up as footsteps approached. She scrambled to her feet and backed away when Siamis reached for the cellar door.

A few moments later, Liere saw the door swing open for the first time in days. She blinked in the bright light as Siamis took hold of her shoulder, drew her out, and said, "Detlev is getting impatient. He's trying to break my wards. I knew you would come in useful."

"Where is she going?" Julian asked, dismayed.

Siamis glanced absently down at her. "Let's see if our young friend here can distract him."

He did not say for what: Liere staggered as the hard fingers let her go, and transfer magic seized her, and flung her back into the world again. She staggered and looked around in fear, finding herself in another bare stone room lit by a single slit near the ceiling.

A door opened. Blue-white light slanted in, bringing in a heavy scent of mimosa.

Liere wanted to run, but where could she run to? She got her trembling legs moving, and ventured out.

Unkind laughter met her. She looked across a low room full of low curved chairs like half-circles in which various people sat. Her attention passed over them, then snagged on the derisive gaze of a brown-haired man.

She knew from Senrid's memories that this was Detlev.

"So this is the famous world-rescuer, Sartora, Queen of Bereth Ferian!" he said, and the people laughed.

Every word stung. She dropped her head forward, shutting her eyes, her mind-shield tight.

"Where is the dyr?" came the amused voice.

She braced for the careless roughness of Siamis's searchers, but no one touched her. She looked up, instinctively putting out the tiniest tendril of mind quest . . . and he was waiting.

Lilith had exhorted her to practice her mind-shield. Liere had exhorted others to practice theirs, and she had what she thought was a good shield against the battering of others' thoughts, but now she learned how very, very inexperienced she really was.

Detlev was there in the surface of her mind. Terror struck through her, knife-sharp in agonized expectation of him tromping through all the corners of her mind, opening and slamming doors into memories. She cowered into as small a ball as she could as his mental voice shouted endlessly, *Where is the dyr? Where is the dyr?* while ignoring her mental voice whimpering *I don't know, I don't know.*

Finally he gave up in disgust. His presence was gone. She snapped her mind-shield around herself so hard she scarcely heard as Detlev turned to the avid watchers. "Meet the mighty mage who defeated my nephew. Are you impressed yet?"

Raucous laughter battered Liere. She collapsed onto the floor, arms wrapped tightly around her knees, her mind shrinking into inward focus. She knew she was isolated, totally without defenses or the possibility of aid.

"Who is going to save the world-saver?" came the scornful voice, followed by excoriating laughter.

But when Detlev shifted to describing in remorseless detail how cowardly, self-centered, and hypocritical her so-called allies were, and how none of them would stir to save her, she thought: *Not Senrid.*

She clung to that thought with all her strength. She knew what Senrid's faults were. He'd told her himself. She'd seen them, but among them cowardice, self-centeredness, and hypocrisy did not number. She knew he would be there if he could—that wherever she was, he'd try to find her.

Then there was Arthur, with his endless patience. And Rel, and Hibern, and even CJ, who believed that 'Sartora' could do miracles—that girls could do miracles. Though CJ had a temper, and struggled with it, she was so fiercely loyal, Liere knew that CJ would come running if she thought another girl was in danger.

Liere hugged those thoughts tightly, deep inside her shell. She even felt a pulse of pity for Detlev, whom everyone hated, even Siamis. He was alone, in the world of the heart.

*I am not alone.*

She did not know how long she could endure, but right now, that thought sustained her.


Abruptly Detlev's mental voice vanished.

Liere kept her head down, but peeked to the side; she half expected the light to be gone, for it felt like she'd been under bombardment for a hundred years. But the square of sunlight on the floor had scarcely shifted.

"She's useless. This," Detlev said contemptuously, "is nothing more than a diversion."

A rough hand seized Liere's arm and drew her to her feet. Pins and needles made standing difficult, and she was dizzy.

"Let us make a little journey," Detlev said.

## Chapter Five

AFTER that soundless impact that reverberated through teeth and bones, Atan paused, her back flat to a wall, as she listened for alarm, shouts, footsteps, any sign that one of the rescuers had been discovered.

Nothing.

The pulse of strong magic was not followed by another. She had to go on.

The rooms she passed now had double doors. They appeared to be libraries. Most were empty. Down one more hall of library rooms she trod until she was startled to hear voices.

They weren't supposed to talk! But as she neared a doorway, she discovered that these voices did not belong to people her age. These were adults, their tones irritated.

"What that spell means is trouble," somebody was saying in Sartoran, "but not for us if we can find that damned book."

Atan put her head down, and peeked out of the sides of her eyes as she walked slowly past the door. Her heart thundered, but the glances cast her way were distracted, uninterested. Several of the adults in there wore the gray uniform tunics of Norsunder, two wore gray mage robes, and one stood out, a small blond woman in a velvet gown.

Atan had seen her before, on a tower, using magic to fight against

Atan when she freed Sartor: that was Dejain, the chief mage of Norsunder Base.

Atan began to suspect that the Norsundrians were also pressed for time, though she had no idea why. She wondered if she ought to try to find out as she turned toward a hall from which enticing smells emanated.

Kitchens! Julian used to raid food from the kitchens, rather than be seen in the dining room, where she might be expected to sit at table and use utensils. Atan was wondering how big the kitchens would be for so large a place when a small figure hurled into her, and she stared down at Julian in wit-flown shock.

Julian was equally startled. "Atan?" She said fiercely, "Go away!"

Julian scampered off. Atan set out after her, but between one turn and another Julian darted into a room or hall and vanished. Atan grimly kept looking until she knew she was lost.

Her eyes stung, sorrow seizing her chest so hard she couldn't breathe. But others were counting on her. She had lost Julian, so it was time to keep her promise and search for the First Witch.

Her eyes were so blinded by tears that she didn't see Julian peering from behind a tapestry until Atan had passed safely by. Everything hurt, especially inside her. She couldn't stop thinking about the sad, afraid face Liere had made before Siamis pushed her into that magic. If he saw Atan, he would do that to her, too!

Julian wasn't mad at Atan any more. Atan never caused bad dreams. She was nice in the dreams. She did keep her promises, even if they were boring ones. She wasn't like Irza, or Mother. And Siamis was just like Mother and Irza, smiling and soft when other people were around, but doing mean things to people, and never keeping promises.

Atan had to go away and be safe!

Julian found who she was looking for: there was the runaway prince at the gate, with a whole lot of warriors ready with bows and arrows and swords and things. But they didn't move, much less spit, so she ran past the rows.

Kessler glanced down at the crimson-faced child who dashed up, trailing her grimy rags. "You said you keep promises," she gasped out, breathing hard.

"If I make them." He glanced down at those eyes shaped so much like his.

Julian looked around, shoving sweaty, matted hair off her cheek, then said in a low voice, "Atan is here."

"Atan?" Sharp interest caused him to wave off the runners waiting for orders. He knelt down. "Atan? On this world? Where?"

"In there." Julian waved impatiently at the palace. "I don't want Siamis to put her in magic, like he did to Liere. She was scared! It was mean. Will you make sure Siamis doesn't do that to Atan?"

Kessler said, "I will take care of Atan. But you must do something for me."

Julian gazed at him in surprise, not unpleased. Nobody asked her to do things, unless it was stupid stuff like putting on princess clothes. "What?"

"Go find Dejain. She's the yellow-haired one, usually in a pink or rose gown. Tell her I want to talk to her, and if she will not come to me, I will come to her. Have you got that right? Repeat it."

Julian repeated it exactly as he'd said.

Kessler gave a brief nod. "Quick."

The child scampered off, bare feet twinkling among the dusty rags. Kessler watched her go, suspecting that if Atan Landis was here, there were surely others from Sartorias-deles. It was actually a clever move on the part of the lighter mages, sacrificing brats who Siamis would never think would turn up, so hadn't warded.

Kessler beckoned to two of his scouts. "You know where they stashed the First Witch."

"Yes."

"Watch without being seen. If anyone suspicious goes near her, you follow them until you find out where they're coming from. Then report back to me." And to the second, "There's at least one Sartoran youth running around. Find out where they're hiding."

One of the most valued of all the architectural professions on Geth was that of the joiner. The best of them did quite well, and were always in demand. Their guild subsequently had a prominent place in the city, as in all cities on Geth; and, as it happened, the First Witch had a brother who was the head of a successful shop.

In a back room, sitting in a rocking chair that moved gently back and forth as if she would go on rocking until the end of time, sat a woman of about sixty-five, with dark hair bound up, not hiding the white streak.

Leander was the one to find her.

When he saw that white stripe, he backed up slowly, then forced himself to compose his face. His body. To walk slowly out into the square with its fountain, across which Norsunder patrols rode frequently.

Leander fell in behind a couple of people carrying empty baskets. Did they think those baskets were filled? The evidence of the enchantment gave him the creeps, but he kept his pace slow, his attention unfocused as he traversed the square in the direction he'd last seen Senrid.

He caught sight of Senrid's middle-aged man guise at the end of a long street. Of course he was moving away, but Leander forced himself to walk slowly, though he increased each step a bit more until finally Senrid turned his head, then moved to one of the benches, and sat down.

When Leander caught up, he explained about the woman in the rocker.

"Just sitting there?"

"Yes."

"Wards or tracers or traps?"

"None that I could discern."

Senrid uttered a soft laugh, then shut his eyes. Leander knew that expression: Senrid was doing his mind thing. Presently he opened his eyes. "Cath knows. I hope that means Lilith is out there listening, and will do whatever it is they planned to do."

"Let's round up the others," Leander suggested.

"Start that. I'll go see if I can sense a trap. If you see Jilo, tell him where I am."

"Right."

Senrid and Leander forced themselves to rise with dreamy slowness, and to shuffle off in opposite directions.

Leander spotted Jilo (in old man form, but as unlike Wan-Edhe as imagination could make him) two streets away, slogging grimly through a row of upholstery and finishing shops. He drifted up, and said low-voiced, "I found her. Senrid's on his way. I'll go warn the others to retreat. Here's the directions to the joiner's shop."

He described the route twice, then Jilo set out at an awkward lope under the low eaves for the joiner's. Senrid spotted him from the other end of a long palm-lined path, and forced himself to move slowly to join him, without looking right or left.

When they reached the shop, they slipped inside—without noticing Kessler's scout watching from the midst of a flowery pocket garden, or the Norsundrian patroller who noted a pair of old men shuffling into the joiner's shop that he knew was supposed to remain empty.

Both patroller and scout went off to report, as inside the shop, Senrid and Jilo separated and began feeling out dark magic wards, tracers, and traps.

Jilo was halfway around the perimeter of the room when Senrid spoke.

"I've found at least two, maybe three traps around her chair," Senrid said to Jilo. "So far. I think we'd better work on these first."

A short time later, "Mirror ward," Jilo sang out.

"You handle that," Senrid said, and began crawling around the room to finish looking for other tracers and traps.

Julian found Dejain, and delivered her message.

The mage stared down at the filthy urchin, fighting the urge to run, to transfer away. The moment she'd dreaded was here.

Her fingers twitched toward the secret pocket in which she'd put the transfer token she'd prepared against disaster, then her hand dropped. She did not want Kessler coming after her. He was unnervingly single-minded when he went on the hunt, and it would only make him angrier. If she pretended cooperation, she might be able to deflect him.

"Show me where he is," she demanded of Julian. To Dejain's annoyance, the child trotted at her heels. "Go on back," Dejain said. "Scat."

"No," Julian said.

"Go pester Siamis."

"I don't like Siamis anymore," Julian retorted.

Dejain uttered a harsh laugh. "No one likes Siamis."

She turned her back and walked faster, forcing the child to pound grimly behind, dragging her load of cloth.

Dejain spotted Kessler standing at his post by the gate, and slowed as she considered her options. She halted in the lee of a flowering jessamine tree and watched as one, then another scout rode up to report.

Dejain hurried her pace, but didn't make it in time to hear either scout make their reports; Kessler saw her, dismissed both his scouts, then gestured to Dejain. "Come with me."

He didn't wait for her corroboration, but scooped up Julian, tucked her under his arm, and took off with rapid step. Dejain lifted her skirts to keep pace, while she reviewed her exit strategies.

Kessler didn't stop until he reached the side entrance to the palace. He set Julian down before the stairway opposite the broom closet. "My spy tells me that you'll find your cousin down that way. Run along. I'll be right behind you." He gave the little girl a push. After one disconcerted look behind her, tear tracks marring her grimy face, Julian ran.

Kessler faced Dejain. "Remove the blood spell."

She stared at him.

He said distinctly, "You enchanted the blade I ordered for someone else. I've known ever since it struck me and threw me straight into Norsunder. Did you really think I did not know?"

Her hand slid toward the secret pocket sewn into the seam of her gown, but Kessler gripped her painfully by the elbow. "Now."

They both knew Detlev and Siamis were involved in a magical struggle. Judging by the impact of powerful magic, it was happening now. Kessler had no more interest in helping the two Ancient Sartorans than Dejain—less, as she still claimed a place at Norsunder Base—and at this moment, they were both unwatched.

She knew Kessler carried at least one hidden weapon. He could kill her in a heartbeat and no one would know. Or care.

She had dreaded this moment so long that it was almost a relief. Without denying or uttering the myriad falsities she'd concocted as excuses, she whispered the long sequence of spells, memorized long ago.

Kessler let her go the moment he was free of Norsunder's hold.

Dejain plunged her hand into her pocket. She had nowhere to go, nothing to be, except chief mage at Norsunder Base. There, precarious as it was, she had power. Anywhere else, she'd have to fight for it, and be on the watch for the greater powers who could be endlessly vindictive. The mere thought made her feel old.

Lesca would make her comfortable until Dejain saw who won. She used her cross-world transfer.

## Chapter Six

THE guards at the gate stood around speculating about why their commander had taken off with the brat and the pretty mage.

"Look," one muttered, causing all heads to turn.

Beyond the open gate, the air shimmered. The smell of mimosa and wild thyme gusted outward in a ring, heat buffeting watching faces, and then a host appeared directly outside the gate. Armed. On horseback. At the center rode Detlev, next to a skinny girl clutching the mane of her horse.

Every mage in the city felt that mass transfer as an inward blow, sharper than the first.

The guards withdrew to either side as Detlev and his force rode slowly in, Liere in the middle, looking blanch-faced and incongruous holding on desperately to the mane of a horse whose reins were held by another rider.

They rode up the street toward the palace.

"What was *that?*" Jilo asked.

Senrid shrugged, and was about to say *Let's get back to work,* when they heard the sound of many footsteps on the pale stone tiles outside the door.

"Who are you?" Armed warriors blocked the door, though as yet they hadn't drawn their weapons. They'd reported the sighting and had been duly ordered to bring in the old men who had entered the shop, but they weren't worried about a fight from a couple of geezers.

Senrid and Jilo avoided looking at each other, knowing that the illusion did not hide their expressions, only distorted their features.

Senrid waggled his hand surreptitiously to Jilo, and rose to his feet as slowly as he could, blocking Jilo from sight as the latter got back to work on breaking the chain of spells.

Hoping he sounded like the enchanted, Senrid said in a monotone, while staring a little above the head of the patrol leader, "I am here to check my sister. I always come to check my sister upon this day."

The patrol leader looked at the others, who looked back. "Nobody's supposed to be here," he said, and when Senrid just stood there, "You can come along and tell Siamis that," he said.

Senrid's thought careened wildly. What to say when he was supposed to be enchanted out of his wits? Of course.

"I am here to check on my sister. I always come to check on my sister this day."

"Yes. Come along." The patrol leader motioned impatiently. Then winced, and cast a troubled look at the window.

Senrid felt the teeth-scraping, burning metal sense of great power building. Behind him, he heard Jilo hiss in his breath.

"Come along!" The Norsundrian's voice sharpened. He took a step toward Senrid, hand going to the hilt of his sword.

Senrid's right hand drifted to his other wrist, though he knew that taking on a patrol with a knife was not going to keep them off longer than a moment or two.

Greenish-white light flashed from horizon to horizon.

Senrid winced; Jilo said, "The ward on the city gates. It's gone." He began whispering, and magical light glittered greenish, smelling of solder.

The patrol leader had interrupted himself to look out into the street. He turned to one of his followers and said, "Find out what that was."

Behind Senrid, Jilo muttered, "First one on her gone." It seemed forever, but was only a moment or two before Jilo said, with satisfaction, "Two, and three."

Senrid was uttering the first phrases of the antidote to Siamis's spell when he remembered he was supposed to catch the victim's attention with a personal object. He cast a despairing look about, glanced at the Norsundrians, and performed the enchantment spell anyway, in the time it took for the patrol leader to draw his sword and advance three steps.

"Lilith," the First Witch murmured on an outgoing breath, gazing into space.

Senrid knew immediately what that meant: Lilith the Guardian had been listening on the mental realm. Oh, yes, the mages were outside the city with their own plans.

But that was pretty much what Lilith had said. At least she played fair. *I did my part, Lilith. Over to you. Now I'm going to find Liere.*

Senrid looked up at the patrol leader, who was motioning impatiently to what he obviously thought were slow old people. The First Witch blinked rapidly, touched Senrid and Jilo to protect them, and spoke several words.

Light slammed into the Norsundrians, freezing them between one step and another.

"That will not last long," she said. "I seem to have little strength. But it ought to be enough to get us past them." She tried to rise, then sank back. "Oh." Her voice was soft, breathless. "*Very* little strength. Will one of you give me an arm?"

Jilo stepped back, expecting Senrid to take care of that, but Senrid was gone, his footsteps rapidly diminishing. So Jilo awkwardly took hold of the old woman's thin arm. She rose with a grunt, and slowly they walked out, Jilo stumbling a little before he found the right pace to match hers.

"There's a shorter way to the palace, up this path," she murmured, pointing to an archway connecting two buildings with what looked like palm-frond roofs. Past Weaver's Row and the Pearl Garden . . . "Let us hurry," she added breathlessly, leaning on Jilo as she increased her pace.

Siamis strolled out the main door to the palace, backed by a company of armed guards, who spread out along the perimeter of the main plaza. They blocked off access from the various tree- and shrub-lined pathways opening onto the plaza, as a small number of vague-faced denizens drifted along oblivious as they went about some habitual task.

The warriors formed up, shield to shield, swords out, as Detlev and his force came riding up the main street from the gate barely visible in the distance.

Siamis gripped his sword by its sheath and sauntered to the center of the plaza.

Detlev reined in, halting his company.

"You're here again," Siamis said as he stepped up to Liere's horse, his back to Detlev.

"I appreciated the diversion," Detlev said, looking down at the top of Siamis's fair hair, his faint smile acerbic. "You knew she was completely ignorant?"

"I thought," Siamis said, "if she did know where the dyr is hidden, you would be the one to discover it, surely." Siamis's lips parted in a smile up at Liere.

Detlev turned his head. His eyes narrowed, and the ring of Siamis's guards surrounding his company stirred. Their patrol leader staggered, then righted himself, saying hoarsely, "Fall back."

Swords rang as they were sheathed again, and shields lowered. The Norsundrians Siamis had ordered to surround Detlev's force now began to line up behind Detlev's warriors—it was clear that Detlev had superseded whatever command they had been given by a mental order to the patrol leader.

As if nothing had happened, Siamis smiled up at Liere, closed his hands around her arms, and lifted her down, keeping his grip on one arm, his other hand still holding the sword.

At that moment Jilo and the First Witch appeared from a side street, as the handful of Isul Demarzal denizens began stirring and looking around with returning awareness. Some sat down abruptly, putting heads in hands, others glanced around bewildered and fearful.

The First Witch tightened her grip on Jilo and raised her voice. "You had better go now. You are not wanted here," she declared. "Your spells are broken. And my allies are coming."

Detlev's head turned sharply. He didn't answer, but raised his hand, and those who knew magic sensed the ingathering of power.

The First Witch struck first, but she was too far away, and too weak, to drop a stone spell around him the way she had around the patrol in the joiner's house.

But her attempt diverted Detlev for a crucial moment. He turned to look for her as the air flickered blue-white and a host of people in layers of bright, filmy fabric appeared.

"Ah," the First Witch said. "I knew the Ones would come."

In the square, a white-haired man wove a spell that raised a wall of virulently glowing green around the Norsundrian warriors. Detlev muttered a spell and struck it down, but the mages united in raising a larger, thicker magical ward.

"Ones?" Jilo asked.

"Help me sit down, young man, will you?" the First Witch asked, pointing to a pretty little bench carved of the shiny wood that looked to Sartorias-deles people like poured chocolate.

In the plaza Detlev raised his hands, which began to glow, but the mages worked together to dissipate the spell he was forming, as the First Witch said, "The Ones is what we call our roaming mages. For a time they give up name, family, home, to wander and do good in the world. They are called simply Ones while they serve."

Detlev turned their way. Jilo hunched down, terrified, as the First Witch called in her cracked, tremulous voice, "You know you do not have the secret of our tunnel transfer. You have only an echo, and we shall break that. I say to you, unwanted enemy, that you had better use it now to remove yourself and these." A gnarled hand dismissively waved at the armed force. "You can fall upon us, and many will die, but we'll—"

Jilo could see that Detlev wasn't listening. His head turned, his eyes searching, and Jilo realized that Siamis had abandoned Detlev. Detlev was alone, facing seven powerful mages, who began to chant in unison. Once again the air shimmered, and the chant became a harsh hum; Jilo started, though the hum was as different from the Great Hum as a scream from a song. But both were products of voice.

The shimmer coalesced into fog, swallowing Detlev and his force, then vanished, blasting the area with a rush of hot air.

At once the newly disenchanted Isul Demarzal people began clamoring for explanations, as more people poured out of the palace, looking about wildly.

Jilo said, "Norsunder was hunting for rift magic, right? But you do it differently here?"

The First Witch looked into his earnest face. "Yes. We call it a chain. For transfer between worlds, the number doesn't matter. Our method is different—it takes several of us to safely chain a transfer."

"So it's not a real tunnel?"

"No, but the word is a way for our minds to grasp how we manipulate space between destinations." By now a couple of younger Geth mages had spotted them, and came hurrying toward their leader. The First Witch rose to greet them, but smiled back at Jilo. "Norsunder will find no cooperation from us now. And that one, he knows it. Thank you for your aid. Go in peace."

Jilo backed away, and anyone who cared to saw a slightly blurry old man loping through the gathering crowds. Inside the palace, it was left turn, left turn, left turns all the way until he reached the stairs.

Glenn was the first one to find his way back to the underground cavern by the dark lake. He'd never had any intention of looking for some old woman. He'd gone straight to spy on Siamis, hoping to be able to kill him for unleashing Henerek on his home, but the fire for vengeance in imagination was doused by the cold splash of reality: Siamis was a fit-looking young man carrying a saber with the absent comfort of one well used to his weapon, and surrounded by guards.

So Glenn had retreated, joined by his sister. She'd lost count of the rooms, which disturbed her so much she intended to start over. But Hibern found her first, and said that Leander had spread the word to retreat.

They descended to the cavern to find the Mearsieans trickling in, having received the news that the First Witch had been found. The ever-growing group of young allies milled around, exchanging stories and speculations about what was going on, as Cath sat silently in their midst, eyes closed.

Then Cath gasped, opened his eyes, and got to his feet as Julian appeared on the stairs. She began to hop from step to step, but tripped as a swathe of her filthy clothes caught underfoot. She pitched out over the stones, but before anyone could do more than exclaim, Rel took two fast steps and caught her midair.

He set her down, and she ran straight to Atan, saying over and over, "I hate him, I hate him, I hate him. I want to go home."

Atan waited, arms kept stiff at her sides until the solid little body collided with her, and then—tentatively, gently—she put her arms around the little girl, who sobbed herself into hiccoughs.

So intent were they all on this reunion that they didn't see Kessler until he appeared at the top of the stairs.

Rel started forward protectively, but Kessler raised a hand as he leaped down, four stairs at time. "Siamis is on the way. I suggest you get out."

Some looked around uncertainly, and Dak turned to his brother, who nodded.

"But we're missing three of our people," Hibern said.

"Two," Atan corrected, pointing to Jilo in old man illusion at the top of the stairs. When he saw Kessler he backed up, looking around wildly.

Kessler glanced up, and said with complete indifference, "Siamis is right behind you."

Jilo looked back and forth in a way that Kessler found comical and

Atan heartbreaking, then he hustled down the stairs, nearly tripping in his haste. He slunk past Kessler, as, at the other end of the cavern, Dak was silently motioning the allies toward the far tunnel. Hibern lingered, hesitant to leave until she saw Senrid safely among them.

Rel pushed past her to confront Kessler. "What are you doing?"

Kessler's sword scraped free of its sheath. "Waiting for him." His smile made Hibern's nerves chill. "I'm going to cut out his heart with the sword named Truth."

Hibern said to Rel in an urgent undervoice that hissed in echoes, "Senrid's missing. And we never did find Liere, so he has to be looking for her."

Cath's young voice echoed from the other end of the tunnel, "Siamis has the girl. The boy is following them."

Rel said, "Let's get out of sight, at least." He indicated the archway.

Hibern followed, glancing back every few steps in hopes of seeing Senrid and Liere.

On her last glance, she saw what she feared most: Siamis appeared at the top of the stairs, gripping Liere with one arm.

He smiled down at Kessler, let Liere free, and drew his sword from its sheath.

Senrid catapulted himself through the entrance at the top of the stairs, then stilled in astonishment at the sight of Siamis, fair hair gleaming in the light slanting down from the stairway, facing a shorter, slight, black-haired fellow in black Norsundrian uniform.

Liere cowered nearby, her drawn, anxious expression lightening to joy when she saw Senrid. He jumped down the stairs, reached her, and their hands met and gripped tight, Liere reassured by Senrid's solid, callus-palmed grip, and he unsettled by how thin her fingers were.

She turned her huge eyes to him, and her thought came, clear as speech: *Siamis said it again, he left the sword as a gift. What can that mean, a gift?*

Senrid grimaced, watching as Siamis and Kessler sized each other up, swordpoints making tiny testing motions. Siamis was taller, wearing a loose, light, open-collared tunic shirt sashed around his hips. He wore forest mocs rather than riding boots, and moved with ease over the smooth stone. Kessler, shorter, reminded Senrid of something with antennae, the way he'd go still, then move so fast he was a blur. Both held their weapons well.

Liere tugged his hand: *Senrid?*

He dragged his gaze away. He hated trying to form words with Dena Yeresbeth—it was too clumsy, with memories and emotions and images leaking into his thoughts, making it difficult to concentrate. But he tried: *Whatever he meant doesn't matter. Because you didn't take it.*

Her response was swift: *But it scares me, Senrid, what he said. I keep thinking, he was twelve when Norsunder took him. I was twelve when I did the Child Spell.*

Senrid's return thought was swift and sarcastic: *He's not twelve now.* Then he got her meaning: *You think he's threatening to make you into a copy of him?*

Clang! The first move in the swordfight was almost too fast to follow. A flurry of exchanges, and the two stepped back, Siamis smiling. Kessler's expression remained blank.

Senrid thought: *What are Detlev and Siamis really after? Did you learn anything while they had you?*

Liere's mental response rocked him back with emotion-charged memory: *They wanted the dyr. Thought I had it.*

Kessler feinted, jabbed, fast as lightning. Siamis sidestepped lightly, just enough for the point to pass uselessly by his ear, and whipped his blade inside Kessler's guard—to find only air.

Senrid's mind ran with images, memories, connections as Kessler and Siamis circled one another on the ancient stone, worn smooth by millennia of flowing water.

The gift. The threat . . . Detlev's *You're not worth my time yet.* "They want us to grow up," Senrid murmured, as maintaining a conversation by Dena Yeresbeth took too much effort.

"Is that it?" Liere whispered, her gaze unwavering. "And then make us into Norsundrians? I never want to grow up, ever."

Senrid watched another flurry of attacks, feints, ripostes from Siamis and Kessler as he struggled against the conflict inside him. There were times when the Child Spell felt like a pair of boots that were too tight, only it was his spirit so confined. One day, he knew, he was going to get rid of the Child Spell.

But if Detlev and Siamis wanted him to do it now, for whatever reason, well, that was easy.

"So we won't," Senrid said, and because he could feel her longing for safety, he cast a fast scan behind them. "Rel's over there," he whispered as Siamis extended his blade in a deceptively leisurely strike, which Kessler evaded with minimal movement. "Let's go."

Liere gave a shaky sigh of relief, and tugged on his hand. Senrid followed, but walking backward. He did not want to miss what so far promised to be the duel of a lifetime. Senrid wasn't all that experienced in training, but he'd watched the academy boys train, and he could see that both Siamis and Kessler were in a class beyond the best the Marlovens had to offer as they circled, upper bodies motionless except for the subtle movements of eye and wrist as they exchanged blows, almost like a conversation.

He let Liere's hand go so he could watch.

Liere ran on a few steps, until she passed the water-carved archway. The illusion made Rel look weird, but she knew he was Rel from the mental plane. She stopped beside him, and shivered, every bruise aching, as she stared at the back of Senrid's head, knowing that Senrid would always stop to watch the duels. *But he will stay a child with me,* she thought. *He won't take the sword gift any more than I will.*

Senrid was not aware that he'd stopped.

Siamis sidestepped an attack, smiled past Kessler, his light gaze reaching across the cavern to meet Senrid's. He deliberately flashed the sword up in a mocking salute, and then returned to the attack.

Kessler's teeth showed at that salute. He had learned three things so far. One, that they were nearly matched in speed and strength. Two, Siamis's training was probably better, or Siamis could read his mind in spite of his mind-shield, because he always knew where Kessler was going to attack.

Third: he was not going to win this match.

But he could try. He flung himself into a risky attack high, low, high, double-bind. The blades rang, bringing a laugh of sheer pleasure from Siamis.

And then came a firm female voice: "The Witches are roused. You know what comes next."

Both swords lifted as the duelists glanced at the new arrival at the top of the stairs. Siamis recognized Lilith the Guardian, as she began whispering a spell. "Late," he said. "Again."

Then he made a motion, a token gleamed briefly, and he vanished: by accident or by intent he was gone before his sword, which stood in mid-air for the single beat of a heart, as if in mockery. Or challenge. Then it, too, was gone.

Kessler lifted his head, his expression disturbingly flat of affect. "Was that for you or for me?"

"I will have to consider," Lilith replied, looking down sadly. Kessler made a sign, murmured, and also vanished.

"Kessler knows magic?" Rel asked, from the cavern archway, where he, too, had been determined to watch that sword duel. "That's bad news. Terrible," he added under his breath.

"It seems he does," Lilith said. "But I believe he's just broken his enforced allegiance to Norsunder. He trusts no one, and with a background like his, who could blame him?"

"I could," CJ whispered from beside Clair.

Rel agreed, but he said nothing as Lilith descended the rest of the stairs. They all began to move, as if released from some kind of spell. Norsunder was truly gone—it began to sink in.

Liere's control gave way at last, and a deep sob shook her as she ran back and cast herself on the Guardian's comfortable bosom. For a time Lilith stood looking down at the tousled head, the unkempt hair hacked so badly, and her smile was tender.

Liere raised teary eyes. "I can't be Sartora. Why can't you stay and teach me?"

"You know my limitations," Lilith said softly. "And there is a world full of wise people who can teach you many things, even if they don't have your talent. But you have to listen to them."

Liere straightened up, aware of the sound of many footsteps as everybody reappeared from the far tunnel and crowded around. She wiped her eyes on her sleeve, and said, "Siamis didn't kill me. I thought he would."

Lilith looked at the space where Siamis had been. "Perhaps he had a trade in mind? Or he didn't want Detlev to keep you? I don't know. He is not your friend, but I wonder if he might be the enemy of your enemy."

Senrid snorted, then cut a fast glance at Liere, whose fingers clutched her elbows in the old worried manner. Moderating his voice, he said, "So why can't we use the dyr against them? It has to be powerful if they want it so badly."

Lilith had been staring at the air where that sword had been, her expression difficult to define, though it wasn't triumphant. Senrid remembered that *Late. Again.* He wondered what history lay behind it— then he remembered that Siamis had once been on the lighter side in the Fall, before he was taken as a child of twelve. Senrid wondered if Siamis was blaming Lilith for not saving him. Then he remembered what she'd said about her daughter, and winced.

Hibern and Rel stepped up to either side of Senrid and Liere as Lilith said, "Ordinarily I am a firm believer in sharing knowledge, and I know how annoying it is to hear 'I can't tell you.' But in this case, really.

Believe me. The less you know about those objects, the better for everyone." She raised her hand, palm out. "Yes, I am aware that to some, my words would act only as a goad. But there are so many better uses of your time, and pursuing the dyra will only bring further trouble."

By then all the others had joined them, Dak and Cath standing a little way away.

"Ah," Lilith said, and turned to Glenn and Tahra. "I wanted to tell you two that the news is perhaps not as dire as you feared. Your mother was taken prisoner. I am sorry to report that we know nothing more than that, but there is one good thing that is definite: your Uncle Roderic escaped from the Norsundrians. He is in Ferdrian now, with what remains of the Knights, busy restoring the city. They need you both."

Liere was saying to Arthur, "Senrid will have to straighten out the mess in his kingdom. Maybe it'll be done by New Year's, when I always visit." She sighed. "I have so much to learn."

Arthur smiled. "One thing about Bereth Ferian. Throw a pen and the ink will splash ten teachers."

Liere smiled at the mild joke, thinking of her quiet room, hot chocolate, books to read, and a walk among the beeches. She no longer wanted to join the Mearsieans, who couldn't seem to see Liere instead of Sartora, but that was all right. They wouldn't have come all this way to help if they didn't think Sartora was their friend, even if she wasn't a very good heroine.

They are all friends, Liere thought. The alliance is real.

Lilith turned her head to survey the gathering and lifted her voice. "All together, I see. Good. The Witches are ready to unite in sending you all home." She looked from one to another. "Siamis's enchantment is gone from Sartorias-deles, and I believe it will be impossible to use it again without its being removed instantly. The antidote is being spread to mages of both worlds."

"Hurray!" the Mearsieans shrieked. "We won! Siamis lost twice, ha ha!"

A noisy cheer went up.

*No, we didn't,* Senrid thought, remembering that mocking salute with the sword named Truth. *That wasn't a battle, it was a scouting foray.*

He didn't say it out loud, but it was heard by all those listening on the mental plane.

## Chapter Seven

*Sartorias-deles*

THE young allies found themselves transferred back to Delfina Valley, from which they all returned to their own homes.

Prince Glenn and Princess Tahra of Everon arrived to a devastated kingdom with only a few months in which to prepare for the winter ahead. The queen was still missing. Roderic Dei had survived his capture, and returned to hold the kingdom for the underage prince and princess. Most of the royal palace had been burned as well as looted, but the Sandrials had been cleaning what they could, and hauling back the things they'd saved. Everyone, from the two royal children to the servants, crowded into a single wing for winter.

Sarendan emerged from the enchantment to be plunged into grief for the loss of the gallant Derek Diamagan. Peitar Selenna, who shared similar personality traits with his exiled uncle as well as physical resemblance, threw himself into mastering magic with all the single-mindedness with which his uncle had once thrown himself into building military might—all to withstand the threat of Norsunder. Peitar understood that though Siamis and Detlev's race to find and control the Geth-deles transfer magic had failed, it was only a temporary setback.

Sartor emerged from the enchantment to discover that the erstwhile commander Bostian had been unable to keep his bored battalion from beginning to sack the city around their oblivious eyes. The guilds were quite angry with the mages for having failed, again, to stop the magic attack—and for having so diminished the Royal Guard that it could not stand against Bostian's invaders.

But at least the invaders themselves were gone: about the time the alliance first transferred to Geth, Siamis had had to drop his search for the source of Geth-deles's transfer magic to return to Eidervaen, which he wanted intact once he was successful.

Since Bostian had proved to have so little control over his command, Siamis confronted him, acidly pointing out that they were completely exposed to a flank attack from, for example, the Marlovens from the other side of the mouth of the Sartoran Sea. They were ordered to plan and drill a defense at the same harbor from which Henerek's army had departed. They marched south and east, and duly planned their defense.

On a wild summer night, they discovered that they *were* being invaded, and a sharp, nasty fight ensued until combatants discovered that they were nominally on the same side. This was Kessler's and Henerek's combined forces, back on the ships they had commandeered, assuming that Sarendan had been raised against them.

By the time the miscommunication was straightened out, orders came down to retreat to Norsunder Base.

Marloven Hess, which had not been invaded, merely had to resume normal life. The horses had enjoyed a splendid summer on the plains their ancestors had come from; the academy had only lost a couple of weeks, which customarily ended with a weeklong wargame in the plains. They had withdrawn deep into the plains, where their instructors taught them to forage, and conducted a protracted game. They returned, sunbrowned and lean, to find that the king was back.

When their families showed up to fetch them, Senrid had to endure questions, silent queries, and a certain amount of oblique chaffing for his having disrupted the entire kingdom for . . . nothing.

He endured it grimly, reflecting that at least he still held his throne.

The least disturbed was Chwahirsland, still in the grip of the glacially disintegrating time binding that Wan-Edhe had laid over Narad, the capital city. To that city, Jilo might never have been gone. To the rest of the kingdom, the season of planting resulted in a slightly more endurable winter than usual, though much bitterness arose in certain army factions at their having had to lower themselves to labors outside of the endless drill they were used to.

Jilo departed Tsauderei's sunlit, beautiful Valley, and transferred back into the toxic grip of that magic, where he got to work.

*Hibern: I promised myself I would inform you when Stefan was cured. Your father succeeded in removing the spells that your meddling made worse. Stefan is himself again, and though your father still refuses to acknowledge you, I asked your brother if he wished to see you home again. I know not what your father said to Stefan during their many wearying magical sessions, but Stefan's bitterness and resentment mirrors your father's.*

*Some day it might be different. I find my own anger abated, especially after many conversations with my own relations. I trust you are learning useful skills, but then you were always an excellent student. I wish you success in your endeavors, my daughter.*

*Tdor Askan*

*Peitar:*

*Lilah will surely tell you how much we talked about your visiting Sartor. I still cannot believe that you have yet to visit Eidervaen. Rel says that when he visits next, he hopes by then Sarendan will be settled, and you and Lilah will come, even if you can be away only for a few days.*

*I say 'by then' partly because I know how much is left to be done after recent events, and that includes a time for grief and memorial. I have made a vow to light a candle each year for Derek, whose gallantry will never be forgotten by any who knew and loved him.*

*But the other reason is because when I arrived back in Eidervaen, it was to discover that the royal Purrad, our labyrinth, which we often talked about showing you, had been destroyed by the parting Norsundrians in a final act of petty malice.*

*I say 'petty' because if the intent was to frighten us, it had the opposite effect. Everybody in the Eidervaen palace, from the smallest curtain runner to Chief Veltos, remembers exactly how it lay, and we have all made a vow to work together until every pebble, every plant, every chime, is replaced exactly the way it was. Their destruction will be erased as if it never happened.*

*Atan*

Atan sent the note and set the new notecase down as Julian entered, almost unrecognizable with her hair cut short to get rid of the impossible mats. Julian wore a neat child's tunic and comfortable riding trousers. Though they were made of unadorned cloth, they fit. What's more, Julian took them off at night, and even put them through the cleaning frame herself. She had decided that baths were the most wonderful thing ever invented, sometimes taking two in a day—one for serious and one for fun.

"What would you like to do?" Atan asked, with a pulse of guilt. But nobody would stop her if she abandoned the tight schedule the high council had bound her to. They were too busy dealing with angry guild leaders and envoys from other parts of the kingdom that the Norsundrians had marched through, taking what they wanted.

"Visit Hannla," Julian said. "She lets me push the broom, and gives me pastry if I do a good job."

"Very well. Maybe she'll let me push the broom, too, and we both can earn a pastry." Atan half-held her hand out, ready to drop it at the first sign of a scowl.

But Julian took that hand, letting out a sigh of contentment as they walked together downstairs.

*Marloven Hess*

Senrid's foot tapped in counterpoint to the enthusiastic thundering of hand drums played by Retren Forthan's old academy friends, gathered from all corners of Marloven Hess for Forthan's wedding to Fenis Senelac.

Fenis was a young bride now, a tall figure in her wedding robe of crimson, edged with shiny black cord and embroidered along hem and cuffs with blue and gold and green figures. It had been made by a many-greats-grandmother and worn by every Senelac bride since.

Senrid watched as she led the singing. Anyone seeing them would take her for Senrid's elder, though they had been born around the same time.

Senrid had survived. The army was back, the garrison as well. On the surface, everything looked normal—he had received a note from Liere, saying that she was now a student at Bereth Ferian's mage school.

Everything looked normal, and yet he knew it wasn't. He forced an attitude of good cheer as he watched Retren Forthan get to his feet, flushed with wine and with the genial, bawdy jokes of his friends. Forthan held his sword high over his head, hilt in one hand, tip balanced on his left fingers, as he began the wedding sword dance.

One by one the other young men joined as Fenis's friends took over the drumming. Men dancing, women watching, and soon they would turn about, making ribald comments—Senrid understood the words, but as yet the meaning was beyond him.

That was fine. He had enough to do, and to think about. Like that last salute of Siamis's. *Gift.* He kept coming back to that. He and Liere were the only ones with Dena Yeresbeth, which was more of a burden than anything else. Siamis's threat about gifts, his salute with the sword, had been aimed specifically at the two of them. Surely being singled out for oblique threat had to do with Dena Yeresbeth. So maybe, once Liere was used to her new school, they should try to seek out some kind of training—

His notecase ticked in his tunic pocket.

He'd gotten pretty good at remembering to check it. Satisfied that nobody was interested in the short figure sitting midway between the old folks and the children trying to gobble all the wedding tarts, he palmed the case from his pocket and unrolled the piece of paper.

*Chwahirsland*

*Senrid:*

*You were correct in what you said about laws that people can point at, that my granting things will look like favoritism and whim if some get what they want and others don't.*

*But we also know that Wan-Edhe could be sent back at any time. I had my first meeting with the army leaders. Uncle Shiam and his third cousins were there with me, as we talked about the future of our kingdom.*

We are agreed that Wan-Edhe will come when he or Norsunder wants, not when we are ready. But until then we shall live as if he will not.

Tsauderei knows about the book, and Mondros wrote to ask where it is. I told him it's stored beyond reach. Now that the secret is no longer a secret, there's no use in trying to discover who blabbed, because after all, it will be the first thing Wan-Edhe demands when he returns.

It reports that Siamis and Detlev are back at Norsunder Base. None of my tracers have alerted me to the presence of Kessler Sonscarna, but the book says he's been here. Twice. I wish I knew what that means.

*Jilo*

# Prelude

*North of Sartor*

**A**ND so the young allies survived their first action. I have endeavored in this, the first record of their alliance, to introduce them before I must introduce their adversaries, as yet unmet.

The last summer storm had washed the sky clear overhead, and left the newly turning leaves bright as jewels. Rel was descending the last of the mountain trail north of Sartor's border when he heard voices echoing through the trees, and a rising shout, "Help!"

Rel slung his pack onto a boulder and unloosed his sword as he splashed through the undergrowth to a clearing. The thud of retreating steps reached him, and a faint, floating laugh on the wind—the laugh of a teenage boy, from the sound—as he stumbled to a stop. There in the middle of the rain-soggy glade lay a boy, bright blotches of color marring the snow all around him.

Rel's gaze snapped to the crimson first, but as that was surrounded by bright splashes of blue and yellow, the fear that the boy's blood had been spilled vanished. It was paint. The boy struggled to rise, and Rel hastened to help him up. He was thin and gangling, in age anywhere from thirteen to eighteen. A pair of wide-set, mild brown eyes gazed out of a thin face half covered by a cloud of curly brown hair, now matted with mud.

"Thank you," the boy said breathlessly. "I don't know what they would have done if you hadn't come along." He looked around, blinking mud off his eyelashes before he wiped a grimy sleeve over his face. "At the very least, they would have smashed all my paints."

Rel looked around. Besides the paints, brushes and other artistic items lay scattered in the snow. "I'll help you." He sheathed his sword and began collecting scattered bits.

"Oh, look at that," the boy mourned. "Demolished my primaries, and it takes so very long to make the blue . . ." He wiped his face again, smearing the mud even worse, then stared in dismay at the splintered remains of little ceramic pots, the colors already soaking into the ground, impossible to retrieve.

Rel said, "There are a few unspilled. See? Three right here."

"Maybe a few more," the boy said with a hopeful air. "They flung them at the trees." He indicated a venerable oak, whose bark had been liberally lightened with a splash of yellow.

In a short time they'd gathered everything they could, and restored it to the boy's travel knapsack, which was full of papers.

"At least they didn't get to your work," Rel said when he discovered the knapsack on the far side of a mossy boulder, where it had obviously been thrown.

"That was probably next." The boy sounded resigned as he dropped the last of the salvaged art materials into the knapsack, then looked up at Rel.

Faint smears of paint streaked his face under the mud. Or maybe those were bruises. "Thank you again. Who are you?"

"Name's Rel. You?"

"Adam." His Sartoran was so good that Rel couldn't quite tell the origin of his accent, except that Adam didn't sound like the Sartorans. Nobody outside of those born in Sartor did, their accent being separated from the rest of the world's use of the language by a hundred years. "Are you going north toward the port city, by any chance?"

"Going through there, yes," Rel said. And, as was considered polite on the Wander, "Want company?"

Adam's relief was unmistakable.

Rel glanced behind them, then said, "Weren't you heading south toward Sartor?"

"I was," Adam admitted. "Someone warned me about brigands, but I didn't believe it. Someone else warned me that the Sartorans probably won't want itinerant art students. Maybe that warning is as good as the first. I can always go back some other time," he said. "That is, if the brigands don't do me in first."

"Have a weapon?" Rel asked as he started back along the path to retrieve his pack. "Any training?"

Adam held his muddy hands away from his sides, his grin rueful.

"I'll walk with you to the next town. You can report what happened."

Adam shrugged into his knapsack, then fell in step beside Rel. "Will it do any good?" he asked.

"Probably not, if you mean, will they go searching. I've been in this area before when brigands attacked, and they didn't do anything then. But there's always hope that the next report will convince someone they've had enough."

"If that's so, I guess I've a duty to be the next."

Adam talked cheerfully as they proceeded up the road, readily answering Rel's questions, not that he asked many. The etiquette of the Wander, Puddlenose had told Rel when they met on Rel's first journey, was not to delve into people's backgrounds unless they offered the information. But a few questions were considered permissible—What's your name? Where do you come from? Have any skills? If the answers were vague, then you dropped the questions, but if detail was offered, you could ask more.

Adam didn't seem interested in origins or whereabouts, anyway. He was far more enthusiastic about his artwork, something he clearly loved talking about.

By the time they glimpsed a market town beyond the last hill, Rel had learned that there were thirty basic sketch techniques, the benefits and drawbacks of dry watercolor versus wet on wet, and the difficulties of making color. "I shall have to start again," Adam finished ruefully. "Remaking my primaries." Then he ran off to a rocky bluff to catch sight of some winter bird, whose plumage he compared to the same sort of bird, but with slightly different plumage, as found farther north.

They stopped once when Adam spotted what he thought an artistically twisted tree, sat on a rock, and pulled out a rumpled sheet of sketch paper.

Rel watched him sketch, impressed. Adam had the shape of the entire tree suggested with no more than three quick, assured lines, then used the pencil to demonstrate a great many of those thirty techniques as he roughed in a bit of the corrugated bark, the gnarled shape, the shadows, the piny spines, the cones, and how the shadow lay on the piled-up leaves left from the recent storm.

Adam had an astonishing eye for detail, so when they reached the town and found the local magistrate, Rel expected such an exact description of the brigands that the miscreants could easily be identified.

What the magistrate got was a confused blur of contradictory facts, all of those hazy. Her exasperation manifested itself in gusty sighs as Adam dithered. "No . . . the leader was not as tall as Rel. Or maybe he was, but he was bent, some. And I was on the ground, so my perspective was distorted. How many? Well, that I'm not certain of. It felt like a gang, but there couldn't have been more than four or five. Three, at the very least."

The magistrate put down her pen. "That will do."

Adam said anxiously, "Is that enough? I am so sorry I don't seem to remember more. But I was so frightened, and then my face was in the mud . . ."

"No, no. It happens. The most assured witness can't always recollect the details, especially when you are taken by surprise," she said, and as Adam walked out, the woman caught Rel by the arm. "Look, you. I don't want to cast aspersions on our duchas, but as Sartor has not kept the old treaty, he's saying if he has to mount and pay for patrollers, then he ought to have a king's treasury, if you catch my meaning."

"I do," Rel said.

The magistrate nicked her chin in Adam's direction. "Your friend there clearly couldn't defend himself against a kitten. You had better see him to wherever he's going."

"I will," Rel said, and had a happy thought. Atan and Hibern were both determined to keep the alliance communicating, which meant a visit to Thad and Karhin Keperi in Colend. Hibern seemed to think that putting someone besides a bunch of busy young rulers in charge of communication was better than leaving everything haphazard.

Rel had agreed; any excuse to visit the Keperis was fine by him. He could see Adam fitting right in with Thad and Karhin. And everybody agreed, the alliance needed more members, if they really wanted it to be effective against Norsunder.

"Would you like to see some of Colend?" Rel asked. "I've friends there."

Adam hefted his knapsack. "I would like to meet them," he said.

# THE NURSE'S REFERENCE LIBRARY®

# Procedures

*Nursing83* Books™
Intermed Communications, Inc.
Springhouse, Pa.

*NURSING83*
BOOKS™

# Intermed Communications Book Division

**CHAIRMAN**
Eugene W. Jackson

**PRESIDENT**
Daniel L. Cheney

**VICE-PRESIDENT**
Timothy B. King

**RESEARCH DIRECTOR**
Elizabeth O'Brien

**PRODUCTION AND PURCHASING DIRECTOR**
Bacil Guiley

© 1983 by Intermed Communications, Inc., 1111 Bethlehem Pike, Springhouse, Pa. 19477

All rights reserved. Reproduction in whole or part by any means whatsoever without written permission of the publisher is prohibited by law. Patient-teaching aids in this book may be reproduced by office copier for distribution to patients. Written permission is required for any other use or to copy any other material in this book. Printed in the United States of America.

NRL5-01 12 82

**Library of Congress Cataloging in Publication Data**
Main entry under title:

Procedures.

    (The Nurse's reference library; 5)
    "Nursing83 books."
    Includes bibliographies and index.
    1. Nursing.  I. Series.    [DNLM: 1. Nursing
process—Methods.    WY 100 P96204]
RT41.P856   1983   610.73   82-15643
ISBN 0-916730-40-9

# NURSE'S REFERENCE LIBRARY® SERIES

## Staff for this volume

**EDITORIAL DIRECTOR**
Helen Klusek Hamilton

**CLINICAL DIRECTOR**
Minnie Bowen Rose, RN, BSN, MEd

**Senior Editorial Manager:** Matthew Cahill

**Editorial Manager:** Martin DiCarlantonio

**Senior Clinical Editor:** Regina Daley Ford, RN, BSN, MA

**Clinical Coordinator:** Susan M. Glover, RN, BSN

**Clinical Editors:** Joanne Patzek DaCunha, RN; Judith A. Schilling McCann, RN, BSN; Anne Moraca-Sawicki, RN, MSN; Anna Marie Seroka, RN, BSN, MEd, CCRN

**Drug Information Editor:** Larry N. Gever, RPh, PharmD

**Senior Editors:** Peter Johnson, Jerome Rubin

**Associate Editors:** June F. Gomez, William James Kelly, Patricia Minard, Alan M. Rubin

**Assistant Editors:** Holly Ann Burdick, H. Nancy Holmes, Patricia E. McCulla

**Graphics Coordinator:** Lisa Z. Cohen

**Production Coordinator:** Patricia Hamilton

**Copy Chief:** Jill Lasker

**Copy Editors:** Barbara Hodgson, Jo Lennon, David R. Moreau

**Contributing Copy Editors:** Andrea F. Barrett, Nancy L. Mack, Ruth A. Older, Barbara F. Ritter, Rebecca S. Van Dine

**Senior Associate Designer:** Kathaleen Motak Singel

**Associate Designer:** Linda Jovinelly Franklin

**Assistant Designers:** Jacalyn M. Bove, Christopher Laird

**Contributing Designers:** Marsha Drummond, Robert Walsh

**Illustrators:** Len Epstein, Robert Jackson, Dimitri Karentnikov, George Retseck

**Art Production Manager:** Robert Perry

**Art Assistants:** Virginia Crawford, Diane Fox, Don Knauss, Sandra Simms, Craig T. Simon, Louise Stamper, Joan Walsh, Ron Yablon

**Typography Manager:** David C. Kosten

**Typography Assistants:** Nancy Merz Ballner, Janice Haber, Ethel Halle, Diane Paluba, Nancy Wirs

**Production Manager:** Wilbur D. Davidson

**Quality Control Manager:** Robert L. Dean

**Editorial Assistants:** Maree E. DeRosa, Bernadette M. Glenn, Sally Johnson

**Researcher:** Vonda Heller

Special thanks to the following, no longer on the staff, who assisted in preparation of this volume: Brenda L. Moyer; Janet C. Stolar, RN, MSN; Pauline L. Wollack.

# Contents

™

# NURSE'S REFERENCE LIBRARY® SERIES

This volume is part of a new series conceived by the publishers of *Nursing83*® magazine and written by hundreds of nursing and medical specialists. This series, the NURSE'S REFERENCE LIBRARY, is the most comprehensive reference set ever created exclusively for the nursing profession. Each volume brings together the most up-to-date clinical information and related nursing practice. Each volume informs, explains, alerts, guides, educates. Taken together, the NURSE'S REFERENCE LIBRARY provides today's nurse with the knowledge and the skills that she needs to be effective in her daily practice and to advance in her career.

## *Other volumes in the series:*

Diseases
Diagnostics
Drugs
Assessment

## *Other publications:*

### NURSING SKILLBOOK® SERIES

Reading EKGs Correctly
Dealing with Death and Dying
Managing Diabetics Properly
Assessing Vital Functions Accurately
Helping Cancer Patients Effectively
Giving Cardiovascular Drugs Safely
Giving Emergency Care Competently

Monitoring Fluid and Electrolytes Precisely
Documenting Patient Care Responsibly
Combatting Cardiovascular Diseases Skillfully
Coping with Neurologic Problems Proficiently
Using Crisis Intervention Wisely
Nursing Critically Ill Patients Confidently

### NURSING PHOTOBOOK™ SERIES

Providing Respiratory Care
Managing I.V. Therapy
Dealing with Emergencies
Giving Medications
Assessing Your Patients
Using Monitors
Providing Early Mobility
Giving Cardiac Care
Performing GI Procedures
Implementing Urologic Procedures

Controlling Infection
Ensuring Intensive Care
Coping with Neurologic Disorders
Caring for Surgical Patients
Working with Orthopedic Patients
Nursing Pediatric Patients
Helping Geriatric Patients
Attending Ob/Gyn Patients
Aiding Ambulatory Patients
Carrying Out Special Procedures

### *Nursing83* DRUG HANDBOOK™

# Advisory Board

*At the time of publication, the advisors, contributors, and clinical consultants held the following positions:*

**Lillian S. Brunner, RN, MSN, ScD, FAAN,** Consultant in Nursing, Presbyterian–University of Pennsylvania Medical Center, Philadelphia.

**Donald C. Cannon, MD, PhD,** Professor, Pathology and Laboratory Medicine, Medical School, University of Texas Health Science Center, Houston.

**Luther Christman, RN, PhD,** Dean, Rush College of Nursing; Vice-President, Nursing Affairs, Rush University, Chicago.

**Kathleen A. Dracup, RN, MN, CCRN,** Research Fellow, Medicine/Cardiology, University of California, Los Angeles.

**Stanley J. Dudrick, MD,** Professor, Department of Surgery, University of Texas Medical School at Houston; St. Luke's Episcopal Hospital, Houston.

**Halbert E. Fillinger, MD,** Assistant Medical Examiner, Philadelphia County, Pa.

**M. Josephine Flaherty, RN, PhD,** Principal Nursing Officer, Department of National Health and Welfare, Ottawa.

**Joyce LeFever Kee, RN, MSN,** Associate Professor, College of Nursing, University of Delaware, Newark.

**Dennis E. Leavelle, MD,** Director, Mayo Medical Laboratories, Department of Laboratory Medicine, Mayo Clinic, Rochester, Minn.

**Roger M. Morrell, MD, PhD, FACP,** Professor, Neurology and Immunology/Microbiology, Wayne State University, School of Medicine, Detroit, Mich.; Chief, Neurology Service, Veterans Administration Medical Center, Allen Park, Mich.

**Ara G. Paul, PhD,** Dean, College of Pharmacy, University of Michigan, Ann Arbor.

**Rose Pinneo, RN, MS,** Associate Professor of Nursing and Clinician II, University of Rochester, N.Y.

**Thomas E. Rubbert, JD, LLB, BSL,** Attorney-at-Law, Los Angeles.

**Maryanne Schreiber, RN, BA,** Product Manager, Patient Monitoring, Hewlett Packard Co., Waltham Division, Waltham, Mass.

**Frances J. Storlie, RN, PhD, ANP,** Adult Nurse Practitioner, Vancouver, Wash.

**Claire L. Watson, RN,** Supervisor, Systems Support Department, IVAC Corporation, San Diego.

# Contributors

**Therese Altier, RN, BSN,** Assistant Head Nurse, Spine Unit, Rush-Presbyterian-St. Luke's Medical Center, Chicago.

**Iris Arnell, RN, BS, ET,** Educator I, Mount Sinai Medical Center, Miami Beach, Fla.

**Edward Averill, RN, BSN,** Head Nurse, Coronary Critical Care Unit, Veterans' Administration Hospital, Portland, Ore.

**Charold L. Baer, RN, PhD,** Professor, Chairperson, Department of Adult Health and Illness, School of Nursing, Oregon Health Sciences University, Portland.

**Mary M. Bailey, RN,** Emergency Department Staff Nurse, Inservice Coordinator, Fitzgerald Division, Mercy Catholic Medical Center, Darby, Pa.

**Amanda S. Baker, RN, PhD,** Associate Dean, College of Nursing, University of Florida, Gainesville.

**Jay Ellen Barrett, RN, BSN, MBA,** Former Coordinator of Staff Development, New England Baptist Hospital, Boston.

**Vicki Schwartz Beaver, RN, MS,** Assistant Professor, Vanderbilt University School of Nursing; Clinical Specialist, Vanderbilt University Medical Center, Nashville, Tenn.

**Diana R. Billman, RN, BSN,** Critical Care Instructor, Muhlenberg Medical Center, Bethlehem, Pa.

**Debra L. Blomstrann, RN,** Clinical Coordinator, Evanston (Ill.) Hospital.

**Heather Boyd-Monk, RN, SRN, BSN,** Educational Coordinator, Nursing Education, Wills Eye Hospital, Philadelphia.

**Peggy Boyle, RN,** Unit Leader, I.V. Therapy Department, Doylestown (Pa.) Hospital.

**Ann Marie Briggs, RN, MSN, FAAN,** Pulmonary Clinical Nurse Specialist, George Washington University Hospital, Washington, D.C.

**Dorothy A. Brooten, RN, PhD,** Chairperson, Health Care of Women and the Childbearing Family Section, School of Nursing, University of Pennsylvania, Philadelphia.

**Lorraine E. Buchanan, RN, MSN,** Project Coordinator, Regional Spinal Cord Injury Center of Delaware Valley, Thomas Jefferson University Hospital, Philadelphia.

**Priscilla A. Butts, RN, MSN,** Doctoral Candidate, New York University; Part-time Lecturer, Perinatal Division, University of Pennsylvania, Philadelphia.

**Carol A. Calianno, RN,** Staff, Warminster (Pa.) General Hospital.

**Mary Castle, RN, MPH,** Infection Control Consultant; Editor, *American Journal of Infection Control,* Denver.

**Glynis Smith Chadwick, RN, BSN,** Former Coordinator, Division of Clinical Nursing Education, Anne Arundel General Hospital, Annapolis, Md.

**Anita Jones Chinnici, RN, MSN,** Former Instructor, School of Nursing, West Virginia University, Charleston.

**Elizabeth K. Clay, RN, BA,** Former Director, Psychiatric Nursing Services, Warminster (Pa.) General Hospital.

**Susan Corbett, RN,** Dermatology Nurse, Skin and Cancer Hospital, Philadelphia.

**Joanne Patzek DaCunha, RN,** Clinical Editor, Nurse's Reference Library, Intermed Communications, Inc., Springhouse, Pa.; Staff, Critical Care Unit, Doylestown (Pa.) Hospital.

**Jane B. Daddario, RN, MSN,** Clinical Nurse Specialist of Obstetrics, Vanderbilt University Medical Center, Nashville, Tenn.

**Janet S. D'Agostino, RN, MSN,** Pulmonary Clinician, St. Elizabeth's Hospital, Brighton, Mass.

**Deborah Dalrymple, RN, BSN,** Staff, Doylestown (Pa.) Hospital; Clinical Instructor, Montgomery County Community College, Blue Bell, Pa.

**Helen Hahler D'Angelo, RN, MSN,** Clinical Consultant, Nurse's Reference Library, Intermed Communications, Inc., Springhouse, Pa.

**Kathy Kirk Davidson, RN, C, BSN,** Director of Regional Perinatal Education, Vanderbilt University Medical Center, Nashville, Tenn.

**Catherine Davis, RN, MSN,** Assistant Professor of Nursing, Hahnemann College of Allied Health Professions, Philadelphia.

**Margaret Copp Dawson, RN, BA, BS,** Nurse Clinician I, Burn Center, University of Michigan Hospital, Ann Arbor.

Janice M. Didich, RN, BSN, MA, Clinical Instructor, Northeast Missouri State University, Kirksville.

Marianne L. Dietrick-Gallagher, RN, MSN, Staff Development Instructor, Hospital of the University of Pennsylvania, Philadelphia.

Susan Dodds, RN, BSN, Head Nurse, Homestead Nursing Home, Willow Grove, Pa.

Susan Donahue, RN, BSN, Staff, Critical Care Unit, Rolling Hill Hospital, Elkins Park, Pa.

Diane K. Dressler, RN, MSN, Clinical Nurse Specialist, Milwaukee.

L. Ruth Driscoll, RN, Former Instructor, School of Practical Nursing, Anne Arundel General Hospital, Annapolis, Md.

Catherine E. Egea, RN, Head Nurse, Outpatient Renal Dialysis Unit, BioMedical Applications, Abington, Pa.

Shirley L. Egger, RegN, Teacher, Intensive Care Nursing, Toronto Western Hospital.

Barbara Boyd Egoville, RN, MSN, Former Instructor, Critical Care Nursing, Lankenau Hospital School of Nursing, Philadelphia.

DeAnn M. Englert, RN, MSN, Assistant Professor, Louisiana State University Medical Center School of Nursing, New Orleans.

Peggy Felice, ET, Enterostomal Therapist, Crozer-Chester Medical Center, Chester, Pa.

Kathy A. Fonda, RN, BSN, Head Nurse, General Hospital of Virginia Beach, Va.

Jane Geer Frankenfield, RN, BSN, Former Staff, Hale Makua Home Health Services, Kahului, Hawaii.

Patricia L. Fuchs, CRTT, RRT, Pediatric and Critical Care Respiratory Therapist, Hartford (Conn.) Hospital.

Kathleen E. Viall Gallagher, RN, MSN, Clinical Consultant, Nurse's Reference Library, Intermed Communications, Inc., Springhouse, Pa.

Susan M. Glover, RN, BSN, Clinical Coordinator, Nurse's Reference Library, Intermed Communications, Inc., Springhouse, Pa.

Carol Ann Gramse, RN, PhD, Assistant Professor of Nursing, Hunter-Bellevue School of Nursing, New York.

Margaret J. Griffiths, RN, MSN, Assistant Professor, Department of Baccalaureate Nursing, Thomas Jefferson University, Philadelphia.

Mary J. Hall, RN, MA, Author, Editor, Consultant, Philadelphia.

Winifred Still Hayes, RN, C, MS, ANP-C, Doctoral Candidate, School of Hygiene and Public Health, Johns Hopkins University, Baltimore.

Jane Ellen Helfant, RN, BA, Clinical Education Manager, Therapeutic Plasma Exchange, Cobe Laboratories, Inc., Lakewood, Colo.

Denise A. Hess, RN, Supervisor, Cardiac and Nuclear Cardiac Exercise Laboratories, Hospital of the University of Pennsylvania, Philadelphia.

Nancy E. Hilt, RN, MSN, Editor, Orthopedic Nursing; Writer, Consultant, Charlottesville, Va.

Sheila Scannell Jenkins, RN, BSN, Graduate Student, University of Connecticut School of Nursing, Storrs; Instructor, Nursing of Children, Bridgeport (Conn.) Hospital School of Nursing.

Gail Johnson, RN, Staff, Neonatal Unit, Hamilton Memorial Hospital, Dalton, Ga.

Sue M. Jones, RN, C, MSN, FNC, Assistant Professor, Community Health Nursing, Vanderbilt University, Nashville, Tenn.

Bonnie Joyce Kaplan, RN, MS, Assistant Professor, Department of Nursing, Anne Arundel Community College, Arnold, Md.

Nancy Kennedy, RN, MSN, Assistant Director of Nursing for Staff Development, General Hospital of Virginia Beach, Va.

Joanne Rossman Keys, RN, BSN, Staff, Postpartum Unit, Anne Arundel General Hospital, Annapolis, Md.

Kristen Kindel, RN, Staff, Neurosurgical Intensive Care Unit, Duke University Medical Center, Durham, N.C.

Kristine M. Kroner, RN, BSN, Head Nurse, Urology, Albert Einstein Medical Center—Northern Division, Philadelphia.

Rochelle Druker Kuhn, RN, MS, Assistant Professor, Hahnemann College of Allied Health Professions, Philadelphia.

Angela D. Lehman, RN, Staff, Doylestown (Pa.) Hospital.

Judith A. Schilling McCann, RN, BSN, Clinical Editor, Nurse's Reference Library, Intermed Communications, Inc., Springhouse, Pa.

Ellen A. McFadden, RN, MS, Assistant Professor, School of Nursing, University of Maryland, Baltimore.

Dianne Monkowski Magnuson, RN, BSN, Staff, Doylestown (Pa.) Hospital.

Catherine A. Maguire, RN, BSN, Instructor in Critical Care, Saint Francis Hospital, Wilmington, Del.

Maria Maiaroto-Gross, RN, BSN, Former Director of Nursing, Dialysis Unit, BioMedical Applications, Abington, Pa.

Eileen M. Markmann, RN, Staff, Critical Care Unit, Doylestown (Pa.) Hospital.

**Sue Dullea Markus, RN, BSN,** Chemotherapy Research Nurse, Baltimore (Md.) Cancer Research Center.

**Patricia Gonce Miller, RN, MS,** Instructor, University of Maryland School of Nursing, Baltimore.

**Royanne A. Moore, RN, MSN,** Nurse Coordinator, Fetal Intensive Care Unit, Vanderbilt University Hospital, Nashville, Tenn.

**Anne Moraca-Sawicki, RN, MSN,** Clinical Editor, Nurse's Reference Library, Intermed Communications, Inc., Springhouse, Pa.

**Kathryn M. Murray, RN,** Nurse Manager, Obstetrics, Doylestown (Pa.) Hospital.

**Susan A. Murray, RN, BSN,** Nurse Epidemiologist, New England Medical Center, Boston.

**Elaine M. Musial, RN, CS, MSN,** Dialysis/ Transplant Patient Care Consultant, Thomas Jefferson University Hospital, Philadelphia.

**Patrice M. Nasielski, RN,** Staff, Los Robles Regional Medical Center, Thousand Oaks, Calif.

**Barbara R. Nassberg, RN, BSN, ET,** Enterostomal Therapist, Mt. Sinai Medical Center, Miami Beach, Fla.

**Helene Ritting Nawrocki, RN,** Director of Education and Training, Delaware Valley Medical Center, Bristol, Pa.

**Paula Stephens Okun, RN, MSN,** Instructor, Gwynedd-Mercy College, Gwynedd Valley, Pa.

**Neal L. Peyser, MA, CCC-A,** Audiologist, Lecturer, Northwestern University, Chicago.

**Phyllis Pletz, RN, MSN,** Assistant Professor, Community College of Allegheny County, Pittsburgh.

**Alice F. Prieto, RN, BSN,** Former Industrial Representative, Bux-Mont Emergency Care Center, Warminster, Pa.

**Nancy Redfern, RN, MSN,** Clinical Nurse Specialist, Orthopedics, Children's Hospital of Philadelphia.

**Mary M. Faut Rodts, RN, MS,** Nurse Practitioner; Assistant Professor, Rush College of Nursing, Rush University, Chicago.

**Loretta Romano, RN,** Infection Control Coordinator, Doylestown (Pa.) Hospital.

**Marie J. Rose, RN, MSN, CCRN,** Senior Clinical Nurse, Cardiac Progressive Care Unit, Walter Reed Army Medical Center, Washington, D.C.

**Dennis G. Ross, RN, MSN,** Assistant Professor of Nursing, Castleton (Vt.) State College.

**Nancy Roth, RPT, MMSc,** Administrative Supervisor, Physical Therapy, Emory University Hospital, Atlanta.

**Valerie Saad, RN, BS,** Staff, Operating Room, Allentown (Pa.) and Sacred Heart Hospital Center.

**Sheron L. Salyer, RN, C, BSN,** Perinatal Research Nurse, Vanderbilt University Hospital, Nashville, Tenn.

**Jean L. Sawyer, RN, BSN, MA,** Instructor, Coordinator, Sophomore Medical-Surgical Nursing, Creighton University, Omaha.

**Anna M. Seroka, RN, MEd, CCRN,** Clinical Editor, Nurse's Reference Library, Intermed Communications, Inc., Springhouse, Pa.

**Suzanne Marr Skinner, RN, MS,** Lecturer, University of Maryland School of Nursing, Baltimore.

**Dorothy W. Smith, RN, EdD, FAAN,** Professor of Nursing, Rutgers University, Newark, N.J.

**Rae Nadine Smith, RN, MS,** Clinical Nursing Specialist, Sorenson Research Company, Salt Lake City.

**Sharon Spilker, RD, BS,** Dietician, Thomas Jefferson University Hospital, Philadelphia.

**Janet C. Stolar, RN, MSN,** Former Clinical Editor, Nurse's Reference Library, Intermed Communications, Inc., Springhouse, Pa.

**Frances J. Storlie, RN, PhD, ANP,** Adult Nurse Practitioner, Vancouver, Wash.

**Arlene Strong, RN, MSN, ANP,** Cardiac Clinical Specialist, Veterans' Administration Medical Center, Portland, Ore.

**Karen Sweet, RN, LLB,** Student-At-Law, Gottlieb, Hoffman, Chaiton, and Kumer, Toronto.

**Maryellyn Tison, RN, BS,** Clinical Instructor, Emergency Nurse Training Program, San Francisco General Hospital.

**Robin Tourigian, RN, MSN,** Nurse Clinician, Oncology Unit, Thomas Jefferson University Hospital, Philadelphia.

**Karen Dyer Vance, RN, BSN,** Clinical Consultant, Nurse's Reference Library, Intermed Communications, Inc., Springhouse, Pa.

**Susan Vigeant, RN, BSN,** Staff, Department of Corrections, Bucks County Health Department, Warrington, Pa.

**Connie A. Walleck, RN, MS, CNRN,** Nurse Clinician II, Research Assistant, University of Maryland Hospital, Baltimore.

**Lois J. Wendorf, RN, ET,** Supervisor of Nurses, Colon and Rectal Surgery, Mayo Clinic, Rochester, Minn.

**Gayle R. Whitman, RN, MSN, CCRN,** Cardiothoracic Clinical Specialist, Cleveland Clinic Hospital.

**Sandi Wind, RN, ET,** Enterostomal Therapist, Hahnemann Medical College and Hospital, Philadelphia.

# Clinical Consultants

**Lucy Jo Atkinson, RN, MS,** Director of Educational Services, Ethicon, Inc., Somerville, N.J.

**Garfield W. AuCoin, RN,** Surgical and Clinical Assistant, Bradenton (Fla.) Orthopaedic Associates.

**Kimberly S. Baker, RN, BSN,** Staff Nurse, Critical Care Units, Medical City Dallas Hospital.

**Cynthia L. Balin, RN, MSN, CCRN,** Clinical Specialist, Wilmington (Del.) Medical Center.

**Marilyn J. Bayne, RN, BSN, MS,** Assistant Professor, Junior Year Faculty, University of Maryland School of Nursing, Baltimore.

**Majorie Davis Beck, RN,** Charge Nurse, Gastrointestinal Procedure Unit, Abington (Pa.) Memorial Hospital.

**Diana R. Billman, RN, BSN,** Critical Care Instructor, Muhlenberg Medical Center, Bethlehem, Pa.

**Debra C. Broadwell, RN, MN, ET,** Program Director, Enterostomal Therapy Educational Program, Emory University School of Medicine, Atlanta.

**Glynis Smith Chadwick, RN, BSN,** Former Coordinator, Division of Clinical Nursing Education, Anne Arundel General Hospital, Annapolis, Md.

**Francis J. Connelly, Jr., BS,** Ocularist, Philadelphia.

**Sue Crow, RN, MSN,** Infection Control Nurse, Louisiana State University Medical Center Hospital, Shreveport.

**Helen Hahler D'Angelo, RN, MSN,** Clinical Consultant, Nurse's Reference Library, Intermed Communications, Inc., Springhouse, Pa.

**Jeanne Dupont, RN,** Head Nurse, Emergency Department, Massachusetts Eye and Ear Infirmary, Boston.

**Barbara Boyd Egoville, RN, MSN,** Former Instructor, Critical Care Nursing, Lankenau Hospital School of Nursing, Philadelphia.

**Deborah J. Fleischmann, RN, BSN,** Nurse Clinician II, Nursing Supervisor, SIDS Institute, University of Maryland School of Medicine, Baltimore.

**Maj. Loretta Forlaw, ANC, MSN,** Clinical Nurse Specialist, Nutritional Support, Walter Reed Army Medical Center, Washington, D.C.

**Jody Foss, RN, MSN, CEN,** Nurse Educator, Project Director, Emergency Nurse Training Program, Trauma Center Foundation, San Francisco General Hospital.

**Janis A. Gallagher, RN,** Coordinator, I.V. Therapy, New England Deaconess Hospital, Boston.

**Kathleen E. Viall Gallagher, RN, MSN,** Clinical Consultant, Nurse's Reference Library, Intermed Communications, Inc., Springhouse, Pa.

**Susan M. Gerhart, RN, MN,** Pediatric Patient Unit Coordinator, Milton S. Hershey Medical Center of Pennsylvania State University, Hershey.

**Sheila A. Glennon, RN, MA, CCRN,** Clinical Supervisor, Neurosurgery, Mount Sinai Hospital and Medical Center, New York.

**Mary Chapman Gyetvan, RN, BSEd,** Clinical Consultant, Nurse's Reference Library, Intermed Communications, Inc., Springhouse, Pa.

**Mary J. Hall, RN, MA,** Author, Editor, Consultant, Philadelphia.

**Elizabeth Ridgely Hayter, RN, CCRN,** Senior Clinician, Surgical Intensive Care Unit, Johns Hopkins University Hospital, Baltimore.

**Rebecca Umbower Hones, RN, BSN, MS,** Staff, Sacred Heart Hospital, Norristown, Pa.

**Maribeth Inturrisi, RN, MS,** Obstetrical Clinical Specialist, University of California Medical Center, San Francisco.

**Capt. Betty C. Jones, ANC, BSN,** Clinical Head Nurse, Adult Respiratory Disease Unit, Walson Army Hospital, Fort Dix, N.J.

**Claudella Jones,** Administrator, National Institute for Burn Medicine, Ann Arbor, Mich.

**Lynda G. Kramer, RN, BSN,** Health Facilities Surveyor, West Virginia Department of Health, Charleston.

**Suzanna Joy Kravitz, RN, BA,** Community Health Nurse, Philadelphia.

**Jeannette P. LaChat, RN, BSN,** Head Nurse, Shady Grove Dialysis Center, Rockville, Md.

**Angela D. Lehman, RN,** Staff, Critical Care Unit, Doylestown (Pa.) Hospital.

**Linda A. Lewandowski, RN, MS,** Pediatric Clinical Nurse Specialist, Yale–New Haven Hospital; Assistant Professor, Yale University School of Nursing, New Haven, Conn.

**Ann D. McClure, RN, BA, MSN,** Former Instructor of Nursing, Montgomery County Community College, Blue Bell, Pa.

**Dianne Monkowski Magnuson, RN, BSN,** Staff, Doylestown (Pa.) Hospital.

**Judith E. Meissner, RN, MSN,** Senior Associate Professor, Bucks County Community College, Newtown, Pa.

**Susan Nevins, RN, CNRN, MA,** Clinical Instructor, Neurosurgical Unit, Mount Sinai Medical Center, New York.

**Susan Oehme, RN, BSN,** Former Staff Nurse, Loudoun Memorial Hospital, Leesburg, Va.

**Paula Stephens Okun, RN, MSN,** Instructor, Gwynedd-Mercy College, Gwynedd Valley, Pa.

**Betsy Ovitt, RN, BSN, CCRN,** Nursing Director, St. Mary's Hospital Burn Center, Milwaukee.

**Maureen Quinn-McKeown, RN, MA,** Assistant Director of Nursing, Magee Rehabilitation Hospital, Philadelphia.

**Lisa Sehrt Rodriquez, RN, BSN,** Instructor, Coordinator of Staff Development in Medical-Surgical Areas, Ochsner Hospital, New Orleans.

**Leslie K. Sampson, RN, CCRN,** Assistant Director of Continuing Nursing Education for Critical Care, Medical College of Pennsylvania, Philadelphia.

**Nancy J. Scott, BSN,** Former Pediatric Supervisor, Anne Arundel General Hospital Annapolis, Md.

**Norma J. Selders, RN, BSN,** Head Nurse, Pharmacy Technician Training and Management, Ohio State University Hospitals, Columbus.

**Barbara Gorham Slaymaker, RN, BSN, CRNP,** Adult Nurse Practitioner, Doylestown, Pa.

**Helen Toman, RN, CCRN,** Senior Clinical Nurse, SICU, Johns Hopkins Hospital, Baltimore.

**Karen Uleckas, RN,** Staff, Anne Arundel General Hospital, Annapolis, Md.

**Karen Dyer Vance, RN, BSN,** Clinical Consultant, Nurse's Reference Library, Intermed Communications, Inc., Springhouse, Pa.

**Susan Vigeant, RN, BSN,** Staff, Department of Corrections, Bucks County Health Department, Warrington, Pa.

**Elaine Gilligan Whelan, RN, MA, MSN,** Assistant Professor of Nursing, Bergen Community College, Paramus, N.J.

**Johnsie Whitt Woody, RN,** Respiratory Nurse Clinician, Duke University Medical Center, Durham, N.C.

# Foreword

Ministrations, acts of aid or service to the patient, are the heart and soul of nursing. Sweeping changes may transform the face of the profession—the emergence of unions, nurses entering private practice—but they can't shake the simple, timeless truth that nurses take care of people.

Yet there has never been a reference book to which nurses could turn for information that combines the details of technique with specific rationale when describing those daily acts of aid or service—those ministrations—which occupy so much of our time.

We often rely on hospital procedure manuals for such information. These manuals are useful but are likely to have important limitations. Committees assigned to updating them may not find time to keep them current. Parochialism inevitably creeps in, making it difficult to recognize commonalities applicable to varied clinical settings.

This latest volume in the Nurse's Reference Library overcomes these problems and superbly fills the long-standing need for a definitive book on nursing procedures. An excellent and exhaustive resource, PROCEDURES emphasizes the practical aspects of nursing care. In precise, step-by-step fashion, it details the correct method for performing many nursing tasks—from the relatively simple, like making an occupied bed, to the complex, such as intraaortic balloon pumping.

The book is divided into two parts. The first covers fundamental nursing skills—facilitating mobility, for example, and controlling infection—that may be used for virtually all patients. The second discusses procedures for diagnosing, monitoring, and treating patients with disorders or conditions associated with various body systems. Chapters on neonatal and pediatric procedures round out the book. Throughout, scores of helpful illustrations, charts, and diagrams clarify and augment the text. A special full-color section summarizes recent advances in equipment. The inside front cover provides a useful guide to priorities in cardiac arrest. The inside back cover provides an index of the procedures that are most often used in emergency situations.

Each chapter begins with a brief introduction that offers general information relevant to the procedures that follow. Each entry begins with a concise introduction describing the procedure and its purpose, the various indications for its use, specific nursing responsibilities, and any contraindications that may exist. The entry continues with *Equipment*, a complete list of equipment and supplies needed to perform the procedure and, when applicable, instructions on how to prepare them.

*Essential Steps*, the core of each entry, then takes the reader through the procedure one step at a time, explaining how the necessary equipment is used and, as appropriate, presenting the rationale for each step in graphically highlighted form.

This emphasis on the rationale is especially helpful. Remembering how to do a procedure correctly is easier when the underlying reason for doing it that way is clear. Moreover, understanding the scientific foundations for a procedure makes devising reasonable variations easier. The nurse who understands *why* certain steps are done also understands when they can be safely varied or omitted; she can then vary the procedure according to changing circumstances, instead of doing it in a mechanical way.

Throughout, a special graphic device, the Nursing Alert, calls attention to conditions and parts of the procedure that involve particular hazard to the patient. A discussion of *Special Considerations* follows with significant precautions, potential complications, and any other relevant information. Finally, *Documentation* specifies aspects of the procedure and associated observations that must be recorded.

The material is presented clearly in a no-nonsense style, with the underlying assumption that the reader is a competent professional who can take the information and adapt it to her own institution's unique requirements.

Realistically, no nurse can be expected to be intimately familiar with every step of every procedure that might confront her during her practice. This book will help the nurse to master new and unfamiliar tasks and will serve as a refresher for procedures performed only infrequently. For students, PROCEDURES will prove an indispensable companion, smoothing their entrance into the profession with reliable guidelines for the successful performance of initially bewildering clinical techniques.

Practicing nurses in any clinical setting will find this volume a useful reference.

DOROTHY W. SMITH, RN, EdD, FAAN

# Overview

An old Zen story tells of the impertinent disciple who, after sharing a simple meal with his master, asked the meaning of life.

The master replied with a question of his own: "Are you finished eating?"

"Yes," said the disciple.

"Then clean your bowl," said the master.

Life, in other words, often holds no deeper meaning than doing what is necessary. Perhaps that's deep enough.

Nursing too has its "unwashed bowls," which we sometimes tend to push aside unthinkingly, intent on exploring larger matters that we deem worthier of our attention. We call them "procedures." They're not terribly exciting to think about and even less thrilling to do. All that step-by-step, first-you-do-this-then-you-do-that business: inserting intravenous lines, administering enemas.

But procedures are *necessary*. There's no getting around them; somebody's got to do them, and 9 times out of 10 that somebody will be a nurse. Good patient care demands that we perform countless procedures daily. And they must be done correctly, professionally, with strict attention to detail.

The challenge is to find a way to make the successful completion of a procedure—no matter how mundane—personally rewarding, to discover the meaning of nursing in these repetitive, often monotonous tasks. How to meet this challenge?

**Step One: Look for Principles**

We can start by recognizing that every nursing procedure owes its existence to certain fundamental principles. For example, the principle behind lubricating a nasogastric tube before insertion is simple but extremely important to patient comfort: Rubbing one dry surface against another produces friction, which in turn produces pain in the patient. Lubricating the tube with jelly, ice, or water allows it to pass smoothly along the nasal and esophageal mucosa without damaging the delicate membranes.

Consider endotracheal tubes. Why do you inflate the cuff on an endotracheal tube for the patient on a ventilator?

Answer: You inflate the cuff with just enough air to close the space between the tube itself and the tracheal mucosa so that the alveoli will receive precisely the right mixture of gases, as controlled by the ventilator. Air can't enter the lungs by any other means. Also, the inflated cuff secures the tube in place, making it impossible for the patient to extubate himself while coughing or retching.

For every nursing procedure there is an underlying anatomic or physiologic premise. Taking the time to consider this premise before performing a procedure not only makes an unappealing task more interesting, but also helps you avoid mistakes. Most procedural errors, I believe, result from failure to comprehend the rationale behind the procedure.

**Step Two: Know Your Equipment**
Equipment, of course, is the nuts and bolts of procedures, and therein lies another nursing problem. Over the years the equipment needed for most nursing procedures has undergone continuous revamping and remodeling. The earliest blood pressure apparatus, to take an extreme example, obviously had to be modified since most nurses would find it cumbersome to lug a 6-foot water column from bedside to bedside.

Today's nurse must work with a whole new generation of sophisticated machines, some of which must be adjusted frequently according to patient responses. With the modern volume-cycled ventilators, for example, the patient's color, respiratory rate, and effort in breathing tell the nurse which settings on the equipment must be changed. Nurses must know about negative and positive pressures, flow rates, and sighing ratios. They must take all these things into account when caring for a patient maintained on ventilatory assistance.

The problem is that equipment invariably separates the patient from the nurse. A recent patient of mine illustrates this point. Jack, age 65, had severe left ventricular disease and needed a coronary artery bypass graft. I wanted to explain the operation to him, but every time I entered Jack's room I first had to survey the equipment that was keeping him alive. There were the four intravenous solutions that must not be allowed to run out, the balloon pump to be monitored, and pressure readouts and EKG strips to be studied.

It took me 3 to 5 minutes to go through this ritual. Meanwhile, Jack, the patient, waited. A less experienced nurse may have needed as much as 15 minutes to conduct the same surveillance!

The only way to bridge this gap between you and the patient is to become so familiar with the intervening equipment that you can perform whatever procedure is necessary in the absolute minimum of time. This is the soundest argument yet for the so-called technical school of nursing, which tends to emphasize the ability to work smoothly and competently with devilishly intricate equipment over more humanistic nursing responsibilities, such as empathizing with the patient and allowing him to express his fears and concerns. Ideally, what we want are nurses who can do both—handle the equipment without tying themselves in knots, yet never lose sight of the human being at the other end of all that marvelous machinery and fancy tubing.

**Step Three: Thank Heaven for Kits**
Fortunately, kits have simplified the task of assembling equipment, reducing the amount of time it takes to perform many nursing procedures. Where once we gathered the cotton balls, the catheter, the drainage bag, the antiseptic solution, and so on, before inserting a urinary catheter, now we just take a kit containing all the essential equipment from the shelf. We can use ready-made kits for inserting chest tubes, for performing a lumbar puncture, and for emergency tracheostomy, to name a few.

The drawback to kits, besides the cost, is the need to memorize a whole roster of brand names—the Cobe clamp, the Jackson-Pratt drainage system, the

Swan-Ganz catheter, for example. The list goes on and on. But surely this is a small price to pay for the convenience of working with preassembled equipment that's ready for immediate use.

### Step Four: Put Yourself in the Patient's Shoes

The patient, however, doesn't care how long it *used to* take a nurse to perform such-and-such a procedure. All he knows is how many minutes—anxious minutes, for him—it takes to do it now. Often he imagines himself a victim of all these contraptions. We've all heard patients tell their relatives or friends: "I guess I must be worse. They put this tube in my nose again." Or, "They're taking my blood pressure every half hour now. I wonder what's going on."

Subtly or openly, the patient measures his progress, or lack of it, as much by the procedures performed on him as by anything his doctor might tell him. This only reinforces the nurse's obligation to know modern medical equipment inside and out, and to become so expert in performing procedures that she can virtually do them with her eyes closed. The more familiar you are with a procedure, the better prepared you'll be to explain its significance to the patient in clear, simple language he can understand. And, needless to say, the patient's confidence in your ability to care for him competently will be given a real boost. No one wants to be cared for by a nurse who "doesn't know which end is up," as I once heard a patient complain.

### Step Five: Clean Bowl

Procedures, in short, needn't be dull or intimidating. By looking for underlying principles, we can learn much from them. By becoming proficient with equipment that inevitably accompanies so many everyday nursing tasks, we can actually move closer to the patient. And the closer we get to him, the nearer we draw to the heart of nursing.

So, with apologies to the old Zen master, we can well imagine the following exchange in response to any impertinent questions about the meaning of nursing:

"Do you have a procedure to do?"

"Yes."

"Then do it."

FRANCES J. STORLIE, RN, PhD

# 1

# Basic Care Procedures

# Basic Care Procedures

## Introduction

According to American Hospital Association statistics, about 37 million patients are admitted to U.S. hospitals every year. Except for women who are admitted for childbirth, most patients face hospitalization reluctantly and rightly so. Hospitalization implies an illness or condition that requires professional management and also carries various potential stressors. For example, the hospital's distance from the patient's home can discourage visits by family and friends, who usually provide comfort and support and, at times, assist with care. The size and type of hospital can also color the patient's response: admission to a large teaching hospital usually carries different connotations than admission to a small community hospital. Previous hospitalizations can shape the patient's reaction to his present stay; familiarity with hospital routines and equipment usually helps ease anxiety, but previous negative experiences exaggerate it. The circumstances of admission profoundly affect the patient's response; scheduled admission for a relatively benign condition surely causes less stress than emergency admission.

Perhaps most important, hospitalization challenges the patient's sense of privacy and control of his life. Inevitably, the patient relinquishes at least part of his normal routine. Illness may also force him to depend on others for his fundamental needs for nutrition, elimination, and personal hygiene. To counteract this invasion of privacy, the patient may establish territorial "ownership" of his area of the room, his supplies, and his bed. Respect the patient's territorial rights by knocking before entering the room and by asking permission to rearrange equipment or his possessions. Carefully handle his valued possessions and any assistive devices. If possible, involve the patient in planning and implementing his care, to promote independence and enhance self-image.

### Promoting a comfortable environment

Physical factors in the patient's environment—temperature, humidity, lighting—can affect his comfort, condition, and, at times, response to treatment. A room temperature of 68° to 72° F. (20° to 22° C.) and a relative humidity of 30% to 60% is usually comfortable for most patients, but elderly patients often prefer a warmer temperature. Proper artificial or natural lighting helps orient the patient to day and night. Keeping lights on or window shades raised during the day and lights out (except night-lights) during the night duplicates the day-night cycle. A night-light that illuminates the floor around the bed without shining in the patient's eyes is best for comfort and safety. Darkening the patient's room for daytime naps aids sleep.

## Providing sensory stimulation

Sensory stimulation informs the patient about his environment and contributes to his well-being. Although the amount and type of stimulation varies with each patient, accurate assessment of his needs helps prevent sensory overload or deprivation. When evaluating stimuli in the patient's environment, remember that illness induces stress and may intensify the patient's response, especially to noise and odors. Minimize irritating noise by keeping conversation at the nurses' station and in corridors at a subdued level. Minimize odors by promptly removing and cleaning bedpans, changing soiled linens, and disposing of withered flowers.

Touching the patient during routine care furnishes stimulation and conveys concern that provides comfort and eases feelings of isolation. Remember, however, that patients vary greatly in their capacity to give and receive touch. To use therapeutic touch effectively, first recognize your own feelings about touching and then develop sensitivity to the patient's response.

## Promoting patient safety

Besides weakening the patient, illness and any accompanying treatment may impair his judgment and contribute to accidents. Be alert to hazards in the patient's environment and, when possible, teach the patient and his family to recognize them.

*To prevent falls:*
• Wipe up spilled liquids and powders immediately. Post signs and instruct the patient to avoid freshly washed or waxed floors.
• Tell the patient to wear shoes or slippers with low heels and nonslip soles.
• Keep the patient's bed in a low position except when giving care. For the confused or pediatric patient, always keep bed side rails raised. For most other patients, raise side rails at night.
• Before patient transfer, lock the wheels of the bed, stretcher, wheelchair, or commode. After transfer, secure safety straps, if appropriate.
• Keep the call button, the telephone, and personal items within the patient's sight and reach.
• If ordered or necessary, apply appropriate restraints to the confused, restless, or combative patient.

*To prevent electrical hazards:*
• If the patient brings an electrical appliance from home, follow hospital policy regarding its use. (Many hospitals prohibit use of ungrounded personal appliances.)
• Inspect the power cord and plug of all electrical equipment. Immediately report frayed cords, exposed wiring, or loose wall outlets. Use three-pronged plugs to ground equipment.
• If you feel a tingling sensation when handling equipment, cords, or metal objects, report this immediately, because it may signal current leakage. Watch for sparks, smoke, or overheating during equipment use.

*To prevent fires:*
• Enforce smoking regulations. Post signs and inform visitors of ongoing oxygen therapy.
• Never allow a disoriented or sedated patient to smoke without supervision.
• In areas where smoking is allowed, provide ashtrays.
• Become familiar with the location and operation of fire extinguishers. Know your hospital's fire codes and evacuation procedure.

*To prevent scalds and burns:*
• Check the water temperature before the patient enters a bathtub or shower.
• Before filling a hot-water bottle, test the water temperature; after filling it, tightly secure its cap and check for leaks. Always insert a hot-water bottle, heating pad, or aquamatic pad in a protective cover before use. During infrared lamp treatment, evaluate tissue condition frequently to avoid overexposure.

Despite these safety measures, incidents may still occur. When they do, prompt reporting and thorough documentation safeguards the patient, the hospital, and the nursing staff.

SUSAN M. GLOVER, RN, BSN

## ADMISSION CARE

# Admission Procedures

*Admission to the nursing unit prepares the patient for his hospital stay. Whether admission is scheduled or follows emergency room treatment, effective admission procedures should accomplish the following goals: verify the patient's identity and assess his clinical status, make him as comfortable as possible in his new and sometimes threatening environment, introduce him to the persons who will share his space or manage his daily care, provide supplies and special equipment needed for daily care, and show personal concern for his well-being.*

*Because admission procedures can color the patient's perception of the hospital environment, they have significant implications for subsequent treatment. Admission routines that are efficient and show appropriate concern for the patient ease anxiety and promote cooperation and receptivity to treatment. In the opposite situation, admission routines that the patient perceives as careless, inefficient, or excessively impersonal can exaggerate anxiety, diminish cooperation, inhibit response to treatment, and even aggravate symptoms.*

## Equipment

Hospital gown □ thermometer □ emesis basin □ bedpan and/or urinal □ bath basin □ water pitcher, cup, and tray □ urine specimen container, if needed.

An admission pack usually contains soap, comb, toothbrush, toothpaste, mouthwash, water pitcher, cup, tray, lotion, tissues, and a thermometer (if an electronic thermometer is not used). Because the patient pays for this pack, he can take it home at the end of his hospital stay. An admission pack helps prevent cross-contamination and increases nursing efficiency by providing basic items at each patient's bedside.

The central supply department provides the other equipment.

## Preparation of equipment

Obtain a gown and admission pack for the patient. Then prepare the patient's room. Position the bed as the patient's condition requires. If the patient is ambulatory, place the bed in low position; if he is arriving on a stretcher, place the bed in high position. Fold down the top linens.

Next, adjust the lights, temperature, and ventilation in the room. If the patient requires emergency or special equipment, such as oxygen or suction, prepare it for use.

## Essential steps

• When the patient arrives on the unit, greet him by name and introduce yourself and any staff present. Be sure to speak slowly and clearly.

• Compare the name and hospital number on the patient's identification bracelet with that listed on the admission form. Verify the name and its spelling with the patient. Notify admission office of any corrections.

• Quickly review the admission form and the doctor's orders. Note the reason for admission, any restrictions on activity or diet, and any orders for specimens for laboratory analysis. Institute stat orders as indicated.

• Escort the patient to his room and, if he's not in great distress, introduce him to his roommate. Then, wash your hands and help him change into a hospital gown or pajamas; if the patient is sharing a room, provide privacy. Itemize all valuables, clothing, and prostheses on the nursing assessment form; if your hospital doesn't use such a form, itemize the patient's belongings in your notes. Encourage the patient to store valuables or large sums of money in the hospital safe or, preferably, to send them home. Show the ambulatory patient where the bathroom and closets are.

● Next, take and record the patient's vital signs, and collect a urine specimen, if ordered. Measure the patient's height and weight if his condition allows it. Don't ask the patient for this information. If the patient can't stand, use a chair or bed scale and ask him his height. *Knowing the patient's height and weight is important for planning treatment and diet and for calculating dosages of medication and anesthetic.*

● Show the patient how to use the equipment in his room. Be sure to include the call system, intercom, emergency call button, bed controls, TV controls, telephone, and lights.

● Explain the hospital routine. Tell the patient when to expect meals, checks of vital signs, and medications. Inform him of the visiting hours and of any restrictions on visiting.

● Take a complete patient history. Include all previous hospitalizations, illnesses, surgeries, current drugs, and food or drug allergies. Ask the patient to tell you why he came to the hospital. Record the answers, in the patient's own words, as the chief complaint. Follow up with a physical assessment, emphasizing complaints. If you discover any marks, bruises, or discolorations, record them on the nursing assessment form. Take as few notes as possible when with the patient; jot down key words, then complete the assessment form outside the room.

● After assessing the patient, inform him of any tests that have been ordered and when they are scheduled. Describe what he should expect.

● Before leaving the patient's room, make sure he's comfortable and safe. Adjust his bed, and place the call button and other equipment (such as water pitcher and cup, emesis basin, and tissues) within easy reach.

● Notify the doctor of his patient's arrival.

### EMERGENCY ADMISSION

For the patient admitted through the emergency room, treating his special needs overshadows routine admission procedures. After treatment is given, the patient arrives on the nursing unit with a temporary identification bracelet, a doctor's order sheet, and a record of emergency room treatment. Read this record, and then talk to the nurse who cared for the patient in the emergency room, to ensure continuity of care and to gain insight into the patient's condition and behavior.

Next, record any ongoing treatment, such as I.V. infusion, in your notes. Take and record vital signs, give ordered medication as needed, and follow the doctor's orders for treatment. If the patient is conscious and not in great distress, carefully explain any treatment orders. Otherwise, delay your explanation. If family members accompany the patient, ask them to wait in the lobby while you assess and begin treatment of the patient. Then, allow them to visit the patient after he's settled in his room. After the patient's condition improves, proceed with routine admission procedures.

### Special considerations

If the patient doesn't speak English and isn't accompanied by a bilingual family member, contact the appropriate resource (usually social service) to secure an interpreter.

If the patient brings medication from home, take an inventory and record this information on the nursing assessment form. Instruct the patient not to take any medication unless authorized by the doctor. Send authorized medication to the hospital pharmacy for identification and relabeling. Send other medication home with a responsible family member, or store it in the designated area outside the patient's room until he's discharged. *Use of unauthorized medication may interfere with treatment or cause overdose.*

Find out the patient's normal routine, and ask him if he would like any adjustments to the hospital regimen; for instance, he may prefer to shower at night instead of in the morning. *By accommodating the patient with such adjustments whenever possible, you can ease his anxiety and help him feel more in control of his situation.*

## Documentation

After leaving the patient's room, complete the nursing assessment form or your notes. The completed form should include the patient's vital signs, height, weight, allergies, and drug and health history; a list of his belongings; the results of physical assessment; and a record of laboratory specimens.

JOANNE PATZEK DACUNHA, RN

---

# Patient Identification

---

*The fundamental means for verifying the patient's identity, the identification bracelet helps prevent errors in patient care. The permanent bracelet, usually issued during scheduled admission, contains the patient's hospital identification number, full name, room and bed numbers, and doctor's name. The temporary bracelet, issued before emergency room treatment, contains the same information plus the number of the patient's emergency room record. Whether permanent or temporary, the bracelet must be checked before every treatment, surgery, diagnostic test, and administration of medication.*

## Equipment

Plastic identification bracelet □ paper tab (designed to slip inside bracelet).

Most bracelets are waterproof to protect the paper tab from spills, which can blur detail. Some hospitals imprint patient information on a plastic bracelet, eliminating the paper tab.

## Essential steps

● When the patient arrives on the nursing unit, check to see if he's wearing an identification bracelet. If he's not, obtain the patient's hospital iden-

tification number, full name, room and bed numbers, and doctor's name from the admission office. Record this information on the bracelet, then secure the bracelet on the patient's wrist. Don't fasten it too tightly, *because this may constrict circulation and interfere with I.V. therapy or taking radial pulse.*

If the patient is wearing a bracelet, verify the information on it. If you discover an error, return the bracelet to the admission office for correction.

● Always check the patient's bracelet before every treatment, surgery, diagnostic test, and administration of medication. Compare the patient's hospital identification number with that listed on the medication cardex or the request slip, *because two patients may have the same name.*

## Special considerations

In many hospitals, the nursing unit is responsible for updating the patient's identification bracelet. If the patient is transferred to another bed or to a different doctor's care, remove and discard the outdated bracelet, and issue a corrected one. Include all unchanged information, such as the patient's hospital identification number.

If the identification bracelet is damaged or lost, replace it.

If you must remove the bracelet, immediately place a new one on a different wrist or ankle. Never tape a bracelet to the bed, because the patient's identity can't be verified if he is moved.

Avoid fastening the bracelet to an arm that requires surgery or that is likely to swell, because the bracelet will then have to be removed.

JOANNE PATZEK DACUNHA, RN

---

# Care of the Patient's Belongings

---

*Proper care of the patient's valuables, clothing, and personal possessions be-*

gins at admission and continues throughout the patient's hospital stay. Documenting all belongings at admission and encouraging the patient to store valuables in the hospital safe or, preferably, to send them home helps prevent loss or damage and protects you and the hospital from claims of negligence or theft.

Documentation of belongings during emergency room treatment proves especially important, because valuables may have been lost or damaged before admission. Such documentation should be witnessed by the patient (if possible), the nurse, and another staff member.

### Equipment
Personal property form □ envelope for valuables □ pen.

### Essential steps
• Explain to the patient that you will record his belongings and store them safely, then gather his valuables, clothing, and personal possessions.
• First, encourage the patient to send home all unnecessary belongings and valuables. Then, urge him to store those valuables not sent home in the hospital safe until discharge, to prevent loss or damage.
• Itemize and fully describe all remaining belongings on the patient's personal property list. Then, ask the patient to read and sign the list to protect yourself and the hospital against charges of negligence or theft.
• Store personal items, such as glasses and clothing, in the bedside stand or closet to prevent loss or damage.
• Place valuables in a secure valuables envelope, and list the contents on the outside. Seal the envelope, have the patient sign it, and send it to be placed in the hospital safe, usually located in the business office.
• According to hospital policy, update the patient's personal property list whenever items are brought from home, sent home, or discarded.
• On discharge, help the patient gather his belongings and, if applicable, retrieve his valuables from the hospital safe. Tell him he must sign a statement verifying receipt of his valuables.

### Special considerations
If the patient wears dentures, place them in a container labeled with its contents, the patient's name, and his room number. Don't wrap the dentures in paper or place them on the patient's meal tray, because they may be mistakenly discarded. If the patient was admitted from the ED, his clothing was placed in a properly labeled bag. When this bag arrives on the nursing unit, you can ask the patient's family to take it home. If no one accompanied the patient at admission, store the bag in the patient's closet until he can send it home. In the latter case, include this bag on the personal property list, the cardex, or in your notes, so the patient won't forget it at discharge.

### Documentation
Itemize and clearly describe all the patient's belongings on the personal property list. Update this list when items are brought from home, sent home, or discarded.
JOANNE PATZEK DACUNHA, RN

## VITAL SIGNS & PHYSICAL EXAM

# Temperature

Body temperature, one of the vital signs, represents the balance between heat produced by metabolism, muscular activity, and other factors and heat lost through the skin, lungs, and body wastes. A stable temperature pattern promotes proper function of cells, tissues, and organs; a change in this pattern usually signals onset of illness.

Temperature can be measured with a mercury, electronic, or chemical-dot thermometer. Oral temperature in adults normally ranges from 97° to 99.5° F. (36.1° to 37.5° C.); rectal temperature, the most accurate reading, is generally 1° F. higher; axillary temperature, the least accurate, 1° to 2° F. lower. Temperature normally fluctuates with rest and activity, with lowest readings generally recorded in the early morning between 4 and 5 a.m.; the highest, between 4 and 8 p.m. Other factors also influence temperature: sex—women normally have higher temperatures than men, especially during ovulation; age—normal temperature is highest in newborns and lowest in the elderly; emotion—heightened emotions raise temperature, depressed emotions lower it; and external environment—heat raises temperature, cold lowers it.

Oral measurement is contraindicated in patients who are unconscious, disoriented, or seizure-prone; in young children and infants; and in patients with oral or nasal impairment that necessitates mouth breathing. Rectal measurement is contraindicated in patients with diarrhea, recent rectal or prostatic surgery or injury (because it may injure inflamed tissue), or recent myocardial infarction (because anal manipulation may stimulate the vagus nerve, causing bradycardia or other rhythm disturbance).

## Equipment
With mercury thermometer (oral, stubby, or rectal): water-soluble lubricant or petrolatum (for rectal temperature) □ tissue □ disposable thermometer sheath (optional) □ alcohol sponge.

With electronic thermometer: oral or rectal probe □ disposable probe cover □ water-soluble lubricant or petrolatum (for taking rectal temperature) □ tissue.

Disposable chemical-dot thermometer.

## Preparation of equipment
A thermometer may be included as part of the admission pack. If it is, keep it at the patient's bedside and, on discharge, allow him to take it home. Otherwise, obtain a thermometer from the nurse's station or central supply department, and bring it to the patient's bedside.

## Essential steps
• Explain the procedure to the patient, and then wash your hands.

For mercury thermometers:
• With your thumb and forefinger, grasp the thermometer at the end opposite the bulb.
• If the thermometer has been soaking in a disinfectant, rinse it in cold water. Rinsing removes chemicals that may irritate mucous membranes of the mouth or rectum, or the skin of the axilla. Avoid using hot water. Hot water causes the mercury to expand and may break the thermometer. Using a twisting motion, wipe the thermometer from the bulb upward.
• Then, quickly snap your wrist to shake down the mercury. Shaking causes the mercury to recede into the bulb. When temperature is taken, the mercury expands in response to heat and rises in the thermometer. If the thermometer isn't shaken, the mercury remains at the previous reading because of constriction above the mercury tip of the thermometer. When shaking down the mercury, be careful not to strike the thermometer against your uniform or on nearby furniture or equipment.
• Next, hold the thermometer at eye level in good light and rotate it slowly until the mercury line becomes visible. A reading of 95° F. (35° C.) contributes to accurate measurement.
• To use disposable sheaths over the mercury thermometer, disinfect the thermometer with an alcohol sponge. Insert it into the disposable sheath opening, then twist to tear the seal at the dotted line. Pull apart. Using sheaths decreases contamination and reduces

# TYPES OF THERMOMETERS

| TYPE | MECHANISM OF ACTION | ADVANTAGES | DISADVANTAGES |
|------|---------------------|------------|---------------|
| **Mercury** <br> Oral <br> Rectal <br> Stubby | Heat expands mercury | • Easy to store <br><br> • Inexpensive <br><br> • Readily available | • Accuracy varies despite manufacturers' efforts to standardize. <br><br> • Risk of breakage and cross-contamination <br><br> • Temperature recorded more slowly than with other thermometers. <br><br> • Mercury column difficult to read. |
| **Electronic** <br> Oral, rectal | Heat alters the amount of current running through a resistor | • Rapid recording and easy-to-read temperature <br><br> • Extremely accurate when properly charged and calibrated <br><br> • Reduces risk of glass breakage. <br><br> • Easy to store <br><br> • Eliminates risk of cross-contamination | • Equipment is expensive, but nursing time saved may offset cost. <br><br> • Recalibration required occasionally. |
| **Chemical dot** | Heat initiates a chemical reaction | • Eliminates risk of cross-contamination and breakage <br><br> • Records temperature faster than mercury thermometer | • Improper storage may cause inaccuracy. <br><br> • Adapter needed for rectal use. <br><br> • Plastic strip in patient's mouth may cause discomfort. |

*cleansing time of thermometers.*
*To take oral temperature:*
• Before inserting the thermometer, ask the patient if he has drunk hot or cold liquids, chewed gum, or smoked within the past 15 to 20 minutes. If he

has, delay taking his temperature for 30 minutes, *because these factors may affect the reading.*

• Then, position the bulb of the thermometer under the patient's tongue, as far back as possible, on either side of the frenulum linguae. *Placing the bulb in this area promotes contact with abundant superficial blood vessels and contributes to an accurate reading.*

• Instruct the patient to close his lips but to avoid biting down with his teeth. *Biting can break the thermometer, cutting the mouth or lips or causing ingestion of broken glass.*

• Leave the thermometer in place for 8 to 10 minutes to register the temperature of the tissues.

• Then, grasp the end of the thermometer, and carefully remove it from the patient's mouth.

• Using a twisting motion, wipe the thermometer with a tissue, to remove mucus that may obscure the mercury column. Or, remove and discard the disposable sheath, if used.

• Read the thermometer at eye level. Then, shake down the mercury.

*To take rectal temperature:*
• Position the patient on his side, with his top leg flexed, and drape him to provide privacy. Then, fold back the bed linens to expose the anus.

• Lubricate about ½″ (1.5 cm) of the bulb of the thermometer for an infant, about 1½″ (4 cm) for an adult. *Squeeze the lubricant onto a wipe to prevent contamination of the lubricant supply. Lubrication reduces friction and thus eases insertion.* This step is unnecessary when using disposable rectal sheaths, because they're prelubricated.

• Next, lift the patient's upper buttock, and insert the thermometer about ½″ for an infant, 1½″ for an adult. Gently direct the thermometer along the rectal wall toward the umbilicus *to avoid perforating the anus or rectum or breaking the thermometer and to ensure an accurate reading (the thermometer will then register the temperature of the hemorrhoidal artery instead of any feces present).* Feces

may increase temperature *because of the heat given off during decomposition.*

• Hold the thermometer in place for 3 minutes. *Holding it prevents damage to the rectal tissues caused by displacement or loss of the thermometer into the rectum.*

• Carefully remove the thermometer, and wipe it with a tissue, using a twisting motion. *Wiping removes fecal matter, which may obscure the mercury column.* Or, remove and discard the disposable sheath, if used.

• Read the thermometer at eye level. Then, shake down the mercury.

• Wipe the patient's anal area to remove any lubricant or feces.

*To take axillary temperature:*
• Position the patient supinely, with the axilla exposed.

• Gently pat the axilla dry with a tissue, because moisture conducts heat. Avoid harsh rubbing, which generates heat.

• Then, ask the patient to place his hand over his chest and to grasp his opposite shoulder, lifting his elbow.

• Next, position the thermometer in the axilla, with the bulb pointing toward the patient's head.

• Tell the patient to continue grasping his shoulder and to lower his elbow and hold it against his chest. *This promotes contact of the thermometer with the skin.*

• Leave the thermometer in place for 11 minutes. *Axillary temperature takes longer to register than oral or rectal temperatures, because the thermometer isn't enclosed in a body cavity.*

• Then, grasp the end of the thermometer and remove it from the axilla.

• Wipe the thermometer with a tissue, using a twisting motion. *Wiping removes sweat, which may obscure the mercury column.* Or, remove and discard the disposable sheath, if used.

• Read the thermometer at eye level. Then, shake down the mercury.

*To clean mercury thermometers:*
• After taking temperature, examine the thermometer for residual mucus,

# CONTINUOUS TEMPERATURE MONITORING

A continuous temperature monitoring device detects body temperature through various sensors—tympanic, nasopharyngeal, esophageal, rectal, skin, or urinary catheter—and sounds an alarm when it deviates from preset limits. This portable, battery-powered device is especially useful in critical-care units where temperature changes can be crucial. It can also monitor temperature during surgery and help detect postoperative recovery. After sensors are in place, ready the device as follows:
• Set the on-off knob to °F. or °C.
• Set the high-low limits for each temperature site (1, 2, and 3). First, set the temperature site knob to 1. Next, simultaneously press the high alarm button and the increase or decrease alarm set button to adjust the limit. Do the same with the low alarm button. Turn the temperature site knob to 2 and then 3, repeating for each setting. To check limits after setting them, press the high or low alarm button.
• After setting the limits, connect the cable(s) to the three-temperature site connector. Secure the alligator clip on the connector to the patient's surgical drape or gown to avoid strain on sensor wires.
• Next, using the toggle, open the cable connector and insert the flat sensor end into the cable connector. Press the front of the toggle to secure the connection.
• Turn the temperature site knob to the desired number; the reading will be displayed after 10 seconds. For multisite monitoring, rotate the temperature site knob and allow 10 seconds between readings. If the room is dark, press the display light button to illuminate the readout.
• When temperature deviates from preset limits, the temperature reading flashes, ALARM appears on the display, and an alarm sounds. To silence the alarm, press the alarm off button at the back of the device.

---

sweat, or stool, all of which *can hinder the action of the disinfectant.*
• Apply soap or detergent solution to loosen debris and promote cleansing.
• Then, rinse the thermometer in cold water to remove debris and soap. *Soap residue can interfere with the action of the disinfectant.*
• Dry the thermometer well, *because water can dilute the disinfectant.*
• Next, place the thermometer in the disinfectant and allow it to soak, as indicated. Soaking time varies with the disinfectant and its concentration.
• After disinfection, rinse the thermometer in cold water.
• Store the thermometer according to hospital policy. Thermometers usually don't have to be kept sterile, because they are used in unsterile body cavities.
*To take oral temperature with an electronic thermometer:*
• Insert the oral probe into the disposable probe cover.
• Position the probe under the patient's tongue, as far back as possible, on either side of the frenulum linguae.
• Then, instruct the patient to close his lips.
• Leave the probe in place until the maximum temperature appears on the digital display. In some units, a buzzer sounds when the maximum temperature is reached; in others, a light goes on.
• After noting temperature, remove the probe from the patient's mouth.
*To take rectal temperature with an electronic thermometer:*
• Insert the rectal probe into the disposable probe cover.
• Position the patient on his side, with his top leg flexed. Then, drape him to provide privacy.
• Lubricate the probe cover *to reduce friction and ease insertion.*
• Next, lift the patient's upper buttock, and gently insert the probe into the anus.
• Leave the probe in place until the

maximum temperature appears on the digital display.

• After noting temperature, carefully remove the probe. Wipe any lubricant or feces from the anal area.

• Remove the probe cover with a tissue or press the button on the probe to eject the cover. Return the probe to its holder.

*To use a disposable chemical-dot thermometer:*

• Remove the thermometer from its protective dispenser case. To do so, grasp the handle end with your thumb and forefinger. Then, move the handle up and down to break the seal. Next, pull the handle straight out. Be sure to keep the thermometer sealed until use, *because opening it activates the dye dots.*

• Position the thermometer tip under the patient's tongue, as far back as possible, on either side of the frenulum linguae.

• Then, instruct the patient to close his lips.

• Leave the thermometer in place for at least 45 seconds.

• Grasp the thermometer and remove it from the patient's mouth. Read the temperature as the last dye dot that has changed color, or fired.

• Discard the thermometer and its dispenser case.

### Special considerations

Use the same thermometer for repeated temperature-taking, to avoid spurious variations caused by equipment differences.

Rinse mercury thermometers in cold water to prevent breakage. Also, never use an oral thermometer to take rectal temperature. Unlike the blunt bulb of the rectal thermometer, the long, slender bulb of the oral thermometer may puncture or injure rectal tissues.

Return electronic thermometers to their chargers so they'll be ready for use when needed again.

Store chemical-dot thermometers in a cool area, because exposure to heat activates the dye dots.

Don't delay or refrain from taking

oral temperature of the patient receiving nasal oxygen, because oxygen administration raises oral temperature only about 0.3° F.

Don't take an axillary temperature immediately after bathing the axilla, because the water temperature and the friction of washing and drying can affect the temperature.

### Documentation

Record the time, route, and temperature on the patient's chart.

JOANNE PATZEK DACUNHA, RN

# Pulse

*The arterial pulse is a recurring fluid wave that courses through the arteries when blood is pumped into an already full aorta during ventricular contraction, flaring its walls. It's most easily detected by palpation where an artery crosses over bone or firm tissue. Common pulse sites are the temporal, carotid, brachial, radial, femoral, and dorsalis pedis arteries. In adults and children over age 3, the radial artery is usually most accessible and can be easily compressed against the radius, so the radial pulse is usually taken; in infants and children under age 3, the apical pulse is best.*

*An apical-radial pulse is taken by simultaneously counting apical and radial beats—the first by auscultation at the apex of the heart, the second by palpation at the radial artery. Some heartbeats detected at the apex aren't strong enough to be detected at peripheral sites. When this occurs, the apical pulse rate is higher than the radial; the difference between the two rates is the pulse deficit.*

*Because the pulse reveals heart function, it's considered a vital sign and is routinely taken to assess overall health. Pulse-taking involves determining the rate (number of beats per minute), rhythm (pattern or regularity of the beats), and volume (amount of blood pumped with each beat).*

### Equipment
Watch with second hand □ stethoscope (for apical pulse) □ alcohol sponge.

### Preparation of equipment
If you're not using your own stethoscope, disinfect the earpieces with an alcohol sponge before and after use, to prevent cross-contamination.

### Essential steps
● Wash your hands, and tell the patient you will take his pulse.
*For radial pulse:*
● Place the patient in a sitting or supine position, with his arm at his side or across his chest. Make sure the patient is comfortable and relaxed, *because an awkward, uncomfortable position may affect the heart rate.*
● Gently press your index, middle, and ring fingers on the radial artery, inside the patient's wrist. You should feel a pulse with only moderate pressure; *excessive pressure may obstruct blood flow distal to the pulse site.* Don't use your thumb to take the patient's pulse, *because its own strong pulse may be confused with the patient's.*
● After you've located the pulse, count the beats for 30 seconds if the rhythm is regular. Then, multiply by 2 to determine the rate. While counting the rate, assess pulse rhythm and volume by noting the pattern and strength of the beats.
● If the patient's pulse is irregular, count for a full 60 seconds. *Counting for a longer period provides a more accurate picture of irregularities.* Repeat the count, if necessary, because pulse irregularities are important signs. If doubt remains, take an apical pulse.
*For apical pulse:*
● Position the patient supinely and drape him.
● Warm the diaphragm of the stethoscope in your hand before applying it to the patient's chest. *Placing a cold diaphragm against the skin may startle the patient and momentarily increase the heart rate.*
● Place the diaphragm of the stethoscope over the apex of the heart, located at the fifth intercostal space, left midclavicular line. Then, insert the earpieces in your ears.
● Move the diaphragm to the site of the loudest beats. Count the beats for 60 seconds, and note their rhythm and volume. Also evaluate the intensity (loudness) of heart sounds.
● Remove the stethoscope and make the patient comfortable.
*For apical-radial pulse:* Two nurses work together to obtain the apical and radial pulses; one palpates the radial pulse while the other auscultates the apical pulse with a stethoscope; both must use the same watch when count-

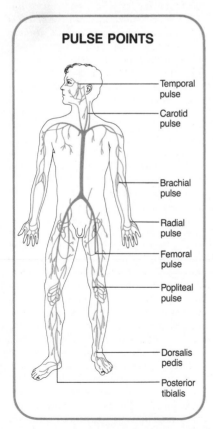

**PULSE POINTS**

Temporal pulse
Carotid pulse
Brachial pulse
Radial pulse
Femoral pulse
Popliteal pulse
Dorsalis pedis
Posterior tibialis

## IDENTIFYING PULSE PATTERNS

| TYPE OF PULSE RATE AND RHYTHM | CAUSES AND INCIDENCE |
|---|---|
| **Normal pulse rate:** 60 to 80 beats/minute; in newborns, 120 to 140 beats/minute | • Varies with such factors as age, physical activity, and sex (men usually have lower pulse rates than women) |
| **Tachycardia:** pulse rate above 100 beats/minute | • Accompanies stimulation of the sympathetic nervous system by emotional stress—anger, fear, anxiety—or certain drugs, such as caffeine<br>• May result from exercise and conditions, such as congestive heart failure, anemia, and fever (which increases oxygen requirements and therefore pulse rate) |
| **Bradycardia:** pulse rate below 60 beats/minute | • Accompanies stimulation of the parasympathetic nervous system by drugs—especially digitalis—and such conditions as cerebral hemorrhage and heart block<br>• May also be present in fit athletes |
| **Irregular pulse:** uneven time intervals between beats (for example, periods of regular rhythm interrupted by pauses or premature beats) | • *Premature beats:* occasional—may occur normally; frequent—may indicate cardiac irritability, hypoxia, digitalis overdose, potassium imbalance, or sometimes more serious arrhythmias |

*Note:* Strips represent 3 seconds.

ing beats.
• Position the patient supinely and drape him.
• Next, locate the apical and radial pulses.
• Determine a time to begin counting. Then, count beats at the same time for 60 seconds.

### Special considerations

When the peripheral pulse is irregular, take an apical pulse to measure the heartbeat more directly.

If a second nurse is not available to help take an apical-radial pulse, you can hold the stethoscope in place with the hand that holds the watch while palpating the radial pulse with the other hand. You can then feel any discrepancies between the apical and radical pulses.

### Documentation

Record pulse rate, rhythm, and volume and the time of measurement. Full or bounding describes a pulse of increased volume; weak or thready, decreased volume. When recording apical pulse, include intensity of heart sounds. When recording apical-radial pulse,

# DETECTING BLOOD FLOW WITH DOPPLER ULTRASOUND

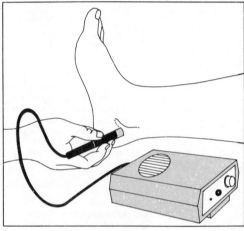

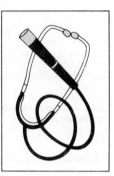

More sensitive than palpation for determining pulse rate, the Doppler ultrasound blood flow detector is especially useful when pulse is faint or weak. Unlike palpation, which detects arterial wall expansion and retraction, this instrument detects the motion of red blood cells.

**To use the Doppler:**
• Apply a small amount of coupling gel— *not* EKG paste or cream—to the ultrasonic probe, which resembles a microphone.
• Position the probe on the skin directly over the selected artery: in the illustration directly above, the probe is over the posterior tibial.
• When using a Doppler model as shown in the illustration at left, turn the instrument on and, moving counterclockwise, set the volume control to the lowest setting. If the Doppler doesn't have a speaker, plug in the earphones and slowly raise the volume. Some Dopplers, like the one shown in the illustration at right, have neither speakers nor earphones: for these, the binaural is needed to hear the sound. If you're trying to detect pulse in deep, small, or obstructed arteries, turn the volume control near maximum.
• To obtain the best signals, tilt the probe 45° from the artery, making sure there is gel between the skin and the probe. Slowly move the probe in a circular motion to locate the center of the artery and the Doppler signal—a hissing noise at heartbeat. Avoid rapid movement of the probe, which distorts the signal.
• Count the signals for 60 seconds to determine pulse rate.
• Next, clean the probe with a soft cloth soaked in antiseptic solution or soapy water. *Don't immerse the probe or bump it against a hard surface.*

chart the rate according to the pulse site, for example, A/R pulse of 80/76.

JOANNE PATZEK DACUNHA, RN

# Respiration

*Controlled by the respiratory center in the lateral medulla oblongata, respi-ration is the exchange of oxygen and carbon dioxide between the atmosphere and body cells. External respiration or breathing, accomplished by the diaphragm and chest muscles, delivers oxygen to the lower respiratory tract and the alveoli. If the major respiratory muscles—the diaphragm and the external intercostal muscles—weaken and fail to provide sufficient ventilation to meet the body's oxygen*

## IDENTIFYING RESPIRATORY PATTERNS

| TYPE OF RESPIRATION | PATTERN | POSSIBLE CAUSES |
|---|---|---|
| **Apnea:** absence of breathing may be periodic | | • Mechanical airway obstruction<br>• Conditions affecting the brain's respiratory center |
| **Apneustic:** prolonged, gasping inspiration, followed by extremely short inefficient expiration | | • Lesions of the lateral medulla oblongata |
| **Biot's:** fast, deep respirations marked by abrupt pauses. Each breath has the same depth. | | • Spinal meningitis or other central nervous system condition |
| **Bradypnea:** slow, regular respirations | | • Conditions affecting the respiratory center in the lateral medulla oblongata: tumors, metabolic disorders, respiratory decompensation; use of opiates and alcohol<br>• Normal pattern during sleep |
| **Cheynes-Stokes:** fast, deep respirations, punctuated by a period of apnea. Respirations increase and decrease for 30 to 170 seconds and stop for 20 to 60 seconds. | | • Increased intracranial pressure, severe congestive heart failure, renal failure, meningitis, drug overdose, cerebral anoxia |
| **Eupnea:** normal rate and rhythm. Rate varies with age: adult, usually 15 to 17 breaths/minute (bpm); teenagers, usually 12 to 20 bpm; ages 2 to 12, usually 20 to 30 bpm; infants, usually 30 to 50 bpm. Two or three deep breaths normally occur each minute. | | • Normal respiration |
| **Hyperpnea:** deep respirations, normal rate | | • Strenuous exercise |
| **Kussmaul's:** fast (over 20 breaths/minute), deep (resembling sighs), labored respirations without pause | | • Renal failure or metabolic acidosis, particularly diabetic ketoacidosis |
| **Tachypnea:** rapid respirations. Rate rises with body temperature—about four breaths/minute for every degree Fahrenheit above normal. | | • Fever, as the body tries to rid itself of excess heat<br>• Pneumonia, compensatory respiratory alkalosis, respiratory insufficiency, lesions of the lateral medulla oblongata, and salicylate poisoning |

*demands, then accessory muscles, such as the scalene, sternocleidomastoid, trapezius, and latissimus dorsi, attempt to compensate.*

*Four measures of respiration—rate, rhythm, depth, and sound—reflect the body's metabolic state, diaphragm and chest muscle condition, and airway patency. Respiratory rate is recorded as the number of cycles (inspiration and expiration) per minute; rhythm, as the regularity of these cycles; depth, as the volume of air inhaled and exhaled with each respiration; and sound, as the audible digression from normal, effortless breathing.*

### Equipment
Watch with second hand.

### Essential steps
The best time to assess your patient's respirations is immediately after taking the pulse rate. Keep your fingertips over the radial artery, and don't tell the patient you're counting respirations. If

you tell the patient, *he'll become conscious of his respirations, changing the rate.*

• Count respirations by observing the rise and fall of the patient's chest as he breathes. Or, position the patient's opposite arm across his chest and count respirations by feeling its rise and fall. Consider one rise and one fall as one respiration.

For children and adults, count respirations for 30 seconds, then multiply by two to obtain the rate per minute; if the rate appears abnormal, count respirations for 60 seconds. For infants, count respirations for 60 seconds *to account for normal variations in their respiratory rate and pattern.*

• Observe chest movements for depth of respiration. If the patient inhales a small volume of air, record this as shallow; if he inhales a large volume, record this as deep.

• Watch chest movements and listen to breathing *to determine the rhythm and sound of respiration.*

### Special considerations
Generally, respirations below 8 and above 40 are considered abnormal; report sudden onset of such rates promptly. Observe for signs of dyspnea, such as anxious facial expression, flaring nostrils, heaving chest wall, and cyanosis. To detect cyanosis, look for characteristic bluish discoloration in the nail beds or the lips, under the tongue, in the buccal mucosa, or in the conjunctiva.

### Documentation
Record the rate, depth, rhythm, and sound of the patient's respirations.
   JOANNE PATZEK DACUNHA, RN

---

### BREATH SOUNDS

As you count respirations, be alert for and record the following breath sounds:
• **Stertor:** snoring sound resulting from secretions in the trachea and large bronchi. Listen for it in patients with neurologic disorders or in those who are comatose.
• **Stridor:** inspiratory crowing sound; occurs with upper airway obstruction in laryngitis, croup, or the presence of a foreign body. When listening for stridor in infants and children with croup, also observe for sternal, substernal, or intercostal retractions.
• **Wheeze:** caused by partial obstruction in the smaller bronchi and bronchioles. This high-pitched, musical sound is common in patients with emphysema or asthma.
• **Expiratory grunt:** in infants, indicates imminent respiratory distress; in older patients, may result from partial airway obstruction or neuromuscular reflex.
   To detect other breath sounds, such as rales and rhonchi, or the absence of sound in the lungs, you will need a stethoscope.

# Blood Pressure

*Blood pressure, the lateral force exerted by blood on the arterial walls,*

TROUBLESHOOTING

## CORRECTING PROBLEMS OF BLOOD PRESSURE MEASUREMENT

| PROBLEM AND POSSIBLE CAUSE | NURSING ACTION |
|---|---|
| **Falsely high reading**<br>• Cuff too small | • Make sure the cuff bladder is 20% wider than the circumference of the arm or leg being used for measurement. |
| • Cuff wrapped too loosely, reducing its effective width | • Tighten the cuff. |
| • Slow cuff deflation, causing venous congestion in the arm or leg | • Never deflate the cuff more slowly than 2 mmHg/heartbeat. |
| • Tilted mercury column | • Read pressures with the mercury column vertical. |
| • Poorly timed measurement—after patient had eaten, ambulated, appeared anxious, or flexed arm muscles | • Postpone blood pressure measurement or help the patient relax before taking pressures. |
| **Falsely low readings**<br>• Incorrect position of arm or leg | • Make sure arm or leg is level with the patient's heart. |
| • Mercury column below eye level | • Read the mercury column at eye level. |
| • Failure to notice auscultatory gap (sound fades out for 10 to 15 mmHg, then returns) | • Estimate systolic pressure by palpation before actually measuring it. Then, check this pressure against the measured pressure. |
| • Inaudibility of low-volume sounds | • Before reinflating the cuff, instruct the patient to raise the arm or leg *to decrease venous pressure and amplify low-volume sounds.* After inflating the cuff, tell the patient to lower the arm or leg. Then, deflate the cuff and listen. If you still fail to detect low-volume sounds, chart the palpated systolic pressure. |

depends on the force of ventricular contractions, arterial wall elasticity, peripheral vascular resistance, and blood volume and viscosity. Systolic, or maximum, pressure occurs during left ventricular contraction and reflects the integrity of heart, arteries, and arterioles. Diastolic, or minimum, pressure occurs during left ventricular relaxation and directly indicates blood vessel resistance. Pulse pressure, the difference between systolic and dia-

stolic pressures, varies inversely with arterial elasticity. Rigid vessels, incapable of distention and recoil, produce high systolic pressure and low diastolic pressure. The difference between them, the pulse pressure, is higher than normal—usually over 30 mmHg.

Blood pressure is measured in millimeters of mercury with a sphygmomanometer and a stethoscope, usually at the brachial artery (less often at the popliteal or radial artery). Lowest in *the neonate, blood pressure rises with age, weight gain, continued stress, and anxiety. Normal blood pressure ranges from 110/60 to 140/90 in adults and from 50/40 to 80/58 in infants.*

*Frequent blood pressure measurement is critical after serious injury, surgery, or anesthesia and during any illness or condition that threatens cardiovascular stability. Regular mea-*

## USING AN ELECTRONIC VITAL SIGNS MONITOR

An electronic vital signs monitor (shown below) noninvasively and automatically registers systolic, diastolic, and mean arterial pressure and heart rate at intervals from 1 to 16 minutes. To use this monitor:
• First, collect the necessary equipment: the monitor, dual air hose, and specially fitted pressure cuff that's 40% wider and 20% longer than the circumference of the arm or leg being monitored. Then, place the monitor on a firm, immobile surface near the patient's bed. Make sure the back of the monitor is unobstructed *to permit heat dissipation.*
• Explain the procedure to the patient. Describe the alarm system, so he won't be frightened if it's triggered.
• Make sure the power switch is off. Then, plug the monitor into a properly grounded wall outlet. Next, secure the dual air hose to the back of the monitor by slipping the metal tips of each hose into the cuff connector bracket, squeezing the two metal prongs on the metal tips, and pressing the tips firmly into the bracket.
• Screw the pressure cuff's tubing into the other ends of the dual air hose, and tighten the screws *to prevent air leaks.*

Keep the air hose away from the patient *to avoid accidental dislodging.*
• Squeeze all air from the cuff, and loosely wrap it around the patient's arm or leg, allowing 2 fingerbreadths between cuff and arm or leg. *Important:* Never apply the cuff to an arm or leg that has an I.V. line in place.
• Make sure the mode switch is in the *auto* position. Then, move the alarm limit switch to the *on* position *to ensure an audible signal when the monitor detects abnormal mean arterial pressure (MAP).*
• To set the cuff inflation interval, depress the appropriate add minute levers. If you wish to measure blood pressure every minute, depress all four levers.
• Turn the power switch to the *on* position; after 20 seconds, the monitor will begin to inflate the cuff for the first reading. If, at a later time, you need to record pressures without waiting for the next inflation, depress the *manual read* lever; the monitor will then inflate the cuff, display pressures, and automatically return to its preset interval.
• If your patient's condition requires, change the monitor's preset alarm limits. To increase the high alarm limit of 140 mmHg for MAP, move the *alarm limit* lever toward the high position; the alarm limit will then rise in 5-mmHg increments until you release the lever. To change the low alarm limit of 50 mmHg for MAP, move the alarm limit lever toward the low position and follow the same procedure. To return the monitor to its preset limits, turn the power switch off and then on again.
• Because the monitor can display pressures in millimeters of mercury or kilopascals, raise and release the *select function* lever *to change units of measure.*

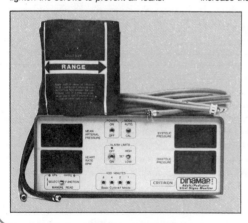

*surement is indicated for patients with a history of hypertension or hypotension.*

## Equipment
Mercury or aneroid sphygmomanometer □ stethoscope □ alcohol sponge.

The sphygmomanometer consists of an inflatable compression cuff linked to a simple air pump and a mercury manometer or an aneroid gauge. The mercury sphygmomanometer is more accurate and requires calibration less frequently than the aneroid model but is larger and heavier. To obtain an accurate reading, its gauge must rest on a level surface and be viewed with the meniscus at eye level; an aneroid gauge can rest in any position but must be viewed directly from the front. Some mercury manometers have specially designed cases that open to form a level surface; others must be attached to a wall or to a base unit that stands on the floor.

Hook, bandage, snap, or Velcro cuffs come in six standard sizes ranging from newborn to extra large adult. Disposable cuffs are available.

## Preparation of equipment
Carefully choose the appropriate cuff size for the patient. An excessively narrow cuff may cause a falsely high pressure reading; an excessively wide one, a falsely low reading. If you're not using your own stethoscope, disinfect its earpieces with an alcohol sponge before placing them in your ears *to avoid cross-contamination.*

## Essential steps
• Tell the patient you will take his blood pressure.
• The patient can lie supine or sit erect during blood pressure measurement. His arm should be extended and well supported at heart level. To obtain an accurate measurement, be sure the patient is relaxed and comfortable when you take his blood pressure.
• If necessary, connect the appropriate tube to the rubber bulb air pump and

the other tube to the manometer. Then, insert the earpieces of the stethoscope in your ears.
• Locate the brachial pulse by palpation. Then, center the diaphragm of the stethoscope over the artery where you detect the strongest beats, and hold it in place with one hand.
• Using the thumb and index finger of your other hand, turn the thumbscrew on the rubber bulb of the air pump clockwise to close the valve.
• Then, pump air into the cuff while auscultating the sound over the brachial artery *to compress and, eventually, occlude arterial blood flow.* When the sound disappears, pump air until the mercury column or aneroid gauge registers 160 mmHg or at least 10 mmHg above the level of the last audible sound.
• Carefully open the valve of the air pump and slowly deflate the cuff—no faster than 5 mmHg/second. While releasing air, watch the mercury column or aneroid gauge and auscultate the sound over the artery.
• When you hear the first beat or clear tapping sound, note the pressure on the column or gauge. This is the systolic pressure. (The beat or tapping sound is the first of five Korotkoff sounds. The second sound resembles a murmur or swish; the third sound, crisp tapping; the fourth sound, a soft, muffled tone; and the fifth, the last sound heard.)
• Continue to release air gradually while auscultating the sound over the artery.
• Record the diastolic pressure—the fourth Korotkoff sound. If you continue to hear sounds as the column or gauge falls to zero (common in children), record the pressure at the beginning of the fourth sound.
• Rapidly deflate the cuff. Wait 15 to 30 seconds, then repeat the procedure, and record pressures *to confirm your original findings.* After doing so, remove and fold the cuff, and return it to storage.

## Special considerations
If you can't auscultate blood pressure sound, you may estimate systolic pres-

sure. To do this, first palpate the brachial or radial pulse. Then, inflate the cuff until you no longer detect the pulse. Slowly deflate the cuff and when you detect the pulse again, record the pressure as the estimated systolic pressure. When measuring blood pressure in the popliteal artery, position the patient on his abdomen; wrap a cuff around the middle of the thigh, and proceed with blood pressure measurement.

If your patient is a crying child, delay blood pressure measurement, if possible, until the child becomes calm *to avoid falsely elevated readings.* If your patient requires frequent blood pressure readings, you may leave the cuff in place; however, be sure to fully deflate the cuff between readings. You can do this by disconnecting the cuff from the tube that leads to the manometer. Before each reading, make sure the cuff hasn't slipped out of position.

If your hospital considers the fourth and fifth Korotkoff sounds as the first and second diastolic pressures, record both pressures.

Remember that malfunction in an aneroid sphygmomanometer can be identified only by checking it against a mercury manometer of known accuracy. Be sure to check your aneroid manometer this way periodically. Malfunction in a mercury manometer is evident in abnormal behavior of the mercury column. Don't attempt to repair either type of sphygmomanometer yourself; instead, send it to the appropriate service department.

Occasionally, blood pressure must be measured in both arms, or with the patient in two different positions (such as lying and standing, or sitting and standing). Then, it's necessary to observe and record any significant difference between the two readings and to record both the blood pressure and the extremity or position used.

### Documentation
On the patient's chart, record blood pressure as systolic over diastolic pressures, such as 120/78; if necessary, record systolic over the two diastolic pressures, such as 120/78/20. If required by your hospital, chart blood pressures on a graph, using dots or checkmarks. Also, if applicable, document extremity used and patient position.

JOANNE PATZEK DACUNHA, RN

# Height and Weight Measurements

*Height and weight measurements are routine for most patients at admission to the hospital. Knowing exact height and weight is essential for calculating dosages of drugs, anesthetics, and radiopaque dyes for X-rays; assessing nutritional status; and determining the height-weight ratio. And because body weight provides the best overall picture of fluid status, monitoring body weight daily proves important for patients receiving sodium-retaining or diuretic medications. Rapid weight gain in such patients signals fluid retention; rapid weight loss, diuresis.*

*Weight can be measured with a standing, chair, or bed scale; height, with the measuring bar on a standing scale.*

### Equipment
Scale—standing (with measuring bar), chair, or bed □ wheelchair (if needed to transport patient).

### Preparation of equipment
Select the appropriate scale—usually, a standing scale for the ambulatory patient, a chair or bed scale for the acutely ill or debilitated patient. Then, check scale balance. Standing scales and, to a lesser extent, bed scales may become unbalanced when transported.

### Essential steps
• Explain the procedure to the patient.
*For the standing scale:*

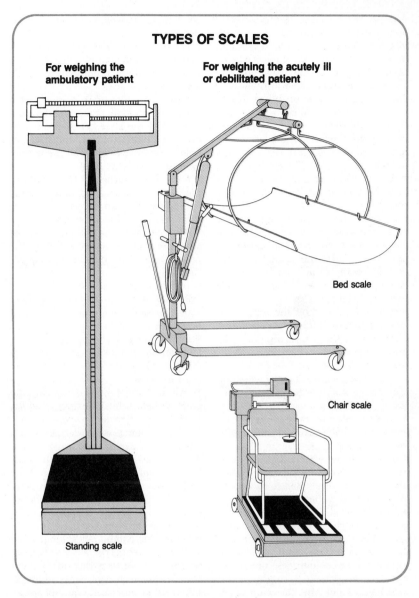

## TYPES OF SCALES

**For weighing the ambulatory patient**

**For weighing the acutely ill or debilitated patient**

Bed scale

Chair scale

Standing scale

• Place a paper towel on the scale's platform.
• Tell the patient to remove his robe and slippers or shoes *to ensure accurate measurement of height and weight.* If the scale has wheels, lock them before the patient steps on. Assist the patient onto the scale *to prevent falls.*
• If you're using the *upright balance (gravity) scale,* slide the lower rider to the groove representing the largest increment below the patient's estimated weight (50, 100, 150, 200 lb, or 25, 50, 75, 100 kg). Then, slide the small upper rider until the beam balances. Add the upper and lower rider figures *to determine the weight.* (Upper-rider calibration is in eighths of a pound.)

• If you're using the *multiple-weight scale,* move the appropriate ratio weights onto the weight holder to balance the scale; ratio weights are labeled 200, 100, and 50 lb (100, 50, and 25 kg). Add ratio weights until the next weight causes the main beam to fall. Then, adjust the main beam poise until the scale balances. Next, add the sum of the ratio weights to the figure on the main beam *to obtain the patient's weight.*

• Return ratio weights to their rack and the weight holder to its proper place.

• If you're measuring height, tell the patient to stand erect on the platform of the scale. Then, raise the measuring bar, extend it to the horizontal position, and depress it until it touches the top of the patient's head. Then, read the patient's height.

• Help the patient off the scale, and give him his robe and slippers or shoes. Then, return the measuring bar to its initial position.

*For the chair scale:*

• Transport the patient to the weighing area or the scale to the patient's bedside.

• Lock the scale in place *to prevent its movement during positioning or weighing the patient.*

• If you're using a scale with a swing-away chair arm, unlock the arm. When unlocked, the arm swings back 180° to permit easy patient access.

• Position the scale beside the patient's bed or wheelchair, with the chair arm open. Then, transfer the patient onto the scale, swing the chair arm to the front of the scale, and lock it in place.

• Weigh the patient by adding ratio weights and adjusting the main beam poise. Then, unlock the swing-away chair arm as before, and transfer the patient to his bed or wheelchair.

• Lock the main beam *to avoid damaging the scale during transport.* Unlock the wheels and remove the scale from the patient's room.

*For the multiple-weight bed scale:*

• Provide privacy, and tell the patient

you're about to weigh him on a special bed scale.

• Position the scale next to the patient's bed and lock the scale's wheels. Then, turn the patient on his side, facing away from the scale.

• Release the stretcher frame to the horizontal position, and pump the hand lever until the stretcher is positioned over the mattress. Lower the stretcher onto the mattress, and roll the patient onto the stretcher.

• Raise the stretcher 2″ (5 cm) above the mattress. Then, add ratio weights and adjust the main beam poise as for the standing and chair scales.

• After weighing the patient, lower the stretcher onto the mattress. Return the patient to the bed in a comfortable position.

*For the digital bed scale:*

• Provide privacy, and tell the patient you're about to weigh him on a special bed scale.

• Release the stretcher to the horizontal position, then lock it in place. Turn the patient on his side, facing away from the scale.

• Roll the base of the scale beneath the patient's bed. Adjust the lever *to widen the base of the scale, providing stability.* After doing so, lock the scale's wheels.

• Center the stretcher above the bed, lower it onto the mattress, and roll the patient onto the stretcher. Then, position the circular weighing arms of the scale over the patient, and attach them securely to the stretcher bars.

• Pump the handle with long, slow strokes *to raise the patient a few inches off the bed.* Ensure that the patient doesn't lean on or touch the headboard, side rails, or other bed equipment, *because this will affect weight measurement.*

• Depress the operate button, and read the patient's weight on the digital display panel. Then, press in the scale's handle *to lower the patient onto the bed.*

• Detach the circular weighing arms from the stretcher bars, roll the patient

back off the stretcher, and position him comfortably in bed.
• Release the wheel lock and withdraw the scale. Return the stretcher to its vertical position for storage.

**Special considerations**
Weigh the patient at the same time each day (usually before breakfast), in similar clothing, using the same scale. If the patient uses crutches, weigh him with the crutches. Then, weigh the crutches and subtract their weight from the total to determine the patient's weight. If the patient is markedly obese, check scale capacity. (Although some newer scales can accommodate up to 600 lb or 270 kg, most scales can measure a maximum of 250 lb or 112.5 kg.) You may have to weigh the patient on a large commercial scale (usually located on the loading dock or in the dietary department).

Before using a bed scale, cover its stretcher with a draw sheet *to avoid stains from perspiration, drainage, or excretions.* Balance the scale with the draw sheet in place *to ensure accurate weighing.* When rolling the patient onto the stretcher, be careful not to dislodge I.V. lines, indwelling catheters, and other supportive equipment.

**Documentation**
Record the patient's height and weight on the nursing assessment form and other medical records, as required by your hospital.
JOANNE PATZEK DACUNHA, RN

# Physical Examination

*The nurse's role in adult physical examination usually entails collecting equipment, preparing and supporting the patient, and assisting the doctor. Collection of the appropriate equipment requires understanding the rea-*

*son for the examination, because a routine physical normally employs more and a larger variety of equipment than an examination inspired by the patient's chief complaint. Patient preparation includes a clear explanation of the examination beforehand and proper positioning and draping during the examination. Besides recognition of and respect for the patient's feelings (particularly embarrassment and anxiety), patient support includes comfort measures and adherence to safety precautions. Assistance comprises anticipation of the doctor's needs for equipment and supplies, disposal or sterilization of used equipment, and handling of specimens for laboratory analysis.*

**Equipment**
Although equipment varies with the kind of examination, the following may be included: urine specimen container and laboratory request slip (if ordered) □ scale with height measurement bar □ sphygmomanometer □ stethoscope □ thermometer □ gown (for patient) □ examining table (with stirrups, if necessary) □ clean gloves □ drapes (sheet or bath blanket, towel) □ adhesive tape □ flashlight □ spotlight or gooseneck lamp □ laryngeal mirror □ tongue blades □ Snellen chart □ ophthalmoscope □ otoscope □ ear specula □ tuning fork □ tape measure □ percussion (reflex) hammer □ sigmoidoscope □ occult blood test kit □ linen-saver pad □ water-soluble lubricant □ tissues □ cotton-tipped applicators □ cotton balls in antiseptic solution, or prepackaged antiseptic swabs □ Papanicolaou test slides and laboratory request slip (if needed) □ vaginal speculum (small size for children and adolescents, medium size for most women, large size for obese and multiparous women) □ Pap stick □ fixative □ container for soiled instruments.

**Preparation of equipment**
Adjust the temperature in the examining room and close the doors *to pre-*

# POSITIONING AND DRAPING THE PATIENT FOR PHYSICAL EXAMINATION

| POSITION AND DRAPING | EXAMINATION | NURSING ACTION |
|---|---|---|
| **Dorsal recumbent** | Pelvic (without vaginal examination) | Instruct the patient to lie on her back, with her knees flexed. |
| **Jackknife** | Rectal for ambulatory males | Turn the patient's gown upward. Instruct him to bend over the bed or specially designed table, with his hips flexed. |
| **Knee-chest** | Rectal | Instruct the patient to kneel, using her head, chest, and arms for support. |
| **Lithotomy** | Vaginal, pelvic | Make sure the patient's buttocks rest at the edge of the table. Then, place a pillow beneath her head. Just before the examination, place her feet in the stirrups and comfortably secure her heels. |
| **Sims'** | Rectal for nonambulatory males and for females receiving a rectal but not a vaginal examination | Place the patient on her left side, with her buttocks close to the edge of the table. Make sure the patient's left leg is straight and that her right leg and hip are flexed. |

*vent drafts.* Cover the examining table with a clean sheet or disposable paper. Then, assemble the appropriate equipment for the scheduled examination.

### Essential steps
• Explain the examination to the patient and answer any questions.
• Instruct the patient to void, if possible. Collect a urine specimen at this time, if ordered. *Emptying the bladder increases patient comfort during examination of the abdomen and genitalia.*
• Help the patient undress, and provide a gown if necessary. Then, measure and record the patient's height and weight. Next, take and record the patient's vital signs.
• Assist the patient onto the examining table *to prevent his falling,* and prepare him for the examination, as appropriate. During a routine physical examination, the doctor usually proceeds from head to toe. Observe the patient closely during the examination, and provide emotional support. When necessary, help the patient change position, *to prevent falls.* Keep the patient adequately draped during position changes, *to reduce exposure and ensure privacy.*

*For a head and neck examination:*
• Instruct the patient to sit upright on the edge of the examining table, and drape a sheet across the top of his legs.
• After the doctor palpates the patient's head and neck, hand the doctor the ophthalmoscope. During the eye examination, turn off the room lights.
• Assemble the otoscope, and gather ear specula and tuning fork. After the doctor completes the ear examination, carefully cleanse the specula with alcohol sponges *to remove cerumen.*
• Hand the doctor the tongue blade and flashlight *to examine the patient's mouth.*

*For a chest examination:*
• Instruct the patient to remain seated on the edge of the table, and loosen the ties on his gown.
• After the doctor auscultates the an-terior and posterior chest with a stethoscope, assist the patient to the supine position.
• If the patient is a female, fold back the top of her gown, and drape a small towel across her breasts *to provide privacy.*
• After the doctor examines the chest, replace the patient's gown.

*For an abdominal examination:*
• Instruct the patient to remain supine, with arms relaxed at his sides. Drape a sheet over his lower body, beginning just above the pubis.
• If the patient is especially tense, place a pillow beneath the knees. *Slight flexing of the knees helps relax abdominal muscles.*
• The doctor then auscultates and palpates the abdomen.

*For a rectal examination:*
• Instruct the ambulatory male patient to stand and lean over the examining table, or place him in the jackknife position. Assist the ambulatory female patient into Sims's position, unless a vaginal examination is also being performed. Assist nonambulatory patients into Sims's position. Or, if ordered, assist the patient into the knee-chest position, which is usually difficult to assume and maintain.
• Drape the perineum by placing a hand towel just below the patient's anus and taping it to the thighs.
• Gather clean gloves, lubricant, sigmoidoscope, and slides for a specimen (if ordered). Then, inform the patient that this examination stimulates the anal sphincter, causing him to feel an urge to defecate. Assure him that this response is normal and will quickly subside.

*For a pelvic examination:*
• If the doctor doesn't plan to perform a vaginal examination, place the patient in the dorsal recumbent position. Cover her to her knees with a sheet.
• The doctor then palpates the pelvic area. Hand the doctor a clean glove. He inserts one finger into the vagina and palpates the pelvic area with the other hand.

*For a vaginal examination:*
• Raise the stirrups on the examining table, and pad them with washcloths.
• Place the patient in the lithotomy position, with her buttocks at the edge of the table. Drape the patient with a sheet, covering her body to the knees. Then, place her heels in the stirrups.
• Warm the speculum under running water, and hand it to the doctor. When he's ready, give him a Pap stick, glass slides, and fixative (a commercial spray, or 95% ethyl alcohol solution in a jar).
*For all examinations:*
• After the examination, help the patient from the table, and allow time to regain balance. If the doctor performed a rectal, vaginal, or pelvic examination, provide tissues *to wipe off residual lubricant.*
• After the patient leaves the examining area, clean soiled instruments and place them in a disinfectant. Restock discarded supplies.

**Documentation**
Record on the patient's chart the time, date, and type of physical examination; the patient's height, weight, and vital signs; the patient's response to the examination; and the doctor's name.
            ELLEN A. McFADDEN, RN, MSN

# SAFETY AND BED-MAKING

# Patient-care Reminders

*Patient-care reminders enhance safety and effective care by drawing attention to the patient's special needs through posted cards or signs. These reminders can outline fluid and dietary restrictions, detail posttest or postoperative care, provide instructions for collecting or handling specimens (such as collect all urine for 24 hours or test all stools for occult blood), and emphasize any information affecting the patient's welfare (such as deafness, blindness, and other communication barriers). Using these reminders helps maintain consistent care by communicating specific needs to the hospital staff and to the patient's family and other visitors.*

**Equipment**
Some hospitals have special cards for use as patient-care reminders. If these are not available, you can make them from plain pieces of paper.

**Essential steps**
• Identify the patient's specific care need(s).
• Clearly write or print the patient's name, room and bed numbers, and specific care need(s) on the card.

## ALLERGY DOCUMENTATION

If the patient is hypersensitive to certain foods (such as strawberries, milk, or eggs) or drugs (most commonly penicillin), exposure to these substances in the hospital can cause minor reactions or, more significantly, anaphylaxis. To prevent such reactions, be sure to notify appropriate hospital personnel of the patient's allergies. After reviewing the allergy history on the patient's admission form, correlate it with his past medical records (if available) for completeness. Then, record these allergies in red on the nursing care cardex and on the medication cardex. Attach a label listing the allergies to the outside of the patient's chart. If the allergies are food related, notify the dietitian; if they're drug related, notify the pharmacy. Make sure you also alert the attending doctor to the patient's allergies.

• Before posting a card, explain to the conscious patient that it helps the staff remember his special needs.
• Post the card prominently on the wall behind the patient's bed or on the headboard or footboard, depending on your hospital's preference.

### Special considerations

Make your instructions positive, not negative. For example, say, "Use left arm only for blood pressure" instead of "Don't use right arm for blood pressure." Never violate the patient's privacy by including diagnosis, details about surgery, or any information he might find embarrassing. If the patient's family or other visitors need to be aware of such a reminder, avoid abbreviations that they may not understand (such as NPO). Write the patient's special needs on the nursing-care plan, with your ideas for meeting them. Discuss these ideas with other staff members, reevaluate them frequently, and update the patient-care reminder when they change. Be sure to review patient-care reminders in your verbal shift report to other staff members.

JOANNE PATZEK DACUNHA, RN

# Soft Restraints

*Various soft restraints limit movement to prevent the confused, disoriented, or combative patient from injuring himself or others. Vest and belt restraints, used to prevent falls from a bed or a chair, permit full movement of arms and legs. Limb restraints, used to prevent removal of supportive equipment, such as I.V. lines, indwelling catheters, and nasogastric tubes, allow only slight limb motion. Like limb restraints, mitts prevent removal of supportive equipment, discourage the scratching of skin rashes or sores, and prevent the combative patient from injuring himself or*

## TIPS FOR USING VEST AND MITT RESTRAINTS

*For the patient confined to a wheelchair, the vest restraint (shown crisscrossed in the photograph above) supports the trunk, prevents forward sliding, and helps hold the patient against the chair.*
  *Mitt restraints (shown in the photograph below), made of transparent Dacron mesh, allow assessment of hand circulation.*

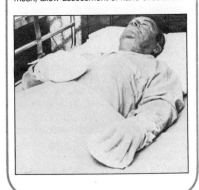

*the nursing staff. Body restraints, used to control the combative or hysterical patient, immobilize all or most of the body.*
  *Restraints are contraindicated in seizure-prone patients because they*

*exaggerate the risk of fracture and trauma. And because restraints can cause skin irritation and restrict blood flow, they are contraindicated over wounds or intravenous catheters. Vest restraints should be used with caution in patients with congestive heart failure or other respiratory disorders. Such restraints can tighten with movement, further limiting respiratory function.*

### Equipment
Soft restraint (vest, limb, mitt, belt, body) □ gauze sponges (for padding, if needed).

Disposable restraints made of heavy gauze are also available.

### Preparation of equipment
Obtain the restraint(s) from the central supply department or other appropriate source.

### Essential steps
● Obtain a doctor's order for the restraint, if required. However, never leave a confused or combative patient unattended or unrestrained while attempting to secure the order.
● Tell the patient what you're about to do and describe the restraint(s) to him. Assure him that they are being used to protect him from injury rather than to punish him.
*To place a vest restraint:*
● Assist the patient to a sitting position, if his condition permits. Then, slip the vest over his gown. Crisscross the cloth flaps at the front, placing the V-shaped opening at the patient's throat. Never crisscross the flaps in the back, *because this may cause the patient to choke if he tries to squirm out of the vest.*
● Pass the tab on one flap through the slot on the opposite flap. Then, adjust the vest for the patient's comfort. You should be able to slip your fist between the vest and the patient. Avoid wrapping the vest too tightly, *because this may restrict respiration.*
● Tie the vest straps securely to the bedframe or wheelchair, out of the patient's reach. Use a bow or a knot that

can be released quickly and easily in an emergency. Never tie a regular knot to secure the straps. Leave 1″ to 2″ (2.5 to 5 cm) of slack in the straps *to allow room for movement.*
● After applying the vest, check the patient's respiratory rate and breath sounds regularly. Be alert for signs of respiratory distress. Also, make sure the vest hasn't tightened with the patient's movement. Loosen the vest frequently, if possible, *so the patient can stretch, turn, and breathe deeply.*
*To place a limb restraint:*
● Pad the patient's wrist or ankle with gauze sponges *to reduce friction between the patient's skin and the restraint, helping to prevent irritation and skin breakdown.* Then, wrap the restraint around the gauze sponge.
● Pass the strap on the narrow end of the restraint through the slot in the broad end, and adjust for a snug fit. Or, fasten the buckle or Velcro cuffs to fit the restraint. You should be able to slip one or two fingers between the restraint and the patient's skin. Avoid fitting the restraint too tightly, *because this may impair circulation distal to the restraint.*
● Tie the restraint's long strap ends securely to the bedframe or a chair, out of the patient's reach. Flex the patient's arm or leg slightly before securing the straps, and leave 1″ to 2″ of slack. *This allows room for movement and helps prevent frozen joints and dislocations.* When securing the straps, never use a regular knot. Tie a bow or a knot that can be released quickly and easily in an emergency.
● After applying limb restraints, be alert for signs of impaired circulation in the extremity distal to the restraint. If the skin appears blue or feels cold, or if the patient complains of a tingling sensation or numbness, loosen the restraint. Perform range-of-motion exercises regularly *to stimulate circulation and prevent contractures and resultant loss of mobility.*
*To place a mitt restraint:*
● Wash and dry the patient's hands.

• Roll up a washcloth or gauze pad, and place it in the patient's palm. Then, have him form a loose fist, if possible, pull the mitt over it, and secure the closure.

• *To restrict the patient's arm movement,* attach the strap to the mitt and tie it securely to the bedframe. Use a bow or a knot that can be released quickly and easily in an emergency. Never tie a regular knot to secure the straps.

• When using mitts made of transparent mesh, check hand movement and skin color frequently *to assess circulation.* Remove the mitts regularly *to stimulate circulation,* and perform passive range-of-motion exercises *to prevent contractures.*

*To place a belt restraint:*

• Center the flannel pad of the belt on the bed. Then, wrap the short strap of the belt around the bedframe and fasten it under the bed.

• Position the patient on the pad. Then, have him roll slightly to one side while you guide the long strap around his waist and through the slot in the pad.

• Wrap the long strap around the bedframe and fasten it under the bed.

• After applying the belt, slip your hand between the patient and the belt *to ensure a secure but comfortable fit. A loose belt can be raised to chest level; a tight one can cause abdominal discomfort.*

*To place a body (Posey net) restraint:*

• Place the restraint flat on the bed, with arm and wrist cuffs facing down and the shoulder V at the head of the bed.

• Place the patient in the prone position on top of the restraint.

• Lift the V over the patient's head. Thread the chest belt through one of the loops in the V *for a snug fit.*

• Secure the straps around the patient's chest, thighs, and legs. Then, turn the patient on his back.

• Secure the straps to the bedframe *to anchor the restraint.* Then, secure the straps around the patient's arms and wrists.

## KNOTS FOR SECURING SOFT RESTRAINTS

When securing soft restraints, use knots that can be released quickly and easily, like those below. Remember, never secure restraints to the side rails, because the rails might be inadvertently lowered, causing patient discomfort.

### FOR SECURING RESTRAINT TO BEDFRAME

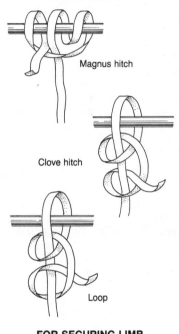

Magnus hitch

Clove hitch

Loop

### FOR SECURING LIMB RESTRAINT TO PATIENT

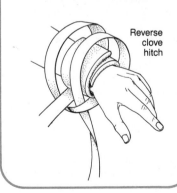

Reverse clove hitch

## Special considerations

Because your authority to use restraints varies from one hospital to another, know your hospital's policy. Also be sure to know your state's regulations governing such restraints. You should know, for instance, that some states prohibit the use of four-point restraints.

When the patient is at high risk for aspiration, restrain him on his side. Never secure all four restraints to one side of the bed, because the patient may fall out of bed.

After assessing the patient's behavior and condition, you may decide to use a two-point restraint, which should restrain one arm and the opposite leg— for example, the right arm and the left leg. Never restrain just one side, because this can cause a patient to fall out of bed.

Don't apply a limb restraint above an I.V. site, because this may occlude the infusion or cause infiltration into surrounding tissue.

Never secure restraints to the side rails, because someone might inadvertently lower the rail before noticing the attached restraint. This may jerk the patient's limb or body, causing him discomfort.

When using washable restraints, place them in the laundry as your hospital directs. Many hospitals separate restraints from other linens to avoid losing them.

## Complications

Excessively tight limb restraints can reduce peripheral circulation; tight vest restraints can impair respiration. So apply restraints carefully and check them regularly.

Skin breakdown can occur under limb restraints. To prevent this, pad the patient's wrists and ankles, frequently loosen or remove restraints, and provide regular skin care.

## Documentation

Record the patient's behavior that necessitated the restraints, when the restraints were applied and removed, and the type of restraints used. If you expect a continued need for restraints, document their use in the cardex.

SUSAN DONAHUE, RN, BSN

# Leather Restraints

*When soft restraints prove ineffective and sedation is dangerous, leather restraints effectively restrict the patient's limb movement to prevent injury to himself or others.*

*Depending on the patient's behavior, these restraints may be applied to all limbs (four-point restraints) or to one arm and one leg (two-point restraints). The duration of such restraint is governed by state law and by hospital policy.*

*Because a patient rarely submits readily to restraints, safe and speedy application requires teamwork by several co-workers, the availability of all equipment, proper patient positioning, and a brief, clear explanation of the procedure to the patient. After application, observe the patient frequently to ensure his safety, to assess the need for continued use of restraints, and to assure him that he's not being punished.*

## Equipment

Two wrist and two ankle leather restraints □ four straps □ key □ large, padded gauze sponges (for padding each extremity).

## Preparation of equipment

Before entering the patient's room, make sure the restraints are the correct size. Because these restraints aren't labeled by size, use the patient's build and weight as a guide. If the restraints are too loose and you haven't access to smaller ones, build up the available restraints with gauze or washcloths taped down securely. After checking the size of the restraints, be sure the straps are unlocked and that the key fits the locks.

### Essential steps

● Obtain adequate assistance to restrain the patient before entering his room. Enlist the aid of several coworkers and organize their effort, giving each person a specific task: for example, one person explains the procedure to the patient and applies the restraints, while the others immobilize the patient's arms and legs.

● Position the patient supine on the bed, with each arm and leg securely held down, *to best control the combative patient and to prevent injury to the patient and others.* Pin the patient's arms and legs at the joints—knee, ankle, shoulder, and wrist—*to minimize his movement without exerting excessive force.*

● As you begin to apply the restraints, calmly explain why they are needed, *to help relieve the patient's anxiety and fear.* Assure him that they are being used to protect him from injury, not to punish him. Tell him that the restraints will be removed when he regains control of his behavior.

● Pad the patient's wrists and ankles *to reduce friction between his skin and the leather, preventing skin irritation and breakdown.*

● Wrap the restraint around the padding. Then, insert the metal loop through the hole that gives the best fit. Apply restraints securely but not too tightly. You should be able to slip one or two fingers between the restraint and the patient's skin. *A tight restraint can compromise circulation; a loose one can be slipped off or moved up the patient's arm or leg, causing skin irritation and breakdown.*

● Thread the strap through the metal loop on the restraint, close the metal loop, and secure the strap to the bedframe, out of the patient's reach.

● Lock the restraint by pushing in the button on the side of the metal loop, and tug it gently to be sure it's secure. Once the restraint is secure, the co-worker can release the arm or leg. Never secure restraints to the side rails, *because inadvertent lowering of the rails could injure the patient.* Flex the patient's arm or leg slightly before locking the strap, *to allow room for movement and to prevent frozen joints and dislocations.*

● Place the key in an accessible location at the nurse's station.

● After applying leather restraints, observe the patient regularly *to give emotional support and to reassess the need for continued use of the restraint.* Check his pulse rate and vital signs at least every 2 hours. Remove or loosen restraints, one at a time, every 2 hours, and perform passive range-of-motion exercises, if possible. To unlock the restraint, insert the key into the metal loop, opposite the locking button. This releases the lock, and the metal loop can be opened. Watch for signs of impaired peripheral circulation, such as cool, cyanotic skin.

### Special considerations

Although hospital policies for using restraints vary, most require a doctor's order for their use. However, you may apply restraints in an emergency. If you do, obtain a doctor's written order as soon as possible afterward (usually within 6 hours), and have the order renewed every 24 hours, if necessary. Become familiar with your state's mental health law, which specifies the legal time limit for restraint and the schedule for reevaluating the need for restraints. As ordered, administer a major tranquilizer (usually, chlorpromazine or haloperidol) I.M. as soon as possible, to calm the violent patient. When the patient becomes drowsy, remove the restraints. If you repeatedly administer I.M. doses of a tranquilizer, monitor the patient's vital signs closely.

Don't restrain a patient in prone position. This position limits his field of vision, intensifies feelings of helplessness and vulnerability, and makes maintaining an airway difficult, especially if the patient has been sedated.

If the patient is disposed to aspiration, restrain him on his side. After assessing the patient's behavior and his potential for hurting himself or others, you may decide to use four-point or two-point restraints. Never restrain one side only with two-point restraint, because the patient may fall out of bed.

Because the restrained patient has limited mobility, his nutrition, elimination, and positioning become your responsibility. To prevent decubiti, reposition the patient regularly, and massage and pad bony prominences and other vulnerable areas.

## Complications
Because most patients resist restraint by biting, kicking, scratching, or head-butting, injury to the patient or to others is the most common complication. Skin breakdown is common during prolonged restraint. To prevent or minimize it, apply sufficient padding around the wrists and ankles, as well as proper skin care—cleansing and drying, followed by the application of lotion.

## Documentation
Record the patient's behavior that necessitated the restraints, when the restraints were applied and removed, the number and location of restraints used, your notification of the doctor, and patient care during restraint. Note skin condition under the restraints and any signs of reduced peripheral circulation. Describe your frequent evaluations of the patient's mental status, because this justifies continued use of restraints. Record vital signs before and after sedation, and note an extreme hypotensive reaction.

JANET C. STOLAR, RN, MSN

# Unoccupied Bed

*Although considered routine, daily changing and periodic straightening of bed linens promotes patient comfort and prevents skin breakdown. When preceded by thorough handwashing, performed cleanly, and followed by proper handling and disposal of soiled linens, this procedure helps control nosocomial infections. In open-bed technique, performed during the ambulatory patient's hospitalization, bed-making entails folding top linens to the foot of the bed to permit easy patient access. In closed-bed technique, performed after patient discharge, bed-making entails keeping top linens unfolded and even with the top of the mattress until the next patient admission.*

## Equipment
Two sheets (one fitted, if available) □ pillowcase □ spread □ draw sheet (optional) □ blanket (optional) □ laundry bag (optional).

## Preparation of equipment
Obtain clean linen, which should be folded in half lengthwise and then folded again, creating a center crease that makes it easier to position the sheet on the bed. If the linen isn't folded properly, refold the bottom sheets with the smooth side of the hem facing inward; refold the top sheets with the rough side of the hem facing inward. This ensures that the rough side doesn't rub against the patient's heels when the bottom sheet is placed on the bed, helping to prevent skin irritation, and that the smooth side can be turned down on the spread, giving the bed a finished appearance.

## Essential steps
• Wash your hands thoroughly, and bring clean linen to the patient's bedside.
• Move furniture away from the bed *to provide ample working space,* if necessary.
• Lower the head of the bed *to make the mattress level and ensure tight-fitting, wrinkle-free linens.* Then, raise the bed to a comfortable working height

# MAKING A POSTOPERATIVE BED

Postoperative bedmaking permits easy patient transfer and promotes cleanliness and comfort. To make a postoperative bed:

• Assemble two clean sheets (one fitted, if available), a draw sheet, a bath blanket, a spread or sheet, a pillowcase, tissues, a trash bag, and linen-saver pads. Prepare linens as you would in making an unoccupied bed. Raise the bed to a comfortable working height to prevent backstrain.

• Make the foundation of the bed, including the draw sheet.

• Place an open bath blanket about 15″ (38 cm) from the head of the bed, with its center fold in the middle of the bed. *The blanket warms the patient and counteracts the decreased body temperature caused by the anesthetic.*

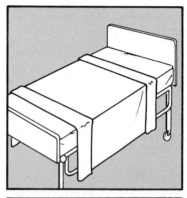

• Place a sheet or spread on the bed, and position it in the same way as the bath blanket. Then, fold the blanket and sheet one quarter down from the top, so that the blanket shows over the sheet. Similarly fold the sheet and blanket from the bottom (as illustrated above).

• On the side of the bed where you'll be receiving the patient (usually the side nearest the door), pick up corner A (as illustrated at center), and make a right angle at the center of the bed. Pick up corner B (at center), and fold it parallel to the first corner. Pick up point C (at bottom), and fanfold the linens back to the opposite side of the bed. Now, the linens won't interfere with the patient transfer from stretcher to bed, and by pulling from point C, they can easily cover the patient. After covering the patient, tuck in the linens at the foot of the bed and miter the corners.

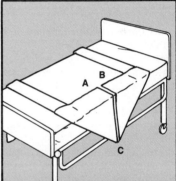

• Slip the pillow into a clean case, and place it on a nearby table or chair. After the patient is in the bed, position the pillow for his comfort and safety.

• To make the patient comfortable and to prevent unnecessary movement and linen changes, anticipate his special needs.

If you anticipate nausea, keep an emesis basin, tissues, and linen-saver pads at the bedside. If you expect bleeding or discharge, place one or more pads on the bed.

Keep extra pillows handy to elevate arms and legs and to promote circulation, thereby preventing edema. If necessary, have ready I.V. equipment, suction apparatus, other special equipment, or a roller for patient transfer.

• Raise the bed to the high position, if it is not already in this position. Then, lock

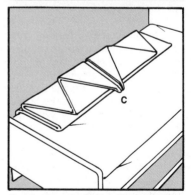

the wheels on the bed, and leave it in the high position, with rails down. Be sure side rails work properly. Move the bedside stand and other objects out of the stretcher's path to facilitate easy transfer when the patient returns.

*to prevent backstrain.*

• Remove the pillowcase and place it in the laundry bag. Or, use the pillowcase, hooked over the back of a chair, as a laundry bag. Then, place the pillow on the bedside stand or a chair.

• Lift the mattress edge slightly and work around the bed, untucking the linens. If you plan to reuse the top linens, fold the top hem of the spread down to the foot hem. Then, pick up the hemmed corners, fold the spread into quarters, and hang it over the back of the chair. Do the same for the top sheet. Otherwise, carefully remove and place the top linens in the laundry bag or pillowcase. *To avoid spreading microorganisms,* don't fan the linen, hold it against your uniform, or place it on the floor.

• Remove the soiled bottom linens, and place them in the laundry bag.

• When stripping the bed, watch for the patient's eyeglasses, dentures, or other belongings that may have fallen between the sheets.

• Push the mattress to the head of the bed; *adjusting it after bed-making loosens the linens.*

• Place the bottom sheet with its center fold in the middle of the mattress. Then, secure the top and bottom corners of the contour (fitted) sheet over the mattress corners on the side nearest you. Or, align the end of the flat sheet with the foot of the mattress, and miter the top corner *to keep the sheet firmly tucked under the mattress.* To miter the corner, first tuck the top end of the sheet evenly under the mattress at the head of the bed. Then, lift the side edge of the sheet about 12″ (30 cm) from the mattress corner and hold it at a right angle to the mattress. Next, tuck in the bottom edge of the sheet hanging below the mattress. Finally, drop the top edge and tuck it under the mattress.

• After tucking under one side of the bottom sheet, place the draw sheet (if needed) about 15″ (38 cm) from the top of the bed, with its center fold in the middle of the bed. Then, tuck in the entire edge of the draw sheet on the

side of the bed nearest you.

• Place the top sheet with its center fold in the middle of the bed and its wide hem even with the top of the bed. Position the rough side of the hem away from the bed, *so the finished side shows after folding.* Allow enough sheet at the top of the bed to form a cuff over the spread.

• Then, place the spread over the top sheet, with its center fold in the middle of the bed.

• Make a 3″ (7.5 cm) toe pleat, or vertical tuck, in the top linens *to allow room for the patient's feet and to prevent pressure that can cause discomfort, skin breakdown, and footdrop.*

• Tuck the top sheet and spread under the foot of the mattress. Then, miter the bottom corners.

• Move to the opposite side of the bed and repeat the procedure. *Completion of one side of the bed at a time promotes efficiency.*

• After fitting all corners of the bottom sheet or tucking them under the mattress, pull the sheet at an angle from the head toward the foot of the bed. *This tightens the linens, making the bottom sheet taut and wrinkle-free and promoting patient comfort.*

• Fold the top sheet over the spread at the head of the bed to form a cuff and to give the bed a finished appearance. When making an open bed, fanfold the top linens to the foot of the bed *to allow easy patient access.*

• Slip the pillow into a clean case, tucking its corners well into the case *to ensure a smooth fit.* Then, place the pillow with its seam at the top of the bed, *to prevent it from rubbing against the patient's neck, causing irritation,* and its open edge facing away from the door, *to give the bed a neat appearance.*

• Lower the bed and lock its wheels *to ensure patient safety.*

• Return furniture to its proper place, and place the call button within the patient's easy reach. Carry soiled linens from the room in outstretched arms *to avoid contaminating your uniform.*

• After disposing of the linens, wash

your hands thoroughly *to prevent the spread of microorganisms.*

### Special considerations

Because a hospital mattress is usually covered with plastic to protect it from drainage and excretions and to facilitate cleaning between patients, a flat bottom sheet tends to loosen and become untucked. Use a fitted sheet, if available, to prevent this.

### Documentation

Although the linen change isn't usually documented, record its time and date in your notes for the patient with incontinence, excessive wound drainage, or diaphoresis.

L. RUTH DRISCOLL, RN

# Occupied Bed

*For the bedridden patient, daily linen changes promote comfort and prevent skin breakdown and nosocomial infection. Such changes necessitate the use of side rails to prevent the patient from rolling out of bed and, depending on his condition, the use of a turning sheet to roll him from side to side.*

*Making an occupied bed may require more than one person and entails loosening the bottom sheet on one side and fanfolding it to the center of the mattress, instead of loosening the bottom sheet on* both *sides and removing it. It also requires completion of the base before* application *of the top sheet, instead of completion of both base and top on one side before their completion on the other side.*

### Equipment

Two sheets (one fitted, if available) □ pillowcase □ spread □ one or two draw sheets □ one or two blankets □ laundry bag (optional) □ sheepskin or other comfort device □ linen-saver pad (optional).

### Preparation of equipment

Obtain clean linen, which should be folded in half lengthwise and then folded again, creating a center crease that makes it easier to position on the bed. If the linen isn't folded properly, refold the bottom sheets with the smooth side of the hem facing inward; refold the top sheets with the rough side of the hem facing inward. This ensures that the rough side doesn't rub against the patient's heels when the bottom sheet is placed on the bed, helping to prevent skin irritation, and that the smooth side can be turned down on the spread, giving the bed a finished appearance.

### Essential steps

• Wash your hands, and bring clean linen to the patient's room.
• Tell the patient you will change his bed linens, and provide privacy.
• Move furniture away from the bed, if necessary, *to provide ample working space.*
• Raise the rail on the far side of the bed *to prevent falls.* Then, adjust the bed to a comfortable working height *to prevent backstrain.*
• If the patient's condition permits, lower the head of the bed *to ensure tight-fitting, wrinkle-free linens.*
• Cover the patient with a bath blanket *to avoid exposure and provide warmth and privacy.* Then, fanfold the top sheet and spread from beneath the bath blanket and bring them back over the blanket. Loosen the top linens at the foot of the bed and remove them separately. If you plan to reuse the top linens, fold each piece neatly and hang it over the back of the chair. Otherwise, place the soiled linen in the laundry bag. *To avoid dispersing microorganisms,* don't fan the linens, hold them against your uniform, or place them on the floor.
• When stripping the bed, watch for the patient's eyeglasses, dentures, and other belongings that may have fallen between the sheets.
• Pull the mattress to the head of the bed, or if the patient is able, ask him to

## MAKING A TRACTION BED

When making the bed of a patient in traction, obtain assistance from a co-worker. Work from head to toe *to minimize the risk of traction misalignment*, and follow the procedure below:

• Wash your hands, bring clean linen to the patient's room, and arrange it in the order of use on the bedside stand or a chair. Then, explain the procedure to the patient, provide privacy, and remove unnecessary furniture and equipment from the vicinity of the bed.

• Lower the rails on both sides of the bed. Stand near the headboard on one side of the bed, and have a co-worker stand near the headboard on the opposite side, facing you.

• Gently pull the mattress to the head of the bed. Avoid sudden movement, which can misalign traction and cause patient discomfort.

• Remove the pillow from the bed. Loosen the bottom linens, and roll them from the headboard toward the patient's head. Then, remove the soiled pillowcase and replace it with a clean one.

• Fold a clean bottom sheet crosswise, with the rough side of the hem facing inward. Then, place the sheet across the head of the bed. Tell the patient to raise his head and upper shoulders by grasping the trapeze above his bed (see illustration at right). Working with a co-worker, quickly fanfold the bottom sheet from the head of the bed under the patient's shoulders, so that it meets the soiled linen. Tuck at least 12″ (30 cm) of the bottom sheet tightly under the head of the mattress. Miter the corners and tuck in the sides as far down as possible.

• Tell the patient to pull higher on the trapeze and to raise his buttocks. As a team, move toward the foot of the bed and, in one movement, quickly and carefully roll soiled linens and clean linens under the patient's buttocks.

• Instruct the patient to release the trapeze and rest. Place a pillow under his head for comfort.

• If allowed, remove any pillows from under the patient's extremity. If pillow removal is contraindicated, continue to move linens toward the foot of the bed, under the patient's legs and traction, while the assisting co-worker lifts the pillows and supports the patient's extremity.

• Put soiled linens in a laundry bag or pillowcase.

• Securely tuck the remaining loose linens under the mattress. To ensure a tight bottom sheet, have the patient raise his weight off the bed by simultaneously grasping the trapeze and raising his buttocks while you pull the sheet tight. As needed, place a draw sheet, linen-saver pad, or sheepskin under the patient's buttocks. After the foundation is made, you can complete the bed-making alone.

• If the bottom sheet doesn't cover the foot of the mattress, pull the draw sheet up to cover it. Miter its corners and tuck in the sides. If the patient's body doesn't touch this sheet frequently, you needn't change it as often.

• Replace the pillows under the patient's extremity, then cover him with a clean top sheet. Fold over the top hem of the sheet approximately 8″ (20 cm). If one or both legs are in traction, fit the lower end of the sheet loosely over the leg(s) in traction; avoid applying unnecessary pressure to the traction ropes. To secure the sheet, tuck the corner of the sheet opposite the traction under the foot of the bed and miter the corner. Neatly tuck in the lower corner of the sheet on the traction side to expose the leg and foot.

• If the traction equipment exposes the

grasp the head of the bed and pull with you; otherwise, ask a co-worker to help you. *Adjusting the mattress after the bed is made loosens the linens.*

• Roll the patient to the far side of the bed, and position the pillow lengthwise under the head *to support the neck.*

• Loosen the soiled bottom linens on the side of the bed nearest you. Then, roll the linens toward the patient's back in the middle of the bed.

• Place a clean bottom sheet on the bed, with its center fold in the middle of the mattress. If you're using a fitted sheet, secure the top and bottom corners over the side of the mattress nearest you. Or, if you're using a flat sheet, place its end even with the foot of the mattress, and miter the top corner *to keep linens firmly tucked under the mattress, preventing wrinkling.* To miter the corner, first tuck the top end of the sheet evenly under the mattress at the

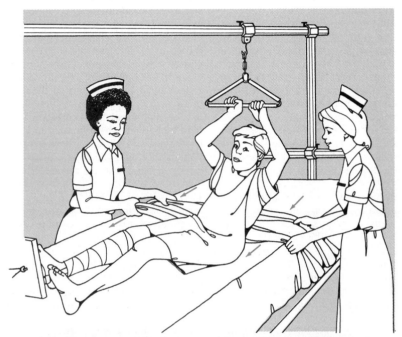

patient's sides, place a draw sheet across the bed. Avoid using a full sheet or spread, because either is too cumbersome.
• Lower the bed, but don't allow the traction weights to touch the floor. Raise the side rails *to prevent falls*. Or, if allowed, leave one side rail down so the patient can reach the bedside stand.
• Check the patient and the traction alignment. Ensure that the traction weights hang freely and that the patient's extremity is free of pressure from knots or tape. Before pulling up the mattress, make sure

that no weights have slipped below the lower edge of the footboard. If they have, upward movement can produce a sudden pull on the traction, causing painful tension.
• To help maintain alignment, follow these precautions: Place a pillow between the foot of the mattress and the foot of the bed *to prevent mattress slippage*. Also, place a pillow or bedroll at the foot of the bed on the unaffected side *to prevent the patient from sliding downward*. Or, use shock blocks to elevate the foot of the bed.

head of the bed. Then, lift the side edge of the sheet about 12″ (30 cm) from the mattress corner, and hold it at a right angle to the mattress. Next, tuck in the bottom edge of the sheet hanging below the mattress. Finally, drop the top edge and tuck it under the mattress.
• Fanfold the remaining clean bottom sheet toward the patient, and place the draw sheet (if needed) about 15″ (38 cm) from the top of the bed, with its center fold in the middle of the mattress. Then

tuck in the entire edge of the draw sheet on the side nearest you. Fanfold the remaining draw sheet toward the patient.
• If necessary, position a linen-saver pad on the draw sheet *to absorb excretions or surgical drainage*, and fanfold it toward the patient.
• Raise the side rail, and roll the patient over the soiled and fanfolded linen to the clean side of the bed.
• Move to the unfinished side of the

bed and lower the side rail. Then, loosen and remove the soiled bottom linens separately and place them in the laundry bag.

• Pull the clean bottom sheet taut. Secure a fitted sheet over the mattress corners or place the end of a flat sheet even with the foot of the bed, and miter the top corner. Then, pull the draw sheet taut and tuck it tightly under the mattress. Unfold and smooth the linen-saver pad, if used.

• Assist the patient to the supine position, if his condition permits.

• Remove the soiled pillowcase, and place it in the laundry bag. Then, slip the pillow into a clean case, tucking its corners well into the case *to ensure a smooth fit.* Then, place the pillow beneath the patient's head. Place the pillow's seam at the top of the bed *to prevent it from rubbing against the patient's neck, causing irritation.* Face the pillow's open edge away from the door *to give the bed a neat appearance.*

• Unfold the clean top sheet over the patient. Face the rough side of the hem away from the bed *to avoid irritating the patient's skin.* Allow enough sheet at the top of the bed to form a cuff over the spread.

• Remove the bath blanket from beneath the sheet, and place and center the spread over the top sheet.

• Make a 3″ (7.5 cm) toe pleat, or vertical tuck, in the top linens *to allow room for the patient's feet and prevent pressure that can cause discomfort, skin breakdown, and footdrop.*

• Tuck the top sheet and spread under the foot of the bed, and miter the bottom corners. Then, fold the top sheet over the spread to give the bed a finished appearance.

• Raise the head of the bed to a comfortable position for the patient, and lower the bed and lock its wheels *to ensure patient safety.* Return furniture to its proper place, and place the call button within the patient's easy reach. Then, remove the laundry bag from the room.

• Wash your hands thoroughly *to pre-* *vent the spread of nosocomial infections.*

## Special considerations

Use a fitted bottom sheet, when available, because a flat sheet easily pulls out from under the mattress, especially with the newer plastic-coated mattresses. Prevent the patient from sliding down in bed by tucking a tightly rolled pillow under the top linens at the foot of the bed. Provide additional comfort for the diaphoretic or bedridden patient by folding a bath blanket in half lengthwise and placing it between the bottom sheet and the plastic mattress cover; the blanket acts as a cushion and helps absorb moisture. *To help prevent sheet burns on the heels, elbows, and bony prominences, center a bath blanket or sheepskin over the bottom sheet; tuck the blanket securely under the mattress.*

If the patient can't help you move or turn him, devise a turning sheet to facilitate bed-making and repositioning of the patient. First, fold a draw sheet or bath blanket, and place it under the buttocks. Make sure the sheet extends from shoulders to knees, so it supports most of the patient's weight. Then, roll the sides of the sheet to form handles. Next, ask a co-worker to help you lift and move the patient. With one person holding each side of the sheet, you can move the patient without wrinkling the bottom linens. If you can't get help and must turn the patient yourself, stand at the side of the bed. Turn the patient toward the rail and, if he's able, ask him to grasp the rail to assist in turning. Then, reach over the patient and firmly grasp the opposite rolled edge of the sheet. Then, pull the rolled edge carefully toward you, turning the patient.

## Documentation

Although a linen change isn't usually documented, record its time and date in your notes for the patient with incontinence, excessive wound drainage, or diaphoresis.

L. RUTH DRISCOLL, RN

# Supplemental Bed Equipment

*Although supplemental bed equipment doesn't replace meticulous skin care, frequent turning, or range-of-motion exercises, it promotes the bedridden patient's comfort and helps prevent decubiti and other complications of immobility. The wooden or hard plastic footboard prevents footdrop by maintaining proper alignment and keeps the bed linens off the patient's feet. The foot cradle, an arch or horizontal bar positioned over the end of the bed, keeps bed linens off the patient's feet, preventing skin irritation and breakdown, especially in patients with peripheral vascular disease or neuropathy. The bedboard, made of wood or wood covered with canvas, firms the mattress and is especially useful for the patient with spinal injuries. The metal basic frame and the metal trapeze, a triangular piece attached to this frame, allow the patient with arm mobility and strength to lift himself off the bed, facilitating bed-making and bedpan positioning. The metal overbed cradle, a cagelike frame positioned on top of the mattress, keeps bed linens off the patient with burns, open wounds, or a wet cast.*

*The vinyl water mattress and the foam mattress, used to prevent or treat decubiti, exert less pressure on the skin than the standard hospital mattress. Although the alternating pressure pad (a vinyl pad divided into chambers filled with air or water and attached to an electric pump) serves the same purpose, it also stimulates circulation by continuous inflation and deflation of its chambers.*

## Equipment
● Footboard □ footboard cover □ draw sheet □ bath blanket □ safety pins □ foot cradle □ bedboard □ basic frame with trapeze □ overbed cradle □ rolled gauze □ water mattress □ stretcher □ alternating pressure pad □ pump and tubing □ footstool □ linen-saver pad □ foam mattress (such as an egg crate mattress) □ plastic protective sleeve for foam mattress (partial or full length).

All supplemental bed equipment is optional, depending on the patient's needs. Both reusable and disposable water mattresses are available. The reusable water mattress replaces the standard hospital mattress and rests on a sheet of heavy cardboard placed over the bedsprings; the smaller, less bulky disposable mattress rests on top of the standard hospital mattress.

## Preparation of equipment
If supplemental bed equipment isn't available on the unit, order it from the central supply department and request delivery to the patient's room, as needed.

If you're preparing a footboard for use, place a cover over it to provide padding. Or, pad it with a folded draw sheet or bath blanket: Bring the top and side edges of the sheet or blanket to the back of the footboard, miter the corners, and secure them at the center with safety pins. Padding cushions the patient's feet against pressure from the hard footboard, helping to prevent skin irritation and breakdown.

## Essential steps
● Tell the patient what you're about to do and describe the equipment.
● Wash your hands.
*To place a footboard:*
● Move the patient up in bed *to allow room for the footboard.* Loosen the top linens at the foot of the bed, then fold them back over the patient to expose his feet.
● Lift the mattress at the foot of the bed, and place the lip of the footboard between the mattress and the bedsprings. Or, secure the footboard under both sides of the mattress.
● Adjust the footboard so the patient's feet rest comfortably against it. If the footboard isn't adjustable, tuck a folded

# TYPES OF SUPPLEMENTAL BED EQUIPMENT

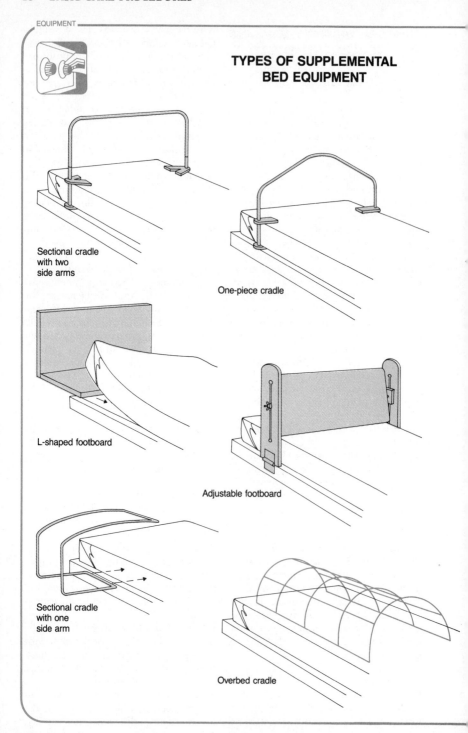

Sectional cradle with two side arms

One-piece cradle

L-shaped footboard

Adjustable footboard

Sectional cradle with one side arm

Overbed cradle

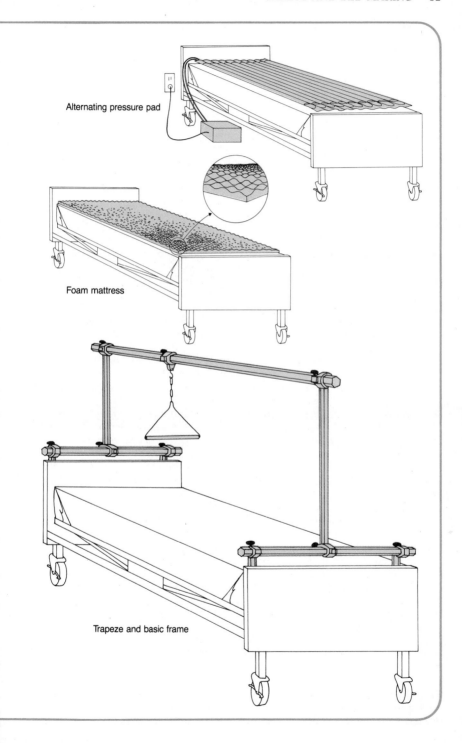

Alternating pressure pad

Foam mattress

Trapeze and basic frame

bath blanket between the board and the patient's feet.

• Unless the footboard has side supports, place a sandbag, a folded bath blanket, or a pillow alongside each foot *to maintain 90° foot alignment.*

• Fold the top linens over the footboard, tuck them under the mattress, and miter the corners.

• Adjust the top linens at the head of the bed *to cover the patient's shoulders.* Apply a second sheet if the linens don't cover the patient adequately.

*To place a foot cradle:*

• Loosen the top linens at the foot of the bed, and fold them over the patient or to one side.

• When using a one-piece cradle, place one side arm under the mattress, carefully extend the arch over the bed, and place the other side arm under the mattress on the opposite side. Then, adjust the tension rods so they rest securely over the edge of the mattress.

When using a sectional cradle with two side arms, first place the side arms under the mattress. Secure the tension rods over the edge of the mattress. Then, carefully place the arch over the bed and connect it to the side arms.

When using a sectional cradle with one side arm, connect the side arm and horizontal cradle bar before placement. Then, place the side arm under the mattress on one side of the bed.

• Cover the cradle with the top linens, tuck them under the mattress at the foot of the bed, and miter the corners.

• Adjust the top linens at the head of the bed *to cover the patient's shoulders.* Apply a second sheet, if the linens don't cover the patient adequately.

*To place an overbed cradle:*

• Loosen and remove the top linens.

• Carefully lower the cradle onto the patient's bed and secure it in place. Wrap roller gauze around both sides of the cradle. Then, pull the gauze taut and attach it to the bedsprings.

• Cover the cradle with the top linens, tuck them under the mattress at the foot of the bed, and miter the corners.

• Adjust the top linens at the head of

the bed *to cover the patient's shoulders.* Apply a second sheet if the linens don't cover the patient adequately.

*To place a bedboard:*

• Transfer the patient from his bed to a stretcher or a chair. Obtain assistance, if necessary.

• Strip the linens from the bed. If you plan to reuse them, fold each piece neatly and hang it over the back of a chair. Otherwise, discard soiled linens in a laundry bag.

• If the bedboard consists of wooden slats encased in canvas, lift the mattress at the head of the bed and center the board over the bedsprings *to prevent it from jutting out and causing accidental injury.* Unroll the slats to cover the bedsprings at the head of the bed. Then, lift the mattress at the foot of the bed and unroll the remaining slats.

If the bedboard consists of one solid or two hinged pieces of wood, lift the mattress on one side of the bed, and center the board over the bedsprings.

• After positioning the bedboard, replace the linens. Then, return the patient to bed.

*To place a basic frame with trapeze:*

• If an orthopedic technician isn't available to secure the frame and trapeze to the patient's bed, get assistance to attach these devices, as necessary. (See "Mechanical Traction," in Chapter 13.) Hang the trapeze within the patient's easy reach.

*To place a portable water mattress:*

• This mattress is heavy and bulky, so you'll need several co-workers to help you transfer it from the stretcher to the patient's bed. Because its weight may rule out use on some electric beds, check with the maintenance department before transferring the mattress. Also, ensure that the patient isn't disposed to motion sickness *because the movement of the water in the mattress may cause nausea.*

• Position the mattress on the bed, and place the protective cover over it. Then, place a bottom sheet over the cover and tuck it in loosely.

• Place a sheepskin, linen-saver pad, or draw sheet over the bottom sheet, as needed. Adding these doesn't decrease the effectiveness of this mattress.
• Position the patient comfortably on the mattress. Then, cover him with the top linens, and tuck them in loosely.
• Check the water mattress daily *to ensure adequate flotation.* To do so, place your hand under the patient's thighs. If you can feel the bottom of the mattress, arrange to have water added.

*To place an alternating pressure pad:*
• If possible, transfer the patient from his bed to a stretcher or a chair. Obtain assistance, if necessary.
• Strip the linens from the bed. Then, inspect the plug and electrical cord of the alternating pressure pad for evidence of frayed or broken wires.
• Unfold the pad on top of the mattress, with the appropriate side facing up.
• Place the motor on a linen-saver pad on the floor or on a footstool near the mattress outlets. Connect the tubing securely to the motor and to the mattress outlets, and plug the cord into an electrical outlet. Turn the motor on.
• After several minutes, observe the emptying and filling of the pad's chambers, and check the tubing for kinks that could interfere with the pad's function.
• Place a bottom sheet over the pad, and tuck it in loosely. *To avoid tube constriction,* don't miter the corner where the tubing is attached.
• Position the patient comfortably on the pad, cover him with the top linens, and tuck them in loosely.
• If the pad becomes soiled, clean it with a damp cloth and mild soap, then dry well. *To avoid damaging the pad's surface,* don't use alcohol.
• When the patient no longer needs the pad or is discharged, turn the motor off, disconnect the tubing, and unplug the cord from the wall outlet. Remove the pad from the patient's bed, and fold and discard it. Or, if applicable, give the pad to the patient to take home. Inform him that the motor needed to power the pad can usually be rented

from a surgical supply store.
• Coil the tubing and electrical cord, then strap them to the motor. Return the motor unit to the central supply department.

*To place a foam mattress:*
• If possible, transfer the patient from his bed to a stretcher or a chair. Obtain assistance, if necessary.
• Strip the linens from the bed. Then, place the foam mattress on top of the standard mattress, wavy side up.
• Slip the protective sleeve over the foam mattress at the patient's buttock level *to prevent the absorption of excretions into the mattress.* If necessary, use a full-length sleeve.
• Place a bottom sheet over the foam mattress, and tuck it in loosely. *Tucking it too tightly can decrease the cushioning effect.*
• Position the patient comfortably on the mattress. Then, cover him with the top linens, and tuck them in loosely.
• When the patient no longer needs the mattress or is discharged, discard the mattress or let him take it home.

## Special considerations
Because a plastic-covered mattress slides off a bedboard easily, be sure a co-worker is standing on the opposite side of the bed when you're transferring the patient from stretcher to bed. Help the patient who is ambulatory into and out of bed so the mattress doesn't shift beneath him.

Place the patient in bed before positioning and securing an overbed or foot cradle *to ensure its proper placement and to prevent patient injury.* Similarly, remove the cradle before the patient gets out of bed. When turning or positioning the patient on his side, be sure the foot cradle's tension rod doesn't rest against his skin, because this may cause pressure and predispose him to skin breakdown.

Exercise caution when turning the obese patient on a water mattress, *because turning displaces a large volume of water.* Be sure to keep the side rails raised during turning *to prevent falls.*

Avoid placing excessive layers of draw sheets or linen-saver pads between the alternating pressure pad and the patient, because these decrease the pad's effectiveness. Avoid using pins or sharp instruments near an alternating pressure pad or water mattress *to prevent accidental puncture.*

To position an alternating pressure pad or foam mattress in an occupied bed, first raise the side rail, and roll the patient to the far side of the bed. Then, center the inflated pad or foam mattress on the bed, and fold it against the patient's back. Roll the patient back over the fold, and straighten the pad or mattress. If the patient is in traction, unroll the pad or mattress from head to foot.

Use up to three foam mattresses on the bed, as the patient's condition requires. Place one mattress on the bed to prevent decubiti, two or three mattresses to treat them. You can decrease the pressure exerted on the bony prominences by increasing the number of mattresses.

If the bottom bedsheet isn't wide enough to cover both the standard and the foam mattresses, use two bottom sheets. Cover the standard mattress with one sheet, then cover the foam mattress with a second sheet and tuck it between the standard and foam mattresses.

Because a foam mattress is tightly rolled for storage, it may need to be unrolled on a clean empty bed and allowed to recover its original springiness before use.

Don't use a foam mattress to lift the patient, because the mattress may tear, causing the patient to fall.

**Documentation**
In your notes and care plan, record the type of supplemental bed equipment used, the time and date of use, and patient response to treatment.

L. RUTH DRISCOLL, RN

## HYGIENE AND COMFORT

# Bed Bath

*A complete bed bath cleanses the skin, stimulates circulation, provides mild exercise, and promotes comfort. Bathing also allows assessment of skin color and condition, joint mobility, and muscle strength. Depending on overall condition and duration of hospitalization, the patient may have a complete or partial bath daily. A partial bath—taking in the hands, face, axillae, back, genitalia, and anal region—can replace the complete bath for the patient with dry, fragile skin or extreme weakness, and can supplement the complete bath for the diaphoretic or incontinent patient.*

## Equipment
Bath basin □ bath blanket □ soap □ bath towel □ washcloth □ skin lotion □ orangewood stick □ deodorant □ bath oil (optional) □ powder (optional) □ ABD pad (optional) □ linen-saver pad (optional).

## Preparation of equipment
Adjust the temperature in the patient's room, and close the windows and doors to prevent drafts. Find out the patient's preference for soap and other hygiene aids; some patients are allergic to soap and some prefer bath oils or lotions. Then, assemble the equipment on an overbed table or bedside stand.

## Essential steps
● Tell the patient you will give him a bath, and provide privacy. If the patient's condition permits, encourage him to assist with bathing *to provide exercise and promote independence.*
● Raise the patient's bed to a comfort-

able working height *to avoid tiring your back.* Then, position the patient supine, if possible, and offer a bedpan or urinal.

• Fill the bath basin two-thirds full with warm water (about 115° F. or 46° C.) and bring it to the patient's bedside. Be sure the water temperature is comfortable *to avoid burning or chilling the patient.*

• If the bed is to be changed, remove the top linen. If not, fanfold it to the foot of the bed.

• Remove the patient's gown and other articles, such as elastic stockings, elastic bandages, and restraints. Cover him with a bath blanket *to provide warmth and privacy.*

• Place a towel under the patient's chin. Then, wash his face. Begin with his eyes, working from the inner to the outer canthus without soap. Use a separate section of the washcloth for each eye *to avoid spreading ocular infection.*

• If the patient can use soap, apply it to the cloth, and wash the rest of his face, ears, and neck, using firm, gentle strokes. Rinse thoroughly, because *residual soap can cause itching and dryness.* Then, dry the area thoroughly. Observe the skin for irritation, scaling, or other abnormalities.

• Turn down the bath blanket, and drape the patient's chest with a bath towel. While washing, rinsing, and drying the chest and axillae, observe respiration. Use firm strokes *to avoid tickling the patient.* If the patient can use a deodorant, apply it.

• Place a bath towel beneath the patient's arm farthest from you. Then, bathe this arm, using long, smooth strokes and moving from wrist to shoulder *to stimulate venous circulation.* If possible, soak the patient's hand in the basin *to remove dirt and soften nails.* If necessary, clean the patient's fingernails with an orangewood stick. Observe the color of his hand and nail beds *to assess peripheral circulation.* Bathe the opposite arm and hand in the same manner.

• Turn down the bath blanket to expose the patient's abdomen and groin, keeping a bath towel across the chest *to avoid chills.* Bathe, rinse, and dry the abdomen and groin while checking for abdominal distention or tenderness. Then, turn back the bath blanket to cover the patient's chest and abdomen.

• Uncover the leg farthest from you, and place a bath towel beneath it. Flex this leg and bathe it, using long, smooth strokes and moving from ankle to hip *to stimulate venous circulation;* do not massage the leg, *to prevent dislodgment of an existing thrombus, possibly causing a pulmonary embolus.* Rinse and dry the leg.

If possible, place a basin on the patient's bed, flex the leg at the knee, and place the foot in the basin. Allow the foot to soak, wash it with soap, and rinse thoroughly. Then, remove the foot from the basin, dry it, and clean the toenails. Observe skin condition and color during cleansing *to assess peripheral circulation.* Repeat the procedure on the other leg and foot.

• Cover the patient with the bath blanket *to prevent chilling.* Then, lower the bed and raise the side rails *to ensure the patient's safety,* while you change the bath water. Next, turn the patient on his side or stomach, place a towel beneath him, and drape him *to prevent chilling.* Bathe, rinse, and dry his back and buttocks.

• Massage the patient's back with lotion, giving attention to bony prominences. Check for redness, abrasions, and decubiti.

• Bathe the rectal area from front to back *to avoid contaminating the perineum.* Rinse and dry the area well.

• Observing safety precautions, change the bath water again. Then, turn the patient on his back and bathe the genital area thoroughly but gently, using a different section of the washcloth for each downward stroke. Bathe from front to back, avoiding the rectal area. Rinse thoroughly and pat dry.

• Perform indwelling catheter care, if applicable. Apply perineal pads or scrotal supports, as needed. Replace

the patient's gown and any elastic stockings, bandages, or restraints removed before the bath.
• Remake the bed or change the linens, and remove the bath blanket.
• Place a bath towel beneath the patient's head, then brush and comb his hair. *The towel catches loose hair.*
• Return the bed to its initial position, and make the patient comfortable.
• Carry soiled linens to the hamper with outstretched arms. Don't let the soiled linens touch your uniform *to prevent the spread of organisms.*

### Special considerations
When bathing the patient, fold the washcloth around your hand to form a mitt; *this keeps the cloth warm longer and prevents its loose ends from dribbling water onto the patient.* Change bath water as often as necessary to keep it comfortable, warm, and clean.

Carefully dry creased areas—under breasts, in the groin area, and between fingers, toes, and buttocks. Dust these areas lightly with powder after drying *to reduce friction.* Avoid too heavy dusting, *which can cause caking and irritation.*

If the patient has very dry skin, use bath oil instead of soap; no rinsing is necessary. However, if the patient wears elastic stockings, don't use bath oil or powder on the legs, *because both reduce elasticity.*

Warm the lotion for the back massage before use, because *cold lotion can startle the patient and cause muscle tension and vasoconstriction.*

Move the body joints through their full range of motion during the bath *to improve circulation, maintain joint mobility, and preserve muscle tone.*

If the patient is incontinent, loosely tuck an ABD pad between his buttocks and place a linen saver pad beneath it *to absorb fecal drainage.* Together, these pads help prevent skin irritation and reduce the number of linen changes.

### Documentation
Record the time and date of the bed bath on the flowchart. Document any unusual findings on the nursing-care plan, and report such findings to the charge nurse.

L. RUTH DRISCOLL, RN

# Tub Baths and Showers

*Tub baths and showers satisfy the patient's need for personal hygiene, stimulate circulation, and reduce tension. They also allow you to observe skin condition and assess joint mobility and muscle strength. If not precluded by the patient's condition or safety considerations, privacy during bathing promotes the patient's sense of well-being by allowing him to assume responsibility for his own care.*

*Patients who are recovering from recent surgery, who are emotionally unstable, or have casted extremities or dressings in place usually require the doctor's permission for a tub bath or shower.*

### Equipment
One or two washcloths □ one bath towel □ bath blanket □ soap (or nonallergenic equivalent) □ rubber bath mat (if the tub doesn't have nonskid strips) □ towel mat □ bath thermometer □ chair or stool (optional) □ clean clothing or hospital gown □ shower cap (optional) □ patient's toiletries (optional)—deodorant, powder, body lotion □ bath oil (optional) □ shampoo or mild castile soap (optional).

### Preparation of equipment
Prepare the bathing area before the patient arrives. Close the doors and windows and adjust the room temperature *to avoid chilling the patient.* If necessary, clean the bathtub or shower. Then, assemble bathing articles and observe the following safety measures:

*For a bath,* position a chair next to

the tub to help the patient get into and out of the tub and to provide a seat if he becomes weak. Place a bath blanket over the chair to cover the patient who becomes chilled. Fill the tub halfway with water, and test temperature with a bath thermometer; water temperature should range from 100° to 110° F. (37.8° to 43.3° C.). Aside from the obvious risk of scalding the patient, excessively hot water can cause cutaneous vasodilation, *which alters blood flow to the brain and may lead to dizziness or fainting.*

*For a shower,* place a special or nonskid chair in the shower to provide support; the chair also allows the patient to sit down to wash his legs and feet, reducing the risk of falling.

Make sure nonskid mats or rubber strips cover the bottom of the tub or shower. If they're not in place, cover the bottom with a rubber mat. Next, place a towel mat next to the bathing area. Remove electrical appliances, such as hair dryers and heaters, from the patient's reach to prevent electrical accidents. Adjust water flow and temperature just before the patient gets in.

### Essential steps

- Escort the patient to the bathing area, and help him undress as necessary. Have a shower cap available for the female patient to keep her hair dry, if she doesn't wish to wash it. Otherwise, provide shampoo or mild castile soap.
- Assist the patient into the tub or shower. If the patient has dry skin, add bath oil after the patient enters the tub, *because oil makes the tub slick and increases the risk of falling.*
- Being careful to respect his privacy, help the patient bathe, as needed; many patients appreciate help washing their backs.
- If you can safely leave the patient alone, place the call button within easy reach and show the patient how to use it. *Tell the patient to leave the door unlocked for his own safety, but assure him you'll post an "occupied" sign on the door.* Stay nearby in case of emer-

## HYDRAULIC BATH-LIFT BATHING SYSTEM

For the debilitated patient who can't take a shower or bath independently, a bath lift can facilitate patient transfer and eliminate strain on the nurse's back. A portable hose allows you to rinse the patient's hair. These lifts are most commonly found in rehabilitation or geriatric centers.

To allow for patient transfer, the lift (chair or stretcher) lowers to the patient's bed level. The lift can then lower the patient into a height-adjustable tub, set at the working height most comfortable for the nurse. Because the patient remains on the lift throughout the bath, the process is simply reversed when taking the patient out of the tub.

The patient who's using a hydraulic lift for the first time is apt to feel insecure and fearful. However, it's worthwhile using, because once the patient uses the lift, he'll probably find the bath both therapeutic and relaxing.

gency, and check on the patient every 5 to 10 minutes.
- When the patient finishes bathing, drain the tub or turn off the shower.
- Assist the patient onto the bath mat *to prevent his falling.* Then, help him dry off and dress, as necessary.
- Escort the patient to his room.
- Cleanse and disinfect the bathing area. Dry the floor well *to prevent slipping.*
- Dispose of soiled linens and return the patient's personal belongings to his bedside.

### Special considerations

If you don't have a bath thermometer, test the temperature by immersing your elbow in the water.

If you're giving a tub bath to a patient with a cast or dressing on an arm or leg, wrap the arm or leg in a clear plastic bag. Secure the bag with tape, being careful not to constrict circulation. Instruct the patient to dangle the arm or leg over the edge of the tub, and keep it out of the water.

Encourage the patient to use safety devices, bars, and rails when bathing. Because bathing in warm water causes vasodilation, the patient may feel faint. If so, open the drain or turn off the shower. Cover the patient's shoulders and back with a towel, and instruct him to lean forward in the tub, lowering his head; or, assist him out of the shower onto a chair, lower his head, and summon help. If you have an ampul of aromatic spirits of ammonia readily available, wave it under the patient's nostrils. Never leave the patient unattended to obtain an ampul. When the patient recovers, escort him to bed and monitor vital signs.

**Documentation**
Describe the patient's skin condition and record any discoloration or redness of skin and any adverse reactions in your notes.

ALICE F. PRIETO, RN, BSN

# Hair Care

*Hair care includes combing, brushing, styling, and shampooing. Combing and brushing stimulate scalp circulation, remove dead cells and debris, and distribute hair oils to produce a healthy sheen. Shampooing removes dirt and old oils and helps prevent skin irritation.*

*Frequency of hair care depends on the length and texture of the patient's hair, the duration of hospitalization, and the patient's condition. Usually, hair should be combed and brushed daily and shampooed according to the patient's normal routine, but at least once every 1 to 2 weeks. Shampooing is contraindicated in patients with cra-*

*nial injury, such as recent craniotomy, depressed skull fracture, or conditions necessitating intracranial pressure monitoring.*

**Equipment**
Comb, brush, and towel □ shampoo tray with tubing □ liquid shampoo (or mild soap, such as castile) □ three bath towels □ two bath blankets □ pail or plastic wastebasket □ two large pitchers or other large containers □ one small pitcher or beaker □ basin □ linen-saver pads.

Optional equipment includes hair conditioner or rinse, alcohol, oil, rubber bands (or ribbon or gauze), scissors, footstool, and draw sheet.

**Preparation of equipment**
The patient may bring his own comb and brush to the hospital. The comb and brush should be clean. The comb should have dull, even teeth to prevent scratching the scalp; the brush, stiff bristles to enhance vigorous brushing and stimulation of circulation.

Before shampooing the patient's hair, adjust room temperature and close off drafts to prevent chilling the patient. If necessary, wash the comb and brush in hot, soapy water. Next, obtain a shampoo tray from the storage area or devise a trough, if necessary. Then, assemble the equipment on the patient's bedside stand.

**Essential steps**
*To comb and brush hair:*
• Tell the patient you're going to comb and brush his hair. If practical, encourage him to care for his own hair, and provide assistance as necessary.
• Adjust the bed to a comfortable working height *to prevent backstrain.* Then, if the patient's condition allows, help him to a sitting position by raising the head of the bed.
• Provide privacy, and drape a towel over the patient's pillow and shoulders *to catch loose hair and dirt.*
• For short hair, comb and brush one side at a time.

• For long or curly hair, turn the patient's head away from you, then part his hair down the middle from front to back. If it's tangled, rub alcohol or oil on the hair strands to loosen them. Comb and vigorously brush the hair on the side facing up. Then, turn the patient's head toward you, and comb and brush the opposite side. Part hair into small sections for easier handling. Comb one section at a time, working from the ends toward the scalp to remove tangles. Hold each section above the section being combed, *to avoid pulling the patient's scalp.* After combing, brush vigorously.

• Style hair as the patient prefers. Braiding long or curly hair helps prevent snarling. To braid, part hair down the middle of the scalp and begin braiding near the face. Don't braid too tightly, *to avoid patient discomfort.* Fasten the ends of the braids with rubber bands, ribbon, or gauze. Then, pin the braids across the top of the patient's head or leave them down, as the patient desires, *so the finished braids don't press against the patient's scalp.*

• After styling, carefully remove the towel by folding it inward. *This prevents loose hairs and debris from falling onto the pillow or into the patient's bed.*

To shampoo hair of the patient confined to bed rest:

• Cover the patient with a bath blanket. Then, fanfold the linens to the foot of the bed, or remove them if changing is necessary.

• Place a pail or plastic container on a linen-saver pad on the floor or on a footstool near the head of the bed. The pail or container catches waste water from the shampoo tray.

• Fill large pitchers or containers with comfortable warm water and place them on the overbed table.

• Next, lower the head of the bed until it's horizontal, and remove the patient's pillow, if allowed.

• Fold the second bath blanket and tuck it under the patient's shoulders *to improve water drainage.*

EQUIPMENT

## HOW TO MAKE A SHAMPOO TROUGH

To make a trough, roll a bath blanket, towel, or sheet into a log. Shape the log into a U and place it in a large plastic bag, such as that used for contaminated waste. Arrange the bag under the patient's head, with the end of the bag extending over the edge of the bed and into a bucket on the floor (as illustrated below).

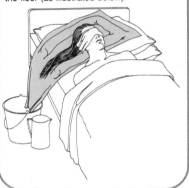

• Cover the bath blanket and the head of the bed with a linen-saver pad *to protect them from moisture.*

• Then, place a bath towel and linen-saver pad together, and place it around the patient's neck and over his shoulders. *This protects the patient from moisture and pads his neck against the pressure of the shampoo tray.*

• Place the shampoo tray under the patient's head, positioning the neck in the U-shaped opening. Arrange the bath blanket and towel so the patient is comfortable.

• Adjust the shampoo tray to carry waste water away from the patient's head, and place the drainage hose in the pail. Tuck a folded towel or draw sheet under the opposite side of the shampoo tray to promote drainage, if necessary.

When shampooing, place a wet washcloth over the patient's eyes to prevent soapy water from splashing in them; place cotton in his ears to prevent moisture from collecting in the canals.
• Fill the small container by dipping it into the large pitcher. Carefully pour water over the patient's hair. Don't overload the tray *to avoid spills.*
• Then, with your fingertips, rub shampoo into the patient's hair. Massage his scalp well *to emulsify hair oil. Vigorous rubbing stimulates the scalp and also helps the patient relax.*
• Using the small container, pour water over the patient's hair until it's free of shampoo. Then, apply shampoo and rinse again. Apply conditioner or a rinse, if necessary.
• Remove the shampoo tray, and wrap

---

## HAIR CARE FOR BLACK PATIENTS

Hair-care principles are unchanging for all people, but hair-care techniques vary with hair type. Many black people have thick, curly hair. The curl results from the angle at which hair is set in the scalp. Very curly or spiraled hair is set at a large angle, causing it to stand out from the head. Although spiraled hair may look strong and wiry, its shafts aren't as strong as those of straight hair and can be easily broken. Even when straightened, spiraled hair retains a tendency to become easily tangled, causing severe matting or even knotting. In the bedridden patient, matting usually occurs in hair on the back and sides of the head.

**Removing tangles**
Before removing tangles, you may need to apply a conditioner or lubricant to correct dryness. Make sure to obtain your patient's permission before applying it. After conditioning, weave your spread fingers through the hair to lift and free hair strands. You can also move your fingers in a semi–rotary-combing fashion, while gently lifting the hair until it's tangle-free. Or,

you can insert a natural long-toothed comb (pic) into hair ends and gently lift and fluff the hair (as shown above) to make it tangle-free. Repeat, each time inserting the comb farther into the hair and untangling it until you reach the scalp.

If you use a regular comb to remove tangles, first part the hair into sections, then comb each section separately. If the tangles are in the ends of the hair, hold the hair securely at the base of the section. Gently ease the tangles free with the comb until the entire section is combed.

**Combing natural (Afro) styles**
Using a large, natural open-toothed comb (pic), begin at the neckline, and lift and

fluff the hair outward. Continue fluffing, moving upward until the whole head is covered.

You can also divide your patient's hair into halves, from the forehead to the neckline. Begin combing out one half, starting at the neckline and working upward to the forehead. Repeat the procedure on the other half.

**Shampooing natural styles**
Begin at the scalp, and work outward to the ends of the hair in a comblike manner. Don't use a circular motion; it only tangles hair. To prevent tangles, you may want to apply a detangling solution first. Hair that's styled in cornrows doesn't have to be unbraided for washing.

the patient's hair in a towel. Remove the linen-saver pad from the bed, and return the bed to its initial position.
• Dry the patient's hair by gently rubbing it with a towel.
• Remove and empty the pail. Cleanse the shampoo tray, and return it to storage. Remove pitchers from the bedside, and return the shampoo to the bedside stand.
• Comb and brush the patient's hair.
• Remake the bed or change the linens, if needed, and remove the bath blanket.
• Reposition the patient comfortably.

**Special considerations**
When giving hair care, check the patient's scalp carefully for signs of scalp disorders or skin breakdown, particularly in bedridden patients. Make sure each patient has his own comb and brush *to avoid contamination.*

When a shampoo tray isn't available, devise a trough (see *How to Make a Shampoo Trough,* page 49). Or, place pillows under the patient's shoulders to elevate his head and use a standard basin. Because a standard basin doesn't have a drainage spout, empty it frequently to prevent overflow.

When shampooing the hair of a patient in a body cast, drape the upper cast completely to prevent loose hairs from falling inside; don't raise the patient's shoulders too high, to avoid chest pressure from the top of the cast. Or, you can shampoo the patient in a body cast by placing him on a stretcher. Then, devise a plastic trough to drain into a sink or hopper by covering the end of the stretcher with plastic. Extend the patient's head slightly over the end of the stretcher to facilitate drainage. If the patient's hair is severely matted, obtain a doctor's order and written permission from the patient or a responsible family member before cutting it. Use dry shampoo instead of liquid shampoo to clean the hair of an acutely ill patient.

**Documentation**
Record the date and time of shampoo

on the flowchart and any scalp abnormalities in your notes.

L. RUTH DRISCOLL, RN

# Shaving

*Performed with a straight, safety, or electric razor, shaving is usually part of the male patient's daily care. Besides reducing bacterial growth on the face, shaving promotes patient comfort by removing whiskers that often itch and irritate the skin and produce an unkempt appearance. Because nicks and cuts occur most frequently with a straight or a safety razor, shaving with an electric razor is indicated for the patient with a clotting disorder or undergoing anticoagulant therapy. Shaving is contraindicated in the patient with a facial skin disorder or wound.*

**Equipment**
Safety razor □ soap or shaving cream □ bath towel □ washcloth □ basin. *Optional:* mirror □ after-shave lotion □ talcum powder.

A shaving kit containing a razor, and soap container is also available.

*With an electric razor:* bath towel. *Optional:* pre-shave and after-shave lotions □ mirror.

**Preparation of equipment**
If you're using a straight or a safety razor, make sure the blade is sharp, clean, even, and free of rust; if necessary, insert a new blade securely in the razor. (A razor can be used more than once but only by the same patient.) If the patient is bedridden, assemble the equipment on the bedside stand or overbed table; if he is ambulatory, assemble it at the sink. When the patient is ready to shave, fill the basin or sink with warm water.

If you're using an electric razor, check its cord for fraying or other damage presenting an electrical hazard. If the razor isn't double-insulated or battery-operated, use a grounded (three-pronged) plug. Then, examine the razor head for sharp edges and cleanliness. Read the manufacturer's instructions, if available, and assemble the equipment at the bedside.

### Essential steps
● Tell the patient you're about to shave him, and provide privacy. Ask him to assist you as much as possible *to promote patient independence.*
● Unless contraindicated, place the conscious patient in the high Fowler's or semi-Fowler's position. If the patient is unconscious, elevate the head *to prevent soap and water from dribbling behind it.*
● Direct bright light onto the patient's face, but not into his eyes.
*To shave with a straight razor:*
● Drape a towel around the patient's shoulders, and tuck it under the chin *to protect the bed from moisture and to catch falling whiskers.*
● Using the washcloth, wet the patient's entire beard with warm water. Then, let the warm cloth soak the beard for at least 1 minute *to soften whiskers.*
● Apply shaving cream to the beard. Or, if you're using soap, rub to form a lather.
● Gently pull the patient's skin taut with one hand and shave with the other, holding the razor firmly. Ask the patient to puff his cheeks or turn his head, as necessary, to shave hard-to-reach areas.
Begin at the sideburns and work toward the chin using short, firm, downward strokes in the direction of hair growth. *This reduces skin irritation and helps prevent nicks and cuts.*
● Rinse the razor often *to remove whiskers.* Apply more warm water or shaving cream to the face, as needed, *to maintain a good lather.*
● Shave across the chin and up the neck and throat. Use short, gentle strokes for the neck and the area around the nose and mouth *to avoid skin irritation.*
● Change the water, and rinse any remaining lather and whiskers from the

patient's face. Then, dry the face and, if the patient desires, apply after-shave lotion or talcum powder.
● Rinse the razor and basin, then return the razor to its storage area.
*To shave with an electric razor:*
● Plug in the razor, and apply preshave lotion, if available, *to remove skin oils.* If the razor head is adjustable, select the appropriate setting.
● Using a circular motion and pressing the razor firmly against the skin, shave each area of the patient's face until smooth.
● If the patient desires, apply talcum powder or after-shave lotion.
● Clean the razor head, and return the razor to its storage area.

### Special considerations
If the patient is conscious, find out his usual shaving routine. Although shaving in the direction of hair growth is most common, the patient may prefer the opposite direction.
Don't interchange patients' shaving equipment *to prevent cross-contamination.*

### Complications
Cuts and abrasions are the most common complications of shaving and can require application of antiseptic lotion.

### Documentation
If applicable, record nicks or cuts resulting from shaving.
NANCY KENNEDY, RN, MSN

# Eye Care

*When paralysis or coma impairs or erases the corneal reflex, frequent eye care aims to keep the exposed cornea moist, preventing ulceration and inflammation. Application of gauze pads saturated with saline solution over the eyelids moistens the eyes. Commercially available eye ointments and ar-*

*tificial tears also lubricate the corneas, but a doctor's order is required for their use.*

*Although eye care isn't a sterile procedure, asepsis should be observed as closely as possible.*

## Equipment

Sterile basin □ sterile towel □ sterile cotton balls □ sterile saline solution □ mineral oil □ gauze or eyepads □ nonallergenic tape.

## Preparation of equipment

Assemble the equipment at the patient's bedside. Then, pour a small amount of saline solution into the basin.

## Essential steps

• Wash your hands thoroughly, and tell the patient what you're about to do, even if he is comatose or appears unresponsive.

• To remove secretions or crusts adhering to the eyelids and eyelashes, first soak a cotton ball in saline solution. Then, gently wipe the patient's eye with the moistened cotton ball, working from the inner canthus to the outer canthus *to prevent debris and fluid from entering the nasolacrimal duct. To prevent cross-contamination,* use a fresh cotton ball for each swipe until the eye is clean. Repeat the procedure for the other eye.

• After cleaning the eye, instill artificial tears or apply eye ointment, as ordered, *to keep the eye moist.*

• Close the patient's eyelids. Then, dab a small amount of mineral oil on each lid *to lubricate and protect fragile skin.*

• Soak gauze pads in saline solution, place them over the eyelids, and secure with nonallergenic tape. Change gauze pads, as necessary, *to keep them well saturated.*

• After giving eye care, cover the basin with a sterile towel. Change the setup (basin, towel, and saline solution) at least daily.

## Documentation

Record the time and type of eye care in your notes. If applicable, chart administration of eye drops or ointment in the patient's medication record.

JOANNE PATZEK DACUNHA, RN

# Contact Lens Care

*Contact lenses—thin curved disks made of hard or soft plastic to correct visual defects—float on the tear layer in the eye. Hard contact lenses cover part of the cornea, touching the eye surface only during blinking. In contrast, soft lenses cover the entire cornea and, because they're pliable, mold themselves to the eyes for a firmer fit.*

*Although a patient can normally care for his own contact lenses, illness or emergency treatment may require that you remove or insert them for him. Proper handling of contact lenses helps prevent eye injury and loss or damage of the lenses.*

## Equipment

Saline eye drops (if needed) □ lens storage case (or two small medicine cups and adhesive tape) □ suction cup (optional) □ flashlight (if needed).

*For hard lenses:* wetting, cleaning, and soaking solutions.

*For soft lenses:* with heat disinfection—normal saline solution (salt tablet and distilled water) □ cleaning solution (enzymatic cleaning tablet and distilled water) □ plastic or glass vials □ disinfecting unit; with chemical disinfection—cleaning, rinsing, storage, and disinfection solutions.

## Preparation of equipment

If a commercial storage case isn't available, place a few drops of normal saline solution in two small medicine cups. To prevent switching lenses, mark one cup L and the other cup R.

## Essential steps

• Tell the patient what you're about to

do, and wash your hands *to help prevent ocular infection.*

*To insert hard lenses:*
• Wet one lens with solution, and gently rub it between your thumb and index finger, or place it on your palm and rub it with your index finger.
• Place the lens, convex side down, on the tip of your right index finger (if right-handed).
• Instruct the patient to gaze upward slightly. Separate the eyelids with your left thumb and index finger, and place the lens directly on the cornea. Using the same procedure, insert the opposite lens.

*To insert soft lenses:*
• Flex one lens between your thumb and index finger. If its edge points slightly inward, the lens is in the correct position; if its edge points outward, the lens is inside out and must be reversed.
• Wet the lens with fresh saline solution, and rub it gently between your thumb and index finger, or place it on your palm and rub it with your index finger.
• Place the lens, convex side down, on the tip of your right index finger.
• Instruct the patient to gaze upward slightly. Separate the eyelids with your left thumb and index finger, and place the lens on the sclera, just below the cornea. Then, slide the lens up with your finger and center it on the cornea. Using the same procedure, insert the opposite lens.

*To remove hard lenses:*
• Before removing a lens, position the patient supine. *This prevents the lens from popping out onto the floor, causing loss or damage.*
• Using your thumb or middle finger, stretch the patient's upper eyelid toward the temporal bone.
• Place your middle finger on the upper eyelid and your thumb on the lower lid. Gently move the lids toward each other *to trap the lens edge and break the suction.* Cup your other hand below the eye to catch the lens when it pops out *to prevent loss of lens.*

• Place the lens in the appropriate well of the storage case with a few drops of soaking solution. Or, place the lens in the labeled medicine cup, and secure adhesive tape over the top of the cup *to prevent loss of the lens.*
• Remove and care for the opposite lens using the same technique.

*To remove soft lenses:*
• Position the patient supine. Then, raise the upper eyelid and hold it against the orbital rim.
• Lightly place the thumb and forefinger of your opposite hand on the lens. Then, pinch the lens; it should pop off the cornea.
• Place the lens in the appropriate well of the storage case with a few drops of normal saline solution. Or, place the lens in the labeled medicine cup, and secure adhesive tape over the top of the cup *to prevent loss of the lens.*
• Remove and care for the opposite lens using the same technique.

*To clean hard lenses:*
• Place a few drops of cleaning solution on one lens. Then, rub the lens gently between your thumb and index finger, or place it on your palm and rub it with your index finger *to remove dirt and film.* If the lens remains soiled, clean it with a stronger cleaning solution.
• Rinse the lens thoroughly with tap water.
• After cleansing the opposite lens, place both lenses in soaking solution or, if the doctor recommends, store them dry.

*To clean soft lenses by heat disinfection:*
• Place a few drops of fresh normal saline solution on each lens. Then, rub each lens gently between your thumb and index finger, or place it on your palm and rub it with your index finger.
• After cleaning the lenses, place each one in the appropriate well of the disinfecting case, and fill each well with fresh saline solution.
• Close the case caps and wipe the case dry. Then place the case in the disinfecting unit and close the cover tightly.
• Place the unit on a formica, ceramic

## REMOVING CONTACT LENSES WITH A SUCTION CUP

In an emergency or a difficult removal, a rubber suction cup can aid contact lens removal. To remove a lens:

• First, make sure the suction cup is clean. Then, wet the cup with normal saline solution.
• Gently pull down the patient's lower eyelid. Don't pull down the lid too far, because the upper lid will then descend, making lens removal more difficult.
• Press the suction cup to the center of the lens (see photograph at right), not to the eye. (If you mistakenly press it to the eye, release suction by sliding the cup to the eye's outer corner and turning the cup gently.) Then check that all edges of the suction cup are touching the lens.
• Release suction pressure on the lens. Next, break the suction at the lower scleral area by pulling the lens from the bottom in a rocking motion. Be sure to break the suction before pulling the lens forward. (If you have difficulty with this step, raise the patient's upper eyelid and break the suction at the upper scleral area. Pull up-

ward and outward to remove the lens from under the lower eyelid.)
• Pull the lens out and down.
• Wash the cup in warm soapy water.

---

tile, or other heat-resistant surface.
• Plug the disinfecting unit into an electrical outlet and turn it on. After cleaning, the unit shuts off automatically.
• In addition to routine heat disinfection, soft lenses need weekly cleansing with an enzymatic solution *to dissolve protein deposits.* First rinse and fill the plastic or glass vials of the lens storage case with distilled water, and drop an enzymatic cleaning tablet in each vial. Then, put one lens in each vial and fasten the caps. Shake the vials *to dissolve the tablets.*
• Let the lenses soak 6 to 12 hours or overnight. Then, remove and rinse them thoroughly with fresh saline solution. Next, place the lenses in the disinfecting unit and proceed as above.

Discard the solution in the vials, rinse the vials with tap water, and allow them to air-dry.

*To clean soft lenses by chemical disinfection:*
• Place a few drops of cleaning solution on one lens. Then, rub the lens gently between your thumb and forefinger, or place it on your palm and rub it with your index finger.
• Position the lens on the palm side of your index and middle fingers, and rinse it thoroughly with solution.
• Place the lens in the correct well of the storage case, fill the well with storage and disinfectant solution, and close its cap tightly. Repeat the procedure for the other lens.
• Store the lenses overnight or for at least 4 hours.
• Before inserting the lenses, clean and rinse them again as described above. After storage, empty the solution from the wells and rinse them with hot water. Then, flush the wells with rinsing solution and air-dry.

### Special considerations

If the patient's eyes appear dry, instill several drops of sterile saline solution, and wait a few minutes before removing the lens, *to prevent corneal damage.*

If you can't easily remove a lens, notify an ophthalmologist.

Avoid instillation of eye medication while the patient is wearing soft lenses. The lenses can combine chemically with the medication, possibly causing eye irritation or lens damage.

Don't allow soft lenses, which are 40% to 60% water, to dry out. If they do, soak them in saline solution to return them to their natural shape.

If an unconscious patient is admitted to the emergency department, check for contact lenses by opening each eyelid and searching with a small flashlight. If you detect lenses, remove them immediately, because tears cannot circulate freely beneath the lenses with eyelids closed, causing corneal ulcers and occasionally blindness after prolonged lens retention. Advise the wearer to carry appropriate identification to speed lens removal and ensure proper care in an emergency.

**Documentation**

Record eye condition before and after removal of lenses; the time of lens insertion, removal, and cleaning; the location of stored lenses; and, if applicable, the removal of lenses from the hospital by a family member.

JOANNE PATZEK DACUNHA, RN

# Prosthetic Eye Care

*An eye prosthesis—a durable, plastic globe fashioned to resemble the patient's natural eye—can usually be cared for by the patient unless injury or paralysis impairs his mobility. In the unconscious patient, the prosthesis can remain in place unless excessive secretions occur or surgery is scheduled.*

*Prosthetic eye care depends largely on the patient's preference and routine, but daily removal and cleansing isn't necessary. If the patient's socket becomes irritated and dry, or when discharge accompanies a cold, removal of the prosthesis and irrigation of the socket with normal saline solution or ophthalmic irrigating solution can increase patient comfort. Although not a sterile procedure, removal of the prosthesis requires good handwashing technique, careful handling, and proper storage of the device in water or saline solution.*

**Equipment**

Suction cup (optional) □ storage container for prosthesis □ normal saline solution or ophthalmic irrigating solution □ irrigation set (if saline solution is used) □ container of water □ emesis basin □ gauze □ towel.

**Preparation of equipment**

Assemble the equipment at the patient's bedside. Provide a mirror for the bedridden patient capable of performing self-care.

**Essential steps**

● Wash your hands *to avoid introducing bacteria into the eye socket.* Then, explain the procedure to the patient. Place the patient in the sitting or supine position, as his condition allows, and provide privacy.

*To remove the prosthesis:*

● Line the bottom of the storage container with gauze *to cushion the prosthesis and prevent scratches.* Then, fill the container with water.

● Gently pull down on the patient's lower lid with your left middle finger (if right-handed).

● Using your right hand, squeeze the suction cup *to create a vacuum,* and place its tip on the prosthesis. Pull the prosthesis downward and out of the socket. If a suction cup isn't available, apply slight pressure under the lower edge of the prosthesis with your right thumb. Cup your left hand under the prosthesis *to catch it when it slips out.*

● After removing the prosthesis, carefully cleanse it with water or irrigating solution; avoid using alcohol, *which dulls plastic.* Then, immerse the prosthesis in

## HOW TO REMOVE A PROSTHESIS

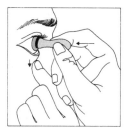  

With your dominant hand, place the tip of the suction cup on the patient's prosthesis; with your other hand, depress the lower lid (as illustrated at left). Pull out and downward, sliding the prosthesis over the lower lid (at middle). Finally, slide the prosthesis out from under the upper lid (at right).

the water-filled storage container.

*To irrigate the eye socket:*
• Drape a towel over the patient's shoulders to protect the gown. Then, instruct the sitting patient to hold an emesis basin next to the eye socket, or tuck the basin beneath the supine patient's cheek.
• Moisten the gauze with normal saline or irrigating solution. Then, wipe the patient's eyelids *to remove secretions or crusts adhering to the lashes.*
• Using your left hand, gently separate the patient's eyelids with your index and middle fingers or thumb and index fingers.
• Irrigate the eye socket thoroughly, directing solution from the inner canthus to the outer canthus. Then, pat the eyelids dry with gauze.
• Remove and discard the towel. Clean the emesis basin, and return it to the patient's bedside stand.

*To insert the prosthesis:*
• Moisten the prosthesis with saline solution or water *to reduce friction and ease insertion.*
• Squeeze the suction cup *to create a vacuum,* and center its tip on the prosthesis. Or, hold the prosthesis between your right thumb and index finger.
• Using your left index and middle fingers, gently pull upward on the patient's upper lid. Then, slip the upper

edge of the prosthesis under the upper lid, pointing the narrow end of the prosthesis toward the patient's nose.
• While supporting the prosthesis with your left fingers, gently pull the lower lid down with your right middle finger, and slip the lower edge of the prosthesis under the lower lid.
• Squeeze the suction cup to release the prosthesis, if applicable.
• Be sure the prosthesis is correctly positioned in the socket.

### Special considerations

Find out the patient's routine care of the prosthesis; some patients may remove and wash the prosthesis daily and irrigate the socket with saline solution. Assist the patient to follow his usual routine, as necessary.

If the patient doesn't wear eyeglasses, suggest that he obtain a pair of glasses with clear plastic lenses *to help protect the remaining natural eye from trauma.*

If the patient experiences itching around the prosthesis, instruct him to close the eye and rub toward the bridge of the nose. *This prevents the prosthesis from spinning in the socket and possibly popping out.*

### Documentation

Record the patient's care routine for the

prosthesis on the cardex, and the time, date, and type of care in your notes. Record redness, discharge, or other signs of irritation in the eye socket.

JOANNE PATZEK DACUNHA, RN

# Hearing Aid Care

*The hearing aid—a battery-powered device consisting of a microphone, amplifier, receiver, and earmold—amplifies sound to a volume audible to the hearing-impaired. Its microphone first picks up sound and converts it into electrical energy; then its amplifier magnifies this energy electronically; next, the receiver converts the amplified energy back into sound energy; and finally, the earmold directs the amplified sound into the user's ear.*

*Proper hearing aid function requires careful handling during insertion and removal, regular cleaning of the earmold to prevent wax buildup, and prompt replacement of dead batteries. When properly fitted, worn, and cared for, the hearing aid provides a critical link between the hearing-impaired patient and his environment.*

## Equipment

Appropriate hearing aid □ battery (if needed).

## Essential steps

• Wash your hands, and tell the patient what you're about to do.

*To insert the hearing aid:*

• First, be sure the hearing aid is turned off and that the volume is turned all the way down.

• Then, examine the earmold and the patient's external ear *to determine how the mold fits the ear.* Some earmolds fill only the ear canal and concha, whereas others fill all contours of the external ear. Use the canal portion, a long part common to all earmolds, as a guide. Also, ask the patient to help

you distinguish right and left earmolds, if necessary.

• Hold the earmold next to the patient's ear, with its parts in line with corresponding parts of the external ear. Then, rotate the earmold slightly forward, and insert the canal portion. Next, gently push the earmold into the ear while rotating it backward. Adjust the folds of the ear over the earmold, if necessary. When properly inserted, the earmold fits snugly. Ask the patient if the earmold feels comfortable and secure.

• After inserting the earmold, adjust other parts of the hearing aid as needed. Place a behind-the-ear aid over the patient's ear. Or, clip a body aid to the patient's shirt pocket, undergarment, or hearing aid harness carrier.

• Finally, set the switch to the *on* position, usually labeled M, and turn the volume halfway up. Ask the patient if the volume is suitable, and adjust it as necessary.

*To remove a hearing aid:*

• First, set the switch to the *off* position and lower the volume. Then, remove the earmold by rotating it forward and pulling outward. Next, remove or unclip the hearing aid case.

• After removal, store the hearing aid in a safe *to prevent loss or damage.*

*To care for a hearing aid:*

• Keep the earmold clean and free of excess wax *to prevent infection and promote efficient hearing aid performance.* For a body aid, detach the earmold from the receiver; for the behind-the-ear or eyeglass aid, detach the earmold where its tubing meets the hook of the hearing aid case, if possible. Don't remove the earmold if glue or a small metal split ring secures the earmold tubing to the hearing aid case.

• After detaching the earmold, soak it in a mild soapy solution. Then, rinse it and dry well. Blow excess moisture through the earmold opening. If the opening is clogged with wax or debris, use a pipe cleaner or toothpick to remove it. Then, replace the dry, clean earmold in the hearing aid case.

## COMMON TYPES OF HEARING AIDS

**Behind-the-ear aid** (most widely used type) fits neatly over the ear. The hearing aid case houses the microphone, the amplifier, and the receiver. A small plastic tube connects the case to an earmold.

**Body hearing aid** (used for most severe hearing loss) clips onto a shirt pocket, an undergarment, or a hearing aid harness carrier. The hearing aid case houses the microphone—covered by a grill—and the amplifier. A cord connects the case to the receiver and transmits the amplified sound. An earmold, which fits into the ear, snaps into the receiver.

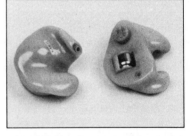

**Eyeglass aid** (hearing aid may be in one or both temples) resembles the behind-the-ear aid, except that its components are contained in an eyeglass temple. In some eyeglass aids, tubing inserted into the ear canal substitutes for an earmold.

**In-the-ear aid** (most compact type) consists of one piece fashioned like an earmold, which houses the microphone, the amplifier, and the receiver.

• For an in-the-ear aid and an aid with an unremovable earmold, wipe the mold with a damp cloth. Use a pipe cleaner or toothpick *to unclog the earmold opening.* Avoid pushing debris into the opening.

### Special considerations

Because the hearing aid is a delicate electronic instrument, avoid exposing it to heat and humidity, and never immerse it in water. When caring for the aid, limit cleaning to the earmold. Don't insert sharp objects into the microphone or receiver opening of the hearing aid; only an audiologist or hearing aid dealer should clean these parts.

If the hearing aid fails to operate,

## TROUBLESHOOTING HEARING AID PROBLEMS

| PROBLEM AND POSSIBLE CAUSE | NURSING INTERVENTION |
|---|---|
| **No sound or weak sound**<br>• Improper battery insertion<br>• Dead battery<br>• Clogged earmold opening<br>• Twisted plastic tubing<br>• Switch on *off* or on *T* for use with telephone<br>• Volume not turned high enough | • Reinsert the battery.<br>• Try a new battery.<br>• Unclog earmold opening.<br>• Untwist plastic tubing.<br>• Switch to *on* or *M* position.<br>• Turn volume control at least one half full rotation. |
| **Whistling or squealing sound**<br>• Improper earmold insertion<br>• Volume turned too high<br>• With a body hearing aid, earmold is not securely snapped to receiver. (A whistling sound is normal when the earmold is not inserted and the hearing aid is turned on. Such whistling indicates that the hearing aid is working and that the battery is inserted properly.) | • Reinsert earmold.<br>• Turn down volume.<br>• Secure earmold to receiver. |

Note: If problems persist, consult an audiologist.

consult the patient, because long-time hearing aid users usually know how to solve problems with their aids, or review instructions in the operating manual. If you still need help, contact the audiologist or dealer who dispensed the aid or the hospital audiologist.

Replace a dead battery with a new one of the same type. When inserting the battery, match negative ( − ) and positive ( + ) signs. If the hearing aid won't be used for several days, remove the battery *to prevent possible corrosion from battery leakage.*

When communicating with the patient who wears a hearing aid, be sure to get his attention before speaking. Then, face him directly and speak clearly and naturally as you would in normal conversation, without shouting or over-enunciating words. Keep your hands and other objects away from your face, so the patient can see lip movements, facial expressions, and other gestures that aid communication. If the patient fails to understand you, rephrase your sentences instead of repeating the same words.

If the patient's scheduled for diagnostic studies, insert his hearing aid beforehand, so he feels more secure and can follow directions accurately. Remove the aid before the patient goes to surgery.

### Documentation
In your notes, record any problems the patient has with the hearing aid and the location of the aid when not in use.

NEAL L. PEYSER, MA, CCC-A

# Mouth Care

*Given during morning or bedtime care or after meals, oral care entails brush-*

*ing and flossing the teeth and inspecting the mouth. It removes soft plaque deposits and calculus from the teeth, massages the gums, reduces mouth odor, and helps prevent infection. By freshening the patient's mouth, oral care also enhances appreciation of food, thereby contributing to good nutrition.*

*Although the ambulatory patient can usually perform oral care alone, the bedridden patient may require partial to full assistance. The comatose patient always requires full assistance, including the use of suction equipment to prevent aspiration during oral care.*

## Equipment

Towel or tissues □ emesis basin □ trash bag □ mouthwash □ toothbrush and dentifrice □ pitcher and glass □ drinking straw □ dental floss □ dental floss holder, if available □ small mirror (if necessary).

For the comatose or debilitated patient, also have ready the following equipment (as needed): linen-saver pad, bite-block, petrolatum, cotton-tipped swabs, oral suction equipment or gauze sponges. Optional equipment includes lemon-glycerin swabs, tongue blade, 4″ x 4″ gauze sponges, and adhesive tape.

Use unwaxed dental floss, if available. *Waxed floss can leave a residue on the teeth and promote retention of plaque.*

## Preparation of equipment

Fill a pitcher with water and bring it and other equipment to the patient's bedside. If suction equipment is not already available for the comatose patient, order it from the central supply department. When it arrives on the unit, bring it to the patient's room. Connect the tubing to the suction bottle and suction catheter, insert the plug into an outlet, and check for correct operation. If necessary, devise a bite-block to protect yourself from biting during the procedure. Wrap a gauze sponge over the end of a tongue blade, fold the edge in, and secure it with adhesive tape.

## Essential steps

● Wash your hands thoroughly, explain the procedure to the patient, and provide privacy.

*If the bedridden patient is capable of self-care:*

● If allowed, place the patient in Fowler's position. Place the overbed table across the bed, and arrange the equipment on it. Open the table and set up the built-in mirror, if available, or position a small mirror on the table.

● Next, drape a towel over the patient's chest to protect his gown. Then, instruct him to floss his teeth while looking into the mirror.

● If the patient is flossing incorrectly, instruct him to wrap the floss around the second or third fingers of both hands. Starting with the back teeth, have him insert the floss as far as possible into the interproximal space without injuring the gums, and clean the surfaces of adjacent teeth by pulling the floss up and down against the side of each tooth. Then, instruct him to wrap the floss around the back of each tooth (forming a C), and pull the floss up and down over the tooth. After the patient flosses a pair of teeth, remind him to use a clean 1″ (2.5 cm) section of floss for the next pair.

● After the patient flosses, mix mouthwash and water in a glass, place a straw in the glass, and position the emesis basin nearby. Then, instruct the patient to brush his teeth while looking into the mirror. Encourage him to rinse frequently during brushing, and provide tissues to wipe the mouth.

*If the conscious patient is incapable of self-care:*

● Raise the bed to a comfortable working height *to prevent backstrain.* Then, lower the head of the bed, and position the patient on his side, with his face extended over the edge of the pillow *to facilitate drainage and prevent fluid aspiration.* Place a linen-saver pad under the patient's chin and an emesis basin near his cheek *to absorb or catch drainage.*

● Next, arrange the equipment on the

# USING THE WATER PIK

The water pik directs a pulsating jet of water around the teeth to massage gums and remove debris and food particles. It's especially useful for cleaning areas missed by brushing, such as around bridgework, crowns, and dental wires. Because the water pik enhances oral hygiene, it benefits patients undergoing head and neck irradiation, which can damage teeth and cause severe caries. The water pik also promotes oral hygiene in a patient with a fractured jaw or with mouth injuries that limit standard mouth care.

**To use the water pik**
• Assemble the following equipment: water pik machine, towel, emesis basin, pharyngeal suction setup, and if ordered, salt solution and mouthwash.
• Position the patient on his side *to prevent aspiration of water.* Then, place a towel under the chin and an emesis basin next to the cheek *to absorb or catch drainage.*
• Insert the water pik's plug into a nearby electrical outlet.
• Remove the cover of the water pik. Then, turn the water pik upside down and fill it with lukewarm water or with a mouthwash or salt solution, as ordered. When using a salt solution, dissolve the salt beforehand in a separate container. Then, pour the solution into the cover.
• Secure the cover to the base of the water pik. Then, remove the water hose handle from the base, and snap the jet tip into place. If necessary, wet the grooved end of the tip *to ease insertion.*
• Adjust the pressure dial to

the setting most comfortable for the patient. If his gums are tender and prone to bleeding, choose a low setting.
• Adjust the knurled knob on the handle *to direct the water jet,* place the jet tip in the patient's mouth, and turn on the water pik. Instruct the alert patient to keep his lips partially closed *to avoid splashing water.*
• Direct the water at a right angle to the gum line of each tooth (as shown below). Avoid directing water under the patient's tongue, *because this may traumatize sensitive tissue.*
• After irrigating each tooth, pause briefly and instruct the patient to expectorate water or solution into the emesis basin; if he can't, suction it from the sides of the mouth.
• After irrigating all teeth, turn off the water pik, and remove the jet tip from the patient's mouth.
• Empty the remaining water or solution from the cover, remove the jet tip from the handle, and return the handle to the base. Clean the jet tip with soap and water, and rinse the cover. Dry the jet tip and cover, and return them to their storage positions.

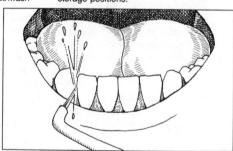

overbed table or bedside stand.
• Lubricate the patient's lips with petrolatum *to prevent dryness and cracking.* Reapply lubricant, as needed, during oral care.
• Use a floss holder *to clean between the patient's teeth.* Hold the floss close to the tooth and direct it as close to the gum as possible without injuring the

sensitive tissues around the tooth.
• After flossing the patient's teeth, mix mouthwash and water in a glass and place the straw in it.
• Then, wet the toothbrush with water. If necessary, use hot water *to soften the bristles.*
• Brush the patient's lower teeth from the gum line up; the upper teeth, from

the gum line down. Place the brush at a 45° angle to the gum line, and press the bristles gently into the gingival sulcus. Using short, gentle strokes *to prevent gum damage,* brush the facial surfaces (toward the cheek) and the lingual surfaces (toward the tongue) of the bottom teeth; use just the tip of the brush for the lingual surfaces of the front teeth. Then, using the same technique, brush the facial and lingual surfaces of the top teeth. Next, brush the biting surfaces of the bottom and top teeth, using a back-and-forth motion. Have the patient rinse frequently during brushing by taking the mouthwash solution through the straw. Hold the emesis basin steady under the patient's cheek, and wipe the mouth and cheeks with tissues, as needed.

• After brushing the patient's teeth, dip a mouth swab into the mouthwash solution. Press the swab against the side of the glass to remove excess moisture. Then, gently stroke the gums, buccal surfaces, palate, and tongue *to clean the mucosa and stimulate circulation.* Replace the swab as necessary for thorough cleaning. Avoid inserting the swab too deeply *to prevent gagging and vomiting.*

*If the patient is comatose:*

• Adjust the bed to a comfortable working height. Then, position the patient as described above *to facilitate drainage and prevent fluid aspiration.* Place a linen-saver pad under the chin and an emesis basin near the cheek *to absorb or catch drainage.*

• Next, arrange equipment on the overbed table. Turn on the suction machine. As necessary during the procedure, insert the suction catheter into the patient's mouth *to remove saliva, dentifrice, and mouthwash.* If a suction machine isn't available, swab the inside of the patient's mouth frequently with a gauze sponge.

• Lubricate the patient's lips with petrolatum *to prevent dryness and cracking.* Reapply lubricant, as needed, during oral care.

• Insert the bite-block *to hold the pa-*

*tient's mouth open during care.*

• Use a floss holder *to clean between the patient's teeth.* Hold the floss close to the tooth, and direct it as close to the gum as possible without injuring sensitive tissue.

• After flossing, wet the toothbrush, apply dentifrice, and brush the teeth.

• Mix mouthwash and water in a glass. Then, dip a cotton-tipped swab into the mouthwash solution, and gently stroke the oral membranes *to clean the mucosa and stimulate circulation.*

*After completing oral care:*

• Examine the patient's mouth for cleanliness and for tooth and tissue condition. Then, rinse the toothbrush and clean the emesis basin and glass. If necessary, empty and clean the suction bottle and place a clean suction catheter on the tubing. Return reusable equipment to the appropriate storage location and properly dispose of disposable equipment.

### Special considerations

Use cotton-tipped swabs to clean the teeth of a patient with sensitive gums. Swabs produce less friction than a toothbrush but don't clean as well.

Clean the mouth of the edentulous comatose patient by wrapping gauze around your forefinger, moistening it with mouthwash, and gently swabbing oral tissues. If necessary, moisten gauze in a equal mixture of hydrogen peroxide and water *to remove tenacious mucus.*

Because mucous membranes dry quickly in the patient breathing through the mouth or receiving oxygen therapy, regularly moisten the mouth and lips with mineral oil, lemon-glycerin swabs, or water. If you use water as the lubricant, place a short straw in a glass of water and stop the open end with your finger. Remove the straw from the water and, with your finger in place, position it in the patient's mouth. Release your finger slightly to let the water flow out gradually. If the patient is comatose, suction excess water to prevent aspiration.

## DENTURE CARE

Dentures—prostheses made of plastic or vulcanite—replace some or all natural teeth. Like natural teeth, dentures require proper care to remove soft plaque deposits and calculus and to reduce mouth odor. Such care involves removing and rinsing dentures after meals, daily brushing, and to remove tenacious deposits, soaking in a commercial denture cleaner.

Dentures must be removed from the comatose or presurgical patient to prevent possible airway obstruction. To remove dentures:

• First, assemble this equipment at the patient's bedside: emesis basin, properly labeled denture cup, toothbrush or denture brush, toothpaste, commercial denture cleaner, paper towel, mouthwash, and adhesive denture liner (optional).

• To remove a full upper denture, grasp the front and palatal surfaces of the denture with your thumb and forefinger. Position the index finger of your opposite hand over the upper border of the denture, and press *to break the seal of the denture from the palate.* For easy removal, grasp the denture with gauze, because *saliva can make it slippery.*

• To remove a full lower denture, grasp the front and lingual surfaces of the denture with your thumb and index finger, and gently lift up.

• To remove partial dentures, exert equal pressure on the border of each side of the denture. Avoid lifting the clasps, *which easily bend or break.*

• After removing dentures, place them in a properly labeled denture cup. Add warm water and a commercial denture cleaner *to remove stains and hardened deposits.* Follow the directions on the package. Avoid soaking dentures with metal parts overnight, *because this can cause corrosion.* Also, avoid soaking dentures in mouthwash, *because this may pit the denture material.*

• Instruct the patient to rinse with mouthwash *to remove food particles and reduce mouth odor.* Then, stroke the palate, buccal surfaces, gums, and tongue with a soft toothbrush or cotton swab *to clean the mucosa and stimulate circulation.* Watch for irritated areas or sores, which may indicate a poorly fitting denture.

• Carry the denture cup, emesis basin, toothbrush, and toothpaste to the sink. After lining the basin with a paper towel, fill it with water *to cushion the dentures if you should drop them.* Then, hold the dentures over the basin, wet them with warm water, and apply toothpaste to a denture brush or long-bristled toothbrush. Clean the dentures, using only moderate pressure *to prevent scratches* and warm water *to prevent distortion.*

• Clean the denture cup, and place the dentures in it. Rinse the brush, and clean and dry the emesis basin. Return these articles to the patient's bedside stand.

• *To insert dentures:* If the patient desires, apply adhesive liner to the dentures. Moisten the dentures with water, if necessary, *to reduce friction and ease insertion.*

• Encourage the patient to wear dentures *to enhance his appearance, to facilitate eating and speaking, and to prevent changes in the gum line that may affect denture fit.*

### Documentation

Record the time and date of oral care in your notes. Also document any unusual conditions, such as bleeding, edema, mouth odor, excessive secretions, or plaques on the tongue.

L. RUTH DRISCOLL, RN

# Back Care

*Regular bathing and massage of the neck, back, buttocks, and upper arms promotes patient relaxation and allows assessment of skin condition. Particularly important for the bedridden patient, massage causes cutaneous vasodilation, helping to prevent decubiti caused by prolonged pressure on bony prominences or by perspiration. Gentle back massage can be performed after myocardial infarction but may be contraindicated in patients with rib fractures, surgical incisions, or other recent back trauma.*

### Equipment

Basin □ soap □ bath blanket □ bath towel □ washcloth □ back lotion with lanolin base □ talcum powder (optional).

## Preparation of equipment
Fill the basin two-thirds full with warm water. Then, place the lotion bottle in the basin to warm the lotion. *Application of warmed lotion prevents chilling or startling the patient, thereby reducing muscle tension and vasoconstriction.*

Assemble the equipment at the patient's bedside.

## Essential steps
• Explain the procedure to the patient, and provide privacy. Ask him to tell you if you're applying too much or too little pressure.

• Adjust the bed to a comfortable working height and lower the head of the bed, if allowed.

• Place the patient in the prone position, if possible, or on his side. Position him along the edge of the bed nearest you *to prevent backstrain.*

• Untie the patient's gown, and expose his back, shoulders, and buttocks. Then, drape the patient's genitalia, legs, lower arms, and chest with a bath blanket *to prevent chills and minimize exposure.* Place a towel next to or under the patient's side *to protect bed linens from moisture.*

• Fold the washcloth around your hand to form a mitt. *This prevents the loose ends of the cloth from dripping water on the patient, causing chills, and also keeps the cloth warm longer.*

• Using long, firm strokes, bathe the patient's back, beginning at the neck and shoulders and moving downward to the buttocks. Rinse and dry well, *because moisture trapped between the buttocks can cause chafing and predispose to decubiti formation.* While giving care, closely examine the patient's back, especially the bony prominences of the shoulders, the scapulae, and the coccyx, for redness or abrasions.

• Remove the warmed lotion bottle from the basin, and pour a small amount of lotion into your palm. Rub your hands together *to divide the lotion.* Then, apply the lotion to the patient's back, using long, firm strokes. *Lotion reduces friction, making back massage easier.*

• Massage the patient's back, beginning at the base of the spine and moving upward to the shoulders. Alternate the three basic strokes: effleurage, friction, and petrissage (see *Giving a Back Massage*, page 66). For a relaxing effect, massage slowly; for a stimulating effect, massage quickly. Add lotion, as needed, keeping one hand on the patient's back *to avoid interrupting the massage.*

• Compress, squeeze, and lift trapezius muscle *to help relax the patient.*

• Finish the massage by using long, firm strokes, and blot any excess lotion from the patient's back with a towel. Then, retie the patient's gown and straighten or change the bed linens, as necessary.

• Empty and clean the basin. Return equipment to the appropriate storage area. Return the bed to its initial position, and make the patient comfortable.

## Special considerations
Before giving back care, assess the patient's body structure and skin condition, and tailor the duration and strength of the massage accordingly. If you're giving back care at bedtime, have the patient ready for bed beforehand, so the massage can help him fall asleep.

Use separate lotion for each patient to prevent cross-contamination. If the patient has oily skin, substitute a powder or lotion of the patient's choice. However, don't use powder if the patient has an endotracheal or tracheal tube in place, to prevent aspiration. Also, avoid using powder and lotion together as this may lead to skin maceration. When massaging, stand with one foot slightly forward and your knees bent slightly *to allow effective use of your arm and shoulder muscles.* Give special attention to bony prominences, because these areas are disposed to

## GIVING A BACK MASSAGE

Three strokes—friction, effleurage, and petrissage—can be used in back massage. When using effleurage and friction, keep your hands parallel to the vertebrae to avoid tickling the patient. When using any stroke, maintain a regular rhythm to help the patient relax.

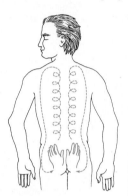

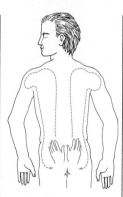

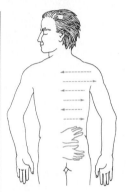

**Friction**
Using a circular thumb stroke, massage from the buttocks to the shoulders, then, using a smooth stroke, return to the buttocks.

**Effleurage**
Using your palm, stroke from the buttocks up to the shoulders, over the upper arms, and back to the buttocks. Use slightly less pressure on the downward strokes.

**Petrissage**
Using your thumb and forefinger, knead and stroke half the back and upper arms, starting at the buttocks and moving toward the shoulder. Then, knead and stroke the other half of the back, rhythmically alternating your hands.

---

decubiti formation. Don't massage the patient's legs unless ordered. Reddened legs can signal clot formation; massage can dislodge the clot, causing emboli. Develop a turning schedule and give back care at each position change.

**Documentation**
Chart back care on the flowsheet. Record redness, abrasion, or change in skin condition in your notes.

L. RUTH DRISCOLL, RN

# Perineal Care

*Bathing the perineal area—the external genitalia and the rectal area—during the daily bath and, if necessary, at bedtime and after urination and bowel movements, promotes cleanliness, prevents infection, and removes irritating and odorous secretions, such as smegma—a cheeselike substance that collects under the foreskin of the penis or on the inner surface of the labia. For the patient with perineal skin breakdown, frequent bathing followed by application of an ointment or cream aids healing. Perineal care should always be given with due consideration for the patient's privacy.*

**Equipment**
Clean disposable gloves □ washcloths (as many as necessary) □ clean basin □ mild soap □ bath towel □ bath blanket □ toilet tissue □ linen-saver pad □ trash bag.

Optional equipment includes disposable washcloths, bedpan, peri bottle, petrolatum, zinc oxide cream, and vitamins A and D ointment.

## Preparation of equipment
Obtain ointment or cream, as needed. Then, fill the basin two-thirds full with warm water. Also, fill the peri bottle with warm water, if needed. Assemble the equipment at the patient's bedside.

## Essential steps
• Wash your hands thoroughly, and tell the patient what you're about to do.
• Adjust the bed to a comfortable working height *to prevent backstrain,* and lower the head of the bed, if allowed.
• Provide privacy, and position the patient supine. Place a linen-saver pad under the buttocks *to protect the bed from stains and moisture.*
*To give perineal care to the female patient:*
• To minimize the patient's exposure and embarrassment, place the bath blanket over her with corners head to foot and side to side. Wrap each leg with a side corner, tucking it under the hip. Then, fold back the corner between the legs to expose the perineum.
• Put on clean disposable gloves *to prevent the spread of microorganisms.*
• Ask the patient to bend her knees slightly and to spread her legs. Separate her labia with one hand, and bathe with the other, using gentle downward strokes from front to back of the perineum *to prevent intestinal organisms from contaminating the urethra.* Avoid the area around the rectum, and use a clean section of washcloth for each stroke by folding each used section inward. *This prevents the spread of contaminated secretions or discharge.*
• Using a clean washcloth, rinse thoroughly from front to back, *because soap residue can cause skin irritation.* Pat the area dry, *because moisture can also cause skin irritation and discomfort.*
• Apply ordered ointments or creams.

• Turn the patient on her side to Sims's position, if possible, *to expose the rectal area.*
• Cleanse, rinse, and dry the rectal area, wiping from front to back, beginning at the posterior vaginal opening.
*To give perineal care to the male patient:*
• Drape the patient's legs to minimize exposure and embarrassment, and expose the genital area.
• Put on clean disposable gloves *to prevent the spread of microorganisms.*
• Hold the shaft of the penis with one hand and bathe with the other, beginning at the tip and working in a circular motion from the center to the periphery *to avoid introducing microorganisms into the urethra.* Use a different section of washcloth for each stroke *to prevent the spread of contaminated secretions or discharge.*
• Rinse thoroughly, using the same circular motion.
• For the uncircumcised patient, gently retract the foreskin and cleanse beneath it. Rinse well but don't dry, *because moisture provides lubrication and prevents friction in replacing the foreskin.* Replace the foreskin *to avoid constriction of the penis, resulting in edema and tissue damage.*
• Wash the remainder of the penis, using downward strokes toward the scrotum. Rinse well and pat dry.
• Cleanse the top and sides of the scrotum; rinse and pat dry. *Handle the scrotum gently to avoid causing discomfort.*
• Turn the patient on his side. Cleanse the bottom of the scrotum and the rectal area. Rinse well and pat dry.
*After providing perineal care:*
• Reposition the patient and make him comfortable. Remove the bath blanket and linen-saver pad, then replace the bed linens.
• Clean and return the basin and dispose of soiled articles.

## Special considerations
Give perineal care to a patient of the

opposite sex in a matter-of-fact way to minimize embarrassment.

If the patient is incontinent, first remove excess feces with toilet tissue. Then, position her on a bedpan, and add a small amount of antiseptic soap to a peri bottle to eliminate odor. Irrigate the perineal area to remove any remaining fecal matter. After cleansing the perineum, apply ointment or cream (petrolatum, zinc oxide cream, or vitamins A and D ointment) *to prevent skin breakdown by providing a barrier between the skin and excretions.* To reduce the number of linen changes, tuck an ABD pad between the patient's buttocks to absorb oozing feces.

## Documentation

Record perineal care and any special treatment in your notes. Document the need for continued treatment, if necessary, in your care plan. Describe perineal skin condition and any odor or discharge.

L. RUTH DRISCOLL, RN

# Foot Care

*Proper foot care—daily bathing of feet and regular trimming of toenails—promotes cleanliness, prevents infection, controls odor by removing debris between toes and beneath toenails, and stimulates peripheral circulation. It's especially important for bedridden patients and others who are especially susceptible to foot infection because of peripheral vascular disease, diabetes mellitus, or any condition that impairs peripheral circulation. In such patients, proper foot care should include meticulous cleanliness and regular observation for signs of skin breakdown. Toenail-trimming is contraindicated in patients with toe infections, diabetes mellitus, and peripheral vascular disease, unless performed by a doctor or podiatrist.*

## Equipment

Bath blanket □ large basin □ soap □ towel □ linen-saver pad □ washcloth □ toenail clippers □ orangewood stick □ emery board □ cotton-tipped swab □ lotion □ water-absorbent powder □ bath thermometer.

## Preparation of equipment

Fill the basin halfway with warm water. Test water temperature with a bath thermometer. Remember, some patients have diminished peripheral sensation. Such patients could painlessly immerse their feet in hot water over 105° F. (40.6° C.), resulting in burns.

Assemble the equipment at the patient's bedside.

## Essential steps

● Tell the patient you will wash his feet.
● Cover the patient with a bath blanket. Then, fanfold the top linen to the foot of the bed.
● Place a linen-saver pad and a towel under the feet on the bed to keep the bottom linen dry. Then, position the basin on the pad.
● Insert a pillow beneath the patient's knee *to provide support,* and cushion the rim of the basin with the edge of the towel *to prevent pressure.*
● Immerse one foot in the basin. Wash it with soap, then allow it to soak for about 10 minutes. *Soaking softens skin and toenails, loosens debris beneath toenails, and comforts and refreshes the patient.*
● After soaking, rinse the foot, remove it from the basin, and place it on the towel.
● Dry the foot thoroughly, especially between the toes, *to avoid skin breakdown.* Blot gently to dry, *because harsh rubbing may damage the skin.*
● Empty the basin, refill it with warm water, and clean and soak the other foot.
● While one foot is soaking, give the other foot a pedicure. Using the cotton-tipped swab, carefully clean the toenails. Using an orangewood stick, gently remove any dirt beneath the toenails;

## PATIENT-TEACHING AID

### DIABETIC FOOT CARE

Dear Patient:

Because you have diabetes, your feet require meticulous daily care. Diabetes can reduce blood supply to your feet, so normally minor foot injuries, such as an ingrown toenail or a blister, can lead to dangerous infection. Because diabetes also reduces sensation in your feet, you can burn or chill your feet without feeling it.

To prevent foot problems, follow this care routine:

• Soak your feet in warm soapy water for 5 minutes every day. To prevent burns, check the water temperature before immersing your feet.

• Dry your feet gently and thoroughly by blotting them with a towel. Be sure to dry between the toes.

• Apply oil or lotion to your feet immediately after drying, to prevent evaporating water from drying your skin. Lotion will keep your skin soft.

• If your feet perspire heavily, use a mild foot powder. Sprinkle it lightly between your toes and in your socks and shoes.

• Don't cut your nails. Instead, file them even with the end of your toes. Don't corner nails or file them shorter than the ends of your toes. If your nails are too thick, tough, or misshapen to file, consult a podiatrist.

• Exercise your feet daily to improve circulation. Sitting on the edge of the bed, point your toes upward, then downward, 10 times. Then, make a circle with each foot 10 times.

• Make sure your shoes are properly fitted. Break in new shoes gradually, increasing wearing time by half an hour each day. Check worn shoes frequently for rough spots in the lining.

• Wear clean socks daily. Don't wear socks with holes or darns with rough, irritating seams.

• Consult a podiatrist for treatment of corns and calluses. Self-treatment or application of caustic agents may be harmful.

• If your feet are cold, wear warm socks or slippers and use extra blankets. Avoid using heating pads and hot-water bottles, which may cause burns.

• Regularly check the skin of your feet for cuts, cracks, blisters, or red, swollen areas.

• If you cut your foot, no matter how slightly, contact the doctor. Meanwhile, wash the cut thoroughly and apply a *mild* antiseptic. Avoid harsh antiseptics, such as iodine, which can cause tissue damage.

• Don't wear tight-fitting garments or engage in activities that can decrease circulation. Especially avoid wearing elastic garters, sitting with knees crossed, picking at sores or rough spots on your feet, walking barefoot, or applying adhesive tape to the skin of your feet.

---

*avoid injuring subungual skin.*

• Trim nails, if needed, by cutting straight across *to prevent ingrown toenails.* Clip small sections of the nail at a time, starting at one edge and working across. Then, file trimmed toenails with an emery board to smooth rough edges. *Keeping the toenails trimmed and filed prevents scratching and injury to the skin on the opposite leg.*

• Rinse the foot that has been soaking, dry it thoroughly, and give it a pedicure.

• Apply lotion to moisten dry skin, or lightly dust powder between the toes

to absorb moisture.

• Remove and clean all equipment.

### Special considerations

While providing foot care, observe the color, shape, and texture of the toenails. If you see redness, drying, cracking, blisters, discoloration, or other signs of trauma, especially in patients with impaired peripheral circulation, notify the doctor. Because such patients are vulnerable to infection and gangrene, they need prompt treatment.

If a patient's toenail grows inward at the corners, tuck a wisp of cotton

## TREATING CORNS AND CALLUSES

Friction, pressure, faulty weight-bearing, or deformity may produce common foot disorders, such as corns and calluses. *Calluses,* broad-based areas of hyperkeratotic tissue, may occur on any area of constant friction or irritation, usually on the base of the foot. *Corns,* traumatic keratoses containing a firm, central core, commonly appear on the fourth or fifth toe over a joint or on a bony prominence; they usually have a conical shape.

Generally, your care of corns and calluses provides temporary comfort and reduces excessive scaliness. A podiatrist or doctor then debrides these lesions to effect complete healing.

A pumice stone is contraindicated if the patient has pain, erythema, broken skin, infection, diabetes, or peripheral vascular disease.

If your institution's protocol allows, follow these steps to treat corns and calluses:
• First, soak the patient's foot in warm water (105° F. or 40.5° C.) for 10 minutes, then blot the unaffected areas. Don't use excessive friction, which may irritate and damage skin or dry affected areas.
• To make the patient comfortable and reduce scaliness, remove the top layers of keratosis with a pumice stone. Holding the stone in your palm and working in a circular motion, apply gentle friction to each corn and callus. Don't try to remove all the hyperkeratotic tissue; otherwise, you may irritate or damage skin.
• Rinse the pumice stone as often as necessary to remove debris. After finishing treatment, blot the foot dry. Then, repeat the procedure for the other foot.
• To soften the skin after the treatment, apply a small amount of lanolin-containing cream or lotion to both feet.
• To reduce pressure, you can apply commercially available protective aids, such as an oval corn pad, a foam toe cap, or a corn shield. Don't apply adhesive directly to keratoses, and remember that these temporary measures do not replace podiatric care.
• Teach the patient how to perform these procedures at home, if appropriate. Remember, diabetic patients and those with peripheral vascular disease may need additional foot-care instructions.
• Record size, number, location, and type of keratoses on the patient's chart.

ANNE MORACA-SAWICKI, RN, MSN

under it to relieve pressure on the toe.

When giving the bedridden patient foot care, unless contraindicated, perform range-of-motion exercises to stimulate circulation and prevent foot contractures or muscle atrophy. Tuck folded 2″ x 2″ gauze pads between overlapping toes to protect the skin from the toenails. Apply heel protectors to prevent skin breakdown.

**Documentation**
Record the date and time of bathing and toenail-trimming in your notes.

JOANNE PATZEK DACUNHA, RN

# H.S. (Hour of Sleep) Care
*[Evening care, P.M. care]*

*H.S. (hour of sleep) care meets the patient's physical and psychological needs in preparation for sleep. It includes providing for the patient's hygiene needs, making the bed clean and comfortable, and ensuring his safety. For example, raising bed side rails can prevent the drowsy or sedated patient from falling. H.S. care also provides an opportunity to answer the patient's questions about the next day's upcoming tests and procedures and to discuss his worries and concerns.*

*Effective H.S. care prepares the patient for a good night's sleep; ineffective care may contribute to sleeplessness, which can intensify patient anxiety and interfere with treatment and recuperation.*

**Equipment**
Bedpan, urinal, or commode □ basin □ soap □ washcloth □ towel □ toothbrush and toothpaste □ denture cup and commercial denture cleaner, if necessary □ lotion □ clean linens, if necessary □ blankets □ soft restraints, if necessary.

## Preparation of equipment

Assemble the equipment at the patient's bedside. For the ambulatory patient who is capable of self-care, assemble soap, a washcloth, a towel, and oral hygiene items at the sink.

## Essential steps

• Tell the patient you will help him prepare for sleep, and provide privacy.
• Offer the patient on bed rest a bedpan, urinal, or commode. Or, assist the ambulatory patient to the bathroom.
• Fill the basin with warm water, and bring it to the patient's bedside. Immerse the lotion in the basin *to warm it for back massage.* Then, wash the patient's face and hands, and dry them well. Encourage the patient to do this himself, if possible, *to promote independence.*
• Provide toothpaste or a properly labeled denture cup and commercial denture cleaner. Assist the patient with oral hygiene, as necessary. If the patient prefers to wear dentures until bedtime, leave denture-care items within easy reach.
• After providing oral care, turn the patient on his side or stomach. Wash, rinse, and dry the patient's back and buttocks. Then, massage well with lotion *to help relax the patient.* While providing back care, observe the skin for redness, cracking, or other signs of breakdown. If the patient's gown is soiled or damp, provide or help him put on a clean one.
• Check dressings, binders, antiembolism stockings, or other aids, changing or readjusting them as needed.
• Refill the water container, and place it and a box of tissues within the patient's easy reach *to prevent falls if patient needs to reach for these things.*
• *Straighten or change bed linens, as necessary, and fluff the patient's pillow. Cover him with a blanket or place one within his easy reach to prevent chills during the night.* Then, position him comfortably. If he appears distressed, restless, or in pain, give ordered drugs, as needed.

## PROMOTING GOOD SLEEP

In addition to H.S. care provided by the evening staff, other nursing shifts can help promote good sleep by following these suggestions:

### Day staff

• Encourage naps in the morning rather than in the afternoon. Morning naps are usually a continuation of rapid-eye-movement sleep, and because it's a light sleep, it normally leaves the patient feeling refreshed. Also, if your patient naps in the morning, he will more likely feel tired enough by evening to fall asleep.
• If your patient's condition permits, try to keep him as active as possible during the day.
• Check your patient's history for unresolved anxiety—situations at home that may be worrying him in the hospital; such as financial problems or invalid spouse at home. Help alleviate the worry by getting your patient in touch with a hospital social worker or clergyman.

### Night staff

• Find out who isn't sleeping and why.
• Be sure unit lights are dim and unnecessary lights are out.
• When checking on your patient, be as quiet as possible.
• Avoid loud discussions in the hallways during rounds.
• After establishing a successful sleep plan for your patient, write it down on the nursing-care plan so it can be followed again.

• After making the patient comfortable, evaluate his mental and physical condition. Then, if ordered and in accord with hospital policy, apply soft restraints *to prevent falls.* Place the bed in a low position and raise the side rails. Place the call button within the patient's easy reach, and instruct him to call you whenever necessary. Next, straighten the patient's unit: Move all breakables from the overbed table out of his reach, and remove any equipment and supplies that could cause falls should the patient get up during the night. Finally, turn off the overhead light and put on the night-light.

## Special considerations

Ask the patient about his sleep routine at home, and whenever possible, let him follow it. Also try to observe certain rituals, such as a bedtime snack, which can aid sleep. A back massage, a tub bath, or a shower also help relax the patient and promote a restful night. If the patient normally bathes or showers before bedtime, let him do so in the hospital if his condition and doctor's orders permit it.

## Documentation

Record the time and type of H.S. care in your notes. Include application of soft restraints and any other special procedures.

JOANNE PATZEK DACUNHA, RN

# Bed Rest

*[Complete care]*

*Whether ordered by the doctor or instituted independently by the nurse to limit the patient's mobility, bed rest helps reduce stress on fractures, wounds, and other injured tissues; promotes healing; helps relieve pain; and supports faltering body systems. The degree of bed rest varies with the patient's condition: complete bed rest prohibits all physical activity; bed rest with bathroom privileges allows the patient to walk to the bathroom. Prolonged bed rest can lead to contractures, skin breakdown, and other complications unless they're prevented by frequent range-of-motion exercises, meticulous skin care, coughing and deep-breathing exercises, and regular position changes.*

## Equipment

Care of the patient on bed rest requires varied equipment to meet basic needs and, at times, to perform specialized procedures. Before entering the patient's room, assess his immediate needs and gather necessary equipment. Pillows and blankets are generally available and may be used as supports.

For the patient on prolonged bed rest, obtain supplemental bed equipment—foam mattress, sheepskin pad, footboard, or other equipment—from the nursing unit or the central supply department. If ordered, procure or arrange patient transfer to a CircOlectric bed, an air-fluidized bed, or a Stryker frame to prevent or treat complications of bed rest.

## Essential steps

● Explain the purpose of bed rest to the alert patient. Review the prescribed physical limitations, and instruct the patient to follow them closely.
● At the beginning of your shift, take and record vital signs *to establish a baseline,* and check peripheral circulation. Then, offer the patient the bedpan, urinal, or commode.
● Examine skin color and integrity at the sacrum, coccyx, heels, elbows, and other areas vulnerable to breakdown. Also, watch for sacral edema, which increases the risk of breakdown. Record any redness, discoloration, or blistering. Apply lotion to reddened areas or carry out other ordered treatments. Then, inspect these areas at least every 2 hours.
● Instruct the patient to practice coughing and deep-breathing exercises *to expand the lungs and help loosen secretions, thereby helping to prevent pulmonary complications, such as pneumonia.* Have him perform incentive spirometry or implement inhalation or respiratory therapy, as ordered.
● Bathe the patient, if indicated, and administer back care *to promote relaxation and stimulate circulation.* Avoid rubbing the back with alcohol *because it dries the skin.*
● Afterward, change the patient's gown if it's soiled or damp. Replace bed linens, if necessary, or straighten them *to remove wrinkles.*
● Position the patient comfortably, us-

ing extra pillows or blankets for support. Add or adjust supplemental bed equipment as needed. Reposition the patient at least every 2 hours *to promote circulation and reduce pressure on the bony prominences.* If indicated, post a care reminder over the bed, listing the time and to which side the patient is to be turned. Record the turning schedule on the cardex *to ensure continuity of care.*

• Perform passive range-of-motion exercises—or, if the patient's condition permits, encourage active range-of-motion exercises—at least three times daily *to maintain joint mobility and help prevent contractures.* Perform passive exercises slowly and smoothly, supporting each joint with a cupped hand while taking it through its full range of motion. Observe the patient for fatigue, and pause between the different exercises *to let him rest.*

• If applicable, remove antiembolism stockings twice daily *to facilitate circulation and give foot care.* At least every 8 hours, check for Homans' sign— pain behind the knee on forced dorsiflexion of the foot—*to detect thrombophlebitis.*

• Find out the patient's food preferences *to promote good nutrition.* Ensure intake that's high in protein and vitamin C—nutrients that aid tissue growth and repair. Encourage adequate fluid intake, *to help promote urine production, thereby decreasing the risk of infection and urinary calculus formation.* Offer prune juice *to help prevent constipation.* Provide small, frequent meals if the patient cannot ingest three large meals daily. After meals, encourage the patient to remain in a sitting position or to lie on his right side, if possible, for at least 1 hour. *This prevents a feeling of fullness against the diaphragm, reduces nausea, aids passage of food through the gastrointestinal tract, and reduces the risk of vomiting and aspiration.*

• *To help prevent constipation from leading to fecal impaction,* monitor the patient's bowel movements.

## Special considerations

Elevate the foot of the bed, if allowed, *to prevent the patient from sliding toward the foot of the bed.* Never gatch the bed or tuck pillows under the patient's knees, *because this decreases blood flow below the knees and predisposes to thrombophlebitis.* If the patient's condition permits, have him assist with care *to promote independence.* Also, provide reading material or suggest other appropriate activities *to help prevent boredom and depression.*

## Complications

Prolonged bed rest may promote formation of decubiti on bony prominences and other areas subject to constant pressure. Inactivity decreases muscle strength, tone, and size, and triggers release of minerals from bone; it may lead to stiff joints, contractures, and osteoporosis. Subsequently, it may lead to formation of renal calculi as the kidneys filter this increased mineral load. Prolonged bed rest can also contribute to urinary tract infection and formation of calculi as a result of urinary stasis. Patients commonly have difficulty voiding in the recumbent position.

Similarly, bed rest tends to cause constipation, stemming from decreased intestinal peristalsis or difficulty using the bedpan and, when prolonged, can cause fecal impaction. Prolonged bed rest commonly leads to thrombophlebitis and dependent edema, resulting from decreased tissue perfusion or venous stasis. It also leads to pneumonia and possibly atelectasis, resulting from pooling and thickening of pulmonary secretions in dependent areas of the lungs.

## Documentation

Record care of the bedridden patient in your notes or on the flowsheet. Include the patient's response to bed rest, and your observations on his physical and emotional status.

SUSAN DONAHUE, RN, BSN

## NUTRITION

# Feeding

*Confusion, upper-extremity immobility, injury, weakness, or restrictions on activities or positions may prevent a patient from feeding himself. Feeding the patient then becomes a key nursing responsibility. Injured or debilitated patients may experience depression and subsequent anorexia. Meeting such patients' nutritional needs requires determining food preferences, conducting the feeding in a friendly, unhurried manner, encouraging self-feeding to promote independence and dignity, and documenting intake and output.*

### Equipment
Meal tray □ overbed table □ linen-saver pad or towel □ flexible straws □ feeding syringe.

### Essential steps
• Because most adults consider being fed demeaning, be sure to allow the patient some control over mealtime. For example, let the patient set the pace of the meal or determine the order in which he eats the various foods.
• Raise the head of the bed, if allowed. *The Fowler's or semi-Fowler's position makes swallowing easier and reduces the risk of aspiration and choking.*
• Before the meal tray arrives, give the patient soap, a basin of water or a wet washcloth, and a hand towel to clean his hands. If necessary, you may wash his hands for him.
• Wipe the overbed table with soap and water or alcohol, especially if a urinal or bedpan had been placed on it.
• When the meal tray arrives, compare the name on the tray with the name on the patient's identification bracelet. Check the tray to be sure it contains foods appropriate for the patient's condition.
• Tuck the napkin or towel under the

patient's chin to protect his gown from spills. If necessary, use a linen-saver pad or towel to protect bed linens.
• Position a chair next to the patient's bed so you can sit comfortably while feeding him.
• Set up the patient's tray, remove the plate from the tray warmer, and discard all plastic wrappings. Then, cut the food into bite-sized pieces and prepare it, as necessary.
• Ask the patient which food he prefers to eat first. *Some patients prefer to eat one food at a time; others prefer to alternate foods.*
• If the patient has difficulty swallowing, offer liquids carefully with a spoon or feeding syringe *to help prevent aspiration.* (Pureed or soft foods, such as custard or flavored gelatin, may be easier to swallow than liquids.) If the patient doesn't have difficulty swallowing, use a flexible straw *to reduce the risk of spills.*
• Ask the patient to indicate when he's ready for another mouthful. Pause between courses and whenever the patient wants to rest. During the meal, wipe the patient's mouth and chin, as necessary.
• When the patient finishes eating, remove the tray. If necessary, clean up spills and change the bed linens. Provide mouth care.

### Special considerations
Don't feed the patient too quickly; *this can upset him and impair digestion.*
   If the patient is restricted to the prone position, feed him foods that he can easily chew. If he's restricted to the supine position, feed him liquids carefully and only after he has swallowed any food in his mouth *to reduce the risk of aspiration.* If the patient is restricted to the prone or the supine position but can use his arms and hands, encourage him to try foods he can pick up, such as sandwiches. If the patient can assume the Fowler's or semi-

# ASSISTIVE FEEDING DEVICES

Various devices can help the patient with limited arm mobility, grasp, range of motion, or coordination to feed himself.

Before introducing your patient to an assistive feeding device, assess his ability to master it. Don't introduce a device he can't manage. If his condition is progressively disabling, encourage him to use the device only until his mastery of it falters.

Introduce the assistive device before mealtime, with the patient seated in a natural position. Explain its purpose, show the patient how to use it, and encourage him to practice using it.

After meals, wash the device thoroughly and store it in the patient's bedside stand so it doesn't get misplaced. Document the patient's progress and share breakthroughs with staff and family members to help reinforce the patient's independence. Devices you can use include:

• **Plate guards** help all patients who have difficulty feeding themselves. The guard blocks food from spilling off the plate, allowing it to be picked up with a fork or spoon. Attach the guard to the side of the plate opposite the hand the patient uses to feed himself. Guiding the patient's hand, show him how to push food against the guard to secure it on the utensil. Then have him try again with food of a different consistency. When the patient tires, feed him the rest of the meal. At subsequent meals, encourage the patient to feed himself for progressively longer periods until he can feed himself an entire meal.

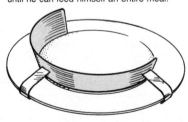

• **Swivel spoons** can help the patient with limited range of motion in his forearm. They can be used with universal cuffs.

• **Universal cuffs** help the patient with flail hands or diminished grasp. The cuff contains a slot that holds a fork or spoon. Attach it to the hand the patient uses to feed himself. Then, place a fork or spoon in the cuff slot. If necessary, bend the utensil to facilitate feeding.

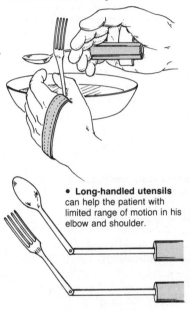

• **Long-handled utensils** can help the patient with limited range of motion in his elbow and shoulder.

• **Utensils with built-up handles** can help the patient with diminished grasp. They are commercially available but can also be improvised by wrapping tape around the handle of a fork or spoon.

Fowler's position but has limited use of his arms or hands, instruct him in the use of assistive feeding devices (see *Assistive Feeding Devices*, page 75), and encourage him to feed himself.

If the patient's food intake is inadequate because of chronic poor eating habits or anorexia, offer small, frequent meals *to provide a well-balanced diet.* If the patient won't eat, try to find out why; for example, recheck his food preferences. Also, make sure the patient isn't in pain at mealtimes or that he hasn't received any upsetting or nauseating treatments immediately before meals. Of course, clear the bedside of emesis basins, urinals, bedpans, and similar articles at mealtimes.

Establish a pattern for feeding the patient, and share this information with the rest of the nursing staff. If you don't, the patient will repeatedly have to instruct staff members on the best way to feed him or will have to endure their attempts to find the best way.

If the patient and his family are willing, suggest that family members assist with feeding. This will make the patient feel more comfortable at mealtimes and may facilitate discharge planning.

**Complications**

Aspiration of food and choking can occur if the patient is fed too quickly or is given excessively large mouthfuls.

**Documentation**

Describe the feeding technique used in the nursing-care plan to ensure continuity of care. In your notes, record the amount of food and fluid consumed; also note the fluids consumed on the intake and output record, if required. Note which foods the patient consistently fails to eat, then try to find the reason. For the blind patient, record the pattern of feeding on the nursing-care plan (see *Arranging Food for the Blind or Visually Impaired Patient*).

LORRAINE BUCHANAN, RN, MSN

---

## ARRANGING FOOD FOR THE BLIND OR VISUALLY IMPAIRED PATIENT

To help the blind or visually impaired patient feed himself, at every meal, tell the patient how the different foods on his plate correspond to the hours on a clock face. The platter in the illustration shows meat at 12 o'clock, a vegetable at 6 o'clock, and rice at 9 o'clock.

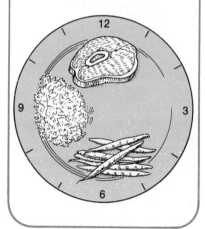

---

# Intake and Output

*Accurate intake and output records help evaluate a patient's fluid balance, suggest various diagnoses, and influence the choice of therapy. These records are mandatory for patients with burns, renal failure, electrolyte imbalance, congestive heart failure, or severe diarrhea, and for those receiving diuretics or corticosteroids. Intake and output records are also significant in monitoring patients with nasogastric or nasoenteric tubes, drainage collection devices, or those receiving I.V. infusions.*

*Intake comprises all fluids taken by mouth, including foods that are liquid at room temperature, such as gelatin, custard, and ice cream. Also consid-*

## HOW TO PERFORM A CALORIE COUNT

Counting a patient's caloric intake over a 24-hour period reveals the nutritional adequacy of his diet. It helps to determine the need for supplemental feeding (oral, tube, or parenteral) or total nutritional support. A calorie count is particularly useful during the transition from tube feeding or parenteral hyperalimentation to oral feeding. To perform a calorie count:

• Notify the dietitian, and explain the procedure to the patient *to ensure an accurate record.*
• Post a patient-care reminder in the patient's room. The reminder should state: "*Calorie count*—Please record the amount and type of all foods and fluids consumed by the patient."
• When the patient's meal tray arrives, make sure all the items on his menu are on his tray.
• After the patient finishes each meal, record the amount of food and fluid consumed next to the corresponding item on his menu or on a form provided by the dietitian. Record the amount of food consumed as "¼, ½, ¾, all," or "none"; record the amount of fluid in milliliters. Because hospital food portions are standardized, the dietitian can calculate a calorie count from your notations on the menu or form.

Make your calorie record as specific as possible, especially when recording amounts for combination dishes. For a cottage cheese and fruit platter, for example, you might record: "cottage cheese, ¼; fruit, all." (If the patient is receiving tube feeding in addition to regular meals, note this also.)

• Ask the patient if he has consumed any food or fluids between this and the previous meal. If he has, record the type of intake and the amount on the menu or form.
• At the end of the 24-hour period, send the completed menu or form to the food service department. The dietitian will then calculate the calorie count and record the amount on the patient's chart daily.

SHARON SPILKER, BS, RD

---

ered as intake are gastrointestinal tract instillations (such as gastric gavage), any body cavity instillation (bladder irrigation, for example), and parenteral infusions. Output includes urine, vomitus, and drainage (such as from a nasogastric or nasoenteric tube or from a wound). Aspirated fluids, blood loss, diarrhea or stool, and perspiration are also recorded as output.

### Equipment
Fluid collection devices, as needed (urinal, bedpan, commode, toilet specimen pan, catheter or drainage collection bag, wound suction apparatus, emesis basin, suction collection container) □ graduated measuring container □ reference chart of standard hospital container volumes, if available □ two patient-care reminders □ bedside (working) intake and output record □ permanent intake and output record □ pencil and paper.

### Preparation of equipment
Post an intake and output record, with a pencil, near the patient's bedside. If possible, place a graduated measuring container in the patient's room or bathroom.

### Essential steps
• Explain the procedure to the patient and his family. Stress the importance of their cooperation in recording all intake and output. If the patient is alert and dependable, teach him to keep the intake and output record. Give him paper and a pencil, a graduated measuring container, and a reference chart of standard hospital container volumes.
• Place patient-care reminders over the patient's bed and in the bathroom. Also, note the procedure on the nursing-care cardex *to help ensure an accurate record.* Notify any hospital personnel who have contact with the patient.

*To measure intake:*
• Total the amount of fluid consumed with each meal, and record it on the bedside intake and output sheet before removing the tray from the room. Also,

record the amount of fluid consumed with medications and between meals.

• Record the amount of fluid intake by instillation—gastric gavage, nasogastric or nasoenteric tube irrigation, or peritoneal dialysis, for example—and tube feedings, when given. Chart the amount of intake by continuous I.V. or intraarterial infusion after each bottle infused and at the end of each 8-hour shift.

*To measure output:*
• Instruct the patient to void into the collection device (bedpan, urinal, commode, or toilet specimen pan). Tell him not to discard any urine or put toilet tissue in the collection device. Measure and record the amount of urine after each voiding. If the patient has a catheter drainage bag or other drainage collection device in place, empty it at the end of each shift and record the amount.
• Measure and record any unformed stools; count formed stools.
• Measure and record any vomitus.
• To measure nasogastric drainage, disconnect the collection container from the suction setup, empty its contents into the graduated container, and record the amount. Rinse the container, replace it, and turn on the suction apparatus. Measure nasogastric drainage at the end of each shift.
• If the patient requires a portable wound suction device, empty and measure drainage at the end of each shift. Be sure to compress and reseal the container properly *to ensure adequate suction.* If the patient has an ileostomy or colostomy pouch, empty it at the end of each shift or as necessary.
• Collect T tube drainage in a glass bottle or catheter collection bag. Empty and measure drainage at the end of each shift. Or, if the doctor prefers not to have drainage emptied, mark the drainage level on the bottle or bag with tape. Document chest tube drainage in this way.
• Record the amount of any body fluids aspirated for diagnostic or therapeutic purposes, as in procedures such as

thoracentesis and paracentesis.
• To record blood loss from wounds or menstruation, count the number of gauze sponge or sanitary pad changes and estimate the amount of blood (small, moderate, large) on each.
• Note and estimate the amount of diaphoresis. Remember that one necessary bed change equals about 1 qt (1 liter) of perspiration.

**Special considerations**
Whenever possible, measure—don't estimate—fluids. Use calibrated cups to measure small amounts of fluid accurately. (Remember that a full glass of ice, when melted, equals a half glass of water.)

For the infant or young child wearing diapers, record the weight of each wet diaper. Or, record the number of diaper changes, with an estimate of the amount of urine (small, moderate, large). For the patient who is incontinent, record the number of voidings and estimate the amount of urine. Weigh urine-soaked linen-saver pads, if possible.

When measuring hourly urinary output to assess kidney function, notify the doctor if output falls below 30 ml. Also, contact the doctor if, after monitoring for 24 hours, intake and output differ significantly.

Evaluate the type, amount, and route of fluid intake and output *to help determine electrolyte imbalance.* Excessive nasogastric drainage may deplete hydrochloric acid and predispose to alkalosis; severe diarrhea may deplete bicarbonate and predispose to acidosis.

**Documentation**
At the end of each 8-hour shift, calculate the total intake and output. Enter these amounts on the bedside record, and chart them on the permanent record. After three consecutive shifts, chart the 24-hour total. Record hourly urinary output on the patient's chart, if applicable.

JOANNE PATZEK DACUNHA, RN

## ELIMINATION

# Bedpan and Urinal

*These devices permit elimination by the bedridden patient and accurate observation and measurement of urine and stool. The bedpan is used by the female patient for defecation and urination and by the male patient for defecation; the urinal, by the male patient for urination. Either device should be offered frequently—before meals, visiting hours, morning and evening care, and any treatments or procedures. Whenever possible, allow the patient to use a bedpan or urinal in privacy.*

### Equipment

Bedpan/urinal with cover □ toilet tissue □ two washcloths □ soap □ towel □ linen-saver pad □ optional: air freshner, talcum powder.

Available in both adult and pediatric sizes, the bedpan may be disposable or permanent; the latter type requires sterilization before use by another patient. The fracture pan, a type of bedpan, is used when spinal injuries, body casts, or other conditions prohibit or restrict turning.

Available in male and female models, the urinal may also be disposable or permanent. The male urinal has a cylindrical neck; the female urinal, which is infrequently used, has a wide, spout-shaped neck.

### Preparation of equipment

Remove the bedpan or urinal from the patient's bedside stand or obtain one from the central supply department. If you're using a metal bedpan, warm it under running water *to avoid startling the patient and stimulating muscle contraction, which hinders elimination.* Then, dry the bedpan thoroughly and test its temperature, *because metal retains heat.* If necessary, lightly sprinkle talcum powder on the edge of the

bedpan *to reduce friction during placement and removal.* For the thin patient, place a linen-saver pad at the edge of the bedpan *to minimize pressure on the coccyx.*

### Essential steps

● If the patient's condition permits, provide privacy *to minimize embarrassment.*

*To place a bedpan:*

● If allowed, elevate the head of the bed slightly *to prevent hyperextension of the spine when the patient raises the buttocks.*

● Rest the bedpan on the edge of the bed. Then, turn down the corner of the top linens and draw up the patient's gown. Ask him *to raise the buttocks by flexing the knees and pushing down on the heels.* While supporting the patient's lower back with one hand, center the curved, smooth edge of the bedpan beneath the buttocks.

● After positioning the bedpan, elevate the head of the bed further, if allowed, until the patient is sitting erect. *Because this position resembles the normal elimination posture, it aids defecation and urination.*

If elevating the head of the bed is contraindicated, tuck a small pillow or folded bath blanket under the patient's back *to cushion the sacrum against the edge of the bedpan and support the lumbar region.*

● If the patient can be left alone, place the bed in a low position and raise the side rails *to ensure his safety.* Place toilet tissue and the call button within the patient's easy reach, and instruct him to push the button after elimination. If the patient is weak or disoriented, stay with him during elimination.

● Before removing the bedpan, lower the head of the bed slightly. Then, ask the patient to raise the buttocks off the bed. Support the lower back with one hand, and gently remove the bedpan

## USING A COMMODE

An alternative to a bedpan, a commode is a portable chair made of wood, plastic, or metal, with a large opening in the center of the seat. It may have a bedpan or bucket that slides underneath the opening, or it may slide directly over the toilet, adding height to the standard toilet seat. Unlike a bedpan, a commode allows the patient to assume his normal elimination posture, which aids defecation.

Before the commode is to be used, inspect its condition and clean it if necessary. Then, roll or carry the commode to the patient's room. Place it parallel and as close as possible to the patient's bed, and secure its brakes or wheel locks; if necessary, block its wheels with sandbags. Assist the patient onto the commode, provide toilet tissue, and place the call button within easy reach. Instruct the patient to push the call button when he has finished.

If necessary, assist the patient with cleansing. Help him into bed and make him comfortable. Offer the patient soap, water, and a towel to wash his hands. Then, close the lid of the commode or cover the bucket. Roll the commode or carry the bucket to the bathroom or hopper room. If ordered, observe and measure the contents before disposal. Rinse and clean the bucket; then spray or wipe the bucket and commode seat with disinfectant.

NANCY KENNEDY, RN, MSN

with the other *to avoid skin injury caused by friction.* Cover the bedpan and place it on the chair.

• After defecation, assist with cleaning the rectal and perineal area, as necessary, *to prevent irritation and infection.* Turn the patient on his side, wipe carefully with toilet tissue, cleanse the area with a damp washcloth and soap, and dry well. For the female patient, cleanse from front to back *to avoid introducing rectal contaminants through the vaginal or urinary meatus.*

*To place a urinal:*

• Lift the corner of the top linens, hand

the urinal to the patient, and have him position it.

• If the patient can't position the urinal himself, spread his legs slightly and hold the urinal in place *to prevent spills.*

• After the patient voids, carefully withdraw the urinal.

*After the patient has used a bedpan or urinal:*

• Give the patient a clean damp washcloth for his hands. Then, check the bed linens for wetness or soiling, and straighten or change them, if needed. Next, make the patient comfortable. Place the bed in the low position and raise the side rails.

• Take the bedpan or urinal to the bathroom or hopper room, and observe the color, odor, amount, and consistency of its contents. If ordered, measure urinary output or liquid stool, or obtain a specimen for laboratory analysis.

• Empty the bedpan or urinal into the toilet or hopper. Rinse with cold water and clean it thoroughly, using a disinfectant solution. Then dry and return it to the patient's bedside stand.

• Use an air freshener, if necessary, *to eliminate offensive odors and reduce the patient's embarrassment.*

• Wash your hands.

### Special considerations

Explain to the patient that drug treatment and changes in environment, diet, and activity may disrupt his usual elimination schedule. Try to anticipate elimination needs, and offer the bedpan or urinal frequently *to help reduce embarrassment and minimize the risk of incontinence.* Avoid placing a bedpan or urinal on top of the bedside stand or overbed table *to avoid contamination of clean equipment and food trays.* Similarly, avoid placing it on the floor *to prevent the spread of microorganisms from the floor to the patient's bed linens when the device is used.*

If the patient can't raise the buttocks from the bed, roll him on his side, and position the bedpan against the buttocks. Then, holding the bedpan in place, roll the patient on his back. Adjust the bedpan, as necessary. After elimination, hold the bedpan securely *to avoid spills*, have the patient roll to one side, and remove the pan. If necessary, ask a co-worker to help you position and remove the bedpan.

If the patient feels pain during turning or discomfort on a standard bedpan, use a fracture pan. Unlike the standard bedpan, the fracture pan is slipped under the buttocks from the front rather than the side. Because it's shallower than the standard bedpan, you need only lift the patient slightly to position it. If the patient is obese or otherwise difficult to lift, ask a co-worker to help you.

If the patient has an indwelling catheter in place, carefully position and remove the bedpan *to avoid tension on the catheter, which could dislodge the catheter or cause irritation.* After the patient defecates, wipe, cleanse, and dry the anal region, taking care to avoid catheter contamination. Then, if necessary, cleanse the urinary meatus with povidone-iodine solution.

**Documentation**
Record the time, date, and type of elimination on the flowsheet and the amount of urinary output or liquid stool on the intake and output record, as needed. In your notes, document the presence of blood, pus, or other abnormal characteristics in urine or stool.

L. RUTH DRISCOLL, RN

# Male Incontinence Device

*[Condom catheter, Texas catheter]*

Used in place of an indwelling catheter for a male patient who is incontinent,

*a male incontinence device reduces the risk of urinary tract infection, promotes bladder retraining (when possible), and improves the patient's self-image. The device consists of a condom*

EQUIPMENT

## HOW TO APPLY A MALE INCONTINENCE DEVICE

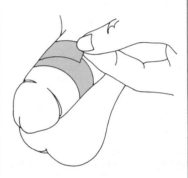

Apply an adhesive strip midway up the shaft of the penis (illustrated above). Then, roll the condom catheter onto the end of the penis (illustrated below).

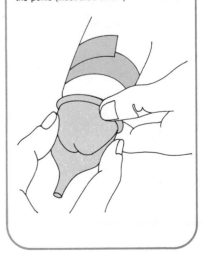

# CUNNINGHAM CLAMP

The Cunningham clamp, commonly used alternately with other male incontinence devices, prevents urine leakage by exerting light pressure on the urethral canal and compressing the urethral lumen. To apply the Cunningham clamp, follow these instructions:

• Select the appropriate size clamp, and gather a washcloth, a towel, soap, and water. Explain the procedure to the patient *to ensure cooperation,* wash your hands thoroughly, and provide privacy.
• Cleanse the penis, and observe for skin breakdown and edema.
• Mold the upper part of the Cunningham clamp to fit the shape of the penis. Then position the clamp so its hump rests on the underside of the penis (see illustration below) *to exert sufficient pressure on the urethral canal.* For regular- and large-sized clamps, adjust pressure using the ratchet catch; for infant- and juvenile-sized clamps, adjust pressure using snap buttons. Don't secure the clamp too tightly, *to avoid constricted circulation.*
• Release the clamp every 3 to 4 hours *to allow urine drainage.* On regular- and large-sized clamps, press inward on both spring-wire loops; on infant- and juvenile-sized clamps, unsnap the buttons. Follow the same procedure to remove the clamp.
• After removing the clamp, check for edema and skin breakdown.
• If applicable, teach the patient how to apply the clamp.

*catheter secured to the shaft of the penis and connected to a leg bag or straight drainage bag. It has no contraindications but can cause skin irritation and edema.*

## Equipment
Condom catheter □ drainage bag □ extension tubing □ hypoallergenic tape or incontinence sheath holder □ commercial adhesive strip or skin-bond cement □ elastic adhesive or Velcro, if needed □ razor, if needed □ basin □ soap □ washcloth □ towel.

## Preparation of equipment
Fill the basin with lukewarm water. Then, bring the basin and the remaining equipment to the patient's bedside.

## Essential steps
• Explain the procedure to the patient, wash your hands thoroughly, and provide privacy.
   *To apply the incontinence device:*
• If the patient is circumcised, wash the penis with soap and water, rinse well, and pat dry with a towel. If the patient is uncircumcised, gently retract the foreskin and cleanse beneath it. Rinse well but don't dry, *because moisture provides lubrication and prevents friction during foreskin replacement.* Replace the foreskin *to avoid penile constriction.* Then, shave the base and shaft of the penis *to prevent the adhesive strip or skin-bond cement from pulling pubic hair.*
• If you're using a precut commercial adhesive strip, insert the glans penis through its opening, and position the strip 1″ (2.5 cm) from the scrotal area; or, if you're using uncut adhesive, cut a strip to fit around the shaft of the penis, and apply it in a spiral, starting 1″ (2.5 cm) from the scrotal area and working toward the glans penis. Remove the protective covering from one side of the adhesive strip and press this side firmly to the penis *to enhance adhesion.* Then, remove the covering from the other side of the strip.
   If a commercial adhesive strip isn't

available, apply skin-bond cement and let it dry for a few minutes.

• Position the rolled condom catheter at the tip of the penis, with its drainage opening at the urinary meatus. Be sure this opening clears the tip of the penis by about ½″ (1 cm) *to prevent irritation of the glans penis.* Then, unroll the catheter upward, past the adhesive strip on the shaft of the penis. Next, gently press the catheter until it sticks to the adhesive strip.

• After the condom catheter is in place, secure it with hypoallergenic tape or a sheath holder.

• Using extension tubing, connect the condom catheter to the leg bag or straight drainage bag.

*To remove the incontinence device:*

• Simultaneously roll the condom catheter and adhesive strip off the penis and discard them. If you've used skin-bond cement rather than an adhesive strip, remove it with solvent.

• Cleanse the penis with lukewarm water, rinse thoroughly, and dry. Observe for swelling or signs of skin breakdown.

• Remove the leg bag by closing the drain clamp, unlatching the leg straps, and disconnecting the extension tubing at the top of the bag.

### Special considerations

If hypoallergenic tape or a sheath holder isn't available, secure the condom with a strip of elastic adhesive or Velcro. Apply the strip snugly but not too tightly, *to prevent circulatory constriction.*

Inspect the condom catheter for twists and the extension tubing for kinks *to prevent obstruction of urine flow, which can lead to a balloon effect of urine at the end of the condom and result in displacement of the condom catheter.*

### Documentation

Record the date and time of application and removal of the incontinence device. Also note skin condition and the patient's response to the device.

JOANNE PATZEK DACUNHA, RN

## Credé's Maneuver

*When lower motor neuron damage impairs the voiding reflex, the bladder may become flaccid or areflexic. Because the bladder fails to contract properly, urine collects within it, causing distention. Credé's maneuver— application of manual pressure over the lower abdomen—promotes complete emptying of the bladder. After appropriate instruction, the patient can perform this maneuver himself, unless he cannot reach the lower abdomen or lacks sufficient strength and dexterity in his hands. Even when performed properly, Credé's maneuver isn't always successful and doesn't always eliminate the need for catheterization.*

*Although Credé's maneuver has no contraindications, it is not used after abdominal surgery if the incision is not completely healed. When using Credé's maneuver, close monitoring of urinary output is necessary to prevent possible infection from accumulation of residual urine.*

### Equipment
Bedpan, urinal, or bedside commode.

### Essential steps

• Explain the procedure to the patient, and wash your hands.

• If allowed, place the patient in the Fowler's position and position the bedpan beneath the buttocks, or the urinal between the legs. Or, if the patient's condition permits, assist him onto the bedside commode.

• Place your hands flatly just below the umbilicus. Ask the female patient to bend forward at the hips. Then, firmly stroke downward to the bladder about six times *to stimulate the voiding reflex.*

• Then, place one hand on top of the other above the pubic arch. Press firmly inward and downward *to compress the bladder and expel residual urine.*

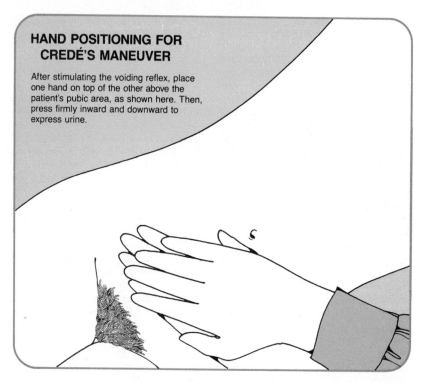

**HAND POSITIONING FOR CREDÉ'S MANEUVER**

After stimulating the voiding reflex, place one hand on top of the other above the patient's pubic area, as shown here. Then, press firmly inward and downward to express urine.

## Special considerations

After the patient has learned the procedure and can use Credé's maneuver successfully, measuring the expelled urine may not be necessary after each voiding. The patient may then void into the toilet.

## Documentation

Record the date and time of the procedure and the amount of expelled urine.

JOANNE PATZEK DACUNHA, RN

# Digital Removal of Fecal Impaction

*Fecal impaction—a large, hard, dry mass of stool present in the folds of the rectum and, at times, the sigmoid co-* *lon—results from prolonged retention and accumulation of stool. Usually, its causes include poor bowel habits, inactivity, dehydration, improper diet (especially inadequate fluid intake), constipation-inducing drugs, and incomplete bowel cleansing after a barium enema or barium swallow. Digital removal of fecal impaction—when oil retention and cleansing enemas, suppositories, and laxatives fail to clear the impaction—may require a doctor's order.*

*This procedure is contraindicated in pregnancy; after rectal, genitourinary, abdominal, perineal, or gynecologic reconstructive surgery; in patients with myocardial infarction, coronary insufficiency, pulmonary embolus, congestive heart failure, heart block, and Stokes-Adams syndrome (without pacemaker treatment); and in gastrointestinal or vaginal bleeding, hemorrhoids, rectal polyps, and blood dyscrasias.*

## Equipment
Clean gloves □ linen-saver pad □ bedpan □ plastic disposal bag □ soap □ water-filled basin □ towel □ washcloth □ water-soluble lubricant.

## Essential steps
• Explain the procedure to the patient and provide privacy.
• Position the patient on the left side and flex the knees *to allow easier access to the sigmoid colon and the rectum.* Then, drape the patient, and place a linen-saver pad beneath the buttocks *to prevent soiling the bed linens.*
• Put on gloves, and moisten one index finger with water-soluble lubricant *to reduce friction during insertion, thereby avoiding injury to sensitive tissue.*
• Instruct the patient to breathe deeply *to promote relaxation.* Then, gently insert the lubricated index finger beyond the anal sphincter until you touch the impaction. Rotate the finger gently around the stool *to dislodge and break it into small fragments.* Then, work the fragments downward to the end of the rectum, and remove each one separately.
• Before removing the finger, gently stimulate the anal sphincter with a circular motion two or three times *to increase peristalsis and encourage evacuation.*
• Remove the finger and take off the gloves. Then, cleanse the anal area with soap and water and lightly pat dry with the towel.
• Offer the patient the bedpan or commode, *because digital manipulation stimulates the urge to defecate.*
• Place disposable items in the plastic bag, and discard properly. If necessary, clean the bedpan and return it to the bedside stand.
• Wash your hands.

## Special considerations
If the patient experiences pain, nausea, rectal bleeding, changes in pulse rate or skin color, diaphoresis, or syncope, stop the procedure and notify the doctor immediately.

## Complications
Digital removal of fecal impaction can stimulate the vagus nerve and may cause rapid heartbeat and syncope.

## Documentation
Record the time and date of the procedure, the patient's response, and stool color, consistency, and odor.
JOANNE PATZEK DACUNHA, RN

## SPIRITUAL CARE

# Spiritual Care

The patient's religious beliefs can profoundly influence his recovery rate, attitude toward treatment, and overall response to hospitalization. In certain religious groups, beliefs can preclude diagnostic tests and therapeutic treatments, entail dietary restrictions, and prohibit organ donation and artificial prolongation of life.

Consequently, effective patient care requires that you recognize and respect the patient's religious beliefs. Recognizing his religious beliefs and need for spiritual care may require close attention to the patient's nonverbal cues or seemingly casual remarks that express his spiritual concerns. Respecting his beliefs may require that you set aside your own personal beliefs, accepting the patient's beliefs in a nonjudgmental way. Providing spiritual care may then require that you contact an appropriate clergyman in the hospital or community, assist him in performing rites and administering sacraments by gathering the necessary equipment, and prepare the patient for the clergyman's visit.

# BELIEFS AND PRACTICES OF VARIOUS RELIGIONS

| RELIGION | BIRTH AND DEATH RITUALS | DIETARY RESTRICTIONS | PRACTICES IN HEALTH CRISIS |
|---|---|---|---|
| **Adventist** (Seventh-Day Adventist, Church of God, Advent Christian Church) | None (baptism of adults only) | Alcohol, coffee, tea, narcotics, stimulants; in many groups, meat prohibited also | Communion and baptism performed. Some members believe in divine healing, anointing with oil, and prayer. Some regard Saturday as Sabbath. |
| **Baptist** (27 different groups) | At birth, none (baptism of believers only); before death, counseling by clergy and prayer | Alcohol; in some groups, coffee and tea prohibited also | Some believe in healing by laying on of hands. Resistance to medical therapy occasionally approved. |
| **Church of Christ** | None (baptism at age 8 or older) | Alcohol discouraged | Communion, anointing with oil, laying on of hands, and counseling by minister |
| **Church of Christ, Scientist** (Christian Scientist) | At birth, none; before death, counseling by Christian Science practitioner | Alcohol, coffee, and tobacco prohibited | Many members refuse all treatment, including drugs, biopsies, physical examination, and blood transfusions. Vaccination only when required by law. Alteration of thoughts believed to cure illness. Hypnotism and psychotherapy prohibited. (Christian Science nurses and nursing homes honor these beliefs.) |
| **Church of Jesus Christ of Latter-Day Saints** (Mormon) | At birth, none (baptism at age 8 or older); before death, baptism and gospel preaching | Alcohol, tobacco, tea, and coffee prohibited; meat intake limited | Divine healing through the laying on of hands; communion on Sunday; some members may refuse medical treatment. Many wear special undergarment. |
| **Eastern Orthodox Churches** (Albanian, Bulgarian, Cypriot, Czechoslovakian, Egyptian, Greek, Polish, Rumanian, Russian, Syrian, Turkish) | At birth, baptism and confirmation; before death, last rites. For members of the Russian Orthodox Church, arms are crossed after death, fingers set in cross, and unembalmed body clothed in natural fiber. | For members of the Russian Orthodox Church and usually the Greek Orthodox Church, no meat or dairy products on Wednesday, Friday, and during Lent. | Anointing of the sick. For members of the Russian Orthodox Church, cross necklace replaced immediately after surgery and no shaving of male patients except in preparation for surgery. For members of the Greek Orthodox Church, communion and Sacrament of Holy Unction. |
| **Episcopalian** | At birth, baptism; before death, occasional last rites | For some members, abstention from meat on Friday, fasting before communion (which may be daily) | Communion, prayer, and counseling by minister |

Note: Because religious beliefs may vary within particular sects, individual practices may differ from those described here.

| RELIGION | BIRTH AND DEATH RITUALS | DIETARY RESTRICTIONS | PRACTICES IN HEALTH CRISIS |
|---|---|---|---|
| **Islam** (Muslim) | If abortion occurs before 130 days, fetus treated as discarded tissue; after 130 days, as a human being. Before death, confession of sins with family present; after death, only relatives or friends may touch the body | Pork prohibited; daylight fasting during ninth month of Muhammadan calendar | Faith healing for the patient's morale only; conservative members reject medical therapy. |
| **Jehovah's Witnesses** | None | Abstention from foods to which blood has been added. | Generally, no blood transfusion; may require court order for emergency transfusion |
| **Judaism** | Ritual circumcision after birth; burial of dead fetus; ritual washing of dead; burial (including organs and other body tissues) occurs as soon as possible; no autopsy | For Orthodox and Conservative Jews, kosher dietary laws (for example, pork and shellfish prohibited); for Reform Jews, usually no restrictions | Donation or transplantation of organs requires rabbinical consultation. For Orthodox and Conservative Jews, medical procedures may be prohibited on Sabbath—from sundown Friday to sundown Saturday—and special holidays. |
| **Lutheran** | Baptism usually performed 6 to 8 weeks after birth | None | Communion, prayer, and counseling by minister |
| **United Methodist** | None (baptism of children and adults only) | None | Communion before surgery or similar crisis; donation of body parts encouraged |
| **Pentecostal** (Assembly of God, Foursquare Church) | None (baptism only after age of accountability) | Abstention from alcohol, tobacco, meat slaughtered by strangling, any food to which blood has been added, and sometimes pork | Divine healing through prayer, anointing with oil, and laying on of hands |
| **Orthodox Presbyterian** | Infant baptism; scripture reading and prayer before death | None | Communion, prayer, and counseling by minister |
| **Roman Catholic** | Infant baptism, including baptism of aborted fetus without sign of clinical death (tissue necrosis); before death, anointing of the sick | Fasting or abstention from meat on Ash Wednesday and on Friday during Lent; this practice usually waived for the hospitalized | Burial of major amputated limb (sometimes) in consecrated ground; donation or transplantation of organs allowed if benefit to recipient is proportionate to the donor's potential harm. |

## Equipment

Clean towel (one or two) □ teaspoon, or 1 oz (30 ml) medicine cup (for baptism) □ container of water (for emergency baptism).

Some hospitals, particularly those with a religious affiliation, provide baptism trays. The clergyman may bring holy water, holy oil, and other religious articles to minister to the patient.

## Preparation of equipment

For baptism, cover a small table with a clean towel. Fold a second towel and place it on the table, along with the teaspoon or medicine cup. For communion and anointing, cover the bedside stand with a clean towel. For circumcision of a Jewish infant, sterilize the ceremonial instruments, if requested by the mohel (a specialist who is certified by rabbinic authorities to perform circumcision).

## Essential steps

• Check the patient's admission record *to determine religious affiliation.* Remember that the patient may claim no religious beliefs. And, even if a patient states that he is agnostic, this may not rule out his need for spiritual or pastoral care. Such patients may also wish to speak with a clergyman, so watch and listen carefully for subtle expressions of such desire.

• Evaluate the patient's behavior for signs of loneliness, anxiety, or fear— emotions that may signal his need for spiritual counsel. Also consider if the patient is facing a health crisis. Such a crisis commonly precedes childbirth, surgery, chronic illnesses, and impending death. Remember that a patient may feel acutely distressed because of inability to participate in religious observances. Help such a patient verbalize his beliefs *to relieve stress.* Listen to the patient, and let him express his concerns, but carefully refrain from imposing your beliefs on him *to avoid conflict and further stress.* If the patient requests, arrange a visit by an appropriate clergyman. Consult this clergyman if you need more information about the patient's beliefs.

• If your patient faces the possibility of abortion, amputation, transfusion, or other medical procedures with important religious significance or implications, try to discover his spiritual attitude.

• Also, try to determine your patient's attitude about the importance of laying on of hands, confession, communion, observance of holy days (including the Sabbath), and restrictions in diet or physical appearance. Helping the patient continue his normal religious practices during hospitalization can greatly *help reduce stress.*

• If the patient is pregnant, find out her beliefs concerning infant baptism and circumcision, and after delivery, comply with them.

If a neonate is in critical condition, call an appropriate clergyman immediately. To administer emergency baptism, the clergyman pours a small amount of holy water into a teaspoon or a medicine cup. He then sprinkles a few drops of water over the infant's head and says, "(Name of child), I baptize you in the name of the Father, the Son, and the Holy Spirit. Amen." In an extreme emergency, you can administer Roman Catholic baptism, using any water available. If you do, be sure to notify the priest, *because this sacrament is administered only once.*

• If a Jewish patient delivers a male infant prematurely or by cesarean birth, ask her if she plans to observe the rite of circumcision (Brith), a significant ceremony performed on the eighth day after birth. (Because a patient who vaginally deliver a healthy, full-term baby is usually discharged after 3 or 4 days, this ceremony is normally performed outside the hospital.)

For a Brith, ensure privacy and, if requested, sterilize the instruments.

• If the patient requests communion, prepare him for it before the clergyman arrives. First, place him in the Fowler's or semi-Fowler's position, if his condition permits; otherwise, allow him to remain supine. Tuck a clean towel under his chin, and straighten the bed linens.

• If a terminally ill patient requests last rites or special treatment of his body after death, call an appropriate clergyman. For the Roman Catholic patient, call a priest to administer the Sacrament of Anointing of the Sick, even if the patient is unresponsive or comatose. To prepare the patient for this sacrament, uncover the arms and fold back the top linens to expose the feet. After the clergyman anoints the patient's forehead, eyes, nose, mouth, hands, and feet, straighten and retuck the bed linens.

### Special considerations

Handle the patient's religious articles carefully to avoid damage or loss. Become familiar with religious resources in your hospital. Some institutions employ one or more clergymen, who counsel both patients and staff and link patients to other community clergymen.

If the patient tries to convert you to his personal beliefs, tell him that you respect his beliefs but are content with your own.

### Documentation

Complete a baptismal form and attach it to the patient's record; send a copy of the form to the appropriate clergyman. Record the rite of circumcision and anointing in your notes. Also, record anointing in red on the cardex so it won't be repeated unnecessarily.

JOANNE PATZEK DACUNHA, RN

# TRANSFER, DISCHARGE, & TERMINAL CARE

## Transfer Procedures

*Patient transfer—whether within the hospital or to another care facility— requires thorough preparation and careful documentation. Preparation includes an explanation of the transfer to the patient and his family, discussion of the patient's condition and care plan with the staff at the receiving unit or facility, and arrangements for transportation, if necessary. Documentation of the patient's condition before and during transfer and adequate communication between nursing staffs ensure continuity of nursing care and provide legal protection for the transferring hospital and its staff.*

### Equipment

Admissions inventory of belongings □ patient's chart, medication, cardex □ bag or suitcase.

### Essential steps

• Explain the transfer to the patient and his family. Assess his physical condition *to determine the means of transfer,* such as a wheelchair or a stretcher.

• Using the admissions inventory of belongings as a checklist, collect the patient's property. Be sure to check the entire room, including the closet, the bedside stand, the overbed table, and the bathroom.

• Gather the patient's medications from the cart and the refrigerator. If the patient is being transferred to another unit, send them to the receiving unit; if he's being transferred to another facility, return them to the hospital pharmacy.

• Notify the hospital's business office and other appropriate departments of the transfer.

• Contact the nursing staff on the receiving unit and review the patient's condition, drug regimen, and other treatments with them *to ensure conti-*

*nuity of care.*

*Transfer within the hospital:*
• If the patient is being transferred from or to an intensive care unit, your hospital may require new care orders from the patient's doctor. If it does, review the new orders with the nursing staff at the receiving unit.

• Send the patient's chart, laboratory request slips, cardex, and other required information to the receiving unit.

• Use a wheelchair to transport the ambulatory patient to the newly assigned room unless it's on the same unit as his present one, in which case he may be allowed to walk. Use a stretcher to transport the bedridden patient. (To eliminate the need for terminal cleaning of the bed, your hospital may prefer to transfer the patient in his bed and merely exchange the unoccupied bed from the newly assigned room.)

• Introduce the patient to the nursing staff at the receiving unit. Then, take the patient to his room and, depending on his condition, place him in the bed or a chair. Introduce him to his new roommate, if appropriate, and tell him about any unfamiliar equipment in the room.

*Transfer to an extended-care facility:*
• Make sure the patient's doctor has written the transfer order on the patient's chart and has completed the special transfer form in duplicate. This form should include the patient's diagnosis, care summary, drug regimen, and special care instructions, such as diet and physical therapy.

• Complete the nursing summary in duplicate. Include the patient's assessment, progress, required nursing treatments, and special needs to ensure continuity of care.

• Keep one copy of the transfer form and the nursing summary with the patient's chart, and forward the other copies to the receiving facility. Don't send the patient's medications, cardex, or chart to the receiving facility.

*Transfer to an acute-care facility:*
• Make sure the doctor has written the transfer order on the patient's chart and has completed the transfer form as discussed above. Then, complete the nursing summary in duplicate.

• Depending on the doctor's instructions, send one copy of the transfer form and the nursing summary and photocopies of the pertinent excerpts from the patient's chart—such as laboratory test and X-ray results, patient history and physical progress notes, and vital signs records—to the receiving facility with the patient. Or, with the doctor's permission, substitute a written summary of the patient's condition and hospital history for the excerpts from the patient's chart. *This information legally protects the transferring hospital and its staff and completes the patient's chart.*

**Special considerations**
If the patient requires an ambulance to take him to another facility, arrange transportation with the hospital's social services department. If you'll be accompanying the patient, assemble the necessary equipment to provide care during transport.

**Documentation**
Record the time and date of transfer, the patient's condition during transfer, the name of the receiving unit or facility, and the means of transportation.

JOANNE PATZEK DACUNHA, RN

# Discharge Procedures

*Although discharge from the hospital is usually considered routine, effective discharge requires careful planning and continuing assessment of the patient's needs during his hospitalization. Ideally, discharge planning begins after admission and takes into account the patient's understanding of his condi-*

tion. *Discharge planning aims to teach the patient and his family about his disease and its effect on his life-style; to provide instructions for performing at-home procedures; to communicate dietary or activity restrictions; and to explain the purpose, side effects, and scheduling of drug treatment. It can also include arranging for transportation on discharge and for follow-up care, if necessary, and contacting hospital or community service agencies for home health care.*

### Equipment
Wheelchair, unless the patient leaves by ambulance □ patient's chart □ patient instruction sheet □ discharge summary sheet □ plastic bag or patient's suitcase for personal belongings.

### Essential steps
● Before the day of discharge, inform the patient's family of the time and date of discharge. If his family can't arrange transportation, notify the social services department. (Always confirm arranged transportation on the day of discharge.)
● Obtain a written discharge order from the doctor. If the patient discharges himself against medical advice, obtain the appropriate hospital form (see *Discharge Against Medical Advice*).
● If the patient requires at-home medical care, confirm arrangements with the appropriate community agency or hospital department.
● On the day of discharge, review the patient's discharge care plan, initiated on admission and modified during his hospitalization, with the patient and his family. List prescribed drugs on the patient instruction sheet, with the dosage, prescribed time schedule, and significant side effects to be reported to the doctor. Ensure that the drug schedule doesn't unnecessarily conflict with the patient's life-style *to prevent improper administration and promote patient compliance.*
● Review procedures the patient or his

> ## DISCHARGE AGAINST MEDICAL ADVICE
>
> Occasionally, the patient or his family may demand discharge against the doctor's advice. If this occurs, notify the doctor immediately. If the doctor fails to convince the patient to remain in the hospital, he'll ask the patient to sign a form releasing the hospital from legal responsibility for any medical problems the patient may experience after discharge.
>
> If the doctor isn't available, discuss the discharge form with the patient and obtain his signature. If the patient refuses to sign the form, don't detain him: *This violates his legal rights.* After the patient leaves, document the incident thoroughly in your notes and notify the doctor.

family is required to perform at home. If necessary, demonstrate these procedures and provide written instructions.
● List dietary and activity restrictions, if applicable, on the patient instruction sheet, and review the reasons for the restrictions. If bed rest is ordered, make sure the patient's family can provide daily care.
● Check with the doctor about the patient's next office appointment; inform the patient of the date, time, and location. If scheduling is your responsibility, make an appointment with the doctor, outpatient clinic, physical therapy or X-ray department, or other health services. If the patient can't arrange transportation, notify the social services department.
● Retrieve the patient's valuables from the hospital safe and review each item with him. Then, obtain the patient's signature *to verify receipt of his valuables.*
● Obtain from the pharmacy any drugs the patient brought to the hospital and any new prescription.
● If appropriate, take and record the patient's vital signs on the discharge summary form.
● Help the patient to dress, if necessary.
● Collect the patient's personal belong-

ings, compare them to the admission inventory of belongings, and help place them in his suitcase or a plastic bag.
• After checking the room for misplaced belongings, help the patient into the wheelchair, and escort him to the hospital's exit; or, if the patient leaves by ambulance, help him onto the litter. If the patient's family hasn't already made arrangements for payment, stop at the business office.
• After the patient has left the area, strip the bed linens and notify the housekeeping staff that the room is ready for terminal cleaning.

### Special considerations
Whenever possible, involve the patient's family in discharge planning, *so they can better understand and perform patient-care procedures.* Before the patient is discharged, perform a physical assessment. If you detect abnormal signs or the patient develops new symptoms, notify the doctor and delay discharge until he's seen the patient.

### Documentation
Although hospital policy determines the extent and form of discharge documentation, you'll usually record the time and date of discharge, the patient's physical condition, special dietary or activity instructions, type and frequency of at-home procedures, the patient's drug regimen, the date of follow-up appointments, the mode of departure and the name of the patient's escort, and a summary of the patient's hospitalization (if necessary).

JOANNE PATZEK DACUNHA, RN

# Care of the Dying Patient

*Care of the dying patient aims to provide physical and emotional comfort.*

*Such a patient needs intensive physical support as he develops the signs of impending death: reduced respiratory rate and depth, decreased or absent blood pressure, weak or erratic pulse rate, lowered skin temperature, decreased level of consciousness, diminished senses and neuromuscular control, diaphoresis, and pallor.*

*The dying patient also needs emotional support but at this final stage such support most often means simple reassurance and someone's physical presence to ease any fear and loneliness. More intense emotional support is important at much earlier stages, especially in patients with long-term progressive illness who can work through the stages of dying (see The Five Stages of Dying). Keep in mind that emotional care requires respect for the patient's wishes about extraordinary means of supporting life. The patient may have signed a living will. This document, legally binding in some states, states the wish for a natural death unimpeded by artificial support by defibrillators, respirators, auxiliary hearts, life-sustaining drugs, and so on. If the patient has signed such a document, respect his wishes and communicate the doctor's "no code" order to all staff members.*

### Equipment
Clean bed linens □ clean gowns □ water-filled basin □ soap □ washcloth □ towels □ lotion □ linen-saver pads □ indwelling catheter (optional) □ petrolatum □ lemon-glycerin swabs □ suction and resuscitation equipment, as necessary.

### Essential steps
*To meet the dying patient's physical needs:*
• Take vital signs often, and observe for pallor, diaphoresis, and decreased level of consciousness.
• Reposition the patient in bed at least every 2 hours, *because sensation, reflexes, and mobility diminish first in the legs and gradually in the arms.*

Make sure the bedsheets cover him loosely *to reduce discomfort caused by pressure on arms and legs.*

• When the patient's vision and hearing start to fail, turn his head toward the light and speak to him from near the head of the bed. *Because hearing may remain acute despite loss of consciousness,* avoid whispering or speaking inappropriately about the patient in his presence.

• Change the bed linens and the patient's gown as necessary, *because his body temperature may rise, causing diaphoresis.* Provide skin care during gown changes, and adjust the room temperature for patient comfort, if necessary.

• Observe for incontinence or anuria, *the result of diminished neuromuscular control or decreased renal function.* If necessary, obtain an order to catheterize the patient, or place linensaver pads beneath the patient's buttocks. Provide perineal care *to prevent irritation and discomfort.*

• Suction the patient's mouth and upper airway *to remove secretions.* Elevate the head of the bed *to decrease respiratory resistance.* As the patient's condition deteriorates, he may breathe mostly through his mouth.

• Offer fluids frequently, and lubricate the patient's lips and mouth with petrolatum or lemon-glycerin swabs *to counteract dryness.*

• If the comatose patient's eyes are open, provide appropriate eye care *to prevent corneal ulceration.* Such ulcerations can cause blindness and prevent the use of these tissues for transplant should the patient not recover.

• Provide ordered pain medication, as needed.

*To meet the dying patient's emotional needs:*

• Fully explain all care and treatments to the patient (even if he's unconscious, because he may still be able to hear). Answer the patient's questions as candidly as possible, without extinguishing hope.

• Allow the patient to express his feel-

## THE FIVE STAGES OF DYING

According to Elisabeth Kübler-Ross, author of *On Death and Dying*, the dying patient may progress through five psychological stages in preparation for death. Although each patient experiences these stages differently, understanding them will help you meet your patient's needs.

**1 Denial.** When the patient first learns of his terminal illness, he'll refuse to accept the diagnosis. He may experience physical symptoms similar to a stress reaction—shock, fainting, pallor, sweating, tachycardia, nausea, and gastrointestinal disorders. During this stage, be honest with the patient but not blunt or callous. Maintain communication with him so he can discuss his feelings when he accepts the reality of death.

**2 Anger.** Once the patient stops denying his death, he may show deep resentment to those who will live on after his death—to you, to the hospital staff, and to his own family. Although you may instinctively draw back from the patient or even resent him for his behavior, remember that he's dying and has a right to be angry. After you accept his anger, you can help him find different ways to express it and can help his family to understand it.

**3 Bargaining.** Although the patient accepts impending death, he attempts to bargain for more time with God or fate. The patient will probably strike his bargain secretly. If he does confide in you, don't urge him to keep his promises.

**4 Depression.** First, the patient may experience regrets about his past; then he grieves about his current condition. He may withdraw from his friends, family, doctor, and from you. You may find him sitting alone, in tears. Accept the patient's sorrow, and if he talks to you, listen. Provide comfort by touch, as appropriate. Resist the temptation to make optimistic remarks or cheerful small talk.

**5 Acceptance.** In this last stage, the patient accepts the inevitability and imminence of his death—without emotion. He may simply desire the quiet company of a family member or friend. If, for some reason, a family member or friend can't be there, stay with the patient to satisfy his final need.

## DONATION OF BODY PARTS

Because of the passage of the Uniform Anatomical Gift Act (United States) and the Human Tissues Gift Act (Canada), donation of organs for transplantation only requires written and witnessed documents.

According to the American Medical Association, about 25 kinds of tissues and organs are being transplanted. To assure a successful transplantation, certain problems must be overcome: lack of suitable donors, tissue preservation, wound infection, operative technique, and—the major difficulty—rejection of grafted tissue.

Types of transplants include kidney and structural body tissues. More experimental transplants include the heart, lung, liver, pancreas, and bone marrow.

For successful *kidney transplantation*, living members of the patient's immediate family with a compatible blood and HLA type are preferred to cadaver donors. Cadaver donors for kidney transplantation should be under age 60, have no history of hypertension, renal disease, or cancer (except for brain tumors), and must be free of infection.

Usually, cadaver donors have suffered clinical brain death as a result of accident or intracerebral hemorrhage. A pulsatile perfusion machine can maintain kidneys from such donors until a suitable recipient is found. A national computer network system helps in this search.

For successful *corneal transplantation*, the donor should have no history of corneal infection, glaucoma, intraocular surgery, penetrating trauma, or hereditary disease of the cornea. The success rate for these transplants is 85% to 90%. Donated eyes must be removed 6 to 8 hours after death and immediately preserved in a special tissue culture medium, which can preserve them for up to 72 hours.

After discovering a potential donor, the doctor should notify the appropriate transplant center. At this time, your awareness of the patient's or his family's religious beliefs can help you provide comfort and support.

EILEEN M. MARKMANN, RN

ings, which may range from anger to loneliness. Take time to talk with the patient. When you do, sit near the head of the bed. Avoid looking rushed or unconcerned.

• Notify family members, if not present, when the patient wishes to see them. Let the patient and his family discuss death at their own pace. Give them opportunities to express their feelings, but avoid encouraging them if they seem unwilling.

• Offer to contact a member of the clergy or social services department, if appropriate.

### Special considerations

If the patient has signed a living will, the doctor will write a "no code" order on his progress notes and order sheets. Know your state's policy regarding the living will. If it's legal, transfer the "no code" order to the patient's chart or cardex and, at the end of your shift, inform the incoming staff of this order.

If family members remain with the patient, show them the location of bathrooms, lounges, and cafeterias. Explain the patient's needs, treatments, and care plan to them. If appropriate, offer to teach them specific skills so they can take part in nursing care. Emphasize that their efforts are important and effective. As the patient's death approaches, give them emotional support.

### Documentation

Record changes in the patient's vital signs, intake and output, and level of consciousness. Note the times of cardiac arrest and the end of respiration.

NANCY KENNEDY, RN, MSN

# Postmortem Care

*Postmortem care includes cleansing and preparing the deceased patient for family viewing, arranging transportation to the morgue or funeral home, and determining the disposition of his belongings. In addition, postmortem care entails comforting and supporting the patient's family and providing for their privacy. Usually, postmortem care begins after a doctor certifies the patient's death; if the patient died violently or under suspicious circumstances, postmortem care may be postponed until the medical examiner completes an autopsy.*

## Equipment

Gauze or soft string ties □ chin straps □ ABD pads □ plastic shroud or body wrap □ three identification tags □ plastic bag (for patient's belongings) □ adhesive bandages to cover wounds or punctures □ soap □ water-filled basin □ towels □ washcloths □ stretcher.

A commercial morgue pack usually contains gauze or string ties, chin straps, a shroud, and identification tags.

## Essential steps

• Document any auxiliary equipment, such as a respirator, attached to the body.

• Place the body in the supine position, arms at the sides and his head on a pillow. Then, elevate the head of the bed slightly *to prevent discoloration from blood settling in the face.*

• If the patient wore dentures and hospital policy permits, gently insert them, then close his mouth. Then close the eyes by gently pressing on the lids with your fingertips. If they don't stay closed, place moist cotton balls on the eyelids for a few minutes, and then try again to close them. Place a folded towel under the chin *to keep the jaw closed.*

• Remove all indwelling catheters, tubes, and tape, and apply adhesive bandages to puncture sites. Replace soiled dressings.

• Collect all the patient's valuables *to prevent loss.* If you're unable to remove a ring, cover it with gauze, tape it in place, and tie the gauze to the wrist *to prevent slippage and subsequent loss.*

• Cleanse the body thoroughly. Place one or more ABD pads between the buttocks to absorb rectal discharge or drainage.

• Cover the body up to the chin with a clean sheet.

• Offer comfort and emotional support to the family. Ask if they wish to see the body. If they do, allow them to do so in privacy.

• After the family leaves, remove the towel from under the chin of the deceased patient. Wrap chin straps under the chin and tie them on top of the head. Then, pad the wrists and ankles *to prevent bruises,* and tie them together with gauze or soft string.

• Fill out the three identification tags. Each tag should include the deceased patient's name, room and bed numbers, date and time of death, and doctor's name. Tie one tag to the deceased patient's hand or foot, but don't remove his hospital identification bracelet *to ensure correct identification.*

• Place the shroud or body wrap on the morgue stretcher and, after obtaining assistance, transfer the body to the stretcher. Wrap the body, and tie the shroud or wrap with the string provided. Then, attach another identification tag, and cover the shroud or wrap with a clean sheet. (If a shroud or wrap isn't available, dress the deceased patient in a clean gown and cover the body with a sheet.)

• Place the deceased patient's personal belongings, including valuables, in a bag and attach the third identification tag.

• Close the doors of adjoining rooms, if possible. Then, take the body to the morgue. Use corridors that aren't crowded and, if possible, a service elevator.

## Special considerations

Give the deceased patient's personal belongings to his family or bring them to the morgue. If you give the family jewelry or money, make sure a coworker is present as a witness. Obtain a signature of an adult family member *to verify receipt of valuables.*

## Documentation

Although the extent of documentation may vary between hospitals, always record the disposition of the patient's possessions, especially jewelry and money. Also, note the date and time the deceased patient was transported to the morgue.

NANCY KENNEDY, RN, MSN

# 2 Mobility

# Mobility

## Introduction

Mobility is often the first patient activity limited or lost when illness strikes. Loss of mobility—even temporarily, as a result of bed rest restrictions—affects all body systems and can have effects as devastating as the primary disorder. Its combined physical and psychological effects can hamper patient recovery and rehabilitation. For example, prolonged bed rest can lead to footdrop, contractures, and other deformities, as well as to depression and a negative body image.

Whenever a patient's condition impairs or prevents mobility, nursing goals are to promote independence through motivation and goal-setting, to prevent injury and the complications of immobility, to provide patient teaching, and to foster a positive body image, especially in the patient with long-term or permanent immobility. You can achieve the first three goals through realistic assessment of the patient, adherence to proper body mechanics, transfer techniques and scheduled physical care measures, and effective patient teaching. You can achieve the last goal by offering the patient acceptance, encouragement, and praise during all interactions.

### Nursing process and immobility

Begin your care of the patient by assessing both his physical and mental condition. Determine the extent of his physical capabilities and sensory deficits. Find out what he knows about his condition and prognosis. Determine his willingness and motivation to achieve greater independence, if possible.

Check the patient's care plan to determine if the doctor or physical therapist has given specific care instructions. Review the patient's medical history, because this may reveal his attitude toward his condition and possible rehabilitation. Then, talk to the patient's family to learn about his home life and financial concerns, their expectations of the patient, and their willingness to help.

After determining the patient's capabilities and expectations, find out if impaired mobility is a problem. Then, establish short- and long-term rehabilitation goals with the patient. Above all, be realistic, even if the patient or his family has unrealistic expectations. Avoid placing an absolute deadline on short- or long-term goals, because failure to meet a scheduled goal can cause frustration—possibly leading to depression and loss of motivation to meet later goals. Make sure short-term goals are easily attainable. Meeting these will bolster the patient's confidence and provide motivation to work toward long-term goals.

After formulating rehabilitation goals, help the patient achieve them. Evaluate his progress periodically, and revise the goals, if necessary.

### Avoid injury

When giving care to the immobilized

patient, you must often give the patient partial to complete assistance during moving, lifting, and transport. Performing these procedures with good body mechanics and appropriate assistive devices can prevent injury, fatigue, and patient discomfort. Performing them incorrectly can result in injury to you and the patient.

The following guidelines can help you carry out safe transfer of the immobile patient. Before transfer, assess the patient's capabilities, limitations, and physical condition to determine the number of staff members needed to perform the procedure safely. Then explain the procedure to the patient to ensure his understanding and cooperation. If you're using unfamiliar equipment to facilitate the transfer, read the manufacturer's instructions carefully to promote efficiency and safety. During the transfer, be alert for changes in the patient's condition, such as increasing weakness or confusion. Failure to recognize these changes contributes to incidents and injuries.

**Prevent complications**
For the bedridden patient, immobility poses special hazards, such as pressure on bony prominences; venous, pulmonary, and urinary stasis; and disuse of muscles and joints. These can lead to such troublesome, dangerous, and sometimes irreversible complications as decubiti, thrombi, phlebitis, pneumonia, urinary calculi, and contractures. Although contractures, decubitus ulcers, and pneumonia are perhaps the most common complications, prolonged immobility can affect all body systems. To prevent complications, correct positioning, meticulous skin care, and regular turning and range-of-motion exercises are essential.

Various devices are also helpful in preventing the complications of immobility. For example, hand rolls help prevent finger contractures and keep the hands and wrists in a functional position. Sheepskins provide soft padding to prevent pressure on the bony prominences, which can lead to decubitus ulcer formation. Antiembolism stockings prevent pooling of blood in the lower leg, reducing the risk of thrombi. Special beds, such as the CircOlectric and Roto Rest models, allow automatic turning and repositioning to stimulate circulation and prevent multisystem complications; the air fluidized bed reduces surface pressure and minimizes trauma.

**Promote rehabilitation**
Planning for rehabilitation should begin at admission and continue throughout hospitalization, always accurately reflecting the patient's condition and ability. The first step toward rehabilitation is often progressive ambulation, which should begin as soon as possible—if necessary using such assistive devices as a cane, crutches, or a walker.

Effective rehabilitation also requires teaching of positioning, transfer, and mobilization techniques to the patient and his family. Teaching these techniques effectively depends on your ability to demonstrate each technique and clearly communicate instructions for carrying it out. Demonstrating a technique, such as transfer from bed to wheelchair, during hospitalization helps the patient and his family to understand it. Allowing them to practice it under your supervision gives them the confidence to perform it at home.

When teaching rehabilitation techniques, encourage and answer all questions. Anticipate problems, such as inability to cope with physical limitations, altered financial circumstances, and changes in self-concept. Be ready to work out practical solutions with them. Make sure the family understands the importance of observing for changes in the patient's physical status, which may signal deterioration or developing complications. Encourage them to provide positive reinforcement to motivate the patient to work toward his goals.

ANNE MORACA-SAWICKI, RN, MSN

# BODY MECHANICS & TRANSFER TECHNIQUES

## Body Mechanics

*Following the three principles of correct body mechanics in all daily activities helps prevent musculoskeletal injury and fatigue.*
1. Keeping a low center of gravity *by flexing the hips and knees instead of bending at the waist distributes weight evenly between the upper and lower body and helps maintain balance.*
2. Using a wide base of support *by spreading the feet apart provides lateral stability and lowers the center of gravity.*
3. Maintaining proper body alignment *by moving the feet to avoid twisting and bending at the waist keeps the center of gravity directly over the base of support.*

*Besides using correct body mechanics, you must recognize your physical limitations and ask for help when needed to prevent musculoskeletal injury and fatigue.*

### Essential steps
*To sit correctly:*
● Position the buttocks against the back of the chair. *The ischial tuberosities, not the sacrum, then provide the base of support, promoting proper spinal alignment.*
● Place the feet flat on the floor at a 90° angle to the lower legs. Flex the hips slightly, so the knees are higher than the ischial tuberosities, *to reduce lower back strain.*
● Flex the lumbar spine slightly *to maintain the natural spinal curve and prevent vertebral column ligament strain.*
● If the chair has arms, flex the elbows and place the forearms on the armrests *to avoid shoulder strain.*
*To stand correctly:*

● Keep the feet parallel, 6″ to 8″ (15 to 20 cm) apart. Place equal weight on both legs *to minimize strain on weight-bearing joints.*
● Flex the knees slightly, but don't lock them. Retract the buttocks and abdomen, tilt the pelvis back slightly, and move the chest slightly out and the shoulders back. Keep the neck straight and the chin pointed slightly downward.
*To walk correctly:*
● Assume the correct standing position. Step forward a comfortable distance with one leg, tilting the pelvis slightly forward and downward. Touch the floor first with the heel, then with the ball of the foot, and finally with the toes. During this sequence advance the other leg and arm *to promote balance and stability.*
*To push and pull correctly:*
● Stand close to the object, and place one foot slightly ahead of the other, as in a walking position. Tighten the leg muscles and set the pelvis by simultaneously contracting the abdominal and gluteal muscles.
● To push, place your hands on the object and flex the elbows. Lean into the object by shifting weight from the back leg to the front leg, and apply smooth continuous pressure.
● To pull, grasp the object, and flex the elbows. Lean away from the object by shifting weight from the front leg to the back leg. Pull smoothly, avoiding sudden, jerky movements.
● After you've started to move the object, keep it in motion; stopping and starting use more energy.
*To stoop correctly:*
● Stand with your feet 10″ to 12″ (25 to 30 cm) apart and one foot slightly ahead of the other *to widen the base of support.*
● Lower yourself by flexing the knees, and place more weight on the front foot

than on the back foot. Keep the upper body straight by not bending at the waist.

• To stand up again, straighten the knees, keeping the back straight.

*To lift and carry correctly:*

• Assume the stooping position directly in front of the object *to minimize back flexion and avoid spinal rotation when lifting.*

• Grasp the object, and tighten your abdominal muscles.

• Stand up by straightening the knees, using the leg and hip muscles. Always keep the back straight *to maintain a fixed center of gravity.*

• Carry the object close to your body at waist height—near the body's center of gravity—*to avoid straining the back muscles.*

### Special considerations

Wear shoes with low heels, flexible nonslip soles, and closed backs *to promote correct body alignment, facilitate good body mechanics, and prevent accidents.* When possible, pull rather than push an object, *because the elbow flexors are stronger than the extensors.* When doing heavy lifting or moving, remember to use assistive or mechanical devices, if available.

LORRAINE E. BUCHANAN, RN, MSN

# Patient Transfer from Bed to Stretcher

*Transfer from bed to stretcher, one of the most common transfers, can require the help of one or more coworkers, depending on the patient's size and condition. Techniques for achieving this transfer include the straight lift, carry lift, lift sheet, and roller board.*

*In the straight, or patient-assisted, lift—used to move the pediatric or very* light patient, or the patient who can assist transfer—the members of the transfer team place their hands and arms beneath the patient's buttocks and, if necessary, the shoulders. In the carry lift, they roll the patient onto their upper arms and hold him against their chests. In the lift sheet transfer, they place a sheet under the patient and lift or slide him onto the stretcher. In the roller board transfer, two team members slide the patient onto the stretcher.

### Equipment

Stretcher □ roller board or lift sheet, if necessary.

### Preparation of equipment

Adjust the bed to the same height as the stretcher.

### Essential steps

• Tell the patient you will move him from the bed to the stretcher, and place him in the supine position.

• Instruct team members to remove their rings and watches *to avoid scratching the patient during transfer.*

*To perform the four-person straight lift:*

• Place the stretcher parallel to the bed, and lock the wheels of both *to ensure patient safety.*

• Stand at the center of the stretcher, and have another team member stand at the patient's head. The two other team members should stand next to the bed, on the other side—one at the center and the other at the patient's feet. (Occasionally, two team members may kneel on the stretcher to facilitate the transfer, but correct body mechanics are difficult to observe in this position.)

• Slide your arms, palms up, beneath the patient, while the other team members do the same. In this position, you and the team member directly opposite support the patient's buttocks and hips; the team member at the head of the bed supports the patient's head and shoulders; the one at the foot supports the patient's legs and feet.

• On a count of three, the team members lift the patient several inches, move him onto the stretcher, and slide their arms out from under him. Keep movements smooth *to minimize patient discomfort and avoid muscle strain by team members.*

*To perform the four-person carry lift:*

• Place the stretcher perpendicular to the bed, with the head of the stretcher at the foot of the bed. Lock the bed and stretcher wheels *to ensure patient safety.*

• Raise the bed to a comfortable working height.

• Line up all four team members on the same side of the bed as the stretcher, with the tallest member at the patient's head; the shortest at his feet. The member at the patient's head is the leader of the team and gives the lift signals.

• Tell the team members to flex their knees and slide their hands, palms up, under the patient until he rests securely on their upper arms. Make sure the patient is adequately supported at the head and shoulders, buttocks and hips, and legs and feet.

• On a count of three, the team straighten their knees and roll the patient onto his side, against their chests. *This reduces strain on the lifters* and allows them to hold the patient for several minutes if necessary.

• Together the team step back, with the member supporting the feet moving the farthest, to bring the patient's legs around to the foot of the stretcher. On a count of three, the team lower the patient onto the stretcher by bending at the knees, and slide their arms out from under the patient.

*To perform the four-person lift sheet transfer:*

• Position the bed, stretcher, and team members as for the straight lift. Then, instruct the team to grasp the edges of the sheet under the patient, rolling them close to the patient *to obtain a firm grip, provide stability, and spare the patient undue sensations of instability.*

• On a count of three, the team lift or slide the patient onto the stretcher in a smooth, continuous motion *to avoid muscle strain and minimize patient discomfort.*

*To perform the roller board transfer:*

• Place the stretcher parallel to the bed, and lock the wheels of both *to ensure patient safety.*

• Stand next to the bed, and instruct a co-worker to stand next to the stretcher.

• Reach over the patient and pull the far side of the bedsheet toward you to turn the patient slightly on his side. Your co-worker then places the roller board beneath the patient, making sure the board bridges the gap between stretcher and bed.

• Ease the patient onto the roller board and release the sheet. Your co-worker then grasps the near side of the sheet at the patient's hips and shoulders and pulls him onto the stretcher in a smooth, continuous motion. She then reaches over the patient, grasps the far side of the sheet, and logrolls him toward her.

• Remove the roller board as your co-worker returns the patient to the supine position.

*After all transfers:*

• Position the patient comfortably on the stretcher, apply safety straps, and raise and secure side rails.

## Special considerations

When transferring a helpless or markedly obese patient from bed to stretcher, first lift and move the patient in increments, to the edge of the bed. Then, rest for a few seconds, repositioning the patient if necessary, and lift him onto the stretcher. If the patient can bear weight on the arms or legs, two or three co-workers can perform this transfer: one can support the buttocks and guide the patient, another can stabilize the stretcher by leaning over it and guiding the patient into position, and a third can transfer any attached equipment. If the patient is light, three co-workers can perform the carry lift; however, with either three or four team members, one stabilizes the head if the patient can't support it himself or has cervical instability, injury, or surgery.

Depending on the patient's size and condition, lift sheet transfer can require two to seven co-workers.

**Documentation**
Record the time and, if necessary, the type of transfer in your notes. Complete other required forms, as necessary.

LORRAINE E. BUCHANAN, RN, MSN

# Patient Transfer from Bed to Wheelchair

*For the patient with diminished or absent lower-body sensation or one-sided weakness, immobility, or injury, transfer from bed to wheelchair may require partial support to full assistance—initially by at least two persons. Subsequent transfer of the patient with generalized weakness may be performed by one nurse. After transfer, proper positioning helps prevent excessive pressure on bony prominences, which predisposes the patient to skin breakdown.*

**Equipment**
Wheelchair with locks □ pajama bottoms (or robe) □ shoes or slippers with nonslip soles.

If a wheelchair isn't available, a sturdy chair can be used instead.

**Essential steps**
*For the patient with generalized weakness:*
● Explain the procedure to the patient and demonstrate his role.
● Place the wheelchair adjacent and at a 45° angle to the bed, and lock its wheels. Make sure bed wheels are also locked. Raise the footrests *to avoid interfering with the transfer.*
● If necessary, check pulse rate and blood pressure with the patient supine, *to assess cardiovascular stability.* Then, help him put on the pajama bottoms and slippers or shoes with nonslip soles *to prevent falls.*
● Raise the head of the bed in 20° to 30° increments *to allow for patient adjustment to posture changes.*
● When the patient is upright, allow him to rest briefly. Then, bring him to the dangling position (see "Progressive Ambulation" in this chapter).
● Tell the patient to move toward the edge of the bed and, ideally, to place his feet flat on the floor. Stand in front of the patient, blocking his toes with your feet and his knees with yours *to prevent his knees from buckling.*
● Flex your knees slightly, place your arms around the patient's waist, and tell him to place his hands on the edge of the bed. Avoid bending at your waist *to prevent back strain.*
● Ask the patient to push himself off the bed and to support as much of his own weight as possible, as you stand by straightening your knees and hips, bringing the patient with you.
● Supporting the patient as needed, pivot toward the wheelchair, keeping your knees next to his. Tell the patient to grasp the farthest armrest of the wheelchair with his closest hand.
● Help the patient lower himself into the wheelchair by flexing your hips and knees, but not your back. Instruct him to reach back and grasp the other wheelchair armrest as he sits, *to avoid abrupt contact with the seat.* Fasten the seat belt *to prevent falls,* and if necessary, check pulse rate and blood pressure *to assess cardiovascular stability.*
● If the patient can't position himself correctly, help him move the buttocks against the back of the chair, *so the ischial tuberosities, not the sacrum, provide the base of support.*
● Place the patient's feet flat on the footrests, pointed straight ahead. Then, position the knees and hips with the correct amount of flexion and in appropriate alignment. If appropriate,

## USING A TRANSFER BOARD

For the patient who can't stand, a transfer board allows safe transfer from bed to wheelchair. To perform this transfer:
• First explain and demonstrate the procedure. Eventually, the patient may become proficient enough to perform transfer independently or with some supervision.

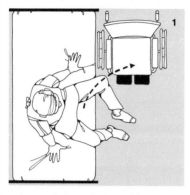

• Help the patient put on pajama bottoms or a robe, and shoes or slippers.
• Place the wheelchair parallel to and facing the foot of the bed. Lock the wheels, and remove the armrest closest to the patient. Make sure the bed is flat, and adjust its height so it's level with the wheelchair seat.
• Assist the patient to a sitting position on the edge of the bed, with his feet resting on the floor. Make sure the front edge of the wheelchair seat is aligned with the back of the patient's knees (see illustration #1). *Although it's important that the patient have an even surface on which to transfer, he may find it easier to*

*transfer to a slightly lower surface.*
• Ask the patient to lean away from the wheelchair while you slide one end of the transfer board under him.
• Now, place the other end of the transfer board on the wheelchair seat, and help the patient return to the upright position.
• Stand in front of the patient *to prevent him from sliding forward.* Tell him to push down with both arms, lifting the buttocks up and onto the transfer board. The patient then repeats this maneuver, edging along the board, until he's seated in the wheelchair. If the patient can't use his arms to assist with the transfer, stand in front of him, put your arms around his waist, and gradually slide him across the

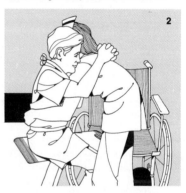

board until he's safely in the chair (see illustration #2). If necessary, apply a seat belt *to prevent falls.*
• Then, remove the transfer board, replace the wheelchair armrest, and reposition the patient in the chair.

use elevating legrests to position the patient's hips in more than 90° of flexion; *this position relieves pressure on the popliteal space and places more secure weight bearing on the ischial tuberosities.*
• Position the patient's arms on the wheelchair's armrests with shoulders abducted, elbows slightly flexed, forearms pronated, and wrists and hands in neutral position. If necessary, support or elevate the patient's hands and forearms with a pillow *to prevent dependent edema.*

### Special considerations

If the patient starts to fall during transfer, ease him to the closest surface—the bed, floor, or chair. *Never* stretch to finish the transfer. Doing so can cause loss of balance, falls, muscle strain, and other injuries—to you and the patient.

If the patient has one-sided weakness, follow the preceding essential steps, but place the chair on the unaffected side. Instruct the patient to pivot and bear as much weight as possible on the unaffected side. Support the affected side, because the patient will tend to lean to this side. Use pillows to support the hemiplegic patient's affected side to prevent slumping in the wheelchair.

### Documentation
If necessary, record the time of transfer and the extent of assistance in your notes.

LORRAINE E. BUCHANAN, RN, MSN

---

# Patient Transfer with a Hydraulic Lift

*Using a hydraulic lift to raise the immobile patient from the supine to the sitting position allows safe, comfortable transfer between bed and chair. It's indicated for the obese or immobile patient for whom manual transfer poses the potential for nurse or patient injury. Although most models of hydraulic lift can be operated by one person, it's preferable to have two staff members present during transfer to stabilize and support the patient.*

### Equipment
Hydraulic lift, with sling and chains (or straps) □ hooks/chair or wheelchair.

### Preparation of equipment
Because models of hydraulic lift may vary in weight capacity, check the manufacturer's specifications before attempting patient transfer. Make sure the bed and wheelchair wheels are locked before beginning the transfer.

### Essential steps
● Explain the procedure to the patient, and reassure him that the hydraulic lift can safely support his weight and won't tip over.
● Make sure the side rail opposite you is raised and secure. Then, roll the patient toward you, onto his side, and

raise the side rail. Walk to the opposite side of the bed and lower the side rail.
● Place the sling under the patient's buttock, with its lower edge below the greater trochanter. Then fanfold the far side of the sling against the back and buttocks.
● Roll the patient toward you onto the sling, and raise the side rail. Then, lower the opposite side rail.
● Slide your hands under the patient and pull the sling from beneath him, smoothing out all wrinkles. Then, roll the patient onto his back and center him on the sling.
● Place the appropriate chair next to the head of the bed, facing the foot.
● Lower the side rail next to the chair, and raise the bed only until the base of the lift can extend under the bed. *To avoid alarming and endangering the patient,* don't raise the bed completely.
● Set the lift's adjustable base to its widest position *to ensure added stability.* Then, move the lift so its arm lies perpendicular to the bed, directly over the patient.
● Connect one end of the chains (or straps) to the side arms on the lift; the other, hooked end to the sling. Face the hooks away from the patient *to prevent slippage and to avoid injury from their pointed edges.* The patient may place his arms inside or outside the chains (or straps) or may grasp them once the slack is gone (to avoid injury).
● Tighten the turnscrew on the lift. Then, depending on the type of lift, pump the handle or turn it clockwise, until the patient assumes a sitting position and his buttocks clear the bed surface by 1″ or 2″ (2.5 or 5 cm). Momentarily suspend the patient above the bed *until he feels secure that the lift can bear his weight.*
● Holding the patient's knees or shoulders with one hand, move the lift away from the bed and position it so its legs straddle the chair. (Or, have another co-worker guide the patient's body while you move the lift.) Depending on the type of lift, the arm should now rest in front or to one side of the chair.

## USING THE TRANS-AID® HYDRAULIC LIFT

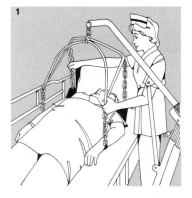

**1** After placing the patient supine in the center of the sling, position the hydraulic lift above him, as shown here. Then, attach the chains to the hooks on the sling.

**2** Turn the lift handle clockwise to raise the patient to the sitting position. If he's positioned properly, continue to raise him until he's suspended just above the bed.

**3** After positioning the patient above the wheelchair, turn the lift handle counter-clockwise to lower him onto the seat. When the chains become slack, stop turning and unhook the sling from the lift.

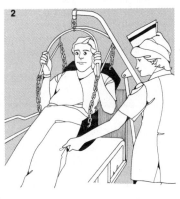

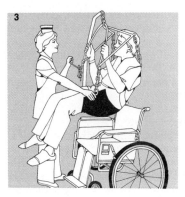

● Release the turnscrew. Then, depress the handle or turn it counterclockwise *to lower the patient into the chair.* While lowering the patient, push gently on his knees *to maintain correct sitting posture.* After lowering the patient into the chair, fasten the seat belt *to ensure his safety.*

● Remove the hooks or straps from the sling, but leave the sling in place for later transfer from chair to bed. Then, move the lift away from the patient.

● To return the patient to bed, reverse the procedure.

## Special considerations

Before transferring the patient with an altered center of gravity (caused by a halo vest or a lower-extremity cast), obtain help from a co-worker. If the patient will require lift transfers after discharge, teach his family how to use this device correctly and allow supervised practice.

## Documentation

If necessary, record the time of transfer in your notes.

LORRAINE E. BUCHANAN, RN, MSN

# Patient Repositioning with a Turning Sheet

*A turning sheet allows scheduled position changes with a minimum of strain on patient and nurse. Usually performed by two persons, this procedure is commonly used for the patient who can't or is forbidden to turn himself. But after the turning sheet is in place, depending on the patient's size, one person can reposition the patient.*

## Equipment
Turning sheet.

## Preparation of equipment
If a commercial turning sheet isn't available, fold a standard hospital sheet in half crosswise and then in half again. In either case, the turning sheet must have double thickness *to ensure its strength for safe repositioning.*

## Essential steps
- Explain the procedure to the patient.
- Stand at the side of the bed. Instruct your co-worker to stand on the opposite side; ensure that the side rail is raised and secure. Then, turn the supine patient away from you, onto his side.
- Place the turning sheet behind the patient so that its near side extends just over the edge of the bed from slightly above the shoulders to slightly below the buttocks. *This arrangement allows enough sheet on the near side of the bed for subsequent repositioning.*
- Fanfold the turning sheet as close to the patient's body as possible. Then, raise the near side rail, and tell your co-worker to roll the patient across the folded sheet, toward you. Your co-worker than grasps the folded turning sheet, pulls it firmly toward herself *to remove all the fanfolds from under the patient,* and then smooths any wrinkles *to avoid skin irritation, which can contribute to skin breakdown.*
- Together, grasp the sheet under the patient's shoulders and hips, and on a count of three, lift him to the opposite side of the bed.
- To turn the patient toward you, reach over him and grasp the sheet, and gently pull it toward you.
- While you're holding the patient with the sheet, your co-worker places pillows behind the shoulders and hips, arranging them lengthwise with one edge under the patient and the opposite edge wedged under the first *to provide maximum support and maintain the lateral position.*
- Align the patient's extremities.

## Special considerations
If the patient has spinal injury or instability, always use the logroll technique for turning; if he's helpless, support his head during turning.

## Documentation
Record regular position changes on the flowsheet and the patient's chart.

LORRAINE E. BUCHANAN, RN, MSN

# BODY POSITION AND MOBILITY

# Patient Positioning and Alignment

*Proper positioning and alignment are necessary for all patients but especially for those with impaired mobility. When combined with scheduled position changes and range-of-motion exercises, proper positioning can promote comfort, maintain and help restore body function, and help prevent contractures and formation of decubiti.*

## THREE COMMON POSITIONS

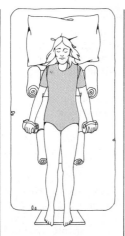

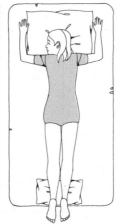

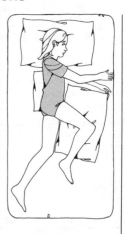

### Supine

Place the patient on her back, with her face upward. Use shoulder, hand, and trochanter rolls and footboard to position and align the patient's extremities.

### Prone

Place the patient on her stomach, with her face to the side.

### Lateral

Place the patient on one side, with her head aligned with her spine and her body straight.

---

*These measures can help the patient regain mobility and shorten duration of hospitalization.*

### Equipment
Standard adjustable hospital bed □ footboard □ standard bed pillows (large and small) □ flat, firm pillow □ sandbag (optional) □ blankets □ towels □ two washcloths.

Various commercially available devices, usually made from shaped sponge rubber, can help maintain position and alignment.

### Preparation of equipment
Position the footboard 2″ to 3″ (5 to 7.5 cm) beyond the end of the mattress. Roll the blankets or towels into an appropriate form for use as supports (such as trochanter rolls), or fold them for use as pads. Fold the washcloths in half, and shape them for use as hand

rolls; apply adhesive tape to secure their shape.

### Essential steps
● When first positioning the patient, explain that proper positioning prevents skin irritation and formation of decubitus ulcers. Emphasize the importance of his cooperation during position changes. Tell him the schedule and position changes you will use.

*To position the patient supine:*
● Place a flat, firm pillow under the patient's head so that the neck is straight but not hyperextended. *This prevents neck stiffness and excessive occipital pressure, which can contribute to decubitus formation.*
● Lift the patient's heels slightly off the mattress by placing a thin blanket under the calves or by extending the heels over the edge of the mattress *to prevent excess pressure on the heels, which can*

## ASSESSING FOR NEUROVASCULAR COMPROMISE AT PRESSURE POINTS

Every time you reposition a patient, check for cardiovascular and neurologic changes, such as numbness and tingling, caused by prolonged pressure at vulnerable sites.
• Inspect the patient's skin over bony prominences for erythema and irritation. Test reddened skin for blanching, which indicates unimpaired circulation. If redness—a normal response to pressure— doesn't disappear within 30 minutes and the area is warmer than surrounding skin, don't reposition the patient on this area for a while.
• Ask the patient if he feels numbness or tingling distal to the reddened areas on his extremities. Ulnar neuropathy commonly follows the use of the elbows to support and stabilize the upper body; peroneal neuropathy commonly follows incorrect placement of a supportive roll that compresses the common peroneal nerve (at the fibular head, just lateral to the patella). Both neuropathies are preventable, but they are rarely detected until they cause functional impairment.
• Check for palsies in the ulnar and peroneal nerves. Palsies begin as paresthesias and can lead to functional impairment.
• Document your findings and any recommendations for changes in the patient's turning and positioning schedule.

contribute to *decubitus formation*. Avoid placing pillows under the knees, *because this may cause flexion contractures of the hips and knees*. If the patient already has hip contractures, you may need to place pillows under the knees, as necessary, because a flat position can aggravate back pain.
• Position a trochanter roll firmly against each hip and thigh *to prevent external hip rotation*. Keep the rolls away from the sides of the knees, because this *can cause peroneal nerve compression, possibly resulting in footdrop*.
• Place the plantar surface of both feet against the footboard at a 90° angle to the legs. Then, position the arms in partial abduction *to prevent flexion contractures of the shoulders*.
• With the patient's forearms pronated slightly, flex each elbow slightly. Then, place a small towel or pillow under each upper arm above the elbow *to avoid compression of the ulnar nerves*.
• Arrange the patient's wrists in the neutral position, with the fingers partially flexed in the natural relaxed position. If necessary, place the fingers around a hand roll, with the thumb abducted in opposition, *to maintain normal position of hands and fingers*.
*To position the patient laterally:*
• Use a turning sheet to position the patient on his side. Then, arrange two bed pillows under the sheet and behind the patient *to support the shoulders, upper torso, buttocks, and hips*.
• Place a flat, firm pillow under the head, so the neck is straight.
• Extend the bottom leg in a straight line with the back and shoulders. Flex the top leg at the hip and knee, and support it with a bed pillow from the groin to slightly above the ankle *to avoid contact with the bottom leg and maintain hip alignment. This helps prevent lower back strain and formation of decubiti over the bony prominences.*
• If necessary, place a firm pillow or sandbag against the plantar surface of each foot *to maintain dorsiflexion and prevent footdrop*.
• Externally rotate and partially extend the bottom arm. Place the top arm, with elbow flexed and shoulder abducted, on a bed pillow *to prevent drag on the shoulder and wristdrop*.
*To position the patient prone:*
• If a linen-saver pad is being used to absorb drainage, center it on the bed so that the patient turns onto it. Then, use a turning sheet and obtain assistance, if necessary, to turn the patient onto the abdomen.
• Turn the patient's head to the side he prefers. Then, place the legs in slight abduction, with the knees and hips extended.
• Position the feet over the end of the

mattress, against the footboard. Place a thin rolled blanket or a flat pillow under the anterior ankles *to avoid pressing the toes against the bedsprings.*

● Abduct the arms slightly and flex the elbows, raising the forearms slightly and resting the palms on the bed, with fingers extended. Or, *maintain normal finger flexion with hand rolls.*

### Special considerations
Because correct positioning and alignment alone can't prevent joint contractures and decubitus formation, change the patient's position and assess skin condition at least every 2 hours, on an established schedule. Base this schedule on the doctor's orders and the patient's condition. Ensure that all shifts know and adhere to this schedule—and to the range-of-motion exercise schedule—*to help prevent joint contractures, loss of muscle tone, and formation of decubiti.*

### Documentation
Record the patient's tolerance for various positions in his progress notes, and use this information to develop a turning and positioning program.

LORRAINE E. BUCHANAN, RN, MSN

---

# Devices to Maintain Alignment and Reduce Pressure

---

*Various assistive devices are used to maintain correct body positioning and to help prevent complications of prolonged bed rest. These devices fall into four main categories:* cradle boots *to protect the heels and help prevent skin breakdown, footdrop, and (some types) external hip rotation;* abduction pillows *to help prevent internal hip rotation after femoral fracture, hip fracture, or surgery;* trochanter rolls *to help prevent external hip rotation;*

*and* hand rolls *to help prevent hand contractures. Cradle boots and trochanter and hand rolls are especially useful when caring for patients with loss of sensation, mobility, or consciousness.*

### Equipment
Cradle boots or substitute □ abduction pillow □ trochanter rolls □ hand rolls.

The cradle boot is made of sponge rubber and has a space cut out for the ankle and foot. Other commercial boots are available but not all help to prevent external hip rotation. Footboards with antirotation blocks help prevent footdrop and external hip rotation but not heel pressure. High-topped sneakers may be used to help prevent footdrop but they do not prevent external hip rotation or heel pressure.

The abduction pillow is a wedge-shaped piece of sponge rubber with lateral indentations for the patient's thighs. Its straps wrap around the thighs *to maintain correct positioning.* Although a properly shaped bed pillow may temporarily substitute for the commercial abduction pillow, it's hard to apply and fails to maintain the correct lateral alignment.

The commercial trochanter roll is made of sponge rubber but can also be improvised from a rolled blanket or towel.

The hand roll, available in both hard and soft materials, is held in place by fixed or adjustable straps. It can be improvised from a rolled washcloth secured with adhesive tape.

### Preparation of equipment
If you're using a device that's available in different sizes, select the appropriate size for the patient.

### Essential steps
*To apply cradle boots:*
● Open the slit on the superior surface of the boot. Then, place the patient's heel in the circular cutout area. If the patient is positioned laterally, you may apply the boot only to the bottom foot

## COMMONLY USED COMMERCIAL DEVICES

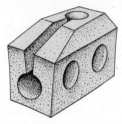

**Hand roll:** prevents hand contractures

**Cradle boot:** prevents footdrop, skin breakdown, and external hip rotation

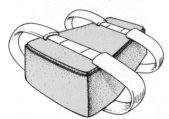

**Abductor pillow:** prevents internal hip rotation

**Trochanter roll:** prevents external hip rotation

and support the flexed top foot with a pillow.
• If appropriate, insert the other heel in the second boot.
• Position the patient's legs properly *to prevent strain on hip ligaments and pressure on bony prominences.*

*To apply an abduction pillow:*
• Place the pillow between the supine patient's legs. Slide it toward the groin so it touches the legs all along its length.
• Place the upper part of both legs in the pillow's lateral indentations, and secure the straps *to prevent slippage.*

*To apply trochanter rolls:*
• Position one roll along the outside of the thigh, from the iliac crest to mid-thigh. Then, place another roll along the other thigh. Make sure neither roll extends as far as the knee *to avoid peroneal nerve compression and palsy, which can lead to footdrop.*
• If you've fashioned trochanter rolls from a towel, leave several inches unrolled and tuck this under the thigh *to hold the device in place and maintain patient position.*

*To apply hand rolls:*
• Place one roll in the patient's hand to maintain the neutral position. Then, secure the strap, if present, or apply gauze and secure with hypoallergenic or adhesive tape.
• Similarly apply the second roll to the other hand.

### Special considerations
Remember that the use of assistive devices does not preclude regularly scheduled patient positioning, range-of-motion exercises, and skin care.

*To prevent contractures and formation of decubiti,* remove a soft hand roll every 4 hours (every 2 hours if the patient has hand spasticity); remove a hard hand roll every 2 hours.

### Documentation
Record the use of assistive devices in the patient's chart and the nursing-care plan. Evaluate the effect of these on your patient-care goals.

LORRAINE E. BUCHANAN, RN, MSN

# Passive Range-of-Motion Exercises

*Passive range-of-motion (ROM) exercises, used to move the patient's joints through as full a range of motion as possible, improve or maintain joint mobility and help prevent contractures. Performed by a nurse, physical therapist, or member of the patient's family, these exercises are indicated for the patient with temporary or permanent loss of mobility, sensation, or consciousness. Performed properly, passive ROM exercises require recognition of the patient's limits of motion and support of all joints during movement.*

*Passive ROM exercises are contraindicated in patients with septic joints, acute thrombophlebitis, severe arthritic joint inflammation, or recent trauma with possible occult fractures or internal injuries.*

### Essential steps

• Before starting passive ROM exercises, assess the patient for disability and weakness. Determine the joints that need ROM exercises, and consult the doctor or physical therapist about limitations or precautions for specific exercises. The exercises below treat all joints, but they don't have to be performed in the order given or all at once. You can schedule them over the course of a day, whenever the patient is in the most convenient position. Remember, perform all exercises slowly, gently, and to the end of the normal range of motion or to the point of pain. Never force a joint to move beyond resistance or continue movement beyond the point of pain.

• When you're ready to perform ROM exercises, raise the bed to a comfortable working height.

*To exercise the neck:*

• *Extension-flexion.* Position the patient supine on the bed, without a pillow. Support the back of the head with one hand and the chin with the other. To perform extension, bend the neck backward, so the patient looks at the ceiling; to perform flexion, bend the head forward at the neck, bringing the chin toward the chest. Ideally, the patient should be able to rest the chin on the chest.

• *Lateral flexion.* Place one hand on each side of the patient's face. Tilt the head laterally, bringing the right ear toward the right shoulder, then slowly tilt the head back toward the left shoulder.

• *Rotation.* With your hands in the same position as for lateral flexion, turn the patient's head from right to left, as if he were looking over his shoulder.

*To exercise the shoulders:*

• *Extension-flexion.* If possible, place the patient in the prone, side-lying, or sitting position. Or, remove the headboard and slide the patient down in bed. These exercises are most effective when the patient is in the prone, side-lying, or sitting position. Then, with the patient's arm in the natural extended position (at his side, palm facing his body), place one hand under the elbow and grasp the wrist with the other. Keeping the patient's elbow straight, bring the arm straight up until it reaches the ear (flexion). If necessary, bend the elbow so the forearm reaches above the head.

• *Vertical abduction-adduction.* Assume the same starting position as for extension-flexion. Then, swing the patient's arm outward from the side, staying in the plane of the body (abduction). Return the arm to the side, and then direct it across the midline toward the other arm (adduction.) To achieve full range of motion, externally rotate the arm at the shoulder, bring the arm up to the ear, and then return it to the starting position.

• *Horizontal abduction-adduction.* Place the patient's arm in vertical abduction, and then bend the elbow (hor-

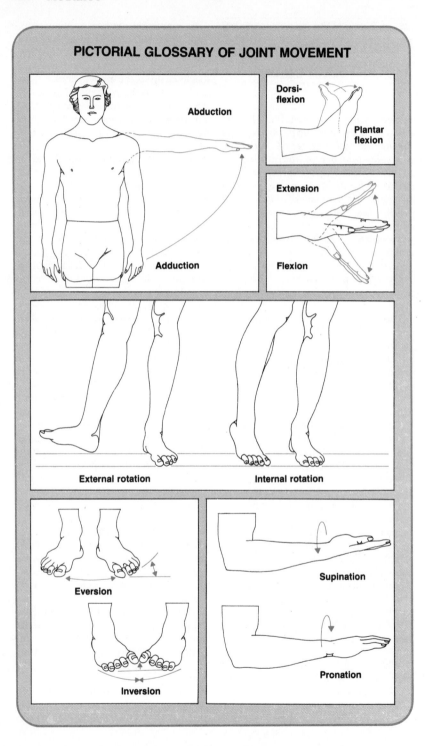

# PICTORIAL GLOSSARY OF JOINT MOVEMENT

Abduction

Adduction

Dorsi-flexion

Plantar flexion

Extension

Flexion

External rotation

Internal rotation

Eversion

Inversion

Supination

Pronation

izontal abduction). Grasp the elbow with one hand and the wrist with the other. Carry the patient's arm across the body so the hand touches the opposite shoulder (horizontal adduction).

• *Internal-external rotation.* Place the patient's arm in horizontal abduction. Grasp the wrist with one hand and the elbow, bent at a 90° angle, with the other. Keeping the shoulder at a 90° angle to the mattress, gently lower the forearm until the palm touches the bed (internal rotation). Return to the starting position, then gently push the dorsal forearm toward the mattress so the back of the hand touches the bed (external rotation).

*To exercise the elbow:*

• *Extension-flexion.* Place the patient's arm at his side, with the palm facing upward (extension). Grasp the wrist so the hand won't droop. Keeping the upper arm on the bed, bring the hand up toward the shoulder (flexion).

*To exercise the forearm:*

• *Supination-pronation.* With the patient's arm in the natural extended position, lift the hand into the air, keeping the elbow on the bed. Grasp his wrist with one hand and his hand with your other hand. Twist the hand to bring the palm up (supination). Then, twist it back again to bring the palm down (pronation).

*To exercise the wrist:*

---

## HOW TO PERFORM ISOMETRIC EXERCISES

Isometric exercises, which strengthen and increase muscle tone, contract muscles against resistance (from other muscles or from a stationary object, such as a bed or a wall) but without joint movement. Performed anywhere—while standing, sitting, or lying down—these exercises require only a comfortable position and proper body alignment. Hold each contraction for 2 to 5 seconds and repeat it three to four times daily—below peak contraction level for the first week; thereafter at peak level.

**Neck rotators.** Place the heel of the hand above one ear. Push the head toward the hand as forcefully as possible, without moving the head, neck, or arm. Repeat the exercise on the other side.

**Neck flexors.** Place both palms on the forehead. Without moving the neck, push the head forward while resisting with the palms.

**Neck extensors.** Clasp your fingers behind your head. Push your head against your hands without moving the neck.

**Shoulder elevators.** Holding your right arm straight down at your side, grasp the right wrist with the left hand. Try to shrug the right shoulder, but prevent it from moving by holding the arm in place. Alternate arms.

**Shoulder, chest, and scapular musculature.** Place your right fist in your left palm, and raise both arms to shoulder height. Push your fist into the palm as forcefully as possible without moving either arm. Then, with the arms in the same position, clasp the fingers and try to pull the hands apart. Repeat the pattern beginning with the left fist in the right palm.

**Elbow flexors and extensors.** With the right elbow bent at 90° and the right palm facing upward, place the left fist against the right palm. Try to bend the right elbow further while resisting with the left fist. Repeat the pattern, bending the left elbow.

**Abdomen.** Assume a sitting position, and bend slightly forward, with your hands in front of the middle of the thighs. Try to bend forward further, resisting by pressing the palms against the thighs.

Or, in the supine position, clasp your hands behind the head. Then, raise the shoulders about an inch, holding this position for a few seconds.

**Back extensors.** In a sitting position, bend forward and place your hands under the buttocks. Try to stand up, resisting with both hands.

**Hip abductors.** While standing, squeeze the inner thighs together as tightly as possible. Placing a pillow between the knees supplies resistance and increases the effectiveness of this exercise.

**Hip extensors.** Squeeze the buttocks together as tightly as possible.

**Knee extensors.** Straighten the knee fully. Then, vigorously tighten the muscle above the knee, so it moves the kneecap upward. Alternate legs.

**Ankle flexors and extensors.** Pull the toes upward, holding briefly. Then, push them down as far as possible, again holding briefly.

# PATIENT-TEACHING AID

## HOW TO PERFORM ACTIVE RANGE-OF-MOTION EXERCISES

Dear Patient:

Your doctor has prescribed active range-of-motion exercises to help you maintain joint mobility and prevent contractures. You can do these exercises while lying down, sitting, or standing. Repeat each exercise three to five times at first, increasing the number gradually as your activity tolerance increases. Remember to exercise slowly.

**Neck.** Move your head backward and forward, as far as possible, as if you were nodding "yes."

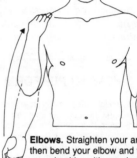

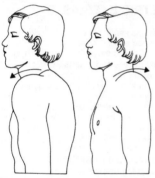

**Shoulders.** Raise your shoulders and move them forward in a circular motion. Then, move them backward in a circular motion.

**Elbows.** Straighten your arm, and then bend your elbow and touch your shoulder with your hand. Then, straighten your arm slowly. Repeat this pattern with the other arm.

**Wrist and hand.** With your forearms resting on the arms of a chair, palms down, bend your wrists slowly up and down.

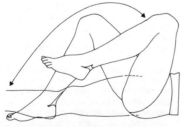

**Hips and knees.** Keeping one foot flat on the bed and knee bent, bend the other leg, bringing it as far as possible toward your chest. Slowly stretch this leg out again, straightening the knee and hip. Relax. Repeat the pattern with the other leg.

**Ankle.** Make a circle with your foot, moving first clockwise and then counter-clockwise. Repeat with the other foot.

• *Extension-flexion.* With the patient's arm in the same position as for forearm exercises, bend the hand back toward the dorsal forearm (extension); then bend it forward (flexion).

• *Lateral flexion.* In the same position as for extension-flexion, rock the hand sideways.

• *Circumduction.* In the same position as for extension-flexion, rotate the hand in a circular motion.

To exercise the fingers and thumb:

• *Extension-flexion.* Keep the arm in the same position as for the forearm exercises. Grasp the palm and wrist with one hand, and gently straighten the fingers with the other (extension). Then, place your hand on the back of the patient's fingers, and gently bend his hand into a fist (flexion). Repeat these two motions with each finger, individually flexing each joint.

• *Abduction-adduction.* In the same position as for extension-flexion, spread two adjoining fingers apart (abduction) and then bring them together (adduction). Repeat this exercise for all fingers and thumbs.

• *Opposition.* In the same position as for extension-flexion, pinch the thumb and each fingertip together, one at a time.

• *Circumduction.* In the same position as for extension-flexion, rotate the thumb in a circle.

To exercise the hip and knee:

• *Extension-flexion.* With the patient's leg flat on the bed in the natural extended position, place one hand under the ankle and the other hand under the knee. Bend the hip and knee toward the chest, sliding your hand out from under the knee to allow full joint flexion.

• *Abduction-adduction.* Place your hands under the ankle and knee. Move the leg sideways, out and away from the other leg (abduction), and then back, over, and across it (adduction).

• *Internal-external rotation.* With the patient's leg flat on the bed, grasp its dorsal side above the ankle and at the knee. Roll the leg toward the midline (internal rotation), and then away from the midline (external rotation).

To exercise the ankle:

• *Dorsiflexion-plantar flexion.* Place one hand under the heel and the other on the ball of the foot. Push the foot toward the head and pull the heel back (dorsiflexion). Then, move your hand from the ball to the dorsal surface. Pull the foot down toward the bed and push the heel back (plantar flexion).

• *Circumduction.* Place one hand under the ankle, and grasp the foot with the other hand. Then, rotate the ankle in a circular motion.

To exercise the foot:

• *Inversion-eversion.* Maintaining the starting position as for ankle circumduction, hold the ankle securely. Twist the foot with the sole toward the midline (inversion), and then away from the midline (eversion).

To exercise the toes:

• *Extension-flexion.* Hold the ankle securely with one hand, and curl the toes toward the sole with the other hand (flexion). Then, straighten and stretch the toes back toward the dorsal surface of the foot (extension).

• *Abduction-adduction.* Spread two adjoining toes apart (abduction) and then bring them together (adduction). Repeat for all toes.

## Special considerations

Because joints begin to stiffen within 24 hours of disuse, start passive ROM exercises as soon as possible, and perform them at least once a shift, particularly during bathing or turning the patient. Use good body mechanics, and repeat each exercise at least three times but more often if necessary. When possible, encourage the patient to assist with the exercises. After completing them, reposition the patient correctly.

If the disabled patient requires long-term rehabilitation after discharge, teach a family member to perform passive ROM exercises.

## Documentation

Record the joints exercised, the presence of edema or pressure areas, any pain resulting from the exercises, and the patient's tolerance of them.

NANCY ROTH, RPT, MMSc

# Progressive Ambulation

*Progressive ambulation is the gradual return to full ambulation begun 1 to 2 days after surgery or after 2 or more days of bed rest. Early ambulation helps prevent the common complications of bed rest: respiratory stasis and hypostatic pneumonia; circulatory stasis, thrombophlebitis, and emboli; urinary stasis, retention, infection, and calculus formation; abdominal distention, constipation, and decreased appetite. It also helps restore the patient's sense of equilibrium and enhances his self-confidence and self-image.*

*Progressive ambulation begins with dangling feet over the edge of the bed and progresses to sitting in an armchair or a wheelchair, walking in the room, then walking in the halls. The patient's progress depends on his condition and the doctor's orders. Successful return to full ambulation requires good communication between patient and nurse, correct body mechanics, and careful patient observation.*

## Equipment
Robe □ slippers for sitting, hard-soled shoes for walking □ chair or wheelchair □ walking belt (optional) □ assistive device (cane, crutches, walker), if necessary.

## Preparation of equipment
If the patient requires an assistive device, the physical therapist or rehabilitation nurse usually selects the appropriate one and teaches its use.

## Essential steps
● Check the patient's history, diagnosis, and therapy regimen. Ask him if he feels pain or weakness; if necessary, give medication for pain, and wait for it to take effect before attempting ambulation. Remember that the medicated patient may overestimate his capabilities or develop hypotension or dizziness.
● Find out the patient's attitude and expectations for ambulation. Then, taking his response into account, explain the immediate goal of ambulation and the way you'll help him achieve it. Provide encouragement, because he may be hesitant or fearful; reassure him that he needn't attempt more than he can reasonably do. If he fears pain in an incision, show him how to support it by placing a hand alongside or gently over the dressing site.
● Remove equipment or other objects to provide a clear path *to prevent falls.*

*To dangle the patient's legs correctly:*
● Position the bed horizontally and the patient laterally, facing you. Move his legs over the side of the bed and grasp his shoulders, standing with a wide base of support. Ask the patient to help by pushing up from the bed with his arms. Then, shift your weight from the foot closest to the patient's head to the other foot as you steadily and deliberately raise the patient to the sitting position. Pull with your whole body, not just your arms, *to avoid straining your back and jostling the patient.*
Alternately, you can raise the head of the bed to a 45° angle *to allow easier elevation of the patient.* Use this method only if the patient has good enough sitting balance *to prevent falls.*
● While the patient adjusts to an upright position, continue to stand facing him to prevent falls, and observe him closely. Be alert for signs and symptoms of orthostatic hypotension: fainting, dizziness, and complaints of blurred vision. If desired, check pulse rate and blood pressure.

*To assist the patient to a standing position:*

## POSITIONING THE PATIENT FOR DANGLING, SITTING, AND WALKING

**Dangling:** To help the patient support himself in a dangling position, move an overbed table in front of him and place a pillow on it.

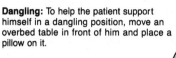
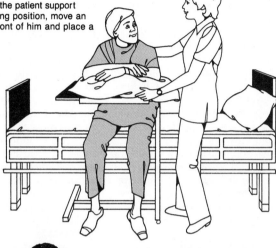

**Sitting:** Seat the patient in a chair with armrests and a straight back. Position his lower back against the rear of the chair, keeping his feet flat on the floor, hips and knees at right angles, and upper body straight. Rest his forearms on the armrests.

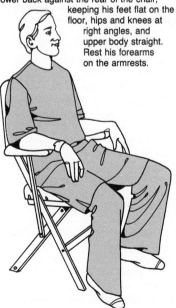

**Walking:** Provide a path unimpeded by equipment and other objects, and avoid overexertion. If necessary, hold the patient so you can control his upper and lower body and any lateral movements.

• After the patient can dangle his legs successfully and can support his weight on them, attempt the standing position.
• Help the patient put on a robe and slippers or shoes. If you plan to use a walking belt, apply it now.
• If the patient is alert and has fair to good strength, place his feet flat on the floor and allow him to stand by himself. As he stands, place one hand under his axilla and the other hand around his waist *to prevent falls.* Help him stand fully erect *to promote good balance and correct breathing.*

If the patient needs help standing, position your knees to either side of his. Bend your knees, put your arms around his waist, and instruct him to push up from the bed with the arms. Then straighten your knees and pull the patient with you while rising to an erect position. This technique helps you *avoid back muscle strain.*

*To help the patient sit and walk:*
• Once the patient stands, you can pivot and lower him into an armchair or wheelchair, or you can begin to walk with him.
• If you've decided to seat him, place the lower back against the rear of the chair and the feet flat on the floor. Position the hips and knees at right angles, and keep the upper body straight. Then, flex the elbows, and place the forearms on the arms of the chair.
• If the patient can walk safely only with your assistance, stand behind him, placing one hand under the axilla and the other hand around the waist. *This allows you to control the upper and lower body as well as lateral deviation.*

If you can't support the patient, ask a co-worker to help you. Stand to one side of the patient, and place your hand under the arm or on the elbow, or grasp the walking belt. Standing on the other side of the patient, the assisting co-worker supports the patient similarly.
• Give the patient verbal and tactile cues *to encourage him during walking.* Stay close to a railed wall or other supportive structure and, if necessary, allow the patient to rest in a chair before attempting to walk back to his room. If he can't walk back, tell him to remain seated while you summon assistance or obtain a wheelchair. Don't leave the patient unattended if you have any reason to think he may fall. If you can't find a chair nearby, have the patient lean against the wall and just call for assistance as you help support him.

## Special considerations
Assess your patient's abilities carefully. Some patients resist ambulation, while others are too eager to begin and overestimate their capabilities. Set daily or weekly goals to help motivate the patient. If early ambulation is impossible, encourage bed exercises. Don't let the use of catheters and infusion bottles discourage ambulation, because these are easily portable; but check dressings and tubes carefully afterward for proper position and changes in drainage. If appropriate, take pulse, respirations, and blood pressure. When leaving the patient sitting up in a chair, make certain he has a call button or signal device. Restrain the confused patient to prevent falls.

If the patient begins to fall, *don't* try to catch him. Instead, break his fall as best you can by easing him to the bed, chair, or floor, making sure he doesn't strike his head. Then summon help. *Don't* leave the patient alone—he needs your comfort and reassurance.

If the patient experiences dyspnea, diaphoresis, or orthostatic hypotension, stabilize his position and take vital signs. Place him in the semi-Fowler's position to facilitate breathing. If his condition doesn't improve rapidly, notify the doctor.

## Documentation
Record the type of transfer and assistance required; the duration of sitting, standing, or walking; the distance walked, if appropriate; the patient's response to ambulation; and any significant changes in blood pressure, pulse, and respirations.

NANCY ROTH, RPT, MMSc

# Tilt Table

*The tilt table, a padded table or board that can be gradually raised from horizontal to vertical position, can help prevent the complications of prolonged bed rest. Used for the patient with a spinal cord injury, brain damage, orthostatic hypotension, or other condition that prevents free standing, the tilt table increases tolerance of the upright position, conditions the cardiovascular system, stretches muscles, and helps prevent contractures, bone demineralization, and urinary calculus formation.*

### Equipment
Tilt table with footboard and restraining straps □ sphygmomanometer □ stethoscope □ antiembolism stockings or elastic bandages □ abdominal binder (optional).

### Preparation of equipment
Common types of tilt tables include the electric table, which moves at a slow, steady rate; the manual table, which is raised by a handle; and the spring-assisted table, which is raised by a pedal.

### Essential steps
• Explain the use and benefits of the tilt table to the patient.
• Apply antiembolism stockings *to restrict the vascular walls and help prevent pooling of blood and development of edema.* If necessary, apply an abdominal binder, *to avoid pooling of blood in the splanchnic region, which contributes to insufficient cerebral circulation and orthostatic hypotension.*

Obtain assistance and place the patient on a stretcher for transport to the location of the tilt table (usually in the physical therapy department).
• Make sure the tilt table is locked in the horizontal position. Then, transfer the patient to the table, placing him in the supine position, with feet flat against the footboard.
• If the patient can't bear weight on one leg, place a wooden block between the footboard and the weight-bearing foot, permitting the non–weight-bearing leg to dangle freely.
• Fasten the safety straps, then take the patient's blood pressure and pulse.
• Tilt the table slowly in 15° to 30° increments, evaluating the patient constantly. Take blood pressure every 3 to 5 minutes, *because movement from the supine to the upright position decreases systolic pressure.* Be alert for signs and symptoms of insufficient cerebral circulation: dizziness, nausea, pallor, diaphoresis, tachycardia, change in mental status. If any of these signs or symptoms, hypotension, or seizure occurs, immediately return the table to the horizontal position.
• If the patient tolerates the upright position well, continue to tilt the table until reaching the desired angle, usually between 45° and 80°. A 60° tilt gives the patient the physiologic effects and sensations of standing upright.
• Gradually return the patient to horizontal position, and check vital signs. Then, obtain assistance, and transfer the patient onto the stretcher for transport back to his room.

### Special considerations

Never leave the patient unattended on the tilt table, because marked physiologic changes can occur suddenly.

Let the patient's response determine the angle of tilt and duration of elevation, but avoid prolonged upright positioning, *which may lead to venous stasis.*

### Documentation
Record the angle and duration of elevation; changes in the patient's pulse, blood pressure, and physical and mental status; and his response to treatment.

NANCY ROTH, RPT, MMSc

# Canes

*Indicated for the patient with one-sided weakness or injury, occasional loss of balance, or increased joint pressure, the cane provides balance and support for walking and reduces fatigue and strain on weight-bearing joints. Available in various sizes, the cane should extend from the greater trochanter to the floor and have a rubber tip to prevent slippage.*

*Canes are contraindicated for the patient with bilateral weakness; such a patient should use crutches or a walker.*

## Equipment
Rubber-tipped cane.

Although wooden canes are available, three types of aluminum canes are used most frequently. The standard aluminum cane—used by the patient requiring only slight assistance to walk—provides the least support; its half-circle handle allows it to be hooked over chairs. The T-handle cane—used by the patient with hand weakness—has a straight, shaped handle with grips and a bent shaft. It provides greater stability than the standard cane. The quad (broad-based) cane—used by the patient with poor balance or the cerebrovascular accident patient with one-sided weakness and inability to hold onto a walker with both hands—has a base with four additional supports in a rectangular array. The quad cane provides greater stability than a standard cane but considerably less than a walker.

## Preparation of equipment
Ask the patient to hold the cane on the uninvolved side 4″ to 6″ (10 to 15 cm) from the base of the little toe. If the cane is made of aluminum, adjust its height by pushing in the metal button on the shaft and raising or lowering the shaft; it it's wooden, the rubber tip is removed and the excess is sawed off. At the correct height, the handle of the cane is level with the greater trochanter *and allows approximately 15° flexion at the elbow.* If the cane is too short, the patient will have to drop the shoulder to lean on the cane; if the cane is too long, he'll have to raise the shoulder and will have difficulty supporting his weight.

## Essential steps
● Explain the mechanics of cane-walking to the patient. Tell him to hold the cane on the uninvolved side *to promote a reciprocal gait pattern and to distribute weight away from the involved side.*
● Instruct the patient to hold the cane close to the body *to prevent leaning,* and to move the cane and the involved leg simultaneously, followed by the uninvolved leg.
● Encourage the patient to keep the stride length of each leg and the timing of each step (cadence) equal.

---

### TEACHING SAFE USE OF A CANE

To teach the patient to sit down, stand by his affected side and tell him to place the backs of his legs against the edge of the chair seat. Then, tell him to move the cane out from his side and to reach back with both hands to grasp the chair's armrests. Supporting his weight on the armrests, he can then lower himself onto the seat. While he's seated, he should keep the cane hooked on the armrest or the chair back.

To teach the patient to get up, stand by his affected side and tell him to unhook the cane from the chair and hold it in his stronger hand, as he grasps the armrests. He then should move the uninvolved foot slightly forward, lean slightly forward, and push against the armrests to raise himself upright.

Warn the patient against leaning on the cane when sitting or rising from the chair *to prevent loss of balance and falls.*

Supervise your patient each time he gets in or out of a chair until you're both certain he can do it alone.

• Instruct the patient to always use a railing, if present, when negotiating stairs. Tell him to hold the cane with the other hand or to keep it in the hand grasping the railing. To ascend stairs, the patient should lead with the uninvolved leg and follow with the involved leg; to descend, he should lead with the involved leg and follow with the uninvolved one. Help the patient remember by telling him to use this mnemonic device: The good goes up, and the bad goes down.

To negotiate stairs without a railing, the patient should use the walking technique to ascend and descend the stairs, but move the cane just before the involved leg. Thus, to ascend stairs, the patient should hold the cane on the uninvolved side, step with the uninvolved leg, advance the cane, then the involved leg. To descend, he should hold the cane on the uninvolved side, lead with the cane, then the involved leg, and finally the uninvolved leg.

### Special considerations

After instructing the patient, demonstrate correct cane-walking. Then, have him practice in front of you before allowing him to walk alone. When he's ready to climb stairs, advise him that he'll need considerable practice (in the physical therapy department) to learn to shift his weight correctly.

To prevent falls during the learning period, guard the patient carefully by standing behind him slightly to his stronger side and putting one foot between his feet and your other foot to the outside of the uninvolved leg. If necessary, use a walking belt. Decrease your guarding as the patient gains competence. Encourage and praise his efforts to raise his self-esteem and provide motivation.

### Documentation

Record the type of cane used, the amount of guarding required, the distance walked, and the patient's understanding and tolerance of cane-walking.

NANCY ROTH, RPT, MMSc

# Crutches

*Crutches remove weight from one or both legs, enabling the patient to support himself with the hands and arms. Typically prescribed for the patient with lower-extremity injury or weakness, successful use of crutches requires balance, stamina, and upper-body strength. Crutch selection and walking gait depend on the patient's condition. The patient who can't use crutches may be able to use a walker.*

### Equipment

Crutches with axillary pads, handgrips, and rubber suction tips □ walking belt (optional).

Three types of crutches are commonly used. Standard aluminum or wooden crutches—used by the patient with a sprain, strain, cast, or pinning—require stamina and upper-body strength. Aluminum Lofstrand, or forearm, crutches—used by the paraplegic or other patient using the swing-through gait—employ a collar that fits around the forearm and a horizontal handgrip that provides support. Platform crutches—used by the arthritic patient with an upper-extremity deficit that prevents weight-bearing through the wrist—provide padded surfaces for the upper extremities.

### Preparation of equipment

After choosing the appropriate crutches, adjust their height with the patient standing or, if necessary, recumbent. Position the crutches so they extend from a point 4″ to 6″ (10 to 15 cm) to the side and 4″ to 6″ in front of the patient's feet to 1½″ to 2″ (4 to 5 cm) below the axillae. Then, adjust the handgrips so the patient's elbows are flexed at a 15° angle when he's standing with the crutches in resting position.

### Essential steps

• Consult with the patient's doctor and

physical therapist *to coordinate reha-bilitation orders and teaching.*

• Describe the gait you will teach and the reason for your choice. Then, demonstrate the gait, as necessary.

• Place a walking belt around the patient's waist, if necessary, *to help prevent falls.* Tell the patient to position the crutches and to shift his weight from side to side. Then, place the patient in front of a full-length mirror to facilitate learning and coordination.

• Teach the four-point gait to the patient who can bear weight on both legs. Although this is the safest gait, *because three points are always in contact with the floor,* it requires greater coordination than others due to its constant shifting of weight. Use the sequence right crutch, left foot, left crutch, right foot. Suggest counting *to help develop rhythm,* and make sure each short step is of equal length. If the patient gains proficiency at this gait, teach the faster two-point gait.

• Teach the two-point gait to the patient with weak legs but good coordination and arm strength. This is the most natural crutch-walking gait, *because it mimics walking, with alternating swings of the arms and legs.* Instruct the patient to advance the right crutch and left foot simultaneously, followed by the left crutch and the right foot.

• Teach the three-point gait to the patient who can bear only partial or no weight on one leg. Instruct him to advance both crutches 6″ to 8″ (15 to 20 cm) along with the involved leg. Then, tell him to bring the uninvolved leg forward and to bear the bulk of his weight on the crutches but some of it on the involved leg, if possible. Stress the importance of taking steps of equal length and duration, with no pauses.

• Teach the swing-to or swing-through gaits—the fastest ones—to the patient with complete paralysis of the hips and legs. When used with chronic conditions, *these gaits can lead to atrophy of the hips and legs if appropriate therapeutic exercises are not performed*

*routinely.* Instruct the patient to advance both crutches simultaneously and to swing the legs parallel to (swing-to) or beyond the crutches (swing-through).

• To teach the patient who uses crutches to get up from a chair, tell him to hold both crutches in one hand, with the tips resting firmly on the floor. Then, instruct him to push up from the chair with his free hand, supporting himself with the crutches.

To sit down, the patient reverses the process: Tell him to support himself with the crutches in one hand and lower himself with the other.

• To teach the patient to ascend stairs using the three-point gait, tell him to lead with the uninvolved leg and to follow with both the crutches and the involved leg. To descend stairs, he should lead with the crutches and the involved leg and follow with the good leg. He may find it helpful to remember "The good goes up, the bad goes down."

### Special considerations

Encourage arm and shoulder strengthening exercises to prepare the patient for crutch-walking. Teach crutch-walking by demonstrating correct technique. If possible, teach two techniques—one fast and one slow—*so the patient can alternate between them to prevent excessive muscle fatigue and can adjust more easily to various walking conditions.* When the patient is ready to walk, stand behind him and hold onto the walking belt with your palm facing upward *to provide support.* Make sure he maintains good posture *to prevent loss of balance and falls.* Also, warn him against habitually leaning on the crutches, *because prolonged pressure on the axillae can damage the brachial nerves, causing brachial nerve palsy.*

### Documentation

Record the type of gait the patient used, the amount of assistance required, the distance walked, and the patient's tolerance of the crutches and gait.

NANCY ROTH, RPT, MMSc

# Walkers

*A walker consists of a metal frame with handgrips, four legs, and one open side. Because this device provides greater stability and security than other ambulatory aids, it's recommended for the patient with insufficient strength and balance to use crutches or a cane, or with weakness requiring frequent rest periods. Attachments for standard walkers and modified walkers help meet special needs.*

## Equipment

Walker with attachments, as necessary.

Various types of walkers are available. The standard walker—used by the patient with unilateral or bilateral

---

## TEACHING SAFE USE OF A WALKER

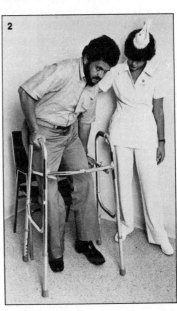

**To teach the patient to sit down:**
• First, tell the patient to stand with the back of his stronger leg against the front of the chair, with his weaker leg slightly off the floor, and the walker directly in front.
• Tell him to grasp the armrest with the hand on the weaker side and then shift his weight to the stronger leg and the hand grasping the armrest. (See photograph #1, in which the patient has left leg weakness.)
• Tell the patient to lower himself into the chair and slide backward. After he is seated, he should place the walker beside the chair.

**To teach the patient to get up:**
• After bringing the walker back to the front of his chair, tell the patient to slide forward in the chair. Placing the back of his stronger leg against the seat, he then advances the weaker leg.
• Next, placing both hands on the armrests, he can push himself to a standing position. Supporting his weight with the stronger leg and the opposite hand, have the patient grasp the walker's handgrip with the free hand. (See photograph #2, in which the patient shows left leg weakness.)
• Next, the patient grasps the free handgrip with his other hand.

weakness or inability to bear weight on one leg—requires good arm strength and balance. Platform attachments may be added to this walker for the patient with arthritic arms or a casted arm and who can't bear weight directly on the hand, wrist, or forearm. With the doctor's approval, wheels may be placed on the front legs of the standard walker to allow the extremely weak or poorly coordinated patient to roll the device forward, instead of lifting it. However, wheels are infrequently applied, for safety reasons.

The stair walker—used by the patient who must negotiate stairs without bilateral handrails—requires good arm strength and balance. Its extra set of handles extend toward the patient on the open side. The rolling walker—used by the patient with very weak legs—has four wheels and a seat. The reciprocal walker—used by the patient with very weak arms—allows one side to be advanced ahead of the other.

### Preparation of equipment
Obtain the appropriate walker. Adjust it to the patient's height: His elbows should be flexed at a 15° angle when standing comfortably within the walker with his hands placed on the grips. To adjust the walker, turn it upside down, and change leg length by pushing in the button on each shaft and releasing it when the leg is in the correct position. Make sure the walker is level before the patient attempts to use it.

### Essential steps
• Tell the patient you will teach him how to use a walker correctly.
• Help the patient stand within the walker, and instruct him to hold the handgrips firmly and equally.
• If the patient has one-sided leg weakness, tell him to advance the walker 6" to 8" (15 to 20 cm) and to step forward with the involved leg, supporting himself on the arms, and to follow with the uninvolved leg. If he has equal strength in both legs, instruct him to advance the walker 6" to 8" and to step forward with either leg. If he can't use one leg, tell him to advance the walker 6" to 8" and to swing onto it, supporting his weight on the hands.
• If the patient is using a reciprocal walker, teach him the two-point or four-point gait (see "Crutches" in this chapter). If the patient is using a wheeled or stair walker, reinforce the physical therapist's instructions. Stress the need for caution when using a stair walker.

### Special considerations
When the patient first practices with the walker, stand behind him, closer to the involved leg. Encourage him to take equal strides, *overcoming the tendency to favor the involved leg by taking longer steps with it than with the uninvolved leg.* If he starts to fall, support the hips and shoulders *to help maintain an upright position, if possible.*

### Documentation
Record the type of walker and attachments used, the degree of guarding required, the distance walked, and the patient's tolerance of ambulation.

NANCY ROTH, RPT, MMSc

# SPECIAL BEDS

## Turning Frames
### [Stryker and Orthopedic Equipment Company]

Indicated for the patient with spinal injury or surgery requiring immobility, turning frames—Stryker and Orthopedic Equipment Company (OEC)—allow frequent turning between supine and prone positions without disturbing spinal alignment. Both manufacturers' models consist of a support, an anterior frame for prone positioning,

## TURNING THE PATIENT WITH THE STRYKER WEDGE FRAME

First, remove the armboards. Then, arrange the anterior frame over the patient and lock it at the head end. Replace the anterior half of the ring, if removed, and close it over the patient until it locks automatically.

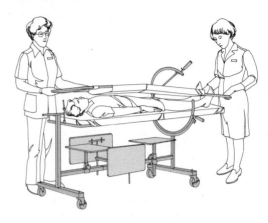

Next, place the patient's arms around the anterior frame, if he is able to grasp it. Pull out the locking pin, release the lock, and turn the patient.

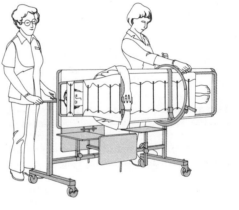

and a posterior frame for supine positioning. During turning, the anterior and posterior frames secure the patient between them, and then pivot.

Operation of a Stryker or OEC frame requires considerable training and experience for at least one member of the turning team. Use of these frames may be contraindicated for the patient who is obese.

### Equipment

Turning frames □ armboards □ special sheets (with ties) designed to fit each frame □ footboard.

The OEC turning frame allows cervical and pelvic traction; the Stryker frame allows cervical traction.

### Preparation of equipment

Place sheets on the anterior and posterior frames. Tie sheet corners to the frame, and secure the remainder of each sheet to the nearest fastener. Make sure the perineal opening on the posterior frame is in correct position. Secure the posterior frame to the bed and lock it in place. Then, turn the bed *to check that it's working properly*. Next, lock its wheels.

## Essential steps

• Obtain assistance from several co-workers to accomplish the initial patient transfer to the frame.

• Explain the use of the turning frame to the patient. Tell him that he may feel confined when the frames are in place, and that he may experience a floating sensation during turning. Reassure him that the frames will hold him securely and that the top frame will be removed after turning.

• Transfer the patient to the supine position on the posterior frame, taking care to maintain spinal alignment. Attach and adjust the armboards *for comfort and support.* Make sure the patient's hands are in a functional position *to prevent deformity.* Use hand rolls, if desired.

• Support the feet in the correct position with a footboard *to prevent footdrop.* Apply cradle boots *to reduce heel pressure,* if desired.

• Make sure all tubings are properly positioned *to maintain their function.*

*To turn the patient from the supine to the prone position:*

• Obtain assistance from one or more co-workers.

• Remove the top sheet, if present. Then, place a pillow lengthwise over the anterior legs *to act as a pad during turning.*

• Detach the armboards, and store them on the shelf beneath the bed.

• Carefully remove the nuts at both ends of the posterior frame, and position the anterior frame so its face support fits over the patient's face and its upper portion extends from the shoulders to the symphysis pubis, with the 4″ (10-cm) opening over the perineum. Make sure the lower portion of the frame extends to the ankles, allowing the feet to extend over the end of the frame in the prone position.

• After adjusting the anterior frame, securely lock it in place at both ends.

• Place the patient's arms at his sides. Or, if possible, have him put them around and grasp the anterior frame *for a sense of security during turning.*

• Place two or three safety belts around the turning frames *to promote safety and prevent the patient's arms and legs from slipping during turning.* If necessary, position I.V., Foley, or chest tubing appropriately *to prevent dislodgement or entanglement during turning.* Then, tell the patient the direction of turning.

• With one co-worker positioned at each end of the bed, simultaneously remove the locking pins, release the locks, and on a count of three, turn the patient quickly and smoothly, maintaining cervical traction. If other co-workers are present, ask them to stand beside the frames during turning *to reassure the patient, who may be anxious and fear falling.*

• Close both locks and replace the pins before releasing your grip on the frame. Then, remove the safety belts and the posterior frame.

• Position the patient properly. Make sure all tubing and equipment are properly positioned and adjusted.

• Replace and adjust the armboards, if necessary. Change linen, if necessary.

• Assess skin for redness or pressure areas, and give skin care or other prescribed treatments.

• Follow the same procedure to return the patient to the supine position.

## Special considerations

Turn the patient at least every 2 hours. Between turnings, perform appropriate range-of-motion exercises, as ordered. If the patient finds the prone position uncomfortable, administer prescribed pain medication before turning *to promote comfort.* If he has Crutchfield or Gardner-Wells tongs in place, turn cautiously *to avoid dislodging them.* If he's connected to a respirator, disconnect the device immediately before turning and reconnect it immediately afterward.

Remove the perineal section of the frame for bedpan use, but always replace it immediately afterward *to prevent spinal misalignment from inadequate support of the patient's buttock in the supine position.* Provide appropriate diversion *to counteract boredom.* Adjust the reading board for meals and reading, and provide adequate light *to prevent eyestrain.*

## Complications
Complications resulting from the proper use of turning frames are unusual.

## Documentation
Record the time of turning, the patient's tolerance of turning, any treatments, and your observations on the patient's condition.

ANNE MORACA-SAWICKI, RN, MSN

# CircOlectric Bed
*[Circle bed]*

The *CircOlectric bed permits frequent turning of the severely injured or immobilized patient with minimal trauma and extraneous movement. Its multiple intermediate positions help prevent or treat decubiti as well as respiratory and circulatory complications. Because of its narrow mattress, the bed permits close contact between patient and nurse, allowing better body mechanics and preventing back strain. Because this bed is portable, it eliminates potentially traumatic patient transfer. However, its complexity requires special equipment orientation; safe operation requires the presence of at least two persons.*

*The CircOlectric bed is contraindicated in a patient with spinal instability, because the feet bear much of the weight during turning, placing pressure on the spine.*

## Equipment
CircOlectric bed □ fitted sheets □ sheepskin □ bedpan.

## Preparation of equipment
In some hospitals with low doorways, you may have to remove the upper half of the frame to get the bed onto an elevator and into the patient's room. To do so, simply remove the connecting bolts; after the bed is in the patient's room, reassemble the frame.

Place a specially fitted sheet over the turning frame and the bottom mattress *to ensure patient comfort and help prevent decubiti.* If necessary, secure the bedpan below the perineal opening of the bottom mattress.

Before placing the patient in the bed, examine the electrical cord and plug for defects, and place the cord where it won't be caught or severed during turning. Then, plug the cord into an electrical outlet and check the mechanical function. Lock the bed's wheels before transferring the patient onto it.

## Essential steps
● Because the size and appearance of the CircOlectric bed may initially alarm the patient, describe its major parts and advantages beforehand. Describe the turning procedure to the patient, and reassure him that the bed will hold him securely.

*To place the patient supine on the bed:*
● Obtain assistance and transfer the patient from the hospital bed or stretcher to the CircOlectric bed. Be sure to position him correctly over the perineal opening.
● Position the bed's footboard against the feet *to help prevent footdrop and promote body alignment.* Place sheepskin under the heels *to help prevent formation of decubiti.* If necessary, place supports under the lower legs to raise the heels off the bed. To secure the footboard, press the buttons and slide the unit toward the feet until it reaches the desired position. (When using the turning frame, press the buttons and slide the footboard toward the end of the bed.)
● Install the canvas-covered side rails *to ensure patient safety and provide a sense of security.* Loosen the stabilizing bolts in the square holders on

either side of the bed. Then, select the correct counterpiece on the side rail; the straight counterpiece keeps the side rail upright for protection at night and during supine positioning, and the 90° counterpiece keeps it level for prone positioning and for use as an armrest. After each side rail is in position, tighten its stabilizing bolt.

*To turn the patient to the prone position:*

• Before turning the patient, straighten the bed, if necessary, and its wheels *to prevent movement.* Then, release the footboard, and move it away from the patient's feet. Leave enough room for placement of a footboard on the turning frame.

• If the patient is in traction, secure the traction guide equipment to the mobile portion of the frame. Because the weights will hang freely to the side of the circular frame, they won't change during turning.

• With assistance from a co-worker, lift the turning frame over the patient. (At least two persons should always participate in turning *to ensure patient safety.*) Remove the nuts on the bolts at both ends of the mattress. Slip the holes in the turning frame over the bolts and replace the nuts, turning them as tightly as possible. If you can't secure the nuts tightly, place a turning key in the small holes of the nuts and tighten them.

• Pad and position the footboard on the turning frame. Depress the buttons to adjust it properly. Be sure the footboard rests securely against the pa-

## THE CIRCOLECTRIC BED

To ensure patient safety, as one nurse turns the bed, the other nurse watches and reassures the patient.

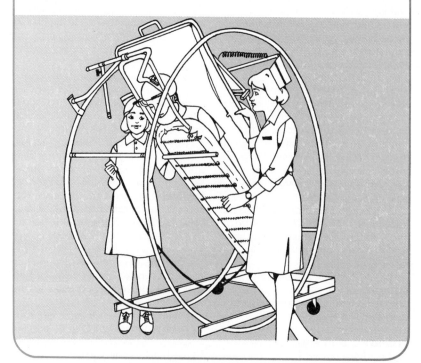

tient's feet, *because it will bear his weight when he's upright.*

• Apply the head restraint *to support and immobilize the head during the turning and prone positioning.* Make sure it's sufficiently padded *to help prevent facial decubiti.* Observe for pressure areas to determine the best position for the head support. (Some beds have slings instead of metal bars.) Secure the headrest by adjusting the clamps.

• Tuck in the sheets at the head of the mattress *so they don't rub against the patient's neck, causing ulcerations or occluding a tracheostomy.* Tell the patient to cross his hands over his chest or to grasp the sides of the turning frame *to protect his hands.* If the patient is paralyzed, place the arms at the sides and fasten the safety straps around the turning and posterior frames. *This promotes safety and keeps the arms at the sides and between the frames during turning.*

• Remove the bedpan if it's in place. Free I.V. lines, traction weights, Foley drainage bag, and any other attachments, and position them *to prevent dislodgement, entanglement, or complications during turning.*

• Unclamp the control switch from the bedframe. Hold it so you can operate the switch with your thumb. While a co-worker watches and reassures the patient, turn the bed with *continuous pressure* on the control switch, *to minimize patient nausea and vertigo.*

• After the patient is positioned correctly (safety latches prevent the bed from turning too far in either direction), release the nut from the front of the main mattress. Free the mattress frame from the bolt and replace the nut. Pull forward on the release bar at the top of the frame. A series of springs raises the mattress up, off the patient's back, and a catch in the frame locks the mattress in the raised position. While the patient is prone, provide back care and change bedsheets on the main mattress. If the patient's feet are lower than the head, check feet and ankles for dependent edema.

*To return the patient to the supine position:*

• Release the catch by pulling the release bar forward. Pull the mattress into place and bolt it. Remove the armrests and bedpan; correctly position I.V. lines, traction weights, Foley drainage bag, and other tubing or attachments for turning. Hold the control switch in the reverse position until the bed is level. When the bed is in position, release the nuts, remove the turning frame, and replace the nuts. Position the patient comfortably and adjust the footboard appropriately.

*To place the patient in the upright or sitting position:*

• If the patient is at a stage of rehabilitation that requires periodic standing, flip the safety latch forward *to stop the bed in the upright position.* Be sure to return the latch to its normal position before returning the patient to horizontal position.

• If the patient requires periodic sitting, push forward on the lever at the side of the mattress. Apply safety straps, if necessary. *To return the patient to the supine position,* pull back on the lever.

## Special considerations

Provide extra skin care and padding for the feet, occiput, chin, and forehead, because *these areas receive added pressure.* Before turning the patient, be sure that it won't put traction on any tubing support system, such as a Foley catheter or I.V. tubing. If the patient has a tracheostomy and is connected to a respirator, use a hand-held resuscitator, such as an Ambu bag, during turning. If the patient is receiving oxygen, temporarily disconnect it during turning.

During turning, the patient may experience nausea, vertigo, fear of falling, or spatial disorientation. *To minimize nausea and vertigo,* be sure to complete the turn without interruption. *To minimize spatial disorientation,* place an overbed table within the patient's field of vision.

Watch carefully for signs of cardiac arrest, particularly during the patient's first few turnings. If the patient has neurologic damage, a doctor should be present during the first few turnings.

After turning and positioning are completed, provide prism glasses or attach a mirror to the upper part of the bed *to increase the patient's field of vision.*

If electrical failure occurs, you can turn the bed with the handcrank stored in the tray at the head of the bed. Keep the end stud nuts on the appropriate frame bar when not in use *to prevent losing them.*

## Complications
Decubiti may form on the feet, occiput, chin, and forehead after prolonged positioning, and on the heels of the patient with diminished lower-extremity sensation.

## Documentation
Record the date and time the patient was placed on the bed, the frequency of turning, and the patient's progress and psychological response.

JOANNE PATZEK DACUNHA, RN

# Roto Rest Bed
*[Kinetic treatment table]*

*The Roto Rest bed rotates mechanically from side to side in a cradlelike motion, achieving a maximum elevation of 62° and full side-to-side turning approximately every 4½ minutes. Its constant motion promotes postural drainage and peristalsis and helps prevent the complications of immobility, such as pressure areas and decubitus formation, deep vein thrombi, bone demineralization and formation of renal calculi, and orthostatic hypotension. Because the bed holds the patient motionless during turning, it's especially recommended for the patient with spinal cord injury, multiple trauma, cerebrovascular accident, multiple sclerosis, coma, severe burns, hypostatic pneumonia, atelectasis, or other unilateral lung involvement causing poor ventilation and perfusion. Lateral positioning, with the affected lung in a superior position, improves blood-gas exchange dramatically.*

*Operation of the Roto Rest bed requires considerable training and experience. Patient transfer and positioning on the bed should be performed by at least two persons to ensure safety.*

*The Roto Rest bed is contraindicated for the patient with severe claustrophobia or an unstable cervical fracture without neurologic deficit and without the complications of immobility. Because the bed stimulates comatose patients and peristalsis, it should be used cautiously for patients in the extreme agitation phase of coma and in those with severe uncontrollable diarrhea.*

## Equipment
Roto Rest bed with appropriate accessories □ pillowcases or linen-saver pads □ flat sheet or padding.

The Roto Rest bed can accommodate cervical traction devices and tongs. The Mark I model has access hatches on its bottom for the rectal, cervical, and thoracic areas; the Mark III model has an access hatch for the rectal area. Both models have arm and leg hatches that fold down to allow range-of-motion exercises. Other features include variable rotation (40° or 62° from side to side, or 40° to one side and 62° to the other); supports and clips for chest tubes, catheters, and drains; a fan; and access for X-rays. Racks beneath the bed hold plates in place for chest and spinal films.

The rotation of this bed doesn't interfere with pressure monitoring. Transducers can be mounted at the head of the bed.

## Preparation of equipment
Carefully inspect the bed and run it

through a complete cycle in both automatic and manual modes to ensure it is in proper working order. If you're using the Mark I model, check the tightness of the set screws at the head of the bed.

To prepare the bed for the patient, remove the counterbalance weights from the keel and place them in the base frame storage area. Then, release the connecting arm by pulling down on the cam handle and depressing the lower side of the footboard. Next, lock the table in horizontal position, and place all side supports in the extreme lateral position by loosening the cam handles on the underside of the table. Slide the supports off the bed. (To facilitate reassembly, all supports and packs are labeled *right* or *left* on the bottom.)

Remove the knee packs by depressing the snap button and rotating and pulling the packs from the tube. Then, remove the abductor packs (the Mark III model has one pack) by depressing and sliding them toward the head of the bed. Next, loosen the foot and knee assemblies by lifting the cam handle at its base and sliding them to the foot of the bed. Now, loosen the shoulder clamp assembly hand knobs, swing the shoulder clamps to the vertical position, and retighten them.

If you're using the Mark I model, remove the cervical, thoracic, and rectal packs. Cover them with pillowcases or linen-saver pads, smooth all wrinkles, and replace the packs. If you're using the Mark III model, remove the rectal pack, cover, and replace.

Cover the upper half of the bed, which is a solid unit, with a sheet or padding. Install new disposable foam cushions for the head, shoulders, and foot packs.

### Essential steps

● If possible, show the patient the bed before use. Explain and demonstrate its operation and reassure the patient that the bed will hold him securely during operation.

*To position the patient on the bed:*

● Make sure the bed is turned off. Then, place and lock the bed in horizontal position, out of gear. Latch all hatches and lock the wheels.
● Obtain assistance and transfer the patient. Gently slide him to the center of the bed *to prevent contact with the pillar posts and to ensure proper balance during bed operation.* Smooth the pillowcase or linen-saver pad beneath the hips. Then, place any tubings through the appropriate notches and ensure that any traction weights hang free of the bed.
● Place the patient's arms at a 90° angle to the sides, and insert the thoracic side supports in their posts. Adjust the patient's longitudinal position to allow a 1″ (2.5-cm) space between the axillae and the supports, *thereby avoiding pressure on the axillary blood vessels and brachial plexus.* Push the supports against the chest and lock the cam arms securely, *to provide support and ensure patient safety.*
● Place the disposable supports under the legs so the heels extend over the edge, *to prevent pressure and resultant decubitus formation.*
● Install and adjust the foot supports so the feet lie in the normal anatomic position, *thereby helping to prevent footdrop.* Remember, the foot supports should be in position for only 2 hours of every shift *to prevent excessive pressure on the soles and toes and resultant decubitus formation.*
● Place the abductor pack(s) in the appropriate supports, allowing a 6″ (15-cm) space between the packs and the groin. Tighten the knobs on the bed's underside at the base of the support tubes.
● Install the leg side supports snugly against the hips, and tighten the cam arms. Position the knee assemblies slightly above the knees and tighten the cam arms. Then, place your hand on the patient's knee and move the knee pack until it rests lightly on the top of your hand. Repeat for the other knee.
● Loosen the retaining rings on the crossbar, and slide the head and shoul-

der assembly laterally. *The retaining rings maintain correct lateral position of the shoulder clamp assembly and head support pack.*

• Carefully lower the head and shoulder assembly into place and slide it to touch the head.

• Place your hand on the patient's shoulder, and move the shoulder pack until it touches your hand. Tighten it in place. Then, repeat for the other shoulder. The 1″ clearance between the shoulders and the packs *prevents excess pressure, which can lead to decubitus formation.*

• Place the head pack close to but not touching the ears (or tongs).

• Tighten the head and shoulder assembly securely, *so it won't lift off the bed.* Position the restraining rings next to the shoulder assembly bracket and tighten them.

• Place the patient's arms on the disposable supports. The best types of supports keep the hands in functional position without pressure on the ulnar nerve. Then, install the side arm supports and secure the safety straps. Place one safety strap across the shoulder assembly; place the other strap over the thoracic supports. If necessary, cover the patient with a flat sheet.

*To balance the bed:*

• Place one hand on the footboard *to steady the bed and prevent rapid turning if it's unbalanced.* Then, remove the locking pin. If the bed rotates to one side, reposition the patient in its center; if it tilts to the right, gently turn it slightly to the left and slide the right packs toward the patient; if it tilts to the left, reverse the preceding step. If a large imbalance exists, you may have to adjust the packs on both sides.

• After the patient is centered, gently turn the bed to the 62° position.

• Measure the space between the chest, 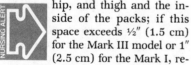 hip, and thigh and the inside of the packs; if this space exceeds ½″ (1.5 cm) for the Mark III model or 1″ (2.5 cm) for the Mark I, return the bed to horizontal position,

lock it in place, and slide the packs inward on both sides. If the space appears too tight, proceed as above but slide both packs outward. *Excessively loose packs cause the patient to slide from side to side during turning, possibly resulting in unnecessary movement at fracture sites, skin irritation from shearing force, and bed imbalance. Overly tight packs can place pressure on the patient during turning.*

• After adjusting the packs, check the bed; balance and correct it, if necessary.

• If you're using the Mark III model bed and the patient weighs more than 160 lb (72 kg), the bed may become top-heavy. To correct this, place counterbalance weights in the appropriate slots in the keel of the bed. Add one weight for every 20 lb (9 kg) over 160, but remember that placement of weights doesn't replace correct patient positioning.

If you're using the Mark I model, it may be necessary to add weights for the patient weighing considerably less than 160 lb. Place one weight for each 20 lb less than 160 in the proper bracket at the *foot* of the bed.

*To start automatic bed rotation:*

• Ensure that all packs are securely in place. Then, hold the footboard firmly and remove the locking pin *to start the bed's motor.* The bed then continues to rotate until the pin is reinserted.

• Raise the connecting arm cam handle until the connecting assembly snaps into place, locking the bed into automatic rotation.

• Remain with the patient for at least three complete turns from side to side *to ensure his comfort and safety.* Observe the operation of the bed and offer the patient psychological support.

## Special considerations

 If the patient develops cardiac arrest while on the bed, perform cardiopulmonary resuscitation after taking the bed out of gear, locking it in horizontal position, removing the side arm support and the thoracic pack, lifting the shoulder assembly, and dropping the arm pack. Doing all these steps takes only 5 to 10 seconds. You won't need a cardiac board because of the bed's firm surface.

If power failure occurs, lock the bed in horizontal or lateral position and rotate it manually every ½ hour *to prevent pressure areas and subsequent formation of decubiti.* If the patient is an amputee, you may need to balance the bed by placing sandbags in the appropriate area. If cervical traction causes the patient to slide upward, place the bed in the reverse Trendelenburg position. If this fails to secure the patient, place one shoulder pack firmly against the shoulder. Alternate shoulder packs every hour *to prevent pressure areas from developing.* If extremity traction causes the patient to migrate toward the foot of the bed, use the Trendelenburg position.

If the patient develops high fever, you may sponge him with water or alcohol, as ordered. Or, sponge the patient with water, cover him with a sheet, and turn on the fan attachment; the fan blows beneath the sheet, cooling the patient by evaporation.

Bathe the patient daily, thoroughly rinsing soap residue from the skin *to prevent irritation and dermatitis.* Lock the bed in the extreme lateral position for access to the back of the head, thorax, and buttocks through the appropriate hatches. Clean the mattress and nondisposable packs during patient care, and rinse them thoroughly to remove all soap residue.

Expect increased drainage from any decubiti for the first few days the patient is on the bed, because the motion *helps debride necrotic tissue and improves local circulation.*

Perform or schedule daily range-of-motion exercises, as ordered, because the bed allows full access to all extremities without disturbing spinal alignment. Drop the arm hatch for shoulder rotation, remove the thoracic packs for shoulder abduction, and drop the leg hatch and remove leg and knee packs for hip rotation and full leg motion.

Control leg spasticity with packs. If the patient has knee flexion, you may be able to minimize it by applying gentle pressure over the knee packs, but relieve this pressure every 2 hours.

Prevent urinary or fecal soiling of the bed, because the number of cushions makes the bed hard to clean. Diaper the diarrheic patient because *the bed's motion accelerates peristalsis, exacerbating this problem.* For female patients, tape a Foley catheter to the thigh before bringing it through the rectal hatch. For the male patient with spinal cord lesions, tape the catheter to the abdomen and then to the thigh *to facilitate gravity drainage.* Hang the drainage bag on the clips provided, and make sure it doesn't catch between the bedframes during rotation.

If the patient has a tracheal or endotracheal tube and is receiving mechanical ventilation, attach the tub⌐ support bracket between the cervicₐ pack and the arm packs. Tape the con necting T tubing to the support and run it beside the patient's head and off the center of the table *to help prevent reflux of condensation.* If the patient has a chest tube, make sure it's long enough *to prevent tension during bed rotation.* Expect the bed's motion to increase drainage in the patient with pulmonary congestion or pneumonia; suction more often during the patient's first 12 to 24 hours on the bed. A vibrator unit is available for use under the thoracic hatch of the Mark I to help mobilize pulmonary secretions faster.

### Complications
If the patient, accessories, and supportive apparatus are positioned correctly, no complications should occur.

### Documentation
Record changes in the patient's condition in your progress notes. Note turning times and ongoing care on the, flowchart.

JOANNE PATZEK DaCUNHA, RN

# Clinitron Therapy

*Originally called the air fluidized bed and designed for managing burns, Clinitron therapy is now used for patients with diverse debilities. It supports the patient on a thick layer of minute silicone beads, or microspheres. A monofilament polyester filter sheet covers the microspheres but allows warmed air, propelled by a blower beneath the therapy unit, to pass through it. The resultant fluidlike surface of the unit reduces pressure on the skin sufficiently to avoid obstruction of capillary blood flow, thereby helping to prevent formation of decubiti. In Clinitron therapy, small amounts of wound drainage can flow into the mi-crospheres, where the drainage is rendered nonharmful, obviating the need for most dressings. Use of this therapy also permits harmless contact with grafted sites, promoting comfort and healing.*

*Because of the therapy unit's complexity, its use requires special training. It may be contraindicated for the patient who can't mobilize pulmonary secretions, because the absence of back support impairs productive coughing.*

## Equipment

Clinitron therapy unit with microspheres (approximately 1,650 lb/742.5 kg) □ filter sheet □ six aluminum rails (for restraining and sealing filter sheet) □ flat sheet □ elastic cord.

The unit can be defluidized to form a firm surface, molded to the patient's body. Its air temperature is adjustable to help control hypothermia and hyperthermia.

## Preparation of equipment

Usually, the manufacturer or trained hospital staff prepare the therapy unit. However, if you must help prepare the unit for use, be sure the microspheres are placed to within ½" (1.5 cm) of its top. Then, position the filter sheet on the unit with its printed side facing upward. Match the holes in the sheet to the holes in the edge of the unit's frame. Next, place the aluminum rails on the frame, with the studs in the proper holes. Depress the rails firmly, and secure them by tightening the knurled knobs to seal the filter sheet tightly. Place a flat hospital sheet over the filter sheet, and secure it with the elastic cord to prevent billowing.

Turn on the air current to fluidize the unit. Then defluidize the unit to be sure it's working properly.

## Essential steps

• Explain and, if possible, demonstrate the operation of the Clinitron therapy unit for the patient. Tell him the reason for its use and the sensations associated with it. Then, defluidize the unit.

---

## HOW CLINITRON THERAPY WORKS

Clinitron therapy uses silicone-coated microspheres (50 to 150 microns) of lime glass, suspended by air currents, to create a fluidlike environment. Because the microspheres don't contain free silica, there's no danger of silicosis.

Besides the microspheres and their containing tank, the basic components of the therapy unit are a sieve to catch clumped microspheres, a temperature-regulated air compressor and blower system, and a special monofilament polyester filter sheet that retains the microspheres in the tank but allows air to filter through.

Clinitron therapy usually eliminates the need to dress wounds with minimal drainage. Such wounds can be exposed to the air and allowed to drain into the unit; however, extensive or copiously draining wounds require dressings, because large amounts of fluid impair the unit's fluidization and temperature control. When wound drainage passes through the filter sheet, it clumps together with the microspheres, raising the pH to 9.0 or 10.0, thereby suppressing bacterial growth. The air circulating through the unit then dries these clumps, isolating any cells present. These heavy clumps sink into the sieve, where they can be removed.

• Using good body mechanics and with the help of three or more co-workers, transfer the patient to the unit, using a lift sheet.

• Refluidize the unit, and remove the lift sheet.

• Adjust the air temperature of the unit, as necessary. Because the unit usually operates within 10° to 12° F. of the ambient temperature, set room temperature to 75° F. (23.89° C.). If the temperature of the microspheres reaches 105° F. (40.56° C.), the unit automatically shuts off. It restarts automatically after 30 minutes.

• To position a bedpan, roll the patient away from you, place the bedpan on the flat sheet, and push it into the microspheres. Then, reposition the patient. To remove the bedpan, hold it steady and roll the patient away from you. Defluidize the unit and remove the bedpan. Then, refluidize the unit and reposition the patient.

### Special considerations

Monitor the patient's fluid and electrolyte status because the warm, dry air circulated by the Clinitron therapy unit increases evaporative water loss, possibly requiring modifications in oral or I.V. intake. If the patient experiences excessive respiratory dryness, use a humidifier and mask, as ordered.

Encourage coughing and deep breathing *to help prevent pulmonary complications.* After prolonged Clinitron therapy, watch for hypocalcemia and hypophosphoremia. If not contraindicated and the patient wishes to smoke, defluidize the therapy unit.

Cover any copiously draining wound with a porous dressing to absorb some of the drainage. Keep petrolatum or silver-based topical applications covered with an impervious dressing, *to minimize or prevent their absorption by the microspheres.* Avoid using wet dressings or soaks, *because the excess fluid causes the microspheres to clump, impairing fluidization.* Because of this drying effect, always cover a mesh graft for the first 2 to 8 days, as ordered.

Because the unit restarts automatically if defluidized for 30 minutes, unplug it to perform cardiopulmonary resuscitation or other procedures.

Don't wear a watch when handling the microspheres, because they are small enough to penetrate and damage the mechanism. Don't secure the filter sheet with pins or clamps *to prevent release of microspheres.* Repair any holes or tears with iron-on patching tape.

Sieve the microspheres between patients or monthly to remove clumped microspheres. Handle them carefully to avoid spills, because they are extremely slippery on floors and can cause falls. Treat a soiled filter sheet and clumped microspheres as contaminated items and handle according to hospital policy. Change the filter sheet, and operate the unit unoccupied for 24 hours between patients.

### Documentation

Record the duration and response to management on the defluidized therapy unit.

CATHERINE A. MAGUIRE, RN, BSN

## Selected References

Gragg, Shirley H., and Rees, Olive M. *Scientific Principles in Nursing.* St. Louis: C.V. Mosby Co., 1970.

Hilt, Nancy, and Cogburn, Shirley B. *Manual of Orthopedics.* St. Louis: C.V. Mosby Co., 1980.

Krusen, Frank H., Kottke, Frederic J., and Ellwood, Paul M., eds. *Handbook of Physical Medicine and Rehabilitation.* Philadelphia: W.B. Saunders Co., 1971.

Larson, Carroll B., and Gould, Marjorie. *Orthopedic Nursing.* St. Louis: C.V. Mosby Co., 1974.

Rantz, Marilyn J., and Courtial, Donald. *Lifting, Moving, and Transferring Patients.* St. Louis: C.V. Mosby Co., 1977.

# 3 Infection Control

# Infection Control

## Introduction

Until the late 19th century, when Koch, Pasteur, and other pioneer microbiologists discovered the causative role of bacteria in infection, contagion was minimally understood, standards of cleanliness were primitive, and sterile technique unknown. Hospitals housed all kinds of patients together in large wards. Surgeons operated without washing their hands or cleaning their instruments. Under these conditions, hospital treatment itself sometimes threatened the patient's survival more than his primary illness.

Only after health-care workers found effective ways to eliminate or limit the spread of pathogens did the death rates from hospital-related infections begin to decline. Today we expect hospital treatment to promote, not retard, recovery. Despite this progress, hospital infections still pose a real problem.

### Nosocomial infections

Despite stringent regulations designed to control infections and imposed by government and medical authorities, nosocomial infections still significantly threaten hospitalized patients. Every year, about 5% of all patients admitted to hospitals in the United States acquire infections there; about 3% of these infections are fatal. Of the patients with nosocomial infection, 18% develop more than one type of infection. Nosocomial infection costs patients and insurance companies about $1 billion a year.

The most common nosocomial infections are urinary tract infection, pneumonia, and bacteremia. Urinary tract infections are more common in women than in men; infections in other sites are more common in men. All nosocomial infections are three times more common in surgical patients than in nonsurgical patients; they are especially common in patients who have received mechanical ventilation or catheterization. The risk of such infections rises with the patient's age and is related to duration of preoperative and total hospitalization and the duration and site of surgery.

Not all nosocomial infections can be prevented. For example, in patients who are immunodeficient or who are receiving immunosuppressive therapy, infection may develop despite all precautions.

### Infection-control programs

According to recommendations first issued in 1958 by the Joint Commission on Accreditation of Hospitals and the American Hospital Association, every accredited hospital must have an infection-control committee and a surveillance system as part of a formal infection-control program. Such a program is designed to reduce the rate of infection by keeping the hospital staff continuously aware of the risk of hospital infection and by encouraging them to take personal responsibility for preventing it.

In most hospitals, infection-control practitioners, usually registered nurses, assume daily responsibility for surveillance and other aspects of infection control. Although their specific responsibilities may vary among hospitals, typical activities include:

• teaching the hospital staff the importance of correct handwashing between patient contact (a simple, but probably the most effective, way to reduce infection risk)

• assessing patients for infection and taking proper precautionary measures against contamination and spread of infection

• showing patient-care providers how to collect and handle laboratory specimens

• developing infection-control guidelines, instructing the staff, and monitoring isolation procedures.

This chapter provides detailed procedures for handwashing and isolation. Other aspects of infection control are included when relevant to specific patient-care procedures.

## Isolation as prevention

Although most isolation procedures aim to prevent transmission of disease from infected patients to other patients, to hospital staff, or to visitors, protective isolation procedures shield susceptible patients with impaired physiologic defenses from contact with other persons. (In this case, emphasis is on isolating the patient from the pathogen.) Formerly, infected patients were set apart from the rest of the hospital community and given minimal human contact; in some areas, special hospitals existed solely to treat patients with contagious diseases. Today, most patients with communicable infections are effectively managed without such separation by nurses who are taught special skills for protecting themselves from infection and for containing the pathogens, while giving as much human contact as possible during patient care.

SUSAN M. GLOVER, RN, BSN

---

## THE INFECTION CHAIN

The infection chain has three basic links: the *infectious agent's source* (infection-causing pathogen), the *mode of transmission,* and a *susceptible host.* Infection-control procedures attempt to break the chain by eliminating or minimizing the sources and by interrupting infection transmission.

The *agent* must have a reservoir, such as water, I.V. fluids, or human tissue, in which to grow; it must be able to leave a reservoir through a *portal of exit,* such as the gastrointestinal, respiratory, or genitourinary tract.

The *mode of transmission* bridges the gap between the agent and its host by *contact* (direct: touching infected site or person; or indirect: touching inanimate object contaminated by infected person), a *common vehicle* (such as multidose medicine vial, dirty needle, or blood), a *vector* (transmitted by a nonhuman carrier, such as an insect or animal), or an *airborne contaminant* (contacting or breathing in droplets from person who sneezes).

The *host* is infected when the agent traverses his defenses through a *portal of entry*—such as a natural body orifice (nose, mouth, anus, and so forth), any skin break, or placement of an invasive device into a body orifice or an artificial opening.

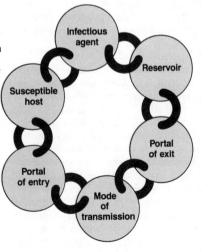

# GENERAL PRINCIPLES

# Handwashing

*Your hands serve as the common vehicle in almost every transfer of potential pathogens from one patient to another, from a contaminated article to the patient, or from yourself to the patient. Because of this, handwashing is the single most important measure for preventing the spread of infection. Thorough handwashing requires a vigorous lather and usually takes only about 10 seconds. To protect your patients from nosocomial infections, you should wash your hands routinely between every patient contact and after handling contaminated articles. Because this may be impractical, you should base your handwashing needs on the actual risk of contamination with pathogens that could be transferred to a susceptible patient. Handwashing is always essential after handling contaminated articles and before caring for susceptible patients and handling invasive devices.*

*Clean, healthy hands with smooth skin, short fingernails, and no rings minimize the risk of contamination. Bacteria are even more difficult to remove from rough or chapped hands.*

## Equipment
Soap or detergent □ warm running water □ paper towels □ optional: antiseptic cleansing agent, nail file, orangewood stick, and fingernail brush.

## Essential steps
• Remove all rings, *because these harbor dirt and skin organisms.* Wear your watch well above the wrist.
• Wet your hands and wrists with warm water and apply soap. Hold your hands below elbow level *to avoid contaminating clean areas.* For a routine 10-second handwashing, wash vigorously with soap under a stream of water; *this*

*removes most transient flora.*
• Avoid splashing water on yourself or the floor, because pathogens spread more easily on wet surfaces and slippery floors are dangerous. Avoid touching the sink or faucets, *which are considered contaminated.*
• Rinse bar soap before returning it to the soap dish.
• Work up a lather by rubbing your hands together vigorously. If you can't remove your wedding band, move it up and down the finger to clean beneath the ring. Soap and warm water reduce surface tension and this, aided by friction, removes surface organisms, which wash away in the lather. The more vigorously you rub your hands when washing, the more contaminants you remove.
• Pay special attention to the area under fingernails and around cuticles and the thumbs, knuckles, and sides of hands, *because organisms thrive in these protected or overlooked areas.*
• Rinse hands and wrists well, *because running water flushes suds, soil, and pathogens away.* Keep your hands down in the sink, *to prevent residue from running back up your forearms.*
• Pat hands and wrists dry with a paper towel. Avoid rubbing, *which can cause abrasion and chapping.*
• If the sink is not equipped with knee or foot controls, turn off the faucets by gripping them with a dry paper towel, *to avoid recontaminating your hands.*

## Special considerations
Wash your hands before starting any sterile procedure or whenever your hands are grossly contaminated. At such times wash your forearms also, and with a fingernail, disposable sponge brush, or plastic cuticle stick clean under the fingernails and in and around the cuticles. Remember that brushes, metal files, or other hard objects may injure your skin and, if reused, may be

a source of contamination.

Some cleansing agents are more appropriate in certain nursing situations than others. Soaps and detergents suspend easily removable soil and microorganisms from superficial skin layers, whereas antiseptics control or kill microorganisms on deeper skin layers. Neither agent sterilizes the skin.

Wash with *soap* before coming on duty; before and after direct or indirect patient contact; before and after performing any bodily functions, such as blowing your nose or using the bathroom; before preparing or serving food; before preparing or administering medications; after direct or indirect contact with a patient's excretions, secretions, or blood; and after completing your shift.

Use an *antiseptic* when you must reliably eliminate microorganisms from your hands, such as before and after handling invasive devices and performing wound care and dressing changes, and after hands have been contaminated with virulent pathogens. Antiseptics are also recommended for handwashing in isolation rooms, newborn nurseries, and before caring for any highly susceptible patient. If you're putting on clean or sterile gloves, wash before and after with an antiseptic, *so bacteria will not grow under the gloves or in case the gloves are torn or punctured.*

## Complications

Because it causes loss of natural skin oils, frequent handwashing may result in dryness, cracking, and irritation. These effects are probably more common after repeated use of antiseptics, especially in persons with sensitive skin.

If your hands are dry, cracked, or develop dermatitis, apply an emollient hand cream after each washing or switch to a different cleansing agent. If you have a skin irritation that causes you to wash your hands less often, you'll become a dangerous reservoir for bacteria.

MARY CASTLE, RN, MPH

# Isolation Equipment
*[Gowns, gloves, caps, and masks; isolation cart; isolation cards]*

*Essential to the success of an infection-control program for patients who require isolation is a supply of barrier clothing—such as gowns, gloves, caps, and masks—for the patient-care team, with each member trained in their correct use; an isolation cart containing extra isolation equipment, used when the patient's room has no anteroom and usually situated outside the room; a system of color-coded cards stating the type of isolation and alerting staff to precautions and equipment needed, for marking the patient's door; and a method of containing contagion from used articles from the isolation area, called double-bagging. (See* Double-bagging Technique, *page 142.) Correctly done, this last measure protects you and other hospital personnel from nosocomial infections.*

*Isolation to contain infection may require one or all three barriers, depending on how an infectious agent is transmitted. In protective, or reverse, isolation, isolation garb protects an immunosuppressed patient from infection by organisms from care-providers or from the hospital environment. In all other types of isolation, isolation garb protects you from the patient's infection and prevents you from transmitting it to other patients.*

## Equipment
The isolation cart may be a covered, wheeled utility table or may be specially designed. It should include a work area (such as a pull-out shelf), drawers or cabinet for isolation supplies, and possibly a pole on which to hang coats or jackets. Supplies for the cart or anteroom should be stocked according to the isolation category and the patient's individual needs. In strict

isolation, for example, the cart should contain gloves, gowns, caps, and masks; appropriate signs; labels and tape; specially marked laundry bags (and water-soluble laundry bags, if used); and plastic trash bags.

*For gowning, gloving, and masking:* gowns ☐ gloves ☐ caps ☐ masks.

### Preparation of equipment

Remove the cover from the isolation cart if the cart is a wheeled utility table, and set up the work area. Check isolation cart or anteroom supplies to ensure that correct and sufficient supplies are in place for the designated isolation category.

Pour antiseptic agent into a basin so it is available for handwashing if an isolation cart is used.

### Essential steps

*To put on isolation garb:*
• Remove your watch and rings.
• Wash your hands with an antiseptic agent *to prevent growth of microorganisms when skin is gloved.*
• Put the gown on. Wrap it around the back of your uniform, and tie the strings or fasten the snaps or pressure-sensitive tabs at the neck.
• Make sure your uniform is completely covered, and secure the gown at the waist.
• Put the cap on, making sure all hair is contained. Place the mask snugly over your nose and mouth. Secure ear loops around the ears or tie the strings behind your head, high enough so the mask won't slip off. If the mask has a metal strip, squeeze it to fit your nose firmly but comfortably. If you wear eyeglasses, tuck the mask under their lower edge.
• Put on the gloves. Cover the edges of the gown sleeves by pulling the gloves over the cuffs. If the sleeves are short, tape them to the gloves. *This will prevent the gown sleeves from riding up while you care for the patient.*
• If you'll need a watch while in the room, place it in a plastic bag to prevent contamination.

---

## THE ISOLATION CARD SYSTEM

The Centers for Disease Control of the Department of Health and Human Services have devised a system using color-coded ready reference cards to identify the five major categories of isolation. Each isolation category is represented by a color: yellow, *strict;* red, *respiratory;* blue, *protective* (reverse); brown, *enteric precautions;* green, *wound and skin precautions.* Many hospitals also use cards printed in the same format, but without warning colors, to signify secretion and blood precautions.

As soon as isolation is ordered, these cards, which have a pressure-sensitive backing, are posted on the patient's door, chart, bed, bathroom, and other areas, as needed, and are not removed until after the patient vacates the room and terminal cleaning is performed. The cards specify necessary equipment and precautions and remind visitors to report to the nurse's station before entering the patient's room so they may be properly instructed and prepared. The card's backing lists the communicable diseases included in the isolation category.

Cards should be issued with the isolation cart or a supply kept in the patient's anteroom or at the nurse's station.

---

*To remove isolation garb:*
• Remember that the outside surfaces of your barrier clothes are contaminated.
• With the gloves on, untie the gown's waiststrings, *which are considered contaminated.*
• With your gloved right hand, remove the left glove by pulling on the cuff, turning the glove inside out as you pull. Don't touch any skin with your right glove. Then, remove the right glove by wedging one or two fingers of your left hand inside the glove and pulling it off, turning it inside out also as you remove it. Discard the gloves in the trash container.
• Untie your mask, holding it only by the strings. Remove the cap and discard both cap and mask in the trash container. If the patient has a disease that is spread by airborne pathogens,

## DOUBLE-BAGGING TECHNIQUE

Safe removal of contaminated articles, such as soiled linen, from an isolation room requires double-bagging to contain contamination and limit the spread of infection. This procedure isn't necessary in protective isolation, because the patient isn't the contamination source.

When you need to remove articles from an isolation room, get another person to help you. After providing care in the patient's room, you're considered contaminated; your "clean" partner stands outside the isolation room and sets up clean containers just outside the room (or in the anteroom if this is available) to receive contaminated containers and materials without contaminating the clean containers' outer surfaces. For example, she would set up a clean laundry bag, open and ready, in a clean laundry hamper, or hang it over a chair back, facing the isolation room door.

When caring for the isolated patient, put used items into appropriate containers: disposables in impervious wastebags, reusables in paper or plastic bags, linen in water-soluble bags. Wrap dry linens around the wet linens to keep them from dissolving the water-soluble bag before it reaches the washing machine. If you bag glass containers, leave their lids off to prevent explosions during incineration or sterilization.

Replace waste containers when they are about three-quarters full; full containers are hard to double-bag and likely to spill over, increasing the risk of spreading

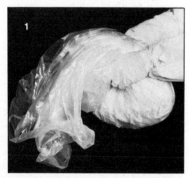

infection. When closing a plastic bag, point the bag's opening away from you and gently expel excess air. (See photograph #1.) This makes the bag easier to double-bag and prevents a water-soluble bag

from rupturing when it's dropped down the laundry chute. Secure the top of the bag by closing it with plastic ties or twist tapes, or by rolling it down and sealing it with isolation tape. If you must work alone, put the sealed "dirty" bag in the

outside container, which you've hung on an outside chair, as described. (See photograph #2.) Then remove your isolation garb correctly, and dispose of it in the new trash receptacle; seal the outside bag and prepare it for pickup by the housekeeping staff.

If you have a partner outside, have her hold a clean bag away from her body, with her hands protected from contamination under a cuff formed by folding down the bag's top edge. Put the contaminated bag into this clean bag, making sure it touches only the inside of the clean bag.

This done, your partner then closes the clean bag, without touching the inside of the bag or its contents, by unfolding the cuff, expelling any air from the bag, rolling the top down, and securing the bag firmly with isolation tape. She should clearly mark the bag's contents on the outside so the housekeeping staff can deal with it properly. Finally, she should wash her hands.

you may prefer to remove the mask last.
- Untie the neck straps of your gown. Grasp the outside of the gown at the back of the shoulders and pull the gown down over your arms, turning it inside out as you remove it, to ensure containment of the pathogens.
- Holding the gown well away from your uniform, fold it inside out. Discard it in the laundry or trash container, depending on whether the gown is cloth or paper.
- If the sink is inside the patient's room, wash your hands and forearms with antiseptic before leaving the room. Turn off the faucet, using a paper towel; dispose of the towel. Grasp the door handle with a clean paper towel to open it; discard the towel in the trash container inside the room, closing the door from the outside with your bare hand.
- If the sink is in an anteroom, wash your hands and forearms with antiseptic after leaving the room.

### Special considerations

Use gowns, gloves, caps, and masks only once, and discard them in the appropriate container before leaving a contaminated area. Gowns, caps, and masks lose their effectiveness when wet, *because moisture permits organisms to seep through the material.* Change the gown, cap, and mask as soon as moisture is noticeable, or within 20 minutes, whichever occurs first.

Wash your hands after touching the patient's drainage, secretions, or excretions, even if you haven't finished his care, *to avoid contaminating the patient with his own flora.*

At the end of your shift, replace items used *to ensure a continuous supply of necessary items.*

When the patient is transferred to another unit or discharged, return the isolation cart to the appropriate area for cleaning and restocking of supplies. If an anteroom is available, it is carefully cleaned and then restocked by central supply.

MARY CASTLE, RN, MPH

# Reportable Diseases

*Certain contagious diseases must be reported to local and state public health officials and, ultimately, to the Centers for Disease Control. Generally, these diseases fall into two categories: those reported individually on definitive or suspected diagnosis, and those reported by the number of cases per week. The list of reportable diseases is long and varies from state to state, but the most commonly reported ones include hepatitis, viral meningitis, meningococcal infection, encephalitis, salmonellosis, shigellosis, syphilis, and gonorrhea.*

*In most states, the patient's doctor must report communicable diseases to health officials. In hospitals, the infection-control practitioner (ICP) or epidemiologist reports such diseases. Nevertheless, it's helpful for you to know the reporting requirements and the procedure. Fast, accurate reporting helps health officials identify and control probable infection sources, prevent possible epidemics, and guide public-health planning and policy.*

### Equipment

Nursing procedure or infection-control manual □ disease-reporting form, if available.

### Essential steps

- Make sure reportable diseases are listed and available to all shifts.
- Know your hospital's protocol for reporting diseases. Generally, you'll contact the ICP or epidemiologist. If the responsible person isn't available, contact your supervisor or the infectious-disease doctor on call.

### Documentation

Document any disease reported to the ICP, the ICP's name, and the date and time of the report.

MARY CASTLE, RN, MPH

## GUIDE TO REPORTABLE DISEASES AND CONDITIONS*

### CATEGORY I: REPORT IMMEDIATELY

Amebiasis

Animal bites

Anthrax (pulmonary or cutaneous)

Botulism (food-borne, infant)

Brucellosis

Cholera

Diphtheria (pharyngeal or cutaneous)

Encephalitis (primary or postinfectious)

Gastroenteritis (institutional outbreaks)

Guillain-Barré syndrome

Hepatitis Type A (include suspected source)

Hepatitis Type B (include suspected source)

Hepatitis, unspecified (include suspected source)

Legionellosis (Legionnaire's disease)

Leprosy

Leptospirosis

Malaria

Meningitis (specify etiology)

Meningococcal disease

Mumps

Pertussis

Plague (pneumonic or bubonic)

Poliomyelitis

Psittacosis

Rabies

Reye's syndrome

Rocky Mountain spotted fever

Rubella

Rubella, congenital syndrome

Rubeola

Salmonellosis

Sexually transmitted diseases

Shigellosis

Smallpox

Staphylococcal infections (neonatal)

Tetanus

Toxic shock syndrome

Trichinosis

Tuberculosis

Tularemia

Typhoid fever

Typhus

Yellow fever

### CATEGORY II: REPORT WEEKLY BY NUMBER OF CASES

Chicken pox

Group A beta-hemolytic streptococcal infections (including scarlet fever)

Influenza

Mumps

*This listing varies from state to state and is updated periodically.

# GUIDELINES

## Strict Isolation
### [Complete isolation, total isolation]

Strict isolation prevents the spread of communicable diseases that are transmitted by contact and airborne routes. It's required for such diseases as chicken pox and congenital rubella syndrome. It's recommended for Staphylococcus aureus; for group A streptococcal infections on wounds, burns, and extensive dermatitis when drainage cannot be contained by the dressing; and for pneumonia caused by S. aureus or group A streptococci.

Strict isolation requires a private

room with toilet facilities; good handwashing technique; and use of gowns,
gloves, caps, and masks by hospital
staff and visitors.

## Equipment

The patient's anteroom or the isolation
cart should contain gowns □ gloves □
masks □ caps □ specially marked laundry bags □ water-soluble laundry bags
□ plastic bags □ isolation cards □ isolation tape or labels.

Gather additional supplies, such as
a bedpan, urinal, thermometer, stethoscope, and blood pressure cuff, so you
don't have to leave the room unnecessarily.

## Preparation of equipment

Keep uncontaminated supplies in the
patient's anteroom or in the isolation
cart outside the patient's room.

## Essential steps

• Place the patient in a private room
with private toilet facilities and an

### CONDITIONS REQUIRING STRICT ISOLATION

| CONDITION | PERIOD OF ISOLATION |
|---|---|
| **Anthrax, pulmonary** | Duration of illness |
| **Chicken pox** | In the normal patient, 7 days after eruptions appear (duration of illness); in the asymptomatic susceptible patient, 3 weeks after exposure |
| **Diphtheria** | After two cultures from nose, throat, and any skin lesions, taken at least 24 hours apart after cessation of antimicrobial therapy, are negative for *Corynebacterium diphtheriae* |
| **Lassa fever** | Duration of illness |
| **Marburg virus disease** | Duration of illness |
| **Neonatal vesicular disease** (*Herpesvirus hominis*) | Duration of illness |
| **Pneumonia** with group A streptococcal infection | 24 hours after starting effective therapy |
| **Pneumonia** with *Staphylococcus aureus* | Duration of illness |
| **Pneumonic plague** | After completion of antibiotic regimen and negative culture findings |
| **Rabies** | Duration of illness |
| **Rubella, congenital** | Duration of illness |
| **Skin infections (major) or major burn wounds** infected with *Staphylococcus aureus* or group A streptococcal infection | Duration of illness |
| **Vaccinia** (generalized and progressive and eczema vaccinatum) | Duration of illness |

anteroom, where possible. Explain the isolation procedure to him *to allay his fears and promote his cooperation.*

• Keep the patient's door closed at all times. Put strict isolation cards on the patient's door.

• Wash your hands with an antiseptic soap before donning gloves, *to prevent bacterial growth on covered skin.* Wash gloved hands with an antiseptic soap if they become contaminated during patient care. Wash hands well with an antiseptic soap after leaving the room.

• Put on a clean gown, gloves, cap, and mask each time you enter the room, and use proper technique to take them off.

• Tape an impervious bag to the patient's bedside for tissues and oral secretions, and teach him to dispose of tissues correctly.

• Instruct hospital staff and visitors to put on gowns, gloves, caps, and masks before entering the isolation room and to use proper technique for taking them off.

**Special considerations**

Keep the patient's chart outside the isolation room *to avoid contaminating it.* Handle dressings of patients in strict isolation with "no-touch" technique. Handle dirty dressings with one set of sterile gloves and instruments; remove gloves and wash your hands with antiseptic; then use a new set of sterile gloves and instruments to provide care and apply new dressings (see "Wound Management" in Chapter 5).

Empty bedpans and urinals in the toilet.

All items that come in contact with the patient must be double-bagged, sealed, and marked with isolation tape before removal. Send reusable supplies to the central supply department for decontamination. Remember that nothing used in strict isolation can be reused before it's been correctly cleaned and sterilized by the central supply department.

Permanent fixtures in the isolation room should be cleaned routinely and after patient discharge by housekeeping staff. They should put on gowns, gloves, caps, and masks and only use cleaning equipment that remains in the isolation room until terminal disinfection. Cleaning water must be emptied in the room and buckets disinfected with each use *to eliminate a potential reservoir for bacterial growth.*

Dietary supplies, such as cups, utensils, and plates, are usually disposable. Used supplies and uneaten food that can't be flushed down the patient's toilet must be double-bagged and marked ISOLATION for incineration. If the patient requests nondisposable silverware and dishes, they must be washed after each meal, wrapped in towels, and left in the patient's room. When he leaves isolation, nondisposables are double-bagged, marked ISOLATION, and sent to the central supply department for sterilization before being returned to the kitchen. Dishes used to transport food to the patient's room *but not taken inside* are not contaminated and require only routine cleaning.

**Documentation**

Record the need for strict isolation on the nursing-care plan.

MARY CASTLE, RN, MPH

# Respiratory Isolation

*Respiratory isolation prevents the spread of infectious diseases that may be transmitted by direct or indirect contact or by airborne pathogens that are breathed, sneezed, or coughed into the environment. Effective respiratory isolation requires a private room, the use of masks by anyone entering the room, good handwashing technique, and proper handling and disposal of articles contaminated by respiratory tract secretions. When handling infants who require respiratory isolation, good technique requires the use of masks* and *gowns to prevent contamination of clothing by respiratory tract secretions.*

### Equipment
Masks □ gowns, if necessary □ plastic bags □ isolation card □ isolation tape or labels.

Gather any additional supplies, such as a thermometer, stethoscope, and blood pressure cuff, *so you don't have to leave the isolation room unnecessarily.*

### Preparation of equipment
Keep respiratory isolation supplies *outside* the patient's room.

### Essential steps
• Locate the patient in a private room with private toilet facilities and an anteroom, if possible. If necessary, two patients with the same infection may share a room.
• Keep the patient's door closed at all times *to isolate the patient's air supply;* put a respiratory isolation card on the door.
• Wash your hands before entering and after leaving the room and during patient care if you must handle respiratory tract secretions.

• Pick up your mask by the top strings, adjust it around your nose and mouth, and tie the strings for a comfortable fit. (If the mask has a flexible noseband, adjust it to fit firmly but comfortably.) Don't touch the front of the mask while wearing it, *because it is a contaminated surface.*
• Instruct the patient to cover his mouth with a tissue while coughing or sneezing, *to control the spread of airborne droplets.*
• Tape an impervious bag to the patient's bedside, and teach him to dispose of tissues correctly.
• Place all sputum specimens from respiratory isolation patients in impervious, labeled containers and send them to the laboratory.
• Ensure that all visitors wear masks and, if necessary, gowns.
• Double-bag all items that have come in direct contact with the patient, such as linens, trash, and nondisposable utensils or instruments, before removal from the room, *to prevent contagion.*

### Special considerations
Before removing your mask, wash your hands. Untie the strings and dispose of the mask, handling it by the strings only. If the patient has a highly con-

## DISEASES REQUIRING RESPIRATORY ISOLATION

| DISEASE | PERIOD OF ISOLATION |
| --- | --- |
| Meningitis, meningo-coccal | 24 hours after start of effective therapy |
| Meningococcemia | 24 hours after start of effective therapy |
| Mumps | 9 days after onset of swelling |
| Pertussis | 7 days after start of therapy or 3 weeks after onset of paroxysms, if untreated |
| Rubella | 5 days after onset of rash |
| Rubeola | 4 days after onset of rash |
| Tuberculosis, pulmonary | 2 weeks after start of effective therapy |

tagious respiratory disease, you may discard the mask in a lined, covered receptacle outside the patient's room. Thus, you'll be outside the room (with the door shut behind you) before removing your protective garb. Remember to discard the mask right at the door. *Carrying it away from the patient's immediate area spreads the contamination.* When the outside receptacle is full, double-bag its contents for disposal.

During terminal cleaning of the room, remind the housekeeping staff to wear masks.

### Documentation
Record the need for respiratory isolation on the nursing-care plan.

MARY CASTLE, RN, MPH

# Protective Isolation
## *[Reverse isolation]*

*Unlike other isolation procedures, protective isolation guards the patient with seriously impaired resistance to infection against contact with potential pathogens. This procedure is used for patients with extensive noninfected burns and for those who have leukopenia or are receiving immunosuppressive treatments.*

*Protective isolation requires a private room equipped with positive air pressure, if possible, to force suspended particles down and out of the room. It also requires use of gowns, gloves, caps, and masks by hospital staff and visitors, and good handwashing technique using antiseptic agents. For care of patients with temporary high susceptibility, such as those who have undergone bone marrow transplantation, protective isolation may also require a patient-isolator unit and use of sterile linens, gowns, gloves, and head and shoe coverings. In such cases, all other items taken into the room should also be sterilized.*

### Equipment
Gowns □ gloves □ masks □ caps □ shoe covers, if required □ plastic bags □ protective isolation cards.

Gather any additional supplies, such as a thermometer, stethoscope, and blood pressure cuff, *so you don't have to leave the isolation room unnecessarily.*

### Preparation of equipment
Keep supplies in a clean enclosed cart or in an anteroom outside the room.

### Essential steps
• After locating the patient in a private room, explain isolation procedures to him *to ease anxiety and promote cooperation.*

• Keep the door to the room closed at all times; place protective isolation cards on the door.

• Wash your hands with an antiseptic agent before putting on gloves, *to prevent bacterial growth on gloved skin;* wash gloves with antiseptic if they become contaminated during patient care; and wash your hands again after leaving the room.

• Put on a clean gown, mask, cap, and gloves each time you enter the patient's room.

• Don't allow visits by anyone known to be infected or ill. Show all visitors how to put on gowns, gloves, caps, and masks before entering the patient's room, and tell them to remove them only after leaving the room.

### Special considerations
Don't perform invasive procedures, such as urethral catheterization, unless absolutely necessary, *because their use risks serious infection in the patient with impaired resistance.* Avoid transporting the patient out of the room; if he must be moved, gown and mask him first.

Instruct the housekeeping staff to put on gowns, gloves, caps, and masks before entering the patient's room; they should not enter if they are ill or infected.

The room should be cleaned with new or scrupulously clean equipment. Because the patient does not have a contagious disease, materials leaving the room need no special precautions, and the room requires no special cleaning precautions after the patient has been discharged.

**Documentation**
Record the need for protective isolation on the nursing-care plan.

MARY CASTLE, RN, MPH

# Enteric Precautions

*Enteric precautions prevent the spread of gastrointestinal infections caused by infectious organisms transmitted by the fecal-oral route through direct or indirect contact with feces or articles heavily contaminated with feces. Effective enteric precautions require careful handwashing and use of gowns and gloves by all who have direct contact with the patient or his excretions.*

*Children must be placed in private rooms. Contagious and noncontagious adults can safely share rooms if they avoid direct contact and wash their hands well after using the bathroom and before eating. An adult patient may require a private room because of hospital policy, doctor's preference, fecal incontinence, or a behavior problem.*

*If you suspect your patient has infectious diarrhea, collect a stool specimen for culture and begin enteric precautions immediately, without waiting for test results.*

**Equipment**
Gowns □ gloves □ plastic bags □ specially marked laundry bags □ water-soluble laundry bags □ isolation cards □ isolation tape or labels.

**Preparation of equipment**
Keep clean (unused) enteric isolation

## CONDITIONS OR TREATMENTS REQUIRING PROTECTIVE ISOLATION

| CONDITION OR TREATMENT | PERIOD OF ISOLATION |
| --- | --- |
| **Agranulocytosis** | Until remission |
| **Burns,** noninfected, extensive | Until skin surface is substantially healed |
| **Dermatitis,** noninfected vesicular, bullous, or eczematous disease (when severe and extensive) | Until skin surface is substantially healed |
| **Immunosuppressive therapy** | Until patient defenses are considered adequate |
| **Lymphomas and leukemia,** especially in late stages of Hodgkin's disease or acute leukemia | Until clinical improvement is substantial |

supplies *outside* the patient's room.

**Essential steps**
• Explain the enteric precautions to the patient *to ease anxiety and ensure cooperation.*
• If necessary, locate the adult in a private room; locate the child in a private room *to prevent fecal-oral cross-contamination.*
• Put an enteric precaution card on the patient's door.
• Put on a gown and gloves before direct contact with the patient or his excretions.
• Wash your hands before giving the patient care. Use soap if you're not going to wear gloves, an antiseptic agent if you are. Wash gloved or ungloved hands with antiseptic if they are contaminated, and wash them again with antiseptic after giving care.
• Teach the patient to wash his hands before eating and after elimination.

## CONDITIONS REQUIRING ENTERIC PRECAUTIONS

| CONDITION | PERIOD OF ISOLATION |
|---|---|
| Cholera | Duration of illness |
| Diarrhea, and acute illness caused by suspected infection | Duration of illness |
| Enterocolitis, staphylococcal | Until completion of antibiotic therapy and negative culture findings |
| Gastroenteritis | |
| Enteropathogenic *Escherichia coli* | Until three consecutive stool cultures or fluorescent antibody test, taken after completion of antibiotic therapy, prove negative |
| Enterotoxic *E. coli* | Duration of illness |
| *Salmonella* species (except *Salmonella typhi*) | Duration of illness |
| *S. typhi* | Until three consecutive stool cultures, taken after completion of antibiotic therapy, prove negative |
| *Shigella* species | Until three consecutive stool cultures, taken after completion of antibiotic therapy, prove negative |
| *Yersinia enterocolitica* | Duration of illness |
| Hepatitis Type A, Type B, or unspecified | Duration of hospitalization |

• If the patient is using a bedpan or urinal, empty the contents directly into the toilet. Then properly clean the container and return it to the bedside stand. When the patient is discharged, place the nondisposable bedpan or urinal in a plastic bag, close it securely, label it with isolation tape, and send it to the central supply department for decontamination and sterilization.

• Discard liquids and soft flushable foods in the toilet. Wrap and discard solid leftover food and disposable dishes and utensils in a wastebasket. Nondisposable utensils, dishes, and trays should be cleaned, put in a plastic bag labeled with isolation tape, and sent to the central supply department for decontamination before return to the kitchen.

• Change bedclothes and linens daily,

and immediately if soiled. Bag used linens first in a water-soluble laundry bag, taking care to wrap wet linen with dry, and then in a specially marked laundry bag. Close the bag, and label it with isolation tape.

• Collect laboratory specimens in appropriate, properly labeled containers with secure covers. Send specimen containers to the laboratory in plastic bags marked ISOLATION.

• Tell visitors and housekeeping staff to put on gowns and gloves before entering the patient's room if they will be in direct contact with the patient or his excretions.

### Special considerations
When caring for a patient with viral hepatitis, use disposable needles and syringes. Discard used needles in a

punctureproof, rigid container.

*To prevent infection,* be especially careful not to puncture yourself accidentally with the needle when giving injections, starting I.V. infusions, or drawing blood. Never bend, break, or recap used needles. If you must use nondisposable needles or syringes, rinse the used needles under cold water *to prevent clogging the lumen with coagulated protein,* and place them in a punctureproof, rigid container.

Double-bag the container, label the bag HEPATITIS, and send it to the central supply department. Tape an impervious bag to the bed for tissues and oral secretions. For disposal, double-bag it and mark it HEPATITIS.

Housekeeping staff must wear gowns and gloves while cleaning the toilet bowl and sink in an enteric precautions room, especially if the patient has hepatitis.

**Documentation**

Record the need for enteric precautions on the nursing-care plan.

MARY CASTLE, RN, MPH

# Wound and Skin Precautions

*Wound and skin precautions prevent transmission of organisms by direct wound contact or by handling of heavily contaminated articles. They are required for extensive skin infections; for wound infections that are not covered by dressings or that have copious purulent drainage not contained by dressings (except group A streptococcal and* Staphylococcus aureus *infections, which require strict isolation); and for wound and skin infections covered by dressings that adequately contain the infection, including* S. aureus *and group A streptococcal infections.*

*Wound and skin precautions do not*

*require a private room. They require gowns and gloves during direct wound contact, use of masks during dressing changes, careful handwashing, and "no touch" handling of dressings, linens, and contaminated instruments.*

**Equipment**

Routine care requires no special equipment, but it requires special techniques when care results in wound contact or the handling of contaminated equipment.

Gowns □ gloves □ masks □ plastic

## CONDITIONS REQUIRING WOUND AND SKIN PRECAUTIONS

| CONDITION | PERIOD OF ISOLATION |
|---|---|
| **Bubonic plague** | Until completion of antibiotic therapy and negative culture results |
| **Gas gangrene** (from *Clostridium perfringens*) | Duration of illness |
| **Herpes zoster, localized** | Duration of illness |
| **Melioidosis** (extrapulmonary, with draining sinuses) | Duration of illness |
| **Puerperal sepsis** (with group A streptococcal infection; vaginal discharge) | Duration of illness |
| **Wound and skin infections** Other than *Staphylococcus aureus* or group A streptococcal infections when uncovered. | Duration of illness |
| Covered by dressings that contain discharge, including *S. aureus* or group A streptococcal infections | Duration of illness |

bags □ wound and skin precaution cards □ specially marked laundry bags □ water-soluble laundry bags □ isolation tape or labels.

### Preparation of equipment
Keep clean supplies *outside* the room. Don't bring the dressing cart into the room; have one person hand clean materials in to the person working in the room, *to prevent contamination of the cart.* Use disposable materials and instruments whenever possible.

### Essential steps
• Locate the patient in a private room only if required by hospital policy, the doctor, or the patient's condition. Explain the precautions and the reasons for them to the patient. Place wound and skin precaution cards on the door.
• Wash your hands with soap and warm water before entering; with an antiseptic after you leave the room, before gloving, and when changing gloves during direct contact with the wound or its drainage or for a dressing change.
• Put on a gown and gloves for direct contact with wounds and a mask for dressing changes. Instruct other staff and visitors to avoid contact with the wound, drainage, dressings, or linens.

### Special considerations
Double-bagging technique (see *Double-Bagging Technique,* page 142) is required for all items that come in direct contact with the patient's wound—such as dressings, disposable instruments, and linens (for decontamination and sterilization)—*to contain contaminants and prevent contagion.*

When taking swabs or aspirating specimens for culture, avoid contaminating the outside of the container. Double-bag the specimen, label the container with isolation tape, and send it to the laboratory immediately.

### Documentation
Record the need for wound and skin precautions in the nursing-care plan.

MARY CASTLE, RN, MPH

# Blood Precautions

*Blood precautions help prevent cross-contamination of patients and hospital staff by infected blood, or by equipment or specimens contaminated by infected blood. Precautions generally include storing used needles and syringes in a punctureproof container and proper disposal of contaminated equipment and supplies. A gown and gloves are recommended for any procedure that may expose you to contamination with blood from a spurting vessel, such as venipuncture or arterial line insertion.*

*Blood precautions must be observed rigorously during care of patients with viral hepatitis (types A, B, or unspecified); malaria; or arthropod-borne viruses, such as dengue, yellow fever, or Colorado tick fever.*

### Equipment
Routine care requires no special equipment, but it requires special techniques when care involves contact with blood or contaminated articles.

Blood precautions card □ punctureproof container (for syringe and needle disposal) □ clear plastic biohazard bags □ gloves □ gowns □ water-soluble laundry bags □ specially marked laundry bags □ marking pen □ isolation tape or labels.

### Preparation of equipment
Bring all necessary supplies to the patient's room, *to avoid interruptions and unnecessary glove changes.*

### Essential steps
• Put a blood precautions card on the door and bed *to notify staff to observe blood precautions.*
• Wash your hands for 10 to 15 seconds with antiseptic soap *to avoid spreading microorganisms.*
• Wear clean gloves if the procedure involves possible contact with infected blood. Place used needles and syringes

in the punctureproof container after handling them carefully and as little as possible; don't bend or resheath the needle before disposing of it *to avoid an accidental puncture and possible infection.* When the procedure is complete, remove gloves by turning them inside out *to avoid touching contaminated surfaces,* and dispose of them properly (see "Isolation Equipment" in this chapter).

• Place blood specimens in an impervious bag, close it with isolation tape, and label the bag with the patient's name, diagnosis, and the words BLOOD PRECAUTIONS *to alert staff and prevent accidental contamination.*

• Place contaminated bed linens in a water-soluble laundry bag, and then place this inside a specially marked laundry bag.

• Place disposable equipment and supplies in a plastic bag and label it with isolation tape. Incinerate all burnable trash; place nonburnable trash in an impervious bag marked ISOLATION, and send it to the central supply department for decontamination before it can be discarded.

• Wash all nondisposable supplies in soap and water *to remove protein matter.* Always leave instruments in the open position, place them in a clear plastic biohazard bag *to help the central supply department personnel choose the appropriate decontamination method,* and send the double-bagged items to the central supply department. Never mix glass, plastic, metal, or rubber items, because each material requires a different decontamination method.

• After you've completed the pr( :edure and disposed of trash and equipment properly, wash your hands with antiseptic soap.

## Special considerations
If applicable, inform other hospital departments—such as radiology, the laboratory, operating room, and physical therapy—of the need to observe blood precautions.

## Documentation
Record the need for blood precautions on the nursing-care plan.

LORETTA ROMANO, RN, BS

---

# Lesion Secretion Precautions

---

*These precautions protect the patients and hospital personnel from cross-contamination by secretions from infected, draining wounds and from secretion-contaminated articles. Although the risk of cross-contamination from a lesion is slight, such precautions should be maintained until discharge stops or culture reports prove negative. Lesion secretion precautions require "no-touch" technique during dressing changes, thorough handwashing before and after patient contact, and double-bagging of soiled articles and equipment.*

## Equipment
Routine care requires no special equipment, but it requires special techniques when care involves contact with contaminated articles.

Sterile gloves □ sterile forceps, if needed □ clear plastic biohazard bag □ sterile dressings, if needed □ water-soluble laundry bags □ specially marked laundry bags □ sterile equipment for irrigating, cleaning, or medicating wounds, if necessary (see "Wound Management" in Chapter 5) □ marking pen □ isolation tape or labels □ lesion secretion precaution cards.

## Preparation of equipment
If wound care or dressing changes are to be performed, collect the required equipment and bring it into the patient's room.

## Essential steps
• Place a lesion secretion precaution

## CONDITIONS REQUIRING LESION
## SECRETION PRECAUTIONS

| CONDITION | PERIOD OF PRECAUTION |
|---|---|
| **Actinomycosis** (draining lesion) | Duration of drainage |
| **Anthrax, cutaneous** | Until negative culture results |
| **Brucellosis** (draining lesion) | Duration of drainage |
| **Candidiasis, mucocutaneous** | Duration of illness |
| **Coccidioidomycosis** (draining lesion) | Duration of drainage |
| **Conjunctivitis, acute bacterial** (including gonococcal) | Until 24 hours after start of effective therapy |
| **Conjunctivitis, viral** | Duration of illness |
| **Gonorrhea** | Until 24 hours after start of effective therapy |
| **Granuloma inguinale** | Duration of illness |
| **Herpes simplex** (except disseminated neonatal disease) (For disseminated neonatal disease, see "Strict Isolation"; for oral herpes, see "Oral Secretion Precautions," both in this chapter.) | Duration of illness |
| **Keratoconjunctivitis, epidemic** | Duration of illness |
| **Listeriosis** | Duration of illness |
| **Lymphogranuloma venereum** | Duration of illness |
| **Nocardiosis** (draining lesion) | Duration of illness |
| **Ophthalmia neonatorum, gonococcal** | Until 24 hours after start of effective therapy |
| **Orf** | Duration of illness |
| **Skin, burn, and wound infections, minor** (*Staphylococcus aureus* or group A streptococcal) | Duration of drainage |
| **Syphilis, mucocutaneous** | Until 24 hours after start of effective therapy |
| **Trachoma, acute** | Duration of illness |
| **Tuberculosis** (extrapulmonary draining lesion) | Duration of drainage |
| **Tularemia** (draining lesion) | Duration of drainage |

card on the door *to alert staff to observe lesion precautions.*

• Explain the procedure to the patient *to ease anxiety and promote cooperation.* Tell him to refrain from touching the wound or dressing *to avoid self-contamination.*

If wound care or dressing changes are to be performed, proceed with the following steps:

• Open the plastic bag for use in holding soiled dressings and disposable equipment.

• Wash your hands for 10 to 15 seconds with antiseptic soap and put on gloves.

• Remove the old dressing and place it in the plastic bag, being careful not to touch the outside of the bag. Remove your gloves by turning them inside out *to avoid touching contaminated sur-*

*faces;* discard them in the plastic bag.
- Put on sterile gloves to cleanse, irrigate, or medicate the wound, as ordered.
- With sterile gloves or sterile forceps, redress the patient's wound (see "Wound Management" in Chapter 5).
- Wash all nondisposable supplies with soap and water *to remove protein matter,* leave them in the open position, and place them in a clear plastic biohazard bag *to help the central supply department choose the appropriate method of decontamination and sterilization.* Send the double-bagged items to the central supply department. Never mix glass, plastic, metal, or rubber items, because each material requires different decontamination.
- Place contaminated disposable items in the same bag with soiled dressings. Seal the bag and mark it with isolation tape.
- Place contaminated linens in a water-soluble laundry bag; then place this inside a specially marked isolation laundry bag and send it to the laundry.
- Wash your hands with antiseptic soap *to avoid spreading organisms.*

### Special considerations
If the patient is receiving physical therapy, notify the department that he is on lesion secretion precautions, *because they may need to clean and disinfect their equipment after his treatment.*

### Documentation
Record the start of lesion secretion precautions and the time and date of wound care, if applicable, on the patient's care plan and chart.

LORETTA ROMANO, RN, BS

# Oral Secretion Precautions

*These precautions help protect patients and hospital staff from direct contact* *with an infected patient's oral secretions. Oral secretion precautions include proper patient instruction for coughing, sneezing, and expectorating and correct handling and disposal of contaminated tissues and equipment.*

*Despite the minimal risk of cross-contamination, oral secretion precautions are required for any patient with copious oral secretions, even if no infectious organism has been identified.*

## DISEASES REQUIRING ORAL SECRETION PRECAUTIONS

| DISEASE | PERIOD OF PRECAUTION |
|---|---|
| **Herpangina** | Duration of hospitalization |
| **Herpes oralis** | Duration of illness |
| **Melioidosis, pulmonary** | Duration of illness |
| **Mononucleosis, infectious** | Duration of illness |
| **Pharyngitis, streptococcal** | Until 24 hours after start of effective therapy |
| **Pneumonia, bacterial and mycoplasmal** | Duration of illness |
| **Psittacosis** | Duration of illness (patient who is coughing and raising sputum may need respiratory isolation) |
| **Q fever** | Duration of illness |
| **Respiratory disease, acute and infectious** | Duration of illness |
| **Scarlet fever** | Until 24 hours after start of effective therapy |
| **Tuberculosis, chronic** | Prophylactic during active, chronic disease |

## Equipment

Routine care requires no special equipment, but it requires special techniques when care involves contact with contaminated articles.

Plastic bag □ tissues □ adhesive tape □ large safety pin □ lined trash receptacle □ oral secretion precaution card.

## Essential steps

• Place oral secretion precaution card on the door.
• Explain the procedure to the patient *to ease anxiety and promote cooperation.*
• Attach the plastic bag to the side rail within the patient's easy reach, and secure it with adhesive tape.
• Tell the patient to hold a tissue close to his mouth before coughing, sneezing, or expectorating and to deposit the tissue immediately into the bedside bag.
• When the plastic bag is three-quarters full, remove it from the side rail, seal it, and place it in a lined trash receptacle; then seal the trash bag, mark it with isolation tape, and send it to the incinerator.
• Wash your hands for 10 to 15 seconds with antiseptic soap after handling and disposing of the trash bag, *to prevent spreading microorganisms.*
• Replace the patient's tissue bag as needed. Follow your hospital's routine if it has established a minimum-change schedule, such as once every shift.

## Special considerations

If the patient has had nasotracheal suctioning or has a tracheostomy, place the contaminated suction catheter and gloves in an impervious bag, seal it, and mark it with isolation tape for disposal. Follow your hospital's policy for appropriate disposal of utensils, dishes, and trays. Nondisposable equipment, such as thermometers, must be sent to the central supply department for sterilization before reuse.

## Documentation

On the nursing-care plan, record the characteristics and amount of secretions; note the presence of blood, pus, tissue, or foul odors and any significant changes in color, viscosity, or amount.

LORETTA ROMANO, RN, BS

# Terminal Cleaning of the Isolation Room

*An isolation room or other room prepared for isolation purposes must be thoroughly cleaned and disinfected before use by another patient.*

*Nursing responsibilities for terminal cleaning vary but usually include stripping the bed, double-bagging all supplies and removing them from the room, and cleaning bedside equipment. Normally, the housekeeping staff is responsible for cleaning the rest of the room. Special cleaning is unnecessary if the patient is found to be free of infection and is removed from isolation. Depending on the type of isolation, terminal cleaning of a contaminated room requires use of gowns, gloves, or masks by housekeeping personnel and special cleaning of housekeeping equipment after the room is cleaned.*

## Equipment

*Depending on type of isolation:* gowns □ gloves □ caps □ masks □ plastic bags □ water-soluble laundry bags □ specially marked laundry bags □ germicide.

## Preparation of equipment

Keep terminal cleaning equipment in the isolation room.

## Essential steps

• Put on appropriate isolation garb.
• Empty nondisposable receptacles (such as ashtrays, thermometer holders, drainage bottles, urinals, and bedpans) into the toilet, wipe them with disinfectant solution, double-bag them,

and mark the bags with isolation tape for decontamination in the central supply department. If the receptacles are disposable, empty them; then double-bag and discard them with other disposables.

• Clean other patient-care supplies, such as reusable equipment, with disinfectant solution. Always clean from the cleanest to the dirtiest areas of the room *to avoid spreading organisms from possible reservoirs of infectious organisms.*

• Depending on the type of isolation, double-bag the blood pressure cuff and any respiratory equipment, mark it ISOLATION, and send it to the central supply department for decontamination and sterilization. If there is a needle disposal box, tape it shut with isolation tape and double-bag it for incineration.

• Clean larger items (such as wheelchairs) and fixed equipment (such as the sphygmomanometer holder) with disinfectant solution.

• When you've completed your part of terminal cleaning, label all double-bagged articles with isolation tape and note contents on the outside *to alert other hospital personnel to follow appropriate decontamination and sterilization procedures.* Then remove the isolation card from the door.

**Special considerations**

Don't disinfect the isolation room by

## CLEANING, DISINFECTING, AND STERILIZING

Although often incorrectly used interchangeably, these terms have different specific meanings in infection control.

*Cleaning* removes dirt and debris from a surface, usually with water and with or without detergents. It physically removes organisms from a surface but doesn't kill them. Equipment must be cleaned before sterilization.

*Disinfecting* provides an intermediate state between clean and sterile. It kills only certain kinds of microorganisms but doesn't kill spores. Equipment can be disinfected by pasteurization, by exposure to ultraviolet rays, or by soaking in a disinfectant solution. The equipment to be disinfected must be as clean as possible, because disinfectants cannot penetrate deposits of pus, blood, or other organic substances and may even be neutralized by them.

*Sterilizing* destroys all microorganisms—including bacteria, viruses, fungi, parasites, and their spores—through use of pressurized steam, gas (ethylene oxide), liquid (actuated glutaraldehyde), or dry heat. Boiling water does *not* kill spores.

fogging; this is ineffective. Generally, you don't have to air the room after patient discharge, *because the air conditioning system changes the air rapidly.* If the ventilation system malfunctions in a strict or respiratory isolation room, open the windows and close the doors for 1 or 2 hours before you begin terminal cleaning.

SUSAN M. GLOVER, RN, BSN

## Selected References

Brunner, Lillian S., and Suddarth, Doris S. *Textbook of Medical-Surgical Nursing,* 4th ed. Philadelphia: J.B. Lippincott Co., 1980.

*Controlling Infection.* Nursing Photobook™ Series. Springhouse, Pa.: Intermed Communications, Inc., 1981.

Dison, Norma. *Clinical Nursing Techniques,* 4th ed. St. Louis: C.V. Mosby Co., 1979.

Haley, Robert W., et al. "Nosocomial Infections in U.S. Hospitals, 1975-1976: Estimated Frequency by Selected Character-

istics of Patients," *The American Journal of Medicine* 70:947, April 1981.

*Isolation Techniques for Use in Hospitals,* 2nd ed. Atlanta: Centers for Disease Control, 1975.

King, Eunice M., et al. *Illustrated Manual of Nursing Techniques.* Philadelphia: J.B. Lippincott Co., 1976.

Kozier, Barbara B., and Erb, Glenora L. *Fundamentals of Nursing: Concepts & Procedures.* New York: Addison-Wesley Publishing Co., 1979.

# 4 Diagnostic Tests

# Diagnostic Tests

## Introduction

In any clinical setting, diagnostic testing is likely a large part of your professional responsibility. Your duties may routinely include patient care before, during, and after the test; performing or assisting with the test or, at times, teaching the patient how to perform it; and collecting and labeling specimens and ensuring their timely delivery to the laboratory. (See *Common Diagnostic Tests and Procedures,* page 160.) In some settings, nurses may be solely responsible for performing and interpreting diagnostic tests and procedures. For example, specially trained nurses may routinely perform arterial puncture to obtain a sample for blood gas analysis; in some oncology centers, nurses now perform bone marrow aspiration. In every case, nursing responsibility for diagnostic tests depends on the clinical setting, hospital policy, and guidelines provided in state or provincial nurse practice acts.

### Patient care

Clear explanation of a diagnostic test helps minimize a patient's anxiety, fosters cooperation, and thus promotes more reliable results; it's also essential for obtaining informed consent. When preparing a patient for a diagnostic test, make your explanations clear, honest, and as complete as appropriate. For example, before a difficult procedure, such as lumbar puncture, you should warn the patient about any discomfort he may feel. Letting the patient know exactly what to expect helps him withstand even rigorous procedures. Such preparation should include telling the patient how long the procedure takes and how soon results will be available.

If you're assisting the doctor during a diagnostic procedure, talk to the patient throughout to comfort and encourage him. Afterward, watch for side effects or complications, and be prepared to implement appropriate posttest care.

### Informed consent

Rising standards of medical care and patients' rising expectations have led to recognition of fundamental patient-care standards and legal principles on which are based a body of patients' rights. One of the most important of these rights is expressed in the doctrine of informed consent, which states that the patient (or if the patient is legally incompetent, a responsible family member) must clearly understand what will be done during a test, surgery, or any medical procedure and must understand its risks and implications *before* he can legally consent to it.

Explaining a procedure, how it will be performed, and its potential benefits and risks is primarily the doctor's responsibility. The nurse generally reinforces the doctor's explanations and verifies the patient's ability to comprehend them. She is responsible for witnessing and sometimes for obtaining written consent. Written consent is not always necessary; informed verbal con-

## COMMON DIAGNOSTIC TESTS AND PROCEDURES

| TEST/PROCEDURE | PURPOSE | PERFORMED BY |
|---|---|---|
| Venipuncture | To obtain venous blood sample | STN |
| Blood culture | To isolate and identify pathogens in bacteremia or septicemia | STN |
| Reagent strip tests (blood) | To determine approximate blood glucose levels | N, P |
| Arterial puncture | To obtain arterial blood sample for blood gas analysis | STN |
| Allen's test | To assess ulnar artery function | N |
| Intravascular line aspiration | To obtain arterial or venous blood samples for laboratory analysis | STN |
| Urine collection (clean-catch midstream, timed, catheter) | To obtain urine specimen for laboratory analysis | N, P |
| Reagent strip and tablet tests (urine) | To determine glucose or acetone levels | N, P |
| Urine specific gravity | To determine urine concentration | N |
| Urine pH (reagent strips) | To determine acidity/alkalinity | N, P |
| Straining urine | To detect calculi | N, P |
| Sputum collection | To identify pulmonary pathogens | N, P |
| Stool collection | To obtain a sample for analysis | N, P |
| Fecal occult blood (Hemoccult) | To detect blood in stool | N, P |

KEY: **N** = Nurse, **STN** = Specially trained nurse, **P** = Patient

sent is often considered adequate. The patient retains the legal right to withdraw consent—whether written or not—at any time and for any reason and to *refuse* care or treatment.

### Patient teaching

Depending on the test, your teaching may have to exceed what's necessary to obtain informed consent. Some tests require more detailed instructions to promote cooperation and ensure more accurate sample collection. For example, you may have to instruct the patient to observe a special diet, to discontinue certain medications for a specified time before a test, or to learn a special collection technique.

Whenever possible, reinforce your verbal explanations with appropriate printed information. Make sure the patient has a copy in time to read it before physical preparation for the test or procedure begins. Many institutions also have videocassettes, telelectures, and films available to augment the patient-teaching process.

ANNE MORACA-SAWICKI, RN, MSN

# BLOOD SPECIMENS

## Venipuncture

*Venipuncture, piercing a vein with a needle to obtain a venous sample, is commonly performed at the antecubital fossa; less commonly, on veins in the wrist, the dorsum of the hand or foot, or, if necessary, almost any other vein. Use of leg veins for venipuncture increases the risk of thrombophlebitis and embolism and should be avoided, if possible. Venipuncture should be performed cautiously in patients with clotting disorders or in those receiving anticoagulant therapy.*

*To obtain a blood sample, the needle may be attached to a syringe or to the needle holder of an evacuated collection tube. Diagnostic venipuncture is commonly performed by a laboratory technician and occasionally by a nurse.*

*Venipuncture is also performed with different equipment to implement intravenous therapy (see Chapter 6, INTRAVASCULAR THERAPY).*

### Equipment
Tourniquet □ 70% ethyl alcohol or povidone-iodine sponges □ sterile syringes or evacuated tubes and needle holder □ sterile needles: 20G or 21G for the forearm; 25G for the wrist, hand, or ankle or for children □ color-coded tubes containing appropriate additives □ labels □ 2″ x 2″ gauze pads □ adhesive bandage.

### Preparation of equipment
If you're using an evacuated tube, open the needle packet, attach the needle to its holder, and select the appropriate vacuum collection tube. If you're using a syringe, attach the appropriate needle to it. Be sure to choose a syringe large enough to hold all the blood that is required for the test. Label all collection tubes clearly with the patient's name and room number, the doctor's name, and the date and time of collection.

### Essential steps
● Wash your hands thoroughly *to prevent cross-contamination.*
● Tell the patient you're about to take a blood sample, and explain the procedure *to ease anxiety and ensure his cooperation.*
● If the patient is on bed rest, ask him to lie supine, with his head slightly elevated and his arms at his sides. If he is ambulatory, ask him to sit in a chair and to support his arm securely on an armrest or table.
● Assess the patient's veins *to determine the best puncture site.* Observe the skin for the vein's blue color, or palpate the vein for a firm rebound sensation.
● Tie a tourniquet proximal to the area chosen. If you've selected the antecubital vein, tie the tourniquet on the upper arm. *The tourniquet prevents venous return to the heart, causing the vein to dilate.* The tourniquet should be tight enough to impede venous flow without stopping arterial flow. If arterial perfusion is maintained, you'll be able to feel the radial pulse. (If the tourniquet fails to dilate the vein, have the patient open and close his fist repeatedly. Then ask him to close his fist as you insert the needle and to open it again when the needle is in place.)
● Cleanse the venipuncture site with an alcohol or povidone-iodine sponge. Wipe in a circular motion, spiraling outward from the site *to avoid introducing normal skin flora into the patient's vascular system during the procedure.* Allow the skin to dry before performing the venipuncture.
● If you palpate the vein over the venipuncture site before inserting the needle, be sure to cleanse the finger you use with alcohol or povidone-iodine, *to prevent cross-contamination.* Immo-

bilize the vein by pressing just below the venipuncture site with your thumb and drawing the skin taut.

• Hold the needle holder or syringe with the needle bevel up and the shaft parallel to the path of the vein, at a 15° angle to the arm. Insert the needle into the vein. If you use a syringe, venous blood will appear in the hub; withdraw the blood slowly, pulling the plunger of the syringe gently, to create steady suction until you obtain the required sample. *Pulling the plunger too forcibly may cause the vein to collapse.* If you use an evacuated tube, a drop of blood will appear just inside the needle holder. Grasp the holder securely, and push down on the collection tube until the needle punctures the rubber stopper; blood will flow into the tube automatically.

• Remove the tourniquet as soon as the blood flow is adequate, *to prevent stasis and hemoconcentration, which can impair test results.* If the flow is sluggish, leave the tourniquet in place longer, but *always* remove it before withdrawing the needle.

• After you've drawn the sample, place a gauze pad over the puncture site, and slowly and gently remove the needle from the vein. When using an evacuated tube, remove the collection tube from the end of the needle inside the needle holder before withdrawing the needle, *to release the vacuum.*

• Apply gentle pressure to the puncture site for 2 or 3 minutes or until bleeding stops. *This prevents extravasation into the surrounding tissue, which causes a hematoma.*

• After bleeding stops, apply an adhesive bandage.

• If you use a syringe, transfer the sample to a collection tube. Detach the needle from the syringe, open the collection tube, and gently empty the sample into the tube, being careful to avoid foaming, *which may cause hemolysis.*

• Before leaving the patient's bedside, check the venipuncture site to make sure a hematoma hasn't developed. If a hematoma occurs, apply warm soaks.

**Special considerations**

Never draw a venous sample from an arm or leg that is being used for I.V. therapy, blood administration, or I.V. drug administration, *because this may affect test results;* nor should a venous sample be drawn from a site of infection, *because this risks the introduction of pathogens into the patient's vascular system.*

If you use a blood pressure cuff as a tourniquet, inflate it to a range between the patient's systolic and diastolic pressures *to allow for venous distention without constricting arterial flow.* If the patient has large, distended, highly visible veins, perform venipuncture without a tourniquet *to minimize the risk of hematoma.*

If the patient has a clotting disorder or is receiving anticoagulant therapy, maintain pressure on the venipuncture site for at least 5 minutes after withdrawing the needle *to prevent a hematoma.*

**Complications**

A hematoma at the venipuncture site is the most common complication. Infection may result from poor technique.

**Documentation**

Record the date, time, and site of venipuncture; the time the sample was sent to the laboratory; and any adverse effects the patient may experience, such as a hematoma or anxiety.

JOANNE PATZEK DACUNHA, RN

# Blood Culture

*Although blood is normally bacteria-free, it is susceptible to infection through infusion lines, as well as from thrombophlebitis, infected shunts, or bacterial endocarditis from prosthetic heart valve replacements. Bacteria may also invade the vascular system from local tissue infections through the lymphatic system and the thoracic duct.*

*Blood cultures are performed to detect bacterial invasion (bacteremia) and the systemic spread of such an infection (septicemia) in the bloodstream. In this procedure, a laboratory technician or a nurse collects a venous blood sample by venipuncture at the patient's bedside. The sample is inoculated into two bottles, one containing an anaerobic medium and the other an aerobic medium. These samples are incubated to grow and isolate the causative organisms. Blood cultures can identify about 67% of pathogens within 24 hours and up to 90% within 72 hours. A new collection system, called the Isolator, speeds detection of septicemia. It consists of an evacuated tube containing a substance that lyses blood cells. The lysate-blood mixture is then centrifuged and plated directly onto culture plates (see* The Isolator Blood-culturing System*).*

*Although some consider the timing of culture collections debatable and possibly irrelevant, other authorities advocate drawing three blood samples at least 1 hour apart. The first of these should be collected at the earliest sign of suspected bacteremia or septicemia. To check for suspected bacterial endocarditis, three or four samples may be collected at 5- to 30-minute intervals before starting antibiotic therapy.*

### Equipment

Tourniquet □ sterile gloves (optional) □ alcohol sponges □ povidone-iodine sponges □ 10-ml syringe for an adult; 6-ml syringe for a child □ three or four sterile needles □ two or three blood culture bottles (50-ml bottles for adults, 20-ml bottles for infants and children) with sodium polyethanol sulfonate (SPS) added (one aerobic bottle containing a suitable medium, such as Trypticase soy broth with 10% carbon dioxide atmosphere; one anaerobic bottle with prereduced medium; and possibly one hyperosmotic bottle with 10% sucrose medium) □ small adhesive bandages □ 2″ x 2″ gauze pads.

## THE ISOLATOR BLOOD-CULTURING SYSTEM

The Isolator, a single-tube blood-culturing system based on lysis-centrifugation, helps diagnose bacterial infection and measure the effectiveness of antibacterial drug therapy.

When the blood sample is drawn into the Isolator tube, the red blood cells are lysed. Then the sample is centrifuged, concentrating any bacteria or other organisms present onto an inert cushioning pad, and the concentrate is plated directly onto four agar plates.

The Isolator system has several advantages over the conventional blood-culturing system. It eliminates the bottle method's lengthy incubation period, providing faster results; improves bacterial survival, resulting in more true positives through direct plating, which dilutes any antibiotic present in the sample to a greater degree; detects more yeast and polymicrobial infections; improves the laboratory's ability to detect organisms that are difficult to grow; and is easier to use at the patient's bedside and to transport because the blood is drawn directly into the Isolator tube.

### Preparation of equipment
Check culture bottle expiration dates and replace outdated bottles.

### Essential steps
● Tell the patient you will collect a series of blood samples to check for bacterial infection. Explain the procedure *to ease anxiety and promote cooperation.* Explain that the procedure usually requires three separate blood samples drawn at specified times.
● Wash your hands.
● Cleanse the venipuncture site, first with a povidone-iodine sponge and then with an alcohol sponge, starting at the site and working outward in a circular motion. Wait 30 to 60 seconds for the iodine solution to dry and disinfect the area; then wipe with the alcohol *to prevent a possible allergic reaction to the povidone-iodine solution.*
● Put on a sterile glove or prepare the skin on the finger you will use to pal-

pate the vein, *to prevent cross-contamination.*

• Perform a venipuncture, drawing 10 ml of blood from an adult or 2 to 6 ml from a child.

• Wipe the diaphragm tops of the culture bottles with a povidone-iodine sponge, and change the needle on the syringe used to draw the blood.

• Inject 5 ml of blood into each 50-ml bottle or 2 ml into a 20-ml pediatric culture bottle. (Although bottle size varies depending on the hospital's protocol, sample dilution should always be 1:10.)

• Label the culture bottles with the patient's name and room number, the doctor's name, and the date and time of collection. Indicate the suspected diagnosis and the patient's temperature, and note on the laboratory slip any recent antibiotic therapy. Send the samples to the laboratory immediately.

### Special considerations
After disinfecting the venipuncture site, don't probe it with your finger unless you're wearing sterile gloves or have prepared your finger as thoroughly as the venipuncture site.

### Complications
The most common complication of venipuncture is formation of a hematoma. If a hematoma develops, apply warm soaks.

### Documentation
In your notes, record the date and time of blood sample collection, the amount of blood collected, the number of bottles used, the patient's temperature, and any adverse reactions to the procedure.

JOANNE PATZEK DACUNHA, RN

---

## PREPARING YOUR PATIENT FOR THE ORAL GLUCOSE TOLERANCE TEST

The oral glucose tolerance test (OGTT) is the most sensitive test for detecting borderline diabetes mellitus. Although you usually won't collect the five blood and five urine specimens required for this test, you'll be responsible for preparing the patient for the test and monitoring his physical condition during the test.

Begin by explaining the OGTT to the patient. Then, tell him he will receive a high-carbohydrate diet for 3 days and then be required to fast for 10 to 16 hours before the test. The patient must not smoke, drink coffee or alcohol, or exercise strenuously for 8 hours before or during the test. Tell him who will perform the venipunctures and when, and that he may feel slight discomfort from the needle punctures and the pressure of the tourniquet. Reassure him that collecting each blood sample usually takes less than 3 minutes. As ordered, withhold drugs that may affect test results. Remind the patient not to discard the first voided urine specimen on awaking in the morning.

During the test period, watch for signs and symptoms of hypoglycemia—weakness, restlessness, nervousness, hunger, and sweating—and report these to the doctor immediately. Encourage the patient to drink plenty of water to promote adequate urine excretion. Provide a bedpan, urinal, or specimen container when necessary.

---

# Reagent Strip Tests for Blood Glucose
*[Dextrostix®, reflectance photometer, reflectance colorimeter]*

*The rapid, easy-to-perform reagent strip test uses a drop of capillary blood obtained by fingerstick, heelstick, or earlobe puncture to detect or monitor elevated blood glucose levels in patients with diabetes; to screen for diabetes mellitus and neonatal hypoglycemia; and to help distinguish diabetic coma from nondiabetic coma. In this test, a patch of reagents implanted in a handheld plastic strip reacts with glucose in the blood sample, causing a color change. Comparing this color change with a standardized color chart pro-*

*vides a semiquantitative measurement of blood glucose levels; inserting the strip in a portable reflectance photometer or colorimeter provides quantitative measurements that are comparable in accuracy with other laboratory tests.*

*These tests can be performed in the hospital or the doctor's office or at home.*

## Equipment

Reagent strips □ reflectance photometer or colorimeter, if available □ sterile gauze sponges □ alcohol sponges □ disposable lancets □ small adhesive bandage □ watch or clock with a second hand.

## Essential steps

• Explain the procedure to the patient or to an infant's parents.
• Select the puncture site—usually the fingertip or earlobe for an adult and the heel or great toe for an infant.
• If necessary, dilate the capillaries by applying warm, moist compresses to the area for approximately 10 minutes.
• Wipe the puncture site with an alcohol sponge and dry it thoroughly with another gauze sponge.
• To draw a sample from the fingertip with a disposable lancet (smaller than 2 mm), make the puncture perpendicular to the lines of the patient's fingerprints. Pierce the skin sharply and quickly *to minimize pain.*
• Wipe away the first drop of blood *to avoid diluting the sample with tissue fluid.* For the same reason, avoid squeezing the puncture site.
• Now, touch a drop of blood to the reagent area on the strip; make sure you cover the entire reagent spot.
• After collecting the blood sample, briefly apply pressure to the puncture site *to prevent painful extravasation of blood into subcutaneous tissues.* Ask the adult patient to hold a gauze sponge firmly over the puncture site until bleeding stops.
• Leave blood on the strip for exactly 60 seconds, and then quickly wash it

off with a strong stream of water from a wash bottle. *Do not* hold the strip under a faucet. (Some reagent strips require only that the blood be wiped off, without washing.)
• Immediately after washing, compare the color change on the strip with the standardized color chart on the product container. If you're using a reflectance colorimeter (such as the Dextrometer™), insert the strip in the unit, reagent side down, immediately after washing. Close the lid and push the MEASURE button; the blood glucose level, in mg/dl, will appear on the digital display.
• If you're using a reflectance photometer (such as the Glucometer™), press the TIME button on the unit *before* applying blood to the reagent strip. When the buzzer sounds, apply blood to the strip. When the buzzer sounds again, after 60 seconds, wash the excess blood off the strip, blot it, and put it in the test chamber, reagent side down. Press the READ button to obtain the glucose level.
• After bleeding has stopped, you may apply a small adhesive bandage to the puncture site.

## Special considerations

Before using reagent strips, check the expiration date on the package and replace outdated strips. The reagent area of a fresh strip should match the color on the "0" block on the color chart. Protect the strips from light, heat, and moisture.

Avoid cold, cyanotic, or swollen puncture sites *to ensure an adequate blood sample.* If you can't obtain a capillary sample, perform venipuncture and place a large drop of venous blood on the reagent strip. If you want to test blood from a refrigerated sample, allow the blood to return to room temperature before testing.

If the patient will use the reagent system at home, teach him the proper use of the lancet, the reagent strips, and, if necessary, the portable reflectance photometer or colorimeter.

## Documentation

Record the reading from the reagent strip or from the reflectance photometer or colorimeter in the nurse's notes or on a special flowsheet, if available. Also record the time and date of the test.

JOANNE PATZEK DACUNHA, RN

# Arterial Puncture for Blood Gas Analysis

*Blood gas analysis of an arterial sample obtained by percutaneous puncture of the brachial, radial, or femoral artery or drawn from an arterial line, evaluates ventilation by measuring the partial pressures of oxygen ($PaO_2$) and carbon dioxide ($PaCO_2$), and blood pH. $PaO_2$ indicates the amount of oxygen the lungs deliver to the blood, $PaCO_2$ reflects the lungs' capacity to eliminate carbon dioxide, and pH shows the blood's acid-base balance. Arterial blood gas (ABG) samples can also be analyzed for oxygen content, oxygen saturation, and bicarbonate values.*

*Commonly ordered for patients with chronic obstructive pulmonary disease, pulmonary edema, acute respiratory distress syndrome, myocardial infarction, or pneumonia, arterial puncture is also performed during shock and after coronary artery bypass surgery, resuscitation from cardiac arrest, changes in respiratory therapy or status, and prolonged anesthesia.*

*Most ABG samples can be collected by a doctor or a specially trained nurse. Collection from the femoral artery, however, is usually performed by a doctor.*

## Equipment

10-ml glass syringe or plastic Luer-Lok syringe specially made for drawing blood gases □ 1-ml ampul of aqueous heparin (1:1,000) □ 1½" 20G needle □ 1" 22G needle □ alcohol sponge □ povidone-iodine sponge □ two 2" x 2" gauze pads □ rubber cap for syringe hub or rubber stopper for needle □ ice-filled plastic bag □ label □ adhesive bandage.

A commercial kit containing the necessary equipment for arterial puncture (except adhesive bandage and ice) is widely available. If your hospital doesn't have such a kit, obtain a sterile syringe specially made for drawing blood gases and use a clean emesis basin filled with ice, instead of the plastic bag, to transport the sample to the laboratory.

## Preparation of equipment

Prepare the collection equipment outside the patient's room. Wash your hands thoroughly; then open the ABG kit and remove the specimen label and the plastic bag. Record on the label the patient's name and room number, the date, and the doctor's name. Fill the plastic bag with ice and set it aside.

*To heparinize the syringe*, first attach the 20G needle to the syringe. Then, open the ampul of heparin. To prevent the sample from clotting, draw all the heparin into the syringe. Hold the syringe upright, and pull the plunger back slowly to about the 7-ml mark. Rotate the barrel while pulling the plunger back, *to allow the heparin to coat the inside surface of the syringe.* Then, slowly force the heparin toward the hub of the syringe, and expel all but about 0.1 ml of heparin.

*To heparinize the needle*, first replace the 20G needle with the 22G needle. Then, hold the syringe upright, tilt it slightly, and eject the remaining heparin. *Excess heparin in the syringe alters pH and $PaO_2$ results.*

## Essential steps

• Tell the patient you will collect an arterial blood sample, and explain the procedure *to help ease anxiety and promote cooperation.*

• Before attempting a radial puncture, perform the Allen's test *to assess the adequacy of the blood supply to the patient's hand (see How to Perform the*

## HOW TO PERFORM THE ALLEN'S TEST

Before drawing blood from a radial artery, perform the Allen's test. This test tells you whether or not the patient will receive enough blood through the ulnar artery to supply her hand if occlusion of the radial artery occurs.

First, have the patient rest her arm on the mattress or bedside stand, supporting her wrist with a rolled towel (see photograph #1). Ask her to clench her fist. Then, using your index and middle fingers, exert pressure on both the radial and ulnar arteries. Hold this position for a few seconds.

Without removing your fingers from the patient's arteries, ask the patient to unclench her fist and hold her hand in a relaxed position (see photograph #2). The palm will be blanched, because you've impaired the normal blood flow with your fingers.

Now, release the pressure on the patient's ulnar artery. If the hand becomes flushed, indicating the rush of oxygenated blood to the hand, you can safely proceed with the radial artery puncture (see photograph #3). If it doesn't, repeat the test on the other arm. If neither arm produces a positive result, use the brachial artery for arterial puncture.

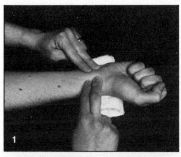

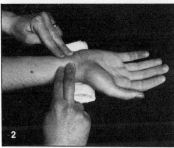

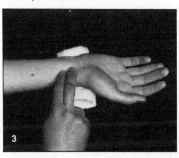

*Allen's Test,* illustrated above).
- Place a rolled towel under the patient's wrist, for support. Locate the artery, and palpate it for a strong pulse.
- Using a circular motion, cleanse the area, starting in the center of the site and spiraling outward, first with a povidone-iodine sponge, which is allowed to dry, and then with an alcohol sponge. Allow the skin to dry.
- Cleanse your index finger with a povidone-iodine sponge, and then an alcohol sponge; palpate the artery again, and choose the puncture site.
- Hold the needle, bevel facing upward, at a 45° angle over the radial artery. (When puncturing the brachial artery, hold the needle at a 60° angle.)

- Puncture the skin and the arterial wall in one motion, following the path of the artery.
- Watch for blood backflow in the syringe. Don't pull back on the plunger, *because arterial blood should enter the syringe automatically.* Fill the syringe to the 5-ml mark.
- After collecting the sample, press a gauze pad firmly over the puncture site until bleeding stops—at least 5 minutes. If the patient is receiving anticoagulant therapy, apply pressure for 10 to 15 minutes; if necessary, ask a co-worker to hold the gauze pad in place while you prepare the sample for transport to the laboratory. Don't ask the patient to hold the pad. If he fails

to apply sufficient pressure, *a large, painful hematoma may form, hindering future arterial punctures at this site.*

• Check the syringe for air bubbles, *because these can alter PaO₂ results.* If air bubbles appear, remove them by holding the syringe upright and slowly ejecting some of the blood onto a 2″ x 2″ gauze pad.

• Insert the needle into a rubber stopper, or remove the needle and place a rubber cap directly on the needle hub. *This prevents the sample from leaking and keeps air out of the syringe.*

• Put the labeled sample in the ice-filled plastic bag. Attach a properly completed laboratory request slip, and send the sample to the laboratory immediately.

• When bleeding stops, apply a small adhesive bandage to the site.

**Special considerations**
If the patient is receiving oxygen, make sure this therapy has been underway for at least 15 minutes before drawing arterial blood. Unless ordered, don't turn off the oxygen before drawing arterial blood samples, and indicate the amount and type of oxygen therapy on the laboratory slip. If the patient isn't receiving oxygen, indicate that he's breathing room air. If he has just received intermittent positive pressure breathing treatment, wait about 20 minutes before drawing the sample.

Do not use a plastic syringe of any kind if the sample will not be tested within an hour of collection, *because plastic syringes are permeable.*

If you use too much force when attempting to puncture the artery, you may cause the needle to touch the periosteum of the bone, causing the patient considerable pain; or, you may advance the needle through the opposite wall of the artery. If this happens, slowly pull the needle back slightly. If blood still fails to enter the syringe, withdraw the needle completely and start with a fresh, heparinized needle. Do not make more than two attempts to withdraw blood from the same site.

If arterial spasm occurs, blood will not flow into the syringe and you won't be able to collect the sample. If this happens, replace the needle with a smaller one and attempt the puncture again. *A smaller-bore needle is less likely to cause arterial spasm.*

If necessary, you may anesthetize the puncture site with 1% lidocaine. Consider such use of lidocaine carefully, because it delays the procedure, the patient may be allergic to the drug, or resulting vasoconstriction may prevent successful puncture.

When filling out an ABG request form, include the following information *to help the laboratory calibrate equipment and evaluate results correctly:* the patient's current temperature, latest hemoglobin determination, current respiratory rate, amount and type of oxygen therapy (if applicable), and FIO₂ and tidal volume (if the patient is on a ventilator).

**Documentation**
Record the time the sample was drawn, the site of puncture, and the type and amount of oxygen therapy.

JOANNE PATZEK DACUNHA, RN

# Aspiration of an Intravascular Line

*In addition to supplying fluids, electrolytes, or medication to many hospital patients, intravascular lines permit safe aspiration of blood samples for laboratory analysis without the discomfort and risks of repeated venous and arterial punctures. In addition, these lines permit repeated blood samples from patients with few usable veins.*

*Central venous lines, usually inserted in patients with poor peripheral circulation, can provide venous blood* samples only if the line isn't being used for hyperalimentation.

Heparin locks, inserted to keep venous access routes open for administering intermittent or emergency I.V. medication, allow frequent aspiration of venous blood samples. Arterial lines, often inserted in patients with respiratory distress or during weaning from a respirator, allow repeated aspiration of arterial samples (for blood gas analysis) and direct monitoring of arterial blood pressure while reducing the risk of embolus and thrombus formation.

## Equipment

For aspiration from a heparin lock: 3-ml syringe □ 10-ml syringe □ two 18G or 20G needles □ appropriate collection tubes □ two alcohol sponges □ 1-ml syringe with 1-ml ampul of aqueous heparin (1:1,000)

For aspiration from a central venous line: two 10-ml syringes □ appropriate collection tubes □ two sterile 4″ x 4″ gauze sponges □ sterile gloves □ sterile occlusive dressing □ adhesive tape □ two povidone-iodine sponges □ povidone-iodine ointment. (A commercial kit for redressing central venous lines is available.)

For aspiration from an arterial line: 5-ml syringe □ 10-ml glass syringe □ 1-ml ampul of aqueous heparin (1:1,000) □ 1″ 22G needle □ alcohol sponges □ rubber cap for syringe hub □ ice-filled plastic bag □ 2″ x 2″ gauze pad. (A commercial kit is available.)

## Essential steps

● Explain the procedure to the patient to ease anxiety and promote cooperation. Emphasize that this procedure is painless.

● Wash your hands thoroughly.

To aspirate from a heparin lock:
● Cleanse the injection port with an alcohol sponge and allow to dry. Then, connect an 18G or 20G needle to the 3-ml syringe and insert it into the injection port.

● Aspirate 2 ml of blood into the sy-ringe by pulling back gently on the plunger to clear it of heparin flush solution. Remove the syringe and needle and discard them.

● Cleanse the injection port with an alcohol sponge and allow to dry. Then, insert a 10-ml syringe with an 18G or 20G needle into the injection port.

● Aspirate the required amount of blood by pulling back gently on the plunger, and then remove the syringe and needle. Cleanse the injection port with an alcohol sponge and allow to dry.

● Insert the 1-ml heparin syringe, and inject this into the heparin lock to remove blood cells from the indwelling catheter and heparinize the catheter to prevent clotting. Then, remove the syringe.

● Remove the needle from the specimen syringe, and remove the stopper from the collection tube; inject the blood sample into the tube gently to prevent foaming and hemolysis.

● Replace the stopper on the collection tube; label it with the date, time, patient's name and room number, and doctor's name; and send it to the laboratory immediately.

To aspirate from a central venous line:
● Place the patient in slight Trendelenburg position.

● Maintaining sterility, open the prepackaged equipment, dressing, gloves, syringes, and ointment packages. Tear the tape, and discard any excess paper to clear the sterile field.

● Wash your hands thoroughly.

● Apply a small amount of povidone-iodine ointment to the prepared dressings or a sterile 4″ x 4″ gauze sponge, maintaining sterile technique.

● Remove and discard dressings around the insertion site, exposing the catheter hub and I.V. tubing connection.

● Put on sterile gloves.

● Every time you open the system to the air, ask the patient to bear down or hold his breath, to increase intrathoracic pressure and prevent air emboli.

● Loosen the I.V. tubing on the catheter, but do not remove it. Hold an empty, sterile 10-ml syringe in the palm of one hand, and secure the catheter hub between the thumb and index finger of your other hand. Then, remove the tubing from the catheter, and replace it immediately with the syringe. Turn the syringe gently until it's locked in place.

• Gently aspirate 5 to 10 ml of blood.

• Loosen the syringe slightly; have ready the other empty, sterile 10-ml syringe in the palm of your hand. Disconnect and discard the filled syringe, and replace it with the empty syringe.

• Gently aspirate the required amount of blood from the line. If you're aspirating more than 10 ml of blood, use a larger syringe or several 10-ml syringes. *Don't refill a single syringe.*

• Remove the collection syringe from the catheter hub, and replace it immediately with the sterile I.V. tubing.

• Transfer blood to a collection tube, label it properly, and send it to the laboratory immediately.

• Using povidone-iodine sponges, thoroughly cleanse the insertion site from its center to beyond the suture line *to avoid recontaminating an already cleansed area.*

• Apply povidone-iodine ointment and a sterile dressing to the insertion site. Make sure the dressing covers the connection site of the catheter and tubing.

• Tape the venous line to the patient, and secure all connections *to prevent accidental breaks in the system.* Adjust the infusion rate, if necessary.

• Place the other sterile 4″ x 4″ gauze sponge on the site, and tape the dressing securely to the skin. Then, initial and date the new dressing.

*To aspirate from an arterial line:*
• Wash your hands thoroughly.

• Heparinize the glass syringe. Then, turn the stopcock handle toward the syringe port, and activate the fast-flush release of the continuous flush device *to flush the arterial line.*

• Unscrew the stopcock cap, and attach the unheparinized 5-ml syringe.

• Turn the stopcock handle back toward the continuous flush device *to initiate arterial blood flow.* Aspirate 5 ml of blood by pulling back gently on the plunger.

• Turn the stopcock handle toward the syringe port *to shut off arterial blood flow.* Then, remove and discard the syringe.

• Secure the heparinized 10-ml glass syringe to the syringe port. Make sure the syringe is free of air bubbles, *which could alter test results.*

• Turn the stopcock handle back toward the continuous flush device *to initiate arterial blood flow.* Arterial pressure automatically forces blood into the syringe without having to pull the plunger back. (This applies *only* to a glass syringe, not a plastic syringe.)

• Withdraw 3 to 5 ml of blood.

• Turn the stopcock handle straight up again and remove the syringe. Hold the barrel and plunger of the syringe securely *to avoid spilling the sample.* Place the rubber cap on the syringe, and place it in the ice-filled plastic bag. Label the bag properly, and send it to the laboratory immediately.

• Place a 2″ x 2″ gauze pad over the syringe port. Turn the stopcock handle toward the patient. Then, activate the fast-flush release of the continuous flush device *to allow I.V. solution to clear blood from the syringe port.*

• Replace the cap on the syringe port, and then turn the stopcock handle so it points straight up. Activate the fast-flush release again *to flush the arterial line completely.*

## Special considerations

Before aspirating samples, determine the amount of blood needed for laboratory testing. Select the appropriate blood collection tube beforehand.

Aspirate venous samples from a central line during tubing replacement or after changes in therapy. Whenever possible, schedule aspirations of required daily samples simultaneously with a timed sample *to avoid unnecessary reopening of the I.V. line and reduce the risk of contamination.*

## Complications

Existing I.V. lines are subject to clotting in the cannula, may propagate air emboli, and may result in fluid extravasation, hematoma, phlebitis, and infection.

## Documentation

In your notes, record the time, date, and site of sample collection; laboratory test to be performed; condition of the sample; and dressing changes.

SUSAN DONAHUE, RN, BSN

# URINE SPECIMENS

# Urine Specimen Collection

*[Random, clean-catch midstream, and indwelling catheter specimen collection]*

*The random urine specimen, usually collected as part of the physical examination or at various times during hospitalization, permits laboratory screening for urinary and systemic pathologies. The clean-catch midstream specimen, originally used only to confirm urinary tract infection, is now replacing random collection for many other purposes, because it provides a virtually uncontaminated specimen without inserting a catheter into the patient's bladder.*

*The indwelling catheter specimen— obtained by clamping the drainage tube and emptying the accumulated urine into a container, or by aspirating with a syringe inserted through a sampling port in the tube or through the rubber catheter—requires sterile technique to prevent catheter contamination and urinary tract infection. This method is contraindicated in patients who have recently undergone genitourinary surgery.*

## Equipment

*For random specimen:* bedpan or urinal with cover, if necessary □ graduated container □ specimen container with lid □ label □ laboratory request slip.

*For clean-catch midstream specimen:* basin □ soap and water □ towel □ sterile gloves □ three sterile 2″ x 2″ gauze pads □ povidone-iodine solution □ sterile specimen container with lid □ label □ bedpan or urinal, if necessary □ laboratory request slip. (Commercial clean-catch kits containing antiseptic towelettes, sterile specimen container with lid and label, and instructions for use in several languages are widely used.)

*For indwelling catheter specimen:* 10-ml syringe □ 21G or 22G 1½″ needle □ tube clamp □ sterile specimen cup with lid □ alcohol sponge □ label □ laboratory request slip.

## Essential steps

● Tell the patient you will collect a urine specimen for laboratory analysis. Explain the procedure to him and to members of his family *to promote cooperation and to prevent accidental disposal of specimens.*

*To collect a random specimen:*

● Provide privacy. Instruct the patient on bed rest to void into a clean bedpan or urinal, or ask the patient who is ambulatory to void into either one in the bathroom.

● Pour at least 120 ml into the specimen container, and cap the container securely. If the patient's urinary output must be measured and recorded, pour the remaining urine into the graduated container. Otherwise, discard the remaining urine. If you inadvertently spill urine on the outside of the container, clean and dry it *to prevent possible cross-contamination.*

● Label the container with the patient's name and room number and the date

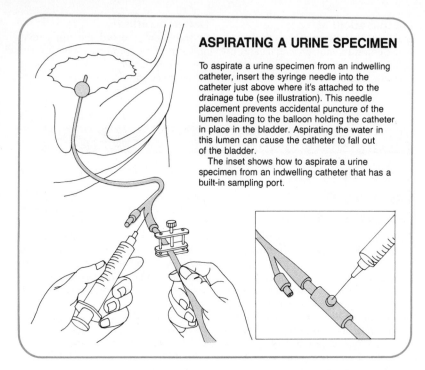

### ASPIRATING A URINE SPECIMEN

To aspirate a urine specimen from an indwelling catheter, insert the syringe needle into the catheter just above where it's attached to the drainage tube (see illustration). This needle placement prevents accidental puncture of the lumen leading to the balloon holding the catheter in place in the bladder. Aspirating the water in this lumen can cause the catheter to fall out of the bladder.

The inset shows how to aspirate a urine specimen from an indwelling catheter that has a built-in sampling port.

and time of collection, and send it to the laboratory immediately.

• Clean the graduated container and urinal or bedpan, and return these to their proper storage. Discard disposable items.

• Wash your hands thoroughly *to prevent cross-contamination.* Offer the patient a washcloth and soap and water to wash his hands.

*To collect a clean-catch midstream specimen:*

• Because this method is used to collect a virtually uncontaminated specimen, explain the procedure to the patient carefully. Provide illustrations to emphasize correct collection technique, if possible.

• Tell the patient first to cleanse the periurethral area (tip of the penis, or labial folds, vulva, and urethral meatus) with soap and water. Then, wipe the area three times, each time with a fresh 2″ x 2″ gauze pad soaked in povidone-iodine solution or, if you're using a commercial kit, with the wipes provided. Instruct the female patient to separate her labial folds with the thumb and forefinger; to wipe down one side with the first pad and discard it; to wipe the other side with the second pad and discard it; and finally, to wipe down the center over the urinary meatus with the third pad and discard it. Stress the importance of cleansing from front to back *to prevent contamination of the genital area with fecal matter.* For the uncircumcised male patient, emphasize the need to retract his foreskin *to effectively cleanse the meatus* and to keep it retracted during voiding.

• Tell the female patient to straddle the bedpan or toilet *to allow labial spreading.* She should continue to keep her labia separated with her fingers while voiding.

• Instruct the patient to begin voiding into the bedpan, urinal, or toilet, *because the urinary stream washes bacteria from the urethra and urinary meatus.* Then, tell the patient to void directly into the sterile container, collecting about 30 to 50 ml at the midstream portion of the voiding. The patient can then finish voiding into the bedpan, urinal, or toilet. Emphasize that the first and the last portions of the voiding are discarded. (If the patient's urinary output must be measured, pour the remaining urine into a graduated container. Be sure to include the amount in the specimen container when recording the amount voided.)

• Take the sterile container from the patient, and cap it securely. Avoid touching the inside of the container or the lid. If the container is soiled, clean it and wipe it dry.

• Wash your hands thoroughly *to prevent cross-contamination,* and tell the patient to do the same.

• Label the container with the patient's name and room number, type of specimen, collection time, and suspected diagnosis, if known. If a urine culture is to be performed, note any current antibiotic therapy on the laboratory request slip. Send the container to the laboratory immediately, or place it on ice *to prevent specimen deterioration and altered test results.*

*To collect an indwelling catheter specimen:*

• About 30 minutes before collecting the specimen, clamp the collection tube *to allow urine to accumulate.*

• If the drainage tube has a sampling port, wipe the port with an alcohol sponge. Uncap the needle on the syringe, and insert the needle into the sampling port at a 90° angle to the tubing. Aspirate the specimen into the syringe.

• If the drainage tube doesn't have a sampling port and the catheter is made of rubber, obtain the specimen from the catheter. *Other types of catheters will leak after you withdraw the needle.* To withdraw the specimen from a rubber catheter, wipe the catheter with an alcohol sponge just above the point where it connects to the drainage tube. Insert the needle into the rubber catheter at a 45° angle and withdraw the specimen. Never insert the needle into the shaft of the catheter, *because this may puncture the lumen leading to the catheter balloon.*

• Transfer the specimen to a sterile container, label the container, and send it to the laboratory immediately or place it on ice. If a urine culture is to be performed, be sure to list any antibiotic therapy on the laboratory request slip.

 Make sure you unclamp the drainage tube after collecting the specimen *to prevent urine backup that may cause bladder distention and infection.*

If the catheter is not made of rubber or has no sampling port, wipe the area where the catheter joins the drainage tube with an alcohol sponge. Disconnect the catheter, and allow urine to drain into the sterile specimen container. Avoid touching the catheter to the inside of the sterile container, and don't touch the catheter drainage tube to anything *to avoid contaminating it.* When you have the specimen, wipe both connection sites with an alcohol sponge and join them. Cap the specimen container, label it, and send it to the laboratory immediately or place it on ice.

### Documentation
Record the times of specimen collection and of transport to the laboratory. Note the appearance, odor, color, and any unusual characteristics of the specimen. If necessary, record the volume on the patient's intake and output chart.

JOANNE PATZEK DACUNHA, RN

# Timed Urine Specimens

*Because hormones, proteins, and electrolytes are excreted in small, variable amounts in urine, urine specimens for measuring these substances must often be collected over an extended time to yield quantities of diagnostic value. A 24-hour specimen is the most commonly used, because it provides an average excretion rate for substances eliminated during this period. Timed specimens may also be collected for shorter periods, such as 2 or 12 hours, depending on the specific information desired. A timed urine specimen may also be collected after administering a challenge dose of a chemical—inulin, for example—to detect various renal disorders.*

### Equipment
Large collection bottle with cap or stopper, or commercial plastic container □ preservative, if necessary □ bedpan or urinal, if patient does not have an indwelling catheter □ graduated container, if patient is on intake and output measurement □ ice-filled container, if a refrigerator isn't available □ label □ laboratory request slip □ four patient-care reminders. Check with the laboratory to see what preservatives may be needed in the urine specimen.

### Essential steps
• Explain the procedure to the patient and his family members *to enlist their cooperation and prevent accidental disposal of urine during the collection period.* Emphasize that loss of even *one* urine specimen during the collection time invalidates the collection and requires that the collection begin again.
• Place patient-care reminders over the patient's bed, in his bathroom, on the bedpan hopper in the utility room, and on the urinal or indwelling catheter collection bag. Include the patient's name and room number, the date(s), and the collection interval.
• Instruct the patient to save all urine during the collection period, to notify you after each voiding, and to avoid contaminating the urine with stool or toilet tissue. (If the patient is to continue the urine collection at home, provide necessary, written instructions for the appropriate method.) Explain any dietary or drug restrictions.

*For a 2-hour collection:*
• If possible, instruct the patient to drink two to four glasses (20 oz or 600 ml) of water about 30 minutes before collection begins. After 30 minutes, tell him to void. Discard this specimen, *so the patient starts the collection time with an empty bladder.*
• If ordered, administer a challenge dose of medication (such as glucose solution or ACTH), and record the time.
• If possible, offer the patient a glass of water at least every hour during the collection period *to stimulate urine production.* After each voiding, add the specimen to the collection bottle.
• Instruct the patient to void, if possible, 15 minutes before the end of the collection period, and add this specimen to the collection bottle.
• At the end of the collection period, send the appropriately labeled collection bottle to the laboratory immediately, along with a properly completed laboratory request slip.

*For 12- and 24-hour collections:*
• Ask the patient to void. Then, discard this urine *so he starts the collection time with an empty bladder.* Record the time.
• After pouring the first urine specimen into the collection bottle, add the required preservative. Then, refrigerate the bottle or keep it on ice until the next voiding.
• Collect all urine voided during the prescribed period. Just before the collection period ends, ask the patient to void again, if possible. Add this last specimen to the collection bottle, pack it in ice *to inhibit deterioration of the specimen,* and immediately send it to the laboratory. Include a properly completed laboratory request slip.

### Special considerations
Before beginning collection of a timed specimen, make sure the laboratory will be open when the collection period

ends *to help ensure fast, accurate test-ing.* If you accidentally discard a specimen during the collection period, restart the collection. Never store a specimen in a refrigerator containing food or medication *to avoid spreading contagion.*

If the patient has an indwelling catheter in place, put the collection bag in an ice-filled container at his bedside.

Accidentally discarding a specimen during a test period may result in an additional day of hospitalization, possibly causing the patient personal and financial hardship. Therefore, it's important to communicate the need to save all the patient's urine during the collection period to all persons involved in his care, as well as to family or other visitors.

**Documentation**
In the cardex and in your notes, record the date(s) and interval of collection and the disposition of the specimen.

JOANNE PATZEK DACUNHA, RN

# Reagent Tests for Urine Glucose and Ketones

*Reagent strip and tablet tests permit fast, accurate monitoring of urine glucose and ketone levels and provide reliable, rapid screening for diabetes. Urine ketone tests, which detect the by-products of fat metabolism, monitor fat metabolism, help diagnose carbohydrate deprivation and diabetic ketoacidosis, and help distinguish between diabetic and nondiabetic coma.*

*The copper reduction test (Clinitest) measures the concentration of reducing substances in the urine through the reactions of such substances with a tablet composed of sodium hydroxide, cupric sulfate, and other reagents. When this tablet is added to a test tube con-taining drops of water and urine, the heat generated by the reaction of sodium hydroxide with water causes a color change because of the reduction of cupric ions in the presence of glucose. Comparison of this test color with a standardized color chart gives the approximate level of urine glucose. Similarly, the Acetest tablet test produces a color reaction that allows an estimate of urine ketone levels by comparison to a standardized chart. Glucose oxidase tests (such as Clinistix, Diastix, Tes-Tape, and Chemstrip G strips) also produce color changes when patches of reagents implanted in hand-held plastic strips react with glucose in the patient's urine; urine ketone strip tests (such as Chemstrip K, Ketostix, and Keto-Diastix) are similar. All these test results are read by comparing color changes against a standardized reference chart.*

## Equipment
*For tablet tests:* specimen container □ 10-ml test tube □ medicine dropper □ Clinitest or Acetest tablets □ Clinitest or Acetest color chart.

*For strip tests:* specimen container □ glucose or ketone test strips □ reference color chart.

## Essential steps
● Explain the test to the patient, and, if he's a newly diagnosed diabetic, teach him to perform the test himself. Check his history for drugs that may interfere with test results.

*To perform the Clinitest tablet test:*
● Ask the patient to void, and then ask him to drink a glass of water, if possible. Collect a second-voided urine specimen 30 to 45 minutes later.
● Perform the 5-drop test: With the medicine dropper, transfer 5 drops of urine from the specimen container to the test tube. Rinse the dropper, and add 10 drops of water to the test tube.
● Add one Clinitest tablet to the tube. Don't touch the tablet with your fingers, *because it contains caustic soda, which can burn your skin.*

• Hold the test tube near the top during the reaction, *because the test solution will come to a boil.* Observe the color change that occurs during the reaction—the pass-through phase.
• Fifteen seconds after effervescence subsides, shake the tube gently. Observe the solution's color, and compare it with the Clinitest color chart. Record the result. *Ignore any changes that develop after 15 seconds.*
• If color changes rapidly in the 5-drop test, record the result as "over 2%" glucose. Or, perform the 2-drop test: Transfer 2 drops of urine from the specimen container to the test tube, and then add 10 drops of water and a Clinitest tablet. After the reaction, observe the color of the test solution, and compare it with the chart. Record the result. Rapid color change in the pass-through phase in the 2-drop test measures glycosuria up to 5%.

*To perform the Acetest tablet test:*
• Collect a second-voided specimen, as for the Clinitest tablet test.
• Place the Acetest tablet on a piece of white paper, and add 1 drop of urine to the tablet.
• After 30 seconds, compare the tablet's color (white, lavender, or purple) with the Acetest color chart. Record the result.

*To perform glucose oxidase strip tests:*
• Explain the test to the patient, and if he's a newly diagnosed diabetic, teach him to perform it himself. Check his drug history for drugs that may interfere with test results.
• Instruct the patient to void, ask him to drink a glass of water, if possible, and collect a second-voided specimen after 30 to 45 minutes.
• If you're using *Clinistix,* dip the reagent end of the strip in urine for 2 seconds. Remove excess urine by tapping the strip against the container's side, time the strip for *exactly 10 seconds,* and then compare its color with the color chart on the container. *Ignore color changes that occur after 10 seconds.* Record the result.

• If you're using a *Diastix* strip, dip the reagent end of the strip in the urine for 2 seconds. Tap off excess urine, time the strip for *exactly 30 seconds,* and then compare its color with the standardized color chart on the container. *Ignore color changes that occur after 30 seconds.* Record the result.
• If you're using a *Tes-Tape* strip, pull about 1½" (3.8 cm) of the reagent strip from the dispenser, and dip one end about ¼" (0.6 cm) into the specimen for 2 seconds. Tap off excess urine, wait *exactly 60 seconds,* and then compare the darkest part of the tape with the standardized color chart. If the test result exceeds 0.5%, wait an additional 60 seconds and make a final comparison. Record the result.

*To perform ketone strip tests:*
• Explain the procedure to the patient, and if he's a newly diagnosed diabetic, teach him to perform the test. Check his drug history. If he's receiving phenazopyridine or levodopa or has recently received sulfobromophthalein, use Acetest tablets instead, *because reagent strips will give inaccurate results.*
• Collect a second-voided midstream specimen.
• If you're using *Ketostix,* dip the reagent end of the strip into the specimen and remove it immediately. Wait *exactly 15 seconds,* and then compare the color of the strip with the standardized color chart on the container. *Ignore color changes that occur after 15 seconds.* Record the result.
• If you're using *Keto-Diastix,* dip the reagent end of the strip into the specimen and remove it immediately. Tap off excess urine, and hold the strip horizontally *to prevent mixing of chemicals between the two reagent squares.* Wait *exactly 15 seconds,* and then compare the color of the ketone part of the strip with the standardized color chart.[1] After 30 seconds, compare the color of the glucose part of the strip with the chart. Record the results.

**Special considerations**
Keep reagent strips in a cool, dry place

(below 86° F., or 30° C.), but don't refrigerate them. Keep their containers tightly closed. Don't use discolored or outdated strips.

Because Clinitest tablets contain caustic soda, keep their container tightly closed and in a dry place. If you must handle these tablets, keep your fingers dry to prevent the tablet from leaving a deposit, which could then be accidentally ingested or brought into contact with eyes, skin, mucous membranes, or clothing, *causing caustic burns.*

Instruct the patient not to contaminate the urine specimen with stool or toilet tissue. Test the urine specimen immediately after the patient voids.

### Documentation
In your notes, record color changes according to the information on the charts on the reagent containers, or use special flowcharts designed to record this information. If you're teaching a patient how to perform the test, keep a record of his progress.

JOANNE PATZEK DACUNHA, RN

# Urine Specific Gravity

*The kidneys maintain homeostasis of body fluids and electrolytes by varying urinary output and its concentration of dissolved salts. Urine specific gravity measures the concentration of urine solutes, which reflects renal capacity to concentrate urine. Capacity to concentrate urine is among the first functions to be lost because of renal tubular damage.*

*Urine specific gravity is determined by comparing the weight of a urine specimen with that of an equivalent volume of distilled water, which is 1.000. Because urine contains dissolved salts and other substances, it's heavier than 1.000. Urine specific grav-*

*ity ranges from 1.003 (very dilute) to 1.035 (highly concentrated); normal values range from 1.010 to 1.025. Specific gravity is measured with a calibrated hydrometer (or urinometer), an instrument designed to float in a cylinder of urine. The more concentrated the urine, the higher the hydrometer floats—and the higher the specific gravity. Although urine specific gravity is commonly measured in a random urine specimen, more accurate measurement is possible in a controlled specimen collected after fluids are withheld for 12 to 24 hours.*

### Equipment
Calibrated hydrometer □ cylinder for urine □ graduated specimen container.

### Essential steps
● Explain the procedure to the patient, and tell him when you will need the

EQUIPMENT

## USING A URINOMETER

The urinometer (a specially calibrated hydrometer) shown here floats in a cylinder, indicating the patient's urine specific gravity. Elevated specific gravity reflects an increased concentration of urine solutes. Specific gravity rises in conditions causing renal hypoperfusion and may indicate congestive heart failure, dehydration, hepatic disorders, or nephrosis. Low specific gravity reflects failure to reabsorb water and concentrate urine; it may indicate hypercalcemia, hypokalemia, alkalosis, acute renal failure, pyelonephritis, glomerulonephritis, or diabetes insipidus.

specimen. If you will be using a controlled specimen, explain why you're withholding fluids and for how long, *to ensure his cooperation.*

• Collect a random urine specimen. Allow it to come to room temperature (71.6° F., or 22° C.) before testing, *because this is the temperature at which most hydrometers are calibrated.*

• Fill the cylinder about three-fourths full of urine. Then, gently drop the hydrometer into the cylinder.

• When the hydrometer stops bobbing, read the specific gravity directly from the scale marked on the calibrated stem of the hydrometer. Make sure the instrument floats freely and doesn't touch the sides of the cylinder. Read the scale at the lowest point of the meniscus, *to ensure an accurate reading.*

• Discard the urine, and rinse the cylinder and hydrometer in cool water. *Warm water coagulates proteins in urine, causing them to stick to the instrument.*

• Wash your hands thoroughly *to prevent cross-contamination.*

### Special considerations

Test the hydrometer in distilled water at room temperature *to check its calibration* (1.000). If necessary, correct the hydrometer reading for temperature effects: add 0.001 to your observed reading for every 5.4° F. (3° C.) above the calibration temperature (71.6° F., or 22° C.); subtract 0.001 for every 5.4° F. below 71.6° F.

### Documentation

Record the volume, color, odor, and appearance of the collected urine specimen, as well as its specific gravity.

JOANNE PATZEK DACUNHA, RN

# Urine pH

*The pH of urine—its alkalinity or acidity—reflects renal capacity to maintain a normal hydrogen ion concentration in plasma and extracellular fluids. Normal hydrogen-ion concentration of urine varies from pH 4.6 to 8.0 but averages around 6.0. The simplest test procedure for pH consists of dipping a reagent strip (such as a Combistix) into a fresh specimen of the patient's urine and comparing the resultant color change with a standardized scale. An alkaline pH (above 7.0), resulting from a diet low in meat but high in vegetables, dairy products, and citrus fruits, causes turbidity and formation of phosphate, carbonate, and amorphous crystals. Alkaline urine may also result from urinary tract infection and metabolic or respiratory alkalosis.*

*An acid pH (below 7.0), resulting from a high-protein diet, also causes turbidity, with formation of oxalate, cystine, amorphous urate, and uric acid crystals. Acid urine may also result from renal tuberculosis, phenylketonuria, alkaptonuria, pyrexia, and all forms of acidosis. Measuring urine pH can also help monitor some medications, such as methenamine, that are active only at certain pH levels.*

### Equipment

Urine specimen container ▢ reagent strips ▢ color chart. (Reagent strip carries a pH indicator as part of a battery of indicators on the same strip.)

### Essential steps

• Wash your hands thoroughly.
• Provide the patient with a specimen container, and instruct him to collect a clean-catch midstream specimen (see "Urine Specimen Collection" in this chapter). Dip the reagent strip in the urine, remove it, and tap off the excess urine from the strip.
• Hold the strip horizontally, *to avoid mixing reagents from adjacent test areas on the strip.* Then, compare the color on the strip with the standardized color chart on the strip package. This comparison can be made up to 60 seconds after immersing the strip.

• Discard the urine specimen. If you're monitoring the patient's intake and output, measure the amount of urine discarded.
• Wash your hands thoroughly *to prevent cross-contamination.*

### Special considerations
Use only a *fresh* urine specimen, *because bacterial growth at room temperature changes the pH.* Avoid letting a drop of urine run off the pH reagent onto adjacent reagent spots on the strip, *because these other reagents will change the pH result.*

### Documentation
Record the results of the test, time of voiding, and the amount voided, if necessary.

JOANNE PATZEK DACUNHA, RN

---

# Straining Urine for Calculi

*Urinary calculi, or urinary stones, may develop anywhere in the urinary tract. They may be excreted with the urine or may become lodged in the urinary tract to cause hematuria, urinary re-* *tention, renal colic, and possibly hydronephrosis. Ranging from microscopic to several centimeters in size, calculi are formed when mineral salts—principally calcium oxalate or calcium phosphate—collect around a nucleus of bacterial cells, blood clots, or other particles. Other substances involved in calculus formation include uric acid, xanthine, and ammonia.*

*Renal calculi result from many causes, including hypercalcemia, which may occur with hyperparathyroidism, excessive dietary intake, prolonged immobility, abnormal urine pH levels, dehydration, hyperuricemia associated with gout, and some hereditary disorders. Most commonly, calculi form as a result of urinary stasis stemming from dehydration (which concentrates urine), benign prostatic hypertrophy, neurologic disorders, or urethral stricture.*

*Testing for calculi requires careful straining of* all *the patient's urine through a gauze pad or fine-mesh sieve and, at times, quantitative laboratory analysis of questionable specimens. Such testing usually continues until the patient passes them or until after surgery, as ordered.*

### Equipment
Fine-mesh sieve or gauze pad □ urinal

---

## HOW TO MAKE A STRAINER

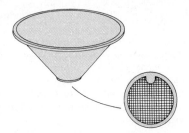

If a commercial strainer (as shown at left) isn't available, unfold a 4″ x 4″ gauze sponge and place it over the top of a graduated measuring device, securing it with a rubber band (as shown at right). To strain urine for stones, slowly pour it from a urinal or bedpan through the gauze into a container.

## TYPES OF CALCULI

**Calcium oxalate calculi** usually result from idiopathic hypercalciuria, a condition that reflects absorption of calcium from the bowel.

**Calcium phosphate calculi** usually result from primary hyperparathyroidism, which causes excessive resorption of calcium from bone.

**Cystine calculi** result from primary cystinuria, an inborn error of metabolism that prevents renal tubular reabsorption of cystine.

**Urate calculi** result from gout, dehydration (causes elevated uric acid levels), acidic urine (pH 5.0), or hepatic dysfunction.

**Magnesium ammonium phosphate calculi** result from the presence of urea-splitting organisms, such as *Proteus,* which raise ammonia concentration and make urine alkaline.

or bedpan □ graduated container □ patient-care reminders □ specimen container (for use if calculi are found).

### Essential steps

• Explain the procedure to the patient and his family, if possible, *to ensure cooperation and to stress the importance of straining all his urine.* Post a patient-care reminder stating STRAIN ALL URINE over his bed, in his bathroom, and on the collection container.
• Tell the patient to notify you after each voiding.
• Place the strainer over the mouth of the collection container, and pour the specimen through the strainer. If the patient has an indwelling catheter in place, strain all urine from the collection bag before discarding it.
• Examine the strainer for calculi. If you detect any calculi or if the filtrate looks questionable, notify the doctor, place the filtrate in a specimen container, and send it to the laboratory.
• Rinse the strainer carefully, and reuse it if intact. If it has become damaged through use discard it and replace it with a new strainer.

### Special considerations

Save any small or suspicious-looking residue left in the specimen container, because even tiny calculi can cause hematuria and pain. Calculi may also appear in various colors, which have diagnostic value.

### Documentation

Chart the times of specimen collection and transport to the laboratory, if necessary. Describe any filtrate passed, and note any pain or hematuria that occurred during voiding.

JOANNE PATZEK DaCUNHA, RN

# STOOL, SPUTUM, AND OTHER SPECIMENS

## Stool Collection

*Stool is collected to determine the presence of blood, ova and parasites, bile, fat, pathogens, or such substances as ingested drugs. Gross examination of stool characteristics, such as color, consistency, and odor, can reveal such conditions as gastrointestinal bleeding and steatorrhea. Stool specimens are collected randomly or for specific periods, such as 72 hours. Because stool specimens can't be obtained on demand, their proper collection necessitates careful instructions to the patient to ensure an uncontaminated specimen.*

### Equipment

Specimen container with lid □ two tongue blades □ paper towel or paper bag □ bedpan or portable commode □

patient-care reminders (for timed specimens) □ gloves.

## Essential steps

• Explain the procedure to the patient and to family members, if possible, *to ensure their cooperation and prevent inadvertent disposal of timed stool specimens.*

• When a timed specimen is required, place a patient-care reminder stating SAVE ALL STOOL over the patient's bed and in his bathroom.

• Tell the patient to notify you when he has the urge to defecate. Have him defecate into a clean, dry bedpan or commode. Instruct him not to contaminate the specimen with urine or toilet tissue, *because urine inhibits fecal bacterial growth and toilet tissue contains bismuth, which interferes with test results.*

• Put on clean gloves.

• Using a tongue blade, transfer the most representative stool specimen from the bedpan to the container, and cap the container. If the patient passes blood, mucus, or pus with the stool, be sure to include this with the specimen.

• Remove your gloves, and wash your hands thoroughly *to prevent cross-contamination.* Wrap the tongue blade in a paper towel and discard it.

• Label the specimen container with the patient's name and room number and the date and time of collection. Send it to the laboratory immediately, *because a fresh specimen provides the most accurate results.* Refrigerate the specimen if it can't be transported to the laboratory immediately. (*Do not* refrigerate stool collected to confirm presence of ova and parasites; such a specimen must be examined immediately or discarded.)

*To collect a timed specimen:*

• Collect the first defecation, and include this in the total specimen.

• Obtain the timed specimen the same way as a random specimen, except that all the stool should be transferred into the specimen container.

• As ordered, send each specimen to the laboratory immediately, or if permitted, refrigerate the specimens collected during the test period and send them when collection is complete.

• Make sure the patient is comfortable after the procedure and that he has the opportunity to thoroughly cleanse his hands and perianal area. Perineal care may be necessary for some patients.

## Special considerations

Never place a stool specimen in a refrigerator that contains food or medication, *to prevent contamination.* Notify your team leader, head nurse, or the doctor if the stool appears unusual.

## Documentation

Record the time of specimen collection and transport to the laboratory. Note stool color, odor, consistency, and any unusual characteristics; also note if the patient had difficulty passing the stool.

JOANNE PATZEK DACUNHA, RN

# Fecal Occult Blood Tests

*[Hematest or Hemoccult tests]*

*Fecal occult blood tests are valuable for determining the presence of occult blood (for detecting hidden gastrointestinal bleeding) and for distinguishing between true melena and melenalike stools. Certain medications, such as iron supplements and bismuth compounds, can cause stools resembling melena.*

*Two common occult blood screening tests are Hematest (an orthotolidin reagent tablet) and the Hemoccult slide (filter paper impregnated with guaiac). Both tests produce a blue reaction in a fecal smear if occult blood loss exceeds 5 ml/day.*

*Occult blood tests are particularly important for early detection of colorectal cancer, because 80% of patients with this disorder test positive. How-*

*ever, a single positive test result does not necessarily confirm gastrointestinal bleeding or indicate colorectal cancer. For a confirmed positive result, this test must be repeated at least three times while the patient is on a meatless, high-residue diet. But a confirmed positive test doesn't necessarily indicate colorectal cancer. It does indicate the need for further diagnostic studies, because gastrointestinal bleeding can result from many causes, such as ulcers, diverticula, or cancer. These tests are easily performed on collected specimens or smears from digital rectal examination.*

### Equipment
Hematest or Hemoccult test kit □ glass or porcelain plate □ tongue blade or other wooden applicator □ clean gloves.

### Essential steps
*To perform the Hematest reagent tablet test:*
- Collect a stool specimen. Put on clean gloves, and using a wooden applicator, smear a bit of the specimen on the filter paper supplied with the kit. Or, after digital rectal examination, wipe the examining finger on a square of the filter paper.
- Place the filter paper with the stool smear on a glass plate.
- Remove a reagent tablet from the bottle, and immediately replace the cap tightly. Then, place the tablet in the center of the stool smear on the filter paper.
- Add one drop of water to the tablet, and allow it to soak in for 5 to 10 seconds. Add a second drop, letting it run from the tablet onto the specimen and filter paper. If necessary, tap the plate gently to dislodge any water from the top of the tablet.
- After *2 minutes,* the filter paper will turn blue if the test is positive. *Do not read the color that appears on the tablet itself or develops on the filter paper after the 2-minute test period.*
- Note the results, and discard the filter paper.

- Remove and discard your gloves, and wash your hands thoroughly.
  *To perform the Hemoccult slide test:*
- Collect a stool specimen. Put on clean gloves, open the flap on the slide packet, and, using a wooden applicator, apply a thin smear of the stool specimen to the guaiac-impregnated filter paper exposed in the box marked A. Apply a second smear from another part of the specimen to box B, *because some parts of the specimen may not contain blood.*
- Open the flap at the rear of the slide package, and place 2 drops of Hemoccult developing solution on the paper over each smear. A blue reaction will appear in 30 to 60 seconds if the test is positive.
- Note the results, and discard the slide package.
- Remove and discard your gloves, and wash your hands thoroughly.
- If repeated testing is necessary after a positive screening test, explain the test to the patient. Instruct him to maintain a high-fiber diet and to refrain from eating red meat, poultry, fish, turnips, and horseradish for 48 to 72 hours before the test as well as throughout the collection period, *because these substances may alter test results.*
- As ordered, have the patient discontinue use of iron preparations, bromides, iodides, rauwolfia derivatives, indomethacin, colchicine, salicylates, phenylbutazone, oxyphenylbutazone, bismuth compounds, steroids, and ascorbic acid for 48 hours before the test and during it, *to ensure accurate test results and to avoid possible bleeding some of these compounds may cause.*

### Special considerations
Make sure stool specimens aren't contaminated with urine, and test them as soon as possible after collection. Also, test specimens from several different portions of the same specimen, because occult blood from the upper gastrointestinal tract isn't always evenly dispersed throughout the formed stool; likewise, blood from colorectal bleed-

ing may occur mostly on the outer stool surface.

Check the condition of the reagent tablets and note their expiration date. Use only fresh tablets and discard outdated ones. Protect Hematest tablets from moisture, heat, and light.

If the patient will use the Hemoccult slide packet at home, advise him to complete the label on the slide packet *before* collecting the specimen for the test.

**Documentation**
Record the time and date of the test, the result, and any unusual characteristics of the stool tested. Report positive results to the doctor.

JOANNE PATZEK DACUNHA, RN

# Sputum Specimens

*Sputum—a mucous secretion produced by the mucous membranes that line the bronchioles, bronchi, and trachea—helps protect the respiratory tract from infection. When expelled from the respiratory tract, sputum carries with it saliva, nasal and sinus secretions, dead cells, and normal oral bacteria. Sputum specimens are often cultured for identification of respiratory pathogens.*

*The usual method of sputum specimen collection is expectoration, which may require ultrasonic nebulization, hydration, or chest percussion and postural drainage. Less common methods include tracheal suctioning and, rarely, bronchoscopy. Tracheal suctioning is contraindicated in patients with esophageal varices and should be performed cautiously in patients with cardiac disease, because it may precipitate cardiac arrhythmias.*

**Equipment**
*For expectoration:* sterile specimen container with tight-fitting cap □ label

□ aerosol (10% sodium chloride [NaCl], propylene glycol, acetylcysteine, or sterile or distilled water) to induce coughing, as ordered □ tissues □ cup with mouthwash □ emesis basin.

*For tracheal suctioning:* size 16 or 18 French sterile suction catheter □ water-soluble lubricant □ sterile gloves □ sterile in-line specimen trap (Lukens trap) □ 3-ml syringe, if necessary □ normal saline solution □ portable suction machine, if wall unit is unavailable □ oxygen therapy equipment. (Commercial suction kits are available and contain all equipment except the suction machine and an in-line specimen container.)

**Essential steps**
● Tell the patient you will collect a sputum specimen, and explain the procedure *to ease anxiety and promote cooperation.* If possible, collect the specimen in the early morning, before breakfast, *to obtain an overnight accumulation of secretions.*

*To collect a sputum specimen by expectoration:*
● Instruct the patient to sit on a chair or at the edge of the bed. If he can't sit up, place him in high Fowler's position.
● Ask the patient to rinse his mouth with mouthwash, *to reduce specimen contamination by oral bacteria and food particles.* Then, tell him to cough deeply and expectorate directly into the specimen container. Collect at least 15 ml of sputum, if possible.
● Cap the container and, if necessary, clean its exterior *to prevent cross-contamination.* Label the container with the patient's name and room number, the doctor's name, date and time of collection, and initial diagnosis. Also include on the laboratory slip the current antibiotic therapy the patient is receiving and note whether sputum was induced, *because such specimens commonly appear watery and may resemble saliva.* Send the specimen to the laboratory immediately.

*To collect a sputum specimen by tra-*

## HOW TO ATTACH A SPECIMEN TRAP TO A SUCTION CATHETER

**1** Push the suction tubing onto the male adapter of the in-line trap.

**2** Put on a sterile glove; with the gloved hand, insert the suction catheter into the rubber tubing of the trap.

**3** After suctioning, disconnect the in-line trap from the suction tubing and catheter. To seal the container, connect the rubber tubing to the male adapter of the trap.

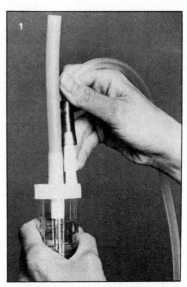

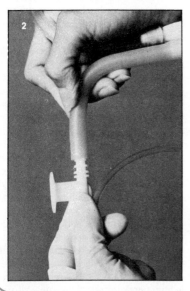

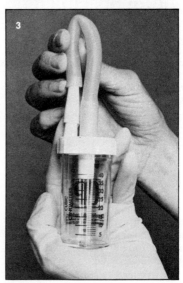

*cheal suctioning* (if the patient can't produce a coughed specimen):
• Check the suction machine to be sure it's functioning properly. Then, place the patient in high or semi-Fowler's position.
• Administer oxygen to the patient be-

fore beginning the procedure.
• Wash your hands thoroughly. Connect the suction tubing to the male adapter of the in-line trap. Then, put on a sterile glove, and with your gloved hand, attach the sterile suction catheter to the rubber tubing of the trap.

• Tell the patient to tilt his head back slightly. Then, lubricate the catheter with normal saline solution, and gently pass it through the patient's nostril, *without suction*.

• When the catheter reaches the larynx, the patient will cough. As he does, quickly advance the catheter into the trachea. Tell the patient to take several deep breaths through his mouth *to help ease insertion*.

• To obtain the specimen, apply suction for 5 to 10 seconds but never longer than 15 seconds, *because prolonged suctioning can cause hypoxia*. Then, discontinue the suction, gently remove the catheter, and administer oxygen.

• Detach the catheter from the in-line specimen trap, gather it up in your gloved hand, and pull the glove cuff inside out and down around the used catheter to enclose it for disposal.

• Detach the specimen trap from the tubing connected to the suction machine. Seal the trap container tightly by connecting the rubber tubing to the male adapter of the trap. Label the container as for an expectorated specimen, and send it to the laboratory immediately.

• Offer the patient a glass of water.

### Special considerations

If you cannot obtain a sputum specimen through tracheal suctioning, instill 2 to 3 ml of normal saline solution into the catheter when it is positioned in the trachea. To do this, disconnect the sterile catheter from the in-line specimen container, and instill the saline solution with a 3-ml syringe. Reattach the in-line specimen trap, and suction for 5 to 10 seconds.

Before sending the specimen to the laboratory, examine it to make sure it is actually sputum, not saliva, *because saliva will produce inaccurate test results*.

Because expectorated sputum is contaminated by normal mouth flora, tracheal suctioning provides a more reliable specimen for diagnosis.

Because the patient may cough vio-

lently during suctioning, wear a mask *to prevent contamination*. If the patient becomes hypoxic or cyanotic during suctioning, remove the catheter immediately and administer oxygen.

If the patient has asthma or chronic bronchitis, watch for aggravated bronchospasms with use of more than a 10% concentration of sodium chloride or acetylcysteine in an aerosol. If he has suspected tuberculosis, don't use more than 20% propylene glycol with water when inducing a sputum specimen, *because a higher concentration inhibits growth of the pathogen and causes erroneous test results*. If propylene glycol isn't available, use 10% to 20% acetylcysteine with water or sodium chloride.

### Complications

Patients with cardiac disease may develop cardiac arrhythmias during the procedure as a result of coughing, especially when the specimen is obtained by suctioning.

### Documentation

In your notes, record the method used to obtain the specimen, the time and date of collection, how the patient tolerated the procedure, and the disposition of the specimen.

JOANNE PATZEK DACUNHA, RN

# Swab Specimens
*[Throat, nasopharyngeal, wound, ear, eye, and rectal specimens]*

*Correct collection and handling of swab specimens helps the laboratory staff identify pathogens accurately, with a minimum of contamination from normal bacterial flora. Collection normally involves sampling inflamed tissues and exudates with sterile swabs of cotton or other absorbent material. Such swabs are immediately placed in a sterile tube containing a transport medium and, in the case of sampling for anaerobes, an inert gas.* These specimens are usually collected to identify pathogens and sometimes to identify asymptomatic carriers of certain easily transmitted disease organisms.

## Equipment

*For throat culture:* sterile swab □ tongue blade □ penlight □ sterile culture tube with transport medium (or commercial collection kit) □ label.

*For nasopharyngeal culture:* flexible cotton-tipped wire swab □ small open-ended Pyrex tube or nasal speculum (optional) □ penlight □ tongue blade □ sterile culture tube with transport medium □ label.

*For wound culture:* sterile gloves □ sterile forceps □ sterile swabs □ alcohol or povidone-iodine sponges □ sterile culture tube with transport medium (or commercial collection kit for aerobic culture) □ labels □ sterile swabs or sterile 10-ml syringe with 21G needle □ special culture tube containing carbon dioxide or nitrogen (for anaerobic culture) □ rubber stopper for needle (optional) □ necessary dressings to redress the wound.

*For ear culture:* clean gloves □ sterile swabs □ sterile culture tube with transport medium □ sterile normal saline solution □ two 2″ x 2″ gauze pads □ label □ 10-ml syringe and 22G 1″ needle (for tympanocentesis).

*For eye culture:* sterile gloves □ sterile swabs □ sterile wire culture loop (for corneal scraping) □ sterile culture tube with transport medium □ sterile normal saline solution □ two 2″ x 2″ gauze pads □ label.

*For rectal culture:* clean gloves □ sterile swab □ sterile culture tube with transport medium □ label.

## Essential steps

• Explain the procedures to the patient *to ease anxiety and ensure his cooperation.*

*To collect a specimen for throat culture:*

• Tell the patient he may gag during the swabbing but that the procedure takes less than a minute.

• Instruct him to sit erect at the edge of the bed or on a chair, facing you. Wash your hands.

• Ask the patient to tilt his head back. Depress his tongue with the tongue blade, and illuminate his throat with the penlight *to check for inflamed areas.*

• If the patient starts to gag, withdraw the tongue blade and tell him to breathe deeply. Once he's relaxed, reinsert the tongue blade but not as deeply as before.

• Swab the tonsillar areas from side to side, including any inflamed or purulent sites. Don't touch the tongue, cheeks, or teeth with the swab *to avoid contaminating it with oral bacteria.*

• Withdraw the swab and immediately place it in the culture tube. If you're using a commercial kit, crush the ampul of culture medium at the bottom of the tube, and push the swab into the medium *to keep the swab moist.*

• Wash your hands.

• Label the specimen with the patient's name and room number, the doctor's name, and the date, time, and site of collection. On the laboratory request form, indicate if any organism is strongly suspected, especially *Corynebacterium diphtheriae* (requires two swabs and special growth medium), *Bordetella pertussis* (requires a nasopharyngeal culture and special growth medium), and *Neisseria meningitidis* (requires enriched selective media).

• Send the specimen to the laboratory immediately *to prevent growth or deterioration of microbes.*

*To collect a specimen for nasopharyngeal culture:*

• Tell the patient he may gag or feel the urge to sneeze during the swabbing but that the procedure takes less than 1 minute.

• Instruct him to sit erect at the edge of the bed or on a chair, facing you. Wash your hands.

• Ask him to blow his nose *to clear his nasal passages.* Then, check his nos-

## ANAEROBIC SPECIMEN COLLECTOR

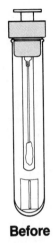

Because most anaerobes die when exposed to oxygen, they must be transported in tubes filled with carbon dioxide or nitrogen. The anaerobic specimen collector shown here includes a rubber-stoppered tube filled with carbon dioxide, a small inner tube, and a swab attached to a plastic plunger.

Before specimen collection, the small inner tube containing the swab is held in place with the rubber stopper (left). After collecting the specimen, quickly replace the swab in the inner tube and depress the plunger to separate the inner tube from the stopper (right), forcing it into the larger tube and exposing the specimen to a $CO_2$-rich environment.

**Before**

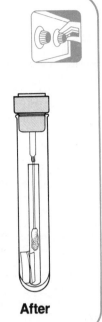

**After**

trils for patency with a penlight.
• Tell the patient first to occlude one nostril and then the other as he exhales. Note the more patent nostril. *You'll insert the swab through this nostril.*
• Ask the patient to cough *to bring organisms to the nasopharynx for a better specimen.*
• Open the package containing the sterile swab, and bend the wire in a curve.
• Ask the patient to tilt his head back, and gently pass the swab through the more patent nostril about 3″ to 4″ (8 to 10 cm) into the nasopharynx, keeping the swab near the septum and the floor of the nose. Rotate the swab quickly and remove it. Or, place the Pyrex tube in the patient's nostril, and carefully pass the swab through the tube into the nasopharynx. Rotate the swab for 5 seconds, and then withdraw it and remove the Pyrex tube.
• Or, using another method, depress the patient's tongue with a tongue blade, and pass the bent wire swab up behind the uvula. Rotate the swab and withdraw it.
• Remove the cap from the culture tube, insert the swab, and break off the contaminated end. Close the tube tightly, label it as for a throat culture, and send it to the laboratory immediately. If you're collecting the specimen to isolate a possible virus, check with the laboratory for the recommended collection technique.
   *To collect a specimen for wound culture:*
• Wash your hands, prepare a sterile field, and put on sterile gloves. With sterile forceps, remove the dressing to expose the wound. Dispose of the soiled dressings properly.
• Cleanse the area around the wound with an alcohol or povidone-iodine sponge *to reduce the risk of contaminating the specimen with skin bacteria.* Allow the area to dry.
• For an *aerobic* culture: Using a sterile cotton-tipped swab, collect as much exudate as possible, or insert the swab

deeply into the wound and gently rotate it. Remove the swab from the wound and immediately place it in the aerobic culture tube. Never collect exudate from the skin and then insert the same swab into the wound; *this could contaminate the wound with skin bacteria.*

• For an *anaerobic* culture: Insert the sterile cotton-tipped swab deeply into the wound, rotate it gently, remove it, and immediately place it in the anaerobic culture tube (see *Anaerobic Specimen Collector,* page 187). Or, insert a sterile 10-ml syringe, without a needle, into the wound, and aspirate 1 to 5 ml of exudate into the syringe. Attach the 21G needle to the syringe, and immediately inject the drainage into the anaerobic culture tube. If a rubber stopper is available, attach the needle to the syringe, gently push all the air out of the syringe by pressing on the plunger, stick the needle tip into the rubber stopper, and send the syringe of aspirate to the laboratory immediately.

*To collect a culture specimen from the ear:*
• Wash your hands, and put on clean gloves.
• Gently clean excess debris from the patient's ear with sterile normal saline solution and gauze pads.
• Insert the swab into the ear canal, and rotate it gently along the walls of the canal.
• Withdraw the swab, being careful not to touch other surfaces *to prevent contaminating the specimen.*
• Place the swab in the culture tube with transport medium.
• Remove the gloves and dispose of them properly. Wash your hands.
• Label the specimen as for throat culture, and send it to the laboratory immediately.

*To collect a culture specimen from the middle ear:*
• Cleanse the outer ear with sterile normal saline solution and gauze pads. After the doctor punctures the eardrum with a needle and aspirates fluid into the syringe, replace the cap on the needle, label the syringe, and send it

to the laboratory immediately.

*To collect a culture specimen from the eye:*
• Wash your hands, and put on sterile gloves.
• Gently clean excess debris from the outside of the eye with sterile normal saline solution and gauze pads, wiping from the inner to the outer canthus.
• Retract the lower eyelid *to expose the conjunctival sac.* Gently rub the sterile swab over the conjunctiva, being careful not to touch other surfaces *to avoid contaminating the specimen.* Hold the swab parallel to the eye, rather than pointed directly at it, *to prevent accidental injury caused by sudden movement.* (If a corneal scraping is required, this procedure is performed by a doctor using a wire culture loop.)
• Place the swab or wire loop immediately in the culture tube with transport medium.
• Remove the gloves and dispose of them properly. Wash your hands.
• Label the specimen as for throat culture, and send it to the laboratory immediately.

*To collect a specimen for rectal culture:*
• Wash your hands, and put on clean gloves.
• Clean the area around the patient's anus with soap and water.
• Insert the swab, moistened with sterile normal saline solution or sterile broth medium, through the anus and advance it about ⅜" (1 cm) for infants or 1½" (4 cm) for adults. While withdrawing the swab, gently rotate it against the walls of the lower rectum to sample a large area of the rectal mucosa.
• Place the swab in a culture tube with transport medium. Then, label the tube as for throat culture, and send it to the laboratory immediately.
• Remove your gloves and dispose of them properly. Wash your hands.

**Special considerations**
Note recent antibiotic therapy on the laboratory slip.

*For a nasopharyngeal specimen:* Because certain organisms, such as *C. diphtheriae* and *B. pertussis*, require special growth media, inform the laboratory if you suspect these are present.

*For a wound specimen:* Although you would normally cleanse the area around a wound to prevent contamination by normal skin flora, don't cleanse a perineal wound with alcohol, *to avoid irritating sensitive tissues.* Also, make sure antiseptic doesn't enter the wound. Because most anaerobes are destroyed by oxygen, place the specimen in the culture tube quickly. Ensure that no air enters the tube and that the double stoppers on the anaerobic collection tube are secure.

*For an ear specimen:* Insert the swab in the ear gently. Then, rotate it carefully *to avoid damaging the eardrum.* Restrain a child or uncooperative patient *to prevent ear trauma from sudden movement.* When sending a specimen in a syringe to the laboratory, secure its cap.

*For an eye specimen:* Don't use an antiseptic before culturing, *to avoid irritating the eye and inhibiting growth of organisms in culture.* Swab the eye carefully *to avoid corneal irritation or trauma.* If the patient is a child or an uncooperative adult, ask a co-worker to restrain the patient's head *to prevent eye trauma from sudden movement.*

## Documentation

Record the time, date, and site of specimen collection and recent or current antibiotic therapy. Note any unusual appearance and odor of the specimen.

SUSAN A. MURRAY, RN, BSN

# Intravenous Catheter Cultures

*Intravenous catheters breach or bypass intact skin and can introduce* bacterial flora directly into a blood vessel, causing pain, redness, swelling, and warmth at the entry site and loss of catheter function from clots or purulent drainage. Prolonged catheterization of the vein increases the risk of infection. Catheter cultures are appropriate when the catheter is a suspected cause of septicemia.

## Equipment

Sterile forceps ◻ sterile scissors ◻ sterile gloves ◻ 70% alcohol sponges ◻ sterile specimen container with lid ◻ labels.

## Essential steps

● Explain the procedure to the patient *to ease his anxiety and ensure his cooperation.*

● Remove the patient's dressings and dispose of them properly.

● Wash your hands thoroughly, put on sterile gloves, and if necessary, remove the sutures holding the catheter in place. Then, wipe the skin around the puncture site with 70% alcohol sponges *to cleanse the area of any blood or antimicrobial ointment.*

● Using sterile forceps, withdraw the catheter carefully. Be sure to direct the removed portion of the catheter upward, *to keep it away from the patient's skin.* Hold it directly over the specimen container, and with sterile scissors, cut about 2″ to 3″ (5 to 8 cm) from the distal end of the catheter and drop it in the container. If a longer catheter is used, cut a second segment of the same length, if ordered, from the proximal end (which was inserted just below the skin surface).

● Close the specimen container lid tightly. Label the container with the patient's name and room number, the doctor's name, and the date and time of collection. Note if more than one segment of the catheter is sent for culture, and identify the proximal and the distal specimens. Send the container to the laboratory immediately.

## Special considerations

Any purulent drainage from the puncture site that appears after catheter removal must be cultured and sent to the laboratory. If I.V. fluid is the suspected source of infection, send the fluid container and I.V. tubing to the laboratory. Restrict other bottles of the same stock number from use. Immediately notify the ICP and the infectious-disease doctor on call.

**Documentation**

Record the procedure and the appearance of the site. Note any drainage.

MARY CASTLE, RN, MPH

---

## MISCELLANEOUS TEST

# Bone Marrow Aspiration and Biopsy

*A specimen of bone marrow—the major site of blood cell formation—may be obtained by aspiration or needle biopsy to evaluate overall blood composition by studying blood elements and precursors as well as abnormal or malignant cells. Such aspiration removes cells through a needle inserted into the marrow cavity of the bone; a biopsy removes a small, solid core of marrow tissue through the needle. Both procedures are usually performed by a doctor, but some hospitals are authorizing specially trained chemotherapy nurses or nurse clinicians to perform the procedures, with the aid of an assistant.*

*Aspirates are valuable in diagnosing various disorders and cancers, such as oat cell carcinoma, leukemia, and such lymphomas as Hodgkin's disease. Biopsies are often performed simultaneously to determine the stage of the disease and to monitor response to treatment.*

**Equipment**

*For aspiration:* prepackaged bone marrow set, which includes povidone-iodine sponges, two sterile drapes (one fenestrated, one plain), ten 4" x 4" gauze sponges, ten 2" x 2" gauze pads, two 12-ml syringes, one 22G ⅝" needle, a scalpel, specimen containers, and bone marrow needles. You will also need 70% isopropyl alcohol □ 1% lidocaine (unopened bottle) □ adhesive tape □ sterile gloves □ glass slides and cover slips □ labels.

*For biopsy* (in addition to above equipment): Vim-Silverman, Jamshidi, Illinois, or Westerman-Jensen needle □ Zenker's acetic acid solution or formaldehyde.

**Essential steps**

● Tell the patient the doctor will collect a bone marrow specimen, and explain the procedure *to ease anxiety and ensure his cooperation.* Make sure the patient or a responsible family member understands the procedure and implications of this test and signs a consent form.

● Inform the patient that the procedure normally takes 5 to 10 minutes, that test results usually are available in 1 day, and that more than one marrow specimen may be required.

● Check the patient's history for hypersensitivity to the local anesthetic. Tell him which bone—sternum or anterior or posterior iliac crest—will be sampled. Inform him that he will receive a local anesthetic and will feel pressure from insertion of the biopsy or aspiration needle, as well as a brief, pulling sensation on removal of the marrow specimen.

● Provide a sedative, as ordered, before the test.

● Position the patient according to the selected puncture site (see *Common Sites of Bone Marrow Aspiration and Biopsy,* opposite).

# COMMON SITES OF BONE MARROW ASPIRATION AND BIOPSY

The **posterior superior iliac crest** is the preferred site, free of nearby vital organs or vessels. For aspiration of bone marrow from this site, the patient is placed in the lateral position with one leg flexed or in the prone position. The needle is inserted several centimeters lateral to the iliosacral junction, either entering the bone plane crest with the needle directed downward and toward the anterior inferior spine, or entering a few centimeters below the crest at a right angle to the bone's surface.

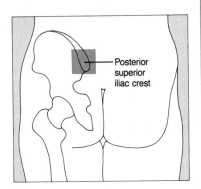

Posterior superior iliac crest

For aspiration from the **anterior iliac crest,** the patient is placed in the supine or side-lying position. The needle is inserted ¾" (2 cm) behind and below the anterior iliac spine and at a right angle to the bone's surface.

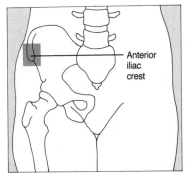

Anterior iliac crest

Aspiration from the **sternum** involves the greatest risk but is commonly used because this site is near the surface, the cortical bone is thin, and the marrow cavity contains numerous cells and relatively little fat or supporting bone. With the patient supine, a small pillow is placed beneath the shoulders to elevate the chest and lower the head. The needle guard is secured 3 to 4 mm from the tip of the needle to prevent accidental puncture of the heart or a major vessel. Then, it's inserted at the midline of the sternum at the second intercostal space. A preliminary chest X-ray is desirable to detect any anatomic abnormalities. The sternum is generally not used for biopsy because of its small size and proximity to vital organs.

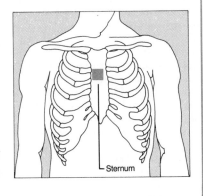

Sternum

• Using sterile technique, the puncture site is cleansed with povidone-iodine solution and allowed to dry; then the area is draped.

• To anesthetize the site, the doctor infiltrates it with 1% lidocaine, first injecting a small amount intradermally, and then using a larger 22G 1″

to 2″ needle to anesthetize the tissue down to the bone.

• When the needle tip reaches the bone, the doctor anesthetizes the periosteum by injecting a small amount of lidocaine in a circular area about ¾″ (2 cm) in diameter. The needle should be withdrawn from the periosteum after each injection.

• After allowing about 1 minute for the lidocaine to take effect, a scalpel may be used to make a small stab incision in the patient's skin to accommodate the bone marrow needle. *This technique avoids pushing skin into the bone marrow and also helps avoid unnecessary skin tearing to help reduce the risk of infection.*

*To perform aspiration:*

• The doctor inserts the bone marrow needle at the selected site and lodges it firmly in the bone cortex. If the patient feels sharp pain instead of pressure when the needle first touches bone, the needle was probably inserted outside the anesthetized area. If this happens, the needle should be lifted slightly and moved to the anesthetized area.

• The needle is advanced by applying an even, downward force with the heel of the hand or the palm, while twisting it back and forth slightly. A crackling sensation means the needle has entered the marrow cavity.

• The inner cannula is then removed, the syringe attached to the needle, the required specimen (usually about 1 ml) aspirated, and the needle withdrawn.

• Pressure should be applied to the site with a gauze pad for 5 minutes to control bleeding, while an assistant prepares the marrow slides. The area is then cleansed with alcohol to remove the povidone-iodine, the skin dried thoroughly with a 4″ x 4″ gauze sponge, and a sterile pressure dressing applied.

*To perform a biopsy:*

• The doctor inserts the biopsy needle into the periosteum and advances it steadily until the outer needle passes through the bone cortex into the marrow cavity.

• The biopsy needle is directed into the marrow cavity by alternately rotating the inner needle clockwise and counterclockwise. Then, a plug of tissue is removed, the needle assembly withdrawn, and the marrow specimen expelled into a properly labeled specimen bottle containing Zenker's acetic acid solution or formaldehyde.

• The area around the biopsy site is cleansed with alcohol to remove the povidone-iodine solution, a sterile 2″ x 2″ gauze pad firmly pressed against the incision to control bleeding, and a sterile pressure dressing applied.

## Special considerations

The force needed to advance a needle into the marrow cavity depends on the patient's bone density. If he has osteoporosis or myeloma or is elderly, only minimal effort is necessary. If he has osteopetrosis, a surgical procedure using a drill may be needed.

Faulty needle placement may yield too little aspirate. If the procedure fails to produce a specimen, the needle must be withdrawn from the bone (but not from the overlying soft tissue), the stylet replaced, and the needle reinserted into a second site within the anesthetized field. Bone marrow specimens should not be collected from irradiated areas, *because radiation may have altered or destroyed the marrow.*

## Complications

Bleeding and infection are potentially life-threatening complications that may result from aspiration or biopsy at any site. Complications of sternal needle puncture are uncommon but include puncture of the heart and major vessels, causing severe hemorrhage; puncture of the mediastinum, causing mediastinitis or pneumomediastinum; and puncture of the lung, causing pneumothorax.

## Documentation

Chart the time, date, location, and patient's tolerance of the procedure and the specimen obtained.

SUSAN MARKUS, RN, BSN

# Selected References

Arndt, Kenneth A. *Manual of Dermatologic Therapeutics*, 2nd ed. Boston: Little, Brown & Co., 1978.

Beeson, Paul B., et al. *Cecil Textbook of Medicine*, 15th ed. Philadelphia: W.B. Saunders Co., 1979.

Brundage, Dorothy. *Nursing Management of Renal Problems*, 2nd ed. St. Louis: C.V. Mosby Co., 1980.

Brunner, Lillian S., and Suddarth, Doris S. *Textbook of Medical-Surgical Nursing*, 4th ed. Philadelphia: J.B. Lippincott Co., 1980.

*Controlling Infection.* Nursing Photobook™ Series. Springhouse, Pa.: Intermed Communications, Inc., 1981.

Cosgriff, James H. *Atlas of Diagnostic and Therapeutic Procedures for Emergency Personnel.* Philadelphia: J.B. Lippincott Co., 1979.

*Diagnostics.* The Nurse's Reference Library™ Series. Springhouse, Pa.: Intermed Communications, Inc., 1981.

*Diseases.* The Nurse's Reference Library™ Series. Springhouse, Pa.: Intermed Communications, Inc., 1981.

DeGroot, Leslie J., ed. *Endocrinology.* New York: Grune & Stratton, Inc., 1979.

Duane, Thomas D., ed. *Clinical Ophthalmology.* New York: Harper & Row Publishers, Inc., 1978.

Duarte, Cristobal G. *Renal Function Tests.* Boston: Little, Brown & Co., 1980.

*Giving Medications.* Nursing Photobook™ Series. Springhouse, Pa.: Intermed Communications, Inc., 1980.

Harrison, J. Hartwell, et al. *Campbell's Urology*, 4th ed. Philadelphia: W.B. Saunders Co., 1978.

Henry, John B. *Todd-Sanford-Davidsohn Clinical Diagnosis and Management by Laboratory Methods*, 16th ed. Philadelphia: W.B. Saunders Co., 1979.

Hudak, Carolyn M., et al., eds. *Critical Care Nursing*, 3rd ed. Philadelphia: J.B. Lippincott Co., 1982.

*Implementing Urologic Procedures.* Nursing Photobook™ Series. Springhouse, Pa.: Intermed Communications, Inc., 1981.

King, Eunice M., et al. *Illustrated Manual of Nursing Techniques*, 2nd ed. Philadelphia: J.B. Lippincott Co., 1981.

Kunin, Calvin M. *Detection, Prevention and Management of Urinary Tract Infections*, 3rd ed. Philadelphia: Lea & Febiger, 1979.

Luckmann, Joan, and Sorenson, Karen C. *Medical-Surgical Nursing: A Psychophysiologic Approach*, 2nd ed. Philadelphia: W.B. Saunders Co., 1980.

*Managing I.V. Therapy.* Nursing Photobook™ Series. Springhouse, Pa.: Intermed Communications, Inc., 1980.

Marchiondo, Kathleen. "Collecting culture specimens," *Nursing79* 9:34, April 1979.

McGuckin, Maryanne. "Getting better urine specimens with the clean-catch midstream technique, *Nursing81* 11:72, January 1981.

Merrill, Vinita. *Atlas of Roentgenographic Positions and Standard Radiologic Procedures*, 4th ed. St. Louis: C.V. Mosby Co., 1975.

*Monitoring Fluid and Electrolytes Precisely.* Nursing Skillbook® Series. Springhouse, Pa.: Intermed Communications, Inc., 1978.

*Performing GI Procedures.* Nursing Photobook™ Series. Springhouse, Pa.: Intermed Communications, Inc., 1981.

*Providing Respiratory Care.* Nursing Photobook™ Series. Springhouse, Pa.: Intermed Communications, Inc., 1979.

Rambo, Beverly J., and Wood, Lucile A. *Nursing Skills for Clinical Practice*, 3rd ed. Philadelphia: W.B. Saunders Co., 1982.

Ravel, Richard. *Clinical Laboratory Medicine*, 3d ed. Chicago: Year Book Medical Publishers, 1978.

Smith, Donald R. *General Urology*, 9th ed. Los Altos, Ca.: Lange Medical Publications, 1978.

Spitler, L.E. "Delayed hypersensitivity skin testing," *Manual of Clinical Immunology*, 2nd ed. Edited by Noel R. Rose. Washington, D.C.: American Society for Microbiology, 1980.

Thompson, Ella M., and Rosdahl, Caroline B. *Textbook of Basic Nursing*, 3d ed. Philadelphia: J.B. Lippincott Co., 1981.

Tietz, Norbert W., ed. *Fundamentals of Clinical Chemistry*, 2nd ed. Philadelphia: W.B. Saunders Co., 1976.

Wallach, Jacques B. *Interpretation of Diagnostic Tests: A Handbook Synopsis of Laboratory Medicine*, 3d ed. Boston: Little, Brown & Co., 1978.

Williams, William J., et al. *Hematology*, 2nd ed. New York: McGraw-Hill Book Co., 1977.

# 5 Physical Treatments

# Physical Treatments

## Introduction

Used effectively for centuries, many physical treatments have become fundamental nursing procedures. The principles behind such treatments as application of heat and cold—and often the techniques for performing them—remain essentially unchanged. Because of this, these treatments may be considered routine and may be performed with less care and less understanding of their purposes than more involved and specialized procedures, such as measuring pulmonary artery pressures. Consequently, improper application of such procedures may increase patient discomfort and anxiety, aggravate the risk of infection, and delay healing time.

### Treatments effective

Most physical treatments have endured procedurally intact because of their effectiveness. Some stimulate or support normal physiologic processes. For example, application of heat enhances healing because the warmth causes vasodilation, thereby increasing blood supply to the affected area and making more nutrients available for tissue growth. Antiembolism stockings support blood vessels, increasing venous return and thereby reducing the risk of deep vein thrombosis. Drains supply wound secretions with an outlet to the surface from underlying tissue, thus assisting the healing process.

Other physical treatments prevent a pathologic response or reduce and inhibit a full-blown response. For ex-

ample, cold applications produce vasoconstriction and increase blood viscosity, thereby reducing inflammation, bleeding, and localized tissue edema. Medicated baths lessen pathologic response by relieving itching and reducing the irritation of various skin disorders. Wound irrigations performed with an antiseptic solution inhibit bacterial growth.

### Use of disposables increased

Improvements in physical treatments have resulted from equipment advances. Particularly, single-use or single-patient disposable products have heightened efficiency and safety. Hot-water bottles and ice collars, sterile gauze dressings, presaturated sterile swabs, and aquamatic K pads are all available for single use. The number and types of disposable items and the variety of prepackaged procedure setup trays available continue to expand. One of the latest such products is the single-patient hyperthermia-hypothermia blanket. This disposable, lightweight vinyl blanket connects to a conventional control module for use both under and over the patient.

A portable fiberglass tub makes it possible to bathe rather than sponge patients on bed rest. The full-sized tub stands as high as the bed, rolls easily on casters, and fills and empties at bedside through a hose that attaches to any faucet.

A vinyl pressure cuff improves on the well-known and effective antiembolism stockings. This portable system simulates the normal pumping action of leg muscles by inflating intermittently from the ankle to above the calf, assisting venous return and preventing blood backflow.

Silicon-foam dressing has improved the care of open, granulating wounds. Poured into the wound in liquid form, this new packing quickly molds into an absorbent rubber pad with the exact contour of the wound, but it permits air circulation and doesn't cause irritation. Easily cleaned with tap water and antiseptic solution, it's reusable until the wound's changing shape necessitates new packing.

Nonallergenic adhesive gauze covers the entire wound site with a single sheet of air- and exudate-permeable adhesive gauze. This type of dressing is particularly well suited for large or curved body areas and holds dressings securely without tape or straps. The gauze can be lifted off easily and painlessly for examination of the wound—even on skin that is sensitive or hairy—and then can be pressed back into place.

The new disposables save nursing time because they're easier to use than the equipment they replace. And nursing time saved means fewer delays in delivering patient care. Before the use of disposable razors, for instance, an entire hospital floor might compete for the use of a single steel razor. Now, supplies are centrally located and readily available when needed. Disposables also save time at the end of a procedure, because they eliminate the time previously spent cleaning, sterilizing, and returning equipment to storage.

Another major advantage of disposable products is that reducing multipatient use of equipment also reduces the spread of nosocomial infection. Disposables also enhance patient comfort, because the equipment is new for each use.

## Skin care emphasized

A growing awareness of the important role meticulous skin care plays in the healing process has resulted from ostomy care. This awareness has evolved from the difficulties experienced by early ostomates—difficulties ranging from simple questions of comfort and convenience to more complex problems of skin excoriation and severe tissue breakdown that delay or prevent stomal healing and full recovery.

As a result, enterostomal therapy is an accepted nursing specialty whose influence extends beyond ostomy care to embrace all types of wound management and general patient care. It includes not only a new body of skin-care knowledge but also a complete line of patient-care supplies. The full range of ostomy products, which is still expanding, has been adapted for all types of patient care. Such products include paper and silk tape and other nonallergenic items that minimize skin reactions, ostomy pouches to collect caustic secretions from any draining wound, karaya seals for fitting pouches to outsized or irregularly shaped wounds, and a variety of other skin protectants useful for preventative or therapeutic treatments.

JUDITH A. SCHILLING MCCANN, BSN

## WOUND-CLOSURE STRIPS

Wound-closure strips are an example of the trend toward improved methods of patient care. This nonallergenic, porous adhesive, illustrated at right, is an alternative to sutures for many types of minor surgery. It also can be used to support sutures or to provide reinforcement for a wound that still requires closure after suture removal.

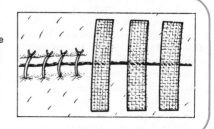

# TREATMENT WITH HEAT AND COLD

## Direct Heat Application

The direct application of heat raises tissue temperature and enhances the inflammatory process as it causes vasodilation and increases local circulation, promoting leukocytosis, suppuration, drainage, and healing. Heat also increases tissue metabolism, reduces pain caused by muscular spasm, and decreases congestion in deep visceral organs.

Directly applied heat may be moist or dry. Moist heat softens crusts and exudates, penetrates deeper than dry heat, doesn't dry the skin, produces less perspiration, and is usually more comfortable for the patient. Devices for applying moist heat include warm compresses for small body areas and warm packs for large areas. Dry heat may be delivered at a higher temperature and for a longer time with less risk of burns than moist heat. Devices for applying dry heat include the hot-water bag, electric heating pad, aquamatic K pad, and chemical hot pack.

Direct heat treatment is contraindicated when hemorrhage is possible and in patients with known or suspected malignancy, because it may encourage cell growth; for a sprained joint during the acute stage, because vasodilation would increase pain and swelling; and for conditions associated with acute inflammation, such as appendicitis. Direct heat should be applied cautiously in patients with impaired renal, cardiac, or respiratory function; arteriosclerosis and atherosclerosis; and impaired sensation, as well as in very young or elderly patients. It should be applied with extreme caution to heat-sensitive areas, such as scar tissue or stomas. Because of the danger of burns and possible systemic effects, such as increased respiratory rate and hypotension, direct heat should be applied only when the doctor specifies its use.

### Equipment
Patient thermometer □ towel □ adhesive tape or roller gauze.

*Hot-water bag:* hot tap water □ pitcher □ bath (utility) thermometer □ absorbent, protective cloth covering.

*Electric heating pad:* absorbent, protective cloth covering.

*Aquamatic K pad:* distilled water □ temperature-adjustment key □ absorbent, protective cloth covering.

*Chemical hot pack* (disposable): absorbent, protective cloth covering.

*Warm compress or pack:* basin of hot tap water or container of sterile water or normal saline or other solution, as ordered □ hot-water bag, aquamatic K pad, or chemical hot pack □ linen-saver pad.

The following items may be sterile or nonsterile, depending on the type of procedure required: compress material (flannel, 4″ x 4″ gauze sponges) or pack material (absorbent towels, ABD pads) □ cotton-tipped applicator □ petrolatum □ forceps □ bowl or basin □ bath (utility) thermometer □ waterproof covering □ towel □ dressing.

### Preparation of equipment
*Hot-water bag:* Fill the bag with hot tap water *to detect leaks and warm the bag,* and then empty it. Run hot tap water into a pitcher and measure the water temperature with the bath thermometer. Adjust the water temperature as ordered, usually to 115° to 125° F. (46.1° to 51.7° C.) for adults and 105° to 115° F. (40.6° to 46.1° C.) for children under age 2 and the elderly. Next, pour hot water into the bag, filling it one-half to two-thirds full. *Partially filling the bag keeps it lightweight and flexible to mold to the treatment area.* Squeeze

## PATIENT-TEACHING AID

### HOW TO RELIEVE MUSCLE SPASM

Dear Patient:

To relieve your muscle spasm, apply moist heat to the painful area. Moist heat is less drying to the skin, less likely to burn, doesn't cause sweating with excessive fluid and salt loss, and penetrates more deeply than dry heat. Apply heat for 20 to 30 minutes, as follows:
• Place a moist towel over the painful area.
• Cover the towel with a hot-water bottle.
• Remove the hot-water bottle and wet pack after 20 to 30 minutes. Never continue application for longer than 30 minutes, at which point therapeutic value decreases.

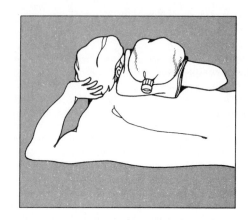

This patient-teaching aid may be reproduced by office copier for distribution to patients.
© 1982, Intermed Communications, Inc.

the bag until the water reaches the neck, *to expel any air that would make the bag inflexible and reduce heat conduction.* Fasten the top, and cover the bag with an absorbent, protective cloth *to provide insulation and absorb the patient's perspiration.* Secure the cover with tape or gauze.

*Electric heating pad:* Check the cord for frayed or damaged insulation. Then, plug in the pad, and adjust the control switch to the desired setting. Wrap the pad in a cloth covering, and secure the cover with tape or gauze.

*Aquamatic K pad:* Check the cord for safety, as above, and fill the control unit two-thirds full with distilled water. Do not use tap water, *because it leaves mineral deposits in the unit.* Check for leaks, and then tilt the unit in several directions *to clear the pad's tubing of air, which could interfere with even heat conduction.* Tighten the cap, and then loosen it a quarter turn *to allow heat expansion within the unit.* After making sure the hoses between the control unit

and the pad are free of tangles, place the unit on the bedside table, slightly above the patient *so gravity can assist water flow.* If the central supply department has not preset the temperature on the control unit, use the key provided to make this adjustment it (usual temperature is 105° F., or 40.6° C.). Then, place the pad in a cloth covering, and secure the cover with tape or gauze. Next, plug in the unit, turn it on, and allow the pad to warm for 2 minutes.

*Chemical hot pack:* Select the correct size pack. Then, follow the manufacturer's directions (strike, squeeze, or knead) *to activate the chemicals that produce the heat.* Place the pack in a cloth covering, and secure the cover with tape or gauze.

*Sterile warm compress or pack:* Warm the container of sterile water or solution by setting it in a sink or basin of hot water. Measure the temperature of the solution with a sterile bath thermometer. If a sterile thermometer is unavailable, pour some heated sterile solution into a clean container, check the temperature with a regular bath thermometer, and then discard the tested solution. Adjust the temperature of the sterile solution by adding hot or cold water to the sink or basin until the solution reaches 131° F. (55° C.) for adults or 105° F. (40.6° C.) for children and the elderly and for an eye compress. Pour the heated solution into a sterile bowl or basin. Then, using sterile technique, soak the compress or pack in the heated solution. If necessary, prepare a hot-water bag, aquamatic K pad, or chemical hot pack *to keep the compress or pack warm.*

*Nonsterile warm compress or pack:* Fill a bowl or basin with hot tap water or other solution, and measure the temperature of the fluid with a bath thermometer. Adjust the temperature as ordered, usually to 131° F. (55° C.) for adults or 105° F. (40.6° C.) for children and the elderly and for an eye compress. Then, soak the compress or pack in the hot liquid. If necessary, prepare a hot-water bag, aquamatic K pad, or chemical hot pack *to keep the compress or pack warm.*

### Essential steps
● Check the doctor's order, and assess the patient's condition.
● Explain the procedure to the patient, and tell him not to lean or lie directly on the heating device, *because this reduces air space and increases the risk of burns.* Warn the patient against adjusting the temperature of the heating device or adding hot water to a hot-water bag, even if he feels he can tolerate a higher temperature. Advise him to report pain or discomfort immediately and to remove the device himself if necessary.
● Provide privacy, and make sure the room is warm and free of drafts. Wash your hands thoroughly.
● Take the patient's temperature, pulse, and respiration *to serve as a baseline.* If heat treatment is being applied to raise the patient's body temperature, monitor temperature, pulse, and respiration throughout the application.
● Expose only the treatment area, *because vasodilation will make the patient chilly.*
● Before applying a hot-water bag, electric heating pad, or chemical hot pack, press the heating device against the inner aspect of your forearm *to test its temperature and heat distribution.* If it is not heating evenly, obtain a new device.
● Apply the device to the treatment area, and if necessary, secure it with tape or gauze. Begin timing the application.
● Assess skin condition frequently, and remove the device if you observe increased swelling or excessive redness, blistering, maceration, or pronounced pallor, or if the patient reports pain or discomfort. Refill a hot-water bag as necessary, *to maintain the correct temperature.*
● Remove the device after 20 to 30 minutes or as ordered.
● Dry the patient's skin with a towel, and redress the site, if necessary. Take the patient's temperature, pulse, and respiration *for comparison with baseline.* Position him comfortably in bed.
● If the treatment is to be repeated, store the equipment in the patient's room, out of his reach; otherwise, return the equipment to its proper place.

*To use a warm compress or pack:*
● Place a linen-saver pad beneath the treatment area.
● Spread petrolatum (sterile, if necessary) over the affected area. Avoid applying it directly to any areas of skin breakdown or to eye tissues. (You may use sterile cotton-tipped applicators for a sterile procedure.) *The petrolatum reduces maceration and the risk of burns by decreasing the rate of heat penetration.*
● Remove the warm compress or pack from the bowl or basin. (Use sterile forceps for a sterile procedure.)
● Wring excess solution from the compress or pack (using sterile forceps for a sterile procedure). *Excess moisture increases the risk of burns.*

● Apply the compress gently to the affected site (using forceps, if warranted). After a few seconds, lift the compress (with forceps, if needed) and check the skin for excessive redness, maceration, or blistering. When you're sure the compress isn't causing a burn, mold it firmly to the skin *to keep out air, which reduces the temperature and effectiveness of the compress.* Work quickly, *so the compress retains its heat.*

● Apply a waterproof covering (sterile, if warranted) to the compress. Secure the covering with tape or gauze *to prevent slippage.*

● Apply a hot-water bag, aquamatic K pad, or chemical hot pack *to maintain the correct temperature.* Begin timing the application.

● Check the patient's skin every 5 minutes for signs of tissue intolerance. Remove the device if the skin shows excessive redness, maceration, or blistering or if the patient feels pain or discomfort. Change the compress as necessary to maintain temperature.

● After 15 or 20 minutes or as ordered, remove the compress. (Use forceps, if warranted; then discard the compress into a waterproof wastebag.)

● Dry the patient's skin with a towel (sterile, if necessary). Note the condition of the skin, and redress the area, if necessary. Take the patient's temperature, pulse, and respiration *for comparison with baseline.* Then, make sure the patient is comfortable.

● Discard liquids and disposable equipment. Return used sterile equipment to the central supply department for sterilization. Clean remaining equipment, and if the treatment will be repeated, store it in the patient's room, out of the way. Otherwise, return it to storage.

### Special considerations

To maintain the patient's comfort during the procedure, make sure he is positioned in proper alignment. Keep the call button within the patient's easy reach, and make sure he is in a position

to remove the heating device if he experiences discomfort.

Unless ordered otherwise, discontinue heat treatments after 45 minutes, *because by this time maximum vasodilation has occurred; vasoconstriction then follows, reversing the effects of the heat treatment.* Also, allow at least 1 hour between treatments *to avoid vasoconstriction.*

Because the temperature of a chemical hot pack varies from 101° to 114° F. (38.3° to 45.6° C.), use a different heating device for treatments requiring a specific or higher temperature.

Don't use an electric heating device near oxygen, *because a spark from a frayed wire could cause explosion and fire. To prevent electric shock,* refrain from using an electric heating pad near liquid (including on a patient who is incontinent) or from handling any electric device with wet hands. When securing a heating device, avoid using safety pins, *because heated metal can cause burns or electric shock, and accidental puncture of an aquamatic K pad or chemical hot pack can cause fluid leakage, resulting in burns.* Avoid crushing or creasing the wires in the electric heating pad, *because this may cause portions of the pad to overheat, leading to burns or fire.*

If the patient is unconscious, anesthetized, irrational, neurologically impaired, or insensitive to heat for any reason, stay with him throughout the treatment, and check the site frequently to avoid such complications as edema, maceration, blotchy redness, and blisters.

When direct heat is ordered to decrease congestion within internal organs, the application must cover a large area *to increase blood volume at the skin's surface.* For relief of pelvic organ congestion, for example, apply heat over the patient's lower abdomen, hips, and thighs. For local relief, concentrate heat only over the specified area.

When applying moist heat to an open wound or to a lesion expected to open during treatment, use sterile technique.

When applying moist heat to both eyes, use separate sterile equipment for each eye *to prevent cross-contamination.*

You may alternately use sterile gloves instead of sterile forceps for application of sterile moist compresses or packs. As an alternate method of applying sterile moist compresses, use a bedside sterilizer to sterilize the compresses. Saturate the compress with tap water or other solution and wring it dry. Then, place it in the bedside sterilizer at 275° F. (135° C.) for 15 minutes. Remove the compress with sterile forceps, and wring out the excess. Then place the compress in a sterile bowl and measure its temperature with a sterile thermometer. Apply the compress as instructed above.

Commercial premoistened sterile compresses may be used as an alternative. Refer to the instructions on the package insert, and follow the same general observations and precautions mentioned above.

### Documentation
Record the time and date of heat application; the type, temperature or heat setting, duration, and site of application; the temperature, pulse, respiration, and skin condition before, during, and after treatment; signs of complications; and the patient's tolerance of and reaction to treatment.

KAREN DYER VANCE, RN, BSN

# Radiant Heat Application

*Radiant heat—dry heat directed to a body area—can improve circulation, decrease wound exudation, prevent maceration, and promote healing. Indicated for patients with stasis or slow-healing wounds, this treatment can be applied during dressing changes and wound debridement.*

*No specific conditions contraindicate radiant heat treatment. However, scar tissue and stomas must be covered during such treatment, and heat-insensitive patients—such as the very young or elderly and debilitated patients—must be monitored frequently to prevent burns. Infrared and ultraviolet treatments—excluded here—also involve radiant heat, but these treatments are usually applied by specially trained personnel.*

### Equipment
Patient thermometer.
*Heat lamp:* light bulb □ yardstick or tape measure.
*Heat cradle:* light bulb(s) □ sheet □ bath blanket(s).

The heat lamp and heat cradle deliver radiant heat. The heat lamp, called a gooseneck lamp because of its long flexible neck, holds a single light bulb of 25 to 100 watts and conducts heat to a localized treatment area. Bulb wattage and the distance between the lamp and the patient regulate the amount of heat delivered. The heat cradle, a metal frame with one or more sockets for 25-watt bulbs, radiates heat to larger areas, such as the legs or abdomen. The cradle fits over the treatment site, and the distance between site and cradle varies less than with a heat lamp. The cradle's construction permits little control over the distance between the patient and the heat source. The number of 25-watt bulbs used and the type and amount of covering tented over the cradle during treatment control the amount of heat delivered. Some cradles are equipped with thermostats that give temperature readings of the amount of heat projected.

### Preparation of equipment
Check the doctor's order, and insert the prescribed wattage light bulb(s) in the heat lamp or heat cradle. If you're using the heat lamp, place it at bedside, plug it into an outlet, and turn it on a few minutes before exposing the patient, *to warm the lamp and prevent needlessly*

*chilling the patient.* If you're using the heat cradle, don't prewarm it, *to prevent burns when positioning it over the patient.*

### Essential steps

• Assess the patient's condition, explain the procedure to him, and assist him to a comfortable position.

• Provide privacy, and make sure the room is warm and free of drafts. Wash your hands thoroughly.

• Remove any metal objects from the patient, such as jewelry and orthopedic braces, before starting the treatment. Ask him if he has any metal prostheses, pins, or plates within the treatment area. *Metal objects—whether internal or external—heat rapidly and may cause discomfort or burns.*

• Take the patient's temperature, pulse, and respiration *to serve as a baseline.*

• Expose only the treatment area *to reduce body heat loss and to avoid chilling the patient.*

• Make sure the patient's skin is clean and dry *to reduce the risk of burns.*

*To use a heat lamp:*

• Position the prewarmed lamp at the patient's side, not over him, so if it drops down, it doesn't fall on and burn him.

• Using a yardstick or cloth measuring tape as a guide, adjust the neck of the lamp so the light bulb is the correct distance from the patient's skin. To determine the correct distance, consider the wattage of the light bulb and the patient's physical condition, skin pigmentation, and ability to tolerate heat. In most cases, allow 14″ (35.6 cm) between the bulb and the patient's skin for a 25-watt bulb, 18″ (45.7 cm) for a 40-watt bulb, and 24″ to 30″ (61 to 76.2 cm) for a 60-watt or higher bulb.

• Continue the procedure as outlined below.

*To use a heat cradle:*

• Place the cradle on the bed, directly over or to the side of the treatment site. Plug in the cord, and turn on the device.

• Cover the cradle with a sheet *to prevent drafts and to concentrate the heat on the treatment site. To prevent a fire,* make sure the sheet doesn't touch the bulb(s).

• Continue the procedure as outlined below.

*To use either device:*

• Time the application.

• Check lamp position and the patient's skin every 5 minutes *to make sure the patient can tolerate the treatment.* If the patient can't tolerate the heat at the prescribed distance, discontinue the treatment and notify the doctor.

• For cradles equipped with thermostats, maintain the heat at 86° to 90° F. (30° to 32.2° C.) or as ordered.

• Turn off the heating device as ordered, usually after 10 to 15 minutes for the first treatment and after 20 to 30 minutes for subsequent treatments.

• Dry the patient's skin, redress the treatment area if necessary, and obtain temperature, pulse, and respiration *for comparison with baseline.* Make sure the patient is comfortable.

• If the treatment is to be repeated, store the equipment in the patient's room, out of his reach; otherwise, return it to storage.

### Special considerations

Avoid application of creams or ointments to the exposed area before the treatment, *because these may increase the risk of burns.*

Never enclose the heat lamp and exposed body part under sheets or blankets. *Doing so increases heat intensity and the risk of burns or fire.* The heat cradle can safely support covers only if the covers don't touch the light bulb(s).

*To prevent fire or explosion,* protect the hot light bulb from paper, cloth, liquids, sprays, and mists.

Caution the patient not to touch the heat lamp or heat cradle, *to prevent burns.* If the patient is very young, elderly, unconscious, anesthetized, neurologically impaired, or otherwise insensitive to heat, stay with him during the treatment, and watch for signs of heat intolerance: redness, pain, extreme chills, and changes in vital signs.

## Complications
Despite usual precautions, radiant heat treatment can cause burns in the patient with extremely sensitive skin.

## Documentation
For heat lamp treatment, record the time, date, and duration of treatment; light bulb wattage; distance of the lamp from the patient's skin; temperature, pulse, and respiration before and after treatment; appearance of the treatment site before and after; and the patient's tolerance for treatment. For heat cradle treatments, in addition to the above information, record the number of light bulbs and the number and type of cradle covers used.

KAREN DYER VANCE, RN, BSN

# Application of Cold

*The application of cold stimulates vasoconstriction; inhibits local circulation, suppuration, and tissue metabolism; relieves congestion; slows bacterial activity in infections; reduces body temperature; and acts as a temporary anesthetic. Because cold also relieves inflammation, prevents edema, and stops bleeding, it's an effective initial treatment after trauma—such as eye injuries, strains, sprains, bruises, and muscle spasms—and is the recommended first aid for burns. Cold does not reduce existing edema, because it inhibits reabsorption of excess fluid.*

*Cold may be applied in dry or moist forms. Moist application is more penetrating than dry, because moisture facilitates conduction. Devices for application of dry cold include the ice bag or collar, aquamatic K pad (which can produce cold or heat), and chemical cold packs and ice packs. Devices for application of moist cold include cold compresses for small body areas and cold packs for large areas.*

*Cold application should be used cautiously in patients with impaired circulation, because of the risk of ischemic tissue damage. Unless ordered, it should not be used in elderly, arthritic, or very young patients.*

## Equipment
Patient thermometer □ towel □ adhesive tape or roller gauze.
*Ice bag or collar:* tap water □ ice chips □ absorbent, protective cloth covering.
*Aquamatic K pad:* distilled water □ temperature-adjustment key □ absorbent, protective cloth covering.
*Cold compress or pack:* container of tap water □ basin of ice chips □ bath (utility) thermometer □ compress material (4″ x 4″ gauze sponges or washcloths) or pack material (towels or flannel) □ linen-saver pad □ waterproof covering.

Single-use packs are available for applications of dry cold. These lightweight plastic packs contain a chemical that, when activated, produces a controlled temperature of 50° to 80° F. (10° to 26.7° C.). Reusable, sealed cold packs, filled with an alcohol-based solution, are also available. These packs are stored frozen until use and, after exterior disinfection, may be refrozen for subsequent use.

## Preparation of equipment
*Ice bag or collar:* Select the correct size device, fill it with cold tap water, and check for leaks. Then, empty the device and fill it about halfway with crushed ice. *Using small pieces of ice keeps the device flexible for molding to the patient's body.* Squeeze the device to expel air that might reduce thermal conduction. Fasten the cap, and wipe any moisture from the outside of the device. Wrap the bag or collar in a cloth covering, and secure the cover with tape or gauze. *The protective cover prevents tissue trauma and absorbs condensation.*

# PATIENT-TEACHING AID

## HOW TO RELIEVE A SPRAIN

Dear Patient:

To relieve pain in the first 24 to 72 hours after a sprain, apply cold to the painful area for 20 to 30 minutes four times daily. Put crushed ice sufficient to cover the painful area in a pillowcase (illustrated at right) or other type of cloth, or in a plastic bag covered with a cloth. For later applications, you can place a tongue blade or ice pop stick in a water-filled paper cup, freeze the cup, and then peel the paper off the ice.

• If you're using ice that is not covered with cloth, place a cold cloth over the painful area to avoid frostbite and cold shock. *Never apply ice directly to the skin.*
• Rub the ice back and forth over cloth-covered skin. Note: Applying cold eases the pain of a joint that has begun to stiffen, but don't let the analgesic effect make you overconfident about using the joint.
• Discontinue applying cold after 24 to 72 hours, when heat, redness, and swelling have subsided or when cold no longer helps. Then begin applying heat.

*Aquamatic K pad:* Check the cord for frayed or damaged insulation. Then, fill the control unit two-thirds full with distilled water. Do not use tap water, *because it leaves mineral deposits in the unit.* Check for leaks, and then tilt the unit several times *to clear the pad's tubing of air, which could interfere with thermal conduction.* Tighten the cap. After ensuring that the hoses between the control unit and pad are free of tangles, place the unit on the bedside table, slightly above the patient *so gravity can assist water flow.* If the central supply department has not preset the temperature on the control unit, use the key provided to adjust it to the lowest temperature. Cover it with an absorbent, protective cloth covering, and secure the cover with tape or gauze. Plug the pad in and turn it on. Allow the pad to cool for 2 minutes before placing it on the patient.

*Chemical cold pack:* Select the cor-rect size pack, and follow the manufacturer's directions (strike, squeeze, or knead) *to activate the chemicals that produce the cold.* Wrap the pack in a cloth cover, and secure the cover with tape or gauze.

*Cold compress or pack:* Cool the tap water by placing the container of water in a basin of ice or by adding ice to the water. Using a bath thermometer for guidance, adjust the water temperature to 59° F. (15° C.) or as ordered. Immerse the compress material or pack material in the water.

### Essential steps
• Check the doctor's order, and assess the patient's condition.
• Explain the procedure to the patient, provide privacy, and make sure the room is warm and free of drafts. Wash your hands thoroughly.
• Take the patient's temperature, pulse, and respirations *to serve as a baseline.*

• Expose only the treatment area *to avoid chilling the patient.*

*To use an ice bag or collar, aquamatic K pad, or chemical cold pack:*
• Place the covered cold device on the treatment site and begin timing the application.
• Observe the site frequently for signs of tissue intolerance: blanching, mottling, graying, cyanosis, maceration, or blisters. Also, be alert for shivering and for patient complaints of burning or numbness. If any of these develop, discontinue treatment and notify the doctor.
• Refill or replace the cold device as necessary *to maintain correct temperature.* Change the protective cover when it becomes wet.
• Remove the device after the prescribed treatment period (usually 30 minutes).

*To use a cold compress or pack:*
• Place a linen-saver pad beneath the treatment area.
• Remove the compress or pack from the water, and wring it *to prevent dripping.* Apply it to the patient, and begin timing the application.
• Cover the compress or pack with a waterproof covering *to provide insulation and to keep the surrounding area dry.* Secure the covering with tape or gauze *to prevent slippage.*
• Check the application site frequently for signs of tissue intolerance. Also note patient complaints of burning or numbness. If such signs develop, discontinue treatment and notify the doctor.
• Change the compress or pack as necessary *to maintain correct temperature.* Remove it after the prescribed treatment period (usually 20 minutes).

*To conclude all cold applications:*
• Dry the patient's skin and redress the treatment site according to the doctor's orders. Then, position the patient comfortably, and take his temperature, pulse, and respiration *for comparison with baseline.*
• Dispose of liquids and soiled materials properly. If treatment is to be re-peated, clean and store the equipment in the patient's room, out of his reach; otherwise, return it to storage.

## Special considerations

Apply cold immediately after an injury *to prevent edema.* Although colder temperatures can be tolerated for a longer time when the treatment area is small, don't continue any application for longer than 1 hour *to prevent reflexive vasodilation.* Similarly, wait at least 1 hour between cold applications *to prevent vasodilation.*

When applying cold to an open wound or to a lesion that may open during treatment, use sterile technique. Also, maintain sterile technique during eye treatment, with separate sterile equipment for each eye when both are treated, *because the conjunctiva is highly susceptible to infection.*

Avoid securing cooling devices with pins, *because an accidental puncture can cause fluid leakage and burns.*

If the patient is unconscious, anesthetized, neurologically impaired, irrational, or otherwise insensitive to cold, stay with him throughout the treatment and check the application site frequently for complications. Warn the patient against placing ice directly on his skin, *because the extreme cold can cause burns.*

## Complications

Thrombi may result from hemoconcentration; pain, burning, or numbness, from intense cold.

## Documentation

Record the time, date, and duration of cold application; type of device used (ice bag or collar, aquamatic K pad, or chemical cold pack) and site of application; temperature or temperature setting; temperature, pulse, and respiration before and after application; skin appearance before, during, and after application; any signs of complications; and the patient's tolerance for treatment.

KAREN DYER VANCE, RN, BSN

# Hyperthermia/ Hypothermia Blanket

*Operated manually or automatically, this blanket-sized aquamatic K pad raises, lowers, or maintains body temperature through conductive heat or cold transfer between blanket and patient.*

*In manual operation, the nurse or doctor sets the temperature on the unit. The blanket reaches and maintains this temperature, regardless of the patient's temperature. If a different unit temperature setting is desired, adjustment is necessary. The nurse monitors the patient's body temperature, using a conventional thermometer. In automatic operation, the unit directly and continually monitors the patient's temperature by means of a thermistor probe (rectal, skin, or esophageal) and alternates heating and cooling cycles as necessary to achieve and maintain the desired body temperature. The thermistor probe may also be used in conjunction with manual operation but is not essential.*

*The blanket is most commonly used to reduce high fever when more conservative measures, such as baths, ice packs, and antipyretics, are unsuccessful. Its other uses include maintaining normal temperature during surgery or shock; inducing hypothermia during surgery to decrease metabolic activity and thereby reduce oxygen requirements; reducing intracranial pressure; controlling bleeding and intractable pain in patients with amputations, burns, or cancer; and providing warmth in severe hypothermia.*

*The blanket should be used cautiously in patients with impaired circulation because of the possibility of severe tissue damage, and in patients connected to other electrical equipment, such as EKG monitors, because of the risk of electric shock.*

## Equipment

Hyperthermia-hypothermia unit □ operation manual □ fluid for the control unit (distilled water or distilled water and 20% ethyl alcohol) □ thermistor probe (rectal, skin, or esophageal) □ one or two hyperthermia-hypothermia blankets □ one or two disposable blanket covers (or one or two sheets or bath blankets) □ lanolin or lanolin–cold cream mixture □ patient thermometer (for manual mode) □ adhesive tape □ sphygmomanometer □ towel □ optional: protective wraps for the patient's hands and feet.

Disposable hyperthermia-hypothermia blankets are available for single-patient use.

## Preparation of equipment

First read the operation manual. Inspect the unit and the blanket(s) for leaks and the plug and connecting wires for broken prongs and fraying. If you detect or suspect malfunction, don't use the equipment.

Review the doctor's order, and prepare one or two blankets by covering them with disposable covers (or use a sheet or a bath blanket when positioning the blanket on the patient). *The cover absorbs perspiration and condensation, which could cause tissue breakdown if left on the skin.* Connect the blanket(s) to the control unit, and set the controls for manual or automatic operation and for the desired blanket or body temperature. Make sure the machine is properly grounded. Turn on the machine and add liquid to the unit reservoir, if necessary, as fluid fills the blanket(s). Allow the blanket(s) to preheat or precool, *so the patient receives immediate thermal benefit.* Place the control unit at the foot of the bed.

## Essential steps

● Assess the patient's condition, and

explain the procedure to him. Provide privacy, and make sure the room is warm and free of drafts. Check hospital policy and, if necessary, make sure the patient or a responsible family member has signed a consent form.

• Wash your hands thoroughly. If the patient is not already wearing a hospital gown, ask him to put one on. Use a gown with cloth ties, not metal snaps or pins, *because the latter could cause heat or cold injury.*

• Take the patient's temperature, pulse, respiration, and blood pressure *to serve as a baseline,* and assess level of consciousness, pupil reaction, limb strength, and skin condition.

• Keeping the bottom bedsheet in place and the patient recumbent, roll the patient to one side and slide the blanket halfway under him, so its top edge aligns with his neck. Then, roll the patient back, and pull and flatten the blanket across the bed. Place a pillow under the patient's head. If the blanket has no ready-made cover, use a sheet or bath blanket as insulation between the patient and the blanket.

• In automatic operation, insert the thermistor probe in the patient's rectum and tape it in place *to prevent accidental dislodgement.* If rectal insertion is contraindicated, tuck a skin probe deep into the axilla, and secure it with tape. If the patient is comatose or anesthetized, insert an esophageal probe. Plug the other end of the probe into the correct jack on the control panel.

• Place a sheet or, if ordered, the second hyperthermia-hypothermia blanket over the patient. *This increases thermal benefit by trapping cooled or heated air.*

• Apply lanolin or lanolin–cold cream mixture to the patient's skin where it touches the blanket *to help protect the skin from heat or cold sensation.*

• Wrap the patient's hands and feet, if he wishes, *to minimize chilling and promote comfort.* Also make sure the patient's head doesn't lie directly on the blanket, *because the blanket's rigid surface may be uncomfortable and the*

*heat or cold may lead to tissue breakdown.*

• Monitor vital signs and perform a neurologic assessment every 5 minutes until the desired body temperature is reached; then every 15 minutes until temperature is stable or as ordered.

• Check intake, output, and specific gravity hourly or as ordered. Observe the patient regularly for color changes in skin, lips, and nail beds, and for edema, induration, inflammation, pain, or sensory impairment. If these occur, discontinue the procedure and notify the doctor.

• Reposition the patient every 30 minutes to 1 hour, unless contraindicated, *to prevent skin breakdown.* Keep the patient's skin, bedclothes, and blanket cover free of perspiration and condensation, and reapply cream to exposed body parts as needed.

• After turning off the machine, follow the manufacturer's directions. *Some units must remain plugged in for at least 30 minutes to allow the condenser fan to remove water vapor from the mechanism.* Continue to monitor the patient's temperature until it stabilizes, *because body temperature can fall as much as 5° F. (2.8° C.) after this procedure.*

• Remove all equipment from the bed. Dry the patient and make him comfortable. Supply a fresh hospital gown, if necessary. Cover the patient lightly.

• Continue to perform neurologic checks and monitor vital signs, intake, output, specific gravity, and general condition every 30 minutes until stable for 2 hours and then hourly or as ordered.

• Clean the thermistor probe by wiping it. *Washing or sterilizing it could damage the outer covering or the sensor wires.*

• Return the equipment to the central supply department for cleaning, servicing, and storage.

### Special considerations

If the patient's condition warrants caution, have the following emergency equipment readily available: suction machine and catheters; cutdown tray and I.V. equipment; oxygen, face mask, and airway. If oxygen is being used, place the hyperthermia-hypothermia control unit at least 3' (91 cm) from the patient and the oxygen.

If excessive shivering occurs during hypothermia, discontinue the procedure and notify the doctor immediately. *Shivering increases metabolism and results in elevated body temperature.*

Avoid using pins to secure catheters, tubes, or blanket covers *because an accidental puncture can result in fluid leakage and burns.*

With hyperthermia or hypothermia therapy, the patient may experience a secondary defense reaction (vasoconstriction or vasodilation, respectively) that causes the body temperature to rebound and thus defeats the treatment's purpose. Rebound may occur up to several days after treatment, but continuing careful monitoring of vital and neurologic signs helps detect it.

If the patient is in isolation, place the blanket, blanket cover, and probe in a plastic bag clearly marked with the type of isolation, *so the central supply department can give it special handling.* If the blanket is disposable, discard it using appropriate precautions.

### Complications
Using a hyperthermia-hypothermia blanket can cause sharp changes in vital signs, shivering, increased intracranial pressure, respiratory distress or arrest, cardiac arrest, oliguria, and anuria.

### Documentation
Record temperature, pulse, respiration, blood pressure, neurologic signs, intake, output, specific gravity, skin condition, and position changes. Also document the type of hyperthermia-hypothermia unit used; control settings (manual or automatic, and temperature settings); date, time, duration, and patient's tolerance of treatment; and any signs of complications.

KAREN DYER VANCE, RN, BSN

# Sponge Bath
*[Alcohol sponge bath, tepid sponge bath]*

The sponge bath—using tepid water, alcohol, or a mixture of the two—is used to reduce fever. It causes superficial blood vessels to dilate and release heat, thereby lowering body temperature. An alcohol sponge bath effects the fastest reduction in temperature, because alcohol evaporates faster than water and thus removes heat more rapidly from skin surfaces; however, it is also more drying. The tepid water sponge bath, with or without alcohol, may lower systemic temperature when routine fever treatments fail, particularly in infants and children, whose temperatures tend to rise very high, very quickly. This treatment is most commonly used in non-hospital settings, because febrile hospitalized patients usually receive antibiotics or antipyretics and, if needed, treatment with hypothermia blankets, which lower and maintain body temperature more effectively.

### Equipment
Basin of tepid water, approximately 80° to 93° F. (26° to 34° C.) ☐ isopropyl rubbing alcohol 70%, if prescribed ☐ bath (utility) thermometer ☐ washcloths ☐ linen-saver pad ☐ bath blanket ☐ patient thermometer ☐ hot-water bag and cover ☐ ice bag and cover ☐ towel ☐ clean pajamas.

### Preparation of equipment
Prepare a hot-water bag and an ice bag. Then, place the bath thermometer in a basin, and run water over it until the temperature reaches the high end of the tepid range, *because the water will cool during the bath.* Add alcohol, if prescribed, at room temperature in a 1:1 proportion. Immerse the washcloths in the tepid solution until saturated.

## Essential steps

- Check the doctor's order, and assess the patient's condition.
- Check the medication cardex for recent administration of an antipyretic, *because this can affect patient response to the bath.*
- Explain the procedure to the patient, provide privacy, and make sure the room is warm and free of drafts. Wash your hands thoroughly.
- Place a linen-saver pad under the patient *to catch any spills* and a bath blanket over him for privacy. Then, remove his pajamas. Also remove the top bed linen *to avoid wetting it.*
- Take the patient's temperature, pulse, and respiration *to serve as a baseline.*
- Place the hot-water bag with protective covering on the patient's feet *to reduce the sensation of chilliness.* Place the covered ice bag on his head *to prevent headache and nasal congestion that occur as the rest of the body cools.*
- Wring out each washcloth before sponging the patient, *so it doesn't drip and cause discomfort.*
- Place moist washcloths over the major superficial blood vessels in the axillae, groin, and popliteal areas *to accelerate cooling.* Change the cloths as they warm.
- Bathe each extremity separately for about 5 minutes; then sponge the chest and abdomen for 5 minutes. Turn the patient, and bathe the back and buttocks for 5 to 10 minutes. Keep the patient covered except for the body part you're sponging.
- Add warm water to the basin as necessary *to maintain the desired water temperature.*
- Check the patient's temperature, pulse, and respiration every 10 minutes. Notify the doctor if the patient's temperature doesn't fall within 30 minutes. End the bath when the patient's temperature is 1° to 2° F. above the desired level, *because his temperature will drift down naturally.* Continue to monitor temperature until it stabilizes.
- Observe the patient for chills, shivering, pallor, mottling, cyanosis of the lips or nail beds, and changes in vital sign—especially a rapid, weak, or irregular pulse—*because such signs may indicate an emergency.* If any of these signs occur, discontinue the bath, cover the patient lightly, and notify the doctor.
- If no adverse effects occur, bathe the patient for at least 30 minutes *to produce a temperature reduction.*
- Pat each area dry after sponging, but avoid rubbing with the towel, *because rubbing increases cell metabolism and produces heat.*
- After the bath, make sure the patient is dry and comfortable. Dress him in fresh pajamas, and cover him lightly.
- Dispose of liquids and soiled materials properly. If the treatment is to be repeated, clean and store the equipment in the patient's room, out of his reach; otherwise, return items to storage.
- Take temperature, pulse, and respiration 30 minutes after the bath *to determine the treatment's effectiveness.*

## Special considerations

If ordered, administer an antipyretic 15 to 20 minutes before the sponge bath *to achieve more rapid fever reduction.* If you're giving an alcohol sponge bath, observe the patient's skin for excessive dryness. Also, keep an emesis basin readily available, *because alcohol vapors may cause nausea and vomiting.*

Consider covering the patient's trunk with a wet towel for 15 minutes to speed cooling. Resaturate the towel as necessary.

Refrain from bathing the breasts of the postpartum patient *to prevent drying the nipples and causing painful fissures.*

Take rectal temperature, unless contraindicated, *for accuracy.* Axillary temperatures are unreliable *because the cool compresses applied to these areas alter the readings.* If you must take oral temperature, do so cautiously, *because chills may cause the patient to bite and shatter the thermometer.* If possible, use an electronic thermometer to take oral temperature, *because it gives a faster reading and isn't covered with glass.*

## Complications

Accelerated temperature reduction can provoke seizure activity.

## Documentation

Record the date, time, and duration of the bath; type and temperature of solution; temperature, pulse, and respiration before, during, and after; complications; and tolerance for treatment.

KAREN DYER VANCE, RN, BSN

# TREATMENT WITH SOAKS & BATHS

## Sitz Bath

### [Hip bath]

*A sitz bath is the immersion of the pelvic area in tepid or hot water. Used to relieve discomfort, especially after surgery or childbirth, the bath promotes wound healing by cleansing the perineum and anus, increasing circulation, and reducing inflammation. It also helps relax local muscles.*

*Performed correctly, the sitz bath requires frequent checks of water temperature to ensure therapeutic effects, frequent monitoring of the patient's pulse to prevent adverse reaction, and correct draping of the patient during the bath and prompt dressing after to prevent vasoconstriction.*

*The sitz bath is contraindicated in nonambulatory, debilitated patients to prevent further weakness, fainting, and cardiovascular stress.*

## Equipment

Sitz tub, portable sitz bath, or regular bathtub □ cloth bathmat □ rubber mat □ bath (utility) thermometer □ towels □ two bath blankets □ hospital gown □ optional: rubber ring, footstool, overbed table, I.V. pole (to hold irrigation bag), wheelchair, dressings.

A disposable sitz bath kit is available for single-patient use. It includes a plastic basin that fits over a commode and an irrigation bag with tubing and clamp.

## Preparation of equipment

To prepare for a sitz bath, clean and disinfect the sitz tub, portable sitz bath, or regular bathtub *to prevent the spread of infection.* Or, obtain a disposable sitz bath kit from the central supply department.

Position the cloth bathmat next to the bathtub, sitz tub, or commode. If you're using a tub, place the rubber mat on its surface *to prevent falls.* Place the rubber ring on the bottom of the tub *to serve as a seat for the patient,* and cover the ring with a towel, *for comfort. Keeping the patient elevated improves water flow over the wound site and avoids unnecessary pressure on tender tissues.*

If you're using a commercial kit, open the package and familiarize yourself with the equipment.

For a sitz tub, set the automatic temperature control at the prescribed level (usually 110° to 115° F. or 43.3° to 46.1° C. for a heat application and 94° to 98° F. or 34.4° to 36.7° C. for relaxation or wound cleansing and healing). Measure the temperature of the water with a bath thermometer to confirm the accuracy of the automatic control. Fill the tub one-third to one-half full of water, so the water will reach the seated patient's umbilicus.

If you're using a regular bathtub, fill it one-third to one-half full of water and measure its temperature with the bath thermometer. Run the water slightly warmer than desired, because it will cool as the patient prepares for the bath.

If you're using a commercial kit, measure water temperature with the bath thermometer, and fill the basin to the specified line. Place the basin under the commode seat. Clamp the irrigation tubing *to block water flow,* and fill the irrigation bag with water of the same temperature as that in the basin. *To create flow pressure,* hang the bag above the patient's head on a hook, towel rack, or I.V. pole.

### Essential steps

• Check the doctor's order, and assess the patient's condition.

• Explain the procedure to the patient. Wash your hands thoroughly.

• Have the patient void. Then, take his pulse *to serve as baseline in gauging response to treatment.*

• Assist the patient to the bath area, provide privacy, and make sure the bath area is warm and free of drafts. Help the patient undress, as needed.

• Remove and dispose of any soiled dressings. If a dressing adheres to a wound, allow it to soak off in the tub. Wash your hands thoroughly.

• Help the patient into the tub or onto the commode, as needed. Instruct him to use the safety rail for balance. Explain that initially the sensation in the wound area may be unpleasant *because of tenderness already present.* Assure him that this discomfort will soon be relieved by the warm water.

• For any apparatus except a regular bathtub, if the patient's feet do not reach the floor and the weight of his legs presses against the edge of the equipment, place a small stool under the patient's feet. *This decreases pressure on local blood vessels.* Also place a folded towel against the patient's lower back *to prevent discomfort and promote correct body alignment.*

• Drape the patient's shoulders and knees with bath blankets *to avoid chills that cause vasoconstriction.*

• If you're using the commercial kit, open the clamp on the irrigation tubing *to allow a continuous flow of warm water over the wound site.* Refill the bag with water of the correct temperature as needed, and encourage the patient to regulate the flow himself.

Place the patient's overbed table in front of him *to provide support and comfort.*

• Using the bath thermometer, check the water temperature frequently. If the water temperature drops significantly, you'll need to add warm water. For maximum safety, first help the patient stand up slowly *to prevent dizziness and loss of balance.* Then, with the patient holding the safety rail *for support,* run warm water into the device while checking water temperature with the bath thermometer until the water reaches the correct temperature. Next, help the patient sit down again to resume the bath.

• If necessary, stay with the patient during the bath. If you must leave, show him how to use the call button, and ensure his privacy.

• Check the patient's pulse, color, and general condition frequently. If the patient feels weak, faint, or nauseated or shows signs of cardiovascular distress, discontinue the bath and help the patient back to bed. Use the wheelchair to transport the patient back to his room if he's away from it. Notify the doctor.

• When the prescribed bath time has elapsed—usually 15 to 20 minutes—tell the patient to use the safety rail for balance and help him slowly to a standing position *to prevent dizziness and to allow him to regain his equilibrium.*

• If necessary, help the patient to dry. Redress the wound as needed, and assist the patient to dress and to return to bed or back to his room.

• Instruct the patient to lie in bed for 30 minutes *to allow his circulation to return to normal.* Continue to monitor pulse.

• Dispose of soiled materials properly. Empty, cleanse, and disinfect the sitz tub, bathtub, or portable sitz bath. Return the commercial kit to the patient's bedside for later use.

### Special considerations

Use a regular bathtub only if a special sitz tub, portable sitz bath, or commercial sitz bath kit is unavailable. *Because application of heat to the extremities causes vasodilation and draws blood away from the perineal area,* a regular bathtub is less effective for local treatment than a sitz device. Tell the patient never to touch an open wound, *because of the risk of infection.* Carefully monitor the patient's pulse throughout the bath, *because this sign directly reflects the patient's tolerance for the treatment.*

### Complications
Weakness or faintness can result from heat or the exertion of changing position. Irregular or accelerated pulse may indicate cardiovascular distress.

### Documentation
Record the date, time, and duration of the bath; wound condition before and after treatment, including color, odor, and amount of drainage; pulse before, during, and after the bath; any complications; and the patient's tolerance for treatment.

ALICE F. PRIETO, RN, BSN

# Therapeutic Baths
## [Balneotherapy]

*Therapeutic baths combine water with oatmeal, starch, oil, alkaline salts, or tar preparations to cleanse the skin; relieve inflammation and pruritus; soften and remove crusts, scales, and old medications; and soothe and relax the patient. Used primarily for their antipruritic and emollient action, these baths relieve pruritus by coating irritated skin with a soothing, protective film; they reduce inflammation by producing vasoconstriction in surface blood vessels.*

*The colloid bath—using instant oatmeal or oatmeal powder, cornstarch, or laundry starch—has a drying effect on eczematous lesions. The oil bath—using mineral or cottonseed oil or commercial bath oils—has an antipruritic and emollient effect that helps treat acute and subacute eczematous lesions and also soothes dry skin. The alkaline bath—using alkaline salts, such as sodium bicarbonate—has a cooling effect that helps relieve pruritus. The medicated tar bath leaves a film of tar on the skin that works with ultraviolet light to inhibit the rapid cell turnover characteristic of psoriasis.*

*The bedridden patient may benefit from a local soak using the therapeutic additive instead of a therapeutic tub bath.*

### Equipment
Bathtub ▢ cloth bathmat ▢ rubber mat ▢ bath (utility) thermometer ▢ therapeutic additive ▢ measuring device ▢ colander or sieve for oatmeal powder ▢ two washcloths ▢ two towels ▢ hospital gown or loose-fitting cotton pajamas ▢ lubricating cream or ointment, if ordered.

### Preparation of equipment
Assemble supplies and draw the bath before bringing the patient to the bath area, *to prevent chilling him.* Begin by cleaning and disinfecting the tub, *because the patient with skin breakdown is particularly vulnerable to infection.* Place the cloth bathmat next to the tub and the rubber mat on the bottom of the tub *to prevent falls, because the therapeutic additive may make the tub slippery.* Fill the tub with 6″ to 8″ (15.2 to 20.3 cm) of water no hotter than 95° to 100° F. (35° to 37.8° C.) *to prevent vasodilation, which could aggravate pruritus.*

Measure the correct amount of therapeutic additive, according to the doctor's order or package instructions. As the tub is filling, thoroughly mix the additive into the water. Add most substances directly to the water, but place oatmeal powder in a sieve or colander under the tub faucet *to help it dissolve.* Regulate the thickness of the oatmeal bath by adding more water or more oatmeal or oatmeal powder as needed. When giving a tar bath, wear a plastic apron or protective gown, *because tar preparations stain clothing.*

**Essential steps**
• Check the doctor's order, and assess the patient's condition.
• Explain the procedure to the patient, and have him void. Wash your hands thoroughly, and then escort the patient to the bath area. Close the door *to provide privacy and eliminate drafts.*
• Assist the patient to undress, and help him into the tub, if necessary. Advise him to use the safety rails to prevent falls.
• Tell him the bath may feel unpleasant at first, *because his skin is irritated,* but assure him that the medication will soon coat and soothe his skin.
• Ask the patient to stretch out in the tub and submerge his body up to the chin. If he's capable, give him a washcloth to apply the bath solution gently to his face and other body areas not immersed. *Note:* If the patient is taking a tar preparation bath, tell him not to get the bath solution in his eyes, *because tar is an eye irritant.*
• Warn the patient against scrubbing his skin, *to prevent further irritation.*
• Add warm water to the bath as needed *to maintain a comfortable temperature.*
• Allow the patient to soak for 15 to 30 minutes. If you must stay with him, pull the bath curtain; *this gives him some privacy and protects him from drafts.* If you must leave the room, show the patient how to use the call button, and ensure his privacy.
• After the bath, help the patient from the tub. Have him use the safety rails *to prevent falls.*
• Help the patient pat his skin dry with towels. *Don't rub the skin, because rubbing produces friction, which increases pruritus.*
• Apply lubricating cream or ointment, if ordered, *to increase hydration while the skin is moist and most permeable.*
• Provide a fresh hospital gown or loose-fitting cotton pajamas. Advise the patient to avoid wearing pajamas, underwear, or other clothing that isn't cotton and loose fitting. *Tight clothing and scratchy or synthetic materials can aggravate skin conditions by causing friction and increasing perspiration.*
• Escort the patient to his room, and make sure he's comfortable.
• Drain the bath water, clean and disinfect the tub, and dispose of soiled materials properly. *If you have given an oatmeal powder bath, rinse the tub immediately after draining it or the powder will cake, making later removal difficult.*

**Special considerations**
*Because pruritus seems worse at night,* give a therapeutic bath before bedtime, unless ordered otherwise, *to promote restful sleep. Because the patient with a skin disorder may be self-conscious,* maintain eye contact during conversation and avoid staring at his skin. Also, avoid nonverbal expressions and gestures that show revulsion. If the patient wishes, allow him to talk about his condition and how it affects his self-esteem.

Refrain from using soap during a therapeutic bath, *because its drying effect counteracts the bath emollient.*

*Because the patient with skin breakdown chills easily,* protect him from drafts. After the bath, avoid covering or dressing him too warmly, *because perspiration aggravates pruritus.* Instruct the patient not to scratch his skin, *to prevent excoriation and infection.*

If the patient is confined to bed, you can place the therapeutic additive in a basin of water (95° to 100° F., or 35° to 37.8° C.) and apply it with a washcloth, using light, gentle strokes.

**Documentation**
Record the date, time, and duration of the bath; water temperature; type and amount of additive; skin appearance before and after the bath; patient's tol-

erance for treatment; and effectiveness of the bath.

KAREN DYER VANCE, RN, BSN

# Soaks (Immersion)

*A soak is the immersion of a body part in warm water or a medicated solution. This treatment helps soften exudates, facilitate debridement, enhance suppuration, cleanse wounds or burns, apply medication to infected areas, and increase local blood supply and circulation.*

*Most soaks are applied with clean tap water and clean technique but require sterile solution and sterile equipment for treating wounds, burns, or other breaks in the skin.*

## Equipment
Basin, or arm or foot tub □ bath (utility) thermometer □ hot tap water or prescribed solution □ cup □ pitcher □ linen-saver pad □ overbed table □ footstool □ pillows □ towels, gauze sponges, and other dressing materials, if needed.

## Preparation of equipment
Clean and disinfect the basin or tub. Run hot tap water into a pitcher, or heat the prescribed solution, as applicable. Measure the water or solution temperature with a bath thermometer. If the temperature is not within the prescribed range (usually 105° to 110° F., or 40.6° to 43.3° C.), add hot or cold water or reheat or cool the solution, as applicable. If you're preparing the soak away from the patient's room, heat the liquid slightly above the correct temperature *to allow for cooling during transport.* If the solution for a medicated soak isn't premixed, prepare the dilution and heat it.

## Essential steps
● Check the doctor's order, and assess the patient's condition.

● Explain the procedure to the patient, and if necessary, check his history for previous allergic reaction to the medicated solution. Provide privacy, and wash your hands thoroughly.

● If the soak basin or tub will be placed in bed, make sure the bed is flat beneath it *to prevent spills.* For an arm soak, have the patient sit erect. For a leg or foot soak, tell him to lie down and bend the appropriate knee. For a foot soak in the sitting position, tell him to sit on the edge of the bed or transfer him to a chair.

● Place a linen-saver pad under the treatment area, and if necessary, cover the pad with a towel *to absorb spillage.*

● Expose the treatment area. Remove any dressing and dispose of it properly. If the dressing is encrusted and stuck to the wound, leave it in place and proceed with the soak. After a few minutes, remove the dressing.

● Position the soak basin under the treatment area on the bed, overbed table, footstool, or floor, as appropriate. Pour the heated liquid into the soak basin or tub. Then, gradually lower the arm or leg into the basin *to allow adjustment to the temperature change.* Make sure the soak solution covers the treatment area.

● Support other body parts with pillows or towels as needed *to prevent discomfort and muscle strain.* Make the patient comfortable, and ensure good body alignment.

● Check the temperature of the soak solution with the bath thermometer every 5 minutes. If the temperature drops below the prescribed range, remove some of the cooled solution with a cup. Then, lift the patient's arm or leg from the basin *to avoid burns,* and add hot water or solution to the basin. Mix the liquid thoroughly, and then check its temperature. If the temperature is within the prescribed range, lower the patient's arm or leg into the basin.

● Observe the patient for signs of tissue intolerance: extreme redness at the treatment site, excessive drainage, bleeding, or maceration. If such signs develop or the patient complains of pain, discontinue the treatment and notify the doctor.

• After 15 to 20 minutes or as ordered, lift the patient's arm or leg from the basin and remove the basin.

• Dry the arm or leg thoroughly with a towel. If the patient has a wound, dry the skin around it without touching the wound.

• While the skin is hydrated from the soak, use gauze sponges to remove loose scales or crusts.

• Observe the treatment area for general appearance, degree of swelling, debridement, suppuration, and healing. Redress the wound, if appropriate.

• Remove the towel and linen-saver pad, and make the patient comfortable in bed.

• Discard the soak solution, dispose of soiled materials properly, and clean and disinfect the basin. If the treatment is to be repeated, store the equipment in the patient's room, out of his reach; otherwise, return it to the central supply department.

**Special considerations**

To treat large areas, particularly burns, a soak may be administered in a whirlpool or Hubbard tank.

**Documentation**

Record the date, time, and duration of the soak; treatment area; solution and its temperature; skin and wound appearance before, during, and after treatment; and the patient's tolerance for treatment.

KAREN DYER VANCE, RN, BSN

# TREATMENT WITH SUPPORTIVE DEVICES

## Antiembolism Stockings

*Elastic antiembolism stockings help prevent deep vein thrombosis (DVT) and pulmonary embolism by compressing superficial leg veins and the soleus muscle. This compression increases venous return by forcing blood into the deep venous system rather than allowing it to pool in the legs and form clots.*

*Antiembolism stockings can provide equal pressure over the entire leg or a graded pressure that is greatest at the ankle and decreases over the length of the leg. Usually indicated for postoperative, bedridden, elderly, or other patients at risk for DVT, these stockings should not be used in patients with dermatoses or open skin lesions, gangrene, congestive heart failure, severe arteriosclerosis or other ischemic vascular disease, pulmonary or any massive edema, recent vein ligation, and vascular or skin graft.*

### Equipment

Tape measure □ antiembolism stockings in correct size and length □ talcum powder.

Various types of antiembolism stockings are available in knee, thigh, and waist lengths.

### Preparation of equipment

*Before applying a knee-length stocking,* measure the circumference of the patient's calf at its widest point and the leg length from the bottom of the heel to the back of the knee. *Before applying a thigh-length stocking,* measure the circumference of the calf and thigh at their widest points and the leg length from the bottom of the heel to the gluteal fold. *Before applying a waist-length stocking,* measure the circumference of the calf and thigh and the leg length

## OPERATING THE THROMBO-GARD™ PRESSURE CUFF

The Thrombo-Gard pressure cuff system is designed to reduce the incidence of deep vein thrombosis (DVT) in immobilized patients during surgery and throughout the postoperative period in patients with chronic venous disease and other patients at risk for DVT. This system consists of a pump with two connecting hoses and two cuffs. Wrapped from ankle to knee on each leg (shown at right), the cuffs imitate normal leg pumping action by sequentially inflating and deflating a series of air cells from the ankle proximally. This milking action propels blood toward the heart, preventing congestion in venous muscle sinuses and valve pockets and preventing blood backflow. To prevent irritation, the cuffs are foam-lined and adjustable.

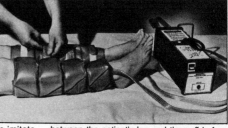

**To operate the pressure cuffs**
• Connect the tubing to the first cuff: attach the ankle connector to the two tubes on the cuff marked *ankle,* and attach the knee connector to the two tubes on the cuff marked *knee.* Now, connect the tubing to the second cuff the same way. Both cuffs must be connected before use. If you're applying one cuff to an amputee, place vinyl caps over the unused connectors to prevent a hissing noise.
• Place the first cuff on the patient's leg so its shortest cell is at his ankle, its padding is against his leg, and its connector is on the side of the leg. To avoid securing the cuff too tightly, place two fingers

between the patient's leg and the cuff before fastening it. Then, put on and fasten the second cuff. Repeat the procedure for the other leg.
• Plug the Thrombo-Gard into a grounded outlet and turn the unit on.
• Observe cuff filling for at least the first two cycles (approximately 3 or 4 minutes), *to ensure correct operation.* Only one cuff should fill at a time, in this order: first cell (closest to ankle), second cell, third cell, fourth cell (closest to knee). Then, all cells should deflate simultaneously. The second cuff then follows the same sequence. If the sequence isn't correct and you're sure the cuffs have been properly applied, remove the cuffs and have the system checked for malfunction. Also, remove them and check for malfunction if the pump indicator light turns on at any time.
• At least once every 8 hours, check the patient's skin color, temperature, sensation, and ability to move. If you notice any significant changes, remove the cuffs and notify the doctor immediately.

from the bottom of the heel to the waist along the side of the body.

Obtain the correct size stocking according to the manufacturer's specifications. If the patient's measurements are not within the range indicated by the manufacturer or if his legs are extremely deformed or edematous, ask the doctor if he wants to order custom-made stockings.

### Essential steps
• Check the doctor's order, and assess

the patient's condition. If his legs are cold or cyanotic, notify the doctor before proceeding.
• Explain the procedure to the patient, provide privacy, and wash your hands thoroughly.
• Have the patient lie down. Then, dust the ankle with talcum powder *to ease application.*

*To apply a knee-length stocking:*
• Insert your hand into the stocking from the top, and grab the heel pocket from the inside. Holding the heel, turn

the stocking inside out so the foot's inside the stocking leg. *This method allows easier application than gathering the entire stocking and working it up over the foot and ankle.*

• With the heel pocket down, hook the index and middle fingers of both your hands into the foot section. Facing the patient, ease the stocking over the toes, stretching it sideways as you move it up the foot. Ask the patient to point the toes, if possible, *to ease application.*

• Support the patient's ankle with one hand, and use the other hand to pull the heel pocket under the heel. Center

the heel in the pocket. *With the foot completely covered, the remainder of the stocking easily slides over it.*

• Gather the loose portion of the stocking up to the toes, and pull only this section over the heel. Gather the loose material at the ankle, and slide the rest of the stocking up over the heel with short pulls, alternating front and back.

• Insert your index and middle fingers into the gathered stocking at the ankle, and ease the fabric up the leg to the knee.

• Supporting the patient's ankle with one hand, use your other hand to stretch

EQUIPMENT

## APPLYING ANTIEMBOLISM STOCKINGS: THREE KEY STEPS

After covering the heel, gather the loose part of the stocking up to the toes (illustration #1) and carry only this portion over the heel. Then, gather the loose part of the stocking at the ankle and bring it over the heel with short, alternating front and back pulls (illustration #2). Next, using both hands, insert your index and middle fingers into the gathered part of the stocking at the ankle and carry the stocking to the top by rocking it slightly up and down (illustration #3).

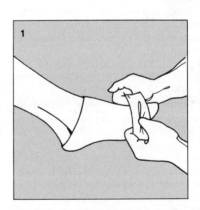

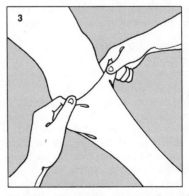

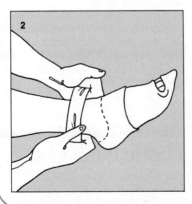

the stocking toward the knee, front and back, *to distribute the material evenly.* The stocking top should be 1″ or 2″ (2.5 or 5 cm) below the bottom of the patella.

• Gently snap the fabric around the ankle *to ensure a tight fit and eliminate gaps that could reduce pressure.*

• Adjust the foot section *for fabric smoothness and toe comfort* by tugging on the toe section. If the stocking has a toe window, make sure it's properly positioned.

• Repeat the procedure for the second stocking, if ordered.

*To apply a thigh-length stocking:*

• Follow the procedure for applying a knee-length stocking, taking care to distribute the fabric evenly below the knee before continuing the procedure.

• With the patient's leg straight, stretch the rest of the stocking over the knee.

• Flex the patient's knee, and pull the stocking over the thigh until the top rests 1″ to 3″ (2.5 to 7.6 cm) below the gluteal fold.

• Stretch the stocking from the top, front and back, *to distribute the fabric evenly over the thigh.*

• Gently snap the fabric behind the knee *to eliminate gaps that could reduce pressure.*

*To apply a waist-length stocking:*

• Follow the procedure for applying knee-length and thigh-length stockings, and extend the stocking top to the gluteal fold.

• Fit the patient with the adjustable belt that accompanies the stockings. Make sure that neither the waistband nor the fabric interferes with any incision, drainage tube, catheter, or other external device.

### Special considerations

Apply the stockings in the morning, if possible, *before swelling occurs.* If the patient has been ambulating, tell him to lie down and elevate his legs for 15 to 30 minutes before applying the stockings *to facilitate venous return.*

Don't allow the stockings to roll or turn down at the top or toe, *because*

*the excess pressure could cause venous strangulation.* Have the patient wear the stockings in bed and during ambulation, *to provide continuous prophylaxis against thrombosis.*

Check the patient's toes at least once every 4 hours and more often in the patient with faint pulse or edema. Note skin color and temperature, sensation, swelling, and ability to move. If complications occur, remove the stockings and notify the doctor immediately.

Be alert for an allergic reaction, *because some patients cannot tolerate the sizing in new stockings.* Laundering the stockings before applying them reduces the risk. Remove the stockings at least once daily *to bathe the skin and observe for irritation and breakdown.*

Using warm water and mild soap, wash the stockings at least every 3 days. Keep two pairs of stockings handy, *one for the patient to wear while the other pair is being laundered.*

Teach the patient how to apply the stockings correctly.

### Complications

Obstruction of arterial blood flow—characterized by cold, bluish toes; dusky toenail beds; decreased or absent pedal pulses; and leg pain or cramps—can result from application of antiembolism stockings. Less serious complications, such as allergic reaction and skin irritation, can also occur.

### Documentation

Record the date and time of stocking application and removal, stocking length and size, condition of leg before and after treatment, condition of toes during treatment, any complications, and tolerance for treatment.

KAREN DYER VANCE, RN, BSN

# Elastic Bandages

*Elastic bandages apply gentle, even pressure to a body part. By supporting lower-extremity blood vessels, these rolled bandages promote venous return and prevent pooling of blood in the legs. They're often used for postoperative or otherwise bedridden patients to prevent thrombophlebitis and pulmonary embolism, because such patients can't stimulate venous return by muscular activity.*

*Elastic bandages also minimize joint swelling after trauma to the musculoskeletal system. Used with a splint, they immobilize a fracture during healing. They can also provide hemostatic pressure and anchor dressings over a fresh wound or after surgical procedures, such as vein stripping.*

## Equipment
Appropriate width elastic bandage □ tape or pins □ gauze sponges or absorbent cotton.

Bandages usually come in 2″ to 6″ (5- to 15-cm) widths and 4′ and 6′ (1.2- and 1.8-m) lengths, with the 3″ (7.6-cm) width adaptable to most applications.

## Preparation of equipment
Select a bandage that completely wraps the affected body part without much excess. Generally, use a narrower bandage for wrapping the foot, lower leg, hand, or arm and a wider bandage for the thigh or trunk. The bandage should be clean and rolled before application.

## Essential steps
● Check the doctor's order, and examine the area to be wrapped for evidence of lesions or skin breakdown. If these conditions are present, consult the doctor before applying the elastic bandage.
● Explain the procedure to the patient, provide privacy, and wash your hands thoroughly. Place the patient in a comfortable position, with the body part to be bandaged in normal functioning position to promote circulation and prevent deformity and discomfort.
● Avoid applying a bandage to a dependent extremity. If you're wrapping an extremity, elevate it for 15 to 30 minutes before application *to facilitate venous return.*
● Apply the bandage so two skin surfaces do not remain in contact when wrapped. Place gauze or absorbent cotton as needed between skin surfaces, such as between toes and fingers or under breasts and arms, *to prevent skin irritation.*
● Hold the bandage with the roll facing upward in one hand and the initial part of the bandage in the other hand. Hold the bandage roll close to the part being bandaged *to ensure even tension and pressure.*
● Unroll the bandage as you wrap the body part in a spiral or spiral-reverse method. Never unroll the entire bandage and then wrap, *because this could produce uneven pressure, which interferes with blood circulation and cell nourishment.*
● Overlap each layer of bandage by one half to two thirds the width of the strip.
● Wrap firmly but not too tightly. As you wrap, ask the patient to tell you if the bandage feels comfortable. If he complains of tingling, itching, numbness, or pain, loosen the bandage.
● When wrapping an extremity, anchor the bandage initially by circling the body part twice. *To prevent the bandage from slipping out of place on the foot,* wrap in a figure eight around the foot, the ankle, and then the foot again before continuing. The same technique works on any joint, such as knee, wrist, or elbow. Include the heel when wrapping the foot, but never wrap the toes (or fingers) unless absolutely necessary, *because the distal extremity is used to detect impaired circulation.*
● When finished wrapping, secure the end of the bandage with tape or pins, being careful not to scratch or pinch the patient. Avoid using metal clips, *because they often don't hold when the patient moves and may get lost in the bed linens and injure him.*
● Check distal circulation after the bandage is in place, *because the elastic*

## TYPES OF BANDAGING TECHNIQUES

**Circular:** Each turn encircles previous turn, completely covering it. Use this turn for anchoring a bandage.

**Spiral:** Each turn partially overlaps previous turn. Use this turn to wrap a long, straight body part or a body part of increasing circumference.

**Spiral-reverse:** Anchor first, and then bandage reverses direction halfway through each spiral turn. Use this turn to accommodate increasing body part circumference.

**Figure eight:** Anchor first below joint, and then use alternating ascending and descending turns to form a figure eight. Use this turn around joints.

**Recurrent:** Bandage includes a combination of several turn types, such as circular, spiral, and spiral-reverse. Use this turn for bandaging a stump or the scalp.

*may tighten as you wrap.*
- Elevate a wrapped extremity for 15 to 30 minutes *to facilitate venous return.*
- Check distal circulation once or twice every 8 hours, *because an elastic bandage that is too tight may result in neurovascular damage.* Lift the distal end of the bandage and assess the color, temperature, and integrity of the skin underneath.
- Remove the bandage every 8 hours or whenever it's loose and wrinkled. Roll it up as you unwrap *to ready it for reuse.* Observe the area and give skin care before rewrapping the bandage.

- Change the bandage at least once daily. Bathe the skin and observe for irritation and breakdown before applying a fresh bandage.

### Special considerations
Wrap the bandage from the distal area to the proximal area *to promote venous return.* Avoid leaving gaps in bandage layers or skin surfaces exposed, *because this may result in uneven pressure on the body part.*

Observe the patient for an allergic reaction, *because some patients cannot tolerate the sizing in a new bandage.* Laundering it reduces this risk.

Launder the bandage daily or whenever it becomes limp, *because laundering restores its elasticity.* Always keep two bandages handy, *so one can be applied while the other bandage is being laundered.*

When using an elastic bandage after a surgical procedure on an extremity, such as vein stripping, or with a splint to immobilize a fracture, remove it only as ordered rather than regularly every 8 hours.

If the patient will be using the wrap at home, teach him or a family member how to apply the bandage correctly and to assess for restricted circulation.

## Complications
Arterial obstruction—characterized by decreased or absent distal pulse, blanching of skin or bluish discoloration and dusky nail beds, numbness and tingling or pain and cramping, and cold skin—can result from elastic bandage application. Edema can occur from obstruction of venous return. Less serious complications include allergic reaction and skin irritation.

## Documentation
Record the date and time of bandage application and removal, site of application, bandage size, skin condition before application, skin care given after removal, any complications, the patient's tolerance for treatment, and any patient teaching.

JOANNE PATZEK DACUNHA, RN

# Binders

*Binders—broad flannel or muslin bandages that circle the chest, abdomen, or groin—provide support, keep dressings in place (especially for patients allergic to tape), reduce tension on wounds and suture lines, and reduce breast engorgement for the nonnursing mother. There are no contraindications to their application.*

## Equipment
Binder of appropriate size and type □ safety pins.

Commercial elastic binders with Velcro closings are replacing the standard cotton straight and scultetus binders that require pins. Disposable T-binders are available, and scrotal supports for the male patient often replace binders, although not after abdominal-perineal resection. For the nonnursing mother, a good support brassiere is usually recommended over a breast binder.

## Preparation of equipment
Measure the area the binder must fit, and obtain the proper size and type of binder from the central supply department.

## Essential steps
• Check the doctor's order, and assess the patient's condition.
• Explain the procedure to the patient, provide privacy, and wash your hands thoroughly.
• Raise the patient's bed to its highest position *to avoid muscle strain during application of the binder.*
• Change the dressing and inspect the wound or suture line, if appropriate.
*To apply a straight abdominal binder:*
• Accordion-fold half the binder, slip it under the patient, and pull it through from the other side. Make sure the binder is straight, free of wrinkles, and evenly distributed under the patient. Its lower edge should extend well below the hips.
• Overlap one side snugly onto the other. Then, insert one finger under the binder's edge *to ensure a snug fit that's still loose enough to avoid impaired circulation and patient discomfort.*
• Starting at the lower edge, pin the binder together with safety pins spaced about 2″ (5 cm) apart. Slip your finger under the binder as you insert the pins, *to avoid pricking the patient.* Place the pins horizontally, *so they don't interfere with body movement.*

# TYPES OF BINDERS

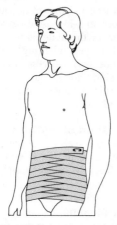

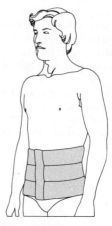

### Scultetus binder
- Keeps suture line intact after abdominal surgery so patient can move more freely
- Provides abdominal support after delivery or paracentesis

### Straight abdominal binder
- Keeps suture line intact after abdominal surgery so patient can move more freely
- Provides abdominal support after delivery or paracentesis

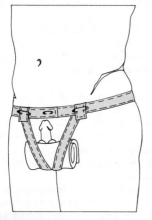

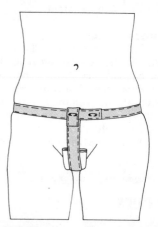

### Double T-binder
- Keeps perineal dressings in place for the male patient or for the female patient requiring a bulky dressing

### Single T-binder
- Keeps perineal dressings in place for the female patient

- Make darts in the binder as needed *to provide even snugness.* Avoid too tight application around the diaphragm, *which may interfere with breathing.*

*To apply a scultetus binder:*
- Slide the binder under the patient's hips and buttocks so its top aligns with the waist and its lowest tail crosses the

extreme lower abdomen.

• Adjust the binder so its solid portion is centered under the patient and its tails are evenly distributed on either side. Spread the tails out flat on the bed *so you can easily pick them up.*

• Beginning at the lower edge of the binder, bring one tail straight across the patient's abdomen. If the tail is too long, fold it over flat at the end. Then, hold this tail snugly in place as you bring the opposite tail across on top of it, overlapping the first tail's upper half.

• Alternating sides, bring one tail at a time straight across the abdomen, each time overlapping the preceding tail by half its width.

• Secure the top strap, using two safety pins placed horizontally *so they won't interfere with body movement.*

*To apply a T-binder:*

• Slip the T-binder under the patient's waist with its tails extending below the buttocks. Smooth the waistband and tails *to remove twists, which can chafe and create pressure on the patient's skin.*

• Pull the waistband snugly into position at the patient's waistline or, if he prefers, lower across the abdomen. Then, fasten it with a safety pin. Next, bring the free tail(s) up between the patient's legs over the dressing or perineal pad.

• For the female patient, bring the single tail up to the center of the waist, loop it behind and over the waistband, and secure it to the waistband by pinning through all layers of material. For the male patient, bring the two tails up on either side of the penis *to provide even support for the testicles.* Loop the ends behind and over the waistband on either side of the midline, and fasten them to the waistband by pinning through all layers of material. *Pinning through multiple layers keeps the straps from slipping sideways as the patient moves.*

• Instruct the patient to call you when he wishes to urinate or defecate, *because the binder must be unfastened and then reapplied.*

*To apply a breast binder:*

• Slip the binder under the patient's chest so its lower edge aligns with the waist. Straighten the binder to distribute it evenly on either side of the body.

• Pull the binder's edges snugly together and begin pinning upward from the waist. Slip your finger under the binder as you insert the pins *to avoid pricking the patient.* Use at least six pins, and place them horizontally *so they won't interfere with body movement.*

• Place the binder so the patient's nipples are centered in the breast tissue. *This ensures good breast alignment and proper support, and produces faster tissue involution.*

• Make darts in the binder wherever necessary *to provide a snug fit.* Do this by overlapping the material horizontally and pinning it perpendicularly.

• Adjust the shoulder straps to the proper fit and secure with safety pins.

*When applying any binder:*

• Ask the patient if the binder feels comfortable. Tell him it may feel tight initially but should feel comfortable shortly. Instruct him to notify you immediately if the binder feels too tight or too loose or comes apart.

• If the patient can ambulate, ask him to do so *to evaluate the fit of the binder.*

## Special considerations

*For maximum support,* wrap the binder so it applies even pressure across the body section. Eliminate all wrinkles and avoid placing pressure over bony prominences.

In surgical applications, fasten straight and scultetus binders from the bottom upward *to relieve gravitational pull on the wound.* In obstetric applications, fasten from the top downward *to direct the uterus into the pelvis,* and observe the patient closely for precipitate delivery, *because this places extra pressure on weak abdominal muscles.* For the obstetric patient, pin the last two straps of the scultetus binder on *both* sides; for the extremely large patient, pin *all* straps.

Be careful not to compress any tubes, drains, or catheters, or to position them so they're working against gravity. Also, don't allow binder placement to interfere with elimination.

Use a double T-binder on a female patient after extensive surgery that requires a large dressing. Use a straight or scultetus binder as a breast binder, if necessary. Pin straps onto the upper front and back for additional support over the shoulders. Observe the patient and check binder placement every 8 hours. Reapply the binder when a dressing needs changing, when the binder becomes loose or too tight, and at other times according to the doctor's orders. When changing the binder, observe the skin for signs of irritation. Give appropriate skin care before reapplying the binder.

**Complications**
Irritation of the underlying skin can result from perspiration or friction.

**Documentation**
Record the date and time of binder application, reapplication, and removal; type and location; purpose of application; skin condition before and after application; dressing changes or skin care; any complications; and the patient's tolerance and comments.

KAREN DYER VANCE, RN, BSN

# Pressure Dressing

*Most effective in controlling capillary or small-vein bleeding, a pressure dressing may be applied as a temporary emergency treatment, usually in a nonhospital setting, to slow bleeding from an external wound. A pressure dressing requires frequent checks for wound drainage to determine its effectiveness in controlling bleeding.*

**Equipment**
Two or more sterile gauze sponges □ roller gauze □ adhesive tape □ pen.

**Preparation of equipment**
Obtain the pressure dressing quickly *to avoid excessive blood loss.* Use clean cloth for the dressing if sterile gauze sponges are unavailable.

**Essential steps**
● Quickly explain the procedure to the patient *to help decrease his anxiety.*
● Elevate the injured body part *to help reduce bleeding.*
● Place enough gauze sponges over the wound to cover it. Don't cleanse the wound; *you can do this when the bleeding stops.*
● For an extremity or trunk wound, hold the dressings firmly over the wound and wrap the roller gauze tightly across them and around the body part *to provide pressure on the wound.* Secure the bandage with adhesive tape.
● To apply a dressing to neck, shoulder, or other wounds that can't be tightly wrapped, don't use roller gauze. Instead, apply tape directly over the dressings *to provide the necessary pressure at the wound site.*
● Check pulse, temperature, and skin condition distal to the wound site *because excess pressure can obstruct normal circulation.*
● Check the dressing frequently *to monitor wound drainage.* At each check, circle the drainage and write the time directly on the dressing *for later reference.*
● If the dressing becomes saturated, do not remove it, *because this will interfere with the maintenance of pressure.* Instead apply an additional dressing over the initial dressing and continue to monitor and record drainage.
● Obtain additional medical care as soon as possible.

**Special considerations**
Apply pressure directly to the wound with your hand if sterile gauze sponges and clean cloth are unavailable.

Avoid using an elastic bandage to bind the dressing, *because it won't wrap tightly enough to pressure the wound site.*

## Complications

Excessively tight application of a pressure dressing can cause impaired circulation.

## Documentation

Record the date and time of dressing application, the presence or absence of distal pulses, the integrity of distal skin, the amount of wound drainage, and any complications.

SUZANNE MARR SKINNER, RN, MS

---

## WOUND CARE

# Preoperative Skin Preparation

*Preoperative skin preparation is an attempt to render the skin as free as possible of microorganisms, thereby reducing the risk of infection at the incision site. It does not duplicate or replace the full sterile preparation that immediately precedes surgery. Preoperative preparation can involve a bath, shower, or local scrub with an antiseptic detergent solution, and removal of hair in a wide area surrounding the operative site. The area of preparation is always much larger than the expected incision site to minimize the number of microorganisms in the areas adjacent to the proposed incision and to allow surgical draping of the patient without contamination.*

## Equipment

Antiseptic soap solution □ tap water □ two clean basins □ bath blanket □ linen-saver pad □ adjustable light □ scissors □ sterile razor with sharp new blade □ 4″ x 4″ gauze sponges, if needed □ cotton-tipped applicators, if needed □ acetone or nail polish remover, if needed □ orangewood stick, if needed □ trash bag □ towel □ optional: clean examination gloves.

Disposable skin-scrub and shave kits are available.

## Preparation of equipment

Use warm tap water *because heat reduces the skin's surface tension and facilitates removal of soil and hair.* Dilute the antiseptic detergent solution with warm tap water in one basin *for washing,* and pour plain warm water into the second basin *for rinsing.*

## Essential steps

● Check the doctor's order and explain the procedure to the patient, including the reason for the extensiveness of the preparation *to avoid causing undue anxiety.* Provide privacy, wash your hands thoroughly, and put on gloves if desired.

● Place the patient in a comfortable position, drape him with the bath blanket, and expose the preparation area. For most surgeries, this area extends 12″ (30 cm) in each direction from the expected incision site. However, *to ensure privacy and avoid chilling the patient,* expose only a small area at a time while performing skin preparation.

● Position a linen-saver pad beneath the patient *to catch spillage and avoid linen changes.* Adjust the light to illuminate the preparation area *because a strong light helps detect fine body hairs.*

● Assess skin condition in the preparation area and report any rash, abrasion, or cut to the doctor before beginning the procedure. Any break in the skin increases the risk of infection and could cause cancellation of planned surgery.

● Have the patient remove all jewelry that may be present on the operative site.

● Begin removal of hair from the preparation area by clipping any long hairs

# SKIN PREPARATION OF SURGICAL SITES

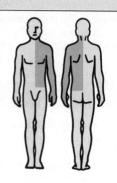

### Shoulder and upper arm

On operative side, shave from fingertips to hairline and from center chest to center spine, extending to iliac crest and including the axilla. If surgery is for upper arm, trim and clean fingernails.

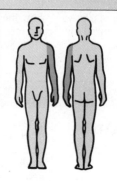

### Forearm, elbow, and hand

On operative side, shave from fingertips to shoulder. Include the axilla, unless surgery is for hand. Trim and clean fingernails.

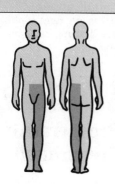

### Hip

On operative side, shave toes to nipple line and at least 3″ (7.6 cm) beyond midline back and front, including the pubis. Clean and trim toenails.

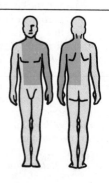

### Chest

Shave from chin to iliac crests and nipple line on unaffected side to midline of back on operative side (2″, or 5 cm, beyond midline of back for thoracotomy). On this side, include axilla and entire arm to elbow.

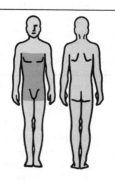

### Abdomen

Shave from 3″ (7.6 cm) above the nipple to upper thighs, including the pubis.

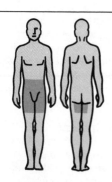

### Lower abdomen

Shave from 2″ (5 cm) above the umbilicus to midthigh, including the pubic area. For femoral ligation, shave to midline of thigh in back. For hernia and embolectomy, shave to costal margin and down to knee, as ordered.

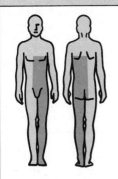

### Thigh

On operative side, shave from toes to 3″ (7.6 cm) above the umbilicus and from midline front to midline back, including the pubis. Clean and trim toenails.

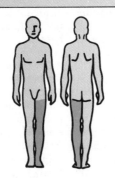

### Knee and lower leg

On operative side, shave from toes to groin. Clean and trim toenails.

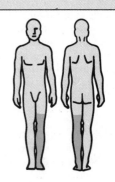

### Ankle and foot

On operative side, shave from toes to 3″ (7.6 cm) above the knee. Clean and trim toenails.

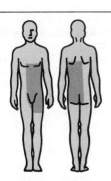

### Flank

On operative side, shave from nipple line to pubis, 3″ (7.6 cm) beyond the midline in back, and 2″ (5 cm) past the abdominal midline. Include pubic area and, on affected side, upper thigh and axilla.

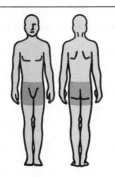

### Perineum

Shave pubis, perineum, and perianal area. Shave from the waist to at least 3″ (7.6 cm) below the groin in front and at least 3″ below the buttocks in back.

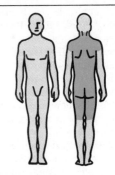

### Spine

Shave entire back, including shoulders and neck to hairline, and down to both knees. Include axillae.

with scissors. Then shave all remaining hair within the area *to remove microorganisms.* Use only a sterilized or sterile disposable razor with a sharp new blade *to avoid the risk of hepatitis from a contaminated razor.*

• Use a gauze sponge to spread liquid soap over the shave site, or use the sponge provided in the disposable kit.

• Pull the skin taut in the direction opposite to the way the hair slants *because this makes the hair rise and shaving easier.*

• Holding the razor at a 45° angle, shave with short strokes in the direction of hair growth *to avoid skin irritation and achieve a smooth clean shave.*

• If possible, avoid lifting the razor from the skin and placing it down again *to minimize the risk of cuts.* Also avoid applying pressure *because this can cause abrasion, particularly over bony prominences.*

• Rinse the razor frequently and reapply the liquid soap to the skin as needed *to keep the area moist.*

• Shave the entire preparation area, even if no hair is visible, *to ensure removal of small hairs.* Reshave where necessary.

• Change the rinse water if necessary. Then, rinse the soap solution and loose hair from the preparation area, and inspect the skin. Immediately notify the doctor of any new nicks, cuts, or abrasions, and file a report if your institution requires it.

• Proceed with a 10-minute scrub *to ensure a clean preparation area.* Wash the area with a gauze sponge dipped in the antiseptic soap solution. Using a circular motion, start at the expected incision site and work outward toward the periphery of the area *to avoid recontaminating the clean area.* Apply light friction while washing *to improve the antiseptic effect of the solution.* Replace the gauze sponge as necessary.

• Carefully cleanse skin folds and crevices, *because they harbor greater numbers of microorganisms.* Scrub the perineal area last, if it's part of the preparation area, for the same reason. Pull loose skin taut. If necessary, use cotton-tipped applicators to clean the umbilicus and an orangewood stick to clean the nails. Be sure to remove any nail polish, *because the anesthetist uses nail-bed color to determine adequate oxygenation.*

• Dry the area with a clean towel and remove the linen-saver pad.

• Give the patient any special instructions for care of the prepared area, and remind him to keep the area clean for surgery. Make sure the patient is comfortable.

• Properly dispose of solutions and trash bag, and clean or dispose of soiled equipment and supplies according to institutional policy.

## Special considerations

When preparing a large area, wash and shave it in small sections, beginning with the expected incision site. *This keeps your work area moist and avoids chilling the patient.* After you've finished all sections, rinse and dry the entire preparation area.

Avoid shaving facial or neck hair on women and children unless ordered. *Never shave eyebrows because this disrupts normal hair growth and the new growth may prove unsightly.* Scalp shaving is usually performed in the operating room, but if you're required to prepare the patient's scalp, retain all hair in a plastic or paper bag with the patient's possessions.

If the patient won't hold still for shaving, remove hair with a depilatory cream. Although this method produces a clean, intact skin without risking cuts or abrasions, it can cause skin irritation or rash, especially in the groin area. If possible, cut long hairs with scissors before applying the cream, *because removal of remaining hair then requires less cream.* Then, use a glove to apply the cream in a layer ½" thick; after about 10 minutes, remove the cream with moist gauze sponges. Next, wash the area with antiseptic soap solution, rinse, and pat dry.

## Complications
Rashes, nicks, cuts, and abrasions are the most common complications of skin preparation.

## Documentation
Record the date, time, and area of preparation; skin condition before and after preparation; any complications; and the patient's tolerance for it. If your institution requires it, complete an incident report if the patient suffers nicks, cuts, or abrasions during skin preparation.

JAY ELLEN BARRETT, RN, BSN, MBA

# Suturing

*Suturing closes a wound with the edges approximated, thereby promoting healing and minimizing tissue scarring. Doctors perform most suturing. However, nurses may suture simple cuts if state regulations and institutional policy permit; such suturing involves relatively clean superficial wounds less than 12 hours old. Nurses rarely suture facial wounds, deep wounds requiring layered sutures, joint wounds, or potentially infected wounds.*

*Performed properly, suturing requires thorough wound preparation and cleansing, sterile technique during wound closure, and careful approximation of wound margins. Usually, this procedure requires assistance from another nurse.*

## Equipment
Adjustable light □ sterile gloves □ sterile towels □ sterile forceps with teeth □ sterile needle holder for curved or straight needle □ sterile cutting-edge needle, curved or straight □ sterile suture material, as ordered □ sterile scissors □ local anesthetic □ topical anesthetic, if needed □ sterile 18G needle □ sterile 25G needle □ sterile 5-ml syringe □ sterile razor with sharp new blade □ materials as needed to irrigate, cleanse, and dress the wound □ restraints, if needed □ waterproof trash bag □ ice pack with cover.

The cutting-edge needle creates a path through tissue for the suture to follow. A straight cutting-edge needle is usually recommended for simple suturing *because it requires less movement of thin traumatized skin tissue.* A curved needle more effectively sutures deep wounds with thicker edges and avoids puncturing underlying tissue layers.

Prepackaged, sterile suture sets are available.

## Preparation of equipment
Assemble all supplies at the patient's bedside. Check the expiration date on each sterile package and inspect for tears. Open the waterproof trash bag and place it nearby. Position the bag *to avoid reaching across the sterile field or the wound when disposing of soiled articles.* Form a cuff by turning down the top of the trash bag *to provide a wide opening and prevent contamination of instruments and gloves by touching the bag's edge.*

## Essential steps
● Explain the procedure to the patient and ask if he's allergic to any anesthetics, adhesive tape, and povidone-iodine or other topical solutions or medications. Tell him that the anesthetic may sting momentarily when injected (unless you're also applying a topical anesthetic), but that it quickly numbs the area.
● Provide privacy, position the patient as necessary, and adjust the light to shine directly on the wound *for maximum visibility.* Restrain the injured part, if necessary.
● Wash your hands thoroughly. Put on sterile examination gloves.
● Shave hair from the immediate area of the wound site, if necessary.
● Cleanse the surrounding skin with soap and water or a mild antiseptic solution *to reduce the number of sur-*

# SUTURE MATERIALS AND METHODS

The type of suture material used to close a wound varies according to the suturing method. Nonabsorbable sutures are commonly used to close the skin surface, providing strength and immobility with minimal tissue irritation. Nonabsorbable suture materials include:
- *silk*
- *cotton*
- *stainless steel*
- *dermal synthetics*, such as nylon.

Absorbable sutures are commonly used when it is undesirable to remove the sutures, for example, in *underlying tissue layers*. Absorbable materials include:
- *chromic catgut*—natural catgut treated with chromium trioxide for strength and prolonged absorption time
- *plain catgut*—absorbed faster than chromic catgut and tends to cause more tissue irritation
- *synthetics*, such as polyglycolic acid, which are replacing catgut because they are stronger and more durable, cause less tissue irritation, and may prove more effective in an infected area.

## Methods for suturing

**Plain interrupted suture:** individual sutures, each using a separate piece of thread and tied independently, with half its length crossing under the suture line and the other half visible above the skin surface

**Plain continuous or continuous running suture:** a series of connected stitches with a knot only at the beginning and end of the series

**Mattress interrupted suture:** independent stitches tunneling completely under the incision line, except for a tiny portion visible on the skin surface at each side of the wound

**Mattress continuous suture:** a series of connected mattress stitches with a knot only at the beginning and end of the series

**Blanket continuous suture:** a series of looped stitches with a knot only at the beginning and end of the series

*face organisms and the risk of infection.* Cleanse to at least 2″ (5 cm) beyond the wound edges in each direction. Assess the patient's wound; then remove and discard your gloves.
- Establish a sterile field with all the equipment and supplies you'll need for suturing and for wound and skin care. Put on sterile gloves, expose the wound, and drape the patient *to decrease the risk of contamination.*
- Unwind the suture and inspect the needle for rough edges.
- Attach the 18G needle to the syringe.

With another nurse holding the anesthetic bottle, withdraw the proper amount of anesthetic. Have the assisting nurse remove the needle. Then, replace it with the sterile 25G needle.

● If needed, also spray or swab a small amount of topical anesthetic into the open wound, and wait until it takes effect. Then, make several lateral injections into the wound edges, holding the syringe parallel to the skin surface. You may use the same needle for all injections *because the area is considered sterile.* With each insertion, first pull back slightly on the plunger *to aspirate for blood and avoid injecting the anesthetic into a blood vessel.*

● Allow the anesthetic to take effect. Then, irrigate the wound *to remove all foreign matter, blood, and drainage.*

● Approximate the wound with your gloved fingers *to judge the alignment.* Then, use sterile forceps to grasp the tissue at one end of the wound in preparation for suturing. Avoid grasping the very edges of the wound *because the forceps may crush the tissue.* If the surface layer is too thin and fragile to hold safely, grasp the subcutaneous tissue to pull the wound together.

● With the forceps holding the tissue, grasp the needle with the needle holder at the end closest to the suture material. However, don't grasp a swaged needle where it's fused to the suture material *because this weakens the juncture.*

● With forceps holding the edge of the wound, evert the tissue *to make needle insertion easier.*

● Position the needle so it enters and exits perpendicular to the skin surface. *Placing the needle at a flatter angle may cause the wound edges to turn under and the sutures to tear through the skin.*

● Insert the needle and angle it to exit the opposite side of the tissue layer. When the needle is visible underneath and enough is showing to grasp with the needle holder, release the entrance part of the needle and grasp the exit tip. Pull the needle through, following the line or curve of the needle itself *to*

*prevent lateral tissue tears.*

● Release the forceps grip on the tissue and use the forceps to grasp the opposite wound edge. Keeping in mind the principles just mentioned, insert the needle on the tissue underside and push it up to the surface.

● Pull the suture tight enough to close the wound without buckling the skin. If you are using plain interrupted sutures, secure the stitch with a square knot (see *How to Tie a Square Knot*, page 232); if you are using continuous sutures, move on to the next stitch. Do not pull the sutures too tightly, *because edema that normally results from tissue trauma will cause them to become even tighter and risk tearing the skin and reopening the wound.*

● Insert each suture close to the wound's edge but far enough away *so it won't tear through the tissue when tightened.*

● To cut the suture after tying it, pull it straight up from the wound and hold it taut. With the scissors held parallel to the skin surface and nearly closed, and with your index finger pressed against the top blade *to stabilize it,* slide the cutting edge of one blade down along the suture to the knot. When you feel the knot's resistance, lift up the blade's cutting edge about ¼"; (0.65 cm) and clip the suture. This prevents the knot from becoming undone and facilitates grasp when removing sutures.

● Once you've completed suturing, cleanse the area again *to reduce skin irritation by removing any blood or drainage.*

● Apply an antiseptic and a sterile dressing, if ordered. If not, ask the doctor about using a collodion solution or spray. Application of a dressing or antiseptic depends on the type of wound, its previous exposure to infectants, and the doctor's preference.

● Make sure the patient is comfortable. Have him rest briefly and then stand slowly *to prevent fainting.*

● Discard your gloves. Properly dispose of solutions and trash bag, and clean or dispose of soiled equipment

## HOW TO TIE A SQUARE KNOT

**1** After drawing a suture through both sides of a wound, leave a short end on one side, and remove the needle from the holder. With the long end of the suture, make a loop around the needle holder.

**2** Maintaining the loop around the needle holder, grasp the short opposite end of the suture with the holder tip.

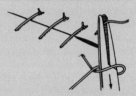

**3** Draw the short end through the loop, and tighten the first part of the knot by pulling the suture ends in opposite directions.

**4** To complete the knot, again loop the long end of the suture around the needle holder and grasp the short suture end opposite.

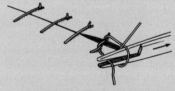

**5** Pull the short end through the loop, and tighten the knot by pulling the ends apart.

and supplies according to institutional policy.

• When the anesthetic wears off, apply an ice pack to the wound and elevate the sutured part above heart level *to minimize pain and swelling.* Use an ice pack with a waterproof cover *to keep the dressing dry.*

• Give an outpatient proper wound-care instructions; tell him how to detect early signs of infection, when and how to change the dressing, and when to return for suture removal. Tell him to report any signs of infection, such as discharge, redness, or swelling, to the doctor.

## Special considerations

If you must suture a small child's cut, immobilize him completely *to avoid any movement that would endanger him or interfere with sterile technique.* Assess the situation, if your institution has no policy, in deciding whether to permit a child's parents to stay with him or to ask them to leave the room during the procedure.

*To reduce the risk of side effects,* use the least amount and lowest concentration of anesthetic needed to numb the injured part.

When selecting the type of stitch to use, consider the risks associated with continuous or running sutures. Although these can be more quickly and easily applied than plain interrupted sutures, *a break in the suture line requires complete resuturing of the wound.* Also, avoid using continuous sutures on jagged wounds and on thick calloused skin *because these won't hold as well as interrupted sutures and may pucker the skin.*

## Documentation

Record the date and time of suturing; type and number of sutures; method of suturing; type, concentration, and amount of anesthetics; wound appearance and care; and the patient's tolerance for treatment. Sign the patient's record and ask the doctor to cosign it to avoid legal complications.

JAY ELLEN BARRETT, RN, BSM, MBA

# Suture-line Care

*Suture-line care involves the aseptic removal of cell debris and drainage from wounds to prevent contamination that can lead to infection. It promotes proper wound healing by stimulating circulation and preventing skin breakdown.*

*This procedure is usually performed daily, or more often for a draining wound. It should not be performed on an incision secured with butterfly adhesive strips.*

## Equipment

Waterproof trash bag □ clean examination gloves, if needed □ sterile gloves □ gown, if indicated □ prescribed antiseptic skin cleanser, sterile saline solution, or sterile water □ sterile container □ sterile 4" x 4" gauze sponges □ sterile cotton-tipped applicator, if needed □ sterile forceps □ materials as needed for irrigating, culturing, and dressing the wound.

Prepackaged dressing sets, with or without instruments, and prepackaged sterile swabs saturated with povidone-iodine are available.

## Preparation of equipment

Assemble all equipment in the patient's room. Check the expiration date on each sterile package and inspect for tears. Open the waterproof trash bag and place it near the patient's bed. Position the bag *to avoid reaching across the sterile field or the wound when disposing of soiled articles.* Form a cuff by turning down the top of the trash bag *to ensure a wide opening and prevent contamination of instruments or gloves by touching the bag's edge.*

## Essential steps

● Check the doctor's order for specific wound-care instructions. Note the location of surgical drains *to avoid displacing them during the procedure.*

● Check for patient allergies, especially to adhesive tape and povidone-iodine or other topical solutions or medications.

● Explain the procedure to the patient and reassure him that it causes no discomfort. Provide privacy and position the patient as necessary.

● Wash your hands thoroughly. Put on a gown, if necessary, *to prevent wound drainage from contaminating your uniform.*

● If the patient's wound has a dressing, put on clean examination gloves and carefully remove it. Discard the dressing and the gloves in the waterproof trash bag. Culture the wound, if ordered.

• Establish a sterile field with all the equipment and supplies you'll need for suture-line care and dressing change. If ointment is ordered, squeeze the needed amount onto the sterile field. If you're using an antiseptic from an unsterile bottle, pour the antiseptic skin cleanser into a sterile container *so you won't contaminate your gloves.* Then put on sterile gloves. If you won't be using prepackaged sterile povidone-iodine swabs to cleanse the wound, saturate sterile gauze sponges with the prescribed cleansing agent. Avoid using cotton balls, *because these may shed particles in the wound, causing irritation, infection, or adhesion.*

• Pick up the moistened gauze sponge with sterile forceps and squeeze out excess solution.

• Working from the top of the incision line, swab once to the bottom and then discard the gauze sponge. With a second moistened gauze sponge, swab from top to bottom in a vertical path next to the incision line.

• Continue to work outward from the incision in lines running parallel to it. Always swab from the clean area toward the less clean area, usually top to bottom. Use each gauze or swab for only one stroke *to avoid tracking wound exudate and normal body flora from the surrounding skin to the clean areas.* Remember that the suture line is cleaner than the adjacent skin, and the top of the suture line is the cleanest, *because more drainage collects at the bottom of the wound.* Avoid cleaning from bottom to top *to prevent further wound contamination.*

• Use sterile cotton-tipped applicators for efficient cleaning of tight-fitting wire sutures, deep and narrow wounds, or wounds with pockets. *Because the cotton on the swab is tightly wrapped, it isn't as likely to leave particles in the wound as a cotton ball.* Remember to wipe only once with each applicator.

• If the patient has a surgical drain, clean the drain's surface last. *Because moist drainage facilitates growth of bacteria,* the drain is considered the most contaminated. Cleanse the skin around the drain by swabbing in half or full circles from the drain site outward.

• Cleanse all areas of the wound *to wash away debris, pus, blood, and necrotic material.* Try not to disturb sutures or irritate the incision line. Cleanse to at least 1″ (2.5 cm) beyond the end of the new dressing. If you aren't applying a dressing, cleanse to at least 2″ (5 cm) beyond the incision line.

• Observe the incision line for good approximation of its edges, and check for signs of infection (heat, redness, swelling, odor), dehiscence, or evisceration. If you observe such signs or the patient reports pain at the wound site, notify the doctor.

• Irrigate the wound, if ordered. Then blot dry with gauze sponges, working from top to bottom and using a new sponge for each wipe. Discard the forceps, if they're disposable.

• Apply antiseptic/bactericidal ointment or other prescribed ointment, if ordered, using a sterile applicator. Apply a minimal amount *because excessive ointment may harbor infectious organisms.*

• Apply a sterile dressing or leave the wound open to the air, as ordered. Remove and discard your gloves.

• Make sure the patient is comfortable.

• Properly dispose of solutions and trash bag, and clean or dispose of soiled equipment and supplies according to institutional policy.

### Special considerations

Try to coordinate suture-line care with the doctor's visit, *so he can observe the incision line without having to dislodge the dressing.* Try to arrange suture-line care to avoid interrupting the patient when he has visitors.

Cleanse the incision line only with solutions prescribed by the doctor or with sterile saline solution or sterile water. *The use of alcohol, peroxide, and other agents is controversial.*

If the incision line is 24 hours old, clean and dry (not draining), and well approximated with sutures, check with the doctor about leaving it open to the air. *This facilitates healing by preventing skin breakdown caused by dressing friction and by wet bulky dressings that hold heat and moisture and promote infection.*

**Complications**
Allergic reactions to the antiseptic or tape may develop.

**Documentation**
Record the date and time of suture-line care; cleansing agent; any additional procedures, such as wound irrigation; appearance of the incision line; characteristics and amount of wound drainage; any signs of wound complications; dressing changes; and the patient's tolerance for treatment.

SUSAN DONAHUE, RN, BSN

# Suture Removal

*The goal of this procedure is to remove skin sutures from a healed wound without damaging newly formed tissue. The timing of suture removal depends on the shape, size, and location of the sutured incision; the absence of inflammation, drainage, and infection; and the patient's general condition. Sutures are usually removed within 7 to 10 days after insertion, for a sufficiently healed wound. Techniques for removal depend on the method of suturing, but all require sterile procedure to prevent contamination. Although a doctor usually removes sutures, a nurse may remove them on the doctor's order if institutional policy permits.*

**Equipment**
Waterproof trash bag □ adjustable light

□ clean examination gloves, if needed □ sterile forceps or sterile hemostat □ sterile suture scissors □ materials as needed to cleanse and dress the suture line □ optional: adhesive butterfly strips or paper tapes and compound benzoin tincture or other skin protectant.

Prepackaged, sterile suture-removal trays and sterile cleaning sponges saturated with povidone-iodine are available.

**Preparation of equipment**
Assemble all equipment in the patient's room. Check the expiration date on each sterile package and inspect for tears. Open the waterproof trash bag and place it near the patient's bed. Position the bag *to avoid reaching across the sterile field or the suture line when disposing of soiled articles.* Form a cuff by turning down the top of the trash bag *to provide a wide opening and prevent contamination of instruments or gloves by touching the bag's edge.*

**Essential steps**
• If your institution allows you to remove sutures, check the doctor's order *to confirm the exact timing and details of this procedure.*
• Check for patient allergies, especially to adhesive tape and povidone-iodine or other topical solutions or medications.
• Tell the patient you're about to remove the stitches from his wound. Assure him that this is generally painless, although he may feel a tickling sensation as the stitches come out. Reassure him that because his wound is healing properly, removing the stitches won't weaken the incision.
• Provide privacy, and position the patient so he's comfortable without undue tension on the suture line. *Some patients experience nausea or dizziness during the procedure,* so have the patient recline if possible. Adjust the light so it shines directly on the suture line.
• Wash your hands thoroughly. If the patient's wound has a dressing, put on

clean examination gloves and carefully remove it. Discard the dressing and the gloves in the waterproof trash bag.

● Observe the patient's wound for gaping, drainage, inflammation, signs of infection, or embedded sutures. Notify the doctor if the wound has failed to heal properly.

● Establish a sterile work area with all the equipment and supplies you'll need for suture removal and wound care. Put on sterile gloves.

● Observing sterile technique, cleanse the suture line *to decrease the number of microorganisms and reduce the risk of infection.*

● Then proceed as follows, according to the type of suture you're removing. *Because the visible part of a suture is exposed to skin bacteria and is considered contaminated,* be sure, whenever possible, to cut sutures at the skin edge on one side of the visible part. Remove the suture by lifting the visible end off the skin *to avoid drawing this contaminated portion through subcutaneous tissue.*

*To remove plain interrupted sutures:*
● Use sterile forceps to grasp the knot of the first suture and gently raise it off the skin, exposing a small portion of the suture that was below skin level.

● Place the rounded tip of the sterile suture scissors against the skin and cut through the suture's exposed portion.

● Still holding the knot with the forceps, pull the cut suture up and out of the skin in a smooth, continuous movement *to minimize pain.* Discard the suture.

● Continue this process, at first removing every other suture, *to maintain suture-line support and to observe the wound for gaping.* If gaping occurs, leave the remaining sutures in place and notify the doctor.

*To remove plain continuous sutures:*
● Cut the first suture on the side opposite the knot. Next, cut the same side of the next suture in line. Then, lift the first suture out in the direction of the knot.

● Repeat the process down the suture line, grasping each suture where you'd usually grasp the knot.

*To remove mattress interrupted sutures:*
● If possible, remove the small visible portion of the suture opposite the knot by cutting it at each visible end and lifting the small piece away from the skin *to prevent pulling it through and contaminating subcutaneous tissue.*

● Then remove the rest of the suture by pulling it out in the direction of the knot.

● If the visible portion is too small to cut twice, cut it once and pull the entire suture out in the opposite direction.

● Repeat this process for the remaining sutures.

*To remove mattress continuous sutures:*
● Follow the procedure for removing mattress interrupted sutures, first removing the small visible portion, if possible, *to prevent pulling it through and contaminating subcutaneous tissue,* and then extracting the rest of the suture in the direction of the knot.

● As you work down the wound, remember to cut each suture on both sides of the incision line *to separate it from adjacent sutures.*

*To remove blanket continuous sutures:*
● Cut the thread opposite the edge with the looped stitch and draw the suture out in the direction of the loop.

*After removing sutures:*
● Wipe the incision line gently with gauze sponges soaked in an antiseptic skin cleanser or with a prepackaged swab. Apply a light sterile gauze dressing, if desired, *to prevent infection and irritation from clothing.* Then discard your gloves.

● Make sure the patient is comfortable. According to the doctor's preference, inform the patient that he can shower in 1 or 2 days if the incision line is dry and heals well. Tell him how to remove the dressing and care for the wound, and instruct him to call the doctor immediately if he observes wound discharge or any other abnormal change.

Tell him that the redness surrounding the incision should gradually disappear and show only a thin line after a few weeks.
• Properly dispose of solutions and trash bag, and clean or dispose of soiled equipment and supplies according to institutional policy.

### Special considerations
Be sure to check the doctor's order for timing of suture removal. Usually, you'll remove sutures on the head and neck 3 to 5 days after insertion; sutures on the chest and abdomen, 5 to 7 days after insertion; on the lower extremity, 7 to 10 days after insertion. However, if the patient has interrupted sutures or an incompletely healed suture line, remove only those sutures specified by the doctor. He may want to leave some sutures in place for an additional day or two *to support the suture line.*

If the patient has both retention and regular sutures in place, check the doctor's order for the sequence in which they are to be removed. *Because retention sutures link underlying fat and muscle tissue and give added support to the obese or slow-healing patient,* these usually remain in place for 14 to 21 days.

Be particularly careful to cleanse the suture line before attempting to remove mattress sutures. *This decreases the risk of infection when the visible, contaminated part of the stitch is too small to cut twice for sterile removal and must be pulled through the tissue.* After you have removed mattress sutures this way, observe the suture line carefully *for subsequent infection.*

If the wound dehisces during suture removal, apply butterfly adhesive strips or paper tapes to support and approximate the edges and call the doctor immediately to make repairs.

Apply butterfly adhesive strips or paper tapes after any suture removal, if desired, *to give added support to the incision line and prevent lateral tension on the wound from forming a wide scar.* Use a small amount of compound benzoin tincture or other skin protectant *to ensure adherence.* Leave the strips in place for 3 to 5 days, or as ordered.

### Documentation
Record the date and time of suture removal, type and number of sutures, appearance of the suture line, any signs of wound complications, any dressings or butterfly strips applied, and the patient's tolerance for treatment.

JAY ELLEN BARRETT, RN, BSN, MBA

# Removal of Skin Staples and Clips

*Skin staples or clips are commonly used in place of standard sutures for closure of lacerations and operative wounds. Because they can secure a wound faster than sutures, they often substitute for surface sutures when cosmetic results are not a prime consideration, such as in abdominal closure. When properly placed, staples and clips distribute tension evenly along the suture line with minimal tissue trauma and compression, facilitating healing and minimizing scarring. Because staples and clips are made from surgical stainless steel, tissue reaction to them is minimal. Doctors usually remove skin staples and clips, but some institutions permit qualified nurses to perform this procedure.*

*Skin staples and clips are contraindicated when wound location requires good cosmetic results or when the incision site makes it impossible to maintain at least a 5-mm distance between the staple and underlying bones, vessels, or internal organs.*

### Equipment
Waterproof trash bag □ adjustable light □ clean examination gloves, if needed □ sterile gloves □ sterile staple or clip

## REMOVING A STAPLE

To remove a staple, first position the extractor beneath the staple's span. Squeeze the extractor's handles until they close completely, and then lift the staple (as shown below).

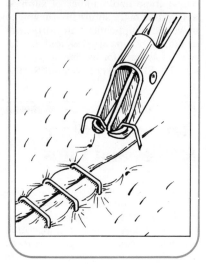

extractor □ materials as needed to cleanse and dress the incision line □ optional: butterfly adhesive strips or paper tapes and compound benzoin tincture or other skin protectant.

Prepackaged, sterile, disposable staple or clip extractors are available.

**Preparation of equipment**
Assemble all equipment in the patient's room. Check the expiration date on each sterile package and inspect for tears. Open the waterproof trash bag and place it near the patient's bed. Position the bag *to avoid reaching across the sterile field or the wound when disposing of soiled articles.* Form a cuff by turning down the top of the bag *to provide a wide opening and prevent contamination of instruments or gloves by touching the bag's edge.*

**Essential steps**
• If your institution allows you to remove skin staples and clips, check the

doctor's order *to confirm the exact timing and details of this procedure.*
• Check for patient allergies, especially to adhesive tape and povidone-iodine or other topical solutions or medications.
• Explain the procedure to the patient. Tell him that he may feel a slight pulling or tickling sensation, but little discomfort, during removal of staples. Reassure him that because his incision is healing properly, removing the supporting staples or clips won't weaken the incision line.
• Provide privacy, and place the patient in a comfortable position without undue tension on the incision line. *Because some patients experience nausea or dizziness during the procedure,* have the patient recline, if possible. Adjust the light to shine directly on the incision line.
• Wash your hands thoroughly.
• If the patient's wound has a dressing, put on clean examination gloves and carefully remove it. Discard the dressing and the gloves in the waterproof trash bag.
• Assess the patient's incision line and notify the doctor if gaping, drainage, inflammation, or other signs of infection are present.
• Establish a sterile work area with all the equipment and supplies you'll need for removing staples or clips, and for cleansing and dressing the incision line. Open the package containing the sterile staple or clip extractor, maintaining asepsis. Put on sterile gloves.
• Wipe the incision line gently with sterile gauze sponges soaked in an antiseptic skin cleanser, or with prepackaged sterile swabs, *to remove surface encrustations.*
• Pick up the sterile staple or clip extractor. Then, starting at one end of the incision line, position the extractor's lower jaws beneath the span of the first staple or clip.
• Squeeze the handles until they're completely closed; then lift the staple or clip away from the skin. *The extractor reforms the shape of the staple*

or clip and pulls the prongs out of the intradermal tissue.
- Hold the extractor over the trash bag, and release the handle to discard the staple or clip.
- Repeat the procedure for each staple or clip until all are removed.
- Apply a light sterile gauze dressing, if desired, to prevent infection and irritation from clothing. Then, discard your gloves.
- Make sure the patient is comfortable. According to the doctor's preference, inform the patient that he can shower in 1 or 2 days if the incision line is dry and healing well. Tell him how to remove the dressing and care for the wound, and instruct him to call the doctor immediately if he observes wound discharge or any other abnormal change. Tell him the redness surrounding the incision should gradually disappear, and that after a few weeks only a thin line should show.
- Properly dispose of solutions and trash bag, and clean or dispose of soiled equipment and supplies according to institutional policy.

### Special considerations

Carefully check the doctor's order for the timing and extent of staple or clip removal. The doctor may want you to remove only alternate staples or clips initially and leave the others in place for an additional day or two to support the incision.

When removing a staple or clip, place the extractor's jaws carefully between the patient's skin and the staple or clip to avoid patient discomfort. Because staples or clips placed too deeply within the skin or left in place too long may resist removal, notify the doctor if extraction is difficult.

If the wound dehisces after the procedure, apply butterfly adhesive strips or paper tapes to approximate and support the edges, and call the doctor immediately to make repairs.

Apply butterfly adhesive strips or paper tapes after removing staples or clips, if desired, to give added support to the incision line and prevent lateral tension from forming a wide scar. Use a small amount of compound benzoin tincture or other skin protectant to ensure adherence. Leave the strips in place for 3 to 5 days.

### Documentation

Record the date and time of staple or clip removal, number of staples or clips removed, appearance of the incision line, any dressings or butterfly strips applied, any signs of wound complications, and the patient's tolerance for treatment.

SUSAN M. GLOVER, RN, BSN

# Wound Management

*Wound management promotes cleanliness to prevent infection by barring pathogens from entering the wound. Correct wound management also protects the skin surface from maceration and excoriation by contact with irritating drainage; it also allows measurement of wound drainage to monitor fluid and electrolyte balance; finally, it promotes patient comfort.*

*The two principal methods for managing a draining wound are dressing and pouching. Dressings are the best choice when skin integrity is not compromised by caustic or excessive drainage. Application of dressings directly follows surgical incision, insertion of a central line, or other invasive procedure. Lightly seeping wounds with drains as well as wounds with minimal purulent drainage can usually be managed with packing and gauze dressings. Dressing the wound necessitates sterile technique and sterile supplies to prevent wound contamination. Such dressings should be changed frequently enough to keep the skin dry.*

*When wound drainage is copious and excoriating, pouching is indicated to protect the skin.*

## RECURRENT BANDAGE TECHNIQUE FOR DIFFICULT AREAS

The recurrent bandage technique helps secure a dressing over difficult-to-bandage sites, such as a finger, a toe, a fist, a stump, or the head. This technique involves two circular turns, additional turns perpendicular to the first ones to cover the desired area, and finally, additional circular turns to secure the bandage. Although the procedure detailed below is for bandaging a finger, you can easily adapt it to bandage any difficult area.

• First, select an elastic bandage, roller gauze, or elastic gauze dressing in the appropriate width. For finger application, you'll need a 1"-wide bandage; for a stump or the head, a 3" or 4" width.

• Secure the bandage at the bottom of the finger with two circular turns (see illustration #1).

• With your index and middle fingers, hold the bandage at the bottom, where it is

secured. Take the bandage over the fingertip to the other side of the finger (see illustration #2).

• Now, using your thumb to hold the other side of the bandage, bring the bandage back and forth until the finger is covered with several layers of bandage (see illustration #3).

• To keep the bandage in place, start at the bottom and wrap the bandage in circles up the finger and back to the bottom (see illustration #4).

• To finish securing the bandage, apply a piece of tape (approximately 6" or 15 cm long) up one side of the finger, over the fingertip, and down the other side. Avoid securing the dressing with a *circle* of tape. Because tape doesn't stretch with swelling of the area as the elastic wrap does, a circle of tape can become a tourniquet, impairing circulation.

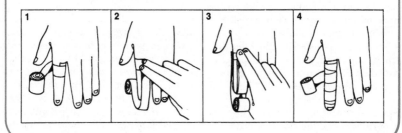

## Equipment

Waterproof trash bag □ clean examination gloves □ gown, if indicated □ sterile 4" x 4" gauze sponges □ ABD pads, if needed □ topical medication, if ordered □ adhesive or other tape □ materials as needed for cleansing, irrigating, culturing, and packing the wound □ optional: skin protectant, Telfa™ pads, acetone, sterile normal saline solution, Montgomery straps or T-binder, and graduated container.

*For a wound with a drain:* sterile scissors and sterile 4" x 4" gauze sponges without cotton lining.

*For pouching a wound:* collection pouch with drainage port.

Sterile cleansing swabs saturated with povidone-iodine are available. Foam dressing is available for managing open granulating wounds. Commercial adhesive gauze is available for dressing application. Prepackaged, sterile dressing sets, with or without instruments, are also available.

## Preparation of equipment

Check the existing dressing *to estimate the amount of gauze needed for the new dressing,* or calculate the amount from previous dressing changes. Assemble all equipment in the patient's room. Check the expiration date on each sterile package and inspect for tears. Open the waterproof trash bag and place it near the patient's bed. Position the bag *to avoid reaching across the sterile field or the wound when disposing of soiled articles.* Form a cuff by turning down the top of the trash bag *to provide a wide opening and prevent contamination of instruments or gloves by touching the bag's edge.*

## Essential steps

● Check the doctor's order for specific wound-care and medication instructions. Be sure to note the location of surgical drains *to avoid dislodging them during the procedure.* Assess the patient's condition.

● Check for patient allergies, especially to adhesive tape and povidone-iodine or other topical solutions or medications.

● Explain the procedure to the patient, provide privacy, and position the patient as necessary. Expose only the wound site *to avoid chilling the patient.*

● Wash your hands thoroughly. Put on a gown, if necessary, *to shield your uniform from wound drainage and prevent its transferrence to others.* Put on clean examination gloves.

● Loosen the soiled dressing by holding the patient's skin and pulling the tape toward the wound. *This protects the newly formed tissue and prevents stress on the incision line.* Moisten the tape with acetone or baby oil, if necessary, *to make removal less painful, particularly from hairy skin.*

● Slowly remove the soiled dressing. If the gauze adheres to the wound, loosen it by moistening with sterile normal saline solution.

● Observe the dressing for the amount, type, color, and odor of drainage.

● Discard the dressing and the examination gloves in the waterproof trash bag.

● Establish a sterile field with all the equipment and supplies you'll need for wound care.

● Put on sterile gloves. Obtain a culture, if ordered; then cleanse the wound.

● Observe the wound *for approximation of the incision line and for signs of infection, such as excessive redness, heat, swelling, and odor.* If such signs occur or the patient reports sudden, new, or progressing pain, notify the doctor.

● Irrigate the wound, if ordered. Apply any prescribed topical medication.

● If ordered, pack the wound with gauze sponges folded to fit. Avoid using cotton-lined gauze sponges, *because cotton fibers can adhere to the wound surface and cause complications.*

● Apply a skin protectant, if warranted.

● To apply the new dressing, begin by gently placing sterile 4″ x 4″ gauze sponges at the wound center and moving progressively outward to the edges of the wound site. Extend the gauze at least 1″ (2.5 cm) beyond the incision line in each direction, and cover the wound evenly with enough sterile dressings (usually two or three layers) to absorb all drainage until the next dressing change. Use ABD pads for outer layers, if needed for added absorbency.

● When the dressing is in place, remove and discard your gloves, *because the tape readily sticks to them and proves difficult to apply.*

● Secure the edges of the dressing to the patient's skin with strips of tape *to maintain sterility of the wound site.* Or, secure the dressing with a T-binder or Montgomery straps *to prevent skin excoriation from repeated removal of tape necessitated by frequent dressing changes.*

● Make sure the patient is comfortable.

● Properly dispose of solutions and trash bag, and clean or dispose of soiled equipment and supplies according to institutional policy. If the patient's wound is draining purulent material, don't return unopened sterile supplies to the sterile supply cabinet, *to prevent cross-contamination of other supplies.*

● For the recently postoperative patient or a patient with complications, check the dressing every 30 minutes or as ordered. For the patient with a properly healing wound, check it at least once every 8 hours.

*To apply a simple dry sterile dressing:*

● Cleanse the wound with an antisep-

## WET DRESSING

Apply a wet dressing, as ordered, to partially healed wounds, wounds without copious drainage, and wounds with small amounts of ischemic-necrotic tissue. This dressing prevents wound desiccation, painful removal, and removal of viable cells along with debris that can occur with a dry dressing. However, a wet dressing won't debride a wound covered by a hard eschar.

Use the same technique for application of a wet dressing as for a dry dressing, with one exception—soak the gauze pad in a wetting solution or medication for a few moments before placing it on the wound. The most commonly used wetting solutions and medications include:

• **isotonic solutions,** such as sterile normal saline or lactated Ringer's solution, which aid mechanical debridement

• **hydrogen peroxide** (commonly used half strength), which irrigates the wound and aids mechanical debridement. Its foaming action also warms the wound, promoting vasodilation and reducing inflammation.

• **acetic acid,** which treats *Pseudomonas* infection

• **sodium hypochlorite** (Dakin's solution), which is an antiseptic that also slightly dissolves necrotic tissue. This solution is unstable and must be freshly prepared every 24 hours.

• **povidone-iodine,** which is a broad-spectrum, fast-acting antimicrobial. Watch for patient sensitivity to it. Also, protect the surrounding skin from contact, because this solution can dry and stain the skin.

• **antibiotic solutions** containing neomycin, chloramphenicol, gentamicin, and carbenicillin. Their use is controversial, because some clinicians believe they cause overgrowth of resistant organisms.

• **enzymatic agents** (collagenase, sutilains, and fibrinolysin and desoxyribonuclease), which digest and liquefy necrotic debris. Their use is controversial, because some clinicians consider their effectiveness unproven.

---

tic skin cleanser *to remove all blood, pus, necrotic tissue, and foreign matter.*

• Layer sterile 4″ x 4″ gauze sponges over the wound.

• Tape the dressing to the patient's skin.

*To dress a wound with a drain:*

• Prepare a drain dressing by using sterile scissors to cut a slit in a sterile 4″ x 4″ gauze sponge. Fold the sponge in half, and cut inward from the center of the folded edge. Don't use a cotton-lined gauze sponge, *because cutting the gauze opens the lining and releases cotton fibers into the wound.* Prepare a second gauze sponge the same way.

• Gently press one folded sponge close to the skin around the drain so the tubing slides into the slit. Press the second folded sponge around the drain from the opposite direction, so the two sponges encircle the tubing.

• Layer as many uncut sterile 4″ x 4″ gauze sponges and/or ABD pads around the tubing as needed *to absorb expected drainage.* Tape the dressing in place, or use a T-binder or Montgomery straps.

*To pouch a heavily draining wound or a wound draining highly caustic fluids:*

• Measure the wound, and cut an opening ⅛″ (0.3 cm) larger in the collection pouch's facing.

• Apply a skin protectant, as needed (see information on ostomy care in Chapter 10, MANAGING GASTROINTESTINAL DISTURBANCES). Some protectants are incorporated with the collection pouch and also provide adhesion.

• Make sure the drainage port at the bottom of the pouch is firmly closed *to prevent leaks.* Then gently press the contoured pouch opening around the wound, beginning at its lower edge, *to catch any drainage.*

*To empty a pouch:*

• Insert the bottom half of the pouch into a graduated collection container and open the drainage port. Note the color, consistency, odor, and amount of fluid. Obtain a culture sample, if ordered, and send it to the laboratory immediately. Remember to follow isolation precautions when handling infectious drainage.

• Wipe the bottom of the pouch and the drainage port with a gauze sponge *to remove any spillage that could irritate the patient's skin or cause an odor.* Then reseal the port. Change the pouch only when it is leaking or is no longer adhesive. *More frequent changes are unnecessary and only irritate the patient's skin.*

### Special considerations

Because many doctors prefer to change the first postoperative dressing themselves *to check the incision line,* avoid changing the first dressing, without specific instructions. If no order exists and drainage is evident on the dressing, reinforce the dressing with fresh sterile gauze. Request an order to change the dressing, or ask the doctor to change the dressing as soon as possible. A reinforced dressing shouldn't remain in place longer than 24 hours, *because it's an excellent medium for bacterial growth.*

Replace any dressing that becomes wet from the outside, as from spilled drinking water, bath water, or urine as soon as possible, *to prevent wound contamination.*

Use acetone to remove any adhesive tape residue. If the doctor wants to avoid debriding the wound, place Telfa™ pads directly over the incision line before applying gauze sponges, *because gauze adheres to the wound and debrides it.*

If the patient has two wounds in the same area, cover each separately with layers of sterile 4″ x 4″ gauze sponges. Then cover both sites with an ABD pad secured to the patient's skin with tape. Don't eliminate the gauze sponges and use the ABD pad alone to cover both sites, *because the single pad quickly saturates with drainage, promoting cross-contamination.*

*To save time when dressing a wound with a drain,* use precut tracheostomy pads or drain sponges instead of custom-cutting gauze sponges to fit around the drain. If the patient is sensitive to adhesive tape, use paper or silk tape, *because these cause less skin reaction and peel off more easily than adhesive tape.* Use a surgical mask to cradle a chin or jawline dressing; *this provides a secure dressing and avoids*

---

## MONTGOMERY STRAPS

Secure an abdominal dressing requiring frequent changes with Montgomery straps. If ready-made straps aren't available at your hospital, follow these steps to make your own:

• Cut four to six strips of 2″ or 3″ wide tape of sufficient length to allow the tape to extend about 6″ beyond the wound on each side. (The length of the tape varies, depending on the patient's size and the type and amount of dressing.)

• Fold one end of each strip 2″ or 3″ over on itself, sticky side in. Then, fold each end again in half, and cut a small semicircle into it. (When using 3″ tape, cut two small semicircles in each end.) To make circles from the semicircles, open the ends of the tape.

• Cleanse the patient's skin to prevent irritation. After the skin dries, apply a skin protective. Then apply the sticky part of each tape to the skin, so the circle of one strip faces the circle of another strip on the opposite side of the dressing. Thread a separate piece, about 12″ (30.5 cm), of gauze, umbilical tape, or twill string through each pair of holes in the straps and tie each thread as you would a shoelace.

• Repeat this procedure according to the number of Montgomery straps needed.

• Replace Montgomery straps whenever they become soiled (every 2 or 3 days). If skin maceration occurs, place new tapes about 1″ (2.5 cm) away from any irritation.

---

*shaving the patient's hair.*

If ordered, use a collodion spray or other similar topical protectant instead of a gauze dressing; *this moisture- and contaminant-proof covering dries in a clear impermeable film that leaves the wound visible for observation and avoids the friction of a dressing.* It peels off or dissolves with special solvent after the wound heals. Particularly useful for children who are active and heal quickly, it isn't recommended for draining wounds *because of its impermeability.*

If a sump drain isn't adequately collecting wound secretions, reinforce it with an ostomy pouch or other collection bag. Use waterproof tape to strengthen a spot on the front of the pouch near the adhesive opening; then cut a small X in the tape. Feed the drain catheter into the pouch through the X cut. Seal the cut around the tubing with more waterproof tape, and then connect the tubing to the suction pump. *This method frees the drainage port at the bottom of the pouch so you don't have to remove the tubing to empty the pouch.* If you use more than one collection pouch for a wound or wounds, be sure to record the volume of drainage separately for each pouch. Avoid using waterproof material over the dressing, *because it reduces air circulation and therefore predisposes the wound to infection from accumulation of heat and moisture.*

## Complications

Allergy to antiseptic skin-cleansing solution, prescribed topical medication, or adhesive tape may result in skin redness, rash, or excoriation.

## Documentation

Record the date, time, and type of wound management procedure; amount of soiled dressing and packing removed; wound appearance and odor, if present; type, color, consistency, and amount of drainage for each wound; presence and location of drains; any additional procedures, such as irrigation, packing, or application of a topical medication; type and amount of new dressing or pouch applied; and the patient's tolerance.

Record special or detailed wound-care instructions on the nursing-care plan. Record the color and amount of measurable drainage on the intake and output sheet.

SUSAN DONAHUE, RN, BSN
PEGGY FELICE, ET
SANDI WIND, RN, ET

# Wound Irrigation

*Irrigation, the flushing of an area, cleanses tissues and removes cell de-* *bris and excess drainage from an open wound. Irrigation with an antiseptic or antibiotic solution helps the wound heal properly from the inside tissue layers outward to the skin surface; it helps prevent premature surface healing over an abscess pocket or infected tract. Performed properly, wound irrigation requires strict sterile technique. After irrigation, open wounds are usually packed to absorb additional purulent drainage.*

## Equipment

Waterproof trash bag □ linen-saver pad □ emesis basin □ clean examination gloves □ sterile gloves □ gown, if indicated □ prescribed irrigant, such as sterile normal saline, hydrogen peroxide, or antibiotic solutions □ sterile water or sterile saline solution □ soft rubber catheter □ 50- to 60-ml piston syringe □ sterile container □ materials as needed for wound care.

Prepackaged, disposable, sterile irrigation and dressing sets are available. Sterile cleansing swabs saturated with povidone-iodine are available.

## Preparation of equipment

Assemble all equipment in the patient's room. Check the expiration date on each sterile package and inspect for tears. Check the sterilization date and the date of first opening on each bottle of irrigating solution; don't use any solution that's been opened longer than 24 hours.

Using aseptic technique, dilute the prescribed irrigant to the correct proportions with sterile water or sterile saline solution, if necessary. Let the solution stand until it reaches room temperature, or warm it to 90° to 95° F. (32.2° to 35° C.).

Open the waterproof trash bag and place it near the patient's bed *to avoid reaching across the sterile field or the wound when disposing of soiled articles.* Form a cuff by turning down the top of the trash bag *to provide a wide opening and prevent contamination by touching the bag's edge.*

## Essential steps

• Check the doctor's order, and assess the patient's condition.
• Check for patient allergies, especially to povidone-iodine or other topical solutions or medications.
• Explain the procedure to the patient, provide privacy, and position the patient correctly for the procedure. Place the linen-saver pad under the patient *to catch any spills and avoid linen changes.* Place the emesis basin below the wound *so the irrigating solution flows into it from the wound.*
• Wash your hands thoroughly. If necessary, put on a gown *to protect your uniform from wound drainage and contamination.* Put on clean examination gloves.
• Remove the soiled dressing; then discard the dressing and gloves in the trash bag.
• Establish a sterile field with all the equipment and supplies you'll need for irrigation and wound care. Pour the prescribed amount of irrigating solution into a sterile container, *so you won't contaminate your sterile gloves later by picking up unsterile containers.* Put on sterile gloves.
• Fill the syringe with the irrigating solution; then connect the rubber catheter to the syringe. Use a soft rubber catheter *to minimize tissue trauma, irritation, and bleeding.*
• Gently insert the catheter into the wound until you feel resistance. Avoid forcing the catheter into the wound, *to prevent tissue damage or, in an abdominal wound, intestinal perforation.*
• Gently instill a slow, steady stream of irrigating solution into the wound until the syringe empties. Make sure the solution flows from the clean to the dirty area of the wound *to prevent contamination of clean tissue by exudate.* Be sure the solution reaches all areas of the wound.
• Pinch the catheter closed as you withdraw the syringe *to prevent aspirating drainage and contaminating the equipment.*
• Refill the syringe, reconnect it to the catheter, and repeat the irrigation.
• Continue to irrigate the wound until you've administered the prescribed amount of solution or until the solution returns clear. Note the amount of solution administered. Then, remove and discard the catheter and syringe in the waterproof trash bag.
• Keep the patient positioned *to allow further wound drainage into the basin.*
• Cleanse the area around the wound *to promote local circulation and help prevent skin breakdown and infection.*
• Pack the wound, if ordered, and apply a sterile dressing. Remove and discard your gloves and gown.
• Make sure the patient is comfortable.
• Properly dispose of drainage, solutions, and trash bag, and clean or dispose of soiled equipment and supplies according to institutional policy. *To prevent contamination of other supplies,* don't return unopened sterile supplies to the sterile supply cabinet.

## Special considerations

Try to coordinate wound irrigation with the doctor's visit *so he can inspect the wound.* Use only the irrigant specified by the doctor, *because others may be erosive or otherwise harmful.* When using an irritating irrigant, such as Dakin's solution, spread sterile petrolatum around the wound site *to protect the patient's skin.* Remember to follow your institution's policy concerning wound and skin precautions when appropriate. Irrigate with a bulb syringe only if a piston syringe is unavailable; *the piston syringe reduces the risk of aspirating drainage.* If the wound is not particularly small or deep, you may want to use just the syringe for irrigation.

## Documentation

Record the date and time of irrigation, amount and type of irrigant, appearance of the wound, any sloughing tissue or exudate, amount of solution returned, and the patient's tolerance of the treatment.

SUSAN DONAHUE, RN, BSN

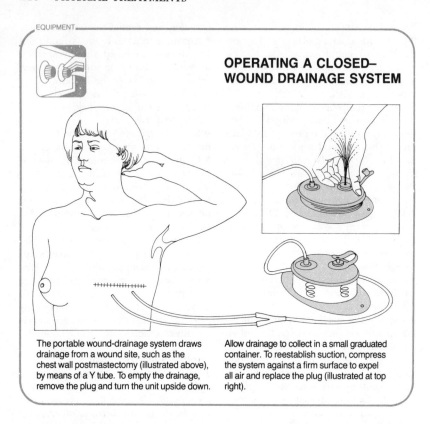

## OPERATING A CLOSED–WOUND DRAINAGE SYSTEM

The portable wound-drainage system draws drainage from a wound site, such as the chest wall postmastectomy (illustrated above), by means of a Y tube. To empty the drainage, remove the plug and turn the unit upside down.

Allow drainage to collect in a small graduated container. To reestablish suction, compress the system against a firm surface to expel all air and replace the plug (illustrated at top right).

# Closed–Wound Drain
### [Hemovac™]

*Usually inserted during surgery in anticipation of substantial postoperative drainage, Hemovac—one type of closed-wound drainage system—promotes healing and prevents swelling by suctioning the serosanguineous fluid that accumulates at the trauma site. By removing this fluid, the drain helps reduce the risk of infection and skin breakdown and the number of dressing changes. A closed wound drain consists of perforated tubing connected to a portable vacuum unit. The tubing lies within the wound and usually leaves the body from a site secondary to the primary suture line to preserve the integrity of wound closure. The exit site is treated as a surgical wound, because the drain is usually sutured to the skin.*

*If wound drainage is heavy, the closed drain may be left in place for longer than 1 week. Frequent emptying and measurement of the contents is required to maintain maximum suction and prevent strain on the suture line.*

## Equipment
Measuring cup or graduated cylinder □ sterile laboratory container, if needed □ sterile alcohol sponges □ materials for drain-suture care.

## Essential steps
• Check the doctor's order, and assess the patient's condition.
• Explain the procedure to the patient, provide privacy, and wash your hands.
• Unclip the vacuum unit from the pa-

tient's bed or gown.
- Using aseptic technique, release the vacuum by removing the spout plug on the collection chamber. The container expands completely as it draws in air.
- Empty the unit's contents into a graduated container, and note the amount and appearance of the drainage. If diagnostic tests will be performed on the fluid sample, pour the drainage directly into a sterile container, note the amount and appearance, and send it to the laboratory.
- Maintaining aseptic technique, use a sterile alcohol sponge to cleanse the unit's spout and plug.
- *To reestablish the vacuum that creates the drain's suction power,* fully compress the vacuum unit. With one hand holding the unit compressed *to maintain the vacuum,* replace the spout plug with your other hand.
- Check the patency of the equipment. Make sure the tubing is free of twists, kinks, and leaks, *because the drainage system must be airtight to work properly.* The vacuum unit should remain compressed when you release manual pressure; rapid reinflation indicates an air leak. If this occurs, reprime the unit and make sure the spout plug is secure.
- Secure the vacuum unit to the patient's bedding or, if he is ambulatory, to his gown. Fasten it below wound level *to promote drainage.* Do not apply tension on drainage tubing when fastening it *to prevent possible dislodgement.* Wash your hands thoroughly.
- Observe the sutures that secure the drain to the patient's skin, looking for signs of pulling or tearing of the suture, and for swelling or infection of surrounding skin. Gently cleanse the sutures with sterile gauze sponges soaked in an antiseptic skin cleanser or with a prepackaged antiseptic swab.
- Properly dispose of drainage, solutions, and trash bag, and clean or dispose of soiled equipment and supplies according to institutional policy.

### Special considerations
Be careful not to mistake chest tubes for closed-wound drains, *because the vacuum of a chest tube should never be released.*

Empty the system and measure its contents once a shift if drainage has accumulated or more often if drainage is excessive. *Removing excess drainage maintains maximum suction and avoids strain on the drain's suture line.*

If the patient has more than one closed drain, number the drains *so the drainage from each site can be recorded.*

### Complications
Occlusion of the tubing by fibrin, clots, or other particles can reduce or obstruct drainage.

### Documentation
Record the date and time you empty the system, the appearance of the drain site and presence of swelling or signs of infection, any equipment malfunction and resultant nursing action, and the patient's tolerance of the treatment. On the intake and output sheet, record drainage color, consistency, type, and amount. If more than one closed drain is present, number the drains and record the above information separately for each drainage site.

SUSAN DONAHUE, RN, BSN

---

### Selected References

Brunner, Lillian S., and Suddarth, Doris S. *The Lippincott Manual of Nursing Practice,* 3rd ed. Philadelphia: J.B. Lippincott Co., 1982.

Kozier, Barbara, and Erb, Glenora Lea. *Fundamentals of Nursing: Concepts and Procedures.* Menlo Park, Calif.: Addison-Wesley Publishing Co., 1979.

Wood, Lucile, A., and Rambo, Beverly J., eds. *Nursing Skills for Allied Health Services,* 2nd ed. Philadelphia: W.B. Saunders Co., vol. 1 and 2, 1977; vol. 3, 1980.

# 6 Intravascular Therapy

# Intravascular Therapy

## Introduction

Although the basic idea is more than 300 years old, intravascular therapy did not become widely accepted until the 1920s, when a way was found to rid intravenous (I.V.) fluids of pyrogens. This made it possible to safely infuse normal saline and dextrose solutions. Later, the development of plastic and silicone catheters heralded a series of equipment advances that have further reduced the risk of complications and made fluid administration more efficient. Today, more than 25% of all patients receive some form of intravascular therapy during hospitalization, and more than 200 commercially prepared I.V. fluids are available.

### Nurse's role

Although the nurse doesn't necessarily insert all types of intravascular lines, she is responsible for maintaining these lines and preventing complications throughout the patient's therapy. Nurses must be sufficiently trained before being allowed to perform intravascular insertions.

A doctor performs venesections and inserts central venous and arterial lines. These are minor surgical procedures that are routinely performed at bedside, thereby permitting therapy to begin quickly.

### Nursing-care plan

The decision to implement intravascular therapy is a medical one. However, nursing assessment of the patient may help the doctor decide whether or not to start intravascular therapy. Once this is decided, a nursing-care plan must focus on properly preparing the patient, maintaining appropriate aseptic technique, and preventing potential complications through meticulous maintenance of the line and insertion site. Intravascular therapy always carries the risk of complications, including infection, phlebitis, emboli, extravasation with or without tissue necrosis, and exsanguination. Any lapse of aseptic technique can introduce pathogens into the circulatory system.

Routine care during intravascular therapy, such as daily tubing changes and regular site rotation, help prevent complications and are less costly and debilitating—and less time-consuming, in the long run—than the treatments complications may require. Daily site care and dressing changes permit observation of the insertion site for signs of inflammation or infection, the most common complications.

### Team concept

Intravascular therapy is developing into a nursing subspecialty. Recent studies have shown that fewer complications develop when the same nurse consistently manages a patient's intravascular therapy. The Centers for Disease Control recommend use of intravascular teams. In some institutions, this team concept has been revived and designated nurses manage specific aspects of intravascular therapy. This system offers the advantage of continuity of care and allows the staff nurse to concentrate on the patient's other needs.

ANNE MORACA-SAWICKI, RN, MSN

## PERIPHERAL LINES

# Preparation for I.V. Therapy

*Before initiation of I.V. therapy, proper selection and assembly of equipment is necessary to ensure accurate delivery of an I.V. solution. Selection of an I.V. administration set reflects the rate and type of infusion and the type of I.V. solution container. Two types of drip system are available: the macrodrip and the microdrip set. The macrodrip set can deliver a solution in large quantities and at rapid rates because it delivers a larger amount of solution with each drop than the microdrip set. The microdrip set, used for pediatric and certain adult patients requiring small or closely regulated amounts of I.V. solution, delivers a smaller quantity of solution with each drop. Administration tubing with a secondary injection port permits separate or simultaneous infusion of two solutions; tubing with a piggyback port and a backcheck valve permits intermittent infusion of a secondary solution and, on its completion, automatic return to infusion of the primary solution. Vented I.V. tubing is selected for a solution contained in a nonvented bottle; nonvented tubing, for a solution contained in a bag or vented bottle.*

*Assembly of I.V. equipment requires aseptic technique to prevent contamination, which can cause local or systemic infection.*

### Equipment

I.V. solution □ I.V. administration set □ filter, if needed □ I.V. pole □ alcohol sponges □ medication and label, if necessary.

### Preparation of equipment

Verify the type, volume, and expiration date of the I.V. solution. Discard any outdated solution. If the solution is con-tained in a glass bottle, inspect for chips or cracks; if it is in a plastic bag, squeeze to detect leaks. Examine the I.V. solution for particles, abnormal discoloration, and cloudiness. If present, discard the solution and notify the pharmacy or dispensing department. If ordered, add medication to the solution, and place a completed medication-added label on the container. Remove the administration set from its box and observe for cracks, holes, and missing clamps.

### Essential steps

● Wash your hands thoroughly *to prevent introducing contaminants during the procedure.*
● Slide the flow clamp of the administration set close to the drip chamber or injection port, and close the clamp.

*To prepare a nonvented bottle:*
● Remove the bottle's metal cap and inner disk, if present.
● Place the bottle on a stable surface, and wipe the rubber stopper with an alcohol sponge.
● Remove the protective cap from the administration set spike, and push the spike through the center of the bottle's rubber stopper. Avoid twisting or angling the spike *to prevent pieces of the stopper from breaking off and falling into the solution.*
● Invert the bottle. If its vacuum is intact, you'll hear a hissing sound and see air bubbles rise (this may not occur if you've already added medication). If it is not intact, discard the bottle.
● Hang the bottle on the I.V. pole, and squeeze the drip chamber until it is half full.

*To prepare a vented bottle:*
● Remove the bottle's metal cap and latex diaphragm *to release the vacuum.* If the vacuum is not intact (except after medication has been added), discard the bottle.
● Place the bottle on a stable surface, and wipe the rubber stopper with an

alcohol sponge.
- Remove the protective cap from the administration set spike, and push the spike through the insertion port next to the air vent tube opening.
- Hang the bottle on the I.V. pole, and squeeze the drip chamber until it is half full.

*To prepare a bag:*
- Place the bag on a flat, stable surface or hang it on an I.V. pole. Then, remove the protective cap or tear tab from the tubing insertion port, and wipe the port with an alcohol sponge.
- Remove the protective cap from the administration set spike.
- Holding the port carefully and firmly with one hand, quickly insert the spike with your other hand.
- Hang the bag, if not already done, and squeeze the drip chamber until it is half full.

*To prime the I.V. tubing and conclude preparation:*
- If desired, attach a filter to the opposite end of the I.V. tubing, and follow the manufacturer's instructions for filling and priming.
- If you're not using a filter, remove the protective cap on the tubing. Then, while maintaining the sterility of the end of the tubing, hold it over a wastebasket or sink, and open the flow clamp.
- Leave the clamp open until I.V. solution flows through the entire length of tubing, forcing out all air. Invert all Y-injection sites and backcheck valves, and tap them, if necessary, *to fill them with solution.*
- After priming the tubing, close the clamp and replace the protective cover. Then, loop the tubing over the I.V. pole.
- Label the container with the patient's name and room number, the date and time, the container number, the ordered duration of infusion, and your initials.

### Special considerations
Always use aseptic technique when preparing I.V. components. If you contaminate the administration set or container, replace it with a new one *to prevent introducing contaminants into the system.*

## GUIDELINES FOR USING IN-LINE I.V. FILTERS

An in-line I.V. filter, such as the 0.22-micron model, removes pathogens and particles from I.V. solutions, helping to reduce the risk of infusion phlebitis. Because a filter is expensive and its installation in an I.V. line is cumbersome and time-consuming, it is not routinely used. Consequently, many institutions require use of a filter only when an admixture is being administered. However, if you're unsure whether or not to use a filter, follow these guidelines.

**Use in-line I.V. filters:**
- for any infusion to an immunodeficient patient
- for hyperalimentation
- when using additives comprising many separate particles, such as antibiotics requiring reconstitution, or when administering several additives
- when using rubber injection sites or plastic diaphragms frequently
- when phlebitis is likely to occur.
 Be sure to change in-line I.V. filters at least every 24 hours. If you don't, bacteria trapped in the filter release endotoxin, a pyrogen small enough to pass through the filter into the bloodstream.

**Avoid using in-line I.V. filters:**
- when administering solutions with large particles that will clog the filter and stop I.V. flow, for example, blood and its components, suspensions (such as amphotericin B), emulsions (such as Liposyn), and high–molecular-volume plasma expanders (such as Dextran)
- when administering a small dosage of a drug (5 mg or less) because the filter may absorb it.

If necessary, you can use vented tubing with a vented bottle. To do this, don't remove the latex diaphragm. Instead, insert the spike into the larger indentation in the diaphragm.

Change I.V. tubing every 48 hours, or more frequently if the solution is running too slowly, and change the filter every 24 hours or sooner if it becomes clogged.

### Documentation
None.

HELENE RITTING NAWROCKI, RN

# Use of a Volume-control Set

*A volume-control set—an I.V. line with a chamber—delivers precise amounts of fluid and shuts off when the fluid is exhausted, preventing air from entering the I.V. line. This device is especially useful for continuous infusion of fluids or medication in children or for intermittent infusion of medication to adults already receiving I.V. therapy.*

## Equipment
Volume-control set □ I.V. solution □ 20G to 22G 1″ needle □ I.V. pole (for setting up a primary I.V. line) □ alcohol sponges □ medication in labeled syringe and 20G to 22G 1″ needle, if needed.

Although various models of volume-control sets are available, each set consists of a graduated chamber (120 to 250 ml), with a spike and filtered air line on its top and administration tubing underneath. The hinged latex valve and floating latex diaphragm sets have a valve at the bottom that closes when the chamber empties; the membrane filter set has a filter at the bottom that prevents the passage of air as long as it is wet.

## Preparation of equipment
Inspect the equipment carefully *to ensure its sterility and the absence of flaws.* Take the equipment to the patient's bedside.

## Essential steps
• Wash your hands, and explain the procedure to the patient. If an I.V. line is already in place, observe its insertion site for signs of infiltration or infection.
• Remove the volume-control set from its box, and close all the clamps.
• Remove the guard from the volume-control set spike, insert the spike into the I.V. solution container, and hang the container on the I.V. pole. If desired, spike a new solution bag after hanging it.

• Open the air vent clamp. Then, open the lower clamp on the I.V. tubing and slide it upward until it's positioned slightly below the drip chamber. Next, close the clamp.
• If you're using a volume-control set with a hinged latex valve or floating latex diaphragm, open the upper clamp until the fluid chamber fills with about 30 ml of solution. Then, close the clamp and carefully squeeze the drip chamber until it is half full.

If you're using a volume-control set with a membrane filter, open the upper clamp until the fluid chamber fills with about 30 ml of solution, and then close the clamp. Open the lower clamp, and squeeze the drip chamber flat with two fingers of your opposite hand. *If you squeeze the drip chamber with the lower clamp closed, you'll damage the membrane filter.* Keeping the drip chamber flat, close the lower clamp. Now, release and reshape the drip chamber, so it fills halfway.
• Open the lower clamp, prime the tubing, and close the clamp. To use as a primary line, insert adapter into the catheter or needle hub. To use as a secondary line, attach a needle to the adapter on the volume-control set. Wipe the Y-injection port of the primary tubing with an alcohol sponge, and insert the needle. Then, tape the connection.
• To add medication, wipe the injection port on the volume-control set with an alcohol sponge, and inject the medication. Place a label on the chamber, and indicate the dosage and the date. Avoid using a felt-tip marker, *because the plastic chamber absorbs ink.*
• Open the upper clamp, fill the fluid chamber with the prescribed amount of solution, and close the clamp. Gently rotate the chamber to mix the medication.
• If present, turn off the primary solution or set the line on a low drip rate *to maintain an open line.*
• Open the lower clamp on the volume-control set, and adjust the drip rate as ordered. After completion of the infusion, open the upper clamp and let 10 ml of I.V. solution flow into the chamber and

# VOLUME-CONTROL SETS

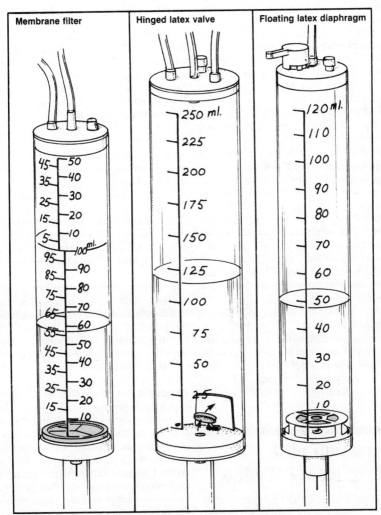

**Membrane filter**

**Hinged latex valve**

**Floating latex diaphragm**

Because of differences in their structures, the three types of volume-control sets—the membrane filter, the hinged latex valve, and the floating latex diaphragm—have different air lock mechanisms.

The membrane filter, shown in device at left, is rigid and remains stationary at the bottom of the fluid chamber. As long as the filter stays wet, it prevents air from entering drip chamber. The hinged latex valve, shown in center device, and the floating latex diaphragm, shown in device at right, rise when the fluid chamber is full and fall to cover the opening in the bottom of the fluid chamber when it's empty, preventing air from entering drip chamber.

through the tubing *to flush them.*
• If you're using the volume-control set as a secondary I.V. line, close the lower clamp and reset the flow rate on the primary line. If you're using the set as a primary I.V. line, close the lower clamp, refill the chamber to prescribed amount, and begin the infusion again.

### Special considerations
Always check compatibility of medication with the I.V. solution. If you're using a membrane filter set, avoid administering suspensions, emulsions, blood, or blood components through it.

If you're using a latex diaphragm set, the diaphragm may stick after repeated use. If it does, close the air vent and upper clamp, invert the drip chamber, and squeeze it. If the diaphragm opens, reopen the clamp and continue to use the set.

If the drip chamber of a hinged latex valve or floating latex diaphragm set overfills, immediately close the upper clamp and air vent, invert the chamber, and squeeze the excess fluid from the drip chamber back into the graduated chamber.

### Documentation
If you add a drug to the volume-control set, record the amount and type of medication, the amount of fluid used to dilute it, and the time of infusion.

HELENE RITTING NAWROCKI, RN

# Insertion of a Peripheral I.V. Line

*One of the most commonly performed procedures, insertion of a peripheral I.V. line involves selection of a cannula and insertion site, application of a tourniquet, preparation of the site, and venipuncture. Selection of a cannula and site depends on the type of solution; the frequency and duration of infusion; the patient's age, size, and condition; and the* patency and location of available veins. The most favorable venipuncture sites are the cephalic, basilic, and antebrachial veins in the lower arm and the veins in the dorsum of the hand; the least favorable are the leg and foot veins because of the increased risk of thrombophlebitis.

Use of a peripheral line allows administration of fluids, medication, blood, and blood components and maintenance of an open vein. Insertion at a particular site is contraindicated in a sclerotic vein and in the presence of burns or an arteriovenous fistula.

### Equipment
Alcohol sponges □ povidone-iodine sponges and ointment □ tourniquet (such as soft rubber tubing or blood pressure cuff) □ two I.V. needles or I.V. catheter devices □ sterile 2″ x 2″ gauze sponges □ 1″ nonallergenic tape □ I.V. solution, with attached and primed administration set □ I.V. pole □ optional: armboard, 2″ roller gauze, and small adhesive bandage.

Commercial venipuncture kits are available with or without an I.V. needle or I.V. catheter device. In many hospitals, venipuncture equipment is kept on a tray or cart, allowing choice of the correct needle or catheter and easy replacement of contaminated items.

### Preparation of equipment
Check the information on the label of the I.V. solution container, including the patient's name and room number, the type of solution, the time and date of its preparation, the preparer's name, and the ordered infusion rate. Compare the doctor's orders with the solution label *to ensure the correct infusion.* Then, select the smallest-gauge cannula possible for the infusion unless subsequent therapy will require a larger cannula; *smaller gauges cause less trauma to veins and allow greater blood flow around their tips, thereby reducing the risk of clotting.*

### Essential steps
• Place the I.V. pole in the proper slot

in the patient's bed. If you're using a portable I.V. pole, position it close to the patient.

• Hang the I.V. solution with attached primed administration set on the I.V. pole.

• Verify the patient's identity by comparing the information on the solution container with the patient's wristband.

• Wash your hands thoroughly *to prevent infection.* Then, explain the procedure to the patient *to ensure cooperation and reduce anxiety, which can cause a vasomotor response resulting in venous constriction.*

---

EQUIPMENT

## NEEDLES AND CATHETERS FOR PERIPHERAL LINES

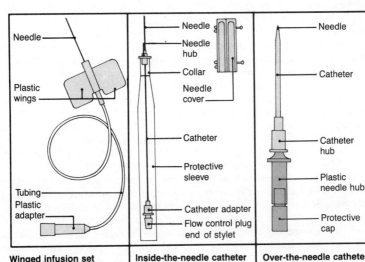

**Winged infusion set**
*Purpose:* short-term therapy for any cooperative adult patient; therapy of any duration for an infant or child or for an elderly patient with fragile or sclerotic veins
*Advantages:* lower incidence of infection and phlebitis than with catheters; easy to insert and secure
*Disadvantage:* risk of irritation or puncture of vein from movement

**Inside-the-needle catheter**
*Purpose:* long-term therapy for the active or agitated patient; also used for central venous insertion
*Advantages:* puncture of vein less likely than with a needle; more comfortable for the patient once it's in place; available in many lengths; most plastic catheters contain radiopaque thread, permitting easy location
*Disadvantages:* greater incidence of infection and phlebitis than with a needle or shorter over-the-needle catheter; some hospitals may not allow nurses to insert it; catheter easily severed; kinking possible due to joint flexion

**Over-the-needle catheter**
*Purpose:* long-term therapy for the active or agitated patient
*Advantages:* puncture of vein less likely than with a needle; is more comfortable for the patient once it's in place; contains radiopaque thread for easy location; easy to insert
*Disadvantages:* greater incidence of infection and phlebitis than with a needle; kinking possible due to joint flexion

• If you're using a winged infusion set, connect the adapter to the administration set, and unclamp the line until fluid flows from the open end of the needle cover. Then, clamp the line and place the needle on a sterile surface, such as the inside of its packaging.

• If you're using a catheter, open its package *to allow easy access.*

• Select the puncture site—preferably a vein in the nondominant arm, but never one in an edematous or impaired arm or leg. For fluid replacement, choose a small vein unless a large vein will be needed for subsequent therapy; this leaves the large veins available for emergency infusion. If long-term therapy is anticipated, start with a vein at the most distal site so you can move upward as needed for further I.V. insertion sites. For infusion of a caustic medication, choose a site away from joints, with plenty of subcutaneous tissue. Be sure the vein can accommodate the cannula if used.

• Wrap the tourniquet 4″ to 8″ (10 to 20 cm) above the intended puncture site *to dilate the vein.* Check for distal pulse. If it is not present, release the tourniquet and reapply with less tension *to prevent arterial occlusion.*

• Lightly palpate the vein with your index and middle fingers. If it rolls or feels hard or ropelike, select another vein.

• If the vein is easily palpable but not sufficiently dilated, one or more of the following techniques may help raise the vein: Tap gently with your finger over the vein, place the extremity in a dependent position for several seconds, or if you have selected a vein in the arm or hand, tell the patient to open and close his fist several times.

• Cleanse the venipuncture site with an alcohol sponge and then the povidone-iodine, working in a circular motion outward from the site to a diameter of 2″ to 4″ (5 to 10 cm) *to remove flora that would otherwise be introduced into the vascular system with the venipuncture.* Allow the povidone-iodine to dry.

• Grasp the needle or catheter. If you're using a *winged infusion set,* hold the short edges of the wings, with the bevel facing upward, between the thumb and forefinger of your dominant hand. Then, squeeze the wings together.

If you're using an *over-the-needle catheter,* grasp the plastic hub with your dominant hand, remove the cover, and examine the catheter tip. If the edge isn't smooth, discard and replace the device.

If you're using an *inside-the-needle catheter,* grasp the needle hub with one hand, and unsnap the needle cover. Then, rotate the catheter device until the bevel faces upward.

• Using the thumb of your opposite hand, stretch the skin taut below the puncture site *to stabilize the vein.*

• Hold the needle at a 45° angle 4″ (10 cm) below and slightly to one side of the puncture site, with the needle pointing in the direction of venous flow.

• Push the needle through the skin until you meet resistance, but avoid penetrating the vein. Lower the needle to a 15° to 20° angle, and slowly pierce the vein; you should feel it pop.

• When you observe blood flashback behind the needle, tilt the needle slightly upward and advance it farther into the vein *to prevent puncture of the posterior vein wall.*

• If you're using a *winged infusion set,* advance the needle fully, if possible, and hold it in place. Release the tourniquet, open the administration set clamp slightly, and check for free flow or infiltration. Then, tape the winged infusion set and tubing in place, using the chevron method (see *Three Methods of Taping a Venipuncture Site,* page 264), *to prevent movement of the needle, which could cause irritation and phlebitis.* Place a long strip of tape, with its adhesive side facing upward, under the infusion set tubing, directly above the wings, and loop it over and onto the wings and then the skin.

If you're using an *over-the-needle catheter,* pull back on the needle with one hand and advance the catheter fully with your opposite hand. Then, apply pressure to the vein beyond the catheter tip *to prevent blood leakage,* and remove the needle. Release the tourniquet, and attach the administration set to the catheter hub. Then, open the administration set clamp slightly, and check for free flow or infiltration. Using the chevron method, tape the catheter, attaching the tape to the catheter hub.

If you're using an *inside-the-needle catheter*, remove the tourniquet, hold the needle in place with one hand, and, with your opposite hand, grasp the catheter through the protective sleeve. Then, slowly thread the catheter through the needle until the hub is within the needle collar. *Never* pull back on the catheter without pulling back on the needle *to avoid severing and releasing the catheter into the circulation, causing an embolus.* If you feel resistance from a valve, withdraw the catheter and needle slightly and reinsert them, rotating the catheter as you pass the valve. Then, withdraw the metal needle, and cover it with the protector. Remove the stylet and protective sleeve, and attach the administration set to the catheter hub. Open the administration set clamp slightly, and check for free flow or infiltration. Use the chevron method to tape the catheter, attaching the tape to the needle hub.

• Apply antimicrobial ointment at the insertion site, and cover with a sterile gauze sponge or small adhesive bandage.
• Loop the I.V. tubing on the extremity, and secure the tubing with tape. *The loop allows some slack to prevent dislodgement of the catheter from tension on the line.*
• Label the last piece of tape with the type and gauge of needle or catheter, the date and time of insertion, and your initials. Adjust the flow rate, as ordered.
• If the puncture site is near a movable joint, secure an armboard with roller gauze or tape over the joint *to provide stability, because excessive movement can dislodge the needle or catheter and increase the risk of thrombophlebitis.*

**Special considerations**
If the patient is elderly, apply the tourniquet carefully *to avoid pinching the skin.* If necessary, apply it over the patient's gown. If routine methods fail to

## REMOVING A PERIPHERAL I.V. LINE

Performed on completion of therapy, for needle or catheter changes, and when infection or infiltration is suspected, removal of a peripheral I.V. line usually requires an alcohol sponge, a sterile gauze pad, and an adhesive bandage. To remove the I.V. line, first clamp the I.V. tubing to stop the flow of solution. Then, gently remove all tape from the skin. Using aseptic technique, open the alcohol sponge, gauze pad, and adhesive bandage, and place them within reach. Hold the sterile gauze pad over the puncture site, and use your other hand to withdraw the needle or catheter slowly and smoothly, keeping it parallel to the skin. (Inspect the catheter tip; if it's not smooth, notify the doctor immediately.) Using the gauze pad, apply firm pressure over the puncture site for 2 to 3 minutes after removing a winged-tip needle and for 5 minutes after removing a catheter or until bleeding has stopped. Cleanse the site with alcohol and apply the adhesive bandage. Or, if blood oozes from the site, apply a pressure bandage. If the site is infected, culture the tip of the cannula and any drainage, according to hospital policy. Then, cleanse the area and apply antiseptic ointment and a sterile dressing. Be sure to document the appearance of the site and any nursing intervention.

dilate the vein sufficiently, apply warm, moist compresses for 3 to 5 minutes. Make sure skin preparation materials are at room temperature, *to avoid vasoconstriction resulting from lower temperatures.* If the patient is allergic to iodine-containing compounds, scrub the skin vigorously with alcohol alone.

If you're penetrating a large vein and institutional policy permits, inject 0.1 to 0.3 ml of lidocaine with a tuberculin syringe around the site; this causes a wheal (which may obscure a smaller vein) but increases patient comfort. Then, hold the needle at a 15° to 20° angle directly over the vein, and pierce the skin and vein in one motion.

If you fail to see blood flashback after entering the vein, pull back slightly and rotate the cannula. If you still fail to see flashback, remove the cannula and try

## MANAGING COMPLICATIONS OF I.V. THERAPY

| COMPLICATION | POSSIBLE CAUSES | SIGNS AND SYMPTOMS |
|---|---|---|
| **Infiltration** | • Needle or catheter displacement<br>• Puncture of the vein | • Cool skin, swelling, and discomfort around site<br>• Edema of entire arm or leg<br>• Absence of blood flashback<br>• Sluggish flow rate |
| **Phlebitis** | • Injury to vein (during venipuncture or from needle movement)<br>• Irritation to vein | • Edema along the course of the affected vein<br>• Sore, hard, cordlike, and warm vein; possibly a red line above the venipuncture site |
| **Circulatory overload** | • Excessive or too rapid administration | • Increased blood pressure and central venous pressure<br>• Venous dilatation, especially of neck veins<br>• Rapid breathing, shortness of breath, rales |
| **Air embolism** (more common with a central venous line than with a peripheral line) | • Empty solution container<br>• Air in tubing<br>• Loose connections, allowing air to enter tubing | • Decreased blood pressure<br>• Weak, rapid pulse<br>• Cyanosis<br>• Loss of consciousness |
| **Catheter embolism** (most common with inside-the-needle catheters) | • Removal of the catheter before the needle<br>• Attempting to rethread the catheter with a needle<br>• Unsecured catheter | • Discomfort along the vein<br>• Cyanosis<br>• Decreased blood pressure<br>• Weak, rapid pulse<br>• Loss of consciousness |
| **Allergic reaction** | • Hypersensitivity to I.V. solution or additive | • Generalized rash, itching<br>• Shortness of breath, tachycardia (uncommon) |
| **Infection at insertion site** | • Poor technique during insertion, cleansing of site, or tubing changes | • Swelling and tenderness at site |
| **Sepsis** (usually develops immediately or shortly after the infusion begins) | • Pathogens entering the bloodstream through the I.V. line | • Abrupt rise in temperature, chills<br>• Nausea and vomiting<br>• Backache<br>• Generalized malaise |

| INTERVENTION | PREVENTION |
|---|---|
| • Discontinue the infusion, and remove the needle or catheter immediately.<br>• If infiltration is detected within 30 minutes of onset and swelling is slight, apply ice. Otherwise, apply warm, wet compresses to promote absorption, and elevate the affected arm or leg. (See also "Management of Extravasation" in Chapter 7.) | • Stabilize the needle or catheter with a splint if the site lies over a joint or the patient is active.<br>• Palpate occasionally to confirm proper needle position.<br>• Check the I.V. site and flow rate frequently. |
| • Discontinue the infusion, and remove the needle or catheter immediately.<br>• Apply warm, moist compresses.<br>• Notify the doctor.<br>• *Important: To prevent further damage to the vein and formation of clots or emboli, do not* rub or massage the affected arm or leg. | • If you must use an irritating additive in an I.V. infusion, administer it through a large vein with good blood flow.<br>• Maintain the infusion at the prescribed rate. |
| • Slow the infusion to a keep-vein-open rate.<br>• Raise the patient's head, and keep him warm.<br>• Monitor vital signs.<br>• Administer oxygen, if permitted.<br>• Notify the doctor. | • Know the patient's cardiovascular status and history.<br>• Carefully monitor intake and output. |
| • Turn the patient to the left side *so any small air bubbles entering the heart can be absorbed in the pulmonary artery.*<br>• Administer oxygen, if permitted.<br>• Notify the doctor immediately.<br>• Check the system for leaks. | • Change the solution container before it empties.<br>• Clear the tubing of air before starting the infusion.<br>• Keep the insertion site below heart level.<br>• Secure all connections. |
| • Discontinue the infusion.<br>• Apply a tourniquet above the insertion site *to impede venous return and prevent further migration of the catheter.* Be careful not to apply the tourniquet too tightly, because it may obstruct arterial blood flow.<br>• Arrange for an X-ray, to locate the catheter. | • Withdraw the needle and catheter together after an unsuccessful venipuncture attempt.<br>• Take special care when taping or withdrawing an inside-the-needle catheter. |
| • Slow the infusion to a keep-vein-open rate.<br>• Notify the doctor. | • Before beginning the infusion, check the patient's drug history for allergies. |
| • Discontinue the infusion.<br>• Culture the needle or catheter.<br>• Clean site and apply antimicrobial ointment.<br>• Cover the site with a sterile dressing. | • Always use aseptic technique when giving care at or near an I.V. insertion site. |
| • Discontinue the infusion.<br>• Culture cannula and samples of solution.<br>• Record lot number of solution and additives.<br>• Save remaining solution for lab analysis.<br>• Notify the doctor immediately. | • Always use aseptic technique when handling I.V. solutions and equipment. |

again. If you still don't succeed, ask another nurse to perform the venipuncture. If you suspect that the cannula is in the vein, try these measures to facilitate blood flashback: pinch the tubing several times; position the I.V. container below needle level; insert the needle and syringe into the injection port closest to the puncture site; then, close the clamp on the I.V. tubing and attempt to aspirate. If the cannula is tightly in place or the patient is extremely dehydrated or hypovolemic, you may not see blood flashback.

### Complications

Peripheral line complications can result from the needle or catheter (infection, phlebitis, embolism) or from the solution (circulatory overload, infiltration, sepsis, allergic reaction). See *Managing Complications of I.V. Therapy,* pages 258 to 259, for further information.

### Documentation

In your notes or on the appropriate I.V. sheets, record the type and gauge of needle or catheter, the location of the insertion site, the type and flow rate of the I.V. solution, the name and amount of medication in the solution (if any), the date and time, and your initials.

HELENE RITTING NAWROCKI, RN

---

# Insertion of an Intermittent Infusion Set
[*Insertion of a heparin lock*]

*An intermittent infusion set consists of a winged-tip needle with tubing ending in a resealable rubber injection port. Filled with dilute heparin to prevent blood clot formation, the device maintains venous access in patients receiving I.V. medication regularly or intermittently but not requiring continuous infusion of fluids. It proves superior to a keep-vein-open line, because it minimizes the risk of fluid overload and electrolyte imbalance; cuts costs; reduces the risk of contamination by eliminating I.V. solution containers and administration sets; increases patient comfort and mobility; reduces patient anxiety; and allows collection of blood samples without repeated venipuncture.*

*Use of an intermittent infusion set is contraindicated in patients with clotting disorders or uncontrolled bleeding.*

### Equipment

Intermittent infusion set □ dilute heparin solution in a 1-ml syringe □ 25G needle □ povidone-iodine sponges □ alcohol sponges □ venipuncture equipment, dressing, and tape.

Some institutions use a 100 U/ml heparin flush; others use 10 U/ml; and still others use normal saline solution in place of heparin. Prefilled heparin cartridges are available in both dosages for use in a syringe cartridge holder.

### Essential steps

● Wash your hands thoroughly *to prevent contamination of the venipuncture site.*
● Explain the procedure to the patient, and describe the purpose of the intermittent infusion set.
● Remove the set from its packaging, wipe the port with an alcohol sponge, and inject a dilute heparin solution to fill the tubing and needle. *This removes air from the system, preventing formation of an air embolus.*
● Select a venipuncture site, and cleanse it first with povidone-iodine sponges and then with alcohol, wiping outward from the site in a circular motion.
● Perform the venipuncture, and ensure correct needle placement in the vein. Then, release the tourniquet.
● Tape the set in place, using the chevron method (see "Dressing, Tubing, and Solution Changes" in this chapter) or an accepted alternative. Loop the tubing so the injection port is free and easily accessible.
● Apply a sterile dressing. On the last piece of tape used to secure the dressing,

write the time, date, and your initials.
• Flush the set with the remaining heparin *to prevent clot formation.*
• Inject 1 ml of dilute heparin solution every 6 to 12 hours *to maintain the patency of the intermittent infusion set.*

**Special considerations**
If ordered, obtain a blood sample for activated partial thromboplastin time before inserting the intermittent infusion set, because small amounts of heparin can alter the results of this test. If the patient feels a burning sensation during injection of heparin, stop the injection and check needle placement. If the needle is in the vein, inject the heparin at a slower rate, *to minimize irritation.* If the needle is not in the vein, remove and discard it. Then, select a new venipuncture site and, using fresh equipment, restart the procedure.

Change the sterile dressing every 24 hours; the infusion set, every 72 hours, using a new venipuncture site. Some institutions use a polyurethane dressing to cover the entire device. This allows more patient freedom and better observation of the injection site.

**Complications**
Use of an intermittent infusion set has the same potential complications as the use of a peripheral I.V. line. See *Managing Complications of I.V. Therapy,* pages 258 to 259, for further information.

**Documentation**
Record the date and time of insertion, the type and gauge of needle, and the date and time of each heparin flush.
HELENE RITTING NAWROCKI, RN

---

# Venesection
**[Cutdown]**

*Performed by a doctor with a nurse assisting, venesection is the sterile insertion of a catheter into the basilic or*

EQUIPMENT

## TYPES OF MALE ADAPTER PLUGS

Male adapter plugs allow conversion of an existing I.V. line to an intermittent infusion set. To do this, prime the male adapter plug with dilute heparin. Then, clamp the I.V. tubing, remove the administration set from the catheter or needle hub, and insert the male adapter plug. Next, inject the remaining dilute heparin to fill the line and to prevent clot formation.

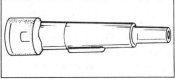

This long male adapter plug slides into place.

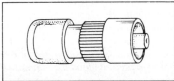

This short male adapter plug twists into place.

*cephalic veins of the antecubital fossa— or, less frequently, into the femoral and saphenous veins because of the risk of phlebitis and emboli—after surgical exposure and incision. After insertion, the catheter is used for the same purposes as a peripheral I.V. line.*

*Venesection is indicated when a vein can't be entered percutaneously—the result of obesity, collapse or sclerosis of the vein, or peripheral vasoconstriction from massive, rapid blood loss.*

**Equipment**
Cutdown tray □ cutdown catheter □ povidone-iodine sponges and ointment □ sterile gown, gloves, and mask for doctor □ sterile drape □ alcohol sponge □ 3-ml syringe with 25G needle □ 1% or 2%

lidocaine injectable □ I.V. solution and administration set ready for use □ silk-suture pack □ sterile 4″ x 4″ gauze sponges □ sterile roller gauze □ 1″ wide tape.

Most institutions have prepared cut-down trays. These usually include scal-pel, blades, scissors, curved and straight hemostats, and retractors.

### Preparation of equipment

If you have not already done so, set up the I.V. solution and administration set. Confirm catheter size and type with the doctor. Then, bring at least two catheters to the patient's room.

### Essential steps

• Supplement the doctor's explanation of the procedure, as necessary, *to reduce the patient's anxiety and ensure his co-operation.* Make sure the patient has signed a consent form.

• Wash your hands thoroughly *to reduce the risk of bacterial contamination of the sterile field.*

• Position the patient so the surgical site is fully exposed and accessible. Then, place a linen-saver pad under the ex-tremity *to prevent blood leakage onto the bed.*

• Place the cutdown tray on a table in the position preferred by the doctor, and open the exterior wrap without touching the inside.

• Assist the doctor to put on gown, gloves, and mask.

• Swab the top of the local anesthetic container with an alcohol sponge, and invert it *so the doctor can fill the syringe.* He then injects the anesthetic and pre-pares and drapes the area.

• While the doctor makes the incision and prepares the vein, open the catheter package using sterile technique and, when requested, present the package to him so he can remove the catheter observing sterile technique.

• After the doctor inserts the catheter, attach the I.V. line to the catheter hub and allow the solution to flow freely for a few minutes *to flush blood from the catheter, thereby preventing clot for-mation.* The doctor then sutures the in-cision and the catheter.

• If it's your responsibility to dress the incision site, put on sterile gloves and apply povidone-iodine ointment. Then, place a 4″ x 4″ gauze sponge over the site, wrap with roller gauze, and tape the edge of the gauze *to secure the dress-ing.*

• Label the last piece of tape "cutdown," and indicate the size of the catheter, the time, and the date.

• Adjust the I.V. flow rate, as ordered.

### Special considerations

If the insertion site is the antecubital fossa, immobilize the extremity with an arm-board, as necessary. Check distal pulses, skin temperature, and nail-bed color *to detect blood flow obstruction.* Observe the puncture site for redness, inflam-mation, and drainage; if present, notify the doctor. If venesection was performed on a lower extremity, watch for signs of phlebitis or pulmonary emboli, *because this area is more vulnerable to infection and clot formation.*

If the patient experiences pain at the incision site after the local anesthetic wears off, offer an analgesic, if ordered.

### Complications

Phlebitis, infection, infiltration, and thrombus formation are the most com-mon complications of venesection.

### Documentation

Record the time and date of the proce-dure, the doctor's name, the type and gauge of catheter, and the type and rate of I.V. solution.

HELENE RITTING NAWROCKI, RN

# Dressing, Tubing, and Solution Changes

*Dressing, tubing, and solution changes reduce the risk of colonization of equip-*

*ment by pathogens. Typically, I.V. dressings are changed every 24 hours; I.V. tubing, every 48 hours; and I.V. solution, every 24 hours or as needed. Dressing changes allow assessment of the venipuncture site for signs of infection, infiltration, and thrombophlebitis. Simultaneous tubing and solution changes reduce the risk of contamination.*

## Equipment
*For dressing change:* povidone-iodine sponges and ointment □ alcohol sponges □ adhesive bandage or sterile 2″ × 2″ gauze pad □ 1″ adhesive tape.

*For tubing change:* I.V. administration set □ sterile 2″ x 2″ gauze pad.

*For solution change:* solution container □ alcohol sponge.

Commercial kits containing the equipment for dressing changes are available.

## Preparation of equipment
If your hospital keeps I.V. equipment and dressings in a tray or cart, have it close by, if possible, because you may have to select a new venipuncture site, depending on the condition of the current site. If you're changing both the solution and the tubing, attach and prime the I.V. administration set before entering the patient's room.

## Essential steps
● Wash your hands thoroughly *to prevent the spread of microorganisms.*
● Explain the procedure to the patient *to allay his fears and ensure cooperation.*

*To change the dressing:*
● Hold the needle or catheter in place with your nondominant hand *to prevent accidental movement or dislodgment, causing puncture of the vein and infiltration.* Then, gently remove the tape and the dressing.
● Assess the venipuncture site for signs of infection (redness and pain at the puncture site), infiltration (coolness, blanching, and edema at the site), and thrombophlebitis (redness, firmness, pain along the path of the vein, and edema). If any such signs are present,

apply pressure to the area with a sterile 2″ x 2″ gauze pad or alcohol sponge and remove the catheter or needle. Maintain pressure on the area until the bleeding stops, and apply an adhesive bandage. Then, using fresh equipment and solution, start the I.V. in another appropriate site.
● If the venipuncture site is intact, hold the needle or catheter and carefully cleanse around the puncture site with a povidone-iodine or alcohol sponge. Work in a circular motion outward from the site *to avoid introducing bacteria into the cleansed area.*
● Apply povidone-iodine ointment and cover with an adhesive bandage or sterile 2″ x 2″ gauze pad. Then, retape the site.

*To change the solution:*
● If you're replacing a bottle, remove the cap and seal from the new bottle, and swab its stopper with alcohol. Clamp the line, remove the spike from the old bottle, and quickly insert the spike into the new bottle. Then, hang the new bottle and adjust the flow rate.
● If you're replacing a bag, remove the seal or tab from the new bag, wipe the stopper with an alcohol sponge, and hang the bag. Reduce the I.V. flow rate, remove the old bag from the pole, and invert it. Remove the spike, quickly insert it into the new bag, and adjust the flow rate.

*To change the tubing:*
● Reduce the I.V. flow rate and remove the old spike from the container, and place the cover of the new spike loosely over it.
● Keeping the old spike in an upright position above the patient's heart level, insert the new spike into the I.V. container and prime the system. Clamp the old tubing; then, follow the steps for changing the tubing and solution.

*To change the tubing and solution together:*
● Hang the new I.V. container and primed set on the pole, and grasp the new adapter in one hand. Then, stop the flow rate in the old tubing.
● Place a sterile gauze pad under the needle or catheter hub *to create a sterile field.* Gently disconnect the old tubing,

# THREE METHODS OF TAPING A VENIPUNCTURE SITE

| Chevron method | U method | Two-tape method |
| --- | --- | --- |
| 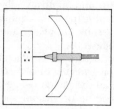 | 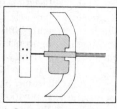 | 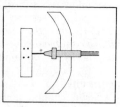 |

**1** Cover the venipuncture site with an adhesive strip or a 2″ x 2″ sterile gauze pad. Then, cut a long strip of ½″ tape. Place one strip, sticky side up, *under* the needle, parallel to the short strip of tape.

**1** Cover the venipuncture site with a 2″ x 2″ sterile gauze pad or an adhesive strip. Then, cut three strips of ½″ tape. With the sticky side up, place one strip *under* the tubing.

**1** Cover the venipuncture site with an adhesive strip or a 2″ x 2″ gauze pad. Then, place a 2″ strip of ½″ tape, sticky side up, *under* the needle.

| 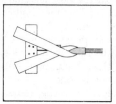 | 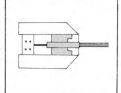 | 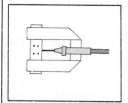 |
| --- | --- | --- |

**2** Cross the end of the tape over the opposite side of the needle, so the tape sticks to the patient's skin.

**2** Bring each side of the tape up, folding it over the wings of the needle, as shown here. Press it down, parallel to the tubing.

**2** Fold the tape ends over and affix them to the patient's skin in a U-shape, as shown here.

| 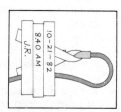 | 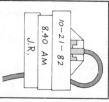 | 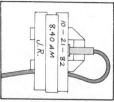 |
| --- | --- | --- |

**3** Apply a piece of 1″ tape across the two wings of the chevron.
Loop the tubing and secure it with another piece of 1″ tape. On the last piece of tape you apply, write the date and time of insertion and your initials.

**3** Loop the tubing and secure it with a piece of 1″ tape. On the last piece of tape you apply, write the date and time of insertion and your initials.

**3** Place a second strip of ½″ tape, sticky side down, over the needle hub. On the last piece of tape you apply, write the date and time of insertion and your initials.
With this method, you can remove the upper strip of tape to check the insertion site while the lower strip anchors the needle.

remove the protective cap from the new tubing, and connect the new adapter to the needle or catheter. Hold the hub securely *to prevent dislodging the needle or catheter tip.*

• Observe for blood backflow into the new tubing *to verify that the needle or catheter is still in place.*

• Adjust the clamp to a slow flow rate *to prevent clot formation.*

• Retape the needle or catheter hub and I.V. tubing, and adjust the I.V. flow rate.

• Label the new tubing with the date and time.

### Special considerations
Check the prescribed I.V. flow rate before each solution change *to prevent errors.* If you have difficulty disconnecting the tubing from the needle or catheter hub,

use a hemostat, but be careful not to crack the tubing adapter or needle or catheter hub. If you crack the adapter or hub (or if you accidentally dislodge the needle or catheter from the vein), remove the needle or catheter. Apply pressure and an adhesive bandage to stop any bleeding. Perform venipuncture at another site, and restart the I.V. The use of transparent dressings on peripheral lines is increasing, allowing inspection of the I.V. site without removing the dressing.

### Documentation
Record the time, date, and rate and type of solution on the I.V. flowchart. Also record this information, dressing or tubing change, and appearance of the site in the cardex and in your notes.

HELENE RITTING NAWROCKI, RN

---

## CENTRAL VENOUS & ARTERIAL LINES

# Insertion and Removal of a Central Venous Line

*Performed by a doctor with a nurse assisting, insertion of a central venous line is the sterile threading of an inside-the-needle catheter through the subclavian vein or, less commonly, the jugular vein into the superior vena cava. Once in place, the central venous line allows monitoring of vena cava blood pressure, which indicates blood volume or pump efficiency, and aspiration of blood samples for diagnostic tests. It also allows administration of I.V. fluids when decreased peripheral circulation causes peripheral venous collapse, when prolonged I.V. therapy reduces the number of usable peripheral veins, and when adequate dilution is necessary (for large fluid volumes or for irritating or hypertonic fluids, such as hyperalimentation solutions).*

*Removal of a central venous line, performed by a nurse on completion of ther-*

*apy or onset of complications, is also a sterile procedure and often requires suture removal. If infection is suspected, the procedure includes collection of a specimen of the catheter tip for culture.*

### Equipment
*For insertion of a central venous line:* shave preparation kit, if necessary □ sterile gloves □ sterile drapes □ masks □ povidone-iodine sponges and ointment □ alcohol sponges □ 3-ml syringe with 25G 1″ needle □ 1% or 2% lidocaine injectable □ two radiopaque inside-the-needle catheters □ 10-ml syringe with Luer-Lok tip □ I.V. solution, with administration set prepared for use □ sterile 4″ x 4″ gauze sponges □ 1″ adhesive tape □ sterile scissors.

Some institutions have prepared trays containing most of the equipment necessary for insertion.

*For removal of a central venous line:* sterile suture-removal set □ sterile gloves □ two masks, if necessary for suspected infection □ sterile drape □ alcohol sponges □ povidone-iodine ointment □ sterile 4″ x 4″ gauze sponges □ sterile, plastic adhesive-backed dressing □ sterile culture tube and sterile scissors for a culture, if necessary.

## Preparation of equipment

Before insertion of a central venous line, confirm catheter size with the doctor; usually, a 14G or 16G catheter is selected. Set up the I.V. solution and prime the administration set. As ordered, notify the radiology department that a portable X-ray machine will be needed.

## Essential steps

• Wash your hands thoroughly *to prevent the spread of microorganisms.*

*To assist with insertion of a central venous line:*

• Reinforce the doctor's explanation of the procedure, and answer the patient's questions. Ensure that the patient has signed a consent form, if necessary, and check his history for hypersensitivity to local anesthetic.

• Establish a sterile field on a table, using a sterile towel or the wrapping from the instrument tray.

• Place the patient in the Trendelenburg position *to dilate veins and reduce the risk of air embolism.*

• *For subclavian insertion,* place a rolled blanket lengthwise between the shoulders *to increase venous distention. For jugular insertion,* place a rolled blanket under the opposite shoulder *to extend the neck, making anatomic landmarks more visible.* Place a linen-saver pad under the appropriate area *to prevent soiling the bed.*

• Turn the patient's head away from the site *to prevent possible contamination from airborne pathogens and to make the site more accessible.* Or, if dictated by hospital policy, mask the patient unless this increases his anxiety or is contraindicated due to his respiratory status.

• Cleanse the insertion site with soap and water *to remove dirt and body oils.* If necessary, shave the area. Then, put on a mask and gloves and cleanse the area around the insertion site with povidone-iodine, working in a circular motion outward from the site to avoid

reintroducing contaminants.

• After the doctor puts on a sterile mask and gloves and drapes the area to create a sterile field, open the packaging of the 3-ml syringe and needle and present it to the doctor using sterile technique.

• Wipe the top of the lidocaine vial with alcohol and invert it. The doctor then fills the 3-ml syringe and injects the anesthetic into the site.

• Open the packaging of the catheter and the 10-ml syringe and present them to the doctor using sterile technique. The doctor then attaches the catheter needle to the syringe, punctures the skin, and inserts the catheter. During this time, prepare the I.V. administration set for immediate attachment to the catheter hub. Ask the patient to perform Valsalva's maneuver while the doctor attaches the I.V. line to the catheter hub. *This increases intrathoracic pressure, reducing the possibility of an air embolus.*

• After the doctor attaches the I.V. line to the catheter hub, set the flow rate, as ordered. The doctor then sutures the catheter in place.

• As ordered, put on sterile gloves, apply povidone-iodine ointment over the site, and apply a sterile 4″ x 4″ gauze dressing.

• After an X-ray confirms correct catheter placement, secure the catheter with tape, reapply the sterile dressing, and tape it to the skin. Label the dressing with the time and date of catheter insertion and catheter length (if not imprinted on the catheter).

*To remove a central venous line:*

• Explain the procedure to the patient and wash your hands. Note the length of the catheter, which should be imprinted on the catheter or written on the dressing. Open the suture-removal set, and use the inside surface of the wrap to establish a sterile field.

• Using sterile technique, open two gauze sponges and one alcohol sponge and drop them onto the sterile field. Squeeze povidone-iodine ointment onto one gauze sponge. Then, loosen and carefully remove the dressing. If a culture of the catheter is to be taken because of suspected infection, put masks on yourself and the patient before dressing removal *to prevent contamination by airborne organisms.*

• Close the flow clamp on the I.V. tubing, and put on sterile gloves.

• Remove any sutures securing the catheter, taking care not to cut the catheter. If you're removing a cutdown catheter, avoid cutting any skin sutures.

• Grasp the needle or catheter hub and slowly and carefully withdraw it from the vein. If the catheter can't easily be retracted, allow the patient to relax; then try again. Avoid forceful retraction, *because venous spasm may be causing the resistance.* If resistance continues, tape the catheter in place and notify the doctor.

• After you've removed the catheter, apply pressure with a gauze sponge *to stop bleeding.* Carefully inspect the tip of the catheter, taking care to prevent contamination. The tip should appear round and smooth. If it is ragged or damaged, notify the doctor immediately, *because a severed catheter can cause an embolus.* If the catheter appears severed, place it on the sterile field and measure its length.

• After bleeding stops, inspect the insertion site for signs of infection, and collect a specimen of any drainage for culture. Cleanse the area around the insertion site with an alcohol sponge *to remove dried blood and adhesive,* then apply povidone-iodine ointment to the area. Place a sterile, plastic adhesive-backed dressing *to prevent exposure of the incision to air.*

• If a culture specimen from the catheter is required, prepare the site with alcohol before catheter removal as ordered, and use sterile scissors to cut a 1″ (2.5 cm) segment from the tip of the removed catheter. Then, place the specimen in the sterile culture tube, and send it to the laboratory immediately.

## Special considerations

As soon as possible after insertion, check catheter placement with a portable X-ray machine or, depending on his condition, send the patient to the radiology department. If hyperalimentation fluid is ordered, begin this infusion only after the X-ray confirms correct catheter placement *because this hypertonic solution could cause problems if the catheter is misplaced.* When catheter placement is in doubt, infuse another I.V. solution such as 10% dextrose in water until correct placement is assured. Be alert for such signs of air embolism as sudden onset of pallor, cyanosis, dyspnea, coughing, and tachycardia, progressing to syncope and shock. If any of these signs occur, place the patient on his left side in the Trendelenburg position, and notify the doctor. Also, after insertion, watch for signs of pneumothorax: shortness of breath, tachycardia, and chest pain. Notify the doctor immediately if such signs appear. Change the dressing and tubing every 24 hours or according to hospital policy while the central venous line is in place. Dressing changes for a central venous line should be done using sterile technique. This is especially important when hyperalimentation solution is being infused.

## Complications

With subclavian vein insertion, pneumothorax is the most common complication. With jugular vein insertion, the catheter may be misdirected toward the brain instead of into the vena cava; a chest X-ray will show this. At either site, air embolism is a possible complication. Other complications are those associated with peripheral lines and inside-the-needle catheters (see *Managing Complications of I.V. Therapy,* pages 258 to 259).

## Documentation

Record the time and date of insertion, the length and location of the catheter, the solution infused, the doctor's name, and the patient's response. Also document the time of the X-ray, its results, and your notification of the doctor.

After removing the central venous line, record the time and date of removal and the type of antimicrobial ointment and dressing applied. Note the condition of the catheter insertion site and collection of a culture specimen.

HELENE RITTING NAWROCKI, RN

# Insertion and Removal of an Arterial Line

*Insertion and removal of an arterial line are sterile procedures performed primarily by a doctor, with a nurse assisting. During insertion, a catheter is introduced into the brachial, the radial, or occasionally the femoral artery. The brachial site, which is easily observed and maintained, may provide more accurate blood pressure readings than the radial site, because it is closer to the heart. However, this site necessitates splinting the elbow to stabilize the catheter. The radial site, also easily observed and located, may entail difficult and painful catheter insertion because of the artery's small lumen. Catheter insertion into the femoral artery, the easiest to locate and puncture in an emergency, carries a high risk of thrombosis. Once in place at any of these sites, an arterial line allows frequent monitoring of blood pressure and sampling of arterial blood for blood gas determination. The patency of the line is maintained by a continuous flush of heparinized saline solution administered under pressure to reduce the risk of clot formation. Because an arterial line carries the risk of bleeding and thrombosis, its insertion is contraindicated in patients with severe coagulopathy, unless the potential benefits outweigh the risks.*

*Removal of an arterial line is usually performed on completion of therapy or onset of complications.*

## Equipment

*For insertion of an arterial line:* I.V. pole □ 500-ml bag of normal saline solution □ heparin, 1 to 2 units/ml of saline solution □ pressure bag □ medication-added label □ two 3-ml syringes (one with a 21G to 25G 1″ needle for heparin insertion into saline solution, one with a 25G

1″ needle for the doctor to use for injection of local anesthetic) □ alcohol sponges □ nonvented I.V. administration set with microdrip chamber □ 6″ extension pressure tubing □ continuous flush device □ three-way stopcock □ dead-end stopcock caps □ povidone-iodine sponges and ointment □ sterile gloves (for doctor) □ □ 1% or 2% lidocaine injectable □ linensaver pad □ sterile towel □ 16G to 20G catheter (type and length depend on site, patient's size, and other possible uses of the line) □ sterile adhesive bandage □ sterile 4″ x 4″ gauze sponges □ 1″ adhesive tape □ optional: suture material, sterile scissors, and splint or armboard.

*For removal of an arterial line:* two sterile 4″ x 4″ gauze sponges □ povidone-iodine ointment □ adhesive bandage □ sterile suture-removal set, if needed □ small sandbag (for removal from a femoral artery) □ alcohol sponges □ optional: sterile container and sterile scissors.

Most institutions use prepackaged arterial line sets containing dead-end caps, connected extension pressure tubing, continuous flush device, and stopcock.

## Preparation of equipment

*For insertion of an arterial line:* Wash your hands thoroughly, and maintain asepsis when setting up the equipment. Inflate the pressure bag to 300 mmHg, check for air leaks, and release the pressure. Then, squeeze the bag of normal saline solution, and check for leaks; if none are present, label the bag with the amount of heparin to be added, and wipe the injection port with an alcohol sponge. Inject the prescribed amount of heparin, and gently rotate the bag to mix the solution. Wipe the main port with an alcohol sponge, and insert the administration set spike. Invert the bag, open the flow clamp, and squeeze the air from the bag *to reduce the risk of introducing air into the line.* Then, close the clamp, place the pressure bag on the I.V. bag, and hang it on the I.V. pole.

Connect the administration set tubing to the continuous flush device's tubing. Secure a stopcock to the patient's side of the device, and attach the pressure tubing to the opposite side of the stopcock. (The transducer is connected to the other port of the continuous flush device.) Then, replace open cap on transducer port with dead-end cap *to prevent leakage of arterial blood.* Gently squeeze the drip chamber until it is about ¼ full of solution. When the bag is pressurized, the chamber will fill further. Remove the cover from the end of the pressure tubing, set the stopcock to the upright (middle) position, and raise the end of the tubing *to expel residual air.* Then, open the flow clamp and activate the fast-flush release; the saline solution should run through the system, flushing all air. Tap the continuous flush device to release any air bubbles. Replace the cover, remove the dead-end cap from the stopcock port that vents to air, and open the stopcock to air and the saline solution. Hold this stopcock port upright until solution flows from it, replace the dead-end cap, and close the stopcock port.

Remove the cover from the end of the transducer port, turn the stopcock so the saline solution enters the transducer port, and activate the continuous flush device to remove all air. Replace the dead-end cap. Set the stopcock in upright position. Close the flow clamp. Inflate the pressure bag to 300 mmHg, but avoid overfilling the drip chamber. If it does overfill, release the pressure bag, invert the drip chamber, squeeze some solution into the I.V. bag, and repressurize the pressure bag.

**Essential steps**
*To assist with insertion of an arterial line:*
● Reinforce the doctor's explanation of the procedure, as needed. Check patient history for hypersensitivity to the local anesthetic.
● Confirm the insertion site with the doctor, and position the patient so the site is well-lighted and accessible.
● Place a linen-saver pad and sterile towel under the arm or leg *to create a sterile field and to prevent blood from soiling the area.*

● After the doctor puts on sterile gloves, open the wrappings of a povidone-iodine sponge and an alcohol sponge. Using sterile technique, the doctor takes the sponges and cleanses the insertion site.
● Open the packaging and present the 3-ml syringe to the doctor *maintaining sterile technique.* Then, wipe the rubber stopper of the lidocaine bottle with alcohol and invert the bottle *to allow the doctor to withdraw the anesthetic.* He then injects the anesthetic into the site.
● Open the catheter packaging. Using sterile technique, the doctor grasps the catheter, flushes it with saline solution, inserts it into the artery, and attaches the administration set.
● Open the flow clamp and activate the fast-flush release *to flush blood from the catheter.*
● If the doctor intends to suture the catheter, temporarily tape the tubing to the patient's arm to keep it in place during suturing. If he doesn't suture the catheter, tape it securely in place.
● Apply povidone-iodine ointment to the insertion site and cover with dressing.
● If necessary, apply an armboard or splint *to immobilize the insertion site.*
● Tape the solution tubing to the patient's arm.
*To assist removal of an arterial line:*
● Wash your hands and explain the procedure to the patient. The doctor gently removes the dressing *to avoid dislodging the catheter,* and removes any sutures.
● Turn off the flow clamp *to prevent fluid leakage,* and open the sterile gauze sponge, being careful not to contaminate it. The doctor withdraws the catheter with a gentle, steady motion, keeping it parallel to the artery *to reduce the risk of trauma.* The doctor or the nurse then immediately applies pressure with a gauze sponge for at least 7 minutes to a brachial site, 5 minutes to a radial site, and 10 minutes to a femoral site or until bleeding ceases.
● Apply povidone-iodine ointment to the site, fold a gauze sponge in half, place it over the site, and cover it with an adhesive bandage to apply pressure. Check distal pulse *to detect arterial obstruc-*

## MANAGING ARTERIAL LINE COMPLICATIONS

| COMPLICATION | POSSIBLE CAUSES | SIGNS AND SYMPTOMS |
|---|---|---|
| Thrombosis | • Arterial damage<br>• Sluggish rate of flush solution<br>• Inadequately heparinized flush solution<br>• Failure to flush catheter when necessary<br>• Irrigation of clotted catheter with syringe | • Loss or weakening of pulse below site<br>• Loss of warmth, sensation, and mobility below site |
| Bleeding and hematoma | • Dislodged catheter<br>• Disconnected line<br>• Blood leakage around catheter | • Bloody dressing; blood flowing from disconnected line<br>• Ecchymosis at the insertion site or of the limb |
| Air embolism | • Empty I.V. container<br>• Air in the tubing<br>• Loose connections | • Decreased blood pressure<br>• Weak, rapid pulse<br>• Cyanosis<br>• Loss of consciousness |
| Systemic infection | • Poor aseptic technique<br>• Contaminated equipment, solution, or medication | • Sudden rise in temperature and pulse rate<br>• Chills, shaking<br>• Changes in blood pressure |
| Arterial spasm | • Traumatic catheter insertion<br>• Arterial irritation after catheter insertion | • Intermittent loss or weakening of pulse below the insertion site |

tion from an overly tight bandage.
• Periodically check the site for a hematoma or bleeding. Place a small sandbag, covered with a washcloth or pillowcase, over a femoral site to prevent delayed bleeding. Check for bleeding under it at least every 15 minutes for the first hour, every 30 minutes for the second, and then every hour for 6 hours.
• Watch for changes in pulse intensity, skin color, and temperature of the arm or leg, which can indicate thrombus formation. Notify the doctor immediately if you observe any of these signs, or signs of pulmonary embolus: dyspnea, chest pain, tachycardia, coughing, or blood-tinged sputum.
• Change the pressure dressing to an adhesive bandage after 2 hours for a brachial or radial site and after 8 hours for a femoral site. Then, deflate the pressure bag, clean it, and return it to its place.

### Special considerations
If the doctor selects the radial artery as the insertion site, perform the Allen's test (see How to Perform the Allen's Test, page 167) to assess blood supply to the hand. After insertion at any site, ensure that all connections are tight, because a patient with normal cardiac output can lose 300 to 500 ml of blood/

| INTERVENTION | PREVENTION |
|---|---|
| • Notify the doctor. He may remove the line or remove the clot by arteriotomy and Fogarty catheterization. | • Check distal pulse and flow rate hourly.<br>• Tape the catheter securely, and splint the arm or leg.<br>• Heparinize the flush solution. Flush the catheter hourly and after collecting blood samples.<br>• Never irrigate an arterial catheter with a syringe. |
| • If catheter is pulled out of the skin, apply direct pressure to the site.<br>• If the line is disconnected, replace the contaminated equipment.<br>• Notify the doctor. | • Frequently check the line connections and insertion site.<br>• Tape the catheter securely, and splint the arm or leg. |
| • Turn patient to his left side, *so any small air bubbles entering the heart can be absorbed in the pulmonary artery.*<br>• Check the line for leaks.<br>• Notify the doctor immediately, and check vital signs.<br>• Administer oxygen, if ordered. | • Expel all air from the line before starting the infusion.<br>• Secure all connections and check them routinely.<br>• Change the I.V. container before it runs out. |
| • Evaluate for other sources of infection. Collect samples of urine, sputum, blood, and I.V. solution for cultures, as ordered.<br>• Notify the doctor. | • Use aseptic technique.<br>• Avoid contaminating the site when bathing the patient.<br>• If the line is accidentally disconnected, replace contaminated equipment. |
| • Notify the doctor.<br>• Prepare an injection of lidocaine. The doctor may inject it into the catheter to relieve the spasm. *Important:* Make sure lidocaine doesn't contain epinephrine. | • Tape the catheter securely and splint the arm or leg. |

minute from an 18G catheter.

Avoid obscuring the catheter hub connection with the dressing; the connection must be visible and accessible at all times. Flush the line every hour or according to hospital policy. Also check the pressure bag *to ensure a constant reading of 300 mmHg.* Also check pulses distal to the insertion site every 2 hours *to detect circulatory impairment.* Change the dressing, tubing, continuous flush device, and I.V. bag every 24 to 48 hours, according to hospital policy.

If you suspect infection, cleanse the insertion site with an alcohol sponge before catheter removal. After the catheter is removed, cut off its tip, using sterile scissors, place it in a sterile container, and send it to the laboratory for culture.

### Complications
See information on the complications of arterial lines in the chart above.

### Documentation
At insertion, record the time, date, doctor's name, insertion site, and the type, gauge, and length of catheter. At removal, record the time, date, doctor's name, condition of the insertion site, and any catheter specimens sent for culture.

HELENE RITTING NAWROCKI, RN

TROUBLESHOOTING

## TROUBLESHOOTING PROBLEMS WITH ARTERIAL LINES

| MECHANICAL PROBLEM | INTERVENTION | PREVENTION |
|---|---|---|
| **Air bubbles in the line** | • Check for leaks and loose connections in the line.<br>• Flush air through an open stopcock port. | • Flush all air from the line when setting up equipment.<br>• Avoid rapid, repeated pulling of the pigtail on fast-flush valve. |
| **Blood clot in the catheter or stopcock** | • Flush the catheter, using the fast-flush valve. *Important:* Never flush an arterial line with a syringe.<br>• Notify the doctor and prepare to replace the line. | • Maintain the flow rate of the heparinized flush solution at 3 to 4 ml/hour.<br>• Flush the catheter, using the fast-flush valve, after aspirating blood samples. |
| **Catheter displacement** | • Attempt to aspirate blood. If you can't, notify the doctor and prepare to replace the line. *Note:* Bloody drainage at the insertion site may indicate catheter displacement. | • Tape the catheter securely.<br>• Splint the arm or leg to stabilize the insertion site. |
| **Blood backup in line** | • Check the position of all stopcocks.<br>• Check for loose connections.<br>• Flush the catheter, using the fast-flush valve.<br>• Replace the dome if blood backs up into it. | • Always maintain 300 mmHg of pressure. |
| **Inability to flush the line** | • Check the position of all stopcocks, the bag pressure, and the condition of tubing.<br>• If line still can't be flushed, notify the doctor and prepare to replace it. | • Always maintain 300 mmHg of pressure. |

# FLOW RATE MANAGEMENT

## Flow Rate Calculation and Management

Calculated from a doctor's orders, flow rate is usually expressed as the total volume of I.V. solution infused over a prescribed interval or as the total volume given in mililiters per hour. When regulated by a clamp, flow rate requires close monitoring and correction because such factors as venous spasm, venous pressure changes, patient movement or manipulation of the clamp, and bent or kinked tubing can cause the rate to vary markedly. When regulated by a clamp *or controller, flow rate is usually measured in drops per minute; by a volumetric pump, in milliliters per hour. With any device, flow rate can be easily monitored by using a time tape, which indicates the prescribed solution level at hourly intervals.*

## Equipment
I.V. administration set with clamp for adjusting flow rate □ watch with second hand □ 1″ paper or adhesive tape (or

## CALCULATING FLOW RATES

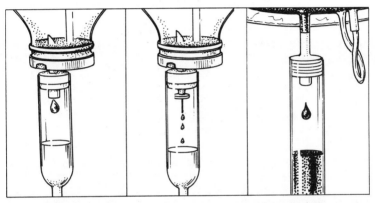

When calculating the flow rate of I.V. solutions, remember that the number of drops required to deliver 1 ml varies with the type of administration set used and the manufacturer. The illustration at left shows a standard (macrodrip) set, which delivers from 10 to 20 drops/ml. The illustration in the center shows a pediatric (microdrip) set, which delivers about 60 drops/ml. The illustration at right shows a blood transfusion set, which delivers about 10 drops/ml.

To calculate the flow rate, it is necessary to know the calibration of the drip rate for each manufacturer's product. As a quick guide, refer to the chart below. Use this formula to calculate specific drip rates.

$$\frac{\text{Volume of infusion (in ml)}}{\text{time of infusion (in minutes)}} \times \text{drop factor in drops/ml} = \text{drops/min}$$

| CO. NAME | DROPS/ ML | DROPS/MINUTE TO INFUSE | | | | | |
|---|---|---|---|---|---|---|---|
| | | 500 ml/ 24 hr 21 ml/hr | 1,000 ml/ 24 hr 42 ml/hr | 1,000 ml/ 20 hr 50 ml/hr | 1,000 ml/ 10 hr 100 ml/hr | 1,000 ml/ 8 hr 125 ml/hr | 1,000 ml/ 6 hr 166 ml/hr |
| Abbott-Baxter | 15 | 5 gtts | 10 gtts | 12 gtts | 25 gtts | 31 gtts | 42 gtts |
| Travenol | 10 | 3 gtts | 7 gtts | 8 gtts | 17 gtts | 21 gtts | 28 gtts |
| Cutter | 20 | 7 gtts | 14 gtts | 17 gtts | 34 gtts | 42 gtts | 56 gtts |
| IVAC | 20 | 7 gtts | 14 gtts | 17 gtts | 34 gtts | 42 gtts | 56 gtts |
| McGaw | 13 | 4 gtts | 9 gtts | 11 gtts | 22 gtts | 27 gtts | 36 gtts |
| Microdrip | 60 | 21 gtts | 42 gtts | 50 gtts | 100 gtts | 125 gtts | 166 gtts |

premarked time tape) ☐ drip rate chart, as necessary ☐ pen.

Two types of flow-regulating clamps are available. The screw clamp provides greater accuracy, but the roller clamp, used for standard fluid therapy, is faster and easier to use. Standard macrodrip sets deliver 10 to 20 drops/ml, depending on the manufacturer; microdrip sets, 60 drops/ml; and blood

TROUBLESHOOTING

## TROUBLESHOOTING I.V. FLOW RATE DEVIATIONS

| PROBLEM AND CAUSE | SOLUTION |
|---|---|
| **Flow rate too fast**<br>• Patient manipulates the clamp | • Instruct the patient not to touch the clamp, and place tape over it. Restrain the patient or administer the I.V. with an infusion pump or a controller, if necessary. |
| • Tubing disconnected from the catheter | • Wipe the distal end of the tubing with alcohol, reinsert firmly into catheter hub, and tape at connection site. |
| • Change in patient position or blood pressure | • Administer the I.V. with an infusion pump or a controller to ensure correct flow rate. |
| • Positional cannulation | • Manipulate cannula, and place a 2″ × 2″ gauze pad under or over the catheter hub to change the angle. Reset the flow clamp at the desired rate. If necessary, remove the cannula and reinsert. |
| • Flow clamp drifting as a result of patient movement | • Place tape below the clamp. |
| **Flow rate too slow**<br>• Venous spasm after insertion | • Apply warm soaks over site. |
| • Venous obstruction from bending arm | • Secure with armboard, if necessary. |
| • Head pressure change (decreasing fluid in bottle causes solution to run slower due to decreasing pressure) | • Readjust the flow rate. |
| • Elevated blood pressure | • Readjust the flow rate. Use an infusion pump or a controller to ensure correct flow rate. |
| • Cold solution | • Allow the solution to warm to room temperature before hanging. |
| • Change in solution viscosity from medication added | • Readjust the flow rate. |
| • I.V. container too low or patient's arm or leg too high | • Hang the container higher or remind the patient to keep the arm below heart level. |
| • Bevel against vein wall (positional cannulation) | • Withdraw the needle slightly or place a folded 2″ × 2″ gauze pad over or under the catheter hub to change the angle. |
| • Excess tubing dangling below insertion site | • Replace the tubing with a shorter piece or tape the excess tubing to the I.V. pole, below the flow clamp (make sure tubing is not kinked). |
| • Cannula too small | • Remove cannula in use and insert larger-bore cannula. |
| • Infiltration or clotted cannula | • Remove the cannula in use and reinsert cannula. |
| • Kinked tubing | • Check the tubing over its entire length, and unkink. |
| • Clotted filter | • Remove and replace with new filter. |
| • Tubing memory (tubing compressed at area clamped) | • Massage or milk the tubing by pinching and wrapping it around a pencil four or five times. Quickly pull the pencil out of the coiled tubing. |

transfusion sets, 10 drops/ml. A commercially available adapter can convert a macrodrip set to a microdrip system.

### Essential steps
*To calculate and set the drip rate:*
• Use the formula on p. 273.
• After calculating the desired drip rate, remove your watch and hold it next to the drip chamber *to allow simultaneous observation of the watch and the drops.*
• Release the clamp to the approximate drip rate. Then count drops for 1 minute *to account for flow irregularities.*
• Adjust the clamp, as necessary, and count drops for 1 minute. Continue to adjust the clamp and count drops until achieving the correct rate.

*To make a time tape:*
• Calculate the number of milliliters to be infused per hour. Place a piece of tape vertically on the container alongside the volume-increment markers.
• Starting at the current solution level, move down the number of milliliters to be infused in 1 hour, and mark the appropriate time and a horizontal line on the tape at this level. Then, continue to mark 1-hour intervals until you reach the bottom of the container.
• Check the flow rate every 15 minutes until it's stable. Then recheck it every hour, and adjust as necessary.

### Special considerations
If the infusion rate slows significantly, avoid increasing the rate to catch up; simply adjust the infusion to the ordered rate. When infusing drugs, use an I.V. pump or controller, if possible, *to avoid flow rate inaccuracies.*

### Complications
An excessively slow flow rate may cause insufficient intake of fluids, drugs, and nutrients; an excessively rapid rate of fluid or drug infusion may cause circulatory overload, possibly leading to congestive heart failure and pulmonary edema, and drug side effects.

### Documentation
Usually, the flow rate is recorded when setting up a peripheral line. However, if you adjust the rate, record the change, the date and time, and your initials.

HELENE RITTING NAWROCKI, RN

# Use of I.V. Controllers and Pumps

*Various types of controllers and pumps electronically regulate the flow of I.V. solution or drugs when extreme accuracy is required, for example during infusion of hyperalimentation solutions and of chemotherapeutic and cardiovacscular agents. Controllers regulate gravity flow by counting drops and achieve the desired infusion rate by compressing the I.V. tubing. However, because controllers simply count drops, which aren't always of equal size, these devices fail to achieve the accuracy of volumetric pumps, which measure flow rate in milliliters per hour.*

*Volumetric pumps, used for high-pressure infusion of drugs or for accurate delivery of fluids or drugs, have mechanisms to propel the solution at the desired rate under pressure. The peristaltic pump applies pressure to the I.V. tubing to force the solution through it. (Not every peristaltic pump is volumetric; some count drops.) The piston-cylinder pump, often called a volumetric pump, pushes the solution through special disposable cassettes; most operate at high pressures (up to 45 psi) and can deliver 1 to 999 ml/ hour with a 97% to 98% accuracy. The portable syringe pump, another type of volumetric pump, delivers very small amounts of fluid over a long duration. It's used for administering fluids to infants and for delivering intraarterial drugs.*

*Both controllers and pumps have various detectors and alarms that automatically signal or respond to the completion of an infusion, the presence of air in line, low battery power, and occlusion or inability to deliver at the set*

## SYRINGE INFUSION PUMPS

Syringe infusion pumps can deliver very small amounts of fluid or medication and are often used in pediatric- and critical-care settings. They can also be used to administer chemotherapeutic agents, oxytocin, insulin, and heparin during hemodialysis.

The body of the pump holds the syringe—which can be as large as 60 ml—and a sliding plate or block moves the plunger. The flow rate is determined by the rate at which the plunger is set to advance and the size of the syringe. The most sophisticated syringe infusion pumps have all the alarm features of an electronic infusion pump and variable flow rates of 0.1 to 99 ml/hour. The simplest versions have no alarms and a single speed.

Originally designed as tabletop units for in-hospital use, some syringe infusion pumps can now be attached to I.V. poles, and miniature pumps can be carried in a pocket or strapped to a patient's arm for continuous medication infusion.

BONNIE JOYCE KAPLAN, RN, MS

rate. *Depending on the problem, these devices may sound or flash an alarm, shut off, or switch to a keep-vein-open rate.*

### Equipment

Controller or pump □ I.V. pole □ I.V. solution □ sterile administration set □ sterile peristaltic tubing or cassette, if needed □ alcohol sponges □ adhesive tape.

Tubing and cassette vary with each manufacturer.

### Preparation of equipment

*To set up a controller,* first attach the controller to the I.V. pole. Then, swab the port on the I.V. container with alcohol, insert the administration set spike, and fill the drip chamber no more than halfway *to avoid miscount of the drops.* Rotate the chamber so the fluid touches all sides *to remove any vapor that could interfere with correct drop counting.* Now, prime the tubing and clamp it closed. Position the drop sensor above the fluid level in the drip chamber and below the drop port *to ensure correct drop count-*

*ing.* Insert the tubing into the controller, close the door, and completely open the flow clamp.

*To set up a volumetric pump,* first attach the pump to the I.V. pole. Then, swab the port on the I.V. container with alcohol, insert the administration set spike, and completely fill the drip chamber *to prevent air bubbles from entering the tubing.* Next, prime the tubing and clamp it closed. Now, follow the manufacturer's instructions for placement of tubing. If you're using a peristaltic pump, you'll usually place the tubing behind the door. If you're using a piston-cylinder pump, attach the tubing to the cassette.

To set up a nonvolumetric peristaltic pump, follow the steps for setting up a controller.

### Essential steps

• Position the controller or pump on the same side of the bed as the I.V. or anticipated venipuncture site *to avoid crisscrossing I.V. lines over the patient.* If necessary, perform venipuncture.
• Plug in the machine and attach its tubing to the needle or catheter hub. If you're using a controller, position the drip chamber 30″ (76.2 cm) above the infusion site *to ensure accurate gravity flow.*
• Depending on the machine, set the appropriate dials on the front panel to the desired infusion rate and volume. Always set the volume dial 50 ml less than the prescribed volume or 50 ml less than the volume in the container, *so you can hang a new container before the old one empties completely.* Then, turn on the machine and press the start button.
• Check the patency of the I.V. line and watch for infiltration. If you're using a controller, monitor the accuracy of the infusion rate.
• Tape all connections and, if necessary, dress the I.V. site. Monitor the drip rate of the controller again, *because taping may alter it.*
• Turn on the alarm switches. Then, explain the alarm system to the patient *to prevent apprehension when a change in the infusion activates the alarm.*

## Special considerations

Frequently monitor the pump or controller and the patient *to ensure the device's correct operation and maintenance of the prescribed flow rate and to detect infiltration and such complications as infection and air embolism.*

If electrical failure occurs, the pumps will automatically switch to battery power. Avoid administering opaque fluids, such as blood, because with some pumps opaque fluids cannot be picked up by the drop detector and with other pumps hemolysis of infused blood may occur.

Move the tubing in controllers and peristaltic pumps every few hours *to prevent permanent compression or tubing damage.* Change the tubing and cassette every 48 hours.

## Complications

Complications with the use of I.V. controllers and pumps are the same as those associated with peripheral lines. (See *Managing Complications of I.V. Therapy,* pages 258 to 259.) Keep in mind that infiltration can develop rapidly with infusion by a volumetric pump.

## Documentation

In addition to the routine documentation of the I.V. infusion, record the use of the controller or pump on the I.V. record and in your notes.

HELENE RITTING NAWROCKI, RN

# PARENTERAL NUTRITION

# Equipment Preparation and Site Care for Intravenous Hyperalimentation
[*Total parenteral nutrition*]

*Intravenous hyperalimentation (IVH) is the parenteral administration of a solution of dextrose, proteins, electrolytes, vitamins, and trace elements in amounts that exceed the patient's energy expenditure, thereby achieving anabolism. Because this solution has about six times the solute concentration of blood, it requires dilution by delivery into a high-flow central vein to avoid injury to the peripheral vasculature. Typically, the solution is delivered to the superior vena cava through an indwelling subclavian vein catheter inserted by the infraclavicular approach or, less commonly, by the supraclavicular, internal jugular, or antecubital fossa approach. IVH may benefit patients with severe burns, acute pancreatitis, short bowel syndrome, enterocutaneous fistula, inflammatory bowel disease, ulcerative colitis, acute renal failure, mild to moderate hepatic failure, cardiac disease or surgery, and cancer.*

*Because the IVH solution is a good medium for bacterial growth and the central venous line gives systemic access, contamination and sepsis are always a risk. Strict surgical asepsis is required during solution, dressing, tubing, and filter changes.*

## Equipment

Infusion pump □ sterile tubing □ two pairs of sterile gloves □ organic solvent (such as 10% acetone or 70% alcohol) □ antimicrobial solution (such as povidone-iodine) □ povidone-iodine ointment (or substitute) □ sterile 4″ x 4″ gauze sponges □ antiseptic adhesive balsam □ nonallergenic tape □ optional: two face masks, sterile scissors, and 0.22-micron cellulose membrane filter.

Prepackaged dressing kits are available commercially.

## Preparation of equipment

Remove the IVH solution from the refrigerator 30 minutes before use, *because delivery of a chilled solution can*

> **THE FOLLOWING ARE CONTRAINDICATED WHEN USING A CENTRAL VENOUS LINE FOR HYPERALIMENTATION**
>
> • Infusion of blood or blood products
> • Bolus injection of drugs
> • Simultaneous administration of I.V. solutions
> • Measurement of central venous pressure
> • Aspiration of blood for routine laboratory tests
> • Addition of medication to an intravenous hyperalimentation solution container
> • Use of three-way stopcocks

*cause pain, hypothermia, venous spasm, and venous constriction.*

Compare the contents of the solution with the doctor's orders. Then, observe the solution for cloudiness, turbidity, and particles and the container for cracks; if any of these are present, return the solution to the pharmacy.

Wash your hands. Connect, in sequence, the pump tubing, filter (if applicable), and extension tubing. Tape the tubing connections *to prevent accidental separation, which can lead to air embolism, exsanguination, and sepsis.* Using strict aseptic technique, insert the pump tubing spike into the port of the IVH container, and start the flow of solution *to prime the tubing and remove air.* Gently tap the tubing *to dislodge air bubbles trapped in the Y-injection sites.*

### Essential steps
• Explain the procedure and clean the patient's overbed table with isopropyl alcohol (if you aren't using a cart).
• If required, put on a mask, and position the patient supine, with his head turned away from the catheter insertion site. If hospital policy dictates and the patient can tolerate it, place a mask over his nose and mouth. Place a sterile drape over the patient who is connected to a ventilator.
• Remove the dressing carefully, pull-

ing the tape gently from the skin *to minimize trauma.* Then, inspect the skin for signs of infection and the catheter for leakage or other mechanical problems.
• Put on sterile gloves, and cleanse the catheter insertion site with sterile sponges or swabs soaked in an organic solvent, such as 10% acetone or 70% alcohol. Work in a circular motion, moving from the insertion site outward to the edge of the adhesive border *to avoid introducing contaminants from the uncleansed area.* Don't allow the organic solvent to touch the tubing *to prevent damage.*
• Working in a circular motion, as before, cleanse the insertion site and the catheter for 2 minutes with the povidone-iodine solution.
• Instruct the patient to perform Valsalva's maneuver or to hold his breath on deep inspiration as you change the I.V. tubing. If the patient is connected to a ventilator, change the tubing immediately after the machine delivers a breath. *These measures increase intrathoracic pressure and prevent air embolism.*
• Ensure that the junction of the catheter tubing is secure, remove the contaminated gloves, and put on a sterile pair.
• Continue to cleanse the skin with povidone-iodine solution for 3 minutes. Avoid removing this solution from the skin *because its antimicrobial effects are long-lasting and continue after drying.*
• Using a sterile swab or sponge, apply povidone-iodine ointment to the skin at the insertion site and to the hub of the catheter at the catheter-tubing junction, being careful not to loosen the connections.
• Arrange the sterile dressing sponges *to shield the catheter and skin from airborne contaminants.* A pre-cut drain sponge may be used around the catheter.
• Apply adhesive balsam to the skin at the perimeter of the dressing sponges.
• With the patient's arm abducted, tape

the dressing securely and occlusively to the skin.

• Write the catheter insertion date, the date of the dressing change, and your initials on a strip of tape and apply this to the dressing.

• Loop and tape the administration tubing (but not the filter) over the intact dressing *to prevent tension on the catheter and its inadvertent removal if the tubing is pulled.*

### Special considerations

If the patient is allergic to iodine, use 70% alcohol for the antimicrobial treatment, increase skin preparation time to 10 minutes, and substitute a combination of antimicrobial and antifungal ointments for the povidone-iodine ointment.

When using a filter, position it between the pump tubing and the extension tubing *to avoid disturbing the underlying dressing.*

If the patient develops a fever, discontinue the IVH solution and replace it with dextrose 10% in water. Change the I.V. tubing and dressing, and notify the doctor, who'll order bacterial and fungal cultures of the IVH solution, tubing, and blood. Reduction of fever 4 to 6 hours after withdrawal implicates the solution or the delivery apparatus. If the fever persists, suspect catheter-related sepsis and again notify the doctor, who will then order blood and urine cultures to help determine the cause of infection. If necessary, the doctor will remove the catheter and order fungal and bacterial cultures. Fever usually subsides within 12 to 24 hours after catheter removal.

Observe the patient for signs of thrombosis or thrombophlebitis, such as erythema and edema at the catheter insertion site; ipsilateral swelling of the arm, neck, or face; pain along the course of the vein; and other systemic manifestations. If such signs occur, notify the doctor immediately; he will remove the catheter and start heparin infusion at a peripheral site.

Be alert for swelling at the catheter insertion site, indicating extravasation of the IVH solution, which can cause necrosis. Check the catheter tubing for leaks from mechanical or chemical disruption.

Watch for signs of air embolism: dyspnea, apprehension, chest pain, tachycardia, hypotension, cyanosis, seizures, loss of consciousness, and cardiopulmonary arrest. If you suspect air embolism, position the patient in the left Trendelenburg position (Durant maneuver) *to allow air to pass from the pulmonary artery,* and administer supplemental oxygen. It may take several minutes for the air to dissipate.

### Complications

Catheter-related sepsis is the most serious complication of IVH. Although uncommon, subclavian or jugular vein thrombosis can result from a malpositioned catheter and can precede septicemia. Air embolism, a potentially fatal complication, can occur during tubing replacement, from inadvertent disconnection of tubing and from undetected hairline cracks in the tubing. Extravasation of IVH solution can cause necrosis, with sequential sloughing of the epidermis and dermis.

### Documentation

Record the times of dressing, filter, and solution changes; the condition of the catheter insertion site; your observations on the patient's condition; and any complications and resulting treatments.

DEANN M. ENGLERT, RN, MSN

# Patient Monitoring During Intravenous Hyperalimentation

*Intravenous hyperalimentation (IVH) necessitates careful patient monitoring to assess the response to the nutrient solu-*

# COMPLICATIONS OF INTRAVENOUS HYPERALIMENTATION (IVH)

| CONDITION | CAUSE | SIGNS AND SYMPTOMS | TREATMENT |
|---|---|---|---|
| Hyperglycemia | Too rapid IVH delivery rate, lowered glucose tolerance, excessive total dextrose load | Glycosuria, nausea, vomiting, diarrhea, confusion, headache, and lethargy; untreated hyperosmolar hyperglycemic dehydration can lead to convulsions, coma, and death. | Add insulin to the IVH solution. |
| Hypoglycemia | Excess endogenous insulin production after abrupt termination of IVH solution, or excessive delivery of exogenous insulin | Muscle weakness, anxiety, confusion, restlessness, diaphoresis, vertigo, pallor, tremors, and palpitations | If possible, give carbohydrates orally; infuse dextrose 10% in water, or administer dextrose 50% in water by I.V. bolus. |
| Fluid deficit | Hyperglycemia, vomiting, diarrhea, fistula output, large burns, inadequate fluid replacement, electrolyte imbalance | Fatigue, dry skin and mucous membranes, lengthwise wrinkles in tongue, depressed anterior fontanelle (in infants), tachycardia, tachypnea, decreased urinary output, normal or subnormal temperature, decreased central venous pressure, acute weight loss, hemoconcentration | Increase fluid intake. |
| Fluid excess | Fluid overload, electrolyte imbalance | Puffy eyelids, peripheral edema, elevated central venous pressure, ascites, acute weight gain, pulmonary edema, pleural effusion, moist rales | Decrease fluid intake. |
| Hypokalemia | Muscle catabolism, loss of gastric secretions from vomiting or suction, diarrhea; may occur when anabolism is achieved, with its accompanying intracellular movement of potassium | Malaise, lethargy, loss of deep tendon reflexes, muscle cramping, paresthesia, atrial and ventricular arrhythmias, decreased intensity of heart sounds, weak pulse, hypotension, and complete heart block | Increase potassium intake. Malnourished patient may require an initial dose of 60 to 100 mEq/1,000 calories. |
| Hypophosphatemia | Phosphate deficiency; infusion of glucose causes phosphate ions to shift at start of IVH or within 48 hours of inadequate phosphate intake | Serum $PO_4$ levels < 1 mg/dl cause lethargy, weakness, paresthesia, glucose intolerance. Severe hypophosphatemia can cause acute hemolytic anemia, convulsions, coma, and death. | Add phosphates to the IVH solution. |

tion and to detect early signs of complications. Because the patient is frequently in a protein-wasting state, IVH causes marked changes in fluid and electrolyte status and in glucose, amino acid, mineral, and vitamin levels.

Assessment of the patient's nutritional status includes physical examination, anthropometric measurements, biochemical determinations, and tests of cell-mediated immunity. Assessment of the patient's condition to detect complications requires recognition of the signs and symptoms of the various possible complications, understanding of laboratory test results, and careful

| CONDITION | CAUSE | SIGNS AND SYMPTOMS | TREATMENT |
|---|---|---|---|
| **Hypocalcemia** | Increased doses of phosphates administered to correct hypophosphatemia, without supplemental calcium; may also result from hypoalbuminemia or excess free water | Nausea, vomiting, diarrhea, hyperactive reflexes, tingling at fingertips and mouth, carpopedal spasm, arrhythmias, tetany, and convulsions | Add calcium to the IVH solution. |
| **Hypomagnesemia** | Inadequate intake of magnesium; severe diarrhea and vomiting exacerbate hypomagnesemia | Lethargy, tremors, athetoid or choreiform movements, positive Chvostek's sign or Trousseau's sign, painful paresthesia, convulsions, and tetany | Add magnesium to the IVH solution. |
| **Essential fatty acid deficiency** | Absent or inadequate fat intake for an extended period | Alopecia, brittle nails, desquamating dermatitis, increased capillary fragility, indolent wound healing, reduced prostaglandin synthesis, increased platelet aggregation, thrombocytopenia, enhanced susceptibility to infection, fatty liver infiltration, lipid accumulation in pulmonary macrophages, notching of R waves on EKG, growth retardation (in children), triene to tetraene ratio greater than 0.4. | For the adult patient, infuse two or three bottles of 10% or 20% fat emulsion daily. |
| **Zinc deficiency** | Altered requirements associated with stress, the degree of intracellular zinc deficit, and induced zinc deficiencies from redistribution during the anabolism | Diarrhea, apathy, confusion, depression, eczematoid dermatitis (initially in nasolabial and perioral areas), alopecia, decreased libido, hypogonadism, indolent wound healing, acute growth arrest, and hypogeusesthesia (diminished sense of taste) | Add zinc to the IVH solution. |
| **Hypocupremia** | Long-term administration of IVH, without addition of copper sulfate; infection, high-output enterocutaneous fistulas, and diarrhea predispose to copper deficiency | Neutropenia and hypochromic microcytic anemia | Add copper to the IVH solution. |

record keeping. Appropriate changes in the IVH regimen then aim to preclude or alleviate complications.

Because the hyperalimentation solution is high in glucose content, the infusion must start slowly to allow the patient's pancreatic beta cells to adapt to it by increasing insulin output. Usually, if the adult patient tolerates the IVH solution well the first day, the doctor increases the intake to 1 liter every 12 hours for at least 2 days. Within the first 3 to 5 days of IVH, the typical adult patient can usually tolerate 3 liters of solution per day without adverse effects.

**Equipment**

Test kit for urine glucose and ketone □ stethoscope □ sphygmomanometer □ watch with second hand □ scale □ input and output chart □ time tape □ additional equipment for nutritional assessment, as ordered.

If the patient is receiving cephalosporins, methyldopa, aspirin, or large doses of ascorbic acid, TesTape should be used in place of Clinitest reagent tablets to avoid false positive results in urine glucose and ketone determinations.

**Preparation of equipment**

For preparation of the infusion pump and hyperalimentation solution, see "Equipment Preparation and Site Care for Intravenous Hyperalimentation" and "Use of I.V. Controllers and Pumps" in this chapter. Attach a time tape to the IVH container to allow approximate measurement of fluid intake.

**Essential steps**

• Explain the procedure to the patient *to diminish his anxiety and ensure cooperation.* Instruct him to inform you if he experiences any unusual sensations during the infusion. Begin the infusion at a slow rate (usually 40 ml/ hour), as ordered, *to reduce the risk of hyperglycemia.* Then, as ordered, increase the adult patient's infusion rate (usually in 40 ml/hour increments) *to allow the pancreatic beta cells to increase endogenous insulin production, and to establish carbohydrate and water tolerances.*

• Check the infusion pump's volume meter and the time tape every 30 minutes, or more often if necessary, *to avoid an irregular flow rate, which can cause disturbances in glucose metabolism.*

• Record vital signs every 4 hours, or more often if necessary, *because increased temperature is one of the earliest signs of catheter-related sepsis.*

• Collect a double-voided urine specimen every 6 hours and test for glucose and acetone. Notify the doctor if observed glycosuria equals or exceeds ¼% ( + + ).

• Accurately record daily fluid intake and output. Specify the volume and type of each fluid, and calculate the daily caloric intake. *This record is a diagnostic tool for prompt, precise replacement of fluid and electrolyte deficits.*

• Physically assess the patient daily. If ordered, measure arm circumference and skinfold thickness over the triceps. Also weigh him at the same time each morning (after voiding), in similar clothing, using the same scale. Suspect fluid imbalance if the patient gains more than 1.1 lb (0.5 kg) per day.

• Monitor the results of routine laboratory tests and report abnormal findings to the doctor *to allow appropriate changes in the IVH solution.* Laboratory tests usually include serum electrolytes, BUN, and blood glucose at least three times a week; and liver function studies, complete blood count and differential, and serum albumin, phosphorus, calcium, magnesium, and creatinine every week. Less frequently ordered studies include serum transferrin, creatinine-height index, nitrogen balance, total lymphocyte count, and skin tests.

• Monitor the patient for signs and symptoms of disturbances of glucose metabolism, fluid and electrolyte imbalances, and nutritional aberrations. Remember that some patients may require supplementary insulin for the duration of IVH; the pharmacy usually adds this directly to the IVH solution.

• When discontinuing IVH, decrease the infusion rate slowly, depending on the patient's current glucose intake, *to minimize the risk of hyperinsulinemia and resulting hypoglycemia.* Weaning usually takes place over 24 to 48 hours but can be completed in 4 to 6 hours if the patient receives sufficient oral or I.V. carbohydrates.

**Complications**

Disturbances of glucose metabolism and fluid and electrolyte balances, and nutritional aberrations can occur during IVH. See *Complications of Intravenous Hyperalimentation Solution Infusion,* pages 280 to 281, for the causes, signs, and symptoms of these complications.

**Documentation**
Record serial monitoring indices on the appropriate flowchart to determine the patient's progress and response. Note any abnormal, adverse, or altered responses.

DEANN M. ENGLERT, RN, MSN

# Preparation for Home Parenteral Nutrition

*Made possible by numerous technical advancements within the last decade, home parenteral nutrition (HPN) enables prolonged or indefinite intravenous hyperalimentation. This technique has dramatically improved the health of patients with such chronic conditions as Crohn's disease and malabsorption syndrome, and with such acute conditions as incomplete bowel obstruction and antineoplastic therapy. It has also decreased the duration of hospitalization.*

*To prepare for parenteral nutrition, a barium-impregnated silicone rubber catheter with a Dacron cuff is implanted in the superior vena cava. Its entrance site is on the anterior abdomen, about ¾" to 1½" (2 to 4 cm) inferior and lateral to the xiphoid process, to allow the patient to care for the catheter. The catheter's extravascular portion is reinforced with Teflon to reduce the risk of inadvertent catheter fracture. About 2 to 3 weeks after implantation, firm tissue covers the catheter cuff to provide a physical barrier to microbial contamination.*

*Preparation for HPN usually necessitates 10 days to 2 weeks of extensive patient teaching and, when possible, of instructing the patient's family.*

*Usually, HPN patients can ingest part of their caloric requirements, requiring 10 to 14 hours of infusion nightly to supply the remaining nutrients. If all the patient's nutrition must be received intravenously, a continuous infusion may be necessary. For both intermittent and continuous infusion, the patient teaching must include various techniques for proper care (see* Preparing the Patient for Home Parenteral Nutrition: A Checklist, *page 285).*

**Equipment**
Teaching aids, as available □ I.V. infusion apparatus □ dressings □ intravenous hyperalimentation (IVH) solution □ volumetric infusion pump □ portable I.V. pole or ambulatory hyperalimentation vest.

IVH solution is available in either premixed or component form. Not every patient is trained to mix the solution, because it requires precision and absolute aseptic and sterile technique to prevent contamination and subsequent sepsis.

**Essential steps**
● Assess the patient's ability to perform the care routines necessary for HPN, and determine if family members or friends can assist with or perform them. Consider the patient's motivation, mental aptitude, job or other daily activities, home environment, and the accessibility of hospitals, home nursing services, and other health-care support systems.
● Formulate a teaching plan based on this assessment and on the patient's expectations. Be sure the plan incorporates goals, specifies criteria for meeting them, and proceeds from simple to complex tasks *to allow the patient to develop confidence.* Avoid placing time limits on goals, *because learning ability and mastery of tasks requiring manual dexterity vary from patient to patient.*
● If desired, develop a written contract between you and the patient that specifies the goals of HPN and the means to achieve them. Revise the contract as

# AMBULATORY HYPERALIMENTATION VEST

The ambulatory hyperalimentation vest, illustrated at right, allows continuous delivery of parenteral nutrition without restricting the patient's mobility. Made from lightweight, polyester mesh, each vest is adjusted to individual specifications. Its breast pockets accommodate bags of nutrient solution, which are attached to the front of each shoulder by means of swiveled garnet hooks. These pockets vary with the size of the patient and of the nutrient bags (for children, the bags are designed to hold 250 ml; for women and small men, 500 ml; for large men, 1,000 ml). Y-tubing connects these bags to a portable volumetric pump, located in a zippered pocket in the vest's lower right quadrant. To provide balance and enhance patient comfort, the pump empties both bags at the same rate.

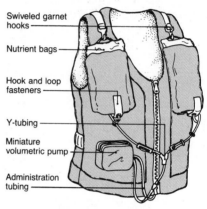

Swiveled garnet hooks

Nutrient bags

Hook and loop fasteners

Y-tubing

Miniature volumetric pump

Administration tubing

When the patient is wearing the vest, the 6' (1.8-m) administration tubing is coiled in one of the pockets. When he's not wearing it, the nutrient bags can hang from a clothes hanger.

necessary *to reflect changes in the patient's needs and performance. Use of the contractual relationship enhances the patient's independence, minimizes conflict and frustration between patient and nurse, encourages open communication, and promotes a cooperative patient-nurse relationship.*

• Implement teaching sessions based on the goals specified in the contract. Conduct these sessions in a quiet area, and if possible, arrange to have a family member present. *When the family member understands the patient's pathophysiology, medical management, and progress, he tends to be less anxious, more satisfied with the quality of health care, and able to acknowledge the limitations and constraints of HPN.*

• Use a variety of teaching-learning materials *to accommodate differences in the ability of the learner.* When teaching the mature learner, use an extensively illustrated manual that includes the goals, equipment, procedures (with rationales), suggested learning activities, and evaluation of equipment for HPN. Demonstrate simulation with mannequins and real equipment *to involve the patient actively and reduce anxiety about performing the HPN tasks.* Stimulate the patient's interest with audiovisual teaching aids.

• Offer positive feedback during all teaching phases.

• Before discharge, critically evaluate the patient's ability to perform HPN tasks and ensure that all essential learning goals have been met.

• Remind the patient to change the catheter site dressing three times a week or whenever it becomes soiled or nonocclusive and to change administration tubing as scheduled. Tell the patient that after the implanted catheter has been in place for 1 month or longer, he may be allowed to remove his dressing and bathe or shower.

Also remind the patient to prevent

contact of the catheter with granular or lint-producing surfaces *to avoid local tissue reaction from airborne particles and surface contaminants.*

• Confirm a suitable IVH schedule with the patient, considering his nutritional needs as well as his life-style. Emphasize his adherence to the prescribed schedule and volume *to prevent glucose imbalance.*

• As ordered, arrange for a home referral service *to help the patient adjust to HPN and resolve any difficulties.*

• At discharge, provide the patient with supplies for HPN, such as dressings, tubing, and IVH solution, and tell him how and where to obtain these supplies. Arrange for a follow-up physical examination and for obtaining specimens for laboratory analysis to detect fluid, electrolyte, and nutrient imbalances.

### Special considerations

When communicating with the HPN patient, be alert for ambivalent feelings toward you. Although the patient may overtly show admiration, respect, and gratitude, he may resent feeling helpless and dependent. Provide opportunities for conversation, and allow the patient to express mixed emotions.

During teaching and treatment, recognize that conflicts can arise between you and the patient unless lines of authority and expectations are clear. Arrange nursing conferences to evaluate the patient's adaptation, to discuss counseling techniques for use during periods of maladaptation or crisis, and to provide management of expected stress in the patient.

Suggest that the patient wear a Medic-Alert bracelet or subscribe to another medical alert service. Ensure that at least one nurse from the home health-care team is always available to the patient in case of emergency.

Because the financial burden of long-term or permanent HPN can be devastating—even for the patient with health insurance—provide the patient with the names of hospitals and philanthropies that provide services or financial support. Inform the elderly patient that Medicare may assume the cost of supplies and pharmaceuticals if he meets eligibility requirements.

---

## PREPARING THE PATIENT FOR HOME PARENTERAL NUTRITION: A CHECKLIST

### BASIC PROCEDURES

Catheter heparinization
Destruction of needles and syringes
Dressing changes
Drug administrations
Handwashing
I.V. fat emulsion administration
I.V. tubing changes
Pump operation
Self-monitoring (intake and output, daily weight, urine testing, temperature, diet record if patient is allowed partial oral intake)
Solution preparation
Use of sterile equipment (packages, gloves, syringes)

### SPECIAL TOPICS

Detection of complications
Financial support, home referral, medical alert, and networking services
Follow-up appointments
Performance of necessary procedures when traveling
Procurement and storage of supplies
Schedule for infusion and free time
Troubleshooting (air embolism; infection; thrombosis; clotted catheter; catheter fracture; pump malfunction; metabolic complications, such as deficiency and excess symptoms; broken I.V. container; contaminated solution or fat emulsion bottle)
Weaning

**Documentation**

Record the patient's learning progress.

DEANN M. ENGLERT, RN, MSN

# Peripheral Vein Nutrition

*Using a combination of an amino acid–dextrose (5% to 10%) solution and a fat emulsion, peripheral vein nutrition can supply full caloric needs without the risks associated with use of a central venous catheter. Because this combined solution has a lower tonicity than an intravenous hyperalimentation solution, the success of peripheral vein nutrition depends on the patient's tolerance of the large volumes of fluid necessary to supply full nutritional needs. Peripheral vein nutrition that includes a fat emulsion is associated with a lower incidence of phlebitis than an amino acid–dextrose solution infused alone. Duration of peripheral vein nutrition is normally limited to less than 3 weeks, because patients with nutritional and metabolic aberrations usually have poor peripheral venous access and require higher caloric intake than can be delivered peripherally to achieve weight gain.*

*Peripheral vein nutrition is contraindicated in patients with malnutrition or disorders of fat metabolism, such as pathologic hyperlipemia, lipid nephrosis, and acute pancreatitis accompanied by hyperlipemia. This technique should be used cautiously in patients with severe hepatic damage, coagulation disorders, anemia, and pulmonary disease and in those who are at increased risk of fat embolism. In the premature or low–birth-weight infant, peripheral vein nutrition with fat emulsion may cause lipid accumulation in the lungs.*

## Equipment

Amino acid–dextrose solution □ fat emulsion □ two controllers □ Y-type nonphthalate administration set □ alcohol sponges □ I.V. pole and venipuncture equipment, if necessary.

The only additive allowed to the fat emulsion is sodium heparin (in a small dosage), which activates lipase, the enzyme needed to oxidize fatty acids and enhance clearance of fat from the blood. An excessive amount of sodium heparin can deplete the body's stores of lipase.

Nonphthalate administration set, designed especially for simultaneous infusion of fat emulsion and amino acid–dextrose solution, consists of two lines in a Y configuration. The vented line is used for the fat emulsion; the nonvented line, containing a filter, for the amino acid–dextrose solution. This special nonphthalate tubing is necessary because lipids can extract small amounts of phthalates from phthalate-plasticized polyvinyl chloride tubing.

Controllers which can accommodate the special tubing are needed to ensure the correct infusion rate, because the risk of phlebitis is smaller when two components are administered at approximately the same rate.

## Preparation of equipment

Inspect the fat emulsion for opacity and consistency of color and texture. If the emulsion looks frothy, oily, or contains particles, or if its stability or sterility is questionable, return the bottle to the pharmacy. Avoid excessive shaking of the bottle *to prevent aggregation of fat globules.* Similarly, inspect the amino acid–dextrose solution for cloudiness, turbidity, and particles and the bottle for cracks; if any of these are present, return the bottle to the pharmacy.

Wash your hands and, using aseptic technique, take the nonphthalate tubing from its package. Remove the protective cap from the fat emulsion bottle, and wipe the rubber stopper with an alcohol sponge. Hold the bottle upright, and insert the vented spike through the inner circle of the rubber stopper. Invert the bottle, and squeeze the drip chamber until it fills to the level indicated in the tubing package instructions. Open the flow clamp, allow fat emulsion to flow through to the Y-connector, and then close the clamp.

Remove the protective cap from the container of amino acid–dextrose solution, and wipe the rubber stopper with an alcohol sponge. Hold the bottle upright, and insert the nonvented spike. Invert the bottle, and squeeze the drip chamber until the fluid reaches the desired level. Hold the filter with the Y-connector facing upward and the air vent downward, and open the clamp. Start the solution flow *to remove air from the filter and line.* Then, close the clamp.

If you're initiating the infusion, hang the bottles after inserting the spikes. Then, attach the controllers to the I.V. pole, and prepare them according to manufacturer's instructions.

**Essential steps**

• Explain the procedure to the patient *to ease his anxiety and promote his cooperation.*

• Obtain baseline vital signs, as ordered. If necessary, perform venipuncture.

*To start the infusion:*

• Connect the administration set to the I.V. needle or catheter hub. Then, turn on the controllers and set them to the desired flow rate. Next, completely open the flow clamps *to allow the controllers to regulate the flow rate.*

• Monitor vital signs every 10 minutes for the first 30 minutes and every hour thereafter.

*To change the solutions and tubing:*

• Hang the new solution bottle and tubing alongside the old ones.

• Examine the skin above the insertion site for signs of phlebitis: redness, warmth, and pain. If such signs are present, remove the existing I.V. line and start a line in a different vein.

• Turn off the controllers, and close the flow clamps on the old tubing. Disconnect the tubing from the needle or catheter hub, and connect the new tubing.

• Open the flow clamps on the new

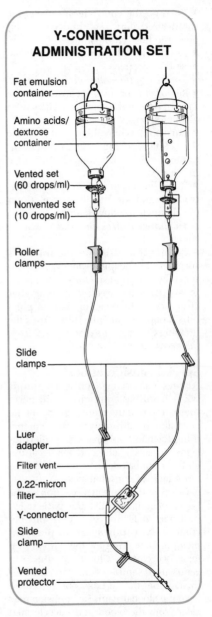

**Y-CONNECTOR ADMINISTRATION SET**

Fat emulsion container

Amino acids/ dextrose container

Vented set (60 drops/ml)

Nonvented set (10 drops/ml)

Roller clamps

Slide clamps

Luer adapter

Filter vent

0.22-micron filter

Y-connector

Slide clamp

Vented protector

bottles to equal, slow flow rates *to prevent clot formation in the needle or catheter while you're inserting the tubing into the controllers.*

• Remove the old tubing from controllers, and insert new tubing according to the manufacturer's instructions.

• Turn on the controllers, set them to the desired flow rate, and completely open the flow clamps.

• Remove the old equipment and dispose of it properly.

*To change the solutions:*

• Remove the protective caps, and wipe the stoppers of the solution bottles with alcohol sponges.

• Turn off the controllers, and close the flow clamps. Using strict aseptic technique, remove each spike and insert it in the new bottle.

• Hang the bottles, turn on the controllers, and set the flow rate. Completely open the flow clamps.

*To change a dressing and needle or catheter:*

• Change the dressing at intervals specified by hospital policy, and inspect the insertion site for signs of phlebitis. Change the needle or catheter after 48 hours or the onset of signs of phlebitis. Loop and tape the tubing over the dressing *to prevent its dislodgment from the needle or catheter hub.*

## Special considerations

Always use strict aseptic technique when handling equipment, and never reuse a partially empty bottle of fat emulsion, because it is an excellent medium for bacterial growth. Be alert for signs of sepsis: elevated temperature, chills, malaise, leukocytosis, and altered level of consciousness.

Observe the patient's reaction to the fat emulsion; usually, the patient experiences a feeling of satiety but occasionally reports an unpleasant metallic taste. Monitor the patient's fat tolerance closely. Cloudy plasma in a centrifuged sample of citrated blood indicates that the fat hasn't been cleared from the bloodstream. Fat emulsion may clear from the blood at an accelerated rate in a patient with full-thickness burns, multiple trauma, and metabolic imbalance, because catecholamines, adrenocortical hormones, thyroxine, and growth hormone enhance lipolysis and mobilization of fatty acids.

Check serum triglyceride levels; these should return to normal within 18 hours after infusion of a bottle of fat emulsion. As ordered, obtain blood samples for laboratory analysis; typically, SGOT, SGPT, alkaline phosphatase, cholesterol, triglyceride, plasma free fatty acid, and coagulation tests are performed weekly *to monitor the patient's response.*

*Because lipase synthesis increases insulin requirements,* increase the insulin dosage of the patient with diabetes, as ordered. For the patient with hypothyroidism, administer thyroid-stimulating hormone—which affects lipase activity—as ordered, *to prevent intravascular accumulations of triglycerides.*

## Complications

Immediate or early adverse reactions to fat emulsion therapy, which reportedly occur in fewer than 1% of patients, include fever, dyspnea, cyanosis, nausea, vomiting, headache, flushing, diaphoresis, lethargy, syncope, chest and back pain, slight pressure over the eyes, irritation at the infusion site, hyperlipemia, hypercoagulability, and thrombocytopenia. Thrombocytopenia has been reported in infants receiving 20% I.V. fat emulsion.

Delayed but uncommon complications associated with prolonged administration of fat emulsion include hepatomegaly, splenomegaly, jaundice secondary to central lobular cholestasis, and blood dyscrasias (thrombocytopenia, leukopenia, and transient increases in liver function studies). For unknown reasons, a few patients receiving 20% I.V. fat emulsion have developed brown pigmentation (I.V. fat pigment) in the reticuloendothelial system.

## Documentation

Record the dates and times of all dressing and cannula changes; the duration and amount of each infusion; and the patient's condition and response to therapy.

DEANN M. ENGLERT, RN, MSN

# BLOOD AND BLOOD COMPONENTS

## Transfusion of Whole Blood and Packed Cells

*Whole blood transfusion replenishes both the volume and the oxygen-carrying capacity of the circulatory system. Transfusion of packed cells, in which 80% of the plasma is removed, restores only the oxygen-carrying capacity. Both types of transfusion treat decreased hemoglobin and hematocrit levels. Whole blood is usually transfused only when decreased levels result from hemorrhage; packed cells are transfused when such depressed levels accompany normal blood volume to avoid possible fluid and circulatory overload. Both whole blood and packed cells contain cellular debris, necessitating in-line filtration during administration.*

*Depending on hospital policy, transfusion may require identification of the patient and blood product by two nurses before administration to prevent errors and a possibly fatal reaction. It always requires a signed consent form from the patient. If the patient is a Jehovah's Witness, transfusion requires special written permission.*

### Equipment

Blood recipient set (filter and tubing with drip chamber for blood, or combined set) □ whole blood or packed cells □ 250 ml of normal saline solution □ I.V. pole □ plasma transfer set (for transfusing packed cells with a straight set) □ informed consent form □ venipuncture equipment, if necessary.

Both straight and Y-type blood administration sets are commonly used. Although both mesh and microaggregate filters are available, the latter type is the preferred type especially when transfusing multiple units of blood.

### Preparation of equipment

Prepare the normal saline solution for infusion: Insert the tubing spike, and prime the filter and tubing according to the manufacturer's instructions. Avoid obtaining whole blood or packed cells until you're ready to begin the transfusion *because red cells deteriorate after 2 hours when stored at room temperature.*

### Essential steps

● Explain the procedure to the patient. Ensure that he has signed a consent form before transfusion therapy.
● Take the patient's vital signs *to serve as baseline values.*
● If the patient doesn't have an I.V. line in place, perform venipuncture, preferably using an 18G catheter or 19G needle. Avoid using an existing line if the needle or catheter lumen is smaller than 20G.
● Attach the saline solution to the catheter or needle hub, and start the infusion at a keep-vein-open rate (about 10 drops/minute).
● Obtain whole blood or packed cells from the blood bank. Check the expiration date on the blood bag, and observe for abnormal color, red cell clumping, gas bubbles, and extraneous material. Return outdated or abnormal blood to the blood bank.
● Compare the name and number on the patient's wristband with that on the blood bag label. Check the blood bag identification number and ABO and Rh compatibility. Also, compare the patient's blood bank identification number, if present, with the number on the blood bag. Ask another nurse to verify all information *to prevent transfusion error and a possibly fatal reaction.*
● If you're administering packed cells with a straight set, use a plasma transfer set to add 50 ml of saline solution to the bag. With the flow clamp closed, insert one spike into the blood bag and the second spike into the saline container.

# TRANSFUSING BLOOD UNDER PRESSURE

Transfuse blood under pressure *only* when rapid replacement is necessary. Begin this procedure by selecting the proper equipment—a pressure cuff or a positive-pressure set. The *pressure cuff,* which resembles a sleeve, is placed over the blood bag and inflated; a pressure gauge, attached to the cuff, is calibrated in millimeters of mercury. The *positive-pressure set* is a gravity administration set containing a built-in pressure chamber that increases the flow rate when manual pressure is applied externally to the chamber.

Prepare the patient and set up equipment in the same way as with a standard administration set. Prime the filter and tubing to remove all air from the administration set. Connect tubing to the needle or catheter hub. Throughout transfusion, watch the patient closely for complications, such as infiltration or extravasation, which can occur quite rapidly.

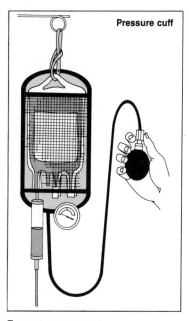

**Pressure cuff**

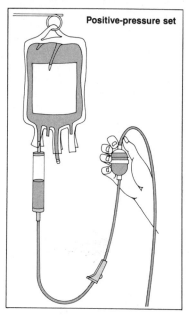

**Positive-pressure set**

**To use a pressure cuff**
• Insert your hand into the pressure cuff sleeve and pull the blood bag upward through the center opening. Then, grasp one loop of the sleeve, slip it through the blood bag loop, and pull the other sleeve loop through it.
• Hang the blood bag on the I.V. pole. Open the flow clamp on the tubing.
• To set the flow rate, turn the screw clamp on the pressure cuff counterclockwise. Compress the pressure bulb of the cuff to inflate the bag until you achieve the desired flow rate. Then, turn the screw clamp clockwise *to maintain this constant flow rate. Note:* As the blood bag empties, the pressure decreases, so check the flow rate regularly and adjust the pressure in the pressure cuff as necessary *to maintain*

*a consistent flow rate.* But don't allow the cuff needle to exceed 300 mmHg, because excessively high pressure may cause hemolysis of red blood cells.

**To use a positive-pressure set**
• Open the upper and lower flow clamps on the administration set. Manually compress and release the pump chamber to force blood down the tubing and into the patient. Allow the pump chamber to refill completely before compressing it again. Continue to compress and release the chamber until the blood bag empties or until rapid administration is no longer necessary. To discontinue transfusion under pressure, stop compressing the chamber and adjust the flow rate as for standard administration.

PEGGY BOYLE, RN

# USING BLOOD-WARMING DEVICES

Use the blood-warming devices shown below for massive, rapid blood transfusions and for exchange transfusions of the newborn, according to hospital policy, because rapid transfusion of cold blood can lead to hypothermia. You can also use these devices for transfusions of the patient with cold agglutinins. Both devices maintain a constant temperature of 98.6° F. (37° C.).

To use either blood warmer, first plug in the device. Then, prepare the patient and equipment as you would if using a straight-line set (for the blood-warming coil) or a Y-set (for the dry-heat warmer). After the administration set is free of air, close the flow-control clamp.

**Blood-warming coil**

**Dry-heat warmer**

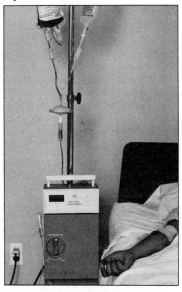

**To use a blood-warming coil**
• Turn on the machine.
• Using aseptic technique, remove the coil from its sterile wrapper and close the clamps. Attach the blood line's male adapter to the coil's female adapter. Then, attach the needle to the opposite end of the coil.
• Immerse the coil in a basin of water warmed to 98.6° F. Keep the adapters dry *to prevent water from entering the tubing and contaminating the entire setup.*
• When the administration set and coil are fully flushed with blood, proceed as you would for straight-line administration. When the blood bag empties, flush the coil with normal saline solution *to remove blood from the line.* Replace the coil after 24 hours.

**To use a dry-heat warmer**
• Insert the warming bag into the blood warmer. Match the bottom lead (for the blood line) and the top lead (for the patient) to the corresponding openings in the blood warmer. *Note:* The top lead has a special outlet chamber attached to it. Mount the warming bag on the support pins, keeping the bag flat against the back panel. Then, secure the pins.
• Close the blood warmer's door and secure the latch. Turn the machine on, and allow it to operate for at least 2 minutes to warm the blood to 98.6° F. Avoid opening the door until completion of the transfusion, *to prevent loss of vacuum and mandatory replacement of the warming bag.*
• While the blood is warming, connect the blood line's adapter to the female adapter on the bottom lead. When the desired temperature is reached, open the saline line clamp and the main flow clamp *to fill the blood-warming bag with saline solution.* Squeeze the outlet chamber on the top lead until it is flat, and continue to hold the chamber. When saline solution appears in the top lead chamber, close the main flow clamp and release the chamber. The chamber then automatically fills halfway with saline solution.
• Remove the adapter cover on the top lead and open the clamp. Expel residual air from the line. Then, close the clamp and recap the line. Next, proceed as you would when administering blood with a Y-set.

Lower the packed cells, open the flow clamp, and allow 50 ml of saline solution to flow into the packed cells. Close the flow clamp, and gently rotate the bag *to mix the saline solution and the cells.* Then, insert the straight set spike into the other port on the blood bag. Leave the plasma transfer set in place during the transfusion.

If you're administering packed cells with a Y-type set, add saline solution to the bag *to dilute the cells* by closing the clamp between the patient and the drip chamber and opening the clamp from the blood. Then, lower the blood bag below the saline container and let 30 to 50 ml of saline flow into the packed cells. Finally, close the clamp to the blood bag, rehang the bag, rotate it gently *to mix the cells and saline solution,* and close the clamp to the saline container.

If you're administering whole blood, gently invert the bag several times *to mix the cells.*

• Open all clamps between the blood bag and the patient, and adjust the flow clamp closest to the patient to deliver 25 to 30 drops/minute; the patient then receives about 50 ml of blood over 30 minutes *to minimize any transfusion reaction, which usually occurs within this period.*

• Remain with the patient, and watch for signs of transfusion reaction. If such signs develop, take and record vital signs. If no signs of a reaction appear within 30 minutes, adjust the flow clamp to the ordered infusion rate. Raising and lowering the blood bag *to adjust the rate reduces the risk of hemolysis from pressure on the tubing.*

• After the completion of the transfusion, flush the filter and tubing with saline solution, if recommended by the manufacturer. Then, reconnect the original I.V. fluid or discontinue the I.V.

• Return the empty blood bag to the blood bank, and discard the tubing and filter.

• Take and record the patient's vital signs.

**Special considerations**
Although some microaggregate filters can be used for up to 10 units of blood, always replace the filter if more than 1 hour elapses between transfusions. Avoid piggybacking blood, because the secondary set can become dislodged from the injection site, causing contamination of the transfused blood. When administering multiple units of blood under pressure, use a blood warmer *to avoid hypothermia.*

**Complications**
Despite increasingly accurate cross-matching precautions, transfusion reactions can occur; despite donor screening, hepatitis can be transmitted. Circulatory overload and hemolytic, allergic, febrile, and pyrogenic reactions can result from any transfusion. Coagulation disturbances, citrate intoxication, hyperkalemia, acid-base imbalance, loss of 2,3-diphosphoglycerate, ammonia intoxication, and hypothermia can result from massive transfusion.

**Documentation**
Record the date and time of transfusion, the type and amount of transfused blood, the patient's vital signs, and your check of all identifying data. Document any transfusion reaction and treatment.

PEGGY BOYLE, RN

# Transfusion of Plasma and Plasma Fractions

*Transfusion of plasma and its fractions serves a variety of therapeutic purposes. For example, transfusion of platelets, which are suspended in 30 to 50 ml of plasma, is ordered to correct an extremely low platelet count (below 10,000 mm³), which can occur in patients with hematologic diseases, such as aplastic anemia and leukemia, and in those receiving antineoplastic chemotherapy. Platelet transfusion is not indicated in disseminated intravascular* coagulation and in disorders causing rapid platelet destruction, such as idiopathic thrombocytopenic purpura. Usually, a large quantity of platelets—typically 4 or more units for an adult—are required to prevent or control bleeding.

Transfusion of fresh or fresh frozen plasma (FFP), which contains most clotting factors but no platelets, is ordered to treat an undetermined clotting factor deficiency, a specific factor deficiency when that factor alone isn't available, and factor deficiencies resulting from hepatic disease or blood dilution. Transfusion of FFP is the only treatment for Factor V deficiency.

Although plasma functions as a blood volume expander, plasma protein fraction (PPF)—a 5% solution of selected proteins (albumin and some globulins) from pooled plasma in a buffered, stabilized saline diluent—and albumin—extracted from plasma, heat-treated, chemically processed, and available in 5% (isotonic) and 25% (hypertonic) preparations—are used more frequently. Both preparations also treat hypoproteinemia and hypoalbuminemia. Hypertonic albumin also reduces cerebral edema by drawing large amounts of extravascular fluid into the vascular system. Albumin transfusion is contraindicated in severe anemia because of the risk of cellular dehydration and should be administered cautiously in cardiac and pulmonary disease because of the risk of congestive heart failure from circulatory overload.

Transfusion of cryoprecipitate, which forms when FFP thaws slowly, replaces missing clotting factors in hemophilia A, von Willebrand's disease, and fibrinogen and Factor XIII deficiencies. However, transfusion of Factor VIII (antihemophilia) concentrate, a lyophilized preparation, is the long-term treatment of choice for hemophilia A, because the amount of Factor VIII per vial varies less than with cryoprecipitate. Prothrombin complex (factors II, VII, IX, and X), obtained through chemical fractionation of pooled plasma, can be used to treat he-

mophilia B, severe liver disease, and acquired deficiencies of factors II, VII, IX, and X. However, it is used infrequently because of the associated high risk of transmitting hepatitis. Transfusion of gamma globulin, the antibody-containing portion of plasma that is obtained by chemical fractionation of pooled plasma, is used to prevent infectious hepatitis (Type A), rubeola, mumps, pertussis, and tetanus (if given before clinical symptoms develop) and to treat hypogammaglobulinemia and agammaglobulinemia. Transfusion of gamma globulin is contraindicated in patients with known hypersensitivity to it or an antiimmunoglobulin antibody (IgA).

## Equipment
Plasma or plasma fraction □ administration set (see *Transfusion Sets*, page 294) □ normal saline solution □ alcohol sponge □ 18G to 20G 1″ needle □ adhesive tape □ venipuncture equipment, if necessary.

## Preparation of equipment
Obtain the necessary unit of plasma or plasma fraction from the blood bank just before transfusion. Check the expiration date, and carefully inspect the plasma for cloudiness and turbidity, and the plastic bag for leaks. Be sure to use FFP within 4 hours, *because it doesn't contain preservatives.* When transfusing a *Factor VIII or prothrombin preparation,* carefully reconstitute it according to the manufacturer's directions, if you did not receive it already prepared by the pharmacy. For administration of Factor VIII concentrate, avoid using a glass syringe to prevent binding to ground glass surfaces.

## Essential steps
● Positively identify the patient by carefully comparing the name and number of his wristband with the information on the laboratory slip.
● Explain the procedure to the patient to ease his anxiety and promote cooperation. Make sure the patient has signed a consent form.

# TRANSFUSION SETS

**The component syringe set** contains two side clamps: one located slightly below the bag spike, the other slightly below the Y-connector (as shown at right). After you have connected the set to the patient, draw the platelets into the syringe and depress the plunger. Control the administration rate by depressing the plunger at various speeds.

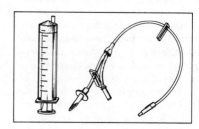

**The component drip set** contains tubing, a drip chamber, and filter (as shown at right). Prepare for transfusion by compressing the drip chamber until the filter is completely covered. Then, close the flow rate clamp, hang the set, and connect the I.V. line to it. Control the administration rate by adjusting the flow clamp.

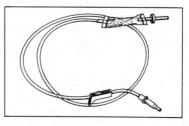

• Obtain baseline vital signs.
• Wash your hands. If an I.V. line is already in place, check the insertion site for inflammation and the line for patency. If the primary solution can't be interrupted or the patient doesn't have an I.V. in place, perform a venipuncture and start the saline infusion at a keep-vein-open (KVO) rate.
• If you're using an existing I.V., replace the infused solution with saline, and adjust the flow to a KVO rate. Insert a sterile plug in the original solution container *to prevent its contamination*.

*To administer plasma, FFP, albumin, Factor VIII concentrate, or prothrombin complex:*
• Attach the administration set to the plasma or plasma product and the needle to the tubing. Then, prime the system.
• Using an alcohol sponge, wipe the Y-injection port of the primary administration set. Then, insert the needle from the plasma product administration set into the injection port, stop the saline infusion, and adjust the flow rate of the

plasma or plasma product, as ordered (see *Administering Plasma and Plasma Fractions*).

*To administer platelets or cryoprecipitate with a component drip set:*
• Open the port of the platelet or cryoprecipitate bag by pulling back the tabs. Then, remove the protective cover of the administration set spike.
• Close the flow clamp and, using a twisting motion, insert the administration set spike into the port. Hang the bag, compress the drip chamber until fluid fully covers the filter, and open the clamp. Then, prime the tubing and close the clamp.
• Using an alcohol sponge, wipe the Y-injection port of the primary administration set. Then, insert the needle from the component drip set into the injection port and stop the saline infusion.
• Completely open the flow clamp on the component drip set *to administer the platelets or cryoprecipitate rapidly, preventing clumping or loss of activity*.

*To administer platelets or cryoprecip-*

*itate with a component syringe set:*
• Close both clamps on the syringe set. Then, open the port of the platelet or cryoprecipitate bag by pulling back the tabs. Next, remove the protective cover of the administration set spike.
• Using a twisting motion, insert the administration set spike into the port.

Then, attach the syringe to the Luer-tip port.
• Open the clamp above the Y-connection, aspirate the contents of the bag into the syringe, and close the clamp. Then, open the clamp below the Y-connection, hold the syringe upright, prime the tubing, and close the clamp.

## ADMINISTERING PLASMA AND PLASMA FRACTIONS

| COMPONENT | METHOD OF ADMINISTRATION | USUAL RATE OF ADMINISTRATION | COMPLICATIONS |
|---|---|---|---|
| Platelets | Component drip set or component syringe set with a nonwettable filter | Rapidly, 1 unit/10 min | Hepatitis, allergic reaction, febrile reaction, circulatory overload |
| Plasma, fresh frozen plasma | Plasma administration set, standard blood administration set with a standard blood filter (microaggregate recipient set unnecessary) | 1 unit in less than 1 hour for hypovolemia | Hepatitis, allergic reaction, febrile reaction, circulatory overload |
| Plasma protein fraction | Standard blood administration set with a standard blood filter (microaggregate recipient set unnecessary) | Usually 5 to 10 ml/min, depending on patient's condition and response | Circulatory overload, hypotension |
| Albumin | Albumin administration set (supplied by manufacturer) | Rapidly for shock; 5 to 10 ml/min for hypoproteinemia | Circulatory overload, pyrogenic reaction, microbial contamination, hepatitis (uncommon) |
| Cryoprecipitate | Component drip set or component syringe set | Rapidly, 10 ml/min | Hepatitis |
| Factor VIII concentrate | Plastic syringe for I.V. injection; plastic syringe and infusion set (provided by manufacturer) for I.V. infusion | 10 to 20 ml/3 min | Hepatitis |
| Prothrombin complex | Standard blood administration set with filter | Varies greatly but usually 1 vial/5 min | Hepatitis (very high risk) |
| Gamma globulin | I.M. injection | Not applicable | Allergic reaction, especially in the patient with anti-IgA antibody |

• Using an alcohol sponge, wipe the Y-injection port of the primary administration set.

• Insert the needle from the syringe set into the injection port, and stop the saline infusion. Depress the syringe plunger and rapidly administer the platelets or cryoprecipitate *to prevent clumping or loss of activity.*

• With either set, administer subsequent bags of platelets by removing the administration set spike and inserting it in a new bag. Remember, if you are using a drip set, close the clamp and attach a new bag before the drip chamber empties and air enters the line. If you are using a syringe set, close the clamp closest to the patient before aspiration.

• After completion of the infusion, flush the line with 20 to 30 ml of saline solution, and discontinue the I.V. unless therapy is scheduled to continue; then, if appropriate, hang the original I.V. solution and adjust the flow rate, as ordered.

*To administer gamma globulin:*

• Follow the manufacturer's instructions. If you're injecting more than 5 ml, divide it into two doses, administered at different sites.

• Discard equipment after use or return it to the blood bank, according to hospital policy.

**Special considerations**
Because platelet transfusion can be time-consuming, schedule your daily patient-care duties around it. During the transfusion therapy, check frequently for bleeding, and instruct the patient to report even slight bleeding.

If the patient requires whole blood or packed cells after plasma transfusion, first administer the plasma with a blood set. Then, maintain the I.V. with saline solution at a KVO rate until you are ready to transfuse blood.

If you have difficulty establishing the flow of an albumin infusion, suspect an air lock in the vent on the tubing spike. To correct this, wipe the container's rubber stopper with an alcohol sponge and insert a 20G 1″ needle. If unsuccessful,

change the tubing. If still unsuccessful, obtain a new container of albumin and administration set and return the defective set. If albumin has been diluted or added to another solution, use it as soon as possible *to prevent bacterial growth.*

Always use an administration set supplied by the manufacturer, because it contains a small concealed filter that removes particles and other contaminants.

**Complications**
For complications associated with transfusion of plasma and its fractions, see *Administering Plasma and Plasma Fractions,* page 295.

**Documentation**
Record the type and amount of plasma or plasma fraction administered, duration of transfusion, baseline vital signs, and any adverse reactions.

PEGGY BOYLE, RN

# Management of Transfusion Reactions

*Transfusion reaction can result from a single or massive transfusion of blood or blood products. Although many reactions occur during or shortly after transfusion, hepatitis can develop as long as 6 months after transfusion.*

*Transfusion reaction requires immediate recognition and prompt nursing actions to prevent further complications and, possibly, death—particularly if the patient is unconscious or so heavily sedated that he can't report the common symptoms.*

**Equipment**
Normal saline solution □ I.V. administration set □ sterile urine specimen container □ needle, syringe, and tubes for blood samples □ transfusion reaction report form.

## Essential steps

• As soon as you suspect an adverse reaction, stop the transfusion and start the saline infusion at a keep-vein-open rate *to maintain venous access.* Don't discard the blood bag or administration set.

• Notify the doctor.

• Monitor vital signs every 15 minutes or as indicated by the severity and type of reaction.

• Compare the labels on all blood containers to corresponding patient identification forms *to ensure transfusion was the correct blood or blood product.*

• Notify the blood bank of a possible transfusion reaction and collect blood samples, as ordered. Immediately send these samples, all transfusion containers (even if empty), and the administration set to the blood bank. The blood bank will test these materials to further evaluate the reaction.

• Collect the first posttransfusion urine specimen, mark the collection slip "Possible Transfusion Reaction," and send it to the laboratory immediately. *The laboratory tests this specimen for the presence of hemoglobin, which indicates a hemolytic reaction.*

• Closely monitor intake and output. Note evidence of oliguria or anuria, *because hemoglobin deposition in the renal tubules can cause renal damage.*

• If ordered, administer oxygen, epinephrine, or other drugs. If ordered, give an alcohol bath or apply a hypothermia blanket *to reduce fever.*

• Make the patient as comfortable as possible and provide reassurance as necessary.

## TYPES OF TRANSFUSION REACTION

| TYPE | CAUSE | SIGNS AND SYMPTOMS |
|------|-------|--------------------|
| Hemolytic | Antibodies in the recipient's plasma react with antigens in donor red blood cells. This leads to donor cell agglutination and capillary occlusion, blocking oxygen and blood flow to vital organs. Eventually, the red cells break down and release free hemoglobin into plasma and urine. This free hemoglobin may block the renal tubules, resulting in renal failure. | Chills, fever, backache, headache, restlessness, anxiety, nausea, vomiting, chest pain, tachycardia, dyspnea, hypotension, cyanosis, hemoglobinemia, hemoglobinuria, oliguria, anuria, jaundice, vascular collapse |
| Allergic | Although its mechanism is unknown, it probably results from the reaction of allergens in donor blood with antibodies in recipient blood. | Urticaria, pruritus, chills, nausea, vomiting, headache, nasal congestion, wheezing; in more severe reactions: bronchospasm, severe dyspnea, laryngeal edema, circulatory collapse |
| Febrile | Recipient sensitivity to donor leukocytes or platelets | Fever, chills, flushing, back pain, malaise, tachycardia, headache, confusion, nausea, vomiting |
| Bacterial | Bacterial contamination of donor blood, usually by gram-negative organisms | Fever, chills, abdominal and extremity pain, vomiting, hypotension, bloody diarrhea |
| Circulatory overload | Rate or volume of transfusion exceeds the circulatory system's capacity. | Cough, chest pain, dyspnea, distended neck veins, tachycardia, cyanosis, frothy sputum, pleural rales, hemoptysis |

## COMPLICATIONS OF MASSIVE TRANSFUSION

If refrigerated properly, whole blood preserved with citrate-phosphate-dextrose (CPD) is suitable for transfusion within 21 days of collection; blood preserved with CPD-adenine is usable for 35 days. During storage, whole blood undergoes changes that can cause complications in the patient receiving blood volume replacement (8 to 10 units for an adult) within 24 hours. These complications include the following:

• *Coagulation disturbances.* These may result from poor survival of platelets, Factor V, and Factor VIII.

• *Citrate intoxication.* This rare reaction may result from the binding of citrate (present in the anticoagulant-preservative solution) to serum calcium, causing hypocalcemia. It occurs with too rapid, massive transfusion of citrated blood and, most commonly, in the patient with existing hepatic or renal dysfunction, because citrate is metabolized in the liver and excreted by the kidneys.

• *Hyperkalemia.* This complication may result from the release of potassium into the plasma during red cell lysis, thereby elevating potassium levels. It is rare except in patients with conditions causing potassium retention, such as renal failure.

• *Acid-base imbalance.* Gradual acidification of stored blood occurs and may result in metabolic acidosis. Particularly at risk is the patient with existing acidosis associated with decreased tissue perfusion. Such an imbalance precedes delayed metabolic alkalosis, caused by rapid citrate metabolism and the resulting bicarbonate excess.

• *Loss of 2, 3-diphosphoglycerate.* This can lead to tighter binding of oxygen to hemoglobin, resulting in a shift of the oxygen dissociation curve to the left. The seriously ill patient may then experience inadequate tissue oxygenation.

• *Ammonia intoxication.* This complication results from increased levels of ammonia in stored blood and primarily affects the patient with hepatic impairment.

• *Hypothermia.* Rapid infusion of large amounts of cold blood can cause hypothermia, which may decrease cardiac output and rate and reduce blood pH.

• *Circulatory overload.* This complication results when transfusion volume exceeds circulatory system capacity, particularly in the debilitated or elderly patient.

• *Bacterial or viral infection.* Although this complication can occur with single or multiple blood transfusions, its risk increases with each transfused unit because various donors are involved. Viral hepatitis, the most common infection transmitted by transfusion, occurs despite screening for hepatitis antigens.

### Special considerations

Treat all transfusion reactions seriously until proven otherwise. If the doctor anticipates a transfusion reaction, such as in leukemia patients, he may order prophylactic treatment with antihistamines or antipyretics to precede blood administration.

### Documentation

Record the time and date of transfusion reaction, the type and amount of infused blood or blood products, the clinical signs of transfusion reaction in order of occurrence, the patient's vital signs, any specimens which were sent to the laboratory for analysis, any treatment, and patient's response to treatment. If required by hospital policy, complete the transfusion reaction form.

PATRICIA GONCE MILLER, RN, MS

# Therapeutic Plasma Exchange
[*Plasmapheresis*]

*In therapeutic plasma exchange (TPE), blood withdrawn from a patient's vein (usually in the antecubital fossa) flows to a cell separator, where it is separated into plasma and formed elements (red cells, white cells, platelets) by centrifugation or by microporous membrane filtration. This plasma is then collected in a container for disposal, and the formed elements are mixed with a plasma replacement fluid (proteins, fluid, and electrolytes) and returned to the patient through an-*

*other vein. In a newer method of TPE, the plasma is separated, filtered to remove the disease mediator, then returned to the patient.* In both methods, the extracorporeal circuit contains 150 to 400 ml of blood during plasma exchange, necessitating the patient's tolerance of decreased blood volume. *TPE may benefit patients with immune-related disorders, such as multiple myeloma, rapidly progressive glomerulonephritis, systemic lupus erythematosus, and rheumatoid arthritis, or with a neuromuscular disorder, such as myasthenia gravis. It is commonly combined with steroid immunosuppressant therapy to suppress pathologic immune responses, thereby preventing further organ or system destruction. The procedure can be performed at the bedside or in a special unit and requires a specially trained technician or nurse to operate the cell separator, another nurse to monitor and maintain the patient, and a specialized doctor to be in the facility.*

### Equipment
Vascular access needles, if not in place ☐ gloves ☐ sterile gauze pads ☐ aids to help maintain blood flow, such as a rolled ABD pad, blood pressure cuff, or heating pad ☐ bedpan ☐ heparin (optional).

The technician or specially trained nurse usually provides all equipment necessary to operate the cell separator.

### Preparation of equipment
Using sterile technique, the technician or specially trained nurse assembles all necessary equipment and primes the extracorporeal circuit with normal saline solution *to remove air bubbles, preventing formation of an air embolus.* Then, she adds an anticoagulant, usually anticoagulant-citrate-dextrose (ACD), which prevents clotting by citrate binding to the blood's ionized (free) calcium; ACD only works in the extracorporeal circuit and is neutralized on return to the patient. The doctor may order the addition of calcium gluconate to the plasma replacement solution *to prevent*

*hypocalcemic reactions, because albumin in this solution can also bind the returned blood's ionized calcium.*

### Essential steps
● Explain the procedure to the patient, and verify that he has signed a consent form. Tell him the procedure usually takes 1 to 2 hours but may take longer, depending on the volume of plasma exchanged. Advise him to eat lightly before the procedure.
● Instruct the patient to urinate before the procedure and during the procedure, as necessary. *A full bladder may cause mild hypotension because of fluid shift or vasovagal reaction.*
● Tell the patient to report any symptoms of hypocalcemic paresthesias—tingling of mouth, chin, or fingers—during treatment.
● Take vital signs *to serve as baseline values.* Put on gloves *to prevent transmission of hepatitis or disease mediator in the contaminated plasma.*
● If an I.V. line is not in place, perform venipunctures *to establish vascular access routes.* Use large-bore needles *to minimize resistance and prevent damage to blood cells.* Obtain blood samples, as ordered. If ordered, administer 2,000 to 3,000 units of heparin I.V. just before TPE *to prevent clot formation in the vascular access sites.*
● The technician or specially trained nurse then connects the patient to the cell separator and starts it. While the machine is operating, observe all solutions *to avoid an air embolus from an empty container.*
● Monitor the patient for signs of hypotension, hypocalcemia, or allergic reaction, which may result from the replacement solution. Temporary reduction of blood flow rate relieves paresthesias from hypocalcemia.
● Take one or more of the following measures *to optimize blood flow,* as necessary: Place the patient in an elevated, semi-Fowler's position *to promote gravity drainage,* and hyperextend the arm on a firm surface, with the wrist supported *to bring large veins to the skin*

*surface.* Instruct the patient to squeeze a small, rolled ABD pad *to promote venous blood flow and prevent vessel collapse.* Apply a tourniquet or blood pressure cuff above the vascular sites *to provide pressure and increase blood pooling.* Place heating pads over the access sites *to dilate the vessels,* but observe for reddening skin, especially in the elderly patient with diminished heat sensitivity. Slightly withdraw or shift the needle *to augment blood flow.*

• After plasma exchange is completed, remove the needles (while wearing gloves) and elevate the affected extremities slightly.

• Firmly hold sterile gauze pads over the puncture sites until bleeding stops. Then, apply sterile pressure dressings. Avoid bending the extremities *to prevent vessel scarring and to allow use of the veins for further treatment.* If necessary, note on the patient's chart that the veins shouldn't be used for other purposes between TPE treatments.

• Mark all disposable equipment and plasma bags as contaminated, and dis-

---

### THERAPEUTIC PLASMA EXCHANGE AFTERCARE

After therapeutic plasma exchange (TPE), the patient may experience fatigue for 1 or 2 days as a result of decreased plasma protein levels. Advise him to rest frequently during this period and to reschedule strenuous activities, if possible. Unless contraindicated, tell him to maintain a high-protein diet to replace lost proteins and to take multivitamins with iron daily. If the patient is receiving steroids and requires a low-sodium diet, emphasize the importance of observing the diet.

Because plasmapheresis and concurrent therapy can cause immunosuppression, advise the patient to avoid persons with colds and other illnesses. Tell him to notify the doctor if any symptoms of an infection develop—even a scratchy throat—so the schedule for TPE and other therapy can be altered, if necessary. Also, advise the patient to notify the doctor of any muscle weakness or cramping.

DEBRA L. BLOMSTRANN, RN

---

card according to institutional policy.

### Special considerations

If possible, withhold drugs until completion of the procedure *to prevent their removal from the blood.* If the unstable patient with myasthenia gravis is undergoing TPE, have emergency equipment available. Monitor such a patient's blood pressure and pulse rate at least every 30 minutes. As ordered, give pyridostigmine bromide only if the patient experiences dysphagia or respiratory difficulty.

If the patient is receiving TPE treatments frequently, he may require transfusions of fresh frozen plasma *to replace the normal clotting factors removed from his plasma.* As ordered, give deep I.M. injections of gamma globulin in divided doses for 3 days after the procedure, *to replace normal immunoglobulins also removed in the plasma, which are needed to resist infection.* If permitted by hospital policy, mix 2 ml of 2% lidocaine with 10 ml of gamma globulin *to promote patient comfort during injection.*

If the patient is receiving immunosuppressant or steroid therapy, watch for signs of infection and an abnormally low WBC count.

### Complications

Hypotension can result from fluid shifts without protein replacement or from decreased blood volume. In the elderly patient, diminished cardiac output may cause hypotension after the procedure. Hypocalcemia can result from the binding of ionized calcium by citrate; hypomagnesemia can follow repeated TPEs, producing severe, prolonged muscle cramping and tetany. Any allergic reaction can result from the protein replacement solution, particularly from the plasma protein fraction. In a patient with myasthenia gravis, cholinergic crisis is possible. In a patient connected to a respirator, increased respiratory secretions can occur for 1 to 2 days after treatment.

### Documentation

Record the time of the procedure, the

patient's vital signs, the vascular access sites, the volume of exchanged plasma, the replacement solution, any adverse reactions, and any administration of drugs. Determine the patient's fluid balance from the following formula, and note it on the intake and output sheet.

Replacement solutions

$$\frac{+ \text{ ACD solution}}{\text{Volume removed}} \times 100 = \% \text{ return.}$$

JANE ELLEN HELFANT, RN, BA

# Autotransfusion

*Autotransfusion is the collection, filtration, and reinfusion of the patient's own blood. Although first performed successfully in 1914, this blood-conserving procedure only gained acceptance after technological advances in the 1970s. Currently, autotransfusion techniques are used after traumatic injury and before, during, and after surgery. The trauma technique, most commonly used for hemothorax, can also be used in primary injuries of the lungs, liver, chest wall, heart, pulmonary vessels, spleen, kidneys, inferior vena cava, and iliac, portal, and subclavian veins. In this technique, the collection system uses citrate-phosphate-dextrose (CPD) to prevent clotting of the collected blood. The preoperative technique, performed primarily for the patient with a rare blood type before major surgery or for whom isoimmunization may complicate future transfusion needs, follows standard blood bank donation and transfusion procedures. The intraoperative technique, used most often for thoracic and cardiovascular surgery, can also be used in hip resection, spinal fusion, liver resection, and ruptured ectopic pregnancy. In this technique, a commercial cell washer-processor reduces anticoagulated collected whole blood to washed, packed RBCs for later reinfusion. The postoperative technique is used solely to collect shed mediastinal blood after cardiac surgery.*

*Autotransfusion has several advantages over transfusion of bank blood. Most important, because autotransfused blood is autologous, it eliminates disease transmission, transfusion reactions, isoimmunization and, in the postoperative system, the addition of anticoagulants. This transfusion method can overcome the objections of certain religious groups who oppose transfusion. Unlike bank blood, autologous blood contains normal levels of 2,3-diphosphoglycerate (2,3-DPG)— advantageous for tissue oxygenation— potassium, ammonia, and clotting factors (except for fibrinogen); has a normal pH; and appears to have viable platelets. Occasionally, it causes transient hemoglobinuria, resulting from RBC trauma during collection.*

*This procedure is contraindicated in malignant neoplasms, intrathoracic or systemic infections and infestations, coagulopathies, enteric contamination, excessive hemolysis, and use of an antibiotic at the site that isn't suitable for I.V. administration.*

## Equipment

*For the trauma system:* I.V. pole or floor stand □ 500-ml bottle of CPD □ chest tubes for hemothorax □ trauma drainage tubing set □ volume-control set (usually 150 ml) □ Receptal canister □ 1,900-ml sterile disposable trauma blood liner, with 170-micron filter □ microemboli filter with recipient set.

*For the intraoperative system:* I.V. pole or floor stand □ two connected Receptal canisters □ 1,900-ml sterile disposable autotransfusion liner, with 170-micron filter □ 1,900-ml sterile disposable overflow liner □ double-lumen aspiration tubing with autotransfusion liner connector and administration set with macrodrip chamber □ suction wand □ anticoagulant solution (CPD or heparin) □ cell washer □ overflow shutoff valve (optional).

Liners and double-lumen tubing with administration set are available as kits.

*For the postoperative system:* Receptal canister □ sterile disposable mediastinal liner □ recipient set with microemboli filter □ mediastinal drainage tubing set.

## Preparation of equipment

*To set up the trauma system:* Remove the sterile liner from the package and extend it to its full length, *so it expands in the canister when the vacuum is applied.* Avoid contaminating the sterile spacer that caps the drainage port. Insert the liner in the canister and snap

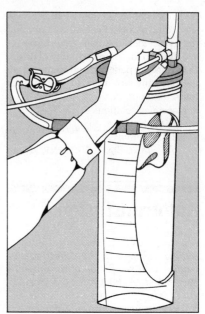

the lid securely in place, with the thumb tab directly over the canister tee *to facilitate connection to suction.* Connect the liner lid tubing with the sterile spacer to the canister tee (shown above). *The sterile spacer prevents contamination of the port by the nonsterile canister tee.* Attach the vacuum tubing to the opposite end of the canister tee. Temporarily occlude the tubing between the vacuum regulator and canister *to set the vacuum pressure between 10 and 30 mmHg. A higher setting increases hemolysis.*

Remove the protective cap from the patient port, and attach the yellow sterile proximal end of the drainage tubing with the anticoagulant connector to the patient port of the liner. Insert the volume-control set spike into the CPD bottle. Hang the bottle and prime the administration set. Remove the yellow cap from the anticoagulant connector, and attach the anticoagulant administration line (shown above). Run 100 ml of CPD into the liner *to prevent clotting of any blood.*

*To set up the intraoperative system:* Open the outer sterile wrap of the equipment, and gently drop the inner package onto the sterile field. Using sterile technique, remove the inner wrap. Remove the overflow liner (orange lid) from the sterile field and extend it to its full length, *so it expands in the canister when vacuum is applied.* Insert the orange-lidded liner in the left canister and connect its tubing to the canister's tee or shutoff valve. *The shutoff valve prevents aspiration of overflow blood into the vacuum line.* Snap the orange lid in place, with the thumb tab directly over the tee.

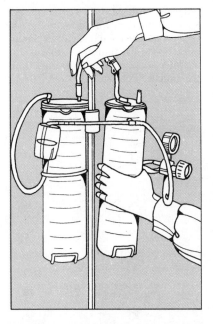

Remove the red-lidded liner from the sterile field, extend it to its full length, insert it in the right canister, and snap it securely in place, with the thumb tab placed directly over the canister tee.

Remove the white protective cap from the orange-lidded patient port, and connect this port to the tubing with the orange connector, which originates at the red lid (shown at left). Connect the vacuum tubing to the canister tee on the canister with the red-lidded liner. Temporarily occlude the tubing between the regulator and the canister *to set the vacuum pressure between 30 and 60 mmHg.* Label the red lid with pertinent patient information *to prevent misidentification when the patient's blood is removed to the cell processor.* Remove the red connector end of the aspiration tubing from the sterile field, and attach it to the patient port on the red lid. The clear end of the aspiration tubing remains within the sterile field for connection to the suction wand. Close the roller clamp on the administration set (shown below), insert the spike into the anticoagulant container, and prime the tubing. Check that all components are securely in place, *because any break in the system interferes with vacuum suction.*

*To set up the postoperative system:* Remove sterile liner from the package

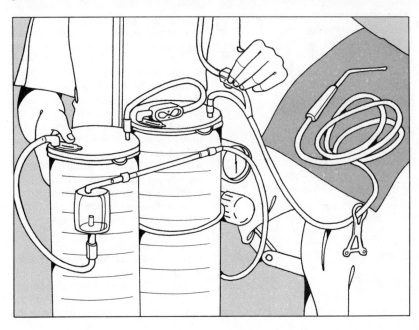

and extend it to its full length, *so it expands in the canister when the vacuum is applied.* Insert liner in the canister, and snap the lid securely into place, with thumb tab placed directly over the canister tee. Connect the liner lid tubing with the sterile spacer to the canister tee. Attach vacuum tubing to the opposite end of the canister tee. Temporarily occlude the tubing between the vacuum regulator and canister *to set the vacuum pressure between 15 mmHg and 30 mmHg.* Remove the protective cap on the patient port, and connect the drainage tubing to the port.

### Essential steps
*To perform the trauma technique:*
• To collect blood, attach the proximal end of the drainage tubing to the chest drainage catheter. During drainage, add one part CPD to seven parts blood.
• To transfuse collected blood, clamp the patient's line *to prevent pneumothorax when the vacuum is lost.* Then, disconnect the patient and anticoagulant lines from the liner lid.
• Disconnect the liner lid tubing and sterile spacer from the canister tee, and

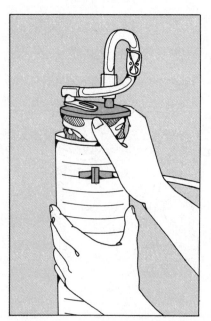

remove and discard the sterile spacer.
• Attach the liner lid tubing to the patient port, close the white cricket clamp, push up on the thumb tab *to unsnap the liner lid,* and remove the liner from the canister (shown at bottom left).

• Invert the liner and raise the recessed stem at the bottom of the liner, remove the yellow cap, and using a twisting motion, insert the microemboli filter set into the liner port.
• Hold the filter and recipient set upright, open the clamp, and gently compress the bag *to remove all air* (shown above). Close the clamp. Next, hang the liner, open the clamp, partly fill the drip chamber, and prime the tubing.
• Transfuse blood in the usual way. If you're using a pressure cuff, avoid exceeding a pressure of 150 mmHg.
  *To perform intraoperative technique:*
• When collecting blood, ensure that the anticoagulant flow rate is sufficient to prevent clotting.
• To transfuse collected blood, disconnect the aspiration tubing from the redlidded patient port. Then, disconnect the tubing from the orange connector on the orange lid, and connect it to the

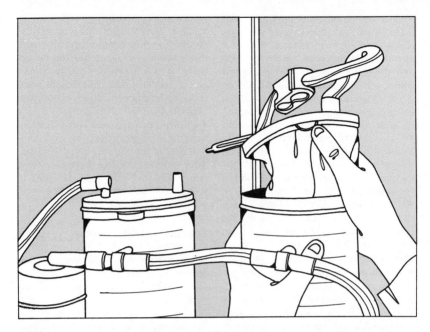

red-lidded patient port. Close the white cricket clamp, and remove and discard the orange adapter from the orange lid.
• Push upward on the red-lidded thumb tab *to unsnap it,* and remove the liner from the canister (shown above).
• To collect additional blood, insert a new red-lidded liner into the canister and make the connections to the orange lid and aspiration tubing.

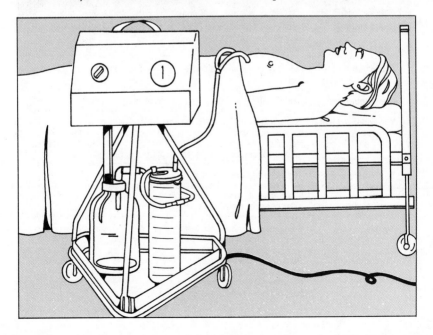

● Place the blood collected in the red-lidded liner in the blood processor, and follow the manufacturer's instruction for operation. The processor washes the blood and the saline solution and packs red cells to a hematocrit of 60% to 75%.

● Transfuse the washed, packed RBCs, using proper equipment and technique.

*To perform postoperative technique:*
● To collect blood, attach the sterile drainage tubing to the thoracic catheters, release the chest tube clamp with the vacuum on, and collect up to 800 ml of blood (shown at bottom of p. 305).

● To transfuse collected blood, clamp the chest drainage tube, disconnect the liner lid tubing and sterile spacer from the canister lid, and remove and discard the spacer.

● Attach the liner lid tubing to the patient port. Push upward on the thumb tab *to unsnap the liner lid,* and remove the liner from the canister. (To collect additional blood, insert a new liner and secure all connections.)

● Place your thumb under or behind the liner's white port *to facilitate valve closure as you separate the liner's sections.* If blood remains in the upper section of the liner, alternately compress both upper and lower sections *to transfer it to the lower one.*

● Clamp recipient set line. Using a twisting motion, insert the microemboli filter in the bottom port of the liner.

● As recommended in the trauma system technique, compress the liner *to remove all air,* prime the line, and transfuse the blood.

**Special considerations**

Cover canisters and avoid unwrapping sterile components until ready to use. Secure all connections and clamp the chest drainage system before stopping suction *to prevent pneumothorax.* If suction fails, place a Heimlich valve between the canister tee and the vacuum. Avoid

---

## COMPLICATIONS OF AUTOTRANSFUSION

| COMPLICATION | CAUSE |
| --- | --- |
| Blood clotting | Insufficient anticoagulant added to collected blood in trauma and intraoperative systems (postoperative system doesn't use anticoagulant) |
| Hemolysis | Blood trauma from turbulence, possibly caused by excess vacuum pressure |
| Coagulopathies | Same as those associated with bank blood |
| Thrombocytopenia | Insufficient platelets in the transfused blood; less common than with bank blood, because autotransfused blood contains some viable platelets. If patient receives more than 4,000 ml of blood, he may require transfusion of fresh frozen plasma or platelet concentrate. |
| Particulate and air emboli | Microaggregate debris causes particulate emboli. When microemboli filters remove this debris, adult respiratory distress syndrome occurs less frequently than with bank blood. Air emboli can occur with a roller pump or pressure system. |
| Sepsis | Breakdown in aseptic technique or use of blood with known enteric contamination or pulmonary infection |
| Citrate toxicity | Rare and unpredictable complication; occurs as frequently in the trauma system as in bank blood transfusion. Citrate-phosphate-dextrose is removed during cell washing in the intraoperative system; none is used in postoperative system. |

excessively high suction pressure, which can collapse the tubing.

If the liner fails to expand after turning on the vacuum, check for leaks at the canister tee, liner lid, and suction connections. If the liner still fails to expand, remove it from the canister, extend it fully, and return it to the canister. In the trauma and intraoperative systems, periodically agitate the liner, *to mix the blood and anticoagulant thoroughly.* Avoid storing blood in a liner; transfuse it within 4 hours of the start of collection.

Monitor the volume of collected blood *to prevent overflow and estimate blood loss;* precise measurement isn't critical, because the blood is returned to the patient. Don't be concerned if clots become trapped in the 170-micron liner filter, because these won't interfere with transfusion. Change the microemboli filter after collecting 1,900 ml.

If you're using the trauma system, remember to vent the volume-control set. If you anticipate heavy bleeding, set up two canisters *to eliminate changing liners.* For selected patients, auto-transfused blood can be washed and processed before reinfusion.

If you're using the intraoperative system, remember that the orange-lidded liner functions only as an overflow trap. Because this liner doesn't contain a 170-micron filter or a spike port, overflow blood collected within it isn't auto-transfused. An overflow shutoff valve prevents the aspiration of blood from this liner into the vacuum system.

## Complications
For a summary of the complications associated with autotransfusion, see the chart on the opposite page.

## Documentation
Record the duration of collection, suction pressure, and the type and amount of anticoagulant. Also note the duration of transfusion and the use of a blood filter or washed cells. Record the amount and characteristics of drainage and any complications.

RAE NADINE SMITH, RN, MS

---

## Selected References

Allen, J.R. "Guidelines for Changing Administration Sets for Intravenous Fluid Therapy," *NITA* 3(5):175, 1980.

Berkman, Eugene, and Umlas, Joel. *Therapeutic Hemapheresis.* Washington, D.C.: American Association of Blood Banks, 1980.

Brunner, Lillian S., and Suddarth, Doris S. *Lippincott Manual of Nursing Practice,* 3rd ed. Philadelphia: J.B. Lippincott Co., 1982.

Englert, D.M. "The Role of the Nurse in Intravenous Hyperalimentation in the United States," in *Symposia: Second European Congress of Parenteral and Enteral Nutrition.* Edited by P. Wright. Stockholm: Almovist and Wiksell Periodical Co., 1981.

Gahart, Betty L. *Intravenous Medications: A Handbook for Nurses and Other Allied Personnel.* St. Louis: C.V. Mosby Co., 1980.

Hauer, J.M., et al. "Autotransfusion," in *Proceedings of the First International Autotransfusion Symposium.* Amsterdam: Elsevier/North Holland, 1981.

"Hyperalimentation Standards of Practice of the National Intravenous Therapy Association (NITA)," *NITA* 3(6):234, 1980.

*Managing I.V. Therapy.* Nursing Photobook™ Series. Springhouse, Pa.: Intermed Communications, Inc., 1980.

Masoorlie, Susan. "Trouble-Free I.V. Starts," *RN* 44:20, February 1981.

Sager, Diane Proctor, and Bomar, Suzanne Kovarovic. *Intravenous Medications.* Philadelphia: J.B. Lippincott and Co., 1980.

*Standards for Blood Banks and Transfusion Services,* 9th ed. Washington, D.C.: American Association of Blood Banks, 1978.

Wong, E.S., et al. "Guidelines for the Prevention and Control of Nosocomial Infections," *Infection Control* 2:119, March-April 1981.

# 7 Drug Administration

# Drug Administration

## Introduction

Drugs may be administered by many different routes. The *oral* route is the most common. The *parenteral* route, often used to describe injections, actually refers to all routes other than oral, and includes the sublingual, inhalational, topical, transdermal, vaginal, and rectal routes.

More than any other factor, the route of administration determines the onset of drug effect. For example, intramuscularly administered drugs act almost immediately because they are immediately accessible in the bloodstream; consequently, they are commonly used to produce a rapid response. Antibiotics, for example, are often given intravascularly to provoke a quick, continuous response. Other drugs must be given intravascularly because they're ineffective or dangerous by other routes. However, some drugs are contraindicated for intravascular use. For example, certain nonaqueous or suspension medications, such as NPH insulin or procaine penicillin, can't be administered by this route because they obstruct blood flow. Drugs administered intrathecally, such as spinal anesthesia, also act rapidly. However, drugs administered by noninjection parenteral routes must be absorbed into the bloodstream before they can take effect. Because their peak effects are therefore delayed, noninjection parenteral routes are used most often when the patient's condition doesn't urgently require an immediate drug effect.

The route of drug administration also affects patient comfort and safety. Drugs administered by noninjection routes generally cause less discomfort—with less risk of dangerous side effects—than those administered by injection.

The recommended route also depends on the drug's intended target organ or system. Skin disorders, for example, often require topical medications; gastrointestinal disorders are commonly treated with oral drugs.

### Drug-distribution systems

Most hospitals use a combination of the *floor-stock* and the *individual prescription order systems* to distribute drugs. In the floor-stock system, each nursing unit has its own supply of drugs, with most of the medications needed for routine patient care stored at the nursing station. The hospital pharmacy stocks only special medications, such as chemotherapeutic drugs, diagnostic agents, and certain antibiotics. With the individual prescription order system, the pharmacist dispenses medications, usually a 5-day supply, according to each patient's prescription.

The *unit-dose system* has proven safer, more convenient, and more economical than the traditional distribution systems. Under the unit-dose system, the pharmacist dispenses a one day supply of labeled, unit-dose packages containing the prescribed medication in the dose ordered, ready for administration to the patient.

### "Five rights" of drug administration

Before you administer any medication,

always compare the doctor's order with the order on the patient's medication record. Then mentally check off the "five rights": *right patient, right drug, right dose, right route, and right time.* If the doctor's order and the patient's medication record match, then compare the label on the medication to the medication record. If this comparison reveals any discrepancies, withhold the medication and verify the order with the doctor or consult with the pharmacist. If a patient questions or doubts any of his medications, always double-check the orders and the medication dose before administering the medication.

Some drugs—such as narcotics, barbiturates, and other controlled substances—have automatic stop dates, mandated by law. Check your institution's policy on how to handle outdated orders. Some medications, such as antibiotics, have automatic stop dates determined by institutional policy.

### Patient response and drug interactions

Assessing a patient's response to medication requires a thorough understanding of his condition and the drug's desired or expected effect. If a patient is receiving quinidine, for example, but continues to have premature ventricular contractions, you should notify the doctor because the drug is not having the desired effect. When assessing the patient's response to therapy, also consider the results of laboratory tests which can indicate either a therapeutic effect, side effect, or toxic level. For example, prothrombin times help evaluate the therapeutic effect of warfarin sodium. Low serum potassium levels can indicate a side effect of certain diuretics. And, serum levels of certain drugs, such as digoxin or phenytoin, can indicate therapeutic or toxic blood levels. Remember to monitor the patient's condition carefully; such changes as weight loss or gain can affect the action of some drugs. Other factors—such as the patient's age, body build, and emotional state—also may affect the patient's response to drug therapy.

Because many patients receive multiple drug therapy, you should also understand drug *interactions.* A drug interaction is a change in drug absorption, distribution, metabolism, and excretion that may occur when one drug is administered with, or shortly after, another drug. A desirable interaction is the basis for combination therapy, which may be used for additive effect, to help maintain an effective blood level and to minimize or prevent side effects. Some interactions, however, can have undesirable results, such as weakening a drug's desired effect or exaggerating its toxicity. For example, the interactions of certain drugs and foods are known to alter absorption and response. Certain foods interfere with the therapeutic effect of antibiotics. This undesirable interaction with food requires that certain antibiotics always be given on an empty stomach for optimum effect.

### Observing for untoward effects

When you administer drugs, you also need to recognize and identify side effects, toxic reactions, and drug allergies. A *side effect* is any drug effect that is not intended. Some side effects are transient and subside as the patient develops a tolerance to the drug. In some patients, adjusting the drug dosage may control undesirable side effects; but in some, side effects will contraindicate the use of a drug altogether.

*Toxic reactions* to a drug can be acute, resulting from excessive doses, or chronic, resulting from progressive accumulation of the drug in the body . Toxic reactions can also result from impaired metabolism or excretion that can cause elevated blood levels.

*Drug allergy* (hypersensitivity) results from an antigen-antibody immune reaction in susceptible patients. Such a reaction can range from mild urticaria to potentially fatal anaphylaxis. Therefore, always be sure to check for allergies before administering medications.

JEANNE L. SAWYER, BSN, MA

# ORAL ADMINISTRATION

## Oral Administration of Drugs

*Because oral administration of drugs is generally safest, most convenient, and least expensive, most drugs are commonly administered by this route. Drugs for oral administration are available in many different forms: tablets, enteric-coated tablets, capsules, syrups, elixirs, oils, liquids, suspensions, powders, and granules. Some require special preparation before administration, such as mixing with juice to make them more palatable; oils, powders, and granules most often require such preparation.*

*Oral drugs are sometimes prescribed in higher dosages than their parenteral equivalents because after absorption through the gastrointestinal system, they are immediately broken down by the liver before they reach the systemic circulation. Nausea, vomiting, inability to swallow, and unconsciousness may contraindicate oral administration.*

### Equipment
Patient's medication record and chart □ prescribed medication □ medication cup □ optional: appropriate vehicle (jelly or applesauce) for crushed pills (common practice for administration to children or the elderly) or liquid (juice, water, or milk); straw.

### Essential steps
● Verify the order on the patient's medication record by checking it against the doctor's order.
● Wash your hands.
● Check the label on the medication three times before administering it *to make sure you'll be giving the prescribed medication:* when you take the container from the shelf or drawer, just before pouring the medication into the medication cup, and before returning the container to the

shelf or drawer. If you're administering a unit-dose medication, check the label for the final time immediately after pouring the medication, before discarding the wrapper. (Remember: Don't open a unit-dose medication until you're at the patient's bedside.)
● Confirm the patient's identity by asking his name and checking the name, room number, and bed number on his wristband.
● Give the patient his medication and, as needed, an appropriate liquid *to aid swallowing, minimize side effects, or promote absorbtion.* For example, cyclophosphamide is given with fluids to minimize side effects; antitussive cough syrup is given without a fluid to avoid diluting its soothing effect on the throat.
● Stay with the patient until he has swallowed the drug. If he seems confused or disoriented, check his mouth *to make sure he has swallowed it.*
● If you're using a medication tray instead of a cart, turn over the patient's medication card.

### Special considerations
Make sure you have a written order for every medication given. Verbal orders should be signed by the doctor within the specified time. (Hospitals usually require a signature within 24 hours; long-term care facilities, within 48 hours.)

To pour liquids, hold the medication cup at eye level. Use your thumb to mark off the correct level on the cup. When pouring the medication into the cup, read the level at the bottom of the meniscus *to ensure accuracy.* (If a liquid is measured in drops, use only the dropper that comes with it.) Hold the container so you can pour away from the label *to avoid smearing it.* Remove drips with an alcohol wipe. Avoid touching the lip of the bottle.

Don't give medication from a poorly labeled or unlabeled container. Don't attempt to label or reinforce drug labels yourself—this is a pharmacist's function.

Never give a medication poured by someone else. Never have your medication cart or tray out of your sight: *This prevents anyone from rearranging the medications or taking one without your knowledge.* Never return unused medications to stock containers. Instead, dispose of them and notify the pharmacy. Keep in mind that the disposal of any narcotic drug must be cosigned by another nurse, as mandated by law.

If the patient has questions about his medication or the dosage, check his medication record again. If the medication is correct, reassure him. Make sure you tell him about any changes in his medication or dosage. Instruct him, as appropriate, about possible side effects. Ask him to report any changes that he feels may be a side effect.

To avoid damaging or staining the patient's teeth, give acid or iron preparations through a straw. An unpleasant-tasting liquid can usually be made more palatable if taken through a straw because the liquid then contacts fewer taste buds.

If the patient can't swallow a whole tablet or capsule, ask the pharmacist if the drug is available in liquid form or if it can be administered by another route. If not, ask him if you can crush the tablet or open the capsule and mix it with food. Remember to contact the doctor for an order to change the route of administration when necessary.

## Documentation
Note the drug administered, the dose, the date and time, and the patient's reaction, if any, on his medication record (and in the nurse's notes and cardex, if necessary). If the patient refuses a drug, document the refusal and notify the charge nurse and the patient's doctor, as needed. Also note if a drug was omitted or withheld for other reasons, such as radiology or laboratory tests. Sign out all narcotics given on the appropriate narcotics central record.

CAROL A. CALIANNO, RN, AD

# Instillation Through a Nasogastric Tube

*Besides providing an alternate means of nourishment, the nasogastric tube allows direct instillation of medication into the gastrointestinal system of patients who can't ingest it orally. Before instillation, the patency and positioning of the tube must be carefully checked, since this procedure is contraindicated if the tube is obstructed, improperly positioned, the patient is vomiting around the tube, or has absent bowel sounds.*

*Oily medications and enteric-coated or sustained-release tablets are contraindicated for instillation through a nasogastric tube. Oily medications cling to the sides of the tube and resist mixing with the irrigating solution. Crushing enteric-coated or sustained-release tablets destroys their intended effect.*

## Equipment
Patient's medication record and chart □ prescribed medication □ towel or linen-saver pad □ 50- or 60-ml piston type, catheter tip syringe □ two 4″ x 4″ gauze sponges □ stethoscope □ diluting liquid □ cup for mixing medication and fluid □ spoon □ 50 ml of water □ rubber band □ optional: pill-crushing equipment (mortar and pestle, for example), clamp (if not already attached to tube).

*For maximum control of suction,* use a piston syringe instead of a bulb type. The liquid for diluting the medication can be juice, water, or a nutritional supplement.

## Preparation of equipment
Gather necessary equipment for use at the patient's bedside. Liquids should be at room temperature. *Administering cold liquid through the nasogastric tube can cause abdominal cramping.* Although this is not a sterile procedure, make sure the cups, syringe, spoon, and gauze are clean.

## HOW TO INSTILL MEDICATION
## THROUGH A NASOGASTRIC TUBE

With the patient in Fowler's or semi-Fowler's position (as shown), hold the tube slightly above the level of the patient's nose. Tilt the tube slightly to prevent air from entering. Then, slowly pour the medication into the syringe.

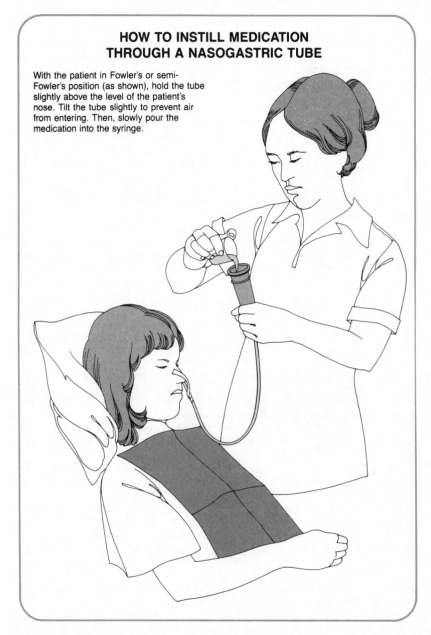

### Essential steps
• Verify the order on the patient's medication record by checking it against the doctor's order.
• Wash your hands.
• Check the label on the medication three times before preparing it for administration *to make sure you'll be giving the prescribed medication*
• If the prescribed medication is in tablet form, crush the tablets to ready them for mixing with the diluting liquid. Bring

the medication and equipment to the patient's bedside.

• Explain the procedure to the patient, if necessary, and provide privacy.

• Confirm the patient's identity by asking his name and checking the name, room number, and bed number on his wristband.

• Unpin the tube from the patient's gown and remove any dressing at the end of the tube. *To avoid soiling the sheets during the procedure,* fold back the bed linens to the patient's waist and drape his chest with the towel or linen-saver pad.

• Elevate the head of the bed so the patient is in Fowler's or semi-Fowler's position.

• After removing the clamp from the tube, take the syringe and create a 10-cc air space in its chamber. Then attach the syringe to the end of the tube.

• Auscultate the patient's abdomen about 3″ (8 cm) below the sternum with the stethoscope. Then, gently insert the 10 cc of air into the tube. You should hear the air bubble entering the stomach. If you hear this sound, gently draw back on the piston of the syringe. The appearance of gastric contents confirms that the tube is patent and in the stomach. If no gastric contents appear when you draw back on the piston of the syringe, the tube may have risen into the patient's esophagus, in which case you'll have to advance it before proceeding.

• If you meet resistance when aspirating for stomach contents, stop the procedure. Resistance may indicate a nonpatent tube or improper tube placement. If the tube seems to be in the stomach, resistance probably means the tube is lying against the stomach wall. *To relieve resistance,* withdraw the tube slightly.

• After you have established tube patency and correct positioning, replace the clamp on the tube, detach the syringe, and lay the end of the tube on the 4″ x 4″ gauze sponge.

• Mix the crushed tablets with the diluting liquid. If the medication is in capsule form, open the capsules and empty their contents into the liquid. Pour liquid medications directly into the diluting liquid. Stir well with the spoon. (If the medication was in tablet form, make sure the particles are small enough to pass through the eyes at the distal end of the tube.)

• Reattach the syringe, without the piston, to the end of the tube and remove the clamp.

• Holding the tube at a level slightly above the patient's nose (see illustration page 313), pour 30 ml of the diluted medication into the syringe barrel. *To prevent air from entering the patient's stomach,* hold the tube at a slight angle. If necessary, raise the tube slightly higher *to increase the flow rate.*

• If the medication flows smoothly, slowly add more until the entire dose has been given. *To prevent air from entering the patient's stomach,* add more medication before the syringe empties completely.

• If the medication doesn't flow properly, don't force it. It may be too thick to flow through the tube. If so, dilute it with water. If you suspect tube placement is inhibiting flow, stop the procedure and reevaluate the placement.

• Watch the patient's reaction throughout the instillation. If he shows any sign of discomfort, stop the procedure immediately.

• As the last of the medication flows out of the syringe, start to irrigate the tube by adding the 50 ml of water. Irrigation clears medication from the sides of the tube and from the distal end, *reducing the risk of clogging.*

• When the water stops flowing, quickly clamp the tube. Detach the syringe from the tube and dispose of it properly.

• Cover the end of the tube with the other 4″ x 4″ sponge and secure it with the rubber band.

• Repin the nasogastric tube to the patient's gown.

• Remove the towel or linen-saver pad and replace bed linens.

• Leave the patient in Fowler's or semi-Fowler's position for at least 30 minutes after the procedure *to facilitate the downward flow of medication into his stomach and prevent reflux into the esophagus.*

## Special considerations

*To prevent instillation of too much fluid* (more than 400 ml of liquid at one time for an adult) plan the drug instillation, if possible, so it doesn't coincide with the patient's regular tube feeding. When you must schedule both simultaneously, give the medication first to ensure that the patient receives prescribed drug therapy even if he can't tolerate an entire feeding. Remember to avoid giving the patient foods that interact adversely with the medication.

If possible, teach the patient who requires long-term treatment to instill medication through his nasogastric tube. Have him observe the procedure several times before allowing him to try it. Stay with him when he performs the procedure for the first few times so you can answer any questions. Provide any assistance he may need and give him positive reinforcement.

## Documentation

Record the installation of the medication, the date, time instilled, the dose and the patient's tolerance of the procedure on the patient's record. Note the amount of fluid instilled on his intake and output sheet.

CAROL A. CALIANNO, RN, AD

# Instillation Through a Gastrostomy Tube

*A gastrostomy tube provides a means for administering nutrients and medications to patients who can't ingest them orally. A gastrostomy tube, surgically inserted directly into the stomach, eliminates the risk of fluid aspiration into the lungs, a constant danger with a nasogastric tube. It also allows long-term use, which is the general indication for this procedure. Before medication is instilled through a gastrostomy tube, the tube should be tested for patency and the fluids should be warmed or cooled to room temperature. This procedure is contraindicated in patients with absent bowel sounds or an obstructed tube.*

## Equipment

Patient's medication record and chart (and intake and output sheet) □ prescribed medication □ diluting liquid □ spoon □ towel or linen-saver pad □ catheter tip syringe or tube-feeding funnel □ water (at least 100 ml) □ cup for mixing medication and fluid □ three 4" x 4" gauze sponges □ rubber band □ tape □ clamp (optional, if not already attached to tube).

Use a piston syringe instead of a bulb type *for maximum control of suction.* The diluting liquid can be juice, water, or a nutritional supplement.

## Preparation of equipment

Make sure all liquids are at room temperature. *Pouring cold liquid into the tube can cause abdominal cramping.* Bring all equipment to the patient's bedside. This is not a sterile procedure, but make sure the cups, syringe or funnel, spoon, and gauze are clean.

## Essential steps

● Verify the order on the patient's medication record by checking it against the doctor's order.
● Wash your hands.
● Check the label on the medication three times before administering it *to make sure you'll be giving the prescribed medication.* (Remember: Don't open a unit-dose medication until you're at the patient's bedside.)
● Crush the tablet or open the capsule *to prepare the medication for mixing with the diluting liquid.* Mix the medication with the appropriate amount of diluting liquid (usually 30 ml) and stir with the spoon.
● Confirm the patient's identity by asking his name and checking the name, room number, and bed number on his wristband.
● After closing the door or drawing the curtain *to ensure privacy,* explain the procedure to the patient.
● *To avoid soiling the sheets during the*

*procedure,* fold the bedlinens below the gastrostomy tube and drape the patient's chest with the towel or linen-saver pad.

● *To facilitate digestion and prevent fluid reflux into the esophagus,* elevate the head of the bed before instilling any medication.

● Remove the dressing that covers the tube. Then remove the dressing at the tip of the tube and attach the syringe or funnel to the tip.

● Release the clamp and instill about 10 ml of water into the tube through the syringe *to check for patency.* If the water flows in easily, the tube is patent. If it flows in slowly, raise the funnel to increase pressure. If the water still doesn't flow properly, stop the procedure and notify the doctor.

● Pour the medication into the syringe or funnel at the rate of 30 ml at a time. Tilt the tube *to allow air to escape as the fluid flows downward.*

● After the medication drains through the syringe or funnel, pour in about 30 ml of water *to irrigate the tube.*

● Tighten the clamp, then place one 4″ x 4″ gauze sponge on the end of the tube and secure it with the rubber band.

● Cover the tube with the other two 4″ x 4″ gauze sponges and secure it firmly with tape.

● Remove the towel or linen-saver pad and replace the bed linens.

● Keep the head of the bed elevated for at least 30 minutes after the procedure *to aid digestion.*

### Special considerations

Sometimes Montgomery straps or an abdominal binder, applied gently, are used *to hold the tube in place and prevent accidental dislodgment.*

Before pouring medication into the tube, gently lift the dressings around the tube *to assess the skin for irritation caused by gastric secretions.* Report any redness or irritation to the doctor.

### Complications

If the patient's stomach is already full, the liquid instilled can cause cramping and abdominal discomfort. Some pa-

tients may experience an allergic reaction to the medication.

### Documentation

Document the medication on the medication record and the patient's chart. Note the fluid instilled on the patient's intake and output sheet.

CAROL A. CALIANNO, RN, AD

# Buccal and Sublingual Drug Administration

*Buccal and sublingual administration of certain drugs prevents their destruction or transformation in the stomach or small intestine. These medications take effect very quickly because the oral mucosa's thin epithelium and abundant vasculature allow direct absorption into the bloodstream. Only a few drugs, however, are given this way (see* Most Commonly Used Buccal and Sublingual Drugs, *page 317). The patient must be observed carefully to make sure he doesn't swallow the drug or suffer localized mucosal irritation.*

### Equipment

Patient's medication record and chart □ prescribed medication □ medication cup.

### Essential steps

● Verify the order on the patient's medication record by checking it against the doctor's order on his chart.

● Wash your hands. Explain the procedure to the patient if he's never taken a drug buccally or sublingually before.

● Check the label on the medication three times before administering it *to make sure you'll be giving the prescribed medication:* When you take the container from the shelf or drawer, just before pouring the medication into the medication cup, and before returning the container to the shelf or drawer. If you're administering a unit-dose medication , check the label for the third time immediately after pouring the medication, and again before discarding the wrapper. (Remember: Don't open a unit-dose medication until you're at the patient's bedside.)

• Confirm the patient's identity by asking his name and checking the name, room number, and bed number on his wristband.

*For buccal administration:*

• Place the tablet in the upper or lower buccal pouch, between the cheek and gum.

*For sublingual administration:*

• Place the tablet under the patient's tongue.

*Then:*

• Instruct the patient to keep the medication in place until it dissolves completely *to ensure absorption.*

• Caution the patient against chewing the tablet or touching it with his tongue *to prevent accidental swallowing.*

• Tell the patient not to smoke before the medication has dissolved *because nicotine's vasoconstrictive effects slow absorption.*

**Special considerations**

Don't give liquids with either form of medication. Some buccal tablets may take up to 1 hour to be absorbed. In that case, the patient should rinse the mouth with water *between* doses. Teach the patient to take sublingual nitroglycerine at the first sign of angina. Tablet should be wet with saliva and placed under the tongue until completely absorbed.

---

**MOST COMMONLY USED BUCCAL AND SUBLINGUAL DRUGS**

**Buccal**
erythrityl tetranitrate (Cardilate)
methyltestosterone (Oreton Methyl)
testosterone (Oreton Propionate)

**Sublingual**
ergotamine tartrate (Ergomar)
erythrityl tetranitrate (Cardilate)
isoproterenol hydrochloride (Isuprel Glossets)
isosorbide dinitrate (Sorbitrate)
nitroglycerin (Nitrostat)

---

**Complications**

Some buccal medications may cause mucosal irritation. Alternate sides of the mouth for repeat doses *to prevent continuous irritation of the same site.* Sublingual medications—erythrityl tetranitrate, for example—may cause a tingling sensation under the tongue. (If the patient finds this annoying, erythrityl tetranitrate can be placed in the buccal pouch instead, another acceptable route for administering this drug.)

**Documentation**

Record the medication administered and the dose, the date and time, and the patient's reaction, if any, on his medication record and chart.

CAROL A. CALIANNO, RN, AD

---

## TOPICAL ADMINISTRATION

# Application and Removal of Ointments

Ointments have a fatty base, such as petrolatum or oil, which distinguishes them from other topical medications. This makes them an ideal medium for therapeutic drugs, most commonly antimicrobials and antiseptics. Ointments also make natural lubricators, protective coatings, and softeners for skin and mucous membranes.

Ointments usually have to be applied two or three times daily to achieve their therapeutic effects. Ointments shouldn't be applied, however, to moist, creased, or folded skin because they can cause *irritation in such instances. To check for sensitivity to an ointment before beginning treatment, a doctor may order a test application on a small patch of skin.*

## Equipment

Patient's medication record and chart □ tube or jar of ointment □ tongue depressors □ 4″ x 4″ gauze sponges □ tape □ solvent (such as cottonseed oil) □ gloves.

The tongue depressors and gauze sponges should be sterile.

## Essential steps

• Verify the order on the patient's medication record by checking it against the doctor's order on his chart.

• Make sure the label on the ointment agrees with the medication order. Read the label again before you open the ointment and as you remove the ointment from the container.

• Confirm the patient's identity by asking his name and checking the name, room number, and bed number on his wristband.

• Provide privacy.

• Explain the procedure thoroughly to the patient *because, after discharge, he may have to apply the ointment himself.*

• Wash your hands *to prevent cross-contamination.*

• Expose the area to be treated. Make sure the skin or mucous membrane is intact (unless the ointment has been ordered to treat a skin lesion such as an ulcer). Application of ointment to broken or abraded skin may cause systemic absorption.

• Help the patient assume a comfortable position that provides access to the area to be treated.

• Open the container of ointment. Place the lid upside down *to prevent contamination of the inside.*

• Remove a tongue depressor from its sterile wrapper and cover one end with ointment from the tube, or lift out a dollop from the jar. Then, transfer the ointment from the tongue depressor to your gloved hand.

• Apply the ointment to the affected area with long, smooth strokes that follow the direction of hair growth. *This prevents medication from being forced into hair follicles, which can cause irritation and lead to folliculitis.* Avoid excessive pressure, *which could abrade the skin.*

• *To prevent contamination of the ointment,* use a new tongue depressor each time you remove ointment from the container.

• *To protect the applied ointment and keep it from soiling the patient's clothes and bedding,* tape an appropriate amount of sterile gauze over the treated area. If you're applying ointment to the patient's hands or feet, cover the site with white cotton gloves or terrycloth scuffs. If you're applying ointment to his entire body, have him wear a loose cotton gown or pajamas.

*To remove ointment:*

• Wash your hands.

• Rub the solvent on your hands and apply it liberally to the treated area in the direction of hair growth, or saturate a sterile gauze sponge with the solvent and use this to gently remove the ointment. Repeat this procedure until you've removed all the ointment.

• Remove excess oil by gently wiping the area with the sterile gauze sponge. Don't rub too hard; *this could irritate the skin.*

• Assess the patient's skin condition for signs of irritation, allergic reaction, or skin breakdown.

## Special considerations

Never apply ointment without first removing previously applied ointment, *to prevent skin irritation from an accumulation of ointment.*

If the patient has an infectious skin condition, use sterile gloves and dispose of old dressings according to institution policy.

Be sure to wear gloves to prevent absorption by your own skin.

Don't apply ointments to mucous membranes as liberally as you would to skin, *since mucous membranes are usually moist and absorb ointment more quickly than skin does.* Also, don't apply too much ointment to any skin area. *It may cause irritation and discomfort, stain clothing and bedding, and make removal difficult.*

Never apply ointment to the eyelids or ear canal unless ordered. *The ointment may congeal and occlude the tear duct or ear canal.*

Inspect the treated area frequently for side effects such as signs of an allergic reaction.

## Complications

Skin irritation, a rash, or an allergic reaction may occur.

## Documentation

Record the ointment applied, the time and date of application, and the condition of the skin at the time. Note subsequent effects of the ointment, if any.

JOANNE PATZEK DACUNHA, RN

# Application of Transdermal Drugs

*Through an adhesive disk or measured dose of ointment applied to the skin, transdermal drugs supply constant, controlled medication directly into the bloodstream for prolonged systemic effect. The only medications currently available in transdermal form are nitroglycerin, used to control angina, and scopolamine, used to treat motion sickness; most other drugs have molecules too large for absorption through the skin. Nitroglycerin ointment dilates coronary vessels for up to 4 hours; a nitroglycerin disk can produce the same effect for as long as 24 hours. The scopolamine disk can relieve motion sickness for as long as 72 hours.*

*Contraindications for transdermal application include skin allergies or skin reactions to the drug. Transdermal drugs should not be applied to broken or irritated skin because they would increase irritation; or to scarred or calloused skin,*

*which may impair absorption.*

## Equipment

Patient's medication record and chart □ prescribed medication (disk or ointment) □ application strip or measuring paper (for nitroglycerin ointment) □ adhesive tape □ plastic wrap (optional for nitroglycerin ointment).

## Essential steps

• Verify the order on the patient's medication record by checking it against the doctor's order.

• Wash your hands.

• Check the label on the medication *to make sure you'll be administering the correct drug in the correct dose.*

• Confirm the patient's identity by asking his name and checking the name, room number, and bed number on his wristband.

• Explain the procedure to the patient and provide privacy.

*To apply transdermal ointments:*

• Place the prescribed amount of ointment on the application strip or measuring paper, taking care not to get any on your skin.

• Apply the strip to any dry, hairless area of the body. Don't rub the ointment into the skin.

• Tape the application strip and ointment to the skin.

• If desired, cover the application strip with the plastic wrap, and tape the wrap in place.

*To apply transdermal disks:*

• Open the package and remove the disk.

• Without touching the adhesive surface, remove the clear-plastic backing.

• Apply the disk to a dry, hairless area (scopolamine is usually applied behind the ear).

*After applying transdermal medications:*

• Store the medication as ordered.

• Instruct the patient to keep the area around the disk or ointment as dry as possible.

• Wash your hands immediately after applying the disk or ointment *to avoid absorbing the drug yourself.*

## PATIENT-TEACHING AID

### APPLYING A NITROGLYCERIN DISK

Dear Patient:

Your doctor has prescribed nitroglycerin for your angina. Nitroglycerin relieves anginal pain by temporarily dilating (widening) veins and arteries. This brings more blood and oxygen to the heart when it needs it most. This way your heart doesn't have to work so hard.

The nitroglycerin your doctor has prescribed comes in a disk. The disk consists of a gel-like substance attached to an adhesive bandage. (See the illustration below, which shows the different layers of the disk.) When applied to the skin, the disk allows nitroglycerin to be absorbed through the skin into the bloodstream. A single application lasts 24 hours.

Apply the disk to any convenient skin area—preferably on the upper arm or chest—without touching the gel or surrounding tape. Use a different site every day to avoid skin irritation. If necessary, you can shave an appropriate site. Avoid any area that may cause uneven absorption, such as skin folds, scars, and calluses, or any irritated or damaged skin areas. Also, don't apply the disk below the elbow or knee.

After application, wash your hands to remove any nitroglycerin that may have rubbed off.

Try not to get the disk wet when you shower. If the disk should leak or fall off, throw it away. Then, clean the site and apply a new disk at a different site.

To ensure 24-hour coverage, apply the nitroglycerin disk at the same time every day. Bedtime application is ideal, because body movement is at a minimum during the night. Also, to ensure continuous nitroglycerin therapy, apply a new disk about 30 minutes before removing the old one.

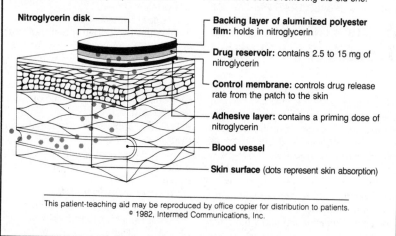

Nitroglycerin disk

**Backing layer of aluminized polyester film:** holds in nitroglycerin

**Drug reservoir:** contains 2.5 to 15 mg of nitroglycerin

**Control membrane:** controls drug release rate from the patch to the skin

**Adhesive layer:** contains a priming dose of nitroglycerin

**Blood vessel**

**Skin surface** (dots represent skin absorption)

## Special considerations

Reapply daily transdermal medications at the same time every day *to ensure a continuous effect,* but alternate the application sites *to avoid skin irritation.* Before reapplying nitroglycerin ointment, remove the plastic wrap, application strip, and any remaining ointment from the patient's skin.

When applying a scopolamine disk, instruct the patient not to drive or operate machinery until his response to the drug has been determined.

Monitor the patient for drug effectiveness.

## Complications

Skin irritation, such as pruritus or a rash, may occur. The patient may also suffer side effects of the drug administered. For example, transdermal nitroglycerin medications may cause headaches and, in the elderly, postural hypotension. Scopolamine has various side effects; dry mouth and drowsiness are the most common.

## Documentation

Record the type of medication, the date and time of application, and the dose on the patient's medication record and chart. Also note any side effects and the patient's response.

JOANNE PATZEK DACUNHA, RN

---

# Medicated Shampoos

---

*Medicated shampoos include keratolytic and cytostatic agents, coal tar preparations, and lindane (gamma benzene hexachloride) solutions. They can be used to treat such conditions as dandruff, psoriasis, and head lice.*

*Keratolytic and cytostatic shampoos are commonly used to treat dandruff. Concentrated formulas, and frequent or extended use, increase their effectiveness. Coal tar shampoos are generally used as an antipruritic in the treatment of psoriasis. However, they are recommended only for a refractory condition because they may cause photosensitivity and retard wound healing. Lindane (gamma benzene hexachloride) solutions are used most often to treat head lice. Such therapy requires disposal of linens, gown, and gloves to prevent the spread of infestation.*

*Medicated shampoos are contraindicated in patients with broken or abraded skin.*

## Equipment

Patient's medication record and chart □ prescribed medicated shampoo □ two bath towels □ comb □ optional: gown, gloves, surgical cap (if desired) and tweezers or fine-tooth comb (for head lice).

## Essential steps

● Verify the order on the patient's med-

ication record by checking it against the doctor's order on the patient's chart.
● Wash your hands.
● Compare the label on the shampoo to the medication record *to make sure you'll be applying the prescribed shampoo.*
● Explain the procedure to the patient and provide privacy.
*For a keratolytic or cytostatic shampoo:*
● Shake the bottle of shampoo well *to mix the solution evenly.*
● Wet the patient's hair thoroughly.
● Apply the proper amount of shampoo, as directed on the label.
● Work the shampoo into a lather, adding water as necessary.
● If the shampoo is a cytostatic agent, rinse the hair immediately. If it's a keratolytic agent, leave it on the scalp and hair for as long as instructed (usually 5 to 10 minutes) *to soften and loosen scales.* Then rinse the hair thoroughly.
● Apply the same amount of shampoo again and lather and rinse.
● Towel dry the patient's hair and comb out any tangles.
*For coal tar shampoos:*
● Wet the patient's hair thoroughly.
● Massage the shampoo into the scalp.
● Rinse completely.
● Massage the shampoo into the scalp again, but this time leave it on for 5 to 10 minutes, as directed on the label.
● Rinse completely.
● Towel dry the patient's hair and comb out any tangles.
*For lindane (gamma benzene hydrochloride) solutions:*
● Put on the gown and gloves before entering the patient's room. If desired you may protect your own hair with a surgical cap.
● Apply the correct amount of the shampoo to dry hair, starting at the scalp and working through to the ends. Pay special attention to obviously infested areas.
● After the shampoo has thoroughly coated the scalp and hair, add small amounts of water and work the shampoo into a lather.
● Lather the scalp and hair for 4 to 6 minutes.

• Rinse completely. Don't repeat the procedure.

• Towel-dry the patient's hair.

• After the hair is dry, comb the hair with a fine-tooth comb to remove nits or nit shells. If necessary, remove dead lice or nits with tweezers.

• Remove your gown and gloves (and cap, if worn) and dispose of them and the towels according to institution policy, *to prevent the spread of lice.*

**Special considerations**
Since instructions may vary among brands, check the label on the shampoo before starting the procedure to ensure use of the correct amount. Keep the shampoo away from the patient's eyes. If any shampoo should accidentally get in his eyes, irrigate promptly with water. Selenium sulfide, used in cytostatic agents, is extremely toxic if ingested.

**Complications**
Repeated shampooing with gamma benzene hydrochloride may cause skin irritation and, possibly, systemic toxicity, especially in children. Warn patients not to use it repeatedly or excessively.

**Documentation**
Record the type of shampoo used on the medication record and chart. Note the effects of the treatment in the nurse's notes.

SUSAN DONAHUE, RN, BSN

# Administration of Eye Medications

*Eye medications—drops, ointments, and disks—serve both diagnostic and therapeutic purposes. During an eye examination, eye drops can be used to anesthetize the eye, dilate the pupil to facilitate refraction, and stain the cornea to identify corneal abrasions or scars. Eye medications can also be used to lubricate the eye, treat certain eye condi-* *tions (such as glaucoma and infections), protect the vision of neonates, and lubricate the eye socket for insertion of an artificial eye. Administration of eye medications requires sterile technique to avoid irritation or infection.*

*Understanding the ocular effects of medications is important because certain drugs may cause eye disorders or have serious ocular side effects. For example, anticholinergics, which are often used during eye examinations, can precipitate acute glaucoma in persons predisposed to that condition.*

**Equipment**
Prescribed eye medication □ patient's medication record and chart □ cotton balls □ warm water or normal saline solution □ gauze pads □ tissues □ eye dressing (optional).

All equipment and medication should be sterile.

**Preparation of equipment**
Make sure the medication is labeled for ophthalmic use. Then check the expiration date. Remember to date the container the first time you use the medication. Usually, an eye medication may be used for a maximum of 2 weeks.

Inspect eye solutions for cloudiness, discoloration, and precipitation, but remember that some eye medications are suspensions and normally appear cloudy. Don't use any solution that appears abnormal. If the tip of an eye ointment tube has crusted, turn the tip on a sterile gauze pad to remove the crust.

**Essential steps**
• Verify the order on the patient's medication record by checking it against the doctor's order on his chart.

• Wash your hands.

• Check the medication label against the medication record.

• Make sure you know which eye to treat. Different medications or doses may be ordered for each eye.

• Confirm the patient's identity by asking his name and checking the name, room number, and bed number on his

## INSERTING AND REMOVING AN EYE MEDICATION DISK

A medication disk inserted into the eye can release medication for up to 1 week. Pilocarpine, for example, can be administered this way to treat glaucoma. The small, flexible oval disk consists of three layers: two soft outer layers and a middle layer containing the medication. Floating between the eyelids and the sclera, the disk stays in the eye while the patient sleeps and even during swimming and athletic activities. Once the disk is in place, the fluid in the eye moistens it, releasing the medication. Eye moisture or contact lenses don't adversely affect the disk. Eye medication disks offer the advantage of continuous release of medication. The patient never has to worry about forgetting to instill his eye drops. Contraindications include conjunctivitis, keratitis, retinal detachment, and any condition where constriction of the pupil should be avoided.

### To insert an eye medication disk

• Arrange to insert the disk before the patient goes to bed. *This minimizes the problems caused by the blurring that occurs immediately after the disk is inserted.*
• Wash your hands.
• Press your fingertip against the oval disk so its length lies horizontally across your fingertip. It should stick to your finger. Lift it out of its packet.
• Evert the patient's lower eyelid and place the disk in the conjunctival sac. It should lie horizontally, not vertically. The disk will automatically stick to the eye.
• Pull the lower eyelid out, up, and over the disk. Tell the patient to blink several times. If the disk is still visible, lift the lower lid out and over the disk again. Tell the patient that once the disk is in place, he can adjust its position by *gently* pressing his finger against his closed lid. Caution him against rubbing his eye or moving the disk across the iris.
• If the disk falls out, wash your hands, rinse the disk in cool water, and reinsert it. If the disk bends out of shape, replace it. If both of the patient's eyes are being treated with medication disks, replace both

disks at the same time, *so both eyes receive medication at the same rate.*
• If the disk continually slips out of position, reinsert the disk under the upper eyelid. To do this, gently lift and evert the upper eyelid and insert the disk in the conjunctival sac. Then, gently pull the lid back into position and tell the patient to blink several times. To adjust the disk to the most comfortable position, have the patient gently press on the closed lid. The more the patient uses the disk, the easier it should be for him to retain it. If he can't, notify the doctor.
• Before discharge, if the patient will continue therapy with an eye medication disk, teach him to insert and remove it himself. To check his mastery of these skills, have him insert and remove it for you.
• Also, teach the patient about possible side effects. Foreign-body sensation in the eye, mild tearing or redness, increased mucous discharge, eyelid redness, and itchiness can occur with the use of disks. Blurred vision, stinging, swelling, and headaches can occur with pilocarpine, specifically. Mild symptoms are common but should subside within the first 6 weeks of use. Tell the patient to report persistent or severe symptoms to his doctor.

### To remove an eye medication disk

• You can remove an eye medication disk with one or two fingers. To use *one finger,* evert the lower eyelid with one hand so you expose the disk. Then, use the forefinger of your other hand to slide the disk onto the lid and out of the patient's eye. To use *two fingers,* evert the lower lid with one hand to expose the disk. Then, pinch the disk with the thumb and forefinger of your other hand and remove it from the eye.
• If the disk is in the upper eyelid, apply long circular strokes to the patient's closed eyelid with your finger until you can see the disk in the corner of the patient's eye. Once the disk is visible, place your finger directly on the disk and move it to the lower sclera. Then remove it as you would a disk in the lower lid.

identification bracelet.
• Explain the procedure to the patient and provide privacy.
• If the patient is wearing an eye dressing, remove it by gently pulling it down and away from his forehead. Take care not to contaminate your hands.

• Remove any discharge by cleansing around the eye with cotton balls moistened with warm water or normal saline solution. With the patient's eye closed, cleanse from the inner canthus to the outer canthus, using a fresh cotton ball for each stroke.

● To remove crusted secretions around the eye, moisten a gauze pad with warm water or normal saline solution. Ask the patient to close the eye, then place the gauze pad over it for a minute or two. Remove the pad, then reapply moist sterile gauze pads, as necessary, until the secretions are soft enough to be removed without traumatizing the mucosa.

● Have the patient sit or lie in the supine position. Instruct him to tilt his head back and toward the side of the affected eye *so excess solution can flow away from the tear duct, preventing systemic absorption through the nasal mucosa.*

● Remove the dropper cap from the medication container. Be careful to avoid contaminating the bottle top. Fill the dropper, as necessary.

● Before instilling the eye drops, instruct the patient to look up and away. *This moves the cornea away from the lower lid and minimizes the risk of touching the cornea with the dropper if the patient blinks.*

● Gently pull down the lower lid *to expose the conjunctival sac.*

*To instill eye drops:*

● Steady the hand in which you are holding the dropper against the patient's forehead. Then, with your other hand, gently pull down the lower lid of the affected eye and instill the drops in the conjunctival sac. Never instill eye drops directly onto the eyeball.

*To apply eye ointment:*

● Squeeze a small ribbon of medication on the conjunctival sac from the inner to the outer canthus. Cut off the ribbon by turning the tube. If you wish, you can steady the hand holding the medication tube by bracing it against the patient's forehead or cheek.

*For both eye drops and ointments:*

● Instruct the patient to close his eyes gently, without squeezing the lids shut. If you instilled eye drops, tell the patient to blink; if you applied ointment, tell him to roll his eyes, *to help distribute the medication over the surface of the eyeball.*

● Remove any excess solution or ointment surrounding the eye with a clean tissue. Use a separate tissue for each eye.

● Apply a new eye dressing, if necessary.

● Return the medication to the storage area. Make sure you store it according to the label's instructions.

● Wash your hands.

*To insert an eye disk:*

● See *Inserting and Removing an Eye Medication Disk,* page 323.

## Special considerations

When administering an eye medication that may be absorbed systemically (such as atropine), gently place your thumb over the inner canthus for 1 to 2 minutes after instilling drops while the patient closes his eyes. *This helps prevent medication from flowing into the tear duct.*

Discard any solution remaining in the dropper before returning it to the bottle. If the dropper has become contaminated, discard it and obtain another sterile dropper. *To avoid cross-infection, never use a container of eye medication for more than one patient.*

## Complications

Instillation of some eye medications may cause transient burning, itching, and redness.

## Documentation

Record the medication instilled or applied, the eye(s) treated, and the date, time, and dose on the patient's medication record and chart. Note any side effects and the patient's response.

SUSAN VIGEANT, RN, BSN

# Instillation of Ear Drops

*Ear drops may be instilled to treat infection and inflammation, to soften cerumen for later removal, to produce local anesthetic effects, or to facilitate removal of an insect trapped in the ear by immobilizing and smothering it. Instillation of ear drops is usually* contraindicated if the patient has a perforated eardrum; however, it may be permitted with certain medications, but then requires sterile technique. Other conditions may also prohibit instillation of certain other medications into the ear. For instance, instillation of drops containing hydrocortisone is contraindicated if the patient has herpes, another viral infection, or a fungal infection.

## Equipment
Prescribed ear drops □ bowl of warm water □ patient's medication record and chart □ light source □ tissue or cotton-tipped applicator □ cotton ball (optional).

## Preparation of equipment
Verify the order on the patient's medication record by checking it against the doctor's order. Check the label on the ear drops when you take them from the shelf or drawer to make sure you'll be administering the correct medication. To avoid side effects (such as vertigo, nausea, and pain) resulting from instillation of ear drops that are too cold, warm the medication to body temperature in the bowl of warm water or carry it in your pocket for 30 minutes before administration. If necessary, test the temperature of the medication by placing a drop on your wrist. (If the medication is too hot, it may burn the patient's eardrum or, at the very least, be ineffective.) Before using a glass dropper, make sure it's not chipped to avoid injury to the ear canal.

## Essential steps
• Wash your hands.
• Confirm the patient's identity by asking his name and checking the name, room number, and bed number on his wristband.
• Provide privacy, if possible. Explain the procedure to the patient.
• Position the patient to lie on his side opposite the affected ear.
• Straighten the patient's ear canal. For an adult, pull the auricle of the ear up and back. For an infant or child under age 3, gently pull the auricle down and

back (the ear canal is straighter at this age).
• Using the light source, examine the ear canal for drainage. If you find any drainage, clean it with the tissue or cotton-tipped applicator because drainage can interfere with the effectiveness of the medication.
• Compare the label on the ear drops to the order on the patient's medication record. Check the label again while drawing the medication into the dropper. Check the label for the final time before returning the ear drops to the shelf or drawer.
• To avoid damaging the ear canal with the dropper, gently support the hand holding the dropper against the patient's head. Straighten the patient's ear canal once again and instill the number of drops ordered. To avoid patient discomfort, direct the drops to fall against the sides of the ear canal, not on the eardrum.
• Instruct the patient to remain on his side for 5 to 10 minutes to allow the medication to run down into the ear canal.
• If ordered, tuck the cotton ball loosely into the opening of the ear canal to prevent the medication from leaking out. Be careful not to insert it too deeply into the canal because this would prevent drainage of secretions and increase pressure on the eardrum.
• Clean and dry the outer ear.
• If ordered, repeat the procedure in the other ear after 5 to 10 minutes.
• Assist the patient into a comfortable position.
• Wash your hands.

## Special considerations
Remember that some conditions make the normally tender ear canal even more sensitive, so be especially gentle when performing this procedure. Remember, to prevent injury to the eardrum, never insert a cotton-tipped applicator into the ear canal past the point where you can see the tip.

Remember to always wash your hands before and after caring for the patient's ear and between caring for both ears.

Strict asepsis is especially vital if the patient's middle or inner ear has been opened by surgery or trauma.

After applying ear drops to soften cerumen, irrigate the ear as ordered *to facilitate cerumen removal.*

If the patient has vertigo, keep the side rails of his bed up and assist him during the procedure, as necessary. Also, move slowly and unhurriedly *to avoid exacerbating his vertigo.*

Teach the patient to instill the ear drops correctly, so he can continue treatment at home, if necessary. Review the procedure and let the patient try it himself while you observe.

## Documentation

Record the medication, ear(s) treated, and the date, time, and number of ear drops instilled on the patient's medication record and chart. Also note any signs observed during the procedure, such as drainage, redness, vertigo, nausea, or pain.

SUSAN VIGEANT, RN, BSN

# Hand-held Oropharyngeal Inhalers

*Hand-held inhalers include the metered-dose nebulizer, the turbo-inhaler, and the nasal inhaler (see* Types of Inhalers, *page 327). These devices deliver topical medications to the respiratory tract, producing both local and systemic effects. The mucosal lining of the respiratory tract absorbs the inhalant almost immediately. Examples of common inhalants are bronchodilators, used to facilitate mucous drainage, and mucolytics, which attain a high local concentration to liquefy tenacious bronchial secretions.*

*Use of a hand-held inhaler may be contraindicated in patients who can't form an airtight seal around the device, and in patients who lack the coordina-*

*tion or clear vision necessary to assemble a turbo-inhaler. Contraindications for specific inhalant drugs are also possible. For example, tachycardia—or a history of cardiac arrythmias associated with tachycardia—contraindicates the use of bronchodilators.*

## Equipment

Patient's medication record and chart □ inhaler (metered-dose nebulizer, turbo-inhaler, or nasal inhaler) □ prescribed medication □ normal saline solution (or another appropriate solution) for gargling □ emesis basin (optional).

## Essential steps

• Verify the order on the patient's medication record by checking it against the doctor's order.

• Wash your hands.

• Check the label on the inhaler against the order on the medication record.

• Confirm the patient's identity by asking his name and by checking his name, room number, and bed number on his wristband.

• Explain the procedure to the patient.

*To use the metered-dose nebulizer:*

• Remove the mouthpiece and cap from the bottle.

• Insert the metal stem on the bottle into the small hole on the flattened portion of the mouthpiece. Then, turn the bottle upside down.

• Have the patient exhale, and then place the mouthpiece in his mouth and tell him to close his lips around it.

• Instruct him to inhale slowly as you firmly push the bottle down against the mouthpiece once. *To draw the medication into his lungs,* tell him to continue inhaling until his lungs feel full.

• Remove the mouthpiece from the patient's mouth, and tell him to hold his breath for several seconds *to allow the medication to reach the alveoli.* Then, instruct him to exhale slowly through pursed lips *to keep the distal bronchioles open, allowing increased absorption and diffusion of the drug and better gas exchange.*

• Have the patient gargle with normal

## TYPES OF INHALERS

| Nasal inhaler | Metered-dose nebulizer | Turbo-inhaler |
|---|---|---|

 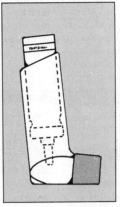 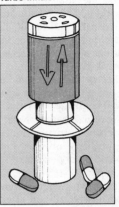

saline solution, if desired, *to remove medication from the mouth and back of the throat.* (The lungs retain only about 10% of the inhalant; most of the remainder is exhaled, but substantial amounts may remain in the oropharynx.)

• Rinse the mouthpiece thoroughly with warm water *to prevent accumulation of residue.*

*To use a turbo-inhaler:*

• Hold the mouthpiece in one hand, and with the other hand slide the gray sleeve away from the mouthpiece as far as it will go.

• Unscrew the tip of the mouthpiece by turning it counterclockwise.

• Firmly press the colored portion of the medication capsule into the propeller stem of the mouthpiece.

• Screw the inhaler together again securely.

• Holding the inhaler with the mouthpiece at the bottom, slide the gray sleeve all the way down and then up again *to puncture the capsule and release the medication.* Do this only once.

• Have the patient exhale completely and tilt his head back. Then, instruct him to place the mouthpiece in his mouth, close his lips around it, and inhale once, quickly and deeply, through the mouthpiece.

• Tell the patient to hold his breath for several seconds *to allow the medication to reach the alveoli.* (Instruct him not to exhale through the mouthpiece.)

• Remove the inhaler from the patient's mouth, and tell him to exhale as much air as possible.

• Repeat the procedure until all the medication in the device is inhaled.

• Have the patient gargle with normal saline solution, if desired, *to remove medication from the mouth and back of the throat.* Be sure to provide an emesis basin if needed.

• Discard the empty medication capsule, put the inhaler in its can, and secure the lid. Rinse the inhaler with warm water at least once a week.

*To use a nasal inhaler:*

• Have the patient blow his nose *to clear his nostrils.*

• Insert the medication cartridge in the

adapter. (When inserting a refill cartridge, first remove the protective cap from the stem.)

• Shake the inhaler well, and remove the protective cap.

• Hold the inhaler with your index finger on top of the cartridge and your thumb under the nasal adapter. The adapter tip should be pointing toward the patient.

• Have the patient tilt his head back. Then, tell him to place the adapter tip into one nostril, while occluding the other nostril with his finger.

• Instruct the patient to inhale gently as he presses the adapter and the cartridge together firmly *to release a measured dose of medication.* Note: Follow manufacturer's instructions. With some medications inhaling during administration is not desirable (Turbinaire, for example).

• Tell the patient to remove the inhaler from his nostril and to exhale through his mouth.

• Shake the inhaler, and have the patient repeat the procedure in the other nostril.

• Have the patient gargle with normal saline solution *to remove medication from the mouth and throat.*

• Remove the medication cartridge from the nasal inhaler, and wash the nasal adapter in lukewarm water. Let the adapter dry thoroughly before reinserting the cartridge.

**Special considerations**
When using a turbo-inhaler or a nasal inhaler, make sure the pressurized cartridge isn't punctured or incinerated. Store the medication cartridge below 120° F. (48.9° C.).

If you're using a turbo-inhaler, keep the medication capsules wrapped until needed *to keep them from deteriorating.*

Teach the patient how to use the inhaler *so he can continue treatments himself after discharge,* if necessary. Explain that overdosage—which is common—can cause the medication to lose its effectiveness. Tell him to record the date and time of each inhalation and his response, *to prevent overdosage and to help the doctor determine the drug's effectiveness.*

Also, note if the patient uses an unusual amount of medication—more than one metered cartridge every 3 weeks, for example, with the metered-dose nebulizer. Inform the patient of possible side effects.

**Documentation**
On the patient's medication record, record the inhalant administered, the dose and the time. Note any significant change in the patient's heart rate after bronchodilation, and any other side effects.

PATRICE M. NASIELSKI, RN

# Instillation of Nasal Medications

*Nasal medications may be instilled by means of drops, a spray (atomizer), or an aerosol (nebulizer). Most drugs instilled by these methods produce local rather than systemic effects. Drops can be directed at a specific area; sprays and aerosols diffuse medication throughout the nose.*

*Most nasal medications, such as phenylephrine, are vasoconstrictors, which relieve nasal congestion by coating and shrinking swollen mucous membranes. Because vasoconstrictors may be absorbed systemically, they are usually contraindicated in hypertensive patients. Other classifications of nasal medications are antiseptics, anesthetics, and corticosteroids. Local anesthetics may be administered to promote patient comfort during rhinolaryngologic examination, laryngoscopy, bronchoscopy, and endotracheal intubation. Corticosteroids reduce inflammation in allergic or inflammatory conditions and in nasal polyps.*

**Equipment**
Prescribed medication □ patient's medication record and chart □ emesis basin (with nose drops only) □ facial tissues □ optional: pillow, small piece of soft rubber or plastic tubing, rubber nipple from baby bottle.

## Preparation of equipment

Verify the order on the patient's medication record by checking it against the doctor's order. Check the label on the medication when you take it from the shelf or drawer *to make sure you'll be administering the correct medication.* Note the concentration of the medication. Phenylephrine (Neosynephrine), for example, is available in various concentrations from 0.125% to 1%.

## Essential steps

• Wash your hands.
• Check the medication label against the medication record.
• Confirm the patient's identity by asking his name and checking the name, room number, and bed number on his wristband.
• Explain the procedure to the patient and provide privacy.
*To instill nose drops:*
• When possible, position the patient so the drops flow back into the nostrils, toward the affected area. *If you want the drops to reach the eustachian tube opening,* position the patient in supine, with his head tilted slightly to the affected side. *To reach the ethmoidal and the sphenoidal sinuses,* place the patient in the Proetz position (with his head hanging over the edge of the bed). *To reach the maxillary and the frontal sinuses and the nasal passages,* place the patient in the Parkinson position (with his head toward the affected side and hanging slightly over the edge of the bed). *To prevent undue strain on the patient's neck muscles,* support his head with one hand.
• If the patient can't assume either the Proetz or the Parkinson position, position him supine, and put a large pillow under the shoulders so the head tilts back over the shoulders. Tilt the head as far back as possible *to prevent the drops from running into the throat.*
• Draw up some medication into the dropper.
• Push up the tip of the patient's nose slightly. Position the dropper just above the nostril, and direct its tip toward the midline of the nose, *so the drops flow*

*toward the back of the nasal cavity rather than toward its base, where they would flow down the throat.*
• Insert the dropper about ⅜" (1 cm) into the nostril. Make sure the dropper doesn't touch the sides of the nostril, because *this would contaminate the dropper and could cause the patient to sneeze.* (Besides, you have to see the dropper tip to count the drops.)
• Instill the prescribed number of drops, observing the patient carefully for any signs of discomfort.
• *To prevent the drops from leaking out of the nostrils,* ask the patient to keep his head tilted back for at least 5 minutes and to breathe through his mouth. *This also allows sufficient time for the medication to constrict mucous membranes.*
• Keep an emesis basin handy, *so the patient can expectorate any medication that flows into the oropharynx and mouth.* Use a facial tissue to wipe any excess medication from the patient's nostrils and face.
• Clean the dropper by separating the plunger and pipette and flushing them with warm water. Allow to air-dry.
*To use a nasal spray:*
• Have the patient sit upright, with his head tilted back slightly.
• Remove the protective cap from the atomizer.
• *To prevent air from entering the nasal cavity and to allow the medication to flow in properly,* occlude one nostril with your finger. Insert the atomizer tip into the open nostril.
• Instruct the patient to inhale, and as he does so, squeeze the atomizer once, quickly and firmly. Use just enough force to coat the inside of the patient's nose with medication.
• If ordered, spray the nostril again. Then, repeat the procedure in the other nostril.
• Instruct the patient to keep his head tilted back for several minutes and to breathe slowly through his nose *so the medication has time to work.* Tell him not to blow his nose.
• Rinse the atomizer tip with warm water *to prevent contamination of the medication with nasal secretions.*

*To use a nasal aerosol:*

• Instruct the patient to clear his nostrils by gently blowing his nose.

• Insert the medication cartridge according to the manufacturer's directions. With some models, you'll fit the medication cartridge over a small hole in the adapter. (When inserting a refill cartridge, first remove the protective cap from the stem.)

• Shake the aerosol well immediately before each use, and remove the protective cap from the adapter tip.

• Hold the aerosol between your thumb and index finger, with your index finger on top of the medication cartridge.

• Tilt the patient's head back, and carefully insert the adapter tip in one nostril, while occluding the other nostril with your finger.

• Press the adapter and cartridge together firmly to release one measured dose of medication.

• Shake the aerosol, and repeat the procedure to instill medication into the other nostril.

• Remove the medication cartridge and wash the nasal adapter in lukewarm water daily. Allow the adapter to dry thoroughly before reinserting the cartridge.

### Special considerations

Before instilling nose drops in a young child or an uncooperative patient, attach a small piece of tubing to the end of the dropper *to prevent damage to mucous membranes.*

When using an aerosol, be careful not to puncture or incinerate the pressurized cartridge. Store it at temperatures below 120° F. (48.9° C.).

*To prevent the spread of infection,* label the medication bottle so you can be sure to use it again only for that patient.

Ideally, a nasal spray should be self-administered by the patient. Teach the patient how to instill nasal medications correctly *so he can continue treatment after discharge,* if necessary. Caution him against using nasal medications longer than prescribed, *because they may cause a rebound effect that wors-*

ens *the condition.* During rebound, the medication loses its effectiveness and relaxes the vessels in the nasal turbinates, producing a stuffiness that can be relieved only by discontinuing the medication.

Inform the patient of possible side effects. For example, explain that when receiving corticosteroids by aerosol therapy, therapeutic effects may not appear for 2 days to 2 weeks.

### Complications

Some nasal medications may cause restlessness, palpitations, nervousness, and other systemic effects. For example, excessive use of corticosteroid aerosols may cause hyperadrenocorticism and adrenal suppression.

### Documentation

Record the medication instilled and its concentration, the number of drops or instillations administered, and whether the medication was instilled in one or both nostrils. Also note the time, date, and any resulting side effects.

SUSAN VIGEANT, RN, BSN

# Insertion of a Rectal Suppository

*A rectal suppository is a small, solid, medicated mass—usually cone-shaped—with a cocoa butter or glycerin base. It may be inserted to stimulate peristalsis and defecation or to relieve pain, vomiting, and local irritation. Rectal suppositories commonly contain drugs that reduce fever, induce relaxation, are impaired by digestive enzymes, or have a taste too offensive for oral use. Rectal suppositories melt at body temperature and are absorbed slowly.*

*Because insertion of a rectal suppository may stimulate the vagus nerve, this procedure is contraindicated in patients with potential cardiac dysrhythmias. It may have to be avoided in patients with recent rectal or prostate surgery because of the risk of local trauma or discomfort during insertion.*

## Equipment

Rectal suppository ☐ patient's medication record and chart ☐ clean finger cot (or glove) ☐ water-soluble lubricant ☐ bedpan (optional).

## Preparation of equipment

Keep rectal suppositories stored in the refrigerator until needed *to prevent softening and possible decreased effectiveness of medication.* A softened suppository is also difficult to handle and insert. To harden it again, hold the suppository (in its wrapper) under cold running water.

## Essential steps

* Verify the order on the patient's medication record by checking it against the doctor's order on his chart.
* Wash your hands.
* Confirm the patient's identity by asking his name and checking the name, room number, and bed number on his wristband.
* Explain the procedure and the purpose of the medication to the patient.
* Provide privacy.
* Place the patient on his left side in the Sims' position. Drape him with the bedcovers to expose only the rectal area.
* Put the finger cot on the index finger of your dominant hand. (If a finger cot is not readily available, use a glove).
* Remove the suppository from its wrapper, and lubricate it with water-soluble lubricant.
* Lift the patient's upper buttock with your nondominant hand *to expose the anus.*
* Instruct the patient to take several deep breaths through his mouth *to help relax the anal sphincters and reduce anxiety or discomfort during insertion.*
* Using the index finger of your dominant hand, insert the suppository— tapered end first—about 1″ to 1½″ (2.5 to 3.8 cm), until you feel it pass the internal anal sphincter. Try to direct

the tapered end toward the side of the rectum, *so it contacts the membranes.*
* Ensure the patient's comfort. Encourage him to lie quietly and, if applicable, to retain the suppository for the appropriate length of time. A suppository administered to relieve constipation should be retained as long as possible (at least 20 minutes) to be effective.
* Discard the used equipment.

## Special considerations

Because the intake of food and fluid stimulates peristalsis, a suppository for relieving constipation should be inserted about 30 minutes before mealtime *to help soften the feces in the rectum and facilitate defecation.* A medicated retention suppository should be inserted between meals. Tell the patient to avoid expelling it, but if the patient has difficulty retaining the suppository, place him on a bedpan immediately after the procedure.

Make sure the patient's call button is handy and watch for his signal, *because he may be unable to suppress the urge to defecate long enough to wait for the bedpan.* For example, a patient with proctitis has a highly sensitive rectum and may not be able to retain a suppository very well. Advise the patient that the suppository may discolor his next bowel movement. Anusol suppositories, for example, give feces a silvergray pasty appearance.

## Documentation

On the medication record, note the time, the dose, and the patient's response.

SUSAN VIGEANT, RN, BSN

# Insertion of Vaginal Medications

*Vaginal medications include suppositories, creams, gels, and ointments. These medications can be inserted as topical treatment for infection (particularly* Trichomonas *vaginitis and monilial vaginitis) or inflammation, or as a contraceptive. Suppositories have a cocoa butter base, which allows them to melt when they contact the vaginal mucosa and then diffuse topically, as effectively as creams, gels, and ointments. (For information on vaginal irrigation see Chapter 16.)*

*Vaginal medications usually come with a disposable applicator that enables placement of medication in the anterior and posterior fornices. Vaginal administration is most effective when the patient can remain lying down afterward and retain the medication.*

### Equipment
Clean gloves □ prescribed medication and applicator, if necessary □ water-soluble lubricant □ small sanitary pad.

### Essential steps
● Verify the order on the patient's medication cardex by checking it against the doctor's order.
● Confirm the patient's identity by asking her name and checking the name, room number, and bed number on her wristband.
● Wash your hands, explain the procedure to the patient, and provide privacy.
● Ask the patient to void.
● Ask the patient if she would rather insert the medication herself. If so, provide appropriate instructions. If not, proceed with the following steps.
● Help her into the lithotomy position.
● Expose only the perineum.
*To insert a suppository:*
● Remove the suppository from the wrapper, and lubricate it with water-soluble lubricant.
● Put on gloves and expose the vagina.
● With the forefinger of your free hand, insert the suppository about 2″ (5 cm) into the vagina. *To ensure patient comfort,* direct your finger *down* initially (toward the spine), and then *up* and *back* (toward the cervix).
● If the suppository is small, insert it in the tip of an applicator. Then, lu-

bricate the applicator, hold it by the cylinder, and insert it into the vagina. When the suppository reaches the distal end of the vagina, depress the plunger. Remove the applicator while the plunger is still depressed.
*To insert ointments, creams, or gels:*
● Insert the plunger into the applicator. Then, fit the applicator to the tube of medication.
● Gently squeeze the tube to fill the applicator with the prescribed amount of medication. Lubricate the applicator.
● Put on gloves and expose the vagina.
● Insert the applicator as you would a small suppository and administer the medication.
*After vaginal insertion:*
● Remove and discard the gloves.
● Wash the applicator with soap and warm water and store it, unless it is disposable. If the applicator can be used again, label it *so it will be used only for the same patient.*
● *To prevent the medication from soiling the patient's clothing and bedding,* provide a sanitary pad.
● Help her return to a comfortable position.
● Wash your hands thoroughly.

### Special considerations
Refrigerate vaginal suppositories that melt at room temperatures. If possible, teach the patient how to insert vaginal medication. She may have to administer it herself after discharge. Give her a patient-instruction chart if one is available. Instruct the patient not to wear a tampon after inserting vaginal medication, *because it would absorb the medication and decrease its effectiveness.*

### Complications
Vaginal medications may cause local irritation.

### Documentation
Record the medication administered, the time, the date, and your initials on the medication record. Note any other pertinent information.

PATRICE M. NASIELSKI, RN

INJECTIONS

# Cartridge-injection System

## [*Tubex; Carpuject*]

*A cartridge-injection system, such as the Tubex or Carpuject, is a convenient, easy-to-use method of injection that facilitates both accuracy and sterility. It consists of a metal (usually chrome-plated brass) or plastic cartridge holder syringe and a prefilled medication cartridge with needle attached. In this system the medication is premixed and premeasured, which saves time and helps ensure an exact dose. Because it is a closed system, the medication remains sealed in the cartridge until the injection is administered, maintaining sterility.*

*The disadvantage of this system is that not all drugs are available in cartridge form. Compatible drugs can be added to partially filled cartridges.*

### Equipment

Metal or plastic cartridge holder syringe □ medication-filled cartridge-needle unit □ sterile alcohol sponge □ additional medication, if prescribed.

Metal syringes are available in both 1-ml and 2-ml cartridge sizes. The 2-ml syringe can be adapted to fit a 1-ml cartridge. Plastic syringes can be used with cartridges of any size.

### Essential steps

- Wash your hands.

*To use a metal syringe (Tubex):*

- Grasp the barrel of the syringe in one hand. With the other hand, pull back on the plunger rod and swing the handle down, so it hangs at a right angle to the barrel (see *Loading Cartridge-injection Syringes*, page 334).
- Make sure the medication and dose are correct, as prescribed, before loading the syringe. Then, slide the cartridge-needle unit—needle end first—into the barrel.
- Hold the metal syringe barrel (not the glass cartridge), and swing the plunger rod back into place. *To fully engage the rod,* turn it clockwise until you hear a click at the front end of the syringe. Both ends of the cartridge-needle unit should be engaged in the syringe before injection.
- Explain the procedure to the patient and provide privacy.
- Remove the rubber sheath covering the needle just before the injection. A popping sound indicates the seal was secure. Expel any air bubbles from the syringe cartridge, and administer the medication, as prescribed.
- After the injection, rest the syringe against the palm of one hand, needle pointing up. Holding the rubber sheath between the thumb and forefinger of the other hand, slide it over the tip of the needle. Shake the syringe gently *to allow gravity to cause the sheath to fall back into position.* Pull down on the bottom of the sheath *to cover the needle completely.*
- Hold the glass cartridge with one hand, and with the other hand rotate the plunger rod counterclockwise to disengage it. Pull the plunger rod back, and open the syringe. *Be careful that you don't pull back on the plunger rod before disengaging it or it will jam.*
- Disengage the glass cartridge by rotating it counterclockwise, and remove it from the syringe. Discard the cartridge and sheath-covered needle according to institution policy.

*To use a plastic syringe (Carpuject):*

- Make sure the medication and dosage are correct before loading the syringe.
- Grasp the barrel of the syringe, with the open side facing you, and pull back the plunger rod as far as possible.
- Disengage the locking screw by turning it counterclockwise.
- Insert the cartridge-needle unit—needle end first—into the open side of the syringe (see *Loading Cartridge-injection*

EQUIPMENT

## LOADING CARTRIDGE-INJECTION SYRINGES

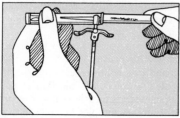

To load a metal cartridge-injection syringe, swing the handle section down, so it hangs at a right angle to the barrel, as shown here. Then, slide the sterile cartridge-needle unit—needle-end first—into the barrel, swing the plunger rod back into place, and engage the plunger into the cartridge.

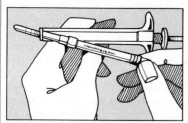

To load a plastic cartridge-injection syringe, insert the cartridge-needle unit—needle-end first—into the open side of the barrel, and engage the plunger into the cartridge by tightening.

*Syringes,* above). Advance and engage the locking screw, and turn it clockwise beyond its initial resistance until it will no longer rotate.

• Advance the plunger rod and screw clockwise onto the threaded insert in the rubber plunger.

• Remove the rubber sheath, expel excess air from the cartridge, and proceed to the patient's room to give the injection.

• After the injection, replace the sheath. Disengage the plunger rod from the plunger by rotating it counterclockwise

and pulling it back as far as possible.

• Disengage the locking screw by rotating it counterclockwise. Turn the syringe over, and remove the cartridge-needle unit. Discard the unit according to institution policy.

*To use a 2-ml syringe with a 1-ml cartridge-needle unit:*

• Insert a 1-ml cartridge-needle unit into the syringe, and engage it in the usual manner.

• Push the number tab at the base of the plunger rod through the syringe to the number 1 position.

• Proceed with the injection.

• Disengage the cartridge-needle unit and discard it. The syringe automatically resets itself for a 2-ml unit.

*To add a compatible medication to a partially filled cartridge:*

• Hold the cartridge with the needle end up. Pull back the plunger rod so the surface of the rubber piston in contact with the medication is set at the 2.5-ml mark.

• Wipe the diaphragm of the vial containing the compatible medication with an alcohol sponge.

• Insert the needle into the single-dose vial. Depress the plunger rod to inject into the vial an amount of air equal to the prescribed amount of medication to be withdrawn from the vial. Pull the rod back to withdraw the medication.

• Remove the needle from the vial, expel excess air, and replace the rubber sheath.

• Proceed to the patient's room to give the injection. Discard the equipment according to institution policy.

### Special considerations

Before combining drugs in a cartridge, check appropriate sources for incompatibilities and contraindications. After mixing the drugs, check again for signs of incompatibility, such as discoloration and precipitation. If combining drugs involves the use of a multidose vial, you may want to use a separate needle and syringe to inject air *to prevent contaminating the vial with the cartridge medication.* If combining drugs involves the use of an ampul, you don't have to inject air into it, *because an ampul doesn't contain a vacuum.*

Empty cartridges can be obtained and used for medications not readily available in the prefilled cartridge form.

Never use a cartridge-needle unit for successive injections or as a multidose container. Discard the unit after one injection.

*To maintain sterility,* keep the rubber sheath or needle guard in place until just before the injection.

For patients in isolation, disposable syringes are recommended instead of the cartridge-injection system. If the cartridge-injection system is used under such circumstances, the syringe should be kept in the patient's room and must be cleaned properly before removing it from the room. Once removed from the room it should be sterilized before reuse for other patients.

**Documentation**

Although no specific documentation concerning the use of this equipment is necessary, record the medications administered, the injection site, the time of administration, and your signature on the patient's medication record. Describe any subsequent effects of the medications.

JOANNE PATZEK DACUNHA, RN

# Combining Drugs in a Syringe

*Combining two drugs in one syringe avoids the discomfort of two separate injections. Usually, drugs can be mixed in a syringe in one of three ways. They may be combined from two multidose vials (regular and long-acting insulin, for example, can be combined this way). They can also be combined from one multidose vial and one ampul, or from two ampuls.*

*Such combinations are contraindicated when the drugs aren't compatible, and when the combined doses exceed the* *amount of solution that can be absorbed from a single injection site.*

**Equipment**

Prescribed drugs □ patient's medication record and chart □ sterile alcohol sponges □ sterile syringe and needle □ optional: cartridge-injection system and filter needle.

The type and size of the syringe and needle depend on the prescribed medications and the patient's body build. Medications which come in prefilled glass syringe cartridges require a cartridge-injection system.

**Essential steps**

● Verify that the drugs to be administered agree with the patient's medication record and the doctor's orders.
● Calculate the dose to be given.
● Wash your hands.

*To mix drugs from two multidose vials:*
● Using an alcohol sponge, wipe the rubber stopper on the first vial. *This decreases the possibility of introducing microorganisms into the medication as you insert the needle into the vial.*
● Pull back the syringe plunger until the volume of air drawn into the syringe equals the volume to be withdrawn from the drug vial.
● Without inverting the vial, insert the needle into the top of the vial, making sure that the bevel's tip doesn't touch the solution. Inject the air into the vial and withdraw the needle. This replaces air in the vial *to prevent creation of a partial vacuum when the drug is withdrawn.*
● Repeat the above steps for the second vial. Then, after injecting the air into the second vial, invert the vial, withdraw the prescribed dose, and then withdraw the needle.
● Wipe the rubber stopper of the first vial again and insert the needle, taking care not to depress the plunger. Invert the vial, withdraw the prescribed dose, and then withdraw the needle.

*To mix drugs from one multidose vial and one ampul:*
● Using an alcohol sponge, clean the vial's rubber stopper.

## COMPATIBILITY TABLE OF DRUGS COMBINED IN A SYRINGE

| | atropine | butorphanol | chlorpromazine | codeine | diazepam | glycopyrrolate | hydromorphone | hydroxyzine | meperidine | morphine | nalbuphine | pentobarbital | phenobarbital | promethazine | scopolamine | secobarbital | sodium bicarbonate | thiopental |
|---|---|---|---|---|---|---|---|---|---|---|---|---|---|---|---|---|---|---|
| atropine | | compatible | provisionally compatible | no data | not compatible | compatible | no data | provisionally compatible | provisionally compatible | provisionally compatible | compatible | provisionally compatible | no data | provisionally compatible | provisionally compatible | no data | not compatible | no data |
| butorphanol | compatible | | provisionally compatible | no data | not compatible | compatible | no data | compatible | no data | no data | no data | not compatible | not compatible | compatible | compatible | not compatible | no data | not compatible |
| chlorpromazine | provisionally compatible | provisionally compatible | | no data | not compatible | compatible | no data | provisionally compatible | provisionally compatible | provisionally compatible | no data | not compatible | not compatible | provisionally compatible | provisionally compatible | not compatible | not compatible | not compatible |
| codeine | no data | no data | no data | | not compatible | compatible | no data | provisionally compatible | no data | no data | no data | not compatible | no data | no data | no data | no data | not compatible | no data |
| diazepam | not compatible | not compatible | not compatible | not compatible | | not compatible | not compatible | not compatible | not compatible | not compatible | not compatible | not compatible | not compatible | not compatible | not compatible | not compatible | not compatible | not compatible |
| glycopyrrolate | compatible | compatible | compatible | compatible | not compatible | | compatible | compatible | compatible | compatible | compatible | not compatible | no data | compatible | compatible | not compatible | not compatible | not compatible |
| hydromorphone | no data | no data | no data | no data | not compatible | compatible | | no data | no data | no data | no data | no data | no data | no data | no data | no data | not compatible | not compatible |
| hydroxyzine | provisionally compatible | compatible | provisionally compatible | provisionally compatible | not compatible | compatible | no data | | provisionally compatible | provisionally compatible | compatible | not compatible | not compatible | provisionally compatible | provisionally compatible | no data | not compatible | no data |
| meperidine | provisionally compatible | no data | provisionally compatible | no data | not compatible | compatible | no data | provisionally compatible | | not compatible | no data | not compatible | not compatible | provisionally compatible | provisionally compatible | no data | not compatible | not compatible |
| morphine | provisionally compatible | no data | provisionally compatible | no data | not compatible | compatible | no data | provisionally compatible | not compatible | | no data | conflicting reports | not compatible | conflicting reports | provisionally compatible | no data | not compatible | not compatible |
| nalbuphine | compatible | no data | no data | no data | not compatible | compatible | no data | compatible | no data | no data | | not compatible | no data | conflicting reports | compatible | no data | no data | no data |
| pentobarbital | provisionally compatible | not compatible | not compatible | not compatible | not compatible | not compatible | no data | not compatible | not compatible | conflicting reports | not compatible | | no data | not compatible | provisionally compatible | no data | conflicting reports | provisionally compatible |
| phenobarbital | no data | not compatible | not compatible | no data | not compatible | no data | no data | not compatible | not compatible | not compatible | no data | no data | | not compatible | no data | no data | no data | compatible |
| promethazine | provisionally compatible | compatible | provisionally compatible | no data | not compatible | compatible | no data | provisionally compatible | provisionally compatible | conflicting reports | conflicting reports | not compatible | not compatible | | provisionally compatible | no data | no data | not compatible |
| scopolamine | provisionally compatible | compatible | provisionally compatible | no data | not compatible | compatible | no data | provisionally compatible | provisionally compatible | provisionally compatible | compatible | provisionally compatible | no data | provisionally compatible | | not compatible | not compatible | compatible |
| secobarbital | no data | not compatible | not compatible | no data | not compatible | not compatible | no data | no data | no data | no data | no data | no data | no data | no data | not compatible | | no data | no data |
| sodium bicarbonate | not compatible | no data | not compatible | not compatible | not compatible | not compatible | not compatible | not compatible | not compatible | not compatible | no data | conflicting reports | no data | no data | not compatible | no data | | not compatible |
| thiopental | no data | not compatible | not compatible | no data | not compatible | not compatible | not compatible | no data | not compatible | not compatible | no data | provisionally compatible | compatible | not compatible | compatible | no data | not compatible | |

KEY

- compatible
- not compatible
- provisionally compatible; use within 15 minutes of preparation
- no available data on compatibility.
- conflicting reports on compatibility; mixing not recommended

• Pull back on the syringe plunger until the volume of air drawn into the syringe equals the volume to be withdrawn from the drug vial.

• Insert the needle into the top of the vial and inject the air. Then, invert the vial and withdraw the prescribed dose. Put the sterile needle cover over the needle.

• Wrap the ampul neck with a piece of sterile gauze or an alcohol sponge *to protect yourself from injury in case the glass splinters.* Break open the ampul, directing the force away from you.

• If desired, switch to the filter needle at this point *to filter out any glass splinters.*

• Insert the needle into the ampul. Be careful not to touch the outside of the ampul with the needle. Draw the correct dose into the syringe.

• If you switched to the filter needle, change back to a regular needle *to administer the drugs.*

*To mix drugs from two ampuls:*

• An opened ampul doesn't contain a vacuum. To mix drugs from two ampuls in a syringe, calculate the prescribed doses and open both ampuls, using aseptic technique. If desired, use a filter needle to draw up the drugs. Then, change to a regular needle to administer them.

## Special considerations

 Never combine two drugs if you're unsure of their compatibility. Although drug incompatibility often causes a visible reaction, such as clouding, bubbling, or precipitation, some incompatible combinations produce no visible reactions even though they alter the chemical nature and action of the drugs. Check with appropriate references and a pharmacist when you're unsure about specific compatibility. When in doubt, administer two separate injections. Never try to combine more than two drugs.

Some medications are compatible for only a brief time after being combined and should be administered within 15 minutes after mixing. After this time, environmental factors—such as temperature, exposure to light, and humidity—may alter compatibility.

Insert a needle through the vial's rubber stopper at a slight angle, bevel up, and exert slight lateral pressure. *This way you won't cut a piece of rubber out of the stopper, which can then be pushed into the vial.*

When mixing drugs from multidose vials, be careful not to contaminate the second drug with the first. Ideally, the needle should be changed after drawing the first medication into the syringe. This isn't always possible, because many disposable syringes do not have removable needles. *To reduce the risk of contamination,* most hospitals dispense parenteral medications in single-dose vials.

Insulin is one of the few drugs that still comes in multidose vials. Be careful when mixing regular and long-acting insulin. Draw up the regular insulin first *to avoid contamination by the long-acting suspension. If a minute amount of the regular insulin is accidentally mixed with the long-acting insulin, it won't appre-*

ciably change the effect of the long-acting insulin. Because the issue of which insulin should be drawn up first is controversial, check institution policy regarding this matter.

When using a cartridge-injection system and a multidose vial, a separate needle and syringe is used to inject the air into the multidose vial. *This prevents possible contamination of the multidose vial by the cartridge-injection system.*

## Documentation

Record the drugs administered, the injection site, time of administration, and your signature on the patient's medication record. Describe drug effects or other pertinent information in the nurse's notes.

PATRICE M. NASIELSKI, RN

# Titration from Parenteral to Oral Analgesics

*Titration determines the dose and frequency of an oral narcotic analgesic necessary to provide analgesia equal to that of the parenteral form. Although parenterally administered narcotics are most commonly used to treat moderate to severe pain, oral administration is desirable for reasons of convenience and patient comfort, and to give patients more control over their medication regimen. Oral analgesics are also preferred for maintenance in patients who require continuous pain relief after discharge and in those with tissue damage from repeated injections.*

*The doctor orders the specific oral medication for titration, as well as its dose and frequency, based on the patient's needs. But careful and constant monitoring by the nurse can help determine the least amount of oral medication necessary to achieve optimal analgesia. The nurse can suggest changes in the medication regimen based on observa-*

*tions of the patient and the data in equianalgesic charts, which provide a general guide for converting from parenteral to oral drugs. Titration to oral drugs is contraindicated in patients with poor gastrointestinal absorption.*

### Equipment
Flowchart for recording subjective and objective data.

### Preparation of equipment
Set up these columns on the flowchart: *date, time, dose, vital signs,* and *patient response.*

### Essential steps
● Obtain the doctor's order, and explain the procedure to the patient.
● *To determine patient response,* develop a uniform system (a numerical scale or set of verbal descriptions, for example) for rating severity of pain.

● Make sure all staff members are aware of the rating system. *This helps in establishing reliable guidelines for this subjective area of assessment and helps ensure the consistent monitoring necessary to titrate doses according to patient need.*
● Obtain baseline vital signs. These provide objective data and are vital components of the overall patient assessment. Particularly note respiratory status during future evaluations. This is the easiest vital sign to evaluate—without disturbing the patient—and is an important indicator of the effect of respiratory depression induced by narcotic overdosage.
● Although procedures for titrating analgesic dosage vary, a common initial method is to administer half the parenteral dose, and then give the equivalent of the remaining half in oral form. For example, a patient receiving 3 mg of I.M. hydromorphone (Dilaudid) would have this dose cut in half to 1.5 mg and would be given the equivalent of the remaining 1.5 mg in an oral form—perhaps 7.5 mg of hydromorphone—as indicated on one standard equianalgesic chart. After several such doses, the total dose is converted to an oral dose.

● Another approach is to administer a "loading dose" of the oral drug. This is an initial dose higher than anticipated need; for example, 15 mg of oral hydromorphone to replace a 2 mg I.M. dose. This may initially produce some sedation but should convince the patient that the oral drug can relieve pain. This initial oral dose is then titrated down, based on the patient's response, to perhaps 14 mg of hydromorphone, then 12 mg, then 10 mg, until a dose is reached that provides satisfactory analgesia with minimal side effects and stable vital signs.
● The total oral dose is then titrated down in 2- to 4-mg increments to the minimum dose necessary to achieve satisfactory analgesia, completing titration.

### Special considerations
The initial oral dose may seem high, but remember that oral medications aren't absorbed into the bloodstream as efficiently as parenteral medications. Indeed, with some drugs, the equianalgesic oral dose may be two (levorphanol tartrate [Levo-Dromoran]) to six times (morphine) the parenteral drug dose. Moreover, a patient in chronic pain can usually tolerate large analgesic doses without experiencing some of the common side effects, such as sedation.

Administer an analgesic drug on a regular schedule *to maintain a constant blood level of analgesia and prevent breakthrough of severe pain.* A carefully controlled drug regimen may also help prevent development of a psychological dependence for a drug and subsequent addiction in a predisposed patient. However, fear of causing drug addiction should not prevent administration of effective doses of analgesics to patients with terminal diseases or intractable pain.

You may want to include staff observations on the flowchart in a column headed *degree of sedation.* This can be determined, for example, by the amount of time the patient is asleep and his ability to perform activities of daily living, such as eating, bathing, and talking.

## Documentation
After each dose, record the appropriate data in each of the flowchart's columns.

SUSAN M. GLOVER, RN, BSN

# Subcutaneous Injections

*Injection into the adipose tissues (fatty layer) beneath the skin delivers a drug into the bloodstream more rapidly than oral administration. Subcutaneous injection allows slower, more sustained drug administration than intramuscular injection; it also causes minimal tissue trauma and carries little risk of striking large blood vessels and nerves.*

*Absorbed mainly through the capillaries, drugs recommended for subcutaneous injection are nonirritating aqueous solutions and suspensions contained in fluid volumes of 0.5 to 2.0 ml. Heparin and insulin, for example (see Nursing Tips for Insulin and Heparin Injections), are usually administered subcutaneously. Drugs and solutions for subcutaneous injection are injected through a relatively short needle, using meticulous sterile technique.*

*The most common subcutaneous injection sites are the outer aspect of the upper arm, anterior thigh, loose tissue of the lower abdomen, buttocks, and upper back. Injection is contraindicated in sites that are inflamed, edematous, scarred, or covered with moles, birthmarks, or other lesions. It may also be contraindicated in patients with impaired coagulation mechanisms.*

## Equipment
Prescribed medication □ patient's medication record and chart □ sterile disposable 25G ⅝″ needle □ prepackaged sterile disposable 1- to 3-ml syringe □ sterile alcohol sponges □ optional: antiseptic skin preparation, filter needle, insulin syringe.

## NURSING TIPS FOR INSULIN AND HEPARIN INJECTIONS

### Insulin
● To establish more consistent blood levels, rotate insulin injection sites within anatomic regions. Absorption varies from one region to another. Preferred insulin injection sites are the arms, abdomen, thighs, and buttocks.
● Make sure the type of insulin, unit dosage, and syringe are correct.
● When combining insulins in a syringe, make sure they are compatible. Regular insulin can be mixed with *all* types. Prompt insulin zinc suspension (Semilente) *cannot* be mixed with NPH insulin. Follow institutional policy as to which insulin to draw up first.
● Before drawing up insulin suspension, gently roll and invert the bottle to ensure even drug particle distribution. *Don't shake the bottle, because this can cause foam or bubbles to develop, changing the potency and altering the dosage.*

### Heparin
● The preferred site for heparin injections is the lower abdominal fat pad, 2″ (5 cm) beneath the umbilicus, from iliac crest to crest. Injecting heparin into this area, which isn't involved in muscular activity, reduces the risk of local capillary bleeding. Always rotate the sites from one side to the other.
● Don't administer any injections within 2″ of a scar, a bruise, or the umbilicus.
● Don't aspirate to check for blood return *because this may cause bleeding into the tissues at the site.*
● Don't rub or massage the site after the injection. Rubbing can cause localized minute hemorrhages or bruises.
● If the patient bruises easily, apply ice to the site for the first 5 minutes after the injection to minimize local hemorrhage.

## Preparation of equipment
Verify the order on the patient's medication record by checking it against the doctor's order.

Inspect the medication to make sure it's not abnormally discolored or cloudy and that it doesn't contain precipitates.

Wash your hands. Select a needle of the right gauge and length. An average adult patient requires a 25G ⅝″ needle; an infant, a child, or an elderly or thin patient, a 25G to 27G ½″ needle.

Remember to check the label on the

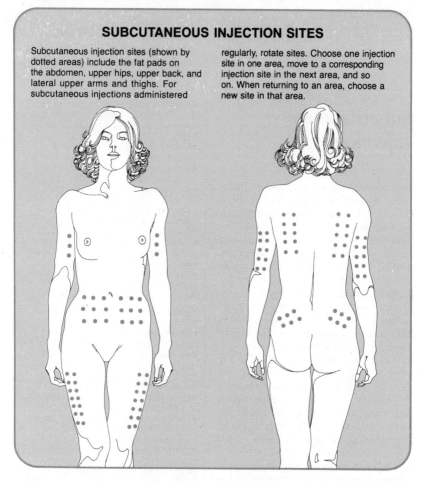

## SUBCUTANEOUS INJECTION SITES

Subcutaneous injection sites (shown by dotted areas) include the fat pads on the abdomen, upper hips, upper back, and lateral upper arms and thighs. For subcutaneous injections administered regularly, rotate sites. Choose one injection site in one area, move to a corresponding injection site in the next area, and so on. When returning to an area, choose a new site in that area.

medication against the medication record. Read the label as you draw up the medication for subcutaneous injection.

*For single-dose ampuls:* Wrap the neck in an alcohol sponge, and snap off the top, directing the force away from your body. If desired, attach a filter needle to the needle and withdraw the medication. Tap the syringe to clear air from it. Cover the needle with the needle sheath. Before discarding the ampul, check the label against the patient's medication record. Discard the filter needle and the ampul. Attach the appropriate needle to the syringe.

*For single-dose or multidose vials:* Reconstitute powdered drugs according to the label's instructions. Make sure all crystalline particles have dissolved in the solution. Warming the vial by holding it and rolling it between your palms may help the drug dissolve faster. Clean the vial's rubber stopper with the sterile alcohol sponge. Pull the syringe plunger back until the volume of air in the barrel equals the volume of drug to be withdrawn.

Insert the needle into the vial. Inject the air, invert the vial, and keep the needle bevel below the level of the solution as you withdraw the prescribed amount. Cover the needle with the needle sheath. Tap the syringe to clear any air from it. Check the drug label against the patient's medication record before returning the multidose vial to the shelf or drawer or before discarding the single-dose vial.

### Essential steps
• Confirm the patient's identity by asking his name and checking the name, room number, and bed number on his wristband.
• Explain the procedure to the patient and provide privacy.
• Select an appropriate injection site (see *Subcutaneous Injection Sites*). Rotate sites according to a planned schedule for patients who require repeated injections. Use different areas of the body unless contraindicated by the specific drug. (Heparin, for example, can be injected only in certain sites.)
• Position and drape the patient.
• Cleanse the injection site with a sterile alcohol sponge, beginning at the center of the site and moving outward in a circular motion. Allow the skin to dry before injecting the drug *to avoid a stinging sensation from introducing alcohol into subcutaneous tissues.*
• Loosen the protective needle sheath.
• With your nondominant hand, grasp the skin around the injection site firmly to elevate the subcutaneous tissue, forming a 1″ (2.5-cm) fat fold.
• Holding the syringe in your dominant hand, insert the loosened needle sheath between the fourth and fifth fingers of your other hand, still pinching the skin around the injection site. Pull back the syringe with your dominant hand to uncover the needle by grasping the syringe like a pencil. Don't touch the needle.
• Position the needle with its bevel up.
• Tell the patient he'll feel a prick as the needle is inserted.
• Insert the needle at a 45° or 90° angle to the skin surface, depending upon the amount of subcutaneous tissue present at the site and the needle length. Some medications, such as heparin, should always be injected at a 90° angle.
• Insert the needle quickly, in one motion. Release the patient's skin *to avoid injecting into compressed tissue and irritating nerve fibers.*

• Pull back the plunger slightly *to aspirate for blood return.* If none appears, begin injecting the drug slowly. If blood appears upon aspiration, withdraw the needle, prepare another syringe, and repeat the procedure.
• After injection, remove the needle gently but quickly at the same angle used for insertion.
• Cover the site with an alcohol sponge, and massage the site gently (unless you have injected a drug that contraindicates massage, such as heparin) *to distribute the drug and facilitate absorption.*
• Remove the sponge, and check the injection site for bleeding or bruising.
• Dispose of injection equipment according to institution policy.

### Special considerations
If the medication is available in prefilled syringes, adjust the angle and depth of insertion according to needle length.

### Complications
Concentrated or irritating solutions may cause sterile abscesses to form. A natural immune response, this complication can be minimized by rotating injection sites. Repeated injections in the same site as that used in insulin-dependent patients can cause lipodystrophy.

### Documentation
Record the time and date of the injection, the medication administered and the dosage, the injection site and route, and the patient's reaction to the medication (for example, pain relief following administration of an analgesic).

SUSAN DONAHUE, RN, BSN

# Intramuscular Injections

*Intramuscular (I.M.) injections deposit medication deep into muscle tissue, where a large network of blood vessels can absorb it readily and quickly. This route*

## LOCATING I.M. INJECTION SITES

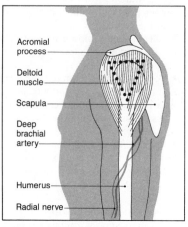

Acromial process

Deltoid muscle

Scapula

Deep brachial artery

Humerus

Radial nerve

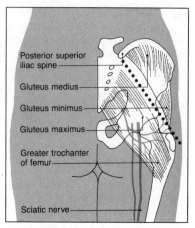

Posterior superior iliac spine

Gluteus medius

Gluteus minimus

Gluteus maximus

Greater trochanter of femur

Sciatic nerve

**Deltoid.** To locate the densest area of muscle and avoid major nerves and blood vessels, first find the lower edge of the acromial process and the point on the lateral arm in line with the axilla. Insert the needle 1″ to 2″ (2.5 to 5 cm) below the acromial process, usually 2 to 3 fingerbreadths, at a 90° angle or angled slightly toward the process.
*Standard ml injected:* 0.5 (range 0.5 to 2)

**Dorsogluteal** (upper outer corner of the gluteus maximus). Restrict injections to the area above and outside the diagonal line drawn from the posterior superior iliac spine to the greater trochanter of the femur. Another method is to divide the buttock into quadrants and inject in the upper outer quadrant, about 2″ to 3″ (5 to 7.6 cm) below the iliac crest. Insert the needle at a 90° angle to the muscle.
*Standard ml injected:* 2 to 4 (range 1 to 5)

---

of administration is preferred when rapid systemic action is desired and when relatively large doses (up to 5 ml in appropriate sites) are necessary. I.M. injections are recommended for patients who can't take medication orally and for drugs that are changed by digestive juices. And because muscle tissue has few sensory nerves, I.M. injection allows less painful administration of irritating drugs.

The site for an I.M. injection must be chosen carefully, taking into account the patient's general physical status and the purpose of the injection. I.M. injections should not be administered at inflamed, edematous, or irritated sites or those containing moles, birthmarks, scar tissue, or other lesions. I.M. injections may also be contraindicated in patients with impaired coagulation mechanisms, and in patients with occlusive peripheral vascular disease, edema, and shock, because these conditions impair peripheral absorption. I.M. injections require sterile technique to maintain the integrity of muscle tissue.

### Equipment

Patient's medication record and chart □ prescribed medication □ 3- to 5-ml prepackaged sterile disposable syringe □ 20G to 25G 1″ to 3″ disposable needle (depending on the medication and injection site) □ alcohol sponges.

The prescribed medication must be sterile. The needle may be packaged separately or already attached to the syringe. Needles used for I.M. injections are longer than subcutaneous needles because they

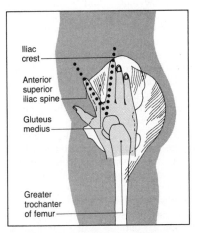

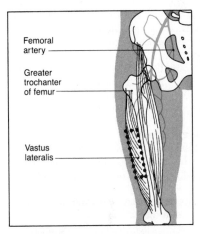

**Ventrogluteal** (gluteus medius and gluteus minimus). First, locate the greater trochanter of the femur with the heel of your hand. Then, spread your index and middle fingers to form a V from the anterior superior iliac spine to the farthest point along the iliac crest that you can reach. Insert the needle into the area between the two fingers at a 90° angle to the muscle. Remove your hand before inserting the needle.
*Standard ml injected:* 1 to 4 (range 1 to 5)

**Vastus lateralis.** Use the lateral muscle of the quadriceps group, along that length of the muscle from a handbreadth below the greater trochanter to a handbreadth above the knee. Insert the needle into the middle third of the muscle on a plane parallel to the surface on which the patient is lying. You may have to bunch the muscle before inserting the needle.
*Standard ml injected:* 1 to 4 (1 to 5; 1 to 3 for infants)

must reach deep into the muscle. Needle length also depends on the injection site, the patient's size, and the amount of subcutaneous fat covering the muscle. Needle gauge should be larger for additional tensile strength and easy transport of viscous solutions and suspensions.

## Preparation of equipment
Verify the order on the patient's medication record by checking it against the doctor's order. Also note if the patient has any allergies, especially before the first dose. Wash your hands; then check the prescribed medication for color and clarity. Never use medication that is cloudy or discolored, or that contains a precipitate, unless the manufacturer's instructions say that doing so is not harmful. Remember that for some drugs (such as suspensions) the presence of drug particles is normal. Observe for abnormal changes in the drugs. If in doubt, check with the pharmacist. Choose equipment appropriate to the prescribed medication and the injection site and make sure it works properly. The plunger rod should slide easily into the barrel. The needle hub should fit securely on the syringe; the needle should be straight, smooth, and free of burrs.

Draw up the prescribed amount of medication using the 3-label check system—read the label as you select the medication, as you draw up the medication, and after you have completed drawing up the medication to assure correct dosage. Then draw about 0.2 cc of air into the syringe. When the syringe is inverted during the injection, the air bubble rises to the plunger end of the syringe and follows the medication into the injection site. *The air clears the needle of medication and helps prevent leakage into the subcutaneous tissue following injection by creating an air block that reduces reflux (tracking) along the needle path.*

Cover the needle with its protective sheath. Dispose of waste properly. Gather all necessary equipment and proceed to the patient's room.

## Essential steps

• Confirm the patient's identity by asking his name and checking his wristband for name, room number, and bed number.

• Provide privacy and explain the procedure to the patient.

• Select an appropriate injection site. The gluteal muscles (gluteus medius and minimus, and the upper outer corner of the gluteus maximus) are most commonly used for healthy adults, although the deltoid muscle may be used for a small-volume injection (2 ml or less). For infants and children, the vastus lateralis muscle of the thighs is used most often, because it's usually the best developed and contains no large nerves or blood vessels, minimizing the risk of serious injury. The rectus femoris muscle may also be used in infants but is usually contraindicated in adults. Remember to always rotate injection sites for patients who require repeated injections.

• Position and drape the patient appropriately, making sure the site is well exposed and that lighting is adequate.

• Loosen the protective needle sheath, but don't remove it.

• After locating the injection site (see *Locating I.M. Injection Sites*, pages 342-343), cleanse the skin at the site with an alcohol sponge. Move the sponge outward in a circular motion, to a circumference of about 2" (5.1 cm) from the injection site. Then allow the skin to dry (the antiseptic will evaporate readily) *to prevent the alcohol from being introduced into the muscle tissue as the needle is inserted,* causing pain or burning when

it reaches the sensory nerve endings of subcutaneous tissue. Keep the alcohol sponge for later use.

• With the thumb and index finger of your nondominant hand, gently stretch the skin of the injection site taut.

• Holding the syringe in your dominant hand, remove the needle sheath by slipping it between the free fingers of your nondominant hand and then drawing back the syringe.

• Position the syringe at a 90° angle to the skin surface, with the needle a couple of inches from the skin. Tell the patient that he will feel a prick as you insert the needle. Then, as you say this, quickly and firmly thrust the needle through the skin and subcutaneous tissue, deep into the muscle.

• Support the syringe with your nondominant hand, if desired. Pull back slightly on the plunger with your dominant hand to aspirate for blood. If no blood appears, place your thumb on the plunger rod and *slowly* inject the medication into the muscle. *A slow, steady injection rate allows the muscle to distend gradually and accept the medication under minimal pressure.* You should feel little or no resistance against the force of the injection. The air bubble in the syringe should follow the medication into the injection site.

 • If blood appears in the syringe on aspiration, the needle is in a blood vessel. If this occurs, stop the injection, withdraw the needle, prepare another injection with new equipment, and inject another site. Don't inject the bloody solution.

• After the injection, gently but rapidly remove the needle at a 90° angle.

• Cover the injection site immediately with the used alcohol sponge, apply gentle pressure, and, unless contraindicated, massage the relaxed muscle *to help distribute the drug and promote absorption.*

• Remove the alcohol sponge and inspect the injection site for signs of active bleeding or bruising. If bleeding continues, apply pressure to the site; if bruising occurs, you may apply ice.

● Discard all equipment appropriately.

## Special considerations

To slow absorption, some drugs for I.M. administration are dissolved in oil or other special solutions. Mix these preparations well before drawing them into the syringe.

Never use the gluteal muscles, which develop from walking, as the injection site for a child under age 3 or who has been walking for less than a year. Never inject sensitive muscles, especially those which twitch or tremble when you assess site landmarks and tissue depth with your fingertips. Injections in these trigger areas may cause sharp or referred pain, such as the pain caused by nerve trauma.

Keep a rotation record that lists all available injection sites, divided into various body areas, for patients who require repeated injections. Rotate from a site in the first area to a site in each of the other areas. Then return to a site in the first area that is at least 1″ (2.5 cm) away from the previous injection site in that area.

If the patient has experienced pain or emotional trauma from repeated injections, consider numbing the area before cleansing it by holding ice on it for several seconds. If you must inject more than 5 ml of solution, divide the solution and inject it at two separate sites.

Always encourage the patient to relax the muscle you'll be injecting, *because injections into tense muscles are more painful than usual and may bleed more readily.*

I.M. injections can traumatize local muscle cells, causing elevated serum levels of enzymes (creatine phosphokinase, CPK) that can be confused with the elevated enzymes resulting from damage to cardiac muscle, as in myocardial infarction. To distinguish between skeletal and cardiac muscle damage, diagnostic tests for suspected myocardial infarction must identify the isoenzyme of CPK specific to cardiac muscle (CPK-MB/CPK$_2$) and include tests for lactic dehydrogenase (LDH) and serum glutamic-oxaloacetic transaminase (SGOT).

Oral or I.V. routes are preferred for administration of drugs that are poorly absorbed by muscle tissue, such as phenytoin, digoxin, chlordiazepoxide, diazepam, and haloperidol.

## Complications

Accidental injection of concentrated or irritating medications into subcutaneous tissue, or other areas where it can't be fully absorbed, can cause sterile abscesses. Such abscesses result from a natural immune response in which phagocytes attempt to remove the foreign matter.

Failure to rotate sites in patients who require repeated injections can lead to deposits of unabsorbed drugs. Such deposits can reduce the desired pharmacologic effect and may lead to abscess formation or tissue fibrosis.

## Documentation

Chart the drug administered, dosage, date, time, route of administration, and injection site. Also, note the patient's tolerance of injection and its effects, including any side effects.

SUSAN DONAHUE, RN, BSN

# Z-track Injection

*The Z-track method of intramuscular injection prevents leakage (tracking) into subcutaneous tissue. It is used with certain drugs—primarily iron preparations, such as iron dextran—that irritate and discolor subcutaneous tissue. Lateral displacement of the skin during the injection helps seal the drug in the muscle. This procedure requires careful attention to technique, because leakage into subcutaneous tissue can cause patient discomfort and may permanently stain some tissues.*

## Equipment

Patient's medication record and chart □

two 20G needles at least 2″ long □ prescribed medication □ 3- to 5-ml syringe □ two sterile alcohol sponges.

## Preparation of equipment

Verify the order on the patient's medication record by checking it against the doctor's order. Wash your hands. Attach one needle to the syringe, and draw up the prescribed medication. Then, draw 0.2 to 0.5 cc of air (depending on hospital policy) into the syringe. Remove the first needle, and attach the second *to prevent leakage into subcutaneous tissue as the needle is inserted.*

## Essential steps

• Confirm the patient's identity, explain the procedure, and provide privacy.
• Place the patient in the lateral position, exposing the opposite gluteal muscle to be used as the injection site. The patient may also be placed in the prone position.
• Cleanse an area on the upper outer quadrant of the patient's buttock with a sterile alcohol sponge.
• Displace the skin laterally by pulling it about ½″ (1 cm) away from the injection site.
• Insert the needle into the muscle at a 90° angle.
• Aspirate for blood return; if none appears, inject the drug slowly, followed by the air. *Injecting air after the drug helps clear the needle and prevents tracking of the medication through subcutaneous tissues as the needle is withdrawn.*
• Wait 10 seconds before withdrawing the needle *to ensure dispersion of the medication.*
• Withdraw the needle slowly. Then, release the displaced skin and subcutaneous tissue *to seal the needle track.*
• Encourage the patient to walk or to move about in bed *to facilitate absorption from the injection site.*
• Discard the needles and syringe according to hospital policy.

## Special considerations

Never inject more than 5 ml into a single site, using the Z-track method.

Don't massage the injection site, because it might force the drug into the subcutaneous tissue. Alternate gluteal sites for repeat injections. If the patient is on bed rest, encourage active range-of-motion exercises or perform passive range-of-motion exercises *to facilitate absorption from the injection site.*

## Documentation

Record the medication, dosage, date, time, and site of injection on the patient's medication record. Include the patient's response to the injected drug in the nurse's notes if necessary.

SUSAN DONAHUE, RN, BSN

# Intraarticular Injection

*An intraarticular injection delivers drugs directly to the synovial cavity of a joint to relieve pain, help preserve function and prevent contractures, and delay muscle atrophy. Drugs commonly administered intraarticularly include corticosteroids, anesthetics, and lubricants. Rarely, antiseptics, analgesics, and counterirritants may be injected by this route. Before intraarticular injection, synovial fluid may be withdrawn to relieve pressure or for laboratory analysis.*

*Usually performed by a doctor with a nurse assisting, an intraarticular injection requires sterile technique. Such an injection is contraindicated in patients with joint infection, joint instability or fracture, or systemic fungal infection.*

## Equipment

Patient's medication record and chart □ 3-ml and 5- or 10-ml syringes □ prescribed medication □ pillows □ sterile towel, gloves, cotton balls, and gauze pads □ sterile emesis basin □ antiseptic solution □ sterile fenestrated drape □ local anesthetic □ 25G ⅝″ needle □ 18G 1½″ needle □ adhesive bandage □ op-

## COMMON INTRAARTICULAR INJECTION SITES

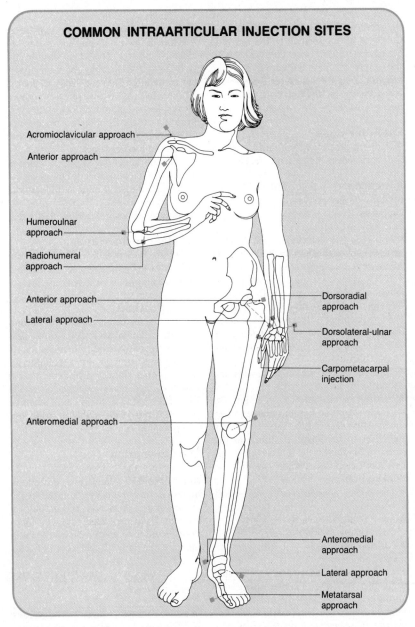

Acromioclavicular approach

Anterior approach

Humeroulnar approach

Radiohumeral approach

Anterior approach

Lateral approach

Anteromedial approach

Dorsoradial approach

Dorsolateral-ulnar approach

Carpometacarpal injection

Anteromedial approach

Lateral approach

Metatarsal approach

tional: sterile test tubes for synovial fluid aspiration, with appropriate additives and specimen labels, and 10- or 20-ml syringe for aspirating synovial fluid specimen.

Sterile povidone-iodine sponges may be used instead of the antiseptic solution and the sterile cotton balls or gauze pads.

### Preparation of equipment

Verify the order on the patient's medication record by checking it against the doctor's order. Wash your hands. Draw the prescribed amount of medication into the 5- or 10-ml syringe before entering the patient's room. Label the syringe with the name of the medication and the amount. Take the container from which you drew the medication with you *so the doctor can verify the syringe contents.*

## Essential steps

• Confirm the patient's identity, explain the procedure to the patient, and provide privacy.
• Position the patient comfortably. The joint to be injected should be stabilized, supported (with pillows, if necessary), and fully exposed.
• Using aseptic technique, open the sterile towel and place it on the bedside table *to create a sterile field.*
• Using aseptic technique, open the syringes, needles, and cotton balls or gauze pads and drop them onto the sterile field.
• After putting on the sterile gloves, the doctor picks up the sterile cotton balls or gauze pads and holds them over the emesis basin.
• Pour the antiseptic solution over the cotton balls or gauze pads.
• The doctor cleanses the injection site with the saturated cotton balls or gauze pads. After draping the site, he checks the label on the local anesthetic as the nurse holds the bottle. Then turn it upside down so the doctor can fill the 3-ml syringe.
• The doctor anesthetizes the skin and subcutaneous tissue at the injection site, using the 25G ⅝″ needle.
*To aspirate synovial fluid:*
• Position the sterile test tubes in the correct order.
• The doctor withdraws synovial fluid with the 18G 1½″ needle, using the 10-ml syringe. The needle is left in the joint *for the subsequent injection of medication.* The syringe with the specimen can be set aside until after the procedure.
• After completing the intraarticular injection, the doctor will attach a needle to the specimen syringe and insert appropriate specimens into the test tubes. Label the test tubes appropriately and send them to the laboratory.

*To perform intraarticular injection:*
• Hand the 5- or 10-ml medication syringe—with an 18G 1½″ needle attached—to the doctor, who then injects the medication into the synovial cavity. (If synovial fluid was aspirated, remove the needle and hand the doctor the medication syringe. He attaches the syringe to the needle already in the joint and injects the medication.)
• After the injection, apply pressure to the site and (if appropriate) massage the area gently for 1 or 2 minutes *to facilitate absorption.*
• Apply an adhesive bandage to the site.

## Special considerations

Advise the patient to avoid excessive use of the affected joint, *because the injected medications may mask pain.*

## Complications

Because the medication may infiltrate and initially irritate surrounding tissue, local joint pain may actually increase for 24 to 48 hours after an intraarticular injection. This should subside within a couple of days. However, fever, persistent increased pain, redness, and swelling may indicate septic arthritis, a serious complication caused by contamination.

## Documentation

Record that the doctor injected medication, the dose, date, time and site of injection, and the doctor's name in the nurse's notes. Also note the amount of synovial fluid aspirated and any laboratory studies requested (if applicable). Describe the patient's tolerance of the injection.

MARGARET J. GRIFFITHS, RN, MSN

# Intrathecal Injection

*An intrathecal injection allows direct administration of medication into the subarachnoid space of the spinal canal.*

Certain drugs—such as anti-infectives, or antineoplastics used to treat meningeal leukemia—are administered by this route because they can't readily penetrate the subdural membrane through the bloodstream. Intrathecal injection may also be used to deliver anesthetics such as lidocaine hydrochloride to achieve regional anesthesia as in spinal anesthesia or epidural block.

An invasive procedure performed by a doctor under sterile conditions, with the nurse assisting, intrathecal injection requires informed patient consent. The injection site is usually between the third and fourth (or fourth and fifth) lumbar vertebrae, well below the spinal cord, preventing the risk of paralysis. This procedure may be preceded by the withdrawal of spinal fluid for laboratory analysis. Contraindications to intrathecal injection include inflammation or infection at the puncture site, septicemia, and spinal deformities (especially when considered as an anesthesia route).

## Equipment

Lumbar puncture tray □ fenestrated drape (if not on the lumbar puncture tray) □ antiseptic solution □ povidone-iodine sponges (or cotton balls or gauze pads) □ sterile disposable gloves □ local anesthetic □ alcohol sponges □ 3- or 5-ml syringe □ 25G ⅝" needle □ syringe containing prescribed drug □ adhesive bandage □ optional: pillows, shave preparation tray, specimen containers with labels.

The lumbar puncture tray, drape, disposable gloves, and cotton balls or gauze pads should all be sterile.

## Essential steps

• Wash your hands.
• Make sure the patient or a responsible family member has signed the consent form.
• Reinforce the doctor's explanation of the procedure to the patient. Tell him that he may experience a stinging sensation when the anesthetic is injected.
• Tell the patient to void just before the procedure, *because he may have to stay*

in bed several hours afterward.
• Provide privacy. If necessary, shave the injection site.
• Place the patient in the right or left lateral position, as directed by the doctor. Use pillows, if permissible, to make him comfortable. Be sure the puncture site is exposed.
• Using aseptic technique, open the lumbar puncture tray and the fenestrated drape. The tray serves as the sterile field.
• If povidone-iodine sponges are not available, pour the antiseptic solution over the cotton balls or gauze pads.
• The doctor puts on the sterile gloves and cleanses the injection site with the povidone-iodine sponges or the saturated cotton balls or gauze pads.
• He drapes the patient with the fenestrated drape so that the area surrounding the third and fourth lumbar vertebrae (or other appropriate site, as directed) is exposed.
• Wipe the diaphragm of the anesthetic bottle with the alcohol sponge. Leave the sponge on the bottle. Don't set the bottle on the sterile field.
• Using aseptic technique, open the syringes and needle and drop them onto the sterile field.
• Show the doctor the label on the local anesthetic to verify its type and strength. Then, turn the bottle upside down, *so the doctor can fill the 3- or 5-ml syringe, using the 25G ⅝" needle, without contaminating the equipment.*
• After the doctor anesthetizes the skin and subcutaneous tissue, he inserts the lumbar puncture needle (from the tray) into the lumbar space. At this point he may collect some spinal fluid for laboratory analysis. If so, label all specimen containers correctly and send them to the laboratory immediately after the procedure.
• Remove the needle from the syringe containing the prescribed medication and hand the syringe to the doctor.
• The doctor attaches the syringe to the lumbar puncture needle and injects the medication into the subarachnoid space.
• After the needle is withdrawn, apply

an adhesive bandage to the site.

• Press gently on the injection site for a couple of minutes, as directed, *to prevent medication seepage.*

• Place the patient in the position ordered by the doctor.

### Special considerations

If you fill the syringe with the prescribed drug, make sure the doctor verifies the drug and the dose before administering the injection.

If the patient can't maintain the correct position, help him maintain back flexion by gently but firmly grasping him behind the neck and knees.

Encourage the patient to drink fluids, as permitted, to help replace any spinal fluid loss.

After injection of chemotherapeutic drugs, be especially alert for specific drug side effects.

### Documentation

Note the time and date of the injection, the dose, any changes in vital signs or neurologic status, fluid leakage or bleeding at the injection site, and the patient's response.

MARGARET J. GRIFFITHS, RN, MSN

---

# INTRAVASCULAR ADMINISTRATION

# Addition of Drugs to an I.V. Solution

*Various transfer devices can be used to add drugs to an I.V. solution. The common syringe and needle are used to draw up medications, reconstitute powdered drugs, and make transfers. A single- or double-headed needle is used to transfer dissolved medication in a vial to an I.V. bottle with intact vacuum. A syringe with a filter needle or filter straw can be used to transfer medication in an ampul to a bottle or bag; an ampul transfer device can be used to add medication only to a bottle with intact vacuum.*

*Before adding any drug to an I.V. solution, it's necessary to establish compatibility of the solution with the drug. Adding drugs to blood is contraindicated because it complicates identifying the source of an adverse reaction.*

### Equipment

Drug to be added □ I.V. solution □ transfer device □ diluent, if necessary □ patient's medication record and chart □ compatibility and stability reference source □ I.V. administration set or sterile I.V. cap □ syringe with filter needle □ labels (to note drug added) □ alcohol sponges □ optional: 250- or 500-ml container; opaque paper or aluminum foil.

You'll also need a needle when using a syringe with a filter needle or filter straw and an ampul transfer device. A 4″ x 4″ gauze sponge helps prevent cuts when you break open an ampul. Always use a small, thin needle (25G 1″) for multiple punctures of a vial, bottle, or bag. A small puncture reseals better.

### Preparation of equipment

Verify the order on the patient's medication record by checking it against the doctor's order. Check hospital policy *to see if you're allowed to add the drug to the I.V. solution.* If so, find out how the drug to be added is packaged, and then obtain the appropriate transfer device and any necessary diluent. Check the compatibility and dosage of the drug, diluent, and I.V. solution. If the drug's stability is limited, mix it in a 100-, 250-, or 500-ml container *to avoid loss of potency and waste.* If the drug becomes unstable after exposure to light, mix it and wrap it with opaque paper or foil. The tubing needn't be covered—only the I.V. bag or bottle.

When you remove the metal cap from an I.V. bottle, you'll see a protective rubber disk. This disk is sterile and needn't be swabbed with alcohol for its first puncture. Drugs can be injected through it with a needle. When you're ready to connect the I.V. tubing, remove the disk *to expose the sterile bottle diaphragm.* You should hear a pop when you remove the disk (unless you've already punctured it), assuring sterility of the container. The bottle top is sterile and needn't be swabbed first.

### Essential steps
• Wash your hands.
• Further verify that you have the correct drug by comparing its label with the order on the medication record. Read the label as you prepare the drug additive and again after you've added it to the solution.
*To use a syringe and needle:*
• Remove the protective metal cap from the drug vial. You don't have to wipe the vial top with alcohol before the first puncture, since it is sterile. After the first puncture, however, wipe the top with a sterile alcohol sponge before each subsequent puncture.
• If the drug to be added is a powder, aspirate the correct amount of diluent into the syringe and inject it into the drug vial. Roll the vial between your hands *to dissolve all particles.*
• If the I.V. container is a bottle, remove the protective metal cap, leaving the rubber seal intact. If the I.V. container is a bag, swab the rubber-stoppered port.
• Inject the drug and gently rotate the bottle or squeeze the bag *to mix the solution.*
*To use a single-headed needle or pin:*
• Remove the protective cap from the needle or pin on top of the drug vial. Then remove the metal cap from the I.V. bottle.
• Invert the medication vial and insert the pin into the I.V. bottle's main port *so the vacuum draws the drug into the bottle.* Remove the vial and gently rotate the bottle *to mix the solution.*
*To use a double-headed needle or pin:*
• Remove the protective cap from the drug vial and swab the rubber seal with

an alcohol sponge, if desired. If you're adding medication to an I.V. bag, remove the protective outer wrapping.
• If the drug to be added is a powder, add the appropriate diluent with a needle and syringe and roll the vial between your hands *to dissolve all particles.*
• Remove the outside cover of the double-headed needle *to expose the shorter needle.* Insert this needle into the drug vial and remove the second half of the needle cover, exposing the longer needle.
• If you're adding medication to an I.V. bottle, remove the protective metal cap. (If you're using an I.V. bag, wipe the rubber-stoppered port with an alcohol sponge.) Invert the medication vial, and insert the longer needle into the center hole of the appropriate seal. The vacuum then draws the drug into the I.V. container. Remove the vial and gently rotate the container *to mix the solution.*
*To use a syringe with a filter needle or straw:*
• If the I.V. container is a bottle, remove the protective metal cap and wipe the seal or port with alcohol, if desired.
• Place the filter needle or straw on the syringe. Then wipe the ampul neck with an alcohol sponge, wrap it in a gauze pad, and snap off the neck, directing the force away from your body.
• Aspirate the ampul contents with the syringe. Then replace the filter needle or straw with a 25G 1″ needle.
• Inject the drug into the I.V. container and rotate the container *to mix the solution.*
*To use an ampul transfer device:*
• Remove the protective metal cap from the I.V. bottle and wipe the rubber seal with an alcohol sponge, if desired.
• Swab the ampul neck with alcohol, wrap it in a gauze pad, and snap it off, directing the force away from your body.
• Attach a 25G 1″ needle to the adapter end of the transfer device. Completely insert the opposite end of the device into the ampul.
• Insert the needle into the injection site on the I.V. bottle's rubber seal. The vacuum draws the drug into the bottle.

- Tilt the ampul to keep the tip of the device covered with the drug. Then rotate the bottle *to mix the solution.*
*After preparing the solution:*
- Recheck the drug dose and I.V. solution *to prevent error.*
- Connect the I.V. administration set or sterile protective cap (provided by the manufacturer) to the I.V. container *to prevent contamination.*
- Fill out the medication-added label and place it on the I.V. container. The label should include the date, drug dose, infusion rate, your initials, and the time the drug was added to the I.V. container.

### Special considerations
Maintain sterile technique throughout this procedure. Since the vacuum of an I.V. bottle remains intact for only one puncture, use a syringe and needle to transfer any other drugs to the bottle. After adding diluent to a powdered drug in a vial, use a filter needle for the transfer, if hospital policy allows.

When making multiple drug transfers, add only one drug at a time. Always add the most concentrated drug first and any colored drugs last. Mix the solution thoroughly and examine it after adding each drug for precipitation, discoloration, or cloudiness.

To add a drug to an I.V. solution that has already been hung, always close the flow clamp *to prevent delivering a bolus of the drug to the patient.* Insert a syringe and needle into the injection site of a vented I.V. bottle or the injection port of an I.V. bag after wiping it with alcohol. Always rotate the container gently *to mix the solution.* Then open the flow clamp and adjust the flow rate.

When administering an I.V. solution with drugs or other additives, watch for signs of drug sensitivity or intolerance.

### Complications
Excessively high drug concentrations in the I.V. solution can cause complications such as sclerosis, thrombosis, hemolysis, or phlebitis. Extravasation of some drugs into subcutaneous tissues can cause tissue necrosis.

### Documentation
As indicated, record the date and time of administration, your initials or name, the drug name and dosage, the amount and type of I.V. solution, and the duration of infusion in the appropriate places on the patient's chart. Depending on policy in your institution, record some or all of the above information in the nurse's notes, the intake and output record, and the I.V. record sheet. Remember to include the amount of fluids infused with I.V. medications on the patient's intake and output record.

PATRICE M. NASIELSKI, RN

# Drug Infusion Through a Secondary I.V. Line

*A secondary I.V. line is a complete I.V. set—container, tubing, and needle—connected to the injection port of a primary line instead of to the I.V. catheter or needle. It can be used for continuous or intermittent drug infusion. When used continuously, a secondary I.V. line permits drug infusion and titration while the primary line maintains a constant total infusion rate. When used intermittently, it's commonly called a piggyback set; in this case, the primary line maintains venous access between drug doses. Antibiotics are most commonly administered by intermittent (piggyback) infusion. You can instantly recognize a true piggyback system since the setup consists of a small infusion bottle for the intermittent drug, with one bottle hung below the other.*

*I.V. pumps may be used to maintain constant infusion rates, especially with a drug such as lidocaine. A pump allows more accurate titration of drug dosage and helps maintain venous access since the drug is delivered under sufficient pressure to prevent clot formation in the I.V. cannula.*

## PIGGYBACK SET

A piggyback set—used solely for intermittent drug infusion—includes a small I.V. bottle, short tubing, and usually a macrodrip system. It connects into a primary line's upper Y-port (piggyback port). For the set to work, you must use an extension hook to position the primary I.V. container below the piggyback container, as shown.

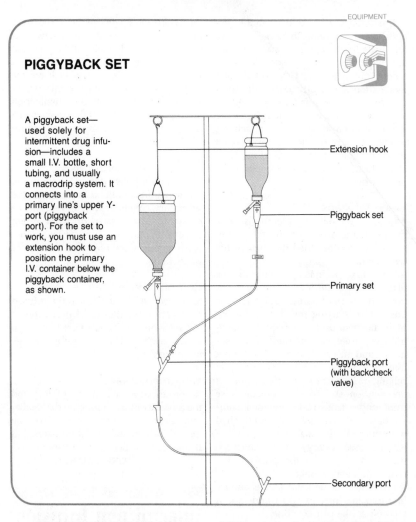

Extension hook

Piggyback set

Primary set

Piggyback port (with backcheck valve)

Secondary port

---

*A secondary I.V. line shouldn't be connected to a hyperalimentation line, because of the risk of contamination.*

### Equipment

Prescribed I.V. medication □ prescribed I.V. solution □ administration set □ 22G 1″ needle □ alcohol sponges □ 1″ adhesive tape □ extension hook and appropriate solution for intermittent piggyback infusion □ saline solution for infusion with incompatible solutions (optional).

For intermittent infusion, the primary line often has a piggyback port with a backcheck valve (see above), which stops the flow from the primary line during drug infusion and returns to the primary flow after infusion. A volume-control set can also be used with an intermittent infusion line.

### Preparation of equipment

Verify the order and wash your hands. Inspect the I.V. container for cracks or leaks and check drug compatibility with the primary solution. See if the primary line has a secondary injection port. If it doesn't, and the medications will be given regularly, replace the I.V. set with a new one that has a secondary injection port.

If necessary, add the drug to the secondary I.V. solution. To do so, remove any seals from the secondary container and wipe the main port with a sterile alcohol sponge. Inject the prescribed medication and gently agitate the solution *to mix the medication thoroughly.* Properly label the I.V. mixture. Insert the administration set spike and attach the needle. Remove the needle cover, open the flow clamp, and prime the line. Then close the flow clamp and replace the needle cover.

### Essential steps

• Confirm the patient's identity by asking his name and checking the name, room number, and bed number on his wristband.
• If the drug is incompatible with the primary I.V. solution, replace the solution with normal saline and flush the line before starting the drug infusion. Many hospital protocols require removing the primary (incompatible) I.V. solution and inserting a sterile I.V. plug into the container until you're ready to rehang it. *This will maintain sterility of the solution* and prevent someone else from inadvertently restarting the incompatible solution before the line is flushed with normal saline solution.
• Hang the secondary container and wipe the injection port of the primary line with an alcohol sponge.
• Insert the needle from the secondary line into the injection port and tape it securely to the primary line.
• *To run the secondary container solely,* lower the primary container with an extension hook. *To run both containers simultaneously,* place them at the same height.
• Open the clamp and adjust the drip rate. *For continuous infusion,* set the secondary solution to the desired drip rate; then adjust the primary solution *to achieve the desired total infusion rate.*
• *For intermittent infusion,* adjust the primary drip rate as required upon completion of the secondary solution. If the secondary solution tubing is being reused, close the clamp on the tubing and follow

the institution's policy: either remove the needle and replace it with a new one, or leave it securely taped in the injection port and label it with the time it was first used. In this case, also leave the empty container in place until you replace it with a new dose of medication at the prescribed time. If the tubing won't be reused, discard it appropriately with the I.V. container.

### Special considerations

If institution policy allows, use a pump for drug infusion. Put a time tape on the secondary container *to help prevent inaccurate administration rate.* When reusing secondary tubing, change it according to hospital policy (usually every 24 to 48 hours).

### Complications

Side effects and reactions to the infused drug can occur. Repeated punctures of the secondary injection port can cause an imperfect seal, with possible leakage or contamination.

### Documentation

Record the amount and type of drug and the amount of I.V. solution on the intake-output and medication records. Note the date, duration, and rate of infusion, and the patient's response, where applicable.

PATRICE M. NASIELSKI, RN

---

# Intermittent Infusion Injection Device
### [*Heparin lock*]

*An intermittent infusion injection device—or heparin lock—eliminates the need for multiple venipunctures or to maintain venous access with a continuous I.V. infusion. It allows intermittent administration through this device by infusion or by the I.V. bolus or I.V. push injection methods. Dilute heparin solution is often injected as the final step in this procedure to prevent clotting in the device. When this is done, the device must be flushed with normal saline solution before and after the prescribed medication is administered in case the heparin and the medication are incompatible. The device may then be reflushed with the heparin solution.*

## Equipment

Patient's medication record and chart □ three 3-ml syringes with 22G 1″ needles □ normal saline solution □ sterile alcohol sponges □ prescribed medication in an I.V. container with administration set and needle (for infusion) or in a syringe with needle (for I.V. bolus or push injection) □ tourniquet □ tape □ dilute heparin solution (optional).

The concentration of dilute heparin solution ranges from 10 to 100 U/ml. The solution is available in a closed cartridge injection system in doses of 10 to 100 U/ml. If this system is used, substitute its syringe for the 3-ml syringe and the heparin cartridge for the heparin solution.

## Preparation of equipment

Verify the order on the patient's medication record by checking it against the doctor's order. Wash your hands, and then wipe the tops of the saline, heparin, and medication containers with sterile alcohol sponges. Fill two of the 3-ml syringes with saline solution; draw 1 ml of heparin solution into the third syringe if necessary. If you'll be infusing medication, insert the administration set spike into the I.V. container, attach the appropriate-sized needle, and prime the line. If you'll be giving an I.V. injection, fill a syringe with the prescribed drug.

## Essential steps

● Confirm the patient's identity by asking his name and checking the name, room number, and bed number on his wristband. Explain the procedure.
● Wipe the injection port of the intermittent infusion device with an alcohol sponge and insert the needle of a saline-filled syringe.
● Aspirate the syringe and observe for blood. If none appears, apply a tourni-

quet slightly above the site, keep it in place for 1 to 2 minutes, and then aspirate again. If blood still doesn't appear, inject the saline solution slowly.

● Stop the injection immediately if you feel any resistance, which indicates that the device is occluded. If this occurs, insert a new intermittent infusion device (heparin lock).
● If you feel no resistance, watch for signs of infiltration (puffiness or pain at the site) as you slowly inject the saline solution. If these signs occur, insert a new intermittent infusion device.
● If blood is aspirated, slowly inject the saline and observe for signs of infiltration. *The saline solution flushes out any residual heparin solution that might be incompatible with the medication.*
● Withdraw the saline syringe and needle.

*To use I.V. bolus or push injections:*
● Insert the needle and syringe for the bolus or push injection into the injection port of the device.
● Inject the medication at the required rate. Then remove the needle from the injection port.
● Insert the needle of the remaining saline-filled syringe into the injection port and slowly inject the saline solution *to flush all medication through the device.*
● Remove the needle and syringe, and insert and inject the heparin flush solution *in order to prevent clotting in the device.*

*To administer an infusion:*
● Insert and tape the needle attached to the administration set.
● Open the infusion line and adjust the flow rate as necessary.
● Infuse medication for the prescribed length of time; then flush the device with saline and heparin, as you would after a bolus or push injection.

## Special considerations

If you're giving a bolus injection of a drug that's incompatible with saline, such as diazepam (Valium), flush the device with bacteriostatic water.

In some institutions, the device is flushed with 2 to 3 ml of normal saline solution instead of heparin flush solution *to prevent clotting in the cannula.*

Intermittent infusion devices should be changed regularly, according to hospital policy (usually every 48 to 72 hours).

### Complications

Infiltration and a specific reaction to the infused drug(s) are the most common complications.

### Documentation

Record the type and amount of drug(s) administered and the time of administration on the medication and intake and output records. Include all I.V. solutions used to dilute the medication and flush the line on the intake record. Document the use of dilute heparin solution on the patient's chart and in the nurse's notes.

MARGARET J. GRIFFITHS, RN, MSN

# I.V. Bolus Injections
### [*I.V. push injections*]

*The I.V. bolus injection method allows rapid intravenous administration of a drug. It may be used in an emergency to provide an immediate drug effect. It can also be used to achieve peak drug levels in the bloodstream, to deliver drugs that can't be diluted (such as diazepam, digoxin, and phenytoin), or to administer drugs that can't be given intramuscularly because they're toxic to muscle tissue or because the patient's ability to absorb them is impaired.*

*The term bolus generally refers to the concentration or amount of a drug. I.V. push is a technique for rapid intravenous injection.*

*Bolus doses of medication may be injected directly into a vein or through an existing I.V. line. The medication administered by these methods takes effect rapidly, so the patient must be monitored for an adverse reaction, such as cardiac arrhythmia. I.V. bolus injections are contraindicated when rapid admin-*istration of a drug could cause life-threatening complications or when the drug requires dilution. For certain drugs, the safe rate of injection is specified by the manufacturer.

### Equipment

Patient's medication record and chart □ prescribed medication □ 20G needle and syringe □ diluent, if necessary □ tourniquet □ povidone-iodine sponge □ sterile alcohol sponge □ sterile 2″ x 2″ gauze pad □ adhesive bandage □ optional: winged-tip needle with catheter and second syringe (and needle) filled with normal saline solution.

The frequent use of a winged-tip needle for this purpose is largely because it can be quickly and easily inserted. This makes it ideal for the repeated administration of drugs, as in weekly or monthly chemotherapy.

### Essential steps

• Verify the doctor's order.
• Know the actions, side effects, and administration rate of the drug to be injected. Draw up the prescribed medication in the syringe; dilute it, if necessary.
• Confirm the patient's identity.
• Explain the procedure to the patient. Observe for drug effects (especially untoward effects) immediately after drug administration.

*To give direct injections:*
• Select the largest vein suitable for an injection. *The larger the vein, the more diluted the drug will become as it travels through it, minimizing vascular irritation.*
• Apply a tourniquet above the injection site to distend the vein.
• Cleanse the injection site with the sterile povidone-iodine sponge. Then cleanse it with the sterile alcohol sponge, working outward from the puncture site in a circular motion *to prevent recontamination with skin bacteria.*
• If you're using the syringe's needle, insert it into the vein at a 30° angle with the bevel upwards. The bevel should reach ¼″ (0.6 cm) into the vein. If you're using a winged-tip needle, insert the needle

(bevel up), tape the butterfly wings in place when you see blood return in the tubing, and attach the syringe containing the drug.
• Pull back on the plunger of the syringe and check for blood backflow, *which indicates that the needle is in the vein.*
• Remove the tourniquet and inject the drug at the appropriate rate.
• Pull back slightly on the plunger of the syringe and check for blood backflow again. *If blood appears, it indicates that the needle remained in place and all of the injected medication entered the vein.*
• If you're using a winged-tip needle, flush the line with the normal saline solution from the second syringe *to ensure delivery of all the medication into the vein.*
• Withdraw the needle and apply pressure to the injection site with the sterile gauze pad for 3 minutes *to prevent hematoma formation.*
• Apply the adhesive bandage to the site after bleeding has stopped.
*To give injections through an existing I.V. line:*
• Check the compatibility of the medication with the I.V. solution.
• Close the flow clamp, wipe the injection port with a sterile alcohol sponge, and inject the drug as you would for direct injection. (Some I.V. lines have a secondary injection port; others have a latex flashbulb at the end of the I.V. tubing where the needle is attached.)
• Open the flow clamp and readjust the flow rate.
• If the drug isn't compatible with the I.V. solution, flush the line with normal saline solution before and after the injection.

### Special considerations
Because drugs administered by I.V. bolus or push injection are delivered directly into the circulatory system and can produce an immediate effect, signs of an acute allergic reaction or anaphylaxis can develop rapidly. If any signs of anaphylaxis occur (dyspnea, cyanosis, convulsions, or increasing respiratory distress), notify the doctor immediately

and begin emergency procedures, as necessary. Also watch for signs of extravasation, such as swelling, the absence of blood backflow, and a sluggish flow rate. If extravasation occurs, stop the injection, estimate the amount of infiltration, and notify the doctor. If you're giving diazepam or chlordiazepoxide hydrochloride through a winged-tip needle or I.V. line, flush with bacteriostatic water instead of saline *to prevent drug precipitation due to incompatibility.*

### Complications
Excessively rapid drug administration may cause adverse effects, depending on the drug administered.

### Documentation
Record the amount and type of drug administered, and duration of the administration in the medication record. Note drug effect and any adverse reactions.
                    PATRICE M. NASIELSKI, RN

# Ready Injectable

*A ready injectable—commercially premeasured medication packaged with a syringe and needle—allows for rapid drug administration in an emergency. Usually, preparing a ready injectable takes only 15 to 20 seconds. Other advantages include the reduced risk of breaking sterile technique during administration and the easy identification of medication and dose.*

*Some ready injectables can be injected directly into an I.V. line; others require dilution in an I.V. solution. Knowing the drug's indications, contraindications, effects, and potential side effects is particularly important, since medications administered intravenously take effect rapidly.*

### Equipment
Prepackaged ready injectable □ sterile alcohol sponge □ I.V. solution for dilu-

tion, if necessary.

## Essential steps

• Identify the medication three times: when taking it from the shelf or drawer; during preparation; and just before administration.
• Read the package directions *to determine if the medication requires dilution.*
• Make sure the patient's I.V. site is patent. Check for good blood return and proper infusion of I.V. fluid; make sure the surrounding skin isn't puffy, red, or inflamed.
• Open the package and ensure that all sterile caps are in place.
• *If the medication is in a vial,* remove the protector caps from the injector and vial. Then thread the vial into the injector and turn it until you meet resistance.
• *If the medication is in the syringe barrel,* thread the rod into the plunger and turn it until you meet resistance.
• Remove the needle guard and expel the air.
• Cleanse the injection site with a sterile alcohol sponge.
• *If the medication requires dilution,* inject it into the appropriate-sized container of compatible I.V. solution.
• *For direct administration,* inject the I.V. bolus into the I.V. line at the injection port or flashbulb.
• Properly dispose of used equipment.

## Special considerations

After administering a drug according to your institution's standing emergency orders, notify the doctor immediately. Monitor the patient for therapeutic response or adverse reactions to the drug.

## Documentation

Document type and amount of drug administered, route of administration, and patient response on the appropriate records. Include monitored rhythm strips to document need for cardiac drugs (such as ventricular arrhythmia necessitating lidocaine bolus according to standing doctor's orders).

ANGELA D. LEHMAN, RN

# Intraarterial Infusion

*Intraarterial infusion can deliver an antineoplastic drug through a catheter in a major artery directly into a localized, inoperable tumor. This procedure allows a high concentration of the drug to reach the tumor with little dilution by the circulatory system and before metabolic breakdown by the liver or kidneys. The intraarterial catheter is directly implanted surgically or threaded through a peripheral artery into branches of the celiac artery for liver tumors, into the external carotid artery for head and neck tumors, and into the internal carotid artery for brain tumors.*

*Intraarterial infusion can also deliver vasopressin to the site of gastrointestinal bleeding. Usually, the catheter is threaded from a peripheral site to the left gastric, celiac, or mesenteric artery, depending on the bleeding site.*

*To prevent blood backflow and clotting, infusion of heparinized saline begins after direct implantation of the catheter in the operating room or after insertion and confirmation of placement in the X-ray department. Equipment for initial infusion must accompany the patient to either location. To allow assessment of response, intraarterial infusion generally begins after the patient returns to the patient-care unit.*

## Equipment

Bag of heparinized saline solution for infusion □ bag of solution with medication for infusion □ I.V. pole □ volumetric infusion pump with tubing and cassette, or pressure cuff with pressure tubing and minidrip chamber □ stopcock □ sterile alcohol sponges □ optional: hemostat and 4″ x 4″ gauze sponge.

The stopcock—placed between the catheter and tubing—prevents blood leakage during bag and tubing changes.

## Preparation of equipment

*To prepare a volumetric infusion pump:* Hang the solution bag. Wipe the tubing insertion port with a sterile alcohol sponge, insert the tubing spike, and fill the drip chamber at least halfway. Then, according to the manufacturer's directions, open the flow clamp and prime the tubing and cassette.

*To prepare a pressure cuff:* Insert the bag through the bottom of the pressure cuff, slip the tab through the hole in the bag, and hang the pressure cuff on the pole. Then wipe the tubing insertion port with an alcohol sponge, insert the tubing spike, and fill the drip chamber only one quarter full *since the drip chamber will continue to fill when the pressure cuff is being pressurized.* Next, open the clamp, prime the tubing, and close the clamp. Inflate the pressure cuff.

## Essential steps

• Assess the patient's understanding of the procedure and correct any misconceptions. Make sure he's aware of the eventual location of the catheter. Tell him that insertion will take place in the operating room or X-ray department and that it takes 1 to 2 hours. If known, tell him how long the catheter will be in place and how it might restrict mobility or activity.

• If ordered, administer analgesics or sedatives.

*To monitor the patient after catheter insertion:*

• If applicable, check the level of the pressure cuff. It should read at least 150 mmHg and must be higher than the patient's systolic blood pressure (but not over 300 mmHg) *to ensure an adequate drip rate for the infused solution.* After checking the pressure, close the inflation flow valve *to prevent air leaks from the pressure cuff.* If leaks do occur, clamp the tubing between the pressure cuff and the bulb with a hemostat and, *to protect the rubber tubing from damage,* wrap a 4″ x 4″ gauze sponge around the tubing before attaching the hemostat.

• Check the infusion tubing *to detect kinks, external obstruction, or blood backflow.* If backflow occurs, increase the pressure in the pressure cuff.

• Monitor the site for bleeding, ecchymosis, hematoma, or catheter movement. Infection can follow catheter insertion, but generally appears several days later.

• Watch for changes in catheter length.

*To change a bag with infusion pump:*

• Stop the infusion, turn the stopcock off, remove the tubing spike from the old bag, and insert it into the new one after cleansing the port with a sterile alcohol sponge.

• Hang the new bag, turn the stopcock on, and start the infusion pump.

*To change the bag with a pressure cuff:*

• Close the flow clamp, turn the stopcock off, and turn the pressure-release valve counterclockwise to deflate the pressure cuff.

• Remove the old bag from the pressure cuff and the tubing spike from the old bag. Put in the new bag and slip the tab through the hole on the top of the bag.

• Wipe the port with an alcohol sponge. Insert the tubing spike and hang the new equipment on the I.V. pole.

• Turn the pressure-release valve clockwise *to prevent air from escaping* and inflate the pressure cuff as necessary—to 150 to 300 mmHg—*to ensure an adequate drip rate.*

• Open the stopcock and the flow clamp and adjust to the desired drip rate.

## Special considerations

*To check the volume remaining in a bag using a pressure cuff,* turn off the stopcock or clamp the line, deflate the pressure cuff, read the fluid level, and reinflate the pressure cuff. When possible, change the tubing every 24 hours with the solution. To do this, assemble new tubing and solution, and a new pressure cuff or pump. Then turn off the stopcock, switch the sets, and start the infusion. Change the dressing every 24 hours or when wet, following hospital policy or using a subclavian dressing kit. Observe the infusion site for catheter displacement, edema, bleeding, ecchymosis, hematoma, and infection.

If both a new bag and new tubing are required, place the new cuff and primed tubing into another pressure bag setup. Then close the flow clamp, inflate the pressure cuff, and turn the stopcock off. Remove the old tubing and setup and replace with the new one. Turn on the stopcock and adjust the flow rate. Follow this same procedure to change an infusion pump, using a new pump setup.

The recent availability of mini-infusion pumps has made it possible for some patients to manage their intra-arterial chemotherapy at home.

**Complications**
Thrombus formation is the most common complication of intraarterial infusion and usually requires removal of the catheter by the doctor. Bleeding can occur at the catheter insertion site. Movement of the catheter, even when sutured in place, requires fluoroscopic confirmation. Catheter-related sepsis may require administration of systemic antibiotics and catheter removal.

**Documentation**
Record drug and fluid infused, tubing and dressing changes, response to infusion, assessment of the catheter site, and signs of complications.

ROBIN TOURIGIAN, RN, MSN

# Management of Intravenous Extravasation

*Extravasation is the leakage of infused solution from a vein into surrounding tissue. The result of a needle puncture of a vascular wall or leakage around a venipuncture site, extravasation causes local pain and itching, edema, blanching, and decreased skin temperature in the affected extremity. Extravasation of intravenous solution is often referred to as infiltration, because the fluid infiltrates the tissues. Extravasation of a small amount of isotonic fluid or a non-irritating drug usually causes only minor discomfort. However, extravasation of some drugs (see Drugs Hazardous on Extravasation) can severely damage tissue through irritative, sclerotic, vesicant, corrosive, or vasoconstrictive action. In these cases, immediate measures must be taken to minimize tissue damage, preventing the need for skin grafts or, rarely, possible amputation.*

*Treatment of extravasations of I.V. solutions and nonirritating drugs involves routine comfort measures, such as application of warm soaks. Treatment of extravasations of corrosive drugs requires emergency treatment to prevent severe tissue necrosis. Treatment of extravasations is controversial, so check your hospital protocol before proceeding.*

**Equipment**
Three 25G ⅝″ needles □ antidote for extravasated drug in appropriate syringe □ two tuberculin syringes □ 5-ml syringe □ sterile alcohol sponge or antiseptic solution □ 4″ x 4″ gauze sponge □ cold and warm compresses □ anti-inflammatory drug (optional).

**Preparation of equipment**
Attach one 25G ⅝″ needle to the syringe containing the antidote. Connect the two remaining 25G ⅝″ needles to the two tuberculin syringes. Then fill one tuberculin syringe with the anti-inflammatory drug, if needed.

**Essential steps**
● Stop the infusion immediately, but *don't* remove the I.V. needle. Carefully estimate the amount of extravasated solution and notify the doctor.
● Disconnect the tubing from the I.V. needle. Attach the 5-ml syringe to the needle and try to withdraw 3 to 5 ml of

blood *to remove any medication or blood in the tubing or needle and provide a path to the infiltrated tissues.*

• Cleanse the area around the extravasation site with an alcohol sponge or gauze sponge soaked in antiseptic solution. Then, insert the needle of the empty tuberculin syringe into the subcutaneous tissue around the site and gently aspirate as much of the solution as possible from the tissue.

• Instill the antidote into the same area. Then, if ordered, slowly instill an anti-inflammatory drug subcutaneously *to help reduce inflammation and edema.*

• Remove the I.V. needle. Note: In some institutions, 5 ml of 8.4% sodium bicarbonate solution is injected through the I.V. needle after extravasation of doxorubicin.

• Apply cold compresses to the affected area for 24 hours, or apply an ice pack for 20 minutes every 4 hours *to cause vasoconstriction that may localize the drug and slow cell metabolism.* After 24 hours, apply warm compresses and elevate the affected extremity *to reduce discomfort and promote fluid reabsorption.* If the extravasated drug is a vasoconstrictor, such as norepinephrine or metaraminol bitartrate, apply warm compresses only.

• Continuously monitor the I.V. site for signs of abscess or necrosis.

### Special considerations

If you're administering a potentially tissue-damaging drug by I.V. bolus or push, first start an I.V. infusion, preferably with normal saline solution. Infuse a small amount of the saline and check for signs of infiltration before injecting the drug.

Know the antidote (if any) for an I.V. drug that can cause tissue necrosis if extravasation occurs. Make sure you're familiar with your institution's policy regarding the administration of such drugs and their antidotes.

Tell the patient to report any discomfort at the I.V. site. During infusion, frequently check the I.V. site for signs of infiltration.

### Documentation

Record the site of the extravasation, the patient's symptoms, the estimated amount of infiltrated solution, nursing treatment, and the time and name of the doctor notified. Continue to document the appearance of the infiltrated site and any associated symptoms.

MARGARET J. GRIFFITHS, RN, MSN

## DRUGS HAZARDOUS ON EXTRAVASATION

The following drugs are commonly associated with tissue necrosis when they extravasate:
amphotericin B (Fungizone)
dactinomycin (actinomycin D, Cosmegen)
daunorubicin (Cerubidine)
dopamine (Intropin)
doxorubicin (Adriamycin)
mechlorethamine, nitrogen mustard (Mustargen)
metaraminol bitartrate (Aramine)
mithramycin (Mithracin)
mitomycin (Mutamycin)
nitroprusside sodium (Nipride)
norepinephrine (Levophed)
potassium chloride
vancomycin (Vancocin)
vinblastine (Velban)
vincristine (Oncovin)

## Selected References

King, Eunice, et al. *Illustrated Manual of Nursing Techniques.* Philadelphia: J.B. Lippincott Co., 1981.
Martin, Eric W. *Drug Interactions Index.* Philadelphia: J.B. Lippincott Co., 1979.
*Nurse's Guide to Drugs.* The Nurse's Reference Library™ Series, Springhouse, Pa.: Intermed Communications, Inc., 1982.
Rodman, Morton, and Smith, Dorothy. *Clinical Pharmacology in Nursing.* Philadelphia: J.B. Lippincott Co., 1980.
Turco, Salvatore, and King, Robert E. *Sterile Dosage Forms,* 2nd ed. Philadelphia: Lea & Febiger, 1979.

# RECENT DEVELOPMENTS IN MEDICAL EQUIPMENT

Recent equipment advances have helped improve medical and nursing care by promoting patient comfort, by increasing the precision of monitoring systems—which enables earlier diagnosis of complications—and by creating more effective and versatile therapeutic aids. This special color section highlights some of these developments.

## Patient comfort

New equipment that promotes increased patient comfort includes:
• *new treatments for immobilized patients*, such as the Roto Rest bed (see pages 130 to 133) and Clinitron therapy (see pages 134 to 135), illustrated in color on pages 368 and 369.
• *the transcutaneous electrical nerve stimulator* (TENS; see pages 642 to 644), which helps control pain by transmitting an electrical current to the patient's nerves, overriding the transmission of pain impulses to the brain. It can replace or minimize use of narcotic analgesics by postsurgical patients with moderate to severe pain and by patients with chronic pain.
• *portable drug infusion pumps*, such as the two types illustrated in color on page 363. These pumps enable patients to enjoy the benefits of continuous drug therapy without confinement to bed and without the discomfort of multiple injections.
• *permeable hypoallergenic adhesive bandages*, which allow air to enter and exudate to escape from wound sites. These bandages adhere securely, lift off easily and painlessly for wound examination, and can be securely replaced after examination. They are also radiotransparent, so they need not be removed for X-rays. These bandages are available in several forms: gauze, surgical dressings, and wound closure strips (see page 196).

## Precise monitoring

New monitoring systems include:
• *cardiac output monitors*, which help assess left ventricular and valve functions by using thermodilution (see pages 400 to 402) to detect the volume of blood ejected from the heart each minute.
• the *Holter monitor* (see pages 381 to 383), a portable cassette recorder worn on a belt, which records the patient's heartbeat over a 24-hour period while he goes about his normal daily activities.
• the *five-lumen pulmonary artery catheter*, illustrated in color on page 367, which can be used for atrial, ventricular, and atrioventricular sequential pacing, expanding the capabilities of the pulmonary catheter (see pages 390 to 397).
• the *transcutaneous pO$_2$ monitor* (see pages 775 to 776), which allows measurement of an infant's blood oxygen tensions, without drawing arterial blood, through a special sensor applied to the infant's skin surface. This method is painless, simple to operate, and easy to read.
• the *electronic vital signs monitor* (see page 18), which allows continuous blood pressure monitoring without insertion of an arterial catheter. It uses an ordinary blood pressure cuff that inflates automatically at preset intervals.

## Therapeutic aids

More effective and versatile therapeutic aids include:
• *autotransfusion equipment* (see pages 301 to 307), illustrated in color on pages 364 and 365, which enables hospital personnel to collect, filter, and reinfuse the patient's own blood before, during, and after surgery, or from a traumatic wound.
• the *halo traction device* (see pages 644 to 647), now available in the four different types illustrated in color on page 370. This device immobilizes the injured cervical spine while allowing the patient to continue most normal daily activities.
• the *intraaortic balloon pump* (see pages 418 to 424), a counterpulsation device that aids left ventricular ejection, helps increase systemic perfusion, increases myocardial oxygenation, and supports a weakened or damaged left ventricle.
• a *programmable pacemaker and its rate controller* (see pages 415 to 418), illustrated in color on page 366. The rate controller adjusts the pacing rate of an implanted programmable pacemaker without surgery.

# PORTABLE INFUSION PUMPS

Portable infusion pumps enable ambulatory patients to receive necessary infusions of medication without unduly disrupting their normal daily activities. The devices are usually worn on the patient's belt, are powered by either a syringe or a peristaltic-action pump, and run on either replaceable or rechargeable batteries.

## The syringe pump

The syringe pump allows either intermittent or continuous drug or fluid infusion. It's ideal for maintaining keep-open lines; administering drugs intravenously, intraarterially, or subcutaneously; and treating medical conditions requiring chronic drug administration, such as cancer and diabetes mellitus. It can also be used to administer blood transfusions, fat emulsions, and nasogastric feedings.

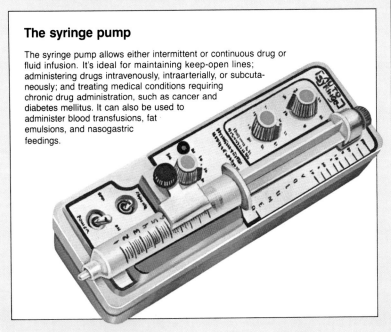

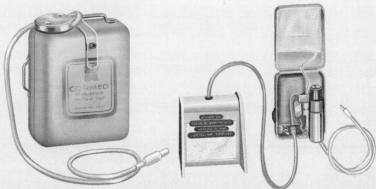

## The peristaltic-action pump

The peristaltic-action pump delivers continuous drug infusion. It's generally used to administer heparin, hyperalimentation, and chemotherapy but can also be used to give other drugs intravenously, intraarterially, or subcutaneously.

# AUTOTRANSFUSION SYSTEMS

## Trauma system

The trauma system, for use in an emergency, allows aspiration of blood from an injury and collection of this blood into a sterile liner enclosed in a canister. When reinfusion is necessary, or when 1,900 ml of blood have been collected, the liner is removed from the canister, a microemboli filter is attached to it, and the blood is quickly and safely reinfused using the gravity-drip method.

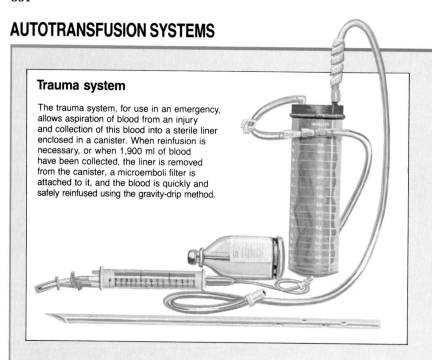

## Postoperative system

The postoperative system, for use after cardiac surgery, allows drainage of blood from the mediastinum and pleural cavity and collection of this blood into a sterile liner enclosed in a canister. When reinfusion is necessary, or when 800 ml of blood have been collected, the liner is removed from the canister, a microemboli filter is attached to it, and the blood is reinfused.

## Intraoperative system

The intraoperative system, for use
during surgery, allows aspiration of blood
from an operative field and collection
of this blood into a sterile liner enclosed
in a canister. When reinfusion is
necessary, or when 1,900 ml of blood
have been collected, the liner is removed
from the canister. The blood is then
processed in a blood washer–processor.
Then, packed red blood cells are
reinfused.

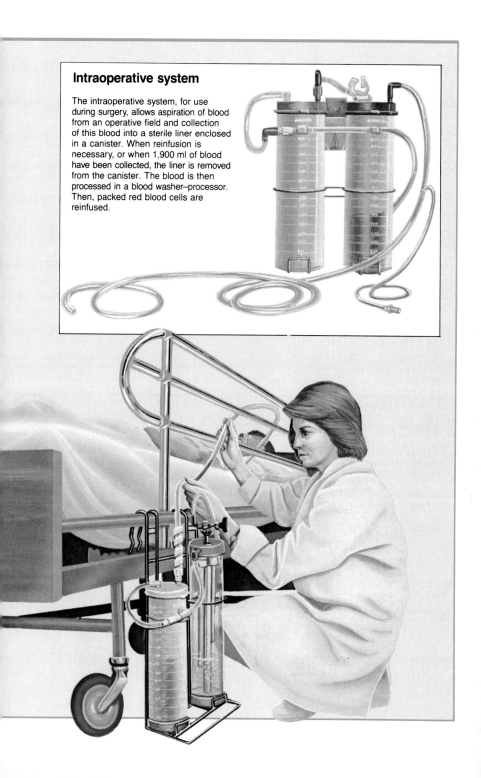

# PROGRAMMABLE PACEMAKER

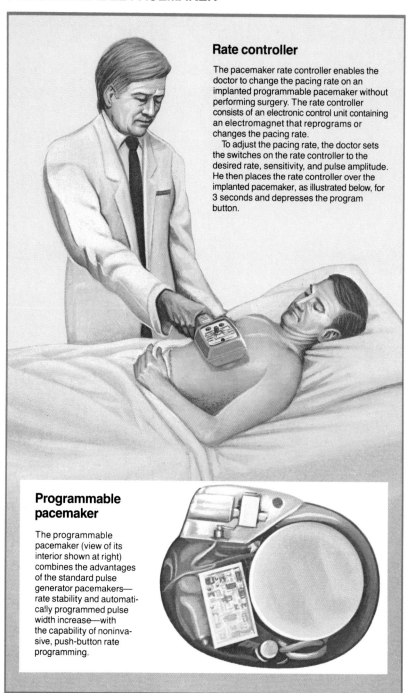

### Rate controller

The pacemaker rate controller enables the doctor to change the pacing rate on an implanted programmable pacemaker without performing surgery. The rate controller consists of an electronic control unit containing an electromagnet that reprograms or changes the pacing rate.

To adjust the pacing rate, the doctor sets the switches on the rate controller to the desired rate, sensitivity, and pulse amplitude. He then places the rate controller over the implanted pacemaker, as illustrated below, for 3 seconds and depresses the program button.

### Programmable pacemaker

The programmable pacemaker (view of its interior shown at right) combines the advantages of the standard pulse generator pacemakers—rate stability and automatically programmed pulse width increase—with the capability of noninvasive, push-button rate programming.

# PULMONARY ARTERY CATHETER

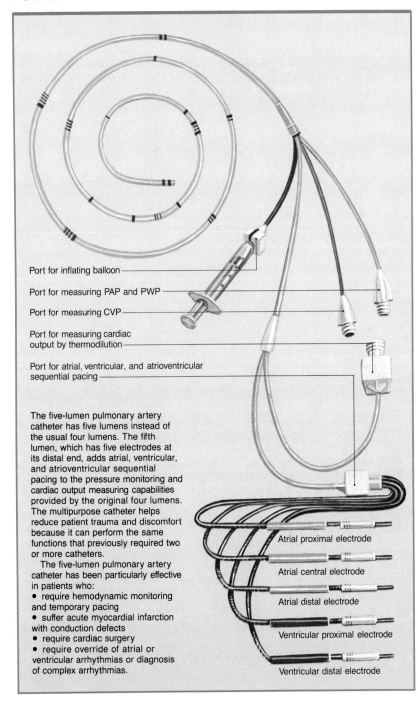

Port for inflating balloon

Port for measuring PAP and PWP

Port for measuring CVP

Port for measuring cardiac output by thermodilution

Port for atrial, ventricular, and atrioventricular sequential pacing

The five-lumen pulmonary artery catheter has five lumens instead of the usual four lumens. The fifth lumen, which has five electrodes at its distal end, adds atrial, ventricular, and atrioventricular sequential pacing to the pressure monitoring and cardiac output measuring capabilities provided by the original four lumens. The multipurpose catheter helps reduce patient trauma and discomfort because it can perform the same functions that previously required two or more catheters.

The five-lumen pulmonary artery catheter has been particularly effective in patients who:
• require hemodynamic monitoring and temporary pacing
• suffer acute myocardial infarction with conduction defects
• require cardiac surgery
• require override of atrial or ventricular arrhythmias or diagnosis of complex arrhythmias.

Atrial proximal electrode

Atrial central electrode

Atrial distal electrode

Ventricular proximal electrode

Ventricular distal electrode

# BEDS FOR IMMOBILIZED PATIENTS

**Clinitron therapy,** originally called the air-fluidized bed, creates a fluidlike environment through silicon-coated microspheres of lime glass, providing all the advantages of true flotation without the disadvantages of instability, patient-positioning difficulties, or immobilization. Advantages include assistance in the control of hypothermia and hyperthermia, minimization of metabolic losses, elimination of maceration and the need for topical remedies and dressings, and increased patient comfort.

Fluidization occurs when compressed air passing through a diffuser board into a microsphere-filled fluidization tank surrounds and suspends each microsphere, enabling it to move independently. The result resembles a dry fluid. Fluid viscosity varies according to microsphere size and air volume.

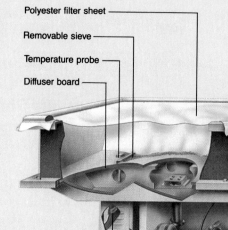

Polyester filter sheet

Removable sieve

Temperature probe

Diffuser board

Control panel

Soundproof lining

Electrical heating element

**The Roto Rest bed,** driven by a silent motor, slowly turns the immobilized patient in a relaxing, continuous motion (more than 300 times a day). This motion provides constant passive exercise and peristaltic stimulation without depriving the patient of sleep or risking further injury. The bed is radiolucent, allowing X-rays to be taken through it without moving the patient; has a built-in fan for cooling the patient and reducing high fever; and allows access for surgery on

## Front view

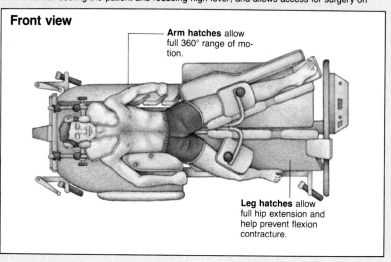

**Arm hatches** allow full 360° range of motion.

**Leg hatches** allow full hip extension and help prevent flexion contracture.

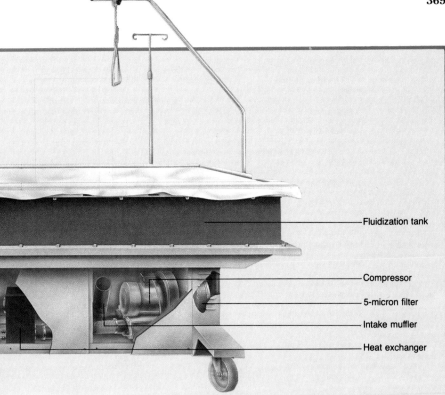

- Fluidization tank
- Compressor
- 5-micron filter
- Intake muffler
- Heat exchanger

multiple-trauma patients without disturbing spinal alignment or traction.

The purpose of each of the bed's hatches is explained in the illustration of the Mark I model shown below. All hatches permit easy accessibility to the most common sites of decubitus ulcer formation. In addition, the arm hatches have holes through which chest tubes can drain, preventing inadvertent reflux and retrograde contamination.

## Back view

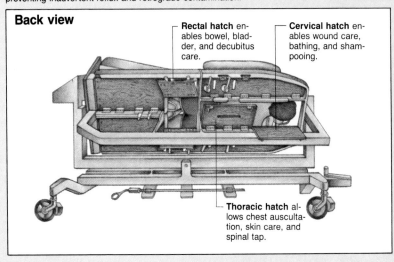

**Rectal hatch** enables bowel, bladder, and decubitus care.

**Cervical hatch** enables wound care, bathing, and shampooing.

**Thoracic hatch** allows chest auscultation, skin care, and spinal tap.

# HALO TRACTION APPARATUS

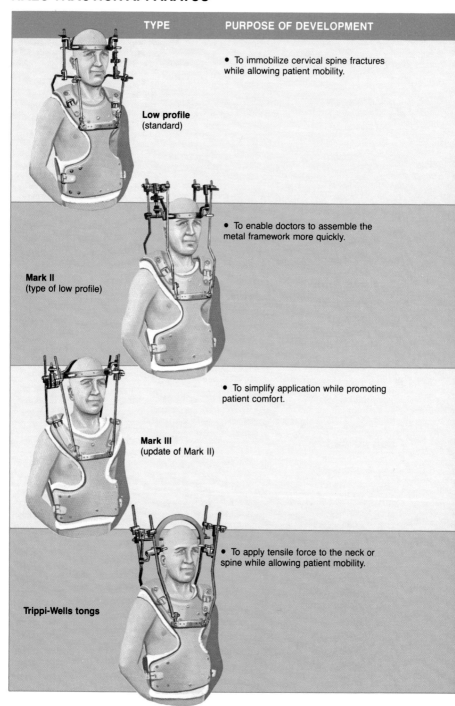

| TYPE | PURPOSE OF DEVELOPMENT |
|------|------------------------|
| **Low profile** (standard) | • To immobilize cervical spine fractures while allowing patient mobility. |
| **Mark II** (type of low profile) | • To enable doctors to assemble the metal framework more quickly. |
| **Mark III** (update of Mark II) | • To simplify application while promoting patient comfort. |
| **Trippi-Wells tongs** | • To apply tensile force to the neck or spine while allowing patient mobility. |

| DESCRIPTION | ADVANTAGES |
|---|---|

- Traction and compression are produced by threaded support rods on either side of the halo ring.
- Flexion and extension are obtained by moving the swivel arm to an anterior or posterior position, depending on the location of the skull pins.

- The swivel arm facilitates surgery of the cervical spine and enables flexion and extension.
- Airway intubation without losing skeletal traction
- Necessary alignment is facilitated by an adjustment at the junction of the threaded support rods and horizontal frame.

- Traction and compression are produced by threaded support rods on either side of the halo ring.
- Flexion and extension are obtained by swivel clamps, which allow the bars to intersect and hold at any angle.

- Allows unobstructed access for anterior-posterior and lateral X-rays of the cervical spine
- Uprights shaped closer to the body allow patient to wear his usual clothing.

- Traction and compression are produced by threaded support rods on either side of the halo.
- Flexion and extension are obtained by a serrated split articulation coupling attached to the halo ring, which can be adjusted in 4° increments.

- The flexible padded strap, which replaces the vest's solid plastic shoulder, eliminates shoulder pressure and discomfort.
- The modified hardware and shorter uprights eliminate many problems of the tall patient and allow unobstructed access for medial-lateral X-rays.

- Traction is produced by four pins that compress the skull.
- Flexion and extension are obtained by adjusting the midline vertical plate.

- Enable changing from mobile to stationary traction without interrupting traction.
- Adjust to three planes for mobile and stationary traction.
- Allow unobstructed access for medial and lateral X-rays.

# 8 Cardiovascular Care

# Cardiovascular Care

## Introduction

The continuing proliferation of diagnostic tests, drugs and therapy, and sophisticated monitoring equipment has made nursing care of patients with cardiovascular disorders as complex as it is commonplace. According to statistics from the American Heart Association, cardiovascular disorders afflict more than 40 million people in the United States alone. Consequently, more nurses than ever before participate in the diagnosis, treatment, and prevention of these disorders. Their responsibilities may include procedures unknown a decade ago. To accommodate these expanding responsibilities, many states have revised their Nurse Practice Acts. Qualified nurses may now routinely perform such complex procedures as carotid massage, cardiopulmonary resuscitation (CPR), and defibrillation; they may also assist with pericardiocentesis and pacemaker implantation. These role changes have expanded nursing accountability. Today, you're legally required to fully understand the doctor's orders, correctly perform ordered procedures, monitor the patient's response to therapy, and know how to use sophisticated equipment.

### Patient teaching

Today, cardiovascular nurses have assumed much of the physical preparation, patient teaching, and psychological preparation necessary to help the patient and his family understand diagnostic tests, monitoring, and treatment. Psychological preparation is especially important when procedures involve the heart because of the inevitable association between the heart and life itself. Before any procedure, give the patient a clear, simple explanation. Even if he fails to understand all the details, your concern and reassurance can improve his prospects for recovery. It also helps ensure his cooperation with diagnostic tests and can improve test reliability as well.

### Monitoring

Cardiac and hemodynamic monitoring techniques have greatly enhanced effective assessment of the patient's cardiovascular status and his response to therapy. Cardiac monitoring includes hardwire monitoring for continuous monitoring of the patient confined to bed, telemetry monitoring for continuous monitoring of the convalescent patient who has some freedom of movement in the hospital, and ambulatory electrocardiography for continuous short-term monitoring of the ambulatory patient. It also guides cardiac drug therapy with pressors and inotropic agents. Hemodynamic monitoring demands strict attention to detailed equipment preparation and a good understanding of cardiovascular anatomy and physiology. Monitoring of central venous pressure, arterial pressure, pulmonary artery and capillary wedge pressure, or cardiac output is frequently performed on the patient with myocardial infarction or congestive heart failure.

Monitoring techniques are being studied and improved to obtain the best results with the least risk to the patient.

## NURSING RESPONSIBILITIES IN PERICARDIOCENTESIS

In pericardiocentesis, a doctor aspirates fluid from the patient's pericardial sac to obtain a specimen or to relieve cardiac tamponade in an emergency. This procedure is performed at the bedside in a critical care unit with an EKG monitor or a portable fluoroscope unit to help the doctor guide the needle. Because pericardiocentesis carries some risk of fatal complications, such as laceration of the myocardium or of a coronary artery, emergency equipment should always be immediately available.

Before the procedure, position the patient supine in the bed, with the head of the bed elevated 60° and his arms supported by pillows, as shown.

During the procedure:

• Encourage the patient by explaining the procedure to him and keeping him informed.

• Assist the doctor as necessary with the procedure.

• Monitor the EKG pattern constantly for PVCs and elevated ST segments, which may indicate the point of the needle has contacted the ventricle; elevated PR segment, which may indicate the needle has touched the atrium; and large, erratic QRS complexes, which may indicate penetration of the myocardium.

• Monitor vital signs every 5 to 15 minutes.

• Note character of aspirated fluid; bloody fluid from pericardial effusion doesn't clot. *A clot in the aspirate means one of the heart's chambers has been punctured.* If this occurs, notify doctor immediately.

• Properly label all specimens and send

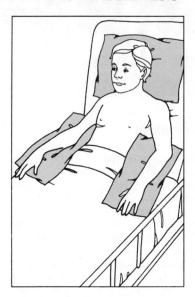

them to the laboratory.

After the procedure, monitor the patient very closely. Be alert for symptoms that may indicate cardiac tamponade: decreased blood pressure, narrowing pulse pressure, increased central venous pressure, distended neck veins, tachycardia, tachypnea, muffled heart sounds, friction and anxiety, and chest pain.

SUSAN VIGEANT, RN, BSN
PAULA STEPHENS OKUN, RN, MSN

---

Nursing research includes determining optimal patient positioning during cardiac output measurement and the effect of different respiration modes (such as breath-holding and ventilators) on pulmonary artery pressure readings.

### Treatment

Advanced life-support techniques are often needed to treat the patient with an impending or overt cardiopulmonary emergency. Selection of specific techniques, such as CPR and defibrillation, depends on the patient's condition, but all emergency techniques require thorough knowledge of cardiovascular anatomy and physiology, familiarity with technical equipment, and well-developed assessment and intervention skills. Knowledge of anatomy and physiology promotes an understanding of the principles of a procedure, regardless of the equipment used. Familiarity with technical equipment is essential to keep pace with rapidly changing technologies that have brought us such devices as intraaortic balloon pumps and cardiac pacemakers. Skillful patient assessment enables you to monitor response to treatments and to correlate this information with results of diagnostic procedures and monitoring to achieve an accurate overview of the patient's condition.

DIANE K. DRESSLER, RN, MSN

# DIAGNOSIS

## Electrocardiography
### [EKG or ECG]

The most frequently used procedure for evaluating cardiac status, electrocardiography detects the presence and location of myocardial infarction (MI), ischemia, conduction delay, chamber enlargement, or arrhythmias, and helps assess the effects of electrolyte disturbances and cardiac drugs. In the 12-lead electrocardiogram (EKG or ECG), five electrodes attached to the patient's arms, legs, and chest measure the electrical potential generated by heartbeats. This potential is analyzed from twelve different views, or leads: three standard bipolar limb leads (I, II, III), three unipolar augmented limb leads ($aV_R$, $aV_L$, $aV_F$), and six unipolar chest leads ($V_1$ to $V_6$). Lead I measures the electrical potential between the left and right arms; lead II, the electrical potential between the left leg and right arm; and lead III, the electrical potential between the left leg and left arm. Using the same electrode placement, leads $aV_R$, $aV_L$, and $aV_F$ measure electrical potential between one augmented limb lead and the electrical midpoint of the remaining two leads (determined electronically by the EKG machine). Both standard and augmented leads view the heart from the front, in the vertical plane. The six unipolar chest leads view it from the horizontal plane, helping to locate pathology in the lateral and posterior walls. The EKG machine averages the electrical potentials of the three limb electrodes (I, II, and III) and compares this with the electrical potential of the chest electrode. Recordings made with the V connection show variations in electrical potential that occur under the chest electrode as its position is changed.

After electrical potentials are transmitted to the EKG machine, these forces are amplified and graphically displayed on a strip chart recorder. The graphic display, or tracing, usually consists of the P wave, the QRS complex, and the T wave. The P wave shows atrial depolarization; the QRS complex, ventricular depolarization; and the T wave, ventricular repolarization.

### Equipment
Single-channel EKG machine with amplifier and strip chart recorder □ recording paper □ five lead wires □ four limb lead electrodes with rubber straps □ one suction cup chest electrode □ electrode gel □ 4" x 4" gauze pads □ alcohol □ disposable razor □ moist cloth towel.

A gauze pad soaked in normal saline solution may be substituted for the electrode gel beneath the limb leads.

### Preparation of equipment
Before using the EKG machine, check the date of its last inspection by the hospital's engineering department. If the period of authorized use has elapsed, avoid using the machine *because even a minute leakage of electric current (10 microamperes or less) may endanger the patient, possibly causing serious and life-threatening dysrhythmias.*

### Essential steps
● Explain the procedure to the patient *to allay his fears and promote his cooperation.* Inform him that he needn't restrict food or fluids beforehand, and that the procedure takes about 15 minutes. Instruct him to relax, lie still, and breathe normally. Advise him not to talk during the procedure *because the sound of his voice may distort the EKG tracing.*
● Check the patient's history for cardiac drugs, and note any current therapy on the test request form.
● Instruct the patient to disrobe to the waist and expose both legs for electrode placement. Drape the female patient's chest until chest leads are applied.
● Place the patient in the supine posi-

tion. However, if he's orthopneic, place him in a semi-Fowler's position. Instruct him to avoid touching the metal handrail of the bed or allowing his feet to touch

## POSITIONING CHEST ELECTRODES AND MARKING EKG STRIPS

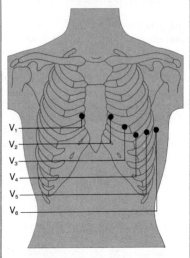

To prevent spurious test results, be sure to position chest electrodes as follows:
$V_1$: fourth intercostal space at right border of sternum
$V_2$: fourth intercostal space at left border of sternum
$V_3$: halfway between $V_2$ and $V_4$
$V_4$: fifth intercostal space at midclavicular line
$V_5$: anterior axillary line (halfway between $V_4$ and $V_6$)
$V_6$: midaxillary line, level with $V_4$.
  Use marking button on the EKG machine to identify chest leads (shown above) and limb leads. Depress button to print a code of long and short dashes (shown below) directly on the EKG strip. (*Note:* Because this code varies, always check the manufacturer's instructions.)

| Limb leads | | Chest leads | |
|---|---|---|---|
| I: | - | $V_1$: | — · |
| II: | -- | $V_2$: | — ·· |
| III: | --- | $V_3$: | — ··· |
| $aV_R$: | · — | $V_4$: | — ···· |
| $aV_L$: | -- — | $V_5$: | — ····· |
| $aV_F$: | --- — | $V_6$: | — ······ |

the footboard, *to prevent current leakage that distorts the EKG tracing.*
● Turn on the EKG machine and set the lead selector to the standby mode *to warm up the stylus mechanism.* Check the paper supply and center the stylus on the paper.
● Cleanse the electrode placement sites with alcohol and shave them, if necessary. Apply electrode gel to the inner aspect of the forearms and the medial aspect of the lower legs. Rub the skin vigorously when applying the electrodes, creating an erythema, *to enhance skin contact with the electrode.*
● Secure the limb electrodes with rubber straps, but avoid overtightening the straps *to prevent circulatory impairment and the onset of muscle spasms, which may distort the recording.* Position the leg electrodes with their connector ends pointing upward *to avoid bending or straining the lead wires.*
● Connect each lead wire to an electrode by inserting the wire prong into the terminal post and tightening the screw. Be sure to match each color-coded lead wire to the corresponding electrode.
● Set the paper-speed selector to 25 mm second, or as ordered. Calibrate the machine by adjusting the sensitivity to normal (usually 10 mm/mV in the vertical plane) and checking the quality and baseline position of the tracing. Remember to calibrate the machine after running each lead *to provide a consistent test standard.*
● Turn the lead selector to lead I. Then, write the lead number on the paper strip, or push the marking button on the machine to identify the lead with a series of dots and dashes (see *Positioning Chest Electrodes and Marking EKG Strips*). Record for 3 to 6 seconds and then return the machine to the standby mode. Repeat the procedure for leads II to $aV_F$.
● After completing the $aV_F$ run, turn the lead selector to a neutral position before running chest leads $V_1$ to $V_6$. *This prevents the stylus from swinging wildly and possibly damaging the paper.*
● Determine proper placement for the chest leads (see illustration at left). If

repeat testing is ordered, use a marking pen to note these positions on the patient's chest *to ensure that future measurements are taken from the same positions.*

• Connect the chest lead wire to the suction cup electrode, apply electrode gel to the chest lead sites, and press the cup firmly to the $V_1$ position. Apply enough gel *to produce efficient suction and low skin resistance.*

• Ask the patient to breathe normally; if his respirations distort the recording, instruct him to hold his breath briefly. Turn the lead selector to V, record a $V_1$ strip for 3 to 6 seconds, and mark it as before.

• Return the lead selector to the neutral position, reposition the electrode to $V_2$, and record. Repeat the procedure through $V_6$, always turning the selector to the neutral position before moving the suction cup.

• After completing $V_6$, run a rhythm strip on lead II for at least 6 seconds. Assess the quality of the whole series and repeat individual lead tracings as needed.

• Disconnect the equipment, remove the electrodes, and wipe the gel from the patient's skin with 4″ x 4″ gauze pads. Then use a moist cloth to remove residual gel. Wash gel from the electrodes and dry them thoroughly.

**Special considerations**
If necessary, replace metal electrodes and straps with suction cups for limb leads *to enhance baseline stability.* Position the cups on the outer aspect of the upper arms instead of the forearms, and on the upper thighs instead of the lower legs.

Before recording, recheck the lead positions and the lead wire and electrode connections *to avoid lead reversal, which produces misleading test results.* Become thoroughly familiar with the appearance of normal EKG tracings *so you can recognize recording errors.* For example, the leads for the right and left arms, when reversed, may falsely indicate myocardial infarction. A normal lead I has a positive deflection; similarly the P waves in lead II normally have a positive deflection. The R waves in the

---

## MULTICHANNEL EKG

Although the single-channel EKG machine is sufficient for most diagnoses, the multichannel EKG machine helps detect complex arrhythmias and ventricular ectopia by simultaneously recording three consecutive leads. When operating this machine, keep in mind these differences from the single-channel machine:

• All electrodes—including the six chest leads—must be in place before running the EKG.

• The machine uses heat- or pressure-sensitive paper and requires no warm-up period.

• The machine automatically records 3 leads at a time until all 12 leads are recorded, without manual lead selection. It also calibrates and standardizes the tracing before recording each lead group.

• The machine can record any lead group in random order, if needed.

---

chest leads should appear increasingly positive as they progress from $V_2$ to $V_6$. Avoid positioning $V_3$ at the same level as $V_4$ to $V_6$ *to prevent a spurious Q wave tracing.*

If the patient's skin is exceptionally oily, scaly, or diaphoretic, rub the electrode site with alcohol and dry it with a cotton ball before applying the gelled electrode. *This may help reduce baseline wander and interference in the tracing.*

If the patient with left ventricular hypertrophy exhibits large R wave tracings that run off the paper, change the sensitivity setting to half-standard, but be sure to mark the run as such. If the patient experiences chest pains during a lead run, note it on the appropriate strip. If he has a pacemaker in place, you can perform electrocardiography with or without a magnet, but be sure to indicate the presence of a pacemaker and the use of the magnet on the strip. (Many pacemakers function only when the heartbeat falls below a preset rate; a magnet makes the pacemaker fire regularly, permitting evaluation of its performance.)

**Documentation**
Label each EKG strip with the patient's

name and room number (if applicable), the date and time of the procedure, and the doctor's name. Include any special information, such as use of a magnet to test pacemaker function. If you send the strips to the EKG department, fill out the request form completely. Include the patient's age, height, weight, blood pressure, diagnosis, and drug regimen.

DENISE A. HESS, RN

# Exercise Electrocardiography
[*Stress EKG*]

*The body responds to exercise by increasing its demand for oxygen—the result of increased respiratory rate, cardiac output, and extraction of oxygen by the tissues. Exercise electrocardiography (EKG) evaluates these changes by monitoring heart rate, blood pressure, and EKG waveforms as the patient walks on a treadmill or pedals a stationary bicycle. This procedure provides diagnostic information that can't be obtained from a resting EKG alone. It's used to diagnose the cause of chest pain, to screen for asymptomatic coronary artery disease, to identify cardiac arrhythmias during exercise, to determine the functional capacity of the heart after surgery or myocardial infarction (MI), to help establish limits for exercise, and to evaluate the effectiveness of antiarrhythmic or antianginal drug therapy.*

*Exercise testing can be performed in single or multiple stages. The single-stage test entails a constant workload throughout the procedure, while the more frequently used multiple-stage test increases the workload at regular intervals until the patient reaches an endpoint, such as a target heart rate or the onset of chest pain or fatigue. Within these protocols, the test may also be submaximal or maximal. The submaximal test doesn't require the patient to reach his highest level of functional aerobic ca-*

*pacity, but stops at an arbitrary endpoint, such as a target heart rate. This test is safer, but yields less diagnostic information than the maximal exercise test.*

*Since exercise electrocardiography places considerable stress on the heart, it may be contraindicated in the patient with dissecting aortic aneurysm, uncontrolled arrhythmias, pericarditis, myocarditis, acute MI, severe anemia, uncontrolled hypertension, unstable angina, congestive heart failure, second- or third-degree heart block, and severe heart valve or coronary artery disease.*

## Equipment
Motor-driven treadmill and controls (or bicycle ergometer with adjustable workload capacity) □ EKG recorder and monitor □ patient cable □ ten electrodes with gel □ elastic bandage or nonallergenic tape to secure electrodes □ cotton-tipped applicators or 4″ × 4″ gauze sponges □ alcohol □ disposable razor (or sterilized nondisposable razor) □ timing device with elapsed time display □ examination table □ crash cart containing emergency drug administration and resuscitation equipment □ I.V. solutions and tubing □ stethoscope □ sphygmomanometer □ optional: skin-deburring device, acetone, gown with opening in front.

## Essential steps
● Explain the procedure to the patient to allay his fears and promote his cooperation. Instruct him not to eat, smoke, or drink alcohol or caffeine-containing beverages for 3 hours before the procedure, but to continue any drug regimen unless the doctor directs otherwise. Tell him this test causes fatigue and slight breathlessness, but assure him that it has few risks. Emphasize that he may stop the test if he feels chest pain or extreme fatigue.
● Make sure the patient or a responsible family member understands and signs a consent form. Check the patient's history for a recent physical examination (within 1 week) and for baseline 12-lead EKG results.

## EKG CHANGES WITH ISCHEMIA

**Resting**

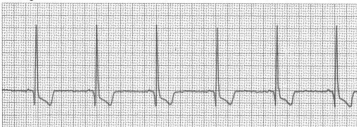

**Angina**

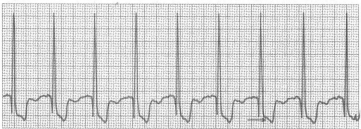

These tracings are from an abnormal exercise EKG obtained during a treadmill test performed on a patient who had recently undergone a triple coronary artery bypass graft. The first tracing shows the heart at rest. In the second tracing, the patient worked up to a 10% grade at 1.7 mph before experiencing ischemia and angina at 2 minutes, 25 seconds. Note the angina tracing shows a depressed ST segment (see arrow above); heart rate was 85.

Tracings courtesy of Arlene Strong, RN, MSN

• Take the patient's vital signs. Instruct the male patient to disrobe to the waist; tell the female patient to keep on her bra and, if she isn't wearing a lightweight, short-sleeved blouse, give her a gown that opens in the front.

• Shave the electrode sites, if necessary, and cleanse the skin with alcohol. Allow the alcohol to dry, and then gently abrade the skin until it reddens *to ensure good electrode contact.* (Some manufacturers include an abrasive patch on the back of the electrode for this purpose; a skin-deburring device such as coarse tissue paper or dry gauze may also be used.)

• Apply chest electrodes according to the desired lead system. Place the patient cable over the patient's shoulder and rest the lead wire junction box on his chest.

Wrap and secure the junction box belt around the patient's chest. Or, if the junction box doesn't have the belt attachment, secure the patient cable by pinning it to the patient's clothing or taping it to his shoulder or back. Then connect the lead wires with nonallergenic tape, or an elastic bandage, if needed.

• Turn on the monitor and obtain a baseline rhythm strip with the patient in the supine position, another with him standing, and a third after a short period of hyperventilation, *to detect changes in the ST segment that may follow position changes and hyperventilation.*

• Take the patient's blood pressure in supine and standing positions. The doctor then examines the rhythm strips and blood pressure measurements for evidence of resting abnormalities and auscultates the chest to detect $S_3$ or $S_4$ gallops, murmurs, or rales.

• *If you're performing the treadmill test,* turn on the machine to a slow speed, and show the patient how to step onto it and use the railing to maintain his balance but *not* to support his weight. Turn off the machine, and then ask the patient to step onto it; turn it on again at slow speed and allow the patient to adjust to walking on it.

• *If you're performing the ergometer test,* ask the patient to sit on the bicycle. If necessary, adjust the seat and handlebars so he can pedal comfortably. Tell him not to grip the handlebars tightly, but to use them only to maintain balance. Instruct him to pedal until he reaches the desired speed, indicated on the speedometer.

• Evaluate the quality of the rhythm strips and the patient's ability to walk or pedal. If either is unsatisfactory, stop the procedure and, if possible, correct the problem.

• Depending on the protocol, increase the workload in stages—usually every 2 to 3 minutes. Start the timer when the patient begins the first stage. Observe the monitor continuously for changes in the heart's electrical activity. Check the rhythm strips at 1-minute intervals for PVC's, arrhythmias, or ST segment changes, and mark each strip with the test level and the time elapsed. Check the patient's blood pressure after each stage, and note any changes.

• Stop the test upon reaching the predetermined endpoint or target heart rate. Tell the patient you will slow the machine and ask him to continue walking or pedaling at the slower rate for several minutes *to prevent nausea and dizzi-*

## SUBMAXIMAL AND MAXIMAL HEART RATES

| AGE GROUP | SUBMAXIMAL HEART RATE* (beats/minute) | MAXIMAL HEART RATE (beats/minute) |
|---|---|---|
| 20 to 24 | 177 | 197 |
| 25 to 29 | 175 | 195 |
| 30 to 34 | 173 | 193 |
| 35 to 39 | 172 | 191 |
| 40 to 44 | 170 | 189 |
| 45 to 49 | 168 | 187 |
| 50 to 54 | 166 | 184 |
| 55 to 59 | 164 | 182 |
| 60 to 64 | 162 | 180 |
| 65 to 69 | 160 | 178 |
| 70 to 74 | 158 | 176 |

*(90% of maximal heart rate)

From *Exercise Testing and Training of Apparently Healthy Individuals: A Handbook for Physicians,* American Heart Association Committee on Exercise (Dallas: American Heart Association, 1972). Used with permission.

*ness.* Then stop the machine and record another rhythm strip, heart rate, and blood pressure. Note the elapsed time.

• Help the patient to the examination table and place him in a supine or semi-Fowler's position, with his legs elevated.

• After the doctor listens to the patient's heart and lungs, record rhythm strip every minute and take blood pressure every 1 to 3 minutes for up to 15 minutes, or until blood pressure returns to baseline.

• Remove the electrodes and allow the patient to wash. However, if the patient wishes to shower, advise him to wait 1 hour and then to use lukewarm water *to prevent dizziness and fainting.*

### Special considerations

Stop the test immediately if the patient experiences nausea, exhaustion, dizziness, or faintness, or if you detect any of the following: three consecutive PVC's on the tracing; decrease in systolic pressure to below the resting level; decrease in the heart rate to 10 beats per minute below the resting level; or onset of severe hypertension, sustained ventricular tachycardia, severe changes in the ST segment, alternating bundle branch pattern or new onset pattern, or any previously undetected rapid arrhythmia. Also, depending on the patient's condition and hospital policy, stop the test if the rhythm strip shows bundle branch block or an ST segment depression exceeding 3 mm. Rarely, persistent ST segment elevation may indicate transmural myocardial ischemia and contraindicates further testing. Avoid stopping the test abruptly if the patient has exercised strenuously *to prevent a possible vasovagal attack.*

Remember that the predictive accuracy of exercise electrocardiography in detecting coronary artery disease varies with the patient's history and sex, and that false-positive results occur in 15% to 20% of all patients. If the patient has an equivocal exercise EKG, an abnormal or uninterpretable resting EKG, left ventricular hypertrophy, or inability to achieve the maximum heart rate, the doctor may order a thallium scan after exercise. Although this test is more accurate than the exercise EKG, it shouldn't be performed on all cardiac patients *since it entails slight exposure to radioactivity and doesn't necessarily supply the needed diagnostic information.*

### Complications

Despite precautions, 2 or 3 of every 10,000 patients develop acute myocardial infarction, respiratory or cardiac arrest, or cerebrovascular accident during or after the exercise EKG.

### Documentation

Document the patient's vital signs, tolerance of the procedure, and any abnormal symptoms. Use a flowchart during the test to document the stage of protocol reached by the patient; the patient's heart rate at each minute of exercise; blood pressure at each progressive stage, and every 3 minutes after exercise; adverse symptoms, if any; EKG changes during exercise; and exercise-induced arrhythmias, if any.

DENISE A. HESS, RN

# Ambulatory Electrocardiography
[*Holter monitoring, ambulatory monitoring*]

*Although standard electrocardiography provides much information about the condition of the heart, it records only about 45 seconds of heart activity. Because of this short test period and the absence during the test of the normal physical and psychological stresses of daily activities, potentially lethal cardiac arrhythmias can remain undetected. Ambulatory electrocardiography can detect these arrhythmias by continuous recording of heart activity. It also helps evaluate chest pains, the effects of antiarrhythmic drug therapy, and patient status after acute myocardial infarction and pacemaker implantation.*

*During Holter monitoring, the patient wears a small reel-to-reel or cassette tape monitor connected to bipolar electrodes applied to his chest, and he keeps a diary of his activities and any associated symptoms, usually for 24 hours (about 100,000 cardiac cycles). After this period, the tape is analyzed by a microcomputer to permit correlation of cardiac irregularities, such as arrhythmias and ST segment changes, with the activities noted in the patient's diary. Other monitors can be worn for 5 to 7 days and are activated by the patient to record cardiac cycles only when he experiences symptoms.*

## Equipment

Monitor, case, and strap □ rechargeable batteries □ reel-to-reel or cassette tape □ electrodes (three to five, depending on the number of recording channels available) □ electrode gel, if necessary □ patient cable with lead wires □ test cable □ EKG machine for recording test strips □ alcohol or acetone □ 4″ × 4″ gauze sponges □ disposable razor □ nonallergenic adhesive tape □ sample and blank patient diaries.

## Preparation of equipment

Make sure the monitor has a new or freshly recharged battery. Load the cassette or tape reels, and attach the patient cable to the monitor securely. Gather all equipment necessary for electrode placement.

## Essential steps

● Because ambulatory electrocardiography is usually performed on an outpatient, carefully explain the procedure to him *to ensure his cooperation, thereby promoting accurate test results.* Tell him he may feel transient discomfort during preparation of the electrode sites. Demonstrate the application of the monitor and show him how to position it when he lies down. Advise him to wear loose-fitting clothing and a front-buttoning top.
● Tell the patient to follow his daily routine during the monitoring period. If he must bathe, advise a sponge bath *to avoid*

*wetting the equipment and dislodging the electrodes.*
● Show the patient a sample diary, and instruct him to log all his daily activities. For example, tell him to include walking, stair climbing, sleep, elimination, intercourse, emotional upset, physical symptoms (dizziness, palpitation, pain, fatigue), and ingestion of medication. Remind him to wear a watch so he can log his activities accurately.
● If applicable, demonstrate how to mark the tape at the onset of symptoms. (If a patient-activated monitor is being used, show the patient how to press the event button to activate the monitor.)
● Tell the patient not to tamper with the monitor or disconnect the lead wires or electrodes. Advise him to avoid magnets, metal detectors, high-voltage areas, and electric blankets *to prevent electrical interference that distorts the recording.* Show him how to check the recorder to make sure it's working properly. Explain that if the monitor light flashes, one of the electrodes may be loose and that he should test each one by depressing its center. Instruct him to return to the hospital or doctor's office if an electrode becomes detached.
● Drape the female patient until you are ready to apply the electrodes.
● Select the appropriate electrode sites. To analyze P waves, QRS complexes, ST segments, and T waves, use a modified $V_4$ or $V_5$ approach: Place the positive ( + ) electrode over the fifth rib in the left midclavicular line, the negative ( − ) electrode over the manubrium, and the ground electrode over the fifth rib in the right midclavicular line.

To analyze cardiac rhythm, set up a modified $V_1$ lead, which produces prominent P waves. Place the positive electrode over the sternum—near the xiphoid process—the negative electrode over the right clavicle or manubrium, and the ground over the fifth rib in the right midclavicular line. Make sure the electrodes are positioned over bone and not over intercostal spaces *to prevent muscle artifact.*
● Shave the electrode sites, if necessary,

and then cleanse the skin of oils with alcohol or acetone. Gently abrade the area until it reddens *to remove dead cells and to promote good skin-electrode contact.*
• Peel the backing from the electrodes and apply them to the prepared sites. (Usually, the electrodes are pregelled.) Be sure to press firmly on the adhesive portion of each electrode to fasten it securely to the skin and to press gently on its gel portion to ensure good contact.
• Attach the patient cable to the monitor, if you haven't already done so. Position the monitor and its case on the patient as he will wear it, and then attach the lead wires to the electrodes. Check that the leads, which are usually coded red ( + ), white ( − ), and green (ground), are matched with the correct electrodes.
• Test the electrode attachment circuit by connecting the monitor to a standard EKG machine and running a rhythm strip. Ask the patient to move his arms and to take several steps *to check for motion artifact.* When you are satisfied that the tracings are of good quality, secure the electrodes, leads, and patient cable to the patient's chest with nonallergenic tape, making sure to tape a loop of the lead wire near the electrode *to avoid placing strain on the electrode itself.*
• Run the patient cable through the front of the patient's shirt or blouse and button the clothing around it. Give the patient a blank diary, and start the first entry with the time and date you started the monitor.
• At the end of the test period, turn off the monitor, remove all electrodes, and clean the application sites. If the patient won't be returning to the doctor's office or the hospital immediately after the monitoring period, show him how to remove and store the equipment. Remind him to bring his diary when he returns.

**Special considerations**
If the procedure is performed on an inpatient whose activity is unrestricted, encourage him to walk about and simulate as many of his normal activities as possible. *Confining such a patient to bed prevents detection of arrhythmias that are precipitated by activity.*

**Documentation**
Record the duration of monitoring an outpatient. If monitoring is performed on an inpatient, enter any treatments, activities, and drug administration in the patient's diary. In the nursing cardex, document ongoing monitoring and convey this information to the next shift.

ANGELA D. LEHMAN, RN

## MONITORING

# Cardiac Monitoring

*Cardiac monitoring is used to continuously observe the heart's electrical activity in patients who may have a symptomatic arrhythmia or any cardiac pathology that may lead to life-threatening arrhythmias. It is also used to evaluate the effects of therapy. Like other forms of electrocardiography, this procedure uses electrodes applied to the patient's chest to pick up patterns of cardiac impulses for display and analysis on a monitor screen. The monitoring is done in several ways. Hardwire monitoring permits continuous observation of a patient directly connected to the monitor console. Telemetry monitoring permits continuous monitoring of an ambulatory patient not connected to a monitor; his cardiac impulses travel from a small transmitter worn by the patient to antenna wires in the ceiling that relay the patterns to the monitor screen.*

*Cardiac monitors usually perform three functions: they display the patient's cardiac rhythm and heart rate; they sound an alarm if heart rate rises above or falls below the allowable per-minute setting; and they provide printouts of cardiac rhythms for documentation.*

## Equipment

Alcohol sponges □ 4" x 4" gauze sponges □ cardiac monitor □ nonallergenic tape □ patient cable □ three lead wires □ three disposable pregelled electrodes. (The number of electrodes varies from three to five, depending on the manufacturer.) Optional: equipment for shaving (razor, basin, warm water, soap, towel, washcloth).

## Preparation of equipment

If necessary, plug the monitor into an electrical outlet and turn it on *to warm up the unit while you prepare the equipment and the patient.* Insert the monitoring end of the patient cable into the appropriate socket in the monitor.

Connect the lead wires to the patient cable: Insert the negative wire into the opening marked ( − ), N, or RA (right arm); the positive wire into the opening marked ( + ), P, LL (left leg) or LA (left arm); and insert the ground wire into the opening marked G, N (neutral), or RL (right leg). Then connect an electrode to each of the lead wires, carefully checking that each lead wire is in its correct outlet.

## Essential steps

● Explain the procedure to the patient and provide privacy. Wash your hands.
● Determine electrode positions on the patient's chest. Select the lead that displays the appropriate QRS complex, P waves, and pacing stimulus. If you select *lead II* (provides a tall, positive QRS complex and a positive P wave), place the negative electrode on the right sternal border at the first intercostal space. Then place the positive electrode at the fourth intercostal space, left of the midclavicular line, and place the ground electrode at the fourth intercostal space, right sternal border.
● If you select a *modified chest lead* (*MCL₁*), which helps determine conduction disturbances or ectopic sites that can't be identified in lead II, place the negative electrode just below the left clavicle in the midclavicular line. Place the positive electrode at the fourth intercostal space at the right sternal border, and place the ground electrode just below the right clavicle in the midclavicular line.
● If necessary, shave an area about 4" (10.16 cm) in diameter around each

---

### SETTING UP FOR TELEMETRY MONITORING

Telemetry monitoring detects arrhythmias precipitated by mild exercise. It's especially useful for the ambulatory patient, because it permits greater freedom than hardwire monitoring and avoids electrical hazards by isolating the monitor system from leakage and accidental shock. To set up telemetry monitoring:
● Insert a battery in the telemetry transmitter, matching the polarity markings on the transmitter case with those on the battery.
● Test the battery's charge by observing the oscilloscope screen, which shows no cardiac activity if the battery is low. In some models, check the battery by pushing the test light button on the back of the transmitter. If the test light fails to go on, replace the battery. Make sure the lead wire cable is securely attached to the transmitter.
● Show the transmitter to the patient and explain how it works. Before proceeding,

answer any questions he may have.
● Apply electrodes to the patient's chest and attach the lead wires to them.
● Place the transmitter in the pouch provided by the manufacturer or in a pouch provided by the hospital. Tie the pouch strings around the patient's neck and waist. Make sure the pouch fits snugly without making the patient uncomfortable. If no pouch is available, place the transmitter in the patient's bathrobe pocket.
● After locating the patient's telemetry monitor in the central console, calibrate it and adjust the heart rate alarms as you would a hardwire monitor.
● Some units have a button that can be pushed if the patient feels symptomatic. This causes the central console to print a rhythm strip. Tell the patient how and when to use this button.
● The transmitter must be removed if the patient takes a shower or bath.

# TROUBLESHOOTING CARDIAC MONITORS

| PROBLEM | POSSIBLE CAUSES | SOLUTIONS |
|---|---|---|
| **False high-rate alarm** | • Monitor interpreting large T waves as QRS complexes, doubling the rate.<br>• Skeletal muscle activity | • Reposition electrodes to lead where QRS complexes are taller than T waves.<br>• Place electrodes away from major muscle masses. |
| **False low-rate alarm** | • Shift in electrical axis from patient movement, making QRS complexes too small to register<br>• Low amplitude of QRS<br>• Poor contact between electrode and skin | • Reapply electrodes. Set *gain* so height of complex is greater than 1 millivolt.<br>• Increase gain.<br>• Reapply electrodes. |
| **Low amplitude** | • Gain dial set too low<br>• Poor contact between skin and electrodes; dried gel; broken or loose lead wires; poor connection between patient and monitor; malfunctioning monitor; physiologic loss of QRS amplitude | • Increase gain.<br>• Check connections on all lead wires and monitoring cable. Replace as necessary. Reapply electrodes, if required. |
| **Wandering baseline** | • Poor position or contact between electrodes and skin<br>• Thoracic movement with respirations | • Reposition or replace electrodes.<br>• Reposition electrodes. |
| **Artifact (waveform interference)** | • Patient experiencing seizures, chills, or anxiety<br><br>• Patient movement<br>• Electrodes applied improperly<br><br>• Static electricity<br><br><br>• Electrical short circuit in lead wires or cable<br><br>• Interference from decreased room humidity | • Notify doctor and treat patient as ordered. Keep patient warm and reassure him.<br>• Help patient relax.<br>• Check electrodes and reapply, if necessary.<br>• Make sure cables do not have exposed connectors. Change static-causing bedclothes.<br>• Replace broken equipment. Use stress loops when applying lead wires.<br>• Regulate humidity to 40%. |
| **Broken lead wires or cable** | • Stress loops not used on lead wires<br>• Cables and lead wires cleaned with alcohol or acetone, causing brittleness | • Replace lead wires and retape them, using stress loops.<br>• Clean cable and lead wires with soapy water. *Do not allow cable ends to become wet.* Replace cable as necessary. |
| **60-cycle interference (fuzzy baseline)** | • Electrical interference from other equipment in room<br><br>• Patient's bed improperly grounded | • Attach all electrical equipment to common ground. Check plugs to make sure prongs aren't loose.<br>• Attach bed ground to the room's common ground. |

electrode site. Clean the area with an alcohol sponge and dry it completely *to remove skin secretions that may interfere with proper electrode function.* Gently abrade the dried area by rubbing it briskly until it reddens *to remove dead skin cells and promote better electrical contact with living cells.* (Some electrodes have a small rough patch for abrading the skin; otherwise, use a dry washcloth or a dry gauze sponge.)

● Remove the backing from the pregelled electrode and test the center of the gel pad for moistness. If it isn't moist, remoisten it with electrode gel or paste, or replace it with a fresh electrode. Then apply the electrode to the site, being careful to firmly press the adhesive part *to ensure a tight seal.*

● Fasten the lead wire receptacle to the patient's gown *to avoid stress on the lead wires during patient movement.* Form a stress loop in each lead wire, tape it to the patient's skin, and leave enough slack between the electrode and the stress loop to allow for patient movement without straining the electrode connection.

● Using the gain control on the monitor, adjust the size of the QRS complexes that appear on the screen. Calibrate the monitor by pushing the calibration button, which causes a waveform 1 mv high to appear. If necessary, adjust the gain control *to make the R wave of the QRS complex higher than the 1-mv waveform.* Then center the waveform on the monitor screen.

● Set the upper and lower limits of the heart rate alarm, based on assessment of each patient's cardiac status. Most monitoring systems allow the rate to be set on the bedside monitor or the central console. Since these are integrated circuits, it will automatically calibrate the whole system. Put the alarm on automatic so that it sounds whenever the patient's heart rate exceeds or falls below the preset limits.

● Make sure the monitor counts each QRS complex. If an audible alarm or flashing light doesn't occur when each complex appears on the screen, increase the gain setting until each complex is sufficiently

high to trigger the audible alarm and the rate light every time.

● Demonstrate the alarm system to the patient and tell him that it may be triggered by movement or a loose electrode, as well as by rhythm disturbances. Emphasize that the machine is not a part of therapy, and that he should feel free to move about in bed despite the alarm.

## Special considerations

Avoid removing the paper backing of the electrodes until just before application *to prevent them from drying out.* Position electrodes on the patient's chest *so they won't interfere with application of defibrillator paddles if emergency defibrillation is required.*

Make sure all electrical equipment and outlets are grounded properly *to avoid electrical shock and artifacts.*

If the patient has an allergic reaction to the monitoring electrodes, secure them with hypoallergenic tape. If the electrode itself is irritating, change its location daily and keep its site as clean and dry as possible. If you use only 3 leads of a 4- or 5-lead cable, unused lead receptacles must be plugged *to prevent interference.*

## Documentation

Record the date and time that monitoring begins and the lead used. Document cardiac rhythm and rate at least every hour, and whenever arrhythmias occur. Mark the rhythm strip with the patient's name, date, time, and the lead used. Document lead changes by running a printout of the new pattern and include reasons for the changes.

PATRICIA GONCE MILLER, RN, MS

# Arterial Pressure Monitoring

*Arterial pressure monitoring provides continuous and accurate arterial pressure readings through a transducer that* converts blood pressure into electrical impulses. These electrical impulses are displayed on a monitor screen and recorded on paper tape. In addition, a visible and audible alarm sounds when pressure exceeds preset limits. Arterial monitoring also shows blood pressure wave configuration, providing information about circulatory system physiology and function.

This procedure is commonly indicated in patients receiving vasoactive drugs and those with an altered hemodynamic status related to variations in cardiac output, hypertensive crisis, dysrhythmias, or shock. The transducer for arterial pressure monitoring may simply be added to an existing arterial line, or all necessary equipment may have to be assembled. Arterial pressure monitoring itself has no contraindications; however, insertion of an arterial line is contraindicated in a patient with severe coagulopathy unless the benefits outweigh the risks of bleeding and thrombosis (see "Arterial Line Insertion" in Chapter 6).

## Equipment

To add a standard transducer: transducer dome □ transducer □ transducer mount □ 3' to 4' pressure tubing □ 2 three-way stopcocks □ monitoring equipment.

To add a miniature transducer: transducer □ three-way stopcock □ monitoring equipment □ isolation dome (optional).

To assemble a complete setup: transducer, dome, and mount (or miniature transducer, with isolation dome, if desired) □ pressure cuff □ 500-ml bag of normal saline solution □ heparin injectable 1:1,000 □ I.V. pole □ 3-ml syringe with 22G 1″ needle □ alcohol sponges □ medication-added label □ nonvented administration set with microdrip chamber □ 3' to 4' pressure tubing (for standard transducer) □ continuous flush device □ 6″ extension pressure tubing □ 5 three-way stopcocks (3 for standard transducer, 2 for miniature transducer) □ male adapter plugs □ dead-end caps □ monitoring equipment.

Prepackaged I.V. equipment is available in various combinations including complete sets. Some sets include two stopcocks, one for each side of the continuous flush device. Isolation units, which act as a dome for the miniature transducer, eliminate the need for sterilization.

## Preparation of equipment

Wash your hands. Turn on the pressure monitor to warm it up while you prepare the equipment. No other special preparation is needed to add a transducer. However, if you're preparing a complete setup, first place the 22G 1″ needle on the 3-ml syringe, clean the top of the heparin bottle with an alcohol sponge, and draw 500 to 1000 U of heparin into the syringe, depending on institution policy. Clean the injection port of the saline bag with an alcohol sponge and inject the heparin. Fill out the medication-added label and place it on the bag. Clean the bag's main port with an alcohol sponge and insert the administration set spike. Invert the bag, open the flow clamp, squeeze air from the bag to minimize the chance of introducing air into the system, and close the clamp. Place the saline bag in the pressure cuff and hang it on the I.V. pole. Squeeze the drip chamber until it's one-quarter full—it will fill further when the bag is pressurized.

If you're using a transducer and transducer dome, attach the dome to the transducer following the manufacturer's instructions. Attach the proper port of the continuous flush device to one of the transducer dome connections (to the 45° connection if there's also a 90° connection). Place a three-way stopcock on the opposite end of the device (the patient's end), and turn it off to the device. Place a stopcock on the opposite dome connection and open it to air and the dome.

Mount the transducer on the I.V. pole, if necessary, and attach the administration set tubing to the short tubing from the continuous flush device. Next, connect the long length of pressure tubing to the stopcock on the continuous flush device; connect the second stopcock to the opposite end of this tubing. Close this

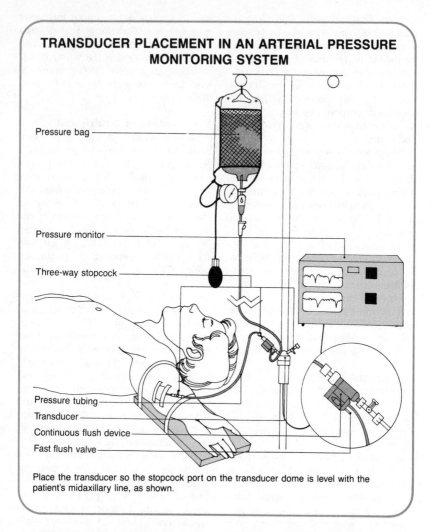

**TRANSDUCER PLACEMENT IN AN ARTERIAL PRESSURE MONITORING SYSTEM**

Pressure bag

Pressure monitor

Three-way stopcock

Pressure tubing
Transducer
Continuous flush device
Fast flush valve

Place the transducer so the stopcock port on the transducer dome is level with the patient's midaxillary line, as shown.

stopcock to the line and air, and connect the 6″ extension tubing to it. Open the flow clamp and run fluid very slowly to the transducer by activating the fast flush release until fluid flows from the stopcock. *This must be done slowly to reduce the risk of introducing air bubbles into the tubing and dome. If necessary, turn and tap the dome to ensure the absence of air bubbles.*

Turn off the stopcock on the transducer dome and place a dead-end cap on both ports *to ensure a closed system and prevent fluid loss and air pocket formation.* Open the stopcock on the continuous flush device to the patient and the device, and open the stopcock on the opposite end of the tubing to the extension tubing. Remove the cap on the extension tubing, activate the fast flush release, and slowly fill the tubing with fluid. Turn both stopcocks to all positions *to expel air.* Close the stopcock at the end of the tubing to the line and air, replace the cap, and place dead-end caps on all stopcock ports venting to air *to prevent contamination and fluid leakage.* Place a male adapter plug on one stopcock port *to allow for the drawing of blood samples while maintaining a closed system.* Inflate the pressure cuff to 300 mmHg and check for leaks.

*If you're using a miniature transducer,* place stopcocks on both sides of the continuous flush device and attach the extension tubing to the stopcock on the patient side. Close this stopcock to air and open it to the fluid line; then shut off the opposite stopcock. Attach the administration set tubing to the short length of tubing from the continuous flush device. Remove the cap from the end of the extension tubing, open the flow clamp, and activate the fast flush release, allowing fluid to flow through the line. When all air is expelled, replace the cap on the extension tubing and open the stopcock to air and the fluid.

Activate the fast flush release and, when the port's filled, place a dead-end cap on it and close the stopcock to this port. Open the opposite stopcock to the fluid line and close it to the parallel port; then activate the fast flush release. When fluid flows from the port perpendicularly to the fluid line, place a dead-end cap on it. Open the stopcock to the fluid line and the opposite port and activate the fast flush release. Attach the miniature transducer to this port when all air is expelled. Inflate the pressure cuff to 300 mmHg *to check for leaks.*

### Essential steps

*To add a standard transducer to an existing arterial line:*
• Explain the procedure to the patient.
• Attach a stopcock to the long length of pressure tubing and activate the fast flush release *to clear the existing line.*
• Turn off the stopcock in the fluid line to the patient and disconnect the continuous flush device. Then connect the stopcock on the pressure tubing to the continuous flush device, open it to the fluid, and activate the fast flush release until the tubing and stopcock fill.
• Turn the stopcock off to the pressure tubing, hold the stopcock port venting to air upright until filled, and put on a dead-end cap. Turn it off to this port.

• Connect the free end of the pressure tubing to the patient and open the distal stopcock to the patient and fluid.
• Attach the transducer dome to the transducer, following the manufacturer's instructions, and mount it on the I.V. pole.
• Place a stopcock on one dome port (the upright one, if present), and open it to air and the dome.
• Plug the transducer into the monitor; then zero and calibrate the monitor according to the manufacturer's instructions.
• Turn the stopcock on the continuous flush device so it's shut off to the patient. Remove the dead-end cap from the device and attach it to the free port on the transducer dome. Then activate the fast flush release and fill the dome with fluid until it flows from the stopcock. Shut off this stopcock so that fluid flows from both ports, and place dead-end caps on these ports.
• Turn the stopcock on the continuous flush device so it's shut off to the free port; then activate the fast flush release to clear the line.
• Adjust the stopcock port on the transducer dome to the height of the right atrium. To do this, first locate the level of the fourth intercostal space at the sternum. Next, measure the depth of the chest at this level and place a mark at one half the anterior-posterior distance (midaxillary line). Finally, adjust the stopcock port on the transducer on the pole to the proper height.

*To add a miniature transducer:*
• Explain the procedure to the patient.
• Plug the transducer into the monitor; then zero and calibrate the monitor according to the manufacturer's instructions.
• Activate the fast flush release *to clear the line;* then shut off the stopcock to the patient. Remove the dead-end cap from the continuous flush device and attach one side port of another stopcock. Open this stopcock's middle port to air and activate the fast flush release until fluid flows from it. Place a dead-end cap on this port, prime the opposite port, and

attach the miniature transducer.

• Open both stopcocks to the line and close them to the free port; then activate the fast flush release to clear the line.

• Make sure the transducer is level with the patient's right atrium.

*To use the fully assembled system:*

• Bring the equipment to the same side of the patient as the anticipated insertion site.

• Place the transducer at the height of the right atrium. Then plug it into the monitor.

• Make sure the stopcock on the dome or closest to the miniature transducer is open to the transducer and air; then zero and calibrate the monitor according to the manufacturer's instructions.

• Close this stopcock to the free port and cap the others (only with a standard transducer), or open the other stopcocks to the patient and transducer.

• Assist the doctor with catheter insertion (see "Arterial Line Insertion" in Chapter 6) and attach the fluid line to the catheter.

*For any assembly:*

• Record systolic, diastolic, and mean pressure readings and obtain strip chart recordings, if desired.

• Observe the pressure waveform on the monitor screen. Notify the doctor of any changes.

• Set the monitor alarms about 20 mmHg above and below the patient's normal pressures, depending on his condition. Keep the alarms on at all times.

• Activate the fast flush release at intervals specified by institution policy *to prevent thrombus formation.* Take pressure readings, as ordered.

• Frequently check the patient's pulse and color, and the temperature of the involved extremity. Notify the doctor of any changes.

**Special considerations**

Always use aseptic technique and observe electrical hazard precautions. Remember that pressure readings can be altered by a clot in the catheter, occlusion of the catheter tip against the artery wall, or the presence of air or a leak in the

system. Prevent these by checking all connections, removing all air from the system, flushing the line at specified intervals, and making sure the pressure cuff reaches 300 mmHg.

Generally, you should recalibrate the monitoring equipment at the beginning of your shift. If there's any doubt as to the accuracy of the monitored arterial pressure, take a cuff pressure reading.

Inspect and redress the insertion site with povidone-iodine ointment every 24 hours, using aseptic technique and gloves. Mark the dressing with the date, time, and your initials. The monitoring apparatus that contacts the I.V. fluid should be replaced every 24 to 48 hours *to aid infection control.*

Dextrose 5% in water is sometimes used as the I.V. solution, *because it's not a plasma expander and doesn't conduct electricity.*

**Documentation**

Begin a flowchart of pressure readings. Record the date and time of monitoring, the type of arterial line, and the arterial wave shape and changes.

MARIE J. ROSE, RN, MSN

# Pulmonary Artery and Capillary Wedge Pressure Monitoring

*This procedure uses a balloon-tipped, flow-directed catheter, connected to a transducer and a monitor, to measure pulmonary artery pressure (PAP) and pulmonary capillary wedge pressure (PCWP). Monitoring these pressures helps assess ventricular capacity to receive and eject blood. It also helps detect complications of acute myocardial infarction, provides information about vascular volume status, and helps evaluate the effect of drug therapy.*

*The pulmonary artery catheter can have two to five lumens for multiple mea-*

*surements and wires for atrial or ventricular pacing. It is inserted by the doctor either percutaneously into the subclavian, jugular, or femoral vein, or through a venous cutdown in the antecubital fossa, and threaded to the junction of the vena cava and right atrium. After the balloon is inflated, venous circulation carries the catheter tip through the right atrium and ventricle to a branch of the pulmonary artery, where the balloon will wedge in a vessel lumen smaller than itself. When the balloon is deflated, the catheter drifts out of this position and into the pulmonary artery, its normal resting place. Catheter progress is usually followed by changes in waveforms on a cardiac monitor; it can also be tracked fluoroscopically. Once the catheter is in place, PAP can be monitored continuously and PCWP taken as required. Pulmonary artery catheterization must be performed carefully in a patient with an implanted pacemaker or left bundle branch block.*

### Equipment

Balloon-tipped, flow-directed pulmonary artery catheter □ pressure cuff □ 500-ml bag of normal saline solution □ heparin injectable 1:1,000 □ 3-ml syringe with 22G 1″ needle □ alcohol sponges □ medication-added label □ nonvented I.V. administration set with microdrip chamber □ 3′ to 4′ pressure tubing □ continuous flush device □ transducer □ transducer dome □ 6″ extension pressure tubing □ 3 three-way stopcocks □ male adapter plug □ two dead-end caps □ I.V. pole with transducer mount □ monitor □ razor, washcloth, basin, and towel (if femoral insertion site is used) □ 250 ml of normal saline solution heparinized with 1 unit heparin, 1:1,000/ml □ introducer, one size larger than catheter □ sterile gowns □ masks □ sterile gloves □ sterile tray containing instruments for procedure □ two 10-ml syringes □ one 5-ml syringe □ povidone-iodine solution □ 1% to 2% lidocaine □ 25G ½″ needle □ 1″ and 3″ tape □ emergency resuscitation equipment □ electrocardiogram (EKG) monitor □ EKG electrodes □ syringe for taking PCWP □ armboard for

antecubital insertion □ lead aprons (if insertion is done under fluoroscopic guidance) □ carbon dioxide for balloon inflation (optional).

Prepackaged equipment for the fluid line is available in various combinations, including complete sets. Some sets incorporate an additional stopcock—one for each side of the continuous flush device. If a miniature transducer is being used, the long length of pressure tubing, one stopcock, and the transducer dome and mount aren't necessary, since the transducer is strapped to the patient's arm, and usually doesn't require a dome. However, transducer domes are now available and are used so the miniature transducer won't require sterilization.

### Preparation of equipment

Turn on the pressure monitor *to allow it to warm up while you prepare the equipment.* Wash your hands. Place the 22G 1″ needle on the 3-ml syringe, cleanse the top of the heparin bottle with an alcohol sponge, and draw 500 to 1,000 U of heparin (depending on the institution's policy) into the syringe. Cleanse the injection port of the 500-ml normal saline solution bag with an alcohol sponge and inject the heparin. Fill out the medication-added label and place it on the bag. Cleanse the bag's main port with an alcohol sponge, and insert the administration set spike. Invert the bag, open the flow clamp, squeeze all the air out of the bag *to minimize the chance of introducing air into the system,* and close the clamp. Place the normal saline solution bag in the pressure cuff and hang it on the I.V. pole. Squeeze the drip chamber until it's one-quarter full; it will fill further when the bag's pressurized.

*If you're using a transducer and transducer dome,* attach the dome to the transducer following the manufacturer's directions. Attach the proper port of the continuous flush device to one of the transducer dome connections (to the 45° connection if there's also a 90° connection). Place a three-way stopcock on the opposite end of the device (the patient's end), and turn it off to the device. Place a stopcock on the opposite transducer dome connection, and open it to air and the dome. Then, mount the transducer on the I.V. pole, if necessary. (Some transducers don't need to be mounted on an I.V. pole; they can be laid on the bed.)

Attach the administration set tubing to the short tubing from the continuous flush device. Connect the long length of pressure tubing to the stopcock on the continuous flush device, and connect the second stopcock to the opposite end of this tubing. Close this stopcock to the line and air, and connect the 6″ extension tubing to it. Open the flow clamp and slowly run fluid to the transducer by activating the fast flush release until fluid flows from the stopcock. *This must be done slowly to reduce the risk of introducing air bubbles into the tubing and dome.* If necessary, turn and tap the transducer dome *to ensure that no air bubbles are present.*

Turn off the stopcock on the transducer dome and place dead-end caps on both ports *to ensure a closed system and prevent fluid loss and air pocket formation.* Open the stopcock on the continuous flush device to the patient and the device; open the stopcock on the opposite end of the tubing to the extension tubing. Remove the cap on the extension tubing, activate the fast flush release, and slowly fill the tubing with fluid. Turn both stopcocks to all positions *to expel air.* Close the stopcock at the end of the tubing to the line and air, replace the cap, and place dead-end caps on all stopcock ports venting to air *to prevent contamination and fluid leakage.* Place a male adapter plug on one stopcock port *to allow for drawing blood samples while maintaining a closed system.* Inflate the pressure cuff to 300 mmHg and check for leaks.

*If you're using a miniature transducer,* place stopcocks on both sides of the continuous flush device, and attach the extension tubing to the stopcock on the patient's end. Turn this stopcock so it's closed to air and open to the fluid line, and shut off the opposite stopcock. Then attach the administration set tub-

ing to the short length of tubing from the continuous flush device. Remove the cap from the end of the extension tubing, open the flow clamp, and activate the fast flush release, allowing fluid to flow through the line. When all air is expelled, replace the cap on the extension tubing and open the stopcock to air and the fluid. Activate the fast flush release and, when the port is filled, place a male adapter plug *to allow for drawing blood samples while maintaining a closed system;* close the stopcock to this port. Turn the other stopcock so it's open to the fluid line and closed to the parallel port, and activate the fast flush release. When fluid flows from the port perpendicularly to the fluid line, place a dead-end cap on it. Then, open the stopcock to the fluid line and the opposite port and activate the fast flush release. Attach the miniature transducer to this port when all air is expelled. Inflate the pressure cuff to 300 mmHg and check for leaks.

### Essential steps

• Explain the procedure to the patient *to allay his fears and promote his cooperation.* Make sure he has signed a consent form and that he understands what it means.

• Place the EKG electrodes on the patient, if they're not already in place, and connect them to the monitor. For a subclavian approach, keep the electrodes on the opposite side of the patient's chest from the insertion site.

• Bring the equipment to the same side of the patient as the insertion site.

*To zero and calibrate the system:*

• Place the transducer dome at the height of the right atrium, and locate the level of the fourth intercostal space at the sternum. Then measure the depth of the chest at this level and place a mark at one-half the anterior-posterior distance (midaxillary line). Next, adjust the transducer on the pole to the proper height. This usually isn't necessary with a miniature transducer as long as it's taped to the patient's arm.

• Plug the transducer cable into the monitor.

- Remove the dead-end cap and open the stopcock on the transducer dome (or, if you're using a miniature transducer, the one closest to it) *to open the transducer to air.*
- Zero and calibrate the monitor according to the manufacturer's directions. Then replace the dead-end cap and close the stopcock to this port.

*To assist with catheter insertion:*
- Make sure emergency resuscitation equipment is readily available. Open the tray containing all the necessary equipment for insertion, maintaining sterile technique.
- Position the patient so the insertion site is visible and accessible. Illuminate the site with an overhead light. For femoral insertion, cleanse and shave an area covering a 3″ (7.6-cm) radius *to help prevent infection and improve tape adhesion.*
- Put on a mask and help the doctor to put on a sterile gown and gloves. If catheter placement is to be guided by fluoroscopy, the doctor must wear a lead apron under the sterile gown. You should also put one on. Place a mask over the patient's nose and mouth, if desired.
- Open the packaging of the syringes and needles and drop them onto the sterile tray, maintaining sterile technique *to prevent contamination.*
- Cleanse the top of the local anesthetic bottle with an alcohol sponge, and invert it *so the doctor can insert the syringe and withdraw the drug.*
- Pour povidone-iodine solution into one of the sterile bowls on the equipment tray.
- Pour 250 ml of heparinized normal saline solution into the other sterile bowl on the equipment tray. *The doctor uses this to test the catheter balloon and to wet the catheter, decreasing the risk of clot formation during insertion.*
- The doctor cleanses the insertion site with povidone-iodine and drapes around the area with sterile drapes.
- Help the doctor attach the distal (pulmonary artery) port of the catheter to the solution line, and then flush the catheter with solution *to remove all air.*
- If a miniature transducer is being used,

the doctor may wish to attach it himself. If so, open its packaging so he can take it, maintaining sterility.
- As the doctor advances the catheter, monitor pressure tracings and EKGs to help locate the catheter if it accidentally moves backward from the pulmonary artery, especially into the right ventricle.
- After the doctor sutures the catheter, apply antiseptic ointment to the insertion site *to reduce the risk of infection.* Place a sterile 4″ x 4″ gauze sponge above and beneath the coiled catheter *to ensure sterility of the catheter insertion site.*
- Apply a dry occlusive dressing to the site. Then use tape to secure the catheter to the dressing *to prevent accidental dislodgment.*
- If the line was inserted into the antecubital fossa, apply a padded armboard to prevent bending the arm.
- Write the date, time, and your initials on a piece of tape and place it on the dressing.
- Remove all used or unnecessary equipment from the room, and throw away all disposable equipment properly. Rinse reusable items in cold water *to remove protein debris* and send them to the central supply department for resterilization.
- Arrange for a chest X-ray at the patient's bedside *to verify correct catheter placement,* if ordered.

*To take a PAP reading:*
- Make sure all the stopcocks are set properly.
- Observe the monitor for pulmonary artery systolic (PAS) and diastolic (PAD) waveforms, and obtain waveform strips *for documentation and for baseline reference.*
- Record PAS, PAD, and mean values (some monitors record this continuously; some require manual setting).

*To take a PCWP reading:*
- Make sure the machine is set to monitor mean pressure.
- To the balloon port, attach a syringe of the size specified on the catheter shaft, filled with the maximum amount of air or carbon dioxide.
- Slowly inject the gas from the syringe

## TROUBLESHOOTING HEMODYNAMIC PRESSURE MONITORING

| PROBLEM | POSSIBLE CAUSES | SOLUTIONS |
|---|---|---|
| **No waveform** | • Power supply turned off.<br>• Monitor screen pressure range set too low.<br><br>• Loose connection in line<br>• Transducer not connected to amplifier.<br>• Stopcock off to patient.<br>• Catheter occluded or out of blood vessel. | • Check power supply.<br>• Raise monitor screen pressure range, if necessary. Rebalance and recalibrate equipment.<br>• Tighten loose connections.<br>• Check and tighten connection.<br><br>• Position stopcock correctly.<br>• Use fast-flush valve to flush line.<br>• Try to aspirate blood from catheter. If the line still won't flush, notify the doctor and prepare to replace the line. |
| **Drifing waveforms** | • Improper warm-up<br><br>• Electrical cable kinked or compressed.<br>• Temperature change in room air or I.V. flush solution. | • Allow monitor and transducer to warm up for 10 to 15 minutes.<br>• Place monitor's cable where it can't be stepped on or compressed.<br>• Routinely zero and calibrate equipment 30 minutes after setting it up. This allows I.V. fluid to warm to room temperature. |
| **Line fails to flush** | • Stopcocks positioned incorrectly.<br><br>• Inadequate pressure from pressure bag<br>• Kink in pressure tubing or blood clot in catheter | • Make sure stopcocks are positioned correctly.<br>• Make sure pressure bag gauge reads 300 mmHg.<br>• Check pressure tubing for kinks.<br>• Try to aspirate the clot with a syringe.<br>• If the line still won't flush, notify the doctor and prepare to replace the line, if necessary. *Important:* Never use a syringe to *flush* a hemodynamic line. |
| **Artifact** (waveform interference) | • Patient movement<br><br>• Electrical interference<br><br>• Catheter fling (tip of pulmonary artery catheter moving rapidly in large blood vessel or heart chamber) | • Wait until the patient is quiet before taking a reading.<br>• Make sure electrical equipment is connected and grounded correctly.<br>• Notify the doctor. He may try to reposition the catheter. |

into the balloon while observing the monitor screen, and inject only until the PA waveform changes to the PCWP waveform. The PCWP waveform often occurs before the maximum amount of gas is injected, but depends on the size of the pulmonary artery. Close the port lock *to hold pressure in the balloon until a mean pressure is obtained.*
• Record the mean pressure.
• Remove the syringe and leave the port lock in the open position *to allow gas to escape and to prevent the balloon from remaining inflated accidentally.*

| PROBLEM | POSSIBLE CAUSES | SOLUTIONS |
|---|---|---|
| **Falsely high readings** | • Transducer balancing port positioned below patient's right atrium.<br>• Flush solution flow rate is too fast.<br>• Air in system<br><br>• Catheter fling (tip of pulmonary artery catheter moving rapidly in large blood vessel or heart chamber) | • Position balancing port level with the patient's right atrium.<br>• Check flush solution flow rate. Maintain it at 3 to 4 ml/hour.<br>• Remove air from the lines and the transducer.<br>• Notify the doctor. He may try to reposition the catheter. |
| **Falsely low readings** | • Transducer balancing port positioned above right atrium.<br>• Transducer imbalance<br><br>• Loose connection | • Position balancing port level with the patient's right atrium.<br>• Make sure the transducer's flow system isn't kinked or occluded and rebalance and recalibrate the equipment.<br>• Tighten loose connections. |
| **Damped waveform** | • Air bubbles<br><br><br>• Blood clot in catheter<br>• Blood flashback in line<br><br><br><br><br><br>• Transducer position<br><br><br><br>• Arterial catheter out of blood vessel or pressed against vessel wall. | • Secure all connections.<br>• Remove air from lines and transducer.<br>• Check for and replace cracked equipment.<br>• Refer to "Line fails to flush" above.<br>• Make sure stopcock positions are correct.<br>• Tighten loose connections and replace cracked equipment.<br>• Flush line with fast-flush valve.<br>• Replace the transducer dome if blood backs up into it.<br>• Make sure the transducer is kept at the level of the right atrium at all times. Improper levels give false high or low pressure readings.<br>• Reposition if the catheter is against vessel wall.<br>• Try to aspirate blood to confirm proper placement in the vessel. If you can't aspirate blood, notify the doctor and prepare to replace the line. *Note:* Bloody drainage at the insertion site may indicate catheter displacement. Notify the doctor immediately. |

• Check on the monitor waveform screen to verify that the catheter has returned to a pulmonary artery position.

• According to hospital policy, activate the fast flush release to flush the catheter, *which helps reposition the catheter tip.*

• Set the high and low rate alarms about 20 mmHg above and below the patient's normal pressures, depending on his condition. Keep the alarms on at *all* times.

• Activate the fast flush release at intervals specified by the institution's policy *to prevent thrombus formation.*

• Take pressure readings, as ordered,

and ensure that the pressure cuff maintains 300 mmHg of pressure. Zero and calibrate the monitor as specified by the manufacturer.

• Frequently check the involved extremity for pulse, color, temperature and sensation, and notify the doctor of any changes.

• Change the catheter dressing when it becomes wet or soiled, or at intervals specified by the institution's policy.

## Special considerations

Use aseptic technique throughout the procedure *to prevent infection.* Prevent exsanguination from a disconnection in the system by using Luer-Loks or other positive locks at all connections, keeping the catheter and all parts of the system unobscured and making sure the monitor is on at all times. Always observe electrical hazard precautions.

Tubing, stopcocks, continuous flush devices, and fluid for infusion should be changed every 24 to 48 hours, depending on the institution's policy, *to aid infection control.*

Positive pressure ventilation may alter the patient's reading in any direction. Pressures should be recorded with the patient on the ventilator.

Dextrose 5% in water is sometimes used as the I.V. solution *because it's not a plasma expander and doesn't conduct an electrical current.*

 During insertion, notify the doctor immediately if the patient experiences arrhythmias, dyspnea, tachypnea, hemoptysis, stridor, or drastic changes in vital signs or pressure readings. These may indicate cardiac perforation, pulmonary artery rupture, hemorrhage, pneumothorax, or hemothorax. Also, notify the doctor of any later arrhythmias.

Note the volume of gas needed to achieve a wedge. Because carbon dioxide diffuses through the balloon at approximately ½ ml/minute, it may be difficult to estimate this, and it may be hard to achieve a wedge. If the volume of gas required for a wedge is significantly be-

low that indicated on the catheter, notify the doctor, *since the catheter may have migrated distally.* You should feel resistance when inflating the balloon. If you don't, notify the doctor immediately—the balloon may have ruptured.

 Never introduce air into a balloon if you suspect it's ruptured; this can cause an air embolus. Prevent balloon rupture by knowing the maximum volume of the balloon, and avoid overinflating the balloon or aspirating from it. Don't leave the balloon wedged for more than 1 to 2 minutes—even less in the elderly patient or one with pulmonary hypertension. Air in the flush system can also cause an embolus.

If the waveform won't return to pulmonary arterial from a wedge, or if it's dampening with low numbers and decreased PAS-PAD differential, check for equipment problems. Then check the patient's blood pressure and pulse. If these aren't changed, the catheter is probably wedged. Because a permanent wedge can cause pulmonary infarct and necrosis, immediately activate the fast flush release, *which can push the catheter tip away from a vessel wall.* Then check for a slowed drip rate and increased pressure readings—signs that the catheter is still wedged. If it is, turn the patient on his right side and instruct him to cough as you flush the line. If the waveform doesn't return to pulmonary arterial, turn the patient onto his left side and repeat the procedure. If there's still no change, notify the doctor immediately.

Large volumes of fluid and drugs should not be given through the distal port, *since vessel spasm or rupture may result.*

## Complications

Thrombosis can result from local irritation from the catheter; the heparinized flush helps prevent thrombus formation. Thromboembolus can occur if a thrombus breaks off and lodges in the circulatory system.

## Documentation

Record the time, size and type of catheter

inserted, insertion site, vital signs, administration of drugs (if any), initial PAP and PCWP readings and tracings, and the patient's tolerance of the procedure. Start a flowsheet of PAP readings and tracings, noting any changes.

ARLENE STRONG, RN, MN
EDWARD AVERILL, RN, BSN

# Central Venous Pressure Monitoring

*Central venous pressure (CVP) measurements are monitored with a manometer connected to a catheter that's threaded through the subclavian or jugular vein (or, less commonly, the basilic, cephalic, or saphenous veins) and placed in or near the right atrium. This procedure allows accurate determination of right atrial blood pressure, which reflects right ventricular pressure; in effect, this indicates the capacity of the right heart to receive and eject blood. CVP is also used to assess blood volume.*

*Because central venous pressure rises only after significant changes have occurred in the left heart or pulmonary venous system, CVP monitoring is being replaced in many hospitals by pulmonary artery (PA) catheterization for assessing rapidly changing cardiovascular status. PA catheterization detects cardiovascular changes before they cause changes in the CVP. However, CVP measurement is still the procedure of choice for postoperative monitoring during hemorrhage, or for assessing hydration status to determine fluid replacement.*

*CVP usually ranges from 3 to 15 $cmH_2O$, but varies with the patient's size, position, and hydration state. Only relative changes in CVP are significant.*

## Equipment

Disposable CVP manometer set with stopcock, extension tubing, and leveling device □ I.V. pole □ container of I.V. solution, as ordered □ I.V. tubing □ optional: nonallergenic tape, indelible marker.

## Preparation of equipment

Gather the appropriate equipment and wash your hands. Clamp the manometer to the I.V. pole, spike the I.V. container, and hang it 30″ to 36″ (76.2 to 91.4 cm) above the insertion site *to prevent blood from backing up in the catheter.* Examine the stopcock *to learn the proper operating positions* (see *Stopcock Positioning and Operation,* page 398). Next, insert the distal end of the tubing into the left side of the stopcock. Turn the stopcock to the *container-to-patient* position, open the flow clamp, and flush the tubing. Then turn the stopcock to the *container-to-manometer* position. Make sure the tubing doesn't contain an in-line filter, which can distort pressure readings. Fill the manometer column with I.V. solution almost to the top; then close the flow clamp on the tubing. Avoid overfilling the manometer *to prevent inactivation of the filter and increased risk of contamination;* also, *if a small plastic ball is used to indicate fluid level in the manometer, it may be forced from the tube and rendered useless.*

## Essential steps

● Explain the procedure to the patient *to allay his fears and promote cooperation.*

● Loosen the protective cover on the distal end of the extension tubing (from the stopcock to the patient), and ask the patient to perform the Valsalva's maneuver *to avoid formation of an air embolus.* Quickly disconnect the existing I.V. tubing, remove the protective covering from the new tubing, and connect it to the patient's catheter.

● If the patient is unconscious, wait until he inhales fully, and then quickly connect the tubing. Lowering the head of the bed is also helpful in preventing an air embolus in a patient who is unable to cooperate. If the patient is intubated, maintain full inflation as you connect the tubing. Finally, adjust the flow clamp to the desired infusion rate.

• Adjust the bed to the horizontal position and place the patient in the supine position. If he's unable to tolerate this position, raise the head of the bed slightly. However, maintain the same position for subsequent CVP readings *to provide an accurate comparison.*

• Adjust the position of the manometer so that the stopcock aligns horizontally with the right atrium.

• *To find the position of the right atrium,* first locate the fourth intercostal space. Then measure the depth of the patient's chest from front to back at this level. Divide the depth in half and mark the site with an indelible marker or a strip of nonallergenic tape. This site becomes the *zero reference point*—the location for all subsequent readings.

• If the manometer has a leveling rod, extend it between the zero reference point and the zero mark at the bottom of the manometer scale. If the rod has a small viewing window, a bubble will appear between two lines in the window when the rod is horizontal. If a leveling rod isn't available, use a yardstick with a level attached. With this you can also watch the bubble for the level.

• When the stopcock of the manometer

## STOPCOCK POSITIONING AND OPERATION

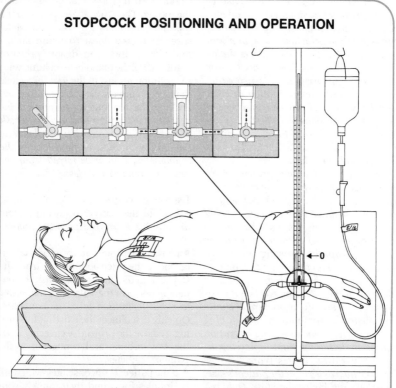

The base of the manometer must be aligned with the right atrium to ensure accurate central venous pressure (CVP) readings. For this reason, the manometer set usually contains a leveling rod to allow you to determine quickly that the base of the manometer is level with the previously determined zero reference point. After adjusting the manometer's position, examine the typical three-way stopcock. By turning it to any position shown, you can control the direction of fluid flow. Four-way stopcocks are also available; the fourth position blocks all openings.

## INTERPRETING CENTRAL VENOUS PRESSURE FINDINGS

To interpret pressure readings correctly, you must establish a normal central venous pressure (CVP) for the patient. The average range is between 5 and 15 cmH$_2$O but varies from patient to patient. To establish a normal range, measure CVP at 15-, 30-, and 60-minute intervals. If a reading differs from the established range by more than 2 cmH$_2$O, double-check it by taking vital signs and assessing the patient's cardiopulmonary status. If these appear stable, check the line for patency and review the measurement procedure. Remember, a blocked line can cause a falsely low reading. If you're sure the abnormal reading is accurate,

however, notify the doctor, according to the range he has set for the patient. Don't rely on vital signs to reflect stable cardiovascular states; regular CVP measurements can detect disorders before changes in vital signs are apparent. For example, a high CVP reading may signal congestive heart failure, hypervolemia, vasoconstriction, or early-stage cardiac tamponade; a low reading may signal peripheral blood pooling, hypovolemia, vasoconstriction, or vasodilation.

If the CVP changes significantly, the doctor will probably order a chest X-ray to detect possible disorders or to determine migration of the catheter tip.

---

is level with the right atrium, tape the manometer set to the I.V. pole *to secure its position.* Recheck the level before each pressure reading. If an adjustment is necessary, first raise or lower the bed and then readjust the manometer on the I.V. pole, if necessary, *to maintain alignment with the atrium.*

• Check the patency of the line by briefly increasing the infusion rate. If the line is not patent, notify the doctor. Never irrigate a clogged CVP line. *This avoids possible release of a thrombus.* If the line is patent, proceed.

• Turn the stopcock to the *container-to-manometer* position *to slowly fill the manometer with I.V. solution, as before.*

• Turn the stopcock to the *manometer-to-patient* position; the fluid level then falls with inspiration, as intrathoracic pressure decreases, and rises slightly with expiration.

• When the fluid column stabilizes (usually between 5 and 15 cmH$_2$O), tap the manometer lightly *to dislodge air bubbles that may distort pressure readings.* Then position yourself so that the top of the fluid column is at eye level. Expect the column to rise and fall slightly during breathing. Note the *lowest* level the fluid reaches, and take your reading from the base of the meniscus. If the manometer has a small ball floating on the fluid surface, take the reading from

the ball's midline. If the fluid fails to fluctuate during breathing, the end of the catheter may be pressed against the vein wall. Ask the patient to cough *to change the catheter's position slightly.*

• Maintain catheter patency by returning the stopcock to the *container-to-patient* position as soon as you take the reading. Then check for blood backflow.

• Readjust the infusion rate and be sure all connections are secure *to minimize the risk of hemorrhage or an air embolus.* (Some hospital policies recommend taping all connections for these reasons.)

• Return the patient to a comfortable position.

### Special considerations

If the patient is connected to a ventilator and is receiving positive end-expiratory pressure (PEEP), expect high CVP readings. *To detect significant changes,* record all pressure readings while the patient is connected to the ventilator. However, if the patient's condition permits, some hospitals allow you to disconnect the ventilator for all CVP readings and reconnect it immediately after the procedure.

Report any deviations from the prescribed CVP range to the doctor. Avoid taking pressure measurements when the patient is sitting up, *since this position causes falsely low results if the patient has been put in a sitting position within 3 minutes of your manometer reading.* Remember that the patient with chronic obstructive pulmonary disease (COPD) usually has a high CVP.

### Documentation
Record the time, date, and pressure reading. If the patient was placed in a special position, note this on the nursing cardex *to ensure consistent readings.*

ARLENE STRONG, RN, MN

# Cardiac Output Measurement

*Measuring cardiac output—the amount of blood ejected from the heart—helps evaluate cardiac function. Normal output is 4 to 8 liters/minute. Low cardiac output can result from decreased myocardial contractility due to myocardial infarction, drugs, acidosis, or hypoxia. Other possible causes are decreased left ventricular filling pressure due to fluid depletion, or increased systemic vascular resistance due to arteriosclerosis or hypertension. Cardiac output can also fall below normal as a result of de-*

*creased blood flow from the ventricles due to valvular heart disease. High cardiac output can occur with some arteriovenous shunts, or from hyperthyroidism or anxiety; it may be normal in athletes.*

*Cardiac output is usually measured indirectly by the thermodilution technique. Two other methods—the Fick technique and the dye dilution test—are used mostly in research and in some cardiac catheterization laboratories (see below). In the thermodilution technique, a balloon-tipped, flow-directed catheter with four or five lumens is inserted into a vein. Normal venous circulation carries the catheter tip through the right side of the heart and into the pulmonary artery. A chilled or room temperature solution is injected into the right atrium through the proximal lumen of the catheter. A minicomputer then calculates cardiac output from temperature changes detected by a thermistor in the catheter tip and the cardiac output is displayed on a digital readout. Two nurses are usually needed to perform this procedure—one to inject the solution, the other to operate the minicomputer. However, this procedure can be done by one nurse, depending on the type of equipment available.*

### Equipment
Cardiac output minicomputer □ centi-

---

## ALTERNATE METHODS OF MEASURING CARDIAC OUTPUT

In the **dye dilution test,** a known volume and concentration of dye is injected into the pulmonary artery and measured by simultaneously sampling the amount of dye in the brachial artery. To calculate cardiac output, these values are entered into a formula or plotted into a time–and–dilution-concentration curve. A minicomputer like the one used for the thermodilution test does the computation. Dye dilution measurements are particularly helpful in detecting intracardiac shunts and valvular regurgitation.

In the **Fick method,** the blood's oxygen content is measured before and after it passes through the lungs. First, blood is removed from the pulmonary and the brachial arteries and is analyzed for oxygen content. Then, a spirometer measures oxygen consumption—the amount of air entering the lungs each minute. After this, cardiac output is calculated by this formula:

$$CO \text{ (liter/min)} = \frac{\text{oxygen consumption (ml/min)}}{\text{arterial oxygen content} - \text{venous oxygen content (ml/min)}}$$

A doctor usually performs this procedure at the patient's bedside, using a pulmonary artery catheter. The Fick method is especially useful in detecting low cardiac output levels.

grade thermometer (if the minicomputer doesn't have a temperature probe) □ basin □ two bags of dextrose 5% in water or normal saline solution □ heparin injectable □ 3-ml syringe with 1″ needle □ straight I.V. administration set □ three-way stopcock □ 10-ml syringe □ large-gauge needle □ alcohol sponges □ gun injector (optional). If desired, an additional piece of I.V. tubing can be used to lengthen the setup. Some new minicomputers measure temperature directly from the pulmonary artery, making it unnecessary to inject a solution unless the patient is connected to a respirator, has an erratic breathing pattern, or has an estimated cardiac output of more than 10 liters/minute.

## Preparation of equipment

Gather all necessary equipment. If necessary, chill the solution in the refrigerator. Then fill the basin with ice and cover the ice with water. If ordered, inject the heparin into one solution bag and label the bag appropriately.

## Essential steps

• Wash your hands.
• Explain the procedure to the patient and provide privacy. Inform him that you're going to inject a solution through the catheter to help evaluate cardiac function. Assure him that he won't experience any discomfort.
• After the doctor inserts the thermodilution catheter, connect the minicomputer cable to the catheter thermistor port. Then take the patient's temperature and record it.
• Immerse both bags of solution (except for the ports) in the ice water.
• Open the main port of the bag without the heparin and pierce it with the large-gauge needle.
• Place the thermometer probe or the centigrade thermometer into the pierced port. *The probe or thermometer determines the baseline temperature of the solution.*
• Using an alcohol sponge, clean the main port of the bag containing the heparin. Insert the administration set spike.

• Attach the sterile stopcock to the opposite end of the tubing and, if desired, add additional tubing to the parallel stopcock port.
• Hold the bag with the port upright, open the flow clamp, and squeeze air from the bag *to avoid introducing an air embolus.*
• Invert the bag and prime the tubing. Then move the stopcock to all positions. Next, connect the additional tubing or the stopcock itself to the catheter's proximal hub.
• Attach the 10-ml syringe to the stopcock's free port and rest it on the minicomputer cart or a table *to avoid straining the line.*
• Turn on the minicomputer and calibrate it according to the manufacturer's instructions.
• When the temperature of the solution reaches 32° F. (0° C.), turn the stopcock toward the patient and fill the syringe with exactly 10 ml of solution. Then turn the stopcock toward the bag of solution.
• Start to inject the solution as your assistant depresses the start button on the minicomputer. Inject the solution within 2 to 3 seconds so it reaches the circulation as a bolus. *Otherwise, the thermistor won't accurately detect the peak temperature change, causing inaccurate results.*
• Record the cardiac output and, after 1 minute, inject more solution. Then record output again, wait 1 minute, and inject more solution.
• After measuring the patient's cardiac output, turn the stopcock off to all positions.

## Special considerations

Place the patient in the supine position or with his head slightly elevated for this procedure. Before injecting the solution, make sure the catheter isn't wedged in the pulmonary artery, *because this can cause false high readings and can also damage the artery.* If ordered, calculate the cardiac index—cardiac output/square meter of body surface area—since it's a more specific and useful measurement than cardiac output.

**Documentation**
Record the average or highest cardiac output, as dictated by institution policy.

Document the amount and type of solution on the input and output sheet.

BARBARA BOYD EGOVILLE, RN, MSN

## TREATMENT

# Cardiopulmonary Resuscitation

*Cardiopulmonary resuscitation (CPR) is an emergency procedure that may restore and maintain a patient's respiration and circulation after his heartbeat and breathing have stopped. CPR must begin as soon as possible after cardiac and respiratory arrest since brain damage or death occurs if circulation isn't restored in 3 to 6 minutes. The patient may not be restored to his previous central nervous system (CNS) status if he's been in arrest for more than 10 minutes. However, if there is any doubt about how long pulse and respirations have been absent, CPR is still performed in an attempt to revive him.*

*The easiest way to remember the basic CPR procedure is to follow the A-B-C scheme: Airway open, Breathing restored, then Circulation restored. After airway, breathing, and circulation have been restored, definitive treatment, including drugs, diagnosis by EKG, or defibrillation, may follow. CPR is contraindicated in "no code" patients.*

## Equipment
Cardiac arrest board, if available. If not available, use any hard, flat surface under the patient.

## Essential steps
● *To verify the patient's unresponsiveness,* gently shake him and, in a loud voice, call out to him (call his name if you know it) and ask if he's all right. Speak directly into each ear *in case he has unilateral deafness.*
● If you're alone, call for help; if you're outside the hospital and other people are around, ask someone to stand by *in case*

*you need help.*
● If the patient isn't lying on a hard surface, place the cardiac arrest board (or the headboard of the bed, if detachable, or some other flat, rigid support) under his back *so that subsequent compression steps will be effective.* If you're outside the hospital, place him on the floor or pavement. If the patient is in a prone position, logroll him into a supine position *to avoid causing any further injury while correctly positioning the patient for CPR.*

*(A) To open the airway:*
● Position yourself on one side of the patient, at his head. Place the hand closer to the patient's head on his forehead; then place your other hand under his neck, close to the back of his head. Tilt his head back while lifting under the neck. *This causes the lower jaw to drop, which makes the tongue fall forward from the back of the throat and opens the airway.*
● Look toward the patient's feet and put your ear over his mouth and nose. *To confirm that the patient has stopped breathing,* watch for chest and stomach movement while listening for sounds of breathing and feeling for breath on your cheek.

*(B) To restore breathing:*
● If the patient is not breathing, use the hand on the patient's forehead to pinch the patient's nostrils closed with your thumb and index finger. Continue to maintain backward pressure on his forehead with the heel and remaining fingers of this hand.
● Take a deep breath, cover the patient's mouth with yours (be sure to seal your mouth tightly over the patient's mouth), and give four breaths in rapid succession *to maintain positive pressure in the patient's lungs and to reopen collapsed al-*

veoli. After each breath, quickly turn your head slightly toward the victim's chest and take a breath of fresh air. Don't let the patient's lungs deflate completely between breaths.

• Move your other hand from under the patient's neck and use it to palpate for the carotid artery on the side of his neck nearest to you. Check carefully for a pulse *since it may be very slow or weak.* Allow 5 to 10 seconds for this step. Use the carotid artery *because it's closest to you*

*and usually accessible,* and *because this pulse is palpable longer than peripheral pulses.*

• At this time, if you're in a hospital, activate the emergency medical system (EMS). If you're outside the hospital and someone is available, have him call an appropriate emergency number; instruct him to report that you have a medical emergency, to give the exact location, and to return immediately so you know he made the call. If you're alone, perform

## HAND POSITIONING FOR CHEST COMPRESSIONS AND THE JAW THRUST

### Hand positioning for chest compressions

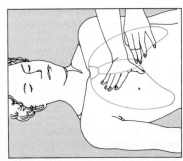

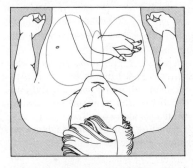

*To position your hands for chest compressions:*
• First, locate the lower margin of the rib cage on the side closer to you, and move your fingers along the lower margin to the xiphoid process.
• Place your middle finger over the process and your index finger next to it. Then, place the heel of your other hand on the lower half of the sternum, next to your index finger, as illustrated top left.
• Remove your first hand from the xiphoid process and place it on top of the hand on the sternum, so both hands are parallel and pointing away from you, as illustrated top right. If you wish, you can interlock the fingers, but always keep them off the patient's chest. You are now ready to start chest compressions.
   *To position your hands for the jaw thrust:*
• Place your thumbs on the mandible near the corners of his mouth, pointing your thumbs toward his feet. Then position the tips of your index fingers at the angles

### Hand positioning for jaw thrust

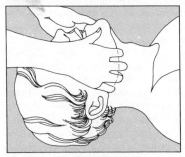

of his jaw, as illustrated above. Push your thumbs down while you lift upward with the tips of your index finger. This action should open the victim's airway.
• For mouth-to-mouth resuscitation, retract the patient's lower lip with your thumb. The head can be tilted back very slightly if attempts to ventilate are unsuccessful.

CPR for 1 minute, then quickly telephone for help if a phone is readily available. If no phone is available, continue with CPR.

*(C) To restore circulation:*
• Remove your hands from the patient's head and neck and position yourself beside his chest. If you're on the floor, place your knees beside the patient's chest; your hands in the correct position for chest compression (see illustration, page 403).
• Lock your elbows, bring your shoulders directly over your hands, and apply firm, downward pressure, compressing the chest 1½″ to 2″ (4 to 5 cm). Count aloud *"one* and *two* and *three,"* and so on. Compress the chest on each number and release the pressure completely on each *and,* without removing your hands from the patient's chest *to prevent position changes between compressions.* Apply compressions at the rate of slightly more than 1/second.
• After 15 compressions, perform the head-tilt/neck-lift maneuver again. Apply your mouth to the patient's and give two full breaths in rapid succession (within a period of 4 to 5 seconds) without allowing full exhalation between breaths. Observe the chest rise.
• Repeat this 15 compressions/two breath cycle three more times.
• Palpate the carotid artery again *to see if the patient's pulse has returned.* Also, put your ear over his mouth and nose again *to check for breathing.*
• Continue this pattern of four cycles of 15 compressions and two breaths, followed by a check for the return of the carotid pulse and breathing. Don't stop for more than 5 seconds unless the patient revives or is being transferred to a stretcher, another person trained in CPR relieves you, a doctor assumes responsibility, or you are unable to continue due to physical exhaustion.
• If another person trained in CPR arrives while you are still able to continue, one of you can perform compressions while the other ventilates the patient and checks his carotid pulse *to monitor the effectiveness of the compressions.* The person doing the ventilations also in-structs the person doing the compressions to stop compressions, checks for spontaneous pulse and respirations, tells the compressor the patient's status, and gives one breath. The compressor then resumes compressions.
• When performing two-person CPR, use a cycle of five compressions (counting "one-one-thousand, two-one-thousand," and so on), followed by one breath, which is given on the release of the fifth compression.
• If the person doing the compression becomes tired, change positions as smoothly as possible. To call for a switch in positions after a 5:1 cycle, say *"Switch-*one-thousand, two-one-thousand..." At this signal, the second person (who's been ventilating the patient) gives a breath at the end of the five compressions and then moves immediately to the chest position. The first person takes his place at the patient's head and takes no more than 5 seconds to check for spontaneous pulse and breathing. Meanwhile, the second person positions himself properly to resume compressions at once. If the patient is pulseless and not breathing, the first person gives one breath and signals the second person to resume compressions. Check the patient's pulse every few minutes and change positions whenever necessary.

**Special considerations**
If respirations are absent but adequate pulse is present, give ventilations alone, without compressions. Do not, however, give compressions without ventilations, *since ventilation is needed to deliver oxygenated blood to tissues.*

If doing CPR alone, perform compressions at the rate of 80 compressions per minute *to compensate for the time you must take to give breaths.* Two-person CPR requires a rate of 60 compressions per minute.

Another way to open the airway is to tilt the head back, place the fingers of the other hand under the lower jaw on the bony part near the chin, and bring the chin forward (the head-tilt/chin-lift maneuver). If you suspect a neck injury,

# ADVANCED LIFE SUPPORT

Advanced life support (ALS) measures support cardiopulmonary resuscitation (CPR) by treating the physical changes and complications that can occur after cardiac arrest. These measures include the use of special techniques and equipment to help establish and maintain ventilation and circulation, the use of cardiac monitors to detect abnormal heart rate and rhythm, the insertion of a peripheral I.V. line, drug therapy, cardiac defibrillation, and the insertion of an artifical pacemaker. When the patient's condition stabilizes, the cause of cardiac arrest can be treated. Many ALS techniques, including defibrillation and drug administration, can be initiated by a specially trained nurse under standing orders; some techniques may be performed only by a doctor.

The techniques and equipment used in ALS depend on the patient's needs and on the setting. Usually, the following sequence of ALS procedures is required:

• First, alert co-workers and obtain a crash cart, which usually contains all equipment necessary for ALS.
• Because CPR requires a firm surface to be effective, place a cardiac arrest board or other flat, rigid support under the patient's back. Start CPR immediately *to ensure oxygenation and perfusion of vital organs.* Continue CPR while other ALS equipment is being set up. During later ALS procedures, avoid interrupting CPR for longer than 15 seconds.
• Set up the EKG machine *to monitor cardiovascular status continuously and to help determine proper therapy.* Because the EKG doesn't indicate the effectiveness of cardiac compression, take central (carotid or femoral) pulses frequently.
• Attempt to obtain a medical history from the patient's family or companion *to learn the probable cause of the arrest and to determine contraindications for resuscitation.*
• Insert a peripheral I.V. line for fluid and emergency drug administration. Use a large blood vessel, such as the brachial vein, *because smaller peripheral vessels tend to collapse quickly during arrest.* Use a large-gauge needle *to prevent dislodgment or injury to the vein, with extravasation and vessel collapse.* Use dextrose 5% in water to start the infusion; other fluids, such as normal saline solution, counteract circulatory collapse caused by hypovolemia and may be ordered as appropriate later.

• Perform defibrillation and administer appropriate drugs, such as epinephrine, isoproterenol, and calcium chloride, which stimulate cardiac pacemaker discharge. These drugs treat asystole without defibrillation but can cause arrhythmias, such as ventricular fibrillation, which require defibrillation. (Although cardiac monitoring should be started before defibrillation, a single countershock delivered to the heart without monitoring isn't harmful, and immediate "blind" defibrillation may prove lifesaving; however, blind defibrillation of children is not recommended.
• If the patient fails to respond quickly to CPR, a single countershock, and basic drug therapy, insert a ventilatory device, such as an endotracheal tube or oxygen cannula. After the device is in place, discontinue mouth-to-mouth breathing, but maintain respiratory assistance with an Ambu bag. Oxygen is used jointly with most of these devices.
• Remove oral secretions with portable or wall suction, and insert a nasogastric tube *to relieve or prevent gastric distention.*
• If the patient responds to the preceding treatments and has severe bradycardia, with reduced cardiac output (as in acute heart block), vasopressors may be given. If these do not sufficiently raise heart rate and cardiac output, the doctor may insert a temporary cardiac pacemaker to boost the heart's faltering electrical activity to a near-normal rate.
• In most cases, when the patient's condition begins to stabilize or when preliminary ALS steps have been taken, he may be transported to a special-care area. If necessary, use a circulatory assist device, such as a manual or automatic chest compressor, *to provide external cardiac compression during transport.* Because the device compresses the sternum 1½" to 2" (3.8 to 5 cm), position the patient carefully *to avoid accidental compression of the ribs or epigastric area, resulting in rib fracture and possible liver laceration.*
• Begin direct therapy as ordered *to treat the underlying cause of the patient's arrest.* For example, if arrest resulted from an acute hypovolemic crisis, replace blood volume and apply Medical Antishock Trousers (MAST) *to redirect circulating blood from the extremities into the central circulation.* Or use acute dialysis to clear endogenous or exogenous toxins that may have caused the arrest.

BARBARA BOYD EGOVILLE, RN, MSN

perform the jaw-thrust maneuver (see illustration, page 403) instead of the head-tilt/neck-lift, *since the jaw-thrust maneuver doesn't hyperextend the neck.*

If the patient has false teeth, leave them in *because they give a better seal around the mouth.* If you can't open the patient's mouth, if the mouth is injured, or if you can't get a tight mouth-to-mouth seal, *give mouth-to-nose ventilations.* Tilt the head back and lift the lower jaw *to close the mouth.* Give a breath through the nose, then remove your mouth *to allow the air to escape and to avoid a buildup of carbon dioxide.*

If the patient has a stoma or temporary tracheostomy, pinch the nostrils with one hand, close the mouth with the other hand, and give mouth-to-stoma or mouth-to-tube ventilations. If the tracheostomy tube has a cuff, inflate it *so you won't have to seal the nose and mouth.*

When performing chest compressions, try to make each compression equal in duration. Quick jabs increase the possibility of injury and result in inadequate blood flow.

If possible, check pupillary reaction too, *to determine the effectiveness of CPR.* If the pupils constrict, oxygenated blood is reaching the brain.

### Complications

The most common complication of CPR, even when performed correctly, is fractured ribs. If a fractured rib punctures a lung, tension pneumothorax or hemothorax may result. Fractures of the sternum can also occur during CPR. Both types of fractures can precipitate fat or bone marrow emboli.

Overzealous compressions can cause cardiac contusions. Compressions of the xiphoid process through improper hand placement can lacerate the liver or spleen.

Gastric distention, another common complication, results when excessive pressure is used to inflate the lungs. This can decrease lung volume and cause regurgitation. If distention occurs, recheck the patient's airway and reposition the airway open. If distention interferes with ventilation and a changed position doesn't

correct it, turn the patient on his side and press gently on the epigastrium *to remove air and prevent aspiration of stomach contents.*

If the patient vomits, turn him on his side, wipe his mouth to remove vomitus, and then return him to the supine position to continue CPR.

### Documentation

Record the time and the reason for starting CPR, as well as the time and the reason for ending it. Document Advanced Life Support (ALS) measures, if any.

CATHERINE DAVIS, MSN

# Cardiac Defibrillation
## [*Direct-current countershock*]

*During defibrillation, a strong electric current is passed through a patient's heart by application of two electrode paddles applied to the chest. The resulting shock, which completely depolarizes the myocardium, usually allows the sinoatrial (SA) node to resume control of a heart that is in coarse ventricular fibrillation. This emergency procedure may also successfully convert ventricular tachycardias that fail to respond to drugs or other therapy; it can also be used to convert other abnormal cardiac rhythms, as in elective cardioversion (see* Assisting with Elective Cardioversion, *page 408).*

*Cardiac defibrillation is most successful when begun as soon as possible after onset of dysrhythmia to minimize acidosis or hypoxia and to restore normal sinus rhythm. Thus, although hospital policy determines who may defibrillate a patient, a specially trained nurse can perform it when necessary since she is often the first person to recognize the need for defibrillation.*

### Equipment

Defibrillator with electrode paddles □

conductive jelly or paste, or saline-soaked 4″ x 4″ gauze sponges □ emergency resuscitation equipment (including resuscitation bag, oxygen and mask; resuscitation board; resuscitation drugs; needles and syringes; suction equipment).

Electrode paddles come in adult and infant sizes, and anterior and anterior-posterior (A/P) types. Anterior infant paddles have 1½″ (3.8 cm) steel disks; anterior adult paddles, 3″ (7.6 cm) steel disks. A/P paddles are usually used for elective cardioversion.

### Essential steps

• The nurse who recognizes the emergency alerts other staff members and performs cardiopulmonary resuscitation (CPR) until the defibrillator is ready *to assure coronary and cerebral arterial blood flow.* (See "Cardiopulmonary Resuscitation," in this chapter.)

• Turn the defibrillator on and be sure the current indicator lights up. If it doesn't, check the battery or other power source. (In some units, the on/off/charge switches are located on the paddle handles; in others, on the front instrument panel.) If the defibrillator can also be used for cardioversion, make sure it's set to defibrillate or is on the asynchronous mode. *If it's set to synchronize, the paddles won't discharge, since there is no R wave in ventricular fibrillation for the synchronous mode to respond to.*

• Set the unit to the prescribed energy level (in joules or watt-seconds) and charge the paddles—to 200 to 400 joules for the adult patient; to 2 to 3.5 joules/kilogram of body weight for the neonatal or pediatric patient. (In severe chest trauma or open heart surgery, when the heart is exposed, the doctor uses special sterile paddles to deliver 5 to 20 joules directly to the myocardium.)

• Make sure the electrode paddles are fully charged. This may be indicated by a light that blinks until full charge is reached, by an audible alarm, by a needle on a panel meter, or by a digital readout.

• Lubricate the paddles *to enhance conduction and prevent burns.* Squeeze a ring of lubricant around one paddle disk,

then rub the disks together to spread the lubricant over the entire disk surface. Or, use a gel-pad or four saline-soaked 4″ x 4″ gauze sponge to lubricate each disk. Be sure to wipe any lubricant from your hands before discharging the paddles *because the electric current can arc from the bottom of the paddles to your hands, causing a shock or burn.* Excessive amounts of the lubricant can also cause the paddles to slip from the patient's chest.

• To position anterior paddles on the patient, put one paddle (sometimes marked "sternum") slightly to the right of the upper sternum and below the clavicle at the level of the second to third intercostal space. For the adult male or pediatric patient, place the other paddle (sometimes marked "apex") slightly to the left of the left nipple at the level of the fifth to sixth intercostal space in the anterior axillary line (corresponding to the $V_5$ chest lead). For the adult female patient, place the left paddle at the mid- or anterior-axillary level, not over the breasts.

When positioning or lubricating the paddles, avoid placing your fingers on the discharge buttons *to prevent an accidental discharge.*

To position A/P paddles, place the flat posterior paddle under the patient's body beneath the heart and immediately below the scapulae (but not under the vertebral column). Place the anterior paddle directly over the heart at the left precordium.

Position infant paddles as you would an adult's.

• Rotate the paddles slightly to spread the lubricant outside the disk diameter, *to help prevent skin burns if electrical current arcs off the sides of the paddles onto the patient's skin.* Make sure that the paddles are correctly positioned before discharge, and that lubricated areas don't touch each other, *to prevent a short circuit.*

• Apply paddles to the chest wall using 20 to 25 pounds of forearm pressure. (Shoulder pressure could cause the paddles to slip, especially when the patient's body jolts during the discharge; insufficient pressure could cause sparks.)

## ASSISTING WITH ELECTIVE CARDIOVERSION

Like defibrillation, elective cardioversion attempts to restore the sinoatrial node to its function as the heart's natural pacemaker. This procedure is performed in much the same way as defibrillation, except that the synchronizer switch is activated and much less energy is needed (25 to 50 joules or watt-seconds). The discharge buttons on the paddles or defibrillator must be held down because the shock isn't triggered until the next QRS complex occurs. This helps prevent ventricular fibrillation, which may result from an improperly timed shock. Usually performed by a doctor, the procedure is elective, requiring the patient's consent; he is then sedated before cardioversion begins.

Cardioversion is used to convert refractory atrial, junctional, and ventricular tachydysrhythmias to normal sinus rhythm. It is contraindicated in patients with digitalis toxicity.

To prepare for cardioversion, assemble all the equipment for defibrillation, including an EKG monitor, I.V. infusion equipment, a cardioverter with synchronizer, an emergency drug cart, and suction equipment. Explain the procedure to the patient and provide privacy. To avoid alarming him, don't use the word "shock" in your explanation. Instead, tell him that cardioversion uses an electric current to slow down the heart rate and relieve symptoms. Make sure he or a responsible

family member understands and signs a consent form. Instruct the patient to abstain from food and fluids for at least 7 or 8 hours, and withhold digitalis for 24 to 36 hours. If you suspect digitalis toxicity, the doctor will probably order the patient's digitalis level taken. Cardioversion usually is delayed until the digitalis level is normal. In many institutions a potassium blood level is obtained and documented prior to this procedure.

Start a peripheral I.V. to administer a sedative or emergency drugs, as ordered. Attach the patient to the EKG monitor and run a 12-lead tracing to detect dysrhythmias. Leave the limb electrodes in place for later recordings. Place chest electrodes in position to obtain the tallest R wave; in most patients this chest lead would be modified lead II or MCL. Make sure the electrodes don't interfere with cardioverter paddle placement. Attach the cardioverter to the monitor and turn on the synchronizer switch or button. Make sure the synchronizer artifact falls on the R wave; *if the cardioverter doesn't recognize the R wave, it won't discharge.* To increase the R wave, increase sensitivity, but make sure not to increase the T wave to the height where the cardioverter recognizes it; or select another lead that shows a larger R wave.

Place the patient in the supine position, and avoid raising the head more than 30°. Have an emergency crash cart ready in case

• If oxygen is being administered, disconnect and shut it off before discharging the paddles *to avoid possible fire hazard.*

• Although some EKG monitors are protected against defibrillator shocks, others may be damaged by the surge of current. If the patient is connected to an EKG monitor, disconnect the patient cable as a precaution, and reconnect it immediately after defibrillation *to record the new heart rhythm.*

• When you're ready to deliver electric shock, instruct staff members to stand clear of the patient and the bed *to avoid the risk of grounding the current and causing a shock.*

• Discharge both paddles by pushing both handle buttons simultaneously, or by pressing the appropriate button on

the paddle or instrument panel of the defibrillator.

• If the first defibrillation fails to convert the rhythm, make sure the paddles are adequately lubricated and fully recharged, and repeat the procedure at the same energy level. If the patient still fails to respond, his heart may be hypoxic, acidotic, or ischemic. Restart CPR, and give supplementary oxygen *to ensure maximum oxygenation of myocardial tissue in case of hypoxia or ischemia,* or administer sodium bicarbonate I.V. *to correct acidosis* and epinephrine I.V. *to stimulate the SA node.* If oxygen is in use, shut it off, then defibrillate again at 360 to 400 joules when the drugs achieve peak action. Continue CPR and oxygen administration *until you detect a carotid pulse. Do not leave oxygen on during* symptomatic bradycardia or ventricular arrhythmias occur. If the patient has loosely fitting dentures, remove them to prevent airway obstruction after sedation. However, if they fit properly, leave them in place to make airway management easier.

Bare the male patient's chest, but cover the female patient's breasts with a towel until paddle electrodes are in position. Administer a sedative, as ordered.

Set the energy level on the cardioverter as ordered (usually 25 or 50 joules). Lubricate the A/P paddle electrodes as for defibrillation. The doctor should now be present to check the patient's sedation level and to perform cardioversion. Make sure the patient is adequately ventilated, and record baseline vital signs prior to cardioversion, *because the sedative may cause apnea or hypotension.*

Make sure the cardioverter is still synchronized with the R wave. Push the charge button to raise the machine to the prescribed energy level. (Most machines have a needle indicator that shows energy level.) Turn on the strip chart recorder *to document the cardioversion.* Also document a strip that validates synchronization of electric impulse with the R wave prior to cardioversion.

If you're performing the procedure, apply A/P paddles. Put the flat paddle under the patient's body, behind the heart and slightly below the left scapula. Place the other paddle over the left precordium,

directly over the heart. Apply 20 to 25 pounds of pressure to the electrodes *to ensure good skin contact and to prevent burns.* Announce "ready stand back," making sure everyone present is away from the bed *to prevent inadvertent grounding and shocks.*

Depress the discharge button on the anterior paddle electrode, and hold that position until the energy is delivered. (You may have to hold the button a second or more.) Remove the paddle electrodes immediately after the shock. Make sure a normal sinus rhythm is present; if it is not, repeat the procedure at a higher energy level, as ordered.

Take a 12-lead EKG and compare it to the preconversion (baseline) EKG. Take the patient's vital signs, immediately after cardioversion and every 15 minutes for at least 1 hour or until stable, and observe his level of consciousness. Make sure his respiratory rate and excursive movements are adequate until he is alert. Observe the cardiac monitor pattern until rhythm stabilizes. Watch for complications of cardioversion: ventricular fibrillation, asystole, rhythm disturbances, skin burns, pulmonary edema or embolus, respiratory depression or arrest, hypotension, and ST segment changes.

When patient is alert and his condition permits, tell him he may begin to eat and move about.

ARLENE STRONG, RN, MSN

*actual defibrillation.*

*After defibrillation:*

• Check carotid pulse, reconnect the EKG cable, and check cardiac rhythm. Reconnect oxygen and continue CPR, if necessary, or prepare to defibrillate again.

• If the paddles have been recharged but not used again, clear the charge by turning off the machine and turning the discharge control to zero, or by pressing the "bleed" button if there is one. Avoid discharging the paddles against each other or into the air.

• Using soap and water, wipe the lubricant from the patient's chest. Treat any burns, as ordered. Clean lubricant from the paddles with soap and water, *to avoid corrosion damage to the disks that can cause arcing.*

• Prepare the defibrillator for imme-

diate reuse. If necessary, restock the machine with more lubricant and other supplies. Be sure to return a battery-powered machine to its recharger.

**Special considerations**

Since defibrillators vary in their setup and operation, familiarize yourself with your institution's equipment. The defibrillator should be checked by the charge nurse at every shift change and inspected regularly by the hospital's engineering department or the manufacturer's service representative.

Remember that the amount of energy required for defibrillation depends on electrode size and placement, the lubricant, the type of waveform (Lown or Edmark), technique (single or multiple shocks), the nature of underlying cardiac disease, and the size and metabolic status of the patient at defibrillation. The larger the patient, the more energy required for defibrillation.

If you carry your stethoscope around your neck, remove it during defibrillation *to prevent shock*. Avoid using distilled water or alcohol to wet gauze sponges for lubricating the paddles; water is a poor conductor, and alcohol may ignite, causing severe burns.

Remember that defibrillation is successful only when a patient's heart shows *coarse* ventricular fibrillation (as opposed to *fine* ventricular fibrillation) on the EKG monitor. If his heart is in *fine* ventricular fibrillation, administer 0.5 mg epinephrine and/or calcium chloride first, *to produce coarse ventricular fibrillation before attempting defibrillation.*

If you have any information about the patient's potassium level, whether hypokalemic or hyperkalemic, inform the doctor responding to the cardiac arrest. Similarly, inform the doctor if you have any knowledge of the patient's digoxin level; patients who have digitalis toxicity will frequently respond well when defibrillated at a lower energy level.

Continue to monitor the patient for dysrhythmias and emergency care instituted if defibrillation is successful; usually the successfully defibrillated patient is admitted to the intensive care unit if he is not already there.

## Complications
Insufficiently lubricated paddles or inadvertent use of alcohol as a lubricant may cause skin burns.

## Documentation
Document the time of cardiac arrest, the personnel performing defibrillation, the amount of energy used (watt-seconds or joules), the number of shocks, and the patient's response. Record the time and response to CPR, and the administration of drugs. Include all monitored rhythm strips taken during the procedure. Note the size and appearance of any burns that may have occurred.

BARBARA BOYD EGOVILLE, RN, MSN

# Carotid Massage

*Carotid massage is the application of manual pressure to the left or right carotid sinus to slow the heart rate. The carotid sinus is located slightly above the bifurcations of the carotid arteries in the neck; its nerve endings respond to pressure as to an increase in blood pressure and relay this message to the vasomotor centers in the brainstem; this, in turn, stimulates the autonomic nervous system to increase vagal tone and slows the heart rate. Peripheral blood vessels then dilate, reducing cardiac output and lowering arterial pressure as much as 20 mmHg in a normal patient.*

*Carotid massage is used to diagnose and treat sinus, atrial, and junctional tachydysrhythmias. Although usually performed by a doctor, it's occasionally done by a specially trained nurse under a doctor's supervision. This procedure requires continuous EKG monitoring as pressure is applied, first to one sinus, and then to the other, each time for no longer than 5 seconds. Pressure should never be applied simultaneously to both sinuses, because this may cause complete asystole and significant impairment of cerebral blood flow. Pressure is released when any sign of rhythm change appears on the EKG monitor.*

*Carotid massage is contraindicated in patients with systolic blood pressure below 100 mmHg, cerebrovascular or carotid artery disease, or hypersensitive carotid sinuses.*

## Equipment
EKG monitor □ crash cart □ I.V. setup with dextrose 5% in water □ cardiotonic drugs, as ordered.

### Essential steps
● Explain the procedure to the patient *to allay his fears and ensure his cooperation*. Place him in the supine position.
● Prepare the patient's skin appropriately and attach EKG electrodes. If ca-

rotid massage is being performed for diagnostic purposes, obtain strip chart recordings, selecting the lead that shows the best P waves. Adjust the position and heat level of the recording stylus, if necessary, *to promote accurate diagnosis of arrhythmias.*

• Start an I.V. line with dextrose 5% in water at a keep-vein-open rate, as ordered, *to provide a route for emergency drug administration.*

• Auscultate both carotid sinuses to detect bruits; *if present, do not perform carotid massage.*

• Locate the bifurcation of the carotid artery on the right side of the patient's neck by turning his head slightly to the left and hyperextending his neck. *This brings the carotid artery closer to the skin and moves the sternocleidomastoid muscle away from the carotid artery.*

• Using a circular motion, gently massage the right carotid sinus between your fingers and the transverse processes of the spine for 3 to 5 seconds. Monitor the EKG throughout the procedure and release the artery as soon as any evidence of a rhythm change appears.

• If this procedure has no effect within 5 seconds, stop massaging the right carotid sinus and massage the left. If this also fails, administer cardiotonic drugs, as ordered.

• Always stop after 5 seconds (or sooner if conversion to sinus rhythm or unacceptable bradycardia occurs) or if the ventricular rate slows sufficiently to permit diagnosis of the rhythm. If severe bradycardia persists, or asystole occurs, be prepared to give emergency treatment.

### Special considerations

Avoid vigorous massage, especially if carotid atherosclerosis is present, *because this procedure may cause embolization of plaque material and cerebrovascular accident.* Although arterial pressure may fall profoundly during massage, especially in the elderly patient with heart disease, it usually rises quickly afterward.

If the procedure is successful, continue to monitor the patient for several hours. Be aware that conversion to normal sinus rhythm may be preceded by brief asystole and several premature ventricular contractions.

### Complications

Although rare, complications include complete heart block with ventricular bradycardia or asystole; cerebral occlusion caused by an embolus, possibly resulting in a cerebrovascular accident; or ventricular fibrillation, especially if digitalis intoxication is present.

### Documentation

Record the date and time of the procedure; your name; frequency and duration of massage; EKG rhythm changes and drug administration, if applicable; and changes in the patient's condition.

ARLENE STRONG, RN, MN

# Temporary Pacemaker Insertion and Care

*When the heart's natural pacemakers fail to maintain a normal heart rate, and cardioactive drugs prove ineffective, an artificial pacemaker may be needed to restore an effective rate. A temporary pacemaker consists of a battery-powered pulse generator which the patient wears on his chest, waist, or upper arm. An electrode catheter transmits electrical impulses from the pacemaker to the patient's heart, and from the heart back to the pacemaker. Pacemakers come in two types:* fixed-rate, *which fire continuously without regard to the patient's heart rate; and* demand, *the more common type, which sense the patient's rate and fire accordingly.*

*Usually aided by a fluoroscope, a doctor inserts the electrode catheter percutaneously into a peripheral vein, through the vena cava and right atrium, and into the apex of the right ventricle. In an emergency, a transthoracic approach may be used. The nurse assists by monitoring catheter insertion with the electrocardiograph (EKG) and by maintaining sterile technique. Femoral insertion is contraindicated in patients with thrombophlebitis, recent pulmonary embolism, or severe coagulopathy.*

## Equipment

Pacemaker pulse generator with battery □ pacemaker catheter □ electrode wires □ EKG monitor with oscilloscope and strip chart recorder □ emergency resuscitation equipment □ alligator clamp □ Velcro strap, elastic bandage, or gauze (for securing the pulse generator to the patient) □ armboard (if necessary) □ tape □ shave preparation kit □ povidone-iodine and benzoin solutions □ 1% lidocaine for anesthesia □ 3- and 5-ml syringes □ 21G and 25G needles □ sterile gloves, gowns, and drapes □ sphygmomanometer □ peripheral I.V. setup □ 4" × 4" sterile gauze sponges □ linen-saver pad.

*For insertion of pacemaker by a doctor:* vein dilators □ large-bore plastic venous catheter □ introducer sheaths □ Cournand needle □ scalpel □ suture □ venesection tray (these supplies may come prepackaged).

## Preparation of equipment

Assemble the necessary equipment. Make sure there's enough paper in the EKG recorder. Alert additional personnel needed for the procedure (such as the X-ray technician).

## Essential steps

● Explain the procedure to the patient. Tell him that he'll feel some local discomfort at the catheter insertion site. Assure him that the catheter will be in place only temporarily. Inform him that when the catheter is withdrawn, it seldom causes discomfort. Ask if he's allergic to local anesthetics.
● Make sure the patient or a responsible family member understands what this procedure involves and signs the consent form.
● Provide sedation, as ordered.
● Establish an I.V. line at a keep-vein-open rate in the patient's left arm *for possible administration of emergency drugs in case of ventricular arrhythmia.*
● Connect the patient to the EKG monitor and turn it on.
● Establish baseline vital signs and a baseline EKG reading.
● Place the linen-saver pad under the catheter insertion site.
● Clean the insertion site with povidone-iodine solution, wiping in a circular motion away from the insertion site *to minimize the risk of infection.* (Some doctors do this themselves.) Usually a 4" × 4" (10 × 10 cm) area is sufficient; in femoral

---

### SETTING THE STIMULATION THRESHOLD

After a pacemaker is inserted, the stimulation threshold must be determined to maintain myocardial contractions. Turn on the EKG monitor and set the pacemaker's sensitivity control to *fixed* or *demand,* as ordered. During this procedure, run EKG monitor strips as needed and note the milliamperes (MA) on each strip as you adjust the MA level. To determine the stimulation threshold:
● Increase the pacemaker rate above the patient's heart rate, as ordered.
● Increase the MA, as ordered, and watch the EKG carefully for "capture" (as indicated by a pacemaker spike followed by a QRS complex). Stop increasing the MA when 100% capture is achieved. Slowly decrease the MA until you lose capture (electrical stimulus fails to generate a QRS complex).
● Record the threshold as *the lowest MA that achieves capture.*
● Set the MA and pacemaker rate as ordered.
   Note the settings on the nursing cardex. As the patient's condition changes, these settings may need to be altered.

KATHRYN HART, RN

insertion, shave and clean a 6″ × 6″ (15 × 15 cm) area.
• Cover the insertion site with a small fenestrated drape. (Some doctors do this after they've cleaned the insertion site.)
• If a venesection is necessary, open the venesection tray.
• The doctor anesthetizes the insertion site and inserts the pacemaker catheter into the vein. Follow the movement of the catheter through the vein on the fluoroscope and watch for arrhythmias. When the catheter reaches the right atrium, large P waves and small QRS complexes will appear; when it reaches the right ventricle, the QRS complexes become very large and the P waves become smaller. When it contacts the right ventricular endocardium, the monitor will show elevated ST segments (injury current).
• Once the catheter is in place, insert the pacemaker leads tightly into their respective slots in the pacemaker generator.
• Check the patient's stimulation threshold (see *Setting the Stimulation Threshold*, opposite). When a 1-to-1 capture is achieved, set the milliamperage (MA) and pacemaker rate as ordered.
• The doctor sutures the catheter to the insertion site. He then makes a stress loop of the remaining lead wire and tapes it to the patient's chest.
• Clean the insertion site, then dress it. (Some institutions and doctors may require that you apply povidone-iodine ointment.) Mark the dressing as required.
• Secure the pulse generator to the patient's chest, waist, or upper arm, using the Velcro strap, elastic bandage, or elastic gauze.
• Place the cap supplied by the manufacturer over the pacer controls *to avoid an accidental change in the setting.*
*After catheter insertion:*
• Make the patient comfortable and administer pain medication as ordered.
• If a femoral or brachial approach was used, immobilize the extremity *to avoid stressing the pacing wires.* The patient should wiggle fingers or toes *to increase circulation and prevent stiffness.*

• The doctor may order postinsertion studies such as an EKG and chest X-ray. Continuously monitor the patient's heart rhythm and take rhythm strips every hour for 24 hours.
• Be sure to note pacemaker settings and include the rate, mode (demand or fixed-rate), and output in milliamperes. Record this information at every shift change; also note if the pacemaker malfunctions or if arrhythmias occur. The doctor should check the pacemaker's output daily *because drugs, electrolyte changes, or ischemia can alter the patient's threshold.*
• Continue to observe the patient for signs and symptoms of pacemaker malfunction, such as *any* change in pulse rate, dyspnea, fatigue, chest pain, vertigo, distended neck veins, and crepitant rales at the base of the lungs.
• Clean the insertion site daily and inspect it for signs of infection, as ordered. Apply povidone-iodine ointment to the site and cover it with a new dressing, as ordered.
• If the catheter wasn't sutured, make sure it's taped securely *to prevent dislodgment.*
• Assess circulation in the extremity below the site of insertion by evaluating the distal pulse, color, temperature, and sensation.
• If the femoral approach was used, check the patient daily for possible thrombosis in the calf veins by observing for Homan's sign (passive dorsiflexion of the patient's foot causes calf pain).
• The doctor will remove the sutures before withdrawing the catheter. Apply povidone-iodine ointment to the site after the catheter is withdrawn, as ordered. Cover it with a pressure dressing *to prevent bleeding.*

### Special considerations

Watch for signs of pacemaker malfunction (see chart on next page).

 Make sure all electrical equipment is grounded with three-pronged plugs inserted in the right receptacles. *This protects the patient from ac-*

TROUBLESHOOTING

# TROUBLESHOOTING
# PACEMAKER PROBLEMS

| PROBLEM | SIGNS | POSSIBLE CAUSES | POSSIBLE SOLUTIONS |
|---|---|---|---|
| **Failure to capture** (pacemaker transmits impulses to heart but fails to stimulate it) | • Apical rate is below pacemaker setting. <br> • Pacemaker spike is not followed by QRS complex on EKG. <br> • Continuous sense/pace dial movement. | • Dislodged catheter <br><br> • Pacemaker end-of-life or premature battery depletion <br> • Fractured lead wire <br><br> • Change in output threshold (stimulation threshold) | • Turn patient on left side to aid catheter contact with myocardium. <br> • Replace the battery. <br><br> • Lead wire replaced by doctor. <br> • Notify doctor and monitor patient closely. Doctor may increase output threshold or reposition catheter. (*Note:* In some institutions, nurse may increase stimulation threshold to reestablish capture before calling doctor.) |
| **Failure to sense** (pacemaker fails to detect ventricular depolarization and functions independently of heart rate) | • Apical rate is higher than pacemaker setting and irregular. <br> • Pacemaker beats follow normal beats at a rate higher than pacemaker setting. <br> • Continuous sense/pacer dial movement. | • Mode dial accidentally set at *fixed* mode <br> • Dislodged catheter <br><br> • Competition between pacemaker's rhythm and patient's rhythm possibly resulting in ventricular fibrillation | • Turn the dial to *demand* mode. <br> • See "Failure to capture." <br> • Turn the pacemaker off. Call the doctor to reposition the catheter. Monitor the patient closely to make sure his heart rate can maintain adequate cardiac output. |
| **Firing loss** (combined failure to sense/capture caused by mechanical failure of the unit) | • No pacing seen <br><br> • No sense/pace dial movement | • Dislodged catheter <br><br> • Pacemaker accidentally turned off <br> • Battery failure <br> • Loose catheter terminals <br><br><br> • Pacemaker generator worn out <br><br><br><br> • Broken catheter wires | • See "Failure to capture." <br> • Turn the pacemaker on. <br> • Replace the battery. <br> • Tighten the terminals, wearing rubber gloves to avoid risk of electric shock for patient. <br> • Replace generator. Monitor patient's apical rate and blood pressure until pacemaker functions correctly. <br> • Catheter wires replaced by the doctor. Monitor the patient closely. |

cidental shocks to the heart that may cause ventricular fibrillation. Also, cover all exposed metal parts of the pacemaker setup, such as electrode connections or pacemaker terminals, with nonconductive tape, or place the pacing unit in a dry rubber surgical glove, to insulate them. Instruct the patient not to use an electric razor or any other nonessential electrical equipment.

If emergency defibrillation should be necessary, make sure the pacemaker can withstand this procedure before starting it; if not, disconnect it to avoid damaging the generator.

Protect the pacemaker and its connections from moisture.

If the patient is disoriented or uncooperative, restrain his arms to prevent accidental removal of pacemaker wires.

If any evidence of infection is present during catheter implantation, culture disposable pacemaker catheter tips after they're removed.

## Complications

Potential complications include: arrhythmias (asystole following abrupt cessation of pacing; ventricular irritability, resulting in ventricular arrhythmias such as ventricular tachycardia); thrombus/embolus (lead-related thrombus or embolism, or inactivity-related thrombus or embolus, both of which may lead to pulmonary embolism); and ventricular rupture (cardiac tamponade resulting from myocardial lead-related hemorrhage may lead to cardiac arrest). Complications at the insertion site may include infection, phlebitis, blood vessel occlusion, hemorrhage, or an allergic reaction to the local anesthetic. Pericarditis may also occur.

## Documentation

Document the type of pacemaker used; date of insertion; doctor's name; control settings used; whether or not the pacemaker successfully treated the patient's arrhythmias, and other pertinent observations. Attach significant portions of the EKG rhythm strip to the record.

PHYLLIS PLETZ, RN, MSN

# Permanent Pacemaker Insertion and Care

Unlike a temporary pacemaker, a permanent pacemaker is self-contained and designed to operate for 3 to 20 years. A surgeon implants a permanent pacemaker in a pocket beneath the patient's skin. This is usually done in the operating room with local or general anesthesia. The nurse assists catheter placement by monitoring the EKG and by maintaining sterile technique.

Permanent pacemakers may be of the fixed or demand type; some with an external hand-held unit can be programmed by the doctor to function in either mode after they have been implanted. Candidates for permanent pacemakers include heart attack victims with persistent bradyarrhythmia, and patients with complete heart block or slow ventricular rates from congenital or degenerative heart disease or after cardiac surgery. Patients who suffer Stokes-Adams attacks, as well as those with Wolff-Parkinson-White syndrome or "sick sinus syndrome," may also benefit from permanent pacemaker implantation.

## Equipment

Sphygmomanometer □ stethoscope □ thermometer □ EKG monitor (with oscilloscope and strip-chart recorder) □ sterile dressing tray □ povidone-iodine ointment □ skin preparation kit with razor □ sterile gauze dressing □ alcohol sponges □ nonallergenic tape □ emergency resuscitation equipment □ scrub gown □ mask.

## Essential steps

• Explain the procedure to the patient. Provide and review with him literature from the manaufacturer or the American Heart Association so he can learn about the pacemaker and how it works. Emphasize that the pacemaker merely augments his natural heart rate, and that he won't be in any grave danger if the pace-

---

## PATIENT-TEACHING AID

### HOW TO CARE FOR YOUR PACEMAKER

Dear Patient:

Your doctor has inserted a pacemaker in your chest to produce the electrical impulses necessary to keep your heart working properly. Now that you have a pacemaker, you must learn how to take care of it. Here are some things you should know about your pacemaker:
• Keep the incision clean and dry until it heals (usually 7 to 10 days). After that, you may wash as usual.
• Wear loose clothing to avoid putting pressure on the pacemaker. For example, a woman with a pacemaker shouldn't wear a tight bra.
• Normally, the implantation bulges slightly. If it reddens, swells, drains, or becomes warm or painful, *notify the doctor immediately.*
• Depending on which type of pacemaker you have, it should give 3 to 4 years service. See the doctor regularly, usually every week during the first month or sooner if you have problems. Call the doctor if you experience chest pain, dizziness, shortness of breath, prolonged hiccups, muscle twitching, nausea, vomiting, or diarrhea, or a *very fast* or *very slow* heart rate. He may have you check your pacemaker periodically by transtelephonic monitoring, which enables you to transmit your EKG over the phone.
• To check your pacemaker, count your pulse at least once a day for a full minute *after you've been at rest for at least 15 minutes.* A good time to take a resting pulse rate is first thing in the morning. Your pulse rate reflects the number of times your heart pumps. The nurse will teach you how to count your pulse and tell you what pulse rate to expect. Report any discrepancy to the doctor immediately. Also, record all your pulse rates; include the number of beats, the date, and the time.
• Take your heart medication, as prescribed. This medication, along with your pacemaker, ensures a regular heart rate. As a reminder, note on a calendar the times when you should take your medication.
• Follow the doctor's orders concerning diet and physical activity. You should exercise every day, but the doctor will tell you how much exercise is right for you. You can participate in any physical activity in accordance with the doctor except a contact sport, such as football. *Don't overdo it.* Be especially careful not to stress the muscles near the pacemaker.
• Don't get too close to gasoline engines, electric motors, or poorly shielded microwave ovens. Don't use an electric shaver directly over the pacemaker. Also, stay away from high-voltage fields created by overhead electric lines. Most other electric equipment won't interfere with your pacemaker.
• If you go to the dentist or any other health-care professional, tell him you're wearing a pacemaker. If you need dental work or surgery is necessary, you might require a prophylactic antibiotic to prevent infections. Consult the doctor before undergoing any procedure that involves electricity, such as cautery or diathermy.
• Always carry your pacemaker emergency card. The card lists your doctor, hospital, type of pacemaker (model, serial number, lead type), and date of implantation.
• You can drive a car after a month has passed since your pacemaker was implanted, but avoid long trips for at least 3 months and when the time for your battery replacement nears. Tell the doctor of your travel plans in advance, and carry a list of doctors and hospitals in the area where you'll be traveling.
• If you're traveling by plane, you must pass through an airport metal detector. Before doing so, be sure to alert the authorities that you have a pacemaker.
• If you have a *nuclear* pacemaker and plan to travel abroad, the Nuclear Regulatory Commission requires that you inform the pacemaker manufacturer of your travel itinerary, your means of travel, and the name of your doctor.
• Periodic short-term hospitalization is usually necessary for battery changes or pacemaker replacement.

---

maker stops working. (see *How to Care For Your Pacemaker*, page 416).

● Make sure the patient or a responsible family member signs a consent form.

● Ask the patient if he's allergic to anesthetics or iodine.

● For transvenous pacemaker insertion, shave the patient's chest from the axilla to the midline and from the clavicle to the nipple line on the side selected by the doctor. If the pacemaker is to be inserted in the axilla, shave that area; for epicardial placement, shave from the nipple line to the umbilicus.

● Establish an I.V. line at a keep-vein-open rate in the patient's left arm *to administer emergency drugs in case of ventricular arrhythmia.*

● Establish baseline vital signs and a baseline EKG recording.

● Provide sedation, as ordered.

*In the operating room:*

● If you will be present during the procedure to monitor arrhythmias, put on a scrub gown and mask.

● Help the patient assume a supine position. Have emergency resuscitation equipment on hand.

● Connect the EKG monitor to the patient and run a baseline rhythm strip. Make sure the machine has enough paper to run additional rhythm strips during the procedure. Leave the monitor screen on throughout the procedure.

● During *endocardial* placement, the doctor, guided by a fluoroscope, passes the electrode catheter through the cephalic or external jugular vein and positions it under the trabeculae in the apex of the right ventricle. He then attaches the catheter to the pulse generator, inserts this into a pocket of muscle in the patient's chest wall, and sutures it closed, leaving a small outlet for a drainage tube.

● During *epicardial* placement, the doctor may apply the electrodes directly to the myocardium after he performs a thoracotomy. In this procedure, the doctor inserts the generator beneath the skin in the subcostal area. If the patient had a temporary pacemaker, the doctor will probably leave it in for 24 hours after the insertion of the permanent implant *in case the new pacemaker doesn't function properly.*

*For postoperative care:*

● Monitor the patient's EKG *to check for arrhythmias.* Record a rhythm strip every hour for 24 hours to check for effective pacemaker function.

● Also monitor the I.V. flow rate; the I.V. line is usually kept in place for 24 to 48 hours postoperatively *to allow for possible emergency treatment of arrhythmias.*

● Check the dressing for signs of bleeding, infection, swelling, redness, or exudate. The doctor may order prophylactic antibiotics for up to 7 days after the implantation.

● Change the dressing and apply povidone-iodine ointment at least once every 24 hours, or according to doctor's orders and institution policy. If the dressing becomes soiled or the site is exposed to air, change the dressing immediately, regardless of when you last changed it.

● Check the patient's vital signs and level of consciousness every 15 minutes for the first hour, every hour for the next 4 hours, every 4 hours for the next 48 hours, and then once every shift. (Confused, elderly patients with second-degree heart block will not show immediate improvement in level of consciousness.)

● Watch for signs and symptoms of a perforated ventricle, with resultant cardiac tamponade: persistent hiccups, distant heart sounds, pulsus paradoxus, hypotension with narrow pulse pressure, increased venous pressure, cyanosis, distended neck veins, decreased urine output, restlessness, or complaints of fullness in the chest. If any of these develop, notify the doctor immediately *because a perforated ventricle requires immediate surgery.*

● Relieve patient discomfort with analgesics, as ordered.

● Teach the patient how to take his own pulse daily before he's discharged from the hospital. Make sure he understands that he must take a resting pulse rate.

Tell him what constitutes an acceptable and unacceptable discrepancy between pulse readings, and whom to call if the discrepancy is unacceptable. The lower rate limit is usually 5 beats per minute below the pulse generator setting; the upper limit is usually 90 to 100 beats per minute.

### Special considerations

If the patient is a hunter, the doctor usually places the pacemaker battery on the side opposite the one where the gun is held *to avoid damaging it during recoil.* If the patient wears a hearing aid, the pacemaker battery is placed on the opposite side accordingly.

Watch for signs of pacemaker malfunction. (See "Temporary Pacemaker Insertion and Care" in this chapter.)

Provide the patient with an identification card that lists the pacemaker type and manufacturer, serial number, pacemaker rate setting, date implanted, and the doctor's name.

### Complications

Complications depend on the surgical approach. After epicardial placement, the patient risks the complications associated with thoracotomy and general anesthesia. Complications of endocardial placement include thrombus and embolus formation and cardiac tamponade due to perforation of the ventricular wall. Both methods of implantation may cause infection or arrhythmia. Other complications involving the pacemaker itself, such as battery failure or a displaced electrode wire, are the same as for a temporary pacemaker.

### Documentation

Document the type of pacemaker used, the serial number and manufacturer's name, the pacing rate, the date of implantation, and the doctor's name. Note whether or not the pacemaker successfully treated the patient's arrhythmias, and include other pertinent observations, such as condition of the incision site.

PHYLLIS PLETZ, RN, MSN

# Intraaortic Balloon Pump Insertion and Care

*The intraaortic balloon pump (IABP) consists of a single-chamber or multichamber polyurethane balloon attached to an external pump console by means of a large-lumen catheter. A surgeon advances the balloon catheter up the patient's descending thoracic aorta to a point just distal to the left subclavian artery. The pumping console inflates the balloon with helium or carbon dioxide during diastole and deflates it during systole. This inflation-deflation cycle, called counterpulsation, is triggered by the patient's electrocardiogram (EKG) projected on the console's oscilloscope. The IABP increases systemic circulation, improves coronary perfusion, and reduces left ventricular workload.*

*The balloon inflates early in diastole, just after the aortic valve closes. Normally, about 70% to 80% of coronary perfusion occurs during diastole. Balloon inflation forces blood toward the aortic valve, which increases pressure in the aortic root and augments diastolic pressure to enhance coronary perfusion. It also forces blood through the brachiocephalic, common carotid, and subclavian arteries arising from the aortic trunk, which increases peripheral circulation.*

*During systole, blood pressure in the left ventricle must exceed that in the aorta to allow the aortic valve to open and eject blood into the system. The aortic resistance that must be overcome is called afterload. The balloon rapidly deflates just before systole, which reduces aortic volume and decreases aortic pressure and afterload. Since aortic pressure is decreased, the left ventricle needn't work as hard to open the aortic valve. This decreased workload reduces the heart's oxygen requirement and, combined with the more efficient myocardial perfusion provided by the IABP, prevents or reduces myocardial ischemia.*

*The IABP console can assist the heart at preset rates—for example, it can inflate/deflate every one to four beats, depending on the patient's need and the type of machine used. It also shuts off automatically in the presence of ventricular arrhythmias.*

*The balloon catheter can be inserted surgically at the patient's bedside, in the operating room, or in a cardiac catheterization laboratory. Or, it can be inserted percutaneously at the patient's bedside with or without fluoroscopic guidance. If insertion is performed in the unit, strict aseptic technique must be followed. In some hospitals, technicians assist the doctor with balloon catheter insertion and removal and troubleshooting problems, and the nurse is usually responsible for patient assessment and management; otherwise, the nurse may care for the patient and operate the IABP machine as well.*

*Before insertion of the balloon catheter, a Swan-Ganz pulmonary artery catheter, a Foley catheter, and an arterial line should be inserted. A peripheral I.V. or subclavian line should also be in place for administering fluids and medications as needed. A transducer connected to the IABP console projects a visible arterial pressure waveform on the oscilloscope. A separate monitor and transducer may be required to display pulmonary artery pressures.*

*Common indications for the IABP include left ventricular failure and cardiogenic shock caused by acute myocardial infarction, unstable or preinfarction angina, and high-risk cardiac surgery. The IABP may also be used to provide preoperative support to the patient undergoing cardiac catheterization.*

*Use of the IABP is contraindicated by the inability to place the catheter through arteriosclerotic vessels, and in patients with irreversible brain damage, cardiomyopathy, incompetent aortic valve, dissecting aortic aneurysm, or ventricular fibrillation.*

## Equipment

IABP console and balloon catheters □ Dacron patch (for surgically inserted balloon) □ EKG electrodes □ gas source for pump (helium or $CO_2$) □ I.V. solution and infusion set □ arterial line catheter □ heparin flush solution, transducer and intraflo setup □ Swan-Ganz pulmonary artery catheter setup □ temporary pacemaker setup □ sterile drape □ sterile gloves □ suture material □ povidone-iodine solution and saline or sterile water for irrigation/suction setup □ oxygen setup and respirator, if necessary □ defibrillator and emergency drugs □ EKG monitor □ Foley catheter □ urimeter □ arterial blood gas (ABG) kits and tubes for laboratory studies □ dressing materials □ iodophor solution or swabs and ointment □ 4"x4" gauze sponges □ disposable razor or commercially available skin preparation kit □ forms necessary for charting frequent measurements.

Three IABP devices are currently in use: the Datascope, Kontron, and SMEC. Each requires its own specific preparation for operation. The information provided here generally applies to all units.

## Preparation of equipment

The doctor tests the balloon catheter for leaks before insertion. The pump console's pressure transducer must be balanced and the oscilloscope monitor on the pump console must be calibrated for accuracy. Depending on hospital policy, balancing and calibration may be performed by the nurse or another specially trained member of the health-care team. Specific procedures differ according to manufacturer's guidelines.

## Essential steps

*To prepare for IABP insertion:*
● Explain the procedure to the patient. Inform him that the balloon catheter temporarily reduces the heart's workload to promote rapid healing of the ventricular muscle, and that it will be removed after his heart can resume an adequate workload again.
● Make sure the patient or responsible

## DIASTOLIC AUGMENTATION

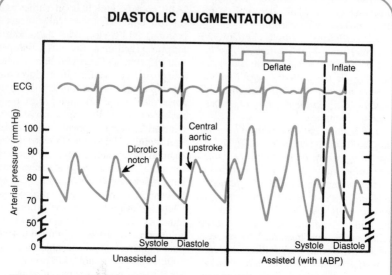

This graph demonstrates how the intraaortic balloon pump (IABP) augments diastolic pressure. The inflation-deflation cycle is synchronized with the R wave on the ECG. The R wave triggers deflation, which begins just before the central aortic upstroke. Inflation begins at the dicrotic notch in early diastole. Note that in an unassisted arterial pressure wave form, peak arterial pressure is during systole. When assisted by the IABP (at right), peak arterial pressure is during diastole, enhancing coronary blood flow. Systolic pressure drops sharply when assisted, decreasing the left ventricle's workload and increasing cardiac output.

family member understands and signs a consent form.

• Obtain baseline vital signs, including pulmonary artery pressures if the line is already inserted. Obtain a baseline EKG.

• Apply chest electrodes in a standard lead II position or in whatever position produces the largest R wave on the oscilloscope needed to trigger the inflation/deflation cycle.

• Assess respiratory status and administer oxygen as necessary.

• Prepare and insert a peripheral I.V. line *to deliver medications as ordered.*

• Prepare for and assist with insertion of an arterial line, as indicated, *to allow arterial pressure monitoring. The augmented pressure waveform demonstrates elevated diastolic and lowered systolic pressure* (see illustration above), and allows you to check proper timing of the inflation/deflation cycle. (Remember, the balloon should inflate during diastole and deflate during systole.)

• Prepare for and assist with insertion of a pulmonary artery line, as indicated, *to allow measurement of pulmonary artery pressure, to permit aspiration of blood samples, and to perform cardiac output studies.* Increased pressures indicate increased myocardial workload and ineffective balloon pumping. Comparison cardiac output studies may be done on and off the IABP to determine patient progress and potential for weaning.

• If bradycardia occurs, give atropine or prepare the patient for pacemaker insertion, as ordered. The balloon pump is ineffective if the patient has bradycardia.

• Obtain specimens for the necessary preoperative laboratory tests, as ordered. These tests usually include blood typing and crossmatching; serum electrolytes and blood glucose to determine homeostatic imbalances; blood urea nitrogen (BUN) and urine creatinine, to assess renal perfusion and function; complete blood count (CBC) and differential; prothrombin time, activated partial thromboplastin time, and a platelet count to detect clotting disorders; arterial blood gas analysis to assess respiratory function; serum cholesterol and triglycerides, to detect arteriosclerotic disease; and sputum and throat cultures and serology to detect infection. (Typing and crossmatch, serum cholesterol and triglycerides, sputum and throat cultures, and serology are usually done for preoperative patients.)

• Insert a Foley catheter *to allow accurate measurement of urinary output and assessment of fluid balance and renal function.*

• Shave the patient from the lower abdomen to the lower thigh bilaterally, including the pubic area, *to reduce the risk of infection.* Although the catheter is usually inserted on the left side, it may be inserted on the right side if the left artery is diseased.

• Attach another set of EKG monitoring

## INTRAARTERIAL BALLOON CATHETER PLACEMENT

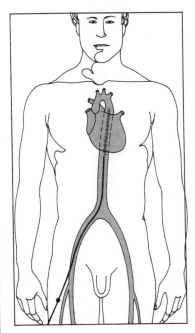

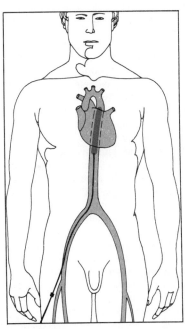

To insert a balloon catheter percutaneously, the doctor punctures the patient's femoral artery with an angiographic needle. He then makes an incision where the needle exits the skin and inserts a dilator to expand the vessel. Next, the doctor removes that dilator and replaces it with the percutaneous introducer dilator and sheath. Just before inserting the balloon catheter, the doctor removes the introducer dilator.

He then feeds the balloon catheter into the sheath and through the femoral artery, as shown at left.
The balloon is tightly wound for insertion. Balloon size varies from patient to patient because the inflated balloon must never completely occlude the artery. Once in place, the balloon is unwound to facilitate inflation, shown at right. Before removal, the balloon must be deflated and rewound.

electrodes to the patient unless the EKG pattern is being transmitted from the patient's monitor to the balloon pump monitor.

● Administer a sedative, as ordered.

● Make sure signed consent forms are on the patient's chart.

*To insert the intraaortic balloon:*

● The surgeon may insert a special intraaortic balloon catheter percutaneously through the femoral artery into the descending thoracic aorta. This simplified procedure may be performed in the unit or in a cardiac catherization laboratory.

● If the surgeon chooses not to insert the catheter percutaneously, he inserts the balloon through a femoral arteriotomy using strict aseptic technique. This procedure is best performed in an operating room.

● After making the incision and isolating the artery, he attaches a Dacron graft to a small opening in the arterial wall, passes the catheter through this graft, and, with optional fluoroscopic guidance, advances it up the descending thoracic aorta and positions the catheter tip between the left subclavian artery and the renal arteries.

● He then sews the Dacron graft around the catheter at the insertion point and connects the other end of the catheter to the pumping console.

*To monitor the patient after IABP insertion:*

● Obtain a chest X-ray to determine correct balloon placement.

● Observe the arterial pressure pattern every 30 minutes for diastolic augmentation, *to verify correctly timed counterpulsation.*

● Measure blood pressure every 15 minutes to 1 hour *to determine the effectiveness of therapy and anticipate the need for vasopressors or vasodilators, such as dopamine or nitroprusside (Nipride).*

● Take apical pulse at least every hour, noting rate and rhythm. *Increased or decreased pulse rate alters the effectiveness of the pump and may require drugs, such as atropine, or pacemaker therapy.*

● Check temperature every hour. If it's

elevated, obtain blood specimens for culture, send them to the laboratory immediately, and notify the doctor.

● Measure intake and output hourly.

● Observe for ischemia in the limbs—especially the affected limb—every hour. Be alert for changes in pulse, color, temperature, and sensation.

 Watch for pump interruptions, which may result from loose EKG electrodes or broken wires, static or 60-cycle interference, kinked catheters, and improper body alignment. Elevate the head of the bed no more than 45°, keeping the patient's leg unflexed at the groin *to prevent catheter kinking or displacement.*

 If the IABP is inadvertently shut off for more than 5 minutes, notify the doctor immediately *to determine the need for heparinization before restarting the balloon. Resumed pumping without adequate anticoagulant precipitates emboli.*

● Observe for optimal timing. Balloon inflation should begin when the aortic valve closes or at the dicrotic notch on the arterial wave form. Deflation should occur just before systole. Improper timing includes late inflation, which reduces coronary artery perfusion, and prolonged deflation, which dangerously increases the resistance against which the left ventricle must pump. In both situations, readjust timing according to the manufacturer's guidelines or notify the person responsible for the balloon pump adjustments.

● Check for gas leaks from the catheter or the balloon. This may be indicated by an alarm on the pump console. If the balloon ruptures, blood will appear in the catheter. If this happens, shut off the pump console and notify the doctor.

 If you suspect balloon rupture, promptly place the patient in Trendelenburg's position *to prevent gas embolus from reaching the brain.*

If the patient is not receiving anticoagulants, the doctor may order I.V. heparin or low-molecular-weight dextran *to prevent platelet aggregation on the quiescent balloon.*

● Measure left arterial pressure and pulmonary capillary wedge pressure (PCWP) every 1 to 2 hours, or as ordered. A rising PCWP indicates increased ventricular pressure and workload; notify the doctor if this occurs. Some patients require the administration of I.V. nitroprusside in addition to the IABP *to reduce preload and afterload.*

● Obtain arterial samples for ABG analysis, as ordered. If the patient is connected to a ventilator, perform ventilation checks, suctioning, and respiratory assessment.

● Monitor electrolytes as ordered, especially sodium *to assess fluid balance* and potassium *to prevent cardiac arrhythmias.*

● Monitor hematologic status. Blood products are usually used to maintain the hematocrit at 30%. Platelets may be required if the platelet count drops. Observe for bleeding gums, blood in urine or stool, or petechiae.

● Monitor the results of clotting tests. As ordered, administer heparin through a pressure infusion to maintain the activated partial thromboplastin time (APTT) at 1½ to 2 times the normal value.

● Turn and position the patient every 2 hours. Provide oral hygiene at least every 4 hours, or as needed. Give pain medication for insertion site discomfort, as ordered.

● Redress the balloon site, as ordered, and observe for signs of inflammation or excessive bleeding. Apply pressure to control bleeding.

● Prevent constipation *to avoid strain on the patient's heart.*

● If angina occurs, notify the doctor immediately, *as the IABP is not effective.*

Watch for signs and symptoms of a dissecting aortic aneurysm, such as a difference in blood pressure between arms; elevated blood pressure; pain in the chest, abdomen, or back; syncope; pallor; diaphoresis; dyspnea; throbbing abdominal mass; and decreased red blood cell count and increased white blood cell count. If you suspect an aortic aneurysm, notify the doctor.

*To wean the patient from the IABP:*

● Assess cardiac index, systemic blood pressure, and PCWP *to evaluate readiness for weaning.*

● To begin weaning, gradually decrease the frequency of balloon augmentation to 1:2, 1:4, and 1:8 as ordered, and measure the cardiac index at each ratio. (Output is frequently measured both on and off the machine.) Some doctors prefer to wean the patient by decreasing balloon volume; however, this must be done cautiously to avoid reducing volume so much that the balloon cannot inflate and deflate forcibly enough to repel platelets. The possibility of increased potential for emboli with this method is controversial, and some doctors choose to administer I.V. heparin or low-molecular-weight dextran when using this method.

*To remove the IABP:*

● The surgeon removes the balloon catheter when augmentation is no longer necessary (such as if cardiac output improves during weaning; or, if angina is absent, PCWP returns to normal, and systolic pressure increases when the machine is turned off). He also removes it if circulation to the limb is seriously compromised; if the patient's condition is diagnosed as inoperable during cardiac catheterization; or if the patient's condition deteriorates beyond recovery. Then he closes the Dacron graft and sutures the insertion site. If a percutaneous catheter is in place, the surgeon usually removes it. Pressure must be applied to the site for 15 to 30 minutes or until bleeding stops; in some hospitals, this is the doctor's responsibility.

● After removal of the IABP, give necessary wound care.

## Complications

Aortic or femoral artery dissection or perforation may occur during balloon insertion. Ischemia or loss of pulses may occur in extremities (especially the legs) due to compromised circulation. Thrombi may form on the balloon, predisposing the patient to emboli. Platelets are destroyed during balloon pumping, causing a decrease in circulating platelets (thrombocytopenia). A gas embolus can occur from balloon rupture. Infection may occur at the balloon insertion site.

### Documentation

Document all aspects of patient assessment and management. If you're responsible for the IABP device, document all routine checks, problems, and troubleshooting measures. If a technician is responsible for the IABP device, record only when and why the technician was notified, as well as the result of his actions on the patient, if any.

PHYLLIS PLETZ, RN, MSN

# Emergency Control of Hemorrhage

*Hemorrhage results from vascular tissue injury—externally from a laceration, amputation, fracture, crush trauma, or nosebleed; internally from a bleeding ulcer, ruptured spleen, or abdominal and chest trauma. Uncontrolled arterial bleeding can rapidly cause shock, and death can occur. In contrast, venous bleeding, even though heavy at first, is usually controlled quickly by clotting unless the patient is receiving anticoagulant therapy or has a bleeding tendency. However, it still requires prompt treatment to prevent heavy blood loss.*

*Direct pressure over a bleeding vessel is the action of choice for external bleeding; it may help stop blood flow long enough to allow clot formation. If this fails to stop bleeding, applying pressure to the major artery proximal to the injury may slow or stop blood flow and perfusion into the tissues. A tourniquet should be used to control bleeding only if all other measures fail, since its use may cause gangrene and possibly necessitate amputation of the affected limb.*

### Equipment

In an emergency, equipment consists of whatever is readily available and adaptable for immediate use. External hemorrhage requires thick pads of sterile gauze, sanitary pads, or clean soft cloths. If dressings aren't available, use your hands to stop excessive bleeding until dressings can be obtained. Tourniquets require a wide fold of cloth or other broad material, such as a belt, blood pressure cuff, scarf, or large handkerchief; a stick or pencil to tighten the tourniquet; and a marking pen or lipstick to identify the patient. Avoid using narrow material (wire or rope) for a tourniquet *to minimize tissue damage.*

### Essential steps

• Explain the procedure to the patient—even if he's comatose or in shock—*to help allay his fears and promote cooperation.*

*To control external bleeding:*

• If necessary, cut the patient's clothing to expose the wound.

• Elevate an affected extremity above heart level *to stop venous and capillary bleeding.*

• Apply steady, direct pressure on the wound with a clean dressing of heavy gauze, a sanitary pad, or clean, soft cloths. If nothing else is available, use your hand. Apply ice to the wound, if possible.

• If direct pressure fails to stop bleeding or cannot be applied because of a fracture, apply digital pressure to the arterial pressure point nearest the wound (see *Locating Arterial Pressure Points,* opposite). If you're not skilled at locating a pressure point precisely, apply pressure with the heel of your hand to cover the area where the pressure point is located. If you've applied pressure correctly, you'll be unable to detect a pulse below the pressure point, and the patient will feel local tingling or numbness.

• If you've controlled the bleeding, apply a compression dressing. Using sterile gauze or clean cloths, prepare a compress six to eight layers thick. Tie the dressing in place with any available cloth, such as a scarf, stocking, or strip of clothing. If blood soaks through the dressing, do not remove it; apply additional dressings over the soaked ones and rebandage.

• If bleeding still persists, prepare to apply a tourniquet. Position the tourniquet on the limb between the site of injury and the heart. Wrap the tourniquet around the extremity, about 2″ (5 cm) above the wound (the tourniquet should not touch the wound edges), tie it with a half knot, then place the stick over the half knot and tie a square knot over it. Tighten the tourniquet by twisting the stick until bleeding stops. Secure the stick in this position with the loose tourniquet ends or an additional piece of cloth. Leave the tourniquet uncovered, and call attention to it by writing a large "T" with a pen or lipstick on the patient's forehead. Indicate tourniquet location and the time of application. Avoid loosening the tourniquet until the patient reaches the hospital. *Doing so may cause a massive hemorrhage that could be lethal to an already hypovolemic patient, and may release dangerous toxins from injured tissues.*

*To control internal bleeding:*
• If you suspect internal bleeding, keep the patient calm. Do not give liquids unless medical attention will be delayed and there is no gastrointestinal bleeding. If possible, apply ice packs to the affected area *to reduce swelling.* Place the patient in Trendelenburg's position to increase cerebral blood flow.
• After any type of hemorrhage, when bleeding is controlled, take vital signs and observe for other major injuries.

### Special considerations
Make sure you apply the tourniquet properly; a loose tourniquet may actually increase blood loss, *since arterial bleeding continues, but the tourniquet prevents venous return.*

Transport the patient to the hospital without delay. If you suspect spinal in-

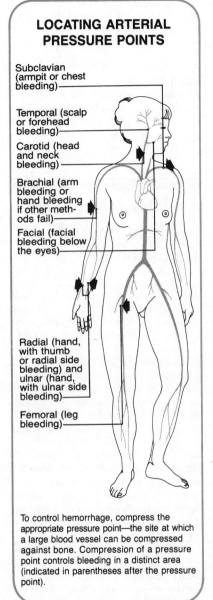

**LOCATING ARTERIAL PRESSURE POINTS**

Subclavian (armpit or chest bleeding)

Temporal (scalp or forehead bleeding)

Carotid (head and neck bleeding)

Brachial (arm bleeding or hand bleeding if other methods fail)

Facial (facial bleeding below the eyes)

Radial (hand, with thumb or radial side bleeding) and ulnar (hand, with ulnar side bleeding)

Femoral (leg bleeding)

To control hemorrhage, compress the appropriate pressure point—the site at which a large blood vessel can be compressed against bone. Compression of a pressure point controls bleeding in a distinct area (indicated in parentheses after the pressure point).

jury, make sure that the patient is tied to a backboard before movement. Handle a partially severed limb with extreme care *to avoid increasing the extent of injury.* A completely severed limb should accompany the patient on transport. Indicate on the tourniquet or the patient's forehead that the severed limb accompanies the victim. (See "Care of a Severed or Partly Severed Body Part" in Chapter 13.)

## Complications

Cardiac arrest can result from hypovolemia with secondary anoxia. Even correct application of a tourniquet may cause gangrene and loss of a limb.

DIANNE MONKOWSKI MAGNUSON, RN, BSN

# Antishock Trousers Application and Removal

*Medical antishock trousers (a MAST suit, also known as a Jobst G Antigravity Suit) are made of inflatable bladders sandwiched between double layers of fabric. When inflated, the suit places external pressure on the lower extremities and abdomen, creating an autotransfusion effect by squeezing blood superiorly and increasing blood volume to the heart, lungs, and brain by up to 30%. The MAST suit is used to treat shock when systolic blood pressure falls below 80 mmHg or below 100 mmHg when accompanied by signs of shock. It can control abdominal and lower extremity hemorrhage by creating internal pressure and external tamponade effects; it can also help stabilize and splint pelvic and femoral fractures.*

*Use of the MAST suit is contraindicated in patients with cardiogenic shock, congestive heart failure, pulmonary edema and tension pneumothorax. It should be used cautiously during pregnancy. The MAST suit must be deflated slowly, with continuous blood pressure monitoring, to prevent potentially irreversible shock from hypovolemia. It shouldn't be removed until the patient's blood volume is restored, the patient's condition is stabilized, or the patient is being prepared for surgery. If necessary, the MAST suit can be deflated by stages in the operating room.*

## Equipment

A MAST suit with footpump is the only necessary equipment. MAST suits come in a pediatric size (for patients 3.5' to 5' [1.05 to 1.5 meters] tall) and an adult size (for patients taller than 5').

## Preparation of equipment

Spread open the MAST suit on a smooth surface or blanket *to avoid puncturing it.* Make sure all the stopcock valves are open. Attach the footpump.

## Essential steps

*To apply a MAST suit:*

● Explain the procedure to the patient *to allay his fears and ensure his cooperation.*

● Take vital signs *to establish baseline measurements.*

● Assess the patient's injuries to determine whether he can be turned from side to side. If the patient can't be turned, slide the MAST suit under him. If the patient can be turned, place the MAST suit next to him and logroll him onto it. You can also set up the MAST suit on a gurney or stretcher and place the patient on it in a supine position.

● Examine the patient for sharp objects, such as pieces of glass or stones, that could injure him or puncture the suit when it's inflated.

● Arrange the MAST suit so the upper edge is just below the patient's rib cage. *Pressure above this area could decrease chest expansion, causing respiratory problems.*

● Fasten the MAST suit around both legs, then around the abdomen. (The suit may not cover a tall patient's lower legs.)

● Doublecheck the stopcocks to make sure they're all open *so the MAST suit will inflate uniformly.*

● Inflate the legs of the MAST suit first, then the abdominal segment, to about 20 to 30 mmHg to start. Monitor the patient's blood pressure and pulse. Continue to inflate the suit slowly while monitoring vital signs. Stop inflating when the patient's systolic blood pressure reaches the desired level, usually 100 mmHg.

• Close all stopcocks *to prevent loss of air and accidental deflation.*

• Monitor the patient's blood pressure, pulse, and respirations every 5 minutes *to determine his response to application of the MAST suit.* Check his pedal pulses and temperature periodically. Notify the doctor if the circulation in his feet appears impaired.

• Make preparations for determining and treating the patient's medical problem, *because the MAST suit is only a temporary treatment.*

To remove a MAST suit:

• Before deflation, make sure that I.V. lines are patent, and that a doctor is in attendance and emergency resuscitation equipment is immediately available. *Removing a MAST suit may cause the patient's blood pressure to drop rapidly.*

• Open the abdominal stopcock and start releasing small amounts of air. Closely monitor the patient's systolic blood pressure as you do this. If it drops 5 mmHg, close the stopcock.

 *Deflating the suit too quickly can allow circulating blood to rush to the abdomen or extremities, causing potentially irreversible shock.*

• If you have to stop deflating the MAST suit because of a drop in blood pressure, increase the flow rate of I.V. solutions *to help stabilize blood pressure.*

• If blood pressure is stable, continue to deflate the MAST suit slowly. After you finish deflating the abdominal section, deflate the legs simultaneously.

• When the MAST suit becomes loose enough, gently pull it off.

• Clean the MAST suit as required, but don't autoclave it or use solvents.

**Special considerations**

Generally, you should see a therapeutic response to treatment when the MAST suit is inflated to 25 mmHg. A so-called morbidity effect, caused by a change in local circulation, occurs at about 50 mmHg. Most types of MAST suits have Velcro straps, pop-off valves, or gauges that prevent inflation beyond 104 mmHg. Normally, the MAST suit shouldn't be left inflated for more than 2 hours, although occasionally it will be used for as long as several days. A range of 25 to 50 mmHg can usually be maintained for up to 48 hours. For prolonged use, the MAST suit may be inflated at a lower pressure than normal.

A MAST suit is radiolucent and allows X-rays while the patient wears it.

**Complications**

Vomiting can result from compression of the abdomen. Anaerobic metabolism, which can result from the MAST suit's pressure being higher than the patient's systolic pressure, can lead to metabolic acidosis. Skin breakdown may follow prolonged use. When used with severe leg fractures for long periods, tissue sloughing and necrosis caused by increased compartmental pressures have necessitated amputation.

**Documentation**

Record the time of application and removal, and the patient's vital signs before application, during treatment, and after removal.

SUZANNE MARR SKINNER, RN, MS

## Selected References

Brunner, Lillian S., and Suddarth, Doris S. *Textbook of Medical-Surgical Nursing,* 4th ed. Philadelphia: W.B. Saunders Co., 1980.

*Diagnostics.* Nurse's Reference Library™ Series. Springhouse, Pa.: Intermed Communications, Inc., 1981.

*Diseases.* Nurse's Reference Library™ Series. Springhouse, Pa.: Intermed Communications, Inc., 1980.

# 9 Respiratory Care

# Respiratory Care

## Introduction

Whether it results from disease or trauma and reflects a primary or secondary response, respiratory impairment generally causes one or all of these physiologic dysfunctions: ineffective airway clearance, ineffective or abnormal breathing patterns, and impaired gas exchange. These physiologic impairments can be corrected or minimized by nursing actions that provide supportive care or assist with implementation or monitoring of medical therapy.

### Primary objectives

Although specific care measures vary depending on the patient's underlying disorder, the objectives of respiratory care are invariably the same: to maintain airway patency, to facilitate normal and effective breathing patterns, and to promote efficient gas exchange. Frequently, achieving one of these objectives helps achieve the others. For example, suctioning thick, tenacious secretions from the airway of a patient with pneumonia increases overall ventilation, thereby improving alveolar gas exchange and reducing the effort required to breathe.

### Diagnostic procedures

A significant part of respiratory care is associated with diagnostic tests to assess pulmonary function. New technology has made such diagnostic studies easier to perform and more likely to be performed at the patient's bedside. For example, the development of fiberoptic bronchoscopy in the mid-60s introduced a new, low-risk method for direct inspection and biopsy of the airways. With fiberoptic equipment, bronchoscopy may still be performed in the operating room or other specially equipped room, but it can be performed with greater ease and less risk to the patient and can yield significantly more information. Fiberoptic equipment is flexible, less traumatic, and can enter distal airways for direct observation of tissues, localization of abnormal tissue, or biopsy. A tissue sample taken from a distorted and discolored airway lining can diagnose lung carcinoma and, in some cases, determine its cell type. Fiberoptic bronchoscopy also facilitates diagnosis of diffuse lung disease, such as interstitial fibrosis and sarcoidosis. Bronchoscopy is useful therapeutically to locate and extract foreign bodies, suction tenacious secretions, and reinflate collapsed bronchi.

When impaired lung mechanics produce inadequate ventilation or perfusion, pulmonary function tests can definitively measure the factors on which ventilatory function depends: lung compliance or elasticity, chest-wall stability, and the adequacy of diaphragmatic and intercostal muscle strength. However, simpler bedside procedures now exist that help monitor changes in the acutely ill patient. Because such changes can occur so frequently, monitoring procedures are usually performed hourly. For example, measurement of negative inspiratory force helps determine the patient's readiness to be weaned from a mechanical ventilator. Bedside measurement of vital capacity and forced expiratory volume can help determine the need for intubation, or evaluate the patient's response to bronchodilator therapy. The information obtained from such diagnostic studies indicates the appropriate nursing care and medical management and provides an objective assessment of respiratory function.

## Monitoring and treatment

Although detecting respiratory dysfunction is not too difficult, monitoring and treating it are more complex and require highly skilled and specially trained personnel. Consider, for example, management of severely impaired gas exchange— the major dysfunction in acute respiratory failure. Therapy formerly consisted of mechanical delivery of oxygen at continuous high concentration and pressure. Today, this therapy includes the use of complex mechanical ventilators. These devices deliver oxygen at variable and precise concentrations and pressures and regulate tidal volume, minute rate, and sighs to support or simulate the patient's normal pattern of respiration. Mechanical ventilators can also deliver nebulizer treatments, regulate weaning, and monitor respiratory status during spontaneous breathing.

Advanced technology now permits more effective monitoring and evaluation of therapeutic results, such as determining the effects of various modes of mechanical ventilation on the heart and cardiovascular system. Sampling arterial and mixed venous blood helps gauge oxygen use by the lungs and other organs. And monitoring the ventilation/perfusion relationship can help direct therapy to maximize the function of healthy lung tissue.

## Airway management

If the lungs are the tree of life, the airways are the vital roots that carry the life substance. They must be kept patent, humidified, and free of bacterial contamination and injury. Management to preserve a patent airway, like most aspects of respiratory care, has changed markedly in the past 10 years. Although

no artificial airway can be considered totally harmless to the tissues, the degree of irreversible damage it now inflicts on the trachea and upper airway has been reduced by emphasizing scrupulous tube care and by improving techniques and equipment for detecting complications and infection.

Advances in the selection and design of endotracheal and tracheostomy tubes, the replacement of rigid tubes with more flexible plastic tubes, and the use of high-volume/low-pressure cuffs and the minimal-leak inflation technique have been especially significant. They have helped eliminate the severe tracheal stenosis and malacia that once commonly followed prolonged compromised arterial and venous circulation in the tracheal wall.

The use of disposable equipment for many respiratory procedures has practically eliminated the potential danger of treating patients with contaminated equipment, especially during emergency. The skilled use of sterile, less traumatic suctioning techniques, maintenance of adequate humidification, and improvements in tracheostomy care have helped minimize the incidence of nosocomial infection in patients with an artificial airway.

In fact, tracheostomy care has improved so dramatically that home management of tracheostomy, unheard of only 10 years ago, is now commonplace. Similarly, the development of patient-teaching programs, community professional and lay support, and such portable equipment as home oxygen units and mechanical ventilators have allowed home care of the patient with severe respiratory impairment.

In all of these patient-care efforts, nursing plays a major role. With skilled assessment of airway patency and clearance, current respiratory patterns, and the effectiveness of gas exchange, you can provide even the most complex respiratory care and can help maintain the physiologic integrity of this vital and delicate system.

ANN MARIE BRIGGS, RN, MSN, FAAN

# DIAGNOSIS
# Bronchoscopy

*Bronchoscopy is the direct observation of the pharynx, larynx, trachea, and bronchi through a rigid or flexible fiber-optic bronchoscope. Although this procedure can be performed at the patient's bedside, it is usually performed in the operating room. Its diagnostic purposes include: specimen collection for bacteriologic and cytologic analysis; determination of the location, extent, and cause of pathology, such as a tumor, bleeding, or tracheal stenosis; determination of the cause of improperly functioning intubation; and detection of tracheobronchial damage after prolonged intubation.*

*Therapeutic purposes of bronchoscopy include removal of a foreign body or localized lesion from the tracheobronchial tree, removal of mucous plugs from the lower airways, prevention or treatment of atelectasis, improvement of bronchial drainage, drainage of abscesses, and the instillation of chemotherapeutic agents.*

*Bronchoscopy may even be performed in the patient with severe respiratory failure who can't breathe adequately by himself. Under these circumstances, the patient can be placed on a ventilator before and during bronchoscopy.*

### Equipment
Bronchoscope with light-source and biopsy attachments □ local anesthetic □ sterile gowns □ sterile gloves □ caps □ surgical masks □ sterile water-soluble lubricant □ sterile drapes □ table (overbed table for bedside bronchoscopy) □ sterile 4″ x 4″ gauze sponges □ emesis basins □ sedatives, as ordered □ suction equipment □ adapter for endotracheal tube □ laboratory request forms.

*Emergency cart:* laryngoscope □ oxygen equipment □ manual resuscitation bag □ oral and endotracheal airways □ tongue blade □ ventilating bronchoscope.

*For biopsy,* optional: sterile container for microbiology specimen, container with 10% formaldehyde for histology specimen, Coplin jar with 95% ethyl alcohol for cytology smears, six glass slides (all frosted, if possible, or with frosted tips).

The fiber-optic bronchoscope is a slender, flexible tube with mirrors, a light, and a suction port at its distal end. It may also have a brush, biopsy forceps, or catheter attachments to obtain specimens for cytologic examination.

Compared to the rigid bronchoscope, the flexible fiber-optic bronchoscope offers many advantages. It's smaller, can be used at the bedside, has a greater range of view of the segmental and subsegmental bronchi, allows good airway access for resuscitation, and reduces the risk of trauma from intubation. However, a large, rigid bronchoscope is necessary to remove foreign objects and excise endobronchial lesions.

Oxygen may be administered through both the flexible and rigid bronchoscopes. A ventilating bronchoscope is used for the patient who has an endotracheal tube or a tracheostomy tube in place and is on a ventilator. This type of bronchoscope is smaller than the flexible bronchoscope and is used because the tubes already present reduce the diameter of the patient's airway.

This procedure deals only with the flexible bronchoscope for bedside use, since the nurse most commonly comes in contact with this equipment.

### Preparation of equipment
Check the doctor's order and assemble all essential and requested equipment, as appropriate. Some doctors may prefer to use their own bronchoscope equipment. If a laryngoscope is requested, check that its light works. If oxygen is requested, set it up. Make sure the emergency cart is properly stocked with equipment and medications. Using sterile technique, open the sterile drapes and place them on the table, then place the

bronchoscope, biopsy attachments, and 4" x 4" gauze sponges on the sterile area. Also, using sterile technique, squeeze the sterile water-soluble lubricant onto the gauze sponges.

## PATIENT CARE AFTER BRONCHOSCOPY

After bronchoscopy, monitor vital signs every 15 minutes or as ordered, until they are stable. Notify the doctor immediately of any complications or deterioration in the patient's condition. Keep resuscitative equipment and tracheotomy tray available for 24 hours after the test.

As ordered, place the conscious patient in the semi-Fowler's position; place the unconscious patient on his side, with the head of the bed slightly elevated to prevent aspiration. Provide an emesis basin, and instruct the patient to spit out saliva rather than swallow it. Observe sputum for blood, and notify the doctor immediately if excessive bleeding occurs. Sputum may be blood tinged, especially after biopsy, but frank bleeding shouldn't be present. Collect sputum for 24 hours immediately following a bronchoscopy for cytologic studies and culture.

Instruct the patient who has had a biopsy to refrain from clearing his throat and coughing, which may dislodge the clot at the biopsy site and cause hemorrhage. Also, advise the patient to avoid smoking for the rest of the day of the procedure, because smoking irritates the tissues and may cause coughing and clot dislodgement.

Restrict food and fluids until after the gag reflex returns (usually in 1½ to 2 hours, although it may take longer in some patients). To test for return of gag reflex, touch the back of his throat with a tongue blade. Also, if the patient has had general anesthesia, check for bowel sounds. Only after bowel sounds and gag reflex have returned should the patient begin to take oral nourishment, as ordered. Usually, you can offer ice chips, then water, and within a few hours, his usual diet. Also, provide medicated lozenges, as ordered, or a local anesthetic, such as lidocaine (Xylocaine Viscous), to ease discomfort. To prevent laryngeal edema, provide humidification, as ordered.

Reassure the patient that hoarseness and sore throat are only temporary, and encourage him to avoid straining his voice. Provide him with alternative means of communication, such as a Magic Slate, letter board, or pad and pencil.

If bronchoscopy is to be performed at the bedside, check the doctor's orders for local anesthetic (usually lidocaine in spray, jelly, or liquid form). Such sedatives as I.V. diazepam (Valium) or meperidine hydrochloride (Demerol) may also be ordered. Check the type and size of the bronchoscopy tube and the size of the gloves needed. Make sure the patient has signed a consent form. Prepare the necessary laboratory request forms *to avoid delay in transporting specimens.*

### Essential steps
*To perform bronchoscopy using a flexible bronchoscope:*
● Assess the patient's condition and obtain baseline vital signs.
● Explain the procedure, even if the patient does not appear to be alert. Provide privacy and wash your hands.
● Administer prescribed medication prior to the procedure, as ordered. Atropine is frequently ordered *to decrease secretions.* A barbiturate or narcotic is usually given intravenously *to allay anxiety and provide sedation or amnesia.*
● If the doctor is using a flexible bronchoscope, place the patient in a supine position on an examination table or bed. Tell him to remain relaxed, hyperextend his neck, place his arms at his sides, and breathe through his nose. Reassure him that he will be able to breathe through and around the tube although fullness in the pharynx may be experienced.
● Help the doctor put on a sterile gown. Then, darken the room *to facilitate fiberoptic viewing during the bronchoscopy.*
● The doctor sprays local anesthetic on the patient's throat and nasal cavity, if this approach will be used. While the anesthetic is taking effect (usually 1 or 2 minutes), the doctor lubricates the bronchoscope *to facilitate insertion.* A laryngoscope may be inserted into the pharynx *to facilitate bronchoscope insertion.* Next, he introduces the bronchoscope through the patient's mouth or nose. When the bronchoscope is just above the vocal cords, the doctor flushes approximately 3 to 4 ml of 2% to 4% lidocaine or other local anesthetic through

the inner channel of the scope *to anesthetize vocal cords and suppress the gag reflex.* Oral suction equipment should be ready in case it's needed. Throughout the procedure, the doctor will instruct the patient in what he is expected to do. The nurse should reinforce the doctor's instructions. During insertion, the patient is told to take a deep breath, hold it briefly, and to try not to cough. *Coughing facilitates movement of the anesthetic over the vocal cords, prolonging laryngeal anesthesia and delaying return of the gag reflex.*

● The bronchoscope is advanced through the larynx into the trachea and bronchi as the doctor inspects the anatomic structure of the trachea, right-lung bronchi, and then left-lung bronchi. He observes the color of the mucosal lining and notes the presence of masses or inflamed areas.

● Throughout the procedure, remind the patient to relax, breathe through his nose, and try not to cough. Reassure the patient by explaining to him what is happening. Also monitor changes in skin color and vital signs, *because this procedure may cause hypoxemia, especially if the patient has pulmonary disease.*

● The doctor may use biopsy forceps to remove tissue specimens from the suspect areas, a bronchial brush to obtain cells from the surface of a lesion, or suction apparatus to remove foreign bodies or mucous plugs. After the necessary specimens or brushings are obtained, the doctor removes the bronchoscope.

● Place specimens for microbiology, histology, and cytology in properly labeled containers. Send the specimens to the laboratory immediately *to ensure accurate test results.*

● Return the patient to bed, if necessary. Make sure he's comfortable.

● Clean the bronchoscope and laryngoscope, if used, and send them to the appropriate area for sterilization.

**Special considerations**

If the doctor is using a rigid bronchoscope, place the patient in the supine position, with his neck fully extended over the end of the examination or operating room table. Whether a rigid or flexible bronchoscope is used, if it is passed through the nose tell the patient to breathe through his mouth. If the patient is on mechanical ventilation, reassure him that no matter what type of bronchoscope is used, a special attachment allows for adequate ventilation throughout the procedure.

Adequate anesthesia of the upper airway is essential. For children and for extremely apprehensive adults, general anesthesia administered in the operating room—by inhalation or the balanced technique of I.V. thiopental sodium followed by curare or succinylcholine chloride—provides an alternative to local anesthesia. Spinal anesthesia is not used, *because it depresses accessory muscles and can cause respiratory failure.*

When a biopsy is to be obtained from the periphery of the lung, bronchoscopy may be performed under fluoroscopy *to pinpoint the lesion and prevent pneumothorax.*

Usually the doctor orders that sputum be collected for 24 hours immediately following bronchoscopy so that the secretions mobilized during this procedure can be sent for cytologic studies and culture.

**Complications**

Hypoxemia may result from patient apprehension, preexisting respiratory disease, or airway occlusion by the bronchoscope. Hemorrhage, more likely to occur when a biopsy has been performed, is indicated by an increase in pulse rate, a decrease in blood pressure, hemoptysis, and symptoms of airway obstruction such as dyspnea, tachypnea, wheezing and stridor. Respiratory distress, characterized by wheezing, dyspnea, cyanosis, tachypnea, hypertension, tachycardia, stridor, and arrhythmia, may occur in adults and especially in children from an adverse reaction to the anesthetic agent or a pneumothorax. Central nervous system stimulation—an adverse reaction to the anesthetic agent characterized by increased pulse rate, excitation, headache, palpitations, elevated blood pressure, rapid, deep respirations, and euphoria—may occur, especially when cocaine is used as the anesthetic. Pneumothorax, typified by dyspnea, cyanosis, and diminished breath sounds on the affected side, can result from the trauma of bronchoscopy or biopsy. Infection is another possible complication.

## Documentation

Record the date and time of the procedure; the dosage, route, and time medications are administered; bronchoscope type and size; the length of time for bronchoscopy; the patient's vital signs; personnel involved in the procedure; the doctor's assessment; laboratory findings; any oxygen administration in liters/minute; patient recovery from the anesthesia and the procedure; necessary aftercare; and any complications and the nursing action taken.

KATHLEEN E. VIALL GALLAGHER, RN, MSN

# Vital Capacity
### [*Wright respirometer*]

*Vital capacity is the maximum volume of air exhaled after maximum inspiration. Usually measuring about 70 ml/ kg of body weight, it may decrease in infection, edema, atelectasis, fibrosis, chest wall disease, pneumothorax, pleural effusion, abdominal distention, neuromuscular disease, and incisional pain, especially after abdominal and thoracic surgery. Pulmonary diseases that decrease vital capacity are restrictive rather than obstructive, limiting the lungs' ability to distend.*

*Measurement of vital capacity helps determine a patient's continued need for ventilatory assistance. A simple, commonly used pulmonary function test, it's performed daily during intubation, to gauge the patient's lung function and readiness for traditional weaning, in-termittent mandatory ventilation (IMV) or extubation. Before extubation, the patient must show a vital capacity of at least 10 to 15 ml/kg of body weight. Below this level, the patient may be limited in his ability to cough, breathe deeply, or maintain adequate ventilatory status for an extended time.*

*While various equipment is available for measuring vital capacity, this procedure describes only the use of the Wright respirometer, most commonly and conveniently used at bedside.*

## Equipment

Wright respirometer □ adapter □ mouthpiece, if indicated □ nose clips, if indicated □ vital capacity predicted-values table □ 4″ x 4″ gauze sponges □ alcohol.

The respirometer dial has two scales: a large peripheral scale and a smaller scale inset in its upper part. Each mark on the large dial equals 1 liter, and one complete revolution of the large hand indicates a volume of 100 liters. Each mark on the small scale equals .10 liters; one complete revolution of the small dial hand marks a volume of 1 liter.

The Wright respirometer measures vital capacity, and can be used to calculate tidal volume (the volume of each breath) and minute volume (the volume of air breathed in a minute, or tidal volume multiplied by respiration rate). The respirometer can be connected to an intubated patient's airway to measure vital capacity, or used with a mouthpiece in a nonintubated patient.

## Preparation of equipment

Check the respirometer for accuracy, then attach the connecting adapter. If you're measuring the vital capacity of a nonintubated patient, attach the mouthpiece to the adapter, or attach a face mask. Turn on the control switch, located on the respirometer's exterior. Press the reset button to return the dial's hands to the zero mark.

## Essential steps

*To assess vital capacity using a Wright respirometer:*

## MEASURING PEAK FLOW RATE

Peak flow rate—the highest flow point during maximal expiration—helps determine the extent of obstructive disease or bronchospasm. Measurement of peak flow rate, however, may precipitate or worsen bronchospasm. This measurement can also be made before and after bronchodilator administration or respiratory therapy *to gauge the effectiveness of treatment.* The patient can also be instructed how to perform this procedure at home, to monitor airway obstruction. A fall in the peak flow rate may indicate that the patient's condition is deteriorating.

To measure peak flow rate, first obtain a flowmeter, disposable mouthpiece, and a predicted values table. Then, wash your hands. Next, attach a clean mouthpiece to the flowmeter, and press the release button behind the mouthpiece to set the pointer on the flowmeter at zero.

● Explain the procedure to the patient *to ensure his cooperation, which is essential to the accurate determination of test results.*
● Have the patient sit upright in a bed or chair. Then, ask him to inhale as deeply as possible. Tell him to insert the mouthpiece and to seal his lips tightly around it.
● Instruct him to exhale forcefully in one short, sharp blast. Complete emptying of the lungs isn't necessary, *because peak flow is achieved within the first half second of expiration.*
● Remove the mouthpiece, and tell the patient to relax. Then, note the reading on the dial (each mark equals 5 liters). Record peak flow as the observed number or the percentage of predicted peak flow.
● Repeat the test twice, after resetting the pointer each time.
● Record any adverse effects during the test, such as wheezing or coughing.

---

● Explain the procedure to the patient, provide privacy, and wash your hands.
● Instruct the patient to sit upright in bed or in a chair, if possible, *to facilitate maximum inspiration.*

*To measure the vital capacity of an intubated patient:*
● Attach the respirometer and adapter to the endotracheal or tracheostomy tube. Instruct the patient to inhale deeply.
● Quickly press the respirometer's reset button to return the dial's hands to the zero mark. Then tell the patient to exhale as quickly, forcefully, and completely as possible.
● Before the patient takes his next breath, turn the control switch to the "off" position *to hold the measurement.* Read the respirometer dial *to determine the volume of exhaled air.*

*To measure the vital capacity of the nonintubated patient:*
● Place clips on the patient's nose *since air leaking through the nose may lower the respirometer reading.* Then instruct him to inhale deeply.
● As the patient reaches peak inspiration, have him insert the respirometer's mouthpiece into his mouth and seal his lips tightly around it. Instruct the patient to exhale as quickly, forcefully, and completely as possible.
● Remove the mouthpiece and read the dial *to determine exhalation volume.*

*After measuring vital capacity:*
● Repeat the procedure twice *to help ensure accurate readings.*
● If necessary, return the patient to bed and make sure he's comfortable.
● Clean the respirometer with alcohol and, if necessary, store the device in the patient's room for later use. If the respirometer won't be used again, return it for sterilization; if it has a one-way valve that prevents contamination and eliminates the need for sterilization, store it appropriately.

### Special considerations
Flow rates above 300 liters/minute can damage the respirometer.

### Complications
Forced expiration can precipitate or worsen bronchospasm and can cause lightheadedness and dizziness in the weak patient.

### Documentation
Record the date and time of the pro-

cedure; the highest vital capacity or the average of the three vital capacity measurements; any adverse effects such as wheezing or coughing and the nursing action taken; and the patient's tolerance for the procedure.

If a commercially available predicted-values table is accessible, record both the patient's measured vital capacity and what percentage of his predicted vital capacity this figure represents. First, find the patient's predicted vital capacity on the chart, based on his age, height, and sex. Then, use the following formula to determine the percentage of predicted vital capacity:

$$\frac{\text{observed VC}}{\text{predicted VC}} \times 100 = \% \text{ predicted VC}$$

A normal value equals at least 80% of the predicted value.

JANET S. D'AGOSTINO, RN, MSN

# Negative Inspiratory Force
## [*Maximal inspiratory force*]

*Negative inspiratory force (NIF), also called maximal inspiratory force (MIF), is the greatest force exerted during inspiration against an artificially occluded airway. A respiratory index used to complement or substitute for measurement of vital capacity, it provides an objective measurement of the patient's muscle strength and ability to cough effectively. During weaning from mechanical ventilation, it helps determine a patient's readiness for extubation.*

*This index is conveyed as a negative number because lung pressure during inspiration is negative, falling below the atmospheric pressure level required to draw air inward as the diaphragm contracts and lung volume increases. Normal inspiratory force usually exceeds −80 cm of water pressure (cmH₂O) within 10 seconds of airway occlusion. While*

*the criteria for extubation may vary from hospital to hospital, an inspiratory force of at least −20 to −25 cmH₂O within 20 seconds usually indicates that a patient can maintain adequate ventilation for a prolonged time without further mechanical assistance.*

*Measurement of inspiratory force also serves as a useful monitor of progressive neuromuscular weakness in the nonintubated patient with myasthenia gravis.*

### Equipment
Inspiratory force meter with manifold tube □ watch with second hand.

### Preparation of equipment
Push the needle-return button to make sure both needles register zero. Connect the manifold to the meter, if it's not already connected.

### Essential steps
• Check the doctor's order and assess the patient's condition before beginning the procedure.
• Explain the procedure to the patient, provide privacy, and wash your hands.
• Make sure the patient's airway is free of secretions. If necessary, perform endotracheal suctioning *to ensure a patent airway,* then allow the patient to rest for several minutes.
• If the patient is using a ventilator, disconnect it.
• Attach the inspiratory force meter's manifold tube to the patient's endotracheal or tracheostomy tube. Make sure the tube cuff is inflated *to prevent inaccurate measurements.*
• Instruct the patient to breathe spontaneously for a few breaths. *Brief, uninterrupted inhalation and exhalation through the manifold safety port helps diminish the patient's anxiety at being removed from the ventilator, and also reveals any obstruction that would affect test results.*
• Cover the manifold safety port with your thumb or fingertip *to occlude the airway.* Maintain the occlusion for 10 to 20 seconds, *sufficient time for the patient to attempt inspiration.*

• If the patient is alert, instruct him to try to inhale while you're blocking his airway. Ask him to attempt the deepest breath possible. The unconscious patient will automatically attempt inspiration during this time.

• Hold a watch with a second hand as close as possible to the meter dial *so you can see both dials at once*. Then, as the patient breathes, note the number of seconds until the red needle on the meter dial rises to the highest point. *This number is the patient's maximal inspiratory force. The black "memory" needle captures this reading, rising higher and locking with each greater exertion so the patient's best effort remains visible.*

### Special considerations

Unlike some other pulmonary function tests, the negative inspiratory force test doesn't require an alert and cooperative patient.

If the patient develops an adverse reaction to airway occlusion—such as arrhythmia, respiratory distress, or a change in vital signs—reestablish an open airway by removing your thumb or finger from the manifold safety port.

If the manifold tube doesn't have a one-way valve, send it to the central supply department for sterilization between patients *to prevent cross-contamination*.

### Documentation

Record the date and time of the procedure; the highest observed inspiratory force in centimeters of water pressure ($cmH_2O$); the time needed to achieve the maximum reading; any adverse reactions and the nursing action taken; the patient's level of consciousness; and tolerance of the procedure.

JANET S. D'AGOSTINO, RN, MSN

# Bedside Spirometry

*Bedside spirometry measures forced vital capacity and forced expiratory vol-*

## INSPIRATORY FORCE METER

The inspiratory force meter performs two functions: its red pointer measures the patient's inspiratory force, and its black memory pointer records the highest inspiratory pressure.

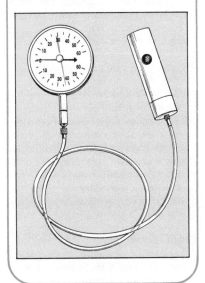

*ume, allowing calculation of other pulmonary function indices, such as timed forced expiratory flow rate. Depending on the type of spirometer, it can also allow direct measurement of vital capacity and tidal volume.*

*Bedside spirometry aids the diagnosis of pulmonary dysfunction before it can be discovered by X-ray or physical examination, evaluation of its severity, and determination of the patient's response to therapy. By assessing the relationship of flow rate to vital capacity, it distinguishes between obstructive and restrictive pulmonary disease. It's also useful for evaluating preoperative anesthesia risk. Because the required breath-*

*ing patterns can aggravate conditions such as bronchospasm, the use of the bedside spirometer requires a review of the patient's history and close observation during testing.*

## Equipment

Spirometer □ disposable mouthpiece □ breathing tube, if required □ spirographic chart, if required □ chart pen, if required □ noseclips □ vital capacity predicted-values table (optional).

Various models of bedside spirometers are commercially available. The results may be recorded on a digital readout, or on a spirogram on an individual chart record, or on a roll of chart paper.

## Preparation of equipment

Review the manufacturer's instructions for assembly and use of the spirometer. If necessary, firmly insert the breathing tube *to ensure a tight connection.* However, if the tube comes preconnected, check the seals for tightness and the tubing for leaks. Check the operation of the recording mechanism, and insert a chart and/or pen, if necessary.

Insert the disposable mouthpiece and make sure it's tightly sealed.

## Essential steps

● Explain the procedure to the patient. Emphasize that his cooperation is essential to ensure accurate results.

● Instruct the patient to remove or loosen any constricting clothing, such as a brassiere, *to prevent alteration of test results from restricted thoracic expansion and abdominal mobility.* Instruct the patient to void *to prevent abdominal discomfort.* Don't perform pulmonary function tests immediately after a large meal, *because the patient will experience abdominal discomfort.*

● If the patient wears dentures that fit poorly, remove them *to prevent incomplete closure of the patient's mouth, causing air leakage around the mouthpiece.* If his dentures fit well, leave them in place *to promote a tight seal.*

● Plug in the machine and set the baseline time, if necessary.

● If desired, allow the patient to practice the required breathing with the breathing tube unhooked. After practice, replace the tube and check the seal.

● Place noseclips on the patient, and have him verify that he can't pass air through his nose.

● *To measure vital capacity,* instruct the patient to inhale as deeply as possible, and then insert the mouthpiece so that his lips are sealed tightly around it *to prevent air leakage and ensure an accurate digital readout or spirogram recording.*

● Instruct the patient to exhale completely. Then quickly remove the mouthpiece *to prevent recording his next inspiration.*

● Allow the patient to rest, and repeat the procedure twice.

● *To measure forced expiratory volume and forced vital capacity,* repeat this procedure with the chart or timer on, but instruct the patient to exhale as quickly and completely as possible. Tell him when to start, and turn on the recorder or timer at the same time.

● Allow the patient to rest, and repeat the procedure twice.

● After completing the procedure, discard the mouthpiece, remove the spirographic chart, and follow the manufacturer's instructions for cleaning and sterilizing the equipment.

## Special considerations

Encourage the patient during the test— this may help him to exhale more forcefully, which can be significant. If the patient coughs during expiration, wait until coughing subsides before repeating the measurement.

Read the vital capacity directly from the readout or spirogram chart. The forced vital capacity is the highest volume recorded on the curve. Accept the highest of the three recorded exhalations as the vital capacity result.

To determine the percentage of predicted vital capacity, first determine the patient's predicted value from the chart. Then, calculate the percentage by using the formula:

$$\frac{\text{observed vital capacity}}{\text{predicted vital capacity}} \times 100$$

To determine the forced expiratory volume for a specified time, mark the point on the spirogram where it crosses the desired time, and draw a straight line from this point to the side of the chart, which indicates volume in liters. This measurement is usually calculated for 1, 2, and 3 seconds and reported as a percentage of vital capacity; a healthy patient will have exhaled 75%, 85%, and 95%, respectively, of his forced vital capacity. Calculate this percentage by using the formula:

$$\frac{\text{observed force}}{\text{observed vital capacity}} \times 100$$

### Complications
Forced exhalation can cause dizziness or lightheadedness, precipitate or worsen bronchospasm, rapidly increase exhaustion possibly to the point of requiring mechanical support, and increase air trapping in the emphysemic patient.

### Documentation
Record the date and time of the procedure; observed and calculated values, including forced expiratory volume at 1, 2, and 3 seconds; any complications and the nursing action taken; and the patient's tolerance for the procedure.

JANET S. D'AGOSTINO, RN, MSN

# Methylene Blue Test

*The methylene blue test detects the aspiration of esophageal contents into the lungs resulting from an absent or impaired swallowing reflex, or a tracheoesophageal fistula that allows communication between the esophagus and the tracheobronchial tree. Such a fistula may be congenital or may be acquired as a result of neoplasm, infection, or* trauma *from such sources as prolonged endotracheal intubation or ingestion of a caustic substance.*

*In this test, which is usually performed by a doctor, a respiratory therapist, or a specially trained nurse, the patient ingests food and/or water colored with methylene blue dye. If aspiration occurs, the suctioned tracheal contents appear blue.*

*The methylene blue test should precede the start of oral feedings in any patient with a tracheostomy tube, to prevent aspiration. In the patient with suspected tracheoesophageal fistula, the test may be performed in the operating room in conjunction with bronchoscopy.*

### Equipment
Suction machine or wall unit with connecting tubing □ sterile suction catheter □ water □ gelatin □ spoon □ methylene blue in ampul or bottled form □ two 10-ml syringes □ syringe needle □ two medication cups □ sterile gloves □ manual resuscitation bag (such as an Ambu bag), or oxygen and nasal cannula □ mouth-care supplies.

Prepackaged tracheal-suction kits are commercially available.

### Preparation of equipment
Assemble all supplies at the patient's bedside and check the expiration date on each sterile package.

Prepare the methylene blue solution and soft, solid dye mixture. If you're using an ampul, open it and draw up 0.5 ml of the dye with a syringe and needle. If you're using bottled dye, use the dropper provided for measuring, or use a syringe and needle. Pour 60 ml of water into a medication cup and add 0.25 ml of the dye to make up the dye solution. To make up the soft, solid dye mixture, place one serving (or an amount equaling at least 2 teaspoons) of gelatin in a medication cup, and add 0.25 ml of dye and enough water to make a soft, solid consistency. Handle the dye carefully *to prevent spills and staining.* Set up and turn on the suction equipment *so it's ready to use during the test.* Using sterile water, test for patency and lubricate the suction tube.

### Essential steps

• Check the doctor's order and assess the patient's condition. Explain the test to the patient, provide privacy, and wash your hands.

• Place the patient so that he's erect in the bed or chair. Avoid performing the test with the patient reclining or with his neck hyperextended *because both positions encourage aspiration.*

• Administer oxygen to the patient *to increase his oxygen reserve.* If he has a tracheostomy tube in place, attach a manual resuscitator to the adapter and administer about four breaths. If the patient doesn't have a tube, instruct him to breathe deeply several times through an oxygen cannula.

• Put on sterile gloves and suction the patient *to eliminate any secretions that might compromise the test.* For the intubated patient with a cuffed tracheostomy tube, suction the trachea through the tracheostomy tube. Then, suction the upper airway through the patient's mouth *to prevent secretions from entering the lower airway after deflation of the tracheostomy tube cuff. To avoid contaminating the trachea with mouth and upper airway bacteria,* do not reverse the order of suctioning.

• Deflate the cuff, if indicated, by withdrawing air with a 10-ml syringe.

• Spoon the tinted gelatin into the patient's mouth; tell him to swallow it.

• Assess the patient's ability to swallow. Watch for coughing, gagging, increased respiratory rate, noisy breathing, or other respiratory changes.

• If the patient can't swallow, or if he chokes, appears cyanotic, or suffers respiratory distress, stop the test immediately and encourage him to cough, if possible. Quickly suction the trachea, using a new, sterile suction catheter, and give oxygen *to relieve dyspnea and hypoxemia.* Observe the suctioned matter *to detect aspiration of the dye-tinted gelatin.*

• If the patient can swallow the gela-

tin, suction the trachea and observe the return *for the presence of dye.* Then administer oxygen to the patient *to restore his oxygen reserve.*

• If the patient has no trouble swallowing the gelatin, repeat the test using the dye-tinted water, *since the patient may be able to tolerate soft solids but be unable to swallow liquids without aspiration.* Observe his ability to swallow water, and immediately stop the test if he experiences difficulty.

• If the patient can swallow approximately 30 ml of the water, suction the trachea and observe the return *for the presence of dye.* Then administer oxygen *to restore oxygen reserve.*

• Reinflate the cuff on the tracheostomy tube, if indicated.

• Give mouth care *to minimize the effect of the dye on oral tissues.* Tell the patient to expect green urine for a few days *as his kidneys eliminate the dye.*

• Dispose of tracheal return and soiled equipment according to institution policy.

• Make sure the patient is comfortable and showing no signs or symptoms of respiratory distress.

• Inform the doctor of test results; he may want to issue new dietary orders for the patient. The test is negative if the patient has no problem swallowing gelatin or water, experiences no respiratory changes, and if no methylene blue is suctioned from the trachea. The test is positive if the patient can't swallow either gelatin or water, shows respiratory changes, or if methylene blue appears in suctioned secretions.

### Special considerations

Perform the methylene blue test with the tracheostomy tube cuff inflated, if desired, *to check for aspiration around the cuff.* If the test is positive when the cuff is deflated, avoid oral feedings. However, if no aspiration occurs when the cuff is inflated, oral feedings can then be given *because the cuff itself prevents aspiration.*

This procedure can give a false positive result for a tracheoesophageal fistula when performed with the cuff inflated. The material suctioned could result from aspiration, not from tracheoesophageal fistula.

## Documentation
Record the date and time of the procedure; the use of water or gelatin or both; cuff inflation or deflation; test results; any complications and the nursing action taken; any change in dietary orders; and the patient's tolerance for the procedure.

JANET S. D'AGOSTINO, RN, MSN

---

# Obstructed Airway Management

Sudden airway obstruction usually results from the presence of a foreign body in the throat or bronchus, but it can also result from laryngeal or vocal cord edema; aspiration of blood, mucus, or vomitus; blockage of the pharynx by the tongue; traumatic injury; bronchoconstriction; and bronchospasm. This emergency procedure deals only with the removal of a foreign body from the upper airway to prevent anoxia, which can lead to brain damage and death within 4 to 6 minutes unless breathing is restored.

An obstruction can be removed by sequentially performing one or more of these maneuvers: the back blow, the Heimlich maneuver, the chest thrust, and the finger sweep. Each maneuver attempts to reestablish airway patency and independent ventilation while preventing or reversing loss of consciousness and anoxia.

The back blow uses direct force to dislodge the foreign body from the patient's airway. The Heimlich maneuver uses an upper abdominal thrust to create sufficient diaphragmatic pressure in the static lung air below the foreign body to expel the obstruction. The chest thrust forces air out of the lungs, creating an artificial cough which expels the obstruction. The finger sweep manually removes the foreign body from the mouth.

These maneuvers are contraindicated in a patient with incomplete or partial airway obstruction, when the patient can maintain adequate ventilation to dislodge the foreign body by effective coughing. However, once the patient is unable to speak, cough, or breathe, immediate action to dislodge the obstruction is necessary. The abdominal thrust is contraindicated for the pregnant woman, the markedly obese patient, and for the patient with recent abdominal surgery. For such patients, the chest thrust, which works on the same principle as the abdominal thrust, is the preferred method.

## Equipment
None.

## Essential steps
• As you perform the following steps, tell the patient you are going to help him. Since this is a very frightening situation for the patient, speak in a controlled and confident manner to help allay his fears.

To perform back blows:
• If the patient is conscious and sitting or standing, stand to his side, slightly behind him. To support the patient's weight, place your weaker hand on his sternum. Then, if possible, lower the patient's head to chest level so that the effects of gravity help to expel the foreign body. With the heel of your hand, deliver four sharp blows to the patient's spine between the scapulae.
• If the patient is lying unconscious, kneel beside him and roll him onto his side so he's facing you with his chest resting against your thighs. With the heel of your stronger hand, deliver four sharp blows to the spine between the scapulae.

To perform the Heimlich maneuver:

## POSITIONS FOR HEIMLICH MANEUVER
### (Abdominal Thrust)

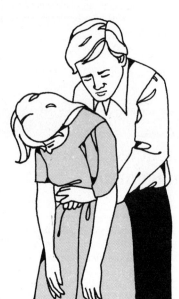

**Standing or sitting positions**
Position your arms around the patient's waist. Then, place your fist against the abdomen, above the navel and below the xiphoid process, as shown. If possible, have the patient bend forward to allow gravity to assist your efforts. Press upward and inward with four quick thrusts.

**Recumbent position (unconscious patient)**
Face the patient and straddle his hips, making sure your shoulders are directly over the abdomen. Place the heel of one hand on top of the other and place both hands on the patient's abdomen, above the navel and below the xiphoid process. Press upward and inward with four quick thrusts.

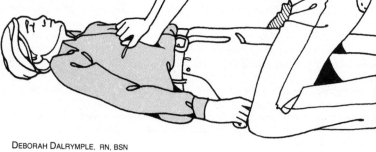

DEBORAH DALRYMPLE, RN, BSN

• *If the patient is sitting or standing,* stand behind him and wrap your arms around his waist. Make a fist, grab it with your other hand, and place the thumb side of your fist against the patient's abdomen above the navel and below the xiphoid process. Press upward and inward with four quick thrusts.

 *Don't place your hands on the xiphoid process or on the lower margins of the rib cage, because the force of your thrusts can cause fractures, or rupture or laceration of the abdominal or thoracic viscera.*

• *If the patient is lying unconscious,* roll him onto his back, then kneel and straddle his hips. This allows proper hand placement to prevent liver or spleen damage from misdirected thrusts. As an alternative you can kneel alongside the patient. *This gives you the freedom to move up close to the head of the patient to recheck airway patency, and remove such obstructors as vomitus, if present.*

• Place the heel of one hand on top of the other. Then, place both hands on the patient's abdomen above the navel and below the xiphoid process. To thrust effectively, make sure your shoulders are directly over the patient's abdomen. Press upward and inward with four quick thrusts.

*To perform the AMA chest thrust:*

• *If the patient is standing or sitting,* stand behind him and wrap your arms around his chest, directly under his armpits. Make a fist, grab it with your opposite hand, and place the thumb side of your fist against the patient's sternum. If possible, lean the patient forward to make use of the effect of gravity. Press backward forcefully into the patient's chest with four quick thrusts.

• *If the patient is lying unconscious,* roll him onto his back, then kneel beside him or straddle his hips. Place the heel of one hand on top of the other. Then, place both hands on the lower half of the patient's sternum, avoiding the xiphoid process. Press downward with four quick thrusts.

*To perform the finger sweep on an* unconscious patient:

• Turn the patient so his head faces upward. Open his mouth with the cross-finger technique by placing your thumb on his upper teeth or gum and your index finger on his lower teeth in the corner of his mouth. Press downward with your thumb and upward with your finger. If necessary, remove loose dentures *to avoid further airway obstruction.*

• Insert the index finger of your opposite hand into the side of the patient's mouth toward the pharynx. If the foreign body is within reach, use a hooking motion from side to side to sweep it forward and out of the mouth. Be careful not to push the object farther into the patient's airway.

• After removing the foreign body, make sure adequate ventilation is restored. Once the patient is alert, instruct him to see a doctor. If you performed this procedure in a hospital, notify the doctor and file an incident report.

## Special considerations

When delivering back blows to an infant or small child, sit with him facedown on your lap or kneel beside him. Use your forearm *to support his ventral body,* and let his arms and head hang forward face down, *to take advantage of gravity in expelling the obstruction.* With the heel or side of your stronger hand, deliver four sharp blows between the scapulae.

The Heimlich Maneuver should not be used on infants and children because of the risk of injuring abdominal organs, especially the liver.

If a patient vomits during the Heimlich maneuver, quickly wipe out his mouth with your fingers and, if he still fails to breathe, resume the maneuver.

*Since skeletal and smooth muscles relax as oxygen deprivation increases,* recognize that previously ineffective maneuvers may now clear an obstructed airway. Use back blows and the Heimlich maneuver in combination *to increase the effectiveness of your efforts.* If all other methods fail, an experienced professional may use forceps to remove the foreign body. Forceps are indicated,

## ASSISTING WITH EMERGENCY CRICOTHYROIDOTOMY

Cricothyroidotomy is the opening or puncture of the trachea through the cricothyroid membrane. It is the procedure of choice when endotracheal intubation or conventional tracheotomy cannot quickly provide an airway, such as in a clinic or a doctor's office. The cricothyroid membrane may be opened with a scalpel or may be punctured with an 11G needle or a special emergency tracheotomy needle. Ideally, this is a sterile procedure. In an emergency situation outside the hospital, maintaining sterile technique may be impossible.

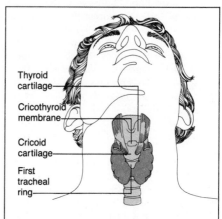

Thyroid cartilage

Cricothyroid membrane

Cricoid cartilage

First tracheal ring

To assist the doctor with this procedure:

• Obtain an emergency tray containing povidone-iodine solution, sterile 4″ x 4″ gauze sponges, a scalpel, and a Delaborde dilator, *or* an 11G needle, *or* a tracheotomy needle, plus a stethoscope.

• Extend the patient's head and neck *to expose the incision site and provide proper tracheal position.*

• Prepare the neck with povidone-iodine solution. The doctor then locates the proper site (see illustration), makes the incision, and inserts a Delaborde dilator *to prevent tissues from closing around the incision.* Or, he may insert an 11G needle into the cricothyroid membrane and direct the needle downward and posteriorly *to avoid damaging the vocal cords.* He then tapes the dilator or needle in place.

• Auscultate bilaterally for breath sounds and take vital signs.

• Once ventilation is achieved, and the patient is in the hospital, blood is drawn for arterial blood gas analysis *to assess the adequacy of ventilation.*

• Immediately following cricothyroidotomy, watch for excessive bleeding at the insertion site, subcutaneous emphysema or inadequate ventilation from incorrect equipment placement, and tracheal or vocal cord damage. Infection may occur several days after this procedure, especially if sterile technique was compromised.

• Document the incident, including date and time, events necessitating the procedure, and the patient's vital signs. If the patient is to be transferred to an ambulance, give the attendant a verbal report.

PATRICIA L. FUCHS, CRTT, RRT

---

however, only when direct visualization of the foreign body is possible. This technique isn't routinely used, *because improper forceps technique can itself be life-threatening, and the availability of the proper forceps in emergency situations is unlikely.* Only a person whose proficiency has been certified by an experienced professional may use forceps to remove a foreign object.

## Complications

Nausea and achiness may develop after the patient regains consciousness and independent ventilation. Serious internal injury may result, signaled by development of ecchymoses over areas exposed to physical trauma from these maneuvers. Such injury includes rupture or laceration of abdominal or thoracic viscera secondary to fractured ribs or sternum, which can result from incorrect placement of the rescuer's hands or in patients with osteoporosis or metastatic lesions.

## Documentation

If this emergency occurs in the hospital setting, record the date and time of the procedure; the patient's activity before the onset of the obstruction; the approximate length of time required to clear the airway; the type and size of the foreign body removed and the patient's vital signs afterward; any complications and the nursing action taken; and the patient's tolerance for the procedure.

Outside the hospital, give a verbal report of the event and your emergency actions to the rescue squad when they arrive.

HELEN HAHLER D'ANGELO, RN, MSN

# Oropharyngeal Airway

*An oropharyngeal airway, a curved rubber or plastic device, is inserted into the mouth to the posterior pharynx to establish or maintain a patent airway. Because the tongue usually obstructs the posterior pharynx of an unconscious patient, insertion of this airway, which conforms to the curvature of the palate, corrects this obstruction and allows air to pass around and through the tube. Use of this airway also facilitates oropharyngeal suctioning. Intended for short-term use only, such as in the immediate postanesthesia stage, the airway is usually replaced by an endotracheal tube if the patient needs further respiratory assistance.*

*The oropharyngeal airway is not the airway of choice for the patient with loose or avulsed teeth or recent oral surgery.*

### Equipment
*For insertion:* oral airway of appropriate size □ adhesive tape or hypoallergenic tape □ tongue blade □ padded tongue blade □ suction equipment (optional).

*For cleansing:* hydrogen peroxide □ water □ basin □ pipe cleaner (optional).

### Preparation of equipment
Select the appropriate-sized airway for your patient, *since an oversized airway*

*can obstruct breathing by depressing the epiglottis into the laryngeal opening.* Usually, select a small size for an infant or child, a medium size for the average adult, and a large size for the large or obese adult. Confirm the correct size by placing the airway flange beside the patient's cheek, parallel to his front teeth. If it's the right size, the airway curve should reach to the angle of the jaw.

### Essential steps
● Explain the procedure to the patient even though he may not appear to be alert. Provide privacy, and wash your hands thoroughly. If the patient is wearing dentures, remove them *so they don't cause further airway obstruction.*
● If necessary, suction the patient.
● Place the patient in the supine position with his neck hyperextended, if this is not contraindicated.
● To insert the airway, use the cross-finger or the tongue blade technique. *For the cross-finger method,* place your thumb

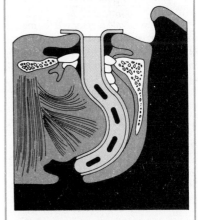

### CORRECT OROPHARYNGEAL AIRWAY PLACEMENT

The flange of the oral airway should extend outside the patient's teeth, and the curved tip should be in the posterior pharynx, as shown.

on the patient's upper teeth and your index finger on his lower teeth. Gently open his mouth by pushing his teeth apart. Next, insert the airway by sliding the tip back over the tongue's surface or by pointing the tip toward the cheek, gently advancing it, and then rotating it so it's pointing downward.

For the tongue blade technique, open the patient's mouth and depress his tongue with the blade. Guide the artificial airway over the back of the tongue as you did for the cross-finger technique, until it's in place.

For either technique, if the patient gags during insertion, hold the airway in place for a few seconds until gagging subsides.

• Use adhesive or hypoallergenic tape to secure the artificial airway to the patient's cheeks and prevent airway dislodgment.

• Position the patient on his side to decrease the risk of aspiration of vomitus.

• Perform mouth care every 2 to 4 hours, as needed. Begin by holding the patient's jaws open with a padded tongue blade and gently removing the airway. Place the airway in a basin and rinse it with hydrogen peroxide followed by water. If secretions remain, use a pipe cleaner to remove them. Complete standard mouth care, reinsert the airway, and secure it with tape.

While the airway is removed for mouth care, observe the mouth's mucous membranes to detect ulceration, because tissue damage can result from prolonged airway use.

• Frequently check the position of the airway for removal or dislodgment.

• When the patient regains consciousness and is able to swallow, remove the airway by pulling it outward and downward, following the mouth's natural curvature. Once the airway is removed, test the patient's cough and gag reflexes to ensure that removal wasn't premature.

### Special considerations

When taping the airway in place, always leave enough room to insert a suction catheter to allow for removal of oral secretions that may obstruct the airway.

Evaluate the patient's behavior to provide the cue for airway removal. The patient is apt to gag or cough as he becomes more alert, indicating that he no longer needs the airway.

### Complications

Tooth damage or loss, tissue damage, and bleeding may result from insertion.

### Documentation

Record the date and time of insertion; size of the airway inserted; removal and cleansing of the airway; condition of mucous membranes; any suctioning; any adverse reactions and the nursing action taken; and the patient's tolerance for the procedure.

HELEN HAHLER D'ANGELO, RN, MSN

# Nasopharyngeal Airway

Insertion of a nasopharyngeal airway, a soft rubber or latex catheter, establishes or maintains a patent airway. It's the airway of choice after recent oral surgery or facial trauma and for the patient with loose, cracked, or avulsed teeth. It's also used to protect the nasal mucosa from injury when frequent nasotracheal suctioning is necessary. The airway follows the curvature of the nasopharynx, passing through the nose and extending from the nostril to the posterior pharynx. The bevel-shaped pharyngeal end of the airway facilitates insertion, and its funnel-shaped nasal end helps prevent slippage.

Insertion of a nasopharyngeal airway is preferred when an oropharyngeal airway is contraindicated or fails to maintain a patent airway. A nasopharyngeal airway is contraindicated in the patient who is receiving anticoagulant therapy, and in the patient with hemorrhagic disorders, sepsis, or pathologic nasopharyngeal deformities.

## Equipment

*For insertion:* nasopharyngeal airway of appropriate size □ tongue blade □ adhesive or hypoallergenic tape □ water-soluble lubricant □ suction equipment (optional).

*For cleansing:* hydrogen peroxide □ water □ basin □ pipe cleaner (optional).

## Preparation of equipment

Measure the diameter of the patient's nostril and the distance from the tip of his nose to his earlobe. Select an airway of slightly smaller diameter than the nostril and of slightly longer length (about 1″, or 2.5 cm, longer) than measured. Lubricate the distal half of the airway's exterior with a water-soluble lubricant *to prevent trauma during insertion.*

## Essential steps

* Wash your hands thoroughly.
* In nonemergency situations, explain the procedure to the patient.
* To insert the airway, hyperextend the patient's neck, if not contraindicated. Then, push up the tip of his nose and pass the airway into his nostril. Avoid pushing against any resistance *to prevent tissue trauma and airway kinking.*
* *To check for correct airway placement,* first close the patient's mouth. Then, place your finger over the tube's opening *to detect air exchange.* Also, depress the patient's tongue with a tongue blade and *look for the airway tip behind the uvula.*
* Apply adhesive or hypoallergenic tape to each side of the airway opening, then secure the tape to the patient's cheeks *to maintain correct airway placement.*
* To prevent mucus from creating obstruction, humidify administered oxygen and instill small amounts of sterile saline into the airway when aspirating secretions.
* Check the airway regularly *to detect dislodgment or obstruction.*
* When the patient's natural airway is patent, remove the airway in one smooth motion. If the airway sticks, apply lubricant around the nasal end of the tube and around the nostril; then gently rotate the airway until it's free.

## Special considerations

If the patient coughs or gags, it may indicate that the tube is too long. If so, remove the airway and insert a shorter one. Once every 8 hours, remove the airway *to check nasal mucous membranes for irritation or ulceration.* Clean the airway by placing it in a basin and rinsing it with hydrogen peroxide and then with water. If secretions remain, use a pipe cleaner to remove them. Reinsert the clean airway into the other nostril, if it's patent, *to avoid skin breakdown.*

*To increase oxygen availability during respiration,* insert a nasal catheter through the airway or place a nasal cannula just under the nose.

## Complications

Sinus infection may result from obstruction of sinus drainage.

## Documentation

Record the date and time of insertion; size of the airway inserted; removal and cleansing of the airway; shifts from one nostril to the other; condition of the mucous membranes; suctioning; complications and nursing action taken; and the patient's reaction to procedure.

HELEN HAHLER D'ANGELO, RN, MSN

# Esophageal Airways

[*Esophageal gastric tube airway and esophageal obturator airway*]

*The esophageal gastric tube airway (EGTA) and the esophageal obturator airway (EOA) are temporary (2-hour maximum) emergency measures used to maintain ventilation in the comatose patient during cardiac or respiratory arrest. These devices prevent tongue obstruction, prevent air from entering the stomach, and keep stomach contents from entering the trachea. They can be inserted only after successful mouth-to-*

*mouth resuscitation has established that the patient's airway is patent.*

*The EGTA and EOA offer an advantage over endotracheal intubation, because personnel with even minimal training can insert them quickly. And, since these devices don't require visualization of the trachea or hyperextension of the neck, they're useful for the patient with suspected spinal injuries. However, neither airway should be used unless the patient is unconscious, since conscious or semiconscious patients will reject them. Both are contraindicated in patients under age 16 (pediatric sizes are not currently available) and in patients who have experienced facial trauma that prevents a snug mask fit. The absence of a strong gag reflex, recent ingestion of toxic chemicals, esophageal disease, or a suspected narcotic overdose that can be reversed by naloxone also contraindicate the use of either airway device.*

## Equipment

Esophageal tube □ face mask □ #16 or #18 French nasogastric tube (for EGTA) □ 35-ml syringe □ stethoscope □ intermittent gastric suction equipment □ oral suction equipment □ optional: manual resuscitation bag such as an Ambu bag, water-soluble lubricant.

The EOA is a single-port esophageal tube with a blind end and a 35-cc inflatable cuff on the exterior portion of the tube just proximal to the blind end. Air exchange occurs in the pharynx through perforations in the tube. The EGTA has twin ports on the face mask—one is for ventilation, the other is an esophageal tube with a one-way valve that blocks the esophagus and prevents air from entering the stomach. An inflatable 35-cc cuff on the exterior portion of the tube is situated at a point in the esophagus just below the tracheal bifurcation. A nasogastric tube can be inserted into the esophageal tube. It passes through the valve at the proximal end, through a small hole at the distal end, and into the stomach, allowing stomach decompression and reducing the risk of aspiration during extubation. Both the EOA and the

EGTA have an inflatable face mask that forms an airtight seal on the face.

## Preparation of equipment

Quickly gather the equipment. Fill the mask with air and check for leaks. Inflate the esophageal tube's cuff with 35 cc of air and check for leaks; then, deflate the cuff. Connect the esophageal tube to the face mask (the lower opening on an EGTA) and listen for the tube to click, indicating proper placement. Lubricate the first inch (2.5 cm) of the tube's distal tip with a water-soluble lubricant, I.V. fluid, the patient's saliva, or tap water. With an EGTA, also lubricate the first inch of the nasogastric tube's distal tip.

## Essential steps

*To insert an esophageal airway:*

● Assess the patient's condition to determine if he's a safe candidate for an esophageal airway.

● If the patient's condition permits, place him supinely with his neck in a neutral or semiflexed position. *Hyperextension of the neck may cause the tube to enter the trachea instead of the esophagus.* Remove dentures, if applicable.

● Insert your thumb deeply into the patient's mouth behind the base of his tongue. Place your index and middle fingers of the same hand under the patient's chin and lift his jaw straight up.

● With your other hand, grasp the esophageal tube just below the mask the same way you'd grasp a pencil. *This promotes gentle maneuvering of the tube and reduces the risk of pharyngeal trauma.*

● Still elevating the patient's jaw with one hand, insert the tip of the esophageal tube into the patient's mouth. Gently guide the airway over the tongue into the pharynx and then into the esophagus, following the natural pharyngeal curve. No force is required for proper insertion; the tube should easily seat itself within 10 seconds. If you encounter resistance, withdraw the tube slightly and readvance it. When the tube is fully advanced, the mask should fit snugly over mouth and nose. If it isn't snug, the mask may need to be inflated more.

• Holding the mask firmly in place, immediately blow into the ventilatory port of the face mask (the upper opening on an EGTA). Watch for chest movement, or auscultate both lungs with a stethoscope.
• If chest movement or breath sounds are

## ESOPHAGEAL AIRWAYS

The **esophageal gastric tube airway** consists of an inflatable face mask and an esophageal tube. The transparent face mask has two ports: a lower port for insertion of an esophageal tube and an upper port for ventilation. The inside of the mask is soft and pliable; it molds to the patient's face and makes a tight seal, preventing air loss.

The proximal end of the esophageal tube has a one-way, nonrefluxing valve that blocks the esophagus. This valve prevents air from entering the stomach, thus reducing the risk of abdominal distention and aspiration. The distal end of the tube has an inflatable cuff that rests in the esophagus just below the tracheal bifurcation, preventing pressure on the noncartilaginous back of the tracheal wall.

During ventilation, air is blown into the upper port in the mask and, with the esophagus blocked, enters the trachea and lungs. (See top illustration.)

A gastric (Levin) tube can be used to suction stomach contents before extubation. It's inserted through the mask's lower port into the esophageal tube, then through a small hole in the end of the tube.

The **esophageal obturator airway** consists of an adjustable, inflatable, transparent face mask with a single port, attached by a snap lock to a blind esophageal tube.

When properly inflated, the transparent mask prevents air from escaping through the nose and mouth. (See bottom illustration.)

The esophageal tube has 16 holes at its proximal end through which air or oxygen, blown into the port of the mask, is transferred to the trachea. The tube's distal end is closed and circled by an inflatable cuff. When the cuff is inflated, it occludes the esophagus, preventing air from entering the stomach and acting as a barrier against vomitus and involuntary aspiration.

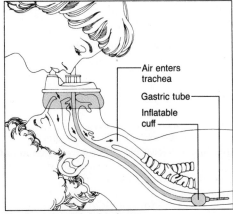

Air enters trachea
Gastric tube
Inflatable cuff

**Esophageal gastric tube airway**

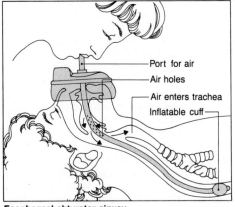

Port for air
Air holes
Air enters trachea
Inflatable cuff

**Esophageal obturator airway**

absent, immediately remove the tube, *because it may be lodged in the trachea.* Reestablish mouth-to-mouth resuscitation for 1 minute, then reinsert the esophageal tube.

• Once the tube is properly in place in the esophagus, draw 35 cc of air into the syringe, connect the syringe to the tube's cuff-inflation valve, and inflate the cuff. Avoid overinflation, *as this can cause esophageal trauma.*

• If you've inserted an EGTA, insert the nasogastric tube through the lower port on the face mask and into the esophageal tube, and advance it to the second marking so it reaches 6″ (15 cm) beyond the distal end of the tube. Suction stomach contents using intermittent gastric suction to decompress the stomach *(particularly necessary after mouth-to-mouth resuscitation, which introduces air to the stomach).* Leave the tube in place during resuscitation.

• For both airways, perform mouth-to-tube ventilation through the face mask port (the upper port on the EGTA), or connect the mask to a manual resuscitation bag or to a mechanical ventilator delivering $FIO_2$ of up to 100%.

• Monitor the patient *to ensure adequate ventilation.* Watch for chest movement, and suction the patient if mucus blocks the EOA tube perforations or in any way interrupts respiration.

*To remove an esophageal airway:*

• Assess the patient's condition *to determine if it's appropriate to remove the airway.* The airway may be removed if respirations are spontaneous and the respiratory rate is 16 to 20 respirations/minute. If 2 hours have elapsed since airway insertion and respirations are not spontaneous and at the normal rate per minute, the patient must be switched to an artificial airway that can be used for long-term ventilation, such as an endotracheal tube.

• Detach the mask from the esophageal tube.

• If the patient is conscious, place him on his left side, if possible, *to avoid aspiration during removal of the esophageal tube.* If he's unconscious and requires an endotracheal tube, insert it and inflate the cuff of the endotracheal tube before removing the esophageal tube. *With the esophageal tube remaining in place, the endotracheal tube is easily placed in the trachea, and stomach contents are less likely to be aspirated when the tube is removed.*

• Deflate the cuff on the esophageal tube by removing the tip of the cuff inflation valve. Don't try to remove the tube with the cuff inflated *because this may cause esophageal perforation.*

• Turn the patient's head to the side, if possible, *to avoid aspiration.*

• If you're using an EOA, insert a nasogastric tube into the esophagus alongside this, if necessary, and decompress the stomach by gravity flow, or connect the nasogastric tube to intermittent gastric suction and suction stomach contents *to prevent aspiration during extubation.*

• Remove the EGTA or EOA in one swift, smooth motion following the natural pharyngeal curve *to avoid esophageal trauma.*

• Perform oropharyngeal suctioning *to remove any residual secretions.*

• Assist the doctor as required in monitoring and maintaining adequate ventilation of the patient.

### Special considerations

Keep EGTAs and EOAs stored in the manufacturer's package until use *to preserve their natural curve.*

For easy insertion, you may prefer to direct the airway along the right side of the patient's mouth *because the esophagus is located to the right of and behind the trachea.* Or, you may advance the tube tip upward toward the hard palate, then invert the tip and glide it along the tongue surface and into the pharynx. *This keeps the tube centered, avoids snagging it on the sides of the throat, and eases insertion in the patient with clenched jaws.*

Watch the unconscious patient as he regains consciousness. Restrain his hands *if he tries to remove the airway.* Explain the procedure to him, if possible, *to reduce his apprehension.* Observe also for retching and, if it occurs, immediately remove the airway, *since the accumulation of vomitus blocked by the airway cuff may cause esophageal perforation.*

Using an EOA or EGTA with a mechanical ventilator isn't as exact in maintaining tidal volume as delivering mechanical ventilation with an endotracheal or tracheostomy tube.

The airway mask and nasogastric tube can be reused often after sterilization; the esophageal tube shouldn't be used more than five times.

## Complications

Insertion of esophageal airways can result in airway obstruction if the tube enters the trachea; pharyngeal trauma; and esophageal perforation, which can lead to abscess formation, mediastinal and subcutaneous emphysema, mediastinitis, hemorrhage, fistula formation, pneumonia, and death.

## Documentation

Record the date and time of the procedure; type of airway inserted; patient's vital signs and level of consciousness; any alternative airway inserted after extubation; any complications and the nursing action taken.

DEBORAH DALRYMPLE, RN, BSN

# Oronasopharyngeal Suction

*Oronasopharyngeal suction removes secretions from the pharynx by means of a suction catheter inserted through the mouth or nostril. Used to maintain a patent airway, this procedure is indicated for the patient who's unable to clear his airway effectively with coughing and expectoration, for example, the unconscious or severely debilitated patient. In such a patient, this procedure promotes pulmonary gas exchange and prevents pneumonia caused by accumulated se-*cretions. *Depending on the patient's condition, suctioning may be required as seldom as once every 8 hours or as often as every 15 minutes.*

*Oronasopharyngeal suction is normally a clean procedure, because the catheter does not progress past the pharynx. However, sterile technique is indicated whenever the patient's oronasopharyngeal mucosa has been impaired, for example, by burns, lesions, or local radiation treatment.*

*This procedure is contraindicated in the patient with nasopharyngeal bleeding or spinal fluid leakage into the nasopharyngeal area.*

## Equipment

Wall suction or portable suction apparatus ☐ collection bottle ☐ connecting tubing ☐ Y-connector (if the catheter has no control valve) ☐ tap water ☐ cup or other disposable container ☐ sterile suction catheter (#12 French or #14 French for adults, #8 French or #10 French for children, pediatric feeding tube for infants) ☐ clean glove.

A sterile catheter, disposable container, and glove are available in a commercially prepared kit.

## Preparation of equipment

Place the suction equipment on the patient's overbed table or bedside stand. Position the table or stand on your preferred side of the bed *to facilitate suctioning.* Attach the collection bottle to the suctioning unit, and attach the connecting tubing to it. Pour 50 to 100 ml of tap water into the cup or disposable container. If the suction catheter doesn't have a control valve, connect the tail of the Y-connector to the connecting tubing.

## Essential steps

● *For nasopharyngeal suction,* check patient history for a deviated nasal septum, broken nose, polyp or other growth, or difficulty breathing through either nostril. Also ask the patient which nostril is more patent.

● Explain the procedure to the patient, provide privacy, and wash your hands.

Let the patient know that suctioning may stimulate the cough or gag reflex.

• Place the patient in semi-Fowler's position *to promote lung expansion and effective coughing.*

• Instruct the patient to cough and breathe slowly and deeply several times before beginning suction. *Coughing helps loosen secretions and may decrease the amount of suctioning necessary, while deep breathing helps minimize or prevent hypoxia.*

• *To facilitate catheter insertion* for oral suctioning, have the patient turn his head toward you; for nasal suctioning, hyperextend the patient's neck.

• Turn on the suction and set the pressure according to hospital policy. In general, the pressure may be set at 100 to 120 mmHg for adults, or 50 to 75 mmHg for infants and children.

• Put on the glove. Use your gloved hand to pick up the catheter and your ungloved hand to hold the connecting tubing. Attach the catheter to the connecting tubing, or to the arm of the Y-connector.

• *For nasal insertion:* Without allowing the catheter to touch the patient, measure the length of the catheter from the tip of the patient's nose to his earlobe *to determine the correct insertion length and ensure that the catheter won't pass into the trachea.* Mark the position on the tube by placing the thumb of your ungloved hand at this point and make a mental note of the length required for proper insertion.

• With your gloved hand, dip the catheter tip into the tap water. With your ungloved hand, place a finger over the catheter's control valve or over the Y-connector's open end, and suction a small amount of water through the catheter *to lubricate the inside to facilitate passage of secretions through the catheter, and to test the suction apparatus.* Dipping the suction catheter tip into the tap water will also lubricate the tip, thereby decreasing trauma during nasal insertion.

• To place the catheter for oropharyngeal suctioning, insert it into the patient's mouth and along one side until it reaches the back of the throat. To place it for nasopharyngeal suctioning, gently insert the catheter through one nostril to the appropriate premeasured distance, directing the tip along the floor of the nasal cavity *to avoid the nasal turbinates.*

• Then, apply suction as you withdraw the catheter. Simultaneously roll the catheter between your thumb and index finger as you remove it, *as this rotating motion prevents tissue trauma.* Apply suction for only 10 to 12 seconds at a time *to minimize or prevent tissue trauma.*

• If secretions are thick, clear the lumen of the catheter by dipping it in water and applying suction.

• Repeat the procedure until respirations are quiet and gurgling or bubbling sounds stop.

• After completing suctioning, instruct the patient to take several slow, deep breaths *to relieve any hypoxia and promote relaxation.*

• Apply suction to clear the connecting tubing; then discard the catheter, the disposable container of water, and the used glove.

• Replace the above items *so they're ready for the next suctioning,* and wash your hands.

• Remove, empty, rinse, and reattach the collection bottle every 8 hours (or more often, as necessary).

## Special considerations

*To facilitate catheter insertion through a nostril,* insert the catheter on a slight downward slant and ask the patient to take slow, deep breaths through his mouth. Avoid inserting the catheter further than the premeasured distance, *because it could enter the trachea or esophagus.* Also, avoid application of suction during insertion *to prevent tissue trauma.*

When using the nasal route, suction cautiously if the patient has a blood dyscrasia or is receiving anticoagulant therapy, *to prevent bleeding.* If the patient has no past history of nasal problems, alternate suctioning between the left and right nostrils *to reduce trauma to one nostril.* If more lubrication is needed, aseptically apply a sterile, water-soluble lubricant to the catheter before insertion into the nostril.

*To facilitate catheter insertion for oropharyngeal suctioning,* depress the tongue with a blade, or ask another nurse to do so. *This makes it easier to see the back of the throat and also prevents the patient from biting the catheter.*

Replace the suction bottle and tubing according to hospital policy.

Don't allow the suction-collection bottle to fill past the three-quarter mark *to avoid damaging the machine.*

Let the patient rest after each 10- to 12-second suctioning period *to reduce the risk of hypoxia.*

## Complications

Increased dyspnea due to hypoxia and anxiety may result from this procedure. Hypoxia can result because oxygen from the oronasopharynx is removed with the secretions. Bloody aspirate can result from prolonged or traumatic suctioning.

## Documentation

Record the date, time, and reason for suctioning; amount, color, consistency, and odor (if any) of the secretions; the patient's respiratory status before and after the procedure; any complications and the nursing action taken; and the patient's tolerance for the procedure.

HELEN HAHLER D'ANGELO, RN, MSN

# Oxygen Administration by Cannula, Catheter, or Mask

*Oxygen is administered by cannula (nasal prongs), catheter, or mask to prevent or reverse hypoxia and improve tissue oxygenation. Hypoxia can result from a disorder in any phase of respiration— ventilation, distribution, diffusion, or perfusion. Unchecked, it affects the brain, adrenal glands, heart, kidneys, and liver in turn.*

*The nasal cannula delivers low-flow oxygen at 22% to 30% concentrations to enrich respiration when accuracy isn't crucial. Inexpensive and easy to use, it interferes less with the patient's movement and other functions than any other device. The nasal catheter also delivers low-flow oxygen, but at higher concentrations of 30% to 35%. It is recommended for short-term treatment, such as for the postsurgical patient whose respiratory rate and depth remain suppressed from anesthesia. An invasive insertion route and the need for frequent changes to alternate nostrils make the catheter more irritating to the patient than other devices. The oxygen mask, depending on the type, can deliver concentrations of up to 100%. It is used when the patient requires high humidity and precise amounts of oxygen, or can breathe only through his mouth. Because the mask is confining, prevents eating, and hampers speech, it may reduce compliance in the patient, who may remove his mask when not in crisis.*

*Regardless of the delivery method, the patient with chronic obstructive pulmonary disease (COPD) should receive only 2 liters of oxygen/minute until arterial blood gases are obtained. Delivering more oxygen than this to COPD patients who chronically retain carbon dioxide may inhibit their hypoxic stimulus to breathe.*

## Equipment

Oxygen source in wall unit or portable cylinder ☐ adapter for wall unit ☐ pressure-reduction gauge for cylinder ☐ flowmeter ☐ cannula, catheter, or mask, as ordered ☐ sterile humidity bottle and appropriate adapters ☐ sterile distilled water ☐ small-diameter connection tubing ☐ flashlight ☐ two OXYGEN PRECAUTION signs ☐ gauze pads (optional).

*For a catheter:* water-soluble lubricant ☐ adhesive or other tape ☐ tongue blade.

*For a high-humidity mask:* large-diameter connection tubing.

# OXYGEN MASKS

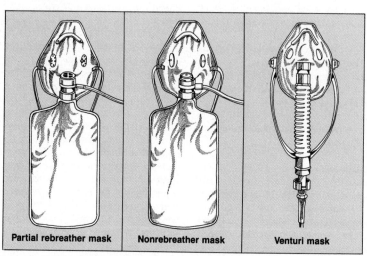

| Partial rebreather mask | Nonrebreather mask | Venturi mask |

The *partial rebreather mask* delivers up to 60% oxygen. It's designed to conserve roughly the first third of a patient's exhaled air, which flows into the reservoir bag. Because this air comes from such passages as the trachea and bronchi, where no gas exchange occurs, the patient essentially rebreathes the same oxygen.

The *nonrebreather mask* delivers up to 90% oxygen. This mask has 3 one-way valves: one located between the reservoir bag and the mask, the others located on the mask itself. These valves prevent room-air entrainment and allow the patient to breathe only the source gas from the bag.

The *Venturi mask* delivers precise oxygen concentrations to within 1%. With this mask, oxygen enters the tubing at a pre-scribed flow rate. When it reaches the Venturi device, it meets a restricted orifice. To maintain the same flow rate, the velocity increases, causing a decrease in pressure on the tubing walls and allowing room air to be drawn in through the ports of entrainment. The amount of air entrained is determined by the size of the orifice: the smaller the orifice, the larger the increase in velocity, the larger the decrease in pressure, and the larger the amount of room air entrained. This results in greater oxygen dilution and lower $FIO_2$.

Disposable cannulas, catheters, and masks, and humidity bottles containing sterile distilled water are commercially available and widely used.

Catheters are available in different sizes. Usually a #8 to #10 French is used for children; #10 to #12 French for adult women; and #12 to #14 French for adult men.

## Preparation of equipment
Assemble the equipment at the patient's bedside. Check the expiration date on each sterile package and inspect for tears. If you're using an oxygen cylinder, transport it only in a cylinder cart. Keep the cylinder secured and away from heat *to prevent breakage and possible explosion.*

If you're using a wall unit, connect the adapter to the unit, check for leaks, and reinsert if necessary. Attach the flow-meter, turn the control switch *to ensure that the meter is working,* and shut it off again.

If you're using a cylinder, check the cylinder gauge *to ensure an adequate supply of oxygen.* Remove the valve cover.* With the oxygen spout pointing away from you, open the valve slightly *to blow any dust from the spout lip;* then immediately shut the valve. Connect the pressure-reduction gauge *to equalize pressure between the oxygen and the atmosphere,* and attach a flowmeter if the pressure gauge lacks one. Then, turn the gauge's flow-control knob counterclockwise *to open it,* and very slowly open the valve on top of the cylinder until the pressure gauge needle stops moving. Next, turn the gauge's flow-control knob clockwise until the flowmeter dial shows the prescribed flow rate in liters/minute. Lastly, turn the flow-control knob counterclockwise until the flowmeter needle falls to zero *to shut it off.*

Now, for both oxygen sources, fill the humidity bottle two-thirds full with sterile distilled water, *because tap water and saline solution leave mineral deposits in the equipment.* Fill the bottle only to the marker, *since overfilling causes water to backflow into the oxygen gauges.* If you're using a prefilled disposable bottle, check that the seal is unbroken; then listen for the rushing sound of the released vacuum as you unseal the bottle. If you fail to hear this sound, discard the bottle, *because it may be unsterile.* Screw the filled humidity bottle to its adapter and connect it to the flowmeter.

Turn on the oxygen to 2 or 3 liters/minute and watch for bubbles in the distilled water *to ensure patency of the humidifier.* Then, place your hand at the bottle opening *to check for the airflow and humidity.* If you're unable to feel the flow of air, increase the flow-control knob setting to 10 or 15 liters/minute and then check again for airflow *to verify patency of the equipment.* Then, return the control knob to the prescribed flow setting.

Attach the cannula, catheter, or mask to the connecting tubing, and attach the tubing to the humidifier port. Test the patency of the cannula, catheter, or mask

by holding it next to your hand or cheek *to feel for airflow and humidity.* Turn up the flow to 10 or 15 liters/minute for a moment to flush the equipment. Then, turn it off until the patient is ready.

## Essential steps

● Check the doctor's order for method of oxygen administration and the prescribed flow rate.

● Assess the patient's condition. In an emergency, verify an open airway before administering oxygen.

● Explain the procedure and the reason for oxygen therapy to the patient before bringing the equipment into his room *to allay his fears, because he may feel that a need for oxygen means his condition has worsened.*

● Check the patient's room for safety of oxygen administration before bringing the equipment into the room. Whenever possible, replace electrical devices with nonelectrical ones, such as substituting a hot water bottle for a heating pad. *Because oxygen supports combustion, the slightest spark can cause fire.*

● Explain oxygen precautions to the patient, his roommate(s), and all visitors. Warn them not to smoke or use an improperly grounded radio, TV, or electric razor while the oxygen is in the room.

● Place an OXYGEN PRECAUTION sign on the outside of the patient's door, and another sign over the patient's bed. Then, bring the equipment to the patient's bedside and prepare it for use.

● Wash your hands. Provide privacy for the patient who will have a nasal catheter inserted.

● Using a flashlight, check the patency of each nostril. As you gently move the tip of the patient's nose, observe for a deviated septum, polyps, edema, or other nasal obstruction. If both nostrils are blocked, you'll have to use a mask to administer oxygen; if only one nostril is blocked, select the device based on the patient's oxygen need. If your choice differs from the doctor's prescribed route, consult him before proceeding.

*To insert a nasal cannula:*

● Set the flow rate, as ordered, but avoid

exceeding the safe limit of 6 liters/minute. If you're using a cylinder, you must also turn on the oxygen.

• Examine the cannula prongs for straight or curved surfaces. Place straight prongs into the patient's nostrils with either surface up, unless one side is flatter and smoother than the other. In this case, place the smoother, flatter side against the skin, *because it produces less friction and pressure in this position.* Direct curved prongs downward toward the floor of the nostrils, thus following the natural curve of the nostrils. *Positioned with the curve facing upward, the mucous membrane can occlude the prong openings and reduce oxygen flow.*

• Hook the cannula tubing behind the patient's ears and under the chin; then slide the adjuster upward under the chin to secure the tubing. When using an elastic strap to secure the cannula, position it over the ears and around the back of the head. Avoid too tight application, *which can result in pressure areas in the nostrils; on the nose, upper lip, and cheeks; behind the ears; and, with cannula tubing, under the chin. Excessively tight application can also occlude the cannula prongs.*

*To insert a nasal catheter:*
• Stretch one end of the catheter in a straight line from the tip of the patient's nose to his earlobe, and mark the spot on the catheter with tape or hold it pinched between thumb and forefinger. *This is the approximate length you'll insert the catheter through one nostril.*

• Lubricate the catheter with sterile distilled water or water-soluble lubricant *to prevent tube curl and nasal irritation during insertion. Respiratory tract mucous membranes safely reabsorb water-soluble lubricant, whereas oily lubricant—aspirated even in small quantities—can cause severe chronic lung irritation and lipid pneumonia.*

• Hyperextend the patient's neck slightly, unless contraindicated.

• Rotate the catheter to determine its natural droop *so you can introduce it in conformity with the natural nasal curve.*

• With the oxygen set at low flow (1 to 2

liters/minute) *to prevent mucus from clogging the catheter ports,* gently insert the catheter through one nostril and into the nasopharynx to the premeasured length, passing it back along the nasal floor *to minimize tissue trauma.*

• Have the patient open his mouth and say "Ahhh." Use a flashlight and tongue blade, if necessary, to help position the catheter directly behind the uvula. At this time, the tip of the catheter should be visible behind the uvula. Now, withdraw the catheter slightly until the tip is no longer visible. If this position causes the patient to choke, gag, or swallow air, again withdraw the catheter slightly. Be sure the catheter doesn't extend beyond the uvula *to prevent gastric distention from misdirected airflow.*

• Using tape, secure the catheter to the nose and cheek. *If not secured at the nose, the catheter may pull out or displace downward and enter the esophagus.* Attaching the catheter to the forehead is less preferable than attaching it to the cheek, *because forehead skin is highly sensitive; the catheter would disturb the patient's vision; and traction at the tip of the nose could produce skin breakdown.*

• Set the flow rate, as ordered, but avoid a rate in excess of 6 liters/minute *to prevent mucosal irritation.*

*To apply a mask:*
• Select the size mask that offers the best fit.

• If ordered, set the flow rate. The doctor usually sets the flow rate for simple masks, but for other masks use these guidelines to help you set the proper rate. Follow the instructions that accompany the Venturi mask, as its operating principle requires precision. Set a rebreathing mask at 10 liters/minute or other rate sufficient to maintain reservoir inflation with the patient's tidal volume. With high-humidity masks, turn up the oxygen until mist flows from the mask. *Flow rates below 5 liters/minute for all but the Venturi mask are inadequate to flush carbon dioxide from the mask.*

• Place the mask over the patient's nose, mouth, and chin, and press its flexible metal edge so it fits the bridge of the nose. Adjust the elastic band around the head *to hold the mask firmly but comfortably over the cheeks, chin, and bridge of the nose.* For the elderly, cachectic, or edentulous patients with sunken cheeks, tape gauze pads to the mask over the cheek area *to create as closely as possible an airtight seal. Without this seal, room air dilutes the oxygen, preventing delivery of the prescribed concentration.*

• If you're using the nonrebreathing mask, make sure the one-way valves or flaps are secure and functioning *to ensure correct delivery of oxygen and exhalation of carbon dioxide. Because this mask excludes room air, valve malfunction can cause buildup of carbon dioxide and lead to suffocation of an unconscious patient.*

• If you're using a nonrebreathing or partial rebreathing mask, observe the reservoir bag as the patient breathes. If it collapses more than slightly during inspiration, raise the flow rate until you see only a slight deflation. *Marked or complete deflation indicates an overly low flow rate.*

• Keep the reservoir bag from twisting or kinking, and make sure it lies outside the gown, sheet, and blankets *so it's completely free to expand.*

### Special considerations

*Since oxygen has no odor, color, and taste,* make sure its source is checked regularly for patency and chemical contamination.

If you're using an oxygen cylinder, keep a second cylinder available *for quick switching when the first cylinder is spent.*

Adequate humidification of oxygen is necessary *to prevent drying and cracking mucous membranes, which interferes with cilial motion and allows bacterial and viral invasion.* Avoid using high humidity with a mask equipped with a reservoir bag unless the equipment has an in-line water trap, *because water tends to collect in the bag.* Make sure the patient is comfortably warm, *since some humidification systems produce a strong chill.* Change the humidity

bottle setup and sterile distilled water daily. Replace all the water in a reusable bottle, instead of just adding water to fill it, *to prevent bacterial growth in the water.* Similarly, discard and replace a commercially prepared bottle.

Using gauze squares, you may pad the tubing and the elastic straps behind the patient's ears and at other pressure points *to prevent skin breakdown.* Tape the pads to the tubing *to ensure their stability and avoid skin irritation from the tape.* If the patient is active, tape cannula tubing to both sides of the face *for security.* And, if the patient is ambulatory, use long tubing *to allow mobility.*

Keep the skin dry under oxygen devices and tubing *to prevent breakdown caused by humidity and perspiration.* Every 2 hours—or more often with high-humidity masks—wipe moisture from the patient's face and mask. Periodically wash and dry the face, but don't use powder, *because the patient may inhale it.* At least every 8 hours, wash the mask with soap and water and dry it thoroughly, and wash the cannula with cotton-tipped applicators dipped in soap and water *to prevent occlusion from mucus and moisture.* If the patient is apprehensive or unable to wait for washing, replace the items immediately with fresh equipment. At least every 8 hours, or more often if the patient produces excess mucus, remove the catheter and insert a fresh one in the opposite nostril, if that nostril is unobstructed. *Rotating the site reduces the risk of skin breakdown on the tip of the nose and decreases mucous membrane irritation and drying.*

At least every 8 hours, check the skin under the tubing or elastic straps *to detect necrosis from pressure, irritation, and moisture.* Remember that discomfort can provoke the patient to resist treatment.

If the patient is confined to bed, encourage position changes every 1 to 2 hours *to promote full ventilation and prevent pneumonia and circulatory problems.*

Check the patient frequently for signs of hypoxia, such as: decreased level of consciousness; increased heart rate and altered rhythm; restlessness; mental confusion; altered blood pressure; perspiration; altered respiratory rate; dyspnea; use of accessory muscles of respiration; full-Fowler's forward-leaning posture; yawning or flared nostrils; skin, nailbed, and buccal membrane cyanosis; and cool, clammy skin. Hypoxia from insufficient oxygen can result from an inadequate prescription or improperly functioning equipment.

Watch also for signs of oxygen toxicity in the patient receiving concentrations above 60% for over 24 hours. *To prevent atelectasis,* which may occur during therapy with high concentrations of oxygen, frequently remind the patient to cough and deep breathe to keep his lungs inflated. *Because prolonged treatment with high concentrations of oxygen can also cause serious lung damage,* make sure arterial blood gases are measured frequently to determine continued use of high concentrations.

Observe the patient for signs of laryngeal ulceration *resulting from inspissation of normal secretions.*

*Because the patient must remove a mask for eating,* suggest that the doctor order a cannula during meals if the patient becomes short of breath without the mask or is a slow eater.

Unless contraindicated, take the rectal temperature of the patient who is receiving oxygen by mask, *because removal of the mask to take an oral temperature can cause the blood oxygen level to drop precipitously.* Check hospital policy concerning oral temperatures when the patient is using a cannula or catheter. Recent studies show that oxygen administration lowers body temperature a maximum of 0.4° F. (0.2° C.). Many hospitals regard this drop as minimal and not worth the discomfort rectal measurement of temperature causes some patients; nor is it worth interruption of oxygen administration during temperature recording.

When oxygen therapy is being discontinued, watch for signs of hypoxia and immediately notify the doctor if these occur. After therapy, discard disposable equipment properly or send reusable equipment to the central supply department for sterilization.

## Documentation

Record the date and time of oxygen administration; mode (cannula, catheter, or mask); flow rate in liters; the patient's condition before and after treatment; your checks of equipment patency; time of oxygen cylinder change; patient, visitor, and roommate instruction about oxygen precautions; and the patient's reaction to oxygen therapy.

KATHLEEN E. VIALL GALLAGHER, RN, MSN

# Humidifiers

*Humidifiers add water vapor to inspired air to prevent drying and irritation of the respiratory mucosa and to help loosen respiratory secretions for easier removal. Some humidifiers also heat the water vapor, thereby enhancing the moisture-carrying capability of the gas and increasing the humidity delivered to the patient.*

*Supplemental humidity must accompany delivery of such medical gases as oxygen, because the gases are totally dry and extremely irritating to mucous membranes. It's used with every oxygen-delivery device except the Venturi mask. If the patient with a Venturi mask requires humidification, the entrained room air is humidified, not the oxygen. Supplemental humidity is also used when secretions are particularly thick and tenacious, and when the patient needs relief from croup or tracheitis.*

*Humidity may be added to a room, using a room humidifier, or combined with inspired-gas lines and delivered directly to the patient. In-line devices include the cold bubble-diffusion humidifier for the patient with an intact upper airway, and the cascade humidifier, which can deliver 100% of needed body hu-*

# HUMIDIFIERS

| TYPE | ADVANTAGES | DISADVANTAGES |
|---|---|---|
| **Cold bubble diffuser**  | • May be used with all oxygen masks, nasal cannulas, and nasal catheters | • Provides only 20% to 40% humidity<br>• Cannot be used for patient with bypassed upper airway |
| **Cascade humidifier**  | • Provides 100% humidity at body temperature<br>• Functions as mainstream humidifier with ventilator<br>• Most effective of all evaporative humidifiers | • Temperature control may become defective from constant use.<br>• If correct water level isn't maintained, patient's mucosa can become irritated from breathing hot, dry air. |
| **Room humidifier (cool mist or steam vaporizer)**  | • May be used with all oxygen masks, nasal cannulas, and nasal catheters. | • Produces humidity inefficiently<br>• Cannot be used for patient with bypassed upper airway |

*midity to the patient when heated and connected to a ventilator.*

## Equipment

*Room humidifier:* humidifier □ sterile distilled water.

*Cold bubble-diffusion humidifier:* humidifier (bubble bottle) □ sterile distilled water □ oxygen source □ flowmeter □ oxygen-delivery device, such as a nasal catheter, nasal cannula, or oxygen mask.

*Cascade humidifier:* humidifier □ sterile distilled water □ oxygen source □ mechanical ventilator.

Many humidifiers are commercially available. In addition, many are at least partially disposable.

## Preparation of equipment

Select the appropriate humidifier, as ordered. Check its cord for fraying or other electrical defects. Use only a three-prong (grounded) plug *to avoid electric shock.* Wash your hands; set up the specified humidifier as described below. Be sure to use only sterile distilled water *to prevent accumulation of mineral deposits and obstruction of tiny openings in the apparatus.*

*To prepare a room humidifier:*
Open the humidifier reservoir. Add sterile distilled water to the fill line, and close the reservoir.

*To prepare a cold bubble-diffusion humidifier:*
Unscrew the humidifier reservoir from the humidifier lid and add sterile distilled water to the fill line on the reservoir. Avoid overfilling the reservoir, *because this can cause condensation to collect in the small-bore oxygen tubing, increasing airflow resistance for the patient.* Screw the reservoir back on to the humidifier. Then, attach the flowmeter to the oxygen source, and connect the humidifier to the bottom of the flowmeter. If you're using a commercially prepackaged humidifier, simply break the seal and attach it to the flowmeter. To prevent the delivery of dry gas to the patient, set the flowmeter to 2 liters/minute. Check humidifier function at this point. To determine if the gas is being delivered to the unit and properly humidified, be sure the flowmeter is set to 2 liters/minute. Bubbling should be visible in the reservoir. To determine if the pressure release system is operating, occlude the port where the oxygen delivery device will be connected to the humidifier and observe for audible release of pressure from the pressure release valve on the humidifier. Decreased bubbling in the reservoir while the port is occluded is another indication that the device is patent.

*To prepare a cascade humidifier:*
Unscrew the bottom of the cascade reservoir, add sterile distilled water to the reservoir's fill line, and reattach it. Remember, the cascade's heater control serves only as a guide; *the in-line thermometer gives a more precise temperature of delivered vapor.* Plug in the heater unit for the cascade and set the temperature dial at midrange (usually at 5). The blue numbers on the cascade (1 through 5) range from room temperature to near body temperature; the white numbers (6 and 7) are in the range of body temperature; the red numbers (8

and 9) are above body temperature. If the temperature is too low at a setting of 5, slowly adjust the dial upward one number at a time. Some temperature dials on cascade humidifiers allow selection of the desired temperature of the delivered gas. Check the in-line thermometer to verify that the desired temperature has been reached. Instead of an in-line thermometer, some ventilators use a probe placed in the line with the thermometer located in the machine itself. *Usually, strive for a reading slightly below body temperature, which results in a relative humidity of 100%.* If you're using the optional temperature alarm *to detect gas temperature changes near the patient,* turn it on and set it slightly above (usually +2° to 3° F.) normal body temperature.

### Essential steps

● Check the doctor's order and assess the patient's respiratory condition.
● Explain the procedure to the patient *to ease his anxiety.* Then, continue the procedure as described below, according to the type of humidifier you're using.

*To use a room humidifier:*
● Position the device on the bedside stand or a nearby table, far enough from walls and furniture *to prevent water damage.*
● Close windows and doors *to maintain the humidity level in the room.*
● Plug the unit in, and direct the humidifier's nozzle toward the patient *to promote effective treatment.* A mist should be visible at the nozzle.
● Frequently check the unit's water level and refill as necessary. When refilling, first unplug the unit *to prevent electric shock.* Discard any water in the reservoir, and refill it with sterile distilled water *to prevent bacterial growth.* Plug in the unit again.
● Continue the treatment for the prescribed length of time.
● Rinse the humidifier reservoir after each use, and return the unit to the central supply department *for sterilization.*

*To use a cold bubble-diffusion humidifier:*
● Attach the oxygen-delivery device to

the bubble-diffusion humidifier.
• Turn the oxygen flowmeter to the prescribed flow rate.
• Position the oxygen-delivery device on the patient.
• Frequently check the unit's reservoir. When water runs low and/or the bubbling stops, discard any remaining water and refill the chamber with fresh sterile distilled water. If you're using a commercially prepackaged humidifier, discard the entire unit and replace it with a fresh one when the water runs low. At low oxygen flow rates, when water is not used rapidly, change the water at least once a day *to prevent bacterial growth.*
• Regularly change the humidifier and its tubing, according to hospital policy, *to prevent respiratory nosocomial infection from bacterial growth in the equipment.*
• When changing the apparatus or discontinuing treatment, return the used equipment to the central supply department for resterilization.
*To use a cascade humidifier:*
• Frequently check the thermometer. The temperature should be slightly below or at body temperature. If at any time you feel that the inspired-gas temperature may be too high for the patient's comfort or safety (when, for example, the tubing or the bottom of the cascade is hot to the touch), turn down the temperature control and call the respiratory therapist for an evaluation. If dangerously hot, dump out the hot water in the cascade and replace it with room temperature distilled water. Remember, the thermometer is only a guide to inspired-gas temperature *because it averages both inspired and expired air temperatures.*
• Arrange the tubing *so that condensation can't flow toward the patient and be aspirated.* If aspiration occurs, immediately suction the patient. Periodically drain condensation from the tubing *to prevent backflow, maintain vapor temperature, and reduce the resistance to oxygen flow.*
• Frequently check the cascade's water level and refill as necessary. When refilling, unscrew the bottom water res-

ervoir. Discard any water left in the cascade reservoir and refill it with sterile distilled water *to prevent bacterial growth in the residual water.* Be sure to keep the cascade's water level well above the minimum line *to prevent the administration of warm, dry air to the patient.*
• Regularly change the cascade and its tubing, according to hospital policy, *to prevent respiratory nosocomial infection from bacterial growth in the equipment. To prevent burns,* let the heater cool off before changing the apparatus.
• When changing the cascade or discontinuing treatment, return the used cascade to the central supply department for resterilization.

### Special considerations
Tell the patient who is using a room humidifier at home that he can fill it with plain tap water, but that he should periodically run the unit with distilled water *to dissolve the mineral deposits left by the tap water.* To clean the humidifier, instruct him to run the unit occasionally with a solution of chlorine bleach and distilled water in the reservoir. This should be done in a well-ventilated room every 5 days *to prevent the otherwise rapid accumulation of mold and bacteria.*

Never allow a heated humidifier to run dry, *because hot, dry gas can severely dry and burn the respiratory mucosa.*

Check thermometer readings regularly *to ensure that inspired air remains at body temperature.* Constant use, flow rates below 1 to 4 liters/minute, and insufficient water in the humidifier can cause the heating device to overheat, raising the temperature of the inspired gas. While water in a heated humidifier container may reach temperatures up to 140° F. (60° C.), it cools and condenses as it passes through the tubing, and should be close to body temperature as the patient breathes it. A range of 90° to 100° F. (32.2° to 37.8° C.) is acceptable.

If you're using a cascade humidifier to treat an oliguric patient, observe him for signs of pulmonary edema and congestive heart failure, *because the system decreases insensible loss.* Notify the doctor immediately if such signs occur.

## Documentation

Record the date and time when humidification began and was discontinued; type of humidifier; flow rate and any other settings, such as respiratory rate and volume; thermometer readings; any complications and the nursing action taken; and the patient's reaction to humidification.

PATRICIA L. FUCHS, CRTT, RRT

# Nebulizers

*Used to deliver moisture or medication, nebulizers produce 100% humidity in a fine aerosol mist of fluid droplets that, ideally, slowly settle deep into the lungs. The large-volume nebulizer, used for long-term therapy, delivers a heated or cool mist. Cool mist can be more comfortable for the recently extubated patient. It is also indicated for the patient with trauma or a recent tracheostomy, because a heated mist may increase bleeding. Heated mist is indicated for the patient with an artificial airway and for the neonate. Cold mist blowing on a neonate can cause a significant decrease in body temperature.*

*The ultrasonic nebulizer is for use in short therapeutic sessions indicated for the patient with thick secretions, to mobilize secretions and facilitate a productive cough. The side-stream nebulizer and the mini-nebulizer deliver aerosolized medication. The side-stream nebulizer attaches to a ventilator or to an intermittent positive-pressure breathing (IPPB) machine, while the mini-nebulizer is hand-held.*

*Nebulization is contraindicated in patients with delicate fluid balance. It should be used cautiously in asthmatic patients with active bronchospasm.*

## Equipment

*For the large-volume nebulizer:* nebulizer □ flowmeter, as necessary □ pressurized gas source □ large-bore oxygen tubing □ appropriate gas-delivery device □ sterile distilled water □ oxygen analyzer, as necessary □ heater, if ordered □ in-line thermometer (for use with a heating device) □ suction equipment, as necessary.

This nebulizer has a 250-ml capacity and can deliver oxygen or room air. Some models have variable fraction of inspired oxygen (FIO$_2$) settings. Prefilled disposable nebulizers are commercially available. The heating device can be a rod immersed in the water, a heating pad wrapped around the container, or a heating plate placed under the container. Nebulizers operating on the Babbington principle are occasionally used in place of the pneumatic reservoir type, because they can deliver almost any oxygen concentration with high humidity without heating. Use of these nebulizers is rare, however, because they contain a fragile glass sphere that is quite expensive to replace.

*For the ultrasonic nebulizer:* nebulizer □ large-bore oxygen tubing □ appropriate gas-delivery device □ sterile distilled water or a sterile distilled water continuous-feed setup □ suction equipment, as necessary.

Two types of ultrasonic nebulizer are available. One has a cup that is filled with sterile distilled water; the other requires a continuous-feed system of sterile distilled water that runs into the nebulizer unit. Both types have internal blower or fan devices.

*For the side-stream nebulizer:* nebulizer □ pressurized gas source □ prescribed drug □ diluent, usually sterile normal saline solution or sterile distilled water □ appropriate-sized syringe and needle □ suction equipment, as necessary.

The nebulizer and tubing are usually connected to the ventilator of an IPPB machine. Use of an IPPB machine also requires a mouthpiece or mask.

*For the mini-nebulizer:* nebulizer cup

EQUIPMENT

# NEBULIZERS

| TYPE | ADVANTAGES | DISADVANTAGES |
|---|---|---|
| **Large-volume nebulizer (heated or cool)**  | • Provides 100% humidity with cool or heated device<br>• Provides both oxygen and aerosol therapy<br>• Is useful for long-term therapy | • Nondisposable units increase risk of bacterial growth.<br>• Condensation can collect in large-bore tubing.<br>• If correct water level in reservoir isn't maintained, mucosal irritation can result from breathing hot, dry air.<br>• Infants easily become overhydrated from mist. |
| **Mini-nebulizer or Maximist** 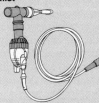 | • Conforms to patient's physiology, allowing him to inhale and exhale on his own power.<br>• Can cause less air trapping than medication administered by intermittent positive-pressure breathing (IPPB)<br>• May be used with compressed air, oxygen, or compressor pump<br>• Compact and disposable | • Procedure takes a long time if patient needs nurse's assistance.<br>• Medication distributed unevenly if patient doesn't breathe properly. |
| **Ultrasonic nebulizer**  | • Provides 100% humidity<br>• 90% of particles reach lower airways<br>• Loosens secretions | • May precipitate bronchospasms in the asthmatic patient.<br>• May cause overhydration. |
| **Side-stream nebulizer** 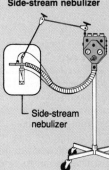<br>— Side-stream nebulizer | • Delivers medication to patient on ventilator or during IPPB therapy | • Those associated with ventilators or IPPB therapy<br>• Adverse reaction to medication |

with lid ☐ pressurized gas source ☐ flowmeter, as necessary ☐ oxygen tubing ☐ T-piece ☐ mouthpiece or mask, or other appropriate gas-delivery device ☐ diluent, usually sterile normal saline solution or sterile distilled water ☐ 5-ml syringe and needle ☐ prescribed medication ☐ suction equipment, as necessary.

Disposable units are commercially available.

## Preparation of equipment

Gather the appropriate equipment and wash your hands. Prepare the nebulizer as described below, according to the type of device you're using, and take the equipment to the patient's bedside.

*To prepare a large-volume nebulizer:* Unscrew the water chamber and fill it to the indicated level with sterile distilled water. Avoid using sterile saline solution, which can cause corrosion. Add a heating device, if ordered. Place a thermometer in-line between the outlet port and the patient, preferably closer to the patient, *to monitor the actual temperature of the inhaled gas and to detect and correct excess heat before the patient can be burned.*

*To prepare an ultrasonic nebulizer:* Fill the nebulizer cup with sterile distilled water or, if using a disposable sterile distilled water container, spike, hang, and attach the container of sterile distilled water to the nebulizer. If using a continuous-feed system, hang the large-volume continuous-feed bag or sterile distilled water on the hook provided on the nebulizer stand. Attach the tubing from the nebulizer bottle to the bag, open the clamp on the tubing, and allow the sterile distilled water to flow into the nebulizer bottle.

*To prepare a side-stream nebulizer:* Draw up the medication and diluent, if required, into the syringe. Or, draw the medication into the syringe and use a premeasured container of sterile saline solution or water.

*To prepare a mini-nebulizer:* Draw up the medication into the syringe and inject it into the medication cup.

Add the prescribed amount of sterile saline solution or water. Keep the cup upright *to prevent spillage.* Attach the T-piece and the mouthpiece, mask, or other gas-delivery device. Attach one end of the oxygen tubing to the nebulizer.

## Essential steps

● Explain the procedure to the patient.

*To use a large-volume nebulizer:*

● Attach the flowmeter to the gas source, and attach the nebulizer to the flowmeter. Turn the flowmeter to 10 to 14 liters/minute, *because these devices require at least 10 liters/minute to operate, and vent as excess any flow above 14 liters/minute.*

● Make sure an ample quantity of mist emanates from the outflow port.

● Set the prescribed $FIO_2$, according to the doctor's order.

● Attach the large-bore tubing to the outlet port and the appropriate delivery device to the distal end of the tubing.

● When giving oxygen, use the oxygen analyzer to evaluate gas flow at the patient's end of the tubing *to ensure delivery of the prescribed percentage of oxygen.*

● If you're using a heater, instruct the patient to report warmth, discomfort, or hot tubing, *because these may indicate a heater malfunction.* Use the in-line thermometer to monitor the temperature of the gas the patient is inhaling. If you turn off the flow for more than 5 minutes, be sure to unplug the heater so the water *doesn't overheat and burn the patient when the flow is turned back on.*

● Attach the delivery device to the patient.

● Encourage and assist the patient to cough and expectorate periodically, or suction him, if necessary.

● Check water level frequently and refill or replace the container *to prevent complications from inhaling dry, hot air, especially in a patient with an artificial airway.* When refilling a reusable container, discard the old water and refill the container to the indicator line with fresh sterile distilled water *to retard bacterial growth.*

● Change the nebulizer unit and tubing daily *to help prevent bacterial contamination.*

*To use an ultrasonic nebulizer:*
• Attach the appropriate large-bore tubing and gas-delivery device.
• Turn on the machine and check the outflow port for proper misting.
• Instruct the patient to breathe slowly and deeply *to provide maximum distribution of the aerosol into the lower bronchial tree.*
• Remain with the patient during the treatment (usually 15 to 20 minutes) and observe for side effects, such as bronchospasm and dyspnea. Take vital signs and auscultate for rales or wheezes, if indicated, *because increased water absorption may cause overhydration and lead to pulmonary edema or increased cardiac workload, conditions that may show up only after extended treatment.*
• Encourage and assist the patient to cough and expectorate, or suction him as necessary, *because secretions may become thin and copious.* Stop suctioning and allow the patient to rest, as necessary.

*To use a side-stream nebulizer:*
• Take vital signs *to establish a baseline.*
• Remove the nebulizer cup, inject the medication, and replace the cup. If using an IPPB machine, attach the mouthpiece or mask to the machine.
• If possible, place the patient in a sitting or high Fowler's position *to encourage full lung expansion and promote aerosol dispersion.* Encourage him to take slow, deep, even breaths. Turn on the machine and check for an ample quantity of mist, indicating proper operation.
• Remain with the patient during treatment (usually 15 to 20 minutes), and take vital signs *to detect adverse reactions to the medication.* If the patient must rest, turn off the nebulizer *to avoid wasting medication.*
• Encourage and assist the patient to cough and expectorate, or suction him as necessary.

*To use a mini-nebulizer:*

• Take the patient's vital signs *to establish a baseline.*
• If possible, place the patient in a sitting or high Fowler's position *to facilitate lung expansion and aerosol dispersion.*
• Attach the free end of the oxygen tubing to the pressurized gas source. Turn on the gas source and check the outflow port for proper misting. If you're administering oxygen, adjust the flowmeter to provide proper misting. Usually a setting of 5 to 6 liters/minute is adequate.
• Instruct the patient to breathe slowly, deeply, and evenly through his mouth, and to hold his breath for 2 to 3 seconds on full inspiration *to receive the full benefit of the medication.*
• If possible, remain with the patient during treatment (usually 15 to 20 minutes). Take vital signs *to detect adverse reactions to the medication.*
• Encourage and assist the patient to cough and expectorate, or suction him as necessary. Briefly stop the treatment if he needs to rest.

*To conclude all nebulizer procedures:*
• Make sure the patient is comfortable and breathing easily before you leave.
• Clean all equipment, as appropriate, and return it to the proper area.

## Special considerations

When using a high-output nebulizer, such as an ultrasonic nebulizer, in the pediatric patient or in the patient with a delicate fluid balance, be alert for signs of overhydration, such as unexplained weight gain over several days after therapy is initiated, pulmonary edema, rales, and electrolyte imbalance.

If a heated nebulizer overheats, unplug the heater and replace the hot water with fresh sterile distilled water. If you're using a T-piece for the patient with an artificial airway, watch for mist at the open end of the tube. If the mist disappears, the patient's inspiratory force exceeds nebulizer output, causing inspiration of room air and, if oxygen is being given, dilution of $FIO_2$. To correct this, add a piece of large-bore oxygen tubing to the open end of the T-piece.

## Complications

With the large-volume nebulizer, pulmonary burns can result from excessive heating due to a short circuit or low water levels. Bacterial contamination can occur. Increased upper airway edema can result from use of a heated aerosol in a patient with laryngeal edema.

With an ultrasonic nebulizer, overhydration can occur, with resultant pulmonary edema or increased cardiac workload. Bronchospasm, a drop in $PaO_2$, or changes in vital signs are also possible.

With a side-stream nebulizer or mininebulizer, adverse reactions to the drug can occur.

## Documentation

Record the date, time, and duration of therapy; type and amount of medication added to the nebulizer; $FIO_2$, if analyzed; baseline and subsequent vital signs; result of the therapy, such as loosened secretions; any complications and the nursing action taken; and the patient's tolerance of the treatment.

PATRICIA L. FUCHS, CRTT, RRT

---

# Incentive Spirometry

*Incentive spirometry uses a breathing device to encourage the patient to achieve maximal ventilation. The device measures respiratory flow or respiratory volume and induces the patient to take a deep breath and hold it for several seconds. This exercise establishes alveolar hyperinflation for a longer time than is possible with a normal deep breath, thus preventing and reversing the alveolar collapse that produces atelectasis and pneumonitis.*

*Incentive spirometry benefits the pa-tient on prolonged bed rest, especially the postoperative patient who may regain his normal respiratory pattern slowly because of such predisposing factors as abdominal or thoracic surgery, advanced age, inactivity, obesity, smoking, and a decreased ability to cough effectively and expel lung secretions.*

## Equipment

Flow or volume incentive spirometer, as indicated, with sterile disposable tube and mouthpiece □ stethoscope □ watch □ tape. Note: The tube and mouthpiece are sterile on first use and clean on subsequent uses.

## Preparation of equipment

Assemble the ordered equipment at the patient's bedside. Read the manufacturer's instructions for spirometer setup and operation. Remove the sterile flow tube and mouthpiece from the package and attach them to the device. Set the flow rate or volume goal, as determined by the doctor or respiratory therapist and based on the patient's preoperative performance. Turn the machine on, if necessary.

## Essential steps

• Assess the patient's condition.
• Explain the procedure to the patient, making sure he understands the importance of performing this exercise regularly *to maintain alveolar inflation and help prevent lung collapse and pneumonia.* Wash your hands.
• Assist the patient to a comfortable sitting or semi-Fowler's position *to promote optimal lung expansion.* If you're using a flow incentive spirometer and the patient is unable to assume or maintain this position, perform the procedure in any position as long as the device remains upright. *Tilting a flow incentive spirometer decreases the required patient effort and reduces the exercise's effectiveness.*
• Auscultate the patient's lungs *to provide a baseline for comparison with post-treatment auscultation.*
• Instruct the patient to insert the

mouthpiece and close his lips tightly around it, *because a weak seal may alter flow or volume readings.*

• Instruct the patient to exhale normally and then inhale to the predetermined level. If you're using a flow spirometer, this inhalation causes one, two, or three balls to rise to the top of the meter, or makes a bellows rise, depending on the type of equipment. If you're using a volume spirometer, in most models inhalation will cause a light to go on.

• When the patient inhales to the set level, instruct him to hold his breath for 3 seconds or, if you're using a volume spirometer, until the light turns off *to achieve maximal alveolar inflation.*

• Tell the patient to remove the mouthpiece and exhale normally. Allow him to relax and take several normal breaths before he attempts another breath with the spirometer.

• Encourage him to cough after each effort, *because deep lung inflation may loosen secretions and facilitate their removal.* Observe any expectorated secretions.

• Have patient take prescribed number of deep breaths. Note the tidal volumes.

• Auscultate patient's lungs and compare findings with first auscultation.

• Instruct the patient to remove the mouthpiece. Wash the device in warm water, and shake it dry. Avoid immersing the spirometer itself, *because this enhances bacterial growth and impairs the internal filter's effectiveness in preventing inhalation of extraneous material.*

• Place the mouthpiece in a plastic storage bag between exercises, and label it and the spirometer, if applicable, with the patient's name *to avoid inadvertent use by another patient.*

### Special considerations
If the patient is scheduled for surgery, make a preoperative assessment of his respiratory pattern and capability to ensure the development of appropriate postoperative goals. Then teach the patient to use the spirometer before surgery *so he can concentrate on your instructions and practice the exercise.* Avoid

exercising at mealtime *to prevent nausea.* If the patient has difficulty breathing only through his mouth, provide a noseclip *to fully measure each breath.* Provide paper and pencil so the patient can note exercise times. Exercise frequency varies with condition and ability.

Immediately after surgery, monitor the exercise frequently *to ensure patient compliance with the instructions and to assess his achievement level.*

### Documentation
Record any preoperative teaching and preoperative flow or volume levels; date and time of the procedure; type of spirometer; flow or volume levels achieved; number of breaths taken; patient's condition before and after the procedure; his tolerance of the procedure; and results of both auscultations.

If you've used a flow incentive spirometer, compute *volume* by multiplying the setting by the duration the patient kept the ball(s) suspended. For example, if the patient suspended the ball(s) for 3 seconds at a setting of 500 cc during each of 10 breaths, multiply 500 cc by 3 seconds and then record this total (1,500 cc) and the number of breaths: 1,500 cc x 10 breaths. If you've used a volume incentive spirometer, take the volume reading directly from the spirometer. For example, record 1,000 cc x 5 breaths.

JAY ELLEN BARRETT, RN, BSN, MBA

# Intermittent Positive-pressure Breathing
[*IPPB*]

*Intermittent positive-pressure breathing (IPPB) delivers room air or oxygen into the lungs at a pressure higher than atmospheric pressure. This delivery ceases when pressure in the mouth or in the breathing circuit tube rises to a predetermined positive pressure.*

*Although IPPB was once the mainstay*

*of pulmonary therapy, its routine use is currently controversial. Its critics contend that this treatment is costly, complicated, and easily replaced by properly performed deep-breathing exercises and incentive spirometry. Despite these claims, IPPB is performed in many institutions by both specially trained nurses and respiratory therapists.*

*Proponents believe that IPPB treatments expand lung volumes more fully and promote an effective cough; deliver aerosolized medications deeper into the air passages; decrease the work of breathing; and assist in the mobilization of secretions.*

*IPPB treatment is contraindicated in uncompensated pneumothorax and tracheoesophageal fistula. Active hemoptysis or recent gastric surgery may also contraindicate this therapy.*

## Equipment

IPPB machine □ breathing circuit tubing □ other necessary tubing (usually one or two sections) □ mouthpiece or mask □ noseclips, if necessary □ source of pressurized gas at 50 pounds/square inch (psi), if necessary □ oxygen, if desired □ prescribed medication, such as isoetharine hydrochloride 1% (Bronkosol) or sterile normal saline solution □ 3-ml syringe with needle □ sphygmomanometer □ stethoscope □ tissues and waste bag, or specimen cup □ suction equipment (optional).

Some IPPB machines have internal compression units, while others require a source of pressurized air or oxygen.

Individual plastic ampuls with premeasured doses of routine IPPB medications are commercially available.

## Preparation of equipment

Check the doctor's order for procedural details and the need for medication. Gather all necessary equipment and take it to the patient's bedside. Attach the breathing circuit tube to the appropriate opening(s), and any other tubes as required, according to the manufacturer's instructions. Draw up the ordered medication in the syringe and inject it into the nebulizer cup, making sure the cup remains upright. Or, snap off the top of the plastic ampul and squeeze its contents into the nebulizer cup.

## Essential steps

• Explain the procedure to the patient *to ensure his cooperation.* Wash your hands.

• Take baseline blood pressure and heart rate, especially if a bronchodilator is to be administered, and listen to breath sounds for comparison with later auscultations.

• If the machine is not already set up, attach the appropriate tubing to the pressure source. Refrain from using a flowmeter, *because the IPPB machine requires a pressure higher than a flowmeter can provide.*

• Check the system for proper operation and leaks. Adjust the pressure as ordered, or to 15 centimeters of water pressure ($cmH_2O$). Remove the mouthpiece or mask and occlude the end of the tubing; then manually cycle the machine on. Check that the machine then cycles off at the desired pressure. If the machine fails to reach pressure, check for a leak in the system—a small hole in the tubing or a disconnection in the circuit or nebulizer.

• Set the nebulizer control, if necessary.

• If you're administering oxygen, set the dilution as ordered. If the patient has chronic obstructive pulmonary disease and can't tolerate increased fraction of inspired oxygen percentage ($FIO_2$), compressed air may be used to power the machine.

• Instruct the patient to sit erect in a chair, if possible, *to allow for optimal lung expansion.* Otherwise, place him in a high Fowler's position.

• Replace the mouthpiece or mask on the tubing. Place it on the patient, or show him how to position it *to achieve a tight seal.*

• Tell the patient to breathe deeply and slowly through his mouth, as if sucking on a straw, allowing the machine to do the work during the treatment. This will cycle the machine and deliver a breath to the patient. When the preset pressure is met, the machine will cycle off, ending inspiration. Instruct him to hold his breath for a few seconds after full inspiration *to allow greater distribution of gas and dispersion of nebulized particles.* Then instruct him to exhale normally.

• While the patient is breathing, adjust the machine settings, as necessary, to match his inspiratory flow pattern. This may include changing the pressure setting or the inspiratory flow, sensitivity, or terminal flow setting, if present. If the patient is unable to maintain a tight seal with the mouthpiece, you may decrease the pressure until he appears comfortable and then gradually increase the pressure; apply a noseclip when using a mouthpiece; or, replace it with a mask.

• During treatment, take the patient's blood pressure and heart rate. *IPPB treatment increases intrathoracic pressure and may temporarily decrease cardiac output and venous return, resulting in tachycardia, hypotension, or headache. Monitoring also detects changes from a reaction to any bronchodilator used.* If you find a sudden change in blood pressure or an elevation in heart rate by 20 or more beats, stop the treatment and notify the doctor immediately.

• If the patient is tolerating the treatment, continue until the medication in the nebulizer is exhausted, usually after 15 to 20 minutes.

• After treatment, or as needed, have the patient expectorate into tissues or a specimen cup, or suction him as necessary. Listen to his breath sounds and compare them to the pretreatment assessment.

• Wash the mouthpiece or mask, the nebulizer, and all other accessories with a warm detergent solution. Rinse and dry them thoroughly *to prevent bacterial growth.* Store the tubing pieces in a clear plastic bag and replace them according to hospital policy, usually every day. Discard soiled tissues in a waste bag and dispose of it properly.

### Special considerations

If possible, avoid administering IPPB treatment immediately before or after a meal *because the treatment may induce nausea, and because a full stomach reduces lung expansion.*

Never give IPPB treatment without medication in the nebulizer *as this could dry the patient's airways and make secretions more difficult to mobilize.* If the purpose of treatment is to mobilize secretions, use a specimen cup to measure the secretions obtained.

If the patient wears dentures, leave them in place *to ensure a proper seal,* but remove them if they slide out of position. If the patient has an artificial airway, use a special adapter, such as mechanical ventilation tubing, to give IPPB treatments. When using a mask to administer treatments, allow the patient frequent rest periods and observe for gastric distention *because it's more likely to occur with a mask.*

If the patient's blood pressure is stable during the initial treatment, you may not need to check it during subsequent treatments unless he has a history of cardiovascular disease, hypotension, or sensitivity to any drug delivered in the treatment.

To assess the treatment appropriately, measure the volume delivered to the patient by IPPB to make sure he's getting a deep breath.

### Complications

Gastric insufflation may result from swallowed air, and occurs more commonly with a mask than with a mouthpiece. Dizziness can result from hyperventilation. The work of breathing can be increased, especially if the patient is uncomfortable with or frightened by the machine. Decreased blood pressure can result from decreased venous return, especially in the patient with hypovolemia or cardiovascular disease. Spontaneous pneumothorax may result from increased intrathoracic pressure; it's rare, but most likely to occur in patients with emphysematous blebs.

### Documentation

Record the date, time, and duration of

treatment; medication administered; pressure used; vital signs; breath sounds before and after treatment; amount of sputum produced; any complications and nursing actions taken; and the patient's tolerance of the procedure.

PATRICIA L. FUCHS, CRTT, RRT

# Chest Physiotherapy

*Chest physiotherapy includes postural drainage, chest percussion and vibration, and coughing and deep breathing exercises. Together, these techniques mobilize and eliminate secretions, reexpand lung tissue, and promote efficient use of respiratory muscles. Of critical importance to the bedridden patient, chest physiotherapy helps prevent or treat atelectasis and pneumonia—respiratory complications that can seriously impede recovery.*

*Postural drainage encourages peripheral pulmonary secretions to empty by gravity into the major bronchi or trachea, and involves sequential repositioning of the patient. Usually, secretions drain best from bronchi positioned perpendicularly to the floor. Lower and middle lobe bronchi usually empty best in the head-down position; upper lobe bronchi, in the head-up position.*

*Indications for chest physiotherapy include the presence of secretions (bronchitis, cystic fibrosis, bronchiectasis, pneumonia); restrictive pulmonary (neuromuscular) disease; chronic obstructive lung disease (emphysema); diseases associated with aspiration (cerebral palsy, muscular dystrophy); postoperative pain associated with impaired breathing (thoracic or abdominal incisions); and prolonged immobility.*

*Contraindications include active pulmonary bleeding with hemoptysis and the immediate posthemorrhage stage; fractured ribs or an unstable chest wall; lung contusions; pulmonary tuberculosis; untreated pneumothorax; acute asthma or bronchospasm; lung abscess or tumor; head injury; and recent myocardial infarction.*

## Equipment
Stethoscope □ pillows □ tilt or postural drainage table (if available) or adjustable hospital bed □ emesis basin □ tissues □ trash bag □ suction equipment, as needed □ equipment for oral care □ sterile specimen container (optional).

## Preparation of equipment
Gather equipment at the patient's bedside. Set up suction equipment, if needed, and test its function. *Suction prevents aspiration of mobilized secretions in the patient who has an ineffective cough reflex as a result of tracheostomy or cerebrovascular accident.*

## Essential steps
● Check the doctor's order for the location of the affected lung area and prescribed type and sequence of procedures.
● Explain the procedure to the patient, provide privacy, and wash your hands.
● Auscultate the patient's lungs *to determine baseline respiratory status.*

*To perform postural drainage:*
● Position the patient as ordered (see the illustrations on pages 472 to 473). The doctor determines position sequence after evaluating chest X-rays and auscultation findings. In generalized disease, drainage usually begins with the lower lobes, continues with the middle lobes, and ends with the upper lobes. In localized disease, drainage begins with the affected lobes, and then proceeds with the other lobes *to avoid spreading the disease to uninvolved areas.*
● Instruct the patient to remain in each position for 10 to 15 minutes. During this time, perform percussion and vibration, as ordered.

*To perform percussion:*
● Instruct the patient to breathe slowly and deeply, using the diaphragm, *to promote relaxation.*
● Hold your hands in a cupped shape, with fingers flexed and thumbs pressed tightly against your index fingers.

• Percuss each segment for 1 to 2 minutes by alternating your hands in a rhythmic manner. Listen for a hollow sound on percussion *to verify correct performance of the technique.*

*To perform vibration:*
• Ask the patient to inhale deeply and then exhale slowly through pursed lips.
• During exhalation, firmly press your hands flat against the chest wall. Tense the muscles of your arms and shoulders in an isometric contraction *to send fine vibrations through the chest wall.*
• Vibrate during five exhalations over each chest segment.

*After completion of postural drainage, percussion or vibration:*
• Instruct the patient to cough *to remove loosened secretions.* First, tell him to inhale deeply through his nose and then exhale in three short huffs. Then have him inhale deeply again and cough through a slightly open mouth. Three consecutive coughs are very effective. An effective cough sounds deep, low, and hollow; an ineffective one, high-pitched. Repeat the exercise two or three times.
• Provide oral hygiene *because secretions may taste foul or have a stale odor.*
• Auscultate the patient's lungs *to evaluate the effectiveness of therapy.*

*To perform deep breathing (diaphragmatic breathing):*
• Place the patient in a sitting position *to promote optimal lung expansion.* Then have him place one hand on the middle of his chest and the other on his abdomen just below his ribs *to feel the rise and fall of the diaphragm.*
• Instruct the patient to inhale slowly and deeply, pushing his abdomen out against his hand *to provide optimal distribution of air to the alveoli.*
• Instruct him to exhale through pursed lips, and to contract his abdomen. *Exhalation through pursed lips improves oxygen diffusion; encourages a slow, deep breathing pattern; and puts back pressure on the airways so that they stay open longer and expel a greater amount of stale air. Abdominal contraction pushes the diaphragm upward, exerts pressure on the lungs, and helps to empty*

*them.* If the patient has chronic obstructive pulmonary disease (COPD), causing chronic retention of carbon dioxide, diaphragmatic breathing and pursed-lip breathing are especially helpful.
• Instruct the patient to perform exercises for 1 minute and then to rest for 2 minutes. Gradually progress to a 10-minute exercise period four times daily.

## Special considerations
For optimal effectiveness as well as safety, modify chest physiotherapy according to the patient's condition. For example, administer supplemental oxygen to the hypoxic patient, or suction the patient with an ineffective cough reflex. If the patient weakens quickly during physiotherapy, divide therapy into shorter sessions, *because fatigue leads to shallow respirations and increased hypoxia.*

Maintain adequate hydration in the patient receiving chest physiotherapy *to help dilute secretions and promote easier mobilization.* Avoid performing postural drainage immediately before or within 1½ hours after meals *to avoid nausea and aspiration of food or vomitus.*

Any adjunct therapy—such as intermittent positive pressure breathing (IPPB), aerosol, or nebulizer—should precede chest physiotherapy.

Refrain from percussing over the spine, liver, kidneys, or spleen *to avoid injury to the spine or internal organs.* Also avoid performing percussion on bare skin or the female patient's breasts. Percuss over the patient's soft clothing (but not over buttons, snaps, or zippers), or place a thin towel over the chest wall. Remember to remove jewelry that might scratch or bruise the patient.

Explain coughing and deep breathing exercises preoperatively, so the patient can practice them when he's free of pain and better able to concentrate. Postoperatively, splint the patient's incision using your hands, or if possible, teach the patient to splint it himself *to minimize pain during coughing.*

## Complications
During postural drainage in head-down

## POSITIONING PATIENTS FOR BRONCHIAL DRAINAGE

To drain *the posterior basal segments of the lower lobes,* elevate the foot of the table 18″ (45 cm), or 30°, or change the elevation of the foot of the bed to simulate the table. Instruct the patient to lie on his abdomen with his head lowered. Then, position pillows as shown here. Percuss his lower ribs on both sides of his spine.

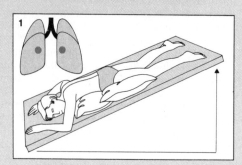

To drain *the lateral basal segments of the lower lobes,* elevate the foot of the table 18″ (45 cm), or 30°. Instruct the patient to lie on his abdomen with his head lowered and his upper leg flexed over a pillow for support. Then have him rotate a quarter turn upward. Percuss his lower ribs on the uppermost portion of his lateral chest wall.

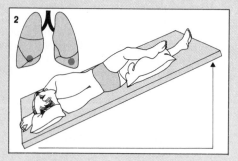

To drain *the anterior basal segments of the lower lobes,* elevate the foot of the table 18″ (45 cm), or 30°. Instruct the patient to lie on his side with his head lowered. Then, place pillows as shown here. Percuss with a slightly cupped hand over his lower ribs just beneath the axilla. *Note:* If an acutely ill patient experiences breathing difficulty in this position, adjust the angle of the bed or table to one he can tolerate. Then, begin percussion.

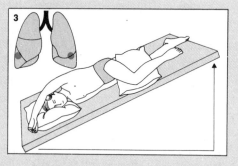

To drain *the superior segments of the lower lobes,* make sure the table is flat. Then, instruct the patient to lie on his abdomen, and place two pillows under his hips. Percuss on both sides of his spine at the lower tip of his scapulae.

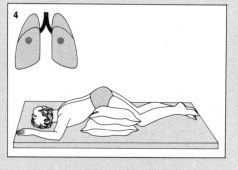

To drain *the medial and lateral segments of the right middle lobe,* elevate the foot of the table 14″ (35 cm), or 15°. Instruct the patient to lie on the left side with his head lowered and his knees flexed. Then, have him rotate a quarter turn backward. Place a pillow beneath him, as shown here. Percuss with your hand moderately cupped over the right nipple. In females cup your hand so its heel is under the armpit and your fingers extend forward beneath the patient's breast.

To drain *the superior and inferior segments of the lingular portion of the left upper lobe,* elevate the foot of the table 14″ (35 cm), or 15°. Have patient lie on right side with head lowered and knees flexed. Then have him rotate a quarter turn backward. Place a pillow behind him, from shoulders to hips. Percuss with your hand moderately cupped over his left nipple. In females, cup your hand so its heel is beneath the armpit and your fingers extend forward beneath the breast.

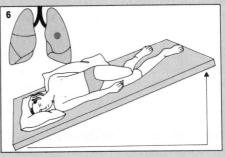

To drain *the anterior segments of the upper lobes,* make sure the table is flat. Instruct the patient to lie on his back with a pillow folded under his knees. Then, have him rotate slightly away from the side being drained. Percuss between his clavicle and nipple.

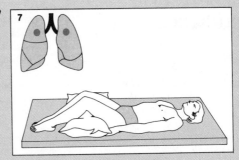

To drain *apical segment of right upper lobe and apical subsegment of apical-posterior segment of left upper lobe,* keep table flat. Have patient lean back on a pillow at a 30° angle against you. Percuss with your hand cupped between his clavicle and the top of each scapula.

To drain *posterior segment of right upper lobe and posterior subsegment of apical-posterior segment of left upper lobe,* keep table flat. Have patient lean over folded pillow at 30° angle. Stand behind him; percuss and clap his upper back on each side.

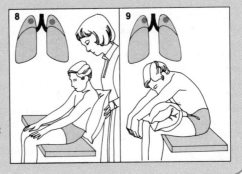

positions, pressure on the diaphragm by abdominal contents can impair respiratory excursion and lead to hypoxia or postural hypotension. Vigorous percussion or vibration can cause rib fracture, especially in the patient with osteoporosis. In an emphysematous patient with blebs, coughing can potentially lead to pneumothorax.

### Documentation

Record the date and time of chest physiotherapy; positions for secretion drainage and length of time each is maintained; chest segments percussed or vibrated; number of coughing and deep breathing exercises; color, amount, odor, and viscosity of secretions produced, and presence of any blood; schedule for chest physiotherapy; any complications and nursing actions taken; and the patient's tolerance of treatment.

CAROL ANN GRAMSE, RN, PhD

# Endotracheal Intubation

*Endotracheal intubation is the oral or nasal insertion of a flexible, cuffed tube through the larynx into the trachea. Performed by a doctor, anesthetist, respiratory therapist, or specially trained nurse, it provides short-term ventilation, usually for 48 to 72 hours, when supplemental oxygen is needed. It's used most frequently in emergency situations, such as respiratory arrest or obstruction; in pulmonary edema when a ventilator is indicated; and in the operating room just before surgery. The patient may be unconscious during intubation. Emergency intubations following verbal orders are common. In nonemergency situations, planning for intubation can include patient teaching and preparation.*

*Endotracheal intubation establishes and maintains a patent airway, provides optimum ventilation in emergency situations, prevents aspiration by sealing off the trachea from the digestive tract, and permits removal of tracheobronchial secretions in the patient who can't cough effectively.*

*Contraindications to endotracheal intubation include acute cervical spinal injury; severe local burns; epiglottitis; and laryngeal obstruction caused by tumor, infection, or vocal cord paralysis. Tracheostomy is the alternative treatment for such patients.*

### Equipment

Cuffed endotracheal tube in the appropriate size, plus spare tube in the same size □ 10-ml syringe □ oral airway or bite block for oral intubation □ lighted laryngoscope with handle and different-sized curved and straight blades □ sedative and local anesthetic spray such as cocaine or lidocaine for the conscious patient □ overbed or other table □ sterile drape □ sterile towel □ sterile gloves (two pairs if intubationist has an assistant) □ sterile water □ sterile basin □ sterile gauze sponge □ water-soluble lubricant □ adhesive or other strong tape □ compound benzoin tincture □ hemostat and small diameter tubing to cover hemostat's teeth □ stethoscope □ suction equipment □ manual resuscitation bag, such as an Ambu bag □ equipment and sterile swivel adapter for administering humidified oxygen □ optional: stylet and Magill forceps.

Laryngoscope blades range from infant to adult sizes. Endotracheal tubes are available in #18 to #30 French for children and #28 to #40 French for adults, with #32 French for adult females and #36 French for adult males the most common sizes.

### Preparation of equipment

Quickly gather supplies. (Many institutions have sterile intubation trays available that contain most of the necessary supplies.) Check the battery-operated light in the laryngoscope handle by snapping the proper-sized blade into place for intubation. If the light fails to flash immediately, replace the laryngoscope or the batteries, whichever is faster.

Using the sterile towel, establish a sterile field on the table. Using sterile technique, open sterile supplies, pour sterile water into the sterile basin, and squeeze water-soluble lubricant onto a sterile gauze sponge.

Put on sterile gloves. Attach the endotracheal tube and its accompanying adapter *so the tube can be attached to a manual resuscitation bag or a mechanical ventilator.* Attach the syringe to the port of the tube's exterior pilot cuff and inflate the cuff slowly, observing for uniform inflation. Check the cuff for leaks or submerge it in the sterile water and watch for air bubbles. Use the syringe *to completely deflate the cuff.* Cover the first inch (2.5 cm) of the tube's distal end with water-soluble lubricant *to ease insertion.* Use only a water-soluble lubricant, *because it's absorbed by mucous membranes.*

Cover the hemostat's teeth with small-diameter tubing *to prevent puncture of the endotracheal tube and air leakage from the cuff.* Use nonallergenic tape if the patient is allergic to adhesive tape, but avoid using paper tape, *which is not strong enough for this purpose.* If you're preparing equipment but not inserting the tube, determine if the intubationist prefers to use a stylet *to stiffen the endotracheal tube for insertion.* Lubricate the entire stylet *so it may be easily removed from the tube after intubation,* and insert it so its distal tip lies about ½" (1 cm) inside the endotracheal tube's distal end. *To prevent vocal cord trauma,* it must not extend beyond the tube. Prepare the humidified oxygen system and the suctioning equipment for immediate use. If the patient is in bed, remove the headboard *to provide easier access.*

### Essential steps
*To orally insert an endotracheal tube:*
● Check the doctor's written order, if one exists, and assess the patient's condition.
● Administer medication, as ordered, *to decrease respiratory secretions, induce amnesia or analgesia, and help calm and relax the conscious patient.* Remove dentures and bridges, if present.
● Administer oxygen until the tube is inserted, *to prevent hypoxia.* Then, suction the patient, if necessary, just before tube insertion *so the intubationist can visualize the structures of the pharynx and the vocal cords.*
● Help the patient into the supine position with the neck hyperextended *to straighten the pharynx and the trachea.*
● Spray local anesthetic into the posterior pharynx *to help quell the gag reflex and reduce patient discomfort during intubation.*
● Put on sterile gloves.
● Standing at the head of the bed, hold the patient's mouth open with your nondominant hand by crossing your index finger over your thumb *for greater leverage.*
● Grasp the laryngoscope handle in your dominant hand and gently slide the blade into the right side of the patient's mouth. Then center the blade, pushing the tongue to the left. Hold the patient's lower lip away from his teeth *to prevent the lip from being caught and traumatized.*
● Advance the blade, bringing the handle toward you, *to expose the epiglottis.* Avoid using the patient's teeth as a pivotal point for the laryngoscope *because you may damage them.*
● Continue to lift the laryngoscope handle toward you *to reveal the vocal cords.*
● Keeping the vocal cords in view, guide the endotracheal tube into the right side of the mouth and down along the laryngoscope blade into the vertical opening of the larynx between the vocal cords. Don't mistake the horizontal opening of the esophagus for the larynx. If the vocal cords are closed in spasm, wait a few seconds for them to relax, then guide the tube gently past them *to avoid trauma.*
● Advance the tube until the cuff disappears beyond the vocal cords. *Further insertion may occlude a major bronchus and precipitate lung collapse.*
● Holding the endotracheal tube in place, quickly remove the stylet, if present.
● Inflate the tube's cuff until resistance

## SECURING AN ENDOTRACHEAL TUBE: THREE METHODS

Before taping the tube in place, make sure the patient's face is clean, dry, and free of beard stubble. If possible, suction his mouth and dry off the tube just before taping. After taping, always check for bilateral breath sounds to ensure the tube hasn't been displaced by manipulation.

**1** Cut two 2″ (5-cm) strips and two 15″ (38-cm) strips of 1″ cloth adhesive tape. Then, cut a 13″ (33-cm) slit in one end of each 15″ strip (see illustration below).

**1**

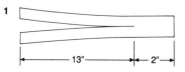

|← 13″ →|← 2″ →|

Apply benzoin to the patient's cheeks.* Place the 2″ strips on his cheeks, creating a new surface on which to anchor the tape securing the endotracheal tube. *When frequent retaping is necessary, this helps preserve the patient's skin's integrity.* If the patient's skin is excoriated or at risk, you can use OP-Site to protect the skin.

Apply benzoin to the tape on the patient's face and to the part of the tube where you will be applying the tape.

On the side of the mouth where the tube will be anchored, place the unslit end of a 15″ strip of tape on top of the tape on the patient's cheek. Just before taping, check the reference mark on the tube to ensure correct placement.

Wrap the top half of the tape around the tube twice, pulling the tape as tightly as possible. Then, directing the tape over the patient's upper lip, place the end of the tape on the patient's other cheek. Cut off any excess tape.

Use the lower half of the tape to secure an oral airway, if necessary (see illustra-

tion below). Or, twist the lower half of the tape around the tube twice and attach

**2**

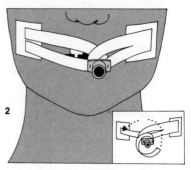

it to the original cheek (see illustration below). *Taping in opposite directions places equal traction on the tube.*

If you've taped in an oral airway or are

**3**

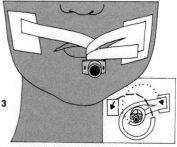

concerned about tube stability, apply the other 15″ strip of tape in the same manner as the first, starting on the other side of the patient's face. If the tape around the tube is too bulky, use only the upper part of the tape and cut off the lower part. If copious oral secretions are present, seal the tape by cutting a 1″ (2.5-cm) piece of paper tape, coating it with benzoin,

---

is felt. Once the patient is on the ventilator you'll use the minimal-leak technique to establish correct inflation of the cuff.

• Remove the laryngoscope and insert an oral airway or bite block *to prevent obstruction of airflow and puncture of the tube by the patient's teeth.*

• *To ensure proper tube placement,* feel the tube's tip for warm exhalations and listen for air movement. If the patient is

breathing spontaneously, observe for chest expansion and auscultate the chest for bilateral breath sounds. If he's unconscious or uncooperative, use a manual resuscitation bag and observe for upper chest movement. If the patient's stomach distends and belching occurs, the tube is in the esophagus. Immediately deflate the cuff, remove the tube, and repeat insertion, using another sterile tube *to prevent contamination of the trachea.*

and placing the paper tape over the adhesive tape.

**2** Cut one piece of 1″ cloth adhesive tape long enough to wrap around the patient's head and overlap in front. Then, cut an 8″ (20-cm) piece of tape and center it on the longer piece, sticky sides

**4**

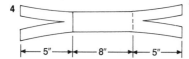

together. Next, cut a 5″ (12.5-cm) slit in each end (see illustration above).

Apply benzoin to the patient's cheeks and under his nose.*

**5**

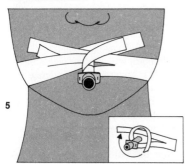

Place the top half of one end of the tape under the patient's nose and wrap the lower half around the endotracheal tube. Place the lower half of the other end of the tape under the patient's nose and wrap the top half around the tube (see illustration above).

**3** Cut a tracheostomy tie in two pieces (one a few inches longer than the other), and cut two 6″ (15-cm) pieces of 1″ cloth

adhesive tape. Then, cut a 2″ slit in one end of both pieces of tape. Fold the other end of the tape so the sticky sides are together and cut a small hole in it (see illustration below).

**6**

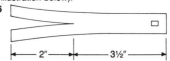

Apply benzoin to the part of the endotracheal tube that will be taped.

Wrap the slit ends of each piece of tape around the tube—one piece on each side. To secure the tape, overlap it.

Apply the free ends of the tape to both sides of the patient's face. Then, insert the tracheostomy ties through the holes on

**7**

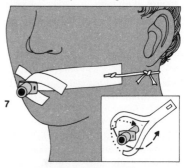

the ends of the tape and knot the ties (see illustration above).

Bring the longer tie behind the patient's neck and tie it to the shorter tie at one side of his neck. *Knotting the ties on the side prevents the patient from lying on the knot and getting a pressure sore.*

---

*Don't spray benzoin directly on the patient's face, because its vapors can be irritating if inhaled and can be harmful to the eyes.

---

● Auscultate bilaterally *to exclude the possibility of endobronchial intubation.* If you fail to hear breath sounds on both sides of the chest, you may have inserted the tube into one of the mainstem bronchi (usually the right one because of its wider angle at the bifurcation); such insertion occludes the other bronchus and lung and results in atelectasis on the obstructed side. Or the tube may be resting on the carina, resulting in dry secretions that obstruct both bronchi. (The patient's coughing and fighting the ventilator will alert you to the problem.) To correct these situations, deflate the cuff, withdraw the tube 1 to 2 mm, auscultate for bilateral breath sounds, and reinflate the cuff.

● Once you've confirmed correct tube placement, administer oxygen, and/or initiate mechanical ventilation, and provide suction.

• *To secure tube position,* apply compound benzoin tincture to each cheek and let it dry *for enhanced tape adhesion.* Tape the tube firmly *to reduce complications* (see *Securing an Endotracheal Tube: Three Methods,* pages 476 to 477). Inflate the cuff by the minimal-leak technique. Attach a 10-ml syringe to the port on the tube's exterior pilot cuff, and place a stethoscope on the side of the patient's neck. Inject small amounts of air with each breath until you hear no leak. Then aspirate 0.1 cc of air from the cuff *to create a minimal air leak.* Record the amount of air needed to inflate the cuff *for subsequent monitoring for tracheal dilation or erosion.*

• Clearly mark the tube's exit point from the mouth with pen or tape. *Periodic monitoring of this mark can reveal tube displacement.*

• Make sure a chest X-ray is taken *to verify tube position.*

• Place a swivel adapter between the tube and the humidified oxygen source *to allow for intermittent suctioning and to reduce tube tension.*

• Place the patient on his side with his head in a comfortable position *to avoid tube kinking and airway obstruction.*

• Auscultate both sides of the chest and check chest movement hourly *to ensure correct tube placement and full lung ventilation.* Give frequent oral care and position the endotracheal tube to avoid excessive pressure on the sides of the mouth *to prevent formation of pressure sores.*

• Suction secretions through the endotracheal tube at least every 1 to 2 hours *to clear secretions and prevent mucous plugs from obstructing the tube.*

## Special considerations

Remember that orotracheal intubation is preferred in emergencies because insertion is easier and faster than with nasotracheal intubation. However, exact tube placement is more difficult, and the tube must be well secured *to avoid kinking and prevent bronchial obstruction or extubation.* Orotracheal intubation is also poorly tolerated by the conscious patient because it stimulates salivation, coughing, and retching.

Recognize that nasotracheal intubation is preferred for elective insertion, particularly for the conscious patient, for long-term intubation, and for the patient with trismus or jaw fracture. Although nasotracheal intubation is more comfortable than oral intubation, it's also more difficult and time-consuming to perform. Because the tube passes blindly through the nasal cavity, the procedure causes greater tissue trauma, increased risk of infection since nasal bacteria are introduced into the trachea, and pressure necrosis of nasal mucosa. However, exact tube placement is easier and the risk of dislodgment lower. The cuff on the endotracheal tube maintains a closed system that permits positive-pressure ventilation and prevents aspiration of secretions and gastric contents.

Although low-pressure cuffs have significantly lowered the incidence of tracheal erosion and necrosis caused by cuff pressure on the tracheal wall, overinflation of a low-pressure cuff can negate this benefit. Use the minimal-leak technique to avoid these complications. Inflating the cuff a bit more to make a complete seal with the least amount of air is the next most desirable method. Always record the volume of air needed to inflate the cuff for either technique. A gradual increase in this volume indicates tracheal dilation or erosion. A sudden increase in volume indicates rupture of the cuff and requires immediate reintubation if the patient is being ventilated, or if he requires continuous cuff inflation to maintain a high concentration of delivered oxygen.

Low-pressure cuffs eliminate the need for hourly deflation of the cuff for 5 minutes; once every 8 hours is sufficient to detect overinflation, tracheal dilation, and erosion. Remember, although you may not be deflating the cuff hourly, secretions that must be removed by oropharyngeal suctioning may collect above the cuff. You can attach the cuff's inflation port to a manometer to obtain the cuff-pressure reading.

## Complications

Endotracheal intubation can result in apnea caused by reflex breath-holding; bronchospasm; aspiration of blood, secretions, or gastric contents; tooth damage or loss; and trauma to the lips, mouth, pharynx, or larynx. It can also result in vocal cord damage; laryngeal edema and erosion; and tracheal stenosis, erosion, and necrosis.

## Documentation

Record the date and time of the procedure; its indication and success or failure; tube type and size; cuff size, amount of inflation, and inflation technique; administration of medication; initiation of supplemental respiratory therapy; results of chest auscultation and results of the chest X-ray; any complications and nursing action taken; and the patient's reaction to the procedure.

KATHLEEN E. VIALL GALLAGHER, RN, MSN

# Endotracheal Tube Care

*After endotracheal tube insertion,, meticulous care is necessary to ensure airway patency and prevent complications until the patient can maintain independent ventilation. This care includes frequent assessment of airway status, maintenance of proper cuff pressure to prevent tissue ischemia and necrosis, careful repositioning of the tube to avoid traumatic manipulation, and constant monitoring for complications. Tube repositioning is done for patient comfort or if a chest X-ray shows improper placement. Move the tube from one side of the mouth to the other to prevent pressure sores.*

## Equipment

*For maintaining the airway:* stethoscope □ suction equipment.
*For repositioning the tube:* 10-ml syringe □ sterile 4″ x 4″ gauze sponges □ compound benzoin tincture □ adhesive or hypoallergenic tape □ suction equipment □ manual resuscitation bag (such as an Ambu bag) with mask in case of accidental extubation □ equipment for measuring cuff pressure (listed below).

*For measuring cuff pressure:* 10-ml syringe □ three-way stopcock □ blood pressure manometer with tubing □ I.V. tubing and connectors, as needed □ stethoscope □ suction equipment.

*For removing the tube:* suction equipment □ supplemental oxygen source with mask □ manual resuscitation bag (such as an Ambu bag) with mask □ equipment for reintubation.

## Preparation of equipment

*For repositioning the endotracheal tube:* Assemble all equipment at the patient's bedside. Using sterile technique, set up the suction equipment.

*For measuring cuff pressure:* Assemble all equipment at the patient's bedside. Attach the syringe to one stopcock port; then attach the tubing from the manometer to another port of the stopcock. Turn the stopcock dial in the "off" position to stopcock port when you'll be connecting the pilot balloon port.

*For extubation:* Assemble all equipment at the patient's bedside. Set up the suction and supplemental oxygen equipment. Have ready all equipment for emergency reintubation.

## Essential steps

• Explain the procedure to the patient even if he doesn't appear to be alert. Provide privacy and wash your hands thoroughly.

*To maintain airway patency:*

• Auscultate the patient's lungs hourly and at any sign of respiratory distress. If you detect an obstructed airway, determine the cause and treat accordingly. If secretions are obstructing the lumen of the tube, suction the secretions from the tube. If the tube has slipped from the trachea into the right or left mainstem bronchus, breath sounds will be absent over one lung. As ordered, obtain a chest X-ray to verify tube placement and, if necessary, reposition the tube. If the inflated cuff has obstructed the opening of the tube, deflate the cuff and notify the doctor.

*To reposition the endotracheal tube:*
• Obtain another nurse's assistance *to prevent accidental extubation if the patient coughs during the procedure.*
• Suction the endotracheal tube to remove any secretions, *which can irritate the bronchi and cause the patient to cough during the procedure. Coughing increases the risk of trauma to the vocal cords and the likelihood of dislodging the tube.* Then, if possible, guide a suction catheter along the tube's exterior *to remove any secretions that may have accumulated above the tube cuff, to help prevent aspiration of secretions during cuff deflation.*
• Deflate the cuff by attaching a 10-ml syringe to the pilot balloon port and aspirating air until you meet resistance and the pilot balloon deflates. Deflate the cuff *before* moving the tube, *because the cuff forms a seal within the trachea and movement of an inflated cuff can damage the tracheal wall and vocal cords.*
• *To prevent traumatic manipulation of the tube,* instruct the assisting nurse to hold it as you carefully untape it. When untaping the tube be sure to locate any identifying landmark, such as a number on the tube, or measure the distance from the patient's mouth to the top of the tube, *so you have a reference point when moving the tube.*
• Reposition the tube as necessary, noting new landmarks or measuring the length. Then, immediately reinflate the cuff. To do this, instruct the patient to inhale, and slowly inflate the cuff using a 10-ml syringe attached to the pilot balloon port. As you do this, use your stethoscope to listen to the patient's neck *to determine the presence of an air leak.* Once air leakage ceases, stop cuff inflation and, while still listening to the patient's neck with your stethoscope, aspirate a small amount of air until you detect a slight leak. *This creates a minimal air leak, which indicates that the cuff is in-*

*flated at the lowest pressure possible to create an adequate seal.* If the patient is attached to a respirator, aspirate to create a minimal air leak during the inspiratory phase of respiration *because the positive pressure of the respirator during inspiration will create a larger leak around the cuff.* Note the number of cubic centimeters of air required to inflate the cuff to achieve a minimal air leak.

Measure cuff pressure (as described below) and compare the reading with previous pressure readings *to prevent overinflation.* Then use benzoin and tape to secure the tube in place.
• Make sure the patient is comfortable and the airway is patent. Properly clean or dispose of equipment.

*To measure cuff pressure:*
• Once the cuff is inflated, measure its pressure at least every 8 hours *to avoid overinflation.*
• Make sure the tube exterior above the cuff is adequately suctioned *since pressure measurement can create a cuff leak, leading to aspiration of any secretions present.*
• Begin with an inflated cuff. Attach the stopcock, manometer, and syringe setup to the pilot balloon cuff port. Be sure the stopcock dial is in the "off" position to the pilot balloon port *to prevent air leakage during equipment setup.* Then, turn the stopcock dial in the "off" position to the syringe *to establish the connection between the cuff and the manometer.*
• Note the pressure reading on the manometer. If the patient is receiving positive-pressure ventilation, record the maximal pressure during inspiration. For spontaneous respiration, measure during exhalation. If the patient coughs, don't record the pressure *as the resulting reading is transient.*
• If you need to adjust the amount of air in the cuff, inflate or deflate the cuff by first turning the stopcock dial off to the manometer. *This establishes the connection between the cuff and the syringe.* Note any additional air required to inflate the cuff to achieve a minimal air leak.

If the pressure exceeds 15 mmHg, notify the doctor. You may need to change to a larger size tube, use higher inflation pressures, or permit a larger air leak. The doctor will decide.

• Disconnect the equipment from the pilot balloon port quickly, *to avoid creating a leak.*

• Make sure the patient is comfortable and the airway is patent. Properly clean or dispose of equipment.

*To remove the endotracheal tube:*

• When you're authorized to remove the tube, obtain another nurse's assistance *to prevent traumatic manipulation of the tube during untaping.*

• Use suction, as before, *to remove secretions both inside and outside the tube.*

• Attach a 10-ml syringe to the pilot balloon port and aspirate air until you meet resistance and the pilot balloon deflates.

• Elevate the head of the patient's bed to approximately 90°. Using a manual resuscitation bag (such as the Ambu bag), give the patient several deep breaths through the endotracheal tube *to hyperinflate his lungs, increase his oxygen reserve, and detect an air leak around the deflated cuff.* If you fail to detect a leak, notify the doctor immediately, and *do not* proceed with extubation. *Absence of an air leak may indicate marked tracheal edema and can result in total airway obstruction if the endotracheal tube is removed.*

• If you detect the proper air leak, untape the endotracheal tube.

• Insert a sterile suction catheter through the endotracheal tube. Then, apply suction and ask the patient to open his mouth fully and pretend to cry out. *This causes abduction of the vocal cords and reduces the risk of laryngeal trauma during withdrawal of the tube.*

• Simultaneously remove the endotracheal tube and the suction catheter in one smooth, outward and downward motion, following the natural curve of the patient's mouth. *Suctioning during extubation removes secretions retained at the end of the tube and prevents aspiration.*

• Give the patient supplemental oxygen.

For highest humidity, use a cool-mist large-volume nebulizer *to help decrease airway irritation, patient discomfort, and laryngeal edema.*

• Encourage the patient to cough, and remind him that his sore throat and hoarseness are to be expected and will gradually subside.

• Make sure the patient is comfortable and the airway is patent. Properly clean or dispose of equipment.

• After extubation, frequently auscultate the patient's lungs and watch for signs of respiratory distress. Be especially alert for stridor or other evidence of upper airway obstruction. If ordered, draw an arterial sample for blood-gas analysis.

## Special considerations

When repositioning a tube, be especially careful in patients with highly sensitive airways. Sedation or direct instillation of 2% lidocaine to numb the airway may be indicated in such patients. Remember, the lidocaine is absorbed systemically, so you must have a doctor's order for its use.

After extubation of a patient who's been intubated for an extended period of time, keep supplies necessary for reintubation readily available for at least 12 hours, or until you're sure the patient can tolerate extubation.

Never extubate a patient unless someone skilled at intubation is readily available.

When measuring cuff pressure, keep the connection between the measuring device and the pilot balloon port tight *to avoid an air leak that could compromise cuff pressure.* If you're using a stopcock, do not leave the manometer in the "off" position, *because if the syringe accidentally comes off, air exchange between the cuff and the atmosphere will result, allowing air to escape from the cuff and creating an air leak.*

Refrain from cutting the pilot balloon to deflate the cuff. However, if you inadvertently cut it, immediately call the person responsible for intubation in your institution, who will remove the damaged endotracheal tube and replace it with one that's intact. Don't remove the tube yourself before assistance arrives, *because a tube with an air leak is better than no assured airway.*

## Complications

Trauma to the larynx or trachea may result from manipulation of the tube, accidental extubation, or slippage of the tube into the right bronchus.

Aspiration of upper airway secretions, underventilation, or coughing spasms may occur if a leak is created during cuff pressure measurement. Airway obstruction, from marked tracheal edema, and ventilatory failure are the gravest possible complications of extubation.

## Documentation

After tube repositioning, record the date and time of the procedure; reason for repositioning, such as malposition shown by chest X-ray or prevention of pressure sores around the mouth; new tube position; total amount of air in the cuff after the procedure; any complications and the nursing action taken; and the patient's tolerance of the procedure.

After cuff pressure measurement, record the date and time of the procedure; cuff pressure, noting spontaneous or positive-pressure breathing; total amount of air in the cuff after the procedure; any complications and the nursing action taken; and the patient's tolerance of the procedure.

After extubation, record the date and time of extubation; presence or absence of stridor or other signs of upper airway edema; type of supplemental oxygen administered; any complications and required subsequent therapy; and the patient's tolerance of the procedure.

PATRICIA L. FUCHS, CRTT, RRT

# Tracheostomy Care

*A tracheostomy is the surgical creation of an external opening into the trachea. It provides and maintains a patent airway, prevents the unconscious or paralyzed patient from aspirating food or secretions, allows removal of tracheobronchial secretions from the patient unable to cough, replaces an endotracheal tube, and permits the use of positive-pressure ventilation.*

*When laryngectomy accompanies a tracheostomy, a laryngectomy tube—a shorter version of a tracheostomy tube—may be inserted by the doctor. In addition, the patient's trachea is sutured to the skin surface. Consequently, with a laryngectomy, accidental tube expulsion doesn't precipitate immediate closure of the tracheal opening. Once healing occurs, the patient has a permanent neck stoma through which respiration takes place. Whether a tracheostomy is performed in an emergency situation or after careful preparation, as a permanent measure or as temporary therapy, postprocedure patient care has the same purposes: to keep the tracheostomy tube free of mucus buildup to ensure airway patency, to maintain mucous membrane and skin integrity, to prevent infection, and to provide psychological support.*

*Tracheostomy care is performed using sterile technique to prevent infection, especially until the stoma has healed (usually 4 days). It may be given as frequently as every ½ hour immediately following tracheotomy, but should never be suspended for more than 8 hours. If the patient will be discharged with a tracheostomy, care measures include teaching him at-home tracheostomy care using clean technique.*

## Equipment

*For sterile single-cannula care:* waterproof trash bag □ two sterile containers □ sterile normal saline solution □ hydrogen peroxide □ sterile gloves □ sterile 4″ x 4″ gauze sponges □ sterile cotton-tipped applicators □ sterile 4″ x 4″ gauze sponge or prepackaged sterile tracheostomy dressing □ equipment and supplies for suctioning and for mouth care □ materials as needed for cuff procedures and changing tracheostomy ties.

*For sterile double-cannula care:* all of the preceding equipment plus sterile forceps □ sterile nylon brush □ sterile 6" (15-cm) pipe cleaners □ a third sterile solution container □ sterile storage container (for the ventilator patient's spare inner cannula).

*For routine tracheostomy care:* Once the stoma has healed, the same sterile solutions and supplies are needed with the exception of sterile gloves. *Strict sterile technique isn't mandatory because the risk of infection is greatly reduced.*

*For emergency tracheostomy care:* sterile tracheal dilator or sterile hemostat □ sterile obturator that fits the tracheostomy tube in use □ extra sterile tracheostomy tube and obturator in appropriate size, plus tube and obturator one size smaller □ suction equipment and supplies. Keep these supplies in full view in the patient's room at all times for easy access in case of emergency. An emergency sterile tracheostomy tube in a sterile wrapper is often taped to the head of the patient's bed for easy access in an emergency.

*For changing tracheostomy ties:* 30" (75-cm) tracheostomy twill tape □ bandage scissors □ hemostat □ sterile glove(s.)

*For cuff procedures:* 5- or 10-ml syringe □ stethoscope □ covered hemostat.

Prepackaged commercial tracheostomy-care sets are readily available.

Three types of tracheostomy tube—metal, plastic, and rubber—are available in various sizes to accommodate infant through adult patients. The metal tube, used mainly for the long-term tracheostomy patient, has three parts—an outer cannula, an inner cannula, and an obturator that serves as a guide for inserting the outer cannula. Some plastic tubes have the same three parts. Most, however, consist of the obturator and one single-walled tube that doesn't require removal for cleaning, because encrustations are less likely to form on nonmetal materials. The red rubber James tube, which doesn't have an inner cannula, is infrequently used because its surface may become roughened

with use and its sterility is difficult to guarantee.

Many tracheostomy tubes have a cuff that's inflated after tube placement. The cuff creates a tracheal seal that blocks aspiration and prevents air leakage, an important consideration immediately after tracheostomy or during positive-pressure ventilation. Some tubes have two cuffs, allowing alternate inflation to reduce tracheal irritation. Cuffs are also commercially available for use on cuffless tracheostomy tubes.

## Preparation of equipment

Wash your hands and assemble all equipment and supplies in the patient's room. Check the expiration date on each sterile package and inspect for tears. Open the waterproof trash bag and place it adjacent to your working area *to avoid reaching across the sterile field or the patient's stoma when disposing of soiled articles.* Form a cuff by turning down the top of the trash bag *to ensure a wide opening and prevent contamination of instruments or glove(s) caused by touching the bag's edge.* Wash your hands thoroughly. Establish a sterile field near the patient's bed (usually on the overbed table), and place equipment and supplies on it. For cleansing, pour sterile normal saline solution, hydrogen peroxide, or a mixture of equal parts of both solutions into one of the sterile containers; then pour sterile normal saline solution into a second container for rinsing. For double-cannula care, you may use the third basin to hold your gauze sponges and swabs saturated with cleansing solution. Prepare new tracheostomy ties from twill tape, if indicated. If using a spare sterile inner cannula, unscrew the cap from the top of the sterile container, but do not remove it.

## Essential steps

● Assess the patient's condition.
● Explain the procedure to the patient, even if he is unresponsive. Provide privacy.
● Unless contraindicated, place the pa-

tient in semi-Fowler's position *to decrease abdominal pressure on the diaphragm, thereby promoting lung expansion.*
- Remove any humidification or ventilation device.
- Using sterile technique, suction the entire length of the tracheostomy tube *to clear the airway of any secretions that may hinder oxygenation.* Follow appropriate suctioning principles.
- Reconnect the patient to the humidifier or ventilator, if necessary.
- Remove and discard the patient's tracheostomy dressing.
- Put a sterile glove on your dominant hand.

*To cleanse a single-cannula tube:*
- With your gloved hand, wet a sterile 4″ x 4″ gauze sponge with the cleansing solution. Squeeze out excess liquid *to prevent accidental aspiration.* Then, wipe the patient's neck under the tracheostomy tube flanges and twill tapes.
- Saturate a second sponge and wipe until the skin surrounding the tracheostomy is cleansed. Use additional sponges or cotton-tipped applicators to cleanse the stoma site and the tube's flanges. Wipe only once with each sponge and then discard it *to prevent contamination of a clean area with a soiled sponge.*
- If encrustations resist removal, cleanse with a sterile cotton-tipped applicator saturated in hydrogen peroxide and pressed to remove excess liquid. Use each applicator only once and wipe gently, *especially if the surrounding skin is excoriated.*
- Rinse debris and any peroxide with one or more sterile 4″ x 4″ gauze sponges dampened in sterile normal saline solution. Dry the area thoroughly with additional sterile gauze sponges. Remove and discard your glove.

*To cleanse a double-cannula tube:*
- With your ungloved hand, disconnect the ventilator and/or humidification device. Then, with the same hand, unlock the tracheostomy tube's inner cannula. Next, with your ungloved hand, remove the inner cannula.

- Place the inner cannula in the container of hydrogen peroxide, and allow it to soak *to remove encrustations.*
- For the ventilator patient, use your ungloved hand to remove the lid from the container with the spare inner cannula. Pick up the cannula with your gloved hand and insert it into the outer cannula of the patient's tracheostomy tube. Use your ungloved hand to reconnect the patient to the ventilator.
- Put a sterile glove on your nondominant hand and cleanse the skin, stoma, and tracheostomy tube flanges with the presoaked gauze sponges and cotton-tipped applicators, as previously described.
- Pick up the inner cannula from the soaking container. Using the sterile nylon brush, scrub the cannula. If the brush doesn't slide easily into the cannula, use a sterile pipe cleaner.
- Immerse the cannula in the container of sterile normal saline solution, and agitate it for about 10 seconds *to rinse it thoroughly and provide a thin film of solution to lubricate it for replacement.*
- Hold the cannula up to the light and inspect it for cleanliness. If encrustations are still present, repeat the cleaning process. If not, grasp the clean cannula and tap it gently against the inside edge of the sterile container *to remove excess liquid, preventing possible aspiration by the patient.* Use three sterile pipe cleaners twisted together, *to dry the inside of the cannula.* Refrain from drying its outer surface *because a thin film of moisture acts as a lubricant during insertion.*
- If the patient is not on a ventilator, gently reinsert the inner cannula into the patient's tracheostomy tube. Lock it in place and then pull on it gently *to ensure secure positioning.* For patients on a ventilator, place the cleaned inner cannula in the sterile storage container.
- Apply a new sterile tracheostomy dressing. If you're not using a commercially prepared dressing, avoid using cotton-filled gauze or a trimmed gauze sponge *because aspiration of lint*

# TRACHEOSTOMY TUBES: ADVANTAGES AND DISADVANTAGES

**PLASTIC**

**METAL**

## Uncuffed tracheostomy tubes

**Advantages**
- Reduces risk of tracheal damage
- Recommended for children because they don't require a cuff
- Permits free flow of air around tube and through larynx

**Disadvantages**
- In adults, lack of cuff pressure increases risk of aspiration and prevents mechanical ventilation.

## Foam-cuffed (Kamen-Wilkinson or Bivona)

**Advantages:**
- Disposable
- Cuff bonded to tube
- Maintains close to atmospheric pressure in tracheostomy tube
- Causes minimal tissue necrosis
- Does *not* require inflating and deflating

**Disadvantages:**
- Those unfamiliar with this device may inject air into cuff or clamp it off, and this prevents proper function.
- Air *must* be aspirated from the cuff to insert this tube. If not, tracheal injury may occur.

## Cuffed

**Advantages**
- Available in small sizes for infants
- Removable inner cannula simplifies cleaning and sterilization.

**Disadvantages**
- Cuff tears easily during removal.
- Cuff slips off easily.
- Inner cannula dislodges easily.
- May need adapter to ventilate patient

## Cuffed

### High pressure

**Advantages**
- Disposable
- Cuff bonded to tube

**Disadvantages**
- More likely to cause tracheal damage or tissue necrosis than low-pressure cuff

### Low-pressure

**Advantages**
- Disposable
- Cuff bonded to tube
- Distributes cuff pressure evenly; no need to deflate periodically to reduce pressure

**Disadvantages**
- More costly than other tubes

and fibers can cause a tracheal abscess. Instead, open a sterile 4″ x 4″ gauze pad to its full length. Fold it in half lengthwise to form a long, thin rectangle. With the folded edge facing downward, find the center of this edge; then fold each side straight up from this point to create a U-shaped pad. Slip this pad under the flanges of the tracheostomy tube so that the pad's flaps encircle and cushion the tube.

• Remove and discard your gloves. Replace and tighten the lid on the container with the cleaned inner cannula, if applicable.

*To conclude tracheostomy care:*
• Replace the tracheostomy ties if they're soiled, loose, or too tight (see below).
• Replace any humidification device.
• Give oral care, as needed, *because the oral cavity can become dry and malodorous or develop sores due to encrusted secretions.*
• Make sure that the patient is comfortable and that he can easily reach the call signal and communication aids.
• Observe soiled dressings and any suctioned secretions for amount, color, consistency, and odor.
• Properly clean or dispose of all equipment, supplies, solutions, and trash, according to hospital policy.
• Replenish any supplies used from the extra tracheostomy-care set, and make sure all necessary supplies are readily available at the bedside.
• Repeat the procedure at least once every 8 hours, or as needed. Change the dressing as often as necessary, whether or not you also perform the entire cleansing procedure, *because a dressing wet with exudate or secretions predisposes the patient to skin excoriation, breakdown, and infection.*

*To change tracheostomy ties:*
• Obtain assistance from another nurse or a respiratory therapist, *because of the risk of accidental tube expulsion during this procedure. Patient movement or coughing can dislodge the tube.*
• Wash your hands thoroughly.
• If you're not using commercially packaged tracheostomy ties, prepare

new ties from a 30″ (75-cm) length of twill tape by folding one end back 1″ (2.5 cm) on itself. Then, with the bandage scissors, cut a ½″ (1.3-cm) slit down the center of the tape from the folded edge. Or, you may fold the end of the tape and cut a small hole at each end of the tie.
• Prepare the other end of the tape in the same way.
• Hold both ends together and, using scissors, cut the resulting circle of tape so that one piece is approximately 10″ (25 cm) long, and the other is about 20″ (50 cm) long.
• Assist the patient into semi-Fowler's position, if possible.
• After your assistant puts on sterile gloves, instruct her to hold the tracheostomy tube in place *to prevent its ejection during replacement of the ties.* However, if you must perform the procedure without assistance, fasten the clean ties in place before removing the old ties *to prevent tube expulsion.*
• With the assistant's gloved fingers holding the tracheostomy tube in place, cut the soiled tracheostomy ties with the bandage scissors or untie them and discard the ties.
• Thread the slit end of one new tie a short distance through the eye of one tracheostomy tube flange from the underside; use the hemostat, if necessary, to pull the tie through. Then, thread the other end of the tie completely through the slit end, and pull it taut so it loops firmly through the tube's flange. *This avoids knots that can cause discomfort and predispose to tissue irritation, pressure, and necrosis at the patient's throat.*
• Fasten the second tie to the opposite flange in the same manner.
• Instruct the patient to flex his neck while you bring the ties around the neck to the *side* and tie them together. *Flexion produces the same neck circumference as coughing and helps prevent an overly tight tie.* Instruct your assistant to place one finger under the tapes as you tie them *to ensure that they're tight enough to avoid slippage but loose*

*enough to prevent choking or jugular vein constriction.* Place the closure on the side *to allow easy access and prevent pressure necrosis at the back of the neck when the patient is recumbent.*
• After securing the ties, cut off the excess tape with the scissors and instruct your assistant to release the tracheostomy tube.
• Make sure the patient is comfortable and can easily reach the call signal and communication aids.
• Frequently check tracheostomy-tie tension on the neck, particularly for the patient with trauma, radical neck dissection, or cardiac failure, *because neck diameter can increase from swelling and cause constriction;* and for the neonatal or restless patient, *because ties can become loosened.*
 *To deflate and inflate a tracheostomy cuff:*
• Check the doctor's order to determine the prescribed schedule for this procedure. *Deflation and inflation are usually ordered at regular intervals, but interval spacing, length of deflation time, and even the need to use this procedure at all when using low-pressure cuffs are controversial.*
• Read the cuff manufacturer's instructions, *because cuff types and procedures vary widely.*
• Assess the patient's condition, explain the procedure to him, and reassure him. Wash your hands thoroughly.
• Help the patient into semi-Fowler's position, if possible, or place him in a supine position, *so secretions above the cuff site will be pushed up into the mouth if the patient is receiving positive-pressure ventilation.*
• Suction the oropharyngeal cavity *to prevent any pooled secretions from descending into the trachea after cuff deflation, causing irritation, abscess, or infection.*
• Release the covered hemostat clamping the cuff inflation tubing, if a hemostat is present.
• Then, insert a 5- or 10-ml syringe into the cuff pilot balloon and very slowly

withdraw all air from the cuff. Leave the syringe attached to the tubing *for later reinflation of the cuff. Slow deflation allows positive lung pressure to push secretions upward from the bronchi. Cuff deflation may also stimulate the patient's cough reflex, producing additional secretions.*
• Remove any ventilation device. Suction the lower airway through any existing tube *to remove all secretions.* Then, return the patient to the ventilation device.
• If ordered, maintain cuff deflation for the prescribed period of time while the patient is off the ventilator, usually 1 to 5 minutes. (Note: With low-pressure cuffs and the minimal-leak technique, it's usually not necessary to maintain cuff deflation.) Observe the patient for adequate ventilation, and suction as necessary. If the patient experiences breathing difficulty, immediately reinflate the cuff by depressing the syringe plunger very slowly. Inject the least amount of air necessary, usually 2 to 5 ml, to achieve an adequate tracheal seal. Keep track of how much air is aspirated and replaced.
• Use a stethoscope during cuff inflation *to help gauge the proper inflation point.* Using the minimal-leak technique, stop inflating when you hear little or no leak from the positive-pressure ventilation. If you're inflating the cuff using cuff-pressure measurement, be careful not to exceed 15 to 20 mmHg. A minimal air leak may facilitate secretion removal from the larynx, whereas overinflation can cause tracheal pressure, dilation, ulceration, fistula formation, and necrosis. Underinflation may permit aspiration of blood, food, or secretions and can cause inadequate ventilation.
• If the tubing doesn't have a one-way valve at the end, clamp the inflation line with a hemostat, covered to protect the tubing, and remove the syringe.
• Check for a leak-free cuff seal. Even with minimal cuff inflation, you should feel no air coming from the patient's mouth, nose, or tracheostomy site, and

a conscious patient shouldn't be able to speak.

• Be alert for air leaks from the cuff itself. Suspect a leak if injection fails to inflate the cuff or increase cuff pressure, if you're unable to inject the amount of air you withdrew, if the patient can speak, if ventilation fails to maintain adequate respiratory movement with pressures or volumes previously considered adequate, and if air escapes during the ventilator's inspiratory cycle.

• Note the exact amount of air used to inflate the cuff *to prevent overinflation in subsequent cuff procedures, and to detect tracheal malacia if more air is consistently needed.*

• Make sure the patient is comfortable and can easily reach the call signal and communication aids.

• Properly clean or dispose of all equipment, supplies, and trash, according to hospital policy.

• Replenish any used supplies and make sure all necessary emergency supplies are at bedside.

• Measure cuff pressure at least once every 8 hours *to avoid overinflation.* Be sure the patient is in the same position for each cuff-pressure reading, *because a change in position can alter the pressure needed to achieve an adequate seal.*

## Special considerations

For immediate use in an emergency, always have ready the following: all equipment and supplies for suctioning, *since the patient may need his airway cleared at any time;* the sterile obturator originally used to insert the patient's tracheostomy tube, *for quick reinsertion if the tube is expelled;* an additional sterile tracheostomy tube (with obturator) of the size currently being used, *to replace a contaminated or expelled tube;* and a spare sterile inner cannula, *to replace a contaminated or expelled inner cannula.* Additional emergency equipment (optional): sterile tracheostomy tube (with obturator) one size smaller than that

currently being used, *to replace an expelled tube when the trachea immediately begins to close, making difficult the insertion of a tube of the original size;* a sterile tracheal dilator or sterile hemostat, *to maintain an open airway before insertion of a new tracheostomy tube.*

Consult the doctor before an emergency about the first-aid measures you can use for your tracheostomy patient. Follow hospital policy regarding procedure if a tracheostomy tube is expelled or if the outer cannula becomes blocked. If the patient's breathing is obstructed—for example, when the tube is blocked with mucus that can't be removed by suctioning or by withdrawing the inner cannula—call the appropriate code and provide manual resuscitation with a manual resuscitation bag, such as an Ambu bag, or reconnect the patient to the ventilator. Or, try to maintain ventilation while someone else calls the doctor to change the tube immediately. Refrain from removing the tracheostomy tube entirely, *because this may completely shut off the airway.* Similarly, refrain from attempting to reinsert an expelled tracheostomy tube yourself *because of the risk of tracheal trauma, perforation, compression, and asphyxiation.* Reassure the patient until the doctor arrives (in such a code or emergency as this it's usually a minute or less). Follow the same procedure for the patient who accidentally expels a tracheostomy tube. If the patient is being discharged with a tracheostomy, start self-care teaching as soon as he's receptive. If he's being discharged with suction equipment (a few patients are), make sure he and his family feel knowledgeable and comfortable about using this equipment.

Refrain from changing tracheostomy ties unnecessarily during the immediate postoperative period before the stoma track is well formed (usually 4 days) *to avoid accidental dislodgment and expulsion of the tube.* Unless secretions or drainage is a problem, ties can be changed once a day.

Refrain from changing a single-cannula tracheostomy tube or the outer cannula of a double-cannula tube. Because of the risk of tracheal complications, the doctor usually changes the cannula, with the frequency of change depending on the patient's condition (once a week or every other week is usual). For patients going home with a metal tracheostomy tube, the usual procedure is to teach the patient to change the tube and clean it daily.

If the patient's neck or stoma is excoriated or infected, apply a water-soluble topical lubricant or antibiotic cream as ordered. Remember not to use a powder or an oil-based substance on or around a stoma *because aspiration can cause infection and abscess.*

Regularly replace all equipment, including solutions, according to hospital policy, *to reduce the risk of nosocomial infections.*

### Complications

The following complications can occur within the first 48 hours after tracheostomy tube insertion: hemorrhage at the operative site, causing drowning; bleeding or edema within the tracheal tissue, causing airway obstruction; aspiration of secretions, resulting in pneumonia; introduction of air into the pleural cavity, causing pneumothorax; hypoxia, acidosis, or sudden electrolyte shifts, triggering cardiac arrest; and introduction of air into surrounding tissues, causing subcutaneous emphysema.

After the first 48 hours, infection at any site distal to and including the stoma can lead to pneumonia from aspirated secretions. Also, secretions can collect under dressings and twill tape, producing skin excoriation and infection. Hardened mucus or a slipped cuff can occlude the cannula opening and obstruct the airway. Tube displacement can stimulate the cough reflex, if the tip rests on the carina, or cause blood vessel erosion and hemorrhage. Just the presence of the tube or cuff pressure can produce tracheal erosion and necrosis.

### Documentation

Record the date and time of the procedure; type of procedure; the amount, consistency, color, and odor of any dressing or suctioned secretions; stomal and skin condition; the patient's respiratory status; change of the tracheostomy tube by the doctor; the duration of any cuff deflation; the amount of any cuff inflation; and cuff pressure readings and specific body position. Note any complications and the nursing action taken; any patient or family teaching and their comprehension and progress; and the patient's tolerance of the treatment.

PATRICIA L. FUCHS, CRTT, RRT

# Tracheal Suction

*Tracheal suction is the removal of secretions from the trachea or bronchi by means of a suction catheter inserted through the mouth, nose, or tracheal stoma, or tracheostomy or endotracheal tube. This procedure helps maintain a patent airway to promote optimal exchange of oxygen and carbon dioxide into and out of the lungs and to prevent pneumonia resulting from the collection of secretions.*

*Laryngospasm and bronchospasm contraindicate this procedure. Nasopharyngeal bleeding, such as that occurring after tonsillectomy, and any local spinal fluid leak contraindicate the nasal approach. Suctioning should be performed cautiously in a patient with a recent tracheostomy, other tracheal or upper respiratory surgery, anticoagulant therapy, or blood dyscrasia, since bleeding is more likely to occur.*

### Equipment

Oxygen source (wall or portable unit, or manual resuscitation bag, such as the

Ambu bag), if applicable □ wall or portable suction apparatus □ collection container □ connecting tube □ Y-connector (if the catheter has no control valve) □ 1-liter bottle of sterile normal saline solution □ sterile suction catheters (usually #12 to #14 French for adults) □ sterile solution container □ sterile glove □ equipment for tracheostomy care and/or mouth care □ waterproof trash bag □ sterile water-soluble lubricant (for nasal insertion) □ optional: sterile towel, 5-ml syringe, 20G needle, vial of sterile normal saline solution.

Various disposable catheters and sets containing catheter, glove, and solution container are commercially available. Normal saline solution for instillation is available in a commercially prepared, plastic 3-ml or 5-ml container.

### Preparation of equipment

Choose the appropriate-sized suction catheter. The diameter should be no larger than half the inside diameter of any tracheostomy or endotracheal tube. Set up the waterproof trash bag. Place the equipment on the patient's overbed table or bedside stand. Position the table or stand on your preferred side of the bed *to facilitate suctioning.* Attach the collection container to the suction unit and the connecting tube to the collection container. If the catheter doesn't have a control valve, connect the tail of the Y-connector to the connecting tubing.

### Essential steps

• Check the doctor's order regarding specifics of suctioning.

• Provide privacy and wash your hands.

• Explain the procedure to the patient, even if he is unresponsive. Tell him that suctioning usually causes transient coughing or gagging, but that coughing is helpful for removal of secretions. If the patient has been suctioned previously, summarize the reasons for suctioning. Continue to reassure the patient throughout the procedure *to minimize anxiety and promote relaxation.*

• Auscultate the patient's lungs bilaterally and take vital signs, if the patient's condition warrants, *to serve as baseline data.*

• Unless contraindicated, place the conscious patient in the semi-Fowler's position *to promote lung expansion and productive coughing.* Place the unconscious patient in the supine position with his head turned toward you; *the supine position helps negate gravitational influence and allows easier aspiration of secretions, while turning the head facilitates catheter insertion.*

• Have the patient cough and breathe slowly and deeply several times, if possible, before you begin to suction. *Coughing helps loosen secretions and may reduce the amount of suctioning, whereas deep breathing helps to minimize or prevent hypoxia.*

• If the patient has an artificial airway, hyperoxygenate his lungs just before suctioning, unless contraindicated. Hyperoxygenate with 100% oxygen, using the sigh mode on the ventilator or a manual resuscitation bag (such as the Ambu bag) for 1 to 2 minutes *to help prevent hypoxia.* If you have an assistant for the procedure, the assistant can manage the patient's oxygen needs while you perform the suctioning.

• Remove the top of the normal saline solution bottle. If you're using an unopened bottle, label it with the date, time, and purpose of the procedure.

• Open the package containing the sterile solution container and, using sterile technique, pour the normal saline solution into the container.

• Place a sterile towel over the patient's chest, if desired, *to provide an additional sterile area.*

• Loosen the adapter on the endotracheal tube prior to gloving *to make it easier to remove with one hand later in the procedure when you are gloved.*

• Open the catheter package (if the catheter is wrapped separately).

• Place the sterile glove on your dominant hand and remove the sterile catheter from its wrapper. Keep it coiled *so it can't touch a nonsterile object.* Attach the sterile catheter to the Y-connector or the connecting tubing. Hold the catheter in your gloved hand and the Y-connector and connecting tubing in your ungloved hand.

• Turn on the suction, and if the unit requires, set the suction pressure according to hospital policy. Generally, the pressure may be set at 100 to 120 mmHg for adults, or 50 to 75 mmHg for infants and children.

• Dip the catheter tip in the sterile saline solution *to lubricate the outside of the catheter and reduce tissue trauma during insertion.*

• With the catheter tip in the sterile saline solution, occlude the control valve with the thumb of your ungloved hand and suction a small amount of solution through the catheter *to test the suction equipment and to lubricate the inside of the catheter to facilitate passage of secretions through it.* For nasal insertion of the catheter, use a sterile, water-soluble lubricant on the tip *to reduce tissue trauma during insertion.*

• Disconnect the oxygen from the patient, if applicable.

• With the catheter's control valve uncovered, gently insert the catheter deep into the trachea (and into a bronchus if indicated) through the patient's tracheostomy tube, stoma, endotracheal tube, mouth, or nostril. Do not apply suction during insertion *to avoid oxygen loss and tissue trauma.*

• Apply suction for 5 to 10 seconds by placing the thumb of your ungloved hand over the control valve. Simultaneously, use your gloved hand to withdraw the catheter as you roll it between your thumb and forefinger. *This rotating motion prevents the catheter from grabbing tissue as it exits, and therefore avoids tissue trauma.* If the catheter does adhere, stop the suction immediately *to protect tracheal tissue.* Even if the patient shows no signs of distress, never suction for more than 5 to 10 seconds at a time *to prevent hypoxia.*

• Withdraw the catheter completely and uncover the control valve to stop the suction.

• If applicable, resume oxygen delivery

after suctioning by reconnecting the source of oxygen or ventilation, and hyperoxygenate the patient's lungs before continuing (unless contraindicated) *to prevent or relieve hypoxia.*

• Observe the patient and allow him to rest for a few minutes before the next suctioning. The timing of each suctioning and the length of each rest period is determined by his tolerance for the procedure and the absence of complications.

• Repeat the above procedure until breathing becomes quiet and relatively effortless.

• If secretions are thick, clear the catheter periodically by dipping the tip in the sterile saline solution and applying suction.

• If the patient's heart rate and rhythm are being monitored, observe for arrhythmias. Should they occur, stop suctioning and ventilate the patient.

• After the procedure is over, hyperoxygenate the patient's lungs for 1 to 2 minutes (unless contraindicated) *to relieve hypoxia and promote relaxation.*

 Remember to decrease the oxygen flow rate to the ordered setting following hyperoxygenation.

• Clear the connecting tubing by aspirating the remaining sterile saline solution. Then, turn off the suction and disconnect the catheter from the connecting tubing. Discard the glove and the catheter in the waterproof trash bag.

• Auscultate lungs bilaterally and take vital signs, if the patient's condition warrants, *to assess the procedure's effectiveness.*

• Perform tracheostomy care and/or mouth care, as indicated.

• Observe the amount, color, and consistency of suctioned secretions. Wash your hands. Replace all used items at the patient's bedside *for possible emergency use.*

## Special considerations

If the patient has an endotracheal or tracheostomy tube, it's not necessary to deflate the cuff for suctioning. Suction the tube first, and then suction above the cuff. If you're deflating the cuff routinely as ordered, however, first suction the secretions above the cuff, and then change the catheter and glove before suctioning the lower airway *to avoid introducing microorganisms into the lower airway.*

*To facilitate insertion of the catheter to suction the right or left bronchus,* ask the patient to turn his head in the direction opposite the bronchus to be suctioned. Also, keep in mind that a straight catheter rather than a coiled catheter can be used more successfully to enter the left bronchus, which diverges from the trachea at a sharper angle (45°) than the right bronchus (25°).

When performing nasotracheal suctioning, ask the patient to take a deep breath as you advance the catheter *to facilitate passage into the trachea.* Also, you can ask him to stick out his tongue *so he will not be able to swallow the catheter during insertion.*

If the patient experiences laryngospasm or bronchospasm (rare complications) during suctioning, disconnect the suction catheter from the connecting tubing and allow the catheter to act as an airway.

*To help liquify tenacious secretions,* 3 to 5 ml of sterile normal saline solution may be instilled into the trachea. Since the effectiveness of this measure remains controversial, a doctor's order is required. If you are going to do this and you are not using a commercially prepared container for this purpose, draw up 3 to 5 ml of saline solution in a syringe and remove the needle. Never use the needle to instill the saline solution because of the danger of accidental needle ejection into the trachea. A manual resuscitation bag, such as the Ambu bag, or the sigh mode on the ventilator may be used to disperse the saline solution.

If for some reason you're unable to suction effectively, notify the doctor.

Empty and rinse the collection container as indicated by hospital policy. Replace the sterile solution, the collection container, and the connecting tubing according to the institution's policy *to minimize the risk of infection from bacterial growth.*

## Complications

Hypoxia and dyspnea can result as oxygen is removed along with secretions and as anxiety produces changes in respiratory pattern. Cardiac arrhythmias, particularly bradycardia or atrioventricular (AV) heart block or reflex tachycardia, and cyanosis can result from hypoxia. Bloody aspirate can result from the underlying disease or from traumatic or prolonged suctioning. Laryngospasm or bronchospasm can be a reflex response to the presence of the suction catheter.

## Documentation

Record the date and time of the procedure and the reason for suctioning; amount, color, consistency, and odor (if any) of the secretions; vital signs and auscultation findings before and after suctioning; use of saline instillation, if ordered; hyperoxygenation before, during, and after suctioning; any complications and the nursing action taken; any inability to suction effectively and notification of the doctor; and pertinent data regarding the patient's subjective response to the procedure.

HELEN HAHLER D'ANGELO, RN, MSN

# Mechanical Ventilation

*Mechanical ventilation artificially controls or assists respiration. It's indicated to correct profound gas transport abnormalities, as evidenced by hypoxia, hypercapnia, and the signs and symptoms of increased work of breathing (nasal flaring, intercostal retraction, hypotension, and diaphoresis). This procedure uses an endotracheal or tracheostomy tube connected to a ventilator to maintain adequate pulmonary blood gas exchange. Maintenance of the mechanically ventilated patient—as well as weaning the patient from ventilation—*

requires continuous care to prevent complications and ensure the treatment's success.

Criteria for successful weaning include nearly normal blood gas levels; partial pressure of oxygen over 70 mmHg with a fraction of inspired oxygen concentration ($FIO_2$) of 40% or less, or partial pressure of carbon dioxide below 50 mmHg; vital capacity of 10 to 15 ml/kg of body weight; negative inspiratory force maneuver (NIFM) greater than $-20$ centimeters of water pressure ($cmH_2O$); peak inspiratory pressure (PIP) above $-20$; ability to double spontaneous resting minute ventilation; evidence of spontaneous respiratory effort; successful discontinuance of any neuromuscular blocking agent; and tidal volume of 3 to 5 cc/kg of body weight. Also, patient should be free of respiratory or other infection, acid-base abnormality, electrolyte abnormality, hyperglycemia, sleep deprivation, energy depletion, fever, cardiac dysrhythmias, renal failure, and shock.

## Equipment

To initiate mechanical ventilation and monitor the patient: oxygen source □ mechanical ventilator □ equipment for setting up ventilator □ sterile distilled water □ endotracheal or tracheostomy tube and oral airway, if needed □ manual resuscitation bag (such as an Ambu bag), with adapter for endotracheal or tracheostomy tube □ oxygen analyzer □ equipment and supplies for tracheal suction □ equipment and supplies for obtaining samples for arterial blood gas (ABG) analysis □ condensation collector □ stethoscope □ respirometer (if using pressure-cycled ventilator) □ sphygmomanometer □ soft restraints (optional).

To set up the ventilator, if necessary: humidifier and heater assembly □ sterile distilled water □ condenser vial and adapter □ nebulizer reservoir □ spirometer □ nebulizer tubing □ green oxygen-connecting tubing □ large-bore corrugated ventilator-circuit tubing with adapter for endotracheal or tracheostomy tube □ oxygen analyzer □ in-line

thermometer.

To wean the patient from the ventilator: heated humidified oxygen setup separate from the mechanical ventilator □ manual resuscitation bag, such as an Ambu bag □ T-piece, tracheostomy collar, or other adapter with exhalation port for endotracheal or tracheostomy tube □ oxygen analyzer □ equipment and supplies for tracheal suction □ equipment and supplies for obtaining samples for ABG analysis □ stethoscope □ sphygmomanometer.

Mechanical ventilators are used as *assisters*, which augment the patient's respiratory effort to provide known tidal volume delivery and allow the patient to determine his minute ventilation requirements; *controllers*, which completely regulate breathing for the patient with paralysis or respiratory arrest; or *assister-controllers*, which encourage the patient's spontaneous breathing but guarantee a minimal level of minute ventilation support through a backup control rate.

Two types of ventilators are commonly used—volume-cycled and pressure-cycled. The volume-cycled ventilator delivers a preset volume of gas before terminating the inspiratory cycle; the pressure-cycled ventilator stops the inspiratory cycle when it achieves the preset pressure. The volume-cycled ventilator, the more accurate for volume delivery, is most useful for patients with such conditions as adult respiratory distress syndrome, because it delivers a constant tidal volume despite changes in airway resistance or lung compliance. The pressure-cycled ventilator is appropriate when excessive inspiratory pressure can result in barotrauma-related damage to the lung, as in the postoperative neonate or infant. The type of ventilator is selected by the doctor.

## Preparation of equipment

Check your institution's policy concerning responsibility for ventilator setup. It is usually the duty of the respiratory therapist. Once the ventilator is set up, prepare the humidifier for use (see *Humidifiers*, page 459).

## Essential steps

*To initiate mechanical ventilation:*
• Verify that the doctor has ordered mechanical ventilation.
• Explain the procedure to the patient, even if he is unresponsive, *to decrease his anxiety.* Be sure to discuss the sensations he'll be experiencing as the machine controls his breathing. Assure him that a nurse will be nearby at all times, and set up a means by which he can signal for immediate assistance.
• Provide privacy, and wash your hands.
• Unless contraindicated, place the patient in semi-Fowler's position *to facilitate lung expansion and help the patient cough more effectively, thus aiding removal of secretions.*
• Check that samples for ABG analysis have been drawn *to serve as baseline indicators.* Also obtain a baseline blood pressure reading, *because a blood pressure sharply falling during ventilation can signal the need to reduce tidal volume.*
• If the patient is not already intubated, an individual trained in endotracheal tube insertion (usually a doctor or an anesthetist) will need to establish an artificial airway by inserting a cuffed endotracheal tube and inflating the cuff. Use an oral airway with an endotracheal tube *to prevent the patient from biting the tube and inhibiting gas flow.* (This is common in a newly intubated patient regaining consciousness after surgery or in a neurologically compromised patient, such as one with status epilepticus.)
• Arrange for a chest X-ray immediately after intubation *to check for proper tube placement.*
• Plug in the ventilator and turn it on. As ordered, adjust such settings as volume control, tidal volume, oxygen concentration, flow rate, and respiratory rate.
• Connect the patient to the ventilator by attaching the adapter end of the machine's corrugated tubing to the patient's endotracheal or tracheostomy tube. Maintain sterility of the inner lumen of both the patient's tube and the machine's tubing.
• Stay with the patient and talk to him *to help him relax. His anxiety, particularly acute at first, can increase his oxygen consumption and cause hypoxia.*
• After the patient has been on the ventilator for about 20 minutes, *the time necessary for gas exchange to equilibrate,* draw an arterial sample for ABG analysis. *The results of the analysis determine the adequacy of oxygenation and ventilation at the prescribed ventilator settings.*
• Adjust the ventilator settings as ordered, based on ABG results, *to prevent such complications as respiratory alkalosis from decreased carbon dioxide levels due to overventilation, respiratory acidosis from increased carbon dioxide levels due to inadequate alveolar ventilation, or atelectasis from an inappropriate tidal volume setting.*
• Make sure the patient is comfortable and relaxed. If he's alert and able to move, see that he can easily reach the call signal and other communication aids.
• Apply soft restraints, if necessary, *to prevent the patient from extubating himself.*

*To monitor the patient:*
• Avoid leaving the patient unattended or unobserved, *because complications leading to respiratory arrest can rapidly occur.* Remember that the patient can't speak—and in some cases can't move—and that he is usually frightened by mechanical ventilation and its attendant noises and lights. Without your reassurance, he may try to fight the machine.
• Wash your hands and perform the following steps regularly every 1 to 2 hours. Be sure to explain each step to the patient *to minimize his anxiety.*
• Check for secure connections at all points, such as between the ventilator and the patient's airway, between the nebulizer and the ventilator tubing, and between plug and socket.
• Ensure that all emergency alarm sys-

tems, especially for the spirometer, are turned on, and that the alert patient can easily reach the call signal and communication aids.

• Ensure that ventilator settings are adjusted as ordered.

• Verify that the ventilator operates according to the settings. For example, if the patient is connected to a volume-cycled ventilator, watch for the appropriate volume to be reached in the spirometer. Count the patient's respirations and compare the number with the machine setting for respiratory rate. At least once every 8 hours, use an oxygen analyzer *to confirm the oxygen concentration reaching the patient.*

If the patient is connected to a pressure-cycled ventilator, monitor exhaled tidal volume with a respirometer *to ensure adequate volume delivery.*

• Check the water level marker in the humidifier and refill the reservoir, if necessary. *Allowing the reservoir to run low risks delivering dry oxygen to the patient; this can cause drying of the respiratory mucosa and can lead to mucosal damage.*

• Disconnect the patient from the ventilator and quickly drain the condensation from the corrugated tubing into a collection container for discard. *Excess condensation in the tubing causes the tubing to dance, increases resistance to incoming air, and may trigger the alarm system.* Be sure to discard the condensation rather than emptying it into the humidifier, *because condensation may be contaminated with the patient's secretions and bacteria, thereby creating or aggravating an infection.*

• If the patient is connected to a volume-cycled ventilator, check the airway pressure gauge for a sudden drop or, particularly, a sudden rise in pressure. If either occurs, report it to the doctor immediately so he can adjust the ventilator settings. Falling pressure may signal a leak in the system; rising pressure may signal a loss of lung compliance.

• If you're using a ventilator that heats

## MASS SPECTROMETER

The mass spectrometer, a noninvasive monitoring instrument, may be used at the patient's bedside, particularly in an intensive care unit, or in a laboratory, usually in a pulmonary function laboratory. At the patient's bedside, it can determine optimal ventilator settings, assess a patient's weaning from a ventilator and postextubation tolerance, and monitor the unstable nonintubated or intubated patient. In the laboratory, it can measure many physiologic parameters, such as oxygen consumption during a pulmonary exercise stress test.

This monitoring instrument can be used in either an automatic or a manual mode. In the automatic mode, it can provide periodic monitoring of 12 to 16 patients at selected time intervals (such as every 10, 20, or 60 minutes) for a selected amount of time (such as 30, 45, or 60 seconds). In the manual mode, it can monitor a single patient for as long as necessary.

The mass spectrometer can reliably measure respired gas tensions, blood gases, metabolic gas exchanges, lung volumes, and other physiologic parameters, including respiratory rate (RR), inspired $O_2$ level, average alveolar $CO_2$ concentration ($PaCO_2$), minute volume, $O_2$ consumption, compliance, end tidal $CO_2$ concentration ($E_TCO_2$), alveolar/arterial $PCO_2$ gradient ($A-aPCO_2$), estimated functional residual capacity (FRC), alveolar dead space, shunt fraction (QS/QT), arterial venous $O_2$ differential, ventilation/perfusion ratio, and cardiac index.

In respiratory monitoring, the mass spectrometer draws in desired gases through tubing connected to the patient's respiratory circuit. In blood gas monitoring, catheters with semipermeable membranes withdraw dissolved gases from the plasma for analysis.

The mass spectrometer can be used with a microprocessor or computer and a recorder to display information at a central location, such as the nurse's station, or at the patient's bedside. It can store information for up to 24 hours.

Before attempting to use this complex instrument, be sure to receive in-depth instruction on its operation and maintenance.

JANET S. D'AGOSTINO, RN, MSN

the artificial air flow, check the temperature gauges to make sure they are set between 95° and 98.6° F. (35° and 37° C.). Also check the in-line thermometer or the thermometer on the ventilator to determine if the temperature of the gas delivered to the patient is within the preset range. If necessary, adjust the temperature gauges to bring the temperature of the gas delivered to the patient within the designated range, and notify the respiratory therapist so he can evaluate the ventilator function. *Overheated air thickens respiratory secretions and can burn the mucosa.*

● *To prevent alveolar collapse and stimulate coughing,* augment the patient's tidal volume with several deep breaths (usually two to three) every hour. If the ventilator doesn't have a built-in sigh mechanism, use a manual resuscitation bag, such as an Ambu bag, connected to an oxygen source.

*Perform the following steps periodically:*

● Draw an arterial sample for ABG analysis, as ordered, and whenever ventilator parameters are changed.

● Have chest X-rays taken, as ordered, *to assess lung condition.*

● Aspirate the trachea as needed (often several times an hour), and observe the suctioned secretions. Notify the doctor if the amount, color, odor, or consistency of the secretions change, *since these can indicate trauma or infection.*

● At least every 4 hours, and perhaps more often depending on the patient's condition, assess the patient for adequate ventilation by inspection, palpation, percussion, and bilateral auscultation. Listen for unilateral breath sounds, especially along the axillary lines of the rib cage, *to distinguish clearly any differences in breath sounds that indicate slippage of the endotracheal or tracheostomy tube into the right bronchus and blockage of the left lung.*

● Precisely record the patient's intake and output as ordered and obtain an exact weight daily *to help determine fluid balance and thus prevent pulmonary edema, especially in the patient with cardiac and/or renal disorders.*

● The humidifier, nebulizer, and all tubing are changed regularly (usually every 24 hours), according to the institution's policy, *to reduce the risk of nosocomial infection.* Often this is performed by the respiratory therapist. Ventilate the patient manually while the equipment is changed and retested.

*To wean the patient:*

● Check the doctor's order for the precise weaning schedule, and assess the patient's respiratory condition.

● Explain the procedure to the patient *to decrease his anxiety.* Warn him that initially he may feel short of breath as his lungs adjust to the increased effort. Assure him that you'll observe him constantly.

● Wash your hands.

● Set up the separate humidified oxygen system, using corrugated tubing to connect it to an endotracheal or tracheostomy tube adapter with an exhalation port, such as a T-piece or tracheostomy collar.

● Adjust the oxygen system to the prescribed flow rate and/or concentration.

● Disconnect the ventilator from the patient, insert the oxygen analyzer, and reattach the ventilator. Place the analyzer as close as possible to the patient *to ensure the most accurate reading of the oxygen delivery.*

● Unless contraindicated, place the patient in semi-Fowler's position *to facilitate lung expansion.*

● Take pulse and respiration, and draw an arterial sample for ABG analysis. *Any sharp change in these baseline conditions may indicate premature weaning.*

● Perform tracheal suctioning *to maximize airway patency.* Do this approximately 15 minutes before disconnecting the patient from the ventilator *to allow time for recovery to the gas levels that existed prior to suctioning.*

● Turn on the humidified oxygen source. Then, detach the patient from the mechanical ventilator and connect his endotracheal or tracheostomy tube to the adapter on the oxygen tubing of the separate humidified oxygen system.

● Turn off the mechanical ventilator.

● Stay with the patient *to reassure him*

*and to monitor his condition.*

• After 1 minute, 5 minutes, and then every 5 minutes thereafter until the patient is returned to the ventilator, take vital signs and observe the patient for skin color, posture, use of accessory muscles, level of consciousness, and subjective complaints. *Any change in these signs may indicate hypoxia.* Also watch the cardiac monitor for tachycardia and extrasystoles, *which can indicate hypoxia and ischemia and lead to decreased kidney perfusion and hypertension.*

• Immediately notify the doctor, draw a blood sample for ABG evaluation, as ordered, and return the patient to the mechanical ventilator if there is a drastic change in any of the above signs of hypoxia. Specific guidelines for returning the patient to mechanical ventilation after drawing a blood sample for ABG evaluation include the following: the patient becomes obtund or abnormally dyspneic, anxious, or tired; respiration rate rises above 30; pulse rate increases more than 20 beats/minute; blood pressure increases or decreases more than 15 mmHg; the ST segment on the EKG is depressed; or the patient develops more than 6 extrasystoles per minute.

• Obtain arterial samples for ABG analysis as ordered, while the patient is breathing spontaneously. The doctor may not request this for the first few weaning sessions, *since these usually last only 5 to 10 minutes, but gas exchange equilibration usually takes 15 to 20 minutes.*

• When the prescribed amount of time has elapsed for the weaning session, return the patient to the mechanical ventilator and turn off the alternate oxygen source.

• Make sure the patient is comfortable and relaxed. If he is alert and able to move, ensure that he can easily reach the call signal or other communication aids. Never leave the patient unattended or unobserved.

• In the absence of complications, continue the weaning schedule as prescribed by the doctor. *The patient's time on the ventilator will decrease as his ability to breathe spontaneously increases, and monitoring frequency is gradually reduced as he adjusts.* Usually the patient returns to the ventilator at night for a few days even if he is able to breathe independently during the day. *This allows him to sleep soundly and conserve his energy for the next day's spontaneous breathing.*

• When the patient has regained the expected use of his lungs and has remained stable for a satisfactory period of time, discontinue mechanical ventilation and the artificial airway, as ordered.

## Special considerations

Provide emotional support to the patient during all phases of mechanical ventilation *to reduce anxiety and promote successful treatment.* Even if the patient is unresponsive, continue to explain all procedures and treatments to him.

Unless contraindicated, turn the patient from side to side every 1 to 2 hours, *to facilitate lung expansion and removal of secretions.* Perform active or passive range-of-motion exercises for all extremities *to reduce the hazards of immobility.* If the patient's condition permits, position him upright at regular intervals *to increase lung expansion.* When moving the patient or the ventilator tubing, be careful to prevent condensation in the tubing from flowing into the lungs, *because aspiration of this moisture can cause tracheal obstruction.* Provide care for the patient's artificial airway as needed.

Administer a sedative or neuromuscular blocking agent, as ordered, *to relax the patient or eliminate spontaneous breathing efforts that can interfere with the ventilator's action.* Remember that the patient receiving a neuromuscular blocking drug requires close observation *because of his inability to move or communicate.*

Ensure that the patient gets adequate rest and sleep, *because fatigue can de-*

*lay weaning from the ventilator.* Provide subdued lighting, safely muffle equipment noises, and restrict staff and visitor access *to provide quiet.*

If the patient fails to progress satisfactorily by traditional weaning methods, the doctor may order intermittent mandatory ventilation (IMV). Now also used as a ventilatory mode and not limited to a weaning mode, IMV allows the patient to breathe spontaneously but also delivers a breath from the ventilator at a preset interval and volume. The number of machine-delivered breaths/minute gradually decreases until the patient's entire minute ventilation is achieved spontaneously.

Synchronized intermittent mandatory ventilation (SIMV) and intermittent demand ventilation (IDV) are alternate methods of weaning the patient by machine. These resemble IMV but require the patient to trigger the machine-controlled breaths. They then synchronize the controlled breaths with the patient's spontaneous respiration. Although the ventilator is preset to deliver a controlled breath at regular intervals, it waits for the patient to initiate that breath and then delivers full volume as he inspires. *This prevents lung overinflation by not forcing a controlled breath into the patient who's just taken his own breath.*

Machine weaning doesn't eliminate observation for signs of hypoxia. And, since the patient may be physiologically but not psychologically ready for weaning, it doesn't replace your bedside support. Also remember that patients are not placed in an IMV mode for weaning and then back on assist-control for mechanical support. IMV is a legitimate mode for continually administering ventilator support.

Schedule weaning to fit in comfortably and realistically with the patient's daily regimen. Avoid scheduling sessions after meals, baths, or diagnostic procedures. Have the patient help you set up the schedule *to give him some sense of control over an often threatening procedure.* As the patient's tolerance for weaning increases, tell him to sit out of bed *to improve breathing and his sense of well-being.* Suggest diversionary activities, *to take his mind off his breathing.*

## Complications

Despite precautions, machine failure, pulmonary barotrauma, decreased cardiac output, and gastric stress ulcers can occur.

## Documentation

During initiation and monitoring, record the date and time of the procedure; type of ventilator; ventilator settings (such as respiratory rate, pressure limits, $FIO_2$, flow rate, positive end-expiratory pressure, if used, and tidal volume). If using a pressure-cycled ventilator, record maximum inspiratory time and the inspiratory to expiratory ratio; any change in ventilator settings; baseline and subsequent determinations of vital signs and ABG status; and auscultation results, including type and location of any adventitious breath sounds. Also note any tracheal suction and the character of suctioned secretions, any range-of-motion exercises performed, intake and output, the patient's weight, any complications and the nursing action taken, and the patient's reaction to treatment.

During weaning, record the date and time of each session and the weaning method (humidified $O_2$ or IMV). Record baseline and subsequent vital signs and ABG status (including duration of independent breathing before arterial puncture), observations of skin color and suctioned secretions, need for tracheal suction, intake and output, the patient's weight, complications and nursing actions, and reaction to weaning. If using the traditional weaning method (humidified $O_2$ with T-piece or tracheostomy collar), note duration of spontaneous breathing and inability to maintain weaning schedule. If using IMV, record control breath rate, each time it's reduced, and spontaneous rate.

KATHLEEN E. VIALL GALLAGHER, RN, MSN

# Manual Ventilation with a Hand-held Resuscitation Bag

*A hand-held resuscitation bag, such as the Ambu bag, is an inflatable device that can be attached to a face mask or directly to an endotracheal or tracheostomy tube to allow manual delivery of oxygen or room air to the lungs of a patient who is unable to ventilate independently. Usually employed in an emergency, manual ventilation with a resuscitation bag can also be performed during temporary disconnection from a mechanical ventilator, such as during a tubing change, during transport, or prior to suctioning. In such instances, use of the manual resuscitation bag maintains ventilation, preventing hypoxia that can lead to brain damage or death. Oxygen administration with a resuscitation bag can help improve the patient's compromised cardiorespiratory status.*

## Equipment

Manual resuscitation bag, such as the Ambu bag □ mask □ oxygen source (wall unit or tank) □ oxygen tubing □ nipple adapter attached to oxygen flowmeter.

A mask, available in adult and pediatric sizes, is used unless the patient has an endotracheal or tracheostomy tube in place, in which case the manual resuscitation bag is attached directly to the tube. It shouldn't be secured with straps, *because quick removal may be necessary to prevent aspiration of vomitus or secretions.*

## Preparation of equipment

Select a mask that fits snugly over the patient's mouth and nose. Attach the mask to the resuscitation bag. If oxygen is readily available, connect the manual resuscitation bag to the oxygen. Attach one end of the tubing to the bottom of the bag and the other end to the nipple adapter on the flowmeter of the oxygen wall unit or tank. Set up suction equipment if time allows.

## Essential steps

• Before using the manual resuscitation bag, check the patient's upper airway for the presence of foreign objects. If present, remove them, *because their removal alone may restore spontaneous respirations in some instances. Also, the presence of foreign matter or secretions can obstruct the airway and impede resuscitation efforts.* If necessary, insert an oropharyngeal or nasopharyngeal airway *to maintain airway patency.* If the patient has a tracheostomy or endotracheal tube in place, suction the tube *to remove any secretions that may obstruct the airway.*

• If appropriate, remove the bed's headboard and stand at the head of the bed *to help maintain the patient's neck in hyperextension and to free space at the side of the bed for such other activities as cardiopulmonary resuscitation.*

• Hyperextend the patient's neck, if not contraindicated, by pulling his jaw forward, *to move the tongue away from the base of the pharynx and prevent obstruction of the airway.*

• Place the mask over the patient's face so that the apex of the triangle covers the bridge of his nose and the base lies between his lower lip and chin. Or, if the patient has a tracheostomy or endotracheal tube in place, remove the mask from the bag and attach the manual resuscitation bag directly to the tube.

• Keeping your nondominant hand on the patient's mask, exert downward pressure *to seal the mask against his face.* For the adult patient, use your dominant hand to compress the bag every 5 seconds *to deliver approximately 1 liter of air.* For a child, the number of compressions should be 15 times per minute, or one compression of the bag every 4 seconds; for the infant, 20 times per minute, or one compression every 3 seconds.

• Observe the patient's chest *to ensure that it rises and falls with each compression.* If ventilation fails to occur, check the fit of the mask and the patency of the patient's airway; if necessary, reposition the patient's head.

## Special considerations

To facilitate neck hyperextension, you may place a rolled towel under the patient's neck. However, avoid neck hyperextension if the patient has a possible cervical injury; instead use the jaw-thrust technique to open the airway. If you need both hands to keep the patient's mask in place and maintain hyperextension, use the lower part of your arm to compress the bag against your side. Observe for vomiting through the clear part of the mask. If vomiting occurs, stop the procedure immediately, lift the mask, wipe and suction vomitus, and resume resuscitation.

## Complications

Aspiration of vomitus can result in pneumonia, and gastric distention may follow forcing of air into the patient's stomach.

## Documentation

In an emergency situation, record the date and time of the procedure; manual ventilation efforts; any complications and the nursing action taken; and the patient's response to treatment, according to the protocol for respiratory arrest in your institution.

In a nonemergency situation, record the date and time of the procedure; reason and length of time the patient is disconnected from mechanical ventilation and receives manual ventilation; any complications and the nursing action taken; and the patient's tolerance for the procedure.

HELEN HAHLER D'ANGELO, RN, MSN

# Thoracentesis

*Thoracentesis is the aspiration of fluid or air from the pleural space. It relieves pulmonary compression and resultant respiratory distress by removing air or fluid accumulations that result from injury or such conditions as tuberculosis or cancer. It also provides a specimen of pleural fluid or tissue for analysis, and allows instillation of chemotherapeutic agents or other medications into the pleural space.*

*Thoracentesis is contraindicated in patients with bleeding disorders.*

## Equipment

Most hospitals have available a prepackaged sterile thoracentesis tray that usually includes sterile gloves, sterile drapes, 70% isopropyl alcohol or povidone-iodine solution, 1% or 2% lidocaine, 5-ml syringe with 21G and 25G needles for anesthetic injection, 17G thoracentesis needle for aspiration, 50-ml syringe, three-way stopcock and tubing, sterile specimen containers, sterile hemostat, and sterile 4″ x 4 ″ gauze sponges.

You'll also need: adhesive tape □ stethoscope □ sphygomomanometer □ laboratory request slips □ drainage bottles □ optional: sterile Teflon catheter, equipment for shaving, biopsy needle, and prescribed sedative with 3-ml syringe and 21G needle, and drainage bottles.

## Preparation of equipment

Assemble all the essential and requested equipment at the patient's bedside or in the treatment area. Check the expiration date on each sterile package and inspect for tears. Prepare the necessary laboratory request slips. Be sure to list current antibiotic therapy on the laboratory slips, *as this will be considered in analyzing the specimens.* Make sure the patient has signed an appropriate consent form. Note any drug allergies, especially to the local anesthetic. Have the patient's chest X-rays available.

## Essential steps

• Explain the procedure to the patient. Tell him it isn't painful, although he may feel pressure during the needle insertion. Provide privacy and wash your hands.

- Administer the prescribed sedative, as ordered.
- Obtain baseline vital signs and assess respiratory function.
- Position the patient. Make sure the patient is firmly supported and comfortable. Although the choice of position is variable, you'll usually seat the patient on the edge of the bed with his legs supported and his head and folded arms resting on a pillow on the overbed table. Or have him straddle a chair backwards and rest his head and folded arms on the chair back. If the patient is unable to sit, turn him on the unaffected side with the arm of the affected side raised above his head. Elevate the head of the bed 30° to 45°, if such elevation isn't contraindicated. *Proper positioning stretches the chest or back and allows easier access to the intercostal spaces.*
- Remind the patient not to cough, breathe deeply, or move suddenly during the procedure *to avoid visceral, pleural, or lung puncture.* If the patient coughs, the doctor will briefly halt the procedure and withdraw the needle slightly *to prevent puncture.*
- Expose the entire chest or back, as appropriate.
- Shave the aspiration site, as ordered.
- Wash your hands again before touching the sterile equipment. Then, using sterile technique, open the thoracentesis tray and assist the doctor as necessary in disinfecting the site.
- If an ampul of local anesthetic does not come in the sterile tray and a multidose vial of local anesthetic is to be used, assist the doctor by wiping the rubber stopper with an alcohol sponge and holding the inverted vial while the doctor withdraws the anesthetic solution.
- After draping the patient and injecting the local anesthetic, the doctor attaches a three-way stopcock with tubing to the aspirating needle and turns the stopcock to prevent air from entering the pleural space through the needle.
- Attach the other end of the tubing to the drainage bottle
- The doctor then inserts the needle into the pleural space and attaches a 50-ml

syringe to the needle's stopcock. A hemostat may be used *to hold the needle in place and prevent pleural tear or lung puncture.* As an alternative, the doctor may introduce a Teflon catheter into the needle, remove the needle, and attach a stopcock and syringe or drainage tubing to the catheter *to reduce the risk of pleural puncture by a needle.*
- Assist the doctor as necessary in specimen collection, fluid drainage, or drug administration.
- Support the patient verbally throughout the procedure and keep him informed of each step. Assess him for signs of anxiety and provide reassurance as necessary.
- Check vital signs regularly during the procedure.

 **NURSING ALERT** Continually observe the patient for such signs of distress as pallor, vertigo, faintness, weak and rapid pulse, decreased blood pressure, dyspnea, tachypnea, diaphoresis, chest pain, blood-tinged mucus, and excessive coughing. Alert the doctor if such signs develop, *because they may indicate complications such as hypovolemic shock or tension pneumothorax.*
- After the doctor withdraws the needle or catheter, apply pressure to the puncture site, using a sterile 4″ x 4″ gauze sponge. Then, apply a sterile gauze dressing and secure it with tape.
- Place the patient in a comfortable position, take his vital signs, and assess his respiratory status.
- Properly label the specimens and send them to the laboratory.
- Discard disposable equipment. Clean nondisposable items and return them for sterilization.
- Continue to check the patient's vital signs and the dressing for drainage every 15 minutes for 1 hour, every 30 minutes for 2 hours, every hour for 4 hours, and every 4 hours for 24 hours.

## Special considerations

To prevent hypovolemic shock, fluid is removed slowly, and no more than 1,200 ml of fluid is removed at one time.

Pleuritic or shoulder pain may indicate pleural irritation by the needle point.

A chest X-ray is usually ordered after the procedure *to detect pneumothorax and evaluate the results of the procedure.*

## Complications

Hypovolemic shock may result from rapid fluid removal as fluid moves from the vascular space to the recently evacuated pleural space. Pneumothorax, possibly leading to mediastinal shift, can occur if needle puncture of the lung allows air to enter the pleural cavity. Pyogenic infection can result from contamination during the procedure.

## Documentation

Record the date and time of thoracentesis; location of the puncture site; volume and description (color, viscosity, odor) of the fluid withdrawn; specimens sent to the laboratory; vital signs and respiratory assessment before, during, and after the procedure; any postprocedural tests, such as chest X-ray; any complications and the nursing action taken; and the patient's reaction to the procedure.

SUSAN VIGEANT, RN, BSN
PAULA STEPHENS OKUN, RN, MSN

# Chest Tube Insertion

*The pleural space normally contains a thin layer of lubricating fluid that allows frictionless movement of the lungs during respiration. An excess of fluid (hemothorax or pleural effusion), air (pneumothorax), or both in this space alters intrapleural pressure and causes partial or complete lung collapse.*

*Chest tube insertion permits the drainage of air or fluid from the pleural space. Performed by a doctor with a nurse assisting, this procedure requires sterile technique. The insertion site varies, depending on the patient's condition and the doctor's judgment. For a pneumo-*

*thorax, the second intercostal space is the usual site, because air rises to the top of the intrapleural space. For a hemothorax or pleural effusion, the sixth to the eighth intercostal spaces are common sites, because fluid settles to the lower levels of the intrapleural space. For removal of both air and fluid, a chest tube is inserted into a high and low site. Following insertion, the chest tube(s) is connected to a thoracic drainage system that provides for the drainage of air and/or fluid out of the pleural space and prevents backflow into that space, thus promoting lung reexpansion.*

## Equipment

Two pairs of sterile gloves □ sterile drape □ povidone-iodine solution □ vial of 1% lidocaine □ 10-ml syringe □ alcohol sponge □ 22G 1″ needle □ 25G ⅝″ needle □ sterile scalpel (usually with #11 blade) □ sterile forceps □ two rubber-tipped clamps for each chest tube inserted □ sterile 4″ x 4″ gauze sponges □ two sterile 4″ x 4″ drain sponges (gauze sponges with slit) □ 3″ or 4″ adhesive or nonallergenic tape, if the patient is allergic to adhesive □ chest tube with trocar □ sterile suture material (usually 2-0 silk with cutting needle) □ thoracic drainage system □ sterile drainage tubing, about 6′ long, and connector □ Y-connector (for two chest tubes on the same side).

Most institutions supply prepackaged chest tube trays that contain all necessary equipment, except for the povidone-iodine solution, alcohol sponges, sterile gloves, lidocaine, and the thoracic drainage system. Check with the doctor to determine which thoracic drainage system will be used.

## Preparation of equipment

Check the expiration date on the sterile packages and inspect for tears. Then, assemble all equipment in the patient's room and set up the thoracic drainage system so it is ready for use. Place it next to the patient's bed so it will be below the chest level to facilitate drainage.

## Essential steps

- Explain the procedure to the patient, provide privacy, and wash your hands.
- Record baseline vital signs.
- Position the patient on his side with the area for chest tube insertion facing upward. (Some doctors prefer the supine position for insertion into the second or third intercostal space; semi-Fowler's position for insertion into the sixth through the eighth intercostal spaces).
- Place the chest tube tray on the overbed table. Open it maintaining sterile technique.
- The doctor puts on gloves and prepares the insertion site by cleansing the area with povidone-iodine solution.
- Wipe the rubber stopper of the lidocaine vial with an alcohol sponge. Then, invert the bottle *and hold it for the doctor to withdraw the anesthetic.*
- After the doctor anesthetizes the site, he makes a small incision and inserts the chest tube. Then, he either immediately connects the chest tube to the thoracic drainage system or momentarily clamps the tube close to the patient's chest until he can connect it to the drainage system. He may then secure the tube to the skin with a suture.
- As the doctor is inserting the chest tube, reassure the patient and assist the doctor as necessary.
- Open the packages containing the 4″ x 4″ drain sponges and gauze sponges, and put on sterile gloves. Place two 4″ x 4″ drain sponges around the insertion site, one from the top and the other from the bottom. Then place several 4″ x 4″ gauze sponges on top of the drain sponges. Tape the dressings, covering them completely.
- Tape the chest tube to the patient's chest distal to the insertion site *to help prevent accidental dislodgment of the tube.*
- Tape the junction of the chest tube and the drainage tube *to prevent their separation.*
- Coil the drainage tubing and secure it to the bed linen with tape and a safety pin, providing enough slack for the patient to move and turn. These measures *prevent the drainage tubing from getting kinked or dropping to the floor, which would impair drainage into the drainage bottle, and they help prevent accidental dislodgment of the chest tube.*
- Immediately after the chest tube is inserted and all connections are made, instruct the patient to take a deep breath, hold it momentarily, and slowly exhale *to assist drainage of the pleural space and lung reexpansion.*
- After insertion, a portable chest X-ray is done *to check tube position.*
- Take the patient's vital signs every 15 minutes for 1 hour, then every hour for 2 hours, or as ordered. Auscultate the patient's lungs at least every 4 hours *to assess air exchange in the affected lung.* Diminished or absent breath sounds indicate that the lung hasn't reexpanded.

## Special considerations

If the patient's chest tube comes out, immediately cover the site with 4″ x 4″ gauze sponges and tape them in place. Stay with the patient and monitor vital signs every 10 minutes. Observe the patient for signs of tension pneumothorax (pallor; vertigo; faintness; weak, rapid pulse; dyspnea; tachypnea; diaphoresis; chest pain; blood-tinged sputum; and excessive coughing). Instruct another staff member to notify the doctor, and gather equipment for reinsertion of the tube.

Place the rubber-tipped clamps at the bedside to clamp the chest tube(s) in case of bottle breakage, cracking of a commercially prepared system, or tubing disconnection. A piece of petrolatum gauze may be wrapped around the chest tube at the insertion site *to make an airtight seal.*

## Documentation

Record the date and time of chest tube insertion, insertion site, drainage system used, presence of drainage and bubbling, vital signs and auscultation findings, any complications, and the nursing action taken.

DEBORAH DALRYMPLE, RN, BSN

# Thoracic Drainage
[*Closed chest drainage, underwater seal drainage*]

*Because the negative pressure within the pleural cavity exerts a suction force that keeps the lungs expanded, any chest trauma that upsets this pressure may cause lung collapse. Consequently, after chest trauma, one or more chest tubes may be surgically inserted and then connected to a thoracic drainage system. Thoracic drainage uses gravity and possibly suction to restore negative pressure and remove any material collected in the pleural cavity. An underwater seal in the drainage system allows air and fluid to escape from the pleural cavity, but doesn't allow air to reenter.*

*Specifically, thoracic drainage may be ordered to remove accumulated air, fluids (blood, pus, chyle, serous fluids, gastric juices), or solids (blood clots) from the pleural cavity; to restore negative pressure in the pleural cavity; and to reexpand a partially or totally collapsed lung.*

## Equipment
Types of thoracic drainage systems include the one-, two-, or three-bottle systems, and commercially prepared systems, such as the Pleur-evac and Argyle systems. While the one- and two-bottle systems are primarily gravity systems, the three-bottle and commercially prepared systems also provide for suction. (Suction is applied through a specifically regulated suction machine or by adding a suction control bottle connected to a suction pump.) If necessary, a two-bottle system can also provide suction if the collection bottle is replaced with a suction control bottle. The water-seal bottle then also serves as the collection bottle. However, the drainage collected in the water-seal bottle submerges more of the water-seal straw than is usually desired and thus creates a resistance to further drainage.

*For all systems:* sterile distilled water (usually 1 liter) □ adhesive tape □ sterile clear plastic tubing □ bottle or system rack □ two rubber-tipped Kelly clamps □ suction source, if ordered.

*For the one-bottle system:* sterile 2-liter bottle □ short sterile glass straw □ long sterile glass straw □ sterile rubber stopper with two holes.

*For the two-bottle system:* two sterile 2-liter bottles □ clear plastic tubing □ three short sterile glass straws □ one long sterile glass straw □ two sterile rubber stoppers, each with two holes.

*For the three-bottle system:* three sterile 2-liter bottles □ sterile clear plastic tubing □ five short sterile glass straws □ two long sterile glass straws □ two sterile rubber stoppers, each with two holes □ one sterile rubber stopper with three holes.

*Note:* The central supply department usually furnishes thoracic drainage systems partially assembled.

*For the Pleur-evac and Argyle systems:* The manufacturer's package contains specific instructions for assembly and the necessary sterile equipment, except for a sterile 50-ml catheter-tip syringe and sterile distilled water. You'll also need adhesive tape and two rubber-tipped Kelly clamps.

## Preparation of equipment
Check the doctor's order to determine the type of drainage system to be used and specific procedural details. If appropriate, request the drainage system from the central supply department. Collect the appropriate equipment and take it to the patient's bedside.

## Essential steps
• Explain the procedure to the patient, and wash your hands.
• Maintain sterile technique throughout the entire procedure, and whenever you make changes in the system or alter any of the connections *to avoid introducing pathogens into the pleural space.*

*To set up any bottle system:*
• Fill the water-seal bottle with approximately 300 ml of sterile distilled water. Stopper the bottle and make sure the long

straw (water-seal straw) is submerged approximately ¾″ (2 cm) *to create the water seal.*

• If you're using a suction control bottle, add sterile distilled water to the suction control bottle until the long straw is submerged to the ordered length.

If you're using a drainage collection bottle, no special preparation is needed; the bottle is stoppered with a rubber stopper which has two short straws in place.

• Place the bottle(s) in a rack on the floor beside the patient's bed to avoid spills or breakage.

• Keep the bottle(s) below the level of the patient's chest *to avoid introducing liquid into the pleural space.*

• Use the clear plastic tubing to make the necessary connections, including to suction if ordered. Attach the tubing to the patient's chest tube, securely taping all connections. Turn on the suction, as ordered. (See pages 506 to 507, for illustrations and further explanation of the bottle system.)

• Place a strip of adhesive tape vertically on the drainage collection bottle. This will be used to note the fluid level at the completion of each shift. In the one-bottle system or the two-bottle system, when the second bottle is used as the suction control bottle, mark the original fluid level.

*To set up the Pleur-evac and Argyle systems:*

• Open the packaged system and place it on the floor in the rack supplied by the manufacturer *to avoid accidentally knocking it over or dislodging the components.* After the system is prepared, it may be hung from the side of the patient's bed.

• Remove the plastic connector from the short tube that's attached to the water-seal chamber. Using a 50-ml catheter-tip syringe, instill sterile distilled water into the water-seal chamber until it reaches the 2-cm mark. Replace the plastic connector. For the Argyle system, fill both water-seal chambers, and replace the plastic connector.

• If suction is ordered, remove the cap

(muffler, atmosphere vent cover) on the suction control chamber *to open the vent.* Next, using the syringe, instill sterile distilled water until it reaches the 20-cm mark or the ordered level, and recap the suction control chamber.

• Using the long tube, connect the patient's chest tube to the closed drainage collection chamber. Secure the connection with tape.

• Connect the short tube on the drainage system to the suction source and turn on the suction. Gentle bubbling should begin in the suction chamber, *indicating that correct suction level has been reached.*

*To care for the patient with closed chest underwater seal drainage:*

• Periodically, note the character, consistency and amount of drainage in the drainage collection chamber or bottle.

• Mark the drainage level in the drainage collection chamber or bottle by noting the time and date at the drainage level on the chamber or bottle every 8 hours, or more often if there is a large amount of drainage.

• Check the water level in the water seal chamber or bottle every 8 hours. If necessary, carefully add sterile distilled water until the water seal straw is submerged ¾″ (2 cm) if a bottle system is being used, or until the water reaches the 2-cm level indicated on the water seal chamber of the commercially prepared system.

• Check for fluctuation in the water seal straw of the bottle or the water seal chamber of the commercially prepared system as the patient breathes. Normal fluctuations of 2″ to 4″ (5 to 10 cm) reflect pressure changes in the pleural space during respiration. With a suction system, the fluid line in the water-seal straw should remain constant. To check for fluctuation when a suction system is being used, momentarily disconnect the suction system so the air vent is opened, and observe for fluctuation.

• Check for intermittent bubbling in the water seal chamber or bottle. This occurs normally when the system is removing air from the pleural cavity. If bubbling isn't readily apparent during

## UNDERWATER SEAL DRAINAGE SYSTEMS

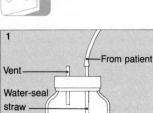

**1**

Vent

Water-seal straw

From patient

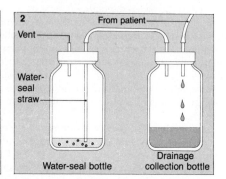

**2**

Vent

Water-seal straw

From patient

Drainage collection bottle

Water-seal bottle

The **one-bottle system,** illustrated at left, is the simplest underwater seal drainage system. The drainage tubing leads to a single 2-liter bottle that serves as both a collection container and a water seal. The bottle has a rubber stopper with two holes in which glass straws can be placed. The short straw acts as an air vent to equalize pressure between the air space of the bottle and the atmosphere. The long straw is attached to tubing leading to the patient for drainage.

The bottle is filled with approximately 300 ml of sterile water so the long drainage straw rests about ¾″ (2 cm) below water level, which rises with inhalation and falls with expiration. This setup creates a water seal that prevents air from reentering the chest, while allowing expulsion of drainage.

However, because the water and drainage share the same bottle, continuous fluid increase eventually decreases the system's effectiveness by creating resistance to further drainage.

In the **two-bottle system,** illustrated at right, liquid drainage falls through a short straw into the collection bottle, and the air flows beyond into the water-seal bottle. This bottle has two holes in its stopper. One hole holds a long, submerged straw that creates the water seal; a second hole holds another short straw, which functions as the air vent.

This setup keeps the water seal at a fixed level, allowing more accurate observation of

quiet breathing, have the patient take a deep breath or cough. Absence of bubbling indicates that the pleural space has sealed.

• Check the water level in the suction control chamber or bottle periodically. Detach the chamber or bottle from the suction source; when bubbling ceases, observe the water level. If necessary, add sterile distilled water to bring the level to the 20-cm line, or as ordered.

• Check for gentle bubbling in the suction control chamber or bottle. Gentle bubbling indicates that the proper suction level has been reached. Vigorous bubbling in this chamber increases the rate of water evaporation.

• Periodically check that the air vent in the system is not occluded. *Occlusion of the air vent results in a buildup of pressure in the system that could cause the patient to develop a tension pneumothorax.*

• Coil the system tubing and secure it to the edge of the bed with a rubber band or tape and a safety pin. Avoid creating dependent loops, kinks, or pressure on the tubing *as they may interfere with chest drainage.*

Avoid lifting drainage bottles above the patient's chest *as this can cause backflow of fluid into the pleural space.*

• Be sure two rubber-tipped clamps have been placed at the bedside. These are

**3**

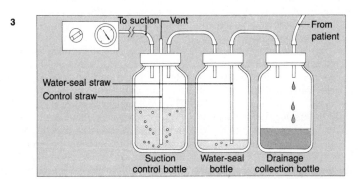

the volume and type of drainage. However, sometimes this system does not supply sufficient suction. If suction is ordered and you're using a suction source with built-in controls, make the connection at the vent stem of the water-seal bottle. Remember, some two-bottle systems don't have a separate collection bottle. In such systems the second bottle is the vacuum control bottle and the first bottle is both the water-seal and drainage collection bottle.

The **three-bottle system**, illustrated above, adds a suction control bottle between the water seal and the suction source. This additional bottle has a long straw in it with the upper end open to the atmosphere, providing another site where air can enter, and the lower end submerged under sterile saline solution. The approximate amount of suction that can be exerted on the drainage system is determined by the depth of a submerged control straw.

*Commercial chest drainage* units duplicate or modify the bottle systems. The popular Pleur-evac, for example, is a one-piece disposable, molded plastic unit with three chambers duplicating the classic three-bottle system—a chamber for drainage, a water seal, and suction control. Special features include a positive pressure-release valve that prevents possible pressure buildup in the pleural space. The Argyle "Double Seal" unit is similar but reads from left to right. It adds a fourth chamber, an additional water seal that's vented to the atmosphere to prevent a possible pressure buildup.

used to clamp the chest tube should a bottle break, the commercially prepared system crack, or to locate an air leak in the system.
• Encourage the patient to cough frequently and breathe deeply *to help drain the pleural space and expand the lungs.*
• Instruct him to sit upright *for optimal lung expansion* and to splint the insertion site while coughing *to minimize pain.*
• Check the rate and quality of the patient's respirations and auscultate the patient's lungs periodically *to assess air exchange in the affected lung.* Diminished or absent breath sounds may indicate that the lung has not reexpanded.
• Tell the patient to report any breathing

difficulty immediately. Notify the doctor immediately if the patient develops cyanosis, rapid, shallow breathing, subcutaneous emphysema, chest pain, or excessive bleeding.
• Milk the tubing as needed *to keep it patent* by squeezing the tubing between the fingers. Strip the tubing only when necessary to remove clots by pinching the tube between your thumb and index finger about 2" (5 cm) from the insertion site. Using the other thumb and index finger, compress the tubing as you slide your fingers down the tube or use a mechanical stripper. After stripping, release the thumb and index finger pinching the tube near the insertion site.

• Check the chest tube dressing at least every 8 hours. Change the dressing as necessary, or according to the institution's policy.

• Encourage active or passive range of motion exercises of the patient's arm or the affected side if he has been splinting the arm. Usually, the thoractomy patient will splint his arm to decrease his discomfort.

• Give ordered pain medication as needed for patient comfort and to help with deep breathing and coughing and range of motion exercises.

• Remind the ambulatory patient to keep the bottles below chest level *and to be careful not to disconnect the tubing to maintain the water seal.* With a suction system, the patient must stay within the range of the length of tubing attached to a wall outlet or portable pump.

## Special considerations

Instruct staff and visitors to avoid touching the equipment *to prevent complications from separated connections and bottle misplacement or breakage.*

When stripping the chest tube with your thumb and index finger, use an alcohol sponge or hand lotion to lubricate the tube.

If excessive continuous bubbling is present in the water seal chamber or bottle, especially if suction is being used, rule out a leak in the drainage system. Try to locate the leak by clamping the tube momentarily at various points along its length. Begin clamping at the tube's proximal end and work down toward the drainage bottles, paying special attention to the seal around the connections. If any connection is loose, push it back together and tape it securely. *The bubbling will stop when a clamp is placed between the air leak and the water seal.* If you clamp along the tube's entire length and the bubbling doesn't stop, the drainage unit may be cracked and need replacement.

If the drainage collection bottle or chamber fills, replace the bottle or the commercially prepared system. To do this, double-clamp the tube close to the insertion site (use two clamps facing in opposite directions), exchange the bottle or system, remove the clamps, and retape the bottle connection. Never leave the tubes clamped for more than a minute or two *to prevent a tension pneumothorax, which may occur when clamping stops air and fluid escape.*

If a bottle breaks, or if the commercially prepared system cracks, clamp the chest tube with the two rubber-tipped clamps at the bedside (placed there at the time of insertion of the chest tube). Place the clamps close to each other near the insertion site; they should face in opposite directions to provide a more complete seal. Stay with the patient and observe him for altered respirations while another staff member brings replacement equipment. Quickly replace the damaged equipment. Unclamp the chest tube and continue to monitor respiratory status (rate, quality and depth of respirations and breath sounds). Submerge the distal end of the tube in a container of sterile normal saline solution *to create a temporary water seal while you replace the bottle.*

Another commercially prepared system, the Ohio thoracic drainage system, also offers gravity or suction-assisted drainage. This system has a self-contained underwater seal that requires no filling. If suction is ordered, the unit connects to a low-vacuum source.

## Complications

Tension pneumothorax may result from excessive accumulation of air and/or drainage which eventually may exert pressure on the heart and aorta, causing a precipitous fall in cardiac output.

## Documentation

Record the date and time thoracic drainage began; type of system; amount of suction applied to the pleural cavity; presence or absence of bubbling and/or fluctuation in the water seal bottle or chamber; initial amount and type of drainage, and the patient's respiratory status.

At the end of each shift, record the

frequency of system inspection; how frequently chest tubes were milked and/or stripped; amount, color, and consistency of drainage; presence or absence of bubbling and/or fluctuation in the water seal bottle or chamber; the patient's respiratory status; condition of the chest dressings; pain medication, if given; and any complications and the nursing action taken.

DEBORAH DALRYMPLE, RN, BSN

# Chest Tube Removal

*Usually performed by a doctor with a nurse assisting, this procedure involves the extraction of a chest tube from the pleural space without introducing air or infectious microorganisms into this space. Because prolonged intubation invites infection along the tube tract, a chest tube is usually removed within 5 to 7 days of insertion. Once a chest X-ray confirms full lung expansion, the tube is clamped with large, smooth, rubber-tipped clamps for up to 24 hours before removal. This allows time to observe the patient for signs of respiratory distress, an indication that air or fluid remains trapped in the pleural space. A chest X-ray is usually taken about 2 hours after clamping; if the patient develops respiratory distress or the X-ray reveals recurrent pneumothorax, the tube clamps can be immediately removed. A chest X-ray is taken again after removal of the chest tube to confirm full lung reexpansion.*

*Chest tube removal is contraindicated when the X-ray shows incomplete lung expansion or when clamping the tube induces respiratory distress.*

## Equipment
Pain medication, if ordered □ 2″ to 3″ (5- to 7.5-cm) wide adhesive or nonallergenic tape □ scissors □ sterile gloves (for removal of tube) □ clean gloves (for removal of dressings) □ sterile petrolatum gauze □ several sterile 4″ x 4″ gauze

sponges □ linen-saver pad □ waterproof trash bag □ specimen collection equipment, if ordered □ sterile suture removal kit with forceps and scissors.

## Preparation of equipment
Assemble all supplies at the patient's bedside. Cut three 6″ (15-cm) strips of adhesive tape (or nonallergenic tape if patient is allergic to adhesive). Check the expiration date on each sterile package and inspect for tears. Open the sterile packages and create a sterile field. Maintaining sterile technique, drop the sterile petrolatum gauze on a sterile gauze sponge for use as an airtight dressing.

## Essential steps
● Assess the depth and quality of the patient's respirations and obtain baseline vital signs.
● Explain the procedure to the patient, provide privacy, and wash your hands. Administer an analgesic, as ordered, 30 minutes before tube removal.
● Place the patient in the semi-Fowler's position or on his unaffected side.
● Place the linen-saver pad under the patient's affected side *to protect the linen from drainage and to provide a place to put the chest tube after removal.*
● Put on clean gloves and remove the chest tube dressings, being careful not to dislodge the chest tube. Discard soiled dressings in the waterproof trash bag.
● The doctor puts on sterile gloves, then holds the chest tube in place with sterile forceps and cuts the suture anchoring the tube.
● Check to be sure the chest tube is securely clamped, and then instruct the patient to *exhale* fully and hold his breath, or *inhale* fully and hold his breath. *This prevents air from being sucked into the pleural space during tube removal.*
● The doctor picks up the airtight dressing *so he can cover the insertion site with it immediately after removing the tube.*
● After the doctor removes the tube and covers the insertion site, secure the dressing with tape strips. Be sure to completely cover the dressing with the tape

to make it as airtight as possible.
- Properly dispose of the chest tube, soiled gloves, and equipment, according to the institution's policy.
- Take vital signs, as ordered, and assess the depth and quality of the patient's respirations.
- For the first few hours after chest tube removal, check the dressing site for sounds of air leakage and observe the patient closely for signs or symptoms of complications, such as recurrent pneumothorax, subcutaneous emphysema, or infection. Signs and symptoms of pneumothorax include dyspnea, chest pain, tachycardia, cyanosis, restlessness, and absent breath sounds in the affected area. Pneumothorax may result from an ineffective seal at the insertion site or from the underlying disease. Subcutaneous emphysema is indicated by a crackling sound heard when the area around the wound is palpated and is caused by a poor seal at the insertion site.

### Special considerations
If the doctor has requested that the chest tube be cultured, he'll hold it as you obtain a swab specimen from its inside.

### Complications
Recurrent pneumothorax, subcutaneous emphysema, or infection may result from chest tube removal.

### Documentation
Record the date and time of tube removal; amount, color, consistency, and odor (if any) of drainage in the bottle; vital signs and depth and quality of the patient's respirations before and after the procedure; and any specimen obtained for culture.

HELEN HAHLER D'ANGELO, RN, MSN

# Phrenic Pacing
[*Diaphragm pacing*]

*Phrenic pacing induces respiration by*

*means of a surgically implanted device, which, when electrically stimulated by an external transmitter and antenna, stimulates the phrenic nerve. This phrenic impulse then causes the diaphragm to descend smoothly, allowing air to be drawn into the lungs.*

*The phrenic pacemaker is most commonly implanted in a patient with chronic dysfunction of the respiratory-control center or with muscle paralysis caused by high cervical spinal-cord trauma or by innervational or synaptic malfunction. A control dysfunction—stemming from tumor, hemorrhage, cerebrovascular accident, or central alveolar hypoventilation (Ondine's curse)—can affect voluntary or involuntary respiration, depending on the site of the cerebral lesion; because the spinal cord is divided into two tracts, voluntary respiration can be maintained after loss of involuntary control. The most common cause of respiratory muscle paralysis is spinal cord damage. Other innervational causes include amyotrophic lateral sclerosis (Lou Gehrig's disease) and Guillain-Barré syndrome; synaptic malfunction can stem from myasthenia gravis. Depending on the cervical or brainstem area affected, the patient with one of these progressive disorders may need partial or total ventilatory support. For successful phrenic pacing, the patient's lungs, diaphragm, and phrenic nerves should be normal, and his anterior horn cells intact from the third to the fifth cervical vertebrae. Phrenic nerve pacing is indicated only to correct chronic respiratory malfunction, not an acute disorder.*

*Loss of involuntary respiratory control usually requires implantation of only one pacemaker, to accomplish breathing during sleep. Loss of both voluntary and involuntary control requires implantation of two pacemakers, one for each phrenic nerve, each operated alternately for 12 hours to prevent diaphragm fatigue. Pacing begins 10 to 14 days after implantation, allowing surgical incisions to heal and edema or other surgical effects on the phrenic nerve to diminish. The pacing schedule varies,*

# SURGICAL IMPLANTATION OF THE PHRENIC PACEMAKER

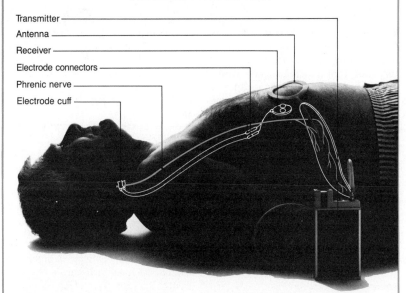

Transmitter
Antenna
Receiver
Electrode connectors
Phrenic nerve
Electrode cuff

A surgeon implants a phrenic pacemaker under local anesthesia. He places the electrode cuff around the phrenic nerve, above the clavicle, usually on the left side. He selects the left side for implantation because any damage on this side will affect pulmonary function less than damage to the right phrenic nerve, which controls ventilation of the larger right lung. The surgeon places the pacemaker in a subcutaneous pocket at the costal margin in the axillary or midaxillary line. Then, before completing surgery, he briefly activates the pacemaker with a sterile antenna to ensure its proper operation and to determine threshold and maximal diaphragmatic contraction. The postoperative orders should include the setting rate.

The pacemaker emits a current that flows from the *transmitter* to the *antenna*, then to the *receiver* through the *electrode connectors* to the *electrode cuff*. This current activates the phrenic nerve, setting the *diaphragm* into motion. The diaphragm pulls air into the lungs resulting in inspiration.

depending on the patient's condition and the underlying disorder. Usually, prolonged dependence on mechanical respiration foreshadows prolonged adaptation to the desired pacing schedule and poor tolerance of initial pacing trials. For example, the patient with central alveolar hypoventilation, in which involuntary respiratory control is lost, may require 3 hours of daily practice for several days before he can switch to regular nocturnal pacing. After 10 to 14 days of successful nocturnal pacing, the patient usually can be discharged with the pacemaker. However, the patient with respiratory-muscle paralysis, such as quadriplegia, must be slowly weaned from mechanical ventilation and eased onto the pacemaker. The schedule begins with short periods of phrenic nerve stimulation to condition a diaphragm weak from inactivity. Conversion from a ventilator to full-time pacing may take several months of gradual buildup.

## Equipment

Pacing antenna □ transmitter □ 9-volt batteries □ battery tester □ adhesive or nonallergenic tape ☐ stethoscope ☐ watch ☐ abdominal binder (optional) ☐ spirometer ☐ 10-ml syringe ☐ suction equipment ☐ sphygmomanometer ☐ mechanical ventilator, as needed.

## Preparation of equipment

Check the doctor's order for the transmitter setting and specific pacing schedule. Wash your hands. Using the battery tester, check the transmitter's battery *to ensure an adequate charge.* If necessary, replace the battery. Adjust the transmitter's amplitude dial to the ordered setting, if necessary. *To ensure that each stimulation is effective,* pacing is usually performed at or slightly above the patient's maximum setting (the setting that produces maximum diaphragmatic contraction) instead of at the threshold setting (the lowest setting that produces any stimulation). Securely tape the dial *to prevent accidental movement.* Have a ventilator available and ready to use if the patient is totally dependent on respiratory support.

## Essential steps

• Assess the patient's condition before beginning the pacing trial.
• Make sure the patient is awake, *because you'll need his cooperation.* Explain the procedure to him, ask if he's allergic to adhesive tape, and provide privacy.
• Feel the patient's chest wall to find the surgically implanted receiver. Apply the antenna to the skin directly over the receiver and tape it securely in place.
• Assist the patient into position, as ordered, usually flat or with the head of the bed elevated 30°. If possible, avoid a sitting position, *which inhibits diaphragmatic movement and causes minute volume to drop sharply.* If the patient must sit, try to counteract this effect by applying an abdominal binder *to elevate the diaphragm to its maximum position.*
• Tell the patient you'll activate the pacemaker after his next expiration. Then, after the expiration, turn on the transmitter.

• Observe the patient's abdomen for respiratory movement, and auscultate his lungs bilaterally for breath sounds.
• Tell the patient the pacemaker induces inspiration 10 to 15 times a minute (faster for an infant or small child) and shuts off automatically during expiration.

*To monitor the patient during initial pacing trials:*
• Frequently turn him from side to side *to prevent atelectasis from diminished respiratory movement on the nonpaced side.*
• Using a spirometer, monitor minute and tidal volumes, as ordered. If the patient has a tracheostomy, use the syringe *to inflate the tracheostomy cuff for minute-volume calculations and to deflate it again for the remainder of pacing time.*
• Closely monitor vital signs. Observe for signs of diaphragm fatigue, such as patient fatigue, decreased tidal volumes and abdominal (diaphragm) movement. Also observe for signs of hypoxia and hypercapnia, such as tachycardia, hypotension, or cyanosis. If any of these symptoms occur, stop phrenic pacing, resume mechanical ventilation or have the patient resume voluntary respiration, and notify the doctor.
• Keep the patient informed of his progress and reassure him that the pacemaker is operating correctly, especially during the initial pacing trials. Occasionally, tell him how long the trials must continue.

*To stop pacing:*
• Tell the patient that you'll turn off the pacemaker after his next expiration, and that he'll have to breathe voluntarily or with the help of a ventilator. Then, after expiration, turn off the transmitter switch. If necessary, connect the patient to the ventilator.
• Watch the patient closely *to ensure adequate ventilation.* Check for abdominal movement and auscultate bilaterally for breath sounds.
• Untape and remove the antenna. Check the antenna site for redness or irritation.
• Store the pacing equipment and supplies in the patient's room in preparation for the next pacing trial.

• Make sure the patient is comfortable and breathing properly before you leave.

## Special considerations

If the pacemaker fails to function properly, first check the battery. If the battery is charged, change the antenna. If the pacemaker still fails to function, switch to a mechanical ventilator, if necessary.

Reduce the dependent patient's fear of pacemaker failure by making sure he has access to an alarm system. For the quadriplegic, this means a system he can activate with his tongue or head in an emergency.

Auscultate the patient's lungs at least several times every 8 hours, and suction as necessary.

Discontinue pacing during times when the patient's intrathoracic pressure changes, such as during vomiting or endotracheal suctioning, *because phrenic stimulation may draw aspirate into the lungs.*

If the patient has trouble swallowing and is being fed through a gastric tube, wait at least 30 minutes after meals before beginning a pacing session. *This reduces the risk of aspiration of gastric contents, which can result from the high intrathoracic pressures generated by pacing.* If the patient is quadriplegic or being paced full-time for some other reason, teach him to swallow food just after the end of inspiration *to prevent aspiration.*

Avoid giving the patient with a phrenic pacemaker tranquilizers, sedatives, or antihistamines, *because these may further depress respiratory drive.*

Caution the patient not to change any of the pacemaker settings, *since these are preset by the doctor according to the results of flow studies.* Tell him to keep the transmitter and antenna dry *to prevent minor electric shock and malfunction.* This will restrict the patient being paced full-time to sponge baths. Instruct him to avoid twisting the antenna connection, *because it could break off.*

Warn the patient not to lean against any large metal surfaces while pacing, *because the conducting surface will di-*rect current from the pacemaker battery, causing the pacemaker to falter or stop.

Begin patient teaching and discharge planning as early as possible. If possible, involve the patient's family.

## Complications

Injury to one or both phrenic nerves prevents the pacemaker from adequately supporting ventilation. Injury may occur during or after surgery and result from damage by the pacemaker's electrode cuff or reduced blood supply to the nerve. The phrenic nerve can recover spontaneously—completely or partially—but recovery is often slow and usually takes a year or more.

Diaphragm fatigue may follow prolonged continual stimulation of the phrenic nerve. Infection at the implant site may occur, indicated by elevated temperature and WBC count, and redness, swelling, and discharge around the operative site.

The implanted receiver may fail mechanically because of seepage of body fluids into its electrical components. Receiver failure may follow a period of erratic pacing or sharp pain over the operative site, but the pacer may also fail without warning.

Upper airway obstruction may result from or be worsened by pacing in patients with central alveolar hypoventilation. Its early symptoms include confusion, restlessness, tachycardia, and diaphoresis. Late symptoms of airway obstruction include stridor, chest wall retractions, and cyanosis.

## Documentation

Record the date and time the patient begins pacing; duration of the pacing session; the side paced; minute and tidal volumes in liters; average minute volume; respiratory rate; the patient's position; use of an abdominal binder; time patient resumes spontaneous or ventilator-assisted breathing; any complications and the nursing action taken; and the patient's tolerance of the procedure.

JANET S. D'AGOSTINO, RN, MSN

# 10 Gastrointestinal Care

# Gastrointestinal Care

## Introduction

Nursing procedures involving the gastrointestinal (GI) tract have varied uses: gastric lavage cleanses the stomach of ingested poisons, whereas giving sodium polystyrene sulfonate (Kayexalate) enemas helps reduce serum potassium. These procedures are used most commonly, however, in the diagnosis and treatment of GI disorders.

GI disturbances affect just about everyone at one time or another. Disorders of this delicate system, so intimately tied to psychological health and stability, range from simple changes in bowel habits, such as constipation, to severe and potentially fatal disorders that may require major surgery, such as colostomy or ileostomy.

### Searching for a cause

Managing a GI disturbance successfully begins with a careful search for the cause—a particularly difficult task with this system. Finding the cause of GI symptoms depends on the answers to many questions: Does the patient have a primary disease of the GI tract or a primary disease of another body system that's causing his GI disorder? What activities of daily living may be contributing factors? Daily stress or poor diet, for example, often induces GI disorders. Psychological factors are often associated with nausea, vomiting, and anorexia—conditions that can affect a patient's appetite, hunger, and satiety. Certain illnesses, drugs, and toxic agents can result in intraabdominal inflammatory disorders or mechanical or neurologic obstruction in the GI tract.

The search for a cause is further complicated by the fact that assessing the GI system requires extraordinary skills. Assessing GI function can be difficult because it produces no obvious normal values, such as pulse rate or respirations, to use as a convenient yardstick. Fortunately, technologic advances in the diagnosis and treatment of GI problems have resulted in the development of sophisticated equipment, such as fiberoptic endoscopes, which allow direct visualization and, at times, treatment of GI pathologies.

### Nursing responsibilities

The nurse's role in managing GI disturbances varies greatly, reflecting the wide spectrum of systemic abnormalities. Nursing responsibilities may be as simple and routine as teaching an elderly patient good health habits and dietary principles that will help him maintain regularity. Or they can be highly specialized, as exemplified by the rigorously precise duties of the nurse who works in a GI laboratory performing and assisting with diagnostic tests.

The nurse also plays a critical role in the management of GI pathologies that require long-term medical treatment and behavior modification. For example, she must help the patient with a chronic duodenal ulcer to become aware of how certain pivotal changes in his life-style, such as giving up cigarettes or curbing a tendency to drink excessively, will help him live more comfortably with his GI disorder. Similarly, she must be prepared to provide appropriate patient teaching and emotional support for patients facing difficult diagnostic tests or invasive GI procedures that often prove to be not only uncomfortable but extremely embarrassing. Helping the patient in this situation to maintain his sense of dignity, while at the same time eliciting his cooperation during the procedure, requires a skillful tempering of compassion with practicality.

### Emerging field

The patient who has undergone major GI surgery usually needs special postoperative support since the surgical procedure will more than likely require that he make permanent and often difficult changes in his life-style. Recognition of the unique problems that confront ostomy patients, for example, has led to the creation of a challenging new field of nursing care—enterostomal therapy. Nurses trained in this field work primarily with colostomy and ileostomy patients to help them meet their physical and psychosocial needs. Enterostomal therapists (ETs) are also trained to manage wound drainage and skin irritation, which frequently plague the ostomy patient. They often encourage such a patient to join an ostomy club, which can help him adjust to necessary changes in his life-style by allowing him to share his fears and concerns with other ostomy patients.

### Team effort

Many different health-care personnel help the nurse care for a patient with a GI disorder. The pharmacist, for example, has contributed much to research efforts to improve patient comfort and reactions to GI disturbances. Simply adding antacids to many drugs has decreased uncomfortable side effects; the formulation of complex acid-base principles has greatly enhanced pharmaceutical management of GI conditions and has eased preoperative preparation of many patients. The sheer number and diversity of GI drugs make the pharmacist a key resource for the nurse in identifying special hazards and side effects and ensuring safe administration and patient comfort.

Research and technology have also produced many advances in nutritional therapy for the management of the GI patient. The benefits of parenteral nutrition (intravenous hyperalimentation) have been widely publicized and are now considered routine in the management of certain digestive disorders or such debilitative conditions as cancer. The clinical success of intravenous hyperalimentation has stimulated renewed interest and research in various methods of gastric and duodenal gavage, bringing significant advances in enteral hyperalimentation. Supplementary enteral feedings provide additional calories, protein, and carbohydrates, whereas maintenance feedings offer the only source of nutrition. Besides advances in feeding techniques, new formulations of nutritional supplements have benefited the patient with malabsorption syndrome.

Doctors have long recognized both the emotional and physical needs of the GI patient. Where to place an abdominal incision and whether or not to remove a diseased GI organ are decisions with important emotional implications for the patient. Knowledge of normal anatomy and physiology, as well as a familiarity with surgical procedures, influences the nursing-care plan for a postoperative GI patient. For example, the nurse who knows that an intestinal obstruction requires immediate decompression of the colon will anticipate a loop colostomy with an initially larger than usual stoma and a larger peristomial surface area. Collaborating with the doctor makes it easier to prepare patients for surgery and to plan postoperative care.

Great progress has been made, in short, by health-care professionals to improve patient compliance and comfort in the diagnosis and treatment of GI disorders. Nursing's unique contribution is providing expert, continuous, and individualized patient care and teaching.

CAROL GRAMSE, RN, PhD

## DIAGNOSIS

# Preparation for Contrast Radiography

*Radiographic studies of the gastrointestinal (GI) tract and associated organs help detect such abnormalities as obstructions, strictures, inflammatory disease, ulcers, and structural changes. Administration of a contrast medium before or during such studies accentuates the densities of abdominal regions and structures, facilitating interpretation of the resulting radiographs. Barium sulfate (an inert nonallergenic substance) is the contrast medium used for radiographic studies of the GI tract; iodine-based contrast media are required for radiographs of the gallbladder, pancreas, spleen, and various ducts.*

*Radiographic studies with iodine-based contrast media require a careful review of the patient's history to detect allergies to iodine, seafood, or iodine-based contrast agents. They also require careful patient preparation before the test and close observation afterward for delayed hypersensitivity reactions (see* Contrast Radiography Fact Sheet, *pages 518 to 519). Certain conditions, such as ulcerative colitis and active GI bleeding, contraindicate the use of laxatives and enemas in preparation for contrast radiography.*

## Equipment

Enema administration equipment (for upper GI and small bowel series, barium enema, oral cholecystography, I.V. cholangiography, and postoperative cholangiography) □ sedative or analgesic (for percutaneous transhepatic cholangiography, endoscopic retrograde cholangiopancreatography, and splenoportography) □ six tablets (500 mg each) of iopanoic acid (for oral cholecystogram) □ 1 g of ampicillin for I.V. administration (for percutaneous transhepatic cholangiography) □ cathartic, such as castor oil (for upper GI and small bowel series, barium enema, and I.V. cholangiography). Some hospitals have commercially prepared barium enema preparation kits.

## Essential steps

● Explain the procedure to the patient *to ease anxiety and aid cooperation.*
● Make sure the patient (or a responsible family member) has signed a consent form.

*Before a barium swallow:*
● Tell the patient that the barium preparation he will be asked to drink looks like a milk shake and tastes chalky.
● Inform patient that stools will appear chalky for 24 to 72 hours after test.
● Withhold all food, fluids, and oral medications, unless ordered otherwise, after midnight on the day of the test.

*Before an upper GI and small bowel series:*
● Tell the patient the barium preparation he will be asked to drink looks like a milkshake and tastes chalky.
● Place the patient on a low-residue diet for 2 to 3 days before the test, *to cleanse his bowel.* Encourage him to drink clear liquids.
● Withhold anticholinergics and narcotics for 24 hours, *because they may decrease peristalsis and impede the elimination of barium from the GI tract after the procedure.*
● Administer a cathartic and a saline or warm tap-water enema the night before the test, if ordered.
● Withhold all food, fluids, and oral medications after midnight on the day of the test, unless otherwise ordered. Also, if the patient is a smoker, withhold cigarettes after midnight on the day of the test *because nicotine stimulates peristalsis and increases gastric secretions, which dilute the contrast agent and can result in inaccurate test results.* If reflux

# CONTRAST RADIOGRAPHY FACT SHEET

| TEST | PURPOSE | POSTTEST CARE |
|---|---|---|
| **Barium swallow** Cineradiography of pharynx and fluoroscopy of esophagus after swallows of barium sulfate. Takes about 30 minutes. Usually part of upper GI series. | To diagnose hiatal hernia, diverticula, and varices; to detect strictures, tumors, polyps, and motility disorders *Contraindications:* intestinal obstruction | • Give ordered cathartic. • Record and describe stools. • Notify the doctor if the patient hasn't expelled barium in 2 to 3 days. • Let the patient resume oral intake when test is done. |
| **Upper gastrointestinal and small bowel series** Fluoroscopy of the esophagus, stomach, and small intestine after ingesting barium. Can take up to 6 hours for full small bowel films. | To detect hiatal hernia, diverticula, varices; aid diagnosis of strictures, ulcers, tumors, regional enteritis, malabsorption syndrome; motility disorders *Contraindications:* digestive tract obstruction or perforation | • Administer a cathartic or enema, if ordered. • Record and describe stools. • Notify the doctor if barium isn't expelled in 2 to 3 days. • Allow the patient to resume his usual diet and medications if more films aren't required. |
| **Barium enema** Fluoroscopic and radiographic examination of the large intestine after a barium sulfate enema, which the patient retains temporarily. In double-contrast technique, the colon is inflated with air, before or after expulsion of the barium. Takes 30 to 45 minutes. | To aid diagnosis of colorectal cancer and inflammatory disease; to detect polyps, diverticula, and structural changes. *Contraindications:* tachycardia, fulminant ulcerative colitis associated with systemic toxicity, toxic megacolon, and suspected perforation or obstruction | • Administer a cathartic, if ordered. • Record and describe the patient's stools. • Notify the doctor if the patient hasn't expelled barium in 2 to 3 days. • Allow the patient to resume his usual diet and medications if more films aren't required. • Encourage bed rest and increased fluid intake. |
| **Hypotonic duodenography** Fluoroscopic examination of the duodenum after instillation of barium sulfate and air through an intestinal catheter. After catheter placement, I.V. glucagon or I.M. anticholinergic induces duodenal hypotonia. Takes about 30 minutes. | To detect small postbulbar duodenal lesions, tumors of the head of the pancreas, and tumors of the ampulla of Vater; to aid diagnosis of chronic pancreatitis *Contraindications:* anticholinergics in patients with severe cardiac disorders or glaucoma | • Watch for side effects after administration of glucagon or an anticholinergic. Anticholinergic can cause urinary retention. • Anticholinergics cause temporary blurred vision. Take safety precautions. • Administer a cathartic, if ordered. • Record and describe stools. • Notify the doctor if barium isn't expelled in 2 to 3 days. • Let the patient resume oral intake when test is done. |
| **Percutaneous transhepatic cholangiography** Fluoroscopic examination of the biliary ducts after injection of contrast agent into a biliary radicle. Takes about 30 minutes. | To distinguish between obstructive and nonobstructive jaundice; to determine the location, extent, and cause of mechanical obstruction *Contraindications:* cholangitis, massive ascites, uncorrectable coagulopathy | • Check the patient's vital signs every 15 minutes for 1 hour, every 30 minutes for 4 hours, every hour for 4 hours, and then every 4 hours until stable. • Enforce bed rest for 6 hours after test, with patient lying on the right side to help prevent hemorrhage. • Check the injection site for bleeding, swelling, tenderness. Watch for signs of peritonitis. • Have patient resume usual diet and medications when test is done. |

## CONTRAST RADIOGRAPHY FACT SHEET (continued)

| TEST | PURPOSE | POSTTEST CARE |
|------|---------|---------------|
| **I.V. cholangiography** Radiography and tomography of the biliary ducts after I.V. infusion of a contrast agent. Also to examine gallbladder unable to concentrate oral contrast agent. Takes 2 to 4 hours. | To detect stones, strictures, and congenital abnormalities of biliary tree *Contraindications:* hyperthyroidism, severe renal or hepatic damage, tuberculosis | • Observe for signs of late hypersensitivity to the dye. • Have the patient resume his usual diet and medications. • Check the I.V. site for redness and swelling. Apply warm compresses, if necessary. |
| **Oral cholecystography** Radiography of the gallbladder 10 to 14 hours after taking contrast agent. May include fat ingestion after gallbladder examination to cause filling of the common bile duct. Takes 30 to 45 minutes. | To detect gallstones; to aid diagnosis of inflammatory disease and tumors of gallbladder *Contraindications:* severe renal or hepatic damage | • Have the patient resume his usual diet and medications after the test. |
| **Postoperative cholangiography** Radiography and fluoroscopy of the biliary ducts (and possibly gallbladder) follows injection of a contrast agent into a T-tube placed in the common bile duct during surgery. Takes about 15 minutes. | To detect calculi, strictures, neoplasms, and fistulas in the biliary ducts *Contraindications:* none | • If T-tube is still in place, attach it to drainage collection container. If T-tube is removed, apply a sterile dressing over the site. Change as needed. • Have the patient resume his usual diet and medications. |
| **Endoscopic retrograde cholangiopancreatography** Radiographic examination of the pancreatic ducts and hepatobiliary tree. Follows injection of a contrast agent into the pancreatic and common bile ducts through an endoscope. After catheter placement, I.V. glucagon or I.M. anticholinergic induces atony and relaxation of the ampullary sphincter. Takes 30 to 60 minutes. | To evaluate obstructive jaundice; to diagnose cancer of the duodenal papilla, pancreas, and biliary ducts; to locate calculi and stenosis in the pancreatic ducts and hepatobiliary tree *Contraindications:* infectious disease, pancreatic pseudocysts, esophageal or duodenal stricture or obstruction, acute pancreatitis, cholangitis, cardiac or respiratory disease, and glaucoma. | • Check vital signs every 15 minutes for 1 hour, every 30 minutes for 4 hours, then as ordered. • Patient may resume oral intake after gag reflex returns. • Observe for signs of cholangitis (hyperbilirubinemia, fever, chills) and pancreatitis (upper left quadrant pain, elevated serum amylase). • Check for signs of urinary retention. If the patient hasn't urinated in 8 hours, notify doctor. • If the patient has a sore throat, soothe with lozenges and warm saline gargles, if ordered. |
| **Splenoportography** Cineradiographic examination of the splenic veins and portal system. Follows injection of a contrast agent into the splenic pulp with a needle inserted percutaneously. Takes 30 to 45 minutes. | To diagnose or assess portal hypertension; to stage cirrhosis *Contraindications:* ascites, uncorrectable coagulopathy, splenomegaly due to infection, markedly impaired liver or kidney function | • Check the patient's vital signs every 15 minutes for 1 hour, every 30 minutes for 4 hours, and every hour for 4 hours until stable. • Observe puncture site for bleeding, swelling, and tenderness. • Have the patient lie on left side for 24 hours *to reduce risk of bleeding.* • Patient may resume usual diet. • Encourage fluid intake. • Draw blood for hematocrit, as ordered. |

is suspected, withhold antacids for several hours before the test.

• Inform the patient that his stools will appear chalky for 24 to 72 hours after the test.

*Before a barium enema:*
• Place the patient on a low-residue diet for 1 to 3 days before the test. If ordered, restrict his diet to clear liquids on the day before the test or for dinner.

• *To ensure adequate hydration,* encourage the patient to drink water or clear liquids 12 to 24 hours before the test.

• Administer a cathartic, such as 1½ to 2 oz (45 to 60 ml) of castor oil, the afternoon before the test, as ordered.

• Give the patient a cleansing enema the night before the test, if ordered.

• About 1 hour before the test, give the patient a light breakfast of toast and black coffee or plain tea, if permitted.

• Inform the patient that his stools will appear chalky for 24 to 72 hours after the test.

*Before hypotonic duodenography:*
• Withhold all food, fluids, and oral medications after midnight on the day of the test, unless otherwise ordered.

• Tell the patient he may belch instilled air or pass flatus during and after the test. Also inform him that his stools will appear chalky for 24 to 72 hours after the test.

• Inform the patient of the possible side effects of the glucagon (nausea, vomiting, hives, flushing) or anticholinergic drug (thirst, dry mouth, tachycardia, blurred vision) that will be used during the procedure.

• Ask the patient to void before going to the radiology department, *because he may experience urinary retention after the procedure as a side effect of the anticholinergic drug.*

*Before oral cholecystography:*
• Check the patient's history for hypersensitivity to iodine, seafood, or any iodine-based contrast agent.

• On the day before the test, instruct the patient to eat a lunch containing simple fats—such as eggs, milk, and butter— *to stimulate the release of bile from the*

*gallbladder* and a fat-free dinner *to inhibit gallbladder contraction and the loss of contrast agent from the gallbladder.*

• Give the patient six tablets (500 mg each) of iopanoic acid (the contrast agent) 2 to 3 hours after dinner, as ordered. Tell him to swallow one tablet every 5 minutes, using no more than two mouthfuls of water each time. Then, withhold all fluids *to help concentrate the contrast agent in the gallbladder.*

• Restrict all fluids, food, oral medications, unless otherwise ordered, and cigarette smoking, after midnight on the day of the test. Cigarettes are withheld because the nicotine causes an increase in peristalsis through the small bowel which stimulates the gallbladder to contract and to empty the contrast agent into the duodenum. This can result in inadequate visualization of the gallbladder, requiring that the test be repeated.

• Administer a cleansing enema in the morning, if ordered.

*Before I.V. cholangiography:*
• Check the patient's history for hypersensitivity to iodine, seafood, or iodine-based contrast agents.

• Place the patient on a low-residue diet the day before the test, *to cleanse his bowel.*

• Provide a dinner high in simple fats (eggs, milk, butter) the night before the test *(to stimulate the release of bile from the gallbladder).* Then, withhold all food. Encourage intake of fat-free liquids, however, *to reduce the risk of renal toxicity from the contrast agent.*

• The night before the test, give the patient 1½ to 2 oz (45 to 60 ml) of castor oil; in the morning, if ordered, administer a cleansing enema.

*Before percutaneous transhepatic cholangiography:*
• Check the patient's history for hypersensitivity to iodine, seafood, or an iodine-based contrast agent. Also note any abnormalities of bleeding, clotting, prothrombin time, and platelet count, *because this test can cause hemorrhaging from the insertion of a needle through the liver and into the hepatic duct.*

• Administer 1 g of ampicillin I.V. every

4 to 6 hours for 24 hours before the test, if ordered, *because this very invasive study is associated with a higher than average rate of infection after the procedure.*
● Withhold all food, fluids, and oral medications for 8 hours before the test.
● Administer a sedative, if ordered, 30 minutes before the test.

*Before postoperative cholangiography:*
● Check the patient's history for hypersensitivity to iodine, seafood, and any iodine-based contrast agent.
● Clamp the T-tube the day before the test, as ordered, *to allow bile to fill the tube and to prevent air bubbles from entering the ducts.*
● Withhold the meal just before the test.
● Administer a cleansing enema 1 hour before the procedure, if ordered.

*Before endoscopic retrograde cholangiopancreatography:*
● Check the patient's history for hypersensitivity to iodine, seafood, and any iodine-based contrast agent.
● Withhold all food, fluids, and oral medications, unless otherwise ordered, after midnight on the day of the test.
● Inform the patient of the possible side effects of the glucagon (nausea, vomiting, hives, flushing) or anticholinergic drug (thirst, dry mouth, tachycardia, blurred vision) that will be used during the test.
● If the patient wears dentures, ask him to remove them.
● Ask the patient to void before going to the radiology department, *because he may experience urinary retention after the procedure as a side effect of the anticholinergic drug.*
● Take the patient's vital signs 30 minutes before the test *to establish baseline data.*

*Before splenoportography:*
● Check the patient's history for hypersensitivity to iodine, seafood, and any iodine-based contrast agent. Also note any abnormalities of bleeding, clotting, prothrombin time, and platelet count. (This test can cause excessive bleeding that may require blood transfusion or,

occasionally, splenectomy.)
● Withhold all food, fluids, and oral medications, unless otherwise ordered, after midnight on the day of the test.
● Administer a sedative and an analgesic before the test, as ordered.
● Take the patient's vital signs 30 minutes before the test *to establish baseline data.*

**Special considerations**
Specific steps in the preparation of patients for contrast radiography may vary; always follow the doctor's orders or the institution's policy.

Before sending the patient to the radiology department, make sure he puts on a hospital gown and removes all jewelry and metal objects that might obscure anatomic detail on the radiograph.

**Documentation**
If the patient is on a special diet, describe it in the nurse's notes. Note when fasting began, if applicable. Record any drugs administered or withheld on the medication record, and in the nurse's notes. Also record in the nurse's notes any enemas given and the results.

KAREN DYER VANCE, RN, BSN

# Endoscopy of the Upper Gastrointestinal Tract

*Endoscopic examination of the upper gastrointestinal (GI) tract allows direct visualization of the esophagus, the stomach, and the duodenum. It may be performed to confirm radiographic findings, to locate and remove foreign bodies, to evaluate complications after gastric and duodenal surgery, and to obtain a biopsy specimen or brushings for cytologic examination. Endoscopy can also help diagnose dyspepsia in the absence of positive radiographic findings and can differentiate ulcers from tumors and intramural from extrinsic lesions. Other indications for this procedure are suspected esophageal stenosis or varices, esophagitis, hiatal hernia, gastritis, polyps, obstructive lesions, and gastric or peptic ulcers.*

*This procedure is executed by the doctor with the nurse assisting. It is best performed in a treatment room, the radiology department, or an operating room, but it can be performed at bedside if the patient can't be moved. This examination is contraindicated in patients with a large aortic aneurysm, acute oral or oropharyngeal inflammation, acute myocardial infarction, and severe cardiac decompensation. Abnormal coagulation studies also contraindicate surgical procedures that can be performed through the endoscope, such as a polypectomy.*

### Equipment

Heparin lock or I.V. infusion equipment □ local anesthetic for throat (spray or gargle) □ emesis basin if gargle is used □ linen-saver pad □ sedatives (usually diazepam or meperidine hydrochloride) □ 3-ml syringe □ appropriate needle □ alcohol sponges □ diluted heparin and tuberculin syringe (to flush heparin lock) □ flexible, fiber-optic endoscope with appropriate attachments (for aspiration, air instillation, biopsy, or photography) □ water-soluble lubricant □ suction machine □ specimen bottles containing 10% formalin for biopsy □ container of 95% ethyl alcohol □ specimen labels □ resuscitation equipment and narcotic antagonists (for emergency use) □ mouthpiece (optional, depending on doctor's preference).

Make sure all equipment is working properly. Keep the resuscitation equipment and narcotic antagonists handy in case of possible severe respiratory depression from sedation.

### Essential steps

*About 1 hour before the procedure:*
● Reinforce the doctor's explanation of the procedure to the patient.

● Make sure the patient or a responsible family member has signed a consent form before he receives a sedative.
● Make sure the patient has had nothing by mouth for at least 6 hours.
● Check the patient's medication record for hypersensitivity to drugs used for premedication.
● Instruct the patient to remove any dentures, partial plates, or detachable caps from his mouth.
● Give him an opportunity to void.
● Provide a hospital gown for him to wear during the procedure.
● Take and record baseline vital signs.
● If ordered, administer a sedative.
● Transport the patient to the assigned room or department on a stretcher.

*To begin the procedure:*
● Wash your hands and provide privacy.
● Place the patient in the supine position on the examining table. (If necessary, this procedure can be performed with the patient on the stretcher.)
● Insert a heparin lock or start an I.V. infusion in an arm vein *for medication administration.*
● Instruct the patient to open his mouth and hold his breath. Spray his throat with a local anesthetic *to suppress the gag reflex.* (The doctor may ask the patient to gargle with a local anesthetic instead.) The anesthetic takes effect in 2 to 3 minutes.
● Place the patient in the left lateral position *to allow for better visualization of the greater curvature of the stomach and easier access to the pylorus.*
● Put a linen-saver pad under cheek.
● If the patient was not sedated before the procedure (or if more sedation is necessary), draw up the prescribed amount of sedative *so the doctor can administer it through the heparin lock or I.V. port.* If a heparin lock is being used, follow the administration of the sedative with diluted heparin according to hospital policy *to maintain patency of the heparin lock.*
● Monitor the patient's blood pressure, pulse, and respirations every few minutes throughout the procedure.
● The doctor may wish to place a mouth-

piece between the patient's teeth *to prevent the patient from biting his fingers or the endoscope.* Reassure the patient that the mouthpiece won't interfere with his breathing.

• The doctor lubricates the endoscope with the water-soluble lubricant.

• Tilt the patient's chin toward his chest, keeping his head in midline, *so the doctor can insert a finger into the patient's mouth and guide the endoscope to the back of the throat.*

• The doctor passes the endoscope in stages, examining each structure as the tube advances. *To obtain the best possible view,* he'll aspirate any mucus or other secretions and instill air to distend structures. Reassure the patient during these steps, and hold his head and shoulders firmly *to help him maintain the proper position,* keeping his chin toward the table *to allow secretions to drain onto the linen-saver pad.* Instruct him to let saliva drain from the side of his mouth and not to try to swallow it.

• *To perform a biopsy,* the doctor passes biopsy forceps through the endoscope to the distal end. If requested, assist him by holding the end of the forceps while he positions the endoscope in the appropriate area, and then by opening and closing the forceps *to obtain tissue specimens.* After removing the specimens, the doctor places them in one or more of the bottles containing 10% formalin.

• *To collect specimens for cytology,* the doctor passes a small brush through the endoscope and brushes suspicious areas of the esophageal or stomach mucosa. He withdraws the brush and places the specimen in the container of 95% ethyl alcohol or places a sample of the specimen on a microscopic slide and applies the spray fixative.

• After the doctor removes the endoscope and mouthpiece, wipe the patient's mouth.

• *After the procedure,* monitor his vital signs every 30 minutes until stable, or as ordered. Remove the heparin lock or I.V. infusion, as ordered.

• Instruct the patient to remain lying down until the effects of the sedative have worn off and you have determined that his vital signs are within normal limits.

• Label each specimen with the patient's name, room number, date, and the site where it was obtained, and then send the specimens to the laboratory.

• Discard all disposable equipment; return reusable equipment to the appropriate department for sterilization.

• Caution the patient not to eat or drink until the effects of the local anesthetic wear off (usually in 30 minutes to 1 hour) and his gag reflex returns (usually 2 to 4 hours). This dictates when the patient can resume liquid intake.

• Tell the patient to inform you if he spits up blood, experiences pain, or has difficulty breathing, *as these are symptoms of complications.*

## Special considerations

Reassure the patient during the procedure *to promote cooperation and ease his anxiety.* If the patient is frightened, he may move suddenly and thus cause trauma or perforation of the upper GI tract by the endoscope.

During the procedure, the doctor may attach a camera to the endoscope to take photographs. The fluoroscope is used during endoscopic retrograde cholangiopancreatography *to visualize the pancreatic ducts and hepatobiliary tree after contrast dye is injected into the duodenal papilla through the endoscope.* Observe the patient for any allergic reactions to the dye.

The local anesthetic sprayed into the patient's mouth tastes bitter and may cause the tongue and throat to feel swollen. If the patient is heavily sedated and has trouble swallowing saliva, turn him on his side and/or suction him *to prevent aspiration of secretions.*

As the endoscope passes the pylorus, the patient may experience some abdominal discomfort or may retch. Advise him to breathe deeply and slowly *to help relax the abdominal muscles.* He also may experience a feeling of fullness or an urge to defecate as air passes into the stomach and duodenum.

The patient may experience a sore

throat after the procedure which may be relieved by drinking liquids or using throat lozenges after the gag reflex returns. Rarely, the patient's throat may be irritated enough to bleed slightly when he coughs.

Advise outpatients to arrange a ride home: *They shouldn't drive for at least 12 hours after the test because of the sedative given during the procedure.*

## Complications

The most common complication associated with endoscopic examination of the upper GI tract is perforation. Esophageal perforation near the cervical area causes difficulty in swallowing, severe discomfort, and neck stiffness with pain aggravated by swallowing; perforation in the thoracic area causes epigastric substernal pain that is exacerbated by breathing and moving; perforation near the diaphragm causes shoulder pain, dyspnea, severe back and abdominal pain, tachycardia, cyanosis, diaphoresis, and hypotension.

Gastric perforation causes severe back and abdominal pain, tachycardia, cyanosis, diaphoresis, and hypotension with a drop in temperature followed by a high fever. After duodenal perforation, vital signs may remain stable initially; then sudden local or general abdominal pain occurs. Although a brief period of improvement follows, peritonitis develops. The patient's abdomen becomes rigid, and he develops a high fever, hypotension, tachycardia, and severe pain that inhibits abdominal movement and the ability to breathe deeply.

Hemorrhage—another complication— may result from trauma or perforation and is indicated by hematemesis, hypotension, and tachycardia.

Other possible complications include adverse reactions to the drugs used.

## Documentation

Record patient preparation, both during and after the procedure, in nurse's notes. Record vital signs on the flowchart or in nurse's notes. Record any medications administered on the medication sheet.

Document in nurse's notes the collection of any specimens, the sites where obtained, and the signs of any complications and subsequent nursing action taken.

CAROL A. CALIANNO, RN, AD

# Endoscopy of the Lower Gastrointestinal Tract

*Proctosigmoidoscopy and colonoscopy are the two endoscopic procedures used to examine the lower gastrointestinal (GI) tract. In both procedures, a doctor inserts an endoscope—a fiber-optic or rigid endoscope for proctosigmoidoscopy; a fiber-optic scope for colonoscopy— through the anus. Proctosigmoidoscopy allows visualization of the distal sigmoid colon, the rectum, and the anal canal. Colonoscopy allows examination of these same structures, as well as the descending, the transverse, and the ascending colon and the cecum.*

*These procedures can confirm radiographic findings. They can also be used to obtain biopsy, cytology, and culture specimens; to perform polypectomy; to locate and coagulate bleeding points; and to diagnose such conditions as cancer, polyps, strictures, ulcerative colitis, and Crohn's disease.*

*Nursing responsibilities and preferred settings for these procedures are the same as for endoscopic examination of the upper gastrointestinal tract. Proctosigmoidoscopy with a rigid scope can be done more easily in the patient's room because the equipment is portable. Endoscopic examination of the lower GI tract is contraindicated in pregnant patients and in those with acute inflammatory disease of the colon, suspected bowel perforation, myocardial infarc-*

tion, and severe cardiac decompensation.

## Equipment

Enema administration equipment □ oral laxative □ hospital gown □ drape □ gloves □ water-soluble lubricant □ endoscope (with biopsy forceps, cytology brush, and culture swab as needed) □ suction machine □ specimen bottles containing 10% formalin □ container with 95% ethyl alcohol or microscopic slide with spray fixative □ culture tubes □ specimen labels □ 4″ x 4″ gauze sponges or tissues □ stretcher if needed □ emergency resuscitation equipment (for both procedures) □ large cotton swabs (for proctosigmoidoscopy) □ optional: (for colonoscopy) heparin lock or I.V. line, sedative, 3-ml syringe, alcohol sponges, appropriate needle; narcotic antagonist.

## Preparation of equipment

Bring all equipment to the area where the procedure will be performed. Make sure all equipment is working properly. Keep resuscitation equipment readily available. For colonoscopy, keep narcotic antagonists handy to counteract possible severe respiratory depression from the sedatives.

## Essential steps

Before the procedure:
• Make sure the patient or a responsible family member has signed an informed consent form. Reinforce the doctor's explanation of the procedure to the patient.
• For colonoscopy, keep the patient on a clear liquid diet for 24 to 48 hours before the procedure, as ordered; administer laxative the evening before the test, as ordered; and about 3 to 4 hours before the procedure, give the patient warm tap-water enemas (1 to 2 liters) until the return is clear.
• About 3 to 4 hours before proctosigmoidoscopy, give the patient two warm tap-water or sodium biphosphate (Fleet) enemas, as ordered.
• Give the patient an opportunity to urinate, and have him put on the hospital gown.

• For colonoscopy, administer a sedative, if ordered. (The doctor will order additional sedation administered through the I.V. line as needed by the patient during the procedure.) Raise the side rails to prevent falls while the patient is sedated.
To begin either procedure:
• Wash your hands, and, if appropriate, help the patient onto the examining table. (If fluoroscopy will be used to confirm the position of the endoscope during colonoscopy, help the patient onto the fluoroscopy table.)
• Record baseline vital signs. Leave the blood pressure cuff in place so you can monitor the patient's blood pressure frequently during the procedure.
• For colonoscopy, insert the heparin lock or start an I.V. infusion, as ordered, to establish an open vein for administering a sedative or emergency medications.
• The doctor injects the sedative, usually diazepam or meperidine (or both). After the sedative is given, monitor the patient's vital signs and observe him closely for respiratory depression and bradycardia.
• Position the patient in the left lateral position with his knees flexed, for colonoscopy, or in the knee-chest or left lateral position, for proctosigmoidoscopy.
• Drape the patient to minimize embarrassment.
• Tell the patient to breathe slowly and deeply as the doctor uses a gloved, lubricated finger to examine the rectum for tenderness and induration and for blood, mucus, and feces.
To perform colonoscopy:
• After the doctor lubricates the colonoscope, instruct the patient to breathe slowly and deeply to relax the anal sphincters and thus facilitate passage of the endoscope.
• Following insertion of the endoscope, the doctor insufflates a small amount of air to help dilate the bowel lumen. Then he advances the instrument into the sigmoid colon. When the colonoscope advances to the descending sigmoid junction, place the patient in the supine or another

position, as ordered, *to facilitate passage through the splenic flexure, the transverse colon, the hepatic flexure, the ascending colon, and the cecum.* (The doctor may use suction at any time during the procedure, to remove blood or secretions that obscure his vision.)

• If ordered, apply gentle pressure to the patient's abdomen *to facilitate passage of the endoscope.*

• After the doctor views the mucosa of the various structures, he may pass the biopsy forceps or a cytology brush through the colonoscope to obtain specimens. Biopsy specimens are placed in the containers of formalin; cytologic specimens are placed in the containers of 95% ethyl alcohol or on a microscopic slide with spray fixative. As the doctor gently withdraws the instrument, he again examines the mucosa.

*To perform proctosigmoidoscopy:*

• After the doctor lubricates the proctosigmoidoscope, tell the patient to breathe slowly and deeply, *so the doctor can pass the instrument more easily.* The doctor lifts the patient's right buttock and inserts the scope into the rectum.

• While the doctor advances the scope to the rectosigmoid junction, he may insufflate air *to facilitate passage into the sigmoid colon.*

• The doctor examines the sigmoid, then the rectal and anal mucosa as he slowly removes the instrument. When using a rigid scope, he may pass a large cotton swab through the instrument or use suction to remove fecal matter, blood, or mucus that blocks his vision. With a flexible scope, only suction is possible.

• If appropriate, the doctor may pass the biopsy forceps, cytology brush, or culture swab through the proctosigmoidoscope to collect specimens. He'll place a specimen for histology in a container with 10% formalin, a specimen for cytology in a container of 95% ethyl alcohol or on a microscopic slide with spray fixative, and a specimen for culture in a culture tube.

*After colonoscopy and proctosigmoidoscopy:*

• If appropriate, help the patient onto a stretcher for return to his room.

• Instruct the patient to remain in bed for 1 to 2 hours until the sedative wears off.

• Label all specimens and send them to the laboratory.

• After colonoscopy, monitor vital signs every 30 minutes until stable, and then remove the heparin lock or I.V. infusion, unless otherwise ordered.

• Observe the patient for signs of complications, such as hemorrhage (which include increased pulse rate, decreased blood pressure, weakness, pallor, rectal bleeding, and possibly abdominal pain and distention). Also look for signs of perforation (which include sudden, severe abdominal pain that becomes generalized, possibly accompanied by abdominal distention, malaise, fever, a change in vital signs, and bloody or mucopurulent rectal drainage).

• Discard disposable equipment; return reusable equipment to the appropriate department for cleaning and disinfection.

## Special considerations

When giving the enemas before the procedure, administer the solution slowly and don't advance the tube too high into the colon. Usually, you shouldn't give more than three enemas without specific orders. If ordered, give an oral electrolyte solution (containing potassium chloride and sodium bicarbonate in 6 to 9 liters of normal saline solution) instead of the enemas over 2 to 3 hours to end about 4 hours before the procedure. *This causes diarrhea and effectively cleans the large intestine;* however, some patients can't tolerate it. If rectal bleeding or severe abdominal pain occurs during any of these preparatory steps, notify the doctor immediately.

Reassure the patient during the procedure *to promote cooperation and ease his anxiety.*

 A frightened patient is more likely to make sudden movements during endoscopy and thus is more susceptible to trauma and perforation.

The endoscope may feel cool when the doctor first inserts it, and the patient may feel the urge to defecate. *To help minimize this effect, warm a rigid scope by holding it under warm running water immediately before insertion.* The patient may also experience cramping as the scope moves through the bowel. If so, breathing slowly and deeply will help relax his abdominal muscles. When the injected air moves down the bowel and escapes, he will experience flatulence. Reassure him that this is normal.

If soreness occurs at the I.V. injection site, you can relieve this with warm compresses. After proctosigmoidoscopy, the patient may resume normal activity within a few minutes.

Administer additional medications during colonoscopy, as ordered. The doctor may order atropine to control bowel spasms or glucagon to paralyze the bowel for a polypectomy. If either is used, monitor the patient closely for hypotension and irregular pulse (expect atropine to increase the pulse rate).

After a polypectomy, the doctor usually orders overnight hospitalization so the patient can be observed for signs of complications, such as pain and bleeding. Also, inform the patient of dietary restrictions, as ordered. (Such restrictions after polypectomy normally include liquids only for the first 24 hours; soft, low-roughage food for the next 24 hours; and regular, low-residue foods for a few weeks.)

### Complications

The most common complications are hemorrhage and perforation.

### Documentation

Record patient preparation, the specific procedure performed, the patient's tolerance of the procedure, the medications administered, and the time and route of administration. Also note the collection of any specimens and transfer to the laboratory. Document the patient's vital signs on the flowchart, and note any complications during the recovery period.

CAROL A. CALIANNO, RN, AD

# Abdominal Paracentesis

*Performed by a doctor with a nurse assisting, abdominal paracentesis is the aspiration of fluid from the peritoneal space through a needle (or a trocar and cannula) inserted in the abdominal wall. This procedure, which may be performed at bedside or in a treatment room, is both diagnostic and therapeutic: It can help determine the cause of ascites and relieve the pressure created by this condition. It can also help diagnose intra-abdominal bleeding following trauma or provide a peritoneal fluid specimen for laboratory analysis.*

*Nursing responsibilities for abdominal paracentesis include preparing the patient, monitoring his condition and providing emotional support during the actual procedure, assisting the doctor, and labeling specimens properly before sending them to the laboratory. This procedure must be performed cautiously in pregnant patients and in patients with bleeding tendencies or unstable vital signs.*

### Equipment

Tape measure □ linen-saver pads □ sterile paracentesis tray □ specimen containers □ large, sterile collection container □ dry, sterile pressure dressing □ laboratory requisition slips □ optional: shave-preparation kit, multidose vial of local anesthetic (if anesthetic not included on tray), alcohol sponge.

The sterile paracentesis tray is prepackaged and usually includes the following: sterile gloves and drapes; local anesthetic (1% or 2% lidocaine); antiseptic (70% alcohol or povidone-iodine); 5-ml syringe with 21G or 25G needle; scalpel; needle holder and suture; scissors; sterile hemostat; aspiration device (either a 16G to 24G sterile spinal needle with a 50-ml Luer-Lok syringe, or a sterile 10G to 24G trocar and cannula); three-way stopcock; drainage tubing; 4″ x 4″

## PATIENT POSITIONING FOR ABDOMINAL PARACENTESIS

Have the patient sit in a chair with his feet flat on the floor. Support his back and arms with pillows. If he can't sit up, place him in a high Fowler's position in bed, as ordered.

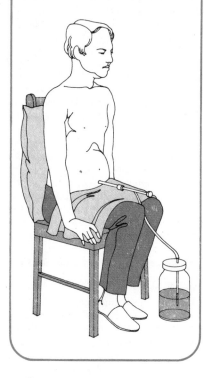

sterile gauze sponges.

### Essential steps

• Explain the procedure to the patient *to ease his anxiety and promote cooperation.* Tell him he will feel a stinging sensation when the local anesthetic is injected, and some pressure when the needle or trocar and cannula are inserted and when abdominal fluid is aspirated.
• Make sure the appropriate consent form has been signed.
• Shave the aspiration site, if ordered.

• Instruct the patient to void before the procedure *to reduce the risk of accidental injury to the bladder when the needle or trocar and cannula are inserted.*
• Record baseline vital signs, weight, and abdominal girth *for posttest comparison.* Use the tape measure to determine the patient's abdominal girth at the umbilical level.
• Have the patient sit in bed or on a chair, with his feet and back firmly supported. *In this position, gravity causes fluid to accumulate in the lower abdominal cavity, and the pressure created by the abdominal organs facilitates fluid flow.*
• Make the patient as comfortable as possible. Keep him covered, except at the puncture site, *to prevent chilling.* Place a linen-saver pad under him.
• Remind the patient to remain as still as possible during the procedure, *to prevent injury from the needle or trocar and cannula.*
• Wash your hands. Then, open the paracentesis tray, using sterile technique.
• If asked, pour the antiseptic onto a sterile 4″ x 4″ gauze sponge held by the doctor.
• As necessary, assist with the injection of the local anesthetic. If the paracentesis tray doesn't contain a sterile ampul of anesthetic, wipe the top of a multidose vial of anesthetic solution with an alcohol sponge, and invert the vial at a 45° angle. *This allows the doctor to insert the sterile 5-ml syringe with the 21G or 25G needle and withdraw the anesthetic without touching the nonsterile vial.*
• The doctor may make a small incision with the scalpel before inserting the needle or trocar and cannula (usually 1″ to 2″, or 2.5 to 5 cm, below the umbilicus). When the needle or trocar pierces the peritoneum, it produces a sound.
• Help the doctor collect the aspirated peritoneal fluid in the appropriate specimen and collection containers. (If drainage of a substantial amount of fluid is ordered, connect the three-way stopcock and tubing to the cannula and run the other end of the tubing to the large sterile collection container.)

• Aspiration of more than 1,500 ml of peritoneal fluid at one time may induce hypovolemic shock because of fluid shift from the circulatory system. Monitor the patient's vital signs every 15 minutes, and observe closely for vertigo, faintness, diaphoresis, pallor, heightened anxiety, tachycardia, dyspnea, and hypotension. If any of these develop, report them to the doctor immediately.

• After the doctor removes the needle or trocar and cannula, he may suture the incision. Apply a sterile pressure dressing to the site, and help the patient assume a comfortable position.

• Monitor the patient's vital signs and check the dressing for drainage every 15 minutes for 1 hour, every 30 minutes for 2 hours, every hour for 4 hours, and then every 4 hours for 24 hours *to detect delayed reactions to the procedure.* Note the color, amount, and character of any drainage.

• Label the specimens, and send them to the laboratory with the appropriate requisition slip. If the patient is receiving antibiotics, note this on the requisition slip. *This information will be considered during fluid analysis.*

• Remove and dispose of all equipment properly.

### Special considerations

Throughout this procedure, explain each step thoroughly to the patient and provide emotional support. If the patient shows any signs of hypovolemic shock, reduce the vertical distance between the needle or the trocar and cannula and the collection bag *to slow the drainage rate.* If necessary, stop the drainage.

If the doctor cannot aspirate peritoneal fluid easily, he may ask you to reposition the patient *to facilitate drainage.*

After the procedure, observe for peritoneal fluid leakage or scrotal edema; if these signs develop, notify the doctor. When the patient's condition allows, record his weight and abdominal girth and compare these measurements with the baseline figures.

### Complications

Hypovolemic shock may result from the sudden shift of fluid from the circulatory system to the peritoneum to replace aspirated fluid. Other possible complications include perforation of abdominal organs by the needle or the trocar and cannula, hepatic coma from decreased systemic circulation and reduced tissue perfusion, and wound infection.

### Documentation

In the nurse's notes, record the date and time of the procedure, the location of the puncture site, and the presence of any sutures. Document the amount, color, viscosity, and odor of aspirated fluid in the nurse's notes and in the intake and output record. Record the patient's vital signs, weight, and abdominal girth measurements before and after the procedure. Also note his reaction to the procedure, vital signs, and any signs and symptoms of complications that may have occurred during the procedure. Record the specimens sent to the laboratory.

SUSAN VIGEANT, RN, BSN
PAULA STEPHENS OKUN, RN, MSN

# Peritoneal Lavage

*Peritoneal lavage can detect free blood in the peritoneal cavity. A catheter is inserted through the abdominal wall into the cavity; peritoneal fluid is then aspirated by syringe. If the aspirated fluid contains no gross blood, a balanced salt solution is infused and then siphoned by gravity drainage. A sample of the siphoned fluid is inspected for gross appearance of blood and then sent to the laboratory for microscopic examination. Strict sterile technique must be maintained throughout this procedure to prevent the introduction of microorganisms into the peritoneum, which could result in peritonitis. Nursing responsibilities during this procedure include preparing the patient and assisting the doctor.*

*Patients who most often need peritoneal lavage are those with histories of blunt abdominal trauma—from a fall or motor vehicle accident, for example. Injuries to the back, flanks, rib cage, and pelvis also may necessitate peritoneal lavage to rule out associated abdominal injury. Peritoneal lavage is contraindicated in pregnant patients and in patients with penetrating abdominal injuries. It should be used cautiously in conditions causing bowel dilatation and in patients with multiple abdominal scars.*

## Equipment

*For patient preparation:* Foley catheter and drainage bag □ nasogastric tube □ gastric suction machine □ shave-preparation kit.

*For lavage:* I.V. pole, macrodrip I.V. tubing, and I.V. solution (1 liter of balanced salt solution, usually lactated Ringer's) □ peritoneal dialysis tray □ sterile gloves □ antiseptic solution (such as povidone-iodine) □ 3-ml syringe with 25G 1″ needle □ bottle of 1% lidocaine with epinephrine □ #14 8″ (20.3 cm) intracatheter, extension tubing, and a small sterile hemostat (to clamp tubing) □ 20-ml syringe □ 30-ml syringe □ one 20G 1½″ needle □ three containers for specimen collection (sterile tube for culture and sensitivity specimen [C & S], large purple-top collection tube, and red-top collection tube) □ appropriate antiseptic ointment □ 4″ x 4″ gauze sponges □ 1″ hypoallergenic tape □ alcohol sponges.

A commercially prepared peritoneal dialysis kit is available. It contains #15 peritoneal dialysis catheter, with trocar and extension tubing with roller clamp. Make sure the macrodrip I.V. tubing doesn't have a reverse flow (or backcheck) valve that would prevent infused fluid from draining out of the peritoneal cavity.

## Essential steps

● Provide privacy, and wash your hands. Reinforce the doctor's explanation of the procedure to the patient, and make sure

he (or a responsible family member) has signed a consent form.
● Catheterize the patient with the Foley catheter, and connect it to the drainage bag. *This reduces the risk of accidental puncture of the bladder during trocar or catheter insertion.*
● Insert the nasogastric tube, and attach it to the gastric suction machine and set on low, or as ordered, to empty the patient's stomach. *This decompresses the stomach—which prevents vomiting and subsequent aspiration—and minimizes the possibility of bowel perforation during trocar or catheter insertion.*
● Open the shave-preparation kit, and shave the patient's abdomen from the umbilicus to the pubic area.
● Set up the I.V. pole. Attach the macrodrip tubing to the I.V. solution container and clear the tubing of air, *to avoid introducing air into the peritoneal cavity during lavage.*
● Open the peritoneal dialysis tray, using sterile technique. After the doctor puts on sterile gloves, he cleanses the patient's abdomen from the costal margin to the pubic area and from flank to flank with the antiseptic solution and drapes the area with sterile towels from the tray *to create a sterile field.* Using sterile technique, hand the doctor the 3-ml syringe and 25G 1″ needle.
● With an alcohol sponge, clean the rubber stopper on the vial of 1% lidocaine with epinephrine, and hold the vial so the doctor can insert the needle and withdraw the anesthetic.
● The doctor injects the patient's skin ¾″ to 1⅛″ (2 to 3 cm) directly below the umbilicus (or at an adjacent site if a surgical scar is present) and administers the anesthetic.
● After the anesthetic has taken effect, he uses the scalpel from the tray to make an incision about ¾″ (2 cm) long through the skin and subcutaneous tissues of the abdominal wall. Then, he retracts the tissue, ligates blood vessels, and uses the 4″ x 4″ gauze sponges to absorb blood in the area *to prevent a false-positive test result.*
● The doctor directs the trocar into the

midline of the pelvis until it enters the peritoneum. The peritoneal dialysis catheter is then advanced over the trocar 6″ to 8″ (15 to 20 cm) into the pelvis, the 20-ml syringe is attached to it, and fluid is aspirated from the peritoneal cavity.
• The presence of unclotted blood, bile, or intestinal contents in the fluid is considered a positive result. If findings are positive, the procedure is terminated, and the patient is prepared for a laparotomy.
• If findings are negative, connect the catheter extension tubing to the I.V. tubing, and instill 500 to 1,000 ml of the I.V. solution into the peritoneal cavity over a 10- to 15-minute period. Then, clamp the tubing. (For pediatric patients, use 10 ml of solution/kg of body weight.)
• Unless contraindicated by the patient's injuries (for example, a spinal cord injury or fractured ribs), gently turn the patient from side to side *to distribute the fluid throughout the peritoneal cavity.* (If turning is contraindicated, the doctor may perform deep, gentle palpation on the sides of the abdomen *to distribute the fluid.*)
• After 10 to 15 minutes, place the I.V. container below the level of the patient's body, and open the clamp on the I.V. tubing. Be careful not to disconnect the tubing from the dialysis catheter. Complete drainage of the peritoneal cavity may take 20 to 30 minutes.
  Be sure to vent glass I.V. containers with a needle *to promote flow.* Such venting is unnecessary with plastic bag containers.
• Using the 30-ml syringe and 20G needle, withdraw 25 to 30 ml of fluid from a port in the I.V. tubing. Clean the top of the specimen containers with an alcohol sponge, and place approximately 10 ml of fluid in the sterile collection tube for C & S, the large purple-top collection tube, and the red-top collection tube. If the specimen for C & S was not obtained first, change the needle *to prevent contamination of the specimen.* Label the specimens, and send them to the laboratory immediately for cell counts, chemistry testing, and an amylase, bile, and

microscopic evaluation of spun-down sediment. Positive test results usually indicate the need for a laparotomy. If the patient's condition is stable, borderline positive results may indicate the need for echography and arteriography. If test results are questionable, the catheter is left in place in case lavage must be repeated.
• If test results are negative, the doctor removes the catheter and sutures the incision.
• Apply the antiseptic ointment. Then, cover the incision with a 4″ x 4″ gauze sponge and secure it with 1″ hypoallergenic tape.
• Discard disposable equipment. Return reusable equipment to the appropriate department for cleaning and resterilization.

## Special considerations
After the lavage, monitor the patient's vital signs, as ordered.
  If abdominal X-rays have been ordered, they should precede peritoneal lavage. *X-rays taken after lavage may be unreliable because of air introduced into the peritoneal cavity.*

## Complications
Bleeding may occur at the incision site or intraabdominally because of laceration of blood vessels. A visceral perforation causes peritonitis and necessitates laparotomy for repair. If the patient is already experiencing respiratory distress, infusion of the balanced salt solution may cause additional stress, precipitating respiratory arrest.

## Documentation
Record the type and size of the peritoneal dialysis catheter used, the type and amount of solution instilled and withdrawn from the peritoneal cavity, the amount and color of the fluid returned, and whether the fluid flowed in and out of the abdomen freely. Note what specimens were obtained and sent to the laboratory. Also note any complications that may have occurred and the nursing action taken.

MARYELLYN TISON, RN, MS

532  GASTROINTESTINAL CARE

# Collection of Pinworm Eggs

*Probably the most common helminthic infection in humans, enterobiasis (pinworm infestation) occurs most commonly in children who live in temperate climates. The adult worm (Enterobius vermicularis) lives in the lower gastrointestinal tract. The female migrates from the anus—usually while the host sleeps—to lay eggs in the perianal and perineal regions. This causes intense itching and scratching, which in turn can lead to reinfestation by the anus-to-finger-to-mouth route.*

*Pinworm eggs are so light they float in the air, usually after being shaken from bedding or clothing, which can lead to infestation through inhalation or ingestion. Retroinfestation can occur when eggs hatch and larvae migrate back into the intestine.*

*The test for enterobiasis involves microscopic identification of eggs collected from the perianal and perineal areas on cellophane tape. The test should be performed early in the morning, before bathing or bowel movement removes the eggs.*

### Equipment
2½″ (6.3 cm) of cellophane tape □ tongue blade □ clean gloves □ glass slide □ laboratory requisition form.

### Essential steps
• Explain the procedure to the patient.
• Make a loop of the tape with the sticky side facing out, and hang it on one end of the tongue blade.
• Put on the gloves *to prevent contaminating your hands.*
• Using the tongue blade, press the sticky surface of the tape against both sides of the perianal and perineal areas *to collect eggs.*
• Place the tape sticky side down on the glass slide, and send it to the laboratory

immediately with the appropriate requisition form.
• Remove the gloves and dispose of them properly. Wash your hands.

### Special considerations
Specimens collected on three successive mornings are usually sufficient to detect eggs.

Explain to the patient or his parents the importance of personal cleanliness and of handwashing before eating. Suggest that all sheets and underwear be changed every day until the infestation clears. Emphasize that all family members should be checked for infestation. If the patient is a child, his school should be notified.

### Documentation
Record the time and date the specimen was collected and sent to the laboratory.
SHEILA SCANNELL JENKINS, RN, BSN

# Abdominal Girth Measurement

*Abdominal girth measurement can detect significant changes in size. Patients with postoperative paralytic ileus or ascites, for example, require repeated measurements for abdominal distention that must be exact. A tape measure is inaccurate, because it can easily be placed in a different spot on the abdomen each time or pulled tighter by one nurse than by another. An abdominal girth gauge— a device made of tongue blades, tape, and rubber bands—can provide accurate measurements, guaranteeing a consistent, uniform procedure.*

### Equipment
Scissors □ 2″ tape □ two tongue blades □ two large rubber bands □ tape measure □ two cotton-tipped applicators □ tincture of benzoin □ felt-tipped pen □ optional: razor, soap and water, basin, washcloth, and towel.

# APPLYING AN ABDOMINAL GIRTH GAUGE

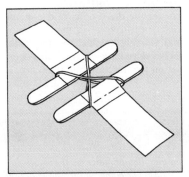

Construct an abdominal girth gauge like the one shown above. Note that the rubber bands form an X between the tongue blades.

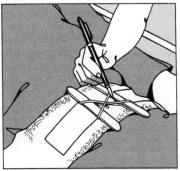

Position the gauge on the patient's abdomen so the midpoint of the X is directly over the patient's umbilicus. Mark the skin of the abdomen with a pen at the inner edges of the tongue blades.

## Preparation of equipment

Cut two 5″ (12.7-cm) pieces of adhesive tape. Place each piece on a flat surface, with its sticky side up. Center the tongue blades vertically across each piece of tape, approximately 1″ (2.5 cm) from the end. Fold the tape over each tongue blade to secure it. Move the tongue blades to within 2″ to 3″ (5 to 7.6 cm) of each other. Then, crisscross the rubber bands over the tongue blades to form an X (as shown in the illustration above ).

## Essential steps

- Explain the procedure to the patient and provide privacy.
- Place the patient in the supine position.
- Center the tape measure directly over the patient's umbilicus, and measure his abdominal girth *to obtain a baseline reading.*
- If the patient has a lot of hair around his umbilicus, wash the area with warm, soapy water and shave it. Be sure to shave a large enough area—approximately 3″ (7.6 cm) on both sides—to allow room

for the tape. Dry the area thoroughly.

- Using the cotton-tipped applicators, apply tincture of benzoin to the areas where the adhesive tape will be applied, *to protect the skin and make the tape stick better.* Allow the preparation to dry.
- Place the abdominal girth gauge, with the sticky side of the tape facing down, over the patient's abdomen. Position it so the middle of the X formed by the rubber bands is directly over the umbilicus. Secure the tape to the skin smoothly.
- Using the felt-tipped pen, draw two lines on the patient's abdomen (one along the inner edge of each tongue blade) *to mark the starting point for abdominal girth measurement.*
- Mark the date, time, girth measurement (as determined with the tape measure), and your initials on the tape. Then, leave the gauge in place until measurement of abdominal distention is no longer necessary.

*For subsequent measurements:*

- Check whether the tongue blades have

moved farther apart from the lines drawn on the patient's abdomen. If they have, draw new lines along the inner edges of the tongue blades.

• Measure the distance between the old and new lines on both sides of the umbilicus. Add the numbers together *to determine how much larger the abdomen has grown since the last measurement.* Add this figure to the last measurement of abdominal girth to get the new measurement, and record this, as above, on the tape.

**Special considerations**

If the patient is ambulatory, cut the tongue blades *to prevent them from poking him when he sits or bends.* Tape the cut edges *to prevent scratches and splinters.*

**Documentation**

Record the date, time, and abdominal girth measurement in the nurse's notes and nursing cardex. Record girth in inches or centimeters (or both), depending on the institution's preference.

JANICE M. DIDICH, RN, BSN, MA

---

## MONITORING

# Insertion and Removal of an Esophageal Tube

*An esophageal tube is inserted to control intraesophageal and/or gastric hemorrhage caused by either esophageal or gastric varices, which typically result from portal hypertension. Usually inserted nasally, the tube is passed through the esophagus and into the stomach. A gastric balloon at the end of the tube is then inflated and drawn tightly against the cardia. This holds the tube in place and exerts pressure on the cardia to control hemorrhage from gastric varices. Most tubes also contain an esophageal balloon to create similar pressure on the esophagus.*

*A doctor inserts an esophageal tube in conjunction with other methods for controlling bleeding, such as iced saline irrigations and vasopressors. These combined methods provide effective, temporary control of acute variceal hemorrhage. Generally, the balloons are deflated after 24 to 48 hours, by which time other measures will have been taken to determine the source of bleeding and to control it. If the esophageal balloon remains inflated longer than 48 hours, pressure necrosis can develop, causing*

*further hemorrhage or perforation.*

*The most commonly used esophageal tubes are the three-lumen Sengstaken-Blakemore tube, the three-lumen Linton tube, and the four-lumen Minnesota esophagogastric tamponade tube (see* Three Types of Esophageal Tubes, *page 537).*

**Equipment**

Traction equipment (football helmet, or Basic frame with pulleys and a 1-lb, or 0.5-kg, weight) □ two drainage bags or two intermittent suction machines with connecting tubes □ disposable irrigation set with 50-ml syringe □ 1 liter of iced normal saline solution □ esophageal tube □ basin of water □ three rubber-shod clamps (two clamps and two plastic plugs for a Minnesota tube) □ blood pressure manometer (mercury manometer for a Minnesota tube) □ waterproof marking pen □ basin of ice □ anesthetizing nasal spray (as ordered) □ water-soluble lubricant □ stethoscope □ sponge rubber nasal cuff □ ½" adhesive tape □ Y-connector tube (for a Sengstaken-Blakemore or Linton tube) □ nasogastric tube (for a Sengstaken-Blakemore tube) □ 50-ml irrigating syringe □ scissors □ cup of water with straw.

**Preparation of equipment**

Attach the traction equipment to the bed, and have it ready to attach to the esophageal tube after insertion. Place the suction machines nearby and plug them in. If you're using drainage bags, remove them from their packages and place them nearby. Open the disposable irrigation set, and fill the container with normal saline solution. Place all other equipment within reach.

Test the balloons on the esophageal tube for air leaks by inflating them and holding them in the basin of water. If no bubbles appear in the water, they are intact. Remove them from the water, deflate them, and clamp their lumens, so they remain deflated during insertion.

To use the *Minnesota* tube, connect the mercury manometer to the gastric pressure monitoring port. Note the pressure when the balloon is inflated with 100, 200, 300, 400, and 500 cc of air.

Check the patency of the aspiration lumens, and make sure they are labeled according to their purpose. If not, label them carefully with the waterproof marking pen.

Chill the tube in a basin of ice *to stiffen it and thus facilitate insertion.*

### Essential steps

- Explain the procedure and its purpose to the patient, and provide privacy. Wash your hands.
- Place the patient in the semi-Fowler's position. *This position makes it easier for the stomach to empty and helps prevent aspiration.*
- The doctor checks the patency of the patient's nostrils.
- *To determine the length of tubing needed,* the doctor places the balloon at the xiphoid process, extends the tube to the ear and forward to the nose, and then marks this point on the tubing with the waterproof marking pen. Next, he sprays the posterior pharynx and nostril with an anesthetic *to minimize discomfort and gagging during intubation.*
- After lubricating the tip of the tube with water-soluble lubricant *to reduce friction and facilitate insertion,* the

━━━ EQUIPMENT

## SECURING ESOPHAGEAL INTUBATION

To reduce the risk of the gastric balloon slipping down from the cardia of the stomach, secure an esophageal tube to the face guard on a football helmet. Tape the tube, as shown, to the face guard, and fasten the chin strap.

If you need to remove the tube quickly, unfasten the chin strap, pull the helmet slightly forward, and cut the tape and the gastric balloon and esophageal balloon lumens while holding the tube near the nostril.

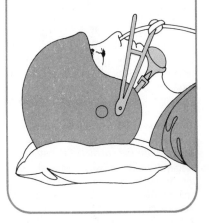

doctor passes the deflated tube through the more patent nostril. As he does, he asks the patient to tilt his chin toward his chest and to swallow when he feels the tip of the tube in the back of his throat. *This helps pass the tube into the esophagus and prevents intubation of the trachea.* (If the tube is introduced through the mouth, the doctor asks the patient to swallow immediately.) As the patient swallows, the doctor quickly pushes the tube forward until it is at least ½″ (1.3 cm) beyond the mark he has made.

- *To confirm tube placement,* the doctor aspirates stomach contents through the gastric port and auscultates the stomach with the stethoscope while injecting air. After inflating the gastric balloon with 20 cc of air, he obtains an abdominal X-ray; the visible outline of the partially inflated gastric balloon verifies correct placement. Using the 50-ml syringe, he irrigates the tube with normal saline solution and empties the stomach as completely as possible. *This prevents regurgitation of gastric contents as the balloon is inflated.*

• After confirming correct placement of the tube, the doctor inflates the gastric balloon with 250 to 500 cc of air (for the *Sengstaken-Blakemore* tube) or 700 to 800 cc of air (for the *Linton* tube) and clamps the tube. For the *Minnesota* tube, he first connects the pressure monitoring port for the gastric balloon lumen to the mercury manometer and then inflates the balloon in 100-cc increments until it is filled with 450 to 500 cc of air. As the air is introduced, the doctor monitors the intragastric balloon pressure. Then, he clamps the pressure monitoring and air inlet ports. For the *Sengstaken-Blakemore* or the *Minnesota* tube, he pulls up on the tube until he feels resistance. *This exerts pressure on the cardia of the stomach.* When the balloon is engaged, the doctor places the sponge rubber nasal cuff around the tube where it emerges from the nostril.

• Tape the cuff in place on the tube *to minimize pressure on the nostril from the traction, thus decreasing the possibility of necrosis.*

• The doctor then attaches traction to the tube with a traction rope and a 1-lb weight; he can also create traction by pulling gently on the tube and taping it securely to the face guard of a football helmet (see *Securing Esophageal Intubation,* page 535).

• If the pulley and weight are used, lower the head of the bed to about 25° *to produce countertraction.*

• Lavage the stomach through the gastric aspiration lumen with iced saline solution until the returns are clear. *This stops hemorrhage through vasoconstriction and empties the stomach; blood detected afterward in the gastric aspirate indicates that bleeding has not been controlled.*

• Attach one of the intermittent suction machines to the gastric aspiration lumen. *This empties the stomach, helps prevent nausea and possible vomiting, and allows continuous observation of the gastric contents for bleeding.*

• As ordered, inflate the esophageal balloon. (Usually, you'll do this immediately to control bleeding.) If a Sengstaken-Blakemore or a Minnesota tube has been used, inflate the esophageal balloon *to directly compress the esophageal varices.* To do this with a *Sengstaken-Blakemore* tube, attach the Y-connector tube to the esophageal lumen. Then, attach a sphygmomanometer inflation bulb to one end of the Y-connector and the manometer to the other end. Inflate the esophageal balloon to about 33 mmHg and clamp the tube. For the *Minnesota* tube, attach the mercury manometer directly to the esophageal pressure monitoring outlet. Then, using the 50-ml syringe and pushing the air slowly into the esophageal balloon port, inflate the esophageal balloon to between 35 and 45 mmHg.

• Set up esophageal suction *to prevent accumulation of secretions that may cause vomiting and pulmonary aspiration.* This is important, because secretions swallowed by a patient can't pass into the stomach with an inflated esophageal balloon in place. To do this with a *Linton* or a *Minnesota* tube, attach an intermittent suction machine to the esophageal aspiration port. For a *Sengstaken-Blakemore* tube, insert a nasogastric tube alongside it, into the esophagus, and then attach suction.

• *To remove the tube,* the doctor uses an irrigating syringe to aspirate the esophageal balloon until it is deflated. If bleeding does not recur, he removes the traction from the gastric tube. Then, he aspirates the gastric balloon to deflate it. The gastric balloon is always deflated just before removing the tube, *because it may ride up into the esophagus or pharynx, obstructing the air-*

# THREE TYPES OF ESOPHAGEAL TUBES

When using esophageal tubes, remember the advantages of each of these three types illustrated below. The *Sengstaken-Blakemore* three-lumen, double-balloon tube provides a gastric aspiration port that allows drainage from below the gastric balloon and also can be used for instilling medication. The *Linton* three-lumen,

single-balloon tube provides ports for esophageal and gastric aspiration and reduces the risk of esophageal necrosis because it doesn't have an esophageal balloon. The *Minnesota* four-lumen, double-balloon tube provides pressure-monitoring ports for both balloons without the need for Y-connectors.

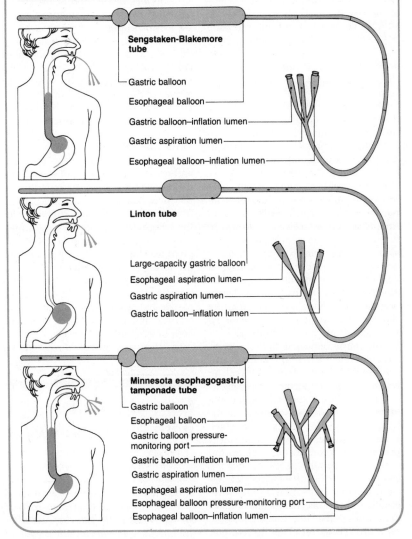

**Sengstaken-Blakemore tube**

Gastric balloon
Esophageal balloon
Gastric balloon–inflation lumen
Gastric aspiration lumen
Esophageal balloon–inflation lumen

**Linton tube**

Large-capacity gastric balloon
Esophageal aspiration lumen
Gastric aspiration lumen
Gastric balloon–inflation lumen

**Minnesota esophagogastric tamponade tube**

Gastric balloon
Esophageal balloon
Gastric balloon pressure-monitoring port
Gastric balloon–inflation lumen
Gastric aspiration lumen
Esophageal aspiration lumen
Esophageal balloon pressure-monitoring port
Esophageal balloon–inflation lumen

*way, or possibly causing asphyxia or rupture.*

• After disconnecting all suction tubes, the doctor gently removes the esophageal tube. If he feels resistance, he aspirates the balloons again. (To remove a *Minnesota* tube, he grasps it near the nostril and cuts all four lumens approximately 3″, or 7.6 cm, below his fingers. This ensures deflation of all balloons.)

### Special considerations

If any signs of cyanosis or airway obstruction develop during intubation, remove the tube immediately, *because it may have entered the trachea instead of the esophagus.* After intubation, keep the scissors taped to the head of the bed. If respiratory distress occurs, cut the tube across all lumens and remove it quickly.

During intubation, the patient can sip water through a straw *to facilitate swallowing as the tube is passed.*

If necessary, a specially trained nurse or technician from the orthopedics department can assist in setting up traction. Never use adhesive tape to secure the tube to the nose, *because the tension resulting from traction can cause necrosis.* As a safety measure, place a wad of adhesive tape or a tongue blade about 1″ (2.5 cm) from the pulley *to prevent the balloon from accidentally slipping into the esophagus, causing asphyxia or esophageal rupture.*

The intraesophageal balloon pressure varies with respirations and esophageal contractions. Baseline pressure is the important pressure.

While inflating the balloon on the *Minnesota* tube, note whether the intragastric balloon pressure rises 15 mmHg higher than the equivalent pressure recorded during preparation of the balloon. *This indicates that the gastric balloon is in the esophagus.* Because further distention could cause esophageal rupture, deflate the balloon and advance the tube further into the stomach. Then, reinflate the balloon

with 450 to 500 cc of air.

The balloon on the *Linton* tube should not remain inflated longer than 48 hours, *because necrosis of the cardia may result.* Generally, the doctor removes the tube only after a trial period of at least 12 hours with the esophageal balloon deflated or with the gastric balloon tension off the cardia. After removal, assist the patient with mouth care.

### Complications

Erosion and perforation of the esophagus and gastric mucosa may result from the tension placed on these areas by the balloons during traction. Inflation of the gastric balloon in the esophagus can cause esophageal rupture. Dislodgment of the tube can cause acute airway occlusion. Aspiration of oral secretions as well as erosions and necrosis of nasal tissues may also occur.

### Documentation

Record the date and time of insertion and removal, the type of tube used, and the name of the doctor who performed the procedure. Also document the intraesophageal balloon pressure (for the Sengstaken-Blakemore or Minnesota tube), the intragastric balloon pressure (for the Minnesota tube), or the amount of air injected (for the Sengstaken-Blakemore and Linton tubes); the amount of fluid used for gastric irrigation; and the color, consistency, and amount of gastric returns, both before and after lavage.

SHIRLEY L. EGGER, RN

# Care of a Patient with an Esophageal Tube

*Although a doctor inserts an esophageal tube, the nurse has the responsibility of caring for the patient during and after intubation. Typically, a patient with an esophageal tube is placed in the intensive care unit, where he is under close observation and receives constant care. He also requires a great deal of emotional support. A quiet environment helps increase the patient's tolerance of the procedure and helps control bleeding. Sedatives are used liberally, when possible, as the patient requires them.*

*Most important, the patient with an esophageal tube in place must be observed closely for esophageal rupture. The fact that varices weaken the esophagus, coupled with the risk of trauma during intubation and inflation of the esophageal balloon, increases the chance of rupture. If rupture occurs, emergency surgery is usually indicated, but the success rate is low.*

### Equipment
Manometer □ two 2-liter bottles of normal saline solution □ irrigation set □ water-soluble lubricant □ several cotton-tipped applicators □ mouth care equipment □ nasopharyngeal suction apparatus □ several #12 French suction catheters □ intake and output record sheets.

### Essential steps
● *To help ease the patient's anxiety,* explain the care you'll be giving. Provide privacy.
● Wash your hands.
● Monitor the patient's vital signs every 5 minutes to 1 hour, as ordered. A change in vital signs may indicate the onset of complications or the recurrence of bleeding.
● If you are using a Sengstaken-Blakemore or a Minnesota tube, check the manometer reading on the esophageal balloon every 15 to 30 minutes *to note any air leakage.*
● Maintain drainage and suction on gastric and esophageal aspiration ports, as ordered. *This is important, because accumulation of fluid in the stomach can cause the patient to regurgitate the tube; accumulation of fluid in the esophagus can cause vomiting and aspiration.*
● Irrigate the gastric aspiration port, as

ordered, using the irrigation set and normal saline solution. *Frequent irrigation prevents clogging in the tube, which could lead to regurgitation of the tube and vomiting.*
● *To prevent pressure sores,* clean the nostrils and lubricate them with water-soluble lubricant frequently. Use warm water to loosen crusted secretions around the nose before applying the lubricant with cotton-tipped applicators.
● Give mouth care frequently *to remove the taste of blood and to relieve dryness from mouth breathing.* Also, provide gentle oral suctioning, using the #12 French catheters, *to help remove secretions.*
● Provide emotional support. Keep the patient as quiet as possible and administer sedatives, as ordered. *This helps control bleeding, so the tube can be deflated as soon as possible.*
● If you are using traction, keep the sponge rubber nasal cuff in position around the nostrils. Change the nasal cuff when it becomes soiled *to make the patient more comfortable and to prevent skin irritation and infection.*
● Be sure the traction weights are suspended from the foot of the bed at all times. Instruct housekeeping and other co-workers not to move them.

 Never place the weights on the bed, *because a reduction in traction could change the position of the tube and cause bleeding.*
● Make sure the patient remains in the semi-Fowler's position *to supply countertraction for the weights and pulleys.*
● Monitor intake and output, as ordered.

### Special considerations
 Observe the patient carefully for esophageal rupture, usually indicated by signs and symptoms of shock, increased respiratory difficulties, and increased bleeding.

Tape a pair of scissors to the head of the bed, *so you can cut the tube quickly to deflate the balloons if the patient develops asphyxia.* When performing this

## SPECIAL USES FOR WIDE-BORE GASTRIC TUBES

As an alternative to the Levin tube and the Salem sump tube, you may use one of the three wide-bore tubes, illustrated at right. These allow large volumes of fluid to pass through faster, making them especially useful when lavaging the stomach of a patient with profuse gastric bleeding or after ingestion of poison. These tubes can't remain inside the patient as long as a Levin tube, because they're usually passed orally. (When absolutely necessary, they can be inserted through the nose.) Insert them only long enough to complete lavage and evacuate stomach contents.

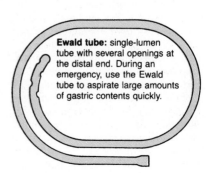

**Ewald tube:** single-lumen tube with several openings at the distal end. During an emergency, use the Ewald tube to aspirate large amounts of gastric contents quickly.

emergency intervention, firmly grasp the tube close to the nostril before cutting.

*Because the constant pressure from the balloons erodes the stomach and the esophagus,* the doctor deflates the balloons one at a time for 5 to 10 minutes every 12 hours.

Be sure to remove traction before deflating either balloon. *Deflating the balloon under tension triggers a rapid release of the entire tube from the nose, resulting in trauma to the mucous membrane, recurrence of bleeding, and possibly airway obstruction.*

An X-ray may be necessary to check the tube's position or to view the chest. To place X-ray films behind the patient's back, lift him in the direction of the pulley. Never roll him from side to side, *because this would exert pressure on the tube.* Move him similarly to make the bed or to place him on the bedpan *to avoid pressure on the tube.*

### Complications

Esophageal rupture, the most life-threatening complication associated with this procedure, can occur at any time, but is most likely during intubation or during inflation of the esophageal balloon. Asphyxia may result if the esophageal balloon moves up the esophagus

and blocks the airway. Aspiration from pooled esophageal secretions may also complicate this procedure.

### Documentation

Record intake and output, vital signs, routine care, and any drugs administered. Also note the color, consistency, and amount of gastric returns; any signs and symptoms of complications; and nursing action taken. Document when the balloons were deflated and by whom.

SHIRLEY L. EGGER, RN

# Insertion and Removal of a Nasogastric Tube

*The nasogastric tube, inserted into the stomach through the nose, has diagnostic and therapeutic uses: It can be used to assess and treat upper gastrointestinal tract bleeding, to collect gastric contents for analysis, to perform gastric lavage, to aspirate gastric secretions, and to administer medications and feedings. The nasogastric tube is also commonly used to prevent vomiting after major*

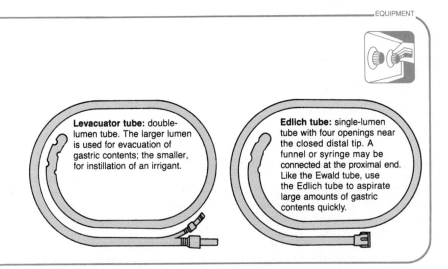

**Levacuator tube:** double-lumen tube. The larger lumen is used for evacuation of gastric contents; the smaller, for instillation of an irrigant.

**Edlich tube:** single-lumen tube with four openings near the closed distal tip. A funnel or syringe may be connected at the proximal end. Like the Ewald tube, use the Edlich tube to aspirate large amounts of gastric contents quickly.

surgery, by decompressing the stomach. Normally, the tube remains in place about 48 to 72 hours after surgery, by which time peristalsis usually returns. A doctor must order the removal of a nasogastric tube.

Insertion of a nasogastric tube, which may be performed by a nurse, requires close observation of the patient while the tube is passed, followed by verification of proper placement. The nurse may also remove the tube; this phase of the procedure necessitates careful handling to prevent injury and aspiration. Insertion must be performed cautiously in pregnant patients and in patients with aortic aneurysm, myocardial infarction, gastric hemorrhage, and esophageal varices. Fluoroscopy may be necessary to check tube position in patients with esophageal cancer and stenosis. Patients with conditions that limit its use must be evaluated carefully to weigh the risks and benefits of intubation.

### Equipment
For insertion of a nasogastric tube: nasogastric tube (usually #14 or #16 French for a normal adult) □ towel or linen-saver pad □ tissues □ emesis basin □ penlight □ ½" or 1" nonallergenic tape □ disposable gloves □ water-soluble lubricant □ glass of water (with straw) □ tongue blade □ 50-ml catheter-tip syringe □ stethoscope □ rubber band □ safety pin □ optional: metal clamp, tincture of benzoin, suction equipment, ice, warm water, Ross-Hanson tape, and pencil.

For removal of a nasogastric tube: stethoscope □ 50-ml catheter-tip syringe □ towel or linen-saver pad □ adhesive remover □ clamp (optional).

The most commonly used nasogastric tubes are the Levin and the Salem sump tubes. Tubes with wider bores are used for special purposes (see *Special Uses for Wide-bore Gastric Tubes*).

### Preparation of equipment
Inspect the tube for defects, such as rough edges or partially closed holes. To facilitate insertion of a limp rubber tube, refrigerate it or place it on ice for about 3 minutes. For easier insertion of a stiff plastic tube, immerse it in warm water to make it more flexible.

### Essential steps
● Provide privacy, wash your hands, and explain the procedure to the patient to ease his anxiety and promote cooperation.
● Place the patient in high Fowler's position.
   To insert the nasogastric tube:
● Stand at the patient's right side if you

are right-handed and at the left side if you are left-handed, *to facilitate tube insertion.*

• Drape the towel or linen-saver pad over the patient's chest *to protect the hospital gown from spills.*

• Place the tissues and emesis basin well within the patient's reach.

• Establish a signal the patient can use if he wants you to stop briefly during the procedure.

• Tell him to blow his nose gently *to clear his nostrils.*

• *To determine which nostril is more patent,* ask the patient if he has ever had nasal surgery, trauma, or a deviated septum. Then, inspect the nostrils with a penlight for any obvious obstruction. Finally, occlude one nostril at a time while the patient breathes through his nose. Choose the nostril with better air flow.

• *To determine the length of tube needed to reach the stomach,* place the end of the tube at the tip of the patient's nose. Then, extend it to the earlobe and down to the xiphoid process. Mark this distance with nonallergenic tape. (Measurements for an average size adult range from 22" to 26," or 55 to 66 cm.)

• Put on the disposable gloves.

• Coil the first 3" to 4" (7.6 to 10 cm) of the tube around your finger *to curve it, which makes it easier to pass.*

• Lubricate the coiled portion of the tube with the water-soluble lubricant *to prevent injury to the nasal passages. Using a water-soluble lubricant prevents oil-aspiration pneumonia if the tube accidentally slips into the trachea.* (Don't occlude the tube with the lubricant.)

• Instruct the patient to tilt his head back slightly.

• Grasp the tube with the curved end down and insert it into the nostril.

• Aim the tube downward and toward the closer ear. Advance it slowly *to avoid pressure on the turbinates,* which could cause pain and bleeding.

• When you feel the tube begin to curve down the pharynx, tell the patient to tilt his head forward *to close the trachea and open the esophagus.*

• Unless contraindicated, give the pa-tient a glass of water, and instruct him to sip the water through the straw. *This helps the tube pass into the esophagus.* (If you are not using water, ask the patient to swallow.) Then, rotate the tube 180° *to redirect the curve, so it won't enter the patient's mouth.*

• As the patient swallows, advance the tube until the tape mark reaches his nostril.

• *To check the placement of the tube,* ask the patient to talk. If he can't, the tube may be coiled in his throat or may have passed through his vocal cords.

• Use the tongue blade and penlight to examine the mouth and throat, especially in an unconscious patient.

• Attach the 50-ml catheter-tip syringe to the tube, and try to aspirate stomach contents. If you can't, position the patient on his left side *to move the contents in the stomach's greater curvature.* Then, attempt to aspirate again. If you still can't aspirate stomach contents, advance the tube 1" to 2" (2.5 to 5 cm) and try again.

• If you're still not sure the tube is in the stomach, place the stethoscope just below the xiphoid process and instill about 15 cc of air. *A whooshing sound means the tube is patent and properly placed in the stomach.* If the patient belches, the tube is in the esophagus.

• If, after these tests, you're still not sure the tube is in the stomach, notify the doctor, who may order X-rays *to confirm correct placement.*

• When correct placement of the tube is confirmed, clamp the tube with a metal clamp or plug it by folding it over and slipping the bend into the tube end.

• If the patient is diaphoretic, apply a small amount of tincture of benzoin to the skin that will be covered by tape.

• Cut a 3" (7.6-cm) length of 1" tape. Tear one end up the center about 1½" (3.8 cm). Tape the untorn end to the nose and crisscross the two free ends around the tube. Apply another piece of tape over the bridge of the nose *to make sure the tube is secure,* or apply ½" tape, using the butterfly technique. Place the middle of the tape at the back of the tube, pull the two ends forward, and crisscross them

over the bridge of the nose. Secure the two ends with a second piece of tape.
• Use the rubber band to tie a slipknot around the tube. Then, secure the rubber band to the patient's gown with a safety pin *to prevent tugging on the tube when the patient moves.*
• Attach the tube to the suction equipment, if ordered. Discard disposable equipment. Place the call button near the patient. Assure him that any discomfort he may feel in his nose and throat will subside as he gets used to the tube.

*To remove the nasogastric tube:*
• Assess bowel function first by auscultating for peristalsis with the stethoscope. (Flatus also indicates proper bowel function.)
• Using the 50-ml catheter-tip syringe, flush the tube with a small amount of air *to clear it of stomach contents that would cause irritation during removal.* You could also clamp the tube or kink it in your hand during removal *to prevent aspiration.*
• Drape a towel or linen-saver pad over the patient's chest *to protect the hospital gown from spills.*
• Untape the tube from the patient's nose, and then unpin it from the gown.
• Instruct the patient to hold his breath *to ensure closure of the epiglottis,* and then withdraw the tube gently and steadily. (When the distal end of the tube reaches the nasopharynx, you can pull it quickly.)
• When possible, quickly cover and remove the tube, *because its sight and odor may nauseate the patient.*
• Assist the patient with good mouth care, and clean the tape residue from his nose with adhesive remover.
• Until you are certain bowel function is normal, monitor the patient continuously for signs of gastrointestinal dysfunction, such as distention and nausea. Such dysfunction may necessitate reinsertion of the tube.

## Special considerations
Before determining the length of tube necessary to reach the stomach, make sure the patient is facing forward, with his neck in a neutral position.

Another way to arrive at the correct distance is by using a Ross-Hanson tape. Place the narrow end of this special measuring tape at the tip of the patient's nose. Then, extend the tape to the tip of the ear and down to the tip of the xiphoid process. Mark this distance on the edge of the tape labeled "nose to ear to xiphoid." The corresponding measurement on the opposite edge indicates the proper insertion length.

If the patient has a nasal condition, such as a deviated septum, that prevents insertion through the nose, pass the tube through the mouth. After removing any dentures, slide the tube over the tongue, and proceed as you would for nasal insertion. When using the oral route, coiling the end of the tube is especially important *to direct it downward at the pharynx.*

If the patient is unconscious, tilt his chin toward his chest *to close the trachea,* and advance the tube between respirations *to make sure it doesn't enter the trachea.* While advancing the tube in the unconscious patient (or in any patient who can't swallow), stroke his neck *to facilitate passage down the esophagus.*

While passing the tube, observe for signs that it has entered the trachea: choking or difficult breathing in a normal, conscious patient and cyanosis in an unconscious patient or one without a cough reflex. If these signs occur, stop immediately and remove the tube. Allow the patient to rest, and try to reinsert the tube.

When checking for proper placement, never place the end of the tube in a container of water. *If the tube is in the trachea, the patient may inhale water; the absence of bubbling doesn't confirm proper placement anyway, because the tube may still be coiled in the trachea or the esophagus.* Don't tape the tube to the patient's forehead, *because the resulting pressure on the nostril can cause necrosis.*

Pain or vomiting after the tube is in place indicates tube obstruction or incorrect placement. Assess immediately to determine the cause.

## Complications

Potential complications of prolonged nasogastric intubation include skin erosion at the nostril, sinusitis, esophagitis, esophagotracheal fistula, gastric ulceration, and pulmonary and oral infection. Additional complications from the use of suction include electrolyte imbalance and dehydration.

## Documentation

Record the type and size of the nasogastric tube and the time and route of tube insertion. Also note the use of suction. For tube removal, record the time and describe the color, consistency, and amount of gastric drainage in the suction bottle.

JAY ELLEN BARRETT, RN, BSN, MBA

# Care of a Patient with a Nasogastric Tube

*Caring for a patient with a nasogastric tube requires careful monitoring of his condition and maintenance of the equipment. Normally, such monitoring involves checking drainage from the tube and assessing gastrointestinal function. Primary procedures for maintaining the equipment are irrigating the tube to ensure patency and prevent mucosal damage and checking for correct tube placement.*

*Specific care varies slightly for the two most commonly used nasogastric tubes: the Levin tube and the Salem sump tube. The Levin tube has only one lumen; the Salem sump tube has a primary suction-drainage lumen and a smaller vent lumen. Air flows through the vent lumen continuously, which prevents a vacuum when the tube adheres to the stomach lining, thus avoiding damage to the delicate gastric mucosa.*

## Equipment

Irrigating solution (usually normal saline solution) □ irrigation container □ bulb syringe □ lemon-glycerin swabs or toothbrush and toothpaste □ petrolatum □ ½″ or 1″ nonallergenic tape □ water-soluble lubricant □ stethoscope □ emesis basin (optional).

Make sure the suction equipment is working properly (see *Gastric Suction Devices*).

When using a Salem sump tube with suction, connect the larger lumen to the suction equipment and select the appropriate setting, as ordered. If the doctor doesn't specify the setting, follow the manufacturer's directions.

Intermittent low suction is recommended for the Levin tube.

## Essential steps

● Explain the procedure to the patient, provide privacy, and wash your hands.

*To irrigate the nasogastric tube:*

● Pour the irrigating solution into the irrigation container.

● Measure the appropriate amount in the bulb syringe *to maintain an accurate intake and output record.*

● When using a Salem sump tube or when using a Levin tube, unclamp the tube or disconnect it from the suction equipment while holding it over an emesis basin *to collect any drainage.*

● Slowly instill the solution into the tube. (When irrigating the Salem sump tube, you may instill small amounts of solution into the vent lumen without interrupting suction; however, you should instill large amounts into the primary lumen.)

● Gently aspirate the solution with the bulb syringe or connect the tube to the suction equipment, as ordered. *Gentle aspiration prevents the exertion of excessive pressure on a suture line and on the delicate gastric mucosa.*

● After attaching the primary lumen of the Salem sump tube to suction, instill 10 to 20 cc of air into the vent lumen *to make sure it is patent.* This air instillation should create a soft hissing sound in the vent. Absence of this sound may indicate a clogged tube; check again by

## GASTRIC SUCTION DEVICES

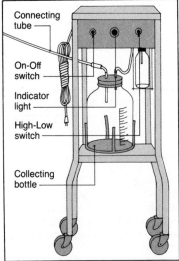

Connecting tube

On-Off switch

Indicator light

High-Low switch

Collecting bottle

*A portable thermotic pump,* such as the Gomco, works like this: a vacuum created intermittently by an electric pump draws gastric contents up the nasogastric tube and into the collecting bottle. A high-low toggle switch controls the suction force.

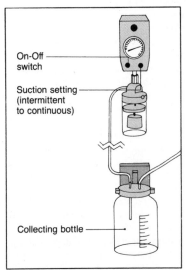

On-Off switch

Suction setting (intermittent to continuous)

Collecting bottle

*A wall-unit suction device* works like a portable thermotic pump, but is fixed to the wall above the patient's bed. This unit provides both intermittent and continuous suction. A high-low knob or dial controls the suction force.

instilling 10 ml of normal saline solution and 10 to 20 cc of air into the vent.
• Measure the amount of drainage and record it in the intake and output record. (Excessive gastric output may result in electrolyte imbalance.)
*To monitor the patient's condition:*
• Provide mouth care once a shift or as necessary. Depending on the patient's condition, use lemon-glycerin swabs to clean his teeth or instruct him to brush them. Coat the lips with petrolatum *to prevent dryness from mouth breathing.*
• Regularly check the tape securing the tube, *because diaphoresis and nasal secretions may loosen it and cause the tube to slide in and out.* If the tape is loose, check for proper tube placement. Remove the tape, cleanse the skin, and ap-

ply fresh tape. Apply water-soluble lubricant to the nostrils, as necessary.
• Assess bowel sounds regularly *to check for gastrointestinal function.*
• Inspect the color, consistency, and odor of gastric drainage. Normal gastric secretions are either colorless or yellow-green from bile and have a mucoid consistency.

A coffee-ground color may indicate bleeding; report it immediately. If you suspect blood in the drainage, use Hematest or a guaiac test. The amount of drainage varies with the underlying disease or condition.

## Special considerations

Irrigate the tube before and after instilling medications. Wait 15 to 20 minutes after instillation before reattaching the suction equipment *to allow sufficient time for the medication to be absorbed.*

When no drainage appears, check for an obstruction by milking the suction tubing. If you suspect the suction equipment isn't working properly, disconnect the nasogastric tube over an emesis basin; with the suction on, place the suction tubing in a container of water. If the apparatus draws the water, the nasogastric tube is clogged or incorrectly positioned. (Remember to note the amount of water on the intake and output record.)

If the nasogastric tube isn't functioning, you may need to reposition the patient or, if possible, rotate the tube and reposition it. If the tube was inserted during surgery don't reposition it *to ensure that it doesn't interfere with gastric or esophageal sutures.* Instead, notify the doctor.

If the patient is ambulatory and suction can be interrupted, disconnect the nasogastric tube from the suction equipment and clamp it *to prevent drainage of stomach contents while the patient is moving around.* (Don't use a serrated clamp, *because it may puncture the plastic tube.)* Instead of using a clamp, you can bend a Levin tube and insert the fold in the tube end, or place the Salem sump pigtail into the suction-drainage lumen.

One disadvantage of the Salem sump tube is reflux of gastric contents into the vent tube when stomach pressure exceeds atmospheric pressure. This problem may result from a clogged suction-drainage lumen or improper setup of the suction system. It occurs most often with wall suction equipment and can be avoided by placing the collection bottle on the floor and attaching it to the suction equipment with a connecting tube. Unless contraindicated, you could also keep the patient's torso elevated higher than 30° and the vent tube above his midline *to prevent a siphoning effect.* Then, place the collection bottle below the patient's midline. (Don't attempt to stop reflux by clamping the vent tube.)

## Complications

Epigastric pain and vomiting indicate a clogged or improperly placed tube. A nasogastric tube may move at any time, and Levin tubes in particular may then aggravate esophagitis, ulcers, or esophageal varices, causing hemorrhage. Dehydration and electrolyte imbalance may result from the removal of fluids and electrolytes through suctioning. Pain, swelling, and absence of salivation may indicate parotitis, which occurs in dehydrated, debilitated patients. Intubation may also cause nasal skin breakdown and discomfort and increased mucous secretions. Aspiration pneumonia may result from gastric reflux.

## Documentation

Keep an accurate record of fluid intake and output, noting the instilled irrigant in fluid input. Record the irrigation schedule and the actual time of each irrigation on the flowchart. Regularly document the color, consistency, and amount of the drainage.

JAY ELLEN BARRETT, RN, BSN, MBA

# Insertion and Removal of a Nasoenteric-decompression Tube

*Longer than a nasogastric tube, the nasoenteric-decompression tube is inserted nasally and passed through the stomach into the intestinal tract. It is used to aspirate intestinal contents for examination and to treat intestinal obstruction. It may also be used to prevent nausea, vomiting, and abdominal distention after gastrointestinal surgery. Only a doctor or a specially trained nurse should perform this procedure.*

*A nasoenteric-decompression tube (see* Nasoenteric-decompression Tubes, *page 548) has a balloon or rubber bag at one end filled with air, mercury, or water to stimulate peristalsis and facilitate passage through the pylorus into the intestinal tract. The type of tube inserted, as well as its length and diameter, depends on the purpose of intubation, on the size of the patient's nostrils, and on the estimated length of time that the tube will remain in place. For example, a tube with a large bore would be used to remove viscous material from the intestinal tract.*

## Equipment

Sterile 10-ml syringe □ 21G needle □ nasoenteric-decompression tube □ basin of water □ 5 to 10 ml of mercury or water, as ordered □ suction equipment □ towel or linen-saver pad □ water-soluble lubricant □ 4″ × 4″ gauze sponge □ ½″ nonallergenic tape □ bulb syringe □ litmus paper □ cotton-tipped applicator □ tincture of benzoin □ rubber band □ safety pin □ clamp □ optional: basin of ice or warm water, penlight, marking pen, glass of water with straw.

## Preparation of equipment

If the tube is too flexible, chill it in a basin of ice *to stiffen it and thus facilitate insertion.* If the tube is too stiff, place it in warm water.

Using the 10-ml syringe, inject air into a *Miller-Abbott tube to test the balloon's capacity.* Then, submerge the inflated balloon in water *to test for leaks.* Deflate it completely before insertion. If you are using a *Cantor* or a *Harris tube*, inject the mercury into the balloon before insertion. (A Miller-Abbott tube should be filled with mercury or water only after it has been passed through the pylorus.)

Set up suction-decompression equipment, if ordered, and make sure it's working properly.

## Essential steps

- Explain the procedure to the patient, and tell him that it will cause some discomfort. Provide privacy and adequate lighting. Wash your hands.
- Place the patient in the semi-Fowler's position, and put the towel or linen-saver

pad over his chest to protect the gown from spills.
- Establish a hand signal the patient can use if he wants to halt the insertion briefly.

*To assist with insertion:*
- The doctor first assesses the patency of the patient's nostrils. For a conscious patient, he determines which nostril is more patent by pinching one nostril and then the other as the patient breathes through his nose. For an unconscious patient, the doctor examines each nostril with a penlight *to check for polyps or a deviated septum.*
- *To determine how far the tube must be inserted to reach the pylorus,* the doctor places the tube's distal end at the tip of the patient's nose, extends the tube to the earlobe and down to the xiphoid process, and then either marks the tube or holds it at this point.
- The doctor applies water-soluble lubricant to the first few centimeters of the tube *to reduce friction and tissue trauma and to facilitate insertion.*
- If the balloon already contains mercury or water, the doctor holds it so the fluid runs to the bottom. Then, he pinches the balloon closed *to keep the fluid there as he begins insertion.*
- Tell the patient to breathe through his mouth or to pant as the doctor inserts the balloon into the nostril. After inserting the balloon, he releases his grasp on the top of it, *so the weight of the fluid helps pull the tube into the nasopharynx.* When the tube reaches the nasopharynx, he instructs the patient to lower his chin to his chest and swallow. The doctor may permit the patient to sip water through a straw *to facilitate swallowing as the tube is advanced;* however, *to prevent aspiration,* he won't allow water until after the tube passes the trachea. Then, the doctor advances the tube slowly *to prevent it from curling or kinking in the stomach.*
- *To confirm the tube's passage into the stomach,* the doctor aspirates stomach contents with a bulb syringe or injects air through the tube while auscultating the patient's stomach with the stethoscope; a whooshing sound confirms

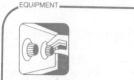

# NASOENTERIC-DECOMPRESSION TUBES

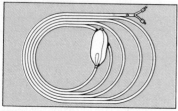

**Miller-Abbott tube**
*Description:* a 10′ long (3-m), double-lumen tube with one inflation lumen and one lumen for injecting mercury or water
*Use:* for bowel obstruction; allows aspiration of intestinal contents

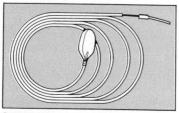

**Cantor tube**
*Description:* a 10′ long (3-m), single-lumen tube with a balloon at the distal tip for injecting mercury
*Use:* for bowel obstruction; allows aspiration of intestinal contents

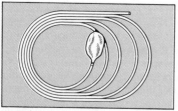

**Harris tube**
*Description:* a 6′ long (1.82-m), single-lumen tube with a balloon for injecting mercury
*Use:* for bowel obstruction; allows lavage of the intestinal tract, usually with a Y-tube attached

proper tube position.

• When proper placement of a *Miller-Abbott* tube is confirmed, the doctor injects the appropriate amount of mercury into the balloon lumen.

• After folding a 4″ × 4″ gauze sponge in half and taping it to the patient's forehead, with the fold nearest to the nose, the doctor slides the tube through the sling, leaving enough slack for the tube to advance.

• Position the patient, as ordered, *to help advance the tube.* Usually, the patient lies on his right side until the tube passes through the pylorus, on his back in the Fowler's position for 30 minutes as the tube passes through the first and second portions of the duodenum, and then on his left side for 2 hours.

• After the tube has passed through the pylorus, the doctor may order you to advance it 2″ to 3″ (5 to 7.6 cm) every hour. If you are advancing the tube manually, tape or fasten it to the patient's nose after each move *to prevent it from being pulled out.* Usually, the tube is allowed to advance on its own, assisted by gravity and peristalsis, once it reaches the duodenum. *To confirm the tube's passage into the duodenum,* aspirate a small amount of fluid with a bulb syringe and test its pH with the litmus paper. (Normally, the pH for intestinal fluid is less than 7.0.)

• After the tube has been inserted the necessary distance, the doctor orders X-rays *to confirm its proper placement in the gastrointestinal tract.* If placement is confirmed, secure the tube *to prevent further advancement.*

• Using a cotton-tipped applicator, apply tincture of benzoin under the appropriate nostril. When it dries, tape the tube over it.

• Loop a rubber band around the tube and pin it to the patient's gown.

• If ordered, attach the tube to intermittent suction.

*To remove the tube:*

• Disconnect the tube from the suction equipment and clamp it. *This prevents aspiration of gastric contents that leak from the tube as you withdraw it.*

• For a *Miller-Abbott tube,* remember to deflate the balloon before slowly withdrawing the tube. While still in the intestines, these tubes should be withdrawn very gradually, 6″ to 8″ (15 to 20 cm) at a time, followed by a 10-minute rest period, *to avoid pulling on the intestines.* After the tube reaches the stomach, withdraw it gently but steadily, as you would a nasogastric tube. Withdraw a *Cantor* or a *Harris tube* completely and gently with the mercury in the bag. An alternative method for the Cantor or Harris tube is to withdraw it gently into the pharynx. Ask the patient to open his mouth, and then grasp the tube and mercury bag. Gently pull the bag outside the patient's mouth and remove the mercury from the bag with a needle and syringe. Pull the rest of the tube through the nose. You may feel slight resistance as you withdraw the tube. If you feel strong resistance, notify the doctor. Send mercury weighted tubes to the central supply department for proper disposal.

## Special considerations

For a *Miller-Abbott tube,* note which lumen is used for inflating the balloon and which is used for drainage. Label them with tape.

Apply a local anesthetic, if ordered, to the nostril or the back of the throat *to dull sensations and the gag reflex for intubation.* Letting the patient gargle with a liquid anesthetic or hold ice chips in his mouth for a few minutes serves the same purpose.

 Don't incinerate a tube containing mercury, *because mercury produces a toxic vapor when burned.* Mercury can be disposed of only by a licensed hazardous-waste disposal company. Put the tube containing mercury in a plastic bag, and send it to the appropriate department for disposal.

## Complications

Indwelling nasogastric decompression tubes may cause reflux esophagitis, inflammation of the nose or mouth, and ulceration of the nose and larynx.

## Documentation

Record the type of tube inserted, the name of the doctor who inserted it, how far it was inserted, how it was advanced, and the position the patient assumed during insertion. Also note whether air, mercury, or water was used to inflate the balloon and how much was used. State whether intestinal contents were withdrawn for laboratory analysis at the time of intubation; if so, describe the amount, color, and consistency.

ELIZABETH K. CLAY, RN, BA

# Care of a Patient with a Nasoenteric-decompression Tube

*The patient who has had a nasoenteric-decompression tube in place requires special care and continuous monitoring. The tube must be checked frequently to make sure it is patent and to ensure that suction and decompression of the bowel are maintained. The patient must be observed for signs or symptoms of fluid and electrolyte imbalances. He must also be observed for signs or symptoms of pneumonia which can result from the presence of the tube in the esophagus. Accurate intake and output records are essential. Frequent mouth and nostril care are also important to ensure patient comfort and prevent skin breakdown.*

## Equipment

Suction-collecting bottle □ intermittent gastric suction machine (wall or portable unit) □ container of water □ mouthwash and water mixture □ lemon-glycerin swabs or petrolatum □ intake and output sheet □ optional: disposable irrigation set and irrigating solution, if irrigation is ordered, and bedside humidifier.

## Preparation of equipment

Attach the suction-collecting bottle to the rubber stopper on the machine. Make sure the seal is tight *to prevent spillage and ensure a vacuum.* Also, make sure the bottle is positioned securely, *so it can't be accidentally knocked over and broken.*

Test the functioning of the machine by turning it on and placing the end of the connecting tube in the container of water. The machine is working properly if water is drawn up into the tube and a red light on the front of the machine goes on.

### Essential steps

• Both the patient and his family should be informed about the purpose of the tube. Answer their questions clearly and thoroughly *to ease their anxiety and promote their cooperation.*

• *To promote passage of the tube,* have the patient lie on his right side for approximately 2 hours, until the tube passes the pylorus, on his back in Fowler's position for about 30 minutes, and on his left side for 2 hours. After the tube has passed the pylorus, the patient may ambulate unless his condition contraindicates this.

• Coil the excess tubing and secure it to the patient's gown or linens with a safety pin attached to a piece of tape on the tubing. *If the tubing is kinked, suction is not maintained.* Do not tape the tube to the nostrils, *because the tube needs to move freely by the aid of gravity and peristalsis.* If ordered, you may advance the tube 2″ to 3″ (5 to 7 cm) every hour *to promote passage of the tube.*

• Allow the patient enough slack in the tubing so he can move about in bed, and show him how far he can move without dislodging the tube.

• After the nasoenteric-decompression tube is secured in place, connect it to the tubing on the suction machine *to begin decompression.*

• Check the functioning of the suction machine every time you enter the room (at least every 2 hours) *to make sure it is working properly and to ensure patency of the nasoenteric tube and decompression of the bowel.* The functioning of intermittent suction machines is difficult to check; look for aspirate in the connecting tube and dripping into the suction-collecting bottle. Empty the bottle every 8 hours and measure its contents.

• After the tube is in the intestines and if the patient isn't nauseated or vomiting, provide a light diet of clear and cream soups, custards, gelatins, milk, and fruit juices, as ordered. These foods are absorbed in the upper part of the small intestine. Clamp the tube for about 1 hour after the patient eats *to allow nutrients to be absorbed.*

• Record intake and output measurements accurately *to monitor the patient's fluid balance.* If you irrigate the tube, its length may prohibit aspiration of the solution, so record the amount of irrigating solution instilled as intake.

• Observe for signs and symptoms of fluid and electrolyte imbalance. Dehydration is indicated by dry skin and mucous membranes, decreased urinary output, lethargy and exhaustion, and fever.

• Observe for signs and symptoms of pneumonia, which can result from the inability to cough effectively because of tube placement. These signs and symptoms include fever, chest pain, tachypnea or labored breathing, and diminished breath sounds over the affected area.

• Observe the amount, color, consistency, and odor of the drainage *to assess abnormalities that require notifying the doctor such as bright red blood in the collection bottle.*

• Provide mouth care at least every 4 hours, *because the tube may remain in place for several days and mouth-breathing causes the lips and tongue to dry and crack.* The patient may brush his teeth or rinse his mouth with a mouthwash and water mixture and lubricate his lips with lemon-glycerin swabs or petrolatum.

• Apply petrolatum to the opening of the nostrils at least every 4 hours *to prevent skin breakdown.*

• Watch for symptoms of the return of peristalsis, such as the presence of bowel sounds, passage of flatus, decreased abdominal distention, and spontaneous bowel movement *which indicate that the tube may be removed.*

## Special considerations

For a *Miller-Abbott tube,* clamp the lumen to the mercury balloon and label "do not touch." Label the other lumen, "suction." This labeling prevents the accidental instillation of irrigation fluid into the wrong lumen and the possible rupture of the mercury balloon.

If the suction machine isn't working properly, replace it immediately. If the machine is working properly but no aspirate is accumulating in the collection bottle, the nasoenteric tube may be obstructed. With a doctor's order, the tube may be irrigated *to clear an obstruction.* Disconnect the tube from the suction source and irrigate it with sterile normal saline solution. Use gravity flow to clear the obstruction unless otherwise ordered. If irrigation doesn't reestablish function, the tube may be kinked or lying against the gastric mucosa. To rectify this, tug slightly on the tube to move it away from the mucosa. If the tube is kinked, it will require further manipulation.

Never reposition or irrigate a nasoenteric - decompression tube without a doctor's order in a patient who has had gastrointestinal surgery, who has had a nasoenteric tube positioned during surgery, or who was difficult to intubate—for instance, one with an esophageal stricture.

If the patient is ambulatory, the suction apparatus can move a short distance with him, or if allowed, it can be disconnected and clamped for a short time.

If the tubing irritates the patient's throat or makes him hoarse, mouthwash, gargles, viscous lidocaine, sour balls, throat lozenges, an ice collar, or gum, as ordered, may provide relief.

If the balloon at the end of the tube begins to protrude from the anus, call the doctor. The tube will be disconnected from suction, the proximal end

cut off, and the rest of the tube gradually removed through the anus manually or with the aid of peristalsis.

## Complications

A fluid-volume deficit and electrolyte imbalance may result from suction of intestinal contents. Pneumonia may occur because intubation interferes with coughing and clearing of the pharynx. The balloon can rupture if it is defective or accidentally irrigated. Such rupture is especially dangerous with a mercury-filled balloon, *because it could possibly cause mercury poisoning.* Also, the weight of the mercury at the end of the tube may cause telescoping of the bowel (intussusception).

## Documentation

Record the frequency and type of mouth and nostril care administered and the presence or absence of a therapeutic effect. Document in the nurse's notes the amount, color, consistency, and odor of the drainage obtained each time the bottle is emptied. Record the amount obtained on the intake and output sheet, as well as any irrigation or fluids introduced through the tube or taken orally by the patient. If applicable, note the length of time the suction machine didn't appear to be functioning and the nursing action taken. Document the amount and character of any vomitus.

ELIZABETH K. CLAY, RN, BA

# Gastric Lavage

*Gastric lavage—the flushing of the stomach and removal of ingested substances through a nasogastric tube—can be used to treat poisoning or drug overdose. This procedure is indicated for patients with central nervous system (CNS) depression, inadequate gag reflex, or an uncooperative attitude, and for those in whom vomiting is contraindicated. Lavage with an iced saline solution possibly augmented with vasoconstrictors, such as norepinephrine, is used to treat gastric or esophageal bleeding.*

*Correct nasogastric tube placement is essential for safe performance of this procedure. Pulmonary misplacement followed by lavage, for example, can be fatal.* This procedure is contraindicated after ingestion of such corrosive substances as lye and some cleaning compounds, because the nasogastric tube may then perforate the esophagus.

### Equipment

Lavage setup (two calibrated containers or bottles, three pieces of large-lumen rubber tubing, Y-connector, and hemostat) □ container of irrigating solution □ I.V. pole □ water-soluble lubricant or anesthetic ointment □ Ewald tube (#28 to #36 French) for poisoning or drug overdose, or Salem sump or Levin tube (#18 French) for gastric or esophageal bleeding □ stethoscope □ ½" nonallergenic tape □ optional: two bath basins or graduated containers filled with ice (for gastric or esophageal bleeding), 50-ml bulb or catheter-tip syringe.

A prepackaged disposable irrigation set is available and can be used for the iced saline lavage. However, the lavage setup should be used to treat poisoning or overdose, *because it's a faster and more effective means of diluting and removing the harmful substance.*

### Preparation of equipment

Prepare the lavage setup by connecting one piece of large-lumen rubber tubing to the container of irrigating solution. Attach the other end of the tubing to the Y-connector, which should be upside down. Then attach the remaining two pieces of rubber tubing to the other ends of the connector.

Place the lower end of one of the two pieces of tubing in one of the calibrated containers or bottles. (Later, you'll connect the other piece of tubing to the patient's nasogastric tube.) Attach the hemostat to the tube attached to the solution container.

Suspend the entire setup from the I.V.

pole, hanging the solution container at the highest level. Before filling the bottle, warm the irrigating solution *to prevent a drop in the patient's body temperature.*

Before iced saline lavage, place the saline in an ice bath.

Lubricate the end of the nasogastric tube with the water-soluble lubricant or anesthetic ointment.

### Essential steps

• Explain the procedure to the patient, provide privacy, and wash your hands.
• Insert the nasogastric tube, and check its position by injecting about 30 cc of air and auscultating the patient's stomach with the stethoscope. If the tube's in place, you'll hear the air being injected into the stomach.
• After making sure the inflow tube is clamped, connect the remaining piece of tubing to the nasogastric tube. Allow stomach contents to empty into the drainage bottle before instilling any irrigating solution. *This confirms proper tube placement and decreases the risk of overfilling the stomach with irrigating solution and inducing vomiting.* If you're using a disposable irrigation set, aspirate stomach contents with a 50-ml bulb or catheter-tip syringe before instilling the solution.
• After confirming proper tube placement, remove the hemostat from the inflow tube and clamp it on the outflow tube.
• Begin gastric lavage by instilling 250 ml of irrigating solution *to evaluate the patient's tolerance and prevent vomiting.* If you're using a syringe, instill 50 ml of solution at a time until you've instilled a total of 250 ml.
• Remove the hemostat from the outflow tube and clamp the inflow tube *to allow the irrigating solution to flow out.* If you're using the disposable irrigation set, aspirate the irrigating solution with the syringe and empty it into a graduated container. Record the amount of outflow to make sure it at least equals the amount of irrigating solution instilled. *This prevents acci-*

dental stomach distention and vomiting. If the amount drained is significantly less than the amount instilled, reposition the tube until sufficient solution flows out.

• Repeat the procedure, increasing the amount of irrigating solution to 500 ml *to flatten the stomach's rugae and ensure that all areas are flushed out.*

• Repeat this inflow-outflow cycle until returned solution becomes clear. *This indicates that the stomach has been emptied of all poisonous or injurious substances or that bleeding has stopped.*

• If ordered, remove the nasogastric tube.

### Special considerations

The doctor may order a vasoconstrictor, such as norepinephrine, added to the iced saline lavage *to control GI bleeding.* If he does, clamp the outflow tube for a prescribed period of time after instilling the solution and before withdrawing it. *This allows time for the mucosa to absorb the drug.*

 Never leave a patient alone during gastric lavage. Observe continuously for any changes in level of consciousness, and monitor vital signs frequently. Remember that a vasovagal response can depress the patient's heart rate. When the nasogastric tube has passed the posterior pharynx, usually the patient is placed in Trendelenburg's position, lying on his left side in a three-quarter prone position. *This position minimizes passage of gastric contents into the duodenum and prevents aspiration of vomitus.* Also keep tracheal suctioning equipment nearby and watch closely for airway obstruction caused by vomiting or excess oral secretions. (Vomiting may occur during tube insertion.) Throughout the procedure, frequent suctioning of the oral cavity may be needed *to prevent aspiration.* For the same reason, in patients with CNS depression or an inadequate gag reflex, the doctor may insert an endotracheal tube before the procedure and inflate the cuff.

When aspirating the stomach for ingested poisons or drugs, save all fluid *for possible laboratory analysis.* If ordered, after lavage for poisons or drug overdose, mix charcoal tablets with saline solution and administer the mixture through the nasogastric tube. The charcoal will remain in the stomach and help absorb any remaining toxic substance.

### Complications

The most common complication of gastric lavage is vomiting with subsequent aspiration, most likely to occur in a groggy patient. Bradyarrhythmias may also occur. After iced saline lavage, the patient's body temperature may drop due to the low temperature of the irrigating fluid.

### Documentation

Record the date and time of lavage; size and type of nasogastric tube inserted; volume and type of irrigating solution used; and volume of gastric contents drained. Record these on an intake and output record and include your observations of gastric contents, such as color and consistency. Also record vital signs and level of consciousness, any drugs instilled through the tube, and the time when the tube was removed.

SUZANNE MARR SKINNER, RN, MS

# Gastrostomy, Duodenostomy, and Jejunostomy Feeding Tubes

*Gastrostomy, duodenostomy, and jejunostomy tubes provide a direct route for administering liquid feedings to the stomach, duodenum, and jejunum, respectively. A surgeon inserts a plastic (Levin) tube or rubber Foley catheter (or mushroom catheter) through a surgical opening into the appropriate portion of the gastrointestinal (GI) tract. The surgical opening is sutured tightly around the catheter or tube to prevent leakage of stomach contents. Used as alternatives to I.V. and nasogastric feeding routes, these tubes allow the patient to feed himself; they also avoid the risk of venous thrombosis and infection associated with parenteral feedings. Because the tube can be removed after several weeks (and then reinserted for feedings), the patient enjoys greater mobility. A prosthesis consisting of internal and external flanges, a 1.6" to 2.4" (4- to 6-cm) shaft, and a screw cap may be used to close the opening between feedings.*

*Postoperative nursing responsibilities include administering the feedings, monitoring the patient's response, and adjusting the feeding schedules. The nurse is also responsible for teaching the patient how to feed himself and care for the tube and peristomal skin.*

#### Equipment
Feeding solution □ large bulb syringe □ 50 ml of water □ graduated containers □ 4" x 4" gauze sponges □ petrolatum or zinc oxide ointment or commercial skin protectant □ sterile basin □ stethoscope □ tape measure.

*For tube insertion:* water-soluble lubricant □ clean gloves □ #18 French whistle-tip catheter or Levin tube □ clamp.

*For tube already inserted:* precut drain sponges □ ABD pads □ Montgomery straps or abdominal binder.

*For a prosthesis:* #18 French whistle-tip catheter or Levin tube □ water-soluble lubricant □ small gauze pad □ nonallergenic tape □ optional: cotton-tipped applicators, hydrogen peroxide, normal saline solution or water.

Commercially prepared, drip-enteral administration sets are available. A patient may prefer this drip method since the gavage container usually holds the entire feeding volume.

#### Preparation of equipment
Always check the label on a commer-cially prepared feeding formula for the expiration date. If the formula has been mixed in the hospital by the pharmacist or another staff member, check the preparation time and date. Discard the solution if it's more than 24 hours old. When mixing a feeding formula, always label it with the time, date, contents, volume, and your initials.

If the patient is permitted solid food, mix it in a blender. *The residue and fiber of a blended, normal diet promotes bowel function, and most patients prefer it to a liquid formula.* Warm the solution to room temperature *to prevent cramps and reduce gas formation.* If it's too thick, dilute it with water.

Measure the feeding solution and water in graduated containers. As the patient's tolerance grows, volume will be increased gradually from about 200 to 800 ml. If you're using a commercially prepared administration set, place the measured solution into the gavage container and flush the tubing *to remove excess air.*

#### Essential steps
● Provide privacy and wash your hands.
● Explain the procedure to the patient.
● Instruct the patient to sit down. If the patient is in bed, unless contraindicated, place him in semi-Fowler's position *to promote digestion and help prevent esophageal reflux of the feeding solution.*
● *If the tube has already been inserted,* attach the bulb syringe to the clamped tube. *This reduces the risk of introducing air into the patient's tract, causing distention and discomfort.* Remove the bulb from the syringe. *To check the patency of the tube,* pour a little water from the graduated container into the syringe and remove the clamp. If water flows in freely, the tube is patent. If it doesn't, notify the doctor.
● *If you have to insert the tube,* first lubricate the distal end; then put on clean gloves. Remove the ostomy dressing and dispose of both the dressing and the gloves properly.

Don't cut the dressings off, *because you may inadvertently cut the gastrostomy tube or the sutures holding it.* If the patient has a prosthesis, remove the cap. Insert the feeding tube into the ostomy opening about 4″ to 6″ (10 to 15 cm). After removing the bulb, attach the syringe to the proximal end of the feeding tube.

• Pour the feeding solution into the syringe. As the solution flows into the stomach, tilt the syringe *to allow air bubbles to escape.*

• Add more solution to the syringe when about one quarter of it remains. Increase or decrease the flow rate by raising or lowering the syringe. Depending on the solution's consistency and the amount, the feeding may take 10 to 20 minutes.

• After administering the ordered amount of feeding solution, flush the tube with about 30 ml of water. *This removes particles and solution from the tube, preserving its patency.*

• Clamp or plug the ostomy tube when it empties *to prevent any leakage from the tube.*

• Remove the syringe.

• If the ostomy tube should be inserted for each feeding, remove it.

• Instruct the patient to remain in a sitting position for 30 minutes *to prevent leakage and gastric reflux into the esophagus and to enhance the normal digestive process.*

• Monitor intake and output *to detect fluid or electrolyte imbalance, which is easily precipitated by diarrhea.*

*To care for the patient:*

• Wash the peristomal skin with soap and water at least once daily, or as necessary.

• If excessive skin irritation is not present, clean encrusted secretions from the tube or skin with cotton-tipped applicators, or use 4″ x 4″ gauze sponges soaked in a mixture of half hydrogen peroxide and half saline or water. Apply the mixture, allow it to soak in, and remove it by wiping from the stoma or from the tube outward. Rinse the area with 4″ x 4″ gauze sponges soaked in water or saline. Then pat dry with additional gauze sponges.

• Apply petrolatum zinc oxide ointment or a commercial skin protectant to the skin near the opening *to prevent or treat skin maceration.*

• Around the tube, apply precut drain sponges designed for gastrostomy openings *to help protect the patient's skin from irritation resulting from gastric juice leakage.*

• Place 4″ x 4″ gauze sponges over the peristomal skin or over the protective ointment.

• Coil the clamped tube once and lay it on the top dressing. *This reduces tension on the suture lines and helps prevent separation if the tube gets pulled accidentally.*

• Cover the coiled tube with ABD pads; secure the pads with Montgomery straps or an abdominal binder.

• Assess bowel sounds before each feeding. At least daily, check abdominal distention by measuring abdominal girth at the umbilicus.

• If the patient complains of thirst, provide water through the tube between feedings *to maintain hydration.* Also provide mouth care.

## Special considerations

If the patient complains of feeling too full after a feeding or experiences regurgitation, try administering smaller, more frequent feedings. If ordered, administer an antidiarrheal agent through the tube. If the patient with duodenostomy or jejunostomy develops dumping syndrome (nausea, vomiting, diarrhea, cramps, pallor, sweating, and fainting), smaller, more frequent feedings and a longer period of postoperative adjustment may alleviate it. This syndrome seems to result from sudden duodenal or jejunal distention and rapid shifting of body fluids to make the intestinal contents isotonic.

## Documentation

On the intake and output record or medication sheet, note the date, time, type, and amount of each feeding and volume of water instilled. In the nurse's notes, document any signs or symptoms of intolerance or improved tolerance. Also, note the patient's progress in learning self-care.

CAROL ANN GRAMSE, RN, PhD

# Insertion and Removal of a Feeding Tube

*Inserting a feeding tube nasally or orally into the stomach or duodenum allows administration of a liquid feeding to a patient who is unable or unwilling to eat or who needs supplemental feedings because of very high nutritional requirements—such as the patient with extensive burns. The nasal route is preferred for insertion of a feeding tube, but the oral route is indicated in patients with such conditions as a grossly deviated septum or a head or nose injury. A duodenal feeding is used when a gastric feeding can't be tolerated or may produce aspiration. This procedure can be performed on a conscious or unconscious patient. Absence of bowel sounds or possible intestinal obstruction contraindicates use of a feeding tube.*

*The newest feeding tubes—made of silicone, polyvinyl chloride, rubber, or polyurethane—have smaller diameters and are softer and more comfortable than the traditional nasogastric tubes. Because of their size and flexibility, these tubes also reduce oropharyngeal irritation, pressure necrosis on the tracheoesophageal wall, distal esophageal irritation, and discomfort from swallowing. To facilitate passage, some feeding tubes are weighted with mercury. However, these tubes require special handling for disposal after being removed. A new radiopaque feeding tube weighted with tungsten requires no special handling.*

## Equipment

*For insertion:* feeding tube with or without guide ☐ linen-saver pad ☐ nonallergenic tape ☐ water-soluble lubricant ☐ tissues ☐ penlight ☐ emesis basin ☐ small cup of water with straw, or ice chips ☐ 50- or 60-ml syringe ☐ stethoscope ☐ tincture of benzoin.

Tube sizes range from #6 French to #18 French, with #8 French the most commonly used. A guide is usually included in the feeding tube package. Because of their small diameter, feeding tubes may curl during insertion, making it necessary to use the guide.

*For removal:* linen-saver pad ☐ tube clamp ☐ bulb syringe ☐ mild soap (optional).

## Preparation of equipment

Have the proper size tube available. Usually, the doctor orders the smallest-bore tube that will allow passage of the liquid feeding formula. Read the instructions on the package carefully, *because certain characteristics vary according to the manufacturer.* (For example, some tubes have marks at the appropriate lengths for gastric, duodenal, and jejunal insertion.) Then, examine the tube *to make sure it's free of defects, such as rough or sharp edges,* and check it for patency by running water through it.

## Essential steps

• Explain the procedure to the patient and show him the tube *so he knows what to expect and can cooperate more fully.*
• Provide privacy and wash your hands.
• Place the patient in the semi- or high Fowler's position. Make sure he doesn't lean forward.
• Drape the portion of the gown covering the patient's chest with the linen-saver pad *to avoid soiling.*
• *To measure the tube length needed to reach the pylorus,* first extend the distal end of the tube from the tip of the patient's nose to his earlobe. Coil this portion of the tube around your finger *so the end will remain curved until you insert it.* Then, extend the uncoiled portion

from the earlobe to the xiphoid process. Use a small piece of nonallergenic tape to mark the total length of these two portions.

• Assess nasal patency by inspecting for a deviated septum or polyps, using the penlight. As the patient breathes through his nose, occlude one nostril, then the other, *to determine which is more patent*. Ask him if he has ever had nasal trauma or surgery.

• Lubricate the curved tip of the tube (and the feeding tube guide, if appropriate) with a small amount of water-soluble lubricant *to prevent tissue trauma during insertion*.

• Ask the patient to hold the emesis basin and tissues in case he needs them.

• *To use the nasal route,* insert the curved, lubricated tip of the tube into the more patent nostril and advance it along the nasal passage toward the ear on the same side. When it passes the nasopharyngeal junction, turn the tube 180° *to aim it down into the esophagus.*

*To use the oral route:*

• Have the patient lower his chin *to close the trachea,* and ask him to open his mouth.

• Place the tip of the tube at the back of the tongue. Then, give the patient the small cup of water with a straw or the ice chips. Tell him to sip the water or suck on the ice and swallow frequently, without clamping his teeth down on the tube, *to facilitate passage of the tube.* Advance the tube as he swallows.

• Keep passing the tube until the tape marking the appropriate length reaches the patient's nostril or lips.

• *To make sure the tube is in the stomach,* attach the 50- or 60-ml syringe filled with 10 cc of air to the end of the tube. Gently inject the air into the tube as you auscultate the patient's abdomen with the stethoscope about 3″ (7.5 cm) below the sternum. If the tube is in the stomach, you'll hear a whooshing sound; if it's coiled in the esophagus, you'll feel resistance when you inject the air, or the patient may belch. If you hear the whooshing sound, try to gently aspirate gastric secretions; if you succeed in doing

this, it confirms correct tube placement. If no gastric secretions return, the tube may be in the esophagus and you'll need to advance it or reinsert it before proceeding.

• After confirming proper tube placement, remove tape marking tube length.

• *To place the tube in the duodenum,* especially a mercury-weighted tube, position the patient on his right side *to aid tube passage through the pylorus by gravity.* Pass the tube 2″ to 3″ (5 to 7.5 cm) per hour until its placement in the duodenum is confirmed. (An X-ray must confirm placement before feeding begins, *because duodenal formula can cause nausea and vomiting if accidentally delivered to the stomach.*)

• Apply the tincture of benzoin to the part of the cheek to be taped. *This will help the tube adhere to the skin and will also prevent irritation.*

• Tape the tube securely to the cheek *to avoid excessive pressure on the nostrils.* (Taping the tube to the forehead causes pressure on the nostrils and nasal irritation.)

*To remove the tube:*

• Place the linen-saver pad over the patient's chest.

• Flush the tube with air, clamp or pinch it *to prevent fluid aspiration during withdrawal,* then withdraw it gently but quickly.

• If the tube will be reused, wash it with mild soap, rinse and flush thoroughly with hot water, and check it for damage. Send it to the appropriate department for sterilization. If it will not be reused, dispose of it properly.

## Special considerations

If the patient is unable to swallow the feeding tube, use a guide *to aid insertion.* (Some hospitals recommend inserting the ends of the feeding tube and a standard nasogastric tube into half of a gelatin capsule and passing both to the patient's stomach. Water is then instilled through the nasogastric tube, causing the gelatin capsule to dissolve and leave the tubes, and allowing the nasogastric tube to be removed.)

Checking for proper placement is especially important, *because small-bore feeding tubes may slide into the trachea without causing immediate signs or symptoms of respiratory distress, such as coughing, choking, gasping, or cyanosis;* however, a patient will usually cough if the tube enters the larynx. To ensure that the tube hasn't entered the larynx, ask the patient to speak. If he can't, the tube is in the larynx and you must withdraw it immediately, *because misplacement can cause instillation of fluid into the respiratory system.*

When checking tube placement by aspiration, pull very gently on the syringe plunger, *because negative pressure may collapse a small-bore feeding tube.* If you meet any resistance during aspiration, stop the procedure, *because resistance may result simply from the tube lying against the stomach wall.* If the tube becomes coiled above the stomach, you will not be able to aspirate stomach contents. To rectify this, change the patient's position or withdraw the tube a few inches, readvance it, and try to aspirate again.

## Documentation

For tube insertion, record the date, time, tube type and size, site of insertion, area of placement, and confirmation of proper placement on the patient's chart and the cardex. For tube removal, record the date, time, and patient tolerance.

CAROL ANN GRAMSE, RN, PhD

# Gastric Tube Feedings
[*Gastric gavage*]

A *gastric tube feeding is a way of administering specially prepared nutrients directly into the stomach. This procedure is indicated for patients who can't eat normally because of dysphagia, oral or* esophageal obstruction, or trauma; and sometimes for patients who are intubated or unconscious, or who have undergone gastrointestinal tract surgery that prohibits normal ingestion of food.

The liquid nutrient solution used for gastric tube feedings comes in various formulas. The solution is administered through a nasogastric tube or one of the newer feeding tubes that cause minimal trauma to gastric tissue when used for a long time. Tube feeding solutions are usually instilled intermittently but may be given continuously at a very slow rate. While less risky than intravenous hyperalimentation, tube feeding is contraindicated in patients with absent bowel sounds and suspected intestinal obstruction.

## Equipment

Feeding formula □ graduated containers □ 50 ml of water □ towel or linen-saver pad □ gavage bag with tubing and flow regulator clamp □ 5- or 10-ml syringe □ stethoscope □ optional: infusion controller and tubing set (for continuous administration), adapter to connect gavage tubing to feeding tube.

Commercially packaged sets, complete with formula, are usually available. If a gavage bag is unavailable, use a bulb syringe or a large catheter-tip syringe. If necessary, improvise with a plastic disposable enema bag.

## Preparation of equipment

The feeding formula should be kept in a refrigerator. Before using the formula, warm the prescribed amount in a basin of hot water, or let it stand for a while until it reaches room temperature.

Never warm the formula over direct heat *because heat, could cause the formula to curdle or even change its chemical composition, and if too warm could cause serious injury when instilled* to the patient.

Pour the appropriate amount of formula into one of the graduated containers. Pour the 50 ml of water into the other container. After closing the gavage tubing clamp, add the formula to the gavage bag or the container that comes in a commercially packaged set. If you're improvising, cut the tubing off an enema bag and insert I.V. tubing (you may need a tubing adapter). Tape the tubing securely to the bag. Then add the formula.

Open the flow clamp on the gavage tubing *to remove air from the lines, which could enter the patient's stomach and cause distention and discomfort.*

### Essential steps
• Inform the patient that you will be administering a tube feeding and explain the procedure to him. Give him a schedule of subsequent feedings. Provide privacy. Then wash your hands. Place the towel or linen-saver pad over the patient's chest *to protect his gown from spillage.*
• Elevate the patient's bed to a high or semi-Fowler's position *to prevent aspiration by gastroesophageal reflux and to facilitate digestion.*
• Remove the cap or plug from the feeding tube. *To check its patency and position,* use the syringe to inject 5 to 10 cc of air through the tube while auscultating the patient's stomach with the stethoscope. Listen for a whooshing sound. Aspirating stomach contents also confirms that the tube is patent and properly positioned.

 Never give a tube feeding until you're sure the tube is properly positioned in the patient's stomach. *Administering a feeding through a misplaced tube can cause the formula to enter the patient's lungs.*
• Connect the gavage bag tubing to the feeding tube. Depending on the types of tubes used, you may need to use an adapter to connect the two.
• If you're using a *bulb or catheter-tip syringe,* remove the bulb or plunger and attach the syringe to the pinched-off feeding tube *to prevent excess air from entering the patient's stomach, causing distention.*
• If you're using an *infusion controller,* thread the tube from the formula con-

tainer through the controller, according to the manufacturer's directions. Purge the tubing of air and attach it to the feeding tube.
• Open the regulator clamp on the gavage bag tubing and adjust the flow rate appropriately. When using a *bulb syringe,* fill the syringe with formula and release the feeding tube *to allow formula to flow through it.* The height at which you hold the syringe will determine flow rate. When the syringe is three-quarters empty, pour more formula into it.

 *To prevent air from entering the tube and the patient's stomach,* never allow the syringe to empty completely. If you're using an *infusion controller,* set the flow rate according to the manufacturer's directions. Always administer a tube feeding slowly—generally 200 to 350 ml over 10 to 15 minutes, depending on the patient's tolerance and the doctor's order—*to prevent sudden stomach distention, which can cause nausea, vomiting, cramps, or diarrhea.*
• After administering the appropriate amount of formula, flush the tubing by adding about 50 ml of water to the gavage bag or bulb syringe. *This maintains the tube's patency by removing excess sticky formula, which could occlude the tube.*
• Depending on the equipment you're using, close the regulator clamp on the gavage bag tubing, disconnect the syringe from the feeding tube, or turn off the infusion controller.
• Cover the end of the feeding tube with its plug or cap, or pinch the tube and insert it into the end. Then wrap it in a piece of gauze and secure it with a rubber band *to prevent leakage and contamination of the tube.*
• Leave the patient in the semi- or high-Fowler's position for at least 30 minutes.
• Rinse all reusable equipment with warm water. Dry it and store it in a convenient place for the next feeding. Change equipment every 24 hours or according to the institution's policy.

### Special considerations
*Never* dilute feeding solutions. Keep so-

lutions prepared by the dietary department refrigerated and use them within 24 hours after preparation. Always shake the container well *to mix the solution thoroughly and eliminate any separation that may occur on standing.* For each feeding, pour only the amount of solution prescribed for the feeding into a graduated container. Be sure to order more solution from the dietary department to avoid running out.

If the feeding solution doesn't initially flow through a bulb syringe, attach the bulb and squeeze it gently to start the flow. Then remove the bulb. Never use the bulb to force the formula through the tube.

Aspirate stomach contents about 2 to 3 hours after the patient's first feeding and before all subsequent feedings *to verify adequate gastric emptying.* Vomiting may occur if the stomach becomes overdistended from overfeeding or delayed gastric emptying.

*To prevent sore throat and mouth odor that can result from prolonged nasogastric intubation,* allow the patient to brush his teeth regularly or provide oral care, using mouthwash or lemon and glycerin swabs. Use petrolatum on dry, cracked lips. (Remember, dry mucous membranes may indicate dehydration, which requires increased fluid intake.) If the patient is unconscious, give good oral care every 4 hours.

During continuous feedings, assess the patient frequently for abdominal distention.

If diarrhea occurs with tube feedings, administer small, frequent, less concentrated feedings. Also, make sure that the feeding isn't cold and that proper storage and sanitation practices have been followed.

The loose stools associated with tube feedings make extra perineal and skin care necessary. The addition of paregoric, tincture of opium, or diphenoxylate hydrochloride may improve the condition.

If constipation occurs, the doctor may increase the fruit, vegetable, or sugar content of the feeding. Also, assess the patient's hydration status, since dehydration may produce constipation. Increase fluid intake, as necessary. If the condition persists, check with a doctor on the administration of an appropriate drug or enema.

Drugs can be administered through the feeding tube. Except for enteric-coated drugs, crush tablets or open and dilute capsules in water before administering them. Be sure to flush the tubing afterward to ensure full instillation of medication.

Reverse peristalsis can obstruct the inflow of solution by causing the tube to "double up" in the esophagus. If you suspect this, withdraw the feeding tube a few inches and reinsert it. Changing the patient's position also may change the position of the tube in the stomach, allowing the solution to flow more freely.

When using a gavage bag, check the flow rate periodically *to determine if the formula is clogging the tubing as it settles. To prevent such clogging,* squeeze the bag frequently to agitate the solution.

Constantly monitor the flow rate of a blended or high-residue feeding *to determine if the tube is clogging as the particles of solution settle.* Also, squeeze the bag frequently *to agitate the solution and prevent clogging.*

As ordered, monitor blood and urine glucose levels *to assess glucose tolerance.* Also, monitor serum electrolytes and other blood studies *to determine response to therapy.*

## Complications

Check your institution's policy on the frequency of changing feeding tubes *to prevent erosion of esophageal, tracheal, nasal, and oropharyngeal mucosa,* which can result if tubes are left in place for a long time. If possible, use the newer smaller-lumen tubes *to prevent such irritation.*

Frequent or large-volume feedings can cause bloating and retention. Dehydration, diarrhea, or vomiting can cause metabolic disturbances. Glycosuria, cramping, and abdominal distention usually indicate intolerance of feedings.

## TROUBLESHOOTING: ENTERAL TUBE COMPLICATIONS

| COMPLICATIONS | NURSING ACTION |
| --- | --- |
| **MECHANICAL** | |
| • **Esophageal erosion** | • Discontinue feeding immediately. |
| • **Tube clogged with solution** | • Flush with water; if still clogged, replace tube. |
| **METABOLIC, FLUID, AND ELECTROLYTE** | |
| • **Hyperglycemia** | • Reduce flow and administer insulin, if ordered. |
| • **Glucosuria** | • Reduce flow and administer insulin, if ordered. |
| • **Hyperosmolar dehydration** | • Discontinue feeding. |
| • **Coma** | • Discontinue feeding. |
| • **Edema** | • Reduce sodium content or slow hyperalimentation rate. |
| • **Hypernatremia** | • Adjust electrolyte content of hyperalimentation. |
| • **Fatty acid deficiency** | • Administer oral linoleic acid supplement or intravenous fat emulsion, as ordered. |

Adapted from American College of Physicians, *Annals of Internal Medicine*, Vol. 90, No. 1, January 1979, with permission.

## Documentation

On the intake and output sheet, record the date, time the feeding began and ended, type and amount of formula administered, and the amount of water given. In your nurse's notes, record the patient's reaction to and tolerance of the feeding, including any cramping, diarrhea, or abdominal distention. Also note the results of blood and urine tests and any drugs given through the tube.

CAROL ANN GRAMSE, RN, PhD

# Enteral Tube Feedings

*Enteral tube feedings deliver a liquid diet directly to the duodenum or proximal jejunum, through a small-caliber, weighted feeding tube. A safe alternative to parenteral hyperalimentation, enteral tube feedings maintain a positive nitrogen balance and promote healing and weight gain in patients who can't receive oral or gastric tube feedings. Continuous-drip alimentation is usually preferred because it ensures a relatively stable blood glucose concentration; this avoids the sporadic hyperosmolarity associated with intermittent enteral feedings. Enteral tube feedings require careful administration of the feeding formula at the ordered flow rate. The administration set must be changed regularly— usually daily, although hospital policies vary. Other important nursing responsibilities include continuous monitoring of the patient and equipment to prevent complications.*

*Enteral tube feeding is contraindicated*

*in patients with absent bowel sounds, intestinal adynamic ileus, and small bowel obstruction or fistula.*

## Equipment

Graduated container □ prescribed feeding formula □ enteral therapy administration sets □ I.V. pole □ sterile 4″ x 4″ gauze sponges □ 30-ml syringe □ container of water □ equipment for oral care □ cotton-tipped applicators □ petrolatum □ optional: ice bag, volumetric infusion pump.

Commercially prepared administration kits containing all the necessary equipment are available. Whether using a prepackaged set or gathering one, it should include a 250- to 1,000-ml gavage container with short tubing, a flow clamp, a drip chamber, and a tube connector or an adapter (to attach the administration tubing to the newer, smaller-caliber feeding tubes). The doctor may order an infusion pump to be used *to ensure accurate delivery of a prescribed amount of formula.* (Some newer, small-lumen tubes require an infusion pump.) The ice bag is necessary if the gavage bag doesn't have an ice pouch.

## Preparation of equipment

Check when the formula was mixed; discard any mixture older than 24 hours. Pour the formula into the gavage bag; open the flow clamp and fill the entire tube *to expel air from the tube and prevent air from entering the intestine.* Close the flow clamp and attach the administration set tube to the feeding tube. Fill the ice pouch or bag with ice. Room temperature formula may be used for short periods, if the patient tolerates it better than iced formula. However, don't hold the formula at room temperature for longer than 10 hours, *since this encourages bacterial growth.*

## Essential steps

• Explain the procedure to the patient, provide privacy, and wash your hands.

*To start a feeding:*

• Elevate the head of the bed and place the patient in low Fowler's position.

• Hang the gavage container on the I.V. pole.

• Open the flow clamp and regulate the flow to the desired rate. To regulate the rate using a volumetric infusion pump, follow the manufacturer's directions for setting up the equipment. (The flow rate is calibrated to deliver the solution in calories/ml of formula/hour. Most patients receive small amounts initially, with volumes increasing gradually once tolerance is established.)

*To change the administration set:*

• Hang the next enteral therapy administration set on the I.V. pole.

• Open the flow clamp *so the formula flows through the tube and expels the air.* Close the clamp and cover the end of the tube with a sterile 4″ x 4″ gauze sponge until you're ready to attach it to the feeding tube *to prevent contamination of the feeding.*

• Close the flow clamp on the old administration set.

• Pinch off the feeding tube *to prevent excess air from entering the intestine and causing abdominal discomfort.*

• Disconnect the old administration set from the feeding tube.

• Uncover the end of the new administration tubing and connect it to the feeding tube.

• Open the flow clamp *to adjust the flow to the desired rate.*

• *To spare the patient the expense of being charged for multiple sets,* you may alternate only two sets, but always make sure they're thoroughly washed and dried before storage.

*To care for and monitor the patient:*

• Give the patient water through the feeding tube, as ordered, *to maintain adequate hydration and prevent hypertonic dehydration.*

• *To reduce oropharyngeal discomfort from the tube,* allow the patient to brush his teeth or care for his dentures regularly, and encourage frequent gargling. If the patient is unconscious, administer oral care with lemon and glycerin swabs.

• Clean the patient's nostrils with cotton-tipped applicators, apply petrolatum along the mucosa, and assess the skin for

signs of breakdown.
- Administer oral medications through the tube, as ordered. Except for enteric-coated drugs, you can crush tablets or open and dilute capsules in water before administering them.
- Encourage the ambulatory patient to walk *to aid absorption of the feeding formula, promote the nutrients' anabolic effects, and foster a sense of well-being.* If using a portable pump, unplug it to convert to battery power and tell the patient to hold the pole securely while walking.
- Weigh the patient daily and maintain accurate intake and output records. *A sudden change in weight indicates altered hydration status and requires an adjustment in the feeding regimen.*
- Check regularly for tube obstruction and esophageal erosion. Try to flush a clogged tube; if you can't, replace the tube. If you suspect esophageal erosion, notify the doctor.
- Monitor frequently for increasing abdominal girth with left upper quadrant pain, *which may result from an excessively high flow rate or inadequate absorption.*
- Frequently monitor the patient's tolerance by assessing for diarrhea, cramps, and nausea, which may indicate an excessive flow rate. *These symptoms may result from the dumping syndrome, in which a large amount of hyperosmotic solution in the duodenum causes excessive diffusion of fluid through the semipermeable membrane. In a patient with low serum albumin, these symptoms may result from reduced oncotic pressure in the duodenal mucosa.*
- If the patient develops diarrhea, provide frequent perineal care.
- Collect urine specimens every 4 to 6 hours and test for glucose.
- *To determine the patient's response to therapy,* collect blood specimens, as ordered, for BUN, serum electrolytes, serum glucose, and serum osmolarity tests. These tests are performed daily for most patients, more often for patients with high carbohydrate intolerance, diabetes, or those receiving steroid therapy.

- Check the flow rate hourly to ensure correct infusion. (With an improvised administration set, use a time tape to record the rate, *because it's difficult to get precise readings from an irrigation container or enema bag.*)

## Special considerations

Always keep the gavage bag closed *to prevent contamination of the formula.* Change and clean the equipment properly. Make sure that the bag always contains formula *because, when it's empty, some pumps will pump air, causing duodenal distention.* Also, maintain a constant flow rate, as ordered, *because a bolus of feeding formula can cause such complications as hyperglycemia, glucosuria, and diarrhea.*

Until the patient acquires a tolerance for the formula, dilution to one-half or three-quarters strength may be required. The concentration of calories/ml is then increased gradually. (A patient with a serum glucose level less than 200mg/100 ml and without glycosuria is considered stable.)

Patients under stress or who are receiving steroids may experience a pseudodiabetic state. Assess them frequently to determine need for insulin.

 *Glycosuria, hyperglycemia, and diuresis can indicate an excessive carbohydrate level, leading to hyperosmotic dehydration, which may be fatal.* Usually, the doctor orders a lactose-free diet, *because stress depletes the lactase needed for lactose hydrolysis in the gastrointestinal tract.* He may order insulin or may add tolbutamide or phenformin to the feeding formula *to maintain a normal glucose level.* As ordered, monitor blood and urine glucose levels *to assess glucose tolerance.*

## Complications

Clogging of the feeding tube is common. Enteral tube feeding may induce metabolic, fluid, and electrolyte abnormalities including hyperglycemia, glycosuria, hyperosmolar dehydration, coma, edema, hypernatremia, essential fatty acid deficiency, and rarely, esophageal erosion. These complications call for specific nursing actions (see *Troubleshooting: Enteral Tube Complications*, page 561).

## Documentation

On the intake and output sheet or medication sheet, note the feeding date and time, type and amount of feeding formula, any drugs, and the volume of water instilled. Record changes of administration sets, flow rate checks, mouth and nose care, ambulation, tube placement checks, and all specimen collections and test results. Note any signs of patient intolerance.

CAROL ANN GRAMSE, RN, PhD

# Care of Patients with T Tubes

*Usually inserted after gallbladder surgery and common bile duct exploration, a T tube (or biliary drainage tube) drains bile until the swelling of the duct resolves. The short end of the tube is inserted into the common bile duct; the long end is brought out through the incision or a separate stab wound and connected to a closed gravity drainage system. Depending on the procedure, the tube remains in place for 10 to 12 days.*

## Equipment

Graduated collection container □ paper bag and waste receptacle □ sterile gloves □ sterile 4″ x 4″ gauze sponges □ sterile normal saline solution □ sterile precut drain sponges □ nonallergenic tape or Montgomery straps □ special skin care aids (optional).

## Essential steps

● Explain the purpose and care of the T tube to the patient. Make sure he understands that the tubing should not be kinked or pulled.

*To empty the T tube:*
● Place the graduated collection container near the outlet valve of the closed gravity system collection bag. Disconnect the cap (or open the clamp) on the bag and empty its contents into the graduated container. (Be especially careful not to contaminate either the outlet valve or the cap.) Recap (or reclamp) the bag. Measure and record the contents.

*To change the dressing around the insertion site:*
● Wash your hands thoroughly *to avoid introducing bacterial contaminants into the incision.*
● Remove the T tube dressings and dispose of them in the paper bag and then into the waste receptacle.
● Inspect the incision for signs of inflammation or infection (such as redness, warmth, edema, tenderness, or induration), dehiscence, and evisceration.
● Put on sterile gloves.
● Clean bile from the skin, using 4″ x 4″ gauze sponges moistened with sterile normal saline solution. If the institution's policy permits, apply a protective agent, such as petrolatum, around the wound *to protect the skin from irritation caused by contact with the bile.*
● Apply a sterile precut drain sponge on each side of the T tube *to facilitate absorption of wound drainage.*
● Apply a sterile 4″ x 4″ gauze sponge over the T tube and the drain sponges. Be careful not to kink the tubing, *which could obstruct drainage.*
● Secure the dressings with the non-allergenic tape or Montgomery straps.

*To let bile flow into the duodenum:*
● Kink the tube and wrap the kink with a rubber band, or clamp the tube with any light clamp that won't put tension on the tube.

 After the tube is clamped, the patient may develop chills, fever, and abdominal discomfort from obstruction to the flow of bile. Report any of these signs immediately.

## Special considerations

Normal bile drainage is 500 to 1,000 ml/day of viscous, green-brown liquid. Bloody or blood-stained bile is normal during the first few hours after surgery. Always keep the drainage bag below the level of the common bile duct *to prevent contamination from backflow.* Provide meticulous skin care and frequent dressing changes. Even though the T tube is connected to a drainage bag, some bile may leak onto the dressings and the skin. This can be especially irritating to the skin. Excessive bile leakage from the wound can indicate a blocked drainage tube. If this occurs, notify the doctor. Check the dressing every hour immediately after surgery and less often as drainage decreases. Use Montgomery straps for frequent dressing changes *to eliminate the need to tear tape from the skin with each dressing change.*

Periodically observe the patient's urine and stools for color changes. Dark urine may indicate bile drainage obstruction; obtain a specimen for laboratory analysis. Stools normally darken as bile drainage to the duodenum increases. Light stools may indicate obstruction of bile drainage. Other signs of obstruction are icteric skin and sclera. Report any of these to the doctor.

After the T tube has drained for several days, the doctor might write an order to clamp the tube. This encourages the flow of bile into the duodenum and promotes digestion.

Occasionally, after prolonged T tube drainage, the patient may have to drink bile to aid digestion. Disguise the bile with fruit juice and, for practical reasons, don't tell the patient what he's drinking.

**Complications**

Obstruction of bile flow resulting from kinking or blockage of the T tube is the most common complication.

**Documentation**

Record the date and time of each dressing change, appearance of the wound and surrounding skin, volume of bile collected, and color of the patient's urine and stools.

CAROL ANN GRAMSE, RN, PhD

# Colostomy Irrigation and Care

*The recommended method of colostomy care depends on its location and the patient's attitude and capabilities. Caring for ascending and right transverse colostomies is very much like caring for ileostomies. Most patients wear a pouch because stool evacuation is irregular and output is unpredictable. However, with left-sided colostomies—involving the descending and sigmoid colons—stools are usually well formed and output is fairly predictable. Pouching is, therefore, not always necessary. Instead, a colostomy irrigation (also known as a colostomy enema) may be the primary method of care. The critical factor is the patient's willingness to learn the procedure and to perform it routinely.*

*Following colostomy surgery, the patient's stoma secretes mucus for 24 to 48 hours; feces aren't visible until approximately 72 hours or longer after surgery. During the first 2 to 3 weeks, as the edema resolves, the stoma shrinks; after approximately 6 months it attains its permanent appearance. Colostomy irrigation is usually first performed between 5 and 7 days after surgery or when bowel sounds return, and it is then repeated daily. If the returns are clear, it may be performed every other day. After 3 to 6 weeks, the patient should be able to regulate elimination by routinely performing irrigation; after several months, he should establish a regular evacuation pattern.*

**Equipment**

Colostomy irrigation set containing an irrigation drain or sleeve, irrigation bag with clamp and tubing, cone or catheter, water-soluble lubricant, ostomy belt (if necessary), and drainage pouch clamp □ 1,000 ml of tap water for irrigation □ I.V. pole or other hook □ plastic or paper bag □ washcloth and towel □ soap and

## ADMINISTERING A BARIUM ENEMA THROUGH A COLOSTOMY

**Before administering a barium enema**
• If ordered, the night before the barium enema provide a clear-liquid diet and administer cleansing irrigations with tepid water, and perhaps a laxative.
• In the morning, you may need to irrigate the colostomy again.

**To administer a barium enema**
• Assemble the following equipment: irrigation bag and tubing; irrigation drain or sleeve, or an open-ended colostomy pouch; 1″ waterproof adhesive tape; bandage scissors; irrigation cone; wire twist tie; straight adapter; water-soluble lubricant; ½″ plastic drainage tubing; I.V. pole; and barium.
• If you're using an irrigation drain or sleeve, apply it over the stoma. If you're using a colostomy pouch, first cut two 1″ (2.5-cm) pieces of adhesive tape and apply them in an X to the front of the colostomy pouch, away from the faceplate. Cut an opening in the center of the X ⅛″ (3 mm) larger than the stoma. Peel the paper backing from the faceplate and slip your hand inside the pouch. Press the adhesive side of the faceplate around the stoma, centering the opening in the tape over the stoma.
*To prevent barium from leaking under the pouch,* smooth out any wrinkles in the

adhesive.
• Attach the adapter to the irrigation cone and apply lubricant to the base of the cone.
• Insert the cone through the bottom of the pouch.
• Center the cone over the stoma and bring out the adapter through the opening in the tape.
• Insert the cone into the stoma.
• Fill the irrigation bag with barium and hang the bag from the I.V. pole.
*To remove all the air from the tubing,* allow the barium to flow down. Then, clamp the tubing and attach it to the adapter. Ask the patient to hold the cone in place by applying gentle pressure with two fingers.
• Insert the drainage tubing 2″ (5 cm) into the bottom of the pouch and secure it with a twist tie.
• Put the end of the drainage tubing into a trash receptacle and unclamp the irrigation tubing. The barium will drain continuously.

**After radiography**
• The doctor may order a laxative and more cleansing irrigations to remove *all* barium from the bowel. *Retained barium can solidify and cause impaction.*

IRIS ARNELL, RN, BS, ET
BARBARA R. NASSBERG, RN, BSN, ET

---

water □ ostomy appliance □ optional: bedpan, chair, linen-saver pad, finger cot or glove.

The tap water for irrigation should be 100° to 105° F. (37.8° to 40.5° C.). If a commercially prepared irrigation set isn't available, adapt a standard enema set by cutting the tip off the end of the catheter and attaching it to a #28 French soft rubber catheter. Substitute a drainable pouch with adhesive backing for the irrigation drain.

You can perform colostomy irrigation through either a cone or a catheter. Whereas a cone is less likely to traumatize the bowel, the irrigation solution may flush back around it during irrigation, especially if it isn't inserted properly. This can occur, for example, if the bowel turns sharply and the cone is stuck against the bowel wall. A catheter is used

if the stoma is stenosed.

Some irrigation drains don't require an ostomy belt, since they fasten with snaps or an adhesive.

## Preparation of equipment

Depending on the patient's condition, colostomy irrigation may be performed in the bathroom, using a toilet, or with the patient in bed, using a bedpan.

Set up the irrigation set at the appropriate site. If you're performing the procedure with the patient in bed, place the bedpan next to the patient and elevate the head of bed 45° to 90°, if permitted. If you're performing the procedure in the bathroom, have the patient sit on the toilet or on a chair facing the toilet, whichever he finds more comfortable. *Assuming the normal body position for bowel evacuation will usually help the patient feel less apprehensive about the procedure.*

Fill the irrigation bag with the warm tap water and hang it on the I.V. pole or hook. The bottom of the bag should be at the patient's shoulder level when he's seated *to prevent fluid from entering the bowel too rapidly.*

## Essential steps

• Explain the procedure to the patient. As you perform the procedure, explain each step again and the rationale behind it, *since he'll eventually be performing it himself.*
• Provide privacy, and wash your hands.
• If the patient is in bed, place a linen-saver pad under him *to protect the sheets from soiling.*
• Remove the ostomy pouch, if applicable. Place the irrigation drain over the stoma and attach the ostomy belt. (If you're using a two-piece system with flanges, snap off the pouch and snap on the irrigation drain; you don't need a belt.)
• Place the bottom open end of the irrigation drain in the toilet or bedpan *to facilitate drainage by gravity.*
• Connect the catheter or cone to the tubing; then insert the catheter or cone into the top opening of the irrigation drain.
• Open the clamp on the irrigation tubing and allow the solution to fill the tubing and the cone or catheter. *This prevents air from entering the bowel.*
• If this is the patient's first colostomy irrigation following surgery, put on a finger cot or glove and gently insert your finger into the stoma *to detect any obstruction and to determine in which direction to insert the catheter.* (The stoma may act as a sphincter at first, tightening around your finger, but it will relax in a few seconds.) Record this information on the chart and nursing-care plan for future reference.
• Lubricate the cone or catheter with the water-soluble lubricant *to avoid irritating the mucous membranes.*
• Gently insert the cone or catheter into the stoma. Insert the tip of the cone so that the stoma is occluded, or insert the catheter about 2″ to 4″ (5 to 10 cm).

• Unclamp the irrigating tubing and allow the water to flow in slowly. The water should enter the colon over a period of 10 to 15 minutes. (If cramping occurs, slow down the flow rate, and ask the patient to take a few deep breaths until the cramps subside.) Cramping during irrigation may indicate that the bowel is ready to empty, the water is too cold, the flow is too fast, or the tube contained air.
• Remove the cone or catheter, fold down the top opening of the irrigation drain, and secure it in the closed position.
• Have the patient sit in front of the toilet for about 15 to 20 minutes so the initial colostomy returns can drain into the toilet. If the patient's on bed rest, allow the colostomy to drain into the bedpan.
• After approximately 15 to 20 minutes, tell the patient he can remain in the bathroom for the duration of the irrigation or he can clamp the bottom of the drain with a rubber band or clip, then ambulate or return to bed. *Ambulating stimulates elimination, producing improved irrigation returns.* Have the non-ambulatory patient lean forward or massage his abdomen *to stimulate returns.*
• Wait approximately 1 hour for the rest of the returns; then remove the irrigation drain from the patient. Using the washcloth, gently clean the area around the stoma with mild soap and water. Be careful not to rub the skin. Rinse and dry the area thoroughly with the towel. Inspect the skin and stoma for any change in appearance. A stoma is normally dark pink to red, but some color variations may occur with a change in the patient's emotions. For example, fear may cause blanching, while anger may produce deep red or purple coloration.

 Notify the doctor of any sustained dark color changes since these may indicate alterations in blood supply to the stoma.

• Apply a clean pouch or dressing, if applicable. If the patient has established a regular pattern of evacuation, apply a small dressing or bandage over the stoma instead of a pouch. Remember to lubricate the stoma first with the water-soluble lubricant *to prevent the dressing or bandage from adhering to the stoma's mucous membranes.*

• Rinse the irrigation drain and store equipment for the next irrigation.

### Special considerations

After you've performed and explained the procedure a few times, permit the patient to perform some of the steps. Gradually, allow him to do more steps of the procedure until he can perform the complete procedure himself.

Before applying a pouch, shave the area aound the stoma, if necessary, *to enhance adherence of the pouch and prevent infection of hair follicles.* When removing an ostomy pouch, you may want to use warm water *to soften the adhesive and reduce skin irritation.*

If the distal portion of the colon was removed, care for the patient's perineal wound after performing colostomy irrigation. Change dressings, as needed, and give sitz baths or irrigations using prescribed solutions, such as 50% normal saline and 50% water or povidone-iodine solution, three or four times a day.

If the patient has had a loop or double-barrel colostomy, he may need a different appliance system. The doctor may order the distal or nonfunctional portion of the bowel irrigated, since it will continue to discharge mucus and possibly necrotic tissue. The returns from this irrigation are through the rectum. Inspect any returns before discarding.

Inform the patient that proper diet and exercise, in addition to irrigation, are required to achieve regulation.

### Complications

Perforation of the bowel may result if the catheter is forced into the stoma. Fluid and electrolyte imbalance may result from excessive water loss through colostomy drainage. Skin irritation may develop as a result of leaking appliances.

### Documentation

Record the date and time care is given; type and amount of irrigating solution used; the stoma's color; and the color, consistency, and amount of drainage. Document patient teaching, the patient's acceptance of self-care, and his learning progress.

SANDY WIND, RN, ET
PEGGY FELICE, RN, ET

# Ileostomy Care

*The ileostomy patient wears an external pouch at all times to collect the watery to pasty feces produced by the small intestine. In addition, this pouch (also known as an appliance or bag) helps control odor and protects the stoma and peristomal skin. A pouch may be worn without changing from 1 to 7 days; it's usually emptied every 4 to 6 hours, or 4 to 5 times a day. Usually, the best time to take care of an ileostomy pouch is just before a meal, 2 to 4 hours after a meal, or just before bedtime, because peristalsis is least active at these times. Skin and stoma care should be performed each time a pouch is changed. Patient teaching is essential, because the patient must care for the pouch, stoma, and peristomal skin himself after discharge.*

*The type of pouch a patient uses depends on several factors, including the stoma's location and construction, the equipment available, the patient's personal preference, and the patient's financial situation, as appliances vary in price.*

### Equipment

Ileostomy appliance (with flange, if applicable) □ skin barrier or skin barrier with flange, if applicable □ stoma measuring guide □ plastic bag □ soap and water □ closure clamp or rubber band □ optional: belt, bedpan, plastic rinse bottle.

Ileostomy appliances are drainable, and may be disposable or reusable, one-piece or two-piece. A *drainable ileostomy pouch* has an opening in the bottom so discharge can be emptied, as necessary. A drainable pouch with a *wide opening* may be used for thick drainage, while one with a *narrow opening* is used for liquid drainage. *Disposable appliances* are used once and discarded, while *reusable pouches* are cleaned and reused. In a *one-piece appliance*, the faceplate or mounting area (the part that supports the pouch and attaches it to the body) is connected to the pouch, whereas these parts are separate in a *two-piece appliance*. Both one-piece and two-piece appliances require a skin barrier between the pouch and skin *to protect the skin and provide a leakproof seal around the stoma*.

Many types and brands of appliances are available. While the procedure for their care is quite similar, these three basic ways to apply pouches distinguish the different types (see *Ostomy Collecting Devices*, pages 570 to 571): a pouch attached to the skin barrier, which adheres to skin; an adhesive-backed pouch added to a separate skin barrier; and a two-piece system with the skin barrier and pouch attached by flanges.

### Preparation of equipment

*To select an appropriate-sized pouch: For a pouch attached to the skin barrier,* measure the stoma with a measuring guide and choose a pouch with an opening that fits snugly around the widest margins of the stoma. Make sure the pouch opening doesn't cover the peristomal skin, *because enzymes in the ileostomy drainage can cause skin irritation and erosion.*

*For an adhesive-backed pouch added to a skin barrier,* trace the hole from the measuring guide that fits around the stoma onto the paper backing of the pouch and cut out the hole. To fit an irregularly shaped stoma, make a pattern. The diameter of the pouch opening should be about 1/8″ larger than the stoma. Then measure and cut a hole in the same fashion on a sheet of skin barrier. This opening should be the same size as the stoma *to prevent peristomal skin erosion from enzymes in ileostomy drainage.* Peel off

the paper backing from the pouch and place the skin barrier over the pouch's opening. Press the aligned openings firmly together. Then, peel off the paper backing from the skin barrier.

*For a two-piece system with flanges,* trace and cut a hole in the skin barrier wafer; make sure the opening doesn't expose the peristomal skin. Select a flange at least 1/4″ larger in diameter than the stoma. Peel off the paper backing from the skin barrier wafer.

### Essential steps

● Provide privacy, and wash your hands.
● Explain the procedure to the patient. As you perform each step, explain what you're doing and why, *because the patient will eventually perform the procedure himself.*
● Remove the old pouch and save the closure clamp. If you're using a skin barrier wafer, also remove the wafer. Hold a tissue or other nonsterile dressing over the stoma to temporarily absorb drainage. Place the old pouch in a plastic bag and discard it.
● Thoroughly wash and dry the peristomal skin with warm water.
*For a pouch attached to the skin barrier:*
● Apply a skin barrier *to prevent peristomal skin erosion*.
● Remove the covering from the skin barrier and the paper backing covering the adhesive (if applicable).
● Center the pouch over the stoma and press gently *to secure the edges*.
● Attach the belt, if desired.
● Press air out of the pouch and attach the closure clamp or secure it with a rubber band. If you're using a rubber band, turn up the bottom of the pouch about 1½″ (3.8 cm) twice, "fanfold" across, and secure it with the rubber band.
*For an adhesive-backed pouch with a separate skin barrier:*
● Apply a skin protector *to prevent peristomal skin erosion*.
● Position the pouch with the attached skin barrier over the stoma and press gently, especially around the inside edge.

## OSTOMY COLLECTING DEVICES

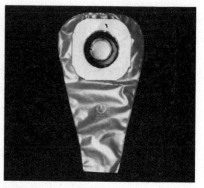

**Type**
Two-piece disposable drainable pouch
with separate skin barrier

**Description**
Transparent or opaque odor-proof plastic
pouch with belt tabs; snaps to skin barrier
with flange

**Indications**
Same as for disposable drainable pouch
with attached skin barrier

**Type**
One-piece disposable drainable pouch attached to skin barrier

**Description**
Transparent or opaque odor-proof plastic
pouch; comes with or without attached adhesive or karaya seal; some pouches have microporous adhesive or belt tabs; bottom opening
allows easy emptying of contents.

**Indications**
For patient who needs to empty pouch frequently—for example, patient with new colostomy or ileostomy, or patient with diarrhea;
may be used permanently or temporarily, until
stoma size stabilizes.

Allow it to set for 1 to 2 minutes. Then
attach the belt, if desired.
• Press air out of the pouch and attach
the closure clamp, close the valve, or
secure with a rubber band.
*For a two-piece system with flanges:*
• Apply a skin barrier to *prevent peristomal skin erosion.*
• Position the skin barrier wafer over
the stoma and press gently, especially
around the inside edge. The patient's body
temperature softens the skin barrier wafer
and molds it to the skin.
• Align the lip of the pouch flange with
the bottom edge of the wafer flange. Gently
press around the circumference of the

pouch flange, beginning at the bottom,
until it's secured to the flange on the
wafer. (The pouch will click into its secured position.) Holding the wafer against
the skin, gently pull down on the pouch
*to confirm that it's secured.*
• Attach the belt, if desired.
• Press air out of the pouch and attach
the closure clamp or secure it with a
rubber band.
*To empty the pouch:*
• *For a pouch with a wide opening,* tilt
the pouch up and remove the closure
clamp. Turn up a cuff on the lower end
of the pouch and allow it to rest in the
bedpan. *This cuff helps keep the end of*

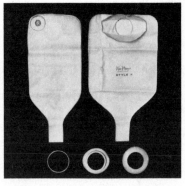

**Type**
One-piece disposable closed-end pouch

**Description**
Transparent or opaque odor-proof plastic
pouch; may include adhesive seal, belt tabs,
skin barrier, or carbon filter for gas release

**Indications**
For the patient with *regulated colostomy;* provides additional security and confidence

**Type**
Two-piece reusable drainable pouch

**Description**
Opaque nonallergenic plastic pouch with
separate custom-made faceplate and
O-ring; some pouches have pressure valve
for gas release; with repeated use, has
1-to 2-month life span; many of these
aren't odor-proof.

**Indications**
Reusable equipment is often indicated
when a firm faceplate is required; less expensive than disposables

---

*the pouch clean for handling.*
● If desired, flush out the inside of the
pouch from the bottom opening with a
plastic rinse bottle filled with tap water.
For the two-piece system with flanges,
the pouch may be unsnapped from the
skin barrier and rinsed into the toilet.
Dry the bottom of the pouch thoroughly.
For a pouch with a wide opening, keep
the cuff turned up while rinsing the pouch,
but turn it down after drying. An odor-
proof pouch doesn't have to be rinsed
after each emptying.

**Special considerations**
After you have performed and explained

the procedure a few times, permit the
patient to perform some of the steps.
Gradually, allow him to do more of the
steps until he can complete the procedure himself.

Special solvents and adhesive remov-
ers help remove adhesive residue from
the skin. They can also thoroughly cleanse
the skin surface of any oils or creams to
improve adherence of the pouch. However, use these solvents carefully, *because they may irritate the skin or
produce allergic reactions in some patients.* Liquid skin sealants can help guard
sensitive skin against irritation from
drainage or adhesives.

To provide extra support of the pouch, reinforce the outside edges with 1″ (2.5-cm) paper tape, applied in picture-frame fashion, laying half of the tape's width on the pouch and the other half on the skin.

If the patient has burning or itching beneath an adhesive appliance or purulent drainage around the stoma, remove the appliance immediately and inspect the area. To help control odor, a commercial deodorant can be placed in the pouch. Since most pouches are odor-proof, odors should be noticeable only when the pouch is emptied. However, if the pouch odor bothers the patient, tell him that he may find it helpful to avoid odor-causing foods, such as fish, eggs, onions, and asparagus. Deodorizers or wick deodorants may be used to control room odor. A well-sealed, odor-proof pouch is ultimately the best protection against odor.

Never make a pinhole in a pouch to release gas *since this destroys the odor-proof seal. To release gas,* remove the closure clamp from the pouch and release the gas from the bottom opening. If a pouch develops a leak, change it immediately.

If the patient wears a reusable appliance, suggest that he own two or more, so he can wear one while cleaning the other. The pouch should be cleaned with soap and water or a commercially available cleansing solution.

## Complications

Failure to center the pouch opening or to wear the belt properly can cause stoma lacerations.

## Documentation

Record the date and time of ileostomy care; note the color, amount, type, and consistency of drainage. Also record the condition of the stoma and surrounding skin. Document the teaching plan, the patient's acceptance and progress in learning self-care, and his learning progress.

SANDI WIND, RN, ET
PEGGY FELICE, RN, ET

# Continent Ileostomy Care
[*Pouch ileostomy*]

*An alternative to a conventional ileostomy, a continent or pouch ileostomy (also known as a Kock ileostomy or ileal pouch) is a surgical procedure that creates an internal reservoir from the terminal ileum. This procedure is used on patients requiring proctocolectomy for chronic ulcerative colitis or multiple polyposis. It can also be done on a patient with a traditional ileostomy stoma. A continent ileostomy is contraindicated for a patient with Crohn's disease or gross obesity. Patients who require emergency surgery and those who are unable to care for the pouch are also poor candidates for this procedure.*

*Preoperative hospitalization may last as long as a few weeks for a proctocolectomy patient with poor nutrition and constant diarrhea, or only 24 hours for a patient with a traditional ileostomy stoma. Preoperative nursing responsibilities during this period include bowel preparation, antibiotic therapy, frequent perineal care if the patient has constant diarrhea, and arranging for supportive counseling. Immediate postoperative care consists of ensuring the patency of the pouch catheter (inserted in the operating room), assessing gastrointestinal function, caring for the stoma and peristomal skin, managing gas pains common to the procedure and, if necessary, continuing perineal skin care. Usually, after about 2 weeks, daily patient teaching on pouch intubation begins. Continuous drainage will be maintained for about 2 to 6 weeks, except during these patient-teaching sessions.*

## Equipment

*For preoperative care:* oral and I.M. antibiotic medication □ optional: intravenous hyperalimentation equipment, perineal skin-care equipment.

*For postoperative care:* drainage equipment □ urinary leg bag □ normal saline solution □ 50-ml catheter-tip syringe □ 20-ml syringe with adapter □ stethoscope □ sterile precut gauze drain sponges □ sterile 4″ × 4″ × 1″ piece of foam □ Montgomery straps □ bandage scissors □ skin ointment with vitamins A and D, lanolin, zinc oxide, or a skin sealant □ antiflatulent □ water-soluble lubricant □ graduated container □ tissues.

### Essential steps

*For preoperative care:*
• Reinforce and, if necessary, supplement the doctor's explanation of a continent ileostomy and its implications for the patient.

*To give preoperative care before a proctocolectomy:*
• Keep the patient on a clear liquid diet and oral antibiotic therapy for 2 to 5 days, as ordered, *to prepare the bowel for surgery.* After midnight on the day of surgery, do not give the patient anything by mouth.
• If ordered by the doctor, maintain intravenous hyperalimentation therapy *to correct the patient's nutritional deficiencies resulting from constant diarrhea.*
• Provide good skin care *since poor nutrition predisposes the patient to skin breakdown.* If the patient has constant diarrhea, also provide perineal skin care.
• Assess the attitudes of the patient and his family toward the operation and the resulting change in the patient's body image. Reassure the patient that the operation will relieve his illness and improve nutritional status.
• Arrange for an enterostomal therapist and a trained representative of a local ostomy group or the American Cancer Society to visit the patient if this is agreeable to him and his doctor.
• On the day of surgery, administer I.M. antibiotics, as ordered.

*To give preoperative care before a pouch conversion:*
• Keep the patient on a clear liquid diet

and antibiotic therapy for 24 hours, as ordered. After midnight on the day of surgery, do not give him anything by mouth.
• On the day of surgery, perform ileal lavage and administer I.M. antibiotics, as ordered.

*To give postoperative care:*
• When the patient returns to his room, attach the catheter to continuous gravity drainage. Usually, this drainage is maintained for 2 to 6 weeks *to allow the suture lines to heal.* Attach a urinary leg bag to the patient's thigh when he's ready to ambulate.
• Irrigate the catheter with 30 ml of normal saline solution every 2 to 4 hours, as ordered and as necessary, *to prevent catheter obstruction and to allow fluid return by gravity.* During the initial postoperative period, the pouch must be kept empty *to allow the suture lines to heal and to prevent rapid pouch expansion.* At first, the drainage will be serosanguinous.
• Monitor fluid intake and output. Replace fluids, orally and intravenously, as necessary. (When gastrointestinal function first returns, output may exceed 2,000 ml/day.)
• During the immediate postoperative period, maintain low, intermittent nasogastric suction and continue to give the patient nothing by mouth, as ordered. *This removes gastric secretions, prevents nausea and vomiting, and enhances healing by allowing the digestive tract to rest.*
• Check bowel sounds regularly *to determine when peristalsis and bowel function return*—usually 3 to 5 days after surgery. When bowel function does return, the patient is normally allowed clear liquids; when fecal drainage appears in the pouch catheter, he's allowed solid food, with some restrictions.
• When the patient can eat solid food, check the catheter frequently *to make sure it's not plugged with mucus or undigested food particles.*
• If the patient complains of abdominal cramping and distention with nausea—symptoms of bowel obstruction—

the catheter may be plugged. Gently irrigate it with 20 to 30 ml of water or normal saline solution until it drains freely. Then move the catheter slightly or rotate it gently *to help clear the obstruction.* If the catheter is still blocked, try milking it. If all these measures fail, notify the doctor.

• Check the stoma frequently for color, edema, and bleeding. Normal color is pink to red; a dark red or blue-red stoma may indicate a compromised blood supply.

• To apply a stoma dressing, slip a precut drain sponge around the catheter and cover the stoma. Then place the 4″ × 4″ × 1″ piece of foam with an opening in the center over the distal end of the catheter and slide it onto the dressing. Secure the foam in place with Montgomery straps. Place the ties of the Montgomery straps across the foam pad; then wrap them around the catheter and tie them.

• Assess the peristomal skin for irritation from moisture.

• Change the dressing over this area every 6 hours or as necessary. Use a skin sealant around the stoma *to prevent skin irritation.* If the skin appears red or irritated, apply a soothing ointment with vitamins A and D, lanolin, or zinc oxide.

• Give medication, as ordered, and encourage ambulation *to reduce gas pains.* Tell the patient he can reduce the amount of air he swallows, and thus minimize gas pains, by chewing his food well, limiting conversation while eating, and not using a straw.

*To intubate the pouch:*

• Provide privacy, carefully explain the procedure to the patient, and wash your hands.

• Tell the patient with a pouch conversion to sit on the toilet *to help him feel more at ease during the procedure.* Have the patient with a perineal wound sit on the side of the bed, *because sitting on the toilet may be painful.*

• Remove the stoma dressing and tie tapes. Disconnect the catheter from the drainage tubing. Remove the catheter from the pouch.

• Rinse the catheter with warm water and insert the distal end in a graduated container.

• Encourage the patient to relax his abdominal muscles *so the tube slides easily into the pouch.*

• Lubricate the catheter tip with the water-soluble lubricant and insert it in the stoma. Gently push the catheter, usually downward, although the direction may vary from patient to patient.

• When the tube is inserted about 2″ to 2½″ (5 to 6 cm), it reaches the nipple valve, and you'll feel resistance. Instruct the patient to take a deep breath as you exert gentle pressure on the tube. If this fails, have the patient rest for a few minutes in the supine position. Then, with the patient still supine, try to insert the tube again.

• Gently insert the catheter to the depth of the suture marking, which the surgeon made during surgery.

• Allow the pouch to drain completely. This usually takes 5 to 10 minutes, but if the drainage is thick or the catheter gets clogged, may take as long as 30 minutes.

• When the tube becomes clogged, use the 50-ml catheter-tip syringe with 30 ml of water to irrigate it. Also, rotate and milk the tube. If these measures fail, then remove, rinse, and reinsert the catheter.

• When drainage is complete, remove the catheter.

• Measure output, noting any water used for irrigation.

• Instruct the patient to bathe or shower. (He may do this with the catheter out of the pouch, but make sure it's not out for more than 20 minutes *to avoid tension on sutures from the accumulating fecal contents in the pouch.*)

• Clean the peristomal skin without soap *to avoid drying.* Thoroughly rinse the catheter with warm water.

• Reinsert the catheter and attach it to the drainage tubing.

• Apply a fresh stoma dressing.

*Before discharge:*

• Be sure the patient is able to properly

intubate the pouch.

• Provide the patient with the appropriate equipment: two catheters, 50-ml catheter-tip syringe, 20-ml syringe with adapter (carried by the patient when he is away from home, and used to flush the catheter if it becomes clogged), dressings, nonallergenic tape, and a bag for carrying supplies.

• Make sure the patient has a schedule for draining the pouch.

• Give him appropriate pamphlets on care of the pouch.

• Make sure the patient knows whom to call when he has questions or problems.

• Tell him where to obtain supplies.

• Refer him to a local ostomy group.

### Special considerations

The doctor may omit orders for enemas as part of the preoperative bowel preparation *since mechanical irritation may rupture an inflamed bowel.*

 Never aspirate fluid from the catheter, *since the resulting negative pressure may cause damage to the inflamed tissue.*

The first few times the pouch is intubated, the patient will be tense and insertion will be difficult. Encourage him to relax. To shorten drainage time, have the patient cough, press gently on his abdomen over the pouch, or suddenly tighten his abdominal muscles and then relax them.

Keep an accurate record of intake and output *to ensure fluid and electrolyte balance.* The average daily output should be 1,000 ml. Report inadequate output *(because the doctor may order additional fluids or I.V. feedings)* and excessive output, over 1,400 ml/day *(because he may order electrolyte monitoring and replacement).* Remember, when peristalsis returns and fecal matter appears in the catheter, output may be as high as 2,000 to 4,000 ml/day.

### Complications

Common postoperative complications include obstruction, fistula, pouch per-

foration, nipple valve dysfunction, abscesses, and bacterial overgrowth in the pouch.

### Documentation

Record the date, time, and all aspects of preoperative and postoperative care including condition of the stoma and peristomal skin, diet, medications, intubations, patient teaching, and discharge planning.

LOIS J. WENDORF, RN, ET

# Enemas
### [*Irrigating enema, Retention enema*]

*Enemas involve the instillation of solution into the rectum and usually into the colon. The retention enema, as its name implies, is held within the rectum or colon longer than the irrigating enema, which is almost completely expelled within 15 minutes. Both types of enema stimulate peristalsis through mechanical distention of the colon and stimulation of the nerves in the rectal wall.*

*Enemas serve to cleanse the lower bowel in preparation for diagnostic or surgical procedures. This cleansing permits direct visualization of the intestinal mucosa in such procedures as sigmoidoscopy and colonoscopy. It also allows instillation of a contrast medium, such as barium, for radiographic examination and reduces contamination of the operative site during certain surgical procedures. Enemas also relieve constipation and are often administered after a barium enema to prevent impaction of retained barium. Certain enemas, such as the Harris flush, relieve gas or distention from a paralytic ileus.*

*The retention enema has additional uses that include acting as an emollient—soothing irritated tissues of the colon—and administering medication. In hepatic coma, a drug-solution enema, such as neomycin sulfate (Mycifradin), reduces blood ammonia levels by decreasing intestinal flora; lactulose (Cephulac), a drug-solution enema, acidifies colon contents and lowers blood ammonia levels. A sodium polystyrene sulfonate (Kayexalate) enema releases sodium ions for exchange by potassium ions in hyperkalemia.*

*Enemas are contraindicated after recent colon or rectal surgery or myocardial infarction, and in the patient with an acute abdominal condition of unknown etiology, such as suspected appendicitis. They should be administered cautiously to a patient with arrhythmia. Sodium polystyrene sulfonate enemas should be given cautiously to the patient with low sodium tolerance.*

## Equipment

Prescribed solution □ bath (utility) thermometer □ enema administration bag with attached rectal tube and clamp □ I.V. pole □ clean examination gloves, if desired □ linen-saver pads □ bath blanket □ two bedpans with covers, or bedside commode □ toilet tissue □ water-soluble lubricant □ diaper for infant or toddler □ optional (for the patient who may have difficulty retaining the solution): plastic rectal tube guard (available with many commercially prepared sets) or a guard made by cutting off the tip of a baby bottle nipple, Foley catheter or Verden rectal catheter with 30-ml balloon and syringe.

Commercially packaged disposable enema administration sets are readily available, as are commercially prepared, small-volume enema solutions in both irrigating and retention types and in a pediatric size.

## Preparation of equipment

Prepare the prescribed type and amount of solution, as indicated. The volume for an irrigating enema is usually 750 to 1,000 ml for an adult; 500 to 1,000 ml for a school-aged child; 500 ml for a toddler or preschooler; and 250 ml or less for an infant or for a retention enema. *Because the ingredients may be mucosal irritants,* make sure the proportions are

correct and the agents are thoroughly mixed *to avoid localized irritation.* Note that some solutions, such as the Mayo and sodium polystyrene sulfonate enemas, require full or partial preparation at bedside immediately before administration.

Warm the solution *to reduce patient discomfort.* Note that some enemas, such as milk-and-molasses and starch, must be heated to high temperatures for proper mixing, and then cooled to 100° to 105° F. (37.8° to 40.6° C.). (See chart, opposite page.) Test the solution's temperature with the bath (utility) thermometer. In the absence of a specific order, administer an adult's enema at 100° to 105° F. and a child's enema at 100° F., *to avoid burning rectal tissues.*

Clamp the tubing and fill the solution bag with the prescribed solution. Unclamp the tubing and allow a small amount of solution to run through the tubing and out the catheter, then reclamp the tubing *to detect leaks and remove air that could cause the patient discomfort if introduced into the colon.* Hang the solution container on the I.V. pole and take all supplies to the patient's room. If you're using a Foley or Verden rectal catheter, fill the syringe for the balloon with 30 ml of water.

## Essential steps

• Check the doctor's order and assess the patient's condition.

• Provide privacy and explain the procedure to the patient. If you're administering an enema to a child, familiarize him with the equipment and allow a parent or another relative to remain with him during the procedure *to provide reassurance.* Instruct the patient to breathe through the mouth *to relax the anal sphincter, which will facilitate catheter insertion.*

• Ask the patient if he's had previous difficulty retaining an enema *to determine the need for a rectal tube guard, Verden rectal or Foley catheter.*

• Wash your hands thoroughly. Put on clean examination gloves, if desired.

• Assist the patient, as necessary, in

## CARMINATIVE, CLEANSING, AND EMOLLIENT ENEMAS

| SOLUTION | PREPARATION | PURPOSE |
|---|---|---|
| **IRRIGATING ENEMAS** | | |
| Harris flush | 1,000 ml of tap water | Cleansing |
| Magnesium sulfate | Add 3 tbsp of magnesium sulfate to 3 tbsp of salt in 1,500 ml of tap water. | Carminative |
| Saline | If a commercially prepared solution isn't available, add 2 tsp of salt to 1,000 ml of tap water. | Cleansing |
| Soap and water | Add 1 packet of mild soap to 1,000 ml of tap water and remove all bubbles before administering. | Cleansing |
| **RETENTION ENEMAS** | | |
| Mayo | Dissolve 60 ml of white sugar in 240 ml of warmed tap water. Add 30 ml of sodium bicarbonate to mixture immediately before administration. | Carminative |
| Milk and molasses | Add 175 to 200 ml of hot milk to 175 to 200 ml of molasses. Heat mixture to 160° F. (71.1° C.) and then cool to 105° F. (40.5° C.). | Carminative |
| Oil | 150 ml of mineral, olive, or cottonseed oil | Cleansing, emollient |
| Olive oil and glycerin | Add 60 ml of olive oil to 60 ml of glycerin. | Cleansing, emollient |
| 1-2-3 | Add 30 ml of magnesium sulfate 50% to 60 ml of glycerin. Add mixture to 90 ml of warm tap water. | Cleansing |
| Starch | Add 1 tsp of powdered starch to 60 ml of cold tap water and add to 160 ml of boiling tap water or add 30 ml of liquid starch mix to the boiling water. Boil the mixture for 2 minutes and then cool to 105° F. (40.5° C.). | Emollient |

putting on a hospital gown. *The gown makes enema administration easier, and the patient worries less about soiling it.*

• If not contraindicated, place the patient in left lateral Sims' position. *This will facilitate the solution's flow by gravity into the descending colon.* If this position is contraindicated or the patient finds it uncomfortable, position him on his back or right side. The instructions on some commercially prepared small-volume solutions recommend the knee-chest position, if it's not contraindicated, *because it helps the solution flow farther into the colon. This ensures the distribution of a small amount of solution over as wide a surface area of the lower colon as possible.*

• Place linen-saver pads under the patient's buttocks *to prevent soiling the linens.* Replace the top bed linens with a bath blanket *to provide privacy and warmth.*

• Have a bedpan or commode nearby so it is available when the patient needs it. If the patient is allowed to use the bathroom, make sure that it will be available when the patient is ready. Have toilet tissue within reach of both the bed and the toilet or commode.

• If necessary, finish preparing the enema solution. For a soapsuds enema, add the soap after the liquid is in the container, and squeeze and invert the bag to mix well. Run the solution through the tubing *to remove air bubbles before enema administration and thus avoid introducing air into the bowel.*

• Lubricate the distal tip of the rectal catheter with water-soluble lubricant *to facilitate rectal insertion and reduce irritation.*

• Separate the patient's buttocks and touch the anal sphincter with the rectal tube *to stimulate contraction.* Then, as the sphincter relaxes, tell the patient to breathe deeply through his mouth as you gently advance the tube in the direction of the umbilicus. Insert the tube about 4″ (10 cm) for an adult, 2″ to 3″ (5 to 7.5 cm) for a child, and 1″ to 1½″ (2.5 to 3.8 cm) for an infant. Avoid forcing the catheter *to prevent rectal wall trauma.* If the tube doesn't advance easily, allow a little solution to flow in *to relax the inner sphincter enough to allow passage.*

• If the patient feels pain or the tube meets continued resistance, notify the doctor: *This may signal an unknown stricture or abscess.* If the patient has poor sphincter control, use a plastic rectal tube guard, or slip the tube through the cut end of a baby bottle nipple. You can also use a Foley catheter as a rectal tube, if the institution's policy permits. Insert the lubricated catheter as you would a rectal tube. Then, gently inflate the catheter's balloon with 20 to 30 ml of water. Gently pull the catheter back against the patient's internal anal sphincter *to seal off the rectum.* If leakage still occurs with the balloon in place, add more water to the balloon in small amounts. Use a Verden rectal catheter with balloon in the same way. When using either catheter, avoid inflating the balloon above 45 ml, *since overinflation can cause compromised blood flow to the rectal tissues.*

• Hold the rectal tube in place throughout the procedure *since bowel contractions and the pressure of the tube against the anal sphincter can promote tube displacement.*

• Hold the solution container slightly above bed level and release the tubing clamp. Then raise the container gradually to start the flow—usually at a rate of 75 to 100 ml/minute for an irrigating enema, but at the slowest possible rate for a retention enema *to avoid stimulating peristalsis and promote retention. Since the height of the solution determines its force,* adjust the flow rate of an irrigating enema by raising or lowering the solution container according to the patient's retention and comfort. However, don't raise it higher than 24″ (70 cm) for an adult and 6″ to 8″ (15 to 20 cm) for a child or infant, *because excessive pressure can force colonic bacteria into the small intestine or rupture the colon.*

• Assess the patient's tolerance frequently during the instillation. If he complains of discomfort, cramps, or the need to defecate, stop the flow by pinching or clamping the tubing. Then, hold the patient's buttocks together or firmly press toilet tissue against the anus. Instruct him to gently massage his abdomen and breathe slowly and deeply through his mouth *to help relax abdominal muscles and promote retention.* Resume administration of the enema at a slower rate of flow after a few minutes when the sensation has passed, but interrupt the flow anytime the patient feels uncomfortable.

• If the flow slows or stops, the catheter tip may be clogged with feces or pressed against the rectal wall. Gently turn the catheter slightly *to free it without stimulating defecation.* If the catheter tip remains clogged, withdraw the catheter, flush with solution, and reinsert.

• After administering most of the prescribed amount of solution, clamp the tubing. Stop the flow before the container empties completely *to avoid introducing air into the bowel.* When performing a Harris flush, stop the flow by lowering the solution container below bed level and allowing gravity to siphon the enema out of the colon. Continue to raise and lower the container until gas bubbles cease or the patient feels more comfortable and abdominal distention subsides. Don't allow the solution container to empty completely before lowering it, *because this may introduce air into the bowel.* If you're using a Foley or Verden rectal catheter, leave the catheter in place *to promote retention.* Or, gently remove the catheter and apply firm pressure with toilet tissue or a rolled washcloth against the anus *to stimulate sphincter contraction and enema retention.*

● For an irrigating enema, instruct the patient to retain the solution for 15 minutes, if possible. For a retention enema, instruct him to avoid defecation for the prescribed length of time or as follows: 30 minutes or longer for oil retention, milk-and-molasses, and Mayo enemas; and 15 to 30 minutes for anthelmintic and emollient enemas. If the patient is apprehensive, position him on the bedpan and allow him to hold the tissue or washcloth against his anus. Place the call signal within his reach. If the patient will be using the bathroom or the commode, instruct him to call for help before attempting to get out of bed, *because the procedure may make the patient—particularly the elderly patient—feel weak or faint.* Also instruct him to call you if he experiences weakness at any time.

● When the solution has remained in the colon for the recommended time or for as long as the patient can tolerate it, deflate the balloon and remove the Foley or Verden rectal catheter, if applicable. Assist the patient onto a bedpan or to the commode or bathroom, as required. Provide privacy while he's expelling the enema. Instruct the patient not to flush the toilet.

● While patient is in the bathroom, remove and discard any soiled linen and linen-saver pads.

● Assist with cleansing, if necessary, and return the patient to bed. Make sure he's clean, comfortable, and can easily reach the call signal. Place a clean linen-saver pad under him *to absorb rectal drainage,* and tell him he may need to expel additional stool or flatus later. Make the patient comfortable in bed and straighten the top linens. Allow him to rest for a while, *since the procedure may tire him.*

● Cover the bedpan or commode and take it to the utility room for observation, or observe the contents of the toilet, as applicable. Carefully note fecal color, consistency, approximate amount (small, medium, or large), and the presence of blood, rectal tissue, worms, pus, mucus, or other unusual matter.

● Rinse the bedpan or commode with cold water, then wash it in hot soapy water. Return it to the patient's bedside.

● Properly dispose of the enema equipment. If additional enemas are scheduled, store clean, reusable equipment in a closed plastic bag in the patient's bathroom. Discard your gloves and wash your hands.

● Ventilate the room or use an air freshener, if necessary.

## Special considerations

To administer a commercially prepared, small-volume enema, first remove the cap over the rectal tube. Insert the rectal tube into the rectum and squeeze the bottle *to deposit the contents in the rectum.* Remove the rectal tube, replace the used enema unit in its original container, and discard.

*Since patients with salt-retention disorders, such as congestive heart failure, may absorb sodium from the saline enema solution,* administer these to such patients with caution and monitor electrolyte status.

Schedule a retention enema before meals, *since a full stomach may stimulate peristalsis and make retention difficult.*

An oil-retention enema is frequently followed 1 hour later by a soap and water enema *to help expel the softened feces completely.*

Administer less solution when giving a hypertonic enema, *since osmotic pull moves fluid into the colon from body tissues, increasing the volume of the colon's contents.*

Alternate means of instilling the solution include using a bulb syringe or a funnel with the rectal tube.

If the patient can tolerate it, place him in Trendelenburg's position to receive the enema. *This allows the solution to reach higher into the colon.* For patients who cannot tolerate a flat position, such as those with shortness of breath, administer the enema with the head of the bed in the lowest position they can safely and comfortably maintain. For bedridden patients using a bedpan to expel the enema, raise the head of the bed to approximate a sitting or squatting position. Don't give an enema to a patient who's in a sitting position, unless absolutely necessary, *because the solution won't flow high enough into the colon and will only distend the rectum and trigger rapid expulsion. In addition, attempting to insert the rectal catheter into a seated patient may injure the rectal wall.*

If the patient has hemorrhoids, instruct him to bear down gently during tube insertion. *This causes the anus to open and facilitates insertion.*

If the patient fails to expel the solution within an hour, *because of diminished neuromuscular response,* you may need to remove the enema solution. First, check the institution's policy, *because you may need a doctor's order.* Whether the hospital requires an order or not, inform the doctor when a patient can't expel an enema spontaneously, *because of possible bowel perforation or electrolyte imbalance.* To siphon the enema solution from the patient's rectum, assist him to a right side-lying position on the bed. Place a bedpan on a bedside chair so it rests below mattress level. Disconnect the tubing from the solution container, place the distal end in the bedpan, and reinsert the rectal end into the patient's anus. If gravity fails to drain the solution into the bedpan, instill 30 to 50 ml of warm water through the tube (105° F., or 40.6° C., for an adult patient; 100° F., or 37.8° C., for a child or infant). Then quickly direct the distal end of the tube into the bedpan. In both cases, measure the return *to be sure all solution has drained.*

In patients with fluid and electrolyte disturbances, measure the amount of expelled solution *to assess for retention of enema fluid.*

Double-bag all enema equipment and label it as isolation equipment if the patient is on enteric precautions.

If the doctor orders enemas until clear, give no more than three *to avoid excessive irritation of the rectal mucosa.* Advise the doctor if the return isn't clear after three administrations.

## Complications

Enemas may produce dizziness or faintness; excessive irritation of the colonic mucosa resulting from repeated administration or from patient sensitivity to enema ingredients; hyponatremia or hypokalemia from repeated administration of hypotonic solutions; colonic water absorption from prolonged retention of hypotonic solutions, which may, in turn, cause hypervolemia or water intoxication; and cardiac dysrhythmias resulting from vasovagal reflex stimulation after insertion of the rectal catheter.

## Documentation

Record the date and time of enema administration; special equipment used; type and amount of solution; retention time; approximate amount returned; color, consistency, and amount of the return; abnormalities within the return; any complications that occurred; and the patient's tolerance for the treatment.

SUSAN M. GLOVER, RN, BSN
KAREN DYER VANCE, RN, BSN

# Insertion of a Rectal Tube

*A rectal tube may relieve the gas and distention that result from gastrointestinal (GI) hypomotility. Such hypomotility can result from many different medical and surgical conditions that decrease peristalsis and may cause paralytic ileus. Intestinal hypomotility can also result from certain habits or patterns of daily living—for example, from eating foods that create flatus (such as onions and cucumbers), from swallowing large amounts of air while eating, drinking, or talking, and from taking drugs that decrease peristalsis (such as atropine sulphate). In all these instances, the bowel fills with gas and distends, preventing the normal release of gas and feces.*

*Insertion of a rectal tube should be easy and painless. The patient should be well informed and relaxed, since his cooperation is essential. Insertion of a rectal tube is contraindicated after recent rectal or prostatic surgery or recent myocardial infarction, and in patients with diseases of the rectal mucosa.*

## Equipment
Stethoscope □ linen-saver pad □ drapes □ #22 French to #32 French rectal tube of soft rubber or plastic □ water-soluble lubricant □ container (emesis basin, plastic bag, or water bottle with vent).

Commercially packaged sterile, prelubricated rectal tubes are available.

## Essential steps
- Bring all necessary equipment to the patient's bedside, and provide privacy.
- Explain the procedure and encourage the patient to relax. Wash your hands.
- Check for abdominal distention; listen for bowel sounds with the stethoscope.
- Place the linen-saver pads under the patient's buttocks *to absorb any rectal drainage that may leak from the tube.*
- Position the patient in Sims position *to facilitate insertion of the rectal tube.*
- Drape to expose patient's buttocks.
- Lubricate the tip of the tube with water-soluble lubricant *to facilitate insertion and prevent rectal irritation.*
- Lift the patient's right buttock *to provide a clear view of the anus.*
- Insert the tip of the rectal tube through the anus and advance it 2″ to 4″ (5 to 10 cm) into the rectum. Direct the tube toward the umbilicus *so it follows the anatomical course of large intestine.*
- Attach the rectal tube to the container and observe for expulsion of gas.
- Remove the tube after 15 to 20 minutes. If no gas has been expelled, tell the patient you will repeat the procedure after 2 to 3 hours, if ordered.
- Clean the patient and replace soiled linens and linen-saver pads as necessary. Make sure the patient is comfortable before you leave him. Again check for abdominal distention and bowel sounds.
- If equipment is to be used by the patient again, clean it and store it in the bedside cabinet; discard disposables.

## Special considerations
As you insert the rectal tube, tell the patient to breathe slowly and deeply, or tell him to bear down as he would for a bowel movement, *to relax the anal sphincter and facilitate insertion.* Explain each step and reasssure him throughout the procedure *to encourage cooperation and help him relax.*

A plastic bag fastened over the end of the tube allows observation of expelled gas. Leaving a rectal tube in place indefinitely does little to promote peristalsis. Repeat insertion periodically to stimulate GI activity. If the tube fails to relieve distention, notify the doctor.

## Documentation
Record the date and time of tube insertion and the amount, color, and consistency of any expelled contents. Describe the patient's abdomen—hard, distended, soft, or drumlike on percussion—and the presence of bowel sounds before and after insertion.

SUSAN DODDS, RN, BSN

# 11 Renal and Urologic Care

# Renal and Urologic Care

## Introduction

Because the renal and urologic systems produce, transport, collect, and excrete urine, their dysfunction usually impairs fluid, electrolyte, and acid-base balance and the elimination of waste products. To restore or facilitate effective function of these systems, treatment of renal and urologic disorders usually involves temporary or permanent insertion of a urinary, peritoneal, or vascular catheter or tube. Catheterization also allows monitoring of renal and urologic systems and aids diagnosis of dysfunctions.

### Helping the patient cope

For the patient with a renal or urologic disorder, nursing care aims to help him accept an invasive procedure or adjust to a new body image. First assess the amount and kind of information he needs and can absorb about the procedure. Then present or reinforce this information and tell him what to expect.

For example, before insertion of an indwelling catheter, tell the patient that he will feel pressure during insertion, that the catheter will cause a sense of fullness or the urge to void, that he must avoid dislodging the catheter, and that the collection bag must be lower than bladder level.

In patients with severe and chronic disorders, treatment usually requires permanent changes, such as urinary diversion, that may severely affect the patient's body image. Managing such a patient effectively requires that you help him cope with distressing changes. Emphasize, and encourage the patient to

recognize, the positive health benefits of treatment. Although initially unappealing, the patient may decide it's easier to live with the stoma than with the disease or symptoms that caused him to seek treatment.

### Managing the procedure

Performing procedures skillfully is only one aspect of successfully managing renal and urologic disorders. You must also thoroughly understand the purpose of each step of the procedure, the physiologic and scientific principles that support it, and the associated indications, contraindications, and clinical ramifications.

For example, if you know how an arteriovenous fistula functions, you won't inadvertently cause it to clot or rupture by taking blood pressure measurements in the affected extremity, drawing blood incorrectly from the vessels, or applying a circumferential constrictive dressing to the extremity. You should also be able to accurately assess the patient's status, plan for the appropriate approach to the procedure, implement the procedure, and evaluate its overall effect on the patient.

Based on the results of continued patient assessment, you should be able to make valid clinical decisions and establish priorities that will contribute to a positive outcome. Your ability to assess a situation, to analyze it critically, and to establish priorities for action probably has the greatest impact on the success of the nursing process.

CHAROLD L. BAER, RN, PhD

# DIAGNOSIS & MONITORING

## Catheterization for Residual Urine

*Catheterization for residual urine detects the presence and amount of urine retained in the bladder after voiding. It provides data on the bladder's condition, capacity, and response to filling. These findings may determine whether the bladder will respond favorably to rehabilitative therapy. Residual urine can become a medium for bacterial growth, which can lead to infection and calculi formation.*

*Catheterization for residual urine may be necessary for postoperative patients and those with urinary incontinence, urethral strictures, cystitis, prostatic obstruction, hypotonic bladder, spinal cord injury, and other neurogenic disorders that interfere with normal bladder function. Because catheterization is a major cause of urinary tract infection, the procedure is always performed using sterile technique.*

### Equipment

Bedpan or urinal □ adjustable light □ sterile graduated measuring container □ washcloth □ soap and water □ sterile fenestrated drape □ sterile cotton balls or swabs □ povidone-iodine or other sterile cleansing solution □ sterile water-soluble lubricant □ sterile straight catheter (#10 to #22 French) □ sterile graduated receptacle □ intake and output sheet □ laboratory request slip □ optional: sterile specimen container (with cover and label), and indwelling catheter.

The most commonly used catheter for adults is the Robinson round-tip, adult #16 French. Commercial kits containing sterile, disposable, urinary catheters are available.

### Essential steps

● Explain the procedure to the patient.

● Tell the patient to notify you the next time he needs to void. When he does so, provide privacy and instruct him to void into the bedpan or urinal. Measure and record the amount of urine.

● If necessary, return the patient to bed.

● Wash your hands thoroughly.

● Position the patient as for indwelling catheterization. Use the washcloth to cleanse the patient's genitalia and perineum, if necessary.

● Direct the adjustable light *to enhance visualization of the urinary meatus.*

● Open the sterile tray using sterile technique, and drape the patient as for indwelling catheterization.

● Saturate the cotton balls or swabs with the cleansing solution and lubricate the catheter tip. Slip the catheter's other end into the notch in the graduated receptacle. If the receptacle isn't notched, anchor the end of the catheter over its edge, using sterile technique. Position the receptacle next to the patient's perineum.

● Wipe the patient's meatus with the cotton balls or swabs saturated with the cleansing solution. Then proceed with catheterization.

● When urine stops flowing, remove the catheter slowly. Cleanse excess lubricant and solution from the area and dry it with cotton balls *to make the patient more comfortable.*

● Measure the volume of residual urine. *A volume of 50 ml or less indicates near-normal or returning bladder function.*

● If ordered, send a specimen of the returned urine in a sterile specimen container to the laboratory for analysis.

● Dispose of all equipment properly.

### Special considerations

Never force a catheter forward. If the catheter meets resistance during insertion, try to maneuver it gently. Tell the patient to cough or bear down during insertion *as this will sometimes ease passage of the catheter.* If you're still unable to insert the catheter, notify

## COLLECTING A URETHRAL SPECIMEN

Gonorrhea affects the epithelium of the urethra and usually causes painful urination and a mucopurulent discharge in men. Diagnosis hinges on identification of *Neisseria gonorrhoeae* in a gram-stained smear or culture of urethral exudate.

*To collect a urethral specimen:*
• Instruct the patient not to urinate for 1 hour before specimen collection *to prevent removal of secretions from the urethra.*
• Wash your hands and provide privacy.
• Position the patient supine on the examining table and expose his penis. Instruct him to grasp and raise his penis *to allow visualization of the urethra.*
• Put on sterile gloves. Insert a sterile thin urogenital alginate swab or a sterile wire bacteriologic loop no more than ⅘" (2 cm) into the urethra, and rotate the swab

or loop from side to side. Leave it in place for 10 to 30 seconds *to absorb organisms.*
• To prepare the specimen for gram staining, gently roll the swab or loop in a circle across the slide. Allow it to dry; then send it to the laboratory. To prepare the specimen for culture, inoculate the medium plate in a Z pattern and immediately cross-streak it *to promote even distribution.* If you're using Transgrow, inoculate the medium with the bottle upright *to prevent loss of carbon dioxide.* After uncapping the bottle, insert the swab at the bottom of the bottle and roll it from side to side. Recap the bottle and send it to the laboratory.
• Assist the patient from the examining table, and allow him to dress.

VICKI SCHWARTZ BEAVER, RN, MS

the doctor. Strictures or spasms of the vesical sphincter may be causing an obstruction. The doctor may have to insert the catheter with the aid of size-graduated sounds or other dilating instruments.

After removing a catheter from an uncircumcised male, be sure to pull the foreskin forward *to prevent inadequate circulation, which may cause painful swelling.*

If continuous bladder drainage is ordered in the event of an excess amount of residual urine, use an indwelling catheter for this procedure, and if necessary, inflate the balloon and leave it in place. *This avoids reinsertion.*

### Complications

Be sure to assess your patient's condition throughout this procedure for any adverse reactions resulting from removal of excessive volumes of residual urine. Check the institution's policy to learn the maximum amount of urine that may be drained at one time (some institutions limit the amount to 700 to 1,000 ml). Whether or not to limit the amount of urine drained is currently controversial.

Bladder atony may result from too rapid bladder decompression.

Urinary tract infection can result from introduction of bacteria into the bladder.

### Documentation

Record the time and date of the procedure, the appearance and volume of voided and residual urine, the transport of any specimens to the laboratory for analysis, and the patient's tolerance of the procedure. Include the urine volumes on the intake and output sheet.

CAROL ANN GRAMSE, RN, PhD

# Insertion of an Indwelling Catheter

*An indwelling catheter (also known as a Foley or retention catheter) remains in the bladder to provide continuous drainage of urine. After insertion of the catheter into the bladder, a balloon at the catheter's proximal end is inflated to prevent it from slipping out. Indwelling catheters are most often used to relieve bladder distention caused by urinary retention and to allow continuous urinary drainage in patients whose meatus is swollen from childbirth, surgery, or local trauma. Other candidates for indwelling catheters include patients whose urinary tracts have been obstructed by tumors or enlarged prostates; those who suffer from urinary retention or infection as a result of neurogenic bladder paralysis caused by spinal cord injury or disease; and critically ill patients whose urinary output must be closely monitored.*

*Insertion of an indwelling catheter should be performed with extreme care to prevent injury and infection. Indwelling catheters can cause trauma to the urethral and bladder mucosa and are a major cause of nosocomial urinary tract infections. Catheters are inserted using sterile technique and only when absolutely necessary.*

## Equipment

Sterile indwelling catheter (latex or silicone #10 to #22 French) □ sterile syringe filled with 5 to 8 ml of sterile normal saline solution □ washcloth □ towel □ soap and water □ two linen-saver pads □ sterile gloves □ sterile fenestrated drape □ povidone-iodine or other sterile cleansing solution □ sterile cotton-tipped applicators (or cotton balls and plastic forceps) □ urine receptacle □ sterile water-soluble lubricant □ sterile drainage collection bag □ adhesive tape □ intake and output sheet □ laboratory request slip □ gooseneck lamp (optional).

Prepackaged sterile disposable kits are readily available. These usually contain all the necessary equipment. The syringes in prepackaged kits are prefilled with sterile saline solution.

## Preparation of equipment

Check the order on the patient's chart *to determine if a size or type of catheter has been specified.*

Select the appropriate equipment and assemble it at the patient's bedside.

## Essential steps

• Explain the procedure to the patient. Check his chart and ask him when he voided last. Percuss and palpate the bladder, and ask if he feels the urge to void.
• Place a lamp next to the patient's bed if room lighting is inadequate *to provide*

*maximum visualization of the urinary meatus.*

• Place the *female patient* in the supine position, with her knees flexed and separated and her feet flat on the bed, about 2' (60 cm) apart. If the patient finds this position uncomfortable, instruct her to flex only one knee and keep the other leg flat on the bed. You may need an assistant to help the patient maintain the necessary position or to hold or direct the light. Place the *male patient* in the supine position with his legs extended and flat on the bed. Ask the patient to maintain the position throughout the procedure *to provide you with a clear view of the urinary meatus and to prevent contamination of the sterile field.*

• Use the washcloth to clean the patient's genitalia and perineum thoroughly with soap and water, if necessary. Dry the area with the towel; then wash your hands.

• Place the linen-saver pads between the patient's legs and tuck them under the hips. *To create the sterile field,* open the prepackaged kit and place it between the legs of the female patient or next to the male patient's hip area. If the sterile gloves are the first item on the top of the tray, put them on. Place the plain drape under the patient's hips. Place the fenestrated drape over the patient, tucking the lower half under the patient's thighs and the upper half over the lower abdomen, exposing only the genitalia. Take care not to contaminate your gloves.

• Open the rest of the prepackaged disposable kit or sterile equipment tray, and, if necessary, add the appropriate-sized catheter and drainage bag to the sterile field. Put on the sterile gloves if you haven't already done so.

• Tear open the packet of cleansing solution and saturate the cotton balls or applicators with it. Be careful not to spill the solution on the equipment.

• Open the packet and apply the water-soluble lubricant to the catheter tip; attach the drainage collection bag to the other end. (If you're using a commercial kit, the drainage bag may already be attached.) Make sure all tubing ends remain sterile, and be sure the clamp at the emptying port of the drainage bag is closed *to prevent leakage of urine from the bag.* Some drainage systems have a chamber that serves as an air lock *to prevent bacteria in urine collected in the drainage bag from ascending the tube to the bladder.*

● Before inserting the catheter, inflate the catheter balloon with the normal saline solution *to inspect it for leaks.* Attach the saline-filled syringe to the Luer-Lok for balloon inflation. Push the plunger and check for seepage as the balloon expands; then aspirate the saline *to deflate the balloon.* Inspect the catheter for resiliency. *Rough, cracked catheters can injure urethral mucosa during insertion, which can predispose to infection.*

● For the *female patient,* separate the labia majora and labia minora as widely as possible with the thumb and middle and index fingers of one hand *so you can obtain a full view of the urinary meatus.* Keep the labia well separated throughout the procedure, so they don't fall back into position and obscure the urinary meatus or contaminate the area once it's cleansed. With your free hand, use a cotton-tipped applicator (or pick up a cotton ball with the plastic forceps) and wipe one side of the urinary meatus with a single downward motion. Wipe the other side with another sterile applicator in the same way. Wipe directly over the meatus with still another sterile applicator. Take care not to contaminate your sterile glove.

● For the *male patient,* grasp the penis with your nondominant hand. If he's uncircumcised, retract the foreskin. With your other hand, use a cotton-tipped applicator or a cotton ball held in forceps to clean the glans in a circular motion, starting at the urinary meatus and working outward. Repeat the procedure with a clean applicator, taking care not to contaminate your sterile glove.

● With your free hand, pick up the catheter.

● Carefully insert the lubricated tip of the catheter into the urinary meatus. *To facilitate catheter insertion,* ask the patient to cough as you insert the catheter.

*This relaxes the sphincter.* Tell the patient to breathe deeply and slowly *to further relax the sphincter and prevent spasms.* Hold the catheter close to its tip *to facilitate insertion and control its direction.*

Never force a catheter forward during insertion. Try gentle maneuvering while having the patient bear down or cough. If you still meet resistance, stop the procedure and notify the doctor immediately. Strictures, spasms of the sphincter, misplacement into the vaginal orifice (in females), or an enlarged prostate (in males) may be causing the resistance or obstruction. The doctor may have to insert the catheter using size-graduated sounds or other dilating instruments.

● For the *female patient,* advance the catheter about 2″ to 3″ (5.1 to 7.6 cm)—while continuing to hold the labia apart—until urine begins to flow. For the *male patient,* gently straighten and stretch the penis *to create slight traction;* then lift it to an angle of 60° to 90°, *to straighten the urethral canal and increase patient comfort during insertion.* Advance the catheter about 6″ to 7″ (15 to 18 cm) until urine begins to flow. If the foreskin was retracted for insertion, be sure to replace it *to prevent compromised circulation and painful swelling.*

● When urine stops flowing, attach the saline-filled syringe to the Luer-Lok. Push the plunger and inflate the balloon *to keep the catheter in place within the bladder.*

Never inflate a balloon without first establishing urine flow, *which assures you that the catheter has been correctly inserted into the bladder,* not into the urethral channel. If you can't establish urine flow, determine if the patient's bladder is empty. If the patient's bladder is empty at the time of insertion, make sure you've advanced the catheter far enough before inflating the balloon *to avoid injuring the urethra.*

● Position the collection bag below bladder level *to prevent reflux of urine into the bladder, which can cause infection, and to facilitate gravity drainage of the bladder.* Make sure the tubing doesn't get tangled in the side rails.

• Tape the catheter to the female patient's thigh *to prevent possible tension on the urogenital trigone.* In males, tape the catheter to the thigh or lower abdomen. *Taping the catheter to the lower abdomen prevents pressure on the urethra at the penoscrotal junction, which can lead to formation of urethrocutaneous fistulae. Taping the catheter also prevents traction on the bladder and alteration in the normal direction of urine flow.*

• Dispose of all used supplies properly.

## Special considerations

Several types of catheter are available with balloons of various sizes. Each has its own method of inflation and closure. For example, in one type of catheter, sterile solution or air is injected through the inflation lumen, then the end of the injection port is folded over itself and fastened with a clamp or rubber band. (Note: Injecting a catheter with air makes identifying leaks difficult and doesn't guarantee deflation of the balloon for removal.) A similar catheter is inflated by penetrating a seal in the end of its inflation lumen with a needle or the tip of the solution-filled syringe. Another type of balloon catheter self-inflates when a prepositioned clamp is loosened. The balloon size determines the amount of solution needed to inflate it. The exact amount is usually printed on the distal extension of the catheter, through which you inflate the balloon.

If necessary, the lateral position (with knees drawn close to the chest) can be used to catheterize the female patient. This position may be especially helpful for elderly or disabled patients, such as those with severe contractures.

If ordered, collect a urine specimen for laboratory analysis from the urine receptacle at the time of catheterization, and connect the drainage bag when urine has stopped flowing.

Inspect the catheter and tubing peri-odically while they're in place *to prevent compression or kinking that may obstruct urine flow.* Explain the basic principles of gravity drainage *so the patient realizes the importance of keeping the drainage tubing and collection bag lower than his bladder at all times.* If necessary, provide the patient with detailed instructions for performing clean intermittent self-catheterization.

Empty the collection bag at least every 8 hours, or more often if indicated, for monitoring purposes. Excessive fluid volume may require more frequent emptying *to prevent traction on the catheter,* which would cause the patient discomfort, and *to safeguard against injury to the urethra and bladder wall.* Some institutions encourage changing catheters at regular intervals, such as every 30 days, if continuous drainage is planned for a prolonged time.

 Observe the patient carefully throughout the procedure for signs of any adverse reactions resulting from removal of excessive volumes of residual urine. Check the institution's policy beforehand to learn the maximum amount of urine that may be drained at one time (some institutions limit the amount of urine drained to 700 to 1,000 ml). Whether or not to limit the amount of urine drained is currently controversial. Clamp the catheter at the first sign of an adverse reaction and notify the doctor.

## Complications

Urinary tract infection can result from the introduction of bacteria into the bladder.

Bladder atony or spasms may result from too rapid decompression of a severely distended bladder.

## Documentation

Record the date, the time, and the size and type of indwelling catheter used (to allow proper changing) in the patient's care plan, the cardex, and your nurse's notes. Also describe in the nurse's notes the amount, color, and other characteristics of the urine emptied from the bladder. Your institution may require only the intake and output sheet for fluid balance data. If large volumes of urine have been emptied, describe the patient's tolerance of the procedure. Note whether a urine specimen was sent for laboratory analysis.

CAROL ANN GRAMSE, RN, PhD

# Daily Care of Indwelling Catheters

*Routine daily care of indwelling catheters is controversial. While some clinical experts believe that it helps prevent infections, some recent studies report that routine catheter care doesn't prevent catheter-related urinary tract infections. So be sure to know and follow hospital policy for catheter care. Catheter equipment should be assessed and the patient's genitalia inspected twice daily. Routine catheter care generally follows the patient's morning bath since it can then immediately follow perineal care. Bedtime catheter care may require preceding perineal care.*

## Equipment

Povidone-iodine (or another appropriate cleansing solution) □ basin □ 4″ x 4″ sterile gauze sponges (about eight) □ sterile gloves □ sterile absorbent cotton balls or cotton-tipped applicators □ adhesive tape □ waste receptacle □ optional: safety pin; rubber band; lamp (preferably gooseneck) or flashlight; specimen container; second basin, soap, and washcloth, if perineal cleansing is necessary; adhesive remover.

Commercially prepared catheter-care kits containing necessary supplies are available.

## Preparation of equipment

Wash your hands and bring all equipment to the patient's bedside. Open the gauze sponges and place several in the basin. Pour some cleansing solution into the first basin over the gauze sponges. Pour only water into the second basin, and moisten three more gauze sponges. If you're using a prepackaged sterile catheter-care kit, open it to create a sterile field.

## Essential steps

● Explain the procedure and its purpose to the patient.

● Provide privacy and make sure that lighting is adequate *to provide maximum visualization of the perineum and catheter tubings.* Place a lamp at the bedside as needed, and perform perineal care, if necessary.

● Inspect the catheter for any problems and the urinary drainage for mucous shreds, blood clots, sediment, and turbidity. Then, pinch the catheter between two fingers *to determine if the catheter's lumen contains any material.* If you notice any of these conditions (or if hospital policy requires it), proceed with the following steps: Obtain a urine specimen (about 6 oz, or 175 ml) and notify the doctor if you suspect a problem.

● Inspect the outside of the catheter where it enters the urinary meatus *for encrusted material and suppurative drainage.* Also, inspect the tissue around the meatus. Normally, several centimeters of sediment accumulate at this site as a result of slight catheter movement at the urethral opening.

● Remove any adhesive tape securing the catheter to the patient's thigh or abdomen. Inspect the area for signs of adhesive burns, such as redness, tenderness, or blisters.

● Put on the sterile gloves. If using a prepackaged kit, open the antiseptic solution and pour it over the cotton balls or applicators. Then use a saturated gauze sponge or the applicators to clean the outside of the catheter and the tissue around the meatus. *To avoid contaminating the urinary tract,* always clean by wiping away from—never toward—the urinary meatus. Use a dry gauze pad to remove encrusted material.

# ATTACHING A LEG BAG

A urinary drainage collection bag attached to the leg provides a catheterized patient with greater mobility. Also, because the collection bag can be worn under clothing it can help a patient feel more comfortable about catheterization. Leg bags are usually worn during the day by patients who require long-term indwelling catheterization and are replaced at night with a standard collection device.

Because some patients will continue to be catheterized after discharge, you must be familiar with this procedure so you can teach them how to attach a leg bag. To perform this procedure, you'll need a leg bag device, which consists of two straps and a drainage collection bag with a short drainage tube. You'll also need an alcohol sponge, a sterile towel, adhesive tape, and a screw clamp or hemostat.

*To prevent infection*, wash the leg bag with soap and water or a bacteriostatic solution before each use. Create a sterile field with the towel *to prevent introducing bacteria into the patient's normally sterile bladder.*

**To attach the leg bag**
• Provide privacy, and explain to the patient that you are going to attach a drainage collection bag to his leg. Describe the advantages of this device, but also explain that a leg bag is smaller than a standard collection device and may have to be emptied more frequently.
• Remove the protective covering from the tip of the drainage tube. Then clean the

tip with an alcohol sponge. Start at the opening, and wipe away from it *to prevent contaminating the tube.* Place the tube on the sterile field, and attach it to the catheter.
• Place the collection bag on the outside of the patient's lower leg, *so it won't interfere with his walking.* Secure the upper strap around the leg, just below the knee; secure the lower strap just below the middle of his calf. *To avoid compromising the patient's circulation,* don't fasten the straps too tightly.
• Tape the catheter to the patient's thigh, leaving some slack *to reduce tension on the urethra.* This also prevents excessive pressure on the trigone of the female patient's bladder and on the male patient's urethra at the penoscrotal junction. Such pressure could eventually cause tissue breakdown.
• Although most leg bags have a valve in the drainage tube that prevents the reflux of urine into the bladder, emphasize to the patient the importance of keeping the drainage bag lower than his bladder at all times, *because the room-temperature urine in the bag is a perfect growth medium for bacteria.*
• *To prevent tension from the weight of a full leg bag, which could damage the patient's bladder wall and urethra,* empty the leg bag frequently. Also, inspect the catheter and drainage tube periodically for compression or kinking, which could obstruct urine flow, resulting in distention of the bladder.

Don't pull on the catheter while you're cleaning it. *This can injure the urethra and the bladder wall. It can also expose a section of the catheter that was inside the urethra, so that when you release the catheter, the newly contaminated section will reenter the urethra, introducing potentially pathogenic organisms.*
• Remove your gloves and tear a piece of tape from the roll.
• *To prevent skin hypersensitivity or irritation,* retape the catheter to the other thigh or opposite side of the abdomen. (Commercial straps are available for this purpose.)

Provide enough slack before securing the catheter *to prevent tension on the tubing that could injure the urethral lumen or bladder wall.*
• Wrap a rubber band around the drainage tubing, insert the safety pin through a loop of the rubber band, and pin the tubing to the sheet below bladder level. Then attach the collection bag, below bladder level, to the bed frame.
• If necessary, cleanse residue from the previous tape site with adhesive remover and dispose of all used supplies.

## Special considerations
Your institution may require the use of

specific cleansing agents for catheter care, to be used routinely or as needed. Check hospital policy before beginning this procedure. A doctor's order may be needed to apply antibiotic ointments to the urinary meatus after cleansing.

In some institutions, catheter care includes wiping the antiseptic cleansing solution from the urinary meatus with a wet sterile gauze sponge *to prevent possible irritation from the presence of the solution.*

Avoid raising the drainage bag above bladder level. *This prevents reflux of urine, an excellent medium for bacterial growth.*

Encourage patients whose fluid intake is not restricted to drink plenty of fluids. *This helps flush the urinary system and reduces sediment formation.*

*To prevent urinary sediment and calculi deposits from obstructing the drainage tube,* some patients are placed on an acid-ash diet to acidify the urine. Cranberry juice, for example, can help to promote urinary acidity.

*To avoid damaging the urethral lumen or bladder wall,* always disconnect the collection bag and tubing from the bed linen and bed frame before helping a patient out of bed.

When possible, attach a leg bag *to allow the patient greater mobility* (see *Attaching a Leg Bag,* opposite).

## Complications

Sediment buildup, such as casts or mucus plugs, can occur anywhere in a catheterization system, especially in bedridden and dehydrated patients. *To prevent sediment buildup,* keep the patient well hydrated, if he's not on fluid restriction. Change indwelling catheter as ordered, or when malfunction, obstruction, or contamination occurs.

Urinary tract infection may result from introduction of endogenous or exogenous bacteria. This can occur during catheter insertion or from intraluminal or extraluminal migration of bacteria up the catheter. Signs and symptoms of such infection vary but may include cloudy urine, hematuria, fever, malaise, tenderness over bladder, or flank pain.

## Documentation

Record the care you performed, any necessary modifications in techniques, any patient complaints or comments, and the condition of the perineum and urinary meatus. Note the character of the urine in the collection bag, any sediment buildup, and whether a specimen was sent for laboratory analysis. Also record fluid intake and output; an hourly record is usually necessary for critically ill patients and those with renal problems.

CAROL ANN GRAMSE, RN, PhD

---

# Catheter Irrigation

Irrigating an indwelling catheter serves several therapeutic purposes. It helps to keep the drainage tube patent by washing out residual urine and bladder sediment and by removing blood clots that may develop after bladder, kidney, or prostate surgery. When necessary, medicated irrigants are used to help soothe irritated bladder tissue and promote healing.

Catheter irrigation requires the strictest aseptic technique to prevent bacteria from entering the bladder. The ends of the catheter and drainage tube and the syringe tip must be kept sterile throughout this procedure. (See also Performing Bladder Instillation, *page 592, a variation of this procedure.*)

## Equipment

Ordered irrigating solution (such as renacidin 10% or sterile normal saline solution) □ sterile graduated receptacle or

## PERFORMING BLADDER INSTILLATION

This procedure introduces medicated irrigating solution into the patient's bladder for a prescribed time, usually to treat bladder infections. To perform bladder instillation in a catheterized patient:
• Gather the prescribed medicated irrigating solution, an irrigation tray, and alcohol sponges.
• Provide privacy, and explain the procedure to the patient.
• Disconnect the catheter and clean it and the drainage tube with an alcohol sponge. Place the sponge over the drainage tube. Hold the end of the catheter with another alcohol sponge.
• Fill the syringe with the prescribed medication. Drain any excess urine from the bladder. Then, slowly introduce the medication into the catheter, and clamp the catheter. Reopen the catheter after the prescribed amount ot time—usually 15 to 30 minutes.
• Clean the ends of the catheter and drainage tube before reconnecting them.
• Document the type and amount of solution used and any pertinent observations.
    If a catheter isn't already inserted, insert one before performing the bladder instillation. Then, remove the catheter. The patient will expel the solution the next time he urinates.

emesis basin □ sterile bulb syringe or 50-ml catheter-tip syringe □ two alcohol sponges □ sterile gloves □ linen-saver pad □ basin of warm water (optional).

Commercially packaged sterile irrigating kits are available; these usually include an irrigating solution container, a graduated receptacle, and a bulb or 50-ml catheter-tip syringe. If the volume of irrigating solution instilled must be measured, use a graduated syringe instead of a noncalibrated bulb syringe.

### Preparation of equipment
If you're using a premixed irrigating solution, check the expiration date on the container. Most solutions are kept refrigerated. *To prevent vesical spasms during instillation of solution,* warm the irrigating solution to room temperature.

Remove the closed container from the refrigerator at least 30 minutes before irrigation or place it in a basin of warm water. Never heat the solution on a burner. *Hot irrigating solution can traumatize the patient's bladder.*

### Essential steps
• Explain the procedure to the patient, wash your hands, and provide privacy.
• Place the linen-saver pad partially under the patient's buttocks *to protect the bed linens.*
• Create the sterile field at the patient's bedside by opening the sterile equipment tray or commercial kit. Using aseptic technique, clean the lip of the solution bottle by pouring a small amount of irrigating solution into a sink or waste receptacle. Then pour the prescribed amount of solution into the graduated receptacle or other solution container.
• Place the tip of the syringe into the solution. Squeeze the bulb or pull back the plunger (depending on the type of syringe), and fill the syringe with the appropriate amount of solution (usually 30 ml).
• Open the alcohol sponges. Then put on the sterile gloves. Clean the juncture of the catheter and drainage tube with an alcohol sponge *to remove as many bacterial contaminants as possible.*
• Disconnect the catheter and drainage tube by twisting them in opposite directions and carefully pulling them apart without creating tension on the catheter. Do not release the catheter; hold it in your nondominant hand. Place the drainage tube on the sterile field or hold it in your nondominant hand in such a way that it won't become contaminated.
• Twist the bulb syringe or catheter-tip syringe into the catheter's distal end.
• Squeeze the bulb or slowly push the plunger of the syringe *to instill the irrigating solution through the catheter.* If necessary, refill the syringe and repeat this step until you've instilled the prescribed amount of irrigating solution.
• Remove the syringe and direct the return flow from the catheter into the graduated receptacle or emesis basin. Don't

let the catheter end touch the collected drainage in the receptacle or become contaminated in any other way.
• Wipe the drainage tube and catheter with the remaining alcohol sponge.
• After the alcohol has evaporated, usually only a few seconds, reattach the drainage tubing to the catheter.
• Dispose of all used supplies properly.

### Special considerations
If you encounter any resistance during instillation of the irrigating solution, do not use excessive pressure to force the solution into the bladder. Stop the procedure and notify the doctor. If an indwelling catheter becomes totally obstructed, remove it and replace it with a new one *to prevent bladder distention, stasis of urine, and subsequent infection.*

If frequent irrigations become necessary, the doctor may order a closed (or continuous) irrigation system. *This decreases the risk of infection by eliminating the need to disconnect the catheter and drainage tube repeatedly.* With a closed system, irrigating solution is instilled into the bladder through a catheter containing a special lumen to which irrigation tubing and solution are attached. When the prescribed amount of solution has been instilled, the tubing is clamped off.

Encourage catheterized patients whose fluid intake is not restricted to drink plenty of fluids *to help flush the urinary system and reduce sediment formation.* An acid-ash diet may also be ordered *to keep the patient's urine acidic, thereby helping to prevent the formation of calculi.* Ascorbic acid (found in citrus fruit juices and dark green and deep yellow vegetables) and cranberry juice especially help to promote such acidity.

### Documentation
Note the amount, color, and consistency of return flow, and document the patient's tolerance of the procedure. Also note any resistance encountered during instillation of the solution. If the return flow volume is less than the prescribed amount of instilled solution, note this on the intake and output balance sheets and in nurse's notes. Record the use of medicated irrigating solutions on the patient's medication record.

CAROL ANN GRAMSE, RN, PhD

# Continuous Bladder Irrigation

*Continuous bladder irrigation can help prevent urinary tract obstruction by flushing out small blood clots that form after prostate or bladder surgery. The continuous flow of irrigating solution through a triple-lumen catheter (see* Setup for Continuous Bladder Irrigation, page 594) *also creates a mild tamponade that may help prevent venous hemorrhaging. The doctor usually inserts the catheter immediately after surgery. This procedure can also be used to treat an irritated, inflamed, or infected bladder lining; in such cases, the catheter is usually inserted at the bedside.*

### Equipment
Two containers of irrigating solution (usually 2,000-ml containers of normal saline or prescribed amount of antibiotic solution) □ Y-type I.V. tubing □ sterile alcohol or povidone-iodine sponge.

*Note:* This type of bladder irrigation requires that a triple-lumen catheter be in place. The irrigation tubing is connected to the third port (or lumen) of the catheter.

Normal saline solution is usually prescribed for bladder irrigation after prostate or bladder surgery. An antibiotic solution may also be ordered postoperatively but is most often used to treat infections. Large volumes of irrigating solution are usually required for continuous bladder irrigation during the first 24 to 48 hours after surgery. This explains the advantage of the Y-type I.V. tubing, which allows immediate irrigation with reserve solution.

## Preparation of equipment

Before starting continuous bladder irrigation, check the irrigating solution against the doctor's order *to make sure you have the right solution.* If the solution is an antibiotic, check its expiration date and the patient's history for allergies.

## Essential steps

- Wash your hands.
- Insert one spike of the Y-type tubing into each container.

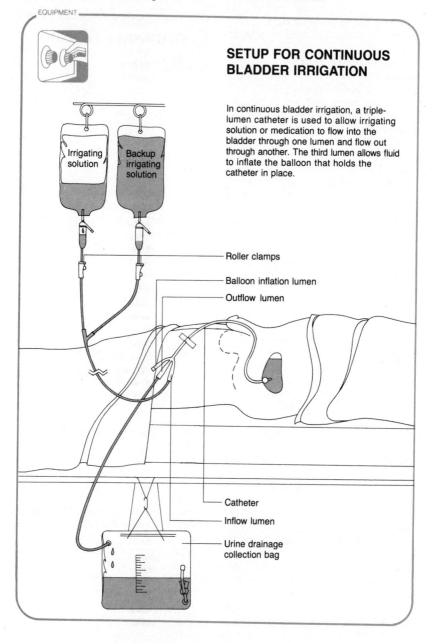

## SETUP FOR CONTINUOUS BLADDER IRRIGATION

In continuous bladder irrigation, a triple-lumen catheter is used to allow irrigating solution or medication to flow into the bladder through one lumen and flow out through another. The third lumen allows fluid to inflate the balloon that holds the catheter in place.

Irrigating solution

Backup irrigating solution

Roller clamps

Balloon inflation lumen

Outflow lumen

Catheter

Inflow lumen

Urine drainage collection bag

• Squeeze the drip chamber on each spike of the tubing.
• Open the flow clamps *to remove air from the tubing that could cause bladder distention.* Then close them.
   *To begin irrigation:*
• Assemble all equipment at the patient's bedside. Explain the procedure to the patient and provide privacy.
• Hang the two containers of irrigating solution on the I.V. pole.
• Clean the opening to the inflow lumen of the catheter with the sterile alcohol or povidone-iodine sponge.
• Insert the distal end of the I.V. tubing securely into the inflow lumen of the catheter. (The outflow lumen should already be attached to tubing leading to the drainage collection bag.)
• Open the flow clamp under one of the containers of irrigating solution, and set the drip rate, as ordered.
   *To use the reserve container:*
• *To prevent air from entering the system,* don't allow the primary container to empty completely. Close the flow clamp under the *near-empty* container and simultaneously open the flow clamp under the reserve container. *This prevents a reflux of irrigation solution from the reserve container into the near-empty one.*
• Adjust the drip rate, as ordered.
• Disconnect the tube from the near-empty container with a twisting motion. Be careful not to contaminate the tip of the tube.
• Hang a new reserve container on the I.V. pole and insert the tubing, maintaining asepsis.
• Discard the empty container appropriately.
• When the first reserve container is nearly empty, repeat the procedure.

**Special considerations**
Always have a second container of irrigating solution available to replace the one that's nearly empty.
   Check the inflow and outflow lines periodically for kinks *to make sure the solution is running freely.* If the flow rate is rapid, check the lines frequently.
   Measure the outflow volume accu-

rately. Outflow volume should equal or, allowing for urine production, slightly surpass inflow volume. If inflow volume exceeds the outflow volume in a postoperative patient, suspect bladder rupture at the suture lines or renal damage, and notify the doctor immediately.
   Also, assess outflow for changes in appearance and blood clots, especially if irrigation is being performed postoperatively to control bleeding. Generally, if drainage is bright red, irrigating solution should be infused rapidly *with the clamp wide open* until drainage clears. Always notify the doctor immediately if you suspect hemorrhage. If drainage is clear, solution is usually given at a rate of 40 to 60 drops/minute. The doctor normally specifies the rate for antibiotic solutions. Be sure to empty drainage collection bags frequently, which may be as often as every 4 hours, or as needed. If the irrigating solution contains an antibiotic, label the container with the drug name, dose, rate, and time added.

**Complications**
Interruptions in a continuous irrigation system can predispose to infection. Obstruction in the catheter's outflow lumen can cause bladder distention.

**Documentation**
After replacing a container of solution, record the time and amount of fluid given on the intake and output record. Also record the time and amount of fluid drained each time you empty the collection bag. Note the time, date, appearance of drainage, and any complaints the patient may have in the nurse's notes.
   CAROL ANN GRAMSE, RN, PhD

# Removal of an Indwelling Catheter

*An indwelling catheter should be removed when bladder decompression is no longer necessary, when the catheter is obstructed, or when the patient can resume voiding. Depending on how long the patient was catheterized, the doctor may order bladder retraining before catheter removal.*

### Equipment

Absorbent cotton □ clean examining gloves □ sterile alcohol sponge □ 10-ml syringe with a Luer-Lok (or a syringe big enough to hold the balloon contents) □ bedpan □ clamp for bladder retraining (optional).

### Essential steps

• Explain to the patient that you're going to remove his catheter and that he may feel slight discomfort. Also tell him that after removing the catheter you will check him periodically during the first 8 to 24 hours *to make sure he resumes voiding.*
  *To retrain the bladder:*
• Clamp the catheter for 2 hours; then release it for 5 minutes *to empty the bladder.*
• Repeat the procedure. (This gradual filling and emptying helps restore the bladder's muscle tone.)
  *To remove the catheter:*
• Wash your hands.
• Provide adequate privacy for the patient so you can expose his genitalia. Place the absorbent cotton alongside the catheter, and put on the examining gloves.
• Clean the inflation port with the alcohol sponge, and attach the syringe to the Luer-Lok mechanism on the catheter.
• *To deflate the balloon,* pull back on the plunger. *This aspirates the fluid injected at the time the catheter was inserted.* (The amount of fluid injected is usually indicated on the tip of the catheter's balloon lumen.) It should also be noted on the cardex and patient's chart.
• Grasp the catheter with the absorbent cotton, and gently remove it from the urethra.
• Offer the patient the bedpan, *because catheter removal often creates a desire to void.*
• Measure the amount of urine in the collection bag before discarding it.

### Special considerations

Encourage fluid intake *to stimulate urine production, to dilute urine, and to help decrease any discomfort the patient may experience when he first starts voiding.*

Within 24 hours, the patient should be voiding normally (300 to 400 ml at a time), depending on fluid intake. If he's voiding small amounts (30 to 100 ml every 30 minutes to 1 hour), he's not emptying his bladder completely. Report this to the doctor.

After catheter removal, assess the patient for voiding difficulty, incontinence or dribbling, urgency, persistent dysuria or bladder spasm, fever, chills, or palpable distention of the bladder. Report any such findings to the doctor.

### Complications

Major complications in removing an indwelling catheter are failure of the balloon to deflate and rupture of the balloon. If the balloon ruptures, cystoscopy is usually performed to ensure removal of all balloon fragments.

### Documentation

*For bladder retraining,* record the date and time the catheter was clamped, the time the catheter was released, and the volume and appearance of urine. *For catheter removal,* record the date and time the catheter was removed and the patient's tolerance of the procedure. Record when and how much the patient voids after catheter removal and any problems associated with voiding.

CAROL ANN GRAMSE, RN, PhD

# Care of Nephrostomy and Cystostomy Tubes

*A nephrostomy tube drains urine directly from a kidney when pathology inhibits the normal flow of urine. A surgeon inserts the tube through the renal cortex and medulla into the renal pelvis from a lateral incision in the flank. The usual indication is obstructive disease, such as calculi in the ureter or ureteropelvic junction. Nephrostomy drainage also allows healing of kidney tissue that has been traumatized by obstructive disease.*

*A cystostomy tube drains urine from the bladder, diverting it from the urethra. The use of this tube is indicated after certain gynecologic procedures, bladder surgery, and prostatectomy, and for severe urethral strictures or trauma. Inserted about 2" (5.1 cm) above the symphysis pubis, a cystostomy tube may be used alone or with an indwelling urethral catheter.*

*Proper care of a nephrostomy or cystostomy tube ensures adequate drainage of the kidney or bladder, helps maintain skin integrity at the insertion site, and may help prevent infection of the urinary system. Dressings around both tubes must be changed when they're wet, and a nephrostomy tube must be periodically irrigated.*

## Equipment

*For dressing changes:* 4" x 4" gauze sponges □ povidone-iodine solution or hydrogen peroxide or povidone-iodine applicators □ sterile cup or emesis basin □ paper bag □ linen-saver pad □ clean gloves (for dressing removal) □ sterile gloves (for new dressing) □ forceps □ precut 4" x 4" drain sponges □ adhesive tape (preferably hypoallergenic).

*For nephrostomy-tube irrigation:* 3-ml syringe □ sterile normal saline solution □ alcohol sponge or povidone-iodine applicator.

Commercially prepared sterile dressing kits with a solution cup, as well as commercially packaged povidone-iodine applicators, are available for use in this procedure.

## Preparation of equipment

Wash your hands and assemble all equipment at the patient's bedside. Open several packages of gauze sponges (or the povidone-iodine applicators). Place the sponges in the sterile cup or basin and pour the povidone-iodine solution over the sponges. If you're using a commercially packaged dressing kit, open it using aseptic technique and fill the cup with antiseptic solution.

Open the paper bag and place it away from the other equipment, *to prevent contamination of the sterile field.*

## Essential steps

*To change dressings:*
● Provide privacy and explain the procedure to the patient. Help him to lie on the side opposite the tube so you can see the tube clearly and change the dressing more easily.
● Place the linen-saver pad under the patient's side *to absorb excess drainage and to keep the patient dry.*
● Put on the clean gloves. Carefully remove the tape around the cystostomy tube; then remove the wet or soiled dressing. Discard them in the paper bag. Remove the gloves and discard them in the bag.
● Put on sterile gloves and, using forceps, pick up a saturated sponge or dip a dry one into the cup of antiseptic solution. (If you're using povidone-iodine applicators, simply pick one up.)
● To clean the wound, make only one wipe with each sponge or applicator, moving from the insertion site outward; discard the used sponge or applicator in the paper bag. Don't touch the paper bag with the forceps *to avoid contaminating them.*
● Pick up a sterile 4" x 4" drain sponge and place it around the tube. If necessary, overlap two sponges around the tube *to provide maximum absorption.*
● Use hypoallergenic tape to secure the dressing in place.
● Dispose of all equipment appropriately. Cleanse the patient as necessary.
*To irrigate a nephrostomy tube:*
● Fill the 3-ml syringe with the sterile normal saline solution.
● Clean the junction of the nephrostomy tube and drainage tube with the alcohol sponge or povidone-iodine applicator and disconnect them.

• Insert the syringe into the nephrostomy tube opening, and instill 2 to 3 ml of solution into the tube.

• Slowly aspirate the solution back into the syringe. *To avoid damaging the tissues of the renal pelvis,* never pull back forcefully on the plunger.

• If the solution doesn't return, remove the syringe from the tube and reattach it to the drainage tubing to allow the solution to drain by gravity.

### Special considerations

 Never irrigate a nephrostomy tube without a doctor's order. Because the capacity of the renal pelvis is about 4 to 8 ml, never irrigate with more than 6 ml of solution. (Remember that the purpose of irrigating the tube is to keep it patent, not to lavage the renal pelvis.)

When necessary, irrigate a cystostomy tube as you would an indwelling catheter. Be sure to perform the irrigation gently *to avoid damaging any suture lines.*

Check a nephrostomy tube frequently for kinks or obstruction. Kinks are likely to occur if the patient lies on the side in which the tube is inserted. Suspect obstructions when you notice a decreasing amount of urine in the drainage bag or increasing urine leakage from the insertion site. Back pressure caused by inadequate drainage can damage nephrons. Gently curve a cystostomy tube *to prevent kinks.* Tape it to the patient's lateral abdomen in at least two places *to prevent tension on the tube.*

To tape a nephrostomy tube directly to the skin, take a wide piece of adhesive tape and cut it twice lengthwise to its midpoint. Apply the uncut end of the tape to the skin so that the midpoint meets the tube. Wrap the middle strip around the tube in spiral fashion. Tape the other two strips to the patient's skin on both sides of the tube. For greater security, you may repeat this step with a second piece of tape, applying it in the reverse direction. You may also wish to apply two more strips of tape perpendicular to and over the first two pieces. In any case, always apply another strip of tape lower down on the tube in the direction of the drainage tube *to further anchor the tube.* Don't place tension on any sutures, which are commonly used *to prevent tube dislocation.*

If a blood clot or mucus plug obstructs a nephrostomy or cystostomy tube, try milking the tube *to restore its patency.* Place the flat side of a closed hemostat under the tube, just above the obstruction. Then pinch the tube against the hemostat and slide both your finger and the hemostat toward you. With your other hand, securely hold the drainage tube above the hemostat *to avoid pulling it out of the incision.*

Cystostomy tubes for postoperative urologic patients are usually checked hourly for 24 hours *to ensure adequate drainage and tube patency.* To check the patency of the tube, note the amount of urine in the drainage bag and check the patient's bladder for distention.

### Complications

Infection may occur because nephrostomy and cystostomy tubes provide a direct opening to the kidney and bladder.

### Documentation

Describe the color and amount of drainage from the nephrostomy or cystostomy tube, and record any color changes as they occur. If the patient has more than one tube, record the drainage from each tube separately. If irrigation is necessary, record the amount and type of irrigant used and whether or not a complete return was obtained.

KRISTINE M. KRONER, RN, BSN

# Care of a Urinary Diversion Stoma

*Urinary diversion stomas provide an alternative route for urine flow when pathology impedes normal drainage. A permanent urinary diversion stoma is indicated in any condition that requires a total cystectomy, such as an invasive bladder tumor; a temporary stoma, in any condition that requires a partial cystectomy. In the latter case, a suprapubic or urethral catheter is usually inserted first to divert the flow of urine temporarily; this catheter remains in place until the bladder incision heals completely. Temporary or permanent urinary diversion stomas may also be indicated in patients with neurogenic bladder, congenital anomaly, trauma to the lower urinary tract, or severe chronic urinary tract infection.*

*Three types of permanent urinary diversion stomas can be created (see Three Types of Urinary Diversion, page 600). Most require the patient to wear a urine-collection appliance. The patient or a family member can learn to care for a urinary diversion stoma at home. However, the patient's emotional adjustment to the stoma must be given special consideration before he can be expected to maintain it properly.*

## Equipment
Basin filled with warm water □ soap □ waste receptacle (such as an impervious or wax-coated bag) □ nonallergenic paper tape □ ruler □ scissors □ urine-collection appliance (with or without antireflux valve) □ graduated cylinder □ cottonless gauze (some rolled, some flat) □ ostomy cement □ skin barrier □ appliance belt □ optional: adhesive solvent, tampon, hair dryer, electric razor, gauze sponge.

Commercially packaged stoma care kits are available.

In place of soap and water, adhesive-remover swabs may be used, if available, or cotton gauze saturated with adhesive solvent.

Some appliances come equipped with a semipermeable skin barrier (impermeable to liquid, but permeable to vapor and oxygen, which is essential to maintaining skin integrity). *Wafer-type* barriers may offer more protection against irritation than adhesive appliances. A

*carbon-zinc* barrier is economical and easy to apply. Its puttylike consistency allows it to be rolled between the palms of the hands to form a "washer" that can encircle the base of the stoma. The carbon-zinc barrier can withstand enzymes, acids, and other damaging discharge material. All of these barriers are easily removed along with the adhesive, causing less damage to the skin. The familiar *karaya* barrier helps protect the skin and stoma from urinary crystal deposits and other irritants. However, urine tends to melt the barrier, limiting its usefulness.

## Preparation of equipment
Take all equipment to the patient's bedside and place it on an overbed table. Attach the waste receptacle to the table with the tape so it's easily accessible. Wash your hands. Provide privacy for the patient. Measure the diameter of the stoma with a ruler. Cut the opening of the appliance with the scissors; it shouldn't be more than ¹/₁₆″ to ⅛″ (0.15 to 0.31 cm) larger than the diameter of the stoma. Moisten the faceplate of the appliance with a small amount of solvent or water *to prepare it for adhesion.* Perform these preliminary steps at the patient's bedside *so you can talk to him about the procedure and demonstrate your skill in handling the equipment, thereby helping him to relax.*

## Essential steps
● Wash your hands again, and take any measures necessary to ensure privacy. Explain the procedure to the patient, offering constant reinforcement and reassurance *to counteract the negative emotional, psychological, and perceptual reactions normally elicited by this procedure.*
● Place the patient's bed in a horizontal position so his abdomen is flat. *This position eliminates skin folds that could cause the appliance to slip or cause irritation.*
● Open the drain valve of the appliance to be replaced *to empty the urine into the graduated cylinder.* Apply soap and water or adhesive solvent as you gently

## THREE TYPES OF URINARY DIVERSION

The three types of permanent urinary diversion with stomas are ureterostomy, ileal conduit, and continent vesicostomy.

In **ureterostomy,** a stoma or stomas are formed when ureters are diverted to the abdominal wall or flank. There are different types of ureterostomy:

• *Loop ureterostomy:* ureters loop as they are brought to skin surface forming a stoma
• *Double-barrel ureterostomy:* both ureters are brought to the skin surface to form side-by-side stomas
• *Transureteroureterostomy:* one ureter is anastomosed to the other, which is then brought to the skin surface to form a stoma
• *Bilateral ureterostomy:* both ureters are brought to the skin surface to form stomas
• *Unilateral ureterostomy:* one ureter is brought to skin surface to form a stoma

In **ileal conduit,** a segment of the ileum is excised, and the two ends of the ileum that result from the excision of the segment are anastomosed. Then, the ureters are dissected from the bladder and anastomosed to the ileal segment. One end of the ileal segment is closed with sutures; the opposite end of the segment is brought through the abdominal wall, thereby forming a stoma.

In **continent vesicostomy,** a tube is formed from part of the bladder wall. One end of the tube is brought to the skin to form the stoma. At the internal end of this tube, a nipple valve is created from the bladder wall so urine won't drain out unless a catheter is inserted through the stoma into the bladder pouch. The urethral neck is sutured closed.

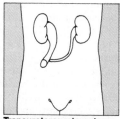

**Flank loop ureterostomy**

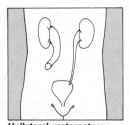

**Double-barrel ureterostomy**

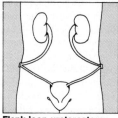

**Transureteroureterostomy**

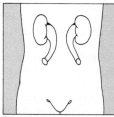

**Bilateral ureterostomy**

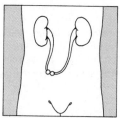

**Unilateral ureterostomy**

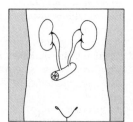

**Ileal conduit**

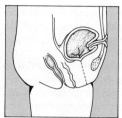

**Continent vesicostomy**

push the skin back from the pouch *to remove the appliance.* If the appliance is disposable, place it in the waste receptacle. If it's reusable, clean and dry it.

 *To prevent burning the patient,* avoid touching the stoma with adhesive solvent. If adhesive remains on the skin, gently rub the area with a dry gauze pad. Place used gauze pads in the waste receptacle. Carefully observe the stoma and peristomal skin for signs of irritation.

• *To prevent the constant flow of urine from seeping out onto the skin while you're changing the appliance,* wick the urine by placing a rolled gauze sponge or tampon in the stoma. Urine will flow up the sponge or tampon by capillary action.

• Use water to carefully wash off any crystal deposits that may have formed around the stoma. If urine has stagnated and has a strong odor, use soap to wash it off, but be sure to rinse the soapy area thoroughly *to remove any oily residue that could cause the appliance to slip.*

• Follow hospital skin-care protocol to treat any minor skin problems.

• Dry the peristomal area thoroughly with a gauze pad *because moisture will keep the appliance from sticking.* Use a hair dryer, if you wish. Remove any hair on the peristomal skin with scissors or an electric razor *to prevent hair follicles from becoming irritated when the pouch is removed, which can cause folliculitis.*

 Never shave the site with a straight-edge razor *because it could cut the skin.*

• Apply a thin layer of ostomy cement around the stoma, and allow it to dry. If you're using an aerosol adhesive, which dries more quickly, either spray it onto a gauze sponge and pat this around the stoma or cover the stoma and spray the adhesive around it. If you're using karaya powder or cornstarch, be sure the skin is completely dry before you apply it.

• Apply the skin barrier, placing it close to the edges of the stoma, *to prevent skin irritation and to make the appliance adhere longer.*

• Remove the sponge or tampon wick, and place it in the waste receptacle.

• When the cement becomes tacky, place the appliance over the stoma, leaving only a small amount (⅜″ to ¾″, or 1 to 2 cm) of skin exposed.

• If hospital protocol allows, secure the faceplate of the appliance to the skin with paper tape, using a picture-framing technique. To do this, place a piece of tape parallel to each edge of the faceplate so it's on both the faceplate and the skin.

• Apply the appliance belt on a level with the stoma. *If the belt is placed above or below the stoma, it can break the bag's seal; it can also rub or traumatize the stoma.* Leave it loose enough so that two fingers can be inserted between the skin and the belt. *If the belt is too tight, it can irritate the skin or cause internal damage.*

• Dispose of the used materials appropriately.

## Special considerations

The patient's attitude toward his urinary diversion stoma plays a big part in determining how well he'll adjust to it. *To encourage a positive attitude,* help the patient get used to the idea of caring for his stoma and the appliance as though it were a natural extension of himself. When teaching him how to perform the procedure, provide positive reinforcement after each step. Suggest that he perform the procedure in the morning when urine flow is slowest. Give him written instructions, if necessary.

Help the patient choose between disposable and reusable appliances by telling him the advantages and disadvantages of each. Emphasize the importance of correct placement of a well-fitted appliance *to prevent seepage of urine onto the skin.* When positioned correctly, most appliances remain in place at least 3 days and as long as 5 days if no leakage occurs. After 5 days, the appliance should be changed for sanitary purposes. With the improved adhesives and pouches available, belts aren't always necessary.

Because urine flow is constant, it accumulates quickly, becoming even heavier than stools. *To prevent the weight of the urine from loosening the seal around the stoma and separating the appliance from the skin,* always empty the bag through the drain valve when it is one-third to one-half full.

Instruct the patient to connect his appliance to a urine-collection container before he goes to sleep. *The continuous flow of urine into the container during the night prevents the urine from accumulating and stagnating in the appliance.*

Teach the patient sanitary and dietary measures that can prolong the usefulness of his stoma and control the odor that often results from alkaline urine, infection, or poor hygiene. Reusable appliances should be washed with soap and lukewarm water, then air-dried thoroughly *to prevent brittleness.* Soaking the appliance in dilute vinegar or placing deodorant tablets in it can dissipate stubborn odors. An acid-ash diet that includes ascorbic acid and cranberry juice raises urinary acidity; this, in turn, reduces bacterial action and fermentation, the underlyng causes of odor. Generous fluid intake also helps to reduce odors by diluting the urine.

Know how to care for the patient

---

## CARING FOR THE PATIENT WITH A CONTINENT VESICOSTOMY

**Before surgery**
• Reinforce and, if necessary, supplement the doctor's explanation of the procedure and its implications to the patient. Inform him that two indwelling catheters will be inserted and left in for 6 weeks, until his stoma heals. He will be discharged from the hospital after the catheters are inserted and then readmitted to have the catheters removed and to learn how to catheterize his stoma.

**Immediately after surgery**
• Monitor intake and output closely. Be alert for decreased output, which may indicate that urine flow is obstructed.
• Watch for common postoperative complications, such as infection. Bladder spasms often occur after a continent vesicotomy and are usually relieved by medication.
• Irrigate the indwelling catheters daily with 30 to 50 ml of sterile normal saline solution. Otherwise, maintain a closed drainage system.
• Cleanse the area around the catheters daily—first with povidone-iodine solution and then with sterile water. Apply a dry sterile dressing to the area. Use precut 4″ x 4″ drain sponges, if possible, around the catheter *to absorb leakage.*
• Teach the patient how to care for the catheters and the catheter insertion sites during the 6 weeks he'll be at home. Also teach him the signs of infection and obstruction.
• *To promote patient mobility and comfort,* connect the catheters to a leg bag. Teach the patient how to do this *so he'll be more comfortable and more mobile at home.*

**After readmittance**
• Teach the patient how to catheterize the stoma. Begin by gathering the following equipment and placing it on a clean towel: rubber catheter (usually #10 French), water-soluble lubricant, povidone-iodine sponge, 4″ x 4″ sterile gauze sponge, nonallergenic adhesive tape, container for collecting urine. Tell the patient he'll need a sterile container if the doctor orders a urine specimen for laboratory analysis.
• Apply water-soluble lubricant to the catheter tip *to facilitate insertion.*
• Remove and discard the gauze pad covering the stoma. Using the povidone-iodine sponge, clean the stoma and the area around it, starting at the stoma and working outward in a circular motion.
• Slowly insert the catheter in the stoma. Urine will begin to flow. When the flow stops, pinch the catheter closed and remove it. Apply gentle suction with an irrigating syringe *to start the flow of urine, if necessary.*
• Dry the skin, if necessary. Apply a sterile gauze sponge over the stoma *to keep it clean.*
• Tell the patient he may reuse a catheter but only after first disinfecting it by rinsing it thoroughly, immersing it in boiling water for 3 minutes, and then thoroughly drying it. Tell him to store it by wrapping it in foil or placing it in a plastic bag.

scheduled for a continent vesicostomy (see page 602).

Tell the patient about ostomy clubs and the American Cancer Society. Members of these organizations routinely visit hospitals. They explain ostomy care and the types of appliances available, and help the patient learn to function normally with his stoma.

## Complications

Because intestinal mucosa is delicate, bleeding may complicate this procedure if the appliance isn't fitted properly. This is especially likely with an ileal conduit, the most common urinary diversion stoma, because a segment of the intestine forms the conduit.

Peristomal skin may become reddened or excoriated from too frequent changing of the bag, or from poor skin care, improper placement of the appliance, or allergic reaction to the appliance or adhesive. Constant leakage around the appliance can result from improper placement or poor skin turgor.

## Documentation

Record the appearance and color of the stoma and whether it's inverted, flush with the skin, or protruding. If it protrudes, note how much it protrudes above the skin. (The normal range is ½″ to ¾″, or 1.3 to 2 cm.) Record the appearance and condition of the peristomal skin. Be sure to note any signs of redness or irritation or patient complaints of itching or burning sensations.

Document the patient's adjustment to the stoma, and note his participation in stoma care and application of the appliance.

CAROL ANN GRAMSE, RN, PhD

# Peritoneal Dialysis

*In patients with acute and chronic renal failure, peritoneal dialysis performs the* *kidneys' function of removing impurities from the blood. Dialysate solution—instilled into the peritoneal cavity by catheter—draws waste products, excess fluid, and electrolytes from the blood through the semi-permeable peritoneal membrane (see* Principles of Peritoneal Dialysis, *page 604). After a prescribed period, the dialysate solution is drained from the peritoneal cavity, removing impurities with it. The dialysis procedure is then repeated, using a new dialysate solution each time, until waste removal is complete and fluid and electrolyte and acid-base balance have been restored.*

*For this procedure, a doctor inserts the peritoneal catheter with a nurse assisting. A specially trained nurse performs the actual dialysis. The insertion may be done at the patient's bedside or in an operating room. Careful monitoring of the patient and his response to treatment throughout the procedure is essential. Peritoneal dialysis is usually contraindicated in patients with a history of extensive abdominal or bowel surgery or extensive abdominal trauma.*

## Equipment

*For catheter placement and dialysis:* prescribed dialysate solution (in 2-liter bottles or bags) □ warmer, heating pad, or water bath □ at least three surgical masks □ medication, if ordered □ dialysis administration set with drainage bag □ I.V. pole □ two pairs of sterile gloves □ fenestrated sterile drape □ vial of lidocaine (1% or 2%) □ alcohol sponge □ 3-ml syringe with 25G 1″ needle □ scalpel (with #11 blade) □ multi-eyed nylon peritoneal catheter □ peritoneal stylet □ sutures or nonallergenic tape □ precut drain sponges □ 4″ x 4″ gauze sponges □ povidone-iodine solution (for doctor to prepare abdomen) □ protective cap for catheter □ small, sterile plastic clamp □ optional: 10-ml syringe with 22G 1½″ needle, specimen container, and label.

*For dressing changes:* one pair of sterile gloves □ ten sterile cotton-tipped applicators or 2″ x 2″ gauze pads □ hydrogen peroxide □ povidone-iodine solution, or

## PRINCIPLES OF PERITONEAL DIALYSIS

Peritoneal dialysis works by a combination of diffusion and osmosis:

**Diffusion** is the movement of particles through a semipermeable membrane from an area of high concentration to an area of low concentration. In peritoneal dialysis, the water-based dialysate solution being infused contains glucose, normal serum electrolytes, and no waste products. Therefore, the waste products and excess serum electrolytes in the blood cross through the semipermeable peritoneal membrane into the dialysate. Removing the waste-filled dialysate and replacing it with fresh solution keeps the waste concentration low and encourages further diffusion. Also, because failing kidneys can't excrete potassium, dialysate potassium levels are kept low.

**Osmosis** is the movement of fluids through a semipermeable membrane from an area of low-solute concentration to an area of high-solute concentration. In peritoneal dialysis, osmosis removes excess water from the patient's blood. Dextrose in the dialysate encourages fluid movement by giving the dialysate a higher solute-particle concentration than the blood.

---

solution of pHisoHex and sterile water or saline solution □ povidone-iodine ointment or triple-antibiotic ointment □ two split drain sponges □ adhesive tape □ two 4″ x 4″ gauze sponges.

All equipment must be sterile. Commercially packaged dialysis kits or trays are available. They contain all the necessary equipment for catheter placement and dressing changes.

### Preparation of equipment

Bring all equipment to the patient's bedside. Make sure the dialysate solution is at body temperature. *This will decrease patient discomfort during the procedure and reduce vasoconstriction of the peritoneal capillaries. To warm the solution before the procedure,* place the container in a warmer or wrap it in a heating pad set at 105° F. (40.6° C.) for 30 to 60 minutes. You can also place the container in a water bath at 98.6° to 100.4° F. (37° to 38° C.) for 30 to 60 minutes, but make sure you change the water at least every 24 hours and add povidone-iodine solution *to discourage bacterial growth.*

### Essential steps

*For catheter placement and dialysis:*
● Explain the procedure to the patient. Weigh him and record his vital signs *to establish baseline levels.* (Weigh the patient daily from this point on *to help you determine how much fluid is being removed during dialysis treatment.*)
● Give the patient the opportunity to urinate. *This reduces the risk of bladder perforation during insertion of the peritoneal catheter and also reduces patient discomfort.* If the patient can't urinate, obtain an order for straight catheterization *to empty his bladder.*
● Place the patient in the supine position, and ask him to put on one of the surgical masks.
● Wash your hands.
● Inspect the warmed dialysate solution, which should appear clear and colorless.
● Add any prescribed medication to the solution after taking the following measures *to prevent contamination of the solution.* Squeeze povidone-iodine solution out of a saturated 4″ x 4″ gauze sponge over the injection port on the bottle or bag and over the rubber stopper on the medication vial. Let the solution stay on for 5 minutes; then clean off excess and draw up the medication and inject it into the bottle or bag. Heparin is often added to the dialysate solution *to prevent the accumulation of fibrin in the catheter.*
● Put on a surgical mask and prepare the dialysis administration set (see *Setup for Peritoneal Dialysis,* page 607). Close the roller clamps on lines A, B, C, D, and E. Place the drainage bag below the patient *to facilitate gravity drainage,* and connect drainage line E to it. Connect dialysate infusion lines A and B to the bottles or bags of dialysate solution. Hang the bottles or bags on the I.V. pole at the patient's bedside. *To prime the tubing,*

open lines A, C, and D, and allow solution to flow until it reaches the first Y-connector. Clamp line A. Open line B *to prime the rest of the tubing with solution.* When the solution reaches the end of line D, close all roller clamps.

• The doctor puts on a mask and a pair of sterile gloves. He cleanses the patient's abdomen with povidone-iodine solution and drapes it with a sterile drape.

• Wipe the stopper of the lidocaine vial with the alcohol sponge. Invert the vial and present it to the doctor so he can withdraw the lidocaine, using the 3-ml syringe with the 25G 1″ needle.

• The doctor anesthetizes a small area of the patient's abdomen below the umbilicus. He then makes a small incision with the scalpel, inserts the catheter into the peritoneal cavity—using the stylet to guide it—and sutures or tapes the catheter in place.

• Connect the catheter to line D of the administration set, using strict aseptic technique *to prevent contamination of the catheter and the solution, which could cause peritonitis.*

• Open the packages containing drain sponges and 4″ x 4″ gauze sponges and put on the other pair of sterile gloves. Then, apply the split drain sponges around the catheter. Cover them with the gauze sponges, and tape them securely.

• Open the roller clamps on lines A, C, and D, and rapidly instill 500 ml of dialysate solution into the peritoneal cavity *to test the catheter's patency.*

• Close the roller clamps on lines A and C. Immediately unclamp line E, and allow fluid to drain into the bag. Outflow should be brisk.

• Having established the catheter's patency, clamp line E and open the clamps on lines A and C *to infuse the prescribed volume of solution from bottle A over a period of 5 to 10 minutes.* As soon as the bottle empties, clamp lines A, C, and D immediately *to prevent air from entering the tubing.*

• Allow the solution to dwell in the peritoneal cavity for the prescribed time (10 minutes to 4 hours) *to let excess fluid, electrolytes, and accumulated wastes move from the blood through the peritoneal membrane and into the dialysate.*

• Warm the solution for the next infusion.

• At the end of the prescribed dwelling time, open the roller clamps on lines D and E, and allow the solution to drain from the peritoneal cavity into the drainage bag.

• Repeat the infusion-dwell-drain cycle—using new solution each time and alternating the bottles or bags attached to lines A and B—until the prescribed amount of solution has been instilled.

• Monitor the patient's vital signs every 2 to 4 hours, or more frequently if necessary. Notify the doctor of any abrupt changes in the patient's condition.

• If the doctor or hospital policy requires a dialysate specimen, collect one after every 10 infusion-dwell-drain cycles (always during the drain phase) or after every 24-hour period. To do this, attach the 10-ml syringe to the 22G 1½″ needle and insert it into the injection port on line E, using strict aseptic technique, and aspirate the drainage sample. Transfer the sample to the specimen container, label it appropriately, and send it to the laboratory for analysis.

• After completing the prescribed number of cycles, put on sterile gloves and clamp the catheter with a small, sterile plastic clamp. Disconnect line D from the peritoneal catheter while holding both lines with sterile 4″ x 4″ gauze sponges. Place the sterile protective cap over the catheter's distal end. (Alternatively, the doctor may remove the catheter and place a Deane's prosthesis in its place *to maintain the patency of the tract and to simplify reinsertion of the catheter for the next dialysis treatment.*)

*For dressing changes:*

• Assemble all equipment at the patient's bedside. Wash your hands.

• Remove the old dressings carefully *to avoid putting tension on the catheter and accidentally dislodging it, and to prevent the introduction of bacteria into the tract through movement of the catheter.*

• Put on the sterile gloves.

• Saturate the sterile applicators or the

2″ x 2″ pads with the hydrogen peroxide, and cleanse the skin around the catheter, moving in concentric circles from the catheter site to the periphery. Remove any crusted material carefully. Repeat this step, using 2″ x 2″ gauze pads saturated with povidone-iodine or pHisoHex solution. If you're using pHisoHex, remove it from the skin with sterile water or saline solution.

• Inspect the catheter site for drainage and the tissue around the site for redness and swelling.

• Apply povidone-iodine ointment or triple-antibiotic ointment to the catheter site with a sterile gauze sponge.

• Place two split drain sponges around the catheter site. Tape the 4″ x 4″ gauze sponges over them to secure the dressing.

### Special considerations
*To reduce the risk of peritonitis,* use strict aseptic technique throughout this procedure. Change the catheter dressing every 24 hours, or whenever it becomes wet or soiled. Frequent dressing changes will also help prevent skin excoriation from any leakage.

*To prevent respiratory distress,* monitor the patient's respiratory status, position the patient for maximal lung expansion, and promote lung expansion through turning, coughing, and deep breathing exercises.

 If respiratory distress is severe, drain the patient's peritoneal cavity and notify a doctor. Closely monitor a patient on peritoneal dialysis who is being weaned from a ventilator.

*To prevent protein depletion* the doctor may order a high protein diet and/or a protein supplement and will monitor serum albumin.

Dialysate solution is available in three concentrations—4.25% dextrose, 2.5% dextrose, and 1.5% dextrose. The 4.25% solution tends to remove the largest amounts of fluid from the blood because its glucose concentration is highest. Monitor patients undergoing dialysis treatment with this concentrated solution carefully *to prevent excess fluid loss.* Also, some of the glucose in the 4.25% solution may enter the patient's bloodstream, causing hyperglycemia. Such hyperglycemia may be severe enough to require administration of insulin by injection or by addition to the dialysate *to control hyperglycemia.*

Patients with low serum potassium levels may require the addition of potassium to the dialysate solution *to prevent further losses.*

Carefully monitor fluid volume balance, blood pressure, and pulse *to help prevent fluid imbalance.* Assess fluid balance at the end of each infusion-dwell-drain cycle. Fluid balance is positive if less than the amount infused was recovered; it is negative if more than the amount infused was recovered. Notify the doctor if the patient retains 500 ml or more of fluid for three consecutive cycles, or if he loses at least 1 liter of fluid for three consecutive cycles.

If it isn't possible to weigh the patient daily when his peritoneal cavity is empty, weigh him during any dwell phase; then, subtract 4.4 lb (2 kg) from his weight for comparison with his baseline weight. Note any variations in the weighing technique next to his weight.

If inflow and outflow is slow or absent, check the tubing for kinks. You can also try raising the I.V. pole or repositioning the patient *to increase the inflow rate.* Applying manual pressure to the lateral aspects of the patient's abdomen may help increase drainage. If these maneuvers fail to affect the flow rate, notify the doctor. Improper positioning of the catheter or an accumulation of fibrin in the catheter's lumen may be causing obstruction.

Always examine outflow fluid (effluent) for color and clarity. Normally, it's clear, pale yellow, but pink-tinged effluent is not uncommon during the first three to four cycles. If the effluent remains pink-tinged, or if it's grossly bloody, suspect bleeding into the peritoneal cavity and notify the doctor. Also notify the doctor if the outflow contains feces, which suggests bowel perforation, or if it is cloudy, which suggests peritonitis. Obtain a sample of abnormal fluid for culture and gram stain.

Patient discomfort at the start of the procedure is normal. If the patient experiences pain during the procedure, determine when it occurs, its quality and duration, and whether it radiates to other body parts, and then notify the doctor. Pain during infusion usually results from a dialysate solution that is too cool or acid. Pain may also result from the rapid inflow; slowing the inflow rate may reduce the pain. Severe, diffuse pain with rebound tenderness (and cloudy effluent) may indicate peritoneal infection. Pain that radiates to the shoulder often results from air accumulation under the diaphragm. Perineal or rectal pain can result from improper catheter placement.

The patient undergoing peritoneal dialysis will require a great deal of assistance in his daily care. *To minimize his discomfort,* perform daily care during a drain phase in the cycle, when the patient's abdomen is less distended. Chronic dialysis patients who return home with dialysis equipment need explicit instructions for daily care.

### Complications

Peritonitis, the most common complication, usually follows contamination of the dialysate solution, but may develop if solution leaks from the catheter and flows back into the catheter tract.

Protein depletion may result from the diffusion of serum protein in the blood into the dialysate solution through the peritoneal membrane. As much as ½ oz (15 g) protein may be lost daily—more in patients with peritonitis.

Respiratory distress may result from the upward pressure on the diaphragm by dialysate solution in the peritoneal cavity, decreasing lung expansion.

Excessive fluid loss from the use of 4.25% solution may cause hypovolemia, hypotension, and shock. Excessive fluid retention may lead to blood volume expansion, hypertension, and pe-

ripheral edema; severe fluid retention may result in pulmonary edema and congestive heart failure. Other pos-

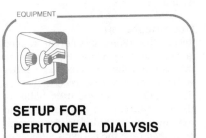

## SETUP FOR PERITONEAL DIALYSIS

To facilitate gravity drainage, the drainage bag is always placed below the patient.

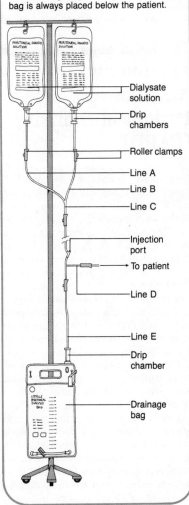

Dialysate solution

Drip chambers

Roller clamps

Line A

Line B

Line C

Injection port

To patient

Line D

Line E

Drip chamber

Drainage bag

sible complications include electrolyte imbalance and hyperglycemia; frequent blood tests can identify them for treatment.

## Documentation

Record the amount of solution infused and drained, any medications added to the solution, and the color and character of effluent. Also record the patient's daily weight and fluid balance. Use a peritoneal dialysis flow sheet to compute total fluid balance after each exchange. Note the patient's vital signs and tolerance of the treatment and any other pertinent observations.

ELAINE M. MUSIAL, RN, MSN, CS

# Continuous Ambulatory Peritoneal Dialysis (CAPD)

*Continuous ambulatory peritoneal dialysis (CAPD) requires the insertion of a Tenchkoff catheter into the peritoneum under local anesthetic, allowing for the continuous presence of dialysate solution in the abdomen. The catheter is sutured in place and its distal portion moved out through a subcutaneous tunnel to the skin's surface. There it serves as an entry and exit port for the dialysate, which is instilled into and drained from the peritoneal cavity by gravity (see* Three Major Steps of Continuous Ambulatory Peritoneal Dialysis, *page 609).*

*For certain patients with end-stage renal failure, CAPD can be a welcome alternative to hemodialysis. Such patients or their family members can usually learn how to perform this procedure after only 2 weeks of training. Because the patient can resume normal daily activities between solution changes, CAPD helps promote independence and a return to near-normal life-style. Another advantage of CAPD is that its cost is*

*less than half that of hemodialysis. Conditions that may prohibit CAPD include recent abdominal surgery, abdominal adhesions, an infected abdominal wall, diaphragmatic tears, ileus, and respiratory insufficiency.*

## Equipment

*To infuse dialysate solution:* prescribed amount of dialysate solution (usually in 2-liter bags) □ water bath or commercial warmer □ three surgical masks □ medication, if ordered □ 42" (106.7 cm) connective tubing with drain clamp □ povidone-iodine sponges □ six to eight packages of sterile 4" x 4 " gauge sponges □ nonallergenic tape □ two sterile waterproof paper barriers (one fenestrated) □ plastic snap-top container □ povidone-iodine solution □ sterile basin □ container of alcohol □ sterile gloves □ optional: syringes (if needed to add medication to solution) and culture specimen container.

*To discontinue dialysis temporarily:* two surgical masks □ three sterile waterproof paper barriers (two fenestrated) □ 4" x 4" gauge sponges (to clean the catheter and for dressings) □ sterile basin □ nonallergenic tape □ povidone-iodine solution □ sterile gloves □ sterile rubber catheter cap □ alcohol sponges.

All equipment—both for infusing the dialysate solution and for discontinuing the procedure—must be sterile.

## Preparation of equipment

Wash your hands. Check the concentration of the dialysate solution against the doctor's orders. Also check its expiration date and appearance; it should be clear, not cloudy. Warm the solution to body temperature by placing it in a sink or basin of hot water; use a commercial warmer if one is available. *To minimize the risk of contaminating the bag's port, leave the dialysate container's wrapper in place. This also keeps the bag dry, which makes examining it for leakage easier after the wrapper is removed.*

Put on a surgical mask. Remove the dialysate container from the warming setup, and remove its protective wrap-

## THREE MAJOR STEPS OF CONTINUOUS AMBULATORY PERITONEAL DIALYSIS

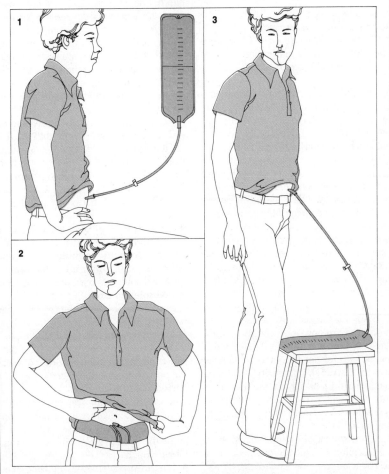

**1** A bag of dialysate is attached to the tube in the patient's abdomen so the fluid flows into the peritoneal cavity.

**2** While the dialysate remains in the peritoneal cavity, the patient can roll up the bag, place it under his shirt, and go about his normal activities.

**3** Unrolling the bag and suspending it below the pelvis allows the dialysate to drain from the peritoneal cavity.

per. Squeeze the bag firmly *to check for leaks.*

If ordered, add any prescribed medication to the dialysate solution, using sterile technique *to avoid contamination.* (The ideal approach is to add medication under a laminar flow hood.)

Insert the connective tubing into the dialysate container. Open the drain clamp *to prime the tube.* Close the clamp.

Wrap a povidone-iodine sponge around the dialysate container's port. Cover it with a dry gauze sponge, and secure it with tape. Remove and discard the surgical mask. Tear tape so it will be ready to secure new dressing.

### Essential steps

*To infuse dialysate solution:*

• Weigh the patient *to establish a baseline level.* Weigh the patient at the same time every day *to help monitor fluid balance.*

• Assemble all equipment at the patient's bedside. Wash your hands and prepare the sterile field. Place a waterproof sterile paper barrier on a dry surface near the patient, being careful to maintain its sterility.

• Fill the snap-top container with povidone-iodine solution, and place it on the sterile field. Place the basin on the sterile field. Then place four pairs of sterile gauze sponges in the sterile basin, and saturate them with the povidone-iodine solution. Drop the remaining gauze sponges on the sterile field. Loosen the cap on the alcohol container, and place it next to the sterile field.

• Put on a clean surgical mask and provide one for the patient.

• Carefully remove tape and discard the dressing covering the peritoneal catheter. Be careful not to touch the catheter or skin. Inspect skin integrity at the catheter site, and look for signs of infection, such as purulent drainage. (If drainage is present, take a swab culture and notify the doctor.)

• Put on the sterile gloves and palpate the insertion site and subcutaneous tunnel route for pain and tenderness. If these signs occur, notify the doctor.

 Don't proceed with the infusion in the presence of drainage, tenderness, or pain without specific orders.

• Wrap one gauze sponge saturated with povidone-iodine solution around the distal end of the catheter, and leave it in place for 5 minutes. Cleanse the catheter and insertion site with the rest of the gauze sponges during this time. Use a circular motion to cleanse the skin, moving outward from the insertion site.

Use straight strokes to cleanse the catheter, beginning at the insertion site and moving outward. Use another area of the sponge each time. Loosen the catheter cap one notch and cleanse the exposed area. Place each used sponge at the base of the catheter *to help support it.* After using the third pair of sponges, place the fenestrated paper barrier around the base of the catheter. Continue cleaning the catheter for another minute with one of the remaining povidone-iodine–soaked sponges.

• Remove the povidone-iodine sponge on the catheter cap, remove the cap, and use the remaining povidone-iodine sponge to cleanse the end of the catheter hub. Attach the connective tubing from the dialysate solution container to the catheter. Secure the junction with adhesive tape.

• Remove the cap from the alcohol container, and pick up a dry 4″ x 4″ gauze sponge. Hold this over the basin, and pour some alcohol over it. Use the alcohol-saturated sponge to remove the povidone-iodine solution from the catheter insertion site, moving from the insertion site outward. Apply a new dressing of 4″ × 4″ gauze sponges and secure it with tape.

• Open the drain clamp on the dialysate container *to allow solution to enter the peritoneal cavity by gravity* over a period of 5 to 10 minutes. Leave a small amount of fluid in the bag *to make folding it easier.* Close the drain clamp.

• Fold the bag and secure it with a belt or in the patient's clothing or a small fabric pouch.

• After the prescribed dwell time (usually 4 to 6 hours), unfold the bag, open the clamp, and allow peritoneal fluid to drain into it by gravity.

• When drainage is complete, attach a new bag of dialysate solution, and repeat the infusion.

*To discontinue dialysis temporarily:*

• Wash your hands, put on a surgical mask, and provide one for the patient.

• Using clean gloves, remove and discard the dressing over the peritoneal catheter and the adhesive tape at the junction of catheter and dialysate tubing.

• Set up a sterile field with a waterproof barrier on a clean, dry surface next to the patient, being sure to maintain its sterility. Place all equipment on the sterile field, and place the 4″ x 4″ gauze sponges in the basin. Saturate them with the povidone-iodine solution. Open the 4″ x 4″ gauze sponges to be used as the dressing, and drop them onto the sterile field. Tear pieces of tape as needed.

• Tape the dialysate tubing to the side rail of the bed *to keep the catheter and tubing off the patient's abdomen.*

• Put on sterile gloves. Then, place one of the fenestrated barriers around the base of the catheter.

• Use a pair of sponges to clean about 6″ (15 cm) of the dialysis tubing for 1 minute, moving in one direction only—away from the catheter. Clean the catheter, moving from the insertion site to the junction of the catheter and dialysis tubing. Place used sponges at the base of the catheter *to prop it up.* Use two more pairs of sponges to clean the junction for a total of 3 minutes.

• Place the second fenestrated paper barrier over the first at the base of the catheter. With the fourth pair of sponges, clean the junction of the catheter and 6″ (15 cm) of the dialysate tubing for another minute. Place it on the second paper barrier.

• Disconnect the dialysate tubing from the catheter. Pick up the rubber catheter cap and fasten it to the catheter, making sure it fits securely over both notches of the hard plastic catheter tip.

• Clean the insertion site and a 2″ (5 cm) radius around it with alcohol sponges, working from the catheter insertion site outward. Let the skin air-dry before applying the dressing.

• Discard used supplies appropriately.

### Special considerations

Because the dialysis patient will be entirely responsible for performing continuous dialysis once he returns home, make sure he understands each step of the procedure thoroughly and can perform each step confidently before his discharge. Teach the patient to use sterile technique throughout each step of the procedure, especially for cleaning and dressing changes, *to prevent such complications as peritonitis.* Make sure the patient is able to recognize the signs and symptoms of peritonitis—fever, abdominal pain, tenderness—and that he realizes the importance of notifying the doctor immediately should any such symptom arise. Alert him to other signs of infection, such as redness and drainage, which he should also report promptly. (Your assessment of the patient's personal hygiene may indicate the need for extra emphasis on the importance of sterile technique.)

Instruct the patient to follow a strict time schedule of fluid exchanges each day *to maintain optimal fluid balance.* Tell him to record his weight daily and to check regularly for swelling of the extremities. Teach him to keep an accurate record of intake and output. Exchanges are usually done at 4- to 6-hour intervals; encourage the patient to resume his normal activities between them. Make sure he knows how to order the necessary equipment.

### Complications

Peritonitis is the most frequent complication. Although treatable, it can permanently scar the peritoneal membrane, decreasing its permeability and reducing dialysis efficiency. Untreated peritonitis can cause septicemia and death.

Protein depletion may result from the diffusion of serum protein from the blood, through the peritoneal membrane, and into the dialysate solution.

Excessive fluid loss may result from the use of the concentrated (4.25%) dialysate solution, mismanagement of the dialysis regimen, or inadequate oral fluid intake. Excessive fluid retention may result from mismanagement of the dialysis regimen or excessive salt and/or oral fluid intake.

### Documentation

Record the type and amount of fluid

instilled and returned for each exchange, the time and duration of the exchange, and any medications that may have been added to the dialysate. Note the appearance of the returned exchange fluid—the presence of mucus, pus, or blood, and the color and clarity of the solution. Note any discrepancy in the balance of fluid intake and output, as well as any signs or symptoms of fluid imbalance, such as weight changes, decreased breath sounds, peripheral edema, ascites, and changes in skin turgor. Record the patient's weight daily after his last fluid exchange, as well as his blood pressure and pulse rate.

ANGELA D. LEHMAN, RN

# Care of an Arteriovenous Shunt

*An arteriovenous (AV) shunt is a U-shaped tube that diverts blood flow from an artery to a vein. Inserted surgically, usually in a forearm or ankle, it provides access to the circulatory system for hemodialysis. After insertion, an AV shunt requires regular assessment for patency and examination of the surrounding skin for signs of infection. Other forms of arteriovenous access, such as fistulas and vein grafts, don't require such continual care.*

*Care of an arteriovenous shunt also includes aseptically cleaning the arterial and venous exit sites, applying antiseptic ointment, and dressing the sites with sterile bandages. When performed daily and just before hemodialysis, this procedure prolongs the life of the shunt, helps prevent infection, and allows for early detection of clotting.*

## Equipment

Drape □ stethoscope □ sterile gloves □ sterile 4″ x 4″ gauze sponges □ sterile cotton-tipped applicators □ antiseptic (usually povidone-iodine solution) □ nonallergenic tape □ optional: swab culture kit, prescribed antimicrobial ointment (usually povidone-iodine), sterile elastic gauze bandage, 2″ x 2″ gauze pads, and hydrogen peroxide.

Kits containing all the necessary equipment can be prepackaged and stored for use.

## Essential steps

• Explain the procedure to the patient, provide privacy, and wash your hands.
• Place the drape on a stable surface—such as a bedside table—*to reduce the risk of trauma to the shunt site.*
• With the patient in a comfortable position, place the extremity with the shunt on the draped surface.
• Remove the two bulldog clamps from the elastic gauze bandage, and unwrap the elastic gauze bandage from the shunt area.
• Carefully take off the gauze dressing covering the shunt. Remove the 4″ x 4″ gauze sponge under the shunt.
• Assess the arterial and venous exit sites for signs of infection, such as erythema, swelling, excessive tenderness, or drainage. Take a swab culture of any purulent drainage. Notify the doctor immediately of any signs of infection.
• Check blood flow through the shunt by inspecting the color of the blood and comparing the warmth of the shunt with that of the surrounding skin. The blood should be bright red; the shunt should feel as warm as the skin.

 If the blood is dark purple or black and the temperature of the shunt is lower than the surrounding skin, clotting is present. Notify the doctor immediately.
• Use the stethoscope to auscultate the shunt between the arterial and venous exit sites. A bruit confirms normal blood flow. Palpate the shunt for a thrill which also indicates normal blood flow.
• Open a few packages of 4″ x 4″ gauze sponges and cotton-tipped applicators and soak them with the antiseptic. Put on the sterile gloves.
• Using a soaked 4″ x 4″ gauze sponge,

start cleaning the skin at one of the exit sites. Wipe away from the site *to remove bacteria and reduce the chance of contaminating the shunt.*

• Use the soaked cotton-tipped applicators to remove any crusted material from the exit site. *This is important because the incrustations provide a medium for bacterial growth.*

• Clean the other exit site, using fresh, soaked 4″ x 4″ gauze sponges and cotton-tipped applicators.

• Clean the rest of the skin that was covered by the gauze dressing with fresh, soaked 4″ x 4″ gauze sponges.

• If ordered, apply antimicrobial ointment to the exit sites *to help prevent infection.*

• Place a dry, sterile 4″ x 4″ gauze sponge under the shunt. *This prevents the shunt from contacting the skin, which could cause skin irritation and breakdown.*

• Cover the exit sites with a dry, sterile 4″ x 4″ gauze sponge, and tape it securely *to keep the exit sites clean and protected.*

• For routine daily care, wrap the shunt with an elastic gauze bandage. Leave a small portion of the shunt cannula exposed *so the patient can check for patency without removing the dressing.*

• Place the bulldog clamps on the edge of the elastic gauze bandage *so the patient can use them quickly to stop hemorrhage in case the shunt separates.*

• For care before hemodialysis, don't redress the shunt, but leave the bulldog clamps in an easily accessible location.

## Special considerations

 Make sure the arteriovenous junction of the shunt is secured with plasticized or nonallergenic tape. *This prevents separation of the two halves of the shunt, minimizing the risk of hemorrhage.*

Always handle the shunt and dressings carefully. Don't use scissors or other sharp instruments to remove the dressing, *because you may accidentally cut the shunt.* Never remove the tape securing the arteriovenous junction during dressing changes.

When cleaning the shunt exit sites, use each 4″ x 4″ gauze sponge only once and avoid wiping any area more than once *to minimize the risk of contamination.* When redressing the site, make sure the tape doesn't kink or occlude the shunt. If the exit sites are heavily encrusted, place a 2″ x 2″ peroxide-soaked gauze pad on the area for about 1 hour *to loosen the crust.* Make sure the patient isn't allergic to iodine before using povidone-iodine solution or ointment. During the procedure, ask the patient how he cares for the shunt at home. Teach proper home care, if necessary.

## Documentation

In the nurse's notes, record that shunt care was administered, the condition of the shunt and surrounding skin, any ointment used, and any instructions given to the patient.

MARIA MAIAROTA-GROSS, RN, BSN

# Hemodialysis

*Hemodialysis is a technique for removing toxic wastes from the blood of patients with renal failure. This procedure removes blood from the body, circulates it through a dialyzer to be purified, then returns the blood to the body. Various access sites can be used for this potentially life-saving procedure (see* Hemodialysis Access Sites, *pages 616-617), but the most common for long-term treatment is an arteriovenous fistula.*

*The underlying mechanism in hemodialysis is differential diffusion across a semipermeable membrane which extracts by-products of protein metabolism (such as urea and uric acid) as well as creatinine and excess body water; this restores or maintains the balance of the body's buffer system and electrolyte level. Hemodialysis thus promotes a rapid return to normal serum values and helps prevent complications commonly associated with uremia.*

*Hemodialysis provides temporary support for patients with acute reversible renal failure; it's also used for regular long-term treatment of patients with chronic end-stage renal failure. A less common indication for hemodialysis is acute poisoning, such as barbiturate or analgesic overdose. The patient's condition and the equipment available determine the number and duration of hemodialysis treatments.*

*Specially trained personnel usually perform this procedure in a hemodialysis unit. However, when necessary—for example, if the patient is acutely ill—hemodialysis can be performed at bedside. Special hemodialysis units are available for use at home. These allow the patient or a family member to perform hemodialysis after proper instruction when the patient is discharged.*

### Equipment

*For preparing the hemodialysis machine:* negative pressure hemodialysis machine □ proper dialyzer □ container of dialysate concentrate □ two 1,000-ml bags of normal saline solution □ I.V. administration set □ arterial and venous line sets □ two transducer filters □ 10-ml syringe □ optional: heparin (if ordered), 3-ml syringe with needle, medication-added label, and metal clamp.

*For hemodialysis with an arteriovenous (AV) shunt:* alcohol sponges □ sterile drape or barrier shield □ sterile gloves □ two sterile shunt adapters □ sterile Teflon connector □ two bulldog clamps □ two 10-ml syringes filled with normal saline solution □ four short strips of adhesive tape □ sterile shunt spreader (optional).

*For hemodialysis with an AV fistula:* two fistula needles (each attached to a 10-ml syringe filled with heparinized normal saline solution) □ linen-saver pad □ sterile povidone-iodine sponges □ 4" x 4" gauze sponges □ tourniquet □ sterile gloves □ two sterile hemostats □ povidone-iodine ointment □ adhesive tape.

*For discontinuing hemodialysis with an AV shunt:* sterile gloves □ two bulldog clamps □ two hemostats □ povidone-

iodine solution □ sterile 4" x 4" gauze sponges □ alcohol sponges □ elastic gauze bandages.

*For discontinuing hemodialysis with an AV fistula:* clean gloves □ four hemostats □ sterile 4" x 4" gauze sponges □ two adhesive bandages.

### Preparation of equipment

When starting hemodialysis with an AV shunt, clean the shunt thoroughly before assembling and preparing equipment at the patient's bedside.

Turn on the hemodialysis machine's cold water tap *to let treated water enter the system.* Turn on the machine and insert the appropriate dialyzer (see *Principles of Hemodialysis,* page 619) into the holder. Open the dialysate concentrate and add it to the proportioning pump, which automatically mixes appropriate amounts of concentrate with the treated water. If ordered, draw up the prescribed amount of heparin in a 3-ml syringe, add it to a 1,000-ml bag of normal saline solution, and prime the dialyzer. Secure the medication-added label to the outside of the bag *to indicate the addition.* If heparin has not been ordered, prime the dialyzer solely with normal saline solution.

Attach the I.V. administration set to the saline solution container, and allow fluid to run through the set *to prime the tubing.* Close the drain clamps and insert the I.V. administration set into the I.V. inlet site of the arterial bloodline. Attach the arterial and venous bloodlines to the hemodialysis machine. Place the patient ends of the arterial and venous lines in the appropriate holders on the machine *to ensure that the saline solution flows into the machine's bucket during priming.* Place the transducer filters on the appropriate arterial and venous line fittings. Attach the monitoring line from the arterial drip chamber to the arterial transducer *to allow monitoring of pressure in the arterial chamber.* Insert the venous drip chamber into the air foam detector and attach the monitoring line from the venous drip chamber to the venous transducer *to allow monitoring of pressure in the venous chamber.* If a heparin pump has been ordered, set it up according to the manufacturer's directions.

Open the cap at the patient end of the arterial line and allow the saline solution to run through by gravity. When this segment of the arterial line is free of air bubbles, occlude the arterial line with the plastic clamp attached to the line.

Invert the dialyzer in its holder so the arterial end is on the bottom. *This decreases the number of air pockets in the dialyzer by allowing air to rise more freely while the dialyzer is being primed and soaked.* Air pockets can cause the patient's blood to clot in the dialyzer; and, by decreasing surface area available for clearance and fluid removal, they can also reduce the dialyzer's efficiency.

Turn the blood pump on, setting the flow at 200 ml/minute. Make sure the roller clamp on the I.V. administration set and the cap on the patient end of the venous line are open. Adjust the fluid in the arterial drip chamber, if present, to approximately midlevel. When the saline solution begins to enter the dialyzer, use your fingers or a metal clamp to milk the arterial line by quickly occluding and releasing it just below its connection to the dialyzer. *This creates pressure behind the saline solution, which will help to flush air out of the dialyzer.* The fluid level in the arterial chamber should rise as the line is occluded. *To prevent forcing saline solution into the isolator,* don't occlude the line for too long.

Allow the saline solution to flow into the dialyzer's venous chamber and adjust the fluid level. Milk the venous line as you did the arterial line. Repeat the procedure until 500 to 1,000 ml of saline solution have been used. Turn the blood pump off and occlude the venous line with the plastic clamp attached to the line. Check the lines carefully for residual air bubbles. Connect the patient end of the venous line securely to the patient end of the arterial line. Open the clamps on both lines. (The roller clamp on the I.V. administration set should still be open.) Turn the blood pump to a setting

of about 275 ml/minute *to allow free recirculation of saline solution through the system.*

With a 10-ml syringe, aspirate a sample of bath solution from the sampling port on the dialysate inlet line *to check its conductivity.* A conductivity reading between 13 and 14 ensures that the machine is properly mixing the bath concentration. Press in the dialysate bypass button. Attach the dialysate *inlet* line to the venous portion of the dialyzer; attach the *outlet* line to the arterial portion. Make sure the connections are secure. Press in the dialysate bypass button again *to allow warm dialysate to circulate through the dialyzer.* Allow the dialyzer to soak in the dialysate and the saline solution to recirculate for at least 10 minutes. *This helps to remove air from the dialyzer and also softens its membranes.* At this point, dialysate pressure should range between 0 and −50.

Check *all* alarms to make sure they're functioning and set properly. Limits on the arterial, venous, and dialysate pressure monitors should be set 50 points above and below the actual reading. The thermostat should be set between 98.6° and 100.4° F. (37° and 38° C.). *A setting that is too high or too low could cause hemolysis.*

Clamp the arterial and venous lines, and disconnect and cap them.

### Essential steps

● Weigh the patient and record his baseline vital signs. (Take the patient's blood pressure *while he's in the supine position and standing.*)

● Help the patient into a comfortable position (usually in the supine position) with the access site well supported and resting on a sterile drape or sterile barrier shield.

● If the patient is undergoing hemodialysis therapy for the first time, explain the procedure in detail.

*To begin hemodialysis with an AV shunt:*

● Remove the bulldog clamps and place them within easy reach on the sterile field. Remove the shunt dressing, and

# HEMODIALYSIS ACCESS SITES

| SITE | ADVANTAGES AND DISADVANTAGES |
| --- | --- |
| **Femoral vein catheterization**<br> | *Advantage:*<br>• Quick access in emergencies<br>*Disadvantages:*<br>• Immobile patient<br>• Risk of infection and femoral artery puncture |
| **Subclavian vein catheterization**<br>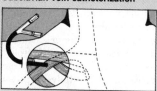 | *Advantages:*<br>• Quick access in emergencies<br>• Mobile patient<br>• Less risk of infection than femoral vein catheterization<br>*Disadvantages:*<br>• Risk of pneumothorax on insertion<br>• Contraindicated with pulmonary hypertension |
| **Arteriovenous shunt**<br>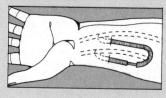 | *Advantages:*<br>• Arterial blood pressure to pump blood<br>• No repeated catheterization or venipuncture<br>*Disadvantages:*<br>• Activity of affected arm or leg restricted<br>• Increased risk of clotting and infection<br>• Chance of accidentally separating, causing severe hemorrhage or death |
| **Arteriovenous fistula**<br>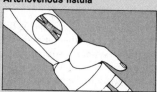 | *Advantages:*<br>• Arterial blood pressure to pump blood<br>• Minimal risk of infection or clotting<br>• Less need for revision than shunt<br>• Unrestricted use of affected arm or leg<br>*Disadvantages:*<br>• Contraindicated in patient with small veins<br>• Possible numbness, tingling, and coldness below fistula site from arterial insufficiency (steal syndome) in atherosclerotic or diabetic patients |
| **Arteriovenous vein graft**<br>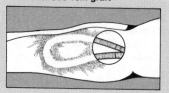 | *Advantages:*<br>• Arterial blood pressure to pump blood<br>• Unrestricted use of grafted arm or leg<br>*Disadvantages:*<br>• Risk of clotting from hypotension<br>• Risk of tissues surrounding graft becoming infected<br>• Risk of steal syndrome as with arteriovenus fistula |

## NURSING CONSIDERATIONS

- Use temporarily (about 1 week).
- To prevent clotting, start hemodialysis immediately after insertion.
- After treatment, flush catheters and fill with heparinized normal saline solution. Cap and cover with sterile dressing.
- Don't allow patient to walk or sit up in bed. He may dislodge catheter, damage vein, or obstruct blood flow.

- Use temporarily (1 to 2 weeks).
- With Y-connector, use venipuncture equipment, which alternately clamps arterial and venous tubes.
- If catheter is used only for outflow, insert over-the-needle catheter into antecubital vein in arm opposite catheter to accommodate venous return.
- Prevent clotting and flush catheter as for femoral vein catheterization.

- Use temporarily or permanently (average 7 to 10 months).
- Have patient keep affected arm or leg straight and elevated for 2 or 3 hours after insertion. For leg shunt, have patient use crutches for 3 weeks. Caution patient to restrict activity in arm or leg.
- Assess shunt site often for good arterial flow. Palpate for thrills and auscultate for bruits.
- Inspect frequently for signs of infection.
- Check blood color in shunt. Bright red indicates normal flow; dark red to purple indicates a clot is forming; purple-red to black (with separation of purple cells and clear serum) indicates clotted shunt.
- Instruct patient to keep shunt clean and dry. Prohibit bathing for 2 to 3 weeks after insertion. Tell patient to protect shunt with plastic once bathing is allowed.
- Don't use affected arm or leg for blood pressure readings or venipuncture.
- Prohibit tight jewelry or clothing over shunt site.

- Use permanently (average 3 to 4 years).
- Keep affected arm elevated immediately after fistula surgery.
- Remove dressings after 2 days; clean suture line with povidone-iodine solution. Apply new sterile dressings daily for 10 to 14 days, until sutures are removed.
- Fistula may require 6 weeks to mature so blood vessels are enlarged and walls thickened. But if necessary, you may perform hemodialysis within 1 week after surgery.
- Assess for blood flow as for arteriovenous shunt.
- Wash affected arm daily with antibacterial soap.
- Don't use affected arm for blood pressure readings or for venipunctures, except for venipunctures when performing hemodialysis.
- Prohibit tight jewelry or clothing over fistula site.

- Use permanently (average 2 years).
- Keep affected arm or leg elevated immediately after grafting.
- Remove dressings after 2 days; clean suture line with povidone-iodine solution. Apply new sterile dressings daily for 10 to 14 days, until sutures are removed.
- Assess for blood flow, as for arteriovenous shunt or fistula. Observe same restrictions regarding blood pressure readings, venipunctures, and wearing of jewelry and clothing. (To prolong graft life, perform venipuncture using single-needle double-lumen catheter.)

clean the shunt as you would for daily care. Clean the bulldog clamps with an alcohol sponge.

• Assemble the shunt adapters according to the manufacturer's directions.

• Clean the arterial and venous shunt tubing with alcohol sponges *to remove bacterial contaminants.* Use a separate sponge for each tubing and wipe in only one direction, moving from the connection site to the insertion sites. Allow the tubing to air-dry.

• Put on the sterile gloves.

• Clamp the arterial side of the shunt with a bulldog clamp *to prevent blood from flowing through it.* Clamp the venous side *to prevent leakage when the shunt is opened.*

• Open the shunt by separating its sides with your fingers or with a sterile shunt spreader, if available. Both sides of the shunt should be exposed. Always inspect the Teflon connector on one side of the shunt *to see if it's damaged or bent.* If necessary, replace it before proceeding. Note which side contains the connector *so you can use the new one to close the shunt after treatment.*

• *To adapt the shunt to the lines of the machine,* attach a shunt adapter and 10-ml syringe filled with about 8 ml of saline solution to the side of the shunt containing the Teflon connector. Attach the new Teflon connector to the other side of the shunt with the second adapter. Attach the second 10-ml syringe filled with about 8 ml of saline solution to the same side.

• Flush the shunt's arterial tubing by releasing its clamp and gently aspirating it with the saline-filled syringe. Then flush the tubing slowly, observing it for signs of fibrin buildup. Repeat the procedure on the venous side of the shunt.

• Secure the shunt to the adapter connection with adhesive tape *to prevent separation during treatment.*

• Connect the arterial and venous lines to the adapters and secure the connections with tape. Tape each line to the patient's arm *to prevent unnecessary strain on the shunt during treatment.*

• Begin hemodialysis according to your unit's protocol.

*To begin hemodialysis with an AV fistula:*

• Flush fistula needles, using attached syringes containing heparinized saline solution, and set them aside.

• Place a linen-saver pad under the patient's arm.

• Clean a 3″ x 10″ (7.6 x 25.4 cm) area of skin over the fistula with povidone-iodine sponges. Discard each sponge after one wipe.

• Apply a tourniquet above the fistula *to distend the veins and facilitate venipuncture.*

• Put on the sterile gloves. Perform the venipuncture with a venous fistula needle. Remove the needle guard and squeeze the wing tips firmly together. Insert the venous needle at least 1″ (2.54 cm) above the fistula, being careful to avoid puncturing the fistula. (If the patient requires frequent hemodialysis, vary the insertion sites.)

• Release the tourniquet and flush the needle with heparinized saline solution *to prevent clotting.* Clamp the venous needle tubing with a hemostat, apply povidone-iodine ointment to the insertion site, and secure the wing tips of the needle to the skin with adhesive tape *to prevent it from dislodging within the vein.*

• Perform another venipuncture with the arterial needle a few inches below the venous needle. Flush the needle with heparinized saline solution. Clamp the arterial needle tubing, apply ointment, and secure the wing tips of the arterial needle as you did the venous needle.

• Remove the syringe from the end of the arterial tubing, uncap the arterial line from the hemodialysis machine, and connect the two lines. Tape the connection securely *to prevent it from separating during the procedure.* Repeat these two steps for the venous line.

• Unclamp the hemostats and start hemodialysis.

*To discontinue hemodialysis with an AV shunt:*

• Wash your hands. Turn the blood pump on the hemodialysis machine to 50 to 100 ml/minute.

• Put on the sterile gloves and remove

# PRINCIPLES OF HEMODIALYSIS

In hemodialysis, blood flows from the patient to an external dialyzer (or artificial kidney) through an arterial access site. Inside the dialyzer, blood and dialysate flow countercurrently, divided by a semipermeable membrane. The dialysate, which contains essential electrolytes in optimal extracellular amounts, is more concentrated than blood. Therefore, through *diffusion*—the process by which concentrated particles cross a membrane to an area of lower concentration—the electrolyte-rich dialysate enters the blood. Simultaneously, the complementary process of *ultrafiltration,* which causes fluids under pressure to move to the side of a membrane under lower pressure, removes excess water—as well as such waste products as urea, creatinine, uric acid, phosphate, and other metabolites—from the blood. Cleansed of impurities, the blood returns to the body through a venous access site.

The most common dialyzer—the *coil* type (top left)—consists of one or more semipermeable membrane tubes or coils wrapped concentrically around a mesh support. Blood passes through coils as the system pumps dialysate between coil layers and through the mesh support at high speed.

A *flat plate,* or *parallel flow-plate,* (top right) dialyzer has two layers of semipermeable membrane, bound by a semirigid or rigid structure. Blood ports are located at both ends of the dialyzer, between the membranes. Blood flows between the membranes, and dialysate flows between the supporting structures and one of the membranes.

A *hollow-fiber, or capillary, dialyzer* (bottom) contains fine capillaries, with a semipermeable membrane enclosed in a plastic cylinder. Blood flows through capillaries as system pumps dialysate in opposite direction on the outside of the capillaries.

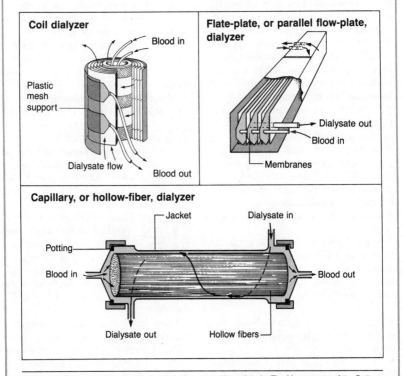

**Coil dialyzer**

Blood in
Plastic mesh support
Dialysate flow
Blood out

**Flate-plate, or parallel flow-plate, dialyzer**

Dialysate out
Blood in
Membranes

**Capillary, or hollow-fiber, dialyzer**

Jacket
Dialysate in
Potting
Blood in
Blood out
Dialysate out
Hollow fibers

Adapted from Constantine L. Hampers, et al., *Long-term Hemodialysis: The Management of the Patient with Chronic Renal Failure* (New York: Grune & Stratton, 1973), and used with permission.

the tape from the connection site of the arterial lines. Clamp the arterial cannula with a bulldog clamp; then disconnect the lines. The blood in the machine's arterial line will continue to flow toward the dialyzer, followed by a column of air. Just before the blood reaches the point where the saline solution enters the line, clamp the bloodline with a hemostat.

• Unclamp the saline solution *to allow a small amount to flow through the line.* Reclamp the saline solution line and unclamp the hemostat on the machine line. *This allows all blood to flow into the dialyzer, where it's circulated through the filter and back to the patient through the venous line.*

• Just before the last volume of blood enters the patient, clamp the venous cannula with a bulldog clamp and the machine's venous line with a hemostat.

• Remove the tape from the connection site of the venous lines. Turn off the blood pump and disconnect the lines.

• Reconnect the shunt cannula. Remove the older of the two Teflon connectors and discard it. Connect the shunt, taking care to position the Teflon connector equally between the two cannulas. Remove the bulldog clamps.

• Secure the shunt connection with plasticized or nonallergenic adhesive tape *to prevent accidental disconnection.*

• Clean the shunt and its site with the gauze sponges soaked with povidone-iodine solution. When the cleansing procedure is finished, remove the povidone-iodine with alcohol sponges.

• Make sure blood flow through the shunt is adequate.

• Apply a dressing to the shunt site and wrap it loosely with elastic gauze bandages. Attach the bulldog clamps to the outside dressing.

*To discontinue hemodialysis with an AV fistula:*

• Wash your hands. Turn the blood pump on the hemodialysis machine to 50 to 100 ml/minute.

• Put on the sterile gloves and remove the tape from the connection site of the arterial lines. Clamp the needle tubing with the hemostat and disconnect the lines. The blood in the machine's arterial line will continue to flow toward the dialyzer, followed by a column of air. Just before the blood reaches the point where the saline solution enters the line, clamp the bloodline with another hemostat.

• Unclamp the saline solution *to allow a small amount to flow through the line.* Reclamp the saline solution line and unclamp the hemostat on the machine line. *This allows all blood to flow into the dialyzer, where it's circulated through the filter and back to the patient through the venous line.*

• Just before the last volume of blood enters the patient, clamp the venous needle tubing and the machine's venous line with hemostats.

• Remove the tape from the connection site of the venous lines. Turn off the blood pump and disconnect the lines.

• Remove the venipuncture needle and apply pressure to the site with a folded 4″ x 4″ gauze sponge for at least 3 to 5 minutes, or until you're sure all bleeding has stopped. Apply an adhesive bandage. Repeat the procedure on the arterial line.

• When hemodialysis is complete, weigh the patient and record his vital signs.

### Special considerations

If home treatment is prescribed, the patient and a family member should receive thorough instruction on the principles of hemodialysis (see page 619) and relevant techniques.

 *To avoid pyrogenic reactions resulting from contamination,* use strict aseptic technique during preparation of the machine. Discard equipment that has fallen to the floor or that has been disconnected and exposed to the air.

Immediately report any machine malfunction or equipment defect.

Avoid unnecessary handling of shunt tubing. However, be sure to inspect the shunt carefully for patency by observing its color, inspecting for the presence of clots and serum and cell separation, and checking the temperature of the silastic tubing. Assess the shunt insertion site for signs of infection, such as bloody or serosanguineous drainage, inflammation, and tenderness, which may indicate the body's rejection of the shunt. Check also to see if the shunt insertion tips have become exposed.

If the ends of the shunt are split, cut off the deteriorated portion behind the split *to prevent leakage.*

Make sure you complete each step in this procedure accurately. *Overlooking a single step or performing it incorrectly can cause unnecessary blood loss or inefficient treatment due to poor clearances or inadequate fluid removal.* For example, never allow a saline solution bag to run dry while priming and soaking the dialyzer. *This can cause air to enter the patient portion of the dialysate system.* Ultimately, failure to perform accurate hemodialysis therapy can lead to patient injury and even death.

If bleeding continues after you remove an AV fistula needle, apply pressure with a Gelfoam sterile sponge. If bleeding persists, apply a Gelfoam sponge soaked in topical thrombin solution.

Throughout hemodialysis, carefully monitor the patient's vital signs. Take blood pressure readings at least hourly and, if necessary, as often as every 15 minutes. Monitor the patient's weight regularly *to ensure adequate ultrafiltration during treatment.* (Many dialysis units are equipped with bed scales.)

Perform periodic tests for clotting time on both the patient's blood samples and samples from the dialyzer. Make sure any meals served to the patient during treatment are small and light.

Continue necessary drug administration during dialysis unless the drug would be removed in the dialysate; if so, administer the drug after dialysis.

If possible, provide a comfortable place to sit and appropriate diversionary activities—such as reading, television, or games—during treatment.

## Complications

Microorganisms in the water used for hemodialysis may cause fever.

Rapid fluid removal and electrolyte changes during hemodialysis can cause early dialysis disequilibrium syndrome. Signs and symptoms of such a reaction may include headaches, muscle cramps, backaches, and seizures.

Excessive removal of fluid during ultrafiltration can cause hypovolemia and hypotension. Diffusion of the sugar and sodium content of the dialysate solution into the blood can cause hyperglycemia and hypernatremia. These conditions, in turn, can cause hyperosmolarity.

*Cardiac arrhythmias* can occur during hemodialysis as a result of electrolyte and pH changes in the blood. They can also develop in patients taking antiarrhythmic drugs as the dialysate removes these drugs during treatment. *Angina* may develop in patients with anemia or preexisting arteriosclerotic cardiovascular disease (ASCVD) because of the physiologic stress on the blood during purification and ultrafiltration.

Some complications of hemodialysis can be fatal. An air embolism, for example, can result if the dialyzer retains air, if tubing connections become loose, or if the saline solution container empties. Hemolysis can result from obstructed flow of the dialysate concentrate or from incorrect setting of the conductivity alarm limits. Hyperthermia, another potentially fatal complication, can result if the dialysate becomes overheated. Exsanguination can result from separations of the bloodlines or from rupture of the bloodlines or dialyzer membrane. Cardiac tamponade may occur during hemodialysis in a patient with pericarditis.

## Documentation

Record the time treatment began and any problems encountered in starting it. Note the patient's baseline vital signs and weight, and vital signs and weight during treatment. Also note the time specimens were taken for blood testing and their results, and any treatment for complications. Record the time the treatment was completed and the patient's response to it.

MARIA MAIAROTO-GROSS, RN, BSN
CATHERINE E. EGEN, RN

# Continuous Slow Ultrafiltration (CSUF)

*Continuous slow ultrafiltration (CSUF) removes fluid (or ultrafiltrate) from patients with oliguric acute renal failure. Usually, fluid is removed from these patients by performing isolated ultrafiltration before, during, or after conventional diffusion dialysis. Isolated ultrafiltration removes 1 to 2 liters of excess fluid in 1 to 2 hours, creating the risk in some patients of hemodynamic instability. CSUF, as its name implies, removes fluid continuously and slowly (about 150 to 200 ml/hour) over at least 24 to 48 hours. With this technique, the patient remains hemodynamically stable; equally important, he needn't restrict his fluid intake to prevent hypervolemia and pulmonary edema. He can take larger and safer dilutions of medications and, if necessary, receive hyperalimentation in full volume to meet nutritional needs.*

*Specially trained dialysis personnel, who may be nurses, usually initiate and discontinue CSUF. Intensive care nurses typically maintain the procedure, which mainly involves monitoring the infusion of heparin, the removal of ultrafiltrate, and patient tolerance throughout the treatment.*

## Equipment

*For dialysis personnel:* two arteriovenous (AV) blood tubing sets □ Amicon Diafilter-20 kidney □ 2 liters of I.V. normal saline solution □ 10,000 units of heparin □ drainage collection bag □ plastic adapter □ sterile scissors □ metal screw clamp.

*For nursing personnel:* 250-ml bag of I.V. normal saline solution □ 10,000 units of heparin □ I.V. infusion pump □ 22G

needle □ elastic gauze dressing □ alcohol sponge □ ½" adhesive tape □ necessary venipuncture equipment needed to determine clotting times.

## Preparation of equipment

Dialysis personnel should cut the AV blood tubing to a length of 7.9" to 9.8" (20 to 25 cm), or as needed, to position the injection-sampling sleeves close to the connection site (see *Setup for CSUF,* opposite). The distal ends of the tubing should then be attached to the Amicon Diafilter-20 kidney. Tubing should be flushed with 2 liters of heparinized saline solution (5,000 units of heparin/1 liter of saline solution) and the drain clamp closed.

Make sure the patient has a functioning AV shunt in his arm or leg before dialysis personnel arrive to start the procedure. Set up 10,000 units of heparin in 250 ml of saline solution on the I.V. infusion pump. (Heparin is an anticoagulant that prevents clots from forming in the artificial kidney during ultrafiltration.) Attach the 22G needle to the I.V. tubing and flush through to the distal end.

## Essential steps

● Explain the procedure in detail to the patient and his family.
● Wash your hands thoroughly *to minimize the danger of infection.* Remove elastic gauze dressing from patient's arm or leg *to expose the AV shunt.*
● Dialysis personnel perform shunt care *to prevent infection* according to hospital policy. The patient ends of the artificial kidney lines are color-coded red (arterial) and blue (venous). The arterial patient line is connected to the arterial limb of the shunt, and the venous patient line is connected to the venous limb of the shunt, using aseptic technique. The drainage collection bag is attached to the port of the ultrafiltrate line with the plastic adapter; the metal screw clamp is placed around the line *to control the flow.* An initial bolus of 500 units of heparin is then infused through the arterial sleeve *to assist in establishing adequate anti-*

## SETUP FOR CONTINUOUS SLOW ULTRAFILTRATION (C.S.U.F.)

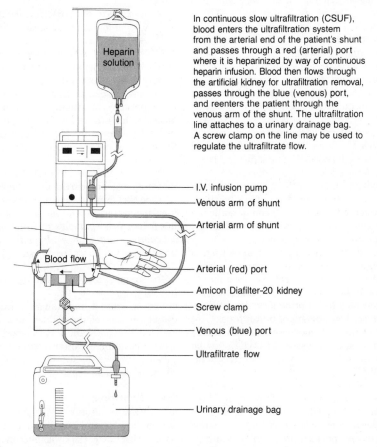

In continuous slow ultrafiltration (CSUF), blood enters the ultrafiltration system from the arterial end of the patient's shunt and passes through a red (arterial) port where it is heparinized by way of continuous heparin infusion. Blood then flows through the artificial kidney for ultrafiltration removal, passes through the blue (venous) port, and reenters the patient through the venous arm of the shunt. The ultrafiltration line attaches to a urinary drainage bag. A screw clamp on the line may be used to regulate the ultrafiltrate flow.

Heparin solution

I.V. infusion pump
Venous arm of shunt
Arterial arm of shunt
Blood flow
Arterial (red) port
Amicon Diafilter-20 kidney
Screw clamp
Venous (blue) port
Ultrafiltrate flow
Urinary drainage bag

*coagulation levels.*

• Secure the artificial kidney to the patient's arm with a new elastic gauze dressing. Leave the arterial, venous, and ultrafiltration ports exposed *to allow infusion of the I.V. solution and the withdrawal of blood when necessary.*

• *To ensure asepsis,* clean the red port of the artificial kidney's arterial sleeve with the alcohol sponge. Insert the 22G needle from the infusion pump into it. Tape the hub of the needle to the tubing.

• Establish the initial rate of heparin infusion on the I.V. infusion pump as ordered by the doctor.

• Adjust the metal screw clamp on the ultrafiltration line to achieve the ordered ultrafiltrate flow rate (usually 150 to 200 ml/hour). Loosen the clamp to increase flow; tighten it to decrease flow.

• Later, titrate the infusion rate of the heparinized solution *to maintain Lee White Clotting Time (LWCT) or other clotting time determinations at the levels ordered.* Continuous LWCT or other clotting time determinations are needed throughout ultrafiltration *to ensure the artificial kidney's patency.*

• Record hourly the volume of ultrafiltrate collected in the drainage collection bag. Also record hourly the LWCT of blood withdrawn from the blue venous port *to indicate the artificial kidney's level of anticoagulation.*

• Dialysis personnel should return at the prescribed time *to disconnect the ultrafiltration line,* reestablish the shunt connection, and perform shunt care.

## Special considerations

*To help prevent infection,* perform shunt care and inspect the shunt insertion sites at least every 24 hours during CSUF. If inflammation or drainage appears at the site, or the patient has a fever or an elevated white blood cell count, notify the doctor. (Site cultures should be done according to hospital policy.)

An I.V. infusion pump can be used to regulate the ultrafiltrate flow accurately. The pump is connected between the ultrafiltrate port and the drainage collection bag and continuously removes the prescribed amount of ultrafiltrate.

Hourly activated clotting times (ACT) may be used instead of LWCT. Results with ACT are less variable than with LWCT.

CSUF is usually continued for as long as the patient benefits from the fluid removal or until diffusion dialysis becomes necessary *to remove toxic substances not removed by ultrafiltration.* Ultrafiltration removes such substances as sodium, potassium, chloride, urea, glucose, and creatinine only in amounts equal to those found in the patient's serum. For example, if the patient's serum potassium level is 6.5 mEq/liter, the potassium level in the ultrafiltrate will be exactly the same. Thus, ultrafiltration does not replace conventional diffusion dialysis to lower the levels of toxic substances that can accumulate in acute renal failure; in such cases, ultrafiltration can be recommended after dialysis.

Because the electrolyte values of serum and ultrafiltrate are identical, send samples of the ultrafiltrate (rather than the serum) to the laboratory for routine electrolyte analysis. *This prevents iatrogenic blood loss resulting from frequent blood sampling.*

 *Because ultrafiltrate levels of total protein, calcium, phosphorus, and enzymes don't reflect serum levels,* serum samples are required for laboratory analysis of these substances.

The patient can sit in a chair during CSUF provided his tubing is securely attached to his arm or leg. If the shunt is in his leg, elevate the leg to the level of the chair by placing it on a stool with pillows.

Obtain bleeding studies (LWCT, prothrombin test, and partial thromboplastin time test) from a vascular access other than the venous or arterial ports of the line *to assess the patient's systemic anticoagulation status at regular intervals,* usually every 8 hours, or as ordered by the doctor.

*To prevent excessive bleeding,* avoid inserting or removing I.V., hyperalimentation, or arterial lines during ultrafiltration. If any of these lines must be inserted, first notify the doctor, who may order I.V. administration of protamine sulfate to reverse the anticoagulant effects of heparin.

## Complications

In addition to infection at the shunt insertion sites, several complications can arise during CSUF. Hypovolemia can follow too rapid removal of fluid; signs of hypovolemia include low filling pressures (such as central venous pressure or pulmonary capillary wedge pressure) and hypotension.

An LWCT above 40 minutes may reflect excessive anticoagulation, resulting in such signs of a clotting disorder as oozing of blood from I.V. sites, hematuria, or guaiac-positive nasogastric drainage. However, bleeding may occur even if the LWCT is within the accepted range (25 to 40 minutes), especially in patients with a history of gastrointestinal bleeding or hepatic dysfunction.

Clotting may occur in the artificial kidney any time the flow is sluggish (which may result from excessive hypotension, or inadequate heparinization as indicated by a subnormal LWCT). A sudden and unexplained decrease in ultrafiltration rate and blood pressure indicate the onset of this condition.

## Documentation

In the nurse's notes, record the patient's vital signs and weight before, during, and after CSUF, as ordered. Describe the condition of the shunt insertion site and shunt care given. Document hourly LWCT (or other clotting time determinations) and hourly heparin infusion rate. Describe the patient's reaction noting complications and nursing actions.

Chart heparin administration in the medication record. Record hourly ultrafiltrate output on the input and output record in a separate column from urine output. *Recording ultrafiltrate output in the urine output column could cause a misleading assessment of the patient's renal status.* Record I.V. infusions as intake on this record.

GAYLE R. WHITMAN, RN, MSN, CCRN

## Selected References

Arenz, Roberta. "Do-It-Yourself Dialysis," *RN* 44:56, July 1981.

Bates, Patricia. "A Troubleshooter's Guide to Indwelling Catheters," *RN* 44:62, March 1981.

Broadwell, Debra C., and Jackson, Bettie S. *Principles of Ostomy Care.* St. Louis: C.V. Mosby Co., 1982.

Brundage, Dorothy J. *Nursing Management of Renal Problems,* 2nd ed. St. Louis: C.V Mosby Co., 1980.

Brunner, Lillian S., and Suddarth, Doris Smith. *The Lippincott Manual of Nursing Practice,* 3rd ed. Philadelphia: J.B. Lippincott Co., 1982.

Brunner, Lillian S., and Suddarth, Doris Smith. *Textbook of Medical-Surgical Nursing,* 4th ed. J.B. Lippincott Co., 1980.

Denniston, Donna Jeanne, and Burns, Kathryn Taylor, "Home Peritoneal Dialysis," *American Journal of Nursing* 80: 2022, November 1980.

*Diseases.* The Nurse's Reference Library™ Series. Springhouse, Pa.: Intermed Communications, Inc., 1981.

Earley, S., and Gottschalk, B., eds. *Strauss and Welt's Diseases of the Kidney,* Vol I & Vol II. Boston: Little, Brown & Co., 1979.

Hampers, Constantine, et al. *Long-term Hemodialysis: The Management of the Patient with Chronic Renal Failure.* New York: Grune & Stratton, 1973.

Harrington, J.D., and Brener, E.R. *Patient Care in Renal Failure.* Philadelphia: W.B. Saunders Co., 1973.

Irwin, Betty C. "Hemodialysis Means Vascular Access...and the Right Kind of Nursing Care," *Nursing79* 9:48, October 1979.

Irwin, Betty C. "Now—Peritoneal Dialysis for Chronic Patients, Too," *RN* 44:49, June 1981.

Killion, Ana. "Reducing the Risk of Infection from Indwelling Urethral Catheters," *Nursing82* 12:84, May 1982.

Kinney, M., et al. *AACN's Clinical Reference for Critical Care Nursing.* New York: McGraw-Hill Book Co., 1981.

Lancaster, Larry E. *The Patient with End Stage Renal Disease.* New York: John Wiley & Sons, 1979.

Lavandero, Ramon, and Davis, Virginia. "Caring for the Catheter Carefully...Before, During and After Peritoneal Dialysis," *Nursing80* 10:73, November 1980.

Millar, Sally, et al., eds. *Methods in Critical Care.* Philadelphia: W.B. Saunders Co., 1980.

*Performing Urologic Procedures.* Nursing Photobook™ Series. Springhouse, Pa.: Intermed Communications, Inc., 1981.

Prowant, Barbara F., and Fruto, Leonor V. "Continuous Ambulatory Peritoneal Dialysis," *Nephrology Nurse* 2:8, January/ February 1980.

Richard, C. J. "Peritoneal Dialysis—A Nursing Update, Part I," *Nephrology Nurse* 2:4, November/December 1980.

Winter, C., and Morel, A. *Nursing Care of Patients with Urologic Diseases,* 4th ed. St. Louis: C.V. Mosby Co., 1977.

# 12 Neurologic Care

# Neurologic Care

## Introduction

The goal of neurologic care is to preserve and restore optimal function of the nervous system. Appropriate supportive care may make restoration possible even after catastrophic illness or injury. Precise nursing skills, meticulously applied, are an indispensable part of such effective care. More and more, these nursing skills require mastery of sophisticated techniques and equipment.

### Neurologic assessment

Appropriate supportive care entails keen observation and documentation of neurologic vital signs, as well as frequent respiratory assessment. The use of specialized charts or flowsheets for recording neurologic vital signs—a common practice in many hospitals—refines documentation and helps prevent misinterpretation of the unstable patient's changing neurologic status. These charts separate and grade components of a neurologic assessment, ensuring clarity and precision—critical factors when even slight and almost imperceptible changes in neurologic vital signs can signal grave deterioration.

Respiratory complications often follow brain or spinal trauma caused by depression of the respiratory control center or paralysis of muscles that accomplish breathing. Brain tissue is especially sensitive to blood levels of oxygen. Inadequate oxygenation can quickly lead to tissue damage—a consequence the neurologic patient can ill afford. Consequently, good pulmonary care complements neurologic care and may include frequent position changes, chest physiotherapy, and tracheal suctioning. Regular assessment of respiratory pattern and breath sounds, along with analysis of arterial blood gases, allows detection of any changes in the patient's respiratory status. Intubation and mechanical ventilation may be necessary to maintain a patent airway and optimal oxygenation of brain tissue.

### Rehabilitation

Rehabilitation of the neurologic patient begins on admission and pervades all aspects of daily care. Neurologic deficit can affect all body systems; it can upset basic body functions and interfere with highly complex thought processes. It can also shatter the patient's sense of identity. Consequently, rehabilitative teaching must address the many psychosocial and physiologic changes associated with the patient's neurologic deficit—a task that requires an enormous investment of time, patience, and energy.

The success of rehabilitation hinges on the patient's ability to adapt to such profound changes. Various factors influence this adaptation: the patient's age, onset of the deficit (traumatic or slowly progressive), and the associated degree of dependency, to name a few.

Obviously, the effects of neurologic deficit vary from patient to patient and can be minimal or extensive. Above all, rehabilitation aims to help the patient lead the most productive and satisfying life possible.

CONNIE A. WALLECK, RN, CNRN

## DIAGNOSIS AND MONITORING

# Neurologic Vital Signs

*Neurologic vital signs supplement the routine measurement of temperature, pulse rate, and respirations by evaluating the patient's level of consciousness, pupillary activity, and sensory and motor function. They provide a simple, indispensable tool for quickly checking the patient's neurologic status.*

*Level of consciousness, or the degree of response to stimuli, reflects brain function and usually provides the first sign of central nervous system (CNS) deterioration. Pupillary activity—pupil size, shape, equality, and response to light—ranks second in heralding increased intracranial pressure. Evaluating muscle strength and tone, reflexes, and posture can also help identify nervous system damage. Finally, ongoing assessment of routine vital signs helps detect neurologic changes or trends. In particular, respiratory rate and pattern can help locate brain lesions and determine their size.*

## Equipment

Penlight □ sterile cotton ball or cotton swab □ thermometer, stethoscope; sphygmomanometer □ pupil size chart.

## Essential steps

● Explain the procedure to the patient, even if he's unresponsive. Then wash your hands and provide privacy.

*To evaluate level of consciousness:*

● Assess the patient's verbal responses and degree of orientation. First, ask the patient his name. If he responds appropriately, assess his orientation to place, time, and date. Ask the patient where he is, and then what day, season, and year it is. (Expect disorientation to affect the sense of date first, then time, place, and finally person.) When the patient responds verbally, note whether the replies are clear, rambling, or garbled.

● Assess the patient's ability to understand and follow simple commands that require a motor response. For example, ask him to open and close his eyes or stick out his tongue.

● If the patient doesn't respond to these commands, apply a painful stimulus. Squeeze Achilles tendons, forearms, and calf muscles with moderate pressure and note response. Check motor responses bilaterally *to rule out monoplegia (paralysis of a single area) and hemiplegia (paralysis of one side of the body).*

*To evaluate pupils and eye movement:*

● Have the patient open his eyes or gently lift his upper lids. Inspect each pupil for size and shape, and compare the two for equality. To evaluate pupil size more precisely, use a scale showing the various pupil sizes (in increments of 1 mm, with the normal diameter from 2 to 6 mm). Remember, pupil size varies considerably, and some patients have normally unequal pupils (anisocoria). Also, see if the pupils are positioned in, or deviated from, the midline.

● Test the patient's direct light response. First, darken the room. Then hold each eyelid open in turn, keeping the other eye covered. Swing the penlight from the patient's ear toward the midline of the face. Shine it directly into the eye. This normally causes immediate pupillary constriction. When you remove the penlight, dilation of the pupil should be similarly prompt.

● Test consensual light response. Hold both eyelids open, but shine the light into one eye only. Watch for constriction in the other pupil, *which indicates proper nerve function at the optic chiasm.*

● Brighten the room and have the conscious patient open his eyes. Observe the lids for ptosis or drooping. Then check extraocular movements. Hold up one finger and ask the patient to follow it with his eyes alone. As you move the finger

## USING THE GLASGOW COMA SCALE

The Glasgow coma scale provides a standard reference for assessing or monitoring a patient with suspected or confirmed brain injury. It measures three faculties' responses to stimuli—*eye opening, motor response,* and *verbal response*—and assigns a number to each of the possible responses within these categories. A score of 3 is the lowest and 15 is the highest. A score of 7 or less indicates coma. This scale is commonly used in the emergency department or at the scene of an accident, and for periodic evaluation of the hospitalized patient.

### THE GLASGOW COMA SCALE

| FACULTY MEASURED | RESPONSE | SCORE |
|---|---|---|
| **Eye opening** | • Spontaneously | 4 |
| | • To verbal command | 3 |
| | • To pain | 2 |
| | • No response | 1 |
| **Motor response** | • To verbal command | 6 |
| | • To painful stimuli (Apply knuckle to sternum; observe arms.) | |
| | Localizes pain | 5 |
| | Flexes and withdraws | 4 |
| | Assumes decorticate posture | 3 |
| | Assumes decerebrate posture | 2 |
| | No response | 1 |
| **Verbal response** (Arouse patient with painful stimuli, if necessary) | • Oriented and converses | 5 |
| | • Disoriented and converses | 4 |
| | • Uses inappropriate words | 3 |
| | • Makes incomprehensible sounds | 2 |
| | • No response | 1 |
| | Total: | 3 to 15 |

*Note:* The *decorticate posture* may indicate a lesion of the frontal lobes, internal capsule, or cerebral penduncles. The *decerebrate posture* may indicate lesions of the upper brain system. *The patient's use of inappropriate words* may indicate either receptive or expressive aphasia. *Incomprehensible sounds* indicate expressive aphasia.

up, down, laterally and obliquely, see if the patient's eyes track together to follow your finger (conjugate gaze). Watch for involuntary jerking or oscillating eye movements (nystagmus).
• Next check for accommodation. Hold up one finger midline to the patient's face and several feet away. Have him focus on your finger. Then gradually bring your finger toward his nose with the patient still focusing on your finger, which should cause convergence of eyes and pupillary constriction.
• Test the corneal reflex by holding the patient's eyelid open and *gently* brushing the cornea with a wisp of cotton or a cotton swab. *Immediate blinking indicates this reflex is intact.* Repeat for the other eye.

Be extremely careful when touching the delicate cornea *to avoid corneal abrasion.* Make sure not to touch the eyelashes with the cotton swab *to avoid blinking unassociated with the corneal reflex.*
• If the patient is unconscious, test the oculocephalic (doll's eye) reflex. Hold the

patient's eyelids open. Then quickly, but gently, turn the patient's head to one side, then the other. If the patient's eyes move in the opposite direction from the side to which you turn the head—eyes move to the right when the head moves to the left—the reflex is intact.

*To evaluate motor function:*
• If the patient is conscious, test his grip strength in both hands at the same time. Extend your hands, ask the patient to squeeze your fingers as hard as he can, and compare grip strength. Grip strength is usually slightly stronger in the dominant hand.
• Test arm strength by having the patient close his eyes and hold his arms straight out in front of him with the palms up. See if either arm drifts downward or pronates, *which indicates muscle weakness.* Then test leg strength by having the patient raise his legs, one at a time. Gently push down on each leg *to evaluate strength.*
• If the patient is unconscious, estimate the strength of spontaneous and reflex movements. Apply a painful stimulus to elicit movement. Exert pressure on each fingernail bed with a pencil or pen. If the patient withdraws from this stimulus, compare the strength of each limb.
• Flex and extend the extremities on both sides *to evaluate muscle tone.*
• Test the plantar reflex in all patients. Stroke the lateral aspect of the sole of the patient's foot with your thumbnail or another moderately sharp object. Normally, this elicits flexion of all toes. Watch for Babinski's sign—dorsiflexion of the great toe with fanning of the other toes—*which indicates an upper motor neuron lesion.*
• Test for Brudzinski's and Kernig's signs in patients suspected of having meningitis.
*To complete the neurologic examination:*
• Take the patient's temperature, pulse, respirations, and blood pressure. Especially note his pulse pressure—the difference between systolic pressure and diastolic pressure—*because widening pulse pressure can indicate increasing intracranial pressure.*

If the previously stable patient suddenly develops a change in neurologic or routine vital signs, further assess his condition and then notify the doctor immediately.

## Special considerations

Watch for decorticate or decerebrate posturing—ominous signs of CNS deterioration—in response to painful stimuli. In decorticate posturing, the patient's arms are adducted and flexed, with the wrists and fingers flexed on the chest. The legs are stiffly extended and internally rotated, with plantar flexion of the feet. In decerebrate posturing, the patient's arms are adducted and extended with the wrists pronated and the fingers flexed. The legs are stiffly extended, with plantar flexion of the feet.

## Documentation

Generally, baseline data requires detailed documentation, whereas subsequent notes can be brief, unless the patient's condition changes. Record the patient's level of consciousness, pupillary activity, motor function, and routine vital signs, as the institution directs. To save time and provide for complete documentation, the institution may permit you to use abbreviations, such as the following: A + O × 4 (alert and oriented to *person, place, time,* and *date*), PERRLA (pupils equal, round, reactive to light and accommodation), PERL (pupils equal, reactive to light), MAEW (moves all extremities well), BLFG (bilateral firm hand grips), EOM (extraocular movements), BLLS (bilateral leg strength). Use standard references, such as the Glasgow coma scale, or descriptive behaviors—difficult to arouse by gentle shaking, sleepy, unresponsive to painful stimuli. Use only commonly understood abbreviations and terms to avoid misinterpretation of patient status. Remember, the neurologic flow chart and patient record are legal documents.

KRISTEN KINDEL, RN

# Tests of Sensory Innervation

*Each of the 31 spinal nerves innervates a segment of the body known as its dermatome. Except for the first cervical vertebra (C₁), which lacks a dorsal root, these nerves transmit sensory stimuli from the skin to the spinal cord. Testing sensory innervation evaluates the patient's ability to perceive and interpret stimuli within the various dermatomes. Sensory testing can help differentiate organic disease from functional or hysterical disorders. It can help identify the cause of referred pain and, when performed periodically, can help monitor progressive disease such as Guillain-Barré syndrome.*

*Assessment of sensory function begins with recognition of the patient's neurologic symptoms, if any. Well-planned testing then avoids undue patient fatigue and inaccurate results. Careful documentation of sensory deficits on a dermatome chart is essential. (See illustration on page 632.)*

*Sensory innervation testing is usually performed to clarify a history of localized pain, numbness or tingling, or motor deficits. It can include evaluation of temperature sense, position sense, two-point discrimination, graphesthesia, point localization, and extinction.*

## Equipment

Two test tubes □ clean, sharp safety pin □ one or two clean cotton balls □ low-pitched tuning fork (128 cycles/second) □ coin, paper clip, or key □ pen or pencil □ two straight pins □ dermatome chart.

Dermatome charts may vary slightly, because segments innervated by the spinal nerves tend to overlap. Always use the chart supplied by the hospital.

## Preparation of equipment

Fill one test tube with cold water and the other with hot water. Avoid temperature extremes that the patient might interpret as pain instead of temperature sensation. Place each test tube against your skin to check the temperature. Then bring all equipment to the bedside.

## Essential steps

● Familiarize yourself with the patient's history and any related sensory abnormalities. Locate abnormalities on the dermatome chart *to guide your testing.*
● Wash your hands, provide privacy, and explain the procedure to the patient. Instruct him to close his eyes and keep them shut throughout the test to ensure accurate results. Reassure the patient *to ease his anxiety.*

*To test pain sense:*
● Open the safety pin and hold it between your fingers. Warn the patient that he will feel slight pin pricks and ask him to describe them as sharp or dull. Then gently press the pin against the patient's skin to elicit a response. You shouldn't puncture the skin. Occasionally, substitute the pin's dull end. Test pain sense on the patient's face, arms, trunk, and legs. If it's abnormal, test temperature sense, which has a closely related neural pathway.

*To test temperature sense:*
● Briefly touch the hot or cold test tube against the patient's skin on his face, arms, trunk, and legs. Ask him to identify hot or cold.

*To test tactile sense:*
● Brush the patient's skin with a wisp of cotton on the face, arms, trunk, and legs. Ask the patient to tell you whenever he feels you touch him. If indicated, check for the extinction phenomenon to further evaluate tactile sense.

*To test extinction:*
● Simultaneously touch corresponding areas on each of the patient's arms with your fingertips. Ask him to tell you where you've touched him. Repeat this test on other corresponding areas on opposite sides of the patient's body. The patient with parietal lobe disease may have normal tactile sense when you touch corresponding areas consecutively, but not simultaneously. On the affected side, the

## USING A DERMATOME CHART FOR REFERENCE

The two figures illustrated at right show the segmental distribution of spinal nerves that transmit pain, temperature, and touch from the skin to the spinal cord.

As you assess your patient for sensory function, use this chart as a reference to document the specific area tested, as well as the test results.

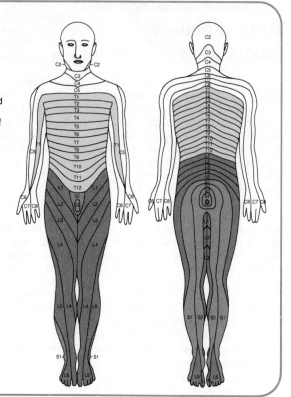

patient will fail to perceive touch.

*To test vibration sense:*

• Vibrate the tuning fork and place it on the distal interphalangeal joint of a finger. Ask the patient to tell you what he's feeling. *To determine if he's feeling pressure or vibration,* leave the fork in place and stop the vibration with your hand. Ask the patient again to tell you what he feels.

• Repeat this test on a finger of the other hand and on the distal interphalangeal joint of both great toes.

• If the vibration sense is abnormal in the fingers and toes, test more proximal bony prominences—wrist, patella, spinous processes.

*To test position sense:*

• Grasp the sides of the great toe between your thumb and index finger. Separate it from the other toes to avoid friction. Then move the toe up and down and ask

the patient to identify the direction in which you're moving the toe.

• Repeat this test for the same toe on the other foot.

• If position sense is abnormal, test more proximal joints—the ankle and knee, for example.

• Test the patient's fingers and, if necessary, his wrists and elbows.

*To test stereognosis:*

• Place a coin, paper clip, or key in the patient's hand and ask him to identify the object.

• Repeat this test for the other hand.

*To test graphesthesia:*

• Grasp the patient's hand, palm facing up. Using the blunt end of a pen or pencil, write a number or letter on his palm. Ask the patient to identify it.

• Repeat this test for the other palm.

*To test two-point discrimination:*

• Hold two straight pins with their points

apart between your fingers. Touch a finger pad with the two pins simultaneously. Ask the patient if he feels one or two pins. Bring the pins closer together and repeat the test. Note the distance at which the patient can no longer distinguish one from two points. On the finger pads, this distance usually ranges from 2 to 3 mm. Occasionally, touch the finger pad with only one pin.
• Repeat this test on a finger pad of the other hand.
• Then test other corresponding areas of the body. Consult a chart to determine normal distances for two-point discrimination. Generally, the less sensitive the area, the greater the distance.

*To test point localization:*
• Touch the patient's hand briefly with your finger. Then have him open his eyes and point to where you've touched him.
• Repeat this test on the other hand and on other corresponding areas of the body.

**Special considerations**
Always check the same area on both sides of the body and compare the patient's responses. When you check an extremity, begin at the most distal point and work your way toward the trunk. Instead of concentrating on only one or two areas, apply stimuli over the entire body to obtain a thorough, accurate assessment. When you find an area of abnormal sensations, map its boundaries carefully.

If the patient has no neurologic signs and symptoms, a screening test of sensory function will usually suffice. This test evaluates pain and vibration sense in the hands and feet, tactile sense on the arms and legs, and stereognosis (identification of objects by touch).

**Documentation**
Record the results of sensory testing on the patient's chart with the time and date. Clearly describe any changes in sensory status. You may want to use these terms to document abnormal sensation: for pain sense, *alganesthesia* or *analgesia* (absent), *hypalgesia* (decreased), and *hyperalgesia* (increased); for temperature sense, *thermanesthesia* (absent), *therm-* *hypesthesia* (decreased), and *thermhyperesthesia* (increased); and for tactile sense, *anesthesia* (absent), *hypesthesia* (decreased), and *hyperesthesia* (increased).

KRISTEN KINDEL, RN

# Intracranial Pressure Monitoring

*Intracranial pressure (ICP) monitoring measures the pressure exerted by brain tissue, blood, and cerebrospinal fluid (CSF) against the skull. Indications for this procedure include head trauma with bleeding or edema, overproduction or insufficient absorption of CSF, cerebral hemorrhage, and space-occupying brain lesions. Such monitoring can detect elevated ICP early, before clinical danger signs develop. Prompt intervention can then help avert or diminish neurologic damage caused by cerebral hypoxia and shifts of brain mass.*

*The three basic ICP monitoring systems use a ventricular catheter, subarachnoid screw, or epidural sensor (see* Three Types of ICP Monitoring, page 634*). Regardless of the devices used, this procedure is always performed by a neurosurgeon in the operating room, emergency room, or critical care unit. Insertion of an ICP monitoring device requires sterile technique to reduce the risk of CNS infection. Setting up equipment for the monitoring systems also requires strict asepsis.*

*Contraindications to ventricular catheter ICP monitoring usually include stenotic cerebral ventricles, cerebral aneurysms in the path of catheter placement, and suspected vascular lesions.*

**Equipment**
*For ventricular catheter or subarachnoid screw monitoring:*
Bedside commercial monitor with transducer ▫ 30-ml vial of sterile normal saline solution ▫ alcohol sponges ▫ 18G

# THREE TYPES OF I.C.P. MONITORING

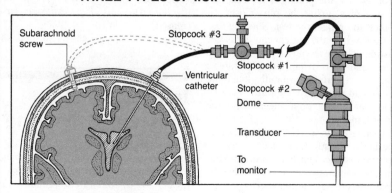

In **ventricular catheter monitoring,** which directly monitors intracranial pressure (ICP), the doctor inserts a small polyethylene or silicone rubber catheter into the lateral ventricle through a twist-drill burr hole. Although this method measures ICP most accurately, it carries the greatest risk of infection. Placing the catheter may be difficult, especially if the ventricle is collapsed, swollen, or displaced. However, this is the only type of ICP monitoring that allows for evaluation of brain compliance and drainage of significant amounts of cerebrospinal fluid (CSF).

**Subarachnoid screw monitoring** involves the insertion of an ICP screw into the subarachnoid space through a twist-drill burr hole in the front of the skull behind the hairline. Placing an ICP screw is easier than placing a ventricular catheter, especially if a computerized axial tomogram (CAT scan) reveals shifting of the cerebrum or collapsed ventricles. This type of ICP monitoring also carries less risk of infection and parenchymal damage

because the screw doesn't penetrate the cerebrum.

In *both* ventricular catheter and sub-arachnoid screw monitoring (see illustration above), a fluid-filled line connects the catheter or screw to a domed transducer. Elevated ICP exerts pressure on the fluid in the line, depressing the dome's diaphragm. The transducer then transmits pressure readings to a monitor for display. If desired, the readings can also be transmitted to a recorder for readout strips.

**Epidural sensor monitoring,** the least invasive method with the lowest incidence of infection, uses a fiber-optic sensor inserted into the epidural space through a burr hole (see illustration below). A cable connects the sensor to a monitor and, if desired, to a recorder. Unlike a ventricular catheter or subarachnoid screw, the sensor can't become occluded with blood or brain tissue. However, the accuracy of epidural monitoring is questionable because it doesn't measure ICP directly from a cranial space filled with CSF.

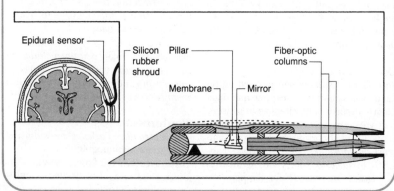

1½" needle □ 20-ml syringe □ plastic transducer dome (disposable or reusable) □ 3 three-way stopcocks □ sterile dead-end caps for stopcock ports □ two packages of sterile 12" (30 cm) high-pressure tubing □ sterile gloves □ commercial ventriculostomy catheter or subarachnoid screw □ commercial ventriculostomy collection bag with drip chamber and pressure tubing (for CSF collection) □ I.V. pole □ optional: cerebrospinal fluid manometer, sterile culture tubes.

*For epidural sensor monitoring:*
Sterile epidural fiberoptic sensor □ ICP monitor unit with sensor switch and cable.

*For all monitoring systems:*
16 to 20 sterile 4" x 4" gauze sponges □ linen-saver pads □ shave preparation tray or hair scissors □ sterile drapes □ povidone-iodine solution □ sterile gown □ surgical mask □ two pairs of sterile gloves □ sterile 3-ml syringe with 25G needle □ bottle of local anesthetic (usually lidocaine 2% solution) □ manual twist drill with screw attachments □ 3-0 suture silk □ povidone-iodine ointment □ collodion solution □ head dressing supplies (two rolls of 4" elastic gauze dressing, one roll of 4" roller gauze, adhesive tape) □ polygraph recorder (optional).

Commercial ventricular monitoring trays are available. The central supply department may also provide prepackaged sterile trays that include everything necessary for catheter or screw insertion except the sterile gloves, gown, drapes, and monitoring equipment. Use a bedside monitor with at least three channels to allow simultaneous monitoring of ICP, electrocardiogram (EKG), and arterial pressure, as ordered. Never select tubing with a continuous flush device: *Excess fluid flushed into the cranial cavity may dangerously spike ICP.* Replace any open stopcock caps with dead-end caps *to maintain sterility.*

## Preparation of equipment
*For ventricular catheter or subarachnoid screw monitoring:*
Connect the transducer to the monitor and turn on the monitor *to let it warm up.* Wash your hands and gather the necessary equipment. Open the equipment tray and use outside sterile wrap to establish a sterile field.

Clean the rubber diaphragm of the vial of saline solution with an alcohol sponge. Draw 20 ml of solution with the 18G 1½" needle attached to the 20-ml syringe. If you're using a disposable dome, eject 1 ml of saline solution onto the transducer diaphragm. (The saline solution acts as a conduction agent, but this priming is necessary only for disposable domes.) Then screw the plastic dome onto the transducer.

Open two of the three-way stopcocks. Consider these stopcocks #1 and #2 (see *Three Types of ICP Monitoring,* opposite). Connect the narrow end of stopcock #1 to one arm of the dome; connect stopcock #2 to the other arm. Tighten all connections securely. Apply the sterile dead-end caps to the stopcock ports.

Open the two packages of 12" high pressure tubing and the remaining stopcock (#3). Using sterile tecnhique, connect one length of tubing to one side port of stopcock #3, and the other length to the opposite side port. Apply a sterile dead-end cap to the top port. Then connect the tubing to stopcock #2.

Remove the needle from the syringe filled with sterile saline solution. Uncap the top port of stopcock #2. Connect the syringe to this port and flush the dome and tubing *to expel all air, since air in the line will dampen the wave, giving an inaccurate ICP reading.* Then flush all stopcock ports. Turn the stopcock to allow flow to the port. Then hold the open port upright *to let air bubbles rise and escape.* After flushing the stopcock, remove the syringe and recap the ports. Place the fluid-filled system on a clean surface.

*To balance the transducer,* turn stopcock #2 off to the pressure tubing, and then turn stopcock #1 open to air. Hold the upright port of stopcock #1 level with the patient's foramen of Monro—the pressure source of ICP readings—located between the lateral end of the eye-

## CALIBRATING AN
## I.C.P. MONITOR

To calibrate an intercranial pressure (ICP) monitor using the *cal factor,* first see if the cal factor is marked on the transducer. If not, obtain it by testing the transducer with a mercury sphygmomanometer, as the operator's manual directs. Depress the "balance" button. If the transducer is balanced properly, you'll get a zero reading. Release the button. Then, depress the "calibrate" button and, while holding this button down, use a screwdriver to turn the screw next to it until the digital reading equals the cal factor.

To use the *electric cal,* depress the "zero" button on the monitor. Make sure the digital readout is zero and the oscilloscope line is at zero. Then depress the "test/cal" button and turn the "sensitivity" knob until the digital reading is 100 mmHg and the line runs on the 100 mmHg level.

To use the *pre-cal,* simply test the function of the monitor and transducer, because they're already calibrated with each other. Depress the "test" button and "zero" button simultaneously and hold them. The digital reading will be zero and the oscilloscope line will be at zero if the equipment's working properly.

Balance and calibrate the transducer and monitor at least once every 4 hours.

brow and the tragus of the ear. Remove the port's sterile dead-end cap.

Depress the monitor's automatic "zero" button or turn the "zero" knob until the monitor reads zero and the oscilloscope line is at zero. Then recap the port. Remember to keep this balancing port level with the foramen of Monro throughout monitoring *to ensure accurate readings.* If the patient moves, reposition and rebalance the transducer accordingly.

Calibrate the monitor to the transducer, according to the institution's policy. Because monitors are varied and complex, the frequency of calibration and personnel involved will differ among institutions. Suspect the need for calibration if pressure readings appear consistently inaccurate. Before calibration, study the operator's manual carefully. Most monitors can be calibrated

by one of three procedures: cal factor, electric cal, or pre-cal (see *Calibrating an ICP Monitor,* at left). After calibrating the monitor, turn stopcock #1 off to the upright balancing port, and open stopcock #2 to the pressure tubing. Turn the knob to "monitor."

No special preparation of equipment is necessary for ICP monitoring with an epidural sensor.

### Essential steps

*To assist with insertion of an ICP monitoring device:*

• Explain the procedure to the patient or his family. Make sure the patient or a responsible family member has signed a consent form.

• Provide privacy if the procedure is being done in an open emergency room or intensive care unit.

• Obtain baseline routine and neurologic vital signs *to aid prompt detection of decompensation during the procedure.*

• Place the patient in the supine position and elevate the head of the bed 30°, or as ordered. Document the number of bed cranks.

• Place linen-saver pads under the patient's head. Shave or clip his hair at the insertion site, as indicated by the doctor, *to decrease the risk of infection.* Carefully fold and remove the linen-saver pads *to avoid spilling loose hair onto the bed.* Drape the patient with sterile drapes. Scrub the insertion site for 2 minutes with povidone-iodine solution.

• The doctor puts on the sterile gown, mask, and sterile gloves. He then opens the interior wrap of the sterile supply tray and proceeds with insertion of the catheter or screw.

• *To facilitate placement of the device,* hold the patient's head in your hands or attach a long strip of 4″ tape to one side rail and bring it across the patient's forehead to the opposite rail. Reassure the conscious patient *to help ease his anxiety.* Talk to him frequently *to assess his level of consciousness and detect signs of deterioration.* Watch for cardiac arrhythmias and abnormal respiratory patterns.

*For ventricular catheter or subarachnoid screw monitoring:*
• Once the catheter or screw is in place, the doctor connects the pressure tubing. Watch the monitor and record the first digital number or *baseline pressure.* The doctor then sutures the catheter or screw to the patient's scalp and connects the drainage system, if needed, to stopcock #3.
• Apply povidone-iodine ointment to the site and a sterile dressing—either a conventional head bandage or two sterile 4″ x 4″ gauze sponges saturated with collodion. (Collodion dries quickly and adheres to the scalp.)
• Place the transducer on a bedside stand or a headboard clip on a level with the cerebral ventricle, located at the foramen of Monro. *This ensures the most accurate pressure readings.*
• If the doctor has set up a drainage system, attach the drip chamber to the headboard or bedside I.V. pole. Position it 2″ to 4″ (5 to 10 cm) above the level of the cerebral ventricle.

 Positioning the drip chamber too high may raise ICP; positioning it too low may cause excessive CSF drainage.

*For monitoring with an epidural sensor:*
• When the sensor is in place, apply povidone-iodine ointment and a sterile dressing to the site.
• Turn the auto-sensor switch on. Then insert the sensor's cable into the cable receptacle.
• Turn on the monitor and let it warm up for 2 to 3 minutes.
• Zero the epidural sensor by adjusting the "zero" knob until the digital reading is between −1 and +2.
• Set the alarm to parameters given by the doctor. Hold down the "patient pressure" switch with one hand. With your other hand, turn the "set alert" knob until the appropriate pressure level appears on the digital reading. Then release the "patient pressure" switch.
• When you release the "patient pressure" switch, the monitor will automat-

ically display the patient's intracranial pressure. Record the first digital number or baseline pressure.

*For all monitoring systems:*
• Inspect the insertion site at least every 24 hours for redness, swelling, and drainage. Clean the site, reapply povidone-iodine ointment, and reapply a sterile dressing. If necessary, remove collodion by softening it with normal saline solution and gently pulling it off. Also, change the equipment setup—stopcocks, pressure tubing, and dome—daily.
• Hourly, or as ordered, assess the patient's clinical status, and take routine and neurologic vital signs. Watch for signs of impending or overt decompensation: papilledema; pupillary dilation (unilateral or bilateral); decreased pupillary response to light; decreasing level of consciousness; rising systolic blood pressure and widening pulse pressure; bradycardia; slowed, irregular respirations; and, in late decompensation, decerebrate posturing.
• Observe digital ICP readings and waves. Remember, the pattern of readings is more significant than any single reading. If you observe continually elevated ICP readings, note how long they're sustained. If they last several minutes, notify the doctor immediately. Finally, record and describe any CSF drainage.

## Special considerations
In infants, ICP monitoring can be performed without penetrating the scalp. In this external method, a photoelectric transducer with a pressure-sensitive membrane is taped to the anterior fontanel. The transducer responds to pressure at the site and transmits readings to a bedside monitor and recording system. The external method is restricted to infants because pressure readings can be obtained only at fontanels—incompletely ossified areas—of the skull.

Various forms of therapy help manage elevated ICP. Osmotic diuretics, such as mannitol by I.V. drip or bolus, reduce cerebral edema by shrinking intracranial contents. The patient may become dehydrated very quickly, however, so monitor serum electrolytes and osmolality closely. Be aware that a rebound increase in ICP may occur.

Fluid restriction, usually 1,500-ml maximum per day, avoids causing or increasing cerebral edema.

Steroids lower elevated ICP by reducing sodium and water concentration in the brain. Since they may also produce peptic ulcer, they're usually given with antacids and cimetidine. Observe for possible gastrointestinal (GI) bleeding. Also monitor urine glucose and acetone levels. Steroids may cause glycosuria in patients with borderline diabetes.

Barbiturate-induced coma depresses the reticular activating system and allows the brain to rest. Reduced demand for oxygen and energy reduces cerebral blood flow, thereby lowering ICP.

Hyperventilation with oxygen, using an Ambu bag or respirator, helps the patient blow off excess carbon dioxide, thus constricting cerebral vessels and reducing cerebral blood volume and ICP. Before tracheal suctioning, hyperventilate the patient with 100% oxygen, as ordered. Apply suction for a maximum of 15 seconds.

Because hyperthermia raises brain metabolism and thus cerebral blood flow, measures to reduce fever—simultaneous administration of acetaminophen, alcohol sponge baths, and a hypothermia blanket—help reduce ICP.

Withdrawal of CSF through the drainage system reduces CSF volume, and thus reduces ICP. Although less commonly used, surgical removal of a skull bone flap provides room for the swollen brain to expand. If this procedure is performed, keep the site clean and dry *to prevent infection* and maintain sterile technique when changing the dressing.

Take measures to prevent a sudden rise in ICP. Position the patient carefully: avoid neck flexion, hip flexion of 90° or greater, the prone position, elevating the head greater than 30°, and lowering the head less than 15°. Be extremely careful when turning the patient. Also discourage Valsalva's maneuver and isometric muscle contractions.

## Complications

CNS infection, the most common hazard of ICP monitoring, can result from contamination of the equipment setup or of the insertion site.

Excessive loss of CSF can result from faulty stopcock placement or a drip chamber that's positioned too low. Such loss can rapidly decompress the cranial contents and damage bridging cortical veins, leading to hematoma formation. Decompression can also lead to rupture of existing hematomas or aneurysms causing hemorrhage since it reduces the tamponade effect.

Excessive loss of CSF may also cause a swift, downward shift of intracranial contents, or herniation of the temporal lobes through the tentorium. This shift of brain mass compresses vital brain stem structures and is fatal. Insertion of the ventricular catheter can create cystic spaces within the brain tissue and cause permanent damage.

## Documentation

Record the time and date of the insertion procedure and the patient's response. Note the insertion site and the type of monitoring system used. Record ICP digital readings and waves hourly in your notes, on a flow chart, or directly on readout strips, depending on the institution's policy. Document any factors that may affect ICP—for example, drug therapy, stressful nursing procedures, or sleep.

Record routine and neurologic vital signs hourly, and describe the patient's clinical status. Note the amount, character, and frequency of any CSF drainage (for example, between 6 p.m. and 7 p.m., 15 drops of blood-tinged CSF).

KRISTEN KINDEL, RN

# Lumbar Puncture

*Lumbar puncture is the insertion of a sterile needle into the subarachnoid space of the spinal canal, usually between the third and fourth lumbar vertebrae. The procedure is performed to detect increased intracranial pressure or the presence of blood in cerebrospinal fluid (CSF), which indicates cerebral hemorrhage; to obtain CSF specimens for laboratory analysis; and to inject dyes or gases to enhance radiologic examination of the brain and spinal cord. Lumbar puncture is also used therapeutically to administer drugs or anesthetics and to relieve intracranial pressure by removing CSF.*

*Performed by a doctor with a nurse assisting, lumbar puncture requires sterile technique and careful patient positioning. This procedure is contraindicated in patients with lumbar deformity or infection at the puncture site. It should be performed cautiously in patients with increased intracranial pressure, because the rapid reduction in pressure that follows withdrawal of fluid can cause cerebellar tonsillar herniation and medullary compression.*

## Equipment

Overbed table □ one or two pairs of sterile gloves for the doctor □ sterile applicators □ povidone-iodine solution □ alcohol sponges □ sterile fenestrated drape □ one 3-ml syringe for local anesthetic □ one 25G ¾" sterile needle for injecting anesthetic □ local anesthetic (usually 1% lidocaine) □ one 18G or 20G 3½" sterile spinal needle with stylet (22G needle for children) □ three-way stopcock □ manometer □ three sterile collection tubes with stoppers □ labels □ laboratory request slips □ small adhesive bandage □ light source, such as a gooseneck lamp.

Disposable lumbar puncture trays containing most of the needed sterile equipment are generally available.

## Essential steps

• Explain the procedure to the patient *to ease anxiety and ensure cooperation.* Be sure a consent form has been signed.
• Inform the patient that he may experience headache after lumbar puncture, but reassure him that his cooperation

during the procedure minimizes such an effect. (Note: Sedatives and analgesics are usually withheld before this test if there is evidence of a central nervous system disorder, *because they may mask important symptoms.*)
• Immediately before the procedure, provide privacy and instruct the patient to void.
• Wash your hands thoroughly.
• Open the equipment tray on an overbed table, being careful not to contaminate the sterile field when you open the wrapper.
• Provide adequate lighting at the puncture site, and adjust the height of the patient's bed *to allow the doctor to perform the procedure comfortably.*
• Position the patient (see *Positioning the Patient for Lumbar Puncture,* page 640), and reemphasize the importance of remaining as still as possible *to minimize discomfort and trauma.*
• The doctor cleanses the puncture site with sterile applicators soaked in povidone-iodine solution, wiping in a circular motion away from the puncture site; he uses three different applicators, *to prevent contamination of spinal tissues by the body's normal skin flora.* After allowing the skin to dry, he wipes the area in a similar manner with three alcohol sponges *to remove the povidone-iodine.* Next, he drapes the area with a fenestrated drape *to provide a sterile field.* (If the doctor uses povidone-iodine sponges instead of sterile applicators, he may remove his sterile gloves and put on another pair *to avoid introducing povidone-iodine into the subarachnoid space with the lumbar puncture needle.*)
• If there is no ampul of anesthetic on the equipment tray, cleanse the injection port of a multidose vial of anesthetic with alcohol, and then invert the vial 45° so the doctor can insert a sterile 25G needle and syringe and withdraw the anesthetic for injection.
• Before the doctor injects the anesthetic, tell the patient he'll experience a transient burning sensation and local pain. Ask him to report any other persistent pain or sensations, *because these*

# POSITIONING THE PATIENT FOR LUMBAR PUNCTURE

Have the patient lie on his side at the edge of the bed, with his chin tucked to his chest and his knees drawn up to his abdomen. Make sure the patient's spine is curved and his back is at the edge of the bed, as shown here. This position widens the spaces between the vertebrae, facilitating insertion of the needle.

To help the patient maintain this position, place one of your hands behind his neck and the other hand behind his knees, and pull gently. Hold the patient firmly in this position throughout the procedure, *to prevent accidental needle displacement.*

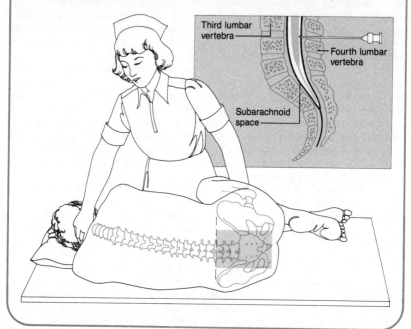

Third lumbar vertebra

Fourth lumbar vertebra

Subarachnoid space

---

may indicate irritation or puncture of a nerve root, requiring repositioning of the needle.

• When the doctor inserts the needle into the subarachnoid space, instruct the patient to remain still and breathe normally. If necessary, hold the patient firmly in position *to prevent sudden movement that may displace the needle.*

• If a lumbar puncture is being performed to administer contrast media for radiologic studies or spinal anesthetic, the doctor injects the dye or anesthetic at this time.

• When the needle is in place, the doctor attaches a manometer with stopcock to the needle hub *to read CSF pressure.* If ordered, help the patient extend his legs to provide a more accurate pressure reading.

• The doctor then detaches the manometer and allows fluid to drain from the needle hub into the collection tubes. When he has collected approximately 2 or 3 ml in each tube, mark the tubes *in sequence,* stopper them securely, and label them properly.

• If the doctor suspects an obstruction in the spinal subarachnoid space, he may check for Queckenstedt's sign. He first takes an initial CSF pressure reading. Then, as ordered, compress the patient's jugular vein for 10 seconds. *This temporarily obstructs blood flow from the cranium, increasing intracranial pressure and, in the absence of a subarach-*

noid block, causing CSF pressure to rise also. The doctor then takes pressure readings every 10 seconds until the pressure stabilizes.

• After the doctor collects the specimens and removes the spinal needle, cleanse the puncture site with povidone-iodine, and apply a small adhesive bandage.

• Send the CSF specimens to the laboratory immediately, with properly completed laboratory request forms.

### Special considerations
During lumbar puncture, watch closely for signs of adverse reaction: elevated pulse rate, pallor, or clammy skin. Alert the doctor immediately to any significant changes.

The patient may be ordered to lie flat for 8 to 12 hours after the procedure. If necessary, place a patient-care reminder on his bed to this effect.

Collected CSF specimens must be sent to the laboratory immediately; they cannot be refrigerated for later transport.

### Complications
Headache is the most common after effect of lumbar puncture. Others may include adverse reaction to the anesthetic, meningitis, epidural or subdural abscess, bleeding into the spinal canal, CSF leakage through the dural defect remaining after needle withdrawal, local pain caused by nerve root irritation, edema or hematoma at the puncture site, transient difficulty in voiding, and fever. The most serious complications of lumbar puncture, though rare, are cerebellar tonsillar herniation and medullary compression.

### Documentation
Record the initiation and completion time of the procedure, the patient's response, the administration of drugs, the number of specimen tubes collected and time of transport to the laboratory, and the color, consistency, and any other characteristics of the collected specimens.

JOANNE PATZEK DACUNHA, RN

## TREATMENT

# Seizure Precautions

*Seizure precautions include padding the side rails, headboard, and footboard of the patient's bed, keeping a padded tongue blade and oral airway handy, and setting up oral suction equipment. These precautions are taken for patients with a history of seizures or a condition that may precipitate seizures, such as hypoglycemia, as well as for patients undergoing therapy, such as electroshock, that may precipitate seizures. Their purpose is to help protect the patient from injury and to maintain a patent airway if a seizure should occur.*

### Equipment
Hospital bed with full-length side rails □ six bath blankets (four for a pediatric crib) □ safety pins □ adhesive tape □ padded tongue blade □ oral airway □ rectal thermometer □ oral suction equipment □ two egg crate mattresses (optional).

### Essential steps
• Explain the reason for the precautions to the patient.

• *To protect the patient's extremities from injury during a seizure,* pad the side rails of the bed with four of the bath blankets. Fold two blankets lengthwise and cover one side rail. (Use one blanket to pad each side rail of a pediatric crib.) Pin the blankets together on the outside of the rail. Then tape the pin *to prevent it from opening accidentally.* Repeat the padding procedure for the opposite side rail. Be sure to keep the padded side rails elevated while the patient is in bed *to prevent falls if he should develop a seizure.*

• *To protect the patient's head from injury during a seizure,* fold the fifth bath blanket into quarters and pad the headboard. Fold the last blanket the same way and pad the footboard *to protect the patient's feet.* Secure the blankets, if necessary, with safety pins or tape. Tape the pins *to prevent them from opening accidentally.*

• Place the padded tongue blade and oral airway at the patient's bedside. Tape them to the headboard or on the wall above the bed *to prevent loss and to keep them handy in an emergency.*

• Take the seizure-prone patient's temperature with a rectal thermometer. *If the patient has a seizure while a thermometer is in his mouth, he could bite and break it, cutting his mouth with glass fragments and possibly—if he should swallow some—injuring his gastrointestinal tract too.*

• Set up the suction equipment. Check equipment daily to make sure it's working properly.

### Special considerations
Make sure you know what to do if the patient has a seizure.

Study the patient's seizure history, if possible. Try to discover what situations, if any, precipitate seizure activity. Find out if the patient experiences an aura that warns him of an impending seizure. The type of aura—auditory, visual, gustatory, olfactory, somatic—helps pinpoint the site in the brain where the seizure originates. The aura may also give the patient time to prepare for the seizure. If you're nearby when the patient experiences an aura, help him into bed and raise the side rails.

Side rails may also be padded with egg crate mattresses. Fold one mattress lengthwise, cover the side rail, and secure the mattress with adhesive tape. Use a second mattress for the other side rail.

### Documentation
Record all seizure precautions taken in the nursing notes.

LORRAINE E. BUCHANAN, RN, MSN

# Transcutaneous Electrical Nerve Stimulator

*A transcutaneous electrical nerve stimulator (TENS) is a portable, battery-powered device that transmits painless electrical impulses to peripheral nerves or directly to a painful area. These impulses block the transmission of pain impulses to the brain. Used for postoperative patients and those with chronic pain, a TENS reduces the need for analgesic drugs and allows the patient to resume normal activities.*

*This device should not be used for patients with cardiac pacemakers, since it can interfere with pacemaker function. A TENS should be used cautiously in all patients with cardiac pathology. This procedure is also contraindicated for pregnant patients because its effect on the fetus is unknown.*

### Equipment
Transcutaneous electrical nerve stimulator □ alcohol sponges □ electrode gel □ electrodes □ adhesive patch or nonallergenic tape □ lead wires □ charged battery pack □ battery recharger.

Commercial TENS kits are available. They include the stimulator, lead wires, electrodes, spare battery pack, battery recharger, and sometimes the adhesive patch. Before the procedure, always test the battery pack to make sure it's fully charged.

### Essential steps
• Wash your hands. Provide privacy. If the patient has never seen a TENS used before, show him the device and explain the procedure.

*Before treatment with TENS:*
• With an alcohol sponge, thoroughly clean the skin where the electrode will be applied. Then dry the skin.
• Apply electrode gel to the bottom of

## HOW T.E.N.S. WORKS

Transcutaneous Electrical Nerve Stimulation (TENS; see photograph) is based on the gate theory of pain, which says painful impulses pass through a so-called gate in the brain. Electrodes placed around the peripheral nerves (or a surgical incision site) transmit a mild electric current, sending painless stimuli to the brain over relatively large nerve fibers. This effectively alters the patient's perception of pain by blocking painful stimuli traveling over smaller fibers. The patient can then determine the amount and frequency of his pain relief by adjusting the intensity and rate controls on the device.

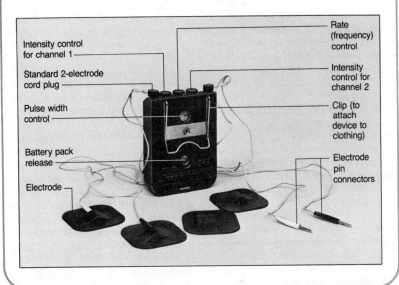

Intensity control for channel 1

Standard 2-electrode cord plug

Pulse width control

Battery pack release

Electrode

Rate (frequency) control

Intensity control for channel 2

Clip (to attach device to clothing)

Electrode pin connectors

each electrode.

• Place the ordered number of electrodes on the skin, leaving at least 2″ (5 cm) between them. Then secure them with the adhesive patch or nonallergenic tape. Tape all sides evenly *so the electrodes are firmly attached to the skin.*

• Plug the pin connectors into the electrode sockets. *To protect the cords,* hold the connectors—not the cords themselves—during insertion.

• Turn the channel controls to the "off" position, or to the position recommended in the operator's manual.

• Plug the lead wires into the jacks in the control box.

• Turn the amplitude and rate dials slowly, as the manual directs. (The patient should feel a tingling sensation.) Then adjust the controls on this device to the prescribed settings or to the settings that are most comfortable.

• Attach the TENS control box to part of the patient's clothing, such as a belt, pocket, or bra.

• *To make sure the device is working effectively,* monitor the patient for signs of excessive stimulation, such as muscular twitches, or signs of inadequate stimulation, signaled by the patient's inability to feel any mild tingling sensation.

*After treatment with TENS:*

• Turn off the controls and unplug the electrode lead wires from the control box.

• If another treatment will be given soon, leave the electrodes in place; if not, remove them.

• Clean the electrodes with soap and water, and cleanse the patient's skin with alcohol sponges. (Don't soak the electrodes in alcohol *since it will damage the rubber.)*

• Remove the battery pack from the unit and replace it with a charged battery pack.

• Recharge the used battery pack *so it's always ready for use.*

### Special considerations

If you must relocate the electrodes during the procedure, turn off the controls first. Follow the doctor's orders regarding electrode placement and control settings. *Incorrect placement of the electrodes will result in inappropriate pain control; setting the controls too high can cause pain, while setting them too low will fail to relieve pain.* Never place the electrodes near the patient's eyes or over the nerves that innervate the carotid sinus or laryngeal or pharyngeal muscles *to avoid interference with critical nerve function.*

Remove the electrodes at least daily *to check for skin irritation and provide skin care.* Also, be sure to keep all equipment clean and out of the reach of children.

If appropriate, let the patient study the operator's manual. Teach him how to place the electrodes properly and how to take care of the TENS unit.

### Documentation

On the patient's medical record and the nursing-care plan, record the electrode sites and the control settings. Also, document the patient's tolerance to treatment and assessment of pain control.

LORRAINE E. BUCHANAN, RN, MSN

# Halo-Vest Traction

*Halo-vest traction immobilizes the head and neck after trauma to the cervical vertebrae, the most common of all spinal injuries. This procedure, which can prevent further injury to the spinal cord, is performed by an orthopedic surgeon with nursing assistance, usually in the emergency department. The halo-vest traction device consists of a metal ring that fits over the the patient's head and metal bars that connect the ring to a plastic vest, which distributes the weight of the entire apparatus around the chest.*

*Once in place, halo-vest traction allows the patient greater mobility than traction with skull tongs. It also carries less risk of infection, because it doesn't require skin incisions and drill holes to position skull pins. There are no contraindications to halo-vest traction, although in life-threatening situations, surgery may be necessary before the apparatus can be applied.*

### Equipment

Halo-vest traction unit □ halo ring □ plastic vest □ cervical collar or sand bags (if needed) □ board or padded headrest □ tape measure □ halo ring conversion chart □ scissors and razor □ 4″ x 4″ gauze sponges □ povidone-iodine solution □ sterile gloves □ Allen wrench □ four positioning pins □ multiple dose vial of 1% lidocaine (with or without epinephrine) □ alcohol sponges □ sterile 3-ml syringe □ sterile 25G needles □ five sterile skull pins (including one spare) □ torque screwdriver □ sheepskin liners □ cotton-tipped applicators □ hydrogen peroxide solution □ sterile water or normal saline solution □ medicated powder or corn-starch □ hair dryer (optional).

Most hospitals supply packaged halo-vest traction units that include software (the jacket, sheepskin liners), hardware (the halo, head pins, upright bars, screws), and tools (torque screwdriver, the two conventional wrenches and the Allen wrench, with screws and bolts). These units don't include sterile gloves, povidone-iodine solution, sterile drapes, cervical collars or equipment for injection of local anesthetic.

### Preparation of equipment

Obtain a halo-vest traction unit with halo rings and plastic vests in several different sizes. Check the expiration date of the prepackaged tray and check outside covering for damage *to assure the sterility of the contents.* Then assemble the equipment at the patient's bedside.

## Essential steps

• Check the support that was applied to the patient's neck on the way to the hospital. If necessary, apply the cervical collar immediately or immobilize the head and neck with sandbags. Keep the cervical collar or sand bags in place until the halo is applied. This support is then carefully removed *to facilitate application of the vest.* Since the patient is likely to be frightened, try to reassure him.

• Remove the headboard and any furniture at the head of the bed *to provide ample working space.* Then carefully place the patient's head on a board or on a padded headrest that extends beyond the edge of the bed.

Never put the patient's head on a pillow before applying the halo *to avoid transection of the spinal cord.*

• Stand at the head of the bed and see if the patient's chin lines up with his midsternum, *indicating proper alignment.* If necessary, support the patient's head in your hands and gently rotate the neck into alignment without flexing or extending it.

*To assist with application of the halo:*

• Ask another nurse to help you with the procedure.

• Explain the procedure to the patient, wash your hands, and provide privacy.

• Hold the patient's head and neck stable while the doctor removes the cervical collar or sand bags. Provide this support until the halo is secure, while another nurse assists with pin insertion.

• The doctor first measures the patient's head and refers to the halo ring conversion chart to determine the correct ring size. (The ring should clear the head by 1.5 cm and fit 1 cm above the bridge of the nose.)

• The doctor selects four pin sites: 1 cm above the lateral one third of each eyebrow and 1 cm above the top of each ear in the occipital area.

• Trim and shave the hair at the pin sites *to facilitate subsequent care and help prevent infection.* Then, use 4″ x 4″ gauze sponges soaked in povidone-iodine solution to cleanse the sites.

---

### TREATING THE PATIENT WITH A SPINAL INJURY

Hasty or improper care of the patient with a spinal injury can cause irreparable cord damage and permanent disability. To help minimize or avoid further injury to the cord and vertebrae, follow these guidelines:

• If the patient has a head or neck injury, or multiple trauma, assume that his spine is also injured until X-rays either rule out or confirm this possibility.

• Immobilize the patient on a board or firm stretcher in the position in which you find him. Use sandbags to immobilize the head and neck. Don't change the patient's position unless his life is endangered (by a fire or imminent explosion, for example).

• Ensure a patent airway and monitor respirations closely. Remember, injury to the cervical spine can affect the diaphragm and the intercostal muscles that control respirations. Watch for rapid, shallow respirations with flaring of the nostrils.

• Once the patient is in the hospital, set up equipment for emergency tracheostomy, mechanical ventilation, and suction.

• Monitor the patient's blood pressure. Anticipate spinal shock—a neurovascular shutdown response to spinal trauma—characterized by hypothermia, flaccid paralysis below the injury level, and hypotension.

• Insert an indwelling catheter, as ordered, because the patient's bladder will be atonic.

• Before X-rays establish the diagnosis, take neurologic vital signs to help assess the severity of the injury. Also, question the patient, his family, or whoever accompanied him about the details of the accident that caused the injury.

LORRAINE E. BUCHANAN, RN, MSN

---

• Open the halo-vest unit using sterile technique *to avoid contamination.* The doctor puts on the sterile gloves and removes the halo and the Allen wrench. He then places the halo over the patient's head and inserts the four positioning pins *to hold the halo in place temporarily.*

• Help the doctor prepare the anesthetic. First, cleanse the injection port of the multiple vial of lidocaine with the alcohol sponge. Then, invert the vial so the doctor can insert a 25G needle attached to the 3-ml syringe, and withdraw the anesthetic.

• The doctor injects the anesthetic at the four pin sites. He may change needles on the syringe after each injection. (If the patient's skin becomes taut, have him close his eyes tightly *to relax the skin.*)

• The doctor removes four of the five skull pins from the sterile setup and firmly screws in each pin at a 90° angle to the skull. When the pins are in place, he removes the positioning pins. He then tightens the skull pins with the torque screwdriver.

*To apply the vest:*

• After the doctor measures the patient's chest and abdomen, he selects on appropriate-sized vest.

• Place the sheepskin liners inside both the front and back of the vest *to make it more comfortable to wear and to help prevent decubiti.*

• Help the doctor carefully raise the patient while another nurse supports the head and neck. Slide the back of the vest under the patient and gently lay him down. The doctor then fastens the front of the vest on the patient's chest using Velcro straps.

• The doctor attaches the metal bars to the halo and vest and tightens each bolt in turn. Once halo-vest traction is in place, X-rays are taken immediately *to check the depth of the skull pins and verify proper alignment.*

*To care for the patient:*

• Take routine and neurologic vital signs at least every 2 hours for 24 hours, and then every 4 hours until stable.

Notify the doctor immediately if your observations include any loss of motor function or any decreased sensation, *which could indicate spinal cord trauma.*

• Gently cleanse the pin sites every 4 hours with the cotton-tipped applicators dipped in hydrogen peroxide solution. Rinse the sites with sterile water or sterile normal saline solution *to remove excess hydrogen perioxde.* Then cleanse the pin sites with povidone-iodine solution. *Meticulous pin site care prevents*

*infection and removes debris that might block drainage and lead to abscess formation.* Watch for signs of infection—a loose pin, swelling or redness, purulent drainage, pain at the site—and notify the doctor if these signs develop.

• The doctor retightens the skull pins with the torque screwdriver 24 hours after the halo is applied. If the patient complains of a headache after the pins are tightened, obtain an order for an analgesic.

• Examine the halo-vest unit every shift *to make sure that everything is secure and that the patient's head is centered within the halo.*

• Wash the patient's chest and back daily. First, loosen the bottom Velcro straps *so you can get to the chest and back.* Then, reaching under the vest, wash and dry the skin. Be careful not to put any stress on the apparatus, *which could knock it out of alignment, and lead to subluxation or severance of the cervical spine.* Check for tender, reddened areas or pressure spots that may develop into decubiti. If necessary, use a hair dryer to dry damp sheepskin *since moisture predisposes the skin to decubitus formation.* Lightly dust the skin with medicated powder or cornstarch *to prevent itching.* If itching persists, check to see if the patient is allergic to sheepskin and if any drug he's taking might cause a skin rash. If the institution's policy allows, change the vest lining, as necessary.

## Special considerations

Keep two conventional wrenches taped to the front of the vest at all times. In the event of cardiac arrest, detach these wrenches, remove the distal anterior bolts, and pull the two upright bars outward. Then unfasten the Velcro straps and remove the front of the vest. Use the sturdy back of the vest as a board for cardiopulmonary resuscitation (CPR). *To prevent subluxating the cervical injury,* start CPR with the jaw thrust, which avoids hyperextension of the neck. Pull the patient's mandible forward, while maintaining proper head and neck alignment. *This pulls the tongue forward to open* the airway for performance of CPR.

Never lift the patient up by the vertical bars. *This could strain or tear the skin at the pin sites, or misalign the traction.*

To prevent falls, walk with the ambulatory patient. Remember, he'll have trouble seeing objects at or near his feet, and the weight of the halo-vest unit may throw him off balance.

### Complications

Manipulating the patient's neck during application of halo-vest traction may cause subluxation, and possible transection of the spinal cord, or it may push a bony fragment into the spinal cord. If the fragment severs the cord at the fourth cervical vertebra, it can paralyze the diaphragm and chest wall, causing fatal respiratory failure unless respiratory support is given immediately.

Inaccurate positioning of the skull pins can lead to a puncture of the dura mater, causing a loss of cerebrospinal fluid and usually a central nervous system infection. Nonsterile technique during application of the halo or inadequate pin site care can also lead to infection at the pin sites. Pressure sores can develop if the vest fits poorly or its edges rub.

### Documentation

Record the date and time the halo-vest traction was applied. Also note the length of the procedure and the patient's response. After application, record routine and neurologic vital signs. Document pin site care and note any signs of infection.

KRISTEN KINDEL, RN

# Care of Skull Tongs

*Applying skeletal traction with skull tongs immobilizes the cervical spine after a fracture or dislocation, invasion by tumor or infection, or surgery. Three types of skull tongs are commonly used: Crutchfield, Gardner-Wells, and Vinke. Once the tongs are in place, traction is created by extending a rope from the center of the tongs over a pulley and attaching weights to it. With the help of X-ray monitoring, the weights are then adjusted to establish reduction, if necessary, and to maintain alignment without excessive tractive force. Nursing care of the patient with skull tongs requires meticulous pin site care to prevent infection and frequent observation of the tractive apparatus to make sure it's working properly.*

### Equipment

Three medicine cups □ one bottle each of hydrogen peroxide, normal saline solution, and povidone-iodine solution □ cotton-tipped applicators □ sandbags or cervical collar (hard or soft) □ strips of fine mesh gauze □ 4″ x 4″ gauze sponge □ sterile gloves □ sterile basin □ sterile scissors.

### Preparation of equipment

Bring the equipment to the patient's room. Place the medicine cups on the bedside table. Fill one cup with a small amount of hydrogen peroxide, one with normal saline solution, and one with povidone-iodine solution. Then set out the cotton-tipped applicators. Keep the sandbags or cervical collar handy for emergency immobilization of the head and neck if the pins in the tongs should slip.

### Essential steps

• Explain the procedure to the patient. Wash your hands. Inform the patient that pin sites usually feel tender for several days after the tongs are applied.

• Before providing care, observe each pin site carefully for signs of infection, such as loose pins, swelling or redness, purulent drainage, or pain. Trim the patient's hair around the pin sites, when necessary, *to facilitate assessment and care.*

• Gently swab each pin site with hydrogen peroxide *to loosen and remove crusty drainage.* Repeat with a fresh cotton-tipped applicator, as needed, for thorough cleansing. Use a separate one for each site *to avoid cross-contamination.*

## SKULL TONGS

All three types of cervical tongs consist of a stainless steel body with a pin (about ⅛" [0.3 cm] in diameter with a sharp tip) attached at each end. The pins on *Crutchfield tongs* are placed about 5" (12.7 cm) apart in line with the long axis of the cervical spine. The pins on the *Gardner-Wells tongs* are farther apart, with the pins inserted slightly above the patient's ears. The pins on *Vinke tongs* are placed at the parietal bones, near the widest transverse diameter of the skull, about 1" (2.54 cm) above the helix.

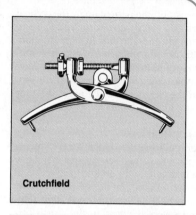

**Crutchfield**

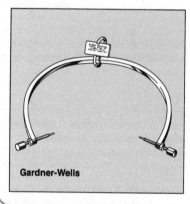

**Gardner-Wells**

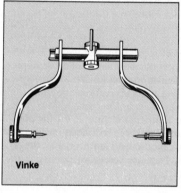

**Vinke**

Swab each site with normal saline solition *to remove excess hydrogen peroxide.* Finally, swab with povidone-iodine *to provide antisepsis at the site and prevent infection.*

● After providing care, discard the medicine cups with any remaining solutions, and used cotton-tipped applicators. Provide pin site care once every shift.

● If the pin sites are infected, apply a povidone-iodine wrap, as ordered. First, obtain strips of fine mesh gauze, or cut a 4" x 4" gauze sponge into strips (using sterile scissors and wearing sterile gloves). Soak the strips in a sterile basin of povidone-iodine solution, and then squeeze out the excess solution. Wrap one strip securely around each pin site. Leave the strip in place to dry until you provide care again. *Removing the dried strip aids debridement and helps clear the infection.*

● Check the tractive apparatus—ropes, weights, pulleys—at the start of each shift, every 4 hours, and as necessary (for example, after position changes). Make sure the rope hangs freely, and that the weights never rest on the floor or become caught under the bed.

### Special considerations

Occasionally, the doctor may prefer an antibacterial ointment for pin site care instead of povidone-iodine solution. *To remove old ointment,* wrap a cotton-tipped applicator with a 4" x 4" gauze sponge, moisten it with hydrogen peroxide, and gently cleanse each site. Keep a box of sterile gauze sponges handy at the patient's bedside.

Watch for signs of loose pins, such as persistent pain or tenderness at pin sites, redness, and drainage. The patient may also report feeling or hearing the pins move. If you suspect a pin has become loose and has slipped, don't turn the patient until the doctor examines the skull tongs and rules this out.

If the pins pull out, carefully remove the traction weights. Immobilize the patient's head and neck with sandbags or apply a cervical collar. Apply manual traction to his head by placing your hands on each side of the mandible and pulling gently, while maintaining proper alignment. Have someone send for the doctor immediately. Once traction is reestablished, take neurologic vital signs.

 Never add or subtract weights to the tractive apparatus without an order by the doctor. *This can cause a neurologic impairment.* Take neurologic vital signs at the beginning of each shift, every 4 hours, and as necessary (for example, after turning or transporting the patient). Carefully assess the function of cranial nerves VI, XI, and XII. These nerve tracts may be impaired by pin placement. To check cranial nerve VI, ask the patient to move his eyes laterally. To check cranial nerve XI, ask him to contract the sternocleidomastoid and trapezius muscles; for cranial nerve XII, ask him to stick out his tongue. Note any asymmetry, deviation or atrophy. Review the patient's chart to determine baseline neurologic vital signs on admission to the hospital and immediately after the tongs were applied.

Monitor respirations closely and keep suction equipment handy. Remember, injury to the cervical spine may affect respirations. So be alert for signs of respiratory distress, such as unequal chest expansion and an irregular or altered respiratory rate or pattern.

Patients with skull tongs may be placed on a turning frame *to facilitate turning without disrupting vertebral alignment.* Establish a turning schedule for the patient—usually a supine position for 2 hours, and then a prone position for 1 hour—*to help prevent complications of immobility.*

## Complications

Infection, excessive tractive force, or osteoporosis can cause the skull pins to slip or pull out. Since this interrupts traction, the patient must receive immediate attention to prevent further injury.

## Documentation

Record the date, time, and type of pin site care, and the patient's response to the procedure in your notes. Describe any signs of infection. Also, note if any weights were added or subtracted. Record neurologic vital signs and the patient's respiratory status. Include the patient's turning schedule and pin site care on the cardex.

THERESE ALTIER, RN, BSN

## Selected References

Barnett, Dale C., and Hair, Barbara. "Use and Effectiveness of Transcutaneous Electrical Nerve Stimulation in Pain Management," *Journal of Neurosurgical Nursing* 13:323, December 1981.

Lyons, Marilyn. "Recognition of Neurological Dysfunction," *Nurse Practitioner* 4:34, September 1979.

Mitchell, Pamela, and Mauss, Nancy. "Intracranial Pressure: Fact and Fancy," *Nursing76* 6:53, June 1976.

Ramirez, Beth. "When You're Faced With a Neuro Patient," *RN* 42:67, January 1979.

Stryker, Ruth. *Rehabilitative Aspects of Acute and Chronic Nursing Care,* 2nd ed. Philadelphia: W.B. Saunders Co., 1977.

Swift, Nancy, with Mabel, Robert M. *Manual of Neurological Nursing.* Boston: Little, Brown & Co., 1978.

Warner, Carmen Germaine. *Emergency Care: Assessment and Intervention.* St. Louis: C.V. Mosby Co., 1978.

Wilson, Susan Fickertt. *Neuronursing.* New York: Springer Publishing Co., 1979.

# 13 Orthopedic Care

# Orthopedic Care

## Introduction

Orthopedics began as a specialty for the prevention and treatment of children's musculoskeletal deformities. However, this branch of medicine has expanded dramatically so that it now includes the prevention, treatment, and care of musculoskeletal conditions affecting patients of all ages.

### Challenges: Old and new

Orthopedic nursing has traditionally required considerable mechanical aptitude for the operation of special mechanical and electrical beds, frames, turning devices, and traction equipment. Now, it also requires that you understand principles of internal and external fixation, prosthetics, orthotics, immobilization, and implantation.

Despite the complex surgical procedures and mechanical devices that characterize modern orthopedic care, some things remain the same. A patient hospitalized for any orthopedic procedure—whether it's cast application, traction, or arthroplasty—is vulnerable to the same complications: *joint stiffness* from immobilization; *decubiti; fractures* from mishandling of osteoporotic extremities; *neurovascular compromise* from pressure over major blood vessels and nerves caused by immobilization devices; *infection* of surgical wounds or skeletal pin tracts; and *prolonged healing time* from failure to observe sound principles of immobilization.

### Consistency: Key consideration

Without exception, these complications can be prevented or minimized by performing the appropriate diagnostic, monitoring, or therapeutic procedure correctly and *consistently*. For example, it's essential to assess the orthopedic patient's neurovascular status at regular intervals; otherwise, signs and symptoms of neurovascular compromise may go undetected until irreversible damage results. Consistent orthopedic care remains the surest way to promote rapid healing and successful rehabilitation.

### Emergency care: Basic steps

A unique aspect of orthopedic nursing care is the high incidence of emergency procedures that you're likely to perform. The first step—always—in administering emergency care at the scene of an accident is immediate assessment for a life-threatening condition. Unless an imminent danger exists, do not move the patient, since this might worsen his injury and pain. If such a danger does threaten the patient, try to check for spinal injury before moving him to a safe area. After assessing for potentially fatal complications, begin the initial assessment of the injury. Always evaluate neurovascular status. (Check for the five P's: *pain, pallor, pulse, paresthesia,* and *paralysis.*) After assessing the injury thoroughly, administer treatment. Apply a clean or sterile dressing to all open wounds to prevent infection. If you suspect bone injury, apply a splint to reduce trauma and immobilize the injury for safe transport.

NANCY E. HILT, RN, BSN, MSN

## DIAGNOSIS AND MONITORING

# Arthrocentesis

*Arthrocentesis is the puncture and aspiration of synovial fluid or blood from a joint, usually the knee, elbow, or shoulder. Performed by a doctor under strict aseptic technique, arthrocentesis may be used to draw a specimen for diagnostic tests, including a culture, cytologic examination, or glucose analysis. When used for diagnosis, arthrocentesis may be performed with two related procedures:* arthrography, *an X-ray that shows joint tissue and structure, and* arthroscopy, *an endoscopic procedure that allows direct visualization of the joint.*

*This procedure may also be performed to relieve pain from fluid accumulation or to administer drugs, especially corticosteroids. A nurse may assist with the procedure, which can be performed in the doctor's office or the patient's bedside. Contraindications for arthrocentesis include infection at the intended puncture site or a septic joint.*

## Equipment

Gloves □ alcohol sponges □ 2″ x 2″ gauze pads □ cotton-tipped applicators □ povidone-iodine solution □ 20G spinal, 18G and 20G 1½″, and 22G 1″ needles for aspiration and drug injection □ disposable 3-, 10-, and 20-ml syringes for aspiration and drug injection □ adhesive strips □ optional: prescribed drugs, local anesthetic (ethyl chloride spray or 1% lidocaine), 25G ½″ needle for anesthetic injection, elastic bandage, Thayer-Martin medium or culture tubes for a culture, plain or heparinized tubes for cytologic examination, tubes with fluoride for glucose analysis, and laboratory slips.

The cotton-tipped applicators, gloves, 2″ x 2″ gauze pads, syringes, and needles must be sterile. The different needles are necessary to ensure that the doctor will have one that is sufficiently long to penetrate the joint capsule.

## Preparation of equipment

If a drug is to be injected, prepare the dosage, as ordered.

## Essential steps

● Explain the procedure to the patient, provide privacy, and wash your hands.
● Position the patient as ordered.
● Open sterile packages and unscrew the bottle cap of the povidone-iodine solution.
● Put on the sterile gloves.
● With the alcohol sponges, clean an area about 3″ (7.6 cm) in diameter at the aspiration site *to reduce the risk of infection.*
● Dry the area with 2″ x 2″ gauze pads.
● With a sterile cotton-tipped applicator, apply the povidone-iodine solution to the same area *to further minimize the risk of infection.*
● Allow the area to dry for about 2 minutes.
● If ordered, spray the area with ethyl chloride *to anesthetize the tissue surrounding the aspiration site.* (The doctor may inject 1% lidocaine instead of ordering an ethyl chloride spray.)
● The doctor then inserts the appropriate needle and aspirates the synovial fluid. To inject a drug, he'll leave the needle in the joint, detach the fluid-filled syringe, attach a syringe containing the drug, and inject it.
● After the doctor withdraws the needle, cleanse the area with povidone-iodine solution.
● Apply direct pressure to the site for 5 minutes; then apply a 2″ x 2″ gauze pad and secure the pad with adhesive strips *to prevent excessive bleeding.* (After aspiration of a large amount of fluid from a weight-bearing joint, apply an elastic bandage *to enhance stability and reduce additional fluid formation.*
● *For synovial fluid analysis,* assist the doctor as he injects fluid into the culture medium or appropriate tube. Note on the laboratory slips and the tubes the

time and date, the joint, the type of fluid, and the tests ordered. Send the specimen to the laboratory immediately.

• Tell the patient to notify the doctor or the nurse if he experiences increased pain, redness, or swelling at the joint.

### Special considerations
Maintain strict aseptic technique during the procedure *to avoid infecting the joint or contaminating the synovial fluid or blood specimen.*

### Complications
Complications after arthrocentesis may include infection, septic arthritis, intra-articular or soft tissue hemorrhage, tendon rupture, and temporary nerve palsy.

### Documentation
In the nurse's notes, record the time and date, the joint, the amount of fluid aspirated, and how well the patient tolerated the procedure. Describe the condition of the aspiration site, noting any swelling, bleeding, or contusions. For synovial fluid analysis, record the tests ordered and the time the specimen was sent to the laboratory. For drug therapy, specify the amount and type of medication given.

KATHY A. FONDA, RN, BSN

# Tissue Pressure Monitoring

*By measuring the pressure in fascia-enclosed compartments, this procedure can detect compartmental syndrome in patients who have experienced soft tissue trauma. Tissue pressure monitoring is indicated when signs and symptoms of compartmental syndrome occur; these include pain, pallor, swelling, paresthesia, tingling, progressive loss of motion, palpable tenderness over the compartment, and especially pain with passive motion. This procedure is particularly* *useful when the patient can't report symptoms of compartmental syndrome or when multiple injuries complicate the clinical picture.*

*Although a specially trained nurse may perform this procedure, a doctor usually performs it, with a nurse assisting. When tissue pressure monitoring confirms compartmental syndrome, the doctor performs an emergency fasciotomy to decompress the compartment. This relieves pressure on microvascular structures and halts destruction of microcirculation and ischemia of nerves and muscles before they cause necrosis.*

### Equipment
Three-way stopcock □ two lengths of I.V. extension tubing □ mercury manometer □ two 18G needles □ 20-ml syringe □ vial of sterile normal saline for injection □ alcohol sponges □ three povidone-iodine sponges □ sterile gloves □ 3-ml syringe with 21G or 23G needle filled with 1% lidocaine □ small adhesive bandage (optional).

### Preparation of equipment
First, make sure the stopcock allows all three ports to be open at the same time. Connect one length of I.V. extension tubing to each of the two opposing ports of the stopcock. Attach the manometer to one length of extension tubing and an 18G needle to the other. Place the 20-ml syringe in the third port of the stopcock. Open the stopcock between the syringe and the extension tubing connected to the needle. Wipe the top of the sterile saline vial with an alcohol sponge and insert the second 18G needle into it as an air vent. Insert the needle attached to the extension tubing through the top of the vial and into the saline. Then pull back on the syringe plunger to withdraw enough saline to fill half of the tubing. The meniscus—the curved line where air and saline meet—should be visible. Open the stopcock to the syringe and both lengths of extension tubing (see *Equipment Setup for Tissue Pressure Monitoring*, page 654).

# EQUIPMENT SETUP FOR TISSUE PRESSURE MONITORING

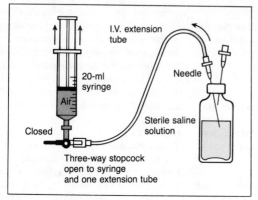

To measure tissue pressure, set up the equipment as shown at left. Insert the needle into the fascia and create a closed system, as shown below, so the air is free to flow into both tubes as the pressure inside the tubes rises.

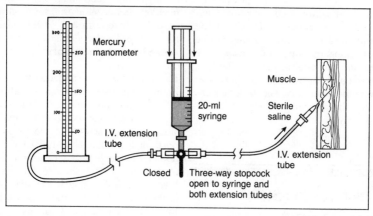

## Essential steps
• Explain the procedure to the patient and wash your hands thoroughly.
• Gently wipe the patient's skin with the povidone-iodine sponges, using a spiral motion from the injection site to its periphery. Allow the skin to air-dry.
• The doctor then puts on the sterile gloves and injects the 1% lidocaine subcutaneously *to anesthetize the area.*
• The doctor removes the needle from the vial and inserts it into the skin at slightly less than a 45° angle to the sur-

face until it reaches the appropriate compartment (see illustration above). The exact site depends on the patient and on the compartment. For the hand, he may use the palmar or dorsal surface of the interosseous muscles; for the forearm, the midarm and midextensor area; for the anterior or deep posterior compartments of the lower leg, the anterior lateral aspect or midline of the lower leg along the distal tibia.
• The doctor slowly depresses the syringe plunger while observing the me-

niscus in the tubing. When the meniscus moves, indicating that a small amount of saline has entered the tissue, he will stop pushing the plunger. If the fluid won't move through the tubing, the needle may be blocked by tissue. The doctor may withdraw the needle and begin again, or he may slowly increase the pressure until it dislodges the tissue. When the meniscus moves, he withdraws the plunger *to avoid injecting too much fluid into the compartment.*

• When the fluid passes into the tissue, read and record the tissue pressure registered on the manometer.

• *To confirm this reading,* the doctor measures the tissue pressure again. He withdraws the plunger slightly *to reduce the pressure,* repositions the needle, and depresses the plunger.

• When fluid begins to move into the compartment again, record the manometer reading.

• After the doctor withdraws the plunger and removes the needle, apply a small adhesive bandage, as needed.

**Special considerations**
Usually, pressures that exceed 30 mmHg in the hand or forearm or 40 to 50 mmHg in the leg and that persist for a few hours indicate the need for emergency fasciotomy. Pressures usually peak about 40 hours after the initial injury. Microcirculation stops completely when tissue pressure equals diastolic blood pressure. Continuous monitoring (for up to 72 hours) using a wick catheter and pressure transducer—such as those used for cranial pressure monitoring—measures interstitial fluid pressure directly. This procedure is performed in a critical care unit or a similarly equipped setting.

**Complications**
Common complications include those associated with intramuscular injections: sterile abscess formation and tissue fibrosis.

**Documentation**
Record the date and time of the procedure, measurement sites, tissue pressure readings, any further treatment, any complications and the nursing action taken, and the patient's tolerance for the procedure.

SUSAN M. GLOVER, RN, BSN

## TREATMENT

# Rigid or Traction Splints

A splint immobilizes the site of an injury so that the patient can be transported without further damage to muscles, nerves, blood vessels, and skin. It also helps avoid excessive bleeding into tissues, restricted blood flow from the pressure of a bone, and paralysis from a spinal cord injury. By minimizing movement, a splint also alleviates pain and allows the injury to heal properly.

A splint can be applied to immobilize a simple or compound fracture, a dislocation, or a subluxation. A rigid splint can be used to immobilize a fracture or dislocation in an extremity. A spineboard, applied for a suspected spinal fracture, is a rigid splint that supports the injured person's entire body. Ideally, two people should apply a rigid splint for an extremity; three people should apply a spineboard. A traction splint immobilizes a fracture and exerts a longitudinal pull, which reduces muscle spasms, pain, and arterial and neural damage. Used primarily for femoral fractures, a traction splint may also be applied for a fractured hip or tibia. Two trained people should apply a traction splint.

No contraindications exist for applying a rigid splint; traction splints are

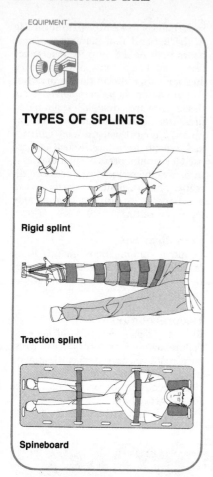

EQUIPMENT

## TYPES OF SPLINTS

**Rigid splint**

**Traction splint**

**Spineboard**

*contraindicated for upper extremity injuries and open fractures. During an emergency, any injury that might be a fracture, dislocation, or subluxation should be splinted.*

### Equipment
Rigid splint, spineboard, or traction splint □ bindings □ padding □ sandbags or rolled towels or clothing □ optional: sterile or clean compresses, ice.

Several commercial splints are available. In an emergency, any long, sturdy object, such as a tree limb, mop handle, or broom—even a magazine or newspaper—can be used to make a rigid splint for an extremity; a door can be used as a spineboard. The most common trac-

tion splints are the Thomas and the Hare. Velcro straps, 2″ roller gauze, or 2″ cloth strips can be used as bindings. When improvising, avoid using twine or rope, if possible, *since they can restrict circulation.*

### Essential steps
• If you're at the scene of an accident, outside the hospital, don't move the patient unless he's in imminent danger, as from a fire or a potential explosion. If possible, check for a spinal injury before moving the patient by asking him to describe and locate the pain. If an imminent danger threatens the patient, move him as though he has a spinal cord injury. Then assess his condition.
• Obtain a complete history of the injury and begin a complete and careful examination by inspecting for obvious deformities, swelling, or bleeding. Determine if the patient can move his extremities. Gently palpate the extremities and spine; inspect for swelling, discoloration, and evidence of fracture or dislocation.
• If an obvious bone malalignment is causing acute distress or severe neurovascular problems, realign the extremity. Check neurovascular integrity distal to the injury site before, during, and after realigning the extremity. Stop the realignment if it causes further neurovascular deterioration. Don't attempt to straighten a dislocation, *because movement may damage displaced vessels and nerves.* Also, don't attempt reduction of a contaminated bone end, *because this may cause additional laceration of soft tissues, vessels, and nerves and gross contamination of deep tissues.*
• Explain the procedure to the patient *to allay his fears.* Remove or cut away clothing from the injury site. For an injured extremity, check neurovascular integrity distal to the injury site.
• Choose a splint that will immobilize the joints above and below the fracture; pad the splint as necessary *to prevent excessive pressure over bony prominences.*
• *For an open wound,* remove only gross

matter on the surrounding skin surface. Don't try to remove debris embedded in the wound. *For an open wound or compound fracture, apply a sterile or clean compress to stop bleeding.* (If one isn't available, use any clean cloth.)

*To apply a rigid splint:*
• Support the injured extremity and apply firm, gentle traction.
• Have an assistant place the splint under, beside, or on top of the extremity.
• Tell the assistant to apply the bindings *to secure the splint.* Make sure they don't obstruct circulation.

*To apply a spineboard:*
• Pad the spineboard (or door) carefully, especially those areas which will support the lumbar region and knees, *to prevent uneven pressure and discomfort.*
• If the patient is in a supine position, logroll him onto the board. Place one hand on each side of his head and apply gentle traction to the head and neck, keeping the head aligned with the body. Have one assistant roll the patient toward him, while another slides the spineboard under the patient. Then instruct the assistants to roll the patient onto the board, while you maintain traction and alignment.
• If the patient is prone, logroll him onto the board in a supine position.
• *To maintain body alignment,* use strips of cloth to secure the patient on the spineboard; *to keep head and neck aligned,* place sandbags or rolled towels or clothes on both sides of the head.

*To apply a traction splint:*
• Place the splint beside the injured leg. Adjust it to the correct length, and then open and adjust the Velcro straps.
• Have an assistant keep the leg motionless, while you pad the ankle and foot and fasten the ankle hitch around them. (You may leave the shoe on.)
• Tell the assistant to lift and support the leg at the injury site, as you apply firm, gentle traction.
• While you maintain traction, instruct the assistant to slide the splint under the leg, pad the groin *to avoid excessive pressure on external geni-*

*talia,* and gently apply the ischial strap.
• Then have the assistant connect the loops of the ankle hitch to the end of the splint.
• Adjust the splint to apply enough traction *to secure the leg comfortably in the corrected position.*
• After applying traction, fasten the Velcro support splints *to secure the leg closely to the splint.*

 Don't use a traction splint for a severely angulated femur or knee fracture. Also, never use a traction splint on an arm, *because the major axillary plexus of nerves and blood*

---

## HOW TO ASSESS NEUROVASCULAR STATUS

Many orthopedic procedures—including splint application, cast care, and arthroplasty care—require that you assess the neurovascular status of the affected extremity. When performing such an assessment, always check the affected extremity for the following characteristics and compare your findings bilaterally:
• Inspect the *color* of the fingers or toes.
• To detect edema, note the *size* of the digits.
• Simultaneously touch the digits of the affected and unaffected extremities and compare the *temperature.*
• Check *capillary refill* by pressing on the distal tip of one digit until it's white. Then release the pressure and note how soon the normal color returns. For both the affected and the unaffected extremities, color should return quickly.
• Check *sensation* by touching the fingers or toes and asking the patient how they feel. Note any numbness or tingling.
• To check *proprioception,* tell the patient to close his eyes; then move one digit and ask him which position it's in.
• To test *movement* of the digits, tell the patient to wiggle his toes or move his fingers.
• Palpate the *distal pulses* to assess vascular patency.

Record your findings for the affected and the unaffected extremities, using standard terminology to avoid ambiguities. Warmth, free movement, rapid capillary refill, and normal color, sensation, and proprioception indicate good neurovascular status.

KATHLEEN GALLAGHER, RN, BSN, MSN

## AIR SPLINT APPLICATION

In an emergency, an air splint can be applied to immobilize a fracture or control bleeding, especially from a forearm or lower leg. Because of its compactness and comfort, this relatively new, soft splint is considered the most convenient splinting device available. Made of double-walled plastic, it provides gentle, diffuse pressure over an injured area; this may actually control bleeding better than a local pressure bandage. The clear plastic simplifies inspection of the affected site for bleeding, pallor, or cyanosis. An air splint also allows the patient to be moved without further damage to the injured limb.

*vessels can't tolerate countertraction.*

### Special considerations

At the scene of an accident, always examine the patient completely for other injuries. Avoid unnecessary movement or manipulation, *since it may cause additional pain or injury.* Base your emergency treatment of multiple injuries on the following priorities: clearing the airway, controlling hemorrhage, managing shock, evaluating neurovascular complications, and immobilizing fractures.

Always consider the possibility of cervical injury in an unconscious patient. If possible, apply the splint before repositioning the patient.

If the patient requires a rigid splint but one isn't available, use another body part as a splint. To splint a leg in this manner, pad its inner aspect and secure it to the other leg with roller gauze or cloth strips.

After applying any type of splint, monitor vital signs frequently, *since bleeding from inside fractured bones and surrounding tissues may cause shock.* Also monitor the neurologic and circulatory status of the fractured limb by assessing skin color and checking for numbness in the fingers or toes. Numbness or paralysis distal to the injury indicates pressure on nerves. Transport the patient as soon as possible to a medical facility. Apply

ice to the injury. Regardless of the apparent extent of the patient's injury, don't allow him to eat or drink anything until the doctor evaluates him.

Indications for removal of a splint include evidence of improper application or vascular impairment. Apply gentle traction and remove the splint carefully under a doctor's direct supervision.

Remember these three rules for treating open soft-tissue wounds: control bleeding, prevent further contamination, and immobilize the area.

### Complications

Multiple transfers and repeated manipulation of a fracture may result in *fat embolism,* indicated by shortness of breath, agitation, and irrational behavior.

### Documentation

On a flow sheet, record the cause of the injury and the circumstances surrounding it. Document the patient's complaints, noting whether or not symptoms are localized. Also, record neurologic and vascular status before and after applying the splint. Note the type of wound and the amount and type of drainage. Document the time of splint application and note if the bone end spontaneously slips into tissue or if transportation causes any change in the degree of dislocation.

DIANA BILLMAN, RN, BSN

# Triangular Slings

*Made from a triangular bandage of muslin, canvas, or cotton, a sling supports and immobilizes an injured arm, wrist, or hand, and thus facilitates healing. It may be applied to restrict movement of a fracture or dislocation or to support a muscle sprain. A sling can also support the weight of a splint or help secure dressings.*

## Equipment

Triangular bandage □ safety pins (tape for children under age 7).

Many commercial slings are available, including models that provide additional support for preexisting conditions, such as paralysis from a cerebrovascular accident.

## Essential steps

• Explain the procedure to the patient and wash your hands thoroughly.

• If the patient is a child, fold the bandage in half—*to make a smaller triangle*—before proceeding.

• Place the apex of the triangular bandage behind the elbow on the affected side. Then, extend one end of the bandage up toward the neck and let the other end hang straight down so the bandage's longest side parallels the midline of the patient's body.

• Take the upper end of the bandage and loop it over the shoulder on the uninjured side and around the back of the patient's neck. Drape it over the shoulder on the injured side.

• Help the patient gently flex his elbow *so the forearm and upper arm form an approximate right angle, with the thumb pointing up.*

• Bring the lower end of the bandage over the forearm and up to the shoulder on the injured side.

• Adjust the bandage so that the forearm and upper arm form an angle of slightly less than 90° *to increase venous return from the hand and forearm* and *to facilitate drainage from swelling.*

• Tie the two bandage ends at the side of the neck *to prevent neck flexion and avoid irritation and pressure over a cervical vertebra.*

• Carefully secure the sling with a safety pin above and behind the elbow. (For a child under age 7, use tape instead of a pin *to avoid the chance of an injury.*)

## Special considerations

If you anticipate prolonged use, pad the area under the knot with gauze *to prevent skin irritation.* Place the sling outside the shirt collar *to reduce direct pressure on the neck and shoulder.*

If the arm requires complete immobilization, apply a swathe after placing the arm in a regular sling. To do this, wrap a folded triangular bandage around the upper arm on the injured side, bringing one end across the upper chest and the other across the upper back. Tie the ends just in front of the axilla on the uninjured side. The swathe should be tight enough to secure the injured arm to the body. At regular intervals, check the sling for proper placement. Also, assess patient comfort and circulation to the fingers.

Give the outpatient an extra triangular bandage and teach him and a family member or friend how to change the sling. Instruct him to have it changed regularly, *because a soiled sling can cause irritation and infection.* Also, tell him to check periodically for axillary skin breakdown.

## Documentation

In the nurse's notes, record the date, time, and location of sling application, and describe the patient's tolerance of the procedure. Also, document circulation to the fingers, especially noting color and temperature.

MARY M. BAILEY, RN

# Clavicle Straps

*A clavicle strap reduces and immobilizes fractures of the clavicle. It does this by elevating, extending, and supporting the shoulders in the proper position for healing, called the position of attention. A commercially available figure-eight strap or a 4" (10-cm) elastic bandage may serve as a clavicle strap. This procedure is contraindicated for an uncooperative patient.*

## Equipment

Powder or cornstarch □ figure-eight clavicle strap or 4" elastic bandage □ tri-

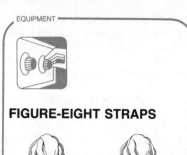

## FIGURE-EIGHT STRAPS

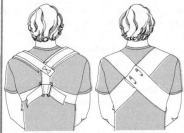

*Commercially made figure-eight straps (illustrated at left) have Velcro attached to the ends for easy fastening. Figure-eight straps (at right) made from a length of elastic bandage are fastened with safety pins.*

angular bandage, if necessary □ safety pins (if necessary) □ tape □ cotton batting or padding □ marking pen □ analgesics, as ordered.

### Essential steps
• Explain the procedure to the patient and provide privacy.
• Help the patient take off his shirt.
• Assess neurovascular integrity by palpating skin temperature; noting the color of the hand and fingers; palpating the radial, ulnar, and brachial pulses bilaterally; and then comparing the affected to the unaffected side (see *How to Assess Neurovascular Status,* page 657). Also, ask the patient about any numbness or tingling distal to the injury, and assess motor function. Determine the patient's degree of comfort and administer analgesics, as ordered.
• Demonstrate how to assume the position of attention.
• Instruct the patient to sit upright and *gradually* assume the position of attention *to minimize pain.*
• Gently apply powder or cornstarch, as

appropriate, to the axillae and shoulder area *to reduce friction from the clavicle strap.* Cornstarch may be used if the patient is allergic to powder.

*To apply a figure-eight strap:*
• Place the apex of the triangle between the scapulae and drape the straps over the shoulders. Bring the strap with the Velcro or buckle end under one axilla d through the loop; then pull the other strap under the other axilla and through the loop.
• Gently adjust the straps so they support the shoulders in the position of attention.
• Bring the straps back under the axillae toward the anterior chest, making sure they maintain the position of attention.

*To apply a 4″ elastic bandage:*
• Roll both ends of the elastic bandage toward the middle, leaving about 12″ to 18″ (30.5 to 45.7 cm) unrolled.
• Place the unrolled portion diagonally across the patient's back, from right shoulder to left axilla.
• Bring the lower end of the bandage under the left axilla and back over the left shoulder; loop the upper end over the right shoulder and under the axilla.
• Pull the two ends together at the center of the back so the bandage supports the position of attention.

*To apply a figure-eight strap or elastic bandage:*
• Secure the ends, using safety pins, Velcro pads, or a buckle, depending on the equipment. Make sure a buckle or any sharp edges face away from the skin. Tape the secured ends to the underlying strap or bandage.
• Place cotton batting or padding under the straps, as well as under the buckle or pins, *to avoid skin irritation.*
• Use the pen to mark the strap at the site of the loop of the figure-eight strap, or the site where the elastic bandage crosses on the patient's back. *If the strap loosens, this mark helps you tighten it to the original position.*
• Assess neurovascular integrity, *which may be impaired by a strap that's too tight.* If neurovascular integrity has changed since your initial assessment, notify the doctor. *He may want to sub-*

stitute another form of treatment.

## Special considerations

If possible, perform the procedure with the patient standing. However, this often isn't feasible, because the pain from the fracture can cause syncope.

An adult with a clavicle strap made from an elastic bandage may require a triangular sling *to help support the weight of the arm, enhance immobilization, and reduce pain* (see "Triangular Slings" in this chapter). For a small child or a confused adult, a well-molded plaster jacket is needed to ensure immobilization. *Inadequate immobilization can result in improper healing.*

Instruct the patient not to remove the clavicle strap. Explain that a family member can provide proper hygiene by lifting segments of the strap to remove the cotton and by washing and powdering the skin daily. Explain that fresh cotton should be applied following cleansing.

For a hospitalized patient, monitor the position of the strap by checking the pen markings every 8 hours. Also, assess neurovascular integrity. Teach an outpatient how to assess his own neurovascular integrity and to recognize symptoms that must be reported to the doctor promptly.

## Documentation

In the nurse's notes section of the emergency department sheet or in the progress notes, record the date and time of strap application, type of clavicle strap, use of powder and padding, bilateral neurovascular integrity before and after the procedure, and instructions to the patient.

MARY M. BAILEY, RN

# Cervical Collars

*A cervical collar may be applied to treat an acute injury (such as a strain of the*

cervical spine muscles) or a chronic condition (such as arthritis or cervical metastasis). It may also be used with such splinting devices as a spineboard to prevent potential cervical spine fracture or cord damage. Designed to hold the neck straight with the chin slightly elevated and tucked in, the collar immobilizes the cervical spine, decreases muscle spasms, and relieves some pain; it also prevents further injury and promotes healing. As symptoms of an acute injury subside, the use of a cervical collar should be gradually discontinued; the patient should alternate periods of application with increasingly longer periods of removal, until application is no longer necessary.

## Equipment

Commercial cervical collar (in the appropriate size).

## Essential steps

● Check the patient's neurovascular status before application.
● Instruct the patient to slowly position his head to face directly forward with his chin slightly elevated and tucked in.
● Place the cervical collar in front of the patient's neck *to ensure that the size is correct.*
● Fit the collar snugly around the neck and attach the Velcro fasteners or buckles at the back of the neck.
● Check the patient's airway and his neurovascular status *to ensure that the collar isn't too tight.*
● If the patient will be using the collar at home, teach him how to apply it, how to perform a neurovascular check, and what symptoms to report to the doctor. Also, if ordered, instruct him to sleep without a pillow.

## Special considerations

For a sprain or a potential cervical spine fracture, make sure the collar isn't too high in front, *because this may hyperextend the neck.* In the patient with a sprain, such hyperextension may cause the ligaments to heal in a shortened position; in the patient with a potential cervical spine fracture, hyperextension may cause serious neurologic damage.

## Documentation
Note the type and size of the cervical collar and the time and date of application. Record the results of neurovascular checks. Document patient comfort and the snugness of the collar's fit. Note all patient instruction.

MARY BAILEY, RN

# Plaster Casts

*A plaster cast is a mold of a body part, usually an extremity, that provides immobilization without discomfort. It can be used to treat injuries (including fractures), to correct orthopedic conditions (such as deformities), or to promote healing after general or plastic surgery, amputation, or nerve and vascular repair. Although many new casting materials have been developed, plaster of paris is still preferred because it's inexpensive, nontoxic, nonflammable, easy to mold, and rarely causes an allergic reaction or skin irritation.*

*A doctor normally applies a cast, with the nurse preparing both the equipment and the patient and assisting during the procedure. Some specially trained nurses may apply or change a standard cast, but an orthopedist must reduce and set the fracture. Of course, an orthopedist must order and apply any specialized cast.*

*Contraindications for casting may include skin diseases, peripheral vascular disease, diabetes mellitus, and a susceptibility to skin irritations. However, these aren't strict contraindications; the doctor must weigh the potential risks and benefits for each patient.*

## Equipment
Tubular stockinette □ plaster rolls □ plaster splints (if necessary) □ bucket of water □ linen-saver pad □ sheet wadding □ sponge or felt padding (if necessary) □ cast knife and cast cutter (if necessary) □ pillows or bath blankets □ optional: plastic gloves, apron, local anesthetic, appropriate-sized syringe and needle, alcohol sponge, cast stand.

Gather the tubular stockinette, plaster rolls, and plaster splints in the appropriate sizes. Tubular stockinettes are available in sizes ranging from 2″ to 12″ (5 to 30 cm) wide; plaster rolls, from 2″ to 6″ (5 to 15 cm) wide; and plaster splints, from 3″ to 6″ (7.6 to 15 cm) wide. Have available a pair of plastic gloves to protect the doctor's hands and an apron for his clothing. (Remember, he may be applying several casts a day.)

### Preparation of equipment
Gently squeeze the packaged plaster rolls *to make sure the plaster envelopes don't have any air leaks.* Humid air penetrating such leaks can cause the plaster to become stale, which could make it set too quickly, form lumps, fail to bond with lower layers, or set as a soft, friable mass. (Baking a stale plaster roll at a medium temperature for 1 hour can make it usable again.)

Follow the manufacturer's directions

---

### CAST CARE

A fiberglass cast dries immediately after application. A plaster extremity cast dries in approximately 24 to 48 hours; a plaster spica or body cast, in 48 to 72 hours. During this drying period, the cast must be properly positioned to prevent a depression in the cast that may cause pressure areas or dependent edema. Neurovascular status must be assessed, drainage monitored, and the condition of the cast checked periodically.

After the cast is completely dry, it looks white and shiny and no longer feels damp or soft. Care consists of monitoring for changes in the drainage pattern, preventing skin breakdown near the cast, and averting the complications of immobility.

Patient teaching must begin immediately after the cast is applied and should continue until the patient or a family member can care for the cast (see *Dos and Don'ts of Cast Care*, page 664).

NANCY REDFERN, RN, MSN

for water temperature. Usually, room temperature or slightly warmer water is recommended, *because it allows the cast to set in about 7 minutes without excessive exothermia.* (Cold water retards the rate of setting and may be used to facilitate difficult molding; warm water speeds the rate of setting and raises skin temperature under the cast.) Place all equipment within the doctor's easy reach.

### Essential steps

• *To allay the patient's fears,* explain the procedure, making sure he understands that heat will build under the cast because of a chemical reaction between the water and plaster. Also, begin explaining some aspects of proper cast care *to prepare him for patient teaching and to assess his knowledge level.*

• Cover the appropriate parts of the patient's bedding and gown with a linen-saver pad.

• Assess the condition of the skin in the affected area, noting any redness, contusions, or open wounds. *This will make it easier to evaluate any complaints the patient may have after the cast is applied.* (If the patient has severe contusions or open wounds, the doctor may administer a local anesthetic.)

• *To establish baseline measurements,* palpate the distal pulses; assess the color, temperature, and capillary refill of the appropriate fingers or toes; and check neurologic function, including sensation and motion in the affected and unaffected extremities (see *How to Assess Neurovascular Status,* page 657).

• Help the doctor position the limb, as ordered. (Usually the limb is immobilized in its natural position.)

• Support the limb in the prescribed position while the doctor applies the tubular stockinette and sheet wadding. The stockinette is placed so it will extend beyond the ends of the cast to pad the edges. (If the patient has an open wound or a severe contusion, the doctor may not use the stockinette.) The limb is then wrapped in sheet wadding, starting at the distal end; extra wadding is applied to the distal and proximal ends of the

## HOW TO REMOVE A CAST

Normally, a cast is removed when a fracture heals or requires further manipulation. Less common indications include cast damage, a pressure sore under the cast, excessive drainage or bleeding, and a constrictive cast.

MARY M. FAUT, RN, MS

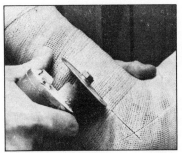

**1** First, cut one side of the cast, and then the other.

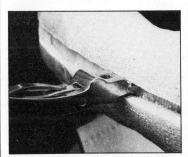

**2** Next, open the cast pieces with a spreader.

**3** Finally, cut through the cast padding with cast scissors.

## PATIENT-TEACHING AID

### DOS AND DON'TS OF CAST CARE

Dear Patient:

To care for your casted arm or leg, follow these guidelines:

**DOS**
• *DO* keep your casted limb elevated above heart level whenever possible to prevent excess swelling. For example, if your leg is in a cast, lie down and elevate your leg with pillows. If your arm is in a cast, prop the arm so your hand and elbow are higher than your shoulder.
• *DO* call your doctor if your fingers or toes become numb or tingle, or if you have difficulty moving them. These signs could indicate a developing infection.
• *DO* call your doctor if you develop a fever, experience unusual pain, or notice a foul odor coming from the cast. These signs could indicate a developing infection.
• *DO* any exercises you've been taught by your doctor, nurses, or physical therapist, to maintain your muscle strength.

• *DO* call your doctor if your cast needs to be repaired (for example, if it becomes loose and slides) or if you have *any* questions at all about caring for it.

**DON'TS**
• *DON'T* get your plaster cast wet; moisture will weaken or destroy it. If your cast is fiberglass, ask your doctor if moisture will affect it.
• *DON'T* insert anything, such as a back scratcher, into your cast to relieve an itch. You could damage your skin and cause an infection.
• *DON'T* put powder, liquid, or lotion in your cast. Use alcohol only on the skin at the cast edges.
• *DON'T* chip, crush, cut, or otherwise break your cast.
• *DON'T* bear weight on your cast unless your doctor tells you to do so.

DENNIS G. ROSS, RN, MSN

---

cast area. As the doctor applies the sheet wadding, help him check for wrinkles and uncovered areas. The doctor may also place an extra layer of sponge or felt padding over any bony prominence and over the area where the cast cutter will be used.
• Assist the doctor by holding the limb in the proper position or preparing the plaster rolls, as ordered. *To assist with plaster preparation,* place a roll on its end in the bucket of water, making sure it is completely submerged. When air bubbles stop rising from the roll, remove it, gently squeeze the excess water from it, and hand it to the doctor, who will begin applying it to the extremity. As he applies the first roll, prepare a second roll in the same manner. (Keep at least one roll ahead of the doctor.)
• After the doctor applies each roll, he'll smooth it to remove wrinkles, spread the plaster into the cloth webbing, and empty

air pockets. If he's using plaster splints, he'll apply them in the middle layers. Before wrapping the last roll, he'll pull the ends of the tubular stockinette over the cast edges *to create padded ends, prevent cast crumbling, and reduce skin irritation.* He then uses the final roll to keep the ends of the stockinette in place.
• Use a cast stand or the palm of your hand to support the cast in the therapeutic position until it becomes firm to the touch (usually 6 to 8 minutes).
• *To check circulation in the casted limb,* palpate the distal pulse and assess the color, temperature, and capillary refill of the fingers or toes. Determine neurologic status by asking the patient if he's experiencing paresthesia in the extremity or decreased motion of the extremity's uncovered joints. Assess the unaffected extremity in the same manner and compare findings with those for the affected extremity.

• Elevate the limb above heart level with pillows or blankets, as ordered, *to facilitate venous return and reduce edema.* To prevent molding, make sure pressure is evenly distributed under the cast.

• The doctor will then send the patient for X-rays *to ensure proper positioning.*

• Instruct the patient to notify the doctor of any pain or burning under the cast. (After the cast hardens, the doctor may cut a window in the cast to inspect the painful or burning area.)

• Pour water into a sink containing a plaster trap. Don't use a regular sink, *because plaster will block the plumbing.*

## Special considerations

Never use the bed or a table to support the cast as it sets, *since molding can result, causing pressure necrosis of underlying tissue.* Also, don't use rubber- or plastic-covered pillows before the cast hardens (usually 24 to 48 hours), as they can trap heat under the cast.

## Complications

Possible complications of improper cast application include palsy, paresthesia, ischemia (which may require amputation), ischemic myositis, pressure necrosis, and eventually misalignment or nonunion of fractured bones.

## Documentation

Record the date and time of cast application; skin condition of the extremity before the cast was applied, noting any contusions, redness, or open wounds; results of neurovascular checks before and after application, for the affected and unaffected extremities; location of any special devices, such as felt pads or plaster splints; and any patient teaching.

DENNIS G. ROSS, RN, MSN

# Mechanical Traction

*Mechanical traction exerts a pulling force on a part of the body—usually the spine,* the pelvis, or the long bones of the arms and legs. It can be used to reduce fractures, to treat dislocations, to correct or prevent deformities, to improve or correct contractures, or to decrease muscle spasms. Depending on the injury or condition, an orthopedist may order skin or skeletal traction. Applied directly to the skin and thus indirectly to the bone, skin traction is ordered when a light, temporary, or noncontinuous pull is required. Contraindications for skin traction include a severe injury with open wounds, an allergy to tape or other skin traction equipment, circulatory disturbances, dermatitis, and varicose veins. In skeletal traction, an orthopedist inserts a pin or wire through the bone and attaches the traction equipment to the pin or wire to exert a direct, constant, longitudinal pull. Indications for skeletal traction include fractures of the tibia, femur, and humerus. Such infections as osteomyelitis contraindicate skeletal traction.

Nursing responsibilities for this procedure include setting up a basic or Balkan traction frame (see Traction Frames, page 666). The design of the patient's bed usually dictates whether to use a claw clamp or I.V.-post-type frame. (However, the claw-type Balkan frame is rarely used.) Setup of the specific traction can be done by a specially trained nurse or by the doctor. Instructions for setting up these specific traction units usually accompany the equipment. After the patient is placed in the specific type of traction as ordered by the orthopedist (see Types of Traction, page 668), the nurse is responsible for preventing complications from immobility; for routinely inspecting the equipment; for adding traction weights, as ordered; and, in patients under skeletal traction, for monitoring the pin insertion sites for signs of infection.

## Equipment

*For setting up the frame:*
Claw-type basic frame—102″ (259-cm) plain bar □ two 66″ (168-cm) swivel-clamp bars □ two upper-panel clamps □

two lower-panel clamps.

*I.V.-type basic frame*—102″ plain bar □ 27″ (69-cm) double-clamp bar □ 48″ (122-cm) swivel-clamp bar □ two 36″ (91-cm) plain bars □ four 4″ (10-cm) I.V. posts with clamps □ cross clamp.

*I.V.-type Balkan frame*—two 102″ plain bars □ two 48″ swivel-clamp bars □ two 27″ double-clamp bars □ five 36″ plain bars □ four 4″ I.V. posts with clamps □ eight cross clamps.

*For all frame types*—trapeze with clamp

## TRACTION FRAMES

**Claw-type basic frame:** Claw attachments secure the uprights to the footboard and headboard.

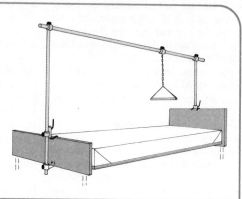

**I.V.-type basic frame:** I.V. posts, placed in I.V. holders, support the horizontal bars across the foot and head of the bed. These horizontal bars then support the two uprights.

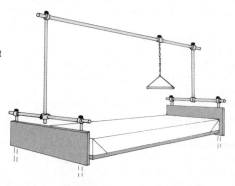

**I.V. Balkan frame:** I.V. posts and horizontal bars, secured in the same manner as those for the I.V. basic frame, support four up-rights.

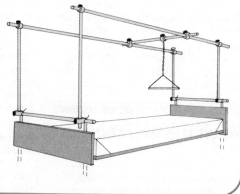

□ wall bumper horns or roller.

*For skeletal traction care:*
Sterile cotton-tipped applicators □ prescribed antiseptic, usually hydrogen peroxide □ sterile gauze sponges □ povidone-iodine solution □ antimicrobial ointment (optional).

Most traction equipment is made of steel or aluminum; the latter is more commonly used because of its lighter weight.

## Preparation of equipment

Arrange with central supply or the appropriate department to have the traction equipment transported to the patient's room on a traction cart. If appropriate, gather the equipment for pin-site care at the patient's bedside.

## Essential steps

• Explain the purpose of traction to the patient. Emphasize the importance of maintaining the proper body alignment after the traction equipment is set up.

*To set up a claw-type basic frame:*
• Attach one lower-panel and one upper-panel clamp to each 66″ swivel-clamp bar.
• Next, fasten one bar to the footboard and one to the headboard by turning the clamp knobs clockwise until they are tight, and then pulling back on the upper clamp's rubberized bar until it is tight.
• Secure the 102″ horizontal plain bar atop the two vertical bars, making sure the clamp knobs point up.
• Using the appropriate clamp, attach the trapeze to the horizontal bar about 2′ (0.6 m) from the head of the bed.

*To set up an I.V.-type basic frame:*
• Attach one 4″ I.V. post with clamp to each end of both 36″ horizontal plain bars.
• Secure an I.V. post in each I.V. holder at the bed corners. Using a cross clamp, fasten the 48″ vertical swivel-clamp bar to the middle of the horizontal plain bar at the foot of the bed.
• Fasten the 27″ vertical double-clamp bar to the middle of the horizontal plain bar at the head of the bed.
• Attach the 102″ horizontal plain bar

to the tops of the two vertical bars, making sure the clamp knobs point up.
• Using the appropriate clamp, attach the trapeze to the horizontal bar about 2′ (0.6 m) from the head of the bed.

*To set up an I.V.-type Balkan frame:*
• Attach one 4″ I.V. post with clamp to each end of two 36″ horizontal plain bars.
• Secure an I.V. post in each I.V. holder at the bed corners.
• Next, attach a 48″ vertical swivel-clamp bar, using a cross clamp, to each I.V. post clamp on the horizontal plain bar at the foot of the bed.
• Fasten one 36″ horizontal plain bar across the midpoints of the two 48″ swivel-clamp bars, using two cross clamps.
• Next, attach a 27″ vertical double-clamp bar to each I.V. post clamp on the horizontal bar at the head of the bed.
• Using two cross clamps, fasten a 36″ horizontal plain bar across the midpoints of two 27″ double-clamp bars.
• Then clamp a 102″ horizontal plain bar onto the vertical bars on each side of the bed, making sure the clamp knobs point up.
• Use two cross clamps to attach a 36″ horizontal plain bar across the two overhead bars, about 2′ from the head of the bed.
• Attach the trapeze to this 36″ horizontal bar.

*After setting up any frame:*
• Attach a wall bumper or roller to the vertical bar or bars at the head of the bed. *This protects the walls from damage from the bed or the equipment.*

*Caring for the traction patient:*
• Show the patient how much movement he's allowed and instruct him not to readjust the equipment. Also, tell him to report any pain or pressure from the traction equipment.
• At least once a shift, make sure that the traction equipment connections are tight and that none of the parts is touching the bedding, the patient, or other inappropriate parts of the equipment. Check for impingements, such as ropes riding on footboard or catching between pulleys. *Friction and impingement reduce the effectiveness of traction.*

# TYPES OF TRACTION

| TYPE | DESCRIPTION AND COMMON USES |
|------|------------------------------|

**Buck's extension**

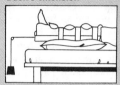

- *Skin traction* usually applied to leg by weight attached to spreader bar below foot, and pulling force is applied with the leg in a straight line.
- Pillow placed under leg keeps pressure off heel.
- *Uses:* dislocated hip after reduction; hip fractures before surgery; after total hip replacement; locked knee; fractured femur before surgical reduction; irritated hip or knee joint.

**Dunlop's**

- Applies lateral traction to elbow; temporary, used for children.
- Using *skin traction,* shoulder is abducted 90° and elbow extended in 45° position *to stretch bicep muscle.*
- Uses two pulling forces: one applied laterally to forearm by skin traction, the other downward by sling hanging from distal portion of upper arm. Forces act on elbow from two directions with different magnitudes, causing pull in a third direction.
- *Uses:* transcondylar and supracondylar fractures of humerus; contracture of elbow.

**Overhead (90°-90°)**

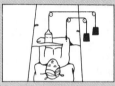

- If applied to arm, upper arm is perpendicular to body, elbow is flexed 90°, and forearm is supported by sling suspended from overhead pulley.
- Usually used with *skeletal application,* with pin insertion through olecranon.
- *Uses:* fracture of humerus or elbow; fracture or injury of shoulder; may also be applied to legs for displaced fractured femur in children, or for lower back pain.

**Russell's**

- *Skin traction* to affected leg and sling placed under knee.
- Uses two pulling forces: one applied by double-pulley system at foot, and the other applied upward by sling under knee attached to single overhead pulley.
- *Uses:* congenital hip dislocation; hip fracture; after total hip replacement; fractured femur; disease of hip or knee.

**Sidearm**

- May be applied by skin or skeletal traction.
- For lateral-longitudinal traction of humerus, shoulder is abducted 90° and externally rotated, elbow is flexed 90° and kept perpendicular to bed.
- *For skin traction,* separate wraps are used on upper arm and forearm.
- *Skeletal traction* applied by pin through olecranon, with forearm traction by adhesive straps and elastic bandage.
- *Uses:* fractures, dislocations, and other pathologies of upper arm and shoulder; tissue injury around elbow (skin traction).

**Balanced suspension with Thomas splint**

- May be used with skin and skeletal traction to suspend leg in splint and permit patient to move freely in bed.
- Distribution of weights exerts traction force, provides countertraction, and suspends leg.
- Pearson attachment is sometimes used with Thomas splint to support lower leg off bed, allowing knee flexion.
- *Uses:* fractures of femoral shaft, hip, and/or lower leg.

• Inspect the traction equipment *to ensure the correct line of pull.*

• Inspect the ropes for fraying, *which can eventually cause a rope to break.*

• Make sure the ropes are positioned properly in the pulley track. *An improperly positioned rope changes the degree of traction.*

• *To prevent tampering and aid stability and security,* make sure that all rope ends are taped above the knot.

• Inspect the equipment regularly to make sure that the traction weights hang freely. *Weights that touch the floor, bed, or each other reduce the amount of traction.*

• About every 2 hours, check the patient for proper body alignment and reposition the patient as necessary. Misalignment causes ineffective traction and may cause a nonuniting fracture.

• *To prevent complications from immobility,* assess neurovascular integrity routinely (see *How to Assess Neurovascular Status,* page 657). The patient's condition, the hospital routine, and the doctor's orders determine the frequency of neurovascular assessments.

• Provide skin care, encourage coughing and deep breathing exercises, and assist with ordered range-of-motion exercises for unaffected extremities. Check elimination patterns and provide laxatives, as ordered.

• For the patient with skeletal traction, make sure that the protruding pin or wire ends are covered with cork *to prevent them from tearing the bedding or injuring the patient and staff.* (The wire ends won't be exposed if the patient has a Hoffman device.)

• Check the pin site and surrounding skin regularly for signs of infection.

• If ordered, clean the pin site and surrounding skin with sterile cotton-tipped applicators dipped in the ordered antiseptic (usually hydrogen peroxide). If ordered, apply antimicrobial ointment to the pin sites, using a sterile cotton-tipped applicator. Then dress them with sterile gauze sponges soaked in povidone-iodine solution. (Some doctors order pin-site care daily to prevent infection; others do not, believing that frequent cleansing and dressing can cause infection.)

### Special considerations

When ordered, apply weights slowly and carefully *to avoid jerking the affected extremity. To avoid injury in case the ropes break,* arrange the weights so they don't hang over the patient.

### Complications

Immobility during traction may result in decubitus ulcers; muscle atrophy, weakness, or contractures; and osteoporosis. Immobility can also cause gastrointestinal disturbances, such as constipation; urinary problems, including stasis and calculi; respiratory problems, such as stasis of secretions and hypostatic pneumonia; and circulatory disturbances, including stasis and thrombophlebitis. Prolonged immobility, especially after trauma, may promote depression or other emotional disturbances. Skeletal traction may cause osteomyelitis originating at the pin or wire sites.

### Documentation

In the nurse's notes, record the amount of traction weight daily, noting the application of additional weights and patient tolerance. Document equipment inspections and patient care, including routine checks of neurovascular integrity, skin condition, respiratory status, and elimination patterns. If applicable, note the condition of the pin site and any care given.

KATHY A. FONDA, RN, BSN

# Care of a Stump and Prosthesis

*Patient care immediately after limb amputation includes monitoring drainage from the stump, positioning the affected extremity, assisting with exercises prescribed by a physical therapist, and wrapping and conditioning the stump.*

*Postoperative care of the stump will vary slightly, depending on the amputation site (arm or leg) and the type of dressing applied to the stump (elastic bandage or plaster-of-paris cast).*

*After the stump heals, it requires only routine daily care, such as proper hygiene and continued muscle-strengthening exercises. The prosthesis—once the patient begins to use it—also requires daily care. Normally, a plastic prosthesis, the most common type, must be cleaned and lubricated and checked for proper fit. As the patient recovers from the physical and psychological trauma of amputation, you must teach correct procedures for routine daily care of both the stump and the prosthesis.*

## Equipment

*For postoperative stump care:*
Pressure dressing □ tourniquet □ ABD pad □ 1″ adhesive tape □ sandbags or trochanter roll (for a leg) □ elastic stump shrinker or 4″ elastic bandage.

*For stump and prosthesis care:*
Alcohol sponges □ stump socks □ two washcloths □ two towels □ appropriate lubricating oil.

## Essential steps

*For postoperative care:*
• Attach the tourniquet to the bed in an obvious place.
• Perform routine postoperative care—frequently assessing respiratory status and level of consciousness, monitoring vital signs and I.V. infusions, checking tube patency, and providing for the patient's comfort and safety.

*To monitor stump drainage:*
• *Because gravity causes fluid to accumulate at the stump,* frequently check the amount of blood and drainage on the dressing. Notify the doctor if accumulations of drainage or blood increase rapidly. If excessive bleeding occurs, notify the doctor immediately and apply a pressure dressing or use the appropriate pressure points. If this doesn't control bleeding, use the tourniquet only as a last resort.
• Tape the ABD pad over the moist part of the dressing, as necessary. *This provides a dry area to help prevent bacterial infection.*
• Monitor the suction drainage equipment and note the amount and type of drainage.

*To position the extremity:*
• *To prevent contractures,* position an arm with the elbow extended and the shoulder abducted.
• *To correctly position a leg,* elevate the foot of the bed slightly and place sandbags or a trochanter roll against the hip *to prevent external rotation.*

 Don't place a pillow under the thigh to flex the hip *because this can cause hip flexion contracture.* For the same reason tell the patient to avoid prolonged sitting.

• After a below-the-knee amputation, maintain knee extension *to prevent hamstring muscle contractures.*
• After any *leg amputation,* place the patient on a firm surface in the prone position for at least 4 hours a day, with his legs close together and without pillows under his stomach, hips, knees, or stump, unless this position is contraindicated. *This position helps prevent hip flexion, contractures, and abduction and stretches the flexor muscles.*

*To assist with prescribed exercises:*
• After *arm amputation,* encourage the patient to exercise the remaining arm *to prevent muscle contractures.* Help the patient perform isometric and range-of-motion exercises for *both* shoulders, as prescribed by the physical therapist, *because use of the prosthesis requires both shoulders.*
• After *leg amputation,* stand behind the patient and, if necessary, support him with your hands at his waist during balancing exercises.
• Instruct the patient to exercise both the affected and unaffected limbs *to maintain muscle tone and increase muscle strength.* The patient with a leg amputation should perform push-ups (in the sitting position, arms at his sides) or pull-ups on the trapeze *to strengthen his arms in preparation for using crutches.*

*To wrap and condition the stump:*
• If the patient doesn't have a rigid cast, apply an elastic stump shrinker *to prevent edema and shape the limb in preparation for the prosthesis.* Wrap the stump so that it narrows toward the distal end. *This helps to ensure maximum comfort when the patient wears the prosthesis.*
• Instead of using an elastic stump shrinker, you can wrap the stump in a 4″ elastic bandage. To do this, stretch the bandage to about two thirds its maximum length as you wrap it diagonally around the stump, with the greatest pressure distally. Make sure the bandage covers all portions of the stump and is smooth *since wrinkles or exposed areas encourage skin breakdown.*
• If the patient experiences throbbing after the stump is wrapped, remove the bandage immediately and reapply it less tightly. *Throbbing indicates impaired circulation.*
• Check the bandage regularly. Rewrap it when it begins to bunch up at the end (usually about every 12 hours for a moderately active patient) or every 24 hours.
• After removing the bandage to rewrap it, massage the stump gently, always pushing *toward* the suture line. *This stimulates circulation and prevents scar tissue from adhering to the bone.*
• When healing begins, instruct the patient to push the stump against a pillow. Then have him progress gradually to push against harder surfaces, such as a padded chair, then a hard chair. *These conditioning exercises will help the patient adjust to experiencing pressure and sensation in the stump.*

*To care for a healed stump:*
• Bathe the stump, but never shave it: *A rash or irritation may result.* If possible, bathe the stump at the end of the day, *since the warm water may cause swelling, making reapplication of the prosthesis difficult.*
• Rub the stump with alcohol daily *to toughen the skin, reducing the risk of skin breakdown.* (Avoid using powders or lotions, *which can soften or irritate the skin.*)

---

## EMERGENCY CARE OF A SEVERED BODY PART

Through microsurgery, reimplantation of a severed body part (such as a hand, foot, digit, or ear) may restore function as well as provide cosmetic repair. Crucial to the success of reimplantation is emergency care of the patient and the injured body part. The part must be wrapped and cooled quickly and properly, but need not be cleaned to avoid further trauma. Irreversible tissue damage occurs after only 6 hours at ambient temperature. However, hypothermic management seldom preserves tissues for more than 24 hours.

To care for the patient with a severed body part:
• Make sure the hemorrhage at the amputation site is controlled.
• Place several sterile gauze sponges and an appropriate amount of sterile roller gauze in a sterile basin, and pour sterile normal saline or sterile lactated Ringer's solution over them. Put on the sterile gloves.
• Place the moist gauze sponges over the stump; then wrap it with moist roller gauze. Put a watertight covering over the stump and place it in an ice-packed plastic bag. Avoid using dry ice *to prevent irreversible tissue damage.*
• Holding the body part in one hand, carefully cover it with the moist gauze sponges. Then wrap it with the moist roller gauze.
• Place the wrapped body part in a watertight plastic bag *to avoid contact between body tissue and ice, which can cause freezing and prevent reimplantation.* Tape the bag closed and put it in the ice-filled container. Label the container with the patient's name and identification number, as well as the date and time.
• Prepare the patient and the body part for transfer to a reimplantation center.

SUSAN M. GLOVER, RN, BSN

---

• Inspect the stump for redness, swelling, irritation, and calluses. Report any of these to the doctor. Tell the patient to avoid putting weight on the stump. (The skin should be firm but not taut over the bony end of the limb.)
• Continue muscle-strengthening exercises, *so the patient can build the strength he'll need to control the prosthesis.*
• Change the patient's stump socks as

necessary *to avoid exposing the skin to excessive perspiration, which can be irritating.* Wash the socks in warm water and gentle nondetergent soap; lay them flat on a towel to dry. *Machine washing or drying may shrink the socks.*

*To care for a plastic prosthesis:*
• Wipe the plastic socket of the prosthesis with a damp cloth and mild soap or alcohol *to prevent bacterial accumulation.*
• Wipe the insert with a dry cloth.
• Dry the prosthesis thoroughly; if possible, allow it to dry overnight.
• Maintain and lubricate the prosthesis, as instructed by the manufacturer's guide.
• Check for malfunctions and adjust or repair the prosthesis as necessary *to prevent further damage.*
• Check the condition of the shoe on a foot prosthesis frequently and change it as necessary.

*To apply a prosthesis:*
• Apply a stump sock. Keep the seams away from bony prominences.
• If the prosthesis has an insert, remove it from the socket, place it over the stump, and insert the stump into the prosthesis.
• If no insert is present, merely slide the prosthesis over the stump. Secure the prosthesis onto the stump according to manufacturer's directions.

### Special considerations
Teach the patient how to care for his stump and prosthesis properly. Make sure he knows the signs and symptoms that indicate problems in the stump. Also, teach him that a 10-lb (4.5-kg) change in body weight will alter his stump size and require a new prosthesis socket *to ensure a correct fit.*

Exercise of the remaining muscles in an amputated limb must begin the day after surgery. A physical therapist will direct these exercises. For example, arm exercises progress from isometrics to assisted range-of-motion to active range-of-motion. Leg exercises include rising from a chair, balancing on one leg, and range-of-motion exercises of the knees and hips.

For a below-the-knee amputation, you may substitute an athletic tube sock for a stump sock by cutting off the elastic band. If the patient has a rigid plaster-of-paris dressing, perform normal cast care. Check the cast frequently to make sure it doesn't slip off. If it does, apply an elastic bandage immediately and notify the doctor *because edema will form rapidly.*

### Complications
The most common postoperative complications include hemorrhage, stump infection, contractures, and a swollen or flabby stump. Complications that can develop at any time after an amputation include skin breakdown or irritation from lack of ventilation; friction from an irritant in the prosthesis; a sebaceous cyst or boil from tight socks; psychological problems, such as denial or withdrawal; and phantom pain caused by stimulation of nerves that once carried sensations from the distal part of the extremity.

### Documentation
Record the date, time, and specific procedures in all postoperative care, including amount and type of drainage, condition of the dressing, need for dressing reinforcement, and appearance of the suture line and surrounding tissue. Also, note any signs of skin irritation or infection, any complications and the nursing action taken, the patient's tolerance for exercises, and his psychological reaction to the amputation.

During routine daily care, document the date, time, type of care given, and condition of the skin and suture line, noting any signs of irritation, such as redness or tenderness.

NANCY ROTH, RN, BS

# Arthroplasty Care

*Care of the patient after arthroplasty— the surgical replacement of a joint or part of a joint—helps restore use of the affected extremity; it also aids prevention of such complications as infection, phlebitis, and respiratory problems. Arthroplasty care includes immobilizing the affected joint, assisting with exercises, and providing routine postoperative care. An equally important nursing responsibility is teaching home care and exercises that may continue for several years, depending on the type of arthroplasty performed and the patient's condition.*

*The two most common arthroplastic procedures are cup arthroplasty and total joint replacement. In* cup arthroplasty, *the surgeon inserts a movable cup between the hip joint surfaces. This procedure is usually indicated for a young patient with rheumatoid arthritis, degenerative joint disease from trauma, or an acetabulum fracture. Total joint replacement (usually of the hip or knee) is commonly performed on elderly patients.*

*Indications for total hip replacement include osteoarthritis and severe crippling rheumatoid arthritis; for total knee replacement, indications include severe pain, joint contractures, and swelling that prohibits full extension or flexion. Nursing care after these operations—as well as care after less common surgical procedures (such as shoulder, elbow, wrist, ankle, or finger joint replacement)—is essentially the same.*

### Equipment

Balkan frame with trapeze □ comfort device (such as foam mattress, alternating pressure mattress, or sheepskin) □ incentive spirometer or intermittent positive-pressure breathing (IPPB) machine □ elastic stocking □ sterile dressings □ hypoallergenic tape □ ice bag □ skin lotion □ crutches or walker □ pillow.

After cup arthroplasty or total hip replacement, balance suspension traction may be applied in the operating room, possibly supplemented by Buck's traction or abduction splints. After total knee replacement, a commercial knee immobilizer or, less commonly, a cast may be applied in the operating room. A cast is applied infrequently because the leg is usually swollen after the operation; if the cast were applied then, it would fail to provide stability once the swelling diminished. A cast also prevents inspection of the suture line.

### Preparation of equipment

After the patient is taken to the operating room, construct a Balkan frame with a trapeze on his bed frame. *This will allow him some mobility after the operation.* Then, make the bed, using a comfort device and clean linen. If postoperative traction is ordered, have the bed taken to the operating room. *This enables direct, immediate placement of the patient on his hospital bed after surgery, instead of necessitating an additional move from his recovery room bed.*

### Essential steps

● Check vital signs every 30 minutes until stable, then every hour for 8 hours, every 2 hours for the next 8 hours, and finally every 4 hours. Report any changes in vital signs, *which may indicate such postoperative complications as infection and hemorrhage.*

● Encourage the patient to perform deep breathing and coughing exercises 10 times hourly. Assist with incentive spirometry or IPPB treatments, as ordered, *to prevent respiratory complications.*

● Assess neurovascular status every 2 hours for the first 48 hours and then every 4 hours *for signs of complications* (see *How to Assess Neurovascular Status,* page 657). Specifically, check the affected leg for color, temperature, toe movement, sensation, edema, capillary filling, and pedal pulse. Also, investigate any complaints of pain, burning, numbness, or tingling.

● Apply the elastic stocking to the unaffected leg, as ordered, *to promote venous return and prevent phlebitis and pulmonary emboli.* Once every 8 hours, remove this stocking, inspect the leg for pressure sores, and reapply the stocking.

● Administer pain medications, as ordered.

● For at least 48 hours after surgery, administer I.V. antibiotics, as ordered, *to minimize the risk of wound infection.* Also, observe the site for such symptoms of phlebitis as warmth, swelling, tenderness, redness, and positive Homans' sign.

• Administer anticoagulant therapy, as ordered, *to minimize the risk of thrombophlebitis and embolus formation.* Observe for bleeding.

• Check dressings for excessive bleeding. Circle any drainage on the dressing and mark it with your initials, the date, and the time. As appropriate, apply more sterile dressings, using hypoallergenic tape. Report any excessive bleeding to the doctor.

• Observe the closed-wound drainage system for discharge color. *Proper drainage prevents hematoma. Purulent discharge and fever may indicate infection.* Empty and measure drainage, as ordered, using aseptic technique *to prevent infection.*

• Monitor fluid intake and output daily, making sure to include wound drainage in the output measurement.

• Apply an ice bag, as ordered, to the affected site for the first 48 hours *to reduce swelling, relieve pain, and control bleeding.*

• Every 2 hours, turn the patient no more than 45° toward the unaffected side and keep him in this position as long as he's comfortable. These changes in position *help prevent respiratory complications and skin breakdown.*

• Help the patient use the trapeze to lift himself every 2 hours. Then provide skin care to the back and buttocks, using warm water and lotion, *to prevent skin breakdown.*

• Instruct the patient to exercise the unaffected extremities *to help maintain muscle strength and range of motion and to help prevent phlebitis.*

• Before ambulation exercises, administer a mild analgesic, as ordered, *because movement is very painful.* Encourage the patient during the exercises.

• Assist the patient with progressive ambulation, using adjustable crutches or a walker when needed for support.

• Before discharge, instruct the patient regarding home care and exercises.

*After cup arthroplasty:*

• Maintain balanced suspension and, if appropriate, Buck's traction *to support the leg, reduce muscle spasms, maintain abduction, and increase patient comfort.*

• Keep the affected leg in abduction and internal rotation *to stabilize the hip and keep the cup and femur head in the acetabulum.* Place a pillow between the patient's legs *to maintain hip abduction.*

• On the day after surgery, instruct the patient to perform exercises, as ordered, *to maintain muscle strength and prepare him for eventual ambulation.* Exercises include quadriceps setting, ankle rotation, and plantar flexion and dorsiflexion of the feet.

*After total hip replacement:*

• Maintain balanced suspension and, if appropriate, Buck's traction *to increase patient comfort, reduce muscle spasms, and maintain hip abduction.* Place a pillow between the patient's legs *to help maintain hip abduction.*

• If the patient desires, elevate the head of the bed 45° for comfort. (Some doctors permit a 60° elevation.) Keep the bed elevated for 30 minutes or less at a time *to prevent excessive hip flexion.*

 Don't let the hip flex past 90°, *because flexion may dislocate the prosthesis.*

• Keep the patient in the supine position, with the affected hip in full extension, for 1 hour three times a day and at night. *This will help prevent hip flexion contracture.*

• On the day after surgery, have the patient begin plantar flexion and dorsiflexion exercises of the foot on the affected leg. When ordered, instruct him to begin quadriceps exercises.

*After total knee replacement:*

• Keep the knee immobilized in full extension immediately after surgery.

• Elevate the affected leg, as ordered, *to reduce swelling.*

• Instruct the patient to begin quadriceps setting exercises and straight leg-raising, when ordered (usually on the second postoperative day). Encourage flexion-extension exercises, when ordered (usually after the first dressing change).

## Special considerations

Before surgery, explain the procedure to the patient. Emphasize that frequent assessment—including the monitoring of vital signs, neurovascular integrity, and wound drainage—is normal after the operation. Inform him that he'll receive I.V. antibiotics for about 2 days. Also, be sure he understands that he'll receive pain medication only if he asks for it. Explain the need for immobilizing the affected leg and exercising the unaffected one.

## Complications

Immobility after arthroplasty may result in such complications as shock, pulmonary embolism, pneumonia, phlebitis, paralytic ileus, bladder retention, and bowel impaction. A deep wound or infection at the prosthesis site is a serious complication that may force removal of the prosthesis. Dislocation of a total hip prosthesis usually occurs only after violent hip flexion. Signs of dislocation include inability to rotate the hip or bear weight, shortening of the leg, and increased pain.

## Documentation

In the nursing notes, record neurovascular status, maintenance of traction (for cup arthroplasty and hip replacement), or knee immobilization (for knee replacement). Also, note the condition of the dressings and the drainage system, and the application of ice bags. Describe the patient's position (especially the position of the affected leg), skin care and condition, respiratory care and condition, and the use of elastic stockings. Document all exercises performed and their effect; also record ambulatory efforts, the type of support used, and the amount of traction weight. Record discharge instructions and how well the patient understands them.

On the appropriate check sheet, record vital signs and fluid intake and output. On the cardex care plan, note the turning and skin care schedule and the current exercise and ambulation program. Also, include the doctor's orders for the amount of traction weight and the degree of flexion permitted; update these orders as necessary.

KATHY FONDA, RN, BSN

## Selected References

Barry, Jeanie, ed. *Emergency Nursing.* New York: McGraw-Hill Book Co., 1978.

Carini, Geraldine K., and Birmingham, Jacqueline. *Traction Made Manageable: A Self Learning Module.* New York: McGraw-Hill Book Co., 1980.

Cavanaugh, Clare Ellen. "Digital Replantation," *Critical Care Update* 8:5, August 1981.

Crossland, Sharon, and Deyerle, William M. "Compartment Syndrome," *Nursing80* 10:51, November 1980.

Glancy, Gerald L. "Compartment Syndromes," *ONA Journal* 2:148, June 1975.

Hilt, Nancy E., and Cogburn, Shirley B. *Manual of Orthopedics.* St. Louis: C.V. Mosby Co., 1980.

Kinney, M.R., et al. *AACN Clinical Reference for Critical Care Nursing.* New York: McGraw-Hill Book Co., 1981.

Larson, Carroll, and Gould, Marjorie. *Orthopedic Nursing,* 9th ed. St. Louis: C.V. Mosby Co., 1978.

Matsen, Frederich A. III, and Frugmire, Richard Jr. "Compartmental Syndromes," *Surgery, Gynecology, and Obstetrics* 147:943, December 1978.

Millar, Sally, ed. *Methods in Critical Care.* Philadelphia: W.B. Saunders Co., 1980.

Miller, Robert H. *Textbook of Basic Emergency Medicine,* 2nd ed. St. Louis: C.V. Mosby Co., 1980.

Mourad, Leona A. *Nursing Care of Adults with Orthopedic Conditions.* New York: John Wiley & Sons, Inc., 1980.

Schwartz, George R. *Principles and Practice of Emergency Medicine,* 2 vols. Philadelphia: W.B. Saunders Co., 1978.

# 14 Skin Care

# Skin Care

## Introduction

The skin protects internal structures from aqueous solutions, bacteria, trauma, and toxic compounds. It regulates body temperature, controls homeostasis, serves as an organ of sensation and excretion, and is extremely important to a person's self-image. It also reflects cellular immune response to the intradermal injection or topical application of antigens. Thus, in caring for the patient with a skin disorder or burns, the main goals are to prevent infection, promote new skin growth, control pain, and provide psychological and emotional support.

### Controlling infection

Because the skin is the body's first line of defense against infection, any damage to its integrity increases the risk of infection, which can delay healing, increase pain, and even threaten the patient's life. Most burn deaths, for example, result from complications secondary to infection rather than from the burns themselves. Controlling infection requires sterile techniques to avoid introducing new pathogens into an already contaminated wound. It's achieved by thorough handwashing with an antiseptic agent and use of sterile equipment during wound care.

### Promoting new skin growth

Promotion of the skin's natural healing processes requires regular changes of dressings (extra changes whenever they become soiled), thorough wound cleansing, and, if necessary, debridement to reduce bacteria and encourage tissue re-

pair. Using warm solutions for wound cleansing increases circulation to the site, promoting transport of oxygen and nutrients needed to support tissue repair.

### Controlling pain

To control pain effectively, the nurse must realize that each patient reacts differently to it and respond to the patient's needs accordingly. If the patient has a minor skin discomfort, such as pruritus, an analgesic or topical medication, reassurance, or distraction technique may relieve it. If he has moderate pain, comfortable positioning and scheduling ample rest may provide relief. However, if he has severe pain, only strong narcotic analgesics may provide relief.

### Psychological support essential

Painful and disfiguring skin disorders may cause the patient to feel depressed, frustrated, or angry. Such a patient needs constant psychological as well as physical support to help him cope successfully with his altered self-image. Severe disfigurement requires long-term psychological support, as in the case of an extensively burned patient whose recovery is always slow, painful, and difficult. The expectation and, later, the actual presence of scars or other evidence of skin injury or disease influences his self-acceptance as well as acceptance by others. Sensitivity to the patient's needs and respect for his manner of coping with his problems is one of nursing's most important challenges.

MARGARET COPP DAWSON, RN, BA, BS

# DIAGNOSIS

# Intradermal Skin Tests

In intradermal tests, recall antigens— those to which the patient has been or may have been previously exposed or sensitized—are injected into the superficial layer of skin with a needle and syringe or a sterile four-pronged lancet to evaluate immune response. Such recall antigens as tuberculin, blastomycin, coccidioidin, and histoplasmin are used to provoke a secondary immune response.

Tuberculin tests (such as the Tine, Aplitest, Mono-Vacc, or Mantoux) produce a delayed hypersensitivity reaction in patients with active or dormant tuberculosis. Recall antigen tests for blastomycosis, coccidioidomycosis, and histoplasmosis produce depressed or negative delayed hypersensitivity reactions in patients with these diseases. Conversely, these recall antigen tests produce positive delayed hypersensitivity reactions in patients capable of maintaining a nonspecific inflammatory response to the antigen.

The primary immune response is evaluated by exposing the patient to new antigens, such as dinitrochlorobenzene (DNCB), which are applied topically as a sensitizing dose, followed by a challenge dose (see "Patch and Scratch Allergy Tests" in this chapter).

Tuberculin tests are contraindicated in patients with current reactions to smallpox vaccinations or with any rash or other skin disorder, and in known tuberculin-positive reactors. Use of recall antigens is contraindicated in persons known to be hypersensitive to the test antigen. Intradermal tests have limited value in infants, because their immune systems are immature and inadequately sensitized.

## Equipment

For blastomycin, coccidioidin, and histoplasmin recall antigen tests: alcohol sponges □ one or two 1-ml tuberculin syringes with 25G or 26G ½" or ⅝" needles □ vial of antigen diluent □ prescribed antigen □ vial of normal saline solution or extra diluent (if a control wheal is ordered) □ millimeter ruler.

For Mantoux test: alcohol sponges □ vial of intermediate-strength purified protein derivative (PPD) □ tuberculin syringe with 25G or 26G ½" or ⅝" needle.

For Tine test, Aplitest, or Mono-Vacc test: multipuncture device □ alcohol sponges □ millimeter ruler.

Have emergency resuscitation equipment and medications readily available in case of rare anaphylactic reaction to the test antigen.

## Preparation of equipment

Check the expiration date and strength of the antigen, to ensure accurate test results.

Check the condition of the lancets in the Tine test or Aplitest device.

The Mantoux antigen (PPD) is already reconstituted; draw up 0.1 ml of solution into the tuberculin syringe. This antigen is adsorbed by plastic. Administer the injection immediately after drawing it up.

Reconstitute recall antigens by drawing up 1 ml of diluent and adding it slowly to the vial of antigen. After reconstitution, draw up 0.1 ml into the tuberculin syringe. (In some hospitals, the pharmacist reconstitutes the antigen before it is sent to the nursing unit. If you are responsible for reconstitution, however, read and follow package insert instructions carefully.)

If a control wheal is ordered, draw up 0.1 ml of normal saline or allergy test diluent into a tuberculin syringe.

## Essential steps

• Explain the procedure to the patient

## GUIDE TO SKIN TEST REACTIONS

| TESTS | TYPE OF REACTION | REACTION | INDURATION | ERYTHEMA |
|---|---|---|---|---|
| **Blastomycosis, coccidioidomycosis, histoplasmosis** | Positive | | ≥ 5 mm | |
| | Borderline | | < 5 mm | > 5 mm |
| | Negative | | None | < 5 mm |
| **Mantoux** (Aplisol) | Significant | | > 10 mm | |
| | Not significant | | None or < 5 mm | |
| **Multiple-puncture device** (Tine and Aplitest) | Significant | | Vesiculation | |
| | Not significant | | 2 mm without vesiculation | |
| | Not significant | | < 2 mm | |

*to ease anxiety and ensure his cooperation.*

• Check the patient's history for hypersensitivity to any of the test antigens or previous reaction to a skin test. If the patient has had any allergic reactions, notify the doctor.

• Tell the patient when to expect reactions to appear. Explain that some antigens (such as DNCB) are readministered after 2 weeks.

• Some tests, such as the DNCB, require the patient's informed consent, because they are used as part of experimental research studies. Be sure the patient has signed the consent form.

• Wash your hands thoroughly. Instruct the patient to sit up and to extend his arm and support it on a flat surface, with the volar surface exposed.

• Cleanse the volar surface of the arm, about 2 or 3 fingerbreadths distal to the antecubital space, with alcohol *to protect the wheal from potential infection.* You may also cleanse the area with acetone *to remove skin oils that may interfere with test results.* Be sure the test site you have chosen has adequate subcutaneous tissue and is free of hair or blemishes. Allow the skin to dry completely before administering the injection, *to avoid inactivating the antigen.*

*To perform the Tine test, Aplitest, and Mono-Vacc test:*

• Remove the protective cap from the unit.

• Hold the patient's forearm with one hand, and stretch taut the cleansed skin area with your fingers. Grasp the unit with your other hand, and firmly depress the tines completely into the patient's skin, without twisting the unit.

• Hold the device in place for at least 1 second. If you have applied sufficient pressure, you'll see four distinct punctures and a circular depression made by the device on the skin. Recap the device and discard it.

• Read Tine test and Aplitest results 48 to 72 hours after injection; Mono-Vacc test results, 48 to 96 hours after injection. Record test results.

*To perform recall antigen and Mantoux tests:*

• Prepare and position the patient's forearm as above.

• With your free hand, hold the needle at a 15° angle to the patient's arm, with its bevel up.

• For each antigen being tested, insert the needle about 3 mm below the epidermis at sites 2″ (5 cm) apart. Stop when the needle bevel is under the skin, and inject the antigen slowly and gently; you should feel some resistance as you do this, and a wheal should form as you inject the antigen. (If the needle moves freely and no wheal forms, you have injected the antigen too deeply; withdraw the needle and administer another test dose at least 2″, or 5 cm, from the first site.)

• Withdraw the needle, and apply gentle pressure to the injection site. Don't rub the site, *to avoid irritating underlying tissues, which may affect test results.*

• Dispose of the needle and syringe properly.

• If a control wheal is required, inject normal saline solution or test diluent into the other arm, following the same procedure.

• Circle each test site with a marking pen, and label each site according to the recall antigen given. Instruct the patient to refrain from washing off the circles until the test is completed.

• After waiting 48 to 72 hours, inspect injection sites for reactivity. Record induration in millimeters. A negative test at this first antigen concentration may be confirmed by retesting with a higher concentration. (If the patient is known to be hypersensitive to skin tests, use a first-strength dose [1 tuberculin unit] in the Mantoux test *to avoid vesiculation, ulceration, and possibly necrosis at the puncture site.*)

### Special considerations

If the patient is an outpatient, instruct him to return at the prescribed time to have the test results read.

Don't perform a skin test in areas with excess hair, acne, dermatitis, or insufficient subcutaneous tissue, such as over a tendon or a bone. Be sure a wheal appears after you inject the antigen; if none appears, repeat the test.

### Complications

A severe anaphylactic response, requiring immediate epinephrine injection and other emergency resuscitation procedures, can result in patients hypersensitive to the test antigens. Other adverse reactions include tissue ulceration and necrosis, which may require topical skin treatment or cold soaks.

### Documentation

Record the patient's name, the date, the strength and type of antigens used, the method of administration, the location of test sites, and the time for reading test results. After reading the results, record the amount of induration, vesiculation, or erythema, if present. Note any adverse reactions, and chart notification of the doctor and any requests for additional tests.

KAREN DYER VANCE, RN, BSN

# Patch and Scratch Allergy Tests

*Patch and scratch skin tests are used to evaluate the immune system's ability to respond to known allergens, which are applied to hairless areas of the patient's body, such as the scapula, the volar surface of the forearm, or the an-*

*terior surface of the thigh. In patch testing, each allergen (a dilute solution, an ointment, or a dry preparation) is applied directly to the skin and covered with gauze secured by tape, or prepared gauze patches impregnated with the antigens are applied to the skin. Test results are read 48 to 72 hours later; erythema, papules, vesicles, or edema indicates a positive reaction.*

*Scratch tests involve scarifying the patient's skin with a special tool or needle and introducing the allergens into the scratched area. Test sites are examined 30 to 40 minutes later and compared with a control site; erythema or edema indicates a positive reaction.*

*Both kinds of tests provoke delayed hypersensitivity reactions mediated by T cells in the patient's immune system. Although minute amounts of test allergens can usually demonstrate an intact immune response, the test may also indicate an anergic (diminished or absent) reaction in patients with acute leukemia, Hodgkin's disease, congenital immunodeficiencies, or overwhelming infections, and in elderly patients.*

*If a patient is thought to be anergic, he may be exposed to a new antigen, such as dinitrochlorobenzene (DNCB), to confirm anergy. In this test, a sensitizing dose of DNCB is applied to the skin and a challenge dose reapplied 10 to 14 days later (see Testing for Dinitrochlorobenzene Sensitization, page 682).*

*Patch and scratch tests are contraindicated in patients with inflammation, skin diseases, or significantly impaired immune response. These tests have limited value in infants because of their immature, poorly sensitized immune system.*

### Equipment

*For patch and scratch tests:* alcohol sponges □ 2″ x 2″ gauze pads □ standard patch tray containing panel of allergens (varies with manufacturer) □ diluents (such as petrolatum, mineral oil, or less preferably, distilled water) □ millimeter ruler □ filter paper disks (patches) □ 1″ nonallergenic adhesive tape (or square of soft cotton gauze and occlusive tape, cellophane tape, or Elastopatch) □ if necessary, specific potential allergens not contained in the commercial kit but brought by the patient, such as soap, perfume, cosmetics, and workplace chemicals (which may have to be mixed with a diluent).

*For the scratch test only:* sterile lancet, sterile darning needle, sterile four-pronged tine, or sterile scarifier (von Pirquet or Robinson type) □ eyedropper □ glycerin-saline control solution □ millimeter ruler.

### Preparation of equipment

If the test requires an allergenic solution, have the laboratory or pharmacist prepare it, *to ensure correct dosage and dilution.*

### Essential steps

● Explain the procedure to the patient *to ease anxiety and ensure his cooperation.* Ask him if adhesive tape irritates his skin. If it does, use paper tape *to prevent a spurious allergic reaction.* Wash your hands.

*To perform a patch test:*

● Thoroughly cleanse the area with alcohol to remove skin bacteria, and allow it to dry; then wipe the area with acetone *to remove oils that may affect test results.* Allow the area to dry.

● Remove the protective cover from the filter paper disk or patch. Apply the allergen directly to the skin or to the gauze or disk (unless these are already impregnated), and secure the patch to the skin with tape. Each test site should be about 2″ (5 cm) apart *to prevent one test result from obscuring another in case of a positive reaction.*

● Leave the patch in place for the prescribed period (usually 48 to 72 hours), and keep the area dry. Then, remove the patch, and wait 30 minutes *to allow any unrelated reaction, such as irritation from tape removal, to subside.*

● Examine the test site for erythema, papules, vesicles, or edema. If such signs are absent, reexamine the site 96 hours after application of the allergens *to de-*

## TESTING FOR DINITROCHLOROBENZENE SENSITIZATION

The patient who shows little or no reaction (anergy) to the panel of test antigens during skin testing may not have been previously exposed to them or may be immunodeficient. In such a patient, the dinitrochlorobenzene (DNCB) sensitization test can verify the presence of cell-mediated immune function.

In the DNCB test, this chemical, when applied to the patient's skin, acts like a "new" antigen, combining with skin proteins to form a substance that stimulates T cell sensitization to DNCB. Ten to fourteen days after this sensitizing dose, a challenge dose should produce a positive reaction, indicating intact cell-mediated immunity. A negative reaction confirms anergy.

To perform this test, wear gloves and a mask *to prevent self-sensitization to the chemical.* You'll need a sterile gauze pad, an adhesive bandage, alcohol sponges, acetone, and cotton-tipped applicators.

• Explain the procedure to the patient, and tell him the DNCB will be reapplied after 2 weeks. Check your hospital's policy on DNCB. This test usually requires a record of informed consent and possibly FDA approval.

• Dissolve the DNCB in acetone, as ordered. Position the patient's arm as for a patch test. Using an alcohol sponge, cleanse a small, hairless area midway between the wrist and elbow and allow it to dry. Then, using a cotton-tipped applicator, apply the prescribed amount of DNCB (sensitizing dose) and allow the DNCB to dry. Cover the area with a sterile gauze pad or adhesive bandage for 24 to 48 hours.

• Tell the patient to watch for a spontaneous flare reaction 10 to 14 days after the first DNCB application. If a reaction occurs, use a smaller dose of test solution for the DNCB challenge dose.

• After 14 days, apply the challenge dose to the same site, using the same procedures; inspect the site 48 to 96 hours later for reactivity. If test results are negative, the challenge dose can be repeated 2 weeks later (1 month after the sensitizing dose).

• Score the patient's response to the test as follows:

**0** = No reaction

**1**$^+$ = Erythema only

**2**$^+$ = Erythema with induration

**3**$^+$ = Vesicles, erythema, and induration

**4**$^+$ = Bullae and/or ulceration.

---

tect a possible delayed reaction.
• Record test results as follows:
? + = doubtful reaction; negative or anergic
+ = weak (nonvesicular) reaction; erythema or papules
+ + = strong (edematous or vesicular) reaction; erythema, papules, and/or small vesicles
+ + + = extreme reaction; all the above, as well as vesicles, bullae, or ulceration
IR = irritant reaction; inflammation, dryness.

*To perform a scratch test:*
• Cleanse the skin as before, and allow it to dry.
• Using your thumb and index finger, stretch the skin taut at the scratch site. Then, make a scratch 1 to 4 mm long and about 2 mm deep with the sterile lancet or tine. If you use a tine, apply pressure for about 1 second *to raise a welt.* If you draw blood, apply an adhesive bandage and scratch another site.
• With an eyedropper, apply a drop of the allergen to the scratch site. If you're applying more than one allergen, space the drops about 2″ (5 cm) apart *to prevent a mixed reaction.* Don't touch the skin with the dropper, *to prevent cross-contamination.*
• Prepare another scratch site as a control, and place a drop of glycerin-saline in it. Be sure to keep this site about 2″ (5 cm) from all other sites.
• Don't wipe the scratch site, *to avoid removing the allergen and invalidating the test.*
• Examine the test site after waiting 30 to 40 minutes for erythema or edema to appear. Then measure the diameter of the reaction, and record the results in millimeters.

## Special considerations

Apply the appropriate amount of allergen to the test sites *to ensure accurate results*. Instruct the patient to keep the test sites dry and to avoid covering them with potentially allergenic materials, such as wool, which may cause itching or sensitivity. Tell him not to rub or scratch the test sites *to avoid invalidating results*.

## Complications

Patch or scratch tests rarely cause an anaphylactic reaction. If they cause persistent itching, notify the doctor; he may order a topical corticosteroid preparation.

## Documentation

Record the time, date, site of administration, and type of antigen. When the test is read, record the time, date, and results: Describe the patient's response to the allergen, and note the size of reaction in millimeters.

WINIFRED STILL HAYES, RN, MS, ANP-C

---

# TREATMENT

# Treatment of Decubitus Ulcers

*Decubitus ulcers (pressure sores, bedsores) result from skin breakdown caused by impaired blood circulation and edema in areas of the patient's body that are subjected to prolonged pressure, warmth, and poor air circulation. The most susceptible pressure points usually lie over bony prominences, such as the sacrum, iliac crests, scapulae, heels, or vertebrae. Decubiti may also form wherever two skin surfaces are in prolonged close contact, such as the abdominal or gluteal folds or beneath the breasts. Untreated pressure sores progress from skin blanching to erythema and inflammation and finally to tissue necrosis involving subcutaneous tissue, fascia, muscle, and bone.*

*Decubiti most commonly result from inadequate skin care and failure to position and turn the patient frequently enough to relieve pressure. Malnourished, immunosuppressed, dehydrated, incontinent, or elderly patients with poor circulation are especially susceptible to pressure sores. Paralyzed patients with muscular atrophy or those who have malabsorption syndrome or such metabolic disorders as diabetes are also at special risk.*

*Treatment aims to relieve pressure and restore circulation to the affected area, to prevent infection and further necrosis, and to promote skin regeneration. Depending on the severity of the wound, treatment may last a year or more and includes cleansing and use of a variety of protective dressings, topical medications to promote healing, and mechanical devices to relieve pressure. Debridement, hydrotherapy, grafting, and nutritional therapy may supplement these measures to promote healing.*

*The nurse usually performs many of the treatments, with a therapist's help, according to hospital policy. (See "Debridement," "Hydrotherapy," and "Autograft Care" in this chapter.) The procedure detailed here includes daily cleaning and care of the ulcer.*

## Equipment

Overbed table □ sterile basin □ sterile gloves □ clean gloves □ sterile normal saline solution or other cleansing agent, as ordered, such as half-strength hydrogen peroxide, aluminum acetate (Burow's solution), boric acid, povidone-iodine solution, or acetic acid □ mild soap or skin cleanser □ sterile 4″ x 4″ gauze sponges □ topical medication, as ordered □ Telfa pads □ hydrophobic paste □ skin adhesive □ antiseptic plastic film spray □ Montgomery straps, or paper or nylon tape (to secure dressings) □ sterile syringe without needle (to apply ointments) □ linen-saver pads □ impervious plastic or wax-coated paper bag.

*Optional equipment, depending on ordered treatment:* irrigation set, heat lamp, topical oxygen therapy equipment, permeable adhesive membrane, jet lavage, whirlpool hydrotherapy bath, skin barrier (such as karaya powder), enzymatic debriding agent, absorbable gelatin sponge, disposable razor (if necessary).

### Preparation of equipment

Assemble needed items at the patient's bedside. Cut tape into strips for securing dressings. Loosen bottle caps for easy removal when needed. Loosen taped edges of dressings before putting on gloves. Tape an impervious bag to the overbed table to receive used dressings and trash.

### Essential steps

• Wash your hands.
• Explain the procedure to the patient *to allay his fears and ensure his cooperation.* Provide privacy.
• Position the patient comfortably, but *make sure that you can reach the ulcer site easily.*
• Cover the bed linens with a linen-saver pad *to prevent soiling.*
• Open the gauze sponge packages. Soak half the sponges by pouring sterile saline solution over them or, using sterile technique, dropping them into a sterile basin of saline solution. Leave the rest of the sponges in their opened packages.
• If a new dressing is applied immediately after wound cleansing and medication, open the dressing packages at this time and leave them in the packages.
• Put on the clean gloves.
• Remove the old dressing to expose the wound, and discard the dressing in the impervious bag.
• Cleanse the skin around the ulcer with mild soap and water or other mild cleanser, working in a spiral pattern from the center outward. (Don't use an oil-based cleanser if you'll be using adhesive bandages, tape, or hydrophobic paste, *because they won't adhere properly.)*

• Use gentle friction during cleansing *to massage the skin and stimulate circulation,* and blot the skin dry with gauze sponges.
• Cleanse the ulcer with gauze sponges soaked in the ordered cleansing solution. Using a spiral motion, begin at the center of the ulcer and work toward the edges, *to avoid contaminating the wound with skin flora.*
• Use a new sterile gauze sponge for each stroke; discard contaminated sponges in the impervious bag.
• If the ulcer is deep and draining, apply the cleansing solution with an irrigating syringe. Be sure to irrigate all areas, especially under skin flaps. Rinse the ulcer thoroughly with sterile normal saline solution, *to remove all cleansing solution.*
• Assess the condition of the skin and the ulcer, noting its color, odor, and amount of drainage, if any.
• Blot the ulcer dry with gauze sponges, working from the center to the edges.
• Remove your gloves and discard them in the impervious bag.
• At this time, perform any ordered therapy, such as topical oxygen or convection heat. If no therapy is ordered, put on sterile gloves and apply medication, such as an antibiotic, *to control infection;* an enzymatic agent *to debride the ulcer;* or a gelatin sponge or dextranomer *to absorb secretions and promote wound granulation.*
• Apply ointments with a sterile syringe (minus needle) *to avoid contaminating the medication tube.*
• If necessary, apply a protective agent, such as tincture of benzoin spray, to the skin around the ulcer *to protect the skin from irritation by wound drainage, tape, urine, or feces.*
• Dress the ulcer with a Telfa pad, plastic side down. *This protects the ulcer from infection without sticking to it, and absorbs drainage.* If the wound is large or draining copiously, place extra gauze sponges or abdominal pads over the Telfa pad.
• Shave any hair around the ulcer *to help the dressing adhere to the skin.*
• Secure the dressing with paper or ny-

## HOW TO PREVENT DECUBITUS ULCERS

Prevention of decubitus ulcers is primarily a nursing responsibility. The most effective means of preventing skin breakdown are relief of pressure on the skin, maintenance of adequate circulation, and an adequate diet. Observe these guidelines to maintain skin integrity:

• Prevent pressure on the skin by turning and repositioning the patient every 1 to 2 hours, depending on his condition, and using pressure-relief aids, such as a water mattress and sheepskin. When you turn the patient, don't drag the hips or shoulders across the sheet, *to prevent skin abrasion.* Use a turning sheet or ask two or three co-workers to help you lift him into a new position.

• Post a turning schedule at the patient's bedside and in the nursing-care plan, noting any positions to be avoided and the frequency of turning.

• Observe the patient for reddened or blanched areas, especially at ear rims and areas of bony prominences that blanch with decreased circulation, such as shoulder blades, elbows, sacrum, hips, inner aspect of knees, outer ankles, and heels. If you detect any redness or blanching, massage the area *to increase circulation* and avoid turning the patient onto this area until the redness or blanching subsides. Pad the area with commercial protectors, sheepskin, gauze, or lamb's wool *to allow air to circulate.* Do not use plastic next to the skin, *because it prevents air circulation and collects moisture, which leads to skin breakdown.*

• Do not raise the head of the bed more than 30° except for a short time, *to prevent shearing pressure.*

• Periodically shift the weight of the patient in a chair or wheelchair *to allow blood to flow into compressed tissue.* Encourage a paraplegic patient to shift his weight by doing push-ups in the wheelchair. If the patient needs your help to shift his weight, sit next to him and help him shift his weight to one buttock while you support him for 60 seconds. Repeat on the other side.

• Make sure appliances, casts, and splints aren't too tight or they'll decrease circulation and pinch the skin. If necessary, pad the appliance or loosen it.

• Encourage active or perform passive range-of-motion exercises *to increase circulation to the extremities.*

• Apply lotion *to decrease friction.* After application, massage the skin *to stimulate circulation and reduce edema.*

• Keep mattress coverings wrinkle-free *to prevent uneven pressure distribution.*

• Use special equipment, such as the foam eggcrate mattress, flotation pad, alternating pressure mattress (see "Supplemental Bed Equipment" in Chapter 1), sheepskin padding, and heel and elbow protectors (see "Devices to Maintain Alignment and Reduce Pressure" in Chapter 2) *to provide special support and minimize direct pressure on the patient's body.* When a patient has severe decubiti, the doctor may prescribe special mattresses or beds, such as the CircOlectric bed, the Stryker frame, and the air-fluidized bed (see "CircOlectric Bed," "Turning Frames," and "Clinitron Therapy," respectively, in Chapter 2).

• Make sure the patient's diet is adequate in protein, vitamin C, and iron *to maintain skin integrity.* Measure his daily dietary intake—not necessarily the amount of food served—in calories. Depending on the patient's condition, the doctor may order enteral or parenteral hyperalimentation.

• Try to prevent diarrhea and control urinary incontinence, *because excretions cause skin maceration.*

---

lon tape. If the dressing must be changed frequently, use a Montgomery strap (see "Wound Management" in Chapter 5). Before applying the Montgomery straps, be sure to coat the skin around the ulcer with tincture of benzoin or aerosol plastic film *to prevent skin trauma when straps are removed.*

• Remove and discard your gloves in the impervious bag, and dispose of the bag according to the hospital's policy.

• Wash your hands and return reusable equipment to proper storage areas.

### Special considerations

A permeable adhesive membrane (permeable to air and moisture but not to bacteria, urine, feces, or other contaminants) can be applied to a clean wound as the only dressing and needs to be changed only every 3 to 7 days. Such dressings are self-sealing. Drainage that accumulates beneath them can be aspirated safely with a needle and syringe.

# QUICK GUIDE TO DECUBITUS ULCER THERAPY

| TREATMENT | NURSING CONSIDERATIONS |
|---|---|
| **TOPICAL AGENTS**<br>**hexachlorophene**<br>(pHisoHex*) | • May cause vasoconstriction, leading to further decubitus ulceration.<br>• Tissues may absorb hexachlorophene.<br>• May produce neurotoxic effects.<br>• Always rinse the area thoroughly after use. |
| **collagenase**<br>(Santyl*) | • Do not use with detergents, hexachlorophene, antiseptics (especially those containing heavy metal ions, such as mercury or silver), iodine, or soaks or acidic solutions containing metal ions, such as aluminum acetate (Burow's solution). These may decrease enzymatic activity of the collagenase.<br>• Apply this debriding ointment in thin layers after cleansing lesion with normal saline solution, neutral buffer solution, or hydrogen peroxide.<br>• Use with caution in debilitated patients, because debriding enzymes may increase risk of bacteremia. Observe for signs and symptoms of systemic infection and protein sensitization (long-term therapy).<br>• Watch for granulation, which may indicate effectiveness.<br>• If enzymatic action must be stopped for any reason, apply Burow's solution.<br>• Avoid getting ointment in the eyes. If this occurs, flush with water immediately. |
| **compound benzoin**<br>**tincture**<br>(Benzoin Spray) | • Do not apply to acutely inflamed areas. Benzoin spray is usually applied only to healthy skin surrounding the decubitus ulcer *to prevent further skin breakdown.*<br>• Observe for inflammation or infection, because protectants are occlusive layers that retain moisture, exclude air, and trap cutaneous bacteria. |
| **dexpanthenol**<br>(Panthoderm Cream*,<br>Panthoderm Lotion) | • Do not apply to lesions of patients with hemophilia.<br>• Thoroughly cleanse the lesion before each application. Works best on dry lesions rather than on oozing lesions. |
| **dextranomer**<br>(Debrisan) | • Do not use dextranomer beads to cleanse nonsecreting wounds. Discontinue treatment when wound is no longer exuding.<br>• Cleanse but do not dry the lesion before applying the dextranomer beads.<br>• Remove the medication when it turns gray-yellow, indicating saturation.<br>• To remove, irrigate with jet lavage using sterile water, a saline solution, or other cleansing solution.<br>• Avoid contact with eyes. |
| **fibrinolysin and des-**<br>**oxyribonuclease**<br>(Elase*) | • Dense, dry eschar must be removed surgically before enzymatic debridement with fibrinolysin.<br>• Lesion should be cleansed, dried, and coated with a thin layer of the enzyme ointment and then covered with a nonadhering dressing at least once a day. |
| **absorbable gelatin**<br>**sponge**<br>(Gelfoam) | • Sponges control oozing when inserted into the deepest portion of the lesion. Do not remove or disturb the sponges already in place, but extra pieces may be added, if necessary.<br>• Do not use with other topical agents. |

## QUICK GUIDE TO DECUBITUS ULCER THERAPY *(continued)*

| TREATMENT | NURSING CONSIDERATIONS |
|---|---|
| **karaya blanket** | • Use only on small, ulcerated areas.<br>• Do not use on areas that require daily cleansing; protective coating should remain on the wound for several days. |
| **scarlet red**<br>*(Decubitex Ointment)* | • Keep ointment in contact with newly forming tissue. Use a thin layer of ointment and cover loosely with dry sterile gauze to allow wound to "breathe."<br>• Change the dressing twice daily, especially where seeping and secretions are present. |
| **silicone**<br>*(Silicone and Zinc Oxide Compound, Silon Spray)* | • Be aware that silicone is difficult to remove from skin; it resists water and soap. Although it is a topical protectant, it does not protect against oils or solvents.<br>• Observe for inflammation or infection, because the protectant is occlusive and retains moisture, excludes air, and traps cutaneous bacteria.<br>• It may be used alone, as a vehicle for medications, or with other topical medications.<br>• Protect eyes against spray. |
| **sutilains**<br>*(Travase*)* | • Do not use with detergents, antiinfectives (such as benzalkonium chloride, hexachlorophene, iodine, and nitrofurazone), and compounds containing metallic ions (such as silver nitrate and thimerosal) which adversely affect enzymatic activity of sutilains. Also, do not use this debriding agent in wounds involving major body cavities or containing exposed nerves or nerve tissue, in fungating neoplastic ulcers, in wounds in women of childbearing age, or in persons with limited cardiac or pulmonary reserves.<br>• Store at 35.6° to 50° F. (2° to 10° C.).<br>• If used with topical antimicrobials, apply sutilains ointment first.<br>• For best response, keep affected area moist.<br>• The doctor may order a mild analgesic to reduce painful reactions, but with doctor's approval, discontinue sutilains if pain is severe. Also discontinue if bleeding or dermatitis develops.<br>• Use cautiously near eyes. If accidental contact occurs, flush eyes repeatedly with large amounts of normal saline solution or sterile water. |
| **PHYSICAL THERAPY**<br>**Topical oxygen therapy** | • Use moisturized oxygen—slightly pressurized—to avoid dry necrosis along the ulcer's edge. You will need an oxygen source (such as wall oxygen), a pressure system for the oxygen (such as an intermittent positive-pressure breathing machine), a method to localize the oxygen directly over the lesion, and tubing for connections.<br>• Apply the oxygen directly over the ulcer, usually for 15 minutes, three or four times daily. |
| **Heat lamp therapy** | • Place the lamp at least 18″ (45.7 cm) away from the patient and to his side *to minimize its intensity.*<br>• Perform this treatment for a 10-minute period three or four times daily.<br>• Check every 5 minutes for redness or pain in the skin around the ulcer. Stay with the patient during therapy, because he may inadvertently move too close to the lamp and burn his skin. |

*Available in U.S. and Canada. All other products (no symbol) available in U.S. only.

Before applying the membrane, defat the surrounding skin with acetone or the manufacturer's suggested solution.

If necessary, the patient is placed on a high-protein diet with extra vitamin C, *to promote healing.* I.V. hypertonic glucose and amino acids and oral crystalline amino acids serve as beneficial aggressive nutritional supports, especially for the patient with large decubiti.

If appropriate, teach the patient to examine his own skin with a mirror for redness, blanching, or any breaks in the skin.

In some hospitals, decubiti are considered contaminated wounds, and wound and skin precautions are enforced (see "Wound and Skin Precautions" in Chapter 3).

### Complications
Notify the doctor at the first signs of infection, which include foul-smelling drainage, persistent pain, severe erythema, and elevated skin and body temperatures. Untreated infections can cause septicemia and osteomyelitis.

### Documentation
Record the date and time of initial and subsequent treatments. Initially document the ulcer's location, size (length, width, depth), and color; amount, odor, and color of drainage; and condition of the surrounding skin. Note the treatment being used on the nursing-care plan, and update daily or as required. Note any change in the condition or size of the ulcer and any elevation of skin temperature on the progress record. Record the patient's temperature daily on the vital signs sheet.

CAROL ANN GRAMSE, RN, PhD

---

# Unna Boot

---

*An Unna boot (or gelatin compression boot) is applied to treat foot or leg con-ditions, such as venous ulcer or stasis dermatitis, that are free of infection and necrotic tissue. The medicated boot promotes healing by exerting even pressure on the veins of the affected extremity while protecting them from additional trauma.*

*A commercially prepared gauze bandage, saturated with Unna paste, is most commonly used to wrap the foot and leg. If such a bandage isn't available, Unna paste may be applied to the extremity, which is then wrapped with lightweight gauze. This procedure is contraindicated only if the patient is allergic to an ingredient in the paste (gelatin, zinc oxide, and glycerin).*

### Equipment
Commercially prepared gauze bandage saturated with Unna paste (or Unna paste and lightweight gauze) □ bandage scissors □ elastic bandage to apply over commercially prepared bandage (optional).

### Essential steps
• Explain the procedure to the patient and provide privacy.
• Wash your hands.
• Clean the affected extremity gently *to remove dirt that may create pressure points after the bandage is applied and to prevent the proliferation of bacteria.*
• Position the patient's leg so the knee is slightly flexed.
• If a commercially prepared bandage isn't available, spread an even coat of Unna paste on the leg and foot; then cover it with the lightweight gauze. Apply three to four layers of paste interspersed with layers of gauze.
• Starting at the inner ankle, wrap the prepared bandage or the lightweight gauze around the patient's foot, making figure-eight turns around the ankle. *To cover the area completely,* make sure each turn overlaps the previous one by half the bandage's width.
• Continue wrapping the patient's leg up to the knee, using firm, even pressure. Mold the boot with your free hand as you apply the bandage *to make it smooth and even.*

• Make a 2″ (5-cm) slit in the boot just below the knee *to avoid constriction as the dressing hardens.*

• If using a commercially prepared bandage, you may cover the boot with an elastic bandage *to protect the patient's clothing and bed linens from the paste.*

• Instruct the patient to remain in bed with his leg outstretched and elevated on a pillow until the paste dries (approximately 30 minutes). Observe the patient's toes for signs of circulatory impairment, such as cyanosis and coolness, especially if he complains of pain and numbness. *This indicates that the bandage has been wrapped too tightly.*

• Leave the boot on for several days, or as ordered. Instruct the patient to walk on it or handle it carefully *to avoid damaging the boot.* Tell him the boot will stiffen, but won't be as hard as a cast.

• Change the boot weekly, or as ordered, *to assess the underlying skin and healing ulcers.* Remove the boot by cutting the dressing with the bandage scissors.

### Special considerations

Never apply the boot when edema is present, *because the boot will loosen as the edema decreases, reducing pressure on the veins.*

Don't make reverse turns while wrapping the bandage. *This could create excessive pressure areas, which may cause discomfort as the bandage hardens.*

Tell the patient not to shower or take a tub bath while wearing the Unna boot *because these could soften and loosen it.*

### Complications

Contact dermatitis may result from an allergic reaction to Unna paste.

### Documentation

Record the date, time, and location of boot application, appearance of the patient's skin before and after application of the boot, equipment used (commercially prepared bandage or Unna paste and lightweight gauze), and any allergic reaction. If you removed the boot and applied a new one, note this too.

SUSAN CORBETT, RN

# Disinfection of Skin Parasites

*Parasitic skin infestations are usually caused by head and body lice* (Pediculus), *pubic lice* (Phthirus), *or scabies mites* (Sarcoptes). *Lice suck blood from the skin and inject a toxin that causes allergic reactions, such as itching, swelling, and excoriation caused by scratching. Mites burrow into the upper skin layers and produce similar allergic symptoms. Body lice infest the hair and scalp as well as the body; they can spread through shared use of combs, clothing, bed linens, and other personal items, and through close contact with the infected individual. Pubic lice is spread primarily through sexual contacts. Scabies mites flourish in warm, protected areas of the body, such as the waistline, axillary folds, flexor surfaces of wrists or elbows, nipples, penis, or buttocks.*

*Treatment for lice and mites is similar and involves application of medicated shampoos, creams, or lotions to the affected areas to kill the parasites and their eggs; other necessary measures include proper laundering, disinfection, or disposal of the contaminated clothing or linens.*

*Pediculicides or scabicides are contraindicated in patients who develop hypersensitivity to them.*

### Equipment

Prescribed medication: shampoo containing copper oleate and tetrahydronaphthalene, gamma benzene hexachloride (gamma BHC, GBH, lindane), pyrethrins, or coal tar derivatives; lotion or cream containing benzyl benzoate, crotamiton, pyrethrins, GBH, or sulfa (6% in petrolatum) □ fine-tooth comb and brush to remove nits and dead lice □ bath towels □ gloves □ gown □ clean gown and linen for the patient □ isolation bags □ topical ointment for skin, if ordered □ surgical cap for nurse (optional).

## Preparation of equipment

Assemble all equipment on a cart or tray. If the patient is in isolation, wash your hands and put on a gown, gloves, and a surgical cap before entering the patient's room (see "Isolation Equipment" in Chapter 3).

## Essential steps

• Explain the procedure to the patient *to allay his fears and ensure his cooperation.* If he will use the medication at home, caution him against its overuse, *which may itself cause pruritus.*

*To remove head lice:*

• Place a small, dry towel or washcloth over the patient's eyes *to protect them from shampoo.*

• Apply the prescribed shampoo according to product directions (it may be left in place for 10 minutes to 24 hours, depending on the product). Then, shampoo the hair and scalp thoroughly, being careful to keep the medication out of the patient's eyes.

• Rinse the hair and scalp with warm water *to remove dead lice and prevent skin irritation from the medication.* If necessary, remove dead lice and nits with a brush or fine-tooth comb dipped in hot vinegar *to loosen nit cement and help remove nits.*

• Place any towels used, the patient's contaminated gown, and his bed linen in a properly labeled isolation bag. All the patient's linen should go in this bag.

• Provide a new, clean gown and linens for the patient, and send the sealed isolation bag to the central supply department for laundering.

• If shampooing is done at home by the patient or his family, instruct them to launder used linens and towels in hot water, separate from all other laundry items.

*To remove body or pubic lice:*

• Provide privacy. Place towels under the patient's hips and axillary areas, and drape the pubic area.

• Apply the medication to the axillary or pubic area and leave in place, as ordered. Then cleanse the treated areas with soap and water *to remove dead lice*

*and prevent skin irritation.*

• Treat contaminated clothes and linens as above.

• Remove body lice by bathing with soap and water or, if the infestation is severe, by applying a medicated cream or lotion.

*To remove scabies mites:*

• Have the patient bathe. Apply the prescribed lotion or cream to the affected area, and leave it in place as ordered (up to 24 hours).

• Cleanse the area with soap and water *to remove the medication and prevent skin irritation.* Explain to the patient that if pruritus recurs, it doesn't mean reinfestation unless living mites are found. Apply topical ointment to relieve pruritus, if ordered.

• Collect all towels and linens and place them in a properly marked isolation bag, as above.

• If the procedure is performed at home, instruct the patient to wash all clothes and linens in very hot water, or have clothing dry-cleaned or pressed with a hot iron *to kill adult mites and eggs.*

## Special considerations

Family members who have been in close contact with the patient should also be examined and treated, if necessary. Ask the patient with pubic lice for a history of recent sexual contacts, so they too may be examined and, if necessary, treated.

Suggest that the patient's family spray upholstery, rugs, bedding, and clothing or other items that may serve as a reservoir for the parasites, *to prevent reinfestation.* Pets don't need treatment, *since the human parasites cannot survive on them.*

*To avoid transmitting parasites to other patients,* practice good hand-washing technique, and thoroughly disinfect the patient's room after he is discharged.

## Complications

Scratching can cause excoriation of the skin and scalp, which may lead to pyoderma and dermatitis or other secondary skin infections. Pruritus may result from an allergic reaction to the medication, or from its excessive use, and may be treated with a topical steroid or other antiinflammatory agent.

## Documentation

Record the date and time of treatment, the medication used, and the patient's reaction to the treatment. Note skin appearance before and after treatment, and record incidence of secondary infection, if any.

SUSAN CORBETT, RN

# Relief of Nail-bed Pressure

*Injuries to the fingers and toes may cause painful hematomas to develop under the nail plate (subungual hematoma). To relieve the pain caused by pressure against the nail bed, the nail may be pierced with a cautery, a hot needle, or a hot paper clip. Although this procedure usually is performed by the nurse, some hospitals allow only a doctor to perform it.*

## Equipment

Large paper clip, sterile 18G needle, or disposable electric cautery □ alcohol lamp (to be used as heat source if cautery is unavailable) □ povidone-iodine solution □ 4″ x 4″ gauze sponges □ basin for soaking finger or toe □ sterile tubular gauze dressing or sterile 2″ x 2″ gauze pads □ adhesive tape □ topical antibiotic ointment, if ordered.

## Essential steps

• Explain the procedure to the patient *to ease his anxiety and promote cooperation.* Then, wash your hands.
• Soak the affected finger or toe for 5 to 15 minutes *to obtain asepsis.*
• Ignite the alcohol lamp or turn on the cautery.
• If you use a paper clip, straighten the longer curved end.
• Hold the paper clip or sterile needle

with a gauze sponge, and heat the point until it is red-hot. If you're using a cautery, wait until the exposed wire tip becomes red-hot.
• Hold the patient's finger or toe firmly *to prevent sudden movement.*
• Hold the paper clip, needle, or cautery over the hematoma, at a right angle to the nail.
• With smooth, steady pressure, burn a hole in the nail until bleeding occurs. Don't force the needle. Reassure the patient that this is painless, *because the nail has no nerve endings.*
• Wipe the area with a dry gauze sponge *to absorb any blood or drainage.* If there is much pressure under the nail, blood may spurt out as soon as the hole is made.
• Gently squeeze the underside of the finger or toe *to express additional blood and reduce the size of the hematoma.*
• Cleanse the area again with a gauze sponge soaked in antiseptic solution, and then dry the area with another gauze sponge. Apply topical antibiotic ointment, if ordered.
• Apply a sterile tubular gauze dressing and secure it with tape. The dressing should be slightly bulky. If tubular gauze is unavailable, use sterile 2″ x 2″ gauze pads and an elastic gauze dressing.
• Inform the patient of the signs and symptoms of infection, and instruct him to call the doctor if infection develops.

## Special considerations

If necessary, have the patient lie down for the procedure, so he won't develop syncope.

## Complications

Infection may develop at the nail puncture site.

## Documentation

Record the date and time the procedure was performed, method used to puncture the nail, estimate of amount of blood drained,. condition of the nail, and the patient's reaction to the treatment. Also note the application of any topical medication.

SUZANNE MARR SKINNER, RN, MS

# Care of Traumatic Wounds

*Because most traumatic wounds are caused by accidental injury in unsterile conditions, they carry a high risk of local infection that can delay healing, increase scar formation, and lead to a systemic infection such as septicemia. Wound care aims to remove bacteria, prevent infection, promote healing, and minimize scarring.*

*While caring for a traumatic wound, the nurse can also assess its condition. The type of wound and degree of contamination usually determine which cleansing technique and cleansing agent will be used. Large, deep, or very dirty wounds may require analgesic medication and such special procedures as debridement and irrigation.*

## Equipment

Sterile basin □ ordered cleansing agent □ sterile normal saline solution □ sterile 4″ x 4″ gauze sponges □ sterile cotton-tipped applicators □ linen-saver pad □ dry sterile dressing, Telfa pad, or petrolatum gauze □ optional: razor, soap and warm water, towel, sterile and clean gloves, 50-ml catheter-tip syringe, surgical scrub brush, jet lavage (such as a Water-Pik), antibiotic ointment, splint, analgesic or anesthetic (as ordered), sterile forceps, sutures and suture set.

## Preparation of equipment

Assemble needed equipment at the patient's bedside. Fill the basin with the ordered cleansing agent and sterile normal saline solution. Make sure the treatment area has enough light to allow careful observation of the wound. Wear sterile or clean gloves *to avoid spreading infection.*

## Essential steps

• Wash your hands.
• Explain the procedure to the patient and provide privacy.
• Assess the patient's pain *to determine if he needs analgesia or anesthesia during wound care.* Administer pain medication, if ordered, except intradermally injected local anesthetics, which are administered by the doctor. Prepare the local anesthetic for injection by withdrawing the correct amount of anesthetic into a 3-ml syringe with a 25G 1″ needle. If ordered, pour a stronger anesthetic solution over a large abrasion before cleansing *to anesthetize the wound.*
• Place a linen-saver pad under the area to be cleansed.
• If necessary, shave the area around the wound *to facilitate cleansing and treatment.*
• Wet a sterile 4″ x 4″ gauze sponge with the ordered cleansing agent. Never cleanse a wound with cotton balls or cotton-filled gauze sponges, *because cotton fibers may be pulled off and left in the wound, causing contamination.* Cleanse the wound gently using a circular motion, working outward from the center of the wound to approximately 2″ (5 cm) past its edge. *This motion removes nearby sources of contamination and stimulates circulation to the wound site.* Discard the soiled gauze sponge and use fresh sponges as necessary.
• Continue cleansing for approximately 5 minutes, or until the wound appears clean.
• Be sure to use a cotton-tipped applicator dipped in the cleansing solution *to cleanse narrow or hard-to-reach parts of the wound.*
• Wet several 4″ x 4″ gauze sponges with the sterile normal saline and rinse the wound with the same circular motion used in cleansing.
• Extremely dirty wounds that require additional cleansing may be scrubbed with a surgical brush or irrigated with jet lavage (such as a 50-ml catheter-tip syringe or a Water-Pik). Don't use a bulb syringe or I.V. tubing *because these can't provide enough force to remove embedded debris.* Wear sterile gloves when you're manually removing embedded debris.

• After the wound has been cleansed, the doctor may debride the wound *to remove dead tissue and to reduce the risk of infection and scarring.*

• If necessary, the doctor may suture the wound edges or apply sterile strips of porous tape, depending on the wound's depth.

• Apply the ordered antibacterial ointment *to help prevent infection.*

• Apply a dry sterile dressing over the wound *to absorb its drainage and to protect the site from bacterial contamination.*

• Apply a nonadhering pad, such as a Telfa pad or petrolatum gauze, on abrasions, *to keep the dressing from sticking to the wound.*

### Special considerations

Do not cleanse a wound with alcohol *because it is very painful and dehydrates tissue.*

The doctor may perform extensive debriding and suturing in the operating room. If this is necessary, pack the wound with gauze sponges soaked in sterile normal saline solution before moving the patient to the operating room. Recognize that a wound in an area subjected to repeated trauma may require splinting *to promote complete healing.*

Check the patient's medical history for previous tetanus immunization and, if ordered, arrange for additional immunization.

Teach the patient how to care for his wound, and, if necessary, inform him when to return to have his sutures removed.

### Complications

The most common complication of traumatic wounds is infection.

### Documentation

Record the date and time of the procedure, the size and condition of the wound, the administration of medications, and specific wound-care measures.

SUZANNE MARR SKINNER, RN, MS

# Burn Care

*The major goals of wound care in the patient with burns are to prevent infection and further destruction of soft tissue, cartilage, or bone; to promote cosmetic healing; and to retain body function.*

*Prevention of infection is the primary and overriding clinical goal and requires meticulous sterile technique in wound care. Infection can cause a partial-thickness burn wound to worsen into a full-thickness injury. It can also cause skin graft rejection; delay wound healing; increase pain; lead to nutritional imbalance; and prolong the duration of hospitalization. In fact, infection is the leading cause of death in patients with severe burns.*

*Other techniques are also essential for effective burn care. For example, careful dressing change techniques help promote healing by ensuring that burned surfaces never touch each other; such techniques also promote debridement of dead skin (eschar) and stimulate circulation. Careful positioning and regular exercising of burned extremities during healing help maintain joint function and prevent contractures and deformities (see* How to Position the Burn Patient to Prevent Deformity, *page 696).*

*Burn dressings generally consist of three layers: a first layer of fine mesh gauze saturated with the ordered topical agent, a second layer of padding, and a third layer of elastic gauze dressing. A burn dressing should protect the wound and absorb fluid to prevent maceration and help keep the topical agent in contact with the skin. Burn dressings are changed daily, or more frequently, if ordered. Although most burn wounds require dressings, some wounds may be treated with a topical medication and exposed to air to limit bacterial growth. While the latter method may be effective in certain circumstances, it presents its own care problems, including possible adhe-*

# ASSESSING BURN EXTENT

When an adult burn patient is admitted to the emergency room, the extent of his burn injury may be determined by using the Rule of Nines: count the head and neck as 9%, each arm as 9%, each leg as 18%, the front of the trunk as 18%, the back of the trunk as 18%, and the perineum as 1%. (Don't use the Rule of Nines for infants and children, since the percentage for the head and neck is higher and the percentage for the legs lower than in adults. For example, in infants the head and neck account for about 21% of total skin surface.)

Later, when time permits, you may want to use the Lund and Browder chart that appears below to make a more accurate evaluation. This method considers proportional size differences for all ages.

After thorough cleansing of the burn injury area and before applying dressings, systematically inspect the patient from head to toe, front to back, shading in all burned areas on the figures by the chart. Circle the numbers corresponding to these shaded areas on the chart. Total the numbers in the column to determine the percentage of burn surface.

Also, consider the depth of injury: first-, second-, or third-degree. Regard second-degree burns as "partial thickness" and third-degree burns as "full thickness."

To determine the percentage of second- and third-degree burns, first record the circled numbers in the appropriate column on the chart. Then total each column.

Finally, assess for circumferential full-thickness injury. A burn wound around an extremity may act as a tourniquet, causing severe edema and cutting off the extremity's distal arterial supply. If the burn wound is located around the chest or neck, it may seriously reduce excursion of the chest wall, thus compromising respiration.

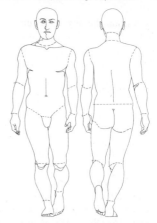

| PERCENTAGE OF BURN AREA | | | | | | | | |
|---|---|---|---|---|---|---|---|---|
| AREA | 1 YEAR | 1 TO 4 YEARS | 5 TO 9 YEARS | 10 TO 14 YEARS | 15 YEARS | ADULT | SECOND-DEGREE | THIRD-DEGREE |
| **Head** | 19 | 17 | 13 | 11 | 9 | 7 | | |
| **Neck** | 2 | 2 | 2 | 2 | 2 | 2 | | |
| **Anterior trunk** | 13 | 13 | 13 | 13 | 13 | 13 | | |
| **Posterior trunk** | 13 | 13 | 13 | 13 | 13 | 13 | | |
| **Rt. buttock** | 2½ | 2½ | 2½ | 2½ | 2½ | 2½ | | |
| **Lt. buttock** | 2½ | 2½ | 2½ | 2½ | 2½ | 2½ | | |
| **Genitalia** | 1 | 1 | 1 | 1 | 1 | 1 | | |
| **Rt. upper arm** | 4 | 4 | 4 | 4 | 4 | 4 | | |
| **Lt. upper arm** | 4 | 4 | 4 | 4 | 4 | 4 | | |
| **Rt. lower arm** | 3 | 3 | 3 | 3 | 3 | 3 | | |
| **Lt. lower arm** | 3 | 3 | 3 | 3 | 3 | 3 | | |
| **Rt. hand** | 2½ | 2½ | 2½ | 2½ | 2½ | 2½ | | |
| **Lt. hand** | 2½ | 2½ | 2½ | 2½ | 2½ | 2½ | | |
| **Rt. thigh** | 5½ | 6½ | 8 | 8½ | 9 | 9½ | | |
| **Lt. thigh** | 5½ | 6½ | 8 | 8½ | 9 | 9½ | | |
| **Rt. leg** | 5 | 5 | 5½ | 6 | 6½ | 7 | | |
| **Lt. leg** | 5 | 5 | 5½ | 6 | 6½ | 7 | | |
| **Rt. foot** | 3½ | 3½ | 3½ | 3½ | 3½ | 3½ | | |
| **Lt. foot** | 3½ | 3½ | 3½ | 3½ | 3½ | 3½ | | |
| **Total** | | | | | | | | |

Adapted with permission from C.P. Artz and J.A. Moncrief. *The Treatment of Burns* (2nd ed.; Philadelphia: W.B. Saunders Co., 1969).

## THE OP-SITE DRESSING

As an alternative to the traditional gauze dressing, the doctor may order a polyurethane Op-Site or Tegaderm dressing for the burn patient. This nonporous, self-adhesive, transparent drape, when used on second-degree burns or abrasions, reduces the risk of infection and does not require the changing or periodic debridement necessary with other dressings.

Op-Site has additional advantages:
• The dressing remains in place until the burn is completely healed. Because the membrane is transparent, you can easily inspect the burn.
• The occlusive film retains the serous exudate, keeps the wound moist, and, consequently, hastens healing.
• By keeping the wound moist, the dressing adheres only to the area surrounding the burn and not to the wound's surface.
• The dressing's elasticity enables you to apply the dressing over a joint without reducing the patient's mobility. It also allows the patient to shower or bathe without removing the dressing.

**To apply the dressing**
• Thoroughly cleanse the area and shave the hair within 2″ (5 cm) of the site. Rub the area with alcohol or acetone to defat the skin and allow it to dry before continuing.
• Ask two or three co-workers to help you, depending on the location and size of the burn.
• Measure the burn and choose the correct dressing size. Apply the polyurethane dressing, leaving 1″ to 1½″ (2.5 to 3.8 cm) around the burn site to ensure total coverage. Don't stretch the dressing too tightly, because a stretched dressing restricts mobility and may cause discomfort.
• Have each helper hold the green tabs attached to the dressing. Press the dressing onto the area and peel back evenly, removing the white backing. Reinforce the dressing by placing porous adhesive tape across the edge of the dressing. As you apply the dressing, explain its advantages to the patient. Tell him not to try to remove it.
• Serum can accumulate under the dressings, so repair dressings frequently, especially on large areas. If the dressing is intact, aspirate the serum and patch the needle hole, or reapply the dressing. Replace any leaking dressing.

---

sion to bed coverings, poor drainage control, or partial loss of the topical agent.

### Equipment
Ordered topical agent □ ordered pain medication □ 4″ x 4″ gauze sponges □ two basins □ two pairs of gloves □ rolls or sheets of fine mesh gauze □ elastic gauze dressing □ cotton-tipped applicators □ soap and water □ normal saline solution □ towels □ scissors □ tissue forceps □ bath blanket □ surgical cap □ mask □ clean or sterile gown. All equipment except cap and mask should be sterile.

### Preparation of equipment
Assemble needed equipment on the dressing table. Make sure the treatment area is adequately illuminated *to allow accurate wound assessment.* Open the packages using sterile technique and arrange them in order of use on a sterile field. Warm the sterile saline by placing the unopened bottles in warm water.

### Essential steps
• Administer the ordered pain medication about 20 minutes before beginning wound care.
• Explain the procedure to the patient and provide privacy.
• Turn on overhead heat lamps to avoid chilling. Check that they aren't too hot.
• Wash your hands.
  *To remove dressings without hydrotherapy:*
• Put on the gown (clean if in a burn unit, sterile if not), mask, and sterile gloves.
• Remove the dressings down to the fine mesh gauze.
• Soak the fine mesh dressings with warm saline or a mixture of two parts normal saline and one part 3% hydrogen peroxide.
• Cut the outer dressings with sterile blunt scissors and lay them open.
• Remove the inner dressings with sterile forceps or your sterile-gloved hand.
• Because soiled dressings are a prime

source of infection, dispose of them carefully in an impervious bag, according to the hospital's policy.

• Gently remove any exudate and the topical agent with 4″ x 4″ gauze sponges moistened with a mild soap and water or saline solution.

• Carefully debride all loose eschar with

## HOW TO POSITION THE BURN PATIENT TO PREVENT DEFORMITY

| AREA BURNED | POTENTIAL DEFORMITY | POSITION OF PREVENTION |
|---|---|---|
| **Neck** | | |
| Anterior aspect or circumferential | • Flexion contracture of neck | • No pillow under head |
| Posterior aspect only | • Extensor contracture of neck | • Prone: pillow under upper chest to flex cervical spine |
| **Axilla** | | |
| Anterior | • Adduction and internal rotation | • Shoulder joint in abduction (100° to 130°) and external rotation |
| Posterior | • Adduction and external rotation | • Shoulder in forward flexion and 100° to 130° abduction |
| **Pectoral region** | • Shoulder protraction | • No pillow; shoulders abducted and externally rotated |
| **Chest or abdomen** | • Kyphosis | • As for pectoral region, with hips neutral (NOT flexed) |
| **Lateral trunk** | • Scoliosis | • Supine; affected arm abducted |
| **Elbow** | | |
| Anterior surface or circumferential | • Flexion and pronation | • Arm extended and supinated |
| **Wrist** | | |
| Total or volar surface | • Flexion | • Splint in 15° extension |
| Dorsal surface | • Extension | • Splint in 15° flexion |
| **Fingers** | • Adhesions of the extensor tendons, loss of palmar grasp | • Metacarpophalangeal joints in maximum flexion; interphalangeal joints in slight flexion; thumb in maximum abduction |
| **Hip** (includes inguinal and perineal burns) | • Internal rotation, flexion, and adduction; possibly joint subluxation if contracture is severe | • Neutral rotation and abduction; maintain extension by prone position or pillow under buttocks |
| **Knee** | | |
| Popliteal surface or circumferential | • Flexion | • Maintain extension using posterior splints; *no pillows* under knees while supine or under ankles while prone |
| **Ankle** | • Plantar flexion if foot muscles are weak or their tendons are divided | • 90° dorsiflexion with splint, if possible, rather than with footboard |

From Claudella A. Jones, RN and Irving Feller, MD, PROCEDURES FOR NURSING THE BURNED PATIENT, National Institute for Burn Medicine, 1975.

sterile forceps and scissors.

• Assess the wound's condition. The wound should be clean, with no debris, loose tissue, purulence, inflammation, or darkened margins.

• Before applying a new dressing remove gown, gloves, and mask, dispose of them properly, and put on a fresh, clean mask, cap, gown (clean if in a burn unit, sterile if not), and sterile gloves.

• Apply the ordered topical agent, if the fine mesh gauze isn't already impregnated with it.

• Cover the wound with fine mesh gauze (or, soak the gauze in the topical agent, and then apply). Cut it to fit only burned areas; do not cover unburned areas.

*For special areas—arms and legs:*
• Wrap the dressings from the distal to the proximal area, *to stimulate circulation and prevent constriction.* Wind the dressings once around the extremity, so the edges overlap slightly, and then cut the bandages. Continue wrapping until you have covered the entire wound.

• Wrap coarse roller gauze (saturated with the same topical agent) over the leg or arm with the same distal to proximal motion as before.

• Apply a dry roller gauze or elastic gauze bandage to hold the two bottom layers in place.

*Hands and feet:*
• Wrap each finger separately with a single layer of fine mesh gauze *to allow the patient to use his hands and to prevent webbing contractures.* Place gauze between the toes.

*Chest, abdomen, and back:*
• Apply a large sheet of gauze and a layer of coarse gauze saturated with the ordered topical agent. Then place a sterile towel on top of the gauze and pin the towels together, front to back; or wrap the area with elastic gauze dressing *to avoid constricting the patient's respiration, especially in infants or children, elderly patients, or those with circumferential injuries.*

*Face:*
• For scalp burns, shave the scalp hair around the burn and clip other hair to about 2″ in length *to prevent contamination of burned areas of the scalp.*

• Make sure the final layer of elastic gauze dressing doesn't cover the eyes, nostrils, or mouth.

*Ears:*
• Shave the hair around the affected ear.

• Remove exudate and crusts with cotton-tipped applicators dipped in saline-peroxide solution.

• Place a layer of fine mesh gauze behind the auricle *to prevent webbing.*

• Apply fine mesh gauze and 4″ x 4″ gauze sponges dampened (but not soaked) with the ordered topical agent *to prevent pooling in the middle ear.* Position the patient's ears properly before bandaging *to avoid damaging auricular cartilage.*

• Don't expose the ear to air until it's completely healed.

• Assess the patient's hearing.

*Eyes:*
• Cleanse the area around the eyes and the eyelids with a cotton-tipped applicator and sterile normal saline every 4 to 6 hours or as needed to remove crusts and drainage.

• Administer the ordered eye ointments or drops.

• If the patient can't close his eyes, apply lubricating ointments or drops, as ordered.

• Make sure the patient's eyes are closed before applying eye pads, *to prevent corneal abrasion.* Don't apply any topical ointments near the eyes or on the lids without a doctor's order.

*Nose:*
• Check the nostrils for inhalation injury, inflamed mucosa, and singed vibrissae.

• Cleanse the nostrils with cotton-tipped applicators dipped in sterile normal saline solution.

• Remove crusts.

• Apply the ordered ointments.

• If the patient has a nasogastric tube, use tracheostomy ties to secure the tube in place.

• Cleanse the area around the tube every 4 to 6 hours.

*Muscles, tendons, and bones:*
• Keep the areas moist to prevent drying and destruction of viable tissue.

• Maintain strict aseptic technique to prevent infection.
• Change dressings every 4 to 6 hours, or as ordered.
• Perform conservative debridement *to minimize tissue destruction.*

### Special considerations
• Observe wound conditions. A very dry wound may indicate dehydration; a purulent, soupy, or malodorous wound indicates frank infection; a green-grey exudate indicates *Pseudomonas* infection; a blue-black discoloration at the wound edge may indicate septicemia; a white, powdery appearance may indicate fungal growth; and redness and swelling at the edges may indicate cellulitis.

Healthy granulation tissue looks *clean,* pinkish, faintly shiny, and free of exudate. If you notice any departure from this, alert the patient's doctor and record it on the patient's chart. If available, use a ceiling-mounted overhead heat lamp or heat shield *to avoid chilling the patient during dressing changes.* Be careful not to overheat the skin surface.

### Complications
Infection is the most common complication.

### Documentation
Record the date and time of care, wound condition, special dressing change techniques, and the patient's tolerance of the procedure.
CATHERINE A. MAGUIRE, RN, BSN

---

# Topical Burn Dressings

---

*Topical medications and dressings are often used together in burn-wound management to prevent infection, and to promote healing and formation of new skin. Topical burn dressings may take the form of soaks (dressings saturated with so-lutions of silver nitrate or povidone-iodine), dry dressings impregnated with ointments or creams, or dry dressings impregnated with antimicrobials and applied over an enzymatic debriding agent.*

*Treatment depends on the nature and extent of the burn, the patient's condition, and the type of pathogens present. Silver sulfadiazine should be used cautiously in patients who are hypersensitive to sulfa preparations; gentamicin—which is nephrotoxic and ototoxic—should be used with care in patients with impaired renal function.*

### Equipment
Large sterile basin □ fine mesh gauze □ elastic gauze dressing □ stockinette (4″, 6″, or 12″) □ sterile scissors □ sterile forceps □ nonallergenic adhesive tape □ clean gloves □ sterile gloves □ mask □ clean or sterile gown or apron □ cap □ ordered topical agent (such as 0.5% to 1% silver nitrate solution, povidone-iodine solution, silver sulfadiazine, mafenide acetate, gentamicin, sutilains, or other enzymatic agent) □ ordered pain medication □ sterile 50-ml catheter-tipped irrigating syringe □ sterile bath blanket.

### Preparation of equipment
Assemble necessary equipment on a dressing cart, at the patient's bedside, or in a treatment room. Make sure the treatment area is sufficiently lighted *to allow accurate assessment of the wound.*

### Essential steps
• Administer an analgesic, as ordered, about 20 minutes before starting the procedure.
• Provide privacy. If the patient is just starting this treatment regimen, explain the procedure *to ease his anxiety and promote cooperation.*
• Wash your hands, and put on sterile gloves, a gown or apron (clean if in a burn unit, sterile if not), cap, and mask.
*To apply a wet dressing:*
• Soak the fine mesh gauze and the elastic gauze dressing in a large sterile basin containing the ordered solution.

• Wring out the fine mesh gauze until it is moist—not dripping—and apply it to the wound. Warn the patient that he may feel some transient pain as the dressing is applied.

• Wring out the elastic gauze dressing, and then wrap the extremities with it *to hold the fine mesh gauze in place.*

• Roll a dry stockinette over the dressing *to keep dressings intact.*

• Cover the patient with a cotton bath blanket *to prevent chilling* and change it if it becomes damp. Overhead heat lamps may also be used.

• Change the dressings frequently to keep the wound moist; this is especially important if silver nitrate is the topical agent used, *because it becomes ineffective and the high concentration of silver ions in this agent may actually damage tissue if dressings are allowed to dry out.* (Some hospitals prefer to irrigate the dressing with solution at least every 4 hours by using a sterile irrigating syringe and irrigating through small slits cut into the outer stockinette layer to rewet the gauze dressing.)

*To apply a dry dressing with a topical agent:*

• Remove dressings. Cleanse the wound (see "Burn Care," "Hydrotherapy," and "Debridement" in this chapter).

• If the fine mesh gauze is not already impregnated with the topical agent, apply the ordered agent to the wound in a thin layer—about 2 to 4 mm thick—using your sterile-gloved hand.

• Apply fine mesh gauze over the wound and wrap with elastic gauze dressing *to hold the fine mesh gauze in place and absorb any drainage.*

*To apply an enzymatic agent:*

• Remove the old dressings and cleanse the wound.

• Apply the enzymatic agent in a layer about 1 to 2 mm thick, using your sterile-gloved hand.

• Cover the enzymatic agent with fine mesh gauze impregnated with the ordered antimicrobial ointment, *because the enzyme alone can't stop or reduce bacterial growth.* Wrap with elastic gauze dressing *to hold the fine mesh gauze in place and absorb drainage.*

## Special considerations

Avoid splashing when wringing out a dressing saturated with silver nitrate, *because this agent permanently stains skin and clothing brown to black on exposure to air.* Povidone-iodine can usually be removed by laundering.

Don't allow two burned surfaces, such as two fingers or two toes, to touch each other when applying dressings or these surfaces may become webbed during healing. Webbing necessitates surgical release of scars to correct deformity, and prolongs therapy.

An enzymatic agent (such as sutilains ointment) should be used with an antibiotic, such as silver sulfadiazine, mafenide acetate, or gentamicin, *because an enzymatic agent may spread infection by opening the blood vessels in a potentially contaminated wound.* Do not use an enzymatic agent concomitantly with hexachlorophene, iodine, nitrofurazone, or silver nitrate.

Enzymatic debridement must begin within 24 hours to be effective.

Do not use an enzymatic agent on more than 15% of the total burn surface at one time, *because it increases fluid loss from the wound.*

## Complications

Each topical agent has various side effects; the most common ones are listed below.

Silver nitrate solution produces serum electrolyte imbalances, especially of sodium, potassium, and calcium. Povidone-iodine solution may cause metabolic acidosis and elevated serum iodine levels; it may also cause pruritus and rash in some patients. Silver sulfadiazine may cause pruritus and rash and may depress granulocyte formation if applied to more than 30% of the total body surface area. Mafenide acetate may impair the patient's renal buffer system and cause metabolic acidosis if used on large areas. Watch for hyperpnea, as the patient attempts to compensate for metabolic acidosis by blowing off carbon dioxide.

Monitor serum electrolytes and arterial blood gases. Mafenide acetate is painful on application. If gentamicin is used, check the patient's serum creatinine and urine creatinine levels. Sutilains ointment may irritate viable tissue around the wound and causes some bleeding or fluid loss from the wound.

### Documentation

As with all dressing changes, record the date and time, treatment, and pertinent wound observations on the patient's chart. Note any patient comfort measures used and how well the patient tolerates the procedure.

CATHERINE A. MAGUIRE, RN, BSN

# Biologic Dressings

*Biologic dressings provide a temporary protective covering for clean partial-thickness burn wounds and areas of clean granulation. They are also used to temporarily secure fresh skin grafts, as well as to protect graft donor sites. Although pigskin is the most commonly used biologic dressing, others include cadaver skin and amniotic membranes, which are usually applied by a doctor in the operating room. These dressings reduce fluid, heat, and electrolyte loss from the wound; relieve pain by covering and immobilizing sensitive nerve endings; help prevent infection; and stimulate new skin growth.*

*Before a biologic dressing is applied, the wound must be cleansed, debrided, or otherwise prepared. The frequency of dressing changes depends on the type of wound and the specific function of the dressing.*

### Equipment

Ordered pain medication □ cap □ mask □ sterile or clean gown □ sterile gloves □ biologic dressing (pig or cadaver skin, or amniotic membrane) □ normal sterile saline solution □ sterile basin □ 18" x 18"

fine mesh gauze (impregnated with a topical agent, if ordered) □ elastic gauze dressing □ stockinette or elastic bandage □ sterile forceps □ sterile scissors □ sterile hemostats.

### Preparation of equipment

Pigskin dressings are available packaged and ready-to-use; frozen, which must be reconstituted in normal sterile saline solution 30 minutes before use; and fresh from a pigskin bank (the most difficult to obtain). Usually, pigskin is packaged as 4" (10 cm) wide strips rolled on fine mesh gauze, which allows it to be rolled directly onto the patient's wound.

Cadaver skin is obtained at autopsy within 24 hours after death and freeze-dried or stored in a special solution. Amniotic membrane is obtained from the delivery room; it must be sterile and the product of an uncomplicated delivery.

Place the pigskin or other biologic dressing in the sterile basin. Using sterile technique, open the packages of sterile dressings. Arrange the equipment on the dressing cart and keep the cart readily accessible. Make sure the treatment area has sufficient lighting *to allow accurate wound assessment and dressing placement.*

### Essential steps

● If this is the patient's first treatment, explain the procedure to him *to allay his fears and ensure his cooperation.* Provide privacy.

● If ordered, administer an analgesic to the patient 20 minutes before beginning the procedure.

● Wash your hands and put on cap, mask, gown (clean if in a burn unit, sterile if not), and sterile gloves.

● Roll the pigskin directly onto the skin with the shiny side down.

● Apply the pigskin strips so the edges touch but don't overlap. Use sterile forceps if necessary.

● Smooth folds and wrinkles out of the pigskin by rolling it with the hemostat handle, the forceps handle, or your sterile gloved hand *to cover the wound completely and ensure complete adherence.*

- Use the scissors to trim the pigskin around the wound *so it fits the wound without overlapping adjacent areas.*
- Place 18″ × 18″ fine mesh gauze (impregnated with a topical agent, if ordered) over the pigskin *to avoid disturbing the pigskin during the first dressing change.*
- Apply the elastic gauze dressing over the 18″ x 18″ fine mesh gauze to keep the pigskin in place.
- Put a stockinette over the entire area or wrap the area with an elastic bandage to protect the pigskin and ensure that it stays in place.
- Position the patient comfortably.
- Remove the dressing cart; take off gloves, gown, mask, and cap; and discard disposable items according to the hospital's policy.

### Special considerations
Handle the biologic dressing as little as possible. The steps for applying cadaver skin or amniotic membrane are similar, but they are applied by a doctor in the operating room.

### Complications
Infection may develop under the pigskin. Observe the wound carefully during dressing changes for signs of such infection. Suspect an allergic reaction to the dressing if the patient develops a fever within 24 hours.

### Documentation
Record the time and date of dressing changes, areas of application, quality of adherence, and the presence of purulent drainage or any other signs of infection. Note the patient's reaction to the dressing.

CATHERINE A. MAGUIRE, RN, BSN

# Hydrotherapy

*Hydrotherapy for the treatment of serious burns involves immersing the pa-tient on a plinth in a tank of warm water, such as a Hubbard tank, or having the patient sit in a hip tub or bathtub. If the patient is ambulatory, he may walk to the tank, step in with assistance, and sit or lie on a plinth; otherwise, he is transferred to the tank on a stretcher covered with the plinth and immersed into the tank by means of a hoist attached to the plinth. Also known as tub-bing, hydrotherapy is performed by nurses, frequently with the aid of physical therapists, and is used to allow relatively atraumatic wound debridement, dressing changes, removal of previously applied topical agents, and general body cleansing. It also permits nearly fric-tionless range-of-motion exercising of all extremities, which is essential to mini-mize contractures.*

*Hydrotherapy is contraindicated in the presence of any sudden changes in the patient's condition, such as electrolyte or fluid imbalance; body temperature over 103° F. (39° C.) or below 98° F. (37° C.); or sudden increase or decrease in res-piration, pulse, or blood pressure. It is also contraindicated for patients who have mending fractures, endotracheal tubes, or tracheostomies, or those who other-wise need respiratory aid. If the patient has had skin grafts, hydrotherapy is discontinued for 3 to 5 days, as ordered, or until the grafts take.*

### Equipment
Hubbard tank □ plastic tub liner □ stretcher □ headrest □ plinth □ hydraulic hoist □ chemical additives, as ordered □ gown □ mask □ cap □ examination gloves (for removing dressings) □ shoulder-length gloves (for tubbing) □ debride-ment instruments (see "Debridement" in this chapter) □ razor, shaving cream, mild soap, shampoo, washcloth (for general cleansing purposes) □ gauze or foam-rubber surgical sponges □ cotton-tipped applicators □ sterile sheets □ warm, ster-ile bath blankets.

### Preparation of equipment
The tub, its equipment, and the tub room must be thoroughly cleaned and disin-

fected before each treatment *to prevent cross-contamination.* After cleaning, place the tub liner in the tub and fill it with water warmed to 98° to 104° F. (36.6° to 40° C.). Attach the headrest to the sides of the tub. Add prescribed chemicals, such as sodium chloride *(to maintain an isotonic level, usually 0.9%, and prevent dialysis and tissue irritation),* potassium chloride *(to prevent potassium loss),* calcium hypochlorite detergent *(to help prevent infection),* and antifoaming agent *(to reduce sudsing when water is agitated).* Warm the sterile blankets. Be sure that the tub room is warm enough to avoid chilling the patient.

### Essential steps

• If this is the patient's first tub treatment, explain the procedure to him *to allay his fears and ensure his cooperation.* If necessary (such as before debridement), administer an analgesic 20 minutes before the procedure.
• Check the patient's vital signs.
• If the patient is receiving an I.V. infusion, see that there is enough I.V. solution to last throughout the procedure.
• Transfer the patient onto a plinth-covered stretcher and transport him to the therapy room. Ambulatory patients may walk to the therapy room unassisted, if the room is nearby.
• Wash your hands and put on gown, gloves, mask, and surgical cap.
• If the patient's dressings are to be changed, remove the outer dressings and dispose of them properly before immersing the patient in the tank. Leave the fine mesh layer on the wound.

Ambulatory patients may walk to the plinth and sit on it for transfer to the tub, or they may be assisted into the tub and situated on the already lowered plinth.
• Attach the plinth to the overhead hoist with a hydraulic lift, ensuring that hoist hooks are securely fastened to it. Use the hoist to transfer the patient to and from the tub.
• Lower the patient into the tank so his head is supported by the headrest. Allow him to soak for 3 to 5 minutes.
• Remove your gloves and put on the shoulder-length tubbing gloves.
• Remove the rest of the gauze dressings, if any, from the patient's wounds.
• If ordered, place the tub's agitator into the water and turn it on. (It may burn out if turned on out of water.) Since agitators are difficult to clean thoroughly, some plinth liners have pierced tubes through which air is driven to create a froth of air bubbles—a more effective and comfortable type of agitation.
• Cleanse all unburned areas first (encourage the patient to do this himself if he can). Wash unburned skin and shave hairy areas near the wound, as well as facial hair; shampoo the scalp and give mouth care. Provide perineal care, and clean inside the patient's nose and the folds of the ears and eyes with cotton-tipped applicators.
• Gently scrub burned areas with gauze pads or sponges *to remove topical agents, exudates, necrotic tissue, and other debris.* Wound debridement may be done at this time, after turning off the agitator.
• Exercise the patient's extremities with active or passive range-of-motion exercises. A physical therapist may work with the patient at this time.
• When treatment is complete, lift the patient from the water (but still over the tub) with the hoist.
• Spray-rinse the patient's entire body *to remove debris from shaving, cleansing, or debridement.*
• Transfer the plinth and the patient to a stretcher covered with a sterile sheet and bath blanket and cover him with a warm, sterile sheet (a blanket may be added for warmth); pat dry unburned areas and warm him to prevent chilling.
• Transfer the patient to a second stretcher covered with a sterile sheet and blanket and cover the patient with a warm, sterile sheet. Remove gown, gloves, and mask, and then transport him to the dressing area for further debridement, if needed, and application of sterile dressing.
• Drain the tank and clean and disinfect it according to the hospital's policy.

### Special considerations

Remain with the patient at all times, *to*

*prevent him from injuring himself in the tub.* Limit hydrotherapy to 20 to 30 minutes, and watch the patient closely for any adverse reactions.

Whenever possible, the patient is weighed during hydrotherapy, using a hoist that has a load cell, or using table scales. Weighing patients helps assess nutritional status, determine electrolyte imbalance, and measure fluid shift. For example, during the emergency period, a 1 kg weight loss equals a 1 liter fluid loss; in the acute period, fluid retention may indicate renal or congestive heart failure.

Although a Hubbard tank is most often used for hydrotherapy of large burn wounds, any kind of hydrotherapy tub can be used, as appropriate for the patient's size and condition.

### Complications
Incomplete disinfection of tank drains and faucets or a cross contamination from members of the tubbing team may cause infection. The patient may chill easily due to decreased resistance to temperature changes. Fluid or electrolyte imbalance may result from a chemical imbalance between the patient and the tub solution; for example, if insufficient sodium chloride is added to create an isotonic solution, dialysis may occur.

### Documentation
Record the date, time, and patient's reaction to hydrotherapy; the patient's condition (vital signs, condition of wound, and presence of infection or bleeding). Note treatments used, such as debridement. Record any special treatments in the nursing-care plan.

CATHERINE A. MAGUIRE, RN, BSN

# Debridement

*Debridement of a burn wound removes eschar (dead tissue) to prevent or control infection, to promote healing, and to prepare the wound surface for grafting. Debridement usually involves careful prying and cutting of loosened eschar with forceps and scissors to separate it from the viable tissue beneath. Ideally, a burn wound should be debrided daily during the dressing change to avoid possible hemorrhaging from excessively forceful debridement and to reduce the need for extensive debridement under anesthesia. Depending on the size and severity of the burn, debridement may be done at the patient's bedside, in the dressing room, or during hydrotherapy, which softens the eschar for easier removal. If necessary, it may be done in the operating room under partial or general anesthesia.*

*There are no contraindications to debridement. However, closed blisters over partial-thickness burns should not be debrided.*

### Equipment
Ordered pain medication □ two pairs of sterile gloves □ two sterile or clean gowns or aprons □ mask □ cap □ sterile scissors □ sterile forceps □ 4" x 4" sterile gauze sponges □ hemostatic agent (such as Oxycell), as ordered.

### Preparation of equipment
Assemble the needed equipment. Sterile supplies are usually delivered daily from the hospital's central supply department or the pharmacy's central service.

Make sure the following equipment is immediately available to the doctor to control hemorrhage: needle holder and gut suture with needle (2.0 or 3.0 chromic).

### Essential steps
• Explain the procedure to the patient *to allay his fears and ensure his cooperation.*
• Provide privacy. Administer an analgesic 20 minutes before the debridement is scheduled to begin.
• Keep the patient warm and avoid exposing large areas of his body *to prevent chilling and fluid and electrolyte loss.*

• Wash your hands and put on cap, mask, gown or apron (clean if in a burn unit, sterile if not), and sterile gloves.

• Remove the burn dressings and cleanse the wound (for detailed information see "Burn Care" in this chapter).

• Remove your gown or apron and dirty gloves, and change to another gown or apron (again, clean if in a burn unit, sterile, if not) and sterile gloves.

• Pick up loosened edges of eschar with forceps, and, with the blunt edge of scissors or forceps, probe the eschar and cut the dead tissue away from the wound with the scissors. Leave a ¼" (0.6 cm) edge on remaining eschar, *to avoid cutting into viable tissue.*

• Since debridement removes only dead tissue, bleeding should be minimal. If bleeding occurs, apply gentle pressure on the wound with 4" x 4" gauze sponges and apply the hemostatic agent. If bleeding persists, notify the doctor and maintain pressure on the wound until he arrives. Excessive bleeding and spurting may require ligation of vessels.

• Perform additional procedures, such as application of topical medications and dressings replacement, if ordered.

• If debridement was performed in a special area, return the patient to his room.

### Special considerations
Work quickly, with an assistant if possible, to complete this painful procedure as quickly as possible. Provide psychological support. Don't debride more than a 4" × 4" (10 cm × 10 cm) area at one time, and limit the procedure to no more than 20 minutes, if possible.

### Complications
Because burns damage or destroy the protective skin barrier, infection may develop despite the use of sterile technique. Some blood may be lost during the debriding process. Debridement may cause bleeding when it inadvertently cuts or erodes a blood vessel.

### Documentation
Record the date and time of debridement, area debrided, medications used, condition of the wound (including signs of infection or skin breakdown), and patient's reaction to the procedure.

CATHERINE A. MAGUIRE, RN, BSN

# Autograft Care

*An autograft is a portion of healthy skin taken from another part of the patient's own body to resurface an area damaged by full-thickness burn injury. Successful autografting depends on clean wound granulation with adequate vascularization; complete contact of the graft with its bed; good aseptic technique; adequate graft immobilization; and skilled postoperative observation and care.*

*The size and depth of the patient's burns determine whether they will require grafting. Grafting usually is done when wound debridement is complete, about 14 to 21 days after the injury. With enzymatic debridement, grafting may be performed 5 to 7 days after debridement is complete; with surgical debridement, grafting can be performed the same day as the surgery.*

*Depending on your hospital's policy, either a doctor or a specially trained nurse may change autograft dressings. Dressings are usually left unchanged for 4 to 5 days after surgery to avoid disturbing the graft.*

### Equipment
Ordered analgesic □ clean and sterile gloves □ cap □ mask □ sterile gown □ sterile forceps □ sterile scissors □ sterile 4" x 4" gauze sponges □ sterile elastic gauze dressing □ sterile fine mesh gauze □ warm, sterile normal saline solution □ moisturizing cream □ topical agent (such as micronized silver sulfadiazine cream) □ sterile cotton-tipped applicators (optional).

### Preparation of equipment
Assemble the equipment on the dressings cart.

## CARE OF A DONOR GRAFT SITE

Autografts are usually taken from another area of the patient's body with a dermatome, which cuts uniform split-thickness slices of skin that are about 0.005″ to 0.02″ (0.013 to 0.05 cm) thick. The donor site is cared for much the same as the autograft, using dressing changes in the initial stages to prevent infection and promote healing. Depending on the thickness of the graft, the site may be used again in as short a time as 10 days.

Consider the donor site a partial-thickness wound that may bleed, drain, and be painful. Scrupulous care of the site is necessary to prevent infection that could convert the wound to full thickness.

• Put on sterile gloves. Apply scarlet red ointment to the donor site, and cover the site with a fine mesh gauze *to prevent infection and promote wound re-epithelialization.* Keep the gauze in place *to promote healing.*

• Apply an elastic gauze bandage soaked in peroxide–normal saline solution to the site every 6 to 8 hours until the dressing or the donor site dries and stops oozing, usually in 3 to 5 days.

• Remove the elastic gauze bandage to expose the donor site dressing, and trim ragged edges, if necessary.

• Peel off and clip the dressing as it dries. When the gauze is thoroughly dry—usually within 10 days—soak it with water *to aid removal.* A dry dressing indicates healing.

• Remove crusts with soap and water and apply a lanolin cream after the dressing is removed. Do not apply a lanolin cream until the dressing is thoroughly dry.

• If evidence of infection is noted (purulence and/or inflammation), soak off the donor site dressing and dress the area with a local antiinfective, such as silver sulfadiazine, as ordered.

• Apply a lanolin cream daily to completely healed donor sites and to healed recipient sites *to keep them pliable and to remove crusts.*

### Essential steps

• Explain the procedure to the patient and provide privacy. Administer an analgesic, as ordered, 20 to 30 minutes before beginning the procedure.

• Wash your hands.

• Put on the sterile gown and the clean mask, cap, and gloves.

• Remove all outer dressings. Then soak the remaining graft dressings with warm saline solution before removing them. Remove all dressings—except the bottom layer of fine mesh gauze—carefully and slowly, *to avoid dislodging the graft.*

• Remove and discard the clean gloves and put on the sterile gloves.

• Assess the condition of the graft. If you observe a purulent drainage, remove the mesh gauze with sterile forceps and cleanse the area gently. If necessary, soak the gauze with the warm saline solution *to facilitate removal.* Remove serous matter from beneath the graft by clipping the bleb with sterile scissors and dabbing the exudate with a gauze sponge or a cotton-tipped applicator. Drain hematomas with a similar technique.

• On large areas, place fresh mesh gauze saturated with the ordered topical agent over the graft *to promote wound healing and prevent infection.* Cover the mesh gauze with elastic gauze dressing.

• Small areas and grafted areas on the patient's face may be left undressed and exposed to air.

• Cleanse any completely healed areas and apply a moisturizing cream to these areas to prevent dryness.

### Special considerations

*To avoid dislodging the graft:* Discontinue hydrotherapy, as ordered, usually for 3 to 4 days after grafting. Avoid using the blood pressure cuff over the graft. Don't use a heat lamp or other source of heat on or near the graft. Don't pull on dressings during dressing changes. Make sure that dressings don't become soaked. Keep the patient from lying on the graft.

### Documentation

Record the time and date of all dressing changes, medications used, condition of the graft, any additional treatment, and the patient's reaction to the graft.

CATHERINE A. MAGUIRE, RN, BSN

# 15 Eye, Ear, and Nose Care

# Eye, Ear, and Nose Care

## Introduction

Because an estimated 70% of all sensory information reaches the brain through the eyes, visual impairment interferes with the ability to function independently, to perceive meaning in the world, and to enjoy much aesthetic pleasure. Untreated hearing loss can drastically impair sound adjustment and interaction; inner ear disorders may also disrupt equilibrium. Nasal disorders can interfere with breathing and cause discomfort and pain.

Since disorders of these organs are as common as they are troublesome, you're likely to perform many of the procedures that follow whether you work in a hospital, school, or industrial setting. You're sure to be called on to assist with or perform diagnostic tests, emergency treatment of trauma, or routine treatments. Nursing procedures affecting these critical organs necessitate the utmost care and precision to prevent infection and injury and preserve function.

Fewer people today lose their sight from infections or injuries than in the past. Nevertheless, the incidence of blindness is rising—primarily because of such diseases as diabetic retinopathy, glaucoma, cataracts, and macular degeneration among the elderly. About 20 million Americans also suffer from some form of hearing loss.

When caring for patients with a sensory loss, remember that they're actually experiencing multiple impairment. Because their sensory ability has been impaired, their perceptual ability has also been diminished. This combined loss significantly alters a person's daily activities and threatens his security.

### Communicate clearly

Performing procedures that diagnose or treat (or even temporarily cause) sensory impairment therefore requires the ability to give clear, simple instructions and explanations. You must also be able to reassure a patient who's sure to be apprehensive about his ability to care for himself and function independently.

In an emergency, effective communication is critical, since you'll be dealing with someone who's suddenly disoriented by sensory and perceptual impairment.

### Patient teaching

The most important contribution you can make in eye, ear, and nose care is to teach preventive health measures by:
- helping the patient recognize the signs and symptoms of sensory disorder.
- stressing the importance of regular examinations to detect problems early.
- advising the patient who works to use safety equipment when applicable.

Always make your explanations thorough. A simple fact or tip that, to you, seems almost too obvious to mention may actually be a valuable insight for the patient.

When the patient leaves you, he should have more than just commonsense guidelines. Let him go with the belief that his ability to understand and enjoy life depends on following them.

MARY J. HALL, RN, MA

# DIAGNOSIS

# Eyelid Eversion

*Eyelid eversion during external eye examinations provides a complete view of the sclera and conjunctiva. It's also useful for irrigating the eye after chemical contamination. Usually, only the lower lids are everted for a screening examination. However, if an abnormal condition is suspected, the upper lid of the affected eye may also be everted (unless swelling prevents manipulation) to inspect the palpebral conjunctiva for foreign objects or inflammation. When chemicals splash into the eyes, upper lid eversion is always indicated to ensure adequate exposure of the cornea, bulbar and palpebral conjunctiva, and the conjunctival fornix, and to permit thorough irrigation of the area. Upper lid eversion for irrigation should be performed with a lid retractor to expose as much of the upper fornix as possible.*

## Equipment
Sterile cotton-tipped applicator (for upper lid eversion) □ sterile lid retractor (for double eversion of the upper lid).

## Preparation of equipment
The lid retractor may be packaged and already sterilized; if it isn't, soak it in an appropriate disinfectant for the indicated time (10 minutes for Cidex; 20 minutes for 70% alcohol). Rinse it thoroughly with sterile water *to prevent chemical burns from the disinfectant.*

## Essential steps
• Explain the procedure to the patient *to help relax him.* Manipulation of the eyelid is easier in a relaxed patient.
• Wash your hands *to prevent contamination of the conjunctiva.*
 *To evert the lower lid:*
• Place your index finger on the lower orbital rim *to avoid pressing the eyeball.*
• With the same finger, gently pull the lower lid downward toward the cheek *to expose the lower conjunctiva.*
• Instruct the patient to look up *to examine the lower lid and the sclera beneath the transparent conjunctiva.*
 *To evert the upper lid:*
• Instruct the patient to look down, keeping his eyes slightly open. *This relaxes the levator muscles; closing the eyes contracts the orbicularis muscle and makes lid eversion more difficult.*
• Grasp the upper eyelashes between your thumb and index finger and pull downward gently. (Pulling the lashes upward or forward causes contractions of the orbicularis muscle.)
• Place the cotton-tipped applicator across the outer surface of the eyelid, about ⅖″ (1 cm) above the lid margin, and use it to push down on the upper lid *so the lid folds over the applicator.*
• Remove the applicator and place it against the upper palpebral surface of the conjunctiva *to keep the lid everted.*
• *To return the upper lid to normal position,* pull the lashes forward and tell the patient to look up and then blink.
 *To double-evert the upper lid with a retractor:*
• After grasping the lashes and pulling them downward, place the retractor with its curved end facing the outer surface of the eyelid and its handle pointing toward the cheek.
• Gently push the retractor down on the upper lid, indenting the lid.
• As the eyelid folds over the curved end of the retractor, raise the handle above the patient's forehead. (The curved end of the retractor should be inside the fold of the lid; the handle, against the brow.)
• *To expose the conjunctival fornix,* pull the eyelid upward with the retractor.
• Return the upper lid to normal position as for upper lid eversion.

## Special considerations
When examining both eyes, wash your hands again before everting the second

lid *to prevent cross-contamination.* Examine the right eye first unless you suspect an infection in that eye.

Make sure the patient looks up during the procedure *to allow adequate visualization of the lower fornix.* If you see signs of eye trauma, especially around the globe of the eye, cover the eye with a sterile dressing and notify the doctor. If, however, you suspect an eye infection, notify the doctor but don't patch the eye.

### Documentation
Record the type of eversion, the eyelid everted, and the indication.

HEATHER BOYD-MONK, RN, SRN, BSN

# Fluorescein Staining

*Fluorescein staining is performed to investigate suspected corneal and conjunctival abrasions, erosion, ulcers, herpes simplex keratitis, and embedded foreign bodies. Because the corneal layers and conjunctiva are transparent, fluorescein staining allows better visualization of these abnormalities than a slit-lamp examination without dye.*

### Equipment
Sterile fluorescein-impregnated strips □ sterile normal saline solution (for eye irrigation) or sterile topical anesthetic (such as proparacaine hydrochloride) □ penlight or cobalt blue light □ tissues.

### Essential steps
- Wash your hands and provide privacy.
- Explain the procedure to the patient. Reassure him that it isn't painful.
- Make sure the patient's head is supported on a headrest or against a wall.
- Remove the sterile fluorescein strip from the package and moisten the tip with a drop of sterile normal saline solution. If applanation tonometry will follow fluorescein staining, moisten the tip with the local anesthetic, as ordered. Gently evert the patient's lower eyelid and touch the lower conjunctival sac with the tip of the fluorescein strip.
- Instruct the patient to gently blink his eyes. *This will spread the dye over the corneal and conjunctival surfaces.*
- If you're staining both eyes, use another sterile fluorescein strip for the second eye *to avoid cross-contamination.* Instruct the patient to look straight ahead.
- Shine the cobalt blue light or penlight from the side of the eye at an oblique angle across the cornea. *This provides better detail than shining the light directly on the cornea.*
- Inspect the cornea under the light. Bright green areas indicate true corneal damage.
- Irrigate thoroughly *to prevent chemical conjunctivitis from the fluorescein.*
- Wipe fluorescein stains off the face.

### Documentation
Note the affected eye and the size and position of the corneal defect—for example, OD (oculus dexter, or right eye), 2 mm abrasion at 7 o'clock.

HEATHER BOYD-MONK, RN, SRN, BSN

## TREATMENT

# Hot and Cold Eye Compresses

*Eye compresses—hot or cold—are soothing and therapeutic. Hot compresses may be used to cleanse the eye*

*and relieve discomfort. Also, because heat increases circulation and thus enhances absorption and decreases inflammation, hot compresses may be applied to promote drainage of superficial infections. Cold compresses can reduce swelling or bleeding, and relieve itching. Cold compresses, which numb sensory fibers,*

## EYE PATCH APPLICATION

Two kinds of eye patches are used: a light patch and a pressure patch. A light patch is usually applied—with or without a plastic or metal shield—to prevent further injury after trauma or surgery, to avoid damage to the eye after administration of a local anesthetic, or for therapeutic use. It's gently applied over the patient's closed eye and secured with two strips of tape. A pressure patch—actually two or three patches—keeps the eyelid closed and thus helps to heal corneal abrasions and control postoperative edema and hemorrhage from trauma. Occasionally, a head dressing may be used with a pressure patch to apply additional pressure or, in burn patients, to secure the patch without tape.

Except in emergencies, an eye patch must be ordered by a doctor, although a nurse usually applies it; a pressure patch requires an ophthalmologist's prescription and supervision. A surface bacterial infection contraindicates an eye patch, because it enhances bacterial growth.

*may also be ordered to ease periorbital discomfort between prescribed doses of pain medication. Usually, hot or cold compresses are applied for a period of 20 minutes, 4 times a day.*

### Equipment
*For hot compresses:*
Prescribed solution, usually tap water or normal saline solution □ sterile bowl □ sterile 4″ x 4″ gauze sponges □ towel.
*For cold compresses:*
Ice chips □ small plastic bag (such as a sandwich bag), or clean examination glove □ ½″ nonallergenic tape □ towel □ sterile 4″ x 4″ gauze sponges □ sterile water, normal saline solution, or prescribed ophthalmic irrigating solution.

### Preparation of equipment
*For hot compresses,* adjust the temperature of the tap water so it's as warm as possible without burning your hand. *To warm a bottle of normal saline solution,* place it in a container of warm water. Run the tap water or pour the normal saline solution into a sterile bowl and

fill it about half-full. Place some gauze sponges in the bowl.

*For cold compresses,* place the ice chips in the plastic bag or the palm of the examination glove. Keep the ice pack small *to avoid excessive pressure on the eye.* Remove excessive air from the bag or glove and knot the open end *so melting ice doesn't spill out.* Cut a piece of nonallergenic tape *to secure the ice pack to the forehead.* Place all equipment on the patient's bedside stand.

### Essential steps
• Explain the procedure to the patient and provide privacy.
• When applying hot compresses, have the patient sit, if possible, so he can help with the procedure. When applying cold compresses, place the patient in the supine position, with his head supported by a pillow and turned slightly to the unaffected side. *This position helps keep the compress in place.*
• Place a towel around the patient's shoulders *to keep his clothing dry.*
*To apply a hot compress:*
• Take two 4″ x 4″ gauze sponges from the basin and wring out the excess solution.
• Tell the patient to close his eyes. Gently apply the sponges—one on top of the other—to the affected eye. (If the patient complains that the compress feels too hot, remove it immediately.)
• Change the compress every few minutes, as necessary, for the prescribed length of time. After removing each compress, check the skin for signs of burning.
*To apply a cold compress:*
• If the patient has an eye patch, remove it.
• Moisten the middle of one of the sterile 4″ x 4″ gauze sponges with the sterile water, normal saline solution, or ophthalmic irrigating solution. *This helps to conduct the cold from the ice pack.* (Keep the edges dry, *so they can absorb excess moisture.*)
• Tell the patient to close his eyes; then place the moist gauze sponge over the affected eye.
• Place the ice pack over the gauze sponge

and tape the knotted end to the forehead. If the patient complains of pain, remove the ice pack. Some patients may have an adverse reaction to cold.

• Remove the tape, ice pack, and gauze sponge after 15 to 20 minutes and discard them.

*After removing an eye compress:*
• Use the remaining sterile 4″ x 4″ gauze sponges to clean and dry the patient's face.

• If ordered, replace the eye patch (see *Eye Patch Application,* opposite).

### Special considerations
When applying hot water compresses, change the water as frequently as necessary *to maintain a constant temperature.*

When teaching a patient to apply warm compresses at home, tell him that he can substitute a clean bowl and facecloth for the sterile equipment.

If ordered to apply moist, cold compresses directly to the eyelid, fill a basin with ice and water and soak 4″ x 4″ gauze sponges in it. Place a compress directly on the lid; change compresses every 2 to 3 minutes.

### Documentation
Record the time and duration of the procedure, the appearance of the eye before and after treatment, and the application of any ointments or dressings.

HEATHER BOYD-MONK, RN, SRN, BSN

# Eye Irrigation
## [*Emergency procedure*]

*Irrigation is used to flush secretions, chemicals, and foreign bodies from the eye. For emergency irrigation, tap water may be used, but it's not preferred because its temperature and pressure are difficult to control.*

*The amount of solution needed to irrigate an eye depends on the contami-nant. Secretions require only small amounts; major chemical burns need copious amounts. Use of I.V. tubing connected to an I.V. bottle or bag of normal saline solution (see* Two Methods of Eye Irrigation, *page 712) ensures that enough solution is available for continuous irrigation of a chemical burn.*

### Equipment
Towels □ retractor □ cotton balls or dry tissues □ proparacaine hydrochloride (optional).

*For moderate irrigation:* prescribed sterile ophthalmic irrigating solution □ cotton-tipped applicators.

*For copious irrigation:* 1,000-ml bottle or bag of normal saline solution □ standard I.V. infusion set without needle.

Commercially prepared bottles of sterile ophthalmic irrigating solution are available. All solutions should be about room temperature; the suggested range is 65° to 72° F. (18° to 22° C.).

### Preparation of equipment
Check the solution for sterility, proper strength, and expiration date. For *moderate irrigation,* remove the cap from the container of sterile ophthalmic irrigating solution and place the container within easy reach. (Be sure to keep the tip of the container sterile.) For *copious irrigation,* use sterile technique to set up the I.V. tubing and the bag or bottle of normal saline solution. Hang the container on an I.V. pole, fill the I.V. tubing with the solution, and adjust the drip regulator valve *to ensure an adequate but not forceful flow.* Place all other equipment within easy reach.

### Essential steps
• Wash your hands and explain the procedure to the patient. If the patient has a chemical burn, ease his anxiety by explaining that irrigation prevents further damage.

• Assist the patient into the supine position, with his head turned to the affected side, *to prevent solution flowing over the nose and into the other eye.*

• Place a towel under the patient's head

## TWO METHODS OF EYE IRRIGATION

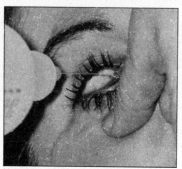

Use the *commercially prepared sterile ophthalmic irrigating solution* method for moderate irrigation procedures, such as removal of eye secretions.

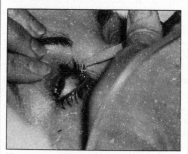

Use the *I.V. tubing* method for heavy irrigation procedures, such as treatment of chemical burns.

and have him hold another towel against his affected side *to catch excess solution.*
• Using the thumb and index finger of your nondominant hand, separate the patient's eyelids.
• If ordered, instill proparacaine hydrochloride eye drops, a topical anesthetic, *as a comfort measure.* Use them only once *because repeated use retards healing.*
• *To irrigate the lower cul-de-sac,* continue holding the eyelids apart with your thumb and index finger. *To irrigate the upper lid (the superior fornix)* use a lid retractor. Steady the hand holding the

retractor by resting it on the patient's forehead. *The retractor prevents the lid from closing involuntarily when solution touches the cornea and conjunctiva.*

*To perform moderate irrigation:*
• Using the bottle of sterile opthalmic irrigating solution, direct a constant, gentle stream at the inner canthus *so the solution flows over the cornea.*
• Evert the lower eyelid and double-evert the upper lid *to inspect for retained chemical particles.* (Double-eversion of the upper lid is especially important when the patient has lime in his eye.)
• Remove any particles by gently sweeping the fornices of the conjunctiva with sterile, wet, cotton-tipped applicators.
• Resume the irrigation until the eye is clean.

*To perform copious irrigation:*
• Open the control valve on the I.V. tubing and direct the stream at the inner canthus, *so the normal saline solution flows across the cornea to the outer canthus.*
• Periodically stop the flow of solution and tell the patient to close the eye *to move secretions from the upper to the lower conjunctival sac. This may also dislodge any particles.*

*After either type of eye irrigation:*
• Dry the eyelids with cotton balls, wiping from the inner to the outer canthus, using a new cotton ball for each wipe. *This reduces the patient's need to rub the eye.*
• When indicated, arrange for follow-up care.
• Wash your hands *to prevent chemical burning from contaminants.*

### Special considerations
When irrigating both eyes, have the patient tilt his head toward the side being irrigated to avoid cross-contamination.

For chemical burns, irrigate each eye with at least 1,000 ml of normal saline solution *to dilute and wash out the harsh chemical.* If the specific chemical is unknown, you can use litmus paper *to determine if the substance is acid or alkali.* (After irrigating any chemical, note the time, date, and chemical for your own reference *in case you develop contact dermatitis.*)

## Documentation
Note the duration of irrigation, as well as the type and amount of solution. Also, record your assessment of the patient before and after irrigation.

HEATHER BOYD-MONK, RN, SRN, BSN

# Eye Cleansing

*A patient's eyes may require cleansing with an irrigating solution when meibomian gland secretions cause his eyelids to stick together during sleep, a normal occurrence. However, this procedure is most commonly performed after eye surgery, when meibomian gland secretions increase, and during eye infections, when exudate combines with these secretions.*

*This is a clean procedure using sterile supplies to minimize the risk of eye infection from contaminated equipment. It may be performed with either a commercial solution in an irrigating bottle or sterile normal saline solution and cotton balls. However, after eye surgery the doctor will specify a cleansing solution and order sterile technique. A special type of eyelid hygiene, using dilute baby shampoo and a cotton-tipped applicator, should be taught to patients with chronic blepharitis.*

## Equipment
Several sterile packages of cotton or rayon balls □ commercial eye cleansing solution or sterile normal saline solution □ optional: sterile gloves (if sterile technique is used), clean gloves (if eye infection is present), sterile cotton-tipped applicators.

## Essential steps
• Explain the procedure to the patient, provide privacy, and wash your hands.
• Open a package of cotton or rayon balls and moisten several with the eye cleansing solution.
• If the doctor has ordered sterile technique, put on sterile gloves. If the patient has an eye infection, put on nonsterile gloves *to protect yourself.*

*To use a commercial solution:*
• Hold a cluster of dry cotton balls at the outer canthus of the appropriate eye.
• Instruct the patient to tilt his head to the side being cleansed.
• With the patient's eyes closed, gently squeeze a stream of cleansing solution across the lids. Direct the stream from the inner to the outer canthus *to avoid contaminating the other eye.*
• Moisten a cotton ball with the cleansing solution, and gently wipe the lids from the inner to the outer canthus *to remove the secretions loosened by the cleansing solution.*

*To use normal saline solution:*
• Moisten a cotton ball with normal saline solution and gently wipe the closed eyelid from the inner to the outer canthus.

*For both methods:*
• Using a fresh cotton ball after each application, repeat the procedure as necessary *to remove all secretions.*
• If the eyelids remain encrusted, moisten a cotton-tipped applicator with the cleansing solution, place it at the eyelid margin, and roll it away from the eye. Then, with a cotton ball also moistened with the cleansing solution, gently wipe the eyelid from the inner to the outer canthus *to remove secretions.* (Repeat this procedure, as necessary.)
• Gently dry the eyelids with a dry cotton ball. *To prevent patient discomfort,* avoid putting pressure on the eyeball; make sure cotton threads don't catch on the eyelashes.

## Special considerations
Since the patient won't be able to watch the procedure, reassure him by explaining each step as you perform it. If neither eye is infected and both require cleansing, always start with the right one. *Then, if you're interrupted, you'll recall which eye has been cleansed.* When one eye is

infected, always clean the uninfected eye first.

## Documentation

Record the condition of the eye before cleansing, noting any drainage. Document the solution used and the condition of the eye after the procedure. On the nursing care plan, note the type of procedure and how often it's required.

HEATHER BOYD-MONK, RN, SRN, BSN

# Ear Irrigation

*Irrigating the ear involves washing the external auditory canal with a stream of solution to cleanse the canal of discharge, to soften and remove impacted cerumen, or to dislodge a foreign body. Ear irrigation must be performed carefully to avoid causing discomfort or vertigo and to prevent maceration of the skin of the canal (which may precipitate otitis externa). Ear irrigation may contaminate the middle ear if the tympanic membrane is ruptured. For this reason, visual examination by the doctor with an otoscope always precedes ear irrigation.*

*This procedure is contraindicated when the auditory canal is obstructed by a vegetable foreign body, such as a pea, a bean, or a kernel of corn. These foreign bodies are hygroscopic—that is, they absorb moisture. Instilling an irrigating solution will cause them to swell, causing intense pain and complicating removal of the object. Ear irrigation is also contraindicated if the patient has a cold, fever, ear infection, or a known injury or rupture of the tympanic membrane.*

## Equipment

Ear irrigation syringe (Pomeroy, bulb, or rubber bulb) □ 500 ml of irrigating solution (normal saline, alcohol, or oil) □ large basin □ otoscope □ linen-saver pad and bath towel □ emesis basin □ cotton balls or cotton-tipped applicators □ 4″ x 4″ gauze sponge □ optional: adjustable light (such as gooseneck lamp), irrigating container, tubing, clamp, and catheter with ear tip.

## Preparation of equipment

Select the appropriate syringe (see *Syringes for Ear Irrigation*) and obtain the prescribed irrigating solution. Put the container of irrigating solution into the large basin, which should be filled with hot water *to warm the solution to body temperature*—95° to 105° F. (35° to 40.6° C.). Avoid extreme temperature changes, which can affect inner ear fluids, causing nausea and dizziness. Test the temperature of the solution by placing a few drops on the inner aspect of your wrist. Inspect all glass syringe or catheter tips for breakage; inspect all metal tips for roughness. (A glass ear tip has two extensions: the solution enters the ear through one and leaves through the other.)

## Essential steps

• Explain the procedure to the patient, provide privacy, and wash your hands.
• If you haven't already done so, use the otoscope to check the auditory canal to be irrigated.
• Assist the patient to a sitting position. *To prevent the solution from running down his neck,* tilt his head slightly forward and toward the affected side. If the patient can't sit, have him lie on his back and tilt his head slightly forward and toward the affected ear. Then, sit in a chair at the side of the bed.
• Make sure you have adequate lighting.
• If the patient is sitting, place the linen-saver pad—covered with the bath towel—on his shoulder and upper arm, under the affected ear. If he's lying down, cover his pillow and the area under the affected ear.
• Have the patient hold the emesis basin close to his head under the affected ear.
• *To avoid getting dirt into the ear canal,* clean the auricle and the meatus of the auditory canal with a cotton ball or cotton-tipped applicator moistened with normal saline or irrigating solution.

• Draw up the irrigating solution into the syringe and expel any air.

• *To facilitate irrigation,* straighten the auditory canal by grasping the helix between the thumb and index finger of your nondominant hand and pulling upward and backward. (For a child, grasp the earlobe and pull it downward and backward.)

• Place the tip of the irrigating syringe at the meatus of the auditory canal. Make sure you don't occlude the meatus *because this will prevent the solution from running back out the ear, causing increased pressure in the canal.*

• Point the tip of the syringe upward and toward the posterior ear canal *so the solution can flow forward and carry debris out of the ear.*

• Begin irrigation by directing a gentle flow of solution against the canal wall. *This avoids damage to the tympanic membrane and also avoids pushing debris further into the canal.*

• Observe the patient for signs of pain or dizziness. If either occurs, stop the procedure immediately.

• When the syringe is empty, remove it and inspect the return flow. Refill the syringe and continue the irrigation until the return flow is clear or until you've used all the solution.

• Remove the syringe and inspect the ear canal *for cleanliness* with the otoscope.

• Dry the patient's auricle and neck.

• Remove the bath towel and linen-saver pad. Help the seated patient lie on his affected side with the 4″ x 4″ gauze sponge under his ear *to facilitate drainage of residual debris.*

### Special considerations

Avoid dropping or squirting solution on the eardrum: *This could startle the patient and cause him discomfort.* Never use more than 500 ml of solution during this procedure.

If you're using an irrigating catheter instead of a syringe, regulate the flow of solution to a steady, comfortable rate with the irrigation clamp. Don't raise the container above 6″ (15 cm). *If the*

EQUIPMENT

## SYRINGES FOR EAR IRRIGATION

The **bulb syringe** (illustrated at top left) is usually preferred because it won't exert excessive force. The **rubber bulb syringe** (illustrated at bottom left) provides insufficient force for adults but is preferred for children. The **Pomeroy syringe** (illustrated at right) exerts the most force, so it must be used with caution.

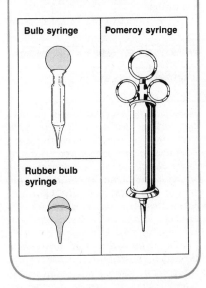

| Bulb syringe | Pomeroy syringe |
| --- | --- |
| Rubber bulb syringe | |

*container is higher, the resulting pressure may damage the tympanic membrane.*

The doctor may order you to place a cotton pledget in the ear canal *to retain some of the solution.* If he does, pack the cotton loosely and instruct the patient not to remove it.

If irrigation doesn't dislodge impacted cerumen, the doctor may order you to instill several drops of glycerin, carbamide peroxide (Debrox), or a similar preparation two to three times daily for 2 to 3 days, and then irrigate the ear again.

## Complications

Possible complications are vertigo, skin maceration, otitis externa, and, if the tympanic membrane is ruptured, otitis media. Forceful instillation of solution can rupture the tympanic membrane.

## Documentation

Record the date and time of the irrigation and which ear was irrigated. Also note the volume and the solution used, the appearance of the canal both before and after irrigation, the appearance of the return flow, the patient's tolerance of the procedure, and any comments he made regarding his condition.

PATRICIA GONCE MILLER, RN, MS

# Nasal Packing

*Nasal packing is necessary when the usual therapeutic measures, such as direct pressure or cautery, fail to control severe epistaxis. An anterior nasal pack—a strip of petrolatum or iodoform gauze—is inserted in horizontal layers into the anterior nostrils, usually near the turbinates. A posterior nasal pack consists of rolled gauze secured with strong silk sutures that help shape the pack. The loose ends of the sutures are brought through the nostrils and are used to provide traction against the bleeding vessels after the pack is inserted into the nasopharynx. The patient with a posterior nasal pack is sedated and hospitalized until the pack is removed, usually in 2 to 5 days.*

*Anterior and posterior nasal packing is performed by a doctor, with a nurse assisting. Foley and nasal balloon catheters may also be used to provide pressure on a posterior bleeding site; the inflated balloon provides traction against the bleeding vessel.*

## Equipment

Headlamp or head mirror □ suction apparatus (with sterile suction connecting tubing and sterile nasal aspirator tip) □ two sterile towels □ local anesthetic spray or vial of local anesthetic solution (usually 5% to 10% cocaine, 0.05% phenylephrine hydrochloride with tetracaine hydrochloride, or 1% lidocaine hydrochloride with 1:100,000 epinephrine solution) □ 10-ml syringe with a 22G 1½″ needle (for withdrawal of anesthetic solution from vial) □ small sterile cup (for vial of anesthetic solution) □ sterile bowl □ sterile normal saline solution □ sterile anterior nasal pack (½″ wide petrolatum or iodoform gauze) or posterior pack (4″ x 4″ sterile gauze sponges tied in a roll and secured with three 18″ heavy silk sutures) □ antibiotic ointment □ three gowns (for patient, doctor, and nurse) □ sedative or tranquilizer □ sterile cotton-tipped applicators □ nasal speculum □ electrocautery or silver nitrate pledgets □ sterile bayonet forceps □ water-soluble lubricant □ two #10 or #12 French catheters (smaller size for child) □ Kelly clamp □ dental roll □ nonallergenic tape □ flashlight, scissors, and hemostat (for use in an emergency) □ sterile gloves (optional).

Commercially made posterior nasal packs are available. Some hospitals carry an ear, nose, and throat (ENT) tray in the central supply department; the tray includes pharyngeal (dental) mirrors, speculums, and forceps. Some doctors may prefer to secure a posterior nasal pack with umbilical cord tape instead of sutures.

## Preparation of equipment

Place all equipment at the patient's bedside. Make sure the headlamp is working properly. Plug the suction apparatus into the wall outlet, attach connecting tubing, and make sure it's working properly. At the bedside, create a sterile field with the two sterile towels or the ENT tray. Using sterile technique, place all sterile equipment on the sterile field.

If you're using a local anesthetic solution instead of a spray, withdraw it from the vial with the 22G 1½″ needle attached to the 10-ml syringe, and place it in the small sterile cup. Open the sterile

# NASAL BALLOON CATHETERS

To control posterior epistaxis, the doctor may use a nasal balloon catheter instead of posterior nasal packing. These catheters are self-retaining and disposable, and can be either single- or double-cuffed. The single-cuffed catheter (see illustration at left) consists of a cuff that, when inflated, compresses the blood vessels, and a soft, collapsible outside bulb that prevents the catheter from slipping out of place posteriorly.

The double-cuffed catheter (see illustration at right) consists of a posterior cuff that, when inflated, secures the catheter in the nasopharynx; an anterior cuff that, when inflated, compresses the blood vessels; and a central airway that helps the patient breathe more comfortably. Each cuff is inflated independently.

Before insertion, the doctor lubricates the catheter with an antibiotic ointment and inserts it through the patient's nostril.

He then inflates the balloon by inserting sterile saline solution into the appropriate valve. (If a double-cuffed catheter is used, the doctor will inflate the posterior cuff first.) He may secure the catheter by taping its anterior tip to the outside of the patient's nose.

To remove the catheter, the doctor deflates the balloon by inserting the hub of a syringe deeply into the valve and withdrawing the solution. He then gently withdraws the catheter from the nostril.

Check the placement of these catheters routinely. With a double-cuffed catheter, you may clean the central airway with a small-gauge suction catheter *to remove clots or secretions.* The doctor may want to deflate the cuff for 10 minutes every 24 hours *to prevent damage to the patient's nasal mucosa.* Expect to find a small amount of discharge around the catheter each day.

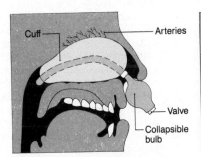

**Single-cuffed catheter inflated in place**

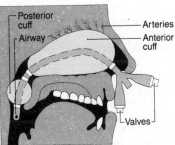

**Double-cuffed catheter inflated in place**

suction-connecting tubing and place it on the sterile field. Fill the sterile bowl with the normal saline solution *so the suction tubing can be flushed as necessary.*

If a commercially made posterior pack isn't available, wash your hands, put on sterile gloves, and make a posterior pack by rolling a sterile 4″ x 4″ gauze sponge. Trim excess gauze with sterile scissors. The pack should be 1½″ wide by 1″ (3.75 cm x 2.5 cm) in diameter. Secure the roll with three silk sutures. Place a

suture at each end and one in the middle of the roll; let the ends of the sutures hang free. Thoroughly lubricate both anterior and posterior nasal packing with the antibiotic ointment.

## Essential steps

● Explain the procedure to the patient and offer reassurance to reduce anxiety. Provide privacy and wash your hands. Put on one of the gowns, and have the patient also put one on.
● Assist the patient to a sitting position.

Have him lean forward *to prevent blood from draining into his throat and choking him.* Have the patient apply pressure to his nostrils *to minimize bleeding while you prepare for the procedure.* If the patient can't apply pressure, apply it yourself or have another nurse do so while you prepare for the procedure.

• Take the patient's vital signs *to check his tolerance of the sitting position.*

• The sedative or tranquilizer is administered, as ordered, *to reduce anxiety.* Continue to monitor the patient's vital signs *because the drug may mask signs of impending hypovolemic shock.*

• The doctor anesthetizes the patient's nasal passages with the anesthetic spray or a cotton-tipped applicator dipped in anesthetic solution. The anesthetic is a vasoconstrictor that may temporarily bring the bleeding under control. (If the doctor wants to wear sterile gloves, he puts them on at this step.)

• Observe the patient for signs of aspiration *because the anesthetic may suppress the gag reflex.*

• As soon as the anesthetic takes effect, the doctor prepares to use suction to clear the patient's nose of any blood clots. *This helps locate the source of the bleeding.* Turn the suction apparatus on. The doctor attaches the nasal aspirator tip to the connecting tubing.

• As soon as the doctor has cleared the patient's nose, he inserts the nasal speculum and uses the headlamp or head mirror to locate the source of the bleeding.

• If the doctor determines that the source of the bleeding is in the anterior nose, he may attempt to control it with electrocautery or silver nitrate pledgets.

• If the anterior nose bleed continues after electrocautery or insertion of silver nitrate pledgets, the doctor inserts a deep anterior pack. Using the bayonet forceps, he layers the ½" petrolatum or iodoform gauze strip horizontally in the nose *to prevent it from falling into the patient's throat. Horizontal layers also ensure uniform pressure in the anterior nostrils.* One end of the gauze is left in the tip of the nostril *to allow easy removal*

of the packing. (If the patient has both anterior and posterior bleeding, the doctor will insert an anterior pack after the posterior pack.)

• If the source of the bleeding is in the posterior nose, the doctor will insert a posterior nasal pack. First, he lubricates the catheters with the water-soluble lubricant. Then, he inserts the catheters into the patient's nostrils and slowly advances them into the nasopharynx. Instruct the patient to pant *to minimize gagging.*

• When the tips of the catheters become visible in the nasopharynx, the doctor pulls them out through the patient's mouth with the Kelly clamp. He then secures the left suture on the nasal pack to the left catheter tip and the right suture to the right catheter tip. The middle suture hangs free.

• The doctor withdraws the catheters through the patient's nose until the sutures tied to the nasal pack emerge from the patient's nostrils. He then attaches the Kelly clamp over both sutures. The middle suture is now hanging out of the patient's mouth. Applying steady traction on the sutures with the Kelly clamps, he pulls the pack into place behind the patient's soft palate, against the posterior end of the septum, and uses the index finger of his free hand to tuck the pack tightly behind the soft palate. The doctor examines the patient's throat *to make sure the uvula hasn't been forced up under the pack.*

• Using the Kelly clamp, tautly hold the sutures that have been drawn through the nose, while the doctor detaches the sutures from the catheters and packs the anterior nose. Make sure you hold the sutures straight out from the centers of the nostrils *to prevent them from cutting the floor of the nose.*

• The doctor maintains pressure on the sutures and secures the posterior pack in place by tying the two sutures hanging from the nostrils around a dental roll, which will rest just under the patient's nose. *This also helps prevent irritation of the nasal septum.* He then tapes the middle suture to the patient's cheek, leaving enough slack for the patient to open and close his mouth and swallow comfortably. *This prevents stress on the suture, which could cut the patient's lip and soft palate.*

● Assist the patient to a comfortable position. If he has difficulty breathing and relaxing, elevate the head of his bed.

● Place emergency equipment (such as a flashlight, scissors, and a hemostat) at the patient's bedside *in case the posterior packing accidentally slips out of place and obstructs the patient's airway.*

● Make sure the patient's call bell is within reach and is working properly, *so the patient can call for help quickly.*

● Take the patient's vital signs after the procedure and continue to monitor them frequently. Notify the doctor immediately if complications develop.

### Special considerations

Avoid tension on the middle suture taped to the patient's cheek *because it may cause the posterior pack to slip down, obstructing the patient's airway.*

 If the nasal pack does slip out of place, obstructing the patient's airway, quickly cut the sutures on the dental roll, untape the middle suture, attach the hemostat to the middle suture, and pull the pack out through the mouth.

If bleeding is significant, a complete blood count is obtained as soon as possible. A type and cross match of blood may also be necessary. Arterial blood gases are checked after insertion of a nasal pack *to detect hypoxia.*

Assess for new bleeding and check the pack periodically. The doctor may have to reposition or remove the pack.

Observe the patient closely, noting his level of consciousness. Monitor his vital signs frequently, and listen to his breath sounds.

 Watch for signs and symptoms of hypoxia (tachycardia, confusion, cyanosis, or restlessness). Notify the doctor if any of these clinical effects develop. Obtain an order for arterial blood gas (ABG) analysis and oxygen

administration. Give the oxygen by mask as soon as the ABG's are drawn.

Maintain an I.V. line and give a mild sedative, if ordered.

After the doctor removes the nasal packs, tell the patient not to blow his nose for at least 48 hours.

As an alternative to a posterior nasal pack, a Foley catheter may be used. *The advantage of this alternate method is the fact that a Foley catheter doesn't have to be drawn from below the palate through the mouth.* Single- and double-cuffed nasal catheters can also be used to apply pressure on a posterior bleeding site (see illustration on page 717).

### Complications

Because a posterior nasal pack depresses the soft palate, thus causing airway resistance, it may lead to carbon dioxide retention and hypoxia. The sedative or tranquilizer used during nasal packing may cause hypertension or hypotension. Severe bleeding and hypovolemia may cause hypotension. The sedated patient may aspirate bloody secretions. A posterior nasal pack that slips out of place may obstruct the airway. A bulky posterior pack may cause difficulty swallowing. Other possible complications include sinusitis, otitis media, hemotympanum, or pressure necrosis.

### Documentation

In the nurse's notes, record the number and type of nasal packs used *to ensure that all packs are removed after treatment.* On the patient's intake and output sheet, record the approximate amount of blood lost, the volume of I.V. fluids administered, liquids taken orally, and any blood transfused. Also note in the nurse's notes the patient's response to the procedure, his vital signs, any drugs administered, whether an I.V. line is in place, and laboratory tests and complications. If a Foley catheter was used, record its size and the amount of fluid in the balloon. If a nasal balloon catheter is used, record the type used and the amount of fluid in the balloon.

SUSAN VIGEANT, RN, BSN

# 16 Obstetric and Gynecologic Care

# Obstetric and Gynecologic Care

## Introduction

Because of its profound implications for the patient's emotional well-being, gynecologic and obstetric care requires expertise that goes beyond the usual clinical skills. Such care must reflect clinical competence combined with sensitivity and good judgment that take into account the patient's sexuality and self-image and recognize the personal implications of changing social attitudes and values. Contemporary nursing care must, for example, cope effectively with such diversely demanding problems as cancer, venereal disease, rape, and childbirth alternatives. The latter surely represents one of the most dramatic, pervasive, and almost universally accepted social and medical changes.

### Childbirth alternatives

Nearly 3.6 million infants were born in the United States in 1981. Many of these births took place with considerably less medical intervention than was customary in the previous decade, primarily because parents today frequently choose to control the circumstances of their child's birth. They question the need for medical management of labor—the routine administration of analgesics and anesthetics, for example—instead of passively accepting it as part of a prescribed childbirth ritual. Consequently, various childbirth alternatives have emerged.

Perhaps the most dramatic change in obstetrics is the burgeoning movement toward prepared childbirth. The philosophy behind prepared childbirth holds that labor and delivery are natural phenomena that should be fully experienced by a woman who is awake and alert. Childbirth classes, often conducted by nurses, prepare the woman to control pain during labor through breathing and relaxation techniques and by encouraging the husband to be present in the labor and delivery rooms to provide support and direction.

The delivery setting is also a matter of choice for today's parents. Although most deliveries still take place in a hospital, home births are becoming increasingly popular. A *birth center,* usually located in the maternity unit of a hospital or operated by a childbirth association, combines the advantages of both delivery settings—a homelike environment with quick medical intervention available in an emergency.

### Midwifery

Although the midwife has always been a fixture in rural or poor communities, she has only lately gained recognition and acceptance as a health professional. Today a registered nurse can receive midwifery training and take an examination for licensure. The current trend is to take advantage of the nurse-midwife's expertise, instead of viewing her as merely an obstetric aide. The nurse-midwife works in cooperation with or under the supervision of the doctor, but some state and federal legislatures are considering bills to permit independent practice. Several states now permit direct payment to the nurse-midwife for her services.

PRISCILLA A. BUTTS, RN, MSN

## DIAGNOSIS

# Specimen Collection to Confirm Gonorrhea

*Gonorrhea, the most common venereal disease, results almost exclusively from sexual transmission of the gram-negative microorganism* Neisseria gonorrhoeae. *A gram-stained smear of genital exudate can confirm gonorrhea in 90% of men (see* Collecting a Urethral Specimen, *page 545). However, a culture is necessary to establish this diagnosis in women, because normal vaginal flora contain gram-negative microorganisms.*

*This procedure, performed by a specially trained nurse, involves the collection of a specimen and inoculation of a medium for culture. Collection sites include the endocervix, urethra, rectum, and oropharynx. The procedure should accompany the pelvic exam for women with previous or possible current infection. Although most infected women remain asymptomatic, some develop a greenish-yellow cervical discharge.*

*Collection of an endocervical specimen is contraindicated in prepubescent children to avoid possible cervical laceration. The specimen may be procured from the vaginal mucosa instead.*

## Equipment

*To collect all culture specimens:* culture medium plates—Modified Thayer-Martin (MTM), Martin-Lewis, or New York City □ laboratory request slips.

*To collect an endocervical specimen for culture:* gloves □ drape □ vaginal speculum □ ring forceps □ cotton balls or large cotton swabs □ long, sterile cotton-tipped applicator □ adjustable light.

*To collect a urethral specimen for culture:* sterile wire bacteriologic loop or thin, sterile, urogenital alginate swab □ sterile cotton-tipped applicator □ sterile gloves.

*To collect a rectal specimen for culture:* sterile cotton-tipped applicator.

*To collect an oropharyngeal specimen for culture:* tongue blade □ sterile cotton-tipped applicator.

The culture medium plate must be refrigerated in an inverted position until ready for use. After specimen collection, the inoculated plate must be placed in a carbon dioxide-rich environment within 15 minutes to promote bacterial growth. Some institutions use a carbon dioxide-generating tablet placed in a special plastic bag. Others use Transgrow, a variant of the MTM medium that comes in a screw-cap bottle containing air and carbon dioxide. When laboratory facilities aren't readily available, this bottle preserves the specimen during transport.

## Preparation of equipment

Remove the medium plate from the refrigerator and allow it to reach room temperature. Keep the plate inverted *to prevent accumulation of excess moisture.* Next, label the plate properly.

## Essential steps

● Explain the procedure to the patient and wash your hands.

*To collect an endocervical specimen:*

● Ask the patient if she has used a vaginal douche within the last 24 hours; if she has, reschedule the procedure. *Douching removes cervical secretions and can lead to an inaccurate culture report.*

● Instruct the patient to void *to reduce discomfort during the procedure.* Then, provide privacy and tell her to undress below the waist and to sit on the examining table. Have her drape the pelvic region.

● Place the patient in the lithotomy position, with her feet in the stirrups and her buttocks extending slightly beyond the edge of the table. Adjust the drape *to minimize exposure.*

● Adjust the light *to allow full visualization of the genital area.* Then, fold

# COLLECTION OF RAPE EVIDENCE

Rape generally refers to sexual intercourse between a man and a woman without the woman's consent. *To care for the rape victim:*

• Take her to a private room and provide support. Offer to contact her family or friends.

• Explain the procedure and answer the patient's questions. Ask her to sign a consent form *to authorize the physical examination, collection of evidence, and treatment.* Obtain her medical history and a description of the rape.

• After the doctor performs a thorough physical examination, help him photograph the patient's injuries. *Photographs are legally admissible in court and offer proof of injury after healing has taken place.*

• Darken the room and examine the patient's clothing and body with the Wood's light. *The ultraviolet rays cause seminal fluid to appear fluorescent blue because of its high acid phosphatase levels.* Circle clothing stains that are Wood's light-positive with a laundry marker.

• Using a clean tongue blade, scrape areas that are Wood's light-positive. *Analysis of the scrapings for acid phosphatase and ABH antigen verifies the presence of semen and helps identify the assailant.*

• Comb the pubic hair *to dislodge any loose hair and foreign material.* Next, cut a few of the patient's pubic hairs. *Loose hair can be cross matched against the patient's pubic hair and that of her assailant.*

• Collect clippings from each fingernail. *Skin cells or dried blood found under nails may match those of the assailant. Fibers from clothing or other material may match evidence found at the scene.*

• Collect venous blood samples—one for RPR, a test for syphilis; one for blood type and Rh factor; and one for a pregnancy test. *The patient's blood type and Rh factor must be compared to the assailant's blood type, identified through nail clippings or semen analysis.*

• Before the pelvic exam, instruct the patient to urinate. Tell her not to wipe the vulva *to avoid removal of any semen.*

• If the patient has inserted a tampon, ask her to remove it; then wrap and label it.

• Place the patient in the lithotomy position and drape her. The doctor examines the external genitalia for injuries and evaluates the state of the hymen.

• The doctor inserts a lubricated speculum and inspects the cervix and vagina for trauma. *The speculum is lubricated with water because commercial lubricants retard sperm motility and interfere with specimen collection and analysis.*

• Using a cotton-tipped applicator, the doctor obtains a specimen from the posterior fornix, smears the specimen on a microscope slide, adds a drop of normal saline solution, and places a coverslip over it. *Discovery of motile sperm on this wet mount verifies sexual intercourse within the past 28 hours.*

• The doctor obtains another specimen from the posterior fornix and smears it on a slide. *Gram's stain is applied to this smear to help identify sperm.*

• The doctor collects two final specimens from the posterior fornix and places each into a test tube with normal saline solution—one to be tested for acid phosphatase, the other for ABH antigen. Store these tubes on ice until they're taken to the laboratory. The acid phosphatase test helps determine the time of the assault, *because a fresh ejaculate (from within the past 12 hours) contains the highest concentration of acid phosphatase. It also verifies the presence of seminal fluid when sperm are absent.* Like other body fluids, semen contains the soluble A, B, and H blood group substances in the 80% of males who are genetic secretors. Thus, blood group A substance in the seminal fluid points to an assailant who is a secretor with blood group A.

• The doctor collects endocervical and urethral specimens for gonorrhea culture, as well as oral and rectal specimens, if necessary. Because collection of an endocervical specimen may dislodge motile sperm from the endocervix, this procedure must follow collection of posterior fornix secretions *to avoid collection of sperm from someone other than the assailant.*

• Carefully label all specimens, and list them in your notes.

• The doctor performs a bimanual examination of the uterus. He also examines the anus if the patient reports penetration there. After this exam, the doctor cleans any cuts and treats lacerations.

• Collect a specimen of the patient's saliva and place it in a test tube filled with normal saline solution. *An ABH antigen test of sputum determines the patient's secretory status, which is compared to that of the alleged assailant.*

• Allow the patient to wash and dress.

• Develop a follow-up care plan to meet the patient's needs. Give her the names and phone numbers of local organizations for counseling rape victims, such as Women Organized Against Rape (WOAR).

SUE M. JONES, RNC, FNC, MSN

back the drape *to expose the perineum.*
• Put on sterile gloves, grasp the speculum, and moisten it with warm water *to provide lubrication.* Avoid using water-soluble lubricants, *since these contaminate the specimen.* Next, insert the vaginal speculum and lock it in place.
• Using cotton balls in the ring forceps, or a large cotton-tipped swab, clean mucus from the cervix.
• Insert a long, sterile cotton-tipped applicator into the endocervical canal, and rotate it from side to side. Leave the cotton-tipped applicator in place for 10 to 30 seconds *to allow absorption of organisms.*
• Unlock the speculum and remove it.
*To collect a urethral specimen:*
• With the patient in the lithotomy position, insert a sterile wire bacteriologic loop or a thin, sterile, urogenital alginate swab no more than ⅘" (2 cm) into the urethra, and rotate the swab or loop from side to side. Leave it in place for 10 to 30 seconds *to allow absorption of organisms.*

Or, you can milk the urethra of secretions to obtain the specimen. Simply press one finger of your gloved hand against the anterior vaginal wall. Then, withdraw your finger *to expel secretions.* Next, collect secretions with a dry, sterile cotton-tipped applicator.
*To collect a rectal specimen:*
• With the patient in the lithotomy position, insert a sterile cotton-tipped applicator about 1" (2.5 cm) into the anal canal. Rotate the applicator from side to side, and leave it in place for 10 to 30 seconds *to allow absorption of organisms.*
• If the cotton-tipped applicator is contaminated with feces, discard it and repeat the procedure using a clean applicator.
*To collect an oropharyngeal specimen:*
• Instruct the patient to sit erect in a chair, to tilt her head backward, and to close her eyes.
• Using a tongue blade, observe the patient's throat for inflammation. Then, use a dry, sterile cotton-tipped applicator to gently stroke the tonsillar areas, including any inflamed or purulent sites. Avoid touching the teeth, cheeks, or tongue with the applicator *to prevent specimen contamination.*
*After all specimen collections:*
• Prepare the culture medium, as ordered. If you're using an MTM plate, roll the swab on it in a Z pattern. Then, using a wire loop, cross-streak the plate *to evenly distribute the specimen.* Then, send the specimen to the laboratory immediately, along with the appropriate slips.

If you're using Transgrow, inoculate the medium with the bottle upright *to prevent loss of carbon dioxide.* Then, arrange for transport of the Transgrow bottle, *since the specimen requires subculturing within 24 to 48 hours to obtain successful growths.*
• Assist the patient from the examining table, and provide privacy for her to dress.
• Carefully dispose of gloves, cotton-tipped applicators, and speculum *to prevent staff exposure to the organism.* Wash your hands.

**Special considerations**
Advise the patient to refrain from sexual activity until test results are available (usually in 24 to 72 hours). If test results confirm gonorrhea, instruct the patient to return for repeat testing 3 to 5 days after completion of treatment. Also offer the patient and, if possible, her partner counseling to deal with the emotional distress caused by the diagnosis of gonorrhea.

**Documentation**
Record the date, time, and site(s) of specimen collection; description of any discharge; and the patient's response to the procedure.

VICKI SCHWARTZ BEAVER, RN, MS

# Papanicolaou Test
[*Pap test, Pap smear*]

*The Papanicolaou test, a cytologic test*

developed in the 1920s by George N. Papanicolaou, allows early detection of cervical cancer. Performed by a doctor or a specially trained nurse, this test involves scraping secretions from the cervix, spreading them on a slide, and immediately coating the slide with fixative spray or solution to preserve specimen cells for nuclear staining. Cytologic evaluation then outlines cell maturity, morphology, and metabolic activity. Although cervical scrapings are the most common test specimen, the Pap test also permits cytologic evaluation of the vaginal pool, prostatic secretions, urine, gastric secretions, cavity fluids, bronchial aspirations, and sputum.

## Equipment
Bivalve vaginal speculum □ gloves □ Pap stick (wooden spatula) □ long cotton-tipped applicator □ three glass microscope slides □ fixative (a commercial spray or 95% ethyl alcohol solution in a jar) □ adjustable lamp □ drape □ laboratory request slips.

## Preparation of equipment
Select the appropriate-sized speculum, and gather the equipment in the examining room. Label the glass slides with the patient's name and E, C, and V to differentiate endocervical, cervical, and vaginal specimens.

## Essential steps
● Explain the procedure to the patient and wash your hands.
● Instruct the patient to void to relax the perineal muscles and facilitate bimanual examination of the uterus.
● Provide privacy and instruct the patient to undress below the waist, but to wear her shoes, if desired, to cushion her feet against the stirrups. Then, instruct her to sit on the examining table and to drape her genital region.
● Place the patient in the lithotomy position, with her feet in the stirrups and her buttocks extended slightly beyond the edge of the table. Adjust the drape.
● Adjust the lamp to fully illuminate the genital area. Then, fold back the corner

of the drape to expose the perineum.
● If you're performing the procedure, first place a glove on your nondominant hand. Then, grasp the speculum with your dominant hand, and moisten it with warm water to ease insertion. Avoid using water-soluble lubricants, which can interfere with accurate laboratory testing.
● Warn the patient that you're about to touch her to avoid startling her. Then, gently separate the labia with the thumb and forefinger of your gloved hand.
● Instruct the patient to take several deep breaths, and insert the speculum into the vagina. Once it's in place, slowly open the blades to expose the cervix. Then, lock the blades in place.
● Insert a cotton-tipped applicator through the speculum ⅕" (0.5 cm) into the cervical os. Rotate it 360° to obtain an endocervical specimen. Then, remove the cotton-tipped applicator and gently roll it in a circle across the slide marked E. Refrain from rubbing the applicator on the slide to prevent cell destruction. Immediately place the slide in a fixative solution or spray it with a fixative to prevent drying of the cells, which interferes with nuclear staining and cytologic interpretation.
● Insert the small curved end of the Pap stick through the speculum and place it directly over the cervical os. Rotate the stick gently but firmly to scrape cells loose. Remove the stick, spread the specimen across the slide marked C, and fix it immediately, as before.
● Insert the opposite end of the Pap stick or a cotton-tipped applicator through the speculum, and scrape the posterior fornix or vaginal pool—an area that collects cells from the endometrium, vagina, and cervix. Remove the stick or applicator, spread the specimen across the slide marked V, and fix it immediately.
● Unlock the speculum to ease removal and avoid accidentally pinching the vaginal wall. Then, withdraw the speculum.
● After the bimanual exam, which usually follows the Pap test, gently remove the patient's feet from the stirrups and assist her to a sitting position. Provide privacy for her to dress.

• Fill out the appropriate laboratory slips, including the date of the patient's last menses.

## Special considerations

Many preventable factors can interfere with the Pap test's accuracy, so provide appropriate patient teaching beforehand. For example, use of a vaginal douche in the 48-hour period before specimen collection washes away cellular deposits and prevents adequate sampling. Instillation of vaginal medications in the same period makes cytologic interpretation difficult. Collection of a specimen during menstruation prevents adequate sampling because menstrual flow washes away cells; ideally, such collection should take place 5 to 6 days before menses or 1 week after it. Application of topical antibiotics promotes rapid, heavy shedding of cells and requires postponement of the Pap test for at least 1 month.

If the patient has had a complete hysterectomy, collect test specimens from the vaginal pool and cuff.

## Complications

Failure to unlock the speculum blades before removal can pinch vaginal tissue. Although slight cramping normally accompanies this exam, rough handling of the speculum can cause severe cramping. Scraping an inflamed cervix with the Pap stick can cause slight bleeding.

## Documentation

On the patient's chart, record the date and time of specimen collection, any complications, and the nursing action taken.

CAROL ANN GRAMSE, RN, PhD

# Endometrial Biopsy

*Biopsy of the endometrium—the mucosal uterine lining that sloughs off and regenerates during each menstrual cycle—determines the causes of intermenstrual bleeding (hyperplasia, carcinoma) or infertility, and detects luteal deficiency. In a premenopausal patient, endometrial biopsy is usually performed on the first day of the menstrual period, to avoid interfering with a possible uterine pregnancy. In a menopausal patient, the biopsy may be performed at any time.*

*The procedure is performed by a gynecologist, with a nurse assisting, in the doctor's office or in an outpatient facility. Biopsy is performed by curettage or by flushing out endometrial cells with a jet washer. The latter technique may be used as a screening test for endometrial carcinoma.*

## Equipment

*For curettage:* drape □ clean gloves □ Papanicolaou (Pap) test kit, if needed □ sterile gloves □ two vaginal specula (one sterile) □ povidone-iodine solution □ sterile sponge sticks □ 4″ x 4″ sterile gauze sponges □ sterile tenaculum □ sterile uterine sound □ sterile 5- or 10-ml syringe □ sterile Novak curette or other type of sterile endometrial biopsy curette □ specimen container with formalin preservative and tight-fitting lid □ peri-pad.

*For jet washing:* disposable sterile Gravlee jet washer □ sterile normal saline solution □ sterile gloves □ povidone-iodine solution □ sterile tenaculum □ vaginal speculum □ water-soluble lubricant □ sterile uterine sound □ sponge sticks □ sterile drapes □ Pap test kit.

## Essential steps

• Instruct the patient to void and to remove all clothing from the waist down. Provide a drape for cover.
• Explain the procedure to the patient and tell her that she may experience discomfort similar to menstrual cramps *because of cervical dilatation.*
• If a Mayo stand is being used, adjust it to a convenient height for the doctor. Carefully open the sterile wrapper from around the instrument tray, using sterile technique. Leave the wrapper on the Mayo stand *to create a sterile field.* Using sterile technique, open the inside wrapper

to expose the necessary instruments. If the instruments are individually wrapped, open them just before use, if the doctor prefers.

• Place the patient in the lithotomy position, with her feet in the stirrups. Adjust the drape *to minimize exposure and to give the doctor an unobstructed view of the perineum.*

*For curettage:*

• Provide the doctor with a pair of clean gloves and a clean speculum. He may perform a Pap test and will examine the uterus bimanually.

• After the bimanual examination, give the doctor the sterile gloves and a sterile speculum.

• The doctor cleanses the cervix and vaginal vault with povidone-iodine solution, using a sterile sponge stick and gauze sponges. Next, he grasps the cervix with the sterile tenaculum and applies traction. He measures the depth of the uterus with a uterine sound *to avoid perforation with the curette.*

• After the doctor withdraws the sound, attach the syringe to the curette and hand it to him. The doctor gently inserts the curette and draws it from back to front in a single swipe, while retracting the plunger of the syringe. When he has collected enough tissue in the curette, he withdraws it, disconnects it from the syringe, and fills the syringe with formalin *to preserve the tissue specimen.* Finally, he reconnects the apparatus and forces the specimen through the curette into the specimen container.

• Close the specimen container, label it, and send it to the laboratory with a completed laboratory request slip.

• Remove the patient's feet from the stirrups and assist her to a sitting position. Give her a peri-pad *to absorb any postprocedure bleeding,* and tell her to report any abnormal bleeding. Provide privacy for her to dress.

*For jet wash (Gravlee):*

• After examining the uterus and performing a Pap test (as explained in curettage), the doctor bends the cannula of the jet washer to fit the curvature of the uterine cavity. Then, he pours 30 ml of

## TWO METHODS OF ENDOMETRIAL BIOPSY

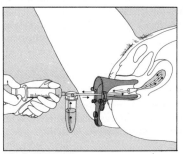

**Gravlee jet wash**
A jet washer (illustrated above) consists of a syringe, a reservoir for saline solution, and a cannula with a rubber plug at the end to prevent leakage of solution during the procedure; a speculum prevents retraction of the vaginal walls. Pushing the plunger of the syringe forces isotonic saline solution into the uterus through the cannula. Then the saline solution, which now contains endometrial cells, returns through the cannula into the syringe.

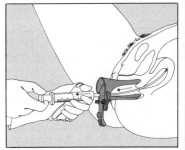

**Curettage**
The Nova curette (illustrated above) is attached to a syringe for insertion; a speculum prevents retraction of the vaginal walls. To draw the collected tissue into the syringe, the doctor pulls back the plunger of the syringe while scraping cell samples from the endometrial walls.

sterile normal saline solution into the reservoir and attaches it to the screw cap on the apparatus (see *Two Methods of Endometrial Biopsy,* above). Next, he gently inserts the cannula into the uterus, making sure the rubber plug is snug in the cervical os *to prevent saline solution from leaking out during the irrigation.*

• When the doctor retracts the plunger of the syringe, saline solution draws into the uterus, irrigates the endometrial tissue, and returns through the cannula into the syringe. When the syringe is filled, the doctor withdraws the device from the uterus, disconnects the syringe, and expels its contents into the reservoir, which now doubles as a specimen container.

• Close the specimen container, label it properly, and send it with a completed request slip to the laboratory. If the specimen can't be sent immediately, add a preservative, such as formalin.

• Remove the patient's feet from the stirrups and assist her to a sitting position. Provide privacy for her to dress.

### Special considerations
If the patient experiences cramps, provide an analgesic such as aspirin, if ordered, or apply heat to the lower abdomen.

### Documentation
In the patient's record, document the procedure, date, doctor's name, and the patient's response.

JOANNE ROSSMAN KEYS, RN, BSN

---

# FETAL EVALUATION

## Fetal Heart Rate

*Used to screen for fetal well-being during gestation and labor, auscultation of fetal heart rate (FHR) involves counting fetal heart beats after placement of a fetoscope or Doppler stethoscope on the maternal abdomen. Simultaneous determination of maternal pulse by palpation prevents confusion of maternal and fetal heart beats. The fetoscope can detect FHR as early as the 18th week of gestation. It's useful during the early stage of labor when contractions are mild and infrequent, but may be less reliable in later stages. The Doppler stethoscope, a more sensitive instrument, can detect FHR as early as the 10th week of gestation, and is useful throughout labor.*

*Because FHR usually ranges from 120 to 160 beats per minute, auscultation yields only an average rate, at best. It can detect gross, but often late, signs of fetal distress (tachycardia, bradycardia) and is thus recommended in the uncomplicated pregnancy. For the high-risk pregnancy, indirect or direct electronic fetal monitoring provides more accurate information on fetal status.*

### Equipment
Fetoscope or Doppler stethoscope with ultrasound transducer □ mineral oil or water-soluble jelly (for Doppler) □ watch or clock with second hand □ drape or sheet.

### Essential steps
• Explain the procedure to the patient, wash your hands, and provide privacy. Assure the patient that detection of the loudest fetal heart sounds can require repeated instrument repositioning.

• Assist the patient to a supine position and drape her appropriately *to minimize exposure.* If you're using the Doppler stethoscope, rub mineral oil or water-soluble jelly on the patient's abdomen *to create an airtight seal between the skin and transducer, thereby promoting optimal ultrasound wave reception.*

*To count FHR during gestation:*
• If the fetus is less than 20 weeks old, place the bell of the fetoscope or the head of the Doppler stethoscope at the midline of the abdomen above the pubic hairline. Later in pregnancy, when fetal position can be determined, palpate for the back of the fetal thorax and position the instrument directly over it. Locate the loudest heart beats, and palpate the maternal pulse.

• Count fetal heart beats for at least 15 seconds, while monitoring maternal pulse. Record FHR/ minute.

*To count FHR during labor:*
• Position the fetoscope or Doppler stethoscope on the abdomen midway between the umbilicus and symphysis pubis for cephalic presentation, or above or at the level of the umbilicus for breech presentation. Locate the loudest heart beats, and palpate the maternal pulse.
• Monitor maternal pulse and count fetal heart beats for 60 seconds during the relaxation period between contractions *to determine baseline FHR.* Then count heart beats for 60 seconds during a contraction and for 30 seconds immediately after it.
• Notify the doctor immediately of marked changes in FHR from the baseline, especially during or immediately after a contraction. Remember that signs of fetal distress most often occur immediately after a contraction. If fetal distress develops, begin indirect or direct electronic fetal monitoring.
• Repeat the procedure, as ordered.

### Special considerations
If you're auscultating FHR with the Doppler stethoscope, be aware that obesity and hydramnios can cause absorption of sound waves, making the procedure difficult to perform accurately. If the doctor orders continuous FHR monitoring, strap the transducer to the maternal abdomen; a microphone within the transducer amplifies FHR.

### Documentation
Record FHR and maternal pulse on the flow sheet.
VICKI SCHWARTZ BEAVER, RN, MS

# Amniocentesis

*Performed by a doctor with a nurse assisting, amniocentesis is the sterile needle aspiration of fluid from the amniotic sac for laboratory analysis. Usually performed between the 14th and 16th weeks*
*of pregnancy, this procedure can detect open neural tube, chromosomal, and genetic defects, as well as certain metabolic disorders; it can also determine the sex of the fetus and assess its health. During the last trimester of pregnancy, amniocentesis can help evaluate fetal lung maturity and monitor Rh hemolytic disease.*

*Indications for amniocentesis include maternal age over 35 (associated with increased risk of Down's syndrome) and a family history of inborn errors of metabolism or of neural tube, chromosomal, or genetic defects. This invasive procedure rarely produces maternal or fetal complications. It may be performed on an outpatient basis in an operating room, a labor and delivery suite, or a treatment room near the labor and delivery suite.*

*Contraindications include an anterior uterine wall completely covered by the placenta and insufficient amniotic fluid.*

### Equipment
Hospital gown □ two pairs of sterile gloves, sterile gowns, and masks □ sphygmomanometer □ stethoscope □ thermometer □ ultrasound transducer □ Doppler stethoscope or fetoscope □ antiseptic solution with sterile container □ sterile 4″ x 4″ gauze sponges □ local anesthetic □ 10-ml syringe □ 22G or 25G needle □ sterile 20G or 22G 4″ spinal needle with stylet □ sterile 20-ml glass syringe □ clean amber glass specimen container (for Rh sensitization and lecithin/sphingomyelin [L/S] ratio tests) □ three sterile glass specimen tubes (for genetic tests) □ adhesive bandage.

Many hospitals provide amniocentesis trays that contain all the necessary equipment.

### Preparation of equipment
If an amber specimen container isn't available, secure adhesive tape or aluminum foil around the outside of a clean test tube or glass container. *Aspirated amniotic fluid must be protected from light to prevent the breakdown of pigments, such as bilirubin.* Properly label all specimen containers or tubes.

## Essential steps

• Explain the procedure to the patient. Make sure she understands that the risk of complications is low; that the doctor may need to repeat the procedure; that amniotic fluid analysis can't rule out all birth defects; and, for a multiple pregnancy, that the procedure provides information only for the fetuses tested.

• Make sure the patient has signed a consent form.

• *To reduce the risk of bladder puncture,* have the patient void just before the procedure.

• Provide privacy and instruct the patient to put on a hospital gown. Assist her to a supine position and obtain baseline maternal vital signs. Next, obtain a baseline fetal heart rate (FHR) with the Doppler stethoscope or fetoscope.

• *To ensure sterility of the needle insertion site,* tell the patient to fold her hands on her chest so you can cover them with the hospital gown, or have her place her hands behind her head. Also, remind the patient to remain still.

• The doctor will use an ultrasound scan to locate the fetus and placenta. When a pocket of amniotic fluid is identified, he determines the appropriate depth for needle insertion. Next, the doctor puts on the sterile gown, sterile gloves, and mask and prepares the skin with an antiseptic solution.

• Clean the diaphragm of the multidose vial of anesthetic solution with alcohol and invert the bottle to allow the doctor to withdraw and administer the anesthetic.

• Scrub, and put on sterile gown, sterile gloves, and mask to assist the doctor in the sterile procedure.

• After the anesthetic takes effect, the doctor inserts the 20G needle with a stylet through the abdomen and uterine wall into the amniotic sac. He removes the stylet and, when a drop of amniotic fluid appears, he attaches the 20-ml glass syringe to the needle and aspirates fluid.

• For a genetic study, open the sterile glass specimen tubes. As soon as the doctor transfers the amniotic fluid to the tubes, using sterile technique, close the tubes. *Contamination of the specimen can cause chromosomal aberrations.* The doctor discards the first 5 ml of fluid because it may contain maternal cells.

• For the Rh sensitization or L/S ratio test, open the amber or covered specimen container *so the doctor can transfer the amniotic fluid.* Then close the container *to protect the fluid from light and prevent the breakdown of pigments,* such as bilirubin.

• When the doctor withdraws the needle, place an adhesive bandage over the insertion site.

• Complete the laboratory request slips and send the specimen(s) to the laboratory immediately. If the amniotic fluid is bloody or meconium-stained, immediate centrifugation preserves the specimen for analysis.

• If the patient is in the third trimester of pregnancy, instruct her to lie on her side *to avoid hypotension from pressure of the gravid uterus on the vena cava.* Monitor maternal vital signs and FHR every 15 minutes for 30 minutes to detect any changes from the baseline measurements.

 Fetal tachycardia or bradycardia may indicate distress. If these signs appear, notify the doctor and monitor FHR until they resolve.

• Instruct the patient to report vaginal discharge of fluid or blood, decreased fetal movement, contractions, or fever and chills.

• Have the outpatient rest until her vital signs are stable. Then assist her to dress in preparation for discharge.

## Special considerations

Provide emotional support to the patient during the procedure, and explain the key steps as the doctor performs them. Also monitor the patient for signs and symptoms of supine hypotension, such as light-headedness, nausea and diaphoresis.

## Complications

Maternal complications of amniocentesis are rare (less than 1%), but may include amniotic fluid embolism, hemorrhage, infection, induced labor, abruptio placentae, bladder or intestinal puncture, and Rh isoimmunization.

Fetal complications, which are also uncommon, include intrauterine fetal death, amnionitis, injury from needle puncture, amniotic fluid leakage, bleeding, abortion, and premature delivery.

## Documentation

Record the doctor's name, the date and time, baseline maternal vital signs and FHR, and changes in baseline data. Note ordered laboratory tests, amount and appearance of the specimen, and time of transport to the laboratory.

SHERON L. SALYER, RNC, BSN

# Antepartal Nonstress Test

*Performed by a specially trained nurse, the nonstress test (NST) evaluates fetal well-being by measuring the fetal heart response to spontaneous uterine contractions or fetal movements; such contractions or movements produce transient accelerations in the heart rate of a healthy fetus. Usually ordered during the third trimester of pregnancy, this noninvasive screening test uses indirect electronic monitoring to record fetal heart rate (FHR) and the duration of uterine contractions. It's indicated for suspected fetal distress or placental insufficiency associated with diabetes mellitus, hyperthyroidism, chronic or pregnancy-induced hypertension, collagen disease, heart disease, chronic renal disease, intrauterine growth retardation, sickle cell disease, Rh sensitization, suspected postmaturity, a history of miscarriage or stillbirth, aspiration of meconium-stained amniotic fluid, or abnormal estriol excretion.*

## Equipment

Electronic fetal monitor □ tocotransdu-cer □ ultrasound transducer, phono-transducer, or abdominal fetal EKG apparatus □ conductive gel □ transducer straps □ monitor printout paper.

The ultrasound transducer is most frequently used to monitor FHR.

## Preparation of equipment

Set up equipment for indirect fetal monitoring (see "Indirect Fetal Monitoring" in this chapter).

## Essential steps

• Explain the procedure to the patient *to reassure her.* Provide privacy and wash your hands.

• Place the patient in a semi-Fowler's or lateral tilt position with a pillow under one hip. Avoid positioning the patient supine, *because pressure on the maternal great vessels from the gravid uterus may cause maternal hypotension and reduce uterine perfusion, leading to fetal hypoxia and inaccurate test results.* Drape the patient to avoid unnecessary exposure, but leave her abdomen uncovered.

• Apply the conductive gel, and position and secure the tocotransducer and FHR transducer to the maternal abdomen. Turn on the fetal monitor.

• Obtain baseline maternal vital signs and record them on the printout paper. Also note on the printout the patient's name, the date and time, and the reason for the test.

• Instruct the patient to depress the monitor's mark or test button when she feels the fetus move. If she's unable to reach the button, tell her to immediately report fetal movement *so you can note it on the printout paper.*

• If you fail to record spontaneous fetal movement within 20 minutes, gently shake the abdomen or apply gentle pressure. *Since the fetus alternates between approximately 20-minute periods of activity and rest, external stimulation may stir him to move.*

• If you record two FHR accelerations that exceed baseline by at least 15 beats per minute, that last longer than 15 seconds, and occur within a 10-minute period, conclude the test. *Such findings, called a reactive NST, indicate that an intact autonomic nervous system controls FHR.* Turn off the fetal monitor, disconnect the transducers, and provide privacy for the patient to dress.

• If you fail to obtain reactive results, monitor the fetus for an additional 40 minutes. If you still fail to obtain these results, perform the contraction stress test (CST), as ordered, *to provide more definitive information on fetal status.*

### Special considerations
Testing is usually performed weekly in high-risk pregnancies.

### Documentation
On the printout paper, record the time of changes in the maternal position and FHR, fetal movement, uterine contractions, and external stimulation.

SHERON L. SALYER, RNC, BSN

# Antepartal Contraction Stress Test
### [*Oxytocin challenge test (OCT)*]

*The antepartal contraction stress test (CST) evaluates the respiratory function of the placenta and identifies the fetus who will be unable to withstand the stress of labor. Performed by a specially trained nurse, this test uses indirect electronic monitoring to measure fetal heart response to spontaneous or oxytocin-induced uterine contractions. Such contractions produce a transient reduction in uteroplacental blood flow, causing a decelerated heart rate in the fetus compromised by placental insufficiency. Similar to the nonstress test (NST), the CST is indicated for the patient with suspected fetal compromise or placental insufficiency because of diabetes mellitus, hyperthyroidism, chronic or pregnancy-*induced hypertension, collagen disease, heart disease, chronic renal disease, sickle-cell disease, intrauterine growth retardation, Rh sensitization, suspected fetal postmaturity, a history of miscarriage or stillbirth, aspiration of meconium-stained amniotic fluid, or abnormal estriol excretion. It's also indicated after a nonreactive NST.*

*Contraindications to the CST include premature labor or membrane rupture, multiple gestation, hydramnios, previous cesarean section, placenta previa, and incompetent cervical os. If the test must be performed, it requires preparation for emergency delivery.*

### Equipment
Electronic fetal monitor □ tocotransducer □ ultrasound transducer □ conductive gel □ transducer straps □ printout paper □ sphygmomanometer □ stethoscope □ continuous infusion pump and tubing □ oxytocin solution, as ordered □ prescribed I.V. solution □ I.V. administration set for primary line □ 20G 1″ needle □ venipuncture equipment.

### Preparation of equipment
Set up the equipment for indirect fetal monitoring (see "Indirect Fetal Monitoring" in this chapter), and check for proper operation of the infusion pump.

### Essential steps
• Explain the procedure to the patient *to reassure her,* and offer emotional support. Make sure that the patient has signed a consent form, if required. Provide privacy and wash your hands.
• Instruct the patient to void *since the test takes 1½ to 2 hours to complete.*
• Assist the patient to a semi-Fowler's or a lateral-tilt position, and put a pillow beneath one hip. Avoid the supine position *since pressure on the maternal great vessels from the gravid uterus may cause maternal hypotension and reduce uterine perfusion, leading to fetal hypoxia and inaccurate test results.* Drape the patient but leave her abdomen uncovered.
• Position and secure the tocotransducer

## LATE DECELERATIONS OF FETAL HEART RATE

Late decelerations of the fetal heart rate (FHR) occur in response to uterine contractions in fetal compromise or placental insufficiency. In such insufficiency, the respiratory function of the placenta is inadequate to supply the fetus with enough oxygen to last through a contraction. As a contraction increases in intensity, blood flow through the uterine muscle to the placenta decreases. At the peak of a contraction blood flow is drastically reduced, but it then gradually returns to normal. Late decelerations usually begin at the peak of a contraction. Baseline FHR then fails to return until after the contraction passes, as shown.

**Fetal heart rate (bpm)**

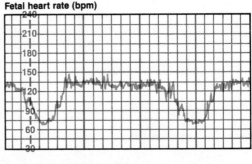

**Uterine contractions (mmHg)**

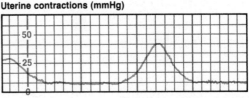

and ultrasound transducer to the abdomen. Turn on the fetal monitor.

● Obtain baseline maternal vital signs and record them on the printout. Also note the patient's name, the date and time, and the reason for the test.

● Record baseline measurements of uterine contractions, fetal movement, and fetal heart rate (FHR) for 20 minutes. If necessary, adjust the equipment *to obtain readable data.*

● If you record three spontaneous uterine contractions within a 10-minute period, conclude the test. If you record a reactive NST (see "Antepartal Nonstress Test" in this chapter), notify the doctor; he may consider the test complete. However, if testing fails to meet the specified criteria, prepare the oxytocin solution for infusion, as ordered, and label the solution container with the dilution.

● Connect one end of the infusion pump tubing to the solution bag and connect the opposite end to the pump. Then attach a 20G 1″ needle to the tubing to piggyback it to the primary I.V. line.

● Start a primary I.V. line, preferably in a peripheral vein, using the prescribed solution *to maintain venous access.*

● Piggyback the oxytocin solution into the primary I.V. line at the Y-injection port closest to the patient. *Piggybacking at this port ensures that the primary line contains the smallest possible concentration of oxytocin, allowing rapid termination of the infusion.*

● Set the drip rate of oxytocin to 1 to 2 mU/minute, or as ordered.

● Every 15 minutes, increase the drip rate 1 to 2 mU/minute, or as ordered, until you record three contractions in 10 minutes with clear FHR tracings. Avoid too rapid infusion *to prevent hyperstimulation of the uterus, resulting in iatrogenic late decelerations and inaccurate test results.*

● After recording the three contractions, stop the oxytocin drip. Continue to monitor the patient for 30 minutes or until the contraction rate returns to baseline.

● Send the printout to the doctor for interpretation. Make sure the patient is comfortable while she waits for the results of the test.

● When the test results are available, discontinue the I.V. line, if ordered. Dis-

## LEOPOLD'S MANEUVERS

Performing the four Leopold's maneuvers helps you determine fetal presentation and position, which are useful for accurate transducer placement for fetal monitoring.

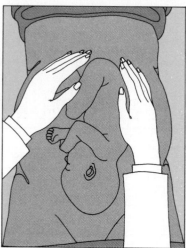

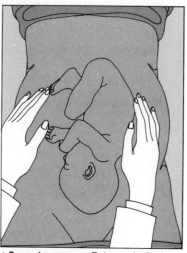

• **First maneuver:** To determine whether the head or buttocks occupies the fundus, face the patient, and palpate the upper abdomen with both hands. If the fetus is in the vertex position—left occiput anterior (LOA)—you'll feel an irregularly shaped, soft part: the fetus' buttocks. If the fetus is in the breech position, you'll feel a hard, round, movable fetal part: the fetus' head.

• **Second maneuver:** To locate the fetal back, palpate both sides of the abdomen separately. To palpate the right side of the abdomen, apply deep but gentle pressure with the palm of your right hand while steadying the uterus with your left hand. Repeat for the left side, using your left hand to palpate and your right one to steady the uterus. On one side you should feel a smooth, hard surface offering resistance: the fetal back. On the other side of the abdomen, expect to feel some irregular knobs or lumps: the fetus' hands, feet, elbows, and knees. If the fetus is in the breech position, its back will be more difficult, if not impossible, to find.

assemble and discard the disposable I.V. equipment.

### Special considerations

During the procedure, monitor the patient's blood pressure before each increase in the oxytocin drip rate. On rare occasions, administration of oxytocin induces hypotension.

If bradycardia, hyperstimulation of the uterus, or prolonged FHR decelerations occur, stop the oxytocin drip, change the patient's position, and use a face mask to administer 6 to 10 liters of oxygen/minute. Then, notify the doctor and continue to monitor FHR. Explain these procedures to the patient as you perform them *to reassure her.*

### Complications

Rarely, the oxytocin challenge test may induce labor.

### Documentation

On the printout, note the time of changes in maternal position and FHR, fetal movement, uterine contractions, incremental increases in oxytocin dosage, and vital signs. Also record this information,

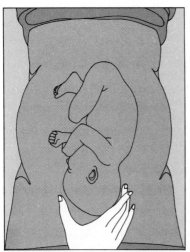 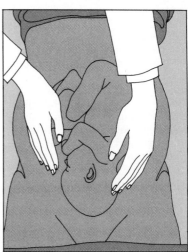

• **Third maneuver:** To determine which fetal part lies over the inlet, spread apart the thumb and fingers of your dominant hand, and gently grasp the lower portion of the abdomen just above the symphysis pubis. If the fetus is in the vertex position, you should feel a hard fetal part: the head. If the fetus is in the breech position, expect to feel a soft part: the fetus' buttocks. This maneuver confirms the findings of the first maneuver.

• **Fourth maneuver:** To assess fetal descent into the pelvis, turn and face the mother's feet; palpate both sides of the lower abdomen, moving toward the pubis. If the fetus is in the vertex position and you feel its head, then the head isn't engaged in the pelvic inlet. But if you have difficulty feeling the head, then it's probably engaged. If the fetus is in the breech position and you feel its hips, the buttocks probably aren't engaged in the pelvic inlet. If you have difficulty feeling the hips, the buttocks are probably engaged.

as well as the type of I.V. needle and solution, on the patient's chart.

SHERON L. SALYER, RNC, BSN

# Indirect Fetal Monitoring
[*External fetal monitoring*]

*This noninvasive procedure uses two devices strapped to the mother's abdomen to evaluate fetal well-being during labor. One, an ultrasound transducer, directs high-frequency sound waves through soft body tissues to the fetal heart, records and amplifies the reflected waves, and relays them to a recording assembly that traces fetal heart beats on a printout. The other, a pressure-sensitive toco-transducer activated by rises of the uterine fundus, simultaneously records the length, but not the intensity, of uterine contractions and traces this information on the same printout.*

*Indirect fetal monitoring is indicated for high-risk pregnancy, during oxytocin-*

*induced labor, and for antepartal non-stress and contraction-stress tests. This procedure has no contraindications, but may be difficult to perform on patients with hydramnios, on obese patients, or on very active or premature fetuses.*

## Equipment

Electronic fetal monitor □ tocotransducer □ ultrasound transducer □ conduction gel □ transducer straps □ printout paper.

Phonotransducers and abdominal electrocardiogram (EKG) transducers are commercially available, but these devices aren't used as frequently as the ultrasound transducer.

## Preparation of equipment

Because fetal monitors are varied and complex, first familiarize yourself with the operator's manual. If the monitor has two paper speeds, set the monitor to 3 cm/minute *to ensure a more readable tracing; a 1-cm/minute tracing is too condensed and can interfere with accurate interpretation of test results.* Next, plug the tocotransducer into the uterine activity input jack and the ultrasound transducer into the phono/ultrasound jack. Attach the straps to the tocotransducer and the ultrasound transducer.

Note the patient's name, the date, maternal vital signs and position, the paper speed, and the number of the strip on the printout paper *to maintain consistent monitoring.*

## Essential steps

• Explain the procedure to the patient, and provide emotional support. Inform her that the monitor may make noise if the uterine tracing is above or below the calibrated strips on the printout paper and that this doesn't indicate fetal distress. Also explain other aspects of the monitor *to help reduce anxiety about her infant's well-being.*
• Make sure the patient has signed a consent form, as required.
• Wash your hands and provide privacy.
• Assist the patient to a semi-Fowler's or a left-lateral position with the abdomen

exposed. The patient should not be in a supine position *because pressure from the gravid uterus on the mother's inferior vena cava may cause maternal hypotension and decrease uterine perfusion, resulting in fetal hypoxia.*
• Palpate the patient's abdomen to locate the fundus—the area of greatest muscle density in the uterus. Then place the tocotransducer over the fundus and secure it with a strap.
• Adjust the pen set controls until you obtain a printout of 20 to 25 mmHg between contractions. *This avoids triggering the alarm that sounds when the tracings drop below the paper's margins.* The proper setting varies among tocotransducers.
• Apply conduction gel to the ultrasound transducer crystals *to promote an airtight seal and optimal transmission of ultrasound.*
• Use Leopold's maneuvers (see illustration, pages 734 to 735) to palpate the fetal back, where fetal heart sounds are most audible.
• Start the monitor. Then, place the ultrasound transducer directly over the site of strongest heart sounds, and strap it in place.
• Press the record control to begin the printout. On the printout paper, note any coughing, position changes, drug administration, vaginal examinations, and blood pressure readings that may affect interpretation of tracings.
• Teach the patient and her coach to time and control a contraction with the monitor. To time contractions, inform them that the distance from one vertical line to the next on the printout paper represents a minute. The coach can use this information to prepare the patient for the onset of a contraction and to guide and slow her breathing as the contraction subsides.

*To monitor the patient:*
• Note the frequency and duration of uterine contractions. Palpate the uterus *to determine the intensity of contractions.*
• Check the baseline fetal heart rate (FHR)—the rate between contractions.

(FHR is usually 120 to 160 beats per minute.)

• Assess periodic accelerations or decelerations from the baseline FHR. Note the shape of the FHR pattern in relation to that of the uterine contraction, the time-relationship between the onset of an FHR deceleration and the onset of a uterine contraction, the time-relationship of the lowest level of an FHR deceleration to the peak of a uterine contraction, and the range of FHR deceleration.

• Move the tocotransducer and the ultrasound transducer *to accommodate changes in maternal or fetal position.* Readjust both transducers every hour and assess the patient's skin for reddened areas caused by the strap pressure.

• Clean the ultrasound transducer periodically with a damp cloth *to remove dried conduction gel that can interfere with ultrasound transmission.* Apply fresh gel, as necessary. After use, place the cover over the ultrasound transducer.

### Special considerations

If the patient reports that contractions aren't being recorded on the monitor, suspect equipment error, palpate for contractions, and readjust the tocotransducer. If the patient reports discomfort in the position that provides the clearest signal, first obtain a 5- or 10-minute tracing in this position. If the tracing is satisfactory, assist the patient to a more comfortable position. As she progresses through the second stage of labor, abdominal pressure increases and the tracings may then exceed the alarm boundaries. When it's time for the patient to push, instruct her to push until she hears the alarm, and then try to keep the alarm sounding by pushing as long as possible. The patient can use this as a positive audible signal *to reinforce her efforts to push.*

### Documentation

Number each sheet of printout paper and label it with the patient's name, the date, the time, and the paper speed. Also note the time of any vaginal examinations, membrane rupture, drug administra-

tion, and maternal or fetal movements. Record maternal vital signs and the intensity of uterine contractions. Include a summary of this information in your notes.

VICKI SCHWARTZ BEAVER, RN, MS

# Direct Fetal Monitoring
## [Internal fetal monitoring]

*Performed only after the amniotic sac ruptures and the cervix dilates about 3 cm, this sterile invasive procedure uses a water-filled intrauterine catheter to measure the frequency, duration, and pressure of uterine contractions, and an electrode secured to the presenting fetal part, usually the scalp, to monitor fetal heart rate (FHR). The uterine catheter also allows aspiration of an amniotic fluid specimen for laboratory analysis.*

*When indirect fetal monitoring provides insufficient or suspicious information regarding fetal well-being, direct monitoring furnishes data on true beat-to-beat variations and allows accurate measurement of intrauterine pressure. Because it provides precise information about fetal well-being and the progress of labor, it helps determine the need for intervention. Direct fetal monitoring is usually performed by a doctor with a nurse assisting, but can be performed by a specially trained nurse.*

*Direct fetal monitoring is contraindicated in maternal blood dyscrasias, suspected fetal immune deficiency, and placenta previa; in face, brow, and breech presentations or when there is uncertainty as to the presenting part; or in the presence of cervical or vaginal herpes lesions.*

### Equipment

Electronic fetal monitor □ printout paper □ strain gauge and bracket □ intrauterine catheter and guide □ 20-ml syringe □ 20G needle □ three-way stopcock □ sterile water □ spiral electrode with drive tube and guide tube □ leg plate □ conduction gel □ nonallergenic tape □ two pairs of sterile gloves □ sterile drape □ antiseptic solution (optional).

Commercially available kits for direct fetal monitoring contain the intrauterine catheter and guide, syringe, and three-way stopcock.

### Preparation of equipment

Because fetal monitors are varied and complex, familiarize yourself with the operator's manual before attempting this procedure. If the monitor has two paper speeds, set the monitor to 3 cm/minute *to ensure a readable tracing; a 1-cm/ minute tracing is too condensed and can interfere with accurate interpretation of test results.* Record the number of the strip, the patient's name, the date, the paper speed, the type of procedure, and the reason for the procedure on the printout paper.

Place the strain gauge on the appropriate mounting bracket. Then attach this bracket to the side of the monitor. Connect the strain-gauge cable to the uterine activity outlet on the monitor.

Wash your hands and open the sterile equipment, maintaining aseptic technique. Fill the 20-ml syringe with sterile water.

### Essential steps

● Explain the procedure to the patient and provide emotional support. Inform her that the monitor may make a noise if the uterine tracing swings off the printout paper, but that this doesn't indicate fetal distress.

● Make sure the patient has signed a consent form, if required.

*To assist with catheter insertion:*

● Assist the patient to the dorsal lithotomy position. The doctor then puts on sterile gloves and performs a vaginal examination *to identify the position of the placenta, uterus, and fetal parts.*

● Drape the perineum with a sterile drape. Then cleanse the perineal area with antiseptic solution according to hospital policy. After the doctor puts on

a fresh pair of sterile gloves, he inserts the uterine end of the catheter into the uncurved end of the catheter guide and slides it through.

● Attach the syringe with 20 ml of sterile water to the monitor end of the catheter. Avoid touching the inside of the catheter *to prevent contamination.* Flush the catheter with about 5 ml of water and leave the syringe in place.

● Secure the three-way stopcock to the angle fitting of the strain gauge. Avoid touching the stopcock ports *to prevent contamination.* Adjust the strain gauge so it's level with the patient's xiphoid process *to ensure a correct reading.* Positioning the strain gauge too low causes an erroneously high reading; if the position of the strain gauge is too high, an erroneously low reading results.

● The doctor inserts the catheter with the guide about ⅘" (2 cm) into the cervical opening. Then, holding the guide in place, he advances the catheter into the uterus until the black mark or the word *stop* on the catheter reaches the introitus. Next, he disconnects the syringe from the catheter, removes the catheter guide, and attaches the catheter to the side fitting on the three-way stopcock.

● Tape the catheter to the patient's inner thigh with the nonallergenic tape.

● Refill the syringe with 20 ml of sterile water and secure the syringe to the upright fitting of the stopcock.

● Turn the stopcock lever to the right *to open the connection between the syringe and catheter.* Inject 5 ml of water *to clear air bubbles from the catheter that prevent accurate pressure measurement.*

● Turn the stopcock lever to the left *to close off the catheter.* Lift the pressure-release cap, and inject water *to flush air bubbles from the strain gauge dome.*

● Check the operation of the monitoring system. First, disconnect the syringe from the stopcock fitting *to open the strain gauge to atmospheric pressure.* Next, turn on the monitor. Observe the bottom of the printout where uterine contractions are recorded. A zero level reading indicates the system is operating properly.

Reconnect the syringe to the stopcock fitting.

• Turn the stopcock lever to the upright position *to open the connection between the strain gauge and catheter and begin monitoring.*

*To assist with electrode application:*

• Apply conduction gel to the leg plate. Then secure the leg plate to the patient's inner thigh with the Velcro straps. Next, plug the leg plate into the electrocardiogram (EKG) outlet on the monitor.

• The doctor then performs a vaginal examination *to confirm the fetal presenting part and determine its level of descent. This second examination prevents attachment of the electrode to fetal suture lines or fontanelles, the face, or the genitalia.*

• After checking for proper engagement of the spiral electrode within the drive tube, the doctor advances the two until the electrode reaches the fetal presenting part. *To secure the electrode,* the doctor applies mild pressure and turns the drive tube clockwise 360°.

• After the doctor removes the locking pin and guide tube, connect the color-coded electrode wires to the posts on the leg plate. Turn on the recorder and note the time on the printout paper.

• Assist the patient to a comfortable position and readjust the strain gauge height.

*To monitor the patient:*

• Note the frequency, duration, and intensity of uterine contractions. (Normal intrauterine pressure is between 8 and 12 mmHg.)

• Check the baseline FHR—the rate between contractions. (FHR is usually 120 to 160 beats per minute.)

• Assess periodic accelerations or decelerations from the baseline FHR. Note the shape of the FHR pattern in relation to that of the uterine contraction; the time between the onset of an FHR deceleration and the onset of a uterine contraction; the time between the lowest level of an FHR deceleration and the peak of a uterine contraction; and the range of FHR deceleration.

• Check for FHR variability, a measure of fetal reserve and neurologic control.

## Special considerations

During labor, clean the leg plate and reapply conduction gel, as necessary. Periodically flush the intrauterine catheter *to remove air and vernix that prevent accurate pressure measurement.* Also flush the catheter if the monitor isn't recording contractions. If the FHR tracing isn't clear, tug gently on the electrode wire *to ensure electrode attachment.*

## Complications

Possible maternal complications include uterine perforation and intrauterine infection. Fetal complications may include scalp abscess and hematoma. However, the risk of such complications is slight.

## Documentation

Number each printout sheet and label it with the patient's name, date, time, paper speed, type of procedure, and reason for the procedure. Note insertion of the catheter and electrode, drug administration, vaginal examinations, or position changes on the printout. Periodically summarize this information in your notes. Check hospital policy for required documentation.

VICKI SCHWARTZ BEAVER, RN, MS

## LABOR AND DELIVERY

# Palpation of Uterine Contractions

*Periodic, involuntary uterine contrac-* *tions characterize normal labor and cause progressive cervical effacement and dilatation, and descent of the fetus. Palpation of the uterus evaluates the progress of labor by determining the frequency, duration, and intensity of contractions*

## UNDERSTANDING UTERINE CONTRACTIONS

When plotted on a graph, a uterine contraction forms a bell-shaped curve. The steepest slope of this curve, denoting the rapid rise in intraamniotic pressure, marks the beginning of a contraction. The *duration* of a contraction is the interval of time from the initial tightening of the uterus to the onset of relaxation. *Relaxation* is the period of time between the end of one contraction and the onset of the next. *Frequency* is the interval between the onset of two consecutive contractions. *Intensity* describes the strength of a contraction, or the degree of uterine muscle tension. It varies considerably during labor and may be mild, moderate, or strong.

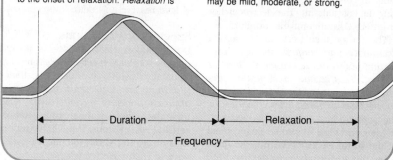

and the relaxation time between them. The character of contractions varies with the stage of labor and the infusion of labor-inducing drugs, such as oxytocin. As labor advances, contractions usually become more frequent and intense, and they last longer. Regular contractions, which occur at 15- to 20-minute intervals and last 10 to 30 seconds, signal the onset of the first stage of labor. Contractions then quicken, arriving every 3 to 5 minutes, and lasting 30 to 45 seconds. At the end of the first stage of labor, when cervical dilatation is complete, contractions occur 1 to 2 minutes apart and last 45 to 60 seconds. In the second stage of labor, which ends with childbirth, contractions are equally close together but last 50 to 90 seconds.

### Equipment

Watch with a second hand □ sheet (for draping).

### Essential steps

• Review the patient's admission history *to determine the onset, frequency, duration, and intensity of contractions*. Also note the location of the strongest contractions or greatest pressure.

• Explain the procedure to the patient, wash your hands, and provide privacy. Warn her before palpating the uterus since she may be ticklish or sensitive to touch.

• Assist the patient to a comfortable position on her side *to remove pressure from the inferior vena cava and promote uteroplacental circulation. This position also relieves direct pressure on the sacral area from the fetal head and eases backache.* Then, drape the patient.

• Place your fingertips on the fundus of the uterus, slightly above the umbilicus, *to assess contractions.* Because the fundus has the greatest proportion of uterine smooth muscle, you'll feel contractions most strongly there. Time the duration and frequency of contractions and the relaxation period between them. Also evaluate the intensity of contractions.

• Assess the patient's breathing and relaxation techniques, and provide emotional support. Observe the patient's response to contractions *to evaluate the need for an analgesic or anesthetic.*

• If appropriate, have the patient palpate a contraction *to decrease her anxiety.*

### Special considerations

Since the patient may become irritable

or panic-stricken during the transition stage of labor—when the cervix dilates from 7 to 10 cm—and abdominal palpation may aggravate her distress, monitor contractions only as necessary. If appropriate, teach her coach to palpate and record contractions.

 If any contraction lasts longer than 90 seconds and isn't followed by uterine muscle relaxation, notify the doctor immediately *to evaluate the effect on maternal and fetal well-being.* Hypertonic contractions can cause uterine rupture and fetal hypoxia.

Also report a short relaxation period between contractions. This period allows the intervillous spaces of the uterus to fill with oxygen and nutrients. Inadequate relaxation between contractions increases the risk of fetal hypoxia and exhausts the mother.

## Documentation

Record the frequency, duration, and intensity of contractions and the relaxation time between them. In your notes, describe the patient's response to contractions.

VICKI SCHWARTZ BEAVER, RN, MS

# Vaginal Examination

*Performed by a doctor or a specially trained nurse, periodic vaginal examination during labor involves palpation of the cervix, the maternal ischial spines, and the fetal presenting part. This sterile procedure monitors the progress of labor by determining cervical dilatation and effacement, fetal presentation and station, and the status of the amniotic membranes. Dilatation is measured in centimeters from 0 to 10; effacement is measured as a percentage from 0 to 100. Usually, a primigravida first experiences effacement and then dilatation; a multigravida experiences both simultaneously (see* Cervical Effacement and Dilatation, *page 742).*

*Palpation through the dilated cervix determines fetal presentation (cephalic, breech, or transverse) and station—the proximity of this presenting part to the level of the maternal ischial spines. Evaluation of amniotic membranes is done to detect membrane rupture.*

*Vaginal examination is contraindicated in patients with excessive vaginal bleeding—a possible indication of placenta previa.*

## Equipment

Sterile glove ☐ sterile water-soluble lubricant.

## Essential steps

● Explain the procedure to the patient, wash your hands, and provide privacy.
● Assist the patient to the lithotomy position and drape her appropriately.
● Put a sterile glove on the hand to be used for the examination. Then apply sterile water-soluble lubricant to the index and middle fingers of the gloved hand *to facilitate the examination.*
● Tell the patient when you are about to touch her *to avoid startling her.* Then gently touch her leg or knee.
● Insert your lubricated fingers into the vagina, palm side downward, *to avoid placing discomforting pressure on the urinary meatus.*
● Place your ungloved hand on the patient's abdomen *to steady the fetus,* and apply gentle downward pressure *to bring the fetal presenting part closer to the cervix for palpation.*
● Palpate for the cervix. In early labor, it may assume a posterior position and be difficult to locate. Once you locate the cervix, note its consistency. Throughout pregnancy, the cervix gradually softens and reaches a butterlike consistency before labor begins.
● During cervical palpation, determine the condition of the amniotic membranes. If you detect a small bulge at the cervix, the membranes are intact. However, if you express amniotic fluid, the membranes have ruptured.
● Estimate cervical dilatation by insert-

## CERVICAL EFFACEMENT AND DILATATION

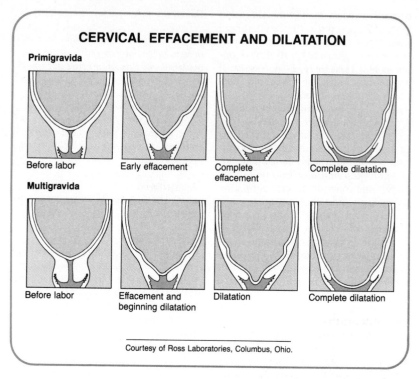

**Primigravida**

Before labor

Early effacement

Complete effacement

Complete dilatation

**Multigravida**

Before labor

Effacement and beginning dilatation

Dilatation

Complete dilatation

Courtesy of Ross Laboratories, Columbus, Ohio.

ing your fingers inside the internal os. Each fingerbreadth of dilatation equals about 1.5 to 2 cm.

• Determine the percentage of effacement by palpating the ridge of tissue around the cervix.

• Determine the fetal presenting part and its station by palpation. To determine station, first locate the ischial spines on the side walls of the pelvis. Then compare the location of the presenting part with the ischial spines. Noted in centimeters, station may be above (expressed as minus), below (expressed as plus), or at the level of the ischial spines (zero), indicating engagement.

• After completing the examination, cleanse excess lubricant from the patient's perineum. Change linens, if necessary, and wash your hands.

• Describe labor progress *to encourage the patient and help reduce anxiety.*

### Special considerations

In early labor, perform the vaginal ex-amination between contractions, focusing primarily on the extent of cervical dilatation and effacement. At the end of the first stage, perform the examination during a contraction, when the uterine muscle pushes the fetus downward, but emphasize evaluation of fetal descent.

If the amniotic membrane ruptures, record the fetal heart rate (FHR). Then note the time and describe the color, odor, and approximate amount of fluid. If FHR becomes unstable, notify the doctor, determine fetal station, and check for umbilical cord prolapse. After the membranes rupture, perform the vaginal examination only when labor changes significantly *to minimize the risk of intrauterine infection.*

### Documentation

After each examination, record the percentage of effacement, dilatation in centimeters, the station of the fetal presenting part, and amniotic membrane status.

VICKI SCHWARTZ BEAVER, RN, MS

# Oxytocin Administration

*The hormone oxytocin stimulates uterine smooth muscle to contract and causes cervical dilatation. Synthetic oxytocin may be administered intravenously to artificially induce or augment labor. This hormone is administered with an infusion pump for optimal regulation of oxytocin dosage, which varies with uterine sensitivity, and to help prevent hyperstimulation of the uterus.*

*The doctor decides whether to use oxytocin during labor; the nurse is responsible for managing the oxytocin infusion and for monitoring maternal-fetal response to its administration, which helps prevent complications. Generally, indications for use of oxytocin during labor include pregnancy-induced hypertension, prolonged gestation, maternal diabetes, Rh sensitization, and premature or prolonged rupture of membranes.*

*Contraindications include situations in which induction or continuation of labor are inadvisable—for example, placenta previa, diagnosed cephalopelvic disproportion, and fetal distress. Oxytocin should be administered cautiously in a patient with an overdistended uterus, or in patients with a history of cervical or uterine surgery or grand multiparity.*

## Equipment

Administration set for primary I.V. line □ infusion pump and tubing □ I.V. solution, as ordered □ equipment for indirect or direct fetal monitoring (see "Indirect Fetal Monitoring" and "Direct Fetal Monitoring" in this chapter) □ oxytocin □ 20G 1″ needle □ medication-added label □ venipuncture equipment, with an 18G over-the-needle catheter.

## Preparation of equipment

Prepare the oxytocin solution, as ordered. Label the I.V. container with the dilution. Then attach the infusion pump tubing to the I.V. container, and connect it to the infusion pump. Review the operator's manual before beginning the procedure *since infusion pumps vary.*

Attach the 20G 1″ needle to the tubing *to piggyback it to the primary intravenous line.* Then, set up the equipment for direct or indirect fetal monitoring.

## Essential steps

● Explain the procedure to the patient and provide privacy. Then wash your hands.

● Assist the patient to a lateral tilt position and place a pillow beneath one hip for support. Don't allow the patient to assume a supine position *since pressure from the gravid uterus on the maternal great vessels may result in maternal hypotension and reduced uterine perfusion.*

● Record a baseline fetal heart rate (FHR) and uterine contractions for 20 minutes *to evaluate fetal status and spontaneous uterine activity.*

● Start the primary I.V. line, preferably in a radial vein, *to maintain venous access. Administration of fluids through this line also supports hydration during labor.* Use the 18G over-the-needle catheter *to allow delivery of blood products if complications, such as uterine rupture resulting from hyperstimulation, should occur.*

● Piggyback the oxytocin solution with the infusion pump to the primary I.V. line at the Y-injection site closest to the patient. *Piggybacking maintains patency of the line if oxytocin is discontinued. Using the Y-injection site nearest the venipuncture ensures that the primary line contains the smallest possible concentration of oxytocin if the drug needs to be promptly discontinued.*

● Initiate the oxytocin infusion at the rate of 1 to 2 milliunits (mU)/minute, or as ordered.

● Increase the rate by 1 to 2 mU/minute

every 10 to 15 minutes, or as ordered, *to achieve optimal uterine activity.*

• Assess maternal-fetal response to the oxytocin. If you're using an *external fetal monitor,* the monitor strip should show contractions occurring every 2 to 3 minutes and lasting about 1 minute. Note the relaxation time on the monitor strip. Also palpate the uterus *to assess the intensity of contractions.* If you're using an *internal monitor,* check for an optimal baseline tone of 5 to 15 mmHg and 180 to 240 Montevideo units/ 10 minutes. To calculate Montevideo units, add the intensities (peak pressure minus baseline tone) of all contractions within a 10-minute period. With optimal uterine activity, the progress of labor approximates the Friedman curve—1 cm dilatation/hour in the active phase of the first stage of labor.

• Every 10 to 15 minutes, evaluate FHR; maternal affective response; and maternal pulse, blood pressure, and respirations. Also assess uterine contractions and the rate of oxytocin infusion. If contractions are less than 2 minutes apart and last 90 seconds or longer, or if the uterus doesn't return to baseline tone between contractions, discontinue or decrease the rate of infusion. Hyperstimulation may have occurred. Also, changing the mother's position and increasing the infusion rate of the primary I.V. line may reduce uterine irritability by increasing uterine blood flow.

• After hyperstimulation has resolved, resume the oxytocin infusion. Depending on maternal-fetal status and your assessment of the clinical situation, select one of the following methods: resume the infusion at 1 to 2 mU/minute and increase the rate, as before; resume the infusion at one half of the last dosage given and increase the rate, as before; or, resume the infusion at the dosage given before signs of hyperstimulation occurred.

• Monitor and record intake and output. At rates of 16 mU/minute and above, oxytocin has an antidiuretic effect. Use an electrolyte-containing I.V. solution *to maintain electrolyte balance.*

## Special considerations

Oxytocin can be given without an infusion pump or electronic fetal monitor. If an infusion pump isn't used, administer oxytocin through a minidrop system (60 gtt/ml) and observe the patient closely. If an electronic fetal monitor isn't used, palpate and evaluate contractions frequently. Auscultate FHR every 5 to 15 minutes (see "Fetal Heart Rate" in this chapter).

Use the following formulas to convert milliliters (ml)/hour or drops (gtt)/ minute to milliunits (mU)/minute. *Conversion to mU/minute gives the actual drug dosage instead of fluid dosage and aids communication between personnel using different dilutions.* The need for applying these formulas varies with the infusion pump. *To determine oxytocin dilution (in mU/ml),* divide the units of drug by the milliliters of fluid and multiply by 1,000. *To convert ml/ hour to mU/minute,* first determine oxytocin dilution, then multiply mU/ ml by ml/hour (60 minutes). *To convert gtts/minute to mU/minute,* divide mU/ ml by gtts/ml to get mU/gtts; then multiply mU/gtts by gtts/minute.

## Complications

Oxytocin can cause hyperstimulation of the uterus, in which contractions occur more often than every 2 minutes, or the uterus fails to relax to baseline tone between contractions. Hyperstimulation may progress to tetanic contractions, which last longer than 2 minutes. It may also lead to fetal distress, abruptio placentae, or rupture of the uterus. Rarely, oxytocin administration leads to maternal convulsions or coma from water intoxication.

## Documentation

Record maternal affective response, as well as maternal blood pressure, pulse, and respirations on the flowchart. Note FHR, uterine activity, oxytocin infusion rate, and intake and output.

KATHY KIRK DAVIDSON, RNC, BSN

# Amniotomy
## [*Membrane rupture*]

*Performed by a doctor or a nurse-midwife, amniotomy is the insertion of a sterile amniohook through the cervical os to rupture the amniotic membranes. This controversial but frequently used procedure causes drainage of the amniotic fluid, thereby shortening uterine muscle fibers and enhancing the intensity, frequency, and duration of contractions. It may be performed to induce labor if the membranes fail to rupture spontaneously after full cervical dilation, to expedite labor after the onset of dilation, or to allow insertion of an intrauterine catheter and a spiral electrode for direct fetal monitoring. Oxytocin infusion may precede amniotomy or follow it by 6 to 8 hours if labor fails to progress. If delivery doesn't occur within 24 hours after amniotomy, cesarean section may be necessary.*

*Maternal and fetal factors that influence the decision to perform amniotomy include the presentation, position, and station of the fetus; the degree of cervical dilation and effacement; the gestational age; the presence of complications; the frequency and intensity of contractions; and maternal and fetal vital signs. A high-risk pregnancy may contraindicate this procedure. Amniotomy is contraindicated if the fetal presenting part is not engaged because of the risk of transverse lie and because amniotomy may cause umbilical cord prolapse. Prolapsed umbilical cord is an obstetric emergency that requires immediate cesarean delivery to prevent fetal death.*

## Equipment

4" x 4" gauze sponges ▫ povidone-iodine solution ▫ linen-saver pads ▫ bedpan ▫ equipment for indirect fetal monitoring, or a fetoscope or Doppler stethoscope ▫ sterile gloves ▫ sterile amniohook ▫ additional linens.

## Preparation of equipment
Gather the equipment at the patient's bedside.

## Essential steps
● Reinforce the doctor or nurse-midwife's explanation of the procedure, and answer the patient's questions. Then wash your hands.
● Cleanse the perineum with soap and water or with the 4" x 4" gauze sponges, moistened with povidone-iodine solution. (Many institutions use only soap and water, because the color of the povidone-iodine solution can cause a misleading assessment when observing amniotic fluid for meconium).
● Place the patient on the bedpan *to provide a receptacle for the amniotic fluid and facilitate its examination.* Then elevate the head of the bed 25° *to tilt the pelvis for easier access to the vagina.*
● Note the baseline fetal heart rate (FHR) *to evaluate fetal status before and after amniotomy.* Use indirect fetal monitoring throughout the procedure, if available.
● Using sterile technique, open the package containing the amniohook. The doctor or nurse-midwife then puts on sterile gloves and removes the amniohook from the package.
● If ordered, apply fundal pressure as the doctor or nurse-midwife inserts the amniohook into the vagina. *This helps to keep the fetal presenting part engaged and reduces the risk of cord prolapse.* The doctor or nurse-midwife then ruptures the membranes at the internal os.
● If indirect fetal monitoring isn't available, use a fetoscope or Doppler stethoscope to evaluate FHR for at least 60 seconds after membrane rupture *to detect bradycardia.* Otherwise, check the monitor tracing for variable or prolonged decelerations in FHR that may indicate cord compression. If these FHR changes occur, the doctor or nurse-midwife will perform a vaginal examination *to check for cord prolapse.*
● Clean and dry the perineal area and remove the bedpan. When necessary, replace the linen-saver pad under the pa-

tient's buttocks *to promote comfort.*
• Observe the amniotic fluid for meconium or blood. Note its color and measure the amount of fluid.
• Take the patient's temperature every 2 hours *to detect possible infection.* If her temperature rises, begin hourly checks. Continue to monitor uterine contractions and the progress of labor.

## Special considerations
When performing a vaginal examination after amniotomy, maintain strict aseptic technique *to prevent uterine infection.* Minimize the number of examinations.

## Complications
Umbilical cord prolapse is an immediate and potentially fatal complication for the fetus. It occurs when the gush of amniotic fluid after membrane rupture sweeps the cord down through the cervix. Intrauterine infection can result from failure to use aseptic technique during amniotomy and during vaginal examination, or from prolonged labor after amniotomy.

## Documentation
Record FHR before and at frequent intervals immediately after amniotomy (every 5 minutes for 20 minutes and then every 30 minutes). Note the presence of meconium or blood in amniotic fluid, and the odor and amount of fluid. Record maternal temperature and the progress of labor after amniotomy.

BONNIE JOYCE KAPLAN, RN, MS

# Emergency Delivery

*Emergency delivery—the unplanned birth of an infant outside of a hospital—may occur when labor progresses very quickly or circumstances prevent the mother from being taken to a medical facility. Skilled assistance during an emergency delivery includes establishing a clean, private delivery area; promoting a slow, controlled delivery; and preventing injury, infection, and hemorrhage.*

## Equipment
Unopened newspaper or large piece of clean cloth (such as a tablecloth, but even a clean towel or curtain will do in this emergency) □ bath towel, blanket, or coat (to support the mother's buttocks) □ at least two small, clean cloths □ clean, sharp object (such as a pen, crochet hook, scissors, new razor blade, sharp knife, or nail file) □ ligating material (such as string, yarn, ribbon, or new shoelaces) □ clean blanket or towel (to cover the infant).

## Preparation of equipment
If possible, boil the ligating and cutting materials for 5 minutes.

## Essential steps
• If possible, have someone call for an ambulance or arrange for transportation for the mother and infant.
• Explain to the mother that you'll deliver her baby. Offer support and reassurance *to ease her fears.* Encourage her to pant during contractions *to promote a slow, controlled delivery.* Then provide privacy and wash your hands.
• Position the mother comfortably on a bed, couch, or the ground. Open the newspaper or the large, clean cloth and place it under the mother's buttocks *to provide a clean delivery area.* (The newspaper is preferred because the ink contains bactericidal components.) Elevate the patient's buttocks slightly with the bath towel, blanket, or coat *to provide additional room for delivery.*
• Check for signs of imminent delivery—bulging perineum, an increase in bloody show, urgency to push, and crowning of the presenting part.
• As the infant's head begins to crown, use one hand to place one of the small, clean cloths under the perineum for support. Apply gentle pressure to the infant's head with the other hand *to promote a slow, controlled delivery. Rapid delivery causes an abrupt pressure change within the fetal skull, which may produce dural*

*or subdural tears, as well as lacerations of the mother's perineum or rectum.*

Never exert excessive pressure on the infant's head, and never attempt to significantly delay delivery by applying pressure. *Unde pressure can cause cephalohematoma or scalp lacerations, head trauma, and vagal stimulation or potential occlusion of the cord that can result in fetal bradycardia, circulatory depression, and hypoxia.*

● Check for the presence of an intact amniotic sac. Tear or puncture intact membranes with the clean, sharp object *to prevent aspiration of amniotic fluid at delivery.*

● As the infant's head emerges, instruct the mother to pant *to slow delivery.* Insert one or two fingers along the back of the infant's head *to check for the umbilical cord.*

If the cord is wrapped loosely around the infant's neck, slip it over his head *to prevent strangulation during delivery.* If it's tightly wrapped, ligate the cord in two places, and then carefully cut between the ligatures.

● Carefully support the infant's head with both hands as it rotates to one side (external rotation). Gently wipe mucus and amniotic fluid from the nose and mouth with a clean, small cloth *to prevent aspiration.*

● Instruct the mother to bear down with the next contraction *to aid delivery of the shoulders.* Position your hands on either side of the infant's head, supporting the neck. Exert gentle downward pressure *to deliver the superior shoulder.* Then exert gentle upward pressure *to deliver the inferior shoulder.*

● Support the infant's body securely after delivery of the shoulders. *Remember that amniotic fluid and vernix make the infant slippery.* Keep him in a slightly head-down position *to encourage mucus drainage from the respiratory tract.* Wipe excess mucus from his face. If he doesn't cry spontaneously, gently stroke the soles of his feet or pat his back. Never suspend an infant by his feet.

● Cover the infant quickly with the blanket or towel *to minimize heat loss.* Cradle him at the level of the uterus until the umbilical cord stops pulsating. *This prevents the infant's blood from flowing to or from the placenta, leading to hypovolemia or hypervolemia, respectively. Hypovolemia can result in circulatory collapse and neonatal death; hypervolemia can cause hyperbilirubinemia.*

● Place the infant on the mother's abdomen in a slightly head-down position.

● Ligate the umbilical cord at two points, 1″ to 2″ (2.54 to 5.08 cm) apart. Place the first ligature 4″ to 6″ (10.16 to 15.24 cm) from the infant. *Ligation prevents autotransfusion in the infant that may cause hemolysis and hyperbilirubinemia.*

● Cut the umbilical cord between the two ligatures.

● Watch for signs of placental separation, such as a slight gush of dark blood from the vagina and a lengthening of the cord. If the uterine fundus grows firm and rises within the abdomen, it also indicates that the placenta has separated from the uterine wall. When these signs occur, usually within 5 minutes after delivery, encourage the mother to bear down *to expel the placenta.* As she does, apply gentle downward pressure on the abdomen *to aid placental delivery.*

Never tug on the cord to initiate or aid placental delivery *because this may invert the uterus or sever the cord from the placenta.*

● After the mother expels the placenta, examine it for intactness. *Retained placental fragments may cause hemorrhage or lead to intrauterine infection.* Place the cord and the placenta inside the towel or blanket covering the infant to provide extra warmth. *This also ensures that the cord and placenta will be transported to the hospital, where they will be examined more closely.*

● Palpate the mother's uterus *to make sure it's firm.* Gently massage the atonic uterus *to encourage contraction and prevent hemorrhage.* Encourage breastfeeding, if appropriate, *to stimulate*

*uterine contraction.*
• Check the mother for excessive bleeding from perineal lacerations. Apply a perineal pad, if available, and instruct her to press her thighs together. Provide comfort and reassurance, and offer fluids, if available. Be sure mother and infant are warm and dry. Arrange for immediate transport to a medical facility.

### Special considerations

Never introduce any object into the vagina to facilitate delivery. *This increases the risk of intrauterine infection as well as trauma to the cervix, uterus, fetus, cord, or placenta.*

In a *breech presentation*, make every attempt to transport the mother to a nearby medical facility. If the mother begins to deliver, carefully support the infant's buttocks with both hands. Gently lift the body to deliver the posterior shoulder. Then lower the infant slightly to deliver the anterior shoulder. Flexion of the head usually follows. Never apply traction to the body *to avoid lodging the head in the cervix.* Allow the infant to rotate and deliver spontaneously.

If the umbilical cord delivers first, elevate the presenting part throughout delivery *to prevent occlusion of the cord, resulting in fetal hypoxia.* Because cesarean section is usually indicated in this obstetric emergency, arrange for immediate transport to a nearby medical facility.

If the infant fails to begin spontaneous respirations after birth, administer artificial respiration. Place your mouth over the infant's nose and mouth and deliver four short puffs of air collected in your cheeks. Next, check the umbilical cord for pulse. If it's absent, begin cardiopulmonary resuscitation (CPR): Place your index and middle fingers over the lower third of the sternum, and apply five compressions for each breath of air delivered. Continue to perform CPR until spontaneous respirations and heart beat resume.

### Documentation

Provide the medical care team with the following information, if possible: the time of delivery, the presentation and position of the infant, and any complications during the delivery, such as the cord being wrapped around the infant's neck. Describe the color, character, and amount of amniotic fluid. Note the time of placental expulsion, the appearance and intactness of the placenta, the amount of postpartum bleeding, the status of uterine contractions, and maternal affect. If known, record the mother's blood type and Rh factor. Document the sex of the infant, an estimate of Apgar score, and any resuscitation measures. Also record the commencement of breast-feeding and any fluids given to the mother.

ROYANNE A. MOORE, RN, MSN

# Cesarean Section

*Cesarean section—the delivery of an infant through an incision of the abdomen and uterus—accounts for about 20% of all births in the United States. It's indicated when labor or vaginal delivery carries unacceptable risk for the mother or fetus, as in cephalopelvic disproportion, placenta previa or abruptio placentae, and transverse lie or other malpresentations. Because most primary cesarean sections aren't anticipated, there's little time for patient preparation. Repeat cesarean sections, on the other hand, are scheduled in advance and allow time for thorough preparation and preoperative teaching. Repeat cesarean sections are usually performed because of the increased risk of uterine rupture during labor.*

*Preparation and aftercare for cesarean section must address the mother's physical and emotional needs.*

### Equipment

Fetoscope or doptone □ examination light □ incentive spirometer □ preoperative checklist □ skin preparation kit □ intake and output sheet □ preoperative medication, as ordered □ I.V. equipment and solution, as ordered □ indwelling catheter and drainage bag □ antacid (optional).

## Essential steps

• Complete routine admissions procedures according to the institution's policy. Make sure the patient has signed a consent form.

• Obtain baseline maternal vital signs and fetal heart rate. Assess maternal and fetal status frequently until delivery, as the institution's policy directs.

• For a scheduled cesarean section, you'll have ample time to discuss the procedure with the patient and her husband as well as provide preoperative teaching. But if the procedure is an emergency or the patient is exhausted from a long, inefficient labor, briefly stress the essential points about the procedure. Also, observe the mother for signs of imminent delivery.

• Explore the patient's feelings about cesarean section. If she expresses guilt or loss of self-esteem, reassure her that cesarean birth provides her infant with the safest, easiest delivery. Describe the equipment in the delivery room or, if possible, show her the room beforehand. Tell her that delivery usually takes about 5 to 10 minutes, although suturing often takes up to 40 minutes.

• Emphasize the importance of ventilating the lungs postoperatively. Demonstrate the incentive spirometer and have the patient practice deep breathing. Also explain incision care and splinting measures for coughing. Note measures to relieve abdominal distention due to gas— plenty of fluids and early ambulation. Show the patient how to move from a lying to a leg-dangling position.

• Restrict food and fluids after midnight, if a general anesthetic is ordered, *to prevent aspiration of vomitus.*

*To prepare the patient for surgery:*
• Scrub and shave the abdomen and the symphysis pubis, as ordered.

• Insert an indwelling catheter, as ordered. Tell the mother that the catheter will remain in place for 24 hours or longer, as needed.

• Notify the pediatrician of the anticipated delivery time, and be sure the nursery is ready to receive the newborn.

• Administer any ordered preoperative medication. Also give the mother an antacid *to help neutralize stomach acid,* if ordered.

• Start an I.V. infusion, if required. Use an 18G or larger cannula *to allow blood administration through the I.V., if needed.* Make sure the doctor has ordered typing and cross matching of the mother's blood and that 2 units of blood are available.

• Be sure the preoperative checklist is complete.

• When appropriate, obtain assistance to transfer the patient to the delivery or operating room.

*To care for the patient after surgery:*
• As soon as possible, allow the mother to see, touch, and hold her baby, either in the delivery room or after she recovers from the general anesthetic. *Contact with the infant promotes bonding.*

• Assess the mother for hemorrhage. Check the perineal pad and abdominal dressing every 15 minutes for 1 hour, then every half hour for 4 hours, every hour for 4 hours, and finally every 4 hours for 24 hours. Perform fundal checks at the same intervals. Monitor vital signs every 5 minutes until stable. Then check vital signs when you evaluate perineal and abdominal drainage.

• Monitor intake and output, as ordered. Expect the mother to receive I.V. fluids for 24 to 48 hours. Often the doctor will order oxytocin mixed in the first 1,000 to 2,000 ml of I.V. fluids infused *to promote uterine contraction and decrease the risk of hemorrhage.*

• Assist the mother to turn from side to side every 1 to 2 hours. Encourage her to cough and deep breathe and use the incentive spirometer *to promote adequate respiratory function.*

• Massage the mother's back *to minimize back discomfort.* Supply pillows for support and provide analgesics, as ordered.

## Special considerations

Try to place cesarean mothers together

so they can share their experiences and ideas. Direct the mother, if she desires, to a community group of cesarean mothers for additional support.

Be aware that the mother undergoing cesarean section may feel cheated and disappointed because she didn't have a vaginal delivery.

## Complications

Incisional discomfort and gas pain are the most common complications of cesarean section. Other complications include infection (endometritis, myometritis, urinary tract, wound, pneumonia, peritonitis, generalized sepsis); hemorrhage; adhesions; fistulas; wound dehiscence; subsequent uterine rupture; injury to ureters, bladder, or bowel; blood transfusion complications; thromboemboli or thrombophlebitis; and aspiration pneumonia or other anesthetic-related complications.

## Documentation

Complete admission forms, according to hospital policy, and document patient teaching. Record maternal and fetal vital signs before delivery. After delivery, record maternal vital signs. Describe the progress of uterine involution and perineal and abdominal drainage. Record intake and output, if ordered.

JANE B. DADDARIO, RN, MSN

# PUERPERIUM

# Fundal Checks

*After delivery, the uterus gradually decreases in size and descends into its prepregnancy position in the pelvis—a process known as involution. Palpation of the uterine fundus evaluates this process by determining uterine size, degree of firmness, and rate of descent, which is measured in fingerbreadths above or below the umbilicus. Involution normally begins immediately after delivery, when the firmly contracted uterus is midway between the umbilicus and the symphysis pubis. Soon the uterus rises to the umbilicus or slightly above it. After the second postpartum day, the uterus begins its descent into the pelvis at the rate of 1 fingerbreadth per day, or slightly less for the patient who has had a cesarean section. By the 10th postpartum day the uterus lies deep in the pelvis, either at or below the symphysis pubis, and cannot be palpated.*

*When the uterus fails to contract or remain firm during involution, uterine bleeding or hemorrhage can result. At delivery, placental separation exposes large uterine blood vessels. Uterine contraction acts as a tourniquet to close these blood vessels at the placental site. Fundal massage, the administration of synthetic oxytocics, or the release of natural oxytocics during breast-feeding helps to maintain or stimulate contraction.*

## Equipment
None.

## Essential steps

• Explain the procedure to the patient, and provide privacy. Wash your hands thoroughly.
• Unless the doctor orders otherwise, perform fundal checks as follows: every 10 to 15 minutes for 60 to 90 minutes in the recovery room; every 30 minutes for the next 2 hours; every hour for the next 3 hours; every 4 hours for the rest of the first postpartum day; and every 8 hours until discharge. Administer prescribed analgesics before fundal checks, if indicated.
• Help the patient urinate, *because bladder distention impairs contraction by pushing the uterus up and to the side.* Catheterize the patient if she is unable to urinate or if the uterus becomes displaced with increased bleeding.

• Lower the head of the bed so the patient is lying supinely. If this position is uncomfortable, especially for the patient who has had a cesarean section, keep the head of the bed slightly elevated. Expose the abdomen for palpation and the perineum for observation of bleeding, clots, and tissue expulsion as you massage the fundus.

• Place one hand on the lower portion of the uterus *to provide stability.* Then place your other hand flat on the abdomen, with your middle finger over the umbilicus and your thumb pointing toward the pubis. Gently palpate for the fundus.

• Once you've located the fundus, count the number of fingerbreadths from the umbilicus to the fundus. One fingerbreadth equals about ½″ (1 cm).

• Cup your hands around the fundus *to evaluate uterine firmness.* If the uterus is soft and boggy, gently massage it with a circular motion until it becomes firm. Simply cupping the uterus between your hands may also stimulate contraction. If the uterus fails to contract and heavy bleeding occurs, notify the doctor immediately. If it becomes firm after massage, keep one hand on the lower uterus and apply gentle pressure toward the pubis *to help expel any clots.*

• Cleanse the perineal area and apply a clean pad. Help the patient assume a comfortable position.

### Special considerations

Because incisional pain makes fundal checks especially uncomfortable for the patient who has had a cesarean section, provide pain medication beforehand, as ordered. If the lochia isn't heavy after 4 hours, the doctor may permit fewer fundal checks than usual, especially if oxytocin is being administered intravenously. Be alert for the absence of lochia, which may indicate that a clot is blocking the cervical os. Sudden heavy bleeding could result if a change of position dislodges the clot.

### Complications

Because the uterus and its supporting

## POSTPARTUM PERINEAL CARE

A vaginal delivery stretches and sometimes tears the perineal muscles, resulting in postpartum edema and tenderness. An episiotomy can also contribute to perineal discomfort. The two goals of postpartum perineal care are promoting patient comfort and healing and preventing infection. Performed after elimination, this procedure involves assessment of the lochia, cleansing and drying of the perineum, and application of a clean perineal pad. Lochia includes blood and debris sloughed from the placental site and the decidua. Immediately after delivery, the discharge is red; it turns maroon in 1 to 2 days and becomes creamy white within 7 to 10 days. It gradually decreases in amount, but may continue for as long as 6 weeks.

Perineal cleansing may be performed with a hand-held peri-bottle or a water-jet irrigation system. If you're using water-jet irrigation, first wash your hands and make sure the wall unit is turned off. Insert the prefilled cartridge of antiseptic or medicated solution into the handle, and push the disposable nozzle into the handle until it clicks into place. Instruct the patient to sit on the commode. Next, place the nozzle parallel to the perineum and turn on the unit. Rinse the perineum for at least 2 minutes from front to back. Then turn off the unit, remove the nozzle, and discard the cartridge. Have the patient stand up before you flush the commode *to avoid spraying the perineum with contaminated water.* Dry the nozzle and set it aside for subsequent use.

Teach the ambulatory patient to perform perineal self-care with a peri-bottle or a water-jet irrigation system. Supervise her the first time she does it. Instruct her to count the number of perineal pads she uses, describe the discharge to you, and inform you of increased bleeding or the onset of bright red bleeding. Provide her with a belt to keep the pads in place; for the patient who has had a cesarean section, offer safety pins to secure the pad to her underpants, because a belt may cause uncomfortable pressure on the incision.

ligaments are usually tender after delivery, pain is the most common complication of fundal massage. Excessive massage can stimulate premature uterine contractions that, in turn, may cause undue muscle fatigue and lead to uterine atony or inversion.

### Documentation

Record fundal height in fingerbreadths, position (midline or off-center), and degree of firmness (firm or soft). Document massage and note passage of any clots. Record excessive bleeding and your notification of the doctor.

JOANNE ROSSMAN KEYS, RN, BSN

# Breast Pumps

*Manual and electric breast pumps produce suction to stimulate milk flow. The electric pump is more effective and efficient than the manual pump.*

Breast pumps can be used to stimulate or maintain milk production while a mother and her infant are separated, or while illness temporarily incapacitates one or the other, or both. These devices can also be used to relieve engorgement or to collect milk either for a premature infant with a weak sucking reflex or for donation to a milk bank. An electric pump has several additional uses. It can reduce pressure on sore or cracked nipples or reestablish maternal milk supply when a weaned infant becomes allergic to formula. It can also be used to collect milk from a mother with inverted nipples or from a mother who has been unable to express milk manually or with a manual pump.

### Equipment

Manual or electric breast pump □ sterile collection bag or bottle (if milk is being saved) □ water-based cream or hydrous lanolin □ breast pads □ warm compresses (optional).

With an electric breast pump, you'll also need a sterile, single-use patient accessory kit, which many electric-pump manufacturers supply. The kit contains shields, milk cups, an overflow bottle, and tubing, and can be washed with soap and water for repeated use.

### Preparation of equipment

Assemble the breast pump according to the manufacturer's instructions. If the milk is to be stored or frozen, sterilize any removable parts the milk will contact.

### Essential steps

• Explain the procedure to the patient.
• Administer an analgesic, if ordered.
• Instruct the patient to urinate *so she won't have to interrupt the procedure for that purpose.* Also tell her to wash her hands *to prevent contamination.*
• Tell the patient to drink a beverage before, during, and after breast pumping. *This ensures sufficient fluid intake to maintain adequate milk production.*
• Encourage the patient to assume a comfortable position, using pillows for support, and to relax. Provide privacy and instruct her to fully expose her breast *to prevent lint and dirt from entering the milk collection container.*
• If the patient's breasts are engorged, have her apply warm compresses to them for 5 minutes or take a warm shower *to dilate the milk ducts and stimulate the letdown reflex.*
• Tell the patient to moisten her breasts near the nipples, as well as the inside of the pump flange or shield, with warm water. *This helps to create a seal that reduces friction.*
  *To use a manual pump:*
• For the *cylinder model,* tell the patient to place the flange or shield against her breast with the nipple in the center of the device. For the *bulb model,* instruct the patient to squeeze the bulb halfway before placing the nipple and areola into the flange, with the nipple slightly off-center. Then tell her to release the suction gently *to draw the nipple and areola into the flange.*
• To use the *cylinder model,* tell the patient to move the outer cylinder of the pump toward and then away from the breast, in a pistonlike motion, *to draw the milk from the breast.* Have her pump each breast in this manner until it's empty.

## PATIENT-TEACHING AID

### HOW TO EXPRESS MILK MANUALLY

**Dear Patient:**

If a breast pump isn't available, you can express milk manually by following these instructions:
• Before expressing milk, urinate, have something to eat or drink, and get some pillows to make yourself comfortable.
• Wash your hands with soap and water, and relax. Fully expose your breasts so that lint and dirt from your clothing won't enter the milk. If your breasts are engorged, apply warm compresses for 5 minutes or take a warm shower *to dilate the milk ducts and increase milk flow.*
• Using the palm of your hand, gently stroke your breast from the chest wall to the nipple, touching all areas.

• Support the massaged breast with one hand. With your other hand, gently but firmly grasp the breast, placing your thumb above and your index finger below your nipple on the edge of the areola. Press toward your chest wall, squeeze your thumb and index finger together gently, and then pull forward slightly. Rotate your hand around the breast *to reach all milk ducts.* Occasionally, you may need to massage your breasts again *to stimulate milk production.*
• When necessary, alternate breasts every few minutes. Be patient; milk may not flow immediately.
• When the milk begins to flow, lean over a sterile measuring cup or jar to collect it.

To use the *bulb model,* tell the patient to squeeze and release the bulb repeatedly *to draw milk from the breast.* Emptying each breast may take as long as 20 minutes, depending on the patient's relaxation, letdown, technique, and the type of manual pump being used.
• Have the patient remove the flange from the breast by inserting a finger between the breast and flange *to break suction.*
• If the milk is to be stored or frozen, tell the mother to fill a sterile bottle with the milk from the cylinder. If the milk is to be given to the baby, instruct the mother to screw a rubber nipple to the cylinder to feed the baby.
*To use an electric breast pump:*
• Make sure the pump is grounded with a three-pronged plug *to prevent electric shock.*
• Instruct the patient to set the suction regulator on low. Tell her to hold the collection unit upright *to prevent milk from being sucked into the machine.* Have her place the shield against the breast with the nipple centered.
• Tell the patient to turn on the machine and adjust the suction regulator to achieve a comfortable pressure. Have her check

the operator's manual to determine the pressure setting at which the pump functions most efficiently.
• Instruct the patient to pump each breast for 5 to 7 minutes or until the spray becomes scant. (Usually, 8 oz, or 240 ml, can be pumped in approximately 15 to 20 minutes.)
• Tell the patient to remove the shield from the breast by inserting a finger between the breast and the shield *to break the suction,* and return the suction regulator to the low setting. Then have her turn off the machine.
• If the milk is to be stored or frozen, tell the patient to empty the milk collection unit into a sterile bottle. If the milk is to be given to the baby, tell the mother to fill a clean, dry container.
• Label the collected milk with the date and time, the amount, and the infant's name, if applicable.
*After breast pumping:*
• Instruct the patient to air-dry her nipples for about 15 minutes.
• If the nipples are sore or irritated, have the patient apply a light layer of hydrous lanolin to the nipples and areolae. If she's allergic to wool, tell her to use water-

based cream, *because hydrous lanolin is a wool derivative.*

• Instruct her to disassemble the removable parts of the pump and wash them according to the manufacturer's directions.

### Special considerations

Provide emotional support *so the mother doesn't become depressed by her infant's absence at feeding time.*

If the patient is to use a breast pump for some time, have her pump her breasts every 2 to 3 hours *because newborns nurse 8 to 12 times every 24 hours.* Remind her to pump her breasts at night *because the breasts need round-the-clock stimulation to produce milk and maintain an adequate supply.* Once the supply is established, some mothers may need to pump once nightly; others find that 6 hours of sleep maintains the supply.

Breast milk can be stored in the refrigerator for 48 hours and in the freezer at 0° F. ($-17.8°$ C.) for up to 6 months.

Outside the hospital, electric pumps can be acquired by making a donation or contribution toward their maintenance and replacement costs. These devices can be obtained through the Childbirth Education Association–Nursing Mothers, La Leche League, or a milk bank. Electric pumps can be expensive, but some insurance plans provide coverage if the doctor prescribes their use. If the milk is to be donated to a milk bank, the pump is supplied free by the milk bank.

### Complications

Common complications include nipple trauma from high suction setting on an electric pump, and contaminated milk due to inadequate cleaning, storage, and sterilization of the equipment. Infection has been a frequent problem with the bulb-type manual pump because the bulb is difficult to clean and sterilize. Also, milk is occasionally pulled into the bulb, contaminating the collected milk.

### Documentation

Record how long the patient pumped each breast, the amount of milk collected, and the patient's reaction to the procedure.

JOANNE ROSSMAN KEYS, RN, BSN

# Breast-feeding Assistance

*Breast-feeding is the safest, simplest, and least expensive method for providing complete infant nutrition. If breast-feeding is to be successful and satisfying for both mother and infant, the mother must learn proper breast care, the physiology of stimulating milk flow, and the technique for placing the infant at her breast. Breast-feeding is contraindicated for a mother with a severe chronic condition, such as active tuberculosis.*

### Equipment

Nursing or support bra □ pillow □ optional: protective cover, such as cloth diaper or small towel; commercially available breast pads without plastic liners, or pads made from sanitary napkins, gauze, cloth diapers, or cotton handkerchiefs; water-based cream or hydrous lanolin; patient-teaching material.

### Essential steps

• Explain the procedure to the mother and provide privacy.

• Have the mother wear a nursing or support bra *to provide breast support and to control engorgement.* Instruct her to drink a beverage before, during, or after breast-feeding. *This ensures adequate fluid intake to maintain milk production.*

• Tell the mother to check the infant's diaper and change it if it's wet or soiled. Next, instruct her to urinate *so she won't have to interrupt the feeding for that purpose.*

• Wash your hands. Also, instruct the mother to wash her hands.

• Help the mother find a comfortable position, such as the madonna or side-lying position (illustrated below), *to aid the letdown reflex.* Have her expose one breast and rest the nape of the infant's neck at the antecubital space of her arm, supporting his back with her forearm.

• Guiding the mother's free hand, have her place her thumb on top of the exposed breast's areola and her first two fingers beneath it.

• Tell the mother to stroke the infant's cheek closer to her exposed breast with the nipple *to stimulate the rooting instinct.* Emphasize that she shouldn't touch the other cheek *because the infant may turn his head away from the breast.* Also instruct her not to turn the infant's face toward the breast, touch both of his cheeks simultaneously, or push the back of his head. *These actions confuse the infant and create resistance to breastfeeding.*

• When the infant turns his head and roots for the nipple, tell the mother to insert the nipple—and as much of the areola as possible—into the infant's mouth *so he can exert sufficient pressure with his lips, gums, and cheek muscles on the milk sinuses below the areola.*

• Check for occlusion of the infant's nostrils by the mother's breast. If the nostrils are occluded, tell the mother to press her finger on her breast below the infant's nose to give him room to breathe.

• Have the mother begin nursing for 5 minutes on each side, then 7 minutes, and finally 10 minutes by the end of 3 days. If she has preconditioned her breasts, she will be able to progress to the 10 to 15 minutes on each side faster. After the infant nurses for this period at one breast, tell the mother to slip a finger into the side of his mouth *to break the seal and remove him from her breast.*

• Tell the mother to gently pat or rub the infant's back *to expel any ingested air.* Have her place a protective cover, such as a cloth diaper, under the infant's chin.

• Tell the mother to feed the infant at the other breast. If she wishes, and the infant

## BREAST-FEEDING POSITIONS

In the **madonna position,** the standard, preferred position, the mother flexes her elbow on the side of her exposed breast *to support the infant.* She places a pillow beneath her elbow *to support her arm,* and then grasps her exposed breast *to facilitate breast-feeding.*

In the **side-lying position,** the mother lies on her side, raises her arm, and flexes it beneath her head. She curves her other arm *to support the infant's back*

*and neck.* She may wish to support her head with a pillow instead of her arm. The infant can then nurse at either breast.

In the **football position,** used for nursing twins, the mother sits in a chair or up against the headboard of a bed and places a pillow on her lap. She then places a pillow beneath each infant and supports each infant's head with the palm of her hand. She then rests each infant under an arm, pointing the infants' feet away from her.

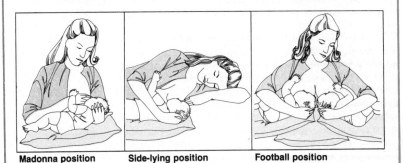

Madonna position     Side-lying position     Football position

# BREAST CARE

Patients planning to breast-feed should prepare their breasts by doing prescribed exercises and by toughening their skin during pregnancy. Have your patient consult her doctor to find out the most appropriate care measures for her.

Postpartum breast care is necessary to maintain breast tissue integrity and also serves to protect the keratin layer buildup on the areola. This layer thickens from breast-feeding. Proper breast care also helps preserve a substance secreted by the Montgomery glands that lubricates the nipples and areolae, and provides antimicrobial protection for the keratin layer.

Although postpartum breast care varies for the breast-feeding and non–breast-feeding mother, both must learn to perform this procedure themselves.

*For the breast-feeding mother:*
- Tell the patient to wash the areola and the nipple with water. She should avoid using a washcloth *to prevent removal of natural oils and keratin.*
- If the nipples are sore or irritated, instruct the patient to apply a light layer of water-based cream or hydrous lanolin to the nipples and areolae. The patient may place breast pads over the nipples *to collect leaking colostrum or milk.*

- Instruct the patient to wear a clean, well-fitting support or nursing bra.
- Tell the breast-feeding mother with engorged breasts to apply warm compresses to her breasts or take a warm shower and express some milk before feeding to dilate the milk ducts and facilitate letdown and make the nipples more pliable.

*For the non–breast-feeding mother:*
- Instruct the patient to cleanse her breasts, using the same technique as the breast-feeding mother but tell her that she may use soap.
- Instruct the patient to wear a support bra *to help minimize engorgement and decrease nipple stimulation.*
- When breast milk comes in (2 to 5 days postpartum), it will be accompanied by a slight temperature elevation and a noticeable change in the breasts—an increase in size, firmness, and warmth. Instruct the mother who isn't breast-feeding to refrain from stimulating the nipples or manually expressing her milk at this time to avoid stimulating further milk production. Instead, provide pain medication, as ordered, or ice packs, or a breast binder if the bra doesn't fit well.
JOANNE ROSSMAN KEYS, RN, BSN

remains awake, she may nurse him longer than 10 minutes (the usual duration for emptying a breast). *A demand feeding routine, in which the infant is fed according to his hunger and desire, establishes an abundant, steady milk supply appropriate for the infant's requirements (milk production increases with more frequent nursing), satisfies the need to suck, and promotes bonding.*
- When the mother finishes nursing, have her place the infant in the prone position, or on his side with a blanket roll at his back *to provide stability.* Instruct her not to place him in the supine position *because the infant may aspirate vomitus.* However, if the mother wishes to hold the infant longer, don't rush her *since touching enhances bonding.*
- Instruct the mother to air-dry her nipples for 15 minutes. Then she may apply a light coat of water-based cream or hy-

drous lanolin to her nipples and areolae *to prevent irritation and cracking or to soothe existing irritation.* Tell her that she doesn't have to wash off the cream before the next feeding.
- If breast milk leaks between or during feeding (a common problem during the first few weeks of breast-feeding), tell the mother to insert breast pads in her bra.
- Encourage the mother's breast-feeding efforts. Also, urge her to eat balanced meals, to drink at least eight glasses of fluid a day, and to nap daily for at least the first 2 weeks postpartum. Answer her questions about breast-feeding and provide patient-teaching material, if available. Before she goes home, refer her to Nursing Mothers, a division of the Childbirth Education Association, or a La Leche League counselor for more breast-feeding information and support.

## Special considerations

Instruct the mother to assume the side-lying position for breast-feeding on the delivery table. This reduces discomfort from the episiotomy. You can also adjust the table so the mother can sit up. Because the mother will probably be exhausted from delivery or drowsy from medication, stay with her during feedings for the first 8 hours.

Inform the mother that infants routinely lose several ounces during the first days of extrauterine life. Advise her that colostrum, her first milk, is yellow, rich in protein and antibodies, and secreted in small amounts; her true milk, which is thin and blue, doesn't appear until several days after delivery. Remind her that there is no standard schedule for breast-feeding and that developing a routine takes time. Tell her to expect uterine cramping during feeding until her uterus returns to its original size. Cramping results from the release of oxytocin, which contracts the uterine muscles and initiates the letdown reflex, thereby allowing milk to flow from the alveoli into the ducts. Advise her that relaxation promotes the letdown reflex, that she may feel a tingling sensation when it occurs, and that milk may drip or spray from her breasts. Tell her to control milk leakage in the nonnursing breast by applying light pressure with her fingers or the palm of her hand to the nipple.

If the infant shows little interest in breast-feeding, reassure the mother that he may need several days to adjust to it. If the infant is sleepy, encourage her to offer the breast frequently, but to refrain from forcing him to breast-feed. Instead, advise her to try rubbing the infant's feet, unwrapping him, changing his diaper, changing her position or the infant's, or manually expressing milk and then allowing the infant to suckle. A balky infant may suck eagerly if milk is already flowing.

If the infant still fails to nurse sufficiently and dehydration seems likely, have the mother give him expressed milk through a medicine dropper or small syringe. Instruct her to avoid frequent use of a bottle *because the infant may become used to the artificial nipple and subsequently reject the mother's.* Only rarely does a breast-fed infant need supplemental glucose and water.

Instruct the mother to start breast-feeding with the breast she used last at the previous feeding. Suggest pinning a safety pin on her bra strap on the side she last used *to serve as a reminder.*

Observe the mother for breast engorgement. If it's severe, have her apply hot compresses to the breasts, massage them, or take a warm shower. Administer an analgesic to relieve discomfort, as indicated. If these measures fail to spur the letdown reflex, notify the doctor; he may order oxytocin, administered I.M., to facilitate milk release.

Observe the mother for signs of mastitis—red, tender, or warm breast, and fever.

## Complications

Breast engorgement may result from venous and lymphatic stasis and alveolar milk accumulation. Mastitis occurs postpartum in about 1% of mothers. It results from the introduction of a pathogen, usually originating in the infant's nose or pharynx, into breast tissue through a cracked or fissured nipple.

## Documentation

After helping the mother to breast-feed, note the areas in which she needs further assistance. Document patient teaching.

JANE GEER FRANKENFIELD, RN, BSN

# RhoGAM Administration

*RhoGAM is a concentrated solution of gamma globulin containing $Rh_0(D)$ antibodies. Intramuscular injection of RhoGAM prevents the Rh-negative mother from producing her own antibodies in* *response to Rh-positive fetal blood cells, which could endanger future Rh-positive infants. Maternal immunization to the Rh antigen commonly results from transplacental hemorrhage during gestation or delivery. During gestation, the unchecked incompatibility of fetal and maternal blood can lead to hemolytic disease in the newborn.*

*RhoGAM injection is indicated for the Rh-negative mother after abortion, ectopic pregnancy, or delivery of an infant who has $Rh_0(D)$-positive or $D^{u}$-positive blood and Coombs'-negative cord blood. The injection should be given within 72 hours to prevent future maternal immunization. Subsequent pregnancies of the Rh-negative mother require screening to detect previous inadequate RhoGAM administration or low Rh-positive antibody titers.*

*Administration of RhoGAM at approximately 28 weeks' gestation can also protect the fetus of the Rh-negative mother. Although common in western Europe, Canada, and Australia, this alternative practice is just now gaining acceptance in the United States. RhoGAM can also be given after amniocentesis or other abdominal trauma that carries the risk of introducing fetal cells into the maternal circulation. In the patient who aborts during the first trimester, a 50-mcg dose effectively prevents Rh sensitization.*

### Equipment
3-ml syringe □ 22G 1½" needle □ alcohol sponges □ RhoGAM vial(s) □ triplicate form and patient ID card (from blood bank or hospital laboratory).

### Essential steps
• Explain the purpose of RhoGAM administration to the patient, and answer her questions. Provide privacy; wash your hands.
• Withdraw the RhoGAM from the vial, cleanse the gluteal injection site, and administer it intramuscularly.
• Complete the triplicate form, as indicated. Attach the top copy to the patient's chart. Send the remaining two copies, along with the empty RhoGAM vial, to the laboratory or blood bank.
• Give the patient the ID card that specifies her Rh-negative status, and instruct her to keep it in her wallet.

### Special considerations
After the procedure, observe the patient for redness and soreness at the injection site.

### Complications
Complications of a single RhoGAM injection are infrequent, mild, and confined to the injection site. After multiple injections (given after Rh mismatch) they may include fever, myalgia, lethargy, splenomegaly, or hyperbilirubinemia.

### Documentation
Record the date and time the packing was removed; the color, amount, and odor of drainage on the packing; the number and type of packings used; and any complications and resulting nursing action.

SUE M. JONES, RNC, FNC, MSN

# MISCELLANEOUS

# Removal of Vaginal Packing

*Vaginal packing is used to administer drugs, absorb uterine blood, and apply pressure to the cervix or the vaginal walls. Removal of the packing usually takes place within 24 hours of insertion and requires a doctor's order. To perform the procedure, you must know why the packing was inserted and the number and type of packings used.*

### Equipment
Clean gloves □ linen-saver pad □ paper

or plastic waste bag □ sheet for draping □ perineal pad

## Preparation of equipment
Place the waste bag near the patient's bed *for immediate disposal of the packing, especially if it has an unpleasant odor.*

## Essential steps
• Explain the procedure to the patient, and inform her that vaginal packing normally has an unpleasant odor after it's removed.
• Provide privacy and wash your hands.
• Assist the patient into the supine position with her knees bent and her feet flat on the bed, or have her press the soles of her feet together. Drape the patient appropriately *to provide privacy and warmth.*
• Place the linen-saver pad under the patient's hips *to prevent soiling the bed linen and to provide a place to put the removed packing.*
• Put on the gloves and separate the labia. Grasp the visible end of the packing and remove it slowly and firmly *to gradually decrease vaginal pressure and reduce the risk of tearing the packing.*
• After removing the packing, place it on the linen-saver pad and examine it carefully *to detect tears, thereby preventing possible vaginal infection from residual packing.* Inspect the drainage on the packing for color, amount, and odor.
• Discard the packing, the linen-saver pad, and your gloves into the waste bag.
• Provide the patient with a perineal pad *to absorb any remaining vaginal drainage.*
• Remove the waste bag from the room and discard it.

## Special considerations
If you're assisting the doctor with this procedure, explain the steps to the patient, and assess drainage on the packing. After removal of the packing, observe the patient for signs and symptoms of vaginitis, such as purulent discharge and pain, and for increased vaginal bleeding.

Notify the doctor if either condition develops.

## Complications
Vaginitis can result from retention of packing fragments. Increased vaginal bleeding can follow removal of a pack used to apply cervical or vaginal pressure.

## Documentation
Record the date and time the packing was removed; the color, amount, and odor of drainage on the packing; the number and type of packings used; and any complications and resulting nursing action.
SUE M. JONES, RNC, FNC, MSN

# Vaginal Irrigation

*Vaginal irrigation is the instillation of fluid into the vaginal cavity to remove odor or foul discharge, to preoperatively disinfect the vagina, or to administer antiseptic drugs. It may also be performed to stop bleeding (using a cold solution) or to relieve pain and inflammation (using a warm solution). When performed after delivery or gynecologic surgery, vaginal irrigation requires aseptic technique. Patient teaching is often necessary, since the patient will frequently have to repeat the procedure herself. This procedure is usually contraindicated during pregnancy; for 4 to 6 weeks after miscarriage or postpartum; or in untreated venereal disease.*

## Equipment
Plastic irrigation container or bag □ tubing □ clamp □ curved plastic vaginal tip □ prescribed solution □ utility bath thermometer □ straight-back chair or short I.V. pole □ pillows □ linen-saver pad □ bedpan with cover □ clean gloves □ water-soluble lubricant □ toilet tissue □ perineal pad □ container to mix douche solution (optional).

Vaginal irrigation sets are available;

they contain the plastic irrigation container or bag, tubing, clamp, curved plastic vaginal tip, and water-soluble lubricant. These sets may be disposable or nondisposable; the latter require sterilization after final use.

### Preparation of equipment
Prepare the prescribed irrigating solution, as ordered. Heat the solution to a temperature between 105° to 110° F. (40.6° to 43.3° C.), as ordered. Avoid overheating *to prevent injury to vaginal mucous membranes and the skin of the meatus.* Hang the irrigation bag, with its tubing clamp closed, on the I.V. pole or straight-back chair.

### Essential steps
• Explain the procedure to the patient, and provide privacy. Wash your hands. Have the patient urinate *to prevent discomfort from a distended bladder and to allow full distention of the vagina with the solution.*
• Lower the head of the bed and help the patient into the dorsal recumbent position. Place a pillow under her head and a linen-saver pad beneath her buttocks.
• Position the patient on the bedpan and drape her as you would for a pelvic examination. Place a pillow under her back *to provide comfort.*
• Adjust the height of the irrigation bag to no more than 2′ (0.6 m) above the level of the vagina *to ensure a slow, steady flow of solution.*
• Put on clean gloves.
• Lubricate the end of the plastic vaginal tip with water-soluble lubricant *to facilitate insertion.*
• Separate the labia and open the tubing clamp *to allow a small amount of solution to flow over the meatus. This reduces the risk of introducing external organisms into the vagina.* Then reclamp the tubing.
• Gently insert the vaginal tip 2″ to 2½″ (5.1 to 6.4 cm) into the vagina at approximately a 45° angle, following the vaginal curvature *to prevent patient discomfort.*

• Open the clamp *to allow solution to flow into the vagina.* Then gently rotate the vaginal tip *to make sure that fluid reaches all areas of the vagina.* If retention of the solution is ordered, clamp the tube and use your free hand to close the labia around the tip for 30 to 60 seconds.
• When the irrigating container is empty, close the clamp and remove the tip from the vagina.
• Help the patient into a sitting position on the bedpan *to allow the solution to drain from the vagina.*
• Remove the bedpan and inspect the return flow.
• Offer the patient toilet tissue *to dry the perineum.* Instruct her to wipe from front to back *to avoid fecal contamination of the urethra and vagina.* Then provide the patient with a perineal pad *to keep the bed dry and promote her comfort.*
• Rinse and dry the equipment, and set it aside for subsequent use. After final use of the equipment, discard the disposable irrigation set or send the nondisposable set to the hospital's central supply department for sterilization.
• Wash your hands.

### Special considerations
If the patient is performing vaginal irrigation, make sure she knows which solution to use. Instruct her not to attempt irrigation while sitting on the toilet or standing in the shower, *because only the supine position ensures thorough vaginal irrigation.* Supervise the patient the first time she performs vaginal irrigation. Also, emphasize to her that irrigation is necessary only in the presence of inflammation, hyperacidity, odorous discharge, pain, or bleeding.

### Documentation
Record the type and amount of irrigating solution, the characteristics of the return flow, the duration of the procedure, and the patient's response.

SUE M. JONES, RNC, FNC, MSN

# Care During Radioactive Implant

Radioactive implants retard or destroy malignant cells in patients with invasive squamous cell carcinoma of the breast, the cervix, or the endometrium. The two types of implants are intracavitary, in which isotopes are placed within a body cavity (such as the uterus), and interstitial, in which isotope needles or seeds are placed within tissue (such as mammary tissue). By destroying malignant cells, radiation therapy can prolong the patient's life, promote comfort, and induce partial or complete remission.

Because the radiation emitted by the encapsulated radioisotope is potentially hazardous, the patient should have a private room with a radiation precaution sign on the door. Observation of precautions against radiation exposure (distance, shielding, and time) is also mandatory (see Working Safely Around Radioactive Implants, page 762).

## Equipment

Radiation precaution sign (RADIATION AREA) for the patient's door and chart □ large isolation trash and linen cans with covers □ film badge or dosimeter □ lead apron and gloves □ long-handled, ring-necked lead forceps □ lead-insulated container □ sterile gloves.

For an intracavitary implant: in addition to the above, foam mattress (such as an eggcrate mattress) □ vaginal irrigation setup □ povidone-iodine solution □ enema setup □ indwelling catheter and continuous drainage bag □ perineal pads.

## Essential steps

● Reinforce the doctor's explanation of the procedure and answer the patient's questions. Remind her that the surgeon implants the holding device (applicator) for the radioisotope in the operating room. Tell her that subsequent X-rays, usually taken in the radiology department, confirm the applicator's position, and that insertion of the radioisotope into the applicator takes place in her room to avoid unnecessary radiation exposure of hospital staff and visitors. Also tell her that hospital staff and visitors will have to limit the time they can spend in her room after the radioisotope is inserted. Encourage her to use the intercom, call system, or telephone freely to minimize her feelings of isolation.

● Inform the patient that she may experience discomfort from the implant, but that she will receive analgesics, as needed.

To prepare the patient for a cervical implant:

● If ordered, perform vaginal irrigation with povidone-iodine solution the evening before the procedure. Administer an enema to reduce the risk of incidental bowel radiation from distention of the sigmoid colon.

● Restrict food and fluids after midnight on the day of the procedure.

● On the morning of the procedure, help the patient shampoo and shower, if possible.

● Insert an indwelling catheter to prevent incidental bladder radiation from distention; then connect the catheter to the drainage bag.

● Immediately before the patient is transported to the operating room, record baseline vital signs.

To prepare the patient for a breast implant:

● Restrict food and fluids after midnight on the day of the procedure.

● On the morning of the procedure, help the patient shampoo and shower, if possible.

● Immediately before the patient is transported to the operating room, instruct her to urinate, and record her baseline vital signs.

To prepare the patient's room for her return:

● Instruct the housekeeping staff to clean the room thoroughly, because they won't be permitted to enter it after the patient returns with the radioisotope in place.

## WORKING SAFELY AROUND RADIOACTIVE IMPLANTS

To minimize your radiation exposure, follow radiation safety precautions of distance, shielding, and time.
• *Distance.* Work as far from the radiation source as possible. The intensity of the radiation decreases by the square of the distance between you and the source.
• *Shielding.* Keep a lead apron and shield between you and the radiation source, whenever possible.
• *Time.* The less time you're near the patient, the less radiation you'll receive. The best way to minimize this time is to work efficiently.

Safe time depends on your proximity to the patient, as illustrated below.

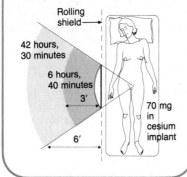

Rolling shield

42 hours, 30 minutes

6 hours, 40 minutes

3'

6'

70 mg in cesium implant

• Place the radiation precaution sign on the patient's door and have large trash and linen cans with covers placed in the room. If the patient is to have a cervical implant, place an eggcrate mattress on the bed *to promote comfort and minimize the risk of decubitus ulcer formation.* Place the long-handled, ring-necked lead forceps and perineal pads near the patient's bed.

*To care for the patient after a cervical implant:*
• Before entering the patient's room, plan to observe radiation precautions and to spend no more than 30 minutes with the patient each day. Put on the film badge or dosimeter *to monitor radiation exposure.*
• Check the placement of the applicator once every 8 hours *to make sure it hasn't become dislodged.*

• Administer analgesics for pain, as ordered.
• Administer antidiarrheal medication, as ordered, *to decrease bowel stimulation, thereby preventing defecation while the radioisotope is in place. Defecation may dislodge the isotope and cause incidental bowel radiation from a distended sigmoid colon.* Also give the patient a low residue diet, as ordered, *to decrease bowel stimulation and fecal bulk.*
• Elevate the head of the bed 10° to 30° and enforce bed rest. Encourage the patient to perform range-of-motion exercises with both arms, as well as plantar flexion and dorsiflexion of the feet *to minimize the respiratory and circulatory complications of prolonged bed rest.* Help the patient logroll from side to side and provide meticulous skin care *to reduce the risk of decubitus ulcer formation.* Teach the patient diaphragmatic breathing exercises, and encourage her to practice them every 2 hours *to promote lung expansion and avoid respiratory complications.* Auscultate her breath sounds.
• Change the perineal pad, as needed. Avoid performing other perineal care or adjusting the indwelling catheter *to reduce the risk of dislodgment of the applicator or radiation source.*
• Assist the patient in bathing her torso, but do not permit a complete bath.
• For the duration of the implant, place all linens, dressings, and trash in the isolation linen or trash cans *to prevent radioactive contamination of regular hospital trash, in case of accidental dislodgment of the implanted isotope.* Discard urine, stool, and vomitus as usual, since these are not radioactive.
• When the radiologist is ready to remove the implant (between 1 and 5 days), remove the indwelling catheter. The radiologist then puts on sterile gloves and, using the long-handled, ring-necked lead forceps, removes the applicator and the vaginal packing.
• When the patient is ready to get out of bed, provide assistance, *because she may be weak or may develop orthostatic hypotension* from prolonged bed rest.

• If ordered, perform vaginal irrigation with a povidone-iodine solution (or plain water) before discharge. Also, administer an enema, if ordered.
• Tell her to expect slight to moderate vaginal bleeding after discharge. Instruct her to notify the doctor if the bleeding increases, persists for more than 48 hours, or has a foul odor; if her temperature rises (a sign of infection); or if she experiences urinary frequency, urgency, incontinence, or hematuria (signs of incidental bladder radiation).
• Explain to the patient that she may resume normal activities but should avoid sexual intercourse and the use of tampons until after her follow-up visit to the doctor (about 6 weeks).

*To care for the patient after a breast implant:*
• Inform the patient that she's permitted out of bed, but not out of the room, *because of the risk of radiation exposure to hospital staff and visitors.*
• For the duration of the implant, place all linens, dressings, and trash in the isolation trash and linen cans *to prevent radioactive contamination of regular hospital trash should the isotope be accidentally dislodged.* Discard urine, stool, and vomitus as usual, because these are not radioactive.
• After the radiologist removes the applicator and the radiation source, tell the patient that she may resume all normal activities, including showering.
• Before discharge, teach the patient how to examine her breasts.

### Special considerations
Remember that the patient undergoing radioactive implantation is under considerable stress because of the diagnosis of cancer, fear of radiation therapy, and anxiety about altered sexual and reproductive functions. Consequently, provide clear explanations about the procedure and offer frequent reassurance.

 A dosimeter or radiation film badge doesn't prevent exposure to radiation. The device simply measures the amount of radiation exposure. Turn in the radiation badge monthly, and be sure to maintain a precise record of your exposure.

Because the developing embryo and fetus are highly susceptible to the potentially damaging effects of ionizing radiation, warn pregnant staff members and visitors not to enter the patient's room. Instruct hospital staff members and visitors to wear lead aprons and gloves in the patient's presence, as hospital policy directs, and caution them to follow all radiation precautions.

 If the radiation source or applicator becomes dislodged, use the long-handled, ring-necked lead forceps to grasp it and place it in the lead-insulated container. Then notify the radiologist immediately. Never grasp the radioactive source or applicator with your hand *to avoid a radiation burn.* Never carry the source or applicator outside the patient's room *to avoid radiation exposure of hospital staff and visitors.*

If the patient dies with the implant in place, contact the radiologist. Be sure to postpone postmortem care until the radiologist removes the radiation source or applicator.

### Complications
Complications related to implantation include dislodgment of the radiation source or applicator, infection or necrosis, radiation-related proctitis, fistula formation, dehydration, vaginal stenosis, and decreased vaginal lubrication during intercourse.

### Documentation
Record all preoperative procedures, as well as the radiation precautions taken and maintained during the implantation period. Record the patient's emotional response to the treatment, any complications and the resulting nursing action, and the date and time the applicator or radiation source was removed. Also keep an accurate intake and output record to detect dehydration.

MARIANNE L. DIETRICK-GALLAGHER, RN, MSN

# 17 Neonatal Care

# Neonatal Care

## Introduction

About 30 to 40 years ago, the trend toward hospital deliveries was firmly established, essentially eliminating home deliveries. This movement and the availability of advanced supportive technology—especially after the introduction of antibiotics—combined to reduce neonatal mortality. Today, 97% of all births occur in hospitals, and the average stay has been reduced from 2 to 3 weeks to 2 to 3 days. Intensive-care nurseries for high-risk neonates have become commonplace, the role of diagnostic testing has expanded, and nursing care has become more technically advanced.

### New knowledge

Neonatal care has improved through better understanding of the pathophysiology and behavior of full-term and premature neonates. Until the 1960s, admission to a premature nursery depended solely on birth weight. The neonate weighing less than 5.5 lb (2.50 kg) was considered premature, and the neonate over this weight was considered full-term. New criteria indicate whether the neonate grew at an appropriate rate in utero. It's now possible, for example, to identify the 8 lb (3.62 kg), 35-week neonate of a diabetic mother as premature and large for gestational age.

New methods of clinical evaluation, combined with new technological and biochemical monitoring systems, have improved neonatal care. To apply these advances, nurses must be familiar with neonatal physiology and use of modern monitoring equipment.

### Regionalized perinatal care

This new potential for successful care of high-risk neonates has changed the structure of health-care services. Regionalized systems now provide universal access to skilled neonatal care. Each region has three types of facilities, ranked according to care level. *Level I* facilities have three major functions: management of normal pregnancy, labor, and delivery; early identification of high-risk pregnancy or high-risk neonates after birth; and providing competent emergency care for unexpected obstetric or neonatal emergencies. *Level II*, or intermediate care, facilities provide full maternal and neonatal care in uncomplicated circumstances, and can manage 75% to 90% of complications. *Level III* facilities provide routine maternal and neonatal care, and can manage the most complex perinatal disorders.

Regionalized neonatal services, improved technology, and skilled care providers have cut neonatal mortality rates in half in many parts of the United States. This is especially true of very low–birth-weight neonates (below 1,500 g). Before 1960, fewer than 20% of this group survived, but their survival rate in Level III units has improved dramatically. Nurses have played a critical role in the development and success of care, monitoring, and treatment of neonates. Their skilled nursing care has significantly influenced the survival, well-being, and development of the especially vulnerable neonates in their care.

DOROTHY A. BROOTEN, RN, PhD

# DIAGNOSIS

# Phenylketonuria Test
[*Guthrie Screening Test*]

*Reflecting an inborn error of amino acid metabolism, phenylketonuria (PKU) results from a deficiency of the liver enzyme that converts phenylalanine to tyrosine. If this condition is not detected early and treated promptly with a special diet, toxic levels of phenylalanine accumulate in the blood and cause cerebral damage and mental retardation.*

*To prevent such retardation, nearly every state requires PKU testing of neonates. For accurate test results, the neonate should receive a protein diet for 24 to 48 hours before being tested for PKU. Traditionally, this test was done on the third to sixth day of life, but this is now often impossible because of the popularity of early hospital discharge. Accordingly, in 1982, the American Academy of Pediatrics Committee on Genetics recommended that the test be performed on all neonates, regardless of age, before they are released from the hospital. A retest before the third week of life is recommended for all neonates who were tested in the first 24 hours after delivery.*

*In the Guthrie screening test, the neonate's capillary blood is analyzed for abnormally high levels of serum phenylalanine. A positive test requires additional testing to confirm phenylketonuria and rule out other causes, such as delayed development of certain enzyme systems, galactosemia, or liver disease.*

## Equipment
Special PKU filter paper (usually provided by state health department) □ alcohol sponges □ sterile lancet □ 2″ x 2″ gauze pads □ adhesive bandage □ laboratory request form □ capillary tubes (optional).

## Essential steps
● Confirm the infant's identity by checking his identification bracelet.
● Explain the procedure to the parents *to reassure them and prevent alarm when they see the adhesive bandage on the neonate's heel.*
● Wash your hands thoroughly to prevent contamination.
● Open an alcohol sponge, uncover one of the neonate's feet (preferably the foot not previously pricked for a blood sample). Then, clean a spot on his heel with the sponge, and dry the spot with a 2″ x 2″ gauze pad. Next, hold the limb in a dependent position *to increase venous pressure.*
● Using aseptic technique, open the lancet and stick the heel gently but firmly. Following directions on the filter paper supplied by your state health department or hospital, dab each place provided on the filter paper with blood, making sure the blood soaks through the paper. Or, draw up blood in a capillary tube and apply it to the filter paper. If necessary, wipe the puncture with an alcohol sponge *to stimulate bleeding.*
● Allow the blood on the filter paper to dry, and send it and the completed request form to the laboratory.

## Special considerations
Treatment for PKU is a controlled low phenylalanine diet, at least during childhood; whether it must continue throughout the patient's life is controversial. A special feeding formula is available for infants. When the infant needs solid food, the diet requires weighing all allowable food and calculating phenylalanine intake.

## Documentation
Record the date and time of the test, and disposition of the samples in your nurse's notes or on the appropriate hospital form, such as the newborn assessment sheet.

ANITA JONES CHINNICI, RN, MSN

# Percutaneous Bladder Aspiration

### [*Suprapubic bladder tap*]

In percutaneous bladder aspiration, a needle is inserted directly into the bladder through the abdominal wall in the suprapubic area. This procedure is used to obtain a sterile urine specimen for culture, or to aid diagnosis of anuria or urinary tract conditions in the neonate with voiding problems.

Performed by a doctor with one or two nurses assisting, percutaneous bladder aspiration requires sterile technique to prevent bladder infection or contamination of the specimen. The neonate's bladder should be distended and palpable above the symphysis pubis; oral or I.V. fluids may be ordered increased by the doctor for an hour before the procedure to increase bladder distension. The procedure is contraindicated in neonates with severe bleeding problems.

## Equipment

Two 21G 1½" sterile needles □ sterile 20-ml syringe □ sterile urine specimen container □ specimen label □ alcohol sponge □ povidone-iodine sponge □ sterile 4" x 4" gauze sponges □ sterile gloves □ small adhesive bandage □ laboratory request form.

## Preparation of equipment

Fill out the specimen label with the patient's name and address, doctor's name, hospital identification number, and method of urine collection. Assemble needed equipment at bedside or in the treatment area. Check the expiration date on each sterile package and inspect for tears. Assist the doctor by handing him the needed equipment during the procedure while another staff member holds the infant in position.

## Essential steps

• Explain the procedure to the parents and reassure them that it is safe.

• Wash your hands thoroughly *to prevent contamination.*

• Place the neonate in a supine position with his head toward you and his legs in the frog position. Hold the neonate gently but firmly in this position *to allow easy access to the aspiration site and to prevent sudden movements that can cause contamination or injury.*

• The doctor cleanses the suprapubic area, first with the povidone-iodine sponge, and then with the alcohol sponge, *to cleanse the area and avoid contaminating the specimen.* He then locates the symphysis pubis through palpation and penetrates the abdominal wall ⅖" to ⅘" (1 to 2 cm) above the symphysis pubis, directing the needle toward the bladder at approximately a 30° angle. He inserts the needle until he feels a change in resistance.

• Continue to hold the neonate in position while the doctor aspirates the urine specimen.

• After he withdraws the needle, gently apply pressure to the puncture site with a gauze sponge for 2 to 3 minutes *to stop internal and external bleeding.*

• Check the aspiration site for signs of bleeding. Apply an adhesive bandage after bleeding stops.

• Rediaper the neonate and comfort him.

• Record the date and time of aspiration, and the amount of urine, on the specimen label. Send the specimen to the laboratory in a sterile container or in the original syringe capped with a new sterile needle cap *to prevent specimen contamination, which produces false-positive results.*

## Special considerations

The doctor may use sonographic equipment to locate the bladder if he can't determine its position by palpation.

Urethral catheterization may be ordered as an alternative to percutaneous bladder aspiration. Procedure for infant catheterization is the same as for an adult. (A #3 French or #5 French feeding tube can be used as a urethral catheter in such cases.)

If the doctor orders strict output measurement after a bladder tap, the infant may have a special neonatal collection bag applied. Output may also be measured (though less accurately) by weighing the diaper before and after voiding.

## Complications
Complications include bleeding at the puncture site and hematuria. Report excessive bleeding immediately. Hematuria may occur normally for as long as two days following aspiration, due to the trauma from the procedure.

## Documentation
On the nurse's notes and the intake and output record, note the amount of urine aspirated.

On the patient's chart, record the date and time of the procedure, specimen delivery to the laboratory, method of collection, color and appearance of the urine specimen, and color and appearance of subsequent voidings. Also note subsequent observations of the puncture site and the neonate's tolerance of the procedure.

GAIL JOHNSON, RN

# MONITORING

# Apgar Scoring

*Developed by anesthesiologist Dr. Virginia Apgar in 1952, Apgar scoring evaluates neonatal heart rate, respiratory effort, muscle tone, reflex irritability, and color. Evaluation of each of the categories is performed 1 minute after birth or after establishment of a clear airway, and again 5 minutes later. Each item has a maximum score of 2 and a minimum score of 0. The final Apgar score is the sum total of the five items; a maximum score is 10.*

*Evaluation at 1 minute quickly indicates the neonate's initial adaptation to extrauterine life and whether or not resuscitation is necessary. The 5-minute score gives a more accurate picture of his overall status, including obvious neurologic impairment or impending death. The Apgar score isn't taken when the neonate needs prompt resuscitation.*

## Equipment
Apgar scoring sheet or newborn assessment sheet □ stethoscope □ alcohol sponges □ clock with second hand, or Apgar score timer.

## Preparation of equipment
If a scoring timer is used, make sure both timers are on at the instant the neonate is completely delivered.

## Essential steps
● Note the time the neonate is delivered.
● At one minute after birth, perform the following:
*Assess heart rate:*
● Count the heart rate for 60 seconds by using the stethoscope or palpating the pulsations of the umbilical cord where it joins the abdomen. Assign a 0 for no heart rate, a 1 for a rate less than 100 beats per minute (bpm) and a 2 for a rate over 100 bpm.
*Assess respiratory effort:*
● Count unassisted respirations for 60 seconds, noting quality and regularity (a normal rate is 30 to 50 respirations per minute). Assign a 0 for no respirations; a 1 for slow, irregular, shallow, or gasping respirations; and a 2 for regular respirations and vigorous crying.
*Assess muscle tone:*
● Observe the extremities for flexion and resistance to extension. This can be done by extending the limbs and observing their rapid return to the neonate's normal state of flexion. Assign a 0 if the neonate is flaccid; a 1 for some flexion and resistance to extension; and a 2 for normal flexion of elbows, knees, and hips, with good resistance to extension.
*Assess reflex irritability:*

## RECORDING THE APGAR SCORE

Use the chart shown here to record the neonatal Apgar score. A score of 7 to 10 indicates that the infant is in good condition; 4 to 6 indicates fair condition—the infant may have moderate central nervous system depression, muscle flaccidity, cyanosis, and poor respirations; 0 to 3 indicates very poor condition—the infant needs immediate resuscitation, as ordered.

### APGAR SCORING SYSTEM

| SIGN | 0 | 1 | 2 | RATING 1 MIN | 5 MIN |
|------|---|---|---|--------------|-------|
| **Heart rate** | Absent | Slow (less than 100 bpm) | More than 100 bpm | | |
| **Respiratory effort** | Absent | Slow, irregular | Good crying | | |
| **Muscle tone** | Flaccid | Some flexion and resistance to extension of extremities | Active motion | | |
| **Reflex irritability** | No response | Grimace or weak cry | Vigorous cry | | |
| **Color** | Pallor, cyanosis | Pink body, blue extremities | Completely pink | | |
| | | | FINAL TOTAL | | |

• Observe the neonate's response while suctioning his nose, or by flicking the sole of his foot. Assign a 0 for no response, a 1 for a grimace or weak cry, and a 2 for a vigorous cry.

*Assess color:*

• Observe skin color, especially at the extremities. Assign a 0 for complete pallor and cyanosis, a 1 for a pink body with blue extremities (acrocyanosis), and a 2 for a completely pink body. To assess color of a dark-skinned neonate, inspect the color of the mucous membranes of the mouth and conjunctiva, the lips, the palms of the hands, and the soles of the feet.

• Total the score and record it.

• Repeat the evaluation and record the score at 5 minutes after birth.

### Special considerations

If possible, discuss Apgar scoring with the parents during early labor, when they will be more receptive to new knowledge if teaching is necessary. *To prevent con-fusion or misunderstanding at delivery,* explain to them what will occur and why, and that this is a routine procedure. If the neonate requires emergency care, make sure that a member of the delivery team offers reassurance to the mother, and the father, if he's present.

Closely observe the neonate whose mother has been heavily sedated just before delivery—he may score high at birth, but may become depressed or unresponsive in the nursery due to secondary effects of the drug(s).

### Documentation

Record the Apgar score on the Apgar scoring sheet and/or the newborn assessment sheet required by your institution, making sure to indicate the total Apgar score and the signs for which points were deducted, in order to guide care of the neonate and allow anticipation of his future needs (see *Recording the Apgar Score,* above).

ANITA JONES CHINNICI, RN, MSN

EQUIPMENT

## AIRWAY CLEARANCE

As soon as the neonate's head presents at delivery, his nose, mouth, and pharynx must be cleared of mucus and amniotic fluid to prevent aspiration and to allow him to start breathing. Although postural drainage with bulb suction usually suffices, negative-pressure mouth suction using a mucus trap suction device, such as a DeLee mucus trap, or mechanical suction, may be required to clear the lower airway and remove blood.

Suctioning should always begin with the neonate's mouth, because stimulating the nose may cause him to inhale and aspirate. After the neonate's first cry, suctioning may again be needed. If, after thorough suctioning, respirations seem inadequate, the neonate should be checked for congenital deformities that prevent normal breathing, and the doctor may begin resuscitation procedures.

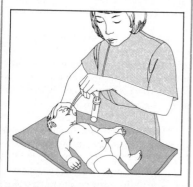

To position a mucus trap, carefully insert the catheter into the neonate's pharynx and place the mouthpiece in your mouth.

GAIL JOHNSON, RN

# Vital Signs

*Frequent and accurate measurement of the neonate's respiration, heart rate, temperature, and sometimes blood pres-* sure is an essential part of neonatal physical assessment. Respiratory rate may be determined by observing respiration rate visually, or by auscultating with a pediatric stethoscope and observing for labored or abnormal breathing. Heart rate is taken apically with a pediatric stethoscope.

The first neonatal temperature is taken rectally, to check for rectal patency; subsequent temperature readings are axillary, to avoid injuring the rectal mucosa. Blood pressure may be checked by palpation, auscultation, flush method, Doppler ultrasound, or with an electronic vital signs monitor.

### Equipment
Pediatric stethoscope □ watch with second hand □ thermometer (mercury or electronic with rectal probe and cover) □ water-soluble lubricant □ sphygmomanometer with 1″ (2.5 cm) cuff □ optional: Doppler ultrasound device with coupling gel or electronic vital signs monitor, gown.

### Preparation of equipment
Assemble needed equipment at the patient's bedside. Shake a mercury thermometer to below 96° F. (35.5° C.). Apply a probe cover to the rectal probe of the electronic thermometer if it is to be used. Lubricate the thermometer or probe cover before taking a rectal temperature.

### Essential steps
• Wash your hands *to prevent contamination.*
• Put on a gown before entering the nursery or mother's room, if required.
  *To determine respiratory rate:*
• Respiration should be observed first, before the neonate becomes disturbed. Observe and count respiratory movements for 1 minute, and record the result. Expect neonatal respirations to be irregular in rate and depth, varying from shallow and slow to rapid and deep and primarily diaphragmatic.
• While counting, observe for marked irregularities, periods of apnea, and signs

of distress, such as nasal flaring, sternal and costal retractions, seesaw movements, or grunting.

*To determine heart rate:*
• Listen with the stethoscope at the level of the third or fourth intercostal space, just outside the midclavicular line.
• Count for 1 minute *to obtain an accurate result and to allow time to note irregularities,* and record the rate.

*To take a rectal temperature:*
• Place the neonate in the supine position and firmly grasp his ankles with your index finger between them *to prevent skin trauma.* Place a diaper over the penis of a male neonate *to avoid becoming wet if he urinates.*
• While continuing to hold his ankles, insert the lubricated thermometer no more than ½"—*any further could cause rectal trauma.* Place the palm of your hand on the neonate's buttocks and hold the thermometer between your index and middle fingers. *This stabilizes the thermometer and prevents breakage if the infant moves suddenly.* To inhibit the defecation response induced by rectal insertion of a thermometer, press the neonate's buttocks together. If you meet resistance during thermometer insertion, withdraw it and notify the doctor.
• Hold a mercury thermometer in place for 3 minutes, an electric thermometer until the temperature registers (see "Temperature," Chapter 1.) Remove the thermometer and read the scale where the mercury stops, or the digital readout, and record the result.

*To take an axillary temperature:*
• Place the thermometer under the neonate's arm at the axillary crease with the thermometer tip toward his head, and allow his arm to rest on top of it.
• Hold the thermometer in place 5 to 7 minutes (for mercury); for an electronic thermometer, hold in place until the temperature registers.
• Record the result.

*To determine blood pressure:*
• Blood pressure readings should be taken when the neonate is quiet.
• Apply the manometer cuff around the neonate's upper arm and inflate it above

## NORMAL NEONATAL VITAL SIGNS

**Respiration**
30 to 50 respirations/minute

**Heart rate** (apical)
110 to 160 beats/minute

**Temperature**
Rectal
96° to 99.5° F. (35.6° to 37.5° C.)
Axillary
97.7° to 98° F. (36.5° to 36.7° C.)

**Blood pressure** (at birth)
Systolic
60 to 80 mmHg
Diastolic
40 to 50 mmHg

systolic pressure.
• Then, decrease the pressure not faster than 5 mmHg/second and use one of the following methods to determine the blood pressure:
*Palpation:* Feel for a radial or brachial pulse, which is systolic blood pressure.
*Auscultation:* Using a pediatric stethoscope and amplification, listen for diastolic and systolic sounds at the brachial artery.

## ADMISSION TO THE NURSERY

When the neonate's condition stabilizes sufficiently after delivery, he is admitted to the nursery for further observation and assessment. The first few hours after birth are medically critical; complications frequently appear during this first period of adjustment outside the mother's womb. Depending on your hospital's protocol, the nursery admission may include an identification check, weighing, placement in a radiant heat warmer, rectal temperature measurement, injection of vitamin K₁, eye treatment, or other procedures.

If a neonate is born outside the hospital, he must be placed in isolation.

## CARE OF THE STILLBORN

A fetus born dead at a gestational age of 16 weeks or more, and measuring 6 ¼" (15.87 cm) or more in length, is considered a stillborn. Delivery of a less mature fetus is considered a spontaneous abortion.

In addition to measuring and weighing the stillborn and preparing it for the morgue, the nurse should provide support to the parents. Because stillbirth can be expected or unexpected, supportive care may vary. When the stillbirth is expected, supportive care centers on helping the mother through an emotionally stressful experience and guiding the parents through the later stages of their grief, because they may have been waiting for the delivery. When a stillbirth is unexpected, supportive care involves helping the parents express their anger and relieve any grief in positive ways.

KATHRYN M. MURRAY, RN

*Flush Method:* To blanch the extremity, apply compression with one hand while inflating the manometer cuff, or securely wrap the distal extremity with an elastic bandage before inflating. *Compression causes complete capillary emptying.* Release compression of the distal extremity before deflating the cuff. As you deflate the cuff, observe for the first flush of returning blood to the blanched extremity; immediately read the pressure on the manometer, which reflects the mean arterial blood pressure (normal range is 30 to 60 mmHg for infants over 5.5 lbs [2,500 g]).

*Ultrasound or electronic vital signs monitor:* Procedure is the same as for adult (see "Blood Pressure," Chapter 1).

### Special considerations

If desired, count respirations while auscultating for heart rate.

When listening to neonatal heart tones immediately after birth, you may hear murmurs because of a delay in the closing of fetal blood shunts. Since taking vital signs may cause the neonate to become restless and cry, findings may be altered—for example, heart rate may be elevated. Therefore, record the neonate's activity with your findings.

### Documentation

Record the measurements in your nurse's notes, a special newborn appraisal form, or a flowchart. Include any observations about the infant's condition.

ANITA JONES CHINNICI, RN, MSN

# Size and Weight Measurements

*Measurement of body dimensions and weight is an important part of the neonate's physical assessment. Besides allowing accurate monitoring of normal growth, these measurements help detect such disorders as failure to thrive, small size for gestational age, hydrocephalus, and intracranial bleeding. The measurements are taken in the nursery, during well-child visits, and sometimes at home at regular intervals; they are then compared to the previous set of measurements and to normal values.*

*The neonate's head circumference is normally greater than or equal to the chest circumference, except during the first 24 hours of life, when head molding may cause head circumference to be slightly smaller than that of the chest. Head contour should return to normal in 2 to 3 days.*

*The neonate's weight varies, depending on sex, gestational age, heredity, and other factors. The firstborn usually weighs less at birth than his siblings. The infant of a diabetic mother tends to be large. The normal neonate loses 5% to 10% of his birth weight during the first few days due to withholding feedings and passage of urine and meconium, but will regain this weight within 10 days. Normal weight gain for the neonate is 5 to 7 oz (142 to 198 g) per week.*

### Equipment

Crib or examining table with a firm surface □ scale with tray □ scale paper, if necessary □ tape measure.

Disposable paper tape measures are available. Cloth tapes aren't recommended because they can stretch, giving inaccurate measurements.

## Preparation of equipment

Place clean paper on the scale, if necessary, and balance the scale to zero, according to the manufacturer's instructions.

## Essential steps

• Explain the procedure to the parents, if present.

• Wash your hands *to avoid contamination.*

• Place the neonate in the supine position on the crib or examining table, and remove all clothing except for the diaper.

*To measure head circumference:*

• Place the tape under the neonate's head at the occiput and wrap it around snugly just above the eyebrows—this should be the point of greatest circumference. Record the measurement. Average neonatal head circumference is 13″ to 14″ (33 to 35 cm).

*To measure the chest circumference:*

• Place the tape under the back and wrap it snugly around the chest at the nipple line. Make sure the tape is at the same level in the back and front. Record the measurement. Average neonatal chest circumference is 12″ to 13″ (30 to 33 cm).

*To measure length:*

• Fully extend the neonate's legs with the toes up and measure from the heel to the top of the head. If possible, have someone extend the legs by pressing down gently on the knees. Record the measurement. Average neonatal length is 19″ to 22½″ (48 to 57 cm).

*To weigh the neonate:*

• Remove his diaper and place him in the middle of the tray on the scale. Balance the scale and note his weight. Keep one hand poised over him at all times *to prevent falls,* and work quickly *to avoid having the scale soiled or wet.* Return the neonate to the crib or examining table. Record the weight. Average weight

of a full-term neonate in the United States is approximately 7½ lb (3,400 g); the normal range is 5½ to 9½ lb (2,500 to 4,300 g).

• When finished, replace the neonate's diaper and clothing, and return him to his crib, if necessary, or hand him to the parent to hold and comfort.

## Special considerations

Another way to measure length is to place the neonate on paper, such as that found on most examining tables, mark the paper at the heel with the toes pointing straight up, and at the head; then measure the distance between the marks.

Various models of scales are available; be sure to learn how to read and operate the one available to you. Most newer models give metric units of measurement. Provide the parents with a table of metric conversions, if necessary, for weighing the infant at home.

## Documentation

Record each weight and size measurement on the nurse's notes or infant assessment sheet.

For well-child visits, the parents usually carry a booklet in which they record weight and size measurements.

ANITA JONES CHINNICI, RN, MSN

# Apnea Monitoring

*Infantile apnea is considered a cause of sudden infant death syndrome (SIDS), a leading cause of neonatal death in the United States. SIDS may result from an abnormality of ventilation control, which causes prolonged periods of apnea with hypoxemia, acid-base imbalances, and cardiac arrhythmias. Because resuscitation is most successful if apneic episodes are detected and treated at their onset, apnea monitors, which sound an alarm when the neonate's breathing rate falls below a preset level, are used in neonates who are vulnerable to apnea.*

## HOW TO OPERATE A PRESSURE TRANSDUCER APNEA MONITOR (APNEA MATTRESS)

If you use the pressure transducer apnea monitor rather than the thoracic impedance type, operate the equipment as follows:
• Assemble the pressure transducer monitor and the pressure transducer pad.
• Plug the monitor into a wall outlet; then plug the cable of the transducer pad into the monitor.
• To make sure the pad is working, touch it. The respiration light on the monitor should blink.
• Follow the manufacturer's instructions for pad placement.

If you have trouble obtaining a signal, place a foam rubber pad under the mattress and position the transducer pad between the foam and the mattress.

*Two basic types of apnea monitors are in use. The thoracic impedance monitor uses chest electrodes to detect conduction changes caused by respirations; some monitors of this type also have an alarm for bradycardia. The apnea mattress monitor detects pressure changes caused by chest movements by means of a transducer connected to a pressure-sensitive pad under the neonate's mattress (see above).*

*Apnea monitors are most commonly prescribed for use in premature infants and those with such neurologic disorders as hydrocephalus, neonatal respiratory distress syndrome (hyaline membrane disease), seizure disorders, congenital heart disease with congestive heart failure, a personal history of sleep-induced apnea, and a family history of SIDS.*

*To guard against potentially life-threatening episodes in neonates who may be vulnerable to prolonged apnea, monitoring begins in the hospital and continues at home. Parents must be instructed as to how to operate the monitor, what to do when the alarm sounds, and how to perform infant cardiopulmonary resuscitation. Crucial steps for*

*correct use of each type of monitor include testing the alarm system, positioning the sensor properly, and setting the selector knobs correctly for the patient. The procedure for use of the thoracic impedance monitor is given below.*

### Equipment
Monitor unit □ electrodes □ lead wires □ electrode belt □ electrode gel, if needed □ stable surface for monitor placement.

Pregelled disposable electrodes are available.

### Essential steps
• Explain the procedure to the parents, if appropriate, and wash your hands.
• Plug in the power cord, attach the lead wires to the electrodes, and then attach the electrodes to the belt. If necessary, apply gel to the electrodes. Or, place the electrodes directly on the neonate's chest after applying electrode gel, and attach the lead wires.
• Wrap the belt snugly but not restrictively around the neonate's chest at the point of greatest movement, optimally at the right and left midaxillary line approximately ¾" (2 cm) below the axilla. Make sure the lead wires are in the appropriate position, according to manufacturer's instructions.
• Connect the lead wires to the patient cable according to the color code, and then connect the patient cable to the proper jack at the rear of the unit.
• Turn the sensitivity knobs to maximum *to allow adjustment of the system.*
• Set the alarm delay to the recommended time.
• Turn on the monitor. The alarms will ring until both sensitivity knobs are adjusted. Reset the apnea and bradycardia alarms according to the manufacturer's instructions. Then, adjust the sensitivity controls so the indicator lights blink with each breath and heart beat.
• If the apnea or bradycardia alarm sounds during monitoring, immediately check the neonate's respirations and skin color, but don't touch or disturb him *until you confirm apnea.*
• If the neonate is still breathing and his

skin color is good, readjust sensitivity controls or reposition the electrodes, if necessary.

• If the neonate isn't breathing but his skin is pink, wait 10 seconds to see if he starts breathing spontaneously. If he doesn't, try to stimulate breathing by using one of the methods given below.

• If he isn't breathing and he's pale, dusky, or blue, try to stimulate him immediately. Sequentially, attempt to stimulate respirations by: placing your hand on the neonate's back, giving him a gentle shake, giving him a vigorous shake, slapping the bottom of his feet. If he doesn't begin to breathe immediately, start cardiopulmonary resuscitation (for detailed instructions see "Cardiopulmonary Resuscitation" in Chapter 18).

### Special considerations

Don't put the monitor on top of any other electrical device; make sure it's on a level surface and can't be easily bumped.

Don't use lotions, oils, or powders on the infant's chest, where they could contact the electrode belt and cause it to slip. Periodically check alarm operation by unplugging the sensor plug: the alarm should sound after the preset time delay.

### Complications

An apneic episode may not trigger the alarm in upper airway obstruction when the neonate continues to make respiratory efforts without gas exchange. However, if the monitor has a bradycardia alarm, it may be triggered in response to the decreased heart rate that results from vagal stimulation accompanying airway obstruction. Also, with thoracic impedance monitors without bradycardia alarms, bradycardia during apnea can be read as shallow breathing, because this type of apnea monitor fails to distinguish between respiratory movement and the large cardiac stroke volume associated with bradycardia. In this case, the alarm won't trigger until the heart rate is less than the apnea limit.

### Documentation

Record all alarm incidents, documenting the time, length of apnea, the infant's skin color, stimulation measures taken, and any other pertinent information.

ANITA JONES CHINNICI, RN, MSN

# Transcutaneous pO₂ Monitoring

*A transcutaneous pO₂ (TcpO₂) monitor, using an electrode containing a transducer system, heating device, and temperature probe, measures the amount of oxygen diffusing through the neonate's skin from capillaries directly beneath the surface. This measurement correlates closely with the neonate's PaO₂, and supplements the established methods of observing skin color and taking periodic arterial blood gas measurements to detect hypoxemia and hyperoxemia.*

*When the electrode is heated to a constant temperature higher than that of the skin, usually 111°F. (44°C.), it significantly increases capillary blood flow and enhances oxygen diffusion through the tissue beneath the electrode for measurement. This procedure is being used widely in intensive care nurseries by staff nurses trained to use the monitor.*

*Since neonatal skin is very thin, with little subcutaneous fat, TcpO₂ monitoring is quite accurate. However, in infants with shock or hypoperfusion, results do not accurately reflect arterial values, because blood is shunted to the heart, brain, and lungs, reducing peripheral blood flow.*

### Equipment

TcpO₂ monitor and electrode □ cotton balls □ soap and water □ alcohol sponge □ adhesive ring for electrode.

TcpO₂ monitors usually have digital readouts and strip chart recorders to show trends. The electrode can be placed on any flat site, preferably with good capillary blood flow, few fatty deposits, and no bony prominences. The neonate's upper chest, abdomen, and inner thigh are common monitoring sites.

## Preparation of equipment

Set up the monitor, and calibrate it, if necessary, following manufacturer's instructions. Ensure that the strip chart recorder is working properly.

## Essential steps

• Wash your hands and select the electrode monitoring site.
• Cleanse the site, first using a cotton ball with soap and water, then an alcohol sponge, *to remove dirt and oils and ensure good electrode contact.*
• Dry the skin, attach the adhesive ring to the electrode, and moisten the monitor site with a drop of water, according to manufacturer's instructions, *to seal out all air.*
• Place the electrode on the site, making sure that the adhesive ring is tight.
• Set alarm switches and electrode temperature according to manufacturer's instructions or hospital policy.
• Make sure that the reading has stabilized in 10 to 20 minutes. The normal range is 50 to 90 mmHg, but may vary with the neonate and the equipment.
• Rotate the electrode site every 4 hours *to prevent skin irritation or breakdown, or burns.*

## Special considerations

Expect the $TcpO_2$ to vary with movement and treatment of the neonate, and to drop markedly whenever the neonate (less than 3 days old) cries vigorously. Be prepared to start resuscitation if a sudden significant drop in $TcpO_2$ occurs. Remember that $TcpO_2$ monitoring doesn't replace arterial blood gases, because it doesn't give information about $PaCO_2$ and pH.

## Complications

Burns and blisters from the electrode and skin reactions to the adhesive ring can occur.

## Documentation

Place graphs or printouts on the neonate's chart. Record the range of values seen during the monitoring in your nurse's notes.

ANITA JONES CHINNICI, RN, MSN

---

## TREATMENT

# Credé's Treatment

Developed by the German gynecologist Karl S.F. Credé in 1884, this treatment is the instillation of a 1% solution of silver nitrate into the neonate's eyes. Its purpose is to prevent gonorrheal conjunctivitis caused by Neisseria gonorrhoeae, *which the neonate may acquire from the mother during passage down the birth canal.*

Before this treatment, gonorrheal conjunctivitis was a common cause of permanent eye damage and blindness. Credé's treatment using silver nitrate is now mandatory in all 50 states; however, some states permit use of such ophthalmic ointments as tetracycline, erythromycin, or penicillin as an alternative to silver nitrate, principally because of the chemical irritation that silver nitrate instillation often causes.

Usually the solution is placed in the conjunctival sac and spread by closing the eye. Although previous practice called for irrigating the eye for about 30 seconds after instillation, the Committee on Ophthalmia Neonatorum of the National Society for the Prevention of Blindness currently does not recommend irrigation, and this view has been endorsed by the American Academy of Pediatrics.

Although silver nitrate may be administered in the delivery room at birth, treatment, which can cause conjunctival swelling (thus disrupting the usual quiet alert state of the neonate at birth), can be delayed for up to an hour to allow initial parent-child bonding.

*Silver nitrate prophylaxis may not be effective if the the infection was acquired in utero due to premature rupture of the membranes.*

### Equipment

Silver nitrate ampul or antibiotic ointment, as ordered □ sterile needle, or pin supplied by silver nitrate manufacturer □ gauze sponges.

### Preparation of equipment

Puncture one end of the wax silver nitrate ampul with the needle or pin or, if using antibiotic ointment, remove the cap from the ointment container.

### Essential steps

• If the parents of the neonate are present, explain that the procedure is required by state law. Tell them that it may temporarily irritate the neonate's eyes and make him cry, but that the effects are transient.

• Shield the infant's eyes from direct light, and tilt his head slightly to the side of the intended instillation.

• Using your nondominant hand, gently raise the neonate's upper eyelid with your index finger and pull down the lower eyelid with your thumb.

• Using your dominant hand, instill 1 drop of the silver nitrate solution into the lower conjunctival sac or apply the antibiotic ointment in a line along the lower conjunctival sac.

• Repeat the procedure for the other eye.

• Manipulate the lids *to spread the medication over the eye.*

• Wait 15 seconds after application, then, *to avoid discoloring the skin,* remove any excess silver nitrate with a gauze pad.

### Special considerations

Instill another drop if the silver nitrate solution touches only the eyelid or eyelid margins *to ensure complete prophylaxis.* If chemical conjunctivitis occurs or if the skin around the neonate's eyes is discolored, reassure the parents that these are temporary and will clear within several days.

### Complications

Especially after instillation of silver nitrate, chemical conjunctivitis may cause redness, swelling, and drainage.

### Documentation

If the procedure is performed in the delivery room, record the treatment on the delivery room form. If performed in the nursery, record it in your nursing notes.

GAIL JOHNSON, RN

# Sponge and Tub Baths

*Daily neonatal bathing removes bacteria, bodily wastes, and environmental contaminants from the skin. It allows for assessment of the neonate's entire body for early detection of problems, such as skin irritation, incipient infection, jaundice, and breathing difficulties. Bathing also allows the neonate to exercise his muscles, and permits the caregiver to provide range-of-motion exercises and pleasurable sensations with firm, gentle stroking motions.*

*The neonate is given sponge baths until he is about 2 weeks old and has shed his umbilical stump; after that, he may be bathed in a small tub. If he has been circumcised, he should be sponged until his penis is completely healed.*

*For a sponge bath, the neonate should be lying in his incubator or crib; for a tub bath, he is supported in a semireclining position while in the water. Bathing procedures are otherwise the same.*

*Bathing is contraindicated until the neonate's temperature stabilizes, and shouldn't be done immediately after feeding, because of the risk of regurgitation and aspiration.*

### Equipment

Basin or other small tub □ flat working surface of convenient height with protective padded cover □ mild soap □ cotton balls □ small, soft washcloth □

## UMBILICAL CORD CARE

The purpose of umbilical cord care is to keep the remaining umbilical stump clean, dry, and free of infection and to detect or prevent bleeding. After the cord is clamped or tied, it is checked for the appropriate number of blood vessels—two arteries and one large vein—and for length—normally 20″ (55 cm)—before being cut. The cord should appear transparent and blue-white, with no odor. After the cord is cut 2″ (5 cm) from the umbilicus, initial care consists of keeping the cord stump clean and dry and exposed to air.

A drying agent (triple dye, alcohol, or povidone-iodine solution) is applied to hasten drying of the cord if an accessible blood vessel is not required and the neonate is stabilized and at least 4 hours old. The cord is then checked regularly. Any oozing or bleeding from the end of the cord should be reported immediately and the cord should be reclamped. The neonate is not given a tub bath until after the cord has separated from the abdomen.

Umbilical cord care is contraindicated in a neonate whose condition requires venous or arterial access through an umbilical vessel. In such an infant, the cord stump is kept moist by wrapping it in sterile gauze soaked in normal saline solution.

ANITA JONES CHINNICI, RN, MSN

receiving blanket □ towel □ diaper □ change of clothing □ petrolatum gauze to redress circumcision □ drying agent for cord care (optional).

## Preparation of equipment

Fill the basin with comfortably warm water, about 98° to 100° F. (36.7° to 37.8° C.). Adjust the water temperature as needed, *to avoid chilling or burning sensitive neonatal skin.*

Prepare a diaper. Fold it for proper fit. (If you're using a cloth diaper, see *Folding a Diaper,* page 779.) Arrange all equipment on a stable surface, within easy reach. Use a folded blanket or towel as protective padding under the neonate *to give him a feeling of security and to help prevent him from rolling off the surface.*

## Essential steps

● Place the neonate in the supine position on the work surface, and remove his shirt *to give clear access to his head and neck.*

● Cover him from the shoulders down with the receiving blanket *to minimize heat loss—neonates have a large surface area compared with their body size.*

● Moisten a cotton ball, and gently wipe from the inner canthus of one eye over the eyelid to the outer canthus, *to remove any accumulated discharge and prevent irritation and contamination of the lacrimal duct.* Repeat with a clean cotton ball on the other eye.

● Wet the washcloth, wring it out, and thoroughly but gently wash his face; move from forehead to chin, and work carefully around his nose and mouth *to remove any collected material.* Be careful not to drag the unused end of the washcloth over the neonate's face, *because this may irritate him.*

● Gently pat his face dry with the towel, again taking care not to drag it across his face.

● Rinse and lightly soap the washcloth, and then wring it out carefully *to avoid dripping soapy water into the neonate's eyes.*

● Gently but firmly wash the neonate's scalp *to help prevent cradle cap (scaling and peeling of skin, a common neonatal skin condition),* and continue with the ears and neck. Be certain to clean between the folds of the neck, behind the ears, and the external part of the ear. *Don't attempt to clean inside the ear canal—regardless of obvious waxy secretions—because this can damage delicate ear structures.* Notify the doctor if you notice an excessive accumulation of wax.

● Thoroughly rinse and wring the washcloth, and wipe over washed areas repeatedly *to remove all soap, which can cause irritation and drying.*

● Pat the areas dry with the towel, paying particular attention to the neck folds, *because residual moisture there can cause intertrigo (irritation from moist friction between two skin surfaces).*

## FOLDING A DIAPER

Careful and frequent diaper changes protect the skin of the genitalia, perineum, and buttocks from irritation, chafing, and excoriation; allow assessment of urinary and fecal elimination; and permit treatment of any irritated areas.

### Square Diaper

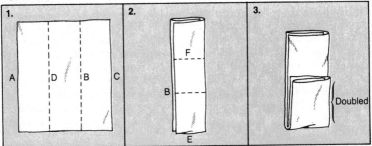

You may use a square or rectangular cloth diaper. *To fold a square diaper,* fold the two ends inward to form a long rectangle—A to B and C to D (#1 above). Then divide the rectangle into thirds, and fold E to F (#2 above). The diaper will now have a double thickness (#3 above) in the front. You can place the diaper under the neonate this way or leave the double thickness in the back.

### Rectangular Diaper

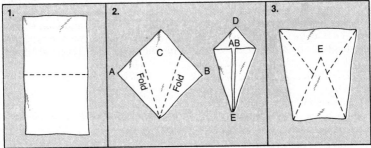

*To fold a rectangular diaper,* first fold the diaper in half to form a square (#1 above). Then rotate the square so that a corner lies at the top (#2 above). Fold the outer corners inward to form a kite shape (#2 above)—A to C and B to C. Next, fold the top corner—D—down and the bottom corner—E—up (#3 above). Place the diaper under the neonate with the long, top edge across his back.

JANE GEER FRANKENFIELD, RN, BSN

---

• Rinse the washcloth, lightly soap it, and uncover the upper portion of the neonate's body.

• Wash his chest, shoulders, axillae, arms, and hands, and wipe between the fingers. Work quickly *to avoid unnecessary chilling,* and use long, firm stroking motions, *which neonates seem to prefer.* Rinse soap off fingers and hands immediately, *to prevent the neonate from getting some in his mouth.*

• Turn him on one side and wash his back.

• Cover him with the blanket, rinse and wring the washcloth, then uncover him and wipe away the soap. Repeat this *to*

*ensure complete removal of soap.*
• Pat the areas dry with a towel.
• Expose the lower portion of the neonate's body, cover the upper half with the blanket, and remove the diaper. If you're using cloth diapers, place your fingers between his skin and the safety pin *to avoid inadvertently pricking him.*
• If he has had a bowel movement, wipe off as much feces as possible with an unsoiled part of the diaper.
• Lightly soap the washcloth; wipe over the abdomen and around the umbilical cord; work down each leg to the foot using long, stroking motions; and wash between all toes. Carefully cleanse each inguinal fold.
• Rinse the washcloth and wipe his body twice, paying special attention to creases.
• Wash his genitalia with cotton balls. Spread apart the female's labia and clean between the folds, using a front-to-back motion *to avoid contaminating the vagina and urinary meatus.* Use each cotton ball for one stroke only.
• When washing an uncircumcised male, gently retract the foreskin, if possible. *Don't* force it back. Then clean the area *to remove smegma and prevent adhesions.* Replace the foreskin *to prevent paraphimosis—retraction and constriction of the foreskin behind the glans penis.* When washing a recently circumcised male, carefully clean any feces from the circumcision area. Cleanse the rest of the genitalia, rinse twice, and pat dry.
• Wash over the perineum, front to back, and then wipe the anus, and between the gluteal fold and buttocks. If the neonate has heavily soiled himself, rinse and resoap the washcloth. Thoroughly rinse the area twice, proceeding in the same order as the washing; then scrupulously pat dry with the towel. Remember to keep the neonate covered during washcloth rinsings and soapings *to prevent chilling.*
• Replace the gauze strip covering the circumcision, and provide umbilical cord care, if indicated (see *Umbilical Cord Care*, page 778). Then rediaper the neonate, keeping the upper part of his body covered.

• Redress the neonate, position him comfortably in his bassinet, and straighten the work area.

## Special considerations
During the bath, provide range-of-motion exercises; for example, turn the neonate's head to clean his ears, or lift his arms to reach the axillae. Work as quickly as possible, but make sure you're gentle and soothing. Remember to always adequately support his head.

Never use cotton-tipped applicators to clean his nose or ears, *since they can easily slip and injure him.*

Never leave a neonate unattended or turn your back without keeping a hand on him, *since he can move himself by kicking or rolling.* If you must move away, place the neonate in a secure area, such as the bassinet.

If the neonate's skin is dry, don't use soap at every bath—once or twice a week is sufficient.

## Documentation
Record any problems observed, such as diaper irritation; unusual drainage; swelling, redness, or discharge of the umbilical cord; or poor healing of the circumcision site.

JANE GEER FRANKENFIELD, RN, BSN

# Thermoregulation

*Because the neonate has a relatively large surface-to-weight ratio, reduced metabolism per unit area, and small amounts of insulating fat, he is very susceptible to hypothermia. The neonate keeps warm by metabolizing brown fat, which has a greater concentration of energy-producing mitochondria in its cells, enhancing its capacity for heat production. This kind of fat is unique to neonates. Brown fat metabolism is effective, but only within a very narrow temperature range. Without careful external thermoregulation, the neonate may become chilled, which can result in hypoxia, acidosis, hypo-*

## THERMOREGULATION EQUIPMENT

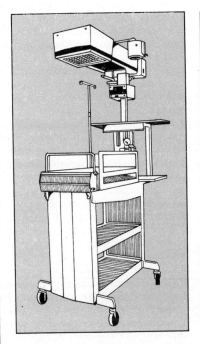

A radiant warmer maintains the neonate's temperature by *radiation*.

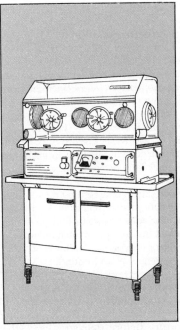

An incubator maintains the neonate's temperature by *conduction* and *convection*.

glycemia, pulmonary vasoconstriction, and even death. The object of thermoregulation is to provide a neutral thermal environment that helps the neonate maintain a normal core temperature with minimal oxygen consumption and caloric expenditure. The core temperature varies with the neonate, but is about 97.7° F. (36.5° C.).

To avoid heat loss, the neonate is first placed under a radiant warmer during suctioning and initial care in the delivery room, then wrapped in a warmed blanket for transport to the nursery. He is placed under another radiant warmer

until his temperature stabilizes; then, he can be placed in a bassinet.

If his temperature does not stabilize, or if he has a condition that effects thermoregulation, he must be placed in a temperature-controlled incubator.

Neonates lose vital body heat in three ways: by evaporation (which can occur when the neonate's wet skin—exposed to the delivery room atmosphere—is cooled by the evaporation of amniotic secretions); by radiation (which can occur when the neonate's body heat is drawn away by cooler objects close to him, such as a cold table surface); and, more obviously, *by conduction (which can occur when the neonate's blanket becomes wet and the water carries warmth directly away from the skin to the blanket). By understanding these mechanisms of heat loss and their effects, you can intervene in many ways to prevent cold stress and its complications.*

## Equipment

Radiant warmer or incubator (if necessary) □ blankets □ washcloths □ skin probe □ adhesive pad □ lubricating jelly □ thermometer □ clothes (including cap for premature infant) □ gooseneck lamp (optional).

Radiant warmers and incubators operate in two ways: *nonservo,* in which the desired temperature must be set manually, and *servo,* in which the temperature is controlled by a probe on the infant's skin. These heating devices also come equipped with alarms. Incubators have the added advantage of providing a closed environment, which reduces the spread of infection and allows control of the oxygen level and humidity.

## Preparation of equipment

Turn on the radiant warmer in the delivery room and set it at the desired temperature before delivery. Place the blankets and washcloths under a heat source to warm.

## Essential steps

*In the delivery room:*
• Place the neonate under the radiant warmer and dry him with the warm washcloths *to prevent heat loss by evaporation.* Pay special attention to his scalp and hair.
• Perform required procedures quickly *to reduce the length of time the neonate is exposed to the cooler air in the delivery room.*
• Wrap him in the warm blankets. If his condition and hospital policy permit, give him to his parents *to promote bonding.*
• Transport the neonate to the nursery in the warm blankets. Use a transport incubator if the nursery is some distance from the delivery room.

*In the nursery:*
• Remove the blankets and place the neonate under the radiant warmer. Use the adhesive pad to apply the probe to his skin, in the upper right abdominal quadrant. *This allows the servo control to keep the neonate's skin temperature between 96.8° and 97.7° F. (36.0° and 36.5° C.).* If you place the infant in the prone position, put the skin probe on his back *to avoid false high readings.* Don't cover the skin probe with anything, *since this could interfere with the servo control.* Make sure the warmer's side panels are up.
• Lubricate the thermometer and take the neonate's rectal temperature on admission *to obtain a core temperature.* Then take axillary temperatures, *which will reflect a temperature drop before the core temperature, and which will also avoid injuring rectal mucosa* (see "Vital Signs" in this chapter). Take axillary temperatures every 15 to 30 minutes until stable, then every 4 hours *to ensure stability.*
• Bathe the neonate in the warmer, after his temperature is stable for 2 to 4 hours. Then, leave him in the warmer until his temperature remains stable for at least 1 to 2 hours. If his temperature doesn't stabilize, take appropriate measures—such as placing him under a plastic heat shield or wrapping him in plastic food wrap—depending on hospital policy. Look for objects, such as a phototherapy unit, that may be blocking the heat source. Also check the neonate for evidence of infection, which can cause hypothermia.
• When the normal neonate's temperature stabilizes, dress him, put him in a bassinet, and cover him with a blanket. For the neonate whose temperature is only barely stabilized, or who requires phototherapy, set up a gooseneck lamp by the bassinet *to provide additional heat.*
• Put a knitted cap on the premature neonate *to reduce heat loss;* then place him in an incubator. (Do the same for a full-term neonate under 4 lb 6 oz, or 2,000 g.) However, respiratory support or other necessary care should be given while the neonate is in the radiant

warmer. Monitor his temperature continuously and remember that insensible water loss is greater under a radiant warmer than in an incubator.

• Apply a skin probe to the neonate in an incubator, as for a neonate in a radiant warmer. Make sure the incubator is away from cool walls or objects.

• Perform all required procedures quickly to maintain a neutral thermal environment. Close portholes or the hood immediately after completing any procedure to reduce heat loss. If procedures must be performed outside the incubator, do them under a radiant warmer.

• Once the neonate's weight is up to about 4 lb 6 oz, wean him from the incubator by slowly reducing its temperature to that of the nursery. Check him periodically for hypothermia. To ensure temperature stability, never discharge the neonate to home directly from an incubator.

### Special considerations

Always warm oxygen before administering it to a neonate to avoid aggravating heat loss from his head and face. Stimulate the neonate in an incubator by stroking him and talking to him and, if possible, by placing a music box in the incubator.

Explain to the mother the importance of maintaining the infant's temperature; instruct her to keep him wrapped in a blanket and out of drafts when he's not in the bassinet.

### Complications

Hypothermia can inhibit weight gain, because the infant is using all his calories to maintain his temperature. Hyperthermia can cause increased oxygen consumption and apnea. Both conditions can result from equipment failures.

### Documentation

Record the heat source and its temperature, as well as the infant's temperature, whenever taken. Document any complications that result from the use of warming equipment.

GAIL JOHNSON, RN

# Bottle-Feeding

*Bottle-feeding is the method of choice when the mother either is unable to or chooses not to breast-feed her infant, or if the infant requires a special diet. Modern formula preparations supply all needed vitamins and nutrients and can be administered by anyone—an advantage over breast-feeding. Usually, ready-to-feed formulas with disposable nipples and caps are used, but some formulas may require advance preparation, as well as sterilization of the formula and equipment.*

*The Committee on Nutrition of the American Academy of Pediatrics has found that adding solid foods, such as cereal or fruit, to the infant's diet during the first 4 to 6 months is no more beneficial for most infants than liquid nourishment (formula or mother's milk) alone.*

*Formulas for the neonate must be sterile and are prepared either by the aseptic method, in which all articles used in formula preparation are sterilized before mixing, or by the terminal heat method, in which the formula is prepared with clean technique and then sterilized using an autoclave or home sterilizer. Most hospitals use commercially prepared formulas that are also available to the mother when she is home.*

*A normal neonate takes 15 to 20 minutes to consume a 1- to 1½-oz bottle portion, and is usually fed every 3 to 4 hours.*

### Equipment

Commercially prepared and sterilized formula, or ingredients and bottle □ nipple and cap □ tissue or cloth □ gown.

Disposable nipples are commonly used in the hospital.

### Preparation of equipment

If you're using commercially packaged formula, screw on the cap and nipple, making sure the seal in the bottle is broken. If you're preparing formula, follow the manufacturer's instructions or the doctor's prescription. The formula should be at room temperature or slightly warmer. If you're sterilizing the bottle and nipple, follow hospital policy.

### Essential steps

• Wash your hands and put on a clean gown.

• Invert the bottle and shake some formula on your wrist *to test the patency of the nipple hole and the temperature of the formula.* The nipple hole should allow formula to drip freely but not run in a stream. *If the hole is too large, the neonate may aspirate formula; if it is too small, he may tire before he has emptied the bottle.*

• Sit comfortably and cradle the neonate in a semireclining position in one arm, to support his head and back. *This allows swallowed air to rise to the top of the stomach where it's more easily expelled.* If he can't be held, sit by him and elevate his head and shoulders slightly.

• Place the nipple in the neonate's mouth, but don't insert it far enough to stimulate the gag reflex. He should then begin to suck, pulling in as much nipple as is comfortable. If he doesn't start to suck, stroke him under the chin or on the side of his cheek, or touch his lips with the nipple *to stimulate his sucking reflex.*

• As the neonate feeds, tilt the bottle upward *to keep the nipple filled with formula and prevent him from swallowing air.* Watch for a steady stream of bubbles in the bottle, which indicates proper venting and flow of formula. If the neonate pushes out the nipple with his tongue, reinsert the nipple, since this is a normal reflex and doesn't necessarily mean that he's satiated.

• Always hold the bottle for a neonate. If left to feed himself, he may aspirate formula or swallow air if the bottle should tilt or empty. *Bottle propping has been linked in older infants with an increased incidence of otitis media and dental caries.*

• Burp (bubble) the neonate after each ½ oz of formula, since he usually swallows air even when fed correctly. Keep a gown on your lap *to avoid soiling your clothing,* and hold the neonate upright in a slightly forward position, with one hand supporting his head and chest. Or, position a clean cloth *to protect your clothing,* and hold the neonate upright over your shoulder or place him face down across your lap. *The change in position helps bring up the bubble.* In each case, rub or gently pat his back until the air is expelled.

• When you've finished feeding and burping the neonate, place him on his stomach or right side *to prevent aspiration if he regurgitates.*

• Discard any remaining formula and properly dispose of all equipment.

### Special considerations

Change the length of feeding by regulating the size of the nipple or the nipple hole, *since the infant tires if he feeds too long, and his sucking needs aren't met if he doesn't feed long enough.*

Be sure to note how much formula is in the bottle before and after the feeding. Use the calibrations along the side of the container to calculate the amount of formula taken.

Be alert for aspiration in the infant with diminished sucking or swallowing reflex, who may have difficulty feeding. Also, take appropriate measures according to hospital policy to feed the neonate with cleft lip and palate.

Teach parents how to properly prepare and sterilize (if required) formula, bottles, and nipples, and how to feed and burp the infant. Although most hospitals have a feeding schedule, advise the mother that she may switch to a more flexible demand-feeding schedule when at home. Warn her that the neonate may not feed well on his first day home because of the activity and changed environment.

### Complications

Bottle propping may allow the nipple to block the infant's air passage, causing suffocation; it may also lead to otitis media or dental caries. Lung infection or death may follow aspiration of regurgitated formula. Regurgitation, which is merely an overflow and often follows feeding, shouldn't be confused with vomiting, which is a more complete emptying of the stomach, is accompanied by other symptoms, and is not associated with feeding.

## Documentation

Record the time of the feeding, the amount taken, how well the neonate fed, if he appeared satisfied, and the occurrence of any regurgitation or vomiting. If the mother feeds him, observe and record how well they interact.

ANITA JONES CHINNICI, RN, MSN

# Gavage-Feeding

*Gavage-feeding involves passing nutrients directly to the neonate's stomach by a tube passed through the nasopharynx or the oropharynx. The procedure is indicated for the neonate who is unable to suck because of prematurity, illness, or congenital deformity. It is also indicated for the infant who risks aspiration because of gastroesophageal reflux or lack of gag reflex, or because he tires easily. In a premature neonate, gavage-feeding is continued until he can begin bottle-feeding.*

*Unless the neonate has problems with the feeding tube, it is inserted before each feeding, usually through his mouth, and then withdrawn after feeding. This intermittent method stimulates the sucking reflex. If the neonate cannot tolerate this, the tube is passed through the nostrils and left in place for 24 to 72 hours.*

*Tube-feeding is contraindicated in the infant with absent bowel sounds, suspected intestinal obstruction, severe respiratory distress, or massive gastroesophageal reflux.*

## Equipment

Feeding tube (#5 or #6 French for nasogastric feeding of premature neonate; #8 French for others) □ feeding reservoir or large (20- to 50-ml) syringe □ prescribed formula or breast milk □ sterile water □ 2- to 5-ml syringe □ tape measure □ tape □ stethoscope □ optional: bowl and pacifier.

A commercial feeding reservoir is available.

## Preparation of equipment

Allow the formula or breast milk to warm to room temperature, if necessary. Wash your hands and open the sterile water, if it comes in a small-sized disposable container, or pour a small amount from a larger container into a bowl. Remove the syringe or reservoir and the feeding tube from the packaging.

## Essential steps

• With a tape measure, *determine the length of tubing needed to ensure placement in the stomach,* according to the institution's policy and the developmental stage of the neonate. Common measurements used are from the bridge of the nose to the xiphoid process; from the tip of the nose to the tip of the earlobe to the midpoint between the xiphoid process and the umbilicus; and, for the premature neonate, from the bridge of the nose to the umbilicus. Mark the tube at the appropriate distance with a piece of tape, measuring from the bottom.

• If possible, support the neonate on your lap in a sitting position *to provide a feeling of warmth and security.* Otherwise, place the neonate in a supine position or tilted slightly to the right, with head and chest slightly elevated.

• Stabilize the neonate's head with one hand and lubricate the feeding tube with sterile water with the other hand.

• Insert the tube smoothly and quickly up to the premeasured mark. For oral insertion, pass the tube toward the back of the throat. For nasal insertion, pass the tube toward the occiput in a horizontal plane.

• Synchronize tube insertion with throat movement if the neonate swallows, *to facilitate its passage into the stomach.* During insertion, watch for choking and cyanosis, signs that the tube has entered the trachea. If these occur, remove the tube and reinsert it. Also, watch for bradycardia and apnea resulting from vagal stimulation. If bradycardia occurs, leave the tube in place for 1 minute and check for return to normal heart rate. If bradycardia persists, remove the tube and notify the doctor.

• If the tube is to remain in place, tape it flat to the neonate's cheek. *To prevent possible nasal skin breakdown,* don't tape the tube to the bridge of his nose.

• Make sure the tube is in the stomach by aspirating residual stomach contents with the syringe. Note the volume obtained, and then reinject it *to avoid altering the neonate's buffer system and electrolyte balance.* If ordered, reduce the volume of the feeding by the residual amount, or prolong the interval between feedings.

• Alternatively, or in addition to the above procedure, check placement of the feeding tube in the stomach by injecting 1 to 2 cc of air into the tube while listening for air sounds in the stomach with the stethoscope.

• If the tube doesn't appear to be in place, insert it several centimeters further and test again. *Don't* begin feeding until you're sure the tube is positioned properly.

• When the tube is in place, fill the feeding reservoir or syringe with the formula or breast milk. Then, inject 1 ml of sterile water into the tube and pinch the top of the tube *to establish gravity flow.* Connect the feeding reservoir or syringe to the top of the tube, and then release the tube *to start the feeding.*

• If the neonate's sitting on your lap, hold the container 4″ (10 cm) above his abdomen. If he's lying down, hold it 6″ to 8″ (15 to 20 cm) above his head. When using a commercial feeding reservoir, observe for air bubbles in the container, indicating passage of formula.

• Regulate flow by raising and lowering the container, so that the feeding takes 15 to 20 minutes, the average time for a bottle feeding. *To prevent stomach distention, reflux, and vomiting,* don't let the feeding proceed too rapidly.

• When the feeding is finished, pinch off

the tubing before air enters the neonate's stomach *to prevent distention, and to avoid leakage of fluid into the pharynx during removal, with possible aspiration.* Then, withdraw the tube smoothly and quickly. If the tube is to remain in place, flush it with several milliliters of sterile water, if ordered.

• Burp the neonate *to decrease abdominal distention.* Hold him upright or in a sitting position, with one hand supporting his head and chest, and gently rub or pat his back until he expels the air.

• Place him on his stomach or right side for 1 hour after feeding *to facilitate gastric emptying and to prevent aspiration if he regurgitates.*

## Special considerations
Use the nasogastric approach for the neonate who must have the feeding tube left in place, *because it's more stable than orogastric insertion.* Alternate the nostril used at each insertion *to prevent skin and mucosal irritation.*

Observe the premature neonate for indications that he's ready to begin bottle-feeding: strong sucking reflex, coordinated sucking and swallowing, alertness before feeding, and sleep after it.

Provide the neonate with a pacifier during feeding *to relax him, to help prevent gagging, and to promote an association between sucking and the feeling of fullness that follows feeding.*

## Complications
Gagging with regurgitation causes loss of nutrients. An indwelling nasogastric tube can cause nasal airway obstruction, irritation of mucous membranes, epistaxis, and stomach perforation. A feeding tube may kink, coil, or knot and become obstructed, preventing feeding.

## Documentation
Record the amount of residual fluid and the amount currently taken. Note the type and amount of any vomitus, and any adverse reactions to tube insertion or feeding.

GAIL JOHNSON, RN

# Circumcision

*Circumcision is the removal of the fore-skin from the neonate's penis. Usually done by a doctor 2 or 3 days after birth, this minor operation is performed for hygienic reasons, to make cleansing the glans easier, and to avoid the risk of phimosis (tightening of the foreskin) in later life. Although some believe circumcision may reduce the future risk of penile cancer, and of cervical cancer in sexual partners, the American Academy of Pediatrics ruled in 1971 that there is no valid medical reason for routine circumcision. Nevertheless, most American males are still circumcised today.*

*In the Jewish religion, circumcision is a religious ritual called a* brith *and is performed by a* mohel *on the eighth day after birth, when the neonate is officially given his name. Since most neonates are sent home before this time, the* brith *is rarely done in the hospital.*

*One method of circumcision involves cutting off the foreskin, using a Yellen clamp to stabilize the penis. With this device, a cone is fitted over the glans to provide a cutting surface and protect the glans penis. In another technique, a plastic circumcision bell (Plastibell) is placed over the glans, and a suture is tied tightly around the base of the foreskin. This method prevents bleeding and is generally considered painless, because stretching of the foreskin inhibits sensory conduction. The resulting ischemia causes the foreskin to drop off after 5 to 8 days.*

*Circumcision is contraindicated in neonates who are ill, or who have bleeding disorders, ambiguous genitalia, or congenital anomalies of the penis, such as hypospadias or epispadias, because the foreskin may be needed for later reconstructive surgery.*

## Equipment

Circumcision tray (contents vary, but usually include circumcision clamps, various size cones, scalpel, probe, scissors, forceps, sterile basin, sterile towel, and sterile drapes) □ povidone-iodine solution □ restraining board with arm and leg restraints □ sterile gloves □ 4" × 4" gauze sponges □ petrolatum gauze □ optional: antibiotic ointment, and hot-water bottle or heating pad to place under the restraining board to warm the neonate.

## Preparation of equipment

*For circumcision using a Yellen clamp:* Assemble the sterile tray and other equipment in the procedure area. Open the sterile tray and pour povidone-iodine solution into the sterile basin. Using sterile technique, place sterile 4" × 4" gauze sponges and petrolatum gauze on the sterile tray. Make sure the area is warm. Arrange the restraining board and direct adequate light on the area.

*For application of a plastic circumcision bell:* A circumcision tray isn't needed. Assemble sterile gloves, suture, restraining board, petrolatum gauze, and, if desired, antibiotic ointment.

A *mohel* usually brings his own equipment.

## Essential steps

*Before circumcision:*
• Make sure the parents understand the procedure and have signed a consent form.
• Make sure that the neonate hasn't been fed for 1 hour before the procedure.
• Place the neonate on the restraining board, and restrain his arms and legs.
• Assist the doctor as necessary throughout the procedure and comfort the neonate as needed.

*For Yellen circumcision:*
• After putting on sterile gloves, the doctor cleans the penis and scrotum with povidone-iodine.
• He then drapes the neonate.
• Next, he applies a circumcision clamp to the penis, loosens the foreskin, inserts the cone under it *to provide a cutting surface and protect the penis,* and cuts off the foreskin.
• When the procedure is complete, he covers the wound with sterile petrola-

tum gauze *to prevent infection and control bleeding.*

*For application of the plastic circumcision bell:*

• The doctor slides the plastic bell device between the foreskin and the glans penis, and he ties a length of suture tightly around the foreskin at the coronal edge of the glans. The foreskin distal to the suture becomes ischemic, then atrophic. After 5 to 8 days, the foreskin drops off with the plastic bell attached, leaving a clean, well-healed line of excision. No special care is required, but you must watch for swelling.

*After circumcision:*

• Remove the neonate from the restraining board. Check for bleeding.

• Cover him with one layer of diaper *to allow observation for bleeding.*

• Show the neonate to his parents *to reassure them that he is all right.*

• Place him in his crib on his side rather than prone, *to keep pressure off the excision area.*

• Change the neonate's diaper as soon as he voids and, if the dressing falls off, cleanse the wound with warm water *to minimize pain from urine on the area.* Don't remove the original dressing until it falls off, which is usually after the first or second voiding.

• Check for bleeding every 15 minutes for the first hour and then every hour for the next 24 hours. If bleeding occurs, apply pressure with sterile gauze sponges; notify the doctor if it continues.

• Continue to diaper the neonate loosely *to prevent irritation.* At each diaper change apply ordered antibiotic ointment, petrolatum, or petrolatum gauze until the wound appears healed.

• Watch for drainage, redness, or swelling. Don't remove the thin yellow-white exudate that forms over the healing area within 1 to 2 days—this is normal, and protects the wound.

## Special considerations

Always make sure the parents have seen the circumcision site before going home so they can ask any questions. Teach them how to care for the area.

## Complications

After a Yellen clamp procedure, infection and bleeding are possible. The skin of the penis shaft can adhere to the glans, resulting in scarring or fibrous bands. The most severe complications are urethral fistulae and edema. Incomplete amputation of the foreskin can follow application of the plastic circumcision bell.

## Documentation

Note the time and date of the circumcision, any parent teaching, and any excessive bleeding.

GAIL JOHNSON, RN

# Phototherapy

*Phototherapy involves exposing the neonate to specific wavelengths of light, which decomposes bilirubin (a by-product of the breakdown of red blood cells) in the neonate's skin by oxidation. This treatment is often necessary in neonates (especially if premature) who cannot completely metabolize and excrete bilirubin in their bile due to immature liver function. This condition, known as neonatal jaundice (hyperbilirubinemia), is not uncommon, because neonates normally have higher bilirubin levels than adults, as a result of their higher red blood cell (RBC) count and a shorter RBC lifespan. Untreated, it can lead to kernicterus (deposition of unconjugated bilirubin in brain cells), which causes permanent brain damage and has a mortality rate approaching 50% in the first month of life.*

*Neonatal jaundice develops 24 hours after delivery in 50% of term neonates (usually day 2 to day 3), and 48 hours after delivery in 80% of premature neonates (usually day 3 to day 5). It usually disappears by day 7 in term neonates and by day 9 or 10 in premature neonates.*

*Phototherapy often begins while the doctor determines the cause of jaundice.*

*It's usually the only treatment necessary, although some neonates (especially those with hemolytic disease) may require exchange transfusions to reduce excessive bilirubin levels (see "Exchange Transfusion" in this chapter).*

## Equipment

Phototherapy unit □ radiometer (or card indicating number of hours the bulbs have been in use) □ cotton balls □ normal saline solution □ methylcellulose ophthalmic drops □ eye pads and eye mask □ Velcro strap or paper tape □ diaper □ bilirubin graph sheet □ optional: surgical face mask, gooseneck lamp.

All equipment needed to cover the neonate's eyes is available prepackaged.

## Preparation of equipment

Set up the phototherapy unit over the neonate's crib or incubator, according to the manufacturer's instructions (see *Phototherapy With an Incubator*). If a radiant warmer with a built-in phototherapy unit is being used, position an additional phototherapy unit to the side of the neonate's bed, making sure that it will be the correct distance from his skin. This additional unit is necessary *to deliver the required therapeutic energy level, because the built-in unit is too far away from the neonate to produce sufficient energy for therapy.* If a radiometer isn't available, check that the bulbs haven't been used longer than specified by the manufacturer or the institution's policy (usually 400 to 500 hours). Replace the bulbs with new ones, if necessary, *to ensure optimum output of radiant energy.* Turn on the unit *to make sure the bulbs are working properly.*

## Essential steps

● Explain the procedure to the parents.
● Record the neonate's initial bilirubin level and take his axillary temperature *to establish baseline measurements.*
● Cleanse the neonate's eyes with the cotton balls moistened with normal saline solution. Then instill 1 drop of methylcellulose in each eye *to prevent drying and corneal abrasion.* Place eye pads

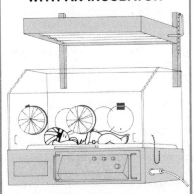

## PHOTOTHERAPY WITH AN INCUBATOR

Plug the phototherapy unit into the outlet found on the neonate's incubator, and position the lamp directly over the incubator's hood as illustrated above. Before exposing the neonate to the light, pad and mask his eyes so they are *completely covered.*

over the eyes *to prevent retinal damage from the phototherapy lights.* Make sure his eyes are shut, *because corneal abrasion can occur if the eyes open beneath the pads.* Finally, place the eye mask over the eye pads and secure it with the Velcro strap or paper tape. Make sure the mask isn't too tight, *because this can cause head molding, particularly in a premature neonate.*
● Undress the neonate *to expose the maximum amount of skin* and lay him on the diaper. If required by the hospital's policy, cover the male neonate's testes with a surgical mask *to protect them.*
● Turn on the phototherapy lights. Make sure there's nothing between the lights and the neonate *to ensure full exposure and to prevent damage to materials, such as plastic, that could melt under the lights.* Always make sure the clear plastic cover is in place on units using fluorescent lights, *because it removes harmful ultraviolet rays and protects the neonate from bulb breakage.*
● Place the radiometer probe in the middle of the crib *to measure the*

*amount of radiant energy being emitted by the lights.* The measurement should be 4 to 6 microwatts per square centimeter per nanometer ($\mu W/cm^2/nm$).

● Take the neonate's axillary temperature every 1 to 2 hours *to prevent hyperthermia and hypothermia.* If needed, provide a heat source, such as a gooseneck lamp with bulb shield, or adjust the temperature of a heated incubator.

● Monitor the number and amount of urinations and bowel movements *to help prevent dehydration, because phototherapy may increase insensible water loss.* Also, monitor specific gravity of urine every 8 hours *to help assess hydration.*

● Cleanse the neonate carefully after each bowel movement, *because the loose, green stools that may result from phototherapy can excoriate the skin.* Don't apply an ointment, *because this can cause burns under the phototherapy lights.*

● Reposition the neonate every few hours.

● Feed the neonate every 3 to 4 hours and offer water between feedings *to ensure adequate hydration;* make sure water intake doesn't replace formula or breast milk. If possible, take him out of the crib and remove his eye mask *to allow visual stimulation and contact,* especially with parents. Check his eyes at this time for signs of irritation or infection.

● Check bilirubin level at least every 24 hours and more often if it's rising significantly. Turn off the phototherapy lights before performing the venipuncture *to prevent false results, since the lights will degrade bilirubin in the sample.*

● Plot bilirubin levels on a bilirubin graph *to be sure the level isn't rising more than 5 mg/day;* a steeper increase indicates the need for additional treatment.

 Notify the doctor if the bilirubin level exceeds 20 mg/100 ml in a full-term neonate, or 15 mg/100 ml if he's premature, *since these levels may result in kernicterus.*

● Check the eye mask frequently *to prevent slippage, exposure of eyes to the lights, or obstruction of the nostrils.* Change the eye pads and the mask daily.

● Review the neonatal and maternal histories for possible causes of the hyperbilirubinemia. Watch for signs of infection and metabolic disorders. Check the neonate's hematocrit for polycythemia. Inspect him for bruising, hematoma, petechiae, and cyanosis. If you're using blue lights, turn them off at this time *because they may mask cyanosis.*

## Special considerations

Use a stocking cap over the eye pads instead of a mask with a very small premature neonate, if desired. If the infant cries excessively during phototherapy, place a blanket roll to each side of him *to provide a quieting feeling of security.*

## Complications

Bronze-baby syndrome—an idiopathic darkening of the skin, serum, and urine—may occur. Changes in feeding, physical activity, and hormonal secretions may follow prolonged therapy.

## Documentation

At least once every 8 hours, record that phototherapy is in progress and that eye pads and a mask are being used. Record the time bilirubin tests are performed and plot bilirubin levels on the appropriate graph. Indicate when pads and mask are changed and eye care given. Record the measured radiant energy at the start of therapy and then every 8 hours. Note how long the infant is removed from under the lights for other procedures or parental contact. Also note the amount of urine and feces passed, the specific gravity of the urine, and fluid intake. Describe any changes in skin, feeding patterns, and level of physical activity.

GAIL JOHNSON, RN

# Exchange Transfusion

*Performed by a doctor with a nurse as-*

*sisting, exchange transfusion is a sterile procedure that replaces a neonate's blood with an equal amount of donor blood to remove excess bilirubin and prevent kernicterus. A two-volume exchange replaces about 85% of the neonate's blood and lowers the bilirubin level by about 50%. However, it doesn't remove any bilirubin in tissue and extravascular spaces, and this bilirubin migrates back into the plasma. Exchange transfusion is usually performed when the bilirubin level increases more than 1 mg/100 ml each hour, or reaches 20 mg/100 ml in a normal full-term neonate, or 15 to 16 mg/100 ml in a premature or weak neonate. It isn't performed when the bilirubin level can be lowered by other treatment, such as phototherapy.*

### Equipment

Umbilical catheter tray with correct size catheters □ exchange transfusion tray □ radiant warmer □ phototherapy unit □ cardiac monitor □ ordered amount and type of blood □ alcohol sponges □ blood warmer □ blood-warming coil □ blood culture tubes (clot and nonclotting) □ feeding tube □ bulb or catheter syringe □ thermometer □ stethoscope □ povidone-iodine solution □ Dextrostix □ infant restraints □ sterile towels □ sterile gloves, gown, and mask □ suction equipment □ resuscitation equipment □ optional: albumin, if ordered; a vial of sterile normal saline solution for injection; manometer; equipment for shielding the infant's eyes.

Most institutions usually have exchange transfusion and umbilical catheter trays prepared.

### Preparation of equipment

Turn on the radiant warmer and set the temperature as prescribed by hospital policy. Place the cardiac monitor at the bedside. Open the trays and, using sterile technique, add any additional items. Obtain banked blood and verify all identifying information with the doctor or another nurse. Hang the blood bag, wipe a port with an alcohol sponge, and insert the spike from the blood tubing. Connect the tubing to the blood warmer, and sta-

bilize the temperature at 98.6° F. (37° C.). Run the blood through to the end of the tubing and remove all air bubbles. Label all laboratory tubes for ordered pre- and postexchange tests. Make sure suction and resuscitation equipment is nearby and working properly.

### Essential steps

● Explain the procedure to the neonate's parents, if possible, and make sure that they have signed a consent form. Positively identify the neonate by checking his identification band.

● Insert a feeding tube and aspirate stomach contents *to prevent aspiration of vomitus.*

● Position the neonate under the radiant warmer *to maintain a stable body temperature and provide an accessible working surface.* If phototherapy will be used during the procedure *to reduce tissue bilirubin,* place eye pads and shields over the neonate's eyes *to prevent retinal damage from the phototherapy lights;* then turn on the lights.

● Tape a skin or rectal thermometer probe in place *to allow continuous temperature monitoring.* Restrain the neonate as necessary.

● Take baseline vital signs. Obtain a blood sample from the neonate's finger and test it with Dextrostix. Avoid collecting blood from an area below his waist *to permit accurate detection of a malpositioned catheter, which often causes mottling of the lower extremities.* Take vital signs and Dextrostix readings every 15 minutes during the procedure.

● Remove the neonate's clothing except for the diaper, *to allow access to his umbilical cord.*

● Connect the neonate to the cardiac monitor.

● Help the doctor put on sterile mask, gown, and gloves, as required. The doctor then cleanses the catheter site; inserts a catheter into the umbilical artery, vein, or both; and attaches stopcocks.

● If ordered, attach a manometer and determine central venous or mean arterial pressure, depending on the vessel(s) catheterized.

• Hang the bag for the neonate's discarded blood lower than the transfusion site in a nonsterile area.

• If ordered, inject albumin, *as it may attract and bind bilirubin, thus facilitating its removal from tissues.* Also, if ordered, hang and connect 10% dextrose in water, and allow it to infuse at the prescribed rate for 30 minutes *to maintain catheter patency and allow the albumin time to work.*

• Assist the doctor, as required, to set up the necessary lines and stopcocks.

• Place the first volume of collected blood into the proper tubes, label the tubes correctly, and send them to the laboratory for blood culture, bilirubin, calcium, glucose, total protein, and CBC or hematocrit determination. Keep the tube for bilirubin determination away from the phototherapy lights, *which decompose bilirubin.* The doctor then alternately removes and transfuses 10 to 15 portions of blood over a period of 1 to 2 hours, to the desired total volume, *to prevent cardiac changes and stress.*

• Record the exact time and amount of collected or transfused blood on the exchange transfusion sheet. *To prevent errors,* repeat each amount after the doctor specifies it.

• During the procedure, observe the neonate for mottling or cyanosis of the lower extremities—possible signs of a malpositioned catheter.

• Alert the doctor each time 100 ml of blood has been exchanged, so he can give calcium gluconate *to prevent tetany from depletion of serum calcium by sodium citrate in the donor blood.* Record the time and amount of calcium gluconate infusion on the exchange transfusion sheet. Auscultate heart rate and watch the cardiac monitor throughout calcium administration *to detect arrhythmias.*

• Alert the doctor when the prescribed amount of blood has been exchanged.

• Place the last sample of collected blood in the proper tubes, label the tubes correctly, and send them to the laboratory for tests, which may include typing and cross matching if another exchange transfusion is required. The doctor then

removes the umbilical catheter or, if he intends to leave it in place, flushes it with sterile normal saline solution.

• If the doctor leaves the catheter in place, begin the prescribed I.V. infusion *to maintain catheter patency and provide nourishment and hydration, because the neonate probably won't be fed for several hours after the procedure.* Follow the hospital's policy for cord care while the catheter is in place.

• After the transfusion has been completed, observe the neonate closely for signs of hypoglycemia, hypocalcemia, acidosis, and sepsis. Take vital signs every 30 minutes for the next 2 hours and then every hour for 4 hours, until stable. If the catheter has been removed, check the umbilical stump for bleeding.

• Notify the parents that the exchange is finished and, if permitted, allow them to visit the neonate.

### Special considerations
If possible, make sure that the neonate isn't fed for several hours before the procedure.

### Complications
Necrotizing enterocolitis can result from compromised bowel circulation from a misplaced or clotted catheter. Hypoglycemia may result from a rebound effect due to increased insulin production in response to glucose in the donor blood. Hypocalcemia can result from calcium depletion by sodium citrate in the donor blood. Other possible complications include infection, air embolism, umbilical vessel perforation, arterial spasms and blood clots, cardiac arrhythmias, splenic rupture, and subsequent portal hypertension from the catheter; blood transfusion reaction; bleeding from the umbilical stump; and cardiac arrest from cardiac overload or decreased cardiac output.

### Documentation
On the exchange transfusion form, record vital signs, including blood pressure; drug administration; the time and amount of blood removal and replace-

ment; the type and Rh factor of transfused blood; infusion of I.V. fluids; collection of blood samples; and the results of laboratory tests. In your notes, record the date and duration of the procedure, the doctor's name, the catheter site, complications and treatment given, the time of catheter removal, postprocedure infusion of I.V. fluids, and any changes in the neonate's behavior.

GAIL JOHNSON, RN

# Oxygen Administration

*Oxygen is administered to relieve neonatal respiratory distress. This distress may be indicated by cyanosis, pallor, tachypnea, nasal flaring, bradycardia, hypothermia, retractions (intercostal, subcostal margin, suprasternal), hypotonia, hyporeflexia, or expiratory grunting. Because of the neonate's size and special respiratory requirements, oxygen administration often requires special techniques and equipment. In emergency situations, oxygen is given through a manual resuscitation bag and mask of appropriate size until more permanent measures can be initiated. When the neonate merely requires additional oxygen above the ambient concentration, it can be delivered by means of an oxygen hood. When the neonate requires continuous positive airway pressure (CPAP) to prevent alveolar collapse at the end of an expiration, as in respiratory distress syndrome (hyaline membrane disease), oxygen is administered through nasal prongs or an endotracheal tube connected to a manometer. If the neonate can't breathe on his own, oxygen must be delivered through a ventilator. Oxygen must be warmed and humidified to prevent hypothermia and dehydration, to which the neonate is especially susceptible.*

*No matter how it's administered, oxygen therapy is potentially hazardous to the neonate. When given in high concentrations and for prolonged periods, it can cause retrolental fibroplasia, which may result in blindness in premature neonates, and can contribute to bronchopulmonary dysplasia.*

## Equipment
Oxygen source, either wall or cylinder □ compressed air source □ flowmeters □ blender or Y-connector □ large- and small-bore oxygen tubing (sterile) □ warming/humidifying device □ blood gas analyzer □ thermometer □ stethoscope □ suction equipment.

*For bag and mask delivery:*
Neonate or premature size mask with manual resuscitation bag □ manometer with connectors.

*For oxygen hood delivery:*
Appropriate-sized oxygen hood.

*For CPAP delivery:*
Nasal prongs or endotracheal tube of appropriate size □ water-soluble lubricant □ nonallergenic tape □ manometer with connectors.

## Preparation of equipment
Wash your hands and gather the necessary equipment.

*To calibrate the oxygen analyzer:* Turn the analyzer on and read room air—this should be 21% oxygen. Check the battery level. Expose the analyzer probe to 100% oxygen and adjust sensitivity as necessary; then recheck the room air reading.

*To set up a manual resuscitation bag and mask:* Place the bag and mask in the crib. Connect the large-bore oxygen tubing to the mask outlet. Connect a manometer to the bag using connectors and small-bore tubing. Connect the free end of the oxygen tubing to the warming/humidifying device. Fill the device with sterile water and turn it on when you're ready to use it, or prepare it according to manufacturer's instructions. Connect another piece of small-bore tubing to the inlet of the warming/humidifing device. Attach a Y-connector to the opposite end of this tubing. Place a piece of small-bore tubing on each end of the

Y-connector, and connect the pieces of tubing to the flowmeters. Place an inline thermometer as close as possible to the delivery end of the apparutus.

To set up an oxygen hood: Bring a clean oxygen hood to the patient's bedside. When a manual resuscitation bag and mask are no longer required, remove the mask and manual resuscitation bag from the connecting tube and attach the oxygen hood to this tubing. Place an inline thermometer as close to the patient as possible whenever using warmed air oxygen.

## Essential steps

To administer emergency oxygen through a manual resuscitation bag and mask:
• Turn on the oxygen and compressed air flowmeters to the prescribed flow rates.
• Apply the mask to the neonate's face, making sure that it doesn't cover his eyes and that air isn't leaking around it because of inadequate pressure or incorrect mask size.
• While stabilizing the neonate, have another staff member notify the doctor immediately.
• Provide 40 breaths per minute with enough pressure to cause a visible rise and fall of the neonate's chest. Provide enough oxygen to keep his nailbeds and mucous membranes pink. If a doctor isn't present when the emergency occurs, deliver the oxygen percentage prescribed by the hospital's emergency policy.
• Watch the neonate's chest movements continuously and check breath sounds. Avoid over-ventilating, as this will blow off too much carbon dioxide and cause apnea.
• Insert a nasogastric tube to keep air out of the stomach.

To administer oxygen through an oxygen hood:
• Remove the connecting tubing from the face mask and connect it to the oxygen hood. Turn on oxygen, and compressed air source, if needed, to the ordered flow rates.
• Place the oxygen hood over the neonate's head.

• Measure the amount of oxygen the neonate is receiving with the oxygen analyzer. Be sure to place the analyzer probe close to the neonate's nose. Adjust the oxygen to the prescribed amount.

To administer oxygen with CPAP:
• Position the neonate on his back with a rolled towel under his neck to keep the airway open but not hyperextend the neck.
• If administering oxygen through nasal prongs, select the correct size for the neonate's nose.
• Apply a small amount of water-soluble lubricant to the outside of the prongs. Turn on the oxygen and compressed air, if necessary. Connect the prongs to the oxygen tubing.
• Insert the prongs into the nose and stabilize them.
• Clean the prongs each shift to ensure patency.
• If you're administering oxygen through an endotracheal tube, obtain the correct size tube and coat it with water-soluble lubricant.
• Turn on the oxygen and compressed air source.
• Assist the doctor in inserting the tube and attaching the oxygen delivery system (as set up for mask and bag delivery).
• Tape the endotracheal tube securely.
• Insert a nasogastric tube and leave it in place to keep the stomach decompressed. Leave it open unless the neonate is receiving gavage-feedings.
• Suction the nasal passages and oropharynx every 2 hours or as needed to maintain an open airway.

To administer oxygen through a ventilator:
• Turn on the ventilator and set the controls, as ordered.
• Assist the doctor with insertion of the endotracheal tube, if not already in place.
• Connect the endotracheal tube to the ventilator and tape the tube securely.
• With any delivery system, carefully watch the manometer to maintain pressure at the prescribed amount; observe the inline thermometer for correct temperature.
• Monitor blood gases every 15 to 20 minutes, or other reasonable interval,

after any alterations of oxygen concentration or pressure. Take samples for arterial blood gases from an umbilical artery catheter, radial artery catheter, or radial artery puncture. If desired, take capillary blood through a warmed heelstick—this gives accurate levels of pH and carbon dioxide, but not oxygen. If ordered, follow oxygen with transcutaneous oxygen monitoring.

• Notify the doctor of arterial blood gas results so he can order appropriate changes in oxygen concentration. Oxygen partial pressure ($PO_2$) is usually maintained between 60 to 90 mmHg arterial and 40 to 60 mmHg capillary.

• Check the neonate's respiratory function with a stethoscope; listen for rales and rhonchi, and bilateral breath sounds.

### Special considerations

Always take electrical precautions when administering oxygen, *to avoid fire or explosion.* As soon as possible, explain the situation and the procedures to the parents. Take measures to keep the neonate warm, *because hypothermia impedes respiration.* Check blood gases at least every hour if the unstable neonate is receiving a high concentration of oxygen, and whenever there's a clinical change. If he doesn't respond to oxygen administration, check for congenital anomalies.

Know how to perform neonatal chest auscultation correctly *to pick up subtle respiratory changes.* Also, be able to identify signs of respiratory distress and perform emergency procedures. If required, perform chest physiotherapy and percussion, as ordered, and follow with suctioning *to remove secretions.* As ordered, discontinue oxygen administration when the neonate's fraction of inspired oxygen ($FIO_2$) is at room air level (20% to 21%) and his arterial oxygen is stable at 60 to 90 mmHg. Repeat blood gases 20 to 30 minutes after discontinuing oxygen, and thereafter as ordered by the doctor or by hospital policy.

### Complications

Retrolental fibroplasia results from constriction of immature retinal blood vessels in response to high concentrations of oxygen for prolonged periods. Although new vessels form in response to the hypoxia, they're fragile. The resulting hemorrhage can cause retinal detachment and eventual blindness, especially in premature infants.

Bronchopulmonary dysplasia (chronic pulmonary lung disease) can result from prolonged ventilation and oxygen therapy. The exact cause of this is unclear, but oxygen damages lung capillaries, resulting in microhemorrhagic changes, diminished mucus flow, and inactivation of surfactant.

Infection or "drowning" can result from overhumidification, which allows water to collect in tubing, where it can suffocate the neonate or provide a growth medium for bacteria. Hypothermia and increased oxygen consumption can result from administration of cool oxygen. Metabolic and respiratory acidosis may follow inadequate ventilation. Pressure sores can form on the neonate's head, face, and around the nose during prolonged oxygen therapy. Pulmonary air leak (pneumothorax, pneumomediastinum, pneumopericardium, interstitial emphysema) can result from forced ventilation or can develop spontaneously in any neonate in respiratory distress. Decreased cardiac output may result from CPAP pressures that are too high.

### Documentation

Note the respiratory distress requiring oxygen administration, the concentration of oxygen given, and the method of administration. Record each alteration in oxygen concentration and the neonate's $FIO_2$, as measured by the oxygen analyzer. Note all routine checks of oxygen concentration. Document all blood gases, the times blood samples were drawn, neonatal condition during therapy, times suctioned, the amount and consistency of mucus, and any complications. Note breath sounds, respiratory rate, and the presence of signs of respiratory distress.

GAIL JOHNSON, RN

# 18 Pediatric Care

# Pediatric Care

## Introduction

Care of the pediatric patient requires an understanding of his distinct physical *and* developmental needs, as well as close communication with his family to meet those needs. Unless nursing care considers both physical and emotional needs, hospitalization can seriously disrupt the child's development, threatening to injure his psyche as it heals his body.

### Physical differences

Managing a child's physical care is not like caring for an adult. The most obvious difference, smaller physical size, greatly reduces the margin for error. Because of this difference, drug dosages and I.V. fluid volumes must be carefully calculated to avoid overdosage and overhydration. The child's physiologic immaturity heightens his response to disorders and his vulnerability to drug reactions. While he recovers from illness more rapidly than an adult, he is more vulnerable to serious complications.

### Developmental needs

A child also differs emotionally and psychologically from the adult; he requires sensory and social stimulation to maintain his sense of security and emotional well-being. Separation from his parents and confrontation with strangers are crucial fears for the child, who is just developing trusting relationships. The young child's heightened sense of fantasy and limited view of life can magnify and distort the unfamiliar hospital setting and events to produce a frightening experience. Because fear and alienation can isolate the child and adversely affect therapy, the nurse needs to interpret and deal constructively with his feelings. She must also promote the child's participation in his own care. She must anticipate his actions and take preventive steps, such as application of restraints, to avoid injury.

### Family-centered care

Contemporary pediatric nursing strives to maintain an optimal environment for the child's continued growth and development within the family unit. It recognizes the parents' role as primary caregivers and protectors, and attempts to support and maintain them in that role. Family-centered care encourages parents to become actively involved in their child's care by allowing open visiting hours and rooming-in policies. It also takes parents' needs into consideration, because a child's illness may precipitate a crisis for the parents. Anxiety about their child's health, the cost of hospitalization, care of siblings, and their own job responsibilities may give them unrealistic expectations of nursing care. Their emotional distress may find expression in anger directed at the staff. The nurse needs to consider the motivation behind such behavior and deal with it in an understanding way.

Increasingly, pediatric nursing is relinquishing the control that shut out parents, attempting instead to make them feel welcome and to create a positive relationship that benefits the child.

AMANDA S. BAKER, RN, PhD

## DIAGNOSIS AND MONITORING

# Urine Collection

*Collection of a urine specimen for laboratory analysis allows screening for urinary tract and renal disease, detection of systemic and metabolic disorders, and evaluation of treatment.*

*Although a child without bladder control can't provide a clean-catch midstream specimen, the urine collection bag is a simple, effective alternative. It offers minimal risk of specimen contamination without resorting to catheterization or suprapubic aspiration, invasive procedures that can introduce bacteria into the bladder. Because the collection bag is secured with adhesive flaps, its use is contraindicated in a child who has extremely sensitive or excoriated perineal skin. Alternate methods of collecting urine from small children use a reversed diaper or a test tube.*

### Equipment

*To collect a random specimen:* pediatric urine collection bag (individually packaged) □ urine specimen container □ two disposable diapers of appropriate size □ scissors □ washcloth □ soap □ water □ towel □ bowl □ linen-saver pad.

*To collect a culture and sensitivity specimen:* sterile pediatric urine collection bag □ sterile urine specimen container □ two disposable diapers of appropriate size □ scissors □ sterile bowl □ sterile or distilled water □ antiseptic skin cleanser □ sterile 4″ x 4″ gauze sponges □ alcohol sponge □ 3-ml syringe with needle □ linen-saver pad.

*To collect a timed specimen:* 24-hour pediatric urine collection bag (individually packaged) with evacuation tubing □ 24-hour urine specimen container □ two disposable diapers of appropriate size □ scissors □ washcloth □ soap □ water □ bowl □ towel □ sterile 4″ x 4″ gauze sponges □ compound benzoin tincture □ small medicine cup □ 35-ml

Luer-Lok syringe or urimeter □ tubing stopper □ clean examination gloves □ limb restraints □ specimen preservative, such as formaldehyde solution □ linen-saver pad.

Kits containing sterile supplies for clean-catch collections are commercially available and may be used to obtain a culture and sensitivity specimen.

### Preparation of equipment

Check the doctor's order for the type of specimen needed and assemble the appropriate equipment. Wash your hands. Complete the laboratory request form *to avoid delay in sending the specimen to the laboratory.* Take the scissors and make a 2″ (5 cm) slit in one diaper, cutting from the center point toward one of the shorter edges. Later, you'll pull the urine collection bag through this slit when you position the bag and diaper on the child. Next, pour water into the bowl; use sterile water and a sterile bowl if you're preparing to collect a specimen for culture and sensitivity.

*If you'll be collecting a culture and sensitivity specimen,* check the expiration date on each sterile package and inspect for tears. Open several packages of sterile 4″ x 4″ gauze sponges.

*If you'll be collecting a timed specimen* using benzoin in liquid form, pour it into the medicine cup. Cut the tubing on the urine collection bag so that only 6″ (15 cm) remain attached. Discard the excess. Place the stopper in the severed end of the tubing. If you're going to use a urimeter for the patient who voids large amounts, don't cut the tubing; simply attach the device.

### Essential steps

*To collect a random specimen:*
• Explain the procedure to the patient—if he's old enough to understand—and to his parents. Provide privacy, especially for the young child.
• Wash your hands.
• Place the child on a linen-saver pad.

## USING A METABOLIC BED

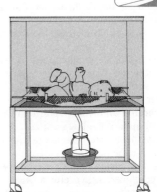

Using a metabolic bed is the preferred method for collecting a 24-hour urine specimen from an infant, *because it prevents urine loss and perineal skin irritation.*

*To prepare for this procedure:*

• Place the metabolic bed in a warm area, away from windows and drafts, *because the infant needs to be partially undressed.*

• Gather the equipment at bedside: filter paper, a 24-hour pediatric urine collection bag, a 24-hour collection container, an ice-filled basin, and two net screens. Using filter paper, cover the hole at the bottom of the bed. Remove the metal rods from their grooves, thread them through the holes in one of the net screens, and reinsert them in their grooves. Write the patient's name, the test, and the duration of collection on the specimen container.

• Insert the container into the ice-filled basin and place it under the hole in the bed. Then attach the 24-hour pediatric urine collecting bag to the hole in the bed, placing the end of its tubing into the 24-hour specimen container.

*To perform this procedure:*

• Wash your hands.

• Undress the infant except for an undershirt. Place him in the bed, on top of the net screen. If necessary, apply restraints. Close the door of the metabolic bed and secure the lock. Provide the infant with toys and activities appropriate for his age.

• Check the collection device connections frequently *to prevent leakage.*

ROCHELLE DRUKER KUHN, RN, MS

• Clean the perineal area with soap, water, and a washcloth, working from the urinary meatus outward *to prevent contamination of the urine specimen with flora from the surrounding skin.* Wipe gently *to prevent tissue trauma and stimulation of urination.* Be sure to separate the labia of the female patient, or to retract the foreskin of the uncircumcised male patient, *to expose the urinary meatus for thorough cleansing.* Thoroughly rinse the area with clear water and dry with a towel. Refrain from using powder, lotion, or cream, *because these counteract the adhesive.*

• Place the patient in the frog position, with his legs separated and knees flexed. If necessary, have the child's parent hold him while you apply the collection bag.

• Remove the protective coverings from the collection bag's adhesive flaps. For the female patient, first separate the labia and gently press the bag's lower rim to the perineum. Then, working upward toward the pubis, attach the rest of the adhesive rim inside the labia majora. For the male patient, place the bag's opening over the penis and scrotum and press the adhesive rim to the skin.

• Once the bag is securely attached, gently pull it through the slit in the diaper *to prevent compression of the bag by the diaper and to allow observation of the specimen immediately after voiding.* Then fasten the diaper on the child.

• When urine appears in the bag, gently remove the diaper and the bag. Hold the bag's bottom port over the collection container, remove the tab from the port, and let the urine flow into the container.

• Measure the output, if necessary.

• Attach the laboratory request slip to the container and send the specimen directly to the laboratory.

• Put the second diaper on the child and make sure he's comfortable.

*To collect a culture and sensitivity specimen:*

• Follow the procedure for collecting a random specimen, with these modifications:

• Use sterile or distilled water, an antiseptic skin cleanser, and sterile 4″ x 4″ gauze sponges to cleanse the perineal area.

• First clean the urinary meatus; then work outward. Wipe only once with each gauze sponge, then discard it.

• After the patient urinates, remove the bag and use an alcohol sponge to clean a small area of the bag's surface. Puncture the clean area with the needle and aspirate urine into the syringe.

• Inject the urine into the sterile specimen container. Be careful to keep the needle from touching the container's sides *to maintain sterility.* Remember, a large volume of urine is unnecessary *because only about 1 ml of urine is needed to perform the culture and sensitivity test.*

*To collect a timed specimen:*

• Check the doctor's order for the duration of collection and the indication for the procedure. Following the steps for random specimen collection, prepare the patient and cleanse the perineum.

• Apply compound benzoin tincture to the perineal area *so the collection bag will adhere better and you won't have to reapply it during the collection period.* If you're using liquid benzoin, dip a gauze sponge into the medicine cup containing the liquid. If desired, wear a clean examination glove *to protect your hand.* If you're using benzoin spray, cover the genitalia with a gauze sponge before spraying *to prevent tissue trauma.*

• Allow the benzoin to dry. Then apply the collection bag, pull the bottom of the bag and the tubing through the slit in the diaper, and fasten the diaper.

• Restrain the child, if necessary, *to prevent dislodgment of the bag and tubing.* Leg restraints usually suffice for an infant, but arm restraints may be necessary for the toddler.

• Check the collection bag and tubing every 30 minutes *to ensure a proper seal, because any leak prevents collection of*

*a complete specimen.*

• When urine appears in the bag, remove the stopper in the bag's tubing, attach the syringe to the end of the tubing, and aspirate the urine. Then remove the syringe and insert the stopper into the tubing.

• Discard the specimen and begin timing the collection.

• When the next urine specimen is obtained, add the preservative to the 24-hour specimen container along with the specimen and refrigerate, if ordered, *to keep the sample stable.*

• Periodically empty the collection bag *to prevent skin breakdown and infection, and dislodgment of the collection bag from the weight of the urine.* Each time you remove urine, add it to the specimen container; then use the syringe to inject a small amount of air into the collection bag *to prevent a vacuum that can block urine drainage.*

• When the prescribed collection period has elapsed (or as nearly as possible), terminate the collection and send the total accumulated specimen to the laboratory.

• Wash the perineal area thoroughly with soap and water *to remove the benzoin;* then put the second diaper on the patient.

**Special considerations**

Whatever the collection method used, avoid forcing fluids *to prevent dilution of the specimen, which can alter test results.*

For a random collection or a culture and sensitivity collection, obtain a first-voided morning specimen, if possible.

If the collection bag becomes dislodged during timed collection, immediately reapply benzoin and attach another collection bag *to prevent loss of the specimen and the need to restart the collection.*

To collect a urine specimen from an infant or young child with extremely sensitive or excoriated perineal skin, use the inside-out disposable diaper method. Place cotton balls in the perineal area of the diaper to absorb urine as the child voids. After he has voided, remove the diaper and squeeze urine from the cotton balls into a specimen cup. Alternately, tape a test tube to a male child's penis to collect urine.

## Complications
Adhesive on the collection bag can cause skin excoriation.

## Documentation
Record the date, time, and method of collection; the amount of output, if necessary; the use of restraints; any complications; the time of specimen transport to the laboratory; and the patient's tolerance for the procedure.

ROCHELLE DRUKER KUHN, RN, MS

# Weight Measurement

*Periodic weight measurement helps evaluate an infant's or child's pattern of growth. It can also detect abnormal changes that indicate a pathologic condition, such as a rapid weight loss from diarrhea or vomiting, or an excessive gain from edema or an endocrine disorder. These changes may have more pronounced effects on a child than on an adult because of the child's smaller size and fluid volume.*

*Weight measurement also allows determination of fluid and nutrient requirements, calculation of drug dosages, and evaluation of response to therapy.*

## Equipment
Platform scale (for infant) or upright scale (for child) □ protective paper or diaper □ alcohol or other antiseptic cleansing solution, according to hospital policy □ 4″ x 4″ gauze sponge.

## Preparation of equipment
Take the scale to the patient's bedside. Place a clean diaper or sheet of protective paper on the platform scale's surface *to prevent cross-contamination between*

*patients.* With the paper or diaper in place, balance the scale according to the manufacturer's instructions.

## Essential steps
• Explain the procedure to the child, if appropriate, and to his parents.
• Check the child's most recent weight *to serve as a baseline for comparison.*
• Make sure the room is warm.
• Wash your hands.
• Undress the infant completely *to allow precise calculation of minor weight changes.* Let the older child keep his underwear or pajamas on *to avoid embarrassing him,* but ask him to take off his shoes or slippers.
• Gently lay or sit the infant on the platform scale. Keep one hand over him, without touching him, at all times *to prevent him from falling.* Instruct the older child to mount the upright scale and stand still while you weigh him.
• If the scale doesn't have a digital readout, adjust the weights until the scale balances. If possible, wait until the infant or child is still before you take the reading, *because movement can alter the measurement.*
• Compare the child's current weight with his most recent one. If the figures differ markedly, rebalance the scale and reweigh the child *to verify his current weight.* You may wish to have another nurse validate the figure.
• Return the infant to his crib and rediaper him, or hand him to his parent for redressing. Help the older child get dressed, if necessary.
• Dispose of the protective paper or diaper. If you've used a platform scale, clean the weighing surface with a 4″ x 4″ gauze sponge moistened in alcohol or other antiseptic cleansing solution, according to the institution's policy, *to prevent cross-contamination between patients.*
• Wash your hands.

## Special considerations
For repeated measurements, weigh the infant or child at the same time of day, using the same scale, and in similar clothing *to ensure accuracy and consis-*

*tency.* Place an extremely active infant on his abdomen *so he won't roll as much.*

If the older infant or toddler is too active for accurate weight measurement on a platform scale, balance an upright scale and weigh yourself on it. Then pick up the child, step onto the scale, read the weight, and subtract your own weight from the combined total *to obtain the child's weight.* Refrain from using this method to weigh an infant, however, *be-* *cause it's less exact than a direct weight obtained in ounces on a platform scale.*

### Documentation

Record the date, time, and weight; any factor affecting weight, such as the presence of a cast, brace, dressing, or I.V. armboard; any verification of unusual weight change; and method used, such as holding the child to weigh him.

ROCHELLE DRUKER KUHN, RN, MS

---

## TREATMENT

# Admission

---

*The admission procedure orients the child and his parents to the hospital setting. It includes a comprehensive nursing interview and physical examination to collect baseline data for use in formulating a nursing-care plan. The admission procedure also gives you the opportunity to establish a friendly, trusting relationship with the child and his family, thereby helping to relieve fears and anxieties that can hinder treatment.*

### Equipment

Thermometer □ stethoscope □ sphygmomanometer with blood pressure cuff of appropriate size □ scale □ identification bracelet □ equipment and supplies, as needed, for collecting blood and urine samples □ health history form or assessment sheet, if available.

### Essential steps

• Introduce yourself to the patient and his parents. Ask the child what name he prefers to be called and establish what he should call you.
• Orient the child and his parents to the unit and room, and introduce them to any roommates. Point out the location of bathrooms for both the child and visitors.
• Explain hospital regulations for visitors—meals, smoking, and use of the television and telephone. Emphasize the unit's positive and reassuring aspects, such as the company of other children, the availability of a playroom, books, toys, and remote control television.
• Explain the hospital's rooming-in policy to the parents. Stress the importance of rooming-in to the parents of an infant or preschooler. If a parent is unable to room-in, tell the child that a nurse is awake all night in case he needs something. Remember that the toddler under 3 years of age may fear separation from his parents, whereas the older child may worry more about what's going to happen to him in the hospital.
• If the child is not wearing an identification bracelet, apply a correctly printed one to his wrist and explain why he must wear it.
• Explain the admission routine and procedures. Allow the child to handle equipment, if appropriate, *to minimize his fears.*
• Collect patient data for use in formulating a nursing care plan. Include information from the child's health history; his growth, development, and psychosocial assessment; a survey of his daily routines; and the physical assessment. Use a health history form or assessment sheet, if provided by your hospital, to compile this information.
*To take the child's health history:*
• Find out the child's reaction to any previous hospitalization.
• Ask the child and his parents about their preparation for, and understanding

of, the current hospitalization. If their answers are vague, explain in nontechnical language the reasons for their child's admission, and refer them to the doctor for further explanation. Reassure the preschool or school-age child that hospitalization is not a punishment for some real or imagined wrongdoing.

• Note the child's past illnesses, immunization record, and any tendency to bleed or bruise easily. Identify any upsetting aspects of his present or past illnesses, such as fear of injections.

• Ask about any allergies to food, medication, or environment.

• Find out if the child currently receives drug therapy. If he does, record the drug's name, dosage, schedule, and route of administration. If the drug is given orally, specify its form as pill, powder, or liquid.

*To collect information on the child's growth, development, and psychosocial adjustment:*

• Observe the interaction between the child and his parents. Ask the parents to describe the child's temperament (friendly, quiet, or aggressive), his reaction to stress, and his coping measures. Inquire about any behavioral problems, such as temper tantrums or breath holding. Find out if the child has previously slept away from home.

• Determine if the child's ethnic or religious background requires any special routines or restrictions.

• Ask the parents about siblings, and determine who will care for them during the child's hospital stay.

*To collect information about the child's daily routine:*

• Record the child's typical diet. Identify his food preferences and dislikes, his facility with utensils, and any feeding problems.

• Ask the parents if the child requires a night-light and whether he sleeps in a bed or a crib. Identify the routine for naps and nighttime sleep, the need of a special toy or blanket to provide reassurance, or any sleeping problems.

• Inquire about the child's elimination needs. If applicable, determine his progress in toilet training and the frequency of bowel movements.

• Ask for and note any special words the child uses to communicate his needs.

• Inquire about particular routines that lessen the child's anxiety, such as bedtime prayers or a drink of water.

• Determine the child's favorite activities and types of playthings. Find out if he attends school. If he attends nursery school, ask how frequently.

*To perform a physical assessment:*

• Take the child's pulse rate and respirations first, *because measurement of temperature is an invasive procedure that can produce anxiety.* Then take blood pressure and temperature, and measure height and weight; if you're weighing an infant, also note his birth weight.

• Examine the child carefully and record pertinent observations. Note his general physical and psychological condition, level of growth and development, and signs and symptoms relating to his present condition. Also note any physical abnormalities or limitations, use of an assistive device, and the presence of a prosthesis.

• Observe the child carefully for rashes, bruises, abrasions, scars, fractures, burns, discharge, or change in level of consciousness that may indicate abuse or an unknown infection.

*After completing the data collection:*

• Instruct the parents and the child on appropriate safety measures.

• Make sure the proper consent forms have been signed.

• If ordered, collect blood and urine specimens, label them, and send them to the laboratory for analysis.

• Solicit further questions from the child and his parents. If necessary, assist the child, or ask the parents to assist him, in putting on pajamas or a hospital gown.

• Give the child's clothing (if appropriate), home medications, and any valuable items to the parents to take home. Label any personal toy or blanket that the child keeps *to prevent its loss.*

## Special considerations
Always include the child's parents in all explanations of hospital routines and

procedures *to avoid any feelings of fear or distrust they may otherwise project to the child.* Similarly, include the child and speak directly to him, when possible, *to enhance his self-image and his sense of control.*

Encourage the parents to participate in the child's care during his hospital stay, and point out the location of items and facilities that may be needed. Explain the aspects of care that you provide and those that the parents may provide.

If possible, initially interview the school-age child alone, and then repeat the interview questions with the parents present *to obtain a complete picture of their individual perceptions, fears, fantasies, and anxieties.* Allow the child to play or watch television, as he wishes, while you talk to his parents.

## Documentation

Record the date and time of admission; all aspects of the nursing history and results of physical assessment; any specimen collections; and the child's reaction to admission.

GLYNIS SMITH CHADWICK, RN, BSN

# Restraining Devices and Positions

*Restraining devices and positions are often used to protect a child from injury, to facilitate examination, and to aid in diagnostic tests and treatment. Because such restraints themselves are likely to make a child cry, a key nursing responsibility before applying restraints, therefore, is explaining to the child—if he's old enough to understand—why they are needed. Parents should also know why restraints are being applied. Restraints should be used only when absolutely necessary for the child's safety; their use in protecting a child from injury doesn't eliminate the need to observe the patient carefully.*

## Equipment

Appropriate restraint (see *Types of Restraints*, page 806; see also "Soft Restraints" in Chapter 1), including, as needed, washcloth or gauze sponges □ baby blanket or crib sheet □ safety pins □ tongue blades □ tape □ elastic gauze dressing.

## Essential steps

• Explain the purpose of the restraining position or technique to the patient (if he's old enough to understand) and to the parent(s). Show them the particular device to be used, if applicable, and assure them that it won't cause any pain or discomfort.

*To apply a jacket restraint:*
• Select the correct size *for maximum safety and comfort.*
• Apply the restraint over the child's pajamas *to reduce skin irritation.*
• Tie the restraint in the back *so the patient can't undo it.*
• Secure the long ties to the bed frame, or around the back of the chair arms, *so the child can't slide them off or untie them.*

*To apply a belt restraint:*
• Select the correct size.
• Apply the restraint over the patient's pajamas. Wrap the flannel-padded area of the belt around his waist, crossing it in back.
• Loop the belt smoothly and secure the ties to the bed frame or around the back of the chair arms.

*For an ankle restraint:*
• Secure both ends of the strap to the crib frame.
• Place padding (washcloths or gauze sponges) around the patient's ankles.
• Use safety pins *to fasten the ankle flaps securely around each ankle.*
• Check the patient's feet and toes frequently for adequate circulation.

*To apply individual wrist or ankle restraints:*
• Select the appropriate-sized restraint.
• Place padding around the patient's wrist or ankle.
• Apply the device and tie the ends to the bed frame.

• Check the patient's fingers or toes frequently for adequate circulation.

*To apply a clove-hitch (figure-eight) restraint:*

• Pad the patient's wrist or ankle with a washcloth or gauze sponges.

• Make a figure-eight loop with the elastic gauze dressing; then place one loop over the other.

• Insert the patient's padded wrist or ankle through the loops and tie the loop ends to the bed frame. When properly tied, the knot won't tighten when drawn taut.

• Check the patient's fingers or toes frequently for adequate circulation.

*To apply a mitten-glove restraint:*

• Trim the patient's fingernails, if necessary. (Check the institution's policy first.)

• Select the appropriate-sized commercial mitten-glove restraint (or use socks, or a stockinette with a knot tied in one end, when necessary).

• Slip the mitten-glove over the patient's hand and pull the drawstring to tighten it, taking care not to restrict circulation. The hand can then be either left free or restrained with an arm or limb restraint.

• Remove the glove at least daily (more often, if necessary) for skin cleansing and drying.

*To apply an elbow restraint:*

• Select the appropriate size for the patient's arm.

• Place the restraint over a long-sleeved shirt and position the elbow in the center of the restraint.

• Fasten the restraint with ties, safety pins, or tape.

• Hold the end of the shirt sleeve over the edge of the restraint and fasten it with safety pins. (A safety pin can also be used to secure the top of the restraint to the shirt.)

• Check the restraint often for proper placement.

*To place a crib net or bubble top:*

• Attach the net over the top of the bed; fasten the ties under the bed so that the side rails can be lowered.

• If a bubble top is used, secure it to the bed frame with four clamps—two at the

head of the bed, two at the foot.

*To apply a mummy restraint:*

• Place a baby blanket or crib sheet on a flat surface and fold one corner.

• Position the patient on the blanket with his shoulders at the fold and his feet toward the opposite corner.

• Straighten the patient's right arm alongside his body. Pull the blanket firmly across the patient's right shoulder, arm, and chest, and then tuck it behind his left side, leaving the left arm free.

• Straighten the patient's left arm alongside his body. Bring the left side of the blanket across his left shoulder and arm, and over his chest. Then tuck it in.

• Fold the lower corner up. Use safety pins, if needed, *to secure the patient's feet inside the blanket.*

• Make sure the patient's arms are aligned with his body and that he's not immobilized in an awkward position.

*To restrain a child for jugular venipuncture:*

• Place the patient in the mummy restraint with the upper part of the restraint low enough for his neck to be freely accessible.

• Position the patient so his head extends slightly over the edge of the bed, table, or pillow, and is supported comfortably. *This position stretches the external jugular vein.*

• Turn the patient's head to the side and stabilize it with your hands. Cup the occiput in the palm of one hand and spread the fingers of the other hand over the patient's face. Be sure the patient's mouth and nose aren't obstructed. Don't block the venipuncture site with your arms.

*To restrain a child for femoral venipuncture:*

• Place the patient on his back with his arms and legs extended in a froglike position. (Cover the male child's genital area with a diaper *in case he urinates during the procedure.*)

• Stand at the patient's head. Place your hands on his knees and drop your forearms over his arms.

*To restrain a child for lumbar puncture:*

• Wrap the patient's legs securely with

# TYPES OF RESTRAINTS

**Jacket**

**Limb restraint**

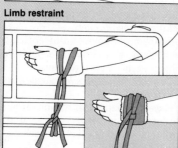

**Belt**

**Mitten-Glove**     **Elbow restraint**

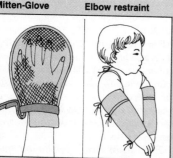

**Restraining board**

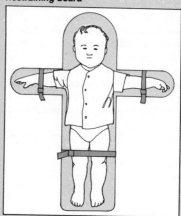

**Crib with net**

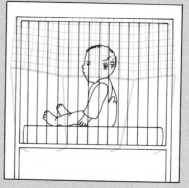

**Crib with bubble top**

a blanket before positioning *to minimize kicking.*

• Place the patient on his side with his back close to the edge of the examination table.

• Place one arm behind the patient's neck and the other behind his thighs, and clasp your hands in front of his abdomen.

• Keep the patient in a flexed position *to enlarge the spaces between the spines of the lumbar vertebrae. Because this position may be especially frightening for the child,* talk to him and reassure him frequently. *This may also help to keep him still and allay his fears.* Observe the child for difficulty in breathing, *because this position may interfere with chest expansion.*

*To restrain a child for ear examination:*

• Have the child sit sideways in your lap with the ear to be examined facing the examiner and with his opposite arm around you.

• Hold the child's head firmly against your chest with one arm, and use your other arm to hug the child, thereby restraining his free arm.

*To restrain a child for nose or throat examination:*

• Place the patient in a supine position.

• Extend his arms over his head and hold them tightly, immobilizing his head between them.

### Special considerations

A doctor's order—as well as a parental release form—may be needed before a restraint can be applied or removed. Always check hospital policy first.

Assess the patient frequently for skin irritation, redness, and impaired circulation. Remove the restraint every 2 to 4 hours, as needed, to permit movement of the affected extremity.

Always tie restraints so they can be untied easily in case of an emergency. Remember, restraining ties that are too short severely limit movement, while ties that are too long may cause the patient to become tangled. Never tie restraints to the bed's side rails; *if the rails are*

accidentally lowered with the restraints still tied, the patient can be injured. Unless absolutely necessary, don't restrict movement of all four limbs. If all extremities must be restrained, release one at a time at regular intervals. While holding a patient in a restraining position, speak to him frequently in a gently reassuring voice.

Avoid the supine position when restraining an unconscious patient or a patient who's just been fed, *because he may regurgitate or aspirate food.*

Never leave a patient alone in a highchair even when a restraint is in place. *An active child can tip the chair over.*

### Documentation

Record the date, type of restraint, time it was applied and removed, and any observations about circulation and skin condition. After diagnostic tests, record the date and time, specimens obtained, and pertinent follow-up observations.

GLYNIS SMITH CHADWICK, RN, BSN

# Drug Administration

*Administering drugs to an infant or child requires extreme accuracy and constant vigilance to ensure optimal effect and minimal toxicity. Not only does drug dosage vary with the size of the patient and the severity of his illness, but the growing child's rapid metabolic changes make his response to drugs faster and more unpredictable than an adult's. Even a slight miscalculation in dosage can produce grave effects; anaphylactic reaction in a child, for instance, is more severe than in an adult—and more likely to result in death. And, because the young child often can't interpret or communicate an adverse reaction, it's the nurse's responsibility to recognize the signs and symptoms.*

*At the same time, the nurse must maintain a good relationship with the child even though she may be causing him discomfort. It's her responsibility to be supportive while helping him learn to control his dislike for medication so he can cooperate when necessary. A firm, positive, consistent, and calm attitude is essential.*

## Equipment
*For oral medications:* prescribed medication □ medication cup or disposable syringe □ spoon, plastic medicine dropper, or straw, as applicable □ baby bottle nipple □ mixer, such as water, syrup, or jelly, as needed, for mixing medication □ fruit juice, as needed, for a chaser □ mortar and pestle, as needed.

*For injections:* prescribed medication □ tuberculin syringe or other syringe □ appropriate-sized needle □ alcohol sponges □ 2″ x 2″ gauze pads □ small adhesive bandage.

*For nose drops:* prescribed medication □ plastic medicine dropper □ infant bulb syringe □ pillow.

*For ear drops:* prescribed medication □ plastic medicine dropper □ cotton.

*For eye drops or ointment:* prescribed medication □ plastic medicine dropper (as needed) □ tissues.

*For rectal medications:* prescribed suppository □ glove or finger cot □ water-soluble lubricant.

*For dermatomucosal medications:* prescribed medication □ soap □ water □ 4″ x 4″ gauze sponges □ mitten or elbow restraints (optional).

## Preparation of equipment
Check the doctor's order for the prescribed drug, dosage, timing, and route. Compare the order to the drug label for correctness of medication and dosage, and check the drug's expiration date. Check the child's chart for drug incompatibilities or allergies. Carefully calculate the dosage. If you're in doubt about the dosage calculation, have another nurse verify it, especially before giving drugs that may be hazardous or lethal, such as insulin, heparin, digoxin, epinephrine, or narcotics. Check hospital policy to learn which drugs must be calculated and checked by two nurses. Then, wash

your hands and prepare the correct dose.

*For oral medications:* Administer drugs to an infant or young child in liquid form, if possible. However, refrain from adding a drug to the child's bottle or other large amount of liquid, *because he may not drink it all and may thus receive inadequate dosage.* If only a tablet is available, crush it in a mortar; then mix with a compatible syrup. Check with the pharmacist or an appropriate drug reference book *to ensure that crushing the tablet doesn't inactivate it.* Use a syringe to measure a liquid medication dose, *because it's more accurate than a medication cup.* If you're using a medication cup, however, place it on a flat surface at eye level *to check the dosage.* If the child takes medicine by spoon at home, use a spoon to administer it, but don't use the spoon to measure the dosage, *because it's inaccurate.* To provide consistent care, check the child's records for information about how he prefers to take medication. Look for such statements as "Mix with jelly," "Takes best for mother," or "Swabs own injection site." Prepare any mixtures the child's records indicate, as long as they are compatible with his prescribed diet.

*For injections:* Prepare injections out of the child's sight *to avoid frightening him.* For intramuscular (I.M.) injections, determine if low platelet count, volume depletion, or other conditions prevent the use of this route, and consult the doctor about any conflict. If you're giving two drugs simultaneously, check their compatibility with any up-to-date compatibility chart. Then, calculate the combined dosage volume, and check the need for divided doses by determining whether the combined volume will be too great for proper absorption from a single I.M. injection site.

*For accurate measurement of small dosage for an infant,* use a tuberculin syringe with a ½″ needle. Remember to inject no more than 0.5 ml at one site for the small infant with small muscle mass, and no more than 1 ml for the larger infant. For the toddler or older child, use a syringe with a 1″ needle to measure dosage.

*For nose and ear drops:* Warm nose drops (for an infant) and ear drops (for any age child) to body temperature by running warm water over the container for several minutes, or by carrying the container in your pocket for 30 minutes. *Cold ear drops can cause pain and vertigo.* Test the temperature of the drops before administering them.

## Essential steps

• Assess the patient's condition.

• Identify the child by comparing his identification bracelet with the medication card or sheet, and by asking the older child to tell you his name.

• Explain the procedure to the child in terms he can understand, and to his parent(s), if present.

• Carefully observe the child for any rash, itch, cough, or other sign of adverse reaction to a previously administered drug.

• Provide privacy, especially for the older child. Then, proceed as follows, according to the type of drug you're administering.

*To administer oral medication to an infant:*

• Use a plastic syringe without a needle, or a plastic medicine dropper, to administer the medication.

• Pick up the infant, raise his head and shoulders, or turn his head to the side *to prevent aspiration.*

• Gently press down on his chin with your thumb *to open his mouth.*

• Place the syringe or medicine dropper alongside the tongue and slowly release the medication. Release only enough to be swallowed at one time *to prevent choking.* For small infants, allow the child to suck on the syringe as you slowly expel the medication, or allow the infant to suck the medication from a baby bottle nipple.

• After all the medication has been administered, give the infant the fruit juice chaser. Then, if he's a small or inactive infant, place him on his side or abdomen *to prevent aspiration.* If the infant is very active, allow him to assume a comfortable position, *because forcing a side-lying*

position may make him agitated.

*To administer oral medication to a toddler:*

• Place the medication in a cup. Then pick up the toddler or elevate his head and shoulders *to prevent aspiration.*

• If possible, enlist the toddler's cooperation by asking him to help hold the cup. If he's unable to drink by himself, hold the cup to his lips, or use a syringe or a spoon, and proceed as described above for an infant, making sure the child drinks all the medication.

• Give the desired chaser.

*To administer oral medication to an older child:*

• If possible, allow the child to choose the mixer and the chaser, for liquid medication.

• If feasible, let the child choose where he'll take the medication, such as sitting in bed or on his parent's lap.

• If the child's old enough (usually age 4 to 6), teach him or review with him the method for swallowing tablets or capsules.

• Have him place the pill on the back of his tongue and immediately swallow it with water or juice. Emphasize swallowing the liquid rather than calling attention to the pill.

• Make sure the child takes sufficient liquid *to swallow the pill and prevent it from lodging in the esophagus.* Have him open his mouth *so you can check to ensure that he's swallowed the pill.*

• If the child is unable to swallow the pill, crush it and place it in the proper mixer, allowing a choice of mixers if possible.

*To give an I.M. injection to an infant:*

• Select the injection site. Usually, you'll choose the vastus lateralis muscle in the anterolateral aspect of the thigh, the largest and most developed muscle in the child under age 2. If necessary, you can use the ventrogluteal muscle, located between the greater trochanter of the femur and the iliac crest, although maintaining the infant's position for this site is sometimes difficult. Avoid using the posterior gluteal muscles in an infant, *because these don't develop until the child has been ambulatory for at least one year.*

• Place the infant in a secure position and have an assistant immobilize him if necessary.

• Cleanse the injection site with an alcohol sponge, moving outward from the center with a spiral motion *to avoid contaminating the clean area.*

• Grasp the skin between your thumb and forefinger *to immobilize it and to create a muscle mass for the injection.* Then, insert the needle with a quick darting motion. If injecting into the ventrogluteal muscle, inject at a 45° angle toward the knee.

• Aspirate the syringe plunger *to ensure that the needle isn't in a blood vessel.* If no blood appears, inject the medication slowly *so the muscle can distend to accommodate the volume.*

• Withdraw the needle and rub the area with a 2″ x 2″ gauze pad *to stimulate circulation and enhance absorption,* unless contraindicated. Place a small adhesive bandage over the injection site.

• Hold and comfort the infant *to reassure him* or, preferably, have his parent do this.

*To give an I.M. injection to a toddler or older child:*

• Explain each step to the child as his level of understanding and cooperation allows. Explain that the injection will help him get better and that it's not a punishment. Allow him to help as much as possible and as he desires.

• Have an assistant standing by *to immobilize the child for the injection, if necessary.*

• Select the injection site. The lateral and anterior aspects of the thigh are the least threatening sites for the toddler or preschooler. The upper outer quadrant of the posterior gluteal muscle may be used for the older school-age child, but accuracy is crucial *because of the danger of damaging the sciatic nerve.* The deltoid muscle may be used for injecting small volumes to older, larger children.

• Cleanse the injection site with an alcohol sponge, working with a spiral motion outward from the center *to avoid contaminating the clean area.*

• Grasp the skin between your thumb and forefinger *to immobilize it and to create a muscle mass for the injection.* Then, insert the needle. For anterior and lateral thigh sites, insert the needle at a 45° angle directed toward the child's knee. For posterior and ventrogluteal sites, insert the needle at an angle perpendicular to the surface the child is lying on, rather than to the skin surface.

• Aspirate for blood. If none appears, slowly inject the medication. Then withdraw the needle, rub the site, unless contraindicated, and cover it with a small adhesive bandage. Hold the child for a few minutes or, preferably, ask his parent to hold him, *to calm and comfort him.*

*To give a subcutaneous injection:*

• Usually, adult sites and techniques can be used (see "Subcutaneous Injections" in Chapter 7). Although some subcutaneous medications, such as heparin and insulin, are given abdominally in adults, this site is not used for infants or small children.

*To instill nose drops:*

• Place a pillow under the patient's shoulders and allow his head to fall back over the edge; have him lie on the bed so his head hangs over the edge; or hold him with your arm under his neck and his head tilted back.

• Draw the warmed medication into the dropper.

• Instill the prescribed number of drops or amount of medication without touching the dropper to the nasal mucosa, *to avoid contaminating the remaining nose drops with bacteria.* For the infant, open his nostrils for instillation by gently pushing up on the tip of his nose.

• Repeat the procedure in the other nostril, if ordered.

• After instillation, keep the child's head tilted backward for 3 to 5 minutes *to achieve full drug absorption.* If the child coughs or shows signs of aspiration, sit him upright and pat his back *to clear the lungs.*

• If you're administering decongestant (saline) drops, give them 20 minutes before mealtime, to make eating easier. If you're giving them to an infant, gently suction the nostrils with an infant bulb syringe before administration *to remove excess mucus,* and suction again approximately 20 minutes after administration.

*To instill ear drops:*
• Have the child lie on his side with the affected ear up.
• Draw the warmed medication into the dropper.
• If the child is under age 3, gently pull the pinna down and straight back before instillation, *because the auditory canal of infants and toddlers differs from that of older children and adults.* For the child over age 3, pull the pinna upward and back.
• Instill the prescribed number of drops. Then, gently massage the area immediately anterior to the ear, if it does not cause the child discomfort, *to facilitate entry of the drops.*
• Maintain the patient's position for 5 minutes *to ensure absorption of medication.* Place a piece of loosely packed cotton in the external canal, if desired, *to keep the drops from running out.*
• Repeat the instillation in the other ear, if ordered.

*To instill eye drops or eye ointment:*
• Use the same technique as for an adult. If necessary, obtain assistance to restrain the child.

*To administer a medicated rectal suppository:*
• Explain the procedure to the child and the reasons for giving the medication this way.
• Take the suppository from the refrigerator and open the suppository package immediately before use *to keep it from melting.*
• Put on a clean examination glove or a finger cot. Then, lubricate the suppository with a water-soluble lubricant.
• Insert the suppository beyond the anal sphincter, withdraw your finger, and hold the child's buttocks together until he no longer feels the urge to defecate.

*To administer dermatomucosal medications:*
• Use the same technique as for an adult.

If applying a medication for dermatitis, you can apply mitten or elbow restraints *to prevent scratching.*

## Special considerations

Because drug dosage for a child is best determined by body weight, use Clark's rule for the closest estimate: child's weight in pounds multiplied by the average adult dose and divided by 150. If you have any doubt about the proper dosage, consult the doctor. Post a list of appropriate emergency drug dosages in all pediatric areas and on emergency equipment *for quick reference.*

Firmly establish that the child has no choice about taking the medication. Support him in his dislike for the procedure, but remind him that the medication will help him get well. If he's receiving a one-time injection, he may want to choose the site, but remember that around-the-clock injections must be rotated in a set pattern. If advisable, and if time permits, allow the child to play at giving medication to a doll with a medication cup or syringe. If possible, let a parent stay with the child during the administration *to provide comfort.* However, don't ask the parent to act as a primary restrainer, *because the child may then view him as your accomplice.*

Make oral medication as palatable as possible but, unless ordered, avoid mixing it with milk or milk products that can hinder absorption or with foods that the child may come to dislike through association.

If an injection site is contaminated with feces, be sure to cleanse it well with soap and water before injection *to avoid introducing pathogens into the site.*

When giving an injection to an older child, don't pretend it won't hurt. Explain instead how brief the hurt will be and the need to hold still so it's over quickly. Explain that an assistant will help the child hold still if necessary.

Don't spend time on lengthy explanations for injections. Instead, unless watching increases the child's sense of control, try to divert the child's attention so his muscle will be more relaxed. If he's old enough, suggest he start counting just as you insert the needle and see if he can reach 10 before you're finished. Or, have him shout "ouch" as loud as he can. Don't scold the child for crying, or allow the parent to scold him. For a gluteal injection site, have the child lie flat on his stomach and point his toes together. *This will relax the muscle and lessen the pain.* Always have a small adhesive bandage ready, *as many children see it as a form of comfort.* Praise the child's good behavior. Give him a paper badge token that says "hero" or that has a happy face drawn on it.

If at any time you observe an adverse reaction, notify the doctor *for a decision on ordering a counteractant.* If your only contact with the child is to give medication, try to have some other more pleasant, less painful contact with him *so he doesn't associate you solely with a disagreeable experience.*

### Complications
Every drug has its specific possible complications and adverse effects. If you must administer an unfamiliar drug, check an appropriate drug reference book for information to help you recognize a drug reaction. This is especially important in treating children, who often can't tell you how they're feeling, but who can suddenly develop severe reactions.

### Documentation
Record the date, time, drug, dosage, and route of administration; the injection site(s); the purpose of administration and observation of result, if a drug is being given for an immediate effect (for example, to relieve pain, wheezing, or restlessness); any complications and the nursing action taken; and the child's tolerance of the procedure.

GLYNIS SMITH CHADWICK, RN, BSN

# Intravenous Therapy

*Intravenous (I.V.) therapy allows admin-*

*istration of drugs, replacement of electrolytes, and maintenance of fluid balance. In an infant, a scalp vein may be the preferred infusion site, because it is more accessible and often larger than a peripheral vein. In an older infant, a toddler, or a child, a peripheral vein in the hand, wrist, or foot is the usual site, because it is easy to stabilize. Intravenous therapy requires the use of a volume-control set with microdrip tubing to prevent fluid overload. The calibrated chamber is filled hourly, and the volume of fluid the patient is receiving is checked by both direct observation of the I.V. setup and assessment of hydration status.*

### Equipment
Parenteral solution, as ordered □ volume-control set (Buretrol or Soluset) with microdrip tubing (to deliver 60 drops/ml) □ tourniquet □ micropore filter □ butterfly needles (21G or 23G) □ ½" and 1" wide adhesive tape □ povidone-iodine sponge □ alcohol sponge □ padded armboard □ large safety pins □ I.V. pole □ identification sticker □ safety razor and rubber band (for infusion into a scalp vein) □ limb or jacket restraints □ sandbag (optional).

### Preparation of equipment
Assemble the equipment outside the patient's room, preferably in a treatment room. Inspect the I.V. solution for clarity and expiration date. Close both clamps on the tubing set. Spike and hang the I.V. solution bag on an I.V. pole. Open the clamp between the bag and the volume-control set, and allow 30 to 50 ml of solution to flow into the calibrated chamber. Then tightly close the clamp and squeeze the drip chamber located below the calibrated chamber. *Squeezing expels air and creates a vacuum that pulls solution into the drip chamber on release.* Release the drip chamber and allow the solution to fill it halfway. Attach the micropore filter to the tubing. Open the clamp on the long tubing below the drip chamber, and allow the solution to flush air from the tubing. When fluid reaches the end of the tubing and all of

the air bubbles have been flushed out, close the clamp tightly. Keep the end of the tubing sterile until you're ready to connect it to the needle's tubing (see also "Use of a Volume Control Set" in Chapter 6).

Cut six 8″ to 10″ (20.3 to 25.4 cm) strips of 1″ adhesive tape and three 4″ (10.2 cm) strips of ½″ tape. Attach the ends of the tape to the counter surface or the I.V. pole *to prevent tangles.* Place an identification sticker—showing the solution, medications added, and the patient's name and room number—on the back of the solution bag.

### Essential steps

• Explain the procedure to the child (if he's old enough to understand) and to his parents. Transport the patient to the treatment room and obtain assistance from *at least* one staff member to help restrain the patient during the procedure.

• Reassure the patient; tell him another staff member is going to help him hold still.

• Wash your hands.

• Select the insertion site for the needle or catheter. (If it is a scalp vein, shave a small area around the site *to provide adequate visualization.* Reassure the parents that the hair will grow back quickly. Then place a rubber band around the patient's head *to help dilate the temporal vein.*)

• Cleanse the insertion site and perform venipuncture in the same manner as for an adult. (see "Insertion of a Peripheral Line" in Chapter 6).

• When you see venous return in the butterfly needle tubing, attach the I.V. infusion tubing and open the clamp on the long tubing *to allow solution to flow into the vein.*

• Secure the wings of the butterfly needle with ½″ adhesive tape, using the crossover technique. To do this, pull a strip of tape into a "V." With the sticky side up, slide the "V" under the wings of the butterfly needle so the arms of the "V" remain exposed approximately 2″ (5 cm), and then press the wings down on the

tape *to secure them.* Next, fold the arms back diagonally so they crisscross over the needle. Finish by placing another strip of tape horizontally across the "X" formed by the bands of tape.

• Tape the patient's arm to the padded armboard with 1″ adhesive tape *to minimize movement, diminish tension on the vein, and decrease the risk of needle dislodgment.* Be sure to back the adhesive with tape or gauze wherever it will touch the skin *to prevent irritation and skin breakdown.*

• Adjust the flow of the solution to the correct rate. Keep the clamp between the solution bag and the chamber closed until you are ready to add solution to the chamber.

• Protect the I.V. site *to prevent accidental needle dislodgment.*

• When the patient is returned to his room, pin the padded armboard to the sheet of his crib or bed, or tape it to a small sandbag pinned to the sheet, *to discourage movement.*

• Position the solution bag at the appropriate height *to maintain a continuous drip.* Keep the clamp on the long infusion tubing closed to the drip chamber.

• Add solution hourly from the I.V. bag to the drip chamber. Also assess the infusion site at least hourly for signs of infiltration (swelling, redness, and warmth).

### Special considerations

You may need to use a mechanical infusion pump to facilitate a more precise flow rate, particularly for very small children and those sensitive to fluid overload, such as patients with cardiac disorders. Always use a volume-control set, even if a pump is used, *to minimize the risk of fluid overload in case of accidental detachment of the tubing from the pump.*

If a child's food and fluid intake is restricted, provide frequent mouth care. Offer a pacifier to an infant. Assess the state of hydration frequently by observing skin turgor, moistness of the oral mucosa, urinary output and specific gravity, and, in an infant, the state of the anterior fontanel (bulging or depressed).

To minimize anxiety, you may want to allow the older child to sit up during I.V. insertion.

Use appropriate restraints *to prevent needle dislodgment*. Usually, if the needle is inserted into an arm vein, restrain the child's other arm. If it is inserted into a foot vein, restrain the other foot and both arms. Check the restraint sites at least hourly and provide meticulous skin care, as needed, *to prevent breakdown*.

For I.V. therapy that continues several days or longer, change the tubing and solution bag regularly in accordance with hospital policy, *to prevent infection*. Label each with the date and time it is replaced. Although the butterfly needle is used for most I.V. infusions in children, a flexible plastic catheter is often used for long-term therapy. In an emergency, if venipuncture is difficult, the doctor may perform a surgical cutdown.

## Documentation

In your notes, record the date and time of insertion, type and amount of parenteral solution, type and gauge of needle, insertion site, and indications of the patient's state of hydration. Document the condition of the infusion site, patency of the I.V. system, and application of restraints. Note the specific gravity of the patient's urine, and record hourly fluid intake and output on the intake and output sheet. Record parenteral infusions on the I.V. record sheet.

SHEILA SCANNELL JENKINS, RN, BSN

# Mist Tents

*A mist tent (Croupette, cool humidity tent) contains a nebulizer that transforms distilled water into mist. Available in two models, it creates a cool, moist environment for the child with an upper respiratory tract infection or inflammation. If ordered, pure oxygen may also* *be supplied. The constant cool humidity helps the patient breathe by decreasing respiratory tract edema, liquefying mucous secretions, and reducing the fever that often accompanies respiratory tract distress. The child must be carefully prepared for treatment within a mist tent so he can cope with such enclosure without extreme anxiety and distress.*

## Equipment

Mist-tent frame and plastic tent ◻ two bed sheets ◻ plastic sheet or linen-saver pad ◻ two bath blankets ◻ humidity jar with filter ◻ sterile distilled water ◻ ice chamber ◻ oxygen flowmeter or air compressor, if ordered, with oxygen analyzer ◻ crushed ice ◻ two towels ◻ optional: infant seat, one or two pillows, cap.

## Preparation of equipment

*For the Universal model:* Set up the mist-tent frame and plastic tent at the head of the crib or the bed. (This is done by the respiratory therapist in some institutions.) Cover the mattress as usual with one of the two bed sheets. Then drape the plastic sheet over the upper half of the bed and tuck the ends under the mattress. (For infants, a linen-saver pad may be used instead of a plastic sheet.) Cover the plastic sheet with one of the bath blankets.

Fill the humidity jar three-quarters full with the sterile distilled water. Make sure the filter is clean and in place on the jar, and then screw it in place on the underside of the ice chamber. If ordered, connect the tent to the oxygen flowmeter or air compressor. Fill the ice chamber with crushed ice, and close off the water outlet valve on the chamber.

Turn on the oxygen flowmeter to the ordered setting, or turn on the air compressor. (The exact percentage of oxygen must be measured by an oxygen analyzer.) Allow the mist to fill the tent for about 2 minutes before the patient enters it. Elevate the head of the bed to a position that will be comfortable for the patient.

*For the Model D:* Using one of the bed

sheets, make the crib (or bed) as usual. Lay the linen-saver pad—plastic side up—lengthwise across the top half of the crib. Place the mist-tent frame on the crib and snap the plastic tent onto the frame. Fold each of the two towels in thirds—first lengthwise, then widthwise—and place one under each of the metal plates at the base of the frame. *This prevents the tent from tilting backward when the ice chamber is filled.*

Lay a folded bath blanket across the bottom bars of the mist-tent frame, tucking the ends under the mattress on each side. Place another folded bath blanket lengthwise in the tent. *As moisture accumulates, only the blankets, not the entire crib linen, will have to be changed.*

Fill the humidity jar three-quarters full of sterile distilled water. Make sure the filter is clean and in place on the jar, and then screw the jar in place on the underside of the ice chamber. Attach the mist tent to the oxygen flowmeter or air compressor, using the outlet on the back of the tent.

Fill the ice chamber with crushed ice, unless contraindicated (as for the young infant who has difficulty maintaining his body temperature). Turn off the water outlet valve on the chamber. Turn the damper valve to the horizontal position, and turn on the flowmeter to the ordered setting or turn on the air compressor. Leave it on for about 2 minutes *to fill the tent with mist;* then turn the damper valve to the vertical position while the tent is being used.

### Essential steps

● Explain the mist tent to the patient in terms he can understand (you might compare it to a teepee, for example). For his parents, you might liken it to a vaporizer, a device with which they're probably already familiar. *A careful explanation relieves the patient's fears and promotes cooperation.*
● Wash your hands.
● Position the patient in the tent. The child is often put in the semi-Fowler's position; an infant seat can be used for a baby. Prop up an older infant or a

toddler with a pillow, but be sure the pillow doesn't obstruct the air outlet.
● Cover the patient with a light blanket and supply a small towel or cap for his head. *A proper covering will prevent the patient from becoming chilled when the mist condenses inside the tent.*
● Stay with the patient, or have his parent(s) stay with him, until he's quiet.
● Close the zippers on the openings of the tent and tuck the sides of the tent under the mattress (under the frame for the Model D). Smooth out all creases or wrinkles *to minimize accumulations of moisture.*
● At the foot of the Model D tent, secure the plastic with a blanket folded lengthwise. *A tight seal prevents leakage of mist and oxygen from the tent.*
● Raise the side rails all the way, *because the tent alone won't stop an infant or small child from falling out of bed.*
● Check on the patient frequently; if possible, place him near the nurse's station. The mist makes observation more difficult. *Remember that a few patients don't improve—and may even worsen—after being placed in a mist tent.*

### Special considerations

Refill the humidity jar, as necessary. Use only sterile distilled water *to prevent bacterial growth.* Clean the humidity jar at least daily. If this isn't done by the respiratory therapist in your institution, remove the filter screw and tube and clean them with a toothbrush. Drain water from the ice chamber into a large bucket and replace the ice, as necessary. Clean the inside of the tent with soap and water.

Give the child toys to play with while he's in the tent *to divert his attention.* For the infant, you can string toys across the top bar of the tent. Avoid new, stuffed animals, *because the patient may be allergic to them.*

 *To avoid the possibility of a fire or an explosion,* don't let the child play with battery-operated toys or games that can create sparks or an electrical shock. For the same reason, don't allow the child access to an electrical call-bell. Provide the older patient with a handbell instead.

*To further minimize the possibility of a fire or an explosion,* prohibit smoking in the vicinity of the mist tent. Make sure any water on the floor is mopped up immediately *to prevent falls and to avoid electrical shock.*

New mist therapy units have self-contained cooling units and don't require ice. Change the patient's linen and clothing often, *because they will quickly become wet from the mist.* A nebulizer can supply additional mist, if needed. If you use a nebulizer, watch the patient closely, especially if he has copious mucous secretions which may loosen quickly, creating the risk of aspiration. Also, *to promote efficient drainage of secretions,* have the patient lie in a prone position, with his head to the side. Suction him, if needed.

Monitor the child's temperature regularly, particularly the small infant's, *because the cool mist may lead to hypothermia.*

If the mist tent is to be used at home, teach the parents how to use it correctly, making sure they fully understand how to clean it in order *to discourage bacterial growth.*

If oxygen is required, the percentage used should be monitored by an oxygen analyzer at least twice a shift. Accurate measurement is necessary for effective therapy.

## Documentation

On the patient's chart, note both his respiratory response and his emotional reaction to the mist therapy. If oxygen is ordered, record in the nurse's notes or on a special flow sheet the percentage the patient is receiving, as monitored by the oxygen analyzer, and the date and time the analysis was taken. Also document in the nurse's notes the date and time the patient was placed in the mist tent, when he was removed, any changes in his respiratory status, and the status of his breathing outside the tent.

ROCHELLE DRUKER KUHN, RN, MS

# Cardiopulmonary Resuscitation

*Cardiopulmonary resuscitation (CPR) attempts to restore effective ventilation and circulation after respiratory or cardiac arrest. The principles of CPR remain the same whether performed on an adult, a child, or an infant; however, different CPR techniques reflect the patient's size and the cause of the arrest. For example, in a child or an infant, arrest rarely results from primary cardiac disturbances or arrhythmias. Usually, the arrest stems from hypoxia—the result of airway obstruction by formula, a foreign object, or aspiration of excess mucus; suffocation by plastic bags; laryngospasm and edema from upper respiratory tract infection; or sudden infant death syndrome. If performed in time, CPR can usually restore ventilation and circulation.*

## Equipment

Cardiac arrest board (optional).

## Essential steps

● Place the infant or child on his back *to allow blood flow to the brain during compression,* and support his head and neck.

*To establish unresponsiveness or respiratory difficulty:*
● Shake the patient, flick the sole of his foot with your finger, or pinch his toes. The unresponsive patient fails to move or cry and has limp extremities.
● Call for help in case advanced life support measures are needed.
● If the patient fails to breathe or breathes laboriously, open his airway by using the neck-lift or chin-lift technique. In the *neck-lift technique,* take the hand (or as many fingers as fit comfortably) closest to the patient's feet and place it under his neck; then place the other hand on his forehead. Lift his neck slightly and gently push his head back; *this maneu-*

ver *usually prevents the tongue from obstructing the airway.* However, unlike the technique for an adult, avoid extreme extension of the neck and head *to prevent airway collapse.*

In the *chin-lift technique,* place one hand on the forehead, and use the fingertips of your other hand to lift forward the bony part of the jaw under the chin, *moving the tongue away from the posterior pharyngeal wall and opening the airway.* However, avoid closing the patient's mouth completely or placing excessive pressure beneath the jaw.

*To check for breathing:*
• Immediately place your ear over the patient's mouth. Observe his chest and abdomen for movement. Listen for exhalation of air, and feel for air issuing from the mouth and nose. Remember that chest movement alone doesn't indicate adequate ventilation.
• If the patient's breathing resumes, maintain airway patency. If it fails to resume or is labored and he is cyanotic, begin rescue breathing.

*To apply rescue breathing:*
• Establish an airtight seal. For an infant or small child, cover the mouth and nose with your mouth; for a larger child, pinch the nostrils closed *to prevent the escape of air during ventilation,* and cover only his mouth with yours.
• Deliver four gentle puffs of air in rapid succession, without permitting full pulmonary deflation between breaths, *to detect airway obstruction and open the small air sacs in the lungs.* Observe for expansion of the chest. If air freely enters the patient's lungs and his chest rises, check his pulse.
• If air fails to enter the lungs freely and his chest doesn't rise, use the chin lift to reposition his head and try again. If air still fails to enter his lungs, suspect airway obstruction. If he has been healthy and has no immediate history of croup or epiglottitis, suspect a foreign object. If he has a progressive airway obstruction resulting from respiratory infection, you won't be able to remove the obstruction, and advanced life support measures will be necessary.

*To clear an obstructed airway:*
• If the object causes only a partial obstruction and the patient begins to cough or cry forcefully, encourage spontaneous coughing and breathing, which may help expel the object. However, if the object causes impaired air exchange (characterized by cyanosis, wheezing, and ineffective coughing) or an absence of air exchange (characterized by cyanosis and unconsciousness), try to expel the obstruction. Turn an infant on his stomach, and place your arm under his abdomen, keeping his head lower than his feet. Cradle your hand around his jaw and chest to provide support, and rest your forearm on your thigh *to further stabilize your arm.* Using the heel of your other hand, deliver four rapid blows between the infant's shoulder blades. Use much less force than you would for an older child or an adult.
• If the infant fails to breathe, sandwich him between both your arms *to support his head, neck, and back;* turn him on his back, place him on your thigh, and hold his head lower than his feet. Using two or three fingers, deliver four rapid chest thrusts midsternum between the nipples.
• Use the same procedure for a small child. However, if the child is too large to turn over on your forearm, kneel on the floor and drape the child over your thighs, keeping his head lower than his trunk.
• Deliver four back blows rapidly with the heel of your hand between his shoulder blades. Then support his head and back, and roll the child onto the floor on his back. Deliver four chest thrusts with the heel of your hand.
• Next, immediately place your thumb over the patient's tongue, wrap your finger around his lower jaw, and lift it forward to open his mouth so it can be examined for the foreign object. If it's visible, remove it by using your finger.

 Always avoid a blind finger sweep, *which risks further airway obstruction by pushing the object down the airway.*

• If the patient fails to breathe, resume rescue breathing. If his chest fails to rise, repeat the series of back blows and chest thrusts. After establishing airway patency and delivering four gentle puffs of air, check his pulse.

*To check circulation:*

• For an infant, palpate for the brachial pulse, located on the inside of his upper arm midway between the shoulder and the elbow. (In an infant, the carotid pulse is difficult to locate because of his short neck, and the precordial pulse provides inaccurate results.)

• For a child, check for the carotid pulse, as you would for an adult.

• If the patient has a pulse but fails to breathe, continue resuscitation at the rate of 20 breaths/minute for the infant and 15 breaths/minute for the child. If he attempts to breathe but is cyanotic, coordinate your rescue breathing with his attempts. As he inhales, breathe into his lungs.

• If there is no pulse, position the patient on his back on a hard surface or cardiac arrest board, and begin external chest compressions coordinated with rescue breathing *to promote oxygen circulation throughout the body.* Be careful not to elevate the patient's head above his heart, *because gravity will reduce or prevent blood flow to the brain during compression.*

• For an infant, place two or three fingers on the midsternum between the nipples, and compress the sternum ½″ to 1″ (1.3 to 2.5 cm). The infant's sternum doesn't require much pressure, because it is pliable.

• Deliver 5 compressions to each breath at the rate of 100 compressions/minute. *This compensates for an infant's heart and respiratory rates, which are typically faster than those of an adult.*

• Place your forearm or your other hand under the infant's neck *to maintain an open airway,* and deliver small puffs of air to expand his chest.

• While compressing, count "one, two, three, four, five," and then give the breath with minimum interruption of the compressions. If you have an assistant, ventilate on the upstroke of each fifth compression.

• For a child, compress the lower half of the sternum 1″ to 1½″ (2.5 to 3.8 cm), using the heel of your hand. Use *only* the heel of your hand; keep your fingers off the chest *to avoid fracturing his ribs.* Deliver 5 compressions to each breath at the rate of 80 compressions/minute. Count compressions like this: "one and two and three and four and five." Then give one breath that's strong enough to raise the chest. Check your hand placement, and repeat the 5 compressions to 1 breath pattern.

• If you have an assistant, the person giving chest compressions should count; the person providing ventilation maintains the open airway and administers the breath on the upstroke of the fifth compression.

• For either an infant or a child, check the patient's pulse after the first minute of CPR and every few minutes thereafter, *to assess the effectiveness of chest compression and to detect the return of a spontaneous heartbeat.*

## Special considerations

Remember that the American Heart Association has set guidelines for administering CPR, and that a patient younger than age 1 is regarded as an infant; a patient between ages 1 and 8, a child. These classifications should be used as general guidelines; in an emergency, knowing the precise age isn't critical.

Since an infant or a small child has a smaller lung capacity than an adult, avoid over-ventilation and possible rupture of alveoli. However, the smaller air passages also offer greater resistance to airflow, so observe for chest expansion. If ventilation doesn't cause the chest to rise, reposition the airway and blow harder.

If an infant is large for his age and three fingers won't compress the sternum adequately, use the heel of one hand, as for the child.

Since gastric distension (which decreases lung capacity) can result from artificial respiration, ventilate using only enough air volume to cause the chest to rise. Attempt gastric decompression only if the distension causes inadequate ventilation because there is a danger that the patient may aspirate vomitus. If necessary, turn the patient onto his side, apply gentle pressure to the abdomen, wipe the vomitus from the mouth, and resume CPR.

Avoid abdominal thrusts in an infant or child, if possible, *because of the risk of injury to abdominal organs, especially the liver.*

Perform CPR on an adolescent as you would for an adult.

## Complications
Fractured ribs and injury to internal organs may result from too vigorous compression or incorrect finger or hand placement.

## Documentation
Record the date, time, and type of arrest as well as the symptoms and events preceding it, if known. Document the treatment and the patient's response. Also record the length of time CPR was administered, the outcome of CPR, and whether advanced life support measures were used. Note if the doctor contacted the patient's parents.

GLYNIS SMITH CHADWICK, RN, BSN

# Bryant's Traction

*Bryant's traction (vertical suspension) is one of six types of lower-limb traction used in the orthopedic management of children. Its primary purpose is to immobilize the legs of the patient with a femoral fracture or a congenital dislocation of the hip. Even if only one leg is affected, traction straps are applied to the thighs of both legs to prevent hip rotation and to place equal stress on the child's bones, ensuring equal bilateral growth. The traction apparatus is applied with the patient in the supine position in a crib, with his legs extended vertically at a 90° angle to his body.*

*A suitable candidate for this type of traction is a child who is under age 2 or who weighs between 25 and 30 pounds. This procedure is contraindicated for a child who weighs more than 30 pounds, because of the chance of positional hypertension.*

## Equipment
Nonsterile glove □ cotton balls □ tincture of benzoin □ traction setup (supplied by the orthopedic department) □ moleskin adhesive traction straps □ elastic bandages □ adhesive tape □ jacket restraint □ optional: soap and water, safety razor.

## Preparation of equipment
Assist the doctor and other members of the orthopedic department with measuring and cutting the moleskin straps and with assembling the traction equipment.

## Essential steps
*Before traction is applied:*
● Explain the procedure to the child (if he's old enough to understand) and to his parents.
● If there is hair on the patient's legs, use soap and water and a safety razor to shave the designated area that will be wrapped with adhesive traction straps. Have someone assist you by holding the patient's legs still. *This will minimize the chance of nicking the skin during shaving.*
● Using the nonsterile glove and the cotton balls, paint the patient's legs with the tincture of benzoin. *This preparation provides better adhesion for the traction straps, reduces itching, and helps prevent skin irritation.*

*After traction is applied:*
● Check the apparatus regularly. Make sure that the correct weights are attached, that no weights have been removed, and that the weights don't touch the crib or floor. Inspect the pulley ropes for fraying; make sure they're in the pulley grooves. Wrap the knots with adhesive tape *to prevent them from slipping.*
● Make sure the elastic bandages are in

## POSITIONING THE PATIENT FOR BRYANT'S TRACTION

In Bryant's traction, the patient's legs are extended vertically at a 90° angle to his body, with both buttocks raised slightly off the bed.

the correct position. With assistance from another person to hold the traction straps in place, remove and rewrap the bandage on the unaffected leg, if ordered, *to provide skin care.* Otherwise, provide skin care to the areas above and below the bandage.

● Check regularly to confirm that the patient's buttocks are *slightly* raised off the mattress. Raising them too high reduces the the effectiveness of traction.

● Apply a jacket restraint, as necessary, *to prevent the patient from turning over and interfering with the traction.*

● Mark the side of the crib or bed with a piece of tape *to show the correct position of the patient's shoulder.*

● If possible, photograph the child in the correct position and tape the picture to the head of the crib. *This will show all staff members how the patient should be positioned.* (If a camera isn't available, a drawing will do.)

● Assess the circulatory status of the patient's legs and feet frequently by checking temperature, pulse, color, sensation,

and movement. If you suspect a circulatory problem, loosen the elastic bandage and notify the doctor immediately.

● Provide skin care for the child's back, elbows, and buttocks every 4 hours. *Prolonged confinement in Bryant's traction can lead to skin irritation and breakdown.* A sheepskin may be placed under the child to help prevent skin problems.

● Make sure the child's daily diet contains plenty of roughage. Ensure adequate fluid intake: for infants, about 130 ml/kg of body weight every 24 hours; for toddlers, about 115 ml/kg every 24 hours.

● Encourage the patient to take deep breaths regularly *to minimize the risk of hypostatic pneumonia from immobilization.*

● As ordered, administer drugs to relieve pain from the fracture or dislocation as needed.

● Make sure the patient has quiet periods *to allow sufficient rest and sleep;* also make sure he has periods of play.

● Provide toys and diversionary activities that are appropriate for the child's age. Encourage the family to visit and to participate in care and recreational activities. *This will make the patient feel more comfortable and help minimize the anxiety of the parents and other family members.*

● *As a safety precaution,* keep the crib side rails in the full upright position whenever you are not at the patient's bedside.

## Special considerations

*To encourage the patient to take regular deep breaths,* have him try the following: blowing on a pinwheel, horn, or whistle; using an incentive spirometer; blowing against a facial tissue held in front of him; and singing.

Some doctors allow the bandages on *both* legs to be rewrapped twice daily *to prevent slipping.* However, many prefer to rewrap the affected leg themselves.

Remember that a very young child may not be able to tell you when he is in pain. Determine his need for relief of pain by observing his expression and his behavioral changes, listening to his crying, and noting any refusal to eat or drink.

If hospital policy permits, have the patient's crib moved to the playroom so he can be with other children and participate in activities, such as playing with dolls and puppets. After moving the crib, always check the traction setup. Also, make sure that other children do not play with the ropes and weights.

After the child has been in Bryant's traction for 2 to 4 weeks, the doctor may decide that the fracture or dislocation has healed well enough for the patient to be immobilized in a hip spica cast and cared for at home. Before discharge, teach parents how to assess circulation in the child's legs and provide cast care.

## Complications
Skin necrosis may occur if the elastic bandage slips over the Achilles tendon. Contractures may result from too tightly wrapped elastic bandages. Immobilization can cause many complications, such as constipation and urinary stasis.

## Documentation
Document the date and time traction was applied, the amount of weight applied, the skin care given, the date and time legs were rewrapped and by whom, the skin condition, the use of restraints, and the measures used to enhance respiration. Record circulatory findings as follows: skin temperature (warm or cool to the touch); pulse (strong, weak, or absent); color (normal, cyanotic, or pale); capillary refilling; sensation (awareness of toes being touched); and movement (ability or inability to wiggle toes when they're touched). In the cardex, record a visual documentation (photograph or drawing) showing the correct position of the patient in the traction setup.

ROCHELLE DRUKER KUHN, RN, MS

# Hip Spica Cast Care

*A hip spica cast is used to immobilize both legs of a child after orthopedic surgery for correction of a fracture or deformity. The cast is applied after the deformity is corrected or the fracture reduced. A hip spica cast may also be the means of treatment for orthopedic deformities not requiring surgery.*

*Nursing care includes protecting the cast from urine and feces, and keeping it dry. Efficient cast hygiene promotes the patient's comfort by minimizing skin irritation and other complications. Although infants usually adapt to this cast more easily than older children, both need psychological support and diversionary activity during prolonged immobility.*

*Most hospitalized patients are discharged with the cast in place, so parents must be taught how to take care of the cast properly at home.*

## Equipment
Waterproof adhesive tape □ bandage scissors □ plastic sheet or wrap □ cotton-tipped applicators □ ballpoint pen □ electric cast cutter □ cotton balls □ soap and water □ optional: disposable diapers, Bradford frame, abrasive cleanser with damp sponge or cloth.

## Essential steps
*Before the cast is applied:*
● Explain the procedure to the child (if he is old enough to understand) and to the parents. For a young child, use a doll with a cast or an elastic gauze dressing wrapped around its trunk and limbs *to demonstrate the procedure.*
● If the doctor will apply the cast in the cast room, accompany the patient *to provide comfort and reassurance.* Remember that application of a spica cast can be a frightening experience for a young child; for an older child or adolescent, it can be embarrassing as well.
*After the cast is applied:*
● Cover the bed pillows with the plastic sheet or wrap. Then, with the assistance of others, position the patient so the casted area is on the plastic-covered pillows *to keep the bed linen dry while the cast is wet.* Inspect inside the edges of the cast

for stray bits of plaster which, if allowed to dry, would be rough and difficult to remove.

• Assess the patient's legs for signs and symptoms of circulatory impairment every 1 to 2 hours while the cast is wet, and every 2 to 4 hours thereafter. Look for swelling, coldness, cyanosis or mottling, weak or absent pulse, inability to move toes, numbness, a tingling or burning sensation, and slow capillary refill.

• *To help the cast dry,* turn the patient every 1 to 2 hours the day the cast is applied, and every 4 hours thereafter. Keep the cast uncovered until it dries. Drape the perineal area with a light covering.

• Once the cast has dried, cut several petal-shaped pieces of the waterproof adhesive tape, roughly 1″ to 1½″ (2.5 to 3.8 cm) wide by 3″ (7.6 cm) long, and place them around the cast's edges and perineal cutout. *The petals overlap one another and will protect the patient's skin from the rough plaster.*

• Give the patient a sponge bath *to remove any pieces of plaster from his skin.* (Clean between his toes with cotton-tipped applicators.)

• For the postoperative patient, check for signs of bleeding or drainage, such as cast staining or discoloration. If such signs occur, outline the stained area on the cast with a ballpoint pen. Label it with the date and time and watch for spreading beyond this area. Expect some bleeding and drainage immediately after surgery; be sure to check for bleeding under the cast as well as on the top and sides.

• Assess the patient's respiratory status, especially his ability to expand his chest.

• Check exposed skin for redness and irritation. As part of daily hygiene, cleanse the skin under the edge of the cast with soap and water. Don't apply lotion or powder to these areas, *because they can cause irritation.*

• Observe the patient for discomfort or pain (evident in the infant by continual crying) caused by pressure-sensitive areas under the cast (hot spots). Also check for a foul odor emanating from the cast,

which can indicate a pressure sore, infection, or both.

• *To minimize itching,* use a bulb syringe or a hair dryer (set on "cool") *to introduce air under the cast.*

 Make sure the older child understands that he should never use a sharp object (such as a ruler or a knitting needle) to relieve itching under the cast, *because he may puncture the skin or disrupt a suture line and cause an infection.* Also, make sure the patient doesn't drop small objects or food under the cast. *This can lead to pressure sores.*

• Provide appropriate toys and diversionary activities. Encourage the family to visit and to participate in his care and recreational activities. *This will make the patient feel more comfortable and will make the parents and other family members feel more useful.*

*Before discharge:*

• Make sure the parents know how to care for the cast, turn and position the child, and are aware of restrictions on the patient's mobility and of the warning signs of cast constriction or infection.

*Before the cast is removed:*

• Explain the procedure to the patient and his parents. Assure them that the electric cast cutter has a vibrating blade that won't cut the skin even if it comes in direct contact with it. If necessary, have the person who will cut the cast demonstrate how the device works by touching his own palm with the vibrating blade.

• Because the noise of the cast cutter can be frightening, tuck cotton balls in the patient's ears if he wishes or, if available, place headphones over his ears and let him listen to music.

• Hold the patient still so the cutting can be finished as quickly as possible.

• Remove sloughed skin and sebaceous debris with repeated washings of soap and water or baby oil.

## Special considerations

*For the incontinent patient or young child who is not yet toilet trained,* prevent soiling of the cast by tucking a folded disposable diaper under the perineal edges of the cast. Fasten a second diaper around the cast *to hold the first one in place.* A Bradford frame can minimize cast soiling. Plastic "petals" are tucked into the cast, which allow urine and feces to be channeled into a bedpan. Keep a small blanket draped over the patient's perineal area for privacy.

*For a continent patient,* insert a plastic sheet or wrap into his cast when he's using a bedpan, *to minimize or prevent soiling.* (Plastic sheets are reusable; plastic wraps are disposable.) If a fracture bedpan is used, the patient's head and shoulders should be raised *to prevent urine or feces from draining into the cast.* A soiled cast can be cleaned with an abrasive cleanser and a damp sponge or cloth.

A hip spica cast dries by evaporation from the outside in. This takes 24 to 48 hours ( 8 to 10 hours with some newer, fast-drying materials). Electric fans may be used to make the cast dry faster, but take precautions so that other children in the pediatric unit can't tamper with them.

When turning the patient to help the cast dry, make sure you turn him to his unaffected side *to prevent undue pressure on the affected side.* One person can safely turn an infant; two people should turn an older child or an adolescent. Don't use the stabilizer bar to turn the patient. Handle the damp cast only with your palms, *because pressure from the fingers can leave indentations in the soft plaster*

*and cause pressure sores.*

Keep a cast cutter handy at all times *to remove the cast quickly in an emergency.*

During mealtimes, older patients may be able to eat and swallow more comfortably if placed on their stomachs.

Make sure that parents practice daily cast care under nursing supervision before the patient is discharged. Parent teaching should include: checking the patient's circulatory status and notifying the doctor if the cast becomes too tight; turning the patient safely; applying adhesive tape or plastic petals to the perineal cutoff; cleaning the cast; making sure the patient eats properly; and, when appropriate, preparing a split-Bradford frame.

## Complications

Long-term immobilization in a hip spica cast can cause constipation, urinary stasis, and a predisposition to kidney stones. These functions must be assessed regularly. Other complications related to immobility may also occur.

## Documentation

On the patient's chart, record the date and time of care; circulatory status of the extremities; any bleeding and drainage (measured in coin size, such as dime-sized or quarter-sized, or measured in centimeters); condition of the skin and cast; skin care given; elimination; and the patient's emotional adjustment.

ROCHELLE DRUKER KUHN, RN, MS

---

# Selected References

American Association of Critical Care Nurses. *Critical Care Nursing of Children and Adolescents.* Edited by Annalee R. Oakes. Philadelphia: W.B. Saunders Co., 1981.

Chow, Marilyn P., et al. *Handbook of Pediatric Primary Care.* New York: John Wiley & Sons, 1979.

Hamilton, Persis M. *Basic Pediatric Nursing,* 3rd ed. St. Louis: C.V. Mosby Co., 1978.

Hilt, Nancy, and Cogburn, Shirley. *Manual of Orthopedics.* St. Louis: C.V. Mosby Co., 1980.

Latham, Helen D., et al. *Pediatric Nursing,* 3rd ed. St. Louis: C.V. Mosby Co., 1977.

Scipien, G., et al. *Comprehensive Pediatric Nursing.* New York: McGraw-Hill Book Co., 1979.

Whaley, Lucille F., and Wong, Donna. *Nursing Care of Infants and Children.* St. Louis: C.V. Mosby Co., 1979.

824

# Acknowledgments

**INSIDE FRONT COVER**    Anna Marie Seroka, RN, BSN, MEd, CCRN, Nursing Workshop on Cardiac Priorities

**CHAPTER 1**    *Basic Care Procedures*
pp. 18, 50, 55—Photography by Paul A. Cohen
p. 27—Courtesy of J.T. Posey Co., Arcadia, Calif.
p. 59—Photography by Thomas Staudenmayer

**CHAPTER 2**    *Mobility*
p. 123—Photography by Paul A. Cohen

**CHAPTER 3**    *Infection Control*
p. 142—Photography by Paul A. Cohen

**CHAPTER 4**    *Diagnostic Tests*
pp. 167, 184—Photography by Paul A. Cohen

**CHAPTER 5**    *Physical Treatments*
p. 216—Courtesy of Gaymar Industries, Inc., Orchard Park, N.Y.

**CHAPTER 6**    *Intravascular Therapy*
p. 291—Photography by Paul A. Cohen

**COLOR PLATES**    *Recent Developments in Medical Equipment*
pp. 368-369—Courtesy of Support Systems International, Inc., Johns Island, S.C.

**CHAPTER 9**    *Respiratory Care*
p. 511—Photography by Paul A. Cohen

**CHAPTER 10**    *Gastrointestinal Care*
pp. 570-571—Photography by Paul A. Cohen

**CHAPTER 12**    *Neurologic Care*
p. 643—Photography by Thomas Staudenmayer

**CHAPTER 13**    *Orthopedic Care*
p. 663—Photography by Thomas Staudenmayer

**CHAPTER 15**    *Eye, Ear, and Nose Care*
p. 712—Photography by Heather Boyd-Monk, RN, Wills Eye Hospital, Philadelphia

# Index

# Index

# Nursing72
# Nursing73
# Nursing74
# Nursing75
# Nursing76
# Nursing77
# Nursing78
# Nursing79
# Nursing80
# Nursing81
# Nursing82
# Nursing83
# Nursing84
# Nursing85

# Year after year, one journal delivers more useful clinical information in less time than any other!

Over half a million nurses rely on their subscriptions to keep up with the flood of new drugs, treatments, equipment, and procedures that are changing nursing practice.

Each monthly issue is packed with thoroughly practical, accurate information in concise articles and departments that are clearly written and illustrated in step-by-step detail. You can read an article in minutes and come away with knowledge you can put to work with assurance.

**Feature articles** focus on demanding problems—ranging from hypertensive crises to cardiogenic shock—that require special skills. You'll quickly learn what to do, how to do it best, when (and when not) to do it.

**Drug updates** give you critical information quickly—indications, dosages, interactions, contraindications... all you need to administer drugs more confidently.

**Assessment aids** help you become more proficient in objectively assessing your patients, their conditions, and responses to nursing care.

**Self-quizzes** bring you the chance to test your knowledge of *current* nursing practices.

**Patient-teaching aids** help you prepare your patients to follow instructions at home.

Enter your own subscription today with the coupon below. It's a solid, career investment that pays big dividends for you and your patients; (it's even tax-deductible).

# INDEX OF *EMERGENCY PROCEDURES*